| | | |
|---|---|---|
| 22 | William Shakespeare "Like as the waves" Read by Sir John Gielgud. | :53 |
| 23 | Wallace Stevens "The Idea of Order at Key West" | 4:46 |
| 24 | Dylan Thomas "Do Not Go Gentle . . ." | 1:33 |
| 25 | Derek Walcott "A Far Cry from Africa" | 2:00 |
| 26 | Richard Wilbur "Love Calls Us to the Things of This World" | 1:58 |
| 27 | William Carlos Williams "This Is Just to Say" | :13 |
| 28 | William Butler Yeats "The Lake Isle of Innisfree" | 1:02 |

### DRAMA

| | | |
|---|---|---|
| 29 | Arthur Miller   Excerpt from Act I of *Death of a Salesman* | 7:53 |
| 30 | George Bernard Shaw   Excerpt from *Pygmalion*, Act 2 | 2:02 |
| 31 | William Shakespeare   *Hamlet*, Act 3, Scene 4 Read by Paul Scofield. | 11:41 |

### FICTION

| | | |
|---|---|---|
| 32 | Jamaica Kincaid "Girl" | 3:52 |

## CD2

### FICTION – continued

TRACK

| | | |
|---|---|---|
| 1 | Raymond Carver "Cathedral" Read by Peter Reigert. | 37:20 |
| 2 | James Joyce "Araby" Read by Colm Meaney. | 13:50 |
| 3 | Eudora Welty "Why I Live at the P.O." | 20:20 |

*The Norton*
*Introduction to Literature*
NINTH EDITION

# THE NORTON INTRODUCTION TO *Literature*

NINTH EDITION

ALISON BOOTH
*University of Virginia*

J. PAUL HUNTER
*Emeritus, University of Chicago*
*University of Virginia*

KELLY J. MAYS
*University of Nevada, Las Vegas*

W. W. NORTON & COMPANY
*New York, London*

W. W. Norton & Company has been independent since its founding in 1923, when William Warder and Mary D. Herter Norton first published lectures delivered at the People's Institute, the adult education division of New York City's Cooper Union. The Nortons soon expanded their program beyond the Institute, publishing books by celebrated academics from America and abroad. By mid-century, the two major pillars of Norton's publishing program—trade books and college texts—were firmly established. In the 1950s, the Norton family transferred control of the company to its employees, and today—with a staff of four hundred and a comparable number of trade, college, and professional titles published each year—W. W. Norton & Company stands as the largest and oldest publishing house owned wholly by its employees.

*Editor:* Peter Simon
*Developmental editor:* Michael Fleming
*Editorial assistants:* Rob Bellinger, Evan Leatherwood, Simone Gubar
*Production manager:* Diane O'Connor
*Photo research:* Stephanie Romeo
*Permissions clearance:* Katrina Washington
*Interior design:* Charlotte Staub
*Managing editor, College:* Marian Johnson

*Composition:* Binghamton Valley Composition
*Manufacturing:* R. R. Donnelley & Sons

Copyright © 2005, 2002, 1998, 1995, 1991, 1986, 1981, 1977, 1973 by W. W. Norton & Company, Inc.

All rights reserved
Printed in the United States of America

Since this page cannot legibly accommodate all the copyright notices, the Permissions Acknowledgments constitute an extension of the copyright page.

Library of Congress Cataloging-in-Publication Data

The Norton introduction to literature / [edited by] Alison Booth, J. Paul Hunter, Kelly J. Mays.—9th ed.
    p. cm.
Includes bibliographical references and index.
           **ISBN 0-393-92614-1**
  1. Literature—Collections.  I. Booth, Alison.  II. Hunter, J. Paul, date.  III. Mays, Kelly J.

PN6014.N67 2005
808—dc22
                                                             2005045087

W. W. Norton & Company, Inc., 500 Fifth Avenue, New York, NY 10110
www.wwnorton.com

W. W. Norton & Company Ltd., Castle House, 75/76 Wells Street, London W1T 3QT

5 6 7 8 9 0

# Brief Contents

## *Fiction*

### Reading, Responding, Writing 12

### Understanding the Text 66

 1  PLOT 66
 2  NARRATION AND POINT OF VIEW 123
 3  CHARACTER 150
 4  SETTING 219
 5  SYMBOL 262
 6  THEME 296
 7  THE WHOLE TEXT 341

### Exploring Contexts 404

 8  THE AUTHOR'S WORK AS CONTEXT: D. H. LAWRENCE AND FLANNERY O'CONNOR 404
 9  LITERARY KIND AS CONTEXT: INITIATION STORIES 504
10  FORM AS CONTEXT: THE SHORT SHORT STORY 535
11  CULTURAL AND HISTORICAL CONTEXT 552
12  CRITICAL CONTEXTS: A FICTION CASEBOOK 592

### Reading More Fiction 634

**BIOGRAPHICAL SKETCHES: FICTION WRITERS 794**

## *Poetry*

### Reading, Responding, Writing 810

### Understanding the Text 835

13  TONE 835
14  SPEAKER 861
15  SITUATION AND SETTING 882
16  LANGUAGE 914
17  THE SOUNDS OF POETRY 969
18  INTERNAL STRUCTURE 997
19  EXTERNAL FORM 1019
20  THE WHOLE TEXT 1050

*Exploring Contexts* 1061

- 21 READING POETRY IN CONTEXT 1061
- 22 THE AUTHOR'S WORK AS CONTEXT: JOHN KEATS AND ADRIENNE RICH 1089
- 23 LITERARY TRADITION AS CONTEXT 1131
- 24 CULTURAL AND HISTORICAL CONTEXTS: THE HARLEM RENAISSANCE 1162
- 25 CRITICAL CONTEXTS: A POETRY CASEBOOK 1203

*Reading More Poetry* 1234

**BIOGRAPHICAL SKETCHES: POETS** 1294

# Drama

*Reading, Responding, Writing* 1312

*Understanding the Text* 1360

- 26 ELEMENTS OF DRAMA 1360
- 27 THE WHOLE TEXT 1534

*Exploring Contexts* 1683

- 28 THE AUTHOR'S WORK AS CONTEXT: WILLIAM SHAKESPEARE 1683
- 29 LITERARY CONTEXT: TRAGEDY AND COMEDY 1838
- 30 CULTURAL AND HISTORICAL CONTEXT 1923
- 31 CRITICAL CONTEXTS: A DRAMA CASEBOOK 2071

*Reading More Drama* 2121

**BIOGRAPHICAL SKETCHES: PLAYWRIGHTS** 2234

*Writing about Literature* 2239

- 32 PARAPHRASE, SUMMARY, AND DESCRIPTION 2239
- 33 THE ELEMENTS OF THE ESSAY 2243
- 34 THE WRITING PROCESS 2252
- 35 THE RESEARCH ESSAY 2265
- 36 QUOTATION, CITATION, AND DOCUMENTATION 2280
- 37 SAMPLE RESEARCH PAPER 2292

*Critical Approaches* 2302

*Glossary* A1

**INDEX OF AUTHORS** A31
**INDEX OF TITLES AND FIRST LINES** A38

# Contents

*Preface* xxv

*Introduction* 1
> WHY LITERATURE MATTERS 3
> "THE CANON" 3
> THINKING CRITICALLY ABOUT LITERATURE 5

## Fiction

### Fiction: Reading, Responding, Writing 12

> ANONYMOUS, *The Elephant in the Village of the Blind* 13
> LINDA BREWER, *20/20* 15
> [CD] RAYMOND CARVER, *Cathedral* 20
> GRACE PALEY, *A Conversation With My Father* 31
> [WEB] A. S. BYATT, *The Thing in the Forest* 35
> SHERMAN ALEXIE, *Flight Patterns* 49
> > **STUDENT WRITING:** NINA SULLIVAN, *The Heart of Storytelling in "A Conversation with My Father" and "Flight Patterns"* 63

### Understanding the Text 66

> **1 PLOT** 66
> > MARGARET ATWOOD, *Happy Endings* 67
> > JOHN CHEEVER, *The Country Husband* 74
> > [WEB] JAMES BALDWIN, *Sonny's Blues* 91
> > [WEB] EDITH WHARTON, *Roman Fever* 113
>
> **2 NARRATION AND POINT OF VIEW** 123
> > EDGAR ALLAN POE, *The Cask of Amontillado* 127
> > [WEB] ERNEST HEMINGWAY, *Hills Like White Elephants* 132
> > LORRIE MOORE, *How* 135
> > PETER CAREY, *"Do You Love Me?"* 142
>
> **3 CHARACTER** 150
> > [CD] EUDORA WELTY, *Why I Live at the P.O.* 155

[WEB] indicates that a work is featured on *LitWeb*. [CD] indicates that a work is featured on the Audio Companion.

[WEB] HERMAN MELVILLE, *Bartleby, the Scrivener* 164
DORIS LESSING, *Our Friend Judith* 189
TONI MORRISON, *Recitatif* 202
    **STUDENT WRITING:** BETHANY QUALLS, *Character and Narration in "Cathedral"* 216

### 4 SETTING 219
ANDREA BARRETT, *The Littoral Zone* 221
RICHARD DOKEY, *Sánchez* 227
[WEB] AMY TAN, *A Pair of Tickets* 236
ANTON CHEKHOV, *The Lady with the Dog* 250

### 5 SYMBOL 262
[WEB] NATHANIEL HAWTHORNE, *Young Goodman Brown* 264
[WEB] FRANZ KAFKA, *A Hunger Artist* 274
[WEB] ANN BEATTIE, *Janus* 280
EDWIDGE DANTICAT, *A Wall of Fire Rising* 284

### 6 THEME 296
ANGELA CARTER, *A Souvenir of Japan* 298
BHARATI MUKHERJEE, *The Management of Grief* 304
NADINE GORDIMER, *Good Climate, Friendly Inhabitants* 316
JHUMPA LAHIRI, *Interpreter of Maladies* 325

### 7 THE WHOLE TEXT 341
JOSEPH CONRAD, *The Secret Sharer* 341
LOUISE ERDRICH, *Love Medicine* 369
[WEB] STEPHEN CRANE, *The Open Boat* 385

## Exploring Contexts 404

### 8 THE AUTHOR'S WORK AS CONTEXT: D. H. LAWRENCE AND FLANNERY O'CONNOR 404
D. H. LAWRENCE, *Odour of Chrysanthemums* 409
  *The Blind Man* 423
  *The Rocking-Horse Winner* 436
  *Passages from Essays and Letters* 446
[WEB] FLANNERY O'CONNOR, *A Good Man Is Hard to Find* 451
  *The Lame Shall Enter First* 462
  *Everything That Rises Must Converge* 487
  *Passages from Essays and Letters* 497

### 9 LITERARY KIND AS CONTEXT: INITIATION STORIES 504
TONI CADE BAMBARA, *Gorilla, My Love* 505
[WEB] ALICE MUNRO, *Boys and Girls* 509
[CD] JAMES JOYCE, *Araby* 519
MICHAEL CHABON, *The Lost World* 524

## 10 FORM AS CONTEXT: THE SHORT SHORT STORY 535

[WEB] KATE CHOPIN, *The Story of an Hour* 536
GABRIEL GARCÍA MÁRQUEZ, *A Very Old Man with Enormous Wings* 538
[CD] JAMAICA KINCAID, *Girl* 543
YASUNARI KAWABATA, *The Grasshopper and the Bell Cricket* 544
WILLIAM CARLOS WILLIAMS, *The Use of Force* 546
URSULA K. LE GUIN, *She Unnames Them* 549

## 11 CULTURAL AND HISTORICAL CONTEXT 552

F. SCOTT FITZGERALD, *Babylon Revisited* 560
From *Echoes of the Jazz Age* 575
MALCOLM COWLEY, From *Exile's Return: A Literary Odyssey of the 1920s* 577
THE NEW YORK TIMES, *Stocks Collapse in 16,410,030-Share Day* 583
*Crowds at Tickers See Fortunes Wane* 584
*Women Traders Going Back to Bridge Games* 585
ERNEST R. GROVES, From *Social Problems of the Family* 585
V. F. CALVERTON, From *The Bankruptcy of Marriage* 587

## 12 CRITICAL CONTEXTS: A FICTION CASEBOOK 592

[WEB] WILLIAM FAULKNER, *A Rose for Emily* 594
LAWRENCE R. RODGERS, "We all said, 'She will kill herself' ": The Narrator/Detective in William Faulkner's "A Rose for Emily" 601
GEORGE L. DILLON, *Styles of Reading* 608
JUDITH FETTERLEY, *A Rose for "A Rose for Emily"* 616
GENE M. MOORE, *Of Time and Its Mathematical Progression: Problems of Chronology in Faulkner's "A Rose for Emily"* 622
**STUDENT WRITING:** WILLOW D. CRYSTAL, *"One of us...": Concepts of the Private and the Public in William Faulkner's "A Rose for Emily"* 630

## *Reading More Fiction* 634

GUY DE MAUPASSANT, *The Jewelry* 634
AMBROSE BIERCE, *An Occurrence at Owl Creek Bridge* 639
HENRY JAMES, *The Jolly Corner* 645
[WEB] CHARLOTTE PERKINS GILMAN, *The Yellow Wallpaper* 667
[WEB] SUSAN GLASPELL, *A Jury of Her Peers* 678
[WEB] KATHERINE MANSFIELD, *Bliss* 692
KATHERINE ANNE PORTER, *Flowering Judas* 701
WILLIAM FAULKNER, *Barn Burning* 710
JORGE LUIS BORGES, *The Garden of Forking Paths* 722
RALPH ELLISON, *King of the Bingo Game* 729
JOYCE CAROL OATES, *The Lady with the Pet Dog* 735
BOBBIE ANN MASON, *Shiloh* 747
MARGARET ATWOOD, *Scarlet Ibis* 757

HA JIN, *In Broad Daylight* 768
SALMAN RUSHDIE, *The Prophet's Hair* 776
CAROL SHIELDS, *Dressing Down* 786

**Biographical Sketches: Fiction Writers** 794

# Poetry

## Poetry: Reading, Responding, Writing 810

### READING 811
ELIZABETH BARRETT BROWNING, *How Do I Love Thee?* 811
JAROLD RAMSEY, *The Tally Stick* 812
LINDA PASTAN, *love poem* 813
EZRA POUND, *The River-Merchant's Wife: A Letter* 815
LIZ ROSENBERG, *Married Love* 816

### RESPONDING 817
BEN JONSON, *On My First Son* 818
HOWARD NEMEROV, *The Vacuum* 819
[WEB] SEAMUS HEANEY, *Mid-Term Break* 820
RITA DOVE, *Fifth Grade Autobiography* 821
[WEB] [CD] ANNE SEXTON, *The Fury of Overshoes* 822

### WRITING 825

### PRACTICING READING: SOME POEMS ON LOVE 825
W. H. AUDEN, [*Stop all the clocks, cut off the telephone*] 825
[WEB] ANNE BRADSTREET, *To My Dear and Loving Husband* 826
[CD] WILLIAM SHAKESPEARE, [*Let me not to the marriage of true minds*] 827
SHARON OLDS, *Last Night* 827
APHRA BEHN, *On Her Loving Two Equally* 828
DENISE LEVERTOV, *Wedding-Ring* 829
MARY, LADY CHUDLEIGH, *To the Ladies* 829
W. B. YEATS, *A Last Confession* 830
**STUDENT WRITING:** STEPHEN BORDLAND, *Response paper on W. H. Auden's "Stop all the clocks, cut off the telephone"* 832

## Understanding the Text 835

### 13 TONE 835
[WEB] MARGE PIERCY, *Barbie Doll* 835
W. D. SNODGRASS, *Leaving the Motel* 836
THOM GUNN, *In Time of Plague* 838
ETHERIDGE KNIGHT, *Hard Rock Returns to Prison from the Hospital for the Criminal Insane* 840
[WEB] [CD] WILLIAM BLAKE, *London* 841

MAXINE KUMIN, *Woodchucks* 843
ADRIENNE RICH, *Aunt Jennifer's Tigers* 844

**MANY TONES: POEMS ABOUT FAMILY RELATIONSHIPS** 845
GALWAY KINNELL, *After Making Love We Hear Footsteps* 845
EMILY GROSHOLZ, *Eden* 846
[WEB] [CD] LI-YOUNG LEE, *Persimmons* 847
PAUL MULDOON, *Milkweed and Monarch* 849
ROBERT HAYDEN, *Those Winter Sundays* 850
DANIEL TOBIN, *The Clock* 850
SEAMUS HEANEY, *Mother of the Groom* 851
AGHA SHAHID ALI, *Postcard from Kashmir* 852
OLIVE SENIOR, *Ancestral Poem* 852
PAT MORA, *Elena* 854
JIMMY SANTIAGO BACA, *Green Chile* 854
KELLY CHERRY, *Alzheimer's* 856
ANDREW HUDGINS *Begotten* 856
  *Mostly My Nightmares Are Dull* 857
SIMON J. ORTIZ, *My Father's Song* 858
ALBERTO ALVARO RÍOS, *Mi Abuelo* 858

**14 SPEAKER: WHOSE VOICE DO WE HEAR?** 861
THOMAS HARDY, *The Ruined Maid* 861
X. J. KENNEDY, *In a Prominent Bar in Secaucus One Day* 863
MARGARET ATWOOD, *Death of a Young Son by Drowning* 864
[WEB] ROBERT BROWNING, *Soliloquy of the Spanish Cloister* 866
TESS GALLAGHER, *Sudden Journey* 868
DOROTHY PARKER, *A Certain Lady* 869
WILLIAM WORDSWORTH, *She Dwelt among the Untrodden Ways* 871
[WEB] AUDRE LORDE, *Hanging Fire* 872
JUDITH ORTIZ COFER, *The Changeling* 873
KAREN CHASE, *Venison* 874
SIR THOMAS WYATT, *They Flee from Me* 875
FRED CHAPPELL, *Recovery of Sexual Desire after a Bad Cold* 875
ROBERT BURNS, *To a Louse* 876
PAT MORA, *La Migra* 877
[WEB] EDNA ST. VINCENT MILLAY, [*Women have loved before...*] 878
  [*I being born a woman*] 879
[WEB] [CD] GWENDOLYN BROOKS, *We Real Cool* 879
KATHERINE PHILIPS, *L'amitié: To Mrs. M. Awbrey* 880
[WEB] WALT WHITMAN, [*I celebrate myself, and sing myself*] 881

**15 SITUATION AND SETTING: WHAT HAPPENS? WHERE? WHEN?** 882
JAMES DICKEY, *Cherrylog Road* 883
JOHN DONNE, *The Flea* 886
RITA DOVE, *Daystar* 887

LINDA PASTAN, *To a Daughter Leaving Home* 888
JOHN MILTON, *On the Late Massacre in Piedmont* 889
SYLVIA PLATH, *Point Shirley* 891
[WEB] MATTHEW ARNOLD, *Dover Beach* 893

**SITUATIONS** 895
EMILY BRONTË, *The Night-Wind* 895
ANDREW MARVELL, *To His Coy Mistress* 896
MARILYN CHIN, *Summer Love* 897
VIRGINIA HAMILTON ADAIR, *Peeling an Orange* 898
MARY JO SALTER, *Welcome to Hiroshima* 899
HOWARD NEMEROV, *A Way of Life* 900

**TIMES** 901
WILLIAM SHAKESPEARE, [*Full many a glorious morning have I seen*] 901
JOHN DONNE, *The Good-Morrow* 902
[WEB] SYLVIA PLATH, *Morning Song* 903
BILLY COLLINS, *Morning* 903
AUGUST KLEINZAHLER, *Aubade on East 12th Street* 904
JONATHAN SWIFT, *A Description of the Morning* 905
LOUISE BOGAN, *Evening in the Sanitarium* 905
ARCHIBALD LAMPMAN, *Winter Evening* 906

**PLACES** 907
JOHN BETJEMAN, *In Westminster Abbey* 907
ELIZABETH ALEXANDER, *West Indian Primer* 908
DEREK WALCOTT, *Midsummer* 909
THOM GUNN, *A Map of the City* 910
MARY OLIVER, *Singapore* 911
EARLE BIRNEY, *Irapuato* 912

# 16 LANGUAGE 914

**PRECISION AND AMBIGUITY** 914
SARAH CLEGHORN, [*The golf links lie so near the mill*] 914
ANNE FINCH, COUNTESS OF WINCHELSEA, *There's No To-morrow* 915
CHARLES BERNSTEIN, *Of Time and the Line* 915
YVOR WINTERS, *At the San Francisco Airport* 917
WALTER DE LA MARE, *Slim Cunning Hands* 919
PAT MORA, *Gentle Communion* 920
[CD] EMILY DICKINSON, [*After great pain, a formal feeling comes—*] 922
THEODORE ROETHKE, *My Papa's Waltz* 923
SHARON OLDS, *Sex Without Love* 924
MARTHA COLLINS, *Lies* 925
[CD] EMILY DICKINSON, [*I dwell in Possibility—*] 926
WILLIAM CARLOS WILLIAMS, *The Red Wheelbarrow* 926
[WEB] [CD] *This Is Just to Say* 927

GERARD MANLEY HOPKINS, *Pied Beauty* 927
E. E. CUMMINGS, *[in Just-]* 928
BOB PERELMAN, *The Masque of Rhyme* 929
BEN JONSON, *Still to Be Neat* 930
ROBERT HERRICK, *Delight in Disorder* 931
JOHN MILTON, From *Paradise Lost* 931

**PICTURING: THE LANGUAGES OF DESCRIPTION** 934
JEANNE MARIE BEAUMONT, *Rorschach* 936
OSCAR WILDE, *Symphony in Yellow* 937
RICHARD WILBUR, *The Beautiful Changes* 938
TED HUGHES, *To Paint a Water Lily* 938
JAMES MERRILL, *body* 939
ANDREW MARVELL, *On a Drop of Dew* 940

**METAPHOR AND SIMILE** 941
[CD] WILLIAM SHAKESPEARE, *[That time of year thou mayst in me behold]* 942
LINDA PASTAN, *Marks* 944
DAVID WAGONER, *My Father's Garden* 944
ROBERT BURNS, *A Red, Red Rose* 945
ADRIENNE RICH, *Two Songs* 947
WILLIAM SHAKESPEARE, *[Shall I compare thee to a summer's day?]* 948
ANONYMOUS, *The Twenty-third Psalm* 949
HENRY KING, *Sic Vita* 949
JOHN DONNE, *[Batter my heart, three-personed God]* 950
  *The Computation* 950
  *The Canonization* 951
DAVID FERRY, *At the Hospital* 952
RANDALL JARRELL, *The Death of the Ball Turret Gunner* 953
FRANCIS WILLIAM BOURDILLON, *The Night Has a Thousand Eyes* 953
MARGARET CAVENDISH, DUCHESS OF NEWCASTLE, *Of the Theme of Love* 953
EMILY DICKINSON, *[Wild Night—Wild Nights!]* 954
GREG DELANTY, *The Blind Stitch* 954

**SYMBOL** 955
SHARON OLDS, *Leningrad Cemetery, Winter of 1941* 956
JAMES DICKEY, *The Leap* 957
EDMUND WALLER, *Song* 960
D. H. LAWRENCE, *I Am Like a Rose* 961
DOROTHY PARKER, *One Perfect Rose* 961
WILLIAM BLAKE, *The Sick Rose* 962
ROBERT FROST, *Fireflies in the Garden* 963
STEPHEN DUNN, *Dancing with God* 963
[WEB][CD] ADRIENNE RICH, *Diving into the Wreck* 965
ROO BORSON, *After a Death* 967

## 17 THE SOUNDS OF POETRY 969

- HELEN CHASIN, *The Word* Plum 969
- MONA VAN DUYN, *What the Motorcycle Said* 970
- KENNETH FEARING, *Dirge* 972
- ALEXANDER POPE, *Sound and Sense* 974
- SAMUEL TAYLOR COLERIDGE, *Metrical Feet* 978
- WENDY COPE, *Emily Dickinson* 978
- ANONYMOUS, [*There was a young girl from St. Paul*] 979
- SIR JOHN SUCKLING, *Song* 979
- JOHN DRYDEN, *To the Memory of Mr. Oldham* 980
- [WEB] EDGAR ALLAN POE, *The Raven* 982
- [CD] WILLIAM SHAKESPEARE, [*Like as the waves . . .*] 985
- JAMES MERRILL, *Watching the Dance* 985
- [CD] GERARD MANLEY HOPKINS, *Spring and Fall* 986
- LEE ANN BROWN, *Foolproof Loofah* 987
- [CD] EMILY DICKINSON, [*A narrow Fellow in the Grass*] 987

### WORDS AND MUSIC 988

- THOMAS CAMPION, *When to Her Lute Corinna Sings* 989
- WILLIAM SHAKESPEARE, *Spring* 990
- AUGUSTUS MONTAGUE TOPLADY, *A Prayer, Living and Dying* 990
- ROBERT HAYDEN, *Homage to the Empress of the Blues* 991
- [CD] MICHAEL HARPER, *Dear John, Dear Coltrane* 992
- BOB DYLAN, *Mr. Tambourine Man* 993
- [CD] WILLIE PERDOMO, *123rd Street Rap* 995

## 18 INTERNAL STRUCTURE 997

- EDWIN ARLINGTON ROBINSON, *Mr. Flood's Party* 997
- HOWARD NEMEROV, *The Goose Fish* 1000
- PHILIP LARKIN, *Church Going* 1002
- PAT MORA, *Sonrisas* 1005
- SHARON OLDS, *The Victims* 1006
- ANONYMOUS, *Sir Patrick Spens* 1008
- WILLIAM CARLOS WILLIAMS, *The Dance* 1009
- EMILY DICKINSON, [*The Wind begun to knead the Grass—*] 1010
- WILLIAM SHAKESPEARE, [*Th'expense of spirit in a waste of shame*] 1011
- CATHY SONG, *Heaven* 1011
- STEPHEN DUNN, *Poetry* 1013
- PERCY BYSSHE SHELLEY, *Ode to the West Wind* 1014
- W. H. AUDEN, *In Memory of W. B. Yeats* 1016

## 19 EXTERNAL FORM 1019

### THE SONNET 1022

- WILLIAM WORDSWORTH, *Nuns Fret Not* 1023
- HENRY CONSTABLE, [*My lady's presence makes the roses red*] 1024

DANTE GABRIEL ROSSETTI, *A Sonnet Is a Moment's Monument* 1025
JOHN KEATS, *On the Sonnet* 1025
GWENDOLYN BROOKS, *First Fight. Then Fiddle.* 1026
EMMA LAZARUS, *The New Colossus* 1027
ROBERT FROST, *Range-Finding* 1027
WILLIAM WORDSWORTH, *London, 1802* 1028
JOHN MILTON, *[When I consider how my light is spent]* 1028
ELIZABETH BARRETT BROWNING, *[When our two souls stand up]* 1029
CHRISTINA ROSSETTI, *In an Artist's Studio* 1029
*Cobwebs* 1030
EDNA ST. VINCENT MILLAY, *[What lips my lips have kissed]* 1030
*[I shall forget you presently, my dear]* 1031
GWEN HARWOOD, *In the Park* 1031
HENRY CONSTABLE, *[Wonder it is, and pity]* 1032
SIR PHILIP SIDNEY, *[Come sleep, Oh sleep]* 1033
BARTHOLOMEW GRIFFIN, *Care-charmer Sleep* 1033
WILLIAM SHAKESPEARE, *[My mistress' eyes are nothing like the sun]* 1034
DIANE ACKERMAN, *Sweep Me through Your Many-Chambered Heart* 1034
HELEN CHASIN, *Joy Sonnet in a Random Universe* 1035
BILLY COLLINS, *Sonnet* 1035

**STANZA FORMS** 1036
DYLAN THOMAS, *Do Not Go Gentle into That Good Night* 1037
MARIANNE MOORE, *Poetry* 1037
ELIZABETH BISHOP, *Sestina* 1039
ISHMAEL REED, *beware: do not read this poem* 1040
ARCHIBALD MACLEISH, *Ars Poetica* 1041

**THE WAY A POEM LOOKS** 1042
E. E. CUMMINGS, *[l(a]* 1042
FRANKLIN P. ADAMS, *Composed in the Composing Room* 1043
E. E. CUMMINGS, *[Buffalo Bill's]* 1044
STEVIE SMITH, *The Jungle Husband* 1045
GEORGE HERBERT, *Easter Wings* 1046
ROGER MCGOUGH, *Here I Am* 1046
EARLE BIRNEY, *Anglosaxon Street* 1047
DAVID FERRY, *Evening News* 1048

**20 THE WHOLE TEXT** 1050
ELIZABETH JENNINGS, *Delay* 1050
ANONYMOUS, *Western Wind* 1052
ROBERT HERRICK, *Upon Julia's Clothes* 1053
W. H. AUDEN, *Musée des Beaux Arts* 1055
GEORGE HERBERT, *The Collar* 1056
ROBERT FROST, *Design* 1057
EDEN PHILLPOTTS, *The Learned* 1058

EMILY DICKINSON, [*My Life had stood—a Loaded Gun—*] 1058
BEN JONSON, *Epitaph on Elizabeth, L. H.* 1059

## *Exploring Contexts* 1061

### 21 READING POETRY IN CONTEXT 1061

JAMES A. EMANUEL, *Emmett Till* 1062
THOMAS HARDY, *Channel Firing* 1063
SANDRA GILBERT, *Sonnet: The Ladies' Home Journal* 1064

**TIMES, PLACES, AND EVENTS** 1067

MILLER WILLIAMS, *Thinking about Bill, Dead of AIDS* 1067
IRVING LAYTON, *From Colony to Nation* 1068
LANGSTON HUGHES, *Harlem* 1068
ROBERT HAYDEN, *Frederick Douglass* 1069
FELICIA DOROTHEA HEMANS, *Casabianca* 1069
[CD] ELIZABETH BISHOP, *Casabianca* 1070
[WEB] WILFRED OWEN, *Dulce et Decorum Est* 1071
DUDLEY RANDALL, *Ballad of Birmingham* 1072

**CONSTRUCTING IDENTITY, EXPLORING GENDER** 1073

ELIZABETH BISHOP, *Exchanging Hats* 1073
MARIE HOWE, *Practicing* 1074
RICHARD LOVELACE, *Song: To Lucasta, Going to the Wars* 1075
WILFRED OWEN, *Disabled* 1075
ROBERT BROWNING, *My Last Duchess* 1076
  *A Woman's Last Word* 1078
ELIZABETH BARRETT BROWNING, *To George Sand [A Desire]* 1079
  *To George Sand [A Recognition]* 1080
YUSEF KOMUNYAKAA, *Tu Do Street* 1080
LADY MARY WORTLEY MONTAGU, *Written the First Year I Was Marry'd* 1082
MARGE PIERCY, *What's That Smell in the Kitchen?* 1082
PAULETTE JILES, *Paper Matches* 1083
ELIZABETH I, *When I Was Fair and Young* 1083
MARILYN HACKER, [*Who would divorce her lover*] 1084
AMY LOWELL, *The Lonely Wife* 1085
LIZ ROSENBERG, *The Silence of Women* 1086
THOM GUNN, *A Blank* 1086

### 22 THE AUTHOR'S WORK AS CONTEXT: JOHN KEATS AND ADRIENNE RICH 1089

**KEATS** 1092

*On First Looking into Chapman's Homer* 1094
*On the Grasshopper and the Cricket* 1094
*On Seeing the Elgin Marbles* 1095

Sonnet to Sleep 1095
From *Endymion* (Book 1) 1096
Ode to a Nightingale 1097
Ode on a Grecian Urn 1099
WEB To Autumn 1100
Passages from Letters and the Preface to *Endymion*
  To Benjamin Bailey (Nov. 22, 1817) 1101
  To George and Thomas Keats (Dec. 21, 1817) 1102
  To John Hamilton Reynolds (Feb. 19, 1818) 1101
  To John Taylor (Feb. 27, 1818) 1105
  Preface to *Endymion* (dated April 10, 1818) 1106
CHRONOLOGY 1106

**RICH** 1107
At a Bach Concert 1109
Storm Warnings 1110
Living in Sin 1111
Snapshots of a Daughter-in-Law 1111
Planetarium 1115
For the Record 1117
[My mouth hovers across your breasts] 1118
History 1118
Modotti 1119
Personal Reflections 1120
  When We Dead Awaken: Writing as Re-Vision 1120
  How Does a Poet Put Bread on the Table? 1122
  A Communal Poetry 1123
  Why I Refused the National Medal for the Arts 1124
CHRONOLOGY 1128

## 23 LITERARY TRADITION AS CONTEXT 1131

**ECHO AND ALLUSION** 1132
  BEN JONSON, [Come, my Celia, let us prove] 1133
  WILLIAM BLAKE, The Lamb 1134
  HOWARD NEMEROV, Boom! 1134
  MARIANNE MOORE, Love in America? 1136
  ROBERT HOLLANDER, You Too? Me Too—Why Not? Soda Pop 1137
  WILLIAM SHAKESPEARE, [Not marble, nor the gilded monuments] 1138

**POETIC "KINDS"** 1138
  CD CHRISTOPHER MARLOWE, The Passionate Shepherd to His Love 1139

**HAIKU** 1140
  CHIYOJO, [Whether astringent] 1141
  BASHŌ, [A village without bells—] 1142
    [This road—] 1142

BUSON, [Coolness—] 1142
[Listening to the moon] 1143
SEIFŪ, [The faces of dolls] 1143
LAFCADIO HEARN, [Old pond—] 1143
CLARA A. WALSH, [An old-time pond] 1143
EARL MINER, [The still old pond] 1144
ALLEN GINSBERG, [The old pond] 1144
BABETTE DEUTSCH, [The falling flower] 1144
ETHERIDGE KNIGHT, [Eastern guard tower] 1144
ALLEN GINSBERG, [Looking over my shoulder] 1145
RICHARD WRIGHT, [In the falling snow] 1145
JAMES A. EMANUEL, Ray Charles 1145

**IMITATING AND ANSWERING** 1145
SIR WALTER RALEGH, [The Nymph's Reply to the Shepherd] 1146
WILLIAM CARLOS WILLIAMS, [Raleigh Was Right] 1147
ALLEN GINSBERG, A Further Proposal 1147
E. E. CUMMINGS, [(ponder, darling, these busted statues] 1148
KENNETH KOCH, Variations on a Theme by William Carlos Williams 1149
DESMOND SKIRROW, Ode on a Grecian Urn Summarized 1149
ANTHONY HECHT, The Dover Bitch 1150
WENDY COPE, [Not only marble, but the plastic toys] 1150

**CULTURAL BELIEF AND TRADITION** 1151
JOHN HOLLANDER, Adam's Task 1152
SUSAN DONNELLY, Eve Names the Animals 1153
MIRIAM WADDINGTON, Ulysses Embroidered 1154
ALFRED, LORD TENNYSON, The Kraken 1155
WEB PHILLIS WHEATLEY, On Being Brought from Africa to America 1155
JUNE JORDAN, Something Like a Sonnet for Phillis Miracle Wheatley 1156
CD MAYA ANGELOU, Africa 1156
CD DEREK WALCOTT, A Far Cry from Africa 1157
ALBERTO ALVARO RIOS, Advice to a First Cousin 1158
LOUISE ERDRICH, Jacklight 1159

## 24 CULTURAL AND HISTORICAL CONTEXTS: THE HARLEM RENAISSANCE 1162

ARNA BONTEMPS, A Black Man Talks of Reaping 1172
WEB COUNTEE CULLEN, Yet Do I Marvel 1172
Saturday's Child 1173
From the Dark Tower 1174
ANGELINA GRIMKE, The Black Finger 1174
Tenebris 1174
WEB LANGSTON HUGHES, The Weary Blues 1175
The Negro Speaks of Rivers 1176
I, Too 1177

HELENE JOHNSON, *Sonnet to a Negro in Harlem* 1177
CLAUDE MCKAY, *Harlem Shadows* 1178
   *If We Must Die* 1178
   *The Tropics in New York* 1179
   *The Harlem Dancer* 1179
   *The White House* 1179
JAMES WELDON JOHNSON, From the Preface to *The Book of American Negro Poetry* 1180
ALAIN LOCKE, From *The New Negro* 1183
RUDOLPH FISHER, *The Caucasian Storms Harlem* 1188
W. E. B. DU BOIS, *Two Novels* 1193
ZORA NEALE HURSTON, *How It Feels to Be Colored Me* 1194
LANGSTON HUGHES, From *The Big Sea* [*Harlem Literati*] 1197

## 25 CRITICAL CONTEXTS: A POETRY CASEBOOK 1203

SYLVIA PLATH, *Daddy* 1204
GEORGE STEINER, From *Dying Is an Art* 1208
IRVING HOWE, From *The Plath Celebration: A Partial Dissent* 1211
A. ALVAREZ, From *Sylvia Plath* 1212
JUDITH KROLL, From *Rituals of Exorcism: "Daddy"* 1214
MARY LYNN BROE, From *Protean Poetic* 1217
MARGARET HOMANS, From *A Feminine Tradition* 1220
PAMELA J. ANNAS, From *A Disturbance in Mirrors* 1221
STEVEN GOULD AXELROD, From *Jealous Gods* 1225

## Reading More Poetry 1234

WILLIAM BLAKE, *The Tyger* 1234
   *Holy Thursday* (1789) 1235
   *Holy Thursday* (1794) 1235
GWENDOLYN BROOKS, *To the Disapora* 1236
ROBERT BROWNING, *Porphyria's Lover* 1236
SAMUEL TAYLOR COLERIDGE, *Kubla Khan* 1238
[WEB] [CD] EMILY DICKINSON, [*Because I could not stop for Death—*] 1239
   [*I stepped from Plank to Plank*] 1240
   [*We do not play on Graves—*] 1240
   [*The Brain—is wider than the Sky—*] 1241
   [*She dealt her pretty words like Blades—*] 1241
JOHN DONNE, [*Death, be not proud*] 1241
   *The Sun Rising* 1242
   *Song* 1243
[WEB]   *A Valediction: Forbidding Mourning* 1244
PAUL LAURENCE DUNBAR, *Sympathy* 1245
   *We Wear the Mask* 1245
T. S. ELIOT, *Journey of the Magi* 1246

[CD] ROBERT FROST, *The Road Not Taken* 1247
    *Stopping by Woods on a Snowy Evening* 1248
ALLEN GINSBERG, *Velocity of Money* 1248
THOMAS GRAY, *Elegy Written in a Country Churchyard* 1249
ROBERT HAYDEN, *The Whipping* 1252
SEAMUS HEANEY, *Digging* 1253
    *Punishment* 1254
GERARD MANLEY HOPKINS, *God's Grandeur* 1255
    *The Windhover* 1256
GALWAY KINNELL, *Blackberry Eating* 1256
[CD] ROBERT LOWELL, *Skunk Hour* 1257
ANDREW MARVELL, *The Garden* 1258
SYLVIA PLATH, *Barren Woman* 1260
    *Black Rook in Rainy Weather* 1260
    *Lady Lazarus* 1261
EZRA POUND, *In a Station of the Metro* 1264
    *A Virginal* 1264
FRANCIS QUARLES, *On Change of Weathers* 1264
JOHN CROWE RANSOM, *Bells for John Whiteside's Daughter* 1265
THEODORE ROETHKE, *I Knew a Woman* 1265
    *The Waking* 1266
[CD] WALLACE STEVENS, *The Idea of Order at Key West* 1267
    *The Emperor of Ice-Cream* 1268
    *Anecdote of the Jar* 1269
    *Sunday Morning* 1269
ALFRED, LORD TENNYSON, *Now Sleeps the Crimson Petal* 1272
    *Tears, Idle Tears* 1273
    *Tithonus* 1273
[WEB]     *Ulysses* 1275
DYLAN THOMAS, *Fern Hill* 1277
WALT WHITMAN, *Facing West from California's Shores* 1278
    *I Hear America Singing* 1279
    *A Noiseless Patient Spider* 1279
[CD] RICHARD WILBUR, *Love Calls Us to the Things of This World* 1280
WILLIAM WORDSWORTH, *Lines Written a Few Miles above Tintern Abbey* 1281
C. K. WILLIAMS, *Alzheimer's: The Wife* 1284
[CD] W. B. YEATS, *The Lake Isle of Innisfree* 1285
    *All Things Can Tempt Me* 1285
    *Easter 1916* 1286
    *The Second Coming* 1288
    *Leda and the Swan* 1289
    *Sailing to Byzantium* 1289

Among School Children 1290
Byzantium 1292

**Biographical Sketches: Poets** 1294

# Drama

**Reading, Responding, Writing** 1312

> [WEB] SUSAN GLASPELL, *Trifles* 1314
> [WEB] TOM STOPPARD, *The Real Inspector Hound* 1326

**Understanding the Text** 1360

> **26 ELEMENTS OF DRAMA** 1360
> [CD] BERNARD SHAW, *Pygmalion* 1370
> AUGUST WILSON, *The Piano Lesson* 1441
> [WEB] MARGARET EDSON, *Wit* 1500
>
> **27 THE WHOLE TEXT** 1534
> TENNESSEE WILLIAMS, *A Streetcar Named Desire* 1539
> ANTON CHEKHOV, *The Cherry Orchard* 1604
> PAULA VOGEL, *How I Learned to Drive* 1642

**Exploring Contexts** 1683

> **28 THE AUTHOR'S WORK AS CONTEXT: WILLIAM SHAKESPEARE** 1683
> *A Midsummer Night's Dream* 1690
> [WEB] [CD] *Hamlet* 1743
>
> **29 LITERARY CONTEXT: TRAGEDY AND COMEDY** 1838
> SOPHOCLES, *Oedipus the King* 1840
> OSCAR WILDE, *The Importance of Being Earnest* 1879
>
> **30 CULTURAL AND HISTORICAL CONTEXT** 1923
> [WEB] LORRAINE HANSBERRY, *A Raisin in the Sun* 1942
> [WEB] WOLE SOYINKA, *Death and the King's Horseman* 2003
> RICHARD WRIGHT, From *Twelve Million Black Voices: A Folk History of the Negro in the United States* 2051
> EARL E. THORPE, From *Africa in the Thought of Negro Americans* 2054
> PHAON GOLDMAN, From *The Significance of African Freedom for the Negro American* 2057
> STOKELY CARMICHAEL AND CHARLES V. HAMILTON, From *Black Power: The Politics of Liberation in America* 2059
> ROBERT BLAUNER, From *Internal Colonialism and Ghetto Revolt* 2062
> HENRY JOHN DREWAL, JOHN PEMBERTON III, AND ROWLAND ABIODUN, From *Yoruba: Nine Centuries of African Art and Thought* 2065

31 **CRITICAL CONTEXTS: A DRAMA CASEBOOK** 2071
   [WEB] SOPHOCLES, *Antigone* 2074
      RICHARD C. JEBB, From *The Antigone of Sophocles* 2105
      MAURICE BOWRA, From *Sophoclean Tragedy* 2106
      BERNARD KNOX, Introduction to *Sophocles: The Three Theban Plays* 2108
      MARTHA C. NUSSBAUM, From *The Fragility of Goodness: Luck and Ethics in Greek Tragedy and Philosophy* 2113
      REBECCA W. BUSHNELL, From *Prophesying Tragedy: Sign and Voice in Sophocles' Theban Plays* 2117
      MARY WHITLOCK BLUNDELL, From *Helping Friends and Harming Enemies: A Study in Sophocles and Greek Ethics* 2118

## Reading More Drama 2121

   [WEB] ARTHUR MILLER, *Death of a Salesman* 2121
      HENRIK IBSEN, *A Doll House* 2186

## Biographical Sketches: Playwrights 2234

## Writing about Literature 2239

   32 **PARAPHRASE, SUMMARY, AND DESCRIPTION** 2239
   33 **THE ELEMENTS OF THE ESSAY** 2243
   34 **THE WRITING PROCESS** 2252
   35 **THE RESEARCH ESSAY** 2265
   36 **QUOTATION, CITATION, AND DOCUMENTATION** 2280
   37 **SAMPLE RESEARCH PAPER:** RICHARD GIBSON, "Keeping the Sabbath Separately: Emily Dickinson's Rebellious Faith" 2292

## Critical Approaches 2302

*Glossary* A1

*Permissions Acknowledgments* A9

*Index of Authors* A31

*Index of Titles and First Lines* A38

# Preface for Instructors

Over the past thirty years, *The Norton Introduction to Literature* has helped students learn to read and enjoy literature. This Ninth Edition—our most extensive revision to date—offers in a single volume a complete course in reading and writing about literature. We have thoroughly reshaped it as a teaching anthology focused on the actual tasks, challenges, and questions typically faced by college students and instructors. It offers practical advice to help students transform their first impressions of literary works into fruitful discussions and meaningful critical essays, and it helps students and instructors together tackle the more complex questions at the heart of literary study. We have revised *The Norton Introduction to Literature* with an eye to providing a book that is as flexible and useful as possible—serving many different teaching styles and individual preferences—and that also conveys the excitement at the heart of literature itself.

## Features of *The Norton Introduction to Literature*

*The Norton Introduction to Literature* has been a classroom favorite for over thirty years, and although this Ninth Edition contains much that is new or refashioned, the essential features of the text have remained consistent over many editions:

### Diverse selections with broad appeal

As in the classroom, the readings remain at the heart of all we do, so we have given high priority to selecting a rich array of representative literary works. Among the 67 stories, 383 poems, and 18 plays in *The Norton Introduction to Literature*, readers will find selections by well-established and emerging voices alike, representing a wide variety of times, places, cultural perspectives, and styles. The readings are excitingly diverse in terms of subject and style as well as authorship and national origin. In selecting and presenting literary texts, our top priority continues to be quality and pedagogical relevance and usefulness. To enhance the latter, and to avoid any form of literary segregation, we have integrated the new with the old and the experimental with the canonical. In this way, we aim to help students and teachers alike approach the unfamiliar by way of the familiar (and vice versa).

### Helpful and unobtrusive editorial matter

As always, the editorial material before and after the selections avoids dictating any interpretation or response, but instead highlights essential terms and concepts while providing students with a way into the literature that follows. Questions and writing suggestions—all of which are new or substantially rewritten in the Ninth Edition—help readers apply general concepts to specific readings in order to develop, articulate, and debate their own responses. We have annotated the works, as in all Norton anthologies, with a light hand, seeking to be informative but not interpretive.

## *An introduction to the study of literature*

To introduce students to fiction, poetry, and drama is to open up a complex field of study with a long history. The expanded Introduction addresses many of the questions students may have about this field, concerning not only the nature of literature but also the practice of criticism. By exploring answers to the question "What do we do with literature?" we clear away some of the mystery about matters of method and approach, and we provide motivated students with a sense of the issues and opportunities that lie ahead if they continue their study of literature. A thoroughly revamped "Critical Approaches" chapter provides an overview of contemporary critical theory and its terminology and is useful as an introduction, a refresher, or a preparation for further study.

## *Helpful guidance for writing about literature*

A new "Writing about Literature" section offers detailed and comprehensive guidance on how to write an essay about literature. As in the book's other sections, the first steps are easy, outlining an essay's basic formal elements—thesis, structure, and so on. Following these steps encourages students to approach the essay both as a distinctive genre with its own specifications and as an accessible form of writing with a clear purpose. From here, we walk students step-by-step through the writing process—how to choose a topic, gather evidence, and develop an argument; we detail the methods of writing a research essay; and we explain the mechanics of effective quotation and responsible citation and documentation. Finally, we include a new sample research paper—annotated by the editors to call attention to important features of good student writing.

## *A comprehensive approach to the contexts of literature*

The Ninth Edition not only offers expanded resources for interpreting and writing about literature, but also extends the perspectives from which students can view particular authors and works. One of the great strengths of *The Norton Introduction to Literature* has been its exploration of the relation between literary texts and a variety of contexts. For several editions, "Author's Work" and "Critical Contexts" chapters have served as mini-casebooks containing all the materials necessary for exciting context-focused reading and writing assignments. The Eighth Edition introduced a "Historical and Cultural Context" chapter—a lively study of F. Scott Fitzgerald and the Jazz Age—that works on the same principle. In the Ninth Edition, we add equally illuminating chapters on the poetry of the Harlem Renaissance and on plays by Lorraine Hansberry and Wole Soyinka.

## *A sensible and teachable organization*

We have chosen to preserve the traditional format of *The Norton Introduction to Literature*, which has worked well for teachers and students for many editions. Each genre is approached in three logical steps. Fiction, for example, is introduced by *Fiction: Reading, Responding, Writing*, which treats the purpose and nature of fiction, the reading experience, and the steps one takes to begin writing about fiction. This is followed by the seven-chapter section called *Understanding the Text*, which concentrates one-by-one on each of the genre's key elements. Next, "The Whole Text" chapter reviews the analytical aids presented in the previous chapters and suggests how to use them to form an interpretation. The third section, *Exploring Contexts*, suggests ways to embrace a work of literature by considering various literary, temporal, and cultural contexts. *Reading More*, the final component in the Fiction section, as in Poetry and Drama, is a reservoir of additional readings for independent study or a different approach.

The book's arrangement allows movement from narrower to broader frameworks, from simpler to more complex questions and issues, mirroring the way people read—wanting to learn more as they experience more. At the same time, no chapter or section depends on any other, so that individual teachers can pick and choose which chapters or sections to tackle and in what order.

# New to the Ninth Edition

## *Fifty-nine new selections*

Of the 67 stories, 383 poems, and 18 plays in *The Norton Introduction to Literature*, 13 stories, 42 poems, and 4 plays are new to this edition. You will find new selections from established and respected writers such as Margaret Atwood, A. S. Byatt, Peter Carey, Countee Cullen, Seamus Heaney, Claude McKay, Toni Morrison, Christina Rossetti, Wole Soyinka, Tom Stoppard, Henry James, Edith Wharton, and Oscar Wilde and from emerging writers such as Sherman Alexie, Andrea Barrett, Michael Chabon, Edwidge Danticat, Margaret Edson, Andrew Hudgins, Pat Mora, and Olive Senior.

## *Two new contextual chapters*

Building on the success and popularity of the chapter on Fitzgerald's "Babylon Revisited" that was added to the Eighth Edition, the Ninth Edition includes two new contextual chapters devoted to culture and history.

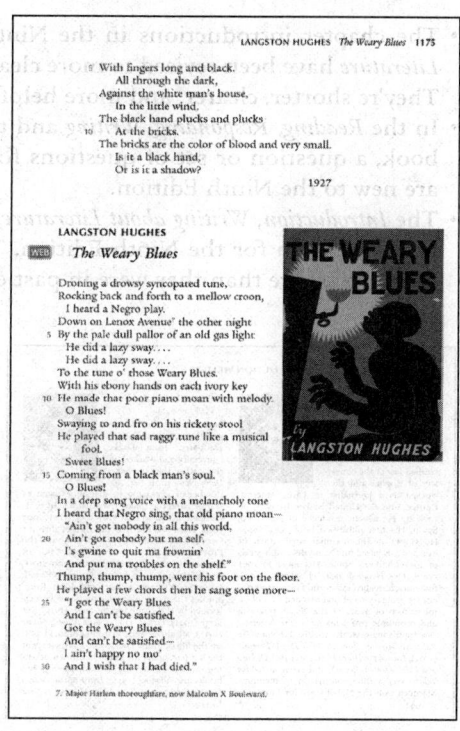

*The Harlem Renaissance:* In the Poetry section, a chapter on the Harlem Renaissance provides not only a compact and teachable selection of some of the best-known poems from this exciting American literary movement, but also prose pieces by Langston Hughes, James Weldon Johnson, Alain Locke, Rudolph Fisher, and Zora Neale Hurston and visual materials to spark student interest and understanding.

*Loraine Hansberry's* A Raisin in the Sun *and Wole Soyinka's* Death and the King's Horseman: This chapter in the Drama section explores the value of reading individual plays within their cultural context and suggests one way of making connections between works when researching cultural and historical context. In addition to the plays, the chapter includes visual resources and nonfiction pieces by Richard Wright, Earl E. Thorpe, Phaon Goldman, Stokely Carmichael, and others.

## Completely Revised Pedagogy

- The chapter introductions in the Ninth Edition of *The Norton Introduction to Literature* have been revised to more clearly introduce major terms and concepts. They're shorter, clearer, and more helpful in this edition.
- In the *Reading, Responding, Writing* and the *Understanding the Text* sections of the book, a question or set of questions follows each piece. All of these questions are new to the Ninth Edition.
- The *Introduction, Writing about Literature,* and *Critical Approaches* sections have all been rewritten for the Ninth Edition. The latter two are now more useful for quick reference than they were in past editions.

 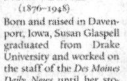 

- To encourage students to use the media that accompanies *The Norton Introduction to Literature*, the Ninth Edition places icons next to the titles of literary works that are featured on the two-CD Audio Companion or on *LitWeb*, the online companion to the anthology.
- Biographical information about the authors whose work is included in the anthology is now gathered at the end of each genre section, and almost all biographical sketches are accompanied by a portrait of the author.

## Accompanying Media

### Free Audio Companion

Because almost all reading experiences can be enhanced by an accompanying listening experience, every new copy of *The Norton Introduction to Literature* comes with two audio CDs that present readings of 28 poems, 4 short stories, and selections from 3 plays. Highlights include Garrison Keillor reading poems by Christopher Marlowe and Emily Dickinson, Lynn Redgrave and Michael Redgrave in a scene from *Pygmalion*, Lee J. Cobb as Willy Loman in *Death of a Salesman*, as well as many authors reading their own works. A complete listing of the tracks on these audio CDs can be found inside the front cover.

### LITWEB *(wwnorton.com/litweb)*

This online companion to *The Norton Introduction to Literature* encourages students to think through their responses to literature in three stages: articulating a personal response, rereading creatively and analytically, and researching contextual and scholarly resources on the Web in order to enrich their own interpretive work. LitWeb's features include:

- **In-Depth Literary Workshops.** Featuring 50 works from the text, these workshops guide students through the reading, rereading, and contextual exploration of a work. Author biographies and a set of related links are included.
- **Online Glossary and Glossary Flashcards.** These flashcards allow students to test and reinforce their knowledge of over 200 literary terms.
- *Writing about Literature*. This substantial section from *The Norton Introduction to Literature* is included online in its entirety.
- Self-Grading **Multiple-Choice Quizzes** on the elements of literature.
- Access to **Norton Poets Online** (*nortonpoets.com*), which features interviews with over 60 contemporary poets, dozens of audio recordings of poets reading their work, essays, online poetry workshops, and an e-mail newsletter.

### Norton Literature Online

In addition to the book-specific resources available in *LitWeb*, every new copy of *The Norton Introduction to Literature* provides students with *free* access to *Norton Literature Online*, the gateway to all Norton's outstanding online literary resources. You can find more information about *Norton Literature Online* inside the back cover of this book.

## Instructor's Resources

### Instructor's Manual

Revised by Barbara Bird and Linda Yakle, both of St. Petersburg College, this thorough guide offers in-depth discussions of nearly all the works in the anthology as well as teaching suggestions and tips for the writing intensive literature course.

*Teaching Poetry: A Handbook of Exercises for Large and Small Classes (Allan J. Gedalof, University of Western Ontario)*

This practical handbook offers a wide variety of innovative in-class exercises to enliven classroom discussion of poetry. Each of these flexible teaching exercises includes straightforward, step-by-step guidelines and suggestions for variation.

*Norton Resource Library (wwnorton.com/nrl)*

The Norton Resource Library offers teachers an online source of instructional content for use in conventional classrooms, course management systems, or distance education environments.

To obtain any of these instructional resources, please contact your local Norton representative.

---

In all our work on this edition, we have been guided by teachers in other English departments and in our own, by students who used the textbook and wrote to us with comments and suggestions, and by students in our own classes. We hope that with such capable help we have been able to offer you a solid and stimulating introduction to the experience of literature.

# Acknowledgments

Our collaboration on this book continually reminds us of why we follow the vocation of teaching literature, which after all is a communal rather than solitary calling. Our own teachers and students as well as our colleagues have shown us how to join private responses to literature with shared learning and interpretation, both in discussion and in writing. We are grateful for the chance to refresh our appreciation of literature with the new as well as the longstanding selections in this book.

We have many people to thank as this edition reaches publication. Of our colleagues and students, we would like to offer special thanks to Gordon Braden and Victor Luftig for opportunities to teach high school English teachers; to Cindy Wall for being an inspirational colleague who also teaches from this text; to Megan Becker-Leckrone, Joseph Clark, Lotta Lofgren, Chip Tucker, Karen Chase, and John O'Brien for help with sources, both literary and pedagogical; to Ellen Malenas, Jill Rappaport, and Chloe Wigston Smith for their expertise as a teaching team in "Introduction to the Major"; and to Richard Gibson for allowing us to reprint his research essay.

*The Norton Introduction to Literature* continues to thrive because teachers and students who use it take the time to provide us with valuable feedback and suggestions for improvement. We thank all of you who do so, and especially the following, whose written comments on the Eighth Edition helped us plan the Ninth: Matt Babcock, Brigham Young University–Idaho; Mary Bayer, Grand Rapids Community College; Brad Bowers, Barry University; Paul Bruss, Eastern Michigan University; Donna Campbell, Gonzaga University; Deany M. Cheramie,

Xavier University; Dean Cooledge, University of Maryland—Eastern Shore; Frances Secco Davidson, Mercer County Community College; Harry Eiss, Eastern Michigan University; Stephen George, Brigham Young University—Idaho; Jerry Gilbert, Jackson State Community College; Atalissa S. Gilfoyle, J. Sargeant Reynolds Community College; Brian Glover, University of Virginia; Kendall Grant, Brigham Young University—Idaho; Anne C. Halligan, Broome Community College; Jack Harrell, Brigham Young University—Idaho; Peter Hawkes, East Stroudsburg University; Rose Hawkins, Community College of Southern Nevada; Pat Heintzelman, Lamar University; Anne Hendricks, Brigham Young University—Idaho; Cynthia Ho, University of North Carolina—Asheville; Caroline Hunt, College of Charleston; Charles Jimenez, Hillsborough Community College; Linda Karch, Norwich University; Alan Kelly, Millersville University; Mary Ann Klein, Quincy University; Dennis P. Kriewald, Laredo Community College; Shawn Liang, Mohawk Valley Community College; David Lipton, Long Beach City College; Nicholas Mason, Brigham Young University; Arch Mayfield, Wayland University; Michael McKeon, Rutgers University; Michael Minassian, Broward Community College; David Mulry, Longview Community College (Odessa); Nancy Nahra, Champlain College; Kelly Owen, College of Charleston; David Paddy, Whittier College; Daniel G. Payne, State University of New York, Oneonta; Velvet Pearson, Long Beach City College; Robert Peltier, Trinity College; Jahan Ramazani, University of Virginia; Catherine Rodriguez, University of Virginia; Phillip A. Snyder, Brigham Young University; Paula Soper, Brigham Young University—Idaho; Darlene Sybert, University of Missouri; Craig Warren, University of Virginia; Sarah Watson, East Texas Baptist University; Sharon Wynkoop, Grand Rapids Community College; and David Zimmerman, Montgomery College.

*The Norton
Introduction to Literature*

NINTH EDITION

# Introduction

## Why Literature Matters

In the opening chapters of Charles Dickens's novel *Hard Times* (1854), the Utilitarian politician Thomas Gradgrind warns the teachers and pupils at his "model" school to avoid using their imaginations. "Teach these boys and girls nothing but Facts. Facts alone are wanted in life," exclaims Mr. Gradgrind to the schoolmaster, Mr. M'Choakumchild. To press his point, Mr. Gradgrind asks "girl number twenty," Sissy Jupe, whose father performs in the circus, to define a horse. When she cannot, Gradgrind turns to Bitzer, a pale, lifeless boy who "looked as though, if he were cut, he would bleed white." A "model" student of this "model" school, Bitzer gives exactly the kind of definition to satisfy Mr. Gradgrind:

> "Quadruped. Graminivorous. Forty teeth, namely, twenty-four grinders, four eye-teeth, and twelve incisive. Sheds coat in spring; in marshy countries, sheds hoofs."

Anyone who has any sense of what a horse is rebels against Bitzer's lifeless version of that animal and against the "Gradgrind" view of reality. Like The Grinch Who Stole Christmas, or like Dickens's own Ebenezer Scrooge in *A Christmas Carol*, Gradgrind wants to kill the irrational spirit; he wants to deal only with material things that can be bought and sold and with qualities that can be measured and counted. As these first scenes of *Hard Times* lead us to expect, in the course of the novel the fact-grinding Mr. Gradgrind learns that human beings cannot live on facts alone; that it is dangerous to stunt the faculties of imagination and feeling; that, in the words of one of the novel's more lovable characters, "People must be amused." Through the downfall of an exaggerated enemy of imagination, Dickens reminds us why we like and even *need* to read literature.

Over the ages, people like Gradgrind have dismissed literature as a luxury, a frivolous pastime, or even a sinful indulgence. Pretending to agree with the Gradgrinds of the world, Oscar Wilde asserted that "all art is quite useless"; but by this Wilde was suggesting that beauty and pleasure are the sole aims of the arts, including imaginative literature. Others (including Dickens himself) have argued for a kind of middle ground between the positions of a Gradgrind and a Wilde, insisting that literature should and does instruct as well as entertain.

> *Writing is not literature unless it gives to the reader a pleasure which arises not only from the things said, but from the way in which they are said.*
> —STOPFORD BROOKE

Wonderfully, instruction and delight often go hand in hand in our experience of literature: we learn from what delights us or what leads us to appreciate new kinds of delight. The pleasure of reading comes in many varieties, however, and sometimes the best pleasures require an effort that beginners tend to call pain. A lot of the writing that is called *literature* is at first difficult for any reader to grasp. But if we read literature only for pleasure, why would we bother with any piece of writing that requires such effort? One answer is that new kinds of pleasure open up through that effort. As we challenge ourselves to read more difficult literature, we become able to extend ourselves further, much like athletes who train for heavier weights or longer jumps with repeated practice.

Another answer came from Wilde himself, for whom literature is of supreme importance precisely because it frees us from the utilitarian preoccupations and activities of daily life. We value literature (all art, really) for breaking the rules of the ordinary. In some kinds of written entertainment, we find immediate "escape," but even imaginative writing that is more difficult to read and understand than a John Grisham or Patricia Cornwell novel offers escape of a sort: it takes us beyond familiar ways of thinking. A realistic story, poem, or play can satisfy a desire for broader experience, even unpleasant experience; we can learn what it might be like to grow up on a Canadian fox farm, for example, or to clean ashtrays in the Singapore airport. We yearn for such knowledge in a very personal way, as though we can know our own identities and experiences only by leaping over the boundaries that usually separate us from other selves and worlds. As even Wilde might have conceded, literature seems extremely *useful* in this respect.

Ultimately, it is impossible to separate knowledge from imagination or instruction from pleasure. For many ages, different peoples have affirmed that while imaginative writing may be like playing, such play is the closest we come to grappling with the complexity of life. Perhaps nothing is more important; perhaps literature is the very thing humanity can least afford to do without. Literature itself provides many examples of characters or even real people who gain a feeling of mastery, meaning, and purpose through learning to read and to write. Take a famous episode in *The Autobiography of Malcolm X* (1964). Malcolm X, in prison, with only an eighth-grade education, realizes he needs to learn standard written and spoken English if he is to succeed as a leader. He begins by copying every word in the dictionary and soon moves to absorbing the books on history and religion in the prison's extensive library. What were the fruits of this labor? "I had never been so truly free in my life. . . . [A] new world opened to me, of being able to read and *understand*." Literacy and a wide knowledge of literature of various kinds can be a sort of franchise, like the vote, and can launch a career.

> *Literature is the human activity that takes the fullest and most precise account of variousness, possibility, complexity, and difficulty.*
> —LIONEL TRILLING

You may already feel the power and pleasure to be gained from a sustained encounter with challenging reading. Then why not simply enjoy it in solitude, on your own free time? Because reading is only one of the activities involved in gaining a full understanding of literature. Literature has a history, and learning that history makes all the difference in the pleasure you can derive from literature. By studying different kinds of literature, or **genres**, as well as different works from various times in history and from various national traditions—by becoming familiar with the conventions of writing a sonnet in seventeenth-century England or of writing a short story in 1920s America—you can come to appreciate and even love works that you might have disliked if you simply read them on your own. Discussing works with your teachers and other students, and writing about them, will give you practice in analyzing them in greater depth. A clear understanding of the aims and designs of a story, poem, or play never falls like a bolt from the blue. Instead, it emerges from a process that often involves comparing this work with other works of its genre, trying to put into words *how* and *why* this work had such an effect on you, and responding to what others say or write about it.

Yet studying literature involves more than cultivating your own skills and insights. Reading can open worlds and change a person's life, but literature also has the potential for political effects. The international best-seller *Uncle Tom's Cabin* (1852), for example, helped create such strong antislavery sentiments before the U.S. Civil War that Abraham Lincoln reportedly described its author, Harriet Beecher Stowe, as "the little lady who started the big war." The personal and the political effects of literature intertwine. A sense of self and an identity as part of a group or a nationality are shaped and reinforced by respected traditions, and many groups and nations now try to recover and protect their own literary traditions rather than be misrepresented by the writings of others. Margaret Atwood has claimed that when Canadian literature was ignored, for instance, Canada itself seemed to have forgotten its identity. Since the 1970s, Canada and many other former colonies of European countries have recovered and developed thriving literatures of their own. Instead of one **canon**—or a single selective list of the most-recognized or most-esteemed works—there are now many canons of literature written in English.

> When other people tell your story, it always comes out crooked.
> —CHIPPEWA ELDER

## "The Canon"

As you begin your college-level study of literature, a debate rages all around you about "the canon." Although this debate has many dimensions, it is often reduced to questions about which authors should be included in literature courses and anthologies: why Dryden and Pope but not Aphra Behn; why Ralph Ellison and not Zora Neale Hurston; why Joseph Conrad or Doris Lessing and not V. S. Naipaul or Bessie Head? *Whom* we publish and teach matters, because our choices convey certain messages about the many kinds of people who have made an art of writing. There are many more people who have expressed themselves in writing than you will be able to read in your lifetime, let alone your college career or this semester. Any anthology, any literature course, leaves out far more than it includes. The anthology you hold in your hands represents a diverse array of authors both ancient and modern, but it does not treat an assortment of types of authors as an end in itself. The works included here are *good*—each after its kind is a splendid creation—but of course such a judgment of quality requires some supporting evidence. As you read, you can gather the most telling evidence, identify your own standards for judging texts, define your own approaches to interpreting them, and finally decide for yourself whether these works belong in the book or in your personal "canon."

Debates about the canon and about whom we should include on the list of literary "greats" won't end soon, largely because such arguments are part of a discussion as old as literature itself. And even the notion of "literature" has had an interesting history.

## What Is Literature?

Before you opened this book, you probably could guess that it would contain the sorts of stories, poems, and plays you have encountered in English classes or in the literature section of a library or bookstore. The three genres of imaginative writing that we select for *The Norton Introduction to Literature* form the heart of literature as it has been defined in schools and universities for over a century. The *Oxford English Dictionary (OED)* defines literature as "writing which has claim to consideration on the ground of beauty of form or emotional effect." The key elements in this definition may be *writing*—after all, the words *literature* and *letters* have roots in common—and *beauty* and *emotion*. But we sometimes use the word *literature* to refer to writing that has little to do with feelings or artful form, as in "scientific literature"—the articles on a particular subject—or "campaign literature." And at least some of the nonfictional works studied in literature classrooms—Martin Luther King Jr.'s "Letter from Birmingham Jail," for example—were originally intended as "campaign literature" of one sort or another.

> *Literature is not things but a way to comprehend things.*
> —NORMAN N. HOLLAND

Could literature, then, include *anything* written? Or could it include works that do not depend on written words, such as staged performances or works recorded on media such as videotape or film? Every society has forms of oral storytelling or poetry, and some peoples do not write down the cherished myths and traditions that are their "literature." If you go on to take more classes in literature or to major in English or another language, you might encounter texts that stretch the concept of literature still further: Web sites or electronic games, for example.

The concept of "literature" as we know it is fairly new. Two hundred years ago, before universities were open to women or people of color, a small male elite studied the ancient classics in Greek and Latin, never dreaming of taking college courses about poetry or fiction or drama written in the modern languages in everyday use. Before modern literature became part of the college curriculum, the word *literature* itself had to be invented. At first, it referred to the cultivation of reading or the practice of writing ("he was a man of much literature"). Only later did it refer to a specialized category of works. Over time, this category narrowed more and more, eventually designating only a special set of imaginative writings, particularly associated with a language and nation (as in "English," "American," or "French" literature). Roughly speaking, by 1900 a college student could take a course in English literature, and the syllabus would exclude most nonfictional forms of writing, from travel writing and journalism to biography, history, or philosophy. Although students at the time would have read widely in these genres of nonfiction, the curriculum in "English literature" had become a walled-in flower garden filled with works of beauty, pleasure, and imagination, and its walls held fast for most of the twentieth century.

> *National literature is now rather an unmeaning term; the epoch of world literature is at hand, and everyone must strive to hasten its approach.*
> —J. W. GOETHE

But now, as you begin this introduction to literature in the twenty-first century, the walls of that garden are coming down. Literature today generally encompasses oral and even visual forms (film and video being closely related to drama, of course), and it takes in, as it did long ago, writings of diverse design and purpose, including nonfiction. As a twenty-first-century student of literature, you may feel the pleasure of reading the best imaginative writings of the past, hoping with the speaker of Keats's "Ode on Melancholy" to "burst Joy's grape against" your "palate fine"—to test your palate or taste for the beauty of language and form. Obviously, the garden reserved for beautiful poetry, fiction, and drama is flourishing; this anthology is testament to its continued health. But the fields beyond the unwalled garden are wild and inviting as well.

Since there has never been absolute, lasting agreement about *what* counts as literature, we might consider instead *how* and *why* we look at particular forms of expression. A song lyric, a screenplay, a supermarket romance, a novel by Toni Morrison or Thomas Mann, and a poem by Walt Whitman or Katherine Philips— each may be interpreted in *literary ways* that yield insights and pleasures. Honing your skills at this kind of interpretation is the primary purpose of this book and most literature courses. By learning to recognize how a story, poem, or play works—not only how it is beautiful and pleasurable but also how it is *effective*— you should gain interpretative skills that you can take with you when you explore zones outside the garden of literature.

## *Thinking Critically about Literature*

From the start of your first encounter with a literary work, you begin the process of **literary criticism** as you formulate questions about the mode (*is this fiction? is it a novel?*), the manner (*who is the narrator? is the style modern, funny?*), and the aims of the text (*is it satiric? is the reader supposed to sympathize with the main character?*). To read the text well, you need to pick up on signals about the way the text is formed, and almost as soon as you have noticed these signals, you begin to explain what they might mean. Your critical reading of a work could start with a simple catalog of its **elements:** you could name the **characters;** retell the **action;** identify the **meter** and **rhyme scheme.** By writing these observations down, you might find new details to observe in the process. Your reading and writing about a work could advance a step further with the help of literary terms, such as **stanza, narrator, metaphor,** because these terms conveniently and quickly identify specific effects and help to connect them to similar techniques or features of other works. A good reader quickly moves from noticing details of a work to interpreting the significance of the way elements are combined in this particular work. A practiced reader, further, compares this work to others, recognizing the characteristics of, say, realist novels or lyrics about love, and noting how this particular example distinguishes itself from others of its genre. Whenever you read, you make crucial assessments of this sort, perhaps even subconsciously.

If you have made a good mental picture of the work and noted your detailed observations, you have laid the foundation of good critical reading and writing. Yet a description of details is not enough for an essay of literary criticism. As a student in a course on literature, you will be discussing works of literature with your class and writing interpretations of these works, to be read by classmates, your instructor, perhaps a parent or friend. Remember that *your* reader will want to learn something from your essay that is not in plain view on a first reading of the literary work. Criticism, in other words, becomes worthwhile when it expresses something unexpected or debatable about a work. This does not mean that good criticism consists of an extreme interpretation based on your own personal feelings. To be persuasive, your critical writing needs to support your impressions with the sort of evidence—such as the details that you have noted in preparation— that will convince others to share your impressions. You will need to argue a case for your interpretation; often the heart of your argument is that the specific evidence you have put forward is a key to a better understanding of the work. Both discussion and writing will help you become a better reader and literary critic in this way. Very often, you will make the text itself seem all the richer and more complex in the process of showing others how it works: its design and the meanings of its effects. Before you venture into this new territory of making your thoughts about works of literature known to your peers and your teacher, however, it might help to review what it means to approach literature from a critical and analytical perspective.

Methods of literary interpretation, like definitions of literature, have varied over time. We may be amused or amazed at the assumptions that guided literary studies in an earlier age, but we should beware of assuming that our own approach is natural, correct, or inevitable. It is good to remember, for instance, that in the early 1800s, many people decried the seductive dangers of novel-reading, especially for young girls. The warnings back then resemble those we hear now about television, video games, and the Internet. Perhaps your children will live in a time when the digital media of the early twenty-first century receives the kind of careful interpretation and appreciation that we grant to novels today.

> *Literature is language charged with meaning. . . . Literature is news that stays news.*
> —EZRA POUND

Every reader has a theory about literature and how to interpret it, whether articulated or not. Over a century ago, an American professor of English, C. T. Winchester, argued in *Some Principles of Literary Criticism* (1902) that "Literary Criticism" should "determine the essential or intrinsic virtues of literature" and measure each work according to those standards. To Winchester, the student's or critic's task is aesthetic "appreciation" of works that have gained "permanence" because of their "appeal to the emotions"; historical or biographical concerns should be kept subordinate to aesthetic judgment. Winchester's plan looked natural or normal in his day, but today it seems unduly limiting. In the late twentieth century, literary scholars questioned nearly every one of Winchester's (and his generation's) underlying assumptions. These more recent scholars called into question the power of language to refer to reality or to express shared values or feelings, the notion that the author consciously intends all or even most of the meanings that can be found in a work, and the near-sacred status that literature had enjoyed for centuries. In the "Critical Approaches" appendix, we provide sketches of some contemporary theories and methods that encourage various ways of seeing literature and culture generally. Knowing a little about these "schools" of literary criticism or theory may help you to recognize and refine your own critical assumptions and methods, and may save you steps in clarifying your views.

Do you need to know anything specialized about literary criticism as you begin to learn how to interpret and write about literature? Your manner of literary criticism rightly will differ from that of a professional literary critic or theorist, as much as the lab work of a student in biology or chemistry differs from the research conducted by the authors of articles in *Science* or *Nature*. Yet just as the student in a lab should be engaged in hands-on discovery, and sometimes has an opportunity to contribute to a published finding, you will be able to develop original and interesting responses to what you read. To offer another metaphor that is even more appropriate to the arts (which have often been called nourishment for the spirit): most of us have thought a great deal about food, yet few of us are farmers, chefs, or restaurant critics. Dining offers greater pleasure, though, when we know the kinds of ingredients that went into each dish, how it has been prepared, and whether the plate before us presents a good example of gumbo or bouillabaisse.

Often students and even teachers of literature object to systems or theories of literary criticism. Too much information about the writer, the work, or the contexts surrounding them, or too many technical terms, can interfere with an original response. Many students wonder not only about the uses of a systematic critical theory, but also about the aims of thorough interpretation or close reading. Why subject the poor text to such probing and questioning? Did the author ever really intend such deep paradoxes or heavy symbolism? Why not content ourselves with our private, unspoiled impressions, and let the text go about its business?

The problem with this understandable wish for an innocent reading and a pure text is that neither of these exist. Three entities must unite in order to produce any act of reading and interpretation: the source of the text (the **author** and other factors that produce it); the **text** itself; and the receiver of the text (the **reader** and other aspects of reception). Your reading and interpretation will be enhanced if you take each of these components into consideration. The most important thing to realize is that each of these three factors, involving real people and their roles or positions, is surrounded by a **historical context**—by external events, cultural and personal values and beliefs, as well as economic constraints and opportunities—that has partly shaped it.

To illustrate the importance of historical context, let's begin by looking at the person with whom you are most familiar: *you*. You undoubtedly sense your uniqueness, and may even see that your uniqueness is determined in part by your beliefs and values as well as by your personal history. But you may not perceive those beliefs, values, and history as having been shaped in turn by many external forces beyond your own or your friends' and family's control. Now and then you may have wondered about the effects of such forces or have been frustrated by the limits they place on you. (Have you ever wished you were born in a different century, or as a different type of person?) At times, you have probably realized that your perceptions of the world depend on who you are—and that someone figuratively standing in a different place would see things from a different point of view.

Nevertheless, it is difficult to maintain this sort of perspective on ourselves and what influences our responses. As a reader, for example, you may feel that you are just reading a poem neutrally, the way you might read a newspaper report about weather on the other side of the world. In any kind of reading, however, you apply your experience with reading similar texts, drawing on your fluency in the language, your ability to read this and other kinds of texts, as well as the information and assumptions that you have been accumulating since birth. You carry the baggage of someone alive today with your particular cultural and family history, and you have particular skills and preconceptions that frame your reading.

Just as you are a unique reader, the story, play, or poem that you read imports its own historical context, and so it actually changes more or less over time. The sequence of words may remain almost identical, from the author's original manuscript to the original published form to the pages of this anthology (although textual scholars would emphasize how much variation there may be between editions). But words in them-

*Literature is the one place in any society where, within the secrecy of our own heads, we can hear voices talking about everything in every possible way.*

—SALMAN RUSHDIE

selves don't create meaning. Think of the puzzlement created by Egyptian hieroglyphs until the Rosetta Stone, found in 1799, provided clues to enable the work of translation. The signs carved in the second century B.C.E. had lost their power to convey meaning until scholars in the 1920s recreated the key, but even then, modern readers could only guess at the nature of the ancient beliefs and practices to which the signs originally referred. Each time we read a text, we become to some extent archeologists or linguists, unearthing and re-creating a sequence of letters, spaces, punctuation marks that has been lying dormant. Most of the literature reprinted here reflects the literary practices and fashions of our own era, yet historical change can be significant over even a few decades, or across different social groups and cultures. When you read, you should be aware of when the work was written and published, since knowing this can help prevent misinterpretations of everything from words that have changed meanings to whether the style was innovative or old-fashioned when the work first came out. Placing a text in its historical and social context can be a rewarding critical method, as suggested by our chapters on Fitzgerald's "Babylon Revisited" (chapter 11), on the poetry of the Harlem Renaissance (chapter 24), and on Lorraine Hansberry's *Raisin in the Sun* and Wole Soyinka's *Death and the King's Horseman* (chapter 30).

If both the reader and the text belong in historical contexts that shape our interpretation, so too does the writer. Contextual issues relating to the author usually concern the career—other works by the same person, relative success and reputation—and what is known about the life. When you read a work in this anthology, the writer's name (or "Anonymous") should be what you notice right after the title. Combined with the publication date, this can provide keys to your reading. The Biographical Sketches following each genre give brief biographies for most of the writers, and you can easily find more information in reference works online or in print, such as *The Dictionary of Literary Biography*. Your instructors may encourage you to read several works by the same author and to learn about the writer's life. Our chapters on Flannery O'Connor, D. H. Lawrence, John Keats, and Adrienne Rich emphasize the benefits of situating stories or poems in the context of other works by the same writer, and of such biographical evidence as letters. Knowing something about the person who wrote the work inevitably shapes interpretation, just as the writer's life was shaped by historical, social, and cultural conditions. Imagine Phillis Wheatley, who had been enslaved as a child in Africa and brought to Boston in 1761, finding time after her housework to write **heroic couplets** with the quill of a bird dipped in homemade ink, by the light of a candle made of animal fat, on paper so expensive that people seldom threw out a "rough draft." Her poetry was of her time, but it was viewed as a curiosity: the first published writing by an African American woman. Most readings of literature draw upon such information about the author's historical context and biography. Yet we cannot return to Boston in the 1770s and interview Wheatley to ask her what she meant in any line of her poetry.

*Literature always anticipates life. It does not copy it, but molds it to its purpose.*
—OSCAR WILDE

Even when a poet or playwright or fiction writer is still alive, it can be misleading to take his or her word about what the work means. Though critics usually do consider what is known about the writer, they prefer to focus on the text itself rather than the creator's statements about what it means. This is precisely because literary works usually intertwine more implications than anyone could consciously intend, and hence remain open to the varied interpretation of others. Further, critics avoid identifying the actual author with the **speaker** of a poem, the **characters** in a play, or the **narrator** of a fictional story. Even very personal or autobiographical writing is an utterance that has been removed from its source, the real person who might write contradictory things in different moods, or would speak differently when just chatting with a friend. Critics have developed the concept of the **implied author,** the designing personality or value system that guides us in this particular text, in order not to confuse the interpretation with too much concern for the biography and intentions of the real author. The implied author will often seem to ask a reader to stand at a distance from the viewpoint of a narrator or speaker: the blandly decent lawyer in "Bartleby, the Scrivener" or the monomaniacal duke in "My Last Duchess," for instance. It is helpful to set aside biography during reading, and to consider whether we are asked to resist the values or behaviors being shown to us. Should we sympathize with Bartleby's nihilism and reproach the lawyer? What sort of future son-in-law would proudly insinuate that he murdered his previous wife? The speaker in a **dramatic monologue** or the narrator who is also a participant in a story should be regarded as akin to a character in a play, that is, as distinct from the poet or author. Because characters in most plays are created to be performed by actors on stage, audiences seldom confuse characters with the playwright, though there may be lines or speeches that seem close to what the playwright would have been likely to say in person. The character L'il Bit in Paula Vogel's play *How I Learned to Drive* at times speaks directly to the audience, like an adult storyteller recalling the events—and very much as we might imagine Vogel herself would speak. But it would have limited the drama if L'il Bit had to be a truthful representative of Vogel's own life, and it hampers interpretation to try to match the fictional world to the facts of biography.

Bearing in mind the various contexts that shape the source, text, and audience will help you develop more persuasive interpretations of literature. You will notice, too, that interpretation is always open to discussion. There will

*And all else is literature.*
—PAUL VERLAINE

always be a variety of respected approaches—generally concentrating on different aspects of the exchange between source, text, and audience—to the study of texts that reward interpretation. You may become acquainted with the variety of schools of literary criticism and theory that, across the generations, have yielded powerful interpretations of literature. Such diversity of methods might suggest that the discussion is pointless: there is no arguing taste, any interpretation will do as well as another. On the contrary, it is quite easy to judge whether any of the various interpretations is reasonably supported by the evidence in the text—the sorts of aspects of the work that this introduction has advised you to look for. That's when the discussion gets interesting. Because there is no single, straight, paved road to the destination of understanding a text, you can explore some of the blazed trails or less-traveled paths. In sharing your interpretations, tested against your peers' responses and guided by the instructor's or other critics' expertise, you will hone your own critical skills, both in discussion and in writing about literature. After the intricate and interactive process of interpretation, you will find that the work has changed when you read it again. What we do with literature alters what it does to us.

# Fiction: Reading, Responding, Writing

**FICTION**

Do you remember the first story you ever heard? The most recent story you told? Even if fairy tales and children's books were never a big part of your life, and even if novels and short stories are only a fraction of your entertainment diet now, you are and have always been immersed in stories — jokes, gossip, news items, television shows, and films. Telling and hearing stories are two of the most common forms of storytelling, and many people who don't usually think of themselves as cooperate in creating stories. Stories also fill and structure our everyday conversations. Of course, these stories tend to begin "You'll never guess what happened . . ." or "So there I was, minding my own business, when . . . ," rather than "Once upon a time . . ." or "Sit-um-tee ("listen to me," as spoken storytellers say). Yet all of these phrases have a similarly magical effect. They alert us that we are about to enter a story, and they ask us to pay a special kind of attention to both the tale and its teller. For all their wonderful variety, too, the stories that follow such phrases have, at their core, much the same shape and perform many of the same functions. Among other things, stories not only create greater intimacy between teller and listener, but they also indirectly connect us to all those who have — in every age and every corner of the world — gathered together to share stories. Most cultures have or had oral storytellers. Many of the stories that we now regard as among the world's greatest were written down only after they had been sung or recited by generations of storytellers.

Of course there are some differences between written and oral stories, and also between the experiences of listening and reading. When we tell a story aloud, for instance, we tend to tell it differently each time, adding and subtracting details, giving it a different "spin." The same process occurs on an even greater scale as a tale passes from one teller to another (as anyone who has ever tracked the progress of a rumor knows well). As a result, oral tales tend to have a fluidity that their written counterparts lack. Many exist in multiple versions. And it's often difficult or impossible to trace a story back to a single "author" or creator. In a sense, then, an oral story is the creation of a whole community (or of many communities), just as oral storytelling tends to be a much more communal event than reading is.

Still, the private experience of reading fiction can be shared and enhanced when you talk with others about what you read, or when you write about it. A literature class will enhance your knowledge and skills in the process of interpretation, and give you a chance to practice talking and writing about literature. This chapter and those that follow, we hope, aid you in that process. As you encounter a diverse array of written fiction and discuss its various elements, you will increase your understanding of the way fiction works and the way readers can make sense of it for themselves and others.

This chapter, in particular, invites you to think further about the shape and function of storytelling, in part by introducing you to a series of stories that

# Fiction: Reading, Responding, Writing

Do you remember the first story you ever heard? The most recent story you told? Even if fairy tales and children's books were never a big part of your life, and even if novels and short stories are only a fraction of your entertainment diet now, you are, and have always been, immersed in stories. Jokes, gossip, news items, television shows, and films are some of our culture's most common forms of storytelling, and many popular video games essentially invite us to cooperate in creating stories. Stories also fill and structure our everyday conversations. Of course, these stories tend to begin "You'll never guess what happened . . ." or "So there I was, minding my own business, when . . . ," rather than "Once upon a time . . ." or *Su-num-twee* ("listen to me," as Spokane storytellers say). Yet all of these phrases have a similarly magical effect. They alert us that we are about to enter a story, and they ask us to pay a special kind of attention to both the tale and its teller. For all their wonderful variety, too, the stories that follow such phrases have, at their core, much the same shape and perform many of the same functions. Among other things, stories not only create greater intimacy between teller and listener, but they also indirectly connect us to all those who have—in every age and every corner of the world—gathered together to share stories. Most cultures have or had oral storytellers. Many of the stories that we now regard as among the world's greatest were written down only after they had been sung or recited by generations of storytellers.

Of course, there are some differences between written and oral stories, and also between the experiences of listening and reading. When we tell a story aloud, for instance, we tend to tell it differently each time, adding and subtracting details, giving it a different "spin." The same process occurs on an even greater scale as a tale passes from one teller to another (as anyone who has ever tracked the progress of a rumor knows well). As a result, oral tales tend to have a fluidity that their written counterparts lack. Many exist in multiple versions. And it's often difficult or impossible to trace a story back to a single "author" or creator. In a sense, then, an oral story is the creation of a whole community (or of many communities), just as oral storytelling tends to be a much more communal event than reading is.

Still, the private experience of reading fiction can be shared and enhanced when you talk with others about what you read, or when you write about it. A literature class will enhance your knowledge and skills in the process of interpretation, and give you a chance to practice talking and writing about literature. This chapter and those that follow will, we hope, aid you in that process. As you encounter a diverse array of written fiction and discuss its various elements, you will increase your understanding of the way fiction works and the way readers can make sense of it for themselves and others.

This chapter, in particular, invites you to think further about the shape and function of storytelling—in part by introducing you to a series of stories that themselves explore just these issues. In a way, this chapter aims to save you some steps on your journey into the world of written fiction by showing how far you have already traveled. The techniques of highly skilled authors and readers of literary fiction have much in common with those we deploy every day. Perhaps without knowing it, you are thus in many ways already expert at both telling stories and interpreting them.

For stories are everywhere: human beings live by stories, and we would find it hard to make sense of our experience if we did not create, share, and compare stories about it. Consider a well-known tale, "The Blind Men and the Elephant," a Buddhist story over two thousand years old. Like other oral stories, this one exists in many versions. Here's our own way of telling it:

## The Elephant in the Village of the Blind

Once there was a village high in the mountains in which everyone was born blind. One day a traveler arrived from far away with many fine things to sell and many tales to tell. The villagers asked, "How did you travel so far and so high carrying so much?" The traveler said, "On my elephant." "What is an elephant?" the villagers asked, having never even heard of such an animal in their remote mountain village. "See for yourself," the traveler replied.

The elders of the village were a little afraid of the strange-smelling creature that took up so much space in the middle of the village square. They could hear it breathing and munching on hay, and feel its slow, swaying movements disturbing the air around them. First one elder reached out and felt its flapping ear. "An elephant is soft but tough, and flexible, like a leather fan." Another grasped its back leg. "An elephant is a rough, hairy pillar." An old woman took hold of a tusk and gasped, "An elephant is a cool, smooth staff." A young girl seized the tail and declared, "An elephant is a fringed rope." A boy took hold of the trunk and announced, "An elephant is a water pipe." Soon others were stroking its sides, which were furrowed like a dry plowed field, and others determined that its head was an overturned washing tub attached to the water pipe.

At first each villager argued with the others on the definition of the elephant, as the traveler watched in silence. Two elders were about to come to blows about a fan that could not possibly be a pillar. Meanwhile the elephant patiently enjoyed the investigations as the cries of curiosity and angry debate mixed in the afternoon sun. Soon someone suggested that a list could be made of all the parts: the elephant had four pillars, one tub, two fans, a water pipe, and two staffs, and was covered in tough, hairy leather or dried mud. Four young mothers, sitting on a bench and comparing impressions, realized that the elephant was in fact an enormous, gentle ox with a stretched nose. The traveler agreed, adding only that it was also a powerful draft horse and that if they bought some of his wares for a good price he would be sure to come that way again in the new year.

It takes very little to make a story. You need a **narrator** or teller and an **audience** of listeners or readers. (In this story as in many others, you don't need to know exactly who is telling or receiving the story. The narrator and the audience could be anyone.) Of course you also need something to tell about, including characters and a potentially problematic situation—here, a village of blind people. Then you need a **plot,** beginning with some event that destabilizes the original situation. (If everything is balanced, nothing happens.) Often such an event is the arrival of an unfamiliar person or thing, in this case an elephant and a traveler. That event creates a **conflict**—here, the misunderstandings about what an elephant is.

It would be easy to change the components of this simple story. Try it yourself. Changing any aspect of the story will inevitably change how it works and what it means to the listener or reader. For example, most versions of this story feature not an entire village of blind people (as our version does), but a small group of blind men who claim to be wiser than their sighted neighbors. These blind men quarrel endlessly because none of them can see; none can put together all the evidence of all their senses or all the elephant's various parts to create a whole. Such traditional versions of the story criticize people who are too proud of what they think they know, and imply that sighted people would know better what an elephant is. We prefer those versions of the tale that, like ours, are set in an imaginary "country" of the blind. (There is an old adage, "In the country of the blind, the one-eyed man is king.") This changes the emphasis of the story from the errors of a few blind wise men to the value and the insufficiency of *any* one person's perspective. For though it's clear that the various members of the community in this version will never agree entirely on one interpretation of (or story about) the elephant, they do not let themselves get bogged down in endless dispute. Instead they compare and combine their various stories and "readings" in order to form a more satisfying, holistic understanding of the wonder in their midst.

*Fiction is not a dream. Nor is it guesswork. It is imagining based on facts, and the facts must be accurate or the work of imagining will not stand up.*
—MARGARET CULKIN BANNING

Perhaps the point of this tale is to show you how to get along when you disagree about a story you have read in a literature classroom! From another angle, it illustrates how any one reader grapples with any one story: by observing one part of the story (or elephant) at a time, a reader tries to understand how those parts work together to form a whole. In reading even the shortest of stories, you read word by word, sentence by sentence, receiving new information one piece at a time. You make sense of each new piece by adding it to those you have already gathered, and as you proceed you form **expectations** about what is yet to come. Thus reading is in itself a kind of storytelling: you project the possible futures of the characters much as you project your own future in the "story" of your own life. Conversely, your expectations for a story will be guided not only by its various features, but also by your unique life "story" and point of view. Just as the blind villagers' individual interpretations of the elephant depend on what previous experiences they bring to bear (of pillars, water pipes, oxen, and dried mud, for example), and also on where (quite literally) they stand in relation to the elephant, so, too, will your response to a work of fiction.

The following short short story is a contemporary work, not a version of a traditional tale. Yet here, too, the writer has given us a minimal amount of information to go on, making each word matter. And here, as in "The Elephant in the Village of the Blind," characters have different perceptions or interpretations of things they have never seen before, in this case the places and objects they encounter on a cross-country car trip. As you read the story, pay attention to your expectations, drawing on your experience of life and on the information you get from this specific story's title and first few sentences. When and how does the story begin to challenge and change your initial expectations?

## LINDA BREWER

## 20/20

By the time they reached Indiana, Bill realized that Ruthie, his driving companion, was incapable of theoretical debate. She drove okay, she went halves on gas, etc., but she refused to argue. She didn't seem to know how. Bill was used to East Coast women who disputed everything he said, every step of the way. Ruthie stuck to simple observation, like "Look, cows." He chalked it up to the fact that she was from rural Ohio and thrilled to death to be anywhere else.

She didn't mind driving into the setting sun. The third evening out, Bill rested his eyes while she cruised along making the occasional announcement.

"Indian paintbrush. A golden eagle."

Miles later he frowned. There was no Indian paintbrush, that he knew of, near Chicago.

The next evening, driving, Ruthie said, "I never thought I'd see a Bigfoot in real life." Bill turned and looked at the side of the road streaming innocently out behind them. Two red spots winked back—reflectors nailed to a tree stump.

"Ruthie, I'll drive," he said. She stopped the car and they changed places in the light of the evening star.

"I'm so glad I got to come with you," Ruthie said. Her eyes were big, blue, and capable of seeing wonderful sights. A white buffalo near Fargo. A UFO above Twin Falls. A handsome genius in the person of Bill himself. This last vision came to her in Spokane and Bill decided to let it ride.

Brewer's title, like all good titles, leads us into the story armed with certain expectations. "20/20" refers to near-perfect eyesight, and it may also remind us of the expression "20/20 hindsight," which suggests that our observations about what has already happened tend to be more accurate than our predictions. (The form of the title "20/20" also reflects the doubleness of the couple's two kinds of vision and of the way they split the driving and expenses.) As a result, the title may initially prepare us for a story that focuses on vision and on the difference between foresight and hindsight, expectation and outcome. This title may alert us to expect the unexpected.

The story itself begins with a potentially difficult situation: two contrasting characters, Bill and Ruthie, alone together for days on a long car trip. Setting is established in a few words: "they reached Indiana." Characters are named, their relationship and different personalities quickly sketched: both are "driving companion[s]," but only one is "incapable of theoretical debate." From our experience of the car trips and relationships that are worth telling about, we expect several possible problems: the car might break down; they might get lost; Bill might begin to hate a woman who refuses to argue with him; Ruthie might be provoked to argue with someone who looks down on easy-going Midwesterners. Then a specific event creates a conflict quite different from (even the opposite of) the one we've been led to expect: Ruthie is driving into the setting sun on the third evening, and she announces that she has seen things that reason and experience tell Bill (and us) she could not have seen in this landscape. The next evening it is worse: she remarks that she just saw a legendary monster, Bigfoot. This must mean that Ruthie is "seeing things" and should not be allowed to drive. But the next phase of the story offers yet another unexpected shift at once comic and romantic: Ruthie's speech and Bill's praise of her eyes show that Bill now admires the imaginative eyesight that leads Ruthie to see him as "a handsome genius." As a result, he will "let it ride," accepting her vision of life because it has endowed the American landscape and Bill himself with mythic grandeur.

Both Bill and Ruthie are telling stories and forming interpretations of what they see and what happened to them on their journey. Ruthie may not argue with Bill, but her statements seem like the beginnings of "tall tales" ("I really saw Bigfoot one evening while I was driving through Nebraska . . ."). We never know what Ruthie privately thinks; what she says and does is reported as Bill would see it, through his point of view. In chapter 2 we will examine the different kinds of narration and point of view used in fiction. The point here is to notice that the development of a fictional story is often a matter of the conflicting stories characters tell. We are all storytellers, just as we are all interpreters of what others tell us. Whenever we report on what we've seen, plan the future, or ponder a personal decision, we are telling stories—forming interpretations, projecting expectations, drawing conclusions. To make sense of experience in these ways, we must also take in and respond to the versions of reality that other people have expressed.

At each point in the story you should both test your initial predictions and formulate new questions or statements about the story, whether in your mind or on paper. This is part of the natural process of hearing stories, as when Bill slowly begins to doubt Ruthie's announcement about Indian paintbrush outside Chicago. He begins to reinterpret her character in light of this new realization: if her observation can't be true, why is she saying it? You may feel it is a very long way from the everyday effort to understand another person to the process of writing an interpretation of a short story for a class. But the steps along that way can be similar and fairly straightforward. Writing a critical essay is just a more committed and systematic way of talking about what you have read.

Thus far we have considered very short forms of storytelling, but in the rest of this and subsequent chapters we turn to longer and more complex fiction. As you proceed you will recognize common qualities and features in the stories, whether long or short. And you will find that all the stories invite you to engage in a similar process of interpretation. In reading most stories, it makes sense to start by responding to the characters and situations almost as if these were real, and to check on your views as the story progresses. In its first few paragraphs, for example, Raymond Carver's "Cathedral" introduces us to three characters: a jealous husband who has a phobia of blind people (and who is also the story's narrator); a wife who likes to write poetry, who has already left one unsatisfying marriage, and who maintains a friendship with a blind man; and a blind man who is sensitive to things the narrator dislikes. Whose side are you on initially? Do you feel sorry for the blind man? Or sorry for the wife, or the husband/narrator? What do you expect to happen? For example, are you worried that the husband will openly insult the blind man?

Answering such questions about the characters and situation can lead you to form a statement about a story, the sort of statement that might eventually become a **thesis** (or debatable claim) in a critical essay. One such statement might be: " 'Cathedral' is a story told by a man who has a problem with sharing feelings who is married to a woman who likes to share her feelings." Until you have read the rest of the story, you don't know if this statement will be true for the whole work, but in most stories such an early, hypothetical statement is a good prediction of what will be important by the end.

Although the design of the story, and the information it provides you should shape your response and expectations, you will also draw on your own knowledge of life and human behavior. You may have unique reasons for reacting more strongly than other readers. You may have lived through similar situations or be related to someone like a character in the story. Everyone is entitled to a personal response, however different it might be from the usual readings of a work. Still, other readers will only be persuaded to share your opinion if you can point to evidence in the text that justifies such a response. The shared interpretation based on the common ground of this particular text is worth the effort of collaboration, as when the villagers try to assemble all the parts of the elephant, or as when generations build a cathedral. Also, like the narrator of Carver's story trying to imagine a cathedral without using the sense of sight, you might in the course of discussing and writing about a story learn something new and change your mind.

As you read, respond, and write about fiction, however, you should draw upon your knowledge of stories (and literature in general) as well as your experience of real life. Your expectations about a particular work of fiction will emerge in great part from knowing that this *is* a work of fiction (and not real life) and that such works share certain tendencies. You already know a lot about the customs or conventions of stories. For instance, you know that stories are generally written in the past tense, and very often in the third person. Both "The Elephant in the Village of the Blind" and "20/20" tell what happened in the past to people who are not telling the story themselves. When a story uses the present tense and the first person, as in the beginning of Grace Paley's "A Conversation with My Father," you should notice this and ask why. Is Paley trying to make us feel as if she is speaking directly to us about a personal experience? Does it make the conversation appear to be happening right now? Why are the stories that the narrator tells her father during this "conversation" told in the third person and past tense? The way a story is told affects how close you feel to the tellers, characters, and events. Yet there are no strict rules about the effects of specific ways of narrating. Sherman Alexie's "Flight Patterns," for example, feels very intimate and recent, even though it is in the third person and past tense. Questions about how a story is narrated can help you measure many of its qualities, but especially how close the audience is expected to feel to the narrator.

> *Fiction is like a spider's web, attached ever so slightly perhaps, but still attached to life at all four corners.*
> —VIRGINIA WOOLF

Yet another principle that you already know is that every detail in a story can offer you clues. This means that an interpretation of any full story can grow out of a question about a single puzzling detail. Titles, as we have already suggested, can provide keys to the whole story. Why is Carver's story called "Cathedral" instead of "The Blind Man"? This might lead you to questions about other details within the story. What difference would it make if the television program they watch were not on cathedrals but on elephants or internal combustion engines? As you notice and interpret such details in the story, you can relate them to characters and actions. Why is it the narrator and not the wife who stays up late and watches TV with the blind man? Does the narrator reveal any handicap in trying to describe the cathedral, the way the blind people do in trying to describe an elephant? Questions about parts of a story help lead you to significant interpretations of the whole.

When reading a story or any kind of literature, you respond to words—that is, to all the choices of wording and sentence structure that make up a **voice** or **style**. This might seem to be one of the more difficult aspects of literature to analyze, and yet if you speak English and the story is written in English you are already attuned to differences of voice or style. Such differences include vocabularies, from plain monosyllables to fancy polysyllables, and manners, from rude to polite. Many modern writers try to capture the patterns of everyday speech of different regions, dialects, or ethnic groups. Grace Paley has commented on the way many writers combine common modes of speech with refined literary style. In an interview at the age of seventy-three (in 1995), Paley claimed that everyone has "two ears. One ear is that literary ear, and it's a good old ear. It's with us when we write in the tradition of English writing, or Western writing that includes Proust and Flaubert. . . . But there is also something else . . . and that is the ear of the language of home, and the language of your street and your own people."[1] This comment also seems fitting for the achievements of both Raymond Carver and Sherman Alexie, who listen closely to the unofficial voices around them and shape these effectively into very artful literary fiction.

You too have ears for different styles. If you were to tell a story about an incident to a friend your own age, to your five-year-old nephew, or to your teacher or parent, you would likely modify the words and the tone you used. Yet your character and behavior would probably come through to each of your listeners. The personality of the narrator in Raymond Carver's "Cathedral" comes through in his speech patterns (we imagine he is speaking to someone he knows as he recalls the visit). "Just amazing. . . . A beard on a blind man! Too much, I say." The voice or writing style conveys a "style" of personality, which makes the reader feel a certain way. It is difficult to describe the precise tone of a style, but by looking closely at words and passages—by quoting selectively as we just did from the narrator of "Cathedral"—you can show how style or voice contributes to the effect of a story.

When you listen to a story you usually wonder about the person who is telling it, based not only on what is told but how it is told, which includes the personality of the teller. William, in Sherman Alexie's "Flight Patterns," listens to the taxi driver's personal history and thinks, "If he was a liar, then he was a magnificent liar." A reader readily becomes curious about the author of a published story or the personality that seems to be telling it. Thus your observations about voice and style may lead you to ask questions about the author. Is Raymond Carver like the sarcastic husband in "Cathedral"? You might consult an entry in a biographical dictionary in your library, on the Web, or in the "Biographical Sketches" in this book, and learn that Carver struggled with substance abuse. But does that make

---

1. "Lit Chat: Grace Paley," *Salon* (www.salon.com/11/departments/litchat1.html).

the story autobiographical? Did Carver share the narrator's prejudice about blind people? The answers to such questions usually should be sought in the work itself. "Cathedral" exposes the narrator's flaws and shows that his prejudice was wrong.

We have found that students of literature often bring up questions about the author's intentions and the relation of the fiction to the author's life. It is difficult to answer such questions without oversimplifying the meaning of the work (or the life), and teachers may therefore warn you away from biographical approaches to literature. Nevertheless, some information about the author "behind" the work can provide a useful context, just as information about when and where a work was first published can be key to a convincing interpretation. Sherman Alexie's "Flight Patterns" was published in 2003 in the United States, in a collection called *Ten Little Indians,* and like the protagonist of the story, the author is a Native American. This does not mean that the character William is just a stand-in for Alexie. Nevertheless, the fact that William has some experiences in common with his creator makes a difference in how we respond—how close we feel to William, how authentic or "real" the story seems to us.

> *The good ended happily, and the bad unhappily. That is what Fiction means.*
> —OSCAR WILDE

Entire essays may be devoted to a story's style, to the author's biography, or to the interaction of both: the voices in the story and the author's personal and social background or historical context. But most of your critical writing will probably concern other matters. When you have read an entire story, you should notice its form or **structure.** Think of form as the blueprint or architectural plan of a story, which provides a general outline of the whole structure as well as details of the design of the parts. Are there any repetitions or patterns that occur throughout the story? Here as elsewhere, you should draw upon your experience of literature and of life to answer such questions. You inevitably have absorbed the standard forms or structures that most stories take. In the stories that follow, we offer some examples of common plans or shapes for stories: the journey to a destination, the return to the past, the shared scene of storytelling. Such structures are effective in fiction because they resemble the forms of storytelling that we know from everyday experience.

One of the most important types of literary knowledge, closely related to form and structure, is the concept of **genre,** or the conventions of different kinds of literature—fiction, poetry, and drama. Your experience of fiction tells you that there are, indeed, different kinds or **subgenres** of fiction, each of which has a slightly different shape. Different kinds of stories have their own conventions: fairy tales begin with "Once upon a time"; in ghost stories and certain other scary stories there is almost always a beautiful young woman threatened by danger; comic stories almost always end happily; and so on. Your expectations as you read a particular story and your sense of how well it worked when it is over are guided by your assumptions about just what kind of story it is.

Just as your response to a character can spark an idea for an essay, your comparative judgment or categorization of a story can generate a thesis. You might, for instance, notice that A. S. Byatt's "The Thing in the Forest" resembles a fairy tale: it begins, "There were once two little girls who saw, or believed they saw, a thing in the forest," and its plot may remind you of "Little Red Riding Hood." You might also notice the ways that it differs from a fairy tale; there is no rescue or "happily ever after" ending. Or perhaps you find it most rewarding to consider

"The Thing in the Forest" as an "initiation" or "coming of age" story like those in chapter 9, as the two girls learn something that changes their lives. Essays about genre can show new ways of seeing a story, as when Lawrence Rodgers interprets William Faulkner's "A Rose for Emily" as a detective story in his essay in chapter 12. You can also prompt interesting questions for an essay by comparing two different stories that use similar generic conventions.

Obviously, there are many ways to approach both reading stories and writing about them, just as there are many varieties of stories on which to feast. Any good story can feed our intellect and our imagination—those two faculties that are contrasted in the story of Bill and Ruthie in "20/20." Fiction helps us extend our knowledge and understanding of the actual world and it prepares us for the extraordinary and unexpected. Effective fiction often presents familiar conditions in such a way that they become unfamiliar. This effect, called defamiliarization, occurs in everyday life when, for example, you return from a trip and see things in your own room as though they were new or not your own. Usually we perceive what habit and convention have told us is "really there," but at certain times none of it looks obvious or natural. Stories, then, may function the way travel does: by taking us out of our world and into another, they enable us to look at things anew much as his car trip with Ruthie helps Bill to do.

Many of us initially prefer literature that reflects our own time and place to literature of other countries and eras. Like Bill, we may want our tales to be small, familiar, and realistic rather than tall, exotic, and fantastic. Indeed, we must find some way to relate any story to our own lives before we can find it intellectually or emotionally meaningful. No one would deny that one of the many things that fiction may be "for" is learning about ourselves and the world around us, with the advantages of artistic enhancement and defamiliarization. But often the last thing we want is a story about people just like ourselves or about a world just like our own. Fiction has the power to be excitingly strange, like a UFO above Twin Falls or Bigfoot loping through Nebraska. It can take us to other places, times, or ways of life, making the unfamiliar more familiar. And whether it focuses on the actual or the extraordinary, all good fiction takes us out of ourselves, beyond the limited vision of our own eyes. It shows us that there are worlds beyond our own immediate experience, and other ways of looking at those worlds.

## RAYMOND CARVER

### *Cathedral*

This blind man, an old friend of my wife's, he was on his way to spend the night. His wife had died. So he was visiting the dead wife's relatives in Connecticut. He called my wife from his in-laws'. Arrangements were made. He would come by train, a five-hour trip, and my wife would meet him at the station. She hadn't seen him since she worked for him one summer in Seattle ten years ago. But she and the blind man had kept in touch. They made tapes and mailed them back and forth. I wasn't enthusiastic about his visit. He was no one I knew. And his being blind bothered me. My idea of blindness came from the movies. In the movies, the blind moved slowly and never laughed. Sometimes they were led by seeing-eye dogs. A blind man in my house was not something I looked forward to.

That summer in Seattle she had needed a job. She didn't have any money. The man she was going to marry at the end of the summer was in officers' training school. He didn't have any money, either. But she was in love with the guy, and he was in love with her, etc. She'd seen something in the paper: HELP WANTED—*Reading to Blind Man,* and a telephone number. She phoned and went over, was hired on the spot. She'd worked with this blind man all summer. She read stuff to him, case studies, reports, that sort of thing. She helped him organize his little office in the county social-service department. They'd become good friends, my wife and the blind man. How do I know these things? She told me. And she told me something else. On her last day in the office, the blind man asked if he could touch her face. She agreed to this. She told me he touched his fingers to every part of her face, her nose—even her neck! She never forgot it. She even tried to write a poem about it. She was always trying to write a poem. She wrote a poem or two every year, usually after something really important had happened to her.

When we first started going out together, she showed me the poem. In the poem, she recalled his fingers and the way they had moved around over her face. In the poem, she talked about what she had felt at the time, about what went through her mind when the blind man touched her nose and lips. I can remember I didn't think much of the poem. Of course, I didn't tell her that. Maybe I just don't understand poetry. I admit it's not the first thing I reach for when I pick up something to read.

Anyway, this man who'd first enjoyed her favors, the officer-to-be, he'd been her childhood sweetheart. So okay. I'm saying that at the end of the summer she let the blind man run his hands over her face, said goodbye to him, married her childhood etc., who was now a commissioned officer, and she moved away from Seattle. But they'd kept in touch, she and the blind man. She made the first contact after a year or so. She called him up one night from an Air Force base in Alabama. She wanted to talk. They talked. He asked her to send him a tape and tell him about her life. She did this. She sent the tape. On the tape, she told the blind man about her husband and about their life together in the military. She told the blind man she loved her husband but she didn't like it where they lived and she didn't like it that he was a part of the military-industrial thing. She told the blind man she'd written a poem and he was in it. She told him that she was writing a poem about what it was like to be an Air Force officer's wife. The poem wasn't finished yet. She was still writing it. The blind man made a tape. He sent her the tape. She made a tape. This went on for years. My wife's officer was posted to one base and then another. She sent tapes from Moody AFB, McGuire, McConnell, and finally Travis, near Sacramento, where one night she got to feeling lonely and cut off from people she kept losing in that moving-around life. She got to feeling she couldn't go it another step. She went in and swallowed all the pills and capsules in the medicine chest and washed them down with a bottle of gin. Then she got into a hot bath and passed out.

But instead of dying, she got sick. She threw up. Her officer—why should he have a name? he was the childhood sweetheart, and what more does he want?— came home from somewhere, found her, and called the ambulance. In time, she put it all on a tape and sent the tape to the blind man. Over the years, she put all kinds of stuff on tapes and sent the tapes off lickety-split. Next to writing a poem every year, I think it was her chief means of recreation. On one tape, she told the blind man she'd decided to live away from her officer for a time. On another tape, she told him about her divorce. She and I began going out, and of course she told her blind man about it. She told him everything, or so it seemed to me. Once she asked me if I'd like to hear the latest tape from the blind man. This was a year ago. I was on the tape, she said. So I said okay, I'd listen to it. I got us drinks and we settled down in the living room. We made ready to listen. First she inserted the tape into the player and adjusted a couple of dials. Then she pushed a lever. The tape squeaked and someone began to talk in this loud voice. She lowered the volume. After a few minutes of harmless chitchat, I heard my own name in the mouth of this stranger, this blind man I didn't even know! And then this: "From all you've said about him, I can only conclude—" But we were interrupted, a knock at the door, something, and we didn't ever get back to the tape. Maybe it was just as well. I'd heard all I wanted to.

Now this same blind man was coming to sleep in my house.

"Maybe I could take him bowling," I said to my wife. She was at the draining board doing scalloped potatoes. She put down the knife she was using and turned around.

"If you love me," she said, "you can do this for me. If you don't love me, okay. But if you had a friend, any friend, and the friend came to visit, I'd make him feel comfortable." She wiped her hands with the dish towel.

"I don't have any blind friends," I said.

10 "You don't have *any* friends," she said. "Period. Besides," she said, "goddamn it, his wife's just died! Don't you understand that? The man's lost his wife!"

I didn't answer. She'd told me a little about the blind man's wife. Her name was Beulah. Beulah! That's a name for a colored woman.

"Was his wife a Negro?" I asked.

"Are you crazy?" my wife said. "Have you just flipped or something?" She picked up a potato. I saw it hit the floor, then roll under the stove. "What's wrong with you?" she said. "Are you drunk?"

"I'm just asking," I said.

15 Right then my wife filled me in with more detail than I cared to know. I made a drink and sat at the kitchen table to listen. Pieces of the story began to fall into place.

Beulah had gone to work for the blind man the summer after my wife had stopped working for him. Pretty soon Beulah and the blind man had themselves a church wedding. It was a little wedding—who'd want to go to such a wedding in the first place?—just the two of them, plus the minister and the minister's wife. But it was a church wedding just the same. It was what Beulah had wanted, he'd said. But even then Beulah must have been carrying the cancer in her glands. After they had been inseparable for eight years—my wife's word, *inseparable*—Beulah's health went into a rapid decline. She died in a Seattle hospital room, the blind man sitting beside the bed and holding on to her hand. They'd married, lived and worked together, slept together—had sex, sure—and then the blind man had to bury her. All this without his having ever seen what the goddamned woman looked like. It was beyond my understanding. Hearing this, I felt sorry for the blind man for a little bit. And then I found myself thinking what a pitiful life this woman must have led. Imagine a woman who could never see herself as she was seen in the eyes of her loved one. A woman who could go on day after day and never receive the smallest compliment from her beloved. A woman whose husband could never read the expression on her face, be it misery or something better. Someone who could wear makeup or not—what difference to him? She could, if she wanted, wear green eye-shadow around one eye, a straight pin in her nostril, yellow slacks and purple shoes, no matter. And then to slip off into death, the blind man's hand on her hand, his blind eyes streaming tears—I'm imagining now—her last thought maybe this: that he never even knew what she looked like, and she on an express to the grave. Robert was left with a small insurance policy and half of a twenty-peso Mexican coin. The other half of the coin went into the box with her. Pathetic.

So when the time rolled around, my wife went to the depot to pick him up. With nothing to do but wait—sure, I blamed him for that—I was having a drink and watching the TV when I heard the car pull into the drive. I got up from the sofa with my drink and went to the window to have a look.

I saw my wife laughing as she parked the car. I saw her get out of the car and shut the door. She was still wearing a smile. Just amazing. She went around to the other side of the car to where the blind man was already starting to get out. This blind man, feature this, he was wearing a full beard! A beard on a blind man! Too much, I say. The blind man reached into the back seat and dragged out a suitcase. My wife took his arm, shut the car door, and, talking all the way, moved him down the drive and then up the steps to the front porch. I turned off the TV. I finished my drink, rinsed the glass, dried my hands. Then I went to the door.

My wife said, "I want you to meet Robert. Robert, this is my husband. I've told you all about him." She was beaming. She had this blind man by his coat sleeve.

The blind man let go of his suitcase and up came his hand.

I took it. He squeezed hard, held my hand, and then he let it go.

"I feel like we've already met," he boomed.

"Likewise," I said. I didn't know what else to say. Then I said, "Welcome. I've heard a lot about you." We began to move then, a little group, from the porch into the living room, my wife guiding him by the arm. The blind man was carrying his suitcase in his other hand. My wife said things like, "To your left here, Robert. That's right. Now watch it, there's a chair. That's it. Sit down right here. This is the sofa. We just bought this sofa two weeks ago."

I started to say something about the old sofa. I'd liked that old sofa. But I didn't say anything. Then I wanted to say something else, small-talk, about the scenic ride along the Hudson. How going *to* New York, you should sit on the right-hand side of the train, and coming *from* New York, the left-hand side.

"Did you have a good train ride?" I said. "Which side of the train did you sit on, by the way?"

"What a question, which side!" my wife said. "What's it matter which side?" she said.

"I just asked," I said.

"Right side," the blind man said. "I hadn't been on a train in nearly forty years. Not since I was a kid. With my folks. That's been a long time. I'd nearly forgotten the sensation. I have winter in my beard now," he said. "So I've been told, anyway. Do I look distinguished, my dear?" the blind man said to my wife.

"You look distinguished, Robert," she said. "Robert," she said. "Robert, it's just so good to see you."

My wife finally took her eyes off the blind man and looked at me. I had the feeling she didn't like what she saw. I shrugged.

I've never met, or personally known, anyone who was blind. This blind man was late forties, a heavy-set, balding man with stooped shoulders, as if he carried a great weight there. He wore brown slacks, brown shoes, a light-brown shirt, a tie, a sports coat. Spiffy. He also had this full beard. But he didn't use a cane and he didn't wear dark glasses. I'd always thought dark glasses were a must for the blind. Fact was, I wished he had a pair. At first glance, his eyes looked like anyone else's eyes. But if you looked close, there was something different about them. Too much white in the iris, for one thing, and the pupils seemed to move around in the sockets without his knowing it or being able to stop it. Creepy. As I stared at his face, I saw the left pupil turn in toward his nose while the other made an effort to keep in one place. But it was only an effort, for that eye was on the roam without his knowing it or wanting it to be.

I said, "Let me get you a drink. What's your pleasure? We have a little of everything. It's one of our pastimes."

"Bub, I'm a Scotch man myself," he said fast enough in this big voice.

"Right," I said. Bub! "Sure you are. I knew it."

He let his fingers touch his suitcase, which was sitting alongside the sofa. He was taking his bearings. I didn't blame him for that.

"I'll move that up to your room," my wife said.

"No, that's fine," the blind man said loudly. "It can go up when I go up."

"A little water with the Scotch?" I said.

"Very little," he said.

"I knew it," I said.

He said, "Just a tad. The Irish actor, Barry Fitzgerald? I'm like that fellow. When I drink water, Fitzgerald said, I drink water. When I drink whiskey, I drink whiskey." My wife laughed. The blind man brought his hand up under his beard. He lifted his beard slowly and let it drop.

I did the drinks, three big glasses of Scotch with a splash of water in each. Then we made ourselves comfortable and talked about Robert's travels. First the long flight from the West Coast to Connecticut, we covered that. Then from Connecticut up here by train. We had another drink concerning that leg of the trip.

I remembered having read somewhere that the blind didn't smoke because, as speculation had it, they couldn't see the smoke they exhaled. I thought I knew that much and that much only about blind people. But this blind man smoked his cigarette down to the nubbin and then lit another one. This blind man filled his ashtray and my wife emptied it.

When we sat down at the table for dinner, we had another drink. My wife heaped Robert's plate with cube steak, scalloped potatoes, green beans. I buttered him up two slices of bread. I said, "Here's bread and butter for you." I swallowed some of my drink. "Now let us pray," I said, and the blind man lowered his head. My wife looked at me, her mouth agape. "Pray the phone won't ring and the food doesn't get cold," I said.

We dug in. We ate everything there was to eat on the table. We ate like there was no tomorrow. We didn't talk. We ate. We scarfed. We grazed that table. We were into serious eating. The blind man had right away located his foods, he knew just where everything was on his plate. I watched with admiration as he used his knife and fork on the meat. He'd cut two pieces of meat, fork the meat into his mouth, and then go all out for the scalloped potatoes, the beans next, and then he'd tear off a hunk of buttered bread and eat that. He'd follow this up with a big drink of milk. It didn't seem to bother him to use his fingers once in a while, either.

We finished everything, including half a strawberry pie. For a few moments, we sat as if stunned. Sweat beaded on our faces. Finally, we got up from the table and left the dirty plates. We didn't look back. We took ourselves into the living room and sank into our places again. Robert and my wife sat on the sofa. I took the big chair. We had us two or three more drinks while they talked about the major things that had come to pass for them in the past ten years. For the most part, I just listened. Now and then I joined in. I didn't want him to think I'd left the room, and I didn't want her to think I was feeling left out. They talked of things that had happened to them—to them!—these past ten years. I waited in vain to hear my name on my wife's sweet lips: "And then my dear husband came into my life"—something like that. But I heard nothing of the sort. More talk of Robert. Robert had done a little of everything, it seemed, a regular blind jack-of-all-trades. But most recently he and his wife had had an Amway distributorship, from which, I gathered, they'd earned their living, such as it was. The blind man was also a ham radio operator. He talked in his loud voice about conversations he'd had with fellow operators in Guam, in the Philippines, in Alaska, and even in Tahiti. He said he'd have a lot of friends there if he ever wanted to go visit those places. From time to time, he'd turn his blind face toward me, put his hand under his beard, ask me something. How long had I been in my present position? (Three years.) Did I like my work? (I didn't.) Was I going to stay with it? (What were the options?) Finally, when I thought he was beginning to run down, I got up and turned on the TV.

My wife looked at me with irritation. She was heading toward a boil. Then she looked at the blind man and said, "Robert, do you have a TV?"

The blind man said, "My dear, I have two TVs. I have a color set and a black-and-white thing, an old relic. It's funny, but if I turn the TV on, and I'm always turning it on, I turn on the color set. It's funny, don't you think?"

I didn't know what to say to that. I had absolutely nothing to say to that. No opinion. So I watched the news program and tried to listen to what the announcer was saying.

"This is a color TV," the blind man said. "Don't ask me how, but I can tell."

"We traded up a while ago," I said.

The blind man had another taste of his drink. He lifted his beard, sniffed it, and let it fall. He leaned forward on the sofa. He positioned his ashtray on the coffee table, then put the lighter to his cigarette. He leaned back on the sofa and crossed his legs at the ankles.

My wife covered her mouth, and then she yawned. She stretched. She said, "I think I'll go upstairs and put on my robe. I think I'll change into something else. Robert, you make yourself comfortable," she said.

"I'm comfortable," the blind man said.

"I want you to feel comfortable in this house," she said.

"I am comfortable," the blind man said.

After she'd left the room, he and I listened to the weather report and then to the sports roundup. By that time, she'd been gone so long I didn't know if she was going to come back. I thought she might have gone to bed. I wished she'd come back downstairs. I didn't want to be left alone with a blind man. I asked him if he wanted another drink, and he said sure. Then I asked if he wanted to smoke some dope with me. I said I'd just rolled a number. I hadn't, but I planned to do so in about two shakes.

"I'll try some with you," he said.

"Damn right," I said. "That's the stuff."

I got our drinks and sat down on the sofa with him. Then I rolled us two fat numbers. I lit one and passed it. I brought it to his fingers. He took it and inhaled.

"Hold it as long as you can," I said. I could tell he didn't know the first thing.

My wife came back downstairs wearing her pink robe and her pink slippers.

"What do I smell?" she said.

"We thought we'd have us some cannabis," I said.

My wife gave me a savage look. Then she looked at the blind man and said, "Robert, I didn't know you smoked."

He said, "I do now, my dear. There's a first time for everything. But I don't feel anything yet."

"This stuff is pretty mellow," I said. "This stuff is mild. It's dope you can reason with," I said. "It doesn't mess you up."

"Not much it doesn't, bub," he said, and laughed.

My wife sat on the sofa between the blind man and me. I passed her the number. She took it and toked and then passed it back to me. "Which way is this going?" she said. Then she said, "I shouldn't be smoking this. I can hardly keep my eyes open as it is. That dinner did me in. I shouldn't have eaten so much."

"It was the strawberry pie," the blind man said. "That's what did it," he said, and he laughed his big laugh. Then he shook his head.

"There's more strawberry pie," I said.

"Do you want some more, Robert?" my wife said.

"Maybe in a little while," he said.

We gave our attention to the TV. My wife yawned again. She said, "Your bed is made up when you feel like going to bed, Robert. I know you must have had a long day. When you're ready to go to bed, say so." She pulled his arm. "Robert?"

He came to and said, "I've had a real nice time. This beats tapes, doesn't it?"

I said, "Coming at you," and I put the number between his fingers. He inhaled, held the smoke, and then let it go. It was like he'd been doing it since he was nine years old.

"Thanks, bub," he said. "But I think this is all for me. I think I'm beginning to feel it," he said. He held the burning roach out for my wife.

"Same here," she said. "Ditto. Me, too." She took the roach and passed it to me. "I may just sit here for a while between you two guys with my eyes closed. But don't let me bother you, okay? Either one of you. If it bothers you, say so. Otherwise, I may just sit here with my eyes closed until you're ready to go to bed," she said. "Your bed's made up, Robert, when you're ready. It's right next to our room at the top of the stairs. We'll show you up when you're ready. You wake me up now, you guys, if I fall asleep." She said that and then she closed her eyes and went to sleep.

The news program ended. I got up and changed the channel. I sat back down on the sofa. I wished my wife hadn't pooped out. Her head lay across the back of the sofa, her mouth open. She'd turned so that her robe had slipped away from her legs, exposing a juicy thigh. I reached to draw her robe back over her, and it was then that I glanced at the blind man. What the hell! I flipped the robe open again.

"You say when you want some strawberry pie," I said.

"I will," he said.

I said, "Are you tired? Do you want me to take you up to your bed? Are you ready to hit the hay?"

"Not yet," he said. "No, I'll stay up with you, bub. If that's all right. I'll stay up until you're ready to turn in. We haven't had a chance to talk. Know what I mean? I feel like me and her monopolized the evening." He lifted his beard and he let it fall. He picked up his cigarettes and his lighter.

"That's all right," I said. Then I said, "I'm glad for the company."

And I guess I was. Every night I smoked dope and stayed up as long as I could before I fell asleep. My wife and I hardly ever went to bed at the same time. When I did go to sleep, I had these dreams. Sometimes I'd wake up from one of them, my heart going crazy.

Something about the church and the Middle Ages was on the TV. Not your run-of-the-mill TV fare. I wanted to watch something else. I turned to the other channels. But there was nothing on them, either. So I turned back to the first channel and apologized.

"Bub, it's all right," the blind man said. "It's fine with me. Whatever you want to watch is okay. I'm always learning something. Learning never ends. It won't hurt me to learn something tonight. I got ears," he said.

We didn't say anything for a time. He was leaning forward with his head turned at me, his right ear aimed in the direction of the set. Very disconcerting. Now and then his eyelids drooped and then they snapped open again. Now and then he put his fingers into his beard and tugged, like he was thinking about something he was hearing on the television.

On the screen, a group of men wearing cowls was being set upon and tormented by men dressed in skeleton costumes and men dressed as devils. The men dressed as devils wore devil masks, horns, and long tails. This pageant was part of a procession. The Englishman who was narrating the thing said it took place in Spain once a year. I tried to explain to the blind man what was happening.

"Skeletons," he said. "I know about skeletons," he said, and he nodded.

The TV showed this one cathedral. Then there was a long, slow look at another one. Finally, the picture switched to the famous one in Paris, with its flying buttresses and its spires reaching up to the clouds. The camera pulled away to show the whole of the cathedral rising above the skyline.

There were times when the Englishman who was telling the thing would shut up, would simply let the camera move around over the cathedrals. Or else the camera would tour the countryside, men in fields walking behind oxen. I waited as long as I could. Then I felt I had to say something. I said, "They're showing the outside of this cathedral now. Gargoyles. Little statues carved to look like monsters. Now I guess they're in Italy. Yeah, they're in Italy. There's paintings on the walls of this one church."

"Are those fresco paintings, bub?" he asked, and he sipped from his drink.

I reached for my glass. But it was empty. I tried to remember what I could remember. "You're asking me are those frescoes?" I said. "That's a good question. I don't know."

The camera moved to a cathedral outside Lisbon. The differences in the Portuguese cathedral compared with the French and Italian were not that great. But they were there. Mostly the interior stuff. Then something occurred to me, and I said, "Something has occurred to me. Do you have any idea what a cathedral is? What they look like, that is? Do you follow me? If somebody says cathedral to you, do you have any notion what they're talking about? Do you know the difference between that and a Baptist church, say?"

He let the smoke dribble from his mouth. "I know they took hundreds of workers fifty or a hundred years to build," he said. "I just heard the man say that, of course. I know generations of the same families worked on a cathedral. I heard him say that, too. The men who began their life's work on them, they never lived to see the completion of their work. In that wise, bub, they're no different from the rest of us, right?" He laughed. Then his eyelids drooped again. His head nodded. He seemed to be snoozing. Maybe he was imagining himself in Portugal. The TV was showing another cathedral now. This one was in Germany. The Englishman's voice droned on. "Cathedrals," the blind man said. He sat up and rolled his head back and forth. "If you want the truth, bub, that's about all I know. What I just said. What I heard him say. But maybe you could describe one to me? I wish you'd do it. I'd like that. If you want to know, I really don't have a good idea."

I stared hard at the shot of the cathedral on the TV. How could I even begin to describe it? But say my life depended on it. Say my life was being threatened by an insane guy who said I had to do it or else.

I stared some more at the cathedral before the picture flipped off into the countryside. There was no use. I turned to the blind man and said, "To begin with, they're very tall." I was looking around the room for clues. "They reach way up. Up and up. Toward the sky. They're so big, some of them, they have to have these supports. To help hold them up, so to speak. These supports are called buttresses. They remind me of viaducts, for some reason. But maybe you don't know viaducts, either? Sometimes the cathedrals have devils and such carved into the front. Sometimes lords and ladies. Don't ask me why this is," I said.

He was nodding. The whole upper part of his body seemed to be moving back and forth.

"I'm not doing so good, am I?" I said.

He stopped nodding and leaned forward on the edge of the sofa. As he listened to me, he was running his fingers through his beard. I wasn't getting through to him, I could see that. But he waited for me to go on just the same. He nodded, like he was trying to encourage me. I tried to think what else to say. "They're really big," I said. "They're massive. They're built of stone. Marble, too, sometimes. In those olden days, when they built cathedrals, men wanted to be close to God. In those olden days, God was an important part of everyone's life. You could tell this from their cathedral-building. I'm sorry," I said, "but it looks like that's the best I can do for you. I'm just no good at it."

"That's all right, bub," the blind man said. "Hey, listen. I hope you don't mind my asking you. Can I ask you something? Let me ask you a simple question, yes or no. I'm just curious and there's no offense. You're my host. But let me ask if you are in any way religious? You don't mind my asking?"

I shook my head. He couldn't see that, though. A wink is the same as a nod to a blind man. "I guess I don't believe in it. In anything. Sometimes it's hard. You know what I'm saying?"

"Sure, I do," he said.

"Right," I said.

The Englishman was still holding forth. My wife sighed in her sleep. She drew a long breath and went on with her sleeping.

"You'll have to forgive me," I said. "But I can't tell you what a cathedral looks like. It just isn't in me to do it. I can't do any more than I've done."

The blind man sat very still, his head down, as he listened to me.

I said, "The truth is, cathedrals don't mean anything special to me. Nothing. Cathedrals. They're something to look at on late-night TV. That's all they are."

It was then that the blind man cleared his throat. He brought something up. He took a handkerchief from his back pocket. Then he said, "I get it, bub. It's okay. It happens. Don't worry about it," he said. "Hey, listen to me. Will you do me a favor? I got an idea. Why don't you find us some heavy paper? And a pen. We'll do something. We'll draw one together. Get us a pen and some heavy paper. Go on, bub, get the stuff," he said.

So I went upstairs. My legs felt like they didn't have any strength in them. They felt like they did after I'd done some running. In my wife's room, I looked around. I found some ballpoints in a little basket on her table. And then I tried to think where to look for the kind of paper he was talking about.

Downstairs, in the kitchen, I found a shopping bag with onion skins in the bottom of the bag. I emptied the bag and shook it. I brought it into the living room and sat down with it near his legs. I moved some things, smoothed the wrinkles from the bag, spread it out on the coffee table.

The blind man got down from the sofa and sat next to me on the carpet.

He ran his fingers over the paper. He went up and down the sides of the paper. The edges, even the edges. He fingered the corners.

"All right," he said. "All right, let's do her."

He found my hand, the hand with the pen. He closed his hand over my hand. "Go ahead, bub, draw," he said. "Draw. You'll see. I'll follow along with you. It'll be okay. Just begin now like I'm telling you. You'll see. Draw," the blind man said.

So I began. First I drew a box that looked like a house. It could have been the house I lived in. Then I put a roof on it. At either end of the roof, I drew spires. Crazy.

"Swell," he said. "Terrific. You're doing fine," he said. "Never thought anything like this could happen in your lifetime, did you, bub? Well, it's a strange life, we all know that. Go on now. Keep it up."

I put in windows with arches. I drew flying buttresses. I hung great doors. I couldn't stop. The TV station went off the air. I put down the pen and closed and opened my fingers. The blind man felt around over the paper. He moved the tips of his fingers over the paper, all over what I had drawn, and he nodded.

"Doing fine," the blind man said.

I took up the pen again, and he found my hand. I kept at it. I'm no artist. But I kept drawing just the same.

My wife opened up her eyes and gazed at us. She sat up on the sofa, her robe hanging open. She said, "What are you doing? Tell me, I want to know."

I didn't answer her.

The blind man said, "We're drawing a cathedral. Me and him are working on it. Press hard," he said to me. "That's right. That's good," he said. "Sure. You got it, bub. I can tell. You didn't think you could. But you can, can't you? You're cooking with gas now. You know what I'm saying? We're going to really have us something here in a minute. How's the old arm?" he said. "Put some people in there now. What's a cathedral without people?"

My wife said, "What's going on? Robert, what are you doing? What's going on?"

"It's all right," he said to her. "Close your eyes now," the blind man said to me.

I did it. I closed them just like he said.

"Are they closed?" he said. "Don't fudge."

"They're closed," I said.

"Keep them that way," he said. He said, "Don't stop now. Draw."

So we kept on with it. His fingers rode my fingers as my hand went over the paper. It was like nothing else in my life up to now.

Then he said, "I think that's it. I think you got it," he said. "Take a look. What do you think?"

But I had my eyes closed. I thought I'd keep them that way for a little longer. I thought it was something I ought to do.

"Well?" he said. "Are you looking?"

My eyes were still closed. I was in my house. I knew that. But I didn't feel like I was inside anything.

"It's really something," I said.

1983

## QUESTIONS

1. In the opening sections of "Cathedral," what do the narrator's remarks about himself, his wife, and the blind man suggest about the kind of person he is? How might Raymond Carver intend for the reader to feel about the narrator at first?
2. At what key moments in the story does the narrator's attitude toward the blind man begin to change? How does this change our view of him?
3. What is the importance of drawing the cathedral, both to the narrator and to the story itself?

GRACE PALEY

## A Conversation with My Father

My father is eighty-six years old and in bed. His heart, that bloody motor, is equally old and will not do certain jobs any more. It still floods his head with brainy light. But it won't let his legs carry the weight of his body around the house. Despite my metaphors, this muscle failure is not due to his old heart, he says, but to a potassium shortage. Sitting on one pillow, leaning on three, he offers last-minute advice and makes a request.

"I would like you to write a simple story just once more," he says, "the kind de Maupassant wrote, or Chekhov, the kind you used to write. Just recognizable people and then write down what happened to them next."

I say, "Yes, why not? That's possible." I want to please him, though I don't remember writing that way. I *would* like to try to tell such a story, if he means the kind that begins: "There was a woman..." followed by plot, the absolute line between two points which I've always despised. Not for literary reasons, but because it takes all hope away. Everyone, real or invented, deserves the open destiny of life.

Finally I thought of a story that had been happening for a couple of years right across the street. I wrote it down, then read it aloud. "Pa," I said, "how about this? Do you mean something like this?"

> Once in my time there was a woman and she had a son. They lived nicely, in a small apartment in Manhattan. This boy at about fifteen became a junkie, which is not unusual in our neighborhood. In order to maintain her close friendship with him, she became a junkie too. She said it was part of the youth culture, with which she felt very much at home. After a while, for a number of reasons, the boy gave it all up and left the city and his mother in disgust. Hopeless and alone, she grieved. We all visit her.

"O.K., Pa, that's it," I said, "an unadorned and miserable tale."

"But that's not what I mean," my father said. "You misunderstood me on purpose. You know there's a lot more to it. You know that. You left everything out. Turgenev[1] wouldn't do that. Chekhov wouldn't do that. There are in fact Russian writers you never heard of, you don't have an inkling of, as good as anyone, who can write a plain ordinary story, who would not leave out what you have left out. I object not to facts but to people sitting in trees talking senselessly, voices from who knows where..."

"Forget that one, Pa, what have I left out now? In this one?"

"Her looks, for instance."

"Oh. Quite handsome, I think. Yes."

"Her hair?"

"Dark, with heavy braids, as though she were a girl or a foreigner."

"What were her parents like, her stock? That she became such a person. It's interesting, you know."

---

1. Ivan Sergeyevich Turgenev (1818–1883); his best-known novel, *Fathers and Sons*, deals with the conflict between generations.

"From out of town. Professional people. The first to be divorced in their county. How's that? Enough?" I asked.

"With you, it's all a joke," he said. "What about the boy's father. Why didn't you mention him? Who was he? Or was the boy born out of wedlock?"

"Yes," I said. "He was born out of wedlock."

"For Godsakes, doesn't anyone in your stories get married? Doesn't anyone have the time to run down to City Hall before they jump into bed?"

"No," I said. "In real life, yes. But in my stories, no."

"Why do you answer me like that?"

"Oh, Pa, this is a simple story about a smart woman who came to N.Y.C. full of interest love trust excitement very up to date, and about her son, what a hard time she had in this world. Married or not, it's of small consequence."

"It is of great consequence," he said.

"O.K.," I said.

"O.K. O.K. yourself," he said, "but listen. I believe you that she's good-looking, but I don't think she was so smart."

"That's true," I said. "Actually that's the trouble with stories. People start out fantastic. You think they're extraordinary, but it turns out as the work goes along, they're just average with a good education. Sometimes the other way around, the person's a kind of dumb innocent, but he outwits you and you can't even think of an ending good enough."

"What do you do then?" he asked. He had been a doctor for a couple of decades and then an artist for a couple of decades and he's still interested in details, craft, technique.

"Well, you just have to let the story lie around till some agreement can be reached between you and the stubborn hero."

"Aren't you talking silly, now?" he asked. "Start again," he said. "It so happens I'm not going out this evening. Tell the story again. See what you can do this time."

"O.K.," I said. "But it's not a five-minute job." Second attempt:

Once, across the street from us, there was a fine handsome woman, our neighbor. She had a son whom she loved because she'd known him since birth (in helpless chubby infancy, and in the wrestling, hugging ages, seven to ten, as well as earlier and later). This boy, when he fell into the fist of adolescence, became a junkie. He was not a hopeless one. He was in fact hopeful, an ideologue and successful converter. With his busy brilliance, he wrote persuasive articles for his high-school newspaper. Seeking a wider audience, using important connections, he drummed into Lower Manhattan newsstand distribution a periodical called *Oh! Golden Horse!*[2]

In order to keep him from feeling guilty (because guilt is the stony heart of nine tenths of all clinically diagnosed cancers in America today, she said), and because she had always believed in giving bad habits room at home where one could keep an eye on them, she too became a junkie. Her kitchen was famous for a while—a center for intellectual addicts who knew what they were doing. A few felt artistic like Coleridge[3] and others were scientific and revolutionary

---

2. *Horse* is slang for heroin.
3. Samuel Taylor Coleridge (1772-1834), English Romantic poet, claimed that his poem "Kubla Khan" recorded what he remembered of a dream stimulated by opium.

like Leary.[4] Although she was often high herself, certain good mothering reflexes remained, and she saw to it that there was lots of orange juice around and honey and milk and vitamin pills. However, she never cooked anything but chili, and that no more than once a week. She explained, when we talked to her, seriously, with neighborly concern, that it was her part in the youth culture and she would rather be with the young, it was an honor, than with her own generation.

One week, while nodding through an Antonioni[5] film, this boy was severely jabbed by the elbow of a stern and proselytizing girl, sitting beside him. She offered immediate apricots and nuts for his sugar level, spoke to him sharply, and took him home.

She had heard of him and his work and she herself published, edited, and wrote a competitive journal called *Man Does Live By Bread Alone*. In the organic heat of her continuous presence he could not help but become interested once more in his muscles, his arteries, and nerve connections. In fact he began to love them, treasure them, praise them with funny little songs in *Man Does Live*...

> *the fingers of my flesh transcend*
> *my transcendental soul*
> *the tightness in my shoulders end*
> *my teeth have made me whole*

To the mouth of his head (that glory of will and determination) he brought hard apples, nuts, wheat germ, and soybean oil. He said to his old friends, From now on, I guess I'll keep my wits about me. I'm going on the natch. He said he was about to begin a spiritual deep-breathing journey. How about you too, Mom? he asked kindly.

His conversion was so radiant, splendid, that neighborhood kids his age began to say that he had never been a real addict at all, only a journalist along for the smell of the story. The mother tried several times to give up what had become without her son and his friends a lonely habit. This effort only brought it to supportable levels. The boy and his girl took their electronic mimeograph and moved to the bushy edge of another borough. They were very strict. They said they would not see her again until she had been off drugs for sixty days.

At home alone in the evening, weeping, the mother read and reread the seven issues of *Oh! Golden Horse!* They seemed to her as truthful as ever. We often crossed the street to visit and console. But if we mentioned any of our children who were at college or in the hospital or dropouts at home, she would cry out, My baby! My baby! and burst into terrible, face-scarring, time-consuming tears. The End.

First my father was silent, then he said, "Number One: You have a nice sense of humor. Number Two: I see you can't tell a plain story. So don't waste time." Then he said sadly, "Number Three: I suppose that means she was alone, she was left like that, his mother. Alone. Probably sick?"

I said, "Yes."

---

4. Timothy Leary (1920–1996), American psychologist, promoted the use of psychedelic drugs.
5. Michelangelo Antonioni (b. 1912), Italian film director (*Blow-Up, Zabriskie Point*). *Nodding:* a slang term referring to the narcotic effect of heroin.

"Poor woman. Poor girl, to be born in a time of fools, to live among fools. The end. The end. You were right to put that down. The end."

I didn't want to argue, but I had to say, "Well, it is not necessarily the end, Pa."

"Yes," he said, "what a tragedy. The end of a person."

"No, Pa," I begged him. "It doesn't have to be. She's only about forty. She could be a hundred different things in this world as time goes on. A teacher or a social worker. An ex-junkie! Sometimes it's better than having a master's in education."

"Jokes," he said. "As a writer that's your main trouble. You don't want to recognize it. Tragedy! Plain tragedy! Historical tragedy! No hope. The end."

"Oh, Pa," I said. "She could change."

"In your own life, too, you have to look it in the face." He took a couple of nitroglycerin.[6] "Turn to five," he said, pointing to the dial on the oxygen tank. He inserted the tubes into his nostrils and breathed deep. He closed his eyes and said, "No."

I had promised the family to always let him have the last word when arguing, but in this case I had a different responsibility. That woman lives across the street. She's my knowledge and my invention. I'm sorry for her. I'm not going to leave her there in that house crying. (Actually neither would Life, which unlike me has no pity.)

Therefore: She did change. Of course her son never came home again. But right now, she's the receptionist in a storefront community clinic in the East Village. Most of the customers are young people, some old friends. The head doctor said to her, "If we only had three people in this clinic with your experiences . . ."

"The doctor said that?" My father took the oxygen tubes out of his nostrils and said, "Jokes. Jokes again."

"No, Pa, it could really happen that way, it's a funny world nowadays."

"No," he said. "Truth first. She will slide back. A person must have character. She does not."

"No, Pa," I said. "That's it. She's got a job. Forget it. She's in that storefront working."

"How long will it be?" he asked. "Tragedy! You too. When will you look it in the face?"

1974

## QUESTIONS

1. What different ideas about stories and storytelling do the narrator and her father seem to have in "A Conversation with My Father"? What might account for their different attitudes?
2. In what ways is the narrator's second version of her story an improvement over the first? Why does her father still reject the story?
3. Why does the narrator's father object so strongly to the jokes in the stories, even though he compliments her "nice sense of humor"? Are jokes out of place in a story about someone facing death?

---

6. Medicine for certain heart conditions.

## A. S. BYATT

## The Thing in the Forest

There were once two little girls who saw, or believed they saw, a thing in a forest. The two little girls were evacuees, who had been sent away from the city by train with a large number of other children.[1] They all had their names attached to their coats with safety pins, and they carried little bags or satchels, and the regulation gas mask. They wore knitted scarves and bonnets or caps, and many had knitted gloves attached to long tapes that ran along their sleeves, inside their coats, and over their shoulders and out, so that they could leave their ten woollen fingers dangling, like a spare pair of hands, like a scarecrow. They all had bare legs and scuffed shoes and wrinkled socks. Most had wounds on their knees in varying stages of freshness and scabbiness. They were at the age when children fall often and their knees were unprotected. With their suitcases, some of which were almost too big to carry, and their other impedimenta, a doll, a toy car, a comic, they were like a disorderly dwarf regiment, stomping along the platform.

The two little girls had not met before, and made friends on the train. They shared a square of chocolate, and took alternate bites at an apple. Their names were Penny and Primrose. Penny was thin and dark and taller, possibly older, than Primrose, who was plump and blond and curly. Primrose had bitten nails, and a velvet collar on her dressy green coat. Penny had a bloodless transparent paleness, a touch of blue in her fine lips. Neither of them knew where they were going, nor how long the journey might take. They did not even know why they were going, since neither of their mothers had quite known how to explain the danger to them. How do you say to your child, I am sending you away, because enemy bombs may fall out of the sky, but I myself am staying here, in what I believe may be daily danger of burning, being buried alive, gas, and ultimately perhaps a gray army rolling in on tanks over the suburbs? So the mothers (who did not resemble each other at all) behaved alike, and explained nothing—it was easier. Their daughters, they knew, were little girls, who would not be able to understand or imagine.

The girls discussed whether it was a sort of holiday or a sort of punishment, or a bit of both. Both had the idea that these were all perhaps not very good children, possibly being sent away for that reason. They were pleased to be able to define each other as "nice." They would stick together, they agreed.

The train crawled sluggishly farther and farther away from the city and their homes. It was not a clean train—the upholstery of their carriage had the dank smell of unwashed trousers, and the gusts of hot steam rolling backward past their windows were full of specks of flimsy ash, and sharp grit, and occasionally fiery sparks that pricked face and fingers like hot needles if you opened the window. It was very noisy, too, whenever it picked up a little speed. The windowpanes were both grimy and misted up. The train stopped frequently, and when it stopped they used their gloves to wipe rounds, through which they peered out

---

1. The story takes place during the Blitz—that is, during the period (1940–41) when British cities were frequently bombed by German warplanes. Many children were evacuated from cities to safer locations in the countryside.

at flooded fields, furrowed hillsides, and tiny stations whose names were carefully blacked out, whose platforms were empty of life.

The children did not know that the namelessness was meant to baffle or delude an invading army. They felt—they did not think it out, but somewhere inside them the idea sprouted—that the erasure was because of them, because they were not meant to know where they were going or, like Hansel and Gretel, to find the way back. They did not speak to each other of this anxiety, but began the kind of conversation children have about things they really dislike, things that upset, or disgust, or frighten them. Semolina pudding with its grainy texture, mushy peas, fat on roast meat. Having your head held roughly back over the basin to have your hair washed, with cold water running down inside your liberty bodice. Gangs in playgrounds. They felt the pressure of all the other alien children in all the other carriages as a potential gang. They shared another square of chocolate, and licked their fingers, and looked out at a great white goose flapping its wings beside an inky pond.

The sky grew dark gray and in the end the train halted. The children got out, and lined up in a crocodile,[2] and were led to a mud-colored bus. Penny and Primrose managed to get a seat together, although it was over the wheel, and both of them began to feel sick as the bus bumped along snaking country lanes, under whipping branches, with torn strips of thin cloud streaming across a full moon.

They were billeted in a mansion commandeered from its owner. The children were told they were there temporarily, until families were found to take them. Penny and Primrose held hands, and said to each other that it would be wizard if they could go to the same family, because at least they would have each other. They didn't say anything to the rather tired-looking ladies who were ordering them about, because, with the cunning of little children, they knew that requests were most often counterproductive—adults liked saying no. They imagined possible families into which they might be thrust. They did not discuss what they imagined, as these pictures, like the black station signs, were too frightening, and words might make some horror solid, in some magical way. Penny, who was a reading child, imagined Victorian dark pillars of severity, like Jane Eyre's Mr. Brocklehurst, or David Copperfield's Mr. Murdstone. Primrose imagined—she didn't know why—a fat woman with a white cap and round red arms who smiled nicely but made the children wear sacking aprons and scrub the steps and the stove. "It's like we were orphans," she said to Penny. "But we're not." Penny said, "If we manage to stick together . . ."

The great house had a double flight of imposing stairs to its front door, and carved griffins and unicorns on its balustrade. There was no lighting, because of the blackout. All the windows were shuttered. The children trudged up the staircase in their crocodile, and were given supper (Irish stew and rice pudding with a dollop of blood-red jam) before going to bed in long makeshift dormitories, where once servants had slept. They had camp beds (military issue) and gray shoddy blankets. Penny and Primrose got beds together but couldn't get a corner. They queued[3] to brush their teeth in a tiny washroom, and both suffered (again without speaking) suffocating anxiety about what would happen if they wanted

---

2. A group of people lined up two by two.  3. Lined up.

to pee in the middle of the night. They also suffered from a fear that in the dark the other children would start laughing and rushing and teasing, and turn themselves into a gang. But that did not happen. Everyone was tired and anxious and orphaned. An uneasy silence, a drift of perturbed sleep, came over them all. The only sounds—from all parts of the great dormitory, it seemed—were suppressed snuffles and sobs, from faces pressed into thin pillows.

When daylight came, things seemed, as they mostly do, brighter and better. The children were given breakfast in a large vaulted room, at trestle tables, porridge made with water, and a dab of the red jam, heavy cups of strong tea. Then they were told they could go out and play until lunchtime. Children in those days—wherever they came from—were not closely watched, were allowed to come and go freely, and those evacuated children were not herded into any kind of holding pen or transit camp. They were told they should be back for lunch at twelve-thirty, by which time those in charge hoped to have sorted out their provisional future lives. It was not known how they would know when it was twelve-thirty, but it was expected that—despite the fact that few of them had wristwatches—they would know how to keep an eye on the time. It was what they were used to.

Penny and Primrose went out together, in their respectable coats and laced shoes, onto the terrace. The terrace appeared to them to be vast. It was covered with a fine layer of damp gravel, stained here and there bright green, or invaded by mosses. Beyond it was a stone balustrade, with a staircase leading down to a lawn. Across the lawn was a sculpted yew hedge. In the middle of the hedge was a wicket gate, and beyond the gate were trees. A forest, the little girls said to themselves.

"Let's go into the forest," said Penny, as though the sentence were required of her.

Primrose hesitated. Most of the other children were running up and down the terrace. Some boys were kicking a ball on the grass.

"O.K.," said Primrose. "We needn't go far."

"No. I've never been in a forest."

"Nor me."

"We ought to look at it, while we've got the opportunity," said Penny.

There was a very small child—one of the smallest—whose name, she told everyone, was Alys. With a "y," she told those who could spell, and those who couldn't, which surely included herself. She was barely out of nappies.[4] She was quite extraordinarily pretty, pink and white, with large pale-blue eyes, and sparse little golden curls all over her head and neck, through which her pink skin could be seen. Nobody seemed to be in charge of her, no elder brother or sister. She had not quite managed to wash the tearstains from her dimpled cheeks.

She had made several attempts to attach herself to Penny and Primrose. They did not want her. They were excited about meeting and liking each other. She said now, "I'm coming, too, into the forest."

"No, you aren't," said Primrose.

"You are too little, you must stay here," said Penny.

"You'll get lost," said Primrose.

---

4. Diapers.

"You won't get lost. I'll come with you," said the little creature, with an engaging smile, made for loving parents and grandparents.

"We don't want you, you see," said Primrose.

"It's for your own good," said Penny.

Alys went on smiling hopefully, the smile becoming more of a mask.

"It will be all right," said Alys.

"Run," said Primrose.

They ran; they ran down the steps and across the lawn, and through the gate, into the forest. They didn't look back. They were long-legged little girls. The trees were silent round them, holding out their branches to the sun.

Primrose touched the warm skin of the nearest saplings, taking off her gloves to feel the cracks and knots. Penny looked into the thick of the forest. There was undergrowth—a mat of brambles and bracken. There were no obvious paths. Dark and light came and went, inviting and mysterious, as the wind pushed clouds across the face of the sun.

"We have to be careful not to get lost," she said. "In stories, people make marks on tree trunks, or unroll a thread, or leave a trail of white pebbles—to find their way back."

"We needn't go out of sight of the gate," said Primrose. "We could just explore a little bit."

They set off, very slowly. They went on tiptoe, making their own narrow passages through the undergrowth, which sometimes came as high as their thin shoulders. They were urban, and unaccustomed to silence. Then they began to hear small sounds. The chatter and repeated lilt and alarm of invisible birds, high up, further in. Rustling in dry leaves. Slitherings, dry coughs, sharp cracks. They went on, pointing out to each other creepers draped with glistening berries, crimson, black, and emerald, little crops of toadstools, some scarlet, some ghostly pale, some a dead-flesh purple, some like tiny parasols—and some like pieces of meat protruding from tree trunks. They met blackberries, but didn't pick them, in case in this place they were dangerous or deceptive. They admired from a safe distance the stiff upright fruiting rods of the lords-and-ladies,[5] packed with fat red berries.

Did they hear it first or smell it? Both sound and scent were at first infinitesimal and dispersed. They gave the strange impression of moving in—in waves—from the whole perimeter of the forest. Both increased very slowly in intensity, and both were mixed, a sound and a smell fabricated of many disparate sounds and smells. A crunching, a crackling, a crushing, a heavy thumping, combining with threshing and thrashing, and added to that a gulping, heaving, boiling, bursting, steaming sound, full of bubbles and farts, piffs and explosions, swallowings and wallowings. The smell was worse, and more aggressive, than the sound. It was a liquid smell of putrefaction, the smell of maggoty things at the bottom of untended dustbins, blocked drains, mixed with the smell of bad eggs, and of rotten carpets and ancient polluted bedding. The ordinary forest smells and sounds were extinguished. The two little girls looked at each other, and took each other's hand. Speechlessly and instinctively, they crouched down behind a fallen tree trunk, and trembled, as the thing came into view.

---

5. Wild arum, a flowering perennial common to southern Britain.

Its head appeared to form, or first become visible in the distance, between the trees. Its face—which was triangular—appeared like a rubbery or fleshy mask over a shapeless sprouting bulb of a head, like a monstrous turnip. Its color was the color of flayed flesh, pitted with wormholes, and its expression was neither wrath nor greed but pure misery. Its most defined feature was a vast mouth, pulled down and down at the corners, tight with a kind of pain. Its lips were thin, and raised, like welts from whip-strokes. It had blind, opaque white eyes, fringed with fleshy lashes and brows like the feelers of sea anemones. Its face was close to the ground and moved toward the children between its forearms, which were squat, thick, powerful, and akimbo, like a cross between a washer-woman's and a primeval dragon's. The flesh on these forearms was glistening and mottled.

The rest of its very large body appeared to be glued together, like still wet papier-mâché, or the carapace of stones and straws and twigs worn by caddis flies underwater. It had a tubular shape, as a turd has a tubular shape, a provisional amalgam. It was made of rank meat, and decaying vegetation, but it also trailed veils and prostheses of man-made materials, bits of wire netting, foul dishcloths, wire-wool full of pan scrubbings, rusty nuts and bolts. It had feeble stubs and stumps of very slender legs, growing out of it at all angles, wavering and rippling like the suckered feet of a caterpillar or the squirming fringe of a centipede. On and on it came, bending and crushing whatever lay in its path, including bushes, though not substantial trees, which it wound between, awkwardly. The little girls observed, with horrified fascination, that when it met a sharp stone, or a narrow tree trunk, it allowed itself to be sliced through, flowed sluggishly round in two or three smaller worms, convulsed, and reunited. Its progress was apparently very painful, for it moaned and whined among its other burblings and belchings. They thought it could not see, or certainly could not see clearly. It and its stench passed within a few feet of their tree trunk, humping along, leaving behind it a trail of bloody slime and dead foliage.

Its end was flat and blunt, almost transparent, like some earthworms.

When it had gone, Penny and Primrose, kneeling on the moss and dead leaves, put their arms about each other, and hugged each other, shaking with dry sobs. Then they stood up, still silent, and stared together, hand in hand, at the trail of obliteration and destruction, which wound out of the forest and into it again. They went back, hand in hand, without looking behind them, afraid that the wicket gate, the lawn, the stone steps, the balustrade, the terrace, and the great house would be transmogrified, or simply not there. But the boys were still playing football on the lawn, a group of girls were skipping and singing shrilly on the gravel. They let go each other's hand, and went back in.

They did not speak to each other again.

The next day, they were separated and placed with strange families. Their stay in these families—Primrose was in a dairy farm, Penny was in a parsonage—did not in fact last very long, though then the time seemed slow motion and endless. Later, Primrose remembered the sound of milk spurting in the pail, and Penny remembered the empty corsets of the Vicar's wife, hanging bony on the line. They remembered dandelion clocks, but you can remember those from anywhere, any time. They remembered the thing they had seen in the forest, on the contrary, in the way you remember those very few dreams—almost all nightmares—that have the quality of life itself. (Though what are dreams if not life itself?) They remembered too solid flesh, too precise a stink, a rattle and a soughing that thrilled the nerves and the cartilage of their growing ears. In the memory, as in such a dream, they felt, I cannot get out, this is a real thing in a real place.

40   They returned from evacuation, like many evacuees, so early that they then lived through wartime in the city, bombardment, blitz, unearthly light and roaring, changed landscapes, holes in their world where the newly dead had been. Both lost their fathers. Primrose's father was in the Army, and was killed, very late in the war, on a crowded troop carrier sunk in the Far East. Penny's father, a much older man, was in the Auxiliary Fire Service, and died in a sheet of flame in the East India Docks on the Thames, pumping evaporating water from a puny coil of hose. They found it hard, after the war, to remember these different men. The claspers of memory could not grip the drowned and the burned. Primrose saw an inane grin under a khaki cap, because her mother had a snapshot. Penny thought she remembered her father, already gray-headed, brushing ash off his boots and trouser cuffs as he put on his tin hat to go out. She thought she remembered a quaver of fear in his tired face, and the muscles composing themselves into resolution. It was not much what either of them remembered.

After the war, their fates were still similar and dissimilar. Penny's widowed mother embraced grief, closed her face and her curtains. Primrose's mother married one of the many admirers she had had before the ship went down, gave birth to another five children, and developed varicose veins and a smoker's cough. She dyed her blond hair with peroxide when it faded. Both Primrose and Penny were only children who now, because of the war, lived in amputated or unreal families. Penny was a good student and in due course went to university, where she chose to study developmental psychology. Primrose had little education. She was always being kept off school to look after the others. She, too, dyed her blond curls with peroxide when they turned mousy and faded. She got fat as Penny got thin. Neither of them married. Penny became a child psychologist, working with the abused, the displaced, the disturbed. Primrose did this and that. She was a barmaid. She worked in a shop. She went to help at various church crèches and Salvation Army gatherings, and discovered she had a talent for storytelling. She became Aunty Primrose, with her own repertoire. She was employed to tell tales to kindergartens and entertain at children's parties. She was much in demand at Halloween, and had her own circle of bright-colored plastic chairs in a local shopping mall, where she kept an eye on the children of burdened women, keeping them safe, offering them just a frisson of fear and terror, which made them wriggle with pleasure.

The house in the country aged differently. During this period of time—while the little girls became women—it was handed over to the nation, which turned it into a living museum. Guided tours took place in it, at regulated times. During these tours, the ballroom and intimate drawing rooms were fenced off with crimson twisted ropes on little brass one-eyed pedestals. The bored and the curious peered in at four-poster beds and pink silk fauteuils,[6] at silver-framed photographs of wartime royalty, and crackling crazing[7] Renaissance and Enlightenment portraits. In the room where the evacuees had eaten their rationed meals, the history of the house was displayed, on posters, in glass cases, with helpful

---

6. Armchairs.   7. Sealed with varnish that, with age, has cracked in patterns.

notices and opened copies of old diaries and records. There was no mention of the evacuees, whose presence appeared to have been too brief to have left any trace.

The two women met in this room on an autumn day in 1984. They had come with a group, walking in a chattering crocodile behind a guide. They prowled around the room, each alone with herself, in opposite directions, each without acknowledging the other's presence. Their mothers had died that spring, within a week of each other, though this coincidence was unknown to them. It had made both of them think of taking a holiday, and both had chosen that part of the world. Penny was wearing a charcoal trouser suit and a black velvet hat. Primrose wore a floral knit long jacket over a shell-pink cashmere sweater, over a rustling long skirt with an elastic waist, in a mustard-colored tapestry print. Her hips and bosom were bulky. Both of them, at the same moment, leaned over an image in a medieval-looking illustrated book. Primrose thought it was a very old book. Penny assumed it was nineteenth-century mock-medieval. It showed a knight, on foot, in a forest, lifting his sword to slay something. The knight shone on the rounded slope of the page, in the light, which caught the gilding on his helmet and sword belt. It was not possible to see what was being slain. This was because, both in the tangled vegetation of the image and in the way the book was displayed in the case, the enemy, or victim, was in shadows.

Neither of them could read the ancient (or pseudo-ancient) black letter of the text beside the illustration. There was a typed description, under the book. They had to lean forward to read it, and to see what was worming its way into, or out of, the deep spine of the book, and that was how each came to see the other's face, close up, in the glass, which was both transparent and reflective. Their transparent reflected faces lost detail—cracked lipstick, pouches, fine lines of wrinkles—and looked both younger and grayer, less substantial. And that is how they came to recognize each other, as they might not have done, plump face to bony face. They breathed each other's names—Penny, Primrose—and their breath misted the glass, obscuring the knight and his opponent. I could have died, I could have wet my knickers, said Penny and Primrose afterward to each other, and both experienced this still moment as pure, dangerous shock. They read the caption, which was about the Loathly Worm, which, tradition held, had infested the countryside and had been killed more than once by scions of that house— Sir Lionel, Sir Boris, Sir Guillem. The Worm, the typewriter had tapped out, was an English worm, not a European dragon, and, like most such worms, was wingless. In some sightings it was reported as having vestigial legs, hands, or feet. In others it was limbless. It had, in monstrous form, the capacity of common or garden worms to sprout new heads or trunks if it was divided, so that two worms, or more, replaced one. This was why it had been killed so often, yet reappeared. It had been reported travelling with a slithering pack of young ones, but these may have been only revitalized segments.

Being English, they thought of tea. There was a tearoom in the great house, in a converted stable at the back. There they stood silently side by side, clutching floral plastic trays spread with briar roses, and purchased scones, superior raspberry jam in tiny jam jars, little plastic tubs of clotted cream. "You couldn't get cream or real jam in the war," said Primrose as they found a corner table. She said wartime rationing had made her permanently greedy, and thin Penny agreed it had—clotted cream was still a treat.

They watched each other warily, offering bland snippets of autobiography in politely hushed voices. Primrose thought Penny looked gaunt, and Penny thought Primrose looked raddled.[8] They established the skein of coincidences—dead fathers, unmarried status, child-caring professions, recently dead mothers. Circling like beaters,[9] they approached the covert thing in the forest. They discussed the great house, politely. Primrose admired the quality of the carpets. Penny said it was nice to see the old pictures back on the wall. Primrose said, Funny really, that there was all that history, but no sign that they, the children, that was, had ever been there. Funny, said Penny, that they should meet each other next to that book, with that picture. "Creepy," said Primrose in a light, light cobweb voice, not looking at Penny. "We saw that thing. When we went in the forest."

"Yes, we did," said Penny. "We saw it."

"Did you ever wonder," asked Primrose, "if we really saw it?"

"Never for a moment," said Penny. "That is, I don't know what it was, but I've always been quite sure we saw it."

50 "Does it change—do you remember all of it?"

"It was a horrible thing, and yes, I remember all of it, there isn't a bit of it I can manage to forget. Though I forget all sorts of things," said Penny, in a thin voice, a vanishing voice.

"And have you ever told anyone of it, spoken of it?" asked Primrose more urgently, leaning forward.

"No," said Penny. She had not. She said, "Who would believe it?"

"That's what I thought," said Primrose. "I didn't speak. But it stuck in my mind like a tapeworm in your gut. I think it did me no good."

55 "It did me no good either," said Penny. "No good at all. I've thought about it," she said to the aging woman opposite, whose face quivered under her dyed goldilocks. "I think, I think there are things that are real—more real than we are—but mostly we don't cross their paths, or they don't cross ours. Maybe at very bad times we get into their world, or notice what they are doing in ours."

Primrose nodded energetically. She looked as though sharing was solace, and Penny, to whom it was not solace, grimaced with pain.

"Sometimes I think that thing finished me off," Penny said to Primrose, a child's voice rising in a woman's gullet, arousing a little girl's scared smile, which wasn't a smile on Primrose's face.

Primrose said, "It did finish her off, that little one, didn't it? She got into its path, didn't she? And when it had gone by—she wasn't anywhere," said Primrose. "That was how it was?"

"Nobody ever asked where she was or looked for her," said Penny.

60 "I wondered if we'd made her up," said Primrose. "But I didn't, we didn't."

"Her name was Alys."

"With a 'y.'"

There had been a mess, a disgusting mess, they remembered, but no particular sign of anything that might have been, or been part of, or belonged to, a persistent little girl called Alys.

Primrose shrugged voluptuously, let out a gale of a sigh, and rearranged her flesh in her clothes.

---

8. Frazzled.   9. Hunters who beat the bushes to drive out game.

"Well, we know we're not mad, anyway," she said. "We've got into a mystery, but we didn't make it up. It wasn't a delusion. So it was good we met, because now we needn't be afraid we're mad, need we—we can get on with things, so to speak?"

They arranged to have dinner together the following evening. They were staying in different bed-and-breakfasts and neither of them thought of exchanging addresses. They agreed on a restaurant in the market square of the local town—Seraphina's Hot Pot—and a time, seven-thirty. They did not even discuss spending the next day together. Primrose went on a local bus tour. Penny took a long solitary walk. The weather was gray, spitting fine rain. Both arrived at their lodgings with headaches, and both made tea with the tea bags and kettle provided in their rooms. They sat on their beds. Penny's had a quilt with blowsy cabbage roses. Primrose's had a black-and-white checked gingham duvet. They turned on their televisions, watched the same game show, listened to the inordinate jolly laughter.

Seven-thirty came and went, and neither woman moved. Both, indistinctly, imagined the other waiting at a table, watching a door open and shut. Neither moved. What could they have said, they asked themselves, but only perfunctorily.

The next day, Penny thought about the wood, put on her walking shoes, and set off obliquely in the opposite direction. Primrose sat over her breakfast, which was English and ample. The wood, the real and imagined wood—both before and after she had entered it with Penny—had always been simultaneously a source of attraction and of discomfort, shading into terror. Without speaking to herself a sentence in her head—"I shall go there"—Primrose decided. And she went straight there, full of warm food, arriving as the morning brightened with the first busload of tourists, and giving them the slip, to take the path they had once taken, across the lawn and through the wicket gate.

The wood was much the same, but denser and more inviting in its new greenness. Primrose's body decided to set off in a rather different direction from the one the little girls had taken. New bracken was uncoiling with snaky force. Yesterday's rain still glittered on limp new hazel leaves and threads of gossamer. Small feathered throats above her whistled and trilled with enchanting territorial aggression and male self-assertion, which were to Primrose simply the chorus. She found a mossy bank, with posies of primroses, which she recognized and took vaguely as a good sign, a personal sign. She was better at flowers than birds, because there had been Flower Fairies in the school bookshelves when she was little, with the flowers painted accurately, accompanied by truly pretty human creatures, all children, clothed in the blues and golds, russets and purples of the flowers and fruits. Here she saw and recognized them, windflower and bryony, self-heal and dead nettle, and had—despite where she was—a lovely lapping sense of invisible, just invisible life swarming in the leaves and along the twigs.

She stopped. She did not like the sound of her own toiling breath. She was not very fit. She saw, then, a whisking in the bracken, a twirl of fur, thin and flaming, quivering on a tree trunk. She saw a squirrel, a red squirrel, watching her from a bough. She had to sit down, as she remembered her mother. She sat on a hummock of grass, rather heavily. She remembered them all, Nutkin and Moldywarp, Brock and Sleepy Dormouse, Natty Newt and Ferdy Frog. Her mother hadn't told stories and hadn't opened gates into imaginary worlds. But she had been good with her fingers. Every Christmas during the war, when toys, and indeed materials, were not to be had, Primrose had woken to find in her stocking a new stuffed creature, made from fur fabric, with button eyes and horny claws. There had been an artistry to them. The stuffed squirrel was the essence of squirrel, the fox was watchful, the newt was slithery. They did not wear anthropomorphic jackets or caps, which made it easier to invest them with imaginary natures. She believed in Father Christmas, and the discovery that her mother had made the toys, the vanishing of magic, had been a breathtaking blow. She could not be grateful for the skill and the imagination, so uncharacteristic of her flirtatious mother. The creatures continued to accumulate. A spider, a Bambi. She told herself stories at night about a girlwoman, an enchantress in a fairy wood, loved and protected by an army of wise and gentle animals. She slept banked in by stuffed creatures, as the house in the blitz was banked in by inadequate sandbags.

Primrose registered the red squirrel as disappointing—stringier and more ratlike than its plump gray city cousins. But she knew it was special, and when it took off from branch to branch, flicking its extended tail like a sail, gripping with its tiny hands, she set out to follow it. It would take her to the center, she thought. It could easily have leaped out of sight, she thought, but it didn't. She pushed through brambles into denser, greener shadows. Juices stained her skirts and skin. She began to tell herself a story about staunch Primrose, not giving up, making her way to "the center." Her childhood stories had all been in the third person. "She was not afraid." "She faced up to the wild beasts. They cowered." She laddered her tights and muddied her shoes and breathed heavier. The squirrel stopped to clean its face. She crushed bluebells and saw the sinister hoods of arum lilies.

She had no idea how far she had come, but she decided that the clearing where she found herself was the center. The squirrel had stopped, and was running up and down a single tree. There was a mossy mound that could have had a thronelike aspect, if you were being imaginative. So she sat on it. "She came to the center and sat on the mossy chair."

Now what?

She had not forgotten what they had seen, the blank miserable face, the powerful claws, the raggle-taggle train of accumulated decay. She had come neither to look for it nor to confront it, but she had come because it was there. She had known all her life that she, Primrose, had really been in a magic forest. She knew that the forest was the source of terror. She had never frightened the littluns she entertained, with tales of lost children in forests. She frightened them with slimy things that came up the plughole, or swarmed out of the U-bend in the lavatory, and were dispatched by bravery and magic. But the woods in her tales bred glamour. They were places where you used words like "spangles" and "sequins" for real dewdrops on real dock leaves. Primrose knew that glamour and the thing they had seen, brilliance and the ashen stink, came from the same place. She made both things safe for the littluns by restricting them to pantomime flats and sweet illustrations. She didn't look at what she knew, better not, but she did know she knew, she recognized confusedly.

Now what?

She sat on the moss, and a voice in her head said, "I want to go home." And she heard herself give a bitter, entirely grownup little laugh, for what was home? What did she know about home?

Where she lived was above a Chinese takeaway. She had a dangerous cupboard-corner she cooked in, a bed, a clothes-rail, an armchair deformed by generations of bottoms. She thought of this place in faded browns and beiges, seen through drifting coils of Chinese cooking steam, scented with stewing pork and a bubbling chicken broth. Home was not real, as all the sturdy twigs and roots in the wood were real. The stuffed animals were piled on the bed and the carpet, their fur rubbed, their pristine stare gone from their scratched eyes. She thought about what one thought was real, sitting there on the moss throne at the center. When Mum had come in, snivelling, to say Dad was dead, Primrose herself had been preoccupied with whether pudding would be tapioca or semolina, whether there would be jam, and, subsequently, how ugly Mum's dripping nose was, how she looked as though she were putting it on.[1] She remembered the semolina and the rather nasty blackberry jam, the taste and the texture, to this day. So was that real, was that home?

She had later invented a picture of a cloudy aquamarine sea under a gold sun, in which a huge fountain of white curling water rose from a foundering ship. It was very beautiful but not real. She could not remember Dad. She could remember the Thing in the Forest, and she could remember Alys. The fact that the mossy tump had lovely colors—crimson and emerald—didn't mean she didn't remember the Thing. She remembered what Penny had said about "things that are more real than we are." She had met one. Here at the center, the spout of water was more real than the semolina, because she was where such things reign. The word she found was "reign." She had understood something, and did not know what she had understood. She wanted badly to go home, and she wanted never to move. The light was lovely in the leaves. The squirrel flirted its tail and suddenly set off again, springing into the branches. The woman lumbered to her feet and licked the bramble scratches on the back of her hands.

Penny walked very steadily, keeping to hedgerows and field-edge paths. She remembered the Thing. She remembered it clearly and daily. But she walked away, noticing and not noticing that her path was deflected by field forms and the lay of the land into a snaking sickle shape. As the day wore on, she settled into her stride and lifted her eyes. When she saw the wood on the horizon, she knew it was the wood, although she was seeing it from an unfamiliar aspect, from where it appeared to be perched on a conical hillock, ridged as though it had been grasped and squeezed by coils of strength. It was almost dusk. She mounted the slope, and went in over a suddenly discovered stile.[2]

Once inside, she moved cautiously. She stood stock-still, and snuffed the air for the remembered rottenness: she listened to the sounds of the trees and the creatures. She smelled rottenness, but it was normal rottenness, leaves and stems mulching back into earth. She heard sounds. Not birdsong, for it was too late in the day, but the odd raucous warning croak. She heard her own heartbeat in the thickening brown air.

It was no use looking for familiar tree trunks or tussocks. They had had a lifetime, her lifetime, to alter out of recognition.

---

1. Pretending.    2. A set of steps for climbing over a fence or hedge.

She began to think she discerned dark tunnels in the undergrowth, where something might have rolled and slid. Mashed seedlings, broken twigs and fronds, none of it very recent. There were things caught in the thorns, flimsy colorless shreds of damp wool or fur. She peered down the tunnels and noted where the scrapings hung thickest. She forced herself to go into the dark, stooping, occasionally crawling on hands and knees. The silence was heavy. She found threadworms of knitting wool, unravelled dishcloth cotton, clinging newsprint. She found odd sausage-shaped tubes of membrane, containing fragments of hair and bone and other inanimate stuffs. They were like monstrous owl pellets, or the gut-shaped hairballs vomited by cats. Penny went forward, putting aside briars and tough stems with careful fingers. It had been here, but how long ago?

Quite suddenly, she came out at a place she remembered. The clearing was larger, the tree trunks were thicker, but the great log behind which they had hidden still lay there. The place was almost the ghost of a camp. The trees round about were hung with pennants and streamers, like the scorched, hacked, threadbare banners in the chapel of the great house, with their brown stains of earth or blood. It had been here, it had never gone away.

Penny moved slowly and dreamily round, looking for things. She found a mock-tortoiseshell hairslide, and a shoe button with a metal shank. She found a bird skeleton, quite fresh, bashed flat. She found ambivalent shards and several teeth, of varying sizes and shapes. She found—spread around, half hidden by roots, stained green but glinting white—a collection of small bones, finger bones, tiny toes, a rib, and finally what might be a brainpan and brow. She thought of putting them in her knapsack, and then thought she could not. She was not an anatomist. The tiny bones might have been badger or fox.

85    She sat down, with her back against the fallen trunk. She thought, Now I am watching myself as you do in a safe dream, but then, when I saw it, it was one of those dreams where you are inside and cannot get out. Except that it wasn't a dream.

It was the encounter with the Thing that had led her to deal professionally in dreams. Something that resembled unreality had lumbered into reality, and she had seen it. She had been the reading child, but after the sight of the Thing she had not been able to inhabit the customary and charming unreality of books. She had become good at studying what could not be seen. She took an interest in the dead, who inhabited real history. She was drawn to the invisible forces that moved in molecules and caused them to coagulate or dissipate. She had become a psychotherapist "to be useful." That was not quite accurate. The corner of the blanket that covered the unthinkable had been turned back enough for her to catch sight of it. She was in its world. It was not by accident that she had come to specialize in severely autistic children, children who twittered, or banged, or stared, who sat damp and absent on Penny's official lap and told her no dreams. The world they knew was a real world. Often Penny thought it was the real world, from which even their desperate parents were at least partly shielded. Somebody had to occupy themselves with the hopeless. Penny felt she could.

All the leaves of the forest began slowly to quaver and then to clatter. Far away, there was the sound of something heavy, and sluggish, stirring. Penny sat very still and expectant. She heard the old blind rumble, she sniffed the old stink. It came from no direction; it was all around; as though the Thing encompassed the wood, or as though it travelled in multiple fragments, as it was described in the old text. It was dark now. What was visible had no distinct color, only shades of ink and elephant.

Now, thought Penny, and just as suddenly as it had begun the turmoil ceased. It was as though the Thing had turned away; she could feel the tremble of the wood recede and become still. Quite rapidly, over the treetops, a huge disk of white gold mounted and hung. Penny remembered her father, standing in the cold light of the full moon, and saying wryly that the bombers would not come tonight, they were safe under a cloudless full moon. He had vanished in an oven of red-yellow roaring, Penny had guessed, or been told, or imagined. Her mother had sent her away before allowing the fireman to speak, who had come with the news. She had been a creep-mouse on stairs and in cubbyholes, trying to overhear what was being imparted. Her mother didn't, or couldn't, want her company. She caught odd phrases of talk—"nothing really to identify," "absolutely no doubt." He had been a tired, gentle man with ash in his trouser turnups. There had been a funeral. Penny remembered thinking there was nothing, or next to nothing, in the coffin his fellow-firemen shouldered. It went up so lightly. It was so easy to set down on the crematorium slab.

They had been living behind the blackout anyway, but her mother went on living behind drawn curtains long after the war was over.

The moon had released the wood, it seemed. Penny stood up and brushed leaf mold off her clothes. She had been ready for it, and it had not come. She felt disappointed. But she accepted her release and found her way back to the fields and her village along liquid trails of moonlight.

The two women took the same train back to the city, but did not encounter each other until they got out. The passengers scurried and shuffled toward the exit, mostly heads down. Both women remembered how they had set out in the wartime dark, with their twig legs and gas masks. Both raised their heads as they neared the barrier, not in hope of being met, for they would not be, but automatically, to calculate where to go and what to do. They saw each other's faces in the cavernous gloom, two pale, recognizable rounds, far enough apart for speech, and even greetings, to be awkward. In the dimness, they were reduced to similarity—dark eyeholes, set mouth. For a moment or two, they stood and simply stared. On that first occasion the station vault had been full of curling steam, and the air gritty with ash. Now the blunt-nosed sleek diesel they had left was blue and gold under a layer of grime. They saw each other through the black imagined veil that grief or pain or despair hangs over the visible world. Each saw the other's face and thought of the unforgettable misery of the face they had seen in the forest. Each thought that the other was the witness, who made the thing certainly real, who prevented her from slipping into the comfort of believing she had imagined it or made it up. So they stared at each other, blankly, without acknowledgment, then picked up their baggage, and turned away into the crowd.

Penny found that the black veil had somehow become part of her vision. She thought constantly about faces, her father's, her mother's, Primrose's face, the hopeful little girl, the woman staring up at her from the glass case, staring at her conspiratorially over the clotted cream. The blond infant Alys, an ingratiating sweet smile. The half-human face of the Thing. She tried to remember that face completely, and suffered over the detail of the dreadful droop of its mouth, the exact inanity of its blind squinnying.[3] Present faces were blank disks, shadowed moons. Her patients came and went. She was increasingly unable to distinguish one from another. The face of the Thing hung in her brain, jealously soliciting her attention, distracting her from dailiness. She had gone back to its place, and had not seen it. She needed to see it. Why she needed it was because it was more real than she was. She would go and face it. What else was there, she asked herself, and answered herself, nothing.

So she made her way back, sitting alone in the train as the fields streaked past, drowsing through a century-long night under the cabbage quilt in the B. and B. This time, she went in the old way, from the house, through the garden gate; she found the old trail quickly, her sharp eye picked up the trace of its detritus, and soon enough she was back in the clearing, where her cairn of tiny bones by the tree trunk was undisturbed. She gave a little sigh, dropped to her knees, and then sat with her back to the rotting wood and silently called the Thing. Almost immediately, she sensed its perturbation, saw the trouble in the branches, heard the lumbering, smelled its ancient smell. It was a grayish, unremarkable day. She closed her eyes briefly as the noise and movement grew stronger. When it came, she would look it in the face, she would see what it was. She clasped her hands loosely in her lap. Her nerves relaxed. Her blood slowed. She was ready.

Primrose was in the shopping mall, putting out her circle of rainbow-colored plastic chairs. She creaked as she bent over them. It was pouring with rain outside, but the mall was enclosed like a crystal palace in a casing of glass. The floor under the rainbow chairs was gleaming dappled marble. They were in front of a dimpling fountain, with lights shining up through the greenish water, making golden rings round the polished pebbles and wishing coins that lay there. The little children collected round her: their mothers kissed them goodbye, told them to be good and quiet and listen to the nice lady. They had little transparent plastic cups of shining orange juice, and each had a biscuit in silver foil. They were all colors—black skin, brown skin, pink skin, freckled skin, pink jacket, yellow jacket, purple hood, scarlet hood. Some grinned and some whimpered, some wriggled, some were still. Primrose sat on the edge of the fountain. She had decided what to do. She smiled her best, most comfortable smile, and adjusted her golden locks. Listen to me, she told them, and I'll tell you something amazing, a story that's never been told before.

95     There were once two little girls who saw, or believed they saw, a thing in a forest. . . .

2000

## QUESTIONS

1. In what ways is "The Thing in the Forest" both like and unlike a traditional fairy tale?
2. What are some indications that the "loathly worm" is supernatural? What do you think it might represent?
3. The names "Penny" and "Primrose" suggest some of the differences between the two characters. How does A. S. Byatt bring out these differences, whether in their appear-

---

3. Squinting.

ance, their family histories, their decisions at the end of the story, or other details? Would the story work as well if either Penny or Primrose saw the worm by herself and the other girl did not? Would it work as well if the girls were more alike?

## SHERMAN ALEXIE

## Flight Patterns

At 5:05 A.M., Patsy Cline fell loudly to pieces on William's clock radio.[1] He hit the snooze button, silencing lonesome Patsy, and dozed for fifteen more minutes before Donna Fargo bragged about being the happiest girl in the whole USA. William wondered what had ever happened to Donna Fargo, whose birth name was the infinitely more interesting Yvonne Vaughn, and wondered *why* he knew Donna Fargo's birth name. Ah, he was the bemused and slightly embarrassed owner of a twenty-first-century American mind.[2] His intellect was a big comfy couch stuffed with sacred and profane trivia. He knew the names of all nine of Elizabeth Taylor's husbands and could quote from memory the entire Declaration of Independence. William knew Donna Fargo's birth name because he *wanted* to know her birth name. He wanted to know all of the great big and tiny little American details. He didn't want to choose between Ernie Hemingway and the Spokane tribal elders, between Mia Hamm and Crazy Horse, between *The Heart Is a Lonely Hunter* and Chief Dan George. William wanted all of it. Hunger was his crime. As for dear Miss Fargo, William figured she probably played the Indian casino circuit along with the Righteous Brothers, Smokey Robinson, Eddie Money, Pat Benatar, RATT, REO Speedwagon, and dozens of other formerly famous rock- and country-music stars. Many of the Indian casino acts were bad, and most of the rest were pure nostalgic entertainment, but a small number made beautiful and timeless music. William knew the genius Merle Haggard played thirty or forty Indian casinos every year, so long live Haggard and long live tribal economic sovereignty. Who cares about fishing and hunting rights? Who cares about uranium mines and nuclear-waste-dump sites on sacred land? Who cares about the recovery of tribal languages? Give me Freddy Fender singing "Before the Next Teardrop Falls" in English and Spanish to 206 Spokane Indians, William thought, and I will be a happy man.

But William wasn't happy this morning. He'd slept poorly—he always slept poorly—and wondered again if his insomnia was a physical or a mental condition. His doctor had offered him sleeping-pill prescriptions, but William declined for philosophical reasons. He was an Indian who didn't smoke or drink or eat processed sugar. He lifted weights three days a week, ran every day, and competed in four triathlons a year. A two-mile swim, a 150-mile bike ride, and a full marathon. A triathlon was a religious quest. If Saint Francis were still around, he'd be a triathlete. Another exaggeration! Theological hyperbole! Rabid self-justification! Diagnostically speaking, William was an obsessive-compulsive workaholic who

---

1. A reference to country music singer Patsy Cline's recording of "I Fall to Pieces" (1961). *Donna Fargo:* American singer (b. 1949) best known for her recording of "Happiest Girl in the Whole U.S.A." (1972).
2. The story contains many references to American popular culture of the post–World War II era.

was afraid of pills. So he suffered sleepless nights and constant daytime fatigue.

This morning, awake and not awake, William turned down the radio, changing Yvonne Vaughn's celebratory anthem into whispered blues, and rolled off the couch onto his hands and knees. His back and legs were sore because he'd slept on the living room couch so the alarm wouldn't disturb his wife and daughter upstairs. Still on his hands and knees, William stretched his spine, using the twelve basic exercises he'd learned from Dr. Adams, that master practitioner of white middle-class chiropractic voodoo. This was all part of William's regular morning ceremony. Other people find God in ornate ritual, but William called out to Geronimo, Jesus Christ, Saint Therese, Buddha, Allah, Billie Holiday, Simon Ortiz, Abe Lincoln, Bessie Smith, Howard Hughes, Leslie Marmon Silko, Joan of Arc and Joan of Collins, John Woo, Wilma Mankiller, and Karl and Groucho Marx while he pumped out fifty push-ups and fifty abdominal crunches. William wasn't particularly religious; he was generally religious. Finished with his morning calisthenics, William showered in the basement, suffering the water that was always too cold down there, and threaded his long black hair into two tight braids—the indigenous businessman's tonsorial special—and dressed in his best travel suit, a navy three-button pinstripe he'd ordered online. He'd worried about the fit, but his tailor was a magician and had only mildly chastised William for such an impulsive purchase. After knotting his blue paisley tie, purchased in person and on sale, William walked upstairs in bare feet and kissed his wife, Marie, good-bye.

"Cancel your flight," she said. "And come back to bed."

5   "You're supposed to be asleep," he said.

She was a small and dark woman who seemed to be smaller and darker at that time of the morning. Her long black hair had once again defeated its braids, but she didn't care. She sometimes went two or three days without brushing it. William was obsessive about his mane, tying and retying his ponytail, knotting and reknotting his braids, experimenting with this shampoo and that conditioner. He greased down his cowlicks (inherited from a cowlicked father and grandfather) with shiny pomade, but Marie's hair was always unkempt, wild, and renegade. William's hair hung around the fort, but Marie's rode on the warpath! She constantly pulled stray strands out of her mouth. William loved her for it. During sex, they spent as much time readjusting her hair as they did readjusting positions. Such were the erotic dangers of loving a Spokane Indian woman.

"Take off your clothes and get in bed," Marie pleaded now.

"I can't do that," William said. "They're counting on me."

"Oh, the plane will be filled with salesmen. Let some other salesman sell what you're selling."

10   "Your breath stinks."

"So do my feet, my pits, and my butt, but you still love me. Come back to bed, and I'll make it worth your while."

William kissed Marie, reached beneath her pajama top, and squeezed her breasts. He thought about reaching inside her pajama bottoms. She wrapped her arms and legs around him and tried to wrestle him into bed. Oh, God, he wanted to climb into bed and make love. He wanted to fornicate, to sex, to breed, to screw, to make the beast with two backs. *Oh, sweetheart, be my little synonym!* He wanted her to be both subject and object. Perhaps it was wrong (and unavoidable) to objectify female strangers, but shouldn't every husband seek to objectify his wife at least once a day? William loved and respected his wife, and delighted in her intelligence, humor, and kindness, but he also loved to watch her lovely ass when she walked, and stare down the front of her loose shirts when she leaned over, and grab her breasts at wildly inappropriate times—during dinner parties and piano recitals and uncontrolled intersections, for instance. He constantly made passes at her, not necessarily expecting to be successful, but to remind her he still desired her and was excited by the thought of her. She was his passive and active.

"Come on," she said. "If you stay home, I'll make you Scooby."

He laughed at the inside joke, created one night while he tried to give her sexual directions and was so aroused that he sounded exactly like Scooby-Doo.

"Stay home, stay home, stay home," she chanted and wrapped herself tighter around him. He was supporting all of her weight, holding her two feet off the bed.

"I'm not strong enough to do this," he said.

"Baby, baby, I'll make you strong," she sang, and it sounded like she was writing a Top 40 hit in the Brill Building, circa 1962. How could he leave a woman who sang like that? He hated to leave, but he loved his work. He was a man, and men needed to work. More sexism! More masculine tunnel vision! More need for gender-sensitivity workshops! He pulled away from her, dropping her back onto the bed, and stepped away.

"Willy Loman," she said, "you must pay attention to me."[3]

"I love you," he said, but she'd already fallen back to sleep—a narcoleptic gift William envied—and he wondered if she would dream about a man who never left her, about some unemployed agoraphobic Indian warrior who liked to cook and wash dishes.

William tiptoed into his daughter's bedroom, expecting to hear her light snore, but she was awake and sitting up in bed, and looked so magical and androgynous with her huge brown eyes and crew-cut hair. She'd wanted to completely shave her head: *I don't want long hair, I don't want short hair, I don't want hair at all, and I don't want to be a girl or a boy, I want to be a yellow and orange leaf some little kid picks up and pastes in his scrapbook.*

"Daddy," she said.

"Grace," he said. "You should be asleep. You have school today."

"I know," she said. "But I wanted to see you before you left."

"Okay," said William as he kissed her forehead, nose, and chin. "You've seen me. Now go back to sleep. I love you and I'm going to miss you."

She fiercely hugged him.

"Oh," he said. "You're such a lovely, lovely girl."

Preternaturally serious, she took his face in her eyes and studied his eyes. Morally examined by a kindergartner!

"Daddy," she said. "Go be silly for those people far away."

She cried as William left her room. Already quite sure he was only an adequate husband, he wondered, as he often did, if he was a bad father. During these mornings, he felt generic and violent, like some caveman leaving the fire to hunt

---

3. A reference to Willy Loman, the protagonist of Arthur Miller's play *Death of a Salesman* (1949); Willy's wife, Linda, says of her husband, "Attention, attention must finally be paid to such a person."

animals in the cold and dark. Maybe his hands were smooth and clean, but they felt bloody.

Downstairs, he put on his socks and shoes and overcoat and listened for his daughter's crying, but she was quiet, having inherited her mother's gift for instant sleep. She had probably fallen back into one of her odd little dreams. While he was gone, she often drew pictures of those dreams, coloring the sky green and the grass blue—everything backward and wrong—and had once sketched a man in a suit crashing an airplane into the bright yellow sun. Ah, the rage, fear, and loneliness of a five-year-old, simple and true! She'd been especially afraid since September 11 of the previous year and constantly quizzed William about what he would do if terrorists hijacked his plane.

"I'd tell them I was your father," he'd said to her before he left for his last business trip. "And they'd stop being bad."

"You're lying," she'd said. "I'm not supposed to listen to liars. If you lie to me, I can't love you."

He couldn't argue with her logic. Maybe she was the most logical person on the planet. Maybe she should be illegally elected president of the United States.

William understood her fear of flying and of his flight. He was afraid of flying, too, but not of terrorists. After the horrible violence of September 11, he figured hijacking was no longer a useful weapon in the terrorist arsenal. These days, a terrorist armed with a box cutter would be torn to pieces by all of the coach-class passengers and fed to the first-class upgrades. However, no matter how much he tried to laugh his fear away, William always scanned the airports and airplanes for little brown guys who reeked of fundamentalism. That meant William was equally afraid of Osama bin Laden and Jerry Falwell wearing the last vestiges of a summer tan. William himself was a little brown guy, so the other travelers were always sniffing around him, but he smelled only of Dove soap, Mennen deodorant, and sarcasm. Still, he understood why people were afraid of him, a brown-skinned man with dark hair and eyes. If Norwegian terrorists had exploded the World Trade Center, then blue-eyed blondes would be viewed with more suspicion. Or so he hoped.

Locking the front door behind him, William stepped away from his house, carried his garment bag and briefcase onto the front porch, and waited for his taxi to arrive. It was a cold and foggy October morning. William could smell the saltwater of Elliott Bay and the freshwater of Lake Washington. Surrounded by gray water and gray fog and gray skies and gray mountains and a gray sun, he'd lived with his family in Seattle for three years and loved it. He couldn't imagine living anywhere else, with any other wife or child, in any other time.

William was tired and happy and romantic and exaggerating the size of his familial devotion so he could justify his departure, so he could survive his departure. He did sometimes think about other women and other possible lives with them. He wondered how his life would have been different if he'd married a white woman and fathered half-white children who grew up to complain and brag about their biracial identities: *Oh, the only box they have for me is Other! I'm not going to check any box! I'm not the Other! I am Tiger Woods!* But William most often fantasized about being single and free to travel as often as he wished— maybe two million miles a year—and how much he'd enjoy the benefits of being a platinum frequent flier. Maybe he'd have one-night stands with a long series of traveling saleswomen, all of them thousands of miles away from husbands and children who kept looking up "feminism" in the dictionary. William knew that was yet another sexist thought. In this capitalistic and democratic culture, talented women should also enjoy the freedom to emotionally and physically abandon their families. After all, talented and educated men have been doing it for generations. Let freedom ring!

Marie had left her job as a corporate accountant to be a full-time mother to Grace. William loved his wife for making the decision, and he tried to do his share of the housework, but he suspected he was an old-fashioned bastard who wanted his wife to stay at home and wait, wait, wait for him.

Marie was always waiting for William to call, to come home, to leave messages saying he was getting on the plane, getting off the plane, checking in to the hotel, going to sleep, waking up, heading for the meeting, catching an earlier or later flight home. He spent one third of his life trying to sleep in uncomfortable beds and one third of his life trying to stay awake in airports. He traveled with thousands of other capitalistic foot soldiers, mostly men but increasing numbers of women, and stayed in the same Ramadas, Holiday Inns, and Radissons. He ate the same room-service meals and ran the same exercise-room treadmills and watched the same pay-per-view porn and stared out the windows at the same strange and lonely cityscapes. Sure, he was an enrolled member of the Spokane Indian tribe, but he was also a fully recognized member of the notebook-computer tribe and the security-checkpoint tribe and the rental-car tribe and the hotel-shuttle-bus tribe and the cell-phone-roaming-charge tribe.

William traveled so often, the Seattle-based flight attendants knew him by first name.

At five minutes to six, the Orange Top taxi pulled into the driveway. The driver, a short and thin black man, stepped out of the cab and waved. William rushed down the stairs and across the pavement. He wanted to get away from the house before he changed his mind about leaving.

"Is that everything, sir?" asked the taxi driver, his accent a colonial cocktail of American English, formal British, and French sibilants added to a base of what must have been North African.

"Yes, it is, sir," said William, self-consciously trying to erase any class differences between them. In Spain the previous summer, an elderly porter had cursed at William when he insisted on carrying his own bags into the hotel. "Perhaps there is something wrong with the caste system, sir," the hotel concierge had explained to William. "But all of us, we want to do our jobs, and we want to do them well."

William didn't want to insult anybody; he wanted the world to be a fair and decent place. At least that was what he wanted to want. More than anything, he wanted to stay home with his fair and decent family. He supposed he wanted the world to be fairer and more decent to his family. We are special, he thought, though he suspected they were just one more family on this block of neighbors, in this city of neighbors, in this country of neighbors, in a world of neighbors. He looked back at his house, at the windows behind which slept his beloved wife and daughter. When he traveled, he had nightmares about strangers breaking into the house and killing and raping Marie and Grace. In other nightmares, he arrived home in time to save his family by beating the intruders and chasing them away. During longer business trips, William's nightmares became more violent as the days and nights passed. If he was gone over a week, he dreamed about mutilating the rapists and eating them alive while his wife and daughter cheered for him.

"Let me take your bags, sir," said the taxi driver.

"What?" asked William, momentarily confused.

"Your bags, sir."

William handed him the briefcase but held on to the heavier garment bag. A stupid compromise, thought William, but it's too late to change it now. God, I'm supposed to be some electric aboriginal warrior, but I'm really a wimpy liberal pacifist. *Dear Lord, how much longer should I mourn the death of Jerry Garcia?*

The taxi driver tried to take the garment bag from William.

"I've got this one," said William, then added, "I've got it, sir."

The taxi driver hesitated, shrugged, opened the trunk, and set the briefcase inside. William laid the garment bag next to his briefcase. The taxi driver shut the trunk and walked around to open William's door.

"No, sir," said William as he awkwardly stepped in front of the taxi driver, opened the door, and took a seat. "I've got it."

"I'm sorry, sir," said the taxi driver and hurried around to the driver's seat. This strange American was making him uncomfortable, and he wanted to get behind the wheel and drive. Driving comforted him.

"To the airport, sir?" asked the taxi driver as he started the meter.

"Yes," said William. "United Airlines."

"Very good, sir."

In silence, they drove along Martin Luther King Jr. Way, the bisector of an African American neighborhood that was rapidly gentrifying. William and his family were Native American gentry! They were the very first Indian family to ever move into a neighborhood and bring up the property values! That was one of William's favorite jokes, self-deprecating and politely racist. White folks could laugh at a joke like that and not feel guilty. But how guilty could white people feel in Seattle? Seattle might be the only city in the country where white people lived comfortably on a street named after Martin Luther King, Jr.

No matter where he lived, William always felt uncomfortable, so he enjoyed other people's discomfort. These days, in the airports, he loved to watch white people enduring random security checks. It was a perverse thrill, to be sure, but William couldn't help himself. He knew those white folks wanted to scream and rage: *Do I look like a terrorist?* And he knew the security officers, most often low-paid brown folks, wanted to scream back: *Define terror, you Anglo bastard!* William figured he'd been pulled over for pat-down searches about 75 percent of the time. Random, my ass! But that was okay! William might have wanted to irritate other people, but he didn't want to scare them. He wanted his fellow travelers to know exactly who and what he was: *I am a Native American and therefore have ten thousand more reasons to terrorize the U.S. than any of those Taliban jerk-offs, but I have chosen instead to become a civic American citizen, so all of you white folks should be celebrating my kindness and moral decency and awesome ability to forgive!* Maybe William should have worn beaded vests when he traveled. Maybe he should have brought a hand drum and sang "Way, ya, way, ya, hey." Maybe he should have thrown casino chips into the crowd.

The taxi driver turned west on Cherry, drove twenty blocks into downtown, took the entrance ramp onto I-5, and headed south for the airport. The freeway was moderately busy for that time of morning.

"Where are you going, sir?" asked the taxi driver.

"I've got business in Chicago," William said. He didn't really want to talk. He needed to meditate in silence. He needed to put his fear of flying inside an imaginary safe deposit box and lock it away. We all have our ceremonies, thought William, our personal narratives. He'd always needed to meditate in the taxi on the way to the airport. Immediately upon arrival at the departure gate, he'd listen to a tape he'd made of rock stars who died in plane crashes. Buddy Holly, Otis Redding, Stevie Ray, "Oh Donna," "Chantilly Lace," "(Sittin' on) The Dock of the Bay." William figured God would never kill a man who listened to such a morbid collection of music. Too easy a target, and plus, God could never justify killing a planeful of innocents to punish one minor sinner.

"What do you do, sir?" asked the taxi driver.

"You know, I'm not sure," said William and laughed. It was true. He worked for a think tank and sold ideas about how to improve other ideas. Two years ago, his company had made a few hundred thousand dollars by designing and selling the idea of a better shopping cart. The CGI prototype was amazing. It looked like a mobile walk-in closet. But it had yet to be manufactured and probably never would be.

"You wear a good suit," said the taxi driver, not sure why William was laughing. "You must be a businessman, no? You must make lots of money."

"I do okay."

"Your house is big and beautiful."

"Yes, I suppose it is."

"You are a family man, yes?"

"I have a wife and daughter."

"Are they beautiful?"

William was pleasantly surprised to be asked such a question. "Yes," he said. "Their names are Marie and Grace. They're very beautiful. I love them very much."

"You must miss them when you travel."

"I miss them so much I go crazy," said William. "I start thinking I'm going to disappear, you know, just vanish, if I'm not home. Sometimes I worry their love is the only thing that makes me human, you know? I think if they stopped loving me, I might burn up, spontaneously combust, and turn into little pieces of oxygen and hydrogen and carbon. Do you know what I'm saying?"

"Yes sir, I understand love can be so large."

William wondered why he was being honest and poetic with a taxi driver. There is emotional safety in anonymity, he thought.

"I have a wife and three sons," said the driver. "But they live in Ethiopia with my mother and father. I have not seen any of them for many years."

For the first time, William looked closely at the driver. He was clear-eyed and handsome, strong of shoulder and arm, maybe fifty years old, maybe older. A thick scar ran from his right ear down his neck and beneath his collar. A black man with a violent history, William thought and immediately reprimanded himself for racially profiling the driver: *Excuse me, sir, but I pulled you over because your scar doesn't belong in this neighborhood.*

"I still think of my children as children," the driver said. "But they are men now. Taller and stronger than me. They are older now than I was when I last saw them."

William did the math and wondered how this driver could function with such fatherly pain. "I bet you can't wait to go home and see them again," he said, following the official handbook of the frightened American male: *When confronted with the mysterious, you can defend yourself by speaking in obvious generalities.*

"I cannot go home," said the taxi driver, "and I fear I will never see them again."

William didn't want to be having this conversation. He wondered if his silence would silence the taxi driver. But it was too late for that.

"What are you?" the driver asked.

"What do you mean?"

"I mean, you are not white, your skin, it is dark like mine."

"Not as dark as yours."

"No," said the driver and laughed. "Not so dark, but too dark to be white. What are you? Are you Jewish?"

Because they were so often Muslim, taxi drivers all over the world had often asked William if he was Jewish. William was always being confused for something else. He was ambiguously ethnic, living somewhere in the darker section of the Great American Crayola Box, but he was more beige than brown, more mauve than sienna.

"Why do you want to know if I'm Jewish?" William asked.

"Oh, I'm sorry, sir, if I offended you. I am not anti-Semitic. I love all of my brothers and sisters. Jews, Catholics, Buddhists, even the atheists, I love them all. Like you Americans sing, 'Joy to the world and Jeremiah Bullfrog!'"

The taxi driver laughed again, and William laughed with him.

"I'm Indian," William said.

"From India?"

"No, not jewel-on-the-forehead Indian," said William. "I'm a bows-and-arrows Indian."

"Oh, you mean ten little, nine little, eight little Indians?"

"Yeah, sort of," said William. "I'm that kind of Indian, but much smarter. I'm a Spokane Indian. We're salmon people."

"In England, they call you Red Indians."

"You've been to England?"

"Yes, I studied physics at Oxford."

"Wow," said William, wondering if this man was a liar.

"You are surprised by this, I imagine. Perhaps you think I'm a liar?"

William covered his mouth with one hand. He smiled this way when he was embarrassed.

"Aha, you do think I'm lying. You ask yourself questions about me. How could a physicist drive a taxi? Well, in the United States, I am a cabdriver, but in Ethiopia, I was a jet-fighter pilot."

By coincidence or magic, or as a coincidence that could willfully be interpreted as magic, they drove past Boeing Field at that exact moment.

"Ah, you see," said the taxi driver, "I can fly any of those planes. The prop planes, the jet planes, even the very large passenger planes. I can also fly the experimental ones that don't fly. But I could make them fly because I am the best pilot in the world. Do you believe me?"

"I don't know," said William, very doubtful of this man but fascinated as well. If he was a liar, then he was a magnificent liar.

On both sides of the freeway, blue-collared men and women drove trucks and forklifts, unloaded trains, trucks, and ships, built computers, televisions, and airplanes. Seattle was a city of industry, of hard work, of calluses on the palms of hands. So many men and women working so hard. William worried that his job—his selling of the purely theoretical—wasn't a real job at all. He didn't build anything. He couldn't walk into department and grocery stores and buy what he'd created, manufactured, and shipped. William's life was measured by imaginary numbers: the binary code of computer languages, the amount of money in his bank accounts, the interest rate on his mortgage, and the rise and fall of the stock market. He invested much of his money in socially responsible funds. Imagine that! Imagine choosing to trust your money with companies that supposedly made their millions through ethical means. Imagine the breathtaking privilege of such a choice. All right, so maybe this was an old story for white men. For most of American history, who else but a white man could endure the existential crisis of economic success? But this story was original and aboriginal for William. For thousands of years, Spokane Indians had lived subsistence lives, using every last part of the salmon and deer because they'd die without every last part, but William only ordered salmon from menus and saw deer on television. Maybe he romanticized the primal—for thousands of years, Indians also died of ear infections—but William wanted his comfortable and safe life to contain more *wilderness*.

"Sir, forgive me for saying this," the taxi driver said, "but you do not look like the Red Indians I have seen before."

"I know," William said. "People usually think I'm a longhaired Mexican."

"What do you say to them when they think such a thing?"

*"No habla español. Indio de Norteamericanos."*

"People think I'm black American. They always want to hip-hop rap to me. 'Are you East Coast or West Coast?' they ask me, and I tell them I am Ivory Coast."

"How have things been since September eleventh?"

"Ah, a good question, sir. It's been interesting. Because people think I'm black, they don't see me as a terrorist, only as a crackhead addict on welfare. So I am a victim of only one misguided idea about who I am."

"We're all trapped by other people's ideas, aren't we?"

"I suppose that is true, sir. How has it been for you?"

"It's all backward," William said. "A few days after it happened, I was walking out of my gym downtown, and this big phallic pickup pulled up in front of me in the crosswalk. Yeah, this big truck with big phallic tires and a big phallic flagpole and a big phallic flag flying, and the big phallic symbol inside leaned out of his window and yelled at me, 'Go back to your own country!' "

"Oh, that is sad and funny," the taxi driver said.

"Yeah," William said. "And it wasn't so much a hate crime as it was a crime of irony, right? And I was laughing so hard, the truck was halfway down the block before I could get breath enough to yell back, 'You first!' "

William and the taxi driver laughed and laughed together. Two dark men laughing at dark jokes.

"I had to fly on the first day you could fly," William said. "And I was flying into Baltimore, you know, and D.C. and Baltimore are pretty much the same damn town, so it was like flying into Ground Zero, you know?"

"It must have been terrifying."

"It was, it was. I was sitting in the plane here in Seattle, getting ready to take off, and I started looking around for suspicious brown guys. I was scared of little brown guys. So was everybody else. We were all afraid of the same things. I started looking around for big white guys because I figured they'd be undercover cops, right?"

"Imagine wanting to be surrounded by white cops!"

"Exactly! I didn't want to see some pacifist, vegan, whole-wheat, free-range, organic, progressive, gray-ponytail, communist, liberal, draft-dodging, NPR-listening wimp! What are they going to do if somebody tries to hijack the plane? Throw a Birkenstock at him? Offer him some pot?"

"Marijuana might actually stop the violence everywhere in the world," the taxi driver said.

"You're right," William said. "But on that plane, I was hoping for about twenty-five NRA-loving, gun-nut, serial-killing, psychopathic, Ollie North, Norman Schwarzkopf, right-wing, Agent Orange, post-traumatic-stress-disorder, CIA, FBI, automatic-weapon, smart-bomb, laser-sighting bastards!"

"You wouldn't want to invite them for dinner," the taxi driver said. "But you want them to protect your children, am I correct?"

"Yes, but it doesn't make sense. None of it makes sense. It's all contradictions."

"The contradictions are the story, yes?"

"Yes."

"I have a story about contradictions," said the taxi driver. "Because you are a Red Indian, I think you will understand my pain."

"*Su-num-twee*," said William.

"What is that? What did you say?"

"*Su-num-twee*. It's Spokane. My language."

"What does it mean?"

"Listen to me."

"Ah, yes, that's good. *Su-num-twee, su-num-twee*. So, what is your name?"

"William."

The taxi driver sat high and straight in his seat, like he was going to say something important. "William, my name is Fekadu. I am Oromo and Muslim, and I come from Addis Ababa in Ethiopia, and I want you to *su-num-twee*."

There was nothing more important than a person's name and the names of his clan, tribe, city, religion, and country. By the social rules of his tribe, William should have reciprocated and officially identified himself. He should have been polite and generous. He was expected to live by so many rules, he sometimes felt like he was living inside an indigenous version of an Edith Wharton[4] novel.

"Mr. William," asked Fekadu, "do you want to hear my story? Do you want to *su-num-twee*?"

"Yes, I do, sure, yes, please," said William. He was lying. He was twenty minutes away from the airport and so close to departure.

"I was not born into an important family," said Fekadu. "But my father worked for an important family. And this important family worked for the family

---

4. American novelist (1862–1937) known for her sophisticated depictions of upper-class mores.

of Emperor Haile Selassie.[5] He was a great and good and kind and terrible man, and he loved his country and killed many of his people. Have you heard of him?"

"No, I'm sorry, I haven't."

"He was magical. Ruled our country for forty-three years. Imagine that! We Ethiopians are strong. White people have never conquered us. We won every war we fought against white people. For all of our history, our emperors have been strong, and Selassie was the strongest. There has never been a man capable of such love and destruction."

"You fought against him?"

Fekadu breathed in so deeply that William recognized it as a religious moment, as the first act of a ceremony, and with the second act, an exhalation, the ceremony truly began.

"No," Fekadu said. "I was a smart child. A genius. A prodigy. It was Selassie who sent me to Oxford. And there I studied physics and learned the math and art of flight. I came back home and flew jets for Selassie's army."

"Did you fly in wars?" William asked.

"Ask me what you really want to ask me, William. You want to know if I was a killer, no?"

William had a vision of his wife and daughter huddling terrified in their Seattle basement while military jets screamed overhead. It happened every August when the U.S. Navy Blue Angels came to entertain the masses with their aerial acrobatics.

"Do you want to know if I was a killer?" asked Fekadu. "Ask me if I was a killer."

William wanted to know the terrible answer without asking the terrible question.

"Will you not ask me what I am?" asked Fekadu.

"I can't."

"I dropped bombs on my own people."

In the sky above them, William counted four, five, six jets flying in holding patterns while awaiting permission to land.

"For three years, I killed my own people," said Fekadu. "And then, on the third of June in 1974, I could not do it anymore. I kissed my wife and sons good-bye that morning, and I kissed my mother and father, and I lied to them and told them I would be back that evening. They had no idea where I was going. But I went to the base, got into my plane, and flew away."

"You defected?" William asked. How could a man steal a fighter plane? Was that possible? And if possible, how much courage would it take to commit such a crime? William was quite sure he could never be that courageous.

"Yes, I defected," said Fekadu. "I flew my plane to France and was almost shot down when I violated their airspace, but they let me land, and they arrested me, and soon enough, they gave me asylum. I came to Seattle five years ago, and I think I will live here the rest of my days."

Fekadu took the next exit. They were two minutes away from the airport. William was surprised to discover that he didn't want this journey to end so soon. He wondered if he should invite Fekadu for coffee and a sandwich, for a

---

5. Haile Selassie (1892–1975), emperor of Ethiopia from 1930 to 1936 and again from 1941 to 1974, when he was overthrown in a violent military coup.

slice of pie, for brotherhood. William wanted to hear more of this man's stories and learn from them, whether they were true or not. Perhaps it didn't matter if any one man's stories were true. Fekadu's autobiography might have been completely fabricated, but William was convinced that somewhere in the world, somewhere in Africa or the United States, a man, a jet pilot, wanted to fly away from the war he was supposed to fight. There must be hundreds, maybe thousands, of such men, and how many were courageous enough to fly away? If Fekadu wasn't describing his own true pain and loneliness, then he might have been accidentally describing the pain of a real and lonely man.

"What about your family?" asked William, because he didn't know what else to ask and because he was thinking of his wife and daughter. "Weren't they in danger? Wouldn't Selassie want to hurt them?"

"I could only pray Selassie would leave them be. He had always been good to me, but he saw me as impulsive, so I hoped he would know my family had nothing to do with my flight. I was a coward for staying and a coward for leaving. But none of it mattered, because Selassie was overthrown a few weeks after I defected."

"A coup?"

"Yes, the Derg[6] deposed him, and they slaughtered all of their enemies and their enemies' families. They suffocated Selassie with a pillow the next year. And now I could never return to Ethiopia because Selassie's people would always want to kill me for my betrayal and the Derg would always want to kill me for being Selassie's soldier. Every night and day, I worry that any of them might harm my family. I want to go there and defend them. I want to bring them here. They can sleep on my floor! But even now, after democracy has almost come to Ethiopia, I cannot go back. There is too much history and pain, and I am too afraid."

"How long has it been since you've talked to your family?"

"We write letters to each other, and sometimes we receive them. They sent me photos once, but they never arrived for me to see. And for two days, I waited by the telephone because they were going to call, but it never rang."

Fekadu pulled the taxi to a slow stop at the airport curb. "We are here, sir," he said. "United Airlines."

William didn't know how this ceremony was supposed to end. He felt small and powerless against the collected history. "What am I supposed to do now?" he asked.

"Sir, you must pay me thirty-eight dollars for this ride," said Fekadu and laughed. "Plus a very good tip."

"How much is good?"

"You see, sometimes I send cash to my family. I wrap it up and try to hide it inside the envelope. I know it gets stolen, but I hope some of it gets through to my family. I hope they buy themselves gifts from me. I hope."

"You pray for this?"

"Yes, William, I pray for this. And I pray for your safety on your trip, and I pray for the safety of your wife and daughter while you are gone."

"Pop the trunk, I'll get my own bags," said William as he gave sixty dollars to Fekadu, exited the taxi, took his luggage out of the trunk, and slammed it shut.

---

6. The brutal military junta that overthrew Haile Selassie in 1974 and ruled Ethiopia until the Derg ("Committee") was itself toppled in 1991.

Then William walked over to the passenger-side window, leaned in, and studied Fekadu's face and the terrible scar on his neck.

"Where did you get that?" William asked.

Fekadu ran a finger along the old wound. "Ah," he said. "You must think I got this flying in a war. But no, I got this in a taxicab wreck. William, I am a much better jet pilot than a car driver."

Fekadu laughed loudly and joyously. William wondered how this poor man could be capable of such happiness, however temporary it was.

"Your stories," said William. "I want to believe you."

"Then believe me," said Fekadu.

Unsure, afraid, William stepped back.

"Good-bye, William American," Fekadu said and drove away.

Standing at curbside, William couldn't breathe well. He wondered if he was dying. Of course he was dying, a flawed mortal dying day by day, but he felt like he might fall over from a heart attack or stroke right there on the sidewalk. He left his bags and ran inside the terminal. Let a luggage porter think his bags were dangerous! Let a security guard x-ray the bags and find mysterious shapes! Let a bomb-squad cowboy explode the bags as precaution! Let an airport manager shut down the airport and search every possible traveler! Let the FAA president order every airplane to land! Let the American skies be empty of everything with wings! Let the birds stop flying! Let the very air go still and cold! William didn't care. He ran through the terminal, searching for an available pay phone, a landline, something true and connected to the ground, and he finally found one and dropped two quarters into the slot and dialed his home number, and it rang and rang and rang and rang, and William worried that his wife and daughter were harmed, were lying dead on the floor, but then Marie answered.

"Hello, William," she said.

"I'm here," he said.

2003

## QUESTIONS

1. In what ways does William represent, and not represent, an "American"? How might William react when Fekadu calls him "William American"?
2. The taxi driver asks William, "The contradictions are the story, yes?" What might this indicate about Sherman Alexie's conception of the reality behind a good story?
3. At the end of "Flight Patterns," does William fully believe Fekadu's story? Does it matter to William whether or not Fekadu's story is factual?

---

## SUGGESTIONS FOR WRITING

1. Citing examples from one or more of the stories in this chapter, write an essay discussing the effects of storytelling on the actions, attitudes, or relationships of the characters.
2. A joke can be ruined if you tell the punchline first. Some stories, however, can begin at the end or interrupt the action to fill in the past. Choose one of the stories in this chapter and look carefully at the order in which events are told. Notice any points that seem out of chronological order or not set in the "present" of the story,

and note whether any long periods of time are skipped or summarized. Would another arrangement work just as well? Write an essay in which you show how time and the order of telling are arranged in this story, and explain why this is an effective way to provide what readers or characters need to know at each stage.
3. Some stories are very specific about when and where they take place, and some allude to history, culture, or social issues. Others are more sparing in details and may seem magical, abstract, or as if they could take place anywhere at any time. Write an essay discussing the significance of setting, historical context, or other references in two of these stories, comparing the ways that the presence or absence of such details contributes to each story's effects.
4. Write a first-person account of "A Conversation with My [Relative]" in which you try to get along with that relative although you are confronting an issue that you disagree about. Or, write a first-person account of a time you met someone you expected to dislike, but instead that person changed your mind or your attitude in some way. Your account may be true or fictitious, and the narrator or speaker may be you or a fictional person. Whether imagined or accurate to your experience, the story should provide details of personality and situation that seem realistic, as if it actually happened.
5. Retell all or part of any story in this chapter in an entirely different way. For example, you might recast "The Elephant in the Village of the Blind" as a newspaper story or retell the after-dinner events of "Cathedral" through the voice of the blind man.

# STUDENT WRITING

The essay below was written by a student in response to the following assignment:

> All of the stories in the "Reading, Responding, Writing" chapter seem to be saying something about the act of storytelling. Write a brief essay that compares any two stories in the chapter, showing how their ideas about storytelling are similar or different.

Nina Sullivan's response to this assignment is a respectable short essay, written without reference to sources outside the stories themselves. Notice how Sullivan grounds her argument in concrete details from the texts.

Nina Sullivan
Professor Hall
English 301
25 January 2004

## The Heart of Storytelling in "A Conversation with My Father" and "Flight Patterns"

At first glance, Grace Paley's "A Conversation with My Father" and Sherman Alexie's "Flight Patterns" seem totally different. One features a white woman and the terminally ill father with whom she is obviously very close. The other focuses on a Native American businessman and a North African cabdriver who are virtual strangers. But if we look closer, the stories start to seem much more alike. Both stories contain stories within stories; in each, one character attempts to tell a story while another attempts to interpret it. In the process, both stories show us that the act of storytelling can lead to illumination. By showing us characters whose perceptions of others are fundamentally altered by the exchange of stories, Paley and Alexie demonstrate the power of stories to influence real lives by opening our minds and our hearts.

In "A Conversation with My Father," the narrator transforms her own and her father's view of a neighbor by turning the woman into a fictional character. At the behest of her father, the narrator tells a story about how the neighbor joined her son in heroin addiction only to be abandoned by him. When the father criticizes this version of the tale, however, calling for more detail, the narrator expands the story. This time, trying to imagine how the neighbor "became such a person" (31; all page references are to the class text, The Norton Anthology of Literature, 9th ed.), she describes both the woman and her son in more positive, sympathetic terms: the mother is "a fine handsome woman" (32) whose "good mothering reflexes remained" despite her drug habit (33); her son is a "hopeful . . . ideologue" who abandons his mother only because he's trying to encourage her to quit heroin (32).

This more detailed version of the story leads the narrator's father to empathize with the neighbor's sad situation: "Poor girl," he says (34); "I suppose that means she was alone, she was left like that, his mother" (33). Moved by his response, the narrator insists that there is hope for the woman and that her story need not end in tragedy. Declaring that now she is "sorry for" her neighbor and that this newfound "pity" won't allow her "to leave her [the neighbor] there in that house crying," the narrator hastily concocts a more hopeful ending in which the woman becomes a receptionist in a community clinic (34). Prior to telling the story, the narrator feels no real emotional tie to the anonymous woman across the street, but by meeting her father's demands that she turn the woman into a character with specific traits and a complex, detailed history, the narrator begins to touch both her father's heart and her own.

At the same time, sharing this story also brings both the narrator and her father face to face with the sad facts that his heart, like all hearts, is a mere "bloody motor" bound to fail sooner or later (31), and that, however different our life stories are, they all have precisely the same tragic ending. This seems to be what the father has in mind when he comments on the way the narrator chooses to conclude the second version of her story. "The end. The end. You were right to put that down. The end," he says (34), implicitly reminding his daughter that his own end is near and that she will be left alone like the mother in the story. Perhaps sensing this, the narrator is suddenly compelled to give the story a happy ending—as much for herself, perhaps, as for her fictional character. Still, as her father recognizes, even this final version of the story, though much less flippant and ironic than the original, is less an act of empathy than another evasion of tragedy. "When will you look it in the face?" her father asks her (34). His question (which is also the final line of Paley's story) reminds us that real life is tragic, and so even a smart, funny story like the narrator's is deficient if it ignores life's tragic dimension. The narrator's earlier comment that "Life . . . unlike me has no pity" (34) implies that she does—deep down, reluctantly—acknowledge this truth.

A comparable set of revelations takes place in Alexie's "Flight Patterns" when a cab driver turns his own life into a story that challenges the preconceptions of the protagonist, William. Despite his own experience with racial prejudice and his strong desire that "the world . . . be a fair and decent place" for all (53), William makes a series of racist assumptions immediately upon meeting his driver. When he notices the man's facial scar, for example, William simply assumes that he is "[a] black man with a violent history" (55). Moments later, when the driver asks, "Are you Jewish?" William wonders whether the driver, like so many "taxi drivers all over the world," is a Muslim (56). Perhaps more important, William simply doesn't want to know anything about the driver and doesn't want to talk to him at all. When the driver begins to speak about his family, William feels both annoyed and "frightened." Not "want[ing] to be having this conversation," he tries to end it, first *by speaking in obvious generalities* and then by retreating into silence, hoping "his silence would silence the taxi driver" (56).

William soon realizes, however, that "it was too late for that" (56). As they make their way to the airport, the taxi driver, Fekadu, tells his story and through it reveals the simplistic and essentially erroneous nature of William's conjectures about him. Rather than the "crackhead addict on welfare" so many people take him to be (57), Fekadu is an Oxford-educated former fighter pilot who defected from Ethiopia when he could no longer tolerate bombing his own people on the government's behalf. Ironically, then, Fekadu does turn out to be the "black man with a violent history" William initially believed him to be. But his complex "story about contradictions" (58) reveals that he was in fact willing to sacrifice everything—home, family, money, security, and status—in order to avoid further violence (59).

Confronted with his false preconceptions, William comes to view Fekadu in a more complex and sympathetic way. Marveling at the courage it would take to do what Fekadu did, and "quite sure he could never be that courageous" himself (59), William suddenly sees Fekadu as an individual as complex as he is and in some ways much more noble. Whereas he once didn't want to talk to Fekadu at all, William is now "surprised to discover" that he actually "want[s] to hear more of this man's stories and learn from them." Not "want[ing] this journey to end," he feels a rush of empathy that makes him want to "invite Fekadu for coffee and a sandwich, for a slice of pie, for brotherhood" (59–60). Once he learns of Fekadu's personal tragedies and sacrifices, William's initial impression of Fekadu as just another "black man with a violent history" gives way to a sense of brotherhood and camaraderie. Fekadu's story leads William to reexamine its teller, to connect Fekadu's experiences as an outsider with his own, and to feel some hope that listening to strangers' stories might help prevent conflict.

Fekadu's story not only leads William to feel an almost familial connection to its teller but also gives William a better appreciation of his own family and relative good fortune. Moved by the story of how Fekadu became separated from his loved ones, William is filled with a new sense of the preciousness of those he has just left behind. Leaving his bags on the curb, he runs into the airport to call his wife and to assure her "I'm here" (61).

Just as in "A Conversation with My Father," where a woman comes to feel sympathy for her neighbor only after trying to capture the woman's life in story form, in "Flight Patterns" a man comes to see a stranger as a brother only after that stranger turns his life into a story. Both protagonists are jolted into seeing the parallels with their own lives, and they emerge from the experience with a renewed sense of sympathy for, and connection to, other people. In both cases, that sympathy comes out of a keener awareness of the things that all people share—the love of family, the pain of solitude, the fact of death.

Interestingly, both stories suggest that storytelling can have this effect on us regardless of whether we try to tell another person's story or we hear it. They also imply that it ultimately doesn't matter much whether the stories are factual or not. As Paley's narrator admits, the "woman [who] lives across the street" is as much a creature of "invention" as of "knowledge" (34). And though Alexie's William initially wonders whether or not Fekadu "was a liar" (56), he couldn't care less by the time the taxi ride is over, for now he is "convinced" that even if "Fekadu's autobiography . . . [were] completely fabricated," even "[i]f Fekadu wasn't describing his own true pain and loneliness," Fekadu's story nonetheless truthfully describes the pain of thousands of "real and lonely m[e]n" (60). What William comes to see is what both these stories affirm: whether fact or fiction, stories have the power to make us all a little less "lonely," a little more "real," and a lot more sympathetic to each other.

# Understanding the Text

## 1 PLOT

It could be said that the heart of any story is an answer to the question, "What happened?" In some stories the outward events may be very slight: "what happened" is minimal. Other stories are more dramatic, with secrets revealed or roles reversed. But whether the work of fiction deals with subtle thoughts or violent crises, you can discover its **plot**. *Plot* simply means the arrangement of the **action**, which may consist of any kind of event or series of events recounted in the story. The questions you ask about plot, or what is happening as you read, will shape your response to a story. What are the opening and concluding circumstances of the story, and how do the beginning and the ending differ? How did earlier events cause characters to behave in certain ways? Why is the sequence of events in a character's life rearranged out of chronological order as the story itself unfolds? Are there particular actions, objects, or other details that provide clues or comments on what happens because of when they are mentioned or the ways they recur or change? Such questions, in various ways relating to matters of cause and effect and of time, will lead to a clearer understanding of a story.

Most stories rely on a standard plot structure: **conflict**—a struggle of some sort—and resolution. The conflict and its resolution may be mild and comic or it may involve such destructive forces as war or racism and the deadening effects of everyday life. Generally, plot follows a five-part pattern: exposition, rising action, turning point (or climax), falling action, and conclusion. The first part of the action, called the **exposition**, introduces the characters, their situation, and, usually, a time and place. It may be as short as a sentence—"Once there was a village high in the mountains in which everyone was born blind"—or it may extend to lengthy paragraphs that set a scene or describe a typical action before the exceptional events of the story begin. Exposition usually reveals some source of conflict and may blend right away into the second phase of the plot, the **rising action**: destabilizing events that break the routine and intensify the conflict. At this point, stories tend to present a **discriminated occasion**—something distinct that happened "one day last November" or "one afternoon in his sixteenth summer." Such occasions may consist of a moment of realization or an encounter, whether remembered or unfolding in the present, that establishes the main characters, as in the early pages of "Cathedral" or "Flight Patterns." The middle, or rising action, of many traditional stories presents a series of similar but steadily intensifying incidents, as in the judgments about the elephant in "The Elephant in the Village of the Blind" or Ruthie's surprising observations in "20/20." The **turning point** or **climax** of the action is the third part of a story, where the incidents and the conflicts they introduce converge on a decisive moment, realization, or action. The final phase of a story presents the outcome, sometimes separated into the **falling action** and the **conclusion**. Thus, at the climax and resolution of "The Elephant" tale, the villagers unite their conflicting opinions of the elephant, and they come to an understanding with each other and with the traveler. All the actions of the story are fulfilled, and the situation that was destabilized at the beginning of the story either becomes stable once more or is replaced by a new stable situation.

This typical arrangement of the action of a story is a guide to your **expectations** or predictions. Yet it is not praise, of course, to call a story "predictable." The interest or special quality of any story depends on how it deviates from or adds to an expected pattern or structure. The reader needs to have a motive for continuing to read. At each step of the way you ask, "What happens next?" or "Where will this end?" Your wonder about these questions may be more or less urgent. As you read you may experience none of the **suspense** or intense curiosity and doubt provoked by mysteries, thrillers, or fiction with "twists" of plot. Yet expectations can motivate us to read on even when we feel the events are familiar and we already know the outcome. Many great stories—the myth of Oedipus, for example—begin after the outcome is well known to the audience. Detective fiction often begins just before or just after the crime is committed, so that the rest of the story concerns the process of explaining what happened and identifying "who done it." The full effect of the story comes as you think back or reread the sequence of hints or clues that you have been given, including false clues or "red herrings" that make you look in the wrong direction. Even in stories that lack such dramatic actions as murder, the big "con," the chase, or the destruction of a villain who would destroy the world, the full impact of the plot may come as you review the whole work after the end.

The effect of a story depends a great deal on your response to plot, which in turn depends on **structure**. Plot structure concerns not only the connections between causes and effects but also the arrangements of moments in time. Events in everyday life have little apparent structure since they follow each other rapidly and in overwhelming quantity; only our attention can select them, sort them out, and make sense of them. Where is the meaning or pattern in the tick, tick, tick of a clock or in a list of all the details that fill a day or a week? As Margaret Atwood's story "Happy Endings" suggests, the story of a life could be "just one thing after another, a what and a what and a what." Stories generally try to avoid that feeling of dull monotony by creating a tension between tick and tock or tock and tick, that is, by lending a meaningful pattern to mere chronology. A sense of purpose comes when you add "How and Why" to "what," as Atwood puts it.

Let's look at "Happy Endings" to see what else Atwood has to say about plot:

## MARGARET ATWOOD

### Happy Endings

John and Mary meet.
What happens next?
If you want a happy ending, try A.

A. John and Mary fall in love and get married. They both have worthwhile and remunerative jobs which they find stimulating and challenging. They buy a charming house. Real estate values go up. Eventually, when they can afford live-in help, they have two children, to whom they are devoted. The children turn out well. John and Mary have a stimulating and challenging sex life and worthwhile friends. They go on fun vacations together. They retire. They both have hobbies which they find stimulating and challenging. Eventually they die. This is the end of the story.

B. Mary falls in love with John but John doesn't fall in love with Mary. He merely uses her body for selfish pleasure and ego gratification of a tepid kind. He comes to her apartment twice a week and she cooks him dinner, you'll notice that he doesn't even consider her worth the price of a dinner out, and after he's eaten the dinner he fucks her and after that he falls asleep, while she does the dishes so he won't think she's untidy, having all those dirty dishes lying around, and puts on fresh lipstick so she'll look good when he wakes up, but when he wakes up he doesn't even notice, he puts on his socks and his shorts and his pants and his shirt and his tie and his shoes, the reverse order from the one in which he took them off. He doesn't take off Mary's clothes, she takes them off herself, she acts as if she's dying for it every time, not because she likes sex exactly, she doesn't, but she wants John to think she does because if they do it often enough surely he'll get used to her, he'll come to depend on her and they will get married, but John goes out the door with hardly so much as a good-night and three days later he turns up at six o'clock and they do the whole thing over again.

Mary gets run-down. Crying is bad for your face, everyone knows that and so does Mary but she can't stop. People at work notice. Her friends tell her John is a rat, a pig, a dog, he isn't good enough for her, but she can't believe it. Inside John, she thinks, is another John, who is much nicer. This other John will emerge like a butterfly from a cocoon, a Jack from a box, a pit from a prune, if the first John is only squeezed enough.

One evening John complains about the food. He has never complained about the food before. Mary is hurt.

Her friends tell her they've seen him in a restaurant with another woman, whose name is Madge. It's not even Madge that finally gets to Mary: it's the restaurant. John has never taken Mary to a restaurant. Mary collects all the sleeping pills and aspirins she can find, and takes them and a half a bottle of sherry. You can see what kind of a woman she is by the fact that it's not even whiskey. She leaves a note for John. She hopes he'll discover her and get her to the hospital in time and repent and then they can get married, but this fails to happen and she dies.

John marries Madge and everything continues as in A.

C. John, who is an older man, falls in love with Mary, and Mary, who is only twenty-two, feels sorry for him because he's worried about his hair falling out. She sleeps with him even though she's not in love with him. She met him at work. She's in love with someone called James, who is twenty-two also and not yet ready to settle down.

John on the contrary settled down long ago: this is what is bothering him.

John has a steady, respectable job and is getting ahead in his field, but Mary isn't impressed by him, she's impressed by James, who has a motorcycle and a fabulous record collection. But James is often away on his motorcycle, being free. Freedom isn't the same for girls, so in the meantime Mary spends Thursday evenings with John. Thursdays are the only days John can get away.

John is married to a woman called Madge and they have two children, a charming house which they bought just before the real estate values went up, and hobbies which they find stimulating and challenging, when they have the time. John tells Mary how important she is to him, but of course he can't leave his wife because a commitment is a commitment. He goes on about this more than is necessary and Mary finds it boring, but older men can keep it up longer so on the whole she has a fairly good time.

One day James breezes in on his motorcycle with some top-grade California hybrid and James and Mary get higher than you'd believe possible and they climb into bed. Everything becomes very underwater, but along comes John, who has a key to Mary's apartment. He finds them stoned and entwined. He's hardly in any position to be jealous, considering Madge, but nevertheless he's overcome with despair. Finally he's middle-aged, in two years he'll be bald as an egg and he can't stand it. He purchases a handgun, saying he needs it for target practice—this is the thin part of the plot, but it can be dealt with later— and shoots the two of them and himself.

Madge, after a suitable period of mourning, marries an understanding man called Fred and everything continues as in A, but under different names.

D. Fred and Madge have no problems. They get along exceptionally well and are good at working out any little difficulties that may arise. But their charming house is by the seashore and one day a giant tidal wave approaches. Real estate values go down. The rest of the story is about what caused the tidal wave and how they escape from it. They do, though thousands drown, but Fred and Madge are virtuous and lucky. Finally on high ground they clasp each other, wet and dripping and grateful, and continue as in A.

E. Yes, but Fred has a bad heart. The rest of the story is about how kind and understanding they both are until Fred dies. Then Madge devotes herself to charity work until the end of A. If you like, it can be "Madge," "cancer," "guilty and confused," and "bird watching."

F. If you think this is all too bourgeois, make John a revolutionary and Mary a counterespionage agent and see how far that gets you. Remember, this is Canada. You'll still end up with A, though in between you may get a lustful brawling saga of passionate involvement, a chronicle of our times, sort of.

You'll have to face it, the endings are the same however you slice it. Don't be deluded by any other endings, they're all fake, either deliberately fake, with malicious intent to deceive, or just motivated by excessive optimism if not by downright sentimentality.

The only authentic ending is the one provided here:

*John and Mary die. John and Mary die. John and Mary die.*

So much for endings. Beginnings are always more fun. True connoisseurs, however, are known to favor the stretch in between, since it's the hardest to do anything with.

That's about all that can be said for plots, which anyway are just one thing after another, a what and a what and a what.

Now try How and Why.

1983

## QUESTIONS

1. In Margaret Atwood's "Happy Endings," why is A so unsatisfying as a story, even though its conclusion ("Eventually they die. This is the end of the story.") is, as Atwood says, the "only authentic ending"?
2. Has the narrator of "Happy Endings" indeed said "about all that can be said for plots" by the end of the story? Are plots no more than "a what and a what and a what"? What else are plots besides a sequence of events?
3. Compare "Happy Endings" with "A Conversation with My Father"; what significant similarities and differences do you see between these two "stories about stories"?

The title of this story and the exposition before part A—"John and Mary meet"—tell you right away to expect a story that mocks romantic clichés, that is, conventions that have been used too much. The rising action in part A—they "fall in love and get married"—raises expectations that something climactic will happen. In part A, however, everything goes nicely, and the story ends with the end of the couple's lives. Clearly, Atwood implies, we don't bother to tell stories with so little conflict or climax. There is not enough change in such an account to make it worth the trouble of telling it. Accordingly, "Happy Endings" offers more advice on how to put a story together, with a succession of alternative plots. A reader does not usually get to determine the outcome in a short story, as one does in a computerized hypertext or one of those long-running plays in which the audience votes to choose victim and murderer. Each section of "Happy Endings" has its complications and crises; for example, after the "thin part of the plot" (a writer would fill in details of how John plans the murder), he shoots his mistress, her lover, and himself. In the falling action and conclusion in part C, the widow Madge (John's wife) recovers and remarries. Other parts of the story take up the thread where another part ended, in a way that resembles real life more than fiction.

The unusual structure of "Happy Endings" calls attention to the choices any writer makes in the course of shaping a story. Rearrangement of chronological order is one of the fundamentals of plot. Many stories are notable for interesting choices about the structure, or the order and interrelation of parts. This can be the key to your interpretation of a story. In life, actions occur one after the other, sequentially. Not all stories, however, describe events chronologically. Even in oral storytelling we often start the main story and then realize we have to back up to explain previous events that have placed people in this situation. In literary fiction, the telling is often out of order to create a sequence of effects on the audience, or to imitate the way a character's memories or responses are developing in the present time of the story. Ask yourself how the story would be different if events in the characters' lives or the paragraphs that you read were rearranged. One reason for altering chronological order is to engage the reader's attention, to make the reader read on.

The difference between chronology and plot resembles the difference between ancient chronicles that list the events of a king's reign and histories that make a meaningful plan out of those events. "The king died and then the queen died," to use one critic's example, is not a plot, for it has not been "tampered with." "The queen died after the king died" includes the same events, but the order in which they are reported has been changed. The reader of the first sentence focuses on the king first; the reader of the second sentence focuses on the queen. Probably there is an additional causal connection between the two events: the queen died *because* her husband had died. While essentially the same thing has been said, the difference in focus and emphasis changes the effect and the meaning. The chronological record has been structured into plot.

The ordering of events, then, provides stories with structure and plot, which shapes our response and interpretation. Like titles, the beginnings of stories are particularly important. Why does a story begin where it does? No event (at least since the Big Bang) is a true beginning; your own life story begins before you were born and even before you were conceived. So to begin a story the author has to select a given point rather than any other. Why does John Cheever's "The Country Husband," in this chapter, open with "To begin at the beginning, the airplane from Minneapolis in which Francis Weed was traveling East ran into heavy weather"? The story could have begun instead with, say, paragraph 11, when the Weeds are preparing to go out on the evening when Francis meets the baby-sitter; or even, with a few adjustments, with paragraph 15, when the baby-sitter opens the door and Francis sees her for the first time, for it is with their encounter that the story truly seems to begin. Yet the brush with death in the crash and Francis's inability to share the experience with anyone he knows provide a context for his brush with the vitality and desire that comprise the rest of the story.

> *Surely it was time someone invented a new plot, or that the author came out from the bushes.*
> —VIRGINIA WOOLF

The point at which a story ends is also a critical aspect of its structure. The destabilization or conflict that initiates the story should be resolved. Thus, a typical ending either reestablishes the old order or establishes a new one. Francis Weed's story ends less than two weeks after the beginning, whereas it would have been possible to "fast forward" to his old age or to the collapse of his first real affair a decade later (as in one of the options in "Happy Endings"). The author's selection of the appropriate ending governs your conclusions about how to interpret the details that have been selected to represent this character's fictional life. Perhaps the narrator of "Happy Endings" is right, and there is only one true end to any life, in fiction as in life: *"John and Mary die. John and Mary die. John and Mary die."* But Atwood herself is not quite serious that all stories must end with death. In fiction, the meaningful shape derives from selecting part of life rather than merely recounting the chronicle of events to the end of the individual's existence. Short fiction is a good form for portraying relatively short periods of time and private experiences, rather than entire lifetimes or extended public events. There can be exceptions to the common structures and patterns of time, as well as exceptions to the common beginnings and endings of short stories. The point is that where the author has made selections and placed emphases determines how a story affects us and what we make of it.

In between the beginning and the end, stories often re-order the time sequence within the fictional world. James Baldwin's "Sonny's Blues" begins, "I read about it in the paper . . . ," and that "it" without antecedent is repeated seven times in the first two paragraphs. This unidentified crisis triggers an intense emotional response in the narrator, a high school teacher who is "scared for Sonny." Read those first two paragraphs and stop. If you try at this point to examine what is going on in your mind, you more than likely will find that you are asking yourself what "it" might refer to, and you probably will have framed for yourself several possible answers. This may be part of the reason that Baldwin begins how and where he does, getting you engaged in the story so that you will read on. To do this, Baldwin "tampers" with chronology, reaching back into the characters' past to dramatize a scene that happened before the fictional present. Thus "Sonny's Blues" uses the technique (familiar from the movies) of **flashback**. By the third paragraph, the narrator begins to tell us about Sonny as a boy, still without identifying the bad news he has read about the adult Sonny. Baldwin relies on such movements from the present to remembered scenes, in a series of flashbacks, partly because the story is about the narrator's changing response to the alarming directions his brother's life has taken at various stages.

You may think that the way to write about the plot of a story is to retell the whole thing in fewer words, removing all the details. But we have already suggested that one principle for interpreting literature is that every detail is significant to the meaning. Indeed, in a short story, partly because of its brevity, every detail, every arrangement or ordering must "count." A summary of the events without the details would therefore miss too much of the real nature of a story. It would also risk leaving the reader cold, because the characters would not seem alive and the situation would seem too abstract. This is essentially the complaint of the dying father in "A Conversation with My Father" when his daughter tells a very short, flat story without developing the characters or complicating the plot. Some stories, like "Happy Endings," deliberately avoid the techniques that create the illusion that the characters, places, and actions are real. When a story defies your expectations that there will be substantial detail, complex characters, and realistic actions of everyday life, you should ask, Is this an intentional effect? The story may be more magical or more philosophical, more about improbable cause and effect or about the questions of what we can know or express about reality, than about the inner experience of people like us.

In order to understand the intended effect of a story, it is a good rule of thumb to be questioning if not suspicious about the slightest matters in it. Descriptions of objects or incidents may turn out to be part of the plot or "what happens." One writer has said that if there is a gun on the wall at the beginning of a story, it must be fired by the end. Usually incidents or details seem less foreboding than a loaded gun, yet a good reading of a story should consider the relevance or significance even of matters that would be left out of a plot summary. In paragraph 9 of "The Country Husband," for example, Francis Weed listens to "the evening sounds of Shady Hill." These include Mr. Nixon's yelling at the squirrels that raid the birdfeeder: "Varmints! Rascals! Avaunt and quit my sight!" And Donald Goslin is playing (badly) Beethoven's *Moonlight Sonata*. These seem like incidental details, yet both sounds reappear in paragraphs 40 and 41. The repetition of such details becomes part of the plot of the story rather than mere decoration of the setting.

As you focus on such details, ask yourself what a particular item adds to the story. What would be lost without it? In what part of the story does the detail appear and is it, or something else like it, repeated elsewhere in the story? Details in fiction can be like colors in a room, a painting, or an outfit of clothes and accessories—hints to make a connection between parts of the whole. As you discuss or write about a story, you may be dazzled by the wide range and complexity of the details contributing to its effect, and even stymied by differing opinions about the significance of any one detail. It may seem strange when classmates ignore details that matter a great deal to you, or notice details that eluded you. These differences of selection and explanation may shed light on why readers respond to, understand, and judge stories differently. That is one of the pleasures of pondering and discussing stories that avoid direct statements of what happened. In order to keep you engaged and alert, a story must make you ask questions about what will happen or what will be revealed next. A good story is a guessing game.

Like all guessing games, from quiz shows to philosophy, the plot game in fiction has certain guidelines. A well-structured plot will play fair with you, offering at appropriate points all the necessary indications or clues to what will happen next, not just springing new and essential information on you at the last minute. It can be a sign of unoriginal or badly made fiction if a story resorts to a sudden rescue, surprise, or twist. Cause and effect, as well as the beginning and ending of the story, should be integrated; the story shouldn't undermine the reader's expectations, as in "Meanwhile, unknown to our hero, the Marines were just on the other side of the hill," or "Susan rolled over in bed and realized the whole thing had been just a dream." Even so, too much uncertainty is frustrating just as knowing too well where it is all heading is wearisome or boring. Readers may expect and want a loaded gun to fire by the last paragraph, but that sort of plot detail can be too predictable. Readers can also be moved and intrigued by changes in feeling that are difficult to express and that lead to no catastrophic action. Many satisfying stories continue to provoke questions long after you have read and reread them. To respond fully to a story you must be alert to its signals and guess along with the author. One way of seeing whether and how your mind is engaged in your reading is to pause at crucial points in the story and consciously explore what you think is coming.

*As regards plots I find real life no help at all. Real life seems to have no plots.*
—IVY COMPTON-BURNETT

Unlike most guessing games, however, the reward in reading short fiction is not for the right guess—anticipating the outcome before the final paragraph—but for the number of guesses, right *and* wrong, that you make, the number of signals you respond to. "Roman Fever" begins in a contemplative, comfortable situation with old friends lunching at a picturesque spot in Rome. The two wealthy American widows are touring with their grown daughters; there are some indications of different personalities and a bit of a generation gap. How many possibilities can you anticipate?

"Roman Fever" is a story with a strong dependence on plot, in the sense that for characters and readers the sequence of thoughts and dialogue and action is essential to understanding. It would ruin the whole if any of the information divulged in the last paragraphs were given away too soon. Yet the ending is well integrated with all the previous details, so that a reader gains further pleasure in rereading for new layers of significance. Knowing the ending, you could go back to any point in the story and, recalling your expectations, gain insight into the characters, the intricacies of the plot, the underlying themes and meanings, and even your own psychology. Short fiction has a great advantage over novels or other longer works in this regard; rereading a short story is a relatively easy thing to do, and among its layered pleasures is the knowledge that with each attempt, you will arrive at a slightly different answer to the question, "What happened?"

## JOHN CHEEVER

### The Country Husband

To begin at the beginning, the airplane from Minneapolis in which Francis Weed was traveling East ran into heavy weather. The sky had been a hazy blue, with the clouds below the plane lying so close together that nothing could be seen of the earth. The mist began to form outside the windows, and they flew into a white cloud of such density that it reflected the exhaust fires. The color of the cloud darkened to gray, and the plane began to rock. Francis had been in heavy weather before, but he had never been shaken up so much. The man in the seat beside him pulled a flask out of his pocket and took a drink. Francis smiled at his neighbor, but the man looked away; he wasn't sharing his pain killer with anyone. The plane began to drop and flounder wildly. A child was crying. The air in the cabin was overheated and stale, and Francis' left foot went to sleep. He read a little from a paper book that he had bought at the airport, but the violence of the storm divided his attention. It was black outside the ports. The exhaust fires blazed and shed sparks in the dark, and, inside, the shaded lights, the stuffiness, and the window curtains gave the cabin an atmosphere of intense and misplaced domesticity. Then the light flickered and went out. "You know what I've always wanted to do?" the man beside Francis said suddenly. "I've always wanted to buy a farm in New Hampshire and raise beef cattle." The stewardess announced that they were going to make an emergency landing. All but the children saw in their minds the spreading wings of the Angel of Death. The pilot could be heard singing faintly, "I've got sixpence, jolly, jolly sixpence. I've got sixpence to last me all my life . . ."[1] There was no other sound.

The loud groaning of the hydraulic valves swallowed up the pilot's song, and there was a shrieking high in the air, like automobile brakes, and the plane hit flat on its belly in a cornfield and shook them so violently that an old man up forward howled, "Me kidneys! Me kidneys!" The stewardess flung open the door, and someone opened an emergency door at the back, letting in the sweet noise of their continuing mortality—the idle splash and smell of a heavy rain. Anxious for their lives, they filed out of the doors and scattered over the cornfield in all directions, praying that the thread would hold. It did. Nothing happened. When it was clear that the plane would not burn or explode, the crew and the stewardess gathered the passengers together and led them to the shelter of a barn. They were not far from Philadelphia, and in a little while a string of taxis took them into the city. "It's just like the Marne,"[2] someone said, but there was surprisingly little relaxation of that suspiciousness with which many Americans regard their fellow travelers.

---

1. Song popular with Allied troops in World War II.
2. On September 8, 1914, over one thousand Paris taxicabs were requisitioned to move troops to the Marne River to halt the encircling Germans.

In Philadelphia, Francis Weed got a train to New York. At the end of that journey, he crossed the city and caught just as it was about to pull out the commuting train that he took five nights a week to his home in Shady Hill.

He sat with Trace Bearden. "You know, I was in that plane that just crashed outside Philadelphia," he said. "We came down in a field . . ." He had traveled faster than the newspapers or the rain, and the weather in New York was sunny and mild. It was a day in late September, as fragrant and shapely as an apple. Trace listened to the story, but how could he get excited? Francis had no powers that would let him re-create a brush with death—particularly in the atmosphere of a commuting train, journeying through a sunny countryside where already, in the slum gardens, there were signs of harvest. Trace picked up his newspaper, and Francis was left alone with his thoughts. He said good night to Trace on the platform at Shady Hill and drove in his secondhand Volkswagen up to the Blenhollow neighborhood, where he lived.

The Weeds' Dutch Colonial house was larger than it appeared to be from the driveway. The living room was spacious and divided like Gaul,[3] into three parts. Around an ell to the left as one entered from the vestibule was the long table, laid for six, with candles and a bowl of fruit in the center. The sounds and smells that came from the open kitchen door were appetizing, for Julia Weed was a good cook. The largest part of the living room centered on a fireplace. On the right were some bookshelves and a piano. The room was polished and tranquil, and from the windows that opened to the west there was some late-summer sunlight, brilliant and as clear as water. Nothing here was neglected; nothing had not been burnished. It was not the kind of household where, after prying open a stuck cigarette box, you would find an old shirt button and a tarnished nickel. The hearth was swept, the roses on the piano were reflected in the polish of the broad top, and there was an album of Schubert waltzes on the rack. Louisa Weed, a pretty girl of nine, was looking out the western windows. Her young brother Henry was standing beside her. Her still younger brother, Toby, was studying the figures of some tonsured monks drinking beer on the polished brass of the woodbox. Francis, taking off his hat and putting down his paper, was not consciously pleased with the scene; he was not that reflective. It was his element, his creation, and he returned to it with that sense of lightness and strength with which any creature returns to his home. "Hi, everybody," he said. "The plane from Minneapolis . . ."

Nine times out of ten, Francis would be greeted with affection, but tonight the children are absorbed in their own antagonisms. Francis had not finished his sentence about the plane crash before Henry plants a kick in Louisa's behind. Louisa swings around, saying, *"Damn you!"* Francis makes the mistake of scolding Louisa for bad language before he punishes Henry. Now Louisa turns on her father and accuses him of favoritism. Henry is always right; she is persecuted and lonely; her lot is hopeless. Francis turns to his son, but the son has justification for the kick—she hit him first; she hit him on the ear, which is dangerous. Louisa agrees with this passionately. She hit him on the ear, and she *meant* to hit him on the ear, because he messed up her china collection. Henry says that this is a lie. Little Toby turns away from the woodbox to throw in some evidence for Louisa. Henry claps his hand over little Toby's mouth. Francis separates the

---

3. Ancient France (Gaul) is so described by Julius Caesar in *The Gallic War*.

two boys but accidentally pushes Toby into the woodbox. Toby begins to cry. Louisa is already crying. Just then, Julia Weed comes into that part of the room where the table is laid. She is a pretty, intelligent woman, and the white in her hair is premature. She does not seem to notice the fracas. "Hello, darling," she says serenely to Francis. "Wash your hands, everyone. Dinner is ready." She strikes a match and lights the six candles in this vale of tears.[4]

This simple announcement, like the war cries of the Scottish chieftains, only refreshes the ferocity of the combatants. Louisa gives Henry a blow on the shoulder. Henry, although he seldom cries, has pitched nine innings and is tired. He bursts into tears. Little Toby discovers a splinter in his hand and begins to howl. Francis says loudly that he has been in a plane crash and that he is tired. Julia appears again from the kitchen and, still ignoring the chaos, asks Francis to go upstairs and tell Helen that everything is ready. Francis is happy to go; it is like getting back to headquarters company.[5] He is planning to tell his oldest daughter about the airplane crash, but Helen is lying on her bed reading a *True Romance* magazine, and the first thing Francis does is to take the magazine from her hand and remind Helen that he has forbidden her to buy it. She did not buy it, Helen replies. It was given to her by her best friend, Bessie Black. Everybody reads *True Romance*. Bessie Black's father reads *True Romance*. There isn't a girl in Helen's class who doesn't read *True Romance*. Francis expresses his detestation of the magazine and then tells her that dinner is ready—although from the sounds downstairs it doesn't seem so. Helen follows him down the stairs. Julia has seated herself in the candlelight and spread a napkin over her lap. Neither Louisa nor Henry has come to the table. Little Toby is still howling, lying face down on the floor. Francis speaks to him gently: "Daddy was in a plane crash this afternoon, Toby. Don't you want to hear about it?" Toby goes on crying. "If you don't come to the table now, Toby," Francis says, "I'll have to send you to bed without any supper." The little boy rises, gives him a cutting look, flies up the stairs to his bedroom, and slams the door. "Oh, dear," Julia says, and starts to go after him. Francis says that she will spoil him. Julia says that Toby is ten pounds underweight and has to be encouraged to eat. Winter is coming, and he will spend the cold months in bed unless he has his dinner. Julia goes upstairs. Francis sits down at the table with Helen. Helen is suffering from the dismal feeling of having read too intently on a fine day, and she gives her father and the room a jaded look. She doesn't understand about the plane crash, because there wasn't a drop of rain in Shady Hill.

Julia returns with Toby, and they all sit down and are served. "Do I have to look at that big, fat slob?" Henry says, of Louisa. Everybody but Toby enters into this skirmish, and it rages up and down the table for five minutes. Toward the end, Henry puts his napkin over his head and, trying to eat that way, spills spinach all over his shirt. Francis asks Julia if the children couldn't have their dinner earlier. Julia's guns are loaded for this. She can't cook two dinners and lay two tables. She paints with lightning strokes that panorama of drudgery in which her youth, her beauty, and her wit have been lost. Francis says that he must be understood; he was nearly killed in an airplane crash, and he doesn't

---

4. Common figurative reference to earthly life (vale is valley); allusion to Bible: "Blessed is the man whose help is from thee: in his heart he hath disposed to ascend by steps, in the vale of tears, in the place which he hath set" (Psalms 83.6–7).   5. That is, like escaping from combat to relative safety behind the lines.

like to come home every night to a battlefield. Now Julia is deeply concerned. Her voice trembles. He doesn't come home every night to a battlefield. The accusation is stupid and mean. Everything was tranquil until he arrived. She stops speaking, puts down her knife and fork, and looks into her plate as if it is a gulf. She begins to cry. "Poor Mummy!" Toby says, and when Julia gets up from the table, drying her tears with a napkin, Toby goes to her side. "Poor Mummy," he says. "Poor Mummy!" And they climb the stairs together. The other children drift away from the battlefield, and Francis goes into the back garden for a cigarette and some air.

It was a pleasant garden, with walks and flower beds and places to sit. The sunset had nearly burned out, but there was still plenty of light. Put into a thoughtful mood by the crash and the battle, Francis listened to the evening sounds of Shady Hill. "Varmints! Rascals!" old Mr. Nixon shouted to the squirrels in his bird-feeding station. "Avaunt and quit my sight!" A door slammed. Someone was cutting grass. Then Donald Goslin, who lived at the corner, began to play the "Moonlight Sonata."[6] He did this nearly every night. He threw the tempo out the window and played it *rubato*[7] from beginning to end, like an outpouring of tearful petulance, lonesomeness, and self-pity—of everything it was Beethoven's greatness not to know. The music rang up and down the street beneath the trees like an appeal for love, for tenderness, aimed at some lovely housemaid—some fresh-faced, homesick girl from Galway, looking at old snapshots in her third-floor room. "Here, Jupiter, here, Jupiter," Francis called to the Mercers' retriever. Jupiter crashed through the tomato vines with the remains of a felt hat in his mouth.

Jupiter was an anomaly. His retrieving instincts and his high spirits were out of place in Shady Hill. He was as black as coal, with a long, alert, intelligent, rakehell face. His eyes gleamed with mischief, and he held his head high. It was the fierce, heavily collared dog's head that appears in heraldry, in tapestry, and that used to appear on umbrella handles and walking sticks. Jupiter went where he pleased, ransacking wastebaskets, clotheslines, garbage pails, and shoe bags. He broke up garden parties and tennis matches, and got mixed up in the processional at Christ Church on Sunday, barking at the men in red dresses.[8] He crashed through old Mr. Nixon's rose garden two or three times a day, cutting a wide swath through the Condesa de Sastagos,[9] and as soon as Donald Goslin lighted his barbecue fire on Thursday nights, Jupiter would get the scent. Nothing the Goslins did could drive him away. Sticks and stones and rude commands only moved him to the edge of the terrace, where he remained, with his gallant and heraldic muzzle, waiting for Donald Goslin to turn his back and reach for the salt. Then he would spring onto the terrace, lift the steak lightly off the fire, and run away with the Goslins' dinner. Jupiter's days were numbered. The Wrightsons' German gardener or the Farquarsons' cook would soon poison him. Even old Mr. Nixon might put some arsenic in the garbage that Jupiter loved. "Here, Jupiter, Jupiter!" Francis called, but the dog pranced off, shaking the hat

---

6. Beethoven's *Sonata Quasi una Fantasia* (1802), a famous and frequently sentimentalized piano composition.   7. With intentional deviations from strict tempo.   8. Probably the choir.
9. Uncommon yellow and red roses, difficult to grow.

in his white teeth. Looking at the windows of his house, Francis saw that Julia had come down and was blowing out the candles.

Julia and Francis Weed went out a great deal. Julia was well liked and gregarious, and her love of parties sprang from a most natural dread of chaos and loneliness. She went through the morning mail with real anxiety, looking for invitations, and she usually found some, but she was insatiable, and if she had gone out seven nights a week, it would not have cured her of a reflective look—the look of someone who hears distant music—for she would always suppose that there was a more brilliant party somewhere else. Francis limited her to two week-night parties, putting a flexible interpretation on Friday, and rode through the weekend like a dory in a gale. The day after the airplane crash, the Weeds were to have dinner with the Farquarsons.

Francis got home late from town, and Julia got the sitter while he dressed, and then hurried him out of the house. The party was small and pleasant, and Francis settled down to enjoy himself. A new maid passed the drinks. Her hair was dark, and her face was round and pale and seemed familiar to Francis. He had not developed his memory as a sentimental faculty. Wood smoke, lilac, and other such perfumes did not stir him, and his memory was something like his appendix—a vestigial repository. It was not his limitation at all to be unable to escape the past; it was perhaps his limitation that he had escaped it so successfully. He might have seen the maid at other parties, he might have seen her taking a walk on Sunday afternoons, but in either case he would not be searching his memory now. Her face was, in a wonderful way, a moon face—Norman or Irish—but it was not beautiful enough to account for his feeling that he had seen her before, in circumstances that he ought to be able to remember. He asked Nellie Farquarson who she was. Nellie said that the maid had come through an agency, and that her home was Trénon, in Normandy—a small place with a church and a restaurant that Nellie had once visited. While Nellie talked on about her travels abroad, Francis realized where he had seen the woman before. It had been at the end of the war. He had left a replacement depot with some other men and taken a three-day pass in Trénon. On their second day, they had walked out to a crossroads to see the public chastisement of a young woman who had lived with the German commandant during the Occupation.

It was a cool morning in the fall. The sky was overcast, and poured down onto the dirt crossroads a very discouraging light. They were on high land and could see how like one another the shapes of the clouds and the hills were as they stretched off toward the sea. The prisoner arrived sitting on a three-legged stool in a farm cart. She stood by the cart while the Mayor read the accusation and the sentence. Her head was bent and her face was set in that empty half smile behind which the whipped soul is suspended. When the Mayor was finished, she undid her hair and let it fall across her back. A little man with a gray mustache cut off her hair with shears and dropped it on the ground. Then, with a bowl of soapy water and a straight razor, he shaved her skull clean. A woman approached and began to undo the fastenings of her clothes, but the prisoner pushed her aside and undressed herself. When she pulled her chemise over her head and threw it on the ground, she was naked. The women jeered; the men were still. There was no change in the falseness or the plaintiveness of the prisoner's smile. The cold wind made her white skin rough and hardened the nipples of her breasts. The jeering ended gradually, put down by the recognition of their common humanity. One woman spat on her, but some inviolable grandeur in her nakedness lasted through the ordeal. When the crowd was quiet, she turned— she had begun to cry—and, with nothing on but a pair of worn black shoes and stockings, walked down the dirt road alone away from the village. The round white face had aged a little, but there was no question but that the maid who passed his cocktails and later served Francis his dinner was the woman who had been punished at the crossroads.

The war seemed now so distant and that world where the cost of partisanship had been death or torture so long ago. Francis had lost track of the men who had been with him in Vésey. He could not count on Julia's discretion. He could not tell anyone. And if he had told the story now, at the dinner table, it would have been a social as well as a human error. The people in the Farquarsons' living room seemed united in their tacit claim that there had been no past, no war— that there was no danger or trouble in the world. In the recorded history of human arrangements, this extraordinary meeting would have fallen into place, but the atmosphere of Shady Hill made the memory unseemly and impolite. The prisoner withdrew after passing the coffee, but the encounter left Francis feeling languid; it had opened his memory and his senses, and left them dilated. Julia went into the house. Francis stayed in the car to take the sitter home.

Expecting to see Mrs. Henlein, the old lady who usually stayed with the children, he was surprised when a young girl opened the door and came out onto the lighted stoop. She stayed in the light to count her textbooks. She was frowning and beautiful. Now, the world is full of beautiful young girls, but Francis saw here the difference between beauty and perfection. All those endearing flaws, moles, birthmarks, and healed wounds were missing, and he experienced in his consciousness that moment when music breaks glass, and felt a pang of recognition as strange, deep and wonderful as anything in his life. It hung from her frown, from an impalpable darkness in her face—a look that impressed him as a direct appeal for love. When she had counted her books, she came down the steps and opened the car door. In the light, he saw that her cheeks were wet. She got in and shut the door.

"You're new," Francis said.

"Yes. Mrs. Henlein is sick. I'm Anne Murchison."

"Did the children give you any trouble?"

"Oh, no, no." She turned and smiled at him unhappily in the dim dashboard light. Her light hair caught on the collar of her jacket, and she shook her head to set it loose.

"You've been crying."

"Yes."

"I hope it was nothing that happened in our house."

"No, no, it was nothing that happened in your house." Her voice was bleak. "It's no secret. Everybody in the village knows. Daddy's an alcoholic, and he just called me from some saloon and gave me a piece of his mind. He thinks I'm immoral. He called just before Mrs. Weed came back."

"I'm sorry."

"Oh, *Lord!*" She gasped and began to cry. She turned toward Francis, and he took her in his arms and let her cry on his shoulder. She shook in his embrace, and this movement accentuated his sense of the fineness of her flesh and bone. The layers of their clothing felt thin, and when her shuddering began to diminish, it was so much like a paroxysm of love that Francis lost his head and pulled her roughly against him. She drew away. "I live on Belleview Avenue," she said. "You go down Lansing Street to the railroad bridge."

"All right." He started the car.

"You turn left at that traffic light.... Now you turn right here and go straight on toward the tracks."

The road Francis took brought him out of his own neighborhood, across the tracks, and toward the river, to a street where the near-poor lived, in houses whose peaked gables and trimmings of wooden lace conveyed the purest feelings of pride and romance, although the houses themselves could not have offered much privacy or comfort, they were all so small. The street was dark, and, stirred by the grace and beauty of the troubled girl, he seemed, in turning into it, to have come into the deepest part of some submerged memory. In the distance, he saw a porch light burning. It was the only one, and she said that the house with the light was where she lived. When he stopped the car, he could see beyond the porch light into a dimly lighted hallway with an old-fashioned clothes tree. "Well, here we are," he said, conscious that a young man would have said something different.

She did not move her hands from the books, where they were folded, and she turned and faced him. There were tears of lust in his eyes. Determinedly—not sadly—he opened the door on his side and walked around to open hers. He took her free hand, letting his fingers in between hers, climbed at her side the two concrete steps, and went up a narrow walk through a front garden where dahlias, marigolds, and roses—things that had withstood the light frosts—still bloomed, and made a bittersweet smell in the night air. At the steps, she freed her hand and then turned and kissed him swiftly. Then she crossed the porch and shut the door. The porch light went out, then the light in the hall. A second later, a light went on upstairs at the side of the house, shining into a tree that was still covered with leaves. It took her only a few minutes to undress and get into bed, and then the house was dark.

30  Julia was asleep when Francis got home. He opened a second window and got into bed to shut his eyes on that night, but as soon as they were shut—as soon as he had dropped off to sleep—the girl entered his mind, moving with perfect freedom through its shut doors and filling chamber after chamber with her light, her perfume, and the music of her voice. He was crossing the Atlantic with her on the old *Mauretania*[1] and, later, living with her in Paris. When he woke from his dream, he got up and smoked a cigarette at the open window. Getting back into bed, he cast around in his mind for something he desired to do that would injure no one, and he thought of skiing. Up through the dimness in his mind rose the image of a mountain deep in snow. It was late in the day. Wherever his eyes looked, he saw broad and heartening things. Over his shoulder, there was a snow-filled valley, rising into wooded hills where the trees dimmed the whiteness like a sparse coat of hair. The cold deadened all sound but the loud, iron clanking of the lift machinery. The light on the trails was blue, and it was harder than it had been a minute or two earlier to pick the turns, harder to judge—now that the snow was all deep blue—the crust, the ice, the bare spots, and the deep piles

---

1. The original *Mauretania* (1907–35), sister ship of the *Lusitania*, which was sunk by the Germans in 1915, was the most famous transatlantic liner of its day.

of dry powder. Down the mountain he swung, matching his speed against the contours of a slope that had been formed in the first ice age, seeking with ardor some simplicity of feeling and circumstance. Night fell then, and he drank a Martini with some old friend in a dirty country bar.

In the morning, Francis' snow-covered mountain was gone, and he was left with his vivid memories of Paris and the *Mauretania*. He had been bitten gravely. He washed his body, shaved his jaws, drank his coffee, and missed the seventy-thirty-one. The train pulled out just as he brought his car to the station, and the longing he felt for the coaches as they drew stubbornly away from him reminded him of the humors of love. He waited for the eight-two, on what was now an empty platform. It was a clear morning; the morning seemed thrown like a gleaming bridge of light over his mixed affairs. His spirits were feverish and high. The image of the girl seemed to put him into a relationship to the world that was mysterious and enthralling. Cars were beginning to fill up the parking lot, and he noticed that those that had driven down from the high land above Shady Hill were white with hoarfrost. This first clear sign of autumn thrilled him. An express train—a night train from Buffalo or Albany—came down the tracks between the platforms, and he saw that the roofs of the foremost cars were covered with a skin of ice. Struck by the miraculous physicalness of everything, he smiled at the passengers in the dining car, who could be seen eating eggs and wiping their mouths with napkins as they traveled. The sleeping-car compartments, with their soiled bed linen, trailed through the fresh morning like a string of rooming-house windows. Then he saw an extraordinary thing; at one of the bedroom windows sat an unclothed woman of exceptional beauty, combing her golden hair. She passed like an apparition through Shady Hill, combing and combing her hair, and Francis followed her with his eyes until she was out of sight. Then old Mrs. Wrightson joined him on the platform and began to talk.

"Well, I guess you must be surprised to see me here the third morning in a row," she said, "but because of my window curtains I'm becoming a regular commuter. The curtains I bought on Monday I returned on Tuesday, and the curtains I bought Tuesday I'm returning today. On Monday, I got exactly what I wanted—it's a wool tapestry with roses and birds—but when I got them home, I found they were the wrong length. Well, I exchanged them yesterday, and when I got them home, I found they were still the wrong length. Now I'm praying to high heaven that the decorator will have them in the right length, because you know my house, you *know* my living-room windows, and you can imagine what a problem they present. I don't know what to do with them."

"I know what to do with them," Francis said.

"What?"

"Paint them black on the inside, and shut up."

There was a gasp from Mrs. Wrightson, and Francis looked down at her to be sure that she knew he meant to be rude. She turned and walked away from him, so damaged in spirit that she limped. A wonderful feeling enveloped him, as if light were being shaken about him, and he thought again of Venus combing and combing her hair as she drifted through the Bronx. The realization of how many years had passed since he had enjoyed being deliberately impolite sobered him. Among his friends and neighbors, there were brilliant and gifted people— he saw that—but many of them, also, were bores and fools, and he had made the mistake of listening to them all with equal attention. He had confused a lack of discrimination with Christian love, and the confusion seemed general and destructive. He was grateful to the girl for this bracing sensation of independence. Birds were singing—cardinals and the last of the robins. The sky shone like enamel. Even the smell of ink from his morning paper honed his appetite for life, and the world that was spread out around him was plainly a paradise.

If Francis had believed in some hierarchy of love—in spirits armed with hunting bows, in the capriciousness of Venus and Eros[2]—or even in magical potions, philters, and stews, in scapulae and quarters of the moon,[3] it might have explained his susceptibility and his feverish high spirits. The autumnal loves of middle age are well publicized, and he guessed that he was face to face with one of these, but there was not a trace of autumn in what he felt. He wanted to sport in the green woods, scratch where he itched, and drink from the same cup.

His secretary, Miss Rainey, was late that morning—she went to a psychiatrist three mornings a week—and when she came in, Francis wondered what advice a psychiatrist would have for him. But the girl promised to bring back into his life something like the sound of music. The realization that this music might lead him straight to a trial for statutory rape at the country courthouse collapsed his happiness. The photograph of his four children laughing into the camera on the beach at Gay Head reproached him. On the letterhead of his firm there was a drawing of the Laocoön,[4] and the figure of the priest and his sons in the coils of the snake appeared to him to have the deepest meaning.

He had lunch with Pinky Trabert. At a conversational level, the mores of his friends were robust and elastic, but he knew that the moral card house would come down on them all—on Julia and the children as well—if he got caught taking advantage of a baby-sitter. Looking back over the recent history of Shady Hill for some precedent, he found there was none. There was no turpitude; there had not been a divorce since he lived there; there had not even been a breath of scandal. Things seemed arranged with more propriety even than in the Kingdom of Heaven. After leaving Pinky, Francis went to a jeweler's and bought the girl a bracelet. How happy this clandestine purchase made him, how stuffy and comical the jeweler's clerks seemed, how sweet the women who passed at his back smelled! On Fifth Avenue, passing Atlas with his shoulders bent under the weight of the world,[5] Francis thought of the strenuousness of containing his physicalness within the patterns he had chosen.

40    He did not know when he would see the girl next. He had the bracelet in his inside pocket when he got home. Opening the door of his house, he found her in the hall. Her back was to him, and she turned when she heard the door close. Her smile was open and loving. Her perfection stunned him like a fine day—a day after a thunderstorm. He seized her and covered her lips with his, and she struggled but she did not have to struggle for long, because just then little Gertrude Flannery appeared from somewhere and said, "Oh, Mr. Weed . . ."

2. Roman name for the goddess of love (Greek: *Aphrodite*) and Greek name for her son (Roman: *Cupid*).
3. Love-inducing and predictive magic. *Scapulae:* small Roman Catholic icons that hang from a ribbon worn around the shoulders.
4. Famous Greek statue, now in the Vatican museum; the "meaning" for Weed seems to reside in the physical struggle, not in the legend (in which the priest and his sons were punished for warning the Trojans about the wooden horse).
5. In Greek legend the Titan Atlas supported the heavens on his shoulders, but he has come to be depicted as bearing the globe; the statue is at Rockefeller Center.

Gertrude was a stray. She had been born with a taste for exploration, and she did not have it in her to center her life with her affectionate parents. People who did not know the Flannerys concluded from Gertrude's behavior that she was the child of a bitterly divided family, where drunken quarrels were the rule. This was not true. The fact that little Gertrude's clothing was ragged and thin was her own triumph over her mother's struggle to dress her warmly and neatly. Garrulous, skinny, and unwashed, she drifted from house to house around the Blenhollow neighborhood, forming and breaking alliances based on an attachment to babies, animals, children her own age, adolescents, and sometimes adults. Opening your front door in the morning, you would find Gertrude sitting on your stoop. Going into the bathroom to shave, you would find Gertrude using the toilet. Looking into your son's crib, you would find it empty, and, looking further, you would find that Gertrude had pushed him in his baby carriage into the next village. She was helpful, pervasive, honest, hungry, and loyal. She never went home of her own choice. When the time to go arrived, she was indifferent to all its signs. "Go home, Gertrude," people could be heard saying in one house or another, night after night. "Go home, Gertrude. It's time for you to go home now, Gertrude." "You had better go home and get your supper, Gertrude." "I told you to go home twenty minutes ago, Gertrude." "Your mother will be worrying about you, Gertrude." "Go home, Gertrude, go home."

There are times when the lines around the human eye seem like shelves of eroded stone and when the staring eye itself strikes us with such a wilderness of animal feeling that we are at a loss. The look Francis gave the little girl was ugly and queer, and it frightened her. He reached into his pockets—his hands were shaking—and took out a quarter. "Go home, Gertrude, go home, and don't tell anyone, Gertrude. Don't—" He choked and ran into the living room as Julia called down to him from upstairs to hurry and dress.

The thought that he would drive Anne Murchison home later that night ran like a golden thread through the events of the party that Francis and Julia went to, and he laughed uproariously at dull jokes, dried a tear when Mabel Mercer told him about the death of her kitten, and stretched, yawned, sighed, and grunted like any other man with a rendezvous at the back of his mind. The bracelet was in his pocket. As he sat talking, the smell of grass was in his nose, and he was wondering where he would park the car. Nobody lived in the old Parker mansion, and the driveway was used as a lovers' lane. Townsend Street was a dead end, and he could park there, beyond the last house. The old lane that used to connect Elm Street to the riverbanks was overgrown, but he had walked there with his children, and he could drive his car deep enough into the brushwoods to be concealed.

The Weeds were the last to leave the party, and their host and hostess spoke of their own married happiness while they all four stood in the hallway saying good night. "She's my girl," their host said, squeezing his wife. "She's my blue sky. After sixteen years, I still bite her shoulders. She makes me feel like Hannibal crossing the Alps."[6]

The Weeds drove home in silence. Francis brought the car up the driveway and sat still, with the motor running. "You can put the car in the garage," Julia

---

[6]. The Carthaginian general (274-183 B.C.E.) attacked the Romans from the rear by crossing the Alps, considered impregnable, with the use of elephants.

said as she got out. "I told the Murchison girl she could leave at eleven. Someone drove her home." She shut the door, and Francis sat in the dark. He would be spared nothing then, it seemed, that a fool was not spared: ravening lewdness, jealousy, this hurt to his feelings that put tears in his eyes, even scorn—for he could see clearly the image he now presented, his arms spread over the steering wheel and his head buried in them for love.

Francis had been a dedicated Boy Scout when he was young, and, remembering the precepts of his youth, he left his office early the next afternoon and played some round-robin squash, but, with his body toned up by exercise and a shower, he realized that he might better have stayed at his desk. It was a frosty night when he got home. The air smelled sharply of change. When he stepped into the house, he sensed an unusual stir. The children were in their best clothes, and when Julia came down, she was wearing a lavender dress and her diamond sunburst. She explained the stir: Mr. Hubber was coming at seven to take their photograph for the Christmas card. She had put out Francis' blue suit and a tie with some color in it, because the picture was going to be in color this year. Julia was lighthearted at the thought of being photographed for Christmas. It was the kind of ceremony she enjoyed.

Francis went upstairs to change his clothes. He was tired from the day's work and tired with longing, and sitting on the edge of the bed had the effect of deepening his weariness. He thought of Anne Murchison, and the physical need to express himself, instead of being restrained by the pink lamps of Julia's dressing table, engulfed him. He went to Julia's desk, took a piece of writing paper, and began to write on it. "Dear Anne, I love you, I love you, I love you . . ." No one would see the letter, and he used no restraint. He used phrases like "heavenly bliss," and "love nest." He salivated, sighed, and trembled. When Julia called him to come down, the abyss between his fantasy and the practical world opened so wide that he felt it affected the muscles of his heart.

Julia and the children were on the stoop, and the photographer and his assistant had set up a double battery of floodlights to show the family and the architectural beauty of the entrance to their house. People who had come home on a late train slowed their cars to see the Weeds being photographed for their Christmas card. A few waved and called to the family. It took half an hour of smiling and wetting their lips before Mr. Hubber was satisfied. The heat of the lights made an unfresh smell in the frosty air, and when they were turned off, they lingered on the retina of Francis' eyes.

Later that night, while Francis and Julia were drinking their coffee in the living room, the doorbell rang. Julia answered the door and let in Clayton Thomas. He had come to pay for some theatre tickets that she had given his mother some time ago, and that Helen Thomas had scrupulously insisted on paying for, though Julia had asked her not to. Julia invited him in to have a cup of coffee. "I won't have any coffee," Clayton said, "but I will come in for a minute." He followed her into the living room, said good evening to Francis, and sat awkwardly in a chair.

50    Clayton's father had been killed in the war, and the young man's fatherlessness surrounded him like an element. This may have been conspicuous in Shady Hill because the Thomases were the only family that lacked a piece; all the other marriages were intact and productive. Clayton was in his second or third year of

college, and he and his mother lived alone in a large house, which she hoped to sell. Clayton had once made some trouble. Years ago, he had stolen some money and run away; he had got to California before they caught up with him. He was tall and homely, wore horn-rimmed glasses, and spoke in a deep voice.

"When do you go back to college, Clayton?" Francis asked.

"I'm not going back," Clayton said. "Mother doesn't have the money, and there's no sense in all this pretense. I'm going to get a job, and if we sell the house, we'll take an apartment in New York."

"Won't you miss Shady Hill?" Julia asked.

"No," Clayton said. "I don't like it."

"Why not?" Francis asked.

"Well, there's a lot here I don't approve of," Clayton said gravely. "Things like the club dances. Last Saturday night, I looked in toward the end and saw Mr. Granner trying to put Mrs. Minot into the trophy case. They were both drunk. I disapprove of so much drinking."

"It was Saturday night," Francis said.

"And all the dovecotes are phony," Clayton said. "And the way people clutter up their lives. I've thought about it a lot, and what seems to me to be really wrong with Shady Hill is that it doesn't have any future. So much energy is spent in perpetuating the place—in keeping out undesirables, and so forth—that the only idea of the future anyone has is just more and more commuting trains and more parties. I don't think that's healthy. I think people ought to be able to dream big dreams about the future. I think people ought to be able to dream great dreams."

"It's too bad you couldn't continue with college," Julia said.

"I want to go to divinity school," Clayton said.

"What's your church?" Francis asked.

"Unitarian, Theosophist, Transcendentalist, Humanist,"[7] Clayton said.

"Wasn't Emerson a transcendentalist?" Julia asked.

"I mean the English transcendentalists," Clayton said. "All the American transcendentalists were goops."

"What kind of job do you expect to get?" Francis asked.

"Well, I'd like to work for a publisher," Clayton said, "but everyone tells me there's nothing doing. But it's the kind of thing I'm interested in. I'm writing a long verse play about good and evil. Uncle Charlie might get me into a bank, and that would be good for me. I need the discipline. I have a long way to go in forming my character. I have some terrible habits. I talk too much. I think I ought to take vows of silence. I ought to try not to speak for a week, and discipline myself. I've thought of making a retreat at one of the Episcopalian monasteries, but I don't like Trinitarianism."

"Do you have any girl friends?" Francis asked.

"I'm engaged to be married," Clayton said. "Of course, I'm not old enough or rich enough to have my engagement observed or respected or anything, but I bought a simulated emerald for Anne Murchison with the money I made cutting lawns this summer. We're going to be married as soon as she finishes school."

---

7. All are deviations from orthodox Christianity and tend to be more human- than God-oriented; the American transcendentalists (see below) tended to change the emphasis from the study of thought to belief in "intuition."

Francis recoiled at the mention of the girl's name. Then a dingy light seemed to emanate from his spirit, showing everything—Julia, the boy, the chairs—in their true colorlessness. It was like a bitter turn of the weather.

"We're going to have a large family," Clayton said. "Her father's a terrible rummy, and I've had my hard times, and we want to have lots of children. Oh, she's wonderful, Mr. and Mrs. Weed, and we have so much in common. We like all the same things. We sent out the same Christmas card last year without planning it, and we both have an allergy to tomatoes, and our eyebrows grow together in the middle. Well, goodnight."

Julia went to the door with him. When she returned, Francis said that Clayton was lazy, irresponsible, affected, and smelly. Julia said that Francis seemed to be getting intolerant; the Thomas boy was young and should be given a chance. Julia had noticed other cases where Francis had been short-tempered. "Mrs. Wrightson has asked everyone in Shady Hill to her anniversary party but us," she said.

"I'm sorry, Julia."

"Do you know why they didn't ask us?"

"Why?"

"Because you insulted Mrs. Wrightson."

"Then you know about it?"

"June Masterson told me. She was standing behind you."

Julia walked in front of the sofa with a small step that expressed, Francis knew, a feeling of anger.

"I did insult Mrs. Wrightson, Julia, and I meant to. I've never liked her parties, and I'm glad she's dropped us."

"What about Helen?"

"How does Helen come into this?"

"Mrs. Wrightson's the one who decides who goes to the assemblies."

"You mean she can keep Helen from going to the dances?"

"Yes."

"I hadn't thought of that."

"Oh. I knew you hadn't thought of it," Julia cried, thrusting hiltdeep into this chink of his armor. "And it makes me furious to see this kind of stupid thoughtlessness wreck everyone's happiness."

"I don't think I've wrecked anyone's happiness."

"Mrs. Wrightson runs Shady Hill and has run it for the last forty years. I don't know what makes you think that in a community like this you can indulge every impulse you have to be insulting, vulgar, and offensive."

"I have very good manners," Francis said, trying to give the evening a turn toward the light.

"Damn you, Francis Weed!" Julia cried, and the spit of her words struck him in the face. "I've worked hard for the social position we enjoy in this place, and I won't stand by and see you wreck it. You must have understood when you settled here that you couldn't expect to live like a bear in a cave."

"I've got to express my likes and dislikes."

"You can conceal your dislikes. You don't have to meet everything head on, like a child. Unless you're anxious to be a social leper. It's no accident that we get asked out a great deal! It's no accident that Helen has so many friends. How would you like to spend your Saturday nights at the movies? How would you like to spend your Sunday raking up dead leaves? How would you like it if your daughter spent the assembly nights sitting at her window, listening to the music from the club? How would you like it—" He did something then that was, after all, not so unaccountable, since her words seemed to raise up between them a wall so deadening that he gagged. He struck her full in the face. She staggered and then, a moment later, seemed composed. She went up the stairs to their room. She didn't slam the door. When Francis followed, a few minutes later, he found her packing a suitcase.

"Julia, I'm very sorry."

"It doesn't matter," she said. She was crying.

"Where do you think you're going?"

"I don't know. I just looked at a timetable. There's an eleven-sixteen into New York. I'll take that."

"You can't go, Julia."

"I can't stay. I know that."

"I'm sorry about Mrs. Wrightson, Julia, and I'm—"

"It doesn't matter about Mrs. Wrightson. That isn't the trouble."

"What is the trouble?"

"You don't love me."

"I do love you, Julia."

"No, you don't."

"Julia, I do love you, and I would like to be as we were—sweet and bawdy and dark—but now there are so many people."

"You hate me."

"I don't hate you, Julia."

"You have no idea of how much you hate me. I think it's subconscious. You don't realize the cruel things you've done."

"What cruel things, Julia?"

"The cruel acts your subconscious drives you to in order to express your hatred of me."

"What, Julia?"

"I've never complained."

"Tell me."

"You don't know what you're doing."

"Tell me."

"Your clothes."

"What do you mean?"

"I mean the way you leave your dirty clothes around in order to express your subconscious hatred of me."

"I don't understand."

"I mean your dirty socks and your dirty pajamas and your dirty underwear and your dirty shirts!" She rose from kneeling by the suitcase and faced him, her eyes blazing and her voice ringing with emotion. "I'm talking about the fact that you've never learned to hang up anything. You just leave your clothes all over the floor where they drop, in order to humiliate me. You do it on purpose!" She fell on the bed, sobbing.

"Julia, darling!" he said, but when she felt his hand on her shoulder she got up.

"Leave me alone," she said. "I have to go." She brushed past him to the closet and came back with a dress. "I'm not taking any of the things you've given me," she said. "I'm leaving my pearls and the fur jacket."

"Oh, Julia!" Her figure, so helpless in its self-deceptions, bent over the suitcase made him nearly sick with pity. She did not understand how desolate her life would be without him. She didn't understand the hours that working women have to keep. She didn't understand that most of her friendships existed within the framework of their marriage, and that without this she would find herself alone. She didn't understand about travel, about hotels, about money. "Julia, I can't let you go! What you don't understand, Julia, is that you've come to be dependent on me."

She tossed her head back and covered her face with her hands. "Did you say that *I* was dependent on *you*?" she asked. "Is that what you said? And who is it that tells you what time to get up in the morning and when to go to bed at night? Who is it that prepares your meals and picks up your dirty clothes and invites your friends to dinner? If it weren't for me, your neckties would be greasy and your clothing would be full of moth holes. You were alone when I met you, Francis Weed, and you'll be alone when I leave. When Mother asked you for a list to send out invitations to our wedding, how many names did you have to give her? Fourteen!"

"Cleveland wasn't my home, Julia."

"And how many of your friends came to the church? Two!"

"Cleveland wasn't my home, Julia."

"Since I'm not taking the fur jacket," she said quietly, "you'd better put it back into storage. There's an insurance policy on the pearls that comes due in January. The name of the laundry and maid's telephone number—all those things are in my desk. I hope you won't drink too much, Francis. I hope that nothing bad will happen to you. If you do get into serious trouble, you can call me."

"Oh, my darling, I can't let you go!" Francis said. "I can't let you go, Julia!" He took her in his arms.

"I guess I'd better stay and take care of you for a little while longer," she said.

Riding to work in the morning, Francis saw the girl walk down the aisle of the coach. He was surprised; he hadn't realized that the school she went to was in the city, but she was carrying books, she seemed to be going to school. His surprise delayed his reaction, but then he got up clumsily and stepped into the aisle. Several people had come between them, but he could see her ahead of him, waiting for someone to open the car door, and then, as the train swerved, putting out her hand to support herself as she crossed the platform into the next car. He followed her through that car and halfway through another before calling her name—"Anne! Anne!"—but she didn't turn. He followed her into still another car, and she sat down in an aisle seat. Coming up to her, all his feelings warm and bent in her direction, he put his hand on the back of her seat—even this touch warmed him—and leaning down to speak to her, he saw that it was not Anne. It was an older woman wearing glasses. He went on deliberately into another car, his face red with embarrassment and the much deeper feeling of having his good sense challenged; for if he couldn't tell one person from another, what evidence was there that his life with Julia and the children had as much reality as his dreams of iniquity in Paris or the litter, the grass smell, and the cave-shaped trees in Lovers' Lane.

Late that afternoon, Julia called to remind Francis that they were going out for dinner. A few minutes later, Trace Bearden called. "Look, fellar," Trace said. "I'm calling for Mrs. Thomas. You know? Clayton, that boy of hers, doesn't seem able to get a job, and I wondered if you could help. If you'd call Charlie Bell—I know he's indebted to you—and say a good word for the kid, I think Charlie would—"

"Trace, I hate to say this," Francis said, "but I don't feel that I can do anything for that boy. The kid's worthless. I know it's a harsh thing to say, but it's a fact. Any kindness done for him would backfire in everybody's face. He's just a worthless kid, Trace, and there's nothing else to be done about it. Even if we got him a job, he wouldn't be able to keep it for a week. I know that to be a fact. It's an awful thing, Trace, and I know it is, but instead of recommending that kid, I'd feel obligated to warn people against him—people who knew his father and would naturally want to step in and do something. I'd feel obliged to warn them. He's a thief. . . ."

The moment this conversation was finished, Miss Rainey came in and stood by his desk. "I'm not going to be able to work for you any more, Mr. Weed," she said. "I can stay until the seventeenth if you need me, but I've been offered a whirlwind of a job, and I'd like to leave as soon as possible."

She went out, leaving him to face alone the wickedness of what he had done to the Thomas boy. His children in their photograph laughed and laughed, glazed with all the bright colors of summer, and he remembered that they had met a bagpiper on the beach that day and he had paid the piper a dollar to play them a battle song of the Black Watch.⁸ The girl would be at the house when he got home. He would spend another evening among his kind neighbors, picking and choosing dead-end streets, cart tracks, and the driveways of abandoned houses. There was nothing to mitigate his feeling—nothing that laughter or a game of softball with the children would change—and, thinking back over the plane crash, the Farquarsons' new maid, and Anne Murchison's difficulties with her drunken father, he wondered how he could have avoided arriving at just where he was. He was in trouble. He had been lost once in his life, coming back from a trout stream in the north woods, and he had now the same bleak realization that no amount of cheerfulness or hopefulness or valor or perseverance could help him find, in the gathering dark, the path that he'd lost. He smelled the forest. The feeling of bleakness was intolerable, and he saw clearly that he had reached the point where he would have to make a choice.

He could go to a psychiatrist, like Miss Rainey; he could go to church and confess his lusts; he could go to a Danish-massage parlor⁹ in the West Seventies that had been recommended by a salesman; he could rape the girl or trust that he would somehow be prevented from doing this; or he could get drunk. It was his life, his boat, and, like every other man, he was made to be the father of thousands, and what harm could there be in a tryst that would make them both feel more kindly toward the world? This was the wrong train of thought, and he came back to the first, the psychiatrist. He had the telephone number of Miss Rainey's doctor, and he called and asked for an immediate appointment. He was insistent with the doctor's secretary—it was his manner in business—and when she said that the doctor's schedule was full for the next few weeks, Francis

---

8. Originally a British Highland regiment that became a line regiment and distinguished itself in battle.
9. Sometimes fronts for houses of prostitution.

demanded an appointment that day and was told to come at five.

The psychiatrist's office was in a building that was used mostly by doctors and dentists, and the hallways were filled with the candy smell of mouthwash and memories of pain. Francis' character had been formed upon a series of private resolves—resolves about cleanliness, about going off the high diving board or repeating any other feat that challenged his courage, about punctuality, honesty, and virtue. To abdicate the perfect loneliness in which he had made his most vital decisions shattered his concept of character and left him now in a condition that felt like shock. He was stupefied. The scene for his *miserere mei Deus*[1] was, like the waiting room of so many doctor's offices, a crude token gesture toward the sweets of domestic bliss: a place arranged with antiques, coffee tables, potted plants, and etchings of snow-covered bridges and geese in flight, although there were no children, no marriage bed, no stove, even, in this travesty of a house, where no one had ever spent the night and where the curtained windows looked straight onto a dark air shaft. Francis gave his name and address to a secretary and then saw, at the side of the room, a policeman moving toward him. "Hold it, hold it," the policeman said. "Don't move. Keep your hands where they are."

"I think it's all right, Officer," the secretary began. "I think it will be—"

"Let's make sure," the policeman said, and he began to slap Francis' clothes, looking for what—pistols, knives, an icepick? Finding nothing, he went off and the secretary began a nervous apology: "When you called on the telephone, Mr. Weed, you seemed very excited, and one of the doctor's patients has been threatening his life, and we have to be careful. If you want to go in now?" Francis pushed open a door connected to an electrical chime, and in the doctor's lair sat down heavily, blew his nose into a handkerchief, searched in his pockets for cigarettes, for matches, for something, and said hoarsely, with tears in his eyes, "I'm in love, Dr. Herzog."

It is a week or ten days later in Shady Hill. The seven-fourteen has come and gone, and here and there dinner is finished and the dishes are in the dish-washing machine. The village hangs, morally and economically, from a thread; but it hangs by its thread in the evening light. Donald Goslin has begun to worry the "Moonlight Sonata" again. *Marcato ma sempre pianissimo!*[2] He seems to be wringing out a wet bath towel, but the housemaid does not heed him. She is writing a letter to Arthur Godfrey.[3] In the cellar of his house, Francis Weed is building a coffee table. Dr. Herzog recommends woodwork as a therapy, and Francis finds some true consolation in the simple arithmetic involved and in the holy smell of new wood. Francis is happy. Upstairs, little Toby is crying, because he is tired. He puts off his cowboy hat, gloves, and fringed jacket, unbuckles the belt studded with gold and rubies, the silver bullets and holsters, slips off his suspenders, his checked shirt, and Levi's, and sits on the edge of his bed to pull off his high boots. Leaving this equipment in a heap, he goes to the closet and takes his space suit off a nail. It is a struggle for him to get into the long tights, but he succeeds. He loops the magic cape over his shoulders and, climbing onto the footboard of his bed, he spreads his arms and flies the short distance to the floor, landing with a thump that is audible to everyone in the house but himself.

---

1. "Have mercy upon me, O God"; first words of Psalm 51.   2. Stressed but always very softly.
3. At the time of the story, host of a daytime radio program especially popular with housewives.

"Go home, Gertrude, go home," Mrs. Masterson says. "I told you to go home an hour ago, Gertrude. It's way past your suppertime, and your mother will be worried. Go home!" A door on the Babcocks' terrace flies open, and out comes Mrs. Babcock without any clothes on, pursued by a naked husband. (Their children are away at boarding school, and their terrace is screened by a hedge.) Over the terrace they go and in at the kitchen door, as passionate and handsome a nymph and satyr as you will find on any wall in Venice. Cutting the last of the roses in her garden, Julia hears old Mr. Nixon shouting at the squirrels in his bird-feeding station. "Rapscallions! Varmints! Avaunt and quit my sight!" A miserable cat wanders into the garden, sunk in spiritual and physical discomfort. Tied to its head is a small straw hat—a doll's hat—and it is securely buttoned into a doll's dress, from the skirts of which protrudes its long, hairy tail. As it walks, it shakes its feet, as if it had fallen into water.

"Here, pussy, pussy, pussy!" Julia calls.

"Here, pussy, here, poor pussy!" But the cat gives her a skeptical look and stumbles away in its skirts. The last to come is Jupiter. He prances through the tomato vines, holding in his generous mouth the remains of an evening slipper. Then it is dark; it is a night where kings in golden suits ride elephants over the mountains.[4]

1958

## QUESTIONS

1. Francis Weed commutes by train "five nights a week to his home in Shady Hill," but "The Country Husband" begins on the night his plane makes an emergency landing and he nearly doesn't make it home. How does this interruption of routine help to prepare for the rest of the story? Why is it significant that everyone else acts as if nothing unusual has happened?
2. Francis "had not developed his memory as a sentimental faculty." Why is memory important in this story? What kinds of memories do people try to ignore and what kinds of memories actually do surface in the story?
3. Consider the story's ending: has Francis's ordered life in Shady Hill been reestablished, or has there been a significant and lasting change in his life?

## JAMES BALDWIN

### Sonny's Blues

I read about it in the paper, in the subway, on my way to work. I read it, and I couldn't believe it, and I read it again. Then perhaps I just stared at it, at the newsprint spelling out his name, spelling out the story. I stared at it in the swinging lights of the subway car, and in the faces and bodies of the people, and in my own face, trapped in the darkness which roared outside.

---

4. Reference to Hannibal; see note 6, p. 83, above. Also, see Sinclair Lewis, *Main Street* (1920), in which the protagonist finds the small town of Gopher Prairie stifling and leaves with her son for Washington, D.C., where, she tells him, " 'We're going to find elephants with golden howdahs from which peep young maharanees with necklaces of rubies....' "

It was not to be believed and I kept telling myself that, as I walked from the subway station to the high school. And at the same time I couldn't doubt it. I was scared, scared for Sonny. He became real to me again. A great block of ice got settled in my belly and kept melting there slowly all day long, while I taught my classes algebra. It was a special kind of ice. It kept melting, sending trickles of ice water all up and down my veins, but it never got less. Sometimes it hardened and seemed to expand until I felt my guts were going to come spilling out or that I was going to choke or scream. This would always be at a moment when I was remembering some specific thing Sonny had once said or done.

When he was about as old as the boys in my classes his face had been bright and open, there was a lot of copper in it; and he'd had wonderfully direct brown eyes, and great gentleness and privacy. I wondered what he looked like now. He had been picked up, the evening before, in a raid on an apartment downtown, for peddling and using heroin.

I couldn't believe it: but what I mean by that is that I couldn't find any room for it anywhere inside me. I had kept it outside me for a long time. I hadn't wanted to know. I had had suspicions, but I didn't name them, I kept putting them away. I told myself that Sonny was wild, but he wasn't crazy. And he'd always been a good boy, he hadn't ever turned hard or evil or disrespectful, the way kids can, so quick, so quick, especially in Harlem. I didn't want to believe that I'd ever see my brother going down, coming to nothing, all that light in his face gone out, in the condition I'd already seen so many others. Yet it had happened and here I was, talking about algebra to a lot of boys who might, every one of them for all I knew, be popping off needles every time they went to the head.[1] Maybe it did more for them than algebra could.

5    I was sure that the first time Sonny had ever had horse,[2] he couldn't have been much older than these boys were now. These boys, now, were living as we'd been living then, they were growing up with a rush and their heads bumped abruptly against the low ceiling of their actual possibilities. They were filled with rage. All they really knew were two darknesses, the darkness of their lives, which was now closing in on them, and the darkness of the movies, which had blinded them to that other darkness, and in which they now, vindictively, dreamed, at once more together than they were at any other time, and more alone.

When the last bell rang, the last class ended, I let out my breath. It seemed I'd been holding it for all that time. My clothes were wet—I may have looked as though I'd been sitting in a steam bath, all dressed up, all afternoon. I sat alone in the classroom a long time. I listened to the boys outside, downstairs, shouting and cursing and laughing. Their laughter struck me for perhaps the first time. It was not the joyous laughter which—God knows why—one associates with children. It was mocking and insular, its intent was to denigrate. It was disenchanted, and in this, also, lay the authority of their curses. Perhaps I was listening to them because I was thinking about my brother and in them I heard my brother. And myself.

One boy was whistling a tune, at once very complicated and very simple, it seemed to be pouring out of him as though he were a bird, and it sounded very cool and moving through all that harsh, bright air, only just holding its own through all those other sounds.

---

1. Lavatory.  2. Heroin.

I stood up and walked over to the window and looked down into the courtyard. It was the beginning of the spring and the sap was rising in the boys. A teacher passed through them every now and again, quickly, as though he or she couldn't wait to get out of that courtyard, to get those boys out of their sight and off their minds. I started collecting my stuff. I thought I'd better get home and talk to Isabel.

The courtyard was almost deserted by the time I got downstairs. I saw this boy standing in the shadow of a doorway, looking just like Sonny. I almost called his name. Then I saw that it wasn't Sonny, but somebody we used to know, a boy from around our block. He'd been Sonny's friend. He'd never been mine, having been too young for me, and, anyway, I'd never liked him. And now, even though he was a grown-up man, he still hung around that block, still spent hours on the street corners, was always high and raggy. I used to run into him from time to time and he'd often work around to asking me for a quarter or fifty cents. He always had some real good excuse, too, and I always gave it to him. I don't know why.

But now, abruptly, I hated him. I couldn't stand the way he looked at me, partly like a dog, partly like a cunning child. I wanted to ask him what the hell he was doing in the school courtyard.

He sort of shuffled over to me, and he said, "I see you got the papers. So you already know about it."

"You mean about Sonny? Yes, I already know about it. How come they didn't get you?"

He grinned. It made him repulsive and it also brought to mind what he'd looked like as a kid. "I wasn't there. I stay away from them people."

"Good for you." I offered him a cigarette and I watched him through the smoke. "You come all the way down here just to tell me about Sonny?"

"That's right." He was sort of shaking his head and his eyes looked strange, as though they were about to cross. The bright sun deadened his damp dark brown skin and it made his eyes look yellow and showed up the dirt in his kinked hair. He smelled funky. I moved a little away from him and I said, "Well, thanks. But I already know about it and I got to get home."

"I'll walk you a little ways," he said. We started walking. There were a couple of kids still loitering in the courtyard and one of them said goodnight to me and looked strangely at the boy beside me.

"What're you going to do?" he asked me. "I mean, about Sonny?"

"Look. I haven't seen Sonny for over a year, I'm not sure I'm going to do anything. Anyway, what the hell *can* I do?"

"That's right," he said quickly, "ain't nothing you can do. Can't much help old Sonny no more, I guess."

It was what I was thinking and so it seemed to me he had no right to say it.

"I'm surprised at Sonny, though," he went on—he had a funny way of talking, he looked straight ahead as though he were talking to himself—"I thought Sonny was a smart boy, I thought he was too smart to get hung."

"I guess he thought so too," I said sharply, "and that's how he got hung. And how about you? You're pretty goddamn smart, I bet."

Then he looked directly at me, just for a minute. "I ain't smart," he said. "If I was smart, I'd have reached for a pistol a long time ago."

"Look. Don't tell *me* your sad story, if it was up to me, I'd give you one." Then

I felt guilty—guilty, probably, for never having supposed that the poor bastard *had* a story of his own, much less a sad one, and I asked, quickly, "What's going to happen to him now?"

He didn't answer this. He was off by himself some place.

"Funny thing," he said, and from his tone we might have been discussing the quickest way to get to Brooklyn, "when I saw the papers this morning, the first thing I asked myself was if I had anything to do with it. I felt sort of responsible."

I began to listen more carefully. The subway station was on the corner, just before us, and I stopped. He stopped, too. We were in front of a bar and he ducked slightly, peering in, but whoever he was looking for didn't seem to be there. The juke box was blasting away with something black and bouncy and I half watched the barmaid as she danced her way from the juke box to her place behind the bar. And I watched her face as she laughingly responded to something someone said to her, still keeping time to the music. When she smiled one saw the little girl, one sensed the doomed, still-struggling woman beneath the battered face of the semi-whore.

"I never *give* Sonny nothing," the boy said finally, "but a long time ago I come to school high and Sonny asked me how it felt." He paused, I couldn't bear to watch him, I watched the barmaid, and I listened to the music which seemed to be causing the pavement to shake. "I told him it felt great." The music stopped, the barmaid paused and watched the juke box until the music began again. "It did."

All this was carrying me some place I didn't want to go. I certainly didn't want to know how it felt. It filled everything, the people, the houses, the music, the dark, quicksilver barmaid, with menace; and this menace was their reality.

"What's going to happen to him now?" I asked again.

"They'll send him away some place and they'll try to cure him." He shook his head. "Maybe he'll even think he's kicked the habit. Then they'll let him loose"—he gestured, throwing his cigarette into the gutter. "That's all."

"What do you mean, that's *all*?"

But I knew what he meant.

"I *mean*, that's *all*." He turned his head and looked at me, pulling down the corners of his mouth. "Don't you know what I mean?" he asked, softly.

"How the hell *would* I know what you mean?" I almost whispered it, I don't know why.

"That's right," he said to the air, "how would *he* know what I mean?" He turned toward me again, patient and calm, and yet I somehow felt him shaking, shaking as though he were going to fall apart. I felt that ice in my guts again, the dread I'd felt all afternoon; and again I watched the barmaid, moving about the bar, washing glasses, and singing. "Listen. They'll let him out and then it'll just start all over again. That's what I mean."

"You mean—they'll let him out. And then he'll just start working his way back in again. You mean he'll never kick the habit. Is that what you mean?"

"That's right," he said, cheerfully. "*You* see what I mean."

"Tell me," I said at last, "why does he want to die? He must want to die, he's killing himself, why does he want to die?"

He looked at me in surprise. He licked his lips. "He don't want to die. He wants to live. Don't nobody want to die, ever."

Then I wanted to ask him—too many things. He could not have answered, or if he had, I could not have borne the answers. I started walking. "Well, I guess it's none of my business."

"It's going to be rough on old Sonny," he said. We reached the subway station. "This is your station?" he asked. I nodded. I took one step down. "Damn!" he said, suddenly. I looked up at him. He grinned again. "Damn it if I didn't leave all my money home. You ain't got a dollar on you, have you? Just for a couple of days, is all."

All at once something inside gave and threatened to come pouring out of me. I didn't hate him any more. I felt that in another moment I'd start crying like a child.

"Sure," I said. "Don't sweat." I looked in my wallet and didn't have a dollar, I only had a five. "Here," I said. "That hold you?"

He didn't look at it—he didn't want to look at it. A terrible, closed look came over his face, as though he were keeping the number on the bill a secret from him and me. "Thanks," he said, and now he was dying to see me go. "Don't worry about Sonny. Maybe I'll write him or something."

"Sure," I said. "You do that. So long."

"Be seeing you," he said. I went on down the steps.

And I didn't write Sonny or send him anything for a long time. When I finally did, it was just after my little girl died, and he wrote me back a letter which made me feel like a bastard.

Here's what he said:

Dear brother,

You don't know how much I needed to hear from you. I wanted to write you many a time but I dug how much I must have hurt you and so I didn't write. But now I feel like a man who's been trying to climb up out of some deep, real deep and funky hole and just saw the sun up there, outside. I got to get outside.

I can't tell you much about how I got here. I mean I don't know how to tell you. I guess I was afraid of something or I was trying to escape from something and you know I have never been very strong in the head (smile). I'm glad Mama and Daddy are dead and can't see what's happened to their son and I swear if I'd known what I was doing I would never have hurt you so, you and a lot of other fine people who were nice to me and who believed in me.

I don't want you to think it had anything to do with me being a musician. It's more than that. Or maybe less than that. I can't get anything straight in my head down here and I try not to think about what's going to happen to me when I get outside again. Sometime I think I'm going to flip and *never* get outside and sometime I think I'll come straight back. I tell you one thing, though, I'd rather blow my brains out than go through this again. But that's what they all say, so they tell me. If I tell you when I'm coming to New York and if you could meet me, I sure would appreciate it. Give my love to Isabel and the kids and I was sure sorry to hear about little Gracie. I wish I could be like Mama and say the Lord's will be done, but I don't know it seems to me that trouble is the one thing that never does get stopped and I don't know what good it does to blame it on the Lord. But maybe it does some good if you believe it.

Your brother,
Sonny

Then I kept in constant touch with him and I sent him whatever I could and I went to meet him when he came back to New York. When I saw him many things I thought I had forgotten came flooding back to me. This was because I had begun, finally, to wonder about Sonny, about the life that Sonny lived inside. This life, whatever it was, had made him older and thinner and it had deepened the distant stillness in which he had always moved. He looked very unlike my baby brother. Yet, when he smiled, when we shook hands, the baby brother I'd never known looked out from the depths of his private life, like an animal waiting to be coaxed into the light.

"How you been keeping?" he asked me.

"All right. And you?"

"Just fine." He was smiling all over his face. "It's good to see you again."

"It's good to see you."

The seven years' difference in our ages lay between us like a chasm: I wondered if these years would ever operate between us as a bridge. I was remembering, and it made it hard to catch my breath, that I had been there when he was born; and I had heard the first words he had ever spoken. When he started to walk, he walked from our mother straight to me. I caught him just before he fell when he took the first steps he ever took in this world.

"How's Isabel?"

"Just fine. She's dying to see you."

"And the boys?"

"They're fine, too. They're anxious to see their uncle."

"Oh, come on. You know they don't remember me."

"Are you kidding? Of course they remember you."

He grinned again. We got into a taxi. We had a lot to say to each other, far too much to know how to begin.

As the taxi began to move, I asked, "You still want to go to India?"

He laughed. "You still remember that. Hell, no. This place is Indian enough for me."

"It used to belong to them," I said.

And he laughed again. "They damn sure knew what they were doing when they got rid of it."

Years ago, when he was around fourteen, he'd been all hipped on the idea of going to India. He read books about people sitting on rocks, naked, in all kinds of weather, but mostly bad, naturally, and walking barefoot through hot coals and arriving at wisdom. I used to say that it sounded to me as though they were getting away from wisdom as fast as they could. I think he sort of looked down on me for that.

"Do you mind," he asked, "if we have the driver drive alongside the park? On the west side—I haven't seen the city in so long."

"Of course not," I said. I was afraid that I might sound as though I were humoring him, but I hoped he wouldn't take it that way.

So we drove along, between the green of the park and the stony, lifeless elegance of hotels and apartment buildings, toward the vivid, killing streets of our childhood. These streets hadn't changed, though housing projects jutted up out of them now like rocks in the middle of a boiling sea. Most of the houses in which we had grown up had vanished, as had the stores from which we had stolen, the basements in which we had first tried sex, the rooftops from which we had hurled tin cans and bricks. But houses exactly like the houses of our past yet dominated the landscape, boys exactly like the boys we once had been found themselves smothering in these houses, came down into the streets for light and air and found themselves encircled by disaster. Some escaped the trap, most didn't. Those who got out always left something of themselves behind, as some animals amputate a leg and leave it in the trap. It might be said, perhaps, that I had escaped, after all, I was a school teacher; or that Sonny had, he hadn't lived in Harlem for years. Yet, as the cab moved uptown through streets which seemed, with a rush, to darken with dark people, and as I covertly studied Sonny's face, it came to me that what we both were seeking through our separate cab windows was that part of ourselves which had been left behind. It's always at the hour of trouble and confrontation that the missing member aches.

We hit 110th Street and started rolling up Lenox Avenue. And I'd known this avenue all my life, but it seemed to me again, as it had seemed on the day I'd first heard about Sonny's trouble, filled with a hidden menace which was its very breath of life.

"We almost there," said Sonny.

"Almost." We were both too nervous to say anything more.

We live in a housing project. It hasn't been up long. A few days after it was up it seemed uninhabitably new, now, of course, it's already rundown. It looks like a parody of the good, clean, faceless life—God knows the people who live in it do their best to make it a parody. The beat-looking grass lying around isn't enough to make their lives green, the hedges will never hold out the streets, and they know it. The big windows fool no one, they aren't big enough to make space out of no space. They don't bother with the windows, they watch the TV screen instead. The playground is most popular with the children who don't play at jacks, or skip rope, or roller skate, or swing, and they can be found in it after dark. We moved in partly because it's not too far from where I teach, and partly for the kids; but it's really just like the houses in which Sonny and I grew up. The same things happen, they'll have the same things to remember. The moment Sonny and I started into the house I had the feeling that I was simply bringing him back into the danger he had almost died trying to escape.

Sonny has never been talkative. So I don't know why I was sure he'd be dying to talk to me when supper was over the first night. Everything went fine, the oldest boy remembered him, and the youngest boy liked him, and Sonny had remembered to bring something for each of them; and Isabel, who is really much nicer than I am, more open and giving, had gone to a lot of trouble about dinner and was genuinely glad to see him. And she's always been able to tease Sonny in a way that I haven't. It was nice to see her face so vivid again and to hear her laugh and watch her make Sonny laugh. She wasn't, or, anyway, she didn't seem to be, at all uneasy or embarrassed. She chatted as though there were no subject which had to be avoided and she got Sonny past his first, faint stiffness. And thank God she was there, for I was filled with that icy dread again. Everything I did seemed awkward to me, and everything I said sounded freighted with hidden meaning. I was trying to remember everything I'd heard about dope addiction and I couldn't help watching Sonny for signs. I wasn't doing it out of malice. I was trying to find out something about my brother. I was dying to hear him tell me he was safe.

"Safe!" my father grunted, whenever Mama suggested trying to move to a neighborhood which might be safer for children. "Safe, hell! Ain't no place safe for kids, nor nobody."

He always went on like this, but he wasn't, ever, really as bad as he sounded, not even on weekends, when he got drunk. As a matter of fact, he was always on the lookout for "something a little better," but he died before he found it. He died suddenly, during a drunken weekend in the middle of the war, when Sonny was fifteen. He and Sonny hadn't ever got on too well. And this was partly because Sonny was the apple of his father's eye. It was because he loved Sonny so much and was frightened for him, that he was always fighting with him. It doesn't do any good to fight with Sonny. Sonny just moves back, inside himself, where he can't be reached. But the principal reason that they never hit it off is that they were so much alike. Daddy was big and rough and loud-talking, just the opposite of Sonny, but they both had—that same privacy.

Mama tried to tell me something about this, just after Daddy died. I was home on leave from the army.

This was the last time I ever saw my mother alive. Just the same, this picture gets all mixed up in my mind with pictures I had of her when she was younger. The way I always see her is the way she used to be on a Sunday afternoon, say, when the old folks were talking after the big Sunday dinner. I always see her wearing pale blue. She'd be sitting on the sofa. And my father would be sitting in the easy chair, not far from her. And the living room would be full of church folks and relatives. There they sit, in chairs all around the living room, and the night is creeping up outside, but nobody knows it yet. You can see the darkness growing against the windowpanes and you hear the street noises every now and again, or maybe the jangling beat of a tambourine from one of the churches close by, but it's real quiet in the room. For a moment nobody's talking, but every face looks darkening, like the sky outside. And my mother rocks a little from the waist, and my father's eyes are closed. Everyone is looking at something a child can't see. For a minute they've forgotten the children. Maybe a kid is lying on the rug, half asleep. Maybe somebody's got a kid in his lap and is absentmindedly stroking the kid's head. Maybe there's a kid, quiet and big-eyed, curled up in a big chair in the corner. The silence, the darkness coming, and the darkness in the faces frighten the child obscurely. He hopes that the hand which strokes his forehead will never stop—will never die. He hopes that there will never come a time when the old folks won't be sitting around the living room, talking about where they've come from, and what they've seen, and what's happened to them and their kinfolk.

But something deep and watchful in the child knows that this is bound to end, is already ending. In a moment someone will get up and turn on the light. Then the old folks will remember the children and they won't talk any more that day. And when light fills the room, the child is filled with darkness. He knows that every time this happens he's moved just a little closer to that darkness outside. The darkness outside is what the old folks have been talking about. It's what they've come from. It's what they endure. The child knows that they won't talk any more because if he knows too much about what's happened to *them*, he'll know too much too soon, about what's going to happen to *him*.

The last time I talked to my mother, I remember I was restless. I wanted to get out and see Isabel. We weren't married then and we had a lot to straighten out between us.

There Mama sat, in black, by the window. She was humming an old church song, *Lord, you brought me from a long ways off.* Sonny was out somewhere. Mama kept watching the streets.

"I don't know," she said, "if I'll ever see you again, after you go off from here. But I hope you'll remember the things I tried to teach you."

"Don't talk like that," I said, and smiled. "You'll be here a long time yet."

She smiled, too, but she said nothing. She was quiet for a long time. And I said, "Mama, don't you worry about nothing. I'll be writing all the time, and you be getting the checks...."

"I want to talk to you about your brother," she said, suddenly. "If anything happens to me he ain't going to have nobody to look out for him."

"Mama," I said, "ain't nothing going to happen to you *or* Sonny. Sonny's all right. He's a good boy and he's got good sense."

"It ain't a question of his being a good boy," Mama said, "nor of his having good sense. It ain't only the bad ones, nor yet the dumb ones that gets sucked under." She stopped, looking at me. "Your Daddy once had a brother," she said, and she smiled in a way that made me feel she was in pain. "You didn't never know that, did you?"

"No," I said, "I never knew that," and I watched her face.

"Oh, yes," she said, "your Daddy had a brother." She looked out of the window again. "I know you never saw your Daddy cry. But *I* did—many a time, through all these years."

I asked her, "What happened to his brother? How come nobody's ever talked about him?"

This was the first time I ever saw my mother look old.

"His brother got killed," she said, "when he was just a little younger than you are now. I knew him. He was a fine boy. He was maybe a little full of the devil, but he didn't mean nobody no harm."

Then she stopped and the room was silent, exactly as it had sometimes been on those Sunday afternoons. Mama kept looking out into the streets.

"He used to have a job in the mill," she said, "and, like all young folks, he just liked to perform on Saturday nights. Saturday nights, him and your father would drift around to different places, go to dances and things like that, or just sit around with people they knew, and your father's brother would sing, he had a fine voice, and play along with himself on his guitar. Well, this particular Saturday night, him and your father was coming home from some place, and they were both a little drunk and there was a moon that night, it was bright like day. Your father's brother was feeling kind of good, and he was whistling to himself, and he had his guitar slung over his shoulder. They was coming down a hill and beneath them was a road that turned off from the highway. Well, your father's brother, being always kind of frisky, decided to run down this hill, and he did, with that guitar banging and clanging behind him, and he ran across the road, and he was making water behind a tree. And your father was sort of amused at him and he was still coming down the hill, kind of slow. Then he heard a car motor and that same minute his brother stepped from behind the tree, into the road, in the moonlight. And he started to cross the road. And your father started to run down the hill, he says he don't know why. This car was full of white men. They was all drunk, and when they seen your father's brother they let out a great whoop and holler and they aimed the car straight at him. They was having fun, they just wanted to scare him, the way they do sometimes, you know. But they was drunk. And I guess the boy, being drunk, too, and scared, kind of lost his head. By the time he jumped it was too late. Your father says he heard his brother scream when the car rolled over him, and he heard the wood of that guitar when it give, and he heard them strings go flying, and he heard them white men shouting, and the car kept on a-going and it ain't stopped till this day. And, time your father got down the hill, his brother weren't nothing but blood and pulp."

Tears were gleaming on my mother's face. There wasn't anything I could say.

"He never mentioned it," she said, "because I never let him mention it before you children. Your Daddy was like a crazy man that night and for many a night thereafter. He says he never in his life seen anything as dark as that road after the lights of that car had gone away. Weren't nothing, weren't nobody on that road, just your Daddy and his brother and that busted guitar. Oh, yes. Your Daddy never did really get right again. Till the day he died he weren't sure but that every white man he saw was the man that killed his brother."

She stopped and took out her handkerchief and dried her eyes and looked at me.

"I ain't telling you all this," she said, "to make you scared or bitter or to make you hate nobody. I'm telling you this because you got a brother. And the world ain't changed."

I guess I didn't want to believe this. I guess she saw this in my face. She turned away from me, toward the window again, searching those streets.

"But I praise my Redeemer," she said at last, "that He called your Daddy home before me. I ain't saying it to throw no flowers at myself, but, I declare, it keeps me from feeling too cast down to know I helped your father get safely through this world. Your father always acted like he was the roughest, strongest man on earth. And everybody took him to be like that. But if he hadn't had me there— to see his tears!"

She was crying again. Still, I couldn't move. I said, "Lord, Lord, Mama, I didn't know it was like that."

"Oh, honey," she said, "there's a lot that you don't know. But you are going to find out." She stood up from the window and came over to me. "You got to hold on to your brother," she said, "and don't let him fall, no matter what it looks like is happening to him and no matter how evil you gets with him. You going to be evil with him many a time. But don't you forget what I told you, you hear?"

"I won't forget," I said. "Don't you worry, I won't forget. I won't let nothing happen to Sonny."

My mother smiled as though she was amused at something she saw in my face. Then, "You may not be able to stop nothing from happening. But you got to let him know you's *there*."

Two days later I was married, and then I was gone. And I had a lot of things on my mind and I pretty well forgot my promise to Mama until I got shipped home on a special furlough for her funeral.

And, after the funeral, with just Sonny and me alone in the empty kitchen, I tried to find out something about him.

"What do you want to do?" I asked him.

"I'm going to be a musician," he said.

For he had graduated, in the time I had been away, from dancing to the juke box to finding out who was playing what, and what they were doing with it, and he had bought himself a set of drums.

"You mean, you want to be a drummer?" I somehow had the feeling that being a drummer might be all right for other people but not for my brother Sonny.

"I don't think," he said, looking at me very gravely, "that I'll ever be a good drummer. But I think I can play a piano."

I frowned. I'd never played the role of the oldest brother quite so seriously before, had scarcely ever, in fact, *asked* Sonny a damn thing. I sensed myself in the presence of something I didn't really know how to handle, didn't understand. So I made my frown a little deeper as I asked: "What kind of musician do you want to be?"

He grinned. "How many kinds do you think there are?"

"Be *serious*," I said.

He laughed, throwing his head back, and then looked at me. "I *am* serious."

"Well, then, for Christ's sake, stop kidding around and answer a serious question. I mean, do you want to be a concert pianist, you want to play classical music and all that, or—or what?" Long before I finished he was laughing again. "For Christ's *sake*, Sonny!"

He sobered, but with difficulty. "I'm sorry. But you sound so—*scared!*" and he was off again.

"Well, you may think it's funny now, baby, but it's not going to be so funny when you have to make your living at it, let me tell you *that*." I was furious because I knew he was laughing at me and I didn't know why.

"No," he said, very sober now, and afraid, perhaps, that he'd hurt me, "I don't want to be a classical pianist. That isn't what interests me. I mean"—he paused, looking hard at me, as though his eyes would help me to understand, and then gestured helplessly, as though perhaps his hand would help—"I mean, I'll have a lot of studying to do, and I'll have to study *everything*, but, I mean, I want to play *with*—jazz musicians." He stopped. "I want to play jazz," he said.

Well, the word had never before sounded as heavy, as real, as it sounded that afternoon in Sonny's mouth. I just looked at him and I was probably frowning a real frown by this time. I simply couldn't see why on earth he'd want to spend his time hanging around nightclubs, clowning around on bandstands, while people pushed each other around a dance floor. It seemed—beneath him, somehow. I had never thought about it before, had never been forced to, but I suppose I had always put jazz musicians in a class with what Daddy called "good-time people."

"Are you *serious?*"

"Hell, *yes*, I'm serious."

He looked more helpless than ever, and annoyed, and deeply hurt.

I suggested, helpfully: "You mean—like Louis Armstrong?"

His face closed as though I'd struck him. "No. I'm not talking about none of that old-time, down home crap."

"Well, look, Sonny, I'm sorry, don't get mad. I just don't altogether get it, that's all. Name somebody—you know, a jazz musician you admire."

"Bird."

"Who?"

"Bird! Charlie Parker!³ Don't they teach you nothing in the goddamn army?"

I lit a cigarette. I was surprised and then a little amused to discover that I was trembling. "I've been out of touch," I said. "You'll have to be patient with me. Now. Who's this Parker character?"

"He's just one of the greatest jazz musicians alive," said Sonny, sullenly, his hands in his pockets, his back to me. "Maybe *the* greatest," he added, bitterly, "that's probably why *you* never heard of him."

"All right," I said, "I'm ignorant. I'm sorry. I'll go out and buy all the cat's records right away, all right?"

"It don't," said Sonny, with dignity, "make any difference to me. I don't care what you listen to. Don't do me no favors."

I was beginning to realize that I'd never seen him so upset before. With another part of my mind I was thinking that this would probably turn out to be one of those things kids go through and that I shouldn't make it seem important by pushing it too hard. Still, I didn't think it would do any harm to ask: "Doesn't all this take a lot of time? Can you make a living at it?"

He turned back to me and half leaned, half sat, on the kitchen table. "Everything takes time," he said, "and—well, yes, sure, I can make a living at it. But what I don't seem to be able to make you understand is that it's the only thing I want to do."

"Well, Sonny," I said gently, "you know people can't always do exactly what they *want* to do—"

"*No*, I don't know that," said Sonny, surprising me. "I think people *ought* to do what they want to do, what else are they alive for?"

"You getting to be a big boy," I said desperately, "it's time you started thinking about your future."

"I'm thinking about my future," said Sonny, grimly. "I think about it all the time."

I gave up. I decided, if he didn't change his mind, that we could always talk about it later. "In the meantime," I said, "you got to finish school." We had already decided that he'd have to move in with Isabel and her folks. I knew this wasn't the ideal arrangement because Isabel's folks are inclined to be dicty⁴ and they hadn't especially wanted Isabel to marry me. But I didn't know what else to do. "And we have to get you fixed up at Isabel's."

There was a long silence. He moved from the kitchen table to the window. "That's a terrible idea. You know it yourself."

"Do you have a *better* idea?"

He just walked up and down the kitchen for a minute. He was as tall as I was. He had started to shave. I suddenly had the feeling that I didn't know him at all.

He stopped at the kitchen table and picked up my cigarettes. Looking at me with a kind of mocking, amused defiance, he put one between his lips. "You mind?"

"You smoking already?"

He lit the cigarette and nodded, watching me through the smoke. "I just wanted to see if I'd have the courage to smoke in front of you." He grinned and

---

3. Charlie ("Bird") Parker (1920–1955), brilliant saxophonist and jazz innovator; working in New York in the mid-1940s, he developed, with Dizzy Gillespie and others, the style of jazz called "bebop." He was a narcotics addict.    4. Snobbish, bossy.

blew a great cloud of smoke to the ceiling. "It was easy." He looked at my face. "Come on, now. I bet you was smoking at my age, tell the truth."

I didn't say anything but the truth was on my face, and he laughed. But now there was something very strained in his laugh. "Sure. And I bet that ain't all you was doing."

He was frightening me a little. "Cut the crap," I said. "We already decided that you was going to go and live at Isabel's. Now what's got into you all of a sudden?"

"*You* decided it," he pointed out. "*I* didn't decide nothing." He stopped in front of me, leaning against the stove, arms loosely folded. "Look, brother. I don't want to stay in Harlem no more, I really don't." He was very earnest. He looked at me, then over toward the kitchen window. There was something in his eyes I'd never seen before, some thoughtfulness, some worry all his own. He rubbed the muscle of one arm. "It's time I was getting out of here."

"Where do you want to *go*, Sonny?"

"I want to join the army. Or the navy, I don't care. If I say I'm old enough, they'll believe me."

Then I got mad. It was because I was so scared. "You must be crazy. You goddamn fool, what the hell do you want to go and join the *army* for?"

"I just told you. To get out of Harlem."

"Sonny, you haven't even finished *school*. And if you really want to be a musician, how do you expect to study if you're in the *army?*"

He looked at me, trapped, and in anguish. "There's ways. I might be able to work out some kind of deal. Anyway, I'll have the G.I. Bill when I come out."

"*If* you come out." We stared at each other. "Sonny, please. Be reasonable. I know the setup is far from perfect. But we got to do the best we can."

"I ain't learning nothing in school," he said. "Even when I go." He turned away from me and opened the window and threw his cigarette out into the narrow alley. I watched his back. "At least, I ain't learning nothing you'd want me to learn." He slammed the window so hard I thought the glass would fly out, and turned back to me. "And I'm sick of the stink of these garbage cans!"

"Sonny," I said, "I know how you feel. But if you don't finish school now, you're going to be sorry later that you didn't." I grabbed him by the shoulders. "And you only got another year. It ain't so bad. And I'll come back and I swear I'll help you do *whatever* you want to do. Just try to put up with it till I come back. Will you please do that? For me?"

He didn't answer and he wouldn't look at me.

"Sonny. You hear me?"

He pulled away. "I hear you. But you never hear anything *I* say."

I didn't know what to say to that. He looked out of the window and then back at me. "OK," he said, and sighed. "I'll try."

Then I said, trying to cheer him up a little, "They got a piano at Isabel's. You can practice on it."

And as a matter of fact, it did cheer him up for a minute. "That's right," he said to himself. "I forgot that." His face relaxed a little. But the worry, the thoughtfulness, played on it still, the way shadows play on a face which is staring into the fire.

But I thought I'd never hear the end of that piano. At first, Isabel would write me, saying how nice it was that Sonny was so serious about his music and how, as soon as he came in from school, or wherever he had been when he was supposed to be at school, he went straight to that piano and stayed there until suppertime. And, after supper, he went back to that piano and stayed there until everybody went to bed. He was at the piano all day Saturday and all day Sunday. Then he bought a record player and started playing records. He'd play one record over and over again, all day long sometimes, and he'd improvise along with it on the piano. Or he'd play one section of the record, one chord, one change, one progression, then he'd do it on the piano. Then back to the record. Then back to the piano.

Well, I really don't know how they stood it. Isabel finally confessed that it wasn't like living with a person at all, it was like living with sound. And the sound didn't make any sense to her, didn't make any sense to any of them—naturally. They began, in a way, to be afflicted by this presence that was living in their home. It was as though Sonny were some sort of god, or monster. He moved in an atmosphere which wasn't like theirs at all. They fed him and he ate, he washed himself, he walked in and out of their door; he certainly wasn't nasty or unpleasant or rude, Sonny isn't any of those things; but it was as though he were all wrapped up in some cloud, some fire, some vision all his own; and there wasn't any way to reach him.

At the same time, he wasn't really a man yet, he was still a child, and they had to watch out for him in all kinds of ways. They certainly couldn't throw him out. Neither did they dare to make a great scene about that piano because even they dimly sensed, as I sensed, from so many thousands of miles away, that Sonny was at that piano playing for his life.

But he hadn't been going to school. One day a letter came from the school board and Isabel's mother got it—there had, apparently, been other letters but Sonny had torn them up. This day, when Sonny came in, Isabel's mother showed him the letter and asked where he'd been spending his time. And she finally got it out of him that he'd been down in Greenwich Village, with musicians and other characters, in a white girl's apartment. And this scared her and she started to scream at him and what came up, once she began—though she denies it to this day—was what sacrifices they were making to give Sonny a decent home and how little he appreciated it.

Sonny didn't play the piano that day. By evening, Isabel's mother had calmed down but then there was the old man to deal with, and Isabel herself. Isabel says she did her best to be calm but she broke down and started crying. She says she just watched Sonny's face. She could tell, by watching him, what was happening with him. And what was happening was that they penetrated his cloud, they had reached him. Even if their fingers had been a thousand times more gentle than human fingers ever are, he could hardly help feeling that they had stripped him naked and were spitting on that nakedness. For he also had to see that his presence, that music, which was life or death to him, had been torture for them and that they had endured it, not at all for his sake, but only for mine. And Sonny couldn't take that. He can take it a little better today than he could then but he's still not very good at it and, frankly, I don't know anybody who is.

The silence of the next few days must have been louder than the sound of all the music ever played since time began. One morning, before she went to work, Isabel was in his room for something and she suddenly realized that all of his records were gone. And she knew for certain that he was gone. And he was. He went as far as the navy would carry him. He finally sent me a postcard from some place in Greece and that was the first I knew that Sonny was still alive. I didn't see him any more until we were both back in New York and the war had long been over.

He was a man by then, of course, but I wasn't willing to see it. He came by the house from time to time, but we fought almost every time we met. I didn't like the way he carried himself, loose and dreamlike all the time, and I didn't like his friends, and his music seemed to be merely an excuse for the life he led. It sounded just that weird and disordered.

Then we had a fight, a pretty awful fight, and I didn't see him for months. By and by I looked him up, where he was living, in a furnished room in the Village, and I tried to make it up. But there were lots of other people in the room and Sonny just lay on his bed, and he wouldn't come downstairs with me, and he treated these other people as though they were his family and I weren't. So I got mad and then he got mad, and then I told him that he might just as well be dead as live the way he was living. Then he stood up and he told me not to worry about him any more in life, that he *was* dead as far as I was concerned. Then he pushed me to the door and the other people looked on as though nothing were happening, and he slammed the door behind me. I stood in the hallway, staring at the door. I heard somebody laugh in the room and then the tears came to my eyes. I started down the steps, whistling to keep from crying, I kept whistling to myself, *You going to need me, baby, one of these cold, rainy days.*

I read about Sonny's trouble in the spring. Little Grace died in the fall. She was a beautiful little girl. But she only lived a little over two years. She died of polio and she suffered. She had a slight fever for a couple of days, but it didn't seem like anything and we just kept her in bed. And we would certainly have called the doctor, but the fever dropped, she seemed to be all right. So we thought it had just been a cold. Then, one day, she was up, playing, Isabel was in the kitchen fixing lunch for the two boys when they'd come in from school, and she heard Grace fall down in the living room. When you have a lot of children you don't always start running when one of them falls, unless they start screaming or something. And, this time, Gracie was quiet. Yet, Isabel says that when she heard that *thump* and then that silence, something happened to her to make her afraid. And she ran to the living room and there was little Grace on the floor, all twisted up, and the reason she hadn't screamed was that she couldn't get her breath. And when she did scream, it was the worst sound, Isabel says, that she'd ever heard in all her life, and she still hears it sometimes in her dreams. Isabel will sometimes wake me up with a low, moaning, strangling sound and I have to be quick to awaken her and hold her to me and where Isabel is weeping against me seems a mortal wound.

I think I may have written Sonny the very day that little Grace was buried. I was sitting in the living room in the dark, by myself, and I suddenly thought of Sonny. My trouble made his real.

One Saturday afternoon, when Sonny had been living with us, or anyway, been in our house, for nearly two weeks, I found myself wandering aimlessly about the living room, drinking from a can of beer, and trying to work up courage to search Sonny's room. He was out, he was usually out whenever I was home, and Isabel had taken the children to see their grandparents. Suddenly I was standing still in front of the living room window, watching Seventh Avenue.

The idea of searching Sonny's room made me still. I scarcely dared to admit to myself what I'd be searching for. I didn't know what I'd do if I found it. Or if I didn't.

On the sidewalk across from me, near the entrance to a barbecue joint, some people were holding an old-fashioned revival meeting. The barbecue cook, wearing a dirty white apron, his conked[5] hair reddish and metallic in the pale sun, and a cigarette between his lips, stood in the doorway, watching them. Kids and older people paused in their errands and stood there, along with some older men and a couple of very tough-looking women who watched everything that happened on the avenue, as though they owned it, or were maybe owned by it. Well, they were watching this, too. The revival was being carried on by three sisters in black, and a brother. All they had were their voices and their Bibles and a tambourine. The brother was testifying[6] and while he testified two of the sisters stood together, seeming to say, amen, and the third sister walked around with the tambourine outstretched and a couple of people dropped coins into it. Then the brother's testimony ended and the sister who had been taking up the collection dumped the coins into her palm and transferred them to the pocket of her long black robe. Then she raised both hands, striking the tambourine against the air, and then against one hand, and she started to sing. And the two other sisters and the brother joined in.

It was strange, suddenly, to watch, though I had been seeing these meetings all my life. So, of course, had everybody else down there. Yet, they paused and watched and listened and I stood still at the window. "*'Tis the old ship of Zion,*" they sang, and the sister with the tambourine kept a steady, jangling beat, "*it has rescued many a thousand!*" Not a soul under the sound of their voices was hearing this song for the first time, not one of them had been rescued. Nor had they seen much in the way of rescue work being done around them. Neither did they especially believe in the holiness of the three sisters and the brother, they knew too much about them, knew where they lived, and how. The woman with the tambourine, whose voice dominated the air, whose face was bright with joy, was divided by very little from the woman who stood watching her, a cigarette between her heavy, chapped lips, her hair a cuckoo's nest, her face scarred and swollen from many beatings, and her black eyes glittering like coal. Perhaps they both knew this, which was why, when, as rarely, they addressed each other, they addressed each other as Sister. As the singing filled the air the watching, listening faces underwent a change, the eyes focusing on something within; the music seemed to soothe a poison out of them; and time seemed, nearly, to fall away from the sullen, belligerent, battered faces, as though they were fleeing back to their first condition, while dreaming of their last. The barbecue cook half shook his head and smiled, and dropped his cigarette and disappeared into his joint. A man fumbled in his pockets for change and stood holding it in his hand impatiently, as though he had just remembered a pressing appointment further up the avenue. He looked furious. Then I saw Sonny, standing on the edge of the crowd. He was carrying a wide, flat notebook with a green cover, and it made him look, from where I was standing, almost like a schoolboy. The coppery sun brought out the copper in his skin, he was very faintly smiling, standing very

---

5. Processed: straightened and greased.   6. Publicly professing belief.

still. Then the singing stopped, the tambourine turned into a collection plate again. The furious man dropped in his coins and vanished, so did a couple of the women, and Sonny dropped some change in the plate, looking directly at the woman with a little smile. He started across the avenue, toward the house. He has a slow, loping walk, something like the way Harlem hipsters walk, only he's imposed on this his own half-beat. I had never really noticed it before.

I stayed at the window, both relieved and apprehensive. As Sonny disappeared from my sight, they began singing again. And they were still singing when his key turned in the lock.

"Hey," he said.

"Hey, yourself. You want some beer?"

"No. Well, maybe." But he came up to the window and stood beside me, looking out. "What a warm voice," he said.

They were singing *If I could only hear my mother pray again!*

"Yes," I said, "and she can sure beat that tambourine."

"But what a terrible song," he said, and laughed. He dropped his notebook on the sofa and disappeared into the kitchen. "Where's Isabel and the kids?"

"I think they went to see their grandparents. You hungry?"

"No." He came back into the living room with his can of beer. "You want to come some place with me tonight?"

I sensed, I don't know how, that I couldn't possibly say no. "Sure. Where?"

He sat down on the sofa and picked up his notebook and started leafing through it. "I'm going to sit in with some fellows in a joint in the Village."

"You mean, you're going to play, tonight?"

"That's right." He took a swallow of his beer and moved back to the window. He gave me a sidelong look. "If you can stand it."

"I'll try," I said.

He smiled to himself and we both watched as the meeting across the way broke up. The three sisters and the brother, heads bowed, were singing *God be with you till we meet again.* The faces around them were very quiet. Then the song ended. The small crowd dispersed. We watched the three women and the lone man walk slowly up the avenue.

"When she was singing before," said Sonny, abruptly, "her voice reminded me for a minute of what heroin feels like sometimes—when it's in your veins. It makes you feel sort of warm and cool at the same time. And distant. And—and sure." He sipped his beer, very deliberately not looking at me. I watched his face. "It makes you feel—in control. Sometimes you've got to have that feeling."

"Do you?" I sat down slowly in the easy chair.

"Sometimes." He went to the sofa and picked up his notebook again. "Some people do."

"In order," I asked, "to play?" And my voice was very ugly, full of contempt and anger.

"Well"—he looked at me with great, troubled eyes, as though, in fact, he hoped his eyes would tell me things he could never otherwise say—"they *think* so. And *if* they think so—!"

"And what do *you* think?" I asked.

He sat on the sofa and put his can of beer on the floor. "I don't know," he said, and I couldn't be sure if he were answering my question or pursuing his thoughts. His face didn't tell me. "It's not so much to *play*. It's to *stand* it, to be able to make it at all. On any level." He frowned and smiled: "In order to keep from shaking to pieces."

"But these friends of yours," I said, "they seem to shake themselves to pieces pretty goddamn fast."

"Maybe." He played with the notebook. And something told me that I should curb my tongue, that Sonny was doing his best to talk, that I should listen. "But of course you only know the ones that've gone to pieces. Some don't—or at least they haven't *yet* and that's just about all *any* of us can say." He paused. "And then there are some who just live, really, in hell, and they know it and they see what's happening and they go right on. I don't know." He sighed, dropped the notebook, folded his arms. "Some guys, you can tell from the way they play, they on something *all* the time. And you can see that, well, it makes something real for them. But of course," he picked up his beer from the floor and sipped it and put the can down again, "they *want* to, too, you've got to see that. Even some of them that say they don't—*some*, not all."

"And what about you?" I asked—I couldn't help it. "What about you? Do *you* want to?"

He stood up and walked to the window and I remained silent for a long time. Then he sighed. "Me," he said. Then: "While I was downstairs before, on my way here, listening to that woman sing, it struck me all of a sudden how much suffering she must have had to go through—to sing like that. It's *repulsive* to think you have to suffer that much."

I said: "But there's no way not to suffer—is there, Sonny?"

"I believe not," he said and smiled, "but that's never stopped anyone from trying." He looked at me. "Has it?" I realized, with this mocking look, that there stood between us, forever, beyond the power of time or forgiveness, the fact that I had held silence—so long!—when he had needed human speech to help him. He turned back to the window. "No, there's no way not to suffer. But you try all kinds of ways to keep from drowning in it, to keep on top of it, and to make it seem—well, like *you*. Like you did something, all right, and now you're suffering for it. You know?" I said nothing. "Well you know," he said, impatiently, "why *do* people suffer? Maybe it's better to do something to give it a reason, *any* reason."

"But we just agreed," I said, "that there's no way not to suffer. Isn't it better, then, just to—take it?"

"But nobody just takes it," Sonny cried, "that's what I'm telling you! *Everybody* tries not to. You're just hung up on the *way* some people try—it's not *your* way!"

The hair on my face began to itch, my face felt wet. "That's not true," I said, "that's not true. I don't give a damn what other people do, I don't even care how they suffer. I just care how *you* suffer." And he looked at me. "Please believe me," I said, "I don't want to see you—die—trying not to suffer."

"I won't," he said flatly, "die trying not to suffer. At least, not any faster than anybody else."

"But there's no need," I said, trying to laugh, "is there? in killing yourself."

I wanted to say more, but I couldn't. I wanted to talk about will power and how life could be—well, beautiful. I wanted to say that it was all within; but was it? or, rather, wasn't that exactly the trouble? And I wanted to promise that I would never fail him again. But it would all have sounded—empty words and lies.

So I made the promise to myself and prayed that I would keep it.

"It's terrible sometimes, inside," he said, "that's what's the trouble. You walk these streets, black and funky and cold, and there's not really a living ass to talk to, and there's nothing shaking, and there's no way of getting it out—that storm inside. You can't talk it and you can't make love with it, and when you finally try to get with it and play it, you realize *nobody's* listening. So *you've* got to listen. You got to find a way to listen."

And then he walked away from the window and sat on the sofa again, as though all the wind had suddenly been knocked out of him. "Sometimes you'll do *anything* to play, even cut your mother's throat." He laughed and looked at me. "Or your brother's." Then he sobered. "Or your own." Then: "Don't worry. I'm all right now and I think I'll *be* all right. But I can't forget—where I've been. I don't mean just the physical place I've been, I mean where I've *been*. And *what* I've been."

"What have you been, Sonny?" I asked.

He smiled—but sat sideways on the sofa, his elbow resting on the back, his fingers playing with his mouth and chin, not looking at me. "I've been something I didn't recognize, didn't know I could be. Didn't know anybody could be." He stopped, looking inward, looking helplessly young, looking old. "I'm not talking about it now because I feel *guilty* or anything like that—maybe it would be better if I did, I don't know. Anyway, I can't really talk about it. Not to you, not to anybody," and now he turned and faced me. "Sometimes, you know, and it was actually when I was most *out* of the world, I felt that I was in it, that I was *with* it, really, and I could play or I didn't really have to *play*, it just came out of me, it was there. And I don't know how I played, thinking about it now, but I know I did awful things, those times, sometimes, to people. Or it wasn't that I *did* anything to them—it was that they weren't real." He picked up the beer can; it was empty; he rolled it between his palms: "And other times—well, I needed a fix, I needed to find a place to lean, I needed to clear a space to *listen*—and I couldn't find it, and I—went crazy, I did terrible things to *me*, I was terrible *for* me." He began pressing the beer can between his hands, I watched the metal begin to give. It glittered, as he played with it like a knife, and I was afraid he would cut himself, but I said nothing. "Oh well. I can never tell you. I was all by myself at the bottom of something, stinking and sweating and crying and shaking, and I smelled it, you know? *my* stink, and I thought I'd die if I couldn't get away from it and yet, all the same, I knew that everything I was doing was just locking me in with it. And I didn't know," he paused, still flattening the beer can, "I didn't know, I still *don't* know, something kept telling me that maybe it was good to smell your own stink, but I didn't think that *that* was what I'd been trying to do—and—who can stand it?" and he abruptly dropped the ruined beer can, looking at me with a small, still smile, and then rose, walking to the window as though it were the lodestone rock. I watched his face, he watched the avenue. "I couldn't tell you when Mama died—but the reason I wanted to leave Harlem so bad was to get away from drugs. And then, when I ran away, that's what I was running from—really. When I came back, nothing had changed, *I* hadn't changed, I was just—older." And he stopped, drumming with his fingers on the windowpane. The sun had vanished, soon darkness would fall. I watched his face. "It can come again," he said, almost as though speaking to himself. Then he turned to me. "It can come again," he repeated. "I just want you to know that."

"All right," I said, at last. "So it can come again. All right."

He smiled, but the smile was sorrowful. "I had to try to tell you," he said.

"Yes," I said. "I understand that."

"You're my brother," he said, looking straight at me, and not smiling at all.

"Yes," I repeated, "yes. I understand that."

He turned back to the window, looking out. "All that hatred down there," he said, "all that hatred and misery and love. It's a wonder it doesn't blow the avenue apart."

We went to the only nightclub on a short, dark street, downtown. We squeezed through the narrow, chattering, jampacked bar to the entrance of the big room, where the bandstand was. And we stood there for a moment, for the lights were very dim in this room and we couldn't see. Then, "Hello, boy," said the voice and an enormous black man, much older than Sonny or myself, erupted out of all that atmospheric lighting and put an arm around Sonny's shoulder. "I been sitting right here," he said, "waiting for you."

He had a big voice, too, and heads in the darkness turned toward us.

Sonny grinned and pulled a little away, and said, "Creole, this is my brother. I told you about him."

Creole shook my hand. "I'm glad to meet you, son," he said, and it was clear that he was glad to meet me *there*, for Sonny's sake. And he smiled, "You got a real musician in *your* family," and he took his arm from Sonny's shoulder and slapped him, lightly, affectionately, with the back of his hand.

"Well. Now I've heard it all," said a voice behind us. This was another musician, and a friend of Sonny's, a coal-black, cheerful-looking man, built close to the ground. He immediately began confiding to me, at the top of his lungs, the most terrible things about Sonny, his teeth gleaming like a lighthouse and his laugh coming up out of him like the beginning of an earthquake. And it turned out that everyone at the bar knew Sonny, or almost everyone; some were musicians, working there, or nearby, or not working, some were simply hangers-on, and some were there to hear Sonny play. I was introduced to all of them and they were all very polite to me. Yet, it was clear that, for them, I was only Sonny's brother. Here, I was in Sonny's world. Or, rather: his kingdom. Here, it was not even a question that his veins bore royal blood.

They were going to play soon and Creole installed me, by myself, at a table in a dark corner. Then I watched them, Creole, and the little black man, and Sonny, and the others, while they horsed around, standing just below the bandstand. The light from the bandstand spilled just a little short of them and, watching them laughing and gesturing and moving about, I had the feeling that they, nevertheless, were being most careful not to step into that circle of light too suddenly; that if they moved into the light too suddenly, without thinking, they would perish in flame. Then, while I watched, one of them, the small black man, moved into the light and crossed the bandstand and started fooling around with his drums. Then—being funny and being, also, extremely ceremonious—Creole took Sonny by the arm and led him to the piano. A woman's voice called Sonny's name and a few hands started clapping. And Sonny, also being funny and being ceremonious, and so touched, I think, that he could have cried, but neither hiding it nor showing it, riding it like a man, grinned, and put both hands to his heart and bowed from the waist.

Creole then went to the bass fiddle and a lean, very bright-skinned brown man jumped up on the bandstand and picked up his horn. So there they were, and the atmosphere on the bandstand and in the room began to change and tighten. Someone stepped up to the microphone and announced them. Then there were all kinds of murmurs. Some people at the bar shushed others. The waitress ran around, frantically getting in the last orders, guys and chicks got closer to each other, and the lights on the bandstand, on the quartet, turned to a kind of indigo. Then they all looked different there. Creole looked about him for the last time, as though he were making certain that all his chickens were in the coop, and then he—jumped and struck the fiddle. And there they were.

All I know about music is that not many people ever really hear it. And even then, on the rare occasions when something opens within, and the music enters, what we mainly hear, or hear corroborated, are personal, private, vanishing evocations. But the man who creates the music is hearing something else, is dealing with the roar rising from the void and imposing order on it as it hits the air. What is evoked in him, then, is of another order, more terrible because it has no words, and triumphant, too, for that same reason. And his triumph, when he triumphs, is ours. I just watched Sonny's face. His face was troubled, he was working hard, but he wasn't with it. And I had the feeling that, in a way, everyone on the bandstand was waiting for him, both waiting for him and pushing him along. But as I began to watch Creole, I realized that it was Creole who held them all back. He had them on a short rein. Up there, keeping the beat with his whole body, wailing on the fiddle, with his eyes half closed, he was listening to everything, but he was listening to Sonny. He was having a dialogue with Sonny. He wanted Sonny to leave the shoreline and strike out for the deep water. He was Sonny's witness that deep water and drowning were not the same thing—he had been there, and he knew. And he wanted Sonny to know. He was waiting for Sonny to do the things on the keys which would let Creole know that Sonny was in the water.

And, while Creole listened, Sonny moved, deep within, exactly like someone in torment. I had never before thought of how awful the relationship must be between the musician and his instrument. He has to fill it, this instrument, with the breath of life, his own. He has to make it do what he wants it to do. And a piano is just a piano. It's made out of so much wood and wires and little hammers and big ones, and ivory. While there's only so much you can do with it, the only way to find this out is to try; to try and make it do everything.

And Sonny hadn't been near a piano for over a year. And he wasn't on much better terms with his life, not the life that stretched before him now. He and the piano stammered, started one way, got scared, stopped; started another way, panicked, marked time, started again; then seemed to have found a direction, panicked again, got stuck. And the face I saw on Sonny I'd never seen before. Everything had been burned out of it, and, at the same time, things usually hidden were being burned in, by the fire and fury of the battle which was occurring in him up there.

Yet, watching Creole's face as they neared the end of the first set, I had the feeling that something had happened, something I hadn't heard. Then they finished, there was scattered applause, and then, without an instant's warning, Creole started into something else, it was almost sardonic, it was *Am I Blue*.[7] And, as though he commanded, Sonny began to play. Something began to happen.

---

7. A favorite jazz standard, brilliantly recorded by Billie Holiday.

And Creole let out the reins. The dry, low, black man said something awful on the drums, Creole answered, and the drums talked back. Then the horn insisted, sweet and high, slightly detached perhaps, and Creole listened, commenting now and then, dry, and driving, beautiful and calm and old. Then they all came together again, and Sonny was part of the family again. I could tell this from his face. He seemed to have found, right there beneath his fingers, a damn brand-new piano. It seemed that he couldn't get over it. Then, for a while, just being happy with Sonny, they seemed to be agreeing with him that brand-new pianos certainly were a gas.

Then Creole stepped forward to remind them that what they were playing was the blues. He hit something in all of them, he hit something in me, myself, and the music tightened and deepened, apprehension began to beat the air. Creole began to tell us what the blues were all about. They were not about anything very new. He and his boys up there were keeping it new, at the risk of ruin, destruction, madness, and death, in order to find new ways to make us listen. For, while the tale of how we suffer, and how we are delighted, and how we may triumph is never new, it always must be heard. There isn't any other tale to tell, it's the only light we've got in all this darkness.

And this tale, according to that face, that body, those strong hands on those strings, has another aspect in every country, and a new depth in every generation. Listen, Creole seemed to be saying, listen. Now these are Sonny's blues. He made the little black man on the drums know it, and the bright, brown man on the horn. Creole wasn't trying any longer to get Sonny in the water. He was wishing him Godspeed. Then he stepped back, very slowly, filling the air with the immense suggestion that Sonny speak for himself.

240   Then they all gathered around Sonny and Sonny played. Every now and again one of them seemed to say, amen. Sonny's fingers filled the air with life, his life. But that life contained so many others. And Sonny went all the way back, he really began with the spare, flat statement of the opening phrase of the song. Then he began to make it his. It was very beautiful because it wasn't hurried and it was no longer a lament. I seemed to hear with what burning he had made it his, and what burning we had yet to make it ours, how we could cease lamenting. Freedom lurked around us and I understood, at last, that he could help us to be free if we would listen, that he would never be free until we did. Yet, there was no battle in his face now, I heard what he had gone through, and would continue to go through until he came to rest in earth. He had made it his: that long line, of which we knew only Mama and Daddy. And he was giving it back, as everything must be given back, so that, passing through death, it can live forever. I saw my mother's face again, and felt, for the first time, how the stones of the road she had walked on must have bruised her feet. I saw the moonlit road where my father's brother died. And it brought something else back to me, and carried me past it, I saw my little girl again and felt Isabel's tears again, and I felt my own tears begin to rise. And I was yet aware that this was only a moment, that the world waited outside, as hungry as a tiger, and that trouble stretched above us, longer than the sky.

Then it was over. Creole and Sonny let out their breath, both soaking wet, and grinning. There was a lot of applause and some of it was real. In the dark, the girl came by and I asked her to take drinks to the bandstand. There was a long pause, while they talked up there in the indigo light and after awhile I saw the girl put a Scotch and milk on top of the piano for Sonny. He didn't seem to notice it, but just before they started playing again, he sipped from it and looked toward me, and nodded. Then he put it back on top of the piano. For me, then, as they began to play again, it glowed and shook above my brother's head like the very cup of trembling.[8]

1957

## QUESTIONS

1. What parts of "Sonny's Blues" correspond to the plot stages of a traditionally told story: exposition, discriminated occasion, rising action, turning point, climax, falling action, conclusion?
2. What is the relationship between the chronology and the plot of "Sonny's Blues"? What does Baldwin gain, or lose, by reordering the events of the story as he does?
3. What is different about the narrative style used to describe the nightclub scene at the story's conclusion? Does this change of style make you reconsider what the story's message might be?

## EDITH WHARTON

## Roman Fever[1]

### I

From the table at which they had been lunching two American ladies of ripe but well-cared-for middle age moved across the lofty terrace of the Roman restaurant and, leaning on its parapet, looked first at each other, and then down on the outspread glories of the Palatine[2] and the Forum,[3] with the same expression of vague but benevolent approval.

As they leaned there a girlish voice echoed up gaily from the stairs leading to the court below. "Well, come along, then," it cried, not to them but to an invisible companion, "and let's leave the young things to their knitting"; and a voice as fresh laughed back: "Oh, look here, Babs, not actually *knitting*—" "Well, I mean figuratively," rejoined the first. "After all, we haven't left our poor parents much else to do . . ." and at that point the turn of the stairs engulfed the dialogue.

The two ladies looked at each other again, this time with a tinge of smiling embarrassment, and the smaller and paler one shook her head and colored slightly.

"Barbara!" she murmured, sending an unheard rebuke after the mocking voice in the stairway.

The other lady, who was fuller, and higher in color, with a small determined 5

---

[8]. See Isaiah 51.17, 22-23: "Awake, awake, stand up, O Jerusalem, which hast drunk at the hand of the Lord the cup of his fury; thou hast drunken the dregs of the cup of trembling, and wrung them out. . . . Behold, I have taken out of thine hand the cup of trembling, even the dregs of the cup of my fury; thou shalt no more drink it again: But I will put it into the hand of them that afflict thee . . ."
1. A type of malaria once thought to be caused by the alternating hot and cool temperatures of the Roman climate. Anglo-American tourists traditionally feared exposure to it at certain times and seasons.
2. One of the seven hills on which the oldest part of Rome was built.
3. The central plaza of ancient Rome.

nose supported by vigorous black eyebrows, gave a good-humored laugh. "That's what our daughters think of us!"

Her companion replied by a deprecating gesture. "Not of us individually. We must remember that. It's just the collective modern idea of Mothers. And you see—" Half guiltily she drew from her handsomely mounted black hand-bag a twist of crimson silk run through by two fine knitting needles. "One never knows," she murmured. "The new system has certainly given us a good deal of time to kill; and sometimes I get tired just looking—even at this." Her gesture was now addressed to the stupendous scene at their feet.

The dark lady laughed again, and they both relapsed upon the view, contemplating it in silence, with a sort of diffused serenity which might have been borrowed from the spring effulgence of the Roman skies. The luncheon-hour was long past, and the two had their end of the vast terrace to themselves. At its opposite extremity a few groups, detained by a lingering look at the outspread city, were gathering up guide-books and fumbling for tips. The last of them scattered, and the two ladies were alone on the air-washed height.

"Well, I don't see why we shouldn't just stay here," said Mrs. Slade, the lady of the high color and energetic brows. Two derelict basket-chairs stood near, and she pushed them into the angle of the parapet, and settled herself in one, her gaze upon the Palatine. "After all, it's still the most beautiful view in the world."

"It always will be, to me," assented her friend Mrs. Ansley, with so slight a stress on the "me" that Mrs. Slade, though she noticed it, wondered if it were not merely accidental, like the random underlinings of old-fashioned letter-writers.

10 "Grace Ansley was always old-fashioned," she thought; and added aloud, with a retrospective smile: "It's a view we've both been familiar with for a good many years. When we first met here we were younger than our girls are now. You remember?"

"Oh, yes, I remember," murmured Mrs. Ansley, with the same undefinable stress—"There's that head-waiter wondering," she interpolated. She was evidently far less sure than her companion of herself and of her rights in the world.

"I'll cure him of wondering," said Mrs. Slade, stretching her hand toward a bag as discreetly opulent-looking as Mrs. Ansley's. Signing to the head-waiter, she explained that she and her friend were old lovers of Rome, and would like to spend the end of the afternoon looking down on the view—that is, if it did not disturb the service? The headwaiter, bowing over her gratuity, assured her that the ladies were most welcome, and would be still more so if they would condescend to remain for dinner. A full moon night, they would remember . . .

Mrs. Slade's black brows drew together, as though references to the moon were out-of-place and even unwelcome. But she smiled away her frown as the head-waiter retreated. "Well, why not? We might do worse. There's no knowing, I suppose, when the girls will be back. Do you even know back from *where*? I don't!"

Mrs. Ansley again colored slightly. "I think those young Italian aviators we met at the Embassy invited them to fly to Tarquinia[4] for tea. I suppose they'll want to wait and fly back by moonlight."

---

4. Now Corneto, Italy, an ancient Etruscan city, 90 km from Rome, the site of well-preserved underground tombs with vivid wall paintings.

"Moonlight—moonlight! What a part it still plays. Do you suppose they're as sentimental as we were?"

"I've come to the conclusion that I don't in the least know what they are," said Mrs. Ansley. "And perhaps we didn't know much more about each other."

"No; perhaps we didn't."

Her friend gave her a shy glance. "I never should have supposed you were sentimental, Alida."

"Well, perhaps I wasn't." Mrs. Slade drew her lids together in retrospect; and for a few moments the two ladies, who had been intimate since childhood, reflected how little they knew each other. Each one, of course, had a label ready to attach to the other's name; Mrs. Delphin Slade, for instance, would have told herself, or any one who asked her, that Mrs. Horace Ansley, twenty-five years ago, had been exquisitely lovely—no, you wouldn't believe it, would you? . . . though, of course, still charming, distinguished . . . Well, as a girl she had been exquisite; far more beautiful than her daughter Barbara, though certainly Babs, according to the new standards at any rate, was more effective—had more *edge,* as they say. Funny where she got it, with those two nullities as parents. Yes; Horace Ansley was—well, just the duplicate of his wife. Museum specimens of old New York. Good-looking, irreproachable, exemplary. Mrs. Slade and Mrs. Ansley had lived opposite each other—actually as well as figuratively—for years. When the drawingroom curtains in No. 20 East 73rd Street were renewed, No. 23, across the way, was always aware of it. And of all the movings, buyings, travels, anniversaries, illnesses—the tame chronicle of an estimable pair. Little of it escaped Mrs. Slade. But she had grown bored with it by the time her husband made his big *coup* in Wall Street, and when they bought in upper Park Avenue had already begun to think: "I'd rather live opposite a speak-easy[5] for a change; at least one might see it raided." The idea of seeing Grace raided was so amusing that (before the move) she launched it at a woman's lunch. It made a hit, and went the rounds—she sometimes wondered if it had crossed the street, and reached Mrs. Ansley. She hoped not, but didn't much mind. Those were the days when respectability was at a discount, and it did the irreproachable no harm to laugh at them a little.

A few years later, and not many months apart, both ladies lost their husbands. There was an appropriate exchange of wreaths and condolences, and a brief renewal of intimacy in the half-shadow of their mourning; and now, after another interval, they had run across each other in Rome, at the same hotel, each of them the modest appendage of a salient daughter. The similarity of their lot had again drawn them together, lending itself to mild jokes, and the mutual confession that, if in old days it must have been tiring to "keep up" with daughters, it was now, at times, a little dull not to.

No doubt, Mrs. Slade reflected, she felt her unemployment more than poor Grace ever would. It was a big drop from being the wife of Delphin Slade to being his widow. She had always regarded herself (with a certain conjugal pride) as his equal in social gifts, as contributing her full share to the making of the exceptional couple they were: but the difference after his death was irremediable. As the wife of the famous corporation lawyer, always with an international case or two on hand, every day brought its exciting and unexpected obligation: the impromptu entertaining of eminent colleagues from abroad, the hurried dashes

---

5. An illegal tavern during the period of Prohibition (1919-31) in the United States.

on legal business to London, Paris or Rome, where the entertaining was so handsomely reciprocated; the amusement of hearing in her wake: "What, that handsome woman with the good clothes and the eyes is Mrs. Slade—*the* Slade's wife? Really? Generally the wives of celebrities are such frumps."

Yes; being *the* Slade's widow was a dullish business after that. In living up to such a husband all her faculties had been engaged; now she had only her daughter to live up to, for the son who seemed to have inherited his father's gifts had died suddenly in boyhood. She had fought through that agony because her husband was there, to be helped and to help; now, after the father's death, the thought of the boy had become unbearable. There was nothing left but to mother her daughter; and dear Jenny was such a perfect daughter that she needed no excessive mothering. "Now with Babs Ansley I don't know that I *should* be so quiet," Mrs. Slade sometimes half-enviously reflected; but Jenny, who was younger than her brilliant friend, was that rare accident, an extremely pretty girl who somehow made youth and prettiness seem as safe as their absence. It was all perplexing—and to Mrs. Slade a little boring. She wished that Jenny would fall in love—with the wrong man, even; that she might have to be watched, outmanoeuvred, rescued. And instead, it was Jenny who watched her mother, kept her out of draughts, made sure that she had taken her tonic...

Mrs. Ansley was much less articulate than her friend, and her mental portrait of Mrs. Slade was slighter, and drawn with fainter touches. "Alida Slade's awfully brilliant; but not as brilliant as she thinks," would have summed it up; though she would have added, for the enlightenment of strangers, that Mrs. Slade had been an extremely dashing girl; much more so than her daughter, who was pretty, of course, and clever in a way, but had none of her mother's—well, "vividness," some one had once called it. Mrs. Ansley would take up current words like this, and cite them in quotation marks, as unheard-of audacities. No; Jenny was not like her mother. Sometimes Mrs. Ansley thought Alida Slade was disappointed; on the whole she had had a sad life. Full of failures and mistakes; Mrs. Ansley had always been rather sorry for her...

So these two ladies visualized each other, each through the wrong end of her little telescope.

II

For a long time they continued to sit side by side without speaking. It seemed as though, to both, there was a relief in laying down their somewhat futile activities in the presence of the vast Memento Mori[6] which faced them. Mrs. Slade sat quite still, her eyes fixed on the golden slope of the Palace of the Caesars,[7] and after a while Mrs. Ansley ceased to fidget with her bag, and she too sank into meditation. Like many intimate friends, the two ladies had never before had occasion to be silent together, and Mrs. Ansley was slightly embarrassed by what seemed, after so many years, a new stage in their intimacy, and one with which she did not yet know how to deal.

Suddenly the air was full of that deep clangor of bells which periodically covers Rome with a roof of silver. Mrs. Slade glanced at her wrist-watch. "Five o'clock already," she said, as though surprised.

---

6. A reminder of human mortality; literally, "Remember that you must die" (Latin).
7. The palace of the Roman emperors is on the Palatine hill.

Mrs. Ansley suggested interrogatively: "There's bridge at the Embassy at five." For a long time Mrs. Slade did not answer. She appeared to be lost in contemplation, and Mrs. Ansley thought the remark had escaped her. But after a while she said, as if speaking out of a dream: "Bridge, did you say? Not unless you want to... But I don't think I will, you know."

"Oh, no," Mrs. Ansley hastened to assure her. "I don't care to at all. It's so lovely here; and so full of old memories, as you say." She settled herself in her chair, and almost furtively drew forth her knitting. Mrs. Slade took sideway note of this activity, but her own beautifully cared-for hands remained motionless on her knee.

"I was just thinking," she said slowly, "what different things Rome stands for to each generation of travellers. To our grandmothers, Roman fever; to our mothers, sentimental dangers—how we used to be guarded!—to our daughters, no more dangers than the middle of Main Street. They don't know it—but how much they're missing!"

The long golden light was beginning to pale, and Mrs. Ansley lifted her knitting a little closer to her eyes. "Yes; how we were guarded!"

"I always used to think," Mrs. Slade continued, "that our mothers had a much more difficult job than our grandmothers. When Roman fever stalked the streets it must have been comparatively easy to gather in the girls at the danger hour; but when you and I were young, with such beauty calling us, and the spice of disobedience thrown in, and no worse risk than catching cold during the cool hour after sunset, the mothers used to be put to it to keep us in—didn't they?"

She turned again toward Mrs. Ansley, but the latter had reached a delicate point in her knitting. "One, two, three—slip two; yes, they must have been," she assented, without looking up.

Mrs. Slade's eyes rested on her with a deepened attention. "She can knit—in the face of *this*! How like her..."

Mrs. Slade leaned back, brooding, her eyes ranging from the ruins which faced her to the long green hollow of the Forum, the fading glow of the church fronts beyond it, and the outlying immensity of the Colosseum.[8] Suddenly she thought: "It's all very well to say that our girls have done away with sentiment and moonlight. But if Babs Ansley isn't out to catch that young aviator—the one who's a Marchese—then I don't know anything. And Jenny has no chance beside her. I know that too. I wonder if that's why Grace Ansley likes the two girls to go everywhere together? My poor Jenny as a foil—!" Mrs. Slade gave a hardly audible laugh, and at the sound Mrs. Ansley dropped her knitting.

"Yes—?"

"I—oh, nothing. I was only thinking how your Babs carries everything before her. That Campolieri boy is one of the best matches in Rome. Don't look so innocent, my dear—you know he is. And I was wondering, ever so respectfully, you understand... wondering how two such exemplary characters as you and Horace had managed to produce anything quite so dynamic." Mrs. Slade laughed again, with a touch of asperity.

Mrs. Ansley's hands lay inert across her needles. She looked straight out at the great accumulated wreckage of passion and splendor at her feet. But her

---

8. The great Roman amphitheater built in the first century C.E., site of lavish spectacles that included wild animals and mortal combat.

small profile was almost expressionless. At length she said: "I think you overrate Babs, my dear."

Mrs. Slade's tone grew easier. "No; I don't. I appreciate her. And perhaps envy you. Oh, my girl's perfect; if I were a chronic invalid I'd—well, I think I'd rather be in Jenny's hands. There must be times . . . but there! I always wanted a brilliant daughter . . . and never quite understood why I got an angel instead."

Mrs. Ansley echoed her laugh in a faint murmur. "Babs is an angel too."

"Of course—of course! But she's got rainbow wings. Well, they're wandering by the sea with their young men; and here we sit . . . and it all brings back the past a little too acutely."

Mrs. Ansley had resumed her knitting. One might almost have imagined (if one had known her less well, Mrs. Slade reflected) that, for her also, too many memories rose from the lengthening shadows of those august ruins. But no; she was simply absorbed in her work. What was there for her to worry about? She knew that Babs would almost certainly come back engaged to the extremely eligible Campolieri. "And she'll sell the New York house, and settle down near them in Rome, and never be in their way . . . she's much too tactful. But she'll have an excellent cook, and just the right people in for bridge and cocktails . . . and a perfectly peaceful old age among her grandchildren."

Mrs. Slade broke off this prophetic flight with a recoil of self-disgust. There was no one of whom she had less right to think unkindly than of Grace Ansley. Would she never cure herself of envying her? Perhaps she had begun too long ago.

She stood up and leaned against the parapet, filling her troubled eyes with the tranquillizing magic of the hour. But instead of tranquillizing her the sight seemed to increase her exasperation. Her gaze turned toward the Colosseum. Already its golden flank was drowned in purple shadow, and above it the sky curved crystal clear, without light or color. It was the moment when afternoon and evening hang balanced in mid-heaven.

Mrs. Slade turned back and laid her hand on her friend's arm. The gesture was so abrupt that Mrs. Ansley looked up, startled.

"The sun's set. You're not afraid, my dear?"

"Afraid—?"

"Of Roman fever or pneumonia? I remember how ill you were that winter. As a girl you had a very delicate throat, hadn't you?"

"Oh, we're all right up here. Down below, in the Forum, it does get deathly cold, all of a sudden . . . but not here."

"Ah, of course you know because you had to be so careful." Mrs. Slade turned back to the parapet. She thought: "I must make one more effort not to hate her." Aloud she said. "Whenever I look at the Forum from up here, I remember that story about a great-aunt of yours, wasn't she? A dreadfully wicked great-aunt?"

"Oh, yes; Great-aunt Harriet. The one who was supposed to have sent her young sister out to the Forum after sunset to gather a nightblooming flower for her album. All our great-aunts and grandmothers used to have albums of dried flowers."

Mrs. Slade nodded. "But she really sent her because they were in love with the same man—"

"Well, that was the family tradition. They said Aunt Harriet confessed it years afterward. At any rate, the poor little sister caught the fever and died. Mother used to frighten us with the story when we were children."

"And you frightened *me* with it, that winter when you and I were here as girls. The winter I was engaged to Delphin."

Mrs. Ansley gave a faint laugh. "Oh, did I? Really frightened you? I don't believe you're easily frightened."

"Not often; but I was then. I was easily frightened because I was too happy. I wonder if you know what that means?"

"I—yes . . ." Mrs. Ansley faltered.

"Well, I suppose that was why the story of your wicked aunt made such an impression on me. And I thought: 'There's no more Roman fever, but the Forum is deathly cold after sunset—especially after a hot day. And the Colosseum's even colder and damper.'"

"The Colosseum—?"

"Yes. It wasn't easy to get in, after the gates were locked for the night. Far from easy. Still, in those days it could be managed; it *was* managed, often. Lovers met there who couldn't meet elsewhere. You knew that?"

"I—I daresay. I don't remember."

"You don't remember? You don't remember going to visit some ruins or other one evening, just after dark, and catching a bad chill? You were supposed to have gone to see the moon rise. People always said that expedition was what caused your illness."

There was a moment's silence; then Mrs. Ansley rejoined: "Did they? It was all so long ago."

"Yes. And you got well again—so it didn't matter. But I suppose it struck your friends—the reason given for your illness, I mean—because everybody knew you were so prudent on account of your throat, and your mother took such care of you . . . You *had* been out late sight-seeing, hadn't you, that night?"

"Perhaps I had. The most prudent girls aren't always prudent. What made you think of it now?"

Mrs. Slade seemed to have no answer ready. But after a moment she broke out: "Because I simply can't bear it any longer—!"

Mrs. Ansley lifted her head quickly. Her eyes were wide and very pale. "Can't bear what?"

"Why—your not knowing that I've always known why you went."

"Why I went—?"

"Yes. You think I'm bluffing, don't you? Well, you went to meet the man I was engaged to—and I can repeat every word of the letter that took you there."

While Mrs. Slade spoke Mrs. Ansley had risen unsteadily to her feet. Her bag, her knitting and gloves, slid in a panic-stricken heap to the ground. She looked at Mrs. Slade as though she were looking at a ghost.

"No, no—don't," she faltered out.

"Why not? Listen, if you don't believe me. 'My one darling, things can't go on like this. I must see you alone. Come to the Colosseum immediately after dark tomorrow. There will be somebody to let you in. No one whom you need fear will suspect'—but perhaps you've forgotten what the letter said?"

Mrs. Ansley met the challenge with an unexpected composure. Steadying herself against the chair she looked at her friend, and replied: "No; I know it by heart too."

"And the signature? 'Only *your* D.S.' Was that it? I'm right, am I? That was the letter that took you out that evening after dark?"

Mrs. Ansley was still looking at her. It seemed to Mrs. Slade that a slow struggle was going on behind the voluntarily controlled mask of her small quiet face. "I shouldn't have thought she had herself so well in hand," Mrs. Slade reflected, almost resentfully. But at this moment Mrs. Ansley spoke. "I don't know how you knew. I burnt that letter at once."

"Yes; you would, naturally—you're so prudent!" The sneer was open now. "And if you burnt the letter you're wondering how on earth I know what was in it. That's it, isn't it?"

Mrs. Slade waited, but Mrs. Ansley did not speak.

"Well, my dear, I know what was in that letter because I wrote it!"

"You wrote it?"

"Yes."

The two women stood for a minute staring at each other in the last golden light. Then Mrs. Ansley dropped back into her chair. "Oh," she murmured, and covered her face with her hands.

Mrs. Slade waited nervously for another word or movement. None came, and at length she broke out. "I horrify you."

Mrs. Ansley's hands dropped to her knee. The face they uncovered was streaked with tears. "I wasn't thinking of you. I was thinking—it was the only letter I ever had from him!"

"And I wrote it. Yes; I wrote it! But I was the girl he was engaged to. Did you happen to remember that?"

Mrs. Ansley's head drooped again. "I'm not trying to excuse myself... I remembered..."

"And still you went?"

"Still I went."

Mrs. Slade stood looking down on the small bowed figure at her side. The flame of her wrath had already sunk, and she wondered why she had ever thought there would be any satisfaction in inflicting so purposeless a wound on her friend. But she had to justify herself.

"You do understand? I'd found out—and I hated you, hated you. I knew you were in love with Delphin—and I was afraid; afraid of you, of your quiet ways, your sweetness... your... well, I wanted you out of the way, that's all. Just for a few weeks; just till I was sure of him. So in a blind fury I wrote that letter... I don't know why I'm telling you now."

"I suppose," said Mrs. Ansley slowly, "it's because you've always gone on hating me."

"Perhaps. Or because I wanted to get the whole thing off my mind." She paused. "I'm glad you destroyed the letter. Of course I never thought you'd die."

Mrs. Ansley relapsed into silence, and Mrs. Slade, leaning above her, was conscious of a strange sense of isolation, of being cut off from the warm current of human communion. "You think me a monster!"

"I don't know... It was the only letter I had, and you say he didn't write it?"

"Ah, how you care for him, still!"

"I cared for that memory," said Mrs. Ansley.

Mrs. Slade continued to look down on her. She seemed physically reduced by the blow—as if, when she got up, the wind might scatter her like a puff of dust. Mrs. Slade's jealousy suddenly leapt up again at the sight. All these years the woman had been living on that letter. How she must have loved him, to treasure the mere memory of its ashes! The letter of the man her friend was engaged to. Wasn't it she who was the monster?

"You tried your best to get him away from me, didn't you? But you failed; and I kept him. That's all."

"Yes. That's all."

"I wish now I hadn't told you. I'd no idea you'd feel about it as you do; I thought you'd be amused. It all happened so long ago, as you say; and you must do me the justice to remember that I had no reason to think you'd ever taken it seriously. How could I, when you were married to Horace Ansley two months afterward? As soon as you could get out of bed your mother rushed you off to Florence and married you. People were rather surprised—they wondered at its being done so quickly; but I thought I knew. I had an idea you did it out of *pique*—to be able to say you'd got ahead of Delphin and me. Girls have such silly reasons for doing the most serious things. And your marrying so soon convinced me that you'd never really cared."

"Yes. I suppose it would," Mrs. Ansley assented.

The clear heaven overhead was emptied of all its gold. Dusk spread over it, abruptly darkening the Seven Hills.[9] Here and there lights began to twinkle through the foliage at their feet. Steps were coming and going on the deserted terrace—waiters looking out of the doorway at the head of the stairs, then reappearing with trays and napkins and flasks of wine. Tables were moved, chairs straightened. A feeble string of electric lights flickered out. Some vases of faded flowers were carried away, and brought back replenished. A stout lady in a dustcoat suddenly appeared, asking in broken Italian if any one had seen the elastic band which held together her tattered Baedeker. She poked with her stick under the table at which she had lunched, the waiters assisting.

The corner where Mrs. Slade and Mrs. Ansley sat was still shadowy and deserted. For a long time neither of them spoke. At length Mrs. Slade began again: "I suppose I did it as a sort of joke—"

"A joke?"

"Well, girls are ferocious sometimes, you know. Girls in love especially. And I remember laughing to myself all that evening at the idea that you were waiting around there in the dark, dodging out of sight, listening for every sound, trying to get in—. Of course I was upset when I heard you were so ill afterward."

Mrs. Ansley had not moved for a long time. But now she turned slowly toward her companion. "But I didn't wait. He'd arranged everything. He was there. We were let in at once," she said.

Mrs. Slade sprang up from her leaning position. "Delphin there? They let you in?—Ah, now you're lying!" she burst out with violence.

Mrs. Ansley's voice grew clearer, and full of surprise. "But of course he was there. Naturally he came—"

"Came? How did he know he'd find you there? You must be raving!"

Mrs. Ansley hesitated, as though reflecting. "But I answered the letter. I told him I'd be there. So he came."

Mrs. Slade flung her hands up to her face. "Oh, God—you answered! I never thought of your answering . . ."

---

9. The ancient center of Rome was built on seven hills beside the Tiber River.

"It's odd you never thought of it, if you wrote the letter."

"Yes. I was blind with rage."

Mrs. Ansley rose, and drew her fur scarf about her. "It is cold here. We'd better go . . . I'm sorry for you," she said, as she clasped the fur about her throat.

The unexpected words sent a pang through Mrs. Slade. "Yes; we'd better go." She gathered up her bag and cloak. "I don't know why you should be sorry for me," she muttered.

Mrs. Ansley stood looking away from her toward the dusky secret mass of the Colosseum. "Well—because I didn't have to wait that night."

Mrs. Slade gave an unquiet laugh. "Yes; I was beaten there. But I oughtn't to begrudge it to you, I suppose. At the end of all these years. After all, I had everything; I had him for twenty-five years. And you had nothing but that one letter that he didn't write."

Mrs. Ansley was again silent. At length she turned toward the door of the terrace. She took a step, and turned back, facing her companion.

"I had Barbara," she said, and began to move ahead of Mrs. Slade toward the stairway.

1936

## QUESTIONS

1. What are the first hints of submerged conflict between Mrs. Slade and Mrs. Ansley? What details in part 1 bring out the differences in their personalities and their lives? How has their relationship changed in the end, and how do the last six paragraphs of the story show the change?
2. Discuss how dramatic irony plays out in "Roman Fever." What is the full story that neither Mrs. Slade nor Mrs. Ansley knows? What is the turning point that prompts the two ladies to reveal what they know to each other?
3. In part 2, Mrs. Slade remembers how earlier generations tried to protect their daughters in Rome. What are the similarities and differences between the older women's memories and the daughters' current experiences of courtship in Italy?

---

## SUGGESTIONS FOR WRITING

1. Write an essay comparing and contrasting the way any two of the stories in this chapter handle the traditional elements of plot: exposition, rising action, discriminated occasion, climax, falling action, conclusion. Consider especially how plot elements contribute to the overall artistic effect.
2. Many stories depict events that do not occur in a simple chronology. For example, "The Thing in the Forest" joins events that are separated by many years, and "Sonny's Blues" makes liberal use of flashbacks that rearrange the order of events. Using any story from this anthology, write an essay discussing the way the author has created a plot from a series of discontinuous events.
3. Reread "Roman Fever" and record the instances when the story prompts you to form expectations that may or may not be borne out by the events to follow. Write an essay in which you analyze the way Wharton has rearranged the chronology of her tale in order to build suspense and stimulate reader engagement with the text.
4. Using Margaret Atwood's "Happy Endings" as a model, write a short story in which the reader is prompted to make choices that can produce a variety of results.
5. Using the characters, settings, and events of "Sonny's Blues," write a narrative that tells the same story from Sonny's point of view.

# 2  NARRATION AND POINT OF VIEW

When we read fiction, our sense of who is telling us the story is as important as our sense of what happens. Unlike drama, in which events occur before us directly, narrative fiction is always mediated; someone is always *between* us and the events—a viewer, a speaker, or both. The way a story is mediated is a key element of fictional structure. This mediation involves both the angle of vision—the point from which the people, events, and other details are viewed—and the words in which the story is embodied. The viewing aspect is called the **focus,** and the verbal aspect the **voice.** Both are generally considered together in the term **point of view.** The teller of a story or novel—the voice that speaks *all* the words we read in it—is called the **narrator.**

Focus acts much as a camera does, choosing what we can look at and the angle at which we can view it, framing, proportioning, emphasizing—even distorting. Whereas plot is a structure that arranges cause and effect as well as time, focus arranges space and measures the distance or closeness of narrator, characters, and readers.

We must pay careful attention to the focus at any given point in a story. Is it fixed or mobile? Does it stay at more or less the same angle to, and at the same distance from, the characters and action, or does it move around or in and out? When the focus centers on a single individual in the story, or relies on that character's voice or thoughts, we say that the point of view is **limited.** When that person leaves the room, the camera must go too, and if we are to know what happens in the room when the focal character is gone, some means of bringing that information must be devised, such as a letter or a report by another character. When stories or novels have several focal characters, the point of view is said to be **unlimited.** The camera is free not only to pull back from a character but may also follow scenes when that character is absent and record the perceptions and internal voices of new characters. **Third-person narrators** ("he" or "she") with unlimited access to the thoughts of more than one character are often called **omniscient** (meaning "all-knowing").

> *The choice of a point of view is the initial act of a culture.*
> —JOSÉ ORTEGA Y GASSET

Identifying the particular kind of narration and point of view an author has chosen for a story is much more than a technical exercise. When you pick up a story or novel, among the first questions you should ask are "Who is telling this?" and "Who sees or knows what?" As you find answers, you begin to locate what makes this story unique. The events in the characters' lives could be presented in a variety of ways, but a different kind of narrator or point of view would change the story utterly. You might want to test this by imagining "The Country Husband" in the first-person voice and focus of Anne, the baby-sitter. Or imagine it still in third-person but focusing through the experience of Francis Weed's wife, Julia.

Point of view may be limited to a **first-person narrator** ("I"), such as Montresor in Edgar Allan Poe's "The Cask of Amontillado." Sometimes such a narrator addresses an **auditor,** an audience within the fiction whose possible reaction is part of the story. Montresor is telling someone what happened one evening fifty years ago. (The beginning of the second sentence, "You, who so well know the nature of my soul," suggests that Montresor is speaking to a friend.) Poe's story is controlled by Montresor's point of view: both what he perceived during his act of revenge and what he says about it years later. We never know what the victim, Fortunato, is thinking. We must rely almost entirely on what Montresor tells his listener about Fortunato in the absence of any witnesses and the victim himself.

Reading a story told in the first person resembles our everyday efforts to understand what people tell us about themselves. In a story, we can find signals that suggest the right mixture of sympathy and distrust to give the speaker. Often a first-person narrator unintentionally reveals herself—the reader can see her flaws—as she tries to be impressive. Sometimes a first-person narrator gives false or distorted information. Some fictions are narrated by villains (Montresor surely counts), insane people, fools, liars, or hypocrites. When we resist a narrator's point of view and judge his or her flaws or misperceptions, we call that narrator **unreliable.** Successful first-person fictions often leave us undecided about the reliability of their narrators or speakers. When you encounter them later in this book, ask yourself how much you trust Sister in Eudora Welty's "Why I Live at the P.O.," the lawyer in Herman Melville's "Bartleby, the Scrivener," the townspeople in William Faulkner's "A Rose for Emily," and the Duke of Ferrara in Robert Browning's poem "My Last Duchess."

> *This is a work of history in fictional form—that is, in personal perspective, which is the only kind of history that exists.*
> —JOYCE CAROL OATES

First-person narration isn't the only type that gives us a limited focus on one character, of course. Readers can gain a privileged insight into one character's experiences through third-person narration as well. Many narratives, from novels to short stories to films, focus on a **centered** or **central consciousness,** filtering things, people, and events through an individual character's perceptions and responses. The modern short story, with its tightly controlled range, often centers on one character's changing state of mind in an ordinary situation during a brief period of time. In third-person narratives, a reader may identify, close-up, with a complex personality but also take in the whole picture, with a bit of distance or perspective on that personality. In John Cheever's "The Country Husband," for example, the narrator slides easily from describing the outer world of a suburban morning to stating the perceptions, feelings, and thoughts of Francis Weed: "The sky shone like enamel. Even the smell of ink from his morning paper honed his appetite for life, and the world that was spread out around him was plainly a paradise." Cheever's story maintains some distance from Francis, though his perceptions dominate the story. Decisions about point of view and narration ensure the right balance of empathy and judgment that the story needs.

Some stories are more interested in setting contradictory versions of reality side by side than in narrating one person's psychological development. The conflict in Edith Wharton's "Roman Fever" depends on our being privileged to overhear Mrs. Slade's hateful thoughts about Mrs. Ansley and to get strategic glimpses of what Mrs. Ansley is thinking about her adversary. Both characters are deceived, the contempt or pity each woman feels for the other being misplaced in light of events that neither fully understood.

Readers quickly learn a story's rules and can tolerate different sorts of rules within one story or among different stories. After all, this is fiction. There are stories in this book, such as William Faulkner's "Barn Burning" and Flannery O'Connor's "The Lame Shall Enter First," in which the point of view shifts—or jumps—from a previously established centered consciousness. The shift may strike us as breaking the rules of the story, or we may need to adjust our understanding of what the story is trying to do. Some stories make a point of asking us to revise our expectations, to bend our rules both for reality and for storytelling. If the narrator refuses to choose what "really" happened, as in Margaret Atwood's "Happy Endings" or Lorrie Moore's "How," we as readers must think about alternatives; the story may be *about* making choices in stories as well as in life. When we read Peter Carey's "Do You Love Me?," we accept the premise that there is a country which must take an annual "census" or "total inventory" during the "Festival of the Corn." The question then becomes not *Is this narrator mad or untrustworthy?* but *How does such an imaginary reality work?* Science fiction or speculative fiction works with such alteration of the familiar rules of our own countries or physical universe. The narrative voice and focus, as in "Do You Love Me?," may seem rational and scientifically objective, like an article in *National Geographic*. A reader should believe the imaginary facts, at least in the first part of the story. Indeed, it adds immeasurably to the pleasure we can derive from stories if we consent, as listeners or readers, to whatever the teller pretends or affirms. Discovering the way the rules work in any story is the first big step to understanding its whole effect, and hence its fresh way of making order out of experience.

Lorrie Moore's "How" has a consistent, limited focus on a central consciousness, but instead of being told in the third person and past tense like "The Country Husband," Moore's story uses **second-person narration**, mostly in the future tense. (Other authors—notably Jay McInerney in his novel *Bright Lights, Big City* [1984]—have employed the second-person voice, creating an effect similar to conversational anecdotes. Contemporary stories often use present tense, but the future tense is extremely rare.) "How" is designed as a parody of a self-help book, offering advice or instructions to "you." At times, you, the flesh-and-blood reader, may identify yourself as the person addressed, even if you are not a young, urban woman who works in an office and seeks relationships other than marriage. At other times, you may imagine "you" as a character. Will the auditor, "you," follow the unidentified narrator's advice? What choices will she make? Is this a clever game played with fiction, or does it convey the difficulty of living out one's own indecisive and conflicted experience?

*There are as many opinions as there are people: each has his own point of view.*
—TERENCE

"How" may be limited to a central consciousness, but that individual is deliberately generic: "you" might be anyone with a similar lifestyle. Ernest Hemingway's "Hills Like White Elephants" takes a different tack by portraying generic characters. Hemingway's third-person narrator takes an unlimited or objective position outside *all* the characters. "Hills Like White Elephants" is a masterpiece of external narration; it seems odd to apply the term *omniscient* to a narrator who knows—or is willing to tell us—so little about the characters. Neither the American nor the girl is a favorite or focal character. True, we see what the girl sees when she looks at the landscape, but we hear only what she says, not what she thinks. In a long paragraph at the end, the narrative camera follows the American as he goes to the bar alone, but it does not report his feelings about the recent argument. The effect of this method is both close-up—as though we too were at the station, eavesdropping on the couple—and remote, almost as out of touch as the lives of these two transients. *Almost,* because minimal, precise clues help us decipher the young woman's pain and the couple's denial. Thus the narration and point of view are exactly right for this incisive but detached story.

> *Narrative teases me. I have little concern in the progress of events.*
> —CHARLES LAMB

To appreciate and enjoy a story, then, you need to find out how it is being told and by whom: you should identify the narrator and the point of view. Sometimes the narrator is a character, like Montresor in Poe's story, and sometimes the narrator has a clear personality even if he or she played no part in the events. At other times, readers may answer the question "Who is telling this story?" with the name of the author. It may seem, for example, that Sherman Alexie himself is the narrator of "Flight Patterns." This can be misleading, however. In most cases, the narrator should not necessarily be identified with the author, even when there is little to distinguish their personalities or experiences from each other. Of course, we can dig up a few facts about the author's life and read them into the story, or, worse, read the character or detail of the story into the author's life, as if a writer has no freedom to invent different people. It is more prudent, however, especially on the basis of a single story, to speak not of the author but of the author's **persona,** the voice or figure of the author who designs the story and creates the narrator who tells it. This persona may or may not resemble in nature or values the actual person of the author. Mary Anne Evans wrote novels under the name George Eliot; her first-person narrator speaks of "himself." That male authorial persona is close to the voice and focus of the masculine narrator of her novels, and neither should be confused with the brilliant, learned Victorian woman with the rather difficult life and poor health. Most authors create such a persona or representative to "write" their stories, wishing perhaps to keep the questions of their own failings or limitations out of the way.

We say *write* the stories. But just as poets write of singing their songs (their poems), so we often speak of telling a story, and we speak of a narrator, which means a teller. There are stories, usually with first-person narrators, that make much of the convention of oral storytelling—Louise Erdrich's "Love Medicine," for example. Stories with auditors, such as "The Cask of Amontillado" or "Why I Live at the P.O.," also have a kind of "oral" feeling. They may remind us of the acts of telling and listening that are so basic to human communities and communication. Children love to hear a story read aloud, even if they have already read it to themselves many times. Older readers, too, enjoy imagining a narrative as a scene of telling. We know that we are only reading words on a page, but we imagine the narrator speaking to us, giving shape, focus, and voice to a particular history.

EDGAR ALLAN POE

# The Cask of Amontillado

The thousand injuries of Fortunato I had borne as I best could, but when he ventured upon insult I vowed revenge. You, who so well know the nature of my soul, will not suppose, however, that I gave utterance to a threat. *At length* I would be avenged; this was a point definitively settled—but the very definitiveness with which it was resolved precluded the idea of risk. I must not only punish but punish with impunity. A wrong is unredressed when retribution overtakes its redresser. It is equally unredressed when the avenger fails to make himself felt as such to him who has done the wrong.

It must be understood that neither by word nor deed had I given Fortunato cause to doubt my good will. I continued, as was my wont, to smile in his face, and he did not perceive that my smile *now* was at the thought of his immolation.

He had a weak point—this Fortunato—although in other regards he was a man to be respected and even feared. He prided himself upon his connoisseurship in wine. Few Italians have the true virtuoso spirit. For the most part their enthusiasm is adopted to suit the time and opportunity, to practice imposture upon the British and Austrian *millionaires*. In painting and gemmary, Fortunato, like his countrymen, was a quack, but in the matter of old wines he was sincere. In this respect I did not differ from him materially;—I was skilful in the Italian vintages myself, and bought largely whenever I could.

It was about dusk, one evening during the supreme madness of the carnival season, that I encountered my friend. He accosted me with excessive warmth, for he had been drinking much. The man wore motley. He had on a tight-fitting parti-striped dress,[1] and his head was surmounted by the conical cap and bells. I was so pleased to see him that I should never have done wringing his hand.

I said to him—"My dear Fortunato, you are luckily met. How remarkably well you are looking to-day. But I have received a pipe[2] of what passes for Amontillado, and I have my doubts."

"How?" said he. "Amontillado? A pipe? Impossible! And in the middle of the carnival!"

"I have my doubts," I replied; "and I was silly enough to pay the full Amontillado price without consulting you in the matter. You were not to be found, and I was fearful of losing a bargain."

"Amontillado!"

"I have my doubts."

"Amontillado!"

"And I must satisfy them."

"Amontillado!"

"As you are engaged, I am on my way to Luchresi. If any one has a critical turn it is he. He will tell me—"

"Luchresi cannot tell Amontillado from Sherry."

"And yet some fools will have it that his taste is a match for your own."

"Come, let us go."

"Whither?"

---

1. Fortunato wears a jester's costume (i.e., motley), not a woman's dress.  2. A large cask.

"To your vaults."

"My friend, no; I will not impose upon your good nature. I perceive you have an engagement. Luchresi—"

"I have no engagement;—come."

"My friend, no. It is not the engagement, but the severe cold with which I perceive you are afflicted. The vaults are insufferably damp. They are encrusted with nitre."

"Let us go, nevertheless. The cold is merely nothing. Amontillado! You have been imposed upon. And as for Luchresi, he cannot distinguish Sherry from Amontillado."

Thus speaking, Fortunato possessed himself of my arm; and putting on a mask of black silk and drawing a *roquelaire*[3] closely about my person, I suffered him to hurry me to my palazzo.

There were no attendants at home; they had absconded to make merry in honour of the time. I had told them that I should not return until the morning, and had given them explicit orders not to stir from the house. These orders were sufficient, I well knew, to insure their immediate disappearance, one and all, as soon as my back was turned.

I took from their sconces two flambeaux,[4] and giving one to Fortunato, bowed him through several suites of rooms to the archway that led into the vaults. I passed down a long and winding staircase, requesting him to be cautious as he followed. We came at length to the foot of the descent, and stood together upon the damp ground of the catacombs of the Montresors.

The gait of my friend was unsteady, and the bells upon his cap jingled as he strode.

"The pipe," said he.

"It is farther on," said I; "but observe the white web-work which gleams from these cavern walls."

He turned towards me, and looked into my eyes with two filmy orbs that distilled the rheum of intoxication.

"Nitre[5]?" he asked, at length.

"Nitre," I replied. "How long have you had that cough?"

"Ugh! ugh! ugh!—ugh! ugh! ugh!—ugh! ugh! ugh!—ugh! ugh! ugh!—ugh! ugh! ugh!"

My poor friend found it impossible to reply for many minutes.

"It is nothing," he said, at last.

"Come," I said, with decision, "we will go back; your health is precious. You are rich, respected, admired, beloved; you are happy, as once I was. You are a man to be missed. For me it is no matter. We will go back; you will be ill, and I cannot be responsible. Besides, there is Luchresi—"

"Enough," he said; "the cough is a mere nothing; it will not kill me. I shall not die of a cough."

"True—true," I replied; "and, indeed, I had no intention of alarming you unneccessarily—but you should use all proper caution. A draught of this Medoc[6] will defend us from the damps."

---

3. Man's heavy, knee-length cloak.   4. That is, two torches from their wall brackets.
5. Potassium nitrate (saltpeter), a white mineral often found on the walls of damp caves, and used in gunpowder.   6. Like De Grâve (below), a French wine.

Here I knocked off the neck of a bottle which I drew from a long row of its fellows that lay upon the mould.

"Drink," I said, presenting him the wine.

He raised it to his lips with a leer. He paused and nodded to me familiarly, while his bells jingled.

"I drink," he said, "to the buried that repose around us."

"And I to your long life."

He again took my arm, and we proceeded.

"These vaults," he said, "are extensive."

"The Montresors," I replied, "were a great and numerous family."

"I forget your arms."

"A huge human foot d'or,[7] in a field azure; the foot crushes a serpent rampant whose fangs are imbedded in the heel."

"And the motto?"

*"Nemo me impune lacessit."*[8]

"Good!" he said.

The wine sparkled in his eyes and the bells jingled. My own fancy grew warm with the Medoc. We had passed through long walls of piled skeletons, with casks and puncheons[9] intermingling, into the inmost recesses of the catacombs. I paused again, and this time I made bold to seize Fortunato by an arm above the elbow.

"The nitre!" I said; "see, it increases. It hangs like moss upon the vaults. We are below the river's bed. The drops of moisture trickle among the bones. Come, we will go back ere it is too late. Your cough——"

"It is nothing," he said; "let us go on. But first, another draught of the Medoc."

I broke and reached him a flaçon of De Grâve. He emptied it at a breath. His eyes flashed with a fierce light. He laughed and threw the bottle upwards with a gesticulation I did not understand.

I looked at him in surprise. He repeated the movement—a grotesque one.

"You do not comprehend?" he said.

"Not I," I replied.

"Then you are not of the brotherhood."

"How?"

"You are not of the masons."[1]

"Yes, yes," I said; "yes, yes."

"You? Impossible! A mason?"

"A mason," I replied.

"A sign," he said, "a sign."

"It is this," I answered producing from beneath the folds of my *roquelaire* a trowel.

"You jest," he exclaimed, recoiling a few paces. "But let us proceed to the Amontillado."

"Be it so," I said, replacing the tool beneath the cloak and again offering him my arm. He leaned upon it heavily. We continued our route in search of the Amontillado. We passed through a range of low arches, descended, passed on,

---

7. Of gold.   8. No one provokes me with impunity.   9. Large casks.
1. Masons or Freemasons, an international secret society condemned by the Catholic Church. Montresor means by mason one who builds with stone, brick, etc.

and descending again, arrived at a deep crypt, in which the foulness of the air caused our flambeaux rather to glow than flame.

At the most remote end of the crypt there appeared another less spacious. Its walls had been lined with human remains, piled to the vault overhead, in the fashion of the great catacombs of Paris. Three sides of this interior crypt were still ornamented in this manner. From the fourth side the bones had been thrown down, and lay promiscuously upon the earth, forming at one point a mound of some size. Within the wall thus exposed by the displacing of the bones, we perceived a still interior crypt or recess, in depth about four feet, in width three, in height six or seven. It seemed to have been constructed for no especial use within itself, but formed merely the interval between two of the colossal supports of the roof of the catacombs, and was backed by one of their circumscribing walls of solid granite.

It was in vain that Fortunato, uplifting his dull torch, endeavoured to pry into the depth of the recess. Its termination the feeble light did not enable us to see.

70   "Proceed," I said; "herein is the Amontillado. As for Luchresi——"

"He is an ignoramus," interrupted my friend, as he stepped unsteadily forward, while I followed immediately at his heels. In an instant he had reached the extremity of the niche, and finding his progress arrested by the rock, stood stupidly bewildered. A moment more and I had fettered him to the granite. In its surface were two iron staples, distant from each other about two feet, horizontally. From one of these depended a short chain, from the other a padlock. Throwing the links about his waist, it was but the work of a few seconds to secure it. He was too much astounded to resist. Withdrawing the key I stepped back from the recess.

"Pass your hand," I said, "over the wall; you cannot help feeling the nitre. Indeed, it is *very* damp. Once more let me *implore* you to return. No? Then I must positively leave you. But I will first render you all the little attentions in my power."

"The Amontillado!" ejaculated my friend, not yet recovered from his astonishment.

"True," I replied; "the Amontillado."

75   As I said these words I busied myself among the pile of bones of which I have before spoken. Throwing them aside, I soon uncovered a quantity of building stone and mortar. With these materials and with the aid of my trowel, I began vigorously to wall up the entrance of the niche.

I had scarcely laid the first tier of the masonry when I discovered that the intoxication of Fortunato had in great measure worn off. The earliest indication I had of this was a low moaning cry from the depth of the recess. It was *not* the cry of a drunken man. There was then a long and obstinate silence. I laid the second tier, and the third, and the fourth; and then I heard the furious vibration of the chain. The noise lasted for several minutes, during which, that I might hearken to it with the more satisfaction, I ceased my labours and sat down upon the bones. When at last the clanking subsided, I resumed the trowel, and finished without interruption the fifth, the sixth, and the seventh tier. The wall was now nearly upon a level with my breast. I again paused, and holding the flambeaux over the mason-work, threw a few feeble rays upon the figure within.

A succession of loud and shrill screams, bursting suddenly from the throat of the chained form, seemed to thrust me violently back. For a brief moment I hesitated, I trembled. Unsheathing my rapier, I began to grope with it about the recess; but the thought of an instant reassured me. I placed my hand upon the solid fabric of the catacombs and felt satisfied. I reapproached the wall. I replied to the yells of him who clamoured. I re-echoed, I aided, I surpassed them in volume and in strength. I did this, and the clamourer grew still.

It was now midnight, and my task was drawing to a close. I had completed the eighth, the ninth and the tenth tier. I had finished a portion of the last and the eleventh; there remained but a single stone to be fitted and plastered in. I struggled with its weight; I placed it partially in its destined position. But now there came from out the niche a low laugh that erected the hairs upon my head. It was succeeded by a sad voice, which I had difficulty in recognizing as that of the noble Fortunato. The voice said—

"Ha! ha! ha!—he! he! he!—a very good joke, indeed—an excellent jest. We will have many a rich laugh about it at the palazzo—he! he! he!—over our wine—he! he! he!"

"The Amontillado!" I said.

"He! he! he!—he! he! he!—yes, the Amontillado. But is it not getting late? Will not they be awaiting us at the palazzo—the Lady Fortunato and the rest? Let us be gone."

"Yes," I said, "let us be gone."

*"For the love of God, Montresor!"*

"Yes," I said, "for the love of God!"

But to these words I hearkened in vain for a reply. I grew impatient. I called aloud—

"Fortunato!"

No answer. I called again—

"Fortunato!"

No answer still. I thrust a torch through the remaining aperture and let it fall within. There came forth in return only a jingling of the bells. My heart grew sick; it was the dampness of the catacombs that made it so. I hastened to make an end of my labour. I forced the last stone into its position; I plastered it up. Against the new masonry I re-erected the old rampart of bones. For the half of a century no mortal has disturbed them. *In pace requiescat!*[2]

1846

## QUESTIONS

1. What can the reader infer about Montresor's social position and character from hints in the text? What evidence does the text provide that Montresor is an unreliable narrator?
2. Who is the auditor, the "You," addressed in the first paragraph of "The Cask of Amontillado"? When is the story being told? Why is it being told? How does your knowledge of the auditor and the occasion influence the effect the story has on you?
3. What devices does Poe use to create and heighten the suspense in the story? Is the outcome ever in doubt?

---

2. May he rest in peace!

ERNEST HEMINGWAY

## Hills Like White Elephants

The hills across the valley of the Ebro[1] were long and white. On this side there was no shade and no trees and the station was between two lines of rails in the sun. Close against the side of the station there was the warm shadow of the building and a curtain, made of strings of bamboo beads, hung across the open door into the bar, to keep out flies. The American and the girl with him sat at a table in the shade, outside the building. It was very hot and the express from Barcelona would come in forty minutes. It stopped at this junction for two minutes and went on to Madrid.

"What should we drink?" the girl asked. She had taken off her hat and put it on the table.

"It's pretty hot," the man said.

"Let's drink beer."

"Dos cervezas," the man said into the curtain.

"Big ones?" a woman asked from the doorway.

"Yes. Two big ones."

The woman brought two glasses of beer and two felt pads. She put the felt pads and the beer glasses on the table and looked at the man and the girl. The girl was looking off at the line of hills. They were white in the sun and the country was brown and dry.

"They look like white elephants," she said.

"I've never seen one," the man drank his beer.

"No, you wouldn't have."

"I might have," the man said. "Just because you say I wouldn't have doesn't prove anything."

The girl looked at the bead curtain. "They've painted something on it," she said. "What does it say?"

"Anis del Toro. It's a drink."

"Could we try it?"

The man called "Listen" through the curtain. The woman came out from the bar.

"Four reales."[2]

"We want two Anis del Toro."

"With water?"

"Do you want it with water?"

"I don't know," the girl said. "Is it good with water?"

"It's all right."

"You want them with water?" asked the woman.

"Yes, with water."

"It tastes like licorice," the girl said and put the glass down.

"That's the way with everything."

"Yes," said the girl. "Everything tastes of licorice. Especially all the things you've waited so long for, like absinthe."

---

1. River in northern Spain.   2. Spanish coins.

"Oh, cut it out."

"You started it," the girl said. "I was being amused. I was having a fine time."

"Well, let's try and have a fine time."

"All right. I was trying. I said the mountains looked like white elephants. Wasn't that bright?"

"That was bright."

"I wanted to try this new drink. That's all we do, isn't it—look at things and try new drinks?"

"I guess so."

The girl looked across at the hills.

"They're lovely hills," she said. "They don't really look like white elephants. I just meant the coloring of their skin through the trees."

"Should we have another drink?"

"All right."

The warm wind blew the bead curtain against the table.

"The beer's nice and cool," the man said.

"It's lovely," the girl said.

"It's really an awfully simple operation, Jig," the man said. "It's not really an operation at all."

The girl looked at the ground the table legs rested on.

"I know you wouldn't mind it, Jig. It's really not anything. It's just to let the air in."

The girl did not say anything.

"I'll go with you and I'll stay with you all the time. They just let the air in and then it's all perfectly natural."

"Then what will we do afterward?"

"We'll be fine afterward. Just like we were before."

"What makes you think so?"

"That's the only thing that bothers us. It's the only thing that's made us unhappy."

The girl looked at the bead curtain, put her hand out and took hold of two of the strings of beads.

"And you think then we'll be all right and be happy."

"I know we will. You don't have to be afraid. I've known lots of people that have done it."

"So have I," said the girl. "And afterward they were all so happy."

"Well," the man said, "if you don't want to you don't have to. I wouldn't have you do it if you didn't want to. But I know it's perfectly simple."

"And you really want to?"

"I think it's the best thing to do. But I don't want you to do it if you don't really want to."

"And if I do it you'll be happy and things will be like they were and you'll love me?"

"I love you now. You know I love you."

"I know. But if I do it, then it will be nice again if I say things are like white elephants, and you'll like it?"

"I'll love it. I love it now but I just can't think about it. You know how I get when I worry."

"If I do it you won't ever worry?"

"I won't worry about that because it's perfectly simple."

"Then I'll do it. Because I don't care about me."

"What do you mean?"

"I don't care about me."

"Well, I care about you."

"Oh, yes. But I don't care about me. And I'll do it and then everything will be fine."

"I don't want you to do it if you feel that way."

The girl stood up and walked to the end of the station. Across, on the other side, were fields of grain and trees along the banks of the Ebro. Far away, beyond the river, were mountains. The shadow of a cloud moved across the field of grain and she saw the river through the trees.

"And we could have all this," she said. "And we could have everything and every day we make it more impossible."

"What did you say?"

"I said we could have everything."

"We can have everything."

"No, we can't."

"We can have the whole world."

"No, we can't."

"We can go everywhere."

"No, we can't. It isn't ours any more."

"It's ours."

"No, it isn't. And once they take it away, you never get it back."

"But they haven't taken it away."

"We'll wait and see."

"Come on back in the shade," he said. "You mustn't feel that way."

"I don't feel any way," the girl said. "I just know things."

"I don't want you to do anything that you don't want to do—"

"Nor that isn't good for me," she said. "I know. Could we have another beer?"

"All right. But you've got to realize—"

"I realize," the girl said. "Can't we maybe stop talking?"

They sat down at the table and the girl looked across at the hills on the dry side of the valley and the man looked at her and at the table.

"You've got to realize," he said, "that I don't want you to do it if you don't want to. I'm perfectly willing to go through with it if it means anything to you."

"Doesn't it mean anything to you? We could get along."

"Of course it does. But I don't want anybody but you. I don't want any one else. And I know it's perfectly simple."

"Yes, you know it's perfectly simple."

"It's all right for you to say that, but I do know it."

"Would you do something for me now?"

"I'd do anything for you."

"Would you please please please please please please please stop talking?"

He did not say anything but looked at the bags against the wall of the station. There were labels on them from all the hotels where they had spent nights.

"But I don't want you to," he said, "I don't care anything about it."

"I'll scream," the girl said.

The woman came out through the curtains with two glasses of beer and put them down on the damp felt pads. "The train comes in five minutes," she said.

"What did she say?" asked the girl.

"That the train is coming in five minutes."

The girl smiled brightly at the woman, to thank her.

"I'd better take the bags over to the other side of the station," the man said. She smiled at him.

"All right. Then come back and we'll finish the beer."

He picked up the two heavy bags and carried them around the station to the other tracks. He looked up the tracks but could not see the train. Coming back, he walked through the barroom, where people waiting for the train were drinking. He drank an Anis at the bar and looked at the people. They were all waiting reasonably for the train. He went out through the bead curtain. She was sitting at the table and smiled at him.

"Do you feel better?" he asked.

"I feel fine," she said. "There's nothing wrong with me. I feel fine."

1927

## QUESTIONS

1. Find the first indication in "Hills Like White Elephants" that the two main characters are not getting along. What is the first clue about the exact nature of their conflict? Why are they going to Madrid? Why do the characters (and the author) refrain from speaking about it explicitly?
2. Point of view includes what characters see. Notice each use of the word "look." What does each person in the story look at, and what does each person seem to understand or feel? Is there anything in the story that none of these people would be able to see or know? How do the different kinds of observation add to the effect of the story?
3. Research the phrase "white elephant." What is the significance of this phrase in the story's title?

## LORRIE MOORE
# How

*So all things limp together for the only possible.* —BECKETT, *Murphy*[1]

Begin by meeting him in a class, in a bar, at a rummage sale. Maybe he teaches sixth grade. Manages a hardware store. Foreman at a carton factory. He will be a good dancer. He will have perfectly cut hair. He will laugh at your jokes.

A week, a month, a year. Feel discovered, comforted, needed, loved, and start sometimes, somehow, to feel bored. When sad or confused, walk uptown to the

---

1. Samuel Beckett (1906-1989), Nobel Prize-winning Irish novelist and playwright who lived in France, perhaps best known today through his play *Waiting for Godot*. This epigraph, from his 1938 novel, *Murphy*, is representative of Beckett's absurdist vision and verbal experimentation.

movies. Buy popcorn. These things come and go. A week, a month, a year.

Make attempts at a less restrictive arrangement. Watch them sputter and deflate like balloons. He will ask you to move in. Do so hesitantly, with ambivalence. Clarify: rents are high, nothing long-range, love and all that, hon, but it's footloose. Lay out the rules with much elocution. Stress openness, nonexclusivity. Make room in his closet, but don't rearrange the furniture.

And yet from time to time you will gaze at his face or his hands and want nothing but him. You will feel passing waves of dependency, devotion, and sentimentality. A week, a month, a year, and he has become your family. Let's say your real mother is a witch. Your father a warlock. Your brothers twin hunchbacks of Notre Dame. They all live in a cave together somewhere.

5    His name means savior. He rolls into your arms like Ozzie and Harriet, the whole Nelson genealogy. He is living rooms and turkey and mantels and Vicks, a nip at the collarbone and you do a slow syrup sink into those arms like a hearth, into those living rooms, well hello Mary Lou.[2]

Say you work in an office but you have bigger plans. He wants to go with you. He wants to be what it is that you want to be. Say you're an aspiring architect. Playwright. Painter. He shows you his sketches. They are awful. What do you think?

Put on some jazz. Take off your clothes. Carefully. It is a craft. He will lie on the floor naked, watching, his arms crossed behind his head. Shirt: brush on snare, steady. Skirt: the desultory talk of piano keys, rocking slow, rambling. Dance together in the dark though it is only afternoon.

Go to a wedding. His relatives. Everyone will compare weight losses and gains. Maiden cousins will be said to have fattened embarrassingly. His mother will be a bookkeeper or a dental hygienist. She will introduce you as his *girl*. Try not to protest. They will have heard a lot about you. Uncles will take him aside and query, What is keeping you, boy? Uncomfortable, everywhere, women in stiff blue taffeta will eye you pitifully, then look quickly away. Everyone will polka. Someone will flash a fifty to dance with the bride and she will hike up her gown and flash back: freshly shaven legs, a wide rolled-out-barrel of a grin. Feel spared. Thought you two'd be doing this by now, you will hear again. Smile. Shrug. Shuffle back for more potato salad.

It hits you more insistently. A restlessness. A virus of discontent. When you pass other men in the street, smile and stare them straight in the eye, straight in the belt buckle.

---

2. A popular song by Ricky Nelson includes the refrain "So hello Mary Lou / Goodbye heart." Ozzie and Harriet were the lead characters in a popular family TV show of the 1950s starring Nelson, his parents, and his brother.

Somehow—in a restaurant or a store—meet an actor. From Vassar or Yale. He can quote Coriolanus's mother.³ This will seem good. Sleep with him once and ride home at 5 a.m. crying in a taxicab. Or: don't sleep with him. Kiss him good night at Union Square and run for your life.

Back at home, days later, feel cranky and tired. Sit on the couch and tell him he's stupid. That you bet he doesn't know who Coriolanus is. That since you moved in you've noticed he rarely reads. He will give you a hurt, hungry-to-learn look, with his James Cagney⁴ eyes. He will try to kiss you. Turn your head. Feel suffocated.

When he climbs onto the covers, naked and hot for you, unleash your irritation in short staccato blasts. Show him your book. Your aspirin. Your clock on the table reading 12:45. He will flop back over to his side of the bed, exasperated. Maybe he'll say something like: Christ, what's wrong? Maybe he won't. If he spends too long in the bathroom, don't ask questions.

The touchiest point will always be this: he craves a family, a neat nest of human bowls; he wants to have your children. On the street he pats their heads. In the supermarket they gather around him by the produce. They form a tight little cluster of cheeks and smiles and hopes. They look like grapes. It will all be for you, baby; reel, sway backward into the frozen foods. An unwitting sigh will escape from your lips like gas. He will begin to talk about a movie camera and children's encyclopedias, picking up size-one shoes in department stores and marveling in one high, amazed whistle. Avoid shopping together.

He will have a nephew named Bradley Bob. Or perhaps a niece named Emily who is always dressed in pink and smells of milk and powder and dirty diapers, although she is already three. At visits she will prance and squeal. She will grab his left leg like a tree trunk and not let go. She will call him nunko. He will know tricks: pulling dimes from her nose, quarters from her ears. She will shriek with glee, flapping her hands in front of her. Leg released, he will pick her up, carry her around like a prize. He is the best nunko in town.

Think about leaving. About packing a bag and slithering off, out the door.
But it is hot out there. And dry. And he can look somehow good to you, like Robert Goulet in a bathing suit.
No, it wouldn't be in summer.⁵

Escape into books. When he asks what you're reading, hold it up without comment. The next day look across to the brown chair and you will see him reading it too. A copy from the library that morning. He has seven days. He will look over the top and wink, saying: Beat you.

---

3. *Coriolanus* is a violent, disturbing tragedy by William Shakespeare; it is rarely produced today.
4. Early Hollywood movie star (1899–1986), more tough guy than romantic lead.
5. Robert Goulet starred as Lancelot in the 1960s musical *Camelot*; the lyrics for one of his character's songs included "If ever I would leave you, / How could it be in summer . . . or winter or fall?"

He will seem to be listening to the classical music station, glancing quickly at you for approval.

At the theater he will chomp Necco wafers loudly and complain about the head in front of him.

He will ask you what *supercilious* means.

He will ask you who Coriolanus is.

He might want to know where Sardinia is located.

What's a *croissant*?

Begin to plot your getaway. Envision possibilities for civility. These are only possibilities.

A week, a month, a year: Tell him you've changed. You no longer like the same music, eat the same food. You dress differently. The two of you are incongruous together. When he tells you that he is changing too, that he loves your records, your teas, your falafel, your shoes, tell him: See, that's the problem. Endeavor to baffle.

Pace around in the kitchen and say that you are unhappy.

But I love you, he will say in his soft, bewildered way, stirring the spaghetti sauce but not you, staring into the pan as if waiting for something, a magic fish, to rise from it and say: That is always enough, why is that not always enough?

You will forget whoever it was that said never trust a thought that doesn't come while walking. But clutch at it. Apartments can shrink inward like drying ponds. You will gasp. Say: I am going for a walk. When he follows you to the door, buzzing at your side like a fly by a bleeding woman, add: *alone*. He will look surprised and hurt and you will hate him. Slam the door, out, down, hurry, it will be colder than you thought, but not far away will be a bar, smoky and dark and sticky with spilled sours. The bartender will be named Rusty or Max and he will know you. A flashy jukebox will blare Jimmy Webb.[6] A balding, purple-shirted man to your left will try to get your attention, mouthing, singing drunkenly. Someone to your right will sniffle to the music. Blink into your drink. Hide behind your hair. Sweet green icing will be flowing down.[7] Flowing, baby, like the Mississippi.

Next: there are medical unpleasantries. Kidneys. He will pee blood. Say you can't believe it. When he shows you later, it will be dark, the color of meat drippings. A huge invisible fist will torpedo through your gut, your face, your pounding heart.

This is no time to leave.

---

6. Jimmy Webb (b. 1946), American songwriter who won many Grammys in the later 1960s for such hits as "By the Time I Get to Phoenix," "Wichita Lineman," "Up, Up and Away," and "MacArthur Park."
7. Webb's "MacArthur Park" includes the lines "MacArthur Park is melting in the dark, / All the sweet green icing flowing down."

There will be doctor's appointments, various opinions. There is nothing conclusive, just an endless series of tests. He will have jarred urine specimens in the refrigerator among the eggs and peanut butter. Some will be in salad dressing bottles. They will be different colors: some green, some purple, some brown. Ask which is the real salad dressing. He will point it out and smile helplessly. Smile back. He will begin to laugh and so will you. Collapse. Roll. Roar together on the floor until you cannot laugh anymore. Bury your face in the crook of his neck. There will be nothing else in the world you can do. That night lie next to each other, silent, stiff, silvery-white in bed. Lie like sewing needles.

Continue to doctor-hop. Await the reports. Look at your watch. If ever you would leave him. Look at your calendar. It wouldn't be in autumn.

There is never anything conclusive, just an endless series of tests.

Once a week you will feel in love with him again. Massage his lower back when it is aching. Lay your cheek against him, feeling, listening for his kidneys. Stay like that all night, never quite falling asleep, never quite wanting to.

The thought will occur to you that you are waiting for him to die.

You will meet another actor. Or maybe it's the same one. Begin to have an affair. Begin to lie. Have dinner with him and his Modigliani-necked mother.[8] She will smoke cigars, play with the fondue, discuss the fallacy of feminine maternal instinct. Afterward, you will all get high.

There is never anything conclusive, just an endless series of tests.

And could you leave him tripping merrily through the snow?

You will fantasize about a funeral. At that you could cry. It would be a study in post-romantic excess, something vaguely Wagnerian.[9] You would be comforted by his lugubrious sisters and his dental hygienist mom. The four of you in the cemetery would throw yourselves at his grave's edge, heaving and sobbing like old Israeli women. You, in particular, would shout, bare your wrists, shake them at the sky, foam at the mouth. There would be no shame, no dignity. You would fly immediately to Acapulco and lounge drunk and malodorous in the casinos until three.

After dinners with the actor: creep home. Your stomach will get fluttery, your steps smaller as you approach the door. Neighbors will be playing music you recall from your childhood—an opera about a pretty lady who was bad and cut a man's hair in his sleep.[1] You recall, recall your grandfather playing it with a

---

8. Amedeo Modigliani (1884–1920), Italian painter famous for nudes with elongated features.
9. Richard Wagner (1813–1883), German composer of massive, stormy operas.
1. Delilah cut the Old Testament hero Samson's hair while he slept, as depicted in the opera *Samson et Dalila*, by Camille Saint-Saëns (1835–1921), first performed in 1877; *Ray pawned off my ten dresses:* an English-speaking child's hearing of *Samson et Dalila's* original French lyric, *réponds à ma tendresse!* ("respond to my affection!"), as sung by Dalila ("Dolly-la").

sort of wrath, his visage laminated with Old Testament righteousness, the violins warming, the scenario unfolding now as you stand outside the door. Ray pawned off my ten dresses: it cascades like a waterfall. Dolly-la, Dolly-la: it is the wail, the next to the last good solo of a doomed man.

Tiptoe. It won't matter. He will be sitting up in bed looking empty. Kiss him, cajole him. Make love to him like never before. At four in the morning you will still be awake, staring at the ceiling. You will horrify yourself.

Thoughts of leaving will move in, bivouac throughout the living room; they will have eyes like rodents and peer out at you from under the sofa, in the dark, from under the sink, luminous glass beads positioned in twos. The houseplants will appear to have chosen sides. Some will thrust stems at you like angry limbs. They will seem to caw like crows. Others will simply sag.

When you go out, leave him with a sinkful of dirty dishes. He will slowly dry them with paper towels, his skin scalded red beneath the wet, flattened hair of his forearms. You will be tempted to tell him to leave them, or to use the terrycloth in the drawer. But you won't. You will put on your coat and hurry away.

When you return, the bathroom light will be on. You will see blouses of yours that he has washed by hand. They will hang in perfect half-inches, dripping, scolding from the shower curtain rod. They will be buttoned with his Cagney eyes, faintly hooded, the twinkle sad and dulled.
Slip quietly under the covers; hold his sleeping hand.
There is never anything conclusive.

At work you will be lachrymose and distracted. You will shamble through the hall like a legume with feet. People will notice.

Nightmares have seasons like hurricanes. Be prepared. You will dream that someone with a violin case is trailing you through the city. Little children come at you with grins and grenades. You may bolt awake with a spasm, reach for him, and find he is not there, but lost in his own sleep, somnambulant, is roaming through the apartment like an old man, babbling gibberish, bumping into tables and lamps, a blanket he has torn from the bed wrapped clumsily around him, toga-style. Get up. Go to him. Touch him. At first he will look at you, wide-eyed, and not see. Put your arms around his waist. He will wake and gasp and cry into your hair. In a minute he will know where he is.

Dream about rainbows, about escapes, about wizards. Your past will fly by you, event by event, like Dorothy's tornadoed neighborhood, past the blown-out window.[2] Airborne. One by one. Wave hello, good-bye. Practice.

Begin to call in sick. Make sure it is after he has already left for work. Sit in a rocking chair. Stare around at the apartment. It will be mid-morning and

---

2. In the film *The Wizard of Oz*, Dorothy dreams of a place "somewhere over the rainbow," and her home is struck by a tornado.

flooded in a hush of sunlight. You rarely see it like this. It will seem strangely deserted, premonitory. There will be apricots shrunk to buttons on the windowsill. A fly will bang stupidly against the panes. The bed will lie open, revealed, like something festering, the wrinkles in the sheets marking time, marking territory like the capillaries of a map. Rock. Hush. Breathe.

On the night you finally tell him, take him out to dinner. Translate the entrees for him. When you are home, lying in bed together, tell him that you are going to leave. He will look panicked, but not surprised. Perhaps he will say, Look, I don't care who else you're seeing or anything: what is your reason?

Do not attempt to bandy words. Tell him you do not love him anymore. It will make him cry, rivulets wending their way into his ears. You will start to feel sick. He will say something like: Well, you lose some, you lose some. You are supposed to laugh. Exhale. Blow your nose. Flick off the light. Have a sense of humor, he will whisper into the black. Have a heart.

Make him breakfast. He will want to know where you will go. Reply: To the actor. Or: To the hunchbacks. He will not eat your breakfast. He will glare at it, stir it around the plate with a fork, and then hurl it against the wall.

When you walk up Third Avenue toward the IRT,[3] do it quickly. You will have a full bag. People will seem to know what you have done, where you are going. They will have his eyes, the same pair, passed along on the street from face to face, like secrets, like glasses at the opera.

This is how you are.
Rushing downstairs into the steamy burn of the subway.
Unable to look a panhandler in the pan.

You will never see him again. Or perhaps you will be sitting in Central Park one April eating your lunch and he will trundle by on roller skates. You will greet him with a wave and a mouth full of sandwich. He will nod, but he will not stop.

There will be an endless series of tests.

A week, a month, a year. The sadness will die like an old dog. You will feel nothing but indifference. The logy whine of a cowboy harmonica, plaintive, weary, it will fade into the hills slow as slow Hank Williams.[4] One of those endings.

1985

---

3. One of the lines of the New York City subway system.
4. (Hiram) Hank Williams (1923–1953), pioneer of American country music, had many hits in his short, hard life, including "Lovesick Blues" (1949) and "Your Cheatin' Heart" (1953).

## QUESTIONS

1. Elaborate on the title. "How" to *what*? Why do you think Lorrie Moore has adapted the mode of an instructional guide to the purpose of storytelling?
2. Who is the narrator, and who is the audience ("you") addressed by the story?
3. From the first paragraph onward, "How" offers alternative "facts" or circumstances as if it is up to you to choose. Which, if any, aspects of character, action, setting, or circumstances are fixed or certain? For instance, could the story be set in a rural village in the 1920s? Could the main characters be in their sixties?

## PETER CAREY

## *"Do You Love Me?"*

### 1. *The Role of the Cartographers*

Perhaps a few words about the role of the Cartographers in our present society are warranted.

To begin with one must understand the nature of the yearly census, a manifestation of our desire to know, always, exactly where we stand. The census, originally a count of the population, has gradually extended until it has become a total inventory of the contents of the nation, a mammoth task which is continuing all the time—no sooner has one census been announced than work on another begins.

The results of the census play an important part in our national life and have, for many years, been the pivot point for the yearly "Festival of the Corn" (an ancient festival, related to the wealth of the earth).[1]

We have a passion for lists. And nowhere is this more clearly illustrated than in the Festival of the Corn which takes place in midsummer, the weather always being fine and warm. On the night of the festival, the householders move their goods and possessions, all furniture, electrical goods, clothing, rugs, kitchen utensils, bathrobes, slippers, cushions, lawnmowers, curtains, doorstops, heirlooms, cameras, and anything else that can be moved into the street so that the census officials may the more easily check the inventory of each household.

5   The Festival of the Corn is, however, much more than a clerical affair. And, the day over and the night come, the householders invite each other to view their possessions which they refer to, on this night, as gifts. It is like nothing more than a wedding feast—there is much cooking, all sorts of traditional dishes, fine wines, strong liquors, music is played loudly in quiet neighborhoods, strangers copulate with strangers, men dance together, and maidens in yellow robes distribute small barley sugar corn-cobs to young and old alike.

And in all this the role of the Cartographers is perhaps the most important, for our people crave, more than anything else, to know the extent of the nation, to know, exactly, the shape of the coastline, to hear what land may have been lost to the sea, to know what has been reclaimed and what is still in doubt. If the Cartographers' report is good the Festival of the Corn will be a good festival.

---

1. Many traditional cultures (American Indian, ancient Greek, etc.) mark the beginning of the harvest season with rituals and feasting. "Corn" can denote any cereal crop, such as wheat or oats.

If the report is bad, one can always sense, for all the dancing and drinking, a feeling of nervousness and apprehension in the revelers, a certain desperation. In the year of a bad Cartographers' report there will always be fights and, occasionally, some property will be stolen as citizens attempt to compensate themselves for their sense of loss.

Because of the importance of their job the Cartographers have become an elite—well-paid, admired, envied, and having no small opinion of themselves. It is said by some that they are overproud, immoral, vain and footloose, and it is perhaps the last charge (by necessity true) that brings about the others. For the Cartographers spend their years traveling up and down the coast, along the great rivers, traversing great mountains and vast deserts. They travel in small parties of three, four, sometimes five, making their own time, working as they please, because eventually it is their own responsibility to see that their team's task is completed in time.

My father, a Cartographer himself, often told me stories about himself or his colleagues and the adventures they had in the wilderness.

There were other stories, however, that always remained in my mind and, as a child, caused me considerable anxiety. These were the stories of the nether regions and I doubt if they were known outside a very small circle of Cartographers and government officials. As a child in a house frequented by Cartographers, I often heard these tales which invariably made me cling closely to my mother's skirts.

It appears that for some time certain regions of the country had become less and less real and these regions were regarded fearfully even by the Cartographers, who prided themselves on their courage. The regions in question were invariably uninhabited, unused for agriculture or industry. There were certain sections of the Halverson Ranges, vast stretches of the Greater Desert,[2] and long pieces of coastline which had begun to slowly disappear like the image on an improperly fixed photograph.

It was because of these nebulous areas that the Fischerscope[3] was introduced. The Fischerscope is not unlike radar in its principle and is able to detect the presence of any object, no matter how dematerialized or insubstantial. In this way the Cartographers were still able to map the questionable parts of the nether regions. To have returned with blanks on the maps would have created such public anxiety that no one dared think what it might do to the stability of our society. I now have reason to believe that certain areas of the country disappeared so completely that even the Fischerscope could not detect them and the Cartographers, acting under political pressure, used old maps to fake-in the missing sections. If my theory is grounded in fact, and I am sure it is, it would explain my father's cynicism about the Festival of the Corn.

## 2. The Archetypal Cartographer

My father was in his fifties but he had kept himself in good shape. His skin was brown and his muscles still firm. He was a tall man with a thick head of gray hair, a slightly less gray mustache and a long aquiline nose. Sitting on a horse

---

2. Fanciful locations.
3. Fischerscope uses x-rays to determine the thickness and hardness of metallic coatings.

he looked as proud and cruel as Genghis Khan.[4] Lying on the beach clad only in bathers and sunglasses he still managed to retain his authoritative air.

Beside him I always felt as if I had betrayed him. I was slightly built, more like my mother.

It was the day before the festival and we lay on the beach, my father, my mother, my girlfriend and I. As was usual in these circumstances my father addressed all his remarks to Karen. He never considered the members of his own family worth talking to. I always had the uncomfortable feeling that he was flirting with my girlfriends and I never knew what to do about it.

People were lying in groups up and down the beach. Near us a family of five were playing with a large beach ball.

"Look at those fools," my father said to Karen.

"Why are they fools?" Karen asked.

"They're fools," said my father. "They were born fools and they'll die fools. Tomorrow they'll dance in the streets and drink too much."

"So," said Karen triumphantly, in the manner of one who has become privy to secret information. "It will be a good Cartographers' report?"

My father roared with laughter.

Karen looked hurt and pouted. "Am I a fool?"

"No," my father said, "you're really quite splendid."

### 3. The Most Famous Festival

The festival, as it turned out, was the greatest disaster in living memory.

The Cartographers' report was excellent, the weather was fine, but somewhere something had gone wrong.

The news was confusing. The television said that, in spite of the good report, various items had been stolen very early in the night. Later there was a news flash to say that a large house had completely disappeared in Howie Street.[5]

Later still we looked out the window to see a huge band of people carrying lighted torches. There was a lot of shouting. The same image, exactly, was on the television and a reporter was explaining that bands of vigilantes were out looking for thieves.

My father stood at the window, a martini in his hand, and watched the vigilantes set alight a house opposite.

My mother wanted to know what we should do.

"Come and watch the fools," my father said, "they're incredible."

### 4. The I.C.I. Incident

The next day the I.C.I.[6] building disappeared in front of a crowd of two thousand people. It took two hours. The crowd stood silently as the great steel and glass structure slowly faded before them.

The staff who were evacuated looked pale and shaken. The caretaker who was amongst the last to leave looked almost translucent. In the days that followed

---

4. Genghis Khan (c. 1162–1227) united the tribes of what is now Mongolia and then turned to conquest; at its height, the Mongol Empire extended from Southeast Asia westward into the Middle East and Eastern Europe, and may have comprised half the world's population.
5. There is a Howie Street in South London (the Royal College of Art is located there), and another in Melbourne, Australia. Peter Carey has lived in both cities.
6. Perhaps the Imperial Chemical Industries, an actual corporation.

he made some name for himself as a mystic, claiming that he had been able to see other worlds, layer upon layer, through the fabric of the here and now.

### 5. Behavior When Confronted with Dematerialization

The anger of our people when confronted with acts of theft has always been legendary and was certainly highlighted by the incidents which occurred on the night of the festival.

But the fury exhibited on this famous night could not compare with the intensity of emotion displayed by those who witnessed the earliest scenes of dematerialization.

The silent crowd who watched the I.C.I. building erupted into hysteria when they realized that it had finally gone and wasn't likely to come back.

It was like some monstrous theft for which punishment must be meted out.

They stormed into the Shell building next door and smashed desks and ripped down office partitions. Reporters who attended the scene were rarely impartial observers, but one of the cooler headed members of the press remarked on the great number of weeping men and women who hurled typewriters from windows and scattered files through crowds of frightened office workers.

Five days later they displayed similar anger when the Shell building itself disappeared.

### 6. Behavior of Those Dematerializing

The first reports of dematerializing people were not generally believed and were suppressed by the media. But these things were soon common knowledge and few families were untouched by them. Such incidents were obviously not all the same but in many victims there was a tendency to exhibit extreme aggression towards those around them. Murders and assaults committed by these unfortunates were not uncommon and in most cases they exhibited an almost unbelievable rage, as if they were the victims of a shocking betrayal.

My friend James Bray was once stopped in the street by a very beautiful woman who clawed and scratched at his face and said: "You did this to me, you bastard, you did this to me."

He had never seen her before but he confessed that, in some irrational way, he felt responsible and didn't defend himself. Fortunately she disappeared before she could do him much damage.

### 7. Some Theories That Arose at the Time

1. The world is merely a dream dreamt by god who is waking after a long sleep. When he is properly awake the world will disappear completely. When the world disappears we will disappear with it and be happy.
2. The world has become sensitive to light. In the same way that prolonged use of say penicillin can suddenly result in a dangerous allergy, prolonged exposure of the world to the sun has made it sensitive to light.

    The advocates of this theory could be seen bustling through the city crowds in their long, hooded black robes.
3. The fact that the world is disappearing has been caused by the sloppy work of the Cartographers and census takers. Those who filled out their census forms incorrectly would lose those items they had neglected to describe. People overlooked in the census by impatient officials would also disappear. A

strong pressure group demanded that a new census be taken quickly before matters got worse.

### 8. My Father's Theory

The world, according to my father, was exactly like the human body and had its own defense mechanisms with which it defended itself against anything that either threatened it or was unnecessary to it. The I.C.I. building and the I.C.I. company had obviously constituted some threat to the world or had simply been irrelevant. That's why it had disappeared and not because some damn fool god was waking up and rubbing his eyes.

"I don't believe in god," my father said. "Humanity is god. Humanity is the only god I know. If humanity doesn't need something it will disappear. People who are not loved will disappear. Everything that is not loved will disappear from the face of the earth. We only exist through the love of others and that's what it's all about."

### 9. A Contradiction

"Look at those fools," my father said, "they wouldn't know if they were up themselves."

### 10. An Unpleasant Scene

The world at this time was full of unpleasant and disturbing scenes. One that I recall vividly took place in the middle of the city on a hot, sultry Tuesday afternoon. It was about one-thirty and I was waiting for Karen by the post office when a man of forty or so ran past me. He was dematerializing rapidly. Everybody seemed to be deliberately looking the other way, which seemed to me to make him dematerialize faster. I stared at him hard, hoping that I could do something to keep him there until help arrived. I tried to love him, because I believed in my father's theory. I thought, I must love that man. But his face irritated me. It is not so easy to love a stranger and I'm ashamed to say that he had the small mouth and close-together eyes that I have always disliked in a person. I tried to love him but I'm afraid I failed.

While I watched he tried to hail taxi after taxi. But the taxi drivers were only too well aware of what was happening and had no wish to spend their time driving a passenger who, at any moment, might cease to exist. They looked the other way or put up their NOT FOR HIRE signs.

Finally he managed to way-lay a taxi at some traffic lights. By this time he was so insubstantial that I could see right through him. He was beginning to shout. A terrible thin noise, but penetrating nonetheless. He tried to open the cab door, but the driver had already locked it. I could hear the man's voice, high and piercing: "I want to go home." He repeated it over and over again. "I want to go home to my wife."

The taxi drove off when the lights changed. There was a lull in the traffic. People had fled the corner and left it deserted and it was I alone who saw the man finally disappear.

I felt sick.

Karen arrived five minutes later and found me pale and shaken. "Are you alright?" she said.

"Do you love me?" I said.

### 11. The Nether Regions

My father had an irritating way of explaining things to me I already understood, refusing to stop no matter how much I said "I know" or "You told me before."

Thus he expounded on the significance of the nether regions, adopting the tone of a lecturer speaking to a class of particularly backward children.

"As you know," he said, "the nether regions were amongst the first to disappear and this in itself is significant. These regions, I'm sure you know, are seldom visited by men and only then by people like me whose sole job is to make sure that they're still there. We had no use for these areas, these deserts, swamps, and coastlines which is why, of course, they disappeared. They were merely possessions of ours and if they had any use at all it was as symbols for our poets, writers and film makers. They were used as symbols of lovelessness, loneliness, uselessness and so on. Do you get what I mean?"

"Yes," I said, "I get what you mean."

"But do you?" my father insisted. "But do you really, I wonder." He examined me seriously, musing on the possibilities of my understanding him. "How old are you?"

"Twenty," I said.

"I knew, of course," he said. "Do you understand the significance of the nether regions?"

I sighed, a little too loudly and my father narrowed his eyes. Quickly I said: "They are like everything else. They're like the cities. The cities are deserts where people are alone and lonely. They don't love one another."

"Don't love one another," intoned my father, also sighing. "We no longer love one another. When we realize that we need one another we will stop disappearing. This is a lesson to us. A hard lesson, but, I hope, an effective one."

My father continued to speak, but I watched him without listening. After a few minutes he stopped abruptly: "Are you listening to me?" he said. I was surprised to detect real concern in his voice. He looked at me questioningly. "I've always looked after you," he said, "ever since you were little."

### 12. The Cartographers' Fall

I don't know when it was that I noticed that my father had become depressed. It probably happened quite gradually without either my mother or me noticing it.

Even when I did become aware of it I attributed it to a woman. My father had a number of lovers and his moods usually reflected the success or failure of these relationships.

But I know now that he had heard already of Hurst and Jamov, the first two Cartographers to disappear. The news was suppressed for several weeks and then, somehow or other, leaked to the press. Certainly the Cartographers had enemies amongst the civil servants who regarded them as overproud and overpaid, and it was probably from one of these civil servants that the press heard the news.

When the news finally broke I understood my father's depression and felt sorry for him.

I didn't know how to help him. I wanted, badly, to make him happy. I had never been able to give him anything or do anything for him that he couldn't do better himself. Now I wanted to help him, to show him I understood.

I found him sitting in front of the television one night when I returned from my office and I sat quietly beside him. He seemed more kindly now and he placed his hand on my knee and patted it.

I sat there for a while, overcome with the new warmth of this relationship and then, unable to contain my emotion any more, I blurted out. "You could change your job."

My father stiffened and sat bolt upright. The pressure of his hand on my knee increased until I yelped with pain, and still he held on, hurting me terribly.

"You are a fool," he said, "you wouldn't know if you were up yourself."

Through the pain in my leg, I felt the intensity of my father's fear.

### 13. Why The World Needs Cartographers

My father woke me at 3:00 a.m. to tell me why the world needed Cartographers. He smelled of whisky and seemed, once again, to be very gentle.

"The world needs Cartographers," he said softly, "because if they didn't have Cartographers the fools wouldn't know where they were. They wouldn't know if they were up themselves if they didn't have a Cartographer to tell them what's happening. The world needs Cartographers," my father said, "it fucking well needs Cartographers."

### 14. One Final Scene

Let me describe a final scene to you: I am sitting on the sofa my father brought home when I was five years old. I am watching television. My father is sitting in a leather armchair that once belonged to his father and which has always been exclusively his. My mother is sitting in the dining alcove with her cards spread across the table, playing one more interminable game of patience.

I glance casually across at my father to see if he is doing anything more than stare into space, and notice, with a terrible shock that he is showing the first signs of dematerializing.

"What are you staring at?" My father, in fact, has been staring at me.

"Nothing."

"Well, don't."

Nervously I return my eyes to the inanity of the television. I don't know what to do. Should I tell my father that he is dematerializing? If I don't tell him will he notice? I feel I should do something but I can feel, already, the anger in his voice. His anger is nothing new. But this is possibly the beginning of a tide of uncontrollable rage. If he knows he is dematerializing, he will think I don't love him. He will blame me. He will attack me. Old as he is, he is still considerably stronger than I am and he could hurt me badly. I stare determinedly at the television and feel my father's eyes on me.

I try to feel love for my father, I try very, very hard.

I attempt to remember how I felt about him when I was little, in the days when he was still occasionally tender towards me.

But it's no good.

Because I can only remember how he has hit me, hurt me, humiliated me and flirted with my girlfriends. I realize, with a flush of panic and guilt, that I don't love him. In spite of which I say: "I love you."

My mother looks up sharply from her cards and lets out a surprised cry.

I turn to my father. He has almost disappeared. I can see the leather of the chair through his stomach.

I don't know whether it is my unconvincing declaration of love or my mother's exclamation that makes my father laugh. For whatever reason, he begins to laugh uncontrollably: "You bloody fools," he gasps, "I wish you could see the looks on your bloody silly faces."

And then he is gone.

My mother looks across at me nervously, a card still in her hand. "Do you love me?" she asks.

1995

## QUESTIONS

1. Characterize the narrative mode of " 'Do You Love Me?' " At what point in the story does the narrator reveal himself as a character?
2. What is the effect of the story's numbered sections and section titles? Why do you think Peter Carey has chosen this device?
3. At what point in " 'Do You Love Me?' " does the reader realize that the story is not a "realistic" depiction of the world? What is the effect of Carey's veiling the story's fantasy element as he does?

## SUGGESTIONS FOR WRITING

1. Write a parody of "The Cask of Amontillado" set in modern times, perhaps on a college campus ("A Barrel of Bud"?).
2. Both Hemingway's "Hills Like White Elephants" and Moore's "How" offer a detached perspective on relationships between men and women at the time the stories were published. Each story is narrated in a specific style and tone, whether removed or close to what a character sees, thinks, or says. Both stories rely on repetition of some ordinary phrases (e.g., "you've got to realize"; "a week, a month, a year"). Write an essay on either story, or a comparison of both stories, in which you show how the voice (style and tone) of the narration and the point of view help to convey the text's perspective on contemporary sexual relationships.
3. In "How," the man that the narrator lives with "craves a family" and plays well with children. Notice other details of his domestic behavior. "You" is referred to as a woman, but does she do some things that are usually thought of as masculine? Write an essay discussing the ways that the story works against expectations about women's and men's roles in relationships.
4. Compare the second-person voice and imperatives in "How" with the choices offered to the reader in Atwood's "Happy Endings." What activities or responses are expected of "you," as reader or auditor in each story? Write an essay commenting on the author/reader relationship suggested in these two stories.
5. Does " 'Do You Love Me?' " have a "plot" in the traditional sense? If so, what is the conflict? What are the exposition, rising action, climax, falling action, and conclusion? Write an essay in which you discuss Carey's approach to storytelling.
6. Carry a notebook or tape recorder for a day or two, and note any stories you tell or hear, such as in daydreams, in conversation, on the phone, through e-mail or instant messaging. Consider what makes stories. Your transcripts may be short and may consist of memories, observations about your own character or those of people around you, plans, or predictions about the future. Choose two of your notes and modify them into plot summaries (no more than a paragraph each), using the first or the third person, the present or the past tense. Add a note about whether a full version of each story should give the inner thoughts of one or more characters, and why.

# 3 CHARACTER

Reading most short stories, your first thoughts may concern *who* as much as *what* and *how*. Character inevitably is a focus of your response to fiction, even if the story goes out of its way to avoid creating the illusion of real people acting in a real world. Stories almost always concern human beings (there may be fables about animals, geometric shapes, flowers), and we are all experts, from our own social experience, at attributing personalities to someone or something with a name and a certain role in the action. As in our assessments of plot, in our response to character we are guided by expectations based on our reading as well as our experience.

A **character** is someone who acts, appears, or is referred to as playing a part in a literary work, usually fiction or drama. **Characterization**—the art and technique of representing fictional personages—depends upon action or plot as well as narration and point of view. Many stories present characters through the medium of a narrator who is offstage, without a body or a personality, a past or a future, who is simply a voice and style and medium for the story. So it is in some of the previous stories in this volume, including "The Country Husband," "The Thing in the Forest," and "Hills Like White Elephants." In other stories, "The Cask of Amontillado" by Edgar Allan Poe, for example, the narrator both tells us the story and plays the central role in the action. Still other stories, such as James Baldwin's "Sonny's Blues" or Herman Melville's "Bartleby, the Scrivener," are narrated in the first person by characters who play an important part in the action, but who serve as witnesses to the experience of the main, title characters. In still another variation, the observing narrator is present in the events in the story but can scarcely be distinguished as a separate personality. This approach is effective in William Faulkner's "A Rose for Emily" and Stephen Crane's "The Open Boat." In short, there can be various combinations of narration and characterization that guide how we perceive the story about the main characters.

> *The sum of tendencies to act in a certain way.*
> —T. H. HUXLEY

The most common term for the character with the leading male role is **hero**, the "good guy," who opposes the **villain**, or "bad guy." The leading female character is the **heroine**. Heroes and heroines are usually larger than life, stronger or better than most human beings, sometimes almost godlike. In most modern fiction, however, the leading character is much more ordinary, more like the rest of us. Such a character is sometimes called an **antihero**, not because he opposes the hero but because he is not heroic in stature or perfection, is not so clearly or simply a "good guy." An older and more neutral term than *hero* for the leading character, a term that does not imply either the presence or the absence of outstanding virtue (and that has the added advantage of referring equally to male and female characters), is **protagonist**, whose opponent is the

**antagonist.** You might get into long and pointless arguments by calling Francis Weed (in John Cheever's "The Country Husband") or Montresor (in "A Cask of Amontillado") a hero, but most would agree that each is his story's protagonist. Some stories, however, leave open to debate the question of which character most deserves to be called the *protagonist*. In "The Thing in the Forest," for example, Penny and Primrose are equally central to what happens.

The **major** or **main characters** are those we see more of over a longer period of time; we learn more about them, and we think of them as more complex and, therefore, frequently more "realistic" than the **minor characters,** the figures who fill out the story. These major characters can grow and change too, sometimes even contradicting expectations.

Yet while minor characters may be less prominent and less complex, they are ultimately just as indispensable to a story as major characters. A very good first question when you set out to write about a character is, "How would this story be different without this character?" Minor characters often play a key role in shaping our interpretations of, and attitudes toward, the major characters, and also in precipitating the changes that major characters undergo. In Herman Melville's "Bartleby, the Scrivener," for example, "flighty" Turkey and "fiery" Nippers help us, as well as the story's narrator, to recognize the uniqueness of the "singularly sedate" Bartleby. Like many a minor character, then, Turkey and Nippers might be described as **foils** to this major character in the sense that they serve as contrasts to the protagonist. "Bartleby the Scrivener" would not absolutely *need* Turkey and Nippers, but these foils to the main character help to bring out what is exceptional about him, his unchanging lack of appetite. In "Sonny's Blues," to take a different example, the "three sisters in black, and a brother" singing spirituals on a street corner do a great deal to foster change in the narrator: helping him to appreciate in a new way the expressive power of music, these characters pave the way for the ultimate transformation of the narrator's attitudes toward both Sonny and the way of life Sonny represents.

Characters that change, develop, or act from conflicting motives are said to be **round characters;** they can "surprise convincingly," as one critic puts it. Simple characters that, like Turkey and Nippers, behave in unchanging or unsurprising ways are called **flat.** But we must be careful not to let terms like *flat* and *round* or *major* and *minor* turn into value judgments. Because flat characters are less complex than round ones, it is easy to assume they are artistically inferior; however, we need only to think of the characters of Charles Dickens, almost all of whom are flat, to realize that this is not always true.

Perhaps you have found that characterization can cause the greatest disagreements about the meaning or quality of a story. Discussion can get wrapped up in whether you liked or disliked so-and-so, or whether you trusted her motives or would have done the same thing in her place. Your teacher will probably warn you not to confuse characters with real people. After all, these are imaginary beings created out of words for certain effects. Yet if a story asks us to suppose the reality of the persons in it, how can we avoid applying our real-life judgments of personality? And don't our opinions about people differ widely in real life?

The very term *character,* when it refers not to a fictional personage but to a combination of qualities in a human being, is somewhat ambiguous. It usually has moral overtones, often favorable (a man of character); it is sometimes neutral but evaluative (character reference). Judgment about character usually involves moral terms like *good* and *bad* and *strong* and *weak*. And individuals and cultures have held conflicting views of what produces character, whether innate factors such as genes or environmental factors such as upbringing. Views differ as well as to whether character is simply a matter of fate, something determined and unchanging, or whether it can change through experience, conversion, or an act of will. Thus the representation of people in fiction can provoke debates that concern the most fundamental values about human nature and varieties of personality—and no one is likely to win such debates any time soon.

> Character is that which reveals moral purpose, exposing the class of things a man chooses or avoids.
> —ARISTOTLE

Nevertheless, such debates can indeed be meaningful, even if irresolvable, insofar as they are provoked by the story that you have read. You can also come to more definite conclusions by focusing more closely upon the characters in a particular story and by remembering that the whole work is an imaginary world—more or less like our own—with its own rules. Rather than asking whether the protagonist is a good or bad person, likable or not, or true to life or not, you should consider whether the characterization is good or bad, whether it is effective in the story's own terms. Just as an actor receives a Best Actor award for playing a character well rather than for playing a good character, so an author may be recognized for good characterization even if we do not like or admire the character the author has created. Often the "bad" or at least morally complex characters interest and teach us the most. Although we should remember that characters exist only in the context of the story, we may learn about real people from characters in fiction or learn to understand fictional characters in part from what we know about real people. Part of the pleasure of many stories is that they afford us an opportunity of seeming to inhabit another person's mind. Even our closest friends would find it hard to convey to us the kinds of intimate details that fiction can express imaginatively.

> It seems that the analysis of character is the highest human entertainment. And literature does it, unlike gossip, without mentioning real names.
> —ISAAC BASHEVIS SINGER

Such better-than-lifelike understanding can be one benefit of interpreting character in fiction. But as we have suggested, some stories and some characters are designed for different effects. Flat or opaque characterization has its place, and so do **stereotypes**: characters based on conscious or unconscious cultural assumptions about what a person's sex, age, ethnicity, nationality, occupation, marital status, and so on will tell us about that person's traits, actions, even values. Any character belongs more or less to a type. One of the chief ways we have of describing or defining is by placing the thing to be defined in a category or class and then distinguishing it from the other members of that class. Characters are almost inevitably identified by category—by sex, age, nationality, occupation, or other characteristics. We learn that the narrator of "Why I Live at the P.O." is a white woman, relatively young, who lives in a small town in Mississippi. The humor of her story may depend on readers' expectations about poor, Southern, uneducated families, and some might object that those expectations are prejudiced. Yet in some stories, characterization exaggerates the conflicts between and among types in order to raise issues about the way people judge and treat each other as types.

Excellent fiction can emerge from the surprises or conflicts created by stereotypical categories. In spite of our best intentions, we function in everyday life by quickly assessing the people we meet, and inevitably categorizing them. It can be wonderful—and it is often a story worth telling to our friends—to discover that a person of a type you really dislike (perhaps a "loser," "bully," "weirdo," or other objectionable type) actually has an individual character and something to say or do that you appreciate. The difference between a stereotype and observed behavior can create a round character, one who can surprise convincingly.

The usual sources of such classifications of people are observations of physical characteristics, which are the stock in trade of narrators of fiction: well-selected, closely observed details of appearance. The physical description of Judith in "Our Friend Judith" makes it possible to visualize her fully, almost to recognize her as an individual:

> Judith is tall, small-breasted, slender. Her light brown hair is parted in the centre and cut straight around her neck. A high straight forehead, straight nose, and full grave mouth are setting for her eyes, which are green, large and prominent. Her lids are very white, fringed with gold, and moulded close over the eyeball....

At the same time, however, the very physical attributes that individualize Judith also encourage us to see her as a certain type of person and, in this case, may convince us that she does conform to our stereotype: "small-breasted" and "slender," with "straight" features, a "grave" mouth, and a severe haircut, Judith does, indeed, *look* as straitlaced, prudish, and conventional as we might expect a "typical English spinster" to be.

In most stories we not only see what characters look like, but also see what they do and hear what they say; we sometimes learn what they think, and what other people think or say about them; we often know what kind of clothes they wear, what and how much they own, treasure, or covet; we may be told about their childhood, parents, or some parts of their past. And all of this information combines to shape our sense of the characters. With the new information of later events or observations, characters may change in our perceptions as well as in their own right. When we first read the physical description of Judith, for example, we probably assign most importance to those features that make her seem straitlaced and rigid, yet by the end of the story we may well both remember and pay more attention to the narrator's remark that those features merely serve as a "setting" for Judith's vibrant green eyes.

A wide range of modern fiction is concerned with encounters between characters who initially cannot accept each other because of prejudice or cultural stereotypes. In Toni Morrison's "Recitatif," two girls are sent to an orphanage. They accept each other right away, although their mothers—Twyla's is a sex worker of some kind (she "dances all night"), and Roberta's is ill—are prejudiced against the race of the other family. The ambiguous details of their characterization, as they grow together and apart in different circumstances through the decades of changing American society, can lead to very different interpretations of this story. Even judgments about what actually happened can be shaped by expectations about people of different classes or races.

Paradoxically, in fiction, as in life, the more groups a character is placed in, the more individual he or she becomes. Sonny, for example, is simultaneously a man, an African American, a blues musician, a heroin addict, a younger brother, an ex-convict, and a resident of an inner-city neighborhood. As a result, our interpretation of Sonny is shaped not only by our assumptions about each of these social groups, but also by our sense of the way that belonging to all of these groups helps to make Sonny who he is. Thus the story asks us to think about how Sonny's choice to be a blues musician relates to the fact that he is African American, about the way inner-city life has shaped Sonny's experience of being African American, and so on.

What we don't know about a character can be as significant and revealing as what we do know. What, for example, is the effect of the fact that we never learn the narrator's name in either "Bartleby, the Scrivener" or "Sonny's Blues"? Or that we know only the nicknames of Nippers and Turkey? As you consider the characterization within a story, pay close attention to the many sorts of things that you are not explicitly told about the characters.

The identification of characters by their social categories is only one aspect of the way stories present imaginary people. Probably action or behavior, and thus plot, is even more important than the typecasting and appearance of characters in guiding your response. As always, it is misleading to isolate the elements of fiction except for purposes of analysis. Throughout a story, plot (or incident) and character are fused. As novelist Henry James wrote,

> What is character but the determination of incident? What is incident but the illustration of character? . . . It is an incident for a woman to stand up with her hand resting on a table and look at you in a certain way; or if it is not an incident I think it will be hard to say what it is. At the same time it is an expression of character. If you say you don't see it, . . . this is exactly what the artist who has reasons of his own for thinking he *does* see it undertakes to show you.

*Character is destiny.*
—GEORGE ELIOT

Though characterization is gradual, taking place sequentially through the story, it is not, as it may seem natural to assume, entirely cumulative. We do not begin with an empty space called Judith or Twyla or William or Primrose and fill it in gradually by adding physical traits, habitual actions, ways of speaking, and so on. Our imagination does not work that way. Rather, just as at each point in the action we project some sort of configuration of how the story will come out or what the world of the story will be like or mean, so we project a more or less complete image of each character at the point at which he or she is first mentioned or appears. The image is based on the initial reference in the text, our reading, and our life experiences and associations. The next time the character appears, we continue to project an image of a complete personality that we might eventually get to know, though we are still only slightly acquainted with this character. Just as in the plot we project a new series of developments and a new outcome at each stage, in characterization we are prepared to be surprised by the traits or qualities that emerge in the course of the action. In other words, rather than assembling a character the way a child attaches the eyes, ears, or hat to a Mr. Potato Head, we overlay a series of impressions of a complete, existing person. Though the final image may be the most enduring, the early images do not all disappear: our view of the character is multidimensional, flickering, like a time-lapse photograph.

Perhaps that is why it is rare that any actor in a film based on a novel or story matches the way we imagined that character if we have read the book or story first—our imagination has not one image but rather a sequence of images associated with that character. It is also why some of us feel that seeing the film before reading the book hobbles the imagination. A particular character's physical attributes, for example, may not be described in a novel until after that character has been involved in some incident; the reader may then need to adjust his or her earlier vision of that character, which is not an option for the viewer of a film. It is thus the reader, rather than a casting director, who finalizes a character in his or her own imagination. Indeed, you may consider yourself a collaborator with the writer in *realizing* the appearance, manner, and personality of the characters described on the page, as the words leave so much to the imagination. For we are all artists representing reality to ourselves. If we study the art of characterization and think about the way we interpret fictional characters, we may become better artists, able to enrich our reading both of fictional texts and of real people and situations.

CD **EUDORA WELTY**

## Why I Live at the P.O.

I was getting along fine with Mama, Papa-Daddy, and Uncle Rondo until my sister Stella-Rondo just separated from her husband and came back home again. Mr. Whitaker! Of course I went with Mr. Whitaker first, when he first appeared here in China Grove, taking "Pose Yourself" photos, and Stella-Rondo broke us up. Told him I was one-sided. Bigger on one side than the other, which is a deliberate, calculated falsehood: I'm the same. Stella-Rondo is exactly twelve months to the day younger than I am and for that reason she's spoiled.

She's always had anything in the world she wanted and then she'd throw it away. Papa-Daddy give her this gorgeous Add-a-Pearl necklace when she was eight years old and she threw it away playing baseball when she was nine, with only two pearls.

So as soon as she got married and moved away from home the first thing she did was separate! From Mr. Whitaker! This photographer with the popeyes she said she trusted. Came home from one of those towns up in Illinois and to our complete surprise brought this child of two.

Mama said she like to make her drop dead for a second. "Here you had this marvelous blonde child and never so much as wrote your mother a word about it," says Mama. "I'm thoroughly ashamed of you." But of course she wasn't.

Stella-Rondo just calmly takes off this *hat*, I wish you could see it. She says, 5 "Why, Mama, Shirley-T.'s adopted, I can prove it."

"How?" says Mama, but all I says was, "H'm!" There I was over the hot stove, trying to stretch two chickens over five people and a completely unexpected child into the bargain without one moment's notice.

"What do you mean—'H'm'?" says Stella-Rondo, and Mama says, "I heard that, Sister."

I said that oh, I didn't mean a thing, only that whoever Shirley-T. was, she was the spit-image of Papa-Daddy if he'd cut off his beard, which of course he'd never do in the world. Papa-Daddy's Mama's papa and sulks.

Stella-Rondo got furious! She said, "Sister, I don't need to tell you you got a lot of nerve and always did have and I'll thank you to make no future reference to my adopted child whatsoever."

"Very well," I said. "Very well, very well. Of course I noticed at once she looks like Mr. Whitaker's side too. That frown. She looks like a cross between Mr. Whitaker and Papa-Daddy."

"Well, all I can say is she isn't."

"She looks exactly like Shirley Temple to me," says Mama, but Shirley-T. just ran away from her.

So the first thing Stella-Rondo did at the table was turn Papa-Daddy against me.

"Papa-Daddy," she says. He was trying to cut up his meat. "Papa-Daddy!" I was taken completely by surprise. Papa-Daddy is about a million years old and's got this long-long beard. "Papa-Daddy, Sister says she fails to understand why you don't cut off your beard."

So Papa-Daddy l-a-y-s down his knife and fork! He's real rich. Mama says he is, he says he isn't. So he says, "Have I heard correctly? You don't understand why I don't cut off my beard?"

"Why," I says, "Papa-Daddy, of course I understand, I did not say any such a thing, the idea!"

He says, "Hussy!"

I says, "Papa-Daddy, you know I wouldn't any more want you to cut off your beard than the man in the moon. It was the farthest thing from my mind! Stella-Rondo sat there and made that up while she was eating breast of chicken."

But he says, "So the postmistress fails to understand why I don't cut off my beard. Which job I got you through my influence with the government. 'Bird's nest'—is that what you call it?"

Not that it isn't the next to smallest P.O. in the entire state of Mississippi.

I says, "Oh, Papa-Daddy," I says, "I didn't say any such a thing, I never dreamed it was a bird's nest, I have always been grateful though this is the next to smallest P.O. in the state of Mississippi, and I do not enjoy being referred to as a hussy by my own grandfather."

But Stella-Rondo says, "Yes, you did say it too. Anybody in the world could of heard you, that had ears."

"Stop right there," says Mama, looking at *me*.

So I pulled my napkin straight back through the napkin ring and left the table.

As soon as I was out of the room Mama says, "Call her back, or she'll starve to death," but Papa-Daddy says, "This is the beard I started growing on the Coast when I was fifteen years old." He would of gone on till nightfall if Shirley-T. hadn't lost the Milky Way she ate in Cairo.

So Papa-Daddy says, "I am going out and lie in the hammock, and you can all sit here and remember my words: I'll never cut off my beard as long as I live, even one inch, and I don't appreciate it in you at all." Passed right by me in the hall and went straight out and got in the hammock.

It would be a holiday. It wasn't five minutes before Uncle Rondo suddenly appeared in the hall in one of Stella-Rondo's flesh-colored kimonos, all cut on the bias, like something Mr. Whitaker probably thought was gorgeous.

"Uncle Rondo!" I says. "I didn't know who that was! Where are you going?"

"Sister," he says, "get out of my way, I'm poisoned."

"If you're poisoned stay away from Papa-Daddy," I says. "Keep out of the hammock. Papa-Daddy will certainly beat you on the head if you come within forty miles of him. He thinks I deliberately said he ought to cut off his beard after he got me the P.O., and I've told him and told him and told him, and he acts like he just don't hear me. Papa-Daddy must of gone stone deaf."

"He picked a fine day to do it then," says Uncle Rondo, and before you could say "Jack Robinson" flew out in the yard.

What he'd really done, he'd drunk another bottle of that prescription. He does it every single Fourth of July as sure as shooting, and it's horribly expensive. Then he falls over in the hammock and snores. So he insisted on zigzagging right on out to the hammock, looking like a half-wit.

Papa-Daddy woke with this horrible yell and right there without moving an inch he tried to turn Uncle Rondo against me. I heard every word he said. Oh, he told Uncle Rondo I didn't learn to read till I was eight years old and he didn't see how in the world I ever got the mail put up at the P.O., much less read it all, and he said if Uncle Rondo could only fathom the lengths he had gone to get me that job! And he said on the other hand he thought Stella-Rondo had a brilliant mind and deserved credit for getting out of town. All the time he was just lying there swinging as pretty as you please and looping out his beard, and poor Uncle Rondo was *pleading* with him to slow down the hammock, it was making him as dizzy as a witch to watch it. But that's what Papa-Daddy likes about a hammock. So Uncle Rondo was too dizzy to get turned against me for the time being. He's Mama's only brother and is a good case of a one-track mind. Ask anybody. A certified pharmacist.

Just then I heard Stella-Rondo raising the upstairs window. While she was married she got this peculiar idea that it's cooler with the windows shut and locked. So she has to raise the window before she can make a soul hear her outdoors.

So she raises the window and says, "*Oh!*" You would have thought she was mortally wounded.

Uncle Rondo and Papa-Daddy didn't even look up, but kept right on with what they were doing. I had to laugh.

I flew up the stairs and threw the door open! I says, "What in the wide world's the matter, Stella-Rondo? You mortally wounded?"

"No," she says, "I am not mortally wounded but I wish you would do me the favor of looking out that window there and telling me what you see."

So I shade my eyes and look out the window.

"I see the front yard," I says.

"Don't you see any human beings?"

"I see Uncle Rondo trying to run Papa-Daddy out of the hammock," I says. "Nothing more. Naturally, it's so suffocating-hot in the house, with all the windows shut and locked, everybody who cares to stay in their right mind will have to go out and get in the hammock before the Fourth of July is over."

"Don't you notice anything different about Uncle Rondo?" asks Stella-Rondo.

"Why, no, except he's got on some terrible-looking flesh-colored contraption I wouldn't be found dead in, is all I can see," I says.

"Never mind, you won't be found dead in it, because it happens to be part of my trousseau, and Mr. Whitaker took several dozen photographs of me in it," says Stella-Rondo. "What on earth could uncle Rondo *mean* by wearing part of my trousseau out in the broad open daylight without saying so much as 'Kiss my foot,' *knowing* I only got home this morning after my separation and hung my negligee up on the bathroom door, just as nervous as I could be?"

"I'm sure I don't know, and what do you expect me to do about it?" I says. "Jump out the window?"

"No, I expect nothing of the kind. I simply declare that Uncle Rondo looks like a fool in it, that's all," she says. "It makes me sick to my stomach."

"Well, he looks as good as he can," I says. "As good as anybody in reason could." I stood up for Uncle Rondo, please remember. And I said to Stella-Rondo, "I think I would do well not to criticize so freely if I were you and came home with a two-year-old child I had never said a word about, and no explanation whatever about my separation."

"I asked you the instant I entered this house not to refer one more time to my adopted child, and you gave me your word of honor you would not," was all Stella-Rondo would say, and started pulling out every one of her eyebrows with some cheap Kress tweezers.

So I merely slammed the door behind me and went down and made some green-tomato pickle. Somebody had to do it. Of course Mama had turned both the Negroes loose; she always said no earthly power could hold one anyway on the Fourth of July, so she wouldn't even try. It turned out that Jaypan fell in the lake and came within a very narrow limit of drowning.

So Mama trots in. Lifts up the lid and says, "H'm! Not very good for your Uncle Rondo in his precarious condition, I must say. Or poor little adopted Shirley-T. Shame on you!"

That made me tired. I says, "Well, Stella-Rondo had better thank her lucky stars it was her instead of me came trotting in with that very peculiar-looking child. Now if it had been me that trotted in from Illinois and brought a peculiar-looking child or two, I shudder to think of the reception I'd of got, much less controlled the diet of an entire family."

"But you must remember, Sister, that you were never married to Mr. Whitaker in the first place and didn't go up to Illinois to live," says Mama, shaking a spoon in my face. "If you had I would of been just as overjoyed to see you and your little adopted girl as I was to see Stella-Rondo, when you wound up with your separation and came on back home."

"You would not," I says.

"Don't contradict me, I would," says Mama.

But I said she couldn't convince me though she talked till she was blue in the face. Then I said, "Besides, you know as well as I do that that child is not adopted."

"She most certainly is adopted," says Mama, stiff as a poker.

I says, "Why, Mama, Stella-Rondo had her just as sure as anything in this world, and just too stuck up to admit it."

"Why, Sister," said Mama. "Here I thought we were going to have a pleasant Fourth of July, and you start right out not believing a word your own baby sister tells you!"

"Just like Cousin Annie Flo. Went to her grave denying the facts of life," I reminded Mama.

"I told you if you ever mentioned Annie Flo's name I'd slap your face," says Mama, and slaps my face.

"All right, you wait and see," I says.

"I," says Mama, "*I* prefer to take my children's word for anything when it's humanly possible." You ought to see Mama, she weighs two hundred pounds and has real tiny feet.

Just then something perfectly horrible occurred to me.

"Mama," I says, "can that child talk?" I simply had to whisper! "Mama, I wonder if that child can be—you know—in any way? Do you realize?" I says, "that she hasn't spoke one single, solitary word to a human being up to this minute? This is the way she looks," I says, and I looked like this.

Well, Mama and I just stood there and stared at each other. It was horrible!

"I remember well that Joe Whitaker frequently drank like a fish," says Mama. "I believed to my soul he drank *chemicals*." And without another word she marches to the foot of the stairs and calls Stella-Rondo.

"Stella-Rondo? O-o-o-o-o! Stella-Rondo!"

"What?" says Stella-Rondo from upstairs. Not even the grace to get up off the bed.

"Can that child of yours talk?" asks Mama.

Stella-Rondo says, "Can she what?"

"Talk! Talk!" says Mama. "Burdyburdyburdyburdy!"

So Stella-Rondo yells back, "Who says she can't talk?"

"Sister says so," says Mama.

"You didn't have to tell me, I know whose word of honor don't mean a thing in this house," says Stella-Rondo.

And in a minute the loudest Yankee voice I ever heard in my life yells out, "OE'm Pop-OE the Sailor-r-r-r Ma-a-an!" and then somebody jumps up and down in the upstairs hall. In another second the house would of fallen down.

"Not only talks, she can tap-dance!" calls Stella-Rondo. "Which is more than some people I won't name can do."

"Why, the little precious darling thing!" Mama says, so surprised. "Just as smart as she can be!" Starts talking baby talk right there. Then she turns on me. "Sister, you ought to be thoroughly ashamed! Run upstairs this instant and apologize to Stella-Rondo and Shirley-T."

"Apologize for what?" I says. "I merely wondered if the child was normal, that's all. Now that she's proved she is, why, I have nothing further to say."

But Mama just turned on her heel and flew out, furious. She ran right upstairs and hugged the baby. She believed it was adopted. Stella-Rondo hadn't done a thing but turn her against me from upstairs while I stood there helpless over the hot stove. So that made Mama, Papa-Daddy, and the baby all on Stella-Rondo's side.

Next, Uncle Rondo.

I must say that Uncle Rondo has been marvelous to me at various times in the past and I was completely unprepared to be made to jump out of my skin, the way it turned out. Once Stella-Rondo did something perfectly horrible to him—broke a chain letter from Flanders Field—and he took the radio back he had given her and gave it to me. Stella-Rondo was furious! For six months we all had to call her Stella instead of Stella-Rondo, or she wouldn't answer. I always thought Uncle Rondo had all the brains of the entire family. Another time he sent me to Mammoth Cave with all expenses paid.

But this would be the day he was drinking that prescription, the Fourth of July.

So at supper Stella-Rondo speaks up and says she thinks Uncle Rondo ought to try to eat a little something. So finally Uncle Rondo said he would try a little cold biscuits and ketchup, but that was all. So *she* brought it to him.

"Do you think it wise to disport with ketchup in Stella-Rondo's flesh-colored kimono?" I says. Trying to be considerate! If Stella-Rondo couldn't watch out for her trousseau, somebody had to.

"Any objections?" asks Uncle Rondo, just about to pour out all of the ketchup.

"Don't mind what she says, Uncle Rondo," says Stella-Rondo. "Sister has been devoting this solid afternoon to sneering out my bedroom window at the way you look."

"What's that?" says Uncle Rondo. Uncle Rondo has got the most terrible temper in the world. Anything is liable to make him tear the house down if it comes at the wrong time.

So Stella-Rondo says, "Sister says, 'Uncle Rondo certainly does look like a fool in that pink kimono!' "

Do you remember who it was really said that?

Uncle Rondo spills out all the ketchup and jumps out of his chair and tears off the kimono and throws it down on the dirty floor and puts his foot on it. It had to be sent all the way to Jackson to the cleaners and re-pleated.

"So that's your opinion of your Uncle Rondo, is it?" he says. "I look like a fool, do I? Well, that's the last straw. A whole day in this house with nothing to do, and then to hear you come out with a remark like that behind my back!"

"I didn't say any such of a thing, Uncle Rondo," I says, "and I'm not saying who did, either. Why, I think you look all right. Just try to take care of yourself and not talk and eat at the same time," I says. "I think you better go lie down."

"Lie down my foot," says Uncle Rondo. I ought to of known by that he was fixing to do something perfectly horrible.

So he didn't do anything that night in the precarious state he was in—just played Casino with Mama and Stella-Rondo and Shirley-T. and gave Shirley-T. a nickel with a head on both sides. It tickled her nearly to death, and she called him "Papa." But at 6:30 A.M. the next morning, he threw a whole five-cent package of some unsold one-inch firecrackers from the store as hard as he could into my bedroom and they every one went off. Not one bad one in the string. Anybody else, there'd be one that wouldn't go off.

Well, I'm just terribly susceptible to noise of any kind, the doctor has always told me I was the most sensitive person he had ever seen in his whole life, and I was simply prostrated. I couldn't eat! People tell me they heard it as far as the cemetery, and old Aunt Jep Patterson, that had been holding her own so good, thought it was Judgment Day and she was going to meet her whole family. It's usually so quiet here.

And I'll tell you it didn't take me any longer than a minute to make up my mind what to do. There I was with the whole entire house on Stella-Rondo's side and turned against me. If I have anything at all I have pride.

So I just decided I'd go straight down to the P.O. There's plenty of room there in the back, I says to myself.

Well! I made no bones about letting the family catch on to what I was up to. I didn't try to conceal it.

The first thing they knew, I marched in where they were all playing Old Maid and pulled the electric oscillating fan out by the plug, and everything got real hot. Next I snatched the pillow I'd done the needlepoint on right off the davenport from behind Papa-Daddy. He went "Ugh!" I beat Stella-Rondo up the stairs and finally found my charm bracelet in her bureau drawer under a picture of Nelson Eddy.[1]

"So that's the way the land lies," says Uncle Rondo. There he was, piecing on the ham. "Well, Sister, I'll be glad to donate my army cot if you got any place to set it up, providing you'll leave right this minute and let me get some peace." Uncle Rondo was in France.

"Thank you kindly for the cot and 'peace' is hardly the word I would select if I had to resort to firecrackers at 6:30 A.M. in a young girl's bedroom," I says to him. "And as to where I intend to go, you seem to forget my position as postmistress of China Grove, Mississippi," I says. "I've always got the P.O."

Well, that made them all sit up and take notice.

I went out front and started digging up some four-o'clocks to plant around the P.O.

"Ah-ah-ah!" says Mama, raising the window. "Those happen to be my four-o'clocks. Everything planted in that star is mine. I've never known you to make anything grow in your life."

"Very well," I says. "But I take the fern. Even you, Mama, can't stand there and deny that I'm the one watered that fern. And I happen to know where I can send in a box top and get a packet of one thousand mixed seeds, no two the same kind, free."

"Oh, where?" Mama wants to know.

But I says, "Too late. You 'tend to your house, and I'll 'tend to mine. You hear things like that all the time if you know how to listen to the radio. Perfectly marvelous offers. Get anything you want free."

So I hope to tell you I marched in and got that radio, and they could of all bit a nail in two, especially Stella-Rondo, that it used to belong to, and she well knew she couldn't get it back, I'd sue for it like a shot. And I very politely took the sewing-machine motor I helped pay the most on to give Mama for Christmas back in 1929, and a good big calendar, with the first-aid remedies on it. The thermometer and the Hawaiian ukulele certainly were rightfully mine, and I stood on the step-ladder and got all my watermelon-rind preserves and every fruit and vegetable I'd put up, every jar. Then I began to pull the tacks out of the bluebird wall vases on the archway to the dining room.

"Who told you you could have those, Miss Priss?" says Mama, fanning as hard as she could.

"I bought 'em and I'll keep track of 'em," I says. "I'll tack 'em up one on each side of the post-office window, and you can see 'em when you come to ask me for your mail, if you're so dead to see 'em."

"Not I! I'll never darken the door to that post office again if I live to be a hundred," Mama says. "Ungrateful child! After all the money we spent on you at the Normal."[2]

"Me either," says Stella-Rondo. "You can just let my mail lie there and *rot*, for all I care. I'll never come and relieve you of a single, solitary piece."

"I should worry," I says. "And who you think's going to sit down and write

---

1. Opera singer (1901–1967) who enjoyed phenomenal popularity in the 1930s and 1940s when he costarred in numerous film musicals with Jeanette MacDonald. The two were known as "America's Singing Sweethearts."   2. That is, normal school (teachers' college).

you all those big fat letters and postcards, by the way? Mr. Whitaker? Just because he was the only man ever dropped down in China Grove and you got him—unfairly—is he going to sit down and write you a lengthy correspondence after you come home giving no rhyme nor reason whatsoever for your separation and no explanation for the presence of that child? I may not have your brilliant mind, but I fail to see it."

So Mama says, "Sister, I've told you a thousand times that Stella-Rondo simply got homesick, and this child is far too big to be hers," and she says, "Now, why don't you just sit down and play Casino?"

Then Shirley-T. sticks out her tongue at me in this perfectly horrible way. She has no more manners than the man in the moon. I told her she was going to cross her eyes like that some day and they'd stick.

"It's too late to stop me now," I says. "You should have tried that yesterday. I'm going to the P.O. and the only way you can possibly see me is to visit me there."

So Papa-Daddy says, "You'll never catch me setting foot in that post office, even if I should take a notion into my head to write a letter some place." He says, "I won't have you reachin' out of that little old window with a pair of shears and cuttin' off any beard of mine. I'm too smart for you!"

"We all are," says Stella-Rondo.

But I said, "If you're so smart, where's Mr. Whitaker?"

So then Uncle Rondo says, "I'll thank you from now on to stop reading all the orders I get on postcards and telling everybody in China Grove what you think is the matter with them," but I says, "I draw my own conclusions and will continue in the future to draw them." I says, "If people want to write their innermost secrets on penny postcards, there's nothing in the wide world you can do about it, Uncle Rondo."

"And if you think we'll ever *write* another postcard you're sadly mistaken," says Mama.

"Cutting off your nose to spite your face then," I says. "But if you're all determined to have no more to do with the U.S. mail, think of this: What will Stella-Rondo do now, if she wants to tell Mr. Whitaker to come after her?"

"Wah!" says Stella-Rondo. I knew she'd cry. She had a conniption fit right there in the kitchen.

"It will be interesting to see how long she holds out," I says. "And now—I am leaving."

"Good-bye," says Uncle Rondo.

"Oh, I declare," says Mama, "to think that a family of mine should quarrel on the Fourth of July, or the day after, over Stella-Rondo leaving old Mr. Whitaker and having the sweetest little adopted child! It looks like we'd all be glad!"

"Wah!" says Stella-Rondo, and has a fresh conniption fit.

"He left *her*—you mark my words," I says. "That's Mr. Whitaker. I know Mr. Whitaker. After all, I knew him first. I said from the beginning he'd up and leave her. I foretold every single thing that's happened."

"Where did he go?" asks Mama.

"Probably to the North Pole, if he knows what's good for him," I says.

But Stella-Rondo just bawled and wouldn't say another word. She flew to her room and slammed the door.

"Now look what you've gone and done, Sister," says Mama. "You go apologize."

"I haven't the time, I'm leaving," I says.

"Well, what are you waiting around for?" asks Uncle Rondo.

So I just picked up the kitchen clock and marched off, without saying, "Kiss my foot," or anything, and never did tell Stella-Rondo good-bye.

There was a girl going along on a little wagon right in front.

"Girl," I says, "come help me haul these things down the hill, I'm going to live in the post office."

Took her nine trips in her express wagon. Uncle Rondo came out on the porch and threw her a nickel.

And that's the last I've laid eyes on any of my family or my family laid eyes on me for five solid days and nights. Stella-Rondo may be telling the most horrible tales in the world about Mr. Whitaker, but I haven't heard them. As I tell everybody, I draw my own conclusions.

But oh, I like it here. It's ideal, as I've been saying. You see, I've got everything cater-cornered, the way I like it. Hear the radio? All the war news. Radio, sewing machine, book ends, ironing board and that great big piano lamp—peace, that's what I like. Butter-bean vines planted all along the front where the strings are.

Of course, there's not much mail. My family are naturally the main people in China Grove, and if they prefer to vanish from the face of the earth, for all the mail they get or the mail they write, why, I'm not going to open my mouth. Some of the folks here in town are taking up for me and some turned against me. I know which is which. There are always people who will quit buying stamps just to get on the right side of Papa-Daddy.

But here I am, and here I'll stay. I want the world to know I'm happy.

And if Stella-Rondo should come to me this minute, on bended knees, and *attempt* to explain the incidents of her life with Mr. Whitaker, I'd simply put my fingers in both my ears and refuse to listen.

1941

## QUESTIONS

1. What is your initial impression of Sister, the story's narrator? At what points in the story do you find yourself reassessing this character? Why?
2. How would you characterize the other members of Sister's family? Which of them (Stella-Rondo, Mama, Papa-Daddy, Uncle Rondo) seem most fully fleshed out, and which seem flat?
3. Is there a realistic way to account for the melodrama of Sister's family life, or is Welty merely exaggerating for comic effect? What clues in the text make "Why I Live at the P.O." believable or unbelievable?

HERMAN MELVILLE

## Bartleby, the Scrivener

A Story of Wall Street

I am a rather elderly man. The nature of my avocations for the last thirty years has brought me into more than ordinary contact with what would seem an interesting and somewhat singular set of men, of whom as yet nothing that I know of has ever been written:—I mean the law-copyists or scriveners. I have known very many of them, professionally and privately, and if I pleased, could relate divers histories, at which good-natured gentlemen might smile, and sentimental souls might weep. But I waive the biographies of all other scriveners for a few passages in the life of Bartleby, who was a scrivener the strangest I ever saw or heard of. While of other law-copyists I might write the complete life, of Bartleby nothing of that sort can be done. I believe that no materials exist for a full and satisfactory biography of this man. It is an irreparable loss to literature. Bartleby was one of those beings of whom nothing is ascertainable, except from the original sources, and in his case those are very small. What my own astonished eyes saw of Bartleby, *that* is all I know of him, except, indeed, one vague report which will appear in the sequel.[1]

Ere introducing the scrivener, as he first appeared to me, it is fit I make some mention of myself, my *employées,* my business, my chambers, and general surroundings; because some such description is indispensable to an adequate understanding of the chief character about to be presented.

Imprimis:[2] I am a man who, from his youth upwards, has been filled with a profound conviction that the easiest way of life is the best. Hence, though I belong to a profession proverbially energetic and nervous, even to turbulence, at times, yet nothing of that sort have I ever suffered to invade my peace. I am one of those unambitious lawyers who never addresses a jury, or in any way draws down public applause; but in the cool tranquillity of a snug retreat, do a snug business among rich men's bonds and mortgages and title-deeds. All who know me, consider me an eminently *safe* man. The late John Jacob Astor,[3] a personage little given to poetic enthusiasm, had no hesitation in pronouncing my first grand point to be prudence; my next, method. I do not speak it in vanity, but simply record the fact, that I was not unemployed in my profession by the late John Jacob Astor; a name which, I admit, I love to repeat, for it hath a rounded and orbicular sound to it, and rings like unto bullion. I will freely add that I was not insensible to the late John Jacob Astor's good opinion.

Some time prior to the period at which this little history begins, my avocations had been largely increased. The good old office, now extinct in the State of New York, of a Master in Chancery[4] had been conferred upon me. It was not a very arduous office, but very pleasantly remunerative. I seldom lose my temper; much

---

1. That is, in the following story.  2. In the first place.
3. New York fur merchant and landowner (1763–1848) who died the richest man in the United States.
4. A court of chancery can temper the law, applying "dictates of conscience" or "the principles of natural justice"; the office of Master was abolished in 1847.

more seldom indulge in dangerous indignation at wrongs and outrages; but I must be permitted to be rash here and declare, that I consider the sudden and violent abrogation of the office of Master in Chancery, by the new Constitution, as a—premature act; inasmuch as I had counted upon a life-lease of the profits, whereas I only received those of a few short years. But this is by the way.

My chambers were up stairs at No. —— Wall Street. At one end they looked upon the white wall of the interior of a spacious skylight shaft, penetrating the building from top to bottom. This view might have been considered rather tame than otherwise, deficient in what landscape painters call "life." But if so, the view from the other end of my chambers offered, at least, a contrast, if nothing more. In that direction my windows commanded an unobstructed view of a lofty brick wall, black by age and everlasting shade; which wall required no spyglass to bring out its lurking beauties, but for the benefit of all near-sighted spectators, was pushed up to within ten feet of my window panes. Owing to the great height of the surrounding buildings, and my chambers being on the second floor, the interval between this wall and mine not a little resembled a huge square cistern.

At the period just preceding the advent of Bartleby, I had two persons as copyists in my employment, and a promising lad as an office-boy. First, Turkey; second, Nippers, third, Ginger Nut. These may seem names the like of which are not usually found in the Directory.[5] In truth they were nicknames, mutually conferred upon each other by my three clerks, and were deemed expressive of their respective persons or characters. Turkey was a short, pursy[6] Englishman of about my own age, that is, somewhere not far from sixty. In the morning, one might say, his face was of a fine florid hue, but after twelve o'clock, meridian— his dinner hour—it blazed like a grate full of Christmas coals; and continued blazing—but, as it were, with a gradual wane—till 6 o'clock, P.M. or thereabouts, after which I saw no more of the proprietor of the face, which gaining its meridian with the sun, seemed to set with it, to rise, culminate, and decline the following day, with the like regularity and undiminished glory. There are many singular coincidences I have known in the course of my life, not the least among which was the fact, that exactly when Turkey displayed his fullest beams from his red and radiant countenance, just then, too, at that critical moment, began the daily period when I considered his business capacities as seriously disturbed for the remainder of the twenty-four hours. Not that he was absolutely idle, or averse to business then; far from it. The difficulty was, he was apt to be altogether too energetic. There was a strange, inflamed, flurried, flighty recklessness of activity about him. He would be incautious in dipping his pen into his inkstand. All his blots upon my documents were dropped there after twelve o'clock, meridian. Indeed, not only would he be reckless and sadly given to making blots in the afternoon, but some days he went further, and was rather noisy. At such times, too, his face flamed with augmented blazonry, as if cannel coal had been heaped on anthracite.[7] He made an unpleasant racket with his chair; spilled his sand-box; in mending his pens, impatiently split them all to pieces, and threw them on the floor in a sudden passion; stood up and leaned over his table, boxing his papers about in a most indecorous manner, very sad to behold in an elderly man like him. Nevertheless, as he was in many ways a most valuable person to me,

---

5. Post Office Directory.  6. Fat, short-winded.
7. A fast, bright-burning coal heaped on slow-burning, barely glowing coal.

and all the time before twelve o'clock, meridian, was the quickest, steadiest creature too, accomplishing a great deal of work in a style not easy to be matched—for these reasons, I was willing to overlook his eccentricities, though indeed, occasionally, I remonstrated with him. I did this very gently, however, because, though the civilest, nay, the blandest and most reverential of men in the morning, yet in the afternoon he was disposed, upon provocation, to be slightly rash with his tongue, in fact, insolent. Now, valuing his morning services as I did, and resolved not to lose them; yet, at the same time made uncomfortable by his inflamed ways after twelve o'clock; and being a man of peace, unwilling by my admonitions to call forth unseemly retorts from him; I took upon me, one Saturday noon (he was always worse on Saturdays), to hint to him, very kindly, that perhaps now that he was growing old, it might be well to abridge his labors; in short, he need not come to my chambers after twelve o'clock, but, dinner over, had best go home to his lodgings and rest himself till tea-time. But no; he insisted upon his afternoon devotions. His countenance became intolerably fervid, as he oratorically assured me—gesticulating with a long ruler at the other end of the room—that if his services in the morning were useful, how indispensable, then, in the afternoon?

"With submission, sir," said Turkey on this occasion, "I consider myself your right-hand man. In the morning I but marshal and deploy my columns; but in the afternoon I put myself at their head, and gallantly charge the foe, thus!"—and he made a violent thrust with the ruler.

"But the blots, Turkey," intimated I.

"True,—but, with submission, sir, behold these hairs! I am getting old. Surely, sir, a blot or two of a warm afternoon is not to be severely urged against gray hairs. Old age—even if it blot the page—is honorable. With submission, sir, we *both* are getting old."

10   This appeal to my fellow-feeling was hardly to be resisted. At all events, I saw that go he would not. So I made up my mind to let him stay, resolving, nevertheless, to see to it, that during the afternoon he had to do with my less important papers.

Nippers, the second on my list, was a whiskered, sallow, and, upon the whole, rather piratical-looking young man of about five and twenty. I always deemed him the victim of two evil powers—ambition and indigestion. The ambition was evinced by a certain impatience of the duties of a mere copyist, an unwarrantable usurpation of strictly professional affairs, such as the original drawing up of legal documents. The indigestion seemed betokened in an occasional nervous testiness and grinning irritability, causing the teeth to audibly grind together over mistakes committed in copying; unnecessary maledictions, hissed, rather than spoken, in the heat of business; and especially by a continual discontent with the height of the table where he worked. Though of a very ingenious mechanical turn, Nippers could never get this table to suit him. He put chips under it, blocks of various sorts, bits of pasteboard, and at last went so far as to attempt an exquisite adjustment by final pieces of folded blotting-paper. But no invention would answer. If, for the sake of easing his back, he brought the table lid at a sharp angle well up towards his chin, and wrote there like a man using the steep roof of a Dutch house for his desk:—then he declared that it stopped the circulation in his arms. If now he lowered the table to his waistbands, and stooped over it in writing, then there was a sore aching in his back. In short, the truth of the matter was, Nippers knew not what he wanted. Or, if he wanted any thing, it was to be rid of a scrivener's table altogether. Among the manifestations of his diseased ambition was a fondness he had for receiving visits from certain ambiguous-looking fellows in seedy coats, whom he called his clients. Indeed I was aware that not only was he, at times, considerable of a ward-politician, but he occasionally did a little business at the Justices' courts, and was not unknown on the steps of the Tombs.[8] I have good reason to believe, however, that one individual who called upon him at my chambers, and who, with a grand air, he insisted was his client, was no other than a dun,[9] and the alleged title-deed, a bill. But with all his failings, and the annoyances he caused me, Nippers, like his compatriot Turkey, was a very useful man to me; wrote a neat, swift hand; and, when he chose, was not deficient in a gentlemanly sort of deportment. Added to this, he always dressed in a gentlemanly sort of way: and so, incidentally, reflected credit upon my chambers. Whereas with respect to Turkey, I had much ado to keep him from being a reproach to me. His clothes were apt to look oily and smell of eating-houses. He wore his pantaloons very loose and baggy in summer. His coats were execrable; his hat not to be handled. But while the hat was a thing of indifference to me, inasmuch as his natural civility and deference, as a dependent Englishman, always led him to doff it the moment he entered the room, yet his coat was another matter. Concerning his coats, I reasoned with him; but with no effect. The truth was, I suppose, that a man with so small an income, could not afford to sport such a lustrous face and a lustrous coat at one and the same time. As Nippers once observed, Turkey's money went chiefly for red ink. One winter day I presented Turkey with a highly-respectable looking coat of my own, a padded gray coat, of a most comfortable warmth, and which buttoned straight up from the knee to the neck. I thought Turkey would appreciate the favor, and abate his rashness and obstreperousness of afternoons. But no. I verily believe that buttoning himself up in so downy and blanket-like a coat had a pernicious effect upon him; upon the same principle that too much oats are bad for horses. In fact, precisely as a rash, restive horse is said to feel his oats, so Turkey felt his coat. It made him insolent. He was a man whom prosperity harmed.

Though concerning the self-indulgent habits of Turkey I had my own private surmises, yet touching Nippers I was well persuaded that whatever might be his faults in other respects, he was, at least, a temperate young man. But indeed, nature herself seemed to have been his vintner,[1] and at his birth charged him so thoroughly with an irritable, brandy-like disposition, that all subsequent potations were needless. When I consider how, amid the stillness of my chambers, Nippers would sometimes impatiently rise from his seat, and stooping over his table, spread his arms wide apart, seize the whole desk, and move it, and jerk it, with a grim, grinding motion on the floor, as if the table were a perverse voluntary agent, intent on thwarting and vexing him; I plainly perceive that for Nippers, brandy and water were altogether superfluous.

It was fortunate for me that, owing to its peculiar cause—indigestion—the irritability and consequent nervousness of Nippers, were mainly observable in the morning, while in the afternoon he was comparatively mild. So that Turkey's paroxysms only coming on about twelve o'clock, I never had to do with their eccentricities at one time. Their fits relieved each other like guards. When Nip-

---

8. Prison in New York City.    9. Bill collector.    1. Wine seller.

pers' was on, Turkey's was off; and *vice versa*. This was a good natural arrangement under the circumstances.

Ginger Nut, the third on my list, was a lad some twelve years old. His father was a carman,[2] ambitious of seeing his son on the bench instead of a cart, before he died. So he sent him to my office as student at law, errand boy, and cleaner and sweeper, at the rate of one dollar a week. He had a little desk to himself, but he did not use it much. Upon inspection, the drawer exhibited a great array of the shells of various sorts of nuts. Indeed, to this quick-witted youth the whole noble science of the law was contained in a nutshell. Not the least among the employments of Ginger Nut, as well as one which he discharged with the most alacrity, was his duty as cake and apple purveyor for Turkey and Nippers. Copying law papers being proverbially a dry, husky sort of business, my two scriveners were fain to moisten their mouths very often with Spitzenbergs[3] to be had at the numerous stalls nigh the Custom House and Post Office. Also, they sent Ginger Nut very frequently for that peculiar cake—small, flat, round, and very spicy—after which he had been named by them. Of a cold morning when business was but dull, Turkey would gobble up scores of these cakes, as if they were mere wafers—indeed they sell them at the rate of six or eight for a penny—the scrape of his pen blending with the crunching of the crisp particles in his mouth. Of all the fiery afternoon blunders and flurried rashnesses of Turkey, was his once moistening a ginger-cake between his lips, and clapping it on to a mortgage for a seal. I came within an ace of dismissing him then. But he mollified me by making an oriental bow, and saying—"With submission, sir, it was generous of me to find you in[4] stationery on my own account."

15    Now my original business—that of a conveyancer and title hunter,[5] and drawer-up of recondite documents of all sorts—was considerably increased by receiving the master's office. There was now great work for scriveners. Not only must I push the clerks already with me, but I must have additional help. In answer to my advertisement, a motionless young man one morning stood upon my office threshold, the door being open, for it was summer. I can see that figure now—pallidly neat, pitiably respectable, incurably forlorn! It was Bartleby.

After a few words touching his qualifications, I engaged him, glad to have among my corps of copyists a man of so singularly sedate an aspect, which I thought might operate beneficially upon the flighty temper of Turkey, and the fiery one of Nippers.

I should have stated before that ground glass folding-doors divided my premises into two parts, one of which was occupied by my scriveners, the other by myself. According to my humor I threw open these doors, or closed them. I resolved to assign Bartleby a corner by the folding-doors, but on my side of them, so as to have this quiet man within easy call, in case any trifling thing was to be done. I placed his desk close up to a small side-window in that part of the room, a window which originally had afforded a lateral view of certain grimy backyards and bricks, but which, owing to subsequent erections, commanded at present no view at all, though it gave some light. Within three feet of the panes was a wall, and the light came down from far above, between two lofty buildings, as

---

2. Driver of wagon or cart that hauls goods.   3. Red-and-yellow American apple.   4. Supply you with.
5. Lawyer who draws up deeds for transferring property, and one who searches out legal control of title deeds.

from a very small opening in a dome. Still further to a satisfactory arrangement, I procured a high green folding screen, which might entirely isolate Bartleby from my sight, though not remove him from my voice. And thus, in a manner, privacy and society were conjoined.

At first Bartleby did an extraordinary quantity of writing. As if long famishing for something to copy, he seemed to gorge himself on my documents. There was no pause for digestion. He ran a day and night line, copying by sunlight and by candlelight. I should have been quite delighted with his application, had he been cheerfully industrious. But he wrote on silently, palely, mechanically.

It is, of course, an indispensable part of a scrivener's business to verify the accuracy of his copy, word by word. Where there are two or more scriveners in an office, they assist each other in this examination, one reading from the copy, the other holding the original. It is a very dull, wearisome, and lethargic affair. I can readily imagine that to some sanguine temperaments it would be altogether intolerable. For example, I cannot credit that the mettlesome poet Byron would have contentedly sat down with Bartleby to examine a law document of, say, five hundred pages, closely written in a crimpy hand.

Now and then, in the haste of business, it had been my habit to assist in comparing some brief document myself, calling Turkey or Nippers for this purpose. One object I had in placing Bartleby so handy to me behind the screen, was to avail myself of his services on such trivial occasions. It was on the third day, I think, of his being with me, and before any necessity had arisen for having his own writing examined, that, being much hurried to complete a small affair I had in hand, I abruptly called to Bartleby. In my haste and natural expectancy of instant compliance, I sat with my head bent over the original on my desk, and my right hand sideways, and somewhat nervously extended with the copy, so that immediately upon emerging from his retreat, Bartleby might snatch it and proceed to business without the least delay.

In this very attitude did I sit when I called to him, rapidly stating what it was I wanted him to do—namely, to examine a small paper with me. Imagine my surprise, nay, my consternation, when without moving from his privacy, Bartleby, in a singularly mild, firm voice, replied, "I would prefer not to."

I sat awhile in perfect silence, rallying my stunned faculties. Immediately it occurred to me that my ears had deceived me, or Bartleby had entirely misunderstood my meaning. I repeated my request in the clearest tone I could assume. But in quite as clear a one came the previous reply, "I would prefer not to."

"Prefer not to," echoed I, rising in high excitement, and crossing the room with a stride. "What do you mean? Are you moon-struck?[6] I want you to help me compare this sheet here—take it," and I thrust it towards him.

"I would prefer not to," said he.

I looked at him steadfastly. His face was leanly composed; his gray eye dimly calm. Not a wrinkle of agitation rippled him. Had there been the least uneasiness, anger, impatience or impertinence in his manner; in other words, had there been anything ordinarily human about him, doubtless I should have violently dismissed him from the premises. But as it was, I should have as soon thought of turning my pale plaster-of-paris bust of Cicero[7] out-of-doors. I stood gazing at

---

6. Crazy.
7. Marcus Tullius Cicero (106–43 B.C.E.), pro-republican Roman statesman, barrister, writer, and orator.

him awhile, as he went on with his own writing, and then reseated myself at my desk. This is very strange, thought I. What had one best do? But my business hurried me. I concluded to forget the matter for the present, reserving it for my future leisure. So calling Nippers from the other room, the paper was speedily examined.

A few days after this, Bartleby concluded four lengthy documents, being quadruplicates of a week's testimony taken before me in my High Court of Chancery. It became necessary to examine them. It was an important suit, and great accuracy was imperative. Having all things arranged I called Turkey, Nippers and Ginger Nut from the next room, meaning to place the four copies in the hands of my four clerks, while I should read from the original. Accordingly Turkey, Nippers and Ginger Nut had taken their seats in a row, each with his document in hand, when I called to Bartleby to join this interesting group.

"Bartleby! quick, I am waiting."

I heard a slow scrape of his chair legs on the uncarpeted floor, and soon he appeared standing at the entrance of his hermitage.

"What is wanted?" said he mildly.

"The copies, the copies," said I hurriedly. "We are going to examine them. There"—and I held towards him the fourth quadruplicate.

"I would prefer not to," he said, and gently disappeared behind the screen.

For a few moments I was turned into a pillar of salt,[8] standing at the head of my seated column of clerks. Recovering myself, I advanced towards the screen, and demanded the reason for such extraordinary conduct.

"*Why* do you refuse?"

"I would prefer not to."

With any other man I should have flown outright into a dreadful passion, scorned all further words, and thrust him ignominiously from my presence. But there was something about Bartleby that not only strangely disarmed me, but in a wonderful manner touched and disconcerted me. I began to reason with him.

"These are your own copies we are about to examine. It is labor saving to you, because one examination will answer for your four papers. It is common usage. Every copyist is bound to help examine his copy. Is it not so? Will you not speak? Answer!"

"I prefer not to," he replied in a flute-like tone. It seemed to me that while I had been addressing him, he carefully revolved every statement that I made; fully comprehended the meaning; could not gainsay the irresistible conclusion; but, at the same time, some paramount consideration prevailed with him to reply as he did.

"You are decided, then, not to comply with my request—a request made according to common usage and common sense?"

He briefly gave me to understand that on that point my judgment was sound. Yes: his decision was irreversible.

It is not seldom the case that when a man is browbeaten in some unprecedented and violently unreasonable way, he begins to stagger in his own plainest faith. He begins, as it were, vaguely to surmise that, wonderful as it may be, all

---

8. Struck dumb; in Genesis 19.26, Lot's wife, defying God's command, "looked back from behind him, and she became a pillar of salt."

the justice and all the reason is on the other side. Accordingly, if any disinterested persons are present, he turns to them for some reinforcement for his own faltering mind.

"Turkey," said I, "what do you think of this? Am I not right?"

"With submission, sir," said Turkey, with his blandest tone, "I think that you are."

"Nippers," said I, "what do *you* think of it?"

"I think I should kick him out of the office."

(The reader of nice perceptions will here perceive that, it being morning, Turkey's answer is couched in polite and tranquil terms, but Nippers replies in ill-tempered ones. Or, to repeat a previous sentence, Nippers's ugly mood was on duty, and Turkey's off.)

"Ginger Nut," said I, willing to enlist the smallest suffrage[9] in my behalf, "what do *you* think of it?"

"I think, sir, he's a little *luny*," replied Ginger Nut, with a grin.

"You hear what they say," said I, turning towards the screen, "come forth and do your duty."

But he vouchsafed no reply. I pondered a moment in sore perplexity. But once more business hurried me. I determined again to postpone the consideration of this dilemma to my future leisure. With a little trouble we made out to examine the papers without Bartleby, though at every page or two, Turkey deferentially dropped his opinion that this proceeding was quite out of the common; while Nippers, twitching in his chair with a dyspeptic nervousness, ground out between his set teeth occasional hissing maledictions against the stubborn oaf behind the screen. And for his (Nippers's) part, this was the first and the last time he would do another man's business without pay.

Meanwhile Bartleby sat in his hermitage, oblivious to everything but his own peculiar business there.

Some days passed, the scrivener being employed upon another lengthy work. His late remarkable conduct led me to regard his ways narrowly. I observed that he never went to dinner; indeed that he never went anywhere. As yet I had never of my personal knowledge known him to be outside of my office. He was a perpetual sentry in the corner. At about eleven o'clock though, in the morning, I noticed that Ginger Nut would advance toward the opening in Bartleby's screen, as if silently beckoned thither by a gesture invisible to me where I sat. The boy would then leave the office jingling a few pence, and reappear with a handful of ginger-nuts which he delivered in the hermitage, receiving two of the cakes for his trouble.

He lives, then, on ginger-nuts, thought I; never eats a dinner, properly speaking; he must be a vegetarian then; but no; he never eats even vegetables, he eats nothing but ginger-nuts. My mind then ran on in reveries concerning the probable effects upon the human constitution of living entirely on ginger-nuts. Ginger-nuts are so called because they contain ginger as one of their peculiar constituents, and the final flavoring one. Now what was ginger? A hot, spicy thing. Was Bartleby hot and spicy? Not at all. Ginger, then, had no effect upon Bartleby. Probably he preferred it should have none.

Nothing so aggravates an earnest person as a passive resistance. If the indi-

---

9. Favorable vote.

vidual so resisted be of a not inhumane temper, and the resisting one perfectly harmless in his passivity; then, in the better moods of the former, he will endeavor charitably to construe to his imagination what proves impossible to be solved by his judgment. Even so, for the most part, I regarded Bartleby and his ways. Poor fellow! thought I, he means no mischief; it is plain he intends no insolence; his aspect sufficiently evinces that his eccentricities are involuntary. He is useful to me. I can get along with him. If I turn him away, the chances are he will fall in with some less indulgent employer, and then he will be rudely treated, and perhaps driven forth miserably to starve. Yes. Here I can cheaply purchase a delicious self-approval. To befriend Bartleby; to humor him in his strange wilfulness, will cost me little or nothing, while I lay up in my soul what will eventually prove a sweet morsel for my conscience. But this mood was not invariable with me. The passiveness of Bartleby sometimes irritated me. I felt strangely goaded on to encounter him in new opposition, to elicit some angry spark from him answerable to my own. But indeed I might as well have essayed to strike fire with my knuckles against a bit of Windsor soap.[1] But one afternoon the evil impulse in me mastered me, and the following little scene ensued:

"Bartleby," said I, "when those papers are all copied, I will compare them with you."

"I would prefer not to."

"How? Surely you do not mean to persist in that mulish vagary?"

No answer.

I threw open the folding-doors near by, and turning upon Turkey and Nippers, exclaimed in an excited manner—

"He says, a second time, he won't examine his papers. What do you think of it, Turkey?"

It was afternoon, be it remembered. Turkey sat glowing like a brass boiler, his bald head steaming, his hands reeling among his blotted papers.

"Think of it?" roared Turkey; "I think I'll just step behind his screen, and black his eyes for him!"

So saying, Turkey rose to his feet and threw his arms into a pugilistic position. He was hurrying away to make good his promise, when I detained him, alarmed at the effect of incautiously rousing Turkey's combativeness after dinner.

"Sit down, Turkey," said I, "and hear what Nippers has to say. What do you think of it, Nippers? Would I not be justified in immediately dismissing Bartleby?"

"Excuse me, that is for you to decide, sir. I think his conduct quite unusual, and indeed unjust, as regards Turkey and myself. But it may only be a passing whim."

"Ah," exclaimed I, "you have strangely changed your mind then—you speak very gently of him now."

"All beer," cried Turkey; "gentleness is effects of beer—Nippers and I dined together today. You see how gentle *I* am, sir. Shall I go and black his eyes?"

"You refer to Bartleby, I suppose. No, not today, Turkey," I replied; "pray, put up your fists."

I closed the doors, and again advanced towards Bartleby. I felt additional incentives tempting me to my fate. I burned to be rebelled against again. I remembered that Bartleby never left the office.

---

1. Scented soap, usually brown.

"Bartleby," said I, "Ginger Nut is away; just step round to the Post Office, won't you? (it was but a three minutes' walk,) and see if there is anything for me."

"I would prefer not to."

"You *will* not?"

"I *prefer* not."

I staggered to my desk, and sat there in a deep study. My blind inveteracy returned. Was there any other thing in which I could procure myself to be ignominiously repulsed by this lean, penniless wight?—my hired clerk? What added thing is there, perfectly reasonable, that he will be sure to refuse to do?

"Bartleby!"

No answer.

"Bartleby," in a louder tone.

No answer.

"Bartleby," I roared.

Like a very ghost, agreeably to the laws of magical invocation, at the third summons, he appeared at the entrance of his hermitage.

"Go to the next room, and tell Nippers to come to me."

"I prefer not to," he respectfully and slowly said, and mildly disappeared.

"Very good, Bartleby," said I, in a quiet sort of serenely severe self-possessed tone, intimating the unalterable purpose of some terrible retribution very close at hand. At the moment I half intended something of the kind. But upon the whole, as it was drawing towards my dinner-hour, I thought it best to put on my hat and walk home for the day, suffering much from perplexity and distress of mind.

Shall I acknowledge it? The conclusion of this whole business was, that it soon became a fixed fact of my chambers, that a pale young scrivener, by the name of Bartleby, had a desk there; that he copied for me at the usual rate of four cents a folio (one hundred words); but he was permanently exempt from examining the work done by him, that duty being transferred to Turkey and Nippers, one of compliment doubtless to their superior acuteness; moreover, said Bartleby was never on any account to be dispatched on the most trivial errand of any sort; and that even if entreated to take upon him such a matter, it was generally understood that he would prefer not to—in other words, that he would refuse point-blank.

As days passed on, I became considerably reconciled to Bartleby. His steadiness, his freedom from all dissipation, his incessant industry (except when he chose to throw himself into a standing revery behind his screen), his great stillness, his unalterableness of demeanor under all circumstances, made him a valuable acquisition. One prime thing was this,—*he was always there;*—first in the morning, continually through the day, and the last at night. I had a singular confidence in his honesty. I felt my most precious papers perfectly safe in his hands. Sometimes to be sure I could not, for the very soul of me, avoid falling into sudden spasmodic passions with him. For it was exceeding difficult to bear in mind all the time those strange peculiarities, privileges, and unheard of exemptions, forming the tacit stipulations on Bartleby's part under which he remained in my office. Now and then, in the eagerness of dispatching pressing business, I would inadvertently summon Bartleby, in a short, rapid tone, to put his finger, say, on the incipient tie of a bit of red tape with which I was about compressing some papers. Of course, from behind the screen the usual answer, "I prefer not to," was sure to come; and then, how could a human creature with the common infirmities of our nature, refrain from bitterly exclaiming upon such perverseness—such unreasonableness? However, every added repulse of this sort which I received only tended to lessen the probability of my repeating the inadvertence.

Here it must be said, that according to the custom of most legal gentlemen occupying chambers in densely-populated law buildings, there were several keys to my door. One was kept by a woman residing in the attic, which person weekly scrubbed and daily swept and dusted my apartments. Another was kept by Turkey for convenience sake. The third I sometimes carried in my own pocket. The fourth I knew not who had.

Now, one Sunday morning I happened to go to Trinity Church, to hear a celebrated preacher, and finding myself rather early on the ground, I thought I would walk round to my chambers for a while. Luckily I had my key with me; but upon applying it to the lock, I found it resisted by something inserted from the inside. Quite surprised, I called out; when to my consternation a key was turned from within; and thrusting his lean visage at me, and holding the door ajar, the apparition of Bartleby appeared, in his shirt sleeves, and otherwise in a strangely tattered dishabille, saying quietly that he was sorry, but he was deeply engaged just then, and—preferred not admitting me at present. In a brief word or two, he moreover added, that perhaps I had better walk round the block two or three times, and by that time he would probably have concluded his affairs.

Now, the utterly unsurmised appearance of Bartleby, tenanting my law-chambers of a Sunday morning, with his cadaverously gentlemanly *nonchalance*, yet withal firm and self-possessed, had such a strange effect upon me, that incontinently I slunk away from my own door, and did as desired. But not without sundry twinges of impotent rebellion against the mild effrontery of this unaccountable scrivener. Indeed, it was his wonderful mildness, chiefly, which not only disarmed me, but unmanned me, as it were. For I consider that one, for the time, is sort of unmanned when he tranquilly permits his hired clerk to dictate to him, and order him away from his own premises. Furthermore, I was full of uneasiness as to what Bartleby could possibly be doing in my office in his shirt sleeves, and in an otherwise dismantled condition of a Sunday morning. Was anything amiss going on? Nay, that was out of the question. It was not to be thought of for a moment that Bartleby was an immoral person. But what could he be doing there?—copying? Nay again, whatever might be his eccentricities, Bartleby was an eminently decorous person. He would be the last man to sit down to his desk in any state approaching to nudity. Besides, it was Sunday; and there was something about Bartleby that forbade the supposition that he would by any secular occupation violate the proprieties of the day.

Nevertheless, my mind was not pacified; and full of a restless curiosity, at last I returned to the door. Without hindrance I inserted my key, opened it, and entered. Bartleby was not to be seen. I looked round anxiously, peeped behind his screen; but it was very plain that he was gone. Upon more closely examining the place, I surmised that for an indefinite period Bartleby must have ate, dressed, and slept in my office, and that too without plate, mirror, or bed. The cushioned seat of a rickety old sofa in one corner bore the faint impress of a lean, reclining form. Rolled away under his desk, I found a blanket under the empty grate, a blacking box[2] and brush; on a chair, a tin basin, with soap and a ragged towel;

---

2. Box of black shoe polish.

in a newspaper a few crumbs of ginger-nuts and a morsel of cheese. Yes, thought I, it is evident enough that Bartleby has been making his home here, keeping bachelor's hall all by himself. Immediately then the thought came sweeping across me, What miserable friendlessness and loneliness are here revealed! His poverty is great; but his solitude, how horrible! Think of it. Of a Sunday, Wall Street is deserted as Petra;[3] and every night of every day it is an emptiness. This building too, which of weekdays hums with industry and life, at nightfall echoes with sheer vacancy, and all through Sunday is forlorn. And here Bartleby makes his home; sole spectator of a solitude which he has seen all populous—a sort of innocent and transformed Marius brooding among the ruins of Carthage![4]

For the first time in my life a feeling of overpowering stinging melancholy seized me. Before, I had never experienced aught but a not-unpleasing sadness. The bond of a common humanity now drew me irresistibly to gloom. A fraternal melancholy! For both I and Bartleby were sons of Adam. I remembered the bright silks and sparkling faces I had seen that day, in gala trim, swan-like sailing down the Mississippi of Broadway; and I contrasted them with the pallid copyist, and thought to myself, Ah, happiness courts the light, so we deem the world is gay; but misery hides aloof, so we deem that misery there is none. These sad fancyings—chimeras, doubtless, of a sick and silly brain—led on to other and more special thoughts, concerning the eccentricities of Bartleby. Presentiments of strange discoveries hovered round me. The scrivener's pale form appeared to me laid out, among uncaring strangers, in its shivering winding sheet.

Suddenly I was attracted by Bartleby's closed desk, the key in open sight left in the lock.

I mean no mischief, seek the gratification of no heartless curiosity, thought I; besides, the desk is mine, and its contents too, so I will make bold to look within. Everything was methodically arranged, the papers smoothly placed. The pigeonholes were deep, and removing the files of documents, I groped into their recesses. Presently I felt something there, and dragged it out. It was an old bandanna handkerchief, heavy and knotted. I opened it, and saw it was a savings' bank.

I now recalled all the quiet mysteries which I had noted in the man. I remembered that he never spoke but to answer; that though at intervals he had considerable time to himself, yet I had never seen him reading—no, not even a newspaper; that for long periods he would stand looking out, at his pale window behind the screen, upon the dead brick wall; I was quite sure he never visited any refectory or eating house; while his pale face clearly indicated that he never drank beer like Turkey, or tea and coffee even, like other men; that he never went anywhere in particular that I could learn; never went out for a walk, unless indeed that was the case at present; that he had declined telling who he was, or whence he came, or whether he had any relatives in the world; that though so thin and pale, he never complained of ill health. And more than all, I remembered a certain

---

3. Once a flourishing Middle Eastern trade center, long in ruins.
4. Gaius (or Caius) Marius (157–86 B.C.E.), Roman consul and general, expelled from Rome in 88 B.C.E. by Sulla; when an officer of Sextilius, the governor, forbade him to land in Africa, Marius replied, "Go tell him that you have seen Caius Marius sitting in exile among the ruins of Carthage," applying the example of the fortune of that city to the change of his own condition. The image was so common that a few years after "Bartleby," Dickens apologizes for using it: "like that lumbering Marius among the ruins of Carthage, who has sat heavy on a thousand millions of similes" ("The Calais Night-Mail," in *The Uncommercial Traveler*).

unconscious air of pallid—how shall I call it?—of pallid haughtiness, say, or rather an austere reserve about him, which had positively awed me into my tame compliance with his eccentricities, when I had feared to ask him to do the slightest incidental thing for me, even though I might know, from his long-continued motionlessness, that behind his screen he must be standing in one of those dead-wall reveries of his.

Revolving all these things, and coupling them with the recently discovered fact that he made my office his constant abiding place and home, and not forgetful of his morbid moodiness; revolving all these things, a prudential feeling began to steal over me. My first emotions had been those of pure melancholy and sincerest pity; but just in proportion as the forlornness of Bartleby grew and grew to my imagination, did that same melancholy merge into fear, that pity into repulsion. So true it is, and so terrible too, that up to a certain point the thought or sight of misery enlists our best affections; but, in certain special cases, beyond that point it does not. They err who would assert that invariably this is owing to the inherent selfishness of the human heart. It rather proceeds from a certain hopelessness of remedying excessive and organic ill. To a sensitive being, pity is not seldom pain. And when at last it is perceived that such pity cannot lead to effectual succor, common sense bids the soul be rid of it. What I saw that morning persuaded me that the scrivener was the victim of innate and incurable disorder. I might give alms to his body; but his body did not pain him; it was his soul that suffered, and his soul I could not reach.

I did not accomplish the purpose of going to Trinity Church that morning. Somehow, the things I had seen disqualified me for the time from churchgoing. I walked homeward, thinking what I would do with Bartleby. Finally, I resolved upon this;—I would put certain calm questions to him the next morning, touching his history, &c., and if he declined to answer them openly and unreservedly (and I supposed he would prefer not), then to give him a twenty-dollar bill over and above whatever I might owe him, and tell him his services were no longer required; but that if in any other way I could assist him, I would be happy to do so, especially if he desired to return to his native place, wherever that might be, I would willingly help to defray the expenses. Moreover, if, after reaching home, he found himself at any time in want of aid, a letter from him would be sure of a reply.

95 The next morning came.

"Bartleby," said I, gently calling to him behind his screen.

No reply.

"Bartleby," said I, in a still gentler tone, "come here; I am not going to ask you to do anything you would prefer not to do—I simply wish to speak to you."

Upon this he noiselessly slid into view.

100 "Will you tell me, Bartleby, where you were born?"

"I would prefer not to."

"Will you tell me *anything* about yourself?"

"I would prefer not to."

"But what reasonable objection can you have to speak to me? I feel friendly towards you."

105 He did not look at me while I spoke, but kept his glance fixed upon my bust of Cicero, which as I then sat, was directly behind me, some six inches above my head.

"What is your answer, Bartleby?" said I, after waiting a considerable time for a reply, during which his countenance remained immovable, only there was the faintest conceivable tremor of the white attenuated mouth.

"At present I prefer to give no answer," he said, and retired into his hermitage.

It was rather weak in me I confess, but his manner on this occasion nettled me. Not only did there seem to lurk in it a certain calm disdain, but his perverseness seemed ungrateful, considering the undeniable good usage and indulgence he had received from me.

Again I sat ruminating what I should do. Mortified as I was at his behavior, and resolved as I had been to dismiss him when I entered my office, nevertheless I strangely felt something superstitious knocking at my heart, and forbidding me to carry out my purpose, and denouncing me for a villain if I dared to breathe one bitter word against this forlornest of mankind. At last, familiarly drawing my chair behind his screen, I sat down and said: "Bartleby, never mind then about revealing your history; but let me entreat you, as a friend, to comply as far as may be with the usages of this office. Say now you will help to examine papers tomorrow or next day: in short, say now that in a day or two you will begin to be a little reasonable:—say so, Bartleby."

"At present I would prefer not to be a little reasonable," was his mildly cadaverous reply.

Just then the folding-doors opened, and Nippers approached. He seemed suffering from an unusually bad night's rest, induced by severer indigestion than common. He overheard those final words of Bartleby.

"*Prefer not,* eh?" gritted Nippers—"I'd *prefer* him, if I were you, sir," addressing me—"I'd *prefer* him; I'd give him preferences, the stubborn mule! What is it, sir, pray, that he *prefers* not to do now?"

Bartleby moved not a limb.

"Mr. Nippers," said I, "I'd prefer that you would withdraw for the present."

Somehow, of late I had got into the way of involuntarily using this word "prefer" upon all sorts of not exactly suitable occasions. And I trembled to think that my contact with the scrivener had already and seriously affected me in a mental way. And what further and deeper aberration might it not yet produce? This apprehension had not been without efficacy in determining me to summary means.

As Nippers, looking very sour and sulky, was departing, Turkey blandly and deferentially approached.

"With submission, sir," said he, "yesterday I was thinking about Bartleby here, and I think that if he would but prefer to take a quart of good ale every day, it would do much towards mending him and enabling him to assist in examining his papers."

"So you have got the word too," said I, slightly excited.

"With submission, what word, sir?" asked Turkey, respectfully crowding himself into the contracted space behind the screen, and by so doing making me jostle the scrivener. "What word, sir?"

"I would prefer to be left alone here," said Bartleby, as if offended at being mobbed in his privacy.

"*That's* the word, Turkey," said I—"*that's* it."

"Oh, *prefer?* oh yes—queer word. I never use it myself. But, sir, as I was saying, if he would but prefer—"

"Turkey," interrupted I, "you will please withdraw."

"Oh certainly, sir, if you prefer that I should."

As he opened the folding-door to retire, Nippers at his desk caught a glimpse of me, and asked whether I would prefer to have a certain paper copied on blue paper or white. He did not in the least roguishly accent the word *prefer*. It was plain that it involuntarily rolled from his tongue. I thought to myself, surely I must get rid of a demented man, who already has in some degree turned the tongues, if not the heads of myself and clerks. But I thought it prudent not to break the dismission at once.

The next day I noticed that Bartleby did nothing but stand at his window in his dead-wall revery. Upon asking him why he did not write, he said that he had decided upon doing no more writing.

"Why, how now? what next?" exclaimed I, "do no more writing?"

"No more."

"And what is the reason?"

"Do you not see the reason for yourself," he indifferently replied.

I looked steadfastly at him, and perceived that his eyes looked dull and glazed. Instantly it occurred to me, that his unexampled diligence in copying by his dim window for the first few weeks of his stay with me might have temporarily impaired his vision.

I was touched. I said something in condolence with him. I hinted that of course he did wisely in abstaining from writing for a while; and urged him to embrace that opportunity of taking wholesome exercise in the open air. This, however, he did not do. A few days after this, my other clerks being absent, and being in a great hurry to dispatch certain letters by the mail, I thought that, having nothing else earthly to do, Bartleby would surely be less inflexible than usual, and carry these letters to the post office. But he blankly declined. So, much to my inconvenience, I went myself.

Still added days went by. Whether Bartleby's eyes improved or not, I could not say. To all appearance, I thought they did. But when I asked him if they did, he vouchsafed no answer. At all events, he would do no copying. At last, in reply to my urgings, he informed me that he had permanently given up copying.

"What!" exclaimed I; "suppose your eyes should get entirely well—better than ever before—would you not copy then?"

"I have given up copying," he answered, and slid aside.

He remained, as ever, a fixture in my chamber. Nay—if that were possible—he became still more of a fixture than before. What was to be done? He would do nothing in the office: why should he stay there? In plain fact, he had now become a millstone[5] to me, not only useless as a necklace, but afflictive to bear. Yet I was sorry for him. I speak less than truth when I say that, on his own account, he occasioned me uneasiness. If he would but have named a single relative or friend, I would instantly have written, and urged their taking the poor fellow away to some convenient retreat. But he seemed alone, absolutely alone in the universe. A bit of wreck in the mid-Atlantic. At length, necessities connected with my business tyrannized over all other considerations. Decently as I could, I told

---

5. Heavy stone for grinding grain. See Matthew 18.6: "But whoso shall offend one of these little ones which believe in me, it were better for him that a millstone were hanged about his neck, and that he were drowned in the depth of the sea."

Bartleby that in six days' time he must unconditionally leave the office. I warned him to take measures, in the interval, for procuring some other abode. I offered to assist him in this endeavor, if he himself would but take the first step towards a removal. "And when you finally quit me, Bartleby," added I, "I shall see that you go not away entirely unprovided. Six days from this hour, remember."

At the expiration of that period, I peeped behind the screen, and lo! Bartleby was there.

I buttoned up my coat, balanced myself; advanced slowly towards him, touched his shoulder, and said, "The time has come; you must quit this place; I am sorry for you; here is money; but you must go."

"I would prefer not," he replied, with his back still towards me.

"You *must*."

He remained silent.

Now I had an unbounded confidence in this man's common honesty. He had frequently restored to me sixpences and shillings[6] carelessly dropped upon the floor, for I am apt to be very reckless in such shirt-button affairs. The proceeding then which followed will not be deemed extraordinary.

"Bartleby," said I, "I owe you twelve dollars on account; here are thirty-two; the odd twenty are yours.—Will you take it?" and I handed the bills towards him.

But he made no motion.

"I will leave them here then," putting them under a weight on the table. Then taking my hat and cane and going to the door I tranquilly turned and added—"After you have removed your things from these offices, Bartleby, you will of course lock the door—since everyone is now gone for the day but you—and if you please, slip your key underneath the mat, so that I may have it in the morning. I shall not see you again; so good-bye to you. If hereafter in your new place of abode I can be of any service to you, do not fail to advise me by letter. Good-bye, Bartleby, and fare you well."

But he answered not a word; like the last column of some ruined temple, he remained standing mute and solitary in the middle of the otherwise deserted room.

As I walked home in a pensive mood, my vanity got the better of my pity. I could not but highly plume myself on my masterly management in getting rid of Bartleby. Masterly I call it, and such it must appear to any dispassionate thinker. The beauty of my procedure seemed to consist in its perfect quietness. There was no vulgar bullying, no bravado of any sort, no choleric hectoring, and striding to and fro across the apartment, jerking out vehement commands for Bartleby to bundle himself off with his beggarly traps.[7] Nothing of the kind. Without loudly bidding Bartleby depart—as an inferior genius might have done—I *assumed* the ground that depart he must; and upon that assumption built all I had to say. The more I thought over my procedure, the more I was charmed with it. Nevertheless, next morning, upon awakening, I had my doubts,—I had somehow slept off the fumes of vanity. One of the coolest and wisest hours a man has is just after he awakes in the morning. My procedure seemed as sagacious as ever,—but only in theory. How it would prove in practice—there was the rub. It was truly a beautiful thought to have assumed Bartleby's departure; but, after all, that assumption was simply my own, and none of Bartleby's. The great point

6. Coins.   7. Personal belongings, luggage.

was, not whether I had assumed that he would quit me, but whether he would prefer so to do. He was more a man of preferences than assumptions.

After breakfast, I walked downtown, arguing the probabilities *pro* and *con*. One moment I thought it would prove a miserable failure, and Bartleby would be found all alive at my office as usual; the next moment it seemed certain that I should see his chair empty. And so I kept veering about. At the corner of Broadway and Canal Street, I saw quite an excited group of people standing in earnest conversation.

"I'll take odds he doesn't," said a voice as I passed.

"Doesn't go?—done!" said I, "put up your money."

I was instinctively putting my hand in my pocket to produce my own, when I remembered that this was an election day. The words I had overheard bore no reference to Bartleby, but to the success or non-success of some candidate for the mayoralty. In my intent frame of mind, I had, as it were, imagined that all Broadway shared in my excitement, and were debating the same question with me. I passed on, very thankful that the uproar of the street screened my momentary absent-mindedness.

As I had intended, I was earlier than usual at my office door. I stood listening for a moment. All was still. He must be gone. I tried the knob. The door was locked. Yes, my procedure had worked to a charm; he indeed must be vanished. Yet a certain melancholy mixed with this: I was almost sorry for my brilliant success. I was fumbling under the door mat for the key, which Bartleby was to have left there for me, when accidentally my knee knocked against a panel, producing a summoning sound, and in response a voice came to me from within—"Not yet; I am occupied."

It was Bartleby.

I was thunderstruck. For an instant I stood like the man who, pipe in mouth, was killed one cloudless afternoon long ago in Virginia, by summer lightning; at his own warm open window he was killed, and remained leaning out there upon the dreamy afternoon, till some one touched him, when he fell.

"Not gone!" I murmured at last. But again obeying that wondrous ascendancy which the inscrutable scrivener had over me, and from which ascendancy, for all my chafing, I could not completely escape, I slowly went downstairs and out into the street, and while walking round the block, considered what I should next do in this unheard-of perplexity. Turn the man out by an actual thrusting I could not; to drive him away by calling him hard names would not do; calling in the police was an unpleasant idea; and yet, permit him to enjoy his cadaverous triumph over me,—this too I could not think of. What was to be done? or, if nothing could be done, was there anything further that I could *assume* in the matter? Yes, as before I had prospectively assumed that Bartleby would depart, so now I might retrospectively assume that departed he was. In the legitimate carrying out of this assumption, I might enter my office in a great hurry, and pretending not to see Bartleby at all, walk straight against him as if he were air. Such a proceeding would in a singular degree have the appearance of a home-thrust.[8] It was hardly possible that Bartleby could withstand such an application of the doctrine of assumptions. But upon second thoughts the success of the plan seemed rather dubious. I resolved to argue the matter over with him again.

---

8. In fencing, a successful thrust to the opponent's body.

"Bartleby," said I, entering the office, with a quietly severe expression, "I am seriously displeased. I am pained, Bartleby. I had thought better of you. I had imagined you of such a gentlemanly organization, that in any delicate dilemma a slight hint would suffice—in short, an assumption. But it appears I am deceived. Why," I added, unaffectedly starting, "you have not even touched that money yet," pointing to it, just where I had left it the evening previous.

He answered nothing.

"Will you, or will you not, quit me?" I now demanded in a sudden passion, advancing close to him.

"I would prefer *not* to quit you," he replied, gently emphasizing the *not*.

"What earthly right have you to stay here? Do you pay any rent? Do you pay my taxes? Or is this property yours?"

He answered nothing.

"Are you ready to go on and write now? Are your eyes recovered? Could you copy a small paper for me this morning? or help examine a few lines? or step round to the post office? In a word, will you do anything at all, to give a coloring to your refusal to depart the premises?"

He silently retired into his hermitage.

I was now in such a state of nervous resentment that I thought it but prudent to check myself at present from further demonstrations. Bartleby and I were alone. I remembered the tragedy of the unfortunate Adams and the still more unfortunate Colt in the solitary office of the latter;[9] and how poor Colt, being dreadfully incensed by Adams, and imprudently permitting himself to get wildly excited, was at unawares hurried into his fatal act—an act which certainly no man could possibly deplore more than the actor himself. Often it had occurred to me in my ponderings upon the subject, that had that altercation taken place in the public street, or at a private residence, it would not have terminated as it did. It was the circumstance of being alone in a solitary office, up stairs, of a building entirely unhallowed by humanizing domestic associations—an uncarpeted office, doubtless, of a dusty, haggard sort of appearance;—this it must have been, which greatly helped to enhance the irritable desperation of the hapless Colt.

But when this old Adam[1] of resentment rose in me and tempted me concerning Bartleby, I grappled him and threw him. How? Why, simply by recalling the divine injunction: "A new commandment[2] give I unto you, that ye love one another." Yes, this it was that saved me. Aside from higher considerations, charity often operates as a vastly wise and prudent principle—a great safeguard to its possessor. Men have committed murder for jealousy's sake, and anger's sake, and hatred's sake, and selfishness' sake, and spiritual pride's sake; but no man that ever I heard of, ever committed a diabolical murder for sweet charity's sake. Mere self-interest, then, if no better motive can be enlisted, should, especially with high-tempered men, prompt all beings to charity and philanthropy. At any rate,

---

9. In 1841, John C. Colt, brother of the famous gunmaker, unintentionally killed Samuel Adams, a printer, when he hit him on the head during a fight.

1. Sinful element in human nature, see e.g., "Invocation of Blessing on the Child," in the *Book of Common Prayer:* "Grant that the old Adam in this child may be so buried, that the new man may be raised up in him." Christ is sometimes called the "new Adam."

2. In John 13.34, where, however, the phrasing is "I give unto . . ."

upon the occasion in question, I strove to drown my exasperated feelings towards the scrivener by benevolently construing his conduct. Poor fellow, poor fellow! thought I, he don't mean anything; and besides, he has seen hard times, and ought to be indulged.

I endeavored also immediately to occupy myself, and at the same time to comfort my despondency. I tried to fancy that in the course of the morning, at such time as might prove agreeable to him, Bartleby, of his own free accord, would emerge from his hermitage, and take up some decided line of march in the direction of the door. But no. Half-past twelve o'clock came; Turkey began to glow in the face, overturn his inkstand, and become generally obstreperous; Nippers abated down into quietude and courtesy; Ginger Nut munched his noon apple; and Bartleby remained standing at his window in one of his profoundest dead-wall reveries. Will it be credited? Ought I to acknowledge it? That afternoon I left the office without saying one further word to him.

Some days now passed, during which, at leisure intervals I looked a little into "Edwards on the Will," and "Priestley on Necessity."[3] Under the circumstances, those books induced a salutary feeling. Gradually I slid into the persuasion that these troubles of mine touching the scrivener, had been all predestinated from eternity, and Bartleby was billeted upon me for some mysterious purpose of an all-wise Providence, which it was not for a mere mortal like me to fathom. Yes, Bartleby, stay there behind your screen, thought I; I shall persecute you no more; you are harmless and noiseless as any of these old chairs; in short, I never feel so private as when I know you are here. At least I see it, I feel it; I penetrate to the predestinated purpose of my life. I am content. Others may have loftier parts to enact; but my mission in this world, Bartleby, is to furnish you with office-room for such period as you may see fit to remain.

I believe that this wise and blessed frame of mind would have continued with me, had it not been for the unsolicited and uncharitable remarks obtruded upon me by my professional friends who visited the rooms. But thus it often is, that the constant friction of illiberal minds wears out at last the best resolves of the more generous. Though to be sure, when I reflected upon it, it was not strange that people entering my office should be struck by the peculiar aspect of the unaccountable Bartleby, and so be tempted to throw out some sinister observations concerning him. Sometimes an attorney having business with me, and calling at my office, and finding no one but the scrivener there, would undertake to obtain some sort of precise information from him touching my whereabouts; but without heeding his idle talk, Bartleby would remain standing immovable in the middle of the room. So after contemplating him in that position for a time, the attorney would depart, no wiser than he came.

Also, when a Reference[4] was going on, and the room full of lawyers and witnesses and business was driving fast; some deeply occupied legal gentleman pres-

---

3. Jonathan Edwards (1703–1758), New England Calvinist theologian and revivalist, in *The Freedom of the Will* (1754), argued that human beings are not in fact free, for though they choose according to the way they see things, that way is predetermined (by biography, environment, and character), and they act out of personality rather than by will. Joseph Priestley (1733–1804), dissenting preacher, scientist, grammarian, and philosopher, in *The Doctrine of Philosophical Necessity* (1777), argued that free will is theologically objectionable, metaphysically incomprehensible, and morally undesirable.
4. Consultation or committee meeting.

ent, seeing Bartleby wholly unemployed, would request him to run round to his (the legal gentleman's) office and fetch some papers for him. Thereupon, Bartleby would tranquilly decline, and yet remain idle as before. Then the lawyer would give a great stare, and turn to me. And what could I say? At last I was made aware that all through the circle of my professional acquaintance, a whisper of wonder was running round, having reference to the strange creature I kept at my office. This worried me very much. And as the idea came upon me of his possibly turning out a long-lived man, and keep occupying my chambers, and denying my authority; and perplexing my visitors; and scandalizing my professional reputation; and casting a general gloom over the premises; keeping soul and body together to the last upon his savings (for doubtless he spent but half a dime a day), and in the end perhaps outlive me, and claim possession of my office by right of his perpetual occupancy: as all these dark anticipations crowded upon me more and more, and my friends continually intruded their relentless remarks upon the apparition in my room; a great change was wrought in me. I resolved to gather all my faculties together, and forever rid me of this intolerable incubus.[5]

Ere revolving any complicated project, however, adapted to this end, I first simply suggested to Bartleby the propriety of his permanent departure. In a calm and serious tone, I commended the idea to his careful and mature consideration. But having taken three days to meditate upon it, he apprised me that his original determination remained the same; in short, that he still preferred to abide with me.

What shall I do? I now said to myself, buttoning up my coat to the last button. What shall I do? what ought I to do? what does conscience say I *should* do with this man, or rather ghost. Rid myself of him, I must; go, he shall. But how? You will not thrust him, the poor, pale, passive mortal,—you will not thrust such a helpless creature out of your door? you will not dishonor yourself by such cruelty? No, I will not, I cannot do that. Rather would I let him live and die here, and then mason up his remains in the wall. What then will you do? For all your coaxing, he will not budge. Bribes he leaves under your own paperweight on your table; in short, it is quite plain that he prefers to cling to you.

Then something severe, something unusual must be done. What! surely you will not have him collared by a constable, and commit his innocent pallor to the common jail? And upon what ground could you procure such a thing to be done?—a vagrant, is he? What! he a vagrant, a wanderer, who refuses to budge? It is because he will *not* be a vagrant, then, that you seek to count him *as* a vagrant. That is too absurd. No visible means of support: there I have him. Wrong again: for indubitably he *does* support himself, and that is the only unanswerable proof that any man can show of his possessing the means so to do. No more then. Since he will not quit me, I must quit him. I will change my offices; I will move elsewhere; and give him fair notice, that if I find him on my new premises I will then proceed against him as a common trespasser.

Acting accordingly, next day I thus addressed him: "I find these chambers too far from the City Hall; the air is unwholesome. In a word, I propose to remove my offices next week, and shall no longer require your services. I tell you this now, in order that you may seek another place."

---

5. Evil spirit.

He made no reply, and nothing more was said.

On the appointed day I engaged carts and men, proceeded to my chambers, and having but little furniture, everything was removed in a few hours. Throughout, the scrivener remained standing behind the screen, which I directed to be removed the last thing. It was withdrawn; and being folded up like a huge folio, left him the motionless occupant of a naked room. I stood in the entry watching him a moment, while something from within me upbraided me.

I re-entered, with my hand in my pocket—and—and my heart in my mouth.

"Good-bye, Bartleby; I am going—good-bye, and God some way bless you; and take that," slipping something in his hand. But it dropped upon the floor, and then,—strange to say—I tore myself from him whom I had so longed to be rid of.

Established in my new quarters, for a day or two I kept the door locked, and started at every footfall in the passages. When I returned to my rooms after any little absence, I would pause at the threshold for an instant, and attentively listen, ere applying my key. But these fears were needless. Bartleby never came nigh me.

I thought all was going well, when a perturbed-looking stranger visited me, inquiring whether I was the person who had recently occupied rooms at No.—— Wall Street.

Full of forebodings, I replied that I was.

"Then sir," said the stranger, who proved a lawyer, "you are responsible for the man you left there. He refuses to do any copying; he refuses to do anything; he says he prefers not to; and he refuses to quit the premises."

"I am very sorry, sir," said I, with assumed tranquillity, but an inward tremor, "but, really, the man you allude to is nothing to me—he is no relation or apprentice of mine, that you should hold me responsible for him."

"In mercy's name, who is he?"

"I certainly cannot inform you. I know nothing about him. Formerly I employed him as a copyist; but he has done nothing for me now for some time past."

"I shall settle him then,—good morning, sir."

Several days passed, and I heard nothing more; and though I often felt a charitable prompting to call at the place and see poor Bartleby, yet a certain squeamishness of I know not what withheld me.

All is over with him, by this time, thought I at last, when through another week no further intelligence reached me. But coming to my room the day after, I found several persons waiting at my door in a high state of nervous excitement.

"That's the man—here he comes," cried the foremost one, whom I recognized as the lawyer who had previously called upon me alone.

"You must take him away, sir, at once," cried a portly person among them, advancing upon me, and whom I knew to be the landlord of No. —— Wall Street. "These gentlemen, my tenants, cannot stand it any longer; Mr. B——" pointing to the lawyer, "has turned him out of his room, and he now persists in haunting the building generally, sitting upon the banisters of the stairs by day, and sleeping in the entry by night. Everybody is concerned; clients are leaving the offices; some fears are entertained of a mob; something you must do, and that without delay."

Aghast at this torrent, I fell back before it, and would fain have locked myself in my new quarters. In vain I persisted that Bartleby was nothing to me—no more than to anyone else. In vain:—I was the last person known to have anything to do with him, and they held me to the terrible account. Fearful then of being exposed in the papers (as one person present obscurely threatened) I considered the matter, and at length said, that if the lawyer would give me a confidential interview with the scrivener, in his (the lawyer's) own room, I would that afternoon strive my best to rid them of the nuisance they complained of.

Going upstairs to my old haunt, there was Bartleby silently sitting upon the banister at the landing.

"What are you doing here, Bartleby?" said I.

"Sitting upon the banister," he mildly replied.

I motioned him into the lawyer's room, who then left us.

"Bartleby," said I, "are you aware that you are the cause of great tribulation to me, by persisting in occupying the entry after being dismissed from the office?"

No answer.

"Now one of two things must take place. Either you must do something, or something must be done to you. Now what sort of business would you like to engage in? Would you like to re-engage in copying for someone?"

"No; I would prefer not to make any change."

"Would you like a clerkship in a drygoods store?"

"There is too much confinement about that. No, I would not like a clerkship; but I am not particular."

"Too much confinement," I cried, "why you keep yourself confined all the time!"

"I would prefer not to take a clerkship," he rejoined, as if to settle that little item at once.

"How would a bartender's business suit you? There is no trying of the eyesight in that."

"I would not like it at all; though, as I said before, I am not particular."

His unwonted wordiness inspirited me. I returned to the charge.

"Well then, would you like to travel through the country collecting bills for the merchants? That would improve your health."

"No, I would prefer to be doing something else."

"How then would going as a companion to Europe, to entertain some young gentleman with your conversation,—how would that suit you?"

"Not at all. It does not strike me that there is anything definite about that. I like to be stationary. But I am not particular."

"Stationary you shall be then," I cried, now losing all patience, and for the first time in all my exasperating connection with him fairly flying into a passion. "If you do not go away from these premises before night, I shall feel bound—indeed I *am* bound—to—to—to quit the premises myself!" I rather absurdly concluded, knowing not with what possible threat to try to frighten his immobility into compliance. Despairing of all further efforts, I was precipitately leaving him, when a final thought occurred to me—one which had not been wholly unindulged before.

"Bartleby," said I, in the kindest tone I could assume under such exciting circumstances, "will you go home with me now—not to my office, but my dwelling—and remain there till we can conclude upon some convenient arrangement for you at our leisure? Come, let us start now, right away."

"No: at present I would prefer not to make any change at all."

I answered nothing; but effectually dodging everyone by the suddenness and rapidity of my flight, rushed from the building, ran up Wall Street toward Broadway, and jumping into the first omnibus was soon removed from pursuit. As soon as tranquillity returned I distinctly perceived that I had now done all that I possibly could, both in respect to the demands of the landlord and his tenants, and with regard to my own desire and sense of duty, to benefit Bartleby, and shield him from rude persecution. I now strove to be entirely carefree and quiescent; and my conscience justified me in the attempt; though indeed it was not so successful as I could have wished. So fearful was I of being again hunted out by the incensed landlord and his exasperated tenants, that, surrendering my business to Nippers, for a few days I drove about the upper part of the town and through the suburbs, in my rockaway;[6] crossed over to Jersey City and Hoboken, and paid fugitive visits to Manhattanville and Astoria. In fact I almost lived in my rockaway for the time.

When again I entered my office, lo, a note from the landlord lay upon the desk. I opened it with trembling hands. It informed me that the writer had sent to the police, and had Bartleby removed to the Tombs as a vagrant. Moreover, since I knew more about him than anyone else, he wished me to appear at that place, and make a suitable statement of the facts. These tidings had a conflicting effect upon me. At first I was indignant; but at last almost approved. The landlord's energetic, summary disposition had led him to adopt a procedure which I do not think I would have decided upon myself; and yet as a last resort, under such peculiar circumstances, it seemed the only plan.

As I afterwards learned, the poor scrivener, when told that he must be conducted to the Tombs, offered not the slightest obstacle, but in his pale unmoving way, silently acquiesced.

Some of the compassionate and curious bystanders joined the party; and headed by one of the constables arm in arm with Bartleby, the silent procession filed its way through all the noise, and heat, and joy of the roaring thoroughfares at noon.

The same day I received the note I went to the Tombs, or to speak more properly, the Halls of Justice. Seeking the right officer, I stated the purpose of my call, and was informed that the individual I described was indeed within. I then assured the functionary that Bartleby was a perfectly honest man, and greatly to be compassionated, however unaccountably eccentric. I narrated all I knew, and closed by suggesting the idea of letting him remain in as indulgent confinement as possible till something less harsh might be done—though indeed I hardly knew what. At all events, if nothing else could be decided upon, the alms-house must receive him. I then begged to have an interview.

Being under no disgraceful charge, and quite serene and harmless in all his ways, they had permitted him freely to wander about the prison, and especially in the inclosed grass-platted yards thereof. And so I found him there, standing all alone in the quietest of the yards, his face towards a high wall, while all around, from the narrow slits of the jail windows, I thought I saw peering out upon him the eyes of murderers and thieves.

"Bartleby!"

"I know you," he said, without looking round,—"and I want nothing to say to you."

---

6. A light, four-wheeled carriage.

"It was not I that brought you here, Bartleby," said I, keenly pained at his implied suspicion. "And to you, this should not be so vile a place. Nothing reproachful attaches to you by being here. And see, it is not so sad a place as one might think. Look, there is the sky, and here is the grass."

"I know where I am," he replied, but would say nothing more, and so I left him.

As I entered the corridor again, a broad meat-like man, in an apron, accosted me, and jerking his thumb over his shoulder said—"Is that your friend?"

"Yes."

"Does he want to starve? If he does, let him live on the prison fare, that's all."

"Who are you?" asked I, not knowing what to make of such an unofficially-speaking person in such a place.

"I am the grub-man. Such gentlemen as have friends here, hire me to provide them with something good to eat."

"Is this so?" said I, turning to the turnkey.

He said it was.

"Well then," said I, slipping some silver into the grub-man's hands (for so they called him). "I want you to give particular attention to my friend there; let him have the best dinner you can get. And you must be as polite to him as possible."

"Introduce me, will you?" said the grub-man, looking at me with an expression which seemed to say he was all impatience for an opportunity to give a specimen of his breeding.

Thinking it would prove of benefit to the scrivener, I acquiesced; and asking the grub-man his name, went up with him to Bartleby.

"Bartleby, this is Mr. Cutlets; you will find him very useful to you."

"Your sarvant, sir, your sarvant," said the grub-man, making a low salutation behind his apron. "Hope you find it pleasant here, sir;—spacious grounds—cool apartments, sir—hope you'll stay with us some time—try to make it agreeable. May Mrs. Cutlets and I have the pleasure of your company to dinner, sir, in Mrs. Cutlets' private room?"

"I prefer not to dine today," said Bartleby, turning away. "It would disagree with me; I am unused to dinners." So saying he slowly moved to the other side of the inclosure, and took up a position fronting the dead-wall.

"How's this?" said the grub-man, addressing me with a stare of astonishment. "He's odd, ain't he?"

"I think he is a little deranged," said I, sadly.

"Deranged? deranged is it? Well now, upon my word, I thought that friend of yourn was a gentleman forger; they are always pale and genteel-like, them forgers. I can't help pity 'em—can't help it, sir. Did you know Monroe Edwards?"[7] he added touchingly, and paused. Then laying his hand pityingly on my shoulder, sighed, "he died of consumption at Sing Sing. So you weren't acquainted with Monroe?"

"No, I was never socially acquainted with any forgers. But I cannot stop longer. Look to my friend yonder. You will not lose by it. I will see you again."

Some few days after this, I again obtained admission to the Tombs, and went

---

7. Famously flamboyant swindler and forger (1808–1847) who died in Sing Sing prison, north of New York City.

through the corridors in quest of Bartleby; but without finding him.

"I saw him coming from his cell not long ago," said a turnkey, "may be he's gone to loiter in the yards."

So I went in that direction.

"Are you looking for the silent man?" said another turnkey passing me. "Yonder he lies—sleeping in the yard there. 'Tis not twenty minutes since I saw him lie down."

The yard was entirely quiet. It was not accessible to the common prisoners. The surrounding walls, of amazing thickness, kept off all sounds behind them. The Egyptian character of the masonry weighed upon me with its gloom. But a soft imprisoned turf grew under foot. The heart of the eternal pyramids, it seemed, wherein, by some strange magic, through the clefts, grass seed, dropped by birds, had sprung.

Strangely huddled at the base of the wall, his knees drawn up, and lying on his side, his head touching the cold stones, I saw the wasted Bartleby. But nothing stirred. I paused; then went close up to him; stooped over, and saw that his dim eyes were open; otherwise he seemed profoundly sleeping. Something prompted me to touch him. I felt his hand, when a tingling shiver ran up my arm and down my spine to my feet.

The round face of the grub-man peered upon me now. "His dinner is ready. Won't he dine today, either? Or does he live without dining?"

"Lives without dining," said I, and closed the eyes.

"Eh!—He's asleep, ain't he?"

"With kings and counsellors,"[8] murmured I.

There would seem little need for proceeding further in this history. Imagination will readily supply the meager recital of poor Bartleby's interment. But ere parting with the reader, let me say, that if this little narrative has sufficiently interested him, to awaken curiosity as to who Bartleby was, and what manner of life he led prior to the present narrator's making his acquaintance, I can only reply, that in such curiosity I fully share, but am wholly unable to gratify it. Yet here I hardly know whether I should divulge one little item of rumor, which came to my ear a few months after the scrivener's decease. Upon what basis it rested, I could never ascertain; and hence, how true it is I cannot now tell. But inasmuch as this vague report has not been without a certain strange suggestive interest to me, however sad, it may prove the same with some others; and so I will briefly mention it. The report was this: that Bartleby had been a subordinate clerk in the Dead Letter Office at Washington, from which he had been suddenly removed by a change in the administration. When I think over this rumor, I cannot adequately express the emotions which seize me. Dead letters! does it not sound like dead men? Conceive a man by nature and misfortune prone to a pallid hopelessness, can any business seem more fitted to heighten it than that of continually handling these dead letters, and assorting them for the flames? For by the cartload they are annually burned. Sometimes from out the folded paper the pale clerk takes a ring:—the finger it was meant for, perhaps, molders in the grave; a banknote sent in swiftest charity:—he whom it would relieve, nor eats nor hungers any more; pardon for those who died despairing; hope for those

---

8. I.e., dead. See Job 3.13–14: "then had I been at rest, With kings and counsellors of the earth, which built desolate places for themselves."

who died unhoping; good tidings for those who died stifled by unrelieved calamities. On errands of life, these letters speed to death.

Ah Bartleby! Ah humanity!

1853

## QUESTIONS

1. By the end of "Bartleby, the Scrivener," what does the reader know for certain about Bartleby? Why do you think Melville provides so little explicit information about this character?
2. The narrator tells us that his clerks' nicknames are "expressive of their respective persons or characters," but he explains only Turkey's nickname in this regard. How would you explain the appropriateness of Nipper's nickname? of Ginger Nut's?
3. One of the few words Bartleby utters is *prefer,* and the other characters find themselves using this "queer word." What can we learn about Bartleby and the others by the ways in which they use the word *prefer?*

## DORIS LESSING

### Our Friend Judith

I stopped inviting Judith to meet people when a Canadian woman remarked, with the satisfied fervour of one who has at last pinned a label on a rare specimen: "She is, of course, one of your typical English spinsters."

This was a few weeks after an American sociologist, having elicited from Judith the facts that she was fortyish, unmarried, and living alone, had enquired of me: "I suppose she has given up?" "Given up what?" I asked; and the subsequent discussion was unrewarding.

Judith did not easily come to parties. She would come after pressure, not so much—one felt—to do one a favour, but in order to correct what she believed to be a defect in her character. "I really ought to enjoy meeting new people more than I do," she said once. We reverted to an earlier pattern of our friendship: odd evenings together, an occasional visit to the cinema, or she would telephone to say: "I'm on my way past you to the British Museum. Would you care for a cup of coffee with me? I have twenty minutes to spare."

It is characteristic of Judith that the word "spinster," used of her, provoked fascinated speculation about other people. There are my aunts, for instance: aged seventy-odd, both unmarried, one an ex-missionary from China, one a retired matron of a famous London hospital. These two old ladies live together under the shadow of the cathedral in a country town. They devote much time to the Church, to good causes, to letter writing with friends all over the world, to the grandchildren and the great-grandchildren of relatives. It would be a mistake, however, on entering a house in which nothing has been moved for fifty years, to diagnose a condition of fossilised late-Victorian integrity. They read every book review in the *Observer* or the *Times,*[1] so that I recently got a letter from Aunt Rose

---

1. Prestigious London newspapers representing roughly the younger, more liberal establishment and the Establishment proper, respectively.

enquiring whether I did not think that the author of *On the Road*[2] was not—perhaps?—exaggerating his difficulties. They know a good deal about music, and write letters of encouragement to young composers they feel are being neglected—"You must understand that anything new and original takes time to be understood." Well-informed and critical Tories, they are as likely to dispatch telegrams of protest to the Home Secretary[3] as letters of support. These ladies, my aunts Emily and Rose, are surely what is meant by the phrase "English spinster." And yet, once the connection has been pointed out, there is no doubt that Judith and they are spiritual cousins, if not sisters. Therefore it follows that one's pitying admiration for women who have supported manless and uncomforted lives needs a certain modification?

5   One will, of course, never know; and I feel now that it is entirely my fault that I shall never know. I had been Judith's friend for upward of five years before the incident occurred which I involuntarily thought of—stupidly enough—as the first time Judith's mask slipped.

A mutual friend, Betty, had been given a cast-off Dior[4] dress. She was too short for it. Also she said: "It's not a dress for a married woman with three children and a talent for cooking. I don't know why not, but it isn't." Judith was the right build. Therefore one evening the three of us met by appointment in Judith's bedroom, with the dress. Neither Betty nor I was surprised at the renewed discovery that Judith was beautiful. We had both often caught each other, and ourselves, in moments of envy when Judith's calm and severe face, her undemonstratively perfect body, succeeded in making everyone else in a room or a street look cheap.

Judith is tall, small-breasted, slender. Her light brown hair is parted in the centre and cut straight around her neck. A high straight forehead, straight nose, a full grave mouth are setting for her eyes, which are green, large and prominent. Her lids are very white, fringed with gold, and moulded close over the eyeball, so that in profile she has the look of a staring gilded mask. The dress was of dark green glistening stuff, cut straight, with a sort of loose tunic. It opened simply at the throat. In it Judith could of course evoke nothing but classical images. Diana, perhaps, back from the hunt, in a relaxed moment? A rather intellectual wood nymph who had opted for an afternoon in the British Museum Reading Room? Something like that. Neither Betty nor I said a word, since Judith was examining herself in a long mirror, and must know she looked magnificent.

Slowly she drew off the dress and laid it aside. Slowly she put on the old cord skirt and woollen blouse she had taken off. She must have surprised a resigned glance between us, for she then remarked, with the smallest of mocking smiles: "One surely ought to stay in character, wouldn't you say?" She added, reading the words out of some invisible book, written not by her, since it was a very vulgar book, but perhaps by one of us: "It does everything *for* me, I must admit."

"After seeing you in it," Betty cried out, defying her, "I can't bear for anyone else to have it. I shall simply put it away." Judith shrugged, rather irritated. In the shapeless skirt and blouse, and without makeup, she stood smiling at us, a

---

2. Jack Kerouac (1922–1969), a leading writer of the Beat Generation, 1950s forerunners of the hippies. Kerouac heroes felt themselves completely cut off from and victimized by American society.
3. Head of the British government department responsible for domestic matters.
4. Famous French designer of high fashions.

woman at whom forty-nine out of fifty people would not look twice.

A second revelatory incident occurred soon after. Betty telephoned me to say that Judith had a kitten. Did I know that Judith adored cats? "No, but of course she would," I said.

Betty lived in the same street as Judith and saw more of her than I did. I was kept posted about the growth and habits of the cat and its effect on Judith's life. She remarked for instance that she felt it was good for her to have a tie and some responsibility. But no sooner was the cat out of kittenhood than all the neighbours complained. It was a tomcat, ungelded, and making every night hideous. Finally the landlord said that either the cat or Judith must go, unless she was prepared to have the cat "fixed."[5] Judith wore herself out trying to find some person, anywhere in Britain, who would be prepared to take the cat. This person would, however, have to sign a written statement not to have the cat "fixed." When Judith took the cat to the vet to be killed, Betty told me she cried for twenty-four hours.

"She didn't think of compromising? After all, perhaps the cat might have preferred to live, if given the choice?"

"Is it likely I'd have the nerve to say anything so sloppy to Judith? It's the nature of a male cat to rampage lustfully about, and therefore it would be morally wrong for Judith to have the cat fixed, simply to suit her own convenience."

"She said that?"

"She wouldn't have to *say* it, surely?"

A third incident was when she allowed a visiting young American, living in Paris, the friend of a friend and scarcely known to her, to use her flat while she visited her parents over Christmas. The young man and his friends lived it up for ten days of alcohol and sex and marijuana, and when Judith came back it took a week to get the place clean again and the furniture mended. She telephoned twice to Paris, the first time to say that he was a disgusting young thug and if he knew what was good for him he would keep out of her way in the future; the second time to apologise for losing her temper. "I had a choice either to let someone use my flat, or to leave it empty. But having chosen that you should have it, it was clearly an unwarrantable infringement of your liberty to make any conditions at all. I do most sincerely ask your pardon." The moral aspects of the matter having been made clear, she was irritated rather than not to receive letters of apology from him—fulsome, embarrassed, but above all, baffled.

It was the note of curiosity in the letters—he even suggested coming over to get to know her better—that irritated her most. "What do you suppose he means?" she said to me. "He lived in my flat for ten days. One would have thought that should be enough, wouldn't you?"

The facts about Judith, then, are all in the open, unconcealed, and plain to anyone who cares to study them; or, as it became plain she feels, to anyone with the intelligence to interpret them.

She has lived for the last twenty years in a small two-roomed flat high over a busy West London street. The flat is shabby and badly heated. The furniture is old, was never anything but ugly, is now frankly rickety and fraying. She has an

---

5. Neutered.

income of two hundred pounds[6] a year from a dead uncle. She lives on this and what she earns from her poetry, and from lecturing on poetry to night classes and extramural university classes.

She does not smoke or drink, and eats very little, from preference, not self-discipline.

She studied poetry and biology at Oxford, with distinction.

She is a Castlewell. That is, she is a member of one of the academic upper-middleclass families, which have been producing for centuries a steady supply of brilliant but sound men and women who are the backbone of the arts and sciences in Britain. She is on cool good terms with her family, who respect her and leave her alone.

She goes on long walking tours, by herself, in such places as Exmoor or West Scotland.

Every three or four years she publishes a volume of poems.

The walls of her flat are completely lined with books. They are scientific, classical and historical; there is a great deal of poetry and some drama. There is not one novel. When Judith says: "Of course I don't read novels," this does not mean that novels have no place, or a small place, in literature; or that people should not read novels; but that it must be obvious she can't be expected to read novels.

I had been visiting her flat for years before I noticed two long shelves of books, under a window, each shelf filled with the works of a single writer. The two writers are not, to put it at the mildest, the kind one would associate with Judith. They are mild, reminiscent, vague and whimsical. Typical English *belles-lettres*, in fact, and by definition abhorrent to her. Not one of the books in the two shelves has been read; some of the pages are still uncut.[7] Yet each book is inscribed or dedicated to her: gratefully, admiringly, sentimentally and, more than once, amorously. In short, it is open to anyone who cares to examine these two shelves, and to work out dates, to conclude that Judith from the age of fifteen to twenty-five had been the beloved young companion of one elderly literary gentleman, and from twenty-five to thirty-five the inspiration of another.

During all that time she had produced her own poetry, and the sort of poetry, it is quite safe to deduce, not at all likely to be admired by her two admirers. Her poems are always cool and intellectual; that is their form, which is contradicted or supported by a gravely sensuous texture. They are poems to read often; one has to, to understand them.

I did not ask Judith a direct question about these two eminent but rather fusty lovers. Not because she would not have answered, or because she would have found the question impertinent, but because such questions are clearly unnecessary. Having those two shelves of books where they are, and books she could not conceivably care for, for their own sake, is publicly giving credit where credit is due. I can imagine her thinking the thing over, and deciding it was only fair, or perhaps honest, to place the books there; and this despite the fact that she would not care at all for the same attention to be paid to her. There is something almost contemptuous in it. For she certainly despises people who feel they need attention.

---

6. About one-third or even one-half of a subsistence income.
7. As recently as the 1960s, many books were still printed on pages that had to be slit apart at the outer edge.

For instance, more than once a new emerging wave of "modern" young poets have discovered her as the only "modern" poet among their despised and well-credited elders. This is because, since she began writing at fifteen, her poems have been full of scientific, mechanical and chemical imagery. This is how she thinks, or feels.

More than once has a young poet hastened to her flat, to claim her as an ally, only to find her totally and by instinct unmoved by words like "modern," "new," "contemporary." He has been outraged and wounded by her principle, so deeply rooted as to be unconscious, and to need no expression but a contemptuous shrug of the shoulders, that publicity seeking or to want critical attention is despicable. It goes without saying that there is perhaps one critic in the world she has any time for. He has sulked off, leaving her on her shelf, which she takes it for granted is her proper place, to be read by an appreciative minority.

Meanwhile she gives her lectures, walks alone through London, writes her poems, and is seen sometimes at a concert or a play with a middleaged professor of Greek, who has a wife and two children.

Betty and I had speculated about this professor, with such remarks as: Surely she must sometimes be lonely? Hasn't she ever wanted to marry? What about that awful moment when one comes in from somewhere at night to an empty flat?

It happened recently that Betty's husband was on a business trip, her children visiting, and she was unable to stand the empty house. She asked Judith for a refuge until her own home filled again.

Afterwards Betty rang me up to report: "Four of the five nights Professor Adams came in about ten or so."

"Was Judith embarrassed?"

"Would you expect her to be?"

"Well, if not embarrassed, at least conscious there was a situation?"

"No, not at all. But I must say I don't think he's good enough for her. He can't possibly understand her. He calls her Judy."

"Good God."

"Yes. But I was wondering. Suppose the other two called her Judy—'little Judy'—imagine it! Isn't it awful? But it does rather throw a light on Judith?"

"It's rather touching."

"I suppose it's touching. But *I* was embarrassed—oh, not because of the situation. Because of how she was, with him. 'Judy, is there another cup of tea in that pot?' And she, rather daughterly and demure, pouring him one."

"Well yes, I can see how you felt."

"Three of the nights he went to her bedroom with her—very casual about it, because she was being. But he was not there in the mornings. So I asked her. You know how it is when you ask her a question. As if you've been having long conversations on that very subject for years and years, and she is merely continuing where you left off last. So when she says something surprising, one feels such a fool to be surprised?"

"Yes. And then?"

"I asked her if she was sorry not to have children. She said yes, but one couldn't have everything."

"One can't have everything, she said?"

"Quite clearly feeling she *has* nearly everything. She said she thought it was a pity, because she would have brought up children very well."

"When you come to think of it, she would, too."

"I asked about marriage, but she said on the whole the role of a mistress suited her better."

"She used the word 'mistress'?"

"You must admit it's the accurate word."

"I suppose so."

"And then she said that while she liked intimacy and sex and everything, she enjoyed waking up in the morning alone and *her own person*."

"Yes, *of course.*"

"Of course. But now she's bothered because the professor would like to marry her. Or he feels he ought. At least, he's getting all guilty and obsessive about it. She says she doesn't see the point of divorce, and anyway, surely it would be very hard on his poor old wife after all these years, particularly after bringing up two children so satisfactorily. She talks about his wife as if she's a kind of nice old charwoman, and it wouldn't be *fair* to sack her, you know. Anyway. What with one thing and another. Judith's going off to Italy soon in order *to collect herself.*"

"But how's she going to pay for it?"

"Luckily the Third Programme's[8] commissioning her to do some arty programmes. They offered her a choice of The Cid—El Thid[9] you know—and the Borgias. Well, the Borghese, then. And Judith settled for the Borgias."

"The Borgias," I said, *"Judith?"*

"Yes, quite. I said that too, in that tone of voice. She saw my point. She says the epic is right up her street, whereas the Renaissance has never been on her wave length. Obviously it couldn't be, all the magnificence and cruelty and *dirt*. But of course chivalry and a high moral code and all those idiotically noble goings-on are right on her wave length."

"Is the money the same?"

"Yes. But is it likely Judith would let money decide? No, she said that one should always choose something new, that isn't up one's street. Well, because it's better for her character, and so on, to get herself unsettled by the Renaissance. She didn't say *that*, of course."

"Of course not."

Judith went to Florence; and for some months postcards informed us tersely of her doings. Then Betty decided she must go by herself for a holiday. She had been appalled by the discovery that if her husband was away for a night she couldn't sleep; and when he went to Australia for three weeks, she stopped living until he came back. She had discussed this with him, and he had agreed that if she really felt the situation to be serious, he would despatch her by air, to Italy, in order to recover her self-respect. As she put it.

I got this letter from her: "It's no use, I'm coming home. I might have known. Better face it, once you're really married you're not fit for man nor beast. And if

---

8. British Broadcasting Corporation public radio service (and now also television channel) specializing in classical music, literature and plays, lectures, etc.
9. Approximate Castilian (standard Spanish) pronunciation of El Cid (rhymes with *steed*), the title of an eleventh-century soldier-hero featured in many works of literature. *Borgias . . . Borghese:* The Borgias were powerful Italian aristocrats, noted especially as patrons of the Catholic Church and the arts during the fifteenth and sixteenth centuries. By correcting herself ("Well, the Borghese, then"), Betty is attempting to render the name in proper Italian; in fact the Borghese were a different Italian Renaissance family.

you remember what I used to be like! *Well!* I moped around Milan. I sunbathed in Venice, then I thought my tan was surely worth something, so I was on the point of starting an affair with another lonely soul, but I lost heart, and went to Florence to see Judith. She wasn't there. She'd gone to the Italian Riviera. I had nothing better to do, so I followed her. When I saw the place I wanted to laugh, it's so much not Judith, you know, all those palms and umbrellas and gaiety at all costs and ever such an ornamental blue sea. Judith is in an enormous stone room up on the hillside above the sea, with grape vines all over the place. You should see her, she's got beautiful. It seems for the last fifteen years she's been going to Soho[1] every Saturday morning to buy food at an Italian shop. I must have looked surprised, because she explained she liked Soho. I suppose because all that dreary vice and nudes and prostitutes and everything prove how right she is to be as she is? She told the people in the shop she was going to Italy, and the *signora*[2] said, what a coincidence, she was going back to Italy too, and she did hope an old friend like Miss Castlewell would visit her there. Judith said to me: 'I felt lacking, when she used the word friend. Our relations have always been formal. Can you understand it?' she said to me. 'For fifteen years,' I said to her. She said: 'I think I must feel it's a kind of imposition, don't you know, expecting people to feel friendship for one.' *Well.* I said: 'You ought to understand it, because you're like that yourself.' 'Am I?' she said. 'Well, think about it,' I said. But I could see she didn't want to think about it. Anyway, she's here, and I've spent a week with her. The widow Maria Rineiri inherited her mother's house, so she came home, from Soho. On the ground floor is a tatty little *rosticceria*[3] patronised by the neighbours. They are all working people. This isn't tourist country, up on the hill. The widow lives above the shop with her little boy, a nasty little brat of about ten. Say what you like, the English are the only people who know how to bring up children, I don't care if that's insular. Judith's room is at the back, with a balcony. Underneath her room is the barber's shop, and the barber is Luigi Rineiri, the widow's younger brother. Yes, I was keeping him until the last. He is about forty, tall dark handsome, a great *bull*, but rather a sweet fatherly bull. He has cut Judith's hair and made it lighter. Now it looks like a sort of gold helmet. Judith is all brown. The widow Rineiri has made her a white dress and a green dress. They fit, for a change. When Judith walks down the street to the lower town, all the Italian males take one look at the golden girl and melt in their own oil like ice cream. Judith takes all this in her stride. She sort of acknowledges the homage. Then she strolls into the sea and vanishes into the foam. She swims five miles every day. *Naturally.* I haven't asked Judith whether she has collected herself, because you can see she hasn't. The widow Rineiri is matchmaking. When I noticed this I wanted to laugh, but luckily I didn't because Judith asked me, really wanting to know: 'Can you see me married to an Italian barber?' (Not being snobbish, but stating the position, so to speak.) 'Well yes,' I said, 'you're the only woman I know who I can see married to an Italian barber.' Because it wouldn't matter who she married, she'd always be her *own person*. 'At any rate, for a time,' I said. At which she said, asperously,[4] 'You can use phrases like for a time in England but not in Italy.' Did you ever see England, at least London, as the home of licence, liberty and free love? No,

---

1. A colorful section of London known for artists and ethnic restaurants as well as prostitutes and pornography.  2. Proprietress.  3. Grill.  4. Sharply, harshly.

neither did I, but of course she's right. Married to Luigi it would be the family, the neighbours, the church and the *bambini*.[5] All the same she's thinking about it, believe it or not. Here she's quite different, all relaxed and free. She's melting in the attention she gets. The widow mothers her and makes her coffee all the time, and listens to a lot of good advice about how to bring up that nasty brat of hers. Unluckily she doesn't take it. Luigi is crazy for her. At mealtimes she goes to the *trattoria*[6] in the upper square and all the workmen treat her like a goddess. Well, a film star then. I said to her, you're mad to come home. For one thing her rent is ten bob[7] a week, and you eat *pasta* and drink red wine till you bust for about one and sixpence. No, she said, it would be nothing but self-indulgence to stay. Why? I said. She said, she's got nothing to stay for. (Ho ho.) And besides, she's done her research on the Borghese, though so far she can't see her way to an honest presentation of the facts. What made these people tick? she wants to know. And so she's only staying because of the cat. I forgot to mention the cat. This is a town of cats. The Italians here love their cats. I wanted to feed a stray cat at the table, but the waiter said no; and after lunch, all the waiters came with trays crammed with leftover food and stray cats came from everywhere to eat. And at dark when the tourists go in to feed and the beach is empty—you know how empty and forlorn a beach is at dusk?—well cats appear from everywhere. The beach seems to move, then you see it's cats. They go stalking along the thin inch of grey water at the edge of the sea, shaking their paws crossly at each step, snatching at the dead little fish, and throwing them with their mouths up on to the dry stand. Then they scamper after them. You've never seen such a snarling and fighting. At dawn when the fishing boats come in to the empty beach, the cats are there in dozens. The fishermen throw them bits of fish. The cats snarl and fight over it. Judith gets up early and goes down to watch. Sometimes Luigi goes too, being tolerant. Because what he really likes is to join the evening promenade with Judith on his arm around and around the square of the upper town. Showing her off. Can you *see* Judith? But she does it. Being tolerant. But she smiles and enjoys the attention she gets, there's no doubt about it.

"She has a cat in her room. It's a kitten really, but it's pregnant. Judith says she can't leave until the kittens are born. The cat is too young to have kittens. Imagine Judith. She sits on her bed in that great stone room, with her bare feet on the stone floor, and watches the cat, and tries to work out why a healthy uninhibited Italian cat always fed on the best from the *rosticceria* should be neurotic. Because it is. When it sees Judith watching it gets nervous and starts licking at the roots of its tail. But Judith goes on watching, and says about Italy that the reason why the English love the Italians is because the Italians make the English feel superior. They have no discipline. And that's a despicable reason for one nation to love another. Then she talks about Luigi and says he has no sense of guilt, but a sense of sin; whereas she has no sense of sin but she has guilt. I haven't asked her if this has been an insuperable barrier, because judging from how she looks, it hasn't. She says she would rather have a sense of sin, because sin can be atoned for, and if she understood sin, perhaps she would be more at home with the Renaissance. Luigi is very healthy, she says, and not neurotic. He

---

5. Children.   6. Inexpensive restaurant.
7. Shillings. There were twenty shillings to the pound; *one and sixpence*, below, is one and a half shillings.

is a Catholic of course. He doesn't mind that she's an atheist. His mother has explained to him that the English are all pagans, but good people at heart. I suppose he thinks a few smart sessions with the local priest would set Judith on the right path for good and all. Meanwhile the cat walks nervously around the room, stopping to lick, and when it can't stand Judith watching it another second, it rolls over on the floor, with its paws tucked up, and rolls up its eyes, and Judith scratches its lumpy pregnant stomach and tells it to relax. It makes *me* nervous to see her, it's not like her, I don't know why. Then Luigi shouts up from the barber's shop, then he comes up and stands at the door laughing, and Judith laughs, and the widow says: Children, enjoy yourselves. And off they go, walking down to the town eating ice cream. The cat follows them. It won't let Judith out of its sight, like a dog. When she swims miles out to sea, the cat hides under a beach hut until she comes back. Then she carries it back up the hill, because that nasty little boy chases it. *Well*. I'm coming home tomorrow thank God, to my dear old Billy, I was mad ever to leave him. There is something about Judith and Italy that has upset me, I don't know what. The point is, what on earth can Judith and Luigi *talk* about? Nothing. How can they? And of course it doesn't matter. So I turn out to be a prude as well. See you next week."

It was my turn for a dose of the sun, so I didn't see Betty. On my way back from Rome I stopped off in Judith's resort and walked up through narrow streets to the upper town, where, in the square with the vine-covered *trattoria* at the corner, was a house with ROSTICCERIA written in black paint on a cracked wooden board over a low door. There was a door curtain of red beads, and flies settled on the beads. I opened the beads with my hands and looked into a small dark room with a stone counter. Loops of salami hung from metal hooks. A glass bell covered some plates of cooked meats. There were flies on the salami and on the glass bell. A few tins on the wooden shelves, a couple of pale loaves, some wine casks and an open case of sticky pale green grapes covered with fruit flies seemed to be the only stock. A single wooden table with two chairs stood in a corner, and two workmen sat there, eating lumps of sausage and bread. Through another bead curtain at the back came a short, smoothly fat, slender-limbed woman with greying hair. I asked for Miss Castlewell, and her face changed. She said in an offended, offhand way: "Miss Castlewell left last week." She took a white cloth from under the counter, and flicked at the flies on the glass bell. "I'm a friend of hers," I said, and she said: *Si*,[8] and put her hands palm down on the counter and looked at me, expressionless. The workmen got up, gulped down the last of their wine, nodded and went. She *ciao*'d[9] them; and looked back at me. Then, since I didn't go, she called: "Luigi!" A shout came from the back room, there was a rattle of beads, and in came first a wiry sharp-faced boy, and then Luigi. He was tall, heavy-shouldered, and his black rough hair was like a cap, pulled low over his brows. He looked good-natured, but at the moment uneasy. His sister said something, and he stood beside her, an ally, and confirmed: "Miss Castlewell went away." I was on the point of giving up, when through the bead curtain that screened off a dazzling light eased a thin tabby cat. It was ugly and it walked uncomfortably, with its back quarters bunched up. The child suddenly let out a "Ssssss" through his teeth, and the cat froze. Luigi said something sharp to the child, and something encouraging to the cat, which sat down, looked

---

8. Yes.   9. Said good-bye to.

straight in front of it, then began frantically licking at its flanks. "Miss Castlewell was offended with us," said Mrs. Rineiri suddenly, and with dignity. "She left early one morning. We did not expect her to go." I said: "Perhaps she had to go home and finish some work."

Mrs. Rineiri shrugged, then sighed. Then she exchanged a hard look with her brother. Clearly the subject had been discussed, and closed forever.

"I've known Judith a long time," I said, trying to find the right note. "She's a remarkable woman. She's a poet." But there was no response to this at all. Meanwhile the child, with a fixed bared-teeth grin, was staring at the cat, narrowing his eyes. Suddenly he let out another "Ssssssss" and added a short high yelp. The cat shot backwards, hit the wall, tried desperately to claw its way up the wall, came to its senses and again sat down and began its urgent, undirected licking at its fur. This time Luigi cuffed the child, who yelped in earnest, and then ran out into the street past the cat. Now that the way was clear the cat shot across the floor, up onto the counter, and bounded past Luigi's shoulder and straight through the bead curtain into the barber's shop, where it landed with a thud.

"Judith was sorry when she left us," said Mrs. Rineiri uncertainly. "She was crying."

"I'm sure she was."

"And so," said Mrs. Rineiri, with finality, laying her hands down again, and looking past me at the bead curtain. That was the end. Luigi nodded brusquely at me, and went into the back. I said goodbye to Mrs. Rineiri and walked back to the lower town. In the square I saw the child, sitting on the running board of a lorry[1] parked outside the *trattoria*, drawing in the dust with his bare toes, and directing in front of him a blank, unhappy stare.

I had to go through Florence, so I went to the address Judith had been at. No, Miss Castlewell had not been back. Her papers and books were still here. Would I take them back with me to England? I made a great parcel and brought them back to England.

I telephoned Judith and she said she had already written for the papers to be sent, but it was kind of me to bring them. There had seemed to be no point, she said, in returning to Florence.

"Shall I bring them over?"

"I would be very grateful, of course."

Judith's flat was chilly, and she wore a bunchy sage-green woollen dress. Her hair was still a soft gold helmet, but she looked pale and rather pinched. She stood with her back to a single bar of electric fire—lit because I demanded it—with her legs apart and her arms folded. She contemplated me.

"I went to the Rineiris' house."

"Oh. Did you?"

"They seemed to miss you."

She said nothing.

"I saw the cat too."

"Oh. Oh, I suppose you and Betty discussed it?" This was with a small unfriendly smile.

"Well, Judith, you must see we were likely to?"

She gave this her consideration and said: "I don't understand why people

1. Truck.

discuss other people. Oh—I'm not criticising you. But I don't see why you are so interested. I don't understand human behaviour and I'm not particularly interested."

"I think you should write to the Rineiris."

"I wrote and thanked them, of course."

"I don't mean that."

"You and Betty have worked it out?"

"Yes, we talked about it. We thought we should talk to you, so you should write to the Rineiris."

"Why?"

"For one thing, they are both very fond of you."

"Fond," she said smiling.

"Judith, I've never in my life felt such an atmosphere of being let down."

Judith considered this. "When something happens that shows one there is really a complete gulf in understanding, what is there to say?"

"It could scarcely have been a complete gulf in understanding. I suppose you are going to say we are being interfering?"

Judith showed distaste. "That is a very stupid word. And it's a stupid idea. No one can interfere with me if I don't let them. No, it's that I don't understand people. I don't understand why you or Betty should care. Or why the Rineiris should, for that matter," she added with the small tight smile.

"Judith!"

"If you've behaved stupidly, there's no point in going on. You put an end to it."

"What happened? Was it the cat?"

"Yes, I suppose so. But it's not important." She looked at me, saw my ironical face, and said: "The cat was too young to have kittens. That is all there was to it."

"Have it your way. But that is obviously not all there is to it."

"What upsets me is that I don't understand at all why I was so upset then."

"What happened? Or don't you want to talk about it?"

"I don't give a damn whether I talk about it or not. You really do say the most extraordinary things, you and Betty. If you want to know, I'll tell you. What does it matter?"

"I would like to know, of course."

"*Of course!*" she said. "In your place I wouldn't care. Well, I think the essence of the thing was that I must have had the wrong attitude to that cat. Cats are supposed to be independent. They are supposed to go off by themselves to have their kittens. This one didn't. It was climbing up on to my bed all one night and crying for attention. I don't like cats on my bed. In the morning I saw she was in pain. I stayed with her all that day. Then Luigi—he's the brother, you know."

"Yes."

"Did Betty mention him? Luigi came up to say it was time I went for a swim. He said the cat should look after itself. I blame myself very much. That's what happens when you submerge yourself in somebody else."

Her look at me was now defiant; and her body showed both defensiveness and aggression. "Yes. It's true. I've always been afraid of it. And in the last few weeks I've behaved badly. It's because I let it happen."

"Well, go on."

"I left the cat and swam. It was late, so it was only for a few minutes. When I came out of the sea the cat had followed me and had had a kitten on the beach. That little beast Michele—the son, you know?—well, he always teased the poor thing, and now he had frightened her off the kitten. It was dead, though. He held it up by the tail and waved it at me as I came out of the sea. I told him to bury it. He scooped two inches of sand away and pushed the kitten in—on the beach, where people are all day. So I buried it properly. He had run off. He was chasing the poor cat. She was terrified and running up the town. I ran too. I caught Michele and I was so angry I hit him. I don't believe in hitting children. I've been feeling beastly about it ever since."

"You were angry."

"It's no excuse. I would never have believed myself capable of hitting a child. I hit him very hard. He went off, crying. The poor cat had got under a big lorry parked in the square. Then she screamed. And then a most remarkable thing happened. She screamed just once, and all at once cats just materialised. One minute there was just one cat, lying under a lorry, and the next, dozens of cats. They sat in a big circle around the lorry, all quite still, and watched my poor cat."

"Rather moving," I said.

"Why?"

"There is no evidence one way or the other," I said in inverted commas,[2] "that the cats were there out of concern for a friend in trouble."

"No," she said energetically. "There isn't. It might have been curiosity. Or anything. How do we know? However, I crawled under the lorry. There were two paws sticking out of the cat's back end. The kitten was the wrong way round. It was stuck. I held the cat down with one hand and I pulled the kitten out with the other." She held out her long white hands. They were still covered with fading scars and scratches. "She bit and yelled, but the kitten was alive. She left the kitten and crawled across the square into the house. Then all the cats got up and walked away. It was the most extraordinary thing I've ever seen. They vanished again. One minute they were all there, and then they had vanished. I went after the cat, with the kitten. Poor little thing, it was covered with dust—being wet, don't you know. The cat was on my bed. There was another kitten coming, but it got stuck too. So when she screamed and screamed I just pulled it out. The kittens began to suck. One kitten was very big. It was a nice fat black kitten. It must have hurt her. But she suddenly bit out—snapped, don't you know, like a reflex action, at the back of the kitten's head. It died, just like that. Extraordinary, isn't it?" she said, blinking hard, her lips quivering. "She was its mother, but she killed it. Then she ran off the bed and went downstairs into the shop under the counter. I called to Luigi. You know, he's Mrs. Rineiri's brother."

"Yes, I know."

"He said she was too young, and she was badly frightened and very hurt. He took the alive kitten to her but she got up and walked away. She didn't want it. Then Luigi told me not to look. But I followed him. He held the kitten by the tail and he banged it against the wall twice. Then he dropped it into the rubbish heap. He moved aside some rubbish with his toe, and put the kitten there and pushed rubbish over it. Then Luigi said the cat should be destroyed. He said she was badly hurt and it would always hurt her to have kittens."

---

2. That is, "I said ironically." In Britain, quotation marks are called "inverted commas."

"He hasn't destroyed her. She's still alive. But it looks to me as if he were right."

"Yes, I expect he was."

"What upset you—that he killed the kitten?"

"Oh no, I expect the cat would if he hadn't. But that isn't the point, is it?"

"What is the point?"

"I don't think I really know." She had been speaking breathlessly, and fast. Now she said slowly: "It's not a question of right or wrong, is it? Why should it be? It's a question of what one is. That night Luigi wanted to go promenading with me. For him, that was *that*. Something had to be done, and he'd done it. But I felt ill. He was very nice to me. He's a very good person," she said, defiantly.

"Yes, he looks it."

"That night I couldn't sleep. I was blaming myself. I should never have left the cat to go swimming. Well, and then I decided to leave the next day. And I did. And that's all. The whole thing was a mistake, from start to finish."

"Going to Italy at all?"

"Oh, to go for a holiday would have been all right."

"You've done all that work for nothing? You mean you aren't going to make use of all that research?"

"No. It was a mistake."

"Why don't you leave it a few weeks and see how things are then?"

"Why?"

"You might feel differently about it."

"What an extraordinary thing to say. Why should I? Oh, you mean, time passing, healing wounds—that sort of thing? What an extraordinary idea. It's always seemed to me an extraordinary idea. No, right from the beginning I've felt ill at ease with the whole business, not myself at all."

"Rather irrationally, I should have said."

Judith considered this, very seriously. She frowned while she thought it over. Then she said: "But if one cannot rely on what one feels, what can one rely on?"

"On what one thinks, I should have expected you to say."

"Should you? Why? Really, you people are all very strange. I don't understand you." She turned off the electric fire, and her face closed up. She smiled, friendly and distant, and said: "I don't really see any point at all in discussing it."

1963

## QUESTIONS

1. "Our Friend Judith" might be thought of as a character study. What is the effect of having Judith's appearance and behavior described by others who can only observe her and can only guess at her thoughts? What does the story gain or lose by the use of this technique?
2. As the images of Judith accumulate throughout the narrative, how does our impression of her change? Is she a flat or a round character? At what point in the story is the narrator herself surprised to learn something new about Judith? Why do you think the narrator and Betty are so fascinated by Judith?
3. Do you agree with Judith that the narrator is "stupid" for using the word *interfere*? What should the reader make of Judith's failure to understand why the narrator, Betty, and the Rineiris "care"?

## TONI MORRISON

### *Recitatif* [1]

My mother danced all night and Roberta's was sick. That's why we were taken to St. Bonny's. People want to put their arms around you when you tell them you were in a shelter, but it really wasn't bad. No big long room with one hundred beds like Bellevue.[2] There were four to a room, and when Roberta and me came, there was a shortage of state kids, so we were the only ones assigned to 406 and could go from bed to bed if we wanted to. And we wanted to, too. We changed beds every night and for the whole four months we were there we never picked one out as our own permanent bed.

It didn't start out that way. The minute I walked in and the Big Bozo introduced us, I got sick to my stomach. It was one thing to be taken out of your own bed early in the morning—it was something else to be stuck in a strange place with a girl from a whole other race. And Mary, that's my mother, she was right. Every now and then she would stop dancing long enough to tell me something important and one of the things she said was that they never washed their hair and they smelled funny. Roberta sure did. Smell funny, I mean. So when the Big Bozo (nobody ever called her Mrs. Itkin, just like nobody ever said St. Bonaventure)—when she said, "Twyla, this is Roberta. Roberta, this is Twyla. Make each other welcome." I said, "My mother won't like you putting me in here."

"Good," said Bozo. "Maybe then she'll come and take you home."

How's that for mean? If Roberta had laughed I would have killed her, but she didn't. She just walked over to the window and stood with her back to us.

5 "Turn around," said the Bozo. "Don't be rude. Now Twyla. Roberta. When you hear a loud buzzer, that's the call for dinner. Come down to the first floor. Any fights and no movie." And then, just to make sure we knew what we would be missing, *"The Wizard of Oz."*

Roberta must have thought I meant that my mother would be mad about my being put in the shelter. Not about rooming with her, because as soon as Bozo left she came over to me and said, "Is your mother sick too?"

"No," I said. "She just likes to dance all night."

"Oh," she nodded her head and I liked the way she understood things so fast. So for the moment it didn't matter that we looked like salt and pepper standing there and that's what the other kids called us sometimes. We were eight years old and got F's all the time. Me because I couldn't remember what I read or what the teacher said. And Roberta because she couldn't read at all and didn't even listen to the teacher. She wasn't good at anything except jacks, at which she was a killer: pow scoop pow scoop pow scoop.

We didn't like each other all that much at first, but nobody else wanted to play with us because we weren't real orphans with beautiful dead parents in the sky. We were dumped. Even the New York City Puerto Ricans and the upstate Indians ignored us. All kinds of kids were in there, black ones, white ones, even

---

1. In classical music such as opera, a vocal passage that is sung in a speechlike manner.
2. Large New York City hospital best known for its psychiatric wards.

two Koreans. The food was good, though. At least I thought so. Roberta hated it and left whole pieces of things on her plate: Spam, Salisbury steak—even jello with fruit cocktail in it, and she didn't care if I ate what she wouldn't. Mary's idea of supper was popcorn and a can of Yoo-Hoo. Hot mashed potatoes and two weenies was like Thanksgiving for me.

It really wasn't bad, St. Bonny's. The big girls on the second floor pushed us around now and then. But that was all. They wore lipstick and eyebrow pencil and wobbled their knees while they watched TV. Fifteen, sixteen, even, some of them were. They were put-out girls, scared runaways most of them. Poor little girls who fought their uncles off but looked tough to us, and mean. God did they look mean. The staff tried to keep them separate from the younger children, but sometimes they caught us watching them in the orchard where they played radios and danced with each other. They'd light out after us and pull our hair or twist our arms. We were scared of them, Roberta and me, but neither of us wanted the other one to know it. So we got a good list of dirty names we could shout back when we ran from them through the orchard. I used to dream a lot and almost always the orchard was there. Two acres, four maybe, of these little apple trees. Hundreds of them. Empty and crooked like beggar women when I first came to St. Bonny's but fat with flowers when I left. I don't know why I dreamt about that orchard so much. Nothing really happened there. Nothing all that important, I mean. Just the big girls dancing and playing the radio. Roberta and me watching. Maggie fell down there once. The kitchen woman with legs like parentheses. And the big girls laughed at her. We should have helped her up, I know, but we were scared of those girls with lipstick and eyebrow pencil. Maggie couldn't talk. The kids said she had her tongue cut out, but I think she was just born that way: mute. She was old and sandy-colored and she worked in the kitchen. I don't know if she was nice or not. I just remember her legs like parentheses and how she rocked when she walked. She worked from early in the morning till two o'clock, and if she was late, if she had too much cleaning and didn't get out till two-fifteen or so, she'd cut through the orchard so she wouldn't miss her bus and have to wait another hour. She wore this really stupid little hat—a kid's hat with ear flaps—and she wasn't much taller than we were. A really awful little hat. Even for a mute, it was dumb—dressing like a kid and never saying anything at all.

"But what about if somebody tries to kill her?" I used to wonder about that. "Or what if she wants to cry? Can she cry?"

"Sure," Roberta said. "But just tears. No sounds come out."

"She can't scream?"

"Nope. Nothing."

"Can she hear?"

"I guess."

"Let's call her," I said. And we did.

"Dummy! Dummy!" She never turned her head.

"Bow legs! Bow legs!" Nothing. She just rocked on, the chin straps of her baby-boy hat swaying from side to side. I think we were wrong. I think she could hear and didn't let on. And it shames me even now to think there was somebody in there after all who heard us call her those names and couldn't tell on us.

We got along all right, Roberta and me. Changed beds every night, got F's in civics and communication skills and gym. The Bozo was disappointed in us, she said. Out of 130 of us state cases, 90 were under twelve. Almost all were real orphans with beautiful dead parents in the sky. We were the only ones dumped and the only ones with F's in three classes including gym. So we got along—what with her leaving whole pieces of things on her plate and being nice about not asking questions.

I think it was the day before Maggie fell down that we found out our mothers were coming to visit us on the same Sunday. We had been at the shelter twenty-eight days (Roberta twenty-eight and a half) and this was their first visit with us. Our mothers would come at ten o'clock in time for chapel, then lunch with us in the teachers' lounge. I thought if my dancing mother met her sick mother it might be good for her. And Roberta thought her sick mother would get a big bang out of a dancing one. We got excited about it and curled each other's hair. After breakfast we sat on the bed watching the road from the window. Roberta's socks were still wet. She washed them the night before and put them on the radiator to dry. They hadn't, but she put them on anyway because their tops were so pretty—scalloped in pink. Each of us had a purple construction-paper basket that we had made in craft class. Mine had a yellow crayon rabbit on it. Roberta's had eggs with wiggly lines of color. Inside were cellophane grass and just the jelly beans because I'd eaten the two marshmallow eggs they gave us. The Big Bozo came herself to get us. Smiling she told us we looked very nice and to come downstairs. We were so surprised by the smile we'd never seen before, neither of us moved.

"Don't you want to see your mommies?"

I stood up first and spilled the jelly beans all over the floor. Bozo's smile disappeared while we scrambled to get the candy up off the floor and put it back in the grass.

She escorted us downstairs to the first floor, where the other girls were lining up to file into the chapel. A bunch of grown-ups stood to one side. Viewers mostly. The old biddies who wanted servants and the fags who wanted company looking for children they might want to adopt. Once in a while a grandmother. Almost never anybody young or anybody whose face wouldn't scare you in the night. Because if any of the real orphans had young relatives they wouldn't be real orphans. I saw Mary right away. She had on those green slacks I hated and hated even more now because didn't she know we were going to chapel? And that fur jacket with the pocket linings so ripped she had to pull to get her hands out of them. But her face was pretty—like always, and she smiled and waved like she was the little girl looking for her mother—not me.

25    I walked slowly, trying not to drop the jelly beans and hoping the paper handle would hold. I had to use my last Chiclet because by the time I finished cutting everything out, all the Elmer's was gone. I am left-handed and the scissors never worked for me. It didn't matter, though; I might just as well have chewed the gum. Mary dropped to her knees and grabbed me, mashing the basket, the jelly beans, and the grass into her ratty fur jacket.

"Twyla, baby. Twyla, baby!"

I could have killed her. Already I heard the big girls in the orchard the next time saying, "Twyyyyyla, baby!" But I couldn't stay mad at Mary while she was smiling and hugging me and smelling of Lady Esther dusting powder. I wanted to stay buried in her fur all day.

To tell the truth I forgot about Roberta. Mary and I got in line for the traipse into chapel and I was feeling proud because she looked so beautiful even in those ugly green slacks that made her behind stick out. A pretty mother on earth is better than a beautiful dead one in the sky even if she did leave you all alone to go dancing.

I felt a tap on my shoulder, turned, and saw Roberta smiling. I smiled back, but not too much lest somebody think this visit was the biggest thing that ever happened in my life. Then Roberta said, "Mother, I want you to meet my roommate, Twyla. And that's Twyla's mother."

I looked up it seemed for miles. She was big. Bigger than any man and on her chest was the biggest cross I'd ever seen. I swear it was six inches long each way. And in the crook of her arm was the biggest Bible ever made.

Mary, simple-minded as ever, grinned and tried to yank her hand out of the pocket with the raggedy lining—to shake hands, I guess. Roberta's mother looked down at me and then looked down at Mary too. She didn't say anything, just grabbed Roberta with her Bible-free hand and stepped out of line, walking quickly to the rear of it. Mary was still grinning because she's not too swift when it comes to what's really going on. Then this light bulb goes off in her head and she says "That bitch!" really loud and us almost in the chapel now. Organ music whining; the Bonny Angels singing sweetly. Everybody in the world turned around to look. And Mary would have kept it up—kept calling names if I hadn't squeezed her hand as hard as I could. That helped a little, but she still twitched and crossed and uncrossed her legs all through service. Even groaned a couple of times. Why did I think she would come there and act right? Slacks. No hat like the grandmothers and viewers, and groaning all the while. When we stood for hymns she kept her mouth shut. Wouldn't even look at the words on the page. She actually reached in her purse for a mirror to check her lipstick. All I could think of was that she really needed to be killed. The sermon lasted a year, and I knew the real orphans were looking smug again.

We were supposed to have lunch in the teachers' lounge, but Mary didn't bring anything, so we picked fur and cellophane grass off the mashed jelly beans and ate them. I could have killed her. I sneaked a look at Roberta. Her mother had brought chicken legs and ham sandwiches and oranges and a whole box of chocolate-covered grahams. Roberta drank milk from a thermos while her mother read the Bible to her.

Things are not right. The wrong food is always with the wrong people. Maybe that's why I got into waitress work later—to match up the right people with the right food. Roberta just let those chicken legs sit there, but she did bring a stack of grahams up to me later when the visit was over. I think she was sorry that her mother would not shake my mother's hand. And I liked that and I liked the fact that she didn't say a word about Mary groaning all the way through the service and not bringing any lunch.

Roberta left in May when the apple trees were heavy and white. On her last day we went to the orchard to watch the big girls smoke and dance by the radio. It didn't matter that they said, "Twyyyyyla, baby." We sat on the ground and breathed. Lady Esther. Apple blossoms. I still go soft when I smell one or the other. Roberta was going home. The big cross and the big Bible was coming to get her and she seemed sort of glad and sort of not. I thought I would die in that room of four beds without her and I knew Bozo had plans to move some other dumped kid in there with me. Roberta promised to write every day, which was really sweet of her because she couldn't read a lick so how could she write anybody. I would have drawn pictures and sent them to her but she never gave me her address. Little by little she faded. Her wet socks with the pink scalloped tops and her big serious-looking eyes—that's all I could catch when I tried to bring her to mind.

I was working behind the counter at the Howard Johnson's on the Thruway just before the Kingston exit. Not a bad job. Kind of a long ride from Newburgh,[3] but okay once I got there. Mine was the second night shift—eleven to seven. Very light until a Greyhound checked in for breakfast around six-thirty. At that hour the sun was all the way clear of the hills behind the restaurant. The place looked better at night—more like shelter—but I loved it when the sun broke in, even if it did show all the cracks in the vinyl and the speckled floor looked dirty no matter what the mop boy did.

It was August and a bus crowd was just unloading. They would stand around a long while: going to the john, and looking at gifts and junk-for-sale machines, reluctant to sit down so soon. Even to eat. I was trying to fill the coffee pots and get them all situated on the electric burners when I saw her. She was sitting in a booth smoking a cigarette with two guys smothered in head and facial hair. Her own hair was so big and wild I could hardly see her face. But the eyes. I would know them anywhere. She had on a powder-blue halter and shorts outfit and earrings the size of bracelets. Talk about lipstick and eyebrow pencil. She made the big girls look like nuns. I couldn't get off the counter until seven o'clock, but I kept watching the booth in case they got up to leave before that. My replacement was on time for a change, so I counted and stacked my receipts as fast as I could and signed off. I walked over to the booth, smiling and wondering if she would remember me. Or even if she wanted to remember me. Maybe she didn't want to be reminded of St. Bonny's or to have anybody know she was ever there. I know I never talked about it to anybody.

I put my hands in my apron pockets and leaned against the back of the booth facing them.

"Roberta? Roberta Fisk?"

She looked up. "Yeah?"

"Twyla."

She squinted for a second and then said, "Wow."

"Remember me?"

"Sure. Hey. Wow."

"It's been a while," I said, and gave a smile to the two hairy guys.

"Yeah. Wow. You work here?"

"Yeah," I said. "I live in Newburgh."

"Newburgh? No kidding?" She laughed then a private laugh that included the guys but only the guys, and they laughed with her. What could I do but laugh too and wonder why I was standing there with my knees showing out from under that uniform. Without looking I could see the blue and white triangle on my head, my hair shapeless in a net, my ankles thick in white oxfords. Nothing could have been less sheer than my stockings. There was this silence that came down right after I laughed. A silence it was her turn to fill up. With introductions, maybe, to her boyfriends or an invitation to sit down and have a Coke. Instead

---

3. City on the Hudson River north of New York City.

she lit a cigarette off the one she'd just finished and said, "We're on our way to the Coast. He's got an appointment with Hendrix." She gestured casually toward the boy next to her.

"Hendrix? Fantastic," I said. "Really fantastic. What's she doing now?"

Roberta coughed on her cigarette and the two guys rolled their eyes up at the ceiling.

"Hendrix. Jimi Hendrix, asshole. He's only the biggest—Oh, wow. Forget it."

I was dismissed without anyone saying goodbye, so I thought I would do it for her.

"How's your mother?" I asked. Her grin cracked her whole face. She swallowed. "Fine," she said. "How's yours?"

"Pretty as a picture," I said and turned away. The backs of my knees were damp. Howard Johnson's really was a dump in the sunlight.

James is as comfortable as a house slipper. He liked my cooking and I liked his big loud family. They have lived in Newburgh all of their lives and talk about it the way people do who have always known a home. His grandmother is a porch swing older than his father and when they talk about streets and avenues and buildings they call them names they no longer have. They still call the A & P[4] Rico's because it stands on property once a mom and pop store owned by Mr. Rico. And they call the new community college Town Hall because it once was. My mother-in-law puts up jelly and cucumbers and buys butter wrapped in cloth from a dairy. James and his father talk about fishing and baseball and I can see them all together on the Hudson in a raggedy skiff. Half the population of Newburgh is on welfare now, but to my husband's family it was still some upstate paradise of a time long past. A time of ice houses and vegetable wagons, coal furnaces and children weeding gardens. When our son was born my mother-in-law gave me the crib blanket that had been hers.

But the town they remembered had changed. Something quick was in the air. Magnificent old houses, so ruined they had become shelter for squatters and rent risks, were bought and renovated. Smart IBM[5] people moved out of their suburbs back into the city and put shutters up and herb gardens in their backyards. A brochure came in the mail announcing the opening of a Food Emporium. Gourmet food it said—and listed items the rich IBM crowd would want. It was located in a new mall at the edge of town and I drove out to shop there one day—just to see. It was late in June. After the tulips were gone and the Queen Elizabeth roses were open everywhere. I trailed my cart along the aisle tossing in smoked oysters and Robert's sauce and things I knew would sit in my cupboard for years. Only when I found some Klondike ice cream bars did I feel less guilty about spending James's fireman's salary so foolishly. My father-in-law ate them with the same gusto little Joseph did.

Waiting in the check-out line I heard a voice say, "Twyla!"

The classical music piped over the aisles had affected me and the woman leaning toward me was dressed to kill. Diamonds on her hand, a smart white summer dress. "I'm Mrs. Benson," I said.

---

4. Supermarket, part of a chain originally known as The Great Atlantic and Pacific Tea Company.
5. The International Business Machine Corporation, which had its executive headquarters in Poughkeepsie, New York.

"Ho. Ho. The Big Bozo," she sang.

For a split second I didn't know what she was talking about. She had a bunch of asparagus and two cartons of fancy water.

"Roberta!"

"Right."

"For heaven's sake. Roberta."

"You look great," she said.

"So do you. Where are you? Here? In Newburgh?"

"Yes. Over in Annandale."

I was opening my mouth to say more when the cashier called my attention to her empty counter.

"Meet you outside." Roberta pointed her finger and went into the express line.

I placed the groceries and kept myself from glancing around to check Roberta's progress. I remembered Howard Johnson's and looking for a chance to speak only to be greeted with a stingy "wow." But she was waiting for me and her huge hair was sleek now, smooth around a small, nicely shaped head. Shoes, dress, everything lovely and summery and rich. I was dying to know what happened to her, how she got from Jimi Hendrix to Annandale, a neighborhood full of doctors and IBM executives. Easy, I thought. Everything is so easy for them. They think they own the world.

"How long," I asked her. "How long have you been here?"

"A year. I got married to a man who lives here. And you, you're married too, right? Benson, you said."

"Yeah. James Benson."

"And is he nice?"

"Oh, is he nice?"

"Well, is he?" Roberta's eyes were steady as though she really meant the question and wanted an answer.

"He's wonderful, Roberta. Wonderful."

"So you're happy."

"Very."

"That's good," she said and nodded her head. "I always hoped you'd be happy. Any kids? I know you have kids."

"One. A boy. How about you?"

"Four."

"Four?"

She laughed. "Step kids. He's a widower."

"Oh."

"Got a minute? Let's have a coffee."

I thought about the Klondikes melting and the inconvenience of going all the way to my car and putting the bags in the trunk. Served me right for buying all that stuff I didn't need. Roberta was ahead of me.

"Put them in my car. It's right here."

And then I saw the dark blue limousine.

"You married a Chinaman?"

"No," she laughed. "He's the driver."

"Oh, my. If the Big Bozo could see you now."

We both giggled. Really giggled. Suddenly, in just a pulse beat, twenty years disappeared and all of it came rushing back. The big girls (whom we called gar girls—Roberta's misheard word for the evil stone faces described in a civics class) there dancing in the orchard, the ploppy mashed potatoes, the double weenies, the Spam with pineapple. We went into the coffee shop holding on to one another and I tried to think why we were glad to see each other this time and not before. Once, twelve years ago, we passed like strangers. A black girl and a white girl meeting in a Howard Johnson's on the road and having nothing to say. One in a blue and white triangle waitress hat—the other on her way to see Hendrix. Now we were behaving like sisters separated for much too long. Those four short months were nothing in time. Maybe it was the thing itself. Just being there, together. Two little girls who knew what nobody else in the world knew—how not to ask questions. How to believe what had to be believed. There was politeness in that reluctance and generosity as well. Is your mother sick too? No, she dances all night. Oh—and an understanding nod.

We sat in a booth by the window and fell into recollection like veterans.

"Did you ever learn to read?"

"Watch." She picked up the menu. "Special of the day. Cream of corn soup. Entrées. Two dots and a wriggly line. Quiche. Chef salad, scallops . . ."

I was laughing and applauding when the waitress came up.

"Remember the Easter baskets?"

"And how we tried to *introduce* them?"

"Your mother with that cross like two telephone poles."

"And yours with those tight slacks."

We laughed so loudly heads turned and made the laughter harder to suppress.

"What happened to the Jimi Hendrix date?"

Roberta made a blow-out sound with her lips.

"When he died I thought about you."

"Oh, you heard about him finally?"

"Finally. Come on, I was a small-town country waitress."

"And I was a small-town country dropout. God, were we wild. I still don't know how I got out of there alive."

"But you did."

"I did. I really did. Now I'm Mrs. Kenneth Norton."

"Sounds like a mouthful."

"It is."

"Servants and all?"

Roberta held up two fingers.

"Ow! What does he do?"

"Computers and stuff. What do I know?"

"I don't remember a hell of a lot from those days, but Lord, St. Bonny's is as clear as daylight. Remember Maggie? The day she fell down and those gar girls laughed at her?"

Roberta looked up from her salad and stared at me. "Maggie didn't fall," she said.

"Yes, she did. You remember."

"No, Twyla. They knocked her down. Those girls pushed her down and tore her clothes. In the orchard."

"I don't—that's not what happened."

"Sure it is. In the orchard. Remember how scared we were?"

"Wait a minute. I don't remember any of that."

"And Bozo was fired."

"You're crazy. She was there when I left. You left before me."

"I went back. You weren't there when they fired Bozo."

"What?"

"Twice. Once for a year when I was about ten, another for two months when I was fourteen. That's when I ran away."

"You ran away from St. Bonny's?"

"I had to. What do you want? Me dancing in that orchard?"

"Are you sure about Maggie?"

"Of course I'm sure. You've blocked it, Twyla. It happened. Those girls had behavior problems, you know."

"Didn't they, though. But why can't I remember the Maggie thing?"

"Believe me. It happened. And we were there."

"Who did you room with when you went back?" I asked her as if I would know her. The Maggie thing was troubling me.

"Creeps. They tickled themselves in the night."

My ears were itching and I wanted to go home suddenly. This was all very well but she couldn't just comb her hair, wash her face and pretend everything was hunky-dory. After the Howard Johnson's snub. And no apology. Nothing.

"Were you on dope or what that time at Howard Johnson's?" I tried to make my voice sound friendlier than I felt.

"Maybe, a little. I never did drugs much. Why?"

"I don't know; you acted sort of like you didn't want to know me then."

"Oh, Twyla, you know how it was in those days: black—white. You know how everything was."

But I didn't know. I thought it was just the opposite. Busloads of blacks and whites came into Howard Johnson's together. They roamed together then: students, musicians, lovers, protesters. You got to see everything at Howard Johnson's and blacks were very friendly with whites in those days. But sitting there with nothing on my plate but two hard tomato wedges wondering about the melting Klondikes it seemed childish remembering the slight. We went to her car, and with the help of the driver, got my stuff into my station wagon.

"We'll keep in touch this time," she said.

"Sure," I said. "Sure. Give me a call."

"I will," she said, and then just as I was sliding behind the wheel, she leaned into the window. "By the way. Your mother. Did she ever stop dancing?"

I shook my head. "No. Never."

Roberta nodded.

"And yours? Did she ever get well?"

She smiled a tiny sad smile. "No. She never did. Look, call me, okay?"

"Okay," I said, but I knew I wouldn't. Roberta had messed up my past somehow with that business about Maggie. I wouldn't forget a thing like that. Would I?

Strife came to us that fall. At least that's what the paper called it. Strife. Racial strife. The word made me think of a bird—a big shrieking bird out of 1,000,000,000 B.C. Flapping its wings and cawing. Its eye with no lid always bearing down on you. All day it screeched and at night it slept on the rooftops. It woke you in the morning and from the *Today* show to the eleven o'clock news it kept you an awful company. I couldn't figure it out from one day to the next. I knew I was supposed to feel something strong, but I didn't know what, and James wasn't any help. Joseph was on the list of kids to be transferred from the junior high school to another one at some far-out-of-the-way place and I thought it was a good thing until I heard it was a bad thing. I mean I didn't know. All the schools seemed dumps to me, and the fact that one was nicer looking didn't hold much weight. But the papers were full of it and then the kids began to get jumpy. In August, mind you. Schools weren't even open yet. I thought Joseph might be frightened to go over there, but he didn't seem scared so I forgot about it, until I found myself driving along Hudson Street out there by the school they were trying to integrate and saw a line of women marching. And who do you suppose was in line, big as life, holding a sign in front of her bigger than her mother's cross? MOTHERS HAVE RIGHTS TOO! it said.

I drove on, and then changed my mind. I circled the block, slowed down, and honked my horn.

Roberta looked over and when she saw me she waved. I didn't wave back, but I didn't move either. She handed her sign to another woman and came over to where I was parked.

"Hi."

"What are you doing?"

"Picketing. What's it look like?"

"What for?"

"What do you mean. 'What for?' They want to take my kids and send them out of the neighborhood. They don't want to go."

"So what if they go to another school? My boy's being bussed too, and I don't mind. Why should you?"

"It's not about us, Twyla. Me and you. It's about our kids."

"What's more *us* than that?"

"Well, it is free country."

"Not yet, but it will be."

"What the hell does that mean? I'm not doing anything to you."

"You really think that?"

"I know it."

"I wonder what made me think you were different."

"I wonder what made me think you were different."

"Look at them," I said. "Just look. Who do they think they are? Swarming all over the place like they own it. And now they think they can decide where my child goes to school. Look at them, Roberta. They're Bozos."

Roberta turned around and looked at the women. Almost all of them were standing still now, waiting. Some were even edging toward us. Roberta looked at me out of some refrigerator behind her eyes. "No, they're not. They're just mothers."

"And what am I? Swiss cheese?"

"I used to curl your hair."

"I hated your hands in my hair."

The women were moving. Our faces looked mean to them of course and they looked as though they could not wait to throw themselves in front of a police car, or better yet, into my car and drag me away by my ankles. Now they surrounded my car and gently, gently began to rock it. I swayed back and forth like a sideways yo-yo. Automatically I reached for Roberta, like the old days in the orchard when they saw us watching them and we had to get out of there, and if one of us fell the other pulled her up and if one of us was caught the other stayed to kick and scratch, and neither would leave the other behind. My arm shot out of the car window but no receiving hand was there. Roberta was looking at me sway from side to side in the car and her face was still. My purse slid from the car seat down under the dashboard. The four policemen who had been drinking Tab in their car finally got the message and strolled over, forcing their way through the women. Quietly, firmly they spoke. "Okay, ladies. Back in line or off the streets."

Some of them went away willingly; others had to be urged away from the car doors and the hood. Roberta didn't move. She was looking steadily at me. I was fumbling to turn on the ignition, which wouldn't catch because the gearshift was still in drive. The seats of the car were a mess because the swaying had thrown my grocery coupons all over it and my purse was sprawled on the floor.

"Maybe I am different now, Twyla. But you're not. You're the same little state kid who kicked a poor old black lady when she was down on the ground. You kicked a black lady and you have the nerve to call me a bigot."

175 The coupons were everywhere and the guts of my purse were bunched under the dashboard. What was she saying? Black? Maggie wasn't black.

"She wasn't black," I said.

"Like hell she wasn't, and you kicked her. We both did. You kicked a black lady who couldn't even scream."

"Liar!"

"You're the liar! Why don't you just go on home and leave us alone, huh?"

180 She turned away and I skidded away from the curb.

The next morning I went into the garage and cut the side out of the carton our portable TV had come in. It wasn't nearly big enough, but after a while I had a decent sign: red spray-painted letters on a white background—AND SO DO CHILDREN ****. I meant just to go down to the school and tack it up somewhere so those cows on the picket line across the street could see it, but when I got there, some ten or so others had already assembled—protesting the cows across the street. Police permits and everything. I got in line and we strutted in time on our side while Roberta's group strutted on theirs. That first day we were all dignified, pretending the other side didn't exist. The second day there was name calling and finger gestures. But that was about all. People changed signs from time to time, but Roberta never did and neither did I. Actually my sign didn't make sense without Roberta's. "And so do children what?" one of the women on my side asked me. Have rights, I said, as though it was obvious.

Roberta didn't acknowledge my presence in any way and I got to thinking maybe she didn't know I was there. I began to pace myself in the line, jostling people one minute and lagging behind the next, so Roberta and I could reach the end of our respective lines at the same time and there would be a moment in our turn when we would face each other. Still, I couldn't tell whether she saw me and knew my sign was for her. The next day I went early before we were scheduled to assemble. I waited until she got there before I exposed my new creation. As soon as she hoisted her MOTHERS HAVE RIGHTS TOO I began to wave my new one, which said, HOW WOULD YOU KNOW? I know she saw that one, but I had gotten addicted now. My signs got crazier each day, and the women on my side decided that I was a kook. They couldn't make heads or tails out of my brilliant screaming posters.

I brought a painted sign in queenly red with huge black letters that said, IS YOUR MOTHER WELL? Roberta took her lunch break and didn't come back for the rest of the day or any day after. Two days later I stopped going too and couldn't have been missed because nobody understood my signs anyway.

It was a nasty six weeks. Classes were suspended and Joseph didn't go to anybody's school until October. The children—everybody's children—soon got bored with that extended vacation they thought was going to be so great. They looked at TV until their eyes flattened. I spent a couple of mornings tutoring my son, as the other mothers said we should. Twice I opened a text from last year that he had never turned in. Twice he yawned in my face. Other mothers organized living room sessions so the kids would keep up. None of the kids could concentrate so they drifted back to *The Price Is Right*[6] and *The Brady Bunch*. When the school finally opened there were fights once or twice and some sirens roared through the streets every once in a while. There were a lot of photographers from Albany. And just when ABC was about to send up a news crew, the kids settled down like nothing in the world had happened. Joseph hung my HOW WOULD YOU KNOW? sign in his bedroom. I don't know what became of AND SO DO CHILDREN \*\*\*\*. I think my father-in-law cleaned some fish on it. He was always puttering around in our garage. Each of his five children lived in Newburgh and he acted as though he had five extra homes.

I couldn't help looking for Roberta when Joseph graduated from high school, but I didn't see her. It didn't trouble me much what she had said to me in the car. I mean the kicking part. I know I didn't do that, I couldn't do that. But I was puzzled by her telling me Maggie was black. When I thought about it I actually couldn't be certain. She wasn't pitch-black, I knew, or I would have remembered that. What I remember was the kiddie hat, and the semicircle legs. I tried to reassure myself about the race thing for a long time until it dawned on me that the truth was already there, and Roberta knew it. I didn't kick her; I didn't join in with the gar girls and kick that lady, but I sure did want to. We watched and never tried to help her and never called for help. Maggie was my dancing mother. Deaf, I thought, and dumb. Nobody inside. Nobody who would hear you if you cried in the night. Nobody who could tell you anything important that you could use. Rocking, dancing, swaying as she walked. And when the gar girls pushed her down, and started roughhousing, I knew she wouldn't scream, couldn't—just like me—and I was glad about that.

We decided not to have a tree, because Christmas would be at my mother-in-law's house, so why have a tree at both places? Joseph was at SUNY New Paltz and we had to economize, we said. But at the last minute, I changed my mind. Nothing could be that bad. So I rushed around town looking for a tree, something small but wide. By the time I found a place, it was snowing and very late. I dawdled like it was the most important purchase in the world and the tree man was fed up with me. Finally I chose one and had it tied onto the trunk of the car. I drove away slowly because the sand trucks were not out yet and the streets could be murder at the beginning of a snowfall. Downtown the streets were wide

---

6. Television game show popular in the 1970s. *The Brady Bunch*: television sitcom popular in the 1970s.

and rather empty except for a cluster of people coming out of the Newburgh Hotel. The one hotel in town that wasn't built out of cardboard and Plexiglas. A party, probably. The men huddled in the snow were dressed in tails and the women had on furs. Shiny things glittered from underneath their coats. It made me tired to look at them. Tired, tired, tired. On the next corner was a small diner with loops and loops of paper bells in the window. I stopped the car and went in. Just for a cup of coffee and twenty minutes of peace before I went home and tried to finish everything before Christmas Eve.

"Twyla?"

There she was. In a silvery evening gown and dark fur coat. A man and another woman were with her, the man fumbling for change to put in the cigarette machine. The woman was humming and tapping on the counter with her fingernails. They all looked a little bit drunk.

"Well. It's you."

190    "How are you?"

I shrugged. "Pretty good. Frazzled. Christmas and all."

"Regular?" called the woman from the counter.

"Fine," Roberta called back and then, "Wait for me in the car."

She slipped into the booth beside me. "I have to tell you something, Twyla. I made up my mind if I ever saw you again, I'd tell you."

195    "I'd just as soon not hear anything, Roberta. It doesn't matter now, anyway."

"No," she said. "Not about that."

"Don't be long," said the woman. She carried two regulars to go and the man peeled his cigarette pack as they left.

"It's about St. Bonny's and Maggie."

"Oh, please."

200    "Listen to me. I really did think she was black. I didn't make that up. I really thought so. But now I can't be sure. I just remember her as old, so old. And because she couldn't talk—well, you know, I thought she was crazy. She'd been brought up in an institution like my mother was and like I thought I would be too. And you were right. We didn't kick her. It was the gar girls. Only them. But, well, I wanted to. I really wanted them to hurt her. I said we did it, too. You and me, but that's not true. And I don't want you to carry that around. It was just that I wanted to do it so bad that day—wanting to is doing it."

Her eyes were watery from the drinks she'd had, I guess. I know it's that way with me. One glass of wine and I start bawling over the littlest thing.

"We were kids, Roberta."

"Yeah. Yeah. I know, just kids."

"Eight."

205    "Eight."

"And lonely."

"Scared, too."

She wiped her cheeks with the heel of her hand and smiled. "Well, that's all I wanted to say."

I nodded and couldn't think of any way to fill the silence that went from the diner past the paper bells on out into the snow. It was heavy now. I thought I'd better wait for the sand trucks before starting home.

210    "Thanks, Roberta."

"Sure."

"Did I tell you? My mother, she never did stop dancing."

"Yes. You told me. And mine, she never got well." Roberta lifted her hands from the tabletop and covered her face with her palms. When she took them away she really was crying. "Oh shit, Twyla. Shit, shit, shit. What the hell happened to Maggie?"

1983

## QUESTIONS

1. From the clues provided by the narrator, how do you figure out the race and class backgrounds of the two main characters, Twyla and Roberta? Why do you think Toni Morrison presents this in the way she does?
2. To what extent are Twyla and Roberta fully rounded characters, and to what extent are they flat, even stereotypical, representatives of their racial or class types? How realistic do you find the two depictions?
3. At the end of "Recitatif," how does Twyla's and Roberta's exploration of the "truth" of what they had seen at St. Bonny's many years earlier affect the reader's sense of the "truth" of later episodes in the story? Is either Twyla or Roberta more reliable than the other?

---

## SUGGESTIONS FOR WRITING

1. Write a first-person narrative in the manner of "Why I Live at the P.O." that makes free use of dialect and exaggeration for comic effect.
2. Write an essay analyzing the character of Bartleby the scrivener. Is Bartleby fully rounded or flat? Does his character change or remain static? Is he best understood as a realistically depicted individual or as a representative of some type or some idea?
3. Write an essay discussing the author's method of characterization in any story you've read so far in this book. How does this method serve the author's storytelling purposes? Are the characters in the story round or flat, individual or stereotypical, distinctly or vaguely depicted, etc.?
4. Write a fictional character exploration in the manner of "Our Friend Judith"—a first-person narrative in which the main character, someone known by the narrator but not very well known, is described through detailed observations as well as reliable or unreliable anecdotes related by other characters.
5. Compare and contrast the methods of characterization Toni Morrison uses in "Recitatif" with those used by A. S. Byatt in "The Thing in the Forest." Do you find one of the stories more effective than the other? Why?

# STUDENT WRITING

The following is a first-draft analysis of character and narration in Raymond Carver's "Cathedral." Read this paper as you would one of your peers' papers, looking for opportunities for the writer to improve her presentation. Is the language consistently appropriate for academic writing? Does the essay maintain its focus? Does it demonstrate a steady progression of well-supported arguments toward a strong, well-earned conclusion? Is there any redundant or otherwise unnecessary material? Are there ideas that need to be developed further?

---

Qualls 1

Bethany Qualls
Professor Netherton
English 301
23 September 2004

Character and Narration in "Cathedral"

    A reader in search of an exciting plot will be pretty disappointed by Raymond Carver's "Cathedral" because the truth is nothing much happens. A suburban husband and wife receive a visit from her former boss, who is blind. After the wife falls asleep, the two men watch a TV program about cathedrals and eventually try to draw one. Along the way the three characters down a few cocktails and smoke a little pot. But that's about as far as the action goes. Instead of focusing on plot, then, the story really asks us to focus on the characters, especially the husband who narrates the story. Through his words even more than his actions the narrator unwittingly shows us why nothing much happens to him by continually demonstrating his utter inability to connect with others or to understand himself.

    The narrator's isolation is most evident in the distanced way he introduces his own story and the people in it. He does not name the other characters or himself, referring to them only by using labels such as "[t]his blind man," "[h]is wife," "my wife" (20; all page references are to the class text, <u>The Norton Introduction to Literature</u>, 9th ed.) and "[t]he man [my wife] was going to marry" (21). Even after the narrator's wife starts referring to their visitor as "Robert," the narrator keeps calling him "the blind man" (23). These labels distance him from the other characters and also leave readers with very little connection to them.

    At least three times the narrator himself notices that this habit of not naming or really acknowledging people is significant. Referring to his wife's "officer," he asks, "why should he have a name? he was the childhood sweetheart, and what more does he want?" (21). Moments later he describes how freaked out he was when he listened to a tape the blind man had sent his wife and "heard [his] own name in the mouth of this . . . blind man . . . [he] didn't even know!" (22). Yet once the blind man arrives and begins to talk with the wife, the narrator finds himself "wait[ing] in vain to hear [his] name on [his] wife's sweet lips" and disappointed to hear "nothing of the sort" (25). Simply using someone's name suggests a kind of intimacy that the narrator avoids and yet secretly yearns for.

Also reinforcing the narrator's isolation and dissatisfaction with it are the awkward euphemisms and clichés he uses, which emphasize how disconnected he is from his own feelings and how uncomfortable he is with other people's. Referring to his wife's first husband, the narrator says it was he "who'd first enjoyed her favors" (21), an antiquated expression even in 1983, the year the story was published. Such language reinforces our sense that the narrator is unable to speak in language that is meaningful or heartfelt, especially when he actually tries to talk about emotions. He describes his wife's feelings for her first husband, for example, by using generic language and then just trailing off entirely: "she was in love with the guy, and he was in love with her, etc." (21). When he refers to the blind man and his wife as "inseparable," he points out that this is, in fact, his "wife's word," not one that he's come up with (22). And even when he admits that he would like to hear his wife talk about him (25), he speaks in language that seems to come from books or movies rather than the heart.

Once the visit actually begins, the narrator's interactions and conversations with the other characters are even more awkward. His discomfort with the very idea of the visit is obvious to his wife and to the reader. As he says in his usual deadpan manner, "I wasn't enthusiastic about his visit" (20). During the visit he sits silent when his wife and Robert are talking and then answers Robert's questions about his life and feelings with the shortest possible phrases: "How long had I been in my present position? (Three years.) Did I like my work? (I didn't.)" (25). Finally, he tries to escape even that much involvement by simply turning on the TV and tuning Robert out (25).

Despite Robert's best attempt to make a connection with the narrator, the narrator resorts to a label again, saying that he "didn't want to be left alone with a blind man" (26). Robert, merely "a blind man," remains a category, not a person, and the narrator can initially relate to Robert only by invoking the stereotypes about that category that he has learned "from the movies" (20). He confides to the reader that he believes that blind people always wear dark glasses, that they never smoke (24), and that a beard on a blind man is "[t]oo much" (23). It follows that the narrator is amazed about the connection his wife and Robert have because he is unable to see Robert as a person like any other. "[W]ho'd want to go to such a wedding in the first place?" (22) he asks rhetorically about Robert's wedding to his wife, Beulah.

Misconceptions continue as the narrator assumes Beulah would "never receive the smallest compliment from her beloved" since the compliments he is thinking about are physical ones (23). Interestingly, when faced with a name that is specific (Beulah), the narrator immediately assumes that he knows what the person with that name must be like ("a colored woman"[22]), even though she is not in the room or known to him. Words fail or mislead the narrator in both directions, as he's using them and as he hears them.

There is hope for the narrator at the end as he gains some empathy and forges a bond with Robert over the drawing of a cathedral. That process seems to begin when the narrator admits to himself, the reader, and Robert that he is "glad for the [Robert's] company" (27) and, for the first time, comes close to disclosing the literally nightmarish loneliness of his life. It culminates in a moment of physical and emotional intimacy that the narrator admits is "like nothing else in my life up to now" (30)—a moment in which discomfort with the very idea of blindness gives way to an attempt to actually experience blindness from the inside. Because the narrator has used words to distance himself from the world, it seems totally right that all this happens only when the narrator *stops* using words. They have a tendency to blind him.

However, even at the very end it isn't completely clear just whether or how the narrator has really changed. He does not completely interact with Robert but has to be prodded into action by him. By choosing to keep his eyes closed, he not only temporarily experiences blindness but also shuts out the rest of the world, since he "didn't feel like [he] was inside anything" (30). Perhaps most important, he remains unable to describe his experience meaningfully, making it difficult for readers to decide whether or not he has really changed. For example, he says, "It was like nothing else in my life up to now" (30), but he doesn't explain why this is true. Is it because he is doing something for someone else? Because he is thinking about the world from another's perspective? Because he feels connected to Robert? Because he is drawing a picture while probably drunk and high? There is no way of knowing.

It's possible that not feeling "inside anything" (30) could be a feeling of freedom from his own habits of guardedness and insensitivity, his emotional "blindness." But even with this final hope for connection, for the majority of the story the narrator is a closed, judgmental man who isolates himself and cannot connect with others. The narrator's view of the world is one filled with misconceptions that the visit from Robert starts to slowly change, yet it is not clear what those changes are, how far they will go, or whether they will last. So a reader is left wondering how much really happens in this story.

# 4 SETTING

All stories, like all individuals, are embedded in a context or **setting**—a time and place. The time can be contemporary, as in Sherman Alexie's "Flight Patterns," or historical, as in Edgar Allan Poe's "The Cask of Amontillado." A story may be set in a mythical past, as in "The Elephant in the Village of the Blind," or an indeterminate future, as in Peter Carey's " 'Do You Love Me?' " Setting can be very limited, recounting the actions of only a few hours (Raymond Carver's "Cathedral"), or it may span several years (James Baldwin's "Sonny's Blues"). The place can be interior and unremarkable (Grace Paley's "A Conversation with My Father"), or it can be a historic and memorable site (Edith Wharton's "Roman Fever"). Although short stories seldom cover as much "ground" in time or space as many novels do, the setting may include several locations, as in Doris Lessing's "Our Friend Judith." Many stories express the sensations of a particular class in a distinct region, as in the American suburbia of John Cheever's "The Country Husband," the rural South of Eudora Welty's "Why I Live at the P.O.," or Harlem during the mid-twentieth century as portrayed in "Sonny's Blues." Other stories convey impressions of locales that are foreign to the reader, where climate, language, and customs create wonder or uneasiness. Just as character and plot are so closely interrelated as to be ultimately indistinguishable, so too are character, plot, and setting. Paradoxically, to see this interpenetration we must think of them first as separable elements. The individuals in the stories are embedded in the specific context, and the more we know of the setting, and of the relationship of the characters to the setting, the more likely we are to understand the characters and the story. Often the setting is a key to discovering interpretations of the story beyond the experience of individual characters and connecting it to traditions, phases of history, and social issues.

A. S. Byatt's "The Thing in the Forest" encompasses the experience of the author's own generation in Britain from World War II to the end of the twentieth century. The important scenes take place at a mansion on a country estate, the sort of place featured in fairy tales and murder mysteries as well as in many classic English novels. The story draws on our expectations

*Fiction depends for its life on place. Place is the crossroads of circumstance, the proving ground of, What happened? Who's here? Who's coming?*
—EUDORA WELTY

about the kind of people and events that belong in such grand settings. Because of the war and the changes of modern life, the house is no longer private and aristocratic, but is open to ordinary children or tourists. Byatt uses realistic description of places as they would appear at different times in the last half century, including one of the new shopping malls where Primrose provides child care. Specific settings add dimensions to the shared experiences not only of the characters but of British society during those decades.

In stories that you have already read as well as in those in this chapter, various settings provide historical and social contexts for the characters' experiences. Thus John Cheever's "The Country Husband" is set in suburban New York not long after World War II; the Weeds and their neighbors are typical of middle-class families in that period, the wife raising Baby-Boomer children, the husband commuting to an office job in the city. While many readers recognize this version of the American Dream from their experience or from movies and television, Cheever's story shows that the suburban setting is less familiar and conflict-free than it seems. Other stories are set at a greater distance from most readers, whether in remote times or foreign countries. "A Cask of Amontillado" might seem improbable if Poe had set it in the Baltimore of his own lifetime, whereas a cruel plot of revenge seems more suited to Renaissance Italy; the characters and plot are Machiavellian, characterized by the unscrupulous cunning described by the Italian Renaissance politician and writer Niccolò Machiavelli (1469–1527). Peter Carey's " 'Do You Love Me?' " appears to be much more specific about history and geography than Poe's tale, but the era and the country with its vanishing map exist only in the imagination. In contrast, Ernest Hemingway's "Hills Like White Elephants" presents a realistic setting in modern Spain, and a situation that at first seems commonplace. Yet something feels very alien about the episode, not only because readers may never have been to Spain. Because they are so sparse, details of the landscape and the bar at the station are magnified in their significance, as if setting alone tells most of the story.

Setting plays a critical role in each of the stories in this chapter as well. Andrea Barrett's "The Littoral Zone" may appear only loosely attached to time and place, as it scarcely refers to historical events or nationality. "Fifteen years ago," in the first sentence, could be any time in our own living memory. Some of the places remain unnamed, yet they might be found on a real map of North America. Both lovers are scientists, and the setting of the beginning of their relationship at a marine biology research station, a kind of working summer camp for professors and students, is inseparable from their experience. The title refers to the scene of their first conversation, which takes place in the shoreline area that is covered at high tide and exposed at low tide. Barrett has woven the material of marine biology into the scenes and the imagery of the story, and the setting becomes a metaphor for the characters' experience.

Other stories may use realistic settings without much apparent significance, yet the time and place can symbolize whole ways of life or value systems. A Mexican village, the Sierra Nevada mountains, and the city of Stockton, California, as presented in Richard Dokey's "Sánchez," offer three very different ways of life and sets of values. In Anton Chekhov's "The Lady with the Dog," as in "The Littoral Zone," a vacation trip to a different place sparks an affair. Yalta, with its fruit, seashore, and semitropical climate, exemplifies a more passionate, pleasurable, exciting life than the cold routine of Moscow. As always, the characters' responses to their environment is integral to the action of the story and its effect on the reader.

Amy Tan's "A Pair of Tickets" adds the dimension of ethnic identity to the effect of traveling from one setting to another. The narrator, who has denied her Chinese heritage while growing up as an American in San Francisco, feels she becomes Chinese when she travels to China. What this means is far from simple, however, as contemporary China includes many features of contemporary global culture, including hamburgers and french fries at the international hotel.

The stories that follow rely on setting in differing ways and to different degrees, but you will see in each of them a revealing portrait of a time and place. Just as our own memories of important experiences include complex impressions of when and where they occurred—the weather, the shape of the room, the music that was playing, even the fashions or the events in the news back then—so stories rely on setting to give substance to the other elements of fiction.

## ANDREA BARRETT

### The Littoral Zone

When they met, fifteen years ago, Jonathan had a job teaching botany at a small college near Albany, and Ruby was teaching invertebrate zoology at a college in the Berkshires.[1] Both of them, along with an ornithologist, an ichthyologist, and an oceanographer, had agreed to spend three weeks of their summer break at a marine biology research station on an island off the New Hampshire coast. They had spouses, children, mortgages, bills; they went, they later told each other, because the pay was too good to refuse. Two-thirds of the way through the course, they agreed that the pay was not enough.

How they reached that first agreement is a story they've repeated to each other again and again and told, separately, to their closest friends. Ruby thinks they had this conversation on the second Friday of the course, after Frank Kenary's slide show on the abyssal fish and before Carol Dagliesh's lecture on the courting behavior of herring gulls. Jonathan maintains that they had it earlier—that Wednesday, maybe, when they were still recovering from Gunnar Erickson's trawling expedition. The days before they became so aware of each other have blurred in their minds, but they agree that their first real conversation took place on the afternoon devoted to the littoral zone.

The tide was all the way out. The students were clumped on the rocky, pitted apron between the water and the ledges, peering into the tidal pools and listing the species they found. Gunnar was in the equipment room, repairing one of the sampling claws. Frank was setting up dissections in the tiny lab; Carol had gone back to the mainland on the supply boat, hoping to replace the camera one of the students had dropped. And so the two of them, Jonathan and Ruby, were left alone for a little while.

They both remember the granite ledge where they sat, and the raucous quarrels of the nesting gulls. They agree that Ruby was scratching furiously at her calves and that Jonathan said, "Take it easy, okay? You'll draw blood."

Her calves were slim and tan, Jonathan remembers. Covered with blotches and scrapes.

I folded my fingers, Ruby remembers. Then I blushed. My throat felt sunburned.

Ruby said, "I know, it's so embarrassing. But all this salt on my poison ivy—God, what I wouldn't give for a bath! They never told me there wouldn't be any *water* here. . . ."

Jonathan gestured at the ocean surrounding them and then they started laughing. *Hysteria*, they have told each other since. They were so tired by then,

[1]. A range of low mountains in western Massachusetts.

twelve days into the course, and so dirty and overworked and strained by pretending to the students that these things didn't matter, that neither of them could understand that they were also lonely. Their shared laughter felt like pure relief.

"No water?" Jonathan said. "I haven't been dry since we got here. My clothes are damp, my sneakers are damp, my hair never dries...."

His hair was beautiful, Ruby remembers. Thick, a little too long. Part blond and part brown.

"I know," she said. "But you know what I mean. I didn't realize they'd have to bring our drinking water over on a boat."

"Or that they'd expect us to wash in the ocean," Jonathan said. Her forearms were dusted with salt, he remembers. The down along them sparkled in the sun.

"And those cots," Ruby said. "Does yours have a sag in it like a hammock?"

"Like a slingshot," Jonathan said.

For half an hour they sat on their ledge and compared their bubbling patches of poison ivy and the barnacle wounds that scored their hands and feet. Nothing healed out here, they told each other. Everything got infected. When one of the students called, "Look what I found!" Jonathan rose and held his hand out to Ruby. She took it easily and hauled herself up and they walked down to the water together. Jonathan's hand was thick and blunt-fingered, with nails bitten down so far that the skin around them was raw. Odd, Ruby remembers thinking. Those bitten stumps attached to such a good-looking man.

They have always agreed that the worst moment, for each of them, was when they stepped from the boat to the dock on the final day of the course and saw their families waiting in the parking lot. Jonathan's wife had their four-year-old daughter balanced on her shoulders. Their two older children were leaning perilously over the guardrails and shrieking at the sight of him. Jessie had turned nine in Jonathan's absence, and Jonathan can't think of her eager face without remembering the starfish he brought as his sole, guilty gift.

Ruby's husband had parked their car just a few yards from Jonathan's family. Her sons were wearing baseball caps, and what Ruby remembers is the way the yellow linings lit their faces. For a minute she saw the children squealing near her sons as faceless, inconsequential; Jonathan later told her that her children had been similarly blurred for him. Then Jonathan said, "That's my family, there," and Ruby said, "That's mine, right next to yours," and all the faces leapt into focus for both of them.

Nothing that was to come—not the days in court, nor the days they moved, nor the losses of jobs and homes—would ever seem so awful to them as that moment when they first saw their families standing there, unaware and hopeful. Deceitfully, treacherously, Ruby and Jonathan separated and walked to the people awaiting them. They didn't introduce each other to their spouses. They didn't look at each other—although, they later admitted, they cast covert looks at each other's families. They thought they were invisible, that no one could see what had happened between them. They thought their families would not remember how they had stepped off the boat and stood, for an instant, together.

On that boat, sitting dumb and miserable in the litter of nets and equipment, they had each pretended to be resigned to going home. Each foresaw (or so they later told each other) the hysterical phone calls and the frenzied, secret meetings. Neither foresaw how much the sight of each other's family would hurt. "Sweetie," Jonathan remembers Ruby's husband saying. "You've lost so much weight." Ruby remembers staring over her husband's shoulder and watching Jessie butt her head like a dog under Jonathan's hand.

For the first twelve days on the island, Jonathan and Ruby were so busy that they hardly noticed each other. For the next few days, after their conversation on the ledge, they sat near each other during faculty lectures and student presentations. These were held in the library, a ramshackle building separated from the bunkhouse and the dining hall by a stretch of wild roses and poison ivy.

Jonathan had talked about algae in there, holding up samples of *Fucus* and *Hildenbrandtia*. Ruby had talked about the littoral zone, that space between high and low watermarks where organisms struggled to adapt to the daily rhythm of immersion and exposure. They had drawn on the blackboard in colored chalk while the students, itchy and hot and tired, scratched their arms and legs and feigned attention.

Neither of them, they admitted much later, had focused fully on the other's lecture. "It was *before*," Ruby has said ruefully. "I didn't know that I was going to want to have listened." And Jonathan has laughed and confessed that he was studying the shells and skulls on the walls while Ruby was drawing on the board.

The library was exceedingly hot, they agreed, and the chairs remarkably uncomfortable; the only good spot was the sofa in front of the fireplace. That was the spot they commandeered on the evening after their first conversation, when dinner led to a walk and then the walk led them into the library a few minutes before the scheduled lecture.

Erika Moorhead, Ruby remembers. Talking about the tensile strength of byssus threads.[2]

Walter Schank, Jonathan remembers. Something to do with hydrozoans.

They both remember feeling comfortable for the first time since their arrival. And for the next few days—three by Ruby's accounting; four by Jonathan's—one of them came early for every lecture and saved a seat on the sofa for the other.

They giggled at Frank Kenary's slides, which he'd arranged like a creepy fashion show: abyssal fish sporting varied blobs of luminescent flesh. When Gunnar talked for two hours about subduction zones[3] and the calcium carbonate cycle, they amused themselves exchanging doodles. They can't remember, now, whether Gunnar's endless lecture came before Carol Dagliesh's filmstrip on the herring gulls, or which of the students tipped over the dissecting scope and sent the dish of copepods to their deaths. But both of them remember those days and nights as being almost purely happy. They swam in that odd, indefinite zone where they were more than friends, not yet lovers, still able to deny to themselves that they were headed where they were headed.

---

2. Fibrous strands with which mollusks attach themselves to rocks or other foreign bodies.
3. Areas where the edge of one tectonic plate of the earth's crust descends below the edge of another; *calcium carbonate cycle:* the natural processes by which calcium carbonate (lime), a whitish mineral dissolved in sea water, is incorporated by mollusks such as clams as the main material of their shells, which are eventually broken down and the calcium carbonate re-dissolved; *copepods:* a subclass of tiny marine crustaceans.

Ruby made the first phone call, a week after they left the island. At eleven o'clock on a Sunday night, she told her husband she'd left something in her office that she needed to prepare the next day's class. She drove to campus, unlocked her door, picked up the phone and called Jonathan at his house. One of his children—Jessie, she thinks—answered the phone. Ruby remembers how, even through the turmoil of her emotions, she'd been shocked at the idea of a child staying up so late.

There was a horrible moment while Jessie went to find her father; another when Jonathan, hearing Ruby's voice, said, "Wait, hang on, I'll just be a minute," and then negotiated Jessie into bed. Ruby waited, dreading his anger, knowing she'd been wrong to call him at home. But Jonathan, when he finally returned, said, "Ruby. You got my letter."

"What letter?" she asked. He wrote to tell me good-bye, she remembers thinking.

"My *letter*," he said. "I wrote you, I have to see you. I can't stand this."

Ruby released the breath she hadn't known she was holding.

"You didn't get it?" he said. "You just called?" It wasn't only me, he remembers thinking. She feels it too.

"I had to hear your voice," she said.

Ruby called, but Jonathan wrote. And so when Jonathan's youngest daughter, Cora, later fell in love and confided in Ruby, and then asked her, "Was it like this with you two? Who started it—you or Dad?" all Ruby could say was, "It happened to both of us."

Sometimes, when Ruby and Jonathan sit on the patio looking out at the hills above Palmyra,[4] they will turn and see their children watching them through the kitchen window. Before the children went off to college, the house bulged with them on weekends and holidays and seemed empty in between; Jonathan's wife had custody of Jessie and Gordon and Cora, and Ruby's husband took her sons, Mickey and Ryan, when he remarried. Now that the children are old enough to come and go as they please, the house is silent almost all the time.

Jessie is twenty-four, and Gordon is twenty-two; Mickey is twenty-one, and Cora and Ryan are both nineteen. When they visit Jonathan and Ruby they spend an unhealthy amount of time talking about their past. In their conversations they seem to split their lives into three epochs: the years when what they think of as their real families were whole; the years right after Jonathan and Ruby met, when their parents were coming and going, fighting and making up, separating and divorcing; and the years since Jonathan and Ruby's marriage, when they were forced into a reconstituted family. Which epoch they decide to explore depends on who's visiting and who's getting along with whom.

"But we were happy," Mickey may say to Ruby, if he and Ryan are visiting and Jonathan's children are absent. "We were, we were fine."

"It wasn't like you and Mom ever fought," Cora may say to Jonathan, if Ruby's sons aren't around. "You could have worked it out if you'd tried."

When they are all together, they tend to avoid the first two epochs and to talk about their first strained weekends and holidays together. They've learned to tolerate each other, despite their forced introductions; Cora and Ryan, whose

---

4. Town in western New York State near the city of Rochester.

birthdays are less than three months apart, seem especially close. Ruby and Jonathan know that much of what draws their youngest children together is shared speculation about what happened on that island.

They look old to their children, they know. Both of them are nearing fifty. Jonathan has grown quite heavy and has lost much of his hair; Ruby's fine-boned figure has gone gaunt and stringy. They know their children can't imagine them young and strong and wrung by passion. The children can't think—can't stand to think—about what happened on the island, but they can't stop themselves from asking questions.

"Did you have other girlfriends?" Cora asks Jonathan. "Were you so unhappy with Mom?"

"Did you know him before?" Ryan asks Ruby. "Did you go there to be with him?"

"We met there," Jonathan and Ruby say. "We had never seen each other before. We fell in love." That is all they will say, they never give details, they say "yes" or "no" to the easy questions and evade the hard ones. They worry that even the little they offer may be too much.

Jonathan and Ruby tell each other the stories of their talk by the tidal pool, their walks and meals, the sagging sofa, the moment in the parking lot, and the evening Ruby made her call. They tell these to console themselves when their children chide them or when, alone in the house, they sit quietly near each other and struggle to conceal their disappointments.

Of course they have expected some of these. Mickey and Gordon have both had trouble in school, and Jessie has grown much too close to her mother; neither Jonathan nor Ruby has found jobs as good as the ones they lost, and their new home in Palmyra still doesn't feel quite like home. But all they have lost in order to be together would seem bearable had they continued to feel the way they felt on the island.

They're sensible people, and very well-mannered; they remind themselves that they were young then and are middle-aged now, and that their fierce attraction would naturally ebb with time. Neither likes to think about how much of the thrill of their early days together came from the obstacles they had to overcome. Some days, when Ruby pulls into the driveway still thinking about her last class and catches sight of Jonathan out in the garden, she can't believe the heavyset figure pruning shrubs so meticulously is the man for whom she fought such battles. Jonathan, who often wakes very early, sometimes stares at Ruby's sleeping face and thinks how much more gracefully his ex-wife is aging.

They never reproach each other. When the tension builds in the house and the silence becomes overwhelming, one or the other will say, "Do you remember . . . ?" and then launch into one of the myths on which they have founded their lives. But there is one story they never tell each other, because they can't bear to talk about what they have lost. This is the one about the evening that has shaped their life together.

Jonathan's hand on Ruby's back, Ruby's hand on Jonathan's thigh, a shirt unbuttoned, a belt undone. They never mention this moment, or the moments that followed it, because that would mean discussing who seduced whom, and any resolution of that would mean assigning blame. Guilt they can handle; they've been living with guilt for fifteen years. But blame? It would be more than either of them could bear, to know the exact moment when one of them precipitated all that has happened to them. The most either of them has ever said is, "How could we have known?"

But the night in the library is what they both think about, when they lie silently next to each other and listen to the wind. It must be summer for them to think about it; the children must be with their other parents and the rain must be falling on the cedar shingles overhead. A candle must be burning on the mantel above the bed and the maple branches outside their window must be tossing against each other. Then they think of the story they know so well and never say out loud.

There was a huge storm three nights before they left the island, the tail end of a hurricane passing farther out to sea. The cedar trees creaked and swayed in the wind beyond the library windows. The students had staggered off to bed, after the visitor from Woods Hole[5] had finished his lecture on the explorations of the *Alvin* in the Cayman Trough, and Frank and Gunnar and Carol had shrouded themselves in their rain gear and left as well, sheltering the visitor between them. Ruby sat at one end of the long table, preparing bottles of fixative for their expedition the following morning, and Jonathan lay on the sofa writing notes. The boat was leaving just after dawn and they knew they ought to go to bed.

The wind picked up outside, sweeping the branches against the walls. The windows rattled. Jonathan shivered and said, "Do you suppose we could get a fire going in that old fireplace?"

"I bet we could," said Ruby, which gave both of them the pretext they needed to crouch side by side on the cracked tiles, brushing elbows as they opened the flue and crumpled paper and laid kindling in the form of a grid. The logs Jonathan found near the lobster traps were dry and the fire caught quickly.

Who found the green candle in the drawer below the microscope? Who lit the candle and turned off the lights? And who found the remains of the jug of wine that Frank had brought in honor of the visitor? They sat there side by side, poking at the burning logs and pretending they weren't doing what they were doing. The wind pushed through the window they'd opened a crack, and the tan window shade lifted and then fell back against the frame. The noise was soothing at first; later it seemed irritating.

Jonathan, whose fingernails were bitten to the quick, admired the long nail on Ruby's right little finger and then said, half-seriously, how much he'd love to bite a nail like that. When Ruby held her hand to his mouth he took the nail between his teeth and nibbled through the white tip, which days in the water had softened. Ruby slipped her other hand inside his shirt and ran it up his back. Jonathan ran his mouth up her arm and down her neck.

They started in front of the fire and worked their way across the floor, breaking a glass, knocking the table askew. Ruby rubbed her back raw against the rug and Jonathan scraped his knees, and twice they paused and laughed at their wild excesses. They moved across the floor from east to west and later from west to east, and between those two journeys, during the time when they heaped their clothes and the sofa cushions into a nest in front of the fire, they talked.

This was not the kind of conversation they'd had during walks and meals since that first time on the rocks: who they were, where they'd come from, how

---

5. The Woods Hole Oceanographic Institute, in southeastern Massachusetts; the *Alvin*: a deep-sea research submarine that has been used to investigate such oceanic trenches as the Cayman Trough, in the Caribbean Sea.

they'd made it here. This was the talk where they instinctively edited out the daily pleasures of their lives on the mainland and spliced together the hard times, the dark times, until they'd constructed versions of themselves that could make sense of what they'd just done.

For months after this, as they lay in stolen, secret rooms between houses and divorces and jobs and lives, Jonathan would tell Ruby that he swallowed her nail. The nail dissolved in his stomach, he'd say. It passed into his villi[6] and out to his blood and then flowed to bone and muscle and nerve, where the molecules that had once been part of her became part of him. Ruby, who always seemed to know more acutely than Jonathan that they'd have to leave whatever room this was in an hour or a day, would argue with him.

"Nails are keratin," she'd tell him. "Like hooves and hair. Like wool. We can't digest wool."

"Moths can," Jonathan would tell her. "Moths eat sweaters."

"Moths have a special enzyme in their saliva," Ruby would say. This was true, she knew it for a fact. She'd been so taken by Jonathan's tale that she'd gone to the library to check out the details and discovered he was wrong.

But Jonathan didn't care what the biochemists said. He held her against his chest and said, "I have an enzyme for you."

That night, after the fire burned out, they slept for a couple of hours. Ruby woke first and watched Jonathan sleep for a while. He slept like a child, with his knees bent toward his chest and his hands clasped between his thighs. Ruby picked up the tipped-over chair and swept the fragments of broken glass onto a sheet of paper. Then she woke Jonathan and they tiptoed back to the rooms where they were supposed to be.

1996

## QUESTIONS

1. Describing one of the earliest encounters between Jonathan and Ruby, Andrea Barrett writes: "They both remember the granite ledge where they sat, and the raucous quarrels of the nesting gulls." What is significant about these details and the fact that they both remember them so clearly? Why is a "littoral zone" such a suitable setting for their meeting?
2. Find instances in the text of memories held only by Ruby, or only by Jonathan. Why do you think Barrett has chosen to tell the story from these two perspectives? How would the effect on the reader change if the story were told from only one character's perspective?
3. At the story's end, Jonathan and Ruby "tiptoed back to the rooms where they were supposed to be." Why is this a fitting ending, despite the fact that the moment comes early in the story's overall chronology?

## RICHARD DOKEY

### Sánchez

That summer the son of Juan Sánchez went to work for the Flotill Cannery in Stockton. Juan drove with him to the valley in the old Ford.

[6]. The tiny, fingerlike projections, through which nutrients are absorbed, that comprise the inner surface of the small intestine.

While they drove, the boy, whose name was Jesús, told him of the greatness of the cannery, of the great aluminum buildings, the marvelous machines, and the belts of cans that never stopped running. He told him of the building on one side of the road where the cans were made and how the cans ran in a metal tube across the road to the cannery. He described the food machines, the sanitary precautions. He laughed when he spoke of the labeling. His voice was serious about the money.

When they got to Stockton, Jesús directed him to the central district of town, the skid row where the boy was to live while he worked for the Flotill. It was a cheap hotel on Center Street. The room smelled. There was a table with one chair. The floor was stained like the floor of a public urinal and the bed was soiled, as were the walls. There were no drapes on the windows. A pall spread out from the single light bulb overhead that was worked with a length of grimy string.

"I will not stay much in the room," Jesús said, seeing his father's face. "It is only for sleep. I will be working overtime, too. There is also the entertainment."

5     Jesús led him from the room and they went out into the street. Next to the hotel there was a vacant lot where a building had stood. The hole which was left had that recent, peculiar look of uprootedness. There were the remains of the foundation, the broken flooring, and the cracked bricks of tired red to which the gray blotches of mortar clung like dried phlegm. But the ground had not yet taken on the opaqueness of wear that the air and sun give it. It gleamed dully in the light and held to itself where it had been torn, as earth does behind a plow. Juan studied the hole for a time; then they walked up Center Street to Main, passing other empty lots, and then moved east toward Hunter Street. At the corner of Hunter and Main a wrecking crew was at work. An iron ball was suspended from the end of a cable and a tall machine swung the ball up and back and then whipped it forward against the building. The ball was very thick-looking, and when it struck the wall the building trembled, spurted dust, and seemed to cringe inward. The vertical lines of the building had gone awry. Juan shook each time the iron struck the wall.

"They are tearing down the old buildings," Jesús explained. "Redevelopment," he pronounced. "Even my building is to go someday."

Juan looked at his son. "And what of the men?" he asked. "Where do the men go when there are no buildings?"

Jesús, who was a head taller than his father, looked down at him and then shrugged in that Mexican way, the head descending and cocking while the shoulders rise as though on puppet strings. "¿Quien sabe?"[1]

"And the large building there?" Juan said, looking across the rows of parked cars in Hunter Square. "The one whose roof rubs the sky. Of what significance?"

10     "That is the new courthouse," Jesús said.

"There are no curtains on the windows."

"They do not put curtains on such windows," Jesús explained.

"No," sighed Juan, "that is true."

They walked north on Hunter past the new Bank of America and entered an old building. They stood to one side of the entrance. Jesús smiled proudly and inhaled the stale air.

15     "This is the entertainment," he said.

Juan looked about. A bar was at his immediate left, and a bald man in a soiled

---

1. Who knows?

apron stood behind it. Beyond the bar there were many thick-wooded tables covered with green material. Men crouched over them and cone-shaped lights hung low from the ceiling casting broad cones of light downward upon the men and tables. Smoke drifted and rolled in the light and pursued the men when they moved quickly. There was the breaking noise of balls striking together, the hard wooden rattle of the cues in the racks upon the wall, the humming slither of the scoring disks along the loose wires overhead, the explosive cursing of the men. The room was warm and dirty. Juan shook his head.

"I have become proficient at the game," Jesús said.

"This is the entertainment," Juan said, still moving his head.

Jesús turned and walked outside. Juan followed. The boy pointed across the parked cars past the courthouse to a marquee on Main Street. "There are also motion pictures," Jesús said.

Juan had seen a movie as a young man working in the fields near Fresno. He had understood no English then. He sat with his friends in the leather seats that had gum under the arms and watched the images move upon the white canvas. The images were dressed in expensive clothes. There was laughing and dancing. One of the men did kissing with two very beautiful women, taking turns with each when the other was absent. This had embarrassed Juan, the embracing and unhesitating submission of the women with so many unfamiliar people to watch. Juan loved his wife, was very tender and gentle with her before she died. He never went to another motion picture, even after he had learned English, and this kept him from the Spanish films as well.

"We will go to the cannery now," Jesús said, taking his father's arm. "I will show you the machines."

Juan permitted himself to be led away, and they moved back past the bank to where the men were destroying the building. A ragged hole, like a wound, had been opened in the wall. Juan stopped and watched. The iron ball came forward tearing at the hole, enlarging it, exposing the empty interior space that had once been a room. The floor of the room teetered at a precarious angle. The wood was splintered and very dry in the noon light.

"I do not think I will go to the cannery," Juan said.

The boy looked at his father like a child who has made a toy out of string and bottle caps only to have it ignored.

"But it is honorable work," Jesús said, suspecting his father. "And it pays well."

"Honor," Juan said. "Honor is a serious matter. It is not a question of honor. You are a man now. All that is needed is a room and a job at the Flotill. Your father is tired, that is all."

"You are disappointed," Jesús said, hanging his head.

"No," Juan said. "I am beyond disappointment. You are my son. Now you have a place in the world. You have the Flotill."

Nothing more was said, and they walked to the car. Juan got in behind the wheel. Jesús stood beside the door, his arms at his sides, the fingers spread. Juan looked up at him. The boy's eyes were big.

"You are my son," Juan said, "and I love you. Do not have disappointment. I am not of the Flotill. Seeing the machines would make it worse. You understand, niño?"[2]

"Sí, Papa," Jesús said. He put a hand on his father's shoulder.

---

2. Son or male child. *Niñito:* dear son. *Querido:* beloved.

"It is a strange world, *niñito*," Juan said.

"I will earn money. I will buy a red car and visit you. All in Twin Pines will be envious of the son of Sánchez, and they will say that Juan Sánchez has a son of purpose."

"Of course, Jesús *mío*," Juan said. He bent and placed his lips against the boy's hand. "I will look for the bright car. I will write regardless." He smiled, showing yellowed teeth. "Goodbye, *querido*," he said. He started the car, raced the engine once too high, and drove off up the street.

35   When Juan Sánchez returned to Twin Pines, he drove the old Ford to the top of Bear Mountain and pushed it over. He then proceeded systematically to burn all that was of importance to him, all that was of nostalgic value, and all else that meant nothing in itself, like the extra chest of drawers he had kept after his wife's death, the small table in the bedroom, and the faded mahogany stand in which he kept his pipe and tobacco and which sat next to the stuffed chair in the front room. He broke all the dishes, cups, plates, discarded all the cooking and eating utensils in the same way. The fire rose in the blue wind carrying dust wafers of ash in quick, breathless spirals and then released them in a panoply of diluted smoke, from which they drifted and spun and fell like burnt snow. The forks, knives, and spoons became very black with a flaky crust of oxidized metal. Then Juan burned his clothing, all that was unnecessary, and the smoke dampened and took on a thick smell. Finally he threw his wife's rosary into the flames. It was a cheap one, made of wood, and disappeared immediately. He went into his room then and lay down on the bed. He went to sleep.

When he woke, it was dark and cool. He stepped outside, urinated, and then returned, shutting the door. The darkness was like a mammoth held breath, and he felt very awake listening to the beating of his heart. He would not be able to sleep now, and so he lay awake thinking.

He thought of his village in Mexico, the baked white clay of the small houses spread like little forts against the stillness of the bare mountains, the men with their great wide hats, their wide, white pants, and their naked, brown-skinned feet, splayed against the fine dust of the road. He saw the village cistern and the women all so big and slow, always with child, enervated by the earth and the unbearable sun, the enervation passing into their very wombs like the acceptance, slow, silent blood. The men walked bent as though carrying the air or sky, slept against the buildings in the shade like old dogs, ate dry, hot food that dried them inside and seemed to bake the moisture from the flesh, so that the men and women while still young had faces like eroded fields and fingers like stringy, empty stream beds. It was a hard land. It took the life of his father and mother before he was twelve and the life of his aunt, with whom he then lived, before he was sixteen.

When he was seventeen he went to Mexicali because he had heard much of America and the money to be obtained there. They took him in a truck with other men to work in the fields around Bakersfield, then in the fields near Fresno. On his return to Mexicali he met La Belleza, as he came to call her: loveliness. He married her when he was nineteen and she only fifteen. The following year she had a baby girl. It was stillborn and the birth almost killed her, for the doctor said the passage was oversmall. The doctor cautioned him (warned him, really) La Belleza could not have children and live, and he went outside into the moonlight and wept.

He had heard much of the liveliness of the Sierra Nevada above what was called the Mother Lode, and because he feared the land, believed almost that it possessed the power to kill him—as it had killed his mother and father, his aunt, was, in fact, slow killing so many of his people—he wanted to run away from it to the high white cold of the California mountains, where he believed his heart would grow, his blood run and, perhaps, the passage of La Belleza might open. Two years later he was taken in the trucks to Stockton in the San Joaquin Valley to pick tomatoes, and he saw the Sierra Nevada above the Mother Lode.

It was from a distance, of course, and in the summer, so that there was no snow. But when he returned he told La Belleza about the blueness of the mountains in the warm, still dawn, the extension of them, the aristocracy of their unmoving height, and that they were only fifty miles away from where he had stood.

He worked very hard now and saved his money. He took La Belleza back to his village, where he owned the white clay house of his father. It was cheaper to live there while he waited, fearing the sun, the dust, and the dry, airless silence, for the money to accumulate. That fall La Belleza became pregnant again by an accident of passion and the pregnancy was very difficult. In the fifth month the doctor—who was an atheist—said that the baby would have to be taken or else the mother would die. The village priest, a very loud, dramatic man—an educated man who took pleasure in striking a pose—proclaimed the wrath of God in the face of such sacrilege. It was the child who must live, the priest cried. The pregnancy must go on. There was the immortal soul of the child to consider. But Juan decided for the atheist doctor, who did take the child. La Belleza lost much blood. At one point her heart had stopped beating. When the child was torn from its mother and Juan saw that it was a boy, he ran out of the clay house of his father and up the dusty road straight into a hideous red moon. He cursed the earth, the sky. He cursed his village, himself, the soulless indifference of the burnt mountains. He cursed God.

Juan was very afraid now, and though it cost more money, he had himself tied by the atheist doctor so that he could never again put the life of La Belleza in danger, for the next time, he knew with certainty, would kill her.

The following summer he went again on the trucks to the San Joaquin Valley. The mountains were still there, high and blue in the quiet dawn, turned to a milky pastel by the heat swirls and haze of midday. Sometimes at night he stepped outside the shacks in which the men were housed and faced the darkness. It was tragic to be so close to what you wanted, he would think, and be unable to possess it. So strong was the feeling in him, particularly during the hot, windless evenings, that he sometimes went with the other men into Stockton, where he stood on the street corners of skid row and talked, though he did not get drunk on cheap wine or go to the whores, as did the other men. Nor did he fight.

They rode in old tilted trucks covered with canvas and sat on rude benches staring out over the slats of the tail gate. The white glare of headlights crawled up and lay upon them, waiting to pass. They stared over the whiteness. When the lights swept out and by, the glass of the side windows shone. Behind the windows sometimes there would be the ghost flash of an upturned face, before the darkness clamped shut. Also, if one of the men had a relative who lived in the area, there was the opportunity to ride in a car.

He had done so once. He had watched the headlights of the car pale, then whiten the back of one of the trucks. He saw the faces of the men turned outward and the looks on the faces that seemed to float upon the whiteness of the light. The men sat forward, arms on knees, and looked over the glare into the darkness. After that he always rode in the trucks.

When he returned to his village after that season's harvest, he knew they could wait no longer. He purchased a dress of silk for La Belleza and in a secondhand store bought an American suit for himself. He had worked hard, sold his father's house, saved all his money, and on a bright day in early September they crossed the border at Mexicali and caught the Greyhound for Fresno.

Juan got up from his bed to go outside. He stood looking up at the stars. The stars were pinned to the darkness, uttering little flickering cries of light, and as always he was moved by the nearness and profusion of their agony. His mother had told him the stars were a kind of purgatory in which souls burned in cold, silent repentance. He had wondered after her death if the earth too were not a star burning in loneliness, and he could never look at them later without thinking this and believing that the earth must be the brightest of all stars. He walked over to the remains of the fire. A dull heat came from the ashes and a column of limp smoke rose and then bent against the night wind. He studied the ashes for a time and then looked over the tall pine shapes to the southern sky. It was there all right. He could feel the dry char of its heat, that deeper, dryer burning. He imagined it, of course. But it was there nevertheless. He went back into the cabin and lay down, but now his thoughts were only of La Belleza and the beautiful Sierra Nevada.

From Fresno all the way up the long valley to Stockton they had been full with pride and expectation. They had purchased oranges and chocolate bars and they ate them laughing. The other people on the bus looked at them, shook their heads, and slept or read magazines. He and La Belleza gazed out the window at the land.

In Stockton they were helped by a man named Eugenio Mendez. Juan had met him while picking tomatoes in the delta. Eugenio had eight children and a very fat but very kind and tolerant wife named Anilla. He had helped them find a cheap room off Center Street, where they stayed while determining their next course of action. Eugenio had access to a car, and it was he who drove them finally to the mountains.

50    It was a day like no other day in his life: to be sitting in the car with La Belleza, to be in this moving car with his Belleza heading straight toward the high, lovely mountains. The car traveled from the flatness of the valley into the rolling brown swells of the foothills, where hundreds of deciduous and evergreen oaks grew, their puffball shapes like still pictures of exploding holiday rockets, only green, but spreading up and out and then around and down in nearly perfect canopies. At Jackson the road turned and began an immediate, constant climb upward.

It was as though his dream about it had materialized. He had never seen so many trees, great with dignity: pines that had gray bark twisted and stringy like hemp; others whose bark resembled dry, flat ginger cookies fastened with black glue about a drum, and others whose bark pulled easily away; and those called redwoods, standing stiff and tall, amber-hued with straight rolls of bark as thick as his fist, flinging out high above great arms of green. And the earth, rich red, as though the blood of scores of Indians had just flowed there and dried. Dark patches of shadow stunned with light, blue flowers, orange flowers, birds, even deer. They saw them all on that first day.

"¿A dónde vamos?" Eugenio had asked. "Where are we going?"

"Bellísima," Juan replied. "Into much loveliness."

They did not reach Twin Pines that day. But on their return a week later they inquired in Jackson about the opportunity of buying land or a house in the mountains. The man, though surprised, told them of the sawmill town of Twin Pines, where there were houses for sale.

Their continued luck on that day precipitated the feeling in Juan that it was indeed the materialization of a dream. He had been able in all those years to save two thousand dollars, and a man had a small shack for sale at the far edge of town. He looked carefully at Juan, at La Belleza and Eugenio and said "One thousand dollars," believing they could never begin to possess such a sum. When Juan handed him the money, the man was so struck that he made out a bill of sale. Juan Sanchez and his wife had their home in the Sierra.

When Juan saw the cabin close up, he knew the man had stolen their money. It was small, the roof slanted to one side, the door would not close evenly. The cabin was gradually falling downhill. But it was theirs and he could, with work, repair it. Hurriedly they drove back to Jackson, rented a truck, bought some cheap furniture and hauled it back to the cabin. When they had moved in, Juan brought forth a bottle of whiskey and for the first time in his life proceeded to get truly drunk.

Juan was very happy with La Belleza. She accepted his philosophy completely, understood his need, made it her own. In spite of the people of the town, they created a peculiar kind of joy. And anyway Juan had knowledge about the people.

Twin Pines had been founded, he learned, by one Benjamin Carter, who lived with his daughter in a magnificent house on the hill overlooking town. This Benjamin Carter was a very wealthy man. He had come to the mountains thirty years before to save his marriage, for he had been poor once and loved when he was poor, but then he grew very rich because of oil discovered on his father's Ohio farm and he went away to the city and became incapable of love in the pursuit of money and power. When he at last married the woman whom he had loved, a barrier had grown between them, for Ben Carter had changed but the woman had not. Then the woman became ill and Ben Carter promised her he would take her West, all the way West away from the city so that it could be as it had been in the beginning of their love. But the woman was with child. And so Ben Carter rushed to the California mountains, bought a thousand acres of land, and hurried to build his house before the rain and snows came. He hired many men and the house was completed, except for the interior work and the furnishings. All that winter men he had hired worked in the snow to finish the house while Ben Carter waited with his wife in the city. When it was early spring they set out for California, Ben Carter, his wife, and the doctor, who strongly advised against the rough train trip and the still rougher climb by horse and wagon from Jackson to the house. But the woman wanted the child born properly, so they went. The baby came the evening of their arrival at the house, and the woman died all night having it. It was this Ben Carter who lived with that daughter now in the great house on the hill, possessing her to the point, it was said about his madness, that he had murdered a young man who had shown interest in her.

Juan learned all this from a Mexican servant who had worked at the great house from the beginning, and when he told the story to La Belleza she wept because of its sadness. It was a tragedy of love, she explained, and Juan—soaring to the heights of his imagination—believed that the town, all one hundred souls, had somehow been infected with the tragedy, as they were touched by the shadow of the house itself, which crept directly up the highway each night when the sun set. This was why they left dead chickens and fish on the porch of the cabin or dumped garbage into the yard. He believed he understood something profound and so did nothing about these incidents, which, after all, might have been the pranks of boys. He did not want the infection to touch him, nor the deeper infection of their prejudice because he was Mexican. He was not indifferent. He was simply too much in love with La Belleza and the Sierra Nevada. Finally the incidents stopped.

60   Now the life of Juan Sánchez entered its most beautiful time. When the first snows fell he became delirious, running through the pines, shouting, rolling on the ground, catching the flakes in his open mouth, bringing them in his cupped hands to rub in the hair of La Belleza, who stood in the doorway of their cabin laughing at him. He danced, made up a song about snowflakes falling on a desert and then a prayer which he addressed to the Virgin of Snowflakes. That night while the snow fluttered like wings against the bedroom window, he celebrated the coming of the whiteness with La Belleza.

He understood that first year in the mountains that love was an enlargement of himself, that it enabled him to be somehow more than he had ever been before, as though certain pores of his senses had only just been opened. Whereas before he had desired the Sierra Nevada for its beauty and contrast to his harsh fatherland, now he came to acquire a love for it, and he loved it as he loved La Belleza; he loved it as a woman. Also in that year he came to realize that there was a fear or dread about such love. It was more a feeling than anything else, something which reached thought now and then, particularly in those last moments before sleep. It was an absolutely minor thing. The primary knowledge was of the manner in which this love seemed to assimilate everything, rejecting all that would not yield. This love was a kind of blindness.

That summer Juan left La Belleza at times to pick the crops of the San Joaquin Valley. He had become good friends with the servant of the big house and this man had access to the owner's car, which he always drove down the mountain in a reckless but confident manner. After that summer Juan planned also to buy a car, not out of material desire, but simply because he believed this man would one day kill himself, and also because he did not wish to be dependent.

He worked in the walnuts near the town of Linden and again in the tomatoes of the rich delta. He wanted very much to have La Belleza with him, but that would have meant more money and a hotel room in the skid row, and that was impossible because of the pimps and whores, the drunks and criminals and the general despair, which the police always tapped at periodic intervals, as one does a vat of fermenting wine. The skid row was a place his love could not assimilate, but he could not ignore it because so many of his people were lost there. He stayed in the labor camps, which were also bad because of what the men did with themselves, but they were tolerable. He worked hard and as often as he could and gazed at the mountains, which he could always see clearly in the morning light. When tomato season was over he returned to La Belleza.

Though the town would never accept them as equals, it came that summer to tolerate their presence. La Belleza made straw baskets which she sold to the townspeople and which were desired for their beauty and intricacy of design.

Juan carved animals, a skill he had acquired from his father, and these were also sold. The activity succeeded so well that Juan took a box of these things to Jackson, where they were readily purchased. The following spring he was able to buy the Ford.

Juan acquired another understanding that second year in the mountains. It was, he believed, that love, his love, was the single greatness of which he was capable, the thing which ennobled him and gave him honor. Love, he became convinced, was his only ability, the one success he had accomplished in a world of insignificance. It was a simple thing, after all, made so painfully simple each time he went to the valley to work with his face toward the ground, every time he saw the men in the fields and listened to their talk and watched them drive off to the skid row at night. After he had acquired this knowledge, the nights he had to spend away from La Belleza were occupied by a new kind of loneliness, as though a part of his body had been separated from the whole. He began also to understand something more of the fear or dread that seemed to trail behind love.

It happened late in the sixth year of their marriage. It was impossible, of course, and he spent many hours at the fire in their cabin telling La Belleza of the impossibility, for the doctor had assured him that all had been well tied. He had conducted himself on the basis of that assumption. But doctors can be wrong. Doctors can make mistakes. La Belleza was with child.

For the first five months the pregnancy was not difficult, and he came almost to believe that indeed the passage of La Belleza would open. He prayed to God. He prayed to the earth and sky. He prayed to the soul of his mother. But after the fifth month the true sickness began and he discarded prayer completely in favor of blasphemy. There was no God and never could be God in the face of such sickness, such unbelievable human sickness. Even when he had her removed to the hospital in Stockton, the doctors could not stop it, but it continued so terribly that he believed that La Belleza carried sickness itself in her womb.

After seven months the doctors decided to take the child. They brought La Belleza into a room with lights and instruments. They worked on her for a long time and she died there under the lights with the doctors cursing and perspiring above the large wound of her pain. They did not tell him of the child, which they had cleaned and placed in an incubator, until the next day. That night he sat in the Ford and tried to see it all, but he could only remember the eyes of La Belleza in the vortex of pain. They were of an almost eerie calmness. They had possessed calmness, as one possesses the truth. Toward morning he slumped sideways on the seat and went to sleep.

So he put her body away in the red earth of the town cemetery beyond the cabin. The pines came together overhead and in the heat of midday a shadow sprinkled with spires of light lay upon the ground so that the earth was cool and clean to smell. He did not even think of taking her back to Mexico, since, from the very beginning she had always been part of that dream he had dreamed. Now she would be always in the Sierra Nevada, with the orange and blue flowers, the quiet, deep whiteness of winter, and all that he ever was or could be was with her.

But he did not think these last thoughts then, as he did now. He had simply performed them out of instinct for their necessity, as he had performed the years of labor while waiting for the infant Jesús to grow to manhood. Jesús. Why had he named the boy Jesús? That, perhaps, had been instinct too. He had stayed after La Belleza's death for the boy, to be with him until manhood, to show him the loveliness of the Sierra Nevada, to instruct him toward true manhood. But Jesús. Ah, Jesús. Jesús the American. Jesús of the Flotill. Jesús understood nothing. Jesús, he believed, was forever lost to knowledge. That day with Jesús had been his own liberation.

For a truth had come upon him after the years of waiting, the ultimate truth that he understood only because La Belleza had passed through his life. Love was beauty, La Belleza and the Sierra Nevada, a kind of created or made thing. But there was another kind of love, a very profound, embracing love that he had felt of late blowing across the mountains from the south and that, he knew now, had always been there from the beginning of his life, disguised in the sun and wind. In this love there was blood and earth and, yes, even God, some kind of god, at least the power of a god. This love wanted him for its own. He understood it, that it had permitted him to have La Belleza and that without it there could have been no Belleza.

Juan placed an arm over his eyes and turned to face the wall. The old bed sighed. An image went off in his head and he remembered vividly the lovely body of La Belleza. In that instant the sound that loving had produced with the bed was alive in him like a forgotten melody, and his body seemed to swell and press against the ceiling. It was particularly cruel because it was so sudden, so intense, and came from so deep within him that he knew it must all still be alive somewhere, and that was the cruelest part of all. He wept softly and held the arm across his eyes.

In the dark morning the people of the town were awakened by the blaze of fire that was the house of Juan Sánchez. Believing that he had perished in the flames, several of the townspeople placed a marker next to the grave of his wife with his name on it. But, of course, on that score they were mistaken. Juan Sánchez had simply gone home.

1981

## QUESTIONS

1. How does Jesús characterize the "skid row" district where he is staying in Stockton? What does the area seem like to Juan? Why does the story begin by showing the way the two characters perceive Stockton?
2. What does the beauty of the Sierra Nevada Mountains represent to Juan? Why do you think this beauty exerts such a powerful hold over him?
3. The story ends, "Juan Sánchez had simply gone home." What are some possible interpretations of this conclusion?

## AMY TAN

### A Pair of Tickets

The minute our train leaves the Hong Kong border and enters Shenzhen, China, I feel different. I can feel the skin on my forehead tingling, my blood rushing through a new course, my bones aching with a familiar old pain. And I think, My mother was right. I am becoming Chinese.

"Cannot be helped," my mother said when I was fifteen and had vigorously denied that I had any Chinese whatsoever below my skin. I was a sophomore at Galileo High in San Francisco, and all my Caucasian friends agreed: I was about as Chinese as they were. But my mother had studied at a famous nursing school in Shanghai, and she said she knew all about genetics. So there was no doubt in her mind, whether I agreed or not: Once you are born Chinese, you cannot help but feel and think Chinese.

"Someday you will see," said my mother. "It's in your blood, waiting to be let go."

And when she said this, I saw myself transforming like a werewolf, a mutant tag of DNA suddenly triggered, replicating itself insidiously into a *syndrome*, a cluster of telltale Chinese behaviors, all those things my mother did to embarrass me—haggling with store owners, pecking her mouth with a toothpick in public, being color-blind to the fact that lemon yellow and pale pink are not good combinations for winter clothes.

But today I realize I've never really known what it means to be Chinese. I am thirty-six years old. My mother is dead and I am on a train, carrying with me her dreams of coming home. I am going to China.

We are going to Guangzhou, my seventy-two-year-old father, Canning Woo, and I, where we will visit his aunt, whom he has not seen since he was ten years old. And I don't know whether it's the prospect of seeing his aunt or if it's because he's back in China, but now he looks like he's a young boy, so innocent and happy I want to button his sweater and pat his head. We are sitting across from each other, separated by a little table with two cold cups of tea. For the first time I can ever remember, my father has tears in his eyes, and all he is seeing out the train window is a sectioned field of yellow, green, and brown, a narrow canal flanking the tracks, low rising hills, and three people in blue jackets riding an ox-driven cart on this early October morning. And I can't help myself. I also have misty eyes, as if I had seen this a long, long time ago, and had almost forgotten.

In less than three hours, we will be in Guangzhou, which my guidebook tells me is how one properly refers to Canton these days. It seems all the cities I have heard of, except Shanghai, have changed their spellings. I think they are saying China has changed in other ways as well. Chungking is Chongqing. And Kweilin is Guilin. I have looked these names up, because after we see my father's aunt in Guangzhou, we will catch a plane to Shanghai, where I will meet my two half-sisters for the first time.

They are my mother's twin daughters from her first marriage, little babies she was forced to abandon on a road as she was fleeing Kweilin for Chungking in 1944. That was all my mother had told me about these daughters, so they had remained babies in my mind, all these years, sitting on the side of a road, listening to bombs whistling in the distance while sucking their patient red thumbs.

And it was only this year that someone found them and wrote with this joyful news. A letter came from Shanghai, addressed to my mother. When I first heard about this, that they were alive, I imagined my identical sisters transforming from little babies into six-year-old girls. In my mind, they were seated next to each other at a table, taking turns with the fountain pen. One would write a neat row of characters: *Dearest Mama. We are alive.* She would brush back her wispy bangs and hand the other sister the pen, and she would write: *Come get us. Please hurry.*

10   Of course they could not know that my mother had died three months before, suddenly, when a blood vessel in her brain burst. One minute she was talking to my father, complaining about the tenants upstairs, scheming how to evict them under the pretense that relatives from China were moving in. The next minute she was holding her head, her eyes squeezed shut, groping for the sofa, and then crumpling softly to the floor with fluttering hands.

So my father had been the first one to open the letter, a long letter it turned out. And they did call her Mama. They said they always revered her as their true mother. They kept a framed picture of her. They told her about their life, from the time my mother last saw them on the road leaving Kweilin to when they were finally found.

And the letter had broken my father's heart so much—these daughters calling my mother from another life he never knew—that he gave the letter to my mother's old friend Auntie Lindo and asked her to write back and tell my sisters, in the gentlest way possible, that my mother was dead.

But instead Auntie Lindo took the letter to the Joy Luck Club and discussed with Auntie Ying and Auntie An-mei what should be done, because they had known for many years about my mother's search for her twin daughters, her endless hope. Auntie Lindo and the others cried over this double tragedy, of losing my mother three months before, and now again. And so they couldn't help but think of some miracle, some possible way of reviving her from the dead, so my mother could fulfill her dream.

So this is what they wrote to my sisters in Shanghai: "Dearest Daughters, I too have never forgotten you in my memory or in my heart. I never gave up hope that we would see each other again in a joyous reunion. I am only sorry it has been too long. I want to tell you everything about my life since I last saw you. I want to tell you this when our family comes to see you in China. . . . ." They signed it with my mother's name.

15   It wasn't until all this had been done that they first told me about my sisters, the letter they received, the one they wrote back.

"They'll think she's coming, then," I murmured. And I had imagined my sisters now being ten or eleven, jumping up and down, holding hands, their pigtails bouncing, excited that their mother—*their* mother—was coming, whereas my mother was dead.

"How can you say she is not coming in a letter?" said Auntie Lindo. "She is their mother. She is your mother. You must be the one to tell them. All these years, they have been dreaming of her." And I thought she was right.

But then I started dreaming, too, of my mother and my sisters and how it would be if I arrived in Shanghai. All these years, while they waited to be found, I had lived with my mother and then had lost her. I imagined seeing my sisters at the airport. They would be standing on their tiptoes, looking anxiously, scanning from one dark head to another as we got off the plane. And I would recognize them instantly, their faces with the identical worried look.

"*Jyejye, Jyejye.* Sister, Sister. We are here," I saw myself saying in my poor version of Chinese.

20   "Where is Mama?" they would say, and look around, still smiling, two flushed and eager faces. "Is she hiding?" And this would have been like my mother, to stand behind just a bit, to tease a little and make people's patience pull a little on their hearts. I would shake my head and tell my sisters she was not hiding.

"Oh, that must be Mama, no?" one of my sisters would whisper excitedly, pointing to another small woman completely engulfed in a tower of presents. And that, too, would have been like my mother, to bring mountains of gifts, food, and toys for children—all bought on sale—shunning thanks, saying the gifts were nothing, and later turning the labels over to show my sisters, "Calvin Klein, 100% wool."

I imagined myself starting to say, "Sisters, I am sorry, I have come alone . . ." and before I could tell them—they could see it in my face—they were wailing, pulling their hair, their lips twisted in pain, as they ran away from me. And then I saw myself getting back on the plane and coming home.

After I had dreamed this scene many times—watching their despair turn from horror into anger—I begged Auntie Lindo to write another letter. And at first she refused.

"How can I say she is dead? I cannot write this," said Auntie Lindo with a stubborn look.

"But it's cruel to have them believe she's coming on the plane," I said. "When they see it's just me, they'll hate me."

"Hate you? Cannot be." She was scowling. "You are their own sister, their only family."

"You don't understand," I protested.

"What I don't understand?" she said.

And I whispered, "They'll think I'm responsible, that she died because I didn't appreciate her."

And Auntie Lindo looked satisfied and sad at the same time, as if this were true and I had finally realized it. She sat down for an hour, and when she stood up she handed me a two-page letter. She had tears in her eyes. I realized that the very thing I had feared, she had done. So even if she had written the news of my mother's death in English, I wouldn't have had the heart to read it.

"Thank you," I whispered.

The landscape has become gray, filled with low flat cement buildings, old factories, and then tracks and more tracks filled with trains like ours passing by in the opposite direction. I see platforms crowded with people wearing drab Western clothes, with spots of bright colors: little children wearing pink and yellow, red and peach. And there are soldiers in olive green and red, and old ladies in gray tops and pants that stop mid-calf. We are in Guangzhou.

Before the train even comes to a stop, people are bringing down their belongings from above their seats. For a moment there is a dangerous shower of heavy suitcases laden with gifts to relatives, half-broken boxes wrapped in miles of string to keep the contents from spilling out, plastic bags filled with yarn and vegetables and packages of dried mushrooms, and camera cases. And then we are caught in a stream of people rushing, shoving, pushing us along, until we find ourselves in one of a dozen lines waiting to go through customs. I feel as if I were getting on a number 30 Stockton bus in San Francisco. I am in China, I remind myself. And somehow the crowds don't bother me. It feels right. I start pushing too.

I take out the declaration forms and my passport. "Woo," it says at the top, and below that, "June May," who was born in "California, U.S.A.," in 1951. I wonder if the customs people will question whether I'm the same person as in the passport photo. In this picture, my chin-length hair is swept back and artfully styled. I am wearing false eyelashes, eye shadow, and lip liner. My cheeks are hollowed out by bronze blusher. But I had not expected the heat in October. And now my hair hangs limp with the humidity. I wear no makeup; in Hong Kong my mascara had melted into dark circles and everything else had felt like layers of grease. So today my face is plain, unadorned except for a thin mist of shiny sweat on my forehead and nose.

Even without makeup, I could never pass for true Chinese. I stand five-foot-six, and my head pokes above the crowd so that I am eye level only with other tourists. My mother once told me my height came from my grandfather, who was a northerner, and may have even had some Mongol blood. "This is what your grandmother once told me," explained my mother. "But now it is too late to ask her. They are all dead, your grandparents, your uncles, and their wives and children, all killed in the war, when a bomb fell on our house. So many generations in one instant."

She had said this so matter-of-factly that I thought she had long since gotten over any grief she had. And then I wondered how she knew they were all dead.

"Maybe they left the house before the bomb fell," I suggested.

"No," said my mother. "Our whole family is gone. It is just you and I."

"But how do you know? Some of them could have escaped."

"Cannot be," said my mother, this time almost angrily. And then her frown was washed over by a puzzled blank look, and she began to talk as if she were trying to remember where she had misplaced something. "I went back to that house. I kept looking up to where the house used to be. And it wasn't a house, just the sky. And below, underneath my feet, were four stories of burnt bricks and wood, all the life of our house. Then off to the side I saw things blown into the yard, nothing valuable. There was a bed someone used to sleep in, really just a metal frame twisted up at one corner. And a book, I don't know what kind, because every page had turned black. And I saw a teacup which was unbroken but filled with ashes. And then I found my doll, with her hands and legs broken, her hair burned off.... When I was a little girl, I had cried for that doll, seeing it all alone in the store window, and my mother had bought it for me. It was an American doll with yellow hair. It could turn its legs and arms. The eyes moved up and down. And when I married and left my family home, I gave the doll to my youngest niece, because she was like me. She cried if that doll was not with her always. Do you see? If she was in the house with that doll, her parents were there, and so everybody was there, waiting together, because that's how our family was."

The woman in the customs booth stares at my documents, then glances at me briefly, and with two quick movements stamps everything and sternly nods me along. And soon my father and I find ourselves in a large area filled with thousands of people and suitcases. I feel lost and my father looks helpless.

"Excuse me," I say to a man who looks like an American. "Can you tell me where I can get a taxi?" He mumbles something that sounds Swedish or Dutch.

"Syau Yen! Syau Yen!" I hear a piercing voice shout from behind me. An old woman in a yellow knit beret is holding up a pink plastic bag filled with wrapped trinkets. I guess she is trying to sell us something. But my father is staring down at this tiny sparrow of a woman, squinting into her eyes. And then his eyes widen, his face opens up and he smiles like a pleased little boy.

"*Aiyi! Aiyi!*"—Auntie Auntie!—he says softly.

"Syau Yen!" coos my great-aunt. I think it's funny she has just called my father "Little Wild Goose." It must be his baby milk name, the name used to discourage ghosts from stealing children.

They clasp each other's hands—they do not hug—and hold on like this, taking turns saying, "Look at you! You are so old. Look how old you've become!" They are both crying openly, laughing at the same time, and I bite my lip, trying not to cry. I'm afraid to feel their joy. Because I am thinking how different our arrival in Shanghai will be tomorrow, how awkward it will feel.

Now Aiyi beams and points to a Polaroid picture of my father. My father had wisely sent pictures when he wrote and said we were coming. See how smart she was, she seems to intone as she compares the picture to my father. In the letter, my father had said we would call her from the hotel once we arrived, so this is a surprise, that they've come to meet us. I wonder if my sisters will be at the airport.

It is only then that I remember the camera. I had meant to take a picture of my father and his aunt the moment they met. It's not too late.

"Here, stand together over here," I say, holding up the Polaroid. The camera flashes and I hand them the snapshot. Aiyi and my father still stand close together, each of them holding a corner of the picture, watching as their images begin to form. They are almost reverentially quiet. Aiyi is only five years older than my father, which makes her around seventy-seven. But she looks ancient, shrunken, a mummified relic. Her thin hair is pure white, her teeth are brown with decay. So much for stories of Chinese women looking young forever, I think to myself.

Now Aiyi is crooning to me: "*Jandale.*" So big already. She looks up at me, at my full height, and then peers into her pink plastic bag—her gifts to us, I have figured out—as if she is wondering what she will give to me, now that I am so old and big. And then she grabs my elbow with her sharp pincerlike grasp and turns me around. A man and a woman in their fifties are shaking hands with my father, everybody smiling and saying, "Ah! Ah!" They are Aiyi's oldest son and his wife, and standing next to them are four other people, around my age, and a little girl who's around ten. The introductions go by so fast, all I know is that one of them is Aiyi's grandson, with his wife, and the other is her granddaughter, with her husband. And the little girl is Lili, Aiyi's great-granddaughter.

Aiyi and my father speak the Mandarin dialect from their childhood, but the rest of the family speaks only the Cantonese of their village. I understand only Mandarin but can't speak it that well. So Aiyi and my father gossip unrestrained in Mandarin, exchanging news about people from their old village. And they stop only occasionally to talk to the rest of us, sometimes in Cantonese, sometimes in English.

"Oh, it is as I suspected," says my father, turning to me. "He died last summer." And I already understood this. I just don't know who this person, Li Gong, is. I feel as if I were in the United Nations and the translators had run amok.

"Hello," I say to the little girl. "My name is Jing-mei." But the little girl squirms to look away, causing her parents to laugh with embarrassment. I try to think of Cantonese words I can say to her, stuff I learned from friends in Chinatown, but all I can think of are swear words, terms for bodily functions, and short phrases like "tastes good," "tastes like garbage," and "she's really ugly." And then I have another plan: I hold up the Polaroid camera, beckoning Lili with my finger.

She immediately jumps forward, places one hand on her hip in the manner of a fashion model, juts out her chest, and flashes me a toothy smile. As soon as I take the picture she is standing next to me, jumping and giggling every few seconds as she watches herself appear on the greenish film.

By the time we hail taxis for the ride to the hotel, Lili is holding tight onto my hand, pulling me along.

In the taxi, Aiyi talks nonstop, so I have no chance to ask her about the different sights we are passing by.

"You wrote and said you would come only for one day," says Aiyi to my father in an agitated tone. "One day! How can you see your family in one day! Toishan is many hours' drive from Guangzhou. And this idea to call us when you arrive. This is nonsense. We have no telephone."

My heart races a little. I wonder if Auntie Lindo told my sisters we would call from the hotel in Shanghai?

Aiyi continues to scold my father. "I was so beside myself, ask my son, almost turned heaven and earth upside down trying to think of a way! So we decided the best was for us to take the bus from Toishan and come into Guangzhou—meet you right from the start."

And now I am holding my breath as the taxi driver dodges between trucks and buses, honking his horn constantly. We seem to be on some sort of long freeway overpass, like a bridge above the city. I can see row after row of apartments, each floor cluttered with laundry hanging out to dry on the balcony. We pass a public bus, with people jammed in so tight their faces are nearly wedged against the window. Then I see the skyline of what must be downtown Guangzhou. From a distance, it looks like a major American city, with highrises and construction going on everywhere. As we slow down in the more congested part of the city, I see scores of little shops, dark inside, lined with counters and shelves. And then there is a building, its front laced with scaffolding made of bamboo poles held together with plastic strips. Men and women are standing on narrow platforms, scraping the sides, working without safety straps or helmets. Oh, would OSHA[1] have a field day here, I think.

Aiyi's shrill voice rises up again: "So it is a shame you can't see our village, our house. My sons have been quite successful, selling our vegetables in the free market. We had enough these last few years to build a big house, three stories, all of new brick, big enough for our whole family and then some. And every year, the money is even better. You Americans aren't the only ones who know how to get rich!"

The taxi stops and I assume we've arrived, but then I peer out at what looks like a grander version of the Hyatt Regency. "This is communist China?" I wonder out loud. And then I shake my head toward my father. "This must be the wrong hotel." I quickly pull out our itinerary, travel tickets, and reservations. I had explicitly instructed my travel agent to choose something inexpensive, in the thirty-to-forty-dollar range. I'm sure of this. And there it says on our itinerary: Garden Hotel, Huanshi Dong Lu. Well, our travel agent had better be prepared to eat the extra, that's all I have to say.

The hotel is magnificent. A bellboy complete with uniform and sharp-creased cap jumps forward and begins to carry our bags into the lobby. Inside, the hotel

---

1. The Occupational Safety and Health Administration, a division of the U.S. Department of Labor.

looks like an orgy of shopping arcades and restaurants all encased in granite and glass. And rather than be impressed, I am worried about the expense, as well as the appearance it must give Aiyi, that we rich Americans cannot be without our luxuries even for one night.

But when I step up to the reservation desk, ready to haggle over this booking mistake, it is confirmed. Our rooms are prepaid, thirty-four dollars each. I feel sheepish, and Aiyi and the others seem delighted by our temporary surroundings. Lili is looking wide-eyed at an arcade filled with video games.

Our whole family crowds into one elevator, and the bellboy waves, saying he will meet us on the eighteenth floor. As soon as the elevator door shuts, everybody becomes very quiet, and when the door finally opens again, everybody talks at once in what sounds like relieved voices. I have the feeling Aiyi and the others have never been on such a long elevator ride.

Our rooms are next to each other and are identical. The rugs, drapes, bedspreads are all in shades of taupe. There's a color television with remote-control panels built into the lamp table between the two twin beds. The bathroom has marble walls and floors. I find a built-in wet bar with a small refrigerator stocked with Heineken beer, Coke Classic, and Seven-Up, mini-bottles of Johnnie Walker Red, Bacardi rum, and Smirnoff vodka, and packets of M & M's, honey-roasted cashews, and Cadbury chocolate bars. And again I say out loud, "This is communist China?"

My father comes into my room. "They decided we should just stay here and visit," he says, shrugging his shoulders. "They say, Less trouble that way. More time to talk."

"What about dinner?" I ask. I have been envisioning my first real Chinese feast for many days already, a big banquet with one of those soups steaming out of a carved winter melon, chicken wrapped in clay, Peking duck, the works.

My father walks over and picks up a room service book next to a *Travel & Leisure* magazine. He flips through the pages quickly and then points to the menu. "This is what they want," says my father.

So it's decided. We are going to dine tonight in our rooms, with our family, sharing hamburgers, french fries, and apple pie à la mode.

Aiyi and her family are browsing the shops while we clean up. After a hot ride on the train, I'm eager for a shower and cooler clothes.

The hotel has provided little packets of shampoo which, upon opening, I discover is the consistency and color of hoisin sauce.[2] This is more like it, I think. This is China. And I rub some in my damp hair.

Standing in the shower, I realize this is the first time I've been by myself in what seems like days. But instead of feeling relieved, I feel forlorn. I think about what my mother said, about activating my genes and becoming Chinese. And I wonder what she meant.

Right after my mother died, I asked myself a lot of things, things that couldn't be answered, to force myself to grieve more. It seemed as if I wanted to sustain my grief, to assure myself that I had cared deeply enough.

But now I ask the questions mostly because I want to know the answers. What was that pork stuff she used to make that had the texture of sawdust? What

---

2. Sweet brownish-red sauce made from soybeans, sugar, water, spices, garlic, and chili.

were the names of the uncles who died in Shanghai? What had she dreamt all these years about her other daughters? All the times when she got mad at me, was she really thinking about them? Did she wish I were they? Did she regret that I wasn't?

---

75    At one o'clock in the morning, I awake to tapping sounds on the window. I must have dozed off and now I feel my body uncramping itself. I'm sitting on the floor, leaning against one of the twin beds. Lili is lying next to me. The others are asleep, too, sprawled out on the beds and floor. Aiyi is seated at a little table, looking very sleepy. And my father is staring out the window, tapping his fingers on the glass. The last time I listened my father was telling Aiyi about his life since he last saw her. How he had gone to Yenching University, later got a post with a newspaper in Chungking, met my mother there, a young widow. How they later fled together to Shanghai to try to find my mother's family house, but there was nothing there. And then they traveled eventually to Canton and then to Hong Kong, then Haiphong and finally to San Francisco. . . .

"Suyuan didn't tell me she was trying all these years to find her daughters," he is now saying in a quiet voice. "Naturally, I did not discuss her daughters with her. I thought she was ashamed she had left them behind."

"Where did she leave them?" asks Aiyi. "How were they found?"

I am wide awake now. Although I have heard parts of this story from my mother's friends.

"It happened when the Japanese took over Kweilin," says my father.

80    "Japanese in Kweilin?" says Aiyi. "That was never the case. Couldn't be. The Japanese never came to Kweilin."

"Yes, that is what the newspapers reported. I know this because I was working for the news bureau at the time. The Kuomintang[3] often told us what we could say and could not say. But we knew the Japanese had come into Kwangsi Province. We had sources who told us how they had captured the Wuchang-Canton railway. How they were coming overland, making very fast progress, marching toward the provincial capital."

Aiyi looks astonished. "If people did not know this, how could Suyuan know the Japanese were coming?"

"An officer of the Kuomintang secretly warned her," explains my father. "Suyuan's husband also was an officer and everybody knew that officers and their families would be the first to be killed. So she gathered a few possessions and, in the middle of the night, she picked up her daughters and fled on foot. The babies were not even one year old."

"How could she give up those babies!" sighs Aiyi. "Twin girls. We have never had such luck in our family." And then she yawns again.

85    "What were they named?" she asks. I listen carefully. I had been planning on using just the familiar "Sister" to address them both. But now I want to know how to pronounce their names.

"They have their father's surname, Wang," says my father. "And their given names are Chwun Yu and Chwun Hwa."

---

3. National People's Party, led by Generalissimo Chiang Kai-shek (1887–1975), which fought successfully against the Japanese occupation before being defeated militarily in 1949 by the Chinese Communist Party, led by Mao Zedong (1893–1976).

"What do the names mean?" I ask.

"Ah." My father draws imaginary characters on the window. "One means 'Spring Rain,' the other 'Spring Flower,'" he explains in English, "because they born in the spring, and of course rain come before flower, same order these girls are born. Your mother like a poet, don't you think?"

I nod my head. I see Aiyi nod her head forward, too. But it falls forward and stays there. She is breathing deeply, noisily. She is asleep.

"And what does Ma's name mean?" I whisper.

"'Suyuan,'" he says, writing more invisible characters on the glass. "The way she write it in Chinese, it mean 'Long-Cherished Wish.' Quite a fancy name, not so ordinary like flower name. See this first character, it mean something like 'Forever Never Forgotten.' But there is another way to write 'Suyuan.' Sound exactly the same, but the meaning is opposite." His finger creates the brushstrokes of another character. "The first part look the same: 'Never Forgotten.' But the last part add to first part make the whole word mean 'Long-Held Grudge.' Your mother get angry with me, I tell her her name should be Grudge."

My father is looking at me, moist-eyed. "See, I pretty clever, too, hah?"

I nod, wishing I could find some way to comfort him. "And what about my name," I ask, "what does 'Jing-mei' mean?"

"Your name also special," he says. I wonder if any name in Chinese is not something special. "'Jing' like excellent *jing*. Not just good, it's something pure, essential, the best quality. *Jing* is good leftover stuff when you take impurities out of something like gold, or rice, or salt. So what is left—just pure essence. And 'Mei,' this is common *mei*, as in *meimei*, 'younger sister.'"

I think about this. My mother's long-cherished wish. Me, the younger sister who was supposed to be the essence of the others. I feed myself with the old grief, wondering how disappointed my mother must have been. Tiny Aiyi stirs suddenly, her head rolls and then falls back, her mouth opens as if to answer my question. She grunts in her sleep, tucking her body more closely into the chair.

"So why did she abandon those babies on the road?" I need to know, because now I feel abandoned too.

"Long time I wondered this myself," says my father. "But then I read that letter from her daughters in Shanghai now, and I talk to Auntie Lindo, all the others. And then I knew. No shame in what she done. None."

"What happened?"

"Your mother running away—" begins my father.

"No, tell me in Chinese," I interrupt. "Really, I can understand."

He begins to talk, still standing at the window, looking into the night.

---

After fleeing Kweilin, your mother walked for several days trying to find a main road. Her thought was to catch a ride on a truck or wagon, to catch enough rides until she reached Chungking, where her husband was stationed.

She had sewn money and jewelry into the lining of her dress, enough, she thought, to barter rides all the way. If I am lucky, she thought, I will not have to trade the heavy gold bracelet and jade ring. These were things from her mother, your grandmother.

By the third day, she had traded nothing. The roads were filled with people, everybody running and begging for rides from passing trucks. The trucks rushed by, afraid to stop. So your mother found no rides, only the start of dysentery pains in her stomach.

Her shoulders ached from the two babies swinging from scarf slings. Blisters grew on the palms from holding two leather suitcases. And then the blisters burst and began to bleed. After a while, she left the suitcases behind, keeping only the food and a few clothes. And later she also dropped the bags of wheat flour and rice and kept walking like this for many miles, singing songs to her little girls, until she was delirious with pain and fever.

Finally, there was not one more step left in her body. She didn't have the strength to carry those babies any farther. She slumped to the ground. She knew she would die of her sickness, or perhaps from thirst, from starvation, or from the Japanese, who she was sure were marching right behind her.

She took the babies out of the slings and sat them on the side of the road, then lay down next to them. You babies are so good, she said, so quiet. They smiled back, reaching their chubby hands for her, wanting to be picked up again. And then she knew she could not bear to watch her babies die with her.

She saw a family with three young children in a cart going by. "Take my babies, I beg you," she cried to them. But they stared back with empty eyes and never stopped.

She saw another person pass and called out again. This time a man turned around, and he had such a terrible expression—your mother said it looked like death itself—she shivered and looked away.

When the road grew quiet, she tore open the lining of her dress, and stuffed jewelry under the shirt of one baby and money under the other. She reached into her pocket and drew out the photos of her family, the picture of her father and mother, the picture of herself and her husband on their wedding day. And she wrote on the back of each the names of the babies and this same message: "Please care for these babies with the money and valuables provided. When it is safe to come, if you bring them to Shanghai, 9 Weichang Lu, the Li family will be glad to give you a generous reward. Li Suyuan and Wang Fuchi."

And then she touched each baby's cheek and told her not to cry. She would go down the road to find them some food and would be back. And without looking back, she walked down the road, stumbling and crying, thinking only of this one last hope, that her daughters would be found by a kindhearted person who would care for them. She would not allow herself to imagine anything else.

She did not remember how far she walked, which direction she went, when she fainted, or how she was found. When she awoke, she was in the back of a bouncing truck with several other sick people, all moaning. And she began to scream, thinking she was now on a journey to Buddhist hell. But the face of an American missionary lady bent over her and smiled, talking to her in a soothing language she did not understand. And yet she could somehow understand. She had been saved for no good reason, and it was now too late to go back and save her babies.

When she arrived in Chungking, she learned her husband had died two weeks before. She told me later she laughed when the officers told her this news, she was so delirious with madness and disease. To come so far, to lose so much and to find nothing.

I met her in a hospital. She was lying on a cot, hardly able to move, her dysentery had drained her so thin. I had come in for my foot, my missing toe, which was cut off by a piece of falling rubble. She was talking to herself, mumbling.

"Look at these clothes," she said, and I saw she had on a rather unusual dress for wartime. It was silk satin, quite dirty, but there was no doubt it was a beautiful dress.

"Look at this face," she said, and I saw her dusty face and hollow cheeks, her eyes shining black. "Do you see my foolish hope?"

"I thought I had lost everything, except these two things," she murmured. "And I wondered which I would lose next. Clothes or hope? Hope or clothes?"

"But now, see here, look what is happening," she said, laughing, as if all her prayers had been answered. And she was pulling hair out of her head as easily as one lifts new wheat from wet soil.

It was an old peasant woman who found them. "How could I resist?" the peasant woman later told your sisters when they were older. They were still sitting obediently near where your mother had left them, looking like little fairy queens waiting for their sedan to arrive.

The woman, Mei Ching, and her husband, Mei Han, lived in a stone cave. There were thousands of hidden caves like that in and around Kweilin so secret that the people remained hidden even after the war ended. The Meis would come out of their cave every few days and forage for food supplies left on the road, and sometimes they would see something that they both agreed was a tragedy to leave behind. So one day they took back to their cave a delicately painted set of rice bowls, another day a little footstool with a velvet cushion and two new wedding blankets. And once, it was your sisters.

They were pious people, Muslims, who believed the twin babies were a sign of double luck, and they were sure of this when, later in the evening, they discovered how valuable the babies were. She and her husband had never seen rings and bracelets like those. And while they admired the pictures, knowing the babies came from a good family, neither of them could read or write. It was not until many months later that Mei Ching found someone who could read the writing on the back. By then, she loved these baby girls like her own.

In 1952 Mei Han, the husband, died. The twins were already eight years old, and Mei Ching now decided it was time to find your sisters' true family. She showed the girls the picture of their mother and told them they had been born into a great family and she would take them back to see their true mother and grandparents. Mei Ching told them about the reward, but she swore she would refuse it. She loved these girls so much, she only wanted them to have what they were entitled to—a better life, a fine house, educated ways. Maybe the family would let her stay on as the girls' amah. Yes, she was certain they would insist.

Of course, when she found the place at 9 Weichang Lu, in the old French Concession, it was something completely different. It was the site of a factory building, recently constructed, and none of the workers knew what had become of the family whose house had burned down on that spot.

Mei Ching could not have known, of course, that your mother and I, her new husband, had already returned to that same place in 1945 in hopes of finding both her family and her daughters.

Your mother and I stayed in China until 1947. We went to many different cities—back to Kweilin, to Changsha, as far south as Kunming. She was always looking out of one corner of her eye for twin babies, then little girls. Later we went to Hong Kong, and when we finally left in 1949 for the United States, I think she was even looking for them on the boat. But when we arrived, she no longer talked about them. I thought, At last, they have died in her heart.

When letters could be openly exchanged between China and the United States, she wrote immediately to old friends in Shanghai and Kweilin. I did not know she did this. Auntie Lindo told me. But of course, by then, all the street names had changed. Some people had died, others had moved away. So it took many years to find a contact. And when she did find an old schoolmate's address and wrote asking her to look for her daughters, her friend wrote back and said this was impossible, like looking for a needle on the bottom of the ocean. How did she know her daughters were in Shanghai and not somewhere else in China? The friend, of course, did not ask, How do you know your daughters are still alive?

So her schoolmate did not look. Finding babies lost during the war was a matter of foolish imagination, and she had no time for that.

But every year, your mother wrote to different people. And this last year, I think she got a big idea in her head, to go to China and find them herself. I remember she told me, "Canning, we should go, before it is too late, before we are too old." And I told her we were already too old, it was already too late.

130  I just thought she wanted to be a tourist! I didn't know she wanted to go and look for her daughters. So when I said it was too late, that must have put a terrible thought in her head that her daughters might be dead. And I think this possibility grew bigger and bigger in her head, until it killed her.

Maybe it was your mother's dead spirit who guided her Shanghai schoolmate to find her daughters. Because after your mother died, the schoolmate saw your sisters, by chance, while shopping for shoes at the Number One Department Store on Nanjing Dong Road. She said it was like a dream, seeing these two women who looked so much alike, moving down the stairs together. There was something about their facial expressions that reminded the schoolmate of your mother.

She quickly walked over to them and called their names, which of course, they did not recognize at first, because Mei Ching had changed their names. But your mother's friend was so sure, she persisted. "Are you not Wang Chwun Yu and Wang Chwun Hwa?" she asked them. And then these double-image women became very excited, because they remembered the names written on the back of an old photo, a photo of a young man and woman they still honored, as their much-loved first parents, who had died and become spirit ghosts still roaming the earth looking for them.

———

At the airport, I am exhausted. I could not sleep last night. Aiyi had followed me into my room at three in the morning, and she instantly fell asleep on one of the twin beds, snoring with the might of a lumberjack. I lay awake thinking about my mother's story, realizing how much I have never known about her, grieving that my sisters and I had both lost her.

And now at the airport, after shaking hands with everybody, waving good-bye, I think about all the different ways we leave people in this world. Cheerily waving good-bye to some at airports, knowing we'll never see each other again.

Leaving others on the side of the road, hoping that we will. Finding my mother in my father's story and saying good-bye before I have a chance to know her better.

Aiyi smiles at me as we wait for our gate to be called. She is so old. I put one arm around her and one arm around Lili. They are the same size, it seems. And then it's time. As we wave good-bye one more time and enter the waiting area, I get the sense I am going from one funeral to another. In my hand I'm clutching a pair of tickets to Shanghai. In two hours we'll be there.

The plane takes off. I close my eyes. How can I describe to them in my broken Chinese about our mother's life? Where should I begin?

"Wake up, we're here," says my father. And I awake with my heart pounding in my throat. I look out the window and we're already on the runway. It's gray outside.

And now I'm walking down the steps of the plane, onto the tarmac and toward the building. If only, I think, if only my mother had lived long enough to be the one walking toward them. I am so nervous I cannot even feel my feet. I am just moving somehow.

Somebody shouts, "She's arrived!" And then I see her. Her short hair. Her small body. And that same look on her face. She has the back of her hand pressed hard against her mouth. She is crying as though she had gone through a terrible ordeal and were happy it is over.

And I know it's not my mother, yet it is the same look she had when I was five and had disappeared all afternoon, for such a long time, that she was convinced I was dead. And when I miraculously appeared, sleepy-eyed, crawling from underneath my bed, she wept and laughed, biting the back of her hand to make sure it was true.

And now I see her again, two of her, waving, and in one hand there is a photo, the Polaroid I sent them. As soon as I get beyond the gate, we run toward each other, all three of us embracing, all hesitations and expectations forgotten.

"Mama, Mama," we all murmur, as if she is among us.

My sisters look at me, proudly. *"Meimei jandale,"* says one sister proudly to the other. "Little Sister has grown up." I look at their faces again and I see no trace of my mother in them. Yet they still look familiar. And now I also see what part of me is Chinese. It is so obvious. It is my family. It is in our blood. After all these years, it can finally be let go.

My sisters and I stand, arms around each other, laughing and wiping the tears from each other's eyes. The flash of the Polaroid goes off and my father hands me the snapshot. My sisters and I watch quietly together, eager to see what develops.

The gray-green surface changes to the bright colors of our three images, sharpening and deepening all at once. And although we don't speak, I know we all see it: Together we look like our mother. Her same eyes, her same mouth, open in surprise to see, at last, her long-cherished wish.

1989

## QUESTIONS

1. Why is the opening scene of "A Pair of Tickets"—the train journey from Hong Kong to Guangzhou—an appropriate setting for June May's remark that she is "becoming Chinese"?
2. When June May arrives in Guangzhou, what are some details that seem familiar to her, and what are some that seem exotic? Why is she so preoccupied with comparing China to America?
3. June May says that "she could never pass for true Chinese," yet by the end of the story she has discovered "the part of me that is Chinese." How does the meaning of "Chinese" evolve throughout the story?

## ANTON CHEKHOV

## *The Lady with the Dog*[1]

### I

It was said that a new person had appeared on the sea-front: a lady with a little dog. Dmitri Dmitritch Gurov, who had by then been a fortnight at Yalta,[2] and so was fairly at home there, had begun to take an interest in new arrivals. Sitting in Verney's pavilion, he saw, walking on the sea-front, a fair-haired young lady of medium height, wearing a *béret*; a white Pomeranian dog was running behind her.

And afterwards he met her in the public gardens and in the square several times a day. She was walking alone, always wearing the same *béret*, and always with the same white dog; no one knew who she was, and every one called her simply "the lady with the dog."

"If she is here alone without a husband or friends, it wouldn't be amiss to make her acquaintance," Gurov reflected.

He was under forty, but he had a daughter already twelve years old, and two sons at school. He had been married young, when he was a student in his second year, and by now his wife seemed half as old again as he. She was a tall, erect woman with dark eyebrows, staid and dignified, and, as she said of herself, intellectual. She read a great deal, used phonetic spelling, called her husband, not Dmitri, but Dimitri, and he secretly considered her unintelligent, narrow, inelegant, was afraid of her, and did not like to be at home. He had begun being unfaithful to her long ago—had been unfaithful to her often, and, probably on that account, almost always spoke ill of women, and when they were talked about in his presence, used to call them "the lower race."

5   It seemed to him that he had been so schooled by bitter experience that he might call them what he liked, and yet he could not get on for two days together without "the lower race." In the society of men he was bored and not himself, with them he was cold and uncommunicative; but when he was in the company of women he felt free, and knew what to say to them and how to behave; and he was at ease with them even when he was silent. In his appearance, in his character, in his whole nature, there was something attractive and elusive which allured women and disposed them in his favour; he knew that, and some force seemed to draw him, too, to them.

Experience often repeated, truly bitter experience, had taught him long ago

---

1. Translated by Constance Garnett.   2. Russian city on the Black Sea; a resort.

that with decent people, especially Moscow people—always slow to move and irresolute—every intimacy, which at first so agreeably diversifies life and appears a light and charming adventure, inevitably grows into a regular problem of extreme intricacy, and in the long run the situation becomes unbearable. But at every fresh meeting with an interesting woman this experience seemed to slip out of his memory, and he was eager for life, and everything seemed simple and amusing.

One evening he was dining in the gardens, and the lady in the *béret* came up slowly to take the next table. Her expression, her gait, her dress, and the way she did her hair told him that she was a lady, that she was married, that she was in Yalta for the first time and alone, and that she was dull there.... The stories told of the immorality in such places as Yalta are to a great extent untrue; he despised them, and knew that such stories were for the most part made up by persons who would themselves have been glad to sin if they had been able; but when the lady sat down at the next table three paces from him, he remembered these tales of easy conquests, of trips to the mountains, and the tempting thought of a swift, fleeting love affair, a romance with an unknown woman, whose name he did not know, suddenly took possession of him.

He beckoned coaxingly to the Pomeranian, and when the dog came up to him he shook his finger at it. The Pomeranian growled: Gurov shook his finger at it again.

The lady looked at him and at once dropped her eyes.

"He doesn't bite," she said, and blushed.

"May I give him a bone?" he asked; and when she nodded he asked courteously, "Have you been long in Yalta?"

"Five days."

"And I have already dragged out a fortnight here."

There was a brief silence.

"Time goes fast, and yet it is so dull here!" she said, not looking at him.

"That's only the fashion to say it is dull here. A provincial will live in Belyov or Zhidra and not be dull, and when he comes here it's 'Oh, the dulness! Oh, the dust!' One would think he came from Grenada."[3]

She laughed. Then both continued eating in silence, like strangers, but after dinner they walked side by side; and there sprang up between them the light jesting conversation of people who are free and satisfied, to whom it does not matter where they go or what they talk about. They walked and talked of the strange light on the sea: the water was of a soft warm lilac hue, and there was a golden streak from the moon upon it. They talked of how sultry it was after a hot day. Gurov told her that he came from Moscow, that he had taken his degree in Arts, but had a post in a bank; that he had trained as an opera-singer, but had given it up, that he owned two houses in Moscow.... And from her he learnt that she had grown up in Petersburg, but had lived in S—— since her marriage two years before, that she was staying another month in Yalta, and that her husband, who needed a holiday too, might perhaps come and fetch her. She was not sure whether her husband had a post in a Crown Department or under the Provincial Council[4]—and was amused by her own ignorance. And Gurov learnt, too, that she was called Anna Sergeyevna.

---

3. Romantic city in southern Spain.
4. That is, a post in a national department, appointed by the czar, or a post in an elective local council.

Afterwards he thought about her in his room at the hotel—thought she would certainly meet him next day; it would be sure to happen. As he got into bed he thought how lately she had been a girl at school, doing lessons like his own daughter; he recalled the diffidence, the angularity, that was still manifest in her laugh and her manner of talking with a stranger. This must have been the first time in her life she had been alone in surroundings in which she was followed, looked at, and spoken to merely from a secret motive which she could hardly fail to guess. He recalled her slender, delicate neck, her lovely grey eyes.

"There's something pathetic about her, anyway," he thought, and fell asleep.

## II

A week had passed since they had made acquaintance. It was a holiday. It was sultry indoors, while in the street the wind whirled the dust round and round, and blew people's hats off. It was a thirsty day, and Gurov often went into the pavilion, and pressed Anna Sergeyevna to have syrup and water or an ice. One did not know what to do with oneself.

In the evening when the wind had dropped a little, they went out on the groyne to see the steamer come in. There were a great many people walking about the harbour; they had gathered to welcome some one, bringing bouquets. And two peculiarities of a well-dressed Yalta crowd were very conspicuous: the elderly ladies were dressed like young ones, and there were great numbers of generals.

Owing to the roughness of the sea, the steamer arrived late, after the sun had set, and it was a long time turning about before it reached the groyne. Anna Sergeyevna looked through her lorgnette at the steamer and the passengers as though looking for acquaintances, and when she turned to Gurov her eyes were shining. She talked a great deal and asked disconnected questions, forgetting next moment what she had asked; then she dropped her lorgnette in the crush.

The festive crowd began to disperse; it was too dark to see people's faces. The wind had completely dropped, but Gurov and Anna Sergeyevna still stood as though waiting to see some one else come from the steamer. Anna Sergeyevna was silent now, and sniffed the flowers without looking at Gurov.

"The weather is better this evening," he said. "Where shall we go now? Shall we drive somewhere?"

She made no answer.

Then he looked at her intently, and all at once put his arm round her and kissed her on the lips, and breathed in the moisture and the fragrance of the flowers; and he immediately looked round him, anxiously wondering whether any one had seen them.

"Let us go to your hotel," he said softly. And both walked quickly.

The room was close and smelt of the scent she had bought at the Japanese shop. Gurov looked at her and thought: "What different people one meets in the world!" From the past he preserved memories of careless, good-natured women, who loved cheerfully and were grateful to him for the happiness he gave them, however brief it might be; and of women like his wife who loved without any genuine feeling, with superfluous phrases, affectedly, hysterically, with an expression that suggested that it was not love nor passion, but something more significant; and of two or three others, very beautiful, cold women, on whose faces he had caught a glimpse of a rapacious expression—an obstinate desire to snatch from life more than it could give, and these were capricious, unreflecting, domineering, unintelligent women not in their first youth, and when Gurov grew cold to them their beauty excited his hatred, and the lace on their linen seemed to him like scales.

But in this case there was still the diffidence, the angularity of inexperienced youth, an awkward feeling; and there was a sense of consternation as though some one had suddenly knocked at the door. The attitude of Anna Sergeyevna—"the lady with the dog"—to what had happened was somehow peculiar, very grave, as though it were her fall—so it seemed, and it was strange and inappropriate. Her face dropped and faded, and on both sides of it her long hair hung down mournfully; she mused in a dejected attitude like "the woman who was a sinner" in an old-fashioned picture.

"It's wrong," she said. "You will be the first to despise me now."

There was a water-melon on the table. Gurov cut himself a slice and began eating it without haste. There followed at least half an hour of silence.

Anna Sergeyevna was touching; there was about her the purity of a good, simple woman who had seen little of life. The solitary candle burning on the table threw a faint light on her face, yet it was clear that she was very unhappy.

"How could I despise you?" asked Gurov. "You don't know what you are saying."

"God forgive me," she said, and her eyes filled with tears. "It's awful."

"You seem to feel you need to be forgiven."

"Forgiven? No. I am a bad, low woman; I despise myself and don't attempt to justify myself. It's not my husband but myself I have deceived. And not only just now; I have been deceiving myself for a long time. My husband may be a good, honest man, but he is a flunkey! I don't know what he does there, what his work is, but I know he is a flunkey! I was twenty when I was married to him. I have been tormented by curiosity; I wanted something better. 'There must be a different sort of life,' I said to myself. I wanted to live! To live, to live! . . . I was fired by curiosity . . . you don't understand it, but, I swear to God, I could not control myself; something happened to me: I could not be restrained. I told my husband I was ill, and came here. . . . And here I have been walking about as though I were dazed, like a mad creature; . . . and now I have become a vulgar, contemptible woman whom any one may despise."

Gurov felt bored already, listening to her. He was irritated by the naïve tone, by this remorse, so unexpected and inopportune; but for the tears in her eyes, he might have thought she was jesting or playing a part.

"I don't understand," he said softly. "What is it you want?"

She hid her face on his breast and pressed close to him.

"Believe me, believe me, I beseech you . . ." she said. "I love a pure, honest life, and sin is loathsome to me. I don't know what I am doing. Simple people say: 'The Evil One has beguiled me.' And I may say of myself now that the Evil One has beguiled me."

"Hush, hush! . . ." he muttered.

He looked at her fixed, scared eyes, kissed her, talked softly and affectionately, and by degrees she was comforted, and her gaiety returned; they both began laughing.

Afterwards when they went out there was not a soul on the sea-front. The town with its cypresses had quite a deathlike air, but the sea still broke noisily on the shore; a single barge was rocking on the waves, and a lantern was blinking sleepily on it.

They found a cab and drove to Oreanda.

"I found out your surname in the hall just now: it was written on the board—Von Diderits," said Gurov. "Is your husband a German?"

"No; I believe his grandfather was a German, but he is an Orthodox Russian himself."

At Oreanda they sat on a seat not far from the church, looked down at the sea, and were silent. Yalta was hardly visible through the morning mist; white clouds stood motionless on the mountain-tops. The leaves did not stir on the trees, grasshoppers chirruped, and the monotonous hollow sound of the sea rising up from below, spoke of the peace, of the eternal sleep awaiting us. So it must have sounded when there was no Yalta, no Oreanda here; so it sounds now, and it will sound as indifferently and monotonously when we are all no more. And in this constancy, in this complete indifference to the life and death of each of us, there lies hid, perhaps, a pledge of our eternal salvation, of the unceasing movement of life upon earth, of unceasing progress towards perfection. Sitting beside a young woman who in the dawn seemed so lovely, soothed and spellbound in these magical surroundings—the sea, mountains, clouds, the open sky—Gurov thought how in reality everything is beautiful in this world when one reflects: everything except what we think or do ourselves when we forget our human dignity and the higher aims of our existence.

A man walked up to them—probably a keeper—looked at them and walked away. And this detail seemed mysterious and beautiful, too. They saw a steamer come from Theodosia, with its lights out in the glow of dawn.

"There is dew on the grass," said Anna Sergeyevna, after a silence.

"Yes. It's time to go home."

They went back to the town.

Then they met every day at twelve o'clock on the sea-front, lunched and dined together, went for walks, admired the sea. She complained that she slept badly, that her heart throbbed violently; asked the same questions, troubled now by jealousy and now by the fear that he did not respect her sufficiently. And often in the square or gardens, when there was no one near them, he suddenly drew her to him and kissed her passionately. Complete idleness, these kisses in broad daylight while he looked round in dread of some one's seeing them, the heat, the smell of the sea, and the continual passing to and fro before him of idle, well-dressed, well-fed people, made a new man of him; he told Anna Sergeyevna how beautiful she was, how fascinating. He was impatiently passionate, he would not move a step away from her, while she was often pensive and continually urged him to confess that he did not respect her, did not love her in the least, and thought of her as nothing but a common woman. Rather late almost every evening they drove somewhere out of town, to Oreanda or to the waterfall; and the expedition was always a success, the scenery invariably impressed them as grand and beautiful.

They were expecting her husband to come, but a letter came from him, saying that there was something wrong with his eyes, and he entreated his wife to come home as quickly as possible. Anna Sergeyevna made haste to go.

"It's a good thing I am going away," she said to Gurov. "It's the finger of destiny!"

She went by coach and he went with her. They were driving the whole day.

When she had got into a compartment of the express, and when the second bell had rung, she said:

"Let me look at you once more . . . look at you once again. That's right."

She did not shed tears, but was so sad that she seemed ill, and her face was quivering.

"I shall remember you . . . think of you," she said. "God be with you; be happy. Don't remember evil against me. We are parting forever—it must be so, for we ought never to have met. Well, God be with you."

The train moved off rapidly, its lights soon vanished from sight, and a minute later there was no sound of it, as though everything had conspired together to end as quickly as possible that sweet delirium, that madness. Left alone on the platform, and gazing into the dark distance, Gurov listened to the chirrup of the grasshoppers and the hum of the telegraph wires, feeling as though he had only just waked up. And he thought, musing, that there had been another episode or adventure in his life, and it, too, was at an end, and nothing was left of it but a memory. . . . He was moved, sad, and conscious of a slight remorse. This young woman whom he would never meet again had not been happy with him; he was genuinely warm and affectionate with her, but yet in his manner, his tone, and his caresses there had been a shade of light irony, the coarse condescension of a happy man who was, besides, almost twice her age. All the time she had called him kind, exceptional, lofty; obviously he had seemed to her different from what he really was, so he had unintentionally deceived her. . . .

Here at the station was already a scent of autumn; it was a cold evening.

"It's time for me to go north," thought Gurov as he left the platform. "High time!"

III

At home in Moscow everything was in its winter routine; the stoves were heated, and in the morning it was still dark when the children were having breakfast and getting ready for school, and the nurse would light the lamp for a short time. The frosts had begun already. When the first snow has fallen, on the first day of sledge-driving it is pleasant to see the white earth, the white roofs, to draw soft, delicious breath, and the season brings back the days of one's youth. The old limes and birches, white with hoar-frost, have a good-natured expression; they are nearer to one's heart than cypresses and palms, and near them one doesn't want to be thinking of the sea and the mountains.

Gurov was Moscow born; he arrived in Moscow on a fine frosty day, and when he put on his fur coat and warm gloves, and walked along Petrovka, and when on Saturday evening he heard the ringing of the bells, his recent trip and the places he had seen lost all charm for him. Little by little he became absorbed in Moscow life, greedily read three newspapers a day, and declared he did not read the Moscow papers on principle! He already felt a longing to go to restaurants, clubs, dinner-parties, anniversary celebrations, and he felt flattered at entertaining distinguished lawyers and artists, and at playing cards with a professor at the doctors' club. He could already eat a whole plateful of salt fish and cabbage. . . .

In another month, he fancied, the image of Anna Sergeyevna would be shrouded in a mist in his memory, and only from time to time would visit him in his dreams with a touching smile as others did. But more than a month passed, real winter had come, and everything was still clear in his memory as though he had parted with Anna Sergeyevna only the day before. And his memories glowed more and more vividly. When in the evening stillness he heard from his study the voices of his children, preparing their lessons, or when he listened to a song or the organ at the restaurant, or the storm howled in the chimney, suddenly everything would rise up in his memory: what had happened on the groyne, and the early morning with the mist on the mountains, and the steamer coming from Theodosia, and the kisses. He would pace a long time about his room, remembering it all and smiling; then his memories passed into dreams, and in his fancy the past was mingled with what was to come. Anna Sergeyevna did not visit him in dreams, but followed him about everywhere like a shadow and haunted him. When he shut his eyes he saw her as though she were living before him, and she seemed to him lovelier, younger, tenderer than she was; and he imagined himself finer than he had been in Yalta. In the evenings she peeped out at him from the bookcase, from the fireplace, from the corner—he heard her breathing, the caressing rustle of her dress. In the street he watched the women, looking for some one like her.

He was tormented by an intense desire to confide his memories to some one. But in his home it was impossible to talk of his love, and he had no one outside; he could not talk to his tenants nor to any one at the bank. And what had he to talk of? Had he been in love, then? Had there been anything beautiful, poetical, or edifying or simply interesting in his relations with Anna Sergeyevna? And there was nothing for him but to talk vaguely of love, of woman, and no one guessed what it meant; only his wife twitched her black eyebrows, and said: "The part of a lady-killer does not suit you at all, Dimitri."

One evening, coming out of the doctors' club with an official with whom he had been playing cards, he could not resist saying:

"If only you knew what a fascinating woman I made the acquaintance of in Yalta!"

The official got into his sledge and was driving away, but turned suddenly and shouted:

"Dmitri Dmitritch!"

"What?"

"You were right this evening: the sturgeon was a bit too strong!"

These words, so ordinary, for some reason moved Gurov to indignation, and struck him as degrading and unclean. What savage manners, what people! What senseless nights, what uninteresting, uneventful days! The rage for card-playing, the gluttony, the drunkenness, the continual talk always about the same thing. Useless pursuits and conversations always about the same things absorb the better part of one's time, the better part of one's strength, and in the end there is left a life grovelling and curtailed, worthless and trivial, and there is no escaping or getting away from it—just as though one were in a madhouse or a prison.

Gurov did not sleep all night, and was filled with indignation. And he had a headache all next day. And the next night he slept badly; he sat up in bed, thinking, or paced up and down his room. He was sick of his children, sick of the bank; he had no desire to go anywhere or to talk of anything.

In the holidays in December he prepared for a journey, and told his wife he was going to Petersburg to do something in the interests of a young friend—and he set off for S——. What for? He did not very well know himself. He wanted to see Anna Sergeyevna and to talk with her—to arrange a meeting, if possible.

He reached S—— in the morning, and took the best room at the hotel, in which the floor was covered with grey army cloth, and on the table was an inkstand, grey with dust and adorned with a figure on horseback, with its hat in its hand and its head broken off. The hotel porter gave him the necessary information; Von Diderits lived in a house of his own in Old Gontcharny Street— it was not far from the hotel: he was rich and lived in good style, and had his own horses; every one in the town knew him. The porter pronounced the name "Dridirits."

Gurov went without haste to Old Gontcharny Street and found the house. Just opposite the house stretched a long grey fence adorned with nails.

"One would run away from a fence like that," thought Gurov, looking from the fence to the windows of the house and back again.

He considered: to-day was a holiday, and the husband would probably be at home. And in any case it would be tactless to go into the house and upset her. If he were to send her a note it might fall into her husband's hands, and then it might ruin everything. The best thing was to trust to chance. And he kept walking up and down the street by the fence, waiting for the chance. He saw a beggar go in at the gate and dogs fly at him; then an hour later he heard a piano, and the sounds were faint and indistinct. Probably it was Anna Sergeyevna playing. The front door suddenly opened, and an old woman came out, followed by the familiar white Pomeranian. Gurov was on the point of calling to the dog, but his heart began beating violently, and in his excitement he could not remember the dog's name.

He walked up and down, and loathed the grey fence more and more, and by now he thought irritably that Anna Sergeyevna had forgotten him, and was perhaps already amusing herself with some one else, and that that was very natural in a young woman who had nothing to look at from morning till night but that confounded fence. He went back to his hotel room and sat for a long while on the sofa, not knowing what to do, then he had dinner and a long nap.

"How stupid and worrying it is!" he thought when he woke and looked at the dark windows: it was already evening. "Here I've had a good sleep for some reason. What shall I do in the night?"

He sat on the bed, which was covered by a cheap grey blanket, such as one sees in hospitals, and he taunted himself in his vexation:

"So much for the lady with the dog . . . so much for the adventure. . . . You're in a nice fix. . . ."

That morning at the station a poster in large letters had caught his eye. "The Geisha"[5] was to be performed for the first time. He thought of this and went to the theatre.

"It's quite possible she may go to the first performance," he thought.

The theatre was full. As in all provincial theatres, there was a fog above the chandelier, the gallery was noisy and restless; in the front row the local dandies were standing up before the beginning of the performance, with their hands behind them; in the Governor's box the Governor's daughter, wearing a boa, was sitting in the front seat, while the Governor himself lurked modestly behind the curtain with only his hands visible; the orchestra was a long time tuning up; the

---

5. Operetta by Sidney Jones (1861–1946) that toured eastern Europe in 1898–99.

stage curtain swayed. All the time the audience were coming in and taking their seats Gurov looked at them eagerly.

Anna Sergeyevna, too, came in. She sat down in the third row, and when Gurov looked at her his heart contracted, and he understood clearly that for him there was in the whole world no creature so near, so precious, and so important to him; she, this little woman, in no way remarkable, lost in a provincial crowd, with a vulgar lorgnette in her hand, filled his whole life now, was his sorrow and his joy, the one happiness that he now desired for himself, and to the sounds of the inferior orchestra, of the wretched provincial violins, he thought how lovely she was. He thought and dreamed.

A young man with small side-whiskers, tall and stooping, came in with Anna Sergeyevna and sat down beside her; he bent his head at every step and seemed to be continually bowing. Most likely this was the husband whom at Yalta, in a rush of bitter feeling, she had called a flunkey. And there really was in his long figure, his side-whiskers, and the small bald patch on his head, something of the flunkey's obsequiousness; his smile was sugary, and in his buttonhole there was some badge of distinction like the number on a waiter.

During the first interval the husband went away to smoke; she remained alone in her stall. Gurov, who was sitting in the stalls, too, went up to her and said in a trembling voice, with a forced smile:

"Good-evening."

90 She glanced at him and turned pale, then glanced again with horror, unable to believe her eyes, and tightly gripped the fan and the lorgnette in her hands, evidently struggling with herself not to faint. Both were silent. She was sitting, he was standing, frightened by her confusion and not venturing to sit down beside her. The violins and the flute began tuning up. He felt suddenly frightened; it seemed as though all the people in the boxes were looking at them. She got up and went quickly to the door; he followed her, and both walked senselessly along passages, and up and down stairs, and figures in legal, scholastic, and civil service uniforms, all wearing badges, flitted before their eyes. They caught glimpses of ladies, of fur coats hanging on pegs; the draughts blew on them, bringing a smell of stale tobacco. And Gurov, whose heart was beating violently, thought:

"Oh, heavens! Why are these people here and this orchestra! . . ."

And at that instant he recalled how when he had seen Anna Sergeyevna off at the station he had thought that everything was over and they would never meet again. But how far they were still from the end!

On the narrow, gloomy staircase over which was written "To the Amphitheatre," she stopped.

"How you have frightened me!" she said, breathing hard, still pale and overwhelmed. "Oh, how you have frightened me! I am half dead. Why have you come? Why?"

95 "But do understand, Anna, do understand . . ." he said hastily in a low voice. "I entreat you to understand. . . ."

She looked at him with dread, with entreaty, with love; she looked at him intently, to keep his features more distinctly in her memory.

"I am so unhappy," she went on, not heeding him. "I have thought of nothing but you all the time; I live only in the thought of you. And I wanted to forget, to forget you; but why, oh, why, have you come?"

On the landing above them two schoolboys were smoking and looking down, but that was nothing to Gurov; he drew Anna Sergeyevna to him, and began kissing her face, her cheeks, and her hands.

"What are you doing, what are you doing!" she cried in horror, pushing him away. "We are mad. Go away to-day; go away at once.... I beseech you by all that is sacred, I implore you.... There are people coming this way!"

Some one was coming up the stairs.

"You must go away," Anna Sergeyevna went on in a whisper. "Do you hear, Dmitri Dmitritch? I will come and see you in Moscow. I have never been happy; I am miserable now, and I never, never shall be happy, never! Don't make me suffer still more! I swear I'll come to Moscow. But now let us part. My precious, good, dear one, we must part!"

She pressed his hand and began rapidly going downstairs, looking round at him, and from her eyes he could see that she really was unhappy. Gurov stood for a little while, listened, then, when all sound had died away, he found his coat and left the theatre.

IV

And Anna Sergeyevna began coming to see him in Moscow. Once in two or three months she left S——, telling her husband that she was going to consult a doctor about an internal complaint—and her husband believed her, and did not believe her. In Moscow she stayed at the Slaviansky Bazaar hotel, and at once sent a man in a red cap to Gurov. Gurov went to see her, and no one in Moscow knew of it.

Once he was going to see her in this way on a winter morning (the messenger had come the evening before when he was out). With him walked his daughter, whom he wanted to take to school: it was on the way. Snow was falling in big wet flakes.

"It's three degrees above freezing-point, and yet it is snowing," said Gurov to his daughter. "The thaw is only on the surface of the earth; there is quite a different temperature at a greater height in the atmosphere."

"And why are there no thunderstorms in the winter, father?"

He explained that, too. He talked, thinking all the while that he was going to see *her*, and no living soul knew of it, and probably never would know. He had two lives: one, open, seen and known by all who cared to know, full of relative truth and of relative falsehood, exactly like the lives of his friends and acquaintances; and another life running its course in secret. And through some strange, perhaps accidental, conjunction of circumstances, everything that was essential, of interest and of value to him, everything in which he was sincere and did not deceive himself, everything that made the kernel of his life, was hidden from other people; and all that was false in him, the sheath in which he hid himself to conceal the truth—such, for instance, as his work in the bank, his discussions at the club, his "lower race," his presence with his wife at anniversary festivities—all that was open. And he judged of others by himself, not believing in what he saw, and always believing that every man had his real, most interesting life under the cover of secrecy and under the cover of night. All personal life rested on secrecy, and possibly it was partly on that account that civilised man was so nervously anxious that personal privacy should be respected.

After leaving his daughter at school, Gurov went on to the Slaviansky Bazaar. He took off his fur coat below, went upstairs, and softly knocked at the door.

Anna Sergeyevna, wearing his favourite grey dress, exhausted by the journey and the suspense, had been expecting him since the evening before. She was pale; she looked at him, and did not smile, and he had hardly come in when she fell on his breast. Their kiss was slow and prolonged, as though they had not met for two years.

"Well, how are you getting on there?" he asked. "What news?"

"Wait; I'll tell you directly.... I can't talk."

She could not speak; she was crying. She turned away from him, and pressed her handkerchief to her eyes.

"Let her have her cry out. I'll sit down and wait," he thought, and he sat down in an arm-chair.

Then he rang and asked for tea to be brought him, and while he drank his tea she remained standing at the window with her back to him. She was crying from emotion, from the miserable consciousness that their life was so hard for them; they could only meet in secret, hiding themselves from people, like thieves! Was not their life shattered?

"Come, do stop!" he said.

It was evident to him that this love of theirs would not soon be over, that he could not see the end of it. Anna Sergeyevna grew more and more attached to him. She adored him, and it was unthinkable to say to her that it was bound to have an end some day; besides, she would not have believed it!

He went up to her and took her by the shoulders to say something affectionate and cheering, and at that moment he saw himself in the looking-glass.

His hair was already beginning to turn grey. And it seemed strange to him that he had grown so much older, so much plainer during the last few years. The shoulders on which his hands rested were warm and quivering. He felt compassion for this life, still so warm and lovely, but probably already not far from beginning to fade and wither like his own. Why did she love him so much? He always seemed to women different from what he was, and they loved in him not himself, but the man created by their imagination, whom they had been eagerly seeking all their lives; and afterwards, when they noticed their mistake, they loved him all the same. And not one of them had been happy with him. Time passed, he had made their acquaintance, got on with them, parted, but he had never once loved; it was anything you like, but not love.

And only now when his head was grey he had fallen properly, really in love—for the first time in his life.

Anna Sergeyevna and he loved each other like people very close and akin, like husband and wife, like tender friends; it seemed to them that fate itself had meant them for one another, and they could not understand why he had a wife and she a husband; and it was as though they were a pair of birds of passage, caught and forced to live in different cages. They forgave each other for what they were ashamed of in their past, they forgave everything in the present, and felt that this love of theirs had changed them both.

In moments of depression in the past he had comforted himself with any arguments that came into his mind, but now he no longer cared for arguments; he felt profound compassion, he wanted to be sincere and tender....

"Don't cry, my darling," he said. "You've had your cry; that's enough.... Let us talk now, let us think of some plan."

Then they spent a long while taking counsel together, talked of how to avoid the necessity for secrecy, for deception, for living in different towns and not seeing each other for long at a time. How could they be free from this intolerable bondage?

"How? How?" he asked, clutching his head. "How?"

And it seemed as though in a little while the solution would be found, and then a new and splendid life would begin; and it was clear to both of them that they had still a long, long road before them, and that the most complicated and difficult part of it was only just beginning.

1899

## QUESTIONS

1. When Gurov and Anna take their first walk together, they discuss "the strange light of the sea: the water was of a soft warm lilac hue, and there was a golden streak from the moon upon it." Why do you think Chekhov waits until this moment to provide descriptive details of the story's setting in Yalta?
2. How do the weather and season described in each section relate to the action in that section?
3. What is Gurov's attitude toward his affair with Anna at the outset? What is Anna's attitude? What are some indications that both Gurov and Anna are unprepared for the relationship that develops between them?

## SUGGESTIONS FOR WRITING

1. In "The Littoral Zone," the island on which Jonathan and Ruby meet and spend three weeks is recalled with great detail and clarity, while the locations where they pass the next fifteen years are barely described. Write an essay in which you discuss how Andrea Barrett uses setting to explore the workings of memory and desire.
2. Richard Dokey's "Sánchez" contains three settings: the San Joaquin Valley towns of Stockton and Linden, Twin Pines in the Sierra Nevada Mountains, and an unnamed village in rural Mexico. Write an essay that considers how each of these locations is used to represent both a certain period in the life of Juan Sánchez and a distinct aspect of his character.
3. In "A Pair of Tickets," Amy Tan provides detailed descriptions of June May's journeys to Guangzhou and Shanghai. In his account of his wife's escape from Kweilin, June May's father says little about the landscape. Write an essay in which you compare and contrast the two very different storytelling techniques used in this story.
4. In each of the stories in this chapter, a place encountered for the first time by a traveler is described with great vividness: the island in "The Littoral Zone," the mountains in "Sánchez," the city of Guangzhou in "A Pair of Tickets," and the city of Yalta in "The Lady with the Dog." Citing examples from these stories, write an essay in which you discuss the effect of new surroundings on our perceptions, emotions, and memories.
5. Write an essay in which you compare and contrast the use of setting in any two stories in this book. You might compare the re-creation of two similar settings, such as landscapes far from home, foreign cities, or stifling suburbs; or you might contrast the treatment of different kinds of settings. Be sure to consider not only the authors' descriptive techniques but also the way the authors use setting to shape plot, point of view, and character.
6. Write a fifth section for "The Lady with the Dog."
7. Write a story in which a newcomer brings a fresh perspective to a familiar setting.

# 5 SYMBOL

One of the aspects of literature that can puzzle both beginners and experts is the use of **figures of speech** or **figurative** language—language that creates imaginative connections between our ideas and our senses or that reveals striking similarities between things we had never associated before. Reading and interpreting a short story does not require that you correctly name its figures of speech, but your skill and appreciation will grow when you learn to recognize the common varieties of figurative language.

When a figure is expressed as an explicit comparison, often signaled by *like* or *as*, it is called a **simile:** "eyes as blue as the sky," for example. An implicit comparison or identification of one thing with another unlike itself, without a verbal signal but just seeming to say "A *is* B," is called a **metaphor:** "Her hair was . . . a soft gold helmet" ("Our Friend Judith") or "His intellect was a big comfy couch" ("Flight Patterns"). Some stories ("The Littoral Zone," for example) employ an **extended metaphor**—a detailed and complex metaphor that stretches through most of a work—to underscore the work's themes.

Another term of figurative language that you have probably encountered is **symbol.** Like other figures of speech, a **symbol** compares or puts together two things that are in some ways *unlike*. In general, you may think of a symbol as a metaphor multiplied. A symbol is a metaphor that has been in use by many people for a long time, or that otherwise has a magnified or many-layered significance. A writer using a symbol expects the audience to recognize it and to have deep or complex associations with what it means, even if this meaning cannot be expressed in words. A symbol usually conveys an abstraction or cluster of abstractions, from the ideal to the imperceptible or the irrational, in a more concrete form. The "stars and stripes"—a descriptive figure of speech for the U.S. flag—stands for the United States; the consensus on what the flag refers to, and the many meanings associated with the vast country it represents, contribute to its richness as a symbol. Other symbols may be more flexible or ambiguous than a flag. A rose can be a symbol of godly love, of romantic desire, of female beauty, of a husband's appreciation for his wife, of the gardens and innocence associated with England or Ireland, of mortality (because the flower wilts) or of hidden cruelty (because it has thorns). The many meanings of a rose throughout civilization are familiar enough to make any mention of a rose in literature or art symbolic. A few symbolic character types, plots, objects, or settings—for example the trickster, the quest, the garden—have become so pervasive and have recurred in so many cultures that they are considered **archetypes** (literary elements that recur in cultural and cross-cultural myth). It is true that literature often invents fresh symbols. If the representative object or concept does not have a familiar association with what it represents, the work must provide clues to its significance. The context of an entire story or poem can guide you in how far to push your own "translation" of what the figure of speech means and whether a metaphor has the deeper significance of a symbol.

But why speak of anything in terms of something else? Why should snakes commonly be symbolic of evil? Sure, some snakes are poisonous, but for some people so are bees, and a lot of snakes are not only harmless but actually helpful ecologically. (In Rudyard Kipling's *The Jungle Book*, the python Ka, while frightening, is on the side of law and order.) The answer is simply that through repeated use over the centuries, the snake has become a traditional symbol of evil—not just danger, sneakiness, and repulsiveness, but absolute spiritual evil. In Nathaniel Hawthorne's "Young Goodman Brown," you will encounter a walking stick carved in the image of a snake, and the context of the rest of the story will support the idea that this is a symbolic reference to the temptation of Adam and Eve by the snake, or Satan, in Paradise. Not only the meaningful names of characters but many other details in the story appear to carry double figurative meanings, and in case there is any doubt, just before the stranger with the walking stick appears, Brown says, "What if the devil himself should be at my very elbow!"

> *A story isn't any good unless it successfully resists paraphrase, unless it hangs on and expands in the mind.*
> —FLANNERY O'CONNOR

However, a single item—even something as traditionally fraught with significance as a snake or a rose—becomes a symbol only when its potentially symbolic meaning is confirmed by something else in the story, just as a point needs a second point to define a line. If the lovers in "The Littoral Zone" had come across a snake on the island, we might have thought it was simply part of the natural habitat, since the story uses few obvious symbols. Yet some readers would suspect that Andrea Barrett put the snake there to give a heavy hint about temptation and sin. It is best to read the entire story and note any and all of the potential symbols before you try to assess the significance of any one of them. Most often, a symbol is a focal point in a story, a single object or situation that draws the attention of one or more characters.

An **allegory** can be regarded as an "extended" symbol that encompasses a whole work. In an allegory, the widely recognized association of one idea with a more concrete or perceptible thing (country and flag, love and rose) is extended, possibly with a variety of other symbols, across a narrative with at least two distinct levels of meaning. *The Pilgrim's Progress* is probably the most famous prose allegory in English; its central character is named Christian; he was born in the City of Destruction and sets out for the Celestial City, passes through the Slough of Despond and Vanity Fair, meets men named Pliable and Obstinate, and so on. Because an allegory sets up series of correspondences rather than using a single well-known symbol, allegories usually help the reader translate these correspondences—*this equals that*—as the obvious names above suggest. The point of an allegory is not to make us hunt for disguised meanings, but to let us enjoy an invented world where everything is especially meaningful, everything corresponds to something else according to a moral or otherwise "correct" plan.

When an entire story, like "Young Goodman Brown" or "A Hunger Artist," is allegorical or symbolic, it is sometimes called a **myth**. *Myth* originally meant a story of communal origin that provided an explanation or religious interpretation of man, nature, the universe, or the relation between them. When members of one culture call the stories of another culture "myths," the word usually implies that the stories are false: we speak of classical myths, but Christians do not speak of

Christian myth. Sometimes we apply the term *myth* to stories by individual modern authors in order to suggest that these stories express experiences or truths that are shared by a community or that extend beyond any one culture or time, whereas a symbolic story may be more personal or private. It is hard to draw the line firmly: "A Hunger Artist" relates to a shared Western myth of art and the artist, and "Young Goodman Brown" refers to broadly held beliefs in early North America, so they have mythic qualities. Ann Beattie's "Janus," a realistic story of our time, scarcely seems mythic, yet it alludes to Janus, a deity in classical mythology. The bowl suggests the emotional emptiness and division in the protagonist's life, but also evokes a long tradition of symbolic vessels or bowls. To recognize this, however, is not to suggest that it is simple to assign meaning to this symbolic object.

In Edwidge Danticat's "A Wall of Fire Rising," the hot-air balloon serves a similar function to that of the bowl in "Janus," though there is no longstanding tradition of symbolic meaning for hot-air balloons. The story gives a matter-of-fact picture of a poor family's struggle to survive in Haiti. But the focus of the climactic action of the story on the father's extraordinary desire to fly in the balloon, and the reference in the title to a line in the revolutionary speech that the son is memorizing, invite readers to look for a figurative meaning; thus the rising of the balloon becomes symbolic. In other stories, the defining situation is obviously imaginary—a literal reading doesn't make sense—so figurative interpretation is called for. In "A Hunger Artist," for instance, as in other stories by Kafka, bizarre circumstances are described in a deadpan factual manner: impossibly long fasts are a popular public spectacle. Because the title and the story itself refer to art and artists, readers are prompted to understand a symbolic comparison between the fictional world of the story and the real world of art. The comparison or analogy is complex and many-layered rather than a simple equation, *this equals that*.

Symbols do not exist solely for the transmission of a meaning we can paraphrase. Like other figures of speech, they are most effective when they cannot be neatly translated into an abstract phrase: when the "something else" that the "something" stands for remains elusive. A good symbol cannot be extracted from the story in which it serves, but it leaves a lasting image of what the story is about. The ultimate unparaphrasable nature of most symbolic images or stories is not vagueness but richness, not disorder but complexity.

## NATHANIEL HAWTHORNE

### Young Goodman Brown

Young goodman Brown came forth, at sunset, into the street of Salem village,[1] but put his head back, after crossing the threshold, to exchange a parting kiss with his young wife. And Faith, as the wife was aptly named, thrust her own

---

1. Salem, Massachusetts, Hawthorne's birthplace (1804), was the scene of the famous witch trials of 1692. Hawthorne's own ancestors were involved in the persecution of witches and Quakers. Hawthorne wrote, "I take shame upon myself for their sakes and pray that any curse incurred by them ... may be now and henceforth removed." *Goodman*: husband, master of household.

pretty head into the street, letting the wind play with the pink ribbons of her cap, while she called to goodman Brown.

"Dearest heart," whispered she, softly and rather sadly, when her lips were close to his ear, "pr'y thee, put off your journey until sunrise, and sleep in your own bed to-night. A lone woman is troubled with such dreams and such thoughts, that she's afeard of herself, sometimes. Pray, tarry with me this night, dear husband, of all nights in the year!"

"My love and my Faith," replied young goodman Brown, "of all nights in the year, this one night must I tarry away from thee. My journey, as thou callest it, forth and back again, must needs be done 'twixt now and sunrise. What, my sweet, pretty wife, dost thou doubt me already, and we but three months married!"

"Then, God bless you!" said Faith, with the pink ribbons, "and may you find all well, when you come back."

"Amen!" cried goodman Brown. "Say thy prayers, dear Faith, and go to bed at dusk, and no harm will come to thee."

So they parted; and the young man pursued his way, until, being about to turn the corner by the meeting-house, he looked back, and saw the head of Faith still peeping after him, with a melancholy air, in spite of her pink ribbons.

"Poor little Faith!" thought he, for his heart smote him. "What a wretch am I, to leave her on such an errand! She talks of dreams, too. Methought, as she spoke, there was trouble in her face, as if a dream had warned her what work is to be done to-night. But, no, no! 't would kill her to think it. Well; she's a blessed angel on earth; and after this one night, I'll cling to her skirts and follow her to Heaven."

With this excellent resolve for the future, goodman Brown felt himself justified in making more haste on his present evil purpose. He had taken a dreary road, darkened by all the gloomiest trees of the forest, which barely stood aside to let the narrow path creep through, and closed immediately behind. It was all as lonely as could be; and there is this peculiarity in such a solitude, that the traveler knows not who may be concealed by the innumerable trunks and the thick boughs overhead; so that, with lonely footsteps, he may yet be passing through an unseen multitude.

"There may be a devilish Indian behind every tree," said goodman Brown, to himself; and he glanced fearfully behind him, as he added, "What if the devil himself should be at my very elbow!"

His head being turned back, he passed a crook of the road, and looking forward again, beheld the figure of a man, in grave and decent attire, seated at the foot of an old tree. He arose, at goodman Brown's approach, and walked onward, side by side with him.

"You are late, goodman Brown," said he. "The clock of the Old South was striking as I came through Boston; and that is full fifteen minutes agone."

"Faith kept me back awhile," replied the young man, with a tremor in his voice, caused by the sudden appearance of his companion, though not wholly unexpected.

It was now deep dusk in the forest, and deepest in that part of it where these two were journeying. As nearly as could be discerned, the second traveler was about fifty years old, apparently in the same rank of life as goodman Brown, and bearing a considerable resemblance to him, though perhaps more in expression than features. Still, they might have been taken for father and son. And yet, though the elder person was as simply clad as the younger, and as simple in manner too, he had an indescribable air of one who knew the world, and would not have felt abashed at the governor's dinner-table, or in king William's[2] court, were it possible that his affairs should call him thither. But the only thing about him, that could be fixed upon as remarkable, was his staff, which bore the likeness of a great black snake, so curiously wrought, that it might almost be seen to twist and wriggle itself, like a living serpent. This, of course, must have been an ocular deception, assisted by the uncertain light.

"Come, goodman Brown!" cried his fellow-traveler, "this is a dull pace for the beginning of a journey. Take my staff, if you are so soon weary."

"Friend," said the other, exchanging his slow pace for a full stop, "having kept covenant by meeting thee here, it is my purpose now to return whence I came. I have scruples, touching the matter thou wot'st of."

"Sayest thou so?" replied he of the serpent, smiling apart. "Let us walk on, nevertheless, reasoning as we go, and if I convince thee not, thou shalt turn back. We are but a little way in the forest, yet."

"Too far, too far!" exclaimed the goodman, unconsciously resuming his walk. "My father never went into the woods on such an errand, nor his father before him. We have been a race of honest men and good Christians, since the days of the martyrs. And shall I be the first of the name of Brown, that ever took this path, and kept"—

"Such company, thou wouldst say," observed the elder person, interpreting his pause. "Good, goodman Brown! I have been as well acquainted with your family as with ever a one among the Puritans; and that's no trifle to say. I helped your grandfather, the constable, when he lashed the Quaker woman so smartly through the streets of Salem. And it was I that brought your father a pitch-pine knot, kindled at my own hearth, to set fire to an Indian village, in king Philip's[3] war. They were my good friends, both; and many a pleasant walk have we had along this path, and returned merrily after midnight. I would fain be friends with you, for their sake."

"If it be as thou sayest," replied goodman Brown, "I marvel they never spoke of these matters. Or, verily, I marvel not, seeing that the least rumor of the sort would have driven them from New-England. We are a people of prayer, and good works, to boot, and abide no such wickedness."

"Wickedness or not," said the traveler with the twisted staff, "I have a very general acquaintance here in New-England. The deacons of many a church have drunk the communion wine with me; the selectmen, of divers towns, make me their chairman; and a majority of the Great and General Court are firm supporters of my interest. The governor and I, too—but these are state-secrets."

"Can this be so!" cried goodman Brown, with a stare of amazement at his undisturbed companion. "Howbeit, I have nothing to do with the governor and council; they have their own ways, and are no rule for a simple husbandman, like me. But, were I to go on with thee, how should I meet the eye of that good

---

2. William III (1650-1702), ruler of England from 1689 to 1702.
3. Metacom or Metacomet, chief of the Wampanoag Indians, known as King Philip, led a war against the New England colonists in 1675-76 that devastated many frontier communities.

old man, our minister, at Salem village? Oh, his voice would make me tremble, both Sabbath-day and lecture-day!"[4]

Thus far, the elder traveler had listened with due gravity, but now burst into a fit of irrepressible mirth, shaking himself so violently, that his snake-like staff actually seemed to wriggle in sympathy.

"Ha! ha! ha!" shouted he, again and again; then composing himself, "Well, go on, goodman Brown, go on; but, pr'y thee, don't kill me with laughing!"

"Well, then, to end the matter at once," said goodman Brown, considerably nettled, "there is my wife, Faith. It would break her dear little heart; and I'd rather break my own!"

"Nay, if that be the case," answered the other, "e'en[5] go thy ways, goodman Brown. I would not, for twenty old women like the one hobbling before us, that Faith should come to any harm."

As he spoke, he pointed his staff at a female figure on the path, in whom goodman Brown recognized a very pious and exemplary dame, who had taught him his catechism, in youth, and was still his moral and spiritual adviser, jointly with the minister and deacon Gookin.

"A marvel, truly, that goody[6] Cloyse should be so far in the wilderness, at night-fall!" said he. "But, with your leave, friend, I shall take a cut through the woods, until we have left this Christian woman behind. Being a stranger to you, she might ask whom I was consorting with, and whither I was going."

"Be it so," said his fellow-traveler. "Betake you to the woods, and let me keep the path."

Accordingly, the young man turned aside, but took care to watch his companion, who advanced softly along the road, until he had come within a staff's length of the old dame. She, meanwhile, was making the best of her way, with singular speed for so aged a woman, and mumbling some indistinct words, a prayer, doubtless, as she went. The traveler put forth his staff, and touched her withered neck with what seemed the serpent's tail.

"The devil!" screamed the pious old lady.

"Then goody Cloyse knows her old friend?" observed the traveler, confronting her, and leaning on his writhing stick.

"Ah, forsooth, and is it your worship, indeed?" cried the good dame. "Yea, truly is it, and in the very image of my old gossip, goodman Brown, the grandfather of the silly fellow that now is. But, would your worship believe it? my broomstick hath strangely disappeared, stolen, as I suspect, by that unhanged witch, goody Cory, and that, too, when I was all anointed with the juice of smallage and cinque-foil and wolf's-bane"[7]—

"Mingled with fine wheat and the fat of a new-born babe," said the shape of old goodman Brown.

"Ah, your worship knows the receipt," cried the old lady, cackling aloud. "So, as I was saying, being all ready for the meeting, and no horse to ride on, I made up my mind to foot it; for they tell me, there is a nice young man to be taken into communion to-night. But now your good worship will lend me your arm, and we shall be there in a twinkling."

---

4. The day for an informal sermon; in the New England colonies, this was usually a Thursday.
5. Just.   6. Short for "goodwife" or housewife.   7. Plants traditionally associated with witchcraft.

"That can hardly be," answered her friend. "I may not spare you my arm, goody Cloyse, but here is my staff, if you will."

So saying, he threw it down at her feet, where, perhaps, it assumed life, being one of the rods which its owner had formerly lent to the Egyptian Magi.[8] Of this fact, however, goodman Brown could not take cognizance. He had cast up his eyes in astonishment, and looking down again, beheld neither goody Cloyse nor the serpentine staff, but his fellow-traveler alone, who waited for him as calmly as if nothing had happened.

"That old woman taught me my catechism!" said the young man; and there was a world of meaning in this simple comment.

They continued to walk onward, while the elder traveler exhorted his companion to make good speed and persevere in the path, discoursing so aptly, that his arguments seemed rather to spring up in the bosom of his auditor, than to be suggested by himself. As they went, he plucked a branch of maple, to serve for a walking-stick, and began to strip it of the twigs and little boughs, which were wet with evening dew. The moment his fingers touched them, they became strangely withered and dried up, as with a week's sunshine. Thus the pair proceeded, at a good free pace, until suddenly, in a gloomy hollow of the road, goodman Brown sat himself down on the stump of a tree, and refused to go any farther.

"Friend," said he, stubbornly, "my mind is made up. Not another step will I budge on this errand. What if a wretched old woman do choose to go to the devil, when I thought she was going to Heaven! Is that any reason why I should quit my dear Faith, and go after her?"

"You will think better of this, by-and-by," said his acquaintance, composedly. "Sit here and rest yourself awhile; and when you feel like moving again, there is my staff to help you along."

Without more words, he threw his companion the maple stick, and was as speedily out of sight, as if he had vanished into the deepening gloom. The young man sat a few moments, by the roadside, applauding himself greatly, and thinking with how clear a conscience he should meet the minister, in his morning-walk, nor shrink from the eye of good old deacon Gookin. And what calm sleep would be his, that very night, which was to have been spent so wickedly, but purely and sweetly now, in the arms of Faith! Amidst these pleasant and praiseworthy meditations, goodman Brown heard the tramp of horses along the road, and deemed it advisable to conceal himself within the verge of the forest, conscious of the guilty purpose that had brought him thither, though now so happily turned from it.

On came the hoof-tramps and the voices of the riders, two grave old voices, conversing soberly as they drew near. These mingled sounds appeared to pass along the road, within a few yards of the young man's hiding-place; but owing, doubtless, to the depth of the gloom, at that particular spot, neither the travelers nor their steeds were visible. Though their figures brushed the small boughs by the way-side, it could not be seen that they intercepted, even for a moment, the faint gleam from the strip of bright sky, athwart which they must have passed.

---

8. In Exodus 7.8–12, the Lord instructs Moses to have his brother Aaron, high priest of the Hebrews, throw down his rod before the pharaoh, whereupon it will be turned into a serpent. The pharaoh has his magicians (magi) do likewise, "but Aaron's rod swallowed up their rods."

Goodman Brown alternately crouched and stood on tip-toe, pulling aside the branches, and thrusting forth his head as far as he durst, without discerning so much as a shadow. It vexed him the more, because he could have sworn, were such a thing possible, that he recognized the voices of the minister and deacon Gookin, jogging along quietly, as they were wont to do, when bound to some ordination or ecclesiastical council. While yet within hearing, one of the riders stopped to pluck a switch.

"Of the two, reverend Sir," said the voice like the deacon's, "I had rather miss an ordination-dinner than to-night's meeting. They tell me that some of our community are to be here from Falmouth[9] and beyond, and others from Connecticut and Rhode-Island; besides several of the Indian powows, who, after their fashion, know almost as much deviltry as the best of us. Moreover, there is a goodly young woman to be taken into communion."

"Mighty well, deacon Gookin!" replied the solemn old tones of the minister. "Spur up, or we shall be late. Nothing can be done, you know, until I get on the ground."

The hoofs clattered again, and the voices, talking so strangely in the empty air, passed on through the forest, where no church had ever been gathered, nor solitary Christian prayed. Whither, then, could these holy men be journeying, so deep into the heathen wilderness? Young goodman Brown caught hold of a tree, for support, being ready to sink down on the ground, faint and overburthened with the heavy sickness of his heart. He looked up to the sky, doubting whether there really was a Heaven above him. Yet, there was the blue arch, and the stars brightening in it.

"With Heaven above, and Faith below, I will yet stand firm against the devil!" cried goodman Brown.

While he still gazed upward, into the deep arch of the firmament, and had lifted his hands to pray, a cloud, though no wind was stirring, hurried across the zenith, and hid the brightening stars. The blue sky was still visible, except directly overhead, where this black mass of cloud was sweeping swiftly northward. Aloft in the air, as if from the depths of the cloud, came a confused and doubtful sound of voices. Once, the listener fancied that he could distinguish the accents of town's-people of his own, men and women, both pious and ungodly, many of whom he had met at the communion-table, and had seen others rioting at the tavern. The next moment, so indistinct were the sounds, he doubted whether he had heard aught but the murmur of the old forest, whispering without a wind. Then came a stronger swell of those familiar tones, heard daily in the sunshine, at Salem village, but never, until now, from a cloud of night. There was one voice, of a young woman, uttering lamentations, yet with an uncertain sorrow, and entreating for some favor, which, perhaps, it would grieve her to obtain. And all the unseen multitude, both saints and sinners, seemed to encourage her onward.

"Faith!" shouted goodman Brown, in a voice of agony and desperation; and the echoes of the forest mocked him, crying—"Faith! Faith!" as if bewildered wretches were seeking her, all through the wilderness.

The cry of grief, rage, and terror, was yet piercing the night, when the unhappy husband held his breath for a response. There was a scream, drowned immedi-

---

9. A port in southern Massachusetts; Salem is in northern Massachusetts.

ately in a louder murmur of voices, fading into far-off laughter, as the dark cloud swept away, leaving the clear and silent sky above goodman Brown. But something fluttered lightly down through the air, and caught on the branch of a tree. The young man seized it, and beheld a pink ribbon.

50 "My Faith is gone!" cried he, after one stupefied moment. "There is no good on earth; and sin is but a name. Come, devil! for to thee is this world given."

And maddened with despair, so that he laughed loud and long, did goodman Brown grasp his staff and set forth again, at such a rate, that he seemed to fly along the forest-path, rather than to walk or run. The road grew wilder and drearier, and more faintly traced, and vanished at length, leaving him in the heart of the dark wilderness, still rushing onward, with the instinct that guides mortal man to evil. The whole forest was peopled with frightful sounds; the creaking of the trees, the howling of wild beasts, and the yell of Indians; while, sometimes, the wind tolled like a distant church-bell, and sometimes gave a broad roar around the traveler, as if all Nature were laughing him to scorn. But he was himself the chief horror of the scene, and shrank not from its other horrors.

"Ha! ha! ha!" roared goodman Brown, when the wind laughed at him. "Let us hear which will laugh loudest! Think not to frighten me with your deviltry! Come witch, come wizard, come Indian powow, come devil himself! and here come goodman Brown. You may as well fear him as he fear you!"

In truth, all through the haunted forest, there could be nothing more frightful than the figure of goodman Brown. On he flew, among the black pines, brandishing his staff with frenzied gestures, now giving vent to an inspiration of horrid blasphemy, and now shouting forth such laughter, as set all the echoes of the forest laughing like demons around him. The fiend in his own shape is less hideous, than when he rages in the breast of man. Thus sped the demoniac on his course, until, quivering among the trees, he saw a red light before him, as when the felled trunks and branches of a clearing have been set on fire, and throw up their lurid blaze against the sky, at the hour of midnight. He paused, in a lull of the tempest that had driven him onward, and heard the swell of what seemed a hymn, rolling solemnly from a distance, with the weight of many voices. He knew the tune; it was a familiar one in the choir of the village meeting-house. The verse died heavily away, and was lengthened by a chorus, not of human voices, but of all the sounds of the benighted wilderness, pealing in awful harmony together. Goodman Brown cried out; and his cry was lost to his own ear, by its unison with the cry of the desert.

In the interval of silence, he stole forward, until the light glared full upon his eyes. At one extremity of an open space, hemmed in by the dark wall of the forest, arose a rock, bearing some rude, natural resemblance either to an altar or a pulpit, and surrounded by four blazing pines, their tops aflame, their stems untouched, like candles at an evening meeting. The mass of foliage, that had overgrown the summit of the rock, was all on fire, blazing high into the night, and fitfully illuminating the whole field. Each pendent twig and leafy festoon was in a blaze. As the red light arose and fell, a numerous congregation alternately shone forth, then disappeared in shadow, and again grew, as it were, out of the darkness, peopling the heart of the solitary woods at once.

55 "A grave and dark-clad company!" quoth goodman Brown.

In truth, they were such. Among them, quivering to-and-fro, between gloom and splendor, appeared faces that would be seen, next day, at the council-board of the province, and others which, Sabbath after Sabbath, looked devoutly heavenward, and benignantly over the crowded pews, from the holiest pulpits in the land. Some affirm, that the lady of the governor was there. At least, there were high dames well known to her, and wives of honored husbands, and widows, a great multitude, and ancient maidens, all of excellent repute, and fair young girls, who trembled, lest their mothers should espy them. Either the sudden gleams of light, flashing over the obscure field, bedazzled goodman Brown, or he recognized a score of the church-members of Salem village, famous for their especial sanctity. Good old deacon Gookin had arrived, and waited at the skirts of that venerable saint, his revered pastor. But, irreverently consorting with these grave, reputable, and pious people, these elders of the church, these chaste dames and dewy virgins, there were men of dissolute lives and women of spotted fame, wretches given over to all mean and filthy vice, and suspected even of horrid crimes. It was strange to see, that the good shrank not from the wicked, nor were the sinners abashed by the saints. Scattered, also, among their pale-faced enemies, were the Indian priests, or powows, who had often scared their native forest with more hideous incantations than any known to English witchcraft.

"But, where is Faith?" thought goodman Brown; and, as hope came into his heart, he trembled.

Another verse of the hymn arose, a slow and solemn strain, such as the pious love, but joined to words which expressed all that our nature can conceive of sin, and darkly hinted at far more. Unfathomable to mere mortals is the lore of fiends. Verse after verse was sung, and still the chorus of the desert swelled between, like the deepest tone of a mighty organ. And, with the final peal of that dreadful anthem, there came a sound, as if the roaring wind, the rushing streams, the howling beasts, and every other voice of the unconverted wilderness, were mingling and according with the voice of guilty man, in homage to the prince of all. The four blazing pines threw up a loftier flame, and obscurely discovered shapes and visages of horror on the smoke-wreaths, above the impious assembly. At the same moment, the fire on the rock shot redly forth, and formed a glowing arch above its base, where now appeared a figure. With reverence be it spoken, the apparition bore no slight similitude, both in garb and manner, to some grave divine of the New-England churches.

"Bring forth the converts!" cried a voice, that echoed through the field and rolled into the forest.

At the word, goodman Brown stept forth from the shadow of the trees, and approached the congregation, with whom he felt a loathful brotherhood, by the sympathy of all that was wicked in his heart. He could have well nigh sworn, that the shape of his own dead father beckoned him to advance, looking downward from a smoke-wreath, while a woman, with dim features of despair, threw out her hand to warn him back. Was it his mother? But he had no power to retreat one step, nor to resist, even in thought, when the minister and good old deacon Gookin, seized his arms, and led him to the blazing rock. Thither came also the slender form of a veiled female, led between goody Cloyse, that pious teacher of the catechism, and Martha Carrier, who had received the devil's promise to be queen of hell. A rampant hag was she! And there stood the proselytes, beneath the canopy of fire.

"Welcome, my children," said the dark figure, "to the communion of your race! Ye have found, thus young, your nature and your destiny. My children, look behind you!"

They turned; and flashing forth, as it were, in a sheet of flame, the fiend-worshippers were seen; the smile of welcome gleamed darkly on every visage.

"There," resumed the sable form, "are all whom ye have reverenced from youth. Ye deemed them holier than yourselves, and shrank from your own sin, contrasting it with their lives of righteousness, and prayerful aspirations heavenward. Yet, here are they all, in my worshipping assembly! This night it shall be granted you to know their secret deeds; how hoary-bearded elders of the church have whispered wanton words to the young maids of their households; how many a woman, eager for widow's weeds, has given her husband a drink at bed-time, and let him sleep his last sleep in her bosom; how beardless youths have made haste to inherit their fathers' wealth; and how fair damsels—blush not, sweet ones!—have dug little graves in the garden, and bidden me, the sole guest, to an infant's funeral. By the sympathy of your human hearts for sin, ye shall scent out all the places—whether in church, bed-chamber, street, field, or forest—where crime has been committed, and shall exult to behold the whole earth one stain of guilt, one mighty blood-spot. Far more than this! It shall be yours to penetrate, in every bosom, the deep mystery of sin, the fountain of all wicked arts, and which, inexhaustibly supplies more evil impulses than human power—than my power, at its utmost!—can make manifest in deeds. And now, my children, look upon each other."

They did so; and, by the blaze of the hell-kindled torches, the wretched man beheld his Faith, and the wife her husband, trembling before that unhallowed altar.

65 "Lo! there ye stand, my children," said the figure, in a deep and solemn tone, almost sad, with its despairing awfulness, as if his once angelic nature could yet mourn for our miserable race. "Depending upon one another's hearts, ye had still hoped, that virtue were not all a dream. Now are ye undeceived! Evil is the nature of mankind. Evil must be your only happiness. Welcome, again, my children, to the communion of your race!"

"Welcome!" repeated the fiend-worshippers, in one cry of despair and triumph.

And there they stood, the only pair, as it seemed, who were yet hesitating on the verge of wickedness, in this dark world. A basin was hollowed, naturally, in the rock. Did it contain water, reddened by the lurid light? or was it blood? or, perchance, a liquid flame? Herein did the Shape of Evil dip his hand, and prepare to lay the mark of baptism upon their foreheads, that they might be partakers of the mystery of sin, more conscious of the secret guilt of others, both in deed and thought, than they could now be of their own. The husband cast one look at his pale wife, and Faith at him. What polluted wretches would the next glance shew them to each other, shuddering alike at what they disclosed and what they saw!

"Faith! Faith!" cried the husband. "Look up to Heaven, and resist the Wicked One!"

Whether Faith obeyed, he knew not. Hardly had he spoken, when he found himself amid calm night and solitude, listening to a roar of the wind, which died heavily away through the forest. He staggered against the rock and felt it chill and damp, while a hanging twig, that had been all on fire, besprinkled his cheek with the coldest dew.

70 The next morning, young goodman Brown came slowly into the street of Salem village, staring around him like a bewildered man. The good old minister

was taking a walk along the graveyard, to get an appetite for breakfast and meditate his sermon, and bestowed a blessing, as he passed, on goodman Brown. He shrank from the venerable saint, as if to avoid an anathema. Old deacon Gookin was at domestic worship, and the holy words of his prayer were heard through the open window. "What God doth the wizard pray to?" quoth goodman Brown. Goody Cloyse, that excellent old Christian, stood in the early sunshine, at her own lattice, catechising a little girl, who had brought her a pint of morning's milk. Goodman Brown snatched away the child, as from the grasp of the fiend himself. Turning the corner by the meeting-house, he spied the head of Faith, with the pink ribbons, gazing anxiously forth, and bursting into such joy at sight of him, that she skipt along the street, and almost kissed her husband before the whole village. But, goodman Brown looked sternly and sadly into her face, and passed on without a greeting.

Had goodman Brown fallen asleep in the forest, and only dreamed a wild dream of a witch-meeting?

Be it so, if you will. But, alas! it was a dream of evil omen for young goodman Brown. A stern, a sad, a darkly meditative, a distrustful, if not a desperate man, did he become, from the night of that fearful dream. On the Sabbath-day, when the congregation were singing a holy psalm, he could not listen, because an anthem of sin rushed loudly upon his ear, and drowned all the blessed strain. When the minister spoke from the pulpit, with power and fervid eloquence, and, with his hand on the open bible, of the sacred truths of our religion, and of saint-like lives and triumphant deaths, and of future bliss or misery unutterable, then did goodman Brown turn pale, dreading, lest the roof should thunder down upon the gray blasphemer and his hearers. Often, awakening suddenly at midnight, he shrank from the bosom of Faith, and at morning or eventide, when the family knelt down at prayer, he scowled, and muttered to himself, and gazed sternly at his wife, and turned away. And when he had lived long, and was borne to his grave, a hoary corpse, followed by Faith, an aged woman, and children and grandchildren, a goodly procession, besides neighbors, not a few, they carved no hopeful verse upon his tomb-stone; for his dying hour was gloom.

1835

## QUESTIONS

1. Why does goodman Brown go into the forest? Why is he surprised to find other people he knows already there?
2. What are some aspects of "Young Goodman Brown" that seem allegorical, and what are some that seem symbolic? Are there images or occurrences in the story that defy such analysis? Why?
3. If there is a "lesson" to be learned from "Young Goodman Brown," what do you think it is? Why do you think that, many years after the main action described in the story, goodman Brown's "dying hour was gloom"?

# FRANZ KAFKA

## A Hunger Artist[1]

During these last decades the interest in professional fasting has markedly diminished. It used to pay very well to stage such great performances under one's own management, but today that is quite impossible. We live in a different world now. At one time the whole town took a lively interest in the hunger artist; from day to day of his fast the excitement mounted; everybody wanted to see him at least once a day; there were people who bought season tickets for the last few days and sat from morning till night in front of his small barred cage; even in the nighttime there were visiting hours, when the whole effect was heightened by torch flares; on fine days the cage was set out in the open air, and then it was the children's special treat to see the hunger artist; for their elders he was often just a joke that happened to be in fashion, but the children stood open-mouthed, holding each other's hands for greater security, marveling at him as he sat there pallid in black tights, with his ribs sticking out so prominently, not even on a seat but down among straw on the ground, sometimes giving a courteous nod, answering questions with a constrained smile, or perhaps stretching an arm through the bars so that one might feel how thin it was, and then again withdrawing deep into himself, paying no attention to anyone or anything, not even to the all-important striking of the clock that was the only piece of furniture in his cage, but merely staring into vacancy with half shut eyes, now and then taking a sip from a tiny glass of water to moisten his lips.

Besides casual onlookers there were also relays of permanent watchers selected by the public, usually butchers, strangely enough, and it was their task to watch the hunger artist day and night, three of them at a time, in case he should have some secret recourse to nourishment. This was nothing but a formality, instituted to reassure the masses, for the initiates knew well enough that during his fast the artist would never in any circumstances, not even under forcible compulsion, swallow the smallest morsel of food: the honor of his profession forbade it. Not every watcher, of course, was capable of understanding this, there were often groups of night watchers who were very lax in carrying out their duties and deliberately huddled together in a retired corner to play cards with great absorption, obviously intending to give the hunger artist the chance of a little refreshment, which they supposed he could draw from some private hoard. Nothing annoyed the artist more than such watchers; they made him miserable; they made his fast seem unendurable; sometimes he mastered his feebleness sufficiently to sing during their watch for as long as he could keep going, to show them how unjust their suspicions were. But that was of little use; they only wondered at his cleverness in being able to fill his mouth even while singing. Much more to his taste were the watchers who sat close up to the bars, who were not content with the dim night lighting of the hall but focused him in the full glare of the electric pocket torch[2] given them by the impresario. The harsh light did not trouble him at all, in any case he could never sleep properly, and he could always drowse a little, whatever the light, at any hour, even when the hall was

---

1. Translated by Edwin and Willa Muir.   2. Flashlight.

thronged with noisy onlookers. He was quite happy at the prospect of spending a sleepless night with such watchers; he was ready to exchange jokes with them, to tell them stories out of his nomadic life, anything at all to keep them awake and demonstrate to them again that he had no eatables in his cage and that he was fasting as not one of them could fast. But his happiest moment was when the morning came and an enormous breakfast was brought them, at his expense, on which they flung themselves with the keen appetite of healthy men after a weary night of wakefulness. Of course there were people who argued that this breakfast was an unfair attempt to bribe the watchers, but that was going rather too far, and when they were invited to take on a night's vigil without a breakfast, merely for the sake of the cause, they made themselves scarce, although they stuck stubbornly to their suspicions.

Such suspicions, anyhow, were a necessary accompaniment to the profession of fasting. No one could possibly watch the hunger artist continuously, day and night, and so no one could produce first-hand evidence that the fast had really been rigorous and continuous; only the artist himself could know that, he was therefore bound to be the sole completely satisfied spectator of his own fast. Yet for other reasons he was never satisfied; it was not perhaps mere fasting that had brought him to such skeleton thinness that many people had regretfully to keep away from his exhibitions, because the sight of him was too much for them, perhaps it was dissatisfaction with himself that had worn him down. For he alone knew, what no other initiate knew, how easy it was to fast. It was the easiest thing in the world. He made no secret of this, yet people did not believe him, at the best they set him down as modest; most of them, however, thought he was out for publicity or else was some kind of cheat who found it easy to fast because he had discovered a way of making it easy, and then had the impudence to admit the fact, more or less. He had to put up with all that, and in the course of time had got used to it, but his inner dissatisfaction always rankled, and never yet, after any term of fasting—this must be granted to his credit—had he left the cage of his own free will. The longest period of fasting was fixed by his impresario at forty days,[3] beyond that term he was not allowed to go, not even in great cities, and there was good reason for it, too. Experience had proved that for about forty days the interest of the public could be stimulated by a steadily increasing pressure of advertisement, but after that the town began to lose interest, sympathetic support began notably to fall off; there were of course local variations as between one town and another or one country and another, but as a general rule forty days marked the limit. So on the fortieth day the flower-bedecked cage was opened, enthusiastic spectators filled the hall, a military band played, two doctors entered the cage to measure the results of the fast, which were announced through a megaphone, and finally two young ladies appeared, blissful at having been selected for the honor, to help the hunger artist down the few steps leading to a small table on which was spread a carefully chosen invalid repast. And at this very moment the artist always turned stubborn. True, he would entrust his bony arms to the outstretched helping hands of the ladies bending over him, but stand up he would not. Why stop fasting at this particular moment, after forty days of it? He had held out for a long time, an illimitably long time; why

---

3. A common biblical length of time; in the New Testament, Jesus fasts for forty days in the desert and has visions of both God and the devil.

stop now, when he was in his best fasting form, or rather, not yet quite in his best fasting form? Why should he be cheated of the fame he would get for fasting longer, for being not only the record hunger artist of all time, which presumably he was already, but for beating his own record by a performance beyond human imagination, since he felt that there were no limits to his capacity for fasting? His public pretended to admire him so much, why should it have so little patience with him; if he could endure fasting longer, why shouldn't the public endure it? Besides, he was tired, he was comfortable sitting in the straw, and now he was supposed to lift himself to his full height and go down to a meal the very thought of which gave him a nausea that only the presence of the ladies kept him from betraying, and even that with an effort. And he looked up into the eyes of the ladies who were apparently so friendly and in reality so cruel, and shook his head, which felt too heavy on its strengthless neck. But then there happened yet again what always happened. The impresario came forward, without a word—for the band made speech impossible—lifted his arms in the air above the artist, as if inviting Heaven to look down upon its creature here in the straw, this suffering martyr, which indeed he was, although in quite another sense; grasped him round the emaciated waist, with exaggerated caution, so that the frail condition he was in might be appreciated; and committed him to the care of the blenching ladies, not without secretly giving him a shaking so that his legs and body tottered and swayed. The artist now submitted completely; his head lolled on his breast as if it had landed there by chance; his body was hollowed out; his legs in a spasm of self-preservation clung close to each other at the knees, yet scraped on the ground as if it were not really solid ground, as if they were only trying to find solid ground; and the whole weight of his body, a feather-weight after all, relapsed onto one of the ladies, who, looking round for help and panting a little—this post of honor was not at all what she had expected it to be—first stretched her neck as far as she could to keep her face at least free from contact with the artist, when finding this impossible, and her more fortunate companion not coming to her aid but merely holding extended on her own trembling hand the little bunch of knucklebones that was the artist's, to the great delight of the spectators burst into tears and had to be replaced by an attendant who had long been stationed in readiness. Then came the food, a little of which the impresario managed to get between the artist's lips, while he sat in a kind of half-fainting trance, to the accompaniment of cheerful patter designed to distract the public's attention from the artist's condition; after that, a toast was drunk to the public, supposedly prompted by a whisper from the artist in the impresario's ear; the band confirmed it with a mighty flourish, the spectators melted away, and no one had any cause to be dissatisfied with the proceedings, no one except the hunger artist himself, he only, as always.

So he lived for many years, with small regular intervals of recuperation, in visible glory, honored by the world, yet in spite of that troubled in spirit, and all the more troubled because no one would take his trouble seriously. What comfort could he possibly need? What more could he possibly wish for? And if some good-natured person, feeling sorry for him, tried to console him by pointing out that his melancholy was probably caused by fasting, it could happen, especially when he had been fasting for some time, that he reacted with an outburst of fury and to the general alarm began to shake the bars of his cage like a wild animal. Yet the impresario had a way of punishing these outbreaks which he rather enjoyed putting into operation. He would apologize publicly for the artist's behavior, which was only to be excused, he admitted, because of the irritability caused by fasting, a condition hardly to be understood by well-fed people; then by natural transition he went on to mention the artist's equally incomprehensible boast that he could fast for much longer than he was doing; he praised the high ambition, the good will, the great self-denial undoubtedly implicit in such a statement; and then quite simply countered it by bringing out photographs, which were also on sale to the public, showing the artist on the fortieth day of a fast lying in bed almost dead from exhaustion. This perversion of the truth, familiar to the artist though it was, always unnerved him afresh and proved too much for him. What was a consequence of the premature ending of his fast was here presented as the cause of it! To fight against this lack of understanding, against a whole world of non-understanding, was impossible. Time and again in good faith he stood by the bars listening to the impresario, but as soon as the photographs appeared he always let go and sank with a groan back on to his straw, and the reassured public could once more come close and gaze at him.

A few years later when the witnesses of such scenes called them to mind, they often failed to understand themselves at all. For meanwhile the aforementioned change in public interest had set in; it seemed to happen almost overnight; there may have been profound causes for it, but who was going to bother about that; at any rate the pampered hunger artist suddenly found himself deserted one fine day by the amusement seekers, who went streaming past him to other more favored attractions. For the last time the impresario hurried him over half Europe to discover whether the old interest might still survive here and there; all in vain; everywhere, as if by secret agreement, a positive revulsion from professional fasting was in evidence. Of course it could not really have sprung up so suddenly as all that, and many premonitory symptoms which had not been sufficiently remarked or suppressed during the rush and glitter of success now came retrospectively to mind, but it was now too late to take any countermeasures. Fasting would surely come into fashion again at some future date, yet that was no comfort for those living in the present. What, then, was the hunger artist to do? He had been applauded by thousands in his time and could hardly come down to showing himself in a street booth at village fairs, and as for adopting another profession, he was not only too old for that but too fanatically devoted to fasting. So he took leave of the impresario, his partner in an unparalleled career, and hired himself to a large circus; in order to spare his own feelings he avoided reading the conditions of his contract.

A large circus with its enormous traffic in replacing and recruiting men, animals and apparatus can always find a use for people at any time, even for a hunger artist, provided of course that he does not ask too much, and in this particular case anyhow it was not only the artist who was taken on but his famous and long-known name as well, indeed considering the peculiar nature of his performance, which was not impaired by advancing age, it could not be objected that here was an artist past his prime, no longer at the height of his professional skill, seeking a refuge in some quiet corner of a circus; on the contrary, the hunger artist averred that he could fast as well as ever, which was entirely credible, he even alleged that if he were allowed to fast as he liked, and this was at once promised him without more ado, he could astound the world by establishing a record never yet achieved, a statement which certainly provoked a smile among the other professionals, since it left out of account the change in public opinion, which the hunger artist in his zeal conveniently forgot.

He had not, however, actually lost his sense of the real situation and took it as a matter of course that he and his cage should be stationed, not in the middle of the ring as a main attraction, but outside, near the animal cages, on a site that was after all easily accessible. Large and gaily painted placards made a frame for the cage and announced what was to be seen inside it. When the public came thronging out in the intervals to see the animals, they could hardly avoid passing the hunger artist's cage and stopping there for a moment, perhaps they might even have stayed longer had not those pressing behind them in the narrow gangway, who did not understand why they should be held up on their way toward the excitements of the menagerie, made it impossible for anyone to stand gazing quietly for any length of time. And that was the reason why the hunger artist, who had of course been looking forward to these visiting hours as the main achievement of his life, began instead to shrink from them. At first he could hardly wait for the intervals; it was exhilarating to watch the crowds come streaming his way, until only too soon—not even the most obstinate self-deception, clung to almost consciously, could hold out against the fact—the conviction was borne in upon him that these people, most of them, to judge from their actions, again and again, without exception, were all on their way to the menagerie. And the first sight of them from the distance remained the best. For when they reached his cage he was at once deafened by the storm of shouting and abuse that arose from the two contending factions, which renewed themselves continuously, of those who wanted to stop and stare at him—he soon began to dislike them more than the others—not out of real interest but only out of obstinate self-assertiveness, and those who wanted to go straight on to the animals. When the first great rush was past, the stragglers came along, and these, whom nothing could have prevented from stopping to look at him as long as they had breath, raced past with long strides, hardly even glancing at him, in their haste to get to the menagerie in time. And all too rarely did it happen that he had a stroke of luck, when some father of a family fetched up before him with his children, pointed a finger at the hunger artist and explained at length what the phenomenon meant, telling stories of earlier years when he himself had watched similar but much more thrilling performances, and the children, still rather uncomprehending, since neither inside nor outside school had they been sufficiently prepared for this lesson—what did they care about fasting?—yet showed by the brightness of their intent eyes that new and better times might be coming. Perhaps, said the hunger artist to himself many a time, things would be a little better if his cage were set not quite so near the menagerie. That made it too easy for people to make their choice, to say nothing of what he suffered from the stench of the menagerie, the animals' restlessness by night, the carrying past of raw lumps of flesh for the beasts of prey, the roaring at feeding times, which depressed him continually. But he did not dare to lodge a complaint with the management; after all, he had the animals to thank for the troops of people who passed his cage, among whom there might always be one here and there to take an interest in him, and who could tell where they might seclude him if he called attention to his existence and thereby to the fact that, strictly speaking, he was only an impediment on the way to the menagerie.

A small impediment, to be sure, one that grew steadily less. People grew familiar with the strange idea that they could be expected, in times like these, to take an interest in a hunger artist, and with this familiarity the verdict went out against him. He might fast as much as he could, and he did so; but nothing could save him now, people passed him by. Just try to explain to anyone the art of fasting! Anyone who has no feeling for it cannot be made to understand it. The fine placards grew dirty and illegible, they were torn down; the little notice board telling the number of fast days achieved, which at first was changed carefully every day, had long stayed at the same figure, for after the first few weeks even this small task seemed pointless to the staff; and so the artist simply fasted on and on, as he had once dreamed of doing, and it was no trouble to him, just as he had always foretold, but no one counted the days, no one, not even the artist himself, knew what records he was already breaking, and his heart grew heavy. And when once in a time some leisurely passer-by stopped, made merry over the old figure on the board and spoke of swindling, that was in its way the stupidest lie ever invented by indifference and inborn malice, since it was not the hunger artist who was cheating; he was working honestly, but the world was cheating him of his reward.

Many more days went by, however, and that too came to an end. An overseer's eye fell on the cage one day and he asked the attendants why this perfectly good cage should be left standing there unused with dirty straw inside it; nobody knew, until one man, helped out by the notice board, remembered about the hunger artist. They poked into the straw with sticks and found him in it. "Are you still fasting?" asked the overseer. "When on earth do you mean to stop?" "Forgive me, everybody," whispered the hunger artist; only the overseer, who had his ear to the bars, understood him. "Of course," said the overseer, and tapped his forehead with a finger to let the attendants know what state the man was in, "we forgive you." "I always wanted you to admire my fasting," said the hunger artist. "We do admire it," said the overseer, affably. "But you shouldn't admire it," said the hunger artist. "Well, then we don't admire it," said the overseer, "but why shouldn't we admire it?" "Because I have to fast, I can't help it," said the hunger artist. "What a fellow you are," said the overseer, "and why can't you help it?" "Because," said the hunger artist, lifting his head a little and speaking, with his lips pursed, as if for a kiss, right into the overseer's ear, so that no syllable might be lost, "because I couldn't find the food I liked. If I had found it, believe me, I should have made no fuss and stuffed myself like you or anyone else." These were his last words, but in his dimming eyes remained the firm though no longer proud persuasion that he was still continuing to fast.

"Well, clear this out now!" said the overseer, and they buried the hunger artist, straw and all. Into the cage they put a young panther. Even the most insensitive felt it refreshing to see this wild creature leaping around the cage that had so long been dreary. The panther was all right. The food he liked was brought him without hesitation by the attendants; he seemed not even to miss his freedom; his noble body, furnished almost to the bursting point with all that it needed, seemed to carry freedom around with it too; somewhere in his jaws it seemed to lurk; and the joy of life streamed with such ardent passion from his throat that for the onlookers it was not easy to stand the shock of it. But they braced themselves, crowded round the cage, and did not want ever to move away.

1924

## QUESTIONS

1. What are some possible symbolic interpretations of the hunger artist? the impresario? How do you interpret the panther that replaces the dead artist at the end of "A Hunger Artist"?
2. Why is fasting such a powerful symbolic art form? What are some of the "hungers" that it might represent?
3. Shortly before he dies, the hunger artist declares that his art shouldn't be admired. Why not? What do you make of his explanation that he simply couldn't find the food that he liked? What "food" might have satisfied him?

## ANN BEATTIE

## *Janus*

The bowl was perfect. Perhaps it was not what you'd select if you faced a shelf of bowls, and not the sort of thing that would inevitably attract a lot of attention at a crafts fair, yet it had real presence. It was as predictably admired as a mutt who has no reason to suspect he might be funny. Just such a dog, in fact, was often brought out (and in) along with the bowl.

Andrea was a real estate agent, and when she thought that some prospective buyers might be dog lovers, she would drop off her dog at the same time she placed the bowl in the house that was up for sale. She would put a dish of water in the kitchen for Mondo, take his squeaking plastic frog out of her purse and drop it on the floor. He would pounce delightedly, just as he did every day at home, batting around his favorite toy. The bowl usually sat on a coffee table, though recently she had displayed it on top of a pine blanket chest and on a lacquered table. It was once placed on a cherry table beneath a Bonnard[1] still life, where it held its own.

Everyone who has purchased a house or who has wanted to sell a house must be familiar with some of the tricks used to convince a buyer that the house is quite special: a fire in the fireplace in early evening; jonquils in a pitcher on the kitchen counter, where no one ordinarily has space to put flowers; perhaps the slight aroma of spring, made by a single drop of scent vaporizing from a lamp bulb.

The wonderful thing about the bowl, Andrea thought, was that it was both subtle and noticeable—a paradox of a bowl. Its glaze was the color of cream and seemed to glow no matter what light it was placed in. There were a few bits of color in it—tiny geometric flashes—and some of these were tinged with flecks of silver. They were as mysterious as cells seen under a microscope; it was difficult not to study them, because they shimmered, flashing for a split second, and then resumed their shape. Something about the colors and their random placement suggested motion. People who liked country furniture always commented on the bowl, but then it turned out that people who felt comfortable with Biedermeier[2] loved it just as much. But the bowl was not at all ostentatious, or even so noticeable that anyone would suspect that it had been put in place deliberately. They

---

1. A work by Pierre Bonnard (1867–1947), French painter.
2. Unpretentious Central European furniture made primarily between 1820 and 1840.

might notice the height of the ceiling on first entering a room, and only when their eye moved down from that, or away from the refraction of sunlight on a pale wall, would they see the bowl. Then they would go immediately to it and comment. Yet they always faltered when they tried to say something. Perhaps it was because they were in the house for a serious reason, not to notice some object.

Once, Andrea got a call from a woman who had not put in an offer on a house she had shown her. That bowl, she said—would it be possible to find out where the owners had bought that beautiful bowl? Andrea pretended that she did not know what the woman was referring to. A bowl, somewhere in the house? Oh, on a table under the window. Yes, she would ask, of course. She let a couple of days pass, then called back to say that the bowl had been a present and the people did not know where it had been purchased.

When the bowl was not being taken from house to house, it sat on Andrea's coffee table at home. She didn't keep it carefully wrapped (although she transported it that way, in a box); she kept it on the table, because she liked to see it. It was large enough so that it didn't seem fragile, or particularly vulnerable if anyone sideswiped the table or Mondo blundered into it at play. She had asked her husband to please not drop his house key in it. It was meant to be empty.

When her husband first noticed the bowl, he had peered into it and smiled briefly. He always urged her to buy things she liked. In recent years, both of them had acquired many things to make up for all the lean years when they were graduate students, but now that they had been comfortable for quite a while, the pleasure of new possessions dwindled. Her husband had pronounced the bowl "pretty," and he had turned away without picking it up to examine it. He had no more interest in the bowl than she had in his new Leica.[3]

She was sure that the bowl brought her luck. Bids were often put in on houses where she had displayed the bowl. Sometimes the owners, who were always asked to be away or to step outside when the house was being shown, didn't even know that the bowl had been in their house. Once—she could not imagine how—she left it behind, and then she was so afraid that something might have happened to it that she rushed back to the house and sighed with relief when the woman owner opened the door. The bowl, Andrea explained—she had purchased a bowl and set it on the chest for safekeeping while she toured the house with the prospective buyers, and she ... She felt like rushing past the frowning woman and seizing her bowl. The owner stepped aside, and it was only when Andrea ran to the chest that the lady glanced at her a little strangely. In the few seconds before Andrea picked up the bowl, she realized that the owner must have just seen that it had been perfectly placed, that the sunlight struck the bluer part of it. Her pitcher had been moved to the far side of the chest, and the bowl predominated. All the way home, Andrea wondered how she could have left the bowl behind. It was like leaving a friend at an outing—just walking off. Sometimes there were stories in the paper about families forgetting a child somewhere and driving to the next city. Andrea had only gone a mile down the road before she remembered.

In time, she dreamed of the bowl. Twice, in a waking dream—early in the morning, between sleep and a last nap before rising—she had a clear vision of it.

---

3. An expensive German camera.

It came into sharp focus and startled her for a moment—the same bowl she looked at every day.

10  She had a very profitable year selling real estate. Word spread, and she had more clients than she felt comfortable with. She had the foolish thought that if only the bowl were an animate object she could thank it. There were times when she wanted to talk to her husband about the bowl. He was a stockbroker, and sometimes told people that he was fortunate to be married to a woman who had such a fine aesthetic sense and yet could also function in the real world. They were a lot alike, really—they had agreed on that. They were both quiet people—reflective, slow to make value judgments, but almost intractable once they had come to a conclusion. They both liked details, but while ironies attracted her, he was more impatient and dismissive when matters became many sided or unclear. But they both knew this; it was the kind of thing they could talk about when they were alone in the car together, coming home from a party or after a weekend with friends. But she never talked to him about the bowl. When they were at dinner, exchanging their news of the day, or while they lay in bed at night listening to the stereo and murmuring sleepy disconnections, she was often tempted to come right out and say that she thought that the bowl in the living room, the cream-colored bowl, was responsible for her success. But she didn't say it. She couldn't begin to explain it. Sometimes in the morning, she would look at him and feel guilty that she had such a constant secret.

Could it be that she had some deeper connection with the bowl—a relationship of some kind? She corrected her thinking: how could she imagine such a thing, when she was a human being and it was a bowl? It was ridiculous. Just think of how people lived together and loved each other... But was that always so clear, always a relationship? She was confused by these thoughts, but they remained in her mind. There was something within her now, something real, that she never talked about.

The bowl was a mystery, even to her. It was frustrating, because her involvement with the bowl contained a steady sense of unrequited good fortune; it would have been easier to respond if some sort of demand were made in return. But that only happened in fairy tales. The bowl was just a bowl. She did not believe that for one second. What she believed was that it was something she loved.

In the past, she had sometimes talked to her husband about a new property she was about to buy or sell—confiding some clever strategy she had devised to persuade owners who seemed ready to sell. Now she stopped doing that, for all her strategies involved the bowl. She became more deliberate with the bowl, and more possessive. She put it in houses only when no one was there, and removed it when she left the house. Instead of just moving a pitcher or a dish, she would remove all the other objects from a table. She had to force herself to handle them carefully, because she didn't really care about them. She just wanted them out of sight.

She wondered how the situation would end. As with a lover, there was no exact scenario of how matters would come to a close. Anxiety became the operative force. It would be irrelevant if the lover rushed into someone else's arms, or wrote her a note and departed to another city. The horror was the possibility of the disappearance. That was what mattered.

15  She would get up at night and look at the bowl. It never occurred to her that

she might break it. She washed and dried it without anxiety, and she moved it often, from coffee table to mahogany corner table or wherever, without fearing an accident. It was clear that she would not be the one who would do anything to the bowl. The bowl was only handled by her, set safely on one surface or another; it was not very likely that anyone would break it. A bowl was a poor conductor of electricity: it would not be hit by lightning. Yet the idea of damage persisted. She did not think beyond that—to what her life would be without the bowl. She only continued to fear that some accident would happen. Why not, in a world where people set plants where they did not belong, so that visitors touring a house would be fooled into thinking that dark corners got sunlight—a world full of tricks?

She had first seen the bowl several years earlier, at a crafts fair she had visited half in secret, with her lover. He had urged her to buy the bowl. She didn't *need* any more things, she told him. But she had been drawn to the bowl, and they had lingered near it. Then she went on to the next booth, and he came up behind her, tapping the rim against her shoulder as she ran her fingers over a wood carving. "You're still insisting that I buy that?" she said. "No," he said. "I bought it for you." He had bought her other things before this—things she liked more, at first—the child's ebony-and-turquoise ring that fitted her little finger; the wooden box, long and thin, beautifully dovetailed, that she used to hold paper clips; the soft gray sweater with a pouch pocket. It was his idea that when he could not be there to hold her hand she could hold her own—clasp her hands inside the lone pocket that stretched across the front. But in time she became more attached to the bowl than to any of his other presents. She tried to talk herself out of it. She owned other things that were more striking or valuable. It wasn't an object whose beauty jumped out at you; a lot of people must have passed it by before the two of them saw it that day.

Her lover had said that she was always too slow to know what she really loved. Why continue with her life the way it was? Why be two-faced, he asked her. He had made the first move toward her. When she would not decide in his favor, would not change her life and come to him, he asked her what made her think she could have it both ways. And then he made the last move and left. It was a decision meant to break her will, to shatter her intransigent ideas about honoring previous commitments.

Time passed. Alone in the living room at night, she often looked at the bowl sitting on the table, still and safe, unilluminated. In its way, it was perfect: the world cut in half, deep and smoothly empty. Near the rim, even in dim light, the eye moved toward one small flash of blue, a vanishing point on the horizon.

1986

## QUESTIONS

1. What might Andrea's bowl symbolize? How might Andrea's own interpretations differ from the author's?
2. In Roman mythology, Janus was the god of doorways and thresholds, usually depicted as having two faces. Why do you think Ann Beattie has titled this story "Janus"?
3. Near the end of the story, Andrea comes to believe that we live in "a world full of tricks." What evidence for this can you find in the story?

## EDWIDGE DANTICAT

### *A Wall of Fire Rising*

"Listen to what happened today," Guy said as he barged through the rattling door of his tiny shack.

His wife, Lili, was squatting in the middle of their one-room home, spreading cornmeal mush on banana leaves for their supper.

"Listen to what happened to *me* today!" Guy's seven-year-old son—Little Guy—dashed from a corner and grabbed his father's hand. The boy dropped his composition notebook as he leaped to his father, nearly stepping into the corn mush and herring that his mother had set out in a trio of half gourds on the clay floor.

"Our boy is in a play." Lili quickly robbed Little Guy of the honor of telling his father the news.

5  "A play?" Guy affectionately stroked the boy's hair.

The boy had such tiny corkscrew curls that no amount of brushing could ever make them all look like a single entity. The other boys at the Lycée Jean-Jacques[1] called him "pepper head" because each separate kinky strand was coiled into a tight tiny ball that looked like small peppercorns.

"When is this play?" Guy asked both the boy and his wife. "Are we going to have to buy new clothes for this?"

Lili got up from the floor and inclined her face towards her husband's in order to receive her nightly peck on the cheek.

"What role do you have in the play?" Guy asked, slowly rubbing the tip of his nails across the boy's scalp. His fingers made a soft grating noise with each invisible circle drawn around the perimeters of the boy's head. Guy's fingers finally landed inside the boy's ears, forcing the boy to giggle until he almost gave himself the hiccups.

10  "Tell me, what is your part in the play?" Guy asked again, pulling his fingers away from his son's ear.

"I am Boukman," the boy huffed out, as though there was some laughter caught in his throat.

"Show Papy your lines," Lili told the boy as she arranged the three open gourds on a piece of plywood raised like a table on two bricks, in the middle of the room. "My love, Boukman is the hero of the play."

The boy went back to the corner where he had been studying and pulled out a thick book carefully covered in brown paper.

"You're going to spend a lifetime learning those." Guy took the book from the boy's hand and flipped through the pages quickly. He had to strain his eyes to see the words by the light of an old kerosene lamp, which that night—like all others—flickered as though it was burning its very last wick.

15  "All these words seem so long and heavy," Guy said. "You think you can do this, son?"

"He has one very good speech," Lili said. "Page forty, remember, son?"

The boy took back the book from his father. His face was crimped in an of-course-I-remember look as he searched for page forty.

---

1. Haiti is French-speaking; Little Guy attends a *lycée* (school) named after Jean-Jacques Dessalines (1758-1806), the founder of independent Haiti. A former slave, Dessalines was declared emperor Jacques I in 1804.

"Bouk-man," Guy struggled with the letters of the slave revolutionary's name as he looked over his son's shoulders. "I see some very hard words here, son."

"He already knows his speech," Lili told her husband.

"Does he now?" asked Guy.

"We've been at it all afternoon," Lili said. "Why don't you go on and recite that speech for your father?"

The boy tipped his head towards the rusting tin on the roof as he prepared to recite his lines.

Lili wiped her hands on an old apron tied around her waist and stopped to listen.

"Remember what you are," Lili said, "a great rebel leader. Remember, it is the revolution."

"Do we want him to be all of that?" Guy asked.

"He is Boukman," Lili said. "What is the only thing on your mind now, Boukman?"

"Supper," Guy whispered, enviously eyeing the food cooling off in the middle of the room. He and the boy looked at each other and began to snicker.

"Tell us the other thing that is on your mind," Lili said, joining in their laughter.

"Freedom!" shouted the boy, as he quickly slipped into his role.

"Louder!" urged Lili.

"Freedom is on my mind!" yelled the boy.

"Why don't you start, son?" said Guy. "If you don't, we'll never get to that other thing that we have on our minds."

The boy closed his eyes and took a deep breath. At first, his lips parted but nothing came out. Lili pushed her head forward as though she were holding her breath. Then like the last burst of lightning out of clearing sky, the boy began.

*"A wall of fire is rising and in the ashes, I see the bones of my people. Not only those people whose dark hollow faces I see daily in the fields, but all those souls who have gone ahead to haunt my dreams. At night I relive once more the last caresses from the hand of a loving father, a valiant love, a beloved friend."*[2]

It was obvious that this was a speech written by a European man, who gave to the slave revolutionary Boukman the kind of European phrasing that might have sent the real Boukman turning in his grave. However, the speech made Lili and Guy stand on the tips of their toes from great pride. As their applause thundered in the small space of their shack that night, they felt as though for a moment they had been given the rare pleasure of hearing the voice of one of the forefathers of Haitian independence in the forced baritone of their only child. The experience left them both with a strange feeling that they could not explain. It left the hair on the back of their necks standing on end. It left them feeling much more love than they ever knew that they could add to their feeling for their son.

"Bravo," Lili cheered, pressing her son into the folds of her apron. "Long live Boukman and long live my boy."

---

2. On the night of August 22, 1791, slaves led by a slave foreman named Boukman (who was secretly a voodoo high priest) built a "wall of fire" that destroyed many plantations in the north of the French colony of Saint-Domingue, marking the beginning of a mass slave revolt that would lead, fourteen years later, to the establishment of independent Haiti.

"Long live our supper," Guy said, quickly batting his eyelashes to keep tears from rolling down his face.

The boy kept his eyes on his book as they ate their supper that night. Usually Guy and Lili would not have allowed that, but this was a special occasion. They watched proudly as the boy muttered his lines between swallows of cornmeal.

The boy was still mumbling the same words as the three of them used the last of the rainwater trapped in old gasoline containers and sugarcane pulp from the nearby sugarcane mill to scrub the gourds that they had eaten from.

When things were really bad for the family, they boiled clean sugarcane pulp to make what Lili called her special sweet water tea. It was supposed to suppress gas and kill the vermin in the stomach that made poor children hungry. That and a pinch of salt under the tongue could usually quench hunger until Guy found a day's work or Lili could manage to buy spices on credit and then peddle them for a profit at the marketplace.

That night, anyway, things were good. Everyone had eaten enough to put all their hunger vermin to sleep.

The boy was sitting in front of the shack on an old plastic bucket turned upside down, straining his eyes to find the words on the page. Sometimes when there was no kerosene for the lamp, the boy would have to go sit by the side of the road and study under the street lamps with the rest of the neighborhood children. Tonight, at least, they had a bit of their own light.

Guy bent down by a small clump of old mushrooms near the boy's feet, trying to get a better look at the plant. He emptied the last drops of rainwater from a gasoline container on the mushroom, wetting the bulging toes sticking out of his sons' sandals, which were already coming apart around his endlessly growing feet.

Guy tried to pluck some of the mushrooms, which were being pushed into the dust as though they wanted to grow beneath the ground as roots. He took one of the mushrooms in his hand, running his smallest finger over the round bulb. He clipped the stem and buried the top in a thick strand of his wife's hair.

The mushroom looked like a dried insect in Lili's hair.

"It sure makes you look special," Guy said, teasing her.

"Thank you so much," Lili said, tapping her husband's arm. "It's nice to know that I deserve these much more than roses."

Taking his wife's hand, Guy said, "Let's go to the sugar mill."

"Can I study my lines there?" the boy asked.

"You know them well enough already," Guy said.

"I need many repetitions," the boy said.

Their feet sounded as though they were playing a wet wind instrument as they slipped in and out of the puddles between the shacks in the shantytown. Near the sugar mill was a large television screen in a iron grill cage that the government had installed so that the shantytown dwellers could watch the state-sponsored news at eight o'clock every night. After the news, a gendarme[3] would come and turn off the television set, taking home the key. On most nights, the people

---

3. French word for policeman or guard.

stayed at the site long after this gendarme had gone and told stories to one another beneath the big blank screen. They made bonfires with dried sticks, corn husks, and paper, cursing the authorities under their breath.

There was a crowd already gathering for the nightly news event. The sugar mill workers sat in the front row in chairs or on old buckets.

Lili and Guy passed the group, clinging to their son so that in his childhood naïveté he wouldn't accidentally glance at the wrong person and be called an insolent child. They didn't like the ambiance of the nightly news watch. They spared themselves trouble by going instead to the sugar mill, where in the past year they had discovered their own wonder.

Everyone knew that the family who owned the sugar mill were eccentric "Arabs," Haitians of Lebanese or Palestinian descent whose family had been in the country for generations. The Assad family had a son who, it seems, was into all manner of odd things, the most recent of which was a hot-air balloon, which he had brought to Haiti from America and occasionally flew over the shantytown skies.

As they approached the fence surrounding the field where the large wicker basket and deflated balloon rested on the ground, Guy let go of the hands of both his wife and the boy.

Lili walked on slowly with her son. For the last few weeks, she had been feeling as though Guy was lost to her each time he reached this point, twelve feet away from the balloon. As Guy pushed his hand through the barbed wire, she could tell from the look on his face that he was thinking of sitting inside the square basket while the smooth rainbow surface of the balloon itself floated above his head. During the day, when the field was open, Guy would walk up to the basket, staring at it with the same kind of longing that most men display when they admire very pretty girls.

Lili and the boy stood watching from a distance as Guy tried to push his hand deeper, beyond the chain link fence that separated him from the balloon. He reached into his pants pocket and pulled out a small pocketknife, sharpening the edges on the metal surface of the fence. When his wife and child moved closer, he put the knife back in his pocket, letting his fingers slide across his son's tightly coiled curls.

"I wager you I can make this thing fly," Guy said.

"Why do you think you can do that?" Lili asked.

"I know it," Guy replied.

He followed her as she circled the sugar mill, leading to their favorite spot under a watch light. Little Guy lagged faithfully behind them. From this distance, the hot-air balloon looked like an odd spaceship.

Lili stretched her body out in the knee-high grass in the field. Guy reached over and tried to touch her between her legs.

"You're not one to worry, Lili," he said. "You're not afraid of the frogs, lizards, or snakes that could be hiding in this grass?"

"I am here with my husband," she said. "You are here to protect me if anything happens."

Guy reached into his shirt pocket and pulled out a lighter and a crumpled piece of paper. He lit the paper until it burned to an ashy film. The burning paper floated in the night breeze for a while, landing in fragments on the grass.

"Did you see that, Lili?" Guy asked with a flame in his eyes brighter than the lighter's. "Did you see how the paper floated when it was burned? This is how that balloon flies."

"What did you mean by saying that you could make it fly?" Lili asked.

"You already know all my secrets," Guy said as the boy came charging towards them.

"Papa, could you play *Lago* with me?" the boy asked.

Lili lay peacefully on the grass as her son and husband played hide-and-seek. Guy kept hiding and his son kept finding him as each time Guy made it easier for the boy.

"We rest now." Guy was becoming breathless.

The stars were circling the peaks of the mountains, dipping into the cane fields belonging to the sugar mill. As Guy caught his breath, the boy raced around the fence, running as fast as he could to purposely make himself dizzy.

"Listen to what happened today," Guy whispered softly in Lili's ear.

"I heard you say that when you walked in the house tonight," Lili said. "With the boy's play, I forgot to ask you."

The boy sneaked up behind them, his face lit up, though his brain was spinning. He wrapped his arms around both their necks.

"We will go back home soon," Lili said.

"Can I recite my lines?" asked the boy.

"We have heard them," Guy said. "Don't tire your lips."

The boy mumbled something under his breath. Guy grabbed his ear and twirled it until it was a tiny ball in his hand. The boy's face contorted with agony as Guy made him kneel in the deep grass in punishment.

Lili looked tortured as she watched the boy squirming in the grass, obviously terrified of the crickets, lizards, and small snakes that might be there.

"Perhaps we should take him home to bed," she said.

"He will never learn," Guy said, "if I say one thing and you say another."

Guy got up and angrily started walking home. Lili walked over, took her son's hand, and raised him from his knees.

"You know you must not mumble," she said.

"I was saying my lines," the boy said.

"Next time say them loud," Lili said, "so he knows what is coming out of your mouth."

That night Lili could hear her son muttering his lines as he tucked himself in his corner of the room and drifted off to sleep. The boy still had the book with his monologue in it clasped under his arm as he slept.

Guy stayed outside in front of the shack as Lili undressed for bed. She loosened the ribbon that held the old light blue cotton skirt around her waist and let it drop past her knees. She grabbed half a lemon that she kept in the corner by the folded mat that she and Guy unrolled to sleep on every night. Lili let her blouse drop to the floor as she smoothed the lemon over her ashen legs.

Guy came in just at that moment and saw her bare chest by the light of the smaller castor oil lamp that they used for the later hours of the night. Her skin had coarsened a bit over the years, he thought. Her breasts now drooped from having nursed their son for two years after he was born. It was now easier for him to imagine their son's lips around those breasts than to imagine his anywhere near them.

He turned his face away as she fumbled for her nightgown. He helped her open the mat, tucking the blanket edges underneath.

Fully clothed, Guy dropped onto the mat next to her. He laid his head on her chest, rubbing the spiky edges of his hair against her nipples.

"What was it that happened today?" Lili asked, running her fingers along Guy's hairline, an angular hairline, almost like a triangle, in the middle of his forehead. She nearly didn't marry him because it was said that people with angular hairlines often have very troubled lives.

"I got a few hours' work for tomorrow at the sugar mill," Guy said. "That's what happened today."

"It was such a long time coming," Lili said.

It was almost six months since the last time Guy had gotten work there. The jobs at the sugar mill were few and far between. The people who had them never left, or when they did they would pass the job on to another family member who was already waiting on line.

Guy did not seem overjoyed about the one day's work.

"I wish I had paid more attention when you came in with the news," Lili said. "I was just so happy about the boy."

"I was born in the shadow of that sugar mill," Guy said. "Probably the first thing my mother gave me to drink as a baby was some sweet water tea from the pulp of the sugarcane. If anyone deserves to work there, I should."

"What will you be doing for your day's work?"

"Would you really like to know?"

"There is never any shame in honest work," she said.

"They want me to scrub the latrines."

"It's honest work," Lili said, trying to console him.

"I am still number seventy-eight on the permanent hire list," he said. "I was thinking of putting the boy on the list now, so maybe by the time he becomes a man he can be up for a job."

Lili's body jerked forward, rising straight up in the air. Guy's head dropped with a loud thump onto the mat.

"I don't want him on that list," she said. "For a young boy to be on any list like that might influence his destiny. I don't want him on the list."

"Look at me," Guy said. "If my father had worked there, if he had me on the list, don't you think I would be working?"

"If you have any regard for me," she said, "you will not put him on the list."

She groped for her husband's chest in the dark and laid her head on it. She could hear his heart beating loudly as though it were pumping double, triple its normal rate.

"You won't put the boy on any lists, will you?" she implored.

"Please, Lili, no more about the boy. He will not go on the list."

"Thank you."

"Tonight I was looking at that balloon in the yard behind the sugar mill," he said. "I have been watching it real close."

"I know."

"I have seen the man who owns it," he said. "I've seen him get in it and put it in the sky and go up there like it was some kind of kite and he was the kite master. I see the men who run after it trying to figure out where it will land. Once I was there and I was one of those men who were running and I actually guessed correctly. I picked a spot in the sugarcane fields. I picked the spot from a distance and it actually landed there."

"Let me say something to you, Guy—"

"Pretend that this is the time of miracles and we believed in them. I watched the owner for a long time, and I think I can fly that balloon. The first time I saw him do it, it looked like a miracle, but the more and more I saw it, the more ordinary it became."

"You're probably intelligent enough to do it," she said.

"I am intelligent enough to do it. You're right to say that I can."

"Don't you think about hurting yourself?"

"Think like this. Can't you see yourself up there? Up in the clouds somewhere like some kind of bird?"

"If God wanted people to fly, he would have given us wings on our backs."

"You're right, Lili, you're right. But look what he gave us instead. He gave us reasons to want to fly. He gave us the air, the birds, our son."

"I don't understand you," she said.

"Our son, your son, you do not want him cleaning latrines."

"He can do other things."

"Me too. I can do other things too."

A loud scream came from the corner where the boy was sleeping. Lili and Guy rushed to him and tried to wake him. The boy was trembling when he opened his eyes.

"What is the matter?" Guy asked.

"I cannot remember my lines," the boy said.

Lili tried to string together what she could remember of her son's lines. The words slowly came back to the boy. By the time he fell back to sleep, it was almost dawn.

The light was slowly coming up behind the trees. Lili could hear the whispers of the market women, their hisses and swearing as their sandals dug into the sharp-edged rocks on the road.

She turned her back to her husband as she slipped out of her nightgown, quickly putting on her day clothes.

"Imagine this," Guy said from the mat on the floor. "I have never really seen your entire body in broad daylight."

Lili shut the door behind her, making her way out to the yard. The empty gasoline containers rested easily on her head as she walked a few miles to the public water fountains. It was harder to keep them steady when the containers were full. The water splashed all over her blouse and rippled down her back.

The sky was blue as it was most mornings, a dark indigo-shaded turquoise that would get lighter when the sun was fully risen.

Guy and the boy were standing in the yard waiting for her when she got back.

"You did not get much sleep, my handsome boy," she said, running her wet fingers over the boy's face.

"He'll be late for school if we do not go right now," Guy said. "I want to drop him off before I start work."

"Do we remember our lines this morning?" Lili asked, tucking the boy's shirt down deep into his short pants.

"We just recited them," Guy said. "Even I know them now."

Lili watched them walk down the footpath, her eyes following them until they disappeared.

As soon as they were out of sight, she poured the water she had fetched into a large calabash, letting it stand beside the house.

She went back into the room and slipped into a dry blouse. It was never too early to start looking around, to scrape together that night's meal.

"Listen to what happened again today," Lili said when Guy walked through the door that afternoon.

Guy blotted his face with a dust rag as he prepared to hear the news. After the day he'd had at the factory, he wanted to sit under a tree and have a leisurely smoke, but he did not want to set a bad example for his son by indulging his very small pleasures.

"You tell him, son," Lili urged the boy, who was quietly sitting in a corner, reading.

"I've got more lines," the boy announced, springing up to his feet. "Papy, do you want to hear them?"

"They are giving him more things to say in the play," Lili explained, "because he did such a good job memorizing so fast."

"My compliments, son. Do you have your new lines memorized too?" Guy asked.

"Why don't you recite your new lines for your father?" Lili said.

The boy walked to the middle of the room and prepared to recite. He cleared his throat, raising his eyes towards the ceiling.

*"There is so much sadness in the faces of my people. I have called on their gods, now I call on our gods. I call on our young. I call on our old. I call on our mighty and the weak. I call on everyone and anyone so that we shall all let out one piercing cry that we may either live freely or we should die."*

"I see your new lines have as much drama as the old ones," Guy said. He wiped a tear away, walked over to the chair, and took the boy in his arms. He pressed the boy's body against his chest before lowering him to the ground.

"Your new lines are wonderful, son. They're every bit as affecting as the old." He tapped the boy's shoulder and walked out of the house.

"What's the matter with Papy?" the boy asked as the door slammed shut behind Guy.

"His heart hurts," Lili said.

After supper, Lili took her son to the field where she knew her husband would be. While the boy ran around, she found her husband sitting in his favorite spot behind the sugar mill.

"Nothing, Lili," he said. "Ask me nothing about this day that I have had."

She sat down on the grass next to him, for once feeling the sharp edges of the grass blades against her ankles.

"You're really good with that boy," he said, drawing circles with his smallest finger on her elbow. "You will make a performer of him. I know you will. You can see the best in that whole situation. It's because you have those stars in your eyes. That's the first thing I noticed about you when I met you. It was your eyes, Lili, so dark and deep. They drew me like danger draws a fool."

He turned over on the grass so that he was staring directly at the moon up in the sky. She could tell that he was also watching the hot-air balloon behind the sugar mill fence out of the corner of his eye.

"Sometimes I know you want to believe in me," he said. "I know you're wishing things for me. You want me to work at the mill. You want me to get a pretty house for us. I know you want these things too, but mostly you want me to feel like a man. That's why you're not one to worry about, Lili. I know you can take things as they come."

"I don't like it when you talk this way," she said.

"Listen to this, Lili. I want to tell you a secret. Sometimes, I just want to take that big balloon and ride it up in the air. I'd like to sail off somewhere and keep floating until I got to a really nice place with a nice plot of land where I could be something new. I'd build my own house, keep my own garden. Just *be* something new."

"I want you to stay away from there."

"I know you don't think I should take it. That can't keep me from wanting."

"You could be injured. Do you ever think about that?"

"Don't you ever want to be something new?"

"I don't like it," she said.

"Please don't get angry with me," he said, his voice straining almost like the boy's.

"If you were to take that balloon and fly away, would you take me and the boy?"

"First you don't want me to take it and now you want to go?"

"I just want to know that when you dream, me and the boy, we're always in your dreams."

He leaned his head on her shoulders and drifted off to sleep. Her back ached as she sat there with his face pressed against her collar bone. He drooled and the saliva dripped down to her breasts, soaking her frayed polyester bra. She listened to the crickets while watching her son play, muttering his lines to himself as he went in a circle around the field. The moon was glowing above their heads. Winking at them, as Guy liked to say, on its way to brighter shores.

Opening his eyes, Guy asked her, "How do you think a man is judged after he's gone?"

How did he expect her to answer something like that?

"People don't eat riches," she said. "They eat what it can buy."

"What does that mean, Lili? Don't talk to me in parables. Talk to me honestly."

"A man is judged by his deeds," she said. "The boy never goes to bed hungry. For as long as he's been with us, he's always been fed."

Just as if he had heard himself mentioned, the boy came dashing from the other side of the field, crashing in a heap on top of his parents.

"My new lines," he said. "I have forgotten my new lines."

"Is this how you will be the day of this play, son?" Guy asked. "When people give you big responsibilities, you have to try to live up to them."

The boy had relearned his new lines by the time they went to bed.

That night, Guy watched his wife very closely as she undressed for bed.

"I would like to be the one to rub that piece of lemon on your knees tonight," he said.

She handed him the half lemon, then raised her skirt above her knees.

Her body began to tremble as he rubbed his fingers over her skin.

"You know that question I asked you before," he said, "how a man is remembered after he's gone? I know the answer now. I know because I remember my father, who was a very poor struggling man all his life. I remember him as a man that I would never want to be."

Lili got up with the break of dawn the next day. The light came up quickly above the trees. Lili greeted some of the market women as they walked together to the public water fountain.

On her way back, the sun had already melted a few gray clouds. She found the boy standing alone in the yard with a terrified expression on his face, the old withered mushrooms uprooted at his feet. He ran up to meet her, nearly knocking her off balance.

"What happened?" she asked. "Have you forgotten your lines?"

The boy was breathing so heavily that his lips could not form a single word.

"What is it?" Lili asked, almost shaking him with anxiety.

"It's Papa," he said finally, raising a stiff finger in the air.

The boy covered his face as his mother looked up at the sky. A rainbow-colored balloon was floating aimlessly above their heads.

"It's Papa," the boy said. "He is in it."

She wanted to look down at her son and tell him that it wasn't his father, but she immediately recognized the spindly arms, in a bright flowered shirt that she had made, gripping the cables.

From the field behind the sugar mill a group of workers were watching the balloon floating in the air. Many were clapping and cheering, calling out Guy's name. A few of the women were waving their head rags at the sky, shouting, "Go! Beautiful, go!"

Lili edged her way to the front of the crowd. Everyone was waiting, watching the balloon drift higher up into the clouds.

"He seems to be right over our heads," said the factory foreman, a short slender mulatto with large buckteeth.

Just then, Lili noticed young Assad, his thick black hair sticking to the beads of sweat on his forehead. His face had the crumpled expression of disrupted sleep.

"He's further away than he seems," said young Assad. "I still don't understand. How did he get up there? You need a whole crew to fly these things."

"I don't know," the foreman said. "One of my workers just came in saying there was a man flying above the factory."

"But how the hell did he start it?" Young Assad was perplexed.

"He just did it," the foreman said.

"Look, he's trying to get out!" someone hollered.

A chorus of screams broke out among the workers.

The boy was looking up, trying to see if his father was really trying to jump out of the balloon. Guy was climbing over the side of the basket. Lili pressed her son's face into her skirt.

Within seconds, Guy was in the air hurtling down towards the crowd. Lili held her breath as she watched him fall. He crashed not far from where Lili and the boy were standing, his blood immediately soaking the landing spot.

The balloon kept floating free, drifting on its way to brighter shores. Young

Assad rushed towards the body. He dropped to his knees and checked the wrist for a pulse, then dropped the arm back to the ground.

"It's over!" The foreman ordered the workers back to work.

Lili tried to keep her son's head pressed against her skirt as she moved closer to the body. The boy yanked himself away and raced to the edge of the field where his father's body was lying on the grass. He reached the body as young Assad still knelt examining the corpse. Lili rushed after him.

"He is mine," she said to young Assad. "He is my family. He belongs to me."

Young Assad got up and raised his head to search the sky for his aimless balloon, trying to guess where it would land. He took one last glance at Guy's bloody corpse, then raced to his car and sped away.

The foreman and another worker carried a cot and blanket from the factory.

Little Guy was breathing quickly as he looked at his father's body on the ground. While the foreman draped a sheet over Guy's corpse, his son began to recite the lines from his play.

"A wall of fire is rising and in the ashes, I see the bones of my people. Not only those people whose dark hollow faces I see daily in the fields, but all those souls who have gone ahead to haunt my dreams. At night I relive once more the last caresses from the hand of a loving father, a valiant love, a beloved friend."

"Let me look at him one last time," Lili said, pulling back the sheet.

She leaned in very close to get a better look at Guy's face. There was little left of that countenance that she had loved so much. Those lips that curled when he was teasing her. That large flat nose that felt like a feather when rubbed against hers. And those eyes, those night-colored eyes. Though clouded with blood, Guy's eyes were still bulging open. Lili was searching for some kind of sign—a blink, a smile, a wink—something that would remind her of the man that she had married.

"His eyes aren't closed," the foreman said to Lili. "Do you want to close them, or should I?"

The boy continued reciting his lines, his voice rising to a man's grieving roar. He kept his eyes closed, his fists balled at his side as he continued with his newest lines.

"There is so much sadness in the faces of my people. I have called on their gods, now I call on our gods. I call on our young. I call on our old. I call on our mighty and the weak. I call on everyone and anyone so that we shall all let out one piercing cry that we may either live freely or we should die."

"Do you want to close the eyes?" the foreman repeated impatiently.

"No, leave them open," Lili said. "My husband, he likes to look at the sky."

1991

## QUESTIONS

1. What do you think the hot-air balloon symbolizes to Assad, its owner? to Guy? to Edwidge Danticat?
2. What is the possible significance of the detail that Little Guy's speech was "written by a European man, who gave to the slave revolutionary Boukman the kind of European phrasing that might have sent the real Boukman turning in his grave"? Is the meaning of the lines affected by the fact that the boy is memorizing them for a

school play about the history of Haiti? Why is Guy skeptical at first, expecting that it would take "a lifetime" to learn the "hard words" in Boukman's speech?
3. What do you think happens at the end of "A Wall of Fire Rising"? Is Guy's plunge to the earth a deliberate suicide or an accident? What are some symbolic interpretations of both possibilities?

---

## SUGGESTIONS FOR WRITING

1. Write an essay in which you argue that "Young Goodman Brown" is either an allegory in which a more or less "correct" interpretation is possible or a symbolic tale that cannot be "decoded" with any certainty. Be sure to use specific details from the story.
2. Write an analysis of the symbolism in either "The Thing in the Forest," "The Country Husband," or "Bartleby, the Scrivener."
3. Write an essay that explores the parallels between specific details in "A Hunger Artist" and art in general.
4. To what extent are the characters in a story "aware" of the symbolism in the story? Write an essay discussing how Andrea in "Janus" is or is not fully aware of the bowl's symbolic importance, and why her degree of awareness is a significant aspect of our understanding of the story.
5. Write an essay in which you compare and contrast the use of symbolism in "Young Goodman Brown" and "A Wall of Fire Rising." Consider specific symbolic techniques used in each story as well as the possible intentions of the authors.
6. Write a parody of any of the stories in this chapter. See if you can make the symbolism deliberately heavy-handed and obvious, or perhaps obscure and puzzling.

# 6 THEME

If you ask what a story is about, an author might answer by telling you the subject. Indeed, a story often announces its subject in the title: "An Occurrence at Owl Creek Bridge." A friend might answer with a short statement: "a man's thoughts as he faces execution for spying during the Civil War." You might answer with a written summary of the plot. A teacher might answer by stating the story's **theme**—its central idea, its thesis, its message—"war destroys dreams." Notice that the theme is far more general than the subject, and consider too that not everyone will agree on a story's theme. While you can usually state a subject and summarize the action after one reading, it sometimes takes several readings to puzzle out a story's theme—deciphering the theme requires paying attention to all the elements of literature: setting, character, plot, symbols, point of view, and language.

Classroom discussions of literature may seem to suggest that we read a work only to figure out its theme. But most themes reflect common wisdom and, stated baldly, they may seem unoriginal. Thus, while we might say that " 'Young Goodman Brown' is about a young husband who finds everyone he thought good and pure attending a witches' meeting," the story's *theme* may be stated: "Everyone partakes of evil." Similarly, the particular experience of love, divorce, and remarriage in "The Littoral Zone" might be condensed into the theme that all passion eventually subsides. Such a thematic statement is far from the end point of reading and interpretation. Instead, it should be a first step toward understanding the work to notice the way each element supports the theme and, perhaps most important, complicates it.

*Ideas are to literature what light is to painting.*
—PAUL BOURGET

Themes are most powerful when they somehow draw on common experience and knowledge. This is not to say that only people who have been directly involved in a war can appreciate the theme of "An Occurrence at Owl Creek Bridge." Nor is it necessary to have been a starving artist to admire and pity the hunger artist and resent the way he is exploited. People with little experience of the lives of married suburban professionals can still grasp that "Janus" shows the conflict between material and emotional success, between living "well" and being really happy. The dream of escaping oppression and hardship is surely accessible to all readers, whether or not their family history resembles that of the Haitians in "A Wall of Fire Rising." To be sure, some familiarity with the historical and cultural context of a story can assist readers in recognizing its theme or themes, and the significance of any story is modified to some extent by the reader's experience of books and life. Yet stories can be an enrichment of experience, inviting readers to travel out of their own immediate circumstances to imagine others. We are able to recognize the common ground of a general theme through the uncommon aspects of experiences different from our own.

Stories, novels, and films often capture our imaginations because they depict ways of life we have never experienced. Since the earliest times, human beings have longed to hear about other lands and other peoples. Although today such forms of nonfiction as ethnography, history, and travel writing can satisfy this longing, fiction remains a uniquely effective way to convey the subtleties of interaction among different people and cultures. When, for example, a person from one country visits another, there are likely to be the kinds of conflicts and revelations that make for a good story. The four stories in this chapter emphasize cultural and social differences, while at the same time pondering estrangement or loss within families or between lovers. Each story conveys both a powerful sense of place and also the great distances between cultures; in each case this is what gives rise to the story's theme. The point of view may be that of an insider who is strangely attracted to a troubled visitor, such as the narrator of Nadine Gordimer's "Good Climate, Friendly Inhabitants," or the focal character Mr. Kapasi in Jhumpa Lahiri's "Interpreter of Maladies." Or the point of view may be that of an outsider, as in Angela Carter's "A Souvenir of Japan," or Bharati Mukherjee's "The Management of Grief."

In distinctive ways, all four stories explore failures to bridge cultural gaps, each story addressing this theme through a subtle use of the elements of fiction. A simple paraphrase or summary of the story would miss what is distinctive about its handling of the idea of cultural differences. Each story has its own specific context in a country with its own history and religious traditions. Aided by footnotes, perhaps, you may interpret the **allusions**—references to history, religion, cultural practices, and so on. You may observe particular metaphors or actions that enhance the meaning of the story and enrich your own restatement of the theme. As always, the title is a key to the rest of the details in a story. In "A Souvenir of Japan," for example, the narrator is a tall, blond, blue-eyed woman who recalls a time when she lived with a younger Japanese man in a Japanese city. From the first half of the first sentence ("When I went outside to see if he was coming home"), we expect a frustrated love story. But the title and the second half of the first sentence turn the reader's attention to the customs of the country, as if offering souvenirs of a tour. The unusual mixture of travelogue and love story calls our attention to the story's theme about the incompatibility of the lovers and their cultures. In "The Management of Grief," the title calls attention to a businesslike way of dealing with death. In this story, a terrorist bombing of an airliner eliminates the family of Mukherjee's narrator, Shaila Bhave, who must serve as go-between and translator as she tries to rebuild a life in a new world, Canada. In Nadine Gordimer's "Good Climate, Friendly Inhabitants," the title sounds like an invitation to move to South Africa, which clashes with the sad story of a gas station clerk, isolated by her age, gender, and racial segregation, who tries to find comfort in telling the story of her dangerous relationship with a drifter. Similarly, in Jhumpa Lahiri's "Interpreter of Maladies," the American-born Mrs. Das seeks relief for her guilt and misery by confessing to the driver who guides their tour in India.

Misunderstandings across great cultural divides—and the self-deceiving stories people tell—are themes in each of these stories. Yet even with their interrelated

> *The meaning of a story has to be embodied in it, has to be made concrete in it. A story is a way to say something that can't be said any other way, and it takes every word in the story to say what the meaning is.*
> —FLANNERY O'CONNOR

themes, these stories differ widely in substance, form, and effect. To locate each theme is not to "close the case," but rather to begin a more searching investigation of the details that make each story vivid and unique. Remember, the theme is an inadequate abstraction from the story; the story and its details do not disappear or lose significance once distilled into theme, nor could you reconstruct a story merely from a statement of its theme. Indeed, theme and story are fused, inseparable. Often difficult to put into words, themes are the common ground that helps you recognize and care about a story, though it seems to be about lives and experiences very different from your own.

## ANGELA CARTER

### A Souvenir of Japan

When I went outside to see if he was coming home, some children dressed ready for bed in cotton nightgowns were playing with sparklers in the vacant lot on the corner. When the sparks fell down in beards of stars, the smiling children cooed softly. Their pleasure was very pure because it was so restrained. An old woman said: "And so they pestered their father until he bought them fireworks." In their language, fireworks are called *hannabi*, which means "flower fire." All through summer, every evening, you can see all kinds of fireworks, from the humblest to the most elaborate, and once we rode the train out of Shinjuku for an hour to watch one of the public displays which are held over rivers so that the dark water multiplies the reflections.

By the time we arrived at our destination, night had already fallen. We were in the suburbs. Many families were on their way to enjoy the fireworks. Their mothers had scrubbed and dressed up the smallest children to celebrate the treat. The little girls were especially immaculate in pink and white cotton kimonos tied with fluffy sashes like swatches of candy floss. Their hair had been most beautifully brushed, arranged in sleek, twin bunches and decorated with twists of gold and silver thread. These children were all on their best behavior, because they were staying up late, and held their parents' hands with a charming propriety. We followed the family parties until we came to some fields by the river and saw, high in the air, fireworks already opening out like variegated parasols. They were visible from far away and, as we took the path that led through the fields towards their source, they seemed to occupy more and more of the sky.

Along the path were stalls where shirtless cooks with sweatbands round their heads roasted corncobs and cuttlefish over charcoal. We bought cuttlefish on skewers and ate them as we walked along. They had been basted with soy sauce and were very good. There were also stalls selling goldfish in plastic bags and others for big balloons with rabbit ears. It was like a fairground—but such a well-ordered fair! Even the patrolling policemen carried colored paper lanterns instead of torches.[1] Everything was altogether quietly festive. Ice-cream sellers wandered among the crowd, ringing handbells. Their boxes of wares smoked with cold and they called out in plaintive voices, "Icy, icy, icy cream!" When young

---

1. Flashlights (British).

lovers dispersed discreetly down the tracks in the sedge, the shadowy, indefatigable salesmen pursued them with bells, lamps and mournful cries.

By now, a great many people were walking towards the fireworks but their steps fell so softly and they chatted in such gentle voices there was no more noise than a warm, continual, murmurous humming, the cozy sound of shared happiness, and the night filled with a muted, bourgeois yet authentic magic. Above our heads, the fireworks hung dissolving earrings on the night. Soon we lay down in a stubbled field to watch the fireworks. But, as I expected, he very quickly grew restive.

"Are you happy?" he asked. "Are you sure you're happy?" I was watching the fireworks and did not reply at first although I knew how bored he was and, if he was himself enjoying anything, it was only the idea of my pleasure—or, rather, the idea that he enjoyed my pleasure, since this would be a proof of love. I became guilty and suggested we return to the heart of the city. We fought a silent battle of self-abnegation and I won it, for I had the stronger character. Yet the last thing in the world that I wanted was to leave the scintillating river and the gentle crowd. But I knew his real desire was to return and so return we did, although I do not know if it was worth my small victory of selflessness to bear his remorse at cutting short my pleasure, even if to engineer this remorse had, at some subterranean level, been the whole object of the outing.

Nevertheless, as the slow train nosed back into the thickets of neon, his natural liveliness returned. He could not lose his old habit of walking through the streets with a sense of expectation, as if a fateful encounter might be just around the corner, for, the longer one stayed out, the longer something remarkable might happen and, even if nothing ever did, the chance of it appeased the sweet ache of his boredom for a little while. Besides, his duty by me was done. He had taken me out for the evening and now he wanted to be rid of me. Or so I saw it. The word for wife, *okusan*, means the person who occupies the inner room and rarely, if ever, comes out of it. Since I often appeared to be his wife, I was frequently subjected to this treatment, though I fought against it bitterly.

But I usually found myself waiting for him to come home knowing, with a certain resentment, that he would not; and that he would not even telephone me to tell me he would be late, either, for he was far too guilty to do so. I had nothing better to do than to watch the neighborhood children light their sparklers and giggle; the old woman stood beside me and I knew she disapproved of me. The entire street politely disapproved of me. Perhaps they thought I was contributing to the delinquency of a juvenile for he was obviously younger than I. The old woman's back was bowed almost to a circle from carrying, when he was a baby, the father who now supervised the domestic fireworks in his evening *déshabillé* of loose, white, crepe drawers, naked to the waist. Her face had the seamed reserve of the old in this country. It was a neighborhood poignantly rich in old ladies.

At the corner shop, they put an old lady outside on an upturned beer crate each morning, to air. I think she must have been the household grandmother. She was so old she had lapsed almost entirely into a somnolent plant life. She was of neither more nor less significance to herself or to the world than the pot of morning glories which blossomed beside her and perhaps she had less significance than the flowers, which would fade before lunch was ready. They kept her very clean. They covered her pale cotton kimono with a spotless pinafore trimmed with coarse lace and she never dirtied it because she did not move. Now and then, a child came out to comb her hair. Her consciousness was quite beclouded by time and, when I passed by, her rheumy eyes settled upon me always with the same, vague, disinterested wonder, like that of an Eskimo watching a train. When she whispered, *Irrasyaimase,* the shopkeeper's word of welcome, in the ghostliest of whispers, like the rustle of a paper bag, I saw her teeth were rimmed with gold.

The children lit sparklers under a mouse-colored sky and, because of the pollution in the atmosphere, the moon was mauve. The cicadas throbbed and shrieked in the backyards. When I think of this city, I shall always remember the cicadas who whirr relentlessly all through the summer nights, rising to a piercing crescendo in the subfusc dawn. I have heard cicadas even in the busiest streets, though they thrive best in the back alleys, where they ceaselessly emit that scarcely tolerable susurration which is like a shrill intensification of extreme heat.

A year before, on such a throbbing, voluptuous, platitudinous, subtropical night, we had been walking down one of these shady streets together, in and out of the shadows of the willow trees, looking for somewhere to make love. Morning glories climbed the lattices which screened the low, wooden houses, but the darkness hid the tender colors of these flowers, which the Japanese prize because they fade so quickly. He soon found a hotel, for the city is hospitable to lovers. We were shown into a room like a paper box. It contained nothing but a mattress spread on the floor. We lay down immediately and began to kiss one another. Then a maid soundlessly opened the sliding door and, stepping out of her slippers, crept in on stockinged feet, breathing apologies. She carried a tray which contained two cups of tea and a plate of candies. She put the tray down on the matted floor beside us and backed, bowing and apologizing, from the room while our uninterrupted kiss continued. He started to unfasten my shirt and then she came back again. This time, she carried an armful of towels. I was stripped stark naked when she returned for a third time to bring the receipt for his money. She was clearly a most respectable woman and, if she was embarrassed, she did not show it by a single word or gesture.

I learned his name was Taro. In a toy store, I saw one of those books for children with pictures which are cunningly made of paper cut-outs so that, when you turn the page, the picture springs up in the three stylized dimensions of a backdrop in Kabuki. It was the story of Momotaro, who was born from a peach. Before my eyes, the paper peach split open and there was the baby, where the stone should have been. He, too, had the inhuman sweetness of a child born from something other than a mother, a passive, cruel sweetness I did not immediately understand, for it was that of the repressed masochism which, in my country, is usually confined to women.

Sometimes he seemed to possess a curiously unearthly quality when he perched upon the mattress with his knees drawn up beneath his chin in the attitude of a pixie on a doorknocker. At these times, his face seemed somehow both too flat and too large for his elegant body which had such curious, androgynous grace with its svelte, elongated spine, wide shoulders and unusually well developed pectorals, almost like the breasts of a girl approaching puberty. There was a subtle lack of alignment between face and body and he seemed almost goblin, as if he might have borrowed another person's head, as Japanese goblins do, in order to perform some devious trick. These impressions of a weird visitor were fleeting yet haunting. Sometimes, it was possible for me to believe he had practiced an enchantment upon me, as foxes in this country may, for, here, a fox can masquerade as human and at the best of times the high cheekbones gave to his face the aspect of a mask.

His hair was so heavy his neck drooped under its weight and was of a black so deep it turned purple in sunlight. His mouth also was purplish and his blunt, bee-stung lips those of Gauguin's Tahitians. The touch of his skin was as smooth as water as it flows through the fingers. His eyelids were retractable, like those of a cat, and sometimes disappeared completely. I should have liked to have had him embalmed and been able to keep him beside me in a glass coffin, so that I could watch him all the time and he would not have been able to get away from me.

As they say, Japan is a man's country. When I first came to Tokyo, cloth carps fluttered from poles in the gardens of the families fortunate enough to have borne boy children, for it was the time of the annual festival, Boys Day. At least they do not disguise the situation. At least one knows where one is. Our polarity was publicly acknowledged and socially sanctioned. As an example of the use of the word *dewa*, which occasionally means, as far as I can gather, "in," I once found in a textbook a sentence which, when translated, read: "In a society where men dominate, they value women only as the object of men's passions." If the only conjunction possible to us was that of the death-defying double-somersault of love, it is, perhaps, a better thing to be valued only as an object of passion than never to be valued at all. I had never been so absolutely the mysterious other. I had become a kind of phoenix, a fabulous beast; I was an outlandish jewel. He found me, I think, inexpressibly exotic. But I often felt like a female impersonator in Japan.

In the department store there was a rack of dresses labeled: "For Young and Cute Girls Only." When I looked at them, I felt as gross as Glumdalclitch.[2] I wore men's sandals because they were the only kind that fitted me and, even so, I had to take the largest size. My pink cheeks, blue eyes and blatant yellow hair made of me, in the visual orchestration of this city in which all heads were dark, eyes brown and skin monotone, an instrument which played upon an alien scale. In a sober harmony of subtle plucked instruments and wistful flutes, I blared. I proclaimed myself like in a perpetual fanfare. He was so delicately put together that I thought his skeleton must have the airy elegance of a bird's and I was sometimes afraid that I might smash him. He told me that when he was in bed with me, he felt like a small boat upon a wide, stormy sea.

We pitched our tent in the most unlikely surroundings. We were living in a room furnished only by passion amongst homes of the most astounding respectability. The sounds around us were the swish of brooms upon *tatami* matting and the clatter of demotic Japanese. On all the window ledges, prim flowers bloomed in pots. Every morning, the washing came out on the balconies at seven. Early one morning, I saw a man washing the leaves of his tree. Quilts and mattresses went out to air at eight. The sunlight lay thick enough on these unpaved alleys to lay the dust and somebody always seemed to be practicing Chopin in one or another of the flimsy houses, so lightly glued together from plywood

---

2. In Jonathan Swift's *Gulliver's Travels*, Glumdalclitch is a giantess of Brobdingnag. She is Gulliver's nurse and, though only nine years old, is nearly forty feet tall.

it seemed they were sustained only by willpower. Once I was at home, however, it was as if I occupied the inner room and he did not expect me to go out of it, although it was I who paid the rent.

Yet, when he was away from me, he spent much of the time savoring the most annihilating remorse. But this remorse or regret was the stuff of life to him and out he would go again the next night, or, if I had been particularly angry, he would wait until the night after that. And, even if he fully intended to come back early and had promised me he would do so, circumstances always somehow denied him and once more he would contrive to miss the last train. He and his friends spent their nights in a desultory progression from coffee shop to bar to *pachinko* parlor to coffee shop again, with the radiant aimlessness of the pure existential hero. They were connoisseurs of boredom. They savored the various bouquets of the subtly differentiated boredoms which rose from the long, wasted hours at the dead end of night. When it was time for the first train in the morning, he would go back to the mysteriously deserted, Piranesi[3] perspectives of the station, discolored by dawn, exquisitely tortured by the notion—which probably contained within it a damped-down spark of hope—that, this time, he might have done something irreparable.

I speak as if he had no secrets from me. Well, then, you must realize that I was suffering from love and I knew him as intimately as I knew my own image in a mirror. In other words, I knew him only in relation to myself. Yet, on those terms, I knew him perfectly. At times, I thought I was inventing him as I went along, however, so you will have to take my word for it that we existed. But I do not want to paint our circumstantial portraits so that we both emerge with enough well-rounded, spuriously detailed actuality that you are forced to believe in us. I do not want to practice such sleight of hand. You must be content only with glimpses of our outlines, as if you had caught sight of our reflections in the looking-glass of somebody else's house as you passed by the window. His name was not Taro. I only called him Taro so that I could use the conceit of the peach boy, because it seemed appropriate.

Speaking of mirrors, the Japanese have a great respect for them and, in old-fashioned inns, one often finds them hooded with fabric covers when not in use. He said: "Mirrors make a room uncozy." I am sure there is more to it than that although they love to be cozy. One must love coziness if one is to live so close together. But, as if in celebration of the thing they feared, they seemed to have made the entire city into a cold hall of mirrors which continually proliferated whole galleries of constantly changing appearances, all marvelous but none tangible. If they did not lock up the real looking-glasses, it would be hard to tell what was real and what was not. Even buildings one had taken for substantial had a trick of disappearing overnight. One morning, we woke to find the house next door reduced to nothing but a heap of sticks and a pile of newspapers neatly tied with string, left out for the garbage collector.

I would not say that he seemed to me to possess the same kind of insubstantiality although his departure usually seemed imminent, until I realized he was as erratic but as inevitable as the weather. If you plan to come and live in Japan, you must be sure you are stoical enough to endure the weather. No, it was not

---

3. Giambattista Piranesi (1720–1778), Italian architect, painter, and engraver famous for exaggerated (oversized), dramatic, mysterious, almost dreamlike prints of Roman architecture and ruins.

insubstantiality; it was a rhetoric valid only on its own terms. When I listened to his protestations, I was prepared to believe he believed in them, although I knew perfectly well they meant nothing. And that isn't fair. When he made them, he believed in them implicitly. Then, he was utterly consumed by conviction. But his dedication was primarily to the idea of himself in love. This idea seemed to him magnificent, even sublime. He was prepared to die for it, as one of Baudelaire's dandies[4] might have been prepared to kill himself in order to preserve himself in the condition of a work of art, for he wanted to make this experience a masterpiece of experience which absolutely transcended the everyday. And this would annihilate the effects of the cruel drug, boredom, to which he was addicted although, perhaps, the element of boredom which is implicit in an affair so isolated from the real world was its principal appeal for him. But I had no means of knowing how far his conviction would take him. And I used to turn over in my mind from time to time the question: how far does a pretense of feeling, maintained with absolute conviction, become authentic?

This country has elevated hypocrisy to the level of the highest style. To look at a samurai, you would not know him for a murderer, or a geisha for a whore. The magnificence of such objects hardly pertains to the human. They live only in a world of icons and there they participate in rituals which transmute life itself to a series of grand gestures, as moving as they are absurd. It was as if they all thought, if we believe in something hard enough, it will come true and, lo and behold! they had and it did. Our street was in essence a slum but, in appearance, it was a little enclave of harmonious quiet and, *mirabile dictu*, it was the appearance which was the reality, because they all behaved so well, kept everything so clean and lived with such rigorous civility. What terrible discipline it takes to live harmoniously. They had crushed all their vigor in order to live harmoniously and now they had the wistful beauty of flowers pressed dry in an enormous book.

But repression does not necessarily give birth only to severe beauties. In its programmed interstices, monstrous passions bloom. They torture trees to make them look more like the formal notion of a tree. They paint amazing pictures on their skins with awl and gouge, sponging away the blood as they go; a tattooed man is a walking masterpiece of remembered pain. They boast the most passionate puppets in the world who mimic love suicides in a stylized fashion, for here there is no such comfortable formula as "happy ever after." And, when I remembered the finale of the puppet tragedies, how the wooden lovers cut their throats together, I felt the beginnings of unease, as if the hieratic imagery of the country might overwhelm me, for his boredom had reached such a degree that he was insulated against everything except the irritation of anguish. If he valued me as an object of passion, he had reduced the word to its root, which derives from the Latin, *patior,* I suffer. He valued me as an instrument which would cause him pain.

So we lived under a disoriented moon which was as angry a purple as if the sky had bruised its eye, and, if we made certain genuine intersections, these only took place in darkness. His contagious conviction that our love was unique and

---

4. Charles Baudelaire (1821–1867), French writer who lived a life of excess and debauchery and who depicted this lifestyle, that of a "dandy," in his infamous poetic work *Les fleurs du mal* (*The Flowers of Evil*) (1857).

desperate infected me with an anxious sickness; soon we would learn to treat one another with the circumspect tenderness of comrades who are amputees, for we were surrounded by the most moving images of evanescence, fireworks, morning glories, the old, children. But the most moving of these images were the intangible reflections of ourselves we saw in one another's eyes, reflections of nothing but appearances, in a city dedicated to seeming, and, try as we might to possess the essence of each other's otherness, we would inevitably fail.

1974

## QUESTIONS

1. How does the narrator's use of pronouns like "he" and "we" in the opening paragraphs serve to immerse the reader in "A Souvenir of Japan"? How does this use of unreferenced pronouns mirror the situation of an outsider plunged into an alien culture?
2. In what ways does this story present a "souvenir of Japan" to an English-speaking outsider? What does the word "souvenir" imply about the narrator's feelings toward Japan and the story she has to tell?
3. How does Angela Carter's use of the word "reflections" at the end of the opening paragraph prefigure many of the images that make up her portrait of Japanese culture? When she uses the same word, "reflections," twice in the final sentence of the story, what additional layers of meaning and thematic significance has the word acquired?

## BHARATI MUKHERJEE

## *The Management of Grief*

A woman I don't know is boiling tea the Indian way in my kitchen. There are a lot of women I don't know in my kitchen, whispering, and moving tactfully. They open doors, rummage through the pantry, and try not to ask me where things are kept. They remind me of when my sons were small, on Mother's Day or when Vikram and I were tired, and they would make big, sloppy omelets. I would lie in bed pretending I didn't hear them.

Dr. Sharma, the treasurer of the Indo-Canada Society, pulls me into the hallway. He wants to know if I am worried about money. His wife, who has just come up from the basement with a tray of empty cups and glasses, scolds him. "Don't bother Mrs. Bhave with mundane details." She looks so monstrously pregnant her baby must be days overdue. I tell her she shouldn't be carrying heavy things. "Shaila," she says, smiling, "this is the fifth." Then she grabs a teenager by his shirttails. He slips his Walkman off his head. He has to be one of her four children, they have the same domed and dented foreheads. "What's the official word now?" she demands. The boy slips the headphones back on. "They're acting evasive, Ma. They're saying it could be an accident or a terrorist bomb."

All morning, the boys have been muttering, Sikh Bomb, Sikh Bomb. The men, not using the word, bow their heads in agreement. Mrs. Sharma touches her forehead at such a word. At least they've stopped talking about space debris and Russian lasers.

Two radios are going in the dining room. They are tuned to different stations. Someone must have brought the radios down from my boys' bedrooms. I haven't gone into their rooms since Kusum came running across the front lawn in her bathrobe. She looked so funny, I was laughing when I opened the door.

The big TV in the den is being whizzed through American networks and cable channels.

"Damn!" some man swears bitterly. "How can these preachers carry on like nothing's happened?" I want to tell him we're not that important. You look at the audience, and at the preacher in his blue robe with his beautiful white hair, the potted palm trees under a blue sky, and you know they care about nothing.

The phone rings and rings. Dr. Sharma's taken charge. "We're with her," he keeps saying. "Yes, yes, the doctor has given calming pills. Yes, yes, pills are having necessary effect." I wonder if pills alone explain this calm. Not peace, just a deadening quiet. I was always controlled, but never repressed. Sound can reach me, but my body is tensed, ready to scream. I hear their voices all around me. I hear my boys and Vikram cry, "Mommy, Shaila!" and their screams insulate me, like headphones.

The woman boiling water tells her story again and again. "I got the news first. My cousin called from Halifax before six A.M., can you imagine? He'd gotten up for prayers and his son was studying for medical exams and he heard on a rock channel that something had happened to a plane. They said first it had disappeared from the radar, like a giant eraser just reached out. His father called me, so I said to him, what do you mean, 'something bad'? You mean a hijacking? And he said, *behn*,[1] there is no confirmation of anything yet, but check with your neighbors because a lot of them must be on that plane. So I called poor Kusum straightaway. I knew Kusum's husband and daughter were booked to go yesterday."

Kusum lives across the street from me. She and Satish had moved in less than a month ago. They said they needed a bigger place. All these people, the Sharmas and friends from the Indo-Canada Society had been there for the housewarming. Satish and Kusum made homemade tandoori on their big gas grill and even the white neighbors piled their plates high with that luridly red, charred, juicy chicken. Their younger daughter had danced, and even our boys had broken away from the Stanley Cup telecast to put in a reluctant appearance. Everyone took pictures for their albums and for the community newspapers—another of our families had made it big in Toronto—and now I wonder how many of those happy faces are gone. "Why does God give us so much if all along He intends to take it away?" Kusum asks me.

I nod. We sit on carpeted stairs, holding hands like children. "I never once told him that I loved him," I say. I was too much the well brought up woman. I was so well brought up I never felt comfortable calling my husband by his first name.

"It's all right," Kusum says. "He knew. My husband knew. They felt it. Modern young girls have to say it because what they feel is fake."

Kusum's daughter, Pam, runs in with an overnight case. Pam's in her McDonald's uniform. "Mummy! You have to get dressed!" Panic makes her cranky. "A reporter's on his way here."

---

1. No.

"Why?"

"You want to talk to him in your bathrobe?" She starts to brush her mother's long hair. She's the daughter who's always in trouble. She dates Canadian boys and hangs out in the mall, shopping for tight sweaters. The younger one, the goody-goody one according to Pam, the one with a voice so sweet that when she sang *bhajans*[2] for Ethiopian relief even a frugal man like my husband wrote out a hundred dollar check, *she* was on that plane. *She* was going to spend July and August with grandparents because Pam wouldn't go. Pam said she'd rather waitress at McDonald's. "If it's a choice between Bombay and Wonderland, I'm picking Wonderland," she'd said.

"Leave me alone," Kusum yells. "You know what I want to do? If I didn't have to look after you now, I'd hang myself."

Pam's young face goes blotchy with pain. "Thanks," she says, "don't let me stop you."

"Hush," pregnant Mrs. Sharma scolds Pam. "Leave your mother alone. Mr. Sharma will tackle the reporters and fill out the forms. He'll say what has to be said."

Pam stands her ground. "You think I don't know what Mummy's thinking? *Why her?* that's what. That's sick! Mummy wishes my little sister were alive and I were dead."

Kusum's hand in mine is trembly hot. We continue to sit on the stairs.

She calls before she arrives, wondering if there's anything I need. Her name is Judith Templeton and she's an appointee of the provincial government. "Multiculturalism?" I ask, and she says, "partially," but that her mandate is bigger. "I've been told you knew many of the people on the flight," she says. "Perhaps if you'd agree to help us reach the others . . . ?"

She gives me time at least to put on tea water and pick up the mess in the front room. I have a few *samosas*[3] from Kusum's housewarming that I could fry up, but then I think, why prolong this visit?

Judith Templeton is much younger than she sounded. She wears a blue suit with a white blouse and a polka dot tie. Her blond hair is cut short, her only jewelry is pearl drop earrings. Her briefcase is new and expensive looking, a gleaming cordovan leather. She sits with it across her lap. When she looks out the front windows onto the street, her contact lenses seem to float in front of her light blue eyes.

"What sort of help do you want from me?" I ask. She has refused the tea, out of politeness, but I insist, along with some slightly stale biscuits.[4]

"I have no experience," she admits. "That is, I have an MSW and I've worked in liaison with accident victims, but I mean I have no experience with a tragedy of this scale—"

"Who could?" I ask.

"—and with the complications of culture, language, and customs. Someone mentioned that Mrs. Bhave is a pillar—because you've taken it more calmly."

At this, perhaps, I frown, for she reaches forward, almost to take my hand. "I hope you understand my meaning, Mrs. Bhave. There are hundreds of people in Metro directly affected, like you, and some of them speak no English. There are some widows who've never handled money or gone on a bus, and there are

---

2. Hymns.   3. Fried turnovers filled with finely chopped meat or vegetables.   4. Cookies.

old parents who still haven't eaten or gone outside their bedrooms. Some houses and apartments have been looted. Some wives are still hysterical. Some husbands are in shock and profound depression. We want to help, but our hands are tied in so many ways. We have to distribute money to some people, and there are legal documents—these things can be done. We have interpreters, but we don't always have the human touch, or maybe the right human touch. We don't want to make mistakes, Mrs. Bhave, and that's why we'd like to ask you to help us."

"More mistakes, you mean," I say.

"Police matters are not in my hands," she answers.

"Nothing I can do will make any difference," I say. "We must all grieve in our own way."

"But you are coping very well. All the people said, Mrs. Bhave is the strongest person of all. Perhaps if the others could see you, talk with you, it would help them."

"By the standards of the people you call hysterical, I am behaving very oddly and very badly, Miss Templeton." I want to say to her, *I wish I could scream, starve, walk into Lake Ontario, jump from a bridge.* "They would not see me as a model. I do not see myself as a model."

I am a freak. No one who has ever known me would think of me reacting this way. This terrible calm will not go away.

She asks me if she may call again, after I get back from a long trip that we all must make. "Of course," I say. "Feel free to call, anytime."

Four days later, I find Kusum squatting on a rock overlooking a bay in Ireland. It isn't a big rock, but it juts sharply out over water. This is as close as we'll ever get to them. June breezes balloon out her sari and unpin her knee-length hair. She has the bewildered look of a sea creature whom the tides have stranded.

It's been one hundred hours since Kusum came stumbling and screaming across my lawn. Waiting around the hospital, we've heard many stories. The police, the diplomats, they tell us things thinking that we're strong, that knowledge is helpful to the grieving, and maybe it is. Some, I know, prefer ignorance, or their own versions. The plane broke into two, they say. Unconsciousness was instantaneous. No one suffered. My boys must have just finished their breakfasts. They loved eating on planes, they loved the smallness of plates, knives, and forks. Last year they saved the airline salt and pepper shakers. Half an hour more and they would have made it to Heathrow.

Kusum says that we can't escape our fate. She says that all those people—our husbands, my boys, her girl with the nightingale voice, all those Hindus, Christians, Sikhs, Muslims, Parsis, and atheists on that plane—were fated to die together off this beautiful bay. She learned this from a swami in Toronto.

I have my Valium.

Six of us "relatives"—two widows and four widowers—choose to spend the day today by the waters instead of sitting in a hospital room and scanning photographs of the dead. That's what they call us now: relatives. I've looked through twenty-seven photos in two days. They're very kind to us, the Irish are very understanding. Sometimes understanding means freeing a tourist bus for this trip to the bay, so we can pretend to spy our loved ones through the glassiness of waves or in sunspeckled cloud shapes.

I could die here, too, and be content.

"What is that, out there?" She's standing and flapping her hands and for a moment I see a head shape bobbing in the waves. She's standing in the water, I, on the boulder. The tide is low, and a round, black, headsized rock has just risen from the waves. She returns, her sari end dripping and ruined and her face is a twisted remnant of hope, the way mine was a hundred hours ago, still laughing but inwardly knowing that nothing but the ultimate tragedy could bring two women together at six o'clock on a Sunday morning. I watch her face sag into blankness.

"That water felt warm, Shaila," she says at length.

"You can't," I say. "We have to wait for our turn to come."

I haven't eaten in four days, haven't brushed my teeth.

"I know," she says. "I tell myself I have no right to grieve. They are in a better place than we are. My swami says I should be thrilled for them. My swami says depression is a sign of our selfishness."

Maybe I'm selfish. Selfishly I break away from Kusum and run, sandals slapping against stones, to the water's edge. What if my boys aren't lying pinned under the debris? What if they aren't stuck a mile below that innocent blue chop? What if, given the strong currents....

Now I've ruined my sari, one of my best. Kusum has joined me, knee-deep in water that feels to me like a swimming pool. I could settle in the water, and my husband would take my hand and the boys would slap water in my face just to see me scream.

"Do you remember what good swimmers my boys were, Kusum?"

"I saw the medals," she says.

One of the widowers, Dr. Ranganathan from Montreal, walks out to us, carrying his shoes in one hand. He's an electrical engineer. Someone at the hotel mentioned his work is famous around the world, something about the place where physics and electricity come together. He has lost a huge family, something indescribable. "With some luck," Dr. Ranganathan suggests to me, "a good swimmer could make it safely to some island. It is quite possible that there may be many, many microscopic islets scattered around."

"You're not just saying that?" I tell Dr. Ranganathan about Vinod, my elder son. Last year he took diving as well.

"It's a parent's duty to hope," he says. "It is foolish to rule out possibilities that have not been tested. I myself have not surrendered hope."

Kusum is sobbing once again. "Dear lady," he says, laying his free hand on her arm, and she calms down.

"Vinod is how old?" he asks me. He's very careful, as we all are. *Is,* not was.

"Fourteen. Yesterday he was fourteen. His father and uncle were going to take him down to the Taj and give him a big birthday party. I couldn't go with them because I couldn't get two weeks off from my stupid job in June." I process bills for a travel agent. June is a big travel month.

Dr. Ranganathan whips the pockets of his suit jacket inside out. Squashed roses, in darkening shades of pink, float on the water. He tore the roses off creepers in somebody's garden. He didn't ask anyone if he could pluck the roses, but now there's been an article about it in the local papers. When you see an Indian person, it says, please give him or her flowers.

"A strong youth of fourteen," he says, "can very likely pull to safety a younger one."

My sons, though four years apart, were very close. Vinod wouldn't let Mithun drown. *Electrical engineering,* I think, foolishly perhaps: this man knows important secrets of the universe, things closed to me. Relief spins me lightheaded. No wonder my boys' photographs haven't turned up in the gallery of photos of the recovered dead. "Such pretty roses," I say.

"My wife loved pink roses. Every Friday I had to bring a bunch home. I used to say, why? After twenty-odd years of marriage you're still needing proof positive of my love?" He has identified his wife and three of his children. Then others from Montreal, the lucky ones, intact families with no survivors. He chuckles as he wades back to shore. Then he swings around to ask me a question. "Mrs. Bhave, you are wanting to throw in some roses for your loved ones? I have two big ones left."

But I have other things to float: Vinod's pocket calculator; a half-painted model B-52 for my Mithun. They'd want them on their island. And for my husband? For him I let fall into the calm, glassy waters a poem I wrote in the hospital yesterday. Finally he'll know my feelings for him.

"Don't tumble, the rocks are slippery," Dr. Ranganathan cautions. He holds out a hand for me to grab.

Then it's time to get back on the bus, time to rush back to our waiting posts on hospital benches.

Kusum is one of the lucky ones. The lucky ones flew here, identified in multiplicate their loved ones, then will fly to India with the bodies for proper ceremonies. Satish is one of the few males who surfaced. The photos of faces we saw on the walls in an office at Heathrow and here in the hospital are mostly of women. Women have more body fat, a nun said to me matter-of-factly. They float better. Today I was stopped by a young sailor on the street. He had loaded bodies, he'd gone into the water when—he checks my face for signs of strength—when the sharks were first spotted. I don't blush, and he breaks down. "It's all right," I say. "Thank you." I had heard about the sharks from Dr. Ranganathan. In his orderly mind, science brings understanding, it holds no terror. It is the shark's duty. For every deer there is a hunter, for every fish a fisherman.

The Irish are not shy; they rush to me and give me hugs and some are crying. I cannot imagine reactions like that on the streets of Toronto. Just strangers, and I am touched. Some carry flowers with them and give them to any Indian they see.

After lunch, a policeman I have gotten to know quite well catches hold of me. He says he thinks he has a match for Vinod. I explain what a good swimmer Vinod is.

"You want me with you when you look at photos?" Dr. Ranganathan walks ahead of me into the picture gallery. In these matters, he is a scientist, and I am grateful. It is a new perspective. "They have performed miracles," he says. "We are indebted to them."

The first day or two the policemen showed us relatives only one picture at a time; now they're in a hurry, they're eager to lay out the possibles, and even the probables.

The face on the photo is of a boy much like Vinod; the same intelligent eyes, the same thick brows dipping into a V. But this boy's features, even his cheeks, are puffier, wider, mushier.

"No." My gaze is pulled by other pictures. There are five other boys who look like Vinod.

The nun assigned to console me rubs the first picture with a fingertip. "When they've been in the water for a while, love, they look a little heavier." The bones under the skin are broken, they said on the first day—try to adjust your memories. It's important.

"It's not him. I'm his mother. I'd know."

"I know this one!" Dr. Ranganathan cries out suddenly from the back of the gallery. "And this one!" I think he senses that I don't want to find my boys. "They are the Kutty brothers. They were also from Montreal." I don't mean to be crying. On the contrary, I am ecstatic. My suitcase in the hotel is packed heavy with dry clothes for my boys.

The policeman starts to cry. "I am so sorry, I am so sorry, ma'am. I really thought we had a match."

With the nun ahead of us and the policeman behind, we, the unlucky ones without our children's bodies, file out of the makeshift gallery.

From Ireland most of us go on to India. Kusum and I take the same direct flight to Bombay, so I can help her clear customs quickly. But we have to argue with a man in uniform. He has large boils on his face. The boils swell and glow with sweat as we argue with him. He wants Kusum to wait in line and he refuses to take authority because his boss is on a tea break. But Kusum won't let her coffins out of sight, and I shan't desert her though I know that my parents, elderly and diabetic, must be waiting in a stuffy car in a scorching lot.

"You bastard!" I scream at the man with the popping boils. Other passengers press closer. "You think we're smuggling contraband in those coffins!"

Once upon a time we were well brought up women; we were dutiful wives who kept our heads veiled, our voices shy and sweet.

In India, I become, once again, an only child of rich, ailing parents. Old friends of the family come to pay their respects. Some are Sikh, and inwardly, involuntarily, I cringe. My parents are progressive people; they do not blame communities for a few individuals.

In Canada it is a different story now.

"Stay longer," my mother pleads. "Canada is a cold place. Why would you want to be all by yourself?" I stay.

Three months pass. Then another.

"Vikram wouldn't have wanted you to give up things!" they protest. They call my husband by the name he was born with. In Toronto he'd changed to Vik so the men he worked with at his office would find his name as easy as Rod or Chris. "You know, the dead aren't cut off from us!"

My grandmother, the spoiled daughter of a rich *zamindar*,[5] shaved her head with rusty razor blades when she was widowed at sixteen. My grandfather died of childhood diabetes when he was nineteen, and she saw herself as the harbinger of bad luck. My mother grew up without parents, raised indifferently by an uncle, while her true mother slept in a hut behind the main estate house and took her food with the servants. She grew up a rationalist. My parents abhor mindless mortification.

---

5. Landowner.

The zamindar's daughter kept stubborn faith in Vedic rituals; my parents rebelled. I am trapped between two modes of knowledge. At thirty-six, I am too old to start over and too young to give up. Like my husband's spirit, I flutter between worlds.

Courting aphasia, we travel. We travel with our phalanx of servants and poor relatives. To hill stations and to beach resorts. We play contract bridge in dusty gymkhana clubs. We ride stubby ponies up crumbly mountain trails. At tea dances, we let ourselves be twirled twice round the ballroom. We hit the holy spots we hadn't made time for before. In Varanasi, Kalighat, Rishikesh, Hardwar, astrologers and palmists seek me out and for a fee offer me cosmic consolations.

Already the widowers among us are being shown new bride candidates. They cannot resist the call of custom, the authority of their parents and older brothers. They must marry; it is the duty of a man to look after a wife. The new wives will be young widows with children, destitute but of good family. They will make loving wives, but the men will shun them. I've had calls from the men over crackling Indian telephone lines. "Save me," they say, these substantial, educated, successful men of forty. "My parents are arranging a marriage for me." In a month they will have buried one family and returned to Canada with a new bride and partial family.

I am comparatively lucky. No one here thinks of arranging a husband for an unlucky widow.

Then, on the third day of the sixth month into this odyssey, in an abandoned temple in a tiny Himalayan village, as I make my offering of flowers and sweetmeats to the god of a tribe of animists, my husband descends to me. He is squatting next to a scrawny *sadhu*[6] in moth-eaten robes. Vikram wears the vanilla suit he wore the last time I hugged him. The *sadhu* tosses petals on a butter-fed flame, reciting Sanskrit mantras and sweeps his face of flies. My husband takes my hands in his.

*You're beautiful,* he starts. Then, *What are you doing here?*

*Shall I stay?* I ask. He only smiles, but already the image is fading. *You must finish alone what we started together.* No seaweed wreathes his mouth. He speaks too fast just as he used to when we were an envied family in our pink split-level. He is gone.

In the windowless altar room, smoky with joss sticks and clarified butter lamps, a sweaty hand gropes for my blouse. I do not shriek. The *sadhu* arranges his robe. The lamps hiss and sputter out.

When we come out of the temple, my mother says, "Did you feel something weird in there?"

My mother has no patience with ghosts, prophetic dreams, holy men, and cults.

"No," I lie. "Nothing."

But she knows that she's lost me. She knows that in days I shall be leaving.

Kusum's put her house up for sale. She wants to live in an ashram in Hardwar. Moving to Hardwar was her swami's idea. Her swami runs two ashrams, the one in Hardwar and another here in Toronto.

"Don't run away," I tell her.

---

6. Hindu holy man.

"I'm not running away," she says. "I'm pursuing inner peace. You think you or that Ranganathan fellow are better off?"

Pam's left for California. She wants to do some modelling, she says. She says when she comes into her share of the insurance money she'll open a yoga-cum-aerobics studio in Hollywood. She sends me postcards so naughty I daren't leave them on the coffee table. Her mother has withdrawn from her and the world.

The rest of us don't lose touch, that's the point. Talk is all we have, says Dr. Ranganathan, who has also resisted his relatives and returned to Montreal and to his job, alone. He says, whom better to talk with than other relatives? We've been melted down and recast as a new tribe.

He calls me twice a week from Montreal. Every Wednesday night and every Saturday afternoon. He is changing jobs, going to Ottawa. But Ottawa is over a hundred miles away, and he is forced to drive two hundred and twenty miles a day. He can't bring himself to sell his house. The house is a temple, he says; the king-sized bed in the master bedroom is a shrine. He sleeps on a folding cot. A devotee.

There are still some hysterical relatives. Judith Templeton's list of those needing help and those who've "accepted" is in nearly perfect balance. Acceptance means you speak of your family in the past tense and you make active plans for moving ahead with your life. There are courses at Seneca and Ryerson[7] we could be taking. Her gleaming leather briefcase is full of college catalogues and lists of cultural societies that need our help. She has done impressive work, I tell her.

"In the textbooks on grief management," she replies—I am her confidante, I realize, one of the few whose grief has not sprung bizarre obsessions—"there are stages to pass through: rejection, depression, acceptance, reconstruction." She has compiled a chart and finds that six months after the tragedy, none of us still reject reality, but only a handful are reconstructing. "Depressed Acceptance" is the plateau we've reached. Remarriage is a major step in reconstruction (though she's a little surprised, even shocked, over *how* quickly some of the men have taken on new families). Selling one's house and changing jobs and cities is healthy.

How do I tell Judith Templeton that my family surrounds me, and that like creatures in epics, they've changed shapes? She sees me as calm and accepting but worries that I have no job, no career. My closest friends are worse off than I. I cannot tell her my days, even my nights, are thrilling.

She asks me to help with families she can't reach at all. An elderly couple in Agincourt whose sons were killed just weeks after they had brought their parents over from a village in Punjab. From their names, I know they are Sikh. Judith Templeton and a translator have visited them twice with offers of money for air fare to Ireland, with bank forms, power-of-attorney forms, but they have refused to sign, or to leave their tiny apartment. Their sons' money is frozen in the bank. Their sons' investment apartments have been trashed by tenants, the furnishings sold off. The parents fear that anything they sign or any money they receive will end the company's or the country's obligations to them. They fear they are selling their sons for two airline tickets to a place they've never seen.

The high-rise apartment is a tower of Indians and West Indians, with a sprinkling of Orientals. The nearest bus stop kiosk is lined with women in saris. Boys

---

7. Seneca College of Applied Arts and Technology, in Willowdale; Ryerson Polytechnical Institute, Toronto.

practice cricket in the parking lot. Inside the building, even I wince a bit from the ferocity of onion fumes, the distinctive and immediate Indianness of frying *ghee*, but Judith Templeton maintains a steady flow of information. These poor old people are in imminent danger of losing their place and all their services.

I say to her, "They are Sikh. They will not open up to a Hindu woman." And what I want to add is, as much as I try not to, I stiffen now at the sight of beards and turbans. I remember a time when we all trusted each other in this new country, it was only the new country we worried about.

The two rooms are dark and stuffy. The lights are off, and an oil lamp sputters on the coffee table. The bent old lady has let us in, and her husband is wrapping a white turban over his oiled, hip-length hair. She immediately goes to the kitchen, and I hear the most familiar sound of an Indian home, tap water hitting and filling a teapot.

They have not paid their utility bills, out of fear and the inability to write a check. The telephone is gone; electricity and gas and water are soon to follow. They have told Judith their sons will provide. They are good boys, and they have always earned and looked after their parents.

We converse a bit in Hindi. They do not ask about the crash and I wonder if I should bring it up. If they think I am here merely as a translator, then they may feel insulted. There are thousands of Punjabi-speakers, Sikhs, in Toronto to do a better job. And so I say to the old lady, "I too have lost my sons, and my husband, in the crash."

Her eyes immediately fill with tears. The man mutters a few words which sound like a blessing. "God provides and God takes away," he says.

I want to say, but only men destroy and give back nothing. "My boys and my husband are not coming back," I say. "We have to understand that."

Now the old woman responds. "But who is to say? Man alone does not decide these things." To this her husband adds his agreement.

Judith asks about the bank papers, the release forms. With a stroke of the pen, they will have a provincial trustee to pay their bills, invest their money, send them a monthly pension.

"Do you know this woman?" I ask them.

The man raises his hand from the table, turns it over and seems to regard each finger separately before he answers. "This young lady is always coming here, we make tea for her and she leaves papers for us to sign." His eyes scan a pile of papers in the corner of the room. "Soon we will be out of tea, then will she go away?"

The old lady adds, "I have asked my neighbors and no one else gets *angrezi*[8] visitors. What have we done?"

"It's her job," I try to explain. "The government is worried. Soon you will have no place to stay, no lights, no gas, no water."

"Government will get its money. Tell her not to worry, we are honorable people."

I try to explain the government wishes to give money, not take. He raises his hand. "Let them take," he says. "We are accustomed to that. That is no problem."

"We are strong people," says the wife. "Tell her that."

"Who needs all this machinery?" demands the husband. "It is unhealthy, the

---

8. English, Anglo.

bright lights, the cold air on a hot day, the cold food, the four gas rings. God will provide, not government."

"When our boys return," the mother says. Her husband sucks his teeth. "Enough talk," he says.

Judith breaks in. "Have you convinced them?" The snaps on her cordovan briefcase go off like firecrackers in that quiet apartment. She lays the sheaf of legal papers on the coffee table. "If they can't write their names, an X will do—I've told them that."

Now the old lady has shuffled to the kitchen and soon emerges with a pot of tea and two cups. "I think my bladder will go first on a job like this," Judith says to me, smiling. "If only there was some way of reaching them. Please thank her for the tea. Tell her she's very kind."

I nod in Judith's direction and tell them in Hindi, "She thanks you for the tea. She thinks you are being very hospitable but she doesn't have the slightest idea what it means."

I want to say, humor her. I want to say, my boys and my husband are with me too, more than ever. I look in the old man's eyes and I can read his stubborn, peasant's message: *I have protected this woman as best I can. She is the only person I have left. Give to me or take from me what you will, but I will not sign for it. I will not pretend that I accept.*

In the car, Judith says, "You see what I'm up against? I'm sure they're lovely people, but their stubbornness and ignorance are driving me crazy. They think signing a paper is signing their sons' death warrants, don't they?"

I am looking out the window. I want to say, *In our culture, it is a parent's duty to hope.*

"Now Shaila, this next woman is a real mess. She cries day and night, and she refuses all medical help. We may have to—"

"—Let me out at the subway," I say.

"I beg your pardon?" I can feel those blue eyes staring at me.

It would not be like her to disobey. She merely disapproves, and slows at a corner to let me out. Her voice is plaintive. "Is there anything I said? Anything I did?"

I could answer her suddenly in a dozen ways, but I choose not to. "Shaila? Let's talk about it," I hear, then slam the door.

A wife and mother begins her new life in a new country, and that life is cut short. Yet her husband tells her: Complete what we have started. We, who stayed out of politics and came halfway around the world to avoid religious and political feuding have been the first in the New World to die from it. I no longer know what we started, nor how to complete it. I write letters to the editors of local papers and to members of Parliament. Now at least they admit it was a bomb. One MP answers back, with sympathy, but with a challenge. You want to make a difference? Work on a campaign. Work on mine. Politicize the Indian voter.

My husband's old lawyer helps me set up a trust. Vikram was a saver and a careful investor. He had saved the boys' boarding school and college fees. I sell the pink house at four times what we paid for it and take a small apartment downtown. I am looking for a charity to support.

We are deep in the Toronto winter, gray skies, icy pavements. I stay indoors, watching television. I have tried to assess my situation, how best to live my life, to complete what we began so many years ago. Kusum has written me from Hardwar that her life is now serene. She has seen Satish and has heard her daughter sing again. Kusum was on a pilgrimage, passing through a village when she heard a young girl's voice, singing one of her daughter's favorite *bhajans*. She followed the music through the squalor of a Himalayan village, to a hut where a young girl, an exact replica of her daughter, was fanning coals under the kitchen fire. When she appeared, the girl cried out, "Ma!" and ran away. What did I think of that?

I think I can only envy her.

Pam didn't make it to California, but writes me from Vancouver. She works in a department store, giving make-up hints to Indian and Oriental girls. Dr. Ranganathan has given up his commute, given up his house and job, and accepted an academic position in Texas where no one knows his story and he has vowed not to tell it. He calls me now once a week.

I wait, I listen, and I pray, but Vikram has not returned to me. The voices and the shapes and the nights filled with visions ended abruptly several weeks ago.

I take it as a sign.

One rare, beautiful, sunny day last week, returning from a small errand on Yonge Street, I was walking through the park from the subway to my apartment. I live equidistant from the Ontario Houses of Parliament and the University of Toronto. The day was not cold, but something in the bare trees caught my attention. I looked up from the gravel, into the branches and the clear blue sky beyond. I thought I heard the rustling of larger forms, and I waited a moment for voices. Nothing.

"What?" I asked.

Then as I stood in the path looking north to Queen's Park and west to the university, I heard the voices of my family one last time. *Your time has come,* they said. *Go, be brave.*

I do not know where this voyage I have begun will end. I do not know which direction I will take. I dropped the package on a park bench and started walking.

1988

## QUESTIONS

1. What words and images in the opening paragraphs of "The Management of Grief" provide the reader with clues to the story's underlying themes of cultural dislocation and the mixing of cultures?
2. Throughout the story Bharati Mukherjee pays close attention to the significance of words and the ways that words express, or fail to express, emotional truths. Find some examples of words and phrases that the narrator and other characters notice as having special significance. Can you think of words in one culture that defy translation into the language of another?
3. Air travel, of course, has greatly increased communication—and, sometimes, friction—between cultures. What is the thematic significance of this story's central event, a plane disaster?

## NADINE GORDIMER

### Good Climate, Friendly Inhabitants

In the office at the garage eight hours a day I wear mauve linen overalls—those snappy uniforms they make for girls who aren't really nurses. I'm forty-nine but I could be twenty-five except for my face and my legs. I've got that very fair skin and my legs have gone mottled, like Roquefort cheese. My hair used to look pretty as chickens' fluff, but now it's been bleached and permed too many times. I wouldn't admit this to anyone else, but to myself I admit everything. Perhaps I'll get one of those wigs everyone's wearing. You don't have to be short of hair, any more, to wear a wig.

I've been years at the garage—service station, as it's been called since it was rebuilt all steel and glass. That's at the front, where the petrol pumps are; you still can't go into the workshop without getting grease on your things. But I don't have much call to go there. Between doing the books you'll see me hanging about in front for a breath of air, smoking a cigarette and keeping an eye on the boys. Not the mechanics—they're all white chaps of course (bunch of ducktails they are, too, most of them)—but the petrol attendants.[1] One boy's been with the firm twenty-three years—sometimes you'd think he owns the place; gets my goat. On the whole they're not a bad lot of natives, though you get a cheeky bastard now and then, or a thief, but he doesn't last long, with us.

We're just off the Greensleeves suburban shopping centre with the terrace restaurant and the fountain, and you get a very nice class of person coming up and down. I'm quite friends with some of the people from the luxury flats round about; they wouldn't pass without a word to me when they're walking their dogs or going to the shops. And of course you get to know a lot of the regular petrol customers, too. We've got two Rolls and any amount of sports cars who never go anywhere else. And I only have to walk down the block to Maison Claude when I get my hair done, or in to Mr. Levine at the Greensleeves Pharmacy if I feel a cold coming on.

I've got a flat in one of the old buildings that are still left, back in town. Not too grand, but for ten quid[2] a month and right on the bus route . . . I was married once and I've got a lovely kid—married since she was seventeen and living in

---

1. The story takes place in 1964 in Johannesburg ("Jo'burg"), a large city in South Africa, under apartheid, a system of laws in effect between 1948 and 1991 that guaranteed white minority rule and disqualified black Africans from civil rights while forcing them to live in "townships," or "homelands." (Those of mixed or Asian descent were also deprived of some rights.) South Africa was a British colony from 1795, though descendants of Dutch settlers, the Boers, went to war (1899-1902) for independence in northern regions that eventually submitted to British rule in the Union of South Africa in 1910. In spite of a large minority of Afrikaans-speaking whites (of Dutch descent), South Africa remained culturally tied to Britain (and part of the Commonwealth of Nations from 1931 to 1961), as the British terms and spellings in this story indicate. The narrator accepts the official line that Africans ("natives") are inferior, childlike, and stupid, and that Europeans must unite in keeping them in their place. The "boys"—in fact, older African men—are given the lower-paying jobs as "petrol" (gas station) attendants, whereas the better-paid job of mechanic is reserved for "white chaps," in this case, young, rude "ducktails," or greasers.
2. A pound in British and South African currency.

Rhodesia;[3] I couldn't stop her. She's very happy with him and they've got twin boys, real little toughies! I've seen them once.

There's a woman friend I go to the early flicks with every Friday, and the Versfelds' where I have a standing invitation for Sunday lunch. I think they depend on me, poor old things; they never see anybody. That's the trouble when you work alone in an office, like I do, you don't make friends at your work. Nobody to talk to but those duckies in the workshop, and what can I have in common with a lot of louts in black leather jackets? No respect, either, you should hear the things they come out with. I'd sooner talk to the blacks, that's the truth, though I know it sounds a strange thing to say. At least they call you missus. Even old Madala knows he can't come into my office without taking his cap off, though heaven help you if you ask that boy to run up to the Greek for a packet of smokes, or round to the Swiss Confectionery. I had a dust-up with him once over it, the old monkey-face, but the manager didn't seem to want to get rid of him, he's been here so long. So he just keeps out of my way and he has his half-crown from me at Christmas, same as the other boys. But you get more sense out of the boss-boy, Jack, than you can out of some whites, believe me, and he can make you laugh, too, in his way—of course they're like children, you see them yelling with laughter over something in their own language, noisy lot of devils; I don't suppose we'd think it funny at all if we knew what it was all about. This Jack used to get a lot of phone calls (I complained to the manager on the quiet and he's put a stop to it, now) and the natives on the other end used to be asking to speak to Mpanza and Makiwane and I don't know what all, and when I'd say there wasn't anyone of that name working here they'd come out with it and ask for Jack. So I said to him one day, why do you people have a hundred and one names, why don't these uncles and aunts and brothers-in-law come out with your name straight away and stop wasting my time? He said, "Here I'm Jack because Mpanza Makiwane is not a name, and there I'm Mpanza Makiwane because Jack is not a name, but I'm the only one who knows who I am wherever I am." I couldn't help laughing. He hardly ever calls you missus, I notice, but it doesn't sound cheeky, the way he speaks. Before they were allowed to buy drink for themselves, he used to ask me to buy a bottle of brandy for him once a week and I didn't see any harm.

Even if things are not too bright, no use grumbling. I don't believe in getting old before my time. Now and then it's happened that some man's taken a fancy to me at the garage. Every time he comes to fill up he finds some excuse to talk to me; if a chap likes me, I begin to feel it just like I did when I was seventeen, so that even if he was just sitting in his car looking at me through the glass of the office, I would know that he was waiting for me to come out. Eventually he'd ask me to the hotel for a drink after work. Usually that was as far as it went. I don't know what happens to these blokes, they are married, I suppose, though their wives don't still wear a perfect size fourteen, like I do. They enjoy talking to another woman once in a while, but they quickly get nervous. They are busi-

---

3. Rhodesia, now Zimbabwe, a country on the northern border of South Africa, gained independence from Britain and political representation for the black majority in 1978-79. (Redistribution of the white-dominated farmlands is a continuing source of conflict.)

nessmen and well off; one sent me a present, but it was one of those old-fashioned compacts, we used to call them flapjacks, meant for loose powder, and I use the solid kind everyone uses now.

Of course you get some funny types, and, as I say, I'm alone there in the front most of the time, with only the boys, the manager is at head office in town, and the other white men are all at the back. Little while ago a fellow came into my office wanting to pay for his petrol with Rhodesian money. Well, Jack, the boss-boy, came first to tell me that this fellow had given him Rhodesian money. I sent back to say we didn't take it. I looked through the glass and saw a big, expensive American car, not very new, and one of those men you recognize at once as the kind who moves about a lot—he was poking out his cheek with his tongue, looking round the station and out into the busy street like, in his head, he was trying to work out his way around in a new town. Some people kick up hell with a native if he refuses them something, but this one didn't seem to; the next thing was he got the boy to bring him to me. "Boss says he must talk to you," Jack said, and turned on his heel. But I said, you wait here. I know Johannesburg; my cash-box was there in the open safe. The fellow was young. He had that very tanned skin that has been sunburnt day after day, the tan you see on lifesavers at the beach. His hair was the thick streaky blond kind, wasted on men. He says, "Miss, can't you help me out for half an hour?" Well, I'd had my hair done, it's true, but I don't kid myself you could think of me as a miss unless you saw my figure, from behind. He went on, "I've just driven down and I haven't had a chance to change my money. Just take this while I get hold of this chap I know and get him to cash a cheque for me."

I told him there was a bank up the road but he made some excuse. "I've got to tell my friend I'm in town anyway. Here, I'll leave this—it's a gold one." And he took the big fancy watch off his arm. "Go on, please, do me a favour." Somehow when he smiled he looked not so young, harder. The smile was on the side of his mouth. Anyway, I suddenly said okay, then, and the native boy turned and went out of the office, but I knew it was all right about my cash, and this fellow asked me which was the quickest way to get to Kensington and I came out from behind my desk and looked it up with him on the wall map. I thought he was a fellow of about twenty-nine or thirty; he was so lean, with a snakeskin belt around his hips and a clean white open-neck shirt.

He was back on the dot. I took the money for the petrol and said, here's your watch, pushing it across the counter. I'd seen, the moment he'd gone and I'd picked up the watch to put it in the safe, that it wasn't gold: one of those Jap fakes that men take out of their pockets and try to sell you on streetcorners. But I didn't say anything, because maybe he'd been had? I gave him the benefit of the doubt. What'd it matter? He'd paid for his petrol, anyway. He thanked me and said he supposed he'd better push off and find some hotel. I said the usual sort of thing, was he here on a visit and so on, and he said, yes, he didn't know how long, perhaps a couple of weeks, it all depended, and he'd like somewhere central. We had quite a little chat—you know how it is, you always feel friendly if you've done someone a favour and it's all worked out okay—and I mentioned a couple of hotels. But it's difficult if you don't know what sort of place a person wants, you may send him somewhere too expensive, or on the other hand you might recommend one of the small places that he'd consider just a joint, such as the New Park, near where I live.

A few days later I'd been down to the shops at lunch hour and when I came by where some of the boys were squatting over their lunch in the sun, Jack said, "That man came again." Thinks I can read his mind; what man, I said, but they never learn. "The other day, with the money that was no good." Oh, you mean the Rhodesian, I said. Jack didn't answer but went on tearing chunks of bread out of half a loaf and stuffing them into his mouth. One of the other boys began telling, in their own language with bits of English thrown in, what I could guess was the story of how the man had tried to pay with money that was no good; big joke, you know; but Jack didn't take any notice, I suppose he'd heard it once too often.

I went into my office to fetch a smoke, and when I was enjoying it outside in the sun Jack came over to the tap near me. I heard him drinking from his hand, and then he said, "He went and looked in the office window." Didn't he buy petrol? I said. "He pulled up at the pump but then he didn't buy, he said he will come back later." Well, that's all right, what're you getting excited about, we sell people as much petrol as they like, I said. I felt uncomfortable, I don't know why; you'd think I'd been giving away petrol at the garage's expense or something.

"You can't come from Rhodesia on those tyres," Jack said. No? I said. "Did you look at those tyres?" Why should *I* look at tyres? "No-no, you look at those tyres on that old car. You can't drive six hundred miles or so on those tyres. Worn out! Down to the tread!" But who cares where he came from, I said, it's his business. "But he had that money," Jack said to me. He shrugged and I shrugged; I went back into my office. As I say, sometimes you find yourself talking to that boy as if he was a white person.

Just before five that same afternoon the fellow came back. I don't know how it was, I happened to look up like I knew the car was going to be there. He was taking petrol and paying for it, this time; old Madala was serving him. I don't know what got into me, curiosity maybe, but I got up and came to my door and said, how's Jo'burg treating you? "Ah, hell, I've had bad luck," he says. "The place I was staying had another booking for my room from today. I was supposed to go to my friend in Berea, but now his wife's brother has come. I don't mind paying for a decent place, but you take one look at some of them . . . Don't you know somewhere?" Well yes, I said, I was telling you that day. And I mentioned the Victoria, but he said he'd tried there, so then I told him about the New Park, near me. He listened, but looking round all the time, his mind was somewhere else. He said, "They'll tell me they're full, it'll be the same story." I told him that Mrs. Douglas who runs the place is a nice woman—she would be sure to fix him up. "You couldn't ask her?" he said. I said well, all right, from my place she was only round the corner, I'd pop in on my way home from work and tell her he'd be getting in touch with her.

When he heard that he said he'd give me a lift in his car, and so I took him to Mrs. Douglas myself, and she gave him a room. As we walked out of the hotel together he seemed wrapped up in his own affairs again, but on the pavement he suddenly suggested a drink. I thought he meant we'd go into the hotel lounge, but he said, "I've got a bottle of gin in the car," and he brought it up to my place. He was telling me about the time he was in the Congo a few years ago, fighting for that native chief, what's-name—Tshombe—against the Irishmen who were sent out there to put old what's-name down. The stories he told about

Elisabethville![4] He was paid so much he could live like a king. We only had two gins each out the bottle, but when I wanted him to take it along with him, he said, "I'll come in for it sometime when I get a chance." He didn't say anything, but I got the idea he had come up to Jo'burg about a job.

15   I was frying a slice of liver next evening when he turned up at the door. The bottle was still standing where it'd been left. You feel uncomfortable when the place's full of the smell of frying and anyone can tell you're about to eat. I gave him the bottle but he didn't take it; he said he was on his way to Vereeniging to see someone, he would just have a quick drink. I had to offer him something to eat, with me. He was one of those people who eat without noticing what it is. He never took in the flat, either; I mean he didn't look round at my things the way it's natural you do in someone else's home. And there was a lovely photo of my kid on the built-in fixture round the electric fire. I said to him while we were eating, is it a job you've come down for? He smiled the way youngsters smile at an older person who won't understand, anyway. "On business." But you could see that he was not a man who had an office, who wore a suit and sat in a chair. He was like one of those men you see in films, you know, the stranger in town who doesn't look as if he lives anywhere. Somebody in a film, thin and burned red as a brick and not saying much. I mean he did talk but it was never really anything about himself, only about things he'd seen happen. He never asked me anything about myself, either. It was queer; because of this, after I'd seen him a few times, it was just the same as if we were people who know each other so well they don't talk about themselves any more.

Another funny thing was, all the time he was coming in and out the flat, I was talking about him with the boy—with Jack. I don't believe in discussing white people with natives, as a rule, I mean, whatever I think of a white, it encourages disrespect if you talk about it to a black. I've never said anything in front of the boys about the behaviour of that crowd of ducktails in the workshop, for instance. And of course I wouldn't be likely to discuss my private life with a native boy. Jack didn't know that this fellow was coming to the flat, but he'd heard me say I'd fix up about the New Park Hotel, and he'd seen me take a lift home that afternoon. The boy's remark about the tyres seemed to stick in my mind; I said to him: That man came all the way from the Congo.

"In that car?" Jack said; he's got such a serious face, for a native. The car goes all right, I said, he's driving all over with it now.

"Why doesn't he bring it in for retreads?"

I said he was just on holiday, he wouldn't have it done here.

20   The fellow didn't appear for five or six days and I thought he'd moved on, or made friends, as people do in this town. There was still about two fingers left in his bottle. I don't drink when I'm on my own. Then he turned up at the garage just at the time I knock off. Again I meant to look at the tyres for myself, but I

---

4. The rich regions of the Congo have changed hands and names many times. Moise-Kapenda Tshombe (1919–1969), a well-educated Methodist teacher as well as a member of tribal royalty, led a movement in Katanga, a southern region just above Zambia, to secede from the newly formed Republic of the Congo in 1960; European and South African mercenaries fought on both sides. Tshombe became president of Katanga in 1960; after defeat and exile, he became prime minister of the united Democratic Republic of Congo in 1964. (From 1971, the country was named Zaire, but it has now returned to the name it held in 1964.) Elisabethville, now Lubumbashi, is on the southern border of Katanga.

forgot. He took me home just like it had been an arranged thing; you know, a grown-up son calling for his mother not because he wants to, but because he has to. We hardly spoke in the car. I went out for pies, which wasn't much of a dinner to offer anyone, but, as I say, he didn't know what he was eating, and he didn't want the gin, he had some cans of beer in the car. He leaned his chair back with all the weight on two legs and said, "I think I must clear out of this lousy dump, I don't know what you've got to be to get along here with these sharks." I said, you kids give up too easy, have you still not landed a job? "A job!" he said. "They owe me *money*, I'm trying to get *money* out of them." What's it all about, I said, what money? He didn't take any notice, as if I wouldn't understand. "Smart alecks and swindlers. I been here nearly three lousy weeks, now." I said, everybody who comes here find Jo'burg tough compared with their home.

He'd had his head tipped back and he lifted it straight and looked at me. "I'm not such a kid." No? I said, feeling a bit awkward because he never talked about himself before. He was looking at me all the time, you'd have thought he was going to find his age written on my face. "I'm thirty-seven," he said. "Did you know that? Thirty-seven. Not so much younger."

Forty-nine. It was true, not so much. But he looked so young, with that hair always slicked back longish behind the ears as if he'd just come out of the shower, and that brown neck in the open-neck shirt. Lean men wear well, you can't tell. He did have false teeth, though, that was why his mouth made him look hard. I supposed he could have been thirty-seven; I didn't know, I didn't know.

It was like the scars on his body. There were scars on his back and other scars on his stomach, and my heart was in my mouth for him when I saw them, still pink and raw-looking, but he said that the ones on his back were from strokes he'd had in a boys' home as a kid and the others were from the fighting in Katanga.

I know nobody would believe me, they would think I was just trying to make excuses for myself, but in the morning everything seemed just the same, I didn't feel I knew him any better. It was just like it was that first day when he came in with his Rhodesian money. He said, "Leave me the key. I might as well use the place while you're out all day." But what about the hotel, I said. "I've taken my things," he says. I said, you mean you've moved out? And something in his face, the bored sort of look, made me ask, you've told Mrs. Douglas? "She's found out by now," he said, it was unusual for him to smile. You mean you went without paying? I said. "Look, I told you I can't get my money out of those bastards."

Well, what could I do? I'd taken him to Mrs. Douglas myself. The woman'd given him a room on my recommendation. I had to go over to the New Park and spin her some yarn about him having to leave suddenly and that he'd left the money for me to pay. What else could I do? Of course I didn't tell *him*.

But I told Jack. That's the funny thing about it. I told Jack that the man had disappeared, run off without paying my friend who ran the hotel where he was staying. The boy clicked his tongue the way they do, and laughed. And I said that was what you got for trying to help people. Yes, he said, Johannesburg was full of people like that, but you learn to know their faces, even if they were nice faces.

I said, you think that man had a nice face?

"You see he has a nice face," the boy said.

I was afraid I'd find the fellow there when I got home, and he was there. I said to him, that's my daughter, and showed him the photo, but he took no interest, not even when I said she lived in Gwelo and perhaps he knew the town himself. I said why didn't he go back to Rhodesia to his job but he said Central Africa was finished, he wasn't going to be pushed around by a lot of blacks running the show—from what he told me, it's awful, you can't keep them out of hotels or anything.[5]

Later on he went out to get some smokes and I suddenly thought, I'll lock the door and I won't let him into the flat again. I had made up my mind to do it. But when I saw his shadow on the other side of the frosty glass I just got up and opened it, and I felt like a fool, what was there to be afraid of? He was such a clean, good-looking fellow standing there; and anybody can be down on his luck. I sometimes wonder what'll happen to me—in some years, of course—if I can't work any more and I'm alone here, and nobody comes. Every Sunday you read in the paper about women dead alone in flats, no one discovers it for days.

He smoked night and day, like the world had some bad smell that he had to keep out of his nose. He was smoking in the bed at the weekend and I made a remark about Princess Margaret when she was here as a kid in 1947—I was looking at a story about the Royal Family, in the Sunday paper. He said he supposed he'd seen her, it was the year he went to the boys' home and they were taken to watch the procession.[6]

One of the few things he'd told me about himself was that he was eight when he was sent to the home; I lay there and worked out that if he was thirty-seven, he should have been twenty in 1947, not eight years old.

But by then I found it hard to believe that he was only twenty-five. You could always get rid of a boy of twenty-five. He wouldn't have the strength inside to make you afraid to try it.

I'd've felt safer if someone had known about him and me but of course I couldn't talk to anyone. Imagine the Versfelds. Or the woman I go out with on Fridays, I don't think she's had a cup of tea with a man since her husband died! I remarked to Jack, the boss-boy, how old did he think the man had been, the one with the Rhodesian money who cheated the hotel? He said, "He's still here?" I said no, no, I just wondered. "He's young, that one," he said, but I should have remembered that half the time natives don't know their own age, it doesn't matter to them the way it does to us. I said to him, wha'd'you call young? He jerked his head back at the workshop. "Same like the mechanics." That bunch of kids! But this fellow wasn't cocky like them, wrestling with each other all over the place, calling after girls, fancying themselves the Beatles when they sing in the washroom. The people he used to go off to see about things—I never saw any of them. If he had friends, they never came round. If only *somebody* else had known he was in the flat!

5. Gwelo is in the center of Zimbabwe (then Rhodesia), approximately five hundred miles from Johannesburg; the distance and bad roads help explain why the narrator would have seen her twin grandsons only once, and why Jack doubts that the treadless tires would have carried the visitor all the way from Rhodesia or the Congo. The young white man complains that "Central Africa" allows more freedom to Africans; indeed, in 1963 African-majority governments won elections in regions of Rhodesia, and in 1964 Northern Rhodesia gained independence as Zambia.
6. England's Princess Margaret (1930–2002), daughter of George VI and sister of the future Queen Elizabeth II (crowned 1953), visited South Africa with her parents and sister in April 1947.

Then he said he was having the car overhauled because he was going off to Durban. He said he had to leave the next Saturday. So I felt much better; I also felt bad, in a way, because there I'd been, thinking I'd have to find some way to make him go. He put his hand on my waist, in the daylight, and smiled right out at me and said, "Sorry; got to push on and get moving sometime, you know," and it was true that in a way he was right, I couldn't think what it'd be like without him, though I was always afraid he would stay. Oh he was nice to me then, I can tell you; he could be nice if he wanted to, it was like a trick that he could do, so real you couldn't believe it when it stopped just like that. I told him he should've brought the car into our place, I'd've seen to it that they did a proper job on it, but no, a friend of his was doing it free, in his own workshop.

Saturday came, he didn't go. The car wasn't ready. He sat about most of the week, disappeared for a night, but was there again in the morning. I'd given him a couple of quid to keep him going. I said to him, what are you mucking about with that car in somebody's back yard for? Take it to a decent garage. Then—I'll never forget it—cool as anything, a bit irritated, he said, "Forget it. I haven't got the car any more." I said, wha'd'you mean, you mean you've sold it?—I suppose because in the back of my mind I'd been thinking, why doesn't he sell it, he needs money. And he said, "That's right. It's sold," but I knew he was lying, he couldn't be bothered to think of anything else to say. Once he'd said the car was sold, he said he was waiting for the money; he did pay me back three quid, but he borrowed again a day or so later. He'd keep his back to me when I came into the flat and he wouldn't answer when I spoke to him; and then just when he turned on me with that closed, half-asleep face and I'd think, this is it, now this is it—I can't explain how finished, done-for I felt, I only know that he had on his face exactly the same look I remember on the face of a man, once, who was drowning some kittens one after the other in a bucket of water—just as I knew it was coming, he would burst out laughing at me. It was the only time he laughed. He would laugh until, nearly crying, I would begin to laugh too. And we would pretend it was kidding, and he would be nice to me, oh, he would be nice to me.

I used to sit in my office at the garage and look round at the car adverts and the maps on the wall and my elephant ear[7] growing in the oil drum and that was the only place I felt: but this is nonsense, what's got into me? The flat, and him in it—they didn't seem real. Then I'd go home at five and there it would all be.

I said to Jack, what's a '59 Chrysler worth? He took his time, he was cleaning his hands on some cotton waste. He said, "With those tyres, nobody will pay much."

Just to show him that he mustn't get too free with a white person, I asked him to send up to Mr Levine for a headache powder for me. I joked, I'm getting a bit like old Madala there, I feel so tired today.

D'you know what that boy said to me then? They've got more feeling than whites sometimes, that's the truth. He said, "When my children grow up they must work for me. Why don't you live there in Rhodesia with your daughter? The child must look after the mother. Why must you stay here alone in this town?"

---

7. A garden plant with particularly large leaves.

Of course I wasn't going to explain to him that I like my independence. I always say I hope when I get old I die before I become a burden on anybody. But that afternoon I did something I should've done long ago, I said to the boy, if ever I don't turn up to work, you must tell them in the workshop to send someone to my flat to look for me. And I wrote down the address. Days could go by before anyone'd find what had become of me; it's not right.

When I got home that same evening, the fellow wasn't there. He'd gone. Not a word, not a note; nothing. Every time I heard the lift[8] rattling I thought, here he is. But he didn't come. When I was home on Saturday afternoon I couldn't stand it any longer and I went up to the Versfelds and asked the old lady if I couldn't sleep there a few days, I said my flat was being painted and the smell turned my stomach. I thought, if he comes to the garage, there are people around, at least there are the boys. I was smoking nearly as much as *he* used to and I couldn't sleep. I had to ask Mr Levine to give me something. The slightest sound and I was in a cold sweat. At the end of the week I had to go back to the flat, and I bought a chain for the door and made a heavy curtain so's you couldn't see anyone standing there. I didn't go out, once I'd got in from work—not even to the early flicks—so I wouldn't have to come back into the building at night. You know how it is when you're nervous, the funniest things comfort you: I'd just tell myself, well, if I shouldn't turn up to work in the morning, the boy'd send someone to see.

Then slowly I was beginning to forget about it. I kept the curtain and the chain and I stayed at home, but when you get used to something, no matter what it is, you don't think about it all the time, any more, though you still believe you do. I hadn't been to Maison Claude for about two weeks and my hair was a sight. Claude advised a soft perm and so it happened that I took a couple of hours off in the afternoon to get it done. The boss-boy Jack says to me when I come back, "He was here."

I didn't know what to do, I couldn't help staring quickly all round. When, I said. "Now-now, while you were out." I had the feeling I couldn't get away. I knew he would come up to me with that closed, half-asleep face—burned as a good-looker lifesaver, burned like one of those tramps who are starving and lousy and pickled with cheap booze but have a horrible healthy look that comes from having nowhere to go out of the sun. I don't know what that boy must have thought of me, my face. He said, "I told him you're gone. You don't work here any more. You went to Rhodesia to your daughter. I don't know which place." And he put his nose back in one of the newspapers he's always reading whenever things are slack; I think he fancies himself quite the educated man and he likes to read about all these blacks who are becoming prime ministers and so on in other countries these days. I never remark on it; if you take any notice of things like that with them, you begin to give them big ideas about themselves.

45  That fellow's never bothered me again. I never breathed a word to anybody about it—as I say, that's the trouble when you work alone in an office like I do, there's no one you can speak to. It just shows you, a woman on her own has always got to look out; it's not only that it's not safe to walk about alone at night because of the natives, this whole town is full of people you can't trust.

1965

---

8. Elevator.

## QUESTIONS

1. What are some clues that the narrator of "Good Climate, Friendly Inhabitants" is much less observant and insightful than the story's author?
2. What does the reader come to understand about the narrator that the narrator fails to understand about herself?
3. How does this irony help to support the story's themes of self-delusion and cultural misreading?

## JHUMPA LAHIRI
### Interpreter of Maladies

At the tea stall Mr. and Mrs. Das bickered about who should take Tina to the toilet. Eventually Mrs. Das relented when Mr. Das pointed out that he had given the girl her bath the night before. In the rearview mirror Mr. Kapasi watched as Mrs. Das emerged slowly from his bulky white Ambassador, dragging her shaved, largely bare legs across the back seat. She did not hold the little girl's hand as they walked to the rest room.

They were on their way to see the Sun Temple at Konarak.[1] It was a dry, bright Saturday, the mid-July heat tempered by a steady ocean breeze, ideal weather for sightseeing. Ordinarily Mr. Kapasi would not have stopped so soon along the way, but less than five minutes after he'd picked up the family that morning in front of Hotel Sandy Villa, the little girl had complained. The first thing Mr. Kapasi had noticed when he saw Mr. and Mrs. Das, standing with their children under the portico of the hotel, was that they were very young, perhaps not even thirty. In addition to Tina they had two boys, Ronny and Bobby, who appeared very close in age and had teeth covered in a network of flashing silver wires. The family looked Indian but dressed as foreigners did, the children in stiff, brightly colored clothing and caps with translucent visors. Mr. Kapasi was accustomed to foreign tourists; he was assigned to them regularly because he could speak English. Yesterday he had driven an elderly couple from Scotland, both with spotted faces and fluffy white hair so thin it exposed their sunburnt scalps. In comparison, the tanned, youthful faces of Mr. and Mrs. Das were all the more striking. When he'd introduced himself, Mr. Kapasi had pressed his palms together in greeting, but Mr. Das squeezed hands like an American so that Mr. Kapasi felt it in his elbow. Mrs. Das, for her part, had flexed one side of her mouth, smiling dutifully at Mr. Kapasi, without displaying any interest in him.

As they waited at the tea stall, Ronny, who looked like the older of the two boys, clambered suddenly out of the back seat, intrigued by a goat tied to a stake in the ground.

"Don't touch it," Mr. Das said. He glanced up from his paperback tour book, which said "INDIA" in yellow letters and looked as if it had been published

---

1. In paragraphs 91–98, the story provides an accurate history and description of the Sun Temple at Konark (or Konarak), still a pilgrimage as well as tourist site near the east coast in the Orissa region of India. According to legend, the temple was built because Samba, son of Lord Krishna, was cured of leprosy by Surya, the sun god.

abroad. His voice, somehow tentative and a little shrill, sounded as though it had not yet settled into maturity.

"I want to give it a piece of gum," the boy called back as he trotted ahead.

Mr. Das stepped out of the car and stretched his legs by squatting briefly to the ground. A clean-shaven man, he looked exactly like a magnified version of Ronny. He had a sapphire blue visor, and was dressed in shorts, sneakers, and a T-shirt. The camera slung around his neck, with an impressive telephoto lens and numerous buttons and markings, was the only complicated thing he wore. He frowned, watching as Ronny rushed toward the goat, but appeared to have no intention of intervening. "Bobby, make sure that your brother doesn't do anything stupid."

"I don't feel like it," Bobby said, not moving. He was sitting in the front seat beside Mr. Kapasi, studying a picture of the elephant god taped to the glove compartment.

"No need to worry," Mr. Kapasi said. "They are quite tame." Mr. Kapasi was forty-six years old, with receding hair that had gone completely silver, but his butterscotch complexion and his unlined brow, which he treated in spare moments to dabs of lotus-oil balm, made it easy to imagine what he must have looked like at an earlier age. He wore gray trousers and a matching jacket-style shirt, tapered at the waist, with short sleeves and a large pointed collar, made of a thin but durable synthetic material. He had specified both the cut and the fabric to his tailor—it was his preferred uniform for giving tours because it did not get crushed during his long hours behind the wheel. Through the windshield he watched as Ronny circled around the goat, touched it quickly on its side, then trotted back to the car.

"You left India as a child?" Mr. Kapasi asked when Mr. Das had settled once again into the passenger seat.

"Oh, Mina and I were both born in America," Mr. Das announced with an air of sudden confidence. "Born and raised. Our parents live here now, in Assansol.[2] They retired. We visit them every couple years." He turned to watch as the little girl ran toward the car, the wide purple bows of her sundress flopping on her narrow brown shoulders. She was holding to her chest a doll with yellow hair that looked as if it had been chopped, as a punitive measure, with a pair of dull scissors. "This is Tina's first trip to India, isn't it, Tina?"

"I don't have to go to the bathroom anymore," Tina announced.

"Where's Mina?" Mr. Das asked.

Mr. Kapasi found it strange that Mr. Das should refer to his wife by her first name when speaking to the little girl. Tina pointed to where Mrs. Das was purchasing something from one of the shirtless men who worked at the tea stall. Mr. Kapasi heard one of the shirtless men sing a phrase from a popular Hindi love song as Mrs. Das walked back to the car, but she did not appear to understand the words of the song, for she did not express irritation, or embarrassment, or react in any other way to the man's declarations.

He observed her. She wore a red-and-white-checkered skirt that stopped above her knees, slip-on shoes with a square wooden heel, and a close-fitting blouse

---

2. Or Asonsol, a city in northeastern India, not far from Calcutta and about three hundred miles from Puri, the coastal city in Orissa that the Das family is visiting. Puri is both a tourist resort and a Hindu holy city, said to be dominated by the forces of both the gods and humanity.

styled like a man's undershirt. The blouse was decorated at chest-level with a calico appliqué in the shape of a strawberry. She was a short woman, with small hands like paws, her frosty pink fingernails painted to match her lips, and was slightly plump in her figure. Her hair, shorn only a little longer than her husband's, was parted far to one side. She was wearing large dark brown sunglasses with a pinkish tint to them, and carried a big straw bag, almost as big as her torso, shaped like a bowl, with a water bottle poking out of it. She walked slowly, carrying some puffed rice tossed with peanuts and chili peppers in a large packet made from newspapers. Mr. Kapasi turned to Mr. Das.

"Where in America do you live?"

"New Brunswick, New Jersey."

"Next to New York?"

"Exactly. I teach middle school there."

"What subject?"

"Science. In fact, every year I take my students on a trip to the Museum of Natural History in New York City. In a way we have a lot in common, you could say, you and I. How long have you been a tour guide, Mr. Kapasi?"

"Five years."

Mrs. Das reached the car. "How long's the trip?" she asked, shutting the door.

"About two and a half hours," Mr. Kapasi replied.

At this Mrs. Das gave an impatient sigh, as if she had been traveling her whole life without pause. She fanned herself with a folded Bombay film magazine written in English.

"I thought that the Sun Temple is only eighteen miles north of Puri," Mr. Das said, tapping on the tour book.

"The roads to Konarak are poor. Actually it is a distance of fifty-two miles," Mr. Kapasi explained.

Mr. Das nodded, readjusting the camera strap where it had begun to chafe the back of his neck.

Before starting the ignition, Mr. Kapasi reached back to make sure the crank-like locks on the inside of each of the back doors were secured. As soon as the car began to move the little girl began to play with the lock on her side, clicking it with some effort forward and backward, but Mrs. Das said nothing to stop her. She sat a bit slouched at one end of the back seat, not offering her puffed rice to anyone. Ronny and Tina sat on either side of her, both snapping bright green gum.

"Look," Bobby said as the car began to gather speed. He pointed with his finger to the tall trees that lined the road. "Look."

"Monkeys!" Ronny shrieked. "Wow!"

They were seated in groups along the branches, with shining black faces, silver bodies, horizontal eyebrows, and crested heads. Their long gray tails dangled like a series of ropes among the leaves. A few scratched themselves with black leathery hands, or swung their feet, staring as the car passed.

"We call them the hanuman," Mr. Kapasi said. "They are quite common in the area."

As soon as he spoke, one of the monkeys leaped into the middle of the road, causing Mr. Kapasi to brake suddenly. Another bounced onto the hood of the car, then sprang away. Mr. Kapasi beeped his horn. The children began to get excited, sucking in their breath and covering their faces partly with their hands.

They had never seen monkeys outside of a zoo, Mr. Das explained. He asked Mr. Kapasi to stop the car so that he could take a picture.

While Mr. Das adjusted his telephoto lens, Mrs. Das reached into her straw bag and pulled out a bottle of colorless nail polish, which she proceeded to stroke on the tip of her index finger.

The little girl stuck out a hand. "Mine too. Mommy, do mine too."

"Leave me alone," Mrs. Das said, blowing on her nail and turning her body slightly. "You're making me mess up."

The little girl occupied herself by buttoning and unbuttoning a pinafore on the doll's plastic body.

"All set," Mr. Das said, replacing the lens cap.

The car rattled considerably as it raced along the dusty road, causing them all to pop up from their seats every now and then, but Mrs. Das continued to polish her nails. Mr. Kapasi eased up on the accelerator, hoping to produce a smoother ride. When he reached for the gearshift the boy in front accommodated him by swinging his hairless knees out of the way. Mr. Kapasi noted that this boy was slightly paler than the other children. "Daddy, why is the driver sitting on the wrong side in this car, too?" the boy asked.

"They all do that here, dummy," Ronny said.

"Don't call your brother a dummy," Mr. Das said. He turned to Mr. Kapasi. "In America, you know . . . it confuses them."

"Oh yes, I am well aware," Mr. Kapasi said. As delicately as he could, he shifted gears again, accelerating as they approached a hill in the road. "I see it on *Dallas*, the steering wheels are on the left-hand side."

"What's *Dallas*?" Tina asked, banging her now naked doll on the seat behind Mr. Kapasi.

"It went off the air," Mr. Das explained. "It's a television show."[3]

They were all like siblings, Mr. Kapasi thought as they passed a row of date trees. Mr. and Mrs. Das behaved like an older brother and sister, not parents. It seemed that they were in charge of the children only for the day; it was hard to believe they were regularly responsible for anything other than themselves. Mr. Das tapped on his lens cap, and his tour book, dragging his thumbnail occasionally across the pages so that they made a scraping sound. Mrs. Das continued to polish her nails. She had still not removed her sunglasses. Every now and then Tina renewed her plea that she wanted her nails done, too, and so at one point Mrs. Das flicked a drop of polish on the little girl's finger before depositing the bottle back inside her straw bag.

"Isn't this an air-conditioned car?" she asked, still blowing on her hand. The window on Tina's side was broken and could not be rolled down.

"Quit complaining," Mr. Das said. "It isn't so hot."

"I told you to get a car with air-conditioning," Mrs. Das continued. "Why do you do this, Raj, just to save a few stupid rupees. What are you saving us, fifty cents?"

Their accents sounded just like the ones Mr. Kapasi heard on American television programs, though not like the ones on *Dallas*.

"Doesn't it get tiresome, Mr. Kapasi, showing people the same thing every

---

3. Reruns of this American television show (1978–91) featuring the rich, dysfunctional Ewing family of Dallas continue worldwide.

day?" Mr. Das asked, rolling down his own window all the way. "Hey, do you mind stopping the car. I just want to get a shot of this guy."

Mr. Kapasi pulled over to the side of the road as Mr. Das took a picture of a barefoot man, his head wrapped in a dirty turban, seated on top of a cart of grain sacks pulled by a pair of bullocks. Both the man and the bullocks were emaciated. In the back seat Mrs. Das gazed out another window, at the sky, where nearly transparent clouds passed quickly in front of one another.

"I look forward to it, actually," Mr. Kapasi said as they continued on their way. "The Sun Temple is one of my favorite places. In that way it is a reward for me. I give tours on Fridays and Saturdays only. I have another job during the week."

"Oh? Where?" Mr. Das asked.

"I work in a doctor's office."

"You're a doctor?"

"I am not a doctor. I work with one. As an interpreter."

"What does a doctor need an interpreter for?"

"He has a number of Gujarati patients. My father was Gujarati, but many people do not speak Gujarati in this area,[4] including the doctor. And so the doctor asked me to work in his office, interpreting what the patients say."

"Interesting. I've never heard of anything like that," Mr. Das said.

Mr. Kapasi shrugged. "It is a job like any other."

"But so romantic," Mrs. Das said dreamily, breaking her extended silence. She lifted her pinkish brown sunglasses and arranged them on top of her head like a tiara. For the first time, her eyes met Mr. Kapasi's in the rearview mirror: pale, a bit small, their gaze fixed but drowsy.

Mr. Das craned to look at her. "What's so romantic about it?"

"I don't know. Something." She shrugged, knitting her brows together for an instant. "Would you like a piece of gum, Mr. Kapasi?" she asked brightly. She reached into her straw bag and handed him a small square wrapped in green-and-white-striped paper. As soon as Mr. Kapasi put the gum in his mouth a thick sweet liquid burst onto his tongue.

"Tell us more about your job, Mr. Kapasi," Mrs. Das said.

"What would you like to know, madame?"

"I don't know," she shrugged, munching on some puffed rice and licking the mustard oil from the corners of her mouth. "Tell us a typical situation." She settled back in her seat, her head tilted in a patch of sun, and closed her eyes. "I want to picture what happens."

"Very well. The other day a man came in with a pain in his throat."

"Did he smoke cigarettes?"

"No. It was very curious. He complained that he felt as if there were long pieces of straw stuck in his throat. When I told the doctor he was able to prescribe the proper medication."

"That's so neat."

"Yes," Mr. Kapasi agreed after some hesitation.

"So these patients are totally dependent on you," Mrs. Das said. She spoke

---

4. Gujarat is a northwestern region of India, on the Arabian Sea. Mr. Kapasi speaks several of India's disparate regional languages—those of Bengal and Orissa, near where he lives, and Gujarati, from the opposite coast—along with the more widespread Hindi and English.

slowly, as if she were thinking aloud. "In a way, more dependent on you than the doctor."

"How do you mean? How could it be?"

"Well, for example, you could tell the doctor that the pain felt like a burning, not straw. The patient would never know what you had told the doctor, and the doctor wouldn't know that you had told the wrong thing. It's a big responsibility."

"Yes, a big responsibility you have there, Mr. Kapasi," Mr. Das agreed.

Mr. Kapasi had never thought of his job in such complimentary terms. To him it was a thankless occupation. He found nothing noble in interpreting people's maladies, assiduously translating the symptoms of so many swollen bones, countless cramps of bellies and bowels, spots on people's palms that changed color, shape, or size. The doctor, nearly half his age, had an affinity for bell-bottom trousers and made humorless jokes about the Congress party.[5] Together they worked in a stale little infirmary where Mr. Kapasi's smartly tailored clothes clung to him in the heat, in spite of the blackened blades of a ceiling fan churning over their heads.

The job was a sign of his failings. In his youth he'd been a devoted scholar of foreign languages, the owner of an impressive collection of dictionaries. He had dreamed of being an interpreter for diplomats and dignitaries, resolving conflicts between people and nations, settling disputes of which he alone could understand both sides. He was a self-educated man. In a series of notebooks, in the evenings before his parents settled his marriage, he had listed the common etymologies of words, and at one point in his life he was confident that he could converse, if given the opportunity, in English, French, Russian, Portuguese, and Italian, not to mention Hindi, Bengali, Orissi, and Gujarati. Now only a handful of European phrases remained in his memory, scattered words for things like saucers and chairs. English was the only non-Indian language he spoke fluently anymore. Mr. Kapasi knew it was not a remarkable talent. Sometimes he feared that his children knew better English than he did, just from watching television. Still, it came in handy for the tours.

He had taken the job as an interpreter after his first son, at the age of seven, contracted typhoid—that was how he had first made the acquaintance of the doctor. At the time Mr. Kapasi had been teaching English in a grammar school, and he bartered his skills as an interpreter to pay the increasingly exorbitant medical bills. In the end the boy had died one evening in his mother's arms, his limbs burning with fever, but then there was the funeral to pay for, and the other children who were born soon enough, and the newer, bigger house, and the good schools and tutors, and the fine shoes and the television, and the countless other ways he tried to console his wife and to keep her from crying in her sleep, and so when the doctor offered to pay him twice as much as he earned at the grammar school, he accepted. Mr. Kapasi knew that his wife had little regard for his career as an interpreter. He knew it reminded her of the son she'd lost, and that she resented the other lives he helped, in his own small way, to save. If ever she

---

5. The Indian National Congress party, founded in 1885, led the movement for independence from Britain (gained in 1947) through the successive leadership of Mohandas Gandhi and Jawaharlal Nehru. The party divided and subdivided, but a faction once led by Indira Gandhi dominated through the 1980s and much of the '90s, despite being constantly accused of corruption and of using violent tactics.

referred to his position, she used the phrase "doctor's assistant," as if the process of interpretation were equal to taking someone's temperature, or changing a bedpan. She never asked him about the patients who came to the doctor's office, or said that his job was a big responsibility.

For this reason it flattered Mr. Kapasi that Mrs. Das was so intrigued by his job. Unlike his wife, she had reminded him of its intellectual challenges. She had also used the word "romantic." She did not behave in a romantic way toward her husband, and yet she had used the word to describe him. He wondered if Mr. and Mrs. Das were a bad match, just as he and his wife were. Perhaps they, too, had little in common apart from three children and a decade of their lives. The signs he recognized from his own marriage were there—the bickering, the indifference, the protracted silences. Her sudden interest in him, an interest she did not express in either her husband or her children, was mildly intoxicating. When Mr. Kapasi thought once again about how she had said "romantic," the feeling of intoxication grew.

He began to check his reflection in the rearview mirror as he drove, feeling grateful that he had chosen the gray suit that morning and not the brown one, which tended to sag a little in the knees. From time to time he glanced through the mirror at Mrs. Das. In addition to glancing at her face he glanced at the strawberry between her breasts, and the golden brown hollow in her throat. He decided to tell Mrs. Das about another patient, and another: the young woman who had complained of a sensation of raindrops in her spine, the gentleman whose birthmark had begun to sprout hairs. Mrs. Das listened attentively, stroking her hair with a small plastic brush that resembled an oval bed of nails, asking more questions, for yet another example. The children were quiet, intent on spotting more monkeys in the trees, and Mr. Das was absorbed by his tour book, so it seemed like a private conversation between Mr. Kapasi and Mrs. Das. In this manner the next half hour passed, and when they stopped for lunch at a roadside restaurant that sold fritters and omelette sandwiches, usually something Mr. Kapasi looked forward to on his tours so that he could sit in peace and enjoy some hot tea, he was disappointed. As the Das family settled together under a magenta umbrella fringed with white and orange tassels, and placed their orders with one of the waiters who marched about in tricornered caps, Mr. Kapasi reluctantly headed toward a neighboring table.

"Mr. Kapasi, wait. There's room here," Mrs. Das called out. She gathered Tina onto her lap, insisting that he accompany them. And so, together, they had bottled mango juice and sandwiches and plates of onions and potatoes deep-fried in graham-flour batter. After finishing two omelette sandwiches Mr. Das took more pictures of the group as they ate.

"How much longer?" he asked Mr. Kapasi as he paused to load a new roll of film in the camera.

"About half an hour more."

By now the children had gotten up from the table to look at more monkeys perched in a nearby tree, so there was a considerable space between Mrs. Das and Mr. Kapasi. Mr. Das placed the camera to his face and squeezed one eye shut, his tongue exposed at one corner of his mouth. "This looks funny. Mina, you need to lean in closer to Mr. Kapasi."

She did. He could smell a scent on her skin, like a mixture of whiskey and rosewater. He worried suddenly that she could smell his perspiration, which he knew had collected beneath the synthetic material of his shirt. He polished off his mango juice in one gulp and smoothed his silver hair with his hands. A bit of the juice dripped onto his chin. He wondered if Mrs. Das had noticed.

She had not. "What's your address, Mr. Kapasi?" she inquired, fishing for something inside her straw bag.

"You would like my address?"

"So we can send you copies," she said. "Of the pictures." She handed him a scrap of paper which she had hastily ripped from a page of her film magazine. The blank portion was limited, for the narrow strip was crowded by lines of text and a tiny picture of a hero and heroine embracing under a eucalyptus tree.

The paper curled as Mr. Kapasi wrote his address in clear, careful letters. She would write to him, asking about his days interpreting at the doctor's office, and he would respond eloquently, choosing only the most entertaining anecdotes, ones that would make her laugh out loud as she read them in her house in New Jersey. In time she would reveal the disappointment of her marriage, and he his. In this way their friendship would grow, and flourish. He would possess a picture of the two of them, eating fried onions under a magenta umbrella, which he would keep, he decided, safely tucked between the pages of his Russian grammar. As his mind raced, Mr. Kapasi experienced a mild and pleasant shock. It was similar to a feeling he used to experience long ago when, after months of translating with the aid of a dictionary, he would finally read a passage from a French novel, or an Italian sonnet, and understand the words, one after another, unencumbered by his own efforts. In those moments Mr. Kapasi used to believe that all was right with the world, that all struggles were rewarded, that all of life's mistakes made sense in the end. The promise that he would hear from Mrs. Das now filled him with the same belief.

When he finished writing his address Mr. Kapasi handed her the paper, but as soon as he did so he worried that he had either misspelled his name, or accidentally reversed the numbers of his postal code. He dreaded the possibility of a lost letter, the photograph never reaching him, hovering somewhere in Orissa, close but ultimately unattainable. He thought of asking for the slip of paper again, just to make sure he had written his address accurately, but Mrs. Das had already dropped it into the jumble of her bag.

They reached Konarak at two-thirty. The temple, made of sandstone, was a massive pyramid-like structure in the shape of a chariot. It was dedicated to the great master of life, the sun, which struck three sides of the edifice as it made its journey each day across the sky. Twenty-four giant wheels were carved on the north and south sides of the plinth. The whole thing was drawn by a team of seven horses, speeding as if through the heavens. As they approached, Mr. Kapasi explained that the temple had been built between A.D. 1243 and 1255, with the efforts of twelve hundred artisans, by the great ruler of the Ganga dynasty, King Narasimhadeva the First, to commemorate his victory against the Muslim army.

"It says the temple occupies about a hundred and seventy acres of land," Mr. Das said, reading from his book.

"It's like a desert," Ronny said, his eyes wandering across the sand that stretched on all sides beyond the temple.

"The Chandrabhaga River once flowed one mile north of here. It is dry now," Mr. Kapasi said, turning off the engine.

They got out and walked toward the temple, posing first for pictures by the pair of lions that flanked the steps. Mr. Kapasi led them next to one of the wheels of the chariot, higher than any human being, nine feet in diameter.

"'The wheels are supposed to symbolize the wheel of life,'" Mr. Das read. "'They depict the cycle of creation, preservation, and achievement of realization.' Cool." He turned the page of his book. "'Each wheel is divided into eight thick and thin spokes, dividing the day into eight equal parts. The rims are carved with designs of birds and animals, whereas the medallions in the spokes are carved with women in luxurious poses, largely erotic in nature.'"

What he referred to were the countless friezes of entwined naked bodies, making love in various positions, women clinging to the necks of men, their knees wrapped eternally around their lovers' thighs. In addition to these were assorted scenes from daily life, of hunting and trading, of deer being killed with bows and arrows and marching warriors holding swords in their hands.

It was no longer possible to enter the temple, for it had filled with rubble years ago, but they admired the exterior, as did all the tourists Mr. Kapasi brought there, slowly strolling along each of its sides. Mr. Das trailed behind, taking pictures. The children ran ahead, pointing to figures of naked people, intrigued in particular by the Nagamithunas, the half-human, half-serpentine couples who were said, Mr. Kapasi told them, to live in the deepest waters of the sea. Mr. Kapasi was pleased that they liked the temple, pleased especially that it appealed to Mrs. Das. She stopped every three or four paces, staring silently at the carved lovers, and the processions of elephants, and the topless female musicians beating on two-sided drums.

Though Mr. Kapasi had been to the temple countless times, it occurred to him, as he, too, gazed at the topless women, that he had never seen his own wife fully naked. Even when they had made love she kept the panels of her blouse hooked together, the string of her petticoat knotted around her waist. He had never admired the backs of his wife's legs the way he now admired those of Mrs. Das, walking as if for his benefit alone. He had, of course, seen plenty of bare limbs before, belonging to the American and European ladies who took his tours. But Mrs. Das was different. Unlike the other women, who had an interest only in the temple, and kept their noses buried in a guidebook, on their eyes behind the lens of a camera, Mrs. Das had taken an interest in him.

Mr. Kapasi was anxious to be alone with her, to continue their private conversation, yet he felt nervous to walk at her side. She was lost behind her sunglasses, ignoring her husband's requests that she pose for another picture, walking past her children as if they were strangers. Worried that he might disturb her, Mr. Kapasi walked ahead, to admire, as he always did, the three life-sized bronze avatars of Surya, the sun god, each emerging from its own niche on the temple facade to greet the sun at dawn, noon, and evening. They wore elaborate headdresses, their languid, elongated eyes closed, their bare chests draped with carved chains and amulets. Hibiscus petals, offerings from previous visitors, were strewn at their gray-green feet. The last statue, on the northern wall of the temple, was Mr. Kapasi's favorite. This Surya had a tired expression, weary after a hard day of work, sitting astride a horse with folded legs. Even his horse's eyes were drowsy. Around his body were smaller sculptures of women in pairs, their hips thrust to one side.

"Who's that?" Mrs. Das asked. He was startled to see that she was standing beside him.

"He is the Astachala-Surya," Mr. Kapasi said. "The setting sun."

"So in a couple of hours the sun will set right here?" She slipped a foot out of one of her square-heeled shoes, rubbed her toes on the back of her other leg.

"That is correct."

She raised her sunglasses for a moment, then put them back on again. "Neat."

Mr. Kapasi was not certain exactly what the word suggested, but he had a feeling it was a favorable response. He hoped that Mrs. Das had understood Surya's beauty, his power. Perhaps they would discuss it further in their letters. He would explain things to her, things about India, and she would explain things to him about America. In its own way this correspondence would fulfill his dream, of serving as an interpreter between nations. He looked at her straw bag, delighted that his address lay nestled among its contents. When he pictured her so many thousands of miles away he plummeted, so much so that he had an overwhelming urge to wrap his arms around her, to freeze with her, even for an instant, in an embrace witnessed by his favorite Surya. But Mrs. Das had already started walking.

"When do you return to America?" he asked, trying to sound placid.

"In ten days."

He calculated: A week to settle in, a week to develop the pictures, a few days to compose her letter, two weeks to get to India by air. According to his schedule, allowing room for delays, he would hear from Mrs. Das in approximately six weeks' time.

The family was silent as Mr. Kapasi drove them back, a little past four-thirty, to Hotel Sandy Villa. The children had bought miniature granite versions of the chariot's wheels at a souvenir stand, and they turned them round in their hands. Mr. Das continued to read his book. Mrs. Das untangled Tina's hair with her brush and divided it into two little ponytails.

Mr. Kapasi was beginning to dread the thought of dropping them off. He was not prepared to begin his six-week wait to hear from Mrs. Das. As he stole glances at her in the rearview mirror, wrapping elastic bands around Tina's hair, he wondered how he might make the tour last a little longer. Ordinarily he sped back to Puri using a shortcut, eager to return home, scrub his feet and hands with sandalwood soap, and enjoy the evening newspaper and a cup of tea that his wife would serve him in silence. The thought of that silence, something to which he'd long been resigned, now oppressed him. It was then that he suggested visiting the hills at Udayagiri and Khandagiri, where a number of monastic dwellings were hewn out of the ground, facing one another across a defile. It was some miles away, but well worth seeing, Mr. Kapasi told them.

"Oh yeah, there's something mentioned about it in this book," Mr. Das said. "Built by a Jain king or something."[6]

"Shall we go then?" Mr. Kapasi asked. He paused at a turn in the road. "It's to the left."

Mr. Das turned to look at Mrs. Das. Both of them shrugged.

"Left, left," the children chanted.

Mr. Kapasi turned the wheel, almost delirious with relief. He did not know

---

6. This site is not a major tourist attraction; "giri" means mountain. Jainism, one of the several main religions of India, is an atheist sect that emerged from Hinduism around 580 B.C.E., at about the same time as Buddhism.

what he would do or say to Mrs. Das once they arrived at the hills. Perhaps he would tell her what a pleasing smile she had. Perhaps he would compliment her strawberry shirt, which he found irresistibly becoming. Perhaps, when Mr. Das was busy taking a picture, he would take her hand.

He did not have to worry. When they got to the hills, divided by a steep path thick with trees, Mrs. Das refused to get out of the car. All along the path, dozens of monkeys were seated on stones, as well as on the branches of the trees. Their hind legs were stretched out in front and raised to shoulder level, their arms resting on their knees.

"My legs are tired," she said, sinking low in her seat. "I'll stay here."

"Why did you have to wear those stupid shoes?" Mr. Das said. "You won't be in the pictures."

"Pretend I'm there."

"But we could use one of these pictures for our Christmas card this year. We didn't get one of all five of us at the Sun Temple. Mr. Kapasi could take it."

"I'm not coming. Anyway, those monkeys give me the creeps."

"But they're harmless," Mr. Das said. He turned to Mr. Kapasi. "Aren't they?"

"They are more hungry than dangerous," Mr. Kapasi said. "Do not provoke them with food, and they will not bother you."

Mr. Das headed up the defile with the children, the boys at his side, the little girl on his shoulders. Mr. Kapasi watched as they crossed paths with a Japanese man and woman, the only other tourists there, who paused for a final photograph, then stepped into a nearby car and drove away. As the car disappeared out of view some of the monkeys called out, emitting soft whooping sounds, and then walked on their flat black hands and feet up the path. At one point a group of them formed a little ring around Mr. Das and the children. Tina screamed in delight. Ronny ran in circles around his father. Bobby bent down and picked up a fat stick on the ground. When he extended it, one of the monkeys approached him and snatched it, then briefly beat the ground.

"I'll join them," Mr. Kapasi said, unlocking the door on his side. "There is much to explain about the caves."

"No. Stay a minute," Mrs. Das said. She got out of the back seat and slipped in beside Mr. Kapasi. "Raj has his dumb book anyway." Together, through the windshield, Mrs. Das and Mr. Kapasi watched as Bobby and the monkey passed the stick back and forth between them.

"A brave little boy," Mr. Kapasi commented.

"It's not so surprising," Mrs. Das said.

"No?"

"He's not his."

"I beg your pardon?"

"Raj's. He's not Raj's son."

Mr. Kapasi felt a prickle on his skin. He reached into his shirt pocket for the small tin of lotus-oil balm he carried with him at all times, and applied it to three spots on his forehead. He knew that Mrs. Das was watching him, but he did not turn to face her. Instead he watched as the figures of Mr. Das and the children grew smaller, climbing up the steep path, pausing every now and then for a picture, surrounded by a growing number of monkeys.

"Are you surprised?" The way she put it made him choose his words with care.

"It's not the type of thing one assumes," Mr. Kapasi replied slowly. He put the tin of lotus-oil balm back in his pocket.

"No, of course not. And no one knows, of course. No one at all. I've kept it a secret for eight whole years." She looked at Mr. Kapasi, tilting her chin as if to gain a fresh perspective. "But now I've told you."

Mr. Kapasi nodded. He felt suddenly parched, and his forehead was warm and slightly numb from the balm. He considered asking Mrs. Das for a sip of water, then decided against it.

"We met when we were very young," she said. She reached into her straw bag in search of something, then pulled out a packet of puffed rice. "Want some?"

"No, thank you."

She put a fistful in her mouth, sank into the seat a little, and looked away from Mr. Kapasi, out the window on her side of the car. "We married when we were still in college. We were in high school when he proposed. We went to the same college, of course. Back then we couldn't stand the thought of being separated, not for a day, not for a minute. Our parents were best friends who lived in the same town. My entire life I saw him every weekend, either at our house or theirs. We were sent upstairs to play together while our parents joked about our marriage. Imagine! They never caught us at anything, though in a way I think it was all more or less a setup. The things we did those Friday and Saturday nights, while our parents sat downstairs drinking tea . . . I could tell you stories, Mr. Kapasi."

As a result of spending all her time in college with Raj, she continued, she did not make many close friends. There was no one to confide in about him at the end of a difficult day, or to share a passing thought or a worry. Her parents now lived on the other side of the world, but she had never been very close to them, anyway. After marrying so young she was overwhelmed by it all, having a child so quickly, and nursing, and warming up bottles of milk and testing their temperature against her wrist while Raj was at work, dressed in sweaters and corduroy pants, teaching his students about rocks and dinosaurs. Raj never looked cross or harried, or plump as she had become after the first baby.

Always tired, she declined invitations from her one or two college girlfriends, to have lunch or shop in Manhattan. Eventually the friends stopped calling her, so that she was left at home all day with the baby, surrounded by toys that made her trip when she walked or wince when she sat, always cross and tired. Only occasionally did they go out after Ronny was born, and even more rarely did they entertain. Raj didn't mind; he looked forward to coming home from teaching and watching television and bouncing Ronny on his knee. She had been outraged when Raj told her that a Punjabi friend,[7] someone whom she had once met but did not remember, would be staying with them for a week for some job interviews in the New Brunswick area.

Bobby was conceived in the afternoon, on a sofa littered with rubber teething toys, after the friend learned that a London pharmaceutical company had hired him, while Ronny cried to be freed from his playpen. She made no protest when the friend touched the small of her back as she was about to make a pot of coffee, then pulled her against his crisp navy suit. He made love to her swiftly, in silence, with an expertise she had never known, without the meaningful expres-

---

7. A person from the Punjab, a northern region of India, near Pakistan.

sions and smiles Raj always insisted on afterward. The next day Raj drove the friend to JFK.[8] He was married now, to a Punjabi girl, and they lived in London still, and every year they exchanged Christmas cards with Raj and Mina, each couple tucking photos of their families into the envelopes. He did not know that he was Bobby's father. He never would.

"I beg your pardon, Mrs. Das, but why have you told me this information?" Mr. Kapasi asked when she had finally finished speaking, and had turned to face him once again.

"For God's sake, stop calling me Mrs. Das. I'm twenty-eight. You probably have children my age."

"Not quite." It disturbed Mr. Kapasi to learn that she thought of him as a parent. The feeling he had had toward her, that had made him check his reflection in the rearview mirror as they drove, evaporated a little.

"I told you because of your talents." She put the packet of puffed rice back into her bag without folding over the top.

"I don't understand," Mr. Kapasi said.

"Don't you see? For eight years I haven't been able to express this to anybody, not to friends, certainly not to Raj. He doesn't even suspect it. He thinks I'm still in love with him. Well, don't you have anything to say?"

"About what?"

"About what I've just told you. About my secret, and about how terrible it makes me feel. I feel terrible looking at my children, and at Raj, always terrible. I have terrible urges, Mr. Kapasi, to throw things away. One day I had the urge to throw everything I own out of the window, the television, the children, everything. Don't you think it's unhealthy?"

He was silent.

"Mr. Kapasi, don't you have anything to say? I thought that was your job."

"My job is to give tours, Mrs. Das."

"Not that. Your other job. As an interpreter."

"But we do not face a language barrier. What need is there for an interpreter?"

"That's not what I mean. I would never have told you otherwise. Don't you realize what it means for me to tell you?"

"What does it mean?"

"It means that I'm tired of feeling so terrible all the time. Eight years, Mr. Kapasi, I've been in pain eight years. I was hoping you could help me feel better, say the right thing. Suggest some kind of remedy."

He looked at her, in her red plaid skirt and strawberry T-shirt, a woman not yet thirty, who loved neither her husband nor her children, who had already fallen out of love with life. Her confession depressed him, depressed him all the more when he thought of Mr. Das at the top of the path, Tina clinging to his shoulders, taking pictures of ancient monastic cells cut into the hills to show his students in America, unsuspecting and unaware that one of his sons was not his own. Mr. Kapasi felt insulted that Mrs. Das should ask him to interpret her common, trivial little secret. She did not resemble the patients in the doctor's office, those who came glassy-eyed and desperate, unable to sleep or breathe or urinate with ease, unable, above all, to give words to their pains. Still, Mr. Kapasi believed it was his duty to assist Mrs. Das. Perhaps he ought to tell her to confess

---

8. John F. Kennedy International Airport, in New York City.

the truth to Mr. Das. He would explain that honesty was the best policy. Honesty, surely, would help her feel better, as she'd put it. Perhaps he would offer to preside over the discussion, as a mediator. He decided to begin with the most obvious question, to get to the heart of the matter, and so he asked, "Is it really pain you feel, Mrs. Das, or is it guilt?"

She turned to him and glared, mustard oil thick on her frosty pink lips. She opened her mouth to say something, but as she glared at Mr. Kapasi some certain knowledge seemed to pass before her eyes, and she stopped. It crushed him; he knew at that moment that he was not even important enough to be properly insulted. She opened the car door and began walking up the path, wobbling a little on her square wooden heels, reaching into her straw bag to eat handfuls of puffed rice. It fell through her fingers, leaving a zigzagging trail, causing a monkey to leap down from a tree and devour the little white grains. In search of more, the monkey began to follow Mrs. Das. Others joined him, so that she was soon being followed by about half a dozen of them, their velvety tails dragging behind.

Mr. Kapasi stepped out of the car. He wanted to holler, to alert her in some way, but he worried that if she knew they were behind her, she would grow nervous. Perhaps she would lose her balance. Perhaps they would pull at her bag or her hair. He began to jog up the path, taking a fallen branch in his hand to scare away the monkeys. Mrs. Das continued walking, oblivious, trailing grains of puffed rice. Near the top of the incline, before a group of cells fronted by a row of squat stone pillars, Mr. Das was kneeling on the ground, focusing the lens of his camera. The children stood under the arcade, now hiding, now emerging from view.

"Wait for me," Mrs. Das called out. "I'm coming."

165 Tina jumped up and down. "Here comes Mommy!"

"Great," Mr. Das said without looking up. "Just in time. We'll get Mr. Kapasi to take a picture of the five of us."

Mr. Kapasi quickened his pace, waving his branch so that the monkeys scampered away, distracted, in another direction.

"Where's Bobby?" Mrs. Das asked when she stopped.

Mr. Das looked up from the camera. "I don't know. Ronny, where's Bobby?"

170 Ronny shrugged. "I thought he was right here."

"Where is he?" Mrs. Das repeated sharply. "What's wrong with all of you?"

They began calling his name, wandering up and down the path a bit. Because they were calling, they did not initially hear the boy's screams. When they found him, a little farther down the path under a tree, he was surrounded by a group of monkeys, over a dozen of them, pulling at his T-shirt with their long black fingers. The puffed rice Mrs. Das had spilled was scattered at his feet, raked over by the monkeys' hands. The boy was silent, his body frozen, swift tears running down his startled face. His bare legs were dusty and red with welts from where one of the monkeys struck him repeatedly with the stick he had given to it earlier.

"Daddy, the monkey's hurting Bobby," Tina said.

Mr. Das wiped his palms on the front of his shorts. In his nervousness he accidentally pressed the shutter on his camera; the whirring noise of the advancing film excited the monkeys, and the one with the stick began to beat Bobby more intently. "What are we supposed to do? What if they start attacking?"

175 "Mr. Kapasi," Mrs. Das shrieked, noticing him standing to one side. "Do something, for God's sake, do something!"

Mr. Kapasi took his branch and shooed them away, hissing at the ones that remained, stomping his feet to scare them. The animals retreated slowly, with a measured gait, obedient but unintimidated. Mr. Kapasi gathered Bobby in his arms and brought him back to where his parents and siblings were standing. As he carried him he was tempted to whisper a secret into the boy's ear. But Bobby was stunned, and shivering with fright, his legs bleeding slightly where the stick had broken the skin. When Mr. Kapasi delivered him to his parents, Mr. Das brushed some dirt off the boy's T-shirt and put the visor on him the right way. Mrs. Das reached into her straw bag to find a bandage which she taped over the cut on his knee. Ronny offered his brother a fresh piece of gum. "He's fine. Just a little scared, right, Bobby?" Mr. Das said, patting the top of his head.

"God, let's get out of here," Mrs. Das said. She folded her arms across the strawberry on her chest. "This place gives me the creeps."

"Yeah. Back to the hotel, definitely," Mr. Das agreed.

"Poor Bobby," Mrs. Das said. "Come here a second. Let Mommy fix your hair." Again she reached into her straw bag, this time for her hairbrush, and began to run it around the edges of the translucent visor. When she whipped out the hairbrush, the slip of paper with Mr. Kapasi's address on it fluttered away in the wind. No one but Mr. Kapasi noticed. He watched as it rose, carried higher and higher by the breeze, into the trees where the monkeys now sat, solemnly observing the scene below. Mr. Kapasi observed it too, knowing that this was the picture of the Das family he would preserve forever in his mind.

1999

## QUESTIONS

1. For centuries philosophers have argued whether "nature" or "nurture" is the main shaping principal in our lives. In "Interpreter of Maladies," what details make the Indian-American Das family seem more "naturally" Indian or more "nurtured" by their American upbringing?
2. How might his encounter with the Das family alter Mr. Kapasi's sense of what it means to be Indian? Why is it important that this encounter has as its background a visit to ancient Indian religious shrines?
3. What is the thematic significance of the secret that Mrs. Das reveals to Mr. Kapasi? What is its relationship to the rest of the story and aspects of human behavior that transcend culture and upbringing?

## SUGGESTIONS FOR WRITING

1. In any one story in this chapter, find five words that have special thematic significance, and write an essay discussing the way each relates to the story as a whole.
2. Sometimes the theme in a work of literature can be expressed as a strong, clear statement: "A always follows from B," or "An X can never be a Y." More often, though, especially in modern literature, authors offer subtler, often ambiguous themes that deliberately undermine our faith in simple absolutes: "A doesn't necessarily always follow B," or "There are times when an X can be a Y." Write an essay in which you argue that one of the four stories in this chapter has an "always" or "never" kind of theme, and contrast it to the more indeterminate theme in one of the other three stories.

3. Write an essay comparing and contrasting the ways that two or more of the authors in this chapter develop the themes of their stories.
4. The great twentieth-century painter Pablo Picasso once said, "One does a whole painting for one peach and people think just the opposite—that that particular peach is but a detail." Is a work of art "about" the details of its surface, or "about" its underlying themes? Write an essay exploring the relationship between details and theme in one or more of the stories in this chapter.
5. Write two versions of a poem or short story. In the first version, be explicit, even obvious, about your theme. In the second, employ any strategies you wish for veiling the theme as much as possible. Then write a brief essay discussing which version is more successful, and why.
6. Choose a story from any other chapter of this book and write an essay exploring its theme.

# 7 THE WHOLE TEXT

Plot, point of view, character, setting, symbol, and theme are useful concepts. But they do not really exist as discrete parts of a finished work. Analyzing a story means thinking about issues smaller than the whole story—focusing on certain particulars before trying to consider the story as a whole. Our analysis may be enhanced by discussing a story in terms of its "elements," but we must remember both the arbitrariness of those distinctions and the integrity of the story as a whole. As you read the stories that follow in this chapter, apply all that you have learned about the history, the structure, and the elements of fiction, but be especially alert to how the various elements interact. Notice how, after taking a story apart in order to analyze it, we can put it back together.

> *For the fiction writer ... the whole story is the meaning, because it is an experience, not an abstraction.*
> —FLANNERY O'CONNOR

## JOSEPH CONRAD

### The Secret Sharer

I

On my right hand there were lines of fishing-stakes resembling a mysterious system of half-submerged bamboo fences, incomprehensible in its division of the domain of tropical fishes, and crazy[1] of aspect as if abandoned for ever by some nomad tribe of fishermen now gone to the other end of the ocean; for there was no sign of human habitation as far as the eye could reach. To the left a group of barren islets, suggesting ruins of stone walls, towers, and blockhouses, had its foundations set in a blue sea that itself looked solid, so still and stable did it lie below my feet; even the track of light from the westering sun shone smoothly, without that animated glitter which tells of an imperceptible ripple. And when I turned my head to take a parting glance at the tug which had just left us anchored outside the bar, I saw the straight line of the flat shore joined to the stable sea, edge to edge, with a perfect and unmarked closeness, in one leveled floor half brown, half blue under the enormous dome of the sky. Corresponding in their insignificance to the islets of the sea, two small clumps of trees, one on each side of the only fault in the impeccable joint, marked the mouth of the

1. Irregular, rickety.

river Meinam[2] we had just left on the first preparatory stage of our homeward journey; and, far back on the inland level, a larger and loftier mass, the grove surrounding the great Paknam pagoda, was the only thing on which the eye could rest from the vain task of exploring the monotonous sweep of the horizon. Here and there gleams as of a few scattered pieces of silver marked the windings of the great river; and on the nearest of them, just within the bar, the tug steaming right into the land became lost to my sight, hull and funnel and masts, as though the impassive earth had swallowed her up without an effort, without a tremor. My eye followed the light cloud of her smoke, now here, now there, above the plain, according to the devious curves of the stream, but always fainter and farther away, till I lost it at last behind the mitre-shaped hill of the great pagoda. And then I was left alone with my ship, anchored at the head of the Gulf of Siam.

She floated at the starting-point of a long journey, very still in an immense stillness, the shadows of her spars flung far to the eastward by the setting sun. At that moment I was alone on her decks. There was not a sound in her—and around us nothing moved, nothing lived, not a canoe on the water, not a bird in the air, not a cloud in the sky. In this breathless pause at the threshold of a long passage we seemed to be measuring our fitness for a long and arduous enterprise, the appointed task of both our existences to be carried out, far from all human eyes, with only sky and sea for spectators and for judges.

There must have been some glare in the air to interfere with one's sight, because it was only just before the sun left us that my roaming eyes made out beyond the highest ridge of the principal islet of the group something which did away with the solemnity of perfect solitude. The tide of darkness flowed on swiftly; and with tropical suddenness a swarm of stars came out above the shadowy earth, while I lingered yet, my hand resting lightly on my ship's rail as if on the shoulder of a trusted friend. But, with all that multitude of celestial bodies staring down at one, the comfort of quiet communion with her was gone for good. And there were also disturbing sounds by this time—voices, footsteps forward; the steward flitted along the main deck, a busily ministering spirit; a handbell tinkled urgently under the poop deck. . . .

I found my two officers waiting for me near the supper table, in the lighted cuddy.[3] We sat down at once, and as I helped the chief mate, I said:

5 "Are you aware that there is a ship anchored inside the islands? I saw her mast-heads above the ridge as the sun went down."

He raised sharply his simple face, overcharged by a terrible growth of whisker, and emitted his usual ejaculations, "Bless my soul, sir! You don't say so!"

My second mate was a round-cheeked, silent young man, grave beyond his years, I thought; but as our eyes happened to meet I detected a slight quiver on his lips. I looked down at once. It was not my part to encourage sneering on board my ship. It must be said, too, that I knew very little of my officers. In consequence of certain events of no particular significance, except to myself, I had been appointed to the command only a fortnight before. Neither did I know much of the hands forward. All these people had been together for eighteen months or so, and my position was that of the only stranger on board. I mention

---

2. The Menan (Chao Phraya) runs through Bangkok, Thailand, into the Gulf of Siam. The Paknam Pagoda stands at the mouth of the river.
3. A small cabin, adjacent to the captain's quarters, beneath the poop deck.

this because it has some bearing on what is to follow. But what I felt most was my being a stranger to the ship; and if all the truth must be told, I was somewhat of a stranger to myself. The youngest man on board (barring the second mate), and untried as yet by a position of the fullest responsibility, I was willing to take the adequacy of the others for granted. They had simply to be equal to their tasks; but I wondered how far I should turn out faithful to that ideal conception of one's own personality every man sets up for himself secretly.

Meantime the chief mate, with an almost visible effect of collaboration on the part of his round eyes and frightful whiskers, was trying to evolve a theory of the anchored ship. His dominant trait was to take all things into earnest consideration. He was of a painstaking turn of mind. As he used to say, he "liked to account to himself" for practically everything that came in his way, down to a miserable scorpion he had found in his cabin a week before. The why and the wherefore of that scorpion—how it got on board and came to select his room rather than the pantry (which was a dark place and more what a scorpion would be partial to), and how on earth it managed to drown itself in the inkwell of his writing-desk—had exercised him infinitely. The ship within the islands was much more easily accounted for; and just as we were about to rise from table he made his pronouncement. She was, he doubted not, a ship from home lately arrived. Probably she drew too much water to cross the bar except at the top of spring tides. Therefore she went into that natural harbor to wait for a few days in preference to remaining in an open roadstead.

"That's so," confirmed the second mate suddenly, in his slightly hoarse voice. "She draws over twenty feet. She's the Liverpool ship *Sephora* with a cargo of coal. Hundred and twenty-three days from Cardiff."

We looked at him in surprise.

"The tugboat skipper told me when he come on board for your letters, sir," explained the young man. "He expects to take her up the river the day after tomorrow."

After thus overwhelming us with the extent of his information he slipped out of the cabin. The mate observed regretfully that he "could not account for that young fellow's whims." What prevented him telling us all about it at once, he wanted to know.

I detained him as he was making a move. For the last two days the crew had had plenty of hard work, and the night before they had very little sleep. I felt painfully that I—a stranger—was doing something unusual when I directed him to let all hands turn in without setting an anchor-watch.[4] I proposed to keep on deck myself till one o'clock or thereabouts. I would get the second mate to relieve me at that hour.

"He will turn out the cook and the steward at four," I concluded, "and then give you a call. Of course at the slightest sign of any sort of wind we'll have the hands up and make a start at once."

He concealed his astonishment. "Very well, sir." Outside the cuddy he put his head in the second mate's door to inform him of my unheard-of caprice to take a five hours' anchor-watch on myself. I heard the other raise his voice incredulously—"What? The captain himself?" Then a few more murmurs, a door closed, then another. A few moments later I went on deck.

My strangeness, which had made me sleepless, had prompted that unconven-

---

4. A detachment of seamen kept on deck while the ship lies at anchor.

tional arrangement, as if I had expected in those solitary hours of the night to get on terms with the ship of which I knew nothing, manned by men of whom I knew very little more. Fast alongside a wharf, littered like any ship in port with a tangle of unrelated things, invaded by unrelated shore people, I had hardly seen her yet properly. Now, as she lay cleared for sea, the stretch of her main deck seemed to me very fine under the stars. Very fine, very roomy for her size, and very inviting. I descended the poop and paced the waist, my mind picturing to myself the coming passage through the Malay Archipelago, down the Indian Ocean, and up the Atlantic. All its phases were familiar enough to me, every characteristic, all the alternatives which were likely to face me on the high seas—everything! ... except the novel responsibility of command. But I took heart from the reasonable thought that the ship was like other ships, the men like other men, and that the sea was not likely to keep any special surprises expressly for my discomfiture.

Arrived at that comforting conclusion, I bethought myself of a cigar and went below to get it. All was still down there. Everybody at the after end of the ship was sleeping profoundly. I came out again on the quarter-deck, agreeably at ease in my sleeping suit on that warm, breathless night, barefooted, a glowing cigar in my teeth, and, going forward, I was met by the profound silence of the fore end of the ship. Only as I passed the door of the forecastle I heard a deep, quiet, trustful sigh of some sleeper inside. And suddenly I rejoiced in the great security of the sea as compared with the unrest of the land, in my choice of that untempted life presenting no disquieting problems, invested with an elementary moral beauty by the absolute straightforwardness of its appeal and by the singleness of its purpose.

The riding-light[5] in the fore-rigging burned with a clear, untroubled, as if symbolic, flame, confident and bright in the mysterious shades of the night. Passing on my way aft along the other side of the ship, I observed that the rope side-ladder, put over, no doubt, for the master of the tug when he came to fetch away our letters, had not been hauled in as it should have been. I became annoyed at this, for exactitude in small matters is the very soul of discipline. Then I reflected that I had myself peremptorily dismissed my officers from duty, and by my own act had prevented the anchor-watch being formally set and things properly attended to. I asked myself whether it was wise ever to interfere with the established routine of duties even from the kindest of motives. My action might have made me appear eccentric. Goodness only knew how that absurdly whiskered mate would "account" for my conduct, and what the whole ship thought of that informality of their new captain. I was vexed with myself.

Not from compunction certainly, but, as it were mechanically, I proceeded to get the ladder in myself. Now a side-ladder of that sort is a light affair and comes in easily, yet my vigorous tug, which should have brought it flying on board, merely recoiled upon my body in a totally unexpected jerk. What the devil! ... I was so astounded by the immovableness of that ladder that I remained stockstill, trying to account for it to myself like that imbecile mate of mine. In the end, of course, I put my head over the rail.

20   The side of the ship made an opaque belt of shadow on the darkling glassy shimmer of the sea. But I saw at once something elongated and pale floating very close to the ladder. Before I could form a guess a faint flash of phospho-

---

5. Special light displayed by a ship while ("riding") at anchor.

rescent light,[6] which seemed to issue suddenly from the naked body of a man, flickered in the sleeping water with the elusive, silent play of summer lightning in a night sky. With a gasp I saw revealed to my stare a pair of feet, the long legs, a broad livid back immersed right up to the neck in a greenish cadaverous glow. One hand, awash, clutched the bottom rung of the ladder. He was complete but for the head. A headless corpse! The cigar dropped out of my gaping mouth with a tiny plop and a short hiss quite audible in the absolute stillness of all things under heaven. At that I suppose he raised up his face, a dimly pale oval in the shadow of the ship's side. But even then I could only barely make out down there the shape of his black-haired head. However, it was enough for the horrid, frost-bound sensation which had gripped me about the chest to pass off. The moment of vain exclamations was past too. I only climbed on the spare spar and leaned over the rail as far as I could, to bring my eyes nearer to that mystery floating alongside.

As he hung by the ladder, like a resting swimmer, the sea-lightning played about his limbs at every stir; and he appeared in it ghastly, silvery, fish-like. He remained as mute as a fish, too. He made no motion to get out of the water, either. It was inconceivable that he should not attempt to come on board, and strangely troubling to suspect that perhaps he did not want to. And my first words were prompted by just that troubled incertitude.

"What's the matter?" I asked in my ordinary tone, speaking down to the face upturned exactly under mine.

"Cramp," it answered, no louder. Then slightly anxious, "I say, no need to call any one."

"I was not going to," I said.

"Are you alone on deck?"

"Yes."

I had somehow the impression that he was on the point of letting go the ladder to swim away beyond my ken—mysterious as he came. But, for the moment, this being appearing as if he had risen from the bottom of the sea (it was certainly the nearest land to the ship) wanted only to know the time. I told him. And he, down there, tentatively:

"I suppose your captain's turned in?"

"I am sure he isn't," I said.

He seemed to struggle with himself, for I heard something like the low, bitter murmur of doubt. "What's the good?" His next words came out with a hesitating effort.

"Look here, my man. Could you call him out quietly?"

I thought the time had come to declare myself. "*I* am the captain."

I heard a "By Jove!" whispered at the level of the water. The phosphorescence flashed in the swirl of the water all about his limbs, his other hand seized the ladder.

"My name's Leggatt."

The voice was calm and resolute. A good voice. The self-possession of that man had somehow induced a corresponding state in myself. It was very quietly that I remarked:

"You must be a good swimmer."

---

6. Light emitted by microscopic plankton; same as "sea lightning," below.

"Yes. I've been in the water practically since nine o'clock. The question for me now is whether I am to let go this ladder and go on swimming till I sink from exhaustion or—to come on board here."

I felt this was no mere formula of desperate speech, but a real alternative in the view of a strong soul. I should have gathered from this that he was young; indeed, it is only the young who are ever confronted by such clear issues. But at the time it was pure intuition on my part. A mysterious communication was established already between us two—in the face of that silent, darkened tropical sea. I was young, too; young enough to make no comment. The man in the water began suddenly to climb up the ladder, and I hastened away from the rail to fetch some clothes.

Before entering the cabin I stood still, listening in the lobby at the foot of the stairs. A faint snore came through the closed door of the chief mate's room. The second mate's door was on the hook, but the darkness in there was absolutely soundless. He, too, was young and could sleep like a stone. Remained the steward, but he was not likely to wake up before he was called. I got a sleeping suit out of my room, and, coming back on deck, saw the naked man from the sea sitting on the main-hatch, glimmering white in the darkness, his elbows on his knees and his head in his hands. In a moment he had concealed his damp body in a sleeping suit of the same gray-stripe pattern as the one I was wearing, and followed me like my double on the poop. Together we moved right aft, barefooted, silent.

"What is it?" I asked in a deadened voice, taking the lighted lamp out of the binnacle, and raising it to his face.

"An ugly business."

He had rather regular features; a good mouth; light eyes under somewhat heavy, dark eyebrows; a smooth, square forehead; no growth on his cheeks; a small, brown mustache, and a well-shaped, round chin. His expression was concentrated, meditative, under the inspecting light of the lamp I held up to his face; such as a man thinking hard in solitude might wear. My sleeping suit was just right for his size. A well-knit young fellow of twenty-five at most. He caught his lower lip with the edge of white, even teeth.

"Yes," I said, replacing the lamp in the binnacle. The warm, heavy tropical night closed upon his head again.

"There's a ship over there," he murmured.

"Yes, I know. The *Sephora*. Did you know of us?"

"Hadn't the slightest idea. I am the mate of her—" He paused and corrected himself. "I should say I *was*."

"Aha! Something wrong?"

"Yes. Very wrong indeed. I've killed a man."

"What do you mean? Just now?"

"No, on the passage. Weeks ago. Thirty-nine south. When I say a man—"

"Fit of temper," I suggested confidently.

The shadowy, dark head, like mine, seemed to nod imperceptibly above the ghostly gray of my sleeping suit. It was, in the night, as though I had been faced by my own reflection in the depths of a sombre and immense mirror.

"A pretty thing to have to own up to for a Conway[7] boy," murmured my double distinctly.

---

7. The wooden battleship *Conway* was used to train young officers for the Royal Navy and merchant service.

"You're a Conway boy?"

"I am," he said, as if startled. Then, slowly... "Perhaps you too..."

It was so; but being a couple of years older I had left before he joined. After a quick interchange of dates a silence fell; and I thought suddenly of my absurd mate with his terrific whiskers and the "Bless my soul—you don't say so" type of intellect. My double gave me an inkling of his thoughts by saying:

"My father's a parson in Norfolk. Do you see me before a judge and jury on that charge? For myself I can't see the necessity. There are fellows that an angel from heaven—And I am not that. He was one of those creatures that are just simmering all the time with a silly sort of wickedness. Miserable devils that have no business to live at all. He wouldn't do his duty and wouldn't let anybody else do theirs. But what's the good of talking! You know well enough the sort of ill-conditioned snarling cur..."

He appealed to me as if our experiences had been as identical as our clothes. And I knew well enough the pestiferous danger of such a character where there are no means of legal repression. And I knew well enough also that my double there was no homicidal ruffian. I did not think of asking him for details, and he told me the story roughly in brusque, disconnected sentences. I needed no more. I saw it all going on as though I were myself inside that other sleeping suit.

"It happened while we were setting a reefed foresail,[8] at dusk. Reefed foresail! You understand the sort of weather. The only sail we had left to keep the ship running; so you may guess what it had been like for days. Anxious sort of job, that. He gave me some of his cursed insolence at the sheet.[9] I tell you I was overdone with this terrific weather that seemed to have no end to it. Terrific, I tell you—and a deep ship. I believe the fellow himself was half crazed with funk. It was no time for gentlemanly reproof, so I turned round and felled him like an ox. He up and at me. We closed just as an awful sea made for the ship. All hands saw it coming and took to the rigging, but I had him by the throat, and went on shaking him like a rat, the men above us yelling. 'Look out! Look out!' Then a crash as if the sky had fallen on my head. They say that for over ten minutes hardly anything was to be seen of the ship—just the three masts and a bit of the forecastle head and of the poop all awash driving along in a smother of foam. It was a miracle that they found us, jammed together behind the fore-bits. It's clear that I meant business, because I was holding him by the throat still when they picked us up. He was black in the face. It was too much for them. It seems they rushed us aft together, gripped as we were, screaming 'Murder!' like a lot of lunatics, and broke into the cuddy. And the ship running for her life, touch and go all the time, any minute her last in a sea fit to turn your hair gray only a-looking at it. I understand that the skipper, too, started raving like the rest of them. The man had been deprived of sleep for more than a week, and to have this spring on him at the height of a furious gale nearly drove him out of his mind. I wonder they didn't fling me overboard after getting the carcass of their precious shipmate out of my fingers. They had rather a job to separate us, I've been told. A sufficiently fierce story to make an old judge and a respectable jury sit up a bit. The first thing I heard when I came to myself was the maddening howling of that endless gale, and on that the voice of the old man. He was

---

8. In severe weather, sails are reduced in size ("reefed") by folding and tying.
9. Rope used to secure the lower corner of a sail.

hanging on to my bunk, staring into my face out of his sou'wester.

"'Mr. Leggatt, you have killed a man. You can act no longer as chief mate of this ship.'"

His care to subdue his voice made it sound monotonous. He rested a hand on the end of the skylight to steady himself with, and all that time did not stir a limb, so far as I could see. "Nice little tale for a quiet tea party," he concluded in the same tone.

One of my hands, too, rested on the end of the skylight; neither did I stir a limb, so far as I knew. We stood less than a foot from each other. It occurred to me that if old "Bless my soul—you don't say so" were to put his head up the companion and catch sight of us, he would think he was seeing double, or imagine himself come upon a scene of weird witchcraft: the strange captain having a quiet confabulation by the wheel with his own gray ghost. I became very much concerned to prevent anything of the sort. I heard the other's soothing undertone:

"My father's a parson in Norfolk," it said. Evidently he had forgotten he had told me this important fact before. Truly a nice little tale.

65 "You had better slip down into my stateroom now," I said, moving off stealthily. My double followed my movements; our bare feet made no sound; I let him in, closed the door with care, and, after giving a call to the second mate, returned on deck for my relief.

"Not much sign of any wind yet," I remarked when he approached.

"No, sir. Not much," he assented sleepily in his hoarse voice, with just enough deference, no more, and barely suppressing a yawn.

"Well, that's all you have to look out for. You have got your orders."

"Yes, sir."

70 I paced a turn or two on the poop and saw him take up his position face forward with his elbow in the ratlines of the mizzen-rigging before I went below. The mate's faint snoring was still going on peacefully. The cuddy lamp was burning over the table on which stood a vase with flowers, a polite attention from the ship's provision merchant—the last flowers we should see for the next three months at the very least. Two bunches of bananas hung from the beam symmetrically, one on each side of the rudder-casing. Everything was as before in the ship—except that two of her captain's sleeping suits were simultaneously in use, one motionless in the cuddy, the other keeping very still in the captain's stateroom.

It must be explained here that my cabin had the form of the capital letter L, the door being within the angle and opening into the short part of the letter. A couch was to the left, the bedplace to the right; my writing-desk and the chronometers' table faced the door. But any one opening it, unless he stepped right inside, had no view of what I call the long (or vertical) part of the letter. It contained some lockers surmounted by a bookcase; and a few clothes, a thick jacket or two, caps, oilskin coat, and such-like, hung on hooks. There was at the bottom of that part a door opening into my bathroom, which could be entered also directly from the saloon. But that way was never used.

The mysterious arrival had discovered the advantage of this particular shape. Entering my room, lighted strongly by a big bulkhead lamp swung on gimbals above my writing-desk, I did not see him anywhere till he stepped out quietly from behind the coats hung in the recessed part.

"I heard somebody moving about, and went in there at once," he whispered. I, too, spoke under my breath.

"Nobody is likely to come in here without knocking and getting permission."

He nodded. His face was thin and the sunburn faded, as though he had been ill. And no wonder. He had been, I heard presently, kept under arrest in his cabin for nearly nine weeks. But there was nothing sickly in his eyes or in his expression. He was not a bit like me, really; yet, as we stood leaning over my bed-place, whispering side by side, with our dark heads together and our backs to the door, anybody bold enough to open it stealthily would have been treated to the uncanny sight of a double captain busy talking in whispers with his other self.

"But all this doesn't tell me how you came to hang on to our side-ladder," I inquired, in the hardly audible murmurs we used, after he had told me something more of the proceedings on board the *Sephora* once the bad weather was over.

"When we sighted Java Head[1] I had had time to think all those matters out several times over. I had six weeks of doing nothing else, and with only an hour or so every evening for a tramp on the quarterdeck."

He whispered, his arms folded on the side of my bedplace, staring through the open port. And I could imagine perfectly the manner of this thinking out—a stubborn if not a steadfast operation; something of which I should have been perfectly incapable.

"I reckoned it would be dark before we closed with the land," he continued, so low that I had to strain my hearing, near as we were to each other, shoulder touching shoulder almost. "So I asked to speak to the old man. He always seemed very sick when he came to see me—as if he could not look me in the face. You know, that foresail saved the ship. She was too deep to have run long under bare poles. And it was I that managed to set it for him. Anyway, he came. When I had him in my cabin—he stood by the door looking at me as if I had the halter round my neck already—I asked him right away to leave my cabin door unlocked at night while the ship was going through Sunda Straits. There would be the Java coast within two or three miles, off Anjer Point. I wanted nothing more. I've had a prize for swimming my second year in the Conway."

"I can believe it," I breathed out.

"God only knows why they locked me in every night. To see some of their faces you'd have thought they were afraid I'd go about at night strangling people. Am I a murdering brute? Do I look it? By Jove! if I had been he wouldn't have trusted himself like that into my room. You'll say I might have chucked him aside and bolted out, there and then—it was dark already. Well, no. And for the same reason I wouldn't think of trying to smash the door. There would have been a rush to stop me at the noise, and I did not mean to get into a confounded scrimmage. Somebody else might have got killed—for I would not have broken out only to get chucked back, and I did not want any more of that work. He refused, looking more sick than ever. He was afraid of the men, and also of that old second mate of his who had been sailing with him for years—a gray-headed old humbug; and his steward, too, had been with him devil knows how long—seventeen years or more—a dogmatic sort of loafer who hated me like poison,

---

1. A famous landmark for clipper ships engaged in the China trade on the western end of Java, the southern entrance to the Sunda Straits mentioned below; the killing thus took place some fifteen hundred miles south of the present scene.

just because I was the chief mate. No chief mate ever made more than one voyage in the *Sephora*, you know. Those two old chaps ran the ship. Devil only knows what the skipper wasn't afraid of (all his nerve went to pieces altogether in that hellish spell of bad weather we had)—of what the law would do to him—of his wife, perhaps. Oh yes! she's on board. Though I don't think she would have meddled. She would have been only too glad to have me out of the ship in any way. The 'brand of Cain'[2] business, don't you see? That's all right. I was ready enough to go off wandering on the face of the earth—and that was price enough to pay for an Abel of that sort. Anyhow, he wouldn't listen to me. 'This thing must take its course. I represent the law here.' He was shaking like a leaf. 'So you won't?' 'No!' 'Then I hope you will be able to sleep on that," I said, and turned my back on him. 'I wonder that *you* can,' cries he, and locks the door.

"Well, after that, I couldn't. Not very well. That was three weeks ago. We have had a slow passage through the Java Sea; drifted about Carimata[3] for ten days. When we anchored here they thought, I suppose, it was all right. The nearest land (and that's five miles) is the ship's destination; the consul would soon set about catching me; and there would have been no object in bolting to these islets there. I don't suppose there's a drop of water on them. I don't know how it was, but tonight that steward, after bringing me my supper, went out to let me eat it, and left the door unlocked. And I ate it—all there was, too. After I had finished I strolled out on the quarterdeck. I don't know that I meant to do anything. A breath of fresh air was all I wanted, I believe. Then a sudden temptation came over me. I kicked off my slippers and was in the water before I had made up my mind fairly. Somebody heard the splash and they raised an awful hullabaloo. "He's gone! Lower the boats! He's committed suicide! No, he's swimming.' Certainly I was swimming. It's not easy for a swimmer like me to commit suicide by drowning. I landed on the nearest islet before the boat left the ship's side. I heard them pulling about in the dark, hailing, and so on, but after a bit they gave up. Everything quieted down and the anchorage became as still as death. I sat down on a stone and began to think. I felt certain they would start searching for me at daylight. There was no place to hide on those stony things—and if there had been, what would have been the good? But now I was clear of that ship I was not going back. So after a while I took off all my clothes, tied them up in a bundle with a stone inside, and dropped them in the deep water on the outer side of that islet. That was suicide enough for me. Let them think what they liked, but I didn't mean to drown myself. I meant to swim till I sank—but that's not the same thing. I struck out for another of these little islands, and it was from that one that I first saw your riding-light. Something to swim for. I went on easily, and on the way I came upon a flat rock a foot or two above water. In the daytime, I dare say, you might make it out with a glass from your poop. I scrambled up on it and rested myself for a bit. Then I made another start. That last spell must have been over a mile."

His whisper was getting fainter and fainter, and all the time he stared straight out through the porthole, in which there was not even a star to be seen. I had not interrupted him. There was something that made comment impossible, in his narrative, or perhaps in himself; a sort of feeling, a quality, which I can't find

---

2. Genesis 4.15.
3. The Karimata Islands in the straits between Borneo and Sumatra, some three hundred miles northeast of the Sunda Straits.

a name for. And when he ceased, all I found was a futile whisper, "So you swam for our light?"

"Yes—straight for it. It was something to swim for. I couldn't see any stars low down because the coast was in the way, and I couldn't see the land, either. The water was like glass. One might have been swimming in a confounded thousand feet deep cistern with no place for scrambling out anywhere; but what I didn't like was the notion of swimming round and round like a crazed bullock before I gave out; and as I didn't mean to go back . . . No. Do you see me being hauled back, stark naked, off one of these little islands by the scruff of the neck and fighting like a wild beast? Somebody would have got killed for certain, and I did not want any of that. So I went on. Then your ladder—"

"Why didn't you hail the ship?" I asked, a little louder.

He touched my shoulder lightly. Lazy footsteps came right over our heads and stopped. The second mate had crossed from the other side of the poop and might have been hanging over the rail, for all we knew.

"He couldn't hear us talking—could he?" My double breathed into my very ear anxiously.

His anxiety was an answer, a sufficient answer, to the question I had put to him. An answer containing all the difficulty of that situation. I closed the porthole quietly, to make sure. A louder word might have been overheard.

"Who's that?" he whispered then.

"My second mate. But I don't know much more of the fellow than you do."

And I told him a little about myself. I had been appointed to take charge while I least expected anything of the sort, not quite a fortnight ago. I didn't know either the ship or the people. Hadn't had the time in port to look about me or size anybody up. And as to the crew, all they knew was that I was appointed to take the ship home. For the rest, I was almost as much of a stranger on board as himself, I said. And at the moment I felt it most acutely. I felt that it would take very little to make me a suspect person in the eyes of the ship's company.

He had turned about meantime; and we, the two strangers in the ship, faced each other in identical attitudes.

"Your ladder—" he murmured, after a silence. "Who'd have thought of finding a ladder hanging over at night in a ship anchored out here! I felt just then a very unpleasant faintness. After the life I've been leading for nine weeks, anybody would have got out of condition. I wasn't capable of swimming round as far as your rudder-chains. And, lo and behold! there was a ladder to get hold of. After I gripped it I said to myself, 'What's the good?' When I saw a man's head looking over I thought I would swim away presently and leave him shouting—in whatever language it was. I didn't mind being looked at. I—I liked it. And then you speaking to me so quietly—as if you had expected me—made me hold on a little longer. It had been a confounded lonely time—I don't mean while swimming. I was glad to talk a little to somebody that didn't belong to the *Sephora*. As to asking for the captain, that was a mere impulse. It could have been no use, with all the ship knowing about me and the other people pretty certain to be round here in the morning. I don't know—I wanted to be seen, to talk with somebody, before I went on. I don't know what I would have said. . . . 'Fine night, isn't it?' or something of the sort."

"Do you think they will be round here presently?" I asked, with some incredulity.

"Quite likely," he said faintly.

He looked extremely haggard all of a sudden. His head rolled on his shoulders.

"H'm. We shall see then. Meantime get into that bed," I whispered. "Want help? There."

It was a rather high bedplace with a set of drawers underneath. This amazing swimmer really needed the lift I gave him by seizing his leg. He tumbled in, rolled over on his back, and flung one arm across his eyes. And then, with his face nearly hidden, he must have looked exactly as I used to look in that bed. I gazed upon my other self for a while before drawing across carefully the two green serge curtains which ran on a brass rod. I thought for a moment of pinning them together for greater safety, but I sat down on the couch, and once there I felt unwilling to rise and hunt for a pin. I would do it in a moment. I was extremely tired, in a peculiarly intimate way, by the strain of stealthiness, by the effort of whispering, and the general secrecy of this excitement. It was three o'clock by now, and I had been on my feet since nine, but I was not sleepy; I could not have gone to sleep. I sat there, fagged out,[4] looking at the curtains, trying to clear my mind of the confused sensation of being in two places at once, and greatly bothered by an exasperating knocking in my head. It was a relief to discover suddenly that it was not in my head at all, but on the outside of the door. Before I could collect myself, the words "Come in" were out of my mouth, and the steward entered with a tray, bringing in my morning coffee. I had slept, after all, and I was so frightened that I shouted, "This way! I am here, steward," as though he had been miles away. He put down the tray on the table next the couch and only then said, very quietly, "I can see you are here, sir." I felt him give me a keen look, but I dared not meet his eyes just then. He must have wondered why I had drawn the curtains of my bed before going to sleep on the couch. He went out, hooking the door open as usual.

I heard the crew washing decks above me. I knew I would have been told at once if there had been any wind. Calm, I thought, and I was doubly vexed. Indeed, I felt dual more than ever. The steward reappeared suddenly in the doorway. I jumped up from the couch so quickly that he gave a start.

"What do you want here?"

"Close your port, sir—they are washing decks."

"It is closed," I said, reddening.

"Very well, sir." But he did not move from the doorway and returned my stare in an extraordinary, equivocal manner for a time. Then his eyes, wavered, all his expression changed, and in a voice unusually gentle, almost coaxingly.

"May I come in to take the empty cup away, sir?"

"Of course!" I turned my back on him while he popped in and out. Then I unhooked and closed the door and even pushed the bolt. This sort of thing could not go on very long. The cabin was as hot as an oven, too. I took a peep at my double, and discovered that he had not moved; his arm was still over his eyes; but his chest heaved, his hair was wet, his chin glistened with perspiration. I reached over him and opened the port.

"I must show myself on deck," I reflected.

Of course, theoretically, I could do what I liked, with no one to say nay to me within the whole circle of the horizon; but to lock my cabin door and take the key away I did not dare. Directly I put my head out of the companion I saw the

---

4. Exhausted.

group of my two officers, the second mate barefooted, the chief mate in long india-rubber boots, near the break of the poop, and the steward half-way down the poop ladder talking to them eagerly. He happened to catch sight of me and dived, the second ran down on the main deck shouting some order or other, and the chief mate came to meet me, touching his cap.

There was a sort of curiosity in his eye that I did not like. I don't know whether the steward had told them that I was "queer" only, or downright drunk, but I know the man meant to have a good look at me. I watched him coming with a smile which, as he got into point-blank range, took effect and froze his very whiskers. I did not give him time to open his lips.

"Square the yards by lifts and braces[5] before the hands go to breakfast."

It was the first particular order I had given on board that ship; and I stayed on deck to see it executed too. I had felt the need of asserting myself without loss of time. That sneering young cub got taken down a peg or two on that occasion, and I also seized the opportunity of having a good look at the face of every foremast man as they filed past me to go to the after braces. At breakfast time, eating nothing myself, I presided with such frigid dignity that the two mates were only too glad to escape from the cabin as soon as decency permitted; and all the time the dual working of my mind distracted me almost to the point of insanity. I was constantly watching myself, my secret self, as dependent on my actions as my own personality, sleeping in that bed, behind that door which faced me as I sat at the head of the table. It was very much like being mad, only it was worse, because one was aware of it.

I had to shake him for a solid minute, but when at last he opened his eyes it was in the full possession of his senses, with an inquiring look.

"All's well so far," I whispered. "Now you must vanish into the bathroom."

He did so, as noiseless as a ghost, and I then rang for the steward, and facing him boldly, directed him to tidy up my stateroom while I was having my bath—"and be quick about it." As my tone admitted of no excuses, he said, "Yes, sir," and ran off to fetch his dustpan and brushes. I took a bath and did most of my dressing, splashing, and whistling softly for the steward's edification, while the secret sharer of my life stood drawn bolt upright in that little space, his face looking very sunken in daylight, his eyelids lowered under the stern, dark line of his eyebrows drawn together by a slight frown.

When I left him there to go back to my room the steward was finishing dusting. I sent for the mate and engaged him in some insignificant conversation. It was, as it were, trifling with the terrific character of his whiskers; but my object was to give him an opportunity for a good look at my cabin. And then I could at last shut, with a clear conscience, the door of my stateroom and get my double back into the recessed part. There was nothing else for it. He had to sit still on a small folding stool, half smothered by the heavy coats hanging there. We listened to the steward going into the bathroom out of the saloon, filling the water-bottles there, scrubbing the bath, setting things to rights, whisk, bang, clatter—out again into the saloon—turn the key—click. Such was my scheme for keeping my second self invisible. Nothing better could be contrived under the circumstances. And there we sat: I at my writing-desk ready to appear busy with some papers, he behind me, out of sight of the door. It would not have been prudent

---

5. Ropes that adjust the position of the yardarms, vertically (lifts) and horizontally (braces).

to talk in daytime; and I could not have stood the excitement of that queer sense of whispering to myself. Now and then, glancing over my shoulder, I saw him far back there, sitting rigidly on the low stool, his bare feet close together, his arms folded, his head hanging on his breast—and perfectly still. Anybody would have taken him for me.

I was fascinated by it myself. Every moment I had to glance over my shoulder. I was looking at him when a voice outside the door said:

"Beg pardon, sir."

"Well!" . . . I kept my eyes on him, and so when the voice outside the door announced, "There's a ship's boat coming our way, sir," I saw him give a start— the first movement he had made for hours. But he did not raise his bowed head.

"All right. Get the ladder over."

I hesitated. Should I whisper something to him? But what? His immobility seemed to have been never disturbed. What could I tell him he did not know already? . . . Finally I went on deck.

## II

The skipper of the *Sephora* had a thin, red whisker all round his face, and the sort of complexion that goes with hair of that color; also the particular, rather smeary shade of blue in the eyes. He was not exactly a showy figure; his shoulders were high, his stature but middling—one leg slightly more bandy than the other. He shook hands, looking vaguely around. A spiritless tenacity was his main characteristic, I judged. I behaved with a politeness which seemed to disconcert him. Perhaps he was shy. He mumbled to me as if he were ashamed of what he was saying; gave his name (it was something like Archbold—but at this distance of years I hardly am sure), his ship's name, and a few other particulars of that sort, in the manner of a criminal making a reluctant and doleful confession. He had had terrible weather on the passage out—terrible—terrible—wife aboard, too.

By this time we were seated in the cabin and the steward brought in a tray with a bottle and glasses. "Thanks! No." Never took liquor. Would have some water, though. He drank two tumblerfuls. Terrible thirsty work. Ever since daylight had been exploring the islands round his ship.

"What was that for—fun?" I asked with an appearance of polite interest.

"No!" He sighed. "Painful duty."

As he persisted in his mumbling and I wanted my double to hear every word, I hit upon the notion of informing him that I regretted to say I was hard of hearing.

"Such a young man too!" he nodded, keeping his smeary, blue, unintelligent eyes fastened upon me. "What was the cause of it—some disease?" he inquired, without the least sympathy and as if he thought that, if so, I'd got no more than I deserved.

"Yes; disease," I admitted in a cheerful tone which seemed to shock him. But my point was gained, because he had to raise his voice to give me his tale. It is not worth while to record that version. It was just over two months since all this had happened, and he had thought so much about it that he seemed completely muddled as to its bearings, but still immensely impressed.

"What would you think of such a thing happening on board your own ship? I've had the *Sephora* for these fifteen years. I am a well-known shipmaster."

He was densely distressed—and perhaps I should have sympathized with him if I had been able to detach my mental vision from the unsuspected sharer of my cabin as though he were my second self. There he was on the other side of the bulkhead, four or five feet from us, no more, as we sat in the saloon. I looked politely at Captain Archbold (if that was his name), but it was the other I saw, in a gray sleeping suit, seated on a low stool, his bare feet close together, his arms folded, and every word said between us falling into the ears of his dark head bowed on his chest.

"I have been at sea now, man and boy, for seven and thirty years, and I've never heard of such a thing happening in an English ship. And that it should be my ship. Wife on board, too."

I was hardly listening to him.

"Don't you think," I said, "that the heavy sea which, you told me, came aboard just then might have killed the man? I have seen the sheer weight of a sea kill a man very neatly, by simply breaking his neck."

"Good God!" he uttered impressively, fixing his smeary blue eyes on me. "The sea! No man killed by the sea ever looked like that." He seemed positively scandalized at my suggestion. And as I gazed at him, certainly not prepared for anything original on his part, he advanced his head close to mine and thrust his tongue out at me so suddenly that I couldn't help starting back.

After scoring over my calmness in this graphic way he nodded wisely. If I had seen the sight, he assured me, I would never forget it as long as I lived. The weather was too bad to give the corpse a proper sea burial. So next day at dawn they took it up on the poop, covering its face with a bit of bunting; he read a short prayer, and then, just as it was, in its oilskins and long boots, they launched it amongst those mountainous seas that seemed ready every moment to swallow up the ship herself and the terrified lives on board of her.

"That reefed foresail saved you," I threw in.

"Under God—it did," he exclaimed fervently. "It was by a special mercy, I firmly believe, that it stood some of those hurricane squalls."

"It was the setting of that sail which—" I began.

"God's own hand in it," he interrupted me. "Nothing less could have done it. I don't mind telling you that I hardly dared give the order. It seemed impossible that we could touch anything without losing it, and then our last hope would have been gone."

The terror of that gale was on him yet. I let him go on for a bit, then said casually—as if returning to a minor subject:

"You were very anxious to give up your mate to the shore people, I believe?"

He was. To the law. His obscure tenacity on that point had in it something incomprehensible and a little awful; something, as it were, mystical, quite apart from his anxiety that he should not be suspected of "countenancing any doings of that sort." Seven and thirty virtuous years at sea, of which over twenty of immaculate command, and the last fifteen in the *Sephora*, seemed to have laid him under some pitiless obligation.

"And you know," he went on, groping shamefacedly amongst his feelings, "I did not engage that young fellow. His people had some interest with my owners. I was in a way forced to take him on. He looked very smart, very gentlemanly, and all that. But do you know—I never liked him, somehow. I am a plain man. You see, he wasn't exactly the sort for the chief mate of a ship like the *Sephora*."

I had become so connected in thoughts and impressions with the secret sharer of my cabin that I felt as if I, personally, were being given to understand that I, too, was not the sort that would have done for the chief mate of a ship like the *Sephora*. I had no doubt of it in my mind.

"Not at all the style of man. You understand," he insisted superfluously, looking hard at me.

145 I smiled urbanely. He seemed at a loss for a while.

"I suppose I must report a suicide."

"Beg pardon?"

"Sui-cide! That's what I'll have to write to my owners directly I get in."

"Unless you manage to recover him before tomorrow," I assented dispassionately.... "I mean, alive."

150 He mumbled something which I really did not catch, and I turned my ear to him in a puzzled manner. He fairly bawled:

"The land—I say, the mainland is at least seven miles off my anchorage."

"About that."

My lack of excitement, of curiosity, of surprise, of any sort of pronounced interest, began to arouse his distrust. But except for the felicitous pretense of deafness I had not tried to pretend anything. I had felt utterly incapable of playing the part of ignorance properly, and therefore was afraid to try. It is also certain that he had brought some ready-made suspicions with him, and that he viewed my politeness as a strange and unnatural phenomenon. And yet how else could I have received him? Not heartily! That was impossible for psychological reasons, which I need not state here. My only object was to keep off his inquiries. Surlily? Yes, but surliness might have provoked a point-blank question. From its novelty to him and from its nature, punctilious courtesy was the manner best calculated to restrain the man. But there was the danger of his breaking through my defense bluntly. I could not, I think, have met him by a direct lie, also for psychological (not moral) reasons. If he had only known how afraid I was of his putting my feeling of identity with the other to the test! But, strangely enough (I thought of it only afterward), I believe that he was not a little disconcerted by the reverse side of that weird situation, by something in me that reminded him of the man he was seeking—suggested a mysterious similitude to the young fellow he had distrusted and disliked from the first.

However that might have been the silence was not very prolonged. He took another oblique step.

155 "I reckon I had no more than a two-mile pull to your ship. Not a bit more."

"And quite enough, too, in this awful heat," I said.

Another pause full of mistrust followed. Necessity, they say, is mother of invention, but fear, too, is not barren of ingenious suggestions. And I was afraid he would ask me point-blank for news of my other self.

"Nice little saloon, isn't it?" I remarked, as if noticing for the first time the way his eyes roamed from one closed door to the other. "And very well fitted out, too. Here, for instance," I continued, reaching over the back of my seat negligently and flinging the door open, "is my bathroom."

He made an eager movement, but hardly gave it a glance. I got up, shut the door of the bathroom, and invited him to have a look round, as if I were very proud of my accommodation. He had to rise and be shown round, but he went through the business without any raptures whatever.

160 "And now we'll have a look at my stateroom," I declared, in a voice as loud

as I dared to make it, crossing the cabin to the starboard side with purposely heavy steps.

He followed me in and gazed around. My intelligent double had vanished. I played my part.

"Very convenient—isn't it?"

"Very nice. Very comf..." He didn't finish, and went out brusquely as if to escape from some unrighteous wiles of mine. But it was not to be. I had been too frightened not to feel vengeful; I felt I had him on the run, and I meant to keep him on the run. My polite insistence must have had something menacing in it, because he gave in suddenly. And I did not let him off a single item: mates' rooms, pantry, storerooms, the very sail-locker, which was also under the poop— he had to look into them all. When at last I showed him out on the quarter-deck he drew a long, spiritless sigh, and mumbled dismally that he must really be going back to his ship now. I desired my mate, who had joined us, to see to the captain's boat.

The man of whiskers gave a blast on the whistle which he used to wear hanging round his neck, and yelled, "*Sephora*'s away!" My double down there in my cabin must have heard, and certainly could not feel more relieved than I. Four fellows came running out from somewhere forward and went over the side, while my own men, appearing on deck too, lined the rail. I escorted my visitor to the gangway ceremoniously, and nearly overdid it. He was a tenacious beast. On the very ladder he lingered, and in that unique, guiltily conscientious manner of sticking to the point:

"I say ... you ... you don't think that—"

I covered his voice loudly.

"Certainly not.... I am delighted. Goodbye."

I had an idea of what he meant to say, and just saved myself by the privilege of defective hearing. He was too shaken generally to insist, but my mate, close witness of that parting, looked mystified and his face took on a thoughtful cast. As I did not want to appear as if I wished to avoid all communication with my officers, he had the opportunity to address me.

"Seems a very nice man. His boat's crew told our chaps a very extraordinary story, if what I am told by the steward is true. I suppose you had it from the captain, sir?"

"Yes. I had a story from the captain."

"A very horrible affair—isn't it, sir?"

"It is."

"Beats all these tales we hear about murders in Yankee ships."

"I don't think it beats them. I don't think it resembles them in the least."

"Bless my soul—you don't say so! But of course I've no acquaintance whatever with American ships, not I, so I couldn't go against your knowledge. It's horrible enough for me.... But the queerest part is that those fellows seemed to have some idea the man was hidden aboard here. They had really. Did you ever hear of such a thing?"

"Preposterous—isn't it?"

We were walking to and fro athwart the quarter-deck. No one of the crew forward could be seen (the day was Sunday), and the mate pursued:

"There was some little dispute about it. Our chaps took offense. 'As if we would harbor a thing like that,' they said. 'Wouldn't you like to look for him in our coal-hole?' Quite a tiff. But they made it up in the end. I suppose he did drown himself. Don't you, sir?"

"I don't suppose anything."

"You have no doubt in the matter, sir?"

"None whatever."

I left him suddenly. I felt I was producing a bad impression, but with my double down there it was most trying to be on deck. And it was almost as trying to be below. Altogether a nerve-trying situation. But on the whole I felt less torn in two when I was with him. There was no one in the whole ship whom I dared take into my confidence. Since the hands had got to know his story, it would have been impossible to pass him off for any one else, and an accidental discovery was to be dreaded now more than ever....

The steward being engaged in laying the table for dinner, we could talk only with our eyes when I first went down. Later in the afternoon we had a cautious try at whispering. The Sunday quietness of the ship was against us; the stillness of air and water around her was against us; the elements, the men were against us—everything was against us in our secret partnership; time itself—for this could not go on for ever. The very trust in Providence was, I supposed, denied to his guilt. Shall I confess that this thought cast me down very much? And as to the chapter of accidents which counts for so much in the book of success, I could only hope that it was closed. For what favorable accident could be expected?

"Did you hear everything?" were my first words as soon as we took up our position side by side, leaning over my bedplace.

He had. And the proof of it was his earnest whisper, "The man told you he hardly dared to give the order."

I understood the reference to be to that saving foresail.

"Yes. He was afraid of it being lost in the setting."

"I assure you he never gave the order. He may think he did, but he never gave it. He stood there with me on the break of the poop after the maintopsail blew away, and whimpered about our last hope—positively whimpered about it and nothing else—and the night coming on! To hear one's skipper go on like that in such weather was enough to drive any fellow out of his mind. It worked me up into a sort of desperation. I just took it into my own hands and went away from him, boiling, and—But what's the use telling you? *You* know!... Do you think that if I had not been pretty fierce with them I should have got the men to do anything? Not it! The boss'en[6] perhaps? Perhaps! It wasn't a heavy sea—it was a sea gone mad! I suppose the end of the world will be something like that; and a man may have the heart to see it coming once and be done with it—but to have to face it day after day... I don't blame anybody. I was precious little better than the rest. Only—I was an officer of that old coal-wagon, anyhow...."

"I quite understand," I conveyed that sincere assurance into his ear. He was out of breath with whispering; I could hear him pant slightly. It was all very simple. The same strung-up force which had given twenty-four men a chance, at least, for their lives had, in a sort of recoil, crushed an unworthy mutinous existence.

But I had no leisure to weigh the merits of the matter—footsteps in the saloon, a heavy knock. "There's enough wind to get under way with, sir." Here was the

---

6. *Bosun* or *boatswain*: a petty officer in charge of the deck crew and of the rigging.

call of a new claim upon my thoughts and even upon my feelings.

"Turn the hands up," I cried through the door. "I'll be on deck directly."

I was going out to make the acquaintance of my ship. Before I left the cabin our eyes met—the eyes of the only two strangers on board. I pointed to the recessed part where the little camp-stool awaited him and laid my finger on my lips. He made a gesture—somewhat vague—a little mysterious, accompanied by a faint smile, as if of regret.

This is not the place to enlarge upon the sensations of a man who feels for the first time a ship move under his feet to his own independent word. In my case they were not unalloyed. I was not wholly alone with my command; for there was that stranger in my cabin. Or, rather, I was not completely and wholly with her. Part of me was absent. That mental feeling of being in two places at once affected me physically as if the mood of secrecy had penetrated my very soul. Before an hour had elapsed since the ship had begun to move, having occasion to ask the mate (he stood by my side) to take a compass bearing of the Pagoda, I caught myself reaching up to his ear in whispers. I say I caught myself, but enough had escaped to startle the man. I can't describe it otherwise than by saying that he shied. A grave, preoccupied manner, as though he were in possession of some perplexing intelligence, did not leave him henceforth. A little later I moved away from the rail to look at the compass with such a stealthy gait that the helmsman noticed it—and I could not help noticing the unusual roundness of his eyes. These are trifling instances, though it's to no commander's advantage to be suspected of ludicrous eccentricities. But I was also more seriously affected. There are to a seaman certain words, gestures, that should in given conditions come as naturally, as instinctively, as the winking of a menaced eye. A certain order should spring on to his lips without thinking; a certain sign should get itself made, so to speak, without reflection. But all unconscious alertness had abandoned me. I had to make an effort of will to recall myself back (from the cabin) to the conditions of the moment. I felt that I was appearing an irresolute commander to those people who were watching me more or less critically.

And, besides, there were the scares. On the second day out, for instance, coming off the deck in the afternoon (I had straw slippers on my bare feet) I stopped at the open pantry door and spoke to the steward. He was doing something there with his back to me. At the sound of my voice he nearly jumped out of his skin, as the saying is, and incidentally broke a cup.

"What on earth's the matter with you?" I asked, astonished.

He was extremely confused. "Beg your pardon, sir. I made sure you were in your cabin."

"You see I wasn't."

"No, sir. I could have sworn I had heard you moving in there not a moment ago. It's most extraordinary . . . very sorry, sir."

I passed on with an inward shudder. I was so identified with my secret double that I did not even mention the fact in those scanty, fearful whispers we exchanged. I suppose he had made some slight noise of some kind or other. It would have been miraculous if he hadn't at one time or another. And yet, haggard as he appeared, he looked always perfectly self-controlled, more than calm—almost invulnerable. On my suggestion he remained almost entirely in the bathroom, which, upon the whole, was the safest place. There could be really no shadow of an excuse for any one ever wanting to go in there, once the steward had done with it. It was a very tiny place. Sometimes he reclined on the floor, his legs bent, his head sustained on one elbow. At others I would find him on the camp-stool, sitting in his gray sleeping suit and with his cropped dark hair like a patient, unmoved convict. At night I would smuggle him into my bedplace, and we would whisper together, with the regular footfalls of the officer of the watch passing and repassing over our heads. It was an infinitely miserable time. It was lucky that some tins of fine preserves were stowed in a locker in my stateroom; hard bread I could always get hold of; and so he lived on stewed chicken, pâté de foie gras, asparagus, cooked oysters, sardines—on all sorts of abominable sham-delicacies out of tins. My early morning coffee he always drank; and it was all I dared do for him in that respect.

Every day there was the horrible maneuvering to go through so that my room and then the bathroom should be done in the usual way. I came to hate the sight of the steward, to abhor the voice of that harmless man. I felt that it was he who would bring on the disaster of discovery. It hung like a sword over our heads.

The fourth day out, I think (we were then working down the east side of the Gulf of Siam, tack for tack,[7] in light winds and smooth water)—the fourth day, I say, of this miserable juggling with the unavoidable, as we sat at our evening meal, that man, whose slightest movement I dreaded, after putting down the dishes ran up on deck busily. This could not be dangerous. Presently he came down again; and then it appeared that he had remembered a coat of mine which I had thrown over a rail to dry after having been wetted in a shower which had passed over the ship in the afternoon. Sitting stolidly at the head of the table I became terrified at the sight of the garment on his arm. Of course he made for my door. There was no time to lose.

"Steward!" I thundered. My nerves were so shaken that I could not govern my voice and conceal my agitation. This was the sort of thing that made my terrifically whiskered mate tap his forehead with his forefinger. I had detected him using that gesture while talking on deck with a confidential air to the carpenter. It was too far to hear a word, but I had no doubt that this pantomime could only refer to the strange new captain.

"Yes, sir," the pale-faced steward turned resignedly to me. It was this maddening course of being shouted at, checked without rhyme or reason, arbitrarily chased out of my cabin, suddenly called into it, sent flying out of his pantry on incomprehensible errands, that accounted for the growing wretchedness of his expression.

"Where are you going with that coat?"

"To your room, sir."

"Is there another shower coming?"

"I'm sure I don't know, sir. Shall I go up again and see, sir?"

"No! never mind."

My object was attained, as of course my other self in there would have heard everything that passed. During this interlude my two officers never raised their eyes off their respective plates; but the lip of that confounded cub, the second mate, quivered visibly.

I expected the steward to hook my coat on and come out at once. He was very slow about it; but I dominated my nervousness sufficiently not to shout after

---

7. By following a zigzag course into the wind.

him. Suddenly I became aware (it could be heard plainly enough) that the fellow for some reason or other was opening the door of the bathroom. It was the end. The place was literally not big enough to swing a cat in. My voice died in my throat and I went stony all over. I expected to hear a yell of surprise and terror, and made a movement, but had not the strength to get on my legs. Everything remained still. Had my second self taken the poor wretch by the throat? I don't know what I could have done next moment if I had not seen the steward come out of my room, close the door, and then stand quietly by the sideboard.

"Saved," I thought. "But, no! Lost! Gone! He was gone!"

I laid my knife and fork down and leaned back in my chair. My head swam. After a while, when sufficiently recovered to speak in a steady voice, I instructed my mate to put the ship round at eight o'clock himself.

"I won't come on deck," I went on. "I think I'll turn in, and unless the wind shifts I don't want to be disturbed before midnight. I feel a bit seedy."

"You did look middling bad a little while ago," the chief mate remarked without showing any great concern.

They both went out, and I stared at the steward clearing the table. There was nothing to be read on that wretched man's face. But why did he avoid my eyes? I asked myself. Then I thought I should like to hear the sound of his voice.

"Steward!"

"Sir!" Startled as usual.

"Where did you hang up that coat?"

"In the bathroom, sir." The usual anxious tone. "It's not quite dry yet, sir."

For some time longer I sat in the cuddy. Had my double vanished as he had come? But of his coming there was an explanation, whereas his disappearance would be inexplicable.... I went slowly into my dark room, shut the door, lighted the lamp, and for a time dared not turn round. When at last I did I saw him standing bolt upright in the narrow recessed part. It would not be true to say I had a shock, but an irresistible doubt of his bodily existence flitted through my mind. Can it be, I asked myself, that he is not visible to other eyes than mine? It was like being haunted. Motionless, with a grave face, he raised his hands slightly at me in a gesture which meant clearly, "Heavens! what a narrow escape!" Narrow indeed. I think I had come creeping quietly as near insanity as any man who has not actually gone over the border. That gesture restrained me, so to speak.

The mate with the terrific whiskers was now putting the ship on the other tack. In the moment of profound silence which follows upon the hands going to their stations I heard on the poop his raised voice: "Hard alee!"[8] and the distant shout of the order repeated on the main deck. The sails, in that light breeze, made but a faint fluttering noise. It ceased. The ship was coming round slowly; I held my breath in the renewed stillness of expectation; one wouldn't have thought that there was a single living soul on her decks. A sudden brisk shout, "Mainsail haul!" broke the spell, and in the noisy cries and rush overhead of the men running away with the main brace we two, down in my cabin, came together in our usual position by the bedplace.

He did not wait for my question. "I heard him fumbling here and just managed to squat myself down in the bath," he whispered to me. "The fellow only

---

8. That is, put the helm all the way over to the side away from the wind.

opened the door and put his arm in to hang the coat up. All the same...."

"I never thought of that," I whispered back, even more appalled than before at the closeness of the shave, and marveling at that something unyielding in his character which was carrying him through so finely. There was no agitation in his whisper. Whoever was being driven distracted, it was not he. He was sane. And the proof of his sanity was continued when he took up the whispering again.

"It would never do for me to come to life again."

It was something that a ghost might have said. But what he was alluding to was his old captain's reluctant admission of the theory of suicide. It would obviously serve his turn—if I had understood at all the view which seemed to govern the unalterable purpose of his action.

"You must maroon me as soon as ever you can get amongst these islands off the Cambodje[9] shore," he went on.

"Maroon you! We are not living in a boy's adventure tale," I protested. His scornful whispering took me up.

"We aren't indeed! There's nothing of a boy's tale in this. But there's nothing else for it. I want no more. You don't suppose I am afraid of what can be done to me? Prison or gallows or whatever they may please. But you don't see me coming back to explain such things to an old fellow in a wig and twelve respectable tradesmen, do you? What can they know whether I am guilty or not—or of *what* I am guilty, either? That's my affair. What does the Bible say? 'Driven off the face of the earth.'[1] Very well. I am off the face of the earth now. As I came at night so I shall go."

"Impossible!" I murmured. "You can't."

"Can't?.... Not naked like a soul on the Day of Judgment. I shall freeze on to this sleeping suit. The Last Day is not yet—and ... you have understood thoroughly. Didn't you?"

I felt suddenly ashamed of myself. I may say truly that I understood—and my hesitation in letting that man swim away from my ship's side had been a mere sham sentiment, a sort of cowardice.

"It can't be done now till next night," I breathed out. "The ship is on the offshore tack and the wind may fail us."

"As long as I know that you understand," he whispered. "But of course you do. It's a great satisfaction to have got somebody to understand. You seem to have been there on purpose." And in the same whisper, as if we two whenever we talked had to say things to each other which were not fit for the world to hear, he added, "It's very wonderful."

We remained side by side talking in our secret way—but sometimes silent or just exchanging a whispered word or two at long intervals. And as usual he stared through the port. A breath of wind came now and again into our faces. The ship might have been moored in dock, so gently and on an even keel she slipped through the water, that did not murmur even at our passage, shadowy and silent like a phantom sea.

At midnight I went on deck, and to my mate's great surprise put the ship round on the other tack. His terrible whiskers flitted round me in silent criticism. I certainly should not have done it if it had been only a question of getting out of that sleepy gulf as quickly as possible. I believe he told the second mate, who

---

9. Cambodian.  1. Genesis 4.14.

relieved him, that it was a great want of judgment. The other only yawned. That intolerable cub shuffled about so sleepily and lolled against the rails in such a slack, improper fashion that I came down on him sharply.

"Aren't you properly awake yet?"

"Yes, sir! I am awake."

"Well, then, be good enough to hold yourself as if you were. And keep a look out. If there's any current we'll be closing with some islands long before daylight."

The east side of the gulf is fringed with islands, some solitary, others in groups. On the blue background of the high coast they seem to float on silvery patches of calm water, arid and gray, or dark green and rounded like clumps of evergreen bushes, with the larger ones, a mile or two long, showing the outlines of ridges, ribs of gray rock under the dank mantle of matted leafage. Unknown to trade, to travel, almost to geography, the manner of life they harbor is an unsolved secret. There must be villages—settlements of fishermen at least—on the largest of them, and some communication with the world is probably kept up by native craft. But all that forenoon, as we headed for them, fanned along by the faintest of breezes, I saw no sign of man or canoe in the field of the telescope I kept on pointing at the scattered group.

At noon I gave no orders for a change of course, and the mate's whiskers became much concerned and seemed to be offering themselves unduly to my notice. At last I said:

"I am going to stand right in. Quite in—as far as I can take her."

The stare of extreme surprise imparted an air of ferocity also to his eyes, and he looked truly terrific for a moment.

"We're not doing well in the middle of the gulf," I continued casually. "I am going to look for the land breezes tonight."

"Bless my soul! Do you mean, sir, in the dark amongst the lot of all them islands and reefs and shoals?"

"Well, if there are any regular land breezes at all on this coast one must get close inshore to find them—mustn't one?"

"Bless my soul!" he exclaimed again under his breath. All that afternoon he wore a dreamy, comtemplative appearance which in him was a mark of perplexity. After dinner I went into my stateroom as if I meant to take some rest. There we two bent our dark heads over a half-unrolled chart lying on my bed.

"There," I said. "It's got to be Koh-ring.[2] I've been looking at it ever since sunrise. It has got two hills and a low point. It must be inhabited. And on the coast opposite there is what looks like the mouth of a biggish river—with some town, no doubt, not far up. It's the best chance for you that I can see."

"Anything. Koh-ring let it be."

He looked thoughtfully at the chart as if surveying chances and distances from a lofty height—and following with his eyes his own figure wandering on the blank land of Cochin-China, and then passing off that piece of paper clean out of sight into uncharted regions. And it was as if the ship had two captains to plan her course for her. I had been so worried and restless running up and down that I had not had the patience to dress that day. I had remained in my sleeping suit, with straw slippers and a soft floppy hat. The closeness of the heat

---

2. Conrad's name for one of a large number of islands at the head of the Gulf of Siam; *Koh* or *Ko* means *island.*

in the gulf had been most oppressive, and the crew were used to see me wandering in that airy attire.

"She will clear the south point as she heads now," I whispered into his ear. "Goodness only knows when, though—but certainly after dark. I'll edge her in to half a mile, as far as I may be able to judge in the dark . . ."

"Be careful," he murmured warningly—and I realized suddenly that all my future, the only future for which I was fit, would perhaps go irretrievably to pieces in any mishap to my first command.

I could not stop a moment longer in the room. I motioned him to get out of sight and made my way on the poop. That unplayful cub had the watch. I walked up and down for a while thinking things out, then beckoned him over.

"Send a couple of hands to open the two quarter-deck ports," I said mildly.

He actually had the impudence, or else so forgot himself in his wonder at such an incomprehensible order, as to repeat:

"Open the quarter-deck ports! What for, sir?"

"The only reason you need concern yourself about is because I tell you to do so. Have them opened wide and fastened properly."

He reddened and went off, but I believe made some jeering remark to the carpenter as to the sensible practice of ventilating a ship's quarter-deck. I know he popped into the mate's cabin to impart the fact to him, because the whiskers came on deck, as it were by chance, and stole glances at me from below—for signs of lunacy or drunkenness, I suppose.

A little before supper, feeling more restless than ever, I rejoined, for a moment, my second self. And to find him sitting so quietly was surprising, like something against nature, inhuman.

I developed my plan in a hurried whisper.

"I shall stand in as close as I dare and then put her round. I shall presently find means to smuggle you out of here into the sail-locker, which communicates with the lobby. But there is an opening, a sort of square for hauling the sails out, which gives straight on the quarterdeck and which is never closed in fine weather, so as to give air to the sails. When the ship's way is deadened in stays[3] and all the hands are aft at the main braces you shall have a clear road to slip out and get overboard through the open quarter-deck port. I've had them both fastened up. Use a rope's end to lower yourself into the water so as to avoid a splash—you know. It could be heard and cause some beastly complication."

He kept silent for a while, then whispered, "I understand."

"I won't be there to see you go," I began with an effort. "The rest . . . I only hope I have understood too."

"You have. From first to last"—and for the first time there seemed to be a faltering, something strained in his whisper. He caught hold of my arm, but the ringing of the supper bell made me start. He didn't though; he only released his grip.

After supper I didn't come below again till well past eight o'clock. The faint, steady breeze was loaded with dew; and the wet, darkened sails held all there was of propelling power in it. The night, clear and starry, sparkled darkly, and the opaque, lightless patches shifting slowly amongst the low stars were the drifting islets. On the port bow there was a big one more distant and shadowily imposing by the great space of sky it eclipsed.

---

3. When the ship's forward progress is slowed or stopped while tacking (changing course) into the wind.

On opening the door I had a back view of my very own self looking at a chart. He had come out of the recess and was standing near the table.

"Quite dark enough," I whispered.

He stepped back and leaned against my bed with a level, quiet glance. I sat on the couch. We had nothing to say to each other. Over our heads the officer of the watch moved here and there. Then I heard him move quickly. I knew what that meant. He was making for the companion; and presently his voice was outside my door.

"We are drawing in pretty fast, sir. Land looks rather close."

"Very well," I answered. "I am coming on deck directly."

I waited till he was gone out of the cuddy, then rose. My double moved too. The time had come to exchange our last whispers, for neither of us was ever to hear each other's natural voice.

"Look here!" I opened a drawer and took out three sovereigns. "Take this, anyhow. I've got six and I'd give you the lot, only I must keep a little money to buy some fruit and vegetables for the crew from native boats as we go through Sunda Straits."

He shook his head.

"Take it," I urged him, whispering desperately. "No one can tell what . . ."

He smiled and slapped meaningly the only pocket of the sleeping jacket. It was not safe, certainly. But I produced a large old silk handkerchief of mine, and tying the three pieces of gold in a corner, pressed it on him. He was touched, I suppose, because he took it at last and tied it quickly round his waist under the jacket, on his bare skin.

Our eyes met; several seconds elapsed, till, our glances still mingled, I extended my hand and turned the lamp out. Then I passed through the cuddy, leaving the door of my room wide open. . . . "Steward!"

He was still lingering in the pantry in the greatness of his zeal, giving a rub-up to a plated cruet stand the last thing before going to bed. Being careful not to wake up the mate, whose room was opposite, I spoke in an undertone.

He looked round anxiously. "Sir!"

"Can you get me a little hot water from the galley?"

"I am afraid, sir, the galley fire's been out for some time now."

"Go and see."

He fled up the stairs.

"Now," I whispered loudly into the saloon—too loudly, perhaps, but I was afraid I couldn't make a sound. He was by my side in an instant—the double captain slipped past the stairs—through a tiny dark passage . . . a sliding door. We were in the sail-locker, scrambling on our knees over the sails. A sudden thought struck me. I saw myself wandering barefooted, bareheaded, the sun beating on my dark poll. I snatched off my floppy hat and tried hurriedly in the dark to ram it on my other self. He dodged and fended off silently. I wonder what he thought had come to me before he understood and suddenly desisted. Our hands met gropingly, lingered united in a steady, motionless clasp for a second. . . . No word was breathed by either of us when they separated.

I was standing quietly by the pantry door when the steward returned.

"Sorry, sir. Kettle barely warm. Shall I light the spirit-lamp?"

"Never mind."

I came out on deck slowly. It was now a matter of conscience to shave the land as close as possible—for now he must go overboard whenever the ship was put in stays. Must! There could be no going back for him. After a moment I walked over to leeward and my heart flew into my mouth at the nearness of the land on the bow. Under any other circumstances I would not have held on a minute longer. The second mate had followed me anxiously.

I looked on till I felt I could command my voice.

"She will weather," I said then in a quiet tone.

"Are you going to try that, sir?" he stammered out incredulously.

290 I took no notice of him and raised my tone just enough to be heard by the helmsman.

"Keep her good full."[4]

"Good full, sir."

The wind fanned my cheek, the sails slept, the world was silent. The strain of watching the dark loom of the land grow bigger and denser was too much for me. I had to shut my eyes—because the ship must go closer. She must! The stillness was intolerable. Were we standing still?

When I opened my eyes the second view started my heart with a thump. The black southern hill of Koh-ring seemed to hang right over the ship like a towering fragment of the everlasting night. On that enormous mass of blackness there was not a gleam to be seen, not a sound to be heard. It was gliding irresistibly towards us and yet seemed already within reach of the hand. I saw the vague figures of the watch grouped in the waist, gazing in awed silence.

295 "Are you going on, sir?" inquired an unsteady voice at my elbow.

I ignored it. I had to go on.

"Keep her full. Don't check her way. That won't do now," I said warningly.

"I can't see the sails very well," the helmsman answered me, in strange, quavering tones.

Was she close enough? Already she was, I won't say in the shadow of the land, but in the very blackness of it, already swallowed up as it were, gone too close to be recalled, gone from me altogether.

300 "Give the mate a call," I said to the young man who stood at my elbow as still as death. "And turn all hands up."

My tone had a borrowed loudness reverberated from the height of the land. Several voices cried out together, "We are all on deck, sir."

Then stillness again, with the great shadow gliding closer, towering higher, without a light, without a sound. Such a hush had fallen on the ship that she might have been a bark of the dead floating in slowly under the very gate of Erebus.[5]

"My God! Where are we?"

It was the mate moaning at my elbow. He was thunderstruck, and as it were deprived of the moral support of his whiskers. He clapped his hands and absolutely cried out, "Lost!"

305 "Be quiet," I said sternly.

He lowered his tone, but I saw the shadowy gesture of his despair. "What are we doing here?"

"Looking for the land wind."

He made as if to tear his hair, and addressed me recklessly.

---

4. That is, keep the ship's sails filled with wind.
5. In Greek mythology, a place of darkness in the underworld.

"She will never get out. You have done it, sir. I knew it'd end in something like this. She will never weather, and you are too close now to stay. She'll drift ashore before she's round. O my God!"

I caught his arm as he was raising it to batter his poor devoted head, and shook it violently.

"She's ashore already," he wailed, trying to tear himself away.

"Is she?... Keep good full there!"

"Good full, sir," cried the helmsman in a frightened, thin, childlike voice.

I hadn't let go the mate's arm and went on shaking it. "Ready about,[6] do you hear? You go forward"—shake—"and stop there"—shake—"and hold your noise"—shake—"and see these head-sheets properly overhauled"—shake, shake—shake.

And all the time I dared not look towards the land lest my heart should fail me. I released my grip at last and he ran forward as if fleeing for dear life.

I wondered what my double there in the sail-locker thought of this commotion. He was able to hear everything—and perhaps he was able to understand why, on my conscience, it had to be thus close—no less. My first order "Hard alee!" re-echoed ominously under the towering shadow of Koh-ring as if I had shouted in a mountain gorge. And then I watched the land intently. In that smooth water and light wind it was impossible to feel the ship coming-to.[7] No! I could not feel her. And my second self was making now ready to slip out and lower himself overboard. Perhaps he was gone already...?

The great black mass brooding over our very mast-heads began to pivot away from the ship's side silently. And now I forgot the secret stranger ready to depart, and remembered only that I was a total stranger to the ship. I did not know her. Would she do it? How was she to be handled?

I swung the mainyard and waited helplessly. She was perhaps stopped, and her very fate hung in the balance, with the black mass of Koh-ring like the gate of the everlasting night towering over her taffrail. What would she do now? Had she way on her[8] yet? I stepped to the side swiftly, and on the shadowy water I could see nothing except a faint phosphorescent flash revealing the glassy smoothness of the sleeping surface. It was impossible to tell—and I had not learned yet the feel of my ship. Was she moving? What I needed was something easily seen, a piece of paper, which I could throw overboard and watch. I had nothing on me. To run down for it I didn't dare. There was no time. All at once my strained, yearning stare distinguished a white object floating within a yard of the ship's side—white, on the black water. A phosphorescent flash passed under it. What was that thing?... I recognized my own floppy hat. It must have fallen off his head... and he didn't bother. Now I had what I wanted—the saving mark for my eyes. But I hardly thought of my other self, now gone from the ship, to be hidden for ever from all friendly faces, to be a fugitive and a vagabond on the earth, with no brand of the curse on his sane forehead to stay a slaying hand... too proud to explain.

And I watched the hat—the expression of my sudden pity for his mere flesh. It had been meant to save his homeless head from the dangers of the sun. And

---

6. That is, be ready to change the ship's direction by shifting the helm and adjusting the set of the sails; *see these head-sheets properly overhauled:* slacken the ropes that secure the sails of the foremast.
7. Coming to a standstill.   8. Was she moving?

now—behold—it was saving the ship, by serving me for a mark to help out the ignorance of my strangeness. Ha! It was drifting forward, warning me just in time that the ship had gathered sternway.[9]

"Shift the helm," I said in a low voice to the seaman standing still like a statue.

The man's eyes glistened wildly in the binnacle light as he jumped round to the other side and spun round the wheel.

I walked to the break of the poop. On the overshadowed deck all hands stood by the forebraces waiting for my order. The stars ahead seemed to be gliding from right to left. And all was so still in the world that I heard the quiet remark, "She's round," passed in a tone of intense relief between two seamen.

"Let go and haul."

The foreyards ran round with a great noise, amidst cheery cries. And now the frightful whiskers made themselves heard giving various orders. Already the ship was drawing ahead. And I was alone with her. Nothing! no one in the world should stand now between us, throwing a shadow on the way of silent knowledge and mute affection; the perfect communion of a seaman with his first command.

Walking to the taffrail, I was in time to make out, on the very edge of a darkness thrown by a towering black mass like the very gateway of Erebus—yes, I was in time to catch an evanescent glimpse of my white hat left behind to mark the spot where the secret sharer of my cabin and of my thoughts, as though he were my second self, had lowered himself into the water to take his punishment: a free man, a proud swimmer striking out for a new destiny.

1912

## QUESTIONS

1. How does the second paragraph of "The Secret Sharer" help to establish setting? Which words in this paragraph might have figurative significance, or should be read as having meaning for the characterization, plot, and theme of the story? Are there words—or details of the setting—in this paragraph that reappear in other parts of the story?
2. How does paragraph 7 contribute to the characterization of the second mate and the narrator, and how does it reveal the relations among people on board the ship? Does this paragraph add to your expectations for the plot? What words or ideas in the narrator's account catch your attention as warnings, rationalizations, or excuses?
3. How does the "unconventional arrangement" of the narrator-captain's standing the first anchor-watch relate to his character? to the plot? to the theme(s)?
4. When the narrator notices that the rope side-ladder has not been hauled in, he blames himself for having disturbed the ship's routine and conjectures about how his conduct will be "accounted" for by the chief mate and members of the crew. It is just then that "the secret sharer" appears at the very end of that same ladder, as "something elongated and pale" (paragraph 20). What other words in paragraphs 20 and 21 convey the narrator's perception of this strange personage? How do these descriptions, which include significant adjectives ("silvery"), metaphors ("corpse"), and similes ("mute as a fish"), contribute to the tone and effect of the story? What is the connection between the captain's worries about managing the ship and his reaction to the apparition?
5. When Leggatt tells his story, there is a shift in the focus and voice. How does this story within a story function in the plot of "The Secret Sharer"? How does it help

---

9. That is, that the ship had begun moving backward.

define the character of Leggatt? How does it relate to the theme of "the double" in the larger story?
6. The captain of the *Sephora* tells his version of Leggatt's crime, but the narrator says, "It is not worth while to record that version. It was just over two months since all this had happened, and . . . he seemed completely muddled" (paragraph 127). Why do you think the narrator seems so eager to discount Captain Archbold's version of what had happened aboard the *Sephora*?
7. Captain Archbold believes Leggatt was too gentlemanly to be chief mate of the *Sephora*, and the narrator, now so identified with Leggatt, thinks Archbold would not consider the narrator himself a suitable chief mate (much less captain). How central to the story is this issue of fitness to lead? What role does Leggatt play in initiating the narrator into leadership or captaincy?
8. There seems to be a turn in the story after Archbold leaves: ironically, Leggatt seems more of a burden to the narrator, who now becomes more aware of his role as captain: "I was not wholly alone with my command; for there was that stranger in my cabin. . . . Part of me was absent" (paragraph 193). What is the effect of this feeling of split identity on the plot? How does it relate to focus?
9. How does the captain's giving Leggatt his hat figure in the plot? What does it suggest about the narrator's character and feelings? Of what, if anything, might it be a symbol?

The story that follows is funnier than "The Secret Sharer," but no less meaningful. It is the title story, or chapter, of a work that calls itself a novel but can also be seen as a collection of related but separable stories (indeed, many of the chapters were first published separately as stories, and an expanded edition of *Love Medicine* adds four new stories or chapters and rearranges the original sequence). The experiences of a Native American reservation and the healing power of "touch" are likely to seem unfamiliar to most readers. Stop reading after paragraph 18, look at the first of the Questions on page 384, and get your bearings.

**LOUISE ERDRICH**

## Love Medicine

I never really done much with my life, I suppose. I never had a television. Grandma Kashpaw had one inside her apartment at the Senior Citizens, so I used to go there and watch my favorite shows. For a while she used to call me the biggest waste on the reservation and hark back to how she saved me from my own mother, who wanted to tie me in a potato sack and throw me in a slough. Sure, I was grateful to Grandma Kashpaw for saving me like that, for raising me, but gratitude gets old. After a while, stale. I had to stop thanking her. One day I told her I had paid her back in full by staying at her beck and call. I'd do anything for Grandma. She knew that. Besides, I took care of Grandpa like nobody else could, on account of what a handful he'd gotten to be.

But that was nothing. I know the tricks of mind and body inside out without ever having trained for it, because I got the touch. It's a thing you got to be born with. I got secrets in my hands that nobody ever knew to ask. Take Grandma Kashpaw with her tired veins all knotted up in her legs like clumps of blue snails. I take my fingers and I snap them on the knots. The medicine flows out of me.

The touch. I run my fingers up the maps of those rivers of veins or I knock very gentle above their hearts or I make a circling motion on their stomachs, and it helps them. They feel much better. Some women pay me five dollars.

I couldn't do the touch for Grandpa, though. He was a hard nut. You know, some people fall right through the hole in their lives. It's invisible, but they come to it after time, never knowing where. There is this woman here, Lulu Lamartine, who always had a thing for Grandpa. She loved him since she was a girl and always said he was a genius. Now she says that his mind got so full it exploded.

How can I doubt that? I know the feeling when your mental power builds up too far. I always used to say that's why the Indians got drunk. Even statistically we're the smartest people on the earth. Anyhow with Grandpa I couldn't hardly believe it, because all my youth he stood out as a hero to me. When he started getting toward second childhood he went through different moods. He would stand in the woods and cry at the top of his shirt. It scared me, scared everyone, Grandma worst of all.

5   Yet he was so smart—do you believe it?—that he *knew* he was getting foolish.

He said so. He told me that December I failed school and come back on the train to Hoopdance. I didn't have nowhere else to go. He picked me up there and he said it straight out: "I'm getting into my second childhood." And then he said something else I still remember: "I been chosen for it. I couldn't say no." So I figure that a man so smart all his life—tribal chairman and the star of movies and even pictured in the statehouse and on cans of snuff—would know what he's doing by saying yes. I think he was called to second childhood like anybody else gets a call for the priesthood or the army or whatever. So I really did not listen too hard when the doctor said this was some kind of disease old people got eating too much sugar. You just can't tell me that a man who went to Washington and gave them bureaucrats what for could lose his mind from eating too much Milky Way. No, he put second childhood on himself.

Behind those songs he sings out in the middle of Mass, and back of those stories that everybody knows by heart, Grandpa is thinking hard about life. I know the feeling. Sometimes I'll throw up a smokescreen to think behind. I'll hitch up to Winnipeg and play the Space Invaders for six hours, but all the time there and back I will be thinking some fairly deep thoughts that surprise even me, and I'm used to it. As for him, if it was just the thoughts there wouldn't be no problem. Smokescreen is what irritates the social structure, see, and Grandpa has done things that just distract people to the point they want to throw him in the cookie jar where they keep the mentally insane. He's far from that, I know for sure, but even Grandma had trouble keeping her patience once he started sneaking off to Lamartine's place. He's not supposed to have his candy, and Lulu feeds it to him. That's *one* of the reasons why he goes.

Grandma tried to get me to put the touch on Grandpa soon after he began stepping out. I didn't want to, but before Grandma started telling me again what a bad state my bare behind was in when she first took me home, I thought I should at least pretend.

I put my hands on either side of Grandpa's head. You wouldn't look at him and say he was crazy. He's a fine figure of a man, as Lamartine would say, with all his hair and half his teeth, a beak like a hawk, and cheeks like the blades of a hatchet. They put his picture on all the tourist guides to North Dakota and even copied his face for artistic paintings. I guess you could call him a monument all of himself. He started grinning when I put my hands on his templates, and I knew right then he knew how come I touched him. I knew the smokescreen was going to fall.

And I was right: just for a moment it fell.

"Let's pitch whoopee," he said across my shoulder to Grandma.

They don't use that expression much around here anymore, but for damn sure it must have meant something. It got her goat right quick.

She threw my hands off his head herself and stood in front of him, overmatching him pound for pound, and taller too, for she had a growth spurt in middle age while he had shrunk, so now the length and breadth of her surpassed him. She glared and spoke her piece into his face about how he was off at all hours tomcatting and chasing Lamartine again and making a damn old fool of himself.

"And you got no more whoopee to pitch anymore anyhow!" she yelled at last, surprising me so my jaw just dropped, for us kids all had pretended for so long that those rustling sounds we heard from their side of the room at night never happened. She sure had pretended it, up till now, anyway. I saw that tears were in her eyes. And that's when I saw how much grief and love she felt for him. And it gave me a real shock to the system. You see I thought love got easier over the years so it didn't hurt so bad when it hurt, or feel so good when it felt good. I thought it smoothed out and old people hardly noticed it. I thought it curled up and died, I guess. Now I saw it rear up like a whip and lash.

She loved him. She was jealous. She mourned him like the dead.

And he just smiled into the air, trapped in the seams of his mind.

So I didn't know what to do. I was in a laundry then. They was like parents to me, the way they had took me home and reared me. I could see her point for wanting to get him back the way he was so at least she could argue with him, sleep with him, not be shamed out by Lamartine. She'd always love him. That hit me like a ton of bricks. For one whole day I felt this odd feeling that cramped my hands. When you have the touch, that's where longing gets you. I never loved like that. It made me feel all inspired to see them fight, and I wanted to go out and find a woman who I would love until one of us died or went crazy. But I'm not like that really. From time to time I heal a person all up good inside, however when it comes to the long shot I doubt that I got staying power.

And you need that, staying power, going out to love somebody. I knew this quality was not going to jump on me with no effort. So I turned my thoughts back to Grandma and Grandpa. I felt her side of it with my hands and my tangled guts, and I felt his side of it within the stretch of my mentality. He had gone out to lunch one day and never came back. He was fishing in the middle of Matchimanito. And there was big thoughts on his line, and he kept throwing them back for even bigger ones that would explain to him, say, the meaning of how we got here and why we have to leave so soon. All in all, I could not see myself treating Grandpa with the touch, bringing him back, when the real part of him had chose to be off thinking somewhere. It was only the rest of him that stayed around causing trouble, after all, and we could handle most of it without any problem.

Besides, it was hard to argue with his reasons for doing some things. Take Holy Mass. I used to go there just every so often, when I got frustrated mostly, because even though I know the Higher Power dwells everyplace, there's something very calming about the cool greenish inside of our mission. Or so I thought, anyway. Grandpa was the one who stripped off my delusions in this matter, for it was he who busted right through what Father calls the sacred serenity of the place.

20   We filed in that time. Me and Grandpa. We sat down in our pews. Then the rosary got started up pre-Mass and that's when Grandpa filled up his chest and opened his mouth and belted out them words.

HAIL MARIE FULL OF GRACE.

He had a powerful set of lungs.

And he kept on like that. He did not let up. He hollered and he yelled them prayers, and I guess people was used to him by now, because they only muttered theirs and did not quit and gawk like I did. I was getting red-faced, I admit. I give him the elbow once or twice, but that wasn't nothing to him. He kept on. He shrieked to heaven and he pleaded like a movie actor and he pounded his chest like Tarzan in the Lord I Am Not Worthies. I thought he might hurt himself. Then after a while I guess I got used to it, and that's when I wondered: how come?

So afterwards I out and asked him. "How come? How come you yelled?"

25   "God don't hear me otherwise," said Grandpa Kashpaw.

I sweat. I broke right into a little cold sweat at my hairline because I knew this was perfectly right and for years not one damn other person had noticed it. God's been going deaf. Since the Old Testament, God's been deafening up on us. I read, see. Besides the dictionary, which I'm constantly in use of, I had this Bible once. I read it. I found there was discrepancies between then and now. It struck me. Here God used to raineth bread from clouds, smite the Phillipines, sling fire down on red-light districts where people got stabbed. He even appeared in person every once in a while. God used to pay attention, is what I'm saying.

Now there's your God in the Old Testament and there is Chippewa Gods as well. Indian Gods, good and bad, like tricky Nanabozho or the water monster, Missepeshu, who lives over in Matchimanito. That water monster was the last God I ever heard to appear. It had a weakness for young girls and grabbed one of the Pillagers off her rowboat. She got to shore all right, but only after this monster had its way with her. She's an old lady now. Old Lady Pillager. She still doesn't like to see her family fish that lake.

Our Gods aren't perfect, is what I'm saying, but at least they come around. They'll do a favor if you ask them right. You don't have to yell. But you do have to know, like I said, how to ask in the right way. That makes problems, because to ask proper was an art that was lost to the Chippewas once the Catholics gained ground. Even now, I have to wonder if Higher Power turned it back, if we got to yell, or if we just don't speak its language.

I looked around me. How else could I explain what all I had seen in my short life—King smashing his fist in things, Gordie drinking himself down to the Bismarck hospitals, or Aunt June left by a white man to wander off in the snow. How else to explain the times my touch don't work, and farther back, to the oldtime Indians who was swept away in the outright germ warfare and dirty-dog killing of the whites. In those times, us Indians was so much kindlier than now.

30   We took them in.

Oh yes, I'm bitter as an old cutworm just thinking of how they done to us and doing still.

So Grandpa Kashpaw just opened my eyes a little there. Was there any sense relying on a God whose ears was stopped? Just like the government? I says then, right off, maybe we got nothing but ourselves. And that's not much, just personally speaking. I know I don't got the cold hard potatoes it takes to understand everything. Still, there's things I'd like to do. For instance, I'd like to help some people like my Grandpa and Grandma Kashpaw get back some happiness within the tail ends of their lives.

I told you once before I couldn't see my way clear to putting the direct touch on Grandpa's mind, and I kept my moral there, but something soon happened to make me think a little bit of mental adjustment wouldn't do him and the rest of us no harm.

It was after we saw him one afternoon in the sunshine courtyard of the Senior Citizens with Lulu Lamartine. Grandpa used to like to dig there. He had his little dandelion fork out, and he was prying up them dandelions right and left while Lamartine watched him.

"He's scratching up the dirt, all right," said Grandma, watching Lamartine watch Grandpa out the window.

Now Lamartine was about half the considerable size of Grandma, but you would never think of sizes anyway. They were different in an even more noticeable way. It was the difference between a house fixed up with paint and picky fence, and a house left to weather away into the soft earth, is what I'm saying. Lamartine was jacked up, latticed, shuttered, and vinyl sided, while Grandma sagged and bulged on her slipped foundations and let her hair go the silver gray of rain-dried lumber. Right now, she eyed the Lamartine's pert flowery dress with such a look it despaired me. I knew what this could lead to with Grandma. Alternating tongue storms and rock-hard silences was hard on a man, even one who didn't notice, like Grandpa. So I went fetching him.

But he was gone when I popped through the little screen door that led out on the courtyard. There was nobody out there either, to point which way they went. Just the dandelion fork quibbling upright in the ground. That gave me an idea. I snookered over to the Lamartine's door and I listened in first, then knocked. But nobody. So I went walking through the lounges and around the card tables. Still nobody. Finally it was my touch that led me to the laundry room. I cracked the door. I went in. There they were. And he was really loving her up good, boy, and she was going hell for leather. Sheets was flapping on the lines above, and washcloths, pillowcases, shirts was also flying through the air, for they was trying to clear out a place for themselves in a high-heaped but shallow laundry cart. The washers and dryers was all on, chock-full of quarters, shaking and moaning. I couldn't hear what Grandpa and the Lamartine was billing and cooing, and they couldn't hear me.

I didn't know what to do, so I went inside and shut the door.

The Lamartine wore a big curly light-brown wig. Looked like one of them squeaky little white-people dogs. Poodles they call them. Anyway, that wig is what saved us from the worse. For I could hardly shout and tell them I was in there, no more could I try and grab him. I was trapped where I was. There was nothing I could really do but hold the door shut. I was scared of somebody else upsetting in and really getting an eyeful. Turned out though, in the heat of the clinch, as I was trying to avert my eyes you see, the Lamartine's curly wig jumped off her head. And if you ever been in the midst of something and had a big change like that occur in the someone, you can't help know how it devastates your basic urges. Not only that, but her wig was almost with a life of its own. Grandpa's eyes were bugging at the change already, and swear to God if the thing didn't rear up and pop him in the face like it was going to start something. He scrambled up, Grandpa did, and the Lamartine jumped up after him all addled looking. They just stared at each other, huffing and puffing, with quizzical expression. The surprise seemed to drive all sense completely out of Grandpa's mind.

40   "The letter was what started the fire," he said. "I never would have done it."
   "What letter?" said the Lamartine. She was stiff-necked now, and elegant, even bald, like some alien queen. I gave her back the wig. The Lamartine replaced it on her head, and whenever I saw her after that, I couldn't help thinking of her bald, with special powers, as if from another planet.
   "That was a close call," I said to Grandpa after she had left.
   But I think he had already forgot the incident. He just stood there all quiet and thoughtful. You really wouldn't think he was crazy. He looked like he was just about to say something important, explaining himself. He said something, all right, but it didn't have nothing to do with anything that made sense.
   He wondered where the heck he put his dandelion fork. That's when I decided about the mental adjustment.

45 Now what was mostly our problem was not so much that he was not all there, but that what was there of him often hankered after Lamartine. If we could put a stop to that, I thought, we might be getting someplace. But here, see, my touch was of no use. For what could I snap my fingers at to make him faithful to Grandma? Like the quality of staying power, this faithfulness was invisible. I know it's something that you got to acquire, but I never known where from. Maybe there's no rhyme or reason to it, like my getting the touch, and then again maybe it's a kind of magic.
   It was Grandma Kashpaw who thought of it in the end. She knows things. Although she will not admit she has a scrap of Indian blood in her, there's no doubt in my mind she's got some Chippewa. How else would you explain the way she'll be sitting there, in front of her TV story, rocking in her armchair and suddenly she turns on me, her brown eyes hard as lake-bed flint.
   "Lipsha Morrissey," she'll say, "you went out last night and got drunk."
   How did she know that? I'll hardly remember it myself. Then she'll say she just had a feeling or ache in the scar of her hand or a creak in her shoulder. She is constantly being told things by little aggravations in her joints or by her household appliances. One time she told Gordie never to ride with a crazy Lamartine boy. She had seen something in the polished-up tin of her bread toaster. So he didn't. Sure enough, the time came we heard how Lyman and Henry went out of control in their car, ending up in the river. Lyman swam to the top, but Henry never made it.
   Thanks to Grandma's toaster, Gordie was probably spared.

50 Someplace in the blood Grandma Kashpaw knows things. She also remembers things, I found. She keeps things filed away. She's got a memory like them video games that don't forget your score. One reason she remembers so many details about the trouble I gave her in early life is so she can flash back her total when she needs to.

Like now. Take the love medicine. I don't know where she remembered that from. It came tumbling from her mind like an asteroid off the corner of the screen.

Of course she starts out by mentioning the time I had this accident in church and did she leave me there with wet overhalls? No she didn't. And ain't I glad? Yes I am. Now what you want now, Grandma?

But when she mentions them love medicines, I feel my back prickle at the danger. These love medicines is something of an old Chippewa specialty. No other tribe has got them down so well. But love medicines is not for the layman to handle. You don't just go out and get one without paying for it. Before you get one, even, you should go through one hell of a lot of mental condensation. You got to think it over. Choose the right one. You could really mess up your life grinding up the wrong little thing.

So anyhow, I said to Grandma I'd give this love medicine some thought. I knew the best thing was to go ask a specialist like Old Lady Pillager, who lives up in a tangle of bush and never shows herself. But the truth is I was afraid of her, like everyone else. She was known for putting the twisted mouth on people, seizing up their hearts. Old Lady Pillager was serious business, and I have always thought it best to steer clear of that whenever I could. That's why I took the powers in my own hands. That's why I did what I could.

I put my whole mentality to it, nothing held back. After a while I started to remember things I'd heard gossiped over.

I heard of this person once who carried a charm of seeds that looked like baby pearls. They was attracted to a metal knife, which made them powerful. But I didn't know where them seeds grew. Another love charm I heard about I couldn't go along with, because how was I suppose to catch frogs in the act, which it required. Them little creatures is slippery and fast. And then the powerfullest of all, the most extreme, involved nail clips and such. I wasn't anywhere near asking Grandma to provide me all the little body bits that this last love recipe called for. I went walking around for days just trying to think up something that would work.

Well I got it. If it hadn't been the early fall of the year, I never would have got it. But I was sitting underneath a tree one day down near the school just watching people's feet go by when something tells me, look up! Look up! So I look up, and I see two honkers, Canada geese, the kind with little masks on their faces, a bird what mates for life. I see them flying right over my head naturally preparing to land in some slough on the reservation, which they certainly won't get off of alive.

It hits me, anyway. Them geese, they mate for life. And I think to myself, just what if I went out and got a pair? And just what if I fed some part—say the goose heart—of the female to Grandma and Grandpa ate the other heart? Wouldn't that work? Maybe it's all invisible, and then maybe again it's magic. Love is a stony road. We know that for sure. If it's true that the higher feelings of devotion get lodged in the heart like people say, then we'd be home free. If not, eating goose heart couldn't harm nobody anyway. I thought it was worth my effort, and Grandma Kashpaw thought so, too. She had always known a good idea when she heard one. She borrowed me Grandpa's gun.

So I went out to this particular slough, maybe the exact same slough I never got thrown in by my mother, thanks to Grandma Kashpaw, and I hunched down in a good comfortable pile of rushes. I got my gun loaded up. I ate a few of these soft baloney sandwiches Grandma made me for lunch. And then I waited. The cattails blown back and forth above my head. Them stringy blue herons was spearing up their prey. The thing I know how to do best in this world, the thing I been training for all my life, is to wait. Sitting there and sitting there was no hardship on me. I got to thinking about some funny things that happened. There was this one time that Lulu Lamartine's little blue tweety bird, a paraclete, I guess you'd call it, flown up inside her dress and got lost within there. I recalled her running out into the hallway trying to yell something, shaking. She was doing a right good jig there, cutting the rug for sure, and the thing is it *never* flown out. To this day people speculate where it went. They fear she might perhaps of crushed it in her corsets. It sure hasn't ever yet been seen alive. I thought of funny things for a while, but then I used them up, and strange things that happened started weaseling their way into my mind.

60    I got to thinking quite naturally of the Lamartine's cousin named Wristwatch. I never knew what his real name was. They called him Wristwatch because he got his father's broken wristwatch as a young boy when his father passed on. Never in his whole life did Wristwatch take his father's watch off. He didn't care if it worked, although after a while he got sensitive when people asked what time it was, teasing him. He often put it to his ear like he was listening to the tick. But it was broken for good and forever, people said so, at least that's what they thought.

Well I saw Wristwatch smoking in his pickup one afternoon and by nine that evening he was dead.

He died sitting at the Lamartine's table, too. As she told it, Wristwatch had just eaten himself a good-size dinner and she said would he take seconds on the hot dish when he fell over to the floor. They turnt him over. He was gone. But here's the strange thing: when the Senior Citizen's orderly took the pulse he noticed that the wristwatch Wristwatch wore was now working. The moment he died the wristwatch started keeping perfect time. They buried him with the watch still ticking on his arm.

I got to thinking. What if some gravediggers dug up Wristwatch's casket in two hundred years and that watch was still going? I thought what question they would ask and it was this: Whose hand wound it?

I started shaking like a piece of grass at just the thought.

65    Not to get off the subject or nothing. I was still hunkered in the slough. It was passing late into the afternoon and still no honkers had touched down. Now I don't need to tell you that the waiting did not get to me, it was the chill. The rushes was very soft, but damp. I was getting cold and debating to leave, when they landed. Two geese swimming here and there as big as life, looking deep into each other's little pinhole eyes. Just the ones I was looking for. So I lifted Grandpa's gun to my shoulder and I aimed perfectly, and *blam! Blam!* I delivered two accurate shots. But the thing is, them shots missed. I couldn't hardly believe it. Whether it was that the stock had warped or the barrel got bent someways, I don't quite know, but anyway them geese flown off into the dim sky, and Lipsha Morrissey was left there in the rushes with evening fallen and his two cold hands empty. He had before him just the prospect of another day of bone-cracking chill in them rushes, and the thought of it got him depressed.

Now it isn't my style, in no way, to get depressed.

So I said to myself, Lipsha Morrissey, you're a happy S.O.B. who could be covered up with weeds by now down at the bottom of this slough, but instead you're alive to tell the tale. You might have problems in life, but you still got the touch. You got the power, Lipsha Morrissey. Can't argue that. So put your mind to it and figure out how not to be depressed.

I took my advice. I put my mind to it. But I never saw at the time how my thoughts led me astray toward a tragic outcome none could have known. I ignored all the danger, all the limits, for I was tired of sitting in the slough and my feet were numb. My face was aching. I was chilled, so I played with fire. I told myself love medicine was simple. I told myself the old superstitions was just that—strange beliefs. I told myself to take the ten dollars Mary MacDonald had paid me for putting the touch on her arthritis joint, and the other five I hadn't spent yet from winning bingo last Thursday. I told myself to go down to the Red Owl store.

And here is what I did that made the medicine backfire. I took an evil shortcut. I looked at birds that was dead and froze.

All right. So now I guess you will say, "Slap a malpractice suit on Lipsha Morrissey."

I heard of those suits. I used to think it was a color clothing quack doctors had to wear so you could tell them from the good ones. Now I know better that it's law.

As I walked back from the Red Owl with the rock-hard, heavy turkeys, I argued to myself about malpractice. I thought of faith. I thought to myself that faith could be called belief against the odds and whether or not there's any proof. How does that sound? I thought how we might have to yell to be heard by Higher Power, but that's not saying it's not *there*. And that is faith for you. It's belief even when the goods don't deliver. Higher Power makes promises we all know they can't back up, but anybody ever go and slap an old malpractice suit on God? Or the U.S. government? No they don't. Faith might be stupid, but it gets us through. So what I'm heading at is this. I finally convinced myself that the real actual power to the love medicine was not the goose heart itself but the faith in the cure.

I didn't believe it, I knew it was wrong, but by then I had waded so far into my lie I was stuck there. And then I went one step further.

The next day, I cleaned the hearts away from the paper packages of gizzards inside the turkeys. Then I wrapped them hearts with a clean hankie and brung them both to get blessed up at the mission. I wanted to get official blessings from the priest, but when Father answered the door to the rectory, wiping his hands on a little towel, I could tell he was a busy man.

"Booshoo,[1] Father," I said. "I got a slight request to make of you this afternoon."

"What is it?" he said.

"Would you bless this package?" I held out the hankie with the hearts tied inside it.

He looked at the package, questioning it.

"It's turkey hearts," I honestly had to reply.

---

1. *Bonjour,* French for "good day" or "hello."

A look of annoyance crossed his face.

"Why don't you bring this matter over to Sister Martin," he said. "I have duties."

And so, although the blessing wouldn't be as powerful, I went over to the Sisters with the package.

I rung the bell, and they brought Sister Martin to the door. I had her as a music teacher, but I was always so shy then. I never talked out loud. Now, I had grown taller than Sister Martin. Looking down, I saw that she was not feeling up to snuff. Brown circles hung under her eyes.

"What's the matter?" she said, not noticing who I was.

"Remember me, Sister?"

She squinted up at me.

"Oh yes," she said after a moment. "I'm sorry, you're the youngest of the Kashpaws. Gordie's brother."

Her face warmed up.

"Lipsha," I said, "that's my name."

"Well, Lipsha," she said, smiling broad at me now, "what can I do for you?"

They always said she was the kindest-hearted of the Sisters up the hill, and she was. She brought me back into their own kitchen and made me take a big yellow wedge of cake and a glass of milk.

"Now tell me," she said, nodding at my package. "What have you got wrapped up so carefully in those handkerchiefs?"

Like before, I answered honestly.

"Ah," said Sister Martin. "Turkey hearts." She waited.

"I hoped you could bless them."

She waited some more, smiling with her eyes. Kindhearted though she was, I began to sweat. A person could not pull the wool down over Sister Martin. I stumbled through my mind for an explanation, quick, that wouldn't scare her off.

"They're a present," I said, "for Saint Kateri's statue."[2]

"She's not a saint yet."

"I know," I stuttered on. "In the hopes they will crown her."

"Lipsha," she said, "I never heard of such a thing."

So I told her. "Well the truth is," I said, "it's a kind of medicine."

"For what?"

"Love."

"Oh Lipsha," she said after a moment, "you don't need any medicine. I'm sure any girl would like you exactly the way you are."

I just sat there. I felt miserable, caught in my pack of lies.

"Tell you what," she said, seeing how bad I felt, "my blessing won't make any difference anyway. But there is something you can do."

I looked up at her, hopeless.

"Just be yourself."

I looked down at my plate. I knew I wasn't much to brag about right then,

---

2. Kateri Kekakwitha (1656–1680), "Lily of the Mohawk," born in what is now upstate New York to a Mohawk father and an Algonquin mother who was a devout Christian. Following the deaths of her parents, Kateri moved to a Jesuit mission near Montreal to spend the rest of her short life in prayer and chastity. Miracles were attributed to her after her death; she was beatified in 1980 and canonized in 1991.

and I shortly became even less. For as I walked out the door I stuck my fingers in the cup of holy water that was sacred from their touches. I put my fingers in and blessed the hearts, quick, with my own hand.

I went back to Grandma and sat down in her little kitchen at the Senior Citizens. I unwrapped them hearts on the table, and her hard agate eyes went soft. She said she wasn't even going to cook those hearts up but eat them raw so their power would go down strong as possible.

I couldn't hardly watch when she munched hers. Now that's true love. I was worried about how she would get Grandpa to eat his, but she told me she'd think of something and don't worry. So I did not. I was supposed to hide off in her bedroom while she put dinner on a plate for Grandpa and fixed up the heart so he'd eat it. I caught a glint of the plate she was making for him. She put that heart smack on a piece of lettuce like in a restaurant and then attached to it a little heap of boiled peas.

He sat down. I was listening in the next room.

She said, "Why don't you have some mash potato?" So he had some mash potato. Then she gave him a little piece of boiled meat. He ate that. Then she said, "Why you didn't never touch your salad yet. See that heart? I'm feeding you it because the doctor said your blood needs building up."

I couldn't help it, at that point I peeked through a crack in the door.

I saw Grandpa picking at that heart on his plate with a certain look. He didn't look appetized at all, is what I'm saying. I doubted our plan was going to work. Grandma was getting worried, too. She told him one more time, loudly, that he had to eat that heart.

"Swallow it down," she said. "You'll hardly notice it."

He just looked at her straight on. The way he looked at her made me think I was going to see the smokescreen drop a second time, and sure enough it happened.

"What you want me to eat this for so bad?" he asked her uncannily.

Now Grandma knew the jig was up. She knew that he knew she was working medicine. He put his fork down. He rolled the heart around his saucer plate.

"I don't want to eat this," he said to Grandma. "It don't look good."

"Why it's fresh grade-A," she told him. "One hundred percent."

He didn't ask percent what, but his eyes took on an even more warier look.

"Just go on and try it," she said, taking the salt shaker up in her hand. She was getting annoyed. "Not tasty enough? You want me to salt it for you?" She waved the shaker over his plate.

"All right, skinny white girl!" She had got Grandpa mad. Oopsy-daisy, he popped the heart into his mouth. I was about to yawn loudly and come out of the bedroom. I was about ready for this crash of wills to be over, when I saw he was still up to his old tricks. First he rolled it into one side of his cheek. "Mmmmm," he said. Then he rolled it into the other side of his cheek. "Mmmmmmm," again. Then he stuck his tongue out with the heart on it and put it back, and there was no time to react. He had pulled Grandma's leg once too far. Her goat was got. She was so mad she hopped up quick as a wink and slugged him between the shoulderblades to make him swallow.

Only thing is, he choked.

He choked real bad. A person can choke to death. You ever sit down at a restaurant table and up above you there is a list of instructions what to do if something slides down the wrong pipe? It sure makes you chew slow, that's for damn sure. When Grandpa fell off his chair better believe me that little graphic illustrated poster fled into my mind. I jumped out the bedroom. I done everything within my power that I could do to unlodge what was choking him. I squeezed underneath his rib cage. I socked him in the back. I was desperate. But here's the factor of decision: he wasn't choking on the heart alone. There was more to it than that. It was other things that choked him as well. It didn't seem like he wanted to struggle or fight. Death came and tapped his chest, so he went just like that. I'm sorry all through my body at what I done to him with that heart, and there's those who will say Lipsha Morrissey is just excusing himself off the hook by giving song and dance about how Grandpa gave up.

Maybe I can't admit what I did. My touch had gone worthless, that is true. But here is what I seen while he lay in my arms.

You hear a person's life will flash before their eyes when they're in danger. It was him in danger, not me, but it was *his* life come over me. I saw him dying, and it was like someone pulled the shade down in a room. His eyes clouded over and squeezed shut, but just before that I looked in. He was still fishing in the middle of Matchimanito. Big thoughts was on his line and he had half a case of beer in the boat. He waved at me, grinned, and then the bobber went under.

Grandma had gone out of the room crying for help. I bunched my force up in my hands and I held him. I was so wound up I couldn't even breathe. All the moments he had spent with me, all the times he had hoisted me on his shoulders or pointed into the leaves was concentrated in that moment. Time was flashing back and forth like a pinball machine. Lights blinked and balls hopped and rubber bands chirped, until suddenly I realized the last ball had gone down the drain and there was nothing. I felt his force leaving him, flowing out of Grandpa never to return. I felt his mind weakening. The bobber going under in the lake. And I felt the touch retreat back into the darkness inside my body, from where it came.

130    One time, long ago, both of us were fishing together. We caught a big old snapper what started towing us around like it was a motor. "This here fishline is pretty damn good," Grandpa said. "Let's keep this turtle on and see where he takes us." So we rode along behind that turtle, watching as from time to time it surfaced. The thing was just about the size of a washtub. It took us all around the lake twice, and as it was traveling, Grandpa said something as a joke. "Lipsha," he said, "we are glad your mother didn't want you because we was always looking for a boy like you who would tow us around the lake."

"I ain't no snapper. Snappers is so stupid they stay alive when their head's chopped off," I said.

"That ain't stupidity," said Grandpa. "Their brain's just in their heart, like yours is."

When I looked up, I knew the fuse had blown between my heart and my mind and that a terrible understanding was to be given.

Grandma got back into the room and I saw her stumble. And then she went down too. It was like a house you can't hardly believe has stood so long, through years of record weather, suddenly goes down in the worst yet. It makes sense, is what I'm saying, but you still can't hardly believe it. You think a person you know has got through death and illness and being broke and living on commodity rice will get through anything. Then they fold and you see how fragile were the stones that underpinned them. You see how instantly the ground can shift you thought was solid. You see the stop signs and the yellow dividing markers of roads you traveled and all the instructions you had played according to vanish. You see how all the everyday things you counted on was just a dream you had been having by which you run your whole life. She had been over me, like a sheer overhang of rock dividing Lipsha Morrissey from outer space. And now she went underneath. It was as though the banks gave way on the shores of Matchimanito, and where Grandpa's passing was just the bobber swallowed under by his biggest thought, her fall was the house and the rock under it sliding after, sending half the lake splashing up to the clouds.

Where there was nothing.

You play them games never knowing what you see. When I fell into the dream alongside of both of them I saw that the dominions I had defended myself from anciently was but delusions of the screen. Blips of light. And I was scot-free now, whistling through space.

I don't know how I come back. I don't know from where. They was slapping my face when I arrived back at Senior Citizens and they was oxygenating her. I saw her chest move, almost unwilling. She sighed the way she would when somebody bothered her in the middle of a row of beads she was counting. I think it irritated her to no end that they brought her back. I knew from the way she looked after they took the mask off, she was not going to forgive them disturbing her restful peace. Nor was she forgiving Lipsha Morrissey. She had been stepping out onto the road of death, she told the children later at the funeral. I asked was there any stop signs or dividing markers on that road, but she clamped her lips in a vise the way she always done when she was mad.

Which didn't bother me. I knew when things had cleared out she wouldn't have no choice. I was not going to speculate where the blame was put for Grandpa's death. We was in it together. She had slugged him between the shoulders. My touch had failed him, never to return.

All the blood children and the took-ins, like me, came home from Minneapolis and Chicago, where they had relocated years ago. They stayed with friends on the reservation or with Aurelia or slept on Grandma's floor. They were struck down with grief and bereavement to be sure, every one of them. At the funeral I sat down in the back of the church with Albertine. She had gotten all skinny and ragged haired from cramming all her years of study into two or three. She had decided that to be a nurse was not enough for her so she was going to be a doctor. But the way she was straining her mind didn't look too hopeful. Her eyes were bloodshot from driving and crying. She took my hand. From the back we watched all the children and the mourners as they hunched over their prayers, their hands stuffed full of Kleenex. It was someplace in that long sad service that my vision shifted. I began to see things different, more clear. The family kneeling down turned to rocks in a field. It struck me how strong and reliable grief was, and death. Until the end of time, death would be our rock.

So I had perspective on it all, for death gives you that. All the Kashpaw children had done various things to me in their lives—shared their folks with me, loaned me cash, beat me up in secret—and I decided, because of death, then and there I'd call it quits. If I ever saw King again, I'd shake his hand. Forgiving somebody else made the whole thing easier to bear.

Everybody saw Grandpa off into the next world. And then the Kashpaws had to get back to their jobs, which was numerous and impressive. I had a few beers with them and I went back to Grandma, who had sort of got lost in the shuffle of everybody being sad about Grandpa and glad to see one another.

Zelda had sat beside her the whole time and was sitting with her now. I wanted to talk to Grandma, say how sorry I was, that it wasn't her fault, but only mine. I would have, but Zelda gave me one of her looks of strict warning as if to say, "I'll take care of Grandma. Don't horn in on the women."

If only Zelda knew, I thought, the sad realities would change her. But of course I couldn't tell the dark truth.

It was evening, late. Grandma's light was on underneath a crack in the door. About a week had passed since we buried Grandpa. I knocked first but there wasn't no answer, so I went right in. The door was unlocked. She was there but she didn't notice me at first. Her hands were tied up in her rosary, and her gaze was fully absorbed in the easy chair opposite her, the one that had always been Grandpa's favorite. I stood there, staring with her, at the little green nubs in the cloth and plastic armrest covers and the sad little hair-tonic stain he had made on the white doily where he laid his head. For the life of me I couldn't figure what she was staring at. Thin space. Then she turned.

145 "He ain't gone yet," she said.

Remember that chill I luckily didn't get from waiting in the slough? I got it now. I felt it start from the very center of me, where fear hides, waiting to attack. It spiraled outward so that in minutes my fingers and teeth were shaking and clattering. I knew she told the truth. She seen Grandpa. Whether or not he had been there is not the point. She had *seen* him, and that meant anybody else could see him, too. Not only that but, as is usually the case with these here ghosts, he had a certain uneasy reason to come back. And of course Grandma Kashpaw had scanned it out.

I sat down. We sat together on the couch watching his chair out of the corner of our eyes. She had found him sitting in his chair when she walked in the door. "It's the love medicine, my Lipsha," she said. "It was stronger than we thought. He came back even after death to claim me to his side."

I was afraid. "We shouldn't have tampered with it," I said. She agreed. For a while we sat still. I don't know what she thought, but my head felt screwed on backward. I couldn't accurately consider the situation, so I told Grandma to go to bed. I would sleep on the couch keeping my eye on Grandpa's chair. Maybe he would come back and maybe he wouldn't. I guess I feared the one as much as the other, but I got to thinking, see, as I lay there in darkness, that perhaps even through my terrible mistakes some good might come. If Grandpa did come back, I thought he'd return in his right mind. I could talk with him. I could tell him it was all my fault for playing with power I did not understand. Maybe he'd forgive me and rest in peace. I hoped this. I calmed myself and waited for him all night.

150 He fooled me though. He knew what I was waiting for, and it wasn't what he was looking to hear. Come dawn I heard a blood-splitting cry from the bedroom and I rushed in there. Grandma turnt the lights on. She was sitting on the edge of the bed and her face looked harsh, pinched-up, gray.

"He was here," she said. "He came and laid down next to me in bed. And he touched me."

Her heart broke down. She cried. His touch was so cold. She laid back in bed after a while, as it was morning, and I went to the couch. As I lay there, falling asleep, I suddenly felt Grandpa's presence and the barrier between us like a swollen river. I felt how I had wronged him. How awful was the place where I had sent him. Behind the wall of death, he'd watched the living eat and cry and get drunk. He was lonesome, but I understood he meant no harm.

"Go back," I said to the dark, afraid and yet full of pity. "You got to be with your own kind now," I said. I felt him retreating, like a sigh, growing less. I felt his spirit as it shrunk back through the walls, the blinds, the brick courtyard of Senior Citizens. "Look up Aunt June," I whispered as he left.

I slept late the next morning, a good hard sleep allowing the sun to rise and warm the earth. It was past noon when I awoke. There is nothing, to my mind, like a long sleep to make those hard decisions that you neglect under stress of wakefulness. Soon as I woke up that morning, I saw exactly what I'd say to Grandma. I had gotten humble in the past week, not just losing the touch but getting jolted into the understanding that would prey on me from here on out. Your life feels different on you, once you greet death and understand your heart's position. You wear your life like a garment from the mission bundle sale ever after—lightly because you realize you never paid nothing for it, cherishing because you know you won't ever come by such a bargain again. Also you have the feeling someone wore it before you and someone will after. I can't explain that, not yet, but I'm putting my mind to it.

"Grandma," I said, "I got to be honest about the love medicine."

She listened. I knew from then on she would be listening to me the way I had listened to her before. I told her about the turkey hearts and how I had them blessed. I told her what I used as love medicine was purely a fake, and then I said to her what my understanding brought me.

"Love medicine ain't what brings him back to you, Grandma. No, it's something else. He loved you over time and distance, but he went off so quick he never got the chance to tell you how he loves you, how he doesn't blame you, how he understands. It's true feeling, not no magic. No supermarket heart could have brung him back."

She looked at me. She was seeing the years and days I had no way of knowing, and she didn't believe me. I could tell this. Yet a look came on her face. It was like the look of mothers drinking sweetness from their children's eyes. It was tenderness.

"Lipsha," she said, "you was always my favorite."

She took the beads off the bedpost, where she kept them to say at night, and she told me to put out my hand. When I did this, she shut the beads inside of my fist and held them there a long minute, tight, so my hand hurt. I almost cried when she did this. I don't really know why. Tears shot up behind my eyelids, and yet it was nothing. I didn't understand, except her hand was so strong, squeezing mine.

The earth was full of life and there were dandelions growing out the window, thick as thieves, already seeded, fat as big yellow plungers. She let my hand go. I got up. "I'll go out and dig a few dandelions," I told her.

Outside, the sun was hot and heavy as a hand on my back. I felt it flow down my arms, out my fingers, arrowing through the ends of the fork into the earth. With every root I prized up there was return, as if I was kin to its secret lesson. The touch got stronger as I worked through the grassy afternoon. Uncurling from me like a seed out of the blackness where I was lost, the touch spread. The spiked leaves full of bitter mother's milk. A buried root. A nuisance people dig up and throw in the sun to wither. A globe of frail seeds that's indestructible.

1982

## QUESTIONS

1. In the first dramatized scene, Lipsha, the narrator, at Grandma Kashpaw's request, tries to "put the touch" on Grandpa. By this time, some seventeen or eighteen paragraphs into the story, focus and voice and the setting and situation have been established. What is your initial impression of Lipsha's character? Given what you have observed of the structure and elements of the story so far, what do you expect to happen?
2. How is "love medicine" related to the plot? to Grandma's and Lipsha's characters? to theme? In what way(s) may it be considered a symbol?
3. When Lipsha thinks of Wristwatch's grave being dug up in two hundred years, the watch still running, and the diggers asking, "Whose hand wound it?" he says he "started shaking like a piece of grass at just the thought" (paragraph 64). Is he shaking with awe and fear or with laughter? Do you find it awesome or funny?
4. Lipsha tells the stories of Lulu's "tweety bird" that disappeared up her dress and of Wristwatch, whose broken watch started keeping time after its owner dropped dead. He then says, "Not to get off the subject or nothing" (paragraph 65). Are these stories off the subject? How do they arouse expectations? How do they function in the plot? What do they tell you of Lipsha's character? of the nature of the people on the reservation? Are they related to the theme? If so, how?
5. Where in the story is there a difference between how you feel and how you believe Lipsha feels? What is the effect? What is the relationship of this difference to plot, character, voice, and the other elements of the story?
6. Lipsha counsels himself to "put your mind to it and figure out how not to be depressed," but then he adds, "I never saw at the time how my thoughts led me astray toward a tragic outcome none could have known" (paragraph 68). There is a death involved. Is it "tragic"? How do you respond to it?
7. Lipsha says he took "an evil shortcut" in practicing love medicine: does that mean that he has discovered that the old beliefs are not "superstitions" or "strange," as he thought at the time?
8. In the final two paragraphs of the story, has Lipsha's "voice" changed? How do you think he has changed in the course of the story?

"The Open Boat" is a very different kind of story. It engages, from the very beginning, a powerful sense of fear and impending tragedy; the story's major effects arise from suspense over whether the four men in a boat can survive their battle with the raging seas. As in "Love Medicine," the effects depend heavily on the narrative point of view, on our knowing events from the "inside" as they happen rather than from a larger, or longer, perspective. As in both "The Secret Sharer" and "Love Medecine," in "The Open Boat" the narrative voice is striking and unusual. Each word seems specially chosen, in these stories, to contribute to a feeling or mood as well as to reveal the attitudes of the narrator. Yet in Stephen Crane's story the narrator is not quite a character in the action, since it is told in the third person. Thinking about the elements of a story—plot, character, setting, symbol, and theme as well as point of view—can be very helpful here in sorting out how the story generates its strong sense of anxiety and potential doom. The plot is, in one sense, very simple—four men in a boat try to get to shore safely after a shipwreck—and the theme can also be phrased simply and in several different ways: *nature is ultimately indifferent to humanity*, for example, or *human beings are capable of noble sacrifice and heroism, even if fate foils them*. And from the first words, the setting—the stormy sea off the coast of Florida—is presented in the bleakest terms. Setting or location, here, *is* fate, or we might say it determines plot and reveals character. (Notice, too, that the setting seems to have a character or personality of its own, through various descriptions that personify nature.) The accident of being in the wrong place at the wrong time, of having to struggle to stay alive, becomes a relentless test of character and a suspension of outcome. The way the waves threaten the small boat from constantly shifting angles seems to symbolize the life-or-death predicament the men must face. Although the necessary basic knowledge about each literary element is presented within the opening paragraphs, take note, as you read, of how details accumulate to enrich and complicate each of the elements as the story proceeds.

**STEPHEN CRANE**

## The Open Boat

A Tale Intended to Be after the Fact:[1] Being the Experience of Four Men from the Sunk Steamer Commodore

### I

None of them knew the color of the sky. Their eyes glanced level and were fastened upon the waves that swept toward them. These waves were of the hue of slate, save for the tops, which were of foaming white, and all of the men knew the colors of the sea. The horizon narrowed and widened, and dipped and rose, and at all times its edge was jagged with waves that seemed thrust up in points like rocks.

Many a man ought to have a bathtub larger than the boat which here rode upon the sea. These waves were most wrongfully and barbarously abrupt and tall, and each froth-top was a problem in small-boat navigation.

The cook squatted in the bottom, and looked with both eyes at the six inches of gunwale which separated him from the ocean. His sleeves were rolled over his fat forearms, and the two flaps of his unbuttoned vest dangled as he bent to bail out the boat. Often he said, "Gawd! that was a narrow clip." As he remarked it he invariably gazed eastward over the broken sea.

The oiler, steering with one of the two oars in the boat, sometimes raised himself suddenly to keep clear of water that swirled in over the stern. It was a thin little oar, and it seemed often ready to snap.

---

1. Crane had an experience very like the one here re-created in fiction. His autobiographical account of his adventure at sea was published in the New York *Press* on January 7, 1897.

The correspondent, pulling at the other oar, watched the waves and wondered why he was there.

The injured captain, lying in the bow, was at this time buried in that profound dejection and indifference which comes, temporarily at least, to even the bravest and most enduring when, willy-nilly, the firm fails, the army loses, the ship goes down. The mind of the master of a vessel is rooted deep in the timbers of her, though he command for a day or a decade; and this captain had on him the stern impression of a scene in the grays of dawn of seven turned faces, and later a stump of a topmast with a white ball on it, that slashed to and fro at the waves, went low and lower, and down. Thereafter there was something strange in his voice. Although steady, it was deep with mourning, and of a quality beyond oration or tears.

"Keep'er a little more south, Billie," said he.

"A little more south, sir," said the oiler in the stern.

A seat in his boat was not unlike a seat upon a bucking broncho, and by the same token a broncho is not much smaller. The craft pranced and reared and plunged like an animal. As each wave came, and she rose for it, she seemed like a horse making at a fence outrageously high. The manner of her scramble over these walls of water is a mystic thing, and, moreover, at the top of them were ordinarily these problems in white water, the foam racing down from the summit of each wave requiring a new leap, and a leap from the air. Then, after scornfully bumping a crest, she would slide and race and splash down a long incline, and arrive bobbing and nodding in front of the next menace.

A singular disadvantage of the sea lies in the fact that after successfully surmounting one wave you discover that there is another behind it just as important and just as nervously anxious to do something effective in the way of swamping boats. In a ten-foot dinghy one can get an idea of the resources of the sea in the line of waves that is not probable to the average experience, which is never at sea in a dinghy. As each slaty wall of water approached, it shut all else from the view of the men in the boat, and it was not difficult to imagine that this particular wave was the final outburst of the ocean, the last effort of the grim water. There was a terrible grace in the move of the waves, and they came in silence, save for the snarling of the crests.

In the wan light the faces of the men must have been gray. Their eyes must have glinted in strange ways as they gazed steadily astern. Viewed from a balcony, the whole thing would, doubtless, have been weirdly picturesque. But the men in the boat had no time to see it, and if they had had leisure, there were other things to occupy their minds. The sun swung steadily up the sky, and they knew it was broad day because the color of the sea changed from slate to emerald-green streaked with amber lights, and the foam was like tumbling snow. The process of the breaking day was unknown to them. They were aware only of this effect upon the color of the waves that rolled toward them.

In disjointed sentences the cook and the correspondent argued as to the difference between a life-saving station and a house of refuge. The cook had said: "There's a house of refuge just north of the Mosquito Inlet Light, and as soon as they see us they'll come off in their boat and pick us up."

"As soon as who see us?" said the correspondent.

"The crew," said the cook.

"Houses of refuge don't have crews," said the correspondent. "As I understand them, they are only places where clothes and grub are stored for the benefit of shipwrecked people. They don't carry crews."

"Oh, yes, they do," said the cook.

"No, they don't," said the correspondent.

"Well, we're not there yet, anyhow," said the oiler, in the stern.

"Well," said the cook, "perhaps it's not a house of refuge that I'm thinking of as being near Mosquito Inlet Light; perhaps it's a life-saving station."

"We're not there yet," said the oiler in the stern.

## II

As the boat bounced from the top of each wave the wind tore through the hair of the hatless men, and as the craft plopped her stern down again the spray slashed past them. The crest of each of these waves was a hill, from the top of which the men surveyed for a moment a broad tumultuous expanse, shining and wind-riven. It was probably splendid, it was probably glorious, this play of the free sea, wild with lights of emerald and white and amber.

"Bully good thing it's an on-shore wind," said the cook. "If not, where would we be? Wouldn't have a show."

"That's right," said the correspondent.

The busy oiler nodded his assent.

Then the captain, in the bow, chuckled in a way that expressed humor, contempt, tragedy, all in one. "Do you think we've got much of a show now, boys?" said he.

Whereupon the three were silent, save for a trifle of hemming and hawing. To express any particular optimism at this time they felt to be childish and stupid, but they all doubtless possessed this sense of the situation in their minds. A young man thinks doggedly at such times. On the other hand, the ethics of their condition was decidedly against any open suggestion of hopelessness. So they were silent.

"Oh, well," said the captain, soothing his children, "we'll get ashore all right."

But there was that in his tone which made them think; so the oiler quoth, "Yes! if this wind holds."

The cook was bailing. "Yes! if we don't catch hell in the surf."

Canton-flannel[2] gulls flew near and far. Sometimes they sat down on the sea, near patches of brown seaweed that rolled over the waves with a movement like carpets on a line in a gale. The birds sat comfortably in groups, and they were envied by some in the dinghy, for the wrath of the sea was no more to them than it was to a covey of prairie chickens a thousand miles inland. Often they came very close and stared at the men with black bead-like eyes. At these times they were uncanny and sinister in their unblinking scrutiny, and the men hooted angrily at them, telling them to be gone. One came, and evidently decided to alight on the top of the captain's head. The bird flew parallel to the boat and did not circle, but made short sidelong jumps in the air in chicken fashion. His black eyes were wistfully fixed upon the captain's head. "Ugly brute," said the oiler to the bird. "You look as if you were made with a jackknife." The cook and the correspondent swore darkly at the creature. The captain naturally wished to

---

2. A plain-weave cotton fabric.

knock it away with the end of the heavy painter,[3] but he did not dare do it, because anything resembling an emphatic gesture would have capsized this freighted boat; and so, with his open hand, the captain gently and carefully waved the gull away. After it had been discouraged from the pursuit the captain breathed easier on account of his hair, and others breathed easier because the bird struck their minds at this time as being somehow gruesome and ominous.

In the meantime the oiler and the correspondent rowed; and also they rowed. They sat together in the same seat, and each rowed an oar. Then the oiler took both oars; then the correspondent took both oars, then the oiler; then the correspondent. They rowed and they rowed. The very ticklish part of the business was when the time came for the reclining one in the stern to take his turn at the oars. By the very last star of truth, it is easier to steal eggs from under a hen than it was to change seats in the dinghy. First the man in the stern slid his hand along the thwart and moved with care, as if he were of Sèvres.[4] Then the man in the rowing-seat slid his hand along the other thwart. It was all done with the most extraordinary care. As the two sidled past each other, the whole party kept watchful eyes on the coming wave, and the captain cried: "Look out, now! Steady, there!"

The brown mats of seaweed that appeared from time to time were like islands, bits of earth. They were travelling, apparently, neither one way nor the other. They were, to all intents, stationary. They informed the men in the boat that it was making progress slowly toward the land.

The captain, rearing cautiously in the bow after the dinghy soared on a great swell, said that he had seen the lighthouse at Mosquito Inlet. Presently the cook remarked that he had seen it. The correspondent was at the oars then, and for some reason he too wished to look at the lighthouse; but his back was toward the far shore, and the waves were important, and for some time he could not seize an opportunity to turn his head. But at last there came a wave more gentle than the others, and when at the crest of it he swiftly scoured the western horizon.

"See it?" said the captain.

"No," said the correspondent, slowly; "I didn't see anything."

"Look again," said the captain. He pointed. "It's exactly in that direction."

At the top of another wave the correspondent did as he was bid, and this time his eyes chanced on a small, still thing on the edge of the swaying horizon. It was precisely like the point of a pin. It took an anxious eye to find a lighthouse so tiny.

"Think we'll make it, Captain?"

"If this wind holds and the boat don't swamp, we can't do much else," said the captain.

The little boat, lifted by each towering sea and splashed viciously by the crests, made progress that in the absence of seaweed was not apparent to those in her. She seemed just a wee thing wallowing, miraculously top up, at the mercy of five oceans. Occasionally a great spread of water, like white flames, swarmed into her.

"Bail her, cook," said the captain, serenely.

"All right, Captain," said the cheerful cook.

---

3. A mooring rope attached to the bow of a boat.   4. A type of fine china.

### III

It would be difficult to describe the subtle brotherhood of men that was here established on the seas. No one said that it was so. No one mentioned it. But it dwelt in the boat, and each man felt it warm him. They were a captain, an oiler, a cook, and a correspondent, and they were friends—friends in a more curiously iron-bound degree than may be common. The hurt captain, lying against the water jar in the bow, spoke always in a low voice and calmly; but he could never command a more ready and swiftly obedient crew than the motley three of the dinghy. It was more than a mere recognition of what was best for the common safety. There was surely in it a quality that was personal and heart-felt. And after this devotion to the commander of the boat, there was this comradeship, that the correspondent, for instance, who had been taught to be cynical of men, knew even at the time was the best experience of his life. But no one said that it was so. No one mentioned it.

"I wish we had a sail," remarked the captain. "We might try my overcoat on the end of an oar, and give you two boys a chance to rest." So the cook and the correspondent held the mast and spread wide the overcoat; the oiler steered; and the little boat made good way with her new rig. Sometimes the oiler had to scull sharply to keep a sea from breaking into the boat, but otherwise sailing was a success.

Meanwhile the lighthouse had been growing slowly larger. It had now almost assumed color, and appeared like a little gray shadow on the sky. The man at the oars could not be prevented from turning his head rather often to try for a glimpse of this little gray shadow.

At last, from the top of each wave, the men in the tossing boat could see land. Even as the lighthouse was an upright shadow on the sky, this land seemed but a long black shadow on the sea. It certainly was thinner than paper. "We must be about opposite New Smyrna,"[5] said the cook, who had coasted this shore often in schooners. "Captain, by the way, I believe they abandoned that life-saving station there about a year ago."

"Did they?" said the captain.

The wind slowly died away. The cook and the correspondent were not now obliged to slave in order to hold high the oar. But the waves continued their old impetuous swooping at the dinghy, and the little craft, no longer underway, struggled woundily over them. The oiler or the correspondent took the oars again.

Shipwrecks are *apropos* of nothing. If men could only train for them and have them occur when the men had reached pink condition, there would be less drowning at sea. Of the four in the dinghy none had slept any time worth mentioning for two days and two nights previous to embarking in the dinghy, and in the excitement of clambering about the deck of a foundering ship they had also forgotten to eat heartily.

For these reasons, and for others, neither the oiler nor the correspondent was fond of rowing at this time. The correspondent wondered ingenuously how in the name of all that was sane could there be people who thought it amusing to row a boat. It was not an amusement; it was a diabolical punishment, and even

---

5. Town on the Florida coast.

a genius of mental aberrations could never conclude that it was anything but a horror to the muscles and a crime against the back. He mentioned to the boat in general how the amusement of rowing struck him, and the weary-faced oiler smiled in full sympathy. Previously to the foundering, by the way, the oiler had worked a double watch in the engine-room of the ship.

"Take her easy, now, boys," said the captain. "Don't spend yourselves. If we have to run a surf you'll need all your strength, because we'll sure have to swim for it. Take your time."

Slowly the land arose from the sea. From a black line it became a line of black and a line of white—trees and sand. Finally the captain said that he could make out a house on the shore. "That's the house of refuge, sure," said the cook. "They'll see us before long, and come out after us."

The distant lighthouse reared high. "The keeper ought to be able to make us out now, if he's looking through a glass," said the captain. "He'll notify the life-saving people."

"None of those other boats could have got ashore to give word of the wreck," said the oiler, in a low voice, "else the life-boat would be out hunting us."

Slowly and beautifully the land loomed out of the sea. The wind came again. It had veered from the northeast to the southeast. Finally a new sound struck the ears of the men in the boat. It was the low thunder of the surf on the shore. "We'll never be able to make the lighthouse now," said the captain. "Swing her head a little more north, Billie."

"A little more north, sir," said the oiler.

Whereupon the little boat turned her nose once more down the wind, and all but the oarsman watched the shore grow. Under the influence of this expansion doubt and direful apprehension were leaving the minds of the men. The management of the boat was still most absorbing, but it could not prevent a quiet cheerfulness. In an hour, perhaps, they would be ashore.

Their backbones had become thoroughly used to balancing in the boat, and they now rode this wild colt of a dinghy like circus men. The correspondent thought that he had been drenched to the skin, but happening to feel in the top pocket of his coat, he found therein eight cigars. Four of them were soaked with sea-water; four were perfectly scatheless. After a search, somebody produced three dry matches; and thereupon the four waifs rode impudently in their little boat and, with an assurance of an impending rescue shining in their eyes, puffed at the big cigars, and judged well and ill of all men. Everybody took a drink of water.

IV

"Cook," remarked the captain, "there don't seem to be any signs of life about your house of refuge."

"No," replied the cook. "Funny they don't see us!"

A broad stretch of lowly coast lay before the eyes of the men. It was of low dunes topped with dark vegetation. The roar of the surf was plain, and sometimes they could see the white lip of a wave as it spun up the beach. A tiny house was blocked out black upon the sky. Southward, the slim lighthouse lifted its little gray length.

Tide, wind, and waves were swinging the dinghy northward. "Funny they don't see us," said the men.

The surf's roar was here dulled, but its tone was nevertheless thunderous and mighty. As the boat swam over the great rollers the men sat listening to this roar. "We'll swamp sure," said everybody.

It is fair to say here that there was not a life-saving station within twenty miles in either direction; but the men did not know this fact, and in consequence they made dark and opprobrious remarks concerning the eyesight of the nation's life-savers. Four scowling men sat in the dinghy and surpassed records in the invention of epithets.

"Funny they don't see us."

The light-heartedness of a former time had completely faded. To their sharpened minds it was easy to conjure pictures of all kinds of incompetency and blindness and, indeed, cowardice. There was the shore of the populous land, and it was bitter and bitter to them that from it came no sign.

"Well," said the captain, ultimately, "I suppose we'll have to make a try for ourselves. If we stay out here too long, we'll none of us have strength left to swim after the boat swamps."

And so the oiler, who was at the oars, turned the boat straight for the shore. There was a sudden tightening of muscles. There was some thinking.

"If we don't all get ashore," said the captain—"if we don't all get ashore, I suppose you fellows know where to send news of my finish?"

They then briefly exchanged some addresses and admonitions. As for the reflections of the men, there was a great deal of rage in them. Perchance they might be formulated thus: "If I am going to be drowned—if I am going to be drowned—if I am going to be drowned, why, in the name of the seven mad gods who rule the sea, was I allowed to come thus far and contemplate sand and trees? Was I brought here merely to have my nose dragged away as I was about to nibble the sacred cheese of life? It is preposterous. If this old ninny-woman, Fate, cannot do better than this, she should be deprived of the management of men's fortunes. She is an old hen who knows not her intention. If she has decided to drown me, why did she not do it in the beginning and save me all this trouble? The whole affair is absurd.... But no; she cannot mean to drown me. She dare not drown me. She cannot drown me. Not after all this work." Afterward the man might have had an impulse to shake his fist at the clouds. "Just you drown me, now, and then hear what I call you!"

The billows that came at this time were more formidable. They seemed always just about to break and roll over the little boat in a turmoil of foam. There was a preparatory and long growl in the speech of them. No mind unused to the sea would have concluded that the dinghy could ascend these sheer heights in time. The shore was still afar. The oiler was a wily surfman. "Boys," he said, swiftly, "she won't live three minutes more, and we're too far out to swim. Shall I take her to sea again, Captain?"

"Yes; go ahead!" said the captain.

This oiler, by a series of quick miracles and fast and steady oarsmanship, turned the boat in the middle of the surf and took her safely to sea again.

There was a considerable silence as the boat bumped over the furrowed sea to deeper water. Then somebody in gloom spoke: "Well, anyhow, they must have seen us from the shore by now."

The gulls went in slanting flight up the wind toward the gray, desolate east. A squall, marked by dingy clouds and clouds brick-red, like smoke from a burning building, appeared from the southeast.

"What do you think of those life-saving people? Ain't they peaches?"

"Funny they haven't seen us."

"Maybe they think we're out here for sport! Maybe they think we're fishin'. Maybe they think we're damned fools."

It was a long afternoon. A changed tide tried to force them southward, but wind and wave said northward. Far ahead, where coast-line, sea, and sky formed their mighty angle, there were little dots which seemed to indicate a city on the shore.

"St. Augustine."

The captain shook his head. "Too near Mosquito Inlet."

And the oiler rowed, and then the correspondent rowed; then the oiler moved. It was a weary business. The human back can become the seat of more aches and pains than are registered in books for the composite anatomy of a regiment. It is a limited area, but it can become the theatre of innumerable muscular conflicts, tangles, wrenches, knots, and other comforts.

"Did you ever like to row, Billie?" asked the correspondent.

"No," said the oiler. "Hang it."

When one exchanged the rowing-seat for a place in the bottom of the boat, he suffered a bodily depression that caused him to be careless of everything save an obligation to wiggle one finger. There was cold sea-water swashing to and fro in the boat, and he lay in it. His head, pillowed on a thwart, was within an inch of the swirl of a wave-crest, and sometimes a particularly obstreperous sea came inboard and drenched him once more. But these matters did not annoy him. It is almost certain that if the boat had capsized he would have tumbled comfortably out upon the ocean as if he felt sure that it was a great soft mattress.

"Look! There's a man on the shore!"

"There? See 'im? See 'im?"

"Yes, sure! He's walking along."

"Now he's stopped. Look! He's facing us!"

"He's waving at us!"

"So he is! By thunder!"

"Ah, now we're all right! Now we're all right! There'll be a boat out here for us in half an hour."

"He's going on. He's running. He's going up to that house there."

The remote beach seemed lower than the sea, and it required a searching glance to discern the little black figure. The captain saw a floating stick, and they rowed to it. A bath towel was by some weird chance in the boat, and, tying this on the stick, the captain waved it. The oarsman did not dare turn his head, so he was obliged to ask questions.

"What's he doing now?"

"He's standing still again. He's looking, I think.... There he goes again— toward the house.... Now he's stopped again."

"Is he waving at us?"

"No, not now; he was, though."

"Look! There comes another man!"

"He's running."

"Look at him go, would you!"

"Why, he's on a bicycle. Now he's met the other man. They're both waving at us. Look!"

"There comes something up the beach."

"What the devil is that thing?"

"Why, it looks like a boat."

"Why, certainly, it's a boat."

"No; it's on wheels."

"Yes, so it is. Well, that must be the life-boat. They drag them along shore on a wagon."

"That's the life-boat, sure."

"No, by God, it's—it's an omnibus."

"I tell you it's a life-boat."

"It is not! It's an omnibus. I can see it plain. See? One of these big hotel omnibuses."

"By thunder, you're right. It's an omnibus, sure as fate. What do you suppose they are doing with an omnibus? Maybe they are going around collecting the life-crew, hey?"

"That's it, likely. Look! There's a fellow waving a little black flag. He's standing on the steps of the omnibus. There comes those other two fellows. Now they're all talking together. Look at the fellow with the flag. Maybe he ain't waving it!"

"That ain't a flag, is it? That's his coat. Why, certainly, that's his coat."

"So it is: it's his coat. He's taken it off and is waving it around his head. But would you look at him swing it!"

"Oh, say, there isn't any life-saving station there. That's just a winter-resort."

"What's that idiot with the coat mean? What's he signaling, anyhow?"

"It looks as if he were trying to tell us to go north. There must be a life-saving station up there."

"No; he thinks we're fishing. Just giving us a merry hand. See? Ah, there, Willie!"

"Well, I wish I could make something out of those signals. What do you suppose he means?"

"He don't mean anything; he's just playing."

"Well, if he'd just signal us to try the surf again, or to go to sea and wait, or go north, or go south, or go to hell, there would be some reason in it. But look at him! He just stands there and keeps his coat revolving like a wheel. The ass!"

"There come more people."

"Now there's quite a mob. Look! Isn't that a boat?"

"Where? Oh, I see where you mean. No, that's no boat."

"That fellow is still waving his coat."

"He must think we like to see him to do that. Why don't he quit? It don't mean anything."

"I don't know. I think he is trying to make us go north. It must be that there's a life-saving station there somewhere."

"Say, he ain't tired yet. Look at 'im wave!"

"Wonder how long he can keep that up. He's been revolving his coat ever since he caught sight of us. He's an idiot. Why aren't they getting men to bring a boat out? A fishing boat—one of those big yawls—could come out here all right. Why don't he do something?"

"Oh, it's all right now."

"They'll have a boat out here for us in less than no time, now that they've seen us."

A faint yellow tone came into the sky over the low land. The shadows on the sea slowly deepened. The wind bore coldness with it, and the men began to shiver.

"Holy smoke!" said one, allowing his voice to express his impious mood, "if we keep on monkeying out here! If we've got to flounder out here all night!"

"Oh, we'll never have to stay here all night! Don't you worry. They've seen us now, and it won't be long before they'll come chasing out after us."

The shore grew dusky. The man waving a coat blended gradually into this gloom, and it swallowed in the same manner the omnibus and the group of people. The spray, when it dashed uproariously over the side, made the voyagers shrink and swear like men who were being branded.

"I'd like to catch the chump who waved the coat. I feel like socking him one, just for luck."

"Why? What did he do?"

"Oh, nothing, but then he seemed so damned cheerful."

In the meantime the oiler rowed, and then the correspondent rowed, and then the oiler rowed. Gray-faced and bowed forward, they mechanically, turn by turn, plied the leaden oars. The form of the lighthouse had vanished from the southern horizon, but finally a pale star appeared, just lifting from the sea. The streaked saffron in the west passed before the all-merging darkness, and the sea to the east was black. The land had vanished, and was expressed only by the low and drear thunder of the surf.

"If I am going to be drowned—if I am going to be drowned—if I am going to be drowned, why, in the name of the seven mad gods who rule the sea, was I allowed to come thus far and contemplate sand and trees? Was I brought here merely to have my nose dragged away as I was about to nibble the sacred cheese of life?"

The patient captain, drooped over the water-jar, was sometimes obliged to speak to the oarsman.

"Keep her head up! Keep her head up!"

"Keep her head up, sir." The voices were weary and low.

This was surely a quiet evening. All save the oarsman lay heavily and listlessly in the boat's bottom. As for him, his eyes were just capable of noting the tall black waves that swept forward in a most sinister silence, save for an occasional subdued growl of a crest.

The cook's head was on a thwart, and he looked without interest at the water under his nose. He was deep in other scenes. Finally he spoke. "Billie," he murmured, dreamfully, "what kind of pie do you like best?"

V

"Pie!" said the oiler and the correspondent, agitatedly. "Don't talk about those things, blast you!"

"Well," said the cook, "I was just thinking about ham sandwiches, and ——"

A night on the sea in an open boat is a long night. As darkness settled finally, the shine of the light, lifting from the sea in the south, changed to full gold. On the northern horizon a new light appeared, a small bluish gleam on the edge of the waters. These two lights were the furniture of the world. Otherwise there was nothing but waves.

Two men huddled in the stern, and distances were so magnificent in the dinghy that the rower was enabled to keep his feet partly warm by thrusting them under his companions. Their legs indeed extended far under the rowing-seat until they touched the feet of the captain forward. Sometimes, despite the efforts of the tired oarsman, a wave came piling into the boat, an icy wave of the night, and the chilling water soaked them anew. They would twist their bodies for a moment and groan, and sleep the dead sleep once more, while the water in the boat gurgled about them as the craft rocked.

The plan of the oiler and the correspondent was for one to row until he lost the ability, and then arouse the other from his sea-water couch in the bottom of the boat.

The oiler plied the oars until his head drooped forward and the overpowering sleep blinded him; and he rowed yet afterward. Then he touched a man in the bottom of the boat, and called his name. "Will you spell me for a little while?" he said meekly.

"Sure, Billie," said the correspondent, awaking and dragging himself to a sitting position. They exchanged places carefully, and the oiler, cuddling down in the sea-water at the cook's side, seemed to go to sleep instantly.

The particular violence of the sea had ceased. The waves came without snarling. The obligation of the man at the oars was to keep the boat headed so that the tilt of the rollers would not capsize her, and to preserve her from filling when the crests rushed past. The black waves were silent and hard to be seen in the darkness. Often one was almost upon the boat before the oarsman was aware.

In a low voice the correspondent addressed the captain. He was not sure that the captain was awake, although this iron man seemed to be always awake. "Captain, shall I keep her making for that light north, sir?"

The same steady voice answered him. "Yes. Keep it about two points off the port bow."

The cook had tied a life-belt around himself in order to get even the warmth which this clumsy cork contrivance could donate, and he seemed almost stove-like when a rower, whose teeth invariably chattered wildly as soon as he ceased his labor, dropped down to sleep.

The correspondent, as he rowed, looked down at the two men sleeping underfoot. The cook's arm was around the oiler's shoulders, and, with their fragmentary clothing and haggard faces, they were the babes of the sea—a grotesque rendering of the old babes in the wood.

Later he must have grown stupid at his work, for suddenly there was a growling of water, and a crest came with a roar and a swash into the boat, and it was a wonder that it did not set the cook afloat in his life-belt. The cook continued to sleep, but the oiler sat up, blinking his eyes and shaking with the new cold.

"Oh, I'm awful sorry, Billie," said the correspondent, contritely.

"That's all right, old boy," said the oiler, and lay down again and was asleep.

Presently it seemed that even the captain dozed, and the correspondent thought that he was the one man afloat on all the ocean. The wind had a voice as it came over the waves, and it was sadder than the end.

There was a long, loud swishing astern of the boat, and a gleaming trail of phosphorescence, like blue flame, was furrowed on the black waters. It might have been made by a monstrous knife.

Then there came a stillness, while the correspondent breathed with open mouth and looked at the sea.

Suddenly there was another swish and another long flash of bluish light, and this time it was alongside the boat, and might almost have been reached with an oar. The correspondent saw an enormous fin speed like a shadow through the water, hurling the crystalline spray and leaving the long glowing trail.

The correspondent looked over his shoulder at the captain. His face was hidden, and he seemed to be asleep. He looked at the babes of the sea. They certainly were asleep. So, being bereft of sympathy, he leaned a little way to one side and swore softly into the sea.

But the thing did not then leave the vicinity of the boat. Ahead or astern, on one side or the other, at intervals long or short, fled the long sparkling streak, and there was to be heard the *whirroo* of the dark fin. The speed and power of the thing was greatly to be admired. It cut the water like a gigantic and keen projectile.

The presence of this biding thing did not affect the man with the same horror that it would if he had been a picnicker. He simply looked at the sea dully and swore in an undertone.

Nevertheless, it is true that he did not wish to be alone with the thing. He wished one of his companions to awake by chance and keep him company with it. But the captain hung motionless over the water-jar and the oiler and the cook in the bottom of the boat were plunged in slumber.

## VI

"If I am going to be drowned—if I am going to be drowned—if I am going to be drowned, why, in the name of the seven mad gods who rule the sea, was I allowed to come thus far and contemplate sand and trees?"

During this dismal night, it may be remarked that a man would conclude that it was really the intention of the seven mad gods to drown him, despite the abominable injustice of it. For it was certainly an abominable injustice to drown a man who had worked so hard, so hard. The man felt it would be a crime most unnatural. Other people had drowned at sea since galleys swarmed with painted sails, but still —

When it occurs to a man that nature does not regard him as important, and that she feels she would not maim the universe by disposing of him, he at first wishes to throw bricks at the temple, and he hates deeply the fact that there are no bricks and no temples. Any visible expression of nature would surely be pelleted with his jeers.

Then, if there be no tangible thing to hoot, he feels, perhaps, the desire to confront a personification and indulge in pleas, bowed to one knee, and with hands supplicant, saying, "Yes, but I love myself."

A high cold star on a winter's night is the word he feels that she says to him. Thereafter he knows the pathos of his situation.

The men in the dinghy had not discussed these matters, but each had, no doubt, reflected upon them in silence and according to his mind. There was seldom any expression upon their faces save the general one of complete weariness. Speech was devoted to the business of the boat.

To chime the notes of his emotions, a verse mysteriously entered the correspondent's head. He had even forgotten that he had forgotten this verse, but it suddenly was in his mind.

> A soldier of the Legion lay dying in Algiers;
> There was lack of woman's nursing, there was dearth of woman's tears;
> But a comrade stood beside him, and he took the comrade's hand,
> And he said, "I never more shall see my own, my native land."[6]

In his childhood the correspondent had been made acquainted with the fact that a soldier of the Legion lay dying in Algiers, but he had never regarded it as important. Myriads of his schoolfellows had informed him of the soldier's plight, but the dinning had naturally ended by making him perfectly indifferent. He had never considered it his affair that a soldier of the Legion lay dying in Algiers, nor had it appeared to him as a matter for sorrow. It was less to him than the breaking of a pencil's point.

Now, however, it quaintly came to him as a human, living thing. It was no longer merely a picture of a few throes in the breast of a poet, meanwhile drinking tea and warming his feet at the grate; it was an actuality—stern, mournful, and fine.

The correspondent plainly saw the soldier. He lay on the sand with his feet out straight and still. While his pale left hand was upon his chest in an attempt to thwart the going of his life, the blood came between his fingers. In the far Algerian distance, a city of low square forms was set against a sky that was faint with the last sunset hues. The correspondent, plying the oars and dreaming of the slow and slower movements of the lips of the soldier, was moved by a profound and perfectly impersonal comprehension. He was sorry for the soldier of the Legion who lay dying in Algiers.

The thing which had followed the boat and waited had evidently grown bored at the delay. There was no longer to be heard the slash of the cutwater, and there was no longer the flame of the long trail. The light in the north still glimmered, but it was apparently no nearer to the boat. Sometimes the boom of the surf rang in the correspondent's ears, and he turned the craft seaward then and rowed harder. Southward, some one had evidently built a watch-fire on the beach. It was too low and too far to be seen, but it made a shimmering, roseate reflection upon the bluff in back of it, and this could be discerned from the boat. The wind came stronger, and sometimes a wave suddenly raged out like a mountain-cat, and there was to be seen the sheen and sparkle of a broken crest.

The captain, in the bow, moved on his water-jar and sat erect. "Pretty long night," he observed to the correspondent. He looked at the shore. "Those life-saving people take their time."

"Did you see that shark playing around?"

"Yes, I saw him. He was a big fellow, all right."

"Wish I had known you were awake."

Later the correspondent spoke into the bottom of the boat. "Billie!" There was a slow and gradual disentanglement. "Billie, will you spell me?"

"Sure," said the oiler.

As soon as the correspondent touched the cold, comfortable seawater in the bottom of the boat and had huddled close to the cook's life-belt he was deep in sleep, despite the fact that his teeth played all the popular airs. This sleep was so good to him that it was but a moment before he heard a voice call his name

---

6. From "Bingen on the Rhine," by Caroline Norton (1808–1877).

in a tone that demonstrated the last stages of exhaustion. "Will you spell me?"

"Sure, Billie."

The light in the north had mysteriously vanished, but the correspondent took his course from the wide-awake captain.

Later in the night they took the boat farther out to sea, and the captain directed the cook to take one oar at the stern and keep the boat facing the seas. He was to call out if he should hear the thunder of the surf. This plan enabled the oiler and the correspondent to get respite together. "We'll give those boys a chance to get into shape again," said the captain. They curled down and, after a few preliminary chatterings and trembles, slept once more the dead sleep. Neither knew they had bequeathed to the cook the company of another shark, or perhaps the same shark.

As the boat caroused on the waves, spray occasionally bumped over the side and gave them a fresh soaking, but this had no power to break their repose. The ominous slash of the wind and the water affected them as it would have affected mummies.

"Boys," said the cook, with the notes of every reluctance in his voice, "she's drifted in pretty close. I guess one of you had better take her to sea again." The correspondent, aroused, heard the crash of the toppled crests.

As he was rowing, the captain gave him some whiskey-and-water, and this steadied the chills out of him. "If I ever get ashore and anybody shows me even a photograph of an oar —"

At last there was a short conversation.

"Billie! . . . Billie, will you spell me?"

"Sure," said the oiler.

## VII

When the correspondent again opened his eyes, the sea and the sky were each of the gray hue of the dawning. Later, carmine and gold was painted upon the waters. The morning appeared finally, in its splendor, with a sky of pure blue, and the sunlight flamed on the tips of the waves.

On the distant dunes were set many little black cottages, and a tall white windmill reared above them. No man, nor dog, nor bicycle appeared on the beach. The cottages might have formed a deserted village.

The voyagers scanned the shore. A conference was held in the boat. "Well," said the captain, "if no help is coming, we might better try a run through the surf right away. If we stay out here much longer we will be too weak to do anything for ourselves at all." The others silently acquiesced in this reasoning. The boat was headed for the beach. The correspondent wondered if none ever ascended the tall wind-tower,[7] and if then they never looked seaward. This tower was a giant, standing with its back to the plight of the ants. It represented in a degree, to the correspondent, the serenity of nature amid the struggles of the individual—nature in the wind, and nature in the vision of men. She did not seem cruel to him then, nor beneficent, nor treacherous, nor wise. But she was indifferent, flatly indifferent. It is, perhaps, plausible that a man in this situation, impressed with the unconcern of the universe, should see the innumerable flaws of his life, and have them taste wickedly in his mind, and wish for another chance. A distinction between right and wrong seems absurdly clear to him, then, in this

---

7. A watchtower for observing weather.

new ignorance of the grave-edge, and he understands that if he were given another opportunity he would mend his conduct and his words, and be better and brighter during an introduction or at a tea.

"Now, boys," said the captain, "she is going to swamp sure. All we can do is to work her in as far as possible, and then when she swamps, pile out and scramble for the beach. Keep cool now, and don't jump until she swamps sure."

The oiler took the oars. Over his shoulders he scanned the surf. "Captain," he said, "I think I'd better bring her about and keep her head-on to the seas and back her in."

"All right, Billie," said the captain. "Back her in." The oiler swung the boat then, and, seated in the stern, the cook and the correspondent were obliged to look over their shoulders to contemplate the lonely and indifferent shore.

The monstrous inshore rollers heaved the boat high until the men were again enabled to see the white sheets of water scudding up the slanted beach. "We won't get in very close," said the captain. Each time a man could wrest his attention from the rollers, he turned his glance toward the shore, and in the expression of the eyes during this contemplation there was a singular quality. The correspondent, observing the others, knew that they were not afraid, but the full meaning of their glances was shrouded.

As for himself, he was too tired to grapple fundamentally with the fact. He tried to coerce his mind into thinking of it, but the mind was dominated at this time by the muscles, and the muscles said they did not care. It merely occurred to him that if he should drown it would be a shame.

There were no hurried words, no pallor, no plain agitation. The men simply looked at the shore. "Now, remember to get well clear of the boat when you jump," said the captain.

Seaward the crest of a roller suddenly fell with a thunderous crash, and the long white comber came roaring down upon the boat.

"Steady now," said the captain. The men were silent. They turned their eyes from the shore to the comber and waited. The boat slid up the incline, leaped at the furious top, bounced over it, and swung down the long back of the wave. Some water had been shipped, and the cook bailed it out.

But the next crest crashed also. The tumbling, boiling flood of white water caught the boat and whirled it almost perpendicular. Water swarmed in from all sides. The correspondent had his hands on the gunwale at this time, and when the water entered at that place he swiftly withdrew his fingers, as if he objected to wetting them.

The little boat, drunken with this weight of water, reeled and snuggled deeper into the sea.

"Bail her out, cook! Bail her out!" said the captain.

"All right, Captain," said the cook.

"Now, boys, the next one will do for us sure," said the oiler. "Mind to jump clear of the boat."

The third wave moved forward, huge, furious, implacable. It fairly swallowed the dinghy, and almost simultaneously the men tumbled into the sea. A piece of life-belt had lain in the bottom of the boat, and as the correspondent went overboard he held this to his chest with his left hand.

The January water was icy, and reflected immediately that it was colder than he had expected to find it off the coast of Florida. This appeared to his dazed mind as a fact important enough to be noted at the time. The coldness of the water was sad; it was tragic. This fact was somehow mixed and confused with his opinion of his own situation, so that it seemed almost a proper reason for tears. The water was cold.

215   When he came to the surface he was conscious of little but the noisy water. Afterward he saw his companions in the sea. The oiler was ahead in the race. He was swimming strongly and rapidly. Off to the correspondent's left, the cook's great white and corked back bulged out of the water, and in the rear the captain was hanging with his one good hand to the keel of the overturned dinghy.

There is a certain immovable quality to a shore, and the correspondent wondered at it amid the confusion of the sea.

It seemed also very attractive; but the correspondent knew that it was a long journey, and he paddled leisurely. The piece of life-preserver lay under him, and sometimes he whirled down the incline of a wave as if he were on a hand-sled.

But finally he arrived at a place in the sea where travel was beset with difficulty. He did not pause swimming to inquire what manner of current had caught him, but there his progress ceased. The shore was set before him like a bit of scenery on a stage, and he looked at it and understood with his eyes each detail of it.

As the cook passed, much farther to the left, the captain was calling to him, "Turn over on your back, cook! Turn over on your back and use the oar."

220   "All right, sir." The cook turned on his back, and, paddling with an oar, went ahead as if he were a canoe.

Presently the boat also passed to the left of the correspondent, with the captain clinging with one hand to the keel. He would have appeared like a man raising himself to look over a board fence if it were not for the extraordinary gymnastics of the boat. The correspondent marvelled that the captain could still hold to it.

They passed on nearer to shore—the oiler, the cook, the captain—and following them went the water-jar, bouncing gaily over the seas.

The correspondent remained in the grip of this strange new enemy, a current. The shore, with its white slope of sand and its green bluff topped with little silent cottages, was spread like a picture before him. It was very near to him then, but he was impressed as one who, in a gallery, looks at a scene from Brittany or Algiers.

He thought: "I am going to drown? Can it be possible? Can it be possible? Can it be possible?" Perhaps an individual must consider his own death to be the final phenomenon of nature.

225   But later a wave perhaps whirled him out of this small deadly current, for he found suddenly that he could again make progress toward the shore. Later still he was aware that the captain, clinging with one hand to the keel of the dinghy, had his face turned away from the shore and toward him, and was calling his name. "Come to the boat! Come to the boat!"

In his struggle to reach the captain and the boat, he reflected that when one gets properly wearied drowning must really be a comfortable arrangement—a cessation of hostilities accompanied by a large degree of relief; and he was glad of it, for the main thing in his mind for some moments had been horror of the temporary agony; he did not wish to be hurt.

Presently he saw a man running along the shore. He was undressing with most remarkable speed. Coat, trousers, shirt, everything flew magically off him.

"Come to the boat!" called the captain.

"All right, Captain." As the correspondent paddled, he saw the captain let himself down to bottom and leave the boat. Then the correspondent performed his one little marvel of the voyage. A large wave caught him and flung him with ease and supreme speed completely over the boat and far beyond it. It struck him even then as an event in gymnastics and a true miracle of the sea. An overturned boat in the surf is not a plaything to a swimming man.

The correspondent arrived in water that reached only to his waist, but his condition did not enable him to stand for more than a moment. Each wave knocked him into a heap, and the undertow pulled at him.

Then he saw the man who had been running and undressing, and undressing and running, come bounding into the water. He dragged ashore the cook, and then waded toward the captain; but the captain waved him away and sent him to the correspondent. He was naked—naked as a tree in winter; but a halo was about his head, and he shone like a saint. He gave a strong pull, and a long drag, and a bully heave at the correspondent's hand. The correspondent, schooled in the minor formulae, said, "Thanks, old man." But suddenly the man cried, "What's that?" He pointed a swift finger. The correspondent said, "Go."

In the shallows, face downward, lay the oiler. His forehead touched sand that was periodically, between each wave, clear of the sea.

The correspondent did not know all that transpired afterward. When he achieved safe ground he fell, striking the sand with each particular part of his body. It was as if he had dropped from a roof, but the thud was grateful to him.

It seems that instantly the beach was populated with men with blankets, clothes, and flasks, and women with coffee-pots and all the remedies sacred to their minds. The welcome of the land to the men from the sea was warm and generous; but a still and dripping shape was carried slowly up the beach, and the land's welcome for it could only be the different and sinister hospitality of the grave.

When it came night, the white waves paced to and fro in the moonlight, and the wind brought the sound of the great sea's voice to the men on the shore, and they felt that they could then be interpreters.

1898

## QUESTIONS

1. When do you become aware that your view of events in "The Open Boat" is limited to things seen and heard by the four men in the boat? In what specific ways is that important to the story's effect? How much of the story's suspense depends on this limited point of view? How would the effect of the story differ if it were told autobiographically through a first-person narrator?
2. Examine the language of the story's first paragraph. How is the contrast between the sky and the sea significant? What specific colors are mentioned or implied here? How much differentiation in color is discernible to the men? What angles of vision are implied by the color imagery? Which specific words and phrases imply details about body posture and fatigue?
3. How much of the basic plot do you know by the end of the third paragraph? What crucial information is, at this point, still unclear? At what point in the text is each additional plot detail presented?
4. Examine paragraphs 3–6; then differentiate the four men as fully as you can. What distinguishing features help you keep them straight as the narrative proceeds? What

facts are provided later about each of the men? How do you account for the general agreeableness of the group toward the individual needs of each other? How does the captain set himself apart from the rest? What details create the sense of hierarchy in the group? How might the plot differ if the makeup of the group were to change?

5. In some ways the story seems almost timeless as the relentless waves threaten the men and the boat. How much time actually passes? How is the passing of time recorded? How are the threats to life different in different parts of the story?

6. At which points in the story does the men's weariness outweigh their sense of danger? How are these points signaled by the language? What functions does the repetitive language perform? Does Crane affect his reader with the monotony experienced by the men in the boat, or does he capture attention by varying the repetitions?

7. Where does the story's perspective "expand" to include larger reflections and generalizations? How are they justified by the narrative point of view? Describe the "voice" in these comments. What is their tone?

8. In which of the men do you become most interested as the story develops? Point to textual indications that the point of view gradually narrows to increasingly suggest an individual voice rather than the collective one of the four men. Why does such a narrowing occur? What effect does this narrowing point of view have on the story's conclusion?

9. How important is it that the threat to the men involves a natural force? How would the story's theme differ if they faced a human threat? How would the symbolism differ? What do the shifting waves symbolize? How does the language in the story support this symbolism?

## SUGGESTIONS FOR WRITING

1. In "The Secret Sharer," when Leggatt is aboard and dressed in the captain's sleeping suit, he is described as looking like the captain's "double." That, plus Leggatt's arriving from the sea naked, looking like a fish, phosphorescent and oblong, together with the title of the story and the narrator's seeing his first command as a test, has led many readers to interpret this story in psychological terms. Write an essay in which you discuss how the narrator-captain and his "double" might represent different aspects of the mind.

2. Can you imagine "The Secret Sharer"—the story of a new captain taking over command of a strange ship, with mates not of his own choosing and not of his own "kind," of the strained relations between the new captain and the other officers, of his emotional state, and of his first daring act of seamanship—without the presence of a Leggatt? Write a 2–3-page synopsis of such a story, and, in the manner of Conrad, an opening or a closing scene. Is there some way in which you might still call your story "The Secret Sharer"? Who has the secret and with whom does he share it?

3. Write a sequel to "The Secret Sharer" recounting what happens to Leggatt after he leaves the ship, using as many of the elements and details of Conrad's story as you can but with a new focus and voice.

4. Voice is a dominant element in "Love Medicine," and it is largely through Lipsha's voice that we infer his character. His language is ungrammatical, and he seems to have a somewhat naive view of reality, or causality. His kindness and good nature show through the errors and naiveté, however, and he is capable of insight and even wisdom. Write an essay that shows how "Love Medicine"'s theme is presented through a character who is not well educated or intellectually profound and how

the character's very limitations contribute meaning and force to the theme.
5. Toward the end of "Love Medicine," Lipsha tells Grandma that it was not "love medicine" that brought Grandpa's ghost back to her but love itself, not magic but feeling. Grandma looks at him tenderly and says, " 'Lipsha, . . . you was always my favorite' " (paragraph 159). Write an essay in which you discuss this passage in terms of the plot (but be sure to remember Lulu); in terms of Lipsha's character; in terms of Grandma's; in terms of theme (and you might even want to think of "love medicine" as symbol).
6. Look carefully at paragraphs in "The Open Boat" in which different "elements" (such as plot, character, language, setting, and so on) seem purposely merged or fused. How is such interaction accomplished? Choose a single paragraph that illustrates the close interaction of different elements, and write a two-page analytical paper showing how the paragraph works to integrate the story's narrative presentation.
7. Amidst all the terrors recounted in "The Open Boat," the narrator pauses to reflect that "there was this comradeship that the correspondent . . . knew even at the time was the best experience of his life" (paragraph 43). Then he adds: "But no one said that it was so. No one mentioned it." Write an essay in which you explain why the correspondent, "who had been taught to be cynical of men," comes to feel this way, and why none of the men talk about it.
8. Write an essay in which you discuss the symbolism of the predicament in "The Open Boat." Consider, for example, the implacable natural force that threatens the men, their defenselessness, the precariousness of the tiny boat, the circling sharks, the maddening nearness to a shore they cannot reach safely. How much does the story's symbolic effect depend upon the traditional "life as voyage" metaphor?
9. In "The Open Boat," Stephen Crane writes: "When it occurs to a man that nature does not regard him as important, and that she feels she would not maim the universe by disposing of him, he at first wishes to throw bricks at the temple, and he hates deeply the fact that there are no bricks and no temples. Any visible expression of nature would surely be pelleted with his jeers" (paragraph 173). Write a short story depicting characters whose lives are imperiled by natural forces beyond their control.

# *Exploring Contexts*

## 8 THE AUTHOR'S WORK AS CONTEXT: D. H. LAWRENCE AND FLANNERY O'CONNOR

Even if it were desirable to read a story as a thing in itself, separate from everything else we have ever read or seen and from everything else the author has written, this is in practice impossible. We can read Faulkner or Welty or Poe for the first time only once. After we read a second and then a third story by an author, we begin to recognize the voice and gain a sense of familiarity, as we would with a growing acquaintance. Each story is part of the author's entire body of work—the **oeuvre** or **canon**—which, taken together, forms something like a single entity, a coherent vision, a unique world, a "superwork."

The author's voice and vision soon create in us certain expectations—of action, setting, structure, characterization, language, worldview. We come to expect short sentences from Hemingway, long ones from Faulkner, and a certain amount of violence from both. We are not surprised if a Conrad story is set in Africa or Asia or aboard a ship, but we are surprised if a Faulkner story takes place outside Mississippi.

When we find an author's vision attractive or challenging, we naturally also want to find out more about it, so we're drawn not only to the literary works in the canon but also to the author's nonfictional prose—essays, letters, anything we can find that promises a fuller or clearer view of that unique way of looking at the world. Such knowledge is certainly helpful—within limits. D. H. Lawrence warned us to trust the tale and not the teller. A writer's statement of beliefs or of intentions is not necessarily the same as what a given work may show or achieve. And writers often embody in their art what they cannot articulate in discursive prose, what indeed may not be directly expressible at all.

In this chapter we will look briefly but closely at the work of two writers, D. H. Lawrence and Flannery O'Connor. We will look at both differences and similarities among works by the same writer.

*I am a man, and alive. . . . For this reason I am a novelist. And being a novelist, I consider myself superior to the saint, the scientist, the philosopher, and the poet, who are all great masters of different bits of man alive, but never get the whole hog.*

—D. H. LAWRENCE

The three short stories and brief selections from Lawrence's letters and criticism in this chapter are meant to make you feel more at home (and interested) in Lawrence's world and to raise questions about the relationship of individual works to an author's work as a whole. Of course, a few short stories and a few pages of nonfiction cannot adequately represent the career of a writer who was a novelist, poet, critic, and essayist as well as short-story writer, nor can three stories represent the richness and variety of the fifty or more that he published over many years. However, since the stories come from three different decades, they do suggest the continuities and changes during his career. "Odour of Chrysanthemums" is set in the coal-mining region of Lawrence's native English Midlands, the scene of many of his novels, including three of the most famous—*Sons and Lovers* (1913), *The Rainbow* (1915), and *Lady Chatterley's Lover* (1928). Though we have included brief excerpts from his essay "Nottingham and the Mining Countryside" and from his "Autobiographical Sketch," there is no way in so few selections to represent both Lawrence's particular emphasis on the Midlands and also the broad range of his settings—his stories take place all over Western Europe, in the Americas, and in Australia. The setting of "The Blind Man" near Oxford (fifty miles northwest of London) and of "The Rocking-Horse Winner" in London only faintly indicates Lawrence's growing cosmopolitanism, social as well as geographical. It also suggests, though superficially, his developing interest in the transcendent, mystical, or mythic—concerns most fully developed in *The Plumed Serpent* (1926) and *The Man Who Died* (1929)—and his movement in content and style away from nineteenth-century notions of realism.

It may be useful to see the first story here (one of Lawrence's very first stories) through the eyes of its first "professional" reader. Not long before World War I, a young woman sent to novelist Ford Madox Ford, then editor of *The English Review*, three poems and a short story written by a schoolmaster friend of hers, the then-unknown D. H. Lawrence. Ford read the story first and, he recalls, knew immediately that he had a genius on his hands, "a big one." The very title, "Odour of Chrysanthemums," Ford noted, "makes an impact on the mind," indicates that the writer is observant (not many people realize that chrysanthemums have an odor), and sets the dark autumnal tone of the story. From the very first sentence, Ford goes on to say,

D. H. Lawrence as a young schoolmaster

> you know that this fellow with the power of observation is going to write whatever he writes about from the inside. The "Number 4" shows that. He will be the sort of fellow who knows that for the sort of people who work about engines, engines have a sort of individuality. He had to give the engine the personality of a number.... "With seven full wagons."... The "seven" is good. The ordinary careless writer would say "some small wagons." This man knows what he wants. He sees the scene of his story exactly. He has an authoritative mind.
>
> "It appeared round the corner with loud threats of speed."... Good writing; slightly, but not *too* arresting.... "But the colt that it startled from among the gorse ... out-distanced it at a canter." Good again. This fellow does not "state." He doesn't say: "It was coming slowly," or—what would have been a little better—"at seven miles an hour." Because even "seven miles an hour" means nothing definite for the untrained mind. It might mean something for a trainer or pedestrian racers. The imaginative writer writes for all humanity; he does not limit his desired readers to specialists.... But anyone knows that an engine that makes a great deal of noise and yet cannot overtake a colt at a canter must be a ludicrously ineffective machine. We know then that this fellow knows his job.
>
> ... [T]his man knows. He knows how to open a story with a sentence of the

right cadence for holding the attention. He knows how to construct a paragraph. He knows the life he is writing about.... You can trust him for the rest.
—from "Before the Wars," *Selected Memories, The Bodley Head Ford Madox Ford* (London, 1962), I, 322–23

In that uncanny story, "The Rocking-Horse Winner," written at the other end of Lawrence's career and published posthumously in 1932, you will find the same precision of detail and the same "inside view," in the first description of Paul's riding the horse, for example; in the picture of the horse's "lowered face" ("Its red mouth was slightly open, its big eye was wide and glassy-bright" [paragraph 42]); and in the precise accounting of the races, the odds, the money.

Ford read "Odour of Chrysanthemums" outside the context available to us. He did not know anything of the author and had read nothing else by him. Ford was an excellent editor (as well as writer) and, to his credit, spotted Lawrence's talent. Lawrence's mastery of detail made Ford trust him; what he trusted him for seems to have been knowledge of the "other ninety-nine hundredths" of the population, the working class. An English writer who commanded respect and yet who was well versed in the ways of the working classes was rare and notable in those prewar days, and Lawrence's early works are full of details of the lives of miners and their families. But Lawrence, we now know, considered not class but the man-woman relationship to be the "great relationship of humanity." If we know that, know of Lawrence's notoriety for describing sexual relations, know his later works in which sexual relations are the fundamental concern, we may focus our attention less on the picture of the working class in "Odour of Chrysanthemums" than on the strange relationship between the Bateses. Though the class element remains prominent in the story, the context of Lawrence's entire canon highlights this other dimension of human relationships. And though "Odour of Chrysanthemums" is not specifically about love, it shows us Lawrence's view of what woman-man love is not: "Was this what it all meant—utter, intact separateness, obscured by heat of living?... There had been nothing between them, and yet they had come together, exchanging their nakedness repeatedly. Each time he had taken her, they had been two isolated beings, far apart as now" (paragraph 218). Similarly, we may see what parent-child love is not in "The Rocking-Horse Winner":

> [W]hen her children were present, she always felt the centre of her heart go hard. This troubled her, and in her manner she was all the more gentle and anxious for her children, as if she loved them very much. Only she herself knew that at the center of her heart was a hard little place that could not feel love, no, not for anybody. Everybody else said of her: "She is such a good mother. She adores her children." Only she herself, and her children themselves, knew it was not so.
> (paragraph 1)

"The Blind Man," however, is directly about man-woman love and even about man-man love or "the passion of friendship" (paragraph 221). With this subject comes the characteristic Lawrentian focus on the contrast between the physical/sensual/animal/blood-consciousness (paragraph 86)—here embodied in the blind man, Maurice—and intellectual/verbal consciousness—here represented by Bertie, whose world of the mind is imperiled by physical contact (paragraph 235). However, we must be careful not to assume that because "blood-prescience" is primary in Lawrence's system of values it is therefore sufficient, or that because intellectual consciousness alone is inadequate it is therefore useless: note how Isabel and Maurice suffer through times of depression and discontent.

Though Ford stressed Lawrence's ability to observe the outside of things, he also says that "this fellow... is going to write whatever he writes about from the inside." It is not just Lawrence's powers of observation, but his penetration to the inside of his characters' beings, to the shockingly original but convincing motives and feelings he finds there, that mark his best work. The essential separateness of Elizabeth and Walter Bates in "Odour of Chrysanthemums" despite their physical intimacy (and perhaps the essential separateness of each of us), the emptiness at the center of Bertie in "The Blind Man" despite his social and professional success, the hardness at the center of the apparently adoring mother's heart in "The Rocking-Horse Winner" all suggest Lawrence's writing "from the inside," his unconventional insights, and his unique vision.

In this chapter we also offer three of Flannery O'Connor's stories, including the title stories of both her first collection, *A Good Man Is Hard to Find* (1955), and her last, *Everything That Rises Must Converge* (published posthumously in 1965). Her career was short, its latter stages hampered by periodic, intensifying, painful, and debilitating bouts of lupus, but her accomplishments were considerable: she died at thirty-nine, having published some thirty-one stories and two novels, as well as numerous essays and reviews.

*When anybody asks what a story is about, the only proper thing is to tell him to read the story.*
—FLANNERY O'CONNOR

O'Connor's world is not as large as Lawrence's eventually became: her settings are most often in the American South, rural or urban, and her characters most often Southerners, white or black. Consequently, her subject is often what she calls "the race business." Like Lawrence, O'Connor has a keen eye for realistic detail and for the truth that lies beneath the surface of language and self-image. Her means of releasing this inner truth is often, as in Faulkner, violence that shocks the reader and, often, the characters themselves into confronting uncomfortable truths. Though O'Connor is a deeply religious and serious writer, her stories are replete with irony and wit and are sometimes downright funny. (It is worth asking what, if anything, is intentionally funny in Lawrence's writings.) Indeed, as you will see, she is not above mixing comedy and horror or using comic pratfalls to achieve serious (even tragic) ends. The central, sometimes obsessive concerns and assumptions that permeate an author's work do more than relate the individual stories to each other, mutually illuminating and enriching them; they also serve as the author's trademark. It is not difficult to recognize or even parody a story by Lawrence or O'Connor.

Flannery O'Connor

Embodying these larger concerns and underlying such larger structures as plot, focus, and voice are the basic characteristics of the author's language, such as **diction**, the choice and use of words; the structure and rhythm of sentences; figures of thought and speech; and imagery—in other words, the author's **style**.

Perhaps because of the uniqueness of style, the vocabulary for discussing stylistic elements is not precise. We can broadly characterize diction as **formal** ("The Cask of Amontillado") or **informal** ("Cathedral" and, in fact, most of the stories in this book), and within the broad term *informal* we can identify a level of language that approximates the speech of ordinary people, which we call **colloquial** ("Why I Live at the P.O."). But to characterize the stylistic features that distinguish one author's work from the work of his or her contemporaries is a difficult task indeed.

Diction and sentence structure contribute to the **tone** of a work, or the implied attitude or stance of the author toward the characters and events, an aspect somewhat analogous to tone of voice. When what is being said and how it is said (tone) are in harmony, it is difficult to separate one from the other; when there seems to be a discrepancy, we have a number of terms that are useful for describing the difference. If the language seems exaggerated, we call it **overstatement**, or **hyperbole**. Sometimes it will be the narrator, sometimes a character, who uses language so intensive or exaggerated that we must read it at a discount, as it were, and judge the speaker's accuracy or honesty in the process. When Julian's mother, in "Everything That Rises Must Converge," says, "I've always had a great respect for my colored friends.... I'd do anything in the world for them" (paragraph 32), we know she protests too much, that she is exaggerating, and we see the racism lurking beneath her language. When Sister in "Why I Live at the P.O." says, "I do not enjoy being referred to as a hussy by my own grandfather," we know that she means to express her dislike of being called a hussy much more forcefully than she does. She is indulging in a bit of obvious **understatement**, or **litotes**. When a word or expression carries not only its literal meaning but a different meaning for the speaker as well, we have an example of **verbal irony**. For example, when Fortunato says, "I shall not die of a cough," Montresor's "True—true" may seem reassuring, but we learn later in the story why it is both accurate and ominous. There are also nonverbal forms of irony, the most common of which is **situational irony,** which occurs when a character holds a position or has an expectation that is reversed or fulfilled in an unexpected way. Knowing her husband's habit of drinking himself into unconsciousness, Elizabeth Bates expects him to be brought home like a log. How is her expectation fulfilled? She had also said bitterly, "But he needn't come rolling in here in his pit-dirt, for *I* won't wash him" (paragraph 78), and yet she does. Why is her determination altered? As you read through or look back over "Odour of Chrysanthemums," watch for other instances of situational irony—of reversed or unexpectedly fulfilled expectations.

A form of situational irony known as **dramatic irony** occurs when a gap opens between what a character believes or expects and what the reader or audience knows. This may be revealed when a character says something that has unintended alternative meanings to a better-informed listener, or that later becomes true in an unintended way. Dramatic irony also may be sustained throughout an entire work by an unreliable first-person narrator, who perceives or tries to "spin" his or her circumstances in a more or less distorted way. In "A Good Man Is Hard to Find," the grandmother's careful attention to her dress, she believes, ensures respect: "In case of an accident, anyone seeing her dead on the highway would know at once that she was a lady" (paragraph 12). She takes this seriously; most readers find it ludicrous or pathetic; hence it is an example of dramatic irony. At the same time, her remark unknowingly foretells the outcome of the story, a form of situational irony. Such ironic statements and outcomes occur throughout O'Connor's stories. Rather than demeaning her characters, O'Connor's ironic treatment testifies to her keen observation of the common limits of human awareness, and the way people tend to rationalize and misconstrue their situations and their own characters.

Another, highly emphasized element of style is **imagery**. In its broadest sense imagery includes any sensory detail indicated in a work. Imagery in this broad sense, however, is so prevalent in literature that it would take exhaustive statistics to differentiate styles by counting the number of sensory elements per hundred or thousand words, categorizing the images as primarily visual, tactile, auditory, and so forth. In a more restricted sense, *imagery* refers to figurative language (see chapter 5, "Symbol"), particularly that which defines an abstraction or any emotional or psychological state through a sensory comparison. The opening paragraph of "Odour of Chrysanthemums" illustrates the broader definition of imagery, and this passage from later in the same story may represent the figurative sense: "Life with its smoky burning gone from him, had left him apart. . . . In her womb was ice of fear" (paragraph 218).

We might say that if an author's vision gives us his or her profile, the style gives us a fingerprint—though the fingerprint is unique and definitive, it is also harder to come by than a glimpse of a profile. Ultimately, however, vision and style are less distinguishable from each other than the profile-fingerprint analogy suggests. For vision and style do more than interact: they are inextricably fused or compounded. Let us look back at the Ford passage. He says this of "the gorse, which still flickered indistinctly in the raw afternoon": "Good too, distinctly good. This is the just-sufficient observation of nature that gives you, in a single phrase, landscape, time of day, weather, season." Is this vision or style? The observation of nature conveys a way of viewing life in general—an author's vision, but expressing that vision economically, tautly, is style. The two merge.

Whatever else this passage accomplishes, it bears Lawrence's unique literary fingerprint. Perhaps it takes more than just these ten words, but surely in a paragraph or two we know we're in his distinctive fictional world. We recognize, too, the unique language he created out of the common language we share.

## D. H. LAWRENCE

### Odour of Chrysanthemums

#### I

The small locomotive engine, Number 4, came clanking, stumbling down from Selston with seven full waggons. It appeared round the corner with loud threats of speed, but the colt that it startled from among the gorse, which still flickered indistinctly in the raw afternoon, outdistanced it at a canter. A woman, walking up the railway line to Underwood, drew back into the hedge, held her basket aside, and watched the footplate of the engine advancing. The trucks thumped heavily past, one by one, with slow inevitable movement, as she stood insignificantly trapped between the jolting black waggons and the hedge; then they curved away towards the coppice where the withered oak leaves dropped noiselessly, while the birds, pulling at the scarlet hips beside the track, made off into the dusk that had already crept into the spinney. In the open, the smoke from the engine sank and cleaved to the rough grass. The fields were dreary and forsaken, and in the marshy strip that led to the whimsey, a reedy pit-pond, the fowls had already abandoned their run among the alders, to roost in the tarred fowl-house. The pit-bank loomed up beyond the pond, flames like red sores licking its ashy sides, in the afternoon's stagnant light. Just beyond rose the tapering chimneys and the clumsy black headstocks of Brinsley Colliery. The two wheels were spinning fast up against the sky, and the winding-engine rapped out its little spasms. The miners were being turned up.

The engine whistled as it came into the wide bay of railway lines beside the colliery, where rows of trucks stood in harbour.

Miners, single, trailing and in groups, passed like shadows diverging home. At the edge of the ribbed level of sidings squat a low cottage, three steps down from the cinder track. A large bony vine clutched at the house, as if to claw down the tiled roof. Round the bricked yard grew a few wintry primroses. Beyond, the long garden sloped down to a bush-covered brook course. There were some twiggy apple trees, winter-crack trees, and ragged cabbages. Beside the path hung dishevelled pink chrysanthemums, like pink cloths hung on bushes. A woman came stooping out of the felt-covered fowl-house, half-way down the garden. She closed and padlocked the door, then drew herself erect, having brushed some bits from her white apron.

She was a tall woman of imperious mien, handsome, with definite black eyebrows. Her smooth black hair was parted exactly. For a few moments she stood steadily watching the miners as they passed along the railway: then she turned towards the brook course. Her face was calm and set, her mouth was closed with disillusionment. After a moment she called:

5   "John!" There was no answer. She waited, and then said distinctly:

"Where are you?"

"Here!" replied a child's sulky voice from among the bushes. The woman looked piercingly through the dusk.

"Are you at that brook?" she asked sternly.

For answer the child showed himself before the raspberry-canes that rose like whips. He was a small, sturdy boy of five. He stood quite still, defiantly.

10   "Oh!" said the mother, conciliated. "I thought you were down at that wet brook—and you remember what I told you—"

The boy did not move or answer.

"Come, come on in," she said more gently, "it's getting dark. There's your grandfather's engine coming down the line!"

The lad advanced slowly, with resentful, taciturn movement. He was dressed in trousers and waistcoat of cloth that was too thick and hard for the size of the garments. They were evidently cut down from a man's clothes.

As they went slowly towards the house he tore at the ragged wisps of chrysanthemums and dropped the petals in handfuls along the path.

15   "Don't do that—it does look nasty," said his mother. He refrained, and she, suddenly pitiful, broke off a twig with three or four wan flowers and held them against her face. When mother and son reached the yard her hand hesitated, and

instead of laying the flower aside, she pushed it in her apron-band. The mother and son stood at the foot of the three steps looking across the bay of lines at the passing home of the miners. The trundle of the small train was imminent. Suddenly the engine loomed past the house and came to a stop opposite the gate.

The engine-driver, a short man with round grey beard, leaned out of the cab high above the woman.

"Have you got a cup of tea?" he said in a cheery, hearty fashion.

It was her father. She went in, saying she would mash.[1] Directly, she returned.

"I didn't come to see you on Sunday," began the little grey-bearded man.

"I didn't expect you," said his daughter.

The engine-driver winced; then, reassuming his cheery, airy manner, he said:

"Oh, have you heard then? Well, and what do you think——?"

"I think it is soon enough," she replied.

At her brief censure the little man made an impatient gesture, and said coaxingly, yet with dangerous coldness:

"Well, what's a man to do? It's no sort of life for a man of my years, to sit at my own hearth like a stranger. And if I'm going to marry again it may as well be soon as late—what does it matter to anybody?"

The woman did not reply, but turned and went into the house. The man in the engine-cab stood assertive, till she returned with a cup of tea and a piece of bread and butter on a plate. She went up the steps and stood near the footplate of the hissing engine.

"You needn't 'a' brought me bread an' butter," said her father. "But a cup of tea"—he sipped appreciatively—"it's very nice." He sipped for a moment or two, then: "I hear as Walter's got another bout on," he said.

"When hasn't he?" said the woman bitterly.

"I heered tell of him in the 'Lord Nelson'[2] braggin' as he was going to spend that b—— afore he went: half a sovereign[3] that was."

"When?" asked the woman.

"A' Sat'day night—I know that's true."

"Very likely," she laughed bitterly. "He gives me twenty-three shillings."

"Aye, it's a nice thing, when a man can do nothing with his money but make a beast of himself!" said the grey-whiskered man. The woman turned her head away. Her father swallowed the last of his tea and handed her the cup.

"Aye," he sighed, wiping his mouth. "It's a settler, it is——"

He put his hand on the lever. The little engine strained and groaned, and the train rumbled towards the crossing. The woman again looked across the metals. Darkness was settling over the spaces of the railway and trucks: the miners, in grey sombre groups, were still passing home. The winding-engine pulsed hurriedly, with brief pauses. Elizabeth Bates looked at the dreary flow of men, then she went indoors. Her husband did not come.

The kitchen was small and full of firelight; red coals piled glowing up the chimney mouth. All the life of the room seemed in the white, warm hearth and the steel fender reflecting the red fire. The cloth was laid for tea; cups glinted in

---

1. Prepare (tea).   2. A public house, pub.
3. A sovereign (a gold coin worth one pound sterling) was about half a week's wage; there are twenty shillings (see below) to the pound.

the shadows. At the back, where the lowest stairs protruded into the room, the boy sat struggling with a knife and a piece of white wood. He was almost hidden in the shadow. It was half-past four. They had but to await the father's coming to begin tea. As the mother watched her son's sullen little struggle with the wood, she saw herself in his silence and pertinacity; she saw the father in her child's indifference to all but himself. She seemed to be occupied by her husband. He had probably gone past his home, slunk past his own door, to drink before he came in, while his dinner spoiled and wasted in waiting. She glanced at the clock, then took the potatoes to strain them in the yard. The garden and fields beyond the brook were closed in uncertain darkness. When she rose with the saucepan, leaving the drain steaming into the night behind her, she saw the yellow lamps were lit along the high road that went up the hill away beyond the space of the railway lines and the field.

Then again she watched the men trooping home, fewer now and fewer.

Indoors the fire was sinking and the room was dark red. The woman put her saucepan on the hob, and set a batter pudding near the mouth of the oven. Then she stood unmoving. Directly, gratefully, came quick young steps to the door. Someone hung on the latch a moment, then a little girl entered and began pulling off her outdoor things, dragging a mass of curls, just ripening from gold to brown, over her eyes with her hat.

Her mother chid her for coming late from school, and said she would have to keep her at home the dark winter days.

40 "Why, mother, it's hardly a bit dark yet. The lamp's not lighted, and my father's not home."

"No, he isn't. But it's a quarter to five! Did you see anything of him?"

The child became serious. She looked at her mother with large, wistful blue eyes.

"No, mother, I've never seen him. Why? Has he come up an' gone past, to Old Brinsley? He hasn't, mother, 'cos I never saw him."

"He'd watch that," said the mother bitterly, "he'd take care as you didn't see him. But you may depend upon it, he's seated in the 'Prince o' Wales.' He wouldn't be this late."

45 The girl looked at her mother piteously.

"Let's have our teas, mother, should we?" said she.

The mother called John to table. She opened the door once more and looked out across the darkness of the lines. All was deserted: she could not hear the winding-engines.

"Perhaps," she said to herself, "he's stopped to get some ripping[4] done."

They sat down to tea. John, at the end of the table near the door, was almost lost in the darkness. Their faces were hidden from each other. The girl crouched against the fender slowly moving a thick piece of bread before the fire. The lad, his face a dusky mark on the shadow, sat watching her who was transfigured in the red glow.

50 "I do think it's beautiful to look in the fire," said the child.

"Do you?" said her mother. "Why?"

"It's so red, and full of little caves—and it feels so nice, and you can fair smell it."

---

4. Coal-mining term for taking down the roof of an underground road in order to make it higher.

"It'll want mending directly," replied her mother, "and then if your father comes he'll carry on and say there never is a fire when a man comes home sweating from the pit.—A public-house is always warm enough."

There was silence till the boy said complainingly: "Make haste, our Annie."

"Well, I am doing! I can't make the fire do it no faster, can I?"

"She keeps wafflin'[5] it about so's to make 'er slow," grumbled the boy.

"Don't have such an evil imagination, child," replied the mother.

Soon the room was busy in the darkness with the crisp sound of crunching. The mother ate very little. She drank her tea determinedly, and sat thinking. When she rose her anger was evident in the stern unbending of her head. She looked at the pudding in the fender, and broke out:

"It is a scandalous thing as a man can't even come home to his dinner! If it's crozzled[6] up to a cinder I don't see why I should care. Past his very door he goes to get to a public-house, and here I sit with his dinner waiting for him——"

She went out. As she dropped piece after piece of coal on the red fire, the shadows fell on the walls, till the room was almost in total darkness.

"I canna see," grumbled the invisible John. In spite of herself, the mother laughed.

"You know the way to your mouth," she said. She set the dustpan outside the door. When she came again like a shadow on the hearth, the lad repeated, complaining sulkily:

"I canna see."

"Good gracious!" cried the mother irritably, "you're as bad as your father if it's a bit dusk!"

Nevertheless she took a paper spill from a sheaf on the mantelpiece and proceeded to light the lamp that hung from the ceiling in the middle of the room. As she reached up, her figure displayed itself just rounding with maternity.

"Oh, mother——!" exclaimed the girl.

"What?" said the woman, suspended in the act of putting the lamp-glass over the flame. The copper reflector shone handsomely on her, as she stood with uplifted arm, turning to face her daughter:

"You've got a flower in your apron!" said the child, in a little rapture at this unusual event.

"Goodness me!" exclaimed the woman, relieved. "One would think the house was afire." She replaced the glass and waited a moment before turning up the wick. A pale shadow was seen floating vaguely on the floor.

"Let me smell!" said the child, still rapturously, coming forward and putting her face to her mother's waist.

"Go along, silly!" said the mother, turning up the lamp. The light revealed their suspense so that the woman felt it almost unbearable. Annie was still bending at her waist. Irritably, the mother took the flowers out from her apron-band.

"Oh, mother—don't take them out!" Annie cried, catching her hand and trying to replace the sprig.

"Such nonsense!" said the mother, turning away. The child put the pale chrysanthemums to her lips, murmuring:

"Don't they smell beautiful!"

Her mother gave a short laugh.

5. Waving.   6. Shriveled.

"No," she said, "not to me. It was chrysanthemums when I married him, and chrysanthemums when you were born, and the first time they ever brought him home drunk, he'd got brown chrysanthemums in his button-hole."

She looked at the children. Their eyes and their parted lips were wondering. The mother sat rocking in silence for some time. Then she looked at the clock.

"Twenty minutes to six!" In a tone of fine bitter carelessness she continued: "Eh, he'll not come now till they bring him. There he'll stick! But he needn't come rolling in here in his pit-dirt, for *I* won't wash him. He can lie on the floor —Eh, what a fool I've been, what a fool! And this is what I came here for, to this dirty hole, rats and all, for him to slink past his very door. Twice last week— he's begun now——"

She silenced herself, and rose to clear the table.

While for an hour or more the children played, subduedly intent, fertile of imagination, united in fear of the mother's wrath, and in dread of their father's home-coming, Mrs. Bates sat in her rocking-chair making a "singlet" of thick cream-coloured flannel, which gave a dull wounded sound as she tore off the grey edge. She worked at her sewing with energy, listening to the children, and her anger wearied itself, lay down to rest, opening its eyes from time to time and steadily watching, its ears raised to listen. Sometimes even her anger quailed and shrank, and the mother suspended her sewing, tracing the footsteps that thudded along the sleepers outside; she would lift her head sharply to bid the children "hush," but she recovered herself in time, and the footsteps went past the gate, and the children were not flung out of their playworld.

But at last Annie sighed, and gave in. She glanced at her waggon of slippers, and loathed the game. She turned plaintively to her mother.

"Mother!"—but she was inarticulate.

John crept out like a frog from under the sofa. His mother glanced up.

"Yes," she said, "just look at those shirtsleeves!"

The boy held them out to survey them, saying nothing. Then somebody called in a hoarse voice away down the line, and suspense bristled in the room, till two people had gone by outside, talking.

"It is time for bed," said the mother.

"My father hasn't come," wailed Annie plaintively. But her mother was primed with courage.

"Never mind. They'll bring him when he does come—like a log." She meant there would be no scene. "And he may sleep on the floor till he wakes himself. I know he'll not go to work tomorrow after this!"

The children had their hands and faces wiped with a flannel.[7] They were very quiet. When they had put on their nightdresses, they said their prayers, the boy mumbling. The mother looked down at them, at the brown silken bush of intertwining curls in the nape of the girl's neck, at the little black head of the lad, and her heart burst with anger at their father who caused all three such distress. The children hid their faces in her skirts for comfort.

When Mrs. Bates came down, the room was strangely empty, with a tension of expectancy. She took up her sewing and stitched for some time without raising her head. Meantime her anger was tinged with fear.

---

7. Washcloth.

## II

The clock struck eight and she rose suddenly, dropping her sewing on her chair. She went to the stairfoot door, opened it, listening. Then she went out, locking the door behind her.

Something scuffled in the yard, and she started though she knew it was only the rats with which the place was overrun. The night was very dark. In the great bay of railway lines, bulked with trucks, there was no trace of light, only away back she could see a few yellow lamps at the pit-top, and the red smear of the burning pit-bank on the night. She hurried along the edge of the track, then, crossing the converging lines, came to the stile by the white gates, whence she emerged on the road. Then the fear which had led her shrank. People were walking up to New Brinsley; she saw the lights in the houses; twenty yards further on were the broad windows of the "Prince of Wales," very warm and bright, and the loud voices of men could be heard distinctly. What a fool she had been to imagine that anything had happened to him! He was merely drinking over there at the "Prince of Wales." She faltered. She had never yet been to fetch him, and she never would go. So she continued her walk towards the long straggling line of houses, standing blank on the highway. She entered a passage between the dwellings.

"Mr. Rigley?—Yes! Did you want him? No, he's not in at this minute."

The raw-boned woman leaned forward from her dark scullery and peered at the other, upon whom fell a dim light through the blind of the kitchen window.

"Is it Mrs. Bates?" she asked in a tone tinged with respect.

"Yes. I wondered if your Master was at home. Mine hasn't come yet."

"'Asn't 'e! Oh, Jack's been 'ome an 'ad 'is dinner an' gone out. 'E's just gone for 'alf an hour afore bedtime. Did you call at the 'Prince of Wales'?"

"No——"

"No, you didn't like——! It's not very nice." The other woman was indulgent. There was an awkward pause. "Jack never said nothink about—about your Mester," she said.

"No!—I expect he's stuck in there!"

Elizabeth Bates said this bitterly, and with recklessness. She knew that the woman across the yard was standing at her door listening, but she did not care. As she turned:

"Stop a minute! I'll just go an' ask Jack if 'e knows anythink," said Mrs. Rigley.

"Oh, no—I wouldn't like to put—!"

"Yes, I will, if you will just step inside an' see as th' childer doesn't come downstairs and set theirselves afire."

Elizabeth Bates, murmuring a remonstrance, stepped inside. The other woman apologized for the state of the room.

The kitchen needed apology. There were little frocks and trousers and childish undergarments on the squab[8] and on the floor, and a litter of playthings everywhere. On the black American cloth[9] of the table were pieces of bread and cake, crusts, slops, and a teapot with cold tea.

"Eh, ours is just as bad," said Elizabeth Bates, looking at the woman, not at the house. Mrs. Rigley put a shawl over her head and hurried out, saying:

"I shanna be a minute."

---

8. Sofa.   9. Enameled oilcloth.

The other sat, noting with faint disapproval the general untidiness of the room. Then she fell to counting the shoes of various sizes scattered over the floor. There were twelve. She sighed and said to herself, "No wonder!"—glancing at the litter. There came the scratching of two pairs of feet on the yard, and the Rigleys entered. Elizabeth Bates rose. Rigley was a big man, with very large bones. His head looked particularly bony. Across his temple was a blue scar, caused by a wound got in the pit, a wound in which the coal-dust remained blue like tattooing.

"'Asna 'e come whoam yit?" asked the man, without any form of greeting, but with deference and sympathy. "I couldna say wheer he is—'e's non ower theer!"—he jerked his head to signify the "Prince of Wales."

"'E's 'appen[1] gone up to th' 'Yew,'" said Mrs. Rigley.

There was another pause. Rigley had evidently something to get off his mind: "Ah left 'im finishin' a stint," he began. "Loose-all[2] 'ad bin gone about ten minutes when we com'n away, an' I shouted, 'Are ter comin', Walt?' an' 'e said 'Go on, Ah shanna be but a 'ef a minnit,' so we com'n ter th' bottom, me an' Browers, thinkin' as 'e wor just behint, an' 'ud come up i' th' next bantle[3]—"

He stood perplexed, as if answering a charge of deserting his mate. Elizabeth Bates, now again certain of disaster, hastened to reassure him:

"I expect 'e's gone up to th' 'Yew Tree,' as you say. It's not the first time. I've fretted myself into a fever before now. He'll come home when they carry him."

"Ay, isn't it too bad!" deplored the other woman.

"I'll just step up to Dick's an' see if 'e *is* theer," offered the man, afraid of appearing alarmed, afraid of taking liberties.

"Oh, I wouldn't think of bothering you that far," said Elizabeth Bates, with emphasis, but he knew she was glad of his offer.

As they stumbled up the entry, Elizabeth Bates heard Rigley's wife run across the yard and open her neighbour's door. At this, suddenly all the blood in her body seemed to switch away from her heart.

"Mind!" warned Rigley. "Ah've said many a time as Ah'd fill up them ruts in this entry, sumb'dy 'll be breakin' their legs yit."

She recovered herself and walked quickly along with the miner.

"I don't like leaving the children in bed, and nobody in the house," she said.

"No, you dunna!" he replied courteously. They were soon at the gate of the cottage.

"Well, I shanna be many minnits. Dunna you be frettin' now, 'e'll be all right," said the butty.[4]

"Thank you very much, Mr. Rigley," she replied.

"You're welcome!" he stammered, moving away. "I shanna be many minnits."

The house was quiet. Elizabeth Bates took off her hat and shawl, and rolled back the rug. When she had finished, she sat down. It was a few minutes past nine. She was startled by the rapid chuff of the winding-engine at the pit, and the sharp whirr of the brakes on the rope as it descended. Again she felt the painful sweep of her blood, and she put her hand to her side, saying aloud, "Good gracious!—it's only the nine o'clock deputy going down," rebuking herself.

---

1. Perhaps.   2. Signal to quit work and come to the surface.
3. An open seat or car of the lift or elevator that takes the miners to the surface.
4. Buddy, fellow worker.

She sat still, listening. Half an hour of this, and she was wearied out.

"What am I working up like this for?" she said pitiably to herself, "I s'll only be doing myself some damage."

She took out her sewing again.

At a quarter to ten there were footsteps. One person! She watched for the door to open. It was an elderly woman, in a black bonnet and a black woollen shawl—his mother. She was about sixty years old, pale, with blue eyes, and her face all wrinkled and lamentable. She shut the door and turned to her daughter-in-law peevishly.

"Eh, Lizzie, whatever shall we do, whatever shall we do!" she cried.

Elizabeth drew back a little, sharply.

"What is it, mother?" she said.

The elder woman seated herself on the sofa.

"I don't know, child, I can't tell you!"—she shook her head slowly. Elizabeth sat watching her, anxious and vexed.

"I don't know," replied the grandmother, sighing very deeply. "There's no end to my troubles, there isn't. The things I've gone through, I'm sure it's enough——!" She wept without wiping her eyes, the tears running.

"But, mother," interrupted Elizabeth, "what do you mean? What is it?"

The grandmother slowly wiped her eyes. The fountains of her tears were stopped by Elizabeth's directness. She wiped her eyes slowly.

"Poor child! Eh, you poor thing!" she moaned. "I don't know what we're going to do, I don't—and you as you are—it's a thing, it is indeed!"

Elizabeth waited.

"Is he dead?" she asked, and at the words her heart swung violently, though she felt a slight flush of shame at the ultimate extravagance of the question. Her words sufficiently frightened the old lady, almost brought her to herself.

"Don't say so, Elizabeth! We'll hope it's not as bad as that; no, may the Lord spare us that, Elizabeth. Jack Rigley came just as I was sittin' down to a glass afore going to bed, an' 'e said, ' 'Appen you'll go down th' line, Mrs. Bates. Walt's had an accident. 'Appen you'll go an' sit wi' 'er till we can get him home.' I hadn't time to ask him a word afore he was gone. An' I put my bonnet on an' come straight down, Lizzie. I thought to myself, 'Eh, that poor blessed child, if anybody should come an' tell her of a sudden, there's no knowin'; what'll 'appen to 'er.' You mustn't let it upset you, Lizzie—or you know what to expect. How long is it, six months—or is it five, Lizzie? Ay!"—the old woman shook her head—"time slips on, it slips on! Ay!"

Elizabeth's thoughts were busy elsewhere. If he was killed—would she be able to manage on the little pension and what she could earn?—she counted up rapidly. If he was hurt—they wouldn't take him to the hospital—how tiresome he would be to nurse!—but perhaps she'd be able to get him away from the drink and his hateful ways. She would—while he was ill. The tears offered to come to her eyes at the picture. But what sentimental luxury was this she was beginning?—She turned to consider the children. At any rate she was absolutely necessary for them. They were her business.

"Ay!" repeated the old woman, "it seems but a week or two since he brought me his first wages. Ay—he was a good lad, Elizabeth, he was, in his way. I don't know why he got to be such a trouble, I don't. He was a happy lad at home, only full of spirits. But there's no mistake he's been a handful of trouble, he has! I hope the Lord'll spare him to mend his ways. I hope so, I hope so. You've had a sight o' trouble with him, Elizabeth, you have indeed. But he was a jolly enough lad wi' me, he was, I can assure you. I don't know how it is. . . ."

The old woman continued to muse aloud, a monotonous irritating sound, while Elizabeth thought concentratedly, startled once, when she heard the winding-engine chuff quickly, and the brakes skirr with a shriek. Then she heard the engine more slowly, and the brakes made no sound. The old woman did not notice. Elizabeth waited in suspense. The mother-in-law talked, with lapses into silence.

"But he wasn't your son, Lizzie, an' it makes a difference. Whatever he was, I remember him when he was little, an' I learned to understand him and to make allowances. You've got to make allowances for them—"

It was half-past ten, and the old woman was saying: "But it's trouble from beginning to end; you're never too old for trouble, never too old for that—" when the gate banged back, and there were heavy feet on the steps.

"I'll go, Lizzie, let me go," cried the old woman, rising. But Elizabeth was at the door. It was a man in pit-clothes.

150 "They're bringin' 'im, Missis," he said. Elizabeth's heart halted a moment. Then it surged on again, almost suffocating her.

"Is he—is it bad?" she asked.

The man turned away, looking at the darkness:

"The doctor says 'e'd been dead hours. 'E saw 'im i' th' lamp-cabin."

The old woman, who stood just behind Elizabeth, dropped into a chair and folded her hands, crying: "Oh, my boy, my boy!"

155 "Hush!" said Elizabeth, with a sharp twitch of a frown. "Be still, mother, don't waken th' children: I wouldn't have them down for anything!"

The old woman moaned softly, rocking herself. The man was drawing away. Elizabeth took a step forward.

"How was it?" she asked.

"Well, I couldn't say for sure," the man replied, very ill at ease. " 'E wor finishin' a stint an' th' butties 'ad gone, an' a lot o' stuff come down atop 'n 'im."

"And crushed him?" cried the widow, with a shudder.

160 "No," said the man, "it fell at th' back of 'im. 'E wor under th' face, an' it niver touched 'im. It shut 'im in. It seems 'e wor smothered."

Elizabeth shrank back. She heard the old woman behind her cry:

"What?—what did 'e say it was?"

The man replied, more loudly: " 'E wor smothered!"

Then the old woman wailed aloud, and this relieved Elizabeth.

165 "Oh, mother," she said, putting her hands on the old woman, "don't waken th' children, don't waken th' children."

She wept a little, unknowing, while the old mother rocked herself and moaned. Elizabeth remembered that they were bringing him home, and she must be ready. "They'll lay him in the parlour," she said to herself, standing a moment pale and perplexed.

Then she lighted a candle and went into the tiny room. The air was cold and damp, but she could not make a fire, there was no fireplace. She set down the candle and looked round. The candlelight glittered on the lustre-glasses,[5] on the

---

5. Glass pendants around the edge of an ornamental vase.

two vases that held some of the pink chrysanthemums, and on the dark mahogany. There was a cold, deathly smell of chrysanthemums in the room. Elizabeth stood looking at the flowers. She turned away, and calculated whether there would be room to lay him on the floor, between the couch and the chiffonier. She pushed the chairs aside. There would be room to lay him down and to step round him. Then she fetched the old red tablecloth, and another old cloth, spreading them down to save her bit of carpet. She shivered on leaving the parlour; so, from the dresser-drawer she took a clean shirt and put it at the fire to air. All the time her mother-in-law was rocking herself in the chair and moaning.

"You'll have to move from there, mother," said Elizabeth. "They'll be bringing him in. Come in the rocker."

The old mother rose mechanically, and seated herself by the fire, continuing to lament. Elizabeth went into the pantry for another candle, and there, in the little penthouse[6] under the naked tiles, she heard them coming. She stood still in the pantry doorway, listening. She heard them pass the end of the house, and come awkwardly down the three steps, a jumble of shuffling footsteps and muttering voices. The old woman was silent. The men were in the yard.

Then Elizabeth heard Matthews, the manager of the pit, say: "You go in first, Jim. Mind!"

The door came open, and the two women saw a collier backing into the room, holding one end of a stretcher, on which they could see the nailed pitboots of the dead man. The two carriers halted, the man at the head stooping to the lintel of the door.

"Wheer will you have him?" asked the manager, a short, white-bearded man.

Elizabeth roused herself and came from the pantry carrying the unlighted candle.

"In the parlour," she said.

"In there, Jim!" pointed the manager, and the carriers backed round into the tiny room. The coat with which they had covered the body fell off as they awkwardly turned through the two doorways, and the women saw their man, naked to the waist, lying stripped for work. The old woman began to moan in a low voice of horror.

"Lay th' stretcher at th' side," snapped the manager, "an' put 'im on th' cloths. Mind now, mind! Look you now—!"

One of the men had knocked off a vase of chrysanthemums. He stared awkwardly, then they set down the stretcher. Elizabeth did not look at her husband. As soon as she could get in the room, she went and picked up the broken vase and the flowers.

"Wait a minute!" she said.

The three men waited in silence while she mopped up the water with a duster.

"Eh, what a job, what a job, to be sure!" the manager was saying, rubbing his brow with trouble and perplexity. "Never knew such a thing in my life, never! He'd no business to ha' been left. I never knew such a thing in my life! Fell over him clean as a whistle, an' shut him in. Not four foot of space, there wasn't—yet it scarce bruised him."

---

6. Structure, usually with a sloping roof, attached to a house.

He looked down at the dead man, lying prone, half naked, all grimed with coal-dust.

"'Sphyxiated,' the doctor said. It *is* the most terrible job I've ever known. Seems as if it was done o' purpose. Clean over him, an' shut 'im in, like a mouse-trap"—he made a sharp, descending gesture with his hand.

The colliers standing by jerked aside their heads in hopeless comment.

The horror of the thing bristled upon them all.

Then they heard the girl's voice upstairs calling shrilly: "Mother, mother—who is it? Mother, who is it?"

Elizabeth hurried to the foot of the stairs and opened the door:

"Go to sleep!" she commanded sharply. "What are you shouting about? Go to sleep at once—there's nothing——"

Then she began to mount the stairs. They could hear her on the boards, and on the plaster floor of the little bedroom. They could hear her distinctly:

"What's the matter now?—what's the matter with you, silly thing?"—her voice was much agitated, with an unreal gentleness.

"I thought it was some men come," said the plaintive voice of the child. "Has he come?"

"Yes, they've brought him. There's nothing to make a fuss about. Go to sleep now, like a good child."

They could hear her voice in the bedroom, they waited whilst she covered the children under the bedclothes.

"Is he drunk?" asked the girl, timidly, faintly.

"No! No—he's not! He's—he's asleep."

"Is he asleep downstairs?"

"Yes—and don't make a noise."

There was silence for a moment, then the men heard the frightened child again:

"What's that noise?"

"It's nothing, I tell you, what are you bothering for?"

The noise was the grandmother moaning. She was oblivious of everything, sitting on her chair rocking and moaning. The manager put his hand on her arm and bade her "Sh-sh!!"

The old woman opened her eyes and looked at him. She was shocked by this interruption, and seemed to wonder.

"What time is it?"—the plaintive thin voice of the child, sinking back unhappily into sleep, asked this last question.

"Ten o'clock," answered the mother more softly. Then she must have bent down and kissed the children.

Matthews beckoned to the men to come away. They put on their caps, and took up the stretcher. Stepping over the body, they tiptoed out of the house. None of them spoke till they were far from the wakeful children.

When Elizabeth came down she found her mother alone on the parlour floor, leaning over the dead man, the tears dropping on him.

"We must lay him out," the wife said. She put on the kettle, then returning knelt at the feet, and began to unfasten the knotted leather laces. The room was clammy and dim with only one candle, so that she had to bend her face almost to the floor. At last she got off the heavy boots and put them away.

"You must help me now," she whispered to the old woman. Together they stripped the man.

When they arose, saw him lying in the naïve dignity of death, the women stood arrested in fear and respect. For a few moments they remained still, looking down, the old mother whimpering. Elizabeth felt countermanded. She saw him, how utterly inviolable he lay in himself. She had nothing to do with him. She could not accept it. Stooping, she laid her hand on him, in claim. He was still warm, for the mine was hot where he had died. His mother had his face between her hands, and was murmuring incoherently. The old tears fell in succession as drops from wet leaves; the mother was not weeping, merely her tears flowed. Elizabeth embraced the body of her husband, with cheek and lips. She seemed to be listening, inquiring, trying to get some connection. But she could not. She was driven away. He was impregnable.

She rose, went into the kitchen, where she poured warm water into a bowl, brought soap and flannel and a soft towel.

"I must wash him," she said.

Then the old mother rose stiffly, and watched Elizabeth as she carefully washed his face, carefully brushing the big blonde moustache from his mouth with the flannel. She was afraid with a bottomless fear, so she ministered to him. The old woman, jealous, said:

"Let me wipe him!"—and she kneeled on the other side drying slowly as Elizabeth washed, her big black bonnet sometimes brushing the dark head of her daughter. They worked thus in silence for a long time. They never forgot it was death, and the touch of the man's dead body gave them strange emotions, different in each of the women; a great dread possessed them both, the mother felt the lie was given to her womb, she was denied; the wife felt the utter isolation of the human soul, the child within her was a weight apart from her.

At last it was finished. He was a man of handsome body, and his face showed no traces of drink. He was blonde, full-fleshed, with fine limbs. But he was dead.

"Bless him," whispered his mother, looking always at his face, and speaking out of sheer terror. "Dear lad—bless him!" She spoke in a faint sibilant ecstasy of fear and mother love.

Elizabeth sank down again to the floor, and put her face against his neck, and trembled and shuddered. But she had to draw away again. He was dead, and her living flesh had no place against his. A great dread and weariness held her: she was so unavailing. Her life was gone like this.

"White as milk he is, clear as a twelve-month baby, bless him, the darling!" the old mother murmured to herself. "Not a mark on him, clear and clean and white, beautiful as ever a child was made," she murmured with pride. Elizabeth kept her face hidden.

"He went peaceful, Lizzie—peaceful as sleep. Isn't he beautiful, the lamb? Ay—he must ha' made his peace, Lizzie. 'Appen he made it all right, Lizzie, shut in there. He'd have time. He wouldn't look like this if he hadn't made his peace. The lamb, the dear lamb. Eh, but he had a hearty laugh. I loved to hear it. He had the heartiest laugh, Lizzie, as a lad——"

Elizabeth looked up. The man's mouth was fallen back, slightly open under the cover of the moustache. The eyes, half shut, did not show glazed in the obscurity. Life with its smoky burning gone from him, had left him apart and utterly alien to her. And she knew what a stranger he was to her. In her womb was ice of fear, because of this separate stranger with whom she had been living as one flesh. Was this what it all meant—utter, intact separateness, obscured by heat of living? In dread she turned her face away. The fact was too deadly. There had been nothing between them, and yet they had come together, exchanging their nakedness repeatedly. Each time he had taken her, they had been two isolated beings, far apart as now. He was no more responsible than she. The child was like ice in her womb. For as she looked at the dead man, her mind, cold and detached, said clearly: "Who am I? What have I been doing? I have been fighting a husband who did not exist. *He* existed all the time. What wrong have I done? What was that I have been living with? There lies the reality, this man."—And her soul died in her for fear: she knew she had never seen him, he had never seen her, they had met in the dark and had fought in the dark, not knowing whom they met nor whom they fought. And now she saw, and turned silent in seeing. For she had been wrong. She had said he was something he was not; she had felt familiar with him. Whereas he was apart all the while, living as she never lived, feeling as she never felt.

In fear and shame she looked at his naked body, that she had known falsely. And he was the father of her children. Her soul was torn from her body and stood apart. She looked at his naked body and was ashamed, as if she had denied it. After all, it was itself. It seemed awful to her. She looked at his face, and she turned her own face to the wall. For his look was other than hers, his way was not her way. She had denied him what he was—she saw it now. She had refused him as himself.—And this had been her life, and his life.—She was grateful to death, which restored the truth. And she knew she was not dead.

220    And all the while her heart was bursting with grief and pity for him. What had he suffered? What stretch of horror for this helpless man! She was rigid with agony. She had not been able to help him. He had been cruelly injured, this naked man, this other being, and she could make no reparation. There were the children—but the children belonged to life. This dead man had nothing to do with them. He and she were only channels through which life had flowed to issue in the children. She was a mother—but how awful she knew it now to have been a wife. And he, dead now, how awful he must have felt it to be a husband. She felt that in her next world he would be a stranger to her. If they met there, in the beyond, they would only be ashamed of what had been before. The children had come, for some mysterious reason, out of both of them. But the children did not unite them. Now he was dead, she knew how eternally he was apart from her, how eternally he had nothing more to do with her. She saw this episode of her life closed. They had denied each other in life. Now he had withdrawn. An anguish came over her. It was finished then: it had become hopeless between them long before he died. Yet he had been her husband. But how little!

"Have you got his shirt, 'Lizabeth?"

Elizabeth turned without answering, though she strove to weep and behave as her mother-in-law expected. But she could not, she was silenced. She went into the kitchen and returned with the garment.

"It is aired," she said, grasping the cotton shirt here and there to try. She was almost ashamed to handle him; what right had she or anyone to lay hands on him; but her touch was humble on his body. It was hard work to clothe him. He was so heavy and inert. A terrible dread gripped her all the while: that he could be so heavy and utterly inert, unresponsive, apart. The horror of the distance between them was almost too much for her—it was so infinite a gap she must look across.

At last it was finished. They covered him with a sheet and left him lying, with his face bound. And she fastened the door of the little parlour, lest the children should see what was lying there. Then, with peace sunk heavy on her heart, she went about making tidy the kitchen. She knew she submitted to life, which was her immediate master. But from death, her ultimate master, she winced with fear and shame.

1914

## D. H. LAWRENCE

## *The Blind Man*

Isabel Pervin was listening for two sounds—for the sound of wheels on the drive outside and for the noise of her husband's footsteps in the hall. Her dearest and oldest friend, a man who seemed almost indispensable to her living, would drive up in the rainy dusk of the closing November day. The trap had gone to fetch him from the station. And her husband, who had been blinded in Flanders,[1] and who had a disfiguring mark on his brow, would be coming in from the outhouses.[2]

He had been home for a year now. He was totally blind. Yet they had been very happy. The Grange was Maurice's own place. The back was a farmstead, and the Wernhams, who occupied the rear premises, acted as farmers. Isabel lived with her husband in the handsome rooms in front. She and he had been almost entirely alone together since he was wounded. They talked and sang and read together in a wonderful and unspeakable intimacy. Then she reviewed books for a Scottish newspaper, carrying on her old interest, and he occupied himself a good deal with the farm. Sightless, he could still discuss everything with Wernham, and he could also do a good deal of work about the place—menial work, it is true, but it gave him satisfaction. He milked the cows, carried in the pails, turned the separator, attended to the pigs and horses. Life was still very full and strangely serene for the blind man, peaceful with the almost incomprehensible peace of immediate contact in darkness. With his wife he had a whole world, rich and real and invisible.

They were newly and remotely happy. He did not even regret the loss of his sight in these times of dark, palpable joy. A certain exultance swelled his soul.

But as time wore on, sometimes the rich glamour would leave them. Sometimes, after months of this intensity, a sense of burden overcame Isabel, a weariness, a terrible ennui, in that silent house approached between a colonnade of tall-shafted pines. Then she felt she would go mad, for she could not bear it. And sometimes he had devastating fits of depression, which seemed to lay waste his whole being. It was worse than depression—a black misery, when his own life was a torture to him, and when his presence was unbearable to his wife. The dread went down to the roots of her soul as these black days recurred. In a kind of panic she tried to wrap herself up still further in her husband. She forced the

---

1. A region of western Belgium and northern France, the scene of fierce fighting during World War I.
2. Buildings separate from the dwelling, such as barns.

old spontaneous cheerfulness and joy to continue. But the effort it cost her was almost too much. She knew she could not keep it up. She felt she would scream with the strain, and would give anything, anything, to escape. She longed to possess her husband utterly; it gave her inordinate joy to have him entirely to herself. And yet, when again he was gone in a black and massive misery, she could not bear him, she could not bear herself; she wished she could be snatched away off the earth altogether, anything rather than live at this cost.

Dazed, she schemed for a way out. She invited friends, she tried to give him some further connection with the outer world. But it was no good. After all their joy and suffering, after their dark, great year of blindness and solitude and unspeakable nearness, other people seemed to them both shallow, prattling, rather impertinent. Shallow prattle seemed presumptuous. He became impatient and irritated, she was wearied. And so they lapsed into their solitude again. For they preferred it.

But now, in a few weeks' time, her second baby would be born. The first had died, an infant, when her husband first went out to France. She looked with joy and relief to the coming of the second. It would be her salvation. But also she felt some anxiety. She was thirty years old, her husband was a year younger. They both wanted the child very much. Yet she could not help feeling afraid. She had her husband on her hands, a terrible joy to her, and a terrifying burden. The child would occupy her love and attention. And then, what of Maurice? What would he do? If only she could feel that he, too, would be at peace and happy when the child came! She did so want to luxuriate in a rich, physical satisfaction of maternity. But the man, what would he do? How could she provide for him, how avert those shattering black moods of his, which destroyed them both?

She sighed with fear. But at this time Bertie Reid wrote to Isabel. He was her old friend, a second or third cousin, a Scotsman, as she was a Scotswoman. They had been brought up near to one another, and all her life he had been her friend, like a brother, but better than her own brothers. She loved him—though not in the marrying sense. There was a sort of kinship between them, an affinity. They understood one another instinctively. But Isabel would never have thought of marrying Bertie. It would have seemed like marrying in her own family.

Bertie was a barrister and a man of letters, a Scotsman of the intellectual type, quick, ironical, sentimental, and on his knees before the women he adored but did not want to marry. Maurice Pervin was different. He came of a good old country family—the Grange was not a very great distance from Oxford. He was passionate, sensitive, perhaps over-sensitive, wincing—a big fellow with heavy limbs and a forehead that flushed painfully. For his mind was slow, as if drugged by the strong provincial blood that beat in his veins. He was very sensitive to his own mental slowness, his feelings being quick and acute. So that he was just the opposite to Bertie, whose mind was much quicker than his emotions, which were not so very fine.

From the first the two men did not like each other. Isabel felt that they *ought* to get on together. But they did not. She felt that if only each could have the clue to the other there would be such a rare understanding between them. It did not come off, however. Bertie adopted a slightly ironical attitude, very offensive to Maurice, who returned the Scotch irony with English resentment, a resentment which deepened sometimes into stupid hatred.

This was a little puzzling to Isabel. However, she accepted it in the course of things. Men were made freakish and unreasonable. Therefore, when Maurice was going out to France for the second time, she felt that, for her husband's sake, she must discontinue her friendship with Bertie. She wrote to the barrister to this effect. Bertram Reid simply replied that in this, as in all other matters, he must obey her wishes, if these were indeed her wishes.

For nearly two years nothing had passed between the two friends. Isabel rather gloried in the fact; she had no compunction. She had one great article of faith, which was, that husband and wife should be so important to one another, that the rest of the world simply did not count. She and Maurice were husband and wife. They loved one another. They would have children. Then let everybody and everything else fade into insignificance outside this connubial felicity. She professed herself quite happy and ready to receive Maurice's friends. She was happy and ready: the happy wife, the ready woman in possession. Without knowing why, the friends retired abashed, and came no more. Maurice, of course, took as much satisfaction in this connubial absorption as Isabel did.

He shared in Isabel's literary activities, she cultivated a real interest in agriculture and cattle-raising. For she, being at heart perhaps an emotional enthusiast, always cultivated the practical side of life, and prided herself on her mastery of practical affairs. Thus the husband and wife had spent the five years of their married life. The last had been one of blindness and unspeakable intimacy. And now Isabel felt a great indifference coming over her, a sort of lethargy. She wanted to be allowed to bear her child in peace, to nod by the fire and drift vaguely, physically, from day to day. Maurice was like an ominous thunder-cloud. She had to keep waking up to remember him.

When a little note came from Bertie, asking if he were to put up a tombstone to their dead friendship, and speaking of the real pain he felt on account of her husband's loss of sight, she felt a pang, a fluttering agitation of re-awakening. And she read the letter to Maurice.

"Ask him to come down," he said.

"Ask Bertie to come here!" she re-echoed.

"Yes—if he wants to."

Isabel paused for a few moments.

"I know he wants to—he'd only be too glad," she replied. "But what about you, Maurice? How would you like it?"

"I should like it."

"Well—in that case—But I thought you didn't care for him—"

"Oh, I don't know. I might think differently of him now," the blind man replied. It was rather abstruse to Isabel.

"Well, dear," she said, "if you're quite sure—"

"I'm sure enough. Let him come," said Maurice.

So Bertie was coming, coming this evening, in the November rain and darkness. Isabel was agitated, racked with her old restlessness and indecision. She had always suffered from this pain of doubt, just an agonizing sense of uncertainty. It had begun to pass off, in the lethargy of maternity. Now it returned, and she resented it. She struggled as usual to maintain her calm, composed, friendly bearing, a sort of mask she wore over all her body.

A woman had lighted a tall lamp beside the table, and spread the cloth. The long dining-room was dim, with its elegant but rather severe pieces of old furniture. Only the round table glowed softly under the light. It had a rich, beautiful effect. The white cloth glistened and dropped its heavy, pointed lace corners almost to the carpet, the china was old and handsome, creamy-yellow, with a blotched pattern of harsh red and deep blue, the cups large and bell-shaped, the teapot gallant. Isabel looked at it with superficial appreciation.

Her nerves were hurting her. She looked automatically again at the high, uncurtained windows. In the last dusk she could just perceive outside a huge fir tree swaying its boughs: it was as if she thought it rather than saw it. The rain came flying on the window panes. Ah, why had she no peace? These two men, why did they tear at her? Why did they not come—why was there this suspense?

She sat in a lassitude that was really suspense and irritation. Maurice, at least, might come in—there was nothing to keep him out. She rose to her feet. Catching sight of her reflection in a mirror, she glanced at herself with a slight smile of recognition, as if she were an old friend to herself. Her face was oval and calm, her nose a little arched. Her neck made a beautiful line down to her shoulder. With hair knotted loosely behind, she had something of a warm, maternal look. Thinking this of herself, she arched her eyebrows and her rather heavy eyelids, with a little flicker of a smile, and for a moment her gray eyes looked amused and wicked, a little sardonic, out of her transfigured Madonna face.

Then, resuming her air of womanly patience—she was really fatally self-determined—she went with a little jerk toward the door. Her eyes were slightly reddened.

She passed down the wide hall, and through a door at the end. Then she was in the farm premises. The scent of dairy, and of farm-kitchen, and of farmyard and of leather almost overcame her: but particularly the scent of dairy. They had been scalding out the pans. The flagged[3] passage in front of her was dark, puddled and wet. Light came out from the open kitchen door. She went forward and stood in the doorway. The farm-people were at tea, seated at a little distance from her, round a long, narrow table, in the center of which stood a white lamp. Ruddy faces, ruddy hands holding food, red mouths working, heads bent over the tea-cups: men, land-girls, boys: it was tea-time, feeding-time. Some faces caught sight of her. Mrs. Wernham, going round behind the chairs with a large black teapot, halting slightly in her walk, was not aware of her for a moment. Then she turned suddenly.

"Oh, is it Madam!" she exclaimed. "Come in, then, come in! We're at tea." And she dragged forward a chair.

"No, I won't come in," said Isabel. "I'm afraid I interrupt your meal."

"No—no—not likely, Madam, not likely."

"Hasn't Mr. Pervin come in, do you know?"

"I'm sure I couldn't say! Missed him, have you, Madam?"

"No, I only wanted him to come in," laughed Isabel, as if shyly.

"Wanted him, did ye? Get up, boy—get up, now—"

Mrs. Wernham knocked one of the boys on the shoulder. He began to scrape to his feet, chewing largely.

"I believe he's in top stable," said another face from the table.

"Ah! No, don't get up. I'm going myself," said Isabel.

"Don't you go out of a dirty night like this. Let the lad go. Get along wi' ye, boy," said Mrs. Wernham.

---

3. Paved with flat stone.

"No, no," said Isabel, with a decision that was always obeyed. "Go on with your tea, Tom. I'd like to go across to the stable, Mrs. Wernham."

"Did ever you hear tell!" exclaimed the woman.

"Isn't the trap late?" asked Isabel.

"Why, no," said Mrs. Wernham, peering into the distance at the tall, dim clock. "No, Madam—we can give it another quarter or twenty minutes yet, good—yes, every bit of a quarter."

"Ah! It seems late when darkness falls so early," said Isabel.

"It do, that it do. Bother the days, that they draw in so," answered Mrs. Wernham. "Proper[4] miserable!"

"They are," said Isabel, withdrawing.

She pulled on her overshoes, wrapped a large tartan shawl around her, put on a man's felt hat, and ventured out along the causeways of the first yard. It was very dark. The wind was roaring in the great elms behind the out-houses. When she came to the second yard the darkness seemed deeper. She was unsure of her footing. She wished she had brought a lantern. Rain blew against her. Half she liked it, half she felt unwilling to battle.

She reached at last the just visible door of the stable. There was no sign of a light anywhere. Opening the upper half, she looked in: into a simple well of darkness. The smell of horses, ammonia, and of warmth was startling to her, in that full night. She listened with all her ears, but could hear nothing save the night, and the stirring of a horse.

"Maurice!" she called, softly and musically, though she was afraid. "Maurice—are you there?"

Nothing came from the darkness. She knew the rain and wind blew in upon the horses, the hot animal life. Feeling it wrong, she entered the stable, and drew the lower half of the door shut, holding the upper part close. She did not stir, because she was aware of the presence of the dark hindquarters of the horses, though she could not see them, and she was afraid. Something wild stirred in her heart.

She listened intensely. Then she heard a small noise in the distance—far away, it seemed—the chink of a pan, and a man's voice speaking a brief word. It would be Maurice, in the other part of the stable. She stood motionless, waiting for him to come through the partition door. The horses were so terrifying near to her, in the invisible.

The loud jarring of the inner door-latch made her start; the door was opened. She could hear and feel her husband entering and invisibly passing among the horses near to her, in darkness as they were, actively intermingled. The rather low sound of his voice as he spoke to the horses came velvety to her nerves. How near he was, and how invisible! The darkness seemed to be in a strange swirl of violent life, just upon her. She turned giddy.

Her presence of mind made her call, quietly and musically:

"Maurice! Maurice—dea-ar!"

"Yes," he answered. "Isabel?"

She saw nothing, and the sound of his voice seemed to touch her.

"Hello!" she answered cheerfully, straining her eyes to see him. He was still

---

4. Downright, thoroughly.

busy, attending to the horses near her, but she saw only darkness. It made her almost desperate.

"Won't you come in, dear?" she said.

"Yes, I'm coming. Just half a minute. *Stand over—now!* Trap's not come, has it?"

"Not yet," said Isabel.

His voice was pleasant and ordinary, but it had a slight suggestion of the stable to her. She wished he would come away. While he was so utterly invisible she was afraid of him.

"How's the time?" he asked.

"Not yet six," she replied. She disliked to answer into the dark. Presently he came very near to her, and she retreated out of doors.

"The weather blows in here," he said, coming steadily forward, feeling for the doors. She shrank away. At last she could dimly see him.

"Bertie won't have much of a drive," he said, as he closed the doors.

"He won't indeed!" said Isabel calmly, watching the dark shape at the door.

"Give me your arm, dear," she said.

She pressed his arm close to her, as she went. But she longed to see him, to look at him. She was nervous. He walked erect, with face rather lifted, but with a curious tentative movement of his powerful, muscular legs. She could feel the clever, careful, strong contact of his feet with the earth, as she balanced against him. For a moment he was a tower of darkness to her, as if he rose out of the earth.

In the house-passage he wavered, and went cautiously, with a curious look of silence about him as he felt for the bench. Then he sat down heavily. He was a man with rather sloping shoulders, but with heavy limbs, powerful legs that seemed to know the earth. His head was small, usually carried high and light. As he bent down to unfasten his gaiters and boots he did not look blind. His hair was brown and crisp, his hands were large, reddish, intelligent, the veins stood out in the wrists; and his thighs and knees seemed massive. When he stood up his face and neck were surcharged with blood, the veins stood out on his temples. She did not look at his blindness.

Isabel was always glad when they had passed through the dividing door into their own regions of repose and beauty. She was a little afraid of him, out there in the animal grossness of the back. His bearing also changed, as he smelled the familiar, indefinable odor that pervaded his wife's surroundings, a delicate, refined scent, very faintly spicy. Perhaps it came from the potpourri bowls.

He stood at the foot of the stairs, arrested, listening. She watched him, and her heart sickened. He seemed to be listening to fate.

"He's not here yet," he said. "I'll go up and change."

"Maurice," she said, "you're not wishing he wouldn't come, are you?"

"I couldn't quite say," he answered. "I feel myself rather on the *qui vive.*"[5]

"I can see you are," she answered. And she reached up and kissed his cheek. She saw his mouth relax into a slow smile.

"What are you laughing at?" she said roguishly.

"You consoling me," he answered.

"Nay," she answered. "Why should I console you? You know we love each other—you know *how* married we are! What does anything else matter?"

5. Alert.

"Nothing at all, my dear."

He felt for her face, and touched it, smiling.

"*You're* all right, aren't you?" he asked, anxiously.

"I'm wonderfully all right, love," she answered. "It's you I am a little troubled about, at times."

"Why me?" he said, touching her cheeks delicately with the tips of his fingers. The touch had an almost hypnotizing effect on her.

He went away upstairs. She saw him mount into the darkness, unseeing and unchanging. He did not know that the lamps on the upper corridor were unlighted. He went on into the darkness with unchanging step. She heard him in the bathroom.

Pervin moved about almost unconsciously in his familiar surroundings, dark though everything was. He seemed to know the presence of objects before he touched them. It was a pleasure to him to rock thus through a world of things, carried on the flood in a sort of blood-prescience. He did not think much or trouble much. So long as he kept this sheer immediacy of blood-contact with the substantial world he was happy, he wanted no intervention of visual consciousness. In this state there was a certain rich positivity, bordering sometimes on rapture. Life seemed to move in him like a tide lapping, lapping, and advancing, enveloping all things darkly. It was a pleasure to stretch forth the hand and meet the unseen object, clasp it, and possess it in pure contact. He did not try to remember, to visualize. He did not want to. The new way of consciousness substituted itself in him.

The rich suffusion of this state generally kept him happy, reaching its culmination in the consuming passion for his wife. But at times the flow would seem to be checked and thrown back. Then it would beat inside him like a tangled sea, and he was tortured in the shattered chaos of his own blood. He grew to dread this arrest, this throw-back, this chaos inside himself, when he seemed merely at the mercy of his own powerful and conflicting elements. How to get some measure of control or surety, this was the question. And when the question rose maddening in him, he would clench his fists as if he would *compel* the whole universe to submit to him. But it was in vain. He could not even compel himself.

Tonight, however, he was still serene, though little tremors of unreasonable exasperation ran through him. He had to handle the razor very carefully, as he shaved, for it was not at one with him, he was afraid of it. His hearing also was too much sharpened. He heard the woman lighting the lamps on the corridor, and attending to the fire in the visitor's room. And then, as he went to his room he heard the trap arrive. Then came Isabel's voice, lifted and calling, like a bell ringing:

"Is it you, Bertie? Have you come?"

And a man's voice answered out of the wind:

"Hello, Isabel! There you are."

"Have you had a miserable drive? I'm so sorry we couldn't send a closed carriage. I can't see you at all, you know."

"I'm coming. No, I liked the drive—it was like Perthshire.[6] Well, how are you? You're looking fit as ever, as far as I can see."

---

6. County in central Scotland.

"Oh, yes," said Isabel. "I'm wonderfully well. How are you? Rather thin, I think—"

"Worked to death—everybody's old cry. But I'm all right, Ciss. How's Pervin?—isn't he here?"

"Oh, yes, he's upstairs changing. Yes, he's awfully well. Take off your wet things; I'll send them to be dried."

"And how are you both, in spirits? He doesn't fret?"

"No—no, not at all. No, on the contrary, really. We've been wonderfully happy, incredibly. It's more than I can understand—so wonderful: the nearness, and the peace—"

"Ah! Well, that's awfully good news—"

They moved away. Pervin heard no more. But a childish sense of desolation had come over him, as he heard their brisk voices. He seemed shut out—like a child that is left out. He was aimless and excluded, he did not know what to do with himself. The helpless desolation came over him. He fumbled nervously as he dressed himself, in a state almost of childishness. He disliked the Scotch accent in Bertie's speech, and the slight response it found on Isabel's tongue. He disliked the slight purr of complacency in the Scottish speech. He disliked intensely the glib way in which Isabel spoke of their happiness and nearness. It made him recoil. He was fretful and beside himself like a child, he had almost a childish nostalgia to be included in the life circle. And at the same time he was a man, dark and powerful and infuriated by his own weakness. By some fatal flaw, he could not be by himself, he had to depend on the support of another. And this very dependence enraged him. He hated Bertie Reid, and at the same time he knew the hatred was nonsense, he knew it was the outcome of his own weakness.

He went downstairs. Isabel was alone in the dining-room. She watched him enter, head erect, his feet tentative. He looked so strong-blooded and healthy, and, at the same time, cancelled. Cancelled—that was the word that flew across her mind. Perhaps it was his scars suggested it.

"You heard Bertie come, Maurice?" she said.

"Yes—isn't he here?"

"He's in his room. He looks very thin and worn."

"I suppose he works himself to death."

A woman came in with a tray—and after a few minutes Bertie came down. He was a little dark man, with a very big forehead, thin, wispy hair, and sad, large eyes. His expression was inordinately sad—almost funny. He had odd, short legs.

Isabel watched him hesitate under the door, and glance nervously at her husband. Pervin heard him and turned.

"Here you are, now," said Isabel. "Come, let us eat."

Bertie went across to Maurice.

"How are you, Pervin?" he said, as he advanced.

The blind man stuck his hand out into space, and Bertie took it.

"Very fit. Glad you've come," said Maurice.

Isabel glanced at them, and glanced away, as if she could not bear to see them.

"Come," she said. "Come to table. Aren't you both awfully hungry? I am, tremendously."

"I'm afraid you waited for me," said Bertie, as they sat down.

Maurice had a curious monolithic way of sitting in a chair, erect and distant.

Isabel's heart always beat when she caught sight of him thus.

"No," she replied to Bertie. "We're very little later than usual. We're having a sort of high tea, not dinner. Do you mind? It gives us such a nice long evening uninterrupted."

"I like it," said Bertie.

Maurice was feeling, with curious little movements, almost like a cat kneading her bed, for his place, his knife and fork, his napkin. He was getting the whole geography of his cover[7] into his consciousness. He sat erect and inscrutable, remote-seeming. Bertie watched the static figure of the blind man, the delicate tactile discernment of the large, ruddy hands, and the curious mindless silence of the brow, above the scar. With difficulty he looked away, and without knowing what he did, picked up a little crystal bowl of violets from the table, and held them to his nose.

"They are sweet-scented," he said. "Where do they come from?"

"From the garden—under the windows," said Isabel.

"So late in the year—and so fragrant! Do you remember the violets under Aunt Bell's south wall?"

The two friends looked at each other and exchanged a smile, Isabel's eyes lighting up.

"Don't I?" she replied. "*Wasn't* she queer!"

"A curious old girl," laughed Bertie. "There's a streak of freakishness in the family, Isabel."

"Ah—but not in you and me, Bertie," said Isabel. "Give them to Maurice, will you?" she added, as Bertie was putting down the flowers. "Have you smelled the violets, dear? Do!—they are so scented."

Maurice held out his hand, and Bertie placed the tiny bowl against his large, warm-looking fingers. Maurice's hand closed over the thin white fingers of the barrister. Bertie carefully extricated himself. Then the two watched the blind man smelling the violets. He bent his head and seemed to be thinking. Isabel waited.

"Aren't they sweet, Maurice?" she said at last, anxiously.

"Very," he said. And he held out the bowl. Bertie took it. Both he and Isabel were a little afraid, and deeply disturbed.

The meal continued. Isabel and Bertie chatted spasmodically. The blind man was silent. He touched his food repeatedly, with quick, delicate touches of his knife-point, then cut irregular bits. He could not bear to be helped. Both Isabel and Bertie suffered: Isabel wondered why. She did not suffer when she was alone with Maurice. Bertie made her conscious of a strangeness.

After the meal the three drew their chairs to the fire, and sat down to talk. The decanters were put on a table near at hand. Isabel knocked the logs on the fire, and clouds of brilliant sparks went up the chimney. Bertie noticed a slight weariness in her bearing.

"You will be glad when your child comes now, Isabel?" he said.

She looked up to him with a quick wan smile.

"Yes, I shall be glad," she answered. "It begins to seem long. Yes, I shall be very glad. So will you, Maurice, won't you?" she added.

"Yes, I shall," replied her husband.

---

7. Place setting.

"We are both looking forward so much to having it," she said.

"Yes, of course," said Bertie.

He was a bachelor, three or four years older than Isabel. He lived in beautiful rooms overlooking the river, guarded by a faithful Scottish manservant. And he had his friends among the fair sex—not lovers, friends. So long as he could avoid any danger of courtship or marriage, he adored a few good women with constant and unfailing homage, and he was chivalrously fond of quite a number. But if they seemed to encroach on him, he withdrew and detested them.

Isabel knew him very well, knew his beautiful constancy, and kindness, also his incurable weakness, which made him unable ever to enter into close contact of any sort. He was ashamed of himself, because he could not marry, could not approach women physically. He wanted to do so. But he could not. At the center of him he was afraid, helplessly and even brutally afraid. He had given up hope, had ceased to expect any more that he could escape his own weakness. Hence he was a brilliant and successful barrister, also *littérateur* of high repute, a rich man, and a great social success. At the center he felt himself neuter, nothing.

Isabel knew him well. She despised him even while she admired him. She looked at his sad face, his little short legs, and felt contempt of him. She looked at his dark gray eyes, with their uncanny, almost child-like intuition, and she loved him. He understood amazingly—but she had no fear of his understanding. As a man she patronized him.

And she turned to the impassive, silent figure of her husband. He sat leaning back, with folded arms, and face a little uptilted. His knees were straight and massive. She sighed, picked up the poker, and again began to prod the fire, to rouse the clouds of soft, brilliant sparks.

"Isabel tells me," Bertie began suddenly, "that you have not suffered unbearably from the loss of sight."

Maurice straightened himself to attend, but kept his arms folded.

"No," he said, "not unbearably. Now and again one struggles against it, you know. But there are compensations."

"They say it is much worse to be stone deaf," said Isabel.

"I believe it is," said Bertie. "Are there compensations?" he added, to Maurice.

"Yes. You cease to bother about a great many things." Again Maurice stretched his figure, stretched the strong muscles of his back, and leaned backwards, with uplifted face.

"And that is a relief," said Bertie. "But what is there in place of the bothering? What replaces the activity?"

There was a pause. At length the blind man replied, as out of a negligent, unattentive thinking:

"Oh, I don't know. There's a good deal when you're not active."

"Is there?" said Bertie. "What, exactly? It always seems to me that when there is no thought and no action, there is nothing."

Again Maurice was slow in replying.

"There is something," he replied. "I couldn't tell you what it is."

And the talk lapsed once more, Isabel and Bertie chatting gossip and reminiscence, the blind man silent.

At length Maurice rose restlessly, a big, obtrusive figure. He felt tight and hampered. He wanted to go away.

"Do you mind," he said, "if I go and speak to Wernham?"

"No—go along, dear," said Isabel.

And he went out. A silence came over the two friends. At length Bertie said:

"Nevertheless, it is a great deprivation, Cissie."

"It is, Bertie. I know it is."

"Something lacking all the time," said Bertie.

"Yes, I know. And yet—and yet—Maurice is right. There is something else, something *there*, which you never knew was there, and which you can't express."

"What is there?" asked Bertie.

"I don't know—it's awfully hard to define it—but something strong and immediate. There's something strange in Maurice's presence—indefinable—but I couldn't do without it. I agree that it seems to put one's mind to sleep. But when we're alone I miss nothing; it seems awfully rich, almost splendid, you know."

"I'm afraid I don't follow," said Bertie.

They talked desultorily. The wind blew loudly outside, rain chattered on the window-panes, making a sharp drum-sound, because of the closed, mellow-golden shutters inside. The logs burned slowly, with hot, almost invisible small flames. Bertie seemed uneasy, there were dark circles round his eyes. Isabel, rich with her approaching maternity, leaned looking into the fire. Her hair curled in odd, loose strands, very pleasing to the man. But she had a curious feeling of old woe in her heart, old, timeless night-woe.

"I suppose we're all deficient somewhere," said Bertie.

"I suppose so," said Isabel wearily.

"Damned, sooner or later."

"I don't know," she said, rousing herself. "I feel quite all right, you know. The child coming seems to make me indifferent to everything, just placid. I can't feel that there's anything to trouble about, you know."

"A good thing, I should say," he replied slowly.

"Well, there it is. I suppose it's just Nature. If only I felt I needn't trouble about Maurice, I should be perfectly content—"

"But you feel you must trouble about him?"

"Well—I don't know—" She even resented this much effort.

The evening passed slowly. Isabel looked at the clock. "I say," she said. "It's nearly ten o'clock. Where can Maurice be? I'm sure they're all in bed at the back. Excuse me a moment."

She went out, returning almost immediately.

"It's all shut up and in darkness," she said. "I wonder where he is. He must have gone out to the farm—"

Bertie looked at her.

"I suppose he'll come in," he said.

"I suppose so," she said. "But it's unusual for him to be out now."

"Would you like me to go out and see?"

"Well—if you wouldn't mind. I'd go, but—" She did not want to make the physical effort.

Bertie put on an old overcoat and took a lantern. He went out from the side door. He shrank from the wet and roaring night. Such weather had a nervous effect on him: too much moisture everywhere made him feel almost imbecile. Unwilling, he went through it all. A dog barked violently at him. He peered in all the buildings. At last, as he opened the upper door of a sort of intermediate barn, he heard a grinding noise, and looking in, holding up his lantern, saw

Maurice, in his shirtsleeves, standing listening, holding the handle of a turnip-pulper. He had been pulping sweet roots, a pile of which lay dimly heaped in a corner behind him.

"That you, Wernham?" said Maurice, listening.

"No, it's me," said Bertie.

A large, half-wild gray cat was rubbing at Maurice's leg. The blind man stooped to rub its sides. Bertie watched the scene, then unconsciously entered and shut the door behind him. He was in a high sort of barn-place, from which, right and left, ran off the corridors in front of the stalled cattle. He watched the slow, stooping motion of the other man, as he caressed the great cat.

Maurice straightened himself.

"You came to look for me?" he said.

"Isabel was a little uneasy," said Bertie.

"I'll come in. I like messing about doing these jobs."

The cat had reared her sinister, feline length against his leg, clawing at his thigh affectionately. He lifted her claws out of his flesh.

"I hope I'm not in your way at all at the Grange here," said Bertie, rather shy and stiff.

"My way? No, not a bit. I'm glad Isabel has somebody to talk to. I'm afraid it's I who am in the way. I know I'm not very lively company. Isabel's all right, don't you think? She's not unhappy, is she?"

"I don't think so."

"What does she say?"

"She says she's very content—only a little troubled about you."

"Why me?"

"Perhaps afraid that you might brood," said Bertie cautiously.

"She needn't be afraid of that." He continued to caress the flattened gray head of the cat with his fingers. "What I am a bit afraid of," he resumed, "is that she'll find me a dead weight, always alone with me down here."

"I don't think you need think that," said Bertie, though this was what he feared himself.

"I don't know," said Maurice. "Sometimes I feel it isn't fair that she's saddled with me." Then he dropped his voice curiously. "I say," he asked, secretly struggling, "is my face much disfigured? Do you mind telling me?"

"There is the scar," said Bertie, wondering. "Yes, it is a disfigurement. But more pitiable than shocking."

"A pretty bad scar, though," said Maurice.

"Oh, yes."

There was a pause.

"Sometimes I feel I am horrible," said Maurice, in a low voice, talking as if to himself. And Bertie actually felt a quiver of horror.

"That's nonsense," he said.

Maurice again straightened himself, leaving the cat.

"There's no telling," he said. Then again, in an odd tone, he added: "I don't really know you, do I?"

"Probably not," said Bertie.

"Do you mind if I touch you?"

The lawyer shrank away instinctively. And yet, out of very philanthropy, he said, in a small voice: "Not at all."

But he suffered as the blind man stretched out a strong, naked hand to him. Maurice accidentally knocked off Bertie's hat.

"I thought you were taller," he said, starting. Then he laid his hand on Bertie Reid's head, closing the dome of the skull in a soft, firm grasp, gathering it, as it were; then, shifting his grasp and softly closing again, with a fine, close pressure, till he had covered the skull and the face of the smaller man, tracing the brows, and touching the full, closed eyes, touching the small nose and the nostrils, the rough, short moustache, the mouth, the rather strong chin. The hand of the blind man grasped the shoulder, the arm, the hand of the other man. He seemed to take him, in the soft, traveling grasp.

"You seem young," he said quietly, at last.

The lawyer stood almost annihilated, unable to answer.

"Your head seems tender, as if you were young," Maurice repeated. "So do your hands. Touch my eyes, will you?—touch my scar."

Now Bertie quivered with revulsion. Yet he was under the power of the blind man, as if hypnotized. He lifted his hand, and laid the fingers on the scar, on the scarred eyes. Maurice suddenly covered them with his own hand, pressed the fingers of the other man upon his disfigured eye-sockets, trembling in every fiber, and rocking slightly, slowly, from side to side. He remained thus for a minute or more, whilst Bertie stood as if in a swoon, unconscious, imprisoned.

Then suddenly Maurice removed the hand of the other man from his brow, and stood holding it in his own.

"Oh, my God," he said, "we shall know each other now, shan't we? We shall know each other now."

Bertie could not answer. He gazed mute and terror-struck, overcome by his own weakness. He knew he could not answer. He had an unreasonable fear, lest the other man should suddenly destroy him. Whereas Maurice was actually filled with hot, poignant love, the passion of friendship. Perhaps it was this very passion of friendship which Bertie shrank from most.

"We're all right together now, aren't we?" said Maurice. "It's all right now, as long as we live, so far as we're concerned."

"Yes," said Bertie, trying by any means to escape.

Maurice stood with head lifted, as if listening. The new delicate fulfillment of mortal friendship had come as a revelation and surprise to him, something exquisite and unhoped-for. He seemed to be listening to hear if it were real.

Then he turned for his coat.

"Come," he said, "we'll go to Isabel."

Bertie took the lantern and opened the door. The cat disappeared. The two men went in silence along the causeways. Isabel, as they came, thought their footsteps sounded strange. She looked up pathetically and anxiously for their entrance. There seemed a curious elation about Maurice. Bertie was haggard, with sunken eyes.

"What is it?" she asked.

"We've become friends," said Maurice, standing with his feet apart, like a strange colossus.

"Friends!" re-echoed Isabel. And she looked again at Bertie. He met her eyes with a furtive, haggard look; his eyes were as if glazed with misery.

"I'm so glad," she said, in sheer perplexity.

"Yes," said Maurice.

He was indeed so glad. Isabel took his hand with both hers, and held it fast. "You'll be happier now, dear," she said.

But she was watching Bertie. She knew that he had one desire—to escape from this intimacy, this friendship, which had been thrust upon him. He could not bear it that he had been touched by the blind man, his insane reserve broken in. He was like a mollusc whose shell is broken.

1922

## D. H. LAWRENCE
### The Rocking-Horse Winner

There was a woman who was beautiful, who started with all the advantages, yet she had no luck. She married for love, and the love turned to dust. She had bonny children, yet she felt they had been thrust upon her, and she could not love them. They looked at her coldly, as if they were finding fault with her. And hurriedly she felt she must cover up some fault in herself. Yet what it was that she must cover up she never knew. Nevertheless, when her children were present, she always felt the centre of her heart go hard. This troubled her, and in her manner she was all the more gentle and anxious for her children, as if she loved them very much. Only she herself knew that at the centre of her heart was a hard little place that could not feel love, no, not for anybody. Everybody else said of her: "She is such a good mother. She adores her children." Only she herself, and her children themselves, knew it was not so. They read it in each other's eyes.

There were a boy and two little girls. They lived in a pleasant house, with a garden, and they had discreet servants, and felt themselves superior to anyone in the neighbourhood.

Although they lived in style, they felt always an anxiety in the house. There was never enough money. The mother had a small income, and the father had a small income, but not nearly enough for the social position which they had to keep up. The father went in to town to some office. But though he had good prospects, these prospects never materialized. There was always the grinding sense of the shortage of money, though the style was always kept up.

At last the mother said: "I will see if *I* can't make something." But she did not know where to begin. She racked her brains, and tried this thing and the other, but could not find anything successful. The failure made deep lines come into her face. Her children were growing up, they would have to go to school. There must be more money, there must be more money. The father, who was always very handsome and expensive in his tastes, seemed as if he never *would* be able to do anything worth doing. And the mother, who had a great belief in herself, did not succeed any better, and her tastes were just as expensive.

And so the house came to be haunted by the unspoken phrase: *There must be more money! There must be more money!* The children could hear it all the time, though nobody said it aloud. They heard it at Christmas, when the expensive and splendid toys filled the nursery. Behind the shining modern rocking-horse, behind the smart doll's-house, a voice would start whispering: "There *must* be more money! There *must* be more money!" And the children would stop playing, to listen for a moment. They would look into each other's eyes, to see if they had all heard. And each one saw in the eyes of the other two that they too had heard. "There *must* be more money! There *must* be more money!"

It came whispering from the springs of the still-swaying rocking-horse, and even the horse, bending his wooden, champing head, heard it. The big doll, sitting so pink and smirking in her new pram,[1] could hear it quite plainly, and seemed to be smirking all the more self-consciously because of it. The foolish puppy, too, that took the place of the teddy-bear, he was looking so extraordinarily foolish for no other reason but that he heard the secret whisper all over the house: "There *must* be more money!"

Yet nobody ever said it aloud. The whisper was everywhere, and therefore no one spoke it. Just as no one ever says: "We are breathing!" in spite of the fact that breath is coming and going all the time.

"Mother," said the boy Paul one day, "why don't we keep a car of our own? Why do we always use uncle's, or else a taxi?"

"Because we're the poor members of the family," said the mother.

"But why *are* we, mother?"

"Well—I suppose," she said slowly and bitterly, "it's because your father has no luck."

The boy was silent for some time.

"Is luck money, mother?" he asked rather timidly.

"No, Paul. Not quite. It's what causes you to have money."

"Oh!" said Paul vaguely. "I thought when Uncle Oscar said *filthy lucker*, it meant money."

"*Filthy lucre* does mean money," said the mother. "But it's lucre, not luck."

"Oh!" said the boy. "Then what *is* luck, mother?"

"It's what causes you to have money. If you're lucky you have money. That's why it's better to be born lucky than rich. If you're rich, you may lose your money. But if you're lucky, you will always get more money."

"Oh! Will you? And is father not lucky?"

"Very unlucky, I should say," she said bitterly.

The boy watched her with unsure eyes.

"Why?" he asked.

"I don't know. Nobody ever knows why one person is lucky and another unlucky."

"Don't they? Nobody at all? Does *nobody* know?"

"Perhaps God. But He never tells."

"He ought to, then. And aren't you lucky either, mother?"

"I can't be, if I married an unlucky husband."

"But by yourself, aren't you?"

"I used to think I was, before I married. Now I think I am very unlucky indeed."

"Why?"

"Well—never mind! Perhaps I'm not really," she said.

The child looked at her, to see if she meant it. But he saw, by the lines of her mouth, that she was only trying to hide something from him.

"Well, anyhow," he said stoutly, "I'm a lucky person."

---

1. Baby carriage.

"Why?" said his mother, with a sudden laugh.

He stared at her. He didn't even know why he had said it.

"God told me," he asserted, brazening it out.

"I hope He did, dear!" she said, again with a laugh, but rather bitter.

"He did, mother!"

"Excellent!" said the mother, using one of her husband's exclamations.

The boy saw she did not believe him; or, rather, that she paid no attention to his assertion. This angered him somewhat, and made him want to compel her attention.

He went off by himself, vaguely, in a childish way, seeking for the clue to "luck." Absorbed, taking no heed of other people, he went about with a sort of stealth, seeking inwardly for luck. He wanted luck, he wanted it, he wanted it. When the two girls were playing dolls in the nursery, he would sit on his big rocking-horse, charging madly into space, with a frenzy that made the little girls peer at him uneasily. Wildly the horse careered, the waving dark hair of the boy tossed, his eyes had a strange glare in them. The little girls dared not speak to him.

When he had ridden to the end of his mad little journey, he climbed down and stood in front of his rocking-horse, staring fixedly into its lowered face. Its red mouth was slightly open, its big eye was wide and glassy-bright.

"Now!" he would silently command the snorting steed. "Now, take me to where there is luck! Now take me!"

And he would slash the horse on the neck with the little whip he had asked Uncle Oscar for. He *knew* the horse could take him to where there was luck, if only he forced it. So he would mount again, and start on his furious ride, hoping at last to get there. He knew he could get there.

"You'll break your horse, Paul!" said the nurse.

"He's always riding like that! I wish he'd leave off!" said his elder sister Joan.

But he only glared down on them in silence. Nurse gave him up. She could make nothing of him. Anyhow he was growing beyond her.

One day his mother and his Uncle Oscar came in when he was on one of his furious rides. He did not speak to them.

"Hallo, you young jockey! Riding a winner?" said his uncle.

"Aren't you growing too big for a rocking-horse? You're not a very little boy any longer, you know," said his mother.

But Paul only gave a blue glare from his big, rather close-set eyes. He would speak to nobody when he was in full tilt. His mother watched him with an anxious expression on her face.

At last he suddenly stopped forcing his horse into the mechanical gallop, and slid down.

"Well, I got there!" he announced fiercely, his blue eyes still flaring, and his sturdy long legs straddling apart.

"Where did you get to?" asked his mother.

"Where I wanted to go," he flared back at her.

"That's right, son!" said Uncle Oscar. "Don't you stop till you get there. What's the horse's name?"

"He doesn't have a name," said the boy.

"Gets on without all right?" asked the uncle.

"Well, he has different names. He was called Sansovino last week."

"Sansovino, eh? Won the Ascot.[2] How did you know his name?"

"He always talks about horse-races with Bassett," said Joan.

The uncle was delighted to find that his small nephew was posted with all the racing news. Bassett, the young gardener, who had been wounded in the left foot in the war[3] and had got his present job through Oscar Cresswell, whose batman[4] he had been, was a perfect blade of the "turf."[5] He lived in the racing events, and the small boy lived with him.

Oscar Cresswell got it all from Bassett.

"Master Paul comes and asks me, so I can't do more than tell him, sir," said Bassett, his face terribly serious, as if he were speaking of religious matters.

"And does he ever put anything on a horse he fancies?"

"Well—I don't want to give him away—he's a young sport, a fine sport, sir. Would you mind asking him himself? He sort of takes a pleasure in it, and perhaps he'd feel I was giving him away, sir, if you don't mind."

Bassett was serious as a church.

The uncle went back to his nephew and took him off for a ride in the car.

"Say, Paul, old man, do you ever put anything on a horse?" the uncle asked.

The boy watched the handsome man closely.

"Why, do you think I oughtn't to?" he parried.

"Not a bit of it! I thought perhaps you might give me a tip for the Lincoln."

The car sped on into the country, going down to Uncle Oscar's place in Hampshire.

"Honour bright?" said the nephew.

"Honour bright, son!" said the uncle.

"Well, then, Daffodil."

"Daffodil! I doubt it, sonny. What about Mirza?"

"I only know the winner," said the boy. "That's Daffodil."

"Daffodil, eh?"

There was a pause. Daffodil was an obscure horse comparatively.

"Uncle!"

"Yes, son?"

"You won't let it go any further, will you? I promised Bassett."

"Bassett be damned, old man! What's he got to do with it?"

"We're partners. We've been partners from the first. Uncle, he lent me my first five shillings, which I lost. I promised him, honour bright, it was only between me and him; only you gave me that ten-shilling note I started winning with, so I thought you were lucky. You won't let it go any further, will you?"

The boy gazed at his uncle from those big, hot, blue eyes, set rather close together. The uncle stirred and laughed uneasily.

"Right you are, son! I'll keep your tip private. Daffodil, eh? How much are you putting on him?"

"All except twenty pounds," said the boy. "I keep that in reserve."

The uncle thought it a good joke.

---

2. A race run at a course of that name in Berkshire. Other races mentioned in the story are Lincolnshire Handicap, then run at Lincoln Downs; the St. Leger Stakes, run at Doncaster; the Grand National Steeplechase, run at Aintree, the most famous steeplechase in the world; the famous Derby, a mile-and-a-half race for three year olds run at Epsom Downs.
3. World War I, 1914–18.    4. British officer's orderly.    5. Dashing young horseplayer.

"You keep twenty pounds in reserve, do you, you young romancer? What are you betting, then?"

"I'm betting three hundred," said the boy, gravely. "But it's between you and me, Uncle Oscar! Honour bright?"

The uncle burst into a roar of laughter.

"It's between you and me all right, you young Nat Gould,"[6] he said, laughing. "But where's your three hundred?"

"Bassett keeps it for me. We're partners."

"You are, are you! And what is Bassett putting on Daffodil?"

"He won't go quite as high as I do, I expect. Perhaps he'll go a hundred and fifty."

"What, pennies?" laughed the uncle.

"Pounds," said the child, with a surprised look at his uncle. "Bassett keeps a bigger reserve than I do."

Between wonder and amusement Uncle Oscar was silent. He pursued the matter no further, but he determined to take his nephew with him to the Lincoln races.

"Now, son," he said, "I'm putting twenty on Mirza, and I'll put five for you on any horse you fancy. What's your pick?"

"Daffodil, uncle."

"No, not the fiver on Daffodil!"

"I should if it was my own fiver," said the child.

"Good! Good! Right you are! A fiver for me and a fiver for you on Daffodil."

The child had never been to a race-meeting before, and his eyes were blue fire. He pursed his mouth tight, and watched. A Frenchman just in front had put his money on Lancelot. Wild with excitement, he flayed his arms up and down, yelling *"Lancelot! Lancelot!"* in his French accent.

Daffodil came in first, Lancelot second, Mirza third. The child, flushed and with eyes blazing, was curiously serene. His uncle brought him four five-pound notes, four to one.

"What am I to do with these?" he cried, waving them before the boy's eyes.

"I suppose we'll talk to Bassett," said the boy. "I expect I have fifteen hundred now; and twenty in reserve; and this twenty."

His uncle studied him for some moments.

"Look here, son!" he said. "You're not serious about Bassett and that fifteen hundred, are you?"

"Yes, I am. But it's between you and me, uncle. Honour bright!"

"Honour bright all right, son! But I must talk to Bassett."

"If you'd like to be a partner, uncle, with Bassett and me, we could all be partners. Only, you'd have to promise, honour bright, uncle, not to let it go beyond us three. Bassett and I are lucky, and you must be lucky, because it was your ten shillings I started winning with...."

Uncle Oscar took both Bassett and Paul into Richmond Park for an afternoon, and there they talked.

"It's like this, you see, sir," Bassett said. "Master Paul would get me talking about racing events, spinning yarns, you know, sir. And he was always keen on knowing if I'd made or if I'd lost. It's about a year since, now, that I put five

---

6. Nathaniel Gould (1857–1919), novelist and journalist who wrote about horse racing.

shillings on Blush of Dawn for him—and we lost. Then the luck turned, with the ten shillings he had from you, that we put on Singhalese. And since that time, it's been pretty steady, all things considering. What do you say, Master Paul?"

"We're all right when we're sure," said Paul. "It's when we're not quite sure that we go down."

"Oh, but we're careful then," said Bassett.

"But when are you *sure?*" smiled Uncle Oscar.

"It's Master Paul, sir," said Bassett, in a secret, religious voice. "It's as if he had it from heaven. Like Daffodil, now, for the Lincoln. That was as sure as eggs."

"Did you put anything on Daffodil?" asked Oscar Cresswell.

"Yes, sir. I made my bit."

"And my nephew?"

Bassett was obstinately silent, looking at Paul.

"I made twelve hundred, didn't I, Bassett? I told uncle I was putting three hundred on Daffodil."

"That's right," said Bassett, nodding.

"But where's the money?" asked the uncle.

"I keep it safe locked up, sir. Master Paul he can have it any minute he likes to ask for it."

"What, fifteen hundred pounds?"

"And twenty! And *forty,* that is, with the twenty he made on the course."

"It's amazing!" said the uncle.

"If Master Paul offers you to be partners, sir, I would, if I were you; if you'll excuse me," said Bassett.

Oscar Cresswell thought about it.

"I'll see the money," he said.

They drove home again, and sure enough, Bassett came round to the garden-house with fifteen hundred pounds in notes. The twenty pounds reserve was left with Joe Glee, in the Turf Commission deposit.

"You see, it's all right, uncle, when I'm *sure!* Then we go strong, for all we're worth. Don't we, Bassett?"

"We do that, Master Paul"

"And when are you sure?" said the uncle, laughing.

"Oh, well, sometimes I'm *absolutely* sure, like about Daffodil," said the boy; "and sometimes I have an idea; and sometimes I haven't even an idea, have I, Bassett? Then we're careful, because we mostly go down."

"You do, do you! And when you're sure, like about Daffodil, what makes you sure, sonny?"

"Oh, well, I don't know," said the boy uneasily. "I'm sure, you know, uncle; that's all."

"It's as if he had it from heaven, sir," Bassett reiterated.

"I should say so!" said the uncle.

But he became a partner. And when the Leger was coming on, Paul was "sure" about Lively Spark, which was a quite inconsiderable horse. The boy insisted on putting a thousand on the horse, Bassett went for five hundred, and Oscar Cresswell two hundred. Lively Spark came in first, and the betting had been ten to one against him. Paul had made ten thousand.

"You see," he said, "I was absolutely sure of him."

Even Oscar Cresswell had cleared two thousand.

"Look here, son," he said, "this sort of thing makes me nervous."

"It needn't, uncle! Perhaps I shan't be sure again for a long time."

"But what are you going to do with your money?" asked the uncle.

"Of course," said the boy, "I started it for mother. She said she had no luck, because father is unlucky, so I thought if *I* was lucky, it might stop whispering."

"What might stop whispering?"

"Our house. I *hate* our house for whispering."

"What does it whisper?"

"Why—why"—the boy fidgeted—"why, I don't know. But it's always short of money, you know, uncle."

"I know it, son, I know it."

"You know people send mother writs, don't you, uncle?"

"I'm afraid I do," said the uncle.

"And then the house whispers, like people laughing at you behind your back. It's awful, that is! I thought if I was lucky . . ."

"You might stop it," added the uncle.

The boy watched him with big blue eyes, that had an uncanny cold fire in them, and he said never a word.

"Well, then!" said the uncle. "What are we doing?"

"I shouldn't like mother to know I was lucky," said the boy.

"Why not, son?"

"She'd stop me."

"I don't think she would."

"Oh!"—and the boy writhed in an odd way—"I *don't* want her to know, uncle."

"All right, son! We'll manage it without her knowing."

They managed it very easily. Paul, at the other's suggestion, handed over five thousand pounds to his uncle, who deposited it with the family lawyer, who was then to inform Paul's mother that a relative had put five thousand pounds into his hands, which sum was to be paid out a thousand pounds at a time, on the mother's birthday, for the next five years.

"So she'll have a birthday present of a thousand pounds for five successive years," said Uncle Oscar. "I hope it won't make it all the harder for her later."

Paul's mother had her birthday in November. The house had been "whispering" worse than ever lately, and, even in spite of his luck, Paul could not bear up against it. He was very anxious to see the effect of the birthday letter, telling his mother about the thousand pounds.

When there were no visitors, Paul now took his meals with his parents, as he was beyond the nursery control. His mother went into town nearly every day. She had discovered that she had an odd knack of sketching furs and dress materials, so she worked secretly in the studio of a friend who was the chief "artist" for the leading drapers. She drew the figures of ladies in furs and ladies in silk and sequins for the newspaper advertisements. This young woman artist earned several thousand pounds a year, but Paul's mother only made several hundreds, and she was again dissatisfied. She so wanted to be first in something, and she did not succeed, even in making sketches for drapery advertisements.

She was down to breakfast on the morning of her birthday. Paul watched her face as she read her letters. He knew the lawyer's letter. As his mother read it, her face hardened and became more expressionless. Then a cold, determined look came on her mouth. She hid the letter under the pile of others, and said not a word about it.

"Didn't you have anything nice in the post for your birthday, mother?" said Paul.

"Quite moderately nice," she said, her voice cold and absent.

She went away to town without saying more.

But in the afternoon Uncle Oscar appeared. He said Paul's mother had had a long interview with the lawyer, asking if the whole five thousand could not be advanced at once, as she was in debt.

"What do you think, uncle?" said the boy.

"I leave it to you, son."

"Oh, let her have it, then! We can get some more with the other," said the boy.

"A bird in the hand is worth two in the bush, laddie!" said Uncle Oscar.

"But I'm sure to *know* for the Grand National; or the Lincolnshire; or else the Derby. I'm sure to know for *one* of them," said Paul.

So Uncle Oscar signed the agreement, and Paul's mother touched the whole five thousand. Then something very curious happened. The voices in the house suddenly went mad, like a chorus of frogs on a spring evening. There were certain new furnishings, and Paul had a tutor. He was *really* going to Eton, his father's school, in the following autumn. There were flowers in the winter, and a blossoming of the luxury Paul's mother had been used to. And yet the voices in the house, behind the sprays of mimosa and almond blossom, and from under the piles of iridescent cushions, simply trilled and screamed in a sort of ecstasy: "There *must* be more money! Oh-h-h; there *must* be more money Oh, now, now-w! Now-w-w—there *must* be more money!—more than ever! More than ever!"

It frightened Paul terribly. He studied away at his Latin and Greek with his tutors. But his intense hours were spent with Bassett. The Grand National had gone by: he had not "known," and had lost a hundred pounds. Summer was at hand. He was in agony for the Lincoln. But even for the Lincoln he didn't "know," and he lost fifty pounds. He became wild-eyed and strange, as if something were going to explode in him.

"Let it alone, son! Don't you bother about it!" urged Uncle Oscar. But it was as if the boy couldn't really hear what his uncle was saying.

"I've got to know for the Derby! I've got to know for the Derby!" the child reiterated, his big blue eyes blazing with a sort of madness.

His mother noticed how overwrought he was.

"You'd better go to the seaside. Wouldn't you like to go now to the seaside, instead of waiting? I think you'd better," she said, looking down at him anxiously, her heart curiously heavy because of him.

But the child lifted his uncanny blue eyes.

"I couldn't possibly go before the Derby, mother!" he said. "I couldn't possibly!"

"Why not?" she said, her voice becoming heavy when she was opposed. "Why not? You can still go from the seaside to see the Derby with your Uncle Oscar, if that's what you wish. No need for you to wait here. Besides, I think you care too much about these races. It's a bad sign. My family has been a gambling family, and you won't know till you grow up how much damage it has done. But it has done damage. I shall have to send Bassett away, and ask Uncle Oscar not to talk racing to you, unless you promise to be reasonable about it; go away to the seaside and forget it. You're all nerves!"

"I'll do what you like, mother, so long as you don't send me away till after the Derby," the boy said.

"Send you away from where? Just from this house?"

"Yes," he said, gazing at her.

"Why, you curious child, what makes you care about this house so much, suddenly? I never knew you loved it."

He gazed at her without speaking. He had a secret within a secret, something he had not divulged, even to Bassett or to his Uncle Oscar.

But his mother, after standing undecided and a little bit sullen for some moments, said:

"Very well, then! Don't go to the seaside till after the Derby, if you don't wish it. But promise me you won't let your nerves go to pieces. Promise you won't think so much about horse-racing and events, as you call them!"

"Oh, no," said the boy casually. "I won't think much about them, mother. You needn't worry. I wouldn't worry, mother, if I were you."

"If you were me and I were you," said his mother, "I wonder what we *should* do!"

"But you know you needn't worry, mother, don't you?" the boy repeated.

"I should be awfully glad to know it," she said wearily.

"Oh, well, you *can*, you know. I mean, you *ought* to know you needn't worry," he insisted.

"Ought I? Then I'll see about it," she said.

Paul's secret of secrets was his wooden horse, that which had no name. Since he was emancipated from a nurse and a nursery-governess, he had had his rocking-horse removed to his own bedroom at the top of the house.

"Surely, you're too big for a rocking-horse!" his mother had remonstrated.

"Well, you see, mother, till I can have a *real* horse, I like to have *some* sort of animal about," had been his quaint answer.

"Do you feel he keeps you company?" she laughed.

"Oh, yes! He's very good, he always keeps me company, when I'm there," said Paul.

So the horse, rather shabby, stood in an arrested prance in the boy's bedroom. The Derby was drawing near, and the boy grew more and more tense. He hardly heard what was spoken to him, he was very frail, and his eyes were really uncanny. His mother had sudden strange seizures of uneasiness about him. Sometimes, for half-an-hour, she would feel a sudden anxiety about him that was almost anguish. She wanted to rush to him at once, and know he was safe.

Two nights before the Derby, she was at a big party in town, when one of her rushes of anxiety about her boy, her first-born, gripped her heart till she could hardly speak. She fought with the feeling, might and main, for she believed in common-sense. But it was too strong. She had to leave the dance and go downstairs to telephone to the country. The children's nursery-governess was terribly surprised and startled at being rung up in the night.

"Are the children all right, Miss Wilmot?"

"Oh, yes, they are quite all right."

"Master Paul? Is he all right?"

"He went to bed as right as a trivet. Shall I run up and look at him?"

"No," said Paul's mother reluctantly. "No! Don't trouble. It's all right. Don't sit up. We shall be home fairly soon." She did not want her son's privacy intruded upon.

"Very good," said the governess.

It was about one o'clock when Paul's mother and father drove up to their house. All was still. Paul's mother went to her room and slipped off her white fur cloak. She had told her maid not to wait up for her. She heard her husband downstairs, mixing a whisky-and-soda.

And then, because of the strange anxiety at her heart, she stole upstairs to her son's room. Noiselessly she went along the upper corridor. Was there a faint noise? What was it?

She stood, with arrested muscles, outside his door, listening. There was a strange, heavy, and yet not loud noise. Her heart stood still. It was a soundless noise, yet rushing and powerful. Something huge, in violent, hushed motion. What was it? What in God's name was it? She ought to know. She felt that she knew the noise. She knew what it was.

Yet she could not place it. She couldn't say what it was. And on and on it went, like a madness.

Softly, frozen with anxiety and fear, she turned the door-handle.

The room was dark. Yet in the space near the window, she heard and saw something plunging to and fro. She gazed in fear and amazement.

Then suddenly she switched on the light, and saw her son, in his green pyjamas, madly surging on the rocking-horse. The blaze of light suddenly lit him up, as he urged the wooden horse, and lit her up, as she stood, blonde, in her dress of pale green and crystal, in the doorway.

"Paul!" she cried. "Whatever are you doing?"

"It's Malabar!" he screamed, in a powerful, strange voice. "It's Malabar!"

His eyes blazed at her for one strange and senseless second, as he ceased urging his wooden horse. Then he fell with a crash to the ground, and she, all her tormented motherhood flooding upon her, rushed to gather him up.

But he was unconscious, and unconscious he remained, with some brain-fever. He talked and tossed, and his mother sat stonily by his side.

"Malabar! It's Malabar! Bassett, Bassett, I *know*! It's Malabar!"

So the child cried, trying to get up and urge the rocking-horse that gave him his inspiration.

"What does he mean by Malabar?" asked the heart-frozen mother.

"I don't know," said the father stonily.

"What does he mean by Malabar?" she asked her brother Oscar.

"It's one of the horses running for the Derby," was the answer.

And, in spite of himself, Oscar Cresswell spoke to Bassett, and himself put a thousand on Malabar: at fourteen to one.

The third day of the illness was critical: they were waiting for a change. The boy, with his rather long, curly hair, was tossing ceaselessly on the pillow. He neither slept nor regained consciousness, and his eyes were like blue stones. His mother sat, feeling her heart had gone, turned actually into a stone.

In the evening, Oscar Cresswell did not come, but Bassett sent a message, saying could he come up for one moment, just one moment? Paul's mother was very angry at the intrusion, but on second thought she agreed. The boy was the same. Perhaps Bassett might bring him to consciousness.

The gardener, a shortish fellow with a little brown moustache, and sharp little brown eyes, tip-toed into the room, touched his imaginary cap to Paul's mother, and stole to the bedside, staring with glittering, smallish eyes, at the tossing, dying child.

"Master Paul!" he whispered. "Master Paul! Malabar came in first all right, a clean win. I did as you told me. You've made over seventy thousand pounds, you have; you've got over eighty thousand. Malabar came in all right, Master Paul."

"Malabar! Malabar! Did I say Malabar, mother? Did I say Malabar? Do you think I'm lucky, mother? I knew Malabar, didn't I? Over eighty thousand pounds! I call that lucky, don't you, mother? Over eighty thousand pounds! I knew, didn't I know I knew! Malabar came in all right. If I ride my horse till I'm sure, then I tell you, Bassett, you can go as high as you like. Did you go for all you were worth, Bassett?"

"I went a thousand on it, Master Paul."

"I never told you, mother, that if I can ride my horse, and *get there*, then I'm absolutely sure—oh absolutely! Mother, did I ever tell you? I *am* lucky!"

"No, you never did," said the mother.

But the boy died in the night.

And even as he lay dead, his mother heard her brother's voice saying to her: "My God, Hester, you're eighty-odd thousand to the good, and a poor devil of a son to the bad. But, poor devil, poor devil, he's best gone out of a life where he rides his rocking-horse to find a winner."

1932

## D. H. LAWRENCE

### Passages from Essays and Letters

#### From "Nottingham and the Mining Countryside" (1930)

I was born ... in Eastwood, a mining village of some three thousand souls, about eight miles from Nottingham.... It is hilly country.... To me it seemed, and still seems, an extremely beautiful countryside, just between the red sandstone and the oaktrees of Nottingham, and the cold lime-stone, the ash-trees, the stone fences of Derbyshire. To me, as a child and a young man, it was still the old England of the forest and agricultural past; there were no motorcars, the mines were, in a sense, an accident in the landscape, and Robin Hood and his merry men were not very far away.

Lawrence's hometown—Eastwood, ca. 1911

... The people lived almost entirely by instinct, men of my father's age could not really read. And the pit did not mechanize men.... My father loved the pit. He was hurt badly, more than once, but he would never stay away. He loved the contact, the intimacy, as men in the war loved the intense male comradeship of the dark days.

Now the colliers had also an instinct for beauty. The colliers' wives had not. The colliers were deeply alive, instinctively. But they had no daytime ambition, and no daytime intellect. They avoided, really, the rational aspect of life.... They didn't even care very profoundly about wages. It was the women, naturally, who nagged on this score.... The collier went to the pub and drank in order to continue the intimacy with his mates.

... Life for him did not consist of facts, but in a flow. Very often he loved his garden. And very often he had a genuine love of the beauty of flowers....

A collier undercutting coal at Brinsley Colliery

... Most women love flowers as possessions, and as trimmings. They can't look at a flower, and wonder a moment, and pass on. If they see a flower that arrests their attention, they must at once pick it, pluck it. Possession! A possession! Something added on to *me!*

### From "Love" (1918)

... [T]he love between a man and a woman ... is dual. It is the melting into pure communion, and it is the friction of sheer sensuality, both. In pure communion I become whole in love. And in pure, fierce passion of sensuality, I am burned into essentiality. I am driven from the matrix unto sheer separate distinction. I become my single self, inviolable and unique, as the gems were perhaps once driven into themselves out of the confusion of earths....

### From "Women Are So Cocksure" (posthumously published in 1936)

... [My mother] was convinced ... that a man ought not to drink beer. This conviction developed from the fact, naturally, that my father drank beer. He sometimes drank too much. He sometimes boozed away the money necessary for the young family: When my father came in tipsy, she saw scarlet.

### From "Art and Morality" (1925)

Apples are always apples! says Vox Populi, Vox Dei.[1]

Sometimes they're sin, sometimes they're a knock on the head, sometimes

---

1. The voice of the people [is] the voice of God.

they're a bellyache, sometimes they're part of a pie, sometimes they're sauce for a goose....

What art has got to do, and will go on doing, is to reveal things in their different relationships. That is to say, you've got to see in the apples the bellyache, Sir Isaac's knock on the cranium, the vast, moist wall through which the insect bores to lay her eggs in the middle, and the untasted, unknown quality which Eve saw hanging on a tree.

### From "Morality and the Novel" (1925)

The business of art is to reveal the relation between man and his circumambient universe, at the living moment. As mankind is always struggling in the toils of old relationships, art is always ahead of the "times," which themselves are always far in the rear of the living moment.

When van Gogh paints sunflowers, he reveals, or achieves, the vivid relation between himself, as man, and the sunflowers, as sunflower, at that quick moment of time. His painting does not represent the sunflower itself. We shall never know what the sunflower itself is. And the camera will *visualize* the sunflower far more perfectly than van Gogh can.

The vision on the canvas is a third thing, utterly intangible and inexplicable, the offspring of the sunflower itself and van Gogh himself....

... The novel is the highest example of subtle interrelatedness that man has discovered. Everything is true in its own time, place, and circumstance, and untrue outside of its own place, time, circumstance. If you try to nail anything down, in the novel, either it kills the novel, or the novel gets up and walks away with the nail.

... Love is a great emotion. But if you set out to write a novel, and you yourself are in the throes of the great predilection for love, love as the supreme, the only emotion worth living for, then you will write an immoral novel.

Because *no* emotion is supreme, or exclusively worth living for. *All* emotions go to the achieving of a living relationship between a human being and the other human being or creature or thing he becomes purely related to. All emotions, including love and hate, and rage and tenderness, go to the adjusting of the oscillating, unestablished balance between two people who amount to anything....

A new relation, a new relatedness hurts somewhat in the attaining; and will always hurt. So life will always hurt....

D. H. with his wife, Frieda Lawrence

Each time we strive to a new relation, with anyone or anything, it is bound to hurt somewhat. Because it means the struggle with and the displacing of old connections, and this is never pleasant. And, moreover, between living things at least, an adjustment means also a fight, for each party, inevitably, must "seek its own" in the other, and be denied. When, in the two parties, each of them seeks his own, her own, absolutely, then it is a fight to the death. And this is true of the thing called "passion." ...

The great relationship for humanity will always be the relation between man and woman. The relation between man and man, woman and woman, parent and child, will always be subsidiary.

And the relation between man and woman will change forever, and will forever be the new central clue to human life. It is the *relation itself* which is the quick and the central clue to life, not the man, nor the woman, nor the children that result from the relationship, as a contingency.

### From "Why the Novel Matters" (posthumously published in 1936)

We have curious ideas of ourselves. We think of ourselves as a body with a spirit in it, or a body with a soul in it, or a body with a mind in it....

It is a funny sort of superstition. Why should I look at my hand, as it so cleverly writes these words, and decide that it is a mere nothing compared to the mind that directs it? Why should I imagine that there is a *me* which is more *me* than my hand is? Since my hand is absolutely alive, me alive...

And that's what you learn, when you're a novelist. And that's what you are liable *not* to know, if you're a parson, or a philosopher, or a scientist, or a stupid person.

Now I absolutely flatly deny that I am a soul, or a body, or a mind, or an intelligence, or a brain, or a nervous system, or a bunch of glands, or any of the rest of these bits of me. The whole is greater than the part. And therefore, I, who am man alive, am greater than my soul, or spirit, or body, or mind, or consciousness, or anything else that is merely a part of me. I am a man, and alive. I am man alive, and as long as I can, I intend to go on being man alive.

For this reason I am a novelist. And being a novelist, I consider myself superior to the saint, the scientist, the philosopher, and the poet, who are all great masters of different bits of man alive, but never get the whole [thing]....

We should ask for no absolutes, or absolute.... There is no absolute good, there is nothing absolutely right. All things flow and change, and even change is not absolute....

... If the one I love remains unchanged and unchanging, I shall cease to love her. It is only because she changes and startles me into change and defies my inertia, and is herself staggered in her inertia by my changing, that I can continue to love her. If she stayed put, I might as well love the pepper-pot....

In life, there is right and wrong, good and bad, all the time. But what is right in one case is wrong in another. And in the novel you see one man becoming a corpse, because of his so-called goodness, another going dead because of his so-called wickedness. Right and wrong is an instinct: but an instinct of the whole consciousness in a man, bodily, mental, spiritual at once. And only in the novel are *all* things given full play, or at least, they may be given full play, when we realize that life itself, and not inert safety, is the reason for living. For out of the full play of all things emerges the only thing that is anything, the wholeness of a man, the wholeness of a woman, man alive, and live woman.

*From "Autobiographical Sketch" (posthumously published in 1967)*

They ask me; "Did you find it very hard to get on and to become a success?" And I have to admit that if I can be said to have got on, and if I can be called a success, then I *did not* find it hard.

I never starved in a garret, nor waited in anguish for the post to bring me an answer from editor or publisher, nor did I struggle in sweat and blood to bring forth mighty works, nor did I ever wake up and find myself famous.

... My father was a collier, and only a collier, nothing praise-worthy about him. He wasn't even respectable, in so far as he got drunk rather frequently, never went near a chapel, and was usually rather rude to his little immediate bosses at the pit. . . .

My mother was, I suppose, superior. She came from town, and belonged really to the lower bourgeoisie. She spoke King's English, without an accent, and never in her life could even imitate a sentence of the dialect which my father spoke, and which we children spoke out of doors. . . .

... I have *wanted* to feel truly friendly with some, at least, of my fellow-men. Yet I have never quite succeeded. Whether I got on *in* the world is a question; but I certainly don't get on very well *with* the world. And whether I am a worldly success or not I really don't know. But I feel, somehow, not much of a human success.

By which I mean that I don't feel there is any very cordial or fundamental contact between me and society, or me and other people. There is a breach. And my contact is with something that is nonhuman, nonvocal. . . .

[Why?] The answer, as far as I can see, has something to do with class. Class makes a gulf, across which all the best human flow is lost. It is not exactly the triumph of the middle classes that has made the deadness, but the triumph of the middle-class *thing*.

As a man from the working class, I feel that the middle class cut off some of my vital vibration when I am with them. I admit them charming and educated and good people often enough. *But they just stop some part of me from working.* . . .

Then why don't I live with my working people? Because their vibration is limited in another direction. They are narrow, but still fairly deep and passionate, whereas the middle class is broad and shallow and passionless. . . .

I cannot make the transfer from my own class into the middle class. I cannot, not for anything in the world, forfeit my passional consciousness and my old blood-affinity with my fellow-men and the animals and the land, for that other thin, spurious mental conceit which is all that is left of the mental consciousness once it has made itself exclusive.

*From the Letters*

To A. D. McLeod, 26 April 1913

I am so sure that only through a readjustment between men and women, and a making free and healthy of this sex, will she [England] get out of her present atrophy. Oh, Lord, and if I don't "subdue my art to a metaphysic," as somebody very beautifully said of Hardy, I do write because I want folk—English folk—to alter, and have more sense.

**To A. D. McLeod, 2 June 1914**

I think the only re-sourcing of art, revivifying it, is to make it more the joint work of man and woman. I think *the* one thing to do, is for men to have courage to draw nearer to women, expose themselves to them, and be altered by them; and for women to accept and admit men. That is the start—by bringing themselves together, men and women—revealing themselves to each other, gaining great blind knowledge and suffering and joy, which it will take a big further lapse of civilisation to exploit and work out. Because the source of all life and knowledge is in man and woman, and the source of all living is in the interchange and the meeting and mingling of these two: man-life and woman-life, man-knowledge and woman-knowledge, man-being and woman-being.

**To J. B. Pinker, 16 December 1915**

... Tell Arnold Bennett[2] that all rules of construction hold good only for novels which are copies of other novels. A book which is not a copy of other books has its own construction, and what he calls faults, he being an old imitator, I call characteristics.

**To Rolf Gardiner, 9 August 1924**

What we need is to smash a few big holes in European suburbanity, let in a little real fresh air.

**To Lady Ottoline Morrell, 5 February 1929**

... Don't you think it's nonsense when Murry says that my world is not the ordinary man's world and that I am a sort of animal with a sixth sense? Seems to me more likely he's a sort of animal with only four senses—the real sense of touch missing. They all seem determined to make a freak of me—to save their own short-failings, and make them "normal."

## FLANNERY O'CONNOR

### A Good Man Is Hard to Find

The grandmother didn't want to go to Florida. She wanted to visit some of her connections in east Tennessee and she was seizing at every chance to change Bailey's mind. Bailey was the son she lived with, her only boy. He was sitting on the edge of his chair at the table, bent over the orange sports section of the *Journal*. "Now look here, Bailey," she said, "see here, read this," and she stood with one hand on her thin hip and the other rattling the newspaper at his bald head. "Here this fellow that calls himself The Misfit is aloose from the Federal Pen and headed toward Florida and you read here what it says he did to these people. Just you read it. I wouldn't take my children in any direction

---

2. An early-twentieth-century novelist (1867–1931) whose major works—*The Old Wives' Tale* (1908) and *The Clayhanger Family* (1910–15)—treat the middle classes in the pottery country of the English Midlands in a naturalistic manner (usually criticizing the money-grubbing, social-climbing selfishness of the society). In his later years he more or less turned into a hack, though a clever one, and it is to Bennett as a very popular, successful hack that Lawrence is referring.

with a criminal like that aloose in it. I couldn't answer to my conscience if I did."

Bailey didn't look up from his reading so she wheeled around then and faced the children's mother, a young woman in slacks, whose face was as broad and innocent as a cabbage and was tied around with a green head-kerchief that had two points on the top like a rabbit's ears. She was sitting on the sofa, feeding the baby his apricots out of a jar. "The children have been to Florida before," the old lady said. "You all ought to take them somewhere else for a change so they would see different parts of the world and be broad. They never have been to east Tennessee."

The children's mother didn't seem to hear her but the eight-year-old boy, John Wesley, a stocky child with glasses, said, "If you don't want to go to Florida, why dontcha stay at home?" He and the little girl, June Star, were reading the funny papers on the floor.

"She wouldn't stay at home to be queen for a day," June Star said without raising her yellow head.

5 "Yes and what would you do if this fellow, The Misfit, caught you?" the grandmother asked.

"I'd smack his face," John Wesley said.

"She wouldn't stay at home for a million bucks," June Star said. "Afraid she'd miss something. She has to go everywhere we go."

"All right, Miss," the grandmother said. "Just remember that the next time you want me to curl your hair."

June Star said her hair was naturally curly.

10 The next morning the grandmother was the first one in the car, ready to go. She had her big black valise that looked like the head of a hippopotamus in one corner, and underneath it she was hiding a basket with Pitty Sing,[1] the cat, in it. She didn't intend for the cat to be left alone in the house for three days because he would miss her too much and she was afraid he might brush against one of the gas burners and accidentally asphyxiate himself. Her son, Bailey, didn't like to arrive at a motel with a cat.

She sat in the middle of the back seat with John Wesley and June Star on either side of her. Bailey and the children's mother and the baby sat in front and they left Atlanta at eight forty-five with the mileage on the car at 55890. The grandmother wrote this down because she thought it would be interesting to say how many miles they had been when they got back. It took them twenty minutes to reach the outskirts of the city.

The old lady settled herself comfortably, removing her white cotton gloves and putting them up with her purse on the shelf in front of the back window. The children's mother still had on slacks and still had her head tied up in a green kerchief, but the grandmother had on a navy blue straw sailor hat with a bunch of white violets on the brim and a navy blue dress with a small white dot in the print. Her collars and cuffs were white organdy trimmed with lace and at her neckline she had pinned a purple spray of cloth violets containing a sachet. In case of an accident, anyone seeing her dead on the highway would know at once that she was a lady.

---

1. Named after Pitti-Sing, one of the "three little maids from school" in Gilbert and Sullivan's operetta *The Mikado* (1885).

She said she thought it was going to be a good day for driving, neither too hot nor too cold, and she cautioned Bailey that the speed limit was fifty-five miles an hour and that the patrolmen hid themselves behind billboards and small clumps of trees and sped out after you before you had a chance to slow down. She pointed out interesting details of the scenery: Stone Mountain; the blue granite that in some places came up to both sides of the highway; the brilliant red clay banks slightly streaked with purple; and the various crops that made rows of green lace-work on the ground. The trees were full of silver-white sunlight and the meanest of them sparkled. The children were reading comic magazines and their mother had gone back to sleep.

"Let's go through Georgia fast so we won't have to look at it much," John Wesley said.

"If I were a little boy," said the grandmother, "I wouldn't talk about my native state that way. Tennessee has the mountains and Georgia has the hills."

"Tennessee is just a hillbilly dumping ground," John Wesley said, "and Georgia is a lousy state too."

"You said it," June Star said.

"In my time," said the grandmother, folding her thin veined fingers, "children were more respectful of their native states and their parents and everything else. People did right then. Oh look at the cute little pickaninny!" she said and pointed to a Negro child standing in the door of a shack. "Wouldn't that make a picture, now?" she asked and they all turned and looked at the little Negro out of the back window. He waved.

"He didn't have any britches on," June Star said.

"He probably didn't have any," the grandmother explained. "Little niggers in the country don't have things like we do. If I could paint, I'd paint that picture," she said.

The children exchanged comic books.

The grandmother offered to hold the baby and the children's mother passed him over the front seat to her. She set him on her knee and bounced him and told him about the things they were passing. She rolled her eyes and screwed up her mouth and stuck her leathery thin face into his smooth bland one. Occasionally he gave her a faraway smile. They passed a large cotton field with five or six graves fenced in the middle of it, like a small island. "Look at the graveyard!" the grandmother said, pointing it out. "That was the old family burying ground. That belonged to the plantation."

"Where's the plantation?" John Wesley asked.

"Gone with the Wind,"[2] said the grandmother. "Ha. Ha."

When the children finished all the comic books they had brought, they opened the lunch and ate it. The grandmother ate a peanut butter sandwich and an olive and would not let the children throw the box and the paper napkins out the window. When there was nothing else to do they played a game by choosing a cloud and making the other two guess what shape it suggested. John Wesley took one the shape of a cow and June Star guessed a cow and John Wesley said, no,

---

2. The title of an immensely popular novel, published in 1936, by Margaret Mitchell (1900–1949); the novel depicts a large, prosperous Southern plantation, Tara, that is destroyed by Northern troops in the American Civil War.

an automobile, and June Star said he didn't play fair, and they began to slap each other over the grandmother.

The grandmother said she would tell them a story if they would keep quiet. When she told a story, she rolled her eyes and waved her head and was very dramatic. She said once when she was a maiden lady she had been courted by a Mr. Edgar Atkins Teagarden from Jasper, Georgia. She said he was a very good-looking man and a gentleman and that he brought her a watermelon every Saturday afternoon with his initials cut in it, E. A. T. Well, one Saturday, she said, Mr. Teagarden brought the watermelon and there was nobody at home and he left it on the front porch and returned in his buggy to Jasper, but she never got the watermelon, she said, because a nigger boy ate it when he saw the initials, E. A. T.! This story tickled John Wesley's funny bone and he giggled and giggled but June Star didn't think it was any good. She said she wouldn't marry a man that just brought her a watermelon on Saturday. The grandmother said she would have done well to marry Mr. Teagarden because he was a gentleman and had bought Coca-Cola stock when it first came out and that he had died only a few years ago, a very wealthy man.

They stopped at The Tower for barbecued sandwiches. The Tower was a part stucco and part wood filling station and dance hall set in a clearing outside of Timothy. A fat man named Red Sammy Butts ran it and there were signs stuck here and there on the building and for miles up and down the highway saying, TRY RED SAMMY'S FAMOUS BARBECUE. NONE LIKE FAMOUS RED SAMMY'S! RED SAM! THE FAT BOY WITH THE HAPPY LAUGH! A VETERAN! RED SAMMY'S YOUR MAN!

Red Sammy was lying on the bare ground outside The Tower with his head under a truck while a gray monkey about a foot high, chained to a small chinaberry tree, chattered nearby. The monkey sprang back into the tree and got on the highest limb as soon as he saw the children jump out of the car and run toward him.

Inside, The Tower was a long dark room with a counter at one end and tables at the other and dancing space in the middle. They all sat down at a board table next to the nickelodeon[3] and Red Sam's wife, a tall burnt-brown woman with hair and eyes lighter than her skin, came and took their order. The children's mother put a dime in the machine and played "The Tennessee Waltz," and the grandmother said that tune always made her want to dance. She asked Bailey if he would like to dance but he only glared at her. He didn't have a naturally sunny disposition like she did and trips made him nervous. The grandmother's brown eyes were very bright. She swayed her head from side to side and pretended she was dancing in her chair. June Star said play something she could tap to so the children's mother put in another dime and played a fast number and June Star stepped out onto the dance floor and did her tap routine.

"Ain't she cute?" Red Sam's wife said, leaning over the counter. "Would you like to come be my little girl?"

"No I certainly wouldn't," June Star said. "I wouldn't live in a broken-down place like this for a million bucks!" and she ran back to the table.

"Ain't she cute?" the woman repeated, stretching her mouth politely.

"Aren't you ashamed?" hissed the grandmother.

---

3. Jukebox.

Red Sam came in and told his wife to quit lounging on the counter and hurry up with these people's order. His khaki trousers reached just to his hip bones and his stomach hung over them like a sack of meal swaying under his shirt. He came over and sat down at a table nearby and let out a combination sigh and yodel. "You can't win," he said. "You can't win," and he wiped his sweating red face off with a gray handkerchief. "These days you don't know who to trust," he said. "Ain't that the truth?"

"People are certainly not nice like they used to be," said the grandmother.

"Two fellers come in here last week," Red Sammy said, "driving a Chrysler. It was a old beat-up car but it was a good one and these boys looked all right to me. Said they worked at the mill and you know I let them fellers charge the gas they bought? Now why did I do that?"

"Because you're a good man!" the grandmother said at once.

"Yes'm, I suppose so," Red Sam said as if he were struck with this answer.

His wife brought the orders, carrying the five plates all at once without a tray, two in each hand and one balanced on her arm. "It isn't a soul in this green world of God's that you can trust," she said. "And I don't count nobody out of that, not nobody," she repeated, looking at Red Sammy.

"Did you read about that criminal, The Misfit, that's escaped?" asked the grandmother.

"I wouldn't be a bit surprised if he didn't attact this place right here," said the woman. "If he hears about it being here, I wouldn't be none surprised to see him. If he hears it's two cent in the cash register, I wouldn't be a tall surprised if he . . ."

"That'll do," Red Sam said. "Go bring these people their Co'-Colas," and the woman went off to get the rest of the order.

"A good man is hard to find," Red Sammy said. "Everything is getting terrible. I remember the day you could go off and leave your screen door unlatched. Not no more."

He and the grandmother discussed better times. The old lady said that in her opinion Europe was entirely to blame for the way things were now. She said the way Europe acted you would think we were made of money and Red Sam said it was no use talking about it, she was exactly right. The children ran outside into the white sunlight and looked at the monkey in the lacy chinaberry tree. He was busy catching fleas on himself and biting each one carefully between his teeth as if it were a delicacy.

They drove off again into the hot afternoon. The grandmother took cat naps and woke up every few minutes with her own snoring. Outside of Toombsboro she woke up and recalled an old plantation that she had visited in this neighborhood once when she was a young lady. She said the house had six white columns across the front and that there was an avenue of oaks leading up to it and two little wooden trellis arbors on either side in front where you sat down with your suitor after a stroll in the garden. She recalled exactly which road to turn off to get to it. She knew that Bailey would not be willing to lose any time looking at an old house, but the more she talked about it, the more she wanted to see it once again and find out if the little twin arbors were still standing. "There was a secret panel in this house," she said craftily, not telling the truth but wishing that she were, "and the story went that all the family silver was hidden in it when Sherman came through but it was never found . . ."

"Hey!" John Wesley said. "Let's go see it! We'll find it! We'll poke all the woodwork and find it! Who lives there? Where do you turn off at? Hey Pop, can't we turn off there?"

"We never have seen a house with a secret panel!" June Star shrieked. "Let's go to the house with the secret panel! Hey Pop, can't we go see the house with the secret panel!"

"It's not far from here, I know," the grandmother said. "It wouldn't take over twenty minutes."

Bailey was looking straight ahead. His jaw was as rigid as a horseshoe. "No," he said.

50   The children began to yell and scream that they wanted to see the house with the secret panel. John Wesley kicked the back of the front seat and June Star hung over her mother's shoulder and whined desperately into her ear that they never had any fun even on their vacation, that they could never do what THEY wanted to do. The baby began to scream and John Wesley kicked the back of the seat so hard that his father could feel the blows in his kidney.

"All right!" he shouted and drew the car to a stop at the side of the road. "Will you all shut up? Will you all just shut up for one second? If you don't shut up, we won't go anywhere."

"It would be very educational for them," the grandmother murmured.

"All right," Bailey said, "but get this: this is the only time we're going to stop for anything like this. This is the one and only time."

"The dirt road that you have to turn down is about a mile back," the grandmother directed. "I marked it when we passed."

55   "A dirt road," Bailey groaned.

After they had turned around and were headed toward the dirt road, the grandmother recalled other points about the house, the beautiful glass over the front doorway and the candle-lamp in the hall. John Wesley said that the secret panel was probably in the fireplace.

"You can't go inside this house," Bailey said. "You don't know who lives there."

"While you all talk to the people in front, I'll run around behind and get in a window," John Wesley suggested.

"We'll all stay in the car," his mother said.

60   They turned onto the dirt road and the car raced roughly along in a swirl of pink dust. The grandmother recalled the times when there were no paved roads and thirty miles was a day's journey. The dirt road was hilly and there were sudden washes in it and sharp curves on dangerous embankments. All at once they would be on a hill, looking down over the blue tops of trees for miles around, then the next minute, they would be in a red depression with the dust-coated trees looking down on them.

"This place had better turn up in a minute," Bailey said, "or I'm going to turn around."

The road looked as if no one had traveled on it in months.

"It's not much farther," the grandmother said and just as she said it, a horrible thought came to her. The thought was so embarrassing that she turned red in the face and her eyes dilated and her feet jumped up, upsetting her valise in the corner. The instant the valise moved, the newspaper top she had over the basket under it rose with a snarl and Pitty Sing, the cat, sprang onto Bailey's shoulder.

The children were thrown to the floor and their mother, clutching the baby, out the door onto the ground; the old lady was thrown into the front seat. The car turned over once and landed right-side-up in a gulch off the side of the road. Bailey remained in the driver's seat with the cat—gray-striped with a broad white face and an orange nose—clinging to his neck like a caterpillar.

As soon as the children saw they could move their arms and legs, they scrambled out of the car, shouting, "We've had an ACCIDENT!" The grandmother was curled up under the dashboard, hoping she was injured so that Bailey's wrath would not come down on her all at once. The horrible thought she had had before the accident was that the house she had remembered so vividly was not in Georgia but in Tennessee.

Bailey removed the cat from his neck with both hands and flung it out the window against the side of a pine tree. Then he got out of the car and started looking for the children's mother. She was sitting against the side of the red gutted ditch, holding the screaming baby, but she only had a cut down her face and a broken shoulder. "We've had an ACCIDENT!" the children screamed in a frenzy of delight.

"But nobody's killed," June Star said with disappointment as the grandmother limped out of the car, her hat still pinned to her head but the broken front brim standing up at a jaunty angle and the violet spray hanging off the side. They all sat down in the ditch, except the children, to recover from the shock. They were all shaking.

"Maybe a car will come along," said the children's mother hoarsely.

"I believe I have injured an organ," said the grandmother, pressing her side, but no one answered her. Bailey's teeth were clattering. He had on a yellow sport shirt with bright blue parrots designed in it and his face was as yellow as the shirt. The grandmother decided that she would not mention that the house was in Tennessee.

The road was about ten feet above and they could see only the tops of the trees on the other side of it. Behind the ditch they were sitting in there were more woods, tall and dark and deep. In a few minutes they saw a car some distance away on top of a hill, coming slowly as if the occupants were watching them. The grandmother stood up and waved both arms dramatically to attract their attention. The car continued to come on slowly, disappeared around a bend and appeared again, moving even slower, on top of the hill they had gone over. It was a big black battered hearselike automobile. There were three men in it.

It came to a stop just over them and for some minutes, the driver looked down with a steady expressionless gaze to where they were sitting, and didn't speak. Then he turned his head and muttered something to the other two and they got out. One was a fat boy in black trousers and a red sweat shirt with a silver stallion embossed on the front of it. He moved around on the right side of them and stood staring, his mouth partly open in a kind of loose grin. The other had on khaki pants and a blue striped coat and a gray hat pulled down very low, hiding most of his face. He came around slowly on the left side. Neither spoke.

The driver got out of the car and stood by the side of it, looking down at them. He was an older man than the other two. His hair was just beginning to gray and he wore silver-rimmed spectacles that gave him a scholarly look. He had a long creased face and didn't have on any shirt or undershirt. He had on blue jeans that were too tight for him and was holding a black hat and a gun. The two boys also had guns.

"We've had an ACCIDENT!" the children screamed.

The grandmother had the peculiar feeling that the bespectacled man was someone she knew. His face was as familiar to her as if she had known him all her life but she could not recall who he was. He moved away from the car and began to come down the embankment, placing his feet carefully so that he wouldn't slip. He had on tan and white shoes and no socks, and his ankles were red and thin. "Good afternoon," he said. "I see you all had you a little spill."

"We turned over twice!" said the grandmother.

"Oncet," he corrected. "We seen it happen. Try their car and see will it run, Hiram," he said quietly to the boy with the gray hat.

"What you got that gun for?" John Wesley asked. "Whatcha gonna do with that gun?"

"Lady," the man said to the children's mother, "would you mind calling them children to sit down by you? Children make me nervous. I want all you all to sit down right together there where you're at."

"What are you telling US what to do for?" June Star asked.

Behind them the line of woods gaped like a dark open mouth. "Come here," said their mother.

"Look here now," Bailey began suddenly, "we're in a predicament! We're in . . . !"

The grandmother shrieked. She scrambled to her feet and stood staring. "You're The Misfit!" she said. "I recognized you at once!"

"Yes'm," the man said, smiling slightly as if he were pleased in spite of himself to be known, "but it would have been better for all of you, lady, if you hadn't of reckernized me."

Bailey turned his head sharply and said something to his mother that shocked even the children. The old lady began to cry and The Misfit reddened.

"Lady," he said, "don't you get upset. Sometimes a man says things he don't mean. I don't reckon he meant to talk to you thataway."

"You wouldn't shoot a lady, would you?" the grandmother said and removed a clean handkerchief from her cuff and began to slap at her eyes with it.

The Misfit pointed the toe of his shoe into the ground and made a little hole and then covered it up again. "I would hate to have to," he said.

"Listen," the grandmother almost screamed, "I know you're a good man. You don't look a bit like you have common blood. I know you must come from nice people!"

"Yes mam," he said, "finest people in the world." When he smiled he showed a row of strong white teeth. "God never made a finer woman than my mother and my daddy's heart was pure gold," he said. The boy with the red sweat shirt had come around behind them and was standing with his gun at his hip. The Misfit squatted down on the ground. "Watch them children, Bobby Lee," he said. "You know they make me nervous." He looked at the six of them huddled together in front of him and he seemed to be embarrassed as if he couldn't think of anything to say. "Ain't a cloud in the sky," he remarked, looking up at it. "Don't see no sun but don't see no cloud neither."

"Yes, it's a beautiful day," said the grandmother. "Listen," she said, "you shouldn't call yourself The Misfit because I know you're a good man at heart. I can just look at you and tell."

"Hush!" Bailey yelled. "Hush! Everybody shut up and let me handle this!" He was squatting in the position of a runner about to sprint forward but he didn't move.

"I pre-chate that, lady," The Misfit said and drew a little circle in the ground with the butt of his gun.

"It'll take a half a hour to fix this here car," Hiram called, looking over the raised hood of it.

"Well, first you and Bobby Lee get him and that little boy to step over yonder with you," The Misfit said, pointing to Bailey and John Wesley. "The boys want to ast you something," he said to Bailey. "Would you mind stepping back in them woods there with them?"

"Listen," Bailey began, "we're in a terrible predicament! Nobody realizes what this is," and his voice cracked. His eyes were as blue and intense as the parrots in his shirt and he remained perfectly still.

The grandmother reached up to adjust her hat brim as if she were going to the woods with him but it came off in her hand. She stood staring at it and after a second she let it fall on the ground. Hiram pulled Bailey up by the arm as if he were assisting an old man. John Wesley caught hold of his father's hand and Bobby Lee followed. They went off toward the woods and just as they reached the dark edge, Bailey turned and supporting himself against a gray naked pine trunk, he shouted, "I'll be back in a minute, Mamma, wait on me!"

"Come back this instant!" his mother shrilled but they all disappeared into the woods.

"Bailey Boy!" the grandmother called in a tragic voice but she found she was looking at The Misfit squatting on the ground in front of her. "I just know you're a good man," she said desperately. "You're not a bit common!"

"Nome, I ain't a good man," The Misfit said after a second as if he had considered her statement carefully, "but I ain't the worst in the world neither. My daddy said I was a different breed of dog from my brothers and sisters. 'You know,' Daddy said, 'it's some that can live their whole life out without asking about it and it's others has to know why it is, and this boy is one of the latters. He's going to be into everything!'" He put on his black hat and looked up suddenly and then away deep into the woods as if he were embarrassed again. "I'm sorry I don't have on a shirt before you ladies," he said, hunching his shoulders slightly. "We buried our clothes that we had on when we escaped and we're just making do until we can get better. We borrowed these from some folks we met," he explained.

"That's perfectly all right," the grandmother said. "Maybe Bailey has an extra shirt in his suitcase."

"I'll look and see terrectly," The Misfit said.

"Where are they taking him?" the children's mother screamed.

"Daddy was a card himself," The Misfit said. "You couldn't put anything over on him. He never got in trouble with the Authorities though. Just had the knack of handling them."

"You could be honest too if you'd only try," said the grandmother. "Think how wonderful it would be to settle down and live a comfortable life and not have to think about somebody chasing you all the time."

The Misfit kept scratching in the ground with the butt of his gun as if he were thinking about it. "Yes'm, somebody is always after you," he murmured.

The grandmother noticed how thin his shoulder blades were just behind his hat because she was standing up looking down on him. "Do you ever pray?" she asked.

He shook his head. All she saw was the black hat wiggle between his shoulder blades. "Nome," he said.

There was a pistol shot from the woods, followed closely by another. Then silence. The old lady's head jerked around. She could hear the wind move through the tree tops like a long satisfied insuck of breath. "Bailey Boy!" she called.

"I was a gospel singer for a while," The Misfit said. "I been most everything. Been in the arm service, both land and sea, at home and abroad, been twict married, been an undertaker, been with the railroads, plowed Mother Earth, been in a tornado, seen a man burnt alive oncet," and looked up at the children's mother and the little girl who were sitting close together, their faces white and their eyes glassy; "I even seen a woman flogged," he said.

110 "Pray, pray," the grandmother began, "pray, pray . . ."

"I never was a bad boy that I remember of," The Misfit said in an almost dreamy voice, "but somewheres along the line I done something wrong and got sent to the penitentiary. I was buried alive," and he looked up and held her attention to him by a steady stare.

"That's when you should have started to pray," she said. "What did you do to get sent to the penitentiary that first time?"

"Turn to the right, it was a wall," The Misfit said, looking up again at the cloudless sky. "Turn to the left, it was a wall. Look up it was a ceiling, look down it was a floor. I forgot what I done, lady. I set there and set there, trying to remember what it was I done and I ain't recalled it to this day. Oncet in a while, I would think it was coming to me, but it never come."

"Maybe they put you in by mistake," the old lady said vaguely.

115 "Nome," he said. "It wasn't no mistake. They had the papers on me."

"You must have stolen something," she said.

The Misfit sneered slightly. "Nobody had nothing I wanted," he said. "It was a head-doctor at the penitentiary said what I had done was kill my daddy but I known that for a lie. My daddy died in nineteen ought nineteen of the epidemic flu and I never had a thing to do with it. He was buried in the Mount Hopewell Baptist churchyard and you can go there and see for yourself."

"If you would pray," the old lady said, "Jesus would help you."

"That's right," The Misfit said.

120 "Well then, why don't you pray?" she asked trembling with delight suddenly.

"I don't want no hep," he said. "I'm doing all right by myself."

Bobby Lee and Hiram came ambling back from the woods. Bobby Lee was dragging a yellow shirt with bright blue parrots in it.

"Thow me that shirt, Bobby Lee," The Misfit said. The shirt came flying at him and landed on his shoulder and he put it on. The grandmother couldn't name what the shirt reminded her of. "No, lady," The Misfit said while he was buttoning it up, "I found out the crime don't matter. You can do one thing or you can do another, kill a man or take a tire off his car, because sooner or later you're going to forget what it was you done and just be punished for it."

The children's mother had begun to make heaving noises as if she couldn't get her breath. "Lady," he asked, "would you and that little girl like to step off yonder with Bobby Lee and Hiram and join your husband?"

125 "Yes, thank you," the mother said faintly. Her left arm dangled helplessly and she was holding the baby, who had gone to sleep, in the other. "Hep that lady

up, Hiram," The Misfit said as she struggled to climb out of the ditch, "and Bobby Lee, you hold onto that little girl's hand."

"I don't want to hold hands with him," June Star said. "He reminds me of a pig."

The fat boy blushed and laughed and caught her by the arm and pulled her off into the woods after Hiram and her mother.

Alone with The Misfit, the grandmother found that she had lost her voice. There was not a cloud in the sky nor any sun. There was nothing around her but woods. She wanted to tell him that he must pray. She opened and closed her mouth several times before anything came out. Finally she found herself saying, "Jesus, Jesus," meaning, Jesus will help you, but the way she was saying it, it sounded as if she might be cursing.

"Yes'm," The Misfit said as if he agreed. "Jesus thown everything off balance. It was the same case with Him as with me except He hadn't committed any crime and they could prove I had committed one because they had the papers on me. Of course," he said, "they never shown me my papers. That's why I sign myself now. I said long ago, you get you a signature and sign everything you do and keep a copy of it. Then you'll know what you done and you can hold up the crime to the punishment and see do they match and in the end you'll have something to prove you ain't been treated right. I call myself The Misfit," he said, "because I can't make what all I done wrong fit what all I gone through in punishment."

There was a piercing scream from the woods, followed closely by a pistol report. "Does it seem right to you, lady, that one is punished a heap and another ain't punished at all?"

"Jesus!" the old lady cried. "You've got good blood! I know you wouldn't shoot a lady! I know you come from nice people! Pray! Jesus, you ought not to shoot a lady. I'll give you all the money I've got!"

"Lady," The Misfit said, looking beyond her far into the woods, "there never was a body that give the undertaker a tip."

There were two more pistol reports and the grandmother raised her head like a parched old turkey hen crying for water and called, "Bailey Boy, Bailey Boy!" as if her heart would break.

"Jesus was the only One that ever raised the dead." The Misfit continued, "and He shouldn't have done it. He thown everything off balance. If He did what He said, then it's nothing for you to do but thow away everything and follow Him, and if He didn't, then it's nothing for you to do but enjoy the few minutes you got left the best way you can—by killing somebody or burning down his house or doing some other meanness to him. No pleasure but meanness," he said and his voice had become almost a snarl.

"Maybe He didn't raise the dead," the old lady mumbled, not knowing what she was saying and feeling so dizzy that she sank down in the ditch with her legs twisted under her.

"I wasn't there so I can't say He didn't," The Misfit said. "I wisht I had of been there," he said, hitting the ground with his fist. "It ain't right I wasn't there because if I had of been there I would of known. Listen lady," he said in a high voice, "if I had of been there I would of known and I wouldn't be like I am now." His voice seemed about to crack and the grandmother's head cleared for an instant. She saw the man's face twisted close to her own as if he were going to cry and she murmured, "Why you're one of my babies. You're one of my own children!" She reached out and touched him on the shoulder. The Misfit sprang back as if a snake had bitten him and shot her three times through the chest. Then he put his gun down on the ground and took off his glasses and began to clean them.

Hiram and Bobby Lee returned from the woods and stood over the ditch, looking down at the grandmother who half sat and half lay in a puddle of blood with her legs crossed under her like a child's and her face smiling up at the cloudless sky.

Without his glasses, The Misfit's eyes were red-rimmed and pale and defenseless-looking. "Take her off and thow her where you thown the others," he said, picking up the cat that was rubbing itself against his leg.

"She was a talker, wasn't she?" Bobby Lee said, sliding down the ditch with a yodel.

140 "She would of been a good woman," The Misfit said, "if it had been somebody there to shoot her every minute of her life."

"Some fun!" Bobby Lee said.

"Shut up, Bobby Lee," The Misfit said. "It's no real pleasure in life."

1953

## FLANNERY O'CONNOR

## *The Lame Shall Enter First*

Sheppard sat on a stool at the bar that divided the kitchen in half, eating his cereal out of the individual pasteboard box it came in. He ate mechanically, his eyes on the child, who was wandering from cabinet to cabinet in the panelled kitchen, collecting the ingredients for his breakfast. He was a stocky blond boy of ten. Sheppard kept his intense blue eyes fixed on him. The boy's future was written in his face. He would be a banker. No, worse. He would operate a small loan company. All he wanted for the child was that he be good and unselfish and neither seemed likely. Sheppard was a young man whose hair was already white. It stood up like a narrow brush halo over his pink sensitive face.

The boy approached the bar with the jar of peanut butter under his arm, a plate with a quarter of a small chocolate cake on it in one hand and the ketchup bottle in the other. He did not appear to notice his father. He climbed up on the stool and began to spread peanut butter on the cake. He had very large round ears that leaned away from his head and seemed to pull his eyes slightly too far apart. His shirt was green but so faded that the cowboy charging across the front of it was only a shadow.

"Norton," Sheppard said, "I saw Rufus Johnson yesterday. Do you know what he was doing?"

The child looked at him with a kind of half attention, his eyes forward but not yet engaged. They were a paler blue than his father's as if they might have faded like the shirt; one of them listed, almost imperceptibly, toward the outer rim.

5 "He was in an alley," Sheppard said, "and he had his hand in a garbage can.

He was trying to get something to eat out of it." He paused to let this soak in. "He was hungry," he finished, and tried to pierce the child's conscience with his gaze.

The boy picked up the piece of chocolate cake and began to gnaw it from one corner.

"Norton," Sheppard said, "do you have any idea what it means to share?"

A flicker of attention. "Some of it's yours," Norton said.

"Some of it's *his*," Sheppard said heavily. It was hopeless. Almost any fault would have been preferable to selfishness—a violent temper, even a tendency to lie.

The child turned the bottle of ketchup upside down and began thumping ketchup onto the cake.

Sheppard's look of pain increased. "You are ten and Rufus Johnson is fourteen," he said. "Yet I'm sure your shirts would fit Rufus." Rufus Johnson was a boy he had been trying to help at the reformatory for the past year. He had been released two months ago. "When he was in the reformatory, he looked pretty good, but when I saw him yesterday, he was skin and bones. He hasn't been eating cake with peanut butter on it for breakfast."

The child paused. "It's stale," he said. "That's why I have to put stuff on it."

Sheppard turned his face to the window at the end of the bar. The side lawn, green and even, sloped fifty feet or so down to a small suburban wood. When his wife was living, they had often eaten outside, even breakfast, on the grass. He had never noticed then that the child was selfish. "Listen to me," he said, turning back to him, "look at me and listen."

The boy looked at him. At least his eyes were forward.

"I gave Rufus a key to this house when he left the reformatory—to show my confidence in him and so he would have a place he could come to and feel welcome any time. He didn't use it, but I think he'll use it now because he's seen me and he's hungry. And if he doesn't use it, I'm going out and find him and bring him here. I can't see a child eating out of garbage cans."

The boy frowned. It was dawning upon him that something of his was threatened.

Sheppard's mouth stretched in disgust. "Rufus's father died before he was born," he said. "His mother is in the state penitentiary. He was raised by his grandfather in a shack without water or electricity and the old man beat him every day. How would you like to belong to a family like that?"

"I don't know," the child said lamely.

"Well, you might think about it sometime," Sheppard said.

Sheppard was City Recreational Director. On Saturdays he worked at the reformatory as a counselor, receiving nothing for it but the satisfaction of knowing he was helping boys no one else cared about. Johnson was the most intelligent boy he had worked with and the most deprived.

Norton turned what was left of the cake over as if he no longer wanted it.

"Maybe he won't come," the child said and his eyes brightened slightly.

"Think of everything you have that he doesn't!" Sheppard said. "Suppose you had to root in garbage cans for food? Suppose you had a huge swollen foot and one side of you dropped lower than the other when you walked?"

The boy looked blank, obviously unable to imagine such a thing.

"You have a healthy body," Sheppard said, "a good home. You've never been taught anything but the truth. Your daddy gives you everything you need and want. You don't have a grandfather who beats you. And your mother is not in the state penitentiary."

The child pushed his plate away. Sheppard groaned aloud.

A knot of flesh appeared below the boy's suddenly distorted mouth. His face became a mass of lumps with slits for eyes. "If she was in the penitentiary," he began in a kind of racking bellow, "I could go to seeeeee her." Tears rolled down his face and the ketchup dribbled on his chin. He looked as if he had been hit in the mouth. He abandoned himself and howled.

Sheppard sat helpless and miserable, like a man lashed by some elemental force of nature. This was not a normal grief. It was all part of his selfishness. She had been dead for over a year and a child's grief should not last so long. "You're going on eleven years old," he said reproachfully.

The child began an agonizing high-pitched heaving noise.

"If you stop thinking about yourself and think what you can do for somebody else," Sheppard said, "then you'll stop missing your mother."

The boy was silent but his shoulders continued to shake. Then his face collapsed and he began to howl again.

"Don't you think I'm lonely without her too?" Sheppard said. "Don't you think I miss her at all? I do, but I'm not sitting around moping. I'm busy helping other people. When do you see me just sitting around thinking about my troubles?"

The boy slumped as if he were exhausted but fresh tears streaked his face.

"What are you going to do today?" Sheppard asked, to get his mind on something else.

The child ran his arm across his eyes. "Sell seeds," he mumbled.

Always selling something. He had four quart jars full of nickels and dimes he had saved and he took them out of his closet every few days and counted them. "What are you selling seeds for?"

"To win a prize."

"What's the prize?"

"A thousand dollars."

"And what would you do if you had a thousand dollars?"

"Keep it," the child said and wiped his nose on his shoulder.

"I feel sure you would," Sheppard said. "Listen," he said and lowered his voice to an almost pleading tone, "suppose by some chance you did win a thousand dollars. Wouldn't you like to spend it on children less fortunate than yourself? Wouldn't you like to give some swings and trapezes to the orphanage? Wouldn't you like to buy poor Rufus Johnson a new shoe?"

The boy began to back away from the bar. Then suddenly he leaned forward and hung with his mouth open over his plate. Sheppard groaned again. Everything came up, the cake, the peanut butter, the ketchup—a limp sweet batter. He hung over it gagging, more came, and he waited with his mouth open over the plate as if he expected his heart to come up next.

"It's all right," Sheppard said, "it's all right. You couldn't help it. Wipe your mouth and go lie down."

The child hung there a moment longer. Then he raised his face and looked blindly at his father.

"Go on," Sheppard said. "Go on and lie down."

The boy pulled up the end of his t-shirt and smeared his mouth with it. Then he climbed down off the stool and wandered out of the kitchen.

Sheppard sat there staring at the puddle of half-digested food. The sour odor reached him and he drew back. His gorge rose. He got up and carried the plate to the sink and turned the water on it and watched grimly as the mess ran down the drain. Johnson's sad thin hand rooted in garbage cans for food while his own child, selfish, unresponsive, greedy, had so much that he threw it up. He cut off the faucet with a thrust of his fist. Johnson had a capacity for real response and had been deprived of everything from birth; Norton was average or below and had had every advantage.

He went back to the bar to finish his breakfast. The cereal was soggy in the cardboard box but he paid no attention to what he was eating. Johnson was worth any amount of effort because he had the potential. He had seen it from the time the boy had limped in for his first interview.

Sheppard's office at the reformatory was a narrow closet with one window and a small table and two chairs in it. He had never been inside a confessional but he thought it must be the same kind of operation he had here, except that he explained, he did not absolve. His credentials were less dubious than a priest's; he had been trained for what he was doing.

When Johnson came in for his first interview, he had been reading over the boy's record—senseless destruction, windows smashed, city trash boxes set afire, tires slashed—the kind of thing he found where boys had been transplanted abruptly from the country to the city as this one had. He came to Johnson's I. Q. score. It was 140. He raised his eyes eagerly.

The boy sat slumped on the edge of his chair, his arms hanging between his thighs. The light from the window fell on his face. His eyes, steel-colored and very still, were trained narrowly forward. His thin dark hair hung in a flat forelock across the side of his forehead, not carelessly like a boy's, but fiercely like an old man's. A kind of fanatic intelligence was palpable in his face.

Sheppard smiled to diminish the distance between them.

The boy's expression did not soften. He leaned back in his chair and lifted a monstrous club foot to his knee. The foot was in a heavy black battered shoe with a sole four or five inches thick. The leather parted from it in one place and the end of an empty sock protruded like a gray tongue from a severed head. The case was clear to Sheppard instantly. His mischief was compensation for the foot.

"Well Rufus," he said, "I see by the record here that you don't have but a year to serve. What do you plan to do when you get out?"

"I don't make no plans," the boy said. His eyes shifted indifferently to something outside the window behind Sheppard in the far distance.

"Maybe you ought to," Sheppard said and smiled.

Johnson continued to gaze beyond him.

"I want to see you make the most of your intelligence," Sheppard said. "What's most important to you? Let's talk about what's important to *you*." His eyes dropped involuntarily to the foot.

"Study it and git your fill," the boy drawled.

Sheppard reddened. The black deformed mass swelled before his eyes. He ignored the remark and the leer the boy was giving him. "Rufus," he said, "you've got into a lot of senseless trouble but I think when you understand why you do these things, you'll be less inclined to do them." He smiled. They had so few friends, saw so few pleasant faces, that half his effectiveness came from nothing more than smiling at them. "There are a lot of things about yourself that I think I can explain to you," he said.

Johnson looked at him stonily. "I ain't asked for no explanation," he said. "I already know why I do what I do."

"Well good!" Sheppard said. "Suppose you tell me what's made you do the things you've done?"

A black sheen appeared in the boy's eyes. "Satan," he said. "He has me in his power."

65     Sheppard looked at him steadily. There was no indication on the boy's face that he had said this to be funny. The line of his thin mouth was set with pride. Sheppard's eyes hardened. He felt a momentary dull despair as if he were faced with some elemental warping of nature that had happened too long ago to be corrected now. This boy's questions about life had been answered by signs nailed on the pine trees: DOES SATAN HAVE YOU IN HIS POWER? REPENT OR BURN IN HELL. JESUS SAVES. He would know the Bible with or without reading it. His despair gave way to outrage. "Rubbish!" he snorted. "We're living in the space age! You're too smart to give me an answer like that."

Johnson's mouth twisted slightly. His look was contemptuous but amused. There was a glint of challenge in his eyes.

Sheppard scrutinized his face. Where there was intelligence anything was possible. He smiled again, a smile that was like an invitation to the boy to come into a school room with all its windows thrown open to the light. "Rufus," he said, "I'm going to arrange for you to have a conference with me once a week. Maybe there's an explanation for your explanation. Maybe I can explain your devil to you."

After that he had talked to Johnson every Saturday for the rest of the year. He talked at random, the kind of talk the boy would never have heard before. He talked a little above him to give him something to reach for. He roamed from simple psychology and the dodges of the human mind to astronomy and the space capsules that were whirling around the earth faster than the speed of sound and would soon encircle the stars. Instinctively he concentrated on the stars. He wanted to give the boy something to reach for besides his neighbor's goods. He wanted to stretch his horizons. He wanted him to *see* the universe, to see that the darkest parts of it could be penetrated. He would have given anything to be able to put a telescope in Johnson's hands.

Johnson said little and what he did say, for the sake of his pride, was in dissent or senseless contradiction, with the clubfoot raised always to his knee like a weapon ready for use, but Sheppard was not deceived. He watched his eyes and every week he saw something in them crumble. From the boy's face, hard but shocked, braced against the light that was ravaging him, he could see that he was hitting dead center.

70     Johnson was free now to live out of garbage cans and rediscover his old ignorance. The injustice of it was infuriating. He had been sent back to the grandfather; the old man's imbecility could only be imagined. Perhaps the boy had by now run away from him. The idea of getting custody of Johnson had occurred to Sheppard before, but the fact of the grandfather had stood in the way. Nothing excited him so much as thinking what he could do for such a boy. First he would

have him fitted for a new orthopedic shoe. His back was thrown out of line every time he took a step. Then he would encourage him in some particular intellectual interest. He thought of the telescope. He could buy a second-hand one and they could set it up in the attic window. He sat for almost ten minutes thinking what he could do if he had Johnson here with him. What was wasted on Norton would cause Johnson to flourish. Yesterday when he had seen him with his hand in the garbage can, he had waved and started forward. Johnson had seen him, paused a split-second, then vanished with the swiftness of a rat, but not before Sheppard had seen his expression change. Something had kindled in the boy's eyes, he was sure of it, some memory of the lost light.

He got up and threw the cereal box in the garbage. Before he left the house, he looked into Norton's room to be sure he was not still sick. The child was sitting cross-legged on his bed. He had emptied the quart jars of change into one large pile in front of him, and was sorting it out by nickels and dimes and quarters.

That afternoon Norton was alone in the house, squatting on the floor of his room arranging packages of flower seeds in rows around himself. Rain slashed against the window panes and rattled in the gutters. The room had grown dark but every few minutes it was lit by silent lightning and the seed packages showed up gaily on the floor. He squatted motionless like a large pale frog in the midst of this potential garden. All at once his eyes became alert. Without warning the rain had stopped. The silence was heavy as if the downpour had been hushed by violence. He remained motionless, only his eyes turning.

Into the silence came the distinct click of a key turning in the front door lock. The sound was a very deliberate one. It drew attention to itself and held it as if it were controlled more by a mind than by a hand. The child leapt up and got into the closet.

The footsteps began to move in the hall. They were deliberate and irregular, a light and then a heavy one, then a silence as if the visitor had paused to listen himself or to examine something. In a minute the kitchen door screeked. The footsteps crossed the kitchen to the refrigerator. The closet wall and the kitchen wall were the same. Norton stood with his ear pressed against it. The refrigerator door opened. There was a prolonged silence.

He took off his shoes and then tiptoed out of the closet and stepped over the seed packages. In the middle of the room, he stopped and remained where he was, rigid. A thin bony-face boy in a wet black suit stood in his door, blocking his escape. His hair was flattened to his skull by the rain. He stood there like an irate drenched crow. His look went through the child like a pin and paralyzed him. Then his eyes began to move over everything in the room—the unmade bed, the dirty curtains on the one large window, a photograph of a wide-faced young woman that stood up in the clutter on top of the dresser.

The child's tongue suddenly went wild. "He's been expecting you, he's going to give you a new shoe because you have to eat out of garbage cans!" he said in a kind of mouse-like shriek.

"I eat out of garbage cans," the boy said slowly with a beady stare, "because I like to eat out of garbage cans. See?"

The child nodded.

"And I got ways of getting my own shoe. See?"

The child nodded, mesmerized.

The boy limped in and sat down on the bed. He arranged a pillow behind him and stretched his short leg out so that the big black shoe rested conspicuously on a fold of the sheet.

Norton's gaze settled on it and remained immobile. The sole was as thick as a brick.

Johnson wiggled it slightly and smiled. "If I kick somebody *once* with this," he said, "it learns them not to mess with me."

The child nodded.

"Go in the kitchen," Johnson said, "and make me a sandwich with some of that rye bread and ham and bring me a glass of milk."

Norton went off like a mechanical toy, pushed in the right direction. He made a large greasy sandwich with ham hanging out the sides of it and poured out a glass of milk. Then he returned to the room with the glass of milk in one hand and the sandwich in the other.

Johnson was leaning back regally against the pillow. "Thanks, waiter," he said and took the sandwich.

Norton stood by the side of the bed, holding the glass.

The boy tore into the sandwich and ate steadily until he finished it. Then he took the glass of milk. He held it with both hands like a child and when he lowered it for breath, there was a rim of milk around his mouth. He handed Norton the empty glass. "Go get me one of them oranges in there, waiter," he said hoarsely.

Norton went to the kitchen and returned with the orange. Johnson peeled it with his fingers and let the peeling drop in the bed. He ate it slowly, spitting the seeds out in front of him. When he finished, he wiped his hands on the sheet and gave Norton a long appraising stare. He appeared to have been softened by the service. "You're his kid all right," he said. "You got the same stupid face."

The child stood there stolidly as if he had not heard.

"He don't know his left hand from his right," Johnson said with a hoarse pleasure in his voice.

The child cast his eyes a little to the side of the boy's face and looked fixedly at the wall.

"Yaketty yaketty yak," Johnson said, "and never says a thing."

The child's upper lip lifted slightly but he didn't say anything.

"Gas," Johnson said. "Gas."

The child's face began to have a wary look of belligerence. He backed away slightly as if he were prepared to retreat instantly. "He's good," he mumbled. "He helps people."

"Good!" Johnson said savagely. He thrust his head forward. "Listen here," he hissed, "I don't care if he's good or not. He ain't *right!*"

Norton looked stunned.

The screen door in the kitchen banged and someone entered. Johnson sat forward instantly. "Is that him?" he said.

"It's the cook," Norton said. "She comes in the afternoon."

Johnson got up and limped into the hall and stood in the kitchen door and Norton followed him.

The colored girl was at the closet taking off a bright red raincoat. She was a tall light-yellow girl with a mouth like a large rose that had darkened and wilted.

Her hair was dressed in tiers on top of her head and leaned to the side like the Tower of Pisa.

Johnson made a noise through his teeth. "Well look at Aunt Jemima," he said.

The girl paused and trained an insolent gaze on them. They might have been dust on the floor.

"Come on," Johnson said, "let's see what all you got besides a nigger." He opened the first door to his right in the hall and looked into a pink-tiled bathroom. "A pink can!" he murmured.

He turned a comical face to the child. "Does he sit on that?"

"It's for company," Norton said, "but he sits on it sometimes."

"He ought to empty his head in it," Johnson said.

The door was open to the next room. It was the room Sheppard had slept in since his wife died. An ascetic-looking iron bed stood on the bare floor. A heap of Little League baseball uniforms was piled in one corner. Papers were scattered over a large roll-top desk and held down in various places by his pipes. Johnson stood looking into the room silently. He wrinkled his nose. "Guess who?" he said.

The door to the next room was closed but Johnson opened it and thrust his head into the semi-darkness within. The shades were down and the air was close with a faint scent of perfume in it. There was a wide antique bed and a mammoth dresser whose mirror glinted in the half light. Johnson snapped the light switch by the door and crossed the room to the mirror and peered into it. A silver comb and brush lay on the linen runner. He picked up the comb and began to run it through his hair. He combed it straight down on his forehead. Then he swept it to the side, Hitler fashion.

"Leave her comb alone!" the child said. He stood in the door, pale and breathing heavily as if he were watching sacrilege in a holy place.

Johnson put the comb down and picked up the brush and gave his hair a swipe with it.

"She's dead," the child said.

"I ain't afraid of dead people's things," Johnson said. He opened the top drawer and slid his hand in.

"Take your big fat dirty hands off my mother's clothes!" the child said in a high suffocated voice.

"Keep your shirt on, sweetheart," Johnson murmured. He pulled up a wrinkled red polka dot blouse and dropped it back. Then he pulled out a green silk kerchief and whirled it over his head and let it float to the floor. His hand continued to plow deep into the drawer. After a moment it came up gripping a faded corset with four dangling metal supporters. "Thisyer must be her saddle," he observed.

He lifted it gingerly and shook it. Then he fastened it around his waist and jumped up and down, making the metal supporters dance. He began to snap his fingers and turn his hips from side to side. "Gonter rock, rattle and roll," he sang. "Gonter rock, rattle and roll. Can't please that woman, to save my doggone soul." He began to move around, stamping the good foot down and slinging the heavy one to the side. He danced out the door, past the stricken child and down the hall toward the kitchen.

A half hour later Sheppard came home. He dropped his raincoat on a chair in the hall and came as far as the parlor door and stopped. His face was suddenly transformed. It shone with pleasure. Johnson sat, a dark figure, in a high-backed pink upholstered chair. The wall behind him was lined with books from floor to ceiling. He was reading one. Sheppard's eyes narrowed. It was a volume of the Encyclopedia Britannica. He was so engrossed in it that he did not look up. Sheppard held his breath. This was the perfect setting for the boy. He had to keep him here. He had to manage it somehow.

"Rufus!" he said, "it's good to see you boy!" and he bounded forward with his arm outstretched.

Johnson looked up, his face blank. "Oh hello," he said. He ignored the hand as long as he was able but when Sheppard did not withdraw it, he grudgingly shook it.

Sheppard was prepared for this kind of reaction. It was part of Johnson's make-up never to show enthusiasm.

"How are things?" he said. "How's your grandfather treating you?" He sat down on the edge of the sofa.

"He dropped dead," the boy said indifferently.

"You don't mean it!" Sheppard cried. He got up and sat down on the coffee table nearer the boy.

"Naw," Johnson said, "he ain't dropped dead. I wisht he had."

"Well where is he?" Sheppard muttered.

"He's gone with a remnant to the hills," Johnson said. "Him and some others. They're going to bury some Bibles in a cave and take two of different kinds of animals and all like that. Like Noah. Only this time it's going to be fire, not flood."

Sheppard's mouth stretched wryly. "I see," he said. Then he said, "In other words the old fool has abandoned you?"

"He ain't no fool," the boy said in an indignant tone.

"Has he abandoned you or not?" Sheppard asked impatiently.

The boy shrugged.

"Where's your probation officer?"

"I ain't supposed to keep up with him," Johnson said. "He's supposed to keep up with me."

Sheppard laughed. "Wait a minute," he said. He got up and went into the hall and got his raincoat off the chair and took it to the hall closet to hang it up. He had to give himself time to think, to decide how he could ask the boy so that he would stay. He couldn't force him to stay. It would have to be voluntary. Johnson pretended not to like him. That was only to uphold his pride, but he would have to ask him in such a way that his pride could still be upheld. He opened the closet door and took out a hanger. An old gray winter coat of his wife's still hung there. He pushed it aside but it didn't move. He pulled it open roughly and winced as if he had seen the larva inside a cocoon. Norton stood in it, his face swollen and pale, with a drugged look of misery on it. Sheppard stared at him. Suddenly he was confronted with a possibility. "Get out of there," he said. He caught him by the shoulder and propelled him firmly into the parlor and over to the pink chair where Johnson was sitting with the encyclopedia in his lap. He was going to risk everything in one blow.

"Rufus," he said, "I've got a problem. I need your help."

Johnson looked up suspiciously.

"Listen," Sheppard said, "we need another boy in the house." There was a genuine desperation in his voice. "Norton here has never had to divide anything in his life. He doesn't know what it means to share. And I need somebody to teach him. How about helping me out? Stay here for a while with us, Rufus. I need your help." The excitement in his voice made it thin.

The child suddenly came to life. His face swelled with fury. "He went in her room and used her comb!" he screamed, yanking Sheppard's arm. "He put on her corset and danced with Leola, he . . ."

"Stop this!" Sheppard said sharply. "Is tattling all you're capable of? I'm not asking you for a report on Rufus's conduct. I'm asking you to make him welcome here. Do you understand?"

"You see how it is?" he asked, turning to Johnson.

Norton kicked the leg of the pink chair viciously, just missing Johnson's swollen foot. Sheppard yanked him back.

"He said you weren't nothing but gas!" the child shrieked.

A sly look of pleasure crossed Johnson's face.

Sheppard was not put back. These insults were part of the boy's defensive mechanism. "What about it, Rufus?" he said. "Will you stay with us for a while?"

Johnson looked straight in front of him and said nothing. He smiled slightly and appeared to gaze upon some vision of the future that pleased him.

"I don't care," he said and turned a page of the encyclopedia. "I can stand anywhere."

"Wonderful." Sheppard said. "Wonderful."

"He said," the child said in a throaty whisper, "you didn't know your left hand from your right."

There was a silence.

Johnson wet his finger and turned another page of the encyclopedia.

"I have something to say to both of you," Sheppard said in a voice without inflection. His eyes moved from one to the other of them and he spoke slowly as if what he was saying he would say only once and it behooved them to listen. "If it made any difference to me what Rufus thinks of me," he said, "then I wouldn't be asking him here. Rufus is going to help me out and I'm going to help him out and we're both going to help you out. I'd simply be selfish if I let what Rufus thinks of me interfere with what I can do for Rufus. If I can help a person, all I want is to do it. I'm above and beyond simple pettiness."

Neither of them made a sound. Norton stared at the chair cushion. Johnson peered closer at some fine print in the encyclopedia. Sheppard was looking at the tops of their heads. He smiled. After all, he had won. The boy was staying. He reached out and ruffled Norton's hair and slapped Johnson on the shoulder. "Now you fellows sit here and get acquainted," he said gaily and started toward the door. "I'm going to see what Leola left us for supper."

When he was gone, Johnson raised his head and looked at Norton. The child looked back at him bleakly. "God, kid," Johnson said in a cracked voice, "how do you stand it?" His face was stiff with outrage. "He thinks he's Jesus Christ!"

II

Sheppard's attic was a large unfinished room with exposed beams and no electric light. They had set the telescope up on a tripod in one of the dormer windows. It pointed now toward the dark sky where a sliver of moon, as fragile as an egg shell, had just emerged from behind a cloud with a brilliant silver edge. Inside, a kerosene lantern set on a trunk cast their shadows upward and tangled them, wavering slightly, in the joints overhead. Sheppard was sitting on a packing box, looking through the telescope, and Johnson was at his elbow, waiting to get at it. Sheppard had bought it for fifteen dollars two days before at a pawn shop.

"Quit hoggin it," Johnson said.

Sheppard got up and Johnson slid onto the box and put his eye to the instrument.

Sheppard sat down on a straight chair a few feet away. His face was flushed with pleasure. This much of his dream was a reality. Within a week he had made it possible for this boy's vision to pass through a slender channel to the stars. He looked at Johnson's bent back with complete satisfaction. The boy had on one of Norton's plaid shirts and some new khaki trousers he had bought him. The shoe would be ready next week. He had taken him to the brace shop the day after he came and had him fitted for a new shoe. Johnson was as touchy about the foot as if it were a sacred object. His face had been glum while the clerk, a young man with a bright pink bald head, measured the foot with his profane hands. The shoe was going to make the greatest difference in the boy's attitude. Even a child with normal feet was in love with the world after he had got a new pair of shoes. When Norton got a new pair, he walked around for days with his eyes on his feet.

Sheppard glanced across the room at the child. He was sitting on the floor against a trunk, trussed up in a rope he had found and wound around his legs from his ankles to his knees. He appeared so far away that Sheppard might have been looking at him through the wrong end of the telescope. He had had to whip him only once since Johnson had been with them—the first night when Norton had realized that Johnson was going to sleep in his mother's bed. He did not believe in whipping children, particularly in anger. In this case, he had done both and with good results. He had had no more trouble with Norton.

The child hadn't shown any positive generosity toward Johnson but what he couldn't help, he appeared to be resigned to. In the mornings Sheppard sent the two of them to the Y swimming pool, gave them money to get their lunch at the cafeteria and instructed them to meet him in the park in the afternoon to watch his Little League baseball practice. Every afternoon they had arrived at the park, shambling, silent, their faces closed each on his own thoughts as if neither were aware of the other's existence. At least he could be thankful there were no fights.

Norton showed no interest in the telescope. "Don't you want to get up and look through the telescope, Norton?" he said. It irritated him that the child showed no intellectual curiosity whatsoever. "Rufus is going to be way ahead of you."

Norton leaned forward absently and looked at Johnson's back.

Johnson turned around from the instrument. His face had begun to fill out again. The look of outrage had retreated from his hollow cheeks and was shored up now in the caves of his eyes, like a fugitive from Sheppard's kindness. "Don't waste your valuable time, kid," he said. "You seen the moon once, you seen it."

Sheppard was amused by these sudden turns of perversity. The boy resisted whatever he suspected was meant for his improvement and contrived when he was vitally interested in something to leave the impression he was bored. Sheppard was not deceived. Secretly Johnson was learning what he wanted him to learn—that his benefactor was impervious to insult and that there were no cracks in his armor of kindness and patience where a successful shaft could be driven. "Some day you may go to the moon," he said. "In ten years men will probably be making round trips there on schedule. Why you boys may be spacemen. Astronauts!"

"Astro-nuts," Johnson said.

"Nuts or nauts," Sheppard said, "it's perfectly possible that you, Rufus Johnson, will go to the moon."

Something in the depths of Johnson's eyes stirred. All day his humor had been glum. "I ain't going to the moon and get there alive," he said, "and when I die I'm going to hell."

"It's at least possible to get to the moon," Sheppard said dryly. The best way to handle this kind of thing was with gentle ridicule. "We can see it. We know it's there. Nobody has given any reliable evidence there's a hell."

"The Bible has give the evidence," Johnson said darkly, "and if you die and go there you burn forever."

The child leaned forward.

"Whoever says it ain't a hell," Johnson said, "is contradicting Jesus. The dead are judged and the wicked are damned. They weep and gnash their teeth while they burn," he continued, "and it's everlasting darkness."

The child's mouth opened. His eyes appeared to grow hollow.

"Satan runs it," Johnson said.

Norton lurched up and took a hobbled step toward Sheppard. "Is she there?" he said in a loud voice. "Is she there burning up?" He kicked the rope off his feet. "Is she on fire?"

"Oh my God," Sheppard muttered. "No no," he said, "of course she isn't. Rufus is mistaken. Your mother isn't anywhere. She's not unhappy. She just isn't." His lot would have been easier if when his wife died he had told Norton she had gone to heaven and that some day he would see her again, but he could not allow himself to bring him up on a lie.

Norton's face began to twist. A knot formed in his chin.

"Listen," Sheppard said quickly and pulled the child to him, "your mother's spirit lives on in other people and it'll live on in you if you're good and generous like she was."

The child's pale eyes hardened in disbelief.

Sheppard's pity turned to revulsion. The boy would rather she be in hell than nowhere. "Do you understand?" he said. "She doesn't exist." He put his hand on the child's shoulder. "That's all I have to give you," he said in a softer, exasperated tone, "the truth."

Instead of howling, the boy wrenched himself away and caught Johnson by the sleeve. "Is she there, Rufus?" he said. "Is she there, burning up?"

Johnson's eyes glittered. "Well," he said, "she is if she was evil. Was she a whore?"

"Your mother was not a whore," Sheppard said sharply. He had the sensation of driving a car without brakes. "Now let's have no more of this foolishness. We were talking about the moon."

"Did she believe in Jesus?" Johnson asked.

Norton looked blank. After a second he said, "Yes," as if he saw that this was necessary. "She did," he said. "All the time."

"She did not," Sheppard muttered.

"She did all the time," Norton said. "I heard her say she did all the time."

"She's saved," Johnson said.

The child still looked puzzled. "Where?" he said. "Where is she at?"

"On high," Johnson said.

"Where's that?" Norton gasped.

"It's in the sky somewhere," Johnson said, "but you got to be dead to get there. You can't go in no space ship." There was a narrow gleam in his eyes now like a beam holding steady on its target.

"Man's going to the moon," Sheppard said grimly, "is very much like the first fish crawling out of the water onto land billions and billions of years ago. He didn't have an earth suit. He had to grow his adjustments inside. He developed lungs."

"When I'm dead will I go to hell or where she is?" Norton asked.

"Right now you'd go where she is," Johnson said, "but if you live long enough, you'll go to hell."

Sheppard rose abruptly and picked up the lantern. "Close the window, Rufus," he said. "It's time we went to bed."

On the way down the attic stairs he heard Johnson say in a loud whisper behind him, "I'll tell you all about it tomorrow, kid, when Himself has cleared out."

The next day when the boys came to the ball park, he watched them as they came from behind the bleachers and around the edge of the field. Johnson's hand was on Norton's shoulder, his head bent toward the younger boy's ear, and on the child's face there was a look of complete confidence, of dawning light. Sheppard's grimace hardened. This would be Johnson's way of trying to annoy him. But he would not be annoyed. Norton was not bright enough to be damaged much. He gazed at the child's dull absorbed little face. Why try to make him superior? Heaven and hell were for the mediocre, and he was that if he was anything.

The two boys came into the bleachers and sat down about ten feet away, facing him, but neither gave him any sign of recognition. He cast a glance behind him where the Little Leaguers were spread out in the field. Then he started for the bleachers. The hiss of Johnson's voice stopped as he approached.

"What have you fellows been doing today?" he asked genially.

"He's been telling me . . ." Norton started.

Johnson pushed the child in the ribs with his elbow. "We ain't been doing nothing," he said. His face appeared to be covered with a blank glaze but through it a look of complicity was blazoned forth insolently.

Sheppard felt his face grow warm, but he said nothing. A child in a Little League uniform had followed him and was nudging him in the back of the leg with a bat. He turned and put his arm around the boy's neck and went with him back to the game.

That night when he went to the attic to join the boys at the telescope, he found Norton there alone. He was sitting on the packing box, hunched over, looking intently through the instrument. Johnson was not there.

"Where's Rufus?" Sheppard asked.

"I said where's Rufus?" he said louder.

"Gone somewhere," the child said without turning around.

"Gone where?" Sheppard asked.

"He just said he was going somewhere. He said he was fed up looking at stars."

"I see," Sheppard said glumly. He turned and went back down the stairs. He searched the house without finding Johnson. Then he went to the living room and sat down. Yesterday he had been convinced of his success with the boy. Today he faced the possibility that he was failing with him. He had been over-lenient, too concerned to have Johnson like him. He felt a twinge of guilt. What difference did it make if Johnson liked him or not? What was that to him? When the boy came in, they would have a few things understood. As long as you stay here there'll be no going out at night by yourself, do you understand?

I don't have to stay here. It ain't nothing to me staying here.

Oh my God, he thought. He could not bring it to that. He would have to be firm but not make an issue of it. He picked up the evening paper. Kindness and patience were always called for but he had not been firm enough. He sat holding the paper but not reading it. The boy would not respect him unless he showed firmness. The doorbell rang and he went to answer it. He opened it and stepped back, with a pained disappointed face.

A large dour policeman stood on the stoop, holding Johnson by the elbow. At the curb a patrol car waited. Johnson looked very white. His jaw was thrust forward as if to keep from trembling.

"We brought him here first because he raised such a fit," the policeman said, "but now that you've seen him, we're going to take him to the station and ask him a few questions."

"What happened?" Sheppard muttered.

"A house around the corner from here," the policeman said. "A real smash job, dishes broken all over the floor, furniture turned upside down..."

"I didn't have a thing to do with it!" Johnson said. "I was walking along minding my own bidnis when this cop came up and grabbed me."

Sheppard looked at the boy grimly. He made no effort to soften his expression.

Johnson flushed. "I was just walking along," he muttered, but with no conviction in his voice.

"Come on, bud," the policeman said.

"You ain't going to let him take me, are you?" Johnson said. "You believe me, don't you?" There was an appeal in his voice that Sheppard had not heard there before.

This was crucial. The boy would have to learn that he could not be protected when he was guilty. "You'll have to go with him, Rufus," he said.

"You're going to let him take me and I tell you I ain't done a thing?" Johnson said shrilly.

Sheppard's face became harder as his sense of injury grew. The boy had failed him even before he had had a chance to give him the shoe. They were to have got it tomorrow. All his regret turned suddenly on the shoe; his irritation at the sight of Johnson doubled.

"You made out like you had all this confidence in me," the boy mumbled.

"I did have," Sheppard said. His face was wooden.

Johnson turned away with the policeman but before he moved, a gleam of pure hatred flashed toward Sheppard from the pits of his eyes.

Sheppard stood in the door and watched them get into the patrol car and drive away. He summoned his compassion. He would go to the station tomorrow and see what he could do about getting him out of trouble. The night in jail would not hurt him and the experience would teach him that he could not treat with impunity someone who had shown him nothing but kindness. Then they would go get the shoe and perhaps after a night in jail it would mean even more to the boy.

The next morning at eight o'clock the police sergeant called and told him he could come pick Johnson up. "We booked a nigger on that charge," he said. "Your boy didn't have nothing to do with it."

Sheppard was at the station in ten minutes, his face hot with shame. Johnson sat slouched on a bench in a drab outer office, reading a police magazine. There was no one else in the room. Sheppard sat down beside him and put his hand tentatively on his shoulder.

230   The boy glanced up—his lip curled—and back to the magazine.

Sheppard felt physically sick. The ugliness of what he had done bore in upon him with a sudden dull intensity. He had failed him at just the point where he might have turned him once and for all in the right direction. "Rufus," he said, "I apologize. I was wrong and you were right. I misjudged you."

The boy continued to read.

"I'm sorry."

The boy wet his finger and turned a page.

235   Sheppard braced himself. "I was a fool, Rufus," he said.

Johnson's mouth slid slightly to the side. He shrugged without raising his head from the magazine.

"Will you forget it, this time?" Sheppard said. "It won't happen again."

The boy looked up. His eyes were bright and unfriendly. "I'll forget it," he said, "but you better remember it." He got up and stalked toward the door. In the middle of the room he turned and jerked his arm at Sheppard and Sheppard jumped up and followed him as if the boy had yanked an invisible leash.

"Your shoe," he said eagerly, "today is the day to get your shoe!" Thank God for the shoe!

240   But when they went to the brace shop, they found that the shoe had been made two sizes too small and a new one would not be ready for another ten days. Johnson's temper improved at once. The clerk had obviously made a mistake in the measurements but the boy insisted the foot had grown. He left the shop with a pleased expression, as if, in expanding, the foot had acted on some inspiration of its own. Sheppard's face was haggard.

After this he redoubled his efforts. Since Johnson had lost interest in the telescope, he bought a microscope and a box of prepared slides. If he couldn't impress the boy with immensity, he would try the infinitesimal. For two nights Johnson appeared absorbed in the new instrument, then he abruptly lost interest in it, but he seemed content to sit in the living room in the evening and read the encyclopedia. He devoured the encyclopedia as he devoured his dinner, steadily and without dint to his appetite. Each subject appeared to enter his head, be ravaged, and thrown out. Nothing pleased Sheppard more than to see the boy slouched on the sofa, his mouth shut, reading. After they had spent two or three evenings like this, he began to recover his vision. His confidence returned. He knew that some day he would be proud of Johnson.

On Thursday night Sheppard attended a city council meeting. He dropped the boys off at a movie on his way and picked them up on his way back. When they reached home, an automobile with a single red eye above its windshield was waiting in front of the house. Sheppard's lights as he turned into the driveway illuminated two dour faces in the car.

"The cops!" Johnson said. "Some nigger has broke in somewhere and they've come for me again."

"We'll see about that," Sheppard muttered. He stopped the car in the driveway and switched off the lights. "You boys go in the house and go to bed," he said. "I'll handle this."

He got out and strode toward the squad car. He thrust his head in the window. The two policemen were looking at him with silent knowledgeable faces. "A house on the corner of Shelton and Mills," the one in the driver's seat said. "It looks like a train run through it."

"He was in the picture show downtown," Sheppard said. "My boy was with him. He had nothing to do with the other one and he had nothing to do with this one. I'll be responsible."

"If I was you," the one nearest him said, "I wouldn't be responsible for any little bastard like him."

"I said I'd be responsible," Sheppard repeated coldly. "You people made a mistake the last time. Don't make another."

The policemen looked at each other. "It ain't our funeral," the one in the driver's seat said, and turned the key in the ignition.

Sheppard went in the house and sat down in the living room in the dark. He did not suspect Johnson and he did not want the boy to think he did. If Johnson thought he suspected him again, he would lose everything. But he wanted to know if his alibi was airtight. He thought of going to Norton's room and asking him if Johnson had left the movie. But that would be worse. Johnson would know what he was doing and would be incensed. He decided to ask Johnson himself. He would be direct. He went over in his mind what he was going to say and then he got up and went to the boy's door.

It was open as if he had been expected but Johnson was in bed. Just enough light came in from the hall for Sheppard to see his shape under the sheet. He came in and stood at the foot of the bed. "They've gone," he said. "I told them you had nothing to do with it and that I'd be responsible."

There was a muttered "Yeah," from the pillow.

Sheppard hesitated. "Rufus," he said, "you didn't leave the movie for anything at all, did you?"

"You make out like you got all this confidence in me!" a sudden outraged voice cried, "and you ain't got any! You don't trust me no more now than you did then!" The voice, disembodied, seemed to come more surely from the depths of Johnson than when his face was visible. It was a cry of reproach, edged slightly with contempt.

"I do have confidence in you," Sheppard said intensely. "I have every confidence in you. I believe in you and I trust you completely."

"You got your eye on me all the time," the voice said sullenly. "When you get through asking me a bunch of questions, you're going across the hall and ask Norton a bunch of them."

"I have no intention of asking Norton anything and never did," Sheppard said gently. "And I don't suspect you at all. You could hardly have got from the picture show downtown and out here to break in a house and back to the picture show in the time you had."

"That's why you believe me!" the boy cried, "—because you think I couldn't have done it."

"No, no!" Sheppard said. "I believe you because I believe you've got the brains and the guts not to get in trouble again. I believe you know yourself well enough now to know that you don't have to do such things. I believe that you can make anything of yourself that you set your mind to."

260   Johnson sat up. A faint light shone on his forehead but the rest of his face was invisible. "And I could have broke in there if I'd wanted to in the time I had," he said.

"But I know you didn't," Sheppard said. "There's not the least trace of doubt in my mind."

There was a silence. Johnson lay back down. Then the voice, low and hoarse, as if it were being forced out with difficulty, said, "You don't want to steal and smash up things when you've got everything you want already."

Sheppard caught his breath. The boy was thanking him! He was thanking him! There was gratitude in his voice. There was appreciation. He stood there, smiling foolishly in the dark, trying to hold the moment in suspension. Involuntarily he took a step toward the pillow and stretched out his hand and touched Johnson's forehead. It was cold and dry like rusty iron.

"I understand. Good night, son," he said and turned quickly and left the room. He closed the door behind him and stood there, overcome with emotion.

265   Across the hall Norton's door was open. The child lay on the bed on his side, looking into the light from the hall.

After this, the road with Johnson would be smooth.

Norton sat up and beckoned to him.

He saw the child but after the first instant, he did not let his eyes focus directly on him. He could not go in and talk to Norton without breaking Johnson's trust. He hesitated, but remained where he was a moment as if he saw nothing. Tomorrow was the day they were to go back for the shoe. It would be a climax to the good feeling between them. He turned quickly and went back into his own room.

The child sat for some time looking at the spot where his father had stood. Finally his gaze became aimless and he lay back down.

270   The next day Johnson was glum and silent as if he were ashamed that he had revealed himself. His eyes had a hooded look. He seemed to have retired within himself and there to be going through some crisis of determination. Sheppard could not get to the brace shop quickly enough. He left Norton at home because he did not want his attention divided. He wanted to be free to observe Johnson's reaction minutely. The boy did not seem pleased or even interested in the prospect of the shoe, but when it became an actuality, certainly then he would be moved.

The brace shop was a small concrete warehouse lined and stacked with the equipment of affliction. Wheel chairs and walkers covered most of the floor. The walls were hung with every kind of crutch and brace. Artificial limbs were stacked on the shelves, legs and arms and hands, claws and hooks, straps and human harnesses and unidentifiable instruments for unnamed deformities. In a small clearing in the middle of the room there was a row of yellow plastic-cushioned chairs and a shoe-fitting stool. Johnson slouched down in one of the chairs and set his foot up on the stool and sat with his eyes on it moodily. What was roughly the toe had broken open again and he had patched it with a piece of canvas; another place he had patched with what appeared to be the tongue of the original shoe. The two sides were laced with twine.

There was an excited flush on Sheppard's face; his heart was beating unnaturally fast.

The clerk appeared from the back of the shop with the new shoe under his arm. "Got her right this time!" he said. He straddled the shoe-fitting stool and held the shoe up, smiling as if he had produced it by magic.

It was a black slick shapeless object, shining hideously. It looked like a blunt weapon, highly polished.

Johnson gazed at it darkly.

"With this shoe," the clerk said, "you won't know you're walking. You'll think you're riding!" He bent his bright pink bald head and began gingerly to unlace the twine. He removed the old shoe as if he were skinning an animal still half alive. His expression was strained. The unsheathed mass of foot in the dirty sock made Sheppard feel queasy. He turned his eyes away until the new shoe was on. The clerk laced it up rapidly. "Now stand up and walk around," he said, "and see if that ain't power glide." He winked at Sheppard. "In that shoe," he said, "he won't know he don't have a normal foot."

Sheppard's face was bright with pleasure.

Johnson stood up and walked a few yards away. He walked stiffly with almost no dip in his short side. He stood for a moment, rigid, with his back to them.

"Wonderful!" Sheppard said. "Wonderful." It was as if he had given the boy a new spine.

Johnson turned around. His mouth was set in a thin icy line. He came back to the seat and removed the shoe. He put his foot in the old one and began lacing it up.

"You want to take it home and see if it suits you first?" the clerk murmured.

"No," Johnson said. "I ain't going to wear it at all."

"What's wrong with it?" Sheppard said, his voice rising.

"I don't need no new shoe," Johnson said. "And when I do, I got ways of getting my own." His face was stony but there was a glint of triumph in his eyes.

"Boy," the clerk said, "is your trouble in your foot or in your head?"

"Go soak your skull," Johnson said. "Your brains are on fire."

The clerk rose glumly but with dignity and asked Sheppard what he wanted done with the shoe, which he dangled dispiritedly by the lace.

Sheppard's face was a dark angry red. He was staring straight in front of him at a leather corset with an artificial arm attached.

The clerk asked him again.

"Wrap it up," Sheppard muttered. He turned his eyes to Johnson. "He's not mature enough for it yet," he said. "I had thought he was less of a child."

The boy leered. "You been wrong before," he said.

That night they sat in the living room and read as usual. Sheppard kept himself glumly entrenched behind the Sunday New York *Times*. He wanted to recover his good humor, but every time he thought of the rejected shoe, he felt a new charge of irritation. He did not trust himself even to look at Johnson. He realized that the boy had refused the shoe because he was insecure. Johnson had been frightened by his own gratitude. He didn't know what to make of the new self he was becoming conscious of. He understood that something he had been was threatened and he was facing himself and his possibilities for the first time. He was questioning his identity. Grudgingly, Sheppard felt a slight return of sympathy for the boy. In a few minutes, he lowered his paper and looked at him.

Johnson was sitting on the sofa, gazing over the top of the encyclopedia. His expression was trancelike. He might have been listening to something far away. Sheppard watched him intently but the boy continued to listen, and did not turn his head. The poor kid is lost, Sheppard thought. Here he had sat all evening, sullenly reading the paper, and had not said a word to break the tension. "Rufus," he said.

Johnson continued to sit, stock-still, listening.

"Rufus," Sheppard said in a slow hypnotic voice, "you can be anything in the world you want to be. You can be a scientist or an architect or an engineer or whatever you set your mind to, and whatever you set your mind to be, you can be the best of its kind." He imagined his voice penetrating to the boy in the black caverns of his psyche. Johnson leaned forward but his eyes did not turn. On the street a car door closed. There was a silence. Then a sudden blast from the door bell.

Sheppard jumped up and went to the door and opened it. The same policeman who had come before stood there. The patrol car waited at the curb.

"Lemme see that boy," he said.

Sheppard scowled and stood aside. "He's been here all evening," he said. "I can vouch for it."

The policeman walked into the living room. Johnson appeared engrossed in his book. After a second he looked up with an annoyed expression, like a great man interrupted at his work.

"What was that you were looking at in that kitchen window over on Winter Avenue about a half hour ago, bud?" the policeman asked.

"Stop persecuting this boy!" Sheppard said. "I'll vouch for the fact he was here. I was here with him."

"You heard him," Johnson said. "I been here all the time."

"It ain't everybody makes tracks like you," the policeman said and eyed the clubfoot.

"They couldn't be his tracks," Sheppard growled, infuriated. "He's been here all the time. You're wasting your own time and you're wasting ours." He felt the *ours* seal his solidarity with the boy. "I'm sick of this," he said. "You people are too damn lazy to go out and find whoever is doing these things. You come here automatically."

The policeman ignored this and continued looking through Johnson. His eyes were small and alert in his fleshy face. Finally he turned toward the door. "We'll get him sooner or later," he said, "with his head in a window and his tail out."

Sheppard followed him to the door and slammed it behind him. His spirits were soaring. This was exactly what he had needed. He returned with an expectant face.

Johnson had put the book down and was sitting there, looking at him slyly. "Thanks," he said.

Sheppard stopped. The boy's expression was predatory. He was openly leering.

"You ain't such a bad liar yourself," he said.

"Liar?" Sheppard murmured. Could the boy have left and come back? He felt himself sicken. Then a rush of anger sent him forward. "Did you leave?" he said furiously. "I didn't see you leave."

The boy only smiled.

"You went up in the attic to see Norton," Sheppard said.

"Naw," Johnson said, "that kid is crazy. He don't want to do nothing but look through that stinking telescope."

"I don't want to hear about Norton," Sheppard said harshly. "Where were you?"

"I was sitting on that pink can by my ownself," Johnson said. "There wasn't no witnesses."

Sheppard took out his handkerchief and wiped his forehead. He managed to smile.

Johnson rolled his eyes. "You don't believe in me," he said. His voice was cracked the way it had been in the dark room two nights before. "You make out like you got all this confidence in me but you ain't got any. When things get hot, you'll fade like the rest of them." The crack became exaggerated, comic. The mockery in it was blatant. "You don't believe in me. You ain't got no confidence," he wailed. "And you ain't any smarter than that cop. All that about tracks—that was a trap. There wasn't any tracks. That whole place is concreted in the back and my feet were dry."

Sheppard slowly put the handkerchief back in his pocket. He dropped down on the sofa and gazed at the rug beneath his feet. The boy's clubfoot was set within the circle of his vision. The pieced-together shoe appeared to grin at him with Johnson's own face. He caught hold of the edge of the sofa cushion and his knuckles turned white. A chill of hatred shook him. He hated the shoe, hated the foot, hated the boy. His face paled. Hatred choked him. He was aghast at himself.

He caught the boy's shoulder and gripped it fiercely as if to keep himself from falling. "Listen," he said, "you looked in that window to embarrass me. That was all you wanted—to shake my resolve to help you, but my resolve isn't shaken. I'm stronger than you are. I'm stronger than you are and I'm going to save you. The good will triumph."

"Not when it ain't true," the boy said. "Not when it ain't right."

"My resolve isn't shaken," Sheppard repeated. "I'm going to save you."

Johnson's look became sly again. "You ain't going to save me," he said. "You're going to tell me to leave this house. I did those other two jobs too—the first one as well as the one I done when I was supposed to be in the picture show."

"I'm not going to tell you to leave," Sheppard said. His voice was toneless, mechanical. "I'm going to save you."

Johnson thrust his head forward. "Save yourself," he hissed. "Nobody can save me but Jesus."

Sheppard laughed curtly. "You don't deceive me," he said. "I flushed that out of your head in the reformatory. I saved you from that, at least."

The muscles in Johnson's face stiffened. A look of such repulsion hardened on his face that Sheppard drew back. The boy's eyes were like distorting mirrors in which he saw himself made hideous and grotesque. "I'll show you," Johnson whispered. He rose abruptly and started headlong for the door as if he could not get out of Sheppard's sight quick enough, but it was the door to the back hall he went through, not the front door. Sheppard turned on the sofa and looked behind him where the boy had disappeared. He heard the door to his room slam. He was not leaving. The intensity had gone out of Sheppard's eyes. They looked flat and lifeless as if the shock of the boy's revelation were only now reaching the center of his consciousness. "If he would only leave," he murmured. "If he would only leave now of his own accord."

The next morning Johnson appeared at the breakfast table in the grandfather's suit he had come in. Sheppard pretended not to notice but one look told him what he already knew, that he was trapped, that there could be nothing now but a battle of nerves and that Johnson would win it. He wished he had never laid eyes on the boy. The failure of his compassion numbed him. He got out of the house as soon as he could and all day he dreaded to go home in the evening. He had a faint hope that the boy might be gone when he returned. The grandfather's suit might have meant he was leaving. The hope grew in the afternoon. When he came home and opened the front door, his heart was pounding.

He stopped in the hall and looked silently into the living room. His expectant expression faded. His face seemed suddenly as old as his white hair. The two boys were sitting close together on the sofa, reading the same book. Norton's cheek rested against the sleeve of Johnson's black suit. Johnson's finger moved under the lines they were reading. The elder brother and the younger. Sheppard looked woodenly at this scene for almost a minute. Then he walked into the room and took off his coat and dropped it on a chair. Neither boy noticed him. He went on to the kitchen.

Leola left the supper on the stove every afternoon before she left and he put it on the table. His head ached and his nerves were taut. He sat down on the kitchen stool and remained there, sunk in his depression. He wondered if he could infuriate Johnson enough to make him leave of his own accord. Last night what had enraged him was the Jesus business. It might enrage Johnson, but it depressed him. Why not simply tell the boy to go? Admit defeat. The thought of facing Johnson again sickened him. The boy looked at him as if he were the guilty one, as if he were a moral leper. He knew without conceit that he was a good man, that he had nothing to reproach himself with. His feelings about Johnson now were involuntary. He would like to feel compassion for him. He would like to be able to help him. He longed for the time when there would be no one but himself and Norton in the house, when the child's simple selfishness would be all he had to contend with, and his own loneliness.

He got up and took three serving dishes off the shelf and took them to the stove. Absently he began pouring the butterbeans and the hash into the dishes. When the food was on the table, he called them in.

They brought the book with them. Norton pushed his place setting around to the same side of the table as Johnson's and moved his chair next to Johnson's chair. They sat down and put the book between them. It was a black book with red edges.

"What's that you're reading?" Sheppard asked, sitting down.

"The Holy Bible," Johnson said.

God give me strength, Sheppard said under his breath.

"We lifted it from a ten cent store," Johnson said.

"We?" Sheppard muttered. He turned and glared at Norton. The child's face was bright and there was an excited sheen to his eyes. The change that had come over the boy struck him for the first time. He looked alert. He had on a blue plaid shirt and his eyes were a brighter blue than he had ever seen them before. There was a strange new life in him, the sign of new and more rugged vices. "So now you steal?" he said, glowering. "You haven't learned to be generous but you have learned to steal."

"No he ain't," Johnson said. "I was the one lifted it. He only watched. He can't sully himself. It don't make any difference about me. I'm going to hell anyway."

Sheppard held his tongue.

"Unless," Johnson said, "I repent."

"Repent, Rufus," Norton said in a pleading voice. "Repent, hear? You don't want to go to hell."

"Stop talking this nonsense," Sheppard said, looking sharply at the child.

"If I do repent, I'll be a preacher," Johnson said. "If you're going to do it, it's no sense in doing it halfway."

"What are you going to be, Norton," Sheppard asked in a brittle voice, "a preacher too?"

There was a glitter of wild pleasure in the child's eyes. "A space man!" he shouted.

"Wonderful," Sheppard said bitterly.

"Those space ships ain't going to do you any good unless you believe in Jesus," Johnson said. He wet his finger and began to leaf through the pages of the Bible. "I'll read you where it says so," he said.

Sheppard leaned forward and said in a low furious voice, "Put that Bible up, Rufus, and eat your dinner."

Johnson continued searching for the passage.

"Put that Bible up!" Sheppard shouted.

The boy stopped and looked up. His expression was startled but pleased.

"That book is something for you to hide behind," Sheppard said. "It's for cowards, people who are afraid to stand on their own feet and figure things out for themselves."

Johnson's eyes snapped. He backed his chair a little way from the table. "Satan has you in his power," he said. "Not only me. You too."

Sheppard reached across the table to grab the book but Johnson snatched it and put it in his lap.

Sheppard laughed. "You don't believe in that book and you know you don't believe in it!"

"I believe it!" Johnson said. "You don't know what I believe and what I don't."

Sheppard shook his head. "You don't believe it. You're too intelligent."

"I ain't too intelligent," the boy muttered. "You don't know nothing about me. Even if I didn't believe it, it would still be true."

"You don't believe it!" Sheppard said. His face was a taunt.

"I believe it!" Johnson said breathlessly. "I'll show you I believe it!" He opened the book in his lap and tore out a page of it and thrust it into his mouth. He fixed his eyes on Sheppard. His jaws worked furiously and the paper crackled as he chewed it.

"Stop this," Sheppard said in a dry, burnt-out voice. "Stop it."

The boy raised the Bible and tore out a page with his teeth and began grinding it in his mouth, his eyes burning.

Sheppard reached across the table and knocked the book out of his hand. "Leave the table," he said coldly.

Johnson swallowed what was in his mouth. His eyes widened as if a vision of splendor were opening up before him. "I've eaten it!" he breathed. "I've eaten it like Ezekiel and it was honey to my mouth!"[1]

"Leave this table," Sheppard said. His hands were clenched beside his plate.

365 "I've eaten it!" the boy cried. Wonder transformed his face. "I've eaten it like Ezekiel and I don't want none of your food after it nor no more ever."

"Go then," Sheppard said softly. "Go. Go."

The boy rose and picked up the Bible and started toward the hall with it. At the door he paused, a small black figure on the threshold of some dark apocalypse. "The devil has you in his power," he said in a jubilant voice and disappeared.

After supper Sheppard sat in the living room alone. Johnson had left the house but he could not believe that the boy had simply gone. The first feeling of release had passed. He felt dull and cold as at the onset of an illness and dread had settled in him like a fog. Just to leave would be too anticlimactic an end for Johnson's taste; he would return and try to prove something. He might come back a week later and set fire to the place. Nothing seemed too outrageous now.

He picked up the paper and tried to read. In a moment he threw it down and got up and went into the hall and listened. He might be hiding in the attic. He went to the attic door and opened it.

370 The lantern was lit, casting a dim light on the stairs. He didn't hear anything. "Norton," he called, "are you up there?" There was no answer. He mounted the narrow stairs to see.

Amid the strange vine-like shadows cast by the lantern, Norton sat with his eye to the telescope. "Norton," Sheppard said, "do you know where Rufus went?"

The child's back was to him. He was sitting hunched, intent, his large ears directly above his shoulders. Suddenly he waved his hand and crouched closer to the telescope as if he could not get near enough to what he saw.

"Norton!" Sheppard said in a loud voice.

The child didn't move.

375 "Norton!" Sheppard shouted.

Norton started. He turned around. There was an unnatural brightness about his eyes. After a moment he seemed to see that it was Sheppard. "I've found her!" he said breathlessly.

"Found who?" Sheppard said.

"Mamma!"

Sheppard steadied himself in the door way. The jungle of shadows around the child thickened.

380 "Come and look!" he cried. He wiped his sweaty face on the tail of his plaid shirt and then put his eye back to the telescope. His back became fixed in a rigid intensity. All at once he waved again.

---

1. Ezekiel 3.1–3. The Lord in a vision told Ezekiel to eat a roll and go speak to the captive Israelites; when he ate, "it was in my mouth as honey for sweetness."

"Norton," Sheppard said, "you don't see anything in the telescope but star clusters. Now you've had enough of that for one night. You'd better go to bed. Do you know where Rufus is?"

"She's there!" he cried, not turning around from the telescope. "She waved at me!"

"I want you in bed in fifteen minutes," Sheppard said. After a moment he said, "Do you hear me, Norton?"

The child began to wave frantically.

"I mean what I say," Sheppard said. "I'm going to call in fifteen minutes and see if you're in bed."

He went down the steps again and returned to the parlor. He went to the front door and cast a cursory glance out. The sky was crowded with the stars he had been fool enough to think Johnson could reach. Somewhere in the small wood behind the house, a bull frog sounded a low hollow note. He went back to his chair and sat a few minutes. He decided to go to bed. He put his hands on the arms of the chair and leaned forward and heard, like the first shrill note of a disaster warning, the siren of a police car, moving slowly into the neighborhood and nearer until it subsided with a moan outside the house.

He felt a cold weight on his shoulders as if an icy cloak had been thrown about him. He went to the door and opened it.

Two policemen were coming up the walk with a dark snarling Johnson between them, handcuffed to each. A reporter jogged alongside and another policeman waited in the patrol car.

"Here's your boy," the dourest of the policemen said. "Didn't I tell you we'd get him?"

Johnson jerked his arm down savagely. "I was waitin for you!" he said. "You wouldn't have got me if I hadn't of wanted to get caught. It was my idea." He was addressing the policemen but leering at Sheppard.

Sheppard looked at him coldly.

"Why did you want to get caught?" the reporter asked, running around to get beside Johnson. "Why did you deliberately want to get caught?"

The question and the sight of Sheppard seemed to throw the boy into a fury. "To show up that big tin Jesus!" he hissed and kicked his leg out at Sheppard. "He thinks he's God. I'd rather be in the reformatory than in his house, I'd rather be in the pen! The Devil has him in his power. He don't know his left hand from his right, he don't have as much sense as his crazy kid!" He paused and then swept on to his fantastic conclusion. "He made suggestions to me!"

Sheppard's face blanched. He caught hold of the door facing.

"Suggestions?" the reporter said eagerly, "what kind of suggestion?"

"Immor'l suggestions!" Johnson said. "What kind of suggestions do you think? But I ain't having none of it, I'm a Christian, I'm . . ."

Sheppard's face was tight with pain. "He knows that's not true," he said in a shaken voice. "He knows he's lying. I did everything I knew how for him. I did more for him than I did for my own child. I hoped to save him and I failed, but it was an honorable failure. I have nothing to reproach myself with. I made no suggestions to him."

"Do you remember the suggestions?" the reporter asked. "Can you tell us exactly what he said?"

"He's a dirty atheist," Johnson said. "He said there wasn't no hell."

"Well, they seen each other now," one of the policemen said with a knowing sigh. "Let's us go."

"Wait," Sheppard said. He came down one step and fixed his eyes on Johnson's eyes in a last desperate effort to save himself. "Tell the truth, Rufus," he said. "You don't want to perpetrate this lie. You're not evil, you're mortally confused. You don't have to make up for that foot, you don't have to ..."

Johnson hurled himself forward. "Listen at him!" he screamed. "I lie and steal because I'm good at it! My foot don't have a thing to do with it! The lame shall enter first![2] The halt'll be gathered together. When I get ready to be saved, Jesus'll save me, not that lying stinking atheist, not that..."

"That'll be enough out of you," the policeman said and yanked him back. "We just wanted you to see we got him," he said to Sheppard, and the two of them turned around and dragged Johnson away, half turned and screaming back at Sheppard.

"The lame'll carry off the prey!" he screeched, but his voice was muffled inside the car. The reporter scrambled into the front seat with the driver and slammed the door and the siren wailed into the darkness.

Sheppard remained there, bent slightly like a man who has been shot but continues to stand. After a minute he turned and went back in the house and sat down in the chair he had left. He closed his eyes on a picture of Johnson in a circle of reporters at the police station, elaborating his lies. "I have nothing to reproach myself with," he murmured. His every action had been selfless, his one aim had been to save Johnson for some decent kind of service, he had not spared himself, he had sacrificed his reputation, he had done more for Johnson than he had done for his own child. Foulness hung about him like an odor in the air, so close that it seemed to come from his own breath. "I have nothing to reproach myself with," he repeated. His voice sounded dry and harsh. "I did more for him than I did for my own child." He was swept with a sudden panic. He heard the boy's jubilant voice. Satan has you in his power.

"I have nothing to reproach myself with," he began again. "I did more for him than I did for my own child." He heard his voice as if it were the voice of his accuser. He repeated the sentence silently.

Slowly his face drained of color. It became almost gray beneath the white halo of his hair. The sentence echoed in his mind, each syllable like a dull blow. His mouth twisted and he closed his eyes against the revelation. Norton's face rose before him, empty, forlorn, his left eye listing almost imperceptibly toward the outer rim as if it could not bear a full view of grief. His heart constricted with a repulsion for himself so clear and intense that he gasped for breath. He had stuffed his own emptiness with good works like a glutton. He had ignored his own child to feed his vision of himself. He saw the clear-eyed Devil, the sounder of hearts, leering at him from the eyes of Johnson. His image of himself shrivelled until everything was black before him. He sat there paralyzed, aghast.

He saw Norton at the telescope, all back and ears, saw his arm shoot up and wave frantically. A rush of agonizing love for the child rushed over him like a transfusion of life. The little boy's face appeared to him transformed; the image of his salvation; all light. He groaned with joy. He would make everything up to

---

2. Perhaps a reference to the Bible, Luke 14.13–14: "And you will be blessed, because they cannot repay you, for you will be repaid at the resurrection of the righteous."

him. He would never let him suffer again. He would be mother and father. He jumped up and ran to his room, to kiss him, to tell him that he loved him, that he would never fail him again.

The light was on in Norton's room but the bed was empty. He turned and dashed up the attic stairs and at the top reeled back like a man on the edge of a pit. The tripod had fallen and the telescope lay on the floor. A few feet over it, the child hung in the jungle of shadows, just below the beam from which he had launched his flight into space.

1965

# FLANNERY O'CONNOR

## Everything That Rises Must Converge

Her doctor had told Julian's mother that she must lose twenty pounds on account of her blood pressure, so on Wednesday nights Julian had to take her downtown on the bus for a reducing class at the Y. The reducing class was designed for working girls over fifty, who weighed from 165 to 200 pounds. His mother was one of the slimmer ones, but she said ladies did not tell their age or weight. She would not ride the buses by herself at night since they had been integrated, and because the reducing class was one of her few pleasures, necessary for her health, and *free,* she said Julian could at least put himself out to take her, considering all she did for him. Julian did not like to consider all she did for him, but every Wednesday night he braced himself and took her.

She was almost ready to go, standing before the hall mirror, putting on her hat, while he, his hands behind him, appeared pinned to the door frame, waiting like Saint Sebastian for the arrows to begin piercing him.[1] The hat was new and had cost her seven dollars and a half. She kept saying, "Maybe I shouldn't have paid that for it. No, I shouldn't have. I'll take it off and return it tomorrow. I shouldn't have bought it."

Julian raised his eyes to heaven. "Yes, you should have bought it," he said. "Put it on and let's go." It was a hideous hat. A purple velvet flap came down on one side of it and stood up on the other; the rest of it was green and looked like a cushion with the stuffing out. He decided it was less comical than jaunty and pathetic. Everything that gave her pleasure was small and depressed him.

She lifted the hat one more time and set it down slowly on top of her head. Two wings of gray hair protruded on either side of her florid face, but her eyes, sky-blue, were as innocent and untouched by experience as they must have been when she was ten. Were it not that she was a widow who had struggled fiercely to feed and clothe and put him through school and who was supporting him still, "until he got on his feet," she might have been a little girl that he had to take to town.

"It's all right, it's all right," he said. "Let's go." He opened the door himself and started down the walk to get her going. The sky was a dying violet and the

---

1. Discovered to be a Christian, Sebastian, Roman commander in Milan, was tied to a tree, shot with arrows, and left for dead. (He recovered, but when he reasserted his faith he was clubbed to death.)

houses stood out darkly against it, bulbous liver-colored monstrosities of a uniform ugliness though no two were alike. Since this had been a fashionable neighborhood forty years ago, his mother persisted in thinking they did well to have an apartment in it. Each house had a narrow collar of dirt around it in which sat, usually, a grubby child. Julian walked with his hands in his pockets, his head down and thrust forward and his eyes glazed with the determination to make himself completely numb during the time he would be sacrificed to her pleasure.

The door closed and he turned to find the dumpy figure, surmounted by the atrocious hat, coming toward him. "Well," she said, "you only live once and paying a little more for it, I at least won't meet myself coming and going."

"Some day I'll start making money," Julian said gloomily—he knew he never would—"and you can have one of those jokes whenever you take the fit." But first they would move. He visualized a place where the nearest neighbors would be three miles away on either side.

"I think you're doing fine," she said, drawing on her gloves. "You've only been out of school a year. Rome wasn't built in a day."

She was one of the few members of the Y reducing class who arrived in hat and gloves and who had a son who had been to college. "It takes time," she said, "and the world is in such a mess. This hat looked better on me than any of the others, though when she brought it out I said, 'Take that thing back. I wouldn't have it on my head,' and she said, 'Now wait till you see it on,' and when she put it on me, I said, 'We-ull,' and she said, 'If you ask me, that hat does something for you and you do something for the hat, and besides,' she said, 'with that hat, you won't meet yourself coming and going.'"

10   Julian thought he could have stood his lot better if she had been selfish, if she had been an old hag who drank and screamed at him. He walked along, saturated in depression, as if in the midst of his martyrdom he had lost his faith. Catching sight of his long, hopeless, irritated face, she stopped suddenly with a grief-stricken look, and pulled back on his arm. "Wait on me," she said. "I'm going back to the house and take this thing off and tomorrow I'm going to return it. I was out of my head. I can pay the gas bill with that seven-fifty."

He caught her arm in a vicious grip. "You are not going to take it back," he said. "I like it."

"Well," she said, "I don't think I ought . . ."

"Shut up and enjoy it," he muttered, more depressed than ever.

"With the world in the mess it's in," she said, "it's a wonder we can enjoy anything. I tell you, the bottom rail is on the top."

15   Julian sighed.

"Of course," she said, "if you know who are you, you can go anywhere." She said this every time he took her to the reducing class. "Most of them in it are not our kind of people," she said, "but I can be gracious to anybody. I know who I am."

"They don't give a damn for your graciousness," Julian said savagely. "Knowing who you are is good for one generation only. You haven't the foggiest idea where you stand now or who you are."

She stopped and allowed her eyes to flash at him. "I most certainly do know who I am," she said, "and if you don't know who you are, I'm ashamed of you."

"Oh hell," Julian said.

20   "Your great-grandfather was a former governor of this state," she said. "Your grandfather was a prosperous land-owner. Your grandmother was a Godhigh."

"Will you look around you," he said tensely, "and see where you are now?" and he swept his arm jerkily out to indicate the neighborhood, which the growing darkness at least made less dingy.

"You remain what you are," she said. "Your great-grandfather had a plantation and two hundred slaves."

"There are no more slaves," he said irritably.

"They were better off when they were," she said. He groaned to see that she was off on that topic. She rolled onto it every few days like a train on an open track. He knew every stop, every junction, every swamp along the way, and knew the exact point at which her conclusion would roll majestically into the station: "It's ridiculous. It's simply not realistic. They should rise, yes, but on their own side of the fence."

"Let's skip it," Julian said.

"The ones I feel sorry for," she said, "are the ones that are half white. They're tragic."

"Will you skip it?"

"Suppose we were half white. We would certainly have mixed feelings."

"I have mixed feelings now," he groaned.

"Well let's talk about something pleasant," she said. "I remember going to Grandpa's when I was a little girl. Then the house had double stairways that went up to what was really the second floor—all the cooking was done on the first. I used to like to stay down in the kitchen on account of the way the walls smelled. I would sit with my nose pressed against the plaster and take deep breaths. Actually the place belonged to the Godhighs but your grandfather Chestny paid the mortgage and saved it for them. They were in reduced circumstances," she said, "but reduced or not, they never forgot who they were."

"Doubtless that decayed mansion reminded them," Julian muttered. He never spoke of it without contempt or thought of it without longing. He had seen it once when he was a child before it had been sold. The double stairways had rotted and been torn down. Negroes were living in it. But it remained in his mind as his mother had known it. It appeared in his dreams regularly. He would stand on the wide porch, listening to the rustle of oak leaves, then wander through the high-ceilinged hall into the parlor that opened onto it and gaze at the worn rugs and faded draperies. It occurred to him that it was he, not she, who could have appreciated it. He preferred its threadbare elegance to anything he could name and it was because of it that all the neighborhoods they had lived in had been a torment to him—whereas she had hardly known the difference. She called her insensitivity "being adjustable."

"And I remember the old darky who was my nurse, Caroline. There was no better person in the world. I've always had a great respect for my colored friends," she said. "I'd do anything in the world for them and they'd . . ."

"Will you for God's sake get off that subject?" Julian said. When he got on a bus by himself, he made it a point to sit down beside a Negro, in reparation as it were for his mother's sins.

"You're mighty touchy tonight," she said. "Do you feel all right?"

"Yes I feel all right," he said. "Now lay off."

She pursed her lips. "Well, you certainly are in a vile humor," she observed. "I just won't speak to you at all."

They had reached the bus stop. There was no bus in sight and Julian, his hands still jammed in his pockets and his head thrust forward, scowled down the empty street. The frustration of having to wait on the bus as well as ride on it began to creep up his neck like a hot hand. The presence of his mother was borne in upon him as she gave a pained sigh. He looked at her bleakly. She was holding herself very erect under the preposterous hat, wearing it like a banner of her imaginary dignity. There was in him an evil urge to break her spirit. He suddenly unloosened his tie and pulled it off and put it in his pocket.

She stiffened. "Why must you look like *that* when you take me to town?" she said. "Why must you deliberately embarrass me?"

"If you'll never learn where you are," he said, "you can at least learn where I am."

"You look like a—thug," she said.

"Then I must be one," he murmured.

"I'll just go home," she said. "I will not bother you. If you can't do a little thing like that for me . . ."

Rolling his eyes upward, he put his tie back on. "Restored to my class," he muttered. He thrust his face toward her and hissed, "True culture is in the mind, the *mind*," he said, and tapped his head, "the mind."

"It's in the heart," she said, "and in how you do things and how you do things is because of who you *are*."

"Nobody in the damn bus cares who you are."

"I care who I am," she said icily.

The lighted bus appeared on top of the next hill and as it approached, they moved out into the street to meet it. He put his hand under her elbow and hoisted her up on the creaking step. She entered with a little smile, as if she were going into a drawing room where everyone had been waiting for her. While he put in the tokens, she sat down on one of the broad front seats for three which faced the aisle. A thin woman with protruding teeth and long yellow hair was sitting on the end of it. His mother moved up beside her and left room for Julian beside herself. He sat down and looked at the floor across the aisle where a pair of thin feet in red and white canvas sandals were planted.

His mother immediately began a general conversation meant to attract anyone who felt like talking. "Can it get any hotter?" she said and removed from her purse a folding fan, black with a Japanese scene on it, which she began to flutter before her.

"I reckon it might could," the woman with the protruding teeth said, "but I know for a fact my apartment couldn't get no hotter."

"It must get the afternoon sun," his mother said. She sat forward and looked up and down the bus. It was half filled. Everybody was white. "I see we have the bus to ourselves," she said. Julian cringed.

"For a change," said the woman across the aisle, the owner of the red and white canvas sandals. "I come on one the other day and they were thick as fleas—up front and all through."

"The world is in a mess everywhere," his mother said. "I don't know how we've let it get in this fix."

"What gets my goat is all those boys from good families stealing automobile tires," the woman with the protruding teeth said. "I told my boy, I said you may not be rich but you been raised right and if I ever catch you in any such mess, they can send you on to the reformatory. Be exactly where you belong."

"Training tells," his mother said. "Is your boy in high school?"

"Ninth grade," the woman said.

"My son just finished college last year. He wants to write but he's selling typewriters until he gets started," his mother said.

The woman leaned forward and peered at Julian. He threw her such a malevolent look that she subsided against the seat. On the floor across the aisle there was an abandoned newspaper. He got up and got it and opened it out in front of him. His mother discreetly continued the conversation in a lower tone but the woman across the aisle said in a loud voice, "Well that's nice. Selling typewriters is close to writing. He can go right from one to the other."

"I tell him," his mother said, "that Rome wasn't built in a day."

Behind the newspaper Julian was withdrawing into the inner compartment of his mind where he spent most of his time. This was a kind of mental bubble in which he established himself when he could not bear to be a part of what was going on around him. From it he could see out and judge but in it he was safe from any kind of penetration from without. It was the only place where he felt free of the general idiocy of his fellows. His mother had never entered it but from it he could see her with absolute clarity.

The old lady was clever enough and he thought that if she had started from any of the right premises, more might have been expected of her. She lived according to the laws of her own fantasy world, outside of which he had never seen her set foot. The law of it was to sacrifice herself for him after she had first created the necessity to do so by making a mess of things. If he had permitted her sacrifices, it was only because her lack of foresight had made them necessary. All of her life had been a struggle to act like a Chestny without the Chestny goods, and to give him everything she thought a Chestny ought to have; but since, said she, it was fun to struggle, why complain? And when you had won, as she had won, what fun to look back on the hard times! He could not forgive her that she had enjoyed the struggle and that she thought *she* had won.

What she meant when she said she had won was that she had brought him up successfully and had sent him to college and that he had turned out so well—good looking (her teeth had gone unfilled so that his could be straightened), intelligent (he realized he was too intelligent to be a success), and with a future ahead of him (there was of course no future ahead of him). She excused his gloominess on the grounds that he was still growing up and his radical ideas on his lack of practical experience. She said he didn't yet know a thing about "life," that he hadn't even entered the real world—when already he was as disenchanted with it as a man of fifty.

The further irony of all this was that in spite of her, he had turned out so well. In spite of going to only a third-rate college, he had, on his own initiative, come out with a first-rate education; in spite of growing up dominated by a small mind, he had ended up with a large one; in spite of all her foolish views, he was free of prejudice and unafraid to face facts. Most miraculous of all, instead of being blinded by love for her as she was for him, he had cut himself emotionally free of her and could see her with complete objectivity. He was not dominated by his mother.

The bus stopped with a sudden jerk and shook him from his meditation. A woman from the back lurched forward with little steps and barely escaped falling in his newspaper as she righted herself. She got off and a large Negro got on. Julian kept his paper lowered to watch. It gave him a certain satisfaction to see injustice in daily operation. It confirmed his view that with a few exceptions there was no one worth knowing within a radius of three hundred miles. The Negro was well dressed and carried a briefcase. He looked around and then sat down on the other end of the seat where the woman with the red and white canvas sandals was sitting. He immediately unfolded a newspaper and obscured himself behind it. Julian's mother's elbow at once prodded insistently into his ribs. "Now you see why I won't ride on these buses by myself," she whispered.

The woman with the red and white canvas sandals had risen at the same time the Negro sat down and had gone further back in the bus and taken the seat of the woman who had got off. His mother leaned forward and cast her an approving look.

Julian rose, crossed the aisle, and sat down in the place of the woman with the canvas sandals. From this position, he looked serenely across at his mother. Her face had turned an angry red. He stared at her, making his eyes the eyes of a stranger. He felt his tension suddenly lift as if he had openly declared war on her.

He would have liked to get in conversation with the Negro and to talk with him about art or politics or any subject that would be above the comprehension of those around them, but the man remained entrenched behind his paper. He was either ignoring the change of seating or had never noticed it. There was no way for Julian to convey his sympathy.

His mother kept her eyes fixed reproachfully on his face. The woman with the protruding teeth was looking at him avidly as if he were a type of monster new to her.

"Do you have a light?" he asked the Negro.

Without looking away from his paper, the man reached in his pocket and handed him a packet of matches.

"Thanks," Julian said. For a moment he held the matches foolishly. A NO SMOKING sign looked down upon him from over the door. This alone would not have deterred him; he had no cigarettes. He had quit smoking some months before because he could not afford it. "Sorry," he muttered and handed back the matches. The Negro lowered the paper and gave him an annoyed look. He took the matches and raised the paper again.

His mother continued to gaze at him but she did not take advantage of his momentary discomfort. Her eyes retained their battered look. Her face seemed to be unnaturally red, as if her blood pressure had risen. Julian allowed no glimmer of sympathy to show on his face. Having got the advantage, he wanted desperately to keep it and carry it through. He would have liked to teach her a lesson that would last her a while, but there seemed no way to continue the point. The Negro refused to come out from behind his paper.

Julian folded his arms and looked stolidly before him, facing her but as if he did not see her, as if he had ceased to recognize her existence. He visualized a scene in which, the bus having reached their stop, he would remain in his seat and when she said, "Aren't you going to get off?" he would look at her as a stranger who had rashly addressed him. The corner they got off on was usually deserted, but it was well lighted and it would not hurt her to walk by herself the four blocks to the Y. He decided to wait until the time came and then decide whether or not he would let her get off by herself. He would have to be at the Y at ten to bring her back, but he could leave her wondering if he was going to show up. There was no reason for her to think she could always depend on him.

He retired again into the high-ceilinged room sparsely settled with large pieces of antique furniture. His soul expanded momentarily but then he became aware of his mother across from him and the vision shriveled. He studied her coldly. Her feet in little pumps dangled like a child's and did not quite reach the floor. She was training on him an exaggerated look of reproach. He felt completely detached from her. At that moment he could with pleasure have slapped her as he would have slapped a particularly obnoxious child in his charge.

He began to imagine various unlikely ways by which he could teach her a lesson. He might make friends with some distinguished Negro professor or lawyer and bring him home to spend the evening. He would be entirely justified but her blood pressure would rise to 300. He could not push her to the extent of making her have a stroke, and moreover, he had never been successful at making any Negro friends. He had tried to strike up an acquaintance on the bus with some of the better types, with ones that looked like professors or ministers or lawyers. One morning he had sat down next to a distinguished-looking dark brown man who had answered his questions with a sonorous solemnity but who had turned out to be an undertaker. Another day he had sat down beside a cigar-smoking Negro with a diamond ring on his finger, but after a few stilted pleasantries, the Negro had rung the buzzer and risen, slipping two lottery tickets into Julian's hand as he climbed over him to leave.

He imagined his mother lying desperately ill and his being able to secure only a Negro doctor for her. He toyed with that idea for a few minutes and then dropped it for a momentary vision of himself participating as a sympathizer in a sit-in demonstration. This was possible but he did not linger with it. Instead, he approached the ultimate horror. He brought home a beautiful suspiciously Negroid woman. Prepare yourself, he said. There is nothing you can do about it. This is the woman I've chosen. She's intelligent, dignified, even good, and she's suffered and she hasn't thought it *fun*. Now persecute us, go ahead and persecute us. Drive her out of here, but remember, you're driving me too. His eyes were narrowed and through the indignation he had generated, he saw his mother across the aisle, purple-faced, shrunken to the dwarf-like proportions of her moral nature, sitting like a mummy beneath the ridiculous banner of her hat.

He was tilted out of his fantasy again as the bus stopped. The door opened with a sucking hiss and out of the dark a large, gaily dressed, sullen-looking colored woman got on with a little boy. The child, who might have been four, had on a short plaid suit and a Tyrolean hat with a blue feather in it. Julian hoped that he would sit down beside him and that the woman would push in beside his mother. He could think of no better arrangement.

As she waited for her tokens, the woman was surveying the seating possibilities—he hoped with the idea of sitting where she was least wanted. There was something familiar-looking about her but Julian could not place what it was. She was a giant of a woman. Her face was set not only to meet opposition but to seek it out. The downward tilt of her large lower lip was like a warning sign: DON'T TAMPER WITH ME. Her bulging figure was encased in a green crepe dress and her feet overflowed in red shoes. She had on a hideous hat. A purple velvet flap came down on one side of it and stood up on the other; the rest of it was green and looked like a cushion with the stuffing out. She carried a mammoth red pocketbook that bulged throughout as if it were stuffed with rocks.

To Julian's disappointment, the little boy climbed up on the empty seat beside his mother. His mother lumped all children, black and white, into the common category, "cute," and she thought little Negroes were on the whole cuter than little white children. She smiled at the little boy as he climbed on the seat.

Meanwhile the woman was bearing down upon the empty seat beside Julian. To his annoyance, she squeezed herself into it. He saw his mother's face change as the woman settled herself next to him and he realized with satisfaction that this was more objectionable to her than it was to him. Her face seemed almost gray and there was a look of dull recognition in her eyes, as if suddenly she had sickened at some awful confrontation. Julian saw that it was because she and the woman had, in a sense, swapped sons. Though his mother would not realize the symbolic significance of this, she would feel it. His amusement showed plainly on his face.

The woman next to him muttered something unintelligible to herself. He was conscious of a kind of bristling next to him, a muted growling like that of an angry cat. He could not see anything but the red pocketbook upright on the bulging green thighs. He visualized the woman as she had stood waiting for her tokens—the ponderous figure, rising from the red shoes upward over the solid hips, the mammoth bosom, the haughty face, to the green and purple hat.

His eyes widened.

The vision of the two hats, identical, broke upon him with the radiance of a brilliant sunrise. His face was suddenly lit with joy. He could not believe that Fate had thrust upon his mother such a lesson. He gave a loud chuckle so that she would look at him and see that he saw. She turned her eyes on him slowly. The blue in them seemed to have turned a bruised purple. For a moment he had an uncomfortable sense of her innocence, but it lasted only a second before principle rescued him. Justice entitled him to laugh. His grin hardened until it said to her as plainly as if he were saying aloud: Your punishment exactly fits your pettiness. This should teach you a permanent lesson.

Her eyes shifted to the woman. She seemed unable to bear looking at him and to find the woman preferable. He became conscious again of the bristling presence at his side. The woman was rumbling like a volcano about to become active. His mother's mouth began to twitch slightly at one corner. With a sinking heart, he saw incipient signs of recovery on her face and realized that this was going to strike her suddenly as funny and was going to be no lesson at all. She kept her eyes on the woman and an amused smile came over her face as if the woman were a monkey that had stolen her hat. The little Negro was looking up at her with large fascinated eyes. He had been trying to attract her attention for some time.

"Carver!" the woman said suddenly. "Come heah!"

When he saw that the spotlight was on him at last, Carver drew his feet up and turned himself toward Julian's mother and giggled.

"Carver!" the woman said. "You heah me? Come heah!"

Carver slid down from the seat but remained squatting with his back against the base of it, his head turned slyly around toward Julian's mother, who was smiling at him. The woman reached a hand across the aisle and snatched him to her. He righted himself and hung backwards on her knees, grinning at Julian's mother. "Isn't he cute?" Julian's mother said to the woman with the protruding teeth.

"I reckon he is," the woman said without conviction.

The Negress yanked him upright but he eased out of her grip and shot across the aisle and scrambled, giggling wildly, onto the seat beside his love.

"I think he likes me," Julian's mother said, and smiled at the woman. It was the smile she used when she was being particularly gracious to an inferior. Julian saw everything was lost. The lesson had rolled off her like rain on a roof.

The woman stood up and yanked the little boy off the seat as if she were snatching him from contagion. Julian could feel the rage in her at having no weapon like his mother's smile. She gave the child a sharp slap across his leg. He howled once and then thrust his head into her stomach and kicked his feet against her shins. "Behave," she said vehemently.

The bus stopped and the Negro who had been reading the newspaper got off. The woman moved over and set the little boy down with a thump between herself and Julian. She held him firmly by the knee. In a moment he put his hands in front of his face and peeped at Julian's mother through his fingers.

"I see yooooooooo!" she said and put her hand in front of her face and peeped at him.

The woman slapped his hand down. "Quit yo' foolishness," she said, "before I knock the living Jesus out of you!"

Julian was thankful that the next stop was theirs. He reached up and pulled the cord. The woman reached up and pulled it at the same time. Oh my God, he thought. He had the terrible intuition that when they got off the bus together, his mother would open her purse and give the little boy a nickel. The gesture would be as natural to her as breathing. The bus stopped and the woman got up and lunged to the front, dragging the child, who wished to stay on, after her. Julian and his mother got up and followed. As they neared the door, Julian tried to relieve her of her pocketbook.

"No," she murmured, "I want to give the little boy a nickel."

"No!" Julian hissed. "No!"

She smiled down at the child and opened her bag. The bus door opened and the woman picked him up by the arm and descended with him, hanging at her hip. Once in the street she set him down and shook him.

Julian's mother had to close her purse while she got down the bus step but as soon as her feet were on the ground, she opened it again and began to rummage inside. "I can't find but a penny," she whispered, "but it looks like a new one."

"Don't do it!" Julian said fiercely between his teeth. There was a streetlight on the corner and she hurried to get under it so that she could better see into her pocketbook. The woman was heading off rapidly down the street with the child still hanging backward on her hand.

"Oh little boy!" Julian's mother called and took a few quick steps and caught up with them just beyond the lamppost. "Here's a bright new penny for you," and she held out the coin, which shone bronze in the dim light.

The huge woman turned and for a moment stood, her shoulders lifted and her face frozen with frustrated rage, and stared at Julian's mother. Then all at once she seemed to explode like a piece of machinery that had been given one ounce of pressure too much. Julian saw the black fist swing out with the red pocketbook. He shut his eyes and cringed as he heard the woman shout, "He don't take nobody's pennies!" When he opened his eyes, the woman was disappearing down the street with the little boy staring wide-eyed over her shoulder. Julian's mother was sitting on the sidewalk.

"I told you not to do that," Julian said angrily. "I told you not to do that!"

He stood over her for a minute, gritting his teeth. Her legs were stretched out in front of her and her hat was on her lap. He squatted down and looked her in the face. It was totally expressionless. "You got exactly what you deserved," he said. "Now get up."

He picked up her pocketbook and put what had fallen out back in it. He picked the hat up off her lap. The penny caught his eye on the sidewalk and he picked that up and let it drop before her eyes into the purse. Then he stood up and leaned over and held his hands out to pull her up. She remained immobile. He sighed. Rising above them on either side were black apartment buildings, marked with irregular rectangles of light. At the end of the block a man came out of a door and walked off in the opposite direction. "All right," he said, "suppose somebody happens by and wants to know why you're sitting on the sidewalk?"

She took the hand and, breathing hard, pulled heavily up on it and then stood for a moment, swaying slightly as if the spots of light in the darkness were circling around her. Her eyes, shadowed and confused, finally settled on his face. He did not try to conceal his irritation. "I hope this teaches you a lesson," he said. She leaned forward and her eyes raked his face. She seemed trying to determine his identity. Then, as if she found nothing familiar about him, she started off with a headlong movement in the wrong direction.

"Aren't you going on to the Y?" he asked.

"Home," she muttered.

"Well, are we walking?"

For answer she kept going. Julian followed along, his hands behind him. He saw no reason to let the lesson she had had go without backing it up with an explanation of its meaning. She might as well be made to understand what had happened to her. "Don't think that was just an uppity Negro woman," he said. "That was the whole colored race which will no longer take your condescending pennies. That was your black double. She can wear the same hat as you, and to be sure," he added gratuitously (because he thought it was funny), "it looked better on her than it did on you. What all this means," he said, "is that the old world is gone. The old manners are obsolete and your graciousness is not worth a damn." He thought bitterly of the house that had been lost for him. "You aren't who you think you are," he said.

She continued to plow ahead, paying no attention to him. Her hair had come undone on one side. She dropped her pocketbook and took no notice. He stooped and picked it up and handed it to her but she did not take it.

"You needn't act as if the world had come to an end," he said, "because it hasn't. From now on you've got to live in a new world and face a few realities for a change. Buck up," he said, "it won't kill you."

She was breathing fast.

"Let's wait on the bus," he said.

"Home," she said thickly.

"I hate to see you behave like this," he said. "Just like a child. I should be able to expect more of you." He decided to stop where he was and make her stop and wait for a bus. "I'm not going any farther," he said stopping. "We're going on the bus."

She continued to go on as if she had not heard him. He took a few steps and caught her arm and stopped her. He looked into her face and caught his breath. He was looking into a face he had never seen before. "Tell Grandpa to come get me," she said.

He stared, stricken.

"Tell Caroline to come get me," she said.

Stunned, he let her go and she lurched forward again, walking as if one leg were shorter than the other. A tide of darkness seemed to be sweeping her from him. "Mother!" he cried. "Darling, sweetheart, wait!" Crumpling, she fell to the pavement. He dashed forward and fell at her side, crying, "Mamma, Mamma!" He turned her over. Her face was fiercely distorted. One eye, large and staring, moved slightly to the left as if it had become unmoored. The other remained fixed on him, raked his face again, found nothing and closed.

"Wait here, wait here!" he cried and jumped up and began to run for help toward a cluster of lights he saw in the distance ahead of him. "Help, help!" he shouted, but his voice was thin, scarcely a thread of sound. The lights drifted farther away the faster he ran and his feet moved numbly as if they carried him nowhere. The tide of darkness seemed to sweep him back to her, postponing from moment to moment his entry into the world of guilt and sorrow.

1961

# FLANNERY O'CONNOR

## Passages from Essays and Letters

### From "The Fiction Writer and His Country" (1957)

... [W]hen I look at stories I have written I find that they are, for the most part, about people who are poor, who are afflicted in both mind and body, who have little—or at best a distorted—sense of spiritual purpose, and whose actions do not apparently give the reader a great assurance of the joy of life.

Yet how is this? For I am no disbeliever in spiritual purpose and no vague believer. I see from the standpoint of Christian orthodoxy. This means that for me the meaning of life is centered in our Redemption by Christ and what I see in the world I see in its relation to that.

Some may blame preoccupation with the grotesque on the fact that here we have a Southern writer and that this is just the type of imagination that Southern life fosters.... I find it hard to believe that what is observable behavior in one section can be entirely without parallel in another. At least, of late, Southern writers have had the opportunity of pointing out that none of us invented Elvis Presley and that that youth is himself probably less an occasion for concern than his popularity, which is not restricted to the Southern part of the country.

When you can assume that your audience holds the same beliefs you do, you can relax a little and use more normal means of talking to it; when you have to assume that it does not, then you have to make your vision apparent by shock—to the hard of hearing you shout, and for the almost-blind you draw large and startling figures.

*From "The Grotesque in Southern Fiction" (written 1960; posthumously published in 1965)*

All novelists are fundamentally seekers and describers of the real, but the realism of each novelist will depend on his view of the ultimate reaches of reality.... If the novelist is in tune with this [modern scientific] spirit, if he believes that actions are predetermined by psychic make-up or the economic situation or some other determinable factor, then he will be concerned above all with an accurate reproduction of the things that most immediately concern man, with the natural forces that he feels control his destiny....

On the other hand, if the writer believes that our life is and will remain essentially mysterious, ... then what he sees on the surface will be of interest to him only as he can go through it into an experience of mystery itself.... [F]or this kind of writer, the meaning of a story does not begin except at a depth where adequate motivation and adequate psychology and the various determinations have been exhausted. Such a writer will be interested in what we don't understand rather than in what we do.

*From "The Nature and Aim of Fiction"[1] (posthumously published in 1972)*

... The beginning of human knowledge is through the senses, and the fiction writer begins where human perception begins. He appeals through the senses, and you cannot appeal to the senses with abstractions.... [F]iction is so very much an incarnational art.

Now the word *symbol* scares a good many people off, just as the word *art* does. They seem to feel that a symbol is some mysterious thing put in arbitrarily by the writer to frighten the common reader—sort of a literary Masonic grip that is only for the initiated. They seem to think that it is a way of saying something that you aren't actually saying, and so ... they approach it as if it were a problem in algebra. Find *x*. And when they do find or think they find this abstraction, *x*, then they go off with an elaborate sense of satisfaction and the notion that they have "understood" the story....

I think for the fiction writer himself, symbols are something he uses simply as a matter of course. You might say that these are details that, while having their essential place in the literal level of the story, operate in depth as well as on the surface, increasing the story in every direction.

People have a habit of saying, "What is the theme of your story?" and they expect you to give them a statement.... And when they've got a statement..., they go off happy and feel it is no longer necessary to read the story..., but for the

---

1. These selections and those that follow (from "Writing Short Stories") are composites, edited from O'Connor manuscripts by Sally and Robert Fitzgerald and published in *Mystery and Manners*.

fiction writer himself the whole story is the meaning, because it is an experience, not an abstraction.

### From "Writing Short Stories" (posthumously published in 1972)

...A story is a complete dramatic action—and in good stories, the characters are shown through the action and the action is controlled through the characters, and the result of this is meaning that derives from the whole presented experience.

...Nothing essential to the main experience can be left out of a short story. All the action has to be satisfactorily accounted for in terms of motivation, and there has to be a beginning, a middle, and an end, though not necessarily in that order.

...I prefer to talk about the meaning in a story rather than the theme of a story. People talk about the theme of a story as if the theme were like the string that a sack of chicken feed is tied with. They think that if you can pick out the theme, the way you pick the right thread in the chicken-feed sack, you can rip the story open and feed the chickens. But this is not the way meaning works in fiction.

O'Connor alongside self-portrait with peacock

When you can state the theme of a story, when you can separate it from the story itself, then you can be sure the story is not a very good one. The meaning of a story has to be embodied in it, has to be made concrete in it. A story is a way to say something that can't be said any other way, and it takes every word in the story to say what the meaning is. You tell a story because a statement would be inadequate.

An idiom characterizes a society, and when you ignore the idiom, you are very likely ignoring the whole social fabric that could make a meaningful character. You can't cut characters off from their society and say much about them as individuals. You can't say anything meaningful about the mystery of a personality unless you put that personality in a believable and significant social context.

### From "On Her Own Work" (posthumously published in 1972)

In most English classes the short story has become a kind of literary specimen to be dissected. Every time a story of mine appears in a Freshman anthology, I have a vision of it, with its little organs laid open, like a frog in a bottle.

I realize that a certain amount of this what-is-the-significance has to go on, but I think something has gone wrong in the process when, for so many students, the story becomes simply a problem to be solved, something which you evaporate to get Instant Enlightenment.

A story isn't any good unless it successfully resists paraphrase, unless it hangs on and expands in the mind. Properly, you analyze to enjoy, but it's equally true that to analyze with any discrimination, you have to have enjoyed already, and I think that the best reason to hear a story read is that it should stimulate that primary enjoyment.

I often ask myself what makes a story work, and what makes it hold up as a story, and I have decided that it is probably some action, some gesture of a character that is unlike any other in the story, one which indicates where the real heart of the story lies. This would have to be an action or a gesture which was both totally right and totally unexpected; it would have to be one that was both in character and beyond character; it would have to suggest both the world and eternity. The action or gesture I'm talking about would have to be on the anagogical level, that is, the level which has to do with the Divine life and our participation in it. It would be a gesture that transcended any neat allegory that might have been intended or any pat moral categories a reader could make. It would be a gesture which somehow made contact with mystery.

. . . [I]n my own stories I have found that violence is strangely capable of returning my characters to reality and preparing them to accept their moment of grace. . . .

We hear many complaints about the prevalence of violence in modern fiction, and it is always assumed that this violence is a bad thing and meant to be an end in itself. With the serious writer, violence is never an end in itself. It is the extreme situation that best reveals what we are essentially. . . .

### From "Novelist and Believer" (written 1963; posthumously published in 1972)

. . . Great fiction . . . is not simply an imitation of feeling. The good novelist not only finds a symbol for feeling, he finds a symbol and a way of lodging it which tells the intelligent reader whether this feeling is adequate or inadequate, whether it is moral or immoral, whether it is good or evil. And his theology, even in its most remote reaches, will have a direct bearing on this.

. . . The artist penetrates the concrete world in order to find at its depths the image of its source, the image of ultimate reality. This in no way hinders his perception of evil but rather sharpens it, for only when the natural world is seen as good does evil become intelligible as a destructive force and a necessary result of our freedom.

### From the Letters

To a Professor of English, 28 March 1961

The meaning of a story should go on expanding for the reader the more he thinks about it, but meaning cannot be captured in an interpretation. If teachers are in the habit of approaching a story as if it were a research problem for which any answer is believable so long as it is not obvious, then I think students will never learn to enjoy fiction. Too much interpretation is certainly worse than too little, and where feeling for a story is absent, theory will not supply it.

To Louise and Tom Gossett, 10 April 1961

I have just read a review of my book [*The Violent Bear It Away*], long and damming [sic], which says it don't give us hope and courage and that all novels should give us hope and courage. I think if the novel is to give us virtue the selection of hope and courage is rather arbitrary—why not charity, peace, patience, joy, benignity, long-suffering and fear of the Lord? Or faith? The fact of the matter is that the modern mind opposes courage to faith. It also demands that the novel provide us with gifts that only religion can give. I don't think the novel can offend against the truth, but I think its truths are more particular than general. But this is a large subject and I ain't no aesthetician.

To Roslyn Barnes, 17 June 1961

Can you tell me if the statement: "everything that rises must converge" is a true proposition in physics? I can easily see its moral, historical and evolutionary significance, but I want to know if it is also a correct physical statement.

To "A," 22 July 1961

I had a story that I had written a first draft sort of on and Caroline thought as usual that it wasn't dramatic enough (and she was right) and told me all the things that I tell you when I read one of yours. She did think the structure was good and the situation. All I got to do is write the story. This one is called "The Lame Shall Enter First."

To "A," 16 September 1961

The thing I am writing now is surely going to convince Jack [the author John Hawkes] that I am of the Devil's party. It is out of hand right now but I am hoping I can bring it into line. It is a composite of all the eccentricities of my writing and for this reason may not be any good, maybe almost a parody. But what you start, you ought to carry through and if it is no good, I don't have to publish it. I am thinking of changing the title to "The Lame Will Carry Off the Prey."

To John Hawkes, 28 November 1961

You haven't convinced me that I write with the Devil's will or belong in the romantic tradition and I'm prepared to argue some more with you on this if I can remember where we left off at. I think the reason we can't agree on this is because there is a difference in our two devils. My Devil has a name, a history and a definite plan. His name is Lucifer, he's a fallen angel, his sin is pride, and his aim is the destruction of the Divine plan. Now I judge that your Devil is co-equal to God, not his creature: that pride is his virtue not his sin; and that his aim is not to destroy the Divine plan because there isn't any Divine plan to destroy. My Devil is objective and yours is subjective. You say one becomes "evil" when one leaves the herd. I say that depends entirely on what the herd is doing.

To "A," 9 December 1961

Some friends of mine in Texas wrote me that a friend of theirs went into a bookstore looking for a paperback copy of *A Good Man*. The clerk said, "We don't have that one but we have another by that author, called *The Bear That Ran Away With It.*" I foresee the trouble I am going to have with "Everything That Rises Must Converge"—"Every Rabbit That Rises Is a Sage."

To Cecil Dawkins, 6 September 1962

About the story ["The Lame Shall Enter First"] I certainly agree that it don't work and have never felt that it did, but in heaven's name where do you get the idea that Sheppard represents Freud? Freud never entered my mind and looking back over it, I can't make him fit now. The story is about a man who thought he was good and thought he was doing good when he wasn't. Freud was a great one, wasn't he, for bringing home to people the fact that they weren't what they thought they were, so if Freud were in this, which he is not, he would certainly be on the other side of the fence from Shepp. The story doesn't work because I don't know, don't sympathize, don't like Mr. Sheppard in the way that I know and like most of my other characters. This is a story, not a statement. I think you ought to look for simpler explanations of why things don't work and not mess around with philosophical ideas where they haven't been intended or don't apply. There's nothing in the story that could possibly suggest that Sheppard represents Freud. This is some theory of which you are possessed. I am wondering if this kind of theorizing could be what is interfering with your getting going on some writing. Don't mix up thought-knowledge with felt-knowledge. If Sheppard represents anything here, it is, as he realizes at the end of the story, the empty man who fills up his emptiness with good works.

To "A," 3 November 1962

...In that story of mine ["The Lame Shall Enter First"]...the little boy wouldn't have been looking for his mother if she hadn't been a good one when she was alive. This of course could be debated, but it's nowhere suggested in the story that she wasn't a good one.

To Marion Montgomery, 16 June 1963

I never wrote and thanked you for innerducing me at Georgia or for the copy of *The Sermon of Introduction,* but I liked them. They made up for my present lack of popularity with the *Atlanta Journal-Constitution* book page, that alert sheet of Sunday criticism. Did you ever see their mention of "Everything That Rises Must Converge"? Unsigned. I suspect somebody from Atlanta U. did it.

To "A," 1 September 1963

The topical is poison. I got away with it in "Everything That Rises" but only because I say a plague on everybody's house as far as the race business goes.

## SUGGESTIONS FOR WRITING

1. The novelist and critic Ford Madox Ford praised the opening paragraph of "Odour of Chrysanthemums" for the precision of its imagery, which, Ford argues, creates a bond of trust between author and reader: "He knows the life he is writing about. ...You can trust him for the rest." (Ford's remarks about Lawrence can be found in the introduction to this chapter.) What do you think Ford means by "the rest"? What might be the larger purpose behind the descriptive details? Write an essay in which you examine the imagery in one or more of the stories by Lawrence in this chapter and discuss the interrelationship among imagery, language, and theme.
2. Each of the stories by Lawrence in this chapter presents flawed or mortally conflicted relationships—the unhappy marriage in "Odour of Chrysanthemums," the dislike between Maurice and Bertie in "The Blind Man," the unloving bond between mother and son in "The Rocking-Horse Winner." What does Lawrence imply about

the reasons for or conequences of the resistance to intimacy? What can you infer about Lawrence's ideals for marriage and for friendship? Drawing from the stories and nonfiction selections in this chapter, write an essay in which you examine Lawrence's negative and positive treatment of physical, emotional, or intellectual intimacy between lovers, family members, or friends.

3. The three stories by Lawrence in this chapter are from different decades of his career—"Odour of Chrysanthemums" (1914), "The Blind Man" (1922), and "The Rocking-Horse Winner" (1932). Citing examples from these stories as well as statements from the "Passages from Letters and Essays," write an essay discussing Lawrence's artistic growth: the evolution of his style, his thematic concerns, his depth of characterization and insight, his vision.

4. Flannery O'Connor wrote that "the beginning of human knowledge is through the senses, and the fiction writer begins where human perception begins." Citing examples from the O'Connor stories and the nonfiction passages in this chapter, write an essay exploring O'Connor's use of imagery as a starting point for depicting human knowledge.

5. In the stories by Flannery O'Connor in this chapter, characters cling fiercely to visions of a better world that can be grasped with the right manners, the right attitudes, the right beliefs. Yet these visions seem at times to be wholly at odds with the realities of the characters' lives. Write an essay in which you discuss the relationship between the actual and the ideal in the O'Connor stories.

6. Flannery O'Connor wrote that "in my own stories I have found that violence is strangely capable of returning my characters to reality and preparing them to accept their moment of grace" and that violence "is the extreme situation that best reveals what we are essentially." Discuss the three stories by O'Connor in this chapter in light of these statements about violence. What "moments of grace" do you see? What "essential" aspects of human character are revealed?

7. Both Lawrence and O'Connor wrote extensively about the purposes and practices of writing fiction. Citing statements from the "Passages from Essays and Letters," write an essay about either the three Lawrence stories or the three O'Connor stories, exploring the degree to which the author's statements about writing are reflected in the author's practice.

8. Research the life of either Flannery O'Connor or D. H. Lawrence. Choose a theme or a social or historical issue in one or more of the stories offered here, and write an essay that discusses the connections between the author's background and the specific treatment of that theme or issue in that story.

9. Write an essay comparing and contrasting Lawrence's and O'Connor's use of characterization, setting, or symbolism in one or more pairs of the stories in this chapter.

10. Write a short story that parodies the style, setting, and subject matter of either D. H. Lawrence or Flannery O'Connor.

# 9 LITERARY KIND AS CONTEXT: INITIATION STORIES

Systems of grouping and classification, used poorly, can blur distinctions and make all members of a group seem the same. Used well, however, they can help to highlight what is unique about each member. Because literary criticism lacks an agreed-upon system of classification, as in biology, its terms are not so fixed as *phylum, genus, species*. In this book, we use the term **genre** for each of the largest commonly agreed-on categories: fiction, poetry, drama. We use the term **subgenre** for each of the divisions within a genre—subgenres of fiction, for example, are novel, novella, short story, and so on. "Genre" comes from the same root word as "genus," and is defined as "kind or type," especially in the context of literature or the arts. Not surprisingly, then, you may find the term applied both broadly (to all fiction, for example) and narrowly (to one type or kind of fiction). Further, within each subgenre we may identify subgroups or **kinds** such as "the mystery novel" or "the utopian novel."

> *There's only one story, the story of your life.*
> —NORTHROP FRYE

One especially common kind of short story is the **initiation story,** in which a character—usually a child or young person—first learns, or is "initiated into," a significant truth about the world, society, people, or himself or herself. Such a subject tends to dictate the main outlines of the story's action: it begins with the protagonist in a state of innocence or mistaken belief (exposition); it leads up to a moment of illumination or the discovery of a truth (rising action to climax or turning point); and it ends usually (but not always) with some indication of the result of that discovery (falling action to conclusion). This pattern is particularly suitable to a short story because it lends itself to brief treatment. The illumination is more or less sudden—there is seldom need for lengthy development, for multiple scenes or settings, for much time to pass, for complex actions or a large cast of characters—yet it can encapsulate a whole life and wide-ranging, significant themes.

If you've been reading this book from the beginning, you have already run into a number of initiation stories, and you may have some idea of what sorts of truths their protagonists discover. The "adult" knowledge into which characters are initiated differs widely, of course, as does their response to that knowledge: one may retreat from the truth physically or psychologically, as does Young Goodman Brown, or remain unchanged, or revert to one's former state. Initiation stories suggest, however, that even if we choose to retreat from a newly perceived truth, we can never completely return to our former innocence.

Since to the young all things seem possible, many of the truths learned in initiation stories have to do with limitation. The girl in Alice Munro's "Boys and Girls" learns that she is "only a girl," the boy in James Joyce's "Araby" that he is merely "a creature driven" by romantic dreams that can never be realized. Sometimes a child learns the difference between words and reality in the adult world, as Hazel does in Toni Cade Bambara's "Gorilla, My Love," or between change and loss, as Nathan Shapiro does in Michael Chabon's "The Lost World."

By the time you finish this chapter, you should have some idea of the variations possible within the initiation story, and, as you look back to such stories as James Baldwin's "Sonny's Blues," John Cheever's "The Country Husband," D. H. Lawrence's "Odour of Chrysanthemums," Flannery O'Connor's "The Lame Shall Enter First," or Toni Morrison's "Recitatif," you should have a still better idea of the range of stories in this kind. Adults may be initiated as well as children and adolescents; the truths may be bitter or pleasing, cosmic or commonplace, social or personal; the initiates may change forever, retreat from knowledge, or just shrug off what they have learned. By seeing all these stories as part of the large group of initiation stories, you may more readily notice the differences among the protagonists, the learning experiences, and the effects of the initiations on the protagonists, whether they are permanent or temporary, life-denying or life-enhancing. You may, in other words, have gone a long way toward defining the unique vision of each story—its particular definitions of illusion and truth, of childlike innocence and adult wisdom. And illuminating such distinctions is the function of classification in the first place.

## TONI CADE BAMBARA

### Gorilla, My Love

That was the year Hunca Bubba changed his name. Not a change up, but a change back, since Jefferson Winston Vale was the name in the first place. Which was news to me cause he'd been my Hunca Bubba my whole lifetime, since I couldn't manage Uncle to save my life. So far as I was concerned it was a change completely to somethin soundin very geographical weatherlike to me, like somethin you'd find in a almanac. Or somethin you'd run across when you sittin in the navigator seat with a wet thumb on the map crinkly in your lap, watchin the roads and signs so when Granddaddy Vale say "Which way, Scout," you got sense enough to say take the next exit or take a left or whatever it is. Not that Scout's my name. Just the name Granddaddy call whoever sittin in the navigator seat. Which is usually me cause I don't feature sittin in the back with the pecans. Now, you figure pecans all right to be sittin with. If you thinks so, that's your business. But they dusty sometime and make you cough. And they got a way of slidin around and dippin down sudden, like maybe a rat in the buckets. So if you scary like me, you sleep with the lights on and blame it on Baby Jason and, so as not to waste good electric, you study the maps. And that's how come I'm in the navigator seat most times and get to be called Scout.

So Hunca Bubba in the back with the pecans and Baby Jason, and he in love. And we got to hear all this stuff about this woman he in love with and all. Which really ain't enough to keep the mind alive, though Baby Jason got no better sense than to give his undivided attention and keep grabbin at the photograph which is just a picture of some skinny woman in a countrified dress with her hand shot up to her face like she shame fore cameras. But there's a movie house in the background which I ax about. Cause I am a movie freak from way back, even though it do get me in trouble sometime.

Like when me and Big Brood and Baby Jason was on our own last Easter and couldn't go to the Dorset cause we'd seen all the Three Stooges they was. And the RKO Hamilton was closed readying up for the Easter Pageant that night. And the West End, the Regun and the Sunset was too far, less we had grownups with us which we didn't. So we walk up Amsterdam Avenue to the Washington and *Gorilla, My Love* playin, they say, which suit me just fine, though the "my love" part kinda drag Big Brood some. As for Baby Jason, shoot, like Granddaddy say, he'd follow me into the fiery furnace if I say come on. So we go in and get three bags of Havmore potato chips which not only are the best potato chips but the best bags for blowin up and bustin real loud so the matron come trottin down the aisle with her chunky self, flashin that flashlight dead in your eye so you can give her some lip, and if she answer back and you already finish seein the show anyway, why then you just turn the place out. Which I love to do, no lie. With Baby Jason kickin at the seat in front, egging me on, and Big Brood mumblin bout what fiercesome things we goin do. Which means me. Like when the big boys come up on us talkin bout Lemme a nickel. It's me that hide the money. Or when the bad boys in the park take Big Brood's Spaudeen[1] way from him. It's me that jump on they back and fight awhile. And it's me that turns out the show if the matron get too salty.

So the movie come on and right away it's this churchy music and clearly not about no gorilla. Bout Jesus. And I am ready to kill, not cause I got anything gainst Jesus. Just that when you fixed to watch a gorilla picture you don't wanna get messed around with Sunday School stuff. So I am mad. Besides, we see this raggedy old brown film *King of Kings*[2] every year and enough's enough. Grownups figure they can treat you just anyhow. Which burns me up. There I am, my feet up and my Havmore potato chips really salty and crispy and two jawbreakers in my lap and the money safe in my shoe from the big boys, and there comes this Jesus stuff. So we all go wild. Yellin, booin, stompin and carryin on. Really to wake the man in the booth up there who musta went to sleep and put on the wrong reels. But no, cause he holler down to shut up and then he turn the sound up so we really gotta holler like crazy to even hear ourselves good. And the matron ropes off the children section and flashes her light all over the place and we yell some more and some kids slip under the rope and run up and down the aisle just to show it take more than some dusty ole velvet rope to tie us down. And I'm flingin the kid in front of me's popcorn. And Baby Jason kickin seats. And it's really somethin. Then here come the big and bad matron, the one they let out in case of emergency. And she totin that flashlight like she gonna use it on somebody. This here the colored matron Brandy and her friends call Thunderbuns. She do not play. She do not smile. So we shut up and watch the simple ass picture.

Which is not so simple as it is stupid. Cause I realized that just about anybody in my family is better than this god they always talkin about. My daddy wouldn't stand for nobody treatin any of us that way. My mama specially. And I can just

---

1. Probably refers to "Spaldeen," the small pink rubber ball made by the Spalding company and used for stick ball.   2. Although there is a 1961 version, this probably refers to the silent movie made in the 1920s.

see it now, Big Brood up there on the cross talkin bout Forgive them Daddy cause they don't know what they doin. And my Mama say Get on down from there you big fool, whatcha think this is, playtime? And my Daddy yellin to Granddaddy to get him a ladder cause Big Brood actin the fool, his mother side of the family showin up. And my mama and her sister Daisy jumpin on them Romans beatin them with they pocketbooks. And Hunca Bubba tellin them folks on they knees they better get out the way and go get some help or they goin to get trampled on. And Granddaddy Vale sayin Leave the boy alone, if that's what he wants to do with his life we ain't got nothin to say about it. Then Aunt Daisy givin him a taste of that pocketbook, fussin bout what a damn fool old man Granddaddy is. Then everybody jumpin in his chest like the time Uncle Clayton went in the army and come back with only one leg and Granddaddy say somethin stupid about that's life. And by this time Big Brood off the cross and in the park playin handball or skully[3] or somethin. And the family in the kitchen throwin dishes at each other, screamin bout if you hadn't done this I wouldn't had to do that. And me in the parlor trying to do my arithmetic yellin Shut it off.

Which is what I was yellin all by myself which make me a sittin target for Thunderbuns. But when I yell We want our money back, that gets everybody in chorus. And the movie windin up with this heavenly cloud music and the smartass up there in his hole in the wall turns up the sound again to drown us out. Then there comes Bugs Bunny which we already seen so we know we been had. No gorilla my nuthin. And Big Brood say Awwww sheeet, we goin to see the manager and get our money back. And I know from this we business. So I brush the potato chips out of my hair which is where Baby Jason like to put em, and I march myself up the aisle to deal with the manager who is a crook in the first place for lyin out there sayin *Gorilla, My Love* playin. And I never did like the man cause he oily and pasty at the same time like the bad guy in the serial, the one that got a hideout behind a push-button bookcase and play "Moonlight Sonata"[4] with gloves on. I knock on the door and I am furious. And I am alone, too. Cause Big Brood suddenly got to go so bad even though my mama told us bout goin in them nasty bathrooms. And I hear him sigh like he disgusted when he get to the door and see only a little kid there. And now I'm really furious cause I get so tired grownups messin over kids cause they little and can't take em to court. What is it, he say to me like I lost my mittens or wet myself or am somebody's retarded child. When in reality I am the smartest kid P.S. 186 ever had in its whole lifetime and you can ax anybody. Even them teachers that don't like me cause I won't sing them Southern songs or back off when they tell me my questions are out of order. And cause my Mama come up there in a minute when them teachers start playin the dozens[5] behind colored folks. She stalks in with her hat pulled down bad and that Persian lamb coat draped back over one hip on account of she got her fist planted there so she can talk that talk which gets us all hypnotized, and teacher be comin undone cause she know this could be her job and her behind cause Mama got pull with the Board and bad by her own self anyhow.

---

3. A basketball game that tests shooting skill and can be played alone or as a contest between two people.
4. Popular name for Beethoven's *Piano Sonata in C Sharp Minor*, Opus 27, No. 2. The "bad guy" who plays this piece is the Phantom of the Opera.
5. Ritualized game or contest in which two participants exchange artfully stylized insults.

So I kick the door open wider and just walk right by him and sit down and tell the man about himself and that I want my money back and that goes for Baby Jason and Big Brood too. And he still trying to shuffle me out the door even though I'm sittin which shows him for the fool he is. Just like them teachers do fore they realize Mama like a stone on that spot and ain't backin up. So he ain't gettin up off the money. So I was forced to leave, takin the matches from under his ashtray, and set a fire under the candy stand, which closed the raggedy ole Washington down for a week. My Daddy had the suspect it was me cause Big Brood got a big mouth. But I explained right quick what the whole thing was about and I figured it was even-steven. Cause if you say Gorilla, My Love, you supposed to mean it. Just like when you say you goin to give me a party on my birthday, you gotta mean it. And if you say me and Baby Jason can go South pecan haulin with Granddaddy Vale, you better not be comin up with no stuff about the weather look uncertain or did you mop the bathroom or any other trickified business. I mean even gangsters in the movies say My word is my bond. So don't nobody get away with nothin far as I'm concerned. So Daddy put his belt back on. Cause that's the way I was raised. Like my Mama say in one of them situations when I won't back down, Okay Badbird, you right. Your point is well-taken. Not that Badbird my name, just what she say when she tired arguin and know I'm right. And Aunt Jo, who is the hardest head in the family and worse even than Aunt Daisy, she say, You absolutely right Miss Muffin, which also ain't my real name but the name she gave me one time when I got some medicine shot in my behind and wouldn't get up off her pillows for nothin. And even Granddaddy Vale—who got no memory to speak of, so sometime you can just plain lie to him, if you want to be like that—he say, Well if that's what I said, then that's it. But this name business was different they said. It wasn't like Hunca Bubba had gone back on his word or anything. Just that he was thinkin bout gettin married and was usin his real name now. Which ain't the way I saw it at all.

So there I am in the navigator seat. And I turned to him and just plain ole ax him. I mean I come right on out with it. No sense goin all around that barn the old folks talk about. And like my mama say, Hazel—which is my real name and what she remembers to call me when she bein serious—when you got somethin on your mind, speak up and let the chips fall where they may. And if anybody don't like it, tell em to come see your mama. And Daddy look up from the paper and say, You hear your Mama good, Hazel. And tell em to come see me first. Like that. That's how I was raised.

So I turn clear round in the navigator seat and say, "Look here, Hunca Bubba or Jefferson Windsong Vale or whatever your name is, you gonna marry this girl?"

"Sure am," he say, all grins.

And I say, "Member that time you was baby-sittin me when we lived at four-o-nine and there was this big snow and Mama and Daddy got held up in the country so you had to stay for two days?"

And he say, "Sure do."

"Well. You remember how you told me I was the cutest thing that ever walked the earth?"

"Oh, you were real cute when you were little," he say, which is supposed to be funny. I am not laughin.

"Well. You remember what you said?"

And Granddaddy Vale squintin over the wheel and axin Which way, Scout. But Scout is busy and don't care if we all get lost for days.

"Watcha mean, Peaches?"

"My name is Hazel. And what I mean is you said you were going to marry *me* when I grew up. You were going to wait. That's what I mean, my dear Uncle Jefferson." And he don't say nuthin. Just look at me real strange like he never saw me before in life. Like he lost in some weird town in the middle of night and lookin for directions and there's no one to ask. Like it was me that messed up the maps and turned the road posts round. "Well, you said it, didn't you?" And Baby Jason lookin back and forth like we playin ping-pong. Only I ain't playin. I'm hurtin and I can hear that I am screamin. And Granddaddy Vale mumblin how we never gonna get to where we goin if I don't turn around and take my navigator job serious.

"Well, for cryin out loud, Hazel, you just a little girl. And I was just teasin."

" 'And I was just teasin,' " I say back just how he said it so he can hear what a terrible thing it is. Then I don't say nuthin. And he don't say nuthin. And Baby Jason don't say nuthin nohow. Then Granddaddy Vale speak up. "Look here, Precious, it was Hunca Bubba what told you them things. This here, Jefferson Winston Vale." And Hunca Bubba say, "That's right. That was somebody else. I'm a new somebody."

"You a lyin dawg," I say, when I meant to say treacherous dog, but just couldn't get hold of the word. It slipped away from me. And I'm crying and crumplin down in the seat and just don't care. And Granddaddy say to hush and steps on the gas. And I'm losin my bearins and don't even know where to look on the map cause I can't see for cryin. And Baby Jason cryin too. Cause he is my blood brother and understands that we must stick together or be forever lost, what with grown-ups playin change-up and turnin you round every which way so bad. And don't even say they sorry.

### QUESTIONS

1. How is Hazel, the narrator of "Gorilla, My Love," characterized? What are some of the methods that Toni Cade Bambara uses to establish Hazel's age, sex, ethnicity, and personality?
2. Some characters in this story, including Hazel, have multiple names. How do these names contribute to characterization? to theme?
3. How and why does Hazel's view of adults change over the course of the story? What truth does she seem to learn?

### ALICE MUNRO

## Boys and Girls

My father was a fox farmer. That is, he raised silver foxes, in pens; and in the fall and early winter, when their fur was prime, he killed them and skinned them and sold their pelts to the Hudson's Bay Company or the Montreal Fur Traders. These companies supplied us with heroic calendars to hang, one on each side of the kitchen door. Against a background of cold blue sky and black pine forests and treacherous northern rivers, plumed adventurers planted the flags of England or of France; magnificent savages bent their backs to the portage.

For several weeks before Christmas, my father worked after supper in the cellar of our house. The cellar was white-washed, and lit by a hundred-watt bulb over the worktable. My brother Laird and I sat on the top step and watched. My father removed the pelt inside-out from the body of the fox, which looked surprisingly small, mean and rat-like, deprived of its arrogant weight of fur. The naked, slippery bodies were collected in a sack and buried at the dump. One time the hired man, Henry Bailey, had taken a swipe at me with this sack, saying, "Christmas present!" My mother thought that was not funny. In fact she disliked the whole pelting operation—that was what the killing, skinning, and preparation of the furs was called—and wished it did not have to take place in the house. There was the smell. After the pelt had been stretched inside-out on a long board my father scraped away delicately, removing the little clotted webs of blood vessels, the bubbles of fat; the smell of blood and animal fat, with the strong primitive odour of the fox itself, penetrated all parts of the house. I found it reassuringly seasonal, like the smell of oranges and pine needles.

Henry Bailey suffered from bronchial troubles. He would cough and cough until his narrow face turned scarlet, and his light blue, derisive eyes filled up with tears; then he took the lid off the stove, and, standing well back, shot out a great clot of phlegm—hsss—straight into the heart of the flames. We admired him for this performance and for his ability to make his stomach growl at will, and for his laughter, which was full of high whistlings and gurglings and involved the whole faulty machinery of his chest. It was sometimes hard to tell what he was laughing at, and always possible that it might be us.

After we had been sent to bed we could still smell fox and still hear Henry's laugh, but these things, reminders of the warm, safe, brightly lit downstairs world, seemed lost and diminished, floating on the stale cold air upstairs. We were afraid at night in the winter. We were not afraid of *outside* though this was the time of year when snowdrifts curled around our house like sleeping whales and the wind harassed us all night, coming up from the buried fields, the frozen swamp, with its old bugbear chorus of threats and misery. We were afraid of *inside*, the room where we slept. At this time the upstairs of our house was not finished. A brick chimney went up one wall. In the middle of the floor was a square hole, with a wooden railing around it; that was where the stairs came up. On the other side of the stairwell were the things that nobody had any use for any more—a soldiery roll of linoleum, standing on end, a wicker baby carriage, a fern basket, china jugs and basins with cracks in them, a picture of the Battle of Balaclava,[1] very sad to look at. I had told Laird, as soon as he was old enough to understand such things, that bats and skeletons lived over there; whenever a man escaped from the county jail, twenty miles away, I imagined that he had somehow let himself in the window and was hiding behind the linoleum. But we had rules to keep us safe. When the light was on, we were safe as long as we did not step off the square of worn carpet which defined our bedroom-space; when the light was off no place was safe but the beds themselves. I had to turn out the light kneeling on the end of my bed, and stretching as far as I could to reach the cord.

---

1. An indecisive Crimean War battle fought on October 25, 1854.

In the dark we lay on our beds, our narrow life rafts, and fixed our eyes on 5 the faint light coming up the stairwell, and sang songs. Laird sang "Jingle Bells," which he would sing any time, whether it was Christmas or not, and I sang "Danny Boy." I loved the sound of my own voice, frail and supplicating, rising in the dark. We could make out the tall frosted shapes of the windows now, gloomy and white. When I came to the part, *When I am dead, as dead I well may be*—a fit of shivering caused not by the cold sheets but by pleasurable emotion almost silenced me. *You'll kneel and say, an Ave there above me*—What was an Ave? Every day I forgot to find out.

Laird went straight from singing to sleep. I could hear his long, satisfied, bubbly breaths. Now for the time that remained to me, the most perfectly private and perhaps the best time of the whole day, I arranged myself tightly under the covers and went on with one of the stories I was telling myself from night to night. These stories were about myself, when I had grown a little older; they took place in a world that was recognizably mine, yet one that presented opportunities for courage, boldness and self-sacrifice, as mine never did. I rescued people from a bombed building (it discouraged me that the real war had gone on so far away from Jubilee). I shot two rabid wolves who were menacing the schoolyard (the teachers cowered terrified at my back). I rode a fine horse spiritedly down the main street of Jubilee, acknowledging the townspeople's gratitude for some yet-to-be-worked-out piece of heroism (nobody ever rode a horse there, except King Billy in the Orangemen's Day[2] parade). There was always riding and shooting in these stories, though I had only been on a horse twice—bareback because we did not own a saddle—and the second time I had slid right around and dropped under the horse's feet; it had stepped placidly over me. I really was learning to shoot, but I could not hit anything yet, not even tin cans on fence posts.

Alive, the foxes inhabited a world my father made for them. It was surrounded by a high guard fence, like a medieval town, with a gate that was padlocked at night. Along the streets of this town were ranged large, sturdy pens. Each of them had a real door that a man could go through, a wooden ramp along the wire, for the foxes to run up and down on, and a kennel—something like a clothes chest with airholes—where they slept and stayed in winter and had their young. There were feeding and watering dishes attached to the wire in such a way that they could be emptied and cleaned from the outside. The dishes were made of old tin cans, and the ramps and kennels of odds and ends of old lumber. Everything was tidy and ingenious; my father was tirelessly inventive and his favourite book in the world was *Robinson Crusoe*.[3] He had fitted a tin drum on a wheelbarrow, for bringing water down to the pens. This was my job in summer, when the foxes had to have water twice a day. Between nine and ten o'clock in the morning, and again after supper, I filled the drum at the pump and trundled it down through the barnyard to the pens, where I parked it, and filled my watering can and went along the streets. Laird came too, with his little cream and green

---

2. The Orange Society is an Irish Protestant group named after William of Orange, who, as King William III of England, defeated the Catholic James II. The society sponsors an annual procession on July 12 to commemorate the victory of William III at the Battle of the Boyne (1690).
3. Novel (1719) by Daniel Defoe about a man shipwrecked on a desert island; it goes into great detail about the ingenious contraptions he fashions from simple materials.

gardening can, filled too full and knocking against his legs and slopping water on his canvas shoes. I had the real watering can, my father's, though I could only carry it three-quarters full.

The foxes all had names, which were printed on a tin plate and hung beside their doors. They were not named when they were born, but when they survived the first year's pelting and were added to the breeding stock. Those my father had named were called names like Prince, Bob, Wally and Betty. Those I had named were called Star or Turk, or Maureen or Diana. Laird named one Maud after a hired girl we had when he was little, one Harold after a boy at school, and one Mexico, he did not say why.

Naming them did not make pets out of them, or anything like it. Nobody but my father ever went into the pens, and he had twice had blood-poisoning from bites. When I was bringing them their water they prowled up and down on the paths they had made inside their pens, barking seldom—they saved that for nighttime, when they might get up a chorus of community frenzy—but always watching me, their eyes burning, clear gold, in their pointed, malevolent faces. They were beautiful for their delicate legs and heavy, aristocratic tails and the bright fur sprinkled on dark down their backs—which gave them their name—but especially for their faces, drawn exquisitely sharp in pure hostility, and their golden eyes.

10  Besides carrying water I helped my father when he cut the long grass, and the lamb's quarter and flowering money-musk, that grew between the pens. He cut with the scythe and I raked into piles. Then he took a pitchfork and threw freshcut grass all over the top of the pens, to keep the foxes cooler and shade their coats, which were browned by too much sun. My father did not talk to me unless it was about the job we were doing. In this he was quite different from my mother, who, if she was feeling cheerful, would tell me all sorts of things— the name of a dog she had had when she was a little girl, the names of boys she had gone out with later on when she was grown up, and what certain dresses of hers had looked like—she could not imagine now what had become of them. Whatever thoughts and stories my father had were private, and I was shy of him and would never ask him questions. Nevertheless I worked willingly under his eyes, and with a feeling of pride. One time a feed salesman came down into the pens to talk to him and my father said, "Like to have you meet my new hired man." I turned away and raked furiously, red in the face with pleasure.

"Could of fooled me," said the salesman. "I thought it was only a girl."

After the grass was cut, it seemed suddenly much later in the year. I walked on stubble in the earlier evening, aware of the reddening skies, the entering silences, of fall. When I wheeled the tank out of the gate and put the padlock on, it was almost dark. One night at this time I saw my mother and father standing talking on the little rise of ground we called the gangway, in front of the barn. My father had just come from the meathouse; he had his stiff bloody apron on, and a pail of cut-up meat in his hand.

It was an odd thing to see my mother down at the barn. She did not often come out of the house unless it was to do something—hang out the wash or dig potatoes in the garden. She looked out of place, with her bare lumpy legs, not touched by the sun, her apron still on and damp across the stomach from the supper dishes. Her hair was tied up in a kerchief, wisps of it falling out. She would tie her hair up like this in the morning, saying she did not have time to do it properly, and it would stay tied up all day. It was true, too; she really did not have time. These days our back porch was piled with baskets of peaches and grapes and pears, bought in town, and onions and tomatoes and cucumbers grown at home, all waiting to be made into jelly and jam and preserves, pickles and chili sauce. In the kitchen there was a fire in the stove all day, jars clinked in boiling water, sometimes a cheesecloth bag was strung on a pole between two chairs, straining blue-black grape pulp for jelly. I was given jobs to do and I would sit at the table peeling peaches that had been soaked in the hot water, or cutting up onions, my eyes smarting and streaming. As soon as I was done I ran out of the house, trying to get out of earshot before my mother thought of what she wanted me to do next. I hated the hot dark kitchen in summer, the green blinds and the flypapers, the same old oilcloth table and wavy mirror and bumpy linoleum. My mother was too tired and preoccupied to talk to me, she had no heart to tell about the Normal School Graduation Dance; sweat trickled over her face and she was always counting under her breath, pointing at jars, dumping cups of sugar. It seemed to me that work in the house was endless, dreary and peculiarly depressing; work done out of doors, and in my father's service, was ritualistically important.

I wheeled the tank up to the barn, where it was kept, and I heard my mother saying, "Wait till Laird gets a little bigger, then you'll have a real help."

What my father said I did not hear. I was pleased by the way he stood listening, politely as he would to a salesman or a stranger, but with an air of wanting to get on with his real work. I felt my mother had no business down here and I wanted him to feel the same way. What did she mean about Laird? He was no help to anybody. Where was he now? Swinging himself sick on the swing, going around in circles, or trying to catch caterpillars. He never once stayed with me till I was finished.

"And then I can use her more in the house," I heard my mother say. She had a dead-quiet, regretful way of talking about me that always made me uneasy. "I just get my back turned and she runs off. It's not like I had a girl in the family at all."

I went and sat on a feed bag in the corner of the barn, not wanting to appear when this conversation was going on. My mother, I felt, was not to be trusted. She was kinder than my father and more easily fooled, but you could not depend on her, and the real reasons for the things she said and did were not to be known. She loved me, and she sat up late at night making a dress of the difficult style I wanted, for me to wear when school started, but she was also my enemy. She was always plotting. She was plotting now to get me to stay in the house more, although she knew I hated it (*because* she knew I hated it) and keep me from working for my father. It seemed to me she would do this simply out of perversity, and to try her power. It did not occur to me that she could be lonely, or jealous. No grown-up could be; they were too fortunate. I sat and kicked my heels monotonously against a feedbag, raising dust, and did not come out till she was gone.

At any rate, I did not expect my father to pay any attention to what she said. Who could imagine Laird doing my work—Laird remembering the padlock and cleaning out the watering-dishes with a leaf on the end of a stick, or even wheeling the tank without it tumbling over? It showed how little my mother knew about the way things really were.

I have forgotten to say what the foxes were fed. My father's bloody apron reminded me. They were fed horsemeat. At this time most farmers still kept horses, and when a horse got too old to work, or broke a leg or got down and would not get up, as they sometimes did, the owner would call my father, and he and Henry went out to the farm in the truck. Usually they shot and butchered the horse there, paying the farmer from five to twelve dollars. If they had already too much meat on hand, they would bring the horse back alive, and keep it for a few days or weeks in our stable, until the meat was needed. After the war the farmers were buying tractors and gradually getting rid of horses altogether, so it sometimes happened that we got a good healthy horse, that there was just no use for any more. If this happened in the winter we might keep the horse in our stable till spring, for we had plenty of hay and if there was a lot of snow—and the plow did not always get our road cleared—it was convenient to be able to go to town with a horse and cutter.[4]

20      The winter I was eleven years old we had two horses in the stable. We did not know what names they had had before, so we called them Mack and Flora. Mack was an old black workhorse, sooty and indifferent. Flora was a sorrel mare, a driver. We took them both out in the cutter. Mack was slow and easy to handle. Flora was given to fits of violent alarm, veering at cars and even at other horses, but we loved her speed and high-stepping, her general air of gallantry and abandon. On Saturdays we went down to the stable and as soon as we opened the door on its cosy, animal-smelling darkness Flora threw up her head, rolled her eyes, whinnied despairingly and pulled herself through a crisis of nerves on the spot. It was not safe to go into her stall; she would kick.

This winter also I began to hear a great deal more on the theme my mother had sounded when she had been talking in front of the barn. I no longer felt safe. It seemed that in the minds of the people around me there was a steady undercurrent of thought, not to be deflected, on this one subject. The word *girl* had formerly seemed to me innocent and unburdened, like the world *child;* now it appeared that it was no such thing. A girl was not, as I had supposed, simply what I was; it was what I had to become. It was a definition, always touched with emphasis, with reproach and disappointment. Also it was a joke on me. Once Laird and I were fighting, and for the first time ever I had to use all my strength against him; even so, he caught and pinned my arm for a moment, really hurting me. Henry saw this, and laughed, saying, "Oh, that there Laird's gonna show you, one of these days!" Laird was getting a lot bigger. But I was getting bigger too.

My grandmother came to stay with us for a few weeks and I heard other things. "Girls don't slam doors like that." "Girls keep their knees together when they sit down." And worse still, when I asked some questions, "That's none of girls' business." I continued to slam the doors and sit as awkwardly as possible, thinking that by such measures I kept myself free.

When spring came, the horses were let out in the barnyard. Mack stood against the barn wall trying to scratch his neck and haunches, but Flora trotted up and down and reared at the fences, clattering her hooves against the rails. Snow drifts dwindled quickly, revealing the hard grey and brown earth, the familiar rise and

4. A small, light sleigh.

fall of the ground, plain and bare after the fantastic landscape of winter. There was a great feeling of opening-out, of release. We just wore rubbers now, over our shoes; our feet felt ridiculously light. One Saturday we went out to the stable and found all the doors open, letting in the unaccustomed sunlight and fresh air. Henry was there, just idling around looking at his collection of calendars which were tacked up behind the stalls in a part of the stable my mother had probably never seen.

"Come to say goodbye to your old friend Mack?" Henry said. "Here, you give him a taste of oats." He poured some oats into Laird's cupped hands and Laird went to feed Mack. Mack's teeth were in bad shape. He ate very slowly, patiently shifting the oats around in his mouth, trying to find a stump of a molar to grind it on. "Poor old Mack," said Henry mournfully. "When a horse's teeth's gone, he's gone. That's about the way."

"Are you going to shoot him today?" I said. Mack and Flora had been in the stable so long I had almost forgotten they were going to be shot.

Henry didn't answer me. Instead he started to sing in a high, trembly, mocking-sorrowful voice, *Oh, there's no more work, for poor Uncle Ned, he's gone where the good darkies go.*[5] Mack's thick, blackish tongue worked diligently at Laird's hand. I went out before the song was ended and sat down on the gangway.

I had never seen them shoot a horse, but I knew where it was done. Last summer Laird and I had come upon a horse's entrails before they were buried. We had thought it was a big black snake, coiled up in the sun. That was around in the field that ran up beside the barn. I thought that if we went inside the barn, and found a wide crack or knothole to look through we would be able to see them do it. It was not something I wanted to see; just the same, if a thing really happened, it was better to see it, and know.

My father came down from the house, carrying the gun.

"What are you doing here?" he said.

"Nothing."

"Go on up and play around the house."

He sent Laird out of the stable. I said to Laird, "Do you want to see them shoot Mack?" and without waiting for an answer led him around to the front door of the barn, opened it carefully, and went in. "Be quiet or they'll hear us," I said. We could hear Henry and my father talking in the stable, then the heavy, shuffling steps of Mack being backed out of his stall.

In the loft it was cold and dark. Thin, crisscrossed beams of sunlight fell through the cracks. The hay was low. It was a rolling country, hills and hollows, slipping under our feet. About four feet up was a beam going around the walls. We piled hay up in one corner and I boosted Laird up and hoisted myself. The beam was not very wide; we crept along it with our hands flat on the barn walls. There were plenty of knotholes, and I found one that gave me the view I wanted—a corner of the barnyard, the gate, part of the field. Laird did not have a knothole and began to complain.

I showed him a widened crack between two boards. "Be quiet and wait. If they hear you you'll get us in trouble."

My father came in sight carrying the gun. Henry was leading Mack by the

---

5. Lines from the Stephen Foster song "Old Uncle Ned."

halter. He dropped it and took out his cigarette papers and tobacco; he rolled cigarettes for my father and himself. While this was going on Mack nosed around in the old, dead grass along the fence. Then my father opened the gate and they took Mack through. Henry led Mack way from the path to a patch of ground and they talked together, not loud enough for us to hear. Mack again began searching for a mouthful of fresh grass, which was not to be found. My father walked away in a straight line, and stopped short at a distance which seemed to suit him. Henry was walking away from Mack too, but sideways, still negligently holding on to the halter. My father raised the gun and Mack looked up as if he had noticed something and my father shot him.

Mack did not collapse at once but swayed, lurched sideways and fell, first on his side; then he rolled over on his back and, amazingly, kicked his legs for a few seconds in the air. At this Henry laughed, as if Mack had done a trick for him. Laird, who had drawn a long, groaning breath of surprise when the shot was fired, said out loud, "He's not dead." And it seemed to me it might be true. But his legs stopped, he rolled on his side again, his muscles quivered and sank. The two men walked over and looked at him in a businesslike way; they bent down and examined his forehead where the bullet had gone in, and now I saw his blood on the brown grass.

"Now they just skin him and cut him up," I said. "Let's go." My legs were a little shaky and I jumped gratefully down into the hay. "Now you've seen how they shoot a horse," I said in a congratulatory way, as if I had seen it many times before. "Let's see if any barn cat's had kittens in the hay." Laird jumped. He seemed young and obedient again. Suddenly I remembered how, when he was little, I had brought him into the barn and told him to climb the ladder to the top beam. That was in the spring, too, when the hay was low. I had done it out of a need for excitement, a desire for something to happen so that I could tell about it. He was wearing a little bulky brown and white checked coat, made down from one of mine. He went all the way up, just as I told him, and sat down on the top beam with the hay far below him on one side, and the barn floor and some old machinery on the other. Then I ran screaming to my father, "Laird's up on the top beam!" My father came, my mother came, my father went up the ladder talking very quietly and brought Laird down under his arm, at which my mother leaned against the ladder and began to cry. They said to me, "Why weren't you watching him?" but nobody ever knew the truth. Laird did not know enough to tell. But whenever I saw the brown and white checked coat hanging in the closet, or at the bottom of the rag bag, which was where it ended up, I felt a weight in my stomach, the sadness of unexorcized guilt.

I looked at Laird who did not even remember this, and I did not like the look on this thin, winter-pale face. His expression was not frightened or upset, but remote, concentrating. "Listen," I said, in an unusually bright and friendly voice, "you aren't going to tell, are you?"

"No," he said absently.

40   "Promise."

"Promise," he said. I grabbed the hand behind his back to make sure he was not crossing his fingers. Even so, he might have a nightmare; it might come out that way. I decided I had better work hard to get all thoughts of what he had seen out of his mind—which, it seemed to me, could not hold very many things at a time. I got some money I had saved and that afternoon we went into Jubilee and saw a show, with Judy Canova,[6] at which we both laughed a great deal. After that I thought it would be all right.

Two weeks later I knew they were going to shoot Flora. I knew from the night before, when I heard my mother ask if the hay was holding out all right, and my father said, "Well, after to-morrow there'll just be the cow, and we should be able to put her out to grass in another week." So I knew it was Flora's turn in the morning.

This time I didn't think of watching it. That was something to see just one time. I had not thought about it very often since, but sometimes when I was busy, working at school, or standing in front of the mirror combing my hair and wondering if I would be pretty when I grew up, the whole scene would flash into my mind: I would see the easy, practised way my father raised the gun, and hear Henry laughing when Mack kicked his legs in the air. I did not have any great feeling of horror and opposition, such as a city child might have had; I was too used to seeing the death of animals as a necessity by which we lived. Yet I felt a little ashamed, and there was a new wariness, a sense of holding-off, in my attitude to my father and his work.

It was a fine day, and we were going around the yard picking up tree branches that had been torn off in winter storms. This was something we had been told to do, and also we wanted to use them to make a teepee. We heard Flora whinny, and then my father's voice and Henry's shouting, and we ran down to the barnyard to see what was going on.

The stable door was open. Henry had just brought Flora out, and she had broken away from him. She was running free in the barnyard, from one end to the other. We climbed up on the fence. It was exciting to see her running, whinnying, going up on her hind legs, prancing and threatening like a horse in a Western movie, an unbroken ranch horse, though she was just an old driver, an old sorrel mare. My father and Henry ran after her and tried to grab the dangling halter. They tried to work her into a corner, and they had almost succeeded when she made a run between them, wild-eyed, and disappeared around the corner of the barn. We heard the rails clatter down as she got over the fence, and Henry yelled, "She's into the field now!"

That meant she was in the long L-shaped field that ran up by the house. If she got around the center, heading towards the lane, the gate was open; the truck had been driven into the field this morning. My father shouted to me, because I was on the other side of the fence, nearest the lane, "Go shut the gate!"

I could run very fast. I ran across the garden, past the tree where our swing was hung, and jumped across a ditch into the lane. There was the open gate. She had not got out, I could not see her up on the road; she must have run to the other end of the field. The gate was heavy. I lifted it out of the gravel and carried it across the roadway. I had it half-way across when she came in sight, galloping straight towards me. There was just time to get the chain on. Laird came scrambling through the ditch to help me.

Instead of shutting the gate, I opened it as wide as I could. I did not make any decision to do this, it was just what I did. Flora never slowed down; she galloped straight past me, and Laird jumped up and down, yelling, "Shut it, shut it!" even after it was too late. My father and Henry appeared in the field a moment

---

6. American comedian (1913–1983) best known for her yodeling in hillbilly movies of the 1940s.

too late to see what I had done. They only saw Flora heading for the township road. They would think I had not got there in time.

They did not waste any time asking about it. They went back to the barn and got the gun and the knives they used, and put these in the truck; then they turned the truck around and came bouncing up the field toward us. Laird called to them, "Let me go too, let me go too!" and Henry stopped the truck and they took him in. I shut the gate after they were all gone.

I supposed Laird would tell. I wondered what would happen to me. I had never disobeyed my father before, and I could not understand why I had done it. Flora would not really get away. They would catch up with her in the truck. Or if they did not catch her this morning somebody would see her and telephone us this afternoon or tomorrow. There was no wild country here for her to run to, only farms. What was more, my father had paid for her, we needed the meat to feed the foxes, we needed the foxes to make our living. All I had done was make more work for my father who worked hard enough already. And when my father found out about it he was not going to trust me any more, he would know that I was not entirely on his side. I was on Flora's side, and that made me no use to anybody, not even to her. Just the same, I did not regret it; when she came running at me and I held the gate open, that was the only thing I could do.

I went back to the house, and my mother said, "What's all the commotion?" I told her that Flora had kicked down the fence and got away. "Your poor father," she said, "now he'll have to go chasing over the countryside. Well, there isn't any use planning dinner before one." She put up the ironing board. I wanted to tell her, but thought better of it and went upstairs and sat on my bed.

Lately I had been trying to make my part of the room fancy, spreading the bed with old lace curtains, and fixing myself a dressing-table with some leftovers of cretonne for a skirt. I planned to put up some kind of barricade between my bed and Laird's, to keep my section separate from his. In the sunlight, the lace curtains were just dusty rags. We did not sing at night any more. One night when I was singing Laird said, "You sound silly," and I went right on but the next night I did not start. There was not so much need to anyway, we were no longer afraid. We knew it was just old furniture over there, old jumble and confusion. We did not keep to the rules. I still stayed awake after Laird was asleep and told myself stories, but even in these stories something different was happening, mysterious alterations took place. A story might start off in the old way, with a spectacular danger, a fire or wild animals, and for a while I might rescue people; then things would change around, and instead, somebody would be rescuing me. It might be a boy from our class at school, or even Mr. Campbell, our teacher, who tickled girls under the arms. And at this point the story concerned itself at great length with what I looked like—how long my hair was, and what kind of dress I had on; by the time I had these details worked out the real excitement of the story was lost.

It was later than one o'clock when the truck came back. The tarpaulin was over the back, which meant there was meat in it. My mother had to heat dinner up all over again. Henry and my father had changed from their bloody overalls into ordinary working overalls in the barn, and they washed their arms and necks and faces at the sink, and splashed water on their hair and combed it. Laird lifted his arm to show off a streak of blood. "We shot old Flora," he said, "and cut her up in fifty pieces."

"Well I don't want to hear about it," my mother said. "And don't come to my table like that."

My father made him go and wash the blood off.

We sat down and my father said grace and Henry pasted his chewing-gum on the end of his fork, the way he always did; when he took it off he would have us admire the pattern. We began to pass the bowls of steaming, overcooked vegetables. Laird looked across the table at me and said proudly, distinctly, "Anyway it was her fault Flora got away."

"What?" my father said.

"She could of shut the gate and she didn't. She just open' it up and Flora run out."

"Is that right?" my father said.

Everybody at the table was looking at me. I nodded, swallowing food with great difficulty. To my shame, tears flooded my eyes.

My father made a curt sound of disgust. "What did you do that for?"

I did not answer. I put down my fork and waited to be sent from the table, still not looking up.

But this did not happen. For some time nobody said anything, then Laird said matter-of-factly, "She's crying."

"Never mind," my father said. He spoke with resignation, even good humour, the words which absolved and dismissed me for good. "She's only a girl," he said.

I didn't protest that, even in my heart. Maybe it was true.

1968

## QUESTIONS

1. There is only one girl character (the narrator) and one boy character (the narrator's younger brother) in "Boys and Girls." Why do you think Alice Munro uses plural words in the title?
2. Find the two occurrences of the phrase "only a girl." Why and how does the meaning of the phrase change in each case?
3. Why does the narrator choose not to shut the gate on Flora? What role does this act play in her initiation?

## JAMES JOYCE

### Araby

North Richmond Street, being blind,[1] was a quiet street except at the hour when the Christian Brothers' School set the boys free. An uninhabited house of two storeys stood at the blind end, detached from its neighbours in a square ground. The other houses of the street, conscious of decent lives within them, gazed at one another with brown imperturbable faces.

The former tenant of our house, a priest, had died in the back drawing-room. Air, musty from having been long enclosed, hung in all the rooms, and the waste

---

1. That is, a dead-end street.

room behind the kitchen was littered with old useless papers. Among these I found a few paper-covered books, the pages of which were curled and damp: *The Abbot*, by Walter Scott, *The Devout Communicant* and *The Memoirs of Vidocq*[2] I liked the last best because its leaves were yellow. The wild garden behind the house contained a central apple-tree and a few straggling bushes under one of which I found the late tenant's rusty bicycle-pump. He had been a very charitable priest; in his will he had left all his money to institutions and the furniture of his house to his sister.

When the short days of winter came dusk fell before we had well eaten our dinners. When we met in the street the houses had grown sombre. The space of sky above us was the colour of ever-changing violet and towards it the lamps of the street lifted their feeble lanterns. The cold air stung us and we played till our bodies glowed. Our shouts echoed in the silent street. The career of our play brought us through the dark muddy lanes behind the houses where we ran the gantlet of the rough tribes from the cottages, to the back doors of the dark dripping gardens where odours arose from the ashpits,[3] to the dark odorous stables where a coachman smoothed and combed the horse or shook music from the buckled harness. When we returned to the street light from the kitchen windows had filled the areas. If my uncle was seen turning the corner we hid in the shadow until we had seen him safely housed. Or if Mangan's sister came out on the doorstep to call her brother in to his tea we watched her from our shadow peer up and down the street. We waited to see whether she would remain or go in and, if she remained, we left our shadow and walked up to Mangan's steps resignedly. She was waiting for us, her figure defined by the light from the half-opened door. Her brother always teased her before he obeyed and I stood by the railings looking at her. Her dress swung as she moved her body and the soft rope of her hair tossed from side to side.

Every morning I lay on the floor in the front parlour watching her door. The blind was pulled down to within an inch of the sash so that I could not be seen. When she came out on the doorstep my heart leaped. I ran to the hall, seized my books and followed her. I kept her brown figure always in my eye and, when we came near the point at which our ways diverged, I quickened my pace and passed her. This happened morning after morning. I had never spoken to her, except for a few casual words, and yet her name was like a summons to all my foolish blood.

Her image accompanied me even in places the most hostile to romance. On Saturday evenings when my aunt went marketing I had to go to carry some of the parcels. We walked through the flaring streets, jostled by drunken men and bargaining women, amid the curses of labourers, the shrill litanies of shopboys who stood on guard by the barrels of pigs' cheeks, the nasal chanting of street-singers, who sang a *come-all-you* about O'Donovan Rossa,[4] or a ballad about the

---

2. The "memoirs" were probably *not* written by François Vidocq (1775–1857), a French criminal who became chief of detectives and who died poor and disgraced for his part in a crime that he solved; the 1820 novel by Sir Walter Scott (1771–1834) is a romance about the Catholic Mary, Queen of Scots (1542–1587), who was beheaded; *The Devout Communicant: or Pious Mediations and Aspirations for the Three Days Before and Three Days After Receiving the Holy Eucharist* (1813) is a Catholic religious tract.
3. Where fireplace ashes and other household refuse were dumped.
4. Jeremiah O'Donovan (1831–1915) was a militant Irish nationalist who fought on despite terms in prison and banishment. *Come-all-you:* a song, of which there were many, that began "Come, all you Irishmen."

troubles in our native land. These noises converged in a single sensation of life for me: I imagined that I bore my chalice safely through a throng of foes. Her name sprang to my lips at moments in strange prayers and praises which I myself did not understand. My eyes were often full of tears (I could not tell why) and at times a flood from my heart seemed to pour itself out into my bosom. I thought little of the future. I did not know whether I would ever speak to her or not or, if I spoke to her, how I could tell her of my confused adoration. But my body was like a harp and her words and gestures were like fingers running upon the wires.

One evening I went into the back drawing-room in which the priest had died. It was a dark rainy evening and there was no sound in the house. Through one of the broken panes I heard the rain impinge upon the earth, the fine incessant needles of water playing in the sodden beds. Some distant lamp or lighted window gleamed below me. I was thankful that I could see so little. All my senses seemed to desire to veil themselves and, feeling that I was about to slip from them, I pressed the palms of my hands together until they trembled, murmuring: *O love! O love!* many times.

At last she spoke to me. When she addressed the first words to me I was so confused that I did not know what to answer. She asked me was I going to *Araby*.[5] I forget whether I answered yes or no. It would be a splendid bazaar, she said; she would love to go.

—And why can't you? I asked.

While she spoke she turned a silver bracelet round and round her wrist. She could not go, she said, because there would be a retreat[3] that week in her convent. Her brother and two other boys were fighting for their caps and I was alone at the railings. She held one of the spikes, bowing her head towards me. The light from the lamp opposite our door caught the white curve of her neck, lit up her hair that rested there and, falling, lit up the hand upon the railing. It fell over one side of her dress and caught the white border of a petticoat, just visible as she stood at ease.

—It's well for you, she said.

—If I go, I said, I will bring you something.

What innumerable follies laid waste my waking and sleeping thoughts after that evening! I wished to annihilate the tedious intervening days. I chafed against the work of school. At night in my bedroom and by day in the classroom her image came between me and the page I strove to read. The syllables of the word *Araby* were called to me through the silence in which my soul luxuriated and cast an Eastern enchantment over me. I asked for leave to go to the bazaar on Saturday night. My aunt was surprised and hoped it was not some Freemason[6] affair. I answered few questions in class. I watched my master's face pass from amiability to sternness; he hoped I was not beginning to idle. I could not call my wandering thoughts together. I had hardly any patience with the serious work of life which, now that it stood between me and my desire, seemed to me child's play, ugly monotonous child's play.

On Saturday morning I reminded my uncle that I wished to go to the bazaar

---

5. A bazaar billed as a "Grand Oriental Fete," Dublin, May 1894.
6. Freemasons—members of an influential, secretive, and highly ritualistic fraternal organization—were considered enemies of the Catholics.

in the evening. He was fussing at the hallstand, looking for the hat-brush, and answered me curtly:

—Yes, boy, I know.

As he was in the hall I could not go into the front parlour and lie at the window. I left the house in bad humour and walked slowly towards the school. The air was pitilessly raw and already my heart misgave me.

When I came home to dinner my uncle had not yet been home. Still it was early. I sat staring at the clock for some time and, when its ticking began to irritate me, I left the room. I mounted the staircase and gained the upper part of the house. The high cold empty gloomy rooms liberated me and I went from room to room singing. From the front window I saw my companions playing below in the street. Their cries reached me weakened and indistinct and, leaning my forehead against the cool glass, I looked over at the dark house where she lived. I may have stood there for an hour, seeing nothing but the brown-clad figure cast by my imagination, touched discreetly by the lamplight at the curved neck, at the hand upon the railings and at the border below the dress.

When I came downstairs again I found Mrs. Mercer sitting at the fire. She was an old garrulous woman, a pawnbroker's widow, who collected used stamps for some pious purpose. I had to endure the gossip of the tea-table. The meal was prolonged beyond an hour and still my uncle did not come. Mrs. Mercer stood up to go: she was sorry she couldn't wait any longer, but it was after eight o'clock and she did not like to be out late, as the night air was bad for her. When she had gone I began to walk up and down the room, clenching my fists. My aunt said:

—I'm afraid you may put off your bazaar for this night of Our Lord.

At nine o'clock I heard my uncle's latchkey in the halldoor. I heard him talking to himself and heard the hallstand rocking when it had received the weight of his overcoat. I could interpret these signs. When he was midway through his dinner I asked him to give me the money to go to the bazaar. He had forgotten.

—The people are in bed and after their first sleep now, he said.

I did not smile. My aunt said to him energetically:

—Can't you give him the money and let him go? You've kept him late enough as it is.

My uncle said he was very sorry he had forgotten. He said he believed in the old saying: *All work and no play makes Jack a dull boy.* He asked me where I was going and, when I had told him a second time he asked me did I know *The Arab's Farewell to his Steed.*[7] When I left the kitchen he was about to recite the opening lines of the piece to my aunt.

I held a florin[8] tightly in my hand as I strode down Buckingham Street towards the station. The sight of the streets thronged with buyers and glaring with gas recalled to me the purpose of my journey. I took my seat in a third-class carriage of a deserted train. After an intolerable delay the train moved out of the station slowly. It crept onward among ruinous houses and over the twinkling river. At Westland Row Station a crowd of people pressed to the carriage doors; but the porters moved them back, saying that it was a special train for the bazaar. I remained alone in the bare carriage. In a few minutes the train drew up beside

---

7. Or *The Arab's Farewell to His Horse*, a sentimental nineteenth-century poem by Caroline Norton. The speaker has sold the horse.   8. A two-shilling piece; thus four times the "sixpenny entrance" fee.

an improvised wooden platform. I passed out on to the road and saw by the lighted dial of a clock that it was ten minutes to ten. In front of me was a large building which displayed the magical name.

I could not find any sixpenny entrance and, fearing that the bazaar would be closed, I passed in quickly through a turnstile, handing a shilling to a weary-looking man. I found myself in a big hall girdled at half its height by a gallery. Nearly all the stalls were closed and the greater part of the hall was in darkness. I recognised a silence like that which pervades a church after a service. I walked into the centre of the bazaar timidly. A few people were gathered about the stalls which were still open. Before a curtain, over which the words *Café Chantant*[9] were written in coloured lamps, two men were counting money on a salver. I listened to the fall of the coins.

Remembering with difficulty why I had come I went over to one of the stalls and examined porcelain vases and flowered tea-sets. At the door of the stall a young lady was talking and laughing with two young gentlemen. I remarked their English accents and listened vaguely to their conversation.

—O, I never said such a thing!

—O, but you did!

—O, but I didn't!

—Didn't she say that?

—Yes. I heard her.

—O, there's a . . . fib!

Observing me the young lady came over and asked me did I wish to buy anything. The tone of her voice was not encouraging; she seemed to have spoken to me out of a sense of duty. I looked humbly at the great jars that stood like eastern guards at either side of the dark entrance to the stall and murmured:

—No, thank you.

The young lady changed the position of one of the vases and went back to the two young men. They began to talk of the same subject. Once or twice the young lady glanced at me over her shoulder.

I lingered before her stall, though I knew my stay was useless, to make my interest in her wares seem the more real. Then I turned away slowly and walked down the middle of the bazaar. I allowed the two pennies to fall against the sixpence in my pocket. I heard a voice call from one end of the gallery that the light was out. The upper part of the hall was now completely dark.

Gazing up into the darkness I saw myself as a creature driven and derided by vanity; and my eyes burned with anguish and anger.

1914

## QUESTIONS

1. How do the first three paragraphs of "Araby" characterize the environment in which the narrator lives?
2. How might the narrator's environment inspire and shape his fascination with Mangan's sister? with Araby?
3. What kind of "vanity" does the narrator attribute to himself at the story's end? Why is he filled with "anguish and anger"?

---

9. Café with music.

MICHAEL CHABON

## The Lost World

One summer night not long after he turned sixteen, Nathan Shapiro drank four tall cans of Old English 800 and very soon found himself sitting in the front seat of a huge, banana-colored Ford LTD, with his friends Buster, Felix, and Tiger Montaine. They had swallowed the malt liquor while bathing in Buster French's hot tub (the Frenches were from Los Angeles) and, as a result, were driving around boiled, steaming drunk, and in various stages of undress. Buster and Felix E. still had on their scant Speedo bathing suits, Tiger Montaine wore only a black mesh tank top and one sanitary sock, and Nathan, through some combination of glee and desperation, was naked from head to toe.

Two weeks before this, his mother, in a modest and homemade little ceremony, had married a man named Ed, a kindly, balding geologist from Idaho whom she had been dating for six months. And then just this evening, an hour before Nathan went over to Buster French's house, Dr. Shapiro had telephoned jubilantly from Boston to announce the first pregnancy of his wife, Anne. Ricky, Nathan's brother, had been living in Boston for a year now, and he went on and on over the phone about the little bubble of life that had blossomed in the vial of Anne's home pregnancy test, which Ricky had taken to his room and placed between his soccer trophy and a photograph of his mother and father and Nathan standing in the wind at Nag's Head.[1]

All of these developments, though he did his best to welcome them, had left Nathan somewhat more than normally confused. He liked his new stepfather, who had been to Antarctica and Peru and Novaya Zemlya[2] and returned with all sorts of hair-raising tales and queer stones; in his own way he was genuinely as excited as Ricky by the prospect of a new baby; and he was old enough to regard these changes as the inevitable outward expansion, as of an empire or a galaxy, of what once had been his family. He was happy for his parents in their new lives, the way he had always been happy for them, all along, as step by step they had dismantled their marriage; and so he was looking for a reason, an excuse to feel so unmoored, at once so angry and nostalgic; and alcohol seemed to be doing the job. He had no idea of where he and his friends were going, and it was not until they had been lurching aimlessly along the empty, fragrant streets of Huxley for what seemed like hours that he understood that they were headed—as Buster French put it—to the crib of Chaya Feldman.

Buster, driving Mrs. French's car, made this declaration just as the drink, the deep velour seats, and the sweet smell of lawns flowing in through the open windows had begun to lull Nathan to sleep, and at the mention of Chaya's name Nathan sat bolt upright. Buster then called Chaya a "skeezer," which meant, as far as Nathan had been able to determine, that she was certain to permit them—all four of them—those dark liberties of which he was still very much ignorant, a notion which filled him only with wonder, and with solicitude for Chaya, whom he had known since he was six years old. She was a quiet girl, with a serious brown face and tangled hair, and her parents dressed her like a doll. He remem-

---

1. Beach town on North Carolina's Outer Banks.   2. Russian islands in the Arctic Ocean.

bered her as someone who was always coming upon orphaned puppies and sparrow chicks with broken wings, in meadows and along roads where anyone else would have found nothing at all, and then trying imperfectly and with an eyedropper full of milk or sugar water to nurse them back to health. Her chief social art—until recently, at least—had been that, upon request, she could draw you an extremely realistic picture of an eyeball, with a sparkle on the iris, and fathomless pupils, and the finest tracery of veins.

They had never really been friends, but from time to time Nathan still thought about one distant afternoon when he and Chaya had somehow ended up playing together, in the fields behind the Huxley Interfaith Plexus. In the tall grass and the weeds they had played a game of Chaya's own invention, called Planet of the Birds. Nathan had been an intergalactic castaway trying to survive in a windy, grassy world, and Chaya's hair had tossed like a crest of feathers as she sang to him in a variety of cries. Chaya even claimed that when she grew up she was going to write a book set on this imaginary planet, whose name, she said, was Jadis;[3] in the dust she scratched a map of its oceans and aeries. As with all of those blissful Sunday afternoons he had ever passed with some child with whom he never played again—every childhood has a dozen or so—his memory of this vanished afternoon was luminous and clear. In the three years since his liberation from Hebrew school he had seen Chaya twice, from a distance, coming out of a movie with her parents and her sister, Mara. Now Nathan was suddenly afraid for her, and he was afraid, for the first time ever, of the raucous bodies of his friends.

"Hey, Buster," said Felix E. Scott, leaning forward so that for an instant his thigh lay smooth and cool against Nathan's, "what you going to do to Chaya Feldman?"

"Don't tell me you don't already know, Felix E.," said Buster, heaving the LTD into a small cul-de-sac which Nathan recognized, from some long-ago car pool, as Chaya's street.

"Cut the engine," suggested Tiger Montaine, who excelled in stealthy behavior. He ran his battered little Fiat on siphoned gasoline, filched cigarettes from the supermarket, and had for several months, with Nathan's shocked connivance, been replacing Mrs. Shapiro's codeine pills with extra-strength Tylenol, one at a time. "Don't be waking up that mean Israelite daddy." Chaya's father, Moshe, an oncologist, had been born and raised in Israel, and was, in fact, the most humorless and stern of the one hundred and five fathers Nathan had known in his life. He had a dense black beard and crazy eyebrows, and it was widely half-believed that he kept an Uzi submachine gun, from his days in the army of Israel, hidden under his bed.

Buster turned off the ignition and the car began to glide silently toward Chaya's house. The sudden calm cast a pall over the party and no one spoke; perhaps they were only being careful. Nathan pictured Chaya, asleep, her legs tangled under a light summer blanket; a skeezer! Then, because the ignition had been cut, the steering wheel locked, automatically, and before Buster could do anything they had hopped up over the curb, and came to a stop halfway across somebody's front lawn.

---

3. French word meaning *in times past, formerly.*

"We're there," said Buster, and everyone laughed. "Now who's going to go knocking on that skeezer's window?"

"I'll go," said Nathan. "I know her."

All of the other boys turned to regard him. Although Nathan felt fairly confident that his friends held him in a certain esteem—his naked presence among them was testimony to that—he had never distinguished himself for his daring, and in fact generally had to be persuaded even to perform minor feats such as dancing with Twanda Woods, or wearing his sneakers without any laces, an affectation which drove his mother out of her mind. And all of the boys knew, for Nathan had been unable, despite himself, to conceal it, that he had never made love to a girl. Emboldened by the malt liquor, he reached out and pushed Felix E. and Tiger in their faces, so that they fell backward into each other.

"I went to Hebrew school with her," he explained.

Perhaps it was only their shock at this uncharacteristic display of fearlessness, but as Nathan stepped out of the car, he noticed a strange look in the eyes of his friends. It was a kind of blank, blinking puzzlement, as though the game had gone awry. Nathan wondered if the whole thing was a lie, if Chaya was not a skeezer at all, and the boys were all of them virgins, and none of them knew what fate awaited him as he began to make his way, naked, barefoot as a child, across the soft grass. He glanced toward the car, toward the three shadowy heads now drawn together in what looked like anxious parley, and almost turned back.

The next moment, however, he felt an entirely new kind of drunkenness; the air was warm against his skin, his lips, his forearms, and—incredibly—moonlight fell upon his penis. He wished that it were a mile to Chaya's house, and not a few short steps, so that he might walk this way a little longer, like a fairy on a moonlit heath. Just this summer—just this month—his body had begun to grow lean, and he strode across the grass with the jangling gait of a young man, delighting in the purpose of his legs. He came to the Feldmans' driveway and zigzagged quickly around to the left side of the house, where he was confronted with a gated, wooden fence. He stopped and contemplated the latticed gate. His breath came quickly now and there was sweat in his eyebrows; a drop spattered against his cheek. Just when he felt the water on his face he saw, through the spaces in the lattice, that a swimming pool, long and unusually narrow, lay beyond. It was not a pool for a pleasure swim; it was a lap pool, no wider than a pair of racing freestylers. Nathan remembered hearing that Dr. Feldman required himself and his family to swim a mile every day.

Pretending for the moment that he was tricksy Tiger Montaine, Nathan held his breath, eased up the steel latch, and slowly let open the gate, without a sound. He walked to the railroad ties that formed the near end of the lap pool and curled his toes over their edge. Thus perched he stood a moment, looking at the reflected moon on the black water and trying to force the tumult in his stomach to abate. He was so nervous that he forgot why he was nervous, and simply hovered at the edge of Chaya's swimming pool, shaking. What was he doing here? Where were his clothes?

He crouched and then slipped, like a deer fleeing a forest fire, into the cool water. He swam across the pool with a light and leisurely stroke. The exercise of his arms and heart in the cold water cleared his thoughts, and left him with a pleasant chlorine sting in his eyes, and when he arrived at the far side of the lap pool, he felt a greater trust in himself and in the general benevolence of a Tuesday night in July. He pulled himself from the pool and tiptoed around to the back of the Feldmans' house. There were some bedsheets, striped pillowcases, and a pair of bath towels hanging from a revolving clothesline in the backyard, and he considered taking a towel and tying it around his waist. But he felt, obscurely, that there was some advantage in his nakedness, an almost magical advantage that Tiger Montaine, for example, would never have surrendered, and he went over to the windows of the daylight basement in which Chaya had always had her room and stood a moment, with his hands on his wet hips, looking into the dark windows, preparing to wake her. The pool water streamed down his chest to his thighs, raising goosebumps along his legs and arms as Nathan drummed lightly on the glass, attempting a sort of suave seductive rhythm that came out, inexorably, as shave-and-a-hair-cut, two-bits.

•

A light snapped on inside. Someone sat up in the bed—in Chaya's bed—and this someone did not appear to be Chaya. She was too tall, and her hair was fuller and darker, and through the armhole of her sheer short nightgown he saw the startling contour of a woman's heavy breast. He turned and began to hightail it out of the backyard, but the door opened almost immediately, and he turned sheepishly back.

"Is, uh, Chaya here?" he said, in a tone which he hoped would make him sound too stupid to be doing something illicit.

"Nathan? Nathan Shapiro?"

"Chaya?"

"What are you doing here? Where are your clothes?"

The light spilling out around her reduced her to a silhouette and he could not tell if she looked angry or merely puzzled. Her voice was a cracked whisper and sounded rather plaintive in the dark, as though she were also afraid of getting into some kind of trouble.

"I swam in your pool," Nathan offered, uncertain if this would explain everything adequately.

"Well, you'd better get out of here. My dad is sleeping and he hasn't been well."

"Okay," said Nathan. "Good-bye. You got so big, Chaya." He was staring.

"Puberty," she said. "Ever hear of it?" She stepped back into the light of her room and smiled a sort of frowny smile she had always had, and then Nathan felt that he recognized her.

"Chaya, I feel so weird," he said. At the sight of her familiar, serious face he was all at once on the verge of tears.

"Well. Okay, come inside. You have to be quiet."

"Okay."

Nathan followed Chaya into her room, which had the drop ceiling and damp-carpet odor of a basement. On one paneled wall there was a print of *The Starry Night*[4] and an El Al[5] poster with a picture of the Old City of Jerusalem; on the other wall was a painting that Chaya herself must have made, a picture of a palm

---

4. A well-known painting by Dutch artist Vincent van Gogh (1853–1890).
5. The national airline of Israel.

tree full of bright parrots under a double sun, and Nathan remembered the day he had spent on the Planet Jadis. Beside the painting was an old mounted deer's head, with a split ear, wearing sunglasses and a purple beret. On the table beside her bed was a squat jug lamp with a green shade, a package of Kool cigarettes, and a book by Erica Jong[6] that Nathan had twice been admonished against reading by his grandfather. The circle of light from the lamp seemed to fall almost entirely on the bed, and Nathan averted his eyes, so intimate was the sight of the exposed white sheets and the deep declivity in the pillow. The imprint of her sleeping head, the whole idea of Chaya asleep, struck him as terribly poignant, and he could not look. He heard the creak of the bedsprings and the rustle of sheets as she climbed back into bed.

"I mean you're not ugly, or anything, Nathan," said Chaya, "but put something on, okay?"

"I'm naked!" said Nathan. He looked down at himself, and knew that he was naked. And he saw, as through Chaya's eyes, that in assuming some of its manly proportions and features, his penis had also begun to take on a concomitant forlorn and humorous aspect, sort of like the Jeep in Popeye cartoons; and he made an apron of his hands and forearms. This did nothing to conceal, however, the whiteness of his thighs, or the soft, sad divot of hair around his left—but not yet his right—nipple.

"There's a towel on the chair."

"I'd better go," said Nathan. He turned and began to walk out the door, attempting now to cover his probably ridiculous-looking rear end.

"It's okay, go ahead, put it on, Nathan," said Chaya.

"They brought me," he said, turning again and crab-walking over to the chair beside Chaya's desk. "The guys. Tiger and Buster and Felix E." Hurriedly he wrapped the towel around his waist and tucked in one end, in the fashion that his grandmother had always referred to, for some reason, as Turkish. It was a scratchy white towel that had been stolen, to judge from the illegible Hebrew lettering that was woven like a pattern into one side, from some hotel in Israel. The lopsided situation of his chest hair remained a keen embarrassment, and the towel was so skimpy that the knot at his hip just barely held.

"Are they out there?"

"Yeah. They sent me in. They said—"

"Your hair is all wet." She folded her hands over her stomach, on the pleat of the bedclothes, and stared at him. She seemed all in all only mildly surprised to see Nathan, as though he were visiting her in a dream. Her face had grown wider, her cheekbones more pronounced, since the last time he had seen her, and with her tawny skin and her thick eyebrows and that big, wild hair Nathan thought she looked beautiful and a little scary. He sat down and hugged himself. His teeth were chattering.

"Okay, now I better go." He stood up again.

"Wait," said Chaya. She patted the sheets and indicated that he sit beside her. He came to sit gingerly at her feet, keeping hold with one hand of the tenuous Turkish knot.

"Nathan Shapiro," she said, shaking her head.

"Chaya Feldman."

---

6. American novelist (b. 1942) best known for her erotically charged first novel, *Fear of Flying* (1973).

"Mrs. Falutnick's class."

"Kvit chewink your gum in fronta da r-radio," said Nathan, repeating a favorite inscrutable admonishment of Mrs. Falutnick's in an accent he had not mimicked for six or seven years. Chaya laughed, but Nathan only snorted once through his nose. It had been so long since the days of Mrs. Falutnick's class! He saw himself sitting in a flecked plastic chair at the back of the droning classroom in the Huxley Interfaith Plexus, defacing with moustaches and monkey's fur the grave photographs of Emma Lazarus and Abraham Cahan[7] in his copy of *Adventures in American Jewry*, furtively folding all ten inches of a stick of grape Big Buddy into his mouth when Mrs. Falutnick turned her enormous back on the class, and at this he was unaccountably saddened, and he sighed, startling Chaya out of her dream.

"I heard your parents got a divorce," she said. She looked down, and her long hair splashed her folded hands.

"Yeah," said Nathan, hugging himself again. The shiver that this word produced in him never lasted more than a second or two.

"Why did they?"

"I don't know," Nathan said.

"You don't?"

He thought about it for a few seconds, then shook his head. "I mean they told me, but I forget what they said."

"It's complicated," Chaya offered, helpfully. "People change."

"I think that was part of it," Nathan said, but he didn't believe that there was really any explanation at all.

"Does your dad still live around here?"

"He moved to Boston."

"That's cool," said Chaya. She lifted the curtain of hair from her face and smiled another crooked smile. "I wish my dad would move to Boston."

Nathan said automatically, "No, you don't." He had hitherto managed to forget about the fearsome doctor and he glanced over his shoulder. In the far corner of the room he noticed three large plastic suitcases and a guitar case, neatly lined up as for an imminent departure.

"Where are you going?" he said, gesturing toward the luggage.

"Jerusalem," said Chaya. "Tomorrow. Today, I guess. Later this morning."

"With your family? Or all alone?"

"All alone."

"Are you ever coming back?"

"Of course I am, you," she said. "My father thinks I've gotten—he just wants me to learn to be an Israeli."

"Oh," said Nathan. He was not certain what this entailed, but he suddenly pictured Chaya operating a crane on the bristling lip of a giant construction site in the desert, lowering a turbine generator or a sheaf of I-beams down into the void, the dust of the Negev[8] blowing around her like a long scarf.

"Did they tell you I put out?" said Chaya. "Those guys?"

"Kind of," said Nathan, taken aback, before it occurred to him that this was

---

7. Abraham Cahan (1860-1951), American novelist known for chronicling the Jewish-American immigrant experience; Emma Lazarus (1849-1887), American poet best known for her sonnet "The New Colossus," written for the dedication of the Statue of Liberty.    8. Desert in southern Israel.

admitting he had come here for sex, when in fact he had come—why had he come? "It was more like a dare, I guess," he said. "They sort of more or less dared me to come."

"None of them's ever sat on my bed the way you are," said Chaya.

Nathan wondered for a moment exactly what she meant by this, and then, in the next moment, leaned toward her and kissed her lips. This was done only on an off chance and he did not expect that she would take such forceful hold of his body. Startled, without a clue of what he ought to do next, he put one hand on the nape of her neck, the other at the small of her back, and then he lay very still in her arms. He could feel the bones of her hips pressing against him, like a pair of fists, and his lips and somehow his breathing became entangled in her hair. The laundered smell of her bedclothes was overpowering and sweet.

"Are you a virgin, Nathan?" she said, her mouth very close to his.

He considered his reply much longer than he needed to, trying to phrase it as ambiguously as he could. "In a manner of speaking," he said at last, blushing in self-congratulation at the urbanity of this reply.

Her grip upon him relaxed, and she drew back slowly and then fell back against her pillow, looking calm again. He had the feeling that she had been hoping for some reply totally other than the one he had given. Then Chaya sighed, in a bored, theatrical way that to Nathan's ears sounded very grown up, and he was afraid, at last, that she really might have become a skeezer, that it really was possible to lose track of someone so completely that they turned into someone else without your knowing about it.

"Can you still draw eyeballs?" he said.

"Eyeballs?" she said, her face blank. "Sure, I can."

"Chaya! Mara!" called Dr. Feldman from somewhere in the house. His voice resounded like an axe-blow. "That's enough!"

They both started, and stared a moment at one another as children or as lovers caught.

"Can I tell you something, Nathan?" she said. "When I get to Israel I'm *not* coming back."

"You have to come back," he said, taking her hand.

"Chaya!" thundered Dr. Feldman from very far away. "Go to sleep."

"I'll write you," said Chaya. "Give me your address."

"Sixty-four twenty-three Les Adieux Circle. Is he going to come down here?"

"No," she said. "He thinks you're my little sister. I'll never remember that address. Let me write it down."

"Oh, that's all right," said Nathan, getting up. "You don't need to write me a letter."

"No, wait. Hold on."

She climbed out of bed again, grinning, and went to a blue wooden desk, under the stairs that led up to the first floor of the house. Nathan watched the play of her nightgown across her little behind as she bent over to open a drawer, and then scrabbled around in it, looking for a pen. She found a sheet of pink stationery and began to scratch across it with a Smurf pencil.

"Chaya, I'd better go," said Nathan. He headed for the door.

"Wait!" said Chaya. She was writing furiously now, in a pointed, ribbony script almost like cursive Hebrew, and he waited, one hand on the knob, for her to finish, and hoped that Dr. Feldman would not call out again. When she put down her pen she took a red, white, and blue airmail envelope from another drawer, folded the slip of pink paper in half, slid it into the envelope, and ran her tongue along the flap. Then she bent over the desk again and, brushing her hair from the face of the envelope, wrote out what Nathan knew even from a distance to be his name and address.

"There, I wrote you a letter from Jerusalem," she said, turning toward him. "Don't read it until tomorrow."

"Okay," said Nathan. "Good-bye." He hugged her awkwardly, afraid that he might get an erection, and then eased open the basement door. "Have fun in Jerusalem."

"But I'm already there," she said, continuing in this teasing and mysterious vein. She put a hand on each of his shoulders and kissed him on the cheek. Nathan took the letter from her, a little uncertainly. Probably it was just a bunch of scribble, or an apology for not wanting to have sex with him.

"I know what you're doing!" said Dr. Feldman, with that weird Yisraeli accent of his, and Nathan went out naked into the night. He was not quite so drunk anymore, and this time the trip around the house, past the swimming pool, did not seem especially fine or ominous. The dog next door to the Feldmans' caught wind of Nathan and began to rail at him, and he ran the rest of the way, all the while trying to determine if Dr. Feldman and his Uzi were in pursuit. As he was running across the Feldmans' yard and into the neighbors', the white towel finally slipped from his waist and fell away, nearly tripping him; he left it to Chaya to explain how it got there, and went naked the rest of the way.

He came around to his side of the car and hesitated with a hand on the door. They were asleep, all three of them, Felix E. and Tiger slumped in opposite corners of the backseat, Buster stretched out across the front seat of the car. The radio played very softly and threw green light across Buster's thighs. They were snoring with the lustiness of children, and Nathan felt a surge of pity for them and wished that they might just keep on sleeping. When he got into the car, he knew, his friends would want to know what, or rather how much, Chaya had given him; and when he showed them the letter, they would want to read what she had written. He was afraid that its contents might somehow embarrass him, and now he looked for somewhere to conceal it.

At first he considered retrieving the discarded towel, but he was afraid to go back, and anyway, if he wrapped the letter in the towel it would make a pretty suspicious bundle. Then he looked around at the lawn on which they were parked, to see if it held any place in which he could hide the letter, but there was only the silver expanse of lawn, an entire neighborhood of grass and flat moonlight. Under the front windows of the neighbors' house stood one small row of bushes, and he tried poking the envelope deep into this, but you could see it from a mile away, reflecting the light of the moon like a shard of mirror glass, and he retrieved it and looked around again.

Just when he was about to give up and try to hide the letter somewhere in the Frenches' car itself, under a mat, or even in the glove compartment, he spotted a bird feeder, about twenty feet away, hanging from the low branch of a young maple tree. It was shaped like a small transparent house, with a peaked plastic roof and glass walls, about half-filled with birdseed. Nathan unhooked it from its wire and turned it over, his hands shaking with fear and with the aptness of his plan. He pulled off the plastic base of the bird feeder and laid the letter within, burying it amid the smooth and rattling seeds. When he returned the little house to its hook, the letter was nearly invisible, and he trotted back, with a certain air of coolness, to the big yellow LTD.

His friends clambered upright when Nathan climbed back into the car; they were sober and embarrassed, and slapped Nathan constantly on the side of his head. They demanded to know what had happened to Nathan in Chaya's room, and as they drove slowly home he made up a story, filled with sophisticated orgasms, and accurate anatomical impressions, and some bits of sexual dialog in half-remembered Hebrew. The other boys seemed on the whole to believe him, although they were surprised, and blamed malt liquor and hormonal agitation, when halfway through the tale Nathan suddenly burst into tears—then stopped, and resumed his lying account.

The next night Nathan sneaked out of the house after his mother and Ed had gone to sleep. He rode half an hour on his bicycle, through the darkness, to retrieve the letter from Jerusalem. There was no moon, and black shapes seemed to dart and loom across his path. He pulled up in front of the Feldmans' house and contemplated it for a moment, straddling the hard bar of his bike. There was no sign of the towel he had dropped. He hated it that Chaya was not there in her house anymore, that she could so quickly be gone. He had a great curiosity to read what she had written him, but when he crept across to open up the little bird feeder, past the two long scars in the lawn from the wheels of the LTD, he found there was nothing inside it anymore but birdseed. The hairs on the back of his neck stood on end, and he whirled, half expecting to see Chaya, with the letter in her hand, laughing at him from behind the curtain in the low side window of her bedroom. He looked around on the grass, in the row of low shrubs, in the branches of the maple, but the letter was nowhere to be found, and after a few more minutes of baffled searching he got back on his bicycle and pedaled home. As he lay in bed that night he tried to imagine what she might have set down in her letter, what professions of love, what unhappiness, what nonsense, what shame, what news of the planet of her childhood. Then he fell asleep.

•

One Saturday a few weeks afterward, Nathan and his stepfather were in the kitchen, trying to work their way out of an incipient argument about whether or not tuna salad ought to be made with chopped gherkins, the way Ed's grandmother had always made it. The dispute was merely the latest and perhaps the most trivial in what was becoming a disheartening routine for Nathan and Ed, and this particular volley of intransigent politeness had just begun to make Nathan's stomach hurt—without inclining him to capitulate—when Mrs. Shapiro-Knipper entered the kitchen, carrying the Saturday mail.

"Two things," she said, handing Nathan two envelopes, one of them tricolor and heartstopping.

"I'm going to put pickles," said Ed. "You'll see. It's an acquired taste."

This time, though everything Ed liked to eat, from raw oysters to pizza with pineapple and ham, seemed to be an acquired taste, Nathan let it pass. He rose from the kitchen table and carried the two letters out into the hallway and down to his bedroom. The second, in a plain business envelope, was evidently from his father, who had never before sent a letter to Nathan, and Nathan sat on his bed for a long time without opening them, just thinking about mailmen, and sealed envelopes, and the mysteries of the post.

He supposed that the neighbor had found Chaya's letter hidden in the bird feeder before Nathan could retrieve it, and had finally gotten around to affixing a stamp to it and sending it along. Since, in the past weeks, Nathan had decided that he was in love with Chaya, and had been busy erecting all the necessary buttresses and towers and fluttering pennants in his imagination, the surprise arrival of her letter, which he had presumed lost, was a delicious addition to the structure, and he delayed as long as he could stand before finally tearing open the envelope.

DEAR NATHAN,

Sometimes it is very hot here. I have a thousand boyfriends.
It is scary if a gun goes off in the night.

You made me laugh a lot of times in class I remember.

"Take it easy."

Love,
CHAYA

He was sharply disappointed. He hated the fact that he had made her laugh, for one; and it angered him, unreasonably, he knew, that all of the other things—and there were so few of them—she had written were hypothetical, as insubstantial as her Planet of the Birds, or as his parents' marriage, or as the baby that was growing in his stepmother's belly. He stuffed the bogus letter back into the envelope and tore it to pieces.

He was still feeling bad when at last he brought himself to open the letter from his father. It was a brief, barely legible note, on a sheet of legal paper. After some facetious chitchat about the Red Sox and Ricky's karate lessons, Nathan's father had written, "Your mother tells me that you have made some new friends and she is a little worried because you're going around with your shoes untied. Tie your shoelaces. Don't be angry with us, Nate. I know that everything seems different now but you have to get used to it. I will always love you as much as I will love any new Shapiros that come along."

"Nathan?" his mother called to him through the door of his room. "Come on and eat."

"I hate it with gherkins," said Nathan, but his heart had gone out of the argument, and he stood up to join his mother and Ed for lunch. Hastily he dried his eyes, and scrambled to gather up the letter from his father and the scraps of Chaya's letter that were scattered across his bed. It was as he laid them carefully in the Roi-Tan cigar box in which he kept his most important papers that he noticed the strange and beautiful postage stamp in the torn corner of the airmail envelope, and the postmark, printed in an alien script.

1990

## QUESTIONS

1. What has Nathan lost in the process of growing up? How might your answer change over the course of "The Lost World"?
2. What are the key symbolic details included in the description of Nathan's journey to Chaya's bedroom?
3. Nathan receives two letters at the end of the story. What is their significance? How might the postmark on the second letter affect its meaning?

## SUGGESTIONS FOR WRITING

1. How is space designated at the farm and in the house in "Boys and Girls"? Write an essay examining how the uses and restrictions of different spaces might indicate stages of growing up or initiation into the proper roles for adult women and men.
2. At the end of "Araby," the upper parts of the hall are darkened, as though to describe the boy's situation and state of mind. Realizations usually are associated with "enlightenment," or the idea of a light turning on. Write an essay discussing how the story associates light or darkness with the initiation of the narrator.
3. Write an essay that identifies and explores the significance of a group of related words or images that recurs in one of the stories in this chapter.
4. Traditional cultures like that of the Masai people of East Africa have highly ritualized methods of inducting young people into adulthood. Might developed Western societies also be said to have ritual forms of initiation? Drawing evidence from at least two stories in this chapter, write an essay exploring how young people in modern Western societies are initiated into adulthood.
5. Choose a story from any other chapter of this book and write an essay explaining why it should be considered an initiation story.
6. Using any story in this chapter as a model, write a first-person narrative of an actual or fictional initiation into adulthood.

# 10 FORM AS CONTEXT: THE SHORT SHORT STORY

The short short story, or "short-short"—a story of anywhere from a few hundred to a few thousand words—has been around for a long time, but has suddenly become popular. Explanations for this phenomenon range from the shrinking attention span "caused" by television, to the hurried, fragmented nature of contemporary life, to our disenchantment with lengthy accounts of behavior by psychologists, politicians, and novelists. There have also been attempts to define the form generically. The boundaries of the "short-short" as a genre have been those of the anecdote, the vignette or sketch, the parable, the prose poem, the short story proper; yet all these borders between genres have been contested.

Such genres can be grouped together because of their recognized principle of brevity. But writing something imaginative that is short—as if to spare the effort of both the writer and the reader—is not really the point. What is important to recognize is that the length of the story contributes significantly to a story's effect and to your consequent response. A very brief story can create certain effects of concentration and simplicity, of suggestiveness, similar to the effects of poetry and yet related to those of longer prose fiction. You rarely read a full-length novel in a single sitting, so not only is there a momentary recapitulation in your mind as you pick up the narrative again—something like the highlights from the previous episode in a television miniseries—but you have lived another period of your own life outside the narrative. When you sit down to read again you are not exactly the same repository of experiences as when you put the book down; you are at a different point in your life, and your mood may have changed drastically. The novel has advantages, however, in its duration and in the times of your readings and departures: you are likely to recall the characters, scenes, and incidents, in one order or another, and in more or less accurate detail, during the period you are away from the text. The novel thereby gets a texture, layers of memories and views from different angles, that is rarely obtained by a short story, and never by a short short story. You usually read a short story in a single sitting, and though it has an immediate and concentrated impact and you pause a moment to savor its emotional and intellectual effects, you can rarely recall all its details; yet rarely, too, do you immediately begin at the beginning and read it through once again. The effect of the short-short is stronger. Even if the aftereffect is of the same duration (and it often is longer, because the story's economy has left so much out that you have to supply a great deal yourself), it is stronger compared to the length of time of your reading. You can readily remember almost all the details. And, if you are strongly impressed, you may read the story again immediately. So novels, short stories, and short short

> *Not that the story need be long, but it will take a long while to make it short.*
> —HENRY DAVID THOREAU

stories differ not merely in length but also in the way we read and respond to them.

Although you may be able to read four or five short short stories in the time it takes to read one short story of a more common length, you will probably find the experience overwhelming rather than satisfying, because the effects of short short stories are so strong and concentrated. You might take a break after each story in this chapter, using the time to rehearse the story in your mind, to recall its details and its language, and to fill in the particulars that the story can only imply. And when one of these stories affects you, you may want to write an account of your emotive and intellectual responses, of the details you recall, and those you have chosen to supply.

> *There are only two or three human stories, and they go on repeating themselves as fiercely as if they had never happened before.*
> —WILLA CATHER

The stories in this chapter demonstrate the range of the short short form. (Other stories in the book that fit or approach the definition are "The Elephant in the Village of the Blind," "20/20," "Happy Endings," "The Cask of Amontillado," "A Conversation with My Father," and "Hills Like White Elephants.") As you read these stories, you will notice that despite their length, short short stories are capable of as many variations as their longer cousins, and they exhibit widely different treatments of physical space and realistic detail. The short short story can be just the right form to achieve either a great concentration or a vast expansion of time. Everything you have learned of history and structure, focus and voice, characterization, symbol, and theme, then, is needed to articulate the explicit and subtle effects achieved by this compact form.

**KATE CHOPIN**

## The Story of an Hour

Knowing that Mrs. Mallard was afflicted with a heart trouble, great care was taken to break to her as gently as possible the news of her husband's death.

It was her sister Josephine who told her, in broken sentences; veiled hints that revealed in half concealing. Her husband's friend Richards was there, too, near her. It was he who had been in the newspaper office when intelligence of the railroad disaster was received, with Brently Mallard's name leading the list of "killed." He had only taken the time to assure himself of its truth by a second telegram, and had hastened to forestall any less careful, less tender friend in bearing the sad message.

She did not hear the story as many women have heard the same, with a paralyzed inability to accept its significance. She wept at once, with sudden, wild abandonment, in her sister's arms. When the storm of grief had spent itself she went away to her room alone. She would have no one follow her.

There stood, facing the open window, a comfortable, roomy armchair. Into this she sank, pressed down by a physical exhaustion that haunted her body and seemed to reach into her soul.

5   She could see in the open square before her house the tops of trees that were all aquiver with the new spring life. The delicious breath of rain was in the air.

In the street below a peddler was crying his wares. The notes of a distant song which some one was singing reached her faintly, and countless sparrows were twittering in the eaves.

There were patches of blue sky showing here and there through the clouds that had met and piled one above the other in the west facing her window.

She sat with her head thrown back upon the cushion of the chair, quite motionless, except when a sob came up into her throat and shook her, as a child who has cried itself to sleep continues to sob in its dreams.

She was young, with a fair, calm face, whose lines bespoke repression and even a certain strength. But now there was a dull stare in her eyes, whose gaze was fixed away off yonder on one of those patches of blue sky. It was not a glance of reflection, but rather indicated a suspension of intelligent thought.

There was something coming to her and she was waiting for it, fearfully. What was it? She did not know; it was too subtle and elusive to name. But she felt it, creeping out of the sky, reaching toward her through the sounds, the scents, the color that filled the air.

Now her bosom rose and fell tumultuously. She was beginning to recognize this thing that was approaching to possess her, and she was striving to beat it back with her will—as powerless as her two white slender hands would have been.

When she abandoned herself a little whispered word escaped her slightly parted lips. She said it over and over under her breath: "free, free, free!" The vacant stare and the look of terror that had followed it went from her eyes. They stayed keen and bright. Her pulses beat fast, and the coursing blood warmed and relaxed every inch of her body.

She did not stop to ask if it were or were not a monstrous joy that held her. A clear and exalted perception enabled her to dismiss the suggestion as trivial.

She knew that she would weep again when she saw the kind, tender hands folded in death; the face that had never looked save with love upon her, fixed and gray and dead. But she saw beyond that bitter moment a long procession of years to come that would belong to her absolutely. And she opened and spread her arms out to them in welcome.

There would be no one to live for her during those coming years; she would live for herself. There would be no powerful will bending hers in that blind persistence with which men and women believe they have a right to impose a private will upon a fellow-creature. A kind intention or a cruel intention made the act seem no less a crime as she looked upon it in that brief moment of illumination.

And yet she had loved him—sometimes. Often she had not. What did it matter! What could love, the unsolved mystery, count for in face of this possession of self-assertion which she suddenly recognized as the strongest impulse of her being!

"Free! Body and soul free!" she kept whispering.

Josephine was kneeling before the closed door with her lips to the keyhole, imploring for admission. "Louise, open the door! I beg; open the door—you will make yourself ill. What are you doing, Louise? For heaven's sake open the door."

"Go away. I am not making myself ill." No; she was drinking in a very elixir of life through that open window.

Her fancy was running riot along those days ahead of her. Spring days, and summer days, and all sorts of days that would be her own. She breathed a quick prayer that life might be long. It was only yesterday she had thought with a shudder that life might be long.

She arose at length and opened the door to her sister's importunities. There was a feverish triumph in her eyes, and she carried herself unwittingly like a goddess of Victory. She clasped her sister's waist, and together they descended the stairs. Richards stood waiting for them at the bottom.

Some one was opening the front door with a latchkey. It was Brently Mallard who entered, a little travel-stained, composedly carrying his grip-sack and umbrella. He had been far from the scene of accident, and did not even know there had been one. He stood amazed at Josephine's piercing cry; at Richards' quick motion to screen him from the view of his wife.

But Richards was too late.

When the doctors came they said she had died of heart disease—of joy that kills.

1891

# GABRIEL GARCÍA MÁRQUEZ

## A Very Old Man with Enormous Wings[1]

### A Tale for Children

On the third day of rain they had killed so many crabs inside the house that Pelayo had to cross his drenched courtyard and throw them into the sea, because the newborn child had a temperature all night and they thought it was due to the stench. The world had been sad since Tuesday. Sea and sky were a single ashgray thing and the sands of the beach, which on March nights glimmered like powdered light, had become a stew of mud and rotten shellfish. The light was so weak at noon that when Pelayo was coming back to the house after throwing away the crabs, it was hard for him to see what it was that was moving and groaning in the rear of the courtyard. He had to go very close to see that it was an old man, a very old man, lying face down in the mud, who, in spite of his tremendous efforts, couldn't get up, impeded by his enormous wings.

Frightened by that nightmare, Pelayo ran to get Elisenda, his wife, who was putting compresses on the sick child, and he took her to the rear of the courtyard. They both looked at the fallen body with mute stupor. He was dressed like a ragpicker. There were only a few faded hairs left on his bald skull and very few teeth in his mouth, and his pitiful condition of a drenched great-grandfather had taken away any sense of grandeur he might have had. His huge buzzard wings, dirty and half-plucked, were forever entangled in the mud. They looked at him so long and so closely that Pelayo and Elisenda very soon overcame their surprise and in the end found him familiar. Then they dared speak to him, and he answered in an incomprehensible dialect with a strong sailor's voice. That was

---

1. Translated by Gregory Rabassa.

how they skipped over the inconvenience of the wings and quite intelligently concluded that he was a lonely castaway from some foreign ship wrecked by the storm. And yet, they called in a neighbor woman who knew everything about life and death to see him, and all she needed was one look to show them their mistake.

"He's an angel," she told them. "He must have been coming for the child, but the poor fellow is so old that the rain knocked him down."

On the following day everyone knew that a flesh-and-blood angel was held captive in Pelayo's house. Against the judgment of the wise neighbor woman, for whom angels in those times were the fugitive survivors of a celestial conspiracy, they did not have the heart to club him to death. Pelayo watched over him all afternoon from the kitchen, armed with his bailiff's club, and before going to bed he dragged him out of the mud and locked him up with the hens in the wire chicken coop. In the middle of the night, when the rain stopped, Pelayo and Elisenda were still killing crabs. A short time afterward the child woke up without a fever and with a desire to eat. Then they felt magnanimous and decided to put the angel on a raft with fresh water and provisions for three days and leave him to his fate on the high seas. But when they went out into the courtyard with the first light of dawn, they found the whole neighborhood in front of the chicken coop having fun with the angel, without the slightest reverence, tossing him things to eat through the openings in the wire as if he weren't a supernatural creature but a circus animal.

Father Gonzaga arrived before seven o'clock, alarmed at the strange news. By that time onlookers less frivolous than those at dawn had already arrived and they were making all kinds of conjectures concerning the captive's future. The simplest among them thought that he should be named mayor of the world. Others of sterner mind felt that he should be promoted to the rank of five-star general in order to win all wars. Some visionaries hoped that he could be put to stud in order to implant on earth a race of winged wise men who could take charge of the universe. But Father Gonzaga, before becoming a priest, had been a robust woodcutter. Standing by the wire, he reviewed his catechism in an instant and asked them to open the door so that he could take a close look at that pitiful man who looked more like a huge decrepit hen among the fascinated chickens. He was lying in a corner drying his open wings in the sunlight among the fruit peels and breakfast leftovers that the early risers had thrown him. Alien to the impertinences of the world, he only lifted his antiquarian eyes and murmured something in his dialect when Father Gonzaga went into the chicken coop and said good morning to him in Latin. The parish priest had his first suspicion of an imposter when he saw that he did not understand the language of God or know how to greet His ministers. Then he noticed that seen close up he was much too human: he had an unbearable smell of the outdoors, the back side of his wings was strewn with parasites and his main feathers had been mistreated by terrestrial winds, and nothing about him measured up to the proud dignity of angels. Then he came out of the chicken coop and in a brief sermon warned the curious against the risks of being ingenuous. He reminded them that the devil had the bad habit of making use of carnival tricks in order to confuse the unwary. He argued that if wings were not the essential element in determining the difference between a hawk and an airplane, they were even less so in the recognition of angels. Nevertheless, he promised to write a letter to his bishop so that the latter would write to his primate so that the latter would write to the Supreme Pontiff in order to get the final verdict from the highest courts.

His prudence fell on sterile hearts. The news of the captive angel spread with such rapidity that after a few hours the courtyard had the bustle of a marketplace and they had to call in troops with fixed bayonets to disperse the mob that was about to knock the house down. Elisenda, her spine all twisted from sweeping up so much marketplace trash, then got the idea of fencing in the yard and charging five cents admission to see the angel.

The curious came from far away. A traveling carnival arrived with a flying acrobat who buzzed over the crowd several times, but no one paid any attention to him because his wings were not those of an angel but, rather, those of a sidereal bat. The most unfortunate invalids on earth came in search of health: a poor woman who since childhood had been counting her heartbeats and had run out of numbers; a Portuguese man who couldn't sleep because the noise of the stars disturbed him; a sleepwalker who got up at night to undo the things he had done while awake; and many others with less serious ailments. In the midst of that shipwreck disorder that made the earth tremble, Pelayo and Elisenda were happy with fatigue, for in less than a week they had crammed their rooms with money and the line of pilgrims waiting their turn to enter still reached beyond the horizon.

The angel was the only one who took no part in his own act. He spent his time trying to get comfortable in his borrowed nest, befuddled by the hellish heat of the oil lamps and sacramental candles that had been placed along the wire. At first they tried to make him eat some mothballs, which, according to the wisdom of the wise neighbor woman, were the food prescribed for angels. But he turned them down, just as he turned down the papal lunches[2] that the penitents brought him, and they never found out whether it was because he was an angel or because he was an old man that in the end he ate nothing but eggplant mush. His only supernatural virtue seemed to be patience. Especially during the first days, when the hens pecked at him, searching for the stellar parasites that proliferated in his wings, and the cripples pulled out feathers to touch their defective parts with, and even the most merciful threw stones at him, trying to get him to rise so they could see him standing. The only time they succeeded in arousing him was when they burned his side with an iron for branding steers, for he had been motionless for so many hours that they thought he was dead. He awoke with a start, ranting in his hermetic language and with tears in his eyes, and he flapped his wings a couple of times, which brought on a whirlwind of chicken dung and lunar dust and a gale of panic that did not seem to be of this world. Although many thought that his reaction had been one not of rage but of pain, from then on they were careful not to annoy him, because the majority understood that his passivity was not that of a hero taking his ease but that of a cataclysm in repose.

Father Gonzaga held back the crowd's frivolity with formulas of maidservant inspiration while awaiting the arrival of a final judgment on the nature of the captive. But the mail from Rome showed no sense of urgency. They spent their time finding out if the prisoner had a navel, if his dialect had any connection

---

2. Expensive, elaborately prepared meals.

with Aramaic, how many times he could fit on the head of a pin, or whether he wasn't just a Norwegian with wings. Those meager letters might have come and gone until the end of time if a providential event had not put an end to the priest's tribulations.

It so happened that during those days, among so many other carnival attractions, there arrived in town the traveling show of the woman who had been changed into a spider for having disobeyed her parents. The admission to see her was not only less than the admission to see the angel, but people were permitted to ask her all manner of questions about her absurd state and to examine her up and down so that no one would ever doubt the truth of her horror. She was a frightful tarantula the size of a ram and with the head of a sad maiden. What was most heart-rending, however, was not her outlandish shape but the sincere affliction with which she recounted the details of her misfortune. While still practically a child she had sneaked out of her parents' house to go to a dance, and while she was coming back through the woods after having danced all night without permission, a fearful thunderclap rent the sky in two and through the crack came the lightning bolt of brimstone that changed her into a spider. Her only nourishment came from the meatballs that charitable souls chose to toss into her mouth. A spectacle like that, full of so much human truth and with such a fearful lesson, was bound to defeat without even trying that of a haughty angel who scarcely deigned to look at mortals. Besides, the few miracles attributed to the angel showed a certain mental disorder, like the blind man who didn't recover his sight but grew three new teeth, or the paralytic who didn't get to walk but almost won the lottery, and the leper whose sores sprouted sunflowers. Those consolation miracles, which were more like mocking fun, had already ruined the angel's reputation when the woman who had been changed into a spider finally crushed him completely. That was how Father Gonzaga was cured forever of his insomnia and Pelayo's courtyard went back to being as empty as during the time it had rained for three days and crabs walked through the bedrooms.

The owners of the house had no reason to lament. With the money they saved they built a two-story mansion with balconies and gardens and high netting so that crabs wouldn't get in during the winter, and with iron bars on the windows so that angels wouldn't get in. Pelayo also set up a rabbit warren close to town and gave up his job as bailiff for good, and Elisenda bought some satin pumps with high heels and many dresses of iridescent silk, the kind worn on Sunday by the most desirable women in those times. The chicken coop was the only thing that didn't receive any attention. If they washed it down with creolin[3] and burned tears of myrrh inside it every so often, it was not in homage to the angel but to drive away the dungheap stench that still hung everywhere like a ghost and was turning the new house into an old one. At first, when the child learned to walk, they were careful that he not get too close to the chicken coop. But then they began to lose their fears and got used to the smell, and before the child got his second teeth he'd gone inside the chicken coop to play, where the wires were falling apart. The angel was no less standoffish with him than with other mortals, but he tolerated the most ingenious infamies with the patience of a dog who had no illusions. They both came down with chicken pox at the same time. The

---

3. A disinfectant.

doctor who took care of the child couldn't resist the temptation to listen to the angel's heart, and he found so much whistling in the heart and so many sounds in his kidneys that it seemed impossible for him to be alive. What surprised him most, however, was the logic of his wings. They seemed so natural on that completely human organism that he couldn't understand why other men didn't have them too.

When the child began school it had been some time since the sun and rain had caused the collapse of the chicken coop. The angel went dragging himself about here and there like a stray dying man. They would drive him out of the bedroom with a broom and a moment later find him in the kitchen. He seemed to be in so many places at the same time that they grew to think that he'd been duplicated, that he was reproducing himself all through the house, and the exasperated and unhinged Elisenda shouted that it was awful living in that hell full of angels. He could scarcely eat and his antiquarian eyes had also become so foggy that he went about bumping into posts. All he had left were the bare cannulae of his last feathers. Pelayo threw a blanket over him and extended him the charity of letting him sleep in the shed, and only then did they notice that he had a temperature at night, and was delirious with the tongue twisters of an old Norwegian. That was one of the few times they became alarmed, for they thought he was going to die and not even the wise neighbor woman had been able to tell them what to do with dead angels.

And yet he not only survived his worst winter, but seemed improved with the first sunny days. He remained motionless for several days in the farthest corner of the courtyard, where no one would see him, and at the beginning of December some large, stiff feathers began to grow on his wings, the feathers of a scarecrow, which looked more like another misfortune of decrepitude. But he must have known the reason for those changes, for he was quite careful that no one should notice them, that no one should hear the sea chanteys that he sometimes sang under the stars. One morning Elisenda was cutting some bunches of onions for lunch when a wind that seemed to come from the high seas blew into the kitchen. Then she went to the window and caught the angel in his first attempts at flight. They were so clumsy that his fingernails opened a furrow in the vegetable patch and he was on the point of knocking the shed down with the ungainly flapping that slipped on the light and couldn't get a grip on the air. But he did manage to gain altitude. Elisenda let out a sign of relief, for herself and for him, when she saw him pass over the last houses, holding himself up in some way with the risky flapping of a senile vulture. She kept watching him even when she was through cutting the onions and she kept on watching until it was no longer possible for her to see him, because then he was no longer an annoyance in her life but an imaginary dot on the horizon of the sea.

1968

## JAMAICA KINCAID

### Girl

Wash the white clothes on Monday and put them on the stone heap; wash the color clothes on Tuesday and put them on the clothesline to dry; don't walk barehead in the hot sun; cook pumpkin fritters in very hot sweet oil; soak your little cloths right after you take them off; when buying cotton to make yourself a nice blouse, be sure that it doesn't have gum on it, because that way it won't hold up well after a wash; soak salt fish overnight before you cook it; is it true that you sing benna[1] in Sunday school?; always eat your food in such a way that it won't turn someone else's stomach; on Sundays try to walk like a lady and not like the slut you are so bent on becoming; don't sing benna in Sunday school; you mustn't speak to wharf-rat boys, not even to give directions; don't eat fruits on the street—flies will follow you; *but I don't sing benna on Sundays at all and never in Sunday school;* this is how to sew on a button; this is how to make a buttonhole for the button you have just sewed on; this is how to hem a dress when you see the hem coming down and so to prevent yourself from looking like the slut I know you are so bent on becoming; this is how you iron your father's khaki shirt so that it doesn't have a crease; this is how you iron your father's khaki pants so that they don't have a crease; this is how you grow okra—far from the house, because okra tree harbors red ants; when you are growing dasheen, make sure it gets plenty of water or else it makes your throat itch when you are eating it; this is how you sweep a corner; this is how you sweep a whole house; this is how you sweep a yard; this is how you smile to someone you don't like too much; this is how you smile to someone you don't like at all; this is how you smile to someone you like completely; this is how you set a table for tea; this is how you set a table for dinner; this is how you set a table for dinner with an important guest; this is how you set a table for lunch; this is how you set a table for breakfast; this is how to behave in the presence of men who don't know you very well, and this way they won't recognize immediately the slut I have warned you against becoming; be sure to wash every day, even if it is with your own spit; don't squat down to play marbles—you are not a boy, you know; don't pick people's flowers—you might catch something; don't throw stones at blackbirds, because it might not be a blackbird at all; this is how to make a bread pudding; this is how to make doukona[2] this is how to make pepper pot; this is how to make a good medicine for a cold; this is how to make a good medicine to throw away a child before it even becomes a child; this is how to catch a fish; this is how to throw back a fish you don't like, and that way something bad won't fall on you; this is how to bully a man; this is how a man bullies you; this is how to love a man, and if this doesn't work there are other ways, and if they don't work don't feel too bad about giving up; this is how to spit up in the air if you feel like it, and this is how to move quick so that it doesn't fall on you; this is how to make ends meet; always squeeze bread to make sure it's fresh; *but what if the baker won't let me feel*

---

1. A Caribbean folk-music style.
2. A spicy pudding, often made from plantain and wrapped in a plantain or banana leaf.

*the bread?;* you mean to say that after all you are really going to be the kind of woman who the baker won't let near the bread?

1983

## YASUNARI KAWABATA

## *The Grasshopper and the Bell Cricket*[1]

Walking along the tile-roofed wall of the university, I turned aside and approached the upper school. Behind the white board fence of the school playground, from a dusky clump of bushes under the black cherry trees, an insect's voice could be heard. Walking more slowly and listening to that voice, and furthermore reluctant to part with it, I turned right so as not to leave the playground behind. When I turned to the left, the fence gave way to an embankment planted with orange trees. At the corner, I exclaimed with surprise. My eyes gleaming at what they saw up ahead, I hurried forward with short steps.

At the base of the embankment was a bobbing cluster of beautiful varicolored lanterns, such as one might see at a festival in a remote country village. Without going any farther, I knew that it was a group of children on an insect chase among the bushes of the embankment. There were about twenty lanterns. Not only were there crimson, pink, indigo, green, purple, and yellow lanterns, but one lantern glowed with five colors at once. There were even some little red store-bought lanterns. But most of the lanterns were beautiful square ones which the children had made themselves with love and care. The bobbing lanterns, the coming together of children on this lonely slope—surely it was a scene from a fairy tale?

One of the neighborhood children had heard an insect sing on this slope one night. Buying a red lantern, he had come back the next night to find the insect. The night after that, there was another child. This new child could not buy a lantern. Cutting out the back and front of a small carton and papering it, he placed a candle on the bottom and fastened a string to the top. The number of children grew to five, and then to seven. They learned how to color the paper that they stretched over the windows of the cutout cartons, and to draw pictures on it. Then these wise child-artists, cutting out round, three-cornered, and lozenge leaf shapes in the cartons, coloring each little window a different color, with circles and diamonds, red and green, made a single and whole decorative pattern. The child with the red lantern discarded it as a tasteless object that could be bought at a store. The child who had made his own lantern threw it away because the design was too simple. The pattern of light that one had had in hand the night before was unsatisfying the morning after. Each day, with cardboard, paper, brush, scissors, penknife, and glue, the children made new lanterns out of their hearts and minds. Look at my lantern! Be the most unusually beautiful! And each night, they had gone out on their insect hunts. These were the twenty children and their beautiful lanterns that I now saw before me.

Wide-eyed, I loitered near them. Not only did the square lanterns have old-

---

1. Translated by Lane Dunlop.

fashioned patterns and flower shapes, but the names of the children who had made them were cut out in squared letters of the syllabary. Different from the painted-over red lanterns, others (made of thick cutout cardboard) had their designs drawn onto the paper windows, so that the candle's light seemed to emanate from the form and color of the design itself. The lanterns brought out the shadows of the bushes like dark light. The children crouched eagerly on the slope wherever they heard an insect's voice.

"Does anyone want a grasshopper?" A boy, who had been peering into a bush about thirty feet away from the other children, suddenly straightened up and shouted.

"Yes! Give it to me!" Six or seven children came running up. Crowding behind the boy who had found the grasshopper, they peered into the bush. Brushing away their outstretched hands and spreading out his arms, the boy stood as if guarding the bush where the insect was. Waving the lantern in his right hand, he called again to the other children.

"Does anyone want a grasshopper? A grasshopper!"

"I do! I do!" Four or five more children came running up. It seemed you could not catch a more precious insect than a grasshopper. The boy called out a third time.

"Doesn't anyone want a grasshopper?"

Two or three more children came over.

"Yes. I want it."

It was a girl, who just now had come up behind the boy who'd discovered the insect. Lightly turning his body, the boy gracefully bent forward. Shifting the lantern to his left hand, he reached his right hand into the bush.

"It's a grasshopper."

"Yes. I'd like to have it."

The boy quickly stood up. As if to say "Here!" he thrust out his fist that held the insect at the girl. She, slipping her left wrist under the string of her lantern, enclosed the boy's fist with both hands. The boy quietly opened his fist. The insect was transferred to between the girl's thumb and index finger.

"Oh! It's not a grasshopper. It's a bell cricket." The girl's eyes shone as she looked at the small brown insect.

"It's a bell cricket! It's a bell cricket!" The children echoed in an envious chorus.

"It's a bell cricket. It's a bell cricket."

Glancing with her bright intelligent eyes at the boy who had given her the cricket, the girl opened the little insect cage hanging at her side and released the cricket in it.

"It's a bell cricket."

"Oh, it's a bell cricket," the boy who'd captured it muttered. Holding up the insect cage close to his eyes, he looked inside it. By the light of his beautiful many colored lantern, also held up at eye level, he glanced at the girl's face.

Oh, I thought. I felt slightly jealous of the boy, and sheepish. How silly of me not to have understood his actions until now! Then I caught my breath in surprise. Look! It was something on the girl's breast which neither the boy who had given her the cricket, nor she who had accepted it, nor the children who were looking at them noticed.

In the faint greenish light that fell on the girl's breast, wasn't the name "Fujio" clearly discernible? The boy's lantern, which he held up alongside the girl's insect cage, inscribed his name, cut out in the green papered aperture, onto her white cotton kimono. The girl's lantern, which dangled loosely from her wrist, did not project its pattern so clearly, but still one could make out, in a trembling patch of red on the boy's waist, the name "Kiyoko." This chance interplay of red and green—if it was chance or play—neither Fujio nor Kiyoko knew about.

Even if they remembered forever that Fujio had given her the cricket and that Kiyoko had accepted it, not even in dreams would Fujio ever know that his name had been written in green on Kiyoko's breast or that Kiyoko's name had been inscribed in red on his waist, nor would Kiyoko ever know that Fujio's name had been inscribed in green on her breast or that her own name had been written in red on Fujio's waist.

25  Fujio! Even when you have become a young man, laugh with pleasure at a girl's delight when, told that it's a grasshopper, she is given a bell cricket; laugh with affection at a girl's chagrin when, told that it's a bell cricket, she is given a grasshopper.

Even if you have the wit to look by yourself in a bush away from the other children, there are not many bell crickets in the world. Probably you will find a girl like a grasshopper whom you think is a bell cricket.

And finally, to your clouded, wounded heart, even a true bell cricket will seem like a grasshopper. Should that day come, when it seems to you that the world is only full of grasshoppers, I will think it a pity that you have no way to remember tonight's play of light, when your name was written in green by your beautiful lantern on a girl's breast.

1988

## WILLIAM CARLOS WILLIAMS

### *The Use of Force*

They were new patients to me, all I had was the name, Olson. Please come down as soon as you can, my daughter is very sick. When I arrived I was met by the mother, a big startled looking woman, very clean and apologetic who merely said, Is this the doctor? and let me in. In the back, she added. You must excuse us, doctor, we have her in the kitchen where it is warm. It is very damp here sometimes.

The child was fully dressed and sitting on her father's lap near the kitchen table. He tried to get up, but I motioned for him not to bother, took off my overcoat and started to look things over. I could see that they were all very nervous, eyeing me up and down distrustfully. As often, in such cases, they weren't telling me more than they had to, it was up to me to tell them; that's why they were spending three dollars on me.

The child was fairly eating me up with her cold, steady eyes, and no expression to her face whatever. She did not move and seemed, inwardly, quiet; an unusually attractive little thing, and as strong as a heifer in appearance. But her face was flushed, she was breathing rapidly, and I realized that she had a high fever. She had magnificent blonde hair, in profusion. One of those picture children often reproduced in advertising leaflets and the photogravure[1] sections of the Sunday papers.

She's had a fever for three days, began the father and we don't know what it comes from. My wife has given her things, you know, like people do, but it don't do no good. And there's been a lot of sickness around. So we tho't you'd better look her over and tell us what is the matter.

As doctors often do I took a trial shot at it as a point of departure. Has she had a sore throat?

Both parents answered me together, No . . . No, she says her throat don't hurt her.

Does your throat hurt you? added the mother to the child. But the little girl's expression didn't change nor did she move her eyes from my face.

Have you looked?

I tried to, said the mother, but I couldn't see.

As it happens we had been having a number of cases of diphtheria in the school to which this child went during that month and we were all, quite apparently, thinking of that, though no one had as yet spoken of the thing.

Well, I said, suppose we take a look at the throat first. I smiled in my best professional manner and asking for the child's first name I said, come on, Mathilda, open your mouth and let's take a look at your throat.

Nothing doing.

Aw, come on, I coaxed, just open your mouth wide and let me take a look. Look, I said opening both hands wide, I haven't anything in my hands. Just open up and let me see.

Such a nice man, put in the mother. Look how kind he is to you. Come on, do what he tells you to. He won't hurt you.

At that I ground my teeth in disgust. If only they wouldn't use the word "hurt" I might be able to get somewhere. But I did not allow myself to be hurried or disturbed but speaking quietly and slowly I approached the child again.

As I moved my chair a little nearer suddenly with one catlike movement both her hands clawed instinctively for my eyes and she almost reached them too. In fact she knocked my glasses flying and they fell, though unbroken, several feet away from me on the kitchen floor.

Both the mother and father almost turned themselves inside out in embarrassment and apology. You bad girl, said the mother, taking her and shaking her by one arm. Look what you've done. The nice man . . .

For heaven's sake, I broke in. Don't call me a nice man to her. I'm here to look at her throat on the chance that she might have diphtheria[2] and possibly die of it. But that's nothing to her. Look here, I said to the child, we're going to look at your throat. You're old enough to understand what I'm saying. Will you open it now by yourself or shall we have to open it for you?

Not a move. Even her expression hadn't changed. Her breaths however were coming faster and faster. Then the battle began. I had to do it. I had to have a throat culture for her own protection. But first I told the parents that it was

1. Process for printing photographs.
2. Bacterial disease that killed millions, mostly children, in the era before antibiotic medicines and effective programs of immunization. The most common sign of infection is a thick, bluish-white membrane coating the tonsils and throat.

entirely up to them. I explained the danger but said that I would not insist on a throat examination so long as they would take the responsibility.

20    If you don't do what the doctor says you'll have to go to the hospital, the mother admonished her severely.

Oh yeah? I had to smile to myself. After all, I had already fallen in love with the savage brat, the parents were contemptible to me. In the ensuing struggle they grew more and more abject, crushed, exhausted while she surely rose to magnificent heights of insane fury of effort bred of her terror of me.

The father tried his best, and he was a big man but the fact that she was his daughter, his shame at her behavior and his dread of hurting her made him release her just at the critical times when I had almost achieved success, till I wanted to kill him. But his dread also that she might have diphtheria made him tell me to go on, go on though he himself was almost fainting, while the mother moved back and forth behind us raising and lowering her hands in an agony of apprehension.

Put her in front of you on your lap, I ordered, and hold both her wrists.

But as soon as he did the child let out a scream. Don't, you're hurting me. Let go of my hands. Let them go I tell you. Then she shrieked terrifyingly, hysterically. Stop it! Stop it! You're killing me!

25    Do you think she can stand it, doctor! said the mother.

You get out, said the husband to his wife. Do you want her to die of diphtheria?

Come on now, hold her, I said.

Then I grasped the child's head with my left hand and tried to get the wooden tongue depressor between her teeth. She fought, with clenched teeth, desperately! But now I also had grown furious—at a child. I tried to hold myself down but I couldn't. I know how to expose a throat for inspection. And I did my best. When finally I got the wooden spatula behind the last teeth and just the point of it into the mouth cavity, she opened up for an instant but before I could see anything she came down again and gripping the wooden blade between her molars she reduced it to splinters before I could get it out again.

Aren't you ashamed, the mother yelled at her. Aren't you ashamed to act like that in front of the doctor?

30    Get me a smooth-handled spoon of some sort, I told the mother. We're going through with this. The child's mouth was already bleeding. Her tongue was cut and she was screaming in wild hysterical shrieks. Perhaps I should have desisted and come back in an hour or more. No doubt it would have been better. But I have seen at least two children lying dead in bed of neglect in such cases, and feeling that I must get a diagnosis now or never I went at it, again. But the worst of it was that I too had got beyond reason. I could have torn the child apart in my own fury and enjoyed it. It was a pleasure to attack her. My face was burning with it.

The damned little brat must be protected against her own idiocy, one says to one's self at such times. Others must be protected against her. It is a social necessity. And all these things are true. But a blind fury, a feeling of adult shame, bred of a longing for muscular release are the operatives. One goes on to the end.

In the final unreasoning assault I overpowered the child's neck and jaws. I forced the heavy silver spoon back of her teeth and down her throat till she gagged. And there it was—both tonsils covered with membrane. She had fought valiantly to keep me from knowing her secret. She had been hiding that sore throat for three days at least and lying to her parents in order to escape just such an outcome as this.

Now truly she was furious. She had been on the defensive before but now she attacked. Tried to get off her father's lap and fly at me while tears of defeat blinded her eyes.

1938

## URSULA K. LE GUIN

## *She Unnames Them*

Most of them accepted namelessness with the perfect indifference with which they had so long accepted and ignored their names. Whales and dolphins, seals and sea otters consented with particular grace and alacrity, sliding into anonymity as into their element. A faction of yaks, however, protested. They said that "yak" sounded right, and that almost everyone who knew they existed called them that. Unlike the ubiquitous creatures such as rats and fleas, who had been called by hundreds or thousands of different names since Babel, the yaks could truly say, they said, that they had a *name*. They discussed the matter all summer. The councils of the elderly females finally agreed that though the name might be useful to others it was so redundant from the yak point of view that they never spoke it themselves and hence might as well dispense with it. After they presented the argument in this light to their bulls, a full consensus was delayed only by the onset of severe early blizzards. Soon after the beginning of the thaw, their agreement was reached and the designation "yak" was returned to the donor.

Among the domestic animals, few horses had cared what anybody called them since the failure of Dean Swift's attempt to name them from their own vocabulary.[1] Cattle, sheep, swine, asses, mules, and goats, along with chickens, geese, and turkeys, all agreed enthusiastically to give their names back to the people to whom—as they put it—they belonged.

A couple of problems did come up with pets. The cats, of course, steadfastly denied ever having had any name other than those self-given, unspoken, effanineffably personal names which, as the poet named Eliot[2] said, they spend long hours daily contemplating—though none of the contemplators has ever admitted that what they contemplate is their names and some onlookers have wondered if the object of that meditative gaze might not in fact be the Perfect, or Platonic, Mouse.[3] In any case, it is a moot point now. It was with the dogs, and with some

---

1. In *Gulliver's Travels* (1726), Part IV, Jonathan Swift (1667-1745), dean of St. Patrick's Cathedral, Dublin, gave the name *Houyhnhnms*—meant to sound like a horse neighing—to a race of rational, talking horses.
2. British (American-born) poet T. S. Eliot (1888-1965), in *The Naming of Cats* (1939), where he coined the word *effanineffable*.
3. That is, the ideal form of a mouse; the Greek philosopher Plato (ca. 428-348 or 347 B.C.E.) argued that archetypes existed for all material things.

parrots, lovebirds, ravens, and mynahs, that the trouble arose. These verbally talented individuals insisted that their names were important to them, and flatly refused to part with them. But as soon as they understood that the issue was precisely one of individual choice, and that anybody who wanted to be called Rover, or Froufrou, or Polly, or even Birdie in the personal sense, was perfectly free to do so, not one of them had the least objection to parting with the lowercase (or, as regards German creatures, uppercase) generic appellations "poodle," "parrot," "dog," or "bird," and all the Linnaean qualifiers[4] that had trailed along behind them for two hundred years like tin cans tied to a tail.

The insects parted with their names in vast clouds and swarms of ephemeral syllables buzzing and stinging and humming and flitting and crawling and tunneling away.

5   As for the fish of the sea, their names dispersed from them in silence throughout the oceans like faint, dark blurs of cuttlefish ink, and drifted off on the currents without a trace.

None were left now to unname, and yet how close I felt to them when I saw one of them swim or fly or trot or crawl across my way or over my skin, or stalk me in the night, or go along beside me for a while in the day. They seemed far closer than when their names had stood between myself and them like a clear barrier: so close that my fear of them and their fear of me became one same fear. And the attraction that many of us felt, the desire to smell one another's smells, feel or rub or caress one another's scales or skin or feathers or fur, taste one another's blood or flesh, keep one another warm—that attraction was now all one with the fear, and the hunter could not be told from the hunted, nor the eater from the food.

This was more or less the effect I had been after. It was somewhat more powerful than I had anticipated, but I could not now, in all conscience, make an exception for myself. I resolutely put anxiety away, went to Adam,[5] and said, "You and your father lent me this—gave it to me, actually. It's been really useful, but it doesn't exactly seem to fit very well lately. But thanks very much! It's really been very useful."

It is hard to give back a gift without sounding peevish or ungrateful, and I did not want to leave him with that impression of me. He was not paying much attention, as it happened, and said only, "Put it down over there, O.K.?" and went on with what he was doing.

One of my reasons for doing what I did was that talk was getting us nowhere, but all the same I felt a little let down. I had been prepared to defend my decision. And I thought that perhaps when he did notice he might be upset and want to talk. I put some things away and fiddled around a little, but he continued to do what he was doing and to take no notice of anything else. At last I said, "Well, goodbye, dear. I hope the garden key turns up."

---

4. Swedish botanist and taxonomist Carolus Linnaeus (1707–1778) originated the modern scientific classification of plants and animals.
5. See Genesis, esp. 2.19 ("So out of the ground the Lord God formed every beast of the field and every bird of the air and brought them to the man to see what he would call them") and 3.20 ("The man called his wife's name Eve, because she was the mother of all living").

He was fitting parts together, and said, without looking around, "O.K., fine, dear. When's dinner?"

"I'm not sure," I said. "I'm going now. With the—" I hesitated, and finally said, "With them, you know," and went on out. In fact, I had only just then realized how hard it would have been to explain myself. I could not chatter away as I used to do, taking it all for granted. My words now must be as slow, as new, as single, as tentative as the steps I took going down the path away from the house, between the dark-branched, tall dancers motionless against the winter shining.

1985

## SUGGESTIONS FOR WRITING

1. Write an essay in which you discuss what is only implied in "The Story of an Hour"—Louise Mallard's feelings about her marriage, as well as the attitudes toward marriage and the roles of husbands and wives implicit in the story as a whole. Be sure to base any assertions you make on specific passages in the text.
2. In "A Very Old Man with Enormous Wings," is the old man a symbol? If so, a symbol of what? Write an essay in which you offer a possible interpretation of Gabriel García Márquez's tale, accounting for both the fantastic and the realistic elements of the story.
3. Write your own short story, "Boy," modeled on Jamaica Kincaid's "Girl," or write your own version of "Girl." Use either your own point of view or that of an unwelcome adviser.
4. Do "art" and "beauty" have a different meaning for children than they do for adults? Citing examples from Yasunari Kawabata's "The Grasshopper and the Bell Cricket," write an essay in which you discuss the role of art in the lives of children.
5. William Carlos Williams gives a very far-reaching title, "The Use of Force," to a short personal account of a seemingly minor incident. What really happens in this story? Does the patient use any kind of power, if not force? Write an essay analyzing the implications of the story's title and what the story reveals about relations of power between people.
6. What changes when something is given a name? What would it be like to live in a world in which nothing has a name? Write either an essay that discusses the significance of inventing words for things, or a short story that explores what a nameless world might be like.

# 11 CULTURAL AND HISTORICAL CONTEXT

Over the past two hundred years, the meaning of the word *culture* has broadened considerably, from "cultivation" (as in *agri*culture) to "the arts or familiarity with the arts" (*high* culture, *a* cultured *person*) to "a whole way of life" (*American* culture, *African American* culture). The fact that we still use the one word for both "the arts" and "a whole way of life" implies a close, even fundamental relationship between the two. The double implications of "culture" suggest both that works of art reflect and help shape the way we live, and also that art in a particular time and place takes the form it does because of the larger cultural context—what nineteenth-century writer William Hazlitt called "the spirit of the age." In this sense, the first definition of *culture*—"cultivation"—informs the other two definitions because, so the theory goes, a particular "way of life" encourages literature, along with the other arts, to grow in a certain way, in part by shaping the personalities and worldviews of both writers and readers.

While we can often achieve a greater, or at least different, understanding of a literary work by reading other works by the same author and thus getting a sense of that author's unique vision (see chapter 8), we also should remember that authors, like the rest of us, live in particular times and particular places. That is, authorial visions, however unique, are inevitably shaped by cultural and historical context, and our understanding of a particular text or of an author's entire canon can sometimes be enhanced by learning more about that context.

This is not to say that texts and authors *merely* reflect their cultural moment. Although authors—their personalities, viewpoints, concerns, and values—are shaped by the times and places in which they live, they often choose to write because they want to comment on, and maybe even change, the way their contemporaries think, feel, and behave. Literature can and sometimes does shape, as well as reflect, history. Testifying to the powerful effect that literature can exercise, one member of the generation born just after World War I noted that Ernest Hemingway's "impact upon us was tremendous. . . . We could follow him, ape his manner"; "we began unconsciously to . . . impose on everything we did and felt the particular emotions [his fiction] aroused in us."

> *Sometimes I don't know whether Zelda and I are real or whether we are characters in one of my novels.*
> —F. SCOTT FITZGERALD

But what happens to either the individual or the "universal" aspects of a literary work as we focus our attention on its relationship to its cultural and historical context? At its best, the process is one of addition rather than subtraction. Reading a text in light of its cultural and historical context simply gives us a different but complementary perspective to that of reading the text on its own terms or in relation to other contexts. Indeed, what makes the study of literature both exciting and enriching is its multilayered, multidimensional quality: the way that Flannery O'Connor's "Everything That Rises Must Converge," for example, at one and the same time embodies its author's unique vision of the association between violence and enlightenment; explores the universal problem of generational conflict; and evaluates the dramatic cultural transformations that shook the American South during the 1960s. The point, then, of reading with an eye toward cultural and historical context is not to foreclose other ways of reading but rather to enrich our experience of the text and, through it, our sense of what is both common to, and different about, human experience across ages and cultures.

F. Scott Fitzgerald and his story "Babylon Revisited" provide a rich opportunity to explore the complex interaction among author, text, and context. The name *Fitzgerald* has become almost synonymous with the spirit of 1920s and '30s America. As literary critic and editor Malcolm Cowley puts it in his autobiographical *Exile's Return: A Literary Odyssey of the 1920s* (excerpted below), Fitzgerald's "novels and stories are in some ways the best record of the whole period."

Born in 1896, F. Scott Fitzgerald was in his twenties as America entered the '20s. After attending Princeton, serving in the army during the final days of World War I, and working briefly in a New York advertising agency, Fitzgerald published his first novel, *This Side of Paradise*, in 1920.

*First you take a drink, then the drink takes a drink, then the drink takes you.*
—F. SCOTT FITZGERALD

On the strength of the eighteen-thousand-dollar advance he received for the novel, Fitzgerald married Zelda Sayre, and soon they had a daughter. Moving between New York City, St. Paul, and Long Island in the early years of their marriage, the Fitzgeralds then lived mainly in Europe between 1924 and 1931, pursuing a nomadic, expensive, bohemian lifestyle saturated in alcohol. Having spent nearly 113 thousand dollars in four years and finding himself five thousand dollars in debt, Fitzgerald sought to supplement the income derived from his novels (*The Beautiful and the Damned* [1922], *The Great Gatsby* [1925]) by writing short stories for American newspapers and magazines. The beginning of the end of this way of life came in 1930 when Zelda had the first of a series of nervous breakdowns. Thus in December 1930, Zelda was in a Swiss sanitarium, nine-year-old daughter Scottie was installed in a Paris apartment with a French nanny, and Fitzgerald was shuttling back and forth between Paris and Switzerland, writing short stories (including "Babylon Revisited") to keep the family afloat financially, and fending off the efforts of Zelda's disapproving sister to assume custody of Scottie. The situation of the families at the center of "Babylon Revisited" thus closely parallels that of the Fitzgeralds, who were by this time being forced to "pay" in various ways for the life they lived in the 1920s. The summer before writing "Babylon Revis-

The Fitzgeralds celebrate Christmas, early 1920s

ited," Fitzgerald—sounding like the story's protagonist, Charlie Wales—reminisced about that life in a letter to Zelda: "You were going crazy and calling it genius—I was going to ruin and calling it anything that came to hand. And I think everyone far enough away to see us outside of our glib presentation of ourselves guessed at your almost meglomaniacal [sic] selfishness and my insane indulgence in drink. Toward the end nothing mattered." Zelda responded, "You were literally eternally drunk."

As "Babylon Revisited" continually reminds us, Charlie Wales's situation is by no means unique, and neither was the Fitzgeralds': their experience was, as one literary critic insists, "a distillation of the social history of the age." Instead of one age, however, there are in fact two ages depicted in "Babylon Revisited." Written and set in a newly sober, subdued 1930, the story nonetheless "revisits" the previous decade, a decade variously referred to (then and now) as the "Roaring Twenties," the "Jazz Age," and the "Age of Excess." Like Charlie Wales, Fitzgerald is thus seeking to understand the past from the point of view of the present, to trace effects back to their causes.

*Life* magazine covers the Jazz Age

The retrospective mood is characteristic of the early 1930s, expressing itself in semiautobiographical works like Fitzgerald's own "Echoes of the Jazz Age" (November 1931; excerpted below) and Cowley's *Exile's Return* (1934), as well as in historical studies such as Frederick Lewis Allen's *Only Yesterday: An Informal History of the Nineteen-Twenties* (1931). For these writers, what separated "today" from "yesterday" was the Great Crash of October 1929, which preceded the writing of "Babylon Revisited" by only fourteen months. As Fitzgerald wrote in "Echoes," the crash represented the "spectacular death" of the Jazz Age, this cataclysmic event ensuring that the previous decade gained a peculiar kind of distinctness in the American psyche.

The story of what happened in October 1929 can be told in part through numbers: on "Black Thursday," October 24, 1929, thirteen million shares of stock were traded in New York; five days later, on Tuesday, October 29, the number of shares sold mounted to over sixteen million, setting a record that would stand for decades. More importantly, on that horrible Tuesday alone, stock values fell a total of fourteen billion dollars. The results were countless individual bankruptcies and a general collapse of the national economy that eventually culminated in what we now call the Great Depression. By April 1930, the government estimated that three million people were unemployed in the U.S.; by January 1931 (one month before the publication of "Babylon Revisited"), the official number was six million, while unofficial (and probably more accurate) estimates hovered around eight million. Though many insisted in 1930 that the situation was temporary, conditions in fact worsened in the coming years: by 1932, the value of U.S. stocks had fallen by 89 percent; approximately nine million savings accounts had been wiped out; eighty-six thousand businesses had failed; and even the lucky few who were employed had seen their wages drop by around 60 percent.

> *Though the Jazz Age continued, it became less and less an affair of youth. The sequel was like a children's party taken over by adults.*
> —F. SCOTT FITZGERALD

Such numbers serve as vivid testimony to the economic effects of the crash. But what they can't capture nearly so well are its emotional, psychological, and cultural effects. As Frederick Allen reminded his readers in 1930,

> Prosperity is more than an economic condition; it is a state of mind. The Big Bull Market had been more than the climax of a business cycle; it had been the climax of a cycle in American mass thinking and mass emotion. There was hardly a man or woman in the country whose attitude toward life had not been affected by it in some degree and was not now affected by the sudden and brutal shattering of hope. With the Big Bull Market gone and prosperity going, Americans were soon to find themselves living in an altered world which called for new adjustments, new ideas, new habits of thought, and a new order of values. The psychological climate was changing; the ever-shifting currents of American life were turning into new channels.

The Postwar Decade had come to its close. An era had ended. Fitzgerald insisted that what died in the fall of 1929 was "the utter confidence which was [the age's] essential prop."

Looking back across that great divide in time, Fitzgerald described the 1920s as "the most expensive orgy in history." He was far from alone in suggesting that 1929 represented the inevitable reaping of what was sown in the previous decade, yet he was also in good company when he mixed condemnation with nostalgia: "after two years the Jazz Age seems as far away as the days before the War. It was borrowed time anyhow—the whole upper tenth of a nation living with the insouciance of grand ducs and the casualness of chorus girls. But moralizing is easy now and it was pleasant to be in one's twenties in such a certain and unworried time."

When Fitzgerald refers to the "upper tenth," he isn't exaggerating: one historian estimates that on the eve of the crash in 1929, the sixty thousand families "at the top of the economic pyramid controlled as much wealth as the twenty-five million families at the bottom"—people like those employed in the North Carolina textile industry, for example, who earned eighteen dollars for a seventy-hour workweek if they were men, half that if they were women. Yet one reason the 1929 crash was so devastating was that during the 1920s the stock market became the province not just of the millionaire few, but also of countless middle- and working-class Americans, who could buy stocks "on margin" by putting down just 10 percent of the purchase price. The New York Times reported in March 1929, "Playing the Stock market has become a major American pastime."

> *Let me tell you about the very rich. They are different from you and me.*
> —F. SCOTT FITZGERALD

> *Yes, they have more money.*
> —ERNEST HEMINGWAY

Ordinary Americans had been drawn into the stock market in part by the desire to participate in a flourishing consumer culture that floated on credit. As one

Wall Street on the day of the Great Crash

historian remarks, "Going into debt for consumer purchases, a practice condemned in previous more frugal eras as the last refuge of the spendthrift incompetent, came to be honored," by economist and layperson alike, "as a way to raise the standard of living and stave off depression." Such unprecedented consumerism was inspired not only by "utter confidence," but also by the aggressive advertising industry, which occasionally employed writers like Fitzgerald and Cowley. American business spent unprecedented amounts of money on advertising in the '20s—about one and a half billion dollars in 1927, 50 percent more than in 1921. The brash consumerism that resulted is perhaps best illustrated by the rise in automobile sales. Once a luxury item far beyond the reach and the aspirations of average people, the automobile became by the mid 1920s something for which they clamored and which, thanks to economy of scale and the installment plan, they were able to get. Whereas a total of two and a half million automobiles plied U.S. roads in 1915, that number had climbed to eight million by 1920, and to an astonishing seventeen million five years later. In one year (1920–21), the Ford Motor Company alone sold 1,250,000 cars.

For many, the vast increase in the ownership and use of automobiles reflected not only an unprecedented, culture-wide dedication to conspicuous consumption, but also a new kind of restlessness and rootlessness. In a textbook on the family published in 1927 (excerpted below), Boston University sociologist Ernest R. Groves remarks upon a rather curious phenomenon—"a new type of gypsy," the "automobile migrants":

"Consumerism" during the Depression

> Some travel in expensive cars, splendidly equipped, because they enjoy the life better than conventional travel, while others take to the car because only so have they hope of satisfying their wanderlust....
>
> There are all sorts of motives behind the wanderer: restlessness, response to advertising, the lure of the romance of the West and South, expectations of a new start in life, the desire to improve or find health, craving for frontier experience, longing to be rid of conventional habits of life, and pure love of automobile travel.

These "automobile migrants" had their upscale counterparts in the thousands of Americans, like Charlie Wales and writers such as Fitzgerald, Hemingway, and Cowley, for whom frequent travel to and across Europe, and particularly France, became almost *de rigueur* in the '20s.

For sociologists and educators like Groves, the peripatetic lifestyles of these expatriates would likely have been as serious a concern as that of the "automobile migrants" because both undermined the foundations of the traditional (or, in Groves's words, "normal") family:

> A real home requires permanent settlement. This is well illustrated by the family life of the gypsy, which, even when strongly knit together, has been necessarily meagre. A wandering family cannot establish the community contacts that form part of the substance of a normal home....
>
> It has become the conviction of social workers familiar with this type of wanderers, that the problem they present is with us permanently. If so, we have a new but serious family instability. Many of the migrants have children who, as they travel from place to place with their parents, are denied not only proper schooling but normal family experience.... It is not to be expected that such individuals upon maturity will find it easy to settle down and maintain normal home life. They are no more likely to take root than the tramp. The children of these auto parties are frequently exploited and suffer not only along lines of health and education but at times also morally.

Nearly a century later, it may be difficult for us to grasp the dramatic cultural transformations reflected in the wanderings of expatriates and automobile enthusiasts and in the manic consumerism of the 1920s. What was involved, as many commentators suggested at the time, was a profound shift in outlook and ethics: the death of the "old morality" and the birth of the "new." The "old," "Puritan" morality—seen by many then as hopelessly outmoded, repressive, and especially damaging to women—emphasized self-control, self-sacrifice, and faithful adherence to rules and traditions. In its place, the new morality instead championed self-expression and even self-indulgence, encouraging men and women alike to flout any rule, law, or tradition that might infringe upon their individual liberty. Whereas the old morality taught one to keep an eye on the future in order to ensure one's self and the country a better tomorrow, the new ethos encouraged every individual to live fully and freely in the here and now, leaving both the country and the future to take care of themselves.

*There are no second acts in American lives.*
—F. SCOTT FITZGERALD

The conflict between these two moralities reached its climax in the struggle over the prohibition of alcohol. Fittingly enough, the moral crisis of the '20s took the form of a confrontation over consumers' rights. Prohibition, which became law when the Eighteenth Amendment to the United States Constitution was ratified in 1919 and put into effect in January 1920, can be seen as a kind of last-ditch effort to enforce the old morality, though its proponents included feminist and other "progressive" groups. The conflict between old and new moralities was also one between rural "heartland" America and the urban "Babylon" America, as suggested by the fact that Congressional representatives for urban areas were by and large anti-Prohibitionists and that pro-Prohibition forces insisted that their fight was against "great city domination," "the rock upon which past civilizations have been wrecked." Cities, though they might be the centers of fashion and culture, were also regarded by traditionalist or provincial observers as harboring mobs of immigrants and other industrial poor who seemed to spawn children, disease, disorderly conduct, and even political rebellion. In one of countless books published on the alcohol question both before and during Prohibition, *King Alcohol Dethroned* (1917), "Dry" advocate Ferdinand Cowle Iglehart, D.D., uses language that connects Christianity and the Prohibition campaign, "the most important moral event in the history of mankind":

> The thirst of the soul which alcohol pretends to satisfy is that for stimulation, illumination and inspiration. This is a God-given appetite which He intended should be satisfied by truth, righteousness, love, by himself, the embodiment of these attributes.... To satisfy this appetite the father of lies, in the person of King Alcohol, offers himself as a substitute instead of God as the inspiration, the life, the joy of the soul. What a failure, what a fraud, what a tragedy is the substitute, and how long-continued and widespread has been his diabolical deception!

Iglehart is quite sure that God's ways are also the ways of business and industry: "Society," he writes, "is putting up a fierce fight against booze" not just because God wants it, but "on account of the inefficiency that it causes in every department of industry."

Though the fight against the devil, alcohol, and industrial inefficiency was ostensibly won with the passage of the Eighteenth Amendment, that triumph was a hollow one at best. Among other things, as Cowley argued, the coming of Prohibition merely "surrounded the new customs with illicit glamour"—it was, in

Illegal beer being poured away during Prohibition

short, the best advertisement of all. Rather than taking their spirits in a respectable public bar as they might have done before Prohibition, for example, New Yorkers in 1929 could sip "King Alcohol" in any of the thirty-two thousand speakeasies that the Police Commissioner estimated were operating in the city; and whereas in 1918 they had probably sipped nothing stronger than beer or wine, by 1929 they were almost certainly indulging in hard liquor. In addition to the obvious allure of defying the law, customers of the speakeasy typically enjoyed two other disreputable, if not illegal, pleasures: listening to a jazz band and engaging in what some called "pelvic dancing." Prohibition also helped turn organized crime into a major, efficient, and profitable, if violent, machine with close links to "legitimate" industry: Al Capone's Chicago-based organization alone made an estimated one hundred million dollars per year during Prohibition, while major industrialists and their trade-union antagonists fought each other with the help or interference of mobsters.

In the early 1920s the conflict between old and new moralities that led to open battle between Treasury agents, rumrunners, and speakeasy clientele was often described in generational terms. For the new morality was associated with "flaming youth," the generation that Gertrude Stein labeled "lost" and that Fitzgerald described in *This Side of Paradise* as "a new generation dedicated more than the last to the fear of poverty and the worship of success; grown up to find all Gods dead, all wars fought, all faiths in man shaken." Not surprisingly, *This Side of Paradise* was often cited by Fitzgerald's contemporaries as a guidebook to "the new morality," as well as a manifesto for what a 1925 book called *The Revolt of Modern Youth*. While the causes for that revolt were multiple, it was only partly a reaction to the national repression and denial symbolized by a federal prohibition of alcohol.

Fitzgerald and many of his contemporaries agreed that World War I exercised a decisive, if complex and multifaceted, influence.

Although the "new morality" was initially associated with bohemian circles and with those who came of age during and just after the war, it soon transformed all sectors of American society. For many, especially experts in the relatively new fields of psychology and sociology, the effects of the new morality, and especially of the dramatic changes in women's roles associated with it, were felt most profoundly in the area of family life. Ernest R. Groves's *Social Problems of the Family* and V. F. Calverton's *The Bankruptcy of Marriage* (both excerpted below) were merely two of the countless books and articles published in the 1920s about what another book labeled "the Marriage Crisis." Fitzgerald's fictional Wales family seems to have broken up in large part because of the death of Helen, Charlie's wife; and widowers like Charlie get some attention in *Social Problems of the Family*. Yet what inspired most commentary was the fact that more American families than ever before were being broken up by divorce: from 1916 to 1922, the number of divorces in the United States increased 33 percent. Perhaps more importantly, the shape of intact middle-class American families and the very concept of marriage were profoundly changing—whether for good (as Calverton has it) or for ill (as Groves argues).

> *Show me a hero and I will write you a tragedy.*
> —F. SCOTT FITZGERALD

As such different assessments of the American family in the 1920s may remind us, the spirit of the Jazz Age, like the spirit of any age, is as much about debate as about consensus, as much about divisions between various groups as about an underlying unity of experience or outlook. Indeed, the work of the African American writers associated with the 1920s Harlem Renaissance—including Countee Cullen, Langston Hughes, and Claude McKay (all of whom are represented in this book)—reflects a very different experience than does that of white Americans such as Fitzgerald, Cowley, and Edna St. Vincent Millay. And however close in spirit Millay's poetry might be to Fitzgerald's fiction, one can't help but wonder how she, as a "new woman" writer, might have depicted her own "Babylon." Like "American culture" itself, then, any cultural moment or context is a tapestry woven out of many diverse threads.

## F. SCOTT FITZGERALD

### Babylon Revisited

I

"And where's Mr. Campbell?" Charlie asked.

"Gone to Switzerland. Mr. Campbell's a pretty sick man, Mr. Wales."

"I'm sorry to hear that. And George Hardt?" Charlie inquired.

"Back in America, gone to work."

5 "And where is the Snow Bird?"

"He was in here last week. Anyway, his friend, Mr. Schaeffer, is in Paris."

Two familiar names from the long list of a year and a half ago. Charlie scribbled an address in his notebook and tore out the page.

"If you see Mr. Schaeffer, give him this," he said. "It's my brother-in-law's address. I haven't settled on a hotel yet."

He was not really disappointed to find Paris was so empty. But the stillness in the Ritz bar was strange and portentous. It was not an American bar any more—he felt polite in it, and not as if he owned it. It had gone back into France. He felt the stillness from the moment he got out of the taxi and saw the doorman, usually in a frenzy of activity at this hour, gossiping with a *chasseur*[1] by the servants' entrance.

Passing through the corridor, he heard only a single, bored voice in the once-clamorous women's room. When he turned into the bar he travelled the twenty feet of green carpet with his eyes fixed straight ahead by old habit; and then, with his foot firmly on the rail, he turned and surveyed the room, encountering only a single pair of eyes that fluttered up from a newspaper in the corner. Charlie asked for the head barman, Paul, who in the latter days of the bull market had come to work in his own custom-built car—disembarking, however, with due nicety at the nearest corner. But Paul was at his country house today and Alix giving him information.

"No, no more," Charlie said, "I'm going slow these days."

Alix congratulated him: "You were going pretty strong a couple of years ago."

"I'll stick to it all right," Charlie assured him. "I've stuck to it for over a year and a half now."

"How do you find conditions in America?"

"I haven't been to America for months. I'm in business in Prague, representing a couple of concerns there. They don't know about me down there."

Alix smiled.

"Remember the night of George Hardt's bachelor dinner here?" said Charlie. "By the way, what's become of Claude Fessenden?"

Alix lowered his voice confidentially: "He's in Paris, but he doesn't come here any more. Paul doesn't allow it. He ran up a bill of thirty thousand francs, charging all his drinks and his lunches, and usually his dinner, for more than a year. And when Paul finally told him he had to pay, he gave him a bad check."

Alix shook his head sadly.

"I don't understand it, such a dandy fellow. Now he's all bloated up—" He made a plump apple of his hands.

Charlie watched a group of strident queens installing themselves in a corner.

"Nothing affects them," he thought. "Stocks rise and fall, people loaf or work, but they go on forever." The place oppressed him. He called for the dice and shook with Alix for the drink.

"Here for long, Mr. Wales?"

"I'm here for four or five days to see my little girl."

"Oh-h! You have a little girl?"

Outside, the fire-red, gas-blue, ghost-green signs shone smokily through the tranquil rain. It was late afternoon and the streets were in movement; the *bistros* gleamed. At the corner of the Boulevard des Capucines he took a taxi. The Place de la Concorde moved by in pink majesty; they crossed the logical Seine, and Charlie felt the sudden provincial quality of the Left Bank.[2]

---

1. Bellhop.
2. The Seine River flows westward through Paris, cutting the city into two sections—the elegant Right Bank (to the north) and the more bohemian Left Bank (to the south). Located on the Right Bank along the Seine, the Place de la Concorde (literally, "place of the peace") is the largest plaza in Paris.

Charlie directed his taxi to the Avenue de l'Opera, which was out of his way. But he wanted to see the blue hour spread over the magnificent façade, and imagine that the cab horns, playing endlessly the first few bars of *La Plus que Lent*, were the trumpets of the Second Empire.[3] They were closing the iron grill in front of Brentano's Book-store, and people were already at dinner behind the trim little bourgeois hedge of Duval's. He had never eaten at a really cheap restaurant in Paris. Five-course dinner, four francs fifty, eighteen cents, wine included. For some odd reason he wished that he had.

As they rolled on to the Left Bank and he felt its sudden provincialism, he thought, "I spoiled this city for myself. I didn't realize it, but the days came along one after another, and then two years were gone, and everything was gone, and I was gone."

He was thirty-five, and good to look at. The Irish mobility of his face was sobered by a deep wrinkle between his eyes. As he rang his brother-in-law's bell in the Rue Palatine, the wrinkle deepened till it pulled down his brows; he felt a cramping sensation in his belly. From behind the maid who opened the door darted a lovely little girl of nine who shrieked "Daddy!" and flew up, struggling like a fish, into his arms. She pulled his head around by one ear and set her cheek against his.

"My old pie," he said.

"Oh, daddy, daddy, daddy, daddy, dads, dads, dads!"

She drew them into the salon, where the family waited, a boy and girl his daughter's age, his sister-in-law and her husband. He greeted Marion with his voice pitched carefully to avoid either feigned enthusiasm or dislike, but her response was more frankly tepid, though she minimized her expression of unalterable distrust by directing her regard toward his child. The two men clasped hands in a friendly way and Lincoln Peters rested his for a moment on Charlie's shoulder.

The room was warm and comfortably American. The three children moved intimately about, playing through the yellow oblongs that led to other rooms; the cheer of six o'clock spoke in the eager smacks of the fire and the sounds of French activity in the kitchen. But Charlie did not relax; his heart sat up rigidly in his body and he drew confidence from his daughter, who from time to time came close to him, holding in her arms the doll he had brought.

"Really extremely well," he declared in answer to Lincoln's question. "There's a lot of business there that isn't moving at all, but we're doing even better than ever. In fact, damn well. I'm bringing my sister over from America next month to keep house for me. My income last year was bigger than it was when I had money. You see, the Czechs—"

His boasting was for a specific purpose; but after a moment, seeing a faint restiveness in Lincoln's eye, he changed the subject:

"Those are fine children of yours, well brought up, good manners."

"We think Honoria's a great little girl too."

---

3. Elected president of the Second French Republic after the Revolution of 1848, Louis-Napoléon Bonaparte (1808–1873), nephew of France's first emperor, Napoléon Bonaparte, founded the Second Empire by declaring himself Emperor Napoléon III in 1852; he was ousted by republicans in 1871. *La plus que Lent* (literally, "more than slow"): piano work composed in 1910 by French "impressionist" composer Claude Debussy (1862–1918).

Marion Peters came back from the kitchen. She was a tall woman with worried eyes, who had once possessed a fresh American loveliness. Charlie had never been sensitive to it and was always surprised when people spoke of how pretty she had been. From the first there had been an instinctive antipathy between them.

"Well, how do you find Honoria?" she asked.

"Wonderful. I was astonished how much she's grown in ten months. All the children are looking well."

"We haven't had a doctor for a year. How do you like being back in Paris?"

"It seems very funny to see so few Americans around."

"I'm delighted," Marion said vehemently. "Now at least you can go into a store without their assuming you're a millionaire. We've suffered like everybody, but on the whole it's a good deal pleasanter."

"But it was nice while it lasted," Charlie said. "We were a sort of royalty, almost infallible, with a sort of magic around us. In the bar this afternoon"—he stumbled, seeing his mistake—"there wasn't a man I knew."

She looked at him keenly. "I should think you'd have had enough of bars."

"I only stayed a minute. I take one drink every afternoon, and no more."

"Don't you want a cocktail before dinner?" Lincoln asked.

"I take only one drink every afternoon, and I've had that."

"I hope you keep to it," said Marion.

Her dislike was evident in the coldness with which she spoke, but Charlie only smiled; he had larger plans. Her very aggressiveness gave him an advantage, and he knew enough to wait. He wanted them to initiate the discussion of what they knew had brought him to Paris.

At dinner he couldn't decide whether Honoria was most like him or her mother. Fortunate if she didn't combine the traits of both that had brought them to disaster. A great wave of protectiveness went over him. He thought he knew what to do for her. He believed in character; he wanted to jump back a whole generation and trust in character again as the eternally valuable element. Everything wore out.

He left soon after dinner, but not to go home. He was curious to see Paris by night with clearer and more judicious eyes than those of other days. He bought a *strapontin* for the Casino and watched Josephine Baker[4] go through her chocolate arabesques.

After an hour he left and strolled toward Montmartre,[5] up the Rue Pigalle into the Place Blanche. The rain had stopped and there were a few people in evening clothes disembarking from taxis in front of cabarets, and *cocottes*[6] prowling singly or in pairs, and many Negroes. He passed a lighted door from which issued music, and stopped with the sense of familiarity; it was Bricktop's, where he had parted with so many hours and so much money. A few doors farther on he found another ancient rendezvous and incautiously put his head inside. Immediately an eager orchestra burst into sound, a pair of professional dancers

---

4. African American jazz singer and dancer (1906–1975) who became one of France's most popular entertainers in the 1920s and '30s, creating a sensation with her *danse sauvage* ("wild dance") and revealing costumes; in 1924 she starred in the Broadway show *Chocolate Dandies*. *Strapontin*: foldaway seat.
5. Hilltop neighborhood in north-central Paris long associated with artists and intellectuals.
6. Prostitutes.

leaped to their feet and a maître d'hôtel swooped toward him, crying, "Crowd just arriving, sir!" But he withdrew quickly.

"You have to be damn drunk," he thought.

Zelli's was closed, the bleak and sinister cheap hotels surrounding it were dark; up in the Rue Blanche there was more light and a local, colloquial French crowd. The Poet's Cave had disappeared, but the two great mouths of the Café of Heaven and the Café of Hell[7] still yawned—even devoured, as he watched, the meager contents of a tourist bus—a German, a Japanese, and an American couple who glanced at him with frightened eyes.

So much for the effort and ingenuity of Montmartre. All the catering to vice and waste was on an utterly childish scale, and he suddenly realized the meaning of the word "dissipate"—to dissipate into thin air; to make nothing out of something. In the little hours of the night every move from place to place was an enormous human jump, an increase of paying for the privilege of slower and slower motion.

He remembered thousand-franc notes given to an orchestra for playing a single number, hundred-franc notes tossed to a doorman for calling a cab.

But it hadn't been given for nothing.

It had been given, even the most wildly squandered sum, as an offering to destiny that he might not remember the things most worth remembering, the things that now he would always remember—his child taken from his control, his wife escaped to a grave in Vermont.

In the glare of a *brasserie*[8] a woman spoke to him. He bought her some eggs and coffee, and then, eluding her encouraging stare, gave her a twenty-franc note and took a taxi to his hotel.

II

He woke upon a fine fall day—football weather. The depression of yesterday was gone and he liked the people on the streets. At noon he sat opposite Honoria at Le Grand Vatel, the only restaurant he could think of not reminiscent of champagne dinners and long luncheons that began at two and ended in a blurred and vague twilight.

"Now, how about vegetables? Oughtn't you to have some vegetables?"

"Well, yes."

"Here's *épinards* and *chou-fleur* and carrots and *haricots*."[9]

"I'd like *chou-fleur*."

"Wouldn't you like to have two vegetables?"

"I usually only have one at lunch."

The waiter was pretending to be inordinately fond of children. *"Qu'elle est mignonne la petite? Elle parle exactement comme une Française."*[1]

"How about dessert? Shall we wait and see?"

The waiter disappeared. Honoria looked at her father expectantly.

"What are we going to do?"

"First, we're going to that toy store in the Rue Saint-Honoré and buy you

---

7. A 1907 guidebook labels the cafés of Montmarte "eccentric, fantastic" and "morbid" and describes "cabarets of Heaven, Hell, and Death, where the waiters are dressed respectively as angels, devils, undertakers."
8. Restaurant, especially one that sells beer.   9. Spinach and cauliflower and carrots and beans.
1. Isn't she a cute little girl? She speaks exactly like a French girl.

anything you like. And then we're going to the vaudeville at the Empire."

She hesitated. "I like it about the vaudeville, but not the toy store."

"Why not?"

"Well, you brought me this doll." She had it with her. "And I've got lots of things. And we're not rich any more, are we?"

"We never were. But today you are to have anything you want."

"All right," she agreed resignedly.

When there had been her mother and a French nurse he had been inclined to be strict; now he extended himself, reached out for a new tolerance; he must be both parents to her and not shut any of her out of communication.

"I want to get to know you," he said gravely. "First let me introduce myself. My name is Charles J. Wales, of Prague."

"Oh, daddy!" her voice cracked with laughter.

"And who are you, please?" he persisted, and she accepted a rôle immediately: "Honoria Wales, Rue Palatine, Paris."

"Married or single?"

"No, not married. Single."

He indicated the doll. "But I see you have a child, madame."

Unwilling to disinherit it, she took it to her heart and thought quickly: "Yes, I've been married, but I'm not married now. My husband is dead."

He went on quickly, "And the child's name?"

"Simone. That's after my best friend at school."

"I'm very pleased that you're doing so well at school."

"I'm third this month," she boasted. "Elsie"—that was her cousin—"is only about eighteenth, and Richard is about at the bottom."

"You like Richard and Elsie, don't you?"

"Oh, yes. I like Richard quite well and I like her all right."

Cautiously and casually he asked: "And Aunt Marion and Uncle Lincoln—which do you like best?"

"Oh, Uncle Lincoln, I guess."

He was increasingly aware of her presence. As they came in, a murmur of "...adorable" followed them, and now the people at the next table bent all their silences upon her, staring as if she were something no more conscious than a flower.

"Why don't I live with you?" she asked suddenly. "Because mamma's dead?"

"You must stay here and learn more French. It would have been hard for daddy to take care of you so well."

"I don't really need much taking care of any more. I do everything for myself."

Going out of the restaurant, a man and a woman unexpectedly hailed him.

"Well, the old Wales!"

"Hello there, Lorraine. ... Dunc."

Sudden ghosts out of the past: Duncan Schaeffer, a friend from college. Lorraine Quarrles, a lovely, pale blonde of thirty; one of a crowd who had helped them make months into days in the lavish times of three years ago.

"My husband couldn't come this year," she said, in answer to his question. "We're poor as hell. So he gave me two hundred a month and told me I could do my worst on that. . . . This your little girl?"

"What about coming back and sitting down?" Duncan asked.

"Can't do it." He was glad for an excuse. As always, he felt Lorraine's passionate, provocative attraction, but his own rhythm was different now.

"Well, how about dinner?" she asked.

"I'm not free. Give me your address and let me call you."

"Charlie, I believe you're sober," she said judicially. "I honestly believe he's sober, Dunc. Pinch him and see if he's sober."

Charlie indicated Honoria with his head. They both laughed.

"What's your address?" said Duncan sceptically.

He hesitated, unwilling to give the name of his hotel.

"I'm not settled yet. I'd better call you. We're going to see the vaudeville at the Empire."

"There! That's what I want to do," Lorraine said. "I want to see some clowns and acrobats and jugglers. That's just what we'll do, Dunc."

"We've got to do an errand first," said Charlie. "Perhaps we'll see you there."

"All right, you snob.... Good-by, beautiful little girl."

"Good-by."

Honoria bobbed politely.

Somehow, an unwelcome encounter. They liked him because he was functioning, because he was serious; they wanted to see him, because he was stronger than they were now, because they wanted to draw a certain sustenance from his strength.

At the Empire, Honoria proudly refused to sit upon her father's folded coat. She was already an individual with a code of her own, and Charlie was more and more absorbed by the desire of putting a little of himself into her before she crystallized utterly. It was hopeless to try to know her in so short a time.

Between the acts they came upon Duncan and Lorraine in the lobby where the band was playing.

"Have a drink?"

"All right, but not up at the bar. We'll take a table."

"The perfect father."

Listening abstractedly to Lorraine, Charlie watched Honoria's eyes leave their table, and he followed them wistfully about the room, wondering what they saw. He met her glance and she smiled.

"I liked that lemonade," she said.

What had she said? What had he expected? Going home in a taxi afterward, he pulled her over until her head rested against his chest.

"Darling, do you ever think about your mother?"

"Yes, sometimes," she answered vaguely.

"I don't want you to forget her. Have you got a picture of her?"

"Yes, I think so. Anyhow, Aunt Marion has. Why don't you want me to forget her?"

"She loved you very much."

"I loved her too."

They were silent for a moment.

"Daddy, I want to come and live with you," she said suddenly.

His heart leaped; he had wanted it to come like this.

"Aren't you perfectly happy?"

"Yes, but I love you better than anybody. And you love me better than anybody, don't you, now that mummy's dead?"

"Of course I do. But you won't always like me best, honey. You'll grow up and meet somebody your own age and go marry him and forget you ever had a daddy."

"Yes, that's true," she agreed tranquilly.

He didn't go in. He was coming back at nine o'clock and he wanted to keep himself fresh and new for the thing he must say then.

"When you're safe inside, just show yourself in that window."

"All right. Good-by, dads, dads, dads, dads."

He waited in the dark street until she appeared, all warm and glowing, in the window above and kissed her fingers out into the night.

III

They were waiting. Marion sat behind the coffee service in a dignified black dinner dress that just faintly suggested mourning. Lincoln was walking up and down with the animation of one who had already been talking. They were as anxious as he was to get into the question. He opened it almost immediately:

"I suppose you know what I want to see you about—why I really came to Paris."

Marion played with the black stars on her necklace and frowned.

"I'm awfully anxious to have a home," he continued. "And I'm awfully anxious to have Honoria in it. I appreciate your taking in Honoria for her mother's sake, but things have changed now"—he hesitated and then continued more forcibly—"changed radically with me, and I want to ask you to reconsider the matter. It would be silly for me to deny that about three years ago I was acting badly—"

Marion looked up at him with hard eyes.

"—but all that's over. As I told you, I haven't had more than a drink a day for over a year, and I take that drink deliberately, so that the idea of alcohol won't get too big in my imagination. You see the idea?"

"No," said Marion succinctly.

"It's a sort of stunt I set myself. It keeps the matter in proportion."

"I get you," said Lincoln. "You don't want to admit it's got any attraction for you."

"Something like that. Sometimes I forget and don't take it. But I try to take it. Anyhow, I couldn't afford to drink in my position. The people I represent are more than satisfied with what I've done, and I'm bringing my sister over from Burlington to keep house for me, and I want awfully to have Honoria too. You know that even when her mother and I weren't getting along well we never let anything that happened touch Honoria. I know she's fond of me and I know I'm able to take care of her and—well, there you are. How do you feel about it?"

He knew that now he would have to take a beating. It would last an hour or two hours, and it would be difficult, but if he modulated his inevitable resentment to the chastened attitude of the reformed sinner, he might win his point in the end.

Keep your temper, he told himself. You don't want to be justified. You want Honoria.

Lincoln spoke first: "We've been talking it over ever since we got your letter last month. We're happy to have Honoria here. She's a dear little thing, and we're glad to be able to help her, but of course that isn't the question——"

Marion interrupted suddenly. "How long are you going to stay sober, Charlie?" she asked.

"Permanently, I hope."

"How can anybody count on that?"

"You know I never did drink heavily until I gave up business and came over here with nothing to do. Then Helen and I began to run around with—"

"Please leave Helen out of it. I can't bear to hear you talk about her like that."

He stared at her grimly; he had never been certain how fond of each other the sisters were in life.

"My drinking only lasted about a year and a half—from the time we came over until I—collapsed."

"It was time enough."

"It was time enough," he agreed.

"My duty is entirely to Helen," she said. "I try to think what she would have wanted me to do. Frankly, from the night you did that terrible thing you haven't really existed for me. I can't help that. She was my sister."

"Yes."

"When she was dying she asked me to look out for Honoria. If you hadn't been in a sanitarium then, it might have helped matters."

He had no answer.

"I'll never in my life be able to forget the morning when Helen knocked at my door, soaked to the skin and shivering, and said you'd locked her out."

Charlie gripped the sides of the chair. This was more difficult than he expected; he wanted to launch out into a long expostulation and explanation, but he only said: "The night I locked her out—" and she interrupted, "I don't feel up to going over that again."

After a moment's silence Lincoln said: "We're getting off the subject. You want Marion to set aside her legal guardianship and give you Honoria. I think the main point for her is whether she has confidence in you or not."

"I don't blame Marion," Charlie said slowly, "but I think she can have entire confidence in me. I had a good record up to three years ago. Of course, it's within human possibilities I might go wrong any time. But if we wait much longer I'll lose Honoria's childhood and my chance for a home." He shook his head, "I'll simply lose her, don't you see?"

"Yes, I see," said Lincoln.

"Why didn't you think of all this before?" Marion asked.

"I suppose I did, from time to time, but Helen and I were getting along badly. When I consented to the guardianship, I was flat on my back in a sanitarium and the market had cleaned me out. I knew I'd acted badly, and I thought if it would bring any peace to Helen, I'd agree to anything. But now it's different. I'm functioning, I'm behaving damn well, so far as—"

"Please don't swear at me," Marion said.

He looked at her, startled. With each remark the force of her dislike became more and more apparent. She had built up all her fear of life into one wall and faced it toward him. This trivial reproof was possibly the result of some trouble with the cook several hours before. Charlie became increasingly alarmed at leaving Honoria in this atmosphere of hostility against himself; sooner or later it would come out, in a word here, a shake of the head there, and some of that distrust would be irrevocably implanted in Honoria. But he pulled his temper down out of his face and shut it up inside him; he had won a point, for Lincoln realized the absurdity of Marion's remark and asked her lightly since when she had objected to the word "damn."

"Another thing," Charlie said: "I'm able to give her certain advantages now. I'm going to take a French governess to Prague with me. I've got a lease on a new apartment—"

He stopped, realizing that he was blundering. They couldn't be expected to accept with equanimity the fact that his income was again twice as large as their own.

"I suppose you can give her more luxuries than we can," said Marion. "When you were throwing away money we were living along watching every ten francs. . . . I suppose you'll start doing it again."

"Oh, no," he said. "I've learned. I worked hard for ten years, you know—until I got lucky in the market, like so many people. Terribly lucky. It didn't seem any use working any more, so I quit. It won't happen again."

There was a long silence. All of them felt their nerves straining, and for the first time in a year Charlie wanted a drink. He was sure now that Lincoln Peters wanted him to have his child.

Marion shuddered suddenly; part of her saw that Charlie's feet were planted on the earth now, and her own maternal feeling recognized the naturalness of his desire; but she had lived for a long time with a prejudice—a prejudice founded on a curious disbelief in her sister's happiness, and which, in the shock of one terrible night, had turned to hatred for him. It had all happened at a point in her life where the discouragement of ill health and adverse circumstances made it necessary for her to believe in tangible villainy and a tangible villain.

"I can't help what I think!" she cried out suddenly. "How much you were responsible for Helen's death, I don't know. It's something you'll have to square with your own conscience."

An electric current of agony surged through him; for a moment he was almost on his feet, an unuttered sound echoing in his throat. He hung on to himself for a moment, another moment.

"Hold on there," said Lincoln uncomfortably. "I never thought you were responsible for that."

"Helen died of heart trouble," Charlie said dully.

"Yes, heart trouble." Marion spoke as if the phrase had another meaning for her.

Then, in the flatness that followed her outburst, she saw him plainly and she knew he had somehow arrived at control over the situation. Glancing at her husband, she found no help from him, and as abruptly as if it were a matter of no importance, she threw up the sponge.

"Do what you like!" she cried, springing up from her chair. "She's your child. I'm not the person to stand in your way. I think if it were my child I'd rather see her—" She managed to check herself. "You two decide it. I can't stand this. I'm sick. I'm going to bed."

She hurried from the room; after a moment Lincoln said:

"This has been a hard day for her. You know how strongly she feels—" His voice was almost apologetic: "When a woman gets an idea in her head."

"Of course."

"It's going to be all right. I think she sees now that you—can provide for the child, and so we can't very well stand in your way or Honoria's way."

"Thank you, Lincoln."

"I'd better go along and see how she is."

"I'm going."

He was still trembling when he reached the street, but a walk down the Rue Bonaparte to the quais set him up, and as he crossed the Seine, fresh and new by the quai lamps, he felt exultant. But back in his room he couldn't sleep. The image of Helen haunted him. Helen whom he had loved so until they had senselessly begun to abuse each other's love, tear it into shreds. On that terrible February night that Marion remembered so vividly, a slow quarrel had gone on for hours. There was a scene at the Florida, and then he attempted to take her home, and then she kissed young Webb at a table; after that there was what she had hysterically said. When he arrived home alone he turned the key in the lock in wild anger. How could he know she would arrive an hour later alone, that there would be a snowstorm in which she wandered about in slippers, too confused to find a taxi? Then the aftermath, her escaping pneumonia by a miracle, and all the attendant horror. They were "reconciled," but that was the beginning of the end, and Marion, who had seen with her own eyes and who imagined it to be one of many scenes from her sister's martyrdom, never forgot.

Going over it again brought Helen nearer, and in the white, soft light that steals upon half sleep near morning he found himself talking to her again. She said that he was perfectly right about Honoria and that she wanted Honoria to be with him. She said she was glad he was being good and doing better. She said a lot of other things—very friendly things—but she was in a swing in a white dress, and swinging faster and faster all the time, so that at the end he could not hear clearly all that she said.

IV

He woke up feeling happy. The door of the world was open again. He made plans, vistas, futures for Honoria and himself, but suddenly he grew sad, remembering all the plans he and Helen had made. She had not planned to die. The present was the thing—work to do and someone to love. But not to love too much, for he knew the injury that a father can do to a daughter or a mother to a son by attaching them too closely: afterward, out in the world, the child would seek in the marriage partner the same blind tenderness and, failing probably to find it, turn against love and life.

It was another bright, crisp day. He called Lincoln Peters at the bank where he worked and asked if he could count on taking Honoria when he left for Prague. Lincoln agreed that there was no reason for delay. One thing—the legal guardianship. Marion wanted to retain that a while longer. She was upset by the whole matter, and it would oil things if she felt that the situation was still in her control for another year. Charlie agreed, wanting only the tangible, visible child.

Then the question of a governess. Charlie sat in a gloomy agency and talked to a cross Béarnaise and to a buxom Breton[2] peasant, neither of whom he could have endured. There were others whom he would see tomorrow.

He lunched with Lincoln Peters at Griffons, trying to keep down his exultation.

"There's nothing quite like your own child," Lincoln said. "But you understand how Marion feels too."

---

2. Native or inhabitant of Brittany, in northwestern France; *Béarnaise*: native or inhabitant of Béarn, in southwestern France.

"She's forgotten how hard I worked for seven years there," Charlie said. "She just remembers one night."

"There's another thing." Lincoln hesitated. "While you and Helen were tearing around Europe throwing money away, we were just getting along. I didn't touch any of the prosperity because I never got ahead enough to carry anything but my insurance. I think Marion felt there was some kind of injustice in it—you not even working toward the end, and getting richer and richer."

"It went just as quick as it came," said Charlie.

"Yes, a lot of it stayed in the hands of *chasseurs* and saxophone players and maîtres d'hôtel—well, the big party's over now. I just said that to explain Marion's feeling about those crazy years. If you drop in about six o'clock tonight before Marion's too tired, we'll settle the details on the spot."

Back at his hotel, Charlie found a *pneumatique*[3] that had been redirected from the Ritz bar where Charlie had left his address for the purpose of finding a certain man.

> Dear Charlie: You were so strange when we saw you the other day that I wondered if I did something to offend you. If so, I'm not conscious of it. In fact, I have thought about you too much for the last year, and it's always been in the back of my mind that I might see you if I came over here. We *did* have such good times that crazy spring, like the night you and I stole the butcher's tricycle, and the time we tried to call on the president and you had the old derby rim and the wire cane. Everybody seems so old lately, but I don't feel old a bit. Couldn't we get together some time today for old time's sake? I've got a vile hang-over for the moment, but will be feeling better this afternoon and will look for you about five in the sweat-shop at the Ritz.
>
> Always devotedly,<br>Lorraine.

His first feeling was one of awe that he had actually, in his mature years, stolen a tricycle and pedalled Lorraine all over the Étoile[4] between the small hours and dawn. In retrospect it was a nightmare. Locking out Helen didn't fit in with any other act of his life, but the tricycle incident did—it was one of many. How many weeks or months of dissipation to arrive at that condition of utter irresponsibility?

He tried to picture how Lorraine had appeared to him then—very attractive; Helen was unhappy about it, though she said nothing. Yesterday, in the restaurant, Lorraine had seemed trite, blurred, worn away. He emphatically did not want to see her, and he was glad Alix had not given away his hotel address. It was a relief to think, instead, of Honoria, to think of Sundays spent with her and of saying good morning to her and of knowing she was there in his house at night, drawing her breath in the darkness.

At five he took a taxi and bought presents for all the Peters—a piquant cloth doll, a box of Roman soldiers, flowers for Marion, big linen handkerchiefs for Lincoln.

He saw, when he arrived in the apartment, that Marion had accepted the

---

3. Message or letter sent by pneumatic tube.
4. Intersection at the northwestern end of the Champs-Élysées, where twelve streets join to form a "star" (or *étoile*).

inevitable. She greeted him now as though he were a recalcitrant member of the family, rather than a menacing outsider. Honoria had been told she was going; Charlie was glad to see that her tact made her conceal her excessive happiness. Only on his lap did she whisper her delight and the question "When?" before she slipped away with the other children.

He and Marion were alone for a minute in the room, and on an impulse he spoke out boldly:

"Family quarrels are bitter things. They don't go according to any rules. They're not like aches or wounds; they're more like splits in the skin that won't heal because there's not enough material. I wish you and I could be on better terms."

"Some things are hard to forget," she answered. "It's a question of confidence." There was no answer to this and presently she asked, "When do you propose to take her?"

"As soon as I can get a governess. I hoped the day after tomorrow."

"That's impossible. I've got to get her things in shape. Not before Saturday."

He yielded. Coming back into the room, Lincoln offered him a drink.

"I'll take my daily whisky," he said.

It was warm here, it was a home, people together by a fire. The children felt very safe and important; the mother and father were serious, watchful. They had things to do for the children more important than his visit here. A spoonful of medicine was, after all, more important than the strained relations between Marion and himself. They were not dull people, but they were very much in the grip of life and circumstances. He wondered if he couldn't do something to get Lincoln out of his rut at the bank.

A long peal at the door-bell; the *bonne à tout faire*[5] passed through and went down the corridor. The door opened upon another long ring, and then voices, and the three in the salon looked up expectantly; Lincoln moved to bring the corridor within his range of vision, and Marion rose. Then the maid came back along the corridor, closely followed by the voices, which developed under the light into Duncan Schaeffer and Lorraine Quarrles.

They were gay, they were hilarious, they were roaring with laughter. For a moment Charlie was astounded, unable to understand how they ferreted out the Peters' address.

"Ah-h-h!" Duncan wagged his finger roguishly at Charlie. "Ah-h-h!"

They both slid down another cascade of laughter. Anxious and at a loss, Charlie shook hands with them quickly and presented them to Lincoln and Marion. Marion nodded, scarcely speaking. She had drawn back a step toward the fire; her little girl stood beside her, and Marion put an arm about her shoulder.

With growing annoyance at the intrusion, Charlie waited for them to explain themselves. After some concentration Duncan said:

"We came to invite you out to dinner. Lorraine and I insist that all this shishi, cagy business 'bout your address got to stop."

Charlie came closer to them, as if to force them backward down the corridor.

"Sorry, but I can't. Tell me where you'll be and I'll phone you in half an hour."

This made no impression. Lorraine sat down suddenly on the side of a chair, and focussing her eyes on Richard, cried, "Oh, what a nice little boy! Come here,

---

5. Maid of all work.

little boy." Richard glanced at his mother, but did not move. With a perceptible shrug of her shoulders, Lorraine turned back to Charlie:

"Come and dine. Sure your cousins won' mine. See you so sel'om. Or solemn."

"I can't," said Charlie sharply. "You two have dinner and I'll phone you."

Her voice became suddenly unpleasant. "All right, we'll go. But I remember once when you hammered on my door at four A.M. I was enough of a good sport to give you a drink. Come on, Dunc."

Still in slow motion, with blurred, angry faces, with uncertain feet, they retired along the corridor.

"Good night," Charlie said.

"Good night!" responded Lorraine emphatically.

When he went back into the salon Marion had not moved, only now her son was standing in the circle of her other arm. Lincoln was still swinging Honoria back and forth like a pendulum from side to side.

"What an outrage!" Charlie broke out. "What an absolute outrage!"

Neither of them answered. Charlie dropped into an armchair, picked up his drink, set it down again and said:

"People I haven't seen for two years having the colossal nerve——"

He broke off. Marion had made the sound "Oh!" in one swift, furious breath, turned her body from him with a jerk and left the room.

Lincoln set down Honoria carefully.

"You children go in and start your soup," he said, and when they obeyed, he said to Charlie:

"Marion's not well and she can't stand shocks. That kind of people make her really physically sick."

"I didn't tell them to come here. They wormed your name out of somebody. They deliberately——"

"Well, it's too bad. It doesn't help matters. Excuse me a minute."

Left alone, Charlie sat tense in his chair. In the next room he could hear the children eating, talking in monosyllables, already oblivious to the scene between their elders. He heard a murmur of conversation from a farther room and then the ticking bell of a telephone receiver picked up, and in a panic he moved to the other side of the room and out of earshot.

In a minute Lincoln came back. "Look here, Charlie. I think we'd better call off dinner for tonight. Marion's in bad shape."

"Is she angry with me?"

"Sort of," he said, almost roughly. "She's not strong and——"

"You mean she's changed her mind about Honoria?"

"She's pretty bitter right now. I don't know. You phone me at the bank tomorrow."

"I wish you'd explain to her I never dreamed these people would come here. I'm just as sore as you are."

"I couldn't explain anything to her now."

Charlie got up. He took his coat and hat and started down the corridor. Then he opened the door of the dining room and said in a strange voice, "Good night, children."

Honoria rose and ran around the table to hug him.

"Good night, sweetheart," he said vaguely, and then trying to make his voice more tender, trying to conciliate something, "Good night, dear children."

V

Charlie went directly to the Ritz bar with the furious idea of finding Lorraine and Duncan, but they were not there, and he realized that in any case there was nothing he could do. He had not touched his drink at the Peters', and now he ordered a whisky-and-soda. Paul came over to say hello.

"It's a great change," he said sadly. "We do about half the business we did. So many fellows I hear about back in the States lost everything, maybe not in the first crash, but then in the second. Your friend George Hardt lost every cent, I hear. Are you back in the States?"

"No, I'm in business in Prague."

"I heard that you lost a lot in the crash."

"I did," and he added grimly, "but I lost everything I wanted in the boom."

"Selling short."[6]

"Something like that."

Again the memory of those days swept over him like a nightmare—the people they had met travelling; then people who couldn't add a row of figures or speak a coherent sentence. The little man Helen had consented to dance with at the ship's party, who had insulted her ten feet from the table; the women and girls carried screaming with drink or drugs out of public places—

—The men who locked their wives out in the snow, because the snow of twenty-nine wasn't real snow. If you didn't want it to be snow, you just paid some money.

He went to the phone and called the Peters' apartment; Lincoln answered.

"I called up because this thing is on my mind. Has Marion said anything definite?"

"Marion's sick," Lincoln answered shortly. "I know this thing isn't altogether your fault, but I can't have her go to pieces about it. I'm afraid we'll have to let it slide for six months; I can't take the chance of working her up to this state again."

"I see."

"I'm sorry, Charlie."

He went back to his table. His whisky glass was empty, but he shook his head when Alix looked at it questioningly. There wasn't much he could do now except send Honoria some things; he would send her a lot of things tomorrow. He thought rather angrily that this was just money—he had given so many people money....

"No, no more," he said to another waiter. "What do I owe you?"

He would come back some day; they couldn't make him pay forever. But he wanted his child, and nothing was much good now, beside that fact. He wasn't young any more, with a lot of nice thoughts and dreams to have by himself. He was absolutely sure Helen wouldn't have wanted him to be so alone.

1931

The following excerpts from texts published in the 1920s and '30s will give you a fuller sense of the events, feelings, moods, concerns, and viewpoints that make

---

6. Selling securities, particularly in anticipation of falling prices, that the seller does not actually possess at the time of sale.

up the cultural and historical context of "Babylon Revisited." They should help you to better understand both Fitzgerald's era and his story's complex and ambiguous commentary on it.

## F. SCOTT FITZGERALD

### Echoes of the Jazz Age (November 1931)

It is too soon to write about the Jazz Age with perspective.... It is as dead as were the Yellow Nineties in 1902. Yet the present writer already looks back to it with nostalgia. It bore him up, flattered him and gave him more money than he had dreamed of, simply for telling people that he felt as they did, that something had to be done with all the nervous energy stored up and unexpended in the War.

The ten-year period that, as if reluctant to die outmoded in its bed, leaped to a spectacular death in October, 1929, began about the time of the May Day riots in 1919.[1] When the police rode down the demobilized country boys gaping at the orators in Madison Square, it was the sort of measure bound to alienate the more intelligent young men from the prevailing order.... If goose-livered business men had this effect on the government, then maybe we had gone to war for J. P. Morgan's loans after all.[2] But, because we were tired of Great Causes, there was no more than a short outbreak of moral indignation.... The events of 1919 left us cynical rather than revolutionary.... It was characteristic of the Jazz Age that it had no interest in politics at all.

•

It was an age of miracles, it was an age of art, it was an age of excess, and it was an age of satire....

The first social revelation created a sensation out of all proportion to its novelty. As far back as 1915 the unchaperoned young people of the smaller cities had discovered the mobile privacy of that automobile given to young Bill at sixteen to make him "self-reliant." At first petting was a desperate adventure even under such favorable conditions, but presently confidences were exchanged and the old commandment broke down. As early as 1917 there were references to such sweet and casual dalliance in any number[3] of the *Yale Record* or the *Princeton Tiger*.

But petting in its more audacious manifestations was confined to the wealthier classes—among other young people the old standard prevailed until after the

---

1. On May Day (May 1), 1919, during a period of heated public controversy over "reds," radicals and unionists organized rallies, mass meetings, and parades throughout the U.S.; riots ensued in several cities, including Boston, Detroit, Cleveland, and New York. Fitzgerald's short story "May Day" focuses partly on these events.
2. John Pierpont Morgan (1867–1943), the most important American financier of his day and head of the banking firm founded by his father, brought together over two thousand American banks to float a total of more than one and a half billion dollars in Allied bonds during World War I.
3. Issue (as of a periodical).

War, and a kiss meant that a proposal was expected.... Only in 1920 did the veil finally fall—the Jazz Age was in flower.

...By 1923 their elders, tired of watching the carnival with ill-concealed envy, had discovered that young liquor will take the place of young blood, and with a whoop the orgy began....

A whole race going hedonistic, deciding on pleasure. The precocious intimacies of the younger generation would have come about with or without prohibition.... But the general decision to be amused that began with the cocktail parties of 1921 had more complicated origins.

The word jazz in its progress toward respectability has meant first sex, then dancing, then music. It is associated with a state of nervous stimulation, not unlike that of big cities behind the lines of a war....

...Society, even in small cities, now dined in separate chambers, and the sober table learned about the gay table only from hearsay. There were very few people left at the sober table....

The gay elements of society had divided into two main streams, one flowing toward Palm Beach[4] and Deauville, and the other, much smaller, toward the summer Riviera. One could get away with more on the summer Riviera, and whatever happened seemed to have something to do with art. From 1926 to 1929, the great years of the Cap d'Antibes, this corner of France was dominated by a group quite distinct from that American society which is dominated by Europeans. Pretty much of anything went at Antibes....

...I remember a fellow expatriate opening a letter from a mutual friend of ours, urging him to come home and be revitalized by the hardy, bracing qualities of the native soil. It was a strong letter and it affected us both deeply, until we noticed that it was headed from a nerve sanitarium in Pennsylvania.

By this time contemporaries of mine had begun to disappear into the dark maw of violence. A classmate killed his wife and himself on Long Island, another tumbled "accidently" from a skyscraper in Philadelphia, another purposely from a skyscraper in New York. One was killed in a speak-easy in Chicago; another was beaten to death in a speak-easy in New York and crawled home to the Princeton Club to die; still another had his skull crushed by a maniac's axe in an insane asylum where he was confined.... [T]hese things happened not during the depression but during the boom.

...Americans were wandering ever more widely.... And by 1928 Paris had grown suffocating. With each new shipment of Americans spewed up by the boom the quality fell off, until toward the end there was something sinister about the crazy boatloads.... [I]t was evident that money and power were falling into the hands of people in comparison with whom the leader of a village Soviet would be a gold-mine of judgment and culture. There were citizens travelling in luxury in 1928 and 1929 who, in the distortion of their new condition, had the human value of Pekinese, bivalves, cretins, goats.... But in those days life was like the race in *Alice in Wonderland*, there was a prize for every one.

---

4. Resort town in Florida that became a popular destination in the 1920s; *Deauville*: fashionable resort town in northern France, located on the English Channel.

... Somebody had blundered and the most expensive orgy in history was over.

It ended two years ago, because the utter confidence which was its essential prop received an enormous jolt, and it didn't take long for the flimsy structure to settle earthward. And after two years the Jazz Age seems as far away as the days before the War. It was borrowed time anyhow—the whole upper tenth of a nation living with the insouciance of grand ducs and the casualness of chorus girls. But moralizing is easy now and it was pleasant to be in one's twenties in such a certain and unworried time. Even when you were broke you didn't worry about money, because it was in such profusion around you....

Now once more the belt is tight and we summon the proper expression of horror as we look back at our wasted youth. Sometimes, though, there is a ghostly rumble among the drums, an asthmatic whisper in the trombones that swings me back into the early twenties when we drank wood alcohol and every day in every way grew better and better, ... and it seemed only a question of a few years before the older people would step aside and let the world be run by those who saw things as they were—and it all seems rosy and romantic to us who were young then, because we will never feel quite so intensely about our surroundings any more.

## MALCOLM COWLEY

## *From* Exile's Return: A Literary Odyssey of the 1920s (1934)

It often seems to me that our years in school and after school, in college and later in the army, might be regarded as a long process of deracination. Looking backward, I feel that our whole training was involuntarily directed toward destroying whatever roots we had in the soil, toward eradicating our local and regional peculiarities, toward making us homeless citizens of the world.

In school, unless we happened to be Southerners, we were divested of any local pride. We studied Ancient History and American History, but not, in my own case, the history of western Pennsylvania. We learned by name the rivers of Siberia—Obi, Yenisei, Lena, Amur—but not the Ohio with its navigable tributaries, or why most of them had ceased to be navigated, or why Pittsburgh was built at its forks. We had high-school courses in Latin, German, Chemistry, good courses all of them, and a class in Civics where we learned to list the amendments to the Constitution and name the members of the Supreme Court; but we never learned how Presidents were really chosen or how a law was put through Congress. If one of us had later come into contact with the practical side of government—that is, if he wished to get a street paved, an assessment reduced, a friend out of trouble with the police or a relative appointed to office—well, fortunately the ward boss[1] wouldn't take much time to set him straight.

Of the English texts we studied, I can remember only one, "The Legend of

---

1. The vote gatherer and dispenser of patronage for his *ward* (small division of a city for representative, electoral, or administrative purposes). Seen as bases for corrupt political machines, wards diminished in stature after the early twentieth century.

Sleepy Hollow,"[2] that gave us any idea that an American valley could be as effectively clothed in romance as Ivanhoe's castle or the London of Henry Esmond.[3] It seemed to us that America was beneath the level of great fiction; it seemed that literature in general, and art and learning, were things existing at an infinite distance from our daily lives. For those of us who read independently, this impression became even stronger: the only authors to admire were foreign authors. We came to feel that wisdom was an attribute of Greece and art of the Renaissance, that glamour belonged only to Paris or Vienna and that glory was confined to the dim past. If we tried, notwithstanding, to write about more immediate subjects, we were forced to use a language not properly our own. A definite effort was being made to destroy all trace of local idiom or pronunciation and have us speak "correctly"—that is, in a standardized Amerenglish as colorless as Esperanto.[4] Some of our instructors had themselves acquired this public-school dialect only by dint of practice, and now set forth its rules with an iron pedantry, as if they were teaching a dead language.

In college the process of deracination went on remorselessly. We were not being prepared for citizenship in a town, a state or a nation; we were not being trained for an industry or profession essential to the common life; instead we were being exhorted to enter that international republic of learning whose traditions are those of Athens, Florence, Paris, Berlin and Oxford....

... School and college had uprooted us in spirit; now[5] we were physically uprooted, hundreds of us, millions, plucked from our own soil as if by a clamshell bucket and dumped, scattered among strange people. All our roots were dead now, even the Anglo-Saxon tradition of our literary ancestors, even the habits of slow thrift that characterized our social class. We were fed, lodged, clothed by strangers, commanded by strangers, infected with the poison of irresponsibility—the poison of travel, too, for we had learned that problems could be left behind us merely by moving elsewhere—and the poison of danger, excitement, that made our old life seem intolerable. Then, as suddenly as it began for us, the war ended.

When we first heard of the Armistice we felt a sense of relief too deep to express, and we all got drunk. We had come through, we were still alive, and nobody at all would be killed tomorrow. The composite fatherland for which we had fought and in which some of us still believed—France, Italy, the Allies, our English homeland, democracy, the self-determination of small nations—had triumphed. We danced in the streets, embraced old women and pretty girls, swore blood brotherhood with soldiers in little bars, drank with our elbows locked in theirs, reeled through the streets with bottles of champagne, fell asleep somewhere. On the next day, after we got over our hangovers, we didn't know what to do, so we got drunk. But slowly, as the days went by, the intoxication passed, and the tears of joy: it appeared that our composite fatherland was dissolving

---

2. Washington Irving's short story (1819–20), set in a Dutch enclave on the Hudson River in New York State.
3. The protagonist of William Makepeace Thackeray's novel *The History of Henry Esmond, Esquire* (1852), which takes place partly amidst London society. *Ivanhoe's castle*: a setting in Sir Walter Scott's historical romance *Ivanhoe* (1819), which concerns the life of Sir Wilfred of Ivanhoe, a fictional Saxon knight.
4. An artificial international language based on common elements of the principal European languages.
5. During World War I.

into quarreling statesmen and oil and steel magnates. Our own nation had passed the Prohibition Amendment as if to publish a bill of separation between itself and ourselves; it wasn't our country any longer. Nevertheless we returned to it: there was nowhere else to go. We returned to New York, appropriately—to the homeland of the uprooted, where everyone you met came from another town and tried to forget it; where nobody seemed to have parents, or a past more distant than last night's swell party, or a future beyond the swell party this evening and the disillusioned book he would write tomorrow.

Greenwich Village was not only a place, a mood, a way of life: like all bohemias, it was also a doctrine. Since the days of Gautier and Murger,[6] this doctrine had remained the same in spirit, but it had changed in several details. By 1920, it had become a system of ideas that could roughly be summarized as follows:

1. The idea of salvation by the child.—Each of us at birth has special potentialities which are slowly crushed and destroyed by a standardized society and mechanical methods of teaching. If a new educational system can be introduced, one by which children are encouraged to develop their own personalities, to blossom freely like flowers, then the world will be saved by this new, free generation.

2. The idea of self-expression.—Each man's, each woman's, purpose in life is to express himself, to realize his full individuality through creative work and beautiful living in beautiful surroundings.

3. The idea of paganism.—The body is a temple in which there is nothing unclean, a shrine to be adorned for the ritual of love.

4. The idea of living for the moment.—It is stupid to pile up treasures that we can enjoy only in old age, when we have lost the capacity for enjoyment. Better to seize the moment as it comes, to dwell in it intensely, even at the cost of future suffering. Better to live extravagantly, gather June rosebuds, "burn my candle at both ends.... It gives a lovely light."[7]

5. The idea of liberty.—Every law, convention or rule of art that prevents self-expression or the full enjoyment of the moment should be shattered and abolished. Puritanism is the great enemy. The crusade against puritanism is the only crusade with which free individuals are justified in allying themselves.

6. The idea of female equality.—Women should be the economic and moral equals of men. They should have the same pay, the same working conditions, the same opportunity for drinking, smoking, taking or dismissing lovers.

7. The idea of psychological adjustment.—We are unhappy because we are maladjusted, and maladjusted because we are repressed. If our individual repressions can be removed—by confessing them to a Freudian psychologist—then we can adjust ourselves to any situation, and be happy in it. (But Freudianism is

---

6. Théophile Gautier (1811–1872) and Louis-Henri Murger (1822–1861), French writers known for celebrating art for art's sake and depicting bohemian life, respectively.
7. Slight misquotation of "First Fig" (1920) by American poet Edna St. Vincent Millay (1892–1950). The full poem reads: "My candle burns at both ends; / It will not last the night; / But ah, my foes, and oh, my friends— / It gives a lovely light!"

only one method of adjustment. What is wrong with us may be our glands, and by a slight operation, or merely by taking a daily dose of thyroid, we may alter our whole personalities. Again, we may adjust ourselves by some such psychophysical discipline as was taught by Gurdjieff.[8] The implication of all these methods is the same—that the environment itself need not be altered. That explains why most radicals who became converted to psychoanalysis or glands or Gurdjieff gradually abandoned their political radicalism.)

8. The idea of changing place—"They do things better in Europe." England and Germany have the wisdom of old cultures; the Latin peoples have admirably preserved their pagan heritage. By expatriating himself, by living in Paris, Capri or the South of France, the artist can break the puritan shackles, drink, live freely and be wholly creative.

All these, from the standpoint of the business-Christian ethic then represented by the *Saturday Evening Post*, were corrupt ideas. This older ethic is familiar to most people, but one feature of it has not been sufficiently emphasized. Substantially, it was a *production* ethic. The great virtues it taught were industry, foresight, thrift and personal initiative. The workman should be industrious in order to produce more for his employer; he should look ahead to the future; he should save money in order to become a capitalist himself; then he should exercise personal initiative and found new factories where other workmen would toil industriously, and save, and become capitalists in their turn.

During the process many people would suffer privations: most workers would live meagerly and wrack their bodies with labor; even the employers would deny themselves luxuries that they could easily purchase, choosing instead to put back the money into their business; but after all, our bodies were not to be pampered; they were temporary dwelling places, and we should be rewarded in Heaven for our self-denial. On earth, our duty was to accumulate more wealth and produce more goods, the ultimate use of which was no subject for worry. They would somehow be absorbed, by new markets opened in the West, or overseas in new countries, or by the increased purchasing power of workmen who had saved and bettered their position.

That was the ethic of a young capitalism, and it worked admirably, so long as the territory and population of the country were expanding faster than its industrial plant. But after the war the situation changed. Our industries had grown enormously to satisfy a demand that suddenly ceased. To keep the factory wheels turning, a new domestic market had to be created. Industry and thrift were no longer adequate. There must be a new ethic that encouraged people to buy, a *consumption* ethic.

It happened that many of the Greenwich Village ideas proved useful in the altered situation. Thus, *self-expression* and *paganism* encouraged a demand for all sorts of products—modern furniture, beach pajamas, cosmetics, colored bathrooms with toilet paper to match. *Living for the moment* meant buying an automobile, radio or house, using it now and paying for it tomorrow. *Female equality*

---

8. George Ivanovitch Gurdjieff (1872–1945), Armenian spiritualist and philosopher, founded a quasi-religious movement that involved dialogue, exercise, and dance. Gurdjieff's Institute for the Harmonious Development of Man, centered in Russia and then France, furthered its influence through performances in U.S. cities during 1924.

was capable of doubling the consumption of products—cigarettes, for example—that had formerly been used by men alone. Even *changing place* would help to stimulate business in the country from which the artist was being expatriated. The exiles of art were also trade missionaries: involuntarily they increased the foreign demand for fountain pens, silk stockings, grapefruit and portable typewriters. They drew after them an invading army of tourists, thus swelling the profits of steamship lines and travel agencies. Everything fitted into the business picture.

I don't mean to say that Greenwich Village was the source of the revolution in morals that affected all our lives in the decade after the war, and neither do I mean that big business deliberately plotted to render the nation extravagant, pleasure worshiping and reckless of tomorrow.

The new moral standards arose from conditions that had nothing to do with the Village. They were, as a matter of fact, not really new. Always, even in the great age of the Puritans, there had been currents of licentiousness that were favored by the immoderate American climate and held in check only by hellfire preaching and the hardships of settling a new country. Old Boston, Providence, rural Connecticut, all had their underworlds. The reason puritanism became so strong in America was perhaps that it had to be strong in order to checkmate its enemies. But it was already weakening as the country grew richer in the twenty years before the war; and the war itself was the puritan crisis and defeat.

All standards were relaxed in the stormy-sultry wartime atmosphere. It wasn't only the boys of my age, those serving in the army, who were transformed by events: their sisters and younger brothers were affected in a different fashion. With their fathers away, perhaps, and their mothers making bandages or tea-dancing[9] with lonely officers, it was possible for boys and girls to do what they pleased. For the first time they could go to dances unchaperoned, drive the family car and park it by the roadside while they made love, and come home after midnight, a little tipsy, with nobody to reproach them in the hallway. They took advantage of these stolen liberties—indeed, one might say that the revolution in morals began as a middle-class children's revolt.

But everything conspired to further it. Prohibition came and surrounded the new customs with illicit glamour; prosperity made it possible to practice them; Freudian psychology provided a philosophical justification and made it unfashionable to be repressed; still later the sex magazines and the movies, even the pulpit, would advertise a revolution that had taken place silently and triumphed without a struggle. In all this Greenwich Village had no part. The revolution would have occurred if the Village had never existed, but—the point is important—it would not have followed the same course. The Village, older in revolt, gave form to the movement, created its fashions, and supplied the writers and illustrators who would render them popular. As for American business, though it laid no plots in advance, it was quick enough to use the situation, to exploit the new markets for cigarettes and cosmetics, and to realize that, in advertising pages and movie palaces, sex appeal was now the surest appeal.

The Greenwich Village standards, with the help of business, had spread

---

9. Dancing and socializing that follows or is accompanied by afternoon tea.

through the country. Young women east and west had bobbed their hair, let it grow and bobbed it again; they had passed through the period when corsets were checked in the cloakroom at dances and the period when corsets were not worn. They were not very self-conscious when they talked about taking a lover; and the conversations ran from mother fixations to birth control while they smoked cigarettes between the courses of luncheons eaten in black-and-orange tea shop[1] just like those in the Village. People of forty had been affected by the younger generation: they spent too much money, drank too much gin, made love to one another's wives and talked about their neuroses. Houses were furnished to look like studios. Stenographers went on parties, following the example of the boss and his girl friend and her husband. The "party," conceived as a gathering together of men and women to drink gin cocktails, flirt, dance to the phonograph or radio and gossip about their absent friends, had in fact become one of the most popular American institutions; nobody stopped to think how short its history had been in this country. It developed out of the "orgies" celebrated by the French 1830 Romantics,[2] but it was introduced into this country by Greenwich Villagers—before being adopted by salesmen from Kokomo and the younger country-club set in Kansas City.

Wherever one turned the Greenwich Village ideas were making their way: even the *Saturday Evening Post*[3] was feeling their influence. Long before Repeal, it began to wobble on Prohibition. It allowed drinking, petting and unfaithfulness to be mentioned in the stories it published; its illustrations showed women smoking. Its advertising columns admitted one after another of the strictly pagan products—cosmetics, toilet tissues, cigarettes—yet still it continued to thunder against Greenwich Village and bohemian immorality. It even nourished the illusion that its long campaign had been successful. On more than one occasion it announced that the Village was dead and buried: "The sad truth is," it said in the autumn of 1931, "that the Village was a flop." Perhaps it was true that the Village was moribund—of that we can't be sure, for creeds and ways of life among artists are hard to kill. If, however, the Village was really dying, it was dying of success. It was dying because it became so popular that too many people insisted on living there. It was dying because women smoked cigarettes on the streets of the Bronx, drank gin cocktails in Omaha and had perfectly swell parties in Seattle and Middletown—in other words, because American business and the whole of middle-class America had been going Greenwich Village.

•

Ever since 1920 there had been no break in the movement toward France. Artists and writers, art photographers, art salesmen, dancers, movie actors, Guggenheim

---

1. Shops serving "exotic" black teas such as English Breakfast, Earl Grey, Darjeeling, Assam, Lapsang Souchong, and Orange Pekoe. (Orange refers to the royal Dutch house of Orange and not the color of the tea.)
2. Prompted by an antiroyalist revolution in July 1830 that yielded the "citizen-king" Louis-Philippe's eighteen-year July Monarchy, French Romantic writers led by the poet, novelist, and playwright Victor Hugo (1802–1855) began a vigorous and long-standing literary battle against Neoclassicists. They viewed the artist as a noble outlaw at war with society, free in both choice and treatment of a subject, dedicated to passionate love.
3. Popular weekly magazine best known for its mainstream content and for many cover illustrations by artist Norman Rockwell (1894–1978). Fitzgerald's "Babylon Revisited" appeared in the *Post* in 1931.

fellows,[4] divorcées dabbling in sculpture, unhappy ex-débutantes wondering whether a literary career wouldn't take the place of marriage—a whole world of people with and without talent but sharing the same ideals happily deserted the homeland. Each year some of them returned while others crowded into their places: the migration continued at a swifter rate. But after the middle of the decade the motives behind it underwent an imperceptible but real change in emphasis. The earlier exiles had been driven abroad by a hatred of American dullness and puritanism, yet primarily they had traveled *in search of* something— leisure, freedom, knowledge, some quality that was offered by an older culture. Their successors felt the same desires, but felt them a little less strongly. Instead of being drawn ahead, they were propelled from behind, pushed eastward by the need for *getting away from* something. They were not so much exiles as refugees.

**THE NEW YORK TIMES**

## Stocks Collapse in 16,410,030-Share Day . . . (October 30, 1929)

Stock prices virtually collapsed yesterday, swept downward with gigantic losses in the most disastrous trading day in the stock market's history. Billions of dollars in open market values were wiped out as prices crumbled. . . .

From every point of view, in the extent of losses sustained, in total turnover, in the number of speculators wiped out, the day was the most disastrous in Wall Street's history. Hysteria swept the country. . . .

•

The market on the rampage is no respecter of persons. It washed fortune after fortune away yesterday and financially crippled thousands of individuals in all parts of the world. . . .

•

The market has now passed through three days of collapse, and so violent has it been that most authorities believe that the end is not far away. . . .

•

Wall Street was a street of vanished hopes, of curiously silent apprehension and of a sort of paralyzed hypnosis yesterday. Men and women crowded the brokerage offices, even those who have been long since wiped out, and followed the figures on the tape. Little groups gathered here and there to discuss the fall in prices in

---

4. Professionals (in the natural sciences, the social sciences, the humanities, and the creative arts, but not the performing arts) who receive fellowships from the John Simon Guggenheim Memorial Foundation.

hushed and awed tones. They were participating in the making of financial history. It was the consensus of bankers and brokers alike that no such scenes ever again will be witnessed by this generation. To most of those who have been in the market it is all the more awe-inspiring because their financial history is limited to bull markets.

## THE NEW YORK TIMES

### Crowds at Tickers See Fortunes Wane (October 30, 1929)

Groups of men, with here and there a woman, stood about inverted glass bowls[1] all over the city yesterday watching spools of ticker tape unwind and as the tenuous paper with its cryptic numerals grew longer at their feet, their fortunes shrunk. Others sat stolidly on tilted chairs in the customers' rooms of brokerage houses and watched a motion picture of waning wealth as the day's quotations moved silently across a screen.

It was among such groups as these, feeling the pulse of a feverish financial world, whose heart is the Stock Exchange, that drama and perhaps tragedy were to be found. On the floor of the Exchange itself there was little to indicate that the butcher, the baker and the candlestick maker, all were dumping holdings upon a market whose buying appetite was sated.

But the crowds about the ticker tapes, like friends about the bedside of a stricken friend, reflected in their faces the story the tape was telling. There were no smiles. There were no tears either. Just the camaraderie of fellow-sufferers. Everybody wanted to tell his neighbor how much he had lost. Nobody wanted to listen. It was too repetitious a tale.

#### CROWDS OUTSIDE EXCHANGE

Crowds gathered about the chaste white building that is the Stock Exchange, drawn by the fascination of being close while financial history was being made, to catch the fever of excitement that emanated from it. Many who stopped at Broad and Wall Streets knew not why they had come or what they had hoped to see. Actually they saw little enough—bankers whom they did not know by sight hurrying in and out of the office of J. P. Morgan & Co. across the way, other sightseers, a special detail of policemen and a few political speakers who addressed the noonday crowds near the Sub-Treasury Building.

Inside the Exchange, from which all visitors have been barred since Thursday's break in prices, the scene was only a little more dramatic.... [T]he scene was not so different from that beneath the grandstand at race meets when bettors hurry to lay their wagers with bookmakers before the bugle sounds.

---

1. Glass-enclosed machines, known as "tickers," that received stock-market information via telegraph and printed this data on paper tape.

**THE NEW YORK TIMES**

## Women Traders Going Back to Bridge Games; Say They Are Through with Stocks Forever (October 30, 1929)

The women who some time ago took up the pastime of high finance seemed yesterday on the verge of returning to bridge. They filled the uptown offices of Stock Exchange firms, irritable and nervous. Toward 3 o'clock the general tenor of their remarks was that they were through forever.

Stock brokers have said that the women speculators are the worst losers. Many of those appearing the most worried yesterday were elderly. They pushed their way into the crowded rooms, asked for the latest quotations and then blamed the brokers for the condition of things. In one office a stout woman with chins asked a harassed manager for a quotation, heard it and then remarked: "You might at least be a gentleman." She went away crying.

Another woman, also elderly, went into the same office and announced loudly that she had lost $10,000.[1] She seemed proud that she had lost it and went around for some time telling her friends. She wore four rings on one hand and smoked a succession of gold-tipped cigarettes from a jewel-studded gold case.

Four women were making the rounds of the offices on upper Broadway, apparently bent on turning catastrophe into a social affair. They drove in a large car with a chauffeur and entered each office regally. One of them, who said she had lost $15,000, remarked of an office that "this place is depressing." They went elsewhere.

The men in the uptown offices gathered around the tickers, sat quietly in their chairs or stood along the walls of the room. They made calculations, they appeared worried, but they said very little.

Shortly after 3 o'clock a small boy wandered into one of the uptown offices, looked around and finally found his mother. Apparently that is where he had been accustomed to meet her after school. They went out together shortly afterward, the boy asking for an ice cream cone and the woman telling a friend of her day's losses.

**ERNEST R. GROVES**

## From Social Problems of the Family (1927)

[The family] does more than minister to the physical needs of children; it serves society by its effect upon the various members of the family who live together within the home, and particularly by its influence upon the personality of the growing child.

Thus the family has become of primary importance as an effective socializing agency. It is chiefly through the family that culture is transmitted from genera-

---

1. A considerable sum of money in 1929, worth about $100,000 today.

tion to generation.... From parent to child the fundamentals of culture, traditions, ... social habits descend, and in this manner the continuity of social life is assured.

•

At a time when family defects and failures have become numerous and obvious there is need of a program which will tend to conserve family welfare. It is impossible to let the family meet its storm and stress with no effort to direct its course....

... [M]odern civilization is stimulating the increase of divorce. A large number of modern men and women express in all sorts of ways a tendency toward social instability as a result of rapid changes in modes of living. The pulsations of life move swiftly, thoughts are discarded, conventions superseded, thrilling experiences not previously dreamed of are provided, former habits loosened, and the formation of new habits accelerated by the momentum of present-day civilization. Marriage is one of the most delicate and sensitive of human relationships, and it would be strange indeed if it did not reflect the general unrest of our times....

A careful investigation recently made regarding divorces granted in Suffolk County (about 90 per cent. of which is the city of Boston) from January, 1900, through December, 1921, shows the effect of the World War upon the increase of divorces within that county. A remarkable increase of divorces appears for the years 1919, 1920 and 1921.... [T]he, essential cause of this phenomenal increase ... was the disrupting influence of the World War; this great conflict was both an expression of the general restlessness which is the bitter fruit of contemporary civilization, and, itself, a source of social discontent. All parts of life felt its upheaval. Nowhere was its effect more clearly registered in disturbing and uprooting influences than in the family.

•

.... War snatches from home the breadwinner, affords opportunity through the absence of fathers for children to drift into delinquency, gives to countless husbands who finally return home restlessness and wanderlust; it brings to both men and women temptations that lead them to deviate from former moral standards, it stimulates and brings to expression neurotic tendencies that might not have developed to the point of hurting the family had there not been the stress of war.... [War] stimulates fatalistic attitudes toward life which lessen the sense of family responsibility.... During the war when the minds of the people are concentrated on the conflict and the general excitement makes sane thinking difficult, the havoc suffered by the family is not keenly felt, but once the war is over its effects appear....

•

No greater tragedy can come to a family than the death of the father or mother, for added to the grief at the parting of the life of the parent beloved, there is in the case of children a broken family of the most serious kind.

Although the surviving parent may double his efforts in his endeavor to make good the loss suffered by the children, in spite of all he or she does, the family circle is at once stripped of its normal atmosphere and the home functions as a broken instrument. There is general agreement that the family that has lost its mother encounters greater trials than if it is the father who has died, for hers is the larger contribution. The father who is left to care for little children because of the death of the mother faces a very difficult problem and one increasingly hard to solve. A generation ago, an unmarried relative offered the commonest and best solution and in cases where there were none to be called upon a housekeeper could usually be had. The new economic opportunities for women have greatly changed this situation; relatives are far less likely to feel it their duty to assume a task that all recognize to be a severe test of character, and efficient housekeepers, at least for men with moderate incomes, are even more scarce than sacrificing relatives.

It is not at all surprising that we find children who have lost their mothers or fathers by death, and who have not been given satisfactory home life by the successful re-marriage of their remaining parent, so often drifting toward some sort of delinquency; their unsuccessful social adjustment bears tribute to the social values of the normal family and reveals in a striking way the misfortunes that must come to children whose family life is mutilated by death.

Many homes whose mothers are employed outside have conditions resembling those in the homes where death has removed the mother.

## V. F. CALVERTON

## *From* The Bankruptcy of Marriage (1928)

Pirouetting to the rhythm of the tango, ravaged by the contortions of the Charleston, or, cigarette in hand, shimmeying to the music of the masses, the New Woman and the New Morality have made their theatric debut upon the modern scene. At nights, in the large cities, life spins itself into melodrama. The mad dance of youth, intoxicated with the swell of its new freedom, has encircled the western world.... The wild, Corybantian[1] antics of the flapper,[2] flinging herself, in this delirium of escape, night after night upon the edge of nervous ecstasy, are no longer peculiar to our nation....

---

1. Like the wild music and dancing associated with the rites of the Corybantes—attendants and priests of Cybele, an ancient Asiatic goddess of nature.
2. Common term for the young women of the 1920s who flouted traditional social norms of dress and behavior.

Jazz has become an accepted institution.... It expresses the spirit of the age. Youth has steeped itself in its intoxications. Repressions have been released, and in the abandonments of modern life, exhibitionism has changed from a vice into a virtue.

In the flapper we find a vivid symbol of this change. This new girl, with all her emptiness of ideas and effusiveness of emotions, is a revolutionary outgrowth on the feminine scene.... Her speech, her dress, her gesture are outspoken evidences of the nature of her insurrection....

In this whirling race of Change, all restraints and restrictions have been sacrificed. The inhibitions once indispensable to feminine virtue have become riddled with scorn. The old sanctity of marriage has been ridiculed by sallies of wit and satire fired at it from every side. Sexual excitements and ecstasies have become experiences to crave and not to constrain. The flapper is consumed by them.... The old conventions that separated the sexes have been shattered. The old waltz has surrendered to the new jazz....

The old family has decayed. The old home has been replaced by the movie, the club, the dance-hall. Home has become a place to dine and die....

... This new girl, this modern flapper, with her lack of respect for the ideals of her predecessors; and this new masculine youth, with his disregard for the old responsibilities, his disdain for marriage, and contempt for virtue—both were born in the fury of their revolt, in the days of the World War and those that have immediately followed.

The jazz age was born in its tornado of intensity from the vortices of the World War and its aftermath....

The World War not only annihilated the flower of European youth, but it left its deeper effects on the youth that remained....

Youth was disillusioned of purpose and aspiration.

... The psychosis of the last fling predominated. The imminence of death drove men to the last extremities of desire. Nothing mattered! ...

The modern dance was an inevitable outgrowth of this war-madness. Modern youth responded to the wild call. What mattered? To live, to live intensely, to live furiously, to seize from life its every thrill. Such became the new motivation.

In Paris, after the war, they danced.... They wanted an escape that was active, dynamic, electrical.... The spirit of tranquillity was alien to the trend of the age.

Every year, every month, the dance takes new forms, assumes new disguises. Each form is more futile than the other. Each change is more sexual. Only the thin division of clothes and the wild cry of the victrola or violin distinguishes the dance from the pageantry of an ancient saturnalia—or the abandonment of the first act in a brothel.

Youth in its revolt has not only turned against the old traditions, but in its search for the new it is dissipating its energies in extravagance and excess....

This World War, then, shot into shreds the old ideals, the old morals, the old customs....

The Age of Innocence is dead.

•

The question—how did we get this way—is ... one of very intricate and complicated character. The World War, after all, was in itself but a sharp climax in the career of modern industrial civilization.... Industrialism brought with it the factory-system of production with mass-economics as its main manifestation; it drew women into industry, destroyed the unity of the home, and brought the family to a rapid ruin. It brought a new social class into power, the bourgeoisie[3]....

One of the important factors that has undermined th[e] old ethics has been the great change that has taken place in the attitude of the bourgeoisie. Not that the private-property concept has become less pervasive, but that its ethics, under the influence of new conditions, has lost its former asceticism and rigor. The bourgeoisie was a moral class.... Now it is not. Only the petty bourgeoisie is moral in this sense of the word.... [T]he bourgeoisie was originally a working class. It did not have a leisure-class attitude. In fact it condemned a leisure-class attitude. Today this has altered. The bourgeoisie who now represent our plutocracy constitute a leisure class. Prosperity has brought us to the billionaire epoch. ... With the centralization of capital, the acceleration of production, and the achievement of absentee-ownership of industry, combined with the inheritance of wealth which frees the larger part of the younger members of this group also from the necessity of toil, a leisure class was an inevitable result. The bourgeois mores, the old morality that is, was never made for a leisure-class ethic. It was an ethic that grew out of hard and trying struggle, an ethic in which asceticism was a virtue and diversion a sin. But a leisure class cannot live upon asceticism, nor exist without diversion.... The old morals had to crack and crumble. And so they have. The upper bourgeoisie, from the point of view of bourgeois morality, is the most immoral class upon the earth. This fact is to be observed everywhere, in divorce-scandals, court trials, newspaper disclosures, and in the novels and dramas devoted to the upper set....

It is only the petty-bourgeoisie, or the lower and poorer middle-class, that still endeavors to observe the old morality in practice....

The release of the new morals is closely connected with the fading of the old conception of marriage. Monogamous marriage is based upon the idea of a lifetime relationship between one man and one woman. This is the religious as well as the social idea....

... If we say that marriage has decayed, we do not mean that people do not still marry, or that they will not marry in the future. In speaking of the bankruptcy of marriage we mean the bankruptcy of modern marriage and the moral foundations upon which it has been constructed. Even under a state of "free love," people may marry, but their marriages may signify nothing more binding than ephemeral affections and alliances of a fortnight.... This theory of free contract is all that the modern revolutionist or free-lover desires. But this attitude is a violation, in fact is the very antithesis, of the *binding-contract* upon which modern marriage has been founded. It is marriage as we know it, therefore, the marriage of modern monogamy, of the binding-contract variety, our system of marriage, in other words, that has broken down, and today is bankrupt.

---

3. The middle class; *petty bourgeoisie:* lower middle class.

In 1887 there was one divorce to every 17.3 marriages; in 1924 there was one divorce to every 6.9 marriages.

Over two divorces... were granted to wives for every one that was granted to husbands [between 1887 and 1906], which signifies... an attitude on the part of woman that is distantly removed from that of her Victorian predecessors.... Women then were not to "take arms against a sea of trouble,"[4] but to accept it with resignation. Such response was supposed to be part of the innate nobility of her nature. Today woman is in a state of protest and revolt....

... [T]here should be nothing bewildering or strangely novel in this recent revolution in ethics. Scores of such revolutions have occurred in the past, ... expressing each in turn fundamental alterations in social and economic structure. With the candor in which sex is now beginning to be treated, there should again be no cause for astonishment. It is merely a return to an older attitude which was far more clean than the one which we have known.

While in the past we have known the costs of repression, it is the future which will introduce to us the costs of freedom. If freedom as a theory is perfect, and as an aspiration is ideal, it is foolish of us, however, to imagine that in practice it will be accompanied by a complete absence of discord. There will still be individual dilemmas, individual difficulties, and individual disasters....

... [T]he present direction of sex attitudes ... holds forth hope as a rich incentive. The escape from the old ethics can only be viewed as an advance.

In order to progress we must hazard new seas.... Until the new ways have been tried and tested, and the rapids conquered in the crossing, movement in this direction and that will be uncertain and insecure. These are the dangers that accompany exploration....

### SUGGESTIONS FOR WRITING

1. Write an essay that examines one aspect of the lifestyle of Americans in Paris as portrayed in F. Scott Fitzgerald's "Babylon Revisited" and that same aspect of the history of the age (the 1920s and '30s) as documented in the short pieces, by Fitzgerald and others, that accompany the story in this chapter. For example, consider how the economic crash affected the getting and the spending of money. Or compare the different models of family or social life depicted and recalled in the story with the writings that discuss social changes in this era. If there are parallels between Charlie Wales's fictional life and the actual trends and events of that time, does the story clearly take sides for or against old-fashioned ways, the "Roaring Twenties" of excess, or the effort to recover in the early 1930s?
2. In "Babylon Revisited" much is implied about the changing roles of women in modern society. Citing specific passages from Fitzgerald's story as well as from the excerpts by Ernest R. Groves and V. F. Calverton, write an essay discussing the way

---

4. *Hamlet* 3.1.59: "Or to take arms against a sea of troubles" (from Hamlet's famous "To be or not to be" soliloquy).

that "Babylon Revisited" depicts girls and women. What conflicts do you see in the story between characters with different notions of the proper female roles?

3. Research the life of F. Scott Fitzgerald and write an essay examining the parallels between the author and his character Charlie Wales in "Babylon Revisited." How are they similar and how are they different, and why do you think Fitzgerald used the medium of fiction in the way he did? Be sure to cite Fitzgerald's *Echoes of the Jazz Age*, excerpted in this chapter.

4. Write an essay in which you connect a theme, action or event, or character in Fitzgerald's story with one or more of the eight revolutionary new values expressed in Malcolm Cowley's *Exile's Return*. How does the story show the limitations or inconsistencies of these new values? For instance, did the Americans in Paris really seek "a change of place," or did they just occupy parts of Paris and make them American? Is Charlie going to correct his own "psychological adjustment," or is he suffering from something wrong with his culture? Address such questions with reference to the biographical and historical information about Fitzgerald and the period provided here or elsewhere.

5. What is the equivalent in our own time of the stock-market crash of 1929? Is it the events of September 11, 2001? the collapse of the "Internet bubble" in 2000–2001? Write a short story in which the lives of your characters reflect the social, economic, and moral upheavals of the present day. You might employ Fitzgerald's method of looking back at one era, however recent, from the standpoint of drastically altered circumstances.

# 12 CRITICAL CONTEXTS: A FICTION CASEBOOK

We have already seen that, although stories may be read as if they stand alone, they are enriched by being situated in authorial, literary, or cultural and historical contexts. Once a work has earned a place in the canon of literature, it has already become surrounded by a critical context—readers who write about the work and others who engage those readers or critics in dialogue about that work. To write critically about a work of literature is to engage not only the text, but also those who have written about the text. It is always advisable, however, to read and reread the story several times until you have come to terms with it—that is, settled in your own mind what you think about the story and how you interpret it. Only then should you go to other critics—"secondary sources"—to expand or corroborate or reconsider your reading of the story. Often when you read criticism before you have made up your own mind, *all* the critics seem "right" (and the most recently read seem the "most clearly right"), and your own responses are dulled or deflected. On the other hand, when you have settled on your own responses to the story, you can read critics and pick up *additional* information or insights that can enhance rather than erase your own response and judgment. Reading criticism will not rob you of, or substitute for, your individual response. Rather, in addition to being informative in various ways, it may provide you with the means to convince someone else to share your opinion of the work.

*A writer is congenitally unable to tell the truth and that is why we call what he writes fiction.*
—WILLIAM FAULKNER

The story that stands here in the middle of critical discussion is William Faulkner's popular, classic, and controversial tale "A Rose for Emily." It is followed by four published analyses of the story and a student essay. There are hundreds of critical essays and commentaries on "A Rose for Emily"—a recent online search of the Modern Language Association bibliography yielded eighty-five studies of the story published just since 1963, published as far away as Costa Rica and Turkey, and in languages as varied as German and Japanese. It is virtually impossible, then, to fully "report" the history of the critical discussion of this fascinating story. The four critical pieces reprinted here are not necessarily the best (and not necessarily not the best), nor do they fully represent the spectrum of comment and argument about the story. They do, instead, suggest the range of approaches that have been applied to the story as well as some of the story's aspects that have often been singled out for analysis, response, and judgment.

Lawrence R. Rodgers's " 'We all said, "She will kill herself" ': The Narrator/Detective in William Faulkner's 'A Rose for Emily,' " situates Faulkner's story in a literary subgenre, the detective story, matching details of the story to generally accepted definitions of the ingredients of detective fiction.

George L. Dillon's "Styles of Reading," though it first appeared in a highly theoretical professional journal, groups a variety of actual student responses into three categories, and many students who have read this essay agree that it represents the way they read and the kinds of questions they ask of a text. The essay is abbreviated here (ellipses indicate our deletions); in its original form it used long passages from other critics to demonstrate that student approaches were analogous to professional critical readings. Its purpose here is to represent various ways that students and professional critics alike read this—or any—story, and to make you more conscious of what you and your classmates are doing and what you might do in reading fiction.

The third piece, Judith Fetterley's "A Rose for 'A Rose for Emily,'" is adapted from her book *The Resisting Reader: A Feminist Approach to American Fiction*. It suggests that what Emily has done seems grotesque primarily because she is a woman—indeed, a lady—in a society with restrictive standards for what a lady might properly do. Faulkner, she says, sees Emily as "a woman victimized and betrayed by the system of sexual politics, who nevertheless has discovered, within the structures that victimize her, sources of power for herself." Faulkner himself has implied this, she says, alluding to (but not quoting) occasional comments of his.

Actual statements from Faulkner interviews, however, scarcely identify him as a feminist. Two such quotations appear, for example, in *The Paris Review Interviews: Writers at Work*, first series (Baltimore: Penguin, 1958). The first of these wryly claims that "the perfect milieu for the artist to work in" is a brothel. The house is quiet in the mornings—the best time to write—the work is easy, and the pay adequate; the job offers him whatever social life he wants, "gives him a certain standing in his society," and "all the inmates of the house are female and would defer to him and call him 'sir' " (124). The second statement is even more provocative: "Success is feminine and like a woman; if you cringe before her, she will override you. So the way to treat her is to show her the back of your hand" (125). This is not to discount Fetterley's feminist reading of the story, but only to make you wary of trusting what an author says about his or her own work—we should trust the tale, not the teller. After all, evidence in Faulkner's stories, letters, and life can support the view that he was a stereotypical Mississippi white racist or, conversely, that he empathized with African Americans and deplored racism. We naturally and properly read stories as if they are communications from another human mind and experience that we are trying to understand (reading, as one critic has suggested, as a member of the "authorial audience"). All readings must begin with this intention. But even our friends sometimes tell us things about themselves, their attitudes and actions, that they do not know they are revealing, and sometimes they claim intentions or accomplishments that we know not to be "true." We must be alert to the possibility that even authors cannot always distinguish between what they mean and what they have said. We must, then, see a work, another critic has said, "as it cannot see itself." It is only proper to acknowledge the profundity and power of an author's vision and art but probably not a good idea to claim to know fully the author's "intention" (even if you can cite a quotation by the author that purports to define that intention).

> *The writer's only responsibility is to his art. He will be completely ruthless if he is a good one.*
> —WILLIAM FAULKNER

When a work has engaged a number of critics, and especially when something

*Time is dead as long as it is being clicked off by little wheels; only when the clock stops does time come to life.*
—WILLIAM FAULKNER

in the work is difficult or controversial, subsequent commentaries need to acknowledge the previous readings and, by contradicting or modifying their conclusions with new evidence or more persuasive argument, justify still another essay on the oft-debated topic. Gene M. Moore's "Of Time and Its Mathematical Progression: Problems of Chronology in Faulkner's 'A Rose for Emily' " is just such an essay. It addresses once again perhaps the most frequently discussed aspect of Faulkner's story: the precise timing of the events (including Emily's dates of birth and death). Moore cuts some knots and tightens others, establishes a new chronology, and, while admitting residual inconsistencies, offers an explanation of how these came about. It serves here as an exemplary critical argument—engaging both the story and its commentators.

### A NOTE ON DOCUMENTATION

Alert readers will notice that these commentaries use different forms of documentation. Dillon's essay was published in 1982, Fetterley's book in 1978. Both cite their references in notes at the end of their article—for example, "1. Brooke-Rose, 'The Readerhood of Man,' in *The Reader in the Text*, ed. Susan R. Suleiman and Inge Crosman (Princeton: Princeton University Press, 1980), 120–48" (Dillon); "See *Faulkner in the University: Class Conferences at the University of Virginia 1957–1958*, edited by Frederick L. Gwynn and Joseph L. Blotner (Charlottesville: University Press of Virginia, 1959), 87–88; *Faulkner at Nagano*, edited by Robert A. Jeliffe (Tokyo: Kenkyusha, 1956), 71" (Fetterley)—and neither gives a bibliography or a list of "works cited." The essays of Rodgers and Moore—published in 1995 and 1992, respectively—give such a list and interpolate the references with the page number(s) in the text parenthetically—for example, "(Going 53)," "(Wilson 56)." The suggested standard form for literary essays and books is set by the Modern Language Association; between the publication of the earlier and the later essays, the MLA changed the form it recommended. Not everyone uses the newer form. But it is not only for that reason that the older form has been left here in the older essays: whenever you do literary research in books and articles from earlier decades, you will run into this earlier form, so it is just as well to be familiar with it. Note that while this documentation is standard for *literary* commentary, critical and scholarly works in other disciplines—psychology, chemistry, and so forth—use other forms. (For more on documentation, see "Writing about Literature," below.)

### WILLIAM FAULKNER

## A Rose for Emily

### I

When Miss Emily Grierson died, our whole town went to her funeral: the men through a sort of respectful affection for a fallen monument, the women mostly out of curiosity to see the inside of her house, which no one save an old manservant—a combined gardener and cook—had seen in at least ten years.

It was a big, squarish frame house that had once been white, decorated with cupolas and spires and scrolled balconies in the heavily lightsome style of the seventies,[1] set on what had once been our most select street. But garages and cotton gins had encroached and obliterated even the august names of that neighborhood; only Miss Emily's house was left, lifting its stubborn and coquettish decay above the cotton wagons and the gasoline pumps—an eyesore among eyesores. And now Miss Emily had gone to join the representatives of those august names where they lay in the cedar-bemused cemetery among the ranked and anonymous graves of Union and Confederate soldiers who fell at the battle of Jefferson.

Alive, Miss Emily had been a tradition, a duty, and a care; a sort of hereditary obligation upon the town, dating from that day in 1894 when Colonel Sartoris, the mayor—he who fathered the edict that no Negro woman should appear on the streets without an apron—remitted her taxes, the dispensation dating from the death of her father on into perpetuity. Not that Miss Emily would have accepted charity. Colonel Sartoris invented an involved tale to the effect that Miss Emily's father had loaned money to the town, which the town, as a matter of business, preferred this way of repaying. Only a man of Colonel Sartoris' generation and thought could have invented it, and only a woman could have believed it.

When the next generation, with its more modern ideas, became mayors and aldermen, this arrangement created some little dissatisfaction. On the first of the year they mailed her a tax notice. February came, and there was no reply. They wrote her a formal letter, asking her to call at the sheriff's office at her convenience. A week later the mayor wrote her himself, offering to call or to send his car for her, and received in reply a note on paper of an archaic shape, in a thin, flowing calligraphy in faded ink, to the effect that she no longer went out at all. The tax notice was also enclosed, without comment.

They called a special meeting of the Board of Aldermen. A deputation waited upon her, knocked at the door through which no visitor had passed since she ceased giving china-painting lessons eight or ten years earlier. They were admitted by the old Negro into a dim hall from which a stairway mounted into still more shadow. It smelled of dust and disuse—a close, dank smell. The Negro led them into the parlor. It was furnished in heavy, leather-covered furniture. When the Negro opened the blinds of one window, a faint dust rose sluggishly about their thighs, spinning with slow motes in the single sun-ray. On a tarnished gilt easel before the fireplace stood a crayon portrait of Miss Emily's father.

They rose when she entered—a small, fat woman in black, with a thin gold chain descending to her waist and vanishing into her belt, leaning on an ebony cane with a tarnished gold head. Her skeleton was small and spare; perhaps that was why what would have been merely plumpness in another was obesity in her. She looked bloated, like a body long submerged in motionless water, and of that pallid hue. Her eyes, lost in the fatty ridges of her face, looked like two small pieces of coal pressed into a lump of dough as they moved from one face to another while the visitors stated their errand.

---

1. The 1870s, the decade following the Civil War between the "Union and Confederate soldiers" mentioned at the end of the paragraph.

She did not ask them to sit. She just stood in the door and listened quietly until the spokesman came to a stumbling halt. Then they could hear the invisible watch ticking at the end of the gold chain.

Her voice was dry and cold. "I have no taxes in Jefferson. Colonel Sartoris explained it to me. Perhaps one of you can gain access to the city records and satisfy yourselves."

"But we have. We are the city authorities, Miss Emily. Didn't you get a notice from the sheriff, signed by him?"

10 "I received a paper, yes," Miss Emily said. "Perhaps he considers himself the sheriff.... I have no taxes in Jefferson."

"But there is nothing on the books to show that, you see. We must go by the—"

"See Colonel Sartoris. I have no taxes in Jefferson."

"But, Miss Emily—"

"See Colonel Sartoris." (Colonel Sartoris had been dead almost ten years.) "I have no taxes in Jefferson. Tobe!" The Negro appeared. "Show these gentlemen out."

II

15 So she vanquished them, horse and foot, just as she had vanquished their fathers thirty years before about the smell. That was two years after her father's death and a short time after her sweetheart—the one we believed would marry her—had deserted her. After her father's death she went out very little; after her sweetheart went away, people hardly saw her at all. A few of the ladies had the temerity to call, but were not received, and the only sign of life about the place was the Negro man—a young man then—going in and out with a market basket.

"Just as if a man—any man—could keep a kitchen properly," the ladies said; so they were not surprised when the smell developed. It was another link between the gross, teeming world and the high and mighty Griersons.

A neighbor, a woman, complained to the mayor, Judge Stevens, eighty years old.

"But what will you have me do about it, madam?" he said.

"Why, send her word to stop it," the woman said. "Isn't there a law?"

20 "I'm sure that won't be necessary," Judge Stevens said. "It's probably just a snake or a rat that nigger of hers killed in the yard. I'll speak to him about it."

The next day he received two more complaints, one from a man who came in diffident deprecation. "We really must do something about it, Judge. I'd be the last one in the world to bother Miss Emily, but we've got to do something." That night the Board of Aldermen met—three gray-beards and one younger man, a member of the rising generation.

"It's simple enough," he said. "Send her word to have her place cleaned up. Give her a certain time to do it in, and if she don't . . ."

"Dammit, sir," Judge Stevens said, "will you accuse a lady to her face of smelling bad?"

So the next night, after midnight, four men crossed Miss Emily's lawn and slunk about the house like burglars, sniffing along the base of the brickwork and at the cellar openings while one of them performed a regular sowing motion with his hand out of a sack slung from his shoulder. They broke open the cellar door and sprinkled lime there, and in all the outbuildings. As they recrossed the lawn, a window that had been dark was lighted and Miss Emily sat in it, the light behind her, and her upright torso motionless as that of an idol. They crept quietly across the lawn and into the shadow of the locusts that lined the street. After a week or two the smell went away.

That was when people had begun to feel really sorry for her. People in our town, remembering how old lady Wyatt, her great-aunt, had gone completely crazy at last, believed that the Griersons held themselves a little too high for what they really were. None of the young men were quite good enough for Miss Emily and such. We had long thought of them as a tableau; Miss Emily a slender figure in white in the background, her father a spraddled silhouette in the foreground, his back to her and clutching a horsewhip, the two of them framed by the back-flung front door. So when she got to be thirty and was still single, we were not pleased exactly, but vindicated; even with insanity in the family she wouldn't have turned down all of her chances if they had really materialized.

When her father died, it got about that the house was all that was left to her; and in a way, people were glad. At last they could pity Miss Emily. Being left alone, and a pauper, she had become humanized. Now she too would know the old thrill and the old despair of a penny more or less.

The day after his death all the ladies prepared to call at the house and offer condolence and aid, as is our custom. Miss Emily met them at the door, dressed as usual and with no trace of grief on her face. She told them that her father was not dead. She did that for three days, with the ministers calling on her, and the doctors, trying to persuade her to let them dispose of the body. Just as they were about to resort to law and force, she broke down, and they buried her father quickly.

We did not say she was crazy then. We believed she had to do that. We remembered all the young men her father had driven away, and we knew that with nothing left, she would have to cling to that which had robbed her, as people will.

III

She was sick for a long time. When we saw her again, her hair was cut short, making her look like a girl, with a vague resemblance to those angels in colored church windows—sort of tragic and serene.

The town had just let the contracts for paving the sidewalks, and in the summer after her father's death they began to work. The construction company came with niggers and mules and machinery, and a foreman named Homer Barron, a Yankee—a big, dark, ready man, with a big voice and eyes lighter than his face. The little boys would follow in groups to hear him cuss the niggers, and the niggers singing in time to the rise and fall of picks. Pretty soon he knew everybody in town. Whenever you heard a lot of laughing anywhere about the square, Homer Barron would be in the center of the group. Presently we began to see him and Miss Emily on Sunday afternoons driving in the yellow-wheeled buggy and the matched team of bays from the livery stable.

At first we were glad that Miss Emily would have an interest, because the ladies all said, "Of course a Grierson would not think seriously of a Northerner, a day laborer." But there were still others, older people, who said that even grief could not cause a real lady to forget *noblesse oblige*—without calling it *noblesse oblige*.[2] They just said, "Poor Emily. Her kinsfolk should come to her." She had

---

2. The obligation, coming with noble or upper-class birth, to behave with honor and generosity toward those less privileged.

some kin in Alabama; but years ago her father had fallen out with them over the estate of old lady Wyatt, the crazy woman, and there was no communication between the two families. They had not even been represented at the funeral.

And as soon as the old people said, "Poor Emily," the whispering began. "Do you suppose it's really so?" they said to one another. "Of course it is. What else could . . ." This behind their hands; rustling of craned silk and satin behind jalousies[3] closed upon the sun of Sunday afternoon as the thin, swift clop-clop-clop of the matched team passed: "Poor Emily."

She carried her head high enough—even when we believed that she was fallen. It was as if she demanded more than ever the recognition of her dignity as the last Grierson; as if it had wanted that touch of earthiness to reaffirm her imperviousness. Like when she bought the rat poison, the arsenic. That was over a year after they had begun to say "Poor Emily," and while the two female cousins were visiting her.

"I want some poison," she said to the druggist. She was over thirty then, still a slight woman, though thinner than usual, with cold, haughty black eyes in a face the flesh of which was strained across the temples and about the eyesockets as you imagine a lighthouse-keeper's face ought to look. "I want some poison," she said.

"Yes, Miss Emily. What kind? For rats and such? I'd recom—"

"I want the best you have. I don't care what kind."

The druggist named several. "They'll kill anything up to an elephant. But what you want is—"

"Arsenic," Miss Emily said. "Is that a good one?"

"Is . . . arsenic? Yes ma'am. But what you want—"

"I want arsenic."

The druggist looked down at her. She looked back at him, erect, her face like a strained flag. "Why, of course," the druggist said. "If that's what you want. But the law requires you to tell what you are going to use it for."

Miss Emily just stared at him, her head tilted back in order to look him eye for eye, until he looked away and went and got the arsenic and wrapped it up. The Negro delivery boy brought her the package; the druggist didn't come back. When she opened the package at home there was written on the box, under the skull and bones: "For rats."

IV

So the next day we all said, "She will kill herself"; and we said it would be the best thing. When she had first begun to be seen with Homer Barron, we had said, "She will marry him." Then we said, "She will persuade him yet," because Homer himself had remarked—he liked men, and it was known that he drank with the younger men in the Elk's Club—that he was not a marrying man. Later we said, "Poor Emily," behind the jalousies as they passed on Sunday afternoon in the glittering buggy, Miss Emily with her head high and Homer Barron with his hat cocked and a cigar in his teeth, reins and whip in a yellow glove.

Then some of the ladies began to say that it was a disgrace to the town and a bad example to the young people. The men did not want to interfere, but at last the ladies forced the Baptist minister—Miss Emily's people were Episcopal—

---

3. Window blinds made of adjustable horizontal slats.

to call upon her. He would never divulge what happened during that interview, but he refused to go back again. The next Sunday they again drove about the streets, and the following day the minister's wife wrote to Miss Emily's relations in Alabama.

So she had blood-kin under her roof again and we sat back to watch developments. At first nothing happened. Then we were sure that they were to be married. We learned that Miss Emily had been to the jeweler's and ordered a man's toilet set in silver, with the letters H. B. on each piece. Two days later we learned that she had bought a complete outfit of men's clothing, including a nightshirt, and we said, "They are married." We were really glad. We were glad because the two female cousins were even more Grierson than Miss Emily had ever been.

So we were not surprised when Homer Barron—the streets had been finished some time since—was gone. We were a little disappointed that there was not a public blowing-off, but we believed that he had gone on to prepare for Miss Emily's coming, or to give her a chance to get rid of the cousins. (By that time it was a cabal, and we were all Miss Emily's allies to help circumvent the cousins.) Sure enough, after another week they departed. And, as we had expected all along, within three days Homer Barron was back in town. A neighbor saw the Negro man admit him at the kitchen door at dusk one evening.

And that was the last we saw of Homer Barron. And of Miss Emily for some time. The Negro man went in and out with the market basket, but the front door remained closed. Now and then we would see her at a window for a moment, as the men did that night when they sprinkled the lime, but for almost six months she did not appear on the streets. Then we knew that this was to be expected too; as if that quality of her father which had thwarted her woman's life so many times had been too virulent and too furious to die.

When we next saw Miss Emily, she had grown fat and her hair was turning gray. During the next few years it grew grayer and grayer until it attained an even pepper-and-salt iron-gray, when it ceased turning. Up to the day of her death at seventy-four it was still that vigorous iron-gray, like the hair of an active man.

From that time on her front door remained closed, save for a period of six or seven years, when she was about forty, during which she gave lessons in china-painting. She fitted up a studio in one of the downstairs rooms, where the daughters and grand-daughters of Colonel Sartoris' contemporaries were sent to her with the same regularity and in the same spirit that they were sent on Sundays with a twenty-five cent piece for the collection plate. Meanwhile her taxes had been remitted.

Then the newer generation became the backbone and the spirit of the town, and the painting pupils grew up and fell away and did not send their children to her with boxes of color and tedious brushes and pictures cut from the ladies' magazines. The front door closed upon the last one and remained closed for good. When the town got free postal delivery Miss Emily alone refused to let them fasten the metal numbers above her door and attach a mailbox to it. She would not listen to them.

Daily, monthly, yearly we watched the Negro grow grayer and more stooped, going in and out with the market basket. Each December we sent her a tax notice, which would be returned by the post office a week later, unclaimed. Now and then we would see her in one of the downstairs windows—she had evidently shut up the top floor of the house—like the carven torso of an idol in a niche, looking or not looking at us, we could never tell which. Thus she passed from generation to generation—dear, inescapable, impervious, tranquil, and perverse.

And so she died. Fell ill in the house filled with dust and shadows, with only a doddering Negro man to wait on her. We did not even know she was sick; we had long since given up trying to get any information from the Negro. He talked to no one, probably not even to her, for his voice had grown harsh and rusty, as if from disuse.

She died in one of the downstairs rooms, in a heavy walnut bed with a curtain, her gray head propped on a pillow yellow and moldy with age and lack of sunlight.

V

The Negro met the first of the ladies at the front door and let them in, with their hushed, sibilant voices and their quick, curious glances, and then he disappeared. He walked right through the house and out the back and was not seen again.

The two female cousins came at once. They held the funeral on the second day, with the town coming to look at Miss Emily beneath a mass of bought flowers, with the crayon face of her father musing profoundly above the bier and the ladies sibilant and macabre; and the very old men—some in their brushed Confederate uniforms—on the porch and the lawn, talking of Miss Emily as if she had been a contemporary of theirs, believing that they had danced with her and courted her perhaps, confusing time with its mathematical progression, as the old do, to whom all the past is not a diminishing road, but, instead, a huge meadow which no winter ever quite touches, divided from them now by the narrow bottleneck of the most recent decade of years.

Already we knew that there was one room in that region above stairs which no one had seen in forty years, and which would have to be forced. They waited until Miss Emily was decently in the ground before they opened it.

The violence of breaking down the door seemed to fill this room with pervading dust. A thin, acrid pall as of the tomb seemed to lie everywhere upon this room decked and furnished as for a bridal: upon the valance curtains of faded rose color, upon the rose-shaded lights, upon the dressing table, upon the delicate array of crystal and the man's toilet things backed with tarnished silver, silver so tarnished that the monogram was obscured. Among them lay a collar and tie, as if they had just been removed, which, lifted, left upon the surface a pale crescent in the dust. Upon a chair hung the suit, carefully folded; beneath it the two mute shoes and the discarded socks.

The man himself lay in the bed.

For a long while we just stood there, looking down at the profound and fleshless grin. The body had apparently once lain in the attitude of an embrace, but now the long sleep that outlasts love, that conquers even the grimace of love, had cuckolded him. What was left of him, rotted beneath what was left of the nightshirt, had become inextricable from the bed in which he lay; and upon him and upon the pillow beside him lay that even coating of the patient and biding dust.

Then we noticed that in the second pillow was the indentation of a head. One of us lifted something from it, and leaning forward, that faint and invisible dust dry and acrid in the nostrils, we saw a long strand of iron-gray hair.

1931

**LAWRENCE R. RODGERS**

## "We all said, 'She will kill herself' ": The Narrator/Detective in William Faulkner's "A Rose for Emily"*

William Faulkner's most famous short story, "A Rose for Emily," is a classic expression of American gothicism. Rich in interpretive possibility and long a critical favorite, this 1929 story is a dark parable of the decline of southern sensibility. Its impact relies on a slow accretion of atmospheric detail, with each new detail further illuminating the many mysteries surrounding the life of confederate matriarch Emily Grierson. The story also may be read within the framework of a related popular genre, the classical detective story, whose American origins are traced to Edgar Allan Poe. It is commonly known that Faulkner learned much about genre-writing from his fellow southerner. He capitalized on Poe's legacy in novels such as *Intruder in the Dust* (1948) and *Knight's Gambit* (1949) as well as in "An Error in Chemistry," his 1946 short story published in *Ellery Queen's Mystery Magazine*. Faulkner's ability to expand and rework the devices of the detective story in these later works makes him a worthy successor to Poe.[1] But it is in the earlier, less straightforward story of detection, "A Rose for Emily," that Faulkner's lifelong interest in shaping his fiction around the theme of detection can be observed in its nascent form, and the important presence of the detective figure throughout his fiction can begin to be more fully appreciated.

While it might initially seem surprising that 20th-century America's premier novelist would draw so freely from the conventions of formula fiction, Faulkner was, to his frustration, well-versed with the necessities of writing with mass publication in mind. Any number of his works betray his willingness to annex popular conventions. His sixth novel, *Sanctuary*, is a case in point.[2] Frustrated by a mounting stack of what he considered brilliant fiction with no press to publish it, he sat down in late January of 1929 and in four months completed the sensational *Sanctuary*, which would remain his bleakest, most unrelentingly ruthless examination of the modern world. As he would later tell an audience, the novel was "basely conceived ... I thought of the most horrific idea I could think of and wrote it" with the goal of making money (qtd. in Minter 107). Shortly after *Sanctuary*'s acceptance, in April 1930, while the near-broke writer was still awaiting royalties, "A Rose for Emily" appeared in *The Forum*. Having already had it rejected by *Scribner's*, Faulkner was thrilled to receive his first short story publication, less for the honor than for the fact that he desperately needed money to pay mounting medical costs and back bills for materials used in restoring his home, Rowen Oak.

Following the example of "A Rose for Emily," the bulk of Faulkner's short

---

* From *Clues: A Journal of Detection* 16 (1995): 117-29.

fiction was produced in assembly-line spurts of productivity and aimed toward quick publication in national magazines, which, in turn, helped finance the slower pace of his more involved, less marketable novels. Biographer Frederick Karl notes that Faulkner earned more from selling four short stories to *Saturday Evening Post* than from the combined royalties of his first four novels (401). Nonetheless, the shy southerner much preferred to don the guise of the solitary romantic artist laboring purely for the sake of his craft. But in light of his lifelong financial difficulties, such a pose merely placated his ongoing taste for self-invention. However much he scorned the popular marketplace in favor of writing what he viewed as Art with a capital A, he always maintained close contact with a broad-based, "nonliterary" readership.[3]

In his well-known discussion of detective story conventions in *Adventure, Mystery and Romance,* John Cawelti provides a useful, simple litmus test for establishing whether a text follows the classical detective formula. In his scheme, there are three conditions that must be met: 1) the story must have a mystery that needs solving; 2) there must be concealed facts that a detective has to explore; and 3) these facts must become clear in the end (132). "A Rose for Emily" easily satisfies these conditions. Homer Barron, a laborer from the North, comes to work in the tightly knit community of Jefferson, Mississippi. After he is seen in the company of Emily, the eccentric daughter of one of Jefferson's finest families, Homer's courtship fuels town gossip. Various loosely related details soon mount up to suggest something is seriously amiss. Homer mysteriously disappears, reappears and then disappears again not long after Miss Emily purchases rat poison. A foul smell emanates from her old home, causing some men from the town to sneak into her yard to sprinkle it with lime. Emily herself goes through profound physical changes, growing fat and grey-headed. Finally, after her death, Homer's disappearance is solved in what Irving Howe has wryly noted makes for a hair-raising conclusion (265). Miss Emily, aware of the town's penchant for judgment, ruled by the codes of etiquette of a once-proud lineage, and unable to fathom the changing conditions of the new South, has indeed poisoned Homer and retreated (with his corpse) into the recesses of her attic, where, liberated from prying eyes, she has been allowed to carry on her illicit love affair in post-mortem privacy. The evidence betraying her necrophilia is a single strand of iron-grey hair lying on a head-shaped indentation next to the corpse, which, much like the values that Emily tried to uphold by removing her affairs from public view, has become a grotesque, rotted perversion of its former self.

In light of all the praise given over to the originality, ambiguity, technical merit, and skillful manipulation of discontinuous, fragmentary narrative time in "A Rose for Emily," it is, within these considerations, an interestingly conventional detective tale. Its pattern of action is ordered around the basic elements of the popular genre: a southern setting circumscribing an eerie, decaying mansion; a curious disappearance; portents of a murder, in this case a poisoning; an unlikely, peculiar suspect, and a mysterious locked room whose assortment of clues turns up a corpse, a murderer and, finally, a solution to a macabre but oddly plausible crime. What appears to be missing here is the detective, the detached figure whose analytic insight allows him (or, more rarely, her) to solve the crime and thus restore rationality and a sense of order to a world of uncertainty.

However, on examination, we find that Faulkner (who made a career of stretching the boundaries of convention, literary and otherwise, to suit his own needs) provides a kind of detective, but with an inventive twist. Cawelti notes that a detective story need not contain a professional crime solver like a Maigret, a Dupin or a Holmes as long as some character "performs the role of successful inquirer" (132).

In "A Rose for Emily" the unnamed narrator that pieces together the fragmented decline of the Grierson lineage plays just such a role. More originally, this narrator/detective is also an unknowing driving force behind Emily's crime. Speaking in the "we" voice, the narrator, an overwhelming presence throughout the narrative, embodies the town's shared sentiments toward Emily. Having spent years not only observing but also commenting and rendering judgment upon the woman described as "a tradition, a duty, and a care,"[4] this *vox populi* is so persistent in assuming its natural right to intrude on Emily's life, that she—obsessively mindful of the need to honor the town's, and her father's, rigid code of genteel behavior—chooses murder rather than a public flouting of the town's values. The dramatic distance on display here provides an ironic layer to the narrative. As the observers of the conflict between the teller-of-tale's desire to solve the curious mysteries that surround Emily's life—indeed, his complicity in shaping them—and his undetective-like detachment from her crimes, readers occupy the tantalizing position of having insight into unraveling the mystery which the narrator lacks.

A classical detective story, quite simply, begins with an unsolved crime and moves toward its solution. Introduced into a world of ambiguity, mystery, and multiple possibilities, the reader is steadily made aware of key details that eventually allow a series of events to be placed into a comprehendable order. In "A Rose for Emily" the air of mystery commences with the first sentence: "When Miss Emily Grierson died, our whole town went to her funeral: the men through a sort of respectful affection for a fallen monument, the women mostly out of curiosity to see the inside of her house, which no one save an old manservant ... had seen in at least ten years" (119). Playing off the detective convention of entering a locked room and delaying the revelation of its contents until the story's conclusion, this teasing beginning invites the reader to participate in unraveling the mysteries that have led up to Emily's funeral. However, making order out of Emily's life is a complicated matter, since the narrator recalls the details through a non-linear filter.

Cloaking an additional layer of mystery on Emily's story, the narrator's disjointed, associational recollection of details has led readers and critics to become the surrogate detectives of Faulkner's world. They have tried to "unscramble" the chronology and thus "solve" the structural ambiguities of the story by reconstructing Faulkner's calendar.[5] With evidence sparse and at times contradictory, these attempts, relying on close reading, conjecture, and extra-textual evidence, have yielded several slightly different time-lines. Although these time-lines claim to be pedagogically useful in allowing students to grasp "the elusive, illusive quality of time that lies at the heart of the story" (Going 53), their more immediate appeal is as a kind of armchair detective's game. They offer the challenge of taking the story's one exact reference to time (the remitting of Colonel Sartoris, taxes "in 1894") and combining it with the two dozen or so more approximate references to come up with a set of dates corresponding to the major events of Emily's life. Since the temporal world of Faulkner's Yoknapatawpha County remains relatively consistent (if inexact) throughout his entire corpus, other texts besides "A Rose for Emily," like his 1929 novel *Sartoris*, also help provide clues. Thus the more familiar the detective-critic becomes with the entire Faulkner corpus, the more equipped he or she is to place the events of Emily's life in the context of Yoknapatawpha County's overall pattern of myth.

But beyond offering superficial clarification about the plot, an exact chronology hardly seems to matter. As is invariably the case with Faulkner, appreciating the text's brilliance only begins with comprehending the plot, however ordered. Reduced to its basic situation, "A Rose for Emily" is fairly standard melodrama, probably loosely based on a conflation of actual odd events that occurred around Oxford in the 1920s (cf. Cullen and Watkins 70-71). Faulkner's plots can be brilliantly imagined, but what infuses this particular story with its force is the *manner* in which the plot is related to us by the purportedly innocuous observer of Emily's life. In other words, Faulkner conceives of "A Rose for Emily" quite cunningly by bending the traditional presentation of the detective. The narrative's overwhelming presence is the narrator himself, speaking as a representative voice of Jefferson (or, in using the "we" pronoun throughout, perhaps even as the collective voice of the town). In culling the data of Emily's life, the narrator/detective's favored posture is, in the classic mode of the genre, one of surveillance and, less classically, one of judgment. From the initial sentence, the narrator demands not just to retell the events of Emily's life, but to relish the manner in which the town intrudes upon them. Town members try to collect her taxes, insist on burying her father, attempt to rid her house of its odor, force the Baptist minister and her Alabama relatives into her home, and, after her death, eagerly break into her mysterious upstairs room.

Fully in keeping with the town's invasive aesthetic of observation, the narrator/detective's willingness to pass judgment on all he witnesses so completely overturns the illusion of objectivity that he speaks, if you will, not as the detached soloist of a Greek chorus, but as a prime participant in the tragic drama he relates. The ways of interpreting Emily's decision to murder Homer are numerous, as the many critical pieces on the story bear out. For simple clarification, they can be summarized along two lines. One group finds the murder growing out of Emily's demented attempt to forestall the inevitable passage of time—toward her abandonment by Homer, toward her own death, and toward the steady encroachment of the North and the New South on something loosely defined as the "tradition" of the Old South. Another view sees the murder in more psychological terms. It grows out of Emily's complex relationship to her father, who, by elevating her above all of the eligible men of Jefferson, insured that to yield to what one commentator called the "normal emotions" associated with desire, his daughter had to "retreat into a marginal world, into fantasy" (O'Connor 184).

These lines of interpretation complement more than critique each other, and collectively they offer an interesting range of views on the story. Together, they de-emphasize the element of detection, viewing the murder and its solution not as the central action but as manifestations of the principal element, the decline of the Grierson lineage and all it represents. Recognizing the way in which the story makes use of the detective genre, however, adds another interpretive layer to the story by making the narrator—or more precisely, the collective sensibility the narrator represents—a central player in the pattern of action. Detective stories typically place less emphasis on the crime, the criminal, and the victim than on the detective. Detectives such as Dupin, Holmes, Poirot, Sergeant Cuff, Dr. Gideon Fell, and Nero Wolfe may be detached from the society they observe but they still rest at the center of the author's narrative world. Faulkner bends his narrator/detective in some obvious ways away from these more traditional examples. Strictly speaking, his detective is no nearer Poe's Dupin than Emily is a re-creation of Minister D, the master criminal of "The Purloined Letter." But the narrative is an ongoing investigation of Emily's life and the narrator is the principal detective in this investigation.

Much of the story's action is centered around the combination of Emily's desire to remain isolated and the narrator and his fellow townsfolk's refusal to honor that desire. Consider, among many examples, the language of intrusion and judgment implied in the following passages.

They were not surprised when the smell developed.

That was when people had begun to feel really sorry for her. People in our town ... believed that the Griersons held themselves a little too high for what they really were.

So when she got to be thirty and was still single, we were not pleased exactly, but vindicated.

When her father died, it got about that the house was all that was left to her; and in a way, people were glad. At last they could pity Miss Emily.

We did not say she was crazy then. We believed she had to do that.

As soon as the old people said, "Poor Emily," the whispering began.

She carried her head high enough—even when we believed that she was fallen.

And finally, the story's most startling and significant statement made shortly after Emily purchases rat poison: "So the next day we all said, 'she will kill herself'; and *we said it would be the best thing*" (my emphasis, 121–26). The town, it is evident, has made Emily its obsession, with every detail of her life subject to discussion, speculation and assessment. Without means by which to carry on her affair in public (and a noticeably diminishing lack of interest on Homer's part, since he "liked men" and was not ready to settle down), Emily insures her isolation in a cunningly ironic and comic verbal reversal on the town's recommendation of suicide; she herself kills Homer Barron, and from the town's point of view, it was the best thing.

"The detective novel features two expulsions of 'bad' or socially unfit characters: the victim and the murderer" (Grella 49). In the context of the genre, as George Grella describes it, Homer is a classic victim because he is guilty of an unpardonable crime against the community. He was born in the North, which in the world of Jefferson, Mississippi, since the days of the Civil War, has been a capital offense. After he disappears, no more attention is paid to him ("that was the last we saw of Homer Barron" [127]). The town's purported lack of interest can be formally explained as a crafty plotting device of Faulkner's to draw suspicion away from the existence of the murder (which is further obscured by the temporal shifts in the narrative). To this end, the narrator casually mentions Homer for the first time in the story as the "sweetheart" who "deserted" Emily.

But it is also significant that as a northerner—as well as a common day-laborer—Homer represents the kind of unwelcomed resident and ineligible mate the town wants to repel if it is to preserve its traditional arrangements. His very proximity to Emily is, according to Jefferson's ladies, "a disgrace to the town and a bad example to the young people" (126). Homer is, to echo Grella's apt phrase, "an exceptionally murderable man" (49)—a victim whose disappearance invites a conspiracy of silence.

The very failure of the narrator and the town to "solve" the crime until the murderer herself has died indicates much about the true nature of the society in which the murder occurred. If we assume that the narrator/detective and other townsfolk know about the crime (although the textual evidence for this can only be ambiguously inferred), we also realize that for the town to reveal Emily's crime and indicate what it will do in response is far more complicated than silently ignoring the entire matter. For the people of Jefferson, the illusion of *noblesse oblige* is to be preserved at all costs, whether it means remitting Emily's taxes, inviting her Alabama kinfolk to come to Jefferson and regulate her embarrassing courtship, or ignoring a murder by passing off the foul smell emanating from her house shortly after Homer's disappearance as "probably just a snake or a rat."

This conveniently evasive speculation comes from Judge Stevens (whose son is likely Gavin Stevens, the detective/lawyer/chess aficionado in *Knight's Gambit*). The statement can be read several ways. It emphasizes Emily's status as a Poe-like "least-likely" criminal, a misfit so unsuited for the role of murderer that the town's leading citizen does not suspect her. In this light, the Judge's pronouncement is not a red herring, but its opposite, a statement that has the effect of allowing a very real clue to be introduced before allowing a purportedly disinterested observer to shift the narrative's emphasis away from the crime. However, it can also be suggested that, given the facts at hand (e.g., Emily's resistance to allowing her father to be buried and Stevens' reluctance to accuse a "lady" of smelling bad), Stevens' statement is not the naive observation of a casual onlooker but a conveniently calculating means on his part of preserving order, glossing over the rather obvious fact that a well-known citizen has a murder victim rotting inside her house. Where the reader stands in relation to the very tangible clue of the smell depends on his or her willingness to accept the judge's explanation at face value. Like the best detective writers, Faulkner is able to offer pieces of information about the crime, thus putting the careful reader on equal footing with characters in the story, but to do so in such a way as to delay the obvious solution until more substantial proof of the murder comes forth.

That proof comes in the story's final three paragraphs, beginning with the one-sentence paragraph: "The man himself lay in the bed." The crime is both confirmed and solved; the detective pattern is compressed into one climactic scene, which inventively re-imagines a version of Poe's "locked room" mystery, "The Murders in the Rue Morgue." In the classic locked-room story, Dupin unravels the story behind a mother and daughter's murder, which has occurred in an apartment where all the windows and doors are sealed from the inside. In Faulkner's version, a victim's body is similarly discovered inside a mysterious upstairs room, whose door has to be broken down to gain admittance. But since the killer's identity and the mechanism of the murder are readily apparent, the narrator's puzzle is not solved simply by answering "who done it" and "how she done it." The narrator has the more challenging goal of comprehending the gruesome spectacle in the context of the town's obsession with Emily's entire life. This is accomplished with the minuscule clue of a single strand of hair, a temporarily "hidden object" that once detected sets Emily's disturbed mind state into stark relief and provides the town with just the kind of hindsight evidence it needs to justify all of the attention it paid to her over the years.

Finally, in a single sentence, Faulkner skillfully brings the mystery to a close and leaves the reader to reflect upon the narrator/detective's involvement in Emily's deranged decision to murder Homer Barron. As an inventive precursor to Faulkner's own later detective characters, this narrator is an example of how the author, rather than simply mimicking other detective stories, re-worked the classical devices of detection to suit his own ends. "A Rose for Emily" is a notable example of Faulkner's talent for taking the raw materials of his surroundings and working them into original forms—whether this meant drawing from his literary antecedents, re-configuring actual events, or delving into his own considerable imagination. John T. Irwin, in his discussion of *Knight's Gambit*, sets Faulkner next to Poe as a "worthy successor" and a "formidable competitor to the [detective] genre's originator" (173). When viewed as a detective story, "A Rose for Emily" helps buttress this claim and thereby furthers our appreciation of Faulkner's lifelong interest in laying out and then solving the many curious mysteries of what he famously termed his "own little postage stamp of native soil" (qtd. in Minter 76).

NOTES

1. For discussions of Faulkner's debt to Poe, see especially Cawelti, 134; Irwin; and Stronks, 11.
2. *Sanctuary* exhibits its own interesting connections to the classical detective story. In his famous 1933 preface to the novel, French novelist André Malraux remarked that *Sanctuary* was "a novel with a detective-story atmosphere but without detectives"; qtd. in Sundquist, 47.
3. For a thorough discussion of Faulkner and popular short fiction see Matthews, 3-37.
4. All subsequent quotes from the primary text are from *Collected Stories of William Faulkner*, 119-30, and will be cited internally by page number.
5. In the Merrill Literary Casebook series for "A Rose for Emily," editor M. Thomas Inge reprints four articles that posit slightly different time-lines, all of which focus on the story's chronology: see 34, 50-53, 83, 84-86, 90-92.

WORKS CITED

Cawelti, John G. *Adventure, Mystery, and Romance: Formula Stories as Art and Popular Culture*. Chicago: U of Chicago P, 1976.
Cullen, John B., and Floyd C. Watkins, *Old Times in the Faulkner Country*. Chapel Hill: U of North Carolina P, 1961.
Faulkner, William. *Collected Stories of William Faulkner*. New York: Vintage, 1977.
Going, William T. "Chronology in Teaching 'A Rose for Emily.'" *A Rose for Emily*. Ed. M. Thomas Inge. Columbus: Merrill, 1970. 50-53.
Grella, George. "Murder and Manners: The Formal Detective Novel." *Dimensions*

of *Detective Fiction*. Ed. Larry N. Landrum, Pat Browne, and Ray B. Browne. Bowling Green, OH: Bowling Green State U Popular P, 1976. 37–57.

Howe, Irving. *William Faulkner: A Critical Study*. New York: Vintage, 1962.

Inge, M. Thomas, ed. *A Rose for Emily*. Columbus: Merrill, 1970.

Irwin, John T. "*Knight's Gambit*: Poe, Faulkner, and the Tradition of the Detective Story." *Faulkner and the Short Story*. Ed. Evans Harrington and Ann J. Abadie. Jackson: U of Mississippi P, 1992. 149–73.

Karl, Frederick R. *William Faulkner: An American Writer*. New York: Weidenfeld and Nicolson, 1989.

Matthews, John T. "Shortened Stories: Faulkner and the Market." *Faulkner and the Short Story*. Ed. Evans Harrington and Ann J. Abadie. Jackson: UP of Mississippi. 3–37.

Minter, David. *William Faulkner: His Life and Work*. Baltimore: Johns Hopkins UP, 1980.

O'Connor, William. "The State of Faulkner Criticism." *Sewanee Review* 60 (1952): 184.

Stronks, James. "A Poe Source for Faulkner? 'To Helen' and 'A Rose for Emily.'" *Poe Newsletter* I (Apr. 1968): 11.

Sundquist, Eric. *Faulkner: The House Divided*. Baltimore: Johns Hopkins UP, 1983.

## GEORGE L. DILLON

### Styles of Reading*

One of the things readers do with stories is to talk about them. These stories have not said it all, and readers derive evident pleasure from completing them, commenting on them, making them their own in various ways. Christine Brooke-Rose has recently called attention to the strategic incompleteness of good stories—spelling everything out treats the reader as stupid—and has suggested a classification of stories according to the tasks they leave to readers, or in which they entangle readers.[1] If we look at actual, published discussions of a story, however, we find no two of them answering the same set of questions, which suggests that we should look for questions (pre)inscribed in the reader as well as the text—the text, it is a matter of fact, has not very narrowly constrained the set of questions the readers have posed. As soon as we raise the matter of the actual performance of readers, however, we encounter a plethora of variables, and it has become something of a fashion in discussions of reading to enumerate them, often, it seems, to frighten scholars back to the study of narrative competence and the ways texts constrain, or should constrain interpretations. . . . If we are concerned with how people actually do read stories, however, these lists outline an area for research. . . . Perhaps there are underlying regularities which *in fact* shape readers' performances; perhaps there are none. In this article, I will examine readings of Faulkner's "A Rose for Emily," and focus initially on one area of variation—the answers readers have given to questions about the chron-

---

* From *Poetics Today* 3.2 (1982): 77–88. Copyright 1982 by The Porter Institute for Poetics and Semiotics, Tel Aviv University. Reprinted by permission.

ological sequence, or "event chain," of the story—to see how wild the variation is and what hope there may be of identifying regularities of performance.

One reason for focusing on event chains is that these have been among the most intensively studied of the many aspects of story comprehension.... Readers employ two basic operations in building event chains: connection and inference. No story I know of spells out all of the terms and connections in an event chain (Miss Emily's motive for murdering Homer Barron, for example, is left for the reader to infer, as is the connection of the arsenic to the murder), and a story that did spell them all out would treat the reader as inconceivably stupid. Two distinctions are in order here: event chains are not precisely chronological, though I think they do correspond closely to ... chronological sequences, that is, a certain sequentiality is implicit in the notions of motive, action, cause, response, and consequence, but not necessarily clock or calendar time, nor do pieces of the overall chain have to be strictly ordered; different sequences may overlap. This point is quite clear in regard to "A Rose for Emily": it seems possible to establish a chronology of the story that orders all of its major incidents, though it is very difficult to do so,[2] and it is not necessary to have worked out such a time scheme in order to get major portions of the event chain straight. Second, event chains are not "plots." ... That is, they are shapeless and open-ended; they do not account for any sense of beginning, climax, or conclusion. ... [E]vent chains are part of the comprehension of all narratives; indeed, of all happenings, not just stories....

When we survey the published criticism of "A Rose for Emily," we find a large and bewildering array of questions about the event chain that have been answered. These include:

1. Why weren't there suitable suitors for Emily?
2. How does Emily respond to being denied suitors?
3. Why does Emily take up with Homer Barron?
4. What happened when he left? Did he abandon her? Why did he come back?
5. Why did she kill him?
6. Why did the smell disappear after only one week?
7. What did Miss Emily think of the men scattering lime around her house?
8. How did the hair come to be on the pillow? How much hair is a *Strand*?
9. What was her relationship to Tobe?
10. Did she lie beside the corpse? How often, for what period of years?
11. Why did she not leave the house for the last decade of her life?
12. Did she not know Colonel Sartoris had been dead ten years when she faced down the Aldermen?
13. How crazy was she (unable to distinguish fantasy from reality)?
14. Why does she allow so much dust in her house?

There is also one question that has been asked but not answered, as far as I know: What transpired when the Baptist minister visited her? As the specialists in story comprehension have noted, once we realize that a Story Comprehender must have the power to carry out inferences in order to comprehend even the simplest story and give it that power, the problem becomes one of limiting the inferences drawn to some "relevant" subset of the possible ones.... [B]ut it is not clear how to apply this principle [of relevance] to the fourteen questions and answers, since every one of those questions was answered by at least one critic who felt the answer was relevant to the interpretation of the story—relevant to determining her motives, naming her actions, and so on. Of course, some of these event-chain inferences are stimulated by the particular interpretation a critic is putting forth, but there does not seem to be any basis on which to separate those inferences that are made independent of an interpretation from those which are not.... People do not agree on the story to then disagree on the interpretation. It is simply not true that, as Wolfgang Iser claims, "On the level of plot, then, there is a high degree of intersubjective consensus," with subjective variation arising at the level of significance.[3] In fact, when we look at the list of questions that have been answered, the construction of event chains seems wildly unconstrained.

If we look at whole readings, however, some system and pattern does emerge. There are two surveys of the criticism of this story, and both find it fairly easy to group the readings into three classes (though the classes are somewhat differently defined).[4] We could group the readings according to what one might call "approaches," suggesting by that term some set of general questions readers taking a particular approach tend to pose of texts they read. This notion can be pushed in two, opposite directions. Taking it one way, we could argue that the variation considered so far does not directly reflect the way readers read but the way critics write about stories when they have an eye toward publication.... Taken the other way, these approaches could be viewed as personal styles or preferences in reading that happen to have acquired some public sanction. We generally have some style of reading before we know much about "approaches," after all, though we may learn other questions to ask when we study literature. In any case, one must have learned the approach in order to use it.... Some light on the matter is shed, I think, by the very copious transcripts of interviews with undergraduate English majors about "A Rose for Emily" published by Norman Holland in *5 Readers Reading*.

Holland's students also show three distinct approaches, and these approaches match up with the types of approaches in the published criticism[, t]hough ... they do seem to be giving what they feel are their own responses and to be responding in somewhat original—but consistent—ways to his questions. Also, ... the criticism they chose to be influenced by as much reflects their cognitive styles as it determines them. Holland's study strongly suggests that there are styles of reading stories, characteristic ways that readers interrogate texts, and that the "approaches" in the criticism are indeed rooted in the critics' own styles of reading and appeal to like-minded readers. I will illustrate this correspondence for three basic styles, which I will call the Character-Action-Moral (CAM) style, the Digger for Secrets style, and the Anthropologist style.

The CAM style differs markedly from the other two in treating the meaning (or significance) as more or less evident in the story: the reader makes the text his own, and makes the reading more apparent, by elaborating the event chain in the direction of the main character's traits, motives, thoughts, responses, and choices. To do this, CAM readers treat the world of the text as an extension or portion of the real world, the characters as real persons, so that we will recognize the experience of characters as being like our own experience; hence it can be understood or explained just as we would understand our own experience. Thus, the inferences they draw are based on commonsense notions of the way the world is, people are, etc. The other two styles appropriate the text not by immersion, but by analytic distance, probing and abstracting behind what is said; they assume that the world of the text is an edited version of our world—a *structure* rather than a glimpse or fragment. The CAM reader works by amalgamating the story into the body of his own beliefs and practical axioms about how life is or should be, the analytic styles by postulating the otherness or strangeness of the text.

The standard CAM reading contains lists of traits that account for the actions of the main character in a straightforward evaluative fashion.... The actions are assumed to be pointers toward relatively permanent and pervasive characteristics, and one often finds "it could be otherwise" speculations in CAM readings (e.g., "A Rose for Emily" could have had a happy outcome if Homer Barron had been a marrying man—West;[5] if another man had proposed to Emily after she finished with Homer, she would have declined the offer because she felt herself already married—Sam, in Holland [pp. 138-39]). That is, the notion of character seems to presuppose the freedom of individuals to choose their responses to their situations, and stories like "A Rose for Emily" are treated as collisions between characters and situations—as *tragedies*, in the traditional Butcher/Bradley sense:

> Perhaps the horrible and the admirable aspects of Miss Emily's final deed arise from the same basic fact of her character: she insists on meeting the world on her own terms. She never cringes, she never begs for sympathy, she refuses to shrink into an amiable old maid, she never accepts the community's ordinary judgments or values. This independence of spirit and pride can, and does in her case, twist the individual into a sort of monster, but, at the same time, this refusal to accept the hero values carries with it a dignity and courage.[6] ...

... We can see here the way the common notion of tragedy directs the reading toward character analysis; it also introduces three other questions, namely, those of awareness, tragic flaw, and moral. The evoking or constructing of character seems to lead directly to inference o[f] the character's thoughts. When done naïvely, the results are fairly obtrusive, as when Holland's Sam says Emily has an awareness that "things were moving on, that things were changing, and yet, a similar awareness that she was unable to change along with them" (p. 137). More subtle is a partial merging of reader's and character's points of view. The reader talks about the character in terms the character himself might use: "She lost her honor, and what else could she do but keep him [Homer] forever, make him hers in the only way she possibly could?" (Sam. p. 137)....

This construction of an inner logic for the character is essential to the drawing of the moral: once we have realized the character's viewpoint, we can see the fatal flaw, the impulses or tendencies in ourselves that we should not give in to. If this immersion and identification with the character (which is plainly the identification of the character with the reader, in terms of himself) fails, ... the CAM reader must direct his attention away from the details that suggest Miss Emily is not "like us" (above all, the questions about sleeping next to the corpse).

In sum, then, the CAM style is not afraid to state the obvious; it does not try to be ingenious or clever, but solid and useful; it does not assume the author is fashioning puzzles for us to solve, or playing tricks on us. The story conceals nothing—it is merely, of necessity, incomplete. For Diggers for Secrets, however, the story enwraps secrets, the narrator hides them[,] ... and the reader must uncover them. The title of Edward Stone's *A Certain Morbidness* suggests how he will read "A Rose for Emily."[7] Diggers for Secrets expect narrators to screen us from the "reality,"

> But when, during her early spinsterhood, her father dies and she refuses for three days to hand his putrefying body over for burial, we are shocked by this irrational action, even though in keeping with his standpoint of noncommitment Faulkner tries to minimize it ("We remembered all the young men her father had driven away, and we knew that with nothing left, she would have to cling to that which had robbed her, as people will"). (Stone, 96)

and expect the author only to give us clues:

> For Faulkner, so far from withholding all clues to Homer Barron's whereabouts, scatters them with a precise prodigality; since his is a story primarily of character, it is to his purpose to saturate our awareness of Miss Emily's abnormality as he goes, so that the last six shocking words merely put the final touch on that purpose. (p. 65)

Sebastian, who is Holland's Digger, also comments on the evenhandedness of the narrator, whom he describes as switching sides (p. 177), and he too finds the maxim about holding on to that which robbed her a screen rather than an explanation: "Shouldn't have put that in, Bill," he says (p. 186). He even proposes to see through the author: "I wanted to see what unconscious things he would reveal about the South" (p. 186).

When Diggers for Secrets explain the psychology of characters, they employ the categories of depth and abnormal psychology ... and frequently "diagnose" motives the characters would not be aware of and in terms they might well not accept. Sebastian uses the terms *sexuality*, *obsession*, and *necrophilia* heavily and confidently, but he still falls short, in eloquence at least, of ... Edward Stone:

> Her passionate, almost sexual relationship with her dead father forces her to distrust the living body of Homer and to kill him so that he will resemble the dead father she can never forget.
> Not only does this obsessed spinster continue for some years to share a marriage bed with the body of the man she poisoned—she evidently derives either erotic gratification or spiritual sustenance (both?) from these ghastly nuptials. She becomes, in short, a necrophile or a veritable saprophytic organism; for we learn that the "slender figure in white" that was the young Miss Emily becomes, as though with the middle-aged propriety that the marriage customarily brings, fat! (Stone, 96)

... In a similar vein, Sebastian draws numerous inferences about the Negro servant Tobe's complicity in Emily's crime, about her "affair" with Homer, about the details of her sleeping with his corpse (how can a woman perform an act of necrophilia on a man?), and so on.

Symbolism being a ready avenue to non-obvious meanings, these readers find symbolic significances and secrets in details that the CAM readers either pass over or handle prosaically: Miss Emily's house for Stone is an isolated fortress, a forbidden, majestic stronghold; ... for Sebastian, the title is richly ironic, "an unforgiveable irony in one sense: 'A Rose by any other name would not smell half as sweet!' There's not much sweetness about *her* rose. So I think the title refers to the decomposition of living matter, and so I take it ironically" (p. 182). ... One expects such ironies from an author presumed to conceal.

An interesting feature of "A Rose for Emily" is that it contains not only a literal hidden secret (which Sebastian objects to as a bit too overt) but a "reader" as well (the narrator). That is, people who habitually look for the dirty reality behind appearances are open to the charge of prurience, a charge that would be easy to level at these readers, and one that the story conveniently allows us to displace onto the narrator ("the community") instead. So the taint of corruption spreads to the town, all these readers say, but, of course, not to *us*.[8] Thus in a sense, the abnormal becomes normal, and the story acquires the universality that raises it from case history to literature. The search for the abnormal and perverse finally leads back to the unacknowledged parts of our selves.

Though the Diggers for Secrets make use of abstractive codes that explain what is going on in the story, their interest in "what's really going on" does, as we have seen, lead to inferences elaborating the event chain. The third group, the Anthropologists, have much less to say about events than either of the first two groups. Their interest, rather, is in identifying the cultural norms and values that explain what characters indisputably do and say. Like Diggers for Secrets, these readers go beneath the surface and state things that are implicit and not said, though what they bring out is not a secret, but the general principles and values which the story illustrates as an example. To some degree, early readings that talk of a conflict in "A Rose for Emily" between the North and the South, or old versus new South, outline this approach, but these readings tended to be brief and schematic, as if critics were not willing to reopen old wounds.[9] And, too, Faulkner was on record as not intending such an interpretation.[10] When a reader is especially engaged in the critique of the norms and values of American society, however, the story takes on interest as an extended exemplum. Thus the two instances of this style of reading, Holland's Shep and Judith Fetterley, are both radicals. For Shep, who is Holland's example of a sixties radical, the characters and events of the story exemplify forces of social struggle—class struggle, racial struggle, and above all the struggle between true and false values. Thus he says Emily's father represents the old code, the dead hand of the past; Homer Barron represents the forces of aimless technology; Emily herself was, he says, "perpetuating the same ethos in which her father lived" (p. 61); "In a way, Miss Emily is a descendant of the culture hero, except that she's a descendant of the culture hero in his waning phase" (p. 166); "They had a very rigid formal code and it was perhaps very much a dead code by the time she got her hands on it, but it represented something which the new people weren't able to offer an adequate substitute for" (p. 161). Proceeding at such a lofty plane, he is fairly indifferent to the detailed goings-on of the event chain, though he does infer Emily's response to the lime-scattering incident—namely, scorn for the men—and he is willing to speculate under Holland's urging. He offers two motives for the murder, first, simple revenge, to keep him from leaving her; but he also evolves a second, mythic explanation, which I quote at some length:

> She can reverse the social decay process by putting her lover, representative of all of them ["the newcomers"] through a physical decay process and coming to relish the sight. This would also give some sort of, quote, explanation, unquote, for her necrophilic hangups. The fact that she wanted her father's body around to . . . preserve it from decay—she was denying the end of the line thing symbolized by putting it underground and letting the earth have it. (p. 171)

... So there is a double or triple pattern of explanation here—commonsense psychology (she wanted revenge), operation of social forces, and mythic patterns; these explanations seem somewhat detached from each other and so the reading is not completely totalized.

If Shep is an example of a sixties radical, then Judith Fetterley, in her book *The Resisting Reader*,[11] represents a kind of seventies version of the same basic style of reading. Fetterley focuses on stating the social norms and codes that explain the events of the story—there is very little in the way of constructive activity of motives, actions, responses, and consequences, except for a brief discussion of the lime-scattering incident. She also offers two motives for the murder: first, that Emily murdered Homer because she had to have a man (thus illustrating the brainwashing of the code); but she also offers the following symbolic/mythic account:

> Having been consumed by her father, Emily in turn feeds off Homer Barron, becoming, after his death, suspiciously fat. Or, to put it another way, it is as if, after her father's death, she has reversed his act of incorporating her by incorporating and becoming him, metamorphosed from the slender figure in white to the obese figure in black whose hair is "a vigorous iron-gray, like the hair of an active man." She has taken into herself the violence in him which thwarted her and has reenacted it upon Homer Barron. (pp. 42–43)

On first reading, this seems very much like Stone's celebration of Faulkner's "ghoulish evolution" of the gothic, but on closer examination, the passage is really suggesting a crude form of retributive justice, a pointed, if lurid, warning to the upholders of patriarchy. It is striking that the same elementary operations—*connecting* her growing fat to Homer's murder and *inferring* a causal link—result in such different explanations.

Like Shep, Fetterley makes heavy use of symbolic interpretation and the logic of example: Emily's confinement by her father represents confinement of women by patriarchy; the remission of taxes signifies continued dependence of women on men; the men's treatment of her, and her ability to buffalo them and commit murder without punishment, are explained in terms of the code of the "lady" who is assumed to be out of touch with reality, and must be kept so; Emily represents the town itself, and in discovering her nature, they discover their own. The focus of Fetterley's interest is in flushing the codes out of hiding and explaining what happens in terms of them, though it is not a totalizing reading in that she doesn't claim to have explained everything in the story in terms of the codes; this treatment represents the extreme of abstraction away from the events and surface of the story toward allegory and parable. That's what it means to be a Resisting Reader: to refuse to give yourself to the work, to accept any of its givens—and in fact, to bring precisely those axioms into question.

Clearly, then, these three styles or approaches are asking different questions of the text, and constructing what are to various degrees different stories in the course of answering them. . . . Readers predisposed to a certain style of reading [however] will, when faced with the same text, come up with some very similar stories along with some very similar explanations.

. . . [T]he notion that these styles are, or can become, general patterns of thinking, rather than a learned decorum of literary criticism, seems to derive support from the consideration that we also exhibit differences of styles in thinking about real people and events. We think of ourselves and others as conscious, moral agents shaping our destinies in situations benign and hostile, but also as mysteries to ourselves and others, and/or as enacting typical social roles and attitudes. There is some basis for concluding that we understand literature and life in the same or similar ways, and that some of the ways we read literature will be applied in reading others of life's texts.

## NOTES

1. Brooke-Rose, "The Readerhood of Man," in *The Reader in the Text*, ed. Susan R. Suleiman and Inge Crosman (Princeton: Princeton University Press, 1980), 120–48.
2. At least five chronologies have appeared in print, all differing: William T. Going, "Chronology in Teaching 'A Rose for Emily.'" *Exercise Exchange* 5 (1958): 8–11; Robert W. Woodward, "The Chronology of 'A Rose for Emily.'" *Exercise Exchange* 13 (1966): 17–19; Paul D. McGlynn, "The Chronology of 'A Rose for Emily,'" *Studies in Short Fiction* 6 (1969): 461–62; Helen E. Nebeker, "Chronology Revisited," *Studies in Short Fiction* 8 (1971): 471–73; and Menakhem Perry, "Literary Dynamics: How the Order of a Text Creates Its Meaning," *Poetics Today* 1 (1979): 35–63; 311–61.
3. Wolfgang Iser, *The Act of Reading* (Baltimore: Johns Hopkins University Press, 1978), 123. Iser's definition of *significance* as "the reader's absorption of the meaning into his own existence" (p. 151) leaves us in need of an intermediate term between it and *plot* (event chains)—something like *explanation*, which is constructed to account for events (e.g., in terms of character traits, maxims of behavior, mythic patterns, etc.) but which is not necessarily the amalgamation of the story into the reader's subjectivity. For one thing, explanation need not be evaluative. I am using *interpretation* in a broad sense here to mean the reader's commentary minus any plot summary, though even the latter is usually tailored to fit the commentary.
4. See Norman Holland, *5 Readers Reading* (New Haven: Yale University Press, 1975), 21–24 (cited in the text as Holland, or Holland's Sam); and Perry, "Literary Dynamics," 62–63 et passim.
5. Ray B. West, "Atmosphere and Theme in Faulkner's 'A Rose for Emily,'" in *William Faulkner: Four Decades of Criticism*, ed. Linda W. Wagner (East Lansing: Michigan State University Press, 1973), 192–98. Cited in the text as West.
6. Cleanth Brooks and Robert Penn Warren, *Understanding Fiction* (New York: Crofts, 1948), ... [413].
7. Stone, *A Certain Morbidness* (Carbondale: Southern Illinois University Press, 1969). Cited in the text as Stone.
8. For Ruth Sullivan, however, the narrator is a prying, probing voyeur, and so are we readers. See "The Narrators in 'A Rose for Emily,'" *Journal of Narrative Technique* 1 (1971): 159–78.
9. Frederick Gwynn and Joseph L. Blotner, *Faulkner in the University* (New York: Vintage Books, 1965), 47–48.
10. There is one style which I find attested only in Holland's interviews (and in some of the papers of David Bleich's students), that we might call the Visualizer style, the style of Holland's Sandra, whose comments ... are strongly weighted to descriptions of characters' expressions and feelings, decors and

other physical details and commentary on the suitability of words, images and tonal effects in the narration. This is perhaps the most surface or craft-conscious of the styles, and the reason it does not appear in the published readings is that it is more a style of appreciation than explanation, or, to put it another way, it is more concerned with explaining the details of the style and presentation . . . than with the story. . . .

11. Fetterley, *The Resisting Reader* (Bloomington and London: Indiana University Press, 1978).

## JUDITH FETTERLEY
### *A Rose for "A Rose for Emily"**

In "A Rose for Emily" . . . grotesque reality . . . becomes explicit. Justifying Faulkner's use of the grotesque has been a major concern of critics who have written on the story. If, however, one approaches "A Rose for Emily" from a feminist perspective, one notices that the grotesque aspects of the story are a result of its violation of the expectations generated by the conventions of sexual politics. The ending shocks us not simply by its hint of necrophilia; more shocking is the fact that it is a woman who provides the hint. It is one thing for Poe to spend his nights in the tomb of Annabel Lee and another thing for Miss Emily Grierson to deposit a strand of iron-gray hair on the pillow beside the rotted corpse of Homer Barron. Further, we do not expect to discover that a woman has murdered a man. . . . To reverse [the] "natural" pattern inevitably produces the grotesque.

Faulkner, however, is not interested in invoking the kind of grotesque which is the consequence of reversing the clichés of sexism for the sake of a cheap thrill. . . . Rather, Faulkner invokes the grotesque in order to illuminate and define the true nature of the conventions on which it depends. "A Rose for Emily" is a story not of a conflict between the South and the North or between the old order and the new; it is a story of the patriarchy North and South, new and old, and of the sexual conflict within it. As Faulkner himself has implied,[1] it is a story of a woman victimized and betrayed by the system of sexual politics, who nevertheless has discovered, within the structures that victimize her, sources of power for herself. . . . "A Rose for Emily" is the story of how to murder your gentleman caller and get away with it. Faulkner's story is an analysis of how men's attitudes toward women turn back upon themselves; it is a demonstration of the thesis that it is impossible to oppress without in turn being oppressed, it is impossible to kill without creating the conditions for your own murder. "A Rose for Emily" is the story of a *lady* and of her revenge for that grotesque identity.

"When Miss Emily Grierson died, our whole town went to her funeral." The public and communal nature of Emily's funeral, a festival that brings the town together, clarifying its social relationships and revitalizing its sense of the past, indicates her central role in Jefferson. Alive, Emily is town property and the subject of shared speculation; dead, she is town history and the subject of legend.

---

* From *The Resisting Reader: A Feminist Approach to American Fiction*, by Judith Fetterley (Bloomington and London: Indiana UP, 1978). Copyright 1978 by Judith Fetterley. Reprinted by permission.

It is her value as a symbol, however obscure and however ambivalent, of something that is of central significance to the identity of Jefferson and to the meaning of its history that compels the narrator to assume a communal voice to tell her story. For Emily... is a man-made object, a cultural artifact, and what she is reflects and defines the culture that has produced her.

The history the narrator relates to us reveals Jefferson's continuous emotional involvement with Emily. Indeed, though she shuts herself up in a house which she rarely leaves and which no one enters, her furious isolation is in direct proportion to the town's obsession with her:... she is the object of incessant attention; her every act is immediately consumed by the town for gossip and seized on to justify their interference in her affairs. Her private life becomes a public document that the town folk feel free to interpret at will, and they are alternately curious, jealous, spiteful, pitying, partisan, proud, disapproving, admiring, and vindicated. Her funeral is not simply a communal ceremony; it is also the climax of their invasion of her private life and the logical extension of their voyeuristic attitude toward her. Despite the narrator's demurral, getting inside Emily's house is the all-consuming desire of the town's population, both male and female; while the men may wait a little longer, their motive is still prurient curiosity: "Already we knew that there was one room in that region above stairs which no one had seen in forty years, and which would have to be forced. They waited until Miss Emily was decently in the ground before they opened it."

In a context in which the overtones of violation and invasion are so palpable, the word "decently" has that ironic ring which gives the game away. When the men finally do break down the door, they find that Emily has satisfied their prurience with a vengeance and in doing so has created for them a mirror image of themselves. The true nature of Emily's relation to Jefferson is contained in the analogies between what those who break open that room see in it and what has brought them there to see it. The perverse, violent, and grotesque aspects of the sight of Homer Barron's rotted corpse in a room decked out for a bridal and now faded and covered in dust reflects back to them the perverseness of their own prurient interest in Emily, the violence implicit in their continued invasions of her life, and the grotesqueness of the symbolic artifact they have made of her—their monument, their idol, their lady. Thus, the figure that Jefferson places at the center of its legendary history does indeed contain the clue to the meaning of that history—a history which began long before Emily's funeral and long before Homer Barron's disappearance or appearance and long before Colonel Sartoris' fathering of edicts and remittances. It is recorded in that emblem which lies at the heart of the town's memory and at the heart of patriarchal culture: "We had long thought of them as a tableau, Miss Emily a slender figure in white in the background, her father a spraddled silhouette in the foreground, his back to her and clutching a horsewhip, the two of them framed by the back-flung front door."

The importance of Emily's father in shaping the quality of her life is insistent throughout the story. Even in her death the force of his presence is felt; above her dead body sits "the crayon face of her father musing profoundly," symbolic of the degree to which he has dominated and shadowed her life, "as if that quality of her father which had thwarted her woman's life so many times had been too virulent and too furious to die." The violence of this consuming relationship is made explicit in the imagery of the tableau. Although the violence is apparently directed outward—the upraised horsewhip against the would-be suitor—the real object of it is the woman-daughter, forced into the background and dominated by the phallic figure of the spraddled father whose back is turned on her and who prevents her from getting out at the same time that he prevents them from getting in. [Emily's] . . . spatial confinement [is] . . . a metaphor for her psychic confinement: her identity is determined by the constructs of her father's mind, and she can no more escape from his creation of her as "a slender figure in white" than she can escape his house.

What is true for Emily in relation to her father is equally true for her in relation to Jefferson: her status as a lady is a cage from which she cannot escape. To them she is always *Miss* Emily; she is never referred to and never thought of as otherwise. In omitting her title from his, Faulkner emphasizes the point that the real violence done to Emily is in making her a "Miss"; the omission is one of his roses for her. Because she is *Miss* Emily *Grierson*, Emily's father dresses her in white, places her in the background, and drives away her suitors. Because she is Miss Emily Grierson, the town invests her with that communal significance which makes her the object of their obsession and the subject of their incessant scrutiny. And because she is a lady, the town is able to impose a particular code of behavior on her ("But there were still others, older people, who said that even grief could not cause a real lady to forget *noblesse oblige*") and to see in her failure to live up to that code an excuse for interfering in her life. As a lady, Emily is venerated, but veneration results in the more telling emotions of envy and spite: "It was another link between the gross, teeming world and the high and mighty Griersons"; "People . . . believed that the Griersons held themselves a little too high for what they really were." The violence implicit in the desire to see the monument fall and reveal itself for clay suggests the violence inherent in the original impulse to venerate.

The violence behind veneration is emphasized through another telling emblem in the story. Emily's position as a hereditary obligation upon the town dates from "that day in 1894 when Colonel Sartoris, the mayor—he who fathered the edict that no Negro woman should appear on the streets without an apron on—remitted her taxes, the dispensation dating from the death of her father on into perpetuity." The conjunction of these two actions in the same syntactic unit is crucial, for it insists on their essential similarity. It indicates that the impulse to exempt is analogous to the desire to restrict, and that what appears to be a kindness or an act of veneration is in fact an insult. Sartoris' remission of Emily's taxes is a public declaration of the fact that a lady is not considered to be, and hence not allowed or enabled to be, economically independent (consider, in this connection, Emily's lessons in china painting; they are a latter-day version of Sartoris' "charity" and a brilliant image of Emily's economic uselessness). His act is a public statement of the fact that a lady, if she is to survive, must have either husband or father, and that, because Emily has neither, the town must assume responsibility for her. The remission of taxes that defines Emily's status dates from the death of her father, and she is handed over from one patron to the next, the town instead of husband taking on the role of father. Indeed, the use of the word "fathered" in describing Sartoris' behavior as mayor underlines the fact that his chivalric attitude toward Emily is simply a subtler and more dishonest version of her father's horsewhip.

The narrator is the last of the patriarchs who take upon themselves the burden of defining Emily's life, and his violence toward her is the most subtle of all. His tone of incantatory reminiscence and nostalgic veneration seems free of the taint of horsewhip and edict. Yet a thoroughgoing contempt for the "ladies" who spy and pry and gossip out of their petty jealousy and curiosity is one of the clearest strands in the narrator's consciousness. Emily is exempted from the general indictment because she is a *real* lady—that is, eccentric, slightly crazy, obsolete, a "stubborn and coquettish decay," absurd but indulged; "dear, inescapable, impervious, tranquil, and perverse"; indeed, anything and everything but human.

Not only does "A Rose for Emily" expose the violence done to a woman by making her a lady; it also explores the particular form of power the victim gains from this position and can use on those who enact this violence. "A Rose for Emily" is concerned with the consequences of violence for both the violated and the violators. One of the most striking aspects of the story is the disparity between Miss Emily Grierson and the Emily to whom Faulkner gives his rose in ironic imitation of the chivalric behavior the story exposes. The form of Faulkner's title establishes a camaraderie between author and protagonist and signals that a distinction must be made between the story Faulkner is telling and the story the narrator is telling. This distinction is of major importance because it suggests, of course, that the narrator, looking through a patriarchal lens, does not see Emily at all but rather a figment of his own imagination created in conjunction with the cumulative imagination of the town: . . . nobody sees *Emily*. And because nobody sees *her*, she can literally get away with murder. Emily is characterized by her ability to understand and utilize the power that accrues to her from the fact that men do not see her but rather their concept of her: "'I have no taxes in Jefferson. Colonel Sartoris explained it to me. . . . Tobe! . . . Show these gentlemen out." Relying on the conventional assumptions about ladies who are expected to be neither reasonable nor in touch with reality, Emily presents an impregnable front that vanquishes the men "horse and foot, just as she had vanquished their fathers thirty years before." In spite of their "modern" ideas, this new generation, when faced with Miss Emily, are as much bound by the code of gentlemanly behavior as their fathers were ("They rose when she entered"). This code gives Emily a power that renders the gentlemen unable to function in a situation in which a lady neither sits down herself nor asks them to. They are brought to a "stumbling halt" and can do nothing when confronted with her refusal to engage in rational discourse. Their only recourse in the face of such eccentricity is to engage in behavior unbecoming to gentlemen, and Emily can count on their continuing to see themselves as gentlemen and her as a lady and on their returning a verdict of helpless noninterference.

It is in relation to Emily's disposal of Homer Barron, however, that Faulkner demonstrates most clearly the power of conventional assumptions about the nature of ladies to blind the town to what is going on and to allow Emily to murder with impunity. When Emily buys the poison, it never occurs to anyone that she intends to use it on Homer, so strong is the presumption that ladies when jilted commit suicide, not murder. And when her house begins to smell, the women blame it on the eccentricity of having a man servant rather than a woman, "as if a man—any man—could keep a kitchen properly." And when they hint that her eccentricity may have shaded over into madness, "remembering how old lady Wyatt, her great aunt, had gone completely crazy at last." The presumption of madness, that preeminently female response to bereavement, can be used to explain away much in the behavior of ladies whose activities seem a bit odd.

But even more pointed is what happens when the men try not to explain but to do something about the smell: " 'Dammit, sir,' Judge Stevens said, 'will you accuse a lady to her face of smelling bad?' " But if a lady cannot be told that she smells, then the cause of the smell cannot be discovered and so her crime is "perfect." Clearly, the assumptions behind the Judge's outraged retort go beyond the myth that ladies are out of touch with reality. His outburst insists that it is the responsibility of gentlemen to make them so. Ladies must not be confronted with facts; they must be shielded from all that is unpleasant. Thus Colonel Sartoris remits Emily's taxes with a palpably absurd story, designed to protect her from an awareness of her poverty and her dependence on charity, and to protect him from having to confront her with it. And thus Judge Stevens will not confront Emily with the fact that her house stinks, though she is living in it and can hardly be unaware of the odor. Committed as they are to the myth that ladies and bad smells cannot coexist, these gentlemen insulate themselves from reality. And by defining a lady as a subhuman and hence sublegal entity, they have created a situation their laws can't touch. They have made it possible for Emily to be extra-legal: " 'Why, of course,' the druggist said, 'If that's what you want. But the law requires you to tell what you are going to use it for.' Miss Emily just stared at him, her head tilted back in order to look him eye for eye, until he looked away and went and got the arsenic and wrapped it up." And, finally, they have created a situation in which they become the criminals: "So the next night, after midnight, four men crossed Miss Emily's lawn and slunk about the house like burglars." Above them, "her upright torso motionless as that of an idol," sits Emily, observing them act out their charade of chivalry. As they leave, she confronts them with the reality they are trying to protect her from: she turns on the light so that they may see her watching them. One can only wonder at the fact, and regret, that she didn't call the sheriff and have them arrested for trespassing.

Not only is "A Rose for Emily" a supreme analysis of what men do to women by making them ladies; it is also an exposure of how this act in turn defines and recoils upon men. This is the significance of the dynamic that Faulkner establishes between Emily and Jefferson. And it is equally the point of the dynamic implied between the tableau of Emily and her father and the tableau which greets the men who break down the door of that room in the region above the stairs. When the would-be "suitors" finally get into her father's house, they discover the consequences of his oppression of her, for the violence contained in the rotted corpse of Homer Barron is the mirror image of the violence represented in the tableau, the back-flung front door flung back with a vengeance. Having been consumed by her father, Emily in turn feeds off Homer Barron, becoming, after his death, suspiciously fat. Or, to put it another way, it is as if, after her father's death, she has reversed his act of incorporating her by incorporating and becoming him, metamorphosed from the slender figure in white to the obese figure in black whose hair is "a vigorous iron-gray, like the hair of an active man." She has taken into herself the violence in him which thwarted her and has reenacted it upon Homer Barron.

That final encounter, however, is not simply an image of the reciprocity of violence. Its power of definition also derives from its grotesqueness, which makes finally explicit the grotesqueness that has been latent in the description of Emily throughout the story: "Her skeleton was small and spare; perhaps that was why what would have been merely plumpness in another was obesity in her. She looked bloated, like a body long submerged in motionless water, and of that pallid hue. Her eyes, lost in the fatty ridges of her face, looked like two small pieces of coal pressed into a lump of dough." The impact of this description depends on the contrast it establishes between Emily's reality as a fat, bloated figure in black and the conventional image of a lady—expectations that are fostered in the town by its emblematic memory of Emily as a slender figure in white and in us by the narrator's tone of romantic invocation and by the passage itself. Were she not expected to look so different, were her skeleton not small and spare, Emily would not be so grotesque. Thus, the focus is on the grotesqueness that results when stereotypes are imposed upon reality. And the implication of this focus is that the real grotesque is the stereotype itself. If Emily is both lady and grotesque, then the syllogism must be completed thus: the idea of a lady is grotesque. So Emily is metaphor and mirror for the town of Jefferson; and when, at the end, the town folk finally discover who and what she is, they have in fact encountered who and what they are.... [T]he efforts to read "A Rose for Emily" as a parable of the relations between North and South, or as a conflict between an old order and a new, or as a story about the human relation to Time, don't work because the attempt to make Emily representative of such concepts stumbles over the fact that woman's condition is not the "human" condition.[2] To understand Emily's experience requires a primary awareness of the fact that she is a woman.

But, more important, Faulkner provides us with an image of retaliation. [Emily] does not simply acquiesce; she prefers to murder rather than to die. In this respect she is a welcome change from the image of woman as willing victim that fills the pages of our literature.... Nevertheless, Emily's action is still reaction. "A Rose for Emily" exposes the poverty of a situation in which turnabout is the only possibility and in which one's acts are neither self-generated nor self-determined but are simply a response to and a reflection of forces outside oneself. Though Emily may be proud, strong, and indomitable, her murder of Homer Barron is finally an indication of the severely limited nature of the power women can wrest from the system that oppresses them.... Emily's act ... is possible only because it can be kept secret; and it can be kept secret only at the cost of exploiting her image as a lady....

Patriarchal culture is based to a considerable extent on the argument that men and women are made for each other and on the conviction that "masculinity" and "feminity" are the natural reflection of that divinely ordained complement. Yet, if one reads..."A Rose for Emily" as [an] analys[i]s of the consequences of a massive differentiation of everything according to sex, one sees that in reality a sexist culture is one in which men and women are not simply incompatible but murderously so.... Emily murders Homer Barron because she must at any cost get a man. The [gap] ... between cultural myth and cultural reality ... suggest[s] that in this disparity is the ultimate grotesque.

NOTES

1. See *Faulkner in the University: Class Conferences at the University of Virginia 1957–1958*, edited by Frederick L. Gwynn and Joseph I. Blotner (Charlottesville: University Press of Virginia, 1959), 87–88; *Faulkner at Nagamo*, edited by Robert A. Jeliffe (Tokyo: Kenkyusha, 1956), 71.
2. For a sense of some of the difficulties involved in reading the story in these terms, I refer the reader to the collection of criticism edited by M. Thomas Inge, *A Rose for Emily* (Columbus, Ohio: Merrill, 1970).

## GENE M. MOORE

### *Of Time and Its Mathematical Progression: Problems of Chronology in Faulkner's "A Rose for Emily"*\*

Over the past 30 years, no fewer than *eight* different chronologies have been proposed to account for the events occurring in William Faulkner's celebrated short story "A Rose for Emily."[1] These chronologies cover a span of 14 years (Miss Emily was born between 1850 and 1864, and died between 1924 and 1938), and they make use of many different kinds of evidence: not only internal temporal references and cross-references in the story, but also historical, biographical, canonical, and even forensic evidence. Given the amount of interest generated by this question and the range of evidence employed in the various arguments, it is remarkable that no one seems ever to have regarded the original manuscript as a possible source of chronological information; in fact, evidence from the manuscript makes it possible to solve some of the problems of Miss Emily's chronology by fixing the date of her father's death.

While critics have recognized the importance of time to a proper understanding of the story[,] ... they have also complained, in strong and vivid language, of the difficulty of establishing a consistent chronology: "Faulkner destroys chronological time in his story" (Magalaner and Volpe, cited in Inge 63); he uses "a complicatedly disjunctive time scheme" (Wilson 56) that "twists chronology almost beyond recognition" (Sullivan 167); his technique is an "abandonment of chronology" (A. M. Wright, cited in Sullivan 167). Yet whether the story of

---

\* From *Studies in Short Fiction* 29 (Spring 1992): 195–204. All notes are Moore's; some of his works cited have been omitted.

1. These chronologies were proposed by—in chronological order—Going (1958), Hagopian et al. (1964), Woodward (1966), McGlynn (1969), Nebeker (1970 and 1971), Wilson (1972), Brooks (1978), and Perry (1979). The first four were reprinted in Inge's 1970 casebook. Cleanth Brooks refers to five chronologies in this casebook (382n), but I have only been able to discover four, and my count is confirmed by the list in one of the suggestions for short papers at the end of Inge's volume (127). Helen E. Nebeker has proposed two different chronologies (the first in "Emily's Rose ...: Thematic Implications" and the second in "Emily's Rose ...: A Postscript" and "Chronology Revised"). Although different evidence is used, Nebeker's second chronology agrees with that proposed by Hagopian et al.

Miss Emily Grierson is to be understood in terms of conflict between the North and the South, between the Old South and the New South, or between the "past" and the "present," for the sake of all these arguments it is vitally important to establish her own chronological place in the historical context of the passing generations. What dates are carved on Miss Emily's tombstone?

The task at hand has never been stated more simply than by William T. Going in the earliest of the chronologies: "By means of internal or external evidence, date the major events of Emily Grierson's life" (8). Yet in practice it is often difficult to distinguish "internal" from "external" evidence. Is evidence from the unrevised manuscript of "A Rose for Emily" internal or external? What about references to Judge Stevens or Colonel Sartoris in other works by Faulkner? In general, what constitutes legitimate chronological evidence? In cases of conflict, what forms of evidence should take precedence over others? The "internal" chronology of a given work may or may not prove to be consistent, and may or may not be attached (consistently or inconsistently) to a variety of "external" chronologies based on information such as references occurring in other works by the same author (*canonical* evidence), or what we know about the author's life (*biographical* evidence) or the context of history in general (*historical* evidence). In each case, specific chronological references can be either *absolute*, in the form of dates (such as the single reference to 1894 in "A Rose for Emily"); *relative* to other references (e.g., "the summer after her father's death," "thirty years before"); or *contextual*, establishing a measure of time with reference to historical or natural codes of temporality outside the text (e.g., allusions to the Civil War signify 1861–65; the graying of Miss Emily's hair is a gradual process; dead bodies decompose at a certain rate under certain conditions, etc.). The discrepancies among the eight chronologies are largely a result of underlying differences of opinion about the relative weights to be accorded these various kinds of evidence.

The specific difficulty of establishing a chronology for Miss Emily arises largely because the first half of her story is told essentially in reverse chronological order, and the events in it are described not in terms of dates or specific historical references, but most often in terms of her age at the time. Anchoring this "internal" chronology in history requires, in effect, that we find at least one point of attachment between "internal" references to Miss Emily's age or activities, and "external" references to dates or known historical events.

Most of the discussion in the eight chronologies has centered upon two problematic events in her life: the remission of her taxes by Colonel Sartoris in 1894 [paragraph 3], and the period of china-painting lessons "when she was about forty" [paragraph 49]. 1894 is the only date mentioned in the story, but its exact position in Miss Emily's life (i.e., her age at the time) is by no means certain. In the third paragraph of the story, reference is made to "that day in 1894 when Colonel Sartoris, the mayor... remitted her taxes, the dispensation dating from the death of her father on into perpetuity."... This means, at the least, that her father died no later than 1894. We are told that at the time of her father's death Miss Emily had "got to be thirty and was still single" [paragraph 25]; and when she buys the poison about two years later, the narrator reminds us that "She was over thirty then" [paragraph 34]. The year 1864 is thus a *terminus ad quem* for Miss Emily's birth, and is respected as such by all the chronologists.

Some, however, have taken 1894 as the point of attachment between Emily's life and historical chronology, assuming that her taxes were remitted immediately following her father's death, and that he accordingly died that same year (McGlynn, Wilson). Her age at the time is taken as 30 (McGlynn) or 32 (Wilson), indicating that she was born in 1862 or 1864 and died in 1936 or 1938. However, "A Rose for Emily" was first published in 1930, creating a "glaring discrepancy" that led Helen E. Nebeker to revise her original chronology ("Chronology Revised" 471), and that in Menakhem Perry's opinion leads to "absurd conclusions" (344n26). Nebeker and Perry take 1930, the date of publication, as a *terminus ad quem* for Miss Emily's death, which means that the year 1856 becomes the corresponding *terminus* for her birth.²

The remission of Miss Emily's taxes is mentioned twice in the story: first as occurring in 1894, and second in connection with the period of her china-painting lessons "when she was about forty": the narrator ends the paragraph describing these lessons with the remark that "Meanwhile her taxes had been remitted" (128). Some chronologists have taken this "Meanwhile" to mean that Miss Emily must have been "about forty" in 1894, and that she was therefore born in 1854 and died in 1928 (Hagopian et al., Nebeker, "Emily's Rose . . . : A Postscript" and "Chronology Revised"). Brooks's chronology is a numerical compromise between those of Going and Hagopian et al., according to which Miss Emily, born in 1852, would have been 42 in 1894. Perry also takes this "Meanwhile" as indicative of simultaneity: "She was exempted from taxation in the period when she gave china-painting lessons" (344n26). In other words, much of the discrepancy among the various chronologies can be understood as a result of the choice of where to attach the historical "anchor" of the remission of taxes in 1894: to the death of Miss Emily's father when she was "over thirty," or to the china-painting period when she was "about forty"?

Surprisingly, what no one seems to have noticed or taken seriously is that in the original manuscript Faulkner assigned a different date to the remission of Miss Emily's taxes and a specific date to her father's death: the corresponding passage in the manuscript speaks of "that day in 1904 when Colonel Sartoris . . . remitted her taxes dating from the death of her father 16 years back, on into perpetuity" (Inge 8).³ One can only speculate about why Faulkner found it necessary to shift the date of Colonel Sartoris's gallant action back ten years from 1904 to 1894, and to delete all reference to the "16 years" since the father's death. Perhaps 16 years seemed too long for Miss Emily to remain actively on the minds of city officials? In any event, it is clear that when Faulkner originally committed the story to paper, her taxes were remitted not in 1894 but in 1904, 16 years after the death of her father in 1888. Restoring Faulkner's alterations and deletions may seem to run counter to the editorial principle of respecting the

---

2. The provisional futurism of a situation in which Miss Emily dies fictionally some years after the announcement of her death in the "real" world, as posited in half of the published chronologies (those of Woodward, McGlynn, Nebeker ["Emily's Rose . . . : Thematic Implications"], and Wilson), is not without literary precedent. . . . In the case of "A Rose for Emily," the "inconvenience" indeed exists only if one claims to identify the fictional world of Miss Emily with the historical world of William Faulkner; but this claim is at the origin of any attempt to set up a chronology.

3. This oversight is all the more remarkable in view of the fact that a quite legible reproduction of the first manuscript page was printed as an illustration in Inge's 1970 casebook, which all the later critics have cited as a reference.

author's final intentions; but keeping the original dates in mind can help untangle the story's chronology.

The altered date and the omission of the reference to "16 years back" in the typescript version need not mean that Faulkner had necessarily changed his mind about the date of Miss Emily's father's death. Had he moved it back the same 10 years, she would have to have been born before 1848 to have been over 30 by 1878, and would thus have been of the same generation as the Civil War veterans who attend her funeral. As Brooks noted,

> The "very old men—some in their brushed Confederate uniforms" who, at the funeral, talked "of Miss Emily as if she had been a contemporary of theirs, believing that they had danced with her and courted her" must have been a number of years older than she. (*WF: Toward Yoknapatawpha and Beyond* 383)[4]

However, in the earliest of the chronologies, William T. Going invoked Faulkner's authority to the effect that Miss Emily was born in 1850 and died in 1924, since 1924 was the date assigned to "A Rose for Emily" in Malcolm Cowley's Viking Portable edition of Faulkner's works (1946), in which Cowley noted editorially that dates were assigned "with the author's consent and later with his advice at doubtful points" (cited in Inge 51).[5] Going set the date of her father's death as early as 1882.

Manuscript evidence cannot solve all the chronological problems, since the china-painting period is defined not only in connection with Miss Emily's being "about forty," but also retrospectively, working backward from later events: the death of Colonel Sartoris, the visit of the tax delegation, and her own death. We are told that no one had seen the house's interior for "at least ten years" before she died [paragraph 1], and that the visit of the tax delegation (which may or may not have been the last visit before her death, but is in any case the only visit we are told about) took place "eight or ten years" after she ceased giving china-painting lessons [paragraph 5] and "almost ten years" after the death of Colonel Sartoris [paragraph 14].[6] In other words, she died at least 18 years after the last lessons were given: 18 years before her death at age 74, Miss Emily would have been 56 years old, so that if the lessons lasted for "a period of six or seven years"[paragraph 49], Miss Emily could not have been "about forty" at the time, but would instead have been about 50. Paul D. McGlynn has attempted to disregard this problem by suggesting that "Of course 'about forty' might well be a genteel euphemism for 'about fifty' " (Inge 91; cf. Wilson 59); but this suggestion still does not explain why the narrator would protect Miss Emily's age only at this particular point and not elsewhere. Would anyone wish to read the narrator's two references to her being "over thirty" as genteel euphemisms for "over forty," or the announcement of her "death at seventy-four" as a coded euphemism for 84? In effect, the chronology to be established by tracing the course of Miss Emily's life forward from the time of her father's death fails to square with the

---

4. On similar historical grounds, one could argue that the Homer Barron episode must be set much later, since the actual streets of Oxford were not paved until the 1920s (Cullen and Watkins 71, cited in Inge 17).
5. Cowley also acknowledged in his Introduction that "As one book leads into another, Faulkner sometimes falls into inconsistencies of detail." He added that "these errors are comparatively few and inconsequential. ...I should judge that most of them are afterthoughts rather than oversights" (Cowley 7–8).
6. In the place of the reference to the china-painting lessons as having ceased "eight or ten years earlier" (120), the unrevised manuscript reads "6 or 7 years ago" (Faulkner, *Manuscripts* 189).

chronology to be derived retrospectively from the time of her own death.

Interpreting the reference to "at least ten years" as possibly allowing for as much as 20 years is also no solution, since the visit of the tax delegation is the peg from which the date of the smell "thirty years before" is hung. Internal references indicate that Homer Barron must have died when Miss Emily was about 33 or 34 years old: at least 40 years before her own death (equal to the "at least ten years" since the last visit plus the 30 years since the smell), and two years after her father's death, which occurred when she was already at least 30. A limit is thereby set to the range of time included in "at least": her last visit had to occur "at least ten years" and at most 12 years before her death, since if it occurred more than 12 years earlier, she would have been under 30 when her father died.

In summary, the chronologies can be divided roughly into two groups: one group—Woodward, McGlynn, Nebeker ("Emily's Rose...: Thematic Implications"), and Wilson—connects the tax remission of 1894 with her father's death (Emily is between 30 and 34 in 1894); while the other—Going, Hagopian et al., Nebeker ("Emily's Rose...: A Postscript" and "Chronology Revised"), Brooks, and Perry—links the reference to 1894 with the period of china-painting (i.e., Emily is "about forty," or between 39 and 42, in 1894). The first group tends to disregard the narrator's reference to the remission of taxes as being retroactive: "the dispensation dating from the death of her father on into perpetuity" [paragraph 3]. Taxes are collected annually—"On the first of the year they mailed her a tax notice" [paragraph 4]—so that if Miss Emily's taxes were remitted the same year her father died, the narrator's reference to the retroactive nature of the remission would appear to be unnecessary.

This much can be determined on the basis of "internal" references alone; but the references to Colonel Sartoris and to Judge Stevens lead us outside the story to look for external canonical evidence in the form of references to these gentlemen in other works by Faulkner. If Judge Stevens was already 80 years old and mayor at the time of the smell (which the chronologies date variously between 1884 and 1896), then he is probably too old to be Judge Lemuel Stevens, the father of Gavin Stevens, who is mentioned in Faulkner's late works: he would have been between 102 and 114 years old at the time of his death in 1918—perhaps not an altogether impossible age, but one remarkable enough to be worth mentioning. Nevertheless, most of the glossaries and indexes have identified the elderly Judge Stevens of "A Rose for Emily" with Judge Lemuel....

Similar problems arise with the reference to a Colonel Sartoris who was mayor in 1894 and who died "almost ten years" before the visit of the tax delegation (and thus about 20 years before Miss Emily's death, when she was about 54). Once again, there is some doubt about which Colonel Sartoris is meant: Faulkner has described the early history of the Sartoris family more thoroughly than that of the Stevenses, so that it appears correspondingly more difficult to imagine a strange new Colonel Sartoris, unique to "A Rose for Emily" and unmentioned elsewhere, who could have been mayor in 1894. Faulkner's works mention two Colonel Sartorises: Colonel John Sartoris, who dies too early to have been Miss Emily's mayor in 1894, and his son Bayard—"the banker with his courtesy title acquired partly by inheritance and partly by propinquity" (*Reivers* 74)—who dies too late....

However, the original date of 1904 for the mayoral edict may help to solve this problem as well, since young Bayard Sartoris could well have been mayor at that time. We are told in *The Reivers* of his propensity for passing edicts, although he is not specifically named as mayor; when his matched carriage horses are startled by a home-made automobile, "by the next night there was formally recorded into the archives of Jefferson a city ordinance against the operation of any mechanically propelled vehicle inside the corporate limits" (27–28); additional information in *The Reivers* makes it possible to date this incident as having occurred in 1904. The Colonel's tendency to govern by radical edict is mentioned in "A Rose for Emily" as well, since it was "he who fathered the edict that no Negro woman should appear on the streets without an apron" (par. 3).

In conclusion, the neglected manuscript evidence, by allowing us to fix the date of the death of Miss Emily's father in 1888, makes it possible to establish a chronology that is different from the eight that have been suggested previously (although it differs from that of Perry by only one year). Perhaps when Faulkner decided to move the time of Miss Emily's tax remission back by ten years, he simply failed to consider the consequences of this alteration for the rest of the chronology. Yet whether the year in question is 1894 or 1904, the internal inconsistency of the period of her china-painting remains, together with the canonical inconsistencies concerning the identities of Judge Stevens and Colonel Sartoris. The ancient Civil War veterans who try to remember Miss Emily are not alone in having to cope with the problem of "confusing time with its mathematical progression."

### APPENDIX: A CHRONOLOGY FOR MISS EMILY GRIERSON

1856: Miss Emily is born; the narrator never mentions her birth directly, but his reference to "the day of her death at seventy-four" (127–28) defines the parameters of any chronology in terms of a span of 74 years.
1870–1879: The Grierson house is built "in the heavily lightsome style of the seventies" (119), thus presumably during the 1870s.
1888: Her father dies after "she got to be thirty" (123).
1889: She meets Homer Barron "the summer after her father's death" (124).
1890: She buys arsenic from the druggist "over a year after they had begun to say 'Poor Emily'.... She was over thirty then" (125). She poisons Homer Barron, who disappears "two years after her father's death"; a smell is noticed "a short time after" (122), which is also "thirty years before" the tax visit (121).
1893–1900: Miss Emily is "about forty"; she gives lessons in china-painting "for a period of six or seven years" (128).
1894: "Meanwhile" (119, 128) Colonel Sartoris, the mayor, remits her taxes.
1920: She is visited by a deputation of the Board of Aldermen "eight or ten years" after she stops giving china-painting lessons (120) and "almost ten years" (121) after the death of Colonel Sartoris.
1930: She dies "at least ten years" (119) since her last visit, presumably from the tax deputation; after her funeral, the room, "which no one had seen in forty years" (129), is opened.

WORKS CITED

Brooks, Cleanth. *William Faulkner: The Yoknapatawpha Country*. New Haven: Yale UP, 1963.

———. *William Faulkner: Toward Yoknapatawpha and Beyond*. New Haven: Yale UP, 1978.

Cowley, Malcolm. Introduction. *The Portable Faulkner*. New York: Viking, 1946. 1–24.

Cullen, John B., and Floyd C. Watkins. "Miss Emily." *Old Times in the Faulkner Country*. Chapel Hill: U of North Carolina P, 1961. 70–71. Rpt. in Inge 17–18.

Faulkner, William. *Collected Stories of William Faulkner*. New York: Random, 1950.

———. *Flags in the Dust*. New York: Random, 1973.

———. *Requiem for a Nun*. New York: Random, 1950.

———. *The Reivers*. New York: Random, 1962.

———. "A Rose for Emily." *Collected Stories* 119–30.

———. *The Unvanquished*. New York: Random, 1938.

———. *William Faulkner Manuscripts: These 13*. Ed. Noel Polk. New York: Garland, 1985. 188–214.

Ford, Margaret Patricia, and Suzanne Kincaid. *Who's Who in Faulkner*. N.p.: Louisiana State UP, 1963.

Going, William T. "Chronology in Teaching 'A Rose for Emily.'" *Exercise Exchange* 5 (February 1958): 8–11. Rpt. in Inge 50–53.

Hagopian, John V., W. Gordon Cunliffe, and Martin Dolch. "A Rose for Emily," *Insight I: Analyses of American Literature*. Frankfurt: Hirschgraben, 1964. 43–50. Rpt. in Inge 76–83.

Inge, M. Thomas. *William Faulkner: A Rose for Emily*. The Charles E. Merrill Literary Casebook Series. Columbus, OH: Merrill, 1970.

Kirk, Robert W., and Marvin Klotz. *Faulkner's People: A Complete Guide and Index to Characters in the Fiction of William Faulkner*. Berkeley: U of California P, 1963.

McGlynn, Paul D. "The Chronology of 'A Rose for Emily.'" *Studies in Short Fiction* 6 (1969): 461–62. Rpt. in Inge 90–92.

Nebeker, Helen E. "Emily's Rose of Love: Thematic Implications of Point of View in Faulkner's 'A Rose for Emily.'" *Bulletin of the Rocky Mountain Modern Language Association* 24 (1970): 3–13.

———. "Emily's Rose of Love: A Postscript." *Bulletin of the Rocky Mountain Modern Language Association* 24 (1970): 190–91.

———. "Chronology Revised." *Studies in Short Fiction* 8 (1971): 471–73.

Perry, Menakhem. "Literary Dynamics: How the Order of a Text Creates its Meanings [With an Analysis of Faulkner's 'A Rose for Emily']." *Poetics Today* 1:1–2 (Autumn 1979): 35–64, 311–61.

Runyan, Harry. *A Faulkner Glossary*. New York: Citadel, 1964.

Sullivan, Ruth. "The Narrator in 'A Rose for Emily.'" *Journal of Narrative Technique* 1 (1971): 159–78.

Wilson, G. R., Jr. "The Chronology of Faulkner's 'A Rose for Emily' Again." *Notes on Mississippi Writers* 5 (Fall 1972): 56, 44, 58–62.

Woodward, Robert H. "The Chronology of 'A Rose for Emily.'" *Exercise Exchange* 8 (March 1966): 17–19. Rpt. in Inge 84–86.

## SUGGESTIONS FOR WRITING

1. William Faulkner's "A Rose for Emily" shares its southern setting with several other stories in this book: one by Eudora Welty ("Why I Live at the P.O.") and three by Flannery O'Connor ("A Good Man Is Hard to Find," "The Lame Shall Enter First," and "Everything That Rises Must Converge"). What makes each of these stories distinctively "southern"? Does "southern" mean the same thing to each of these authors? Write an essay in which you compare and contrast the southern setting of "A Rose for Emily" with the setting of at least one of these other stories.
2. What information can a reader detect, or infer, about the narrator of "A Rose for Emily"? What sort of person or persons could be telling the story (young, old, male, female, black, white, a southern local or a northern visitor)? Does the narrator share all the values of the townspeople, or express any mixed feelings about their views or behavior? Does Faulkner (or the implied author of the story) share all the narrator's attitudes, or does the story place the narrator at a certain ironic distance from author and reader? Write an essay in which you characterize the authority and limitations of the narrator in relation to the society of Jefferson and to the implied author of the story.
3. In his essay "We all said, 'She will kill herself,' " Lawrence R. Rodgers argues that "A Rose for Emily" is, in fact, essentially a detective story. Do you agree? Does it really matter whether or not "A Rose for Emily" is a certain "kind" of fiction? Write an essay in which you either agree or disagree with Rodgers's approach to the story and the significance of that approach.
4. George L. Dillon, in his essay "Styles of Reading," identifies three types of readers: those who read for "Character-Action-Moral," those who are "Diggers for Secrets," and those who are "Anthropologists." Dillon's analysis suggests that, although these types of reader may vary in sophistication, no one type is more or less likely to produce a "correct" interpretation of a given literary text. Apply Dillon's model to any of the stories you have read in this book and suggest three possible readings, each valid in its own right.
5. Judith Fetterley urges a feminist reading of Faulkner's story in her essay "A Rose for 'A Rose for Emily.' " Do you find her arguments persuasive? Write an essay comparing Fetterley's take on "A Rose for Emily" with that of another critic who considers the social subordination of women or the gender of characters or the narrator to be crucial to the meaning of this story.
6. Much has been written about Faulkner's handling of time and chronology in "A Rose for Emily." In his essay "Of Time and Its Mathematical Progression," Gene M. Moore describes a variety of critical attempts to untangle the story's time line. Taking note of the arguments Moore describes, write an essay in which you present your own interpretation of chronology and its importance in "A Rose for Emily."
7. In this chapter you have seen how a single work of literature (Faulkner's "A Rose for Emily") can generate a broad range of critical responses (the accompanying essays by Dillon, Fetterley, Moore, and others). Taken together, these texts represent a kind of ongoing conversation between a "primary text" and "secondary texts," and even among these "secondary texts" themselves. Using secondary texts available to you at a library and on the Internet, write an essay in which you join in the critical "conversation" about any of the stories you have read in this book. Be sure to follow the standard scholarly procedures for documenting your sources properly.

## STUDENT WRITING

Crystal 1

Willow D. Crystal
Professor Akerley
English 1002
23 April 2004

"One of us . . .": Concepts of the Private and the Public in William Faulkner's
"A Rose for Emily"

Throughout "A Rose for Emily," William Faulkner introduces a tension between what is private, or belongs to the individual, and what is public, or the possession of the group. "When Miss Emily Grierson died," the tale begins, "our whole town went to her funeral: the men through a sort of respectful affection for a fallen monument, the women mostly out of curiosity to see the inside of her house . . . " (594). The men of the small town of Jefferson, Mississippi, are motivated to attend Miss Emily's funeral for public reasons; the women, to see "the inside of her house," that private realm which has remained inaccessible for "at least ten years" (595).

This opposition of the private with the public has intrigued critics of Faulkner's tale since the story was first published. Distinctions between the private and the public are central to Lawrence R. Rodgers's argument in his essay " 'We all said, "she will kill herself" ': The Narrator/Detective in William Faulkner's 'A Rose for Emily.' " The very concept of the detective genre demands that "there must be concealed facts that . . . must become clear in the end" (119), private actions which become public knowledge. In her feminist tribute, "A Rose for 'A Rose for Emily,' " Judith Fetterley uses the private-public dichotomy to demonstrate the "grotesque reality" (34) of the patriarchal social system in Faulkner's story. According to Fetterley, Miss Emily's "private life becomes a public document that the town folk feel free to interpret at will" (36). Thus, while critics such as Rodgers and Fetterley offer convincing—if divergent—interpretations of "A Rose for Emily," it is necessary first to understand in Faulkner's eerie and enigmatic story the relationship between the public and the private, and the consequences of this relationship within the story and for the reader.

The most explicit illustration of the opposition between the public and the private occurs in the social and economic interactions between the town of Jefferson, represented by the narrator's "our" and "we," and the reclusive Miss Emily. "Alive," the narrator explains, "Miss Emily had been a tradition, a duty, and a care; a sort of hereditary obligation upon the town, dating from that day in 1894 when Colonel Sartoris, the mayor, . . . remitted her taxes, the dispensation dating from the death of her father on into perpetuity" (595). Ironically (and this is one of the prime examples of the complexity of the relationship of private and public in the story), the price of privacy for Miss Emily becomes the loss of that very privacy. Despite—or perhaps because of—her refusal to buy into the community, the citizens of Jefferson determine that it is their "duty," their "hereditary obligation," to oversee her activities. When, for example, Miss Emily's house begins to emit an unpleasant smell, the town officials decide to solve the problem by dusting her property with lime. When she refuses to provide a reason why she wants to buy poison, the druggist scrawls "For rats" (598) across the package, literally and protectively overwriting her silence.

Arguably, the townspeople's actions serve to protect Miss Emily's privacy—by preserving her perceived gentility—as much as they effectively destroy it with their intrusive zeal. But in this very act of protection they reaffirm the town's proprietary relation to the public "monument" that is Miss Emily and, consequently, reinforce her inability to make decisions for herself.

While the communal narrator and Miss Emily appear to be polar opposites—one standing for the public while the other fiercely defends her privacy—the two are united when an outsider such as Homer Barron appears in their midst. If Miss Emily serves as a representation—an icon, an inactive figure in a "tableau," an "idol"—of traditional antebellum southern values, then Homer represents all that is new and different. A "day laborer" (597) from the North, Homer comes to Jefferson to pave the sidewalks, a task which itself suggests the modernization of the town.

The secret and destructive union between these two representational figures implies a complex relationship between the private and the public. When Miss Emily kills Homer and confines his remains to a room in her attic, where, according to Rodgers, "she has been allowed to carry on her illicit love affair in post-mortem privacy" (119), this grotesque act ironically suggests that she has capitulated to the code of gentility that Jefferson imagines her to embody. This code demands the end of a romantic affair which some residents deemed "a disgrace to the town and a bad example to the young people" (598), thus placing traditions and the good of the community above Miss Emily's own wishes. Through its insistence on Miss Emily's symbolic relation to a bygone era, the town—via the narrator—becomes "an unknowing driving force behind Emily's crime" (Rodgers 120). Her private act is both the result of and a support for public norms and expectations.

At the same time, however, the act of murder also marks Miss Emily's corruption of that very code. By killing Homer in private, Miss Emily deliberately flouts public norms, and by eluding explicit detection until after her own death, she asserts the primacy of the private. The murder of the outsider in their midst thus leads Miss Emily to achieve paradoxically both a more complete privacy—a marriage of sorts without a husband—and a role in the preservation of the community.

Yet the elaborate relationship between Jefferson and Miss Emily is not the only way in which Homer's murder may be understood as a casualty of the tension between the public and the private. When Miss Emily kills Homer, Rodgers contends, "from the town's point of view, it was the best thing. . . . Homer represents the kind of unwelcomed resident and ineligible mate the town wants to repel if it is to preserve its traditional arrangements" (125). The people of Jefferson and Miss Emily join in a struggle to "repel" the outside and to ensure a private, inner order and tradition. This complicity creates intriguing parallels between the illicit, fatal union of Homer and Miss Emily and the reunion of the North and the South following the Civil War. In this reformulation of the private and the public, Miss Emily becomes, as Fetterley notes, a "metaphor and mirror for the town of Jefferson" (43). Miss Emily's honor is the townspeople's honor, her preservation their preservation.

Finally, the parallels between Miss Emily's secretive habits and the narrator's circuitous presentation of the story lead to a third dimension of the negotiations between the private and the public in "A Rose for Emily," a dimension in which Faulkner as author and the collective "we" as narrator confront their public consumers, the readers. Told by the anonymous narrator as if retrospectively, "A Rose for Emily" skips forward and back in time, omitting details and deferring revelations to such a degree that many critics have gone to extreme lengths to establish reliable chronologies for the tale. The much-debated "we" remains anonymous and unreachable throughout the tale—maintaining a virtually unbreachable privacy—even as it invites the public (the reader) to participate in the narrator's acts of detection and revelation. Rodgers observes:

> The dramatic distance on display here provides an ironic layer to the narrative. As the observers of the conflict between the teller-of-tale's desire to solve the curious mysteries that surround Emily's life—indeed, his complicity in shaping them—and his undetective-like detachment from her crimes, readers occupy the tantalizing position of having insight into unraveling the mystery which the narrator lacks. (120–21)

The reader is thus a member of the communal "we"—party to the narrator's investigation and Jefferson's voyeuristic obsession with Miss Emily—but also apart, removed to a plane from which "insight" into and observation of the narrator's own actions and motives become possible. The reader, just like Miss Emily, Homer, and the town of Jefferson itself, becomes a crucial element in the tension between the public and the private.

Thus, public and private are, in the end, far from exclusive categories. And for all of its literal as well as figurative insistence on opposition and either/or structures, Faulkner's "A Rose for Emily" enacts the provocative idea of being "[o]ne of us" (600–601), of being both an individual and a member of a community, both a private entity and a participant in the public sphere.

Works Cited

Faulkner, William. "A Rose for Emily." The Norton Introduction to Literature. 9th ed. Eds. Alison Booth, J. Paul Hunter, and Kelly J. Mays. New York: Norton, 2005. 595–601.

Fetterley, Judith. "A Rose for 'A Rose for Emily.'" The Resisting Reader: A Feminist Approach to American Fiction. Bloomington: Indiana UP, 1978. 34–45.

Moore, Gene M. "Of Time and Its Mathematical Progression: Problems of Chronology in Faulkner's 'A Rose for Emily.'" Studies in Short Fiction 29 (1992): 195–204.

Rodgers, Lawrence R. " 'We all said, "she will kill herself" ': The Narrator/Detective in William Faulkner's 'A Rose for Emily.' " Clues: A Journal of Detection 16 (1995): 117–29.

# Reading More Fiction

## GUY DE MAUPASSANT
### The Jewelry[1]

Having met the girl one evening, at the house of the office-superintendent, M. Lantin became enveloped in love as in a net.

She was the daughter of a country-tutor, who had been dead for several years. Afterward she had come to Paris with her mother, who made regular visits to several bourgeois families of the neighborhood, in hopes of being able to get her daughter married. They were poor and respectable, quiet and gentle. The young girl seemed to be the very ideal of that pure good woman to whom every young man dreams of entrusting his future. Her modest beauty had a charm of angelic shyness; and the slight smile that always dwelt about her lips seemed a reflection of her heart.

Everybody sang her praises; all who knew her kept saying: "The man who gets her will be lucky. No one could find a nicer girl than that."

M. Lantin, who was then chief clerk in the office of the Minister of the Interior, with a salary of 3,500 francs a year,[2] demanded her hand, and married her.

5   He was unutterably happy with her. She ruled his home with an economy so adroit that they really seemed to live in luxury. It would be impossible to conceive of any attentions, tendernesses, playful caresses which she did not lavish upon her husband; and such was the charm of her person that, six years after he married her, he loved her even more than he did the first day.

There were only two points upon which he ever found fault with her—her love of the theater, and her passion for false jewelry.

Her lady-friends (she was acquainted with the wives of several small office holders) were always bringing her tickets for the theaters; whenever there was a performance that made a sensation, she always had her *loge* secured, even for first performances; and she would drag her husband with her to all these entertainments, which used to tire him horribly after his day's work. So at last he begged her to go to the theater with some lady-acquaintances who would consent to see her home afterward. She refused for quite a while—thinking it would not look very well to go out thus unaccompanied by her husband. But finally she yielded, just to please him; and he felt infinitely grateful to her therefor.

Now this passion for the theater at last evoked in her the desire of dress. It was true that her toilette remained simple, always in good taste, but modest; and her sweet grace, her irresistible grace, ever smiling and shy, seemed to take fresh charm from the simplicity of her robes. But she got into the habit of suspending in her pretty ears two big cut pebbles, fashioned in imitation of diamonds; and

---

1. Translated by Lafcadio Hearn.
2. A midlevel bureaucratic wage, perhaps about $30,000 to $40,000 today.

she wore necklaces of false pearls, bracelets of false gold, and haircombs studded with paste-imitations of precious stones.

Her husband, who felt shocked by this love of tinsel and show, would often say—"My dear, when one has not the means to afford real jewelry, one should appear adorned with one's natural beauty and grace only—and these gifts are the rarest of jewels."

But she would smile sweetly and answer: "What does it matter? I like those things—that is my little whim. I know you are right; but one can't make oneself over again. I've always loved jewelry so much!"

And then she would roll the pearls of the necklaces between her fingers, and make the facets of the cut crystals flash in the light, repeating: "Now look at them—see how well the work is done. You would swear it was real jewelry."

He would then smile in his turn, and declare to her: "You have the tastes of a regular Gypsy."

Sometimes, in the evening, when they were having a chat by the fire, she would rise and fetch the morocco box in which she kept her "stock" (as M. Lantin called it)—would put it on the tea-table, and begin to examine the false jewelry with passionate delight, as if she experienced some secret and mysterious sensations of pleasure in their contemplation; and she would insist on putting one of the necklaces round her husband's neck, and laugh till she couldn't laugh any more, crying out: "Oh! how funny you look!" Then she would rush into his arms, and kiss him furiously.

One winter's night, after she had been to the Opera, she came home chilled through, and trembling. Next day she had a bad cough. Eight days after that, she died of pneumonia.

Lantin was very nearly following her into the tomb. His despair was so frightful that in one single month his hair turned white. He wept from morning till night, feeling his heart torn by inexpressible suffering—ever haunted by the memory of her, by the smile, by the voice, by all the charm of the dead woman.

Time did not assuage his grief. Often during office hours his fellow-clerks went off to a corner to chat about this or that topic of the day—his cheeks might have been seen to swell up all of a sudden, his nose wrinkle, his eyes fill with water—he would pull a frightful face, and begin to sob.

He had kept his dead companion's room just in the order she had left it, and he used to lock himself up in it every evening to think about her—all the furniture, and even all her dresses, remained in the same place they had been on the last day of her life.

But life became hard for him. His salary, which, in his wife's hands, had amply sufficed for all household needs, now proved scarcely sufficient to supply his own few wants. And he asked himself in astonishment how she had managed always to furnish him with excellent wines and with delicate eating which he could not now afford at all with his scanty means.

He got a little into debt, like men obliged to live by their wits. At last one morning that he happened to find himself without a cent in his pocket, and a whole week to wait before he could draw his monthly salary, he thought of selling something; and almost immediately it occurred to him to sell his wife's "stock"— for he had always borne a secret grudge against the flash-jewelry that used to annoy him so much in former days. The mere sight of it, day after day, somewhat spoiled the sad pleasure of thinking of his darling.

He tried a long time to make a choice among the heap of trinkets she had left behind her—for up to the very last day of her life she had kept obstinately buying them, bringing home some new thing almost every night—and finally he resolved to take the big pearl necklace which she used to like the best of all, and which he thought ought certainly to be worth six or eight francs, as it was really very nicely mounted for an imitation necklace.

He put it in his pocket, and walked toward the office, following the boulevards, and looking for some jewelry-store on the way, where he could enter with confidence.

Finally he saw a place and went in; feeling a little ashamed of thus exposing his misery, and of trying to sell such a trifling object.

"Sir," he said to the jeweler, "please tell me what this is worth."

The jeweler took the necklace, examined it, weighed it, took up a magnifying glass, called his clerk, talked to him in whispers, put down the necklace on the counter, and drew back a little bit to judge of its effect at a distance.

M. Lantin, feeling very much embarrassed by all these ceremonies, opened his mouth and began to declare—"Oh! I know it can't be worth much"... when the jeweler interrupted him saying:

"Well, sir, that is worth between twelve and fifteen thousand francs; but I cannot buy it unless you can let me know exactly how you came by it."

The widower's eyes opened enormously, and he stood gaping—unable to understand. Then after a while he stammered out: "You said?... Are you sure?" The jeweler, misconstruing the cause of this astonishment, replied in a dry tone—"Go elsewhere if you like, and see if you can get any more for it. The very most I would give for it is fifteen thousand. Come back and see me again, if you can't do better."

M. Lantin, feeling perfectly idiotic, took his necklace and departed; obeying a confused desire to find himself alone and to get a chance to think.

But the moment he found himself in the street again, he began to laugh, and he muttered to himself: "The fool!—oh! what a fool; If I had only taken him at his word. Well, well!—a jeweler who can't tell paste from real jewelry!"

And he entered another jewelry-store, at the corner of the Rue de la Paix. The moment the jeweler set eyes on the necklace, he examined—"Hello! I know that necklace well—it was sold here!"

M. Lantin, very nervous, asked:

"What's it worth?"

"Sir, I sold it for twenty-five thousand francs. I am willing to buy it back again for eighteen thousand—if you can prove to me satisfactorily, according to legal prescriptions, how you came into possession of it"—This time, M. Lantin was simply paralyzed with astonishment. He said: "Well... but please look at it again, sir. I always thought until now that it was... was false."

The jeweler said:

"Will you give me your name, sir?"

"Certainly. My name is Lantin; I am employed at the office of the Minister of the Interior. I live at No. 16, Rue des Martyrs."

The merchant opened the register, looked, and said: "Yes; this necklace was sent to the address of Madame Lantin, 16 Rue des Martyrs, on July 20th, 1876."

And the two men looked into each other's eyes—the clerk wild with surprise; the jeweler suspecting he had a thief before him.

The jeweler resumed:

"Will you be kind enough to leave this article here for twenty-four hours only—I'll give you a receipt."

M. Lantin stuttered: "Yes-ah! certainly." And he went out folding up the receipt, which he put in his pocket.

Then he crossed the street, went the wrong way, found out his mistake, returned by way of the Tuileries, crossed the Seine, found out he had taken the wrong road again, and went back to the Champs-Élysées without being able to get one clear idea into his head. He tried to reason, to understand. His wife could never have bought so valuable an object as that. Certainly not. But then, it must have been a present! . . . A present from whom? What for?

He stopped and stood stock-still in the middle of the avenue.

A horrible suspicion swept across his mind. . . . She? . . . But then all those other pieces of jewelry must have been presents also! . . . Then it seemed to him that the ground was heaving under his feet; that a tree, right in front of him, was falling toward him; he thrust out his arms instinctively, and fell senseless.

He recovered his consciousness again in a drug-store to which some bystanders had carried him. He had them lead him home, and he locked himself into his room.

Until nightfall he cried without stopping, biting his handkerchief to keep himself from screaming out. Then, completely worn out with grief and fatigue, he went to bed, and slept a leaden sleep.

A ray of sunshine awakened him, and he rose and dressed himself slowly to go to the office. It was hard to have to work after such a shock. Then he reflected that he might be able to excuse himself to the superintendent, and he wrote to him. Then he remembered he would have to go back to the jeweler's; and shame made his face purple. He remained thinking a long time. Still he could not leave the necklace there; he put on his coat and went out.

It was a fine day; the sky extended all blue over the city, and seemed to make it smile. Strollers were walking aimlessly about, with their hands in their pockets.

Lantin thought as he watched them passing: "How lucky the men are who have fortunes! With money a man can even shake off grief—you can go where you please—travel—amuse yourself! Oh! if I were only rich!"

He suddenly discovered he was hungry—not having eaten anything since the evening before. But his pockets were empty; and he remembered the necklace. Eighteen thousand francs! Eighteen thousand francs!—that was a sum—that was!

He made his way to the Rue de la Paix and began to walk backward and forward on the sidewalk in front of the store. Eighteen thousand francs! Twenty times he started to go in; but shame always kept him back.

Still he was hungry—very hungry—and had not a cent. He made one brusque resolve, and crossed the street almost at a run, so as not to let himself have time to think over the matter; and he rushed into the jeweler's.

As soon as he saw him, the merchant hurried forward, and offered him a chair with smiling politeness. Even the clerks came forward to stare at Lantin, with gaiety in their eyes and smiles about their lips.

The jeweler said: "Sir, I made inquiries; and if you are still so disposed, I am ready to pay you down the price I offered you."

The clerk stammered: "Why, yes—sir, certainly."

The jeweler took from a drawer eighteen big bills,[3] counted them, and held them out to Lantin, who signed a little receipt, and thrust the money feverishly into his pocket.

Then, as he was on the point of leaving, he turned to the ever-smiling merchant, and said, lowering his eyes: "I have some—I have some other jewelry, which came to me in the same—from the same inheritance. Would you purchase them also from me?"

The merchant bowed, and answered: "Why, certainly, sir—certainly...." One of the clerks rushed out to laugh at his ease; another kept blowing his nose as hard as he could.

Lantin, impassive, flushed and serious, said: "I will bring them to you."

And he hired a cab to get the jewelry.

When he returned to the store, an hour later, he had not yet breakfasted. They examined the jewelry—piece by piece—putting a value on each. Nearly all had been purchased from that very house.

Lantin, now, disputed estimates made, got angry, insisted on seeing the books, and talked louder and louder the higher the estimates grew.

The big diamond earrings were worth 20,000 francs; the bracelets, 35,000; the brooches, rings and medallions, 16,000; a set of emeralds and sapphires, 14,000; solitaire, suspended to a gold neckchain, 40,000; the total value being estimated at 196,000 francs.

The merchant observed with mischievous good nature: "The person who owned these must have put all her savings into jewelry."

Lantin answered with gravity: "Perhaps that is as good a way of saving money as any other." And he went off, after having agreed with the merchant that an expert should make a counter-estimate for him the next day.

When he found himself in the street again, he looked at the Column Vendôme[4] with the desire to climb it, as if it were a May pole. He felt jolly enough to play leapfrog over the Emperor's head—up there in the blue sky.

He breakfasted at Voisin's[5] restaurant, and ordered wine at 20 francs a bottle.

Then he hired a cab and drove out to the Bois.[6] He looked at the carriages passing with a sort of contempt, and a wild desire to yell out to the passers-by: "I am rich, too—I am! I have 200,000 francs!"

The recollection of the office suddenly came back to him. He drove there, walked right into the superintendent's private room, and said: "Sir, I come to give you my resignation. I have just come into a fortune of *three* hundred thousand francs." Then he shook hands all round with his fellow-clerks; and told them all about his plans for a new career. Then he went to dinner at the Café Anglais.

Finding himself seated at the same table with a man who seemed to him quite genteel, he could not resist the itching desire to tell him, with a certain air of coquetry, that he had just inherited a fortune of *four* hundred thousand francs.

For the first time in his life he went to the theater without feeling bored by

---

3. French paper money varies in size; the larger the bill, the larger the denomination.
4. Famous column with a statue of Napoleon at the top.
5. Like the Café Anglais below, a well-known and high-priced restaurant.
6. Large Parisian park where the rich took their outings.

the performance; and he passed the night in revelry and debauch.

Six months after he married again. His second wife was the most upright of spouses, but had a terrible temper. She made his life very miserable.

1883

AMBROSE BIERCE

## An Occurrence at Owl Creek Bridge

### I

A man stood upon a railroad bridge in Northern Alabama, looking down into the swift waters twenty feet below. The man's hands were behind his back, the wrists bound with a cord. A rope loosely encircled his neck. It was attached to a stout cross-timber above his head, and the slack fell to the level of his knees. Some loose boards laid upon the sleepers supporting the metals of the railway supplied a footing for him and his executioners—two private soldiers of the Federal army, directed by a sergeant, who in civil life may have been a deputy sheriff. At a short remove upon the same temporary platform was an officer in the uniform of his rank, armed. He was a captain. A sentinel at each end of the bridge stood with his rifle in the position known as "support," that is to say, vertical in front of the left shoulder, the hammer resting on the forearm thrown straight across the chest—a formal and unnatural position, enforcing an erect carriage of the body. It did not appear to be the duty of these two men to know what was occurring at the centre of the bridge; they merely blockaded the two ends of the foot plank which traversed it.

Beyond one of the sentinels nobody was in sight; the railroad ran straight away into a forest for a hundred yards, then, curving, was lost to view. Doubtless there was an outpost further along. The other bank of the stream was open ground—a gentle acclivity crowned with a stockade of vertical tree trunks, loop-holed for rifles, with a single embrasure through which protruded the muzzle of a brass cannon commanding the bridge. Midway of the slope between bridge and fort were the spectators—a single company of infantry in line, at "parade rest," the butts of the rifles on the ground, the barrels inclining slightly backward against the right shoulder, the hands crossed upon the stock. A lieutenant stood at the right of the line, the point of his sword upon the ground, his left hand resting upon his right. Excepting the group of four at the centre of the bridge not a man moved. The company faced the bridge, staring stonily, motionless. The sentinels, facing the banks of the stream, might have been statues to adorn the bridge. The captain stood with folded arms, silent, observing the work of his subordinates but making no sign. Death is a dignitary who, when he comes announced, is to be received with formal manifestations of respect, even by those most familiar with him. In the code of military etiquette silence and fixity are forms of deference.

The man who was engaged in being hanged was apparently about thirty-five years of age. He was a civilian, if one might judge from his dress, which was that of a planter. His features were good—a straight nose, firm mouth, broad forehead, from which his long, dark hair was combed straight back, falling behind his ears to the collar of his well-fitting frock coat. He wore a moustache and pointed beard, but no whiskers; his eyes were large and dark grey and had a kindly expression which one would hardly have expected in one whose neck was in the hemp. Evidently this was no vulgar assassin. The liberal military code makes provision for hanging many kinds of people, and gentlemen are not excluded.

The preparations being complete, the two private soldiers stepped aside and each drew away the plank upon which he had been standing. The sergeant turned to the captain, saluted and placed himself immediately behind that officer, who in turn moved apart one pace. These movements left the condemned man and the sergeant standing on the two ends of the same plank, which spanned three of the cross-ties of the bridge. The end upon which the civilian stood almost, but not quite, reached a fourth. This plank had been held in place by the weight of the captain; it was now held by that of the sergeant. At a signal from the former, the latter would step aside, the plank would tilt and the condemned man go down between two ties. The arrangement commended itself to his judgment as simple and effective. His face had not been covered nor his eyes bandaged. He looked a moment at his "unsteadfast footing," then let his gaze wander to the swirling water of the stream racing madly beneath his feet. A piece of dancing driftwood caught his attention and his eyes followed it down the current. How slowly it appeared to move! What a sluggish stream!

5  He closed his eyes in order to fix his last thoughts upon his wife and children. The water, touched to gold by the early sun, the brooding mists under the banks at some distance down the stream, the fort, the soldiers, the piece of drift—all had distracted him. And now he became conscious of a new disturbance. Striking through the thought of his dear ones was a sound which he could neither ignore nor understand, a sharp, distinct, metallic percussion like the stroke of a blacksmith's hammer upon the anvil; it had the same ringing quality. He wondered what it was, and whether immeasurably distant or near by—it seemed both. Its recurrence was regular, but as slow as the tolling of a death knell. He awaited each stroke with impatience and—he knew not why—apprehension. The intervals of silence grew progressively longer, the delays became maddening. With their greater infrequency the sounds increased in strength and sharpness. They hurt his ear like the thrust of a knife; he feared he would shriek. What he heard was the ticking of his watch.

He unclosed his eyes and saw again the water below him. "If I could free my hands," he thought, "I might throw off the noose and spring into the stream. By diving I could evade the bullets, and, swimming vigorously, reach the bank, take to the woods, and get away home. My home, thank God, is as yet outside their lines; my wife and little ones are still beyond the invader's farthest advance."

As these thoughts, which have here to be set down in words, were flashed into the doomed man's brain rather than evolved from it, the captain nodded to the sergeant. The sergeant stepped aside.

II

Peyton Farquhar was a well-to-do planter, of an old and highly-respected Alabama family. Being a slave owner, and, like other slave owners, a politician, he was naturally an original secessionist and ardently devoted to the Southern cause. Circumstances of an imperious nature which it is unnecessary to relate here, had prevented him from taking service with the gallant army which had fought the disastrous campaigns ending with the fall of Corinth,[1] and he chafed under the inglorious restraint, longing for the release of his energies, the larger life of the soldier, the opportunity for distinction. That opportunity, he felt, would come, as it comes to all in war time. Meanwhile he did what he could. No service was too humble for him to perform in aid of the South, no adventure too perilous for him to undertake if consistent with the character of a civilian who was at heart a soldier, and who in good faith and without too much qualification assented to at least a part of the frankly villainous dictum that all is fair in love and war.

One evening while Farquhar and his wife were sitting on a rustic bench near the entrance to his grounds, a grey-clad soldier rode up to the gate and asked for a drink of water. Mrs. Farquhar was only too happy to serve him with her own white hands. While she was gone to fetch the water, her husband approached the dusty horseman and inquired eagerly for news from the front.

"The Yanks are repairing the railroads," said the man, "and are getting ready for another advance. They have reached the Owl Creek bridge, put it in order, and built a stockade on the other bank. The commandant has issued an order, which is posted everywhere, declaring that any civilian caught interfering with the railroad, its bridges, tunnels, or trains, will be summarily hanged. I saw the order."

"How far is it to the Owl Creek bridge?" Farquhar asked.

"About thirty miles."

"Is there no force on this side the creek?"

"Only a picket post half a mile out, on the railroad, and a single sentinel at this end of the bridge."

"Suppose a man—a civilian and student of hanging—should elude the picket post and perhaps get the better of the sentinel," said Farquhar, smiling, "what could he accomplish?"

The soldier reflected. "I was there a month ago," he replied. "I observed that the flood of last winter had lodged a great quantity of driftwood against the wooden pier at this end of the bridge. It is now dry and would burn like tow."

The lady had now brought the water, which the soldier drank. He thanked her ceremoniously, bowed to her husband, and rode away. An hour later, after nightfall, he repassed the plantation, going northward in the direction from which he had come. He was a Federal scout.

III

As Peyton Farquhar fell straight downward through the bridge, he lost consciousness and was as one already dead. From this state he was awakened—ages later, it seemed to him—by the pain of a sharp pressure upon his throat, followed by a sense of suffocation. Keen, poignant agonies seemed to shoot from his neck downward through every fibre of his body and limbs. These pains appeared to flash along well-defined lines of ramification, and to beat with an inconceivably rapid periodicity. They seemed like streams of pulsating fire heating him to an intolerable temperature. As to his head, he was conscious of nothing but a feeling of fullness—of congestion. These sensations were unaccompanied by thought. The intellectual part of his nature was already effaced; he had power only to feel,

---

1. Corinth, Mississippi, captured by General Ulysses S. Grant in April 1862.

and feeling was torment. He was conscious of motion. Encompassed in a luminous cloud, of which he was now merely the fiery heart, without material substance, he swung through unthinkable arcs of oscillation, like a vast pendulum. Then all at once, with terrible suddenness, the light about him shot upward with the noise of a loud plash; a frightful roaring was in his ears, and all was cold and dark. The power of thought was restored; he knew that the rope had broken and he had fallen into the stream. There was no additional strangulation; the noose about his neck was already suffocating him, and kept the water from his lungs. To die of hanging at the bottom of a river!—the idea seemed to him ludicrous. He opened his eyes in the blackness and saw above him a gleam of light, but how distant, how inaccessible! He was still sinking, for the light became fainter and fainter until it was a mere glimmer. Then it began to grow and brighten, and he knew that he was rising toward the surface—knew it with reluctance, for he was now very comfortable. "To be hanged and drowned," he thought, "that is not so bad; but I do not wish to be shot. No; I will not be shot; that is not fair."

He was not conscious of an effort, but a sharp pain in his wrist apprised him that he was trying to free his hands. He gave the struggle his attention, as an idler might observe the feat of a juggler, without interest in the outcome. What splendid effort!—what magnificent, what superhuman strength! Ah, that was a fine endeavour! Bravo! The cord fell away; his arms parted and floated upward, the hands dimly seen on each side in the growing light. He watched them with a new interest as first one and then the other pounced upon the noose at his neck. They tore it away and thrust it fiercely aside, its undulations resembling those of a water-snake. "Put it back, put it back!" He thought he shouted these words to his hands, for the undoing of the noose had been succeeded by the direst pang which he had yet experienced. His neck ached horribly; his brain was on fire; his heart, which had been fluttering faintly, gave a great leap, trying to force itself out at his mouth. His whole body was racked and wrenched with an insupportable anguish! But his disobedient hands gave no heed to the command. They beat the water vigorously with quick, downward strokes, forcing him to the surface. He felt his head emerge; his eyes were blinded by the sunlight; his chest expanded convulsively, and with a supreme and crowning agony his lungs engulfed a great draught of air, which instantly he expelled in a shriek!

20   He was now in full possession of his physical senses. They were, indeed, preternaturally keen and alert. Something in the awful disturbance of his organic system had so exalted and refined them that they made record of things never before perceived. He felt the ripples upon his face and heard their separate sounds as they struck. He looked at the forest on the bank of the stream, saw the individual trees, the leaves and the veining of each leaf—the very insects upon them, the locusts, the brilliant-bodied flies, the grey spiders stretching their webs from twig to twig. He noted the prismatic colors in all the dewdrops upon a million blades of grass. The humming of the gnats that danced above the eddies of the stream, the beating of the dragon flies' wings, the strokes of the water spiders' legs, like oars which had lifted their boat—all these made audible music. A fish slid along beneath his eyes and he heard the rush of its body parting the water.

He had come to the surface facing down the stream; in a moment the visible world seemed to wheel slowly round, himself the pivotal point, and he saw the bridge, the fort, the soldiers upon the bridge, the captain, the sergeant, the two privates, his executioners. They were in silhouette against the blue sky. They shouted and gesticulated, pointing at him; the captain had drawn his pistol, but did not fire; the others were unarmed. Their movements were grotesque and horrible, their forms gigantic.

Suddenly he heard a sharp report and something struck the water smartly within a few inches of his head, spattering his face with spray. He heard a second report, and saw one of the sentinels with his rifle at his shoulder, a light cloud of blue smoke rising from the muzzle. The man in the water saw the eye of the man on the bridge gazing into his own through the sights of the rifle. He observed that it was a grey eye, and remembered having read that grey eyes were keenest and that all famous marksmen had them. Nevertheless, this one had missed.

A counter swirl had caught Farquhar and turned him half round; he was again looking into the forest on the bank opposite the fort. The sound of a clear, high voice in a monotonous singsong now rang out behind him and came across the water with a distinctness that pierced and subdued all other sounds, even the beating of the ripples in his ears. Although no soldier, he had frequented camps enough to know the dread significance of that deliberate, drawling, aspirated chant; the lieutenant on shore was taking a part in the morning's work. How coldly and pitilessly—with what an even, calm intonation, presaging and enforcing tranquillity in the men—with what accurately-measured intervals fell those cruel words:

"Attention, company. . . . Shoulder arms. . . . Ready. . . . Aim. . . . Fire."

Farquhar dived—dived as deeply as he could. The water roared in his ears like the voice of Niagara, yet he heard the dulled thunder of the volley, and rising again toward the surface, met shining bits of metal, singularly flattened, oscillating slowly downward. Some of them touched him on the face and hands, then fell away, continuing their descent. One lodged between his collar and neck; it was uncomfortably warm, and he snatched it out.

As he rose to the surface, gasping for breath, he saw that he had been a long time under water; he was perceptibly farther down stream—nearer to safety. The soldiers had almost finished reloading; the metal ramrods flashed all at once in the sunshine as they were drawn from the barrels, turned in the air, and thrust into their sockets. The two sentinels fired again, independently and ineffectually.

The hunted man saw all this over his shoulder; he was now swimming vigorously with the current. His brain was as energetic as his arms and legs; he thought with the rapidity of lightning.

"The officer," he reasoned, "will not make that martinet's error a second time. It is as easy to dodge a volley as a single shot. He has probably already given the command to fire at will. God help me, I cannot dodge them all!"

An appalling plash within two yards of him, followed by a loud rushing sound, *diminuendo*, which seemed to travel back through the air to the fort and died in an explosion which stirred the very river to its deeps! A rising sheet of water, which curved over him, fell down upon him, blinded him, strangled him! The cannon had taken a hand in the game. As he shook his head free from the commotion of the smitten water, he heard the deflected shot humming through the air ahead, and in an instant it was cracking and smashing the branches in the forest beyond.

"They will not do that again," he thought; "the next time they will use a charge of grape. I must keep my eye upon the gun; the smoke will apprise me—the report arrives too late; it lags behind the missile. It is a good gun."

Suddenly he felt himself whirled round and round—spinning like a top. The water, the banks, the forest, the now distant bridge, fort and men—all were commingled and blurred. Objects were represented by their colors only; circular horizontal streaks of color—that was all he saw. He had been caught in a vortex and was being whirled on with a velocity of advance and gyration which made him giddy and sick. In a few moments he was flung upon the gravel at the foot of the left bank of the stream—the southern bank—and behind a projecting point which concealed him from his enemies. The sudden arrest of his motion, the abrasion of one of his hands on the gravel, restored him and he wept with delight. He dug his fingers into the sand, threw it over himself in handfuls and audibly blessed it. It looked like gold, like diamonds, rubies, emeralds; he could think of nothing beautiful which it did not resemble. The trees upon the bank were giant garden plants; he noted a definite order in their arrangement, inhaled the fragrance of their blooms. A strange, roseate light shone through the spaces among their trunks, and the wind made in their branches the music of æolian harps. He had no wish to perfect his escape, was content to remain in that enchanting spot until retaken.

A whizz and rattle of grapeshot among the branches high above his head roused him from his dream. The baffled cannoneer had fired him a random farewell. He sprang to his feet, rushed up the sloping bank, and plunged into the forest.

All that day he travelled, laying his course by the rounding sun. The forest seemed interminable; nowhere did he discover a break in it, not even a woodman's road. He had not known that he lived in so wild a region. There was something uncanny in the revelation.

By nightfall he was fatigued, footsore, famishing. The thought of his wife and children urged him on. At last he found a road which led him in what he knew to be the right direction. It was as wide and straight as a city street, yet it seemed untravelled. No fields bordered it, no dwelling anywhere. Not so much as the barking of a dog suggested human habitation. The black bodies of the great trees formed a straight wall on both sides, terminating on the horizon in a point, like a diagram in a lesson in perspective. Overhead, as he looked up through this rift in the wood, shone great golden stars looking unfamiliar and grouped in strange constellations. He was sure they were arranged in some order which had a secret and malign significance. The wood on either side was full of singular noises, among which—once, twice, and again—he distinctly heard whispers in an unknown tongue.

His neck was in pain, and, lifting his hand to it, he found it horribly swollen. He knew that it had a circle of black where the rope had bruised it. His eyes felt congested; he could no longer close them. His tongue was swollen with thirst; he relieved its fever by thrusting it forward from between his teeth into the cool air. How softly the turf had carpeted the untravelled avenue! He could no longer feel the roadway beneath his feet!

Doubtless, despite his suffering, he fell asleep while walking, for now he sees another scene—perhaps he has merely recovered from a delirium. He stands at the gate of his own home. All is as he left it, and all bright and beautiful in the morning sunshine. He must have travelled the entire night. As he pushes open the gate and passes up the wide white walk, he sees a flutter of female garments; his wife, looking fresh and cool and sweet, steps down from the verandah to meet him. At the bottom of the steps she stands waiting, with a smile of ineffable joy, an attitude of matchless grace and dignity. Ah, how beautiful she is! He springs forward with extended arms. As he is about to clasp her, he feels a stunning blow upon the back of the neck; a blinding white light blazes all about him, with a sound like the shock of a cannon—then all is darkness and silence!

Peyton Farquhar was dead; his body, with a broken neck, swung gently from side to side beneath the timbers of the Owl Creek bridge.

1891

# HENRY JAMES

## The Jolly Corner

### I

"Every one asks me what I 'think' of everything," said Spencer Brydon; "and I make answer as I can—begging or dodging the question, putting them off with any nonsense. It wouldn't matter to any of them really," he went on, "for, even were it possible to meet in that stand-and-deliver way so silly a demand on so big a subject, my 'thoughts' would still be almost altogether about something that concerns only myself." He was talking to Miss Staverton, with whom for a couple of months now he had availed himself of every possible occasion to talk; this disposition and this resource, this comfort and support, as the situation in fact presented itself, having promptly enough taken the first place in the considerable array of rather unattenuated surprises attending his so strangely belated return to America. Everything was somehow a surprise; and that might be natural when one had so long and so consistently neglected everything, taken pains to give surprises so much margin for play. He had given them more than thirty years—thirty-three, to be exact; and they now seemed to him to have organized their performance quite on the scale of that license. He had been twenty-three on leaving New York—he was fifty-six to-day: unless indeed he were to reckon as he had sometimes, since his repatriation, found himself feeling; in which case he would have lived longer than is often allotted to man. It would have taken a century, he repeatedly said to himself, and said also to Alice Staverton, it would have taken a longer absence and a more averted mind than those even of which he had been guilty, to pile up the differences, the newness, the queerness, above all the bignesses, for the better or the worse, that at present assaulted his vision wherever he looked.

The great fact all the while however had been the incalculability; since he *had* supposed himself, from decade to decade, to be allowing, and in the most liberal and intelligent manner, for brilliancy of change. He actually saw that he had allowed for nothing; he missed what he would have been sure of finding, he found what he would never have imagined. Proportions and values were upside-down; the ugly things he had expected, the ugly things of his far-away youth, when he had too promptly waked up to a sense of the ugly—these uncanny phenomena placed him rather, as it happened, under the charm; whereas the "swagger" things, the modern, the monstrous, the famous things, those he had more particularly, like thousands of ingenuous enquirers every year, come over to see, were exactly his sources of dismay. They were as so many set traps for displeasure, above all for reaction, of which his restless tread was constantly pressing the spring. It was interesting, doubtless, the whole show, but it would have been too disconcerting hadn't a certain finer truth saved the situation. He had distinctly not, in this steadier light, come over *all* for the monstrosities; he had come, not only in the last analysis but quite on the face of the act, under an impulse with which they had nothing to do. He had come—putting the thing pompously—to look at his "property," which he had thus for a third of a century not been within four thousand miles of; or, expressing it less sordidly, he had yielded to the humor of seeing again his house on the jolly corner, as he usually, and quite fondly, described it—the one in which he had first seen the light, in which various members of his family had lived and had died, in which the holidays of his overschooled boyhood had been passed and the few social flowers of his chilled adolescence gathered, and which, alienated then for so long a period, had, through the successive deaths of his two brothers and the termination of old arrangements, come wholly into his hands. He was the owner of another, not quite so "good"—the jolly corner having been, from far back, superlatively extended and consecrated; and the value of the pair represented his main capital, with an income consisting, in these later years, of their respective rents which (thanks precisely to their original excellent type) had never been depressingly low. He could live in "Europe," as he had been in the habit of living, on the product of these flourishing New York leases, and all the better since, that of the second structure, the mere number in its long row, having within a twelvemonth fallen in, renovation at a high advance had proved beautifully possible.

These were items of property indeed, but he had found himself since his arrival distinguishing more than ever between them. The house within the street, two bristling blocks westward, was already in course of reconstruction as a tall mass of flats; he had acceded, some time before, to overtures for this conversion—in which, now that it was going forward, it had been not the least of his astonishments to find himself able, on the spot, and though without a previous ounce of such experience, to participate with a certain intelligence, almost with a certain authority. He had lived his life with his back so turned to such concerns and his face addressed to those of so different an order that he scarce knew what to make of this lively stir, in a compartment of his mind never yet penetrated, of a capacity for business and a sense for construction. These virtues, so common all round him now, had been dormant in his own organism—where it might be said of them perhaps that they had slept the sleep of the just. At present, in the splendid autumn weather—the autumn at least was a pure boon in the terrible place—he loafed about his "work" undeterred, secretly agitated; not in the least "minding" that the whole proposition, as they said, was vulgar and sordid, and ready to climb ladders, to walk the plank, to handle materials and look wise about them, to ask questions, in fine, and challenge explanations and really "go into" figures.

It amused, it verily quite charmed him; and, by the same stroke, it amused, and even more, Alice Staverton, though perhaps charming her perceptibly less. She wasn't however going to be better-off for it, as *he* was—and so astonishingly much: nothing was now likely, he knew, ever to make her better-off than she found herself, in the afternoon of life, as the delicately frugal possessor and tenant of the small house in Irving Place[1] to which she had subtly managed to cling through her almost unbroken New York career. If he knew the way to it now better than to any other address among the dreadful multiplied numberings which seemed to him to reduce the whole place to some vast ledger-page, overgrown, fantastic, of ruled and criss-crossed lines and figures—if he had formed, for his consolation, that habit, it was really not a little because of the charm of his having encountered and recognised, in the vast wilderness of the wholesale, breaking through the mere gross generalization of wealth and force and success, a small still scene where items and shades, all delicate things, kept the sharpness of the notes of a high voice perfectly trained, and where economy hung about like the scent of a garden. His old friend lived with one maid and herself dusted her relics and trimmed her lamps and polished her silver; she stood off, in the awful modern crush, when she could, but she sallied forth and did battle when the challenge was really to "spirit," the spirit she after all confessed to, proudly and a little shyly, as to that of the better time, that of *their* common, their quite far-away and antediluvian social period and order. She made use of the street-cars when need be, the terrible things that people scrambled for as the panic-stricken at sea scramble for the boats; she affronted, inscrutably, under stress, all the public concussions and ordeals; and yet, with that slim mystifying grace of her appearance, which defied you to say if she were a fair young woman who looked older through trouble, or a fine smooth older one who looked young through successful indifference; with her precious reference, above all, to memories and histories into which he could enter, she was as exquisite for him as some pale pressed flower (a rarity to begin with), and, failing other sweetnesses, she was a sufficient reward of his effort. They had communities of knowledge, "their" knowledge (this discriminating possessive was always on her lips) of presences of the other age, presences all overlaid, in his case, by the experience of a man and the freedom of a wanderer, overlaid by pleasure, by infidelity, by passages of life that were strange and dim to her, just by "Europe" in short, but still unobscured, still exposed and cherished, under that pious visitation of the spirit from which she had never been diverted.

She had come with him one day to see how his "apartment-house" was rising; he had helped her over gaps and explained to her plans, and while they were there had happened to have, before her, a brief but lively discussion with the man in charge, the representative of the building-firm that had undertaken his work. He had found himself quite "standing-up" to this personage over a failure on the latter's part to observe some detail of one of their noted conditions, and had so lucidly argued his case that, besides ever so prettily flushing, at the time, for sympathy in his triumph, she had afterwards said to him (though to a slightly greater effect of irony) that he had clearly for too many years neglected a real gift. If he had but stayed at home he would have anticipated the inventor of the sky-scraper. If he had but stayed at home he would have discovered his genius in time really to start some new variety of awful architectural hare and run it till it burrowed in a gold-mine. He was to remember these words, while the weeks elapsed, for the small silver ring they had sounded over the queerest and deepest of his own lately most disguised and most muffled vibrations.

It had begun to be present to him after the first fortnight, it had broken out

---

1. A short street in New York's Union Square area, where James spent much of his boyhood.

with the oddest abruptness, this particular wanton wonderment: it met him there—and this was the image under which he himself judged the matter, or at least, not a little, thrilled and flushed with it—very much as he might have been met by some strange figure, some unexpected occupant, at a turn of one of the dim passages of an empty house. The quaint analogy quite hauntingly remained with him, when he didn't indeed rather improve it by a still intenser form: that of his opening a door behind which he would have made sure of finding nothing, a door into a room shuttered and void, and yet so coming, which a great suppressed start, on some quite erect confronting presence, something planted in the middle of the place and facing him through the dusk. After that visit to the house in construction he walked with his companion to see the other and always so much the better one, which in the eastward direction formed one of the corners, the "jolly" one precisely, of the street now so generally dishonored and disfigured in its westward reaches, and of the comparatively conservative Avenue. The Avenue still had pretensions, as Miss Staverton said, to decency; the old people had mostly gone, the old names were unknown, and here and there an old association seemed to stray, all vaguely, like some very aged person, out too late, whom you might meet and feel the impulse to watch or follow, in kindness, for safe restoration to shelter.

They went in together, our friends; he admitted himself with his key, as he kept no one there, he explained, preferring, for his reasons, to leave the place empty, under a simple arrangement with a good woman living in the neighborhood and who came for a daily hour to open windows and dust and sweep. Spencer Brydon had his reason and was glowingly aware of them; they seemed to him better each time he was there, though he didn't name them all to his companion, any more than he told her as yet how often, how quite absurdly often, he himself came. He only let her see for the present, while they walked through the great blank rooms, that absolute vacancy reigned and that, from top to bottom, there was nothing but Mrs. Muldoon's broomstick, in a corner, to tempt the burglar. Mrs. Muldoon was then on the premises, and she loquaciously attended the visitors, preceding them from room to room and pushing back shutters, and throwing up sashes—all to show them, as she remarked, how little there was to see. There was little indeed to see in the great gaunt shell where the main dispositions and the general apportionment of space, the style of an age of ampler allowances, had nevertheless for its master their honest pleading message, affecting him as some good old servant's, some lifelong retainer's appeal for a character,[2] or even for a retiring-pension; yet it was also a remark of Mrs. Muldoon's that, glad as she was to oblige him by her noonday round, there was a request she greatly hoped he would never make of her. If he should wish her for any reason to come in after dark she would just tell him, if he "plased," that he must ask it of somebody else.

The fact that there was nothing to see didn't militate for the worthy woman against what one *might* see, and she put it frankly to Miss Staverton that no lady could be expected to like, could she? "craping up to thim top storeys in the ayvil hours." The gas and the electric light were off the house, and she fairly evoked a gruesome vision of her march through the great grey rooms—so many of them as there were too!—with her glimmering taper. Miss Staverton met her honest

---

2. A character reference.

glare with a smile and the profession that she herself certainly would recoil from such an adventure. Spencer Brydon meanwhile held his peace—for the moment; the question of the "evil" hours in his old home had already become too grave for him. He had begun some time since to "crape," and he knew just why a packet of candles addressed to that pursuit had been stowed by his own hand, three weeks before, at the back of a drawer of the fine old sideboard that occupied, as a "fixture," the deep recess in the dining-room. Just now he laughed at his companions—quickly however changing the subject; for the reason that, in the first place, his laugh struck him even at that moment as starting the odd echo, the conscious human resonance (he scarce knew how to qualify it) that sounds made while he was there alone sent back to his ear or his fancy; and that, in the second, he imagined Alice Staverton for the instant on the point of asking him, with a divination, if he ever so prowled. There were divinations he was unprepared for, and he had at all events averted enquiry by the time Mrs. Muldoon had left them, passing on to other parts.

There was happily enough to say, on so consecrated a spot, that could be said freely and fairly; so that a whole train of declarations was precipitated by his friend's having herself broken out, after a yearning look round: "But I hope you don't mean they want you to pull *this* to pieces!" His answer came, promptly, with his reawakened wrath: it was of course exactly what they wanted, and what they were "at" him for, daily, with the iteration of people who couldn't for their life understand a man's liability to decent feelings. He had found the place, just as it stood and beyond what he could express, an interest and a joy. There were values other than the beastly rent-values, and in short, in short—! But it was thus Miss Staverton took him up. "In short you're to make so good a thing of your sky-scraper that, living in luxury on *those* ill-gotten gains, you can afford for a while to be sentimental here!" Her smile had for him, with the words, the particular mild irony with which he found half her talk suffused; an irony without bitterness and that came, exactly, from her having so much imagination—not, like the cheap sarcasms with which one heard most people, about the world of "society," bid for the reputation of cleverness, from nobody's really having any. It was agreeable to him at this very moment to be sure that when he had answered, after a brief demur, "Well yes: so, precisely, you may put it!" her imagination would still do him justice. He explained that even if never a dollar were to come to him from the other house he would nevertheless cherish this one; and he dwelt, further, while they lingered and wandered, on the fact of the stupefaction he was already exciting, the positive mystification he felt himself create.

He spoke of the value of all he read into it, into the mere sight of the walls, mere shapes of the rooms, mere sound of the floors, mere feel, in his hand, of the old silver-plated knobs of the several mahogany doors, which suggested the pressure of the palms of the dead; the seventy years of the past in fine[3] that these things represented, the annals of nearly three generations, counting his grandfather's, the one that had ended there, and the impalpable ashes of his long-extinct youth, afloat in the very air like microscopic motes. She listened to everything; she was a woman who answered intimately but who utterly didn't chatter. She scattered abroad therefore no cloud of words; she could assent, she

---

3. In short.

could agree, above all she could encourage, without doing that. Only at the last she went a little further than he had done himself. "And then how do you know? You may still, after all, want to live here." It rather indeed pulled him up, for it wasn't what he had been thinking, at least in her sense of the words. "You mean I may decide to stay on for the sake of it?"

"Well, *with* such a home—!" But, quite beautifully, she had too much tact to dot so monstrous an *i*, and it was precisely an illustration of the way she didn't rattle. How could any one—of any wit—insist on any one else's "wanting" to live in New York?

"Oh," he said, "I *might* have lived here (since I had my opportunity early in life); I might have put in here all these years. Then everything would have been different enough—and, I dare say, 'funny' enough. But that's another matter. And then the beauty of it—I mean of my perversity, of my refusal to agree to a 'deal'—is just in the total absence of a reason. Don't you see that if I had a reason about the matter at all it would *have* to be the other way, and would then be inevitably a reason of dollars? There are no reasons here *but* of dollars. Let us therefore have none whatever—not the ghost of one."

They were back in the hall then for departure, but from where they stood the vista was large, through an open door, into the great square main saloon, with its almost antique felicity of brave spaces between windows. Her eyes came back from that reach and met his own a moment. "Are you very sure the 'ghost' of one doesn't, much rather, serve—?"

He had a positive sense of turning pale. But it was as near as they were then to come. For he made answer, he believed, between a glare and a grin: "Oh ghosts—of course the place must swarm with them! I should be ashamed of it if it didn't. Poor Mrs. Muldoon's right, and it's why I haven't asked her to do more than look in."

15        Miss Staverton's gaze again lost itself, and things she didn't utter, it was clear, came and went in her mind. She might even for the minute, off there in the fine room, have imagined some element dimly gathering. Simplified like the death-mask of a handsome face, it perhaps produced for her just then an effect akin to the stir of an expression in the "set" commemorative plaster. Yet whatever her impression may have been she produced instead a vague platitude. "Well, if it were only furnished and lived in—!"

She appeared to imply that in case of its being still furnished he might have been a little less opposed to the idea of a return. But she passed straight into the vestibule, as if to leave her words behind her, and the next moment he had opened the house-door and was standing with her on the steps. He closed the door and, while he re-pocketed his key, looking up and down, they took in the comparatively harsh actuality of the Avenue, which reminded him of the assault of the outer light of the Desert on the traveller emerging from an Egyptian tomb. But he risked before they stepped into the street his gathered answer to her speech. "For me it *is* lived in. For me it *is* furnished." At which it was easy for her to sigh "Ah yes—!" all vaguely and discreetly; since his parents and his favourite sister, to say nothing of other kin, in numbers, had run their course and met their end there. That represented, within the walls, ineffaceable life.

It was a few days after this that, during an hour passed with her again, he had expressed his impatience of the too flattering curiosity—among the people he met—about his appreciation of New York. He had arrived at none at all that was socially producible, and as for that matter of his "thinking" (thinking the better or the worse of anything there) he was wholly taken up with one subject of thought. It was mere vain egoism, and it was moreover, if she liked, a morbid obsession. He found all things come back to the question of what he personally might have been, how he might have led his life and "turned out," if he had not so, at the outset, given it up. And confessing for the first time to the intensity within him of this absurd speculation—which but proved also, no doubt, the habit of too selfishly thinking—he affirmed the impotence there of any other source of interest, any other native appeal. "What would it have made of me, what would it have made of me? I keep for ever wondering, all idiotically; as if I could possibly know! I see what it has made of dozens of others, those I meet, and it positively aches within me, to the point of exasperation, that it would have made something of me as well. Only I can't make out *what*, and the worry of it, the small rage of curiosity never to be satisfied, brings back what I remember to have felt, once or twice, after judging best, for reasons, to burn some important letter unopened. I've been sorry, I've hated it—I've never known what was in the letter. You may of course say it's a trifle—!"

"I don't say it's a trifle," Miss Staverton gravely interrupted.

She was seated by her fire, and before her, on his feet and restless, he turned to and fro between this intensity of his idea and a fitful and unseeing inspection, through his single eye-glass, of the dear little old objects on her chimney-piece. Her interruption made him for an instant look at her harder. "I shouldn't care if you did!" he laughed, however; "and it's only a figure, at any rate, for the way I now feel. *Not* to have followed my perverse young course—and almost in the teeth of my father's curse, as I may say; not to have kept it up, so, 'over there,' from that day to this, without a doubt or a pang; not, above all, to have liked it, to have loved it, so much, loved it, no doubt, with such an abysmal conceit of my own preference: some variation from *that*, I say, must have produced some different effect for my life and for my 'form.' I should have stuck here—if it had been possible; and I was too young, at twenty-three, to judge, *pour deux sous*,[4] whether it *were* possible. If I had waited I might have seen it was, and then I might have been, by staying here, something nearer to one of these types who have been hammered so hard and made so keen by their conditions. It isn't that I admire them so much—the question of any charm in them, or of any charm, beyond that of the rank money-passion, exerted by their conditions *for* them, has nothing to do with the matter: it's only a question of what fantastic, yet perfectly possible, development of my own nature I mayn't have missed. It comes over me that I had then a strange *alter ego* deep down somewhere within me, as the full-blown flower is in the small tight bud, and that I just took the course, I just transferred him to the climate, that blighted him for once and for ever."

"And you wonder about the flower," Miss Staverton said. "So do I, if you want to know; and so I've been wondering these several weeks. I believe in the flower," she continued, "I feel it would have been quite splendid, quite huge and monstrous."

"Monstrous above all!" her visitor echoed; "and I imagine, by the same stroke, quite hideous and offensive."

"You don't believe that," she returned; "if you did you wouldn't wonder. You'd

---

4. "For two cents" (French). That is, I couldn't give even a hasty, two-cent judgment.

know, and that would be enough for you. What you feel—and what I feel *for* you—is that you'd have had power."

"You'd have liked me that way?" he asked.

She barely hung fire. "How should I not have liked you?"

"I see. You'd have liked me, have preferred me, a billionaire!"

"How should I not have liked you?" she simply again asked.

He stood before her still—her question kept him motionless. He took it in, so much there was of it; and indeed his not otherwise meeting it testified to that. "I know at least what I am," he simply went on; "the other side of the medal's clear enough. I've not been edifying—I believe I'm thought in a hundred quarters, to have been barely decent. I've followed strange paths and worshipped strange gods; it must have come to you again and again—in fact, you've admitted to me as much—that I was leading, at any time these thirty years, a selfish frivolous scandalous life. And you see what it has made of me."

She just waited, smiling at him. "You see what it has made of *me*."

"Oh you're a person whom nothing can have altered. You were born to be what you are, anywhere, anyway: you've the perfection nothing else could have blighted. And don't you see how, without my exile, I shouldn't have been waiting till now—?" But he pulled up for the strange pang.

"The great thing to see," she presently said, "seems to me to be that it has spoiled nothing. It hasn't spoiled your being here at last. It hasn't spoiled this. It hasn't spoiled your speaking—" She also however faltered.

He wondered at everything her controlled emotion might mean. "Do you believe then—too dreadfully!—that I *am* as good as I might ever have been?"

"Oh no! Far from it!" With which she got up from her chair and was nearer to him. "But I don't care," she smiled.

"You mean I'm good enough?"

She considered a little. "Will you believe it if I say so? I mean will you let that settle your question for you?" And then as if making out in his face that he drew back from this, that he had some idea which, however absurd, he couldn't yet bargain away: "Oh you don't care either—but very differently: you don't care for anything but yourself."

Spencer Brydon recognised it—it was in fact what he had absolutely professed. Yet he importantly qualified. "*He* isn't myself. He's the just so totally other person. But I do want to see him," he added. "And I can. And I shall."

Their eyes met for a minute while he guessed from something in hers that she divined his strange sense. But neither of them otherwise expressed it, and her apparent understanding, with no protesting shock, no easy derision, touched him more deeply than anything yet, constituting for his stifled perversity, on the spot, an element that was like breatheable air. What she said however was unexpected. "Well, *I've* seen him."

"You—?"

"I've seen him in a dream."

"Oh a 'dream'—!" It let him down.

"But twice over," she continued. "I saw him as I see you now."

"You've dreamed the same dream—?"

"Twice over," she repeated. "The very same."

This did somehow a little speak to him, as it also gratified him. "You dream about me at that rate?"

"Ah about *him*!" she smiled.

His eyes again sounded her. "Then you know all about him." And as she said nothing more: "What's the wretch like?"

She hesitated, and it was as if he were pressing her so hard that, resisting for reasons of her own, she had to turn away. "I'll tell you some other time!"

## II

It was after this that there was most of a virtue for him, most of a cultivated charm, most of a preposterous secret thrill, in the particular form of surrender to his obsession and of address to what he more and more believed to be his privilege. It was what in these weeks he was living for—since he really felt life to begin but after Mrs. Muldoon had retired from the scene and, visiting the ample house from attic to cellar, making sure he was alone, he knew himself in safe possession and, as he tacitly expressed it, let himself go. He sometimes came twice in the twenty-four hours; the moments he liked best were those of gathering dusk, of the short autumn twilight; this was the time of which, again and again, he found himself hoping most. Then he could, as seemed to him, most intimately wander and wait, linger and listen, feel his fine attention, never in his life before so fine, on the pulse of the great vague place: he preferred the lampless hour and only wished he might have prolonged each day the deep crepuscular spell. Later—rarely much before midnight, but then for a considerable vigil—he watched with his glimmering light; moving slowly, holding it high, playing it far, rejoicing above all, as much as he might, in open vistas, reaches of communication between rooms and by passages; the long straight chance or show, as he would have called it, for the revelation he pretended to invite. It was a practice he found he could perfectly "work" without exciting remark; no one was in the least the wiser for it; even Alice Staverton, who was moreover a well of discretion, didn't quite fully imagine.

He let himself in and let himself out with the assurance of calm proprietorship; and accident so far favoured him that, if a fat Avenue "officer" had happened on occasion to see him entering at eleven-thirty, he had never yet, to the best of his belief, been noticed as emerging at two. He walked there on the crisp November nights, arrived regularly at the evening's end; it was as easy to do this after dining out as to take his way to a club or to his hotel. When he left his club, if he hadn't been dining out, it was ostensibly to go to his hotel; and when he left his hotel, if he had spent a part of the evening there, it was ostensibly to go to his club. Everything was easy in fine; everything conspired and promoted: there was truly even in the strain of his experience something that glossed over, something that salved and simplified, all the rest of consciousness. He circulated, talked, renewed, loosely and pleasantly, old relations—met indeed, so far as he could, new expectations and seemed to make out on the whole that in spite of the career, of such different contacts, which he had spoken of to Miss Staverton as ministering so little, for those who might have watched it, to edification, he was positively rather liked than not. He was a dim secondary social success—and all with people who had truly not an idea of him. It was all mere surface sound, this murmur of their welcome, this popping of their corks—just as his gestures of response were the extravagant shadows, emphatic in proportion as they meant little, of some game of *ombres chinoises*.[5] He projected himself all day, in thought, straight over the bristling line of hard unconscious heads and into the other, the

---

5. Chinese shadows (French)—shadow theater.

real, the waiting life; the life that, as soon as he had heard behind him the click of his great house-door, began for him, on the jolly corner, as beguilingly as the slow opening bars of some rich music follow the tap of the conductor's wand.

He always caught the first effect of the steel point of his stick on the old marble of the hall pavement, large black-and-white squares that he remembered as the admiration of his childhood and that had then made in him, as he now saw, for the growth of an early conception of style. This effect was the dim reverberating tinkle as of some far-off bell hung who should say where?—in the depths of the house, of the past, of that mystical other world that might have flourished for him had he not, for weal or woe, abandoned it. On this impression he did ever the same thing; he put his stick noiselessly away in a corner—feeling the place once more in the likeness of some great glass bowl, all precious concave crystal, set delicately humming by the play of a moist finger round its edge. The concave crystal held, as it were, this mystical other world, and the indescribably fine murmur of its rim was the sigh there, the scarce audible pathetic wail to his strained ear, of all the old baffled forsworn possibilities. What he did therefore by this appeal of his hushed presence was to wake them into such measure of ghostly life as they might still enjoy. They were shy, all but unappeasably shy, but they weren't really sinister; at least they weren't as he had hitherto felt them—before they had taken the Form he so yearned to make them take, the Form he at moments saw himself in the light of fairly hunting on tiptoe, the points of his evening-shoes, from room to room and from storey to storey.

That was the essence of his vision—which was all rank folly, if one would, while he was out of the house and otherwise occupied, but which took on the last verisimilitude as soon as he was placed and posted. He knew what he meant and what he wanted; it was as clear as the figure on a cheque presented in demand for cash. His *alter ego* "walked"—that was the note of his image of him, while his image of his motive for his own odd pastime was the desire to waylay him and meet him. He roamed, slowly, warily, but all restlessly, he himself did—Mrs. Muldoon had been right, absolutely, with her figure of their "craping"; and the presence he watched for would roam restlessly too. But it would be as cautious and as shifty; the conviction of its probable, in fact its already quite sensible, quite audible evasion of pursuit grew for him from night to night, laying on him finally a rigour to which nothing in his life had been comparable. It had been the theory of many superficially-judging persons, he knew, that he was wasting that life in a surrender to sensations, but he had tasted of no pleasure so fine as his actual tension, had been introduced to no sport that demanded at once the patience and the nerve of this stalking of a creature more subtle, yet at bay perhaps more formidable, than any beast of the forest. The terms, the comparisons, the very practices of the chase positively came again into play; there were even moments when passages of his occasional experience as a sportsman, stirred memories, from his younger time, of moor and mountain and desert, revived for him—and to the increase of his keenness—by the tremendous force of analogy. He found himself at moments—once he had placed his single light on some mantel-shelf or in some recess—stepping back into shelter or shade, effacing himself behind a door or in an embrasure, as he had sought of old the vantage of rock and tree; he found himself holding his breath and living in the joy of the instant, the supreme suspense created by big game alone.

He wasn't afraid (though putting himself the question as he believed gentlemen on Bengal tiger-shoots or in close quarters with the great bear of the Rockies had been known to confess to having put it); and this indeed—since here at least he might be frank!—because of the impression, so intimate and so strange, that he himself produced as yet a dread, produced certainly a strain, beyond the liveliest he was likely to feel. They fell for him into categories, they fairly became familiar, the signs, for his own perception, of the alarm his presence and his vigilance created; though leaving him always to remark, portentously, on his probably having formed a relation, his probably enjoying a consciousness, unique in the experience of man. People enough, first and last, had been in terror of apparitions, but who had ever before so turned the tables and become himself, in the apparitional world, an incalculable terror? He might have found this sublime had he quite dared to think of it; but he didn't too much insist, truly, on that side of his privilege. With habit and repetition he gained to an extraordinary degree the power to penetrate the dusk of distances and the darkness of corners, to resolve back into their innocence the treacheries of uncertain light, the evil-looking forms taken in the gloom by mere shadows, by accidents of the air, by shifting effects of perspective; putting down his dim luminary he could still wander on without it, pass into other rooms and, only knowing it was there behind him in case of need, see his way about, visually project for his purpose a comparative clearness. It made him feel, this acquired faculty, like some monstrous stealthy cat; he wondered if he would have glared at these moments with large shining yellow eyes, and what it mightn't verily be, for the poor hard-pressed *alter ego*, to be confronted with such a type.

He liked however the open shutters; he opened everywhere those Mrs. Muldoon had closed, closing them as carefully afterwards, so that she shouldn't notice: he liked—oh this he did like, and above all in the upper rooms!—the sense of the hard silver of the autumn stars through the window-panes, and scarcely less the flare of the street-lamps below, the white electric lustre which it would have taken curtains to keep out. This was human actual social; this was of the world he had lived in, and he was more at his ease certainly for the countenance, coldly general and impersonal, that all the while and in spite of his detachment it seemed to give him. He had support of course mostly in the rooms at the wide front and the prolonged side; it failed him considerably in the central shades and the parts at the back. But if he sometimes, on his rounds, was glad of his optical reach, so none the less often the rear of the house affected him as the very jungle of his prey. The place was there more subdivided; a large "extension" in particular, where small rooms for servants had been multiplied, abounded in nooks and corners, in closets and passages, in the ramifications especially of an ample back staircase over which he leaned, many a time, to look far down—not deterred from his gravity even while aware that he might, for a spectator, have figured some solemn simpleton playing at hide-and-seek. Outside in fact he might himself make that ironic *rapprochement*,[6] but within the walls, and in spite of the clear windows, his consistency was proof against the cynical light of New York.

It had belonged to that idea of the exasperated consciousness of his victim to become a real test for him; since he had quite put it to himself from the first that, oh distinctly! he could "cultivate" his whole perception. He had felt it as

---

6. A bringing together, comparison (French).

above all open to cultivation—which indeed was but another name for his manner of spending his time. He was bringing it on, bringing it to perfection, by practice; in consequence of which it had grown so fine that he was now aware of impressions, attestations of his general postulate, that couldn't have broken upon him at once. This was the case more specifically with a phenomenon at last quite frequent for him in the upper rooms, the recognition—absolutely unmistakable, and by a turn dating from a particular hour, his resumption of his campaign after a diplomatic drop, a calculated absence of three nights—of his being definitely followed, tracked at a distance carefully taken and to the express end that he should the less confidently, less arrogantly, appear to himself merely to pursue. It worried, it finally quite broke him up, for it proved, of all the conceivable impressions, the one least suited to his book. He was kept in sight while remaining himself—as regards the essence of his position—sightless, and his only recourse then was in abrupt turns, rapid recoveries of ground. He wheeled about, retracing his steps, as if he might so catch in his face at least the stirred air of some other quick revolution. It was indeed true that his fully dislocalised thought of these manoeuvres recalled to him Pantaloon, at the Christmas farce,[7] buffeted and tricked from behind by ubiquitous Harlequin; but if left intact the influence of the conditions themselves each time he was re-exposed to them, so that in fact this association, had he suffered it to become constant, would on a certain side have but ministered to his intenser gravity. He had made, as I have said, to create on the premises the baseless sense of a reprieve, his three absences; and the result of the third was to confirm the after-effect of the second.

On his return, that night—the night succeeding his last intermission—he stood in the hall and looked up the staircase with a certainty more intimate than any he had yet known. "He's *there*, at the top, and waiting—not, as in general, falling back for disappearance. He's holding his ground, and it's the first time—which is a proof, isn't it? that something has happened for him." So Brydon argued with his hand on the banister and his foot on the lowest stair; in which position he felt as never before the air chilled by his logic. He himself turned cold in it, for he seemed of a sudden to know what now was involved. "Harder pressed?—yes, he takes it in, with its thus making clear to him that I've come, as they say, 'to stay.' He finally doesn't like and can't bear it, in the sense, I mean, that his wrath, his menaced interest, now balances with his dread. I've hunted him till he has 'turned': that, up there, is what has happened—he's the fanged or the antlered animal brought at last to bay." There came to him, as I say—but determined by an influence beyond my notation!—the acuteness of this certainty; under which however the next moment he had broken into a sweat that he would as little have consented to attribute to fear as he would have dared immediately to act upon it for enterprise. It marked none the less a prodigious thrill, a thrill that represented sudden dismay, no doubt, but also represented, and with the selfsame throb, the strangest, the most joyous, possibly the next minute almost the proudest, duplication of consciousness.

"He has been dodging, retreating, hiding, but now, worked up to anger, he'll fight!"—this intense impression made a single mouthful, as it were, of terror and applause. But what was wondrous was that the applause, for the felt fact, was

---

7. Christmas pantomime, an annual comic stage presentation derived from the Italian *commedia dell'arte*, featuring such stock characters as Pantaloon and Harlequin.

so eager, since, if it was his other self he was running to earth, this ineffable identity was thus in the last resort not unworthy of him. It bristled there—somewhere near at hand, however unseen still—as the hunted thing, even as the trodden worm of the adage *must* at last bristle;[8] and Brydon at this instant tasted probably of a sensation more complex than had ever before found itself consistent with sanity. It was as if it would have shamed him that a character so associated with his own should triumphantly succeed in just skulking, should to the end not risk the open; so that the drop of this danger was, on the spot, a great lift of the whole situation. Yet with another rare shift of the same subtlety he was already trying to measure by how much more he himself might now be in peril of fear; so rejoicing that he could, in another form, actively inspire that fear, and simultaneously quaking for the form in which he might passively know it.

The apprehension of knowing it must after a little have grown in him, and the strangest moment of his adventure perhaps, the most memorable or really most interesting, afterwards, of his crisis, was the lapse of certain instants of concentrated conscious *combat*, the sense of a need to hold on to something, even after the manner of a man slipping and slipping on some awful incline; the vivid impulse, above all, to move, to act, to charge, somehow and upon something—to show himself, in a word, that he wasn't afraid. The state of "holding-on" was thus the state to which he was momentarily reduced; if there had been anything, in the great vacancy, to seize, he would presently have been aware of having clutched it as he might under a shock at home have clutched the nearest chairback. He had been surprised at any rate—of this he *was* aware—into something unprecedented since his original appropriation of the place; he had closed his eyes, held them tight, for a long minute, as with that instinct of dismay and that terror of vision. When he opened them the room, the other contiguous rooms, extraordinarily, seemed lighter—so light, almost, that at first he took the change for day. He stood firm, however that might be, just where he had paused; his resistance had helped him—it was as if there were something he had tided over. He knew after a little what this was—it had been in the imminent danger of flight. He had stiffened his will against going; without this he would have made for the stairs, and it seemed to him that, still with his eyes closed, he would have descended them, would have known how, straight and swiftly, to the bottom.

Well, as he had held out, here he was—still at the top, among the more intricate upper rooms and with the gauntlet of the others, of all the rest of the house, still to run when it should be his time to go. He would go at his time—only at his time: didn't he go every night very much at the same hour? He took out his watch—there was light for that: it was scarcely a quarter past one, and he had never withdrawn so soon. He reached his lodgings for the most part at two—with his walk of a quarter of an hour. He would wait for the last quarter—he wouldn't stir till then; and he kept his watch there with his eyes on it, reflecting while he held it that this deliberate wait, a wait with an effort, which he recognised, would serve perfectly for the attestation he desired to make. It would prove his courage—unless indeed the latter might most be proved by his budging at

---

8. The phrase "the worm has turned" is a shortened version of an adage cited by Shakespeare in *3 Henry VI*: "The smallest worm will turn, being trodden on."

last from his place. What he mainly felt now was that, since he hadn't originally scuttled, he had his dignities—which had never in his life seemed so many—all to preserve and to carry aloft. This was before him in truth as a physical image, an image almost worthy of an age of greater romance. That remark indeed glimmered for him only to glow the next instant with a finer light; since what age of romance, after all, could have matched either the state of his mind or, "objectively," as they said, the wonder of his situation? The only difference would have been that, brandishing his dignities over his head as in a parchment scroll, he might then—that is in the heroic time—have proceeded downstairs with a drawn sword in his other grasp.

At present, really, the light he had set down on the mantel of the next room would have to figure his sword; which utensil, in the course of a minute, he had taken the requisite number of steps to possess himself of. The door between the rooms was open, and from the second another door opened to a third. These rooms, as he remembered, gave all three upon a common corridor as well, but there was a fourth, beyond them, without issue save through the preceding. To have moved, to have heard his step again, was appreciably a help; though even in recognising this he lingered once more a little by the chimney-piece on which his light had rested. When he next moved, just hesitating where to turn, he found himself considering a circumstance that, after his first and comparatively vague apprehension of it, produced in him the start that often attends some pang of recollection, the violent shock of having ceased happily to forget. He had come into sight of the door in which the brief chain of communication ended and which he now surveyed from the nearer threshold, the one not directly facing it. Placed at some distance to the left of this point, it would have admitted him to the last room of the four, the room without other approach or egress, had it not, to his intimate conviction, been closed *since* his former visitation, the matter probably of a quarter of an hour before. He stared with all his eyes at the wonder of the fact, arrested again where he stood and again holding his breath while he sounded its sense. Surely it had been *subsequently* closed—that is it had been on his previous passage indubitably open!

He took it full in the face that something had happened between—that he couldn't not have noticed before (by which he meant on his original tour of all the rooms that evening) that such a barrier had exceptionally presented itself. He had indeed since that moment undergone an agitation so extraordinary that it might have muddled for him any earlier view; and he tried to convince himself that he might perhaps then have gone into the room and, inadvertently, automatically, on coming out, have drawn the door after him. The difficulty was that this exactly was what he never did; it was against his whole policy, as he might have said, the essence of which was to keep vistas clear. He had them from the first, as he was well aware, quite on the brain: the strange apparition, at the far end of one of them, of his baffled "prey" (which had become by so sharp an irony so little the term now to apply!) was the form of success his imagination had most cherished, projecting into it always a refinement of beauty. He had known fifty times the start of perception that had afterwards dropped; had fifty times gasped to himself "There!" under some fond brief hallucination. The house, as the case stood, admirably lent itself; he might wonder at the taste, the native architecture of the particular time, which could rejoice so in the multiplication of doors—the opposite extreme to the modern, the actual almost complete proscription of them; but it had fairly contributed to provoke this obsession of the presence encountered telescopically, as he might say, focussed and studied in diminishing perspective and as by a rest for the elbow.

It was with these considerations that his present attention was charged—they perfectly availed to make what he saw portentous. He *couldn't*, by any lapse, have blocked that aperture; and if he hadn't, if it was unthinkable, why what else was clear but that there had been another agent? Another agent?—he had been catching, as he felt, a moment back, the very breath of him; but when had he been so close as in this simple, this logical, this completely personal act? It was so logical, that is, that one might have *taken* it for personal; yet for what did Brydon take it, he asked himself, while, softly panting, he felt his eyes almost leave their sockets. Ah this time at last they *were*, the two, the opposed projections of him, in presence; and this time, as much as one would, the question of danger loomed. With it rose, as not before, the question of courage—for what he knew the blank face of the door to say to him was "Show us how much you have!" It stared, it glared back at him with that challenge; it put to him the two alternatives: should he just push it open or not? Oh to have this consciousness was to *think*—and to think, Brydon knew, as he stood there, was, with the lapsing moments, not to have acted! Not to have acted—that was the misery and the pang—was even still not to act; was in fact *all* to feel the thing in another, in a new and terrible way. How long did he pause and how long did he debate? There was presently nothing to measure it; for his vibration had already changed—as just by the effect of its intensity. Shut up there, at bay, defiant, and with the prodigy of the thing palpably proveably *done*, thus giving notice like some stark signboard—under that accession of accent the situation itself had turned; and Brydon at last remarkably made up his mind on what it had turned to.

It had turned altogether to a different admonition; to a supreme hint, for him, of the value of Discretion! This slowly dawned, no doubt—for it could take its time; so perfectly, on his threshold, had he been stayed, so little as yet had he either advanced or retreated. It was the strangest of all things that now when, by his taking ten steps and applying his hand to a latch, or even his shoulder and his knee, if necessary, to a panel, all the hunger of his prime need might have been met, his high curiosity crowned, his unrest assuaged—it was amazing, but it was also exquisite and rare, that insistence should have, at a touch, quite dropped from him. Discretion—he jumped at that; and yet not, verily, at such a pitch, because it saved his nerves or his skin, but because, much more valuable, it saved the situation. When I say he "jumped" at it I feel the consonance of this term with the fact that—at the end indeed of I know not how long—he did move again, he crossed straight to the door. He wouldn't touch it—it seemed now that he might *if* he would: he would only just wait there a little, to show, to prove, that he wouldn't. He had thus another station, close to the thin partition by which revelation was denied him; but with his eyes bent and his hands held off in a mere intensity of stillness. He listened as if there had been something to hear, but this attitude, while it lasted, was his own communication. "If you won't then—good: I spare you and I give up. You affect me as by the appeal positively for pity: you convince me that for reasons rigid and sublime—what do I know?— we both of us should have suffered. I respect them then, and, though moved and privileged as, I believe, it has never been given to man, I retire, I renounce— never, on my honour, to try again. So rest for ever—and let *me*!"

That, for Brydon was the deep sense of this last demonstration—solemn, measured, directed, as he felt it to be. He brought it to a close, he turned away; and now verily he knew how deeply he had been stirred. He retraced his steps, taking up his candle, burnt, he observed, well-nigh to the socket, and marking again, lighten it as he would, the distinctness of his footfall; after which, in a moment, he knew himself at the other side of the house. He did here what he had not yet done at these hours—he opened half a casement, one of those in the front, and let in the air of the night; a thing he would have taken at any time previous for a sharp rupture of his spell. His spell was broken now, and it didn't matter—broken by his concession and his surrender, which made it idle henceforth that he should ever come back. The empty street—its other life so marked even by the great lamplit vacancy—was within call, within touch; he stayed there as to be in it again, high above it though he was still perched; he watched as for some comforting common fact, some vulgar human note, the passage of a scavenger or a thief, some night-bird however base. He would have blessed that sign of life; he would have welcomed positively the slow approach of his friend the policeman, whom he had hitherto only sought to avoid, and was not sure that if the patrol had come into sight he mightn't have felt the impulse to get into relation with it, to hail it, on some pretext, from his fourth floor.

The pretext that wouldn't have been too silly or too compromising, the explanation that would have saved his dignity and kept his name, in such a case, out of the papers, was not definite to him: he was so occupied with the thought of recording his Discretion—as an effect of the vow he had just uttered to his intimate adversary—that the importance of this loomed large and something had overtaken all ironically his sense of proportion. If there had been a ladder applied to the front of the house, even one of the vertiginous perpendiculars employed by painters and roofers and sometimes left standing overnight, he would have managed somehow, astride of the window-sill, to compass by outstretched leg and arm that mode of descent. If there had been some such uncanny thing as he had found in his room at hotels, a workable fire-escape in the form of notched cable or a canvas shoot, he would have availed himself of it as a proof—well, of his present delicacy. He nursed that sentiment, as the question stood, a little in vain, and even—at the end of he scarce knew, once more, how long—found it, as by the action on his mind of the failure of response of the outer world, sinking back to vague anguish. It seemed to him he had waited an age for some stir of the great grim hush; the life of the town was itself under a spell—so unnaturally, up and down the whole prospect of known and rather ugly objects, the blankness and the silence lasted. Had they ever, he asked himself, the hard-faced houses, which had begun to look livid in the dim dawn, had they ever spoken so little to any need of his spirit? Great built voids, great crowded stillnesses put on, often, in the heart of cities, for the small hours, a sort of sinister mask, and it was of this large collective negation that Brydon presently became conscious—all the more that the break of day was, almost incredibly, now at hand, proving to him what a night he had made of it.

He looked again at his watch, saw what had become of his time-values (he had taken hours for minutes—not, as in other tense situations, minutes for hours) and the strange air of the streets was but the weak, the sullen flush of a dawn in which everything was still locked up. His choked appeal from his own open window had been the sole note of life, and he could but break off at last as for a worse despair. Yet while so deeply demoralised he was capable again of an impulse denoting—at least by his present measure—extraordinary resolution; of retracing his steps to the spot where he had turned cold with the extinction of his last pulse of doubt as to there being in the place another presence than his own. This required an effort strong enough to sicken him; but he had his reason, which overmastered for the moment everything else. There was the whole of the rest of the house to traverse, and how should he screw himself to that if the door he had seen closed were at present open? He could hold to the idea that the closing had practically been for him an act of mercy, a chance offered him to descend, depart, get off the ground and never again profane it. This conception held together, it worked; but what it meant for him depended now clearly on the amount of forbearance his recent action, or rather his recent inaction, had engendered. The image of the "presence," whatever it was, waiting there for him to go—this image had not yet been so concrete for his nerves as when he stopped short of the point at which certainty would have come to him. For, with all his resolution, or more exactly with all his dread, he did stop short—he hung back from really seeing. The risk was too great and his fear too definite: it took at this moment an awful specific form.

He knew—yes, as he had never known anything—that, *should* he see the door open, it would all too abjectly be the end of him. It would mean that the agent of his shame—for his shame was the deep abjection—was once more at large and in general possession; and what glared him thus in the face was the act that this would determine for him. It would send him straight about to the window he had left open, and by that window, be long ladder and dangling rope as absent as they would, he saw himself uncontrollably insanely fatally take his way to the street. The hideous chance of this he at least could avert; but he could only avert it by recoiling in time from assurance. He had the whole house to deal with, this fact was still there; only he now knew that uncertainty alone could start him. He stole back from where he had checked himself—merely to do so was suddenly like safety—and, making blindly for the greater staircase, left gaping rooms and sounding passages behind. Here was the top of the stairs, with a fine large dim descent and three spacious landings to mark off. His instinct was all for mildness, but his feet were harsh on the floors, and, strangely, when he had in a couple of minutes become aware of this, it counted somehow for help. He couldn't have spoken, the tone of his voice would have scared him, and the common conceit or resource of "whistling in the dark" (whether literally or figuratively) have appeared basely vulgar; yet he liked none the less to hear himself go, and when he had reached his first landing—taking it all with no rush, but quite steadily—that stage of success drew from him a gasp of relief.

The house, withal, seemed immense, the scale of space again inordinate; the open rooms, to no one of which his eyes deflected, gloomed in their shuttered state like mouths of caverns; only the high skylight that formed the crown of the deep well created for him a medium in which he could advance, but which might have been, for queerness of colour, some watery under-world. He tried to think of something noble, as that his property was really grand, a splendid possession; but this nobleness took the form too of the clear delight with which he was finally to sacrifice it. They might come in now, the builders, the destroyers—they might come as soon as they would. At the end of two flights he had dropped to another zone, and from the middle of the third, with only one more left, he recognized the influence of the lower windows, of half-drawn blinds, of the occasional gleam of street-lamps, of the glazed spaces of the vestibule. This was the bottom of the sea, which showed an illumination of its own and which he even saw paved—when at a given moment he drew up to sink a long look over the banisters—with the marble squares of his childhood. By that time indubitably he felt, as he might have said in a commoner cause, better; it had allowed him to stop and draw breath, and the ease increased with the sight of the old black-and-white slabs. But what he most felt was that now surely, with the element of impunity pulling him as by hard firm hands, the case was settled for what he might have seen above had he dared that last look. The closed door, blessedly remote now, was still closed—and he had only in short to reach that of the house.

He came down further, he crossed the passage forming the access to the last flight; and if here again he stopped an instant it was almost for the sharpness of the thrill of assured escape. It made him shut his eyes—which opened again to the straight slope of the remainder of the stairs. Here was impunity still, but impunity almost excessive; inasmuch as the sidelights and the high fan-tracery of the entrance were glimmering straight into the hall; an appearance produced, he the next instant saw, by the fact that the vestibule gaped wide, that the hinged halves of the inner door had been thrown far back. Out of that again the *question* sprang at him, making his eyes, as he felt, half-start from his head, as they had done, at the top of the house, before the sign of the other door. If he had left that one open, hadn't he left this one closed, and wasn't he now in *most* immediate presence of some inconceivable occult activity? It was as sharp, the question, as a knife in his side, but the answer hung fire still and seemed to lose itself in the vague darkness to which the thin admitted dawn, glimmering archwise over the whole outer door, made a semicircular margin, a cold silvery nimbus that seemed to play a little as he looked—to shift and expand and contract.

It was as if there had been something within it, protected by indistinctness and corresponding in extent with the opaque surface behind, the painted panels of the last barrier to his escape, of which the key was in his pocket. The indistinctness mocked him even while he stared, affected him as somehow shrouding or challenging certitude, so that after faltering an instant on his step he let himself go with the sense that here *was* at last something to meet, to touch, to take, to know—something all unnatural and dreadful, but to advance upon which was the condition for him either of liberation or of supreme defeat. The penumbra, dense and dark, was the virtual screen of a figure which stood in it as still as some image erect in a niche or as some black-vizored sentinel guarding a treasure. Brydon was to know afterwards, was to recall and make out, the particular thing he had believed during the rest of his descent. He saw, in its great grey glimmering margin, the central vagueness diminish, and he felt it to be taking the very form toward which, for so many days, the passion of his curiosity had yearned. It gloomed, it loomed, it was something, it was somebody, the prodigy of a personal presence.

Rigid and conscious, spectral yet human, a man of his own substance and stature waited there to measure himself with his power to dismay. This only could it be—this only till he recognised, with his advance, that what made the face dim was the pair of raised hands that covered it and in which, so far from being offered in defiance, it was buried as for dark deprecation. So Brydon, before him, took him in; with every fact of him now, in the higher light, hard and acute—his planted stillness, his vivid truth, his grizzled bent head and white masking hands, his queer actuality of evening-dress, of dangling double eye-glass, of gleaming silk lappet and white linen, of pearl button and gold watch-guard and polished shoe. No portrait by a great modern master could have presented him with more intensity, thrust him out of his frame with more art, as if there had been "treatment," of the consummate sort, in his every shade and salience. The revulsion, for our friend, had become, before he knew it, immense—this drop, in the act of apprehension, to the sense of his adversary's inscrutable manœuvre. That meaning at least, while he gaped, it offered him; for he could but gape at his other self in this other anguish, gape as a proof that *he*, standing there for the achieved, the enjoyed, the triumphant life, couldn't be faced in his triumph. Wasn't the proof in the splendid covering hands, strong and completely spread?— so spread and so intentional that, in spite of a special verity that surpassed every other, the fact that one of these hands had lost two fingers, which were reduced to stumps, as if accidentally shot away, the face was effectually guarded and saved.

"Saved," though, *would* it be?—Brydon breathed his wonder till the very impunity of his attitude and the very insistence of his eyes produced, as he felt, a sudden stir which showed the next instant as a deeper portent, while the head raised itself, the betrayal of a braver purpose. The hands, as he looked, began to move, to open; then, as if deciding in a flash, dropped from the face and left it uncovered and presented. Horror, with the sight, had leaped into Brydon's throat, gasping there in a sound he couldn't utter; for the bared identity was too hideous as *his*, and his glare was the passion of his protest. The face, *that* face, Spencer Brydon's?—he searched it still, but looking away from it in dismay and denial, falling straight from his height of sublimity. It was unknown, inconceivable, awful, disconnected from any possibility—! He had been "sold," he inwardly moaned, stalking such game as this: the presence before him was a presence, the horror within him a horror, but the waste of his nights had been only grotesque and the success of his adventure an irony. Such an identity fitted his at *no* point, made its alternative monstrous. A thousand times yes, as it came upon him nearer now—the face was the face of a stranger. It came upon him nearer now, quite as one of those expanding fantastic images projected by the magic lantern of childhood; for the stranger, whoever he might be, evil, odious, blatant, vulgar, had advanced as for aggression, and he knew himself give ground. Then harder pressed still, sick with the force of his shock, and falling back as under the hot breath and the roused passion of a life larger than his own, a rage of personality before which his own collapsed, he felt the whole vision turn to darkness and his very feet give way. His head went round; he was going; he had gone.

III

What had next brought him back, clearly—though after how long?—was Mrs. Muldoon's voice, coming to him from quite near, from so near that he seemed presently to see her as kneeling on the ground before him while he lay looking up at her; himself not wholly on the ground, but half-raised and upheld—conscious, yes, of tenderness of support and, more particularly, of a head pillowed in extraordinary softness and faintly refreshing fragrance. He considered, he wondered, his wit but half at his service; then another face intervened, bending more directly over him, and he finally knew that Alice Staverton had made her lap an ample and perfect cushion to him, and that she had to this end seated herself on the lowest degree of the staircase, the rest of his long person remaining stretched on his old black-and-white slabs. They were cold, these marble squares of his youth; but *he* somehow was not, in this rich return of consciousness—the most wonderful hour, little by little, that he had ever known, leaving him, as it did, so gratefully, so abysmally passive, and yet as with a treasure of intelligence waiting all round him for quiet appropriation; dissolved, he might call it, in the air of the place and producing the golden glow of a late autumn afternoon. He had come back, yes—come back from further away than any man but himself had ever travelled; but it was strange how with this sense of what he had come back *to* seemed really the great thing, and as if his prodigious journey had been all for the sake of it. Slowly but surely his consciousness grew, his vision of his state thus completing itself: he had been miraculously *carried* back—lifted and carefully borne as from where he had been picked up, the uttermost end of an interminable grey passage. Even with this he was suffered to rest, and what had now brought him to knowledge was the break in the long mild motion.

It had brought him to knowledge, to knowledge—yes, this was the beauty of his state; which came to resemble more and more that of a man who has gone to sleep on some news of a great inheritance, and then, after dreaming it away, after profaning it with matters strange to it, has waked up again to serenity of certitude and has only to lie and watch it grow. This was the drift of his patience—that he had only to let it shine on him. He must moreover, with intermissions, still have been lifted and borne; since why and how else should he have known himself, later on, with the afternoon glow intenser, no longer at the foot of his stairs—situated as these now seemed at that dark other end of his tunnel—but on a deep window-bench of his high saloon, over which had been spread, couch-fashion, a mantle of soft stuff lined with grey fur that was familiar to his eyes and that one of his hands kept fondly feeling as for its pledge of truth. Mrs. Muldoon's face had gone, but the other, the second he had recognised, hung over him in a way that showed how he was still propped and pillowed. He took it all in, and the more he took it the more it seemed to suffice: he was as much at peace as if he had had food and drink. It was the two women who had found him, on Mrs. Muldoon's having plied, at her usual hour, her latch-key—and on her having above all arrived while Miss Staverton still lingered near the house. She had been turning away, all anxiety, from worrying the vain bell-handle—her calculation having been of the hour of the good woman's visit; but the latter, blessedly, had come up while she was still there, and they had entered together. He had then lain, beyond the vestibule, very much as he was lying now—quite, that is, as he appeared to have fallen, but all so wondrously without bruise or gash; only in a depth of stupor. What he most took in, however, at present, with the steadier clearance, was that Alice Staverton had for a long unspeakable moment not doubted he was dead.

"It must have been that I *was*." He made it out as she held him. "Yes—I can only have died. You brought me literally to life. Only," he wondered, his eyes rising to her, "only, in the name of all the benedictions, how?"

It took her but an instant to bend her face and kiss him, and something in the manner of it, and in the way her hands clasped and locked his head while he felt the cool charity and virtue of her lips, something in all this beatitude somehow answered everything. "And now I keep you," she said.

"Oh keep me, keep me!" he pleaded while her face still hung over him: in response to which it dropped again and stayed close, clingingly close. It was the seal of their situation—of which he tasted the impress for a long blissful moment in silence. But he came back. "Yet how did you know—?"

"I was uneasy. You were to have come, you remember—and you had sent no word."

"Yes, I remember—I was to have gone to you at one to-day." It caught on to their "old" life and relation—which were so near and so far. "I was still out there in my strange darkness—where was it, what was it? I must have stayed there so long." He could but wonder at the depth and the duration of his swoon.

"Since last night?" she asked with a shade of fear for her possible indiscretion.

"Since this morning—it must have been: the cold dim dawn of to-day. Where have I been," he vaguely wailed, "where have I been?" He felt her hold him close, and it was as if this helped him now to make in all security his mild moan. "What a long dark day!"

All in her tenderness she had waited a moment. "In the cold dim dawn?" she quavered.

But he had already gone on piecing together the parts of the whole prodigy. "As I didn't turn up you came straight—?"

She barely cast about. "I went first to your hotel—where they told me of your absence. You had dined out last evening and hadn't been back since. But they appeared to know you had been at your club."

"So you had the idea of *this*—?"

"Of what?" she asked in a moment.

"Well—of what has happened."

"I believed at least you'd have been here. I've known, all along," she said, "that you've been coming."

" 'Known' it—?"

"Well, I've believed it. I said nothing to you after that talk we had a month ago—but I felt sure. I knew you *would*," she declared.

"That I'd persist, you mean?"

"That you'd see him."

"Ah but I didn't!" cried Brydon with his long wail. "There's somebody—an awful beast; whom I brought, too horribly, to bay. But it's not me."

At this she bent over him again, and her eyes were in his eyes. "No—it's not you." And it was as if, while her face hovered, he might have made out in it, hadn't it been so near, some particular meaning blurred by a smile. "No, thank heaven," she repeated—"it's not you! Of course it wasn't to have been."

"Ah but it *was*," he gently insisted. And he stared before him now as he had been staring for so many weeks. "I was to have known myself."

"You couldn't!" she returned consolingly. And then reverting, and as if to account further for what she had herself done, "But it wasn't only *that*, that you hadn't been at home," she went on. "I waited till the hour at which we had found Mrs. Muldoon that day of my going with you; and she arrived, as I've told you, while, failing to bring any one to the door, I lingered in my despair on the steps. After a little, if she hadn't come, by such a mercy, I should have found means to hunt her up. But it wasn't," said Alice Staverton, as if once more with her fine intention—"it wasn't only that."

His eyes, as he lay, turned back to her. "What more then?"

She met it, the wonder she had stirred. "In the cold dim dawn, you say? Well, in the cold dim dawn of this morning I too saw you."

"Saw *me*—?"

"Saw *him*," said Alice Staverton. "It must have been at the same moment."

He lay an instant taking it in—as if he wished to be quite reasonable. "At the same moment?"

"Yes—in my dream again, the same one I've named to you. He came back to me. Then I knew it for a sign. He had come to you."

At this Brydon raised himself; he had to see her better. She helped him when she understood his movement, and he sat up, steadying himself beside her there on the window-bench and with his right hand grasping her left. "*He* didn't come to me."

"You came to yourself," she beautifully smiled.

"Ah I've come to myself now—thanks to you, dearest. But this brute, with his awful face—this brute's a black stranger. He's none of *me*, even as I *might* have been," Brydon sturdily declared.

But she kept the clearness that was like the breath of infallibility. "Isn't the whole point that you'd have been different?"

He almost scowled for it. "As different as *that*—?"

Her look again was more beautiful to him than the things of this world. "Haven't you exactly wanted to know *how* different? So this morning," she said, "you appeared to me."

"Like *him*?"

"A black stranger!"

"Then how did you know it was I?"

"Because, as I told you weeks ago, my mind, my imagination, had worked so over what you might, what you mightn't have been—to show you, you see, how I've thought of you. In the midst of that you came to me—that my wonder might be answered. So I knew," she went on; "and believed that, since the question held you too so fast, as you told me that day, you too would see for yourself. And when this morning I again saw I knew it would be because you had—and also then, from the first moment, because you somehow wanted me. *He* seemed to tell me of that. So why," she strangely smiled, "shouldn't I like him?"

It brought Spencer Brydon to his feet. "You 'like' that horror—?"

"I *could* have liked him. And to me," she said, "he was no horror. I had accepted him."

" 'Accepted'—?" Brydon oddly sounded.

"Before, for the interest of his difference—yes. And as *I* didn't disown him, as *I* knew him—which you at last, confronted with him in his difference, so cruelly didn't, my dear—well, he must have been, you see, less dreadful to me. And it may have pleased him that I pitied him."

She was beside him on her feet, but still holding his hand—still with her arm supporting him. But though it all brought for him thus a dim light, "You 'pitied' him?" he grudgingly, resentfully asked.

"He has been unhappy, he has been ravaged," she said.

"And haven't I been unhappy? Am not I—you've only to look at me!—ravaged?"

"Ah I don't say I like him *better*," she granted after a thought. "But he's grim, he's worn—and things have happened to him. He doesn't make shift, for sight, with your charming monocle."

"No"—it struck Brydon: "I couldn't have sported mine 'downtown.' They'd have guyed[9] me there."

"His great convex pince-nez[1]—I saw it, I recognised the kind—is for his poor ruined sight. And his poor right hand—!"

"Ah!" Brydon winced—whether for his proved identity or for his lost fingers. Then, "He has a million a year," he lucidly added. "But he hasn't you."

"And he isn't—no, he isn't—*you*!" she murmured as he drew her to his breast.

1909

## CHARLOTTE PERKINS GILMAN

## *The Yellow Wallpaper*

It is very seldom that mere ordinary people like John and myself secure ancestral halls for the summer.

A colonial mansion, a hereditary estate, I would say a haunted house, and reach the height of romantic felicity—but that would be asking too much of fate!

Still I will proudly declare that there is something queer about it.

Else, why should it be let so cheaply? And why have stood so long untenanted?

John laughs at me, of course, but one expects that in marriage.

John is practical in the extreme. He has no patience with faith, an intense horror of superstition, and he scoffs openly at any talk of things not to be felt and seen and put down in figures.

John is a physician, and *perhaps*—(I would not say it to a living soul, of course, but this is dead paper and a great relief to my mind—) *perhaps* that is one reason I do not get well faster.

You see he does not believe I am sick!

And what can one do?

If a physician of high standing, and one's own husband, assures friends and relatives that there is really nothing the matter with one but temporary nervous depression—a slight hysterical tendency—what is one to do?

My brother is also a physician, and also of high standing, and he says the same thing.

So I take phosphates or phosphites—whichever it is, and tonics, and journeys, and air, and exercise, and am absolutely forbidden to "work" until I am well again.

Personally, I disagree with their ideas.

Personally, I believe that congenial work, with excitement and change, would do me good.

But what is one to do?

I did write for a while in spite of them; but it *does* exhaust me a good deal—having to be so sly about it, or else meet with heavy opposition.

---

9. Ridiculed.   1. "Pinch-nose" (French)—eyeglasses that clip onto the nose.

I sometimes fancy that in my condition if I had less opposition and more society and stimulus—but John says the very worst thing I can do is to think about my condition, and I confess it always makes me feel bad.

So I will let it alone and talk about the house.

The most beautiful place! It is quite alone, standing well back from the road, quite three miles from the village. It makes me think of English places that you read about, for there are hedges and walls and gates that lock, and lots of separate little houses for the gardeners and people.

There is a *delicious* garden! I never saw such a garden—large and shady, full of box-bordered paths, and lined with long grape-covered arbors with seats under them.

There were greenhouses, too, but they are all broken now.

There was some legal trouble, I believe, something about the heirs and co-heirs; anyhow, the place has been empty for years.

That spoils my ghostliness, I am afraid, but I don't care—there is something strange about the house—I can feel it.

I even said so to John one moonlight evening, but he said what I felt was a *draught,* and shut the window.

I get unreasonably angry with John sometimes. I'm sure I never used to be so sensitive. I think it is due to this nervous condition.

But John says if I feel so, I shall neglect proper self-control; so I take pains to control myself—before him, at least, and that makes me very tired.

I don't like our room a bit. I wanted one downstairs that opened on the piazza and had roses all over the window, and such pretty old-fashioned chintz hangings! but John would not hear of it.

He said there was only one window and not room for two beds, and no near room for him if he took another.

He is very careful and loving, and hardly lets me stir without special direction.

I have a schedule prescription for each hour in the day; he takes all care from me, and so I feel basely ungrateful not to value it more.

He said we came here solely on my account, that I was to have perfect rest and all the air I could get. "Your exercise depends on your strength, my dear," said he, "and your food somewhat on your appetite; but air you can absorb all the time." So we took the nursery at the top of the house.

It is a big, airy room, the whole floor nearly, with windows that look all ways, and air and sunshine galore. It was nursery first and then playroom and gymnasium, I should judge; for the windows are barred for little children, and there are rings and things in the walls.

The paint and paper look as if a boys' school had used it. It is stripped off—the paper—in great patches all around the head of my bed, about as far as I can reach, and in a great place on the other side of the room low down. I never saw a worse paper in my life.

One of those sprawling flamboyant patterns committing every artistic sin.

It is dull enough to confuse the eye in following, pronounced enough to constantly irritate and provoke study, and when you follow the lame uncertain curves for a little distance they suddenly commit suicide—plunge off at outrageous angles, destroy themselves in unheard of contradictions.

The color is repellant, almost revolting; a smouldering unclean yellow, strangely faded by the slow-turning sunlight.

It is a dull yet lurid orange in some places, a sickly sulphur tint in others.

No wonder the children hated it! I should hate it myself if I had to live in this room long.

There comes John, and I must put this away,—he hates to have me write a word.

We have been here two weeks, and I haven't felt like writing before, since that first day.

I am sitting by the window now, up in this atrocious nursery, and there is nothing to hinder my writing as much as I please, save lack of strength.

John is away all day, and even some nights when his cases are serious.

I am glad my case is not serious!

But these nervous troubles are dreadfully depressing.

John does not know how much I really suffer. He knows there is no *reason* to suffer, and that satisfies him.

Of course it is only nervousness. It does weigh on me so not to do my duty in any way!

I mean to be such a help to John, such a real rest and comfort, and here I am a comparative burden already!

Nobody would believe what an effort it is to do what little I am able,—to dress and entertain, and order things.

It is fortunate Mary is so good with the baby. Such a dear baby!

And yet I *cannot* be with him, it makes me so nervous.

I suppose John never was nervous in his life. He laughs at me so about this wallpaper!

At first he meant to repaper the room, but afterwards he said that I was letting it get the better of me, and that nothing was worse for a nervous patient than to give way to such fancies.

He said that after the wallpaper was changed it would be the heavy bedstead, and then the barred windows, and then that gate at the head of the stairs, and so on.

"You know the place is doing you good," he said, "and really, dear, I don't care to renovate the house just for a three months' rental."

"Then do let us go downstairs," I said, "there are such pretty rooms there."

Then he took me in his arms and called me a blessed little goose, and said he would go down cellar, if I wished, and have it whitewashed into the bargain.

But he is right enough about the beds and windows and things.

It is an airy and comfortable room as any one need wish, and, of course, I would not be so silly as to make him uncomfortable just for a whim.

I'm really getting quite fond of the big room, all but that horrid paper.

Out of one window I can see the garden, those mysterious deep-shaded arbors, the riotous old-fashioned flowers, and bushes and gnarly trees.

Out of another I get a lovely view of the bay and a little private wharf belonging to the estate. There is a beautiful shaded lane that runs down there from the house. I always fancy I see people walking in these numerous paths and arbors, but John has cautioned me not to give way to fancy in the least. He says that with my imaginative power and habit of story-making, a nervous weakness like mine is sure to lead to all manner of excited fancies, and that I ought to use my will and good sense to check the tendency. So I try.

I think sometimes that if I were only well enough to write a little it would relieve the press of ideas and rest me.

But I find I get pretty tired when I try.

It is so discouraging not to have any advice and companionship about my work. When I get really well, John says we will ask Cousin Henry and Julia down for a long visit; but he says he would as soon put fireworks in my pillow-case as to let me have those stimulating people about now.

I wish I could get well faster.

But I must not think about that. This paper looks to me as if it *knew* what a vicious influence it had!

There is a recurrent spot where the pattern lolls like a broken neck and two bulbous eyes stare at you upside down.

I get positively angry with the impertinence of it and the everlastingness. Up and down and sideways they crawl, and those absurd, unblinking eyes are everywhere. There is one place where two breadths didn't match, and the eyes go all up and down the line, one a little higher than the other.

I never saw so much expression in an inanimate thing before, and we all know how much expression they have! I used to lie awake as a child and get more entertainment and terror out of blank walls and plain furniture than most children could find in a toy-store.

I remember what a kindly wink the knobs of our big, old bureau used to have, and there was one chair that always seemed like a strong friend.

I used to feel that if any of the other things looked too fierce I could always hop into that chair and be safe.

The furniture in this room is no worse than inharmonious, however, for we had to bring it all from downstairs. I suppose when this was used as a playroom they had to take the nursery things out, and no wonder! I never saw such ravages as the children have made here.

The wallpaper, as I said before, is torn off in spots, and it sticketh closer than a brother—they must have had perseverance as well as hatred.

Then the floor is scratched and gouged and splintered, the plaster itself is dug out here and there, and this great heavy bed which is all we found in the room, looks as if it had been through the wars.

But I don't mind it a bit—only the paper.

There comes John's sister. Such a dear girl as she is, and so careful of me! I must not let her find me writing.

She is a perfect and enthusiastic housekeeper, and hopes for no better profession. I verily believe she thinks it is the writing which made me sick!

But I can write when she is out, and see her a long way off from these windows.

There is one that commands the road, a lovely shaded winding road, and one that just looks off over the country. A lovely country, too, full of great elms and velvet meadows.

This wallpaper has a kind of sub-pattern in a different shade, a particularly irritating one, for you can only see it in certain lights, and not clearly then.

But in the places where it isn't faded and where the sun is just so—I can see a strange, provoking, formless sort of figure, that seems to skulk about behind that silly and conspicuous front design.

There's sister on the stairs!

Well, the Fourth of July is over! The people are all gone and I am tired out. John thought it might do me good to see a little company, so we just had mother and Nellie and the children down for a week.

Of course I didn't do a thing. Jennie sees to everything now.

But it tired me all the same.

John says if I don't pick up faster he shall send me to Weir Mitchell[1] in the fall.

But I don't want to go there at all. I had a friend who was in his hands once, and she says he is just like John and my brother, only more so!

Besides, it is such an undertaking to go so far.

I don't feel as if it was worth while to turn my hand over for anything, and I'm getting dreadfully fretful and querulous.

I cry at nothing, and cry most of the time.

Of course I don't when John is here, or anybody else, but when I am alone.

And I am alone a good deal just now. John is kept in town very often by serious cases, and Jennie is good and lets me alone when I want her to.

So I walk a little in the garden or down that lovely lane, sit on the porch under the roses, and lie down up here a good deal.

I'm getting really fond of the room in spite of the wallpaper. Perhaps *because* of the wallpaper.

It dwells in my mind so!

I lie here on this great immovable bed—it is nailed down, I believe—and follow that pattern about by the hour. It is as good as gymnastics, I assure you. I start, we'll say, at the bottom, down in the corner over there where it has not been touched, and I determine for the thousandth time that I *will* follow that pointless pattern to some sort of conclusion.

I know a little of the principle of design, and I know this thing was not arranged on any laws of radiation, or alternation, or repetition, or symmetry, or anything else that I ever heard of.

It is repeated, of course, by the breadths, but not otherwise.

Looked at in one way each breadth stands alone, the bloated curves and flourishes—a kind of "debased Romanesque" with *delirium tremens*—go waddling up and down in isolated columns of fatuity.

But, on the other hand, they connect diagonally, and the sprawling outlines run off in great slanting waves of optic horror, like a lot of wallowing seaweeds in full chase.

The whole thing goes horizontally, too, at least it seems so, and I exhaust myself in trying to distinguish the order of its going in that direction.

They have used a horizontal breadth for a frieze, and that adds wonderfully to the confusion.

There is one end of the room where it is almost intact, and there, when the crosslights fade and the low sun shines directly upon it, I can almost fancy radiation after all,—the interminable grotesque seem to form around a common center and rush off in headlong plunges of equal distraction.

It makes me tired to follow it. I will take a nap I guess.

---

1. Silas Weir Mitchell (1829-1914), American physician, novelist, and specialist in nerve disorders, popularized the rest cure.

I don't know why I should write this.
I don't want to.
I don't feel able.
And I know John would think it absurd. But I *must* say what I feel and think in some way—it is such a relief!
But the effort is getting to be greater than the relief.
Half the time now I am awfully lazy, and lie down ever so much.
John says I mustn't lose my strength, and has me take cod liver oil and lots of tonics and things, to say nothing of ale and wine and rare meat.
Dear John! He loves me very dearly, and hates to have me sick. I tried to have a real earnest reasonable talk with him the other day, and tell him how I wish he would let me go and make a visit to Cousin Henry and Julia.
But he said I wasn't able to go, nor able to stand it after I got there; and I did not make out a very good case for myself, for I was crying before I had finished.
It is getting to be a great effort for me to think straight. Just this nervous weakness I suppose.
And dear John gathered me up in his arms, and just carried me upstairs and laid me on the bed, and sat by me and read to me till it tired my head.
He said I was his darling and his comfort and all he had, and that I must take care of myself for his sake, and keep well.
He says no one but myself can help me out of it, that I must use my will and self-control and not let any silly fancies run away with me.
There's one comfort, the baby is well and happy, and does not have to occupy this nursery with the horrid wallpaper.
If we had not used it, that blessed child would have! What a fortunate escape! Why, I wouldn't have a child of mine, an impressionable little thing, live in such a room for worlds.
I never thought of it before, but it is lucky that John kept me here after all, I can stand it so much easier than a baby, you see.
Of course I never mention it to them any more—I am too wise,—but I keep watch of it all the same.
There are things in that paper that nobody knows but me, or ever will.
Behind that outside pattern the dim shapes get clearer every day.
It is always the same shape, only very numerous.
And it is like a woman stooping down and creeping about behind that pattern. I don't like it a bit. I wonder—I begin to think—I wish John would take me away from here!

It is so hard to talk with John about my case, because he is so wise, and because he loves me so.
But I tried it last night.
It was moonlight. The moon shines in all around just as the sun does.
I hate to see it sometimes, it creeps so slowly, and always comes in by one window or another.
John was asleep and I hated to waken him, so I kept still and watched the moonlight on that undulating wallpaper till I felt creepy.
The faint figure behind seemed to shake the pattern, just as if she wanted to get out.
I got up softly and went to feel and see if the paper *did* move, and when I came back John was awake.

"What is it, little girl?" he said. "Don't go walking about like that—you'll get cold."

I thought it was a good time to talk, so I told him that I really was not gaining here, and that I wished he would take me away.

"Why, darling!" said he, "our lease will be up in three weeks, and I can't see how to leave before.

"The repairs are not done at home, and I cannot possibly leave town just now. Of course if you were in any danger, I could and would, but you really are better, dear, whether you can see it or not. I am a doctor, dear, and I know. You are gaining flesh and color, your appetite is better, I feel really much easier about you."

"I don't weigh a bit more," said I, "nor as much; and my appetite may be better in the evening when you are here, but it is worse in the morning when you are away!"

"Bless her little heart!" said he with a big hug, "she shall be as sick as she pleases! But now let's improve the shining hours by going to sleep, and talk about it in the morning!"

"And you won't go away?" I asked gloomily.

"Why, how can I, dear? It is only three weeks more and then we will take a nice little trip of a few days while Jennie is getting the house ready. Really dear you are better!"

"Better in body perhaps—" I began, and stopped short, for he sat up straight and looked at me with such a stern, reproachful look that I could not say another word.

"My darling," said he, "I beg of you, for my sake and for our child's sake, as well as for your own, that you will never for one instant let that idea enter your mind! There is nothing so dangerous, so fascinating, to a temperament like yours. It is a false and foolish fancy. Can you not trust me as a physician when I tell you so?"

So of course I said no more on that score, and we went to sleep before long. He thought I was asleep first, but I wasn't, and lay there for hours trying to decide whether that front pattern and the back pattern really did move together or separately.

On a pattern like this, by daylight, there is a lack of sequence, a defiance of law, that is a constant irritant to a normal mind.

The color is hideous enough, and unreliable enough, and infuriating enough, but the pattern is torturing.

You think you have mastered it, but just as you get well underway in following, it turns a back-somersault and there you are. It slaps you in the face, knocks you down, and tramples upon you. It is like a bad dream.

The outside pattern is a florid arabesque, reminding one of a fungus. If you can imagine a toadstool in joints, an interminable string of toadstools, budding and sprouting in endless convolutions—why, that is something like it.

That is, sometimes!

There is one marked peculiarity about this paper, a thing nobody seems to notice but myself, and that is that it changes as the light changes.

When the sun shoots in through the east window—I always watch for that first long, straight ray—it changes so quickly that I never can quite believe it.

That is why I watch it always.

By moonlight—the moon shines in all night when there is a moon—I wouldn't know it was the same paper.

At night in any kind of light, in twilight, candlelight, lamplight, and worst of all by moonlight, it becomes bars! The outside pattern I mean, and the woman behind it is as plain as can be.

I didn't realize for a long time what the thing was that showed behind, that dim sub-pattern, but now I am quite sure it is a woman.

By daylight she is subdued, quiet. I fancy it is the pattern that keeps her so still. It is so puzzling. It keeps me quiet by the hour.

I lie down ever so much now. John says it is good for me, and to sleep all I can.

Indeed he started the habit by making me lie down for an hour after each meal.

It is a very bad habit I am convinced, for you see I don't sleep.

And that cultivates deceit, for I don't tell them I'm awake—O no!

The fact is I am getting a little afraid of John.

He seems very queer sometimes, and even Jennie has an inexplicable look.

It strikes me occasionally, just as a scientific hypothesis,—that perhaps it is the paper!

I have watched John when he did not know I was looking, and come into the room suddenly on the most innocent excuses, and I've caught him several times *looking at the paper!* And Jennie too. I caught Jennie with her hand on it once.

She didn't know I was in the room, and when I asked her in a quiet, a very quiet voice, with the most restrained manner possible, what she was doing with the paper—she turned around as if she had been caught stealing, and looked quite angry—asked me why I should frighten her so!

Then she said that the paper stained everything it touched, that she had found yellow smooches on all my clothes and John's, and she wished we would be more careful!

Did not that sound innocent? But I know she was studying that pattern, and I am determined that nobody shall find it out but myself!

Life is very much more exciting now than it used to be. You see I have something more to expect, to look forward to, to watch. I really do eat better, and am more quiet than I was.

John is so pleased to see me improve! He laughed a little the other day, and said I seemed to be flourishing in spite of my wallpaper.

I turned it off with a laugh. I had no intention of telling him it was *because* of the wallpaper—he would make fun of me. He might even want to take me away.

I don't want to leave now until I have found it out. There is a week more, and I think that will be enough.

I'm feeling ever so much better! I don't sleep much at night, for it is so interesting to watch developments; but I sleep a good deal in the daytime.

In the daytime it is tiresome and perplexing.

There are always new shoots on the fungus, and new shades of yellow all over it. I cannot keep count of them, though I have tried conscientiously.

It is the strangest yellow, that wallpaper! It makes me think of all the yellow things I ever saw—not beautiful ones like buttercups, but old foul, bad yellow things.

But there is something else about that paper—the smell! I noticed it the moment we came into the room, but with so much air and sun it was not bad. Now we have had a week of fog and rain, and whether the windows are open or not, the smell is here.

It creeps all over the house.

I find it hovering in the dining-room, skulking in the parlor, hiding in the hall, lying in wait for me on the stairs.

It gets into my hair.

Even when I go to ride, if I turn my head suddenly and surprise it—there is that smell!

Such a peculiar odor, too! I have spent hours in trying to analyze it, to find what it smelled like.

It is not bad—at first, and very gentle, but quite the subtlest, most enduring odor I ever met.

In this damp weather it is awful, I wake up in the night and find it hanging over me.

It used to disturb me at first. I thought seriously of burning the house—to reach the smell.

But now I am used to it. The only thing I can think of that it is like is the *color* of the paper! A yellow smell.

There is a very funny mark on this wall, low down, near the mopboard. A streak that runs round the room. It goes behind every piece of furniture, except the bed, a long, straight, even *smooch,* as if it had been rubbed over and over.

I wonder how it was done and who did it, and what they did it for. Round and round and round—round and round and round—it makes me dizzy!

I really have discovered something at last.

Through watching so much at night, when it changes so, I have finally found out.

The front pattern *does* move—and no wonder! The woman behind shakes it!

Sometimes I think there are a great many women behind, and sometimes only one, and she crawls around fast, and her crawling shakes it all over.

Then in the very bright spots she keeps still, and in the very shady spots she just takes hold of the bars and shakes them hard.

And she is all the time trying to climb through. But nobody could climb through that pattern—it strangles so; I think that is why it has so many heads.

They get through, and then the pattern strangles them off and turns them upside down, and makes their eyes white!

If those heads were covered or taken off it would not be half so bad.

I think that woman gets out in the daytime!

And I'll tell you why—privately—I've seen her!

I can see her out of every one of my windows!

It is the same woman, I know, for she is always creeping, and most women do not creep by daylight.

I see her in that long shaded lane, creeping up and down. I see her in those dark grape arbors, creeping all around the garden.

I see her on that long road under the trees, creeping along, and when a carriage comes she hides under the blackberry vines.

I don't blame her a bit. It must be very humiliating to be caught creeping by daylight!

I always lock the door when I creep by daylight. I can't do it at night, for I know John would suspect something at once.

And John is so queer now, that I don't want to irritate him. I wish he would take another room! Besides, I don't want anybody to get that woman out at night but myself.

I often wonder if I could see her out of all the windows at once.

But, turn as fast as I can, I can only see out of one at one time.

And though I always see her, she *may* be able to creep faster than I can turn! I have watched her sometimes away off in the open country, creeping as fast as a cloud shadow in a high wind.

If only that top pattern could be gotten off from the under one! I mean to try it, little by little.

I have found out another funny thing, but I shan't tell it this time! It does not do to trust people too much.

There are only two more days to get this paper off, and I believe John is beginning to notice. I don't like the look in his eyes.

And I heard him ask Jennie a lot of professional questions about me. She had a very good report to give.

She said I slept a good deal in the daytime.

John knows I don't sleep very well at night, for all I'm so quiet!

He asked me all sorts of questions, too, and pretended to be very loving and kind.

As if I couldn't see through him!

Still, I don't wonder he acts so, sleeping under this paper for three months.

It only interests me, but I feel sure John and Jennie are secretly affected by it.

Hurrah! This is the last day, but it is enough. John to stay in town over night, and won't be out until this evening.

Jennie wanted to sleep with me—the sly thing! but I told her I should undoubtedly rest better for a night all alone.

That was clever, for really I wasn't alone a bit! As soon as it was moonlight and that poor thing began to crawl and shake the pattern, I got up and ran to help her.

I pulled and she shook, I shook and she pulled, and before morning we had peeled off yards of that paper.

A strip about as high as my head and half around the room.

And then when the sun came and that awful pattern began to laugh at me, I declared I would finish it to-day!

We go away to-morrow, and they are moving all my furniture down again to leave things as they were before.

Jennie looked at the wall in amazement, but I told her merrily that I did it out of pure spite at the vicious thing.

She laughed and said she wouldn't mind doing it herself, but I must not get tired.

How she betrayed herself that time!

But I am here, and no person touches this paper but me,—not *alive!*

She tried to get me out of the room—it was too patent! But I said it was so quiet and empty and clean now that I believed I would lie down again and sleep all I could; and not to wake me even for dinner—I would call when I woke.

So now she is gone, and the servants are gone, and the things are gone, and there is nothing left but that great bedstead nailed down, with the canvas mattress we found on it.

We shall sleep downstairs to-night, and take the boat home to-morrow.

I quite enjoy the room, now it is bare again.

How those children did tear about here!

This bedstead is fairly gnawed!

But I must get to work.

I have locked the door and thrown the key down into the front path.

I don't want to go out, and I don't want to have anybody come in, till John comes.

I want to astonish him.

I've got a rope up here that even Jennie did not find. If that woman does get out, and tries to get away, I can tie her!

But I forgot I could not reach far without anything to stand on!

This bed will *not* move!

I tried to lift and push it until I was lame, and then I got so angry I bit off a little piece at one corner—but it hurt my teeth.

Then I peeled off all the paper I could reach standing on the floor. It sticks horribly and the pattern just enjoys it! All those strangled heads and bulbous eyes and waddling fungus growths just shriek with derision!

I am getting angry enough to do something desperate. To jump out of the window would be admirable exercise, but the bars are too strong even to try.

Besides I wouldn't do it. Of course not. I know well enough that a step like that is improper and might be misconstrued.

I don't like to *look* out of the windows even—there are so many of those creeping women, and they creep so fast.

I wonder if they all come out of that wallpaper as I did?

But I am securely fastened now by my well-hidden rope—you don't get *me* out in the road there!

I suppose I shall have to get back behind the pattern when it comes night, and that is hard!

It is so pleasant to be out in this great room and creep around as I please!

I don't want to go outside. I won't, even if Jennie asks me to.

For outside you have to creep on the ground, and everything is green instead of yellow.

But here I can creep smoothly on the floor, and my shoulder just fits in that long smooch around the wall, so I cannot lose my way.

Why there's John at the door!

It is no use, young man, you can't open it!

How he does call and pound!

Now he's crying for an axe.

It would be a shame to break down that beautiful door!

"John dear!" said I in the gentlest voice, "the key is down by the front steps, under a plantain leaf!"

That silenced him for a few moments.

Then he said—very quietly indeed, "Open the door, my darling!"

"I can't," said I. "The key is down by the front door under a plantain leaf!"

And then I said it again, several times, very gently and slowly, and said it so often that he had to go and see, and he got it of course, and came in. He stopped short by the door.

"What is the matter?" he cried. "For God's sake, what are you doing!"

265 I kept on creeping just the same, but I looked at him over my shoulder.

"I've got out at last," said I, "in spite of you and Jane. And I've pulled off most of the paper, so you can't put me back!"

Now why should that man have fainted? But he did, and right across my path by the wall, so that I had to creep over him every time!

1892

## SUSAN GLASPELL

### A Jury of Her Peers

When Martha Hale opened the storm door and got a cut of the north wind, she ran back for her big woolen scarf. As she hurriedly wound that round her head her eye made a scandalized sweep of her kitchen. It was no ordinary thing that called her away—it was probably farther from ordinary than anything that had ever happened in Dickson County. But what her eye took in was that her kitchen was in no shape for leaving: her bread all ready for mixing, half the flour sifted and half unsifted.

She hated to see things half done; but she had been at that when the team from town stopped to get Mr. Hale, and then the sheriff came running in to say his wife wished Mrs. Hale would come too—adding, with a grin, that he guessed she was getting scary and wanted another woman along. So she had dropped everything right where it was.

"Martha!" now came her husband's impatient voice. "Don't keep folks waiting out here in the cold."

She again opened the storm door, and this time joined the three men and the one woman waiting for her in the big two-seated buggy.

5 After she had the robes tucked around her she took another look at the woman who sat beside her on the back seat. She had met Mrs. Peters the year before at the county fair, and the thing she remembered about her was that she didn't seem like a sheriff's wife. She was small and thin and didn't have a strong voice. Mrs. Gorman, sheriff's wife before Gorman went out and Peters came in, had a voice that somehow seemed to be backing up the law with every word. But if Mrs. Peters didn't look like a sheriff's wife, Peters made it up in looking like a sheriff. He was to a dot the kind of man who could get himself elected sheriff—a heavy man with a big voice, who was particularly genial with the law-abiding, as if to make it plain that he knew the difference between criminals and non-criminals. And right there it came into Mrs. Hale's mind, with a stab, that this man who was so pleasant and lively with all of them was going to the Wrights' now as a sheriff.

"The country's not very pleasant this time of year," Mrs. Peters at last ventured, as if she felt they ought to be talking as well as the men.

Mrs. Hale scarcely finished her reply, for they had gone up a little hill and could see the Wright place now, and seeing it did not make her feel like talking. It looked very lonesome this cold March morning. It had always been a lonesome-looking place. It was down in a hollow, and the poplar trees around it were lonesome-looking trees. The men were looking at it and talking about what had happened. The county attorney was bending to one side of the buggy, and kept looking steadily at the place as they drew up to it.

"I'm glad you came with me," Mrs. Peters said nervously, as the two women were about to follow the men in through the kitchen door.

Even after she had her foot on the doorstep, her hand on the knob, Martha Hale had a moment of feeling she could not cross that threshold. And the reason it seemed she couldn't cross it now was simply because she hadn't crossed it before. Time and time again it had been in her mind. "I ought to go over and see Minnie Foster"—she still thought of her as Minnie Foster, though for twenty years she had been Mrs. Wright. And then there was always something to do and Minnie Foster would go from her mind. But *now* she could come.

The men went over to the stove. The women stood close together by the door. Young Henderson, the county attorney, turned around and said, "Come up to the fire, ladies."

Mrs. Peters took a step forward, then stopped. "I'm not—cold," she said.

And so the two women stood by the door, at first not even so much as looking around the kitchen.

The men talked for a minute about what a good thing it was the sheriff had sent his deputy out that morning to make a fire for them, and then Sheriff Peters stepped back from the stove, unbuttoned his outer coat, and leaned his hands on the kitchen table in a way that seemed to mark the beginning of official business. "Now, Mr. Hale," he said in a sort of semi-official voice, "before we move things about, you tell Mr. Henderson just what it was you saw when you came here yesterday morning."

The county attorney was looking around the kitchen.

"By the way," he said, "has anything been moved?" He turned to the sheriff. "Are things just as you left them yesterday?"

Peters looked from cupboard to sink; from that to a small worn rocker a little to one side of the kitchen table.

"It's just the same."

"Somebody should have been left here yesterday," said the county attorney.

"Oh—yesterday," returned the sheriff, with a little gesture as of yesterday having been more than he could bear to think of. "When I had to send Frank to Morris Center for that man who went crazy—let me tell you, I had my hands full *yesterday*. I knew you could get back from Omaha by today, George, and as long as I went over everything here myself—"

"Well, Mr. Hale," said the county attorney, in a way of letting what was past and gone go, "tell just what happened when you came here yesterday morning."

Mrs. Hale, still leaning against the door, had that sinking feeling of the mother whose child is about to speak a piece. Lewis often wandered along and got things mixed up in a story. She hoped he would tell this straight and plain, and not say unnecessary things that would just make things harder for Minnie Foster. He didn't begin at once, and she noticed that he looked queer—as if standing in that kitchen and having to tell what he had seen there yesterday morning made him almost sick.

"Yes, Mr. Hale?" the county attorney reminded.

"Harry and I had started to town with a load of potatoes," Mrs. Hale's husband began.

Harry was Mrs. Hale's oldest boy. He wasn't with them now, for the very good reason that those potatoes never got to town yesterday and he was taking them this morning, so he hadn't been home when the sheriff stopped to say he wanted Mr. Hale to come over to the Wright place and tell the county attorney his story there, where he could point it all out. With all Mrs. Hale's other emotions came the fear that maybe Harry wasn't dressed warm enough—they hadn't any of them realized how that north wind did bite.

25 "We come along this road," Hale was going on, with a motion of his hand to the road over which they had just come, "and as we got in sight of the house I says to Harry, 'I'm goin' to see if I can't get John Wright to take a telephone.' You see," he explained to Henderson, "unless I can get somebody to go in with me they won't come out this branch road except for a price I can't pay. I'd spoke to Wright about it once before; but he put me off, saying folks talked too much anyway, and all he asked was peace and quiet—guess you know about how much he talked himself. But I thought maybe if I went to the house and talked about it before his wife, and said all the womenfolks liked the telephones, and that in this lonesome stretch of road it would be a good thing—well, I said to Harry that that was what I was going to say—though I said at the same time that I didn't know as what his wife wanted made much difference to John—"

Now, there he was!—saying things he didn't need to say. Mrs. Hale tried to catch her husband's eye, but fortunately the county attorney interrupted with:

"Let's talk about that a little later, Mr. Hale. I do want to talk about that, but I'm anxious now to get along to just what happened when you got here."

When he began this time, it was very deliberately and carefully:

"I didn't see or hear anything. I knocked at the door. And still it was all quiet inside. I knew they must be up—it was past eight o'clock. So I knocked again, louder, and I thought I heard somebody say 'Come in.' I wasn't sure—I'm not sure yet. But I opened the door—this door," jerking a hand toward the door by which the two women stood, "and there, in that rocker"—pointing to it—"sat Mrs. Wright."

30 Everyone in the kitchen looked at the rocker. It came into Mrs. Hale's mind that the rocker didn't look in the least like Minnie Foster—the Minnie Foster of twenty years before. It was a dingy red, with wooden rungs up the back, and the middle rung was gone, and the chair sagged to one side.

"How did she—look?" the county attorney was inquiring.

"Well," said Hale, "she looked—queer."

"How do you mean—queer?"

As he asked it he took out a notebook and pencil. Mrs. Hale did not like the sight of that pencil. She kept her eye fixed on her husband, as if to keep him from saying unnecessary things that would go into that notebook and make trouble.

35 Hale did speak guardedly, as if the pencil had affected him too.

"Well, as if she didn't know what she was going to do next. And kind of—done up."

"How did she seem to feel about your coming?"

"Why, I don't think she minded—one way or other. She didn't pay much attention. I said, 'Ho' do, Mrs. Wright? It's cold, ain't it!' And she said, 'Is it?'—and went on pleatin' at her apron.

"Well, I was surprised. She didn't ask me to come up to the stove, or to sit down, but just set there, not even lookin' at me. And so I said: 'I want to see John.'

"And then she—laughed. I guess you would call it a laugh.

"I thought of Harry and the team outside, so I said, a little sharp, 'Can I see John?' 'No,' says she—kind of dull like. 'Ain't he home?' says I. Then she looked at me. 'Yes,' says she, 'he's home.' 'Then why can't I see him?' I asked her, out of patience with her now. 'Cause he's dead,' says she, just as quiet and dull—and fell to pleatin' her apron. 'Dead?' says I, like you do when you can't take in what you've heard.

"She just nodded her head, not getting a bit excited, but rockin' back and forth.

" 'Why—where is he?' " says I, not knowing *what* to say.

"She just pointed upstairs—like this"—pointing to the room above.

"I got up, with the idea of going up there myself. By this time I—didn't know what to do. I walked from there to here; then I says: 'Why, what did he die of?'

" 'He died of a rope around his neck,' says she; and just went on pleatin' at her apron."

Hale stopped speaking, and stood staring at the rocker, as if he were still seeing the woman who had sat there the morning before. Nobody spoke; it was as if everyone were seeing the woman who had sat there the morning before.

"And what did you do then?" the county attorney at last broke the silence.

"I went out and called Harry. I thought I might—need help. I got Harry in, and we went upstairs." His voice fell almost to a whisper. "There he was—lying over the—"

"I think I'd rather have you go into that upstairs," the county attorney interrupted, "where you can point it all out. Just go on now with the rest of the story."

"Well, my first thought was to get that rope off. It looked—"

He stopped, his face twitching.

"But Harry, he went up to him, and he said, 'No, he's dead all right, and we'd better not touch anything.' So we went downstairs.

"She was still sitting the same way. 'Has anybody been notified?' I asked. 'No,' says she, unconcerned.

" 'Who did this, Mrs. Wright?' said Harry. He said it business-like, and she stopped pleatin' at her apron. 'I don't know,' she says. 'You don't *know*?' says Harry. 'Weren't you sleepin' in the bed with him?' 'Yes,' says she, 'but I was on the inside.' 'Somebody slipped a rope round his neck and strangled him, and you didn't wake up?' says Harry. 'I didn't wake up,' she said after him.

"We may have looked as if we didn't see how that could be, for after a minute she said, 'I sleep sound.'

"Harry was going to ask her more questions, but I said maybe that weren't our business; maybe we ought to let her tell her story first to the coroner or the sheriff. So Harry went fast as he could over to High Road—the Rivers' place, where there's a telephone."

"And what did she do when she knew you had gone for the coroner?" The attorney got his pencil in his hand all ready for writing.

"She moved from that chair to this one over here"—Hale pointed to a small chair in the corner—"and just sat there with her hands held together and looking down. I got a feeling that I ought to make some conversation, so I said I had come in to see if John wanted to put in a telephone; and at that she started to laugh, and then she stopped and looked at me—scared."

At the sound of a moving pencil the man who was telling the story looked up.

"I dunno—maybe it wasn't scared," he hastened; "I wouldn't like to say it was. Soon Harry got back, and then Dr. Lloyd came, and you, Mr. Peters, and so I guess that's all I know that you don't."

He said that last with relief, and moved a little, as if relaxing. Everyone moved a little. The county attorney walked toward the stair door.

"I guess we'll go upstairs first—then out to the barn and around there."

He paused and looked around the kitchen.

"You're convinced there was nothing important here?" he asked the sheriff. "Nothing that would—point to any motive?"

The sheriff too looked all around, as if to reconvince himself.

"Nothing here but kitchen things," he said, with a little laugh for the insignificance of kitchen things.

The county attorney was looking at the cupboard—a peculiar, ungainly structure, half closet and half cupboard, the upper part of it being built in the wall, and the lower part just the old-fashioned kitchen cupboard. As if its queerness attracted him, he got a chair and opened the upper part and looked in. After a moment he drew his hand away sticky.

"Here's a nice mess," he said resentfully.

The two women had drawn nearer, and now the sheriff's wife spoke.

"Oh—her fruit," she said, looking to Mrs. Hale for sympathetic understanding. She turned back to the county attorney and explained: "She worried about that when it turned so cold last night. She said the fire would go out and her jars might burst."

Mrs. Peters' husband broke into a laugh.

"Well, can you beat the women! Held for murder, and worrying about her preserves!"

The young attorney set his lips.

"I guess before we're through with her she may have something more serious than preserves to worry about."

"Oh, well," said Mrs. Hale's husband, with good-natured superiority, "women are used to worrying over trifles."

The two women moved a little closer together. Neither of them spoke. The county attorney seemed suddenly to remember his manners—and think of his future.

"And yet," said he, with the gallantry of a young politician, "for all their worries, what would we do without the ladies?"

The women did not speak, did not unbend. He went to the sink and began washing his hands. He turned to wipe them on the roller towel—whirled it for a cleaner place.

"Dirty towels! Not much of a housekeeper, would you say, ladies?"

He kicked his foot against some dirty pans under the sink.

"There's a great deal of work to be done on a farm," said Mrs. Hale stiffly.

"To be sure. And yet"—with a little bow to her—"I know there are some Dickson County farmhouses that do not have such roller towels." He gave it a pull to expose its full length again.

"Those towels get dirty awful quick. Men's hands aren't always as clean as they might be."

"Ah, loyal to your sex, I see," he laughed. He stopped and gave her a keen look. "But you and Mrs. Wright were neighbors. I suppose you were friends, too."

Martha Hale shook her head.

"I've seen little enough of her of late years. I've not been in this house—it's more than a year."

"And why was that? You didn't like her?"

"I liked her well enough," she replied with spirit. "Farmers' wives have their hands full, Mr. Henderson. And then"—She looked around the kitchen.

"Yes?" he encouraged.

"It never seemed a very cheerful place," said she, more to herself than to him.

"No," he agreed; "I don't think anyone would call it cheerful. I shouldn't say she had the homemaking instinct."

"Well, I don't know as Wright had, either," she muttered.

"You mean they didn't get on very well?" he was quick to ask.

"No; I don't mean anything," she answered, with decision. As she turned a little away from him, she added: "But I don't think a place would be any the cheerfuler for John Wright's bein' in it."

"I'd like to talk to you about that a little later, Mrs. Hale," he said. "I'm anxious to get the lay of things upstairs now."

He moved toward the stair door, followed by the two men.

"I suppose anything Mrs. Peters does'll be all right?" the sheriff inquired. "She was to take in some clothes for her, you know—and a few little things. We left in such a hurry yesterday."

The county attorney looked at the two women whom they were leaving alone there among the kitchen things.

"Yes—Mrs. Peters," he said, his glance resting on the woman who was not Mrs. Peters, the big farmer woman who stood behind the sheriff's wife. "Of course Mrs. Peters is one of us," he said, in a manner of entrusting responsibility. "And keep your eye out, Mrs. Peters, for anything that might be of use. No telling; you women might come upon a clue to the motive—and that's the thing we need."

Mr. Hale rubbed his face after the fashion of a showman getting ready for a pleasantry.

"But would the women know a clue if they did come upon it?" he said; and, having delivered himself of this, he followed the others through the stair door.

The women stood motionless and silent, listening to the footsteps, first upon the stairs, then in the room above them.

Then, as if releasing herself from something strange, Mrs. Hale began to arrange the dirty pans under the sink, which the county attorney's disdainful push of the foot had deranged.

"I'd hate to have men comin' into my kitchen," she said testily—"snoopin' round and criticizin'."

"Of course it's no more than their duty," said the sheriff's wife, in her manner of timid acquiescence.

"Duty's all right," replied Mrs. Hale bluffly; "but I guess that deputy sheriff that come out to make the fire might have got a little of this on." She gave the roller towel a pull. "Wish I'd thought of that sooner! Seems mean to talk about her for not having things slicked up, when she had to come away in such a hurry."

She looked around the kitchen. Certainly it was not "slicked up." Her eye was held by a bucket of sugar on a low shelf. The cover was off the wooden bucket, and beside it was a paper bag—half full.

Mrs. Hale moved toward it.

"She was putting this in there," she said to herself—slowly.

She thought of the flour in her kitchen at home—half sifted, half not sifted. She had been interrupted and had left things half done. What had interrupted Minnie Foster? Why had that work been left half done? She made a move as if to finish it,—unfinished things always bothered her,—and then she glanced around and saw that Mrs. Peters was watching her—and she didn't want Mrs. Peters to get that feeling she had got of work begun and then—for some reason—not finished.

"It's a shame about her fruit," she said, and walked toward the cupboard that the county attorney had opened, and got on the chair, murmuring: "I wonder if it's all gone."

It was a sorry enough looking sight, but "Here's one that's all right," she said at last. She held it toward the light. "This is cherries, too." She looked again. "I declare I believe that's the only one."

With a sigh, she got down from the chair, went to the sink, and wiped off the bottle.

"She'll feel awful bad, after all her hard work in the hot weather. I remember the afternoon I put up my cherries last summer."

She set the bottle on the table, and, with another sigh, started to sit down in the rocker. But she did not sit down. Something kept her from sitting down in that chair. She straightened—stepped back, and, half turned away, stood looking at it, seeing the woman who sat there "pleatin' at her apron."

The thin voice of the sheriff's wife broke in upon her: "I must be getting those things from the front room closet." She opened the door into the other room, started in, stepped back. "You coming with me, Mrs. Hale?" she asked nervously. "You—you could help me get them."

They were soon back—the stark coldness of that shut-up room was not a thing to linger in.

"My!" said Mrs. Peters, dropping the things on the table and hurrying to the stove.

Mrs. Hale stood examining the clothes the woman who was being detained in town had said she wanted.

"Wright was close!" she exclaimed, holding up a shabby black skirt that bore the marks of much making over. "I think maybe that's why she kept so much to herself. I s'pose she felt she couldn't do her part; and then, you don't enjoy things when you feel shabby. She used to wear pretty clothes and be lively—when she was Minnie Foster, one of the town girls, singing in the choir. But that—oh, that was twenty years ago."

With a carefulness in which there was something tender, she folded the shabby clothes and piled them at one corner of the table. She looked at Mrs. Peters, and there was something in the other woman's look that irritated her.

"She don't care," she said to herself. "Much difference it makes to her whether Minnie Foster had pretty clothes when she was a girl."

Then she looked again, and she wasn't so sure; in fact, she hadn't at any time been perfectly sure about Mrs. Peters. She had that shrinking manner, and yet her eyes looked as if they could see a long way into things.

"This all you was to take in?" asked Mrs. Hale.

"No," said the sheriff's wife; "she said she wanted an apron. Funny thing to want," she ventured in her nervous little way, "for there's not much to get you dirty in jail, goodness knows. But I suppose just to make her feel more natural. If you're used to wearing an apron—. She said they were in the bottom drawer of this cupboard. Yes—here they are. And then her little shawl that always hung on the stair door."

She took the small gray shawl from behind the door leading upstairs, and stood a minute looking at it.

Suddenly Mrs. Hale took a quick step toward the other woman.

"Mrs. Peters!"

"Yes, Mrs. Hale?"

"Do you think she—did it?"

A frightened look blurred the other things in Mrs. Peters' eyes.

"Oh, I don't know," she said, in a voice that seemed to shrink away from the subject.

"Well, I don't think she did," affirmed Mrs. Hale stoutly. "Asking for an apron, and her little shawl. Worryin' about her fruit."

"Mr. Peters says—" Footsteps were heard in the room above; she stopped, looked up, then went on in a lowered voice: "Mr. Peters says—it looks bad for her. Mr. Henderson is awful sarcastic in a speech, and he's going to make fun of her saying she didn't—wake up."

For a moment Mrs. Hale had no answer. Then, "Well, I guess John Wright didn't wake up—when they was slippin' that rope under his neck," she muttered.

"No, it's *strange*," breathed Mrs. Peters. "They think it was such a—funny way to kill a man."

She began to laugh; at sound of the laugh, abruptly stopped.

"That's just what Mr. Hale said," said Mrs. Hale, in a resolutely natural voice. "There was a gun in the house. He says that's what he can't understand."

"Mr. Henderson said, coming out, that what was needed for the case was a motive. Something to show anger—or sudden feeling."

"Well, I don't see any signs of anger around here," said Mrs. Hale. "I don't—"

She stopped. It was as if her mind tripped on something. Her eye was caught by a dish towel in the middle of the kitchen table. Slowly she moved toward the table. One half of it was wiped clean, the other half messy. Her eyes made a slow, almost unwilling turn to the bucket of sugar and the half empty bag beside it. Things begun—and not finished.

After a moment she stepped back, and said, in that manner of releasing herself:

"Wonder how they're finding things upstairs? I hope she had it a little more red-up up there. You know,"—she paused, and feeling gathered,—"it seems kind of *sneaking*; locking her up in town and coming out here to get her own house to turn against her!"

"But, Mrs. Hale," said the sheriff's wife, "the law is the law."

"I s'pose 'tis," answered Mrs. Hale shortly.

She turned to the stove, saying something about that fire not being much to brag of. She worked with it a minute, and when she straightened up she said aggressively:

"The law is the law—and a bad stove is a bad stove. How'd you like to cook on this?"—pointing with the poker to the broken lining. She opened the oven door and started to express her opinion of the oven; but she was swept into her own thoughts, thinking of what it would mean, year after year, to have that stove to wrestle with. The thought of Minnie Foster trying to bake in that oven—and the thought of her never going over to see Minnie Foster—.

She was startled by hearing Mrs. Peters say: "A person gets discouraged—and loses heart."

150 The sheriff's wife had looked from the stove to the sink—to the pail of water which had been carried in from outside. The two women stood there silent, above them the footsteps of the men who were looking for evidence against the woman who had worked in that kitchen. That look of seeing into things, of seeing through a thing to something else, was in the eyes of the sheriff's wife now. When Mrs. Hale next spoke to her, it was gently:

"Better loosen up your things, Mrs. Peters. We'll not feel them when we go out."

Mrs. Peters went to the back of the room to hang up the fur tippet she was wearing. A moment later she exclaimed, "Why, she was piecing a quilt," and held up a large sewing basket piled high with quilt pieces.

Mrs. Hale spread some of the blocks on the table.

"It's log-cabin pattern," she said, putting several of them together. "Pretty, isn't it?"

155 They were so engaged with the quilt that they did not hear the footsteps on the stairs. Just as the stair door opened Mrs. Hale was saying:

"Do you suppose she was going to quilt it or just knot it?"

The sheriff threw up his hands.

"They wonder whether she was going to quilt it or just knot it!"

There was a laugh for the ways of women, a warming of hands over the stove, and then the county attorney said briskly:

160 "Well, let's go right out to the barn and get that cleared up."

"I don't see as there's anything so strange," Mrs. Hale said resentfully, after the outside door had closed on the three men—"our taking up our time with little things while we're waiting for them to get the evidence. I don't see as it's anything to laugh about."

"Of course they've got awful important things on their minds," said the sheriff's wife apologetically.

They returned to an inspection of the blocks for the quilt. Mrs. Hale was looking at the fine, even sewing, and preoccupied with thoughts of the woman who had done that sewing, when she heard the sheriff's wife say, in a queer tone:

"Why, look at this one."

165 She turned to take the block held out to her.

"The sewing," said Mrs. Peters, in a troubled way. "All the rest of them have been so nice and even—but—this one. Why, it looks as if she didn't know what she was about!"

Their eyes met—something flashed to life, passed between them; then, as if with an effort, they seemed to pull away from each other. A moment Mrs. Hale sat there, her hands folded over that sewing which was so unlike all the rest of the sewing. Then she had pulled a knot and drawn the threads.

"Oh, what are you doing, Mrs. Hale?" asked the sheriff's wife, startled.

"Just pulling out a stitch or two that's not sewed very good," said Mrs. Hale mildly.

"I don't think we ought to touch things," Mrs. Peters said, a little helplessly.

"I'd just finish up this end," answered Mrs. Hale, still in that mild, matter-of-fact fashion.

She threaded a needle and started to replace bad sewing with good. For a little while she sewed in silence. Then, in that thin, timid voice, she heard:

"Mrs. Hale!"

"Yes, Mrs. Peters?"

"What do you suppose she was so—nervous about?"

"Oh, *I* don't know," said Mrs. Hale, as if dismissing a thing not important enough to spend much time on. "I don't know as she was—nervous. I sew awful queer sometimes when I'm just tired."

She cut a thread, and out of the corner of her eye looked up at Mrs. Peters. The small, lean face of the sheriff's wife seemed to have tightened up. Her eyes had that look of peering into something. But the next moment she moved, and said in her thin, indecisive way:

"Well, I must get those clothes wrapped. They may be through sooner than we think. I wonder where I could find a piece of paper—and string."

"In that cupboard, maybe," suggested Mrs. Hale, after a glance around.

One piece of the crazy sewing remained unripped. Mrs. Peters' back turned, Martha Hale now scrutinized that piece, compared it with the dainty, accurate sewing of the other blocks. The difference was startling. Holding this block made her feel queer, as if the distracted thoughts of the woman who had perhaps turned to it to try and quiet herself were communicating themselves to her.

Mrs. Peters' voice roused her.

"Here's a birdcage," she said. "Did she have a bird, Mrs. Hale?"

"Why, I don't know whether she did or not." She turned to look at the cage Mrs. Peters was holding up. "I've not been here in so long." She sighed. "There was a man round last year selling canaries cheap—but I don't know as she took one. Maybe she did. She used to sing real pretty herself."

Mrs. Peters looked around the kitchen.

"Seems kind of funny to think of a bird here." She half laughed—an attempt to put up a barrier. "But she must have had one—or why would she have a cage? I wonder what happened to it."

"I suppose maybe the cat got it," suggested Mrs. Hale, resuming her sewing.

"No; she didn't have a cat. She's got that feeling some people have about cats—being afraid of them. When they brought her to our house yesterday, my cat got in the room, and she was real upset and asked me to take it out."

"My sister Bessie was like that," laughed Mrs. Hale.

The sheriff's wife did not reply. The silence made Mrs. Hale turn round. Mrs. Peters was examining the birdcage.

"Look at this door," she said slowly. "It's broke. One hinge has been pulled apart."

Mrs. Hale came nearer.

"Looks as if someone must have been—rough with it."

Again their eyes met—startled, questioning, apprehensive. For a moment neither spoke nor stirred. Then Mrs. Hale, turning away, said brusquely:

"If they're going to find any evidence, I wish they'd be about it. I don't like this place."

"But I'm awful glad you came with me, Mrs. Hale." Mrs. Peters put the birdcage on the table and sat down. "It would be lonesome for me—sitting here alone."

"Yes, it would, wouldn't it?" agreed Mrs. Hale, a certain determined naturalness in her voice. She picked up the sewing, but now it dropped in her lap, and she murmured in a different voice: "But I tell you what I *do* wish, Mrs. Peters. I wish I had come over sometimes when she was here. I wish—I had."

"But of course you were awful busy, Mrs. Hale. Your house—and your children."

"I could've come," retorted Mrs. Hale shortly. "I stayed away because it weren't cheerful—and that's why I ought to have come. I"—she looked around—"I've never liked this place. Maybe because it's down in a hollow and you don't see the road. I don't know what it is, but it's a lonesome place, and always was. I wish I had come over to see Minnie Foster sometimes. I can see now—" She did not put it into words.

"Well, you mustn't reproach yourself," counseled Mrs. Peters. "Somehow, we just don't see how it is with other folks till—something comes up."

"Not having children makes less work," mused Mrs. Hale, after a silence, "but it makes a quiet house—and Wright out to work all day—and no company when he did come in. Did you know John Wright, Mrs. Peters?"

"Not to know him. I've seen him in town. They say he was a good man."

"Yes—good," conceded John Wright's neighbor grimly. "He didn't drink, and kept his word as well as most, I guess, and paid his debts. But he was a hard man, Mrs. Peters. Just to pass the time of day with him—." She stopped, shivered a little. "Like a raw wind that gets to the bone." Her eye fell upon the cage on the table before her, and she added, almost bitterly: "I should think she would've wanted a bird!"

Suddenly she leaned forward, looking intently at the cage. "But what do you s'pose went wrong with it?"

"I don't know," returned Mrs. Peters; "unless it got sick and died."

But after she said it she reached over and swung the broken door. Both women watched it as if somehow held by it.

"You didn't know—her?" Mrs. Hale asked, a gentler note in her voice.

"Not till they brought her yesterday," said the sheriff's wife.

"She—come to think of it, she was kind of like a bird herself. Real sweet and pretty, but kind of timid and—fluttery. How—she—did—change."

That held her for a long time. Finally, as if struck with a happy thought and relieved to get back to everyday things, she exclaimed:

"Tell you what, Mrs. Peters, why don't you take the quilt in with you? It might take up her mind."

"Why, I think that's a real nice idea, Mrs. Hale," agreed the sheriff's wife, as if she too were glad to come into the atmosphere of a simple kindness. "There couldn't possibly be any objection to that, could there? Now, just what will I take? I wonder if her patches are in here—and her things."

They turned to the sewing basket.

"Here's some red," said Mrs. Hale, bringing out a roll of cloth. Underneath that was a box. "Here, maybe her scissors are in here—and her things." She held it up. "What a pretty box! I'll warrant that was something she had a long time ago—when she was a girl."

She held it in her hand a moment; then, with a little sigh, opened it.

Instantly her hand went to her nose.

"Why—!"

Mrs. Peters drew nearer—then turned away.

"There's something wrapped up in this piece of silk," faltered Mrs. Hale.

"This isn't her scissors," said Mrs. Peters in a shrinking voice.

Her hand not steady, Mrs. Hale raised the piece of silk. "Oh, Mrs. Peters!" she cried. "It's—"

Mrs. Peters bent closer.

"It's the bird," she whispered.

"But, Mrs. Peters!" cried Mrs. Hale. "*Look* at it! Its neck—look at its neck! It's all—other side *to.*"

She held the box away from her.

The sheriff's wife again bent closer.

"Somebody wrung its neck," said she, in a voice that was slow and deep.

And then again the eyes of the two women met—this time clung together in a look of dawning comprehension, of growing horror. Mrs. Peters looked from the dead bird to the broken door of the cage. Again their eyes met. And just then there was a sound at the outside door.

Mrs. Hale slipped the box under the quilt pieces in the basket, and sank into the chair before it. Mrs. Peters stood holding to the table. The county attorney and the sheriff came in from outside.

"Well, ladies," said the county attorney, as one turning from serious things to little pleasantries, "have you decided whether she was going to quilt it or knot it?"

"We think," began the sheriff's wife in a flurried voice, "that she was going to—knot it."

He was too preoccupied to notice the change that came in her voice on that last.

"Well, that's very interesting, I'm sure," he said tolerantly. He caught sight of the birdcage. "Has the bird flown?"

"We think the cat got it," said Mrs. Hale in a voice curiously even.

He was walking up and down, as if thinking something out.

"Is there a cat?" he asked absently.

Mrs. Hale shot a look up at the sheriff's wife.

"Well, not *now*," said Mrs. Peters. "They're superstitious, you know; they leave."

She sank into her chair.

The county attorney did not heed her. "No sign at all of anyone having come in from the outside," he said to Peters, in the manner of continuing an interrupted conversation. "Their own rope. Now let's go upstairs again and go over it, piece by piece. It would have to have been someone who knew just the—"

The stair door closed behind them and their voices were lost.

The two women sat motionless, not looking at each other, but as if peering into something and at the same time holding back. When they spoke now it was as if they were afraid of what they were saying, but as if they could not help saying it.

"She liked the bird," said Martha Hale, low and slowly. "She was going to bury it in that pretty box."

"When I was a girl," said Mrs. Peters, under her breath, "my kitten—there was a boy took a hatchet, and before my eyes—before I could get there—" She covered her face an instant. "If they hadn't held me back I would have"—she caught herself, looked upstairs where footsteps were heard, and finished weakly—"hurt him."

Then they sat without speaking or moving.

245 "I wonder how it would seem," Mrs. Hale at last began, as if feeling her way over strange ground—"never to have had any children around?" Her eyes made a slow sweep of the kitchen, as if seeing what that kitchen had meant through all the years. "No, Wright wouldn't like the bird," she said after that—"a thing that sang. She used to sing. He killed that too." Her voice tightened.

Mrs. Peters moved uneasily.

"Of course we don't know who killed the bird."

"I knew John Wright," was Mrs. Hale's answer.

"It was an awful thing was done in this house that night, Mrs. Hale," said the sheriff's wife. "Killing a man while he slept—slipping a thing round his neck that choked the life out of him."

250 Mrs. Hale's hand went out to the birdcage.

"His neck. Choked the life out of him."

"We don't *know* who killed him," whispered Mrs. Peters wildly. "We don't *know.*"

Mrs. Hale had not moved. "If there had been years and years of—nothing, then a bird to sing to you, it would be awful—still—after the bird was still."

It was as if something within her not herself had spoken, and it found in Mrs. Peters something she did not know as herself.

255 "I know what stillness is," she said, in a queer, monotonous voice. "When we homesteaded in Dakota, and my first baby died—after he was two years old—and me with no other then—"

Mrs. Hale stirred.

"How soon do you suppose they'll be through looking for evidence?"

"I know what stillness is," repeated Mrs. Peters, in just that same way. Then she too pulled back. "The law has got to punish crime, Mrs. Hale," she said in her tight little way.

"I wish you'd seen Minnie Foster," was the answer, "when she wore a white dress with blue ribbons, and stood up there in the choir and sang."

260 The picture of that girl, the fact that she had lived neighbor to that girl for twenty years, and had let her die for lack of life, was suddenly more than she could bear.

"Oh, I *wish* I'd come over here once in a while!" she cried. "That was a crime! That was a crime! Who's going to punish that?"

"We mustn't take on," said Mrs. Peters, with a frightened look toward the stairs.

"I might 'a' *known* she needed help! I tell you, it's *queer,* Mrs. Peters. We live close together, and we live far apart. We all go through the same things—it's all just a different kind of the same thing! If it weren't—why do you and I *understand?* Why do we *know*—what we know this minute?"

She dashed her hand across her eyes. Then, seeing the jar of fruit on the table, she reached for it and choked out:

"If I was you I wouldn't *tell* her her fruit was gone! Tell her it *ain't*. Tell her it's all right—all of it. Here—take this in to prove it to her! She—she may never know whether it was broke or not."

She turned away.

Mrs. Peters reached out for the bottle of fruit as if she were glad to take it—as if touching a familiar thing, having something to do, could keep her from something else. She got up, looked about for something to wrap the fruit in, took a petticoat from the pile of clothes she had brought from the front room, and nervously started winding that round the bottle.

"My!" she began, in a high, false voice, "it's a good thing the men couldn't hear us! Getting all stirred up over a little thing like a—dead canary." She hurried over that. "As if that could have anything to do with—with—My, wouldn't they *laugh*?"

Footsteps were heard on the stairs.

"Maybe they would," muttered Mrs. Hale—"maybe they wouldn't."

"No, Peters," said the county attorney incisively; "it's all perfectly clear, except the reason for doing it. But you know juries when it comes to women. If there was some definite thing—something to show. Something to make a story about. A thing that would connect up with this clumsy way of doing it."

In a covert way Mrs. Hale looked at Mrs. Peters. Mrs. Peters was looking at her. Quickly they looked away from each other. The outer door opened and Mr. Hale came in.

"I've got the team round now," he said. "Pretty cold out there."

"I'm going to stay here awhile by myself," the county attorney suddenly announced. "You can send Frank out for me, can't you?" he asked the sheriff. "I want to go over everything. I'm not satisfied we can't do better."

Again, for one brief moment, the two women's eyes found one another.

The sheriff came up to the table.

"Did you want to see what Mrs. Peters was going to take in?"

The county attorney picked up the apron. He laughed.

"Oh, I guess they're not very dangerous things the ladies have picked out."

Mrs. Hale's hand was on the sewing basket in which the box was concealed. She felt that she ought to take her hand off the basket. She did not seem able to. He picked up one of the quilt blocks which she had piled on to cover the box. Her eyes felt like fire. She had a feeling that if he took up the basket she would snatch it from him.

But he did not take it up. With another little laugh, he turned away, saying:

"No; Mrs. Peters doesn't need supervising. For that matter, a sheriff's wife is married to the law. Ever think of it that way, Mrs. Peters?"

Mrs. Peters was standing beside the table. Mrs. Hale shot a look up at her; but she could not see her face. Mrs. Peters had turned away. When she spoke, her voice was muffled.

"Not—just that way," she said.

"Married to the law!" chuckled Mrs. Peters' husband. He moved toward the door into the front room, and said to the county attorney:

"I just want you to come in here a minute, George. We ought to take a look at these windows.

"Oh—windows," said the county attorney scoffingly.

"We'll be right out, Mr. Hale," said the sheriff to the farmer, who was still waiting by the door.

Hale went to look after the horses. The sheriff followed the county attorney into the other room. Again—for one moment—the two women were alone in that kitchen.

Martha Hale sprang up, her hands tight together, looking at that other woman, with whom it rested. At first she could not see her eyes, for the sheriff's wife had not turned back, since she turned away at that suggestion of being married to the law. But now Mrs. Hale made her turn back. Her eyes made her turn back. Slowly, unwillingly, Mrs. Peters turned her head until her eyes met the eyes of the other woman. There was a moment when they held each other in a steady, burning look in which there was no evasion nor flinching. Then Martha Hale's eyes pointed the way to the basket in which was hidden the thing that would make certain the conviction of the other woman—that woman who was not there and yet who had been there with them all through the hour.

For a moment Mrs. Peters did not move. And then she did it. With a rush forward, she threw back the quilt pieces, got the box, tried to put it in her handbag. It was too big. Desperately she opened it, started to take the bird out. But there she broke—she could not touch the bird. She stood helpless, foolish.

There was the sound of a knob turning in the inner door. Martha Hale snatched the box from the sheriff's wife, and got it in the pocket of her big coat just as the sheriff and the county attorney came back into the kitchen.

"Well, Henry," said the county attorney facetiously, "at least we found out that she was not going to quilt it. She was going to—what is it you call it, ladies?"

Mrs. Hale's hand was against the pocket of her coat.

"We call it—knot it, Mr. Henderson."

1917

## KATHERINE MANSFIELD

### Bliss

Although Bertha Young was thirty she still had moments like this when she wanted to run instead of walk, to take dancing steps on and off the pavement, to bowl a hoop,[1] to throw something up in the air and catch it again, or to stand still and laugh at—nothing—at nothing, simply.

What can you do if you are thirty and, turning the corner of your own street, you are overcome, suddenly, by a feeling of bliss—absolute bliss!—as though you'd suddenly swallowed a bright piece of that late afternoon sun and it burned in your bosom, sending out a little shower of sparks into every particle, into every finger and toe? . . .

Oh, is there no way you can express it without being "drunk and disorderly?" How idiotic civilization is! Why be given a body if you have to keep it shut up in a case like a rare, rare fiddle?

"No, that about the fiddle is not quite what I mean," she thought, running

---

1. Play with a rolling hoop.

up the steps and feeling in her bag for the key—she'd forgotten it, as usual—and rattling the letter-box. "It's not what I mean, because—Thank you, Mary"—she went into the hall. "Is nurse back?"

"Yes, M'm."[2]

"And has the fruit come?"

"Yes, M'm. Everything's come."

"Bring the fruit up to the dining-room, will you? I'll arrange it before I go upstairs."

It was dusky in the dining-room and quite chilly. But all the same Bertha threw off her coat; she could not bear the tight clasp of it another moment, and the cold air fell on her arms.

But in her bosom there was still that bright glowing place—that shower of little sparks coming from it. It was almost unbearable. She hardly dared to breathe for fear of fanning it higher, and yet she breathed deeply, deeply. She hardly dared to look into the cold mirror—but she did look, and it gave her back a woman, radiant, with smiling, trembling lips, with big, dark eyes and an air of listening, waiting for something . . . divine to happen . . . that she knew must happen . . . infallibly.

Mary brought in the fruit on a tray and with it a glass bowl, and a blue dish, very lovely, with a strange sheen on it as though it had been dipped in milk.

"Shall I turn on the light, M'm?"

"No, thank you. I can see quite well."

There were tangerines and apples stained with strawberry pink. Some yellow pears, smooth as silk, some white grapes covered with a silver bloom and a big cluster of purple ones. These last she had bought to tone in with the new dining-room carpet. Yes, that did sound rather far-fetched and absurd, but it was really why she had bought them. She had thought in the shop: "I must have some purple ones to bring the carpet up to the table." And it had seemed quite sense at the time.

When she had finished with them and had made two pyramids of these bright round shapes, she stood away from the table to get the effect—and it really was most curious. For the dark table seemed to melt into the dusky light and the glass dish and the blue bowl to float in the air. This, of course in her present mood, was so incredibly beautiful. . . . She began to laugh.

"No, no. I'm getting hysterical." And she seized her bag and coat and ran upstairs to the nursery.

Nurse sat at a low table giving Little B her supper after her bath. The baby had on a white flannel gown and a blue woollen jacket, and her dark, fine hair was brushed up into a funny little peak. She looked up when she saw her mother and began to jump.

"Now, my lovey, eat it up like a good girl," said Nurse, getting her lips in a way that Bertha knew, and that meant she had come into the nursery at another wrong moment.

"Has she been good, Nanny?"

"She's been a little sweet all the afternoon," whispered Nanny. "We went to the park and I sat down on a chair and took her out of the pram and a big dog

---

2. Ma'am.

came along and put its head on my knee and she clutched its ear, tugged it. Oh, you should have seen her."

Bertha wanted to ask if it wasn't rather dangerous to let her clutch at a strange dog's ear. But she did not dare to. She stood watching them, her hands by her side, like the poor little girl in front of the rich little girl with the doll.

The baby looked up at her again, stared, and then smiled so charmingly that Bertha couldn't help crying:

"Oh, Nanny, do let me finish giving her her supper while you put the bath things away."

"Well, M'm, she oughtn't to be changed hands while she's eating," said Nanny, still whispering. "It unsettles her; it's very likely to upset her."

How absurd it was. Why have a baby if it has to be kept—not in a case like a rare, rare fiddle—but in another woman's arms?

"Oh, I must!" said she.

Very offended, Nanny handed her over.

"Now, don't excite her after her supper. You know you do, M'm. And I have such a time with her after!"

Thank heaven! Nanny went out of the room with the bath towels.

"Now I've got you to myself, my little precious," said Bertha, as the baby leaned against her.

She ate delightfully, holding up her lips for the spoon and then waving her hands. Sometimes she wouldn't let the spoon go; and sometimes, just as Bertha had filled it, she waved it away to the four winds.

When the soup was finished Bertha turned round to the fire.

"You're nice—you're very nice!" said she, kissing her warm baby. "I'm fond of you. I like you."

And, indeed, she loved Little B so much—her neck as she bent forward, her exquisite toes as they shone transparent in the firelight—that all her feeling of bliss came back again, and again she didn't know how to express it—what to do with it.

"You're wanted on the telephone," said Nanny, coming back in triumph and seizing *her* Little B.

Down she flew. It was Harry.

"Oh, is that you, Ber? Look here. I'll be late. I'll take a taxi and come along as quickly as I can, but get dinner put back ten minutes—will you? All right?"

"Yes, perfectly. Oh, Harry!"

"Yes?"

What had she to say? She'd nothing to say. She only wanted to get in touch with him for a moment. She couldn't absurdly cry: "Hasn't it been a divine day!"

"What is it?" rapped out the little voice.

"Nothing. *Entendu*,"[3] said Bertha, and hung up the receiver, thinking how more than idiotic civilization was.

They had people coming to dinner. The Norman Knights—a very sound couple—he was about to start a theatre, and she was awfully keen on interior decoration, a young man, Eddie Warren, who had just published a little book of

---

3. Understood (French).

poems and whom everybody was asking to dine, and a "find" of Bertha's called Pearl Fulton. What Miss Fulton did, Bertha didn't know. They had met at the club and Bertha had fallen in love with her, as she always did fall in love with beautiful women who had something strange about them.

The provoking thing was that, though they had been about together and met a number of times and really talked, Bertha couldn't yet make her out. Up to a certain point Miss Fulton was rarely, wonderfully frank, but the certain point was there, and beyond that she would not go.

Was there anything beyond it? Harry said "No." Voted her dullish, and "cold like all blond women, with a touch, perhaps, of anæmia of the brain." But Bertha wouldn't agree with him; not yet, at any rate.

"No, the way she has of sitting with her head a little on one side, and smiling, has something behind it, Harry, and I must find out what that something is."

"Most likely it's a good stomach," answered Harry.

He made a point of catching Bertha's heels with replies of that kind . . . "liver frozen, my dear girl," or "pure flatulence," or "kidney disease," . . . and so on. For some strange reason Bertha liked this, and almost admired it in him very much.

She went into the drawing-room and lighted the fire; then, picking up the cushions, one by one, that Mary had disposed so carefully, she threw them back on to the chairs and the couches. That made all the difference; the room came alive at once. As she was about to throw the last one she surprised herself by suddenly hugging it to her, passionately, passionately. But it did not put out the fire in her bosom. Oh, on the contrary!

The windows of the drawing-room opened on to a balcony overlooking the garden. At the far end, against the wall, there was a tall, slender pear tree in fullest, richest bloom; it stood perfect, as though becalmed against the jade-green sky. Bertha couldn't help feeling, even from this distance, that it had not a single bud or a faded petal. Down below, in the garden beds, the red and yellow tulips, heavy with flowers, seemed to lean upon the dusk. A grey cat, dragging its belly, crept across the lawn, and a black one, its shadow, trailed after. The sight of them, so intent and so quick, gave Bertha a curious shiver.

"What creepy things cats are!" she stammered, and she turned away from the window and began walking up and down. . . .

How strong the jonquils smelled in the warm room. Too strong? Oh, no. And yet, as though overcome, she flung down on a couch and pressed her hands to her eyes.

"I'm too happy—too happy!" she murmured.

And she seemed to see on her eyelids the lovely pear tree with its wide open blossoms as a symbol of her own life.

Really—really—she had everything. She was young. Harry and she were as much in love as ever, and they got on together splendidly and were really good pals. She had an adorable baby. They didn't have to worry about money. They had this absolutely satisfactory house and garden. And friends—modern, thrilling friends, writers and painters and poets or people keen on social questions—just the kind of friends they wanted. And then there were books, and there was music, and she had found a wonderful little dressmaker, and they were going abroad in the summer, and their new cook made the most superb omelettes. . . .

"I'm absurd. Absurd!" She sat up; but she felt quite dizzy, quite drunk. It must have been the spring.

Yes, it was the spring. Now she was so tired she could not drag herself upstairs to dress.

A white dress, a string of jade beads, green shoes and stockings. It wasn't intentional. She had thought of this scheme hours before she stood at the drawing-room window.

Her petals rustled softly into the hall, and she kissed Mrs. Norman Knight, who was taking off the most amusing orange coat with a procession of black monkeys round the hem and up the fronts.

"... Why! Why! Why is the middle-class so stodgy—so utterly without a sense of humor! My dear, it's only by a fluke that I am here at all—Norman being the protective fluke. For my darling monkeys so upset the train that it rose to a man and simply ate me with its eyes. Didn't laugh—wasn't amused—that I should have loved. No, just stared—and bored me through and through."

"But the cream of it was," said Norman, pressing a large tortoiseshell-rimmed monocle into his eye, "you don't mind me telling this, Face, do you?" (In their house and among their friends they called each other Face and Mug.) "The cream of it was when she, being full fed, turned to the woman beside her and said: 'Haven't you ever seen a monkey before?' "

"Oh, yes!" Mrs. Norman Knight joined in the laughter. "Wasn't that too absolutely creamy?"

And a funnier thing still was that now her coat was off she did look like a very intelligent monkey—who had even made that yellow silk dress out of scraped banana skins. And her amber earrings; they were like little dangling nuts.

"This is a sad, sad fall!" said Mug, pausing in front of Little B's perambulator. "When the perambulator comes into the hall—" and he waved the rest of the quotation away.

The bell rang. It was lean, pale Eddie Warren (as usual) in a state of acute distress.

"It *is* the right house, *isn't* it?" he pleaded.

"Oh, I think so—I hope so," said Bertha brightly.

"I have had such a *dreadful* experience with a taximan; he was *most* sinister. I couldn't get him to *stop*. The *more* I knocked and called the *faster* he went. And *in* the moonlight this *bizarre* figure with the *flattened* head *crouching* over the *little* wheel...."

He shuddered, taking off an immense white silk scarf. Bertha noticed that his socks were white, too—most charming.

"But how dreadful!" she cried.

"Yes, it really was," said Eddie, following her into the drawing-room. "I saw myself *driving* through Eternity in a *timeless* taxi."

He knew the Norman Knights. In fact, he was going to write a play for N.K. when the theatre scheme came off.

"Well, Warren, how's the play?" said Norman Knight, dropping his monocle and giving his eye a moment in which to rise to the surface before it was screwed down again.

And Mrs. Norman Knight: "Oh, Mr. Warren, what happy socks!"

"I *am* so glad you like them," said he, staring at his feet. "They seem to have got so *much* whiter since the moon rose." And he turned his lean sorrowful young face to Bertha. "There *is* a moon, you know."

She wanted to cry: "I am sure there is—often—often!"

He really was a most attractive person. But so was Face, crouched before the fire in her banana skins, and so was Mug, smoking a cigarette and saying as he flicked the ash: "Why doth the bridegroom tarry?"[4]

"There he is, now."

Bang went the front door open and shut. Harry shouted: "Hullo, you people. Down in five minutes." And they heard him swarm up the stairs. Bertha couldn't help smiling; she knew how he loved doing things at high pressure. What, after all, did an extra five minutes matter? But he would pretend to himself that they mattered beyond measure. And then he would make a great point of coming into the drawing-room, extravagantly cool and collected.

Harry had such a zest for life. Oh, now she appreciated it in him. And his passion for fighting—for seeking in everything that came up against him another test of his power and of his courage—that, too, she understood. Even when it made him just occasionally, to other people, who didn't know him well, a little ridiculous perhaps. . . . For there were moments when he rushed into battle where no battle was . . . She talked and laughed and positively forgot until he had come in (just as she had imagined) that Pearl Fulton had not turned up.

"I wonder if Miss Fulton has forgotten?"

"I expect so," said Harry. "Is she on the 'phone?"

"Ah! There's a taxi, now." And Bertha smiled with that little air of proprietorship that she always assumed while her women finds were new and mysterious. "She lives in taxis."

"She'll run to fat if she does," said Harry coolly, ringing the bell for dinner. "Frightful danger for blond women."

"Harry—don't," warned Bertha, laughing up at him.

Came another tiny moment, while they waited, laughing and talking, just a trifle too much at their ease, a trifle too unaware. And then Miss Fulton, all in silver, with a silver fillet binding her pale blond hair, came in smiling, her head a little on one side.

"Am I late?"

"No, not at all," said Bertha. "Come along." And she took her arm and they moved into the dining-room.

What was there in the touch of that cool arm that could fan—fan—start blazing—blazing—the fire of bliss that Bertha did not know what to do with?

Miss Fulton did not look at her; but then she seldom did look at people directly. Her heavy eyelids lay upon her eyes and the strange half smile came and went upon her lips as though she lived by listening rather than seeing. But Bertha knew, suddenly, as if the longest, most intimate look had passed between them—as if they had said to each other: "You, too?"—that Pearl Fulton, stirring the beautiful red soup in the grey plate, was feeling just what she was feeling.

And the others? Face and Mug, Eddie and Harry, their spoons rising and falling—dabbing their lips with their napkins, crumbling bread, fiddling with the forks and glasses and talking.

"I met her at the Alpha show—the weirdest little person. She'd not only cut off her hair, but she seemed to have taken a dreadfully good snip off her legs and arms and her neck and her poor little nose as well."

---

4. A reference to Matthew 25.5—"while the bridegroom tarried, they all slumbered and slept."

"Isn't she very *liée*[5] with Michael Oat?"

"The man who wrote *Love in False Teeth*?"

"He wants to write a play for me. One act. One man. Decides to commit suicide. Gives all the reasons why he should and why he shouldn't. And just as he has made up his mind either to do it or not to do it—curtain. Not half a bad idea."

"What's he going to call it—'Stomach Trouble'?"

"I *think* I've come across the *same* idea in a lit-tle French review, *quite* unknown in England."

No, they didn't share it. They were dears—dears—and she loved having them there, at her table, and giving them delicious food and wine. In fact, she longed to tell them how delightful they were, and what a decorative group they made, how they seemed to set one another off and how they reminded her of a play by Chekhov!

Harry was enjoying his dinner. It was part of his—well, not his nature, exactly, and certainly not his pose—his—something or other—to talk about food and to glory in his "shameless passion for the white flesh of the lobster" and "the green of pistachio ices—green and cold like the eyelids of Egyptian dancers."

When he looked up at her and said: "Bertha, this is a very admirable *soufflée!*"[6] she almost could have wept with child-like pleasure.

Oh, why did she feel so tender towards the whole world tonight? Everything was good—was right. All that happened seemed to fill again her brimming cup of bliss.

And still, in the back of her mind, there was the pear tree. It would be silver now, in the light of poor dear Eddie's moon, silver as Miss Fulton, who sat there turning a tangerine in her slender fingers that were so pale a light seemed to come from them.

What she simply couldn't make out—what was miraculous—was how she should have guessed Miss Fulton's mood so exactly and so instantly. For she never doubted for a moment that she was right, and yet what had she to go on? Less than nothing.

"I believe this does happen very, very rarely between women. Never between men," thought Bertha. "But while I am making the coffee in the drawing-room perhaps she will 'give a sign.'"

What she meant by that she did not know, and what would happen after that she could not imagine.

While she thought like this she saw herself talking and laughing. She had to talk because of her desire to laugh.

"I must laugh or die."

But when she noticed Face's funny little habit of tucking something down the front of her bodice—as if she kept a tiny, secret hoard of nuts there, too—Bertha had to dig her nails into her hands—so as not to laugh too much.

It was over at last. And: "Come and see my new coffee machine," said Bertha.

"We only have a new coffee machine once a fortnight," said Harry. Face took her arm this time; Miss Fulton bent her head and followed after.

---

5. "Tied" (French)—that is, linked romantically.   6. A light, baked egg dish.

The fire had died down in the drawing-room to a red, flickering "nest of baby phœnixes," said Face.

"Don't turn up the light for a moment. It is so lovely." And down she crouched by the fire again. She was always cold . . . "without her little red flannel jacket, of course," thought Bertha.

At that moment Miss Fulton "gave the sign."

"Have you a garden?" said the cool, sleepy voice.

This was so exquisite on her part that all Bertha could do was to obey. She crossed the room, pulled the curtains apart, and opened those long windows.

"There!" she breathed.

And the two women stood side by side looking at the slender, flowering tree. Although it was so still it seemed, like the flame of a candle, to stretch up, to point, to quiver in the bright air, to grow taller and taller as they gazed—almost to touch the rim of the round, silver moon.

How long did they stand there? Both, as it were, caught in that circle of unearthly light, understanding each other perfectly, creatures of another world, and wondering what they were to do in this one with all this blissful treasure that burned in their bosoms and dropped, in silver flowers, from their hair and hands?

For ever—for a moment? And did Miss Fulton murmur: "Yes. Just *that*." Or did Bertha dream it?

Then the light was snapped on and Face made the coffee and Harry said: "My dear Mrs. Knight, don't ask me about my baby. I never see her. I shan't feel the slightest interest in her until she has a lover," and Mug took his eye out of the conservatory for a moment and then put it under glass again and Eddie Warren drank his coffee and set down the cup with a face of anguish as though he had drunk and seen the spider.

"What I want to do is to give the young men a show. I believe London is simply teeming with first-chop, unwritten plays. What I want to say to 'em is: 'Here's the theatre. Fire ahead.'"

"You know, my dear, I am going to decorate a room for the Jacob Nathans. Oh, I am so tempted to do a fried-fish scheme, with the backs of the chairs shaped like frying pans and lovely chip potatoes embroidered all over the curtains."

"The trouble with our young writing men is that they are still too romantic. You can't put out to sea without being seasick and wanting a basin. Well, why won't they have the courage of those basins?"

"A *dreadful* poem about a *girl* who was *violated* by a beggar *without* a nose in a lit-tle wood. . . ."

Miss Fulton sank into the lowest, deepest chair and Harry handed round the cigarettes.

From the way he stood in front of her shaking the silver box and saying abruptly: "Egyptian? Turkish? Virginian? They're all mixed up," Bertha realized that she not only bored him; he really disliked her. And she decided from the way Miss Fulton said: "No, thank you, I won't smoke," that she felt it, too, and was hurt.

"Oh, Harry, don't dislike her. You are quite wrong about her. She's wonderful, wonderful. And, besides, how can you feel so differently about someone who means so much to me. I shall try to tell you when we are in bed to-night what has been happening. What she and I have shared."

At those last words something strange and almost terrifying darted into Bertha's mind. And this something blind and smiling whispered to her: "Soon these people will go. The house will be quiet—quiet. The lights will be out. And you and he will be alone together in the dark room—the warm bed...."

She jumped up from her chair and ran over to the piano.

"What a pity someone does not play!" she cried. "What a pity somebody does not play."

For the first time in her life Bertha Young desired her husband.

Oh, she'd loved him—she'd been in love with him, of course, in every other way, but just not in that way. And, equally, of course, she'd understood that he was different. They'd discussed it so often. It had worried her dreadfully at first to find that she was so cold, but after a time it had not seemed to matter. They were so frank with each other—such good pals. That was the best of being modern.

But now—ardently! ardently! The word ached in her ardent body! Was this what that feeling of bliss had been leading up to? But then then—

"My dear," said Mrs. Norman Knight, "you know our shame. We are the victims of time and train. We live in Hampstead. It's been so nice."

"I'll come with you into the hall," said Bertha. "I loved having you. But you must not miss the last train. That's so awful, isn't it?"

"Have a whisky, Knight, before you go?" called Harry.

"No, thanks, old chap."

Bertha squeezed his hand for that as she shook it.

"Good night, good-bye," she cried from the top step, feeling that this self of hers was taking leave of them for ever.

When she got back into the drawing-room the others were on the move.

"... Then you can come part of the way in my taxi."

"I shall be *so* thankful *not* to have to face *another* drive *alone* after my *dreadful* experience."

"You can get a taxi at the rank[7] just at the end of the street. You won't have to walk more than a few yards."

"That's a comfort. I'll go and put on my coat."

Miss Fulton moved towards the hall and Bertha was following when Harry almost pushed past.

"Let me help you."

Bertha knew that he was repenting his rudeness—she let him go. What a boy he was in some ways—so impulsive—so—simple.

And Eddie and she were left by the fire.

"I *wonder* if you have seen Bilks' *new* poem called 'Table d'Hôte,[8]' " said Eddie softly. "It's *so* wonderful. In the last Anthology. Have you got a copy? I'd *so* like to *show* it to you. It beings with an *incredibly* beautiful line: 'Why Must it Always be Tomato Soup?'"

"Yes," said Bertha. And she moved noiselessly to a table opposite the drawing-

---

7. Taxi stand.   8. "Host's table" (French)—complete meal.

room door and Eddie glided noiselessly after her. She picked up the little book and gave it to him; they had not made a sound.

While he looked it up she turned her head towards the hall. And she saw . . . Harry with Miss Fulton's coat in his arms and Miss Fulton with her back turned to him and her head bent. He tossed the coat away, put his hands on her shoulders and turned her violently to him, His lips said: "I adore you," and Miss Fulton laid her moonbeam fingers on his cheeks and smiled her sleepy smile. Harry's nostrils quivered; his lips curled back in a hideous grin while he whispered: "Tomorrow," and with her eyelids Miss Fulton said: "Yes."

"Here it is," said Eddie. " 'Why Must it Always be Tomato Soup?' It's so *deeply* true, don't you feel? Tomato soup is so *dreadfully* eternal."

"If you prefer," said Harry's voice, very loud, from the hall, "I can phone you a cab to come to the door."

"Oh, no. It's not necessary," said Miss Fulton, and she came up to Bertha and gave her the slender fingers to hold.

"Good-bye. Thank you so much."

"Good-bye," said Bertha.

Miss Fulton held her hand a moment longer.

"Your lovely pear tree!" she murmured.

And then she was gone, with Eddie following, like the black cat following the grey cat.

"I'll shut up shop," said Harry, extravagantly cool and collected.

"Your lovely pear tree—pear tree—pear tree!"

Bertha simply ran over to the long windows.

"Oh, what is going to happen now?" she cried.

But the pear tree was as lovely as ever and as full of flower and as still.

1920

# KATHERINE ANNE PORTER

## Flowering Judas

Braggioni sits heaped upon the edge of a straight-backed chair much too small for him, and sings to Laura in a furry, mournful voice. Laura has begun to find reasons for avoiding her own house until the latest possible moment, for Braggioni is there almost every night. No matter how late she is, he will be sitting there with a surly, waiting expression, pulling at his kinky yellow hair, thumbing the strings of his guitar, snarling a tune under his breath. Lupe the Indian maid meets Laura at the door, and says with a flicker of a glance towards the upper room, "He waits."

Laura wishes to lie down, she is tired of her hairpins and the feel of her long tight sleeves, but she says to him, "Have you a new song for me this evening?" If he says yes, she asks him to sing it. If he says no, she remembers his favorite one, and asks him to sing it again. Lupe brings her a cup of chocolate and a plate of rice, and Laura eats at the small table under the lamp, first inviting Braggioni, whose answer is always the same: "I have eaten, and besides, chocolate thickens the voice."

Laura says, "Sing, then," and Braggioni heaves himself into song. He scratches the guitar familiarly as though it were a pet animal, and sings passionately off key, taking the high notes in a prolonged painful squeal. Laura, who haunts the markets listening to the ballad singers, and stops every day to hear the blind boy playing his reed-flute in Sixteenth of September Street,[1] listens to Braggioni with pitiless courtesy, because she dares not smile at his miserable performance. Nobody dares to smile at him. Braggioni is cruel to everyone, with a kind of specialized insolence, but he is so vain of his talents, and so sensitive to slights, it would require a cruelty and vanity greater than his own to lay a finger on the vast cureless wound of his self-esteem. It would require courage, too, for it is dangerous to offend him, and nobody has this courage.

Braggioni loves himself with such tenderness and amplitude and eternal charity that his followers—for he is a leader of men, a skilled revolutionist, and his skin had been punctured in honorable warfare—warm themselves in the reflected glow, and say to each other: "He has a real nobility, a love of humanity raised above mere personal affections." The excess of this self-love has flowed out, inconveniently for her, over Laura, who, with so many others, owes her comfortable situation and her salary to him. When he is in a very good humor, he tells her, "I am tempted to forgive you for being a *gringa. Gringita!*"[2] and Laura, burning, imagines herself leaning forward suddenly, and with a sound backhanded slap wiping the suety smile from his face. If he notices her eyes at these moments he gives no sign.

5   She knows what Braggioni would offer her, and she must resist tenaciously without appearing to resist, and if she could avoid it she would not admit even to herself the slow drift of his intention. During these long evenings which have spoiled a long month for her, she sits in her deep chair with an open book on her knees, resting her eyes on the consoling rigidity of the printed page when the sight and sound of Braggioni singing threaten to identify themselves with all her remembered afflictions and to add their weight to her uneasy premonitions of the future. The gluttonous bulk of Braggioni has become a symbol of her many disillusions, for a revolutionist should be lean, animated by heroic faith, a vessel of abstract virtues. This is nonsense, she knows it now and is ashamed of it. Revolution must have leaders, and leadership is a career for energetic men. She is, her comrades tell her, full of romantic error, for what she defines as cynicism in them is merely "a developed sense of reality." She is almost too willing to say, "I am wrong, I suppose I don't really understand the principles," and afterward she makes a secret truce with herself, determined not to surrender her will to such expedient logic. But she cannot help feeling that she has been betrayed irreparably by the disunion between her way of living and her feeling of what life should be, and at times she is almost contented to rest in this sense of grievance as a private store of consolation. Sometimes she wishes to run away, but she stays. Now she longs to fly out of this room, down the narrow stairs, and into the street where the houses lean together like conspirators under a single mottled lamp, and leave Braggioni singing to himself.

Instead she looks at Braggioni, frankly and clearly, like a good child who understands the rules of behavior. Her knees cling together under sound blue

---

1. Street in Morelia, a city in central Mexico.
2. Diminutive of *gringa:* non-Mexican woman, used pejoratively.

serge, and her round white collar is not purposely nun-like. She wears the uniform of an idea, and has renounced vanities. She was born Roman Catholic, and in spite of her fear of being seen by someone who might make a scandal of it, she slips now and again into some crumbling little church, kneels on the chilly stone, and says a Hail Mary on the gold rosary she bought in Tehuantepec. It is no good and she ends by examining the altar with its tinsel flowers and ragged brocades, and feels tender about the battered doll-shape of some male saint whose white, lace-trimmed drawers hang limply around his ankles below the hieratic dignity of his velvet robe. She has encased herself in a set of principles derived from her early training, leaving no detail of gesture or of personal taste untouched, and for this reason she will not wear lace made on machines. This is her private heresy, for in her special group the machine is sacred, and will be the salvation of the workers. She loves fine lace, and there is a tiny edge of fluted cobweb on this collar, which is one of twenty precisely alike, folded in blue tissue paper in the upper drawer of her clothes chest.

Braggioni catches her glance solidly as if he had been waiting for it, leans forward, balancing his paunch between his spread knees, and sings with tremendous emphasis, weighing his words. He has, the song relates, no father and no mother, nor even a friend to console him; lonely as a wave of the sea he comes and goes, lonely as a wave. His mouth opens round and yearns sideways, his balloon cheeks grow oily with the labor of song. He bulges marvelously in his expensive garments. Over his lavender collar, crushed upon a purple necktie, held by a diamond hoop: over his ammunition belt of tooled leather worked in silver, buckled cruelly around his gasping middle: over the tops of his glossy yellow shoes Braggioni swells with ominous ripeness, his mauve silk hose stretched taut, his ankles bound with the stout leather thongs of his shoes.

When he stretches his eyelids at Laura she notes again that his eyes are the true tawny yellow cat's eyes. He is rich, not in money, he tells her, but in power, and this power brings with it the blameless ownership of things, and the right to indulge his love of small luxuries. "I have a taste for the elegant refinements," he said once, flourishing a yellow silk handkerchief before her nose. "Smell that? It is Jockey Club, imported from New York." Nonetheless he is wounded by life. He will say so presently. "It is true everything turns to dust in the hand, to gall on the tongue." He sighs and his leather belt creaks like a saddle girth. "I am disappointed in everything as it comes. Everything." He shakes his head. "You, poor thing, you will be disappointed too. You are born for it. We are more alike than you realize in some things. Wait and see. Some day you will remember what I have told you, you will know that Braggioni was your friend."

Laura feels a slow chill, a purely physical sense of danger, a warning in her blood that violence, mutilation, a shocking death, wait for her with lessening patience. She has translated this fear into something homely, immediate, and sometimes hesitates before crossing the street. "My personal fate is nothing, except as the testimony of a mental attitude," she reminds herself, quoting from some forgotten philosophic primer, and is sensible enough to add, "Anyhow, I shall not be killed by an automobile if I can help it."

"It may be true I am as corrupt, in another way, as Braggioni," she thinks in spite of herself, "as callous, as incomplete," and if this is so, any kind of death seems preferable. Still she sits quietly, she does not run. Where could she go? Uninvited she has promised herself to this place; she can no longer imagine herself as living in another country, and there is no pleasure in remembering her life before she came here.

Precisely what is the nature of this devotion, its true motives, and what are its obligations? Laura cannot say. She spends part of her days in Xochimilco, near by, teaching Indian children to say in English, "The cat is on the mat." When she appears in the classroom they crowd about her with smiles on their wise, innocent, clay-colored faces, crying "Good morning, my titcher!" in immaculate voices, and they make of her desk a fresh garden of flowers every day.

During her leisure she goes to union meetings and listens to busy important voices quarreling over tactics, methods, internal politics. She visits the prisoners of her own political faith in their cells, where they entertain themselves with counting cockroaches, repenting of their indiscretions, composing their memoirs, writing out manifestoes and plans for their comrades who are still walking about free, hands in pockets, sniffing fresh air. Laura brings them food and cigarettes and a little money, and she brings messages disguised in equivocal phrases from the men outside who dare not set foot in the prison for fear of disappearing into the cells kept empty for them. If the prisoners confuse night and day, and complain, "Dear little Laura, time doesn't pass in this infernal hole, and I won't know when it is time to sleep unless I have a reminder," she brings them their favorite narcotics, and says in a tone that does not wound them with pity, "Tonight will really be night for you," and though her Spanish amuses them, they find her comforting, useful. If they lose patience and all faith, and curse the slowness of their friends in coming to their rescue with money and influence, they trust her not to repeat everything, and if she inquires, "Where do you think we can find money, or influence?" they are certain to answer, "Well, there is Braggioni, why doesn't he do something?"

She smuggles letters from headquarters to men hiding from firing squads in back streets in mildewed houses, where they sit in tumbled beds and talk bitterly as if all Mexico were at their heels, when Laura knows positively they might appear at the band concert in the Alameda on Sunday morning, and no one would notice them. But Braggioni says, "Let them sweat a little. The next time they may be careful. It is very restful to have them out of the way for a while." She is not afraid to knock on any door in any street after midnight, and enter in the darkness, and say to one of these men who is really in danger: "They will be looking for you—seriously—tomorrow morning after six. Here is some money from Vicente. Go to Vera Cruz and wait."

She borrows money from the Roumanian agitator to give to his bitter enemy the Polish agitator. The favor of Braggioni is their disputed territory, and Braggioni holds the balance nicely, for he can use them both. The Polish agitator talks love to her over café tables, hoping to exploit what he believes is her secret sentimental preference for him, and he gives her misinformation which he begs her to repeat as the solemn truth to certain persons. The Roumanian is more adroit. He is generous with his money in all good causes, and lies to her with an air of ingenuous candor, as if he were her good friend and confidant. She never repeats anything they may say. Braggioni never asks questions. He has other ways to discover all that he wishes to know about them.

15    Nobody touches her, but all praise her gray eyes, and the soft, round under lip which promises gayety, yet is always grave, nearly always firmly closed: and they cannot understand why she is in Mexico. She walks back and forth on her

errands, with puzzled eyebrows, carrying her little folder of drawings and music and school papers. No dancer dances more beautifully than Laura walks, and she inspires some amusing, unexpected ardors, which cause little gossip, because nothing comes of them. A young captain who had been a soldier in Zapata's[3] army attempted, during a horseback ride near Cuernavaca, to express his desire for her with the noble simplicity befitting a rude folk-hero: but gently, because he was gentle. This gentleness was his defeat, for when he alighted, and removed her foot from the stirrup, and essayed to draw her down into his arms, her horse, ordinarily a tame one, shied fiercely, reared and plunged away. The young hero's horse careered blindly after his stable-mate, and the hero did not return to the hotel until rather late that evening. At breakfast he came to her table in full charro[4] dress, gray buckskin jacket and trousers with strings of silver buttons down the leg, and he was in a humorous, careless mood. "May I sit with you?" and "You are a wonderful rider. I was terrified that you might be thrown and dragged. I should never have forgiven myself. But I cannot admire you enough for your riding!"

"I learned to ride in Arizona," said Laura.

"If you will ride with me again this morning, I promise you a horse that will not shy with you," he said. But Laura remembered that she must return to Mexico City at noon.

Next morning the children made a celebration and spent their playtime writing on the blackboard, "We lov ar ticher," and with tinted chalks they drew wreaths of flowers around the words. The young hero wrote her a letter: "I am a very foolish, wasteful, impulsive man. I should have first said I love you, and then you would not have run away. But you shall see me again." Laura thought, "I must send him a box of colored crayons," but she was trying to forgive herself for having spurred her horse at the wrong moment.

A brown, shock-haired youth came and stood in her patio one night and sang like a lost soul for two hours, but Laura could think of nothing to do about it. The moonlight spread a wash of gauzy silver over the clear spaces of the garden, and the shadows were cobalt blue. The scarlet blossoms of the Judas tree were dull purple, and the names of the colors repeated themselves automatically in her mind, while she watched not the boy, but his shadow, fallen like a dark garment across the fountain rim, trailing in the water. Lupe came silently and whispered expert counsel in her ear: "If you will throw him one little flower, he will sing another song or two and go away." Laura threw the flower, and he sang a last song and went away with the flower tucked in the band of his hat. Lupe said, "He is one of the organizers of the Typographers Union, and before that he sold corridos[5] in the Merced market, and before that, he came from Guanajuato, where I was born. I would not trust any man, but I trust least those from Guanajuato."

She did not tell Laura that he would be back again the next night, and the next, nor that he would follow her at a certain fixed distance around the Merced market, through the Zócolo, up Francisco I. Madero Avenue, and so along the Paseo de la Reforma to that Chapultepec Park, and into the Philosopher's Foot-

---

3. Emiliano Zapata (1879–1919), Mexican peasant-revolutionary general.
4. Costume worn by peasant horsemen of special status.    5. Popular ballads.

path, still with that flower withering in his hat, and an indivisible attention in his eyes.

Now Laura is accustomed to him, it means nothing except that he is nineteen years old and is observing a convention with all propriety, as though it were founded on a law of nature, which in the end it might well prove to be. He is beginning to write poems which he prints on a wooden press, and he leaves them stuck like handbills in her door. She is pleasantly disturbed by the abstract, unhurried watchfulness of his black eyes which will in time turn easily towards another object. She tells herself that throwing the flower was a mistake, for she is twenty-two years old and knows better; but she refuses to regret it, and persuades herself that her negation of all external events as they occur is a sign that she is gradually perfecting herself in the stoicism she strives to cultivate against that disaster she fears, though she cannot name it.

She is not at home in the world. Every day she teaches children who remain strangers to her, though she loves their tender round hands and their charming opportunist savagery. She knocks at unfamiliar doors not knowing whether a friend or a stranger shall answer, and even if a known face emerges from the sour gloom of that unknown interior, still it is the face of a stranger. No matter what this stranger says to her, nor what her message to him, the very cells of her flesh reject knowledge and kinship in one monotonous word. No. No. No. She draws her strength from this one holy talismanic word which does not suffer her to be led into evil. Denying everything, she may walk anywhere in safety, she looks at everything without amazement.

No, repeats this firm unchanging voice of her blood; and she looks at Braggioni without amazement. He is a great man, he wishes to impress this simple girl who covers her great round breasts with thick dark cloth, and who hides long, invaluably beautiful legs under a heavy skirt. She is almost thin except for the incomprehensible fullness of her breasts, like a nursing mother's, and Braggioni, who considers himself a judge of women, speculates again on the puzzle of her notorious virginity, and takes the liberty of speech which she permits without a sign of modesty, indeed, without any sort of sign, which is disconcerting.

"You think you are so cold, *gringita!* Wait and see. You will surprise yourself some day! May I be there to advise you!" He stretches his eyelids at her, and his ill-humored cat's eyes waver in a separate glance for the two points of light marking the opposite ends of a smoothly drawn path between the swollen curve of her breasts. He is not put off by that blue serge, nor by her resolutely fixed gaze. There is all the time in the world. His cheeks are bellying with the wind of song. "O girl with the dark eyes," he sings, and reconsiders. "But yours are not dark. I can change all that. O girl with the green eyes, you have stolen my heart away!" then his mind wanders to the song, and Laura feels the weight of his attention being shifted elsewhere. Singing thus, he seems harmless, he is quite harmless, there is nothing to do but sit patiently and say "No," when the moment comes. She draws a full breath, and her mind wanders also, but not far. She dares not wander too far.

25   Not for nothing has Braggioni taken pains to be a good revolutionist and a professional lover of humanity. He will never die of it. He has the malice, the cleverness, the wickedness, the sharpness of wit, the hardness of heart, stipulated for loving the world profitably. *He will never die of it.* He will live to see himself

kicked out from his feeding trough by other hungry world-saviors. Traditionally he must sing in spite of his life which drives him to bloodshed, he tells Laura, for his father was a Tuscany[6] peasant who drifted to Yucatan and married a Maya woman: a woman of race, an aristocrat. They gave him the love and knowledge of music, thus: and under the rip of his thumbnail, the strings of the instrument complain like exposed nerves.

Once he was called Delgadito by all the girls and married women who ran after him; he was so scrawny all his bones showed under his thin cotton clothing, and he could squeeze his emptiness to the very backbone with his two hands. He was a poet and the revolution was only a dream then; too many women loved him and sapped away his youth, and he could never find enough to eat anywhere, anywhere! Now he is a leader of men, crafty men who whisper in his ear, hungry men who wait for hours outside his office for a word with him, emaciated men with wild faces who waylay him at the street gate with a timid, "Comrade, let me tell you . . ." and they blow the foul breath from their empty stomachs in his face.

He is always sympathetic. He gives them handfuls of small coins from his own pocket, he promises them work, there will be demonstrations, they must join the unions and attend the meetings, above all they must be on the watch for spies. They are closer to him than his own brothers, without them he can do nothing—until tomorrow, comrade!

Until tomorrow. "They are stupid, they are lazy, they are treacherous, they would cut my throat for nothing," he says to Laura. He has good food and abundant drink, he hires an automobile and drives in the Paseo on Sunday morning, and enjoys plenty of sleep in a soft bed beside a wife who dares not disturb him; and he sits pampering his bones in easy billows of fat, singing to Laura, who knows and thinks these things about him. When he was fifteen, he tried to drown himself because he loved a girl, his first love, and she laughed at him. "A thousand women have paid for that," and his tight little mouth turns down at the corners. Now he perfumes his hair with Jockey Club, and confides to Laura: "One woman is really as good as another for me, in the dark. I prefer them all."

His wife organizes unions among the girls in the cigarette factories, and walks in picket lines, and even speaks at meetings in the evening. But she cannot be brought to acknowledge the benefits of true liberty. "I tell her I must have my freedom, net. She does not understand my point of view." Laura has heard this many times. Braggioni scratches the guitar and meditates. "She is an instinctively virtuous woman, pure gold, no doubt of that. If she were not, I should lock her up, and she knows it."

His wife, who works so hard for the good of the factory girls, employs part of her leisure lying on the floor weeping because there are so many women in the world, and only one husband for her, and she never knows where nor when to look for him. He told her: "Unless you can learn to cry when I am not here, I must go away for good." That day he went away and took a room at the Hotel Madrid.

It is this month of separation for the sake of higher principles that has been spoiled not only for Mrs. Braggioni, whose sense of reality is beyond criticism,

---

6. Region in northern Italy.

but for Laura, who feels herself bogged in a nightmare. Tonight Laura envies Mrs. Braggioni, who is alone, and free to weep as much as she pleases about a concrete wrong. Laura has just come from a visit to the prison, and she is waiting for tomorrow with a bitter anxiety as if tomorrow may not come, but time may be caught immovably in this hour, with herself transfixed, Braggioni singing on forever, and Eugenio's body not yet discovered by the guard.

Braggioni says: "Are you going to sleep?" Almost before she can shake her head, he begins telling her about the May-day disturbances coming on in Morelia, for the Catholics hold a festival in honor of the Blessed Virgin, and the Socialists celebrate their martyrs on that day. "There will be two independent processions, starting from either end of town, and they will march until they meet, and the rest depends . . ." He asks her to oil and load his pistols. Standing up, he unbuckles his ammunition belt, and spreads it laden across her knees. Laura sits with the shells slipping through the cleaning cloth dipped in oil, and he says again he cannot understand why she works so hard for the revolutionary idea unless she loves some man who is in it. "Are you not in love with someone?" "No," says Laura. "And no one is in love with you?" "No." "Then it is your own fault. No woman need go begging. Why, what is the matter with you? The legless beggar woman in the Alameda has a perfectly faithful lover. Did you know that?"

Laura peers down the pistol barrel and says nothing, but a long, slow faintness rises and subsides in her; Braggioni curves his swollen fingers around the throat of the guitar and softly smothers the music out of it, and when she hears him again he seems to have forgotten her, and is speaking in the hypnotic voice he uses when talking in small rooms to a listening, close-gathered crowd. Some day this world, now seemingly so composed and eternal, to the edges of every sea shall be merely a tangle of gaping trenches, of crashing walls and broken bodies. Everything must be torn from its accustomed place where it has rotted for centuries, hurled skyward and distributed, cast down again clean as rain, without separate identity. Nothing shall survive that the stiffened hands of poverty have created for the rich and no one shall be left alive except the elect spirits destined to procreate a new world cleansed of cruelty and injustice, ruled by benevolent anarchy: "Pistols are good, I love them, cannon are even better, but in the end I pin my faith to good dynamite," he concludes, and strokes the pistol lying in her hands. "Once I dreamed of destroying this city, in case it offered resistance to General Ortíz, but it fell into his hands like an overripe pear."

He is made restless by his own words, rises and stands waiting. Laura holds up the belt to him: "Put that on, and go kill somebody in Morelia, and you will be happier," she says softly. The presence of death in the room makes her bold. "Today, I found Eugenio going into a stupor. He refused to allow me to call the prison doctor. He had taken all the tablets I brought him yesterday. He said he took them because he was bored."

"He is a fool, and his death is his own business," says Braggioni, fastening his belt carefully.

"I told him if he had waited only a little while longer, you would have got him set free," says Laura. "He said he did not want to wait."

"He is a fool and we are well rid of him," says Braggioni, reaching for his hat.

He goes away. Laura knows his mood has changed, she will not see him any more for a while. He will send word when he needs her to go on errands into strange streets, to speak to the strange faces that will appear, like clay masks with the power of human speech, to mutter their thanks to Braggioni for his help. Now she is free, and she thinks, I must run while there is time. But she does not go.

Braggioni enters his own house where for a month his wife has spent many hours every night weeping and tangling her hair upon her pillow. She is weeping now, and she weeps more at the sight of him, the cause of all her sorrows. He looks about the room. Nothing is changed, the smells are good and familiar, he is well acquainted with the woman who comes toward him with no reproach except grief on her face. He says to her tenderly: "You are so good, please don't cry any more, you dear good creature." She says, "Are you tired, my angel? Sit here and I will wash your feet." She brings a bowl of water, and kneeling, unlaces his shoes, and when from her knees she raises her sad eyes under her blackened lids, he is sorry for everything, and bursts into tears. "Ah, yes, I am hungry, I am tired, let us eat something together," he says, between sobs. His wife leans her head on his arm and says, "Forgive me!" and this time he is refreshed by the solemn, endless rain of her tears.

Laura takes off her serge dress and puts on a white linen nightgown and goes to bed. She turns her head a little to one side, and lying still, reminds herself that it is time to sleep. Numbers tick in her brain like little clocks, soundless doors close of themselves around her. If you would sleep, you must not remember anything, the children will say tomorrow, good morning, my teacher, the poor prisoners who come every day bringing flowers to their jailor. 1-2-3-4-5—it is monstrous to confuse love with revolution, night with day, life with death—ah, Eugenio!

The tolling of the midnight bell is a signal, but what does it mean? Get up, Laura, and follow me: come out of your sleep, out of your bed, out of this strange house. What are you doing in this house? Without a word, without fear she rose and reached for Eugenio's hand, but he eluded her with a sharp, sly smile and drifted away. This is not all, you shall see—Murderer, he said, follow me, I will show you a new country, but it is far away and we must hurry. No, said Laura, not unless you take my hand, no; and she clung first to the stair rail, and then to the topmost branch of the Judas tree that bent down slowly and set her upon the earth, and then to the rocky ledge of a cliff, and then to the jagged wave of a sea that was not water but a desert of crumbling stone. Where are you taking me, she asked in wonder but without fear. To death, and it is a long way off, and we must hurry, said Eugenio. No, said Laura, not unless you take my hand. Then eat these flowers, poor prisoner, said Eugenio in a voice of pity, take and eat: and from the Judas tree he stripped the warm bleeding flowers, and held them to her lips. She saw that his hand was fleshless, a cluster of small white petrified branches, and his eye sockets were without light, but she ate the flowers greedily for they satisfied both hunger and thirst. Murderer! said Eugenio, and Cannibal! This is my body and my blood. Laura cried No! and at the sound of her own voice, she awoke trembling, and was afraid to sleep again.

1929, 1930

## WILLIAM FAULKNER

### *Barn Burning*

The store in which the Justice of the Peace's court was sitting smelled of cheese. The boy, crouched on his nail keg at the back of the crowded room, knew he smelled cheese, and more: from where he sat he could see the ranked shelves close-packed with the solid, squat, dynamic shapes of tin cans whose labels his stomach read, not from the lettering which meant nothing to his mind but from the scarlet devils and the silver curve of fish—this, the cheese which he knew he smelled and the hermetic meat which his intestines believed he smelled coming in intermittent gusts momentary and brief between the other constant one, the smell and sense just a little of fear because mostly of despair and grief, the old fierce pull of blood. He could not see the table where the Justice sat and before which his father and his father's enemy *(our enemy* he thought in that despair; *ournl mine and hisn both! He's my father!)* stood, but he could hear them, the two of them that is, because his father had said no word yet:

"But what proof have you, Mr. Harris?"

"I told you. The hog got into my corn. I caught it up and sent it back to him. He had no fence that would hold it. I told him so, warned him. The next time I put the hog in my pen. When he came to get it I gave him enough wire to patch up his pen. The next time I put the hog up and kept it. I rode down to his house and saw the wire I gave him still rolled on to the spool in his yard. I told him he could have the hog when he paid me a dollar pound fee. That evening a nigger came with the dollar and got the hog. He was a strange nigger. He said, 'He say to tell you wood and hay kin burn.' I said, 'What?' 'That whut he say to tell you,' the nigger said. 'Wood and hay kin burn.' That night my barn burned. I got the stock out but I lost the barn."

"Where is the nigger? Have you got him?"

5  "He was a strange nigger, I tell you. I don't know what became of him."

"But that's not proof. Don't you see that's not proof?"

"Get that boy up here. He knows." For a moment the boy thought too that the man meant his older brother until Harris said, "Not him. The little one. The boy," and, crouching, small for his age, small and wiry like his father, in patched and faded jeans even too small for him, with straight, uncombed, brown hair and eyes gray and wild as storm scud, he saw the men between himself and the table part and become a lane of grim faces, at the end of which he saw the Justice, a shabby, collarless, graying man in spectacles, beckoning him. He felt no floor under his bare feet; he seemed to walk beneath the palpable weight of the grim turning faces. His father, stiff in his black Sunday coat donned not for the trial but for the moving, did not even look at him. *He aims for me to lie,* he thought, again with that frantic grief and despair. *And I will have to do hit.*

"What's your name, boy?" the Justice said.

"Colonel Sartoris Snopes," the boy whispered.

10  "Hey?" the Justice said. "Talk louder. Colonel Sartoris? I reckon anybody named for Colonel Sartoris in this country can't help but tell the truth, can they?" The boy said nothing. *Enemy! Enemy!* he thought; for a moment he could not even see, could not see that the Justice's face was kindly nor discern that his

voice was troubled when he spoke to the man named Harris: "Do you want me to question this boy?" But he could hear, and during those subsequent long seconds while there was absolutely no sound in the crowded little room save that of quiet and intent breathing it was as if he had swung outward at the end of a grape vine, over a ravine, and at the top of the swing had been caught in a prolonged instant of mesmerized gravity, weightless in time.

"No!" Harris said violently, explosively. "Damnation! Send him out of here!" Now time, the fluid world, rushed beneath him again, the voices coming to him again through the smell of cheese and sealed meat, the fear and despair and the old grief of blood:

"This case is closed. I can't find against you, Snopes, but I can give you advice. Leave this country and don't come back to it."

His father spoke for the first time, his voice cold and harsh, level, without emphasis: "I aim to. I don't figure to stay in a country among people who..." he said something unprintable and vile, addressed to no one.

"That'll do," the Justice said. "Take your wagon and get out of this country before dark. Case dismissed."

His father turned, and he followed the stiff black coat, the wiry figure walking a little stiffly from where a Confederate provost's man's[1] musket ball had taken him in the heel on a stolen horse thirty years ago, followed the two backs now, since his older brother had appeared from somewhere in the crowd, no taller than the father but thicker, chewing tobacco steadily, between the two lines of grim-faced men and out of the store and across the worn gallery and down the sagging steps and among the dogs and half-grown boys in the mild May dust, where as he passed a voice hissed:

"Barn burner!"

Again he could not see, whirling; there was a face in a red haze, moonlike, bigger than the full moon, the owner of it half again his size, he leaping in the red haze toward the face, feeling no blow, feeling no shock when his head struck the earth, scrabbling up and leaping again, feeling no blow this time either and tasting no blood, scrabbling up to see the other boy in full flight and himself already leaping into pursuit as his father's hand jerked him back, the harsh, cold voice speaking above him: "Go get in the wagon."

It stood in a grove of locusts and mulberries across the road. His two hulking sisters in their Sunday dresses and his mother and her sister in calico and sunbonnets were already in it, sitting on and among the sorry residue of the dozen and more movings which even the boy could remember—the battered stove, the broken beds and chairs, the clock inlaid with mother-of-pearl, which would not run, stopped at some fourteen minutes past two o'clock of a dead and forgotten day and time, which had been his mother's dowry. She was crying, though when she saw him she drew her sleeve across her face and began to descend from the wagon. "Get back," the father said.

"He's hurt. I got to get some water and wash his..."

"Get back in the wagon," his father said. He got in too, over the tail-gate. His father mounted to the seat where the older brother already sat and struck the gaunt mules two savage blows with the peeled willow, but without heat. It was not even sadistic; it was exactly that same quality which in later years would

---

1. Military policeman's.

cause his descendants to overrun the engine before putting a motor car into motion, striking and reining back in the same movement. The wagon went on, the store with its quiet crowd of grimly watching men dropped behind; a curve in the road hid it. *Forever* he thought. *Maybe he's done satisfied now, now that he has ... stopping* himself, not to say it aloud even to himself. His mother's hand touched his shoulder.

"Does hit hurt?" she said.

"Naw," he said. "Hit don't hurt. Lemme be."

"Can't you wipe some of the blood off before hit dries?"

"I'll wash to-night," he said. "Lemme be, I tell you."

The wagon went on. He did not know where they were going. None of them ever did or ever asked, because it was always somewhere, always a house of sorts waiting for them a day or two days or even three days away. Likely his father had already arranged to make a crop on another farm before he ... Again he had to stop himself. He (the father) always did. There was something about his wolf-like independence and even courage when the advantage was at least neutral which impressed strangers, as if they got from his latent ravening ferocity not so much a sense of dependability as a feeling that his ferocious conviction in the rightness of his own actions would be of advantage to all whose interest lay with his.

That night they camped, in a grove of oaks and beeches where a spring ran. The nights were still cool and they had a fire against it, of a rail lifted from a nearby fence and cut into lengths—a small fire, neat, niggard almost, a shrewd fire; such fires were his father's habit and custom always, even in freezing weather. Older, the boy might have remarked this and wondered why not a big one; why should not a man who had not only seen the waste and extravagance of war, but who had in his blood an inherent voracious prodigality with material not his own, have burned everything in sight? Then he might have gone a step farther and thought that that was the reason: that niggard blaze was the living fruit of nights passed during those four years in the woods hiding from all men, blue or gray,[2] with his strings of horses (captured horses, he called them). And older still, he might have divined the true reason: that the element of fire spoke to some deep mainspring of his father's being, as the element of steel or of powder spoke to other men, as the one weapon for the preservation of integrity, else breath were not worth the breathing, and hence to be regarded with respect and used with discretion.

But he did not think this now and he had seen those same niggard blazes all his life. He merely ate his supper beside it and was already half asleep over his iron plate when his father called him, and once more he followed the stiff back, the stiff and ruthless limp, up the slope and on to the starlit road where, turning, he could see his father against the stars but without face or depth—a shape black, flat, and bloodless as though cut from tin in the iron folds of the frockcoat which had not been made for him, the voice harsh like tin and without heat like tin:

"You were fixing to tell them. You would have told him." He didn't answer. His father struck him with the flat of his hand on the side of the head, hard but without heat, exactly as he had struck the two mules at the store, exactly as he

---

2. The colors of Union and Confederate Civil War (1861–65) uniforms, respectively.

would strike either of them with any stick in order to kill a horse fly, his voice still without heat or anger: "You're getting to be a man. You got to learn. You got to learn to stick to your own blood or you ain't going to have any blood to stick to you. Do you think either of them, any man there this morning, would? Don't you know all they wanted was a chance to get at me because they knew I had them beat? Eh?" Later, twenty years later, he was to tell himself, "If I had said they wanted only truth, justice, he would have hit me again." But now he said nothing. He was not crying. He just stood there. "Answer me," his father said.

"Yes," he whispered. His father turned.

"Get on to bed. We'll be there tomorrow."

Tomorrow they were there. In the early afternoon the wagon stopped before a paintless two-room house identical almost with the dozen others it had stopped before even in the boy's ten years, and again, as on the other dozen occasions, his mother and aunt got down and began to unload the wagon, although his two sisters and his father and brother had not moved.

"Likely hit ain't fitten for hawgs," one of the sisters said.

"Nevertheless, fit it will and you'll hog it and like it," his father said. "Get out of them chairs and help your Ma unload."

The two sisters got down, big, bovine, in a flutter of cheap ribbons; one of them drew from the jumbled wagon bed a battered lantern, the other a worn broom. His father handed the reins to the older son and began to climb stiffly over the wheel. "When they get unloaded, take the team to the barn and feed them." Then he said, and at first the boy thought he was still speaking to his brother: "Come with me."

"Me?" he said.

"Yes," his father said. "You."

"Abner," his mother said. His father paused and looked back—the harsh level stare beneath the shaggy, graying, irascible brows.

"I reckon I'll have a word with the man that aims to begin to-morrow owning me body and soul for the next eight months."

They went back up the road. A week ago—or before last night, that is—he would have asked where they were going, but not now. His father had struck him before last night but never before had he paused afterward to explain why; it was as if the blow and the following calm, outrageous voice still rang, repercussed, divulging nothing to him save the terrible handicap of being young, the light weight of his few years, just heavy enough to prevent his soaring free of the world as it seemed to be ordered but not heavy enough to keep him footed solid in it, to resist it and try to change the course of its events.

Presently he could see the grove of oaks and cedars and the other flowering trees and shrubs, where the house would be, though not the house yet. They walked beside a fence massed with honeysuckle and Cherokee roses and came to a gate swinging open between two brick pillars, and now, beyond a sweep of drive, he saw the house for the first time and at that instant he forgot his father and the terror and despair both, and even when he remembered his father again (who had not stopped) the terror and despair did not return. Because, for all the twelve movings, they had sojourned until now in a poor country, a land of small farms and fields and houses, and he had never seen a house like this before. *Hit's big as a courthouse* he thought quietly, with a surge of peace and joy whose reason he could not have thought into words, being too young for that: *They are safe from him. People whose lives are a part of this peace and dignity are beyond his touch, he no more to them than a buzzing wasp: capable of stinging for a little moment but that's all; the spell of this peace and dignity rendering even the barns and stable and cribs which belong to it impervious to the puny flames he might contrive* ... this, the peace and joy, ebbing for an instant as he looked again at the stiff black back, the stiff and implacable limp of the figure which was not dwarfed by the house, for the reason that it had never looked big anywhere and which now, against the serene columned backdrop, had more than ever that impervious quality of something cut ruthlessly from tin, depthless, as though, sidewise to the sun, it would cast no shadow. Watching him, the boy remarked the absolutely undeviating course which his father held and saw the stiff foot come squarely down in a pile of fresh droppings where a horse had stood in the drive and which his father could have avoided by a simple change of stride. But it ebbed only for a moment, though he could not have thought this into words either, walking on in the spell of the house, which he could even want but without envy, without sorrow, certainly never with that ravening and jealous rage which unknown to him walked in the ironlike black coat before him: *Maybe he will feel it too. Maybe it will even change him now from what maybe he couldn't help but be.*

They crossed the portico. Now he could hear his father's stiff foot as it came down on the boards with clocklike finality, a sound out of all proportion to the displacement of the body it bore and which was not dwarfed either by the white door before it, as though it had attained to a sort of vicious and ravening minimum not to be dwarfed by anything—the flat, wide, black hat, the formal coat of broadcloth which had once been black but which had now that friction-glazed greenish cast of the bodies of old house flies, the lifted sleeve which was too large, the lifted hand like a curled claw. The door opened so promptly that the boy knew the Negro must have been watching them all the time, an old man with neat grizzled hair, in a linen jacket, who stood barring the door with his body, saying, "Wipe yo foots, white man, fo you come in here. Major ain't home nohow."

"Get out of my way, nigger," his father said, without heat too, flinging the door back and the Negro also and entering, his hat still on his head. And now the boy saw the prints of the stiff foot on the doorjamb and saw them appear on the pale rug behind the machinelike deliberation of the foot which seemed to bear (or transmit) twice the weight which the body compassed. The Negro was shouting "Miss Lula! Miss Lula!" somewhere behind them, then the boy, deluged as though by a warm wave by a suave turn of carpeted stair and a pendant glitter of chandeliers and a mute gleam of gold frames, heard the swift feet and saw her too, a lady—perhaps he had never seen her like before either—in a gray, smooth gown with lace at the throat and an apron tied at the waist and the sleeves turned back, wiping cake or biscuit dough from her hands with a towel as she came up the hall, looking not at his father at all but at the tracks on the blond rug with an expression of incredulous amazement.

"I tried," the Negro cried. "I tole him to . . ."

"Will you please go away?" she said in a shaking voice. "Major de Spain is not at home. Will you please go away?"

45   His father had not spoken again. He did not speak again. He did not even look at her. He just stood stiff in the center of the rug, in his hat, the shaggy

iron-gray brows twitching slightly above the pebble-colored eyes as he appeared to examine the house with brief deliberation. Then with the same deliberation he turned; the boy watched him pivot on the good leg and saw the stiff foot drag round the arc of the turning, leaving a final long and fading smear. His father never looked at it, he never once looked down at the rug. The Negro held the door. It closed behind them, upon the hysteric and indistinguishable woman-wail. His father stopped at the top of the steps and scraped his boot clean on the edge of it. At the gate he stopped again. He stood for a moment, planted stiffly on the stiff foot, looking back at the house. "Pretty and white, ain't it?" he said. "That's sweat. Nigger sweat. Maybe it ain't white enough yet to suit him. Maybe he wants to mix some white sweat with it."

Two hours later the boy was chopping wood behind the house within which his mother and aunt and the two sisters (the mother and aunt, not the two girls, he knew that; even at this distance and muffled by walls the flat loud voices of the two girls emanated an incorrigible idle inertia) were setting up the stove to prepare a meal, when he heard the hooves and saw the linen-clad man on a fine sorrel mare, whom he recognized even before he saw the rolled rug in front of the Negro youth following on a fat bay carriage horse—a suffused, angry face vanishing, still at full gallop, beyond the corner of the house where his father and brother were sitting in the two tilted chairs; and a moment later, almost before he could have put the axe down, he heard the hooves again and watched the sorrel mare go back out of the yard, already galloping again. Then his father began to shout one of the sisters' names, who presently emerged backward from the kitchen door dragging the rolled rug along the ground by one end while the other sister walked behind it.

"If you ain't going to tote, go on and set up the wash pot," the first said.

"You, Sarty!" the second shouted. "Set up the wash pot!" His father appeared at the door, framed against that shabbiness, as he had been against that other bland perfection, impervious to either, the mother's anxious face at his shoulder.

"Go on," the father said. "Pick it up." The two sisters stooped, broad, lethargic; stooping, they presented an incredible expanse of pale cloth and a flutter of tawdry ribbons.

"If I thought enough of a rug to have to git hit all the way from France I wouldn't keep hit where folks coming in would have to tromp on hit," the first said. They raised the rug.

"Abner," the mother said. "Let me do it."

"You go back and git dinner," his father said. "I'll tend to this."

From the woodpile through the rest of the afternoon the boy watched them, the rug spread flat in the dust beside the bubbling wash-pot, the two sisters stooping over it with that profound and lethargic reluctance, while the father stood over them in turn, implacable and grim, driving them though never raising his voice again. He could smell the harsh homemade lye they were using; he saw his mother come to the door once and look toward them with an expression not anxious now but very like despair; he saw his father turn, and he fell to with the axe and saw from the corner of his eye his father raise from the ground a flattish fragment of field stone and examine it and return to the pot, and this time his mother actually spoke: "Abner. Abner. Please don't. Please, Abner."

Then he was done too. It was dusk; the whippoorwills had already begun. He could smell coffee from the room where they would presently eat the cold food remaining from the mid-afternoon meal, though when he entered the house he realized they were having coffee again probably because there was a fire on the hearth, before which the rug now lay spread over the backs of the two chairs. The tracks of his father's foot were gone. Where they had been were now long, water-cloudy scoriations resembling the sporadic course of a Lilliputian mowing machine.

55 It still hung there while they ate the cold food and then went to bed, scattered without order or claim up and down the two rooms, his mother in one bed, where his father would later lie, the older brother in the other, himself, the aunt, and the two sisters on pallets on the floor. But his father was not in bed yet. The last thing the boy remembered was the depthless, harsh silhouette of the hat and coat bending over the rug and it seemed to him that he had not even closed his eyes when the silhouette was standing over him, the fire almost dead behind it, the stiff foot prodding him awake. "Catch up the mule," his father said.

When he returned with the mule his father was standing in the black door, the rolled rug over his shoulder. "Ain't you going to ride?" he said.

"No. Give me your foot."

He bent his knee into his father's hand, the wiry, surprising power flowed smoothly, rising, he rising with it, on to the mule's bare back (they had owned a saddle once; the boy could remember it though not when or where) and with the same effortlessness his father swung the rug up in front of him. Now in the starlight they retraced the afternoon's path, up the dusty road rife with honeysuckle, through the gate and up the black tunnel of the drive to the lightless house, where he sat on the mule and felt the rough warp of the rug drag across his thighs and vanish.

"Don't you want me to help?" he whispered. His father did not answer and now he heard again that stiff foot striking the hollow portico with that wooden and clocklike deliberation, that outrageous overstatement of the weight it carried. The rug, hunched, not flung (the boy could tell that even in the darkness) from his father's shoulder struck the angle of wall and floor with a sound unbelievably loud, thunderous, then the foot again, unhurried and enormous; a light came on in the house and the boy sat, tense, breathing steadily and quietly and just a little fast, though the foot itself did not increase its beat at all, descending the steps now; now the boy could see him.

60 "Don't you want to ride now?" he whispered. "We kin both ride now," the light within the house altering now, flaring up and sinking. *He's coming down the stairs now,* he thought. He had already ridden the mule up beside the horse block; presently his father was up behind him and he doubled the reins over and slashed the mule across the neck, but before the animal could begin to trot the hard, thin arm came round him, the hard, knotted hand jerking the mule back to a walk.

In the first red rays of the sun they were in the lot, putting plow gear on the mules. This time the sorrel mare was in the lot before he heard it at all, the rider collarless and even bareheaded, trembling, speaking in a shaking voice as the woman in the house had done, his father merely looking up once before stooping again to the hame he was buckling, so that the man on the mare spoke to his stooping back:

"You must realize you have ruined that rug. Wasn't there anybody here, any of your women . . ." he ceased, shaking, the boy watching him, the older brother leaning now in the stable door, chewing, blinking slowly and steadily at nothing apparently. "It cost a hundred dollars. But you never had a hundred dollars. You never will. So I'm going to charge you twenty bushels of corn against your crop. I'll add it in your contract and when you come to the commissary you can sign it. That won't keep Mrs. de Spain quiet but maybe it will teach you to wipe your feet off before you enter her house again."

Then he was gone. The boy looked at his father, who still had not spoken or even looked up again, who was now adjusting the logger-head in the hame.

"Pap," he said. His father looked at him—the inscrutable face, the shaggy brows beneath which the gray eyes glinted coldly. Suddenly the boy went toward him, fast, stopping as suddenly. "You done the best you could!" he cried. "If he wanted hit done different why didn't he wait and tell you how? He won't git no twenty bushels! He won't git none! We'll gether hit and hide hit! I kin watch..."

"Did you put the cutter back in that straight stock like I told you?"

"No, sir," he said.

"Then go do it."

That was Wednesday. During the rest of that week he worked steadily, at what was within his scope and some which was beyond it, with an industry that did not need to be driven nor even commanded twice; he had this from his mother, with the difference that some at least of what he did he liked to do, such as splitting wood with the half-size axe which his mother and aunt had earned, or saved money somehow, to present him with at Christmas. In company with the two older women (and on one afternoon, even one of the sisters), he built pens for the shoat and the cow which were a part of his father's contract with the landlord, and one afternoon, his father being absent, gone somewhere on one of the mules, he went to the field.

They were running a middle buster[3] now, his brother holding the plow straight while he handled the reins, and walking beside the straining mule, the rich black soil shearing cool and damp against his bare ankles, he thought *Maybe this is the end of it. Maybe even that twenty bushels that seems hard to have to pay for just a rug will be a cheap price for him to stop forever and always from being what he used to be;* thinking, dreaming now, so that his brother had to speak sharply to him to mind the mule: *Maybe he even won't collect the twenty bushels. Maybe it will all add up and balance and vanish—corn, rug, fire; the terror and grief, the being pulled two ways like between two teams of horses—gone, done with for ever and ever.*

Then it was Saturday; he looked up from beneath the mule he was harnessing and saw his father in the black coat and hat. "Not that," his father said. "The wagon gear." And then, two hours later, sitting in the wagon bed behind his father and brother on the seat, the wagon accomplished a final curve, and he saw the weathered paintless store with its tattered tobacco- and patent-medicine posters and the tethered wagons and saddle animals below the gallery. He mounted the gnawed steps behind his father and brother, and there again was the lane of quiet, watching faces for the three of them to walk through. He saw the man in spectacles sitting at the plank table and he did not need to be told this was a Justice of the Peace; he sent one glare of fierce, exultant, partisan defiance at the man in collar and cravat now, whom he had seen but twice before in his life, and that on a galloping horse, who now wore on his face an expression

---

3. A double moldboard plow that throws a ridge of earth both ways.

not of rage but of amazed unbelief which the boy could not have known was at the incredible circumstance of being sued by one of his own tenants, and came and stood against his father and cried at the Justice: "He ain't done it! He ain't burnt..."

"Go back to the wagon," his father said.

"Burnt?" the Justice said. "Do I understand this rug was burned too?"

"Does anybody here claim it was?" his father said. "Go back to the wagon." But he did not, he merely retreated to the rear of the room, crowded as that other had been, but not to sit down this time, instead, to stand pressing among the motionless bodies, listening to the voices:

"And you claim twenty bushels of corn is too high for the damage you did to the rug?"

75 "He brought the rug to me and said he wanted the tracks washed out of it. I washed the tracks out and took the rug back to him."

"But you didn't carry the rug back to him in the same condition it was in before you made the tracks on it."

His father did not answer, and now for perhaps half a minute there was no sound at all save that of breathing, the faint, steady suspiration of complete and intent listening.

"You decline to answer that, Mr. Snopes?" Again his father did not answer. "I'm going to find against you, Mr. Snopes. I'm going to find that you were responsible for the injury to Major de Spain's rug and hold you liable for it. But twenty bushels of corn seems a little high for a man in your circumstances to have to pay. Major de Spain claims it cost a hundred dollars. October corn will be worth about fifty cents. I figure that if Major de Spain can stand a ninety-five dollar loss on something he paid cash for, you can stand a five-dollar loss you haven't earned yet. I hold you in damages to Major de Spain to the amount of ten bushels of corn over and above your contract with him, to be paid to him out of your crop at gathering time. Court adjourned."

It had taken no time hardly, the morning was but half begun. He thought they would return home and perhaps back to the field, since they were late, far behind all other farmers. But instead his father passed on behind the wagon, merely indicating with his hand for the older brother to follow with it, and crossed the road toward the blacksmith shop opposite, pressing on after his father, overtaking him, speaking, whispering up at the harsh, calm face beneath the weathered hat: "He won't git no ten bushels neither. He won't git one. We'll . . ." until his father glanced for an instant down at him, the face absolutely calm, the grizzled eyebrows tangled above the cold eyes, the voice almost pleasant, almost gentle:

80 "You think so? Well, we'll wait till October anyway."

The matter of the wagon—the setting of a spoke or two and the tightening of the tires—did not take long either, the business of the tires accomplished by driving the wagon into the spring branch behind the shop and letting it stand there, the mules nuzzling into the water from time to time, and the boy on the seat with the idle reins, looking up the slope and through the sooty tunnel of the shed where the slow hammer rang and where his father sat on an upended cypress bolt, easily, either talking or listening, still sitting there when the boy brought the dripping wagon up out of the branch and halted it before the door.

"Take them on to the shade and hitch," his father said. He did so and returned.

His father and the smith and a third man squatting on his heels inside the door were talking, about crops and animals; the boy, squatting too in the ammoniac dust and hoof-parings and scales of rust, heard his father tell a long and unhurried story out of the time before the birth of the older brother even when he had been a professional horsetrader. And then his father came up beside him where he stood before a tattered last year's circus poster on the other side of the store, gazing rapt and quiet at the scarlet horses, the incredible poisings and convolutions of tulle and tights and the painted leers of comedians, and said, "It's time to eat."

But not at home. Squatting beside his brother against the front wall, he watched his father emerge from the store and produce from a paper sack a segment of cheese and divide it carefully and deliberately into three with his pocket knife and produce crackers from the same sack. They all three squatted on the gallery and ate, slowly, without talking; then in the store again, they drank from a tin dipper tepid water smelling of the cedar bucket and of living beech trees. And still they did not go home. It was a horse lot this time, a tall rail fence upon and along which men stood and sat and out of which one by one horses were led, to be walked and trotted and then cantered back and forth along the road while the slow swapping and buying went on and the sun began to slant westward, they—the three of them—watching and listening, the older brother with his muddy eyes and his steady, inevitable tobacco, the father commenting now and then on certain of the animals, to no one in particular.

It was after sundown when they reached home. They ate supper by lamplight, then, sitting on the doorstep, the boy watched the night fully accomplish, listening to the whippoorwills and the frogs, when he heard his mother's voice: "Abner! No! No! Oh, God. Oh, God. Abner!" and he rose, whirled, and saw the altered light through the door where a candle stub now burned in a bottle neck on the table and his father, still in the hat and coat, at once formal and burlesque as though dressed carefully for some shabby and ceremonial violence, emptying the reservoir of the lamp back into the five-gallon kerosene can from which it had been filled, while the mother tugged at his arm until he shifted the lamp to the other hand and flung her back, not savagely or viciously, just hard, into the wall, her hands flung out against the wall for balance, her mouth open and in her face the same quality of hopeless despair as had been in her voice. Then his father saw him standing in the door.

"Go to the barn and get that can of oil we were oiling the wagon with," he said. The boy did not move. Then he could speak.

"What . . ." he cried. "What are you . . ."

"Go get that oil," his father said. "Go."

Then he was moving, running, outside the house, toward the stable: this the old habit, the old blood which he had not been permitted to choose for himself, which had been bequeathed him willy nilly and which had run for so long (and who knew where, battening on what of outrage and savagery and lust) before it came to him. *I could keep on,* he thought. *I could run on and on and never look back, never need to see his face again. Only I can't. I can't,* the rusted can in his hand now, the liquid sploshing in it as he ran back to the house and into it, into the sound of his mother's weeping in the next room, and handed the can to his father.

"Ain't you going to even send a nigger?" he cried. "At least you sent a nigger before!"

This time his father didn't strike him. The hand came even faster than the blow had, the same hand which had set the can on the table with almost excruciating care flashing from the can toward him too quick for him to follow it, gripping him by the back of his shirt and on to tiptoe before he had seen it quit the can, the face stooping at him in breathless and frozen ferocity, the cold, dead voice speaking over him to the older brother, who leaned against the table, chewing with that steady, curious, sidewise motion of cows:

"Empty the can into the big one and go on. I'll catch up with you."

"Better tie him up to the bedpost," the brother said.

"Do like I told you," the father said. Then the boy was moving, his bunched shirt and the hard, bony hand between his shoulder-blades, his toes just touching the floor, across the room and into the other one, past the sisters sitting with spread heavy thighs in the two chairs over the cold hearth, and to where his mother and aunt sat side by side on the bed, the aunt's arms about his mother's shoulders.

"Hold him," the father said. The aunt made a startled movement. "Not you," the father said. "Lennie. Take hold of him. I want to see you do it." His mother took him by the wrist. "You'll hold him better than that. If he gets loose don't you know what he is going to do? He will go up yonder." He jerked his head toward the road. "Maybe I'd better tie him."

"I'll hold him," his mother whispered.

"See you do then." Then his father was gone, the stiff foot heavy and measured upon the boards, ceasing at last.

Then he began to struggle. His mother caught him in both arms, he jerking and wrenching at them. He would be stronger in the end, he knew that. But he had no time to wait for it. "Lemme go!" he cried. "I don't want to have to hit you!"

"Let him go!" the aunt said. "If he don't go, before God, I am going up there myself!"

"Don't you see I can't?" his mother cried. "Sarty! Sarty! No! No! Help me, Lizzie!"

Then he was free. His aunt grasped at him but it was too late. He whirled, running, his mother stumbled forward on to her knees behind him, crying to the nearer sister: "Catch him, Net! Catch him!" But that was too late too, the sister (the sisters were twins, born at the same time, yet either of them now gave the impression of being, encompassing as much living meat and volume and weight as any other two of the family) not yet having begun to rise from the chair, her head, face, alone merely turned, presenting to him in the flying instant an astonishing expanse of young female features untroubled by any surprise even, wearing only an expression of bovine interest. Then he was out of the room, out of the house, in the mild dust of the starlit road and the heavy rifeness of honeysuckle, the pale ribbon unspooling with terrific slowness under his running feet, reaching the gate at last and turning in, running, his heart and lungs drumming, on up the drive toward the lighted house, the lighted door. He did not knock, he burst in, sobbing for breath, incapable for the moment of speech; he saw the astonished face of the Negro in the linen jacket without knowing when the Negro had appeared.

"De Spain!" he cried, panted. "Where's . . ." then he saw the white man too emerging from a white door down the hall. "Barn!" he cried. "Barn!"

"What?" the white man said. "Barn?"
"Yes!" the boy cried. "Barn!"
"Catch him!" the white man shouted.

But it was too late this time too. The Negro grasped his shirt, but the entire sleeve, rotten with washing, carried away, and he was out that door too and in the drive again, and had actually never ceased to run even while he was screaming into the white man's face.

Behind him the white man was shouting, "My horse! Fetch my horse!" and he thought for an instant of cutting across the park and climbing the fence into the road, but he did not know the park nor how high the vine-massed fence might be and he dared not risk it. So he ran on down the drive, blood and breath roaring; presently he was in the road again though he could not see it. He could not hear either: the galloping mare was almost upon him before he heard her, and even then he held his course, as if the very urgency of his wild grief and need must in a moment more find his wings, waiting until the ultimate instant to hurl himself aside and into the weed-choked roadside ditch as the horse thundered past and on, for an instant in furious silhouette against the stars, the tranquil early summer night sky which, even before the shape of the horse and rider vanished, stained abruptly and violently upward: a long, swirling roar incredible and soundless, blotting the stars, and he springing up and into the road again, running again, knowing it was too late yet still running even after he heard the shot and, an instant later, two shots, pausing now without knowing he had ceased to run, crying "Pap! Pap!", running again before he knew he had begun to run, stumbling, tripping over something and scrabbling up again without ceasing to run, looking backward over his shoulder at the glare as he got up, running on among the invisible trees, panting, sobbing, "Father! Father!"

At midnight he was sitting on the crest of a hill. He did not know it was midnight and he did not know how far he had come. But there was no glare behind him now and he sat now, his back toward what he had called home for four days anyhow, his face toward the dark woods which he would enter when breath was strong again, small, shaking steadily in the chill darkness, hugging himself into the remainder of his thin, rotten shirt, the grief and despair now no longer terror and fear but just grief and despair. *Father. My father,* he thought. "He was brave!" he cried suddenly, aloud but not loud, no more than a whisper: "He was! He was in the war! He was in Colonel Sartoris' cav'ry!" not knowing that his father had gone to that war a private in the fine old European sense, wearing no uniform, admitting the authority of and giving fidelity to no man or army or flag, going to war as Malbrouck[4] himself did: for booty—it meant nothing and less than nothing to him if it were enemy booty or his own.

The slow constellations wheeled on. It would be dawn and then sun-up after a while and he would be hungry. But that would be to-morrow and now he was only cold, and walking would cure that. His breathing was easier now and he decided to get up and go on, and then he found that he had been asleep because he knew it was almost dawn, the night almost over. He could tell that from the whippoorwills. They were everywhere now among the dark trees below him, constant and inflectioned and ceaseless, so that, as the instant for giving over to the

---

4. John Churchill, the first duke of Marlborough (1650–1722), an English general whose name became distorted as Malbrough and Malbrouch in English and French popular songs celebrating his exploits.

day birds drew nearer and nearer, there was no interval at all between them. He got up. He was a little stiff, but walking would cure that too as it would the cold, and soon there would be the sun. He went on down the hill, toward the dark woods within which the liquid silver voices of the birds called unceasing—the rapid and urgent beating of the urgent and quiring heart of the late spring night. He did not look back.

1939

JORGE LUIS BORGES

## *The Garden of Forking Paths*[1]

On page 22 of Liddell Hart's *History of World War I* you will read that an attack against the Serre-Montauban line by thirteen British divisions (supported by 1,400 artillery pieces), planned for the 24th of July, 1916, had to be postponed until the morning of the 29th. The torrential rains, Captain Liddell Hart comments, caused this delay, an insignificant one, to be sure.

The following statement, dictated, reread and signed by Dr. Yu Tsun, former professor of English at the *Hochschule* at Tsingtao,[2] throws an unsuspected light over the whole affair. The first two pages of the document are missing.

"... and I hung up the receiver. Immediately afterwards, I recognized the voice that had answered in German. It was that of Captain Richard Madden. Madden's presence in Viktor Runeberg's apartment meant the end of our anxieties and—but this seemed, *or should have seemed,* very secondary to me—also the end of our lives. It meant that Runeberg had been arrested or murdered.[3] Before the sun set on that day, I would encounter the same fate. Madden was implacable. Or rather, he was obliged to be so. An Irishman at the service of England, a man accused of laxity and perhaps of treason, how could he fail to seize and be thankful for such a miraculous opportunity: the discovery, capture, maybe even the death of two agents of the German Reich? I went up to my room; absurdly I locked the door and threw myself on my back on the narrow iron cot. Through the window I saw the familiar roofs and the cloud-shaded six o'clock sun. It seemed incredible to me that that day without premonitions or symbols should be the one of my inexorable death. In spite of my dead father, in spite of having been a child in a symmetrical garden of Hai Feng, was I—now—going to die? Then I reflected that everything happens to a man precisely, precisely *now*. Centuries of centuries and only in the present do things happen; countless men in the air, on the face of the earth and the sea, and all that really is happening is happening to me.... The almost intolerable recollection of Madden's horselike face banished these wanderings. In the midst of my hatred and terror (it means nothing to me now

---

1. Translated by Donald A. Yates.
2. Major port in east China on the Yellow Sea controlled and developed by Germany in the early 1900s. *Hochschule:* university (German).
3. A hypothesis both hateful and odd. The Prussian spy Hans Rabener, alias Viktor Runeberg, attacked with drawn automatic the bearer of the warrant for his arrest, Captain Richard Madden. The latter, in self-defense, inflicted the wound which brought about Runeberg's death. (Editor's note.) [This note is by Borges as "Editor."]

to speak of terror, now that I have mocked Richard Madden, now that my throat yearns for the noose) it occurred to me that that tumultuous and doubtless happy warrior did not suspect that I possessed the Secret. The name of the exact location of the new British artillery park on the River Ancre. A bird streaked across the gray sky and blindly I translated it into an airplane and that airplane into many (against the French sky) annihilating the artillery station with vertical bombs. If only my mouth, before a bullet shattered it, could cry out that secret name so it could be heard in Germany... My human voice was very weak. How might I make it carry to the ear of the Chief? To the ear of that sick and hateful man who knew nothing of Runeberg and me save that we were in Staffordshire[4] and who was waiting in vain for our report in his arid office in Berlin, endlessly examining newspapers... I said out loud: *I must flee.* I sat up noiselessly, in a useless perfection of silence, as if Madden were already lying in wait for me. Something—perhaps the mere vain ostentation of proving my resources were nil—made me look through my pockets. I found what I knew I would find. The American watch, the nickel chain and the square coin, the key ring with the incriminating useless keys to Runeberg's apartment, the notebook, a letter which I resolved to destroy immediately (and which I did not destroy), a crown, two shillings and a few pence, the red and blue pencil, the handkerchief, the revolver with one bullet. Absurdly, I took it in my hand and weighed it in order to inspire courage within myself. Vaguely I thought that a pistol report can be heard at a great distance. In ten minutes my plan was perfected. The telephone book listed the name of the only person capable of transmitting the message; he lived in a suburb of Fenton, less than a half hour's train ride away.

I am a cowardly man. I say it now, now that I have carried to its end a plan whose perilous nature no one can deny. I know its execution was terrible. I didn't do it for Germany, no. I care nothing for a barbarous country which imposed upon me the abjection of being a spy. Besides, I know of a man from England—a modest man—who for me is no less great than Goethe.[5] I talked with him for scarcely an hour, but during that hour he was Goethe.... I did it because I sensed that the Chief somehow feared people of my race—for the innumerable ancestors who merge within me. I wanted to prove to him that a yellow man could save his armies. Besides, I had to flee from Captain Madden. His hands and his voice could call at my door at any moment. I dressed silently, bade farewell to myself in the mirror, went downstairs, scrutinized the peaceful street and went out. The station was not far from my home, but I judged it wise to take a cab. I argued that in this way I ran less risk of being recognized; the fact is that in the deserted street I felt myself visible and vulnerable, infinitely so. I remember that I told the cab driver to stop a short distance before the main entrance. I got out with voluntary, almost painful slowness; I was going to the village of Ashgrove but I bought a ticket for a more distant station. The train left within a very few minutes, at eight-fifty. I hurried; the next one would leave at nine-thirty. There was hardly a soul on the platform. I went through the coaches; I remember a few farmers, a woman dressed in mourning, a young boy who was reading with fervor the *Annals* of Tacitus,[6] a wounded and happy soldier. The coaches jerked

---

4. County in west-central England.
5. Johann Wolfgang von Goethe (1749–1832), German poet and dramatist, author of *Faust*.
6. Cornelius Tacitus (c. 55–c.117 C.E.), Roman historian.

forward at last. A man whom I recognized ran in vain to the end of the platform. It was Captain Richard Madden. Shattered, trembling, I shrank into the far corner of the seat, away from the dreaded window.

From this broken state I passed into an almost abject felicity. I told myself that the duel had already begun and that I had won the first encounter by frustrating, even if for forty minutes, even if by a stroke of fate, the attack of my adversary. I argued that this slightest of victories foreshadowed a total victory. I argued (no less fallaciously) that my cowardly felicity proved that I was a man capable of carrying out the adventure successfully. From this weakness I took strength that did not abandon me. I foresee that man will resign himself each day to more atrocious undertakings; soon there will be no one but warriors and brigands; I give them this counsel: *The author of an atrocious undertaking ought to imagine that he has already accomplished it, ought to impose upon himself a future as irrevocable as the past.* Thus I proceeded as my eyes of a man already dead registered the elapsing of that day, which was perhaps the last, and the diffusion of the night. The train ran gently along, amid ash trees. It stopped, almost in the middle of the fields. No one announced the name of the station. "Ashgrove?" I asked a few lads on the platform. "Ashgrove," they replied. I got off.

A lamp enlightened the platform but the faces of the boys were in shadow. One questioned me, "Are you going to Dr. Stephen Albert's house?" Without waiting for my answer, another said, "The house is a long way from here, but you won't get lost if you take this road to the left and at every crossroads turn again to your left." I tossed them a coin (my last), descended a few stone steps and started down the solitary road. It went downhill, slowly. It was of elemental earth; overhead the branches were tangled; the low, full moon seemed to accompany me.

For an instant, I thought that Richard Madden in some way had penetrated my desperate plan. Very quickly, I understood that that was impossible. The instructions to turn always to the left reminded me that such was the common procedure for discovering the central point of certain labyrinths. I have some understanding of labyrinths: not for nothing am I the great grandson of that Ts'ui Pên who was governor of Yunnan and who renounced worldly power in order to write a novel that might be even more populous than the *Hung Lu Meng*[7] and to construct a labyrinth in which all men would become lost. Thirteen years he dedicated to these heterogeneous tasks, but the hand of a stranger murdered him—and his novel was incoherent and no one found the labyrinth. Beneath English trees I meditated on that lost maze: I imagined it inviolate and perfect at the secret crest of a mountain; I imagined it erased by rice fields or beneath the water; I imagined it infinite, no longer composed of octagonal kiosks and returning paths, but of rivers and provinces and kingdoms...I thought of a labyrinth of labyrinths, of one sinuous spreading labyrinth that would encompass the past and the future and in some way involve the stars. Absorbed in these illusory images, I forgot my destiny of one pursued. I felt myself to be, for an unknown period of time, an abstract perceiver of the world. The vague, living countryside, the moon, the remains of the day worked on me, as well as the slope of the road which eliminated any possibility of weariness. The afternoon was intimate, infinite. The road descended and forked among the now confused

---

7. *The Story of the Stone* (1791), a panoramic Chinese novel that features more than 430 characters.

meadows. A high-pitched, almost syllabic music approached and receded in the shifting of the wind, dimmed by leaves and distance. I thought that a man can be an enemy of other men, of the moments of other men, but not of a country: not of fireflies, words, gardens, streams of water, sunsets. Thus I arrived before a tall, rusty gate. Between the iron bars I made out a poplar grove and a pavilion. I understood suddenly two things, the first trivial, the second almost unbelievable: the music came from the pavilion, and the music was Chinese. For precisely that reason I had openly accepted it without paying it any heed. I do not remember whether there was a bell or whether I knocked with my hand. The sparkling of the music continued.

From the rear of the house within a lantern approached: a lantern that the trees sometimes striped and sometimes eclipsed, a paper lantern that had the form of a drum and the color of the moon. A tall man bore it. I didn't see his face for the light blinded me. He opened the door and said slowly, in my own language: "I see that the pious Hsi P'êng persists in correcting my solitude. You no doubt wish to see the garden?"

I recognized the name of one of our consuls and I replied, disconcerted, "The garden?"

"The garden of forking paths."

Something stirred in my memory and I uttered with incomprehensible certainty, "The garden of my ancestor Ts'ui Pên."

"Your ancestor? Your illustrious ancestor? Come in."

The damp path zigzagged like those of my childhood. We came to a library of Eastern and Western books. I recognized bound in yellow silk several volumes of the Lost Encyclopedia, edited by the Third Emperor of the Luminous Dynasty but never printed.[8] The record on the phonograph revolved next to a bronze phoenix. I also recall a *famille rose* vase and another, many centuries older, of that shade of blue which our craftsmen copied from the potters of Persia . . .

Stephen Albert observed me with a smile. He was, as I have said, very tall, sharp-featured, with gray eyes and a gray beard. He told me that he had been a missionary in Tientsin "before aspiring to become a Sinologist."

We sat down—I on a long, low divan, he with his back to the window and a tall circular clock. I calculated that my pursuer, Richard Madden, could not arrive for at least an hour. My irrevocable determination could wait.

"An astounding fate, that of Ts'ui Pên," Stephen Albert said. "Governor of his native province, learned in astronomy, in astrology and in the tireless interpretation of the canonical books, chess player, famous poet and calligrapher—he abandoned all this in order to compose a book and a maze. He renounced the pleasures of both tyranny and justice, of his populous couch, of his banquets and even of erudition—all to close himself up for thirteen years in the Pavilion of the Limpid Solitude. When he died, his heirs found nothing save chaotic manuscripts. His family, as you may be aware, wished to condemn them to the fire; but his executor—a Taoist or Buddhist monk—insisted on their publication."

"We descendants of Ts'ui Pên," I replied, "continue to curse that monk. Their publication was senseless. The book is an indeterminate heap of contradictory

---

8. A massive encyclopedia commissioned in the early 1400s by the Yung-lo emperor of the Ming dynasty. One copy of the 11,095 manuscript volumes was made in the mid-1500s; the original was destroyed; and only 370 volumes of the copy survive today.

drafts. I examined it once: in the third chapter the hero dies, in the fourth he is alive. As for the other undertaking of Ts'ui Pên, his labyrinth..."

"Here is Ts'ui Pên's labyrinth," he said, indicating a tall lacquered desk.

"An ivory labyrinth!" I exclaimed. "A minimum labyrinth."

"A labyrinth of symbols," he corrected. "An invisible labyrinth of time. To me, a barbarous Englishman, has been entrusted the revelation of this diaphanous mystery. After more than a hundred years, the details are irretrievable; but it is not hard to conjecture what happened. Ts'ui Pên must have said once: *I am withdrawing to write a book.* And another time: *I am withdrawing to construct a labyrinth.* Every one imagined two works; to no one did it occur that the book and the maze were one and the same thing. The Pavilion of the Limpid Solitude stood in the center of a garden that was perhaps intricate; that circumstance could have suggested to the heirs a physical labyrinth. Ts'ui Pên died; no one in the vast territories that were his came upon the labyrinth; the confusion of the novel suggested to me that *it* was the maze. Two circumstances gave me the correct solution of the problem. One: the curious legend that Ts'ui Pên had planned to create a labyrinth which would be strictly infinite. The other: a fragment of a letter I discovered."

Albert rose. He turned his back on me for a moment; he opened a drawer of the black and gold desk. He faced me and in his hands he held a sheet of paper that had once been crimson, but was now pink and tenuous and cross-sectioned. The fame of Ts'ui Pên as a calligrapher had been justly won. I read, uncomprehendingly and with fervor, these words written with a minute brush by a man of my blood: *I leave to the various futures (not to all) my garden of forking paths.* Wordlessly, I returned the sheet. Albert continued:

"Before unearthing this letter, I had questioned myself about the ways in which a book can be infinite. I could think of nothing other than a cyclic volume, a circular one. A book whose last page was identical with the first, a book which had the possibility of continuing indefinitely. I remembered too that night which is at the middle of the Thousand and One Nights[9] when Scheherazade (through a magical oversight of the copyist) begins to relate word for word the story of the Thousand and One Nights, establishing the risk of coming once again to the night when she must repeat it, and thus on to infinity. I imagined as well a Platonic, hereditary work, transmitted from father to son, in which each new individual adds a chapter or corrects with pious care the pages of his elders. These conjectures diverted me; but none seemed to correspond, not even remotely, to the contradictory chapters of Ts'ui Pên. In the midst of this perplexity, I received from Oxford the manuscript you have examined. I lingered, naturally, on the sentence: *I leave to the various futures (not to all) my garden of forking paths.* Almost instantly, I understood: 'The garden of forking paths' was the chaotic novel; the phrase 'the various futures (not to all)' suggested to me the forking in time, not in space. A broad rereading of the work confirmed the theory. In all fictional works, each time a man is confronted with several alternatives, he chooses one and eliminates the others; in the fiction of Ts'ui Pên, he chooses—simultaneously—all of them. *He creates,* in this way, diverse futures, diverse times which themselves also proliferate and fork. Here, then, is the expla-

---

9. Also known as the *Arabian Nights*, a thousand and one tales told by Scheherazade to her husband, Shahrayar, king of Samarkind, to trick him into postponing her execution.

nation of the novel's contradictions. Fang, let us say, has a secret; a stranger calls at his door; Fang resolves to kill him. Naturally, there are several possible outcomes: Fang can kill the intruder, the intruder can kill Fang, they both can escape, they both can die, and so forth. In the work of Ts'ui Pên, all possible outcomes occur; each one is the point of departure for other forkings. Sometimes, the paths of this labyrinth converge: for example, you arrive at this house, but in one of the possible pasts you are my enemy, in another, my friend. If you will resign yourself to my incurable pronunciation, we shall read a few pages."

His face, within the vivid circle of the lamplight, was unquestionably that of an old man, but with something unalterable about it, even immortal. He read with slow precision two versions of the same epic chapter. In the first, an army marches to a battle across a lonely mountain; the horror of the rocks and shadows makes the men undervalue their lives and they gain an easy victory. In the second, the same army traverses a palace where a great festival is taking place; the resplendent battle seems to them a continuation of the celebration and they win the victory. I listened with proper veneration to these ancient narratives, perhaps less admirable in themselves than the fact that they had been created by my blood and were being restored to me by a man of a remote empire, in the course of a desperate adventure, on a Western isle. I remember the last words, repeated in each version like a secret commandment: *Thus fought the heroes, tranquil their admirable hearts, violent their swords, resigned to kill and to die.*

From that moment on, I felt about me and within my dark body an invisible, intangible swarming. Not the swarming of the divergent, parallel and finally coalescent armies, but a more inaccessible, more intimate agitation that they in some manner prefigured. Stephen Albert continued:

"I don't believe that your illustrious ancestor played idly with these variations. I don't consider it credible that he would sacrifice thirteen years to the infinite execution of a rhetorical experiment. In your country, the novel is a subsidiary form of literature; in Ts'ui Pên's time it was a despicable form. Ts'ui Pên was a brilliant novelist, but he was also a man of letters who doubtless did not consider himself a mere novelist. The testimony of his contemporaries proclaims—and his life fully confirms—his metaphysical and mystical interests. Philosophic controversy usurps a good part of the novel. I know that of all problems, none disturbed him so greatly nor worked upon him so much as the abysmal problem of time. Now then, the latter is the only problem that does not figure in the pages of the *Garden*. He does not even use the word that signifies *time*. How do you explain this voluntary omission?"

I proposed several solutions—all unsatisfactory. We discussed them. Finally, Stephen Albert said to me:

"In a riddle whose answer is chess, what is the only prohibited word?"

I thought a moment and replied, "The word *chess*."

"Precisely," said Albert. "*The Garden of Forking Paths* is an enormous riddle, or parable, whose theme is time; this recondite cause prohibits its mention. To omit a word always, to resort to inept metaphors and obvious periphrases, is perhaps the most emphatic way of stressing it. That is the tortuous method preferred, in each of the meanderings of his indefatigable novel, by the oblique Ts'ui Pên. I have compared hundreds of manuscripts, I have corrected the errors that the negligence of the copyists has introduced, I have guessed the plan of this chaos, I have re-established—I believe I have re-established—the primordial organization, I have translated the entire work: it is clear to me that not once does he employ the word 'time.' The explanation is obvious: *The Garden of Forking Paths* is an incomplete, but not false, image of the universe as Ts'ui Pên conceived it. In contrast to Newton and Schopenhauer,[1] your ancestor did not believe in a uniform, absolute time. He believed in an infinite series of times, in a growing, dizzying net of divergent, convergent and parallel times. This network of times which approached one another, forked, broke off, or were unaware of one another for centuries, embraces *all* possibilities of time. We do not exist in the majority of these times; in some you exist, and not I; in others I, and not you; in others, both of us. In the present one, which a favorable fate has granted me, you have arrived at my house; in another, while crossing the garden, you found me dead; in still another, I utter these same words, but I am a mistake, a ghost."

"In every one," I pronounced, not without a tremble to my voice, "I am grateful to you and revere you for your re-creation of the garden of Ts'ui Pên."

"Not in all," he murmured with a smile. "Time forks perpetually toward innumerable futures. In one of them I am your enemy."

Once again I felt the swarming sensation of which I have spoken. It seemed to me that the humid garden that surrounded the house was infinitely saturated with invisible persons. Those persons were Albert and I, secret, busy and multiform in other dimensions of time. I raised my eyes and the tenuous nightmare dissolved. In the yellow and black garden there was only one man; but this man was as strong as a statue... this man was approaching along the path and he was Captain Richard Madden.

"The future already exists," I replied, "but I am your friend. Could I see the letter again?"

Albert rose. Standing tall, he opened the drawer of the tall desk; for the moment his back was to me. I had readied the revolver. I fired with extreme caution. Albert fell uncomplainingly, immediately. I swear his death was instantaneous—a lightning stroke.

The rest is unreal, insignificant. Madden broke in, arrested me. I have been condemned to the gallows. I have won out abominably; I have communicated to Berlin the secret name of the city they must attack. They bombed it yesterday; I read it in the same papers that offered to England the mystery of the learned Sinologist Stephen Albert who was murdered by a stranger, one Yu Tsun. The Chief had deciphered this mystery. He knew my problem was to indicate (through the uproar of the war) the city called Albert, and that I had found no other means to do so than to kill a man of that name. He does not know (no one can know) my innumerable contrition and weariness.

*For Victoria Ocampo*

1941

---

1. Arthur Schopenhauer (1788–1860), German philosopher; Sir Isaac Newton (1642–1727), English mathematician and physicist.

**RALPH ELLISON**

## *King of the Bingo Game*

The woman in front of him was eating roasted peanuts that smelled so good that he could barely contain his hunger. He could not even sleep and wished they'd hurry and begin the bingo game. There, on his right, two fellows were drinking wine out of a bottle wrapped in a paper bag, and he could hear soft gurgling in the dark. His stomach gave a low, gnawing growl. "If this was down South," he thought, "all I'd have to do is lean over and say, 'Lady, gimme a few of those peanuts, please ma'am,' and she'd pass me the bag and never think nothing of it." Or he could ask the fellows for a drink in the same way. Folks down South stuck together that way; they didn't even have to know you. But up here it was different. Ask somebody for something, and they'd think you were crazy. Well, I ain't crazy. I'm just broke, 'cause I got no birth certificate to get a job, and Laura 'bout to die 'cause we got no money for a doctor. But I ain't crazy. And yet a pinpoint of doubt was focused in his mind as he glanced toward the screen and saw the hero stealthily entering a dark room and sending the beam of a flashlight along a wall of bookcases. This is where he finds the trapdoor, he remembered. The man would pass abruptly through the wall and find the girl tied to a bed, her legs and arms spread wide, and her clothing torn to rags. He laughed softly to himself. He had seen the picture three times, and this was one of the best scenes.

On his right the fellow whispered wide-eyed to his companion, "Man, look ayonder!"

"Damn!"

"Wouldn't I like to have her tied up like that..."

"Hey! That fool's letting her loose!"

"Aw, man, he loves her."

"Love or no love!"

The man moved impatiently beside him, and he tried to involve himself in the scene. But Laura was on his mind. Tiring quickly of watching the picture he looked back to where the white beam filtered from the projection room above the balcony. It started small and grew large, specks of dust dancing in its whiteness as it reached the screen. It was strange how the beam always landed right on the screen and didn't mess up and fall somewhere else. But they had it all fixed. Everything was fixed. Now suppose when they showed that girl with her dress torn the girl started taking off the rest of her clothes, and when the guy came in he didn't untie her but kept her there and went to taking off his own clothes? *That* would be something to see. If a picture got out of hand like that those guys up there would go nuts. Yeah, and there'd be so many folks in here you couldn't find a seat for nine months! A strange sensation played over his skin. He shuddered. Yesterday he'd seen a bedbug on a woman's neck as they walked out into the bright street. But exploring his thigh through a hole in his pocket he found only goose pimples and old scars.

The bottle gurgled again. He closed his eyes. Now a dreamy music was accompanying the film and train whistles were sounding in the distance, and he was a boy again walking along a railroad trestle down South, and seeing the train coming, and running back as fast as he could go, and hearing the whistle blowing, and getting off the trestle to solid ground just in time, with the earth trembling beneath his feet, and feeling relieved as he ran down the cinder-strewn embankment onto the highway, and looking back and seeing with terror that the train had left the track and was following him right down the middle of the street, and all the white people laughing as he ran screaming...

"Wake up there, buddy! What the hell do you mean hollering like that? Can't you see we trying to enjoy this here picture?"

He stared at the man with gratitude.

"I'm sorry, old man," he said. "I musta been dreaming."

"Well, here, have a drink. And don't be making no noise like that, damn!"

His hands trembled as he tilted his head. It was not wine, but whiskey. Cold rye whiskey. He took a deep swoller, decided it was better not to take another, and handed the bottle back to its owner.

"Thanks, old man," he said.

Now he felt the cold whiskey breaking a warm path straight through the middle of him, growing hotter and sharper as it moved. He had not eaten all day, and it made him light-headed. The smell of the peanuts stabbed him like a knife, and he got up and found a seat in the middle aisle. But no sooner did he sit than he saw a row of intense-faced young girls, and got up again, thinking, "You chicks musta been Lindy-hopping[1] somewhere." He found a seat several rows ahead as the lights came on, and he saw the screen disappear behind a heavy red and gold curtain; then the curtain rising, and the man with the microphone and a uniformed attendant coming on the stage.

He felt for his bingo cards, smiling. The guy at the door wouldn't like it if he knew about his having *five* cards. Well, not everyone played the bingo game; and even with five cards he didn't have much of a chance. For Laura, though, he had to have faith. He studied the cards, each with its different numerals, punching the free center hole in each and spreading them neatly across his lap; and when the lights faded he sat slouched in his seat so that he could look from his cards to the bingo wheel with but a quick shifting of his eyes.

Ahead, at the end of the darkness, the man with the microphone was pressing a button attached to a long cord and spinning the bingo wheel and calling out the number each time the wheel came to rest. And each time the voice rang out his finger raced over the cards for the number. With five cards he had to move fast. He became nervous; there were too many cards, and the man went too fast with his grating voice. Perhaps he should just select one and throw the others away. But he was afraid. He became warm. Wonder how much Laura's doctor would cost? Damn that, watch the cards! And with despair he heard the man call three in a row which he missed on all five cards. This way he'd never win...

When he saw the row of holes punched across the third card, he sat paralyzed and heard the man call three more numbers before he stumbled forward, screaming,

"Bingo! Bingo!"

"Let that fool up there," someone called.

"Get up there, man!"

He stumbled down the aisle and up the steps to the stage into a light so sharp

1. Dancing.

and bright that for a moment it blinded him, and he felt that he had moved into the spell of some strange, mysterious power. Yet it was as familiar as the sun, and he knew it was the perfectly familiar bingo.

The man with the microphone was saying something to the audience as he held out his card. A cold light flashed from the man's finger as the card left his hand. His knees trembled. The man stepped closer, checking the card against the numbers chalked on the board. Suppose he had made a mistake? The pomade on the man's hair made him feel faint, and he backed away. But the man was checking the card over the microphone now, and he had to stay. He stood tense, listening.

"Under the O, forty-four," the man chanted. "Under the I, seven. Under the G, three. Under the B, ninety-six. Under the N, thirteen!"

His breath came easier as the man smiled at the audience.

"Yes sir, ladies and gentlemen, he's one of the chosen people!"

The audience rippled with laughter and applause.

"Step right up to the front of the stage."

He moved slowly forward, wishing that the light was not so bright.

"To win tonight's jackpot of $36.90 the wheel must stop between the double zero, understand?"

He nodded, knowing the ritual from the many days and nights he had watched the winners march across the stage to press the button that controlled the spinning wheel and receive the prizes. And now he followed the instructions as though he'd crossed the slippery stage a million prize-winning times.

The man was making some kind of joke, and he nodded vacantly. So tense had he become that he felt a sudden desire to cry and shook it away. He felt vaguely that his whole life was determined by the bingo wheel; not only that which would happen now that he was at last before it, but all that had gone before, since his birth, and his mother's birth and the birth of his father. It had always been there, even though he had not been aware of it, handing out the unlucky cards and numbers of his days. The feeling persisted, and he started quickly away. I better get down from here before I make a fool of myself, he thought.

"Here, boy," the man called. "You haven't started yet."

Someone laughed as he went hesitantly back.

"Are you all reet?"

He grinned at the man's jive talk, but no words would come, and he knew it was not a convincing grin. For suddenly he knew that he stood on the slippery brink of some terrible embarrassment.

"Where are you from, boy?" the man asked.

"Down South."

"He's from down South, ladies and gentlemen," the man said. "Where from? Speak right into the mike."

"Rocky Mont," he said. "Rock' Mont, North Car'lina."

"So you decided to come down off that mountain to the U.S.," the man laughed. He felt that the man was making a fool of him, but then something cold was placed in his hand, and the lights were no longer behind him.

Standing before the wheel he felt alone, but that was somehow right, and he remembered his plan. He would give the wheel a short quick twirl. Just a touch of the button. He had watched it many times, and always it came close to double zero when it was short and quick. He steeled himself; the fear had left, and he felt a profound sense of promise, as though he were about to be repaid for all the things he'd suffered all his life. Trembling, he pressed the button. There was a whirl of lights, and in a second he realized with finality that though he wanted to, he could not stop. It was as though he held a high-powered line in his naked hand. His nerves tightened. As the wheel increased its speed it seemed to draw him more and more into its power, as though it held his fate; and with it came a deep need to submit, to whirl, to lose himself in its swirl of color. He could not stop it now. So let it be.

The button rested snugly in his palm where the man had placed it. And now he became aware of the man beside him, advising him through the microphone, while behind the shadowy audience hummed with noisy voices. He shifted his feet. There was still that feeling of helplessness within him, making part of him desire to turn back, even now that the jackpot was right in his hand. He squeezed the button until his fist ached. Then, like the sudden shriek of a subway whistle, a doubt tore through his head. Suppose he did not spin the wheel long enough? What could he do, and how could he tell? And then he knew, even as he wondered, that as long as he pressed the button, he could control the jackpot. He and only he could determine whether or not it was to be his. Not even the man with the microphone could do anything about it now. He felt drunk. Then, as though he had come down from a high hill into a valley of people, he heard the audience yelling.

45    "Come down from there, you jerk!"
"Let somebody else have a chance . . ."
"Ole Jack thinks he done found the end of the rainbow . . ."

The last voice was not unfriendly, and he turned and smiled dreamily into the yelling mouths. Then he turned his back squarely on them.

"Don't take too long, boy," a voice said.

50    He nodded. They were yelling behind him. Those folks did not understand what had happened to him. They had been playing the bingo game day in and night out for years, trying to win rent money or hamburger change. But not one of those wise guys had discovered this wonderful thing. He watched the wheel whirling past the numbers and experienced a burst of exaltation: This is God! This is the really truly God! He said it aloud, "This is God!"

He said it with such absolute conviction that he feared he would fall fainting into the footlights. But the crowd yelled so loud that they could not hear. These fools, he thought. I'm here trying to tell them the most wonderful secret in the world, and they're yelling like they gone crazy. A hand fell upon his shoulder.

"You'll have to make a choice now, boy. You've taken too long."

He brushed the hand violently away.

"Leave me alone, man. I know what I'm doing!"

55    The man looked surprised and held on to the microphone for support. And because he did not wish to hurt the man's feelings he smiled, realizing with a sudden pang that there was no way of explaining to the man just why he had to stand there pressing the button forever.

"Come here," he called tiredly.

The man approached, rolling the heavy microphone across the stage.

"Anybody can play this bingo game, right?" he said.

"Sure, but . . ."

He smiled, feeling inclined to be patient with this slick looking white man with his blue shirt and his sharp gabardine suit.

"That's what I thought," he said. "Anybody can win the jackpot as long as they get the lucky number, right?"

"That's the rule, but after all . . ."

"That's what I thought," he said. "And the big prize goes to the man who knows how to win it?"

The man nodded speechlessly.

"Well then, go on over there and watch me win like I want to. I ain't going to hurt nobody," he said, "and I'll show you how to win. I mean to show the whole world how it's got to be done."

And because he understood, he smiled again to let the man know that he held nothing against him for being white and impatient. Then he refused to see the man any longer and stood pressing the button, the voices of the crowd reaching him like sounds in distant streets. Let them yell. All the Negroes down there were just ashamed because he was black like them. He smiled inwardly, knowing how it was. Most of the time he was ashamed of what Negroes did himself. Well, let them be ashamed for something this time. Like him. He was like a long thin black wire that was being stretched and wound upon the bingo wheel; wound until he wanted to scream; wound, but this time himself controlling the winding and the sadness and the shame, and because he did, Laura would be all right. Suddenly the lights flickered. He staggered backwards. Had something gone wrong? All this noise. Didn't they know that although he controlled the wheel, it also controlled him, and unless he pressed the button forever and forever and ever it would stop, leaving him high and dry, dry and high on this hard high slippery hill and Laura dead? There was only one chance; he had to do whatever the wheel demanded. And gripping the button in despair, he discovered with surprise that it imparted a nervous energy. His spine tingled. He felt a certain power.

Now he faced the raging crowd with defiance, its screams penetrating his eardrums like trumpets shrieking from a juke-box. The vague faces glowing in the bingo lights gave him a sense of himself that he had never known before. He was running the show, by God! They had to react to him, for he was their luck. This is *me*, he thought. Let the bastards yell. Then someone was laughing inside him, and he realized that somehow he had forgotten his own name. It was a sad, lost feeling to lose your name, and a crazy thing to do. That name had been given him by the white man who had owned his grandfather a long lost time ago down South. But maybe those wise guys knew his name.

"Who am I?" he screamed.

"Hurry up and bingo, you jerk!"

They didn't know either, he thought sadly. They didn't even know their own names, they were all poor nameless bastards. Well, he didn't need that old name; he was reborn. For as long as he pressed the button he was The-man-who-pressed-the-button-who-held-the-prize-who-was-the-King-of-Bingo. That was the way it was, and he'd have to press the button even if nobody understood, even though Laura did not understand.

"Live!" he shouted.

The audience quieted like the dying of a huge fan.

"Live, Laura, baby. I got holt of it now, sugar. Live!"

He screamed it, tears streaming down his face. "I got nobody but YOU!"

The screams tore from his very guts. He felt as though the rush of blood to his head would burst out in baseball seams of small red droplets, like a head beaten by police clubs. Bending over he saw a trickle of blood splashing the toe of his shoe. With his free hand he searched his head. It was his nose. God, suppose something has gone wrong? He felt that the whole audience had somehow entered him and was stamping its feet in his stomach and he was unable to throw them out. They wanted the prize, that was it. They wanted the secret for themselves. But they'd never get it; he would keep the bingo wheel whirling forever, and Laura would be safe in the wheel. But would she? It had to be, because if she were not safe the wheel would cease to turn; it could not go on. He had to get away, *vomit* all, and his mind formed an image of himself running with Laura in his arms down the tracks of the subway just ahead of an A train, running desperately *vomit* with people screaming for him to come out but knowing no way of leaving the tracks because to stop would bring the train crushing down upon him and to attempt to leave across the other tracks would mean to run into a hot third rail as high as his waist which threw blue sparks that blinded his eyes until he could hardly see.

He heard singing and the audience was clapping its hands.

> Shoot the liquor to him, Jim, boy!
> Clap-clap-clap
> Well a-calla the cop
> He's blowing his top!
> Shoot the liquor to him, Jim, boy!

Bitter anger grew within him at the singing. They think I'm crazy. Well let 'em laugh. I'll do what I got to do.

He was standing in an attitude of intense listening when he saw that they were watching something on the stage behind him. He felt weak. But when he turned he saw no one. If only his thumb did not ache so. Now they were applauding. And for a moment he thought that the wheel had stopped. But that was impossible, his thumb still pressed the button. Then he saw them. Two men in uniform beckoned from the end of the stage. They were coming toward him, walking in step, slowly, like a tap-dance team returning for a third encore. But their shoulders shot forward, and he backed away, looking wildly about. There was nothing to fight them with. He had only the long black cord which led to a plug somewhere back stage, and he couldn't use that because it operated the bingo wheel. He backed slowly, fixing the men with his eyes as his lips stretched over his teeth in a tight, fixed grin; moved toward the end of the stage and realizing that he couldn't go much further, for suddenly the cord became taut and he couldn't afford to break the cord. But he had to do something. The audience was howling. Suddenly he stopped dead, seeing the men halt, their legs lifted as in an interrupted step of a slow-motion dance. There was nothing to do but run in the other direction and he dashed forward, slipping and sliding. The men fell back, surprised. He struck out violently going past.

"Grab him!"

He ran, but all too quickly the cord tightened, resistingly, and he turned and ran back again. This time he slipped them, and discovered by running in a circle before the wheel he could keep the cord from tightening. But this way he had to flail his arms to keep the men away. Why couldn't they leave a man alone? He ran, circling.

"Ring down the curtain," someone yelled. But they couldn't do that. If they did the wheel flashing from the projection room would be cut off. But they had him before he could tell them so, trying to pry open his fist, and he was wrestling and trying to bring his knees into the fight and holding on to the button, for it was his life. And now he was down, seeing a foot coming down, crushing his wrist cruelly, down, as he saw the wheel whirling serenely above.

"I can't give it up," he screamed. Then quietly, in a confidential tone, "Boys, I really can't give it up."

It landed hard against his head. And in the blank moment they had it away from him, completely now. He fought them trying to pull him up from the stage as he watched the wheel spin slowly to a stop. Without surprise he saw it rest at double-zero.

"You see," he pointed bitterly.

"Sure, boy, sure, it's O.K.," one of the men said smiling.

And seeing the man bow his head to someone he could not see, he felt very, very happy; he would receive what all the winners received.

But as he warmed in the justice of the man's tight smile he did not see the man's slow wink, nor see the bow-legged man behind him step clear of the swiftly descending curtain and set himself for a blow. He only felt the dull pain exploding in his skull, and he knew even as it slipped out of him that his luck had run out on the stage.

1944

# JOYCE CAROL OATES

## The Lady with the Pet Dog

### I

Strangers parted as if to make way for him.

There he stood. He was there in the aisle, a few yards away, watching her.

She leaned forward at once in her seat, her hand jerked up to her face as if to ward off a blow—but then the crowd in the aisle hid him, he was gone. She pressed both hands against her cheeks. He was not there, she had imagined him.

"My God," she whispered.

She was alone. Her husband had gone out to the foyer to make a telephone call; it was intermission at the concert, a Thursday evening.

Now she saw him again, clearly. He was standing there. He was staring at her. Her blood rocked in her body, draining out of her head . . . she was going to faint. . . . They stared at each other. They gave no sign of recognition. Only when he took a step forward did she shake her head *no—no—keep away*. It was not possible.

When her husband returned, she was staring at the place in the aisle where her lover had been standing. Her husband leaned forward to interrupt that stare.

"What's wrong?" he said. "Are you sick?"

Panic rose in her in long shuddering waves. She tried to get to her feet, panicked at the thought of fainting here, and her husband took hold of her. She stood like an aged woman, clutching the seat before her.

At home he helped her up the stairs and she lay down. Her head was like a large piece of crockery that had to be held still, it was so heavy. She was still panicked. She felt it in the shallows of her face, behind her knees, in the pit of her stomach. It sickened her, it made her think of mucus, of something thick and gray congested inside her, stuck to her, that was herself and yet not herself—a poison.

She lay with her knees drawn up toward her chest, her eyes hotly open, while her husband spoke to her. She imagined that other man saying, *Why did you run away from me?* Her husband was saying other words. She tried to listen to them. He was going to call the doctor, he said, and she tried to sit up. "No, I'm all right now," she said quickly. The panic was like lead inside her, so thickly congested. How slow love was to drain out of her, how fluid and sticky it was inside her head!

Her husband believed her. No doctor. No threat. Grateful, she drew her husband down to her. They embraced, not comfortably. For years now they had not been comfortable together, in their intimacy and at a distance, and now they struggled gently as if the paces of this dance were too rigorous for them. It was something they might have known once, but had now outgrown. The panic in her thickened at this double betrayal: she drew her husband to her, she caressed him wildly, she shut her eyes to think about that other man.

A crowd of men and women parting, unexpectedly, and there he stood—there he stood—she kept seeing him, and yet her vision blotched at the memory. It had been finished between them, six months before, but he had come out here ... and she had escaped him, now she was lying in her husband's arms, in his embrace, her face pressed against his. It was a kind of sleep, this love-making. She felt herself falling asleep, her body falling from her. Her eyes shut.

"I love you," her husband said fiercely, angrily.

She shut her eyes and thought of that other man, as if betraying him would give her life a center.

"Did I hurt you? Are you—?" her husband whispered.

Always this hot flashing of shame between them, the shame of her husband's near failure, the clumsiness of his love—

"You didn't hurt me," she said.

II

They had said good-by six months before. He drove her from Nantucket, where they had met, to Albany, New York, where she visited her sister. The hours of intimacy in the car had sealed something between them, a vow of silence and impersonality: she recalled the movement of the highways, the passing of other cars, the natural rhythms of the day hypnotizing her toward sleep while he drove. She trusted him, she could sleep in his presence. Yet she could not really fall asleep in spite of her exhaustion, and she kept jerking awake, frightened, to discover that nothing had changed—still the stranger who was driving her to Albany, still the highway, the sky, the antiseptic odor of the rented car, the sense of a rhythm behind the rhythm of the air that might unleash itself at any second. Everywhere on this highway, at this moment, there were men and women driving together, bonded together—what did that mean, to be together? What did it mean to enter into a bond with another person?

No, she did not really trust him; she did not really trust men. He would glance at her with his small cautious smile and she felt a declaration of shame between them.

Shame.

In her head she rehearsed conversations. She said bitterly, "You'll be relieved when we get to Albany. Relieved to get rid of me." They had spent so many days talking, confessing too much, driven to a pitch of childish excitement, laughing together on the beach, breaking into that pose of laughter that seems to eradicate the soul, so many days of this that the silence of the trip was like the silence of a hospital—all these surface noises, these rattles and hums, but an interior silence, a befuddlement. She said to him in her imagination, "One of us should die." Then she leaned over to touch him. She caressed the back of his neck. She said, aloud, "Would you like me to drive for a while?"

They stopped at a picnic area where other cars were stopped—couples, families—and walked together, smiling at their good luck. He put his arm around her shoulders and she sensed how they were in a posture together, a man and a woman forming a posture, a figure, that someone might sketch and show to them. She said slowly, "I don't want to go back...."

Silence. She looked up at him. His face was heavy with her words, as if she had pulled at his skin with her fingers. Children ran nearby and distracted him— yes, he was a father too, his children ran like that, they tugged at his skin with their light, busy fingers.

"Are you so unhappy?" he said.

"I'm not unhappy, back there. I'm nothing. There's nothing to me," she said.

They stared at each other. The sensation between them was intense, exhausting. She thought that this man was her savior, that he had come to her at a time in her life when her life demanded completion, an end, a permanent fixing of all that was troubled and shifting and deadly. And yet it was absurd to think this. No person could save another. So she drew back from him and released him.

A few hours later they stopped at a gas station in a small city. She went to the women's rest room, having to ask the attendant for a key, and when she came back her eye jumped nervously onto the rented car—why? did she think he might have driven off without her?—onto the man, her friend, standing in conversation with the young attendant. Her friend was as old as her husband, over forty, with lanky, sloping shoulders, a full body, his hair thick, a dark, burnished brown, a festive color that made her eye twitch a little—and his hands were always moving, always those rapid conversational circles, going nowhere, gestures that were at once a little aggressive and apologetic.

She put her hand on his arm, a claim. He turned to her and smiled and she felt that she loved him, that everything in her life had forced her to this moment and that she had no choice about it.

They sat in the car for two hours, in Albany, in the parking lot of a Howard Johnson's restaurant, talking, trying to figure out their past. There was no future. They concentrated on the past, the several days behind them, lit up with a hot, dazzling August sun, like explosions that already belonged to other people, to strangers. Her face was faintly reflected in the green-tinted curve of the windshield, but she could not have recognized that face. She began to cry; she told herself: *I am not here, this will pass, this is nothing.* Still, she could not stop crying. The muscles of her face were springy, like a child's, unpredictable muscles. He stroked her arms, her shoulders, trying to comfort her. "This is so hard ... this is impossible..." he said. She felt panic for the world outside this car, all that was not herself and this man, and at the same time she understood that she was free of him, as people are free of other people, she would leave him soon, safely, and within a few days he would have fallen into the past, the impersonal past....

"I'm so ashamed of myself!" she said finally.

She returned to her husband and saw that another woman, a shadow-woman, had taken her place—noiseless and convincing, like a dancer performing certain difficult steps. Her husband folded her in his arms and talked to her of his own loneliness, his worries about his business, his health, his mother, kept tranquilized and mute in a nursing home, and her spirit detached itself from her and drifted about the rooms of the large house she lived in with her husband, a shadow-woman delicate and imprecise. There was no boundary to her, no edge. Alone, she took hot baths and sat exhausted in the steaming water, wondering at her perpetual exhaustion. All that winter she noticed the limp, languid weight of her arms, her veins bulging slightly with the pressure of her extreme weariness. *This is fate,* she thought, to be here and not there, to be one person and not another, a certain man's wife and not the wife of another man. The long, slow pain of this certainty rose in her, but it never became clear, it was baffling and imprecise. She could not be serious about it; she kept congratulating herself on her own good luck, to have escaped so easily, to have freed herself. So much love had gone into the first several years of her marriage that there wasn't much left, now, for another man.... She was certain of that. But the bath water made her dizzy, all that perpetual heat, and one day in January she drew a razor blade lightly across the inside of her arm, near the elbow, to see what would happen.

Afterward she wrapped a small towel around it, to stop the bleeding. The towel soaked through. She wrapped a bath towel around that and walked through the empty rooms of her home, lightheaded, hardly aware of the stubborn seeping of blood. There was no boundary to her in this house, no precise limit. She could flow out like her own blood and come to no end.

She sat for a while on a blue love seat, her mind empty. Her husband telephoned her when he would be staying late at the plant. He talked to her always about his plans, his problems, his business friends, his future. It was obvious that he had a future. As he spoke she nodded to encourage him, and her heartbeat quickened with the memory of her own, personal shame, the shame of this man's particular, private wife. One evening at dinner he leaned forward and put his head in his arms and fell asleep, like a child. She sat at the table with him for a while, watching him. His hair had gone gray, almost white, at the temples—no one would guess that he was so quick, so careful a man, still fairly young about the eyes. She put her hand on his head, lightly, as if to prove to herself that he was real. He slept, exhausted.

35  One evening they went to a concert and she looked up to see her lover there, in the crowded aisle, in this city, watching her. He was standing there, with his overcoat on, watching her. She went cold. That morning the telephone had rung while her husband was still home, and she had heard him answer it, heard him hang up—it must have been a wrong number—and when the telephone rang again, at 9:30, she had been afraid to answer it. She had left home to be out of the range of that ringing, but now, in this public place, in this busy auditorium, she found herself staring at that man, unable to make any sign to him, any gesture of recognition....

He would have come to her but she shook her head. *No. Stay away.*

Her husband helped her out of the row of seats, saying, "Excuse us, please. Excuse us," so that strangers got to their feet, quickly, alarmed, to let them pass. Was that woman about to faint? What was wrong?

At home she felt the blood drain slowly back into her head. Her husband embraced her hips, pressing his face against her, in that silence that belonged to the earliest days of their marriage. She thought, *He will drive it out of me.* He made love to her and she was back in the auditorium again, sitting alone, now that the concert was over. The stage was empty; the heavy velvet curtains had not been drawn; the musicians' chairs were empty, everything was silent and expectant; in the aisle her lover stood and smiled at her—Her husband was impatient. He was apart from her, working on her, operating on her; and then, stricken, he whispered, "Did I hurt you?"

The telephone rang the next morning. Dully, sluggishly, she answered it. She recognized his voice at once—that "Anna?" with its lifting of the second syllable, questioning and apologetic and making its claim—"Yes, what do you want?" she said.

"Just to see you. Please—"

"I can't."

"Anna, I'm sorry, I didn't mean to upset you—"

"I can't see you."

"Just for a few minutes—I have to talk to you—"

"But why, why now? Why now?" she said.

She heard her voice rising, but she could not stop it. He began to talk again, drowning her out. She remembered his rapid conversation. She remembered his gestures, the witty energetic circling of his hands.

"Please don't hang up!" he cried.

"I can't—I don't want to go through it again—"

"I'm not going to hurt you. Just tell me how you are."

"Everything is the same."

"Everything is the same with me."

She looked up at the ceiling, shyly. "Your wife? Your children?"

"The same."

"Your son?"

"He's fine—"

"I'm glad to hear that. I—"

"Is it still the same with you, your marriage? Tell me what you feel. What are you thinking?"

"I don't know. . . ."

She remembered his intense, eager words, the movement of his hands, that impatient precise fixing of the air by his hands, the jabbing of his fingers.

"Do you love me?" he said.

She could not answer.

"I'll come over to see you," he said.

"No," she said.

What will come next, what will happen?

Flesh hardening on his body, aging. Shrinking. He will grow old, but not soft like her husband. They are two different types: he is nervous, lean, energetic, wise. She will grow thinner, as the tension radiates out from her backbone, wearing down her flesh. Her collarbones will jut out of her skin. Her husband, caressing her in their bed, will discover that she is another woman—she is not there with him—instead she is rising in an elevator in a downtown hotel, carrying a book as a prop, or walking quickly away from that hotel, her head bent and filled with secrets. Love, what to do with it? . . . Useless as moths' wings, as moths' fluttering. . . . She feels the flutterings of silky, crazy wings in her chest.

He flew out to visit her every several weeks, staying at a different hotel each time. He telephoned her, and she drove down to park in an underground garage at the very center of the city.

She lay in his arms while her husband talked to her, miles away, one body fading into another. He will grow old, his body will change, she thought, pressing her cheek against the back of one of these men. If it was her lover, they were in a hotel room: always the propped-up little booklet describing the hotel's many services, with color photographs of its cocktail lounge and dining room and coffee shop. Grow old, leave me, die, go back to your neurotic wife and your sad, ordinary children, she thought, but still her eyes closed gratefully against his skin and she felt how complete their silence was, how they had come to rest in each other.

"Tell me about your life here. The people who love you," he said, as he always did.

One afternoon they lay together for four hours. It was her birthday and she was intoxicated with her good fortune, this prize of the afternoon, this man in her arms! She was a little giddy, she talked too much. She told him about her parents, about her husband. . . . "They were all people I believed in, but it turned out wrong. Now, I believe in you. . . ." He laughed as if shocked by her words. She did not understand. Then she understood. "But I believe truly in you. I can't think of myself without you," she said. . . . He spoke of his wife, her ambitions, her intelligence, her use of the children against him, her use of his younger son's blindness, all of his words gentle and hypnotic and convincing in the late afternoon peace of this hotel room . . . and she felt the terror of laughter, threatening laughter. Their words, like their bodies, were aging.

70  She dressed quickly in the bathroom, drawing her long hair up around the back of her head, fixing it as always, anxious that everything be the same. Her face was slightly raw, from his face. The rubbing of his skin. Her eyes were too bright, wearily bright. Her hair was blond but not so blond as it had been that summer in the white Nantucket air.

She ran water and splashed it on her face. She blinked at the water. Blind. Drowning. She thought with satisfaction that soon, soon, he would be back home, in that house on Long Island she had never seen, with that woman she had never seen, sitting on the edge of another bed, putting on his shoes. She wanted nothing except to be free of him. Why not be free? *Oh*, she thought suddenly, *I will follow you back and kill you. You and her and the little boy. What is there to stop me?*

She left him. Everyone on the street pitied her, that look of absolute zero.

III

A man and a child, approaching her. The sharp acrid smell of fish. The crashing of waves. Anna pretended not to notice the father with his son—there was something strange about them. That frank, silent intimacy, too gentle, the man's bare feet in the water and the boy a few feet away, leaning away from his father. He was about nine years old and still his father held his hand.

A small yipping dog, a golden dog, bounded near them.

Anna turned shyly back to her reading; she did not want to have to speak to these neighbors. She saw the man's shadow falling over her legs, then over the pages of her book, and she had the idea that he wanted to see what she was reading. The dog nuzzled her; the man called him away.

She watched them walk down the beach. She was relieved that the man had not spoken to her.

She saw them in town later that day, the two of them brown-haired and patient, now wearing sandals, walking with that same look of care. The man's white shorts were soiled and a little baggy. His pullover shirt was a faded green. His face was broad, the cheekbones wide, spaced widely apart, the eyes stark in their sockets, as if they fastened onto objects for no reason, ponderous and edgy. The little boy's face was pale and sharp; his lips were perpetually parted.

Anna realized that the child was blind.

The next morning, early, she caught sight of them again. For some reason she went to the back door of her cottage. She faced the sea breeze eagerly. Her heart hammered.... She had been here, in her family's old house, for three days, alone, bitterly satisfied at being alone, and now it was a puzzle to her how her soul strained to fly outward, to meet with another person. She watched the man with his son, his cautious, rather stooped shoulders above the child's small shoulders.

The man was carrying something, it looked like a notebook. He sat on the sand, not far from Anna's spot of the day before, and the dog rushed up to them. The child approached the edge of the ocean, timidly. He moved in short jerky steps, his legs stiff. The dog ran around him. Anna heard the child crying out a word that sounded like "Ty"—it must have been the dog's name—and then the man joined in, his voice heavy and firm.

"Ty—"

Anna tied her hair back with a yellow scarf and went down to the beach.

The man glanced around at her. He smiled. She stared past him at the waves. To talk to him or not to talk—she had the freedom of that choice. For a moment she felt that she had made a mistake, that the child and the dog would not protect her, that behind this man's ordinary, friendly face there was a certain arrogant maleness—then she relented, she smiled shyly.

"A nice house you've got there," the man said.

She nodded her thanks.

The man pushed his sunglasses up on his forehead. Yes, she recognized the eyes of the day before—intelligent and nervous, the sockets pale, untanned.

"Is that your telephone ringing?" he said.

She did not bother to listen. "It's a wrong number," she said.

Her husband calling: she had left home for a few days, to be alone.

But the man, settling himself on the sand, seemed to misinterpret this. He smiled in surprise, one corner of his mouth higher than the other. He said nothing. Anna wondered: *What is he thinking?* The dog was leaping about her, panting against her legs, and she laughed in embarrassment. She bent to pet it, grateful for its busyness. "Don't let him jump up on you," the man said. "He's a nuisance."

The dog was a small golden retriever, a young dog. The blind child, standing now in the water, turned to call the dog to him. His voice was shrill and impatient.

"Our house is the third one down—the white one," the man said.

She turned, startled. "Oh, did you buy it from Dr. Patrick? Did he die?"

"Yes, finally...."

Her eyes wandered nervously over the child and the dog. She felt the nervous beat of her heart out to the very tips of her fingers, the fleshy tips of her fingers: little hearts were there, pulsing. *What is he thinking?* The man had opened his notebook. He had a piece of charcoal and he began to sketch something.

Anna looked down at him. She saw the top of his head, his thick brown hair, the freckles on his shoulders, the quick, deft movement of his hand. Upside down, Anna herself being drawn. She smiled in surprise.

"Let me draw you. Sit down," he said.

She knelt awkwardly a few yards away. He turned the page of the sketch pad. The dog ran to her and she sat, straightening out her skirt beneath her, flinching from the dog's tongue. "Ty!" cried the child. Anna sat, and slowly the pleasure of the moment began to glow in her; her skin flushed with gratitude.

She sat there for nearly an hour. The man did not talk much. Back and forth the dog bounded, shaking itself. The child came to sit near them, in silence. Anna felt that she was drifting into a kind of trance while the man sketched her, half a dozen rapid sketches, the surface of her face given up to him. "Where are you from?" the man asked.

"Ohio. My husband lives in Ohio."

She wore no wedding band.

"Your wife—" Anna began.

"Yes?"

"Is she here?"

"Not right now."

She was silent, ashamed. She had asked an improper question. But the man did not seem to notice. He continued drawing her, bent over the sketch pad. When Anna said she had to go, he showed her the drawings—one after another of her, Anna, recognizably Anna, a woman in her early thirties, her hair smooth and flat across the top of her head, tied behind by a scarf. "Take the one you like best," he said, and she picked one of her with the dog in her lap, sitting very straight, her brows and eyes clearly defined, her lips girlishly pursed, the dog and her dress suggested by a few quick irregular lines.

"Lady with pet dog," the man said.

She spent the rest of that day reading, nearer her cottage. It was not really a cottage—it was a two-story house, large and ungainly and weathered. It was mixed up in her mind with her family, her own childhood, and she glanced up from her book, perplexed, as if waiting for one of her parents or her sister to come up to her. Then she thought of that man, the man with the blind child, the man with the dog, and she could not concentrate on her reading. Someone—probably her father—had marked a passage that must be important, but she kept reading and rereading it: *We try to discover in things, endeared to us on that account, the spiritual glamour which we ourselves have cast upon them; we are disillusioned, and learn that they are in themselves barren and devoid of the charm that they owed, in our minds, to the association of certain ideas....*

She thought again of the man on the beach. She lay the book aside and thought of him: his eyes, his aloneness, his drawings of her.

They began seeing each other after that. He came to her front door in the evening, without the child; he drove her into town for dinner. She was shy and extremely pleased. The darkness of the expensive restaurant released her; she heard herself chatter; she leaned forward and seemed to be offering her face up to him, listening to him. He talked about his work on a Long Island newspaper and she seemed to be listening to him, as she stared at his face, arranging her own face into the expression she had seen in that charcoal drawing. Did he see her like that, then?—girlish and withdrawn and patrician? She felt the weight of his interest in her, a force that fell upon her like a blow. A repeated blow. Of course he was married, he had children—of course she was married, permanently married. This flight from her husband was not important. She had left him before, to be alone, it was not important. Everything in her was slender and delicate and not important.

They walked for hours after dinner, looking at the other strollers, the weekend visitors, the tourists, the couples like themselves. Surely they were mistaken for a couple, a married couple. *This is the hour in which everything is decided,* Anna thought. They had both had several drinks and they talked a great deal. Anna found herself saying too much, stopping and starting giddily. She put her hand to her forehead, feeling faint.

"It's from the sun—you've had too much sun—" he said.

At the door to her cottage, on the front porch, she heard herself asking him if he would like to come in. She allowed him to lead her inside, to close the door. *This is not important,* she thought clearly, *he doesn't mean it, he doesn't love me, nothing will come of it.* She was frightened, yet it seemed to her necessary to give in; she had to leave Nantucket with that act completed, an act of adultery, an accomplishment she would take back to Ohio and to her marriage.

Later, incredibly, she heard herself asking: "Do you . . . do you love me?"

"You're so beautiful!" he said, amazed.

She felt this beauty, shy and glowing and centered in her eyes. He stared at her. In this large, drafty house, alone together, they were like accomplices, conspirators. She could not think: how old was she? which year was this? They had done something unforgivable together, and the knowledge of it was tugging at their faces. A cloud seemed to pass over her. She felt herself smiling shrilly.

Afterward, a peculiar raspiness, a dryness of breath. He was silent. She felt a strange, idle fear, a sense of the danger outside this room and this old, comfortable bed—a danger that would not recognize her as the lady in that drawing, the lady with the pet dog. There was nothing to say to this man, this stranger. She felt the beauty draining out of her face, her eyes fading.

"I've got to be alone," she told him.

He left, and she understood that she would not see him again. She stood by the window of the room, watching the ocean. A sense of shame overpowered her: it was smeared everywhere on her body, the smell of it, the richness of it. She tried to recall him, and his face was confused in her memory: she would have to shout to him across a jumbled space, she would have to wave her arms wildly. *You love me! You must love me!* But she knew he did not love her, and she did not love him; he was a man who drew everything up into himself, like all men, walking away, free to walk away, free to have his own thoughts, free to envision her body, all the secrets of her body. . . . And she lay down again in the bed, feeling how heavy this body had become, her insides heavy with shame, the very backs of her eyelids coated with shame.

"This is the end of one part of my life," she thought.

But in the morning the telephone rang. She answered it. It was her lover: they talked brightly and happily. She could hear the eagerness in his voice, the love in his voice, that same still, sad amazement—she understood how simple life was, there were no problems.

They spent most of their time on the beach, with the child and the dog. He joked and was serious at the same time. He said, once, "You have defined my soul for me," and she laughed to hide her alarm. In a few days it was time for her to leave. He got a sitter for the boy and took the ferry with her to the mainland, then rented a car to drive her up to Albany. She kept thinking: *Now something will happen. It will come to an end.* But most of the drive was silent and hypnotic. She wanted him to joke with her, to say again that she had defined his soul for him, but he drove fast, he was serious, she distrusted the hawkish look of his profile—she did not know him at all. At a gas station she splashed her face with cold water. Alone in the grubby little rest room, shaky and very much alone. In such places are women totally alone with their bodies. The body grows heavier, more evil, in such silence. . . . On the beach everything had been noisy with sunlight and gulls and waves; here, as if run to earth, everything was cramped and silent and dead.

She went outside, squinting. There he was, talking with the station attendant. She could not think as she returned to him whether she wanted to live or not.

She stayed in Albany for a few days, then flew home to her husband. He met her at the airport, near the luggage counter, where her three pieces of pale-brown luggage were brought to him on a conveyer belt, to be claimed by him. He kissed her on the cheek. They shook hands, a little embarrassed. She had come home again.

"How will I live out the rest of my life?" she wondered.

In January her lover spied on her: she glanced up and saw him, in a public place, in the DeRoy Symphony Hall. She was paralyzed with fear. She nearly fainted. In this faint she felt her husband's body, loving her, working its love upon her, and she shut her eyes harder to keep out the certainty of his love—sometimes he failed at loving her, sometimes he succeeded, it had nothing to do with her or her pity or her ten years of love for him, it had nothing to do with a woman at all. It was a private act accomplished by a man, a husband or a lover, in communion with his own soul, his manhood.

Her husband was forty-two years old now, growing slowly into middle age, getting heavier, softer. Her lover was about the same age, narrower in the shoulders, with a full, solid chest, yet lean, nervous. She thought, in her paralysis, of men and how they love freely and eagerly so long as their bodies are capable of love, love for a woman; and then, as love fades in their bodies, it fades from their souls and they become immune and immortal and ready to die.

Her husband was a little rough with her, as if impatient with himself. "I love you," he said fiercely, angrily. And then, ashamed, he said, "Did I hurt you? . . ."

"You didn't hurt me," she said.

Her voice was too shrill for their embrace.

While he was in the bathroom she went to her closet and took out that drawing of the summer before. There she was, on the beach at Nantucket, a lady with a pet dog, her eyes large and defined, the dog in her lap hardly more than a few snarls, a few coarse soft lines of charcoal . . . her dress smeared, her arms oddly limp . . . her hands not well drawn at all. . . . She tried to think: did she love the man who had drawn this? did he love her? The fever in her husband's body had touched her and driven her temperature up, and now she stared at the drawing with a kind of lust, fearful of seeing an ugly soul in that woman's face, fearful of seeing the face suddenly through her lover's eyes. She breathed quickly and harshly, staring at the drawing.

And so, the next day, she went to him at his hotel. She wept, pressing against him, demanding of him, "What do you want? Why are you here? Why don't you let me alone?" He told her that he wanted nothing. He expected nothing. He would not cause trouble.

"I want to talk about last August," he said.

"Don't—" she said.

She was hypnotized by his gesturing hands, his nervousness, his obvious agitation. He kept saying, "I understand. I'm making no claims upon you."

They became lovers again.

He called room service for something to drink and they sat side by side on his bed, looking through a copy of *The New Yorker,* laughing at the cartoons. It was so peaceful in this room, so complete. They were on a holiday. It was a secret holiday. Four-thirty in the afternoon, on a Friday, an ordinary Friday: a secret holiday.

"I won't bother you again," he said.

He flew back to see her again in March, and in late April. He telephoned her from his hotel—a different hotel each time—and she came down to him at once. She rose to him in various elevators, she knocked on the doors of various rooms, she stepped into his embrace, breathless and guilty and already angry with him, pleading with him. One morning in May, when he telephoned, she pressed her forehead against the doorframe and could not speak. He kept saying, "What's wrong? Can't you talk? Aren't you alone?" She felt that she was going insane. Her head would burst. Why, why did he love her, why did he pursue her? Why did he want her to die?

She went to him in the hotel room. A familiar room: had they been here before? "Everything is repeating itself. Everything is stuck," she said. He framed her face in his hands and said that she looked thinner—was she sick?—what was wrong? She shook herself free. He, her lover, looked about the same. There was a small, angry pimple on his neck. He stared at her, eagerly and suspiciously. Did she bring bad news?

"So you love me? You love me?" she asked.

"Why are you so angry?"

"I want to be free of you. The two of us free of each other."

"That isn't true—you don't want that—"

He embraced her. She was wild with that old, familiar passion for him, her body clinging to his, her arms not strong enough to hold him. Ah, what despair!—what bitter hatred she felt!—she needed this man for her salvation, he was all she had to live for, and yet she could not believe in him. He embraced her thighs, her hips, kissing her, pressing his warm face against her, and yet she could not believe in him, not really. She needed him in order to live, but he was not worth her love, he was not worth her dying. . . . She promised herself this: when she got back home, when she was alone, she would draw the razor more deeply across her arm.

The telephone rang and he answered it: a wrong number.

"Jesus," he said.

They lay together, still. She imagined their posture like this, the two of them one figure, one substance; and outside this room and this bed there was a universe of disjointed, separate things, blank things, that had nothing to do with them. She would not be Anna out there, the lady in the drawing. He would not be her lover.

"I love you so much..." she whispered.

"Please don't cry! We have only a few hours, please...."

It was absurd, their clinging together like this. She saw them as a single figure in a drawing, their arms and legs entwined, their heads pressing mutely together. Helpless substance, so heavy and warm and doomed. It was absurd that any human being should be so important to another human being. She wanted to laugh: a laugh might free them both.

She could not laugh.

Sometime later he said, as if they had been arguing, "Look. It's you. You're the one who doesn't want to get married. You lie to me—"

"Lie to you?"

"You love me but you won't marry me, because you want something left over— Something not finished—All your life you can attribute your misery to me, to our not being married—you are using me—"

"Stop it! You'll make me hate you!" she cried.

"You can say to yourself that you're miserable because of *me*. We will never be married, you will never be happy, neither one of us will ever be happy—"

"I don't want to hear this!" she said.

She pressed her hands flatly against her face.

She went to the bathroom to get dressed. She washed her face and part of her body, quickly. The fever was in her, in the pit of her belly. She would rush home and strike a razor across the inside of her arm and free that pressure, that fever.

The impatient bulging of the veins: an ordeal over.

The demand of the telephone's ringing: that ordeal over.

The nuisance of getting the car and driving home in all that five o'clock traffic: an ordeal too much for a woman.

The movement of this stranger's body in hers: over, finished.

Now, dressed, a little calmer, they held hands and talked. They had to talk swiftly, to get all their news in: he did not trust the people who worked for him, he had faith in no one, his wife had moved to a textbook publishing company and was doing well, she had inherited a Ben Shahn[1] painting from her father and wanted to "touch it up a little"—she was crazy!—his blind son was at another school, doing fairly well, in fact his children were all doing fairly well in spite of the stupid mistake of their parents' marriage—and what about her? what about her life? She told him in a rush the one thing he wanted to hear: that she lived with her husband lovelessly, the two of them polite strangers, sharing a bed, lying side by side in the night in that bed, bodies out of which souls had fled. There was no longer even any shame between them.

"And what about me? Do you feel shame with me still?" he asked.

---

1. Socially conscious American realist painter (1898–1969).

She did not answer. She moved away from him and prepared to leave.

Then, a minute later, she happened to catch sight of his reflection in the bureau mirror—he was glancing down at himself, checking himself mechanically, impersonally, preparing also to leave. He too would leave this room: he too was headed somewhere else.

She stared at him. It seemed to her that in this instant he was breaking from her, the image of her lover fell free of her, breaking from her . . . and she realized that he existed in a dimension quite apart from her, a mysterious being. And suddenly, joyfully, she felt a miraculous calm. This man was her husband, truly—they were truly married, here in this room—they had been married haphazardly and accidentally for a long time. In another part of the city she had another husband, a "husband," but she had not betrayed that man, not really. This man, whom she loved above any other person in the world, above even her own self-pitying sorrow and her own life, was her truest lover, her destiny. And she did not hate him, she did not hate herself any longer; she did not wish to die; she was flooded with a strange certainty, a sense of gratitude, of pure selfless energy. It was obvious to her that she had, all along, been behaving correctly; out of instinct.

What triumph, to love like this in any room, anywhere, risking even the craziest of accidents!

"Why are you so happy? What's wrong?" he asked, startled. He stared at her. She felt the abrupt concentration in him, the focusing of his vision on her, almost a bitterness in his face, as if he feared her. What, was it beginning all over again? Their love beginning again, in spite of them? "How can you look so happy?" he asked. "We don't have any right to it. Is it because . . . ?"

"Yes," she said.

1968

## BOBBIE ANN MASON

## *Shiloh*

Leroy Moffitt's wife, Norma Jean, is working on her pectorals. She lifts three-pound dumbbells to warm up, then progresses to a twenty-pound barbell. Standing with her legs apart, she reminds Leroy of Wonder Woman.

"I'd give anything if I could just get these muscles to where they're real hard," says Norma Jean. "Feel this arm. It's not as hard as the other one."

"That's cause you're right-handed," says Leroy, dodging as she swings the barbell in an arc.

"Do you think so?"

"Sure."

Leroy is a truckdriver. He injured his leg in a highway accident four months ago, and his physical therapy, which involves weights and a pulley, prompted Norma Jean to try building herself up. Now she is attending a body-building class. Leroy has been collecting temporary disability since his tractor-trailer jackknifed in Missouri, badly twisting his left leg in its socket. He has a steel pin in his hip. He will probably not be able to drive his rig again. It sits in the backyard, like a gigantic bird that has flown home to roost. Leroy has been home in Kentucky for three months, and his leg is almost healed, but the accident frightened him and he does not want to drive any more long hauls. He is not sure what to do next. In the meantime, he makes things from craft kits. He started by building a miniature log cabin from notched Popsicle sticks. He varnished it and placed it on the TV set, where it remains. It reminds him of a rustic Nativity scene. Then he tried string art (sailing ships on black velvet), a macramé owl kit, a snap-together B-17 Flying Fortress,[1] and a lamp made out of a model truck, with a light fixture screwed in the top of the cab. At first the kits were diversions, something to kill time, but now he is thinking about building a full-scale log house from a kit. It would be considerably cheaper than building a regular house, and besides, Leroy has grown to appreciate how things are put together. He has begun to realize that in all the years he was on the road he never took time to examine anything. He was always flying past scenery.

"They won't let you build a log cabin in any of the new subdivisions," Norma Jean tells him.

"They will if I tell them it's for you," he says, teasing her. Ever since they were married, he has promised Norma Jean he would build her a new home one day. They have always rented, and the house they live in is small and nondescript. It does not even feel like a home, Leroy realizes now.

Norma Jean works at the Rexall drugstore, and she has acquired an amazing amount of information about cosmetics. When she explains to Leroy the three stages of complexion care, involving creams, toners, and moisturizers, he thinks happily of other petroleum products—axle grease, diesel fuel. This is a connection between him and Norma Jean. Since he has been home, he has felt unusually tender about his wife and guilty over his long absences. But he can't tell what she feels about him. Norma Jean has never complained about his traveling; she has never made hurt remarks, like calling his truck a "widow-maker." He is reasonably certain she has been faithful to him, but he wishes she would celebrate his permanent homecoming more happily. Norma Jean is often startled to find Leroy at home, and he thinks she seems a little disappointed about it. Perhaps he reminds her too much of the early days of their marriage, before he went on the road. They had a child who died as an infant, years ago. They never speak about their memories of Randy, which have almost faded, but now that Leroy is home all the time, they sometimes feel awkward around each other, and Leroy wonders if one of them should mention the child. He has the feeling that they are waking up out of a dream together—that they must create a new marriage, start afresh. They are lucky they are still married. Leroy has read that for most people losing a child destroys the marriage—or else he heard this on *Donahue*. He can't always remember where he learns things anymore.

10    At Christmas, Leroy bought an electric organ for Norma Jean. She used to play the piano when she was in high school. "It don't leave you," she told him once. "It's like riding a bicycle."

The new instrument had so many keys and buttons that she was bewildered by it at first. She touched the keys tentatively, pushed some buttons, then pecked out "Chopsticks." It came out in an amplified fox-trot rhythm, with marimba sounds.

---

1. American World War II bomber.

"It's an orchestra!" she cried.

The organ had a pecan-look finish and eighteen preset chords, with optional flute, violin, trumpet, clarinet, and banjo accompaniments. Norma Jean mastered the organ almost immediately. At first she played Christmas songs. Then she bought *The Sixties Songbook* and learned every tune in it, adding variations to each with the rows of brightly colored buttons.

"I didn't like these old songs back then," she said. "But I have this crazy feeling I missed something."

"You didn't miss a thing," said Leroy.

Leroy likes to lie on the couch and smoke a joint and listen to Norma Jean play "Can't Take My Eyes Off You" and "I'll Be Back."[2] He is back again. After fifteen years on the road, he is finally settling down with the woman he loves. She is still pretty. Her skin is flawless. Her frosted curls resemble pencil trimmings.

Now that Leroy has come home to stay, he notices how much the town has changed. Subdivisions are spreading across western Kentucky like an oil slick. The sign at the edge of town says "Pop: 11,500"—only seven hundred more than it said twenty years before. Leroy can't figure out who is living in all the new houses. The farmers who used to gather around the courthouse square on Saturday afternoons to play checkers and spit tobacco juice have gone. It has been years since Leroy has thought about the farmers, and they have disappeared without his noticing.

Leroy meets a kid named Stevie Hamilton in the parking lot at the new shopping center. While they pretend to be strangers meeting over a stalled car, Stevie tosses an ounce of marijuana under the front seat of Leroy's car. Stevie is wearing orange jogging shoes and a T-shirt that says CHATTAHOOCHEE SUPER-RAT. His father is a prominent doctor who lives in one of the expensive subdivisions in a new white-columned brick house that looks like a funeral parlor. In the phone book under his name there is a separate number, with the listing "Teenagers."

"Where do you get this stuff?" asks Leroy. "From your pappy!"

"That's for me to know and you to find out," Stevie says. He is slit-eyed and skinny.

"What else you got?"

"What you interested in?"

"Nothing special. Just wondered."

Leroy used to take speed on the road. Now he has to go slowly. He needs to be mellow. He leans back against the car and says, "I'm aiming to build me a log house, soon as I get time. My wife, though, I don't think she likes the idea."

"Well, let me know when you want me again," Stevie says. He has a cigarette in his cupped palm, as though sheltering it from the wind. He takes a long drag, then stomps it on the asphalt and slouches away.

Stevie's father was two years ahead of Leroy in high school. Leroy is thirty-four. He married Norma Jean when they were both eighteen, and their child Randy was born a few months later, but he died at the age of four months and three days. He would be about Stevie's age now. Norma Jean and Leroy were at

---

2. Hit songs of the 1960s.

the drive-in, watching a double feature (*Dr. Strangelove* and *Lover Come Back*),³ and the baby was sleeping in the back seat. When the first movie ended, the baby was dead. It was the sudden infant death syndrome. Leroy remembers handing Randy to a nurse at the emergency room, as though he were offering her a large doll as a present. A dead baby feels like a sack of flour. "It just happens sometimes," said the doctor, in what Leroy always recalls as a nonchalant tone. Leroy can hardly remember the child anymore, but he still sees vividly a scene from *Dr. Strangelove* in which the President of the United States was talking in a folksy voice on the hot line to the Soviet premier about the bomber accidentally headed toward Russia. He was in the War Room, and the world map was lit up. Leroy remembers Norma Jean catatonically beside him in the hospital and himself thinking: Who is this strange girl? He had forgotten who she was. Now scientists are saying that crib death is caused by a virus. Nobody knows anything, Leroy thinks. The answers are always changing.

When Leroy gets home from the shopping center, Norma Jean's mother, Mabel Beasley, is there. Until this year, Leroy has not realized how much time she spends with Norma Jean. When she visits, she inspects the closets and then the plants, informing Norma Jean when a plant is droopy or yellow. Mabel calls the plants "flowers," although there are never any blooms. She always notices if Norma Jean's laundry is piling up. Mabel is a short, overweight woman whose tight, brown-dyed curls look more like a wig than the actual wig she sometimes wears. Today she has brought Norma Jean an off-white dust ruffle she made for the bed; Mabel works in a custom-upholstery shop.

"This is the tenth one I made this year," Mabel says. "I got started and couldn't stop."

"It's real pretty," says Norma Jean.

30 "Now we can hide things under the bed," says Leroy, who gets along with his mother-in-law primarily by joking with her. Mabel has never really forgiven him for disgracing her by getting Norma Jean pregnant. When the baby died, she said that fate was mocking her.

"What's that thing?" Mabel says to Leroy in a loud voice, pointing to a tangle of yarn on a piece of canvas.

Leroy holds it up for Mabel to see. "It's my needlepoint," he explains. "This is a *Star Trek* pillow cover."

"That's what a woman would do," says Mabel. "Great day in the morning!"

"All the big football players on TV do it," he says.

35 "Why, Leroy, you're always trying to fool me. I don't believe you for one minute. You don't know what to do with yourself—that's the whole trouble. Sewing!"

"I'm aiming to build us a log house," says Leroy. "Soon as my plans come."

"Like *heck* you are," says Norma Jean. She takes Leroy's needlepoint and shoves it into a drawer. "You have to find a job first. Nobody can afford to build now anyway."

Mabel straightens her girdle and says, "I still think before you get tied down y'all ought to take a little run to Shiloh."

"One of these days, Mama," Norma Jean says impatiently.

---

3. A 1963 satire on nuclear war and a 1961 Rock Hudson-Doris Day romantic comedy satirizing the advertising business, respectively.

Mabel is talking about Shiloh, Tennessee. For the past few years, she has been urging Leroy and Norma Jean to visit the Civil War battleground there.[4] Mabel went there on her honeymoon—the only real trip she ever took. Her husband died of a perforated ulcer when Norma Jean was ten, but Mabel, who was accepted into the United Daughters of the Confederacy in 1975, is still preoccupied with going back to Shiloh.

"I've been to kingdom come and back in that truck out yonder," Leroy says to Mabel, "but we never yet set foot in that battleground. Ain't that something? How did I miss it?"

"It's not even that far," Mabel says.

After Mabel leaves, Norma Jean reads to Leroy from a list she has made. "Thing you could do," she announces. "You could get a job as a guard at Union Carbide, where they'd let you set on a stool. You could get on at the lumberyard. You could do a little carpenter work, if you want to build so bad. You could—"

"I can't do something where I'd have to stand up all day."

"You ought to try standing up all day behind a cosmetics counter. It's amazing that I have strong feet, coming from two parents that never had strong feet at all." At the moment Norma Jean is holding on to the kitchen counter, raising her knees one at a time as she talks. She is wearing two-pound ankle weights.

"Don't worry," says Leroy. "I'll do something."

"You could truck calves to slaughter for somebody. You wouldn't have to drive any big old truck for that."

"I'm going to build you this house," says Leroy. "I want to make you a real home."

"I don't want to live in any log cabin."

"It's not a cabin. It's a house."

"I don't care. It looks like a cabin."

"You and me together could lift those logs. It's just like lifting weights."

Norma Jean doesn't answer. Under her breath, she is counting. Now she is marching through the kitchen. She is doing goose steps.

Before his accident, when Leroy came home he used to stay in the house with Norma Jean, watching TV in bed and playing cards. She would cook fried chicken, picnic ham, chocolate pie—all his favorites. Now he is home alone much of the time. In the mornings, Norma Jean disappears, leaving a cooling place in the bed. She eats a cereal called Body Buddies, and she leaves the bowl on the table, with soggy tan balls floating in a milk puddle. He sees things about Norma Jean that he never realized before. When she chops onions, she stares off into a corner, as if she can't bear to look. She puts on her house slippers almost precisely at nine o'clock every evening and nudges her jogging shoes under the couch. She saves bread heels for the birds. Leroy watches the birds at the feeder. He notices the peculiar way goldfinches fly past the window. They close their wings, then fall, then spread their wings to catch and lift themselves. He wonders if they close their eyes when they fall. Norma Jean closes her eyes when they are in bed.

---

4. Where, in April 1862, more than twenty-three thousand troops of the North and South, one-quarter of those who fought there, died. This was the first real indication of how bitter and bloody the war was to be. When Union reinforcements arrived, General Ulysses S. Grant drove the Confederate forces, which had gained an initial victory by a surprise attack, back to their base in Corinth, Mississippi.

She wants the lights turned out. Even then, he is sure she closes her eyes.

He goes for long drives around town. He tends to drive a car rather carelessly. Power steering and an automatic shift make a car feel so small and inconsequential that his body is hardly involved in the driving process. His injured leg stretches out comfortably. Once or twice he has almost hit something, but even the prospect of an accident seems minor in a car. He cruises the new subdivisions, feeling like a criminal rehearsing for a robbery. Norma Jean is probably right about a log house being inappropriate here in the new subdivisions. All the houses look grand and complicated. They depress him.

One day when Leroy comes home from a drive he finds Norma Jean in tears. She is in the kitchen making a potato and mushroom-soup casserole, with grated-cheese topping. She is crying because her mother caught her smoking.

"I didn't hear her coming. I was standing here puffing away pretty as you please," Norma Jean says, wiping her eyes.

"I knew it would happen sooner or later," says Leroy, putting his arm around her.

"She don't know the meaning of the word 'knock,'" says Norma Jean. "It's a wonder she hadn't caught me years ago."

"Think of it this way," Leroy says. "What if she caught me with a joint?"

"You better not let her!" Norma Jean shrieks. "I'm warning you, Leroy Moffitt!"

"I'm just kidding. Here, play me a tune. That'll help you relax."

Norma Jean puts the casserole in the oven and sets the timer. Then she plays a ragtime tune, with horns and banjo, as Leroy lights up a joint and lies on the couch, laughing to himself about Mabel's catching him at it. He thinks of Stevie Hamilton—a doctor's son pushing grass. Everything is funny. The whole town seems crazy and small. He is reminded of Virgil Mathis, a boastful policeman Leroy used to shoot pool with. Virgil recently led a drug bust in a back room at a bowling alley, where he seized ten thousand dollars' worth of marijuana. The newspaper had a picture of him holding up the bags of grass and grinning widely. Right now, Leroy can imagine Virgil breaking down the door and arresting him with a lungful of smoke. Virgil would probably have been alerted to the scene because of all the racket Norma Jean is making. Now she sounds like a hard-rock band. Norma Jean is terrific. When she switches to a latin-rhythm version of "Sunshine Superman," Leroy hums along. Norma Jean's foot goes up and down, up and down.

"Well, what do you think?" Leroy says, when Norma Jean pauses to search through her music.

"What do I think about what?"

His mind has gone blank. Then he says, "I'll sell my rig and build us a house." That wasn't what he wanted to say. He wanted to know what she thought—what she *really* thought—about them.

"Don't start in on that again," says Norma Jean. She begins playing "Who'll Be the Next in Line?"

Leroy used to tell hitchhikers his whole life story—about his travels, his hometown, the baby. He would end with a question: "Well, what do you think?" It was just a rhetorical question. In time, he had the feeling that he'd been telling the same story over and over to the same hitchhikers. He quit talking to hitchhikers when he realized how his voice sounded—whining and self-pitying, like some teenage-tragedy song. Now Leroy has the sudden impulse to tell Norma Jean about himself, as if he had just met her. They have known each other so long they have forgotten a lot about each other. They could become reacquainted. But when the oven timer goes off and she runs to the kitchen, he forgets why he wants to do this.

The next day, Mabel drops by. It is Saturday and Norma Jean is cleaning. Leroy is studying the plans of his log house, which have finally come in the mail. He has them spread out on the table—big sheets of stiff blue paper, with diagrams and numbers printed in white. While Norma Jean runs the vacuum, Mabel drinks coffee. She sets her coffee cup on a blueprint.

"I'm just waiting for time to pass," she says to Leroy, drumming her fingers on the table.

As soon as Norma Jean switches off the vacuum, Mabel says in a loud voice, "Did you hear about the datsun dog that killed the baby?"

Norma Jean says, "The word is 'dachshund.'"

"They put the dog on trial. It chewed the baby's legs off. The mother was in the next room all the time." She raises her voice. "They thought it was neglect."

Norma Jean is holding her ears. Leroy manages to open the refrigerator and get some Diet Pepsi to offer Mabel. Mabel still has some coffee and she waves away the Pepsi.

"Datsuns are like that," Mabel says. "They're jealous dogs. They'll tear a place to pieces if you don't keep an eye on them."

"You better watch out what you're saying, Mabel," says Leroy.

"Well, facts is facts."

Leroy looks out the window at his rig. It is like a huge piece of furniture gathering dust in the backyard. Pretty soon it will be an antique. He hears the vacuum cleaner. Norma Jean seems to be cleaning the living room rug again.

Later, she says to Leroy, "She just said that about the baby because she caught me smoking. She's trying to pay me back."

"What are you talking about?" Leroy says, nervously shuffling blueprints.

"You know good and well," Norma Jean says. She is sitting in a kitchen chair with her feet up and her arms wrapped around her knees. She looks small and helpless. She says, "The very idea, her bringing up a subject like that! Saying it was neglect."

"She didn't mean that," Leroy says.

"She might not have *thought* she meant it. She always says things like that. You don't know how she goes on."

"But she didn't really mean it. She was just talking."

Leroy opens a king-sized bottle of beer and pours it into two glasses, dividing it carefully. He hands a glass to Norma Jean and she takes it from him mechanically. For a long time, they sit by the kitchen window watching the birds at the feeder.

Something is happening. Norma Jean is going to night school. She has graduated from her six-week body-building course and now she is taking an adult-education course in composition at Paducah Community College. She spends her evenings outlining paragraphs.

"First you have a topic sentence," she explains to Leroy. "Then you divide it up. Your secondary topic has to be connected to your primary topic."

To Leroy, this sounds intimidating. "I never was any good in English," he says. "It makes a lot of sense."

"What are you doing this for, anyhow?"

She shrugs. "It's something to do." She stands up and lifts her dumbbells a few times.

"Driving a rig, nobody cared about my English."

"I'm not criticizing your English."

Norma Jean used to say, "If I lose ten minutes' sleep, I just drag all day." Now she stays up late, writing compositions. She got a B on her first paper—a how-to theme on soup-based casseroles. Recently Norma Jean has been cooking unusual foods—tacos, lasagna, Bombay chicken. She doesn't play the organ anymore, though her second paper was called "Why Music Is Important to Me." She sits at the kitchen table, concentrating on her outlines, while Leroy plays with his log house plans, practicing with a set of Lincoln Logs. The thought of getting a truckload of notched, numbered logs scares him, and he wants to be prepared. As he and Norma Jean work together at the kitchen table, Leroy has the hopeful thought that they are sharing something, but he knows he is a fool to think this. Norma Jean is miles away. He knows he is going to lose her. Like Mabel, he is just waiting for time to pass.

One day, Mabel is there before Norma Jean gets home from work, and Leroy finds himself confiding in her. Mabel, he realizes, must know Norma Jean better than he does.

"I don't know what's got into that girl," Mabel says. "She used to go to bed with the chickens. Now you say she's up all hours. Plus her a-smoking. I like to died."

"I want to make her this beautiful home," Leroy says, indicating the Lincoln Logs. "I don't think she even wants it. Maybe she was happier with me gone."

"She don't know what to make of you, coming home like this."

"Is that it?"

Mabel takes the roof off his Lincoln Log cabin. "You couldn't get *me* in a log cabin," she says. "I was raised in one. It's no picnic, let me tell you."

"They're different now," says Leroy.

"I tell you what," Mabel says, smiling oddly at Leroy.

"What?"

"Take her on down to Shiloh. Y'all need to get out together, stir a little. Her brain's all balled up over them books."

Leroy can see traces of Norma Jean's features in her mother's face. Mabel's face has the texture of crinkled cotton, but suddenly she looks pretty. It occurs to Leroy that Mabel has been hinting all along that she wants them to take her with them to Shiloh.

"Let's all go to Shiloh," he says. "You and me and her. Come Sunday."

Mabel throws up her hands in protest. "Oh, no, not me. Young folks want to be by theirselves."

When Norma Jean comes in with groceries, Leroy says excitedly, "Your mama here's been dying to go to Shiloh for thirty-five years. It's about time we went, don't you think?"

"I'm not going to butt in on anybody's second honeymoon," Mabel says.

"Who's going on a honeymoon, for Christ's sake?" Norma Jean says loudly.

"I never raised no daughter of mine to talk that-a-way," Mabel says.

"You ain't seen nothing yet," says Norma Jean. She starts putting away boxes and cans, slamming cabinet doors.

"There's a log cabin at Shiloh." Mabel says, "It was there during the battle. There's bullet holes in it."

"When are you going to *shut up* about Shiloh, Mama?" asks Norma Jean.

"I always thought Shiloh was the prettiest place, so full of history," Mabel goes on. "I just hoped y'all could see it once before I die, so you could tell me about it." Later, she whispers to Leroy, "You do what I said. A little change is what she needs."

"Your name means 'the king,'" Norma Jean says to Leroy that evening. He is trying to get her to go to Shiloh, and she is reading a book about another century.

"Well, I reckon I ought to be right proud."

"I guess so."

"Am I still king around here?"

Norma Jean flexes her biceps and feels them for hardness. "I'm not fooling around with anybody, if that's what you mean," she says.

"Would you tell me if you were?"

"I don't know."

"What does *your* name mean?"

"It was Marilyn Monroe's real name."

"No kidding!"

"Norma comes from the Normans. They were invaders," she says. She closes her book and looks hard at Leroy. "I'll go to Shiloh with you if you'll stop staring at me."

On Sunday, Norma Jean packs a picnic and they go to Shiloh. To Leroy's relief, Mabel says she does not want to come with them. Norma Jean drives, and Leroy, sitting beside her, feels like some boring hitchhiker she has picked up. He tries some conversation, but she answers him in monosyllables. At Shiloh, she drives aimlessly through the park, past bluffs and trails and steep ravines. Shiloh is an immense place, and Leroy cannot see it as a battleground. It is not what he expected. He thought it would look like a golf course. Monuments are everywhere, showing through the thick clusters of trees. Norma Jean passes the log cabin Mabel mentioned. It is surrounded by tourists looking for bullet holes.

"That's not the kind of log house I've got in mind," says Leroy apologetically.

"I know *that*."

"This is a pretty place. Your mama was right."

"It's O.K.," says Norma Jean. "Well, we've seen it. I hope she's satisfied."

They burst out laughing together.

At the park museum, a movie on Shiloh is shown every half hour, but they decide that they don't want to see it. They buy a souvenir Confederate flag for Mabel, and then they find a picnic spot near the cemetery. Norma Jean has brought a picnic cooler, with pimiento sandwiches, soft drinks, and Yodels. Leroy eats a sandwich and then smokes a joint, hiding it behind the picnic cooler. Norma Jean has quit smoking altogether. She is picking cake crumbs from the cellophane wrapper, like a fussy bird.

Leroy says, "So the boys in gray ended up in Corinth. The Union soldiers zapped 'em finally. April 7, 1862."

They both know that he doesn't know any history. He is just talking about some of the historical plaques they have read. He feels awkward, like a boy on a date with an older girl. They are still just making conversation.

"Corinth is where Mama eloped to," says Norma Jean.

They sit in silence and stare at the cemetery for the Union dead and, beyond, at a tall cluster of trees. Campers are parked nearby, bumper to bumper, and small children in bright clothing are cavorting and squealing. Norma Jean wads up the cake wrapper and squeezes it tightly in her hand. Without looking at Leroy, she says, "I want to leave you."

Leroy takes a bottle of Coke out of the cooler and flips off the cap. He holds the bottle poised near his mouth but cannot remember to take a drink. Finally he says, "No, you don't."

"Yes, I do."

"I won't let you."

"You can't stop me."

"Don't do me that way."

Leroy knows Norma Jean will have her own way. "Didn't I promise to be home from now on?" he says.

"In some ways, a woman prefers a man who wanders," says Norma Jean. "That sounds crazy, I know."

"You're not crazy."

Leroy remembers to drink from his Coke. Then he says, "Yes, you *are* crazy. You and me could start all over again. Right back at the beginning."

"We *have* started all over again," says Norma Jean. "And this is how it turned out."

"What did I do wrong?"

"Nothing."

"Is this one of those women's lib things?" Leroy asks.

"Don't be funny."

The cemetery, a green slope dotted with white markers, looks like a subdivision site. Leroy is trying to comprehend that his marriage is breaking up, but for some reason he is wondering about white slabs in a graveyard.

"Everything was fine till Mama caught me smoking," says Norma Jean, standing up. "That set something off."

"What are you talking about?"

"She won't leave me alone—*you* won't leave me alone." Norma Jean seems to be crying, but she is looking away from him. "I feel eighteen again. I can't face that all over again." She starts walking away. "No, it *wasn't* fine. I don't know what I'm saying. Forget it."

Leroy takes a lungful of smoke and closes his eyes as Norma Jean's words sink in. He tries to focus on the fact that thirty-five hundred soldiers died on the grounds around him. He can only think of that war as a board game with plastic soldiers. Leroy almost smiles, as he compares the Confederates' daring attack on the Union camps and Virgil Mathis's raid on the bowling alley. General Grant, drunk and furious, shoved the Southerners back to Corinth, where Mabel and Jet Beasley were married years later, when Mabel was still thin and good-looking. The next day, Mabel and Jet visited the battleground, and then Norma Jean was born, and then she married Leroy and they had a baby, which they lost, and now Leroy and Norma Jean are here at the same battleground. Leroy knows he is leaving out a lot. He is leaving out the insides of history. History was always just names and dates to him. It occurs to him that building a house out of logs is similarly empty—too simple. And the real inner workings of a marriage, like most of history, have escaped him. Now he sees that building a log house is the dumbest idea he could have had. It was clumsy of him to think Norma Jean would want a log house. It was a crazy idea. He'll have to think of something else, quickly. He will wad the blueprints into tight balls and fling them into the lake. Then he'll get moving again. He opens his eyes. Norma Jean has moved away and is walking through the cemetery, following a serpentine brick path.

Leroy gets up to follow his wife, but his good leg is asleep and his bad leg still hurts him. Norma Jean is far away, walking rapidly toward the bluff by the river, and he tries to hobble toward her. Some children run past him, screaming noisily. Norma Jean has reached the bluff, and she is looking out over the Tennessee River. Now she turns toward Leroy and waves her arms. Is she beckoning to him? She seems to be doing an exercise for her chest muscles. The sky is unusually pale—the color of the dust ruffle Mabel made for their bed.

1982

## MARGARET ATWOOD

## *Scarlet Ibis*

Some years ago now, Christine went with Don to Trinidad. They took Lilian, their youngest child, who was four then. The others, who were in school, stayed with their grandmother.

Christine and Don sat beside the hotel pool in the damp heat, drinking rum punch and eating strange-tasting hamburgers. Lilian wanted to be in the pool all the time—she could already swim a little—but Christine didn't think it was a good idea, because of the sun. Christine rubbed sun block on her nose, and on the noses of Lilian and Don. She felt that her legs were too white and that people were looking at her and finding her faintly ridiculous, because of her pinky-white skin and the large hat she wore. More than likely, the young black waiters who brought the rum punch and the hamburgers, who walked easily through the sun without paying any attention to it, who joked among themselves but were solemn when they set down the glasses and plates, had put her in a category; one that included fat, although she was not fat exactly. She suggested to Don that perhaps he was tipping too much. Don said he felt tired.

"You felt tired before," Christine said. "That's why we came, remember? So you could get some rest."

Don took afternoon naps, sprawled on his back on one of the twin beds in the room—Lilian had a fold-out cot—his mouth slightly open, the skin of his face pushed by gravity back down towards his ears, so that he looked tauter, thinner, and more aquiline in this position than he did when awake. Deader, thought Christine, taking a closer look. People lying on their backs in coffins usually—in her limited experience—seemed to have lost weight. This image, of Don encoffined, was one that had been drifting through her mind too often for comfort lately.

It was hopeless expecting Lilian to have an afternoon nap too, so Christine took her down to the pool or tried to keep her quiet by drawing with her, using Magic Markers. At that age Lilian drew nothing but women or girls, wearing very fancy dresses, full-skirted, with a lot of decoration. They were always smiling, with red, curvy mouths, and had abnormally long thick eyelashes. They did not stand on any ground—Lilian was not yet putting the ground into her pictures—but floated on the page as if it were a pond they were spread out on, arms outstretched, feet at the opposite sides of their skirts, their elaborate hair billowing around their heads. Sometimes Lilian put in some birds or the sun, which gave these women the appearance of giant airborne balloons, as if the wind had caught them under their skirts and carried them off, light as feathers, away from everything. Yet, if she were asked, Lilian would say these women were walking.

After a few days of all this, when they ought to have adjusted to the heat, Christine felt they should get out of the hotel and do something. She did not want to go shopping by herself, although Don suggested it; she felt that nothing she tried on helped her look any better, or, to be more precise, that it didn't much matter how she looked. She tried to think of some other distraction, mostly for the sake of Don. Don was not noticeably more rested, although he had a sunburn—which, instead of giving him a glow of health, made him seem angry—and he'd started drumming his fingers on tabletops again. He said he was having trouble sleeping: bad dreams, which he could not remember. Also the air-conditioning was clogging up his nose. He had been under a lot of pressure lately, he said.

Christine didn't need to be told. She could feel the pressure he was under, like a clenched mass of something, tissue, congealed blood, at the back of her own head. She thought of Don as being encased in a sort of metal carapace, like the shell of a crab, that was slowly tightening on him, on all parts of him at once, so that something was sure to burst, like a thumb closed slowly in a car door. The metal skin was his entire body, and Christine didn't know how to unlock it for him and let him out. She felt as if all her ministrations—the cold washcloths for his headaches, the trips to the drugstore for this or that bottle of pills, the hours of tiptoeing around, intercepting the phone, keeping Lilian quiet, above all the mere act of witnessing him, which was so draining—were noticed by him hardly at all: moths beating on the outside of a lit window, behind which someone important was thinking about something of major significance that had nothing to do with moths. This vacation, for instance, had been her idea, but Don was only getting redder and redder.

Unfortunately, it was not carnival season. There were restaurants, but Lilian hated sitting still in them, and one thing Don did not need was more food and especially more drink. Christine wished Don had a sport, but considering the way he was, he would probably overdo it and break something.

"I had an uncle who took up hooking rugs," she'd said to him one evening after dinner. "When he retired. He got them in kits. He said he found it very restful." The aunt that went with that uncle used to say, "I said for better or for worse, but I never said for lunch."

10    "Oh, for God's sake, Christine," was all Don had to say to that. He'd never thought much of her relatives. His view was that Christine was still on the raw side of being raw material. Christine did not look forward to the time, twenty years away at least, when he would be home all day, pacing, drumming his fingers, wanting whatever it was that she could never identify and never provide.

In the morning, while the other two were beginning breakfast, Christine went bravely to the hotel's reception desk. There was a thin, elegant brown girl behind it, in lime green, Rasta beads, and *Vogue* make-up, coiled like spaghetti around the phone. Christine, feeling hot and porous, asked if there was any material on things to do. The girl, sliding her eyes over and past Christine as if she were a minor architectural feature, selected and fanned an assortment of brochures, continuing to laugh lightly into the phone.

Christine took the brochures into the ladies' room to preview them. Not the beach, she decided, because of the sun. Not the boutiques, not the night clubs, not the memories of Old Spain.

She examined her face, added lipstick to her lips, which were getting thin and pinched together. She really needed to do something about herself, before it was too late. She made her way back to the breakfast table. Lilian was saying that the pancakes weren't the same as the ones at home. Don said she had to eat them because she had ordered them, and if she was old enough to order for herself she was old enough to know that they cost money and couldn't be wasted like that. Christine wondered silently if it was a bad pattern, making a child eat everything on her plate, whether she liked the food or not: perhaps Lilian would become fat, later on.

Don was having bacon and eggs. Christine had asked Don to order yoghurt and fresh fruit for her, but there was nothing at her place.

"They didn't have it," Don said.

"Did you order anything else?" said Christine, who was now hungry.

"How was I supposed to know what you want?" said Don.

"We're going to see the Scarlet Ibis," Christine announced brightly to Lilian. She would ask them to bring back the menu, so she could order.

"What?" said Don. Christine handed him the brochure, which showed some red birds with long curved bills sitting in a tree; there was another picture of one close up, in profile, one demented-looking eye staring out from its red feathers like a target.

"They're very rare," said Christine, looking around for a waiter. "It's a preservation."

"You mean a preserve," said Don, reading the brochure. "In a swamp? Probably crawling with mosquitoes."

"I don't want to go," said Lilian, pushing scraps of a pancake around in a pool of watery syrup. This was her other complaint, that it wasn't the right kind of syrup.

"Imitation maple flavouring," Don said, reading the label.

"You don't even know what it is," said Christine. "We'll take some fly dope. Anyway, they wouldn't let tourists go there if there were that many mosquitoes. It's a *mangrove* swamp; that isn't the same as our kind."

"I'm going to get a paper," said Don. He stood up and walked away. His legs, coming out of the bottoms of his Bermuda shorts, were still very white, with an overglaze of pink down the backs. His body, once muscular, was losing tone, sliding down towards his waist and buttocks. He was beginning to slope. From the back, he had the lax, demoralized look of a man who has been confined in an institution, though from the front he was brisk enough.

Watching him go, Christine felt the sickness in the pit of her stomach that was becoming familiar to her these days. Maybe the pressure he was under was her. Maybe she was a weight. Maybe he wanted her to lift up, blow away somewhere, like a kite, the children hanging on behind her in a long string. She didn't know when she had first noticed this feeling; probably after it had been there some time, like a knocking on the front door when you're asleep. There had been a shifting of forces, unseen, unheard, underground, the sliding against each other of giant stones; some tremendous damage had occurred between them, but who could tell when?

"Eat your pancakes," she said to Lilian, "or your father will be annoyed." He would be annoyed anyway: she annoyed him. Even when they made love, which was not frequently any more, it was perfunctory, as if he were listening for something else, a phone call, a footfall. He was like a man scratching himself. She was like his hand.

Christine had a scenario she ran through often, the way she used to run through scenarios of courtship, back in high school: flirtation, pursuit, joyful acquiescence. This was an adult scenario, however. One evening she would say to Don as he was getting up from the table after dinner, "Stay there." He would be so surprised by her tone of voice that he would stay.

"I just want you to sit there and look at me," she would say.

30   He would not say, "For God's sake, Christine." He would know this was serious.

"I'm not asking much from you," she would say, lying.

"What's going on?" he would say.

"I want you to see what I really look like," she would say. "I'm tired of being invisible." Maybe he would, maybe he wouldn't. Maybe he would say he was coming on with a headache. Maybe she would find herself walking on nothing, because maybe there was nothing there. So far she hadn't even come close to beginning, to giving the initial command: "Stay," as if he were a trained dog. But that was what she wanted him to do, wasn't it? "Come back" was more like it. He hadn't always been under pressure.

Once Lilian was old enough, Christine thought, she could go back to work full time. She could brush up her typing and shorthand, find something. That would be good for her; she wouldn't concentrate so much on Don, she would have a reason to look better, she would either find new scenarios or act out the one that was preoccupying her. Maybe she was making things up, about Don. It might be a form of laziness.

• • •

35   Christine's preparations for the afternoon were careful. She bought some mosquito repellant at a drugstore, and a chocolate bar. She took two scarves, one for herself, one for Lilian, in case it was sunny. The big hat would blow off, she thought, as they were going to be in a boat. After a short argument with one of the waiters, who said she could only have drinks by the glass, she succeeded in buying three cans of Pepsi, not chilled. All these things she packed into her bag; Lilian's bag, actually, which was striped in orange and yellow and blue and had a picture of Mickey Mouse on it. They'd used it for the toys Lilian brought with her on the plane.

After lunch they took a taxi, first through the hot streets of the town, where the sidewalks were too narrow or nonexistent and the people crowded onto the road and there was a lot of honking, then out through the cane fields, the road becoming bumpier, the driver increasing speed. He drove with the car radio on, the left-hand window open, and his elbow out, a pink jockey cap tipped back on his head. Christine had shown him the brochure and asked him if he knew where the swamp was; he'd grinned at her and said everybody knew. He said he could take them, but it was too far to go out and back so he would wait there for them. Christine knew it meant extra money, but did not argue.

They passed a man riding a donkey, and two cows wandering around by the roadside, anchored by ropes around their necks which were tied to dragging stones. Christine pointed these out to Lilian. The little houses among the tall cane were made of cement blocks, painted light green or pink or light blue; they were built up on open-work foundations, almost as if they were on stilts. The women who sat on the steps turned their heads, unsmiling, to watch their taxi as it went by.

Lilian asked Christine if she had any gum. Christine didn't. Lilian began chewing on her nails, which she'd taken up since Don had been under pressure. Christine told her to stop. Then Lilian said she wanted to go for a swim. Don looked out the window. "How long did you say?" he asked. It was a reproach, not a question.

Christine hadn't said how long because she didn't know; she didn't know because she'd forgotten to ask. Finally they turned off the main road onto a smaller, muddier one, and parked beside some other cars in a rutted space that had once been part of a field.

"I meet you here," said the driver. He got out of the car, stretched, turned up the car radio. There were other drivers hanging around, some of them in cars, others sitting on the ground drinking from a bottle they were passing around, one asleep.

Christine took Lilian's hand. She didn't want to appear stupid by having to ask where they were supposed to go next. She didn't see anything that looked like a ticket office.

"It must be that shack," Don said, so they walked towards it, a long shed with a tin roof; on the other side of it was a steep bank and the beginning of the water. There were wooden steps leading down to a wharf, which was the same brown as the water itself. Several boats were tied up to it, all of similar design: long and thin, almost like barges, with rows of bench-like seats. Each boat had a small outboard motor at the back. The names painted on the boats looked East Indian.

Christine took the scarves out of her bag and tied one on her own head and one on Lilian's. Although it was beginning to cloud over, the sun was still very bright, and she knew about rays coming through overcast, especially in the tropics. She put sun block on their noses, and thought that the chocolate bar had been a silly idea. Soon it would be a brown puddle at the bottom of her bag, which luckily was waterproof. Don paced behind them as Christine knelt.

An odd smell was coming up from the water: a swamp smell, but with something else mixed in. Christine wondered about sewage disposal. She was glad she'd made Lilian go to the bathroom before they'd left.

There didn't seem to be anyone in charge, anyone to buy the tickets from, although there were several people beside the shed, waiting, probably: two plumpish, middle-aged men in T-shirts and baseball caps turned around backwards, an athletic couple in shorts with outside pockets, who were loaded down with cameras and binoculars, a trim woman in a tailored pink summer suit that must have been far too hot. There was another woman off to the side, a somewhat large woman in a floral print dress. She'd spread a Mexican-looking shawl on the weedy grass near the shed and was sitting down on it, drinking a pint carton of orange juice through a straw. The others looked wilted and dispirited, but not this woman. For her, waiting seemed to be an activity, not something imposed: she gazed around her, at the bank, the brown water, the line of sullen mangrove[1] trees beyond, as if she were enjoying every minute.

This woman seemed the easiest to approach, so Christine went over to her. "Are we in the right place?" she said. "For the birds."

The woman smiled at her and said they were. She had a broad face, with high, almost Slavic cheekbones and round red cheeks like those of an old-fashioned wooden doll, except that they were not painted on. Her taffy-coloured hair was done in waves and rolls, and reminded Christine of the pictures on the Toni home-permanent boxes of several decades before.

"We will leave soon," said the woman. "Have you seen these birds before? They come back only at sunset. The rest of the time they are away, fishing." She smiled again, and Christine thought to herself that it was a pity she hadn't had bands put on to even out her teeth when she was young.

This was the woman's second visit to the Scarlet Ibis preserve, she told Christine. The first was three years ago, when she stopped over here on her way to South America with her husband and children. This time her husband and children had stayed back at the hotel: they hadn't seen a swimming pool for such a long time. She and her husband were Mennonite missionaries, she said. She herself didn't seem embarrassed by this, but Christine blushed a little. She had been raised Anglican, but the only vestige of that was the kind of Christmas cards she favoured: prints of mediaeval or Renaissance old masters. Religious people of any serious kind made her nervous: they were like men in raincoats who might or might not be flashers. You would be going along with them in the ordinary way, and then there could be a swift movement and you would look down to find the coat wide open and nothing on under it but some pant legs held up by rubber bands. This had happened to Christine in a train station once.

"How many children do you have?" she said, to change the subject. Mennonite would explain the wide hips: they liked women who could have a lot of children.

The woman's crooked-toothed smile did not falter. "Four," she said, "but one of them is dead."

"Oh," said Christine. It wasn't clear whether the four included the one dead, or whether that was extra. She knew better than to say, "That's too bad." Such a comment was sure to produce something about the will of God, and she didn't want to deal with that. She looked to make sure Lilian was still there, over by Don. Much of the time Lilian was a given, but there were moments at which she was threatened, unknown to herself, with sudden disappearance. "That's my little girl, over there," Christine said, feeling immediately that this was a callous comment; but the woman continued to smile, in a way that Christine now found eerie.

A small brown man in a Hawaiian-patterned shirt came around from behind

---

1. Tropical trees that grow in shallow coastal waters.

the shed and went quickly down the steps to the wharf. He climbed into one of the boats and lowered the outboard motor into the water.

"Now maybe we'll get some action," Don said. He had come up behind her, but he was talking more to himself than to her. Christine sometimes wondered whether he talked in the same way when she wasn't there at all.

A second man, East Indian, like the first, and also in a hula-dancer shirt, was standing at the top of the steps, and they understood they were to go over. He took their money and gave each of them a business card in return; on one side of it was a coloured picture of an ibis, on the other a name and a phone number. They went single file down the steps and the first man handed them into the boat. When they were all seated—Don, Christine, Lilian, and the pink-suited woman in a crowded row, the two baseball-cap men in front of them, the Mennonite woman and the couple with the cameras at the very front—the second man cast off and hopped lightly into the bow. After a few tries the first man got the motor started, and they putt-putted slowly towards an opening in the trees, leaving a wispy trail of smoke behind them.

It was cloudier now, and not so hot. Christine talked with the pink-suited woman, who had blonde hair elegantly done up in a French roll. She was from Vienna, she said; her husband was here on business. This was the first time she had been on this side of the Atlantic Ocean. The beaches were beautiful, much finer than those of the Mediterranean. Christine complimented her on her good English, and the woman smiled and told her what a beautiful little girl she had, and Christine said Lilian would get conceited, a word that the woman had not yet added to her vocabulary. Lilian was quiet; she had caught sight of the woman's bracelet, which was silver and lavishly engraved. The woman showed it to her. Christine began to enjoy herself, despite the fact that the two men in front of her were talking too loudly. They were drinking beer, from cans they'd brought with them in a paper bag. She opened a Pepsi and shared some with Lilian. Don didn't want any.

They were in a channel now; she looked at the trees on either side, which were all the same, dark-leaved, rising up out of the water, on masses of spindly roots. She didn't know how long they'd been going.

It began to rain, not a downpour but heavily enough, large cold drops. The Viennese woman said, "It's raining," her eyes open in a parody of surprise, holding out her hand and looking up at the sky like someone in a child's picture book. This was for the benefit of Lilian. "We will get wet," she said. She took a white embroidered handkerchief out of her purse and spread it on the top of her head. Lilian was enchanted with the handkerchief and asked Christine if she could have one, too. Don said they should have known, since it always rained in the afternoons here.

The men in baseball caps hunched their shoulders, and one of them said to the Indian in the bow, "Hey, we're getting wet!"

The Indian's timid but closed expression did not change; with apparent reluctance he pulled a rolled-up sheet of plastic out from somewhere under the front seat and handed it to the men. They spent some time unrolling it and getting it straightened out, and then everyone helped to hold the plastic overhead like a roof, while the boat glided on at its unvarying pace, through the mangroves and the steam or mist that was now rising around them.

"Isn't this an adventure?" Christine said, aiming it at Lilian. Lilian was biting her nails. The rain pattered down. Don said he wished he'd brought a paper. The men in baseball caps began to sing, sounding oddly like boys at a summer camp who had gone to sleep one day and awakened thirty years later, unaware of the sinister changes that had taken place in them, the growth and recession of hair and flesh, the exchange of their once-clear voices for the murky ones that were now singing off-key, out of time:

> "They say that in the army,
> the girls are rather fine,
> They promise Betty Grable,
> they give you Frankenstein..."

They had not yet run out of beer. One of them finished a can and tossed it overboard, and it bobbed beside the boat for a moment before falling behind, a bright red dot in the borderless expanse of dull green and dull grey. Christine felt virtuous: she'd put her Pepsi can carefully into her bag, for disposal later.

Then the rain stopped, and after some debate about whether it was going to start again or not, the two baseball-cap men began to roll up the plastic sheet. While they were doing this there was a jarring thud. The boat rocked violently, and the one man who was standing up almost pitched overboard, then sat down with a jerk.

"What the hell?" he said.

The Indian at the back reversed the motor.

"We hit something," said the Viennese woman. She clasped her hands, another classic gesture.

"Obviously," Don said in an undertone. Christine smiled at Lilian, who was looking anxious. The boat started forward again.

"Probably a mangrove root," said the man with the cameras, turning half round. "They grow out under the water." He was the kind who would know.

"Or an alligator," said one of the men in baseball caps. The other man laughed.

"He's joking, darling," Christine said to Lilian.

"But we are sinking," said the Viennese woman, pointing with one outstretched hand, one dramatic finger.

Then they all saw what they had not noticed before. There was a hole in the boat, near the front, right above the platform of loose boards that served as a floor. It was the size of a small fist. Whatever they'd hit had punched right through the wood, as if it were cardboard. Water was pouring through.

"This tub must be completely rotten," Don muttered, directly to Christine this time. This was a role she was sometimes given when they were among people Don didn't know: the listener. "They get like that in the tropics."

"Hey," said one of the men in baseball caps. "You up front. There's a hole in the goddamned boat."

The Indian glanced over his shoulder at the hole. He shrugged, looked away, began fishing in the breast pocket of his sports shirt for a cigarette.

"Hey. Turn this thing around," said the man with the camera.

"Couldn't we get it fixed, and then start again?" said Christine, intending to conciliate. She glanced at the Mennonite woman, hoping for support, but the woman's broad flowered back was towards her.

"If we go back," the Indian said patiently—he could understand English after all—"you miss the birds. It will be too dark."

"Yeah, but if we go forward we sink."

"You will not sink," said the Indian. He had found a cigarette, already half-smoked, and was lighting it.

"He's done it before," said the largest baseball cap. "Every week he gets a hole in the goddamned boat. Nothing to it."

The brown water continued to come in. The boat went forward.

"Right," Don said, loudly, to everyone this time. "He thinks if we don't see the birds, we won't pay him."

That made sense to Christine. For the Indians, it was a lot of money. They probably couldn't afford the gas if they lost the fares. "If you go back, we'll pay you anyway," she called to the Indian. Ordinarily she would have made this suggestion to Don, but she was getting frightened.

Either the Indian didn't hear her or he didn't trust them, or it wasn't his idea of a fair bargain. He didn't smile or reply.

For a few minutes they all sat there, waiting for the problem to be solved. The trees went past. Finally Don said, "We'd better bail. At this rate we'll be in serious trouble in about half an hour."

"I should not have come," said the Viennese woman, in a tone of tragic despair.

"What with?" said the man with the cameras. The men in baseball caps had turned to look at Don, as if he were worthy of attention.

"Mummy, are we going to sink?" said Lilian.

"Of course not, darling," said Christine. "Daddy won't let us."

"Anything there is," said the largest baseball-cap man. He poured the rest of his beer over the side. "You got a jackknife?" he said.

Don didn't, but the man with the cameras did. They watched while he cut the top out of the can, knelt down, moved a loose platform board so he could get at the water, scooped, dumped brown water over the side. Then the other men started taking the tops off their own beer cans, including the full ones, which they emptied out. Christine produced the Pepsi can from her bag. The Mennonite woman had her pint juice carton.

"No mosquitoes, at any rate," Don said, almost cheerfully.

They'd lost a lot of time, and the water was almost up to the floor platform. It seemed to Christine that the boat was becoming heavier, moving more slowly through the water, that the water itself was thicker. They could not empty much water at a time with such small containers, but maybe, with so many of them doing it, it would work.

"This really *is* an adventure," she said to Lilian, who was white-faced and forlorn. "Isn't this fun?"

The Viennese woman was not bailing; she had no container. She was making visible efforts to calm herself. She had taken out a tangerine, which she was peeling, over the embroidered handkerchief which she'd spread out on her lap. Now she produced a beautiful little pen-knife with a mother-of-pearl handle. To Lilian she said, "You are hungry? Look, I will cut in pieces, one piece for you, then one for me, *ja*?" The knife was not really needed, of course. It was to distract Lilian, and Christine was grateful.

There was an audible rhythm in the boat: scrape, dump; scrape, dump. The men in baseball caps, rowdy earlier, were not at all drunk now. Don appeared to be enjoying himself, for the first time on the trip.

But despite their efforts, the level of the water was rising.

"This is ridiculous," Christine said to Don. She stopped bailing with her Pepsi can. She was discouraged and also frightened. She told herself that the Indians wouldn't keep going if they thought there was any real danger, but she wasn't convinced. Maybe they didn't care if everybody drowned; maybe they thought it was Karma. Through the hole the brown water poured, with a steady flow, like a cut vein. It was up to the level of the loose floor boards now.

Then the Mennonite woman stood up. Balancing herself, she removed her shoes, placing them carefully side by side under the seat. Christine had once watched a man do this in a subway station; he'd put the shoes under the bench where she was sitting, and a few minutes later had thrown himself in front of the oncoming train. The two shoes had remained on the neat yellow-tiled floor, like bones on a plate after a meal. It flashed through Christine's head that maybe the woman had become unhinged and was going to leap overboard; this was plausible, because of the dead child. The woman's perpetual smile was a fraud then, as Christine's would have been in her place.

But the woman did not jump over the side of the boat. Instead she bent over and moved the platform boards. Then she turned around and lowered her large flowered rump onto the hole. Her face was towards Christine now; she continued to smile, gazing over the side of the boat at the mangroves and their monotonous roots and leaves as if they were the most interesting scenery she had seen in a long time. The water was above her ankles; her skirt was wet. Did she look a little smug, a little clever or self-consciously heroic? Possibly, thought Christine, though from that round face it was hard to tell.

"Hey," said one of the men in baseball caps, "now you're cooking with gas!" The Indian in the bow looked at the woman; his white teeth appeared briefly.

The others continued to bail, and after a moment Christine began to scoop and pour with the Pepsi can again. Despite herself, the woman impressed her. The water probably wasn't that cold but it was certainly filthy, and who could tell what might be on the other side of the hole? Were they far enough south for piranhas? Yet there was the Mennonite woman plugging the hole with her bottom, serene as a brooding hen, and no doubt unaware of the fact that she was more than a little ridiculous. Christine could imagine the kinds of remarks the men in baseball caps would make about the woman afterwards. "Saved by a big butt." "Hey, never knew it had more than one use." "Finger in the dike had nothing on her." That was the part that would have stopped Christine from doing such a thing, even if she'd managed to think of it.

Now they reached the long aisle of mangroves and emerged into the open; they were in a central space, like a lake, with the dark mangroves walling it around. There was a chicken-wire fence strung across it, to keep any boats from going too close to the Scarlet Ibis' roosting area: that was what the sign said, nailed to a post that was sticking at an angle out of the water. The Indian cut the motor and they drifted towards the fence; the other Indian caught hold of the fence, held on, and the boat stopped, rocking a little. Apart from the ripples they'd caused, the water was dead flat calm; the trees doubled in it appeared black, and the sun, which was just above the western rim of the real trees, was a red disk in the hazy grey sky. The light coming from it was orangy-red and tinted the water. For a few minutes nothing happened. The man with the cameras looked at his watch. Lilian was restless, squirming on the seat. She wanted to draw; she wanted to swim in the pool. If Christine had known the whole thing would take so long she wouldn't have brought her.

"They coming," said the Indian in the bow.

"Birds ahoy," said one of the men in baseball caps, and pointed, and then there were the birds all right, flying through the reddish light, right on cue, first singly, then in flocks of four or five, so bright, so fluorescent that they were like painted flames. They settled into the trees, screaming hoarsely. It was only the screams that revealed them as real birds.

The others had their binoculars up. Even the Viennese woman had a little pair of opera glasses. "Would you look at that," said one of the men. "Wish I'd brought my movie camera."

Don and Christine were without technology. So was the Mennonite woman. "You could watch them forever," she said, to nobody in particular. Christine, afraid that she would go on to say something embarrassing, pretended not to hear her. *Forever* was loaded.

She took Lilian's hand. "See those red birds?" she said. "You might never see one of those again in your entire life." But she knew that for Lilian these birds were no more special than anything else. She was too young for them. She said, "Oh," which was what she would have said if they had been pterodactyls or angels with wings as red as blood. Magicians, Christine knew from Lilian's last birthday party, were a failure with small children, who didn't see any reason why rabbits shouldn't come out of hats.

Don took hold of Christine's hand, a thing he had not done for some time; but Christine, watching the birds, noticed this only afterwards. She felt she was looking at a picture, of exotic flowers or of red fruit growing on trees, evenly spaced, like the fruit in the gardens of mediaeval paintings, solid, clear-edged, in primary colours. On the other side of the fence was another world, not real but at the same time more real than the one on this side, the men and women in their flimsy clothes and aging bodies, the decrepit boat. Her own body seemed fragile and empty, like blown glass.

The Mennonite woman had her face turned up to the sunset; her body was cut off at the neck by shadow, so that her head appeared to be floating in the air. For the first time she looked sad; but when she felt Christine watching her she smiled again, as if to reassure her, her face luminous and pink and round as a plum. Christine felt the two hands holding her own, mooring her, one on either side.

Weight returned to her body. The light was fading, the air chillier. Soon they would have to return in the increasing darkness, in a boat so rotten a misplaced foot would go through it. The water would be black, not brown; it would be full of roots.

"Shouldn't we go back?" she said to Don.

Lilian said, "Mummy, I'm hungry," and Christine remembered the chocolate bar and rummaged in her bag. It was down at the bottom, limp as a slab of bacon but not liquid. She brought it out and peeled off the silver paper, and gave a square to Lilian and one to Don, and ate one herself. The light was pink and dark at the same time, and it was difficult to see what she was doing.

When she told about this later, after they were safely home, Christine put in the swamp and the awful boat, and the men singing and the suspicious smell of the water. She put in Don's irritability, but only on days when he wasn't particularly irritable. (By then, there was less pressure; these things went in phases, Christine decided. She was glad she had never said anything, forced any issues.) She put in how good Lilian had been even though she hadn't wanted to go. She put in the hole in the boat, her own panic, which she made amusing, and the ridiculous bailing with the cans, and the Indians' indifference to their fate. She put in the Mennonite woman sitting on the hole like a big fat hen, making this funny, but admiring also, since the woman's solution to the problem had been so simple and obvious that no one else had thought of it. She left out the dead child.

She put in the rather hilarious trip back to the wharf, with the Indian standing up in the bow, beaming his heavy-duty flashlight at the endless, boring mangroves, and the two men in the baseball caps getting into a mickey[2] and singing dirty songs.

She ended with the birds, which were worth every minute of it, she said. She presented them as a form of entertainment, like the Grand Canyon: something that really ought to be seen, if you liked birds, and if you should happen to be in that part of the world.

1983

# HA JIN

## *In Broad Daylight*

While I was eating corn cake and jellyfish at lunch, our gate was thrown open and Bare Hips hopped in. His large wooden pistol was stuck partly inside the waist of his blue shorts. "White Cat," he called me by my nickname, "hurry, let's go. They caught Old Whore at her home. They're going to take her through the streets this afternoon."

"Really?" I put down my bowl, which was almost empty, and rushed to the inner room for my undershirt and sandals. "I'll be back in a second."

"Bare Hips, did you say they'll parade Mu Ying today?" I heard Grandma ask in her husky voice.

"Yes, all the kids on our street have left for her house. I came to tell White Cat." He paused. "Hey, White Cat, hurry up!"

"Coming," I cried out, still looking for my sandals.

"Good, good!" Grandma said to Bare Hips, while flapping at flies with her large palm-leaf fan. "They should burn the bitch on Heaven Lamp like they did in the old days."

"Come, let's go," Bare Hips said to me the moment I was back. He turned to the door; I picked up my wooden scimitar and followed him.

"Put on your shoes, dear." Grandma stretched out her fan to stop me.

"No time for that, Grandma. I've got to be quick, or I'll miss something and won't be able to tell you the whole story when I get back."

We dashed into the street while Grandma was shouting behind us. "Come back. Take the rubber shoes with you."

We charged toward Mu Ying's home on Eternal Way, waving our weapons above our heads. Grandma was crippled and never came out of our small yard. That was why I had to tell her about what was going on outside. But she knew

---

2. Drunken argument.

Mu Ying well, just as all the old women in our town knew Mu well and hated her. Whenever they heard that she had a man in her home again, these women would say, "This time they ought to burn Old Whore on Heaven Lamp."

What they referred to was the old way of punishing an adulteress. Though they had lived in New China for almost two decades, some ancient notions still stuck in their heads. Grandma told me about many of the executions in the old days that she had seen with her own eyes. Officials used to have the criminals of adultery executed in two different ways. They beheaded the man. He was tied to a stake on the platform at the marketplace. At the first blare of horns, a masked headsman ascended the platform holding a broad ax before his chest; at the second blare of horns, the headsman approached the criminal and raised the ax over his head; at the third blare of horns, the head was lopped off and fell to the ground. If the man's family members were waiting beneath the platform, his head would be picked up to be buried together with his body; if no family member was nearby, dogs would carry the head away and chase each other around until they ate up the flesh and returned for the body.

Unlike the man, the woman involved was executed on Heaven Lamp. She was hung naked upside down above a wood fire whose flames could barely touch her scalp. And two men flogged her away with whips made of bulls' penises. Meanwhile she screamed for help and the whole town could hear her. Since the fire merely scorched her head, it took at least half a day for her to stop shrieking and a day and a night to die completely. People used to believe that the way of punishment was justified by Heaven, so the fire was called Heaven Lamp. But that was an old custom; nobody believed they would burn Mu Ying in that way.

Mu's home, a small granite house with cement tiles built a year before, was next to East Wind Inn on the northern side of Eternal Way. When we entered that street, Bare Hips and I couldn't help looking around tremulously, because that area was the territory of the children living there. Two of the fiercest boys, who would kill without having second thoughts, ruled that part of our town. Whenever a boy from another street wandered into Eternal Way, they'd capture him and beat him up. Of course we did the same thing; if we caught one of them in our territory, we'd at least confiscate whatever he had with him: grasshopper cages, slingshots, bottle caps, marbles, cartridge cases, and so on. We would also make him call every one of us "Father" or "Grandfather." But today hundreds of children and grown-ups were pouring into Eternal Way; two dozen urchins on that street surely couldn't hold their ground. Besides, they had already adopted a truce, since they were more eager to see the Red Guards[1] drag Mu Ying out of her den.

When we arrived, Mu was being brought out through a large crowd at the front gate. Inside her yard there were three rows of colorful washing hung on iron wires, and there was also a grape trellis. Seven or eight children were in there, plucking off grapes and eating them. Two Red Guards held Mu Ying by the arms, and the other Red Guards, about twenty of them, followed behind. They were all from Dalian City and wore home-made army uniforms. God knew how they came to know that there was a bad woman in our town. Though people

---

1. A national student organization sponsored by Mao Zedong as an instrument to start and develop the Great Proletarian Cultural Revolution (1966–76).

hated Mu and called her names, no one would rough her up. Those Red Guards were strangers, so they wouldn't mind doing it.

Surprisingly, Mu looked rather calm; she neither protested nor said a word. The two Red Guards let go of her arms, and she followed them quietly into West Street. We all moved with them. Some children ran several paces ahead to look back at her.

Mu wore a sky-blue dress, which made her different from the other women who always wore jackets and pants suitable for honest work. In fact, even we small boys could tell that she was really handsome, perhaps the best looking woman of her age in our town. Though in her fifties, she didn't have a single gray hair; she was a little plump, but because of her long legs and arms she appeared rather queenly. While most of the women had sallow faces, hers looked white and healthy like fresh milk.

Skipping in front of the crowd, Bare Hips turned around and cried out at her, "Shameless Old Whore!"

She glanced at him, her round eyes flashing; the purple wart beside her left nostril grew darker. Grandma had assured me that Mu's wart was not a beauty-wart but a tear-wart. This meant that her life would be soaked in tears.

20   We knew where we were going, to White Mansion, which was our classroom building, the only two-storied house in the town. As we came to the end of West Street, a short man ran out from a street corner, panting for breath and holding a sickle. He was Meng Su, Mu Ying's husband, who sold bean jelly in summer and sugar-coated haws in winter at the marketplace. He paused in front of the large crowd, as though having forgotten why he had rushed over. He turned his head around to look back; there was nobody behind him. After a short moment he moved close, rather carefully.

"Please let her go," he begged the Red Guards. "Comrade Red Guards, it's all my fault. Please let her go." He put the sickle under his arm and held his hands together before his chest.

"Get out of the way!" commanded a tall young man, who must have been the leader.

"Please don't take her away. It's my fault. I haven't disciplined her well. Please give her a chance to be a new person. I promise, she won't do it again."

The crowd stopped to circle about. "What's your class status?" a square-faced young woman asked in a sharp voice.

25   "Poor peasant," Meng replied, his small eyes tearful and his cupped ears twitching a little. "Please let her go, sister. Have mercy on us! I'm kneeling down to you if you let her go." Before he was able to fall on his knees, two young men held him back. Tears were rolling down his dark fleshy cheeks, and his gray head began waving about. The sickle was taken away from him.

"Shut up," the tall leader yelled and slapped him across the face. "She's a snake. We traveled a hundred and fifty *li*[2] to come here to wipe out poisonous snakes and worms. If you don't stop interfering, we'll parade you with her together. Do you want to join her?"

Silence. Meng covered his face with his large hands as though feeling dizzy.

A man in the crowd said aloud, "If you can share the bed with her, why can't you share the street?"

---

2. Approximately 50 miles.

Many of the grown-ups laughed. "Take him, take him too!" someone told the Red Guards. Meng looked scared, sobbing quietly.

His wife stared at him without saying a word. Her teeth were clenched; a faint smile passed the corners of her mouth. Meng seemed to wince under her stare. The two Red Guards let his arms go, and he stepped aside, watching his wife and the crowd move toward the school.

Of Meng Su people in our town had different opinions. Some said he was a born cuckold who didn't mind his wife's sleeping with any man as long as she could bring money home. Some believed he was a good-tempered man who had stayed with his wife mainly for their children's sake; they forgot that the three children had grown up long before and were working in big cities far away. Some thought he didn't leave his wife because he had no choice—no woman would marry such a dwarf. Grandma, for some reason, seemed to respect Meng. She told me that Mu Ying had once been raped by a group of Russian soldiers under Northern Bridge and was left on the river bank afterwards. That night her husband sneaked there and carried her back. He looked after her for a whole winter till she recovered. "Old Whore doesn't deserve that good-hearted man," Grandma would say. "She's heartless and knows only how to sell her thighs."

We entered the school's playground where about two hundred people had already gathered. "Hey, White Cat and Bare Hips," Big Shrimp called us, waving his claws. Many boys from our street were there too. We went to join them.

The Red Guards took Mu to the front entrance of the building. Two tables had been placed between the stone lions that crouched on each side of the entrance. On one of the tables stood a tall paper hat with the big black characters on its side: "Down with Old Bitch!"

A young man in glasses raised his bony hand and started to address us, "Folks, we've gathered here today to denounce Mu Ying, who is a demon in this town."

"Down with Bourgeois Demons!" a slim woman Red Guard shouted. We raised our fists and repeated the slogan.

"Down with Old Bitch Mu Ying," a middle-aged man cried out with both hands in the air. He was an active revolutionary in our commune. Again we shouted, in louder voices.

The nearsighted man went on, "First, Mu Ying must confess her crime. We must see her attitude toward her own crime. Then we'll make the punishment fit both her crime and her attitude. All right, folks?"

"Right," some voices replied from the crowd.

"Mu Ying," he turned to the criminal, "you must confess everything. It's up to you now."

She was forced to stand on a bench. Staying below the steps, we had to raise our heads to see her face.

The questioning began. "Why do you seduce men and paralyze their revolutionary will with your bourgeois poison?" the tall leader asked in a solemn voice.

"I've never invited any man to my home, have I?" she said rather calmly. Her husband was standing at the front of the crowd, listening to her without showing any emotion, as though having lost his mind.

"Then why did they got to your house and not to others' houses?"

"They wanted to sleep with me," she replied.

"Shameless!" Several women hissed in the crowd.

"A true whore!"

"Scratch her!"

"Rip apart her filthy mouth!"

"Sisters," she spoke aloud. "All right, it was wrong to sleep with them. But you all know what it feels like when you want a man, don't you? Don't you once in a while have that feeling in your bones?" Contemptuously, she looked at the few withered middle-aged women standing in the front row, then closed her eyes. "Oh, you want that real man to have you in his arms and let him touch every part of your body. For that man alone you want to blossom into a woman, a real woman—"

"Take this, you Fox Spirit!" A stout young fellow struck her on the side with a fist like a sledgehammer. The heavy blow silenced her at once. She held her sides with both hands, gasping for breath.

"You're wrong, Mu Ying," Bare Hips's mother spoke from the front of the crowd, her forefinger pointing upward at Mu. "You have your own man, who doesn't lack an arm or a leg. It's wrong to have others' men and more wrong to pocket their money."

"I have my own man?" Mu glanced at her husband and smirked. She straightened up and said, "My man is nothing. He is no good, I mean in bed. He always comes before I feel anything."

All the adults burst out laughing. "What's that? What's so funny?" Big Shrimp asked Bare Hips.

"You didn't get it?" Bare Hips said impatiently. "You don't know anything about what happens between a man and a woman. It means that whenever she doesn't want him to come close to her he comes. Bad timing."

"It doesn't sound like that," I said.

Before we could argue, a large bottle of ink smashed on Mu's head and knocked her off the bench. Prone on the cement terrace, she broke into swearing and blubbering. "Oh, damn your ancestors! Whoever hit me will be childless!" Her left hand was rubbing her head. "Oh Lord of Heaven, they treat their grandma like this!"

"Serves you right!"

"A cheap weasel."

"Even a knife on her throat can't stop her."

"A pig is born to eat slop!"

When they put her back up on the bench, she became another person—her shoulders covered with black stains, and a red line trickling down her left temple. The scorching sun was blazing down on her as though all the black parts on her body were about to burn up. Still moaning, she turned her eyes to the spot where her husband had been standing a few minutes before. But he was no longer there.

"Down with Old Whore!" a farmer shouted in the crowd. We all followed him in one voice. She began trembling slightly.

The tall leader said to us, "In order to get rid of her counterrevolutionary airs, first, we're going to cut her hair." With a wave of his hand, he summoned the Red Guards behind him. Four men moved forward and held her down. The square-faced woman raised a large pair of scissors and thrust them into the mass of the dark hair.

"Don't, don't, please. Help, help! I'll do whatever you want me to—"

"Cut!" someone yelled.

"Shave her head bald!"

The woman Red Guard applied the scissors skillfully. After four or five strokes, Mu's head looked like the tail of a molting hen. She started blubbering again, her nose running and her teeth chattering.

A breeze came and swept away the fluffy curls from the terrace and scattered them on the sandy ground. It was so hot that some people took out fans, waving them continuously. The crowd stank of sweat.

*Wooooo, wooooo, woo, woo.* That was the train coming from Sand County at 3:30. It was a freight train, whose young drivers would toot the steam horn whenever they saw a young woman in a field beneath the track.

The questioning continued. "How many men have you slept with these years?" the nearsighted man asked.

"Three."

"She's lying," a woman in the crowd cried out.

"I told the truth, sister." She wiped off the tears from her cheeks with the back of her hand.

"Who are they?" the young man asked again. "Tell us more about them."

"An officer from the Little Dragon Mountain, and—"

"How many times did he come to your house?"

"I can't remember. Probably twenty."

"What's his name?"

"I don't know. He told me he was a big officer."

"Did you take money from him?"

"Yes."

"How much for each time?"

"Twenty *yuan*."

"How much altogether?"

"Probably five hundred."

"Comrades and Revolutionary Masses," the young man turned to us, "how shall we handle this parasite that sucked blood out of a revolutionary officer?"

"Quarter her with four horses!" an old woman yelled.

"Burn her on Heaven Lamp!"

"Poop on her face!" a small fat girl shouted, her hand raised like a tiny pistol with the thumb cocked up and the forefinger aimed at Mu. Some grown-ups snickered.

Then a pair of old cloth-shoes, a symbol for a promiscuous woman, were passed to the front. The slim young woman took the shoes and tied them together with the laces. She climbed on a table and was about to hang the shoes around Mu's neck. Mu elbowed the woman aside and knocked the shoes to the ground. The stout young fellow picked up the shoes, and jumped twice to slap her on the cheeks with the soles. "You're so stubborn. Do you want to change yourself or not?" he asked.

"Yes, I do," she replied meekly and dared not stir a bit. Meanwhile the shoes were being hung around her neck.

"Now she looks like a real whore," a woman commented.

"Sing us a tune, Sis," a farmer demanded.

"Comrades," the man in glasses resumed, "let us continue the denunciation." He turned to Mu and asked, "Who are the other men?"

"A farmer from Apple Village."

"How many times with him?"
"Once."
"Liar!"
"She's lying!"
"Give her one on the mouth!"

The young man raised his hands to calm the crowd down and questioned her again, "How much did you take from him?"

"Eighty *yuan*."

"One night?"

"Yes."

"Tell us more about it. How can you make us believe you?"

"That old fellow came to town to sell piglets. He sold a whole litter for eighty, and I got the money."

"Why did you charge him more than the officer?"

"No, I didn't. He did it four times in one night."

Some people were smiling and whispering to each other. A woman said that old man must have been a widower or never married.

"What's his name?" the young man went on.

"No idea."

"Was he rich or poor?"

"Poor."

"Comrades," the young man addressed us, "here we have a poor peasant who worked with his sow for a whole year and got only a litter of piglets. That money is the salt and oil money for his family, but this snake swallowed the money with one gulp. What shall we do with her?"

"Kill her!"

"Break her skull!"

"Beat the piss out of her!"

A few farmers began to move forward to the steps, waving their fists or rubbing their hands.

"Hold," a woman Red Guard with a huge Chairman Mao badge on her chest spoke in a commanding voice. "The Great Leader has instructed us: 'For our struggle we need words but not force.' Comrades, we can easily wipe her out with words. Force doesn't solve ideological problems." What she said restrained those enraged farmers, who remained in the crowd.

*Wooo, woo, wooo, woooooooooooo,* an engine screamed in the south. It was strange, because the drivers of the four o'clock train were a bunch of old men who seldom blew the horn.

"Who is the third man?" the nearsighted man continued to question Mu.

"A Red Guard."

The crowd broke into laughter. Some women asked the Red Guards to give her another bottle of ink. "Mu Ying, you're responsible for your own words," the young man said in a serious voice.

"I told you the truth."

"What's his name?"

"I don't know. He led the propaganda team that passed here last month."

"How many times did you sleep with him?"

"Once."

"How much did you make out of him?"

"None. That stingy dog wouldn't pay a cent. He said he was the worker who should be paid."

"So you were outsmarted by him?"

Some men in the crowd guffawed. Mu wiped her nose with her thumb, and at once she wore a thick mustache. "I taught him a lesson, though," she said.

"How?"

"I tweaked his ears, gave him a bleeding nose, and kicked him out. I told him never come back."

People began talking to each other. Some said that she was a strong woman who knew what was hers. Some said the Red Guard was no good; if you got something you had to pay for it. A few women declared that the rascal deserved such a treatment.

"Dear Revolutionary Masses," the tall leader started to speak. "We all have heard the crime Mu Ying committed. She lured one of our officers and one of our poor peasants into the evil water, and she beat a Red Guard black and blue. Shall we let her go home without punishment or shall we teach her an unforgettable lesson so that she won't do it again?"

"Teach her a lesson!" some voices cried out in unison.

"Then we're going to parade her through the streets."

Two Red Guards pulled Mu off the bench, and another picked up the tall hat. "Brothers and sisters," she begged, "please let me off just for once. Don't, don't! I promise I'll correct my fault. I'll be a new person. Help! Oh, help!"

It was no use resisting; within seconds the huge hat was firmly planted on her head. They also hung a big placard between the cloth-shoes lying against her chest. The words on the placard read:

> I am a Broken Shoe
> My Crime Deserves Death

They put a gong in her hands and ordered her to strike it when she announced the words written on the inner side of the gong.

My pals and I followed the crowd, feeling rather tired. Boys from East Street were wilder; they threw stones at Mu's back. One stone struck the back of her head and blood dropped on her neck. But they were stopped immediately by the Red Guards, because a stone missed Mu and hit a man on the shoulder. Old people, who couldn't follow us, were standing on chairs and windowsills with pipes and towels in their hands. We were going to parade her through every street. It would take several hours to finish the whole thing, as the procession would stop for a short while at every street corner.

*Bong*, Mu struck the gong and declared, "I am an evil monster."

"Louder!"

*Dong, bong*—"I have stolen men. I stink for a thousand years."

When we were coming out of the marketplace, Cross Eyes emerged from a narrow lane. He grasped my wrist and Bare Hips's arm and said, "Someone is dead at the train station. Come, let's go there and have a look." The word "dead" at once roused us. We, half a dozen boys, set out running to the train station.

The dead man was Meng Su. A crowd had gathered at the railroad a hundred meters east of the station house. A few men were examining the rail that was stained with blood and studded with bits of flesh. One man paced along the darker part of the rail and announced that the train had dragged Meng at least twenty meters.

Beneath the track, Meng's headless body lay in a ditch. One of his feet was missing, and the whitish shinbone stuck out several inches long. There were so many openings on his body that he looked like a large piece of fresh meat on the counter in the butcher's. Beyond him, ten paces away, a big straw hat remained on the ground. We were told that his head was under the hat.

Bare Hips and I went down the slope to have a glimpse at the head. Other boys dared not take a peep. We two looked at each other, asking with our eyes who should raise the straw hat. I held out my wooden scimitar and lifted the rim of the hat a little with the sword. A swarm of bluebottles charged out, droning like provoked wasps. We bent over to peek at the head. Two long teeth pierced through the upper lip. An eyeball was missing. The gray hair was no longer perceivable, as it was covered with mud and dirt. The open mouth filled with purplish mucus. A tiny lizard skipped, sliding away into the grass.

"Oh!" Bare Hips began vomiting. Sorghum gruel mixed with bits of string beans splashed on a yellowish boulder. "Leave it alone, White Cat."

We lingered at the station, listening to different versions of the accident. Some people said that Meng had gotten drunk and dropped asleep on the track. Some said he hadn't slept at all but laughed hysterically walking in the middle of the track toward the coming train. Some said he had not drunk a drop, as he had spoken with tears in his eyes to a few persons he had run into on his way to the station. In any case, he was dead, torn to pieces.

That evening when I was coming home, I heard Mu Ying groaning in the smoky twilight. "Take me home. Oh, help me. Who can help me? Where are you? Why don't you come and carry me home?"

She was lying at the bus stop, alone.

1993

## SALMAN RUSHDIE

### The Prophet's Hair

Early in the year 19——, when Srinagar[1] was under the spell of a winter so fierce it could crack men's bones as if they were glass, a young man upon whose cold-pinked skin there lay, like a frost, the unmistakable sheen of wealth was to be seen entering the most wretched and disreputable part of the city, where the houses of wood and corrugated iron seemed perpetually on the verge of losing their balance, and asking in low, grave tones where he might go to engage the services of a dependably professional burglar. The young man's name was Atta, and the rogues in that part of town directed him gleefully into ever darker and less public alleys, until in a yard wet with the blood of a slaughtered chicken he was set upon by two men whose faces he never saw, robbed of the substantial bank-roll which he had insanely brought on his solitary excursion, and beaten within an inch of his life.

1. Capital of the Indian state of Jammu and Kashmir.

Night fell. His body was carried by anonymous hands to the edge of the lake, whence it was transported by shikara[2] across the water and deposited, torn and bleeding, on the deserted embankment of the canal which led to the gardens of Shalimar. At dawn the next morning a flower-vendor was rowing his boat through water to which the cold of the night had given the cloudy consistency of wild honey when he saw the prone form of young Atta, who was just beginning to stir and moan, and on whose now deathly pale skin the sheen of wealth could still be made out dimly beneath an actual layer of frost.

The flower-vendor moored his craft and by stooping over the mouth of the injured man was able to learn the poor fellow's address, which was mumbled through lips that could scarcely move; whereupon, hoping for a large tip, the hawker rowed Atta home to a large house on the shores of the lake, where a beautiful but inexplicably bruised young woman and her distraught, but equally handsome mother, neither of whom, it was clear from their eyes, had slept a wink from worrying, screamed at the sight of their Atta—who was the elder brother of the beautiful young woman—lying motionless amidst the funereally stunted winter blooms of the hopeful florist.

The flower-vendor was indeed paid off handsomely, not least to ensure his silence, and plays no further part in our story. Atta himself, suffering terribly from exposure as well as a broken skull, entered a coma which caused the city's finest doctors to shrug helplessly. It was therefore all the more remarkable that on the very next evening the most wretched and disreputable part of the city received a second unexpected visitor. This was Huma, the sister of the unfortunate young man, and her question was the same as her brother's, and asked in the same low, grave tones:

"Where may I hire a thief?"

The story of the rich idiot who had come looking for a burglar was already common knowledge in those insalubrious gullies,[3] but this time the young woman added: "I should say that I am carrying no money, nor am I wearing any jewellery items. My father has disowned me and will pay no ransom if I am kidnapped; and a letter has been lodged with the Deputy Commissioner of Police, my uncle, to be opened in the event of my not being safe at home by morning. In that letter he will find full details of my journey here, and he will move Heaven and Earth to punish my assailants."

Her exceptional beauty, which was visible even through the enormous welts and bruises disfiguring her arms and forehead, coupled with the oddity of her inquiries, had attracted a sizable group of curious onlookers, and because her little speech seemed to them to cover just about everything, no one attempted to injure her in any way, although there were some raucous comments to the effect that it was pretty peculiar for someone who was trying to hire a crook to invoke the protection of a high-up policeman uncle.

She was directed into ever darker and less public alleys until finally in a gully as dark as ink an old woman with eyes which stared so piercingly that Huma

---

2. Boat. The lake referred to is Dal Lake in the city of Srinagar.  3. Narrow alleys.

instantly understood she was blind motioned her through a doorway from which darkness seemed to be pouring like smoke. Clenching her fists, angrily ordering her heart to behave normally, Huma followed the old woman into the gloom-wrapped house.

The faintest conceivable rivulet of candlelight trickled through the darkness; following this unreliable yellow thread (because she could no longer see the old lady), Huma received a sudden sharp blow to the shins and cried out involuntarily, after which she at once bit her lip, angry at having revealed her mounting terror to whoever or whatever waited before her, shrouded in blackness.

She had, in fact, collided with a low table on which a single candle burned and beyond which a mountainous figure could be made out, sitting cross-legged on the floor. "Sit, sit," said a man's calm, deep voice, and her legs, needing no more flowery invitation, buckled beneath her at the terse command. Clutching her left hand in her right, she forced her voice to respond evenly:

"And you, sir, will be the thief I have been requesting?"

Shifting its weight very slightly, the shadow-mountain informed Huma that all criminal activity originating in this zone was well organised and also centrally controlled, so that all requests for what might be termed freelance work had to be channelled through this room.

He demanded comprehensive details of the crime to be committed, including a precise inventory of items to be acquired, also a clear statement of all financial inducements being offered with no gratuities excluded, plus, for filing purposes only, a summary of the motives for the application.

At this, Huma, as though remembering something, stiffened both in body and resolve and replied loudly that her motives were entirely a matter for herself; that she would discuss details with no one but the thief himself; but that the rewards she proposed could only be described as "lavish."

"All I am willing to disclose to you, sir, since it appears that I am on the premises of some sort of employment agency, is that in return for such lavish rewards I must have the most desperate criminal at your disposal, a man for whom life holds no terrors, not even the fear of God.

"The worst of fellows, I tell you—nothing less will do!"

At this a paraffin storm-lantern was lighted, and Huma saw facing her a grey-haired giant down whose left cheek ran the most sinister of scars, a cicatrice in the shape of the letter *sín* in the Nastaliq script.[4] She was gripped by the insupportably nostalgic notion that the bogeyman of her childhood nursery had risen up to confront her, because her ayah had always forestalled any incipient acts of disobedience by threatening Huma and Atta: "You don't watch out and I'll send that one to steal you away—that Sheikh Sín, the Thief of Thieves!"

Here, grey-haired but unquestionably scarred, was the notorious criminal himself—and was she out of her mind, were her ears playing tricks, or had he truly just announced that, given the stated circumstances, he himself was the only man for the job?

---

4. The letter *s* in a cursive Persian script.

Struggling hard against the newborn goblins of nostalgia, Huma warned the fearsome volunteer that only a matter of extreme urgency and peril would have brought her unescorted into these ferocious streets.

"Because we can afford no last-minute backings-out," she continued, "I am determined to tell you everything, keeping back no secrets whatsoever. If, after hearing me out, you are still prepared to proceed, then we shall do everything in our power to assist you, and to make you rich."

The old thief shrugged, nodded, spat. Huma began her story.

Six days ago, everything in the household of her father, the wealthy moneylender Hashim, had been as it always was. At breakfast her mother had spooned khichri[5] lovingly on to the moneylender's plate; the conversation had been filled with those expressions of courtesy and solicitude on which the family prided itself.

Hashim was fond of pointing out that while he was not a godly man he set great store by "living honourably in the world." In that spacious lakeside residence, all outsiders were greeted with the same formality and respect, even those unfortunates who came to negotiate for small fragments of Hashim's large fortune, and of whom he naturally asked an interest rate of over seventy per cent, partly, as he told his khichri-spooning wife, "to teach these people the value of money; let them only learn that, and they will be cured of this fever of borrowing borrowing all the time—so you see that if my plans succeed, I shall put myself out of business!"

In their children, Atta and Huma, the moneylender and his wife had successfully sought to inculcate the virtues of thrift, plain dealing and a healthy independence of spirit. On this, too, Hashim was fond of congratulating himself.

Breakfast ended; the family members wished one another a fulfilling day. Within a few hours, however, the glassy contentment of that household, of that life of porcelain delicacy and alabaster sensibilities, was to be shattered beyond all hope of repair.

The moneylender summoned his personal shikara and was on the point of stepping into it when, attracted by a glint of silver, he noticed a small vial floating between the boat and his private quay. On an impulse, he scooped it out of the glutinous water.

It was a cylinder of tinted glass cased in exquisitely wrought silver, and Hashim saw within its walls a silver pendant bearing a single strand of human hair.

Closing his fist around this unique discovery, he muttered to the boatman that he'd changed his plans, and hurried to his sanctum, where, behind closed doors, he feasted his eyes on his find.

There can be no doubt that Hashim the moneylender knew from the first that he was in possession of the famous relic of the Prophet Muhammad, that revered hair whose theft from its shrine at Hazratbal mosque the previous morning had created an unprecedented hue and cry in the valley.

The thieves—no doubt alarmed by the pandemonium, by the procession through the streets of endless ululating crocodiles of lamentation, by the riots,

---

5. Thick broth prepared with rice and lentils.

the political ramifications and by the massive police search which was commanded and carried out by men whose entire careers now hung upon the finding of this lost hair—had evidently panicked and hurled the vial into the gelatine bosom of the lake.

Having found it by a stroke of great good fortune, Hashim's duty as a citizen was clear: the hair must be restored to its shrine, and the state to equanimity and peace.

But the moneylender had a different notion.

All around him in his study was the evidence of his collector's mania. There were enormous glass cases full of impaled butterflies from Gulmarg, three dozen scale models in various metals of the legendary cannon Zamzama, innumerable swords, a Naga[6] spear, ninety-four terracotta camels of the sort sold on railway station platforms, many samovars, and a whole zoology of tiny sandalwood animals, which had originally been carved to serve as children's bathtime toys.

"And after all," Hashim told himself, "the Prophet would have disapproved mightily of this relic-worship. He abhorred the idea of being deified! So, by keeping this hair from its distracted devotees, I perform—do I not?—a finer service than I would by returning it! Naturally, I don't want it for its religious value ... I'm a man of the world, of this world. I see it purely as a secular object of great rarity and blinding beauty. In short, it's the silver vial I desire, more than the hair.

35 "They say there are American millionaires who purchase stolen art masterpieces and hide them away—they would know how I feel. I must, must have it!"

Every collector must share his treasures with one other human being, and Hashim summoned—and told—his only son Atta, who was deeply perturbed but, having been sworn to secrecy, only spilled the beans when the troubles became too terrible to bear.

The youth excused himself and left his father alone in the crowded solitude of his collections. Hashim was sitting erect in a hard, straight-backed chair, gazing intently at the beautiful vial.

It was well known that the moneylender never ate lunch, so it was not until evening that a servant entered the sanctum to summon his master to the dining-table. He found Hashim as Atta had left him. The same, and not the same—for now the moneylender looked swollen, distended. His eyes bulged even more than they always had, they were red-rimmed, and his knuckles were white.

He seemed to be on the point of bursting! As though, under the influence of the misappropriated relic, he had filled up with some spectral fluid which might at any moment ooze uncontrollably from his every bodily opening.

40 He had to be helped to the table, and then the explosion did indeed take place.

Seemingly careless of the effect of his words on the carefully constructed and fragile constitution of the family's life, Hashim began to gush, to spume long

---

6. Hills in eastern India and northern Burma (now Myanmar); *Zamzama:* from the battle at Zama, North Africa, where Scipio Africanus and Roman troops defeated Hannibal in 202 B.C.E.

streams of awful truths. In horrified silence, his children heard their father turn upon his wife, and reveal to her that for many years their marriage had been the worst of his afflictions. "An end to politeness!" he thundered. "An end to hypocrisy!"

Next, and in the same spirit, he revealed to his family the existence of a mistress; he informed them also of his regular visits to paid women. He told his wife that, far from being the principal beneficiary of his will, she would receive no more than the eighth portion which was her due under Islamic law. Then he turned upon his children, screaming at Atta for his lack of academic ability—"A dope! I have been cursed with a dope!"—and accusing his daughter of lasciviousness, because she went around the city barefaced, which was unseemly for any good Muslim girl to do. She should, he commanded, enter purdah forthwith.

Hashim left the table without having eaten and fell into the deep sleep of a man who has got many things off his chest, leaving his children stunned, in tears, and the dinner going cold on the sideboard under the gaze of an anticipatory bearer.

At five o'clock the next morning the moneylender forced his family to rise, wash and say their prayers. From then on, he began to pray five times daily for the first time in his life, and his wife and children were obliged to do likewise.

Before breakfast, Huma saw the servants, under her father's direction, constructing a great heap of books in the garden and setting fire to it. The only volume left untouched was the Qur'an,[7] which Hashim wrapped in a silken cloth and placed on a table in the hall. He ordered each member of his family to read passages from this book for at least two hours per day. Visits to the cinema were forbidden. And if Atta invited male friends to the house, Huma was to retire to her room.

By now, the family had entered a state of shock and dismay; but there was worse to come.

That afternoon, a trembling debtor arrived at the house to confess his inability to pay the latest instalment of interest owed, and made the mistake of reminding Hashim, in somewhat blustering fashion, of the Qur'an's strictures against usury. The moneylender flew into a rage and attacked the fellow with one of his large collection of bullwhips.

By mischance, later the same day a second defaulter came to plead for time, and was seen fleeing Hashim's study with a great gash in his arm, because Huma's father had called him a thief of other men's money and had tried to cut off the wretch's right hand with one of the thirty-eight kukri knives[8] hanging on the study walls.

These breaches of the family's unwritten laws of decorum alarmed Atta and Huma, and when, that evening, their mother attempted to calm Hashim down, he struck her on the face with an open hand. Atta leapt to his mother's defence and he, too, was sent flying.

---

7. The Koran: the book of revelations made to Muhammad by Allah.
8. Curved knives, broader at the point than at the handle; used by the Gurkhas of India.

50 "From now on," Hashim bellowed, "there's going to be some discipline around here!"

The moneylender's wife began a fit of hysterics which continued throughout that night and the following day, and which so provoked her husband that he threatened her with divorce, at which she fled to her room, locked the door and subsided into a raga of sniffling. Huma now lost her composure, challenged her father openly, and announced (with that same independence of spirit which he had encouraged in her) that she would wear no cloth over her face; apart from anything else, it was bad for the eyes.

On hearing this, her father disowned her on the spot and gave her one week in which to pack her bags and go.

By the fourth day, the fear in the air of the house had become so thick that it was difficult to walk around. Atta told his shock-numbed sister: "We are descending to gutter-level—but I know what must be done."

That afternoon, Hashim left home accompanied by two hired thugs to extract the unpaid dues from his two insolvent clients. Atta went immediately to his father's study. Being the son and heir, he possessed his own key to the moneylender's safe. This he now used, and removing the little vial from its hiding-place, he slipped it into his trouser pocket and re-locked the safe door.

55 Now he told Huma the secret of what his father had fished out of Lake Dal, and exclaimed: "Maybe I'm crazy—maybe the awful things that are happening have made me cracked—but I am convinced there will be no peace in our house until this hair is out of it."

His sister at once agreed that the hair must be returned, and Atta set off in a hired shikara to Hazratbal mosque. Only when the boat had delivered him into the throng of the distraught faithful which was swirling around the desecrated shrine did Atta discover that the relic was no longer in his pocket. There was only a hole, which his mother, usually so attentive to household matters, must have overlooked under the stress of recent events.

Atta's initial surge of chagrin was quickly replaced by a feeling of profound relief.

"Suppose," he imagined, "that I had already announced to the mullahs that the hair was on my person! They would never have believed me now—and this mob would have lynched me! At any rate, it has gone, and that's a load off my mind." Feeling more contented than he had for days, the young man returned home.

Here he found his sister bruised and weeping in the hall; upstairs, in her bedroom, his mother wailed like a brand-new widow. He begged Huma to tell him what had happened, and when she replied that their father, returning from his brutal business trip, had once again noticed a glint of silver between boat and quay, had once again scooped up the errant relic, and was consequently in a rage to end all rages, having beaten the truth out of her—then Atta buried his face in his hands and sobbed out his opinion, which was that the hair was persecuting them, and had come back to finish the job.

60 It was Huma's turn to think of a way out of their troubles.

While her arms turned black and blue and great stains spread across her forehead, she hugged her brother and whispered to him that she was determined to get rid of the hair *at all costs*—she repeated this last phrase several times.

"The hair," she then declared, "was stolen from the mosque; so it can be stolen from this house. But it must be a genuine robbery, carried out by a bona-fide thief, not by one of us who are under the hair's thrall—by a thief so desperate that he fears neither capture nor curses."

Unfortunately, she added, the theft would be ten times harder to pull off now that their father, knowing that there had already been one attempt on the relic, was certainly on his guard.

"Can you do it?"

Huma, in a room lit by candle and storm-lantern, ended her account with one further question: "What assurances can you give that the job holds no terrors for you still?"

The criminal, spitting, stated that he was not in the habit of providing references, as a cook might, or a gardener, but he was not alarmed so easily, certainly not by any children's djinni[9] of a curse. Huma had to be content with this boast, and proceeded to describe the details of the proposed burglary.

"Since my brother's failure to return the hair to the mosque, my father has taken to sleeping with his precious treasure under his pillow. However, he sleeps alone, and very energetically; only enter his room without waking him, and he will certainly have tossed and turned quite enough to make the theft a simple matter. When you have the vial, come to my room," and here she handed Sheikh Sín a plan of her home, "and I will hand over all the jewellery owned by my mother and myself. You will find . . . it is worth . . . that is, you will be able to get a fortune for it . . ."

It was evident that her self-control was weakening and that she was on the point of physical collapse.

"Tonight," she burst out finally. "You must come tonight!"

No sooner had she left the room than the old criminal's body was convulsed by a fit of coughing: he spat blood into an old vanaspati can.[1] The great Sheikh, the "Thief of Thieves," had become a sick man, and every day the time drew nearer when some young pretender to his power would stick a dagger in his stomach. A lifelong addiction to gambling had left him almost as poor as he had been when, decades ago, he had started out in this line of work as a mere pickpocket's apprentice; so in the extraordinary commission he had accepted from the moneylender's daughter he saw his opportunity of amassing enough wealth at a stroke to leave the valley for ever, and acquire the luxury of a respectable death which would leave his stomach intact.

As for the Prophet's hair, well, neither he nor his blind wife had ever had much to say for prophets—that was one thing they had in common with the moneylender's thunderstruck clan.

It would not do, however, to reveal the nature of this, his last crime, to his four sons. To his consternation, they had all grown up to be hopelessly devout

---

9. In Muslim demonology, a spirit (genie) with supernatural powers.
1. Can for vegetable fat used as butter in India.

men, who even spoke of making the pilgrimage to Mecca some day. "Absurd!" their father would laugh at them. "Just tell me how you will go?" For, with a parent's absolutist love, he had made sure they were all provided with a life-long source of high income by crippling them at birth, so that, as they dragged themselves around the city, they earned excellent money in the begging business.

The children, then, could look after themselves.

He and his wife would be off soon with the jewel-boxes of the moneylender's women. It was a timely chance indeed that had brought the beautiful bruised girl into his corner of the town.

75 That night, the large house on the shore of the lake lay blindly waiting, with silence lapping at its walls. A burglar's night: clouds in the sky and mists on the winter water. Hashim the moneylender was asleep, the only member of his family to whom sleep had come that night. In another room, his son Atta lay deep in the coils of his coma with a blood-clot forming on his brain, watched over by a mother who had let down her long greying hair to show her grief, a mother who placed warm compresses on his head with gestures redolent of impotence. In a third bedroom Huma waited, fully dressed, amidst the jewel-heavy caskets of her desperation.

At last a bulbul sang softly from the garden below her window and, creeping downstairs, she opened a door to the bird, on whose face there was a scar in the shape of the Nastaliq letter *sín*.

Noiselessly, the bird flew up the stairs behind her. At the head of the staircase they parted, moving in opposite directions along the corridor of their conspiracy without a glance at one another.

Entering the moneylender's room with professional ease, the burglar, Sín, discovered that Huma's predictions had been wholly accurate. Hashim lay sprawled diagonally across his bed, the pillow untenanted by his head, the prize easily accessible. Step by padded step, Sín moved towards the goal.

It was at this point that, in the bedroom next door, young Atta sat bolt upright in his bed, giving his mother a great fright, and without any warning—prompted by goodness knows what pressure of the blood-clot upon his brain—began screaming at the top of his voice:

80 *"Thief! Thief! Thief!"*

It seems probable that his poor mind had been dwelling, in these last moments, upon his own father; but it is impossible to be certain, because having uttered these three emphatic words the young man fell back upon his pillow and died.

At once his mother set up a screeching and a wailing and a keening and a howling so earsplittingly intense that they completed the work which Atta's cry had begun—that is, her laments penetrated the walls of her husband's bedroom and brought Hashim wide awake.

Sheikh Sín was just deciding whether to dive beneath the bed or brain the moneylender good and proper when Hashim grabbed the tiger-striped swordstick which always stood propped up in a corner beside his bed, and rushed from the room without so much as noticing the burglar who stood on the opposite side of the bed in the darkness. Sín stooped quickly and removed the vial containing the Prophet's hair from its hiding-place.

Meanwhile Hashim had erupted into the corridor, having unsheathed the sword inside his cane. In his right hand he held the weapon and was waving it about dementedly. His left hand was shaking the stick. A shadow came rushing towards him through the midnight darkness of the passageway and, in his somnolent anger, the moneylender thrust his sword fatally through its heart. Turning up the light, he found that he had murdered his daughter, and under the dire influence of this accident he was so overwhelmed by remorse that he turned the sword upon himself, fell upon it and so extinguished his life. His wife, the sole surviving member of the family, was driven mad by the general carnage and had to be committed to an asylum for the insane by her brother, the city's Deputy Commissioner of Police.

Sheikh Sín had quickly understood that the plan had gone awry.

Abandoning the dream of the jewel-boxes when he was but a few yards from its fulfilment, he climbed out of Hashim's window and made his escape during the appalling events described above. Reaching home before dawn, he woke his wife and confessed his failure. It would be necessary, he whispered, for him to vanish for a while. Her blind eyes never opened until he had gone.

The noise in the Hashim household had roused their servants and even managed to awaken the night-watchman, who had been fast asleep as usual on his charpoy by the street-gate. They alerted the police, and the Deputy Commissioner himself was informed. When he heard of Huma's death, the mournful officer opened and read the sealed letter which his niece had given him, and instantly led a large detachment of armed men into the light-repellent gullies of the most wretched and disreputable part of the city.

The tongue of a malicious cat-burglar named Huma's fellow-conspirator; the finger of an ambitious bank-robber pointed at the house in which he lay concealed; and although Sín managed to crawl through a hatch in the attic and attempt a roof-top escape, a bullet from the Deputy Commissioner's own rifle penetrated his stomach and brought him crashing messily to the ground at the feet of Huma's enraged uncle.

From the dead thief's pocket rolled a vial of tinted glass, cased in filigree silver.

The recovery of the Prophet's hair was announced at once on All-India Radio. One month later, the valley's holiest men assembled at the Hazratbal mosque and formally authenticated the relic. It sits to this day in a closely guarded vault by the shores of the loveliest of lakes in the heart of the valley which was once closer than any other place on earth to Paradise.

But before our story can properly be concluded, it is necessary to record that when the four sons of the dead Sheikh awoke on the morning of his death, having unwittingly spent a few minutes under the same roof as the famous hair, they found that a miracle had occurred, that they were all sound of limb and strong of wind, as whole as they might have been if their father had not thought to smash their legs in the first hours of their lives. They were, all four of them, very properly furious, because the miracle had reduced their earning powers by 75 per cent, at the most conservative estimate; so they were ruined men.

Only the Sheikh's widow had some reason for feeling grateful, because although her husband was dead she had regained her sight, so that it was possible for her to spend her last days gazing once more upon the beauties of the valley of Kashmir.

1995

**CAROL SHIELDS**

## *Dressing Down*

You might say that my grandfather carried the idea of "dressing down" to new heights.

He was, of course, a social activist of national reputation and, as well, the first serious nudist in southern Ontario, the founder of Club Soleil, which is still in existence, still thriving, on the shores of Lake Simcoe, just north of Toronto. You'll recognize his name at once if you're up on your twentieth-century history.

His biography came out too late—he had been dead for some years by then—for him to comment on or defend his own beliefs as a naturist, not that he would have done so, not that he would have entertained for two minutes the rude intervention of a press interview. *But how do you carry your wallet, sir? What do you do, sir, about, um, the male body's sudden embarrassments?*

Please, he would have said to the journalists from the *Toronto Star* or the *Globe* or the *Telegram* or whatever, please! The exposure of the skin to the sun and air is a private matter, and your interest in the project, gentlemen, ladies, is—forgive me—entirely prurient.

5   These same questions, I confess, also occurred to me as a young boy. How had my grandfather become a nudist in the first place and what did it mean to him to shuck off his clothes, all his clothes, for one month of the year? Was it so he could feel the gaze of a hot July afternoon spreading across the square lean acreage of his chest, and, in softer shadows, onto those other less talked about areas? And, another question, how did he reconcile his nudist yearnings with his Wesleyan calling, with his eleven-months-a-year job as YMCA director for eastern Canada?

If you drive the highway to Lake Simcoe today, you'll be struck by the variety of signs greeting you left and right between the groves of pine and birch: one by one they gesture toward green-leafed darkness, offering winding trails, gravel roads, pointing the way to countless small hidden lakes, beaches, and stretches of inspirational shore. "Awake-Again Bible Conference." "Bide-a-Wee Housekeeping Cottages, Reasonable Rates." "The Merit Institute. Absolutely Private." "Fish 'n' Fun with Mike and Hank." "STOP AND SAY HELLO—TED AND TINA." "ADX Yoga and More." And, finally, "Club Soleil."

Club Soleil has never, not since its founding in 1926, had more than the most discreet of highway signs, hand-painted, black on white, a single board nailed to the trunk of a long-lived elm, with roughly fashioned arrow tip pointing eastward toward a trail, one that discouraged (yet allowed) wheeled traffic.

Campers at Club Soleil slept in tents in the early years. Meals, vegetarian, were taken beneath the shade of an immense canvas structure known as The Meeting Place. Why vegetarian? Why Carrot Soufflé on Monday, Parsnip Purée on Tuesday, Swiss Chard Pie on Wednesday, and so on and so on? My grandfather was a meat eater for the rest of the year, but in July he lived on leaves, roots, seeds, the only nourishment going at Club Soleil.

The prohibition against the eating of flesh might seem to some visitors a contradiction when human flesh was everywhere displayed on the Club Soleil lawns and on the narrow strip of beach running around a promontory called The Point. The living hams and haunches of middle-aged men made their way between mixed flower and vegetable beds, another of my grandfather's innovations. And so did the necks, shoulders, throats, and bellies of their wives. White jellied breast flesh jiggled in the Ontario sunlight, tested it, defied it. Buttocks. Thighs. Calves. Fragile ankle bones belonging to city lawyers, physicians, charity organizers, household matriarchs. Patrician feet stepped carefully across the beach pebbles and drummed up and down on the grass where a volleyball court had been set up for the young people.

My grandmother had difficulty with all this. It was only after she and my grandfather were married that he told her how he had been taken by friends soon after finishing university to a naturist beach on the Atlantic coast of France. He had greeted the new experience as a door swinging wide open in his existence. Some men are brought to life by the sexual spasm; my grandfather tasted ecstasy for the first time as he lowered his trousers on the slope of a French sand dune, then, more cautiously, dropping his underwear as well, then stepping free. Dry heat and sunlight penetrated his dark manly parts, which since birth had been confined. A hundred other bathers looked on, or rather, they *didn't* look on, that was the wonder of it, that they never so much as glanced in his direction.

He had not expected in his life to feel a breeze pass over his nether regions— this is the untethering miracle he tried to explain to my grandmother, and later to her son, my father. The pleasure was intense and yet subtle. It resonated across the width of his skin, the entire human envelope electrified—here was paradise. And it was in accord with nature's design, as he saw it. It was true; he was able to see nothing perverse about his reaction. How could it be so when he became at that pants-dropping moment larger, stronger, nobler, a man charged with a new range of moral duty? The Protestant God of shame had nodded in response, nodded and smiled and drifted away, and my grandfather, so unexpectedly twitched into life, announced himself an instant convert. He walked straight into the sea, then, where the cold salt water flowed around every mound and recess of his body and completed the arc of liberation.

But how was he to bring the same set of circumstances and appreciations to rigid Ontario? And how, a year later, to explain his passion to his young bride, my gently brought up grandmother?

He was a man, however, who took for granted his right to make his dreams come true. Ever methodical in his dealings, he sent away to the International Naturism Institute in Switzerland for information, then began to look for a piece of well-sheltered lake property which he was able to purchase with part of his inheritance. Next he carefully sounded out a few of his more worldly friends. Might they be interested? Had they discovered for themselves the health-giving benefits of naturism, psychological as well as physical, the mind and body unfettered and fused? Did they know of others who might be interested in the venture? Discretion would rule the day, of course. Privacy, sanctuary, a quiet bond between comrades, an agreement to give one's self up to the pleasures that God Himself had provided.

Yes, my grandmother said, but this is not the sort of thing that remains secret, no matter how circumspect one is.

15     She was right. Word got around. It was inevitable. But her husband's passion for health and sun, his annual indulgence, only enhanced his dignity. It seemed he could do no wrong in those days. The imagined presence of this young, muscular, unclothed body, released to nature, to prelapsarian abandonment, and its contrast to the suited, shirted, necktied manliness he presented to the world as he went about lecturing on social justice or presiding over his YMCA duties—this misalignment only gave him a beguiling, eccentric edge, arousing even in the straitlaced a shrugging admiration and making of him an exceptional being, free-minded, liberal, a man of virility, who also happened to be clever and compelling—especially to women. He became, in the puritanical society he inhabited, rather famous.

My grandmother's disinclination for nudity would not have surprised those who knew her well. Her interest was in covering up, not stripping down. The same week she married my grandfather she'd had curtains and heavy draperies made for the windows of the house they bought on Macklin Avenue. By the following summer slipcovers dressed the wicker porch furniture. Scarves in broiderie anglaise[1] adorned every bureau. Pillows in my grandparents' house were fitted with undercovers as well as overcovers, and she herself sewed a sort of skirt in flowered chintz, which was tied prettily with bias tape around he wringer washing machine when it was not in use. Lace doilies sat on the arms and back of every chair. Woolen throws were flung across the various sofas. Rugs lay scattered everywhere upon the thick carpets. Fullness, plumpness, doubleness. Hers was a house where one could imagine the possibility of suffocation.

Her own clothing, needless to say, comprised layers of underclothes, foundation garments, garters and stockings, brassieres, camisoles, slips, blouses, cardigans, lined skirts, aprons, and even good aprons worn over the everyday aprons. Her mind drifted toward texture, fabric, protection, and warmth, as though she could never burrow deeply enough into the folds of herself.

Which was why she had so much difficulty taking part in the annual July rites at Lake Simcoe. Naturism was not her nature. Nudity was the cross she bore.

At first she tried to make bargains with her husband. "I'll go," she told him, "but don't expect me to go around with *my* clothes off."

20     He reasoned with her gently, reminding her that nudity was an activity that, once established, did not allow abstentions. Nudity implied community. The effort to throw off cultural ignorance was so difficult, he explained, that reinforcement was ever needed. A single clothed person creates a rebuke to the unclothed. One person walking across the Club Soleil lawn in a summer dress and sandals and underpants is enough to unsettle others in the matter of the choice they had taken.

---

1. Decorative fabric popular in the nineteenth century.

But going without clothes was unhygienic, she argued.

No, he said, not at all. (He had read his material from the International Naturalism Institute closely.) Woven cloth habors mites, molds, dust, germs. Whereas nothing is easier to keep clean than human skin, which is, in fact, self-cleaning.

Infection, my grandmother pointed out. From others.

Not a chance, he argued. Not when every camper is issued a clean towel at the beginning of the day, and this towel is used on the various benches and hammocks at Club Soleil, and even carried into the dining hall and spread on the chair before the diner sits down.

"It's different for women," she protested, gesturing awkwardly, miserably. "Women have special problems."

My grandfather explained that when women campers were "having their time," they had only to wear a short pleated skirt, rather like a tennis skirt. No one thought a thing of it, six days, seven days, nature's timetable. There was, of course, no reason to cover the breasts or shoulders.

"I can't imagine Mrs. Archie Hammond going around naked, not with her sags and bags." My grandmother said this with uncharacteristic bitterness.

"Kate and Archie have both signed up."

"Naked? Those two?"

"Of course, naked. Though naked, my love, is not really a word that naturists use."

"Yes, you've told me. A hundred times. But naked is naked."

"Semantics." (My grandfather, it must be remembered, lived in the day when to snort out the word *semantics* was enough to win any quarrel.)

"You do know what people will say, don't you?"

"Of course I know. They'll say that visitors to Camp Soleil are licentious. That we are seekers of sexual pleasure, and that the removal of the artificial barrier of clothing will only inflame our lust. But these people will be wrong."

"I'm not so sure of that," she said. "I know Archie Hammond. I've seen how he looks at women, even with their clothes on."

"Our bodies are God's gifts. There are those who believe that our bodies are holy temples."

"Then why," she asked cannily, "don't you ever see pictures of Jesus without *his* clothes on? He's always got that big brown robe wrapped around him. Even on the cross he had a little piece of cloth—"

"This discussion is going nowhere."

Indeed this discussion would have gone nowhere. It would have vanished into historical silence, except that my grandfather confided its essence to his adult son—my own father—years later, where it was received, as such parental offerings are, with huge embarrassment and rejection. How could such a private argument have taken place between one's own mother and father? Why this mention of the unmentionables between them, infidelities, monthlies—was it really necessary?

"Don't you see," my grandmother, not yet thirty years old, said to her husband, "how humiliating this is for me? A grown-up woman. Playing Adam and Eve at the beach."

He was touched by the Adam and Eve reference. It brought a smile to his lips, threw him off course. This was not what she intended.

"Do it for me," he pleaded. He had a slow, rich, persuasive way of speaking. "Please just try it for me."

"Would you love me less if I refused?"

"No," he replied. But he had let slip a small pause before he spoke, and this was registered on my grandmother's consciousness.

"It's wrong, you know it's wrong. It fans those instincts of ours that belong to, well..."

"To what? Say it."

"To barnyard animals."

"Ah!"

"I can't help it. That's what I think."

"We are animals, my precious love."

"You know what I mean."

"Why don't we make a bargain, then?"

She was suspicious of bargains. She came from a wealthy Ontario family (cheese, walnuts, whiskey) where bad bargains had been made between brother and sister, father and son. "What kind of bargain?" she asked.

"You're crying."

"I have to know. I need to know."

"I propose that during the month of July we abstain."

"Abstain?"

"From sexual intercourse."

"But"—she must have paused at this point, hating this term *sexual intercourse*, and yet shocked that her husband would relinquish so easily their greatest personal pleasure—"why?"

"To prove to you, conclusively, that going unclothed among those we trust has nothing to do with the desires of the flesh."

"I see."

My grandmother was a passionate woman, but probably shy about the verbal expression of passion—and not sure how to show her shocked disappointment in the proposed accommodation. "I don't know what to think," she said, tears lining her lashes, knowing she had somehow been trapped in her own objections.

And so she was now faced with a dilemma. Her husband had countered each of her arguments about Club Soleil, and had even offered the ultimate sacrifice, an abstention from intimate relations during the unclothed month of July. She was cornered. She must respond, somehow, and of course she was at an age when people believe they will become more and not less than they are.

"All right," she said to the proposed bargain. "All right."

Did she say it crossly or tenderly? With a sense of defeat or victory? The particular tone of the story has not come down to me.

And so the long succession of summers began, the humiliation of July first when my grandmother's favorite flowered dresses came off, her girdle, her hose, her underpants. There is a certain sharp irony to be felt when cast in a role one can't quite occupy, and for my grandmother a jolt of anger must surely have accompanied her acquiescence, the beginning of a longer anger. She found a way to walk on the beach with reasonable dignity, but never with ease, and she learned to stand nodding and chatting with Kate Hammond and the other women, blocking out the sight of their bared, softening flesh, discussing the weather, the children, the latest movies and books. She never, apparently, became accustomed to her exposed body with its pale protrusions, its slopes and meadows and damp cavities. Her fair face lightly perspired in the fresh breeze. Always she carried herself with an air of dolefulness, her eyes wary, her hands crossed stiffly over the region of her pubis. Stiff with love and suffering and absence.

This went on for years. My grandparents and the other original members grew older. Some of them retired and moved to Florida, but a new and younger set of naturists joined the ranks. Archie Hammond died of a heart attack, though Kate Hammond remained a loyal summer camper, moving from a tent into one of the newer cabins. The tennis courts were upgraded. A vegetarian chef was brought from Banff.[2]

Then, suddenly one summer, my grandmother refused to take part. The cause of her refusal was me, her ten-year-old grandson, who was to be taken to Club Soleil for the first time. It was one thing, she felt, to take off her clothes in front of her husband and friends; she had hardened herself to the shame of it. But she would not become a naked grandmother, she would not allow herself to surrender to this ultimate indignity. This was asking too much.

She remained in Toronto that summer, and the rupture between herself and my grandfather was never completely mended.

It might be wondered why I was not introduced to Club Soleil until I was ten years old. I loved my grandparents, and had often wondered where they disappeared to each summer. I sensed some reticence, distaste even, on my father's part when it came to discussing the matter. *Soleil* was a French word, he explained carefully, meaning sunshine. Our own vacations—my mother, father, and I, their only child—were taken at Muskoka Lodge, where the wearing of clothes was unquestioned, and indeed may have been part of the reason for going there. It was a fashionable place in those days, and a full wardrobe of "resort apparel" was de rigueur. I remember that my mother possessed a pale peach dress with a little "bolero" that floated behind her as she stood leaning on the porch rail during the evening cocktail hour. My father, of course, ended each day by exchanging his golf clothes for a white dinner jacket.

Then one year they decided to go to Europe instead, and someone suggested that I should stay behind and join my grandparents at Club Soleil. The idea of perpetual *soleil* was appealing, especially since our own Muskoka Lodge summers were often cloudy or rain-soaked.

At this point the real nature of the enterprise was explained to me, and I remember my father's words as he struggled to fill me in. "It is a place," he said, "where people go about in their birthday suits."

I knew what birthday suits meant. It was one of the jokes of the schoolyard. Birthday suits meant buck-naked, stark-naked. Starkers.

"You mean with nothing on?" I was deeply shocked, though I later wondered if part of my shock was rehearsed and just slightly augmented for effect.

My father coughed slightly. "It's believed, you see, to be good for the health. Vitamin D, the sunshine vitamin."

"Not even their swimming suits?" This came out in a theatrical squeal. It seemed important to reach a full understanding at once, to get it over with.

---

2. Mountain-resort town in Alberta, Canada.

"I know it's difficult to imagine." He patted me on the shoulder then, a rare gesture from a man who lacked any real sense of physical warmth.

Oddly, the thought of my grandmother's naked body lay well within my powers of imagination. I had inspected the plump nylon-encased feet and legs of my mother, so rosy, sleek, and unscented, and I'd also seen the statues in the park and at the art gallery, the smooth marble parts of women, unblemished and still and lacking human orifices. What shocked me far more was thinking of my unclothed grandfather, a man who had always seemed to me *more* clothed than other men. His dark business suits were thicker of fabric and more closely woven. And there were his tight collars, black hose, serious oxfords, and the silk scarf he tucked in the neck of his woolen overcoat so that not an inch of flesh, except for his hands and face, was available for scrutiny. But this was my winter grandfather, the only one I had ever seen. Could he possibly have, tucked between his trousered legs, what my father had, what I had?

Yes, it turned out that he did, but instead of hiding these parts behind a bath towel as I was taught to do at home, he strolled the grounds of Club Soleil, an elegant man at home in his own aging, pickled-in-brine skin, a revered ascetic and—it was clear—lord of his own domain, majestic in his entitlement, patting the heads of children and stopping to chat with Kate Hammond at the edge of the archery range. "You must not be afraid," he said to me kindly on the day of my arrival, "to follow the rituals we observe in our summer community."

To be encouraged in such sanctified naughtiness was beyond any dream a ten-year-old boy might have. I learned. I learned fast, but at the same time I understood that the world was subtly spoiled. People with their limbs and creases and folds were more alike than I thought. Skin tones, hairy patches—that was all they had. Take off your clothes and you were left with your dull suit of invisibility.

What I witnessed led me into a distress I couldn't account for or explain, but which involved a feverish disowning of my own naked body and a frantic plummeting into willed blindness. I was launched into the long business of shame, accumulating the mingled secrets of disgust and longing, that eventually formed a kind of rattling carapace that restricted natural movement and ease.

"I'm only sorry," my grandfather said often that summer, "that your grandmother is not here to see how brown and strong you've grown."

When my grandfather died he was buried in a plain pine coffin, just as the instructions in his will outlined.

And his tall and by now greatly withered body was laid out on the bare floor of the coffin without a stitch to conceal his nakedness and not even a blanket or sheet for comfort's sake. This was not his request, but my grandmother's, grimly decreed when the family gathered to discuss the "arrangements." She insisted it would have been what he wanted, and since the coffin was to be closed, what difference did it make. She also insisted that Mrs. Kate Hammond be barred from the funeral.

"It is impossible to bar anyone from a public funeral," my father insisted.

"Then she is not to be invited to stay for coffee afterward," my grandmother said. "She will probably come anyway, but she is not to be explicitly invited." She said this sternly, punitively it seemed to her family, in an attempt to outflank her dead husband, but by then all of us had learned to shrink from the anger that deformed her last years.

Her own death, pneumonia, occurred a mere eighteen months after my grandfather's. She too had specified in her will a plain pine box, with the additional written request that her body be put to rest unclothed and that the coffin be left open at the funeral.

It was as though she had hungered for this lewd indiscretion, as though some large smoldering ugliness had offered itself to her in her last days and she had been unable to resist. That's what I thought at the time.

Now I think of that final gesture differently. (Needless to say, the family did *not* honor her final request, the pine coffin, yes, and yes to the naked body, but the lid was firmly closed.) It seems to me now that an offering was made on her part, heartbreaking in its impropriety and wish for amends. This desire perhaps had acquired a grotesque life of its own, with a vividness that could find no form of expression in the scanable universe. "The unclothed body," she might have said, pouring into that vessel of a word a metaphorical cleansing, "is all we're allowed to take away with us."

The rest must have fallen away in the same moment she wrote down the words of her will: the draperies, the coverings, the fringe and feathers, the wrappings, the linings, the stuffings and stitching. Good-bye, she must have said to what couldn't be helped. Good-bye to the circular life of shame and its infinite regress.

She must have thought she could get everything back by a single act of acquiescence. In the next world, just a breath away, the two of them would greet each other rapturously. Their revealed limbs would flash among the bright vegetation, at home in the green-clothed world, and embracing each other without restraint.

She would have forgotten that nature's substance is gnarled and knotted in its grain, so that no absolutely straight thing can come of it. They should have understood that all along, those two. It might have become one of their perishable secrets, part of the bliss they would one day gladly surrender.

1999

# Biographical Sketches
# Fiction Writers

## SHERMAN ALEXIE
(b. 1966)

Born on an Indian reservation near Spokane, Washington, Sherman Alexie attended high school in nearby Reardan, where he was the only native American other than the school mascot. Shortly after graduating in American Studies from Washington State University, Alexie received the Washington State Arts Commission Poetry Fellowship in 1991 and the National Endowment for the Arts Poetry Fellowship in 1992. The first of nine collections of poetry, *The Business of Fancydancing* (1991) was named a *New York Times* Notable Book of the Year in 1992. *The Lone Ranger and Tonto Fistfight in Heaven* (1993), a collection of short stories, received a PEN/Hemingway Award for Best First Book of Fiction. Alexie is also the author of two novels, *Reservation Blues* (1995) and *Indian Killer* (1996), as well as screenplays: *Smoke Signals* (1998) and *49?* (2004) were both featured at the Sundance Film Festival. A stand-up comedian and four-time champion of the World Heavyweight Poetry Bout, he lives in Seattle, Washington.

## MARGARET ATWOOD
(b. 1939)

Margaret Atwood spent her first eleven years in sparsely populated areas of northern Ontario and Quebec, where her father worked as an entomologist. Educated at the University of Toronto and Harvard, Atwood published her first poem at nineteen and has won numerous prizes for her poetry as well as her fiction. Her many novels include *The Edible Woman* (1969), *Surfacing* (1972), *Life before Man* (1979), *Bodily Harm* (1982), *The Handmaid's Tale* (1985), *Cat's Eye* (1988), *The Robber Bride* (1993), *Alias Grace* (1996), the Booker Prize–winning *The Blind Assassin* (2000), and *Oryx and Crake* (2003); her story collections include *Murder in the Dark* (1983), *Bluebeard's Egg* (1983), *Wilderness Tips* (1991), and *Good Bones* (1992). *Morning in the Burned House* (1995) is her most recent collection of poems. Atwood has also authored two children's books, *For the Birds* (1990) and *Princess Prunella and the Purple Peanut* (1995), a book of critical essays, *Strange Things: The Malevolent North in Canadian Literature* (1995), and *Negotiating with the Dead: A Writer on Writing* (2002).

## JAMES BALDWIN
(1924–1987)

For much of his life, James Baldwin was a leading literary spokesman for civil rights and racial equality in America. Born in New York City but long a resident of France, he first attracted critical attention with two extraordinary novels, *Go Tell It on the Mountain* (1953), drawing upon his past as a teenage preacher in the Fireside Pentecostal Church, and *Giovanni's Room* (1956), which dealt with the anguish of being black and homosexual in a largely white and heterosexual society; other works include the novels *Another Country* (1962) and *If Beale Street Could Talk* (1974), the play *Blues for Mr. Charlie* (1964), and a story collection, *Going to Meet the Man* (1965). Baldwin is perhaps best remembered as a perceptive and eloquent essayist, the author of *Notes of a Native Son* (1955), *Nobody Knows My Name* (1961), *The Fire Next Time* (1963), *No Name in the Street* (1972), and *The Price of a Ticket* (1985).

## TONI CADE BAMBARA
(1939–1995)

Born in New York City, Toni Cade Bambara grew up in Harlem and Bedford-Stuyvesant, two of New York's poorest neighborhoods. She began writing as a child and took her last name from a signature on a sketchbook she found in a trunk belonging to her great-grandmother. (The Bambara are a people of northwest Africa.) After graduating from Queens College, she wrote fiction in "the predawn in-betweens" while studying for her MA at the City College of New York, and working at a great variety of jobs: dancer, social worker, recreation director, psychiatric counselor, college English teacher, literary critic, and film producer. Bambara began to publish her stories in 1962. Her fiction includes two collections of stories, *Gorilla, My Love* (1972) and *The Sea Birds Are Still Alive* (1977), as well as two novels, *The Salt Eaters* (1980) and *If Blessing Comes* (1987). Bambara also edited two anthologies, *The Black Woman* (1970) and *Stories for Black Folks* (1971).

## ANDREA BARRETT
(b. 1955)
Andrea Barrett grew up on Cape Cod, Massachusetts, and earned a B.S. in biology from Union College in Schenectady, New York. She didn't start writing in  earnest until her thirties, not long after she walked away from a Ph.D. program in zoology. Barrett's fascination with the natural world figures prominently in her fiction. *Ship Fever*, a collection of short stories that interweaves historical nineteenth century scientists with fictional characters, won the National Book Award for Fiction in 1996. Her novel *The Voyage of the Narwhal* (1998) narrates a nineteenth-century Arctic expedition, and many of its characters reappear in *Servants of the Map* (2002), a collection of short stories that was a finalist for the Pulitzer Prize. She has been a Fellow at the New York Public Library's Center for Scholars and Writers and in 2001 was granted a MacArthur Fellowship (the so-called "Genius Award"). Barrett teaches at Williams College in Massachusetts and at Warren Wilson College in North Carolina.

## ANN BEATTIE (b. 1947)
Ann Beattie grew up in the Washington suburb of Chevy Chase, Maryland. She received a B.A. from American University and went on to graduate study in English at the University of Connecticut. After publishing "A Rose  for Judy Garland" in 1972, she began placing stories in such magazines as *The New Yorker*, becoming a kind of spokesperson for the generation that came of age in the 1960s. Many of her stories have been collected in *Distortions* (1976), *Secrets and Surprises* (1979), *Jacklighting* (1981), *The Burning House* (1982), *Where You'll Find Me* (1986), *What Was Mine: Stories* (1990), and *Park City: New and Selected Stories* (1999). Her novels are *Chilly Scenes of Winter* (1976), *Falling in Place* (1980), *Love Always* (1985), *Picturing Will* (1990), *Another You* (1995), *My Life, Starring Dara Falcon* (1997), *Park City* (1998), and *Perfect Recall* (2002). In 2000 Beattie received the PEN/Malamud Prize for Excellence in Short Fiction. She teaches writing at the University of Virginia.

## AMBROSE BIERCE
(1842–1914?)
The tenth child of a poor Ohio family, Ambrose Bierce served with distinction in the Union Army during the Civil War, rising to the rank of major.  After the war he worked as a journalist in California and London, where his boisterous western mannerisms and savage wit made him a celebrity and earned him the name "Bitter Bierce." He is probably best known as the author of *The Cynic's Word Book* (1906; later called *The Devil's Dictionary*), but his finest achievement may be his two volumes of short stories, *Tales of Soldiers and Civilians* (1891; later called *In the Midst of Life*) and *Can Such Things Be?* (1893), and *The Monk and the Hangman's Daughter* (1892), an adaptation of a German story. Disillusioned and depressed after his divorce and the deaths of his two sons, Bierce went to Mexico in 1913, where he reportedly rode with Pancho Villa's revolutionaries. He disappeared and is presumed to have died there.

## JORGE LUIS BORGES
(1899–1986)
Often considered Latin America's foremost author, Jorge Luis Borges was born and raised in Argentina, where he spoke both Spanish and English.  Traveling in Europe, his family was trapped in Geneva at the outbreak of World War I, and Borges attended the Collège de Genève, where he learned French, German, and Latin. He

then spent two years in Spain, where he wrote his first poems under the influence of the Ultraists, an "art for art's sake" movement that Borges established in Argentina upon his return in 1921. Despite his persistent and outspoken opposition to the military dictatorship of Juan Perón, he eventually became the director of the national library of Argentina. His many publications include *Ficciones, 1935–1944* (1944), *El Aleph* (1949), *El Libro de Arena* (1955), and *El Libro de los Seres Imaginarios* (1967). English translations of his works include *Labyrinths: Selected Stories and Other Writings* (1988), *Ficciones* (1989), *Collected Fictions* (1999), *Selected Non-Fictions* (1999), and *Selected Poems* (2000).

## LINDA BREWER (b. 1946)

Western writer Linda Brewer grew up in Oregon's Siuslaw and now lives in the Sonora Desert of southern Arizona, where she works in a medical lab and writes features and food articles for a Tucson publication, *The Desert Leaf*. A finalist in the World's Best Short Story Contest, she won the 2002 Raymond Carver Short Story Contest. Her story "20/20" was featured in *Micro Fiction: An Anthology of Really Short Stories* (1996).

## A. S. BYATT (b. 1936)

The oldest of four children (and half-sister of novelist Margaret Drabble), Antonia Susan Byatt was born in Sheffield, Yorkshire, graduated from Newnham College, Cambridge, and worked toward her doctorate in seventeenth-century English literature at Bryn Mawr College in Pennsylvania and at Somerville College, Oxford. In 1964 Byatt began teaching at the University of London, the same year she published her first work, *Shadow of a Sun*, a novel about a young woman attempting to escape the influence of her novelist father. Byatt has drawn on her rich academic background in novels such as *The Game* (1967), *The Virgin in the Garden* (1978), *Still Life* (1985), the Booker Prize–winning *Possession* (1989), *Babel Tower* (1996), *The Biographer's Tale* (2001), and *A Whistling Woman* (2002), and such story collections as *Sugar* (1989) and *Little Black Book of Stories* (2004). She has also published many works of literary criticism, including *Degrees of Freedom* (1965) and *Their Time* (1970), a study of Wordsworth and Coleridge. Byatt lives in London.

## PETER CAREY (b. 1943)

Peter Carey was born in Bacchus Marsh in Victoria, Australia. After flunking college chemistry, Carey became an apprentice at a Volkswagen ad agency—there he discovered writing. Two collections of short stories, *War Crimes* (1979) and *The Fat Man in History* (1980), were followed by novels such as *Bliss* (1981), *Illywhacker* (1985), *The Tax Inspector* (1991), *The Unusual Life of Tristan Smith* (1994), *Jack Maggs* (1997), and *My Life as a Fake* (2003). Carey's novel *Oscar and Lucinda* earned the 1988 Booker Prize for Fiction; he won a second Booker Prize in 2001 with his *True History of the Kelly Gang*. Carey has also published a screenplay, *Until the End of the World* (1992); a children's book, *The Big Bazoohley* (1995); and nonfiction works: *30 Days in Sydney: A Wildly Distorted Account* (2001) and his latest book, *Wrong about Japan* (2005), a memoir of his travels in Japan with his son. He teaches creative writing at New York University.

## ANGELA CARTER
(1940–1992)

Born in Eastbourne, Sussex, England, Angela Carter chose to work as a journalist rather than attend Oxford University, though she later studied medieval literature at the University of Bristol. Her novels include *Shadow Dance* (1966), *The Magic Toyshop* (1967), *Heroes and Villains* (1969), *Several Perceptions* (1968), *The Infernal Desire Machines of Dr. Hoffman* (1973), *The Passion of New Eve* (1977), *Nights at the Circus* (1984), *Black Venus* (1985), *Love* (1988), and *Wise Children* (1991). Her stories are collected in *Burning Your Boats* (1997). Carter's writing gained widespread popularity after the release of the film *The Company of Wolves* (1984), which was based on a story from *The Bloody Chamber* (1979), a collection of macabre and erotic retellings of fairy tales. Her chief nonfiction work is *The Sadeian Woman: An Exercise in Cultural History* (1979). When she died in 1992, novelist Salman Rushdie wrote that "English literature has lost its high sorceress, its benevolent witch queen."

## RAYMOND CARVER
(1938–1988)

Born in the logging town of Clatskanie, Oregon, to a working-class family, Raymond Carver married at nineteen and had two children by the time he was twenty-one. Despite these early responsibilities and a struggle with alcoholism that was to continue for the rest of his life, Carver published his first story in 1961 and graduated from Humboldt State College in 1963. He published his first book, *Near Klamath*, a collection of poems, in 1968, and thereafter supported himself with visiting lectureships at the University of California at Berkeley, Syracuse University, and the Iowa Writer's Workshop, among other institutions. His short-story collections include *What We Talk About When We Talk About Love* (1981), *Will You Please Be Quiet, Please?* (1976), *Cathedral* (1983), *My Father's Life* (1986), and *Where I'm Calling From* (1989). His poetry is collected in *All of Us* (2000).

## MICHAEL CHABON
(b. 1963)

Michael Chabon was still a graduate student at the University of California, Irvine, when his MFA thesis became a bestselling novel, *The Mysteries of Pittsburgh* (1988). Two collections of short stories followed: *A Model World* (1990) and *Werewolves in Their Youth* (1999). Chabon's second novel, *Wonder Boys* (1995), was adapted into a movie starring Michael Douglas. *The Amazing Adventures of Kavalier and Clay* (2000), a novel about two boy geniuses who start a comic-strip business during WWII, earned Chabon the Pulitzer Prize in 2001. His stories have appeared in *The New Yorker, Playboy, Harper's,* and *Esquire*. In 2002 Chabon wrote a novel for children, *Summerland*. His novel *The Final Solution* appeared in 2004. Chabon lives in Berkeley, California.

## JOHN CHEEVER
(1912–1982)

John Cheever was born in Quincy, Massachusetts. His formal education ended when he was expelled from Thayer Academy at seventeen; he moved to New York City and devoted himself to fiction writing, except for brief interludes of writing scripts for television and of teaching at Barnard College and the University of Iowa. Cheever published his first story when he was sixteen, and even after his first novel, *The Wapshot Chronicle*, won the National Book Award in 1958, he was known primarily as a prolific writer of superb short stories. Collections include *The Way Some People Live* (1943), *The Enormous Radio* (1953), and *The Stories of John Cheever* (1978), which won the Pulitzer Prize. Known as "the Chekhov of the suburbs," Cheever was awarded the National Medal for Literature by the American Academy of Arts and Letters in 1982, shortly before he died.

## ANTON CHEKHOV
(1860–1904)

The grandson of an emancipated serf, Anton Chekhov was born in the Russian town of Taganrog. In 1875, his father, a grocer facing bankruptcy and imprisonment, fled to Moscow and soon the rest of the family lost their house to a former friend and lodger, a situation that Chekhov would revisit in his play *The Cherry Orchard*. In 1884, Chekhov received his M.D. from the University of Moscow. He purchased an estate near Moscow in the early 1890s and became both an industrious landowner and doctor to the local peasants. After contributing stories to magazines and journals throughout the 1880s, he began writing for the stage in 1887. His plays, now regarded as classics, were generally ill-received in his lifetime. *The Wood Demon* (later rewritten as *Uncle Vanya*) was performed only a few times in 1889 before closing, while the 1896 premiere of *The Seagull* turned into a riot when an audience expecting comedy was confronted with an experimental tragedy.

## KATE CHOPIN
(1850–1904)

Katherine O'Flaherty was born in St. Louis, Missouri, to a Creole-Irish family that enjoyed a high place in society. Her father died when she was four, and Kate was raised by her mother, grandmother, and great-grandmother. Very well read at a young age, she received her formal education at the St. Louis Academy of the Sacred Heart. In 1870, she married Oscar

Chopin, a Louisiana businessman, and lived with him in Natchitoches parish and New Orleans, where she became a close observer of Creole and Cajun life. Following her husband's sudden death in 1884, she returned to St. Louis, where she raised her six children and began her literary career. In slightly more than a decade she produced a substantial body of work, including the story collections *Bayou Folk* (1894) and *A Night in Acadie* (1897) and the classic novel *The Awakening* (1899), which was greeted with a storm of criticism for its frank treatment of female sexuality.

## JOSEPH CONRAD
(1857–1924)

Jozeph Teodor Konrad Nalecz Korzeniowski was born in Berdyczew, Polish Ukraine. Orphaned at eleven, he eventually made his way to Marseilles and by the age of seventeen had made several trips to the West Indies as an apprentice seaman. After some troubles in France involving gambling debts, he sailed on a British ship, landed in England in 1878, and spent the next sixteen years in the British merchant service, rising to master in 1886, the year he became a British subject. In 1890, he worked on a boat that sailed up the Congo, a trip that would inspire his best-known work, the novella *Heart of Darkness* (1899). Although he began writing in 1889, he did not publish his first novel, *Almayer's Folly*, until 1896, and enjoyed little popular success until the publication of *Chance* in 1913. Among his major novels are *Lord Jim* (1900), *Nostromo* (1904), *The Secret Agent* (1907), *Under Western Eyes* (1910), *Chance* (1913), and *Victory* (1915).

## STEPHEN CRANE
(1871–1900)

One of fourteen children, Stephen Crane and his family moved frequently before settling, after his father's death in 1880, in Asbury Park, New Jersey. Crane sporadically attended various preparatory schools and colleges without excelling at much besides baseball. Determined to be a journalist, he left school for the last time in 1891 and began contributing pieces to New York newspapers. His city experiences led him to write *Maggie: A Girl of the Streets*, a realist social-reform novel published in 1893 at his own expense. His next novel, *The Red Badge of Courage* (1895), presented a stark picture of the Civil War and brought him widespread fame; many of his stories were published in the collections *The Open Boat and Other Tales of Adventure* (1898) and *The Monster and Other Stories* (1899). Crane served as a foreign correspondent, reporting on conflicts in Cuba and Greece, and lived his last years abroad, dying of tuberculosis at the age of 28.

## EDWIDGE DANTICAT
(b. 1969)

When she was twelve, Edwidge Danticat moved from Port-au-Prince, Haiti, to Brooklyn, New York, where her parents had relocated eight years before. Danticat published her first writing in English two years later, a newspaper article about her immigration to the United States that developed into her first novel, *Breath, Eyes, Memory* (1994). Danticat received a degree in French literature from Barnard College and an MFA from Brown University. *Krik? Krak!* (1991), a collection of short stories, was nominated for the National Book Award. Her second novel, *The Farming of Bones* (1998) is based on the 1937 massacre of Haitians at the border of the Dominican Republic. In 2002 Danticat published *After the Dance: A Walk through Carnival in Jacmel, Haiti*, an account of her travels. Most recently she published *The Dew Breaker* (2004), a collection of stories that examine the life of a Haitian torturer. She teaches creative writing at New York University.

## RICHARD DOKEY
(b. 1933)

A native of Stockton, California, and a graduate of the University of California at Berkeley, Richard Dokey has worked as a laborer on a railroad, in a shipyard, for a soft-drink bottling company, and for an ink factory, but he now teaches philosophy at San Joachin Delta College in Stockton, California. His works include *August Heat* (1982), a short-story collection; *Funeral: A Play* (1982); *Sánchez and Other Stories* (1981); *The Adidas Kid* (1993), a novella; *The Hollow Man* (1999), a novel; and *Pale Morning Dun* (2004), a collection of short stories.

## RALPH ELLISON
(1914–1994)

After the early death of his father, Ralph Ellison was raised by his mother and by a close-knit African American community in Oklahoma City. He grew up loving jazz and began to study music at Tuskegee Institute in 1933. In 1936, Ellison moved to New York, where, with the novelist Richard Wright's encouragement, he wrote short stories, essays, and book reviews. In the years after his monumental novel *Invisible Man* (1952) won the National Book Award and earned him international acclaim, Ellison lectured and taught at various institutions, including New York University, and published *Shadow and Act* (1964), a collection of critical essays on the novelist's art. Upon his death from cancer in 1994, the literary world learned that he had been working steadily on a second major novel, begun in 1952, seemingly lost in a fire in 1967. The nearly completed manuscript was edited by Ellison's friend John F. Callahan and published as *Juneteenth* (1999).

## WILLIAM FAULKNER
(1897–1962)

A native of Oxford, Mississippi, William Faulkner left high school without graduating, joined the Royal Canadian Air Force in 1918, and in the mid-1920s lived briefly in New Orleans, where he was encouraged as a writer by Sherwood Anderson. He then spent a few miserable months as a clerk in a New York bookstore, published a collection of poems, *The Marble Faun*, in 1924, and took a long walking tour of Europe in 1925 before returning to Mississippi. With the publication of *Sartoris* in 1929, Faulkner began a cycle of works, featuring recurrent characters and families in fictional Yoknapatawpha County, including *The Sound and the Fury* (1929), *As I Lay Dying* (1930), *Light in August* (1932), *Absalom, Absalom!* (1936), *The Hamlet* (1940), and *Go Down, Moses* (1942). He spent time in Hollywood, writing screenplays for *The Big Sleep* and other films, and lived his last years in Charlottesville, Virginia. Faulkner received the Nobel Prize for Literature in 1950.

## LOUISE ERDRICH
(b. 1954)

Born in Minnesota of German-American and French-Chippewa descent, Louise Erdrich grew up in Wahpeton, North Dakota, as a member of the Turtle Mountain Band of Chippewa. She attended Dartmouth College and received an MFA in creative writing from Johns Hopkins University. Her first novel, *Love Medicine* (1984), a collection of linked stories, won the National Book Critics Circle Award. In her subsequent publications—*The Beet Queen* (1986), *Tracks* (1988), *The Bingo Palace* (1993), and *Tales of Burning Love* (1996)—she pursued her focus on the lives of Native Americans in contemporary North Dakota. In 1991, she jointly authored the best-selling novel *The Crown of Columbus* with her husband, Michael Dorris. Her recent works include the novels *The Antelope Wife* (1998), *The Last Report on the Miracles at Little No Horse* (2001), *The Master Butchers Singing Club* (2003), *Four Souls* (2004), and a novel for young readers, *The Birchbark House* (2002).

## F. SCOTT FITZGERALD
(1896–1940)

Born in Minnesota into a solidly upper-middle-class Catholic family, Francis Scott Key Fitzgerald started writing at a young age and continued even after dropping out of Princeton to join the army. At twenty-one he submitted his first novel for publication; it was rejected, but with the kind of encouragement that led to his revising it for years. In 1918, while stationed in Alabama, he met Zelda Sayre, whom he married after the publication of that first novel, *This Side of Paradise* (1920), which became an immediate best-seller and established Fitzgerald as a spokesperson for his generation. Extravagant living, in New York and later in Europe, took its toll on both of them, as he succumbed to alcoholism and she to mental illness. Much of Fitzgerald's semiautobiographical work depicts the privileged lives of wealthy, aspiring socialites of the Roaring Twenties. His novels include *The Beautiful and the Damned* (1922), *The Great Gatsby* (1925), and *Tender Is the Night* (1934).

## GABRIEL GARCÍA MÁRQUEZ (b. 1928)

Born in Aracataca, Colombia, a remote town near the Caribbean coast, Gabriel García Márquez studied law at the University of Bogotá and then worked as a journalist in Latin America, Europe, and the United States. In 1967, he took up permanent residence in Barcelona, Spain. His first published book, *Leaf Storm* (1955), set in the fictional small town of Macondo, is based on the myths and legends of his childhood home. His most famous novel, *One Hundred Years of Solitude* (1967), fuses magic, reality, fable, and fantasy to present six generations of one Macondo family, a microcosm of many of the social, political, and economic problems of Latin America. Among his many works are *The Autumn of the Patriarch* (1975), *Chronicle of a Death Foretold* (1981), *Love in the Time of Cholera* (1987), *Of Love and Other Demons* (1994), and *Living to Tell the Tale* (2003), a three-volume set of memoirs. Márquez won the Nobel Prize for Literature in 1982.

## SUSAN GLASPELL (1876–1948)

Born and raised in Davenport, Iowa, Susan Glaspell graduated from Drake University and worked on the staff of the *Des Moines Daily News* until her stories began appearing in magazines such as *Harper's* and the *Ladies' Home Journal*. In 1911, Glaspell moved to New York City, where, two years later, she married the theater director George Cram Cook. In 1915, they founded the Provincetown Playhouse on Cape Cod, an extraordinary gathering of actors, directors, and playwrights, including Eugene O'Neill, Edna St. Vincent Millay, and John Reed; among the many plays she wrote to be performed by this company are *Trifles* (1916), *The Verge* (1921), *Bernice* (1924), and *Alison's House* (1931), a Pulitzer Prize–winning drama based on the life of Emily Dickinson. Glaspell spent the last part of her life in Provincetown, devoting herself to writing fiction; among her books are *Visioning* (1911), *Lifted Masks: Stories* (1912), *Fidelity* (1915), and *The Morning Is Near Us* (1940).

## CHARLOTTE PERKINS GILMAN (1860–1935)

Charlotte Anna Perkins was born in Hartford, Connecticut. After a painful, lonely childhood and several years of supporting herself as a governess, art teacher, and designer of greeting cards, Perkins married the artist Charles Stetson. Following Gilman's suffering several extended periods of depression, her husband put her in the care of a doctor who "sent me home with the solemn advice to 'live as domestic a life as ... possible,' to 'have but two hours' intellectual life a day,' and 'never to touch pen, brush, or pencil again' as long as I lived." Three months of this regimen brought her "near the borderline of utter mortal ruin" and inspired her masterpiece, "The Yellow Wallpaper." In 1900, she married George Houghton Gilman, having divorced Stetson in 1892. Her nonfiction works, springing from the early women's movement, include *Women and Economics* (1898) and *Man-Made World* (1911). She also wrote several utopian novels, including *Moving the Mountain* (1911) and *Herland* (1915).

## NADINE GORDIMER (b. 1923)

Nadine Gordimer was born in Springs, South Africa, to an English mother and a Lithuanian father (a jeweler). She attended the University of Witwatersrand in Johannesburg before publishing her first collection of stories, *Face to Face* (1949). Much of her fiction depicts how apartheid warped the supposedly apolitical realms of emotion, self-knowledge, and personal relations for both blacks and whites. Though her books were often banned in South Africa, her novel *Burger's Daughter* (1979) received so much praise that the government lifted the ban on it. Other novels include *The Lying Days* (1953), *The Conservationist* (winner of the Booker Prize in 1974), *The House Gun* (1998), and *The Pickup* (2001). Her short-story collections include *Six Feet of the Country* (1956), *Friday's Footprint* (1960), *Why Haven't You Written?* (1973), *A Soldier's Embrace* (1980), *Jump* (1991), and *Loot and Other Stories* (2003). Gordimer won the 1991 Nobel Prize for Literature. Though traveling widely as a lecturer, she continues to live in Johannesburg.

## HA JIN (b. 1956)

Born Xuefei Jin, Ha Jin grew up in mainland China. During his teenage years, he served in the People's Army. He then worked for a railroad company while teaching himself English, before receiving degrees from Heilongjiang and Shandong universities in China. While earning his Ph.D. from Brandeis, Jin watched television coverage of the Tiananmen Square massacre and decided to remain, with his wife and son, in the United States, where he now teaches English and creative writing at Emory University. He has published the poetry collections *Between Silences* (1990), *Facing Shadows* (1996), and *Wreckage* (2001); the short-story collections *Ocean of Words: Army Stories* (1996), *Under the Red Flag* (1997), and *The Bridegroom* (2000); and the novels *In the Pond* (1998) and *Waiting* (1999), which won both the National Book Award and the 2000 PEN/Faulkner Award for Fiction. Ha Jin's most recent novels are *The Crazed* (2002) and *War Trash* (2004).

## ERNEST HEMINGWAY (1899–1961)

Born in Oak Park, Illinois, Ernest Hemingway became a reporter after graduating from high school. During World War I, he served as an ambulance-service volunteer in France and an infantryman in Italy, where he was wounded and decorated for valor. After the war, he lived for a time in Paris, part of the "Lost Generation" of American expatriates such as Gertrude Stein and F. Scott Fitzgerald. Two volumes of stories, *In Our Time* (1925) and *Death in the Afternoon* (1932), and two major novels, *The Sun Also Rises* (1926) and *A Farewell to Arms* (1929), established his international reputation. Hemingway supported the Loyalists in the Spanish Civil War—the subject of *For Whom the Bell Tolls* (1940)—served as a war correspondent during World War II, and from 1950 until his death lived in Cuba. His novel *The Old Man and the Sea* (1952) won a Pulitzer Prize, and Hemingway was awarded the Nobel Prize for Literature in 1954.

## NATHANIEL HAWTHORNE (1804–1864)

Nathaniel Hawthorne was born in Salem, Massachusetts, a descendant of Puritan immigrants. Educated at Bowdoin College, he was agonizingly slow in winning recognition for his work, and supported himself from time to time in government service—working in the customhouses of Boston and Salem and serving as the United States consul in Liverpool. His early collections of stories, *Twice-Told Tales* (1837) and *Mosses from an Old Manse* (1846), did not sell well, and it was not until the publication of his most famous novel, *The Scarlet Letter* (1850), that his fame spread beyond a discerning few. His other novels include *The House of the Seven Gables* (1851) and *The Blithedale Romance* (1852). Burdened by a deep sense of guilt for his family's role in the notorious Salem witchcraft trials over a century before he was born (one ancestor had been a judge), Hawthorne used fiction as a means of exploring the moral dimensions of sin and the human soul.

## HENRY JAMES (1843–1916)

Son of a writer and religious philosopher and his wife, brother of the philosopher William James, Henry James was born in New York and entered Harvard Law School in 1862, after private study, art school, and study and residence abroad. Thereafter his American home was in Cambridge, Massachusetts, but he lived in England from 1876 until his death forty years later, having become a British subject in 1915. James's fiction often centers on the encounters of Americans with Europeans; he treats America and Europe as much as moral or value systems as geographical settings. Not only his practice but also his theory of fiction, set forth mainly in the prefaces to his novels, dominated fiction criticism for generations. Among his many works are *The American* (1877), *Daisy Miller* (1879), *Washington Square* (1881), *Portrait of a Lady* (1881), *The Bostonians* (1886), *The Turn of the Screw* (1898), *The Wings of the Dove* (1902), *The Ambassadors* (1903), and *The Golden Bowl* (1904).

## JAMES JOYCE
(1882–1941)

In 1902, after graduating from University College, Dublin, James Joyce left Ireland for Paris, returning a year later to teach school. In October 1904, he eloped with Nora Barnacle and settled in Trieste, where he taught English for the Berlitz school. Though he lived as an expatriate for the rest of his life, all of his fiction is set in his native Dublin. Joyce had more than his share of difficulties with publication and censorship. His volume of short stories, *Dubliners*, completed in 1905, was not published until 1914. His novel *Portrait of the Artist as a Young Man*, dated "Dublin 1904, Trieste 1914," appeared first in America, in 1916. His great novel, *Ulysses* (1921), was banned for a dozen years in the United States and as long or longer elsewhere. In addition, Joyce published a play, *Exiles* (1918); two collections of poetry, *Chamber Music* (1907) and *Pomes Penyeach* (1927); and the monumental, experimental, and puzzling novel *Finnegans Wake* (1939).

## FRANZ KAFKA
(1883–1924)

Born into a middle-class Jewish family in Prague, Franz Kafka earned a doctorate in law from the German University in that city and held an inconspicuous position in the civil service for many years. Emotionally and physically ill for the last seven or eight years of his short life, he died of tuberculosis in Vienna, never having married (though he was twice engaged to the same woman and lived with an actress in Berlin for some time before he died) and not having published his three major novels, *The Trial* (1925), *The Castle* (1926), and *Amerika* (1927). Indeed, he ordered his friend Max Brod to destroy them and other works he had left in manuscript. Fortunately, Brod did not; and not long after Kafka's death, his sometimes-dreamlike, sometimes-nightmarish work was known and admired all over the world. His stories in English translation are collected in *The Great Wall of China* (1933), *The Penal Colony* (1948), and *The Complete Stories* (1976).

## YASUNARI KAWABATA
(1899–1972)

Born in Osaka, Japan, to a prosperous family, Yasunari Kawabata graduated from Tokyo Imperial University in 1924 and had his first literary success with the semiautobiographical novella *The Izu Dancer* (1926). He cofounded the journal *Contemporary Literature* in support of the Neosensualist movement, which had much in common with the European literary movements of Dadaism, Expressionism, and Cubism. His best-known works include *Snow Country* (1937), *Thousand Cranes* (1952), *The Sound of the Mountain* (1954), *The Lake* (1955), *The Sleeping Beauty* (1960), *The Old Capital* (1962), and the collection *Palm-of-the-Hand Stories* (translated in 1988). Kawabata was awarded the Nobel Prize for Literature in 1968. After long suffering from poor health, he committed suicide in 1972.

## JAMAICA KINCAID
(b. 1949)

Born in St. John's, Antigua, Elaine Potter Richardson left her native island and her family at seventeen. Changing her name to Jamaica Kincaid, she worked in New York City as an au pair and a receptionist before studying photography at the New School for Social Research, then briefly continuing her studies at Franconia College in New Hampshire. After returning to New York, she became a regular contributor to *The New Yorker*, for which she wrote from 1976 until 1995. Her publications include a collection of short stories, *At the Bottom of the River* (1983); a book-length essay about Antigua, *A Small Place* (1988); a book for children, *Annie, Gwen, Lilly, Pam, and Tulip* (1986); the novels *Annie John* (1985), *Lucy* (1990), and *The Autobiography of My Mother* (1996); the memoir *My Brother* (1997); and a collection of her *New Yorker* pieces, *Talk Stories* (2001). Her most recent novel, *Mr. Potter* (2002), takes place on the island of Antigua.

## JHUMPA LAHIRI
(b. 1967)

Born in London and raised in Rhode Island, Jhumpa Lahiri is the daughter of Bengali parents; much of her fiction addresses the difficulty of reconciling an Indian heritage with life in the United States. Lahiri earned a B.A. from Barnard College and several degrees from Boston University: an M.A. in English, an MFA in creative writing, an M.A. in comparative studies in literature and the arts, and a Ph.D. in Renaissance Studies. She has published many stories in well-known periodicals such as *The New Yorker* and won the 2000 Pulitzer Prize for her first collection, *Interpreter of Maladies* (1999), a best-seller that has been translated into 29 languages. *The Namesake*, her first novel, was published in 2003. Lahiri lives in New York City.

## D. H. LAWRENCE
(1885–1930)

The son of a coal miner and a schoolteacher, David Herbert Lawrence was able to attend high school only briefly. He worked for a surgical-appliance manufacturer, attended Nottingham University College, and taught school in Croydon, near London. After publishing his first novel, *The White Peacock* (1911), he devoted his time exclusively to writing; *Sons and Lovers* (1913) established him as a major literary figure. In 1912, he eloped with Frieda von Richthofen, and in 1914, after her divorce, they were married. During World War I, both his novels and his wife's German nationality gave him trouble: *The Rainbow* was published in September 1915 and suppressed in November. In 1919, the Lawrences left England and began years of wandering: first Italy, then Ceylon, Australia, Mexico, and New Mexico, then back to England and Italy. Lawrence published *Women in Love* in 1920 and *Lady Chatterley's Lover*, his most sexually explicit novel, in 1928. Through it all he suffered from tuberculosis and eventually died from the disease.

## URSULA K. LE GUIN
(b. 1929)

Born in Berkeley, California, to a writer/folklorist mother and an anthropologist father, Ursula Kroeber earned a B.A. from Radcliffe College and an M.A. from Columbia University. In 1952, she married the historian Charles Le Guin. Although she began publishing fiction in the early 1960s, Le Guin established her literary reputation with the philosophical fantasy *A Wizard of Earthsea* (1968), which formed a trilogy with *The Tombs of Atuan* (1971) and *The Farthest Shore* (1972). Read by both adolescents and adults, her work often depicts complex fictional societies with a folklorist's or anthropologist's eye for detail. Her novels include *The Left Hand of Darkness* (1969), *The Dispossessed* (1974), *Malafrena* (1979), *The Compass Rose* (1982), *The Telling* (2000), and *Gifts* (2004). Short story collections include *The Birthday of the World* (2002) and *Changing Planes* (2003). In addition, Le Guin has written essays, children's books, and poetry; she has collaborated on multimedia work and edited collections of science fiction.

## DORIS LESSING (b. 1919)

Born in Persia (now Iran), to English parents, Doris Tayler lived for twenty-five years in Southern Rhodesia (now Zimbabwe), where she left school at fourteen to work as a nursemaid and secretary. After marriages to Frank Wisdom and Gottfried Lessing, she moved to England and soon published her first novel, *The Grass Is Singing* (1950). Some of her work is political, and much of it examines the inner lives of modern women. Her major works of fiction include the five Martha Quest novels, *Children of Violence* (1952–69); *The Golden Notebook* (1962); a five-volume science-fiction collection, *Canopus in Argos: Archives* (1979–83); *The Good Terrorist* (1985); and *The Fifth Child* (1988). She has also published short fiction, plays, poetry, and two volumes of an autobiography. Her most recent works are *Ben, in the World: The Sequel to The Fifth Child* (2000), a novel; *The Grandmothers* (2003), a collection of four novellas; and *Time Bites* (2004), a selection of personal essays.

## KATHERINE MANSFIELD
(1888–1923)

Born in Wellington, New Zealand, Katherine Mansfield Beauchamp was an accomplished cellist who studied music at Queen's College, London. At her parents' urging she returned to New Zealand, where, instead of settling down as they wished, she turned to writing at the age of 20. She moved back to London, dropped her last name, and began publishing story collections including *In a German Pension* (1911); *Bliss* (1920), which established her reputation; *The Garden-Party* (1922); and *The Dove's Nest* (1923). A longtime companion of John Middleton Murry, she was friends with (and a literary rival of) D.H. Lawrence and Virginia Woolf. She died suddenly in 1923, while in France trying to cure her tuberculosis. A final volume of stories, *Something Childish*, was published shortly thereafter. *Novels and Novelists*, a collection of essays, appeared in 1930 and her *Collected Stories* in 1937.

## BOBBIE ANN MASON
(b. 1940)

Bobbie Ann Mason was born and raised in Mayfield, Kentucky, where her parents were dairy farmers. She received a B.A. from the University of Kentucky, an M.A. from the State University of New York at Binghamton, and a Ph.D. in English from the University of Connecticut. After her stories had appeared in such magazines as *The New Yorker* and *Redbook*, Mason published her first collection, *Shiloh and Other Stories* (1982), which won the Ernest Hemingway Foundation Award and established her literary reputation. She has since written two novels, *In Country* (1985) and *Feather Crowns* (1993); a short novel, *Spence and Lila* (1988); three collections of stories: *Love Life* (1989), *Midnight Magic* (1998), and *Zigzagging Down a Wild Trail* (2001); and a memoir, *Clear Springs* (1999), which was a finalist for the Pulitzer Prize. She lives in rural Pennsylvania.

## GUY DE MAUPASSANT
(1850–1893)

Born Henri René Albert in Normandy, France, Maupassant was expelled at sixteen from a Rouen seminary and finished his education at a public high school. After serving in the Franco-Prussian War, he was a government clerk in Paris for ten years. A protégé of Flaubert, he published during the 1880s some three hundred stories, half a dozen novels, and plays. The short stories, which appeared regularly in popular periodicals, sampled military and peasant life, the decadent world of politics and journalism, prostitution, the supernatural, and the hypocrisies of solid citizens; with Chekhov, he may be said to have created the modern short story. His life ended somewhat like one of his own stories: he died of syphilis in an asylum. His novels include *Une Vie (A Life*, 1883), *Bel Ami (Handsome Friend*, 1885), and *Pierre et Jean* (1888). His stories are available in various collections.

## HERMAN MELVILLE
(1819–1891)

When his father died in debt, twelve-year-old Herman Melville's life of privilege became one of struggle. At eighteen, he left his native New York to teach in a backwoods Massachusetts school, then trained as a surveyor; finding no work, he became a sailor in 1839. After five years in the South Seas, he wrote *Typee* (1846) and *Omoo* (1847), sensationalized accounts of his voyages that were wildly popular. They proved the pinnacle of Melville's career in his lifetime, however; *Mardi* (1849) was judged too abstruse, the travel narratives *Redburn* (1849) and *White-Jacket* (1850), too listless. Melville's magnum opus, *Moby-Dick* (1851), was alternately shunned and condemned. His later novels—*Pierre* (1852), *Israel Potter* (1853), and *The Confidence-Man* (1856)—as well as his poetry collection *Battle-Pieces* (1866) were all but ignored. Melville's reputation as one of the giants of American literature was established only after his death; the novel *Billy Budd, Sailor* (not published until 1924), like *Moby-Dick*, was judged a masterpiece.

## LORRIE MOORE
(b. 1957)

Marie Lorena Moore was born in Glens Falls, New York. At nineteen, while attending St. Lawrence University, she published her first story in *Seventeen* magazine; after graduating, she worked as a paralegal in New York City before earning her MFA in creative writing from Cornell. In 1989 her story "You're Ugly, Too" was published in the *New Yorker* and was included in *The Best American Short Stories*. Her first book, *Self-Help* (1985), a collection of short stories, was followed by the novels *Anagrams* (1986) and *Who Will Run the Frog Hospital?* (1994), and the short-story collections *Like Life* (1990) and *Birds of America* (1998). Since 1984, she has been a professor of English at the University of Wisconsin at Madison.

## TONI MORRISON
(b. 1931)

Born in Lorain, Ohio, a steel town on the shores of Lake Erie, Chloe Anthony Wofford was the first member of her family to go to college, graduating from Howard University in 1953 and earning an M.A. from Cornell. She taught at both Texas Southern University and at Howard before becoming an editor at Random House, where she worked for nearly twenty years. In such novels as *The Bluest Eye* (1969), *Sula* (1973), *Song of Solomon* (1977), *Beloved* (1987), and *Paradise* (1998), Morrison traces the problems and possibilities faced by black Americans struggling with slavery and its aftermath in the United States. More recent work includes her eighth novel, *Love* (2003); two picture books for children co-authored with her son, Slade: *The Bog Box* (1999) and *Book of Mean People* (2002); and a book for young adults, *Remember: The Journey to School Integration* (2004). In 1993 she became the first African American author to win the Nobel Prize for literature.

## BHARATI MUKHERJEE
(b. 1940)

Born to wealthy parents in Calcutta, Bharati Mukherjee attended private schools in India, London, and Switzerland before studying at the University of Iowa, where she earned both an MFA in creative writing and a Ph.D. in English and Comparative Literature. At Iowa she met and married Canadian novelist Clark Blaise, with whom she has lived in Canada and the United States, and with whom she wrote *Days and Nights in Calcutta* (1977), an acclaimed account of their visit to her native India in 1972. In addition to her novels *The Tiger's Daughter* (1971), *Wife* (1975), *Jasmine* (1989), *The Holder of the World* (1993), *Leave It to Me* (1997), *Desirable Daughters* (2002), and *The Tree Bride* (2004), Mukherjee has published the short-story collections *Darkness* (1985) and *The Middleman* (1988). She teaches at the University of California at Berkeley.

## ALICE MUNRO (b. 1931)

Widely considered Canada's best short-story writer, Alice Laidlaw was born on a farm in Wingham, Ontario, near Lake Huron. She began publishing stories while attending the University of Western Ontario. When her two-year scholarship ran out, she left the university, married James Munro, and moved to Vancouver. Her stories appeared sporadically during the 1950s, and she did not publish her first collection, the Governor General's Award-winning *Dance of the Happy Shades*, until 1968. Divorced and remarried, she returned to Ontario and went on to publish the novel *Lives of Girls and Women* (1971) and the collections *Something I've Been Meaning to Tell You* (1974), *Who Do You Think You Are?* (1978, published in the US as *The Beggar Maid* in 1979), *The Moons of Jupiter* (1983), *The Progress of Love* (1986), *Friend of My Youth* (1990), *Open Secrets* (1994), *Selected Stories* (1996), *The Love of a Good Woman* (1998), *Hateship, Friendship, Courtship, Loveship, and Marriage* (2001), and *Runaway* (2004).

## JOYCE CAROL OATES
(b. 1938)

A remarkably prolific writer of short stories, poems, novels, and nonfiction, Joyce Carol Oates was born in Lockport, New York, and graduated from Syracuse University. She received an M.A. in English from the University of Wisconsin but abandoned doctoral studies at Rice University in order to devote herself to writing. The recipient of numerous awards, including the O. Henry Award for continuing achievement (1970, 1986), the Rea Award for the Short Story, the Alan Swallow Award for Fiction, and the National Book Award for the novel *them* (1969), Oates has taught at the University of Detroit and the University of Windsor, Ontario, and currently teaches creative writing at Princeton University. Her recent novels include *We Were the Mulvaneys* (1996), *Blonde* (2000), *The Tattooed Girl* (2003), *Rape: A Love Story* (2003), *Take Me, Take Me With You* (2004), and *The Falls* (2004). *The Faith of A Writer: Life, Craft, Art*, a collection of personal essays, was published in 2003.

## FLANNERY O'CONNOR
(1925–1964)

Mary Flannery O'Connor was born in Savannah, Georgia, studied at the Georgia State College for Women, and won a fellowship to the Writer's Workshop of the University of Iowa, from which she received her MFA. In 1950, she was first diagnosed with lupus, a painful autoimmune disorder that had killed her father and would trouble her for the rest of her brief life. Her first novel, *Wise Blood*, was published in 1952, and her first collection of stories, *A Good Man Is Hard to Find*, in 1955. She was able to complete only one more novel, *The Violent Bear It Away* (1960), and a second collection of stories, *Everything That Rises Must Converge* (1965), before dying of lupus, in Milledgeville, Georgia. Her posthumously published *Complete Stories* won the National Book Award in 1972. A collection of letters, edited by Sally Fitzgerald under the title *The Habit of Being*, appeared in 1979.

## GRACE PALEY (b. 1922)

Born to Russian immigrants in the Bronx, New York, Grace Paley attended Hunter College and New York University but never finished college because she was too busy reading and writing poetry before she turned to fiction. Her short stories, first published in *The Little Disturbances of Man: Stories of Men and Women at Love* (1959), *Enormous Changes at the Last Minute* (1974), and *Later the Same Day* (1985), are assembled in *The Collected Stories* (1994); her poetry, in *Begin Again: Collected Poems* (2000); and her essays, reviews, and lectures, in *Just as I Thought* (1998). In 1987, she was awarded a Senior Fellowship by the National Endowment for the Arts, in recognition of her lifetime contribution to literature. In 1988, she was named the first New York State Author. Always politically engaged, she was an outspoken critic of the Vietnam War and has been a lifelong anti-nuclear activist and an outspoken feminist.

## EDGAR ALLAN POE
(1809–1849)

Orphaned before he was three, Edgar Poe was adopted by John Allan, a wealthy Richmond businessman. Poe received his early schooling in Richmond and in England before a brief, unsuccessful stint at the University of Virginia. After serving for two years in the army, he was appointed to West Point in 1830 but was expelled within the year for cutting classes. Living in Baltimore with his grandmother, aunt, and cousin Virginia (whom he married in 1835, when she was thirteen), Poe eked out a precarious living as an editor; his keen-edged reviews earned him numerous literary enemies. His two-volume *Tales of the Grotesque and Arabesque* received little critical attention when published in 1839, but his poem "The Raven" (1845) made him a literary celebrity. After his wife's death of tuberculosis in 1847, Poe, already an alcoholic, became increasingly erratic and two years later he died mysteriously in Baltimore. His poems and stories have been collected in many editions.

## KATHERINE ANNE PORTER (1890–1980)

A native of Indian Creek, Texas, and a descendant of Daniel Boone, Katherine Anne Porter was raised by her grandmother and educated in convent schools. Forced by tuberculosis to abandon an acting career, she worked as a journalist in Denver, Chicago, and Mexico. She published her first short story in 1922; her first collection *Flowering Judas* (1930), won critical acclaim. Porter's only full-length novel, *Ship of Fools* (1962), established her as a major American writer and made her rich. She won numerous awards for her work, including both a Pulitzer Prize and a National Book Award for her *Collected Short Stories* (1965) and a Gold Medal from the National Institute of Arts and Letters. Among her works are the story collections *Pale Horse, Pale Rider* (1939) and *The Leaning Tower and Other Stories* (1944); a volume of essays, *The Days Before* (1952); and an account of the controversial Sacco and Vanzetti murder trial, *The Never-Ending Wrong* (1977).

## SALMAN RUSHDIE
(b. 1947)

Born in Bombay, India, Salman Rushdie was educated in England at Rugby School and Cambridge University. He published his first novel, *Grimus* (1975), while working as an advertising copywriter; his second novel, the Booker Prize-winning *Midnight's Children* (1981), established his literary reputation. Rushdie received international attention when Muslim clerics issued a *fatwa* (death sentence) against him following the publication of his novel *The Satanic Verses* (1988), which allegedly blasphemes Islam. Obliged to go into hiding, Rushdie continued to write and to make unannounced public appearances. In 1998, the Iranian government revoked the *fatwa* and Rushdie ended his hiding. His works include the children's book *Haroun and the Sea of Stories* (1990); the novels *Shame* (1983), *The Moor's Last Sigh* (1995), *The Ground Beneath Her Feet* (1999), and *Fury* (2001); a collection of short stories, *East, West* (1994); and two volumes of essays: *Imaginary Homelands: Essays and Criticism* (1991); and *Step Across This Line: Collected Nonfiction 1992–2002* (2002).

## CAROL SHIELDS
(1935–2003)

Born in Oak Park, Illinois, Carol Shields received her B.A. from Hanover College and her M.A. from the University of Ottawa. She taught at several Canadian universities; in 1996, she became chancellor of the University of Winnipeg. Meanwhile, novels such as *Small Ceremonies* (1976), *The Box Garden* (1977), *Happenstance* (1980), and *A Fairly Conventional Woman* (1982) slowly built her a Canadian readership. With her first story collection, *Various Miracles* (1985), Shields experimented with multiple narrators. She refined this technique in the triumphantly successful novel *The Stone Diaries* (1993), a fictional biography that won the Pulitzer Prize. In addition to such plays as *Thirteen Hands* (1993), her work includes another innovative novel, *Larry's Party* (1997); a collection of stories, *Dressing Up for the Carnival* (2000); the short biography *Jane Austen* (2001); and *Dropped Threads 2: More of What We Aren't Told* (2001), a collection of personal essays. Shields's last novel, *Unless* (2002), was published a year before she died of cancer.

## AMY TAN (b. 1952)

Amy Tan was born in Oakland, California, just two and a half years after her parents immigrated from China. She received her M.A. in linguistics from San Jose State University and has worked on programs for disabled children and as a freelance writer. In 1987, she visited China for the first time—"As soon as my feet touched China, I became Chinese"—and returned to write her first book, *The Joy Luck Club* (1989). Tan has since published three more novels—*The Kitchen God's Wife* (1991), *The Hundred Secret Senses* (1995), and *The Bonesetter's Daughter* (2000)—and has co-authored two children's books. Her first book of nonfiction, *The Opposite of Fate: A Book of Musings* (2003), explores lucky accidents, choice, and memory. Tan is also the lead singer for the Rock Bottom Remainders, a rock band made up of fellow writers, including Stephen King and Dave Barry; they make appearances at benefits that support literacy programs for children.

## EUDORA WELTY
(1909–2001)

Known as the "First Lady of Southern Literature," Eudora Welty was born and raised in Jackson, Mississippi, attended Mississippi State College for Women, and earned a B.A. from the University of Wisconsin. Among the countless awards she received were two Guggenheim Fellowships, six O. Henry Awards, a Pulitzer Prize, the French Legion of Honor, the National Medal for Literature, and the Presidential Medal of Freedom. Although she wrote five novels, including *The Robber Bridegroom* (1942), *Ponder Heart* (1954), and *The Optimist's Daughter* (1972), she is best known for her short stories, many of which have been published in *The Collected Stories of Eudora Welty* (1980). Among her nonfiction works are *One Writer's Beginnings* (1984), *A Writer's Eye: Collected Book Reviews* (1994), and five collections of her photographs, including *One Place, One Time* (1978) and *Photographs* (1989). In 1998 the Library of America published a two-volume edition of her selected works, making her the first living author they had published.

## EDITH WHARTON
(1862–1937)

Edith Jones was born into a distinguished New York family. Educated by private tutors and governesses, she published a book of her poems privately but did not begin to write for a public audience until after her marriage, to Edward Wharton, in 1885. The author of more than fifty volumes of poetry, essays, fiction, travelogues, and criticism, she was the first woman to receive an honorary doctorate from Yale University, in 1923. Although she emigrated to France in 1907 (and later was awarded the

Legion of Honor for her philanthropic work during World War I), she continued to write about the New England of her youth in novels such as the popular *Ethan Frome* (1911). Among her many works are *The Valley of Decision* (1902), *The House of Mirth* (1905), *A Son at the Front* (1923), *Twilight Sleep* (1927), the autobiographical *A Backward Glance* (1934), and *The Buccaneers* (1938). She received a Pulitzer Prize for *The Age of Innocence* (1920).

## WILLIAM CARLOS WILLIAMS (1883–1963)

Born in Rutherford, New Jersey, William Carlos Williams attended school in Switzerland and New York and studied medicine at the University of Pennsylvania and the University of Leipzig in Germany. He spent most of his life in Rutherford, practicing medicine and gradually establishing himself as one of the great figures in American poetry. Early in his writing career he left the European-inspired Imagist movement in favor of a more uniquely American poetic style comprised of vital, local language and "no ideas but in things." His shorter poems have been published in numerous collected editions and other volumes, including the Pulitzer Prize-winning *Brueghel, and Other Poems* (1963); his five-volume philosophical poem, *Paterson,* was published in 1963. Among his other works are plays such as *A Dream of Love* (1948) and *Many Loves* (1950); a trilogy of novels: *White Mules* (1937), *In the Money* (1940), and *The Build-Up* (1952); his *Autobiography* (1951); his *Selected Essays* (1954); and his *Selected Letters* (1957).

# POETRY

# Poetry: Reading, Responding, Writing

If you're a reader of poetry, you already know: poetry reading is not just an intellectual and bookish activity; it is about feeling. Reading poetry well means responding to it: if you respond on a feeling level, you are likely to read more accurately, with deeper understanding, and with greater pleasure. And, conversely, if you read poetry accurately, and with attention to detail, you will almost certainly respond to it—or learn how to respond—on an emotional level. Reading poetry involves conscious articulation through language, and reading and responding come to be, for experienced readers of poetry, very nearly one. But those who teach poetry—and there are a lot of us, almost all enthusiasts about both poetry as a subject and reading as a craft—have discovered something else: writing about poetry helps both the reading and the responding processes. Responding involves remembering and reflecting as well. As you recall your own past and make associations between things in the text and things you already know and feel, you will not only respond more fully to a particular poem, but improve your reading skills more generally. Your knowledge and life experience inform your reading of what is before you and allow you to connect elements within the text—events, images, words, sounds—so that meanings and feelings develop and accumulate. Prior learning creates expectations: of pattern, repetition, association, or causality. Reflecting on the text—and on expectations produced by themes and ideas in the text—re-creates old feelings but directs them in new, often unusual ways. Poems, even when they are about things we have no experience of, connect to things we do know and order our memories, thoughts, and feelings in new and newly challenging ways.

> *Poetry is a way of taking life by the throat.*
> —ROBERT FROST

A course in reading poetry can ultimately enrich your life by helping you become more articulate and more sensitive to both ideas and feelings: that's the larger goal. But the more immediate goal—and the route to the larger one—is to make you a better reader of texts and a more precise and careful writer yourself. Close attention to one text makes you appreciate, and understand, textuality and its possibilities more generally. Texts may be complex and even unstable in some ways; they do not affect all readers the same way, and they work through language that has its own volatilities and complexities. But paying attention to how you read—developing specific questions to ask and working on your reading skills systematically—can take a lot of the guess-work out of reading texts and give you a sense of greater satisfaction in your interpretations.

## READING

Poems, perhaps even more than other texts, can sharpen your reading skills because they tend to be so compact, so fully dependent on concise expressions of feeling. In poems, ideas and feelings are packed tightly into just a few lines. The experiences of life are very concentrated here, and meanings emerge quickly, word by word. Poems often show us the very process of putting feelings into a language that can be shared with others—to *say* feelings in a communicable way. Poetry can be intellectual too, explaining and exploring ideas, but its focus is more often on how people feel than how they think. Poems work out a shareable language for feeling, and one of poetry's most insistent virtues arises from its attempt to express the inexpressible. How can anyone, for example, put into words what it means to be in love or how it feels to lose someone one cares about? Poetry tries, and it often captures a shade of emotion that feels just right to a reader. No single poem can be said to represent all the things that love or death feels like or means, but one of the joys of experiencing poetry occurs when we read a poem and want to say, "Yes, that is just what it is like; I know exactly what that line means but I've never been able to express it so well." Poetry can be the voice of our feelings even when our minds are speechless with grief or joy. Reading is no substitute for living, but it can make living more abundant and more available.

Here are two poems that talk about the sincerity and depth of love between two people. Each is written as if it were spoken by one person to his or her lover, and each is definite and powerful about the intensity and quality of love; but the poems work in quite different ways—the first one asserting the strength and depth of love, the second implying intense feeling by reminiscing about earlier events in the relationship between the two people.

## ELIZABETH BARRETT BROWNING

### *How Do I Love Thee?*

How do I love thee? Let me count the ways.
I love thee to the depth and breadth and height
My soul can reach, when feeling out of sight
For the ends of Being and ideal Grace.
5  I love thee to the level of every day's
Most quiet need, by sun and candlelight.
I love thee freely, as men strive for Right;
I love thee purely, as they turn from Praise;
I love thee with the passion put to use
10  In my old griefs, and with my childhood's faith.
I love thee with a love I seemed to lose
With my lost saints—I love thee with the breath,
Smiles, tears of all my life!—and, if God choose,
I shall but love thee better after death.

1850

JAROLD RAMSEY

## The Tally Stick

Here from the start, from our first of days, look:
I have carved our lives in secret on this stick
of mountain mahogany the length of your arms
outstretched, the wood clear red, so hard and rare.
5 It is time to touch and handle what we know we share.

Near the butt, this intricate notch where the grains
converge and join: it is our wedding.
I can read it through with a thumb and tell you now
who danced, who made up the songs, who meant us joy.
10 These little arrowheads along the grain,
they are the births of our children. See,
they make a kind of design with these heavy crosses,
the deaths of our parents, the loss of friends.

Over it all as it goes, of course, I
15 have chiseled Events, History—random
hashmarks cut against the swirling grain.
See, here is the Year the World Went Wrong,
we thought, and here the days the Great Men fell.
The lengthening runes of our lives run through it all.

20 See, our tally stick is whittled nearly end to end;
delicate as scrimshaw, it would not bear you up.
Regrets have polished it, hand over hand.
Yet let us take it up, and as our fingers
like children leading on a trail cry back
25 our unforgotten wonders, sign after sign,
we will talk softly as of ordinary matters,
and in one another's blameless eyes go blind.

1977

"How Do I Love Thee?" is direct but fairly abstract. It lists several ways in which the poet feels love and connects them to some noble ideas of higher obligations—to justice (line 7), for example, and to spiritual aspiration (lines 2-4). It suggests a wide range of things that love can mean and notices a variety of emotions. It is an ardent statement of feeling and asserts a permanence that will extend even beyond death. It contains admirable thoughts and memorable phrases that many lovers would like to hear said to themselves. What it does not do is say very much about what the relationship between the two lovers is like on an everyday basis, what experiences they have had together, what distinguishes their relationship from that of other devoted or ideal lovers. Its appeal is to our general sense of what love is like and of how intense feelings can be; it does not offer details.

"The Tally Stick" is much more concrete. The whole poem concentrates on a single object that, like "How Do I Love Thee?," "counts" or "tallies" the ways in which this couple love one another. This stick stands for their love and becomes a kind of physical totem for it: its natural features (lines 6, 10, and 12) and the marks carved on it (lines 15-16, 20-21) indicate events in the story of the relationship. We could say that the stick *symbolizes* their love—later on, we will look at terms like this that make it easier to talk about poems—but for now it is enough to notice that the stick serves the lovers as a marker and a reminder of some specific details of their love. It is a special kind of reminder because its language is "secret" (line 2), something they can share privately (except that we as readers of the poem are looking over their shoulders, not intruding but sharing their secret). The poet interprets the particular features of the stick as standing for particular events—their wedding and the births of their children, for example—and carves marks into it as reminders of other events (lines 15 ff.). The stick itself becomes a very personal object, and in the last stanza of the poem it is as if we watch the lovers touching the stick together and reminiscing over it, gradually dissolving into their emotions and each other as they recall the "unforgotten wonders" (line 25) of their lives together.

Both poems are powerful statements of feelings, each in its own way. Various readers will respond differently to each poem; the effect these poems have on their readers will lead some to prefer one and some the other. Personal preference does not mean that objective standards for poetry cannot be found—some poems *are* better than others, and later we will look in detail at features that help us to evaluate poems—but we need no preconceived standards as to what poetry must be or how it must work. Some good poems are quite abstract, others quite specific. Any poem that helps us to articulate and clarify human feelings and ideas has a legitimate claim on us as readers.

Both "How Do I Love Thee?" and "The Tally Stick" are written as if they were addressed to the partner in the love relationship, and both talk directly about the intensity of the love, as does the following poem:

### LINDA PASTAN

### *love poem*

I want to write you
a love poem as headlong
as our creek
after thaw
5   when we stand
on its dangerous
banks and watch it carry
with it every twig
every dry leaf and branch
10  in its path
every scruple
when we see it
so swollen

> with runoff
> 15 that even as we watch
> we must grab
> each other
> and step back
> we must grab each
> 20 other or
> get our shoes
> soaked we must
> grab each other
>
> 1988

The directness and simplicity of this poem suggest how the art and craft of poems work. The poem expresses the desire to write a love poem even as the love poem itself begins to proceed; the desire and the resultant poem exist side by side, and in reading the poem we seem to watch and hear the poet's creative process at work in developing appropriate metaphors and means of expression. The poem must be "headlong" (line 2) to match the power of a love that needs to be compared to the irresistible forces of nature. The poem should, like the love it expresses and the swollen creek it describes, sweep everything along, and it should represent (and reproduce) the sense of watching that the lovers have when they observe natural processes at work. The poem, like the action it represents, has to suggest to readers the kind of desire that grabbing each other means to the lovers.

The lovers in this poem seem, at least to themselves, to own the world they observe, but in fact they are controlled by it. The creek on whose banks they stand is "our creek" (line 3), but what they observe as they watch its rising currents requires them ("must," lines 16, 19, 22) to "grab each other" over and over again. It is as if their love is part of nature itself, which subjects them to forces larger than themselves. Everything—twigs, leaves, branches, scruples—is carried along by the powerful currents after the "thaw" (line 4), and the poem replicates the repeated action of the lovers as if to power along observant readers, just as the lovers are powered along by what they see. But the poem (and their love) admits dangers, too; it is the fact of danger that propels the lovers to each other. The poem suggests that love provides a kind of haven, but the haven hardly involves passivity or peace; instead, it requires the kind of grabbing that means activity and boldness and deep passion. Love here is no quiet or simple matter even if the expression of it in poems can be direct and can stem from a simple observation of experience. The "love poem" itself—linked as it is with the headlong currents of the creek from which the lovers are protecting themselves—even represents that which is beyond love and that which, therefore, both threatens love and at the same time makes it happen. The power of poetry is thus affirmed at the center of the poem, but what poetry is about (love and life) is suggested to be more important. Poetry makes things happen but is not itself a substitute for life, just a means to make life more energetic and meaningful.

The next poem talks only indirectly about the quality and intensity of love. It is written as if it were a letter from a woman to her husband, who has gone on a long journey on business. It directly expresses how much she misses him and indirectly suggests how much she cares about him.

# EZRA POUND

## *The River-Merchant's Wife: A Letter*

*(after Rihaku)*[1]

While my hair was still cut straight across my forehead
I played about the front gate, pulling flowers.
You came by on bamboo stilts, playing horse,
You walked about my seat, playing with blue plums.
5 And we went on living in the village of Chokan:
Two small people, without dislike or suspicion.

At fourteen I married My Lord you.
I never laughed, being bashful.
Lowering my head, I looked at the wall.
10 Called to, a thousand times, I never looked back.

At fifteen I stopped scowling,
I desired my dust to be mingled with yours
For ever and for ever and for ever.
Why should I climb the look out?

15 At sixteen you departed,
You went into far Ku-to-yen, by the river of swirling eddies,
And you have been gone five months.
The monkeys make sorrowful noise overhead.
You dragged your feet when you went out.
20 By the gate now, the moss is grown, the different mosses,
Too deep to clear them away!

The leaves fall early this autumn, in wind.
The paired butterflies are already yellow with August
Over the grass in the West garden;
25 They hurt me. I grow older.
If you are coming down through the narrows of the river Kiang,
Please let me know beforehand,
And I will come out to meet you
    As far as Cho-fu-Sa.

1915

The "letter" tells us only a few facts about the nameless merchant's wife: that she is about sixteen and a half years old, that she married at fourteen and fell in love with her husband a year later, that she is now very lonely. About their relationship we know only that they were childhood playmates in a small Chinese village, that their marriage originally was not a matter of personal choice, and that

---

1. The Japanese name for Li Po, an eighth-century Chinese poet. Pound's poem is a loose paraphrase of one by Li Po.

the husband unwillingly went away on a long journey five months ago. But the words tell us a great deal about how the young wife feels, and the simplicity of her language suggests her sincere and deep longing. The daily noises she hears seem "sorrowful" (line 18), and she worries about the dangers of the faraway place where her husband is, thinking of it in terms of its perilous "river of swirling eddies" (line 16). She thinks of how moss has grown up over the unused gate, and more time seems to her to have passed than actually has (lines 22–25). Nostalgically she remembers their innocent childhood, when they played together without deeper love or commitment (lines 1–6), and contrasts that with her later satisfaction in their love (lines 11–14) and with her present anxiety, loneliness, and desire. We do not need to know the geography of the river Kiang or how far Cho-fu-Sa is to sense that her wish to see him is very strong, that her desire is powerful enough to make her venture beyond the ordinary geographical bounds of her existence so that their reunion will happen sooner. The closest she comes to a direct statement about her love is "I desired my dust to be mingled with yours / For ever and for ever and for ever" (lines 12–13). But her single-minded vision of the world, her perception of even the beauty of nature as only a record of her husband's absence and the passage of time, and her plain, apparently uncalculated language about her rejection of other suitors and her shutting out of the rest of the world all show her to be committed, desirous, nearly desperate for his presence. In a different sense, she too has counted the ways that she loves her man.

Poems can be about the meaning of a relationship or about disappointment just as easily as about emotional fulfillment, and poets are often very good at suggesting the contradictions and uncertainties in relationships. Love does not always go smoothly, and the following poem records (in a kind of monologue, part dream and part waking) the complex longings of a married woman whose attitudes toward marriage are quite different from those of Barrett Browning or the river-merchant's wife.

### LIZ ROSENBERG

## *Married Love*

The trees are uncurling their first
green messages: Spring, and some man
lets his arm brush my arm in a darkened
theatre. Faint-headed, I fight the throb.
5 Later I dream
the gas attendant puts a cool hand
on my breast, asking a question.
Slowly I rise through the surface of the dream,
brushing his hand and my own heat away.
10 Young, I burned to marry. Married,
the smolder goes on underground;
clutching at weeds, writhing everywhere.
I'm trying to talk to a friend on burning

issues, flaming from the feet up,
15 drinking in his breath, touching his wrist.
I want to grab the pretty woman
on the street, seize the falcon
by its neck, beat my way into whistling steam.

I turn to you in the dark, oh husband,
20 watching your lit breath circle the pillow.
Then you turn to me, throwing first one limb
and then another over me, in the easy brotherly
lust of marriage. I cling to you
as if I were a burning ship and you
25 could save me, as if I won't go sliding down
beneath you soon; as if our lives are made of rise
and fall, and we could ride this out forever,
with longing's thunder rolling heavy in our arms.

1986

The initial expectations of springtime and newness here quickly turn into signs, both conscious and unconscious, of desire ("throb") for anonymous sex attraction ("some man"). Reality and fantasy are nearly one here, as the woman tries to reject arousal she does not wish to feel. All the poem, in fact, is full of fire and burning, which the speaker cannot ignore, subdue, or quench; there is hurt here and bewilderment and fear, and the easy habitual comforts of married love are not exactly reassuring ("brotherly lust") nor do they seem to satisfy desire. The woman feels herself to be a burning (and sinking) ship, and her marital clinging seems an act of desperation; she hopes for salvation (or at least a "rid[ing] out"), but "longing's thunder" remains far more powerful than any sense of satisfaction or solution. Poetry does not always celebrate or make us feel better; sometimes, as here, it challenges easy or familiar notions of how feelings are supposed to work, and even the most appealing subjects may be transformed, challenging our assumptions and understanding.

## RESPONDING

The poems we have looked at so far all describe, though in quite different ways, feelings associated with loving or being attached to someone and the expression—either physical or verbal—of those feelings. Watching how poems discover a language for feeling can help us to discover a language for our own feelings, but the process is also reciprocal: being conscious of feelings we already have can lead us into poems more surely and with more satisfaction. Readers with a strong romantic bent—and with strong yearnings or positive memories of desire—will be likely to find "The Tally Stick" and "The River-Merchant's Wife: A Letter" easy to respond to and admire, while those more skeptical of human institutions and male habits may find the wifely despair of "Married Love" more satisfying.

*If I feel physically as if the top of my head were taken off, I know that is poetry.*
—EMILY DICKINSON

Poems can be about all kinds of experiences, and not all the things we find in them will replicate (or even relate to) experiences we may have had individually. But sharing through language will often enable us to uncover feelings—of love or anger, fear or confidence—we did not know we had. The next few poems involve another, far less pleasant set of feelings than those usually generated by love, but even here, where our experience may be limited, we are able to respond, to feel the tug of emotions within us that we may not be fully aware of. In the following poem, a father struggles to understand and control his grief over the death of a seven-year-old son. We don't have to be a father or to have lost a loved one to be aware of—and even share—the speaker's pain, because our own experiences will have given us some idea of what such a loss would feel like. And the words and strategies of the poem may arouse expectations created by our previous experiences.

### BEN JONSON

## *On My First Son*

Farewell, thou child of my right hand,[1] and joy;
My sin was too much hope of thee, loved boy:
Seven years thou wert lent to me, and I thee pay,
Exacted by thy fate, on the just[2] day.
5 O could I lose all father now! for why
Will man lament the state he should envý,
To have so soon 'scaped world's and flesh's rage,
And, if no other misery, yet age?
Rest in soft peace, and asked, say, "Here doth lie
10 Ben Jonson his[3] best piece of poetry."
For whose sake henceforth all his vows be such
As what he loves may never like too much.

1616

This poem's attempts to rationalize the boy's death are quite conventional. Although the father tries to be comforted by pious thoughts, his feelings keep showing through. The poem's beginning—with its formal "farewell" and the rather distant-sounding address to the dead boy ("child of my right hand")—cannot be sustained for long: both of the first two lines end with bursts of emotion. It is as if the father is trying to explain the death to himself and to keep his emotions under control, but cannot quite manage it. Even the punctuation suggests the way his feelings compete with conventional attempts to put the death into some sort of perspective that will soften the grief, and the comma near the end of each of the first two lines marks a pause that cannot quite hold back the overflowing

---

1. A literal translation of the son's name, Benjamin.
2. Exact; the son died on his seventh birthday, in 1603.
3. That is, Ben Jonson's (this was a common Renaissance form of the possessive).

emotion. But finally the only "idea" that the poem supports is that the father wishes he did not feel so intensely; in the fifth line he fairly blurts that he wishes he could lose his fatherly emotions, and in the final lines he resolves never again to "like" so much that he can be this deeply hurt. Philosophy and religion offer their useful counsels in this poem, but they prove far less powerful than feeling. Rather than drawing some kind of moral about what death means, the poem presents the actuality of feeling as inevitable and nearly all-consuming.

The poem that follows also tries to suppress the rawness of feelings about the death of a loved one, but here the survivor is haunted by memories of his wife when he sees a physical object—a vacuum cleaner—that he associates with her.

## HOWARD NEMEROV

### The Vacuum

The house is so quiet now
The vacuum cleaner sulks in the corner closet,
Its bag limp as a stopped lung, its mouth
Grinning into the floor, maybe at my
5  Slovenly life, my dog-dead youth.

I've lived this way long enough,
But when my old woman died her soul
Went into that vacuum cleaner, and I can't bear
To see the bag swell like a belly, eating the dust
10 And the woolen mice, and begin to howl

Because there is old filth everywhere
She used to crawl, in the corner and under the stair.
I know now how life is cheap as dirt,
And still the hungry, angry heart
15 Hangs on and howls, biting at air.

1955

The poem is about a vacuum in the husband's life, but the title refers most obviously to the vacuum cleaner that, like the tally stick we looked at earlier, seems to stand for many of the things that were once important in the life he had together with his wife. The cleaner is a reminder of the dead wife ("my old woman," line 7) because of her devotion to cleanliness. But to the surviving husband buried in the filth of his life it seems as if the machine has become almost human, a kind of ghost of her: it "sulks" (line 2), it has lungs and a mouth (line 3), and it seems to grin, making fun of what has become of him. He "can't bear" (line 8) to see it in action because it then seems too much alive, too much a reminder of her life. The poem records his paralysis, his inability to do more than discover that life is "cheap as dirt" without her ordering and cleansing presence for him. At the end it is *his* angry heart that acts like the haunting machine, howling and biting at air as if he has merged with her spirit and the physical object that memorializes her.

This poem puts a strong emphasis on the stillness of death and the way it makes things seem to stop; it captures in words the hurt, the anger, the inability to understand, the vacuum that remains when a loved one dies and leaves a vacant space. But here we do not see the body or hear a direct good-bye to the dead person; rather we encounter the feeling that lingers and won't go away, recalled through memory by an especially significant object, a mere thing but one that has been personalized to the point of becoming nearly human in itself. (The event described here is, by the way, fictional; the poet's wife did not actually die. Like a dramatist or writer of fiction, the poet may simply *imagine* an event in order to analyze and articulate how such an event might feel in certain circumstances. A work of literature can be *true* without being *actual*.)

Here is another poem about a death:

### SEAMUS HEANEY

### Mid-Term Break

I sat all morning in the college sick bay
Counting bells knelling classes to a close.
At two o'clock our neighbors drove me home.

In the porch I met my father crying—
5 He had always taken funerals in his stride—
And Big Jim Evans saying it was a hard blow.

The baby cooed and laughed and rocked the pram
When I came in, and I was embarrassed
By old men standing up to shake my hand

10 And tell me they were "sorry for my trouble,"
Whispers informed strangers I was the eldest,
Away at school, as my mother held my hand

In hers and coughed out angry tearless sighs.
At ten o'clock the ambulance arrived
15 With the corpse, stanched and bandaged by the nurses.

Next morning I went up into the room. Snowdrops
And candles soothed the bedside; I saw him
For the first time in six weeks. Paler now,

Wearing a poppy bruise on his left temple,
20 He lay in the four foot box as in his cot.
No gaudy scars, the bumper knocked him clear.

A four foot box, a foot for every year.

1966

If, in "The Vacuum," the grief is displaced onto an object left behind, here grief seems almost wordless. The speaker of the poem, the older brother of the dead four-year-old, cannot really articulate his grief and instead provides a lot of meticulous detail, as if giving us information can substitute for an expression of feeling. He is "embarrassed" (line 8) by the attempts of others to say how they feel and to empathize with him. He records the feelings of other family members in detail, but never fully expresses his own feelings, as if he has taken on a kind of deadness of his own that eludes, and substitutes for, articulation. Only when he confronts the bruised body itself can he begin to come to terms with the loss, and even there he resorts to a kind of mathematical formula to displace the feeling so that he doesn't have to talk about it. Though the feelings in the poem are extremely powerful, the power is expressed (as in the Jonson poem above) by suppression. It is not restraint that holds back the young man's grief, but a silence that cannot be put into any words except those of enumerated facts.

Sometimes poems are a way of confronting feelings. Sometimes they explore feelings in detail and try to intellectualize or rationalize them. At other times, poems generate responses by recalling experiences many years in the past. In the following two poems, for example, memories of childhood provide perspective on two very different events. In the first, written as if the person speaking the poem were in the fifth grade, a child's sense of death is portrayed through her exploration of a photograph that makes her grandfather's presence vivid to her memory—a memory that lingers primarily through smell and touch. In the second poem, another childhood memory—this time of overshoes—takes an adult almost physically back into childhood. As you read the two poems, keep track of (or perhaps even jot down) your responses. How much of your feeling is due to your own past experiences? In which specific places? What family photographs do you remember most vividly? What feelings did they evoke that make them so memorable? How are your memories different from those expressed in "Fifth Grade Autobiography"? in "The Fury of Overshoes"? Which feelings expressed in each poem are similar to your own? Where do your feelings differ most strongly? How would you articulate your responses to such memories differently? In what ways does an awareness of your similar—and different—experiences and feelings make you a better reader of the poem?

### RITA DOVE

## *Fifth Grade Autobiography*

I was four in this photograph fishing
with my grandparents at a lake in Michigan.
My brother squats in poison ivy.
His Davy Crockett cap
5  sits squared on his head so the raccoon tail
flounces down the back of his sailor suit.

My grandfather sits to the far right
in a folding chair,
and I know his left hand is on
10  the tobacco in his pants pocket

because I used to wrap it for him
every Christmas. Grandmother's hips
bulge from the brush, she's leaning
into the ice chest, sun through the trees
15 printing her dress with soft
luminous paws.

I am staring jealously at my brother;
the day before he rode his first horse, alone.
I was strapped in a basket
20 behind my grandfather.
He smelled of lemons. He's died—

but I remember his hands.

1989

 **ANNE SEXTON**

## The Fury of Overshoes

They sit in a row
outside the kindergarten,
black, red, brown, all
with those brass buckles.
5 Remember when you couldn't
buckle your own
overshoe
or tie your own
shoe
10 or cut your own meat
and the tears
running down like mud
because you fell off your
tricycle?
15 Remember, big fish,
when you couldn't swim
and simply slipped under
like a stone frog?
The world wasn't
20 yours.
It belonged to
the big people.
Under your bed
sat the wolf
25 and he made a shadow
when cars passed by
at night.
They made you give up

>       your nightlight
>    30 and your teddy
>       and your thumb.
>       Oh overshoes,
>       don't you
>       remember me,
>    35 pushing you up and down
>       in the winter snow?
>       Oh thumb,
>       I want a drink,
>       it is dark,
>    40 where are the big people,
>       when will I get there,
>       taking giant steps
>       all day,
>       each day
>    45 and thinking
>       nothing of it?
>                         1974

There is much more going on in the poems we have glanced at than we have taken time to consider, but even the quickest look at these poems suggests the range of feelings that poems offer—the depth of feeling, the clarity, the experience that may be articulately and precisely shared. Not all poems are as accessible as those we've looked at so far, and even the accessible ones yield themselves to us more readily and more fully if we approach them systematically by developing specific reading habits and skills—just as someone learning to play tennis or to make pottery systematically learns the rules, the techniques, the things to watch out for that are distinctive to the pleasures and hazards of that skill or craft. It helps if you develop a sense of what to expect, and the chapters that follow will show you the things that poets can do—and thus what poems can do for you.

But knowing what to expect isn't everything. As a reader of poetry, you should always be open—to new experiences, new feelings, new ideas. Every poem is a potential new experience, and no matter how sophisticated you become, you can still be surprised (and delighted) by new poems—and by rereading old ones. Good poems bear many, many rereadings, and often one discovers something new with every new reading: there is no such thing as "mastering" a poem, and good poems are not exhausted by repeated readings. Let poems surprise you when you come to them, let them come on their own terms, let them be themselves. If you are open to poetry, you are also open to much more that the world can offer you.

No one can give you a method that will offer you total experience of all poems. But because individual poems often share characteristics with other poems, the following guidelines can prompt you to ask the right questions:

1. *Read the syntax literally.* What the words say literally in normal sentences is only a starting point, but it is the place to start. Not all poems use normal

prose syntax, but most of them do, and you can save yourself embarrassment by paraphrasing accurately (that is, rephrasing what the poem literally says, in plain prose) and not simply free-associating from an isolated word or phrase.

2. *Articulate for yourself what the title, subject, and situation make you expect.* Poets often use false leads and try to surprise you by doing shocking things, but defining expectation lets you become conscious of where you are when you begin.

3. *Identify the poem's situation.* What is said is often conditioned by where it is said and by whom. Identifying the speaker and his or her place in the situation puts what he or she says in perspective.

4. *Find out what is implied by the traditions behind the poem.* Verse forms, poetic kinds, and metrical patterns all have a frame of reference, traditions of the way they are usually used and for what. For example, the **anapest** (two unstressed syllables followed by a stressed one, as in the word *Tennessee*) is usually used for comic poems, and when poets use it "straight" they are probably making a point with this "departure" from tradition.

5. *Use your dictionary, other reference books, and reliable Web sites.* Look up anything you don't understand: an unfamiliar word (or an ordinary word used in an unfamiliar way), a place, a person, a myth, an idea—anything the poem uses. When you can't find what you need or don't know where to look, ask the reference librarian for help.

6. *Remember that poems exist in time, and times change.* Not only the meanings of words, but whole ways of looking at the universe vary in different ages. Consciousness of time works two ways: your knowledge of history provides a context for reading the poem, and the poem's use of a word or idea may modify your notion of a particular age.

7. *Take a poem on its own terms.* Adjust to the poem; don't make the poem adjust to you. Be prepared to hear things you do not want to hear. Not all poems are about your ideas, nor will they always present emotions you want to feel. But be tolerant and listen to the poem's ideas, not only to your wish to revise them for yourself.

8. *Be willing to be surprised.* Things often happen in poems that turn them around. A poem may seem to suggest one thing at first, then persuade you of its opposite, or at least of a significant qualification or variation.

9. *Assume there is a reason for everything.* Poets do make mistakes, but when a poem shows some degree of verbal control it is usually safest to assume that the poet chose each word carefully; if the choice seems peculiar, you may be missing something. Try to account for everything in a poem, see what kind of sense you can make of it, and figure out a coherent **pattern** that explains the text as it stands.

10. *Argue.* Discussion usually results in clarification and keeps you from being too dependent on personal biases and preoccupations that sometimes mislead even the best readers. Talking a poem over with someone else (especially someone who thinks very differently) can expand your perspective.

## WRITING ABOUT POEMS

If you have been keeping notes on your personal responses to the poems you've read, you have already taken an important step toward writing about them. There are many different ways to write about poems, just as there are many different things to say. (The section of the anthology called "Writing about Literature" suggests some ways to come up with a good topic.) But all writing begins with a clear sense of the poem itself and your responses to it, so the first steps (long before formally sitting down to write) are to read the poem several times and keep notes on the things that strike you and the questions that remain.

Formulating a clear series of questions will usually suggest an appropriate approach to the poem and a good topic. Learning to ask the right questions can save you a lot of time. Some questions—the kinds of questions implied in the ten guidelines for reading listed above—are basic and apply, more or less, to all poems. But each poem makes demands of its own, too, because of its distinctive way of going about its business, so you will usually want to list what seem to you the crucial questions for that poem. Here, just to give you an example, are some questions that could lead you to a paper topic about the Aphra Behn poem on p. 828.

1. How does the **title** affect your reading of and response to the poem?
2. What is the poem about?
3. What makes the poem interesting?
4. Who is the **speaker**? What role does the speaker have?
5. What effect does the poem have on you? Do you think the poet intended such an effect?
6. What is distinctive about the poet's use of language? Which words especially contribute to the poem's effect?

What *is* poetry? Let your definition be cumulative as you read more and more poems. No dictionary definition will cover all that you find, and it is better to discover for yourself poetry's many ingredients, its many effects, its many ways of acting. What can it do for you? Wait and see. Add up its effects after you have read carefully—after you have reread and studied—a hundred or so poems; then continue to read new poems or reread old ones.

## PRACTICING READING: SOME POEMS ON LOVE

### W. H. AUDEN

### [*Stop all the clocks, cut off the telephone*]

Stop all the clocks, cut off the telephone,
Prevent the dog from barking with a juicy bone,
Silence the pianos and with muffled drum
Bring out the coffin, let the mourners come.

5 Let aeroplanes circle moaning overhead
Scribbling on the sky the message He Is Dead,
Put crêpe bows round the white necks of the public doves,
Let the traffic policemen wear black cotton gloves.

He was my North, my South, my East and West,
10 My working week and my Sunday rest,
My noon, my midnight, my talk, my song;
I thought that love would last for ever: I was wrong.

The stars are not wanted now: put out every one;
Pack up the moon and dismantle the sun;
15 Pour away the ocean and sweep up the wood;
For nothing now can ever come to any good.

ca. 1936

- Whom does the speaker of this poem seem to be addressing? Why might the poet have proclaimed his grief with such a public declaration as this poem?

### ANNE BRADSTREET

## To My Dear and Loving Husband

If ever two were one, then surely we.
If ever man were loved by wife, then thee;
If ever wife was happy in a man,
Compare with me ye women if you can.
5 I prize thy love more than whole mines of gold,
Or all the riches that the East doth hold.
My love is such that rivers cannot quench,
Nor aught but love from thee give recompense.
Thy love is such I can no way repay;
10 The heavens reward thee manifold, I pray.
Then while we live, in love let's so persever,
That when we live no more we may live ever.

1678

- How does Bradstreet's strategy of characterizing her love through a series of comparisons compare with Barrett Browning's strategy in "How Do I Love Thee?"

**WILLIAM SHAKESPEARE**

## [Let me not to the marriage of true minds]

Let me not to the marriage of true minds
Admit impediments.[1] Love is not love
Which alters when it alteration finds,
Or bends with the remover to remove:
5 Oh, no! it is an ever-fixéd mark,
That looks on tempests and is never shaken;
It is the star to every wandering bark,
Whose worth's unknown, although his height be taken.[2]
Love's not Time's fool, though rosy lips and cheeks
10 Within his bending sickle's compass come;
Love alters not with his brief hours and weeks,
But bears it out even to the edge of doom.
If this be error and upon me proved,
I never writ, nor no man ever loved.

1609

- What might the speaker mean when he says that love doesn't "ben[d] with the remover to remove"?

**SHARON OLDS**

## Last Night

The next day, I am almost afraid.
Love? It was more like dragonflies
in the sun, 100 degrees at noon,
the ends of their abdomens stuck together, I
5 close my eyes when I remember. I hardly
knew myself, like something twisting and
twisting out of a chrysalis,
enormous, without language, all
head, all shut eyes, and the humming
10 like madness, the way they writhe away,
and do not leave, back, back,
away, back. Did I know you? No kiss,
no tenderness—more like killing, death-grip
holding to life, genitals
15 like violent hands clasped tight

---

1. The Marriage Service contains this address to the witnesses: "If any of you know cause or just impediments why these persons should not be joined together...."
2. That is, measuring the altitude of stars (for purposes of navigation) is not a way to measure value.

barely moving, more like being closed
in a great jaw and eaten, and the screaming
I groan to remember it, and when we started
to die, then I refuse to remember,
20 the way a drunkard forgets. After,
you held my hands extremely hard as my
body moved in shudders like the ferry when its
axle is loosed past engagement, you kept me
sealed exactly against you, our hairlines
25 wet as the arc of a gateway after
a cloudburst, you secured me in your arms till I slept—
that was love, and we woke in the morning
clasped, fragrant, buoyant, that was
the morning after love.

1996

- What comparison is the speaker of this poem making between "dragonflies / in the sun" and a night of love-making?

## APHRA BEHN

### *On Her Loving Two Equally*

I

How strongly does my passion flow,
Divided equally twixt[3] two?
Damon had ne'er subdued my heart
Had not Alexis took his part;
5 Nor could Alexis powerful prove,
Without my Damon's aid, to gain my love.

II

When my Alexis present is,
Then I for Damon sigh and mourn;
But when Alexis I do miss,
10 Damon gains nothing but my scorn.
But if it chance they both are by,
For both alike I languish, sigh, and die.

III

Cure then, thou mighty wingéd god,[4]
This restless fever in my blood;
15 One golden-pointed dart take back:
But which, O Cupid, wilt thou take?

---

3. Between.
4. Cupid, who, according to myth, shot darts of lead and of gold at the hearts of lovers, corresponding to false love and true love, respectively.

If Damon's, all my hopes are crossed;
Or that of my Alexis, I am lost.

1684

- What is this poem saying about the nature of love if the speaker's passions are stronger when "divided"?

## DENISE LEVERTOV

### Wedding-Ring

My wedding-ring lies in a basket
as if at the bottom of a well.
Nothing will come to fish it back up
and onto my finger again.
                             It lies
among keys to abandoned houses,
nails waiting to be needed and hammered
into some wall,
telephone numbers with no names attached,
idle paperclips.
                          It can't be given away
for fear of bringing ill-luck.
                          It can't be sold
for the marriage was good in its own
time, though that time is gone.
                          Could some artificer
beat into it bright stones, transform it
into a dazzling circlet no one could take
for solemn betrothal or to make promises
living will not let them keep? Change it
into a simple gift I could give in friendship?

1978

- How does the wedding ring's situation—lying "in a basket / as if at the bottom of a well"—embody the marriage symbolized by the ring?

## MARY, LADY CHUDLEIGH

### To the Ladies

Wife and servant are the same,
But only differ in the name:
For when that fatal knot is tied,

Which nothing, nothing can divide,
5 When she the word *Obey* has said,
And man by law supreme has made,
Then all that's kind is laid aside,
And nothing left but state[5] and pride.
Fierce as an eastern prince he grows,
10 And all his innate rigor shows:
Then but to look, to laugh, or speak,
Will the nuptial contract break.
Like mutes, she signs alone must make,
And never any freedom take,
15 But still be governed by a nod,
And fear her husband as her god:
Him still must serve, him still obey,
And nothing act, and nothing say,
But what her haughty lord thinks fit,
20 Who, with the power, has all the wit.
Then shun, oh! shun that wretched state,
And all the fawning flatterers hate.
Value yourselves, and men despise:
You must be proud, if you'll be wise.
                            1703

- Who do you think is the intended audience for this poem? If the speaker overstates her case to some degree, why might she do so?

## W. B. YEATS

### A Last Confession

What lively lad most pleasured me
Of all that with me lay?
I answer that I gave my soul
And loved in misery,
5 But had great pleasure with a lad
That I loved bodily.

Flinging from his arms I laughed
To think his passion such
He fancied that I gave a soul
10 Did but our bodies touch,
And laughed upon his breast to think
Beast gave beast as much.

I gave what other women gave
That stepped out of their clothes,

---

5. Social position.

15 But when this soul, its body off,
   Naked to naked goes,
   He it has found shall find therein
   What none other knows,

   And give his own and take his own
20 And rule in his own right;
   And though it loved in misery
   Close and cling so tight,
   There's not a bird of day that dare
   Extinguish that delight.

                                    1933

- What distinction is the speaker making between physical and spiritual love? Why would this poem be someone's "last confession"?

---

**SUGGESTIONS FOR WRITING**

1. Of all the love poems in this chapter, which one would you most like to have addressed to you? which least? Write an essay in which you answer the author of either poem you have chosen, explaining what seemed to you most (or least) complimentary in what the poem said about you.
2. Paraphrase—that is, put into different words line by line and stanza by stanza—Behn's "On Her Loving Two Equally" or Yeats's "A Last Confession." Summarize the poem's basic statement in one sentence. How accurately do your paraphrase and summary represent the feelings recorded in the poem? Write an essay in which you discuss the differences between poetry and paraphrases of poetry.
3. Consider your responses to all the marriage poems in this chapter. Which one most accurately expresses your ideal of a good marriage? Why do you think so? What does your choice say about you? Write an essay in which you reflect upon how these poems reinforce, refine, or perhaps even challenge your views of marriage.

# STUDENT WRITING

In the 'response paper' that follows, Stephen Bordland works through Auden's poem "Stop all the clocks, cut off the telephone," more or less line-by-line, writing down whatever ideas come to him. The form of this paper is less important than the process of thinking carefully about the poem's music, emotions, and meanings. As you can see, by the time Stephen reaches the end of his response, he has decided on a topic for the more formal paper that he will write later.

**WEB** For more examples of response papers as well as many first-response exercises, go to LitWeb at *wwnorton.com/introlit/*.

Stephen Bordland
Professor O'Connor
English 157
2 February 2005

Response Paper on
W. H. Auden's "Stop all the clocks, cut off the telephone"

I first heard this poem read aloud when I saw the movie <u>Four Weddings and a Funeral</u> on cable. The character who read the poem was reading it at the funeral of his lover. It was perfectly suited to the story and was very moving. I was struck by the actor's reading because the poem seemed to have a steady rhythm for several lines and then suddenly hit what sounded like a dead end—"I thought that love would last forever: I was wrong." Hearing the actor's reading of this poem made me want to read it myself, to see if the poem would still affect me if I read/heard it outside of the context of an emotional scene in a movie. It did, and I think that the "I was wrong" line is the key—a turning point, I guess.

In the anthology, the poem seems to have no actual title (at least that's how I interpret the fact that the first line is in brackets where the title usually goes), but I did some searching on the Internet and found that this poem was once called "Funeral Blues." If I were reading the poem for the first time under that title, I would at least know that the poem has something to do with death right from the start. But this title makes the poem sound irreverent rather than sincerely painful. I wonder if that would have been true in the 1930s, when Auden wrote the poem. There were lots of blues and jazz songs of that era whose titles ended in "Blues" (like Robert Johnson's "Kindhearted Woman Blues"), so maybe the title wasn't meant to be read the way that I'm reading it. Anyway, I don't know if Auden himself changed the title, or if there's another story there, but I think it's a better poem without the title.

The poem starts with a request to an unknown person (everyone?) to make some common aspects of daily life go away: "Stop all the clocks," presumably because time seems to be standing still; "cut off the telephone," presumably because the speaker wants to be alone and undisturbed, cut off from human contact. I'm not sure what's implied by "Prevent the dog from barking with a juicy bone," mainly because I'm confused about the literal meaning: are we supposed to prevent the dog from barking by giving him a juicy bone (one way to interpret "with a juicy bone"), or are we supposed to prevent the dog with a juicy bone in his mouth (another way of interpreting "with a juicy bone") from barking at all? I don't think I really have a handle on what this line means in relation to the other ones, but I'll leave it for now. In the next line, "Silence the pianos" clearly means that the speaker wants no music now that his lover is dead, except for the "muffled drum" that will accompany the coffin and mourners in the fourth line. It's interesting that all of these things so far are sounds—the tick-tock of the clock, the ring of the telephone, a barking dog, music. They all seem to stand in for something, too—for the passing of time, contact with other people (and with pets?), joy as expressed by music.

The image of "aeroplanes" circling overhead (and "moaning"—that's a really good choice of words) writing "He is Dead" is very strong and would have been a very modern reference at the time of this poem (1936). A Christian Science Monitor article about a "skywriting" pilot says that "Skywriting's heyday was from the 1930s to the early 1950s when Pepsi Cola used skywriting as its main way of advertising" <csmonitor.com/cgi-bin/durableRedirect.pl?/durable/2000/01/25/p22s1.htm>, so the reference here is to a commercial medium being used to make as many people as possible aware of the speaker's loss. If a poet tried to make a reference to something equivalent today, it would have to be a television advertisement or a web log, maybe. I wonder if a modern poet could really pull off a reference to a TV ad and still make it sound sincerely sad.

I'm not sure what the "crepe bows round the white necks of the public doves" means. Would the bows even be visible? Does "crepe" imply a color, or is it just a type of fabric? And what is a public dove? I'm not sure I like the repetition in this line of three adjective/noun pairs: "crepe bows," "white necks," "public doves." It seems too precious or "poetic." The "traffic policemen" that I've seen all wear white gloves so that their hand movements can be seen clearly. The speaker wants them all to wear "black cotton gloves," the appropriate color for mourning, but that would probably create real problems for the drivers trying to see what the policemen are directing them to do. So, I wonder if the bows on doves and black gloves on cops are both there to show us that the speaker is feeling not just the sort of grief that moves him to write poetry, but also the sort of intense pain that makes him want to throw the rest of the world into the same confusion and chaos he's experiencing. Or at least, he's not only asking to be alone, but also wanting the rest of the world to share his grief.

In the next four lines, the speaker turns to himself and his lover: "He was my North, my South, my East and West / My working week and my Sunday rest." These lines flow so smoothly, with a soothing, regular rhythm; they're almost sing-songy. But they don't seem sappy or wrong in this poem; they seem painfully sincere. The author uses place (as described by the compass) and time (the whole week, the reference to noon and midnight) to make very clear, in case we hadn't figured it out from the preceding lines, that his lover was everything to him. In the fourth line of this section, this regular rhythm is interrupted, or even stopped dead: "I thought that love would last for ever: I was wrong." This is a very true and moving conclusion to reach, but it also seems ironic, once we read to the end of the poem. If the speaker was wrong to believe (before the death of his lover) that love would last forever, isn't it possible that he's wrong about the conclusion "nothing now can ever come to any good"—that grief will last forever

I think that Auden probably intended us to be aware of this irony. It seems to me that the poem is broken into three major parts: first, we sympathize with the speaker's grief and sense of loss. Then we're supposed to stop at the point where the speaker makes a judgment about his understanding of the world prior to that loss ("I thought that love would last for ever: I was wrong") and to spend a moment absorbing the meaning of that judgment. Finally, as we read the most extreme expression of the speaker's loss ("Pack up the moon and dismantle the sun"), we can see that although we sympathize and understand, we also know something that the speaker doesn't know at the moment. Just as his love apparently blinded the speaker to love's inevitable end, his profound grief is probably blinding him to grief's inevitable end. Also, it may just be me, but it seems that this last part is almost too dramatic or theatrical, as if maybe the speaker has made some sort of transition from being unself-consciously mournful to being self-consciously aware that the way he's expressing himself is poetic.

Back to the idea about the irony: the poem itself seems to be arguing against the notion that love cannot last forever (or, okay, a very long time). After all, people are still reading this poem, and I bet people will continue to read it for as long as people read poetry. That's about as close to forever as we get on this earth, so even though the lovers of this poem are long dead, their love lives on, in a way. Auden must have been aware of this when he was writing the poem. I wonder if he ever said anything in letters, essays, or speeches about art and immortality? If so, I think I'll write a paper on that topic as addressed in this poem.

# Understanding the Text

## 13 TONE

Poetry is full of surprises. Poems express anger or outrage just as effectively as love or sadness, and good poems can be written about going to a rock concert or having lunch or mowing the lawn, as well as about making love or smelling flowers or listening to Beethoven. Even poems on "predictable" subjects can surprise us with unpredicted attitudes, unusual events, or sudden twists. Knowing that a poem is about some particular subject—love, for example, or death—may give us a general idea of what to expect, but it never tells us altogether what we will find in a particular poem. Responding to a poem fully means being open to the poem and its surprises, letting the poem guide us to its own stances, feelings, and ideas—to an illumination of a topic that may be very different from what we expect or what we have thought before. Letting a poem speak to us means listening to *how* the poem says what it says—hearing the tone of voice implied in the way the words are spoken. *What* a poem says involves its **theme**, a statement about its subject. *How* a poem makes that statement involves its **tone**, the poem's attitude or feelings toward the theme.

The following two poems—one about death and one about love—express attitudes and feelings quite different from those in the poems we have read so far.

### MARGE PIERCY

### *Barbie Doll*

This girlchild was born as usual
and presented dolls that did pee-pee
and miniature GE stoves and irons
and wee lipsticks the color of cherry candy.
5 Then in the magic of puberty, a classmate said:
You have a great big nose and fat legs.

She was healthy, tested intelligent,
possessed strong arms and back,
abundant sexual drive and manual dexterity.
10 She went to and fro apologizing.
Everyone saw a fat nose on thick legs.

She was advised to play coy,
exhorted to come on hearty,
exercise, diet, smile and wheedle.

15 Her good nature wore out
   like a fan belt.
   So she cut off her nose and her legs
   and offered them up.

   In the casket displayed on satin she lay
20 with the undertaker's cosmetics painted on,
   a turned-up putty nose,
   dressed in a pink and white nightie.
   Doesn't she look pretty? everyone said.
   Consummation at last.
25 To every woman a happy ending.

                                    1973

## W. D. SNODGRASS

### *Leaving the Motel*

   Outside, the last kids holler
   Near the pool: they'll stay the night.
   Pick up the towels; fold your collar
   Out of sight.

5  Check: is the second bed
   Unrumpled, as agreed?
   Landlords have to think ahead
   In case of need,

   Too. Keep things straight: don't take
10 The matches, the wrong keyrings—
   We've nowhere we could keep a keepsake—
   Ashtrays, combs, things

   That sooner or later others
   Would accidentally find.
15 Check: take nothing of one another's
   And leave behind

   Your license number only,
   Which they won't care to trace;
   We've paid. Still, should such things get lonely,
20 Leave in their vase

   An aspirin to preserve
   Our lilacs, the wayside flowers
   We've gathered and must leave to serve
   A few more hours;

25  That's all. We can't tell when
    We'll come back, can't press claims,
    We would no doubt have other rooms then,
    Or other names.

1968

The first poem, "Barbie Doll," has the strong note of sadness that characterizes many death poems, but it emphasizes not the girl's death but the disappointments in her life. The only "scene" in the poem (lines 19-23) portrays the unnamed girl at rest in her casket, but the still body in the casket contrasts not with vitality but with frustration and anxiety: her life since puberty (lines 5-6) had been full of apologies and attempts to change her physical appearance and emotional makeup. The "consummation" she achieves in death is not, however, a triumph, despite what people say (line 23). Although the poem's last two words are "happy ending," this girl without a name has died in embarrassment and without fulfillment, and the final lines are ironic, questioning the whole idea of what "happy" means. The cheerful comments at the end lack force and truth because of what we already know; we understand them as ironic because they underline how unhappy the girl was and how false her cosmeticized corpse is to the sad truth of her life.

The poem suggests the falsity and destructiveness of those standards of female beauty that have led to the tragedy of the girl's life. In an important sense, the poem is not really *about* death at all in spite of the fact that the girl's death and her repaired corpse are central to it. As the title suggests, the poem dramatizes how standardized, commercialized notions of femininity and prettiness can be painful and destructive to those whose bodies do not precisely fit the conformist models, and the poem vigorously attacks those conventional standards and the widespread, unthinking acceptance of them.

"Leaving the Motel" similarly goes in quite a different direction from many poems on the subject of love. Instead of expressing assurance about how love lasts and endures, or about the sincerity and depth of affection, this poem describes a parting of lovers after a brief, surreptitious sexual encounter. But it does not emphasize sexuality or eroticism in the meeting of the nameless lovers (we see them only as they prepare to leave), nor does it suggest why or how they have found each other, or what either of them is like as a person. It focuses on how careful they must be not to get caught, how exact and calculating they must be in their planning, how finite and limited their encounter must be, how sealed off this encounter is from the rest of their lives. The poem relates the tiny details the lovers must think of, the agreements they must observe, and the ritual checklist of their duties ("Check ... Keep things straight ... Check ... ," lines 5, 9, 15). Affection and sentiment have their small place in the poem (notice the care for the flowers, lines 19-24, and the thought of "press[ing] claims," line 26), but the emphasis is on temporariness, uncertainty, and limits. Although it is about an illicit, perhaps adulterous, sexual encounter, there is no sex in the poem, only a kind of archaeological record of lust.

Labeling a poem a "love poem" or a "death poem" is primarily a matter of convenience; such categories indicate the **subject** of a poem, or the event or **topic** it chooses to engage. But as the poems we have been looking at suggest, poems that may be loosely called "love poems" or "death poems" may differ widely from one another, express totally different attitudes or ideas, and concentrate on very different aspects of the subject. The main advantages of grouping poems in this way is that a reader can become conscious of individual differences; a reading of two poems side by side may suggest how each is distinctive in what it has to say and how it says it.

The theme of a poem may be expressed in several different ways, and poems often have more than one theme. We could say, for example, that the theme of "Leaving the Motel" is that illicit love is secretive, careful, transitory, and short on emotion and sentiment, or that secret sexual encounters tend to be brief, calculated, and characterized by restrained or hesitant feelings. "Barbie Doll" suggests that commercialized standards destroy humane values; that rigid and idealized notions of normality cripple those who are different; that people are easily and tragically led to accept evaluations thrust upon them by others; that American consumers tend to be conformists, easily influenced in their outlook by advertising and by commercial products; that children who do not conform to middle-class standards and notions don't have a chance. The poem implies each of these ideas, and all are quite central to it. But none of these assertions individually nor all of them together can fully express or explain the poem itself. To state the themes in such a brief and abstract way—though it may help to clarify what the poem does and does not say—cannot do justice to the experience of the poem, the way it works on us as readers, the way we respond. Poems affect us in all sorts of ways—emotional and psychological as well as rational—and often a poem's dramatization of a story, an event, or a moment bypasses our rational responses and affects us far more deeply than a clear and logical argument would.

Here is a poem even more directly about desire and its implications. It too is cautious, even critical, but it represents the appeal of both drugs and sex as powerfully as it depicts the fear of their consequences. The "Plague" is here the AIDS epidemic in America, especially among gay men, in the early 1990s.

### THOM GUNN

## *In Time of Plague*

My thoughts are crowded with death
and it draws so oddly on the sexual
that I am confused
confused to be attracted
5   by, in effect, my own annihilation.
Who are these two, these fiercely attractive men
who want me to stick their needle in my arm?
They tell me they are called Brad and John,
one from here, one from Denver, sitting the same
10   on the bench as they talk to me,
their legs spread apart, their eyes attentive.
I love their daring, their looks, their jargon,
and what they have in mind.

Their mind is the mind of death.
15 They know it, and do not know it,
and they are like me in that
(I know it, and do not know it)
and like the flow of people through this bar.
Brad and John thirst heroically together
20 for euphoria—for a state of ardent life
in which we could all stretch ourselves
and lose our differences. I seek
to enter their minds: am I a fool,
and they direct and right, properly
25 testing themselves against risk,
as a human must, and does,
or are they the fools, their alert faces
mere death's heads lighted glamorously?

I weigh possibilities
30 till I am afraid of the strength
of my own health
and of their evident health.

They get restless at last with my indecisiveness
and so, first one, and then the other,
35 move off into the moving concourse of people
who are boisterous and bright
carrying in their faces and throughout their bodies
the news of life and death.

1992

Delicate subject, sensitive poem. The situation and narrative here are quite clear, and the speaker is plainly attracted by the two men and "what they have in mind" (line 13), but the poem is about a mental state rather than physical action. The tone is carefully poised between excitement and fear—so much so that the two emotions don't just coexist but are nearly one, and a lust for life and attraction to death are very close. The speaker realizes that he is "attracted by . . . my own annihilation" (lines 4–5), and his vacillation about action involves an internal debate ("I weigh possibilities," line 29) between desire and self-protection. The tone of voice here is both excited and cautionary—at the same time.

Poems, then, can differ widely from one another even when they share a common subject. And the subjects of poetry can also vary widely. It isn't true that certain subjects are "poetic" and that others aren't appropriate to poetry. Any human activity, thought, or feeling can be the subject of poetry. Poetry often deals with beauty and the softer, more attractive human emotions, but it can deal with ugliness and unattractive human conduct as well, for poetry seeks to represent human beings and human events, showing us ourselves not only as we would like to be but as we are. Good poetry gets written about all kinds of topics, in all kinds of forms, with all kinds of attitudes. Here, for example, is a poem about a prison inmate—and about the conflict between individual and societal values.

ETHERIDGE KNIGHT

## Hard Rock Returns to Prison from the Hospital for the Criminal Insane

Hard Rock was "known not to take no shit
From nobody," and he had the scars to prove it:
Split purple lips, lumped ears, welts above
His yellow eyes, and one long scar that cut
5   Across his temple and plowed through a thick
Canopy of kinky hair.

The WORD was that Hard Rock wasn't a mean nigger
Anymore, that the doctors had bored a hole in his head,
Cut out part of his brain, and shot electricity
10  Through the rest. When they brought Hard Rock back,
Handcuffed and chained, he was turned loose,
Like a freshly gelded stallion, to try his new status.
And we all waited and watched, like indians at a corral,
To see if the WORD was true.

15  As we waited we wrapped ourselves in the cloak
Of his exploits: "Man, the last time, it took eight
Screws to put him in the Hole."[1] "Yeah, remember when he
Smacked the captain with his dinner tray?" "He set
The record for time in the Hole—67 straight days!"
20  "Ol Hard Rock! man, that's one crazy nigger."
And then the jewel of a myth that Hard Rock had once bit
A screw on the thumb and poisoned him with syphilitic spit.

The testing came, to see if Hard Rock was really tame.
A hillbilly called him a black son of a bitch
25  And didn't lose his teeth, a screw who knew Hard Rock
From before shook him down and barked in his face.
And Hard Rock did *nothing*. Just grinned and looked silly,
His eyes empty like knot holes in a fence.

And even after we discovered that it took Hard Rock
30  Exactly 3 minutes to tell you his first name,
We told ourselves that he had just wised up,
Was being cool; but we could not fool ourselves for long,
And we turned away, our eyes on the ground. Crushed.
He had been our Destroyer, the doer of things
35  We dreamed of doing but could not bring ourselves to do,
The fears of years, like a biting whip,
Had cut grooves too deeply across our backs.

1968

---

1. Solitary confinement. *Screws*: guards.

The picture of Hard Rock as a kind of hero to other prison inmates is established early in the poem through a retelling of the legends circulated about him; the straightforward chronology of the poem sets up the mystery of how he will react after his "treatment" in the hospital. The poem identifies with those who wait; they are hopeful that Hard Rock's spirit has not been broken by surgery or shock treatments, and the lines crawl almost to a stop with disappointment in stanza 4. The *"nothing"* (line 27) of Hard Rock's response to taunting and the emptiness of his eyes ("like knot holes in a fence," line 28) reduce the narrator's hopes to despair. The final stanza recounts the observers' attempts to reinterpret, to hang onto hope that their symbol of heroism can stand up against the best efforts to tame him, but the spirit has gone out of the hero-worshipers, too, and the poem records them as beaten, tamed, deprived of their spirit as Hard Rock has been of his. The poem records the despair of the hopeless, and it protests against the cruel exercise of power that can quash even as defiant a figure as Hard Rock.

The following poem is equally full of anger and disappointment, but it expresses its attitudes in a very different way.

### WILLIAM BLAKE

## *London*

I wander through each chartered street,
Near where the chartered Thames does flow,
And mark in every face I meet
Marks of weakness, marks of woe.

5 In every cry of every man,
In every Infant's cry of fear,
In every voice, in every ban,
The mind-forged manacles I hear.

How the Chimney-sweeper's cry
10 Every black'ning Church appalls;
And the hapless Soldier's sigh
Runs in blood down Palace walls.

But most through midnight streets I hear
How the youthful Harlot's curse
15 Blasts the new-born Infant's tear,
And blights with plagues the Marriage hearse.

1794

The poem gives a strong sense of how London feels to this particular observer; it is cluttered, constricting, oppressive. The wordplay here articulates and connects the strong emotions he associates with London experiences. The repeated words—"every," for example, and "cry"—intensify the sense of total despair in the city and create connections between things not necessarily related, such as the cries of street vendors with the cries for help. The twice-used word "chartered" implies strong feelings, too. The streets, instead of seeming alive with people or bustling with movement, are rigidly, coldly determined, controlled, cramped. Likewise the river seems as if it were planned, programmed, laid out by an oppressor. In actual fact, the course of the Thames through the city had been altered (slightly) by the government before Blake's time, but most important is the word's emotional force, the sense it projects of constriction and artificiality: the speaker experiences London as if human artifice had totally usurped nature. Moreover, according to the poem, people are victimized, "marked" by their confrontations with the city and its faceless institutions: the "Soldier's sigh" that "runs in blood down Palace walls" vividly suggests, through metaphor, both the powerlessness of the individual and the callousness of power. The description of the city has clearly become, by now, a subjective, highly emotional, and vivid expression of how the speaker feels about London and what it represents to him.

> *Poetry makes nothing happen.*
> —W. H. AUDEN

Another thing about "London": at first it looks like an account of a personal experience, as if the speaker is describing and interpreting as he goes along: "I wander through each chartered street." But soon it is clear that he is describing many wanderings, putting together impressions from many walks, re-creating a typical walk—which shows him "every" person in the streets, allows him to generalize about the churches being "appalled" (literally, made white) by the cry of the representative Chimney-sweeper, and leads to his conclusions about soldiers, prostitutes, and infants. We receive not a personal record of an event, but a representation of it in retrospect—not a story, not a narrative or chronological account of events, but a dramatization of self that compresses many experiences and impressions into one.

> *When power leads man toward arrogance, poetry reminds him of his limitations. When power narrows the areas of man's concern, poetry reminds him of the richness and diversity of his existence. When power corrupts, poetry cleanses.*
> —JOHN F. KENNEDY

"London" is somber in spite of the poet's playfulness with words. Wordplay may be witty and funny if it calls attention to its own cleverness, but here it prompts the discovery of unsuspected (but meaningful) connections between things. The tone of the poem is sad, despairing, and angry; reading it aloud, one would try to show in the tone of one's voice the strong feelings that the poem expresses, just as one would try to reproduce tenderness and caring and passion in reading aloud "The Tally Stick" or "How Do I Love Thee?"

The following two poems are "about" animals, although both of them place their final emphasis on human beings: the animal in each case is only the means to the end of exploring human nature. The poems share a common assumption that animal behavior may appear to reflect human habits and conduct and may reveal much about ourselves, and in each case the character central to the poem is revealed to be surprisingly unlike the way she thinks of herself. But the poems are very different. Read each poem aloud, and try to imagine what each main character is like. What tones of voice do you use to help express the character of the "killer" (line 24) in the first poem? What demands on your voice does the second poem make?

MAXINE KUMIN

## Woodchucks

Gassing the woodchucks didn't turn out right.
The knockout bomb from the Feed and Grain Exchange
was featured as merciful, quick at the bone
and the case we had against them was airtight,
5 both exits shoehorned shut with puddingstone,[2]
but they had a sub-sub-basement out of range.

Next morning they turned up again, no worse
for the cyanide than we for our cigarettes
and state-store Scotch, all of us up to scratch.
10 They brought down the marigolds as a matter of course
and then took over the vegetable patch
nipping the broccoli shoots, beheading the carrots.

The food from our mouths, I said, righteously thrilling
to the feel of the .22, the bullets' neat noses.
15 I, a lapsed pacifist fallen from grace
puffed with Darwinian pieties for killing,
now drew a bead on the littlest woodchuck's face.
He died down in the everbearing roses.

Ten minutes later I dropped the mother. She
20 flipflopped in the air and fell, her needle teeth
still hooked in a leaf of early Swiss chard.
Another baby next. O one-two-three
the murderer inside me rose up hard,
the hawkeye killer came on stage forthwith.

25 There's one chuck left. Old wily fellow, he keeps
me cocked and ready day after day after day.
All night I hunt his humped-up form. I dream
I sight along the barrel in my sleep.
If only they'd all consented to die unseen
30 gassed underground the quiet Nazi way.

**1972**

---

2. A mixture of cement, pebbles, and gravel.

ADRIENNE RICH

## Aunt Jennifer's Tigers

Aunt Jennifer's tigers prance across a screen,
Bright topaz denizens of a world of green.
They do not fear the men beneath the tree;
They pace in sleek chivalric certainty.

5 Aunt Jennifer's fingers fluttering through her wool
Find even the ivory needle hard to pull.
The massive weight of Uncle's wedding band
Sits heavily upon Aunt Jennifer's hand.

When Aunt is dead, her terrified hands will lie
10 Still ringed with ordeals she was mastered by.
The tigers in the panel that she made
Will go on prancing, proud and unafraid.

1951

If you read "Woodchucks" aloud, how would your tone of voice change from beginning to end? What tone would you use to read the ending? How does the hunter feel about her increasing attraction to violence? Why does the poem begin by calling the gassing of the woodchucks "merciful" and end by describing it as "the quiet Nazi way"? What names does the hunter call herself? How does the name-calling affect your feelings about her? Exactly when does the hunter begin to *enjoy* the feel of the gun and the idea of killing? How does the poet make that clear?

In the second poem, why are tigers a particularly appropriate contrast to the quiet and subdued manner of Aunt Jennifer? What words describing the tigers seem particularly significant? How is the tiger an opposite of Aunt Jennifer? In what ways does it externalize her secrets? Why are Aunt Jennifer's hands described as "terrified"? What clues does the poem give about why Aunt Jennifer is so afraid? How does the poem make you feel about Aunt Jennifer? about her tigers? about her life? How would you describe the tone of the poem? How does the poet feel about Aunt Jennifer?

Twenty years after writing "Aunt Jennifer's Tigers," Adrienne Rich said this about the poem:

> In writing this poem, composed and apparently cool as it is, I thought I was creating a portrait of an imaginary woman. But this woman suffers from the opposition of her imagination, worked out in tapestry, and her lifestyle, "ringed with ordeals she was mastered by." It was important to me that Aunt Jennifer was a person as distinct from myself as possible—distanced by the formalism of the poem, by its objective, observant tone—even by putting the woman in a different generation. In those years formalism was part of the strategy—like asbestos gloves, it allowed me to handle materials I couldn't pick up bare-handed.[3]

---

3. From "When We Dead Awaken: Writing As Re-Vision," a talk given in December 1971 at the Women's Forum of the Modern Language Association.

Not often do we have such an explicit comment on a poem by its author, and (although such a statement may clarify why the author chose a particular mode of presentation and how the poem fits into the author's own patterns of thinking and growing) we don't actually need the explanation in order to understand and experience the force of the poem. Most poems contain within them all we need to tap the human and artistic resources they offer us.

Subject, theme, and tone: each of these categories gives us a way to begin considering poems and how one poem differs from another. Comparing poems with the same subject or a similar theme or tone can lead to a clearer understanding of each individual poem and can refine our responses to their subtle differences. The title of a poem ("Leaving the Motel," for example) or the way a poem first introduces its subject can often give us a sense of what to expect, but we must be open to surprise, too. No two poems affect us in exactly the same way; the variety of possible poems multiplies when you think of all the possible themes and tones that can be explored within any single subject. Varieties of feeling often coincide with varieties of thinking, and readers open to the pleasures of the unexpected may find themselves learning, growing, becoming more sensitive to ideas and human issues—as well as more articulate about feelings and thoughts they already have.

## MANY TONES: POEMS ABOUT FAMILY RELATIONSHIPS

### GALWAY KINNELL

## *After Making Love We Hear Footsteps*

For I can snore like a bullhorn
or play loud music
or sit up talking with any reasonably sober Irishman
and Fergus will only sink deeper
5   into his dreamless sleep, which goes by all in one flash,
but let there be that heavy breathing
or a stifled come-cry anywhere in the house
and he will wrench himself awake
and make for it on the run—as now, we lie together,
10  after making love, quiet, touching along the length of our bodies,
familiar touch of the long-married,
and he appears—in his baseball pajamas, it happens,
the neck opening so small
he has to screw them on, which one day may make him wonder
15  about the mental capacity of baseball players—
and says, "Are you loving and snuggling? May I join?"
He flops down between us and hugs us and snuggles himself to sleep,
his face gleaming with satisfaction at being this very child.

In the half darkness we look at each other
20  and smile
and touch arms across his little, startlingly muscled body—

this one whom habit of memory propels to the ground of his making,
sleeper only the mortal sounds can sing awake,
this blessing love gives again into our arms.

1980

- How does the language in lines 1–5 establish the poem's tone? Do the last lines (starting with line 22) alter the tone in any way?

## EMILY GROSHOLZ

### *Eden*

In lurid cartoon colors, the big baby
dinosaur steps backwards under the shadow
of an approaching tyrannosaurus rex.
"His mommy going to fix it," you remark,
5 serenely anxious, hoping for the best.

After the big explosion, after the lights
go down inside the house and up the street,
we rush outdoors to find a squirrel stopped
in straws of half-gnawed cable. I explain,
10 trying to fit the facts, "The squirrel is dead."

No, you explain it otherwise to me.
"He's sleeping. And his mommy going to come."
Later, when the squirrel has been removed,
"His mommy fix him," you insist, insisting
15 on the right to know what you believe.

The world is truly full of fabulous
great and curious small inhabitants,
and you're the freshly minted, unashamed
Adam in this garden. You preside,
20 appreciate, and judge our proper names.

Like God, I brought you here.
Like God, I seem to be omnipotent,
mostly helpful, sometimes angry as hell.
I fix whatever minor faults arise
25 with bandaids, batteries, masking tape, and pills.

But I am powerless, as you must know,
to chase the serpent sliding in the grass,
or the tall angel with the flaming sword
who scares you when he rises suddenly
30 behind the gates of sunset.

1992

- How does Grosholz use language to elevate the poem's subject matter from the trivial and childish to the biblical and profound?

**LI-YOUNG LEE**

## *Persimmons*

In sixth grade Mrs. Walker
slapped the back of my head
and made me stand in the corner
for not knowing the difference
5   between *persimmon* and *precision*.
How to choose
persimmons. This is precision.
Ripe ones are soft and brown-spotted.
Sniff the bottoms. The sweet one
10  will be fragrant. How to eat:
put the knife away, lay down newspaper.
Peel the skin tenderly, not to tear the meat.
Chew the skin, suck it,
and swallow. Now, eat
15  the meat of the fruit,
so sweet,
all of it, to the heart.

Donna undresses, her stomach is white.
In the yard, dewy and shivering
20  with crickets, we lie naked,
face-up, face-down.
I teach her Chinese.
Crickets: *chiu chiu*. Dew: I've forgotten.
Naked:    I've forgotten.
25  *Ni, wo:* you and me.
I part her legs,
remember to tell her
she is beautiful as the moon.

Other words
30  that got me into trouble were
*fight* and *fright, wren* and *yarn.*
Fight was what I did when I was frightened,
fright was what I felt when I was fighting.
Wrens are small, plain birds,
35  yarn is what one knits with.
Wrens are soft as yarn.
My mother made birds out of yarn.
I loved to watch her tie the stuff;
a bird, a rabbit, a wee man.

40  Mrs. Walker brought a persimmon to class
and cut it up
so everyone could taste

a *Chinese apple.* Knowing
it wasn't ripe or sweet, I didn't eat
45 but watched the other faces.

My mother said every persimmon has a sun
inside, something golden, glowing,
warm as my face.

Once, in the cellar, I found two wrapped in newspaper,
50 forgotten and not yet ripe.
I took them and set both on my bedroom windowsill,
where each morning a cardinal
sang, *The sun, the sun.*
Finally understanding
55 he was going blind,
my father sat up all one night
waiting for a song, a ghost.
I gave him the persimmons,
swelled, heavy as sadness,
60 and sweet as love.

This year, in the muddy lighting
of my parents' cellar, I rummage, looking
for something I lost.
My father sits on the tired, wooden stairs,
65 black cane between his knees,
hand over hand, gripping the handle.

He's so happy that I've come home.
I ask how his eyes are, a stupid question.
*All gone,* he answers.

70 Under some blankets, I find a box.
Inside the box I find three scrolls.
I sit beside him and untie
three paintings by my father:
Hibiscus leaf and a white flower.
75 Two cats preening.
Two persimmons, so full they want to drop from the cloth.

He raises both hands to touch the cloth,
asks, *Which is this?*

*This is persimmons, Father.*

80 *Oh, the feel of the wolftail on the silk,
the strength, the tense
precision in the wrist.
I painted them hundreds of times
eyes closed. These I painted blind.*
85 *Some things never leave a person:
scent of the hair of one you love,*

*the texture of persimmons,*
*in your palm, the ripe weight.*

1986

- How does the tone shift as the focal point of the poem changes? What key words and phrases mark the tone in each stanza?

PAUL MULDOON

## Milkweed and Monarch

As he knelt by the grave of his mother and father
the taste of dill, or tarragon—
he could barely tell one from the other—

filled his mouth. It seemed as if he might smother.
5 Why should he be stricken
with grief, not for his mother and father,

but a woman slinking from the fur of a sea-otter
in Portland, Maine, or, yes, Portland, Oregon—
he could barely tell one from the other—

10 and why should he now savor
the tang of her, her little pickled gherkin,
as he knelt by the grave of his mother and father?

He looked about. He remembered her palaver
on how both earth and sky would darken—
15 "You could barely tell one from the other"—

while the Monarch butterflies passed over
in their milkweed-hunger: "A wing-beat, some reckon,
may trigger off the mother and father

of all storms, striking your Irish Cliffs of Mohel[1]
20 with the force of a hurricane."
Then: "Milkweed and Monarch 'invented' each other."

He looked about. Cow's-parsley[2] in a samovar.
He'd mistaken his mother's name, "Regan," for "Anger":
as he knelt by the grave of his mother and father
25 he could barely tell one from the other.

1999

- What is the effect of the repeating words "father" and "other" on the tone of the poem? What is the feeling of the poem's final stanza?

---

1. Tall, rocky cliffs on the coast of western Ireland that are constantly buffeted by the Atlantic.
2. Another name for Queen Anne's lace, a flowering plant with small, white blossoms that grows in fields and on roadsides.

## ROBERT HAYDEN
### Those Winter Sundays

Sundays too my father got up early
and put his clothes on in the blueblack cold,
then with cracked hands that ached
from labor in the weekday weather made
5   banked fires blaze. No one ever thanked him.

I'd wake and hear the cold splintering, breaking.
When the rooms were warm, he'd call,
and slowly I would rise and dress,
fearing the chronic angers of that house,

10  Speaking indifferently to him,
who had driven out the cold
and polished my good shoes as well.
What did I know, what did I know
of love's austere and lonely offices?

1966

- Why does the poem begin with the words "Sundays too" (rather than, say, "On Sundays")? What are the "austere and lonely offices" of love in the poem's final line?

## DANIEL TOBIN
### The Clock

Bored with plastic armies,
he climbs onto the parlor loveseat
and watches the wide expression of the clock.
He doesn't know what time is,
5   doesn't know how in no time
those numbers will fill his days
the way water fills a bath
into which an exhausted man
lowers himself, not wanting to rise.
10  Sun and moon gaze back at him
from the glaze of the silver frame,
each with a human face,
his own face mirrored there.
Look closer, his mother says,
15  and you can see the small hand move.
And he leans closer now, steadied

in her arms, the hand a winded runner
lapped on the track. That's hours,
she says, the big hand's minutes, the quick,
20 seconds. And the boy fingers the pivot
anchoring them, his touch
stirs with the machine.
*I'm older now, and now, and now.* The gears
start to tick through every room of that house.

1999

- How do the language and tone shift when the boy touches the clock? What exactly has changed?

**SEAMUS HEANEY**

## Mother of the Groom

What she remembers
Is his glistening back
In the bath, his small boots
In the ring of boots at her feet.
5 Hands in her voided lap,
She hears a daughter welcomed.
It's as if he kicked when lifted
And slipped her soapy hold.

Once soap would ease off
10 The wedding ring
That's bedded forever now
In her clapping hand.

1966

- Which words in the poem appear to have double meanings? How does this use of language affect the poem's tone?

## AGHA SHAHID ALI
### Postcard from Kashmir

(for Pavan Sahgal)

Kashmir shrinks into my mailbox,
my home a neat four by six inches.

I always loved neatness. Now I hold
the half-inch Himalayas in my hand.
This is home. And this the closest
I'll ever be to home. When I return,
the colors won't be so brilliant,
the Jhelum's waters[3] so clean,
so ultramarine. My love
so overexposed.

And my memory will be a little
out of focus, in it
a giant negative, black
and white, still undeveloped.

1987

- What words characterize the speaker's dreams of home in this poem? What words reveal a more realistic attitude?

## OLIVE SENIOR
### Ancestral Poem

I

My ancestors are nearer
than albums of pictures
I tread on heels thrust
into broken-down slippers.

II

My mother's womb impulsed
harvests perpetually. She
deeply breathed country air
when she labored me.

III

The pattern woven by my
father's hands lulled me

---

3. The river Jhelum runs through Kashmir and Pakistan.

to sleep. Certain actions
moved me so: my father
planting.

When my father planted
15 his thoughts took flight.
He did not need to think.
The ritual was ingrained
in the blood, embedded
in the centuries of dirt
20 beneath his fingernails
encased in the memories
of his race.

(Yet the whiplash of my
father's wrath rever-
25 berated days in my
mind with the inten-
sity of tuning forks.
He did not think.
My mother stunned wept
30 and prayed Father
Forgive Them knowing not
what she prayed for.)

One day I did not pray
A gloss of sunlight through
35 the leaves betrayed me so
abstracted me from rituals.
And discarded prayers and
disproven myths
confirmed me freedom.

     IV

40 Now against the rhythms
of subway trains my
heartbeats still drum
worksongs. Some wheels
sing freedom, the others:
45 home.

Still, if I could balance
water on my head I can
juggle worlds
on my shoulders

     1985

- How do the poet's unusual word usages—for example, "My mother's womb impulsed / harvests perpetually" and "when she labored me"—contribute to the poem's tone?

**PAT MORA**

## Elena

My Spanish isn't enough.
I remember how I'd smile
listening to my little ones,
understanding every word they'd say,
5 their jokes, their songs, their plots.
    *Vamos a pedirle dulces a mamá. Vamos.*[4]
But that was in Mexico.
Now my children go to American high schools.
They speak English. At night they sit around
10 the kitchen table, laugh with one another.
I stand by the stove and feel dumb, alone.
I bought a book to learn English.
My husband frowned, drank more beer.
My oldest said, "Mamá, he doesn't want you
15 to be smarter than he is." I'm forty,
embarrassed at mispronouncing words,
embarrassed at the laughter of my children,
the grocer, the mailman. Sometimes I take
my English book and lock myself in the bathroom,
20 say the thick words softly,
    for if I stop trying, I will be deaf
when my children need my help.

1985

- What does the speaker mean by the first line—"My Spanish isn't enough"? What other words in the poem address the inadequacy of language?

**JIMMY SANTIAGO BACA**

## Green Chile

I prefer red chile over my eggs
and potatoes for breakfast.
Red chile *ristras*[5] decorate my door,
dry on my roof, and hang from eaves.
5 They lend open-air vegetable stands
historical grandeur, and gently swing
with an air of festive welcome.
I can hear them talking in the wind,

---

4. Let's go ask mama for sweets. Let's go.  5. Braided strings of peppers.

haggard, yellowing, crisp, rasping
10 tongues of old men, licking the breeze.

    But grandmother loves green chile.
When I visit her,
she holds the green chile pepper
in her wrinkled hands.
15 Ah, voluptuous, masculine,
an air of authority and youth simmers
from its swan-neck stem, tapering to a flowery
collar, fermenting resinous spice.
A well-dressed gentleman at the door
20 my grandmother takes sensuously in her hand,
rubbing its firm glossed sides,
caressing the oily rubbery serpent,
with mouth-watering fulfillment,
fondling its curves with gentle fingers.
25 Its bearing magnificent and taut
as flanks of a tiger in mid-leap,
she thrusts her blade into
and cuts it open, with lust
on her hot mouth, sweating over the stove,
30 bandanna round her forehead,
mysterious passion on her face
and she serves me green chile con carne
between soft warm leaves of corn tortillas,
with beans and rice—her sacrifice
35 to her little prince.
I slurp from my plate
with last bit of tortilla, my mouth burns
and I hiss and drink a tall glass of cold water.

    All over New Mexico, sunburned men and women
40 drive rickety trucks stuffed with gunny-sacks
of green chile, from Belen, Veguita, Willard, Estancia,
San Antonio y Socorro, from fields
to roadside stands, you see them roasting green chile
in screen-sided homemade barrels, and for a dollar a bag,
45 we relive this old, beautiful ritual again and again.

                                                          1989

- What different qualities do the red and green chiles have? Which words in the poem help to personify the chiles? How fully do these words reflect the differences between the speaker and the grandmother?

## KELLY CHERRY

### Alzheimer's

He stands at the door, a crazy old man
Back from the hospital, his mind rattling
Like the suitcase, swinging from his hand,
That contains shaving cream, a piggy bank,
5 A book he sometimes pretends to read,
His clothes. On the brick wall beside him
Roses and columbine slug it out for space, claw the mortar.
The sun is shining, as it does late in the afternoon
In England, after rain.
10 Sun hardens the house, reifies it,
Strikes the iron grillwork like a smithy
And sparks fly off, burning in the bushes—
The rosebushes—
While the white wood trim defines solidity in space.
15 This is his house. He remembers it as his,
Remembers the walkway he built between the front room
And the garage, the rhododendron he planted in back,
The car he used to drive. He remembers himself,
A younger man, in a tweed hat, a man who loved
20 Music. There is no time for that now. No time for music,
The peculiar screeching of strings, the luxurious
Fiddling with emotion.
Other things have become more urgent.
Other matters are now of greater import, have more
25 Consequence, must be attended to. The first
Thing he must do, now that he is home, is decide who
This woman is, this old, white-haired woman
Standing here in the doorway,
Welcoming him in.

1997

- How do phrases like "a crazy old man" and "a book he sometimes pretends to read" indicate the speaker's feelings toward her father? Does her attitude shift at some point? Where?

## ANDREW HUDGINS

### Begotten

I've never, as some children do,
looked at my folks and thought, I *must*
have come from someone else—

rich parents who'd misplaced me, but
who would, as in a myth or novel,
return and claim me. Hell, no. I saw
my face in cousins' faces, heard
my voice in their high drawls. And Sundays,
after the dinner plates were cleared,
I lingered, elbow propped on red
oilcloth, and studied great-uncles, aunts,
and cousins new to me. They squirmed.
I stared till I discerned the features
they'd gotten from the family larder:
eyes, nose, lips, hair? I stared until,
uncomfortable, they'd snap, "Hey, boy—
what are you looking at? At me?"
"No, sir," I'd lie. "No, ma'am." I'd count ten
and then continue staring at them.
I never had to ask, What am I?
I stared at my blood-kin, and thought,
So *this*, dear God, is what I am.

1994

## *Mostly My Nightmares Are Dull*

Mostly my nightmares are dull. On autumn nights
I rake the yard. Brown leaves fall faster, faster.
They swamp my ankles, rise up past my knees,
waist, neck, until I'm drowning in dry leaves.
A bourgeois nightmare, sure. But still
I wake up sweaty, short of breath, surprised
at just how little fear it takes to break me.
And worse, some nights I raise the dead. I say,
*I didn't understand that you were dying,*
but Mother simply waves my guilt away,
left-handed, as though it were tobacco smoke.
Grandmother smiles, forgives my vulgar mouth,
and Sister, dead before my birth, confides
that she too loves Ray Charles. Soon Grandma's talk
of niggers makes me snarl at her. She sulks.
Her sulking makes me yell, Mom cries, Ray sings,
and Sister lapses back into her silence.
I wake, they die again, and I walk out
into a day I'll live as carelessly
as if I'll only—fat chance—live it once.

1991

- What can you infer from the language in "Begotten" and "Mostly My Nightmares Are Dull" about the speaker's attitude toward his life?

**SIMON J. ORTIZ**

## My Father's Song

Wanting to say things,
I miss my father tonight.
His voice, the slight catch,
the depth from his thin chest,
5 the tremble of emotion
in something he has just said
to his son, his song:

We planted corn one Spring at Acu—
we planted several times
10 but this one particular time
I remember the soft damp sand
in my hand.

My father had stopped at one point
to show me an overturned furrow;
15 the plowshare had unearthed
the burrow nest of a mouse
in the soft moist sand.

Very gently, he scooped tiny pink animals
into the palm of his hand
20 and told me to touch them.
We took them to the edge
of the field and put them in the shade
of a sand moist clod.

I remember the very softness
25 of cool and warm sand and tiny alive mice
and my father saying things.

1976

- What are the "things" that the speaker wants to say? Are they the same things he remembers his father saying? Does the poem itself says these things?

**ALBERTO ALVARO RÍOS**

## Mi Abuelo[6]

Where my grandfather is is in the ground
where you can hear the future like an

---

6. My grandfather.

Indian with his ear at the tracks. A
pipe leads down to him so that sometimes
he whispers what will happen to a man
in town or how he will meet the best-
dressed woman tomorrow and how the best
man at her wedding will chew the ground
next to her. Mi abuelo is the man
who talks through all the mouths in my house. An
echo of me hitting the pipe sometimes
to stop him from saying "my hair is a
sieve" is the only other sound. It is a
phrase that among all others is the best,
he says, and "my hair is a sieve" is sometimes
repeated for hours out of the ground
when I let him, but mostly I don't. "An
abuelo should be much more than a man
like you!" He stops then, and speaks: "I am a man
who has served ants with the attitude of a
waiter, who has made each smile as only an
ant who is fat can, and they liked me best,
but there is nothing left." Yet, I know he ground
green coffee beans as a child, and sometimes
he will talk about his wife, and sometimes
about when he was deaf and a man
cured him by mail and he heard ground
hogs talking, or about how he walked with a
cane he chewed on when he got hungry. At best,
mi abuelo is a liar. I see an
old picture of him at nani's with an
off-white yellow center mustache and sometimes
that's all I know for sure. He talks best
about these hills, slowest waves, and where this man
is going, and I'm convinced his hair is a
sieve, that his fever is cool now in the ground.
Mi abuelo is an ordinary man.
I look down the pipe, sometimes, and see a
ripple-topped stream in its best suit, in the ground.

1980

- What is the "pipe" in this poem? What might it mean that "my hair is a sieve"? What are some of the speaker's attitudes toward his grandfather?

## SUGGESTIONS FOR WRITING

1. Both "Eden," by Emily Grosholz, and "The Clock," by Daniel Tobin, use shifts of tone to elevate the poems' subject matter from the narrow concerns of children to the more universal issues that face adults. Where, in each poem, is this shift of tone? How is the shift revealed through language? Write an essay in which you compare and contrast the way each poet accomplishes this broadening of perspective.
2. In what way is precision of language the real subject of Li-Young Lee's "Persimmons"? How does the poem itself embody this subject? Write an essay in which you explore the subtle shifts in tone throughout the poem, and the way these shifts affect a reader's feelings. What, finally, seems to be the poet's attitude toward language as a medium for the precise expression of feeling?
3. What words in Robert Hayden's "Those Winter Sundays" suggest the son's feelings toward his father and his home? What words indicate that the poet's attitudes have changed since the time depicted in the poem? Write an essay in which you compare the speaker's feelings, as a youth and then later as a man, about his father and his home.
4. Kelly Cherry's "Alzheimer's" uses contrasts—especially before and after—to characterize the ravages of Alzheimer's disease. What evidence does the poem provide about what the man used to be like? What specific changes have come about? How does the setting of the poem suggest some of those changes? In what ways do the stabilities of house, landscape, and other people clarify what has happened? Write an essay about the function of the poem's setting.
5. Write an essay in which you consider the use of language to create tone in any grouping of two or more poems in this chapter.

# 14 SPEAKER: WHOSE VOICE DO WE HEAR?

Poems are personal. The thoughts and feelings they express belong to a specific person, and however general or universal their sentiments seem to be, poems come to us as the expression of an individual human voice. That voice is often the voice of the poet. But not always. Poets sometimes create "characters" just as writers of fiction or drama do—people who speak for them only indirectly. A character may, in fact, be very different from the poet, just as a character in a play or story is not necessarily the author, and that person, the **speaker** of the poem, may express ideas or feelings very different from the poet's own. In the following poem, rather than speaking directly to us himself, the poet has created two speakers, both female, each of whom has a distinctive voice, personality, and character.

**THOMAS HARDY**

## *The Ruined Maid*

"O 'Melia,[1] my dear, this does everything crown!
Who could have supposed I should meet you in Town?
And whence such fair garments, such prosperi-ty?"—
"O didn't you know I'd been ruined?" said she.

5 —"You left us in tatters, without shoes or socks,
Tired of digging potatoes, and spudding up docks;[2]
And now you've gay bracelets and bright feathers three!"—
"Yes: that's how we dress when we're ruined," said she.

—"At home in the barton[3] you said 'thee' and 'thou,'
10 And 'thik oon,' and 'theäs oon,' and 't'other'; but now
Your talking quite fits 'ee for high compa-ny!"—
"Some polish is gained with one's ruin," said she.

—"Your hands were like paws then, your face blue and bleak
But now I'm bewitched by your delicate cheek,
15 And your little gloves fit as on any la-dy!"—
"We never do work when we're ruined," said she.

---

1. Short for Amelia.  2. Spading up weeds.  3. Farmyard.

—"You used to call home-life a hag-ridden dream,
And you'd sigh, and you'd sock;[4] but at present you seem
To know not of megrims[5] or melancho-ly!"—
20   "True. One's pretty lively when ruined," said she.

—"I wish I had feathers, a fine sweeping gown,
And a delicate face, and could strut about Town!"—
"My dear—a raw country girl, such as you be,
Cannot quite expect that. You ain't ruined," said she.

1866

    The first voice, that of a young woman who has remained back on the farm, is designated typographically (that is, by the way the poem is printed): there are dashes at the beginning and end of all but the first of her speeches. She speaks the first part of each **stanza** (a stanza is a section of a poem designated by spacing), usually the first three lines. The second young woman, a companion and coworker on the farm in years gone by, regularly gets the last line in each stanza (and in the last stanza, two lines), so it is clear who is talking at every point. Also, the two speakers are just as clearly distinguished by what they say, how they say it, and what sort of person each proves to be. The nameless stay-at-home shows little knowledge of the world, and everything surprises her: seeing her former companion at all, but especially seeing her well clothed, cheerful, and polished; and as the poem develops she shows increasing envy of her more worldly friend. She is the "raw country girl" (line 23) that the other speaker says she is, and she still speaks the country dialect ("fits 'ee," line 11, for example) that she notices her friend has lost (lines 9–11). The "ruined" young woman ('Melia), on the other hand, says little except the refrain about having been ruined, but even the slight variations she plays on that theme suggest her sophistication and amusement at her rural friend, although she still uses a country "ain't" at the end. We are not told the full story of their lives (was the "ruined" young woman thrown out? did she run away from home or work?), but we know enough (that they've been separated for some time, that the stay-at-home did not know where the other had gone) to allow the dialogue to articulate the contrast between them: one is still rural, inexperienced, and innocent; the other is sophisticated, citified—and "ruined." Each speaker's style of speech then does the rest.
    It is equally obvious that there is a speaker (or, in this case, a singer) in stanzas 2 through 9 of the following poem:

---

4. Deliver angry blows.     5. Migraine headaches.

## X. J. KENNEDY

## *In a Prominent Bar in Secaucus One Day*

*To the tune of "The Old Orange Flute" or the tune of
"Sweet Betsy from Pike"*

In a prominent bar in Secaucus[6] one day
Rose a lady in skunk with a topheavy sway,
Raised a knobby red finger—all turned from their beer—
While with eyes bright as snowcrust she sang high and clear:

5 "Now who of you'd think from an eyeload of me
That I once was a lady as proud as could be?
Oh I'd never sit down by a tumbledown drunk
If it wasn't, my dears, for the high cost of junk.

"All the gents used to swear that the white of my calf
10 Beat the down of a swan by a length and a half.
In the kerchief of linen I caught to my nose
Ah, there never fell snot, but a little gold rose.

"I had seven gold teeth and a toothpick of gold.
My Virginia cheroot was a leaf of it rolled
15 And I'd light it each time with a thousand in cash—
Why the bums used to fight if I flicked them an ash.

"Once the toast of the Biltmore,[7] the belle of the Taft,
I would drink bottle beer at the Drake, never draft,
And dine at the Astor on Salisbury steak
20 With a clean tablecloth for each bite I did take.

"In a car like the Roxy[8] I'd roll to the track,
A steel-guitar trio, a bar in the back,
And the wheels made no noise, they turned over so fast,
Still it took you ten minutes to see me go past.

25 "When the horses bowed down to me that I might choose,
I bet on them all, for I hated to lose.
Now I'm saddled each night for my butter and eggs
And the broken threads race down the backs of my legs.

"Let you hold in mind, girls, that your beauty must pass
30 Like a lovely white clover that rusts with its grass.
Keep your bottoms off barstools and marry you young
Or be left—an old barrel with many a bung."

---

6. A small town on the Hackensack River in New Jersey, a few miles west of Manhattan.
7. Like the Taft, Drake, and Astor, a once-fashionable New York hotel.
8. A luxurious old New York theater and movie house, the site of many "world premieres" in the heyday of Hollywood.

"For when time takes you out for a spin in his car
You'll be hard-pressed to stop him from going too far
35 And be left by the roadside, for all your good deeds,
Two toadstools for tits and a face full of weeds."

All the house raised a cheer, but the man at the bar
Made a phonecall and up pulled a red patrol car
And she blew us a kiss as they copped her away
40 From that prominent bar in Secaucus, N.J.

1961

Again, we learn about the character primarily through her own words, although we may not believe everything she tells us about her past. From her introduction in the first stanza we get some general notion of her appearance and condition, but it is she who tells us that she is a junkie (line 8) and a prostitute (line 27) and that her face and figure have seen better days (lines 32, 36). That information could make her a sad case, and the poem might lament her state or allow us to lament it, but instead she presents herself in a light, friendly, and theatrical way. She is anxious to give advice and sound righteous (line 31, for example), but she's also enormously cheerful about herself, and her spirit repeatedly bursts forth through her song. Her performance gives her a lot of pleasure as she exaggerates outrageously about her former luxury and prominence, and even her departure in a patrol car she chooses to treat as a grand exit, throwing a kiss to her audience. The comedy is bittersweet, perhaps, but she is allowed to present herself, through her own words and attitudes, as a likable character—someone who has survived life's disappointments and retained her dignity. The glorious fiction of her life, narrated with energy and polish in the manner of a practiced and accomplished liar, betrays some rather naive notions of good taste and luxurious living (lines 18–26). But this "lady in skunk" has a picturesque and engaging style, a refreshing sense of humor about herself, and a flair for drama. Like the cheap fur she wears, her experiences in what she considers high life satisfy her sense of style and celebration. The self-portrait accumulates, almost completely through how she talks about herself, and the poet develops our attitude toward her by allowing her to recount her story herself, in her own words—or rather in words chosen for her by the author.

Sometimes poets "borrow" a character from history and ask readers to factor in historical facts and contexts. In the following poem, for example, the Canadian poet Margaret Atwood draws heavily upon facts and traditions about a nineteenth-century émigré from Scotland to Canada:

## MARGARET ATWOOD

### *Death of a Young Son by Drowning*

He, who navigated with success
the dangerous river of his own birth
once more set forth

on a voyage of discovery
into the land I floated on
but could not touch to claim.

His feet slid on the bank,
the currents took him;
he swirled with ice and trees in the swollen water

and plunged into distant regions,
his head a bathysphere;
through his eyes' thin glass bubbles

he looked out, reckless adventurer
on a landscape stranger than Uranus
we have all been to and some remember.

There was an accident; the air locked,
he was hung in the river like a heart.
They retrieved the swamped body,

cairn of my plans and future charts,
with poles and hooks
from among the nudging logs.

It was spring, the sun kept shining, the new grass
leapt to solidity;
my hands glistened with details.

After the long trip I was tired of waves.
My foot hit rock. The dreamed sails
collapsed, ragged.

    I planted him in this country
    like a flag.

1970

    The poem comes from a volume called *The Journals of Susanna Moodie: Poems by Margaret Atwood* (1970). A frontier pioneer, Moodie herself had written two books about Canada, *Roughing It in the Bush* and *Life in the Clearings,* and Atwood found their observations rather stark and disorganized. She wrote her Susanna Moodie poems to refocus the "character" and to reconstruct Moodie's actual geographical exploration and self-discovery. To truly understand these thoughts and meditations, then, we need to know something of the history behind them. Read in context, they present very powerful psychological and cultural analyses.

    Some speakers in poems are not, however, nearly so heroic or attractive, and some poems create a speaker we are made to dislike, as the following poem does. Here the speaker, as the title implies, is a monk, but he shows himself to be most unspiritual: mean, petty, self-righteous, and despicable.

## ROBERT BROWNING

### Soliloquy of the Spanish Cloister

    Gr-r-r—there go, my heart's abhorrence!
      Water your damned flower-pots, do!
    If hate killed men, Brother Lawrence,
      God's blood, would not mine kill you!
5  What? your myrtle-bush wants trimming?
      Oh, that rose has prior claims—
    Needs its leaden vase filled brimming?
      Hell dry you up with its flames!

    At the meal we sit together:
10  *Salve tibi!*[9] I must hear
    Wish talk of the kind of weather,
      Sort of season, time of year:
    *Not a plenteous cork-crop: scarcely
      Dare we hope oak-galls,*[1] *I doubt:*
15  What's the Latin name for "parsley"?
      What's the Greek name for Swine's Snout?

    Whew! We'll have our platter burnished,
      Laid with care on our own shelf!
    With a fire-new spoon we're furnished,
20    And a goblet for ourself,
    Rinsed like something sacrificial
      Ere 'tis fit to touch our chaps[2]—
    Marked with L. for our initial!
      (He-he! There his lily snaps!)

25  *Saint,* forsooth! While brown Dolores
      —Squats outside the Convent bank
    With Sanchicha, telling stories,
      Steeping tresses in the tank,
    Blue-black, lustrous, thick like horsehairs,
30    —Can't I see his dead eye glow,
    Bright as 'twere a Barbary corsair's?[3]
      (That is, if he'd let it show!)

    When he finishes refection,
      Knife and fork he never lays
35  Cross-wise, to my recollection,
      As do I, in Jesu's praise.
    I the Trinity illustrate,
      Drinking watered orange-pulp—

---

9. Hail to thee (Latin). Italics usually indicate the words of Brother Lawrence.
1. Abnormal growth on oak trees, used for tanning.   2. Jaws.   3. African pirate's.

In three sips the Arian[4] frustrate;
—While he drains his at one gulp.

Oh, those melons? If he's able
   We're to have a feast! so nice!
One goes to the Abbot's table,
   All of us get each a slice.
How go on your flowers? None double?
   Not one fruit-sort can you spy?
Strange!—And I, too, at such trouble,
   —Keep them close-nipped on the sly!

There's a great text in Galatians,
   Once you trip on it, entails
Twenty-nine distinct damnations,[5]
   One sure, if another fails:
If I trip him just a-dying,
   Sure of heaven as sure can be,
Spin him round and send him flying
   Off to hell, a Manichee?[6]

Or, my scrofulous French novel
   On gray paper with blunt type!
Simply glance at it, you grovel
   Hand and foot in Belial's gripe:[7]
If I double down its pages
   At the woeful sixteenth print,
When he gathers his greengages,
   Ope a sieve and slip it in't?

Or, there's Satan!—one might venture
   Pledge one's soul to him, yet leave
Such a flaw in the indenture
   —As he'd miss till, past retrieve,
Blasted lay that rose-acacia
   We're so proud of! *Hy, Zy, Hine* ...[8]
'St, there's Vespers! *Plena gratiâ*
   *Ave, Virgo.*[9] Gr-r-r—you swine!

1842

Not many poems begin with a growl, and this harsh sound turns out to be fair warning that we are about to meet a real beast, even though he is in the clothing of a religious man. In line 1 he shows himself to hold a most uncharitable attitude toward his fellow monk, Brother Lawrence, and by line 4 he has uttered two pro-

---

4. A heretical sect that denied the Trinity.
5. Galatians 5.15-23 provides a long list of possible offenses, though they do not add up to twenty-nine.
6. A heretic. According to the Manichean heresy, the world was divided into the forces of good and evil, equally powerful.    7. In the clutches of Satan.    8. Possibly the beginning of an incantation or curse.
9. The opening words of the *Ave Maria*, here reversed: "Full of grace, Hail, Virgin" (Latin).

fanities and admitted his intense feelings of hatred and vengefulness. His ranting and roaring is full of exclamation points (four in the first stanza!), and he reveals his own personality and character when he imagines curses and unflattering nicknames for Brother Lawrence or plots malicious jokes on him. By the end, we have accumulated no knowledge of Brother Lawrence that makes him seem a fit target for such rage (except that he is pious, dutiful, and pleasant—perhaps enough to make this sort of speaker despise him), but we have discovered the speaker to be lecherous (stanza 4), full of false piety (stanza 5), malicious in trivial matters (stanza 6), ready to use his theological learning to sponsor damnation rather than salvation (stanza 7), a closet reader and viewer of pornography within the monastery (stanza 8)—even willing to risk his own soul in order to torment Brother Lawrence (last stanza).

The speaker characterizes himself; the details accumulate into a fairly full portrait, and here we do not have even an opening and closing "objective" description (as in Kennedy's "In a Prominent Bar") or another speaker (as in Hardy's "The Ruined Maid") to give us perspective. Except for the moments when the speaker mimics or parodies Brother Lawrence (usually in italic type), we have only the speaker's own words and thoughts. But that is enough; the poet has controlled them so carefully that we know what he thinks of the speaker—that he is a mean-spirited, vengeful hypocrite, a thoroughly disreputable and unlikable character. The whole poem has been about him and his attitudes; the point has been to characterize the speaker and develop in us a dislike of him and what he stands for—hypocrisy.

In reading a poem like this aloud, we would want our voice to suggest all the unlikable features of a hypocrite. We would also need to suggest, through tone of voice, the author's contemptuous mocking of the rage and hypocrisy, and we would want, like an actor, to create strong disapproval in the hearer. The poem's words (the ones the author has given to the speaker) clearly imply those attitudes, and we would want our voice to express them. Usually there is much more to a poem than the characterization of the speaker, but in many cases it is necessary first to identify the speaker and determine his or her character before we can appreciate what else goes on in the poem. And sometimes, as here, in looking for the speaker of the poem, we approach the center of the poem itself.

Sometimes the effect of a poem depends on our recognizing the **temporal setting** as well as the speaker's identity. The following poem, for example, quickly makes plain that a childhood experience is at the center of the action and that the speaker is female:

### TESS GALLAGHER

## *Sudden Journey*

    Maybe I'm seven in the open field—
    the straw-grass so high
    only the top of my head makes a curve
    of brown in the yellow. Rain then.
5  First a little. A few drops on my

wrist, the right wrist. More rain.
My shoulders, my chin. Until I'm looking up
to let my eyes take the bliss.
I open my face. Let the teeth show. I
10 pull my shirt down past the collar-bones.
I'm still a boy under my breast spots.
I can drink anywhere. The rain. My
skin shattering. Up suddenly, needing
to gulp, turning with my tongue, my arms out
15 running, running in the hard, cold plenitude
of all those who reach earth by falling.

1984

The sense of adventure and wonder here has a lot to do with the childlike syntax and choice of words at the beginning of the poem. Sentences are short, observations direct and simple. The rain becomes exciting and blissful and totally absorbing as the child's actions and reactions take over the poem in lines 2–13. But not all of the poem takes place in a child's mind in spite of the precise and impressive re-creation of childish responses and feelings. The opening line makes clear that we are sliding into a supposition of the past; "maybe I'm seven" makes clear that we, as conspiring adults, are pretending ourselves into earlier time. And at the end the word "plenitude"—crucial to interpreting the poem's full effect and meaning— makes clear that we are now encountering an adult perspective on the incident. Elsewhere, too, the adult world gives the incident meaning. In line 12, for example, the joke about being able to drink anywhere depends on an adult sense of what being a boy might mean. The "journey" of the poem's title is not only the little girl's running in the rain, but also the adult's return to a past re-created and newly understood.

The speaker in the following poem positions herself very differently, but we do not get a full sense of her until we are well into the poem. As you read, try to imagine the tone of voice you think this person would use. Exactly when do you begin to know what she sounds like?

**DOROTHY PARKER**

# A Certain Lady

Oh, I can smile for you, and tilt my head,
　　And drink your rushing words with eager lips,
And paint my mouth for you a fragrant red,
　　And trace your brows with tutored finger-tips.
5 When you rehearse your list of loves to me,
　　Oh, I can laugh and marvel, rapturous-eyed.
And you laugh back, nor can you ever see
　　The thousand little deaths my heart has died.
And you believe, so well I know my part,

10   That I am gay as morning, light as snow,
   And all the straining things within my heart
      You'll never know.

   Oh, I can laugh and listen, when we meet,
      And you bring tales of fresh adventurings—
15   Of ladies delicately indiscreet,
      Of lingering hands, and gently whispered things.
   And you are pleased with me, and strive anew
      To sing me sagas of your late delights.
   Thus do you want me—marveling, gay, and true—
20   Nor do you see my staring eyes of nights.
      And when, in search of novelty, you stray,
   Oh, I can kiss you blithely as you go . . .
      And what goes on, my love, while you're away,
         You'll never know.

                                              1937

To whom does the speaker seem to be talking? What sort of person is he? How do you feel about him? Which habits and attitudes of his do you like least? How soon can you tell that the speaker is not altogether happy about his conversation and conduct? In what tone of voice would you read the first twenty-two lines aloud? What attitude would you try to express toward the person spoken to? What tone would you use for the last two lines? How would you describe the speaker's personality? What aspects of her behavior are most crucial to the poem's effect?

It is easy to assume that the speaker in a poem is an extension of the poet, especially when the voice is as distinctively self-assured as in "A Certain Lady." So, is the speaker in this poem Dorothy Parker? Maybe. A lot of Parker's poems present a similar world-weary posture and a wry cynicism about romantic love. But the poem is hardly a case of self-revelation, a giving away of personal secrets. If it were, it would be silly, not to say risky, to address her lover in a way that gives damaging facts about a pose she has been so careful to set up.

In poems such as "The Ruined Maid," "In a Prominent Bar," and "Soliloquy of the Spanish Cloister," we are in no danger of mistaking the speaker for the poet, once we have recognized that poets may create speakers who participate in specific situations, much as in fiction or drama. When there is a pointed discrepancy between the speaker and what we know of the poet—when the speaker is a woman, for example, and the poet is a man—we know we have a created speaker to contend with and that the point (or at least *one* point) in the poem is to observe the characterization carefully. In "A Certain Lady" we may be less sure, and in other poems the discrepancy between speaker and poet may be even more uncertain. What are we to make, for example, of the speaker in "Woodchucks" in the previous chapter? Is that speaker the real Maxine Kumin? At best (without knowing something quite specific about the author) we can only say "maybe" to that question. What we can be sure of is the sort of person the speaker is portrayed to be—someone (a man? a woman?) surprised to discover feelings and attitudes that contradict values apparently held with confidence. And that is exactly what we need to know for the poem to have its effect.

Even when poets present themselves as if they were speaking directly to us in their own voices, their poems present only a partial portrait, something considerably less than the full personality and character of the poet. Even when there is not an obviously created character—someone with distinct characteristics that are different from those of the poet—strategies of characterization are used to present the person speaking in one way and not another. Even in a poem like the following one, which contains identifiable autobiographical details, it is still a good idea to think of the speaker instead of the poet, although here the poet is probably writing about a personal, actual experience, and he is certainly making a character of himself—that is, characterizing himself in a certain way, emphasizing some parts of himself and not others.

## WILLIAM WORDSWORTH

### She Dwelt among the Untrodden Ways

> She dwelt among the untrodden ways
>   Beside the springs of Dove,[1]
> A Maid whom there were none to praise
>   And very few to love:
>
> 5 A violet by a mossy stone
>   Half hidden from the eye!
> —Fair as a star, when only one
>   Is shining in the sky.
>
> She lived unknown, and few could know
> 10   When Lucy ceased to be;
> But she is in her grave, and, oh,
>   The difference to me!

1800

Is this poem more about Lucy or about the speaker's feelings concerning her death? Her simple life, far removed from fame and known only to a few, is said to have been beautiful, but we know little about her beyond her name and where she lived, in a beautiful but then-isolated section of northern England. We don't know if she was young or old, only that the speaker thinks of her as "fair" and compares her to a "violet by a mossy stone." We do know that the speaker is deeply pained by her death, so deeply that he is almost inarticulate with grief, lapsing into simple exclamation ("oh," line 11) and hardly able to articulate the "difference" that her death makes.

Did Lucy actually live? Was she a friend of the poet? We don't know; the poem doesn't tell us, and even biographers of Wordsworth are unsure. What we do know is that Wordsworth was able to represent grief very powerfully. Whether the

---

1. A small stream in the Lake District in northern England, near where Wordsworth lived in Dove Cottage at Grasmere.

speaker is the historical Wordsworth or not, that speaker is a major focus of the poem, and it is his feelings that the poem isolates and expresses. We need to recognize some characteristics of the speaker and be sensitive to his feelings for the poem to work.

The poems we have looked at in this chapter—and the group that follows—all suggest the value of beginning the reading of any poem with simple questions: Who is speaking? What do we know about him or her? What kind of person is she or he? Putting together the evidence that the poem presents in answer to such questions can often take us a long way into the poem. For some poems, such questions won't help a great deal because the speaking voice is too indistinct or the character behind the poem too scantily presented. But starting with such questions will often lead you toward the central experience the poem offers. At the very least, the question of speaker helps clarify the tone of voice, and it often provides guidance to the larger situation the poem explores.

· · ·

## AUDRE LORDE

### *Hanging Fire*

I am fourteen
and my skin has betrayed me
the boy I cannot live without
still sucks his thumb
5  in secret
how come my knees are
always so ashy
what if I die
before morning
10 and momma's in the bedroom
with the door closed.

I have to learn how to dance
in time for the next party
my room is too small for me
15 suppose I die before graduation
they will sing sad melodies
but finally
tell the truth about me
There is nothing I want to do
20 and too much
that has to be done
and momma's in the bedroom
with the door closed.

Nobody even stops to think
25 about my side of it

             I should have been on Math Team
             my marks were better than his
             why do I have to be
             the one
30           wearing braces
             I have nothing to wear tomorrow
             will I live long enough
             to grow up
             and momma's in the bedroom
35           with the door closed.
                              1978

- What, precisely, do we know about the speaker? How does she feel about herself? How can you tell?


**JUDITH ORTIZ COFER**

## *The Changeling*

                        As a young girl
     vying for my father's attention,
     I invented a game that made him look up
     from his reading and shake his head
5    as if both baffled and amused.

     In my brother's closet, I'd change
     into his dungarees—the rough material
     molding me into boy shape; hide
     my long hair under an army helmet
10   he'd been given by Father, and emerge
     transformed into the legendary Ché[2]
     of grown-up talk.

     Strutting around the room,
     I'd tell of life in the mountains,
15   of carnage and rivers of blood,
     and of manly feasts with rum and music
     to celebrate victories *para la libertad*.[3]
     He would listen with a smile
     to my tales of battles and brotherhood
20   until Mother called us to dinner.

---

2. Ernesto "Che" Guevara (1928–1967), Argentinian-born Cuban revolutionary leader.
3. For freedom (Spanish).

　　　　She was not amused
　　　　by my transformations, sternly forbidding me
　　　　from sitting down with them as a man.
　　　　She'd order me back to the dark cubicle
25　　　that smelled of adventure, to shed
　　　　my costume, to braid my hair furiously
　　　　with blind hands, and to return invisible,
　　　　as myself,
　　　　to the real world of her kitchen.
　　　　　　　　　　　　　　　　　　　1993

- Why do you think the speaker's father is amused by her "transformation," and why does her mother forbid it? What does this poem imply about all three of them?


### KAREN CHASE

## *Venison*

　　　　Paul set the bags down, told how they had split
　　　　the deer apart, the ease of peeling it
　　　　simpler than skinning a fruit, how the buck
　　　　lay on the worktable, how they sawed
5　　　　an anklebone off, the smell not rank.
　　　　The sun slipped into night.
　　　　*Where are you* I wondered as I grubbed
　　　　through cupboards for noodles at least.
　　　　Then came venison new with blood,
10　　　stray hair from the animal's fur.
　　　　Excited, we cooked the meat.
　　　　Later, I dreamt against your human chest,
　　　　you cloaked me in your large arms, then
　　　　went for me the way you squander food sometimes.
15　　　By then, I was eating limbs in my sleep, somewhere
　　　　in the snow alone, survivor of a downed plane,
　　　　picking at the freshly dead. Whistles
　　　　of a far-off flute—legs, gristle, juice.
　　　　I cracked an elbow against a rock, awoke.
20　　　Throughout the night, we consumed and consumed.
　　　　　　　　　　　　　　　　　　　2000

- How does the poet characterize the speaker's relationship with Paul?

**SIR THOMAS WYATT**

## They Flee from Me

They flee from me, that sometime did me seek,
With naked foot stalking in my chamber.
I have seen them, gentle, tame, and meek,
That now are wild, and do not remember
5 That sometime they put themselves in danger
To take bread at my hand; and now they range,
Busily seeking with a continual change.

Thankéd be Fortune it hath been otherwise,
Twenty times better; but once in special,
10 In thin array, after a pleasant guise,
When her loose gown from her shoulders did fall,
And she me caught in her arms long and small.[4]
And therewith all sweetly did me kiss
And softly said, "Dear heart, how like you this?"

15 It was no dream, I lay broad waking.
But all is turned, thorough[5] my gentleness,
Into a strange fashion of forsaking;
And I have leave to go, of her goodness,
And she also to use newfangleness.[6]
20 But since that I so kindely[7] am servéd,
I fain[8] would know what she hath deservéd.

                                    1557

- Who are "they" who now "flee" the speaker? What is his explanation for their fleeing?

**FRED CHAPPELL**

## Recovery of Sexual Desire after a Bad Cold

Toward morning I dreamed of the Ace of Spades reversed
And woke up giggling.
New presence in the bedroom, as if it had snowed;
And an obdurate stranger come to visit my body.

5 This is how it all renews itself, floating down
Mothy on the shallow end of sleep;
How Easter gets here, and the hard-bitten dogwood
Flowers, and waters run clean again.

---

4. Slender.   5. Through.   6. Fondness for novelty.   7. That is, in kind.   8. Eagerly.

I am a new old man.
10 As morning sweetens the forsythia and the cats.
Bristle with impudent hungers, I learn to smile.
I am a new baby.

What woman could turn from me now?
Shining like a butter knife, and the fever burned off,
15 My whole skin alert as radar, I can think
Of nothing at all but love and fresh coffee.

1985

- What kind of a man is the speaker in this poem? How does he feel now that he has "recovered"?

**ROBERT BURNS**

## To a Louse

*On Seeing One on a Lady's Bonnet at Church*

Ha! whare ya gaun, ye crowlan ferlie![9]
Your impudence protects you sairly:[1]
I canna say but ye strunt[2] rarely,
    Owre gauze and lace;
5 Tho' faith, I fear ye dine but sparely,
    On sic a place.

Ye ugly, creepan, blastit wonner,[3]
Detested, shunn'd, by saunt an' sinner,
How daur ye set your fit[4] upon her,
10     Sae fine a Lady!
Gae somewhere else and seek your dinner,
    On some poor body.

Swith, in some beggar's haffet squattle;[5]
There ye may creep, and sprawl, and sprattle,[6]
15 Wi'ither kindred, jumping cattle,
    In shoals and, nations;
Whare horn nor bane[7] ne'er daur unsettle,
    Your thick plantations.

Now haud you there ye're out o'sight,
20 Below the fatt'rels,[8] snug and tight,
Na faith ye yet![9] ye'll no be right,
    Till ye've got on it,
The vera tapmost, towrin height
    O' Miss's bonnet.

---

9. Crawling miracle!  1. Sorely.  2. Strut.  3. Wonder.  4. Foot.
5. Swift, in some beggar's hair sprawl.  6. Struggle.  7. Bone.  8. Ribbon ends.  9. No matter!

25  My sooth! right bauld ye set your nose out,
       As plump an' gray as onie grozet:[1]
    O for some rank, mercurial rozet,[2]
       Or fell, red smeddum,[3]
    I'd gie you sic a hearty dose o't,
30        Wad dress your droddum![4]

    I wad na been surpriz'd to spy
       You on an auld wife's flainen toy,[5]
    Or aiblins some bit duddie boy,[6]
       On 's wylecoat;[7]
35  But Miss's fine Lunardi,[8] fye!
       How daur ye do't?

    O Jenny dinna toss your head,
    An' set your beauties a' abroad![9]
    Ye little ken what cursed speed
40        The blastie's[1] makin!
    Thae[2] winks and finger-ends, I dread,
       Are notice takin!

    O wad some Pow'r the giftie gie us
    To see oursels as others see us!
45  It wad frae monie a blunder free us
       An foolish notion:
    What airs in dress an' gait wad lea'e us,
       And ev'n Devotion![3]

                                    1785

- What is the speaker's attitude toward the louse? toward Jenny? What lines best summarize the speaker's main point?

## PAT MORA

### La Migra

I

Let's play *La Migra*[4]
I'll be the Border Patrol.
You be the Mexican maid.
I get the badge and sunglasses.
5  You can hide and run,
but you can't get away
because I have a jeep

---

1. Gooseberry.  2. Rosin.  3. Or sharp, red powder.  4. Buttocks.  5. Flannel cap.
6. Or perhaps some small ragged boy.  7. Undershirt.  8. Bonnet.  9. Abroad.  1. Creature's.
2. Those.  3. Piety.  4. Border patrol agents.

I can take you wherever
I want, but don't ask
10 questions because
I don't speak Spanish.
I can touch you wherever
I want but don't complain
too much because I've got
15 boots and kick—if I have to,
and I have handcuffs.
Oh, and a gun.
Get ready, get set, run.

    II

Let's play *La Migra*
20 You be the Border Patrol.
I'll be the Mexican woman.
Your jeep has a flat,
and you have been spotted
by the sun.
25 All you have is heavy: hat,
glasses, badge, shoes, gun.
I know this desert,
where to rest,
where to drink.
30 Oh, I am not alone.
You hear us singing
and laughing with the wind,
*Agua dulce brota aquí,*
*aquí, aquí,*[5] but since you
35 can't speak Spanish,
you do not understand.
Get ready.

        1993

- Who seems to be the speaker of this poem? What is the game of "hide and run" the speaker proposes? Who will win?

## EDNA ST. VINCENT MILLAY

### [*Women have loved before as I love now*]

Women have loved before as I love now;
At least, in lively chronicles of the past—
Of Irish waters by a Cornish prow
Or Trojan waters by a Spartan mast

---

5. Sweet water springs here, here, here.

5   Much to their cost invaded—here and there,
    Hunting the amorous line, skimming the rest,
    I find some woman bearing as I bear
    Love like a burning city in the breast.
    I think however that of all alive
10  I only in such utter, ancient way
    Do suffer love; in me alone survive
    The unregenerate passions of a day
    When treacherous queens, with death upon the tread,
    Heedless and wilful, took their knights to bed.
                                            1931


## [I, being born a woman and distressed]

   I, being born a woman and distressed
   By all the needs and notions of my kind,
   Am urged by your propinquity to find
   Your person fair, and feel a certain zest
5  To bear your body's weight upon my breast:
   So subtly is the fume of life designed,
   To clarify the pulse and cloud the mind,
   And leave me once again undone, possessed.
   Think not for this, however, the poor treason
10 Of my stout blood against my staggering brain,
   I shall remember you with love, or season
   My scorn with pity,—let me make it plain:
   I find this frenzy insufficient reason
   For conversation when we meet again.
                                            1923

- Do both of these poems by Edna St. Vincent Millay seem to have the same speaker? Why or why not?


## GWENDOLYN BROOKS

### We Real Cool

   THE POOL PLAYERS,
   SEVEN AT THE GOLDEN SHOVEL.

   We real cool. We
   Left school. We

   Lurk late. We
   Strike straight. We

5  Sing sin. We
   Thin gin. We

   Jazz June. We
   Die soon.
                1950

- Who are "we" in this poem? Do you think that the speaker and the poet share the same idea of what is "cool"?

### KATHERINE PHILIPS

## *L'amitié: To Mrs. M. Awbrey*

   Soul of my soul, my Joy, my crown, my friend!
   A name which all the rest doth comprehend;
   How happy are we now, whose souls are grown,
   By an incomparable mixture, One:
5  Whose well acquainted minds are now as near
   As Love, or vows, or secrets can endear.
   I have no thought but what's to thee reveal'd,
   Nor thou desire that is from me conceal'd.
   Thy heart locks up my secrets richly set,
10 And my breast is thy private cabinet.
   Thou shedst no tear but what my moisture lent,
   And if I sigh, it is thy breath is spent.
   United thus, what horror can appear
   Worthy our sorrow, anger, or our fear?
15 Let the dull world alone to talk and fight,
   And with their vast ambitions nature fright;
   Let them despise so innocent a flame,
   While Envy, Pride, and Faction play their game:
   But we by Love sublim'd so high shall rise,
20 To pity kings, and conquerors despise,
   Since we that sacred union have engrossed,
   Which they and all the sullen world have lost.
                1667

- Who is the speaker, and whom does the speaker address? Why does the speaker hold her love above "the sullen world"?

## WALT WHITMAN

### [*I celebrate myself, and sing myself*]

I celebrate myself, and sing myself,
And what I assume you shall assume,
For every atom belonging to me as good belongs to you.
I loafe and invite my soul,
5 I lean and loafe at my ease observing a spear of summer grass.

My tongue, every atom of my blood, form'd from this soil, this air,
Born here of parents born here from parents the same, and their
    parents the same,
I, now thirty-seven years old in perfect health begin,
Hoping to cease not till death.
10 Creeds and schools in abeyance,
Retiring back a while sufficed at what they are, but never forgotten,
I harbor for good or bad, I permit to speak at every hazard,
Nature without check with original energy.

1855, 1881

- What is characteristically American about the speaker of this poem?

## SUGGESTIONS FOR WRITING

1. Several of the poems in this chapter create characters and imply situations, as in drama. Write an essay in which you describe and analyze the speaker of either "The Ruined Maid" by Thomas Hardy, "In a Prominent Bar in Secaucus One Day" by X. J. Kennedy, "Soliloquy of the Spanish Cloister" by Robert Browning, or "A Certain Lady" by Dorothy Parker.
2. Write an essay in which you compare and contrast the speakers in "Sudden Journey" by Tess Gallagher, "Hanging Fire" by Audre Lord, "The Changeling" by Judith Ortiz Cofer, and "We Real Cool" by Gwendolyn Brooks. What kinds of self-image do they have? In each poem, what is the distance between the speaker and the poet?
3. In three of the poems in this chapter—"Venison" by Karen Chase, "They Flee from Me" by Sir Thomas Wyatt, and "Recovery of Sexual Desire after a Bad Cold" by Fred Chappell—the speakers describe dreams. How are these dreams integrated into the poems? How are the dreams similar, or different? Write an essay in which you explore the way these three poems make use of the imagery and emotions of dreams.
4. Choose any of the poems in this or the previous chapter and write an essay about the way a poet can create irony and humor through the use of a speaker who is clearly distinct from the poet him- or herself.

# 15 SITUATION AND SETTING: WHAT HAPPENS? WHERE? WHEN?

Questions about the speaker ("Who" questions) in a poem almost always lead to questions of "Where?" "When?" and "Why?" Identifying the speaker is, in fact, usually part of a larger process of defining the entire imagined **situation** in a poem: What is happening? Where is it happening? Who is the speaker speaking to? Who else is present? Why is this event occurring? In order to understand the dialogue in Hardy's "The Ruined Maid," for example, we need to recognize that the friends are meeting after an extended period of separation, and that they meet in a town setting rather than the rural area in which they grew up together. We infer (from the opening lines) that the meeting is accidental, and that no other friends are present for the conversation. The poem's whole "story" depends on their situation: after leading separate lives for a while they have some catching up to do. We don't know what specific town, year, season, or time of day is involved because those details are not important to the poem's effect. But crucial to the poem are the where and when questions that define the situation and relationship of the two speakers, and the answer to the why question—that the meeting is by chance—is important, too. In another poem we looked at in the previous chapter, Parker's "A Certain Lady," the specific moment and place are not important, but we do need to notice that the "lady" is talking to (or having an imaginary conversation with) her lover and that they are talking about a relationship of some duration.

> *It is difficult / to get the news from poems / yet men die miserably every day / for lack / of what is found there.*
> —WILLIAM CARLOS WILLIAMS

Sometimes a *specific* time and place **(setting)** may be important. X. J. Kennedy's "lady in skunk" sings her life story "in a prominent bar in Secaucus," a working-class town in New Jersey, but on no particular occasion ("one day"). In Browning's "Soliloquy of the Spanish Cloister," the setting (a monastery) adds to the irony because of the gross inappropriateness of such sentiments and attitudes in a supposedly holy place, just as the setting of Betjeman's "In Westminster Abbey" (below, page 907) similarly helps us to judge the speaker's ideas, attitudes, and self-conception.

The title of the following poem suggests that place may be important, and it is, although you may be surprised to discover exactly what exists at this address and what uses the speaker makes of it.

JAMES DICKEY

## Cherrylog Road

Off Highway 106
At Cherrylog Road I entered
The '34 Ford without wheels,
Smothered in kudzu,
5   With a seat pulled out to run
Corn whiskey down from the hills,

And then from the other side
Crept into an Essex
With a rumble seat of red leather
10  And then out again, aboard
A blue Chevrolet, releasing
The rust from its other color,

Reared up on three building blocks.
None had the same body heat;
15  I changed with them inward, toward
The weedy heart of the junkyard,
For I knew that Doris Holbrook
Would escape from her father at noon

And would come from the farm
20  To seek parts owned by the sun
Among the abandoned chassis,
Sitting in each in turn
As I did, leaning forward
As in a wild stock-car race

25  In the parking lot of the dead.
Time after time, I climbed in
And out the other side, like
An envoy or movie star
Met at the station by crickets.
30  A radiator cap raised its head,

Become a real toad or a kingsnake
As I neared the hub of the yard,
Passing through many states,
Many lives, to reach
35  Some grandmother's long Pierce-Arrow
Sending platters of blindness forth

From its nickel hubcaps
And spilling its tender upholstery
On sleepy roaches,
40  The glass panel in between

Lady and colored driver
Not all the way broken out,

The back-seat phone
Still on its hook.
45 I got in as though to exclaim,
"Let us go to the orphan asylum,
John; I have some old toys
For children who say their prayers."

I popped with sweat as I thought
50 I heard Doris Holbrook scrape
Like a mouse in the southern-state sun
That was eating the paint in blisters
From a hundred car tops and hoods.
She was tapping like code,

55 Loosening the screws,
Carrying off headlights,
Sparkplugs, bumpers,
Cracked mirrors and gear-knobs,
Getting ready, already,
60 To go back with something to show

Other than her lips' new trembling
I would hold to me soon, soon,
Where I sat in the ripped back seat
Talking over the interphone,
65 Praying for Doris Holbrook
To come from her father's farm

And to get back there
With no trace of me on her face
To be seen by her red-haired father
70 Who would change, in the squalling barn,
Her back's pale skin with a strop,
Then lay for me

In a bootlegger's roasting car
With a string-triggered 12-gauge shotgun
75 To blast the breath from the air.
Not cut by the jagged windshields,
Through the acres of wrecks she came
With a wrench in her hand,

Through dust where the blacksnake dies
80 Of boredom, and the beetle knows
The compost has no more life.
Someone outside would have seen
The oldest car's door inexplicably
Close from within:

85 I held her and held her and held her,
   Convoyed at terrific speed
   By the stalled, dreaming traffic around us,
   So the blacksnake, stiff
   With inaction, curved back
90 Into life, and hunted the mouse

   With deadly overexcitement,
   The beetles reclaimed their field
   As we clung, glued together,
   With the hooks of the seat springs
95 Working through to catch us red-handed
   Amidst the gray breathless batting

   That burst from the seat at our backs.
   We left by separate doors
   Into the changed, other bodies
100 Of cars, she down Cherrylog Road
   And I to my motorcycle
   Parked like the soul of the junkyard

   Restored, a bicycle fleshed
   With power, and tore off
105 Up Highway 106, continually
   Drunk on the wind in my mouth,
   Wringing the handlebar for speed,
   Wild to be wreckage forever.

                                    1964

---

The *exact* location of the junkyard is not important (there is no Highway 106 near the real Cherrylog Road in North Georgia), but we do need to know that the setting is rural, that the time is summer and the summer is hot, and that moonshine whiskey is native to the area. Following the story is no problem once we have sorted out these few facts, and we are prepared to meet the cast of characters: Doris Holbrook, her red-haired father, and the speaker. About each we learn just enough to appreciate the sense of vitality, adventure, power, and disengagement that constitute the major effects of the poem.

The situation of lovemaking in a setting other than the junkyard would not produce the same effects, and the exotic sense of a forbidden meeting in this unlikely place helps to re-create the speaker's sense of the episode. For him, it is memorable (notice all the tiny details he recalls), powerful (notice his reaction when he gets back on his motorcycle), dreamlike (notice the sense of time standing still, especially in lines 85–89), and important (notice how the speaker perceives his environment as changed by their lovemaking, lines 88–91 and 98–100). The wealth of details about setting also helps us to raise other, related questions. Why does the speaker fantasize about being shot by the father (lines 72–75)? Why, in a poem so full of details, do we find out so little about what Doris Holbrook looks like and thinks about? What gives us the sense that this incident is a composite of episodes, an event that was repeated many times? What gives us the impression that the events occurred long ago? What makes the speaker feel so powerful at the end? What does he mean when he talks of himself as being "wild to be wreckage forever"? All of the poem's attention to the speaker's reactions, reflections, and memories is intricately tied up with the particulars of setting. Making love in a junkyard is crucial to the speaker's sense of both power and wreckage, and to him Doris is merely a matter of excitement, adventure, and pale skin, appreciated because she makes the world seem different and because she is willing to take risks and to suffer for meeting him like this. The more we probe the poem with questions about situation, the more likely we are to get a sense of the speaker and to catch the poem's full effect.

The **plot** of "Cherrylog Road" is fairly easy to sort out, but its effect is more complex than the simple story suggests. The next poem we will look at is initially much more difficult to follow. Part of the difficulty is that the poem comes from an earlier age and its language and sentence structure are a bit unfamiliar, and part is that the action in the poem is so closely connected to what is being said. But its opening lines—addressed to someone who is resisting the speaker's suggestions—disclose the situation, and gradually we figure out the scene: a man, trying to convince a woman that they should make love, uses a nearby flea for an unlikely example; it becomes part of his argument. And once we recognize the situation, we can readily follow (and be amused by) the speaker's witty, intricate, and specious argument.

### JOHN DONNE

## The Flea

Mark but this flea, and mark in this[1]
How little that which thou deny'st me is;
It sucked me first, and now sucks thee,
And in this flea our two bloods mingled be;
5  Thou know'st that this cannot be said
A sin, nor shame, nor loss of maidenhead.
   Yet this enjoys before it woo,
And pampered[2] swells with one blood made of two,
And this, alas, is more than we would do.[3]

10  Oh stay,[4] three lives in one flea spare,
Where we almost, yea more than, married are.
This flea is you and I, and this
Our marriage bed, and marriage temple is;
Though parents grudge, and you, we're met

---

1. Medieval preachers and rhetoricians asked their hearers to "mark" (look at) an object that illustrated a moral or philosophical lesson they wished to emphasize.    2. Fed luxuriously.
3. According to the medical theory of Donne's era, conception involved the literal mingling of the lovers' blood.    4. Desist.

15 And cloistered in these living walls of jet.
    Though use[5] make you apt to kill me,
    Let not to that, self-murder added be,
    And sacrilege, three sins in killing three.

    Cruel and sudden, hast thou since
20 Purpled thy nail in blood of innocence?
    Wherein could this flea guilty be,
    Except in that drop which it sucked from thee?
    Yet thou triumph'st, and say'st that thou
    Find'st not thyself, nor me, the weaker now;
25 'Tis true; then learn how false, fears be;
    Just so much honor, when thou yield'st to me,
    Will waste, as this flea's death took life from thee.

                              1633

The scene in "The Flea" develops, action occurs, even as the poem unfolds. Between stanzas 1 and 2, the woman makes a move to kill the flea (as stanza 2 opens, the speaker is trying to stop her), and between stanzas 2 and 3 she has squashed the flea with her fingernail. Once we make sense of what the speaker says, the action is just as clear from the words as if we had stage directions in the margin. All of the speaker's verbal cleverness and all of his silly arguments follow from the situation, and in this poem (as in Browning's "Soliloquy of the Spanish Cloister") we watch as if we were observing a scene in a play. The speaker is, in effect, giving a dramatic monologue for our benefit.

Neither time nor place is important to "The Flea," except that we assume the speaker and his friend are in the same place and have the leisure for some playfulness. The situation could occur anywhere a man, a woman, and a flea could be together: indoors, outdoors, morning, evening, city, country, in a cottage or a castle, on a boat or in a bedroom. We know, from the date of publication, that Donne was writing about people of almost four centuries ago, but the conduct he describes might occur in any age. Only the habits of language (and perhaps the outmoded medical ideas) date the poem.

The two poems that follow have simpler plots, but in each case the heart of the poem is in the basic situation:

**RITA DOVE**

*Daystar*

She wanted a little room for thinking:
but she saw diapers steaming on the line,
a doll slumped behind the door.

---

5. Habit.

So she lugged a chair behind the garage
5 to sit out the children's naps.

Sometimes there were things to watch—
the pinched armor of a vanished cricket,
a floating maple leaf. Other days
she stared until she was assured
10 when she closed her eyes
she'd see only her own vivid blood.

She had an hour, at best, before Liza appeared
pouting from the top of the stairs.
And just *what* was mother doing
15 out back with the field mice? Why,
building a palace. Later
that night when Thomas rolled over and
lurched into her, she would open her eyes
and think of the place that was hers
20 for an hour—where
she was nothing,
pure nothing, in the middle of the day.

1986

## LINDA PASTAN

## *To a Daughter Leaving Home*

When I taught you
at eight to ride
a bicycle, loping along
beside you
5 as you wobbled away
on two round wheels,
my own mouth rounding
in surprise when you pulled
ahead down the curved
10 path of the park,
I kept waiting
for the thud
of your crash as I
sprinted to catch up,
15 while you grew
smaller, more breakable
with distance,
pumping, pumping
for your life, screaming
20 with laughter,
the hair flapping

behind you like a
handkerchief waving
goodbye.

1988

Both poems involve motherhood, but they take entirely different stances about it and have very different tones. The mother in Dove's "Daystar," overwhelmed by the demands of young children, needs a room of her own. All she can manage, however, is a brief hour of respite. The situation is virtually the whole story here. Nothing really happens except that daily events (washing diapers, picking up toys, looking at crickets and leaves, explaining the world to children, having sex) crowd her brief private hour and make it precious. Being "nothing" (lines 21 and 22) takes on great value in these circumstances, and the poem makes much of the setting: an isolated chair behind the garage. Setting in poems often means something much more specific about a particular culture or social history, but here time and place get their value from the circumstances of the situation for one frazzled mother.

The particulars of time and place in Pastan's "To a Daughter Leaving Home" are even less specific; the incident the poem describes happened a long time ago, and its vividness is a function of memory. The speaker here thinks back nostalgically to a moment when her daughter made an earlier (but briefer) departure. Though we learn very little about the speaker, at least directly, we may infer quite a bit about her—her affection for her daughter, the kind of mother she has been, her anxiety at the new departure that seems to reflect the earlier wobbly ride into the distance. The daughter is now, the poem implies, old enough to "leave" home in a full sense, but we do not know the specific reason or what the present circumstances are. Only the title tells us the situation, and (like "Daystar") the poem is all situation.

Some poems, however, depend heavily on historical specifics. In the preceding chapter, for example, we saw how Margaret Atwood based "Death of a Young Son by Drowning" on an actual person's journal entries. While the following poem refers to a particular event, it also draws on the parallels between that event and circumstances surrounding the poet and his immediate readers:

## JOHN MILTON
### On the Late Massacre in Piedmont

    Avenge, O Lord, thy slaughtered saints, whose bones
    Lie scattered on the Alpine mountains cold;
    Even them who kept thy truth so pure of old
    When all our fathers worshiped stocks and stones,[6]
5 Forget not: in thy book record their groans
    Who were thy sheep and in their ancient fold
    Slain by the bloody Piemontese that rolled
    Mother with infant down the rocks. Their moans

---

6. Idols of wood and stone.

> The vales redoubled to the hills, and they
> 10   To heaven. Their martyred blood and ashes sow
>        O'er all th' Italian fields, where still doth sway
>        The triple tyrant:⁷ that from these may grow
>        A hundredfold, who having learnt thy way
>        Early may fly the Babylonian woe.⁸
>
>        1655

The "slaughtered saints" were members of the Waldensians—a heretical sect that had long been settled in southern France and northern Italy (the Piedmont). Though a minority, the Waldensians were allowed freedom of worship until 1655, when their protection under the law was taken away and locals attacked them, killing large numbers. This poem, then, is not a private meditation, but rather a public statement about a well-known "news" event. To fully understand the poem and respond to it meaningfully, the reader must therefore be acquainted with its historical context, including the massacre itself and the significance it had for Milton and his English audience.

Milton wrote the poem shortly after the massacre became known in England, and implicit in its "meaning" is a parallel Milton's readers would have perceived between events in the Piedmont and current English politics. Milton signals the analogy early on by calling the dead Piedmontese "saints," the term then regularly used by English Protestants of the Puritan stamp to describe themselves and to thereby assert their belief that every individual Christian—not just those few "special" religious heroes singled out in the Catholic tradition—lived a heroic life. By identifying the Waldensians with the English Puritans—their beliefs were in some ways quite similar, and both were minorities in a larger political and cultural context—Milton was warning his fellow Puritans that, if the Stuart monarchy were reestablished, what had just happened to the Waldensians could happen to them as well. Indeed, following the Restoration in 1660, tight restrictions were placed on the Puritan "sects" under the new British monarchy. In lines 12 and 14, the poem alludes to dangers of religious rule by dominant groups by invoking standard images of Catholic power and persecution; the heir to the English throne (who succeeded to the throne as Charles II in 1660) was spending his exile in Catholic Europe and was, because of his sympathetic treatment of Catholic associates and friends, suspected of being a Catholic. Chauvinistic Englishmen, who promoted rivalries with Catholic powers like France, considered him a traitor.

Many poems, like this one, make use of historical occurrences and situations to create a widely evocative set of angers, sympathies, and conclusions. Sometimes a poet's intention in recording a particular moment or event is to commemorate it or comment upon it. A poem written about a specific occasion is usually called an **occasional poem**, and such a poem is **referential**; that is, it *refers* to a certain historical time or event. Sometimes, it is hard to place ourselves fully enough in another time or place to imagine sympathetically what a particular historical moment would have been like, and even the best poetic efforts do not necessarily

---

7. The pope's tiara featured three crowns.
8. In Milton's day, Protestants often likened the Roman Church to Babylonian decadence, calling the church "the whore of Babylon," and they read Revelation 17 and 18 as an allegory of its coming destruction.

transport us there. For such poems we need, at the least, specific historical information—plus a willingness on our part as readers to be transported by a name, a date, or a dramatic situation.

Time or place may, of course, be used much less specifically and still be important to a poem; frequently a poem's setting draws upon common notions of a particular time or place. Setting a poem in a garden, for example, or writing about apples almost inevitably reminds many readers of the Garden of Eden because it is part of the Western heritage of belief or knowledge. Even people who don't read at all or who lack Judeo-Christian religious commitments are likely to know about Eden, and a poet writing in our culture can count on that. An **allusion** is a reference to something outside the poem that carries a history of meaning and strong emotional associations. (For a longer account of allusion, see chapter 23.) For example, gardens may carry suggestions of innocence and order, or temptation and the Fall, or both, depending on how the poem handles the allusion. Well-known places from history or myth may be popularly associated with particular ideas or values or ways of life.

The place involved in a poem is its **spatial setting**, and the time is its **temporal setting**. The temporal setting may be a specific date or an era, a season of the year or a time of day. We tend, for example, to think of spring as a time of discovery and growth, and poems set in spring are likely to make use of that association; morning usually suggests discovery as well—beginnings, vitality, the world fresh and new—even to those of us who in reality take our waking slow. Temporal or spatial setting often influences our expectation of theme and tone, although a poet may surprise us by making something very different of what we had thought was familiar. Setting is often an important factor in creating the mood in poems just as in stories, plays, or films. Often the details of setting have a lot to do with the way we ultimately respond to the poem's subject or theme, as in this poem:

**SYLVIA PLATH**

## Point Shirley

From Water-Tower Hill to the brick prison
The shingle booms, bickering under
The sea's collapse.
Snowcakes break and welter. This year
5   The gritted wave leaps
The seawall and drops onto a bier
Of quahog chips,[9]
Leaving a salty mash of ice to whiten

In my grandmother's sand yard. She is dead,
10  Whose laundry snapped and froze here, who
Kept house against
What the sluttish, rutted sea could do.

---

9. Chips from quahog clamshells, common on the New England coast.

Squall waves once danced
Ship timbers in through the cellar window;
15 A thresh-tailed, lanced
Shark littered in the geranium bed—
Such collusion of mulish elements
She wore her broom straws to the nub.
Twenty years out
20 Of her hand; the house still hugs in each drab
Stucco socket
The purple egg-stones: from Great Head's knob
To the filled-in Gut
The sea in its cold gizzard ground those rounds.

25 Nobody wintering now behind
The planked-up windows where she set
Her wheat loaves
And apple cakes to cool. What is it
Survives, grieves
30 So, over this battered, obstinate spit
Of gravel? The waves'
Spewed relics clicker masses in the wind,
Gray waves the stub-necked eiders ride.
A labor of love, and that labor lost.
35 Steadily the sea
Eats at Point Shirley. She died blessed,
And I come by
Bones, bones only, pawed and tossed,
A dog-faced sea.
40 The sun sinks under Boston, bloody red.

I would get from these dry-papped stones
The milk your love instilled in them.
The black ducks dive.
And though your graciousness might stream,
45 And I contrive,
Grandmother, stones are nothing of home
To that spumiest dove.
Against both bar and tower the black sea runs.

1960

One does not have to know the New England coast by personal experience to find it vividly re-created in Plath's poem. A reader who knows that coast or another like it may have an advantage in being able to respond more quickly to the poem's precise description, but the poem does not depend on the reader's having such knowledge. The exact location of Point Shirley, near Boston, is not especially important, but visualization of the setting is. Crucial to the poem's tone and mood is the sense of the sea as aggressor, a force powerful enough to change the contours of the coast and invade the privacy of yards and homes. The energy, relentlessness, and impersonality of the sea met their match, though only temporarily, in the speaker's grandmother, who "[k]ept house against / What the sluttish, rutted sea could do" (lines 11-12). The grandmother *belonged* in this setting, and it seemed hers, but twenty years of her absence (since her death) now begin to show. Still, the marks of her obstinacy and love remain, although ultimately they are doomed by the sea's more enduring power.

Details—and how they are amassed—matter here rather than historic particulars of time and place. The grays and whites and drab colors of the sea and its leavings provide both a visual sense of the scene and the mood for the poem. The stubbornness that the speaker admired in the grandmother seems a part of that tenacious grayness. Nothing happens rapidly here; things wear down. Even the "bloody red" (line 40) of the sun's setting—an ominous sign that adds a vivid fright to the dullness rather than brightening it—makes promises that seem slow and doomed. The toughness of the boarded-up house is a monument to the grandmother's loving care and becomes a way for the speaker to touch her human spirit, but the poem finally emphasizes the relentless black sea, which runs against the landmarks and fortresses that had been identified with the setting in the very first line.

Queries about situation and setting begin as simple questions of identification, but frequently become more complex when we sort out all the implications. Often it takes only a moment to determine a poem's situation, but it may take much longer to discover all the implications of time and place, for their meanings may depend upon visual details, or upon actual historical occurrences, or upon habitual ways of thinking about certain times and places—or all three at once. As you read the following poem, notice how the setting—another shore—prepares us for the speaker's moods and ideas, and then watch how the movement of his mind is affected by what he sees.

### MATTHEW ARNOLD
## *Dover Beach*[1]

The sea is calm tonight.
The tide is full, the moon lies fair
Upon the straits; on the French coast the light
Gleams and is gone; the cliffs of England stand,
5 Glimmering and vast, out in the tranquil bay.
Come to the window, sweet is the night-air!
Only, from the long line of spray
Where the sea meets the moon-blanched land,
Listen! you hear the grating roar
10 Of pebbles which the waves draw back, and fling,
At their return, up the high strand,
Begin, and cease, and then again begin,

---

1. At the narrowest point on the English Channel. The light on the French coast (lines 3-4) would be about twenty miles away.

With tremulous cadence slow, and bring
The eternal note of sadness in.

15  Sophocles long ago
Heard it on the Aegean, and it brought
Into his mind the turbid ebb and flow
Of human misery;[2] we
Find also in the sound a thought,
20  Hearing it by this distant northern sea.

The Sea of Faith
Was once, too, at the full, and round earth's shore
Lay like the folds of a bright girdle furled.
But now I only hear
25  Its melancholy, long, withdrawing roar,
Retreating, to the breath
Of the night-wind, down the vast edges drear
And naked shingles[3] of the world.

Ah, love, let us be true
30  To one another! for the world, which seems
To lie before us like a land of dreams,
So various, so beautiful, so new,
Hath really neither joy, nor love, nor light,
Nor certitude, nor peace, nor help for pain;
35  And we are here as on a darkling plain
Swept with confused alarms of struggle and flight,
Where ignorant armies clash by night.

ca. 1851

Exactly what is the dramatic situation in "Dover Beach"? How soon are you aware that someone is being spoken to? How much do you learn about the person spoken to? How would you describe the speaker's mood? What does the speaker's mood have to do with time and place? Do any details of present time and place help to account for his tendency to talk repeatedly of the past and the future? How important is it to the poem's total effect that the beach here involves an international border? What particulars of Dover Beach seem especially important to the poem's themes? to its emotional effects?

Not all poems have an identifiable situation or setting, just as not all poems have a speaker who is entirely distinct from the author. Poems that simply present a series of thoughts and feelings directly, in a contemplative, meditative, or reflective way, may not set up any kind of action, plot, or situation at all, preferring to speak directly without the intermediary of a dramatic device. But most poems depend crucially upon a sense of place, a sense of time, and an understanding of human interaction in scenes that resemble the strategies of drama or film. And questions about these matters will often lead you to define not only the "facts" but also the feelings central to the design a poem has upon its readers.

---

2. In Sophocles' *Antigone*, lines 637–46, the chorus compares the fate of the house of Oedipus to the waves of the sea.   3. Pebble-strewn beaches.

# SITUATIONS

### EMILY BRONTË
## The Night-Wind

In summer's mellow midnight,
A cloudless moon shone through
Our open parlor window
And rosetrees wet with dew.

5 I sat in silent musing,
The soft wind waved my hair:
It told me Heaven was glorious,
And sleeping Earth was fair.

I needed not its breathing
10 To bring such thoughts to me,
But still it whispered lowly,
"How dark the woods will be!

"The thick leaves in my murmur
Are rustling like a dream,
15 And all their myriad voices
Instinct[1] with spirit seem."

I said, "Go, gentle singer,
Thy wooing voice is kind,
But do not think its music
20 Has power to reach my mind.

"Play with the scented flower,
The young tree's supple bough,
And leave my human feelings
In their own course to flow."

25 The wanderer would not leave me;
Its kiss grew warmer still—
"O come," it sighed so sweetly,
"I'll win thee 'gainst thy will.

"Have we not been from childhood friends?
30 Have I not loved thee long?
As long as thou hast loved the night
Whose silence wakes my song.

"And when thy heart is laid at rest
Beneath the church-yard stone

---

1. Infused.

35   I shall have time enough to mourn
     And thou to be alone."

September 11, 1840

- What might it mean that the speaker feels tempted by the wind to go wandering in the darkness? What might she find there?

ANDREW MARVELL

## To His Coy Mistress

    Had we but world enough, and time,
This coyness,[2] lady, were no crime.
We would sit down, and think which way
To walk, and pass our long love's day.
5 Thou by the Indian Ganges' side
Shouldst rubies[3] find: I by the tide
Of Humber would complain.[4] I would
Love you ten years before the Flood,
And you should if you please refuse
10 Till the conversion of the Jews.[5]
My vegetable love[6] should grow
Vaster than empires, and more slow;
An hundred years should go to praise
Thine eyes, and on thy forehead gaze;
15 Two hundred to adore each breast,
But thirty thousand to the rest.
An age at least to every part,
And the last age should show your heart.
For, lady, you deserve this state;[7]
20 Nor would I love at lower rate.
    But at my back I always hear
Time's wingèd chariot hurrying near;
And yonder all before us lie
Deserts of vast eternity.
25 Thy beauty shall no more be found,
Nor, in thy marble vault, shall sound
My echoing song; then worms shall try

---

2. Hesitancy, modesty (not necessarily suggesting calculation).
3. Talismans that are supposed to preserve virginity.
4. Write love complaints, conventional songs lamenting the cruelty of love. *Humber:* a river and estuary in Marvell's hometown of Hull.
5. Which, according to popular Christian belief, will occur just before the end of the world.
6. Which is capable only of passive growth, not of consciousness. The "vegetable soul" is lower than the other two divisions of the soul, "animal" and "rational."    7. Dignity.

That long preserved virginity,
And your quaint honor turn to dust,
30 And into ashes all my lust:
The grave's a fine and private place,
But none, I think, do there embrace.
   Now therefore, while the youthful hue
Sits on thy skin like morning dew,[8]
35 And while thy willing soul transpires[9]
At every pore with instant fires,
Now let us sport us while we may,
And now, like am'rous birds of prey,
Rather at once our time devour
40 Than languish in his slow-chapped[1] pow'r.
Let us roll all our strength and all
Our sweetness up into one ball,
And tear our pleasures with rough strife
Thorough[2] the iron gates of life.
45 Thus, though we cannot make our sun
Stand still,[3] yet we will make him run.[4]

1681

- Whom is the speaker trying to persuade in this poem? Is his argument persuasive?

**MARILYN CHIN**

## *Summer Love*

The black smoke rising means that I am cooking
dried lotus, bay oysters scrambled with eggs.
If this doesn't please you, too bad, it's all I have.
I don't mind your staying for breakfast—but, please—do not linger;
5 nothing worse in the morning than last night's love.

Your belly is flat and your skin—milk in the moonlight.
I notice your glimmer among a thousand tired eyes.
When we dance closely, fog thickens, all distinctions falter.
I let you touch me where I am most vulnerable,
10 heart of the vulva, vulva of the heart.

---

8. The text reads "glew." "Lew" (warmth) has also been suggested as an emendation.
9. Breathes forth.
1. Slow-jawed. Chronos (Time), ruler of the world in early Greek myth, devoured all of his children except Zeus, who was hidden. Later, Zeus seized power (see line 46 and note).     2. Through.
3. To lengthen his night of love with Alcmene, Zeus made the sun stand still.
4. Each sex act was believed to shorten life by one day.

Perhaps, I fear, there will not be another like you.
Or you might walk away in the same face of the others—
    —blue with scorn and a troubled life.
But, for now, let the summers be savored and the centuries be forgiven.
15 Two lovers in a field of floss and iris—
where nothing else matters but the dew and the light.

                                                                    1994

- How does the language of this poem (and its title) echo the situation's sexuality, uncertainty, and hope?

### VIRGINIA HAMILTON ADAIR

## *Peeling an Orange*

Between you and a bowl of oranges I lie nude
Reading *The World's Illusion* through my tears.
You reach across me hungry for global fruit,
Your bare arm hard, furry and warm on my belly.
5 Your fingers pry the skin of a navel orange
Releasing tiny explosions of spicy oil.
You place peeled disks of gold in a bizarre pattern
On my white body. Rearranging, you bend and bite
The disks to release further their eager scent.
10 I say "Stop, you're tickling," my eyes still on the page.
Aromas of groves arise. Through green leaves
Glow the lofty snows. Through red lips
Your white teeth close on a translucent segment.
Your face over my face eclipses *The World's Illusion*.
15 Pulp and juice pass into my mouth from your mouth.
We laugh against each other's lips. I hold my book
Behind your head, still reading, still weeping a little.
You say "Read on, I'm just an illusion," rolling
Over upon me soothingly, gently moving,
20 Smiling greenly through long lashes. And soon
I say "Don't stop. Don't disillusion me."
Snows melt. The mountain silvers into many a stream.
The oranges are golden worlds in a dark dream.

                                                                    1996

- How does the suggestion of crying alter your perception of the situation in this poem?

## MARY JO SALTER

### Welcome to Hiroshima

is what you first see, stepping off the train:
a billboard brought to you in living English
by Toshiba Electric. While a channel
silent in the TV of the brain

5  projects those flickering re-runs of a cloud
that brims its risen columnful like beer
and, spilling over, hangs its foamy head,
you feel a thirst for history: what year

it started to be safe to breathe the air,
10  and when to drink the blood and scum afloat
on the Ohta River. But no, the water's clear,
they pour it for your morning cup of tea

in one of the countless sunny coffee shops
whose plastic dioramas advertise
15  mutations of cuisine behind the glass:
a pancake sandwich; a pizza someone tops

with a maraschino cherry. Passing by
the Peace Park's floral hypocenter (where
how bravely, or with what mistaken cheer,
20  humanity erased its own erasure),

you enter the memorial museum
and through more glass are served, as on a dish
of blistered grass, three mannequins. Like gloves
a mother clips to coatsleeves, strings of flesh

25  hang from their fingertips; or as if tied
to recall a duty for us, *Reverence*
*the dead whose mourners too shall soon be dead,*
but all commemoration's swallowed up

in questions of bad taste, how re-created
30  horror mocks the grim original,
and thinking at last *They should have left it all*
you stop. This is the wristwatch of a child.

Jammed on the moment's impact, resolute
to communicate some message, although mute,
35  it gestures with its hands at eight-fifteen
and eight-fifteen and eight-fifteen again

while tables of statistics on the wall
update the news by calling on a roll

of tape, death gummed on death, and in the case
40 adjacent, an exhibit under glass

is glass itself: a shard the bomb slammed in
a woman's arm at eight-fifteen, but some
three decades on—as if to make it plain
hope's only as renewable as pain

45 and as if all the unsung
debasements of the past may one day come
rising to the surface once again—
worked its filthy way out like a tongue

1984

- What arrests the speaker's attention to see beyond the "bad taste" (line 29) of the museum's displays? What is it that "works its filthy way out like a tongue" (line 48)?

## HOWARD NEMEROV

### A Way of Life

It's been going on a long time.
For instance, these two guys, not saying much, who slog
Through sun and sand, fleeing the scene of their crime,
Till one turns, without a word, and smacks
5 His buddy flat with the flat of an axe,
Which cuts down on the dialogue
Some, but is viewed rather as normal than sad
By me, as I wait for the next ad.

It seems to me it's been quite a while
10 Since the last vision of blonde loveliness
Vanished, her shampoo and shower and general style
Replaced by this lean young lunk-
head parading along with a gun in his back to confess
How yestereve, being drunk
15 And in a state of existential despair,
He beat up his grandma and pawned her invalid chair.

But here at last is a pale beauty
Smoking a filter beside a mountain stream,
Brief interlude, before the conflict of love and duty
20 Gets moving again, as sheriff and posse expound,
Between jail and saloon, the American Dream
Where Justice, after considerable horsing around,
Turns out to be Mercy; when the villain is knocked off,
A kindly uncle offers syrup for my cough.

25 And now these clean-cut athletic types
In global hats are having a nervous debate
As they stand between their individual rocket ships
Which have landed, appropriately, on some rocks
Somewhere in Space, in an atmosphere of hate
30 Where one tells the other to pull up his socks
And get going, he doesn't say where; they fade,
And an angel food cake flutters in the void.

I used to leave now and again;
No more. A lot of violence in American life
35 These days, mobsters and cops all over the scene.
But there's a lot of love, too, mixed with the strife,
And kitchen-kindness, like a bedtime story
With rich food and a more kissable depilatory.
Still, I keep my weapons handy, sitting here
40 Smoking and shaving and drinking the dry beer.
                                                    1967

- What does the succession of images represent to the speaker of this poem? Would the situation be different today?

# TIMES

## WILLIAM SHAKESPEARE
## [*Full many a glorious morning have I seen*]

Full many a glorious morning have I seen
Flatter the mountain-tops with sovereign eye,
Kissing with golden face the meadows green,
Gilding pale streams with heavenly alchymy;
5 Anon permit the basest clouds to ride
With ugly rack[1] on his celestial face,
And from the forlorn world his visage hide,
Stealing unseen to west with this disgrace:
Even so my sun one early morn did shine,
10 With all-triumphant splendor on my brow;
But, out! alack! he was but one hour mine,
The region cloud hath mask'd him from me now.
  Yet him for this my love no whit disdaineth;
  Suns of the world may stain when heaven's sun staineth.
                                                    1609

1. Moss.

- What words and phrases mark the shifts of the clouds back and forth across the face of the sun in "Full many a glorious morning"? What distinction is Shakespeare making between "suns of the world" and "heaven's sun"?

## JOHN DONNE

### *The Good-Morrow*

    I wonder, by my troth, what thou and I
        Did, till we loved? were we not weaned till then?
    But sucked on country pleasures, childishly?
    Or snorted we in the Seven Sleepers' den?[2]
5   'Twas so; but[3] this, all pleasures fancies be.
        If ever any beauty I did see,
Which I desired, and got,[4] twas but a dream of thee.

    And now good-morrow to our waking souls,
        Which watch not one another out of fear;
10   For love, all love of other sights controls,
        And makes one little room an everywhere.
    Let sea-discoverers to new worlds have gone,
    Let maps to other,[5] worlds on worlds have shown,
Let us possess one world, each hath one, and is one.

15   My face in thine eye, thine in mine appears,[6]
        And true plain hearts do in the faces rest;
    Where can we find two better hemispheres,
    Without sharp north, without declining west?
Whatever dies was not mixed equally,[7]
20   If our two loves be one, or, thou and I
Love so alike that none do slacken, none can die.

                           1633

- Like so many of Donne's poems, this one attempts to persuade. What is the situation of this poem? What does the speaker wish to demonstrate?

---

2. According to legend, seven Christian youths escaped Roman persecution by sleeping in a cave for 187 years. *Snorted:* snored.   3. Except for.   4. Sexually possessed.   5. Other people.
6. That is, each is reflected in the other's eyes.
7. Perfectly mixed elements, according to scholastic philosophy, were stable and immortal.

**SYLVIA PLATH**

## *Morning Song*

Love set you going like a fat gold watch.
The midwife slapped your footsoles, and your bald cry
Took its place among the elements.

Our voices echo, magnifying your arrival. New statue.
5 In a drafty museum, your nakedness
Shadows our safety. We stand round blankly as walls.

I'm no more your mother
Than the cloud that distils a mirror to reflect its own slow
Effacement at the wind's hand.

10 All night your moth-breath
Flickers among the flat pink roses. I wake to listen:
A far sea moves in my ear.

One cry, and I stumble from bed, cow-heavy and floral
In my Victorian nightgown.
15 Your mouth opens clean as a cat's. The window square

Whitens and swallows its dull stars. And now you try
Your handful of notes;
The clear vowels rise like balloons.

1961

- How does this poem's language emphasize the distinctions between the speaker and her baby? How does the poem's setting in time—morning—affect its meaning?

**BILLY COLLINS**

## *Morning*

Why do we bother with the rest of the day,
the swale of the afternoon,
the sudden dip into evening,

then night with his notorious perfumes,
5 his many-pointed stars?

This is the best—
throwing off the light covers,
feet on the cold floor,
and buzzing around the house on espresso—

10   maybe a splash of water on the face,
     a palmful of vitamins—
     but mostly buzzing around the house on espresso,

     dictionary and atlas open on the rug,
     the typewriter waiting for the key of the head,
15   a cello on the radio,

     and, if necessary, the windows—
     trees fifty, a hundred years old
     out there,
     heavy clouds on the way
20   and the lawn steaming like a horse
     in the early morning.

                                           1998

- What words and phrases help to color the reader's perceptions of the various times of day mentioned in this poem? Why is morning "the best" (line 6)?

## AUGUST KLEINZAHLER

### *Aubade on East 12th Street*

     The skylight silvers
     and a faint shudder from the underground
     travels up the building's steel.

     Dawn breaks across this wilderness
5    of roofs with their old wooden storage tanks
     and caps of louvered cowlings

     moving in the wind. Your back,
     raised hip and thigh
     well-tooled as a rounded baluster
10   on a lathe of shadow and light.

                                           1996

- Paraphrase the simile that concludes this poem. How does "a lathe of shadow and light" figure into the comparison?

JONATHAN SWIFT

## A Description of the Morning

Now hardly here and there a hackney-coach[8]
Appearing, showed the ruddy morn's approach.
Now Betty[9] from her master's bed had flown,
And softly stole to discompose her own.
5 The slip shod 'prentice from his master's door
Had pared the dirt, and sprinkled round the floor.
Now Moll had whirled her mop with dext'rous airs,
Prepared to scrub the entry and the stairs.
The youth with broomy stumps began to trace
10 The kennel-edge[1] where wheels had worn the place.
The small-coal man[2] was heard with cadence deep,
Till drowned in shriller notes of chimney-sweep:
Duns[3] at his lordship's gate began to meet;
And brick-dust Moll had screamed through half the street.[4]
15 The turnkey now his flock returning sees,
Duly let out a-nights to steal for fees.[5]
The watchful bailiffs take their silent stands,[6]
And schoolboys lag with satchels in their hands.

1709

- From the poem's brief descriptions of morning routines, what do we know about its various characters and the kind of community they inhabit? Could a similar poem be written today?


LOUISE BOGAN

## Evening in the Sanitarium[7]

The free evening fades, outside the windows fastened with decorative
   iron grilles.
The lamps are lighted; the shades drawn; the nurses are watching a
   little.
It is the hour of the complicated knitting on the safe bone needles; of
   the games of anagrams and bridge;
The deadly game of chess; the book held up like a mask.

---

8. Hired coach. *Hardly:* scarcely; that is, they are just beginning to appear.
9. A stock name for a servant girl. Moll (lines 7, 14) is a frequent lower-class nickname.
1. Edge of the gutter that ran down the middle of the street. *Trace:* To find old nails [Swift's note].
2. A seller of coal and charcoal.   3. Bill collectors.
4. Selling powdered brick that was used to clean knives.
5. Jailers collected fees from prisoners for their keep and often let them out at night so they could steal to pay expenses.   6. Looking for those on their "wanted" lists.
7. Originally published with the subtitle "Imitated from Auden" [Bogan's note].

5   The period of the wildest weeping, the fiercest delusion, is over.
    The women rest their tired half-healed hearts; they are almost well.
    Some of them will stay almost well always: the blunt-faced woman
        whose thinking dissolved
    Under academic discipline; the manic-depressive girl
    Now leveling off; one paranoiac afflicted with jealousy.
10  Another with persecution. Some alleviation has been possible.

    O fortunate bride, who never again will become elated after childbirth!
    O lucky older wife; who has been cured of feeling unwanted!
    To the suburban railway station you will return, return,
    To meet forever Jim home on the 5:35.
15  You will be again as normal and selfish and heartless as anybody else.

    There is life left: the piano says it with its octave smile.
    The soft carpets pad the thump and splinter of the suicide to be.
    Everything will be splendid: the grandmother will not drink habitually.
    The fruit salad will bloom on the plate like a bouquet
20  And the garden produce the blue-ribbon aquilegia.[8]

    The cats will be glad; the fathers feel justified; the mothers relieved.
    The sons and husbands will no longer need to pay the bills.
    Childhoods will be put away, the obscene nightmare abated.

    At the ends of the corridors the baths are running.
25  Mrs. C. again feels the shadow of the obsessive idea.
    Miss R. looks at the mantel-piece, which must mean something.

                                                                    1941

- Why do you think this poem is set in the evening? How does this setting affect the poem?

### ARCHIBALD LAMPMAN

## Winter Evening

    To-night the very horses springing by
       Toss gold from whitened nostrils. In a dream
    The streets that narrow to the westward gleam
    Like rows of golden palaces; and high
5   From all the crowded chimneys tower and die
    A thousand aureoles. Down in the west
    The brimming plains beneath the sunset rest,
    One burning sea of gold. Soon, soon shall fly
    The glorious vision, and the hours shall feel
10     A mightier master; soon from height to height,
    With silence and the sharp unpitying stars,

---

8. Columbine.

Stern creeping frosts, and winds that touch like steel,
Out of the depth beyond the eastern bars,
Glittering and still shall come the awful night.

1899

- How does this poem's language create a sense of afternoon's warmth and beauty, and then of danger and pain in "the awful night"?

# PLACES

### JOHN BETJEMAN

## In Westminster Abbey[9]

Let me take this other glove off
   As the *vox humana*[1] swells,
And the beauteous fields of Eden
   Bask beneath the Abbey bells.
5 Here, where England's statesmen lie,
   Listen to a lady's cry.

Gracious Lord, oh bomb the Germans.
   Spare their women for Thy Sake,
And if that is not too easy
10   We will pardon Thy Mistake.
But, gracious Lord, whate'er shall be,
   Don't let anyone bomb me.

Keep our Empire undismembered
   Guide our Forces by Thy Hand,
15 Gallant blacks from far Jamaica,
   Honduras and Togoland;
Protect them Lord in all their fights,
   And, even more, protect the whites.

Think of what our Nation stands for,
20   Books from Boots[2] and country lanes,
Free speech, free passes, class distinction,
   Democracy and proper drains.
Lord, put beneath Thy special care
   One-eighty-nine Cadogan Square.[3]

---

9. Gothic church in London in which English monarchs are crowned and many famous Englishmen are buried (see lines 5, 39–40).
1. Organ tones that resemble the human voice.    2. A chain of British pharmacies.
3. Presumably where the speaker lives, in a fashionable section of central London.

25 Although dear Lord I am a sinner,
    I have done no major crime;
Now I'll come to Evening Service
    Whensoever I have the time.
So, Lord, reserve for me a crown,[4]
30 And do not let my shares go down.

I will labor for Thy Kingdom,
    Help our lads to win the war,
Send white feathers to the cowards[5]
    Join the Women's Army Corps,[6]
35 Then wash the Steps around Thy Throne
In the Eternal Safety Zone.

Now I feel a little better,
    What a treat to hear Thy Word
Where the bones of leading statesmen,
40     Have so often been interred.
And now, dear Lord, I cannot wait
Because I have a luncheon date.

                1940

- How do the poem's setting in place—a historic church in London— and time—1940, during the German bombardment of Britain—affect the tone?

## ELIZABETH ALEXANDER

### West Indian Primer

    *for Clifford L. Alexander, Sr.*
    *1898–1989*

"On the road between Spanish Town
and Kingston," my grandfather said,
"I was born." His father a merchant,
Jewish, from Italy or Spain

5 In the great earthquake the ground split
clean, and great-grandfather fell
in the fault with his goat. I don't know
how I got this tale and do not ask.

---

4. Coin worth five shillings (but also an afterlife reward).
5. White feathers were sometimes given or sent to men not in uniform to suggest that they were cowards and should join the armed forces.
6. The speaker uses the old World War I name (Women's Army Auxiliary Corps) of the Auxiliary Territorial Service, an organization that performed domestic (and some foreign) defense duties.

His black mother taught my grand-
10 father figures, fixed codfish cakes
and fried plantains, drilled cleanliness,
telling the truth, punctuality.

"There is no man more honest,"
my father says. Years later
15 I read that Jews passed through my
grandfather's birthplace frequently.

I know more about Toussaint[7]
and Hispaniola[8] than my own
Jamaica and my family tales.
20 I finger the stories like genie

lamps. I write this West Indian primer.

1990

- Why do you think this poem is presented as a "primer"—that is, a basic introduction—for the speaker's native Jamaica? Does the poem fulfill that function?

## DEREK WALCOTT

### *Midsummer*

Certain things here[9] are quietly American—
that chain-link fence dividing the absent roars
of the beach from the empty ball park, its holes
muttering the word umpire instead of empire;
5 the gray, metal light where an early pelican
coasts, with its engine off, over the pink fire
of a sea whose surface is as cold as Maine's.
The light warms up the sides of white, eager Cessnas[1]
parked at the airstrip under the freckling hills
10 of St. Thomas. The sheds, the brown, functional hangar,
are like those of the Occupation in the last war.
The night left a rank smell under the casuarinas,
the villas have fenced-off beaches where the natives walk,
illegal immigrants from unlucky islands
15 who envy the smallest polyp its right to work.
Here the wetback crab and the mollusc are citizens,
and the leaves have green cards. Bulldozers jerk
and gouge out a hill, but we all know that the dust

---

7. Self-educated, Haitian black soldier and liberator (1783–1803).
8. The first island claimed by Columbus for Spain in 1492. Now divided into the nations of Haiti and the Dominican Republic.
9. Trinidad.   1. Small airplanes.

            is industrial and must be suffered. Soon—
20      the sea's corrugations are sheets of zinc
        soldered by the sun's steady acetylene. This
        drizzle that falls now is American rain,
        stitching stars in the sand. My own corpuscles
        are changing as fast. I fear what the migrant envies:
25      the starry pattern they make—the flag on the post office—
        the quality of the dirt, the fealty changing under my foot.

                                                    1984

- What is "American" (line 22) about the images described in this poem? Why does the speaker say he fears "the starry pattern" made by the raindrops in the sand (line 25)?

**THOM GUNN**

## *A Map of the City*

I stand upon a hill and see
A luminous country under me,
Through which at two the drunk must weave;
The transient's pause, the sailor's leave.

5   I notice, looking down the hill,
    Arms braced upon a window sill;
    And on the web of fire escapes
    Move the potential, the grey shapes.

    I hold the city here, complete:
10  And every shape defined by light
    Is mine, or corresponds to mine,
    Some flickering or some steady shine.

    This map is ground of my delight.
    Between the limits, night by night,
15  I watch a malady's advance,
    I recognize my love of chance.

    By the recurrent lights I see
    Endless potentiality,
    The crowded, broken, and unfinished!
20  I would not have the risk diminished.

                                                    1954

- In what way does the speaker's view of a city at night constitute a "map"? How is this map "complete" (line 9)?

**MARY OLIVER**

## Singapore

In Singapore, in the airport,
a darkness was ripped from my eyes.
In the women's restroom, one compartment stood open.
A woman knelt there, washing something in the white bowl.
5 Disgust argued in my stomach
and I felt, in my pocket, for my ticket.

A poem should always have birds in it.
Kingfishers, say, with their bold eyes and gaudy wings.
Rivers are pleasant, and of course trees.
10 A waterfall, or if that's not possible, a fountain rising and
    falling.
A person wants to stand in a happy place, in a poem.

When the woman turned I could not answer her face.
Her beauty and her embarrassment struggled together, and
    neither could win.
She smiled and I smiled. What kind of nonsense is this?
15 Everybody needs a job.

Yes, a person wants to stand in a happy place, in a poem.
But first we must watch her as she stares down at her labor,
    which is dull enough.
She is washing the tops of the airport ashtrays, as big as
    hubcaps, with a blue rag.
Her small hands turn the metal, scrubbing and rinsing.
20 She does not work slowly, nor quickly, but like a river.
Her dark hair is like the wing of a bird.

I don't doubt for a moment that she loves her life.
And I want her to rise up from the crust and the slop and
    fly down to the river.
This probably won't happen.
25 But maybe it will.
If the world were only pain and logic, who would want it?

Of course, it isn't.
Neither do I mean anything miraculous, but only
the light that can shine out of a life. I mean
30 the way she unfolded and refolded the blue cloth,
the way her smile was only for my sake; I mean
the way this poem is filled with trees, and birds.

                                                1990

- What "darkness was ripped" from the speaker's eyes (line 2)? Does it matter that the poem is set in (and named after) a particular city?

**EARLE BIRNEY**

## *Irapuato*[2]

    For reasons any
                 brigadier
                        could tell
this is a favorite nook for
5                   massacre

Toltex by Mixtex Mixtex by Aztex
Aztex by Spanishtex Spanishtex by
Mexitex by Mexitex by Mexitex by Texaco[3]
So any farmer can see how the strawberries
10 are the biggest and reddest
    in the whole damn continent

    but why
        when arranged under
                      the market flies
15 do they look like small clotting hearts?

                          1962

- What connects "Toltex" and "Texaco" in the speaker's mind (lines 6–8)?

---

2. A city in central Mexico, northwest of Mexico City.
3. The Toltec, Mixtec, and Aztec peoples lived in pre-Columbian Mexico.

## SUGGESTIONS FOR WRITING

1. Matthew Arnold's "Dover Beach" is a meditation on history and human destiny derived from the poet's close observation of the ebb and flow of the sea. Write an essay in which you examine the poem's descriptive language and the way this creates a suitable setting for Arnold's philosophical musings.
2. Certain seventeenth-century poets, such as John Donne and Andrew Marvell, have been called "metaphysical poets" for their ingenuity in using apparently far-fetched analogies to create apt and insightful comparisons, usually intended to persuade. What is the line of reasoning in Donne's "The Flea" or Marvell's "To His Coy Mistress?" Who is the intended audience for each poem? Write an essay in which you discuss the way that either or both of these poems uses situation as the basis for comparison and persuasion.
3. Mary Jo Salter's "Welcome to Hiroshima" and Howard Nemerov's "A Way of Life" both use situations—visiting a war museum and watching television, respectively—that present a host of ideas about modern society in general and America in particular. What is each poem saying about our moral and political values? Write an essay in which you examine the way either of these poems uses situation to create an implied commentary on American moral and political values.
4. This chapter contains a number of poems that, in both obvious and subtle ways, associate love with the morning—Shakespeare's "Full many a glorious morning have I seen," Donne's "The Good-Morrow," Sylvia Plath's "Morning Song," and August Kleinzahler's "Aubade on East 12th Street." Write an essay in which you compare and contrast the poetic use of the morning setting in any two of these poems.
5. Choose any of the poems in this or the previous chapters and write an essay about the way a poet can use situation and setting to evoke a rich intermingling of language, subject, and feeling.

# 16 LANGUAGE

Fiction and drama depend upon language just as poetry does, but in a poem almost everything comes down to the particular meanings and implications of individual words. When we read stories and plays, we generally focus our attention on character and plot, and although words determine how we imagine those characters and how we respond to what happens to them, we are not as likely to pause over any one word as we may need to when reading a poem. Because poems are often short, a lot depends on every word in them. Sometimes, as though they were distilled prose, poems contain only the essential words. They say just barely enough to communicate in the most basic way, using elemental signs—with each chosen for exactly the right shade of meaning or feeling or both. But elemental does not necessarily mean simple, and these signs may be very rich in their meanings and complex in their effects. The poet's word choice—the **diction** of a poem—determines not only meaning but just about every effect the poem produces.

## PRECISION AND AMBIGUITY

Let's look first at poems that create some of their effects by examining—or playing with—a single word. Often multiple meanings or shiftiness and uncertainty of a word are at issue. The following short poem, for example, depends almost entirely on the way we use the word *play*.

### SARAH CLEGHORN

### [The golf links lie so near the mill]

The golf links lie so near the mill
That almost every day
The laboring children can look out
And see the men at play.
                    1915

While traveling in the American South, Cleghorn had seen, right next to a golf course, a textile mill that employed quite young children. Her poem doesn't *say* that we expect men to work and children to play; it just assumes our expectation and builds an effect of **dramatic irony**—an incongruity between what we expect and what actually occurs—out of the observation. The poem saves almost all of its devastating effect for the final word, after the situation has been carefully described and the irony set up.

In the following two poems, a word used over and over acquires multiple meanings and refuses to be limited to a single one.

## ANNE FINCH, COUNTESS OF WINCHELSEA

### There's No To-morrow

A Fable imitated from Sir Roger L'Estrange

Two long had Lov'd, and now the Nymph desir'd,
The Cloak of Wedlock, as the Case requir'd;
Urg'd that, the Day he wrought her to this Sorrow,
He Vow'd, that he wou'd marry her To-Morrow.
5 Agen he Swears, to shun the present Storm,
That he, To-Morrow, will that Vow perform.
The Morrows in their due Successions came;
Impatient still on Each, the pregnant Dame
Urg'd him to keep his Word, and still he swore the same.
10 When tir'd at length, and meaning no Redress,
But yet the Lye not caring to confess,
He for his Oath this Salvo chose to borrow,
That he was Free, since there was no To-Morrow;
For when it comes in Place to be employ'd,
15 'Tis then To-Day; To-Morrow's ne'er enjoy'd.
The Tale's a Jest, the Moral is a Truth;
To-Morrow and To-Morrow, cheat our Youth:
In riper Age, To-Morrow still we cry,
Not thinking, that the present Day we Dye;
20 Unpractis'd all the Good we had Design'd;
There's No To-Morrow to a Willing Mind.

1713

## CHARLES BERNSTEIN

### Of Time and the Line

George Burns[1] likes to insist that he always
   takes the straight lines; the cigar in his mouth
   is a way of leaving space between the

---

1. American comedian (1896-1996) who played straight man to his wife, Gracie Allen.

lines for a laugh. He weaves lines together
by means of a picaresque narrative;
not so Hennie Youngman,[2] whose lines are strictly paratactic. My father pushed a
line of ladies' dresses—not down the street
in a pushcart but upstairs in a fact'ry
office. My mother has been more concerned
with her hemline. Chairman Mao[3] put forward
Maoist lines, but that's been abandoned (mostly) for the East-West line of malarkey
so popular in these parts. The prestige
of the iambic line has recently
suffered decline, since it's no longer so
clear who "I" am, much less who *you* are. When
making a line, better be double sure
what you're lining in & what you're lining
out & which side of the line you're on; the
world is made up so (Adam didn't so much
name as delineate). Every poem's got
a prosodic lining, some of which will
unzip for summer wear. The lines of an
imaginary are inscribed on the
social flesh by the knifepoint of history.
Nowadays, you can often spot a work
of poetry by whether it's in lines
or no; if it's in prose, there's a good chance
it's a poem. While there is no lesson in
the line more useful than that of the picket line, the line that has caused the most ad-
versity is the bloodline. In Russia
everyone is worried about long lines;
back in the USA, it's strictly soup-
lines. "Take a chisel to write," but for an
actor a line's got to be cued. Or, as
they say in math, it takes two lines to make
an angle but only one lime to make
a Margarita.

                                        1991

    The Finch poem repeatedly explores the shifting sands of the word "tomorrow," first noting how different people may think of its meanings differently, then showing how these shifts are anchored in time and the whole process of meaning. The Bernstein poem finds a great variety of completely different meanings of the word "line." How many different meanings can you distinguish in the poem? What does "Time" (in the title) have to do with the poem?

---

2. American comedian (1906–1998), stand-up king of the one-liner.
3. Mao Zedong (1893–1976), leader of the revolution that established China as a communist nation.

Here is a far more personal and emotional poem, which uses a single word, "terminal," to explore the changing relationship between two people—a father (who speaks the poem) and daughter.

**YVOR WINTERS**

## At the San Francisco Airport

*to my daughter, 1954*

This is the terminal: the light
Gives perfect vision, false and hard;
The metal glitters, deep and bright.
Great planes are waiting in the yard—
5   They are already in the night.

And you are here beside me, small,
Contained and fragile, and intent
On things that I but half recall—
Yet going whither you are bent.
10  I am the past, and that is all.

But you and I in part are one:
The frightened brain, the nervous will,
The knowledge of what must be done,
The passion to acquire the skill
15  To face that which you dare not shun.

The rain of matter upon sense
Destroys me momently. The score:
There comes what will come. The expense
Is what one thought, and something more—
20  One's being and intelligence.

This is the terminal, the break.
Beyond this point, on lines of air,
You take the way that you must take;
And I remain in light and stare—
25  In light, and nothing else, awake.

1954

In this case, the poem soberly and thoughtfully probes the several possible meanings of its key word. The importance of the word involves its **ambiguity** (its having more than one possible meaning) rather than its **precision** (its exactness).

What does it *mean* to be in a place called a "terminal"? As the parting of father and daughter is explored carefully, the place of parting and the means of transportation take on meanings larger than their simple referential ones. The poem presents contrasts—young and old, light and dark, past and present, security and adventure. The father ("I am the past," line 10) remains in the light, among known objects and experiences familiar to his many years; the daughter is about to depart into the night, the unknown, the uncertain future. But they both share a sense of the necessity of the parting, of the need for the daughter to mature, gain knowledge, acquire experience. Is she going off to school? to college? to her first job? We don't know, but her plane ride clearly means a new departure and a clean break with childhood, dependency, the past.

So much depends upon the word "terminal." It refers to the airport building, of course, but it also implies a boundary, an extremity, a terminus, something that is limited, a junction, a place where a connection may be broken. Important as well is the unambiguous or "dictionary" meaning of certain other words—that is, what these words **denote**. The final stanza is articulated flatly, as if the speaker has recovered from the momentary confusion of stanza 4, when "being and intelligence" are lost in the emotion of the parting itself. The words "break," "point," "way," and "remain" are almost unemotional and colorless; they do not make value judgments or offer personal views, but rather define and describe. The sharp articulation of the last stanza stresses the **denotations** of the words employed, as though the speaker is trying to disengage himself from the emotion of the situation and just give the facts.

Words, however, are more than hard blocks of meaning on whose sense everyone agrees. They also have a more personal side, and they carry emotional force and shades of suggestion. The words we use indicate not only what we mean but how we feel about it, and we choose words that we hope will engage others emotionally and persuasively, in conversation and daily usage as well as in poems. A person who holds office is, quite literally (and unemotionally), an *officeholder*—the word denotes what he or she does. But if we want to convey that a particular officeholder is wise, trustworthy, and deserving of political support we may call that person a *civil servant*, a *political leader*, or an *elected official*, whereas if we want to promote distrust or contempt of that same officeholder we might say *politician* or *bureaucrat* or *political hack*. These latter terms have clear **connotations**—suggestions of emotional coloration that imply our attitude and invite a similar one from our hearers. What words **connote** can be just as important to a poem as what they denote; some poems work primarily through denotation and some more through connotation.

> *A poet is, before anything else, a person who is passionately in love with language.*
> —W. H. AUDEN

"At the San Francisco Airport," certainly, depends primarily on denotation. The speaker tries to *specify* the meanings and implications of the parting with his daughter, and his tendency to split categories neatly for the two of them at first contributes to the sense of clarity and certainty he wants to project. He is the past (line 10) and what remains (line 24); he has age and experience, his life is the known quantity, he stands in the light. She, on the other hand, is committed to the adventure of going into the night; she seems small, fragile, and her identity blurs into the uncertain future. Yet the connotations of some words carry strong emotional force as well as clear definition: that the daughter seems "small" and "fragile" to the speaker suggests his fear for her, something quite different from her own sense of adventure. The neat, clean categories keep breaking down, and the speaker's feelings keep showing through. In stanza 1, the light in the terminal gives "perfect vision," but the speaker also notices, indirectly, its artificial quality: it is "false" and "hard," suggesting the limits of the rationalism he tries to maintain. That artificial light shines over most of the poem and honors the speaker's effort, but the whole poem represents his struggle, and in stanza 4 the signals of disturbance are very strong as, despite an insistence on a vocabulary of calculation, his rational facade collapses completely. If we have observed his verbal strategies carefully, we should not be surprised to find him at the end just *staring* in the artificial light, merely awake, although the poem has shown him to be unconsciously awake to much more than he will candidly admit.

"At the San Francisco Airport" is an unusually intricate and complicated poem, and it offers us, if we are willing to examine precisely its carefully crafted fabric, rich insight into how complex it is to be human and to have human feelings and foibles when we think we must be rational machines.

But connotations can work more simply. The following epitaph, for example, even though it describes the mixed feelings one person has about another, depends heavily on the connotations of fairly common words.

WALTER DE LA MARE
## Slim Cunning Hands

Slim cunning hands at rest, and cozening eyes—
Under this stone one loved too wildly lies;
How false she was, no granite could declare;
   Nor all earth's flowers, how fair.
1950

*What* the speaker in "Slim Cunning Hands" remembers about the dead woman—her hands, her eyes—tells part of the story; her physical presence was clearly important to him. The poem's other nouns—stone, granite, flowers—all remind us of her death and its finality. All these words denote objects having to do with the rituals that memorialize a departed life. Granite and stone connote finality as well, and flowers connote fragility and suggest the shortness of life (which is why they have become the symbolic language of funerals). The way the speaker talks about the woman expresses, in just a few words, the complexity of his love for her. She was loved, he says, too "wildly"—by him perhaps, and apparently by others. The excitement she offered is suggested by the word, and also the lack of control. The words "cunning" and "cozening" help us interpret both her wildness and her falsity; they suggest her calculation, cleverness, and untrustworthiness as well as her skill, persuasiveness, and ability to please. Moreover, coming at the end of the second line the word "lies" has more than one meaning. The body "lies" under the stone, but the woman's falsity has by now become too prominent to ignore as a second meaning. And the word "fair," a simple yet very inclusive word, suggests how totally attractive the speaker finds her: her beauty can no more be expressed by flowers than her fickleness can be expressed by something as permanent as words in stone. But the word "fair," in the emphatic position as the final word, also implies two other meanings that seem to resonate, ironically, with what we have already learned about her from the speaker: "impartial" and "just." "Impartial" she may be in her preferences (as the word "false" suggests), but to the speaker she is hardly "just," and the final defining word speaks both to her appearance and (ironically) to her character. Simple words here tell us perhaps all we need to know of a long story—or at least the speaker's version of it.

Words like "fair" and "cozening" are clearly loaded. They imply more emotionally than they mean literally. They have strong, clear connotations; they tell us what to think, what evaluation to make; and they suggest the basis for the evaluation. Both words in the title of the following poem similarly turn out to be key ones to its meaning and effect:

**PAT MORA**

## *Gentle Communion*

Even the long-dead are willing to move.
Without a word, she came with me from the desert.
Mornings she wanders through my rooms
making beds, folding socks.

5   Since she can't hear me anymore,
Mamande[4] ignores the questions I never knew
to ask, about her younger days, her red
hair, the time she fell and broke her nose
in the snow. I will never know.

10  When I try to make her laugh,
to disprove her sad album face, she leaves
the room, resists me as she resisted
grinning for cameras, make-up, English.

While I write, she sits and prays,
15  feet apart, legs never crossed,
the blue housecoat buttoned high
as her hair dries white, girlish
around her head and shoulders.

She closes her eyes, bows her head,
20  and like a child presses her hands together,
her patient flesh steeple, the skin
worn, like the pages of her prayer book.

Sometimes I sit in her wide-armed
chair as I once sat in her lap.
25  Alone, we played a quiet I Spy.
She peeled grapes I still taste.
She removes the thin skin, places
the luminous coolness on my tongue.

---

4. A child's conflation of *mama grande* (Spanish for "grandmother").

> I know not to bite or chew. I wait
> 30 for the thick melt,
> our private green honey.
>
> 1991

Neither of the words in the title appears in the text itself, but both resonate throughout the poem. "Communion" is the more powerful of the words; here, it comes to imply the close ritualized relationship between the speaker and "Mamande." Mamande has long been dead but now returns, recalling to the speaker a host of memories and providing a sense of history and family identity. To the speaker, the reunion has a powerful value, reminding her of rituals, habits, and beliefs that "place" her and affirm her heritage. The past is strong in the speaker's mind and in the poem. Many details are recalled from album photographs—the blue housecoat (line 16), the sad face (line 11), the white hair that was once red (lines 7–8 and 17), the posture at prayer (lines 19–22), the big chair (lines 23–24), the plain old-fashioned style (line 13)—and the speaker's childhood memories fade into them as she recalls a specific intimate moment.

The full effect of the word "communion"—which describes an intimate moment of union and a ritual—comes only in the final lines, when the speaker remembers the secret of the grapes and recalls their sensuous feel and taste. The moment brings together the experience of different generations and cultures and represents a sacred sharing: the Spanish grandmother had resisted English, modernity, and show (line 13), and the speaker is a poet, writing (and publishing) in English, but the two have a common "private" (line 31) moment ritually shared and forever memorable. At the end, too, the full sense of "gentle" becomes evident—a word that sums up the softness, quietness, and understatedness of the experience, the personal qualities of "Mamande," and the unpretentious but dignified social level of the family heritage. Throughout the text, other words—ordinary, simple, and precise—suggest the sense of personal dignity, revealed identity, and verbal power that the speaker comes to accept as her own. Look especially at the words "move" (line 1), "steeple" (line 21), and "luminous" (line 28).

Words are the starting point for all poetry, of course, and almost every word is likely to be significant, either denotatively or connotatively or both. Poets who know their craft pick each word with care to express exactly what needs to be expressed and to suggest every emotional shade that the poem is calculated to evoke in us. Often individual words qualify and amplify one another—suggestions clarify other suggestions, and meanings grow upon meanings—and thus the way the words are put together can be important, too. Notice, for example, that in "Slim Cunning Hands" the final emphasis is on how *fair* in appearance the woman was; the speaker's last word describes the quality he can't forget in spite of her lack of a different kind of fairness and his distrust of her, the quality that, even though it doesn't justify everything else, mitigates all the disappointment and hurt.

That one word does not stand all by itself, however, any more than any other word in a poem can be considered all alone. Every word exists within larger units of meaning—sentences, patterns of comparisons and contrasts, the whole poem— and where the word is and how it is used are often important. The final word or words may be especially emphatic (as in "Slim Cunning Hands"), and words that are repeated take on a special intensity, as "terminal" does in "At the San Francisco Airport," or as "chartered" and "cry" do in "London" (chapter 12), or "what did I know?" in "Those Winter Sundays" (chapter 13). Certain words often stand out, because they are used in an unusual way (like "chartered" in "London") or because they are given an artificial prominence—through unusual sentence structure, for example, or because the title calls special attention to them.

Sometimes word choice in poems is less dramatic and less obviously "significant" but equally important. Often, in fact, simple appropriateness makes the words in a poem work, and words that do not call special attention to themselves can be the most effective. Precision of denotation may be just as impressive and productive of specific effects as the resonance or ambiguous suggestiveness of connotation. Often poems achieve their power by a combination of verbal effects, setting off elaborate figures of speech (which we will discuss shortly) or other complicated strategies with simple words chosen to mark exact actions, moments, or states of mind. Notice, for example, how carefully the following poem produces its complex description of emotional patterns by delineating and then elaborating precise stages of feeling.

### EMILY DICKINSON

### [*After great pain, a formal feeling comes—*]

After great pain, a formal feeling comes—
The Nerves sit ceremonious, like Tombs—
The stiff Heart questions was it He, that bore,
And Yesterday, or Centuries before?

5   The Feet, mechanical, go round—
Of Ground, or Air, or Ought—
A Wooden way
Regardless grown,
A Quartz contentment, like a stone—

10  This is the Hour of Lead—
Remembered, if outlived,
As Freezing Persons recollect the Snow—
First—Chill—then Stupor—then the letting go—

ca. 1862

As you read the following poem, notice how the title calls upon us to wonder, from the beginning, how playful and how patterned the boy's bedtime romp with his father is. Try to be conscious of the emotional effects created by what seem to be the key words. Which words establish the bond between the two males?

**THEODORE ROETHKE**

## My Papa's Waltz

The whiskey on your breath
Could make a small boy dizzy;
But I hung on like death:
Such waltzing was not easy.

5  We romped until the pans
Slid from the kitchen shelf;
My mother's countenance
Could not unfrown itself.

The hand that held my wrist
10 Was battered on one knuckle;
At every step you missed
My right ear scraped a buckle.

You beat time on my head
With a palm caked hard by dirt,
15 Then waltzed me off to bed
Still clinging to your shirt.

1948

Exactly what is the situation in "My Papa's Waltz"? What are the family's economic circumstances? How can you tell? What indications are there of the family's social class, or of the father's line of work? How would you characterize the speaker? How does the poem indicate his pleasure in the bedtime ritual? Which words suggest the boy's excitement? Which suggest his anxiety? How can you tell the speaker's feelings about his father? What clues are there about what the mother is like? What clues are there in the word choice that an adult is remembering a childhood experience? How scared was the boy at the time? How does the grown adult now evaluate his emotions when he was a boy? In what sense is the poem a tribute to memories of the father? How would you describe the poem's tone?

The subtlety and force of word choice is sometimes very much affected by **word order,** the way the sentences are put together. Some poems employ unusual word order because of the demands of rhyme and meter, but ordinarily poets use word order very much as prose writers do, to create a particular emphasis. When you find an unusual word order, you can be pretty sure that something there merits special attention. Notice the odd constructions in the second and third stanzas of "My Papa's Waltz"—the way the speaker talks about the abrasion of buckle on ear in line 12, for example. He does not say that the buckle scraped his ear, but rather puts it the other way round—a big difference in the kind of effect created, for it avoids placing blame and refuses to specify any unpleasant effect. Had he said that the buckle scraped his ear—the normal way of putting it—we would have to worry about the fragile ear. The **syntax** (sentence structure) of the poem channels our feeling and helps to control what we think of the "waltz."

In the most curious part of the poem, the second stanza, the silent mother appears, and the syntax is peculiar in two places. In lines 5-6, the connection between the romping and the pans falling is stated oddly: "We romped *until* the pans / Slid from the kitchen shelf" (emphasis added). The speaker does not say that they knocked down the pans or imply awkwardness, but he does suggest energetic activity and duration. He implies intensity, almost intention—as though the romping would not be complete until the pans fell. And the sentence about the mother—odd but effective—makes her position clear. A silent bystander in this male ritual, she doesn't seem frightened or angry. She seems to be holding a frown, or to have it molded on her face, as though it were part of her own ritual, and perhaps a facet of her stern character as well. The syntax implies that she *has to* maintain the frown, and the falling of the pans almost seems to be for her benefit. She disapproves, but she remains their audience.

Sometimes poems create, as well, a powerful sense of the way minds and emotions work by varying normal syntactical order in special ways. Listen, for example, in the following poem to the speaker's sudden loss of vocal control in the midst of what seems to be a calm analysis of her feelings about sexual behavior.

### SHARON OLDS

## Sex without Love

How do they do it, the ones who make love
without love? Beautiful as dancers,
gliding over each other like ice-skaters
over the ice, fingers hooked
5   inside each other's bodies, faces
red as steak, wine, wet as the
children at birth whose mothers are going to
give them away. How do they come to the
come to the   come to the   God   come to the
10  still waters, and not love
the one who came there with them, light
rising slowly as steam off their joined
skin? These are the true religious,
the purists, the pros, the ones who will not
15  accept a false Messiah, love the
priest instead of the God. They do not
mistake the lover for their own pleasure,
they are like great runners: they know they are alone
with the road surface, the cold, the wind,
20  the fit of their shoes, their over-all cardio-
vascular health—just factors, like the partner
in the bed, and not the truth, which is the
single body alone in the universe
against its own best time.

1984

The poem starts calmly enough, with a simple rhetorical question implying that the speaker just cannot understand sex without love. Lines 2-4 compare such sexual activity with some distant aesthetic, with two carefully delineated examples, and the speaker—although plainly disapproving—seems coolly in control of the analysis and evaluation. But by the end of the fourth line, something begins to seem odd: "hooked" seems too ugly and extreme a way to characterize the lovers' fingers, however much the speaker may disapprove, and by line 6 the syntax seems to break down. How does "wine" fit the syntax of the line? Is it parallel with "steak," another example of redness? Or is it somehow related to the last part of the sentence, parallel with "faces"? Neither of these possibilities quite works. At best, the punctuation is inadequate; at worst, the speaker's mind is working too fast for the language it generates, scrambling its images. We can't yet be sure what is going on, but by the ninth line the lack of control is manifest with the compulsive repeating (three times) of "come to the" and the interjected "God."

Such verbal behavior—here concretized by the way the poem orders its words—invites us to reevaluate the speaker's moralism relative to her emotional involvement with the issues and with her representation of sexuality itself. The speaker's values, as well as those who have sex without love, become a subject for evaluation.

Words, the basic materials of poetry, come in many kinds and can be used in many different ways and in different—sometimes surprising—combinations. They are seldom simple or transparent, even when we know their meanings and recognize their syntactical combinations as ordinary and conventional. Carefully examining them, individually and collectively, is a crucial part of reading poems, and being able to ask good questions about the words that poems use is one of the most basic—and rewarding—skills a reader of poetry can develop.

• • •

## MARTHA COLLINS

### Lies

Anyone can get it wrong, laying low
when she ought to lie, but is it a lie
for her to say she laid him when we know
he wouldn't lie still long enough to let
5  her do it? A good lay is not a song,
not anymore; a good lie is something
else: lyrics, lines, what if you say *dear sister*
when you have no sister, what if you say *guns*
when you saw no guns, though you know
10  they're there? *She laid down her arms; she lay
down, her arms by her sides.* If we don't know,
do we lie if we say? If we don't say, do we lie
down on the job? To arms! in any case
dear friends. If we must lie, let's not lie around.

1999

- How many different meanings of "lie" and "lay" does this poem contain? What would you say is the poem's real subject?

**EMILY DICKINSON**

## [*I dwell in Possibility*—]

I dwell in Possibility—
A fairer House than Prose—
More numerous of Windows—
Superior—for Doors—

5   Of Chambers as the Cedars—
Impregnable of Eye—
And for an Everlasting Roof
The Gambrels[5] of the Sky—

Of Visitors—the fairest—
10  For Occupation—This—
The spreading wide my narrow Hands
To gather Paradise—

ca. 1862

- What does Dickinson seem to mean by "Possibility"? How does the poem's ending broaden this meaning?

**WILLIAM CARLOS WILLIAMS**

## The Red Wheelbarrow

so much depends
upon

a red wheel
barrow

5   glazed with rain
water

beside the white
chickens.
          1923

- Why do you think the poet has included the details of the "rain / water" and "the white / chickens"?

---

5. Roofs with double slopes.

## This Is Just to Say

    I have eaten
    the plums
    that were in
    the icebox

5   and which
    you were probably
    saving
    for breakfast

    Forgive me
10 they were delicious
    so sweet
    and so cold

              1934

- What is meant by "This" in the poem's title? What is the apparent occasion for this poem?

## GERARD MANLEY HOPKINS

### *Pied Beauty*[6]

    Glory be to God for dappled things—
        For skies of couple-color as a brinded[7] cow;
            For rose-moles all in stipple[8] upon trout that swim;
    Fresh-firecoal chestnut-falls;[9] finches' wings;
5     Landscape plotted and pieced—fold, fallow, and plow;
        And all trades, their gear and tackle and trim.
    All things counter, original, spare, strange;
        Whatever is fickle, freckled (who knows how?)
           With swift, slow; sweet, sour; adazzle, dim;
10 He fathers-forth whose beauty is past change;
        Praise him.

                          1887

- How many ways of expressing mixed color can you find in this poem? How does Hopkins expand the meaning of "pied beauty"?

---

6. Particolored beauty: having patches or sections of more than one color.    7. Streaked or spotted.
8. Rose-colored dots or flecks.    9. Fallen chestnuts as red as burning coals.

### E. E. CUMMINGS
## [in Just-][1]

in Just-
spring    when the world is mud-
luscious the little
lame balloonman

5   whistles    far    and wee

and eddieandbill come
running from marbles and
piracies and it's
spring

10  when the world is puddle-wonderful

the queer
old balloonman whistles
far   and   wee
and bettyandisbel come dancing

15  from hop-scotch and jump-rope and
it's
spring
and
     the
20         goat-footed

balloonMan   whistles
far
and
wee[2]

1923

- What are some connotations of "mud-luscious" and "puddle-wonderful"? What are some of the ways in which this poem challenges a reader's expectations of diction and syntax?

---

1. The first poem in the series *Chansons innocentes*.
2. Pan, whose Greek name means "everything," is traditionally represented with a syrinx (or the pipes of Pan). The upper half of his body is human, the lower half goat, and as the father of Silenus he is associated with the spring rites of Dionysus.

# BOB PERELMAN

## The Masque of Rhyme

Adding my pee to the sea
of rhyme, it's time I admit sameness

is a bit of a hoax.
Yes, my body lies over social oceans

5 like yours and slightly like Rover's,
except he barks to speak and we

speak to bargain and intermingle. All's
translation in love and war. Do you

hear the joke about the marriage of
10 true mind to impediment after impediment?

That's what we call "language," at
least around here. What rhymes with "rhythm"?

"Mythic"? You have to squint to
hear it. Squint and scatter letters to

15 the five senses, shake off circumstance, and
find yourself in words: squatting amid

ashes while the wicked affluent legislators
dress for the ball. Your feet ache

and stink. The thought-track wakes and thinks:
20 novelty again, the same old novelty.

It's almost worse than royalty. My biographic
foot in the glass shoe—fate

or déjà vu? The rhythm of
days produces chill, stupor, and after considerable

25 training, a bunch of personal pronouns.
It's Thursday, history's late as usual. Meanwhile,

some sort of sexual traffic jam
has been goading us all into public

revelation. Offstage, Fact slapped Value on the
30 butt, and said, Break a leg,

make a killing, show these suckers
where to suck. And Value answered, Don't

be vulgar, Fact, unless you're speaking personally.
As for me, where the bee

35 sucks, there suck I, a mean-er,
a be-er, an arriviste tooling down that

divided highway heading where none, they say,
ever returns. And when I don't

come back, say I told you
40 everything about yourself except the future, lie

alone in our bed of roses
whence, they say, poems arise, to amuse

the students when we've gone to prose.
I'd say more but you hear

45 those stuck horns blaring: that's been
my cue ever since I can remember.

1998

- How many puns and tricks of sound can you find in this poem?

### BEN JONSON
## Still to Be Neat[3]

Still[4] to be neat, still to be dressed,
As you were going to a feast;
Still to be powdered, still perfumed;
Lady, it is to be presumed,
5 Though art's hid causes are not found,
All is not sweet, all is not sound.

Give me a look, give me a face
That makes simplicity a grace;
Robes loosely flowing, hair as free;
10 Such sweet neglect more taketh me
Than all th' adulteries of art.
They strike mine eyes, but not my heart.

1609

- What are at least two possible meanings of the poem's assertion that "all is not sound"? What are some connotations of "th' adulteries of art"?

---

3. A song from Jonson's play *The Silent Woman* (1609-10).   4. Continually.

**ROBERT HERRICK**

## Delight in Disorder

A sweet disorder in the dress
Kindles in clothes a wantonness.
A lawn[5] about the shoulders thrown
Into a fine distraction;
5 An erring lace, which here and there
Enthralls the crimson stomacher,[6]
A cuff neglectful, and thereby
Ribbands[7] to flow confusedly;
A winning wave, deserving note,
10 In the tempestuous petticoat;
A careless shoestring, in whose tie
I see a wild civility;
Do more bewitch me than when art
Is too precise[8] in every part.
                    1648

- What are some of the words that this poem uses to indicate "disorder"? Why do you think the speaker finds disorder "sweet"?


**JOHN MILTON**

## From *Paradise Lost*[9]

I

Of man's first disobedience, and the fruit[1]
Of that forbidden tree whose mortal taste
Brought death into the world, and all our woe,
With loss of Eden, till one greater Man
5 Restore us, and regain the blissful seat,
Sing, Heav'nly Muse,[2] that, on the secret top

---

5. Scarf of fine linen.   6. Ornamental covering for the breasts.   7. Ribbons.
8. In the sixteenth and seventeenth centuries, Puritans were often called Precisians because of their fastidiousness.
9. The opening lines of Books I and II and a short passage from Book III. The first passage states the poem's subject, and the second describes Satan's beginning address to the council of fallen angels meeting to discuss strategy; in the third, God is looking down from Heaven at his new human creation and watching Satan approaching the Earth.   1. The apple, but also the consequences.
2. Addressing one of the Muses and asking for aid is a convention for the opening lines of an epic; Milton complicates the standard procedure here by describing sources and circumstances of Judeo-Christian revelation rather than specifically invoking one of the nine classical Muses. Sinai is the spur of Mount Oreb, where Moses ("That shepherd," line 8, who was traditionally regarded as author of the first five books of the Bible) received the Law; Sion hill and Siloa (lines 10-11), near Jerusalem, correspond to the traditional mountain (Helicon) and springs of classical tradition.

　　　　Of Oreb, or of Sinai, didst inspire
　　　　That shepherd who first taught the chosen seed
　　　　In the beginning how the Heav'ns and Earth
10　　Rose out of Chaos: or, if Sion hill
　　　　Delight thee more, and Siloa's brook that flowed
　　　　Fast[3] by the oracle of God, I thence
　　　　Invoke thy aid to my adventurous song,
　　　　That with no middle flight intends to soar
15　　Above th' Aonian mount,[4] while it pursues
　　　　Things unattempted yet in prose or rhyme.
　　　　And chiefly thou, O Spirit,[5] that dost prefer
　　　　Before all temples th' upright heart and pure,
　　　　Instruct me, for thou know'st; thou from the first
20　　Wast present, and, with mighty wings outspread,
　　　　Dovelike sat'st brooding on the vast abyss,
　　　　And mad'st it pregnant: what in me is dark
　　　　Illumine; what is low, raise and support;
　　　　That, to the height of this great argument,[6]
25　　I may assert Eternal Providence,
　　　　And justify the ways of God to men.
　　　　　Say first (for Heav'n hides nothing from thy view,
　　　　Nor the deep tract of Hell), say first what cause
　　　　Moved our grand parents, in that happy state,
30　　Favored of Heav'n so highly, to fall off
　　　　From their Creator, and transgress his will
　　　　For one restraint, lords of the world besides?[7]
　　　　Who first seduced them to that foul revolt?
　　　　Th' infernal serpent; he it was, whose guile
35　　Stirred up with envy and revenge, deceived
　　　　The mother of mankind, what time[8] his pride
　　　　Had cast him out from Heav'n, with all his host
　　　　Of rebel angels, by whose aid, aspiring
　　　　To set himself in glory above his peers,
40　　He trusted to have equaled the Most High,
　　　　If he opposed; and with ambitious aim
　　　　Against the throne and monarchy of God,
　　　　Raised impious war in Heav'n and battle proud,
　　　　With vain attempt. Him the Almighty Power
45　　Hurled headlong flaming from th' ethereal sky,
　　　　With hideous ruin and combustion down
　　　　To bottomless perdition, there to dwell

---

3. Close.　　4. Mount Helicon, home of the classical Muses.
5. The divine voice that inspired the Hebrew prophets. Genesis 1.2 says that "the spirit of God moved upon the face of the waters" as part of the process of Creation; Milton follows tradition in making the inspirational and communicative function of God present in Creation itself. The passage echoes and merges many biblical references to Creation and divine revelation.　　6. Subject.　　7. In all other respects. *For*: because of.
8. When.

In adamantine chains and penal fire,
Who durst defy th' Omnipotent to arms.[9]

* * *

### II

High on a throne of royal state, which far
Outshone the wealth of Ormus and of Ind,[1]
Or where the gorgeous East with richest hand
Show'rs on her kings barbaric pearl and gold,
5  Satan exalted sat, by merit raised
To that bad eminence; and, from despair
Thus high uplifted beyond hope, aspires
Beyond thus high, insatiate to pursue
Vain war with Heav'n, and by success[2] untaught,
10  His proud imaginations thus displayed:
 "Powers and Dominions, Deities of Heav'n,
For since no deep within her gulf can hold
Immortal vigor, though oppressed and fall'n,
I give not Heav'n for lost. From this descent
15  Celestial virtues rising will appear
More glorious and more dread than from no fall,
And trust themselves to fear no second fate.
Me though just right and the fixed laws of Heav'n
Did first create your leader, next, free choice,
20  With what besides, in council or in fight,
Hath been achieved of merit, yet this loss,
Thus far at least recovered, hath much more
Established in a safe unenvied throne
Yielded with full consent. The happier state
25  In Heav'n, which follows dignity, might draw
Envy from each inferior; but who here
Will envy whom the highest place exposes
Foremost to stand against the Thunderer's aim
Your bulwark, and condemns to greatest share
30  Of endless pain? Where there is then no good
For which to strive, no strife can grow up there
From faction; for none sure will claim in hell
Precédence, none, whose portion is so small
Of present pain, that with ambitious mind
35  Will covet more. With this advantage then
To union, and firm faith, and firm accord,
More than can be in Heav'n, we now return
To claim our just inheritance of old,
Surer to prosper than prosperity

---

9. After invoking the Muse and giving a brief summary of the poem's subject, an epic regularly begins *in medias res* ("in the midst of things").
1. India. *Ormus*: Hormuz, an island in the Persian Gulf, famous for pearls.
2. Outcome, either good or bad.

> 40 Could have assured us; and by what best way,
> Whether of open war or covert guile,
> We now debate; who can advise, may speak."
>
> \* \* \*
>
> III
>
> \* \* \*
>
> 56 Now had th' Almighty Father from above,
> From the pure empyrean where he sits
> High throned above all height, bent down his eye,
> His own works and their works at once to view:
> 60 About him all the sanctities of Heav'n[3]
> Stood thick as stars, and from his sight received
> Beatitude past utterance; on his right
> The radiant image of his glory sat,
> His only Son. On earth he first beheld
> 65 Our two first parents, yet the only two
> Of mankind, in the happy garden placed,
> Reaping immortal fruits of joy and love,
> Uninterrupted joy, unrivaled love,
> In blissful solitude. He then surveyed
> 70 Hell and the gulf between, and Satan there
> Coasting the wall of Heav'n on this side Night
> In the dun air sublime,[4] and ready now
> To stoop[5] with wearied wings and willing feet
> On the bare outside of this world, that seemed
> 75 Firm land embosomed without firmament,
> Uncertain which, in ocean or in air.
>
> 1667

- What do you think Milton uses convoluted syntax such as that in, for example, the poem's opening sentence (lines 1–16)? What effects of sound or sense does this make possible?
- In the passage describing Heaven (part III, lines 56–69), what words establish the tone? What words indicate a shift in tone when God looks down upon Satan approaching the Earth (lines 69–76)?

## PICTURING: THE LANGUAGES OF DESCRIPTION

The language of poetry is most often visual and pictorial. Rather than depending primarily on abstract ideas and elaborate reasoning, poems depend mainly on concrete and specific words that create images in our minds. Poems thus help us to see things afresh and anew or to feel them suggestively through our other physical senses, such as hearing or touch. But mostly, poetry uses the sense of

---

3. The hierarchies of angels. 4. Aloft in the twilight atmosphere. 5. Swoop down, like a bird of prey.

sight to help us form, in our minds, visual impressions, images that communicate more directly than concepts. We "see" yellow leaves on a branch, a father and son waltzing precariously, or two lovers sitting together on the bank of a stream, so that our response begins from a vivid impression of exactly what is happening. Some people think that those media and arts that challenge the imagination of a hearer or reader—radio drama, for example, or poetry—allow us to respond more fully than those (such as television or theater) that actually show things more fully to our physical senses. Certainly they leave more to our imagination, to our mind's eye.

Visual applications of language stem from the nature and direction of the poetic process itself, and some of them have to do with how poems are conceived and then, gradually, fleshed out in words. Poems are sometimes quite abstract—they can even be *about* abstractions. But usually, they are quite concrete in what they ask us to see. One reason is that they often begin in a poet's mind with a picture or an image: of a person, a place, an event, or an object of observation. That image may be based on something the poet has seen—that is, it may be a picture of something remembered by the poet—but it may also be totally imaginary and only based on the "real world" in the sense that it draws on the poet's physical sense of what the world is like, including the people and things in it. Sometimes a poet represents an imagined scene or object in a highly stylized or feeling-centered way, as do, for example, impressionist or surrealist painters. But that process often begins from a quite specific image in the poet's mind that he or she then tries to **represent,** in words, in such a way that readers can "see" it, too, through the poet's vivid verbal representation of what he or she has already "seen" (imagined) in the mind.

Think of it this way: a painter or sculptor uses strategies of form, color, texture, viewpoint, and relationship to create a visual idea, and so the viewer begins with an *actual* image, something that can be seen physically (though the viewer's understanding and interpretation may be many steps away). Even when a poet begins with an idea that draws on visual experience, however, the reader still has to *imagine* (through the poem's words) an image, some person or thing or action that the poem describes. The poet must help the reader to flesh out that mental image on the basis of the words he or she uses. In a sense, then, the reader becomes a visual artist, but the poet directs how the visualization is to be done by evoking specific responses through words. *How* that happens can involve quite complicated verbal strategies—or even *visual* ones that draw on the possibilities of print (see chapter 19).

The languages of description are quite varied. The visual qualities of poetry result partly from the two aspects of poetic language described in the previous section: on the one hand, the precision of individual words, and, on the other hand, precision's opposite—the reach, richness, and ambiguity of suggestion that words sometimes accrue. Visualization can also derive from sophisticated rhetorical and literary devices (figures of speech and symbols, for example, as we will see later in this chapter). But often description begins simply with naming—providing the word (noun, verb, adjective, or adverb) that will trigger images familiar from a reader's own experience. A reader can readily imagine a *dog* or *cat* or *house* or *flower* when each word is named, but not all readers will have the same kind of dog or flower come to mind (because of our individual experiences) until the word is qualified in some way. So the poet may specify that the dog is a greyhound or poodle, or that the flower is a daffodil or a lilac or Queen Anne's lace; or the poet may provide colors, sizes, specific movements, or particular identifying features. Such description can involve either narrowing by category or expansion through detail, and often comparisons are either explicitly or implicitly involved. In Richard Wilbur's "The Beautiful Changes," for example, the similarity between wading through flowers in a meadow and wading among waves in the sea helps to suggest how the first experience feels as well as to etch it visually in our minds. More than just a matter of naming, using precise words, and providing basic information, description involves qualification and comparison; sometimes the poet needs to tell us what a picture is not, dissociating what the poem describes from other possible images we may have in mind. Different features in the language of description add up to something that describes a whole—a picture or scene—as well as a series of individualized objects.

Seeing in the mind's eye—the re-creation of visual experience—requires different skills from poets and readers. Poets use all the language strategies they can think of to re-create for us something they have already "seen." Poets depend on our having had a rich variety of visual experiences and try to draw on those experiences by using common, evocative words and then refining the process through more elaborate verbal devices. We as readers inhabit the process the other way around, trying to draw on our previous knowledge so that we can "see" by following verbal clues. In the poems that follow, notice the ways that description leads to specific images, and pay attention to how shape, color, relationship, and perspective become clear, not only through individual words but also through combinations of words and phrases that suggest appearance and motion.

• • •

## JEANNE MARIE BEAUMONT

### *Rorschach*

Snow patches along the creek bank.
*Too simple.* Wings melting there.

The tops of two maples
beside the window of my childhood bedroom.

5  Stain on a linen napkin left by lipstick—why it's called that. *Go on.*

A man's tattered bow tie
put through the wash cycle—by accident.

A dress, haunted by the child who wore it,
10  standing by itself in the center of a room.

A face. *Whose?* A woman's face, lathered up
with soap except around the eyes.

A fluke. *A flute?* A fluke
with two eyes on one side of its head.

15 The cigarette ground into the floor
by Bette Davis in *All About Eve.*

*Next.* A house that can't be seen
from the road—no, what hides it.

Graffiti of the nearsighted
20 painted by mouth.

*And if I say "tree"?*
I'd say—death by wood.

*Cabinet?* Casket.
*Tell me again.*

25 A map. A map of the island
where I asked to be born.

1997

- What is the meaning of the poem's title, "Rorschach"? What does that meaning reveal about the nature of the dialogue that follows?

**OSCAR WILDE**

## Symphony in Yellow

An omnibus across the bridge
   Crawls like a yellow butterfly,
   And, here and there, a passer-by
Shows like a little restless midge.[1]

5 Big barges full of yellow hay
   Are moored against the shadowy wharf,
   And, like a yellow silken scarf,
The thick fog hangs along the quay.

The yellow leaves begin to fade
10    And flutter from the Temple[2] elms,
   And at my feet the pale green Thames
Lies like a rod of rippled jade.

1909

- What can you infer about London and its climate and the season from each of the yellow images in this poem?

1. Tiny mosquito-like insect.  2. The law-courts area of London.

RICHARD WILBUR

## The Beautiful Changes

One wading a Fall meadow finds on all sides
The Queen Anne's Lace[3] lying like lilies
On water; it glides
So from the walker, it turns
5 Dry grass to a lake, as the slightest shade of you
Valleys my mind in fabulous blue Lucernes.[4]

The beautiful changes as a forest is changed
By a chameleon's tuning his skin to it;
As a mantis, arranged
10 On a green leaf, grows
Into it, makes the leaf leafier, and proves
Any greenness is deeper than anyone knows.

Your hands hold roses always in a way that says
They are not only yours; the beautiful changes
15 In such kind ways,
Wishing ever to sunder
Things and things' selves for a second finding, to lose
For a moment all that it touches back to wonder.

                                                        1947

- What part of speech is "Beautiful" in the poem's title and lines 7 and 14? What part of speech is "Changes"? What is meant by "the beautiful changes / In such kind ways" (lines 14–15)?


TED HUGHES

## To Paint a Water Lily

A green level of lily leaves
Roofs the pond's chamber and paves

The flies' furious arena: study
These, the two minds of this lady.

5 First observe the air's dragonfly
That eats meat, that bullets by

Or stands in space to take aim;
Others as dangerous comb the hum

---

3. A plant sometimes called "wild carrot," with delicate, finger-like leaves and flat clusters of small white flowers.
4. Alfalfa, a plant resembling clover, with small purple flowers. Lake Lucerne is famed for its deep blue color and picturesque Swiss setting amid limestone mountains.

Under the trees. There are battle-shouts
10 And death-cries everywhere hereabouts

But inaudible, so the eyes praise
To see the colors of these flies

Rainbow their arcs, spark, or settle
Cooling like beads of molten metal
15 Through the spectrum. Think what worse
Is the pond-bed's matter of course;

Prehistoric bedragonned times
Crawl that darkness with Latin names,

Have evolved no improvements there,
20 Jaws for heads, the set stare,

Ignorant of age as of hour—
Now paint the long-necked lily-flower

Which, deep in both worlds, can be still
As a painting, trembling hardly at all
25 Though the dragonfly alight,
Whatever horror nudge her root.

1960

- What are "the two minds of this lady" (line 4)? Whom do you think the speaker is addressing when he commands, "Now paint the long-necked lily flower" (line 22)?

## JAMES MERRILL

### *body*

Look closely at the letters. Can you see,
entering (stage right), then floating full,
then heading off—so soon—
how like a little kohl-rimmed moon
5 *o* plots her course from *b* to *d*

—as *y*, unanswered, knocks at the stage door?
Looked at too long, words fail,
phase out. Ask, now that *body* shines
no longer, by what light you learn these lines
10 and what the *b* and *d* stood for.

1995

- Why might *y* be described as "unanswered" in the word *body*? What is meant by "Looked at too long, words fail"?

ANDREW MARVELL

## On a Drop of Dew

See how the orient[5] dew
Shed from the bosom of the morn
   Into the blowing roses,
Yet careless of its mansion new
5   For[6] the clear region where 'twas born
   Round in itself incloses,
   And in its little globe's extent
Frames as it can its native element;
   How it the purple flow'r does slight,
10    Scarce touching where it lies,
But gazing back upon the skies,
   Shines with a mournful light
   Like its own tear,
Because so long divided from the sphere.[7]
15   Restless it rolls and unsecure,
   Trembling lest it grow impure,
   Till the warm sun pity its pain,
And to the skies exhale it back again.
   So the soul, that drop, that ray
20 Of the clear fountain of eternal day,
Could it within the human flower be seen,
   Rememb'ring still its former height,
   Shuns the sweet leaves and blossoms green;
   And, recollecting its own light,
25 Does, in its pure and circling thoughts, express
The greater Heaven in an Heaven less.
   In how coy[8] a figure wound,
   Every way it turns away;
   So the world excluding round,
30    Yet receiving in the day:
   Dark beneath, but bright above,
   Here disdaining, there in love.

   How loose and easy hence to go,
   How girt and ready to ascend;
35    Moving but on a point below,
   It all about does upwards bend.
Such did the manna's sacred dew distill,

5. Shining.   6. By reason of.   7. Of heaven.   8. Reserved, withdrawn, modest.

White and entire, though congealed and chill;[9]
Congealed on earth, but does, dissolving, run
Into the glories of th' almighty sun.

1681

- How does the sun "exhale" (line 17) the drop of dew? "Back again" to where? Explain the comparison between the dewdrop and the human soul.

## METAPHOR AND SIMILE

Being visual does not just mean describing, telling us facts, indicating shapes, colors, and specific details, and giving us precise discriminations through exacting verbs, nouns, adverbs, and adjectives. Often the vividness of the picture in our minds depends upon comparisons through **figures of speech**. What we are trying to imagine is pictured in terms of something else familiar to us, and we are asked to think of one thing as if it were something else. Many such comparisons, in which something is pictured or figured forth in terms of something already familiar to us, are taken for granted in daily life. Things we can't see or that aren't familiar to us are imaged as things we already know; for example, God is said to be like a father; Italy is said to be shaped like a boot; life is compared to a forest, a journey, or a sea. When the comparison is explicit—that is, when one thing is directly compared to something else—the figure is called a **simile**. When the comparison is implicit, with something described as if it were something else, it is called a **metaphor**.

Poems use **figurative language** much of the time. A poem may insist that death is like a sunset or sex like an earthquake or that the way to imagine how it feels to be spiritually secure is to think of the way a sheep is taken care of by a shepherd. The pictorialness of our imagination may *clarify* things for us—scenes, states of mind, ideas—but at the same time it stimulates us to think of how those pictures make us *feel*. Pictures, even when they are mental pictures or imagined visions, may be both denotative and connotative, just as individual words are: they may clarify and make precise, and they may evoke a range of feelings. In the poem that follows, the poet helps us visualize the old age and approaching death of the speaker by making comparisons with familiar things—the coming of winter, the approach of sunset, and the dying embers of a fire.

---

9. In the wilderness, the Israelites fed upon manna from heaven (distilled from the dew; see Exodus 16.10-21); manna became a traditional symbol for divine grace.

WILLIAM SHAKESPEARE

## [That time of year thou mayst in me behold]

That time of year thou mayst in me behold
When yellow leaves, or none, or few, do hang
Upon those boughs which shake against the cold,
Bare ruined choirs, where late the sweet birds sang.
5  In me thou see'st the twilight of such day
As after sunset fadeth in the west;
Which by and by[1] black night doth take away,
Death's second self,[2] that seals up all in rest.
In me thou see'st the glowing of such fire,
10  That on the ashes of his youth doth lie,
As the deathbed whereon it must expire,
Consumed with that which it was nourished by.
This thou perceiv'st, which makes thy love more strong,
To love that well which thou must leave ere long.

1609

    The first four lines of "That time of year" evoke images of the late autumn; but notice that the poet does not have the speaker say directly that his physical condition and age make him resemble autumn. He draws the comparison without stating it as a comparison: you can see my own state, he says, in the coming of winter, when almost all the leaves have fallen from the trees. The speaker portrays himself *indirectly* by talking about the passing of the year. The poem uses metaphor; that is, one thing is pictured *as if* it were something else. "That time of year" goes on to another metaphor in lines 5–8 and still another in lines 9–12, and each metaphor contributes to our understanding of the speaker's sense of his old age and approaching death. More important, however, is the way the metaphors give us feelings, an emotional sense of the speaker's age and of his own attitude toward aging. Through the metaphors we come to understand, appreciate, and to some extent share the increasing sense of urgency that the poem expresses. Our emotional sense of the poem depends largely on the way each metaphor is developed and by the way each metaphor leads, with its own kind of internal logic, to another.

    The images of late autumn in the first four lines all suggest loneliness, loss, and nostalgia for earlier times. As in the rest of the poem, the speaker presents our eyes as the main vehicle for noticing his age and condition; in the phrase "thou mayst in me behold" (line 1) he introduces what he is asking us to see, and in both lines 5 and 9 he tells us similarly "In me thou see'st...." The picture of the trees shedding their leaves suggests that autumn is nearly over, and we can imagine trees either with yellow leaves, or without leaves, or with just a trace of foliage remaining—the latter perhaps most feelingly suggesting the bleakness and

---

1. Shortly.    2. Sleep.

loneliness that characterize the change of seasons, the ending of the life cycle. But other senses are invoked, too. The boughs shaking against the cold represent an appeal to our tactile sense, and the next line appeals to our sense of hearing, although only by the silence of birds no longer singing. (Notice how exact the visual representation is of the bare, or nearly bare, limbs, even as the speaker notes the cold and the lack of birds; birds lined up like a choir on risers would have made a striking visual image on the barren limbs one above the other, but now there is only the *reminder* of what used to be. The present is quiet, bleak, and lonely; it is the absence of color, song, and life that underscores the visual impression, a reminder of what formerly was.)

The next four lines have a slightly different tone, and the color changes. From a black-and-white landscape with a few yellow leaves, we come upon a rich and almost warm reminder of a faded sunset. But a somber note enters the poem in these lines through another figure of speech, **personification,** which involves treating an abstraction, such as death or justice or beauty, as if it were a person. As the poem talks about the coming of night and of sleep, Sleep is personified as the "second self" of Death (that is, as a kind of "double" for death). The main emphasis is on how night and sleep close in on the twilight, and only secondarily does a reminder of death enter the poem. But it does enter.

The third metaphor—that of the dying embers of a fire—begins in line 9 and continues to color and warm the bleak cold that the poem began with, but it also sharpens the reminder of death. The three main metaphors in the poem work to make our sense of old age and approaching death more familiar but also more immediate: moving from barren trees, to fading twilight, to dying embers suggests a sensuous increase of color and warmth but also an increasing urgency. The first metaphor involves a whole season, or at least a segment of one, a matter of days or possibly weeks; the second involves the passing of a single day, reducing the time scale to a matter of minutes, and the third draws our attention to that split second when a glowing ember dies into a gray ash. The final part of the fire metaphor introduces the most explicit sense of death so far, as the metaphor of embers shifts into a direct reminder of death. Embers, which had been a metaphor of the speaker's aging body, now themselves become, metaphorically, a deathbed; the vitality that nourishes youth is used up just as a log in a fire is. The urgency of the reminder of coming death has now peaked. It is friendlier but now seems immediate and inevitable, a natural part of the life process, and the final two lines then offer an explicit plea to make good and intense use of the remaining moments of human relationship.

"That time of year" represents an unusually intricate use of images to organize a poem and focus its emotional impact. Not all poems are so skillfully made, and not all depend on such a full and varied use of metaphor. But most poems use metaphors for at least part of their effect, and often a poem fully develops a single metaphor as its statement as in the following poem about the role of a mother and wife.

## LINDA PASTAN

### Marks

My husband gives me an A
for last night's supper,
an incomplete for my ironing,
a B plus in bed.
5   My son says I am average,
an average mother, but if
I put my mind to it
I could improve.
My daughter believes
10  in Pass/Fail and tells me
I pass. Wait 'til they learn
I'm dropping out.

1978

The speaker in "Marks" is obviously less than pleased with the idea of continually being judged, and the metaphor of marks (or grades) as a way of talking about her performance of family duties suggests her irritation. The list of the roles implies the many things expected of her, and the three different systems of marking (letter grades, categories to be checked off on a chart, and pass/fail) detail the difficulties of multiple standards. The poem retains the language of schooldays all the way to the end ("learn," line 11; "dropping out," line 12), and the major effect of the poem depends on the irony of the speaker's surrendering to the metaphor the family has thrust upon her; if she is to be judged as if she were a student, she retains the right to leave the system. Ironically, she joins the system (adopts the metaphor for herself) in order to defeat it.

The following poem depends from the beginning—even from its title—on a single metaphor and the values associated with it.

## DAVID WAGONER

### My Father's Garden

On his way to the open hearth where white-hot steel
Boiled against furnace walls in wait for his lance
To pierce the fireclay and set loose demons
And dragons in molten tons, blazing
5   Down to the huge satanic caldrons,
Each day he would pass the scrapyard, his kind of garden.

In rusty rockeries of stoves and brake drums,
In grottoes of sewing machines and refrigerators,
He would pick flowers for us: small gears and cogwheels

10  With teeth like petals, with holes for anthers,
    Long stalks of lead to be poured into toy soldiers,
    Ball bearings as big as grapes to knock them down.

    He was called a melter. He tried to keep his brain
    From melting in those tyger-mouthed mills
15  Where the same steel reappeared over and over
    To be reborn in the fire as something better
    Or worse: cannons or cars, needles or girders,
    Flagpoles, swords, or plowshares.

    But it melted. His classical learning ran
20  Down and away from him, not burning bright.
    His fingers culled a few cold scraps of Latin
    And Greek, *magna sine laude*,[3] for crosswords
    And brought home lumps of tin and sewer grills
    As if they were his ripe prize vegetables.

                                                1987

This poem pays tribute to the speaker's father and the things the father understands and values in his ordinary, workingman's life. The father, a "melter" (line 13) in the steel mills (lines 14–15), values things made from what he helps produce. His avocation has developed from his vocation: he collects metal objects from the scrapyard and brings them home just as another man might pick flowers for his family. The scrapyard is, says the speaker, "his kind of garden" (line 6). The father has led a hard life, but he shows love for his children in the only way he knows how—by bringing home things that mean something to him and that can be made into toys his children will come to value. Describing these scraps as the products of his garden—"As if they were his ripe prize vegetables" (line 24)—makes them seem homegrown, carefully tended, nurtured by the father into a useful beauty. Instead of crude and ugly pieces of scrap, they become—through the metaphor of the poem—examples of value and beauty corresponding to the warm feelings the speaker has for a father who did what he could with what he knew and what he had.

Sometimes, in poetry as in prose, comparisons are made explicitly, as in the following poem:

**ROBERT BURNS**

## A Red, Red Rose

O, my luve's like a red, red rose
That's newly sprung in June.
O, my luve is like the melodie
That's sweetly played in tune.

---

3. Without great distinction; a reversal of the usual *magna cum laude*.

5   As fair art thou, my bonnie lass,
     So deep in luve am I;
     And I will luve thee still, my dear,
     Till a' the seas gang[4] dry.

     Till a' the seas gang dry, my dear,
10  And the rocks melt wi' the sun;
     And I will luve thee still, my dear,
     While the sands o' life shall run.

     And fare thee weel, my only luve,
     And fare thee weel a while!
15  And I will come again, my luve,
     Though it were ten thousand mile.

                    1796

The first four lines make two explicit comparisons: the speaker says that his love is "like a ... rose" and "like [a] melodie." As we noted earlier, such *explicit* comparisons are called similes, and usually (as here) the comparison involves the word *like* or the word *as*. Similes work much as do metaphors, except that usually they are used more passingly, more incidentally; they make a quick comparison and usually do not elaborate, whereas metaphors often extend over a long section of a poem (in which case they are called **extended metaphors**) or even over the whole poem, as in "Marks" (in which case they are called **controlling metaphors**).

The two similes in "A Red, Red Rose" assume that we already have a favorable opinion of roses and of melodies. Here the poet does not develop the comparison or even remind us of attractive details about roses or tunes. He pays the quick compliment and moves on. Similes sometimes develop more elaborate comparisons than this and occasionally, as in Marvell's "On a Drop of Dew," even govern long sections of a poem (in which case they are called **analogies**). Usually, though, a simile is briefer and relies more fully on something we already know. The speaker in "My Papa's Waltz" says that he hung on "like death"; he doesn't have to explain or elaborate the comparison: we know the anxiety he refers to.

Like metaphors, similes may imply both meaning and feeling; they may both explain something and invoke feelings about it. All figurative language involves an attempt to clarify something *and* to prompt readers to feel a certain way about it. Saying that one's love is like a rose implies a delicate and fragile beauty and invites our senses into play so that we can share sensuously a response to appealing fragrance and soft touch, just as the shivering boughs and dying embers in "That time of year" suggest separation and loss at the same time that they invite us to share both the cold sense of loneliness and the warmth of old friendship.

Once you start looking for them, you will find figures of speech in poem after poem; they are among the most common devices through which poets share their visions with us.

The following poem uses a variety of metaphors to describe sexual experiences:

4. Go.

## ADRIENNE RICH
## *Two Songs*

I
Sex, as they harshly call it,
I fell into this morning
at ten o'clock, a drizzling hour
of traffic and wet newspapers.
5   I thought of him who yesterday
clearly didn't
turn me to a hot field
ready for plowing,
and longing for that young man
10  piercéd me to the roots
bathing every vein, etc.[5]
All day he appears to me
touchingly desirable,
a prize one could wreck one's peace for.
15  I'd call it love if love
didn't take so many years
but lust too is a jewel
a sweet flower and what
pure happiness to know
20  all our high-toned questions
breed in a lively animal.

II
That "old last act"!
And yet sometimes
all seems post coitum triste[6]
25  and I a mere bystander.
Somebody else is going off,
getting shot to the moon.
Or, a moon-race!
Split seconds after
30  my opposite number lands
I make it—
we lie fainting together
at a crater-edge
heavy as mercury in our moonsuits
35  till he speaks
in a different language
yet one I've picked up
through cultural exchanges...

---

5. See the opening lines of the Prologue to Chaucer's *Canterbury Tales*.
6. Sadness after sexual union.

we murmur the first moonwords:
40 *Spasibo.*[7] Thanks. O.K.

1964

The first "song" begins straightforwardly as narration ("Sex . . . I fell into this morning / at ten o'clock"), but the vividness of sex and desire is communicated mostly by figures of speech. The speaker compares her body to "a hot field / ready for plowing" (lines 7–8)—quite unlike her resistant body yesterday—and also describes her longing by metaphor, in this case an elaborate one borrowed from another poem. After so sensual and urgent a beginning, the song turns more thoughtful and philosophical, but even the intellectual sorting between love and lust comes to depend on metaphors: lust is a "jewel" (line 17) and a "flower" (line 18). After the opening pace and excitement, those later figures of speech seem calm and tame, moving the poem from the lust of its beginning to a contemplative reflection on the value and beauty of momentary physical pleasures.

The second song depends on two closely related metaphors, each highly self-conscious and a little comic. The song begins on a plaintive note, considering the classic melancholic feeling after sex; the speaker pictures herself as isolated, left out, "a mere bystander" (line 25), while someone else is having sexual pleasure. She describes the pleasure of others through two colloquial expressions (both metaphors) for sexual climax: "going off" (line 26) and "getting shot to the moon" (line 27). Suddenly the narrator pretends to take sex as space travel seriously and creates a metaphor of her own: sexual partners running a "moon-race" (line 28). In the rest of the poem, she presents the metaphor in the context of the space race between the United States and Russia in the early 1960s, and she describes the race, not exactly even but close enough, in detail. These are international relations—foreign affairs—and the lovers appropriately say their thank-yous separately in Russian and English, then sign off with an international "O.K."

• • •

## WILLIAM SHAKESPEARE
### [Shall I compare thee to a summer's day?]

Shall I compare thee to a summer's day?
Thou art more lovely and more temperate.
Rough winds do shake the darling buds of May,
And summer's lease hath all too short a date.
5 Sometime too hot the eye of heaven shines,
And often is his gold complexion dimmed;
And every fair from fair sometime declines,
By chance or nature's changing course untrimmed.
But thy eternal summer shall not fade,

---

7. Russian for "thanks."

10  Nor lose possession of that fair thou ow'st,
    Nor shall Death brag thou wand'rest in his shade,
    When in eternal lines to time thou grow'st.
       So long as men can breathe or eyes can see,
       So long lives this,[8] and this gives life to thee.
                                              1609

- What sort of promise does the speaker make with this poem? Why can he boast that "thy eternal summer shall not fade"?

ANONYMOUS[9]

## The Twenty-third Psalm

The Lord is my shepherd; I shall not want.
He maketh me to lie down in green pastures: he leadeth me beside
   the still waters.
He restoreth my soul: he leadeth me in the paths of righteousness
   for his name's sake.
Yea, though I walk through the valley of the shadow of death,
   I will fear no evil: for thou art with me;
   thy rod and thy staff they comfort me.
5 Thou preparest a table before me in the presence of mine enemies:
      thou anointest my head with oil; my cup runneth over.
Surely goodness and mercy shall follow me all the days of my life:
   and I will dwell in the house of the Lord for ever.

- What is the controlling metaphor in this poem? At what point in the psalm does the controlling metaphor shift?

**HENRY KING**

## Sic Vita[1]

  Like to the falling of a star,
  Or as the flights of eagles are,
  Or like the fresh spring's gaudy hue,
  Or silver drops of morning dew,
5 Or like a wind that chafes the flood,
  Or bubbles which on water stood:

---

8. This poem.
9. Traditionally attributed to King David. This English translation is from the King James Version of the Bible.   1. Such is life.

Even such is man, whose borrowed light
Is straight called in, and paid to night.

The wind blows out, the bubble dies,
10 The spring entombed in autumn lies,
The dew dries up, the star is shot,
The flight is past, and man forgot.

                    1657

- What is a man's "light"? In what way is it "borrowed"? How many similes are there in this poem?

JOHN DONNE

## [Batter my heart, three-personed God][2]

Batter my heart, three-personed God; for You
As yet but knock, breathe, shine, and seek to mend;
That I may rise and stand, o'erthrow me, and bend
Your force, to break, blow, burn, and make me new.
5 I, like an usurped town, to another due,
Labor to admit You, but Oh, to no end!
Reason, Your viceroy[3] in me, me should defend,
But is captived, and proves weak or untrue.
Yet dearly I love You, and would be loved fain,[4]
10 But am betrothed unto Your enemy:
Divorce me, untie or break that knot again,
Take me to You, imprison me, for I,
Except You enthrall me, never shall be free,
Nor ever chaste, except You ravish me.

                    1633

- In the poem's controlling metaphor, who is the speaker? Who, or what, is God? To whom is the speaker "betrothed"?

## The Computation

For the first twenty years, since yesterday,
I scarce believed thou couldst be gone away;
For forty more, I fed on favors past,
And forty on hopes—that thou wouldst, they might, last.
5 Tears drowned one hundred, and sighs blew out two;
A thousand, I did neither think, nor do,

---

2. *Holy Sonnets*, 14.   3. One who rules as the representative of a higher power.   4. Gladly.

Or not divide, all being one thought of you;
  Or in a thousand more forgot that too.
  Yet call not this long life, but think that I
10 Am, by being dead, immortal. Can ghosts die?

1633

- Who, or what, might be "thou" in the second line? What seems to be the cause of the speaker's "death"?

## The Canonization

For God's sake hold your tongue and let me love!
  Or⁵ chide my palsy or my gout,
  My five gray hairs or ruined fortune flout;
  With wealth your state, your mind with arts improve,
5   Take you a course, get you a place,
    Observe his Honor or his Grace,
  Or the king's real or his stampéd face⁶
    Contemplate; what you will, approve,
    So you will let me love.

10 Alas, alas, who's injured by my love?
    What merchant's ships have my sighs drowned?
    Who says my tears have overflowed his ground?
    When did my colds a forward spring remove?
    When did the heats which my veins fill
15    Add one man to the plaguy bill?⁷
    Soldiers find wars, and lawyers find out still
      Litigious men which quarrels move,
      Though she and I do love.

Call us what you will, we are made such by love.
20  Call her one, me another fly,
  We're tapers too, and at our own cost die;⁸
  And we in us find th' eagle and the dove.⁹
    The phoenix riddle hath more wit¹
    By us; we two, being one, are it.
25 So to one neutral thing both sexes fit,
    We die and rise the same, and prove
      Mysterious by this love.

---

5. Either.   6. On coins.   7. List of plague victims.
8. Tapers—candles—consume themselves. To "die" is Renaissance slang for consummating the sexual act, which was popularly believed to shorten life by one day. *Fly:* a traditional symbol of transitory life.
9. Traditional symbols of strength and purity.
1. Meaning. According to tradition, only one phoenix existed at a time, dying in a funeral pyre of its own making and being reborn from its own ashes. The bird's existence was thus a riddle akin to a religious mystery (line 27), and a symbol sometimes fused with Christian representations of immortality.

We can die by it, if not live by love;
    And if unfit for tombs and hearse
30 Our legend be, it will be fit for verse;[2]
    And if no piece of chronicle we prove,
    We'll build in sonnets pretty rooms[3]
    (As well a well-wrought urn becomes[4]
The greatest ashes, as half-acre tombs),
35   And by these hymns all shall approve
    Us canonized for love.

And thus invoke us: "You whom reverent love
    Made one another's hermitage,
You to whom love was peace, that now is rage,
40 Who did the whole world's soul extract, and drove[5]
    Into the glasses of your eyes
    (So made such mirrors and such spies
That they did all to you epitomize)
    Countries, towns, courts; beg from above
45   A pattern of your love!"

                                                1633

- Whom does the speaker address in the first line, "hold your tongue"? Why does the speaker concede that he and his lover may not "prove" a "piece of chronicle" (line 31)?

# DAVID FERRY

## At the Hospital

She was the sentence the cancer spoke at last,
Its blurred grammar finally clarified.
                            1983

- What, exactly, has "clarified" the cancer's "blurred grammar"?

---

2. That is, if we don't turn out to be an authenticated piece of historical narrative.
3. In Italian, *stanza* means room.    4. Befits.    5. Compressed.

### RANDALL JARRELL
## The Death of the Ball Turret Gunner[6]

From my mother's sleep I fell into the State,
And I hunched in its belly till my wet fur froze.
Six miles from earth, loosed from its dream of life,
I woke to black flak and the nightmare fighters.
When I died they washed me out of the turret with a hose.

1945

- What is meant by "I fell into the State"? What do the words "sleep," "dream," and "nightmare" suggest about the poem's basic situation?

### FRANCIS WILLIAM BOURDILLON
## The Night Has a Thousand Eyes

The night has a thousand eyes,
   And the day but one;
Yet the light of the bright world dies
   With the dying sun.

The mind has a thousand eyes,
   And the heart but one;
Yet the light of a whole life dies
   When the love is gone.

1889

- What are the "thousand eyes" of the night? the single eye of the day? What, exactly, are the comparisons to the mind and the heart?

### MARGARET CAVENDISH, DUCHESS OF NEWCASTLE
## Of the Theme of Love

O Love, how thou art tired out with rhyme!
Thou art a tree whereon all poets climb;
And from thy branches every one takes some

---

6. A ball turret was a plexiglass sphere set into the belly of a B-17 or B-24 and inhabited by two .50 caliber machine-guns and one man, a short, small man. When this gunner tracked with his machine-guns a fighter attacking his bomber from below, he revolved with the turret; hunched upside-down in his little sphere, he looked like the foetus in the womb. The fighters which attacked him were armed with cannon firing explosive shells. The hose was a steam hose. [Jarrell's note]

Of thy sweet fruit, which fancy feeds upon.
5 But now thy tree is left so bare and poor
That they can hardly gather one plum more.

late 17th century

- Why does the speaker complain that "thy tree is left so bare and poor"?

**EMILY DICKINSON**

## [Wild Nights—Wild Nights!]

Wild Nights—Wild Nights!
Were I with thee
Wild Nights should be
Our luxury!

5 Futile—the Winds—
To a Heart in port—
Done with the Compass—
Done with the Chart!

Rowing in Eden—
10 Ah, the Sea!
Might I but moor—Tonight—
In Thee!

ca. 1861

- To what, exactly, does the speaker compare her love? What are some possible, even opposite, interpretations of the line "Done with the Chart"?

**GREG DELANTY**

## The Blind Stitch

I can't say why rightly, but suddenly it's clear once more
   what holds us together as we sit, recumbent in the old ease
of each other's company, chewing the rag about friends,
   a poem we loved and such-like. Your Portuguese skin,
5 set off by a turquoise dress, doesn't hinder either.
   But there's something more than tan-deep between us.
I sew a button to a waistcoat you made me, ravelled years ago.
   You hemmed it with the stitch you mend a frock with now.
Our hands, without thought for individual movement, sew in

10    and out, entering and leaving at one and the same time.
      If truth be told, the thread had frayed between us, unnoticed,
        except for the odd rip. But as we sew, love is
    in the mending, and though nothing's said, we feel it
      in a lightness of mood, our ease, our blind stitch.

2001

- In addition to the title, what other words and phrases in this poem contribute to the sewing metaphor?

# SYMBOL

The word *symbol* is often used sloppily and sometimes pretentiously, but properly used the term suggests one of the most basic things about poems—their ability to get beyond what words signify and to make larger claims about meanings in the verbal world. All words go beyond themselves. They are not simply a collection of sounds: they signify something beyond their sounds, often things or actions or ideas. Words describe not only a verbal universe but also a world in which actions occur, acts have implications, and events have meaning. Sometimes words signify something beyond themselves, say *rock* or *tree* or *cloud*, and symbolize something as well, such as solidity or life or dreams. Words can—when their implications are agreed on by tradition, convention, or habit—stand for things beyond their most immediate meanings or significations and become symbols, and even simple words that have accumulated no special power from previous use may be given special significance in special circumstances—in poetry as in life itself.

A **symbol** is, put simply, something that stands for something else. The everyday world is full of common examples; a flag, a logo, a trademark, or a skull and crossbones all suggest things beyond themselves, and everyone likely understands what their display indicates, whether or not each viewer shares a commitment to what is thus represented. In common usage a prison symbolizes confinement, constriction, and loss of freedom, and in specialized traditional usage a cross may symbolize oppression, cruelty, suffering, death, resurrection, triumph, or an intersection of some kind (as in *crossroads* and *crosscurrents*). The specific symbolic significance depends on the context; for example, a reader might determine significance by looking at contiguous details in a poem and by examining the poem's attitude toward a particular tradition or body of beliefs. A star means one thing to a Jewish poet and something else to a Christian poet, still something else to a sailor or an actor. In a very literal sense, words themselves are all symbols (they stand for objects, actions, or qualities, not just for letters or sounds), but symbols in poetry are said to be those words and phrases that have a range of reference beyond their literal signification or denotation.

Poems sometimes create a symbol out of a thing, action, or event that has no previously agreed-upon symbolic significance. The following poem, for example, gives a seemingly random gesture symbolic significance:

SHARON OLDS

## Leningrad Cemetery, Winter of 1941[1]

That winter, the dead could not be buried.
The ground was frozen, the gravediggers weak from hunger,
the coffin wood used for fuel. So they were covered with something
and taken on a child's sled to the cemetery
5 in the sub-zero air. They lay on the soil,
some of them wrapped in dark cloth
bound with rope like the tree's ball of roots
when it waits to be planted; others wound in sheets,
their pale, gauze, tapered shapes
10 stiff as cocoons that will split down the center
when the new life inside is prepared;
but most lay like corpses, their coverings
coming undone, naked calves
hard as corded wood spilling
15 from under a cloak, a hand reaching out
with no sign of peace, wanting to come back
even to the bread made of glue and sawdust,
even to the icy winter, and the siege.

1979

All of these corpses—frozen, neglected, uncovered—vividly stamp upon our minds a picture of the horrors of war, one likely to stay in our minds long after we have finished reading the poem. Several details are striking, and the poem's language heightens our sense of them. The corpses wound in sheets, for example, are described in "their pale, gauze, tapered shapes" (line 9), and they are compared to cocoons that one day will split and emit new life; and the limbs that dangle loose when the coverings come undone are "hard as corded wood spilling" (line 14). But clearly the most memorable sight is the hand dangling from one corpse that is coming unwrapped, for the poet invests that hand with special significance, giving its gesture *meaning*. The hand is "reaching out ... wanting to come back" (lines 15–16); it is as if the dead can still gesture even if they cannot speak, and the gesture seems to signify the desire of the dead to return at any price. They would be glad to live, even under the grim conditions that attend life in Leningrad during the war. Suddenly the grimness that we—the living—have been witnessing pales by comparison with what the dead have lost simply by being dead. The hand has been made to *symbolize* the desire of the dead to return, to live, to be still among us, anywhere. The hand reaches out in the poem as a gesture that means something; the poet has made it a symbol of desire.

The whole array of dead bodies in the poem might be called symbolic as well. As a group, they stand for the war's human waste, and their dramatic presence provides the poem with a dramatic visualization of how war leaves no time for

---

1. The 900-day siege of Leningrad (now Saint Petersburg) during World War II began in September 1941.

decency, not even the decency of burial. The bodies are a symbol: they stand for what the poem as a whole asserts.

The following poem also arises out of a historical moment. Here, however, the poet gives significance to a personal event by the interpretation he puts upon it.

**JAMES DICKEY**

## The Leap

The only thing I have of Jane MacNaughton
Is one instant of a dancing-class dance.
She was the fastest runner in the seventh grade,
My scrapbook says, even when boys were beginning
5   To be as big as the girls,
But I do not have her running in my mind,
Though Frances Lane is there, Agnes Fraser,
Fat Betty Lou Black in the boys-against-girls
Relays we ran at recess: she must have run

10  Like the other girls, with her skirts tucked up
So they would be like bloomers,
But I cannot tell; that part of her is gone.
What I do have is when she came,
With the hem of her skirt where it should be
15  For a young lady, into the annual dance
Of the dancing class we all hated, and with a light
Grave leap, jumped up and touched the end
Of one of the paper-ring decorations

To see if she could reach it. She could,
20  And reached me now as well, hanging in my mind
From a brown chain of brittle paper, thin
And muscular, wide-mouthed, eager to prove
Whatever it proves when you leap
In a new dress, a new womanhood, among the boys
25  Whom you easily left in the dust
Of the passionless playground. If I said I saw
In the paper where Jane MacNaughton Hill,

Mother of four, leapt to her death from a window
Of a downtown hotel, and that her body crushed-in
30  The top of a parked taxi, and that I held
Without trembling a picture of her lying cradled
In that papery steel as though lying in the grass,
One shoe idly off, arms folded across her breast,
I would not believe myself. I would say
35  The convenient thing, that it was a bad dream
Of maturity, to see that eternal process

>           Most obsessively wrong with the world
>           Come out of her light, earth-spurning feet
>           Grown heavy: would say that in the dusty heels
>     40    Of the playground some boy who did not depend
>           On speed of foot, caught and betrayed her.
>           Jane, stay where you are in my first mind:
>           It was odd in that school, at that dance.
>           I and the other slow-footed yokels sat in corners
>     45    Cutting rings out of drawing paper
>
>           Before you leapt in your new dress
>           And touched the end of something I began,
>           Above the couples struggling on the floor,
>           New men and women clutching at each other
>     50    And prancing foolishly as bears: hold on
>           To that ring I made for you, Jane—
>           My feet are nailed to the ground
>           By dust I swallowed thirty years ago—
>           While I examine my hands.
>                                                                   1967

Memory is crucial to "The Leap." The fact that Jane MacNaughton's graceful leap in dancing class has stuck in the speaker's mind all these years means that this leap was important to him, meant something to him, stood for something in his mind. For the speaker, the leap is an "instant" and the "only thing" he has of Jane. He remembers its grace and ease, and he struggles at several points to articulate its meaning (lines 16–26, 44–50), but even without articulation or explanation it remains in his head as a visual memory, a symbol of something beyond himself, something he cannot do, something he wanted to be. What that leap stood for, or symbolized, was boldness, confidence, accomplishment, maturity, Jane's ability to go beyond her fellow students in dancing class—the transcending of childhood by someone entering adulthood. Her feet now seem "earth-spurning" (line 38) in that original leap, and they separate her from everyone else. Jane MacNaughton was beyond the speaker's abilities and any attempt he could make to articulate his hopes, but she was not beyond his dreams. And even before he could say so, she symbolized a dream.

The leap to her death seems cruelly wrong and ironic after the grace of her earlier leap. In memory she is suspended in air, as if there were no gravity, no coming back to earth, as if life could exist as dream. And so the photograph, re-created in precise detail, is a cruel dashing of the speaker's dream—a detailed record of the ending of a leap, a denial of the suspension in which his memory had held her. His dream is grounded; her mortality is insistent. But the speaker still wants to hang on to that symbolic moment (line 42), which he confronts in a more mature context but which he will never altogether replace or surrender.

The leap is ultimately symbolic in the *poem*, too, not just in the speaker's mind. In the poem (and for us as readers) its symbolism is double: the first leap symbolizes aspiration, and the second symbolizes the frustration and grounding of high hopes; the two are complementary, one impossible to imagine without the other. The poem is horrifying in some ways, a dramatic reminder that human beings don't ultimately transcend their mortality, their limits, no matter how heroic or unencumbered by gravity they may have seemed to an observer. But the poem is not altogether sad and despairing, partly because it still affirms the validity of the original leap and partly because it creates and elaborates another symbol: the paper chain.

The chain connects Jane to the speaker both literally and figuratively. It is, in part, *his* paper chain that she had leaped to touch in dancing class (lines 18-19), and he thinks of her first leap as "touch[ing] the end of something I began" (line 47). He and the other earthbound, "slow-footed yokels" (line 44) made the chain, and it connects them to her original leap, just as a photograph glimpsed in the paper connects the speaker to her second leap. The paper in the chain is "brittle" (line 21), and its creators seem dull artisans compared to the artistic performer that Jane was. They are heavy and "left in the dust" (lines 25, 52-53), but she is "light" (line 16) and able to transcend them, even in transcendence touching their lives and what they can do. And so the paper chain becomes the poem's symbol of linkage, connecting lower accomplishment to higher possibility, the artisan to the artist, material substance to the act of imagination. And at the end the speaker examines the hands that made the chain because those hands certify his connection to her and the imaginative leap she had made for him. The chain thus symbolizes not only the lower capabilities of those who cannot leap like the budding Jane could, but (later) the connection with her leap as both transcendence and mortality. Like the leap itself, the chain has been elevated to special meaning, given symbolic significance, by the poet's treatment of it. A leap and a chain have no necessary significance in themselves to most of us—at least no significance that we have all agreed upon—but they may take on significance in specific circumstances or a specific text.

Other objects and acts have a built-in significance because of past usage in literature, or tradition, or the stories a culture develops to explain itself and its beliefs. Over the years some things have acquired an agreed-upon significance, an accepted value in our minds. They already stand for something before the poet cites them; they are **traditional symbols.** Their uses in poetry have to do with the fact that poets can count on a recognition of their traditional suggestions and meanings outside the poem, and the poem does not have to propose or argue a particular symbolic value. Birds, for example, traditionally symbolize flight, freedom from confinement, detachment from earthbound limits, the ability to soar beyond rationality and transcend mortal limits. Traditionally, birds have also been linked with imagination, especially poetic imagination, and poets often identify with them as pure and ideal singers of songs, as in Keats's "Ode to a Nightingale" (see chapter 22). One of the most traditional symbols, the rose, may be a simple and fairly plentiful flower in its season, but it has so long stood for particular qualities that merely to name it raises predictable expectations. Its beauty, delicacy, fragrance, shortness of life, and depth of color have made it a symbol of the transitoriness of beauty, and countless poets have counted on its accepted symbolism—sometimes to compliment a friend (as Burns does in "A Red, Red Rose") or sometimes to make a point about the nature of symbolism. The following poem draws, in quite a traditional way, on the traditional meanings.

## EDMUND WALLER
### *Song*

    Go, lovely rose!
  Tell her that wastes her time and me
    That now she knows,
  When I resemble[2] her to thee,
5  How sweet and fair she seems to be.

    Tell her that's young,
  And shuns to have her graces spied,
    That hadst thou sprung
  In deserts, where no men abide,
10  Thou must have uncommended died.

    Small is the worth
  Of beauty from the light retired;
    Bid her come forth,
  Suffer herself to be desired,
15  And not blush so to be admired.

    Then die! that she
  The common fate of all things rare
    May read in thee;
  How small a part of time they share
  That are so wondrous sweet and fair!

              1645

    The speaker in "Song" sends the rose to his love in order to have it speak its traditional meanings of not only beauty but also transitoriness. He counts on accepted symbolism to make his point and hurry her into accepting his advances. Likewise, the poet does not elaborate or argue these things because he does not need to; he counts on the familiarity of the tradition (though, of course, readers unfamiliar with the tradition will not respond in the same way—that is one reason it is difficult to fully appreciate texts from another linguistic or cultural tradition).
    Poets may use traditional symbols to invoke predictable responses—in effect using shortcuts to meaning by repeating acts of signification sanctioned by time and cultural habit. But often poets examine the tradition even as they employ it, and sometimes they revise or reverse meanings built into the tradition. Symbols do not necessarily stay the same over time, and poets often turn even the most traditional symbols to their own original uses. Knowing the traditions of poetry—reading a lot of poems and observing how they tend to use certain words, metaphors, and symbols—can be very useful in reading new poems, but traditions evolve and individual poems do highly individual things. Knowing the past never means being able to interpret new texts with confidence. Symbolism makes things

---

2. Compare.

happen, but individual poets and texts determine what will happen and how. The following two poems work important variations on the traditional associations of roses:

### D. H. LAWRENCE
## I Am Like a Rose

I am myself at last; now I achieve
My very self. I, with the wonder mellow,
Full of fine warmth, I issue forth in clear
And single me, perfected from my fellow.

5   Here I am all myself. No rose-bush heaving
Its limpid sap to culmination has brought
Itself more sheer and naked out of the green
In stark-clear roses, than I to myself am brought.

                                                    1917

### DOROTHY PARKER
## One Perfect Rose

A single flow'r he sent me, since we met.
    All tenderly his messenger he chose;
Deep-hearted, pure, with scented dew still wet—
    One perfect rose.

5   I knew the language of the floweret;
    "My fragile leaves," it said, "his heart enclose."
Love long has taken for his amulet
    One perfect rose.

Why is it no one ever sent me yet
10    One perfect limousine, do you suppose?
Ah no, it's always just my luck to get
    One perfect rose.

                                                    1937

Sometimes symbols—traditional or not—become so insistent in the world of a poem that the larger referential world is left almost totally behind. In such cases the symbol is everything, and the poem does not just *use* symbols but becomes a **symbolic poem**, usually a highly individualized one dependent on an internal system introduced by the individual poet.

Here is an example of such a poem:

**WILLIAM BLAKE**

## The Sick Rose[3]

O rose, thou art sick.
The invisible worm
That flies in the night
In the howling storm

5 Has found out thy bed
Of crimson joy,
And his dark secret love
Does thy life destroy.

1794

The poem does not seem to be about a rose, but about what the rose represents—not in this case something altogether understandable through the traditional meanings of *rose*.

We usually associate the rose with beauty and love, often with sex; and here several key terms have sexual connotations: "worm," "bed," and "crimson joy." The violation of the rose by the worm is the poem's main concern; the violation seems to have involved secrecy, deceit, and "dark" motives, and the result is sickness rather than the joy of love. The poem is sad; it involves a sense of hurt and tragedy, nearly of despair. The poem cries out against the misuse of the rose, against its desecration, implying that instead of a healthy joy in sensuality and sexuality, there has been in this case destruction and hurt, perhaps because of misunderstanding and repression and lack of sensitivity.

But to say so much about this poem we have to extrapolate from other poems by Blake, and we have to introduce information from outside the poem. Fully symbolic poems often require that, and thus they ask us to go beyond the formal procedures of reading that we have discussed so far. As presented in this poem, the rose is not part of the normal world that we ordinarily see, and it is symbolic in a special sense. The poet does not simply take an object from our everyday world and give it special significance, making it a symbol in the same sense that the leap or the corpse's hand is a symbol. Here the rose seems to belong to its own world, a world made entirely inside the poem or the poet's head. The rose is not referential, or not primarily so. The whole poem is symbolic; it is not paraphrasable; it lives in its own world. But what is the rose here a symbol of? In general terms, we can say from what the poem tells us; but we may not be as confident as we can be in the more nearly recognizable world of "The Leap" or "Leningrad Cemetery, Winter of 1941." In "The Sick Rose," it seems inappropriate to ask the standard questions: What rose? Where? Which worm? What are the particulars here? In the world of this poem worms can fly and may be invisible. We are altogether in a world of meanings that have been formulated according to a special

---

3. In Renaissance emblem books, the scarab beetle, worm, and rose are closely associated: the beetle feeds on dung, and the smell of the rose is fatal to it.

system of knowledge and code of belief. We will feel comfortable and confident in that world only if we read many poems written by the poet (in this case William Blake) within the same symbolic system.

Negotiation of meanings in symbolic poems can be very difficult indeed. Reading symbolic poems is an advanced skill that depends on special knowledge of authors and of the special traditions they work from. But usually the symbols you will find in poems *are* referential of meanings we all share and you can readily discover these meanings by carefully studying the poems themselves.

• • •

**ROBERT FROST**

## Fireflies in the Garden

Here come real stars to fill the upper skies,
And here on earth come emulating flies,
That though they never equal stars in size,
(And they were never really stars at heart)
5 Achieve at times a very star-like start.
Only, of course, they can't sustain the part.

1928

- What is the tone of this poem? What does the poem say about the limits of symbolism?

**STEPHEN DUNN**

## Dancing with God

At first the surprise
of being singled out,
the dance floor crowded
and me not looking my best,
5 a too-often-worn dress
and the man with me
a budding casualty
of one repetition too much.
God just touched his shoulder
10 and he left.
Then the confirmation of
an old guess.
God was a wild god,
into the most mindless rock,
15 but graceful,

looking—this excited me—
like no one I could love,
cruel mouth, eyes evocative
of promises unkept.
20  I never danced better, freer,
as if dancing were my way
of saying how easily
I could be with him, or apart.
When the music turned slow
25  God held me close
and I felt for a moment
I'd mistaken him,
that he was Death
and this the famous embrace
30  before the lights go out.
But God kept holding me
and I him
until the band stopped
and I stood looking at a figure
35  I wanted to slap
or forgive for something,
I couldn't decide which.
He left then, no thanks,
no sign
40  that he'd felt anything
more than an earthly moment
with someone who could've been
anyone on earth.
To this day I don't know why
45  I thought he was God,
though it was clear
there was no going back
to the man who brought me,
nice man
50  with whom I'd slept
and grown tired,
who danced wrong,
who never again
could do anything right.

                            1989

- Does the poem finally state definitively whether or not the dance partner really was God, at least in the speaker's mind? How does the ambiguity serve the poem?

## ADRIENNE RICH

### *Diving into the Wreck*

First having read the book of myths,
and loaded the camera,
and checked the edge of the knife-blade,
I put on
5 the body-armor of black rubber
the absurd flippers
the grave and awkward mask.
I am having to do this
not like Cousteau[4] with his
10 assiduous team
aboard the sun-flooded schooner
but here alone.

There is a ladder.
The ladder is always there
15 hanging innocently
close to the side of the schooner.
We know what it is for,
we who have used it.
Otherwise
20 it's a piece of maritime floss
some sundry equipment.

I go down.
Rung after rung and still
the oxygen immerses me
25 the blue light
the clear atoms
of our human air.
I go down.
My flippers cripple me,
30 I crawl like an insect down the ladder
and there is no one
to tell me when the ocean
will begin.

First the air is blue and then
35 it is bluer and then green and then
black I am blacking out and yet
my mask is powerful
it pumps my blood with power
the sea is another story
40 the sea is not a question of power

---

4. Jacques-Yves Cousteau (1910–1997), French underwater explorer and writer.

I have to learn alone
to turn my body without force
in the deep element.

And now: it is easy to forget
45 what I came for
among so many who have always
lived here
swaying their crenellated fans
between the reefs
50 and besides
you breathe differently down here.

I came to explore the wreck.
The words are purposes.
The words are maps.
55 I came to see the damage that was done
and the treasures that prevail.
I stroke the beam of my lamp
slowly along the flank
of something more permanent
60 than fish or weed

the thing I came for:
the wreck and not the story of the wreck
the thing itself and not the myth
the drowned face always staring
65 toward the sun
the evidence of damage
worn by salt and sway into this threadbare beauty
the ribs of the disaster
curving their assertion
70 among the tentative haunters.

This is the place.
And I am here, the mermaid whose dark hair
streams black, the merman in his armored body
We circle silently
75 about the wreck
we dive into the hold.
I am she: I am he

whose drowned face sleeps with open eyes
whose breasts still bear the stress
80 whose silver, copper, vermeil cargo lies
obscurely inside barrels
half-wedged and left to rot
we are the half-destroyed instruments
that once held to a course
85 the water-eaten log
the fouled compass

>          We are, I am, you are
>          by cowardice or courage
>          the one who find our way
> 90       back to this scene
>          carrying a knife, a camera
>          a book of myths
>          in which
>          our names do not appear.

1972                                                    1973

- What word or phrase first signals the reader that "Diving into the Wreck" is to be understood symbolically, not literally? What are some possible symbolic interpretations of the wreck and the dive?

**ROO BORSON**

## After a Death

> Seeing that there's no other way,
> I turn his absence into a chair.
> I can sit in it,
> gaze out through the window.
> 5 I can do what I do best
> and then go out into the world.
> And I can return then with my useless love,
> to rest,
> because the chair is there.

                                                        1989

- Why do you think the speaker chooses to symbolize her absent loved one with a chair?

---

**SUGGESTIONS FOR WRITING**

1. Choose one poem you have read in this book in which a single word seems crucial to that poem's total effect. Write an essay in which you work out carefully how the poem's meaning and tone depend on that one word.
2. Compare Dickinson's "I dwell in Possibility—" and "Wild Nights—Wild Nights!" (both in this chapter). What patterns of word use do you see in the two poems? What kinds of vocabulary do they have in common? Syntax? Strategies of organization? Find other poems by Dickinson (there are a number in this book) and look for similar patterns of thought and language. What might her poems be like if they were written "normally"? Write an essay in which you explore Dickinson's unique poetic style.
3. Read aloud the passages from Milton's *Paradise Lost*. Then ask a friend to read the

passages aloud as well. As the friend reads, note which words—and which choices of word order—provide especially useful guides for reading aloud. How would the poem be different if Milton had followed "normal" word order instead of a metrical form designed for reading aloud? Write an essay in which you discuss the way Milton uses a highly specialized diction and syntax to create particular poetic effects.

4. Consider the poems about roses found in this chapter and write a paragraph about each poem showing how it establishes specific symbolism for the rose. What generalizations can you draw about the rose's traditional meanings in poetry? If you can, find other poems about roses outside of this book to determine if your generalizations still apply.

5. Research the design of World War II bombers like the B-17 and the B-24. Try to find a picture of the gunner in the ball turret of such an airplane, and note carefully his body position. Write an essay in which you explain how Randall Jarrell's "The Death of the Ball Turret Gunner" uses visual details to create its fetal and birth metaphors.

6. Is there a "correct" interpretation of Adrienne Rich's "Diving into the Wreck"? If one interpretation seems to fit all the particulars of the poem, does that mean it's better than other possible interpretations? Write an essay in which you explore the poem's symbolism and argue for or against the idea that there is a single best way to understand this poem. Can ambiguity serve a poet's purpose, or does it ultimately undercut a poem's meaning and significance?

# 17 THE SOUNDS OF POETRY

A lot of what happens in a poem happens in your mind's eye, but some of it happens in your "mind's ear" and in your voice. Poems are full of meaningful sounds and silences as well as words and sentences. Besides choosing words for their meanings, poets sometimes choose words because they have certain sounds, and poems use sound effects to create a mood or establish a tone, just as films do. Sometimes the sounds of words are crucial to what is happening in the text of the poem.

Here is a poem that explores the sounds of a particular word, tries them on, and analyzes them in relation to the word itself.

### HELEN CHASIN

## *The Word* Plum

The word *plum* is delicious

pout and push, luxury of
self-love, and savoring murmur
full in the mouth and falling
5   like fruit

taut skin
pierced, bitten, provoked into
juice, and tart flesh

question
10   and reply, lip and tongue
of pleasure.
                    1968

The poem savors the sounds of the word as well as the taste and feel of the fruit itself. It is almost as if the poem is tasting the sounds and rolling them slowly on the tongue. The second and third lines even replicate the *p, l, uh,* and *m* sounds of the word while at the same time imitating the squishy sounds of eating the fruit. Words like "delicious" and "luxury" sound juicy, and other words imitate sounds of satisfaction and pleasure—"murmur," for example. Even the process of eating is in part re-created aurally. The tight, clipped sounds of "taut skin/

pierced" suggest the way teeth sharply break the skin and slice quickly into the soft flesh of a plum, and as they describe the tartness, the words ("provoked," "question") force the lips to pucker and the tongue and palate to meet and hold, as if the mouth were savoring a tart fruit. The poet is having fun here re-creating the sensual appeal of a plum, teasing the sounds and meanings out of available words. The words must mean something appropriate and describe something accurately first of all, of course, but when they can also imitate the sounds and feel of the process, they can do double duty. Not many poems manipulate sound as intensely or as fully as "The Word *Plum*," but many poems at least contain passages in which the sounds of life are reproduced by the human voice reading the poem. To get the full effect of this poem—and of many others—*you must read aloud*; that way, you can attend to the vocal rhythms and articulate the sounds as the poem calls for them to be reproduced by the human voice.

You will almost always enhance a poem's effect by reading aloud, using your voice to pronounce the words so that the poem becomes a spoken communication. Historically, poetry began as an oral phenomenon, and often poems that seem very difficult when looked at silently come alive when turned into sound. Early bards in many cultures chanted or recited their verses, and the music of poetry—its cadences and rhythms—developed from this kind of performance. The presentation of primitive poetry (and some later work as well) was often accompanied by some kind of musical instrument. The rhythms of any poem become clearer when you say or hear them.

Poetry is almost always a vocal art, dependent on the human voice to become its full self (for some exceptions look at the shaped verse in chapter 19). In a sense, it only begins to exist as a real phenomenon when a reader reads and actualizes it. Poems don't really achieve their full meaning when they exist merely on a page; a poem on a page is more a score or set of stage directions for a poem than a poem itself. Sometimes, in fact, it is hard to experience the poem at all unless you hear it; the actual experience of saying the words aloud or hearing them spoken is very good practice for learning to hear in your mind's ear when you read silently. A good poetry reading might easily convince you of the importance of a good voice sensitive to the poem's requirements, but you can also persuade yourself by reading poems aloud in the privacy of your own room. An audience is even better, however—an occasion to share the pleasure in the sounds themselves and what they imply. At its oral best, much poetry is communal.

MONA VAN DUYN

## What the Motorcycle Said

Br-r-r-am-m-m, rackety-am-m, OM, *Am:*
All—r-r-room, r-r-ram, ala-bas-ter—
*Am,* the world's my oyster.

I hate plastic, wear it black and slick,
5 hate hardhats, wear one on my head,
that's what the motorcycle said.

Passed phonies in Fords, knocked down billboards, landed
on the other side of The Gap, and Whee,
bypassed history.

10 When I was born (The Past), baby knew best.
They shook when I bawled, took Freud's path,
threw away their wrath.

R-r-rackety-am-m-m. *Am.* War, rhyme,
soap, meat, marriage, the Phantom Jet
15 are shit, and like that.

Hate pompousness, punishment, patience, am into Love,
hate middle-class moneymakers, live on Dad,
that's what the motorcycle said.

Br-r-r-am-m-m. It's Nowsville, man. Passed Oldies, Uglies,
20 Straighties, Honkies. I'll never be
mean, tired or unsexy.

Passed cigarette suckers, souses, mother-fuckers,
losers, went back to Nature and found
how to get VD, stoned.

25 Passed a cow, too fast to hear her moo, "*I* rolled
our leaves of grass into one ball.
*I* am the grassy All."

Br-r-r-am-m-m, rackety-am-m, OM, *Am:*
All—gr-r-rin, oooohgah, gl-l-utton—
30 *Am,* the world's my smilebutton.

1973

Saying this poem as if you were a motorcycle with the power of speech (sort of) is part of the poem's fun, and the rich, loud sounds of a motorcycle revving up concentrate and intensify the effect and enrich the pleasure. It's a shame not to hear a poem like this aloud; you miss a lot if you don't try to imitate the sounds or to pick up the motor's rhythms. A performance here is clearly worth it: human being as motorcycle, motorcycle as human being.

And it's a good poem, too. It does something interesting, important, and maybe a bit subversive. The speaking motorcycle seems to take on the values of some of its riders, the noisy and obtrusive ones that readers most likely associate with motorcycles. The types of riders made fun of here are themselves somewhat mindless and mechanical; they have cult feelings about their group, they travel in packs, and they seem to have no life beyond their machines. The speaking motorcycle, like such riders, exults in power and speed, lives for the moment, and has little respect for people, the past, institutions, or anything beyond its own small world. It is self-centered, trendy, ignorant, and inarticulate; but it is proud as well, mighty proud, and it glories in the rough thunder of its own sounds. That's what the motorcycle says.

The following poem uses sound effectively, too.

KENNETH FEARING

## Dirge

1-2-3 was the number he played but today the number came 3-2-1;
Bought his Carbide at 30, and it went to 29; had the favorite at Bowie[1] but the track was slow—

O executive type, would you like to drive a floating-power, knee-action, silk-upholstered six? Wed a Hollywood star? Shoot the course in 58? Draw to the ace, king, jack?
O fellow with a will who won't take no, watch out for three cigarettes on the same, single match; O democratic voter born in August under Mars, beware of liquidated rails—

5 Denouement to denouement, he took a personal pride in the certain, certain way he lived his own, private life,
But nevertheless, they shut off his gas; nevertheless, the bank foreclosed; nevertheless, the landlord called; nevertheless, the radio broke,
And twelve o'clock arrived just once too often,
Just the same he wore one gray tweed suit, bought one straw hat, drank one straight Scotch, walked one short step, took one long look, drew one deep breath,
Just one too many,

10 And wow he died as wow he lived,
Going whop to the office and blooie home to sleep and biff got married and bam had children and oof got fired,
Zowie did he live and zowie did he die,

With who the hell are you at the corner of his casket, and where the hell're we going on the right-hand silver knob, and who the hell cares walking second from the end with an American Beauty[2] wreath from why the hell not,

Very much missed by the circulation staff of the New York Evening Post; deeply, deeply mourned by the B.M.T.[3]

15 Wham, Mr. Roosevelt; pow, Sears Roebuck; awk, big dipper; bop, summer rain;
Bong, Mr., bong, Mr., bong, Mr., bong.

1935

---

1. A racetrack in Maryland. *Carbide:* stock in the Union Carbide Corporation.   2. A variety of rose.
3. A New York City subway line.

As the title implies, "Dirge" is a kind of musical lament, in this case for a certain sort of businessman who took many chances and saw his investments and life go down the drain in the depression of the early 1930s. Reading this poem aloud helps a lot, in part because of the expressive cartoon words here that echo the action, words like "oof" and "blooie" (which primarily carry their meaning in their sounds, for they have practically no literal or referential meaning). Reading aloud also helps us notice that the poem employs rhythms much as a song would and that it frequently shifts its pace and mood. Notice how carefully the first two lines are balanced, and then how quickly the rhythm shifts as the "executive type" is addressed directly in line 3. (Line 2 is long and dribbles over in the narrow pages of a book like this; the especially long lines and irregular line lengths here create some of the poem's special sound effects.) In the direct address, the poem first picks up the lingo of advertising, which it recites in rapid-fire order rather like advertising phrases. In stanza 3 here, the rhythm shifts again, but the poem gives us helpful clues about how to read. Line 5 sounds like prose and is long, drawn out, and rather dull (rather like its subject), but line 6 sets up a regular (and monotonous) rhythm with its repeated "nevertheless," which punctuates the rhythm like a drumbeat: "But nevertheless, *tuh-tuh-tuh-tuh-tuh;* nevertheless, *tuh-tuh-tuh-tuh;* nevertheless, *tuh-tuh-tuh-tuh;* nevertheless, *tuh-tuh-tuh-tuh-tuh.*" In the next stanza, the repetitive phrasing comes again, this time guided by the word "one" in cooperation with other words of one syllable: "wore *one* gray tweed suit, bought *one* straw hat, *tuh* one *tuh-tuh,* *tuh* one *tuh-tuh,* *tuh* one *tuh-tuh,* *tuh* one *tuh-tuh.*" And then a new rhythm and a new technique begin in stanza 5, which imitates the language of comic books to describe in violent, exaggerated terms the routine of the businessman's life. You have to say words like "whop" and "zowie" aloud and in the rhythm of the whole sentence to get the full effect of how boring his life is, no matter how he tries to jazz it up with exciting words. And so it goes—repeated words, shifting rhythms, emphasis on routine and averageness—until the final bell ("Bong.... bong ... bong ... bong") tolls rhythmically for the dead man in the final clanging line.

> *There are only three things ... that a poem must reach: the eye, the ear, and what we may call the heart or the mind. It is the most important of all to reach the heart of the reader. And the surest way to reach the heart is through the ear.*
> —ROBERT FROST

Sometimes the sounds in poems just provide special effects, rather like a musical score behind a film, setting mood and getting us into an appropriate frame of mind. But often sound and meaning go hand in hand, and the poet finds words that in their sounds echo the action. A word that captures or approximates the sound of what it describes, such as "splash" or "squish" or "murmur," is an **onomatopoeic** word, and the device itself is **onomatopoeia**. And poets can do similar things with pacing and rhythm, sounds and pauses. The punctuation, the length of vowels, and the combination of consonant sounds help to control the way we read so that we use our voice to imitate what is being described. The poems at the end of this chapter suggest several ways that such imitations of pace and pause may occur: by echoing the lapping of waves on a shore, for example ("Like as the waves"), or reproducing the rhythms of a musical style ("Dear John, Dear Coltrane").

Here is a classic passage in which a skillful poet talks about the virtues of making the sound echo the sense—and shows at the same time how to do it:

## ALEXANDER POPE

## *Sound and Sense*[4]

  But most by numbers[5] judge a poet's song,
And smooth or rough, with them, is right or wrong;
In the bright muse though thousand charms conspire,[6]
340 Her voice is all these tuneful fools admire,
Who haunt Parnassus[7] but to please their ear,
Not mend their minds; as some to church repair,
Not for the doctrine, but the music there.
These, equal syllables[8] alone require,
345 Though oft the ear the open vowels tire,
While expletives[9] their feeble aid do join,
And ten low words oft creep in one dull line,
While they ring round the same unvaried chimes,
With sure returns of still expected rhymes.
350 Where'er you find "the cooling western breeze,"
In the next line, it "whispers through the trees";
If crystal streams "with pleasing murmurs creep,"
The reader's threatened (not in vain) with "sleep."
Then, at the last and only couplet fraught
355 With some unmeaning thing they call a thought,
A needless Alexandrine[1] ends the song,
That, like a wounded snake, drags its slow length along.
Leave such to tune their own dull rhymes, and know
What's roundly smooth, or languishingly slow;
360 And praise the easy vigor of a line,
Where Denham's strength and Waller's[2] sweetness join.
True ease in writing comes from art, not chance,
As those move easiest who have learned to dance.
'Tis not enough no harshness gives offense,
365 The sound must seem an echo to the sense:
Soft is the strain when Zephyr[3] gently blows,
And the smooth stream in smoother numbers flows;
But when loud surges lash the sounding shore,
The hoarse, rough verse should like the torrent roar.

---

4. From *An Essay on Criticism*, Pope's poem on the art of poetry and the problems of literary criticism. The passage excerpted here follows a discussion of several common weaknesses of critics—failure to regard an author's intention, for example, or overemphasis on clever metaphors and ornate style.
5. Meter, rhythm, sound.   6. Unite.
7. A mountain in Greece, traditionally associated with the Muses and considered the seat of poetry and music.   8. Regular accents.   9. Filler words, such as "do."
1. A line of six metrical feet, sometimes used in pentameter poems to vary the pace mechanically. Line 357 is an alexandrine.
2. Sir John Denham and Edmund Waller, seventeenth-century poets credited with perfecting the heroic couplet.   3. The west wind.

370 When Ajax[4] strives, some rock's vast weight to throw,
The line too labors, and the words move slow;
Not so, when swift Camilla[5] scours the plain,
Flies o'er th' unbending corn, and skims along the main.
Hear how Timotheus'[6] varied lays surprise,
375 And bid alternate passions fall and rise!
While, at each change, the son of Libyan Jove[7]
Now burns with glory, and then melts with love;
Now his fierce eyes with sparkling fury glow,
Now sighs steal out, and tears begin to flow:
380 Persians and Greeks like turns of nature[8] found,
And the world's victor stood subdued by sound!
The pow'r of music all our hearts allow,
And what Timotheus was, is DRYDEN now.

1711

A lot of things are going on here simultaneously. The poem uses a number of echoic or onomatopoeic words, and in some lines pleasant and unpleasant consonant sounds underline a particular point or add some mood music. When the poet talks about a particular weakness in poetry, he illustrates it at the same time—by using open vowels (line 345), expletives (line 346), monosyllabic words (line 347), predictable rhymes (lines 350–53), or long, slow lines (line 357). And the good qualities of poetry he talks about and illustrates as well (line 360, for example). But the main effects of the passage come from an interaction of several strategies at once. The effects are fairly simple and easy to spot, but their causes involve a lot of poetic ingenuity. In line 340, for example, Pope achieves a careful cacophonous effect by repeating the o͞o vowel sound and repeating the *l* consonant sound together with (twice) interrupting the rough *f* sound in the middle; no one wants to be caught admiring that music, but the careful harmony of the preceding sounds has set us up beautifully. And the pace of lines 347, 357, and 359 is carefully controlled by clashing consonant sounds as well as by the use of long vowels. Line 347 moves incredibly slowly and seems much longer than it is because almost all the one-syllable words end in a consonant that refuses to blend with the beginning of the next word, making the words hard to say without distinct, awkward pauses between them. In lines 357 and 359, long vowels such as those in "wounded," "snake," "slow," "along," "roundly," and "smooth" help to slow down the pace, and awkward, hard-to-pronounce consonants are again juxtaposed. The commas also provide nearly a full stop in the midst of these lines to slow us down still more. Similarly, the harsh lashing of the shore in lines 368–69 is accomplished partly by onomatopoeia, partly by a shift in the pattern of stress, which creates irregular waves in line 368, and partly by the dominance of rough consonants in

---

4. A Greek hero of the Trojan War, noted for his strength.   5. A woman warrior in Virgil's *Aeneid*.
6. The court musician of Alexander the Great, celebrated in a famous poem by John Dryden (see line 383) for the power of his music over Alexander's emotions.
7. In Greek tradition, the chief god of any people was often given the name Zeus (Jove), and the chief god of Libya (the Greek name for all of Africa) was called Zeus Ammon. Alexander visited his oracle and was proclaimed son of the god.   8. Similar alternations of emotion.

line 369. (In Pope's time, the English *r* was still trilled gruffly so that it could be made to sound extremely rrrough and harrrsh.) Almost every line in this passage demonstrates how to make sound echo sense.

As "Sound and Sense" and "Dirge" suggest, poets most effectively manipulate sound by carefully controlling the rhythm of the voice so that not only are the proper sounds heard, but they are heard at precisely the right moment. Pace and rhythm are as important to a good poem as they are to a good piece of music. The human voice naturally develops certain rhythms in speech; some syllables and some words receive more stress than others. Just as multisyllabic words put more stress on some syllables than others (dictionaries always indicate which syllables are stressed), words in the context of a sentence receive more or less stress, depending on meaning. One-syllable words are thus sometimes stressed and sometimes not. A careful poet controls the flow of stresses so that, in many poems, a certain basic pattern of rhythm (or **meter**) develops almost like a quiet percussion instrument in the background. Not all poems have meter, and not all metered poems follow a single dominant rhythm, but many poems employ one pervasive pattern, and it is useful to look for patterns of stress.

In the Western world, we can thank the ancient Greeks for systematizing an understanding of meter and giving us a vocabulary (including the words *rhythm* and *meter*) that enables us to discuss the art of poetry. *Meter* comes from a Greek word meaning "measure": what we measure in the English language are the patterns of stressed (or "accented") syllables that occur naturally when we speak, and, just as when we measure length, the unit we use in measuring poetry is the **foot**. Most traditional poetry in English uses the accentual-syllabic form of meter—meaning that its rhythmic pattern is based on both a set number of syllables per line and a regular pattern of accents in each line. The most common metrical pattern is **iambic,** in which each foot contains an unstressed syllable followed by a stressed one. Consider, for example, the first two lines of Alexander Pope's "Sound and Sense," here marked to show the stressed syllables:

But móst | by núm- | bers júdge | a pó- | et's sóng,
And smóoth | or róugh, | with thém,| is ríght | or wróng.

These lines, like so many in English literature, provide an example of **iambic pentameter**—that is, the lines are written in a meter consisting of five iambic feet. Notice that there is nothing forced or artificial in the sound of these lines; the words flow easily. In fact, linguists contend that English is naturally iambic, and even the most ordinary, "unpoetic" utterances often fall into this pattern: "Please tell me if you've heard this one before." "They said she had a certain way with words." "The baseball game was televised at nine."

Besides the iamb, other metrical feet include the following:

**trochee**—an accented syllable followed by an unstressed one ("méter," "Hómer")
**anapest**—two unaccented syllables followed by a stressed one ("comprehénd," "after yóu")
**dactyl**—an accented syllable followed by two unstressed ones ("róundabout," "dínnertime")

Line lengths are sometimes described in terms of the number of syllables: a *decasyllabic* line, for example, is ten syllables long; an *octosyllabic* is eight, etc. Much more commonly though, lines are described in terms of the number of feet. It is possible to write regular lines using any of the feet shown above:

**iambic pentameter**—"In sé- | quent tóil | all fór- | wards dó | con- | ténd..." (William Shakespeare)
**trochaic octameter**—"Ónce u- | pón a | mídnight | dréary, | whíle I | póndered, | wéak and | wéary..." (Edgar Allan Poe)
**anapestic tetrameter**—"There are mán- | y who sáy | that a dóg | has his dáy..." (Dylan Thomas)
**dactylic hexameter**—"Thís is the | fórest pri- | méval. The | múrmuring | pínes and the | hémlocks..." (Henry Wadsworth Longfellow)

Notice that this final example is perfectly regular until the final foot, a trochee. Few poems, in fact, are written entirely in regular lines, and substitution of one metrical foot for another—to accommodate idioms and conversational habits or to create a special effect or emphasis—is quite common, especially in the first foot of a line. Shakespeare often begins an iambic line with a trochee:

Líke as | the wáves | make towárds | the péb- | bled shóre...

The poet may introduce a **spondee,** for example—a pair of accented syllables. Consider this line from John Milton's *Paradise Lost,* a poem written mainly in iambic pentameter:

Rócks, cáves, | lákes, féns, | bógs, déns, | and Shádes | of Déath...

Here Milton substitutes three spondees for the first three iambs in a pentameter line. John Dryden's "To the Memory of Mr. Oldham" begins with two spondees:

Fárewéll, tóo líttle, and tóo látely knówn

A **caesura,** a short pause often (though not always) signaled by a mark of punctuation such as a comma, may interrupt a line, as in the example from Poe's "The Raven," above, or in most lines of more than five or six syllables. (Sometimes, other even more elaborate accentual variations are used—*amphybrachs,* for example, involve an unstressed syllable, a stressed one, and then another unstressed one—but such hybrids are seldom used in English verse.)

In traditional metrical poetry, the poet's art, just like the musician's, consists of establishing metrical patterns and then varying the patterns without breaking them. With just the few rhythmic building blocks shown above, poets can create an almost infinite variety of rhythms.

Here is a poem that names and illustrates many of the meters. If someone read it aloud and you charted the stressed (−) and unstressed (⌣) syllables, you would have a chart similar to that done by the poet himself in the text.

## SAMUEL TAYLOR COLERIDGE

### *Metrical Feet*

### Lesson for a Boy

    Trōchĕe trīps frŏm lōng tŏ shōrt;[9]
    From long to long in solemn sort
    Slōw Spōndēe stālks; strŏng foōt! yet ill able
    Ĕvĕr tŏ cōme ŭp wĭth Dāctўl trĭsyllăblĕ.
5  Ĭāmbĭcs mārch frŏm shōrt tŏ lōng—
    Wĭth ă leāp ănd ă boūnd thĕ swĭft Ănăpĕsts thrōng;
    One syllable long, with one short at each side,
    Ămphībrăchўs hāstes wĭth ă stātelў strīde—
    Fīrst ănd lāst bēing lōng, mĭddlĕ shōrt, Amphĭmācer
10 Strīkes hĭs thūndĕrĭng hoōfs līke ă proūd hīgh-brĕd Rācer.
    If Derwent[1] be innocent, steady, and wise,
    And delight in the things of earth, water, and skies;
    Tender warmth at his heart, with these meters to show it,
    With sound sense in his brains, may make Derwent a poet—
15 May crown him with fame, and must win him the love
    Of his father on earth and his Father above.
            My dear, dear child!
    Could you stand upon Skiddaw,[2] you would not from its whole ridge
    See a man who so loves you as your fond S. T. COLERIDGE.

1806

The following poem exemplifies **dactylic** rhythm (– ˘ ˘ or stressed syllable followed by two unstressed ones).

### WENDY COPE

### *Emily Dickinson*

    Higgledy-piggledy
    Emily Dickinson
    Liked to use dashes
    Instead of full stops.

5  Nowadays, faced with such
    Idiosyncrasy,
    Critics and editors
    Send for the cops.

1986

---

9. The long and short marks over syllables are Coleridge's.
1. Written originally for Coleridge's son Hartley, the poem was later adapted for his younger son, Derwent.
2. A mountain in the lake country of northern England (where Coleridge lived in his early years), near the town of Derwent.

Limericks rely on **anapestic** meter (˘ ˘ ‒, or two unstressed syllables followed by a stressed one), although usually the first two syllables are in iambic meter (see below).

### ANONYMOUS

There was a young girl from St. Paul,
Wore a newspaper-dress to a ball.
   The dress caught on fire
   And burned her entire
Front page, sporting section and all.

The following poem is composed in the more common **trochaic** meter (‒ ˘, a stressed syllable followed by an unstressed one).

### SIR JOHN SUCKLING

## Song

Why so pale and wan, fond Lover?
   Prithee why so pale?
Will, when looking well can't move her,
   Looking ill prevail?
5   Prithee why so pale?

Why so dull and mute, young Sinner?
   Prithee why so mute?
Will, when speaking well can't win her,
   Saying nothing do 't?
10   Prithee why so mute?

Quit, quit, for shame, this will not move,
   This cannot take her;
If of her self she will not love,
   Nothing can make her;
15   The Devil take her.

                    1646

Like Pope's "Sound and Sense," the following poem uses the English language's most common poetic meter, **iambic** (⌣ –, an unstressed syllable followed by a stressed one, which some would argue is the most "natural" rhythm for English).

## JOHN DRYDEN

### *To the Memory of Mr. Oldham*[3]

Farewell, too little, and too lately known,
Whom I began to think and call my own;
For sure our souls were near allied, and thine
Cast in the same poetic mold with mine.
5  One common note on either lyre did strike,
And knaves and fools we both abhorred alike.
To the same goal did both our studies drive;
The last set out the soonest did arrive.
Thus Nisus fell upon the slippery place,
10  While his young friend performed and won the race.[4]
O early ripe! to thy abundant store
What could advancing age have added more?
It might (what nature never gives the young)
Have taught the numbers[5] of thy native tongue.
15  But satire needs not those, and wit will shine
Through the harsh cadence of a rugged line.[6]
A noble error, and but seldom made,
When poets are by too much force betrayed.
Thy generous fruits, though gathered ere their prime,
20  Still showed a quickness; and maturing time
But mellows what we write to the dull sweets of rhyme.
Once more, hail and farewell; farewell, thou young,
But ah too short, Marcellus[7] of our tongue;
Thy brows with ivy, and with laurels bound;
25  But fate and gloomy night encompass thee around.

1684

**Scanning** a poem line by line—that is, sorting out its metrical pattern—can be hard work, and few people enjoy the process (which is called **scansion**). Doing it right involves listening carefully to your voice as you read aloud, marking the

---

3. John Oldham (1653–1683), who like Dryden (see lines 3–6) wrote satiric poetry.
4. In Virgil's *Aeneid* (Book 5), Nisus (who is leading the race) falls and then trips the second runner so that his friend Euryalus can win.   5. Rhythms.
6. In Dryden's time, the English *r* was pronounced with a harsh, trilling sound.
7. Nephew of the Roman emperor Augustus who died at twenty, celebrated by Virgil in the *Aeneid*, Book 6.

stressed and unstressed syllables, counting the syllables and feet, and checking the rhyme patterns. Though there is no easy substitute for this work, there is often a major payoff in seeing the subtleties of a poet's craft as well as in hearing the poetry itself more fully and resonantly. If, for example, you chart "To the Memory of Mr. Oldham," you will notice some extraordinary variations in the basic iambic pattern, variations that signal special emphasis on certain key terms and that indicate structural changes and directions. Even the first line is highly irregular—even though no pattern has yet been established in our ears. (Often, in fact, you will need to scan several lines before you can be sure of the "controlling" metrical pattern of a poem.) Possibly as many as seven syllables in this first line are stressed, rather than the expected five in a regular iambic pentameter line, and the effect is both to strongly emphasize Oldham's relatively unknown status (*too lit*-tle *and too late*-ly *known*) and to draw out, lengthily, in conjunction with the use of a series of long vowels, the reading of the line.

Hearing a poem properly involves practice—listening to others read poetry and especially to yourself as you read poems aloud, so that you get used to hearing your voice, so that you become confident about where the stresses fall, and so that the rhythms begin to play themselves out "naturally." Your dictionary will show you the stresses for every word of more than one syllable, and the governing stress of individual words will largely control the patterns in a line: if you read a line for its basic sense (almost, for a moment, as if it were prose), you will usually see the line's basic pattern. But single-syllable words can be a challenge because they may or may not get a stress depending on their syntactic function and the full meaning of the sentence. Normally, important functional words, such as nouns and verbs of one syllable, get stressed (as in normal conversation or in prose); but conjunctions (such as *and* or *but*), prepositions (such as *on* or *with*), and articles (such as *an* or *the*) do not. But you often need to make decisions as you say words aloud, decisions based on what the words actually convey and what the sentence means. Listen to yourself as you read aloud and be prepared for uncertainties. Sometimes you will even find your "normal" pronunciation being influenced or modified by the pattern your voice develops as you hear basic rhythms. The way you actually read a line, once you have "heard" the basic rhythm, is influenced by two factors: normal pronunciations and prose sense (on the one hand) and the predominant pattern of the poem (on the other). Since these two forces are constantly in tension and are sometimes contradictory, you can almost never fully predict the actual reading of a line, and good reading aloud (like every other art) depends less on formula than on subtlety and flexibility.

Because scanning lines is an imprecise craft, sometimes very good readers plausibly disagree about whether or not to stress certain syllables. Then, too, some stresses are stronger than others: the convention of calling syllables "stressed" or "unstressed" fails to measure degrees of stress—and meaning often dictates that some syllables be stressed *much* more heavily than others.

In addition, not every poem relies on a formal pattern of stresses. As we saw in "Sound and Sense" and "To the Memory of Mr. Oldham," a poem dominated by iambic meter might incorporate trochaic, anapestic, spondaic, or dactylic feet in one place or another to create a stylistic effect. Beyond that, a poet tired of or resistant to traditional vocal patterns might follow or create other patterns—or employ patternlessness—to form the sound of a poem. Counting only the number of syllables (and *not* stresses) in a line is one common variation, which early-twentieth-century poets such as Marianne Moore were especially fond of. Even more widespread is **free verse**, which does without any governing pattern of stresses or line lengths.

∴

## EDGAR ALLAN POE

## *The Raven*

    Once upon a midnight dreary, while I pondered, weak and weary,
    Over many a quaint and curious volume of forgotten lore,
    While I nodded, nearly napping, suddenly there came a tapping,
    As of some one gently rapping, rapping at my chamber door.
5  " 'Tis some visitor," I muttered, "tapping at my chamber door—
            Only this, and nothing more."

    Ah, distinctly I remember it was in the bleak December,
    And each separate dying ember wrought its ghost upon the floor.
    Eagerly I wished the morrow;—vainly I had sought to borrow
10  From my books surcease of sorrow—sorrow for the lost Lenore—
    For the rare and radiant maiden whom the angels name Lenore—
            Nameless here for evermore.

    And the silken sad uncertain rustling of each purple curtain
    Thrilled me—filled me with fantastic terrors never felt before;
15  So that now, to still the beating of my heart, I stood repeating
    " 'Tis some visitor entreating entrance at my chamber door;—
    Some late visitor entreating entrance at my chamber door;
            This it is, and nothing more."

    Presently my soul grew stronger; hesitating then no longer,
20  "Sir," said I, "or Madam, truly your forgiveness I implore;
    But the fact is I was napping, and so gently you came rapping,
    And so faintly you came tapping, tapping at my chamber door,
    That I scarce was sure I heard you"—here I opened wide the door;—
            Darkness there, and nothing more.

25  Deep into that darkness peering, long I stood there wondering, fearing,
    Doubting, dreaming dreams no mortal ever dared to dream before;
    But the silence was unbroken, and the darkness gave no token,
    And the only word there spoken was the whispered word, "Lenore!"
    This I whispered, and an echo murmured back the word, "Lenore!"—
30           Merely this, and nothing more.

    Back into the chamber turning, all my soul within me burning,
    Soon I heard again a tapping somewhat louder than before.
    "Surely," said I, "surely that is something at my window lattice;
    Let me see, then, what thereat is, and this mystery explore—

35  Let my heart be still a moment and this mystery explore;—
　　　　　　　　'Tis the wind and nothing more!"

Open here I flung the shutter, when, with many a flirt and flutter,
In there stepped a stately raven of the saintly days of yore;
Not the least obeisance made he; not an instant stopped or stayed he;
40  But, with mien of lord or lady, perched above my chamber door—
Perched upon a bust of Pallas[8] just above my chamber door—
　　　　　　　　Perched, and sat, and nothing more.

Then this ebony bird beguiling my sad fancy into smiling,
By the grave and stern decorum of the countenance it wore,
45  "Though thy crest be shorn and shaven, thou," I said, "art sure no craven,
Ghastly grim and ancient raven wandering from the Nightly shore—
Tell me what thy lordly name is on the Night's Plutonian[9] shore!"
　　　　　　　　Quoth the raven, "Nevermore."

Much I marvelled this ungainly fowl to hear discourse so plainly,
50  Though its answer little meaning—little relevancy bore,
For we cannot help agreeing that no living human being
Ever yet was blessed with seeing bird above his chamber door—
Bird or beast upon the sculptured bust above his chamber door,
　　　　　　　　With such name as "Nevermore."

55  But the raven, sitting lonely on the placid bust, spoke only
That one word, as if his soul in that one word he did outpour.
Nothing farther then he uttered—not a feather then he fluttered—
Till I scarcely more than muttered "Other friends have flown before—
On the morrow *he* will leave me, as my hopes have flown before."
60  　　　　　　　Then the bird said "Nevermore."

Startled at the stillness broken by reply so aptly spoken,
"Doubtless," said I, "what it utters is its only stock and store
Caught from some unhappy master whom unmerciful Disaster
Followed fast and followed faster till his songs one burden bore—
65  Till the dirges of his Hope that melancholy burden bore
　　　　　　　　Of 'Never—nevermore.' "

But the raven still beguiling all my sad soul into smiling,
Straight I wheeled a cushioned seat in front of bird and bust and door;
Then, upon the velvet sinking, I betook myself to linking
70  Fancy unto fancy, thinking what this ominous bird of yore—
What this grim, ungainly, ghastly, gaunt, and ominous bird of yore
　　　　　　　　Meant in croaking "Nevermore."

This I sat engaged in guessing, but no syllable expressing
To the fowl whose fiery eyes now burned into my bosom's core;
75  This and more I sat divining, with my head at ease reclining
On the cushion's velvet lining that the lamplight gloated o'er,

---

8. Athena, the Greek goddess of wisdom.　　9. Dark; Pluto was god of the underworld.

But whose velvet violet lining with the lamplight gloating o'er,
    *She* shall press, ah, nevermore!

Then, methought, the air grew denser, perfumed from an unseen censer
80 Swung by angels whose faint foot-falls tinkled on the tufted floor.
"Wretch," I cried, "thy God hath lent thee—by these angels he hath sent thee
Respite—respite and nepenthe[1] from thy memories of Lenore!
Quaff, oh quaff this kind nepenthe and forget this lost Lenore!"
    Quoth the raven, "Nevermore."

85 "Prophet!" said I, "thing of evil!—prophet still, if bird or devil!—
Whether Tempter sent, or whether tempest tossed thee here ashore,
Desolate, yet all undaunted, on this desert land enchanted—
On this home by Horror haunted—tell me truly, I implore—
Is there—*is* there balm in Gilead?[2]—tell me—tell me, I implore!"
90     Quoth the raven, "Nevermore."

"Prophet!" said I, "thing of evil—prophet still, if bird or devil!
By that Heaven that bends above us—by that God we both adore—
Tell this soul with sorrow laden if, within the distant Aidenn,[3]
It shall clasp a sainted maiden whom the angels name Lenore—
95 Clasp a rare and radiant maiden whom the angels name Lenore."
    Quoth the raven, "Nevermore."

"Be that word our sign of parting, bird or fiend!" I shrieked upstarting—
"Get thee back into the tempest and the Night's Plutonian shore!
Leave no black plume as a token of that lie thy soul hath spoken!
100 Leave my loneliness unbroken!—quit the bust above my door!
Take thy beak from out my heart, and take thy form from off my door!"
    Quoth the raven, "Nevermore."

And the raven, never flitting, still is sitting, still is sitting
On the pallid bust of Pallas just above my chamber door;
105 And his eyes have all the seeming of a demon's that is dreaming,
And the lamp-light o'er him streaming throws his shadow on the floor;
And my soul from out that shadow that lies floating on the floor
    Shall be lifted—nevermore!

                   1844

- Describing the composition of "The Raven," Poe wrote of the need to use sounds "in the fullest possible keeping with that melancholy which I had predetermined as the tone of the poem." List at least five of the sound effects (e.g., rhyme, alliteration, etc.) that Poe uses in "The Raven." How does each of these contribute to the poem's tone of "melancholy"?

---

1. A drug reputed by the Greeks to cause forgetfulness or sorrow (pronounced "ne-PEN-thee").
2. See Jeremiah 8.22.  3. Eden.

## WILLIAM SHAKESPEARE

### [Like as the waves make towards the pebbled shore]

Like as the waves make towards the pebbled shore,
So do our minutes hasten to their end,
Each changing place with that which goes before,
In sequent toil all forwards do contend.[4]
5 Nativity, once in the main[5] of light,
Crawls to maturity, wherewith being crowned,
Crooked[6] eclipses 'gainst his glory fight,
And Time that gave doth now his gift confound.[7]
Time doth transfix[8] the flourish set on youth
10 And delves the parallels[9] in beauty's brow,
Feeds on the rarities of nature's truth,
And nothing stands but for his scythe to mow.
And yet to times in hope[1] my verse shall stand,
Praising thy worth, despite his cruel hand.

1609

- Which lines in this poem vary the basic iambic metric scheme? What is the effect of these variations?

## JAMES MERRILL

### Watching the Dance

#### 1. BALANCHINE'S[2]

Poor savage, doubting that a river flows
But for the myriad eddies made
By unseen powers twirling on their toes,

Here in this darkness it would seem
5 You had already died, and were afraid.
Be still. Observe the powers. Infer the stream.

---

4. Struggle. *Sequent:* successive.   5. High seas. *Nativity:* newborn life.   6. Perverse.   7. Bring to nothing.
8. Pierce.   9. Lines, wrinkles.   1. In the future.
2. George Balanchine (1904–1983), Russian-born ballet choreographer and teacher.

2. DISCOTHÈQUE

Having survived entirely your own youth,
Last of your generation, purple gloom
Investing you, sit, Jonah,[3] beyond speech,
10 And let towards the brute volume VOOM whale mouth
VAM pounding viscera VAM VOOM
A teenage plankton luminously twitch.

1967

- When you read this poem aloud, which lines flow most easily, and which contain abrupt pauses? If the first stanza of the poem is an imitation of a dance choreographed by Balanchine, what might this dance look like?

### GERARD MANLEY HOPKINS

## *Spring and Fall:*

*to a young child*

Márgarét áre you gríeving[4]
Over Goldengrove unleaving?
Leáves, like the things of man, you
With your fresh thoughts care for, can you?
5 Áh! ás the heart grows older
It will come to such sights colder
By and by, nor spare a sigh
Though worlds of wanwood leafmeal[5] lie;
And yet you wíll weep and know why.
10 Now no matter, child, the name:
Sórrow's spríngs áre the same.
Nor mouth had, no nor mind, expressed
What heart heard of, ghost[6] guessed:
It ís the blight man was born for,
15 It is Margaret you mourn for.

1880

- How does this poem's heavy use of alliteration serve its themes of youth and age, life and death?

---

3. According to Jonah 4, Jonah sat in gloom near Nineveh after its residents repented and God decided to spare the city from destruction.    4. Hopkins's own accent markings.
5. Broken up, leaf by leaf (analogous to "piecemeal"). *Wanwood:* pale, gloomy woods.    6. Soul.

**LEE ANN BROWN**

## Foolproof Loofah

Lo! I fill prol pills
Poof! I rail pro lolls
Fool! I ill for lips
O Pale! I foil frail profs
5  Fop! I frill pale roils—
So! I proof oil spills

April Fool's!
                              1999

- Do the lines of this poem have meaning outside of their sound?
  How do the poem's first six lines set up the final one?

**EMILY DICKINSON**

## [A narrow Fellow in the Grass]

A narrow Fellow in the Grass
Occasionally rides—
You may have met Him—did you not
His notice sudden is—

5  The Grass divides as with a Comb—
A spotted shaft is seen—
And then it closes at your feet
And opens further on—

He likes a Boggy Acre
10  A Floor too cool for Corn—
Yet when a Boy, and Barefoot—
I more than once at Noon

Have passed, I thought, a Whip lash
Unbraiding in the Sun
15  When stooping to secure it
It wrinkled, and was gone—

Several of Nature's People
I know, and they know me—
I feel for them a transport
20  Of cordiality—

But never met this Fellow
Attended, or alone

Without a tighter breathing
And Zero at the Bone—

1866

- How does Dickinson use sound devices such as alliteration to underscore the images and themes of the poem?

## WORDS AND MUSIC

People often associate poetry with music, and there are good reasons—both historical and theoretical—for doing so. The word **lyric,** for example—the standard term for a short, harmonious, pleasant, and often romantic poem—derives from the ancient Greeks' practice of reciting or singing (and perhaps composing) certain poems to the accompaniment of a stringed, harplike musical instrument, the lyre. Throughout history, poems have been set to music for voices or instruments, and many "lyrics" have been created specifically to fit musical compositions. Many poems, especially during the Renaissance, were simply called "Song" (or "Chanson" or "Lied" or similar terms in other languages), and some were constructed in hybrid musical-poetic forms such as the madrigal, the dirge, the hymn, and so on.

The most fundamental link between poetry and music involves their almost equal dependence on the principles of rhythm. Both art forms have a basis in mathematics—a regular beat or syncopated sound pattern predicts (and to some extent determines) their phrasing and formal movement. Not all composers of either poetry or music have mathematical knowledge, but their crafts depend on an ability to hear (almost instinctively and certainly habitually) pacings, pauses, alternations, and relationships. Just as good musicians learn to listen and count so easily that it seems "natural," poets often develop an ear for rhythm that makes their sound choices effortless and, seemingly, automatic. Readers, too, can develop such an ear, and hearing the rhythms of poems can be crucial to the total effects they create.

There are movements, of course, in both poetry and music to suppress or ignore regular patterns in favor of "freer" sounds and repetitions, but the tendency of both arts to use rhythm predictably makes some comparisons (and some common terminology) desirable and useful for describing strategies and effects. But the parallels are often *not* precise, the relationships metaphoric rather than actual. Both poetry and music use representational or imitative strategies to create the illusion of sounds—bells, waves, motorcycles, for example—but words operate referentially in a way that sounds normally do not, and their syntax is of a different kind from that in musical composition. Readers can better appreciate sound effects in poetry by hearing musical relationships, but the referential fact of language almost always alters the "pure" effects of sound (except in nonsense lyrics or in poems like "Joy Sonnet in a Random Universe" or "What the Motorcycle Said," where simple sounds or tonal expressions are simply recorded and transliterated).

Poems composed to or for music tend to differ from poems that produce or rely on rhythmic, harmonic, or musical effects created solely by words themselves. Reading the lyrics of a song you know well (so that you, in effect, "hear" the music as you read the words) is quite different from reading words that have for you no musical association or history. You probably cannot stop yourself from hearing the music that accompanies lyrics by, say, the Beatles, and the music thus becomes for you, even when you just *read* the words, part of the total effect. But the "music" (or more exactly the percussive rhythms and patterns of sound) created by a poem itself can work in a similar way when there is no musical "source" or co-creation. To say that a poem makes or uses "music" can mean many different things.

The poems that follow were all written for, in conjunction with, or to imitate music. If you "update" this collection with lyrics from your favorite contemporary singers and groups, you may find that some lyrics that are very good when sung do not work well as "separate" poetic texts, whereas some make very good poems indeed. Can you, in the lyrics you know well, separate the actual musical implications from those of the words alone?

## THOMAS CAMPION

### *When to Her Lute Corinna Sings*

    When to her lute Corinna sings,
    Her voice revives the leaden[1] strings,
    And doth in highest notes appear
    As any challenged[2] echo clear;
5  But when she doth of mourning speak,
    Ev'n with her sighs the strings do break.

    And as her lute doth live or die,
    Led by her passion, so must I:
    For when of pleasure she doth sing,
10  My thoughts enjoy a sudden spring;
    But if she doth of sorrow speak,
    Ev'n from my heart the strings do break.

1601

- How does Campion mimic an "echo" in this poem? What is the effect of this echoing?

1. Heavy.   2. Aroused.

## WILLIAM SHAKESPEARE

### Spring[3]

When daisies pied[4] and violets blue
   And ladysmocks all silver-white
And cuckoobuds of yellow hue
   Do paint the meadows with delight,
5 The cuckoo then, on every tree,
Mocks married men;[5] for thus sings he,
          Cuckoo;
Cuckoo, cuckoo: Oh word of fear,
Unpleasing to a married ear!

10 When shepherds pipe on oaten straws,
   And merry larks are plowmen's clocks,
When turtles tread,[6] and rooks, and daws,
   And maidens bleach their summer smocks,
The cuckoo then, on every tree,
15 Mocks married men; for thus sings he,
          Cuckoo;
Cuckoo, cuckoo: Oh word of fear,
Unpleasing to a married ear!

ca. 1595

- What words or phrases might a singer emphasize in order to enhance this poem's comic effect?

## AUGUSTUS MONTAGUE TOPLADY

### A Prayer, Living and Dying

I

ROCK of ages, cleft for me,
Let me hide myself in Thee!
Let the Water and the Blood,
From thy riven Side which flow'd,
5 Be of sin the double cure;
Cleanse me from its guilt and pow'r.

II

Not the labors of my hands
Can fulfill thy Law's demands:
Could my zeal no respite know,

---

3. A song from *Love's Labour's Lost*.  4. Of varied colors.
5. By the resemblance of its call to the word *cuckold*.  6. Turtledoves copulate.

10　Could my tears for ever flow,
　　All for sin could not atone;
　　Thou must save, and Thou alone.

　　　　III
　　Nothing in my hand I bring;
　　Simply to thy Cross I cling;
15　Naked, come to Thee for dress;
　　Helpless, look to Thee for grace;
　　Foul, I to the Fountain fly:
　　Wash me, SAVIOR, or I die!

　　　　IV
　　While I draw this fleeting breath—
20　When my eye-strings break in death—
　　When I soar to worlds unknown—
　　See Thee on thy judgment-throne—
　　ROCK of ages, cleft for me,
　　Let me hide myself in Thee!
　　　　　　　　1776

- What aspects of this poem might make it suitable for communal singing by untrained singers?

## ROBERT HAYDEN

### *Homage to the Empress of the Blues*[7]

　　Because there was a man somewhere in a candystripe silk shirt,
　　gracile and dangerous as a jaguar and because a woman moaned
　　for him in sixty-watt gloom and mourned him Faithless Love
　　Twotiming Love Oh Love Oh Careless Aggravating Love,

5　　She came out on the stage in yards of pearls, emerging like
　　　a favorite scenic view, flashed her golden smile and sang.

　　Because grey laths began somewhere to show from underneath
　　torn hurdygurdy[8] lithographs of dollfaced heaven;
　　and because there were those who feared alarming fists of snow
10　on the door and those who feared the riot-squad of statistics,

　　　She came out on the stage in ostrich feathers, beaded satin,
　　　and shone that smile on us and sang.
　　　　　　　　　　　　　　　　1962

- How do the two short stanzas beginning with "She came out" complete the thoughts of the longer stanzas that start with "Because"?

7. Bessie Smith (1894 [or 1898?]–1937); legendary blues singer whose theatrical style grew out of the black American vaudeville tradition.　8. A disreputable kind of dance hall.

MICHAEL HARPER

## Dear John, Dear Coltrane

*a love supreme, a love supreme*
*a love supreme, a love supreme*[9]

Sex fingers toes
in the marketplace
near your father's church
in Hamlet, North Carolina—[1]
5 witness to this love
in this calm fallow
of these minds,
there is no substitute for pain:
genitals gone or going,
10 seed burned out,
you tuck the roots in the earth,
turn back, and move
by river through the swamps,
singing: *a love supreme, a love supreme;*
15 what does it all mean?
Loss, so great each black
woman expects your failure
in mute change, the seed gone.
You plod up into the electric city—
20 your song now crystal and
the blues. You pick up the horn
with some will and blow
into the freezing night:
*a love supreme, a love supreme—*
25 Dawn comes and you cook
up the thick sin 'tween
impotence and death, fuel
the tenor sax cannibal
heart, genitals and sweat
30 that makes you clean—
*a love supreme, a love supreme—*

*Why you so black?*
*cause I am*
*why you so funky?*
35 *cause I am*

---

9. Coltrane wrote "A Love Supreme" in response to a spiritual experience in 1957 that also led to his quitting heroin and alcohol. Mainly an instrumental improvisation featuring Coltrane's saxophone, the piece begins with the repeated chant of "a love supreme." The record was released in 1965.
1. Coltrane's birthplace. His family shared a house with Coltrane's grandfather, who was the minister of St. Stephen's AME Zion Church.

*why you so black
cause I am
why you so sweet?
cause I am*
40 *why you so black?
cause I am
a love supreme, a love supreme:*

So sick
you couldn't play *Naima,*[2]
45 so flat we ached
for song you'd concealed
with your own blood,
your diseased liver gave
out its purity,
50 the inflated heart
pumps out, the tenor kiss,
tenor love:
*a love supreme, a love supreme—
a love supreme, a love supreme—*

1970

- In what ways is this poem, as suggested by the title, both a "Dear John" letter and a poem of praise?

# BOB DYLAN

## Mr. Tambourine Man

Hey! Mr. Tambourine Man, play a song for me,
I'm not sleepy and there is no place I'm going to.
Hey! Mr. Tambourine Man, play a song for me,
In the jingle jangle morning I'll come followin' you.

5 Though I know that evenin's empire has returned into sand,
Vanished from my hand,
Left me blindly here to stand but still not sleeping.
My weariness amazes me, I'm branded on my feet,
I have no one to meet
10 And the ancient empty street's too dead for dreaming.

Hey! Mr. Tambourine Man, play a song for me,
I'm not sleepy and there is no place I'm going to.
Hey! Mr. Tambourine Man, play a song for me,
In the jingle jangle morning I'll come followin' you.

---

2. A song Coltrane wrote for and named after his wife, recorded in 1959.

15 Take me on a trip upon your magic swirlin' ship,
My senses have been stripped, my hands can't feel to grip,
My toes too numb to step, wait only for my boot heels
To be wanderin'.
I'm ready to go anywhere, I'm ready for to fade
20 Into my own parade, cast your dancing spell my way,
I promise to go under it.

Hey! Mr. Tambourine Man, play a song for me,
I'm not sleepy and there is no place I'm going to.
Hey! Mr. Tambourine Man, play a song for me,
25 In the jingle jangle morning I'll come followin' you.

Though you might hear laughin', spinnin', swingin' madly across the sun,
It's not aimed at anyone, it's just escapin' on the run
And but for the sky there are no fences facin'.
And if you hear vague traces of skippin' reels of rhyme
30 To your tambourine in time, it's just a ragged clown behind,
I wouldn't pay it any mind, it's just a shadow you're
Seein' that he's chasing.

Hey! Mr. Tambourine Man, play a song for me,
I'm not sleepy and there is no place I'm going to.
35 Hey! Mr. Tambourine Man, play a song for me,
In the jingle jangle morning I'll come followin' you.

Then take me disappearin' through the smoke rings of my mind,
Down the foggy ruins of time, far past the frozen leaves,
The haunted, frightened trees, out to the windy beach,
40 Far from the twisted reach of crazy sorrow.
Yes, to dance beneath the diamond sky with one hand waving free,
Silhouetted by the sea, circled by the circus sands,
With all memory and fate driven deep beneath the waves,
Let me forget about today until tomorrow.

45 Hey! Mr. Tambourine Man, play a song for me,
I'm not sleepy and there is no place I'm going to.
Hey! Mr. Tambourine Man, play a song for me,
In the jingle jangle morning I'll come followin' you.

1964

- How does our familiarity with "Mr. Tambourine Man" as a song affect our sense of it as a poem? Do successful song lyrics necessarily work as poetry?

## WILLIE PERDOMO

### *123rd Street Rap*

A day on
123rd Street

goes a little
something like
5   this:

Automatic bullets bounce
off stoop steps

It's about time to pay
all my debts

10  Church bells bong for
for drunken mourners

Baby men growing on
all the corners

Money that
15  ain't mine

Sun that
don't shine

Trees that
don't grow

20  Wind that
won't blow

Drug posses
ready to rumble

Ceilings starting
25  to crumble

Abuelas[3] close
eyes and pray

While they watch
the children play

30  Not much I
can say

Except day turns
to night

---

3. Grandmothers.

And I can't tell what's
35  wrong from what's right

   on 123rd Street
               1996

- Read "123rd Street Rap" first silently and then aloud. Does it "work" better one way or the other? Listen to the author reading this poem (on the CD). Has your opinion of it changed?

---

## SUGGESTIONS FOR WRITING

1. Read Pope's "Sound and Sense" carefully twice—once silently and once aloud—and then mark the stressed and unstressed syllables. Draw up a chart indicating, line by line, exactly what the patterns of stress are, and then single out all the lines that have major variations from the basic iambic pentameter pattern. Pick out six lines with variations that seem to you worthy of comment, and write a paragraph on each in which you show how the varied metrical pattern contributes to the specific effects achieved in that line.

2. Try your hand at writing limericks in imitation of "There was a young girl from St. Paul"; study the rhythmic patterns and line lengths carefully, and imitate them exactly in your poem. Begin your limerick with "There once was a _____ from _____" (using a place for which you think you can find a comic rhyme).

3. Read Poe's "The Raven" aloud, paying particular attention to pacing. Do you find yourself speeding up as you continue through the poem? Does a quickening pace suit the speaker's growing exasperation and madness? Write an essay in which you examine the way that Poe underlines the poem's story and emotional flow with a range of poetic devices: line length, punctuation, rhyme, meter, and the sounds of words.

4. Pope's "Sound and Sense" contains this advice for poets: "But when loud surges lash the sounding shore, / The hoarse, rough verse should like the torrent roar" (lines 368–69). In other words, he counsels that the sound of the poet's description should match the sense of what the poem is describing. Write an essay in which you examine the sound and sense in Shakespeare's "[Like as the waves make towards the pebbled shore]"—how does the poem achieve a harmony of meaning and sound?

5. Write an essay in which you discuss any of the poems you have read in this book in which sound seems a more important element than anything else, even the meaning of words. What is the point of writing and reading this kind of poetry? Can it achieve its effects through silent reading, or must it be experienced aloud?

6. Is there a meaningful difference between poetry and song lyrics? between poetry and rap? Is hip-hop a form of literature? Write an essay in which you explore the definitions of "poetry" and "lyrics." Be sure to cite enough examples to illustrate your ideas.

# 18 INTERNAL STRUCTURE

"Proper words in proper places": that is how one great writer of English prose, Jonathan Swift, described good writing. A good poet finds appropriate words, and already we have looked at some implications for readers of the verbal choices a poet makes. But the poet must also decide where to put those words—how to arrange them for maximum effect—because individual words, metaphors, and symbols exist not only within phrases and sentences and rhythmic patterns but also within the larger whole of the poem. How should the words be arranged and the poem organized? What comes first and what last? Will the poem have a "plot"? What principle or idea of organization will inform it? How can words, sentences, images, ideas, and feelings be combined into a structure that holds together, seems complete, and affects readers?

Considering these questions from the poet's point of view (What is my plan? Where shall I begin?) can help us notice the effects of structural choices. Every poem works in its own unique way, and therefore every poet must make independent decisions about how to organize an individual poem. But poems do fall into patterns of organization, sometimes because of subject matter, sometimes because of effects intended, sometimes for other reasons. A poet may consciously decide on a particular strategy, may reach instinctively for one, or may happen into one that suits the needs of the moment—a framework onto which words and sentences will hang, one by one and group by group.

When a poem tells a story, the organization may be fairly straightforward. The following poem, for example, tells a simple story largely in chronological order:

### EDWIN ARLINGTON ROBINSON

### *Mr. Flood's Party*

> Old Eben Flood, climbing alone one night
> Over the hill between the town below
> And the forsaken upland hermitage
> That held as much as he should ever know
> 5   On earth again of home, paused warily.
> The road was his and not a native near;
> And Eben, having leisure, said aloud,
> For no man else in Tilbury Town to hear:

"Well, Mr. Flood, we have the harvest moon
10   Again, and we may not have many more;
   The bird is on the wing, the poet says,[1]
   And you and I have said it here before.
   Drink to the bird." He raised up to the light
   The jug that he had gone so far to fill,
15   And answered huskily: "Well, Mr. Flood,
   Since you propose it, I believe I will."

   Alone, as if enduring to the end
   A valiant armor of scarred hopes outworn
   He stood there in the middle of the road
20   Like Roland's ghost winding a silent horn.[2]
   Below him, in the town among the trees,
   Where friends of other days had honored him,
   A phantom salutation of the dead
   Rang thinly till old Eben's eyes were dim.

25   Then, as a mother lays her sleeping child
   Down tenderly, fearing it may awake
   He set the jug down slowly at his feet
   With trembling care, knowing that most things break;
   And only when assured that on firm earth
30   It stood, as the uncertain lives of men
   Assuredly did not, he paced away,
   And with his hand extended paused again:

   "Well, Mr. Flood, we have not met like this
   In a long time; and many a change has come
35   To both of us, I fear, since last it was
   We had a drop together. Welcome home!"
   Convivially returning with himself,
   Again he raised the jug up to the light;
   And with an acquiescent quaver said:
40   "Well, Mr. Flood, if you insist, I might.

   "Only a very little, Mr. Flood—
   For auld lang syne. No more, sir; that will do."
   So, for the time, apparently it did,
   And Eben evidently thought so too;
45   For soon amid the silver loneliness
   Of night he lifted up his voice and sang,
   Secure, with only two moons listening,
   Until the whole harmonious landscape rang—

   "For auld lang syne." The weary throat gave out,
50   The last word wavered, and the song was done.

---

1. Edward FitzGerald, in "The Rubáiyát of Omar Khayyám" (more or less a translation of an Arab original), so describes the "Bird of Time."
2. According to French legend, the hero Roland used his powerful ivory horn to warn his allies of impending attack.

>     He raised again the jug regretfully
>     And shook his head, and was again alone.
>     There was not much that was ahead of him,
>     And there was nothing in the town below—
> 55  Where strangers would have shut the many doors
>     That many friends had opened long ago.
>
>                                             1921

The fairly simple **narrative structure** here is based on the gradual unfolding of the story. After old Eben is introduced and situated in relation to the town and his home, the "plot" unfolds: he sits down in the road, reviews his life, reflects on the present, and has a drink—several drinks, in fact, as he thinks about passing time and growing old; then he sings and considers going "home." Not much happens, really; we get a vignette of Mr. Flood between two places and two times. But there *is* action, and the poem's movement—its organization and structure—depends on it: Mr. Flood in motion, in stasis, and then, again, contemplating motion. This counts as event, and a certain, limited chronological movement. We could say that a spare sort of story takes place, like that in Dickey's "Cherrylog Road" (chapter 15). The poem's organization—its structural principle—involves the passing of time, action moving forward, a larger story being revealed by the few moments depicted here.

"Mr. Flood's Party" presents about as much story as a short poem ever does, but like most poems it doesn't really emphasize the developing action—which all seems fairly predictable once we "get" who Eben is, how old he is, and what place he occupies in the communal memory of Tilbury Town and vice versa. Rather, the movement forward in time dictates the shape of the poem, determines the way it presents its images, ideas, themes. Nearly everything occurs within an easy-to-follow chronology.

But even here, in this most simple narrative structure, we note complications. One complication is in the use of time itself, for "old" time and "present" time seem posed against each other as a structural principle, too, one in tension with the chronological movement: Eben's past, as contrasted with his present and limited future, focuses the poem's attention, and in some ways the contrast between what was and what is seems even more important than the brief movement through present time that gets the most obvious attention in the poem. Then, too, "character"—Eben's character and that of the townspeople of later generations—gets a lot of attention, even as the chronology moves forward. More than one structural principle is at work here. We may identify the main movement of the poem as chronological and its principal structure as narrative, but to be fair and full in our discussion we have to note several other competing organizational forces at work—principles of comparison and contrast, for example, and of descriptive elaboration.

Most poems work with this kind of complexity, and identifying a single structure behind any poem involves a sense of the organizational principle that makes it work, while at the same time recognizing that other principles repeatedly, perhaps continually, compete for our attention. A poem's structure involves its conceptual framework—what principle best explains its organization and movement—and it is often useful to identify one dominating kind of structure, such as narrative structure, that gives the poem its shape. But we need to recognize from the start that most poems follow structural models loosely. Finding an appropriate label to describe the structure of a particular poem can help in analyzing the poem's other aspects, but the label itself has no magic.

> *Back of the idea of organic form is the concept that there is a form in all things (and in our experience) which the poet can discover and reveal.*
>
> —DENISE LEVERTOV

Purely narrative poems are often very long and often include many features that are not, strictly speaking, closely connected to the narrative or linked to a strict chronology. Very often a poem moves from a narrative of an event to some sort of commentary or reflection on it, as in Philip Larkin's "Church Going" (below, in this chapter). Reflection can be included along the way or may be implicit in the way the story is narrated, as in Maxine Kumin's "Woodchucks" (chapter 13), where we focus more on the narrator and her responses than on the events in the story.

Just as poems sometimes take on a structure like that of a story, they sometimes borrow the structures of plays. The following poem has a **dramatic structure**; it consists of a series of scenes, each of which is presented vividly and in detail, as if on stage.

## HOWARD NEMEROV

### *The Goose Fish*

On the long shore, lit by the moon
To show them properly alone,
Two lovers suddenly embraced
So that their shadows were as one.
5 The ordinary night was graced
For them by the swift tide of blood
That silently they took at flood.
And for a little time they prized
Themselves emparadised.

10 Then, as if shaken by stage-fright
Beneath the hard moon's bony light,
They stood together on the sand
Embarrassed in each other's sight
But still conspiring hand in hand,
15 Until they saw, there underfoot,
As though the world had found them out,
The goose fish turning up, though dead,
His hugely grinning head.

There in the china light he lay,
20 Most ancient and corrupt and gray.
They hesitated at his smile,
Wondering what it seemed to say
To lovers who a little while

>     Before had thought to understand,
> 25  By violence upon the sand,
>     The only way that could be known
>        To make a world their own.
>
>     It was a wide and moony grin
>     Together peaceful and obscene;
> 30  They knew not what he would express,
>     So finished a comedian
>     He might mean failure or success,
>     But took it for an emblem of
>     Their sudden, new and guilty love
> 35  To be observed by, when they kissed,
>        That rigid optimist.
>
>     So he became their patriarch,
>     Dreadfully mild in the half-dark.
>     His throat that the sand seemed to choke,
> 40  His picket teeth, these left their mark
>     But never did explain the joke
>     That so amused him, lying there
>     While the moon went down to disappear
>     Along the still and tilted track
> 45     That bears the zodiac.

1955

    The first stanza sets the scene—a sandy shore in moonlight—and presents, in fact, the major action of the poem. The rest of the poem dramatizes the lovers' reactions: their initial embarrassment and feelings of guilt (stanza 2), their attempt to interpret the goose fish's smile (stanza 3), their decision to make him, whatever his meaning, the "emblem" of their love (stanza 4), and their acceptance of the fish's ambiguity and of their own relationship (stanza 5). The five stanzas do not exactly present five different scenes or angles on the action, but they do present separate dramatic moments, even if little time has elapsed between them. Almost like a play of five very short acts, the poem traces the drama of the lovers' discovery of themselves and their coming to terms with the meaning of their action. As in many plays, the central event (their lovemaking) is not the central focus of the drama, although the drama is based upon that event and could not take place without it. The poem depicts that event swiftly but very vividly through figurative language: "they took at flood" the "swift tide of blood." The lovers then briefly feel "emparadised," but the poem concentrates on their later reactions.

    Their sudden discovery of the fish, a rude shock, injects a grotesque, almost macabre, note into the poem. From a vision of paradise, the poem seems for a moment to turn toward gothic horror when the lovers discover that they have, after all, been seen—and by such a ghoulish spectator. The last three stanzas gradually re-create the intruder in their minds, as they admit that their act of love exists not in isolation, but rather as part of a continuum, as part of their relationship to the larger world, even (at the end) within the context of the earth itself, and the moon, and the stars. In retrospect, we can see that even at the moment of passion the lovers were in touch with larger processes controlled by the presiding moon ("the swift *tide* of blood"), but neither they nor we had understood their act as such then, and the poem is about this gradual recognition of their "place" in time and space.

Stages of feeling and knowing rather than specific visual scenes determine the poem's progress, and its dramatic structure depends upon internal perceptions and internal states of mind rather than dialogue and events. Visualization and images help to organize the poem, too. Notice in particular how the two most striking visual features—the fish and the moon—are presented stanza by stanza. In stanza 1, the fish does not appear, and the moon exists plain; it is only mentioned, not described, and its light provides a stage spotlight to assure not center-stage attention, but rather total privacy: the moon serves as a lookout for the lovers. The stage imagery, barely suggested by the light in stanza 1, is articulated in stanza 2, and there the moon is "hard" and its light "bony"; its characteristics seem more appropriate to the fish, which has now become visible. In stanza 3, the moon's light comes to seem fragile ("china") as it exposes the fish directly; the moon's role as lookout and protector seems abandoned, or at least endangered. No moon appears in stanza 4, but the fish's grin is "wide and moony," almost as if the two onlookers, one earthly and dead, the other heavenly and eternal, have merged, as they nearly were by the imagery in stanza 2. And in stanza 5, the fish becomes a friend, a comedian, an optimist, an emblem, and a patriarch of their love—and his new position in collaboration with the lovers is presided over by the moon going about its eternal business. The moon—providing the stage light for the poem and the means by which not only the fish but the meaning of the lovers' act is discovered—has also helped to organize the poem, partly as a dramatic accessory, partly as imagery.

The following dramatic poem represents a composite of several similar experiences (compare Blake's "London" [chapter 13] and Dickey's "Cherrylog Road" [chapter 15]) rather than a single event—a fairly common pattern in dramatic poems:

## PHILIP LARKIN
### *Church Going*

    Once I am sure there's nothing going on
    I step inside, letting the door thud shut.
    Another church: matting, seats, and stone,
    And little books; sprawlings of flowers, cut
5  For Sunday, brownish now; some brass and stuff
    Up at the holy end; the small neat organ;
    And a tense, musty, unignorable silence,
    Brewed God knows how long. Hatless, I take off
    My cycle-clips in awkward reverence,

10  Move forward, run my hand around the font.
    From where I stand, the roof looks almost new—

Cleaned, or restored? Someone would know: I don't.
Mounting the lectern, I peruse a few
Hectoring large-scale verses, and pronounce
15 "Here endeth" much more loudly than I'd meant.
The echoes snigger briefly. Back at the door
I sign the book, donate an Irish sixpence,
Reflect the place was not worth stopping for.

Yet stop I did: in fact I often do,
20 And always end much at a loss like this,
Wondering what to look for; wondering, too,
When churches fall completely out of use
What we shall turn them into, if we shall keep
A few cathedrals chronically on show,
25 Their parchment, plate and pyx in locked cases,
And let the rest rent-free to rain and sheep.
Shall we avoid them as unlucky places?

Or, after dark, will dubious women come
To make their children touch a particular stone;
30 Pick simples[3] for a cancer; or on some
Advised night see walking a dead one?
Power of some sort or other will go on
In games, in riddles, seemingly at random;
But superstition, like belief, must die,
35 And what remains when disbelief has gone?
Grass, weedy pavement, brambles, buttress, sky,

A shape less recognizable each week,
A purpose more obscure. I wonder who
Will be the last, the very last, to seek
40 This place for what it was; one of the crew
That tap and jot and know what rood-lofts[4] were?
Some ruin-bibber,[5] randy for antique,
Or Christmas-addict, counting on a whiff
Of gown-and-bands and organ-pipes and myrrh?
45 Or will he be my representative,

Bored, uninformed, knowing the ghostly silt
Dispersed, yet tending to this cross of ground
Through suburb scrub because it held unspilt
So long and equally what since is found
50 Only in separation—marriage, and birth,
And death, and thoughts of these—for whom was built
This special shell? For, though I've no idea

---

3. Medicinal herbs.
4. Galleries atop the screens (on which crosses are mounted) that divide the naves or main bodies of churches from the choirs or chancels.
5. Literally, ruin-drinker: someone extremely attracted to antiquarian objects.

>     What this accoutered frowsty barn is worth,
>     It pleases me to stand in silence here;
>
> 55  A serious house on serious earth it is,
>     In whose blent[6] air all our compulsions meet,
>     Are recognized, and robed as destinies.
>     And that much never can be obsolete,
>     Since someone will forever be surprising
> 60  A hunger in himself to be more serious,
>     And gravitating with it to this ground,
>     Which, he once heard, was proper to grow wise in,
>     If only that so many dead lie round.
>                                                  1955

Ultimately, Larkin's poem focuses on what it means to visit churches, what it might be that church buildings represent, and what we should make of the fact that "church going" (in the usual sense of the word) has declined so much. The poem uses a *different* sort of church going (visitation by tourists) to consider larger questions about the relationship of religion to culture and history. The poem is, finally, a rather philosophical one about the directions of English culture, and through an enumeration of religious objects and rituals it reviews part of the history of that culture. It tells a kind of story first, through one lengthy dramatized scene, in order to comment later on what the place and the experience may mean, and the larger conclusion derives from the particulars of what the speaker does and touches. By the end of stanza 2 the action is over, but that action, we are told, stands for many such visits to similar churches; after that, the next five stanzas present reflection and discussion.

"Church Going" is a curious poem in many ways. It goes to a lot of trouble to characterize its speaker, who seems a rather odd choice as a commentator on the state of religion. His informal attire (he takes off his cycle-clips at the end of stanza 1) and his less than worshipful behavior do not at first make him seem like a serious philosopher. He is not disrespectful or sacrilegious, and before the end of stanza 1 he has tried to describe the "awkward reverence" he feels; but his overly emphatic imitation of part of the service stamps him as playful, a little satirical. He is a tourist here, not someone who regularly drops in for prayer or meditation in the usual sense. And yet those early details give him credentials, in a way; he knows the names of religious objects and has some history of churches in his grasp. Clearly he does this sort of church going habitually ("Yet stop I did: in fact I often do," line 19) because he wonders seriously what it all means—now—in comparison to what it meant to religious worshipers in times past. Ultimately, he takes the church, its cultural meaning, and its function seriously (lines 55 ff.), and he understands the importance of the church in the history of his culture. Thus the relatively brief drama provides a context for the rambling reflections that grow out of the speaker's dramatic experience.

---

6. Blended.

Sometimes poems are organized by contrasts, and they conveniently set one thing up against another that is quite different. Notice, for example, how the following poem carefully contrasts two worlds:

**PAT MORA**

## Sonrisas

I live in a doorway
between two rooms, I hear
quiet clicks, cups of black
coffee, *click, click* like facts
5  budgets, tenure, curriculum,
from careful women in crisp beige
suits, quick beige smiles
that seldom sneak into their eyes.

I peek
10 in the other room señoras
in faded dresses stir sweet
milk coffee, laughter whirls
with steam from fresh *tamales*
*sh, sh, mucho ruido,*[7]
15 they scold one another,
press their lips, trap smiles
in their dark, Mexican eyes.

1986

Here different words, habits, and values characterize the worlds of the two sets of characters, and the poem is organized largely by the contrasts between them. The meaning of the poem (the difference between the two worlds) is very nearly the same as the structure.

Poems often have **discursive structures**, too; that is, they may be organized like a treatise, an argument, or an essay. "First," they say, "and second . . . and third . . ." This sort of 1–2–3 structure takes a variety of forms depending on what is being enumerated or argued. Discursive structures help organize poems such as Shelley's "Ode to the West Wind" (later in this chapter), where the wind drives a leaf in Part I, a cloud in Part II, a wave in Part III, and then, after a summary and statement of the speaker's ambitious hope in Part IV, is asked to make the speaker a lyre in Part V.

Poems may borrow their organizational strategies from many places, imitating chronological, visual, or discursive shapes in reality or in other works of art. Sometimes poems strive to be almost purely descriptive of someone or something (using **descriptive structures**), in which case poets have to make organizational decisions much as painters or photographers would, deciding first how a whole scene should

---

7. A lot of noise.

look, then putting the parts into proper place for the whole. Of course, poems must present their details sequentially, not all at once as actual pictures more or less can, so poets must decide where to start a description (at the left? center? top?) and what sort of movement to use (linear across the scene? clockwise?). But if using words instead of paint or film has some drawbacks, it also has particular advantages: figurative language can be a part of description, or an adjunct to it. Poets can insert comparisons at any point without necessarily disturbing the unity of their descriptions.

Some poems use **imitative structures,** mirroring as exactly as possible the structure of something that already exists as an object and can be seen—another poem perhaps, as in Koch's "Variations on a Theme by William Carlos Williams" (chapter 23). Other poems use **reflective** (or **meditative**) **structures,** pondering a subject, theme, or event, and letting the mind play with it, skipping (logically or not) from one sound to another, or to related thoughts or objects as the mind encounters them.

Although the following poem employs several organizational principles, it ultimately takes its structure from an important shift in the speaker's attitude as she reviews, ponders, and rethinks events of long ago.

### SHARON OLDS

## *The Victims*

When Mother divorced you, we were glad. She took it and
took it, in silence, all those years and then
kicked you out, suddenly, and her
kids loved it. Then you were fired, and we
5   grinned inside, the way people grinned when
Nixon's helicopter lifted off the South
Lawn for the last time.[8] We were tickled
to think of your office taken away,
your secretaries taken away,
10  your lunches with three double bourbons,
your pencils, your reams of paper. Would they take your
suits back, too, those dark
carcasses hung in your closet, and the black
noses of your shoes with their large pores?
15  She had taught us to take it, to hate you and take it
until we pricked with her for your
annihilation, Father. Now I
pass the bums in doorways, the white
slugs of their bodies gleaming through slits in their
20  suits of compressed silt, the stained
flippers of their hands, the underwater

---

8. When Richard Nixon resigned the U.S. presidency on August 8, 1974, his exit from the White House (by helicopter from the lawn) was televised live.

fire of their eyes, ships gone down with the
lanterns lit, and I wonder who took it and
took it from them in silence until they had
25   given it all away and had nothing
left but this.

1984

"The Victims" divides basically into two parts. In the first two-thirds of the poem (from line 1 to the middle of line 17), the speaker evokes her father (the "you" of lines 1, 3, and so forth), who had been guilty of terrible habits and behavior when the speaker was young and was kicked out suddenly and divorced by the speaker's mother (lines 1–3). He was then fired from his job (line 4) and lost his whole way of life (lines 8–12), and the speaker (taught by the mother, lines 15–17) recalls celebrating every defeat and every loss ("we pricked with her for your annihilation," lines 16–17). The mother is regarded as a victim ("She took it and took it, in silence, all those years" [lines 1–2]), and the speaker forms an indivisible unit with her and the other children ("her kids," lines 3–4). They are the "we" of the first part of the poem. They were "glad" (line 1) at the divorce; they "loved it" (line 4) when the mother kicked out the father; they "grinned" (line 5) when the father was fired; they were "tickled" (line 7) when he lost his job, his secretaries, and his daily life. Only at the end of the first section does the speaker (now older but remembering what it was like to be a child) recognize that the mother was responsible for the easy, childish vision of the father's guilt ("She had taught us to take it, to hate you and take it" [line 15]); nevertheless, all sympathy in this part of the poem is with the mother and her children, while all of the imagery is entirely unfavorable to the father. The family reacted to the father's misfortunes the way observers responded to the retreat in disgrace of Richard Nixon from the U.S. presidency. The father seems to have led a luxurious and insensitive life, with lots of support in his office (lines 8–11), fancy clothes (lines 12–14), and decadent lunches (line 10); his artificial identity seemed haunting and frightening (lines 11–14) to the speaker as child.

But in line 17, the poem shifts its focus and tone. The "you" in the poem is now, suddenly, "Father." A bit of sympathy begins to surface for "bums in doorways" (line 18), who begin to seem like victims, too; their bodies are "slugs" (line 19), their suits are made of residual waste (lines 19–20), and their hands are reduced to nearly useless "flippers" (line 21). Their eyes contain fire (line 22), but it is as if they retain only a spark of life in their submerged and dying state. The speaker has not forgotten the cruelty and insensitivity remembered in the first part of the poem, but the blame seems to have shifted somewhat and the father is not the only villain, nor are the mother and children the only victims. Look carefully at how the existence of street people recalls earlier details about the father, how sympathy for his plight is elicited from us, and how the definition of *victim* shifts.

Imagery, words, attitudes, and narrative are different in the two parts of the poem, and the second half carefully qualifies the first, as if to illustrate the more mature and considered attitudes of the speaker in her older years—a qualification of the easy imitation of the earlier years, when the mother's views dominated and set the tone. Change has governed the poem's structure here; differences in age and attitude are supported by an entirely different point of view and frame of reference.

The paradigms (or models) for organizing poems are, finally, not all that different from those of prose. It may be easier to organize something short rather than something long, but the question of intensity becomes comparatively more important in shorter works. Basically, the problem of how to organize one's material is, for the writer, first of all a matter of deciding what kind of thing one wants to create, of having its purposes and effects clearly in mind. That means that every poem will differ somewhat from every other, but it also means that purposeful patterns—narrative, dramatic, descriptive, imitative, or reflective—may help writers organize and develop their ideas. A consciousness of purpose and effect can help the reader see *how* a poem proceeds toward its goal. And seeing how a poem is organized is, in turn, often a good way of seeing where it is going and what its real concerns and purposes may be. Often a poem's organization helps to clarify the particular effects that the poet wishes to generate. In a good poem, means and ends are closely related, and a reader who is a good observer of one will be rewarded with the other.

• • •

### ANONYMOUS

## Sir Patrick Spens

    The king sits in Dumferling toune,[9]
        Drinking the blude-reid[1] wine:
    "O whar will I get guid sailor,
        To sail this ship of mine?"

5   Up and spake an eldern knicht,
        Sat at the king's richt knee:
    "Sir Patrick Spens is the best sailor
        That sails upon the sea."

    The king has written a braid[2] letter
10    And signed it wi' his hand,
    And sent it to Sir Patrick Spens,
        Was walking on the sand.

    The first line that Sir Patrick read,
        A loud lauch[3] lauched he;
15   The next line that Sir Patrick read,
        The tear blinded his ee.[4]

    "O wha is this has done this deed,
        This il deed done to me,
    To send me out this time o' the year,
20    To sail upon the sea?

---

9. Town.   1. Blood-red.   2. Broad: explicit.   3. Laugh.   4. Eye.

"Make haste, make haste, my merry men all,
    Our guid ship sails the morn."
"O say na sae,⁵ my master dear,
    For I fear a deadly storm.

25 "Late, late yestre'en I saw the new moon
    Wi' the auld moon in her arm,
And I fear, I fear, my dear master,
    That we will come to harm."

O our Scots nobles were richt laith⁶
30   To weet their cork-heeled shoon,⁷
But lang owre a'⁸ the play were played
    Their hats they swam aboon.⁹

O lang, lang, may their ladies sit,
    Wi' their fans into their hand,
35 Or ere they see Sir Patrick Spens
    Come sailing to the land.

O lang, lang, may the ladies stand
    Wi' their gold kems¹ in their hair,
Waiting for their ain² dear lords,
40   For they'll see them na mair.

Half o'er, half o'er to Aberdour
    It's fifty fadom deep,
And there lies guid Sir Patrick Spens
    Wi' the Scots lords at his feet.

probably 13th century

- What event is hinted at in line 32 ("Their hats they swam aboon") and in the poem's final stanza? What is the effect of depicting the poem's principal action indirectly?

**WILLIAM CARLOS WILLIAMS**

## *The Dance*

In Brueghel's great picture, The Kermess,³
the dancers go round, they go round and
around, the squeal and the blare and the
tweedle of bagpipes, a bugle and fiddles
5 tipping their bellies (round as the thick-

---

5. Not so.   6. Right loath: very reluctant.
7. To wet their cork-heeled shoes. Cork was expensive, and, therefore, such shoes were a mark of wealth and status.   8. Before all.   9. Their hats swam above them.   1. Combs.   2. Own.
3. A painting by Pieter Brueghel the Elder (1525?–1569).

    sided glasses whose wash they impound)
    their hips and their bellies off balance
    to turn them. Kicking and rolling about
    the Fair Grounds, swinging their butts, those
10  shanks must be sound to bear up under such
    rollicking measures, prance as they dance
    in Brueghel's great picture, The Kermess.

1944

- Why is it appropriate to the subject, a painting, to begin and end the poem with the same line? In what ways is the poem like the dance it depicts?

**EMILY DICKINSON**

## [The Wind begun to knead the Grass—]

    The Wind begun to knead the Grass—
    As Women do a Dough—
    He flung a Hand full at the Plain—
    A Hand full at the Sky—
5  The Leaves unhooked themselves from Trees—
    And started all abroad—
    The Dust did scoop itself like Hands—
    And throw away the Road—
    The Wagons quickened on the Street—
10  The Thunders gossiped low—
    The Lightning showed a Yellow Head—
    And then a livid Toe—
    The Birds put up the Bars to Nests—
    The Cattle flung to Barns—
15  Then came one drop of Giant Rain—
    And then, as if the Hands
    That held the Dams—had parted hold—
    The Waters Wrecked the Sky—
20  But overlooked my Father's House—
    Just Quartering a Tree—

1864

- What happens in this poem's final line? How is this the work of "the Hands"?

## WILLIAM SHAKESPEARE

### [Th'expense of spirit in a waste of shame]

Th'expense of spirit in a waste[4] of shame
Is lust in action; and, till action, lust
Is perjured, murderous, bloody, full of blame,
Savage, extreme, rude, cruel, not to trust;
5 Enjoyed no sooner but despiséd straight:
Past reason hunted; and no sooner had,
Past reason hated, as a swallowed bait,
On purpose laid to make the taker mad:
Mad in pursuit, and in possession so;
10 Had, having, and in quest to have, extreme;
A bliss in proof;[5] and proved, a very woe;
Before, a joy proposed; behind, a dream.
All this the world well knows; yet none knows well
To shun the heaven that leads men to this hell.

1609

- Paraphrase this poem. What emotional stages accompany the carrying out of a violent or lustful act? Is Shakespeare an insightful psychologist? What is his major insight about how lust works?

## CATHY SONG

### Heaven

He thinks when we die we'll go to China.
Think of it—a Chinese heaven
where, except for his blond hair,
the part that belongs to his father,
5 everyone will look like him.
China, that blue flower on the map,
bluer than the sea
his hand must span like a bridge
to reach it.
10 An octave away.

I've never seen it.
It's as if I can't sing that far.
But look—
on the map, this black dot.
15 Here is where we live,

---

4. Using up; also, desert. *Expense:* expending    5. In the act.

             on the pancake plains
             just east of the Rockies,
             on the other side of the clouds.
             A mile above the sea,
20           the air is so thin, you can starve on it.
             No bamboo trees
             But the alpine equivalent,
             reedy aspen with light, fluttering leaves.
             Did a boy in Guangzhou[6] dream of this
25           as his last stop?
             I've heard the trains at night
             whistling past our yards,
             what we've come to own,
             the broken fences, the whiny dog, the rattletrap cars.
30           It's still the wild west,
             mean and grubby,
             the shootouts and fistfights in the back alley.
             With my son the dreamer
             and my daughter, who is too young to walk,
35           I've sat in this spot
             and wondered why here?
             Why in this short life,
             this town, this creek they call a river?

             He had never planned to stay,
40           the boy who helped to build
             the railroads for a dollar a day.[7]
             He had always meant to go back.
             When did he finally know
             that each mile of track led him further away,
45           that he would die in his sleep,
             dispossessed,
             having seen Gold Mountain,[8]
             the icy wind tunneling through it,
             these landlocked, makeshift ghost towns?

50           It must be in the blood,
             this notion of returning.
             It skipped two generations, lay fallow,
             the garden an unmarked grave.
             On a spring sweater day
55           it's as if we remember him.
             I call to the children.
             We can see the mountains
             shimmering blue above the air.
             If you look really hard

---

6. Usually called Canton, a seaport city in southeastern China.
7. The railroads used immigrant day laborers (mostly Chinese) to lay the tracks in the nineteenth century.
8. Chinese term for America, especially common in the nineteenth century.

60 says my son the dreamer,
   leaning out from the laundry's rigging,
   the work shirts fluttering like sails,
   you can see all the way to heaven.

                                        1988

- Who is "He" in this poem's first line? What family history is recounted in the poem?

## STEPHEN DUNN

### Poetry

It makes no difference where one starts,
doesn't every beginning subvert
the tyrannies of time and place?
New Jersey or Vermont, it's the gray zone
5 where I mostly find myself
with little purpose or design.
An apple orchard, an old hotel—
when I introduce them
I feel I've been taken somewhere
10 I've been before; such comfort,
like the sound of consecutive iambs
to the nostalgic ear.
Yet it helps as well
here in the middle, somewhat amused,
15 to have a fast red car
and a winding, country road.
To forget oneself can be an art.
"Frost was wrong about free verse,"
she said to me. "Tear the net down,
20 turn the court into a dance floor."
She happened to be good looking, too,
which seemed to further enliven her remark.
It always makes a difference
how one ends, aren't endings where you
25 shut but don't lock the door?
Strange music beginning,
the dance floor getting crowded now.

                                         1996

- In what way is this poem an *ars poetica*—that is, a declaration of a poet's aims and practices? What is meant by the final two lines?

## PERCY BYSSHE SHELLEY

### Ode to the West Wind

#### I

O wild West Wind, thou breath of Autumn's being,
Thou, from whose unseen presence the leaves dead
Are driven, like ghosts from an enchanter fleeing,

Yellow, and black, and pale, and hectic red,
5  Pestilence-stricken multitudes: O thou,
Who chariotest to their dark wintry bed

The wingéd seeds, where they lie cold and low,
Each like a corpse within its grave, until
Thine azure sister of the Spring shall blow

10  Her clarion[9] o'er the dreaming earth, and fill
(Driving sweet buds like flocks to feed in air)
With living hues and odors plain and hill:

Wild Spirit, which art moving everywhere;
Destroyer and preserver; hear, oh, hear!

#### II

15  Thou on whose stream, mid the steep sky's commotion,
Loose clouds like earth's decaying leaves are shed,
Shook from the tangled boughs of Heaven and Ocean,

Angels[1] of rain and lightning: there are spread
On the blue surface of thine aëry surge,
20  Like the bright hair uplifted from the head

Of some fierce Maenad,[2] even from the dim verge
Of the horizon to the zenith's height,
The locks of the approaching storm. Thou dirge

Of the dying year, to which this closing night
25  Will be the dome of a vast sepulcher,
Vaulted with all thy congregated might

Of vapors, from whose solid atmosphere
Black rain, and fire, and hail will burst: oh, hear!

#### III

Thou who didst waken from his summer dreams
30  The blue Mediterranean, where he lay,
Lulled by the coil of his crystálline streams,

---

9. Trumpet call.  1. Messengers.
2. A frenzied female votary of Dionysus, the Greek god of vegetation and fertility who was supposed to die in the fall and rise again each spring.

Beside a pumice isle in Baiae's bay,[3]
And saw in sleep old palaces and towers
Quivering within the wave's intenser day,

35 All overgrown with azure moss and flowers
So sweet, the sense faints picturing them! Thou
For whose path the Atlantic's level powers

Cleave themselves into chasms, while far below
The sea-blooms and the oozy woods which wear
40 The sapless foliage of the ocean, know

Thy voice, and suddenly grow gray with fear,
And tremble and despoil themselves:[4] oh, hear!

    IV

If I were a dead leaf thou mightest bear;
If I were a swift cloud to fly with thee;
45 A wave to pant beneath thy power, and share

The impulse of thy strength, only less free
Than thou, O uncontrollable! If even
I were as in my boyhood, and could be

The comrade of thy wanderings over Heaven,
50 As then, when to outstrip thy skyey speed
Scarce seemed a vision; I would ne'er have striven

As thus with thee in prayer in my sore need.
Oh, lift me as a wave, a leaf, a cloud!
I fall upon the thorns of life! I bleed!

55 A heavy weight of hours has chained and bowed
One too like thee: tameless, and swift, and proud.

    V

Make me thy lyre, even as the forest is:
What if my leaves are falling like its own!
The tumult of thy mighty harmonies

60 Will take from both a deep, autumnal tone,
Sweet though in sadness. Be thou, Spirit fierce,
My spirit! Be thou me, impetuous one!

Drive my dead thoughts over the universe
Like withered leaves to quicken a new birth!
65 And, by the incantation of this verse,

---

3. Where Roman emperors had erected villas, west of Naples.
4. The vegetation at the bottom of the sea . . . sympathizes with that of the land in the change of seasons [Shelley's note].

Scatter, as from an unextinguished hearth
Ashes and sparks, my words among mankind!
Be through my lips to unawakened earth

The trumpet of a prophecy! O Wind,
70 If Winter comes, can Spring be far behind?

1820

- What attributes of the West Wind does the speaker want his poetry to embody? In what ways is this poem like the wind it describes?

## W. H. AUDEN

### In Memory of W. B. Yeats

*(d. January, 1939)*

I

He disappeared in the dead of winter:
The brooks were frozen, the airports almost deserted,
And snow disfigured the public statues;
The mercury sank in the mouth of the dying day.
5 What instruments we have agree
The day of his death was a dark cold day.

Far from his illness
The wolves ran on through the evergreen forests,
The peasant river was untempted by the fashionable quays;
10 By mourning tongues
The death of the poet was kept from his poems.

But for him it was his last afternoon as himself,
An afternoon of nurses and rumors;
The provinces of his body revolted,
15 The squares of his mind were empty,
Silence invaded the suburbs,
The current of his feeling failed; he became his admirers.

Now he is scattered among a hundred cities
And wholly given over to unfamiliar affections,
20 To find his happiness in another kind of wood
And be punished under a foreign code of conscience.
The words of a dead man
Are modified in the guts of the living.

But in the importance and noise of tomorrow
25 When the brokers are roaring like beasts on the floor of the Bourse,[5]
And the poor have the sufferings to which they are fairly accustomed,

---

5. The Paris stock exchange.

And each in the cell of himself is almost convinced of his freedom,
A few thousand will think of this day
As one thinks of a day when one did something slightly unusual.
What instruments we have agree
The day of his death was a dark cold day.

## II

You were silly like us; your gift survived it all:
The parish of rich women, physical decay,
Yourself. Mad Ireland hurt you into poetry.
Now Ireland has her madness and her weather still,
For poetry makes nothing happen: it survives
In the valley of its making where executives
Would never want to tamper, flows on south
From ranches of isolation and the busy griefs,
Raw towns that we believe and die in; it survives,
A way of happening, a mouth.

## III

Earth, receive an honored guest:
William Yeats is laid to rest.
Let the Irish vessel lie
Emptied of its poetry.

In the nightmare of the dark
All the dogs of Europe bark,
And the living nations wait,
Each sequestered in its hate;

Intellectual disgrace
Stares from every human face,
And the seas of pity lie
Locked and frozen in each eye.

Follow, poet, follow right
To the bottom of the night,
With your unconstraining voice
Still persuade us to rejoice;

With the farming of a verse
Make a vineyard of the curse,
Sing of human unsuccess
In a rapture of distress;

In the deserts of the heart
Let the healing fountain start,
In the prison of his days
Teach the free man how to praise.

1939

- What is meant by "he became his admirers" (line 17)? What meaning is added to line 36 ("For poetry makes nothing happen . . .") by the poem's final three stanzas?

## SUGGESTIONS FOR WRITING

1. How many different "scenes" can you identify in "Sir Patrick Spens"? Write an essay in which you first summarize the story recounted by the poem, and then discuss the methods of storytelling employed by the poem. Consider the transitions from one scene to another and the almost cinematic "fading" effect between scenes?
2. What is the psychology of passion described in Shakespeare's "Th' expense of spirit in a waste of shame"? Write an essay in which you analyze the way the poem dissects the emotions that come before, during, and after a violent or lustful act. What are the "heaven" and "hell" mentioned in the poem's last line?
3. What words and patterns are repeated in the different stanzas of Shelley's "Ode to the West Wind"? What differences are there from stanza to stanza? What "progress" does the poem make? Write an essay in which you discuss the ways that meaning and structure are intertwined in Shelley's poem.
4. Write an essay in which you explore the structure of Auden's "In Memory of W. B. Yeats." What is the logic of the poem? Why does each of the three parts have its own distinct subject, tone, and poetic approach? What subjects does the poem encompass besides the death of Yeats?
5. Pick out any poem you have read in this book that seems particularly effective in the way it is put together. Write an essay in which you consider how the poem is organized—that is, what structural principles it employs. What do the choices of speaker, situation, and setting have to do with the poem's structure? What other artistic decisions contribute to its structure?

# 19 EXTERNAL FORM

Most poems of more than a few lines are divided into **stanzas**—groups of lines divided from other groups by white space on the page. Putting some space between groupings of lines has the effect of sectioning a poem, giving its physical appearance a series of divisions that often mark turns of thought, changes of scene or image, or other shifts in structure or direction. In Donne's "The Flea" (chapter 15), for example, the stanza divisions mark distinct stages in the action: between the first and second stanzas, the speaker stops his companion from killing the flea; between the second and third stanzas, the companion follows through on her intention and kills the flea. In Nemerov's "The Goose Fish" (chapter 18), the stanzas mark stages in the self-perception of the lovers: each stanza is a more or less distinct scene, and the scenes unfold almost like a series of slides. Not all stanzas are quite so neatly patterned as these, but any formal division of a poem into stanzas is important to consider; what appear to be gaps or silences may be structural markers.

Historically, stanzas have most often been organized by patterns of rhyme, and thus stanza divisions have been a visual indicator of patterns in sound. In most traditional stanza forms, the pattern of rhyme is repeated in stanza after stanza throughout the poem, until voice and ear become familiar with the pattern and come to expect and, in a sense, depend on it. The accumulation of pattern allows us to "hear" deviations from the pattern as well, just as we do in music. The rhyme thus becomes an organizational device in the poem—a formal, external determiner of organization, as distinguished from the internal, structural determiners we considered in chapter 18—and ordinarily the metrical patterns stay constant from stanza to stanza. (That is, a formal rhyme scheme is *external* to the unique inner logic of a poem's narrative, descriptive, or discursive design.) In Shelley's "Ode to the West Wind," for example, the first and third lines in each stanza rhyme, and the middle line then rhymes with the first and third lines of the next stanza. (In indicating rhyme, we conventionally use a different letter of the alphabet to represent each rhyme sound; in the following example, if we begin with "being" as *a* and "dead" as *b*, then "fleeing" is also *a*, and "red" and "bed" are *b*.)

> O wild West Wind, thou breath of Autumn's being,　*a*
> Thou, from whose unseen presence the leaves dead　*b*
> Are driven, like ghosts from an enchanter fleeing,　*a*
>
> Yellow, and black, and pale, and hectic red,　*b*
> Pestilence-stricken multitudes: O thou,　*c*
> Who chariotest to their dark wintry bed　*b*

| | |
|---|---|
| The wingéd seeds, where they lie cold and low, | c |
| Each like a corpse within its grave, until | d |
| Thine azure sister of the Spring shall blow | c |

In this stanza form, known as **terza rima,** the stanzas are linked to each other by a common sound: one rhyme sound from each stanza is picked up in the next stanza, and so on to the end of the poem (though sometimes poems in this form have sections that use varied rhyme schemes). This stanza form was used by Dante in *The Divine Comedy,* written in Italian in the early 1300s. Terza rima is not all that common in English because it is a rhyme-rich stanza form—that is, it requires many rhymes, and thus many different rhyme words—and English is, relatively speaking, a rhyme-poor language (not as rich in rhyme possibilities as Italian or French). One reason for this is that English is derived from so many different language families that it has fewer similar word endings than languages that have remained "pure"—that is, more dependent for vocabulary on the roots and patterns found in a single language family.

Many contemporary poets use rhyme sparingly, finding it neither necessary nor appealing, but until the twentieth century the music of rhyme was central to both the sound and the formal conception of most poems. Because poetry was originally an oral art (and its texts not always written down), various kinds of **memory devices** (sometimes called **mnemonic devices**) were built into poems to help reciters remember them. Rhyme was one such device, and most people still find it easier to memorize poetry that rhymes. The simple pleasure of hearing familiar sounds repeated at regular intervals may also help to account for the traditional popularity of rhyme, and perhaps plain habit (for both poets and hearers) had a lot to do with why rhyme flourished for so many centuries in so many languages as an expected feature of poetry. Rhyme also helps to give poetry a special aural quality that distinguishes it from prose, a significant advantage in ages that worry about decorum and propriety and are anxious to preserve a strong sense of poetic tradition. Some ages have been very concerned that poetry should not in any way be mistaken for prose or made to serve prosaic functions, and the literary critics and theorists in those ages made extraordinary efforts to emphasize the distinctions between poetry, which was thought to be artistically superior, and prose, which was thought to be primarily utilitarian. An elitist pride and a fear that an expanded reading public could ultimately dilute the possibilities of traditional art forms have been powerful cultural forces in Western civilization, and if such forces were not themselves responsible for creating rhyme in poetry, they at least helped to preserve a sense of its necessity. But rhyme and other patterns of repeated sounds are also important, for countless historical and cultural reasons, to non-Western languages and poetic traditions as well.

There are at least two other reasons for rhyme. One is complex and hard to state justly without long explanations. It involves traditional ideas about the symmetrical relationship of different aspects of the world and the function of poetry to reflect the universe as human learning has understood it. Many cultures (especially in earlier centuries) have assumed that rhyme was proper to verse, perhaps even essential. Poets in these ages and cultures would have felt themselves eccentric or even foolish to compose poems any other way. Some English poets (especially in the Renaissance) did experiment—often very successfully—with **blank verse** (that is, verse that did not rhyme but that nevertheless had strict metrical requirements), but the cultural pressure for rhyme was almost constant. Why? As noted above, custom or habit may account in part for the assumption that rhyme was necessary, but there was probably more to it than that. Rather, the poets' sense that poetry was an imitation of larger relationships in the universe made it seem natural to use rhyme to represent or re-create a sense of pattern, harmony, correspondence, symmetry, and order. The sounds of poetry were thus, they reasoned, reminders of the harmonious cosmos, of the music of the spheres that animated the planets, the processes of nature, the interrelationship of all created things and beings. Probably no poet ever thought, "I shall now tunefully emulate the harmony of God's carefully ordered universe," but the tendency to use rhyme and other repetitions or re-echoings of sound (such as **alliteration** or **assonance**) nevertheless stemmed ultimately from basic assumptions about how the universe worked. In a modern world increasingly perceived as fragmented and chaotic, there is less of a tendency to assert a sense of harmony and symmetry. It would be far too easy and too mechanical, of course, to think that rhyme in a poem specifically means that the poet has a firm sense of cosmic order, and that an unrhymed poem testifies to chaos, but cultural assumptions do affect the expectations of both poets and readers, and cultural tendencies create a kind of pressure on the individual creator. If you take a survey course (or a series of related "period" courses) in English or American literature, you will readily notice the diminishing sense that rhyme is an indispensable aspect of poetry. And similarly, other linguistic and national traditions vary usages in different times, depending on their own evolving philosophical and cultural assumptions.

One other reason for using rhyme is that it provides a kind of discipline for the poet, a way of harnessing poetic talents and keeping a rein on the imagination, so that the results are ordered, controlled, put into some kind of meaningful and recognizable form. Robert Frost said that writing poems without rhyme or regular meter was pointless, like playing tennis without a net. Writing good poetry does require a lot of discipline, and Frost speaks for many (perhaps most) traditional poets in suggesting that rhyme or rhythm can be a major source of that discipline. But neither one is the only possible source, and more recent poets have usually felt they would rather play by new rules or invent their own as they go along; they have, therefore, sought their sources of discipline elsewhere, preferring the sparer tones that unrhymed poetry provides. It is not that contemporary poets cannot think of rhyme words or that they do not care about the sounds of their poetry; rather, many recent poets have consciously decided not to work with rhyme and to use instead other aural and metrical devices and other strategies for organizing stanzas, just as they have chosen to work with experimental and variable rhythms instead of writing necessarily in the traditional English meters. Nevertheless, many modern poets have continued to write rhymed verse successfully in a more or less traditional way, finding that, in fact, rhyme can be a useful spur to the imagination—the search for a rhyme word can often lead to unexpected discoveries. It might well be, for example, that the need to find a rhyme for "dirt" led Theodore Roethke to the wonderful final line of "My Papa's Waltz" (chapter 16): "Still clinging to your shirt." A free-verse poet might have judged the poem complete after the previous line: "Then waltzed me off to bed."

*Concentration is the very essence of poetry.*
—AMY LOWELL

The amount and density of rhyme vary widely in stanza and verse forms, from elaborate and intricate patterns of rhyme to more casual or spare sound repetitions. The **Spenserian stanza,** for example, is even more rhyme-rich than terza rima, using only three rhyme sounds in nine rhymed lines, as in Keats's *The Eve of St. Agnes:*

> Her falt'ring hand upon the balustrade, *a*
> Old Angela was feeling for the stair, *b*
> When Madeline, St. Agnes' charmèd maid, *a*
> Rose, like a missioned spirit, unaware: *b*
> With silver taper's light, and pious care, *b*
> She turned, and down the agèd gossip led *c*
> To a safe level matting. Now prepare, *b*
> Young Porphyro, for gazing on that bed; *c*
> She comes, she comes again, like ring dove frayed and fled *c*

On the other hand, the **ballad stanza** (as in "Sir Patrick Spens") has only one set of rhymes in four lines; lines 1 and 3 in each stanza do not rhyme at all:

> The king sits in Dumferling toune, *a*
> Drinking the blude-reid wine: *b*
> "O whar will I get guid sailor, *c*
> To sail this ship of mine?" *b*

Most stanza forms use a metrical pattern as well as a rhyme scheme. Terza rima, for example, involves **iambic meter** (unstressed and stressed syllables alternating regularly), and each line has five beats (**pentameter**). Most of the Spenserian stanza (the first eight lines) is also in iambic pentameter, but the ninth line in each stanza has one extra foot (thus, the last line is in iambic hexameter). The ballad stanza, also iambic, as are most English stanza and verse forms, alternates three-beat and four-beat lines; lines 1 and 3 are unrhymed iambic tetrameter (four beats), and lines 2 and 4 are rhymed iambic trimeter (three beats).

## THE SONNET

The **sonnet,** one of the most persistent verse forms, originated in the Middle Ages as a prominent form in Italian and French poetry. It dominated English poetry in the late sixteenth and early seventeenth centuries and then was revived several times from the early-nineteenth century onward. Except for some early experiments with length, the sonnet has always been fourteen lines long, and it usually is written in iambic pentameter. It is most often printed as if it were a *single* stanza, although it actually has several formal divisions that represent its rhyme schemes and formal breaks. As a popular and traditional verse form in English for more than four centuries, the sonnet has been surprisingly resilient even in ages that largely reject rhyme. It continues to attract a variety of poets, including (curiously) radical and even revolutionary poets, who find its formal demands, discipline, and fixed outcome very appealing. Its uses, although quite varied, can be illustrated fairly precisely. As a verse form, the sonnet is contained, compact, demanding; whatever it does, it must do concisely and quickly. To be effective, it must take advantage of the possibilities inherent in its shortness and its relative rigidity. It is best suited to intensity of feeling and concentration of expression. Not too surprisingly, one subject it frequently discusses is confinement itself.

## WILLIAM WORDSWORTH

### Nuns Fret Not

    Nuns fret not at their convent's narrow room;
    And hermits are contented with their cells;
    And students with their pensive citadels;
    Maids at the wheel, the weaver at his loom,
5  Sit blithe and happy; bees that soar for bloom,
    High as the highest Peak of Furness-fells,[1]
    Will murmur by the hour in foxglove bells:
    In truth the prison, unto which we doom
    Ourselves, no prison is: and hence for me,
10 In sundry moods,'twas pastime to be bound
    Within the sonnet's scanty plot of ground;
    Pleased if some souls (for such there needs must be)
    Who have felt the weight of too much liberty,
    Should find brief solace there, as I have found.

                                        1807

    Most sonnets are structured according to one of two principles of division. On one principle, the sonnet divides into three units of four lines each and a final unit of two lines, and sometimes the line spacing reflects this division. On the other, the fundamental break is between the first eight lines (called an octave) and the last six (called a sestet). The 4-4-4-2 sonnet is usually called the **English** or **Shakespearean sonnet,** and ordinarily its rhyme scheme reflects the structure: the scheme of *abab cdcd efef gg* is the classic one, but many variations from that pattern still reflect the basic 4-4-4-2 division. The 8-6 sonnet is usually called the **Italian** or **Petrarchan sonnet** (the Italian poet Petrarch was an early master of this structure), and its "typical" rhyme scheme is *abbaabba cdecde*, although it too produces many variations that still reflect the basic division into two parts, an **octave** and a **sestet**.

    The two kinds of sonnet structures are useful for two different sorts of argument. The 4-4-4-2 structure works very well for constructing a poem that wants to make a three-step argument (with a quick summary at the end), or for setting up brief, cumulative images. "That time of year thou mayst in me behold" (chapter 16), for example, uses the 4-4-4-2 structure to mark the progressive steps toward death and the parting of friends by using three distinct images, then summarizing. "Let me not to the marriage of true minds" (page 827) works very similarly, following the kind of organization that in chapter 18 was referred to as the 1-2-3 structure—and doing it compactly and economically.

    Here, on the other hand, is a poem that uses the 8-6 pattern:

---

1. Mountains in England's Lake District, where Wordsworth lived.

HENRY CONSTABLE

## [My lady's presence makes the roses red]

My lady's presence makes the roses red,
Because to see her lips they blush for shame.
The lily's leaves, for envy, pale became,
And her white hands in them this envy bred.
5 The marigold the leaves abroad doth spread,
Because the sun's and her power is the same.
The violet of purple colour came,
Dyed in the blood she made my heart to shed.
In brief: all flowers from her their virtue take;
10 From her sweet breath their sweet smells do proceed;
The living heat which her eyebeams doth make
Warmeth the ground and quickeneth the seed.
The rain, wherewith she watereth the flowers,
Falls from mine eyes, which she dissolves in showers.

1594

    The first eight lines argue that the lady's presence is responsible for the color of all of nature's flowers, and the final six lines summarize and extend that argument to smells and heat—and finally to the rain that the lady draws from the speaker's eyes. That kind of two-part structure, in which the octave states a proposition or generalization and the sestet provides a particularization or application of it, has a variety of uses. The final lines may, for example, reverse the first eight and achieve a paradox or irony in the poem, or the poem may nearly balance two comparable arguments. Basically, the 8-6 structure lends itself to poems with two points to make, or to those that wish to make one point and then illustrate it.

    Sometimes the neat and precise structure is altered—either slightly, as in Wordsworth's "Nuns Fret Not," above (where the 8-6 structure is more of an 8½-5½ or 7-7 structure), or more radically as particular needs or effects may demand. And the two basic structures certainly do not define all the structural possibilities within a fourteen-line poem, even if they do suggest the most traditional ways of taking advantage of the sonnet's compact and well-kept container.

    During the Renaissance, poets regularly employed the sonnet for love poems, and many modern sonnets continue to be about love or private life. And many continue to use a personal, apparently open and sincere tone. But poets often find the sonnet's compact form and rigid demands equally useful for many varieties of subject, theme, and tone. Besides love, sonnets often treat other subjects: politics, philosophy, discovery. And tones vary widely too, from the anger and remorse of "Th' expense of spirit in a waste of shame" (chapter 18) and righteous outrage of "On the Late Massacre in Piedmont" (chapter 15) to the tender awe of "How Do I Love Thee?" (page 811). Many poets seem to take the kind of comfort Wordsworth describes in the careful limits of the form, finding in its two basic variations (the English sonnet, such as "That time of year," and the Italian sonnet, such as "On First Looking into Chapman's Homer" [chapter 22]) a sufficiency of ways to organize their materials into coherent structures.

• • •

### DANTE GABRIEL ROSSETTI

## A Sonnet Is a Moment's Monument

    A Sonnet is a moment's monument—
      Memorial from the Soul's eternity
      To one dead deathless hour. Look that it be,
    Whether for lustral[2] rite or dire portent,
5   Of its own arduous fullness reverent.
      Carve it in ivory or in ebony,
      As Day or Night may rule; and let Time see
    Its flowering crest impearled and orient.[3]

    A Sonnet is a coin: its face reveals
10    The soul—its converse, to what Power 'tis due—
    Whether for tribute to the august appeals
      Of Life or dower in Love's high retinue,
    It serve; or 'mid the dark wharf's cavernous breath,
    In Charon's palm it pay the toll to Death.[4]

                           1881

- In Rossetti's metaphor comparing the sonnet to a coin (lines 9–14), what are the two "sides" of a sonnet?

### JOHN KEATS

## On the Sonnet

    If by dull rhymes our English must be chained,
    And like Andromeda,[5] the sonnet sweet
    Fettered, in spite of painèd loveliness,
    Let us find, if we must be constrained,
5   Sandals more interwoven and complete

---

2. Purificatory.   3. Sparkling.
4. In classical myth, Charon was the boatman who rowed the souls of the dead across the river Styx. Ancient Greeks put a small coin in the hand of the dead to pay his fee.
5. According to Greek myth, Andromeda was chained to a rock so that she would be devoured by a sea monster. She was rescued by Perseus, who married her. When she died she was placed among the stars.

To fit the naked foot of Poesy:[6]
Let us inspect the lyre, and weigh the stress
Of every chord,[7] and see what may be gained
By ear industrious, and attention meet;
10 Misers of sound and syllable, no less
Than Midas[8] of his coinage, let us be
Jealous of dead leaves in the bay-wreath crown;[9]
So, if we may not let the Muse be free,
She will be bound with garlands of her own.

1819

- What is the rhyme scheme of this poem? How well does this unusual structure meet the challenge implied by the poem?

## GWENDOLYN BROOKS

### *First Fight. Then Fiddle.*

First fight. Then fiddle. Ply the slipping string
With feathery sorcery; muzzle the note
With hurting love; the music that they wrote
Bewitch, bewilder. Qualify to sing
5 Threadwise. Devise no salt, no hempen thing
For the dear instrument to bear. Devote
The bow to silks and honey. Be remote
A while from malice and from murdering.
But first to arms, to armor. Carry hate
10 In front of you and harmony behind.
Be deaf to music and to beauty blind.
Win war. Rise bloody, maybe not too late
For having first to civilize a space
Wherein to play your violin with grace.

1949

- After advising "First Fight. Then fiddle," the speaker discusses first music, then conflict. Why do you think the poet has arranged her argument this way?

---

6. In a letter that contained this sonnet, Keats expressed impatience with the traditional Petrarchan and Shakespearean sonnet forms: "I have been endeavoring to discover a better sonnet stanza than we have."
7. Lyre string; *Meet:* proper.
8. The legendary king of Phrygia who asked, and got, the power to turn all he touched to gold.
9. The bay tree was sacred to Apollo, god of poetry, and bay wreaths came to symbolize true poetic achievement. The withering of the bay tree is sometimes considered an omen of death. *Jealous:* suspiciously watchful.

**EMMA LAZARUS**

## The New Colossus[1]

Not like the brazen giant of Greek fame,[2]
With conquering limbs astride from land to land;
Here at our sea-washed, sunset gates shall stand
A mighty woman with a torch, whose flame
5 Is the imprisoned lightning, and her name
Mother of Exiles. From her beacon-hand
Glows world-wide welcome; her mild eyes command
The air-bridged harbor that twin cities[3] frame.
"Keep ancient lands, your storied pomp!" cries she
10 With silent lips. "Give me your tired, your poor,
Your huddled masses yearning to breathe free,
The wretched refuse of your teeming shore.
Send these, the homeless, tempest-tost to me,
I lift my lamp beside the golden door!"

November 1883

- What comparison is the speaker making between the old and new worlds?

**ROBERT FROST**

## Range-Finding

The battle rent a cobweb diamond-strung
And cut a flower beside a groundbird's nest
Before it stained a single human breast.
The stricken flower bent double and so hung.
5 And still the bird revisited her young.
A butterfly its fall had dispossessed,
A moment sought in air his flower of rest,
Then slightly stooped to it and fluttering clung.
On the bare upland pasture there had spread
10 O'ernight 'twixt mullein stalks a wheel of thread
And straining cables wet with silver dew.
A sudden passing bullet shook it dry.
The indwelling spider ran to greet the fly,
But finding nothing, sullenly withdrew.

1916

- What is the "battle" of line 1? What is the poem's actual subject?

---

1. The poem was written to commemorate the opening of the Statue of Liberty, in New York harbor.
2. The Colossus of Rhodes, one of the seven wonders of the ancient world, a 100-foot statue of Helios, the sun god.   3. Manhattan and Brooklyn.

## WILLIAM WORDSWORTH

### London, 1802

Milton! thou should'st be living at this hour:
England hath need of thee: she is a fen
Of stagnant waters: altar, sword, and pen,
Fireside, the heroic wealth of hall and bower,
5 Have forfeited their ancient English dower
Of inward happiness. We are selfish men;
Oh! raise us up, return to us again;
And give us manners, virtue, freedom, power.
Thy soul was like a star, and dwelt apart:
10 Thou hadst a voice whose sound was like the sea:
Pure as the naked heavens, majestic, free,
So didst thou travel on life's common way,
In cheerful godliness; and yet thy heart
The lowliest duties on herself did lay.

1802

- What is Wordsworth asserting about the power of poetry in this sonnet? Why do you think he chose the sonnet form for this poem?

## JOHN MILTON

### [When I consider how my light is spent]

When I consider how my light is spent,
   Ere half my days, in this dark world and wide,
   And that one talent which is death to hide[4]
Lodged with me useless, though my soul more bent
5 To serve therewith my Maker, and present
   My true account, lest he returning chide;
   "Doth God exact day-labor, light denied?"
I fondly ask; but Patience to prevent[5]
That murmur, soon replies, "God doth not need
10 Either man's work or his own gifts; who best
   Bear his mild yoke, they serve him best. His state
Is kingly. Thousands at his bidding speed
   And post o'er land and ocean without rest:
   They also serve who only stand and wait."

1652?

- Paraphrase the speaker's question and Patience's reply. Does knowing that Milton was blind alter your interpretation of this poem?

---

4. In the parable of the talents (Matthew 25), the servants who earned interest on their master's money (his talents) while he was away were called "good and faithful"; the one who simply hid the money and then returned it was condemned and sent away.  5. Forestall. *Fondly:* foolishly.

**ELIZABETH BARRETT BROWNING**

## [When our two souls stand up]

When our two souls stand up erect and strong,
Face to face, silent, drawing nigh and nigher,
Until the lengthening wings break into fire
At either curvéd point,—what bitter wrong
5 Can the earth do to us, that we should not long
Be here contented? Think. In mounting higher,
The angels would press on us and aspire
To drop some golden orb of perfect song
Into our deep, dear silence. Let us stay
10 Rather on earth, Belovéd,—where the unfit
Contrarious moods of men recoil away
And isolate pure spirits, and permit
A place to stand and love in for a day,
With darkness and the death-hour rounding it.
                                                1897

- Explain the metaphor of this poem's first four lines. What will cause "the lengthening wings" to "break into fire"?

**CHRISTINA ROSSETTI**

## In an Artist's Studio

One face looks out from all his canvases,
   One selfsame figure sits or walks or leans;
   We found her hidden just behind those screens,
That mirror gave back all her loveliness.
5 A queen in opal or in ruby dress,
   A nameless girl in freshest summer-greens,
   A saint, an angel—every canvass means
The same one meaning, neither more nor less.
He feeds upon her face by day and night,
10   And she with true kind eyes looks back on him
Fair as the moon and joyful as the light:
   Not wan with waiting, not with sorrow dim;
Not as she is, but was when hope shone bright;
   Not as she is, but as she fills his dream.
                                                1856

- What do you think is "The same one meaning" the speaker sees in every portrait in the studio?

### Cobwebs

    It is a land with neither night nor day,
      Nor heat nor cold, nor any wind, nor rain,
      Nor hills nor valleys; but one even plain
    Stretches thro' long unbroken miles away:
5  While thro' the sluggish air a twilight grey
      Broodeth; no moons or seasons wax and wane,
      No ebb and flow are there along the main,
    No bud-time no leaf-falling, there for aye[6]:—
    No ripple on the sea, no shifting sand,
10  No beat of wings to stir the stagnant space,
    No pulse of life thro' all the loveless land:
    And loveless sea; no trace of days before,
      No guarded home, no toil-won resting place,
    No future hope no fear for evermore

1855

- What is the "land" that is described throughout this poem? Why do you think the poem is entitled "Cobwebs"?

### EDNA ST. VINCENT MILLAY

### [What lips my lips have kissed, and where, and why]

    What lips my lips have kissed, and where, and why,
    I have forgotten, and what arms have lain
    Under my head till morning; but the rain
    Is full of ghosts tonight, that tap and sigh
5  Upon the glass and listen for reply,
    And in my heart there stirs a quiet pain
    For unremembered lads that not again
    Will turn to me at midnight with a cry.
    Thus in the winter stands the lonely tree,

---

6. Forever.

10  Nor knows what birds have vanished one by one,
Yet knows its boughs more silent than before:
I cannot say what loves have come and gone;
I only know that summer sang in me
A little while, that in me sings no more.

1923

- What are the poem's principal parts? Why does the Petrarchan model suit this sonnet?

## [I shall forget you presently, my dear]

I shall forget you presently, my dear,
So make the most of this, your little day,
Your little month, your little half a year,
Ere I forget, or die, or move away,
5  And we are done forever; by and by
I shall forget you, as I said, but now,
If you entreat me with your loveliest lie
I will protest you with my favorite vow.
I would indeed that love were longer-lived,
10  And oaths were not so brittle as they are,
But so it is, and nature has contrived
To struggle on without a break thus far,—
Whether or not we find what we are seeking
Is idle, biologically speaking.

1922

- What is the meaning of this poem's final couplet? What does it indicate about the poem's tone?

## GWEN HARWOOD

### In the Park

She sits in the park. Her clothes are out of date.
Two children whine and bicker, tug her skirt.
A third draws aimless patterns in the dirt.
Someone she loved once passes by—too late
5  to feign indifference to that casual nod.
"How nice," et cetera. "Time holds great surprises."
From his neat head unquestionably rises
a small balloon . . . "but for the grace of God . . ."

They stand a while in flickering light, rehearsing
10 the children's names and birthdays. "It's so sweet
to hear their chatter, watch them grow and thrive,"
she says to his departing smile. Then, nursing
the youngest child, sits staring at her feet.
To the wind she says, "They have eaten me alive."

1963

- What is the implication of the "small balloon" that rises from the head of the man who passes by?

**HENRY CONSTABLE**

[*Wonder it is, and pity*]

Wonder it is, and pity is, that she
in whom all beauty's treasure we may find,
that may enrich the body and the mind,
towards the poor should use no charity.
5 My love is gone a-begging unto thee,
and if that Beauty had not been more kind
than Pity, long ere this he had been pined;
but Beauty is content his food to be.
Oh pity have, when such poor orphans beg
10 Love (naked boy) hath nothing on his back;
and though he wanteth neither arm nor leg,
yet maimed he is, sith[7] he his sight doth lack.
And yet (though blind) he beauty can behold,
and yet (though naked) he feels more heat than cold.

1592

- Explain the poem's metaphorical representation of Love.

---

7. Since.

## SIR PHILIP SIDNEY

### [Come sleep! Oh sleep]

Come sleep! Oh sleep, the certain knot of peace,
The bating place[8] of wit, the balm of woe,
The poor man's wealth, the prisoner's release,
The indifferent judge between the high and low;
5 With shield of proof[9] shield me from out the press
Of those fierce darts Despair at me doth throw;
Oh make in me those civil wars to cease;
I will good tribute pay, if thou do so.
Take thou of me smooth pillows, sweetest bed,
10 A chamber deaf to noise and blind to light,
A rosy garland and a weary head;
And if these things, as being thine by right,
Move not thy heavy grace, thou shalt in me,
Livelier than elsewhere, Stella's image see.[1]

1591

- What is the speaker's argument? Why is the speaker invoking sleep?

## BARTHOLOMEW GRIFFIN

### Care-charmer Sleep

Care-charmer sleep, sweet ease in restless misery,
The captive's liberty, and his freedom's song,
Balm of the bruised heart, man's chief felicity,
Brother of quiet death, when life is too, too long!
5 A comedy it is, and now an history—
What is not sleep unto the feeble mind!
It easeth him that toils and him that's sorry,
It makes the deaf to hear, to see the blind.
Ungentle sleep, thou helpest all but me,
10 For when I sleep my soul is vexed most.
It is Fidessa[2] that doth master thee;
If she approach, alas, they power is lost.
But here she is. See, how he runs amain![3]
I fear at night he will not come again.

1596

- Why does the speaker call sleep "Ungentle"?

---

8. Resting point in the course of a journey.  9. Armor of proven strength; *Press:* Crowd.
1. This poem is part of a cycle of sonnets addressed to Stella ("star") by the speaker, Astrophel ("star-lover").
2. The poem is part of a cycle of sonnets addressed to Fidessa ("faith").  3. In haste.

## WILLIAM SHAKESPEARE

### [My mistress' eyes are nothing like the sun]

My mistress' eyes are nothing like the sun;
Coral is far more red than her lips' red;
If snow be white, why then her breasts are dun;[4]
If hairs be wires, black wires grow on her head.
5 I have seen roses damasked[5] red and white,
But no such roses see I in her cheeks;
And in some perfumes is there more delight
Than in the breath that from my mistress reeks.
I love to hear her speak, yet well I know
10 That music hath a far more pleasing sound;
I grant I never saw a goddess go;[6]
My mistress, when she walks, treads on the ground.
And yet, by heaven, I think my love as rare
As any she belied with false compare.

1609

- In addition to the speaker's mistress, what might be another subject of this poem?

## DIANE ACKERMAN

### Sweep Me through Your Many-Chambered Heart

Sweep me through your many-chambered heart
if you like, or leave me here, flushed
amid the sap-ooze and blossom: one more dish
in the banquet called April, or think me hard-
5 won all your days full of women. Weeks
later, till I felt your arms around
me like a shackle, heard all the sundown
wizardries the fired body speaks.
Tell me why, if it was no more than this,
10 the unmuddled tumble, the renegade kiss,
today, rapt in a still life and unaware,
my paintbrush dropped like an amber hawk;
thinking I'd heard your footfall on the stair,
I listened, heartwise, for the knock.

1978

- How does the poet make the poem seem off-balance? How is this technique appropriate to the speaker's state of mind?

4. Mouse-colored. 5. Variegated. 6. Walk.

HELEN CHASIN

## Joy Sonnet in a Random Universe

Sometimes I'm happy: la la la la la la la
la la la la la la la la la la la la la la la la
la la la la. Tum tum ti tum. La la la la la la
la la la la la la la la la la la la la la la la la.
5 Hey nonny nonny. La la la la la la la la la
la la la la la la la la la la. Vo do di o do.
Poo poo pi doo. La la la la la la la la la la
la la la la la la la la la la la la la la la la
la la. Whack a doo. La la la la la la la. Sh-
10 boom, sh-boom. La la la la la la la la la la
la la la la la la la la la la la la la la la la
la la. Dum di dum. La la la la la la la la la
la la la la la la la la la. Tra la la. Tra la la
la la la la la la la la la la. Yeah yeah yeah.

1968

- Is Chasin's poem a sonnet? Why or why not?

BILLY COLLINS

## Sonnet

All we need is fourteen lines, well, thirteen now,
and after this one just a dozen
to launch a little ship on love's storm-tossed seas,
then only ten more left like rows of beans.
5 How easily it goes unless you get Elizabethan
and insist the iambic bongos must be played
and rhymes positioned at the ends of lines,
one for every station of the cross.
But hang on here while we make the turn
10 into the final six where all will be resolved,
where longing and heartache will find an end,
where Laura will tell Petrarch to put down his pen,
take off those crazy medieval tights,
blow out the lights, and come at last to bed.

1999

- In what respects is Collins's poem a traditional sonnet? In what respects is it not?

## STANZA FORMS

Many stanza forms are represented in this book. Some have names, because they have been used over and over by different poets. Others (such as Poe's stanza form for "The Raven" [chapter 17]) were invented for a particular use in a particular poem and may never be repeated again. Most traditional stanzas are based on rhyme schemes, but some use other kinds of predictable sound patterns; early English poetry, for example, used alliteration to construct a balance between the first and second half of each line (see Earle Birney's "Anglosaxon Street" [later in this chapter] for a modern imitation of this principle). Sometimes, especially when poets interact with each other within a strong community, highly elaborate *verse forms* have been developed that set up stanzas as part of a scheme for the whole poem. The poets of medieval Provence were especially inventive, subtle, and elaborate in their construction of complex verse forms, some of which have been copied by poets ever since. The **sestina,** for example, depends on the measured repetition of words (rather than just sounds) in particular places; see, for example, Bishop's "Sestina" (later in this chapter) and try to decipher the pattern. (There are also double and even triple sestinas, tough tests of a poet's ingenuity.) And the **villanelle,** another Provençal form, depends on the patterned repetition of whole lines (see Dylan Thomas's "Do Not Go Gentle into That Good Night" [next page]). Different cultures and different languages develop their own patterns and measures—not all poetries are parallel to English poetry—and they vary from age to age as well as nation to nation.

You can probably deduce the principles involved in each of the following stanza or verse forms by looking carefully at a poem that uses it; if you have trouble, look at the definitions in the glossary.

| | | |
|---|---|---|
| **heroic couplet** | "Sound and Sense" | chapter 17 |
| **tetrameter couplet** | "To His Coy Mistress" | chapter 15 |
| **limerick** | "There was a young girl from St. Paul" | chapter 17 |
| **free verse** | "Dirge" | chapter 17 |
| **blank verse** | from *Paradise Lost* | chapter 16 |

What are stanza forms good for? What use is it to recognize them? Why do poets bother? Matters discussed in this chapter so far have suggested two reasons: (1) Breaks between stanzas provide convenient pauses for reader and writer, something roughly equivalent to paragraphs in prose. The eye thus picks up the places where some kind of pause or break or change of focus occurs. (2) Poets sometimes use stanza forms, as they do rhyme itself, as a discipline: writing in a certain kind of stanza form imposes a shape on the act of imagination. But visual spaces and unexpected print divisions also mean that poems sometimes *look* unusual and require special visual attention, attention that does not always follow the logic of sound patterns or syntax. After the following poems illustrating some common stanza forms, you will find a section on poems that employ special configurations and shapes, using spaces and print in other ways, to establish their meanings and effects.

• • •

### DYLAN THOMAS
## Do Not Go Gentle into That Good Night[1]

    Do not go gentle into that good night,
    Old age should burn and rave at close of day;
    Rage, rage against the dying of the light.

    Though wise men at their end know dark is right,
5  Because their words had forked no lightning they
    Do not go gentle into that good night.

    Good men, the last wave by, crying how bright
    Their frail deeds might have danced in a green bay,
    Rage, rage against the dying of the light.

10 Wild men who caught and sang the sun in flight,
    And learn, too late, they grieved it on its way,
    Do not go gentle into that good night.

    Grave men, near death, who see with blinding sight
    Blind eyes could blaze like meteors and be gay,
15 Rage, rage against the dying of the light.

    And you, my father, there on the sad height,
    Curse, bless, me now with your fierce tears, I pray.
    Do not go gentle into that good night.
    Rage, rage against the dying of the light.

                         1952

- What do the wise, good, wild, and grave men have in common with the speaker's father? Why do you think Thomas chose such a strict form, the villanelle, for such an emotionally charged subject?

### MARIANNE MOORE
## Poetry

    I, too, dislike it: there are things that are important beyond all this
      fiddle.
    Reading it, however, with a perfect contempt for it, one discovers in
      it after all, a place for the genuine.
      Hands that can grasp, eyes
5     that can dilate, hair that can rise
        if it must, these things are important not because a

---

1. Written during the final illness of the poet's father.

high-sounding interpretation can be put upon them but because they are
useful. When they become so derivative as to become unintelligible,
the same thing may be said for all of us, that we
10    do not admire what
we cannot understand: the bat
holding on upside down or in quest of something to

eat, elephants pushing, a wild horse taking a roll, a tireless wolf under
a tree, the immovable critic twitching his skin like a horse that feels a
flea, the base-
15    ball fan, the statistician—
nor is it valid
to discriminate against "business documents and

school-books"[2]; all these phenomena are important. One must make a
distinction
however: when dragged into prominence by half poets, the result is not
poetry,
20    nor till the poets among us can be
"literalists of
the imagination"[3]—above
insolence and triviality and can present

for inspection, "imaginary gardens with real toads in them," shall we
have
25    it. In the meantime, if you demand on the one hand,
the raw material of poetry in
all its rawness and
that which is on the other hand
genuine, you are interested in poetry.

1921

- Is this poem more about the reading or the writing of poetry? What does the poem suggest is the relationship between poetry and "the genuine" (line 3)?

---

2. *Diary of Tolstoy* (Dutton), p. 84. "Where the boundary between prose and poetry lies, I shall never be able to understand. The question is raised in manuals of style, yet the answer to it lies beyond me. Poetry is verse: Prose is not verse. Or else poetry is everything with the exception of business documents and school books" [Moore's note].

3. Yeats, *Ideas of Good and Evil* (A. H. Bullen, 1903), p. 182. "The limitation of [William Blake's] view was from the very intensity of his vision; he was a too literal realist of imagination, as others are of nature; and because he believed that the figures seen by the mind's eye, when exalted by inspiration, were 'eternal existences,' symbols of divine essences, he hated every grace of style that might obscure their lineaments" [Moore's note].

**ELIZABETH BISHOP**

## *Sestina*

September rain falls on the house.
In the failing light, the old grandmother
sits in the kitchen with the child
beside the Little Marvel Stove,
5 reading the jokes from the almanac,
laughing and talking to hide her tears.

She thinks that her equinoctial tears
and the rain that beats on the roof of the house
were both foretold by the almanac,
10 but only known to a grandmother.
The iron kettle sings on the stove.
She cuts some bread and says to the child,

*It's time for tea now;* but the child
is watching the teakettle's small hard tears
15 dance like mad on the hot black stove,
the way the rain must dance on the house.
Tidying up, the old grandmother
hangs up the clever almanac

on its string. Birdlike, the almanac
20 hovers half open above the child,
hovers above the old grandmother
and her teacup full of dark brown tears.
She shivers and says she thinks the house
feels chilly, and puts more wood in the stove.

25 *It was to be,* says the Marvel Stove.
*I know what I know,* says the almanac.
With crayons the child draws a rigid house
and a winding pathway. Then the child
puts in a man with buttons like tears
30 and shows it proudly to the grandmother.

But secretly, while the grandmother
busies herself about the stove,
the little moons fall down like tears
from between the pages of the almanac
35 into the flower bed the child
has carefully placed in the front of the house.

*Time to plant tears,* says the almanac.
The grandmother sings to the marvellous stove
and the child draws another inscrutable house.

1965

- Try to derive from "Sestina" the "rules" that govern the sestina form. Why do you think Bishop chose this form for her poem?

ISHMAEL REED

## *beware : do not read this poem*

    tonite , thriller was
    abt an ol woman , so vain she
    surrounded herself w/
      many mirrors
    it got so bad that finally she
5  locked herself indoors & her
    whole life became the
      mirrors

    one day the villagers broke
10 into her house , but she was too
    swift for them . she disappeared
      into a mirror

    each tenant who bought the house
    after that , lost a loved one to
15  the ol woman in the mirror :
      first a little girl
      then a young woman
      then the young woman/s husband

    the hunger of this poem is legendary
20 it has taken in many victims
    back off from this poem
    it has drawn in yr feet
    back off from this poem
    it has drawn in yr legs
25 back off from this poem
    it is a greedy mirror
    you are into this poem . from
      the waist down
    nobody can hear you can they ?
30 this poem has had you up to here
      belch
    this poem aint got no manners
    you cant call out frm this poem
    relax now & go w/ this poem
35 move & roll on to this poem
    do not resist this poem
    this poem has yr eyes
    this poem has his head

this poem has his arms
40 this poem has his fingers
this poem has his fingertips
this poem is the reader & the
reader this poem

    statistic : the us bureau of missing persons reports
45              that in 1968 over 100,000 people disappeared
               leaving no solid clues
                  nor trace    only
      a space    in the lives of their friends
                                                      1970

- How does the speaker's repeated use of the word *mirror* help to determine the form of this poem? How (and why) does the form evolve in the course of the poem?

## ARCHIBALD MacLEISH

### Ars Poetica[4]

A poem should be palpable and mute
As a globed fruit,

Dumb
As old medallions to the thumb,

5 Silent as the sleeve-worn stone
Of casement ledges where the moss has grown—

A poem should be wordless
As the flight of birds.

A poem should be motionless in time
10 As the moon climbs.

Leaving, as the moon releases
Twig by twig the night-entangled trees,

Leaving, as the moon behind the winter leaves,
Memory by memory the mind—

15 A poem should be motionless in time
As the moon climbs.

A poem should be equal to:
Not true.

For all the history of grief
20 An empty doorway and a maple leaf.

---

4. "The Art of Poetry," title of a poetical treatise by the Roman poet Horace (65–8 B.C.E.).

> For love
> The leaning grasses and two lights above the sea—
>
> A poem should not mean
> But be.
>
> 1926

- Can you summarize this poem's ideas about what poetry should be? How does the poem itself illustrate these principles?

## THE WAY A POEM LOOKS

Stanza breaks and other kinds of print spaces are important, primarily to guide the voice and the mind to a clearer sense of sound and meaning. But sometimes poems are written to be seen rather than heard, and their appearance on the page is crucial to their effect. Cummings's poem "l(a," for example, tries to visualize typographically what the poet asks you to see in your mind's eye.

### E. E. CUMMINGS

### [*l(a*]

> l(a
> le
> af
> fa
> 5  ll
> s)
> one
> l
> iness
>
> 1958

Occasionally, too, poems are composed in a specific shape so that they look like physical objects. The poems that follow in this chapter—some very old, some more recent—illustrate ways in which visual effects may be created. Even though poetry has traditionally been thought of as oral—words to be spoken, sung, or performed rather than looked at—the idea that poems can also be related to painting and the visual arts is an old one. Theodoric in ancient Greece is credited with inventing **technopaegnia**—that is, the construction of poems with visual appeal. Once, the shaping of words to resemble an object was thought to have mystical power, but more recent attempts at **concrete poetry** or **shaped verse** are usually playful exercises (such as Hollander's "You Too? Me Too—Why Not? Soda Pop" [chapter 23]) that attempt to supplement (or replace) verbal meanings with devices from painting and sculpture.

Reading a poem like George Herbert's "Easter Wings" aloud wouldn't make much sense. Seeing is everything for a poem like that. A more frequent poetic device involves asking the eyes to become a guide for the voice. The following poem depends on recognition of some standard typographical symbols and knowledge of their names. We have to say those names to read the poem.

**FRANKLIN P. ADAMS**

*Composed in the Composing Room*

At stated .ic times
I love to sit and — off rhymes
Till ,tose at last I fall
Exclaiming "I don't ∧ all."
5 Though I'm an * objection
By running this in this here §
This ☞ of the Fleeting Hour,
This lofty -ician Tower—
A ¶er's hope dispels
10 All fear of deadly ‖.
You think these [ ] are a pipe?
Well, not on your †eotype.

1914

We create the right terms here when we verbalize, putting the visual signs together with the words or letters printed in the poem, for example making the word "periodic" out of ".ic" or "high Phoenician" out of "-ician" or "daguerreotype" out of "†eotype." Like "Easter Wings," "Composed in the Composing Room" uses typography in an extreme way; here the eyes (and mind) are drawn into a punlike game that offers more puzzle-solving pleasure than emotional effect. More often poets give us—by the visual placement of sounds—a guide to reading, inviting us to regulate the pace of our reading, notice pauses or silences, and pay attention both to the syntax of the poem and to the rhetoric of the voice, thus providing us a kind of musical score for reading.

E. E. CUMMINGS

## [Buffalo Bill 's][1]

>     Buffalo Bill 's
>     defunct
>                 who used to
>                 ride a watersmooth-silver
> 5                               stallion
>     and break onetwothreefourfive pigeonsjustlikethat
>                                               Jesus
>     he was a handsome man
>                           and what i want to know is
> 10  how do you like your blueeyed boy
>     Mister Death

                                                    1923

The unusual spacing of words here, with some run together and others widely separated, provides a guide to reading, regulating both speed and sense, so that the poem can capture aloud some of the excitement and wonder that a boy might have felt for a theatrical act as spectacular as that of Buffalo Bill. A good reader-aloud, with only this typographical guidance, can capture some of the wide-eyed boy's enthusiasm, remembered now in retrospect from a later perspective (notice how the word "defunct" helps to set the time and point of view).

In prose, syntax and punctuation are the main guides to the voice of a reader, providing indicators of emphasis, pace, and speed; in poetry as well they are more conventional and more common guides than extreme forms of typography, such as in "Buffalo Bill." Reading a poem sensitively is in some ways a lot like reading a piece of prose sensitively: one has to pay close attention to the way the sentences are put together and how they are punctuated. A good reader makes use of appropriate pauses as well as thundering emphasis; silence as well as sound is part of any poem, and reading punctuation is as important as knowing how to say the words.

Beyond punctuation, the placement and spacing of lines on the page may be helpful to a reader even when that placement is not as radical as it is in "Buffalo Bill." The fact that poetry looks different from prose is not an accident; decisions to make lines one length instead of another have as much to do with vocal breaks and phrasing as with functions of syntax or meaning. In a good poem, there are few accidents, not even in the way the poem meets the eye, which provides the most direct route to the voice; the eye is our scanner and director, our prompter and guide.

The eye also may help the ear in another way—guiding us to notice repeated sounds by spotting repeated visual patterns in letters. The most common rhymes in poems occur at the ends of lines, and the arrangement of lines (the typography of the poem) often calls attention to the pattern of sounds because of the similar

1. *Portraits* XXI.

appearance of line-ending words, as in sonnets and other traditional verse forms. Not all rhymes have similar spellings, of course, but similarities of appearance seem to imply a relationship of sound, too, and many poems hint at their stanza patterns and verse forms by their spatial arrangements and repeated patterns at ends of lines. The following poem takes advantage of such expectations and plays with them by forcing a letter into arbitrary line relationships, forcing words ("stew," line 2) in order to create rhymes, setting up rhyme patterns and then breaking them (lines 9–11), using false or near rhymes (lines 10–11), and creating long lines with multisyllabic rhymes that seem silly (the final two lines).

**STEVIE SMITH**

## The Jungle Husband

Dearest Evelyn, I often think of you
Out with the guns in the jungle stew
Yesterday I hittapotamus
I put the measurements down for you but they got lost in the fuss
5   It's not a good thing to drink out here
You know, I've practically given it up dear.
Tomorrow I am going alone a long way
Into the jungle. It is all grey
But green on top
10   Only sometimes when a tree has fallen
The sun comes down plop, it is quite appalling.
You never want to go in a jungle pool
In the hot sun, it would be the act of a fool
Because it's always full of anacondas, Evelyn, not looking ill-fed
15   I'll say. So no more now, from your loving husband, Wilfred.
                                                                    1957

Visual devices can be entertainments to amuse, bewilder, or tease readers of poetry whose chief expectations concern sound, but sometimes poets achieve surprising (and lasting) original effects by manipulations of print space. Stanzas—visual breaks in poems that indicate some kind of unit of meaning or measurement—ultimately are more than visual devices, for they point to structural questions and ultimately frame and formalize the content of poems. But they present—as do the similar visual patterns of words that rhyme—part of the "score" of poems, and suggest one more way that sight becomes a guide to sound in many poems.

. . .

## GEORGE HERBERT

### Easter Wings

```
Lord, who createdst man in wealth and store,²
      Though foolishly he lost the same,
           Decaying more and more
                Till he became
                   Most poor:
                   With thee
                O let me rise
           As larks,³ harmoniously,
      And sing this day thy victories:
Then shall the fall further the flight in me.

My tender age in sorrow did begin;
   And still with sicknesses and shame
      Thou didst so punish sin,
           That I became
                Most thin.
                With thee
           Let me combine,
      And feel this day thy victory;
   For, if I imp⁴ my wing on thine,
Affliction shall advance the flight in me.
```

1633

- How do this poem's decreasing and increasing line lengths correspond to the meaning of the words? Why do you think Herbert has chosen to present the poem "sideways"?

## ROGER McGOUGH

### Here I Am

        Here I am
     getting on for seventy
and never having gone to work in ladies' underwear
    Never run naked at night in the rain
5    Made love to a girl I'd just met on a plane

  At that awkward age now between birth and death
    I think of all the outrages unperpetrated
       opportunities missed

      The dragons unchased
10      The maidens unkissed

---

2. In plenty.   3. Which herald the morning.
4. Engraft. In falconry, to engraft feathers in a damaged wing, so as to restore the powers of flight *(OED)*.

                The wines still untasted
                The oceans uncrossed
                The fantasies wasted
                The mad urges lost
15                      Here I am
                as old as Methuselah
                was when he was my age
        and never having stepped outside for a fight

                Crossed on red, pissed[5] on rosé (or white)
20              Pretty dull for a poet, I suppose, eh? Quite.

                                1992

- What does this poem's shape suggest about its meaning?


**EARLE BIRNEY**

## *Anglosaxon Street*

Dawn drizzle ended     dampness steams from
blotching brick and     blank plasterwaste
Faded housepatterns     hoary and finicky
unfold stuttering     stick like a phonograph

5 Here is a ghetto     gotten for goyim
O with care denuded     of nigger and kike
No coonsmell rankles     reeks only cellarrot
Ottar[6] of carexhaust     catcorpse and cookinggrease

Imperial hearts     heave in this haven
10 Cracks across windows     are welded with slogans
There'll Always Be An England     enhances geraniums
and V's for Victory     vanquish the housefly

Ho! with climbing sun     march the bleached beldames[7]
festooned with shopping bags     farded[8] flatarched
15 bigthewed Saxonwives     stepping over buttrivers
waddling back wienerladen     to suckle smallfry

Hoy! with sunslope     shrieking over hydrants
flood from learninghall     the lean fingerlings
Nordic nobblecheeked[9]     not all clean of nose
20 leaping Commandowise     into leprous lanes

What! after whistleblow!     spewed from wheelboat
after daylight doughtiness     dire handplay

---

5. Drunk.    6. Roselike fragrance.    7. Aged women.    8. Rouged.    9. Pimpled.

  in sewertrench or sandpit  come Saxonthegns
  Junebrown Jutekings[1]  jawslack for meat

25 Sit after supper  on smeared doorsteps
  not humbly swearing  hatedeeds on Huns
  profiteers politicians  pacifists Jews

  Then by twobit magic  to muse in movie
  unlock picturehoard  or lope to alehall
30 soaking bleakly  in beer skittleless

  Home again to hotbox  and humid husbandhood
  in slumbertrough adding  sleepily to Anglekin
  Alongside in lanenooks  carling and leman[2]
  caterwaul and clip[3]  careless of Saxonry
35 with moonglow and haste  and a higher heartbeat
  Slumbers now slumtrack  unstinks cooling
  waiting brief for milkmaid  mornstar and worldrise

Toronto 1942, revised 1966

- Read this poem aloud. How does the poem's appearance help to determine the tone and pacing of your reading?

## DAVID FERRY

### *Evening News*

We have been there.
      and seen nothing
Nothing has been there
      for us to see
5 In what a beautiful silence
      the death is inflicted
In a dazzling distance
      in the fresh dews
And morning lights
10      how radiantly
In the glistening
      the village is wasted.
It is by such sights
      the eye is instructed.

        1983

- How are the eye and the voice guided through this poem? How is the poem's appearance part of its content?

---

1. The Jutes were the German tribe that invaded England in the fifth century and spearheaded the Anglo-Saxon conquest. *Saxonthegns:* freemen who provided military services for the Saxon lords.
2. Lover. *Carling:* old woman.  3. Embrace.

## SUGGESTIONS FOR WRITING

1. Chart the rhyme scheme of Keats's "On the Sonnet," and then, after reading the poem aloud, mark the major structural divisions of the poem. At what points do these structural divisions and the breaks in rhyme coincide? At what points do they conflict? Write an essay in which you discuss how these patterns and variations relate to the poem's meaning.
2. Consider carefully the structure of and sequencing in Brooks's "First Fight. Then Fiddle." How do various uses of sound in the poem (rhyme, onomatopoeia, and alliteration, for example) reinforce its themes and tones? Write an essay in which you explore the relationship between "sound and sense" in the poem.
3. Some of the sonnets in this book, such as those by Shakespeare, adhere closely to the classic English model; others, such as Milton's "When I consider how my light is spent," follow the Italian model; and some, such as Helen Chasin's "Joy Sonnet in a Random Universe," bear only slight resemblance to either of the traditional sonnet models. Take any four sonnets found in this book as the basis for an essay in which you compare and contrast the various ways poets have used the sonnet form to achieve their unique artistic purposes.
4. Trace the variations on imagery of light and darkness in Thomas's "Do Not Go Gentle into That Good Night." How do we know that light represents life and darkness death (rather than, say, sight and blindness)? How does the poet use the strict formal requirements of the villanelle to emphasize this interplay of light and darkness? Write an essay in which you discuss the interaction of form and content in "Do Not Go Gentle into That Good Night."
5. Every poem has a structure, whether or not it adheres to a traditional form or to conventional ideas about line, rhythm, or spacing. Examine closely the structure of any poem or group of poems in this book. How does the poet use form to shape sound, emotion, and meaning? Write an essay in which you examine the structural choices that determine both the form and the content of these poems.
6. Research Anglo-Saxon poetry and look at classic examples, such as *Beowulf* and "The Seafarer." What are the principles of sound and the function of poetry that inform these Old English poems? Now consider Birney's "Anglosaxon Street." How successful is Birney in applying these principles to a modern poem? Is Birney's poem "serious"? Is it a parody? Write an essay in which you discuss the sound patterns and the form of "Anglosaxon Street" in light of your findings.

# 20 THE WHOLE TEXT

In the previous seven chapters, we have been thinking about one thing at a time—setting, word choice, symbolism, meter, stanza form, and so on—and we have discussed each poem primarily in terms of a single issue. Learning to deal with one problem at a time is good educational practice and in the long run will make you a more careful and more effective reader of poems. Still, the elements of poems do not work individually but in combination, and in considering even the simplest elements (speaker, for example, or setting) we have noticed how categories overlap—how, for example, the question of setting in Dickey's "Cherrylog Road" quickly merges into questions about the speaker, his state of mind, his personality, his distance from the central events in the poem. Thinking about a single issue never does complete justice to an individual poem; no poem depends for all its effects on just one device or one element of the poet's craft. Poems are complex wholes that demand various kinds of attention, and, ultimately, to read any poem fully and well you need to ask every question about craft, form, and tradition that we've asked so far, and many more questions you may learn to ask after more experience in reading poems. Not all questions are equally relevant to all poems, of course, but moving systematically through your whole repertoire of questions will enable you to get beyond the fragmentation of particular issues in order to approach the whole poem and its multiple effects. In this chapter we will consider how the various elements in poems work together.

Below is a short poem in which several issues we have considered come up almost simultaneously.

### ELIZABETH JENNINGS

### *Delay*

The radiance of that star that leans on me
Was shining years ago. The light that now
Glitters up there my eye may never see
And so the time lag teases me with how

5  Love that loves now may not reach me until
Its first desire is spent. The star's impulse
Must wait for eyes to claim it beautiful
And love arrived may find us somewhere else.

1953

In most poems, several issues arise more or less at once, and the analytic practice of separating issues is a convenience rather than an assertion of priorities. In "Delay," a lot of the basic questions (about speaker, situation, and setting, for example) seem to be put on hold in the beginning, but if we proceed systematically the poem opens itself to us. The first line identifies the "I" (or rather, in this case, "me") of the poem as an observer of the bright star that is the main object in the poem and the principal source of its imagery, its "plot," and its analogical argument. But we learn little about the speaker. She surfaces again in lines 4 and 5 and with someone else ("us") in line 8, but she is always "me" in the objective case—acted on rather than acting. All we know for certain about her is that she can speak about the time it takes a star's light to reach her and that she contemplates deeply about the meaning and effect of such time lags. We know even less about the setting and situation; somewhere the speaker watches a bright star and meditates on the fact that she is seeing it long, long after its light was actually sent forth. Her location is not specified, and the time, though probably night, could be any night (in the age of modern astronomy, that is, because the speaker knows about the speed of light and the distance of the stars from Earth); the only other explicit clues we have about the situation involve the "us" of the final line and the fact that the speaker's concern with time seems oddly personal, something that matters to her emotional life—not merely a matter of scientific knowledge.

The poem's language helps us understand much more about the speaker and her situation, as do the poem's structure and stanza form. The most crucial word in the first stanza is probably the verb "leans" (line 1); certainly it is the poem's most unusual and surprising word. Because a star cannot literally *lean* on its observer, the word seems to suggest the speaker's perception of her relationship to the star. Perhaps she feels that the star impinges on her, that she is somehow *subject* to its influence, though not in the popular, astrological sense. Here the star influences the speaker because she understands something about the way the universe works and can apply her knowledge of light and the vastness of space in an analogical way to her own life: it "leans" because it tells her something about how observers are affected by what they observe. And it is worth noticing how fully the speaker thinks of herself as object rather than actor or agent. Here, as throughout the poem, she is acted upon; things happen *to* her—the star leans on her, the time lag teases her (line 4), love may not reach her (line 5), and she (along with someone else) is the object sought in the final line.

Other crucial words also help clarify the speaker and her situation. The words "radiance" (line 1) and "[g]litters" (line 3) are fairly standard ones to describe stars, but here their standard meanings are carefully qualified by their position in time. The actual radiance of the starlight occurred many eons before and seems to be unavailable to the speaker, who now sees only glitter, something far less warm and resonant. And the word "impulse" in line 6 invokes technical knowledge about light. Rather than being impulsive or quickly spent, a star must "wait" for its reception in the eye of the beholder, where it becomes "beautiful"; in physics, an impulse combines force and duration. Hence, the receiver of light—the beholder, the acted-upon—becomes important, and we begin to see why the speaker always appears as the object: she is the receiver and interpreter, and the light is not complete—its duration not established—until she receives and interprets it. The star does, after all, "lean" on (depend on) her in some objective sense as well as the subjective one in which she first seems to report it.

The stanza form suggests that the poem may have stages and that its meaning may emerge in two parts, a suggestion confirmed by the poem's form and structure. The first stanza is entirely about stars and stargazing, but the second stanza establishes the analogy with love that becomes the poem's central metaphor. Now, too, more becomes clear about the speaker and her situation. Her concern is about delay, "time lag" (line 4), and the fact that "[l]ove that loves now may not reach me until / Its first desire is spent" (lines 5–6), a strong indication that her initial observation of the star is driven by feeling and her emotional context. Her attempt to put the remoteness of feeling into a perspective that will enable understanding and patience becomes the "plot" of the poem, and her final calm recognition about "us"—that "love arrived may find us somewhere else"—is, if not comforting, nevertheless a recognition that patience is important and that some things do last. Even the sounds of the poem—in this case the way rhyme is used—help support the meaning of the poem and the tone it achieves. The rhymes in the first part of the poem reflect perfectly the stable sense of ancient stars, while in the second stanza we find near-rhymes: there is harmony here, but in human life and emotion nothing is quite perfect.

Here is another short poem whose several elements deserve detailed attention:

### ANONYMOUS
## Western Wind

    Western wind, when wilt thou blow,
      The small rain down can rain?
    Christ, if my love were in my arms
      And I in my bed again!

  15th century

Perhaps the most obvious thing here is the poem's structure: its first two lines seem to have little to do with the last two. How can we account for these two distinct and apparently unrelated directions, the calm concern with natural processes in the first part and the emotional outburst about loneliness and lovelessness in the second? The best route to the whole poem is still to begin with the most simple of questions—who? when? where? what is happening?—and proceed to more difficult and complex ones.

As in Jennings's "Delay," the speaker here offers little explicit autobiography. The first two lines provide no personal information, but ask a question that could be delivered quite impersonally: they could be part of a philosophical meditation. The abbreviated syntax at the end of line 1 (the question of causality is not fully stated, and we have to supply the "so that" implied at the end of the line) may suggest strong feeling and emotional upset, but it tells us nothing intimate, only that the time is spring (which is when the western wind blows). No place is indicated, no year, no particulars of situation. But lines 3–4, while remaining inexplicit about exact details, make the speaker's situation clear enough: his love is no longer in his arms, and he wishes she were. (We don't really know genders here, but we can make a guess based on what we know of typical practices in fifteenth-century England.)

The poem's language, a study in contrast, guides us to see the two-part structure clearly. The question asked of the wind in lines 1-2 involves straightforward, steady language, but line 3 bursts with agony and personal despair. The power of the first word of line 3—especially in an age of belief—suggests a speaker ready to bewail his loss in the strongest possible terms, and the parallel statements of loss in lines 3 and 4 suggest not only the speaker's physical relationship to his love but also his displacement from home: he is deprived of both place and love, human contact and contact with his past. His longing for a world ordered according to his past experience is structured to parallel his longing for the spring wind that brings the world back to life. The two parts of the poem both express a desire for return—to life, to order, to causal relationships within the world. Setting has in fact become a central theme in the poem, and what the poem expresses tonally involves a powerful desire for stability and belonging—an effect that grows out of our sense of the speaker's situation and character. Speaker, setting, language, and structure here intertwine to create the intense focus of the poem.

In the following short poem, several elements likewise interrelate:

## ROBERT HERRICK

## Upon Julia's Clothes

>    Whenas in silks my Julia goes
>    Then, then, methinks, how sweetly flows
>    That liquefaction of her clothes.
>
>    Next, when I cast mine eyes, and see
> 5  That brave[1] vibration, each way free,
>    O, how that glittering taketh me!

1648

The poem is unabashed in its admiration of the way Julia looks, and nearly everything in its six short lines contributes to its celebratory tone. Perhaps the most striking thing about the poem is its unusual, highly suggestive use of words. "[G]oes" at the end of line 1 may be the first word to call special attention to itself, though we will return in a minute to the very first word of the poem. "Walks" or "moves" would seem to be more obvious choices; "goes" is more neutral and less specific and in most circumstances would seem an inferior choice, but here the

---

1. Handsome, showy.

point seems to be to describe Julia in a kind of seamless and unspecified motion and from a specific angle, because the poem wants to record the effect of Julia's movement on the speaker (already a second element becomes crucial) rather than the specifics of Julia herself. Another word that seems especially important is "liquefaction" (line 3), also an unusual and suggestive word about motion. Again it implies no specific kind of motion, just smoothness and seamlessness, and it applies not to Julia but to her clothes. Other words that might repay a close look include "vibration" in line 5 (the speaker is finally a little more direct); "brave" and "free," also in line 5; and "glittering" and "taketh" in line 6.

Had we begun conventionally by thinking about speaker, situation, and setting, we would have quickly noticed the precise way that the speaker clothes Julia: "in silks," which move almost as one with her body. And we would have noticed that the speaker positions himself almost as voyeur (standing for us as observers, of course, but also for himself as the central figure in the poem). Not much detail about situation or setting is given (and the speaker is characterized only as a viewer and appreciator), but one thing about the scene is crucial, and this takes us back to the first word of the poem, "whenas." The slightly quaint quality of the word may at first obscure, to a modern reader, just what it tells us about the situation, that it is a *generic* scene rather than a single event. "Whenas" is very close to "whenever"; the speaker's claim seems to be that he responds this way *whenever* Julia dons her silks—apparently fairly often, at least in his memory or imagination.

Most of the speaker's language is sensual and rather provocative (he is anxious to share his responses with others so that *everyone* will know just how "taking" Julia is), but one rather elaborate (though somewhat disguised) metaphor suggests his awareness of his own calculation and its consequences. In the beginning of the second stanza he describes how he "cast" his eyes: it is a metaphor from fishing, a frequent one in love poetry about luring, chasing, and catching. Julia, of course, is the object. The metaphor continues two lines later, but the angler has caught himself: he is taken by the "glittering" lure. This turning of the tables, drawing as it does on a traditional, common image that is then modified to help characterize the speaker, gives a little depth to the show: whatever the slither and glitter, there is not just showing off and sensuality but a catch in this angling.

Many other elements deserve comment, especially because they quickly relate to each other. Consider the way the poet uses sounds, first of all in picking words like "liquefaction" that are themselves almost onomatopoeic, but then also using rhyme very cleverly. There are only two rhyme sounds in the poem, one in the first stanza, the other in the second. The long *ee* of the second becomes almost exclamatory, and the three words of the first seem to become linked in a kind of separate grammar of their own, as if "goes," "flows," and "clothes" were all part of a single action—pretty much what the poem claims on a thematic level. A lot happens in this short and simple poem, and although a reader can get at it step by step by thinking about element after element, the interlocking of the elements is finally the most impressive effect of all. Although the plot reenacts familiar stances of woman as object and man as gazer, our analysis and reading need to be flexible enough to consider not only all the analytical categories, but also the ways in which they work together.

Going back to poems read earlier in the book—with the methods and approaches you have learned since then—can help you see how different elements of poems interrelate. Look, for example, at the stanza divisions in Dickey's "Cherrylog Road" (chapter 15) and consider how the neatly spaced, apparently discrete units work against the sometimes frantic pacing of the poem. Or consider the character of the speaker, or the fundamental metaphor of "wreckage" that sponsors the poem, relative to the idea of the speaker. Go back and read Kumin's "Woodchucks" (chapter 13) while thinking about structural questions; or consider how the effaced speaker works in Rich's "Aunt Jennifer's Tigers" (chapter 13); or think about metaphor in Nemerov's "The Vacuum" (page 819).

Here are several more poems to analyze. As you read them, think about the elements discussed in the previous seven chapters—but rather than thinking about a single element at a time, try to consider relationships, how the different elements combine to make you respond not to a single device but to a complex set of strategies and effects.

• • •

### W. H. AUDEN

### *Musée des Beaux Arts*[2]

About suffering they were never wrong,
The Old Masters: how well they understood
Its human position; how it takes place
While someone else is eating or opening a window or just walking
    dully along;
5  How, when the aged are reverently, passionately waiting
For the miraculous birth, there always must be
Children who did not specially want it to happen, skating
On a pond at the edge of the wood:
They never forgot
10  That even the dreadful martyrdom must run its course
Anyhow in a corner, some untidy spot
Where the dogs go on with their doggy life and the torturer's horse
Scratches its innocent behind on a tree.

In Brueghel's *Icarus*,[3] for instance: how everything turns away
15  Quite leisurely from the disaster; the plowman may
Have heard the splash, the forsaken cry,
But for him it was not an important failure; the sun shone
As it had to on the white legs disappearing into the green
Water; and the expensive delicate ship that must have seen

---

2. The Museum of the Fine Arts, in Brussels.
3. *Landscape with the Fall of Icarus*, by Pieter Brueghel the Elder (1525?–1569), located in the Brussels museum. According to Greek myth, Daedalus and his son, Icarus, escaped from imprisonment by using homemade wings of feathers and wax; but Icarus flew too near the sun, the wax melted, and he fell into the sea and drowned. In the Brueghel painting the central figure is a peasant plowing, and several other figures are more immediately noticeable than Icarus, who, disappearing into the sea, is easy to miss in the lower right-hand corner.

20  Something amazing, a boy falling out of the sky,
    Had somewhere to get to and sailed calmly on.

1938

- Find a reproduction of the painting—*Landscape with the Fall of Icarus*, by Pieter Brueghel the Elder—that is the subject of this poem. How is your interpretation affected by examining the painting?

## GEORGE HERBERT

### *The Collar*

I struck the board[4] and cried, "No more;
    I will abroad!
What? shall I ever sigh and pine?
My lines[5] and life are free, free as the road,
5    Loose as the wind, as large as store.[6]
        Shall I be still in suit?[7]
    Have I no harvest but a thorn
    To let me blood, and not restore
What I have lost with cordial[8] fruit?
10        Sure there was wine
Before my sighs did dry it; there was corn
    Before my tears did drown it.
    Is the year only lost to me?
    Have I no bays[9] to crown it,
15 No flowers, no garlands gay? All blasted?
        All wasted?
    Not so, my heart; but there is fruit,
        And thou hast hands.
Recover all thy sigh-blown age
20 On double pleasures: leave thy cold dispute
Of what is fit, and not. Forsake thy cage,[1]
        Thy rope of sands,
Which petty thoughts have made, and made to thee
    Good cable, to enforce and draw,
25        And be thy law,
While thou didst wink[2] and wouldst not see.
        Away! take heed;

---

4. Table.  5. Lot.  6. A storehouse; that is, abundance.  7. In service to another.
8. Reviving, restorative.  9. Laurel wreaths of triumph.  1. Moral restrictions.
2. That is, close your eyes to the weaknesses of such restrictions.

    I will abroad.
Call in thy death's-head[3] there; tie up thy fears.
30      He that forbears
  To suit and serve his need,
     Deserves his load."
But as I raved and grew more fierce and wild
    At every word,
35 Methought I heard one calling, *Child!*
  And I replied, *My Lord.*
            1633

- How does knowledge of Herbert's profession—clergyman—help you to interpret the title and the rest of the poem? What do the many metaphors in the poem suggest about the speaker's state of mind?

## ROBERT FROST

### Design

  I found a dimpled spider, fat and white,
  On a white heal-all,[4] holding up a moth
  Like a white piece of rigid satin cloth—
  Assorted characters of death and blight
5  Mixed ready to begin the morning right,
  Like the ingredients of a witches' broth—
  A snow-drop spider, a flower like a froth,
  And dead wings carried like a paper kite.

  What had that flower to do with being white,
10  The wayside blue and innocent heal-all?
  What brought the kindred spider to that height,
  Then steered the white moth thither in the night?
  What but design of darkness to appall?—
  If design govern in a thing so small.
            1936

- How does this poem confound our usual preconceptions about "light" and "darkness"? How does its elaborate form complement its theme?

---

3. *Memento mori,* a skull intended to remind people of their mortality.
4. A plant, also called the "all-heal" and "self-heal," with tightly clustered violet-blue flowers.

**EDEN PHILLPOTTS**

## The Learned

The grey beards wag, the bald heads nod,
And gather thick as bees,
To talk electrons, gases, God,
Old nebulae, new fleas.
5 Each specialist, each dry-as-dust
And professional oaf,
Holds up his little crumb of crust
And cries, "Behold the loaf!"

1942

- What light does the simile "thick as bees" cast on this poem as a whole? How does the poem's scheme of rhyme and meter contribute to its tone?


**EMILY DICKINSON**

## [My Life had stood—a Loaded Gun—]

My Life had stood—a Loaded Gun—
In Corners—till a Day
The Owner passed—identified—
And carried Me away—

5 And now We roam in Sovereign Woods—
And now We hunt the Doe—
And every time I speak for Him—
The Mountains straight reply—

And do I smile, such cordial light
10 Upon the Valley glow—
It is as a Vesuvian face
Had let its pleasure through—

And when at Night—Our good Day done—
I guard My Master's Head—
15 'Tis better than the Eider-Duck's
Deep Pillow—to have shared—

To foe of His—I'm deadly foe—
None stir the second time—
On whom I lay a Yellow Eye—
20 Or an emphatic Thumb—

Though I than He—may longer live
He longer must—than I—
For I have but the power to kill,
Without—the power to die—

ca. 1863

- How does Dickinson set up and then defy the reader's expectations through the poem's central metaphor—the speaker's life as a loaded gun? How do the poem's quirks (e.g., the jerky rhythm, the strange syntax, the slant rhymes) contribute to its overall effect?

**BEN JONSON**

## Epitaph on Elizabeth, L. H.

Wouldst thou hear what man can say
In a little? Reader, stay.
Underneath this stone doth lie
As much beauty as could die;
5 Which in life did harbor give
To more virtue than doth live.
If at all she had a fault,
Leave it buried in this vault.
One name was Elizabeth;
10 Th' other, let it sleep with death:
Fitter, where it died, to tell,
Than that it lived at all. Farewell.

1616

- How are lines 4 and 6 expressing more than just common courtliness? In what ways is poetry as much this poem's subject as the beauty and virtue of Elizabeth?

## SUGGESTIONS FOR WRITING

1. Consider the setting of Auden's "Musée des Beaux Arts" in the sense of both the painting and its location in the museum. In what different ways do the two settings become important? How do they function to frame the story of Icarus, or the theme of suffering? Write an essay in which you discuss the way the poem's setting and structure contribute to the overall effect of the poem.
2. Consider both speaker and situation as you analyze Herbert's "The Collar." How does one of these elements illuminate the other? Write an essay in which you examine the way the poem's whole effect arises from an understanding of the speaker and situation.
3. Discussing Dickinson's "My Life had stood—a Loaded Gun," the poet Adrienne Rich has written, "I think it is a poem about possession by the daemon [of artistic creativity], about the dangers and risks of such possession if you are a woman, about the knowledge that power in a woman can seem destructive, and that you cannot live without the daemon once it has possessed you." Write an essay in which you respond to Rich's interpretation of Dickinson's poem.
4. Consider the interrelationships among speaker, structure, stanza form, and tone in Frost's "Design" or any other sonnet you have read in this book. How do the elements combine to create a unique whole? Write an essay in which you closely analyze a sonnet—its structure and language, as well as its subject, situation, imagery, and theme.

# *Exploring Contexts*

## 21  READING POETRY IN CONTEXT

The more you know, the better a reader of poetry you will likely be. And that means general knowledge as well as knowledge of other poetry and literary traditions. Poems often draw on a large fund of human knowledge about all sorts of things, asking us to regard a poem in light of facts and values we have taken on from earlier reading or from our experiences in the world. In the previous nine chapters, we have looked at how practice and specific skills make interpretation easier and better; in this "contextual" section we shift our focus to information you need to read richly and fully: information about authors, about events that influenced them or inspired their writing, and about literary traditions that provide a context for their work. Poets always write in a specific time, under unique circumstances, and with some awareness of the world around them, whether or not they explicitly refer to contemporary matters in a particular poem. In this chapter, we will discuss the cultural and historical events, movements, and ideas that directly influence poets or that poets in some way represent in the poems they write.

Very little that you know will ultimately go to waste in your reading of poetry. The best potential reader of poetry has already read widely and thought deeply about all kinds of things, and is supremely wise—wise enough to know exactly how to apply specific knowledge to a given text. We all strive to be that ideal reader, but none of us can fully measure up. Of course, no poet really expects any reader to be perfect, but poems themselves can make special demands: they may require readers to know as much about history, for example, as about the intricacies of language and form. Poems not only *refer* to people, places, and events—things that exist in time—but they also are reflections of given moments, products of both the potentialities and the limitations of the times in which they are created.

Things that happen every day often find their way into poetry in a natural and yet forceful manner. Making love in a junkyard, as in Dickey's "Cherrylog Road" (chapter 15) is a good example; a reader doesn't need to know what particular junkyard was involved—or imaginatively involved—in order to understand the poem, but that reader does need to know what an auto junkyard was like in the mid-twentieth century, with more or less whole car bodies in various states of disintegration roughly arrayed on a large plot of ground. But what if, over the next generation or two, junkyards completely disappear as we find other ways to dispose of old cars? Already, especially in large cities, many old cars are crushed into small metal blocks. But what if the metal is all melted down, or the junk is blasted into space? If that should happen, readers then may have never seen a junkyard, and they will need a footnote to explain what junkyards were like. The history of junkyards will not be lost—people will have pictures, films, and books about the forms and functions of junkyards, probably even the fact that lovers occasionally visited them—but the public memory of junkyards will soon disappear. No social customs, nothing that is made, no institutions or sites can last forever.

Readers may still be able to experience "Cherrylog Road" when junkyards disappear, but they will need some help, and they may think its particulars a little quaint, much as we regard a story that involves a horse and buggy—or even making love in the back-seat of a parked car—as quaint now. Institutions change, habits change, times change, places and settings change—all kinds of particulars change, even when people's wants, needs, and foibles go on in pretty much the same way. Footnotes never provide a precise or adequate substitute for firsthand knowledge, but they can help our understanding and pave the way for feeling. With the aid of footnotes, poems from earlier times can stimulate in readers a kind of imaginative historical sympathy, for poems that refer to specific contemporary details (which have now become to us, in our own time, *historical* details) often describe human nature and human experiences very much as we still know and live them. Today's poem may need tomorrow's footnote, but the poem need not be tomorrow's puzzle—or just a curiosity or fossil.

The following poem, not that many years old, already requires some explanation. Many readers will not know the factual details of the event that occasioned it, and (even more important) most readers will not recall the powerful reaction throughout the United States to the event.

### JAMES A. EMANUEL

## *Emmett Till*[1]

    I hear a whistling
    Through the water.
    Little Emmett
    Won't be still.
5  He keeps floating
    Round the darkness,
    Edging through
    The silent chill.
    Tell me, please,
10 That bedtime story
    Of the fairy
    River Boy
    Who swims forever,
    Deep in treasures,
15 Necklaced in
    A coral toy.
        1968

---

1. In 1955, Till, a black fourteen-year-old from Chicago, was lynched in Mississippi for allegedly making sexual advances toward a white woman.

How do you know what you need to know? The easiest clue is your own puzzlement. When something that you don't recognize happens in a poem—and yet the poem seems not to clarify it—you have a clue that readers at the time the poem was written must have recognized something that is not now common knowledge. Once you know you don't know, it takes only a little work to find out: most college libraries (and, of course, the Internet) contain far more information than you will ever need, and the trick is to search efficiently. Your ability to find the information will depend upon how well you know the printed reference materials and digital resources available to you. Practice helps. Knowledge accumulates. Most poems printed in textbooks like this one will be annotated for you with basic facts, but often you will need additional information before you can interpret a poem's full meaning and feel its resonance. An editor, trying to satisfy the needs of a variety of readers, may not always write the note you particularly need, so you may have to do some digging in the library for the sake of fully appreciating any poem you read—certainly for those you come upon in old magazines and unannotated collections. Few poets like to annotate their own work (they'd rather let you work a little to appreciate it), and besides, many things that now need notes didn't when they were written.

The two poems that follow both require from the reader some specific "referential" information, but they differ considerably in their emphasis on the particularities of time and place. The first poem concerns a moment just before the outbreak of World War I when British naval forces were preparing for combat by taking gunnery practice in the English Channel. The second represents a longer cultural moment in which attitudes and assumptions, rather than a specific event, are at stake.

**THOMAS HARDY**

## Channel Firing

That night your great guns, unawares,
Shook all our coffins as we lay,
And broke the chancel window squares,[2]
We thought it was the Judgment-day

5 And sat upright. While drearisome
Arose the howl of wakened hounds:
The mouse let fall the altar-crumb,[3]
The worms drew back into the mounds,

The glebe cow[4] drooled. Till God called, "No;
10 It's gunnery practice out at sea
Just as before you went below;
The world is as it used to be:

---

2. The windows near the altar in a church.   3. Breadcrumbs from the sacrament of Communion.
4. Parish cow pastured on the meadow next to the churchyard.

"All nations striving strong to make
Red war yet redder. Mad as hatters
15 They do no more for Christés sake
Than you who are helpless in such matters.

"That this is not the judgment-hour
For some of them's a blessed thing,
For if it were they'd have to scour
20 Hell's floor for so much threatening...

"Ha, ha. It will be warmer when
I blow the trumpet (if indeed
I ever do; for you are men,
And rest eternal sorely need)."

25 So down we lay again. "I wonder,
Will the world ever saner be,"
Said one, "than when He sent us under
In our indifferent century!"

And many a skeleton shook his head.
30 "Instead of preaching forty year,"
My neighbor Parson Thirdly said,
"I wish I had stuck to pipes and beer."

Again the guns disturbed the hour,
Roaring their readiness to avenge.
35 As far inland as Stourton Tower,
And Camelot, and starlit Stonehenge.[5]

April 1914

## SANDRA GILBERT

### *Sonnet: The Ladies' Home Journal*

The brilliant stills of food, the cozy
glossy, bygone life—mashed potatoes
posing as whipped cream, a neat mom
conjuring shapes from chaos, trimming the flame—
5 how we ached for all that,
that dance of love in the living room,
those paneled walls, that kitchen golden
as the inside of a seed: how we leaned

---

5. A circular formation of upright stones dating from about 1600 B.C.E. on Salisbury Plain, Wiltshire; it is thought to have been a ceremonial site for political and religious occasions or perhaps an early astronomical observatory. *Stourton Tower:* a monument in Stourhead Park, Wiltshire, built in the eighteenth century to commemorate King Alfred's ninth-century victory over the Danes. *Camelot:* the legendary site of King Arthur's court, said to have been in Cornwall or Somerset.

>     on those shiny columns of advice,
> 10  stroking the *thank yous,* the firm thighs, the wise
>     closets full of soap.
>
>                    But even then
>     we knew it was the lies we loved, the lies
>     we wore like Dior coats,[6] the clean-cut airtight
>     lies that laid out our lives in black and white.
>
>                                                    1984

"Channel Firing" is not ultimately *about* World War I, for it presumes that human behavior stays the same from age to age, but it begins from a particular historical vantage point. The composition date was recorded by the author on the manuscript and is considered part of the poem, but even with that clue a reader would not be able to make much sense of the poem without recognizing the specific reference—the dramatic situation here (with a waking corpse as the main speaker) is difficult enough to sort out. The firing of the guns has awakened the dead who are buried near the channel, and in their puzzlement they assume it is Judgment Day, time for them to arise, until God enters and tells them what is happening. Much of the poem's effect depends on character portrayal—a God who laughs and sounds cynical, a parson who regrets his selfless life and wishes he had indulged himself more—as well as the sense that nothing ever changes. But particularity of time and place is crucial to this sense of changelessness; even so important a contemporary moment as the beginning of a world war—a moment viewed by most people at the time as unique and world-changing—fades into a timeless parade of moments that stretches over centuries of history. The geographical particulars cited at the end—as the sound of the guns moves inland to be heard in place after place—make the same point. Great moments in history are all encompassed in the sound of the guns and its message about human behavior. Times, places, and events, however important they seem, all become part of some larger pattern that denies individuality or uniqueness.

The particulars in "Sonnet: The Ladies' Home Journal" work differently—not to remind us of a specific time that readers need to identify but to characterize a way of seeing and thinking. The referentiality here is more cultural than historical; it is based more on ideas and attitudes characteristic of a particular period than on a specific moment or location. The pictures in the *Ladies' Home Journal* stand for a whole way of thinking about women that was characteristic of the time—the mid-twentieth century—when this popular magazine flourished. The poem implicitly contrasts the "lies" (line 13) of the magazine with the truth of the present—that women's lives and values don't reside in some fantasized sense of beautiful food, motherhood, social rituals, and commercial products. Two vastly different cultural attitudes—that of the poem's present, with its skeptical view of women's traditional roles, and that of a past in which carefully posed glossy photographs represented an idealized womanhood—are at the heart of the poem. Readers need to know what the *Ladies' Home Journal* was like generally in order to understand the poem; we do not need to know the date or contents of a specific issue, only

---

6. Designer coats by Christian Dior.

that this magazine reflected the attitudes and values of a whole age and culture. The referentiality here involves information about ideas and consciousness—about cultural attitudes and their effects on actual human beings—more than the specifics of time and event.

To get at appropriate factual, cultural, and historical information, we need to ask three kinds of questions. One is obvious: it is the "Do I understand the reference to . . . ?" kind. When events, places, or people unfamiliar to you come up, you will need to find out what, where, or who they are. The second kind of question is more difficult: How do you know, in a poem that does *not* refer specifically to events, people, or ideas that you do not recognize, that you *need* to know more? When a poem has no specific references to look up, no people or events to identify, how do you know that it has a specific context? To deal with this sort of question, you have to trust two people: the poet and yourself. Usually, good poets will not puzzle you more than necessary, so you can safely assume that something not self-explanatory will merit close attention and possibly some digging in the library. (Poets do make mistakes and miscalculations about their readers, but at first we should assume they know what they are doing and why they are doing it.) References that are not in themselves clear provide a strong clue that you need more information. And so you need to trust yourself: when something doesn't click, when the information given you does not seem enough, you need to trust your puzzlement and try to find the missing facts that will allow the poem to make sense. But how? Often the date of the poem helps; sometimes the title gives a clue or a point of departure; sometimes you can uncover, by reading about the author, some of the things he or she was interested in or concerned about. There is no single all-purpose way to discover what to look for, but that kind of research—looking for clues, adding up the evidence—can be interesting in itself and very rewarding when it is successful. Meanwhile, the third question, for every factual reference, is *Why?* Why does the poem refer to this particular person instead of some other? What function does the reference serve?

Beyond simply understanding that a particular poem is about an event or place or idea, you often must develop a full sense of historical context, a sense of the larger significance and resonance of the historical background. A poem may expect you to already have some sense of that significance; just as often the poem works to educate you further, both in your understanding and also on the level of feeling.

What we need to bring to our reading varies from poem to poem. For example, Wilfred Owen's "Dulce et Decorum Est" (in this chapter) needs our knowledge that poison gas was used in World War I; the green tint through which the speaker sees the world in lines 13–14 comes from the green glass in the goggles of the gas mask he has just put on. But some broader issues matter as well, such as the climate of opinion that surrounded the war. To idealists, it would become "the war to end all wars," and many soldiers—as well as politicians and propagandists—considered it a sacred mission, regarding the threat of Germany's expansionist policy as dangerous to Western civilization itself. No doubt you will read the poem more intelligently—and with more feeling—the more you know about the context, and the same is true of any poem conscious of its cultural or historical basis. But at the same time, your sense of these subjects will grow as a result of reading sensitively and thoughtfully the poems themselves. Facts are no substitute for skills. Once you have read each of the poems in this section, try taking a breather; and then in one sitting read them all again. Reading poetry can be a form of gaining knowledge as well as an aesthetic experience. Although we don't generally turn to poetry for information as such, poems often give us more than we expect. The ways to wisdom are paved with facts, and although poetry is not primarily a means of transmitting facts, it often requires us to be aware, sometimes in detail, of its context in the real world.

## TIMES, PLACES, AND EVENTS

### MILLER WILLIAMS

### Thinking about Bill, Dead of AIDS

We did not know the first thing about
how blood surrenders to even the smallest threat
when old allergies turn inside out,

the body rescinding all its normal orders
5  to all defenders of flesh, betraying the head,
pulling its guards back from all its borders.

Thinking of friends afraid to shake your hand,
we think of your hand shaking, your mouth set,
your eyes drained of any reprimand.

10 Loving, we kissed you, partly to persuade
both you and us, seeing what eyes had said,
that we were loving and were not afraid.

If we had had more, we would have given more.
As it was we stood next to your bed,
15 stopping, though, to set our smiles at the door.

Not because we were less sure at the last.
Only because, not knowing anything yet,
we didn't know what look would hurt you least.

1989

## IRVING LAYTON

### From Colony to Nation

A dull people,
but the rivers of this country
are wide and beautiful

A dull people
5   enamoured of childish games,
but food is easily come by
and plentiful

Some with a priest's voice
in their cage of ribs: but
10  on high mountain-tops and in thunderstorms
the chirping is not heard

Deferring to beadle and censor;
not ashamed for this,
but given over to horseplay,
15  the making of money

A dull people, without charm or
ideas,
settling into the clean empty look
of a Mountie or dairy farmer
20  as into a legacy

One can ignore them
(the silences, the vast distances help)
and suppose them at the bottom
of one of the meaner lakes,
25  their bones not even picked for souvenirs.

1956

## LANGSTON HUGHES

### Harlem

What happens to a dream deferred?

   Does it dry up
   like a raisin in the sun?
   Or fester like a sore—
5  And then run?
   Does it stink like rotten meat?
   Or crust and sugar over—
   like a syrupy sweet?

                Maybe it just sags
10              like a heavy load.

                *Or does it explode?*

                                                1951


### ROBERT HAYDEN
## Frederick Douglass

When it is finally ours, this freedom,[1] this liberty, this beautiful
and terrible thing, needful to man as air,
usable as earth; when it belongs at last to all,
when it is truly instinct, brain matter, diastole, systole,
5 reflex action; when it is finally won; when it is more
than the gaudy mumbo jumbo of politicians:
this man, this Douglass, this former slave, this Negro
beaten to his knees, exiled, visioning a world
where none is lonely, none hunted, alien,
10 this man, superb in love and logic, this man
shall be remembered. Oh, not with statues' rhetoric,
not with legends and poems and wreaths of bronze alone,
but with the lives grown out of his life, the lives
fleshing his dream of the beautiful, needful thing.

                                                1966


### FELICIA DOROTHEA HEMANS
## Casabianca[2]

The boy stood on the burning deck
  Whence all but he had fled;
The flame that lit the battle's wreck
  Shone round him o'er the dead.

5 Yet beautiful and bright he stood,
    As born to rule the storm;
  A creature of heroic blood,
    A proud, though childlike form.

---

1. Frederick Douglass (1817–1895), an escaped slave, was involved in the Underground Railroad and became publisher of the famous abolitionist newspaper the *North Star*, in Rochester, New York.
2. Young Casabianca, a boy about thirteen years old, son to the Admiral of the *Orient*, remained at his post (in the Battle of the Nile [1798]) after the ship had taken fire, and all the guns had been abandoned; and perished in the explosion of the vessel, when the flames had reached the powder [Hemans's note].

>     The flames roll'd on—he would not go
> 10  Without his father's word;
>     That father, faint in death below,
>       His voice no longer heard.
>
>     He call'd aloud:—"Say, Father, say
>       If yet my task is done?"
> 15  He knew not that the chieftain lay
>       Unconscious of his son.
>
>     "Speak, Father!" once again he cried,
>       "If I may yet be gone!"
>     And but the booming shots replied,
> 20    And fast the flames roll'd on.
>
>     Upon his brow he felt their breath,
>       And in his waving hair,
>     And look'd from that lone post of death
>       In still, yet brave despair.
>
> 25  And shouted but once more aloud,
>       "My Father! must I stay?"
>     While o'er him fast, through sail and shroud,
>       The wreathing fires made way.
>
>     They wrapt the ship in splendor wild,
> 30    They caught the flag on high,
>     And stream'd above the gallant child,
>       Like banners in the sky.
>
>     There came a burst of thunder sound—
>       The boy—oh! where was he?
> 35  Ask of the winds that far around
>       With fragments strew'd the sea!—
>
>     With mast, and helm, and pennon fair,
>       That well had borne their part,
>     But the noblest thing which perish'd there
> 40    Was that young faithful heart
>
>                                    1829

## ELIZABETH BISHOP

### Casabianca

>     Love's the boy stood on the burning deck
>     trying to recite "The boy stood on
>     the burning deck." Love's the son
>     stood stammering elocution
>  5  while the poor ship in flames went down.

Love's the obstinate boy, the ship,
even the swimming sailors, who
would like a schoolroom platform, too,
   or an excuse to stay
10 on deck. And love's the burning boy.

                                        1946


**WILFRED OWEN**

*Dulce et Decorum Est*[3]

Bent double, like old beggars under sacks,
Knock-kneed, coughing like hags, we cursed through sludge,
Till on the haunting flares we turned our backs
And towards our distant rest began to trudge.
5 Men marched asleep. Many had lost their boots
But limped on, blood-shod. All went lame; all blind;
Drunk with fatigue; deaf even to the hoots
Of disappointed shells that dropped behind.

Gas! Gas! Quick, boys!—An ecstasy of fumbling,
10 Fitting the clumsy helmets just in time;
But someone still was yelling out and stumbling
And floundering like a man in fire or lime.—
Dim, through the misty panes and thick green light
As under a green sea, I saw him drowning.

15 In all my dreams, before my helpless sight,
He plunges at me, guttering, choking, drowning.

If in some smothering dreams you too could pace
Behind the wagon that we flung him in,
And watch the white eyes writhing in his face,
20 His hanging face, like a devil's sick of sin;
If you could hear, at every jolt, the blood
Come gargling from the froth-corrupted lungs,
Obscene as cancer, bitter as the cud
Of vile, incurable sores on innocent tongues,—
25 My friend, you would not tell with such high zest
To children ardent for some desperate glory,
The old Lie: Dulce et decorum est
Pro patria mori.

1917

---

3. Part of a phrase from Horace (Roman poet and satirist, 65–8 B.C.E.), quoted in full in the last lines: "It is sweet and proper to die for one's country."

DUDLEY RANDALL

## Ballad of Birmingham

(On the bombing of a church in Birmingham, Alabama, 1963)

"Mother dear, may I go downtown
Instead of out to play,
And march the streets of Birmingham
In a Freedom March today?"

5  "No, baby, no, you may not go,
For the dogs are fierce and wild,
And clubs and hoses, guns and jails
Aren't good for a little child."

"But, mother, I won't be alone.
10 Other children will go with me,
And march the streets of Birmingham
To make our country free."

"No, baby, no, you may not go,
For I fear those guns will fire.
15 But you may go to church instead
And sing in the children's choir."

She has combed and brushed her night-dark hair,
And bathed rose petal sweet,
And drawn white gloves on her small brown hands,
20 And white shoes on her feet.

The mother smiled to know her child
Was in the sacred place,
But that smile was the last smile
To come upon her face.

25 For when she heard the explosion,
Her eyes grew wet and wild.
She raced through the streets of Birmingham
Calling for her child.

She clawed through bits of glass and brick,
30 Then lifted out a shoe.
"Oh, here's the shoe my baby wore,
But, baby, where are you?"

1969

## CONSTRUCTING IDENTITY, EXPLORING GENDER

### ELIZABETH BISHOP
### *Exchanging Hats*

Unfunny uncles who insist
in trying on a lady's hat,
—oh, even if the joke falls flat,
we share your slight transvestite twist

5  in spite of our embarrassment.
Costume and custom are complex.
The headgear of the other sex
inspires us to experiment.

Anandrous[1] aunts, who, at the beach
10 with paper plates upon your laps,
keep putting on the yachtsmen's caps
with exhibitionistic screech,

the visors hanging o'er the ear
so that the golden anchors drag,
15 —the tides of fashion never lag.
Such caps may not be worn next year.

Or you who don the paper plate
itself, and put some grapes upon it,
or sport the Indian's feather bonnet,
20 —perversities may aggravate

the natural madness of the hatter.
And if the opera hats collapse
and crowns grow drafty, then, perhaps,
he thinks what might a miter matter?

25 Unfunny uncle, you who wore a
hat too big, or one too many,
tell us, can't you, are there any
stars inside your black fedora?

Aunt exemplary and slim,
30 with avernal[2] eyes, we wonder
what slow changes they see under
their vast, shady, turned-down brim.

1956

---

1. Literally, "husbandless."   2. Infernal.

MARIE HOWE

## Practicing

I want to write a love poem for the girls I kissed in seventh grade,
a song for what we did on the floor in the basement

of somebody's parents' house, a hymn for what we didn't say but
    thought:
*That feels good* or *I like that*, when we learned how to open each other's
    mouths

how to move our tongues to make somebody moan. We called it
5    practicing, and
one was the boy, and we paired off—maybe six or eight girls—and
    turned out

the lights and kissed and kissed until we were stoned on kisses, and
    lifted our
nightgowns or let the straps drop, and, Now you be the boy:

concrete floor, sleeping bag or couch, playroom, game room, train room,
    laundry.
10 Linda's basement was like a boat with booths and portholes

instead of windows. Gloria's father had a bar downstairs with stools
    that spun,
plush carpeting. We kissed each other's throats.

We sucked each other's breasts, and we left marks, and never spoke of it
    upstairs
outdoors, in daylight, not once. We did it, and it was

practicing, and slept, sprawled so our legs still locked or crossed, a hand
15    still lost
in someone's hair . . . and we grew up and hardly mentioned who

the first kiss really was—a girl like us, still sticky with the moisturizer
    we'd
shared in the bathroom. I want to write a song

for that thick silence in the dark, and the first pure thrill of unreluctant
    desire,
20 just before we made ourselves stop.

1998

**RICHARD LOVELACE**

## Song: To Lucasta, Going to the Wars

Tell me not, sweet, I am unkind,
   That from the nunnery
Of thy chaste breast and quiet mind
   To war and arms I fly.

5 True: a new mistress now I chase,
   The first foe in the field;
And with a stronger faith embrace
   A sword, a horse, a shield.

Yet this inconstancy is such
10   As you too shall adore;
I could not love thee, dear, so much,
   Loved I not honor more.

1649

**WILFRED OWEN**

## Disabled

He sat in a wheeled chair, waiting for dark,
And shivered in his ghastly suit of grey,
Legless, sewn short at elbow. Through the park
Voices of boys rang saddening like a hymn,
5 Voices of play and pleasure after day,
Till gathering sleep had mothered them from him.

About this time Town used to swing so gay
When glow-lamps budded in the light blue trees,
And girls glanced lovelier as the air grew dim,—
10 In the old times, before he threw away his knees.
Now he will never feel again how slim
Girls' waists are, or how warm their subtle hands;
All of them touch him like some queer disease.

There was an artist silly for his face,
15 For it was younger than his youth, last year.
Now, he is old; his back will never brace;
He's lost his color very far from here,
Poured it down shell-holes till the veins ran dry,
And half his lifetime lapsed in the hot race,
20 And leap of purple spurted from his thigh.

One time he liked a blood-smear down his leg,
After the matches,[3] carried shoulder-high
It was after football, when he'd drunk a peg,[4]
He thought he'd better join.—He wonders why.
25 Someone had said he'd look a god in kilts,
That's why; and may be, too, to please his Meg;
Aye, that was it, to please the giddy jilts
He asked to join. He didn't have to beg;
Smiling they wrote his lie; aged nineteen years.

30 Germans he scarcely thought of; all their guilt,
And Austria's, did not move him. And no fears
Of Fear came yet. He thought of jeweled hilts
For daggers in plaid socks; of smart salutes;
And care of arms; and leave; and pay arrears;
35 *Esprit de corps;* and hints for young recruits.
And soon, he was drafted out with drums and cheers.

Some cheered him home, but not as crowds cheer Goal.
Only a solemn man who brought him fruits
*Thanked* him; and then inquired about his soul.
40 Now, he will spend a few sick years in Institutes,
And do what things the rules consider wise,
And take whatever pity they may dole.
Tonight he noticed how the women's eyes
Passed from him to the strong men that were whole.
45 How cold and late it is! Why don't they come
And put him into bed? Why don't they come?

1917

## ROBERT BROWNING

### My Last Duchess

Ferrara[5]

That's my last Duchess painted on the wall,
Looking as if she were alive. I call
That piece a wonder, now: Frà Pandolf's hands[6]
Worked busily a day, and there she stands.
5 Will't please you sit and look at her? I said
"Frà Pandolf" by design, for never read
Strangers like you that pictured countenance,

---

3. Soccer games.   4. A drink, usually brandy and soda.
5. Alfonso II, duke of Ferrara in Italy in the mid-sixteenth century, is the presumed speaker of the poem, which is loosely based on historical events. The duke's first wife—whom he had married when she was fourteen—died under suspicious circumstances at seventeen, and he then negotiated through an agent (to whom the poem is spoken) for the hand of the niece of the count of Tyrol in Austria.
6. Frà Pandolf is, like Claus (line 56), fictitious.

　　　　The depth and passion of its earnest glance,
　　　　But to myself they turned (since none puts by
　10　The curtain I have drawn for you, but I)
　　　　And seemed as they would ask me, if they durst,
　　　　How such a glance came there; so, not the first
　　　　Are you to turn and ask thus. Sir, 'twas not
　　　　Her husband's presence only, called that spot
　15　Of joy into the Duchess' cheek: perhaps
　　　　Frà Pandolf chanced to say "Her mantle laps
　　　　Over my lady's wrist too much," or "Paint
　　　　Must never hope to reproduce the faint
　　　　Half-flush that dies along her throat": such stuff
　20　Was courtesy, she thought, and cause enough
　　　　For calling up that spot of joy. She had
　　　　A heart—how shall I say?—too soon made glad,
　　　　Too easily impressed; she liked whate'er
　　　　She looked on, and her looks went everywhere.
　25　Sir, 'twas all one! My favor at her breast,
　　　　The dropping of the daylight in the West,
　　　　The bough of cherries some officious fool
　　　　Broke in the orchard for her, the white mule
　　　　She rode with round the terrace—all and each
　30　Would draw from her alike the approving speech,
　　　　Or blush, at least. She thanked men,—good! but thanked
　　　　Somehow—I know not how—as if she ranked
　　　　My gift of a nine-hundred-years-old name
　　　　With anybody's gift. Who'd stoop to blame
　35　This sort of trifling? Even had you skill
　　　　In speech—which I have not—to make your will
　　　　Quite clear to such an one, and say, "Just this
　　　　Or that in you disgusts me; here you miss,
　　　　Or there exceed the mark"—and if she let
　40　Herself be lessoned so, nor plainly set
　　　　Her wits to yours, forsooth, and made excuse,
　　　　—E'en then would be some stooping; and I choose
　　　　Never to stoop. Oh sir, she smiled, no doubt,
　　　　Whene'er I passed her; but who passed without
　45　Much the same smile? This grew; I gave commands;
　　　　Then all smiles stopped together. There she stands
　　　　As if alive. Will't please you rise? We'll meet
　　　　The company below, then. I repeat,
　　　　The Count your master's known munificence
　50　Is ample warrant that no just pretense
　　　　Of mine for dowry will be disallowed;
　　　　Though his fair daughter's self, as I avowed
　　　　At starting, is my object. Nay, we'll go
　　　　Together down, sir. Notice Neptune, though,
　55　Taming a sea-horse, thought a rarity,
　　　　Which Claus of Innsbruck cast in bronze for me!
　　　　　　　　　　　　　　　　　　　1842

## A Woman's Last Word

### 1
Let's contend no more, Love,
   Strive nor weep.
All be as before, Love,
   —Only sleep!

### 2
5 What so wild as words are?
   I and thou
In debate, as birds are,
   Hawk on bough!

### 3
See the creature stalking
10    While we speak!
Hush and hide the talking
   Cheek on cheek!

### 4
What so false as truth is,
   False to thee?
15 Where the serpent's tooth is
   Shun the tree—

### 5
Where the apple reddens
   Never pry—
Lest we lose our Edens,
20    Eye and I

### 6
Be a god and hold me
   With a charm!
Be a man and fold me
   With thine arm!

### 7
25 Teach me, only teach, Love!
   As I ought
I will speak thy speech, Love,
   Think thy thought—

            8
    Meet, if thou require it,
30      Both demands,
    Laying flesh and spirit
        In thy hands.

            9
    That shall be tomorrow
        Not tonight:
35  I must bury sorrow
        Out of sight:

            10
    —Must a little weep, Love
        (Foolish me!),
    And so fall asleep, Love,
40      Loved by thee.

                    1855

**ELIZABETH BARRETT BROWNING**

## To George Sand

A Desire

Thou large-brained woman and large-hearted man,
Self-called George Sand[7] whose soul, amid the lions
Of thy tumultuous senses, moans defiance
And answers roar for roar, as spirits can:
5   I would some mild miraculous thunder ran
Above the applauded circus,[8] in appliance
Of thine own nobler nature's strength and science,
Drawing two pinions, white as wings of swan,
From thy strong shoulders, to amaze the place
10  With holier light! that thou to woman's claim
And man's, mightst join beside the angel's grace
Of a pure genius sanctified from blame,
Till child and maiden pressed to thine embrace
To kiss upon thy lips a stainless fame.

                    1844

---

7. Pseudonym of Amandine-Aurore-Lucie (or -Lucille) Dupin, baronne Dudevant (1804–1876), French Romantic novelist, famous for her unconventional ideas and behavior.
8. Roman spectacle involving gladiatorial games, brutal athletic contests, and the killing of Christian slaves by lions.

## *To George Sand*

### A Recognition

True genius, but true woman! dost deny
The woman's nature with a manly scorn,
And break away the gauds and armlets worn
By weaker women in captivity?
5 Ah, vain denial! that revolted cry
Is sobbed in by a woman's voice forlorn,—
Thy woman's hair, my sister, all unshorn
Floats back dishevelled strength in agony,
Disproving thy man's name: and while before
10 The world thou burnest in a poet-fire,
We see thy woman-heart beat evermore
Through the large flame. Beat purer, heart, and higher,
Till God unsex thee on the heavenly shore
Where unincarnate spirits purely aspire!

1844

### YUSEF KOMUNYAKAA

## *Tu Do Street*

Searching for love, a woman,
someone to help ease down the cocked hammer
of my nerves & senses. The music
divides the evening into black
5 & white—soul, country & western,
acid rock, & Frank Sinatra.
I close my eyes & can see
men drawing lines in the dust,
daring each other to step across.
10 America pushes through the membrane
of mist & smoke, & I'm a small boy
again in Bogalusa[9] skirting tough talk
coming out of bars with *White Only*
signs & Hank Snow. But tonight,
15 here in Saigon, just for the hell of it,
I walk into a place with Hank Williams
calling from the jukebox. The bar girls
fade behind a smokescreen, fluttering

---

9. Industrial city in southeastern Louisiana.

          like tropical birds in a cage, not
20     speaking with their eyes & usual
          painted smiles. I get the silent
          treatment. We have played Judas
          for each other out in the boonies
          but only enemy machinegun fire
25     can bring us together again.
          When I order a beer, the mama-san
          behind the counter acts as if she
          can't understand, while her
          eyes caress a white face;
30     down the street the black GIs
          hold to their turf also.
          An off-limits sign pulls me
          deeper into alleys; I look
          for a softness behind these voices
35     wounded by their beauty & war.
          Back in the bush at Dak To
          & Khe Sahn, we fought
          the brothers of these women
          we now run to hold in our arms.
40     There's more than a nation divided
          inside us, as black & white
          soldiers touch the same lovers
          minutes apart, tasting
          each other's breath,
45     without knowing these rooms
          run into each other like tunnels
          leading to the underworld.

                                                                1988

**LADY MARY WORTLEY MONTAGU**

## Written the First Year I Was Marry'd

While thirst of power, and desire of fame,
In every age is every woman's aim;
Of beauty vain, of silly toasters proud,
Fond of a train, and happy in a crowd,
5 On every fop bestowing a kind glance,
Each conquest owing to some loose advance,
Affect to fly, in hopes to be persu'd,
And think they're virtuous, if not grossly lewd:
Let this sure maxim be my virtue's guide,
10 In part to blame she is, who has been try'd;
Too near he has approach'd, who is deny'd.

1712–13


**MARGE PIERCY**

## What's That Smell in the Kitchen?

All over America women are burning dinners.
It's lambchops in Peoria; it's haddock
in Providence; it's steak in Chicago;
tofu delight in Big Sur; red
5 rice and beans in Dallas.
All over America women are burning
food they're supposed to bring with calico
smile on platters glittering like wax.
Anger sputters in her brainpan, confined
10 but spewing out missiles of hot fat.
Carbonized despair presses like a clinker
from a barbecue against the back of her eyes.
If she wants to grill anything, it's
her husband spitted over a slow fire.
15 If she wants to serve him anything
it's a dead rat with a bomb in its belly
ticking like the heart of an insomniac.
Her life is cooked and digested,
nothing but leftovers in Tupperware.
20 Look, she says, once I was roast duck
on your platter with parsley but now I am Spam.
Burning dinner is not incompetence but war.

1983

PAULETTE JILES

## Paper Matches

My aunts washed dishes while the uncles
squirted each other on the lawn with
   garden hoses. Why are we in here,
I said, and they are out there.
5   That's the way it is,
   said Aunt Hetty, the shrivelled-up one.
   I have the rages that small animals have,
being small, being animal.
   Written on me was a message,
10 "At Your Service" like a book of
paper matches. One by one we were
taken out and struck.
   We come bearing supper,
our heads on fire.

                                 1973

ELIZABETH I[1]

## When I Was Fair and Young

When I was fair and young, and favor graced me,
   Of many was I sought, their mistress for to be;
But I did scorn them all, and answered them therefore,
   "Go, go, go, seek some otherwhere,
5      Importune me no more!"

How many weeping eyes I made to pine with woe,
   How many sighing hearts, I have no skill to show;
Yet I the prouder grew, and answered them therefore,
   "Go, go, go, seek some otherwhere,
10     Importune me no more!"

Then spake fair Venus' son, that proud victorious boy,[2]
   And said: "Fine dame, since that you be so coy,
I will so pluck your plumes that you shall say no more,
   'Go, go, go, seek some otherwhere,
15     Importune me no more!' "

---

1. The attribution of this poem to Queen Elizabeth I of England (1533–1603) is likely but not certain.
2. Cupid.

When he had spake these words, such change grew in my breast
    That neither night nor day since that, I could take any rest.
Then lo! I did repent that I had said before,
    "Go, go, go, seek some otherwhere,
20        Importune me no more!"

ca. 1585?

## MARILYN HACKER

### [Who would divorce her lover]

Who would divorce her lover with a phone
call? You did. Like that, it's finished, done—
or is for you. I'm left with closets of
grief (you moved out your things next day). I love
5 you. I want to make the phone call this
time, say, pack your axe,[3] cab uptown, kiss
me, lots. I'll run a bubble bath; we'll sing
in the tub. We worked for love, loved it. Don't sling
that out with Friday's beer cans, or file-card it
10 in a drawer of anecdotes: "My Last
Six Girlfriends: How a Girl Acquires a Past."
I've got "What Becomes of the Broken-Hearted"
run on a loop, unwanted leitmotif.
Lust, light, love, life all tumbled into grief.
15 You closed us off like a parenthesis
and left me knowing just enough to miss.

1986

---

3. Musicians' slang for a musical instrument.

AMY LOWELL

## The Lonely Wife[5]

The mist is thick. On the wide river, the water-plants float smoothly.
No letters come; none go.
There is only the moon, shining through the clouds of a hard, jade-green sky,
Looking down at us so far divided, so anxiously apart.
All day, going about my affairs, I suffer and grieve, and press the thought of you closely to my heart.
My eyebrows are locked in sorrow, I cannot separate them.
Nightly, nightly, I keep ready half the quilt,
And wait for the return of that divine dream which is my Lord.

Beneath the quilt of the Fire-Bird, on the bed of the Silver-Crested Love-Pheasant,
Nightly, nightly, I drowse alone.
The red candles in the silver candlesticks melt, and the wax runs from them,
As the tears of your so Unworthy One escape and continue constantly to flow.
A flower face endures but a short season,
Yet still he drifts along the river Hsiao and the river Hsiang.
As I toss on my pillow, I hear the cold, nostalgic sound of the water-clock:
Shêng! Shêng! it drips, cutting my heart in two.

I rise at dawn. In the Hall of Pictures
They come and tell me that the snow-flowers are falling.
The reed-blind is rolled high, and I gaze at the beautiful, glittering, primeval snow,
Whitening the distance, confusing the stone steps and the courtyard.
The air is filled with its shining, it blows far out like the smoke of a furnace.
The grass-blades are cold and white, like jade girdle pendants.
Surely the Immortals in Heaven must be crazy with wine to cause such disorder,
Seizing the white clouds, crumpling them up, destroying them.

1921

---

5. A translation/adaptation of a poem by the Chinese poet Li Po (701-762 C.E.).

**LIZ ROSENBERG**

## *The Silence of Women*

Old men, as time goes on, grow softer, sweeter,
while their wives get angrier.
You see them hauling the men across the mall
or pushing them down on chairs,
5 "Sit there! and don't you move!"
A lifetime of *yes* has left them
hissing bent as snakes.
It seems even their bones will turn
against them, once the fruitful years are gone.
10 Something snaps off the houselights,
and the cells go dim;
the chicken hatching back into the egg.

Oh lifetime of silence!
words scattered like a sibyl's leaves.
15 Voice thrown into a baritone storm—
whose shrilling is a soulful wind
blown through an instrument
that cannot beat time

but must make music
20 any way it can.

1994

**THOM GUNN**

## *A Blank*

The year of griefs being through, they had to merge
In one last grief, with one last property;
To view itself like loosened cloud lose edge,
And pull apart, and leave a voided sky.

5 Watching Victorian porches through the glass,
From the 6 bus, I caught sight of a friend
Stopped on a corner-kerb to let us pass,
A four-year-old blond child tugging his hand,
Which tug he held against with a slight smile.
10 I knew the smile from certain passages
Two years ago, thus did not know him well,
Since they took place in my bedroom and his.

A sturdy-looking admirable young man.
He said "I chose to do this with my life."

15  Casually met he said it of the plan
    He undertook without a friend or wife.

    Now visibly tugged upon by his decision,
    Wayward and eager. So this was his son!
    What I admired about his self-permission
20  Was that he turned from nothing he had done,
    Or was, or had been, even while he transposed
    The expectations he took out at dark
    —Of Eros playing, features undisclosed—
    Into another pitch, where he might work
25  With the same melody, and opted so
    To educate, permit, guide, feed, keep warm,
    And love a child to be adopted, though
    The child was still a blank then on a form.

    The blank was flesh now, running on its nerve,
30  This fair-topped organism dense with charm,
    Its braided muscle grabbing what would serve,
    His countering pull, his own devoted arm.

                                            1992

---

## SUGGESTIONS FOR WRITING

1. Consider "Harlem" by Langston Hughes and "Frederick Douglass" by Robert Hayden. Does Hughes's poem, written in 1951, predict the violent upheavals of the civil rights movement in the 1960s? Why does Hayden's poem, written in 1966, promise that Douglass "shall be remembered," as though Douglass had only recently died? Write an essay in which you explore the way these two poems speak about their own times by pointing to the future.
2. Generations of American schoolchildren were made to memorize and recite Felicia Dorothea Hemans's "Casabianca," a fact reflected by the references to "stammering elocution" and "a schoolroom platform" in Elizabeth Bishop's "Casabianca." Write an essay in which you discuss Bishop's poem in light of Hemans's original. What made Hemans's poem suitable as a recitation piece? How does Bishop's poem "answer" Heman's? How does each poem demonstrate a sense of what poetry is, or what it is for?
3. Research the use of poison gas in World War I and then write an essay in which you analyze Wilfred Owen's "Dulce et Decorum Est." How does the poem dramatize the effects of gas? What statement does it make about this new form of warfare?
4. Write an essay in which you first present a detailed narrative of the 1963 Birmingham bombing, based on research. Then analyze Dudley Randall's "Ballad of Birmingham" in light of this history. To what extent is Randall's poem based on established facts? To what extent is the poem fictitious? How effective is this mingling of fact and fiction?
5. Write an essay in which you analyze either Robert Browning's "My Last Duchess" or his "A Woman's Last Word." Who is the speaker? Who is being addressed? What is the situation? How do details gradually reveal character and "plot"? What is the advantage to the poet in using this form, the dramatic monologue? How does Browning integrate the poetic elements of language and form into the dramatic monologue?

6. Research the life of the nineteenth-century novelist George Sand, and then write an essay in which you discuss the two sonnets that Elizabeth Barrett Browning dedicated to her. How do these poems, taken together, reveal Barrett Browning's conception of artistic genius, especially when embodied in a woman?
7. How are images of fire and burning used in "What's That Smell in the Kitchen" by Marge Piercy and "Paper Matches" by Paulette Jiles? What common threads of meaning inform the images in these poems? Write an essay in which you compare and contrast Piercy's and Jiles's use of imagery, and also their cultural assumptions about the gender roles of men and women.
8. Which poems in this chapter's "Constructing Identity, Exploring Gender" section most effectively describe how men choose to act like men, and women choose to act like women? Choose at least three poems from this section and analyze how they present the ways that women and men construct their gender identities.
9. Choose any poem in this book and research the historical or cultural background that informs it. Write an essay in which you discuss how the poem illuminates its context, and vice versa.

## 22 THE AUTHOR'S WORK AS CONTEXT: JOHN KEATS AND ADRIENNE RICH

Even though all poets share the medium of language and usually have some common notions about their craft, they put the unique resources of their individual personalities, experiences, and outlooks into every poem they create. A poet may rely on tradition extensively and use devices that others have developed without surrendering his or her individuality, just as any individual shares certain characteristics with others—political affiliations, religious beliefs, tastes in clothes and music—without compromising his or her integrity and uniqueness. Sometimes a person's uniqueness is hard to define. But it is always there, and we recognize and depend on it in our relationships with other people. And so with poets: most don't make a conscious effort to put an individual stamp on their work; they don't have to. The stamp is there in the very subjects, words, images, and forms they choose. Every individual's unique consciousness marks what it records and imagines.

Experienced readers can often identify a poem as the distinctive work of an individual poet even though they may never have seen that poem before, much as experienced listeners can identify a new piece of music as the work of a particular composer, singer, or group after hearing only a few phrases. This ability depends on a lot of reading or a lot of listening to music, and any reasonably sensitive reader can learn, over time, to do it with remarkable accuracy. Yet this ability is not really an end in itself; rather, it is a by-product of learning to appreciate the particular, distinctive qualities of any poet's work. Once you've read several poems by the same poet, you will usually see some features that the poems all share, and gradually you may come to think of those features as characteristic. Many people have favorite poets, just as they have favorite rock groups or rap artists. In both cases, we are attracted to the artist's work precisely because, consciously or not, we recognize and appreciate that artist's distinctive style and outlook.

To perform an experiment, consult the Index of Authors at the back of this book to locate the following poems by Howard Nemerov: "The Vacuum," "The Goose Fish," and "Boom!" (You can also do this experiment with other poets whose work appears in the book several times, such as Emily Dickinson and John Donne.) After reading these poems, list the similarities you find, perhaps by concentrating on each of the literary elements in turn. Then look at Nemerov's "A Way of Life." In what ways is "A Way of Life" like the other Nemerov poems?

The concern with contemporary life, the tendency to concentrate on modern conveniences and luxuries, and the interest in isolating and defining aspects of a distinctively modern sensibility are all characteristic of Nemerov. So, too, is the tendency to create a short drama, with a speaker who is not altogether admirable. Several of Nemerov's poems also share an attitude that seems deeply imbedded in "A Way of Life"—a kind of antiromanticism that emerges when someone tries to sound or feel *too* proud or cheerful and is shown, by events in the poem, to be part of a grimmer reality instead. The concentration upon one or more physical objects is also characteristic, and often (as in "The Vacuum") the main object is a mechanical one that symbolizes modernity and our modern dependency on things. Americanness is emphasized here, too, through a concern with defining not only our time, but also our culture, its habits, and its values. The mood of loneliness is typical of Nemerov, and so is the poem's witty conversational style. The verbal wit here—although not as prominent as the puns and double entendres of "Boom!"—is characteristically informal. Often it seems to derive from the language of commercials and street speech, and Nemerov's undercutting of this language—having a paranoid and simpleminded speaker talk about a gangster in "a state of existential despair"—resembles the strategy of "Boom!" or "The Vacuum." The regular stanzas, rhymed though not in a traditional or regular way and using a number of near-rhymes, are also typical. (Compare, for example, "The Goose Fish.") In short, "A Way of Life" encapsulates Nemerov's thematic interests and ideas, his verbal style, and his cast of mind.

The work of any writer will display a characteristic way of thinking. It will have certain identifiable *tendencies*. But this does not mean that every poem by a particular author will be predictable and contain all of the same features. Poets test their talents and their views—as well as their readers—by experimenting with various subjects and points of view, formal structures and devices. Like all of us, poets also grow and change over time. As readers, then, we want to strive to recognize differences, as well as similarities, among individual poems and to appreciate the ways an author's work does and doesn't change over time.

You will find both continuity and change, similarities and differences, in the work of any good poet, and this chapter introduces you to two great ones. The first, John Keats, enjoyed the briefest of lives and careers, publishing his first poem a mere five years before his death at age 25 (in 1821). As a result, according to one Victorian reviewer, "all Keats's poems are early productions, and there is nothing beyond them but the thought of what he might have become." Thanks to her longevity, the other poet featured in this chapter—Adrienne Rich—gives us the chance to see such "becoming" in action. Indeed, Rich (born in 1929) remains an active, prolific poet, and many readers and critics regard her as the best poet writing today. A careful reader of her work will find similarities of interest and strategy from her earliest poems—published shortly after World War II, in 1951—to her newest ones. A distinctive mind and orientation are at work. And we can speak about characteristic features of Rich's poetry just as surely as we do about characteristic features of Keats's work, even though Rich has written many more poems over a much longer period of time.

But over the years Rich's voice has changed quite a lot, too, and she has modified her views on a number of issues. Such changes were the result both of her personal experiences and of those shared experiences that help to define her era. Many of the changes in Rich's ideas and attitudes, for example, reflect changing concerns among American intellectuals (especially women) in the second half of the twentieth century, and her poems represent both changed social conditions and sharply altered social, political, and philosophical attitudes. But her poems also reflect altered personal circumstances. Rich married in her early twenties and had three children by the time she was thirty; many of her early poems are about heterosexual love, and some of them are quite explicitly about sex. (See, for example, "Two Songs," chapter 16.) More recently, she has been involved in a long-term lesbian relationship and has written, again quite explicitly, about sex between women. (See, for example, "My mouth hovers across your breasts," this chapter.) In Rich's poems, then, we may not only trace the contours of an evolving personal life and outlook, but also—and even more importantly for the study of poetry generally—see how changes *within* the poet and *in her social and cultural context* alter the subjects and themes of her poetry, as well as its formal structure.

Just as information about an author's life and times can help us in this enterprise, so, too, can the essays, letters, and interviews in which an author reflects on the character and aims of his or her poetry and on the subjects the poetry explores. In the case of Rich, we have a bounty of such material from a poet who has also been a remarkably prolific and articulate prose writer. Gathered at the end of the Rich section of this chapter are excerpts from these writings, including both essays that express the author's outlook at a particular moment and retrospective pieces in which the poet gives us her interpretation of the character and development of her work over time. Though Keats wrote no essays of this type, he did leave behind hundreds of letters which both illuminate the ideas about literature and life that animate his poems and vividly display the unique sensibility that produced them.

> *The fear of poetry is an indication that we are cut off from our own reality.*
> —MURIEL RUKEYSER

But before you launch into the poetry and prose of these two great poets, it's worth pausing a moment to ask and answer a key question: of what practical use is it to learn to recognize and understand the distinctive voice and mind of a particular poet? One use is the pleasant surprise that occurs when you recognize something familiar. Reading a new poem by a familiar poet can be like meeting an old friend whose face or conversation reminds you of experiences you have had together. Just as novelty—meeting something or someone altogether new to you—provides one kind of pleasure, so revisiting the familiar provides another, equal and opposite kind. Just *knowing* and *recognizing* often feel good in and of themselves.

In addition, just as you learn from watching other people, seeing how they react and respond to various people, situations, and events, so you can learn from watching poets at work—seeing how they learn and develop, how they change their minds or test alternative points of view, how they discover the reach and limits of their imaginations and talents, how they find their distinctive voices and come to terms with their own identities. Watching a poet at work over a period of years is a little like watching an autobiography unfold, except that the individual poems exist separately and for themselves at the same time that they record the evolution of a distinctive artistic consciousness as it confronts a world that is itself perpetually changing.

Finally, the more you know about a poet and the more of his or her poems you read, the better a reader you will likely be of any individual poem by the poet. External facts of the writer's life may inform whatever he or she writes—be it a poem, an essay, a letter, or an autobiography. But beyond that, when you grow accustomed to a writer's habits and manners and means of expression, you learn what to expect. Coming to a new poem by a poet you already know, you know what to look for and have clear expectations about what the poem will be like. At the same time, you are better prepared to appreciate the surprises each poem holds in store.

## JOHN KEATS

Given the brevity of Keats's life and career, readers new to his work may be surprised by the number and variety, as well as the sheer quality, of his poems. In his four short years as a working poet, he completed numerous sonnets (four are included in this book), one of the most haunting of English ballads ("La Belle Dame sans Merci"), and a handful of longer narrative poems. (The most ambitious of these is *Endymion*, the four-book, 4000-line "poetic romance" that Keats undertook just after abandoning medicine for poetry.) Perhaps even more impressive, Keats wrote the sequence of six great odes—including "Ode to a Nightingale," "Ode on a Grecian Urn," and "To Autumn"—in a mere nine months, between April and September 1819. In addition, Keats left behind the 251 letters that T. S. Eliot described as "the most important ever written by any English poet."

John Keats

To nineteenth-century readers, such achievements were all the more surprising because of Keats's relatively humble upbringing and education. (As one Victorian reviewer marveled, "here is a surgeon's apprentice . . . rivaling in aesthetic perceptions of antique life and thought the most careful scholars of his time and country, and reproducing these impressions in a phraseology as complete and unconventional as if he has mastered the whole history and frequent variations of the English tongue.") Yet it would be a mistake to see Keats as either the "vulgar Cockney" or the untutored genius his contemporaries sometimes took him to be. Well-versed in English poetry past and present, Keats was heavily influenced by poets as diverse as Edmund Spenser, William Shakespeare, John Milton, and William Wordsworth, and was intimately familiar with the literature of ancient Rome (which he read in the original Latin) and ancient Greece (which he read in translation).

Indeed, as you begin to look for patterns in Keats's poems, you may notice that many of them focus on encounters with classical art (a translation of Homer's epics, a group of statues, a funereal urn); take their subjects from classical sources (a fable by Aesop, the myth of Endymion); or allude to classical literature and myth ("Lethe-wards," "Bacchus and his pards"). (Perhaps for this reason, poet Percy Bysshe Shelley declared, "He was a Greek!") As you explore Keats's poetry, then, you may well want to think further about just what the effects of these choices are and what the poems define as most characteristic and attractive about ancient art, life, and thought. Likewise, you will want to think about the implications of Keats's choice to work with traditional poetic forms, especially the sonnet and the ode. (Keats himself somewhat jokingly suggested that he needed such forms in order "to restrain the headlong impetuosity of [his] Muse.")

Ancient artifacts, as well as traditional poetic forms, seem to rank high on Keats's list of "thing[s] of beauty" (*Endymion*). In part this is because their very ancientness shows that they have withstood "the rude / Wasting of old Time," as he says of the Elgin marbles. As a result, they promise not only to remain "a joy forever," but also to grant a kind of immortality both to their subjects and to their creators. Indeed, one of the things that Keats's speakers seems to find so enchanting and so troubling about the various objects they contemplate is that these objects offer at least temporary escape from individual consciousness (or "sole self"), from the constraints of time and space, and from the mutability and mortality to which all living things are subject.

Yet Keats's poetry just as powerfully evokes the beauty of ordinary, living, natural things—of "the sun, the moon, / Trees," and "simple sheep"; of daffodils and musk-rose blooms (*Endymion*, lines 13–14, 15, 19); of nightingales, grasshoppers, and crickets; of "the stubble-plains" and "barred clouds" of a "soft-dying" autumn day ("To Autumn," lines 25–26). And this evocation of natural beauty flows, in part, from a vivid, complex blend of physically rooted "sensations"—of sight, sound, smell, touch, and taste—that define our everyday experience and "bind us to the earth" (*Endymion*, line 7). Through rhythm and rhyme, as well as alliteration, assonance, and onomatopoeia ("The murmurous haunt of flies on summer eves"), Keats not only captures physical sensation in language, but also draws our attention to the sensual—visual, tactile, auditory—qualities of words themselves.

> *Poetry should surprise by a fine excess and not by singularity—it should strike the reader as wording of his own highest thoughts, and appear almost a remembrance.*
> 
> –JOHN KEATS

One of the reasons the odes are so often singled out for praise and commentary is the fact that they focus so relentlessly on this characteristically Keatsian contrast, even conflict, between the actual, sensual world and the ideal world of art and imagination. Literary critic Miriam Allott suggests that the odes, like "all Keats's major poetry," trace the same singular "movement of thought and feeling," which "at first carries the poet . . . into an ideal world of beauty and permanence, and finally returns him to what is actual and inescapable." Echoing Allott, another critic describes the "recurrent pattern" of the odes as "one of dream and awakening, flight on the wings of imagination into a higher order of reality followed by a disillusioned return to the ordinary, everyday world." Yet as you read these and other of Keats's poems, you will see that each offers a unique perspective on the nature and significance of this contrast and on the desirability of escape. Here, as in any poet's work, then, you will want to look for differences as well as similarities, for evolution and change as well as continuity.

## On First Looking into Chapman's Homer[1]

Much have I traveled in the realms of gold,
And many goodly states and kingdoms seen;
Round many western islands have I been
Which bards in fealty to Apollo[2] hold.
5 Oft of one wide expanse had I been told
That deep-browed Homer ruled as his demesne;
Yet did I never breathe its pure serene[3]
Till I heard Chapman speak out loud and bold:
Then felt I like some watcher of the skies
10 When a new planet swims into his ken;[4]
Or like stout Cortez[5] when with eagle eyes
He stared at the Pacific—and all his men
Looked at each other with a wild surmise—
Silent, upon a peak in Darien.

1816

## On the Grasshopper and the Cricket

The poetry of earth is never dead:
When all the birds are faint with the hot sun,
And hide in cooling trees, a voice will run
From hedge to hedge about the new-mown mead;
5 That is the grasshopper's—he takes the lead
In summer luxury—he has never done
With his delights; for when tired out with fun
He rests at ease beneath some pleasant weed.
The poetry of earth is ceasing never:
10 On a lone winter evening, when the frost
Has wrought a silence, from the stove there shrills
The cricket's song, in warmth increasing ever,
And seems to one in drowsiness half lost,
The grasshopper's among some grassy hills.

December 30, 1816

---

1. George Chapman's were among the most famous Renaissance translations; he completed his *Iliad* in 1611, his *Odyssey* in 1616. Keats wrote the sonnet after being led to Chapman by a former teacher and reading the *Iliad* all night long.
2. Greek god of poetry and music. *Fealty:* literally, the loyalty owed by a vassal to his feudal lord.
3. Atmosphere. 4. Range of vision.
5. Actually, Balboa; he first viewed the Pacific from Darien, in Panama.

## On Seeing the Elgin Marbles[6]

My spirit is too weak—mortality
Weighs heavily on me like unwilling sleep,
And each imagined pinnacle and steep
Of godlike hardship tells me I must die
5 Like a sick eagle looking at the sky.
Yet 'tis a gentle luxury to weep
That I have not the cloudy winds to keep
Fresh for the opening of the morning's eye.
Such dim-conceivéd glories of the brain
10 Bring round the heart an indescribable feud;
So do these wonders a most dizzy pain,
That mingles Grecian grandeur with the rude
Wasting of old Time—with a billowy main—
A sun—a shadow of a magnitude.

1817

## Sonnet to Sleep

O soft embalmer of the still midnight,
   Shutting with careful fingers and benign
Our gloom-pleas'd eyes, embower'd from the light,
   Enshaded in forgetfulness divine:
5 O soothest[7] Sleep! if so it please thee, close,
   In midst of this thine hymn, my willing eyes,
Or wait the Amen ere thy poppy[8] throws
   Around my bed its lulling charities.
Then save me or the passed day will shine
10    Upon my pillow, breeding many woes:
Save me from curious[9] conscience, that still hoards
   Its strength for darkness, burrowing like the mole;
Turn the key deftly in the oiled wards,[1]
   And seal the hushed casket of my soul.

Apr. 1819                                                      1838

---

6. Figures and friezes from the Athenian Parthenon, they were taken from the site by Lord Elgin, brought to England in 1806, and then sold to the British Museum, where Keats saw them.
7. Softest.    8. Opium is made from the dried juice of the opium poppy.    9. Scrupulous.
1. The ridges in a lock that correspond to the notches of the key.

## From *Endymion* (Book 1)[2]

A thing of beauty is a joy for ever:
Its loveliness increases; it will never
Pass into nothingness; but still will keep
A bower quiet for us, and a sleep
5 Full of sweet dreams, and health, and quiet breathing.
Therefore, on every morrow, are we wreathing
A flowery band to bind us to the earth,
Spite of despondence, of the inhuman dearth
Of noble natures, of the gloomy days,
10 Of all the unhealthy and o'er-darkened ways
Made for our searching: yes, in spite of all,
Some shape of beauty moves away the pall
From our dark spirits. Such the sun, the moon,
Trees old, and young sprouting a shady boon
15 For simple sheep; and such are daffodils
With the green world they live in; and clear rills
That for themselves a cooling covert make
'Gainst the hot season; the mid forest brake,[3]
Rich with a sprinkling of fair musk-rose blooms:
20 And such too is the grandeur of the dooms[4]
We have imagined for the mighty dead;
All lovely tales that we have heard or read:
An endless fountain of immortal drink,
Pouring unto us from the heaven's brink.
25   Nor do we merely feel these essences
For one short hour; no, even as the trees
That whisper round a temple become soon
Dear as the temple's self, so does the moon,
The passion poesy, glories infinite,
30 Haunt us till they become a cheering light
Unto our souls, and bound to us so fast,
That, whether there be shine, or gloom o'ercast,
They always must be with us, or we die.

1817

---

2. Keats's long poem about the myth of a mortal (Endymion) loved by the goddess of the moon.
3. Thicket.   4. Judgments.

## Ode to a Nightingale

### I

My heart aches, and a drowsy numbness pains
  My sense, as though of hemlock I had drunk,
Or emptied some dull opiate to the drains
  One minute past, and Lethe-wards[5] had sunk:
5 'Tis not through envy of thy happy lot,
  But being too happy in thine happiness,
    That thou, light-wingèd Dryad[6] of the trees,
      In some melodious plot
Of beechen green, and shadows numberless,
10   Singest of summer in full-throated ease.

### II

O, for a draught of vintage! that hath been
  Cooled a long age in the deep-delvèd earth,
Tasting of Flora[7] and the country green,
  Dance, and Provençal song,[8] and sunburnt mirth!
15 O for a beaker full of the warm South,
  Full of the true, the blushful Hippocrene,[9]
    With beaded bubbles winking at the brim,
      And purple-stainèd mouth;
That I might drink, and leave the world unseen,
20   And with thee fade away into the forest dim:

### III

Fade far away, dissolve, and quite forget
  What thou among the leaves hast never known,
The weariness, the fever, and the fret
  Here, where men sit and hear each other groan;
25 Where palsy shakes a few, sad, last gray hairs,
  Where youth grows pale, and specter-thin, and dies;
    Where but to think is to be full of sorrow
      And leaden-eyed despairs,
Where Beauty cannot keep her lustrous eyes,
30   Or new Love pine at them beyond tomorrow.

### IV

Away! away! for I will fly to thee,
  Not charioted by Bacchus and his pards,[1]
But on the viewless[2] wings of Poesy,

---

5. Toward the river of forgetfulness (Lethe) in Hades.    6. Wood nymph.    7. Roman goddess of flowers.
8. The medieval troubadours of Provence were famous for their love songs.
9. The fountain of the Muses on Mt. Helicon, whose waters bring poetic inspiration.
1. The Roman god of wine was sometimes portrayed in a chariot drawn by leopards.    2. Invisible.

            Though the dull brain perplexes and retards:
35      Already with thee! tender is the night,
            And haply the Queen-Moon is on her throne,
                Clustered around by all her starry Fays;[3]
                    But here there is no light,
            Save what from heaven is with the breezes blown
40          Through verdurous glooms and winding mossy ways.

                            V

        I cannot see what flowers are at my feet,
            Nor what soft incense hangs upon the boughs,
        But, in embalmèd[4] darkness, guess each sweet
            Wherewith the seasonable month endows
45      The grass, the thicket, and the fruit-tree wild;
            White hawthorn, and the pastoral eglantine;[5]
                Fast fading violets covered up in leaves;
                    And mid-May's eldest child,
            The coming musk-rose, full of dewy wine,
50          The murmurous haunt of flies on summer eves.

                            VI

        Darkling[6] I listen; and, for many a time
            I have been half in love with easeful Death,
        Called him soft names in many a musèd rhyme,
            To take into the air my quiet breath;
55      Now more than ever seems it rich to die,
            To cease upon the midnight with no pain,
                While thou art pouring forth thy soul abroad
                    In such an ecstasy!
            Still wouldst thou sing, and I have ears in vain—
60          To thy high requiem become a sod.

                            VII

        Thou wast not born for death, immortal Bird!
            No hungry generations tread thee down;
        The voice I hear this passing night was heard
            In ancient days by emperor and clown:
65      Perhaps the selfsame song that found a path
            Through the sad heart of Ruth,[7] when, sick for home,
                She stood in tears amid the alien corn;
                    The same that ofttimes hath
            Charmed magic casements, opening on the foam
70          Of perilous seas, in faery lands forlorn.

                            VIII

        Forlorn! the very word is like a bell
            To toll me back from thee to my sole self!

---

3. Fairies.   4. Fragrant, aromatic.   5. Sweetbriar or honeysuckle.   6. In the dark.
7. A virtuous Moabite widow who, according to the Old Testament Book of Ruth, left her own country to accompany her mother-in-law, Naomi, back to Naomi's native land. She supported herself as a gleaner.

Adieu! the fancy cannot cheat so well
    As she is famed to do, deceiving elf.
75 Adieu! adieu! thy plaintive anthem fades
    Past the near meadows, over the still stream,
        Up the hillside; and now 'tis buried deep
            In the next valley-glades:
    Was it a vision, or a waking dream?
80      Fled is that music:—Do I wake or sleep?

May 1819

## Ode on a Grecian Urn

I

Thou still unravished bride of quietness,
    Thou foster-child of silence and slow time,
Sylvan historian, who canst thus express
    A flowery tale more sweetly than our rhyme:
5 What leaf-fringed legend haunts about thy shape
    Of deities or mortals, or of both,
        In Tempe or the dales of Arcady?[8]
What men or gods are these? What maidens loath?
    What mad pursuit? What struggle to escape?
10      What pipes and timbrels? What wild ecstasy?

II

Heard melodies are sweet, but those unheard
    Are sweeter; therefore, ye soft pipes, play on;
Not to the sensual[9] ear, but, more endeared,
    Pipe to the spirit ditties of no tone:
15 Fair youth, beneath the trees, thou canst not leave
    Thy song, nor ever can those trees be bare;
        Bold Lover, never, never canst thou kiss,
Though winning near the goal—yet, do not grieve;
    She cannot fade, though thou hast not thy bliss,
20      For ever wilt thou love, and she be fair!

III

Ah, happy, happy boughs! that cannot shed
    Your leaves, nor ever bid the Spring adieu;
And, happy melodist, unwearièd,
    For ever piping songs for ever new;

---

8. Arcadia. Tempe is a beautiful valley near Mt. Olympus in Greece, and the valleys ("dales") of Arcadia a picturesque section of the Peloponnesus; both came to be associated with the pastoral ideal.
9. Of the senses, as distinguished from the "ear" of the spirit or imagination.

25  More happy love! more happy, happy love!
       For ever warm and still to be enjoyed,
          For ever panting, and for ever young;
    All breathing human passion far above,
       That leaves a heart high-sorrowful and cloyed,
30        A burning forehead, and a parching tongue.

                IV
    Who are these coming to the sacrifice?
       To what green altar, O mysterious priest,
    Lead'st thou that heifer lowing at the skies,
       And all her silken flanks with garlands dressed?
35  What little town by river or sea shore,
       Or mountain-built with peaceful citadel,
          Is emptied of this folk, this pious morn?
    And, little town, thy streets for evermore
       Will silent be; and not a soul to tell
40        Why thou art desolate, can e'er return.

                V
    O Attic shape! Fair attitude! with brede[1]
       Of marble men and maidens overwrought,[2]
    With forest branches and the trodden weed;
       Thou, silent form, dost tease us out of thought
45  As doth eternity: Cold Pastoral!
       When old age shall this generation waste,
          Thou shalt remain, in midst of other woe
    Than ours, a friend to man, to whom thou say'st,
       Beauty is truth, truth beauty[3]—that is all
50        Ye know on earth, and all ye need to know.

May 1819


## To Autumn

              I
    Season of mists and mellow fruitfulness,
       Close bosom-friend of the maturing sun;
    Conspiring with him how to load and bless
       With fruit the vines that round the thatch-eves run;
 5  To bend with apples the mossed cottage-trees,
       And fill all fruit with ripeness to the core;
          To swell the gourd, and plump the hazel shells

---

1. Woven pattern. *Attic:* Attica was the district of ancient Greece surrounding Athens.
2. Ornamented all over.
3. In some texts of the poem "Beauty is truth, truth beauty" is in quotation marks and in some texts it is not, leading to critical disagreements about whether the last line and a half are also inscribed on the urn or spoken by the poet.

With a sweet kernel; to set budding more,
      And still more, later flowers for the bees,
10 Until they think warm days will never cease,
      For Summer has o'er-brimmed their clammy cells.

            II
   Who hath not seen thee oft amid thy store?
      Sometimes whoever seeks abroad may find
   Thee sitting careless on a granary floor,
15    Thy hair soft-lifted by the winnowing wind;[4]
   Or on a half-reaped furrow sound asleep,
      Drowsed with the fume of poppies, while thy hook[5]
      Spares the next swath and all its twinéd flowers:
   And sometimes like a gleaner thou dost keep
20    Steady thy laden head across a brook;
   Or by a cider-press, with patient look,
      Thou watchest the last oozings hours by hours.

            III
   Where are the songs of Spring? Ay, where are they?
      Think not of them, thou hast thy music too—
25 While barréd clouds bloom the soft-dying day,
      And touch the stubble-plains with rosy hue;
   Then in a wailful choir the small gnats mourn
      Among the river sallows, borne aloft
         Or sinking as the light wind lives or dies;
30 And full-grown lambs loud bleat from hilly bourn;[6]
   Hedge-crickets sing; and now with treble soft
      The red-breast whistles from a garden-croft;[7]
      And gathering swallows twitter in the skies.

September 19, 1819

# PASSAGES FROM LETTERS AND THE PREFACE TO *ENDYMION*

## From *Letter to Benjamin Bailey, November 22, 1817*[1]

... I am certain of nothing but of the holiness of the Heart's affections and the truth of Imagination—What the imagination seizes as Beauty must be truth—whether it existed before or not—for I have the same Idea of all our Passions as

---

4. Which sifts the grain from the chaff.   5. Scythe or sickle.   6. Domain.
7. An enclosed garden near a house.
1. Keats's private letters, often carelessly written, are reprinted here uncorrected.

of Love they are all in their sublime, creative of essential Beauty.... The Imagination may be compared to Adam's dream[2]—he awoke and found it truth. I am the more zealous in this affair, because I have never yet been able to perceive how any thing can be known for truth by consequitive reasoning—and yet it must be—Can it be that even the greatest Philosopher ever ~~when~~ arrived at his goal without putting aside numerous objections—However it may be, O for a Life of Sensations rather than of Thoughts! It is "a Vision in the form of Youth" a Shadow of reality to come—and this consideration has further conv[i]nced me for it has come as auxiliary to another favorite Speculation of mine, that we shall enjoy ourselves here after by having what we called happiness on Earth repeated in a finer tone and so repeated—And yet such a fate can only befall those who delight in sensation rather than hunger as you do after Truth—Adam's dream will do here and seems to be a conviction that Imagination and its empyreal reflection is the same as human Life and its spiritual repetition. But as I was saying—the simple imaginative Mind may have its rewards in the repeti[ti]on of its own silent Working coming continually on the spirit with a fine suddenness—to compare great things with small—have you never by being surprised with an old Melody—in a delicious place—by a delicious voice, fe[l]t over again your very speculations and surmises at the time it first operated on your soul—do you not remember forming to yourself the singer's face more beautiful that [*for* than] it was possible and yet with the elevation of the Moment you did not think so—even then you were mounted on the Wings of Imagination so high—that the Prototype must be here after—that delicious face you will see—What a time! I am continually running away from the subject—sure this cannot be exactly the case with a complex Mind—one that is imaginative and at the same time careful of its fruits—who would exist partly on sensation partly on thought—to whom it is necessary that years should bring the philosophic Mind—such an one I consider your's and therefore it is necessary to your eternal Happiness that you not only ~~have~~ drink this old Wine of Heaven which I shall call the redigestion of our most ethereal Musings on Earth; but also increase in knowledge and know all things....

## From *Letter to George and Thomas Keats,* December 21, 1817

...I spent Friday evening with Wells[3] & went the next morning to see *Death on the Pale horse.*[4] It is a wonderful picture, when West's age is considered; But there is nothing to be intense upon; no women one feels mad to kiss, no face swelling into reality, the excellence of every Art is its intensity, capable of making all disagreeables evaporate, from their being in close relationship with Beauty & Truth—Examine King Lear & you will find this examplified throughout; but in this picture we have unpleasantness without any momentous depth of specula-

---

2. In *Paradise Lost* 7.460–90.   3. Charles Wells (1800–1879), an author.
4. By Benjamin West (1738–1820), American painter and president of the Royal Academy; *Christ Rejected* (mentioned below) is also by West.

tion excited, in which to bury its repulsiveness—
The picture is larger than Christ rejected—I dined
with Haydon the sunday after you left, & had a
very pleasant day, I dined too (for I have been out
too much lately) with Horace Smith & met his
two Brothers with Hill & Kingston & one Du
Bois,[5] they only served to convince me, how superior humour is to wit in respect to enjoyment—
These men say things which make one start,
without making one feel, they are all alike; their
manners are alike; they all know fashionables;
they have a mannerism in their very eating &
drinking, in their mere handling a Decanter—
They talked of Kean[6] & his low company—Would I were with that company
instead of yours said I to myself! I know such like acquaintance will never do
for me & yet I am going to Reynolds, on wednesday—Brown & Dilke walked
with me & back from the Christmas pantomime. I had not a dispute but a
disquisition with Dilke, on various subjects; several things dovetailed in my mind, & at once it
struck me, what quality went to form a Man of
Achievement especially in Literature & which
Shakespeare posessed so enormously—I mean
*Negative Capability,* that is when man is capable
of being in uncertainties, Mysteries, doubts,
without any irritable reaching after fact & reason—Coleridge, for instance, would let go by a
fine isolated verisimilitude caught from the Penetralium of mystery, from being incapable of
remaining content with half knowledge. This
pursued through Volumes would perhaps take us
no further than this, that with a great poet the
sense of Beauty overcomes every other consideration, or rather obliterates all consideration.

George Keats

Thomas Keats

## *Letter to John Hamilton Reynolds, February 19, 1818*

I have an idea that a Man might pass a very pleasant life in this manner—let him
on any certain day read a certain Page of full Poesy or distilled Prose and let him
wander with it, and muse upon it, and reflect from it, and bring home to it, and
prophesy upon it, and dream upon it—untill it becomes stale—but when will it
do so? Never—When Man has arrived at a certain ripeness in intellect any one
grand and spiritual passage serves him as a starting post towards all "the two-and-thirty Pallaces"[7] How happy is such a "voyage of conception," what delicious
diligent Indolence! A doze upon a Sofa does not hinder it, and a nap upon Clover

---

5. Thomas Hill (1760–1840), a book collector, and Edward duBois (1774–1850), a journalist.
6. Edmund Kean (1789–1833), a famous Shakespearean actor.  7. "Places of delight" in Buddhism.

engenders ethereal finger-pointings—the prattle of a child gives it wings, and the converse of middle age a strength to beat them—a strain of musick conducts to "an odd angle of the Isle",[8] and when the leaves whisper it puts a "girdle round the earth",[9] Nor will this sparing touch of noble Books be any irreverance to their Writers—for perhaps the honors paid by Man to Man are trifles in comparison to the Benefit done by great Works to the "Spirit and pulse of good" by their mere passive existence. Memory should not be called knowledge—Many have original minds who do not think it—they are led away by Custom—Now it appears to me that almost any Man may like the Spider spin from his own inwards his own airy Citadel—the points of leaves and twigs on which the Spider begins her work are

John Hamilton Reynolds

few and she fills the Air with a beautiful circuiting: man should be content with as few points to tip with the fine Webb of his Soul and weave a tapestry empyrean—full of Symbols for his spiritual eye, of softness for his spiritual touch, of space for his wandering of distinctness for his Luxury—But the Minds of Mortals are so different and bent on such diverse Journeys that it may at first appear impossible for any common taste and fellowship to exist bettween between two or three under these suppositions—It is however quite the contrary—Minds would leave each other in contrary directions, traverse each other in Numberless points, and all [*for* at] last greet each other at the Journeys end—An old Man and a child would talk together and the old Man be led on his Path, and the child left thinking—Man should not dispute or assert but whisper results to his neighbor, and thus by every germ of Spirit sucking the Sap from mould ethereal every human might become great, and Humanity instead of being a wide heath of Furse[1] and Briars with here and there a remote Oak or Pine, would become a grand democracy of Forest Trees. It has been an old Comparison for our urging on—the Bee hive—however it seems to me that we should rather be the flower than the Bee—for it is a false notion that more is gained by receiving than giving—no, the receiver and the giver are equal in their benefits—The f[l]ower I doubt not receives a fair guerdon from the Bee—its leaves blush deeper in the next spring—and who shall say between Man and Woman which is the most delighted? Now it is more noble to sit like Jove that [*for* than] to fly like Mercury—let us not therefore go hurrying about and collecting honey bee like, buzzing here and there impatiently from a knowledge of what is to be arrived at; but let us open our leaves like a flower and be passive and receptive—budding patiently under the eye of Apollo and taking hints from every noble insect that favors us with a visit—sap will be given us for Meat and dew for drink—I was led into these thoughts, my dear Reynolds, by the beauty of the morning operating

---

8. *The Tempest* 1.2.224.
9. *A Midsummer Night's Dream* 2.1.175-76: "I'll put a girdle round about the earth / In forty minutes."
1. *The Tempest* 1.1.58-59: "Now would I give a thousand furlongs of sea for an acre of barren ground: long heath, broom, furze, anything." (Heather, broom, and furze are all shrubs that grow in poor soil.)

on a sense of Idleness—I have not read any Books—the Morning said I was right—
I had no Idea but of the Morning, and the Thrush said I was right—seeming to
say—

> O thou whose face hath felt the Winter's wind,
> Whose eye has seen the snow-clouds hung in mist,
> And the black elm tops 'mong the freezing stars,
> To thee the spring will be a harvest-time.
> O thou, whose only book has been the light
> Of supreme darkness which thou feddest on
> Night after night when Phœbus was away,
> To thee the spring shall be a triple morn.
> O fret not after knowledge—I have none,
> And yet my song comes native with the warmth.
> O fret not after knowledge—I have none,
> And yet the Evening listens. He who saddens
> At thought of idleness cannot be idle,
> And he's awake who thinks himself asleep.

Now I am sensible all this is a mere sophistication, however it may neighbor to any truths, to excuse my own indolence—so I will not deceive myself that Man should be equal with jove—but think himself very well off as a sort of scullion-Mercury, or even a humble Bee—It is not [for no] matter whether I am right or wrong either one way or another, if there is sufficient to lift a little time from your Shoulders.

## From *Letter to John Taylor*, February 27, 1818

... It is a sorry thing for me that any one should have to overcome Prejudices in reading my Verses—that affects me more than any hyper-criticism on any particular Passage. In *Endymion* I have most likely but moved into the Go-cart from the leading strings. In Poetry I have a few Axioms, and you will see how far I am from their Centre. 1st I think Poetry should surprise by a fine excess and not by Singularity—it should strike the Reader as a wording of his own highest thoughts, and appear almost a Remembrance—2nd Its touches of Beauty should never be half way therby making the reader breathless instead of content: the rise, the progress, the setting of imagery should like the Sun come natural natural too him—shine over him and set soberly although in magnificence leaving him in the Luxury of twilight—but it is easier to think what Poetry should be than to write it—and this leads me on to another axiom. That if Poetry comes not as naturally as the Leaves to a tree it had better not come at all. However it may be with me I cannot help looking into new countries with "O for a Muse of fire to ascend!"[2]—If Endymion serves me as a Pioneer perhaps I ought to be content. I have great reason to be content, for thank God I can read and perhaps understand Shakspeare to his depths, and I have I am sure many friends, who, if I fail, will attribute any change in my Life and Temper to Humbleness rather than to

---

2. *Henry V* Prologue 1: "O for a muse of fire, that would ascend."

Pride—to a cowering under the Wings of great Poets rather than to a Bitterness that I am not appreciated. I am anxious to get Endymion printed that I may forget it and proceed....

## From the Preface to *Endymion*, dated April 10, 1818

The imagination of a boy is healthy, and the mature imagination of a man is healthy; but there is a space of life between, in which the soul is in a ferment, the character undecided, the way of life uncertain, the ambition thick-sighted: thence proceeds mawkishness, and all the thousand bitters which those men I speak of must necessarily taste in going over the following pages.

I hope I have not in too late a day touched the beautiful mythology of Greece, and dulled its brightness: for I wish to try once more, before I bid it farewell.

## CHRONOLOGY

1795  John Keats born October 31 at Finsbury, just north of London, the eldest child of Thomas and Frances Jennings Keats. Thomas Keats was head ostler at a livery stable.

1797–1803  Birth of three brothers and sisters: George in 1797, Thomas in 1799, Frances Mary (Fanny) in 1803.

1803  With George, begins school in Enfield.

1804  Father killed by a fall from his horse, April 15. On June 27 his mother remarries, and the children go to live with their maternal grandparents at Enfield. The grandfather dies a year later, and the children move with their grandmother to Lower Edmonton.

1809  Begins a literary friendship with Charles Cowden Clarke, the son of the headmaster at the Enfield school, and develops a strong interest in reading.

1810  Mother dies of tuberculosis, after a long illness.

1811  Leaves school to become apprenticed to an apothecary-surgeon in Edmonton; completes a prose translation of the *Aeneid*, begun at school.

1814  Earliest known attempts at writing verse. In December his grandmother dies, and the family home is broken up.

1815  In October moves to next stage of his medical training at Guy's Hospital, south of the Thames in London.

1816  On May 5 his first published poem, "O Solitude," appears in Leigh Hunt's *Examiner*. In October writes "On First Looking into Chapman's Homer," published in December. Meets Hunt, Benjamin Haydon, John Hamilton Reynolds, and Shelley. By the spring of 1817, gives up the idea of medical practice.

1817  In March, moves with brothers to Hampstead, sees the Elgin Marbles with Haydon, and publishes his first collection, *Poems*. Composes *Endymion* between April and November. Reads Milton, Shakespeare, and Coleridge; rereads Wordsworth during the year.

1818 *Endymion* published in April, unfavorably reviewed in September, defended by Reynolds in October. During the summer goes on walking tour of the Lake Country and Scotland, but returns to London in mid-August with a sore throat and severe chills. His brother Tom is also seriously ill by late summer, dying on December 1. In September, Keats first meets Fanny Brawne (eighteen years old), with whom he arrives at an "understanding" by Christmas.

1819 Writes *The Eve of St. Agnes* in January, revises it in September. In April Fanny Brawne and her mother move into the other half of the double house in which Keats lives. During April and May writes "La Belle Dame sans Merci" and all the major odes except "To Autumn," written in September. Rental arrangements force separation from Fanny Brawne during the summer (Keats on Isle of Wight from June to August), and in the fall he tries to break his dependence on her, but they become engaged by Christmas. Earlier in December suffers a recurrence of his sore throat.

1820 In February has a severe hemorrhage and in June an attack of blood-spitting. In July his doctor orders him to Italy for the winter; he sails in September and finally arrives in Rome on November 15. In July a volume of poems published, *Lamia, Isabella, The Eve of St. Agnes and Other Poems*. Fanny Brawne nurses him through the late summer.

1821 Dies at 11 P.M., February 23. Buried in the English Cemetery at Rome.

## ADRIENNE RICH

It is fitting that two of Adrienne Rich's books—*A Change of World* (1951) and *The Will to Change* (1971)—bear titles that prominently feature the word *change*. For change has, indeed, been both a continuing concern of her poetry and a hallmark of her poetic career. Published when their author was just twenty-one, poems such as "At a Bach Concert," "Storm Warnings," and "Aunt Jennifer's Tigers" seem, at first glance, preternaturally mature. With their tightly controlled structure, their regular rhythm (and, often, rhyme), and their coolly observant tone, these early poems both embody and celebrate the "discipline" that "masters feelings" and the "proud restraining purity" by which art lends order to life ("At a Bach Concert"). (Versions of the word *master*, in fact, appear in all three poems.) Explaining why he chose *A Change of World* for the Yale Younger Poets Series, poet W. H. Auden singled out just such qualities and attitudes, praising Rich for a "craftsmanship" based in that "capacity for detachment from the self and its emotions without which no art is possible." If "poems are analogous to persons," Auden continued, then these poems are "neatly and modestly dressed, speak quietly but do not mumble, respect their elders but are not cowed by them, and do not tell fibs."

> By 1956, I had begun dating each of my poems by year. I did this because I was finished with the idea of a poem as a single, encapsulated event, a work of art complete in itself; I knew my life was changing, my work was changing, and I needed to indicated to readers my sense of being engaged in a long, continuous process.
> —ADRIENNE RICH

Less than a decade later, however, Rich began to see the very "neatness" and "detachment" of these poems as itself a kind of "fib." As she put it in 1964, the early poems, "even the ones I liked best and in which I felt I'd said most, were queerly limited; . . . in many cases I . . . suppressed, omitted, falsified even, certain disturbing elements to gain the perfection of order." From this point forward, Rich's work is very much an attempt to do the very opposite—to, in Matthew Arnold's words, "see life steadily and see it whole," in all its disturbing, disorderly imperfection. Indeed, one of the major themes of the later poems is both the necessity and the difficulty of breaking through the web of "myth" and illusion in order to get to "the thing itself" ("Diving into the Wreck").

In its attempt to do just that, Rich's work has itself become less neat and orderly, less quiet, modest, and respectful. Beginning with *Snapshots of a Daughter-in-Law* and its title poem, the poems speak in many radically different voices and tones and are cast in many different forms. Rich's evolution as a poet has not been a matter of pursuing any kind of single-minded mastery over her materials. "I find that I can no longer go to write a poem with a neat handful of materials and express those materials according to a prior plan," Rich explained in 1964; "the poem itself engenders new sensations, new awareness in me as it progresses." What results are "poems that *are* experiences" rather than "poems *about* experiences."

Adrienne Rich circa 1970

In becoming more informal, exploratory, and emotional, Rich's poems have also become more personal and autobiographical, more willing to enter and lay bare what "Storm Warnings" calls the "troubled regions" of the poet's own life, heart, and mind. In fact, Rich has suggested that her artistic growth has been, in part, a matter of closing the gap between "the woman in the poem and the woman writing the poem." And in "Roofwalker," a 1961 poem that articulates her new poetic ideal, Rich compares herself both to a roofer standing atop a half-built house and to "a naked man fleeing / across" those very roofs. Like both, she now dares to be "exposed, larger than life, / and due to break my neck."

At the same time, Rich's work has also become steadily more social, political, and historical. "History" is, in fact, the title of one poem in this chapter and the subject of many others. Quite a few allude to, or take as their focus, specific women in history—from poet Emily Dickinson to astronomer Caroline Herschel and photographer Tina Modotti. As early as 1956, moreover, Rich began to insist upon the historicity of her own poems by dating each one. "It seems to me now that this was an oblique political statement," Rich insists in the 1984 essay "Blood, Bread, and Poetry": "It was a declaration that placed poetry in a historical continuity, not above or outside history." "For Rich," as one critic argues, "a deepening subjectivity does not mean withdrawal, as it did for [Emily] Dickinson, but, on the contrary, a more searching engagement with people and with social forces."

In Rich's life, as in her work, the movement into the self has fueled the movement outward—into the world and back into the past—and vice versa. On the one hand, it was in part her personal feelings and experiences—the fact that she felt "unfit, disempowered, adrift" as a housewife and mother in the mid-1950s—that sent her to the work of "political" writers like Mary Wollstonecraft, Simone de Beauvoir, and James Baldwin, and, later, into the anti-war, civil rights, and women's movements. On the other hand, it was these writers and movements that eventually encouraged her to see her "private turmoil"—indeed, her consciousness itself—as the product of historically specific social and political forces. As she explains in "Blood, Bread, and Poetry,"

> my personal world view ... was ... created by political conditions. I was not a man; I was white in a white-supremacist society; I was ... educated from the perspective of a particular class; my father was an "assimilated" Jew in an anti-Semitic world, my mother a white southern Protestant; there were particular historical currents on which my consciousness would come together, piece by piece.... My personal world view, which like so many young people I carried as a conviction of my own uniqueness, was not original with me, but was, rather, my untutored and half-conscious rendering of the facts of blood and bread, the social and political forces of my time and place.

Rich's mature poetry is, in many ways, an attempt to scrutinize the "social and political forces" that shape our lives and our relationships with each other and with the planet we inhabit. In this way, "the personal is political" for and in Rich—and so, too, is the literary. Yet her poetry works as poetry largely because in it the converse is always equally and palpably true. Her "poems compel us," as critic Albert Gelpi suggests, "precisely because ... the politics [are] not abstracted and depersonalized but tested on the nerve-ends."

Despite—or even because of—all the changes, Rich's work also demonstrates a real and rare sort of consistency. From the very beginning of her career, Rich has conceived poems with a powerful sense of functional structure and cast them in lyric modes that sensitively reflect their moods and tones. She has engaged readers viscerally and intellectually through vivid images. And in fact certain images and objects—knives and coffee pots, ruins and rubble, maps and monsters, wintry weather—recur in multiple poems, binding the poems together even as they help us to track a process of evolution and change which, Rich reminds us, isn't either simple or complete. "If you think you can grasp me, think again," she warns us in "Delta"; "my story flows in more than one direction."

## At a Bach Concert

Coming by evening through the wintry city
We said that art is out of love with life.
Here we approach a love that is not pity.

This antique discipline, tenderly severe,
5 Renews belief in love yet masters feeling,
Asking of us a grace in what we bear.

Form is the ultimate gift that love can offer—
The vital union of necessity
With all that we desire, all that we suffer.
10  A too-compassionate art is half an art.
Only such proud restraining purity
Restores the else-betrayed, too-human heart.

                          1951

## Storm Warnings

The glass has been falling all the afternoon,
And knowing better than the instrument
What winds are walking overhead, what zone
Of gray unrest is moving across the land,
5  I leave the book upon a pillowed chair
And walk from window to closed window, watching
Boughs strain against the sky

And think again, as often when the air
Moves inward toward a silent core of waiting,
10  How with a single purpose time has traveled
By secret currents of the undiscerned
Into this polar realm. Weather abroad
And weather in the heart alike come on
Regardless of prediction.

15  Between foreseeing and averting change
Lies all the mastery of elements
Which clocks and weatherglasses cannot alter.
Time in the hand is not control of time,
Nor shattered fragments of an instrument
20  A proof against the wind; the wind will rise,
We can only close the shutters.

I draw the curtains as the sky goes black
And set a match to candles sheathed in glass
Against the keyhole draught, the insistent whine
25  Of weather through the unsealed aperture.
This is our sole defense against the season;
These are the things that we have learned to do
Who live in troubled regions.

                          1951

## Living in Sin

She had thought the studio would keep itself;
no dust upon the furniture of love.
Half heresy, to wish the taps less vocal,
the panes relieved of grime. A plate of pears,
5 a piano with a Persian shawl, a cat
stalking the picturesque amusing mouse
had risen at his urging.
Not that at five each separate stair would writhe
under the milkman's tramp; that morning light
10 so coldly would delineate the scraps
of last night's cheese and three sepulchral bottles;
that on the kitchen shelf among the saucers
a pair of beetle-eyes would fix her own—
envoy from some village in the moldings...
15 Meanwhile, he, with a yawn,
sounded a dozen notes upon the keyboard,
declared it out of tune, shrugged at the mirror,
rubbed at his beard, went out for cigarettes;
while she, jeered by the minor demons,
20 pulled back the sheets and made the bed and found
a towel to dust the table-top,
and let the coffee-pot boil over on the stove.
By evening she was back in love again,
though not so wholly but throughout the night
25 she woke sometimes to feel the daylight coming
like a relentless milkman up the stairs.

1955

## Snapshots of a Daughter-in-Law

1

You, once a belle in Shreveport,
with henna-colored hair, skin like a peachbud,
still have your dresses copied from that time,
and play a Chopin prelude
5 called by Cortot: *"Delicious recollections*
*float like perfume through the memory."*

Your mind now, mouldering like wedding-cake,
heavy with useless experience, rich
with suspicion, rumor, fantasy,
10 crumbling to pieces under the knife-edge
of mere fact. In the prime of your life.

Nervy, glowering, your daughter
wipes the teaspoons, grows another way.

### 2

Banging the coffee-pot into the sink
15 she hears the angels chiding, and looks out
past the raked gardens to the sloppy sky.
Only a week since They said: *Have no patience.*

The next time it was: *Be insatiable.*
Then: *Save yourself; others you cannot save.*[1]
20 Sometimes she's let the tapstream scald her arm,
a match burn to her thumbnail,

or held her hand above the kettle's snout
right in the woolly steam. They are probably angels,
since nothing hurts her any more, except
25 each morning's grit blowing into her eyes.

### 3

A thinking woman sleeps with monsters.
The beak that grips her, she becomes. And Nature,
that sprung-lidded, still commodious
steamer-trunk of *tempora* and *mores*[2]
30 gets stuffed with it all:   the mildewed orange-flowers,
the female pills, the terrible breasts
of Boadicea[3] beneath flat foxes' heads and orchids.

Two handsome women, gripped in argument,
each proud, acute, subtle, I hear scream
35 across the cut glass and majolica
like Furies[4] cornered from their prey:
The argument *ad feminam,*[5] all the old knives
that have rusted in my back, I drive in yours,
*ma semblable, ma soeur!*[6]

### 4

40 Knowing themselves too well in one another:
their gifts no pure fruition, but a thorn,
the prick filed sharp against a hint of scorn . . .
Reading while waiting

---

1. According to Matthew 27.42, the chief priests, scribes, and elders mocked the crucified Jesus by saying, "He saved others; himself he cannot save."   2. Times and customs.
3. Queen of the ancient Britons. When her husband died, the Romans seized the territory he ruled and scourged Boadicea; she then led a heroic but ultimately unsuccessful revolt. *Female pills:* medicines for menstrual ailments.
4. In Roman mythology, the three sisters were the avenging spirits of retributive justice.
5. To the woman (Latin). The *argumentum ad hominem* (literally, argument to the man) is (in classical rhetoric) an argument aimed at a person's individual prejudices or special interests.
6. My mirror-image (or "double"), my sister. Baudelaire, in the prefatory poem to *Les Fleurs du Mal,* addresses (and attacks) his "hypocrite reader" as "mon semblable, mon frère" (my double, my brother).

             for the iron to heat,
45   writing, *My Life had stood—a Loaded Gun—*[7]
     in that Amherst pantry while the jellies boil and scum,
     or, more often,
     iron-eyed and beaked and purposed as a bird,
     dusting everything on the whatnot every day of life.

             5

50   *Dulce ridens, dulce loquens,*[8]
     she shaves her legs until they gleam
     like petrified mammoth-tusk.

             6

     When to her lute Corinna sings[9]
     neither words nor music are her own;
55   only the long hair dipping
     over her cheek, only the song
     of silk against her knees
     and these
     adjusted in reflections of an eye.

60   Poised, trembling and unsatisfied, before
     an unlocked door, that cage of cages,
     tell us, you bird, you tragical machine—
     is this *fertilisante douleur?*[1] Pinned down
     by love, for you the only natural action,
65   are you edged more keen
     to prise the secrets of the vault? has Nature shown
     her household books to you, daughter-in-law,
     that her sons never saw?

             7

     *"To have in this uncertain world some stay*
70   *which cannot be undermined, is*
     *of the utmost consequence."*[2]
                         Thus wrote
     a woman, partly brave and partly good,
     who fought with what she partly understood.
75   Few men about her would or could do more,
     hence she was labeled harpy, shrew and whore.

---

7. "My Life had stood—a Loaded Gun—" [Poem No. 754], Emily Dickinson, *Complete Poems*, ed. T. H. Johnson, 1960, p. 369 [Rich's note]. It is reprinted in chapter 20.
8. Sweet laughter, sweet chatter. The phrase (slightly modified here) concludes Horace's *Ode* 1.22, describing the appeal of a mistress.
9. The opening line of a lyric by Thomas Campion (1567–1620). It is reprinted in chapter 17.
1. Enriching pain (French).
2. "...is of the utmost consequence," from Mary Wollstonecraft, *Thoughts on the Education of Daughters*, London, 1787 [Rich's note].

### 8

"You all die at fifteen," said Diderot,[3]
and turn part legend, part convention.
Still, eyes inaccurately dream
80 behind closed windows blankening with steam.
Deliciously, all that we might have been,
all that we were—fire, tears,
wit, taste, martyred ambition—
stirs like the memory of refused adultery
85 the drained and flagging bosom of our middle years.

### 9

*Not that it is done well, but
that it is done at all?*[4] Yes, think
of the odds! or shrug them off forever.
This luxury of the precocious child,
90 Time's precious chronic invalid,—
would we, darlings, resign it if we could?
Our blight has been our sinecure:
mere talent was enough for us—
glitter in fragments and rough drafts.

95 Sigh no more, ladies.
                Time is male
and in his cups drinks to the fair.
Bemused by gallantry, we hear
our mediocrities over-praised,
100 indolence read as abnegation,
slattern thought styled intuition,
every lapse forgiven, our crime
only to cast too bold a shadow
or smash the mould straight off.

105 For that, solitary confinement,
tear gas, attrition shelling.
Few applicants for that honor.

### 10

                Well,
she's long about her coming, who must be

---

3. "Vous mourez toutes a quinze ans," from the *Lettres à Sophie Volland,* quoted by Simone de Beauvoir in *Le Deuxième Sexe,* vol. II, pp. 123-4 [Rich's note]. Editor of the *Encyclopédie* (the central document of the French Enlightenment), Denis Diderot (1713-1784) became disillusioned with the traditional education of women and undertook an experimental education for his own daughter.
4. Samuel Johnson's comment on women preachers: "Sir, a woman's preaching is like a dog's walking on his hinder legs. It is not done well, but you are surprised to find it done at all" (Boswell's *Life of Johnson,* ed. L. F. Powell and G. B. Hill [Oxford: Clarendon, 1934-64], 1.463).

110 more merciless to herself than history.[5]
Her mind full to the wind, I see her plunge
breasted and glancing through the currents,
taking the light upon her
at least as beautiful as any boy
115 or helicopter,
          poised, still coming,
her fine blades making the air wince

but her cargo
no promise then:
120 delivered
palpable
ours.

1958–60

In her 1972 essay "When We Dead Awaken," Rich describes her consciousness during the time she was writing this poem:

> Over two years I wrote a 10-part poem called "Snapshots of a Daughter-in-Law," in a longer, looser mode than I've ever trusted myself with before. It was an extraordinary relief to write that poem. It strikes me now as too literary, too dependent on allusion; I hadn't found the courage yet to do without authorities, or even to use the pronoun "I"—the woman in the poem is always "she." One section of it, #2, concerns a woman who thinks she is going mad; she is haunted by voices telling her to resist and rebel, voices which she can hear but not obey.

## *Planetarium*

    (*Thinking of Caroline Herschel, 1750–1848, astronomer, sister of William; and others*)

A woman in the shape of a monster
a monster in the shape of a woman
the skies are full of them

a woman    "in the snow
5 among the Clocks and instruments
or measuring the ground with poles"

in her 98 years to discover
8 comets

---

5. Cf. *Le Deuxième Sexe*, vol. II, p. 574: "... elle arrive du fond des ages, de Thèbes, de Minos, de Chichen Itza; et elle est aussi le totem planté au coeur de la brousse africaine; c'est un helicoptère et c'est un oiseau; et voilà la plus grande merveille: sous ses cheveux peints le bruissement des feuillages devient une pensée et des paroles s'échappent de ses seins" [Rich's note].

>           she whom the moon ruled
> 10    like us
>           levitating into the night sky
>           riding the polished lenses
>
>           Galaxies of women, there
>           doing penance for impetuousness
> 15    ribs chilled
>           in those spaces     of the mind
>
>           An eye,
>                   "virile, precise and absolutely certain"
>                        from the mad webs of Uranisborg[6]
> 20                                              encountering the NOVA
>           every impulse of light exploding
>           from the core
>           as life flies out of us
>
>                   Tycho whispering at last
> 25           "Let me not seem to have lived in vain"
>
>           What we see, we see
>           and seeing is changing
>
>           the light that shrivels a mountain
>           and leaves a man alive
> 30    Heartbeat of the pulsar
>           heart sweating through my body
>
>           The radio impulse
>           pouring in from Taurus
>                   I am bombarded yet     I stand
>
> 35    I have been standing all my life in the
>           direct path of a battery of signals
>           the most accurately transmitted most
>           untranslatable language in the universe
>           I am a galactic cloud so deep     so invo-
> 40    luted that a light wave could take 15
>           years to travel through me     And has
>           taken     I am an instrument in the shape
>           of a woman trying to translate pulsations
>           into images     for the relief of the body
> 45    and the reconstruction of the mind.
>
> 1968

---

6. Actually Uraniborg, the elaborate palace-laboratory-observatory of Danish astronomer Tycho Brahe (1546–1601), whose cosmology tried to fuse the Ptolemaic and Copernican systems. Brahe discovered and described (in *De Nova Stella*, 1574) a new star in what had previously been considered a fixed-star system.

## For the Record

The clouds and the stars didn't wage this war
the brooks gave no information
if the mountain spewed stones of fire into the river
it was not taking sides
the raindrop faintly swaying under the leaf
had no political opinions

and if here or there a house
filled with backed-up raw sewage
or poisoned those who lived there
with slow fumes, over years
the houses were not at war
nor did the tinned-up buildings

intend to refuse shelter
to homeless old women and roaming children
they had no policy to keep them roaming
or dying, no, the cities were not the problem
the bridges were non-partisan
the freeways burned, but not with hatred

Even the miles of barbed-wire
stretched around crouching temporary huts
designed to keep the unwanted
at a safe distance, out of sight
even the boards that had to absorb
year upon year, so many human sounds

so many depths of vomit, tears
slow-soaking blood
had not offered themselves for this
The trees didn't volunteer to be cut into boards
nor the thorns for tearing flesh
Look around at all of it

and ask whose signature
is stamped on the orders, traced
in the corner of the building plans
Ask where the illiterate, big-bellied
women were, the drunks and crazies,
the ones you fear most of all: ask where you were.

1983

## [*My mouth hovers across your breasts*][7]

My mouth hovers across your breasts
in the short grey winter afternoon
in this bed      we are delicate
and tough     so hot with joy we amaze ourselves
5   tough      and delicate      we play rings
around each other      our daytime candle burns
with its peculiar light      and if the snow
begins to fall outside      filling the branches
and if the night falls      without announcement
10  these are the pleasures of winter
sudden, wild and delicate      your fingers
exact      my tongue exact at the same moment
stopping to laugh at a joke
my love      hot on your scent      on the cusp of winter

                                                        1986


## *History*[8]

Should I simplify my life for you?
Don't ask how I began to love men.
Don't ask how I began to love women.
Remember the forties songs, the slowdance numbers
5   the small sex-filled gas-rationed Chevrolet?
Remember walking in the snow and who was gay?
Cigarette smoke of the movies, silver-and-gray
profiles, dreaming the dreams of he-and-she
breathing the dissolution of the wisping silver plume?
10  Dreaming that dream we leaned applying lipstick
by the gravestone's mirror when we found ourselves
playing in the cemetery. In Current Events she said
the war in Europe is over, the Allies
and she wore no lipstick have won the war
15  and we raced screaming out of Sixth Period.

Dreaming that dream
we had to maze our ways through a wood
where lips were knives breasts razors and I hid
in the cage of my mind scribbling
20  *this map stops where it all begins*
into a red-and-black notebook.

---

7. This is poem 3 in Rich's series "Tracking Poems."
8. This is poem 4 in Rich's series "Inscriptions."

Remember after the war when peace came down
as plenty for some and they said we were saved
in an eternal present and we knew the world could end?
25 —remember after the war when peace rained down
on the winds from Hiroshima Nagasaki Utah Nevada?[9]
and the socialist queer Christian teacher jumps from the hotel window?[1]
and L.G. saying *I want to sleep with you but not for sex*
and the red-and-black enamelled coffee-pot dripped slow through the
dark grounds
30 —appetite terror power tenderness
the long kiss in the stairwell the switch thrown
on two Jewish Communists[2] married to each other
the definitive crunch of glass at the end of the wedding?
*(When shall we learn, what should be clear as day,*
35 *We cannot choose what we are free to love?)*

1995

## Modotti[3]

Your footprints of light on sensitive paper
that typewriter you made famous
my footsteps following you up stair-
wells of scarred oak and shredded newsprint
5 these windowpanes smeared with stifled breaths
corridors of tile and jaundiced plaster
if this is where I must look for you
then this is where I'll find you

From a streetlamp's wet lozenge bent
10 on a curb plastered with newsprint
the headlines aiming straight at your eyes
to a room's dark breath-smeared light
these footsteps I'm following you with
down tiles of a red corridor
15 if this is a way to find you
of course this is how I'll find you

---

9. Sites of atom bomb explosions, the first two in Japan near the end of World War II, the last two at test sites in the American desert.
1. This line alludes to the critic Francis Otto Matthiessen (1902-1950), who taught at Harvard while Rich was an undergraduate there.
2. Julius and Ethel Rosenberg, executed as spies by the United States in 1953.
3. Tina Modotti (1896-1942): photographer, political activist, revolutionary. Her most significant artistic work was done in Mexico in the 1920s, including a study of the typewriter belonging to her lover, the Cuban revolutionary Julio Antonio Mella. Framed for his murder by the fascists in 1929, she was expelled from Mexico in 1930. After some years of political activity in Berlin, the Soviet Union, and Spain, she returned incognito to Mexico, where she died in 1942.

In my search for Modotti I had to follow clues she left; I did not want to iconize her but to imagine critically the traps and opportunities of her life and choices [Rich's note].

       Your negatives pegged to dry in a darkroom
       rigged up over a bathtub's lozenge
       your footprints of light on sensitive paper
20  stacked curling under blackened panes
       the always upstairs of your hideout
       the stern exposure of your brows
       —these footsteps I'm following you with
       aren't to arrest you

25  The bristling hairs of your eyeflash
       that typewriter you made famous
       your enormous will to arrest and frame
       what was, what is, still liquid, flowing
       your exposure of manifestos, your
30  lightbulb in a scarred ceiling
       well if this is how I find you
       Modotti so I find you

       In the red wash of your darkroom
       from your neighborhood of volcanoes
35  to the geranium nailed in a can
       on the wall of your upstairs hideout
       in the rush of breath a window
       of revolution allowed you
       on this jaundiced stair in this huge lashed eye these
40
       footsteps I'm following you with

1996                                                                             1999

## PERSONAL REFLECTIONS

## From *When We Dead Awaken:*
## *Writing as Re-Vision*[1]

Most, if not all, human lives are full of fantasy—passive daydreaming which need not be acted on. But to write poetry or fiction, or even to think well, is not to fantasize, or to put fantasies on paper. For a poem to coalesce, for a character or an action to take shape, there has to be an imaginative transformation of reality which is in no way passive. And a certain freedom of the mind is needed—freedom to press on, to enter the currents of your thought like a glider pilot, knowing that your motion can be sustained, that the buoyancy of your attention will not be suddenly snatched away. Moreover, if the imagination is to transcend

---

1. First published in *College English* in 1972; this version, slightly revised, is included in *On Lies, Secrets, and Silence: Selected Prose: 1966–1978* (1979).

Adrienne Rich in 1978

and transform experience it has to question, to challenge, to conceive of alternatives, perhaps to the very life you are living at that moment. You have to be free to play around with the notion that day might be night, love might be hate, nothing can be too sacred for the imagination to turn into its opposite or to call experimentally by another name. For writing is re-naming. Now, to be maternally with small children all day in the old way, to be with a man in the old way of marriage, requires a holding-back, a putting-aside of that imaginative activity, and demands instead a kind of conservatism. I want to make it clear that I am *not* saying that in order to write well, or think well, it is necessary to become unavailable to others, or to become a devouring ego. This has been the myth of the masculine artist and thinker; and I do not accept it. But to be a female human being trying to fulfill traditional female functions in a traditional way *is* in direct conflict with the subversive function of the imagination. The word traditional is important here. There must be ways, and we will be finding out more and more about them, in which the energy of creation and the energy of relation can be united. But in those earlier years I always felt the conflict as a failure of love in myself. I had thought I was choosing a full life: the life available to most men, in which sexuality, work, and parenthood could coexist. But I felt, at twenty-nine, guilt toward the people closest to me, and guilty toward my own being.

I wanted, then, more than anything, the one thing of which there was never enough: time to think, time to write. The fifties and early sixties were years of rapid revelations: the sit-ins and marches in the South, the Bay of Pigs, the early antiwar movement, raised large questions—questions for which the masculine world of the academy around me seemed to have expert and fluent answers. But I needed to think for myself—about pacifism and dissent and violence, about poetry and society, and about my own relationship to all these things. For about ten years I was reading in fierce snatches, scribbling in notebooks, writing poetry in fragments; I was looking desperately for clues, because if there were no clues then I thought I might be insane. I wrote in a notebook about this time:

> Paralyzed by the sense that there exists a mesh of relationships—e.g., between my anger at the children, my sensual life, pacifism, sex (I mean sex in its broadest significance, not merely sexual desire)—an interconnectedness which, if I could see it, make it valid, would give me back myself, make it possible to function lucidly and passionately. Yet I grope in and out among these dark webs.

I think I began at this point to feel that politics was not something "out there" but something "in here" and of the essence of my condition.

In the late fifties I was able to write, for the first time, directly about experiencing myself as a woman. The poem was jotted in fragments during children's naps, brief hours in a library, or at 3 A.M. after rising with a wakeful child. I despaired of doing any continuous work at this time. Yet I began to feel that my fragments and scraps had a common consciousness and a common theme, one which I would have been very unwilling to put on paper at an earlier time because I had been taught that poetry should be "universal," which meant, of course, nonfemale. Until then I had tried very much *not* to identify myself as a female poet.

## How Does a Poet Put Bread on the Table?[2]

But how does a poet put bread on the table? Rarely, if ever, by poetry alone. Of the four lesbian poets at the Nuyorican Poets Café about whose lives I know something, one directs an underfunded community arts project, two are untenured college teachers, one an assistant dean of students at a state university. Of other poets I know, most teach, often part time, without security but year round; two are on disability; one does clerical work; one cleans houses; one is a paid organizer; one has a paid editing job. Whatever odd money comes in erratically from readings and workshops, grants, permissions fees, royalties, prizes can be very odd money indeed, never to be counted on and almost always small: checks have to be chased down, grants become fewer and more competitive in a worsening political and economic climate. Most poets who teach at universities are untenured, without pension plans or group health insurance, or are employed at public and community colleges with heavy teaching loads and low salaries. Many give unpaid readings and workshops as part of their political "tithe."

Inherited wealth accounts for the careers of some poets: to inherit wealth is to inherit time. Most of the poets I know, hearing of a sum of money, translate it not into possessions, but into time—that precious immaterial necessity of our lives. It's true that a poem can be attempted in brief interstitial moments, pulled out of the pocket and worked on while waiting for a bus or riding a train or while children nap or while waiting for a new batch of clerical work or blood samples to come in. But only certain kinds of poems are amenable to these conditions. Sometimes the very knowledge of coming interruption dampens the flicker. And there is a difference between the ordinary "free" moments stolen from exhausting family strains, from alienating labor, from thought chained by material anxiety, and those other moments that sometimes arrive in a life being lived at its height though under extreme tension; perhaps we are waiting to initiate some act we believe will catalyze change but whose outcome is uncertain; perhaps we are facing personal or communal crisis in which everything unimportant seems to fall away and we are left with our naked lives, the brevity of life itself, and words. At such times we may experience a speeding-up of our imaginative powers, images and voices rush together in a kind of inevitability, what was externally fragmented is internally recognized, and the hand can barely keep pace.

But such moments presuppose other times: when we could simply stare into the wood grain of a door, or the trace of bubbles in a glass of water as long as

---

2. From *What Is Found There: Notebooks on Poetry and Politics* (1993).

we wanted to, *almost* secure in the knowledge that there would be no interruption—times of slowness, or purposelessness.

Often such time feels like a luxury, guiltily seized when it can be had, fearfully taken because it does not seem like work, this abeyance, but like "wasting time" in a society where personal importance—even job security—can hinge on acting busy, where the phrase "keeping busy" is a common idiom, where there is, for activists, so much to be done.

Most, if not all, of the names we know in North American poetry are the names of people who have had some access to freedom in time—that privilege of some which is actually a necessity for all. The struggle to limit the working day is a sacred struggle for the worker's freedom in time. To feel herself or himself, for a few hours or a weekend, as a free being with choices—to plant vegetables and later sit on the porch with a cold beer, to write poetry or build a fence or fish or play cards, to walk without a purpose, to make love in the daytime. To sleep late. Ordinary human pleasures, the self's re-creation. Yet every working generation has to reclaim that freedom in time, and many are brutally thwarted in the effort. Capitalism is based on the abridgment of that freedom.

Poets in the United States have either had some kind of private means, or help from people with private means, have held full-time, consuming jobs, or have chosen to work in low-paying, part-time sectors of the economy, saving their creative energies for poetry, keeping their material wants simple. Interstitial living, where the art itself is not expected to bring in much money, where the artist may move from a clerical job to part-time, temporary teaching to subsistence living on the land to waitressing or doing construction or translating, typesetting, or ghostwriting. In the 1990s this kind of interstitial living is more difficult, risky, and wearing than it has ever been, and this is a loss to all the arts—as much as the shrinkage of arts funding, the censorship-by-clique, the censorship by the Right, the censorship by distribution.

## *A Communal Poetry*[3]

One day in New York in the late 1980s, I had lunch with a poet I'd known for more than twenty years. Many of his poems were—are—embedded in my life. We had read together at the antiwar events of the Vietnam years. Then, for a long time, we hardly met. As a friend, he had seemed to me withheld, defended in a certain way I defined as masculine and with which I was becoming in general impatient; yet often, in their painful beauty, his poems told another story. On this day, he was as I had remembered him: distant, stiff, shy perhaps. The conversation stumbled along as we talked about our experiences with teaching poetry, which seemed a safe ground. I made some remark about how long it was since last we'd talked. Suddenly, his whole manner changed: *You disappeared! You simply disappeared.* I realized he meant not so much from his life as from a landscape of poetry to which he thought we both belonged and were in some sense loyal.

3. From *What Is Found There: Notebooks on Poetry and Politics* (1993).

If anything, those intervening years had made me feel more apparent, more visible—to myself and to others—as a poet. The powerful magnet of the women's liberation movement—and the women's poetry movement it released—had drawn me to coffeehouses where women were reading new kinds of poems; to emerging "journals of liberation" that published women's poems, often in a context of political articles and the beginnings of feminist criticism; to bookstores selling chapbooks and pamphlets from the new women's presses; to a woman poet's workshops with women in prison; to meetings with other women poets in Chinese restaurants, coffee shops, apartments, where we talked not only of poetry, but of the conditions that make it possible or impossible. It had never occurred to me that I was disappearing—rather, that I was, along with other women poets, beginning to appear. In fact, we were taking part in an immense shift in human consciousness.

Adrienne Rich in the 1990s

My old friend had, I believe, not much awareness of any of this. It was, for him, so off-to-the-edge, so out-of-the-way; perhaps so dangerous, it seemed I had sunk, or dived, into a black hole. Only later, in a less constrained and happier meeting, were we able to speak of the different ways we had perceived that time.

He thought there had been a known, defined poetic landscape and that as poetic contemporaries we simply shared it. But whatever poetic "generation" I belonged to, in the 1950s I was a mother, under thirty, raising three small children. Notwithstanding the prize and the fellowship to Europe that my first book of poems had won me, there was little or no "appearance" I then felt able to claim as a poet, against that other profound and as yet unworded reality.

## *Why I Refused the National Medal for the Arts*[4]

July 3, 1997

Jane Alexander, Chair
The National Endowment for the Arts
1100 Pennsylvania Avenue
Washington, D.C. 20506

Dear Jane Alexander,

I just spoke with a young man from your office, who informed me that I had been chosen to be one of twelve recipients of the National Medal for the Arts at

---

4. From *Arts of the Possible: Essays and Conversations* (2001).
  After the text of my letter to Jane Alexander, then chair of the National Endowment for the Arts, had been fragmentarily quoted in various news stories, Steve Wasserman, editor of the *Los Angeles Times Book Review*, asked me for an article expanding on my reasons. Herewith the letter and the article [Rich's note].

a ceremony at the White House in the fall. I told him at once that I could not accept such an award from President Clinton or this White House because the very meaning of art, as I understand it, is incompatible with the cynical politics of this administration. I want to clarify to you what I meant by my refusal.

Anyone familiar with my work from the early sixties on knows that I believe in art's social presence—as breaker of official silences, as voice for those whose voices are disregarded, and as a human birthright. In my lifetime I have seen the space for the arts opened by movements for social justice, the power of art to break despair. Over the past two decades I have witnessed the increasingly brutal impact of racial and economic injustice in our country.

There is no simple formula for the relationship of art to justice. But I do know that art—in my own case the art of poetry—means nothing if it simply decorates the dinner table of power that holds it hostage. The radical disparities of wealth and power in America are widening at a devastating rate. A president cannot meaningfully honor certain token artists while the people at large are so dishonored.

I know you have been engaged in a serious and disheartening struggle to save government funding for the arts, against those whose fear and suspicion of art is nakedly repressive. In the end, I don't think we can separate art from overall human dignity and hope. My concern for my country is inextricable from my concerns as an artist. I could not participate in a ritual that would feel so hypocritical to me.

Sincerely,
Adrienne Rich

cc: President Clinton

---

The invitation from the White House came by telephone on July 3. After several years' erosion of arts funding and hostile propaganda from the religious right and the Republican Congress, the House vote to end the National Endowment for the Arts was looming. That vote would break as news on July 10; my refusal of the National Medal for the Arts would run as a sidebar story alongside in the *New York Times* and the *San Francisco Chronicle*.

In fact, I was unaware of the timing. My refusal came directly out of my work as a poet and essayist and citizen drawn to the interfold of personal and public experience. I had recently been thinking and writing about the shrinking of the social compact, of whatever it was this country had ever meant when it called itself a democracy: the shredding of the vision of *government of the people, by the people, for the people.*

"We the people—still an excellent phrase," said the playwright Lorraine Hansberry in 1962, well aware who had been excluded, yet believing the phrase might someday come to embrace us all. And I had for years been feeling both personal and public grief, fear, hunger, and the need to render this, my time, in the language of my art.

Whatever was "newsworthy" about my refusal was not about a single individual—not myself, not President Clinton. Nor was it about a single political party.

Both major parties have displayed a crude affinity for the interests of corporate power, while deserting the majority of the people, especially the most vulnerable. Like so many others, I've watched the dismantling of our public education, the steep rise in our incarceration rates, the demonization of our young black men, the accusations against our teen-age mothers, the selling of health care—public and private—to the highest bidders, the export of subsistence-level jobs in the United States to even lower-wage countries, the use of below-minimum-wage prison labor to break strikes and raise profits, the scapegoating of immigrants, the denial of dignity and minimal security to working and poor people. At the same time, we've witnessed the acquisition of publishing houses, once risk-taking conduits of creativity, by conglomerates driven single-mindedly to fast profits, the acquisition of major communications and media by those same interests, the sacrifice of the arts and public libraries in stripped-down school and civic budgets, and, most recently, the evisceration of the National Endowment for the Arts. Piece by piece the democratic process has been losing ground to the accumulation of private wealth.

There is no political leadership in the White House or the Congress that has spoken to and for the people who, in a very real sense, have felt abandoned by their government.

Lorraine Hansberry spoke her words about government during the Cuban missile crisis, at a public meeting in New York to abolish the House Un-American Activities Committee. She also said in that speech, "My government is wrong." She did not say, I abhor all government. She claimed her government as a citizen, African American, and female, and she challenged it. (I listened to her words again, on an old vinyl recording, this past Fourth of July.)

In a similar spirit many of us today might wish to hold government accountable, to challenge the agendas of private power and wealth that have displaced historical tendencies toward genuinely representative government in the United States. We might still wish to claim our government, to say, *This belongs to us—* we, the people, as we are now.

We would have to start asking questions that have been defined as nonquestions—or as naive, childish questions. In the recent official White House focus on race, it goes consistently unsaid that the all-embracing enterprise of our early history was the slave trade, which left nothing, no single life, untouched, and was, along with the genocide of the native population and the seizure of their lands, the foundation of our national prosperity and power. Promote dialogues on race? apologize for slavery? We would need to perform an autopsy on capitalism itself.

Marxism has been declared dead. Yet the questions Marx raised are still alive and pulsing, however the language and the labels have been co-opted and abused. What is social wealth? How do the conditions of human labor infiltrate other social relationships? What would it require for people to live and work together in conditions of radical equality? How much inequality will we tolerate in the world's richest and most powerful nation? Why and how have these and similar questions become discredited in public discourse?

And what about art? Mistrusted, adored, pietized, condemned, dismissed as entertainment, commodified, auctioned at Sotheby's, purchased by investment-seeking celebrities, it dies into the "art object" of a thousand museum basements. It's also reborn hourly in prisons, women's shelters, small-town garages, community-college workshops, halfway houses, wherever someone picks up a pencil, a wood-burning tool, a copy of *The Tempest,* a tag-sale camera, a whittling knife, a stick of charcoal, a pawnshop horn, a video of *Citizen Kane,* whatever lets you know again that this deeply instinctual yet self-conscious expressive language, this regenerative process, could help you save your life. "If there were no poetry on any day in the world," the poet Muriel Rukeyser wrote, "poetry would be invented that day. For there would be an intolerable hunger." In an essay on the Caribbean poet Aimé Césaire, Clayton Eshleman names this hunger as "the desire, the need, for a more profound and ensouled world." There is a continuing dynamic between art repressed and art reborn, between the relentless marketing of the superficial and the "spectral and vivid reality that employs all means" (Rukeyser again) to reach through armoring, resistances, resignation, to recall us to desire.

Art is both tough and fragile. It speaks of what we long to hear and what we dread to find. Its source and native impulse, the imagination, may be shackled in early life, yet may find release in conditions offering little else to the spirit. For a recent document on this, look at Phyllis Kornfeld's *Cellblock Visions: Prison Art in America,* notable for the variety and emotional depth of the artworks reproduced, the words of the inmate artists, and for Kornfeld's unsentimental and lucid text. Having taught art to inmates for fourteen years, in eighteen institutions (including maximum-security units), she sees recent incarceration policy as rapidly devolving from rehabilitation to dehumanization, including the dismantling of prison arts programs.

Art can never be totally legislated by any system, even those that reward obedience and send dissident artists to hard labor and death; nor can it, in our specifically compromised system, be really free. It may push up through cracked macadam, by the merest means, but it needs breathing space, cultivation, protection to fulfill itself. Just as people do. New artists, young or old, need education in their art, the tools of their craft, chances to study examples from the past and meet practitioners in the present, get the criticism and encouragement of mentors, learn that they are not alone. As the social compact withers, fewer and fewer people will be told *Yes, you can do this; this also belongs to you.* Like government, art needs the participation of the many in order not to become the property of a powerful and narrowly self-interested few.

Art is our human birthright, our most powerful means of access to our own and another's experience and imaginative life. In continually rediscovering and recovering the humanity of human beings, art is crucial to the democratic vision. A government tending further and further away from the search for democracy will see less and less "use" in encouraging artists, will see art as obscenity or hoax.

In 1987, the late Justice William Brennan spoke of "formal reason severed from the insights of passion" as a major threat to due-process principles. "Due process asks whether government has treated someone fairly, whether individual dignity has been honored, whether the worth of an individual has been acknowledged. Officials cannot always silence these questions by pointing to rational action taken according to standard rules. They must plumb their conduct more deeply, seeking answers in the more complex equations of human nature and experience."

It is precisely where fear and hatred of art join the pull toward quantification and abstraction, where the human face is mechanically deleted, that human dignity disappears from the social equation. Because it is to those "complex equations of human nature and experience" that art addresses itself.

In a society tyrannized by the accumulation of wealth as Eastern Europe was tyrannized by its own false gods of concentrated power, recognized artists have, perhaps, a new opportunity: to work out our connectedness, *as artists,* with other people who are beleaguered, suffering, disenfranchised—precariously employed workers, trashed elders, rejected youth, the "unsuccessful," and the art they too are nonetheless making and seeking.

I wish I didn't feel the necessity to say here that none of this is about imposing ideology or style or content on artists; it's about the inseparability of art from acute social crisis in this century and the one now approaching.

We have a short-lived model, in our history, for the place of art in relation to government. During the Depression of the 1930s, under New Deal legislation, thousands of creative and performing artists were paid modest stipends to work in the Federal Writers Project, the Federal Theatre Project, the Federal Art Project. Their creativity, in the form of novels, murals, plays, performances, public monuments, the providing of music and theater to new audiences, seeded the art and the consciousness of succeeding decades. By 1939 this funding was discontinued.

Federal funding for the arts, like the philanthropy of private arts patrons, can be given and taken away. In the long run art needs to grow organically out of a social compost nourishing to everyone, a literate citizenry, a free, universal, public education complex with art as an integral element, a society honoring both human individuality and the search for a decent, sustainable common life. In such conditions, art would still be a voice of hunger, desire, discontent, passion, reminding us that the democratic project is never-ending.

For that to happen, what else would have to change?

## CHRONOLOGY

1929   Born in Baltimore, Maryland, May 16. Began writing poetry as a child under the encouragement and supervision of her father, Dr. Arnold Rich, from whose "very Victorian, pre-Raphaelite" library, Rich later recalled, she read Tennyson, Keats, Arnold, Blake, Rossetti, Swinburne, Carlyle, and Pater.

1951   A.B., Radcliffe College. *A Change of World* chosen by W. H. Auden for publication in the Yale Younger Poets series.

1952–53   Guggenheim Fellowship; travel in Europe and England. Marriage to Alfred H. Conrad, an economist who taught at Harvard. Residence in Cambridge, Massachusetts, 1953–66.

1955   Birth of David Conrad. Publication of *The Diamond Cutters and Other Poems.*

1957   Birth of Paul Conrad.

1959   Birth of Jacob Conrad.

1960   National Institute of Arts and Letters Award for poetry.

1961–62   Guggenheim Fellowship; residence with family in the Netherlands.

1962   Bollingen Foundation grant for translation of Dutch poetry.

1962–63   Amy Lowell Travelling Fellowship.

1963   *Snapshots of a Daughter-in-Law* published. Bess Hokin Prize of *Poetry* magazine.

1966 *Necessities of Life* published. Move to New York City; residence there from 1966 on. Increasingly active politically in protests against the war in Vietnam.
1966–68 Lecturer at Swarthmore College.
1967–69 Adjunct Professor of Writing in the Graduate School of the Arts, Columbia University.
1968 Began teaching in the SEEK and Open Admissions Programs at City College of New York.
1969 *Leaflets* published.
1970 Death of Alfred Conrad.
1971 *The Will to Change* published. Increasingly active in the women's movement.
1972–73 Fannie Hurst Visiting Professor of Creative Literature at Brandeis University.
1973 *Diving into the Wreck* published.
1974 National Book Award for *Diving into the Wreck*. Rich rejects the award as an individual, but accepts it, in a statement written with Audre Lorde and Alice Walker, two other nominees, in the name of all women. Professor of English, City College of New York.
1975 *Poems: Selected and New* published.
1976 Professor of English at Douglass College. *Of Woman Born: Motherhood as Experience and Institution* published. *Twenty-one Love Poems* published.
1978 *The Dream of a Common Language: Poems 1974–1977* published.
1979 *On Lies, Secrets, and Silence: Selected Prose 1966–1978* published. Leaves Douglass College and New York City; moves to Montague, Massachusetts; edits, with Michelle Cliff, the lesbian-feminist journal *Sinister Wisdom*.
1981 *A Wild Patience Has Taken Me This Far: Poems 1978–1981* published.
1984 *The Fact of a Doorframe: Poems Selected and New 1950–1984* published. Moves to Santa Cruz, California. Professor of English, San Jose State University.
1986 *Blood, Bread, and Poetry: Selected Prose 1979–1985* published. Professor of English, Stanford University.
1989 *Time's Power: Poems 1985–1988* published.
1991 *An Atlas of the Difficult World: Poems 1988–1991* published.
1992 Wins *Los Angeles Times* Book Prize for *An Atlas of the Difficult World: Poems 1988–1991*, the Lenore Marshall/*Nation* Prize for Poetry, and Nicholas Roerich Museum Poet's Prize; is co-winner of the Frost Silver Medal for distinguished lifetime achievement.
1993 *What Is Found There: Notebooks on Poetry and Politics* published.
1994 Awarded MacArthur fellowship.
1995 *Dark Fields of the Republic: Poems 1991–1995* published.
1996 Awarded the Dorothea Tanning Prize, given by the Academy of American Poets.
1999 Elected a chancellor of the Academy. Received Lannan Foundation's Lifetime Achievement Award. *Midnight Salvage: Poems 1995–1998* published.
2001 *Fox: Poems 1998–2000* and *Arts of the Possible: Essays and Conversations* published.
2002 *The Fact of a Doorframe: Poems Selected and New 1950–2000* published.
2005 *The School among the Ruins: Poems 2000–2004* published.

## SUGGESTIONS FOR WRITING

1. Write an essay in which you analyze one of Keats's sonnets, either "On First Looking into Chapman's Homer," "On the Grasshopper and the Cricket," or "On Seeing the Elgin Marbles." Which sonnet form does the poem employ, and why is this appropriate? What sound effects does Keats use, and why does this enhance the poem? How does Keats use poetic technique to support the poem's theme?
2. John Keats lost both of his parents and his brother while he was still young, and he knew that he was dying of tuberculosis during the final year of his life, when he wrote many of his greatest poems. Write an essay in which you explore the themes of life and death, mortality and immortality, as they reveal themselves in the selections in this chapter. How does Keats's poetry exemplify the Latin dictum *Vita brevis est, ars longa*—"Life is short, art is long"?
3. Write an essay in which you analyze the poetic techniques Keats employs in the passage from *Endymion* in this chapter. What are the relationships between rhymed words? What is the effect of the rhyme scheme? How does Keats create tension with the combination of rhymed couplets and enjambment—the continuation of sentences past the end of a poetic line?
4. Write an essay in which you present a close reading of one of the odes in this chapter. What is the tone, and how is this achieved? What is the relationship between the poem's form (stanzas, rhyme scheme, etc.) and the development of its argument? How does Keats use observed particulars to point to larger themes?
5. What is the relationship between Keats's poems and his theories about poetry? Write an essay in which you discuss how his poems are illuminated by the ideas he expresses in the letters in this chapter.
6. In her 1951 poem "At a Bach Concert," Adrienne Rich wrote that "Form is the ultimate gift that love can offer." What, exactly, is the case for the "discipline" of formalist art argued by this poem? How has Rich's later work both embodied and rejected formalism? Considering as evidence the selections of poetry in this and previous chapters, and prose in this chapter, write an essay in which you discuss how Rich's thoughts about formalism have evolved throughout her career.
7. Carefully considering plot, characterization, and structure, write an essay in which you detail the ways "Diving into the Wreck" (chapter 16) is and is not typical of Rich's work.
8. In poems such as "Snapshots of a Daughter-in-Law," "Planetarium," and "Modotti," Rich considers the creative accomplishments of women throughout history. What role do these women play, separately and together? How is that role both constrained and unconstrained by men? Write an essay in which you examine the way Rich has portrayed creative women. Are they role models in her work, or something else?
9. Rich once said of her college days in the late 1940s, "I had no political ideas of my own, only the era's vague and hallucinatory anti-Communism and the encroaching privatism of the 1950s. Drenched in invisible assumptions of my class and race, unable to fathom the pervasive ideology of gender, I felt 'politics' as distant, vaguely sinister, the province of powerful older men or of people I saw as fanatics. It was in poetry that I sought a grasp on the world and on interior events, 'ideas of order,' even power." Using the poems by Rich included in this book, write an essay that charts the development of the poet's political consciousness.
10. In her prose writings included in this chapter, Rich describes and defends the political passions that, she says, animate her life as an artist. How fully do Rich's poems embody her political beliefs, particularly her commitment to feminism? Write an essay in which you explore Rich's poetry in light of her feminist politics.

# 23 LITERARY TRADITION AS CONTEXT

The more poetry you read, the better a reader of poetry you will likely become. This is not just because your skills will improve and develop, but also because you will come to know more about poetic traditions and thus understand more fully how poets influence each other. Poets are conscious of other poets, and often they refer to each other's work or use it as a starting point for their own in ways that may not be immediately obvious to an outsider. Poetry can be thought of as a form of argument: poets agree or disagree over basic matters. Sometimes a quiet (or even noisy) competitiveness underlies their concern with what other poets do; at other times, playfulness and a sense of humor take over, and the competitiveness dwindles to poetic fun and games. And often poets simply want to share in the bounty of our artistic heritage. In any case, a poet's consciousness of what others have done leads to a sense of tradition that is often hard to articulate but is nevertheless very important to the effects of poetry—and this sense of tradition may present a problem for a new reader of poetry. How can I possibly read this poem intelligently, we are likely to ask sometimes in exasperation, until I've read all the other poems that inspired it? The problem is real. Poets don't expect their readers to have PhD's in literature, but sometimes it *seems* as if they do. For some poets—John Milton, T. S. Eliot, and Richard Wilbur, for example—it does help if one has read practically everything.

Why are poets so dependent on each other? What is the point of their relentless consciousness of what has already been done by others? Why do they repeatedly answer, allude to, and echo other poems? Why does tradition matter to them?

A sense of common task, a communality of purpose, accounts for some traditional poetic practice, as does the competitive desire of individual poets to achieve a place in the poetic **tradition**—the ever-growing body of poetic customs and practices. One way of establishing that place is to define the relationship between one's own work and that of others whose place is already secure. Poets may share and wish to pass on a serious and abiding cultural tradition, but they may also share a sense of playfulness, a kind of poetic gamesmanship. Making words dance on the page or in our heads provides in itself a satisfaction and delight for many writers—pride in craft that is like the pride of a painter or potter or tennis player. Often poets set themselves a particular task to see what they can do. One way of doing that is to introduce a standard **motif** (a recurrent device, formula, or situation that deliberately connects a poem with traditional thought), and then to play variations on it much as a musician might do. Another way is to provide an alternative answer to a question that has repeatedly been asked and answered in a traditional way. Poetic playfulness by no means excludes serious intention—the poems in this chapter often make important state-

*The truest poetry is the most feigning.*
—WILLIAM SHAKESPEARE

ments about their subjects, however humorous they may be in their method. Some teasing of the tradition and of other poets is pure fun, a kind of kidding among good friends; some is harsher and represents an attempt to see the world very differently—to define and articulate a very different set of attitudes and values.

The Anglophone poetic tradition is a rich and varied heritage, and individual poets draw upon it in countless ways. You have probably noticed, in the poems you have read so far, a number of allusions—glances at the tradition or at individual expressions of it. The more poems you read, the more such allusions you will notice and the more you will become a comfortable member of the audience poets write for. Poets expect a lot from readers—not always, but often enough to make a new reader feel nervous and even, sometimes, inadequate. The discomfort fades when you begin to notice things that other readers don't. The poems in this chapter illustrate some of the ways that the tradition energizes individual poets to make the most of their heritage.

## ECHO AND ALLUSION

The poems in this group employ the familiar poetic strategy of echoing or alluding to other texts as a way of importing meaning into a poem, similar to the strategy of "sampling" words or sounds in contemporary music. An **echo** may simply recall a word, phrase, or sound in another text as a way of associating what is going on in *this* poem with something in another, already familiar text. The familiarity itself may sometimes be the point: writers often like to associate what they do with what has already been done, especially if their work sounds like a text that is already much admired. Echoes of Shakespeare, for example, may imply that this new text shares concerns (and, therefore, insight or quality?) with Shakespeare. An **allusion** more insistently connects a particular word, phrase, or section of a poem with some similar formulation in a previous text; it explicitly *invokes* the reader's recognition of the previous text and asks for interpretation based on the implied similarity.

Strategies of echo and allusion can be very complicated, for the question of just how much of one text can carry over—or be forcibly brought over—into another one cannot be answered categorically.

Often poets quote—or echo with variations—a passage from another text in order to suggest some thematic, ideological, tonal, or stylistic link. Sometimes the purpose is simply to invoke an idea or attitude from another text, another place, or another culture. In "Two Songs" (chapter 16), for example, Adrienne Rich employs Chaucer's familiar formulation of the rites of spring (with its description of all things coming to life, their vital juices flowing, as they follow the natural progress of the seasons) to suggest the way the sap rises in ordinary lusty human beings. The quotation thus puts the speaker's attraction to a lover into a larger human perspective, and her sense of herself as a subject and object of lust comes to seem natural, part of the ordinary course of events.

The first poem in "Echo and Allusion" belongs, uncomfortably, in the *carpe diem* ("seize the day") tradition; but unlike ordinary *carpe diem* poems, it is moralistic. It undercuts the speaker by having him allude to familiar biblical passages that imply a condemnation of live-for-today attitudes and ideas. By echoing Satan's tempting addresses to Eve in Genesis, the speaker in Jonson's "Come, my

Celia" condemns himself in the eyes of readers and becomes a seducer-villain instead of a libertine-hero. The other poems here variously recall individual lines, passages, poems, ideas, or traditions in order to establish a particular stance or attitude. The meaning of each poem derives primarily from interpreting the allusion.

Poems certainly do not need earlier texts in order to exist or have meaning, but prior texts may set up what happens in a particular poem or govern how we construe it. Allusion—the strategy of using one text to comment on and influence the interpretation of another—is one of the most popular and familiar poetic strategies.

## BEN JONSON

### [Come, my Celia, let us prove][1]

Come, my Celia, let us prove,[2]
While we can, the sports of love;
Time will not be ours forever:
He at length our good will sever.
5 Spend not, then, his gifts in vain;
Suns that set may rise again,
But if once we lose this light,
'Tis with us perpetual night.
Why should we defer our joys?
10 Fame and rumor are but toys.
Cannot we delude the eyes
Of a few poor household spies?
Or his easier ears beguile,
Thus removéd by our wile?
15 'Tis no sin love's fruits to steal,
But the sweet thefts to reveal;
To be taken, to be seen,
These have crimes accounted been.

1606

---

1. A song from *Volpone,* sung by the play's villain and would-be seducer. Part of the poem paraphrases Catullus, poem 5.   2. Experience.

## WILLIAM BLAKE

### The Lamb

    Little Lamb, who made thee?
    Dost thou know who made thee?
Gave thee life, and bid thee feed
By the stream and o'er the mead;
5 Gave thee clothing of delight,
    Softest clothing woolly bright;
    Gave thee such a tender voice,
Making all the vales rejoice?
    Little Lamb, who made thee?
10 Dost thou know who made thee?

    Little Lamb, I'll tell thee!
    Little Lamb, I'll tell thee:
He is callèd by thy name,
For he calls himself a Lamb,
15 He is meek and he is mild;
    He became a little child.
    I a child and thou a lamb,
We are callèd by his name.
    Little Lamb, God bless thee!
20 Little Lamb, God bless thee!

1789

## HOWARD NEMEROV

### Boom!

#### Sees Boom in Religion, too

*Atlantic City, June 23, 1957 (AP)—President Eisenhower's pastor said tonight that Americans are living in a period of "unprecedented religious activity" caused partially by paid vacations, the eight-hour day and modern conveniences.*

    *"These fruits of material progress," said the Rev. Edward L. R. Elson of the National Presbyterian Church, Washington, "have provided the leisure, the energy, and the means for a level of human and spiritual values never before reached."*

Here at the Vespasian-Carlton,[3] it's just one
religious activity after another; the sky

---

3. Vespasian was emperor of Rome 69–79 C.E., shortly after the reign of Nero. In French, *vespasienne* means "public toilet."

is constantly being crossed by cruciform
airplanes, in which nobody disbelieves
for a second and the tide, the tide
of spiritual progress and prosperity
miraculously keeps rising, to a level
never before attained. The churches are full,
the beaches are full, and the filling-stations
are full, God's great ocean is full
of paid vacationers praying an eight-hour day
to the human and spiritual values, the fruits,
the leisure, the energy, and the means, Lord,
the means for the level, the unprecedented level,
and the modern conveniences, which also are full.
Never before, O Lord, have the prayers and praises
from belfry and phonebooth, from ballpark and barbecue
the sacrifices, so endlessly ascended.

It was not thus when Job in Palestine
sat in the dust and cried, cried bitterly;[4]
when Damien kissed the lepers on their wounds
it was not thus;[5] it was not thus
when Francis worked a fourteen-hour day
strictly for the birds;[6] when Dante took
a week's vacation without pay and it rained
part of the time,[7] O Lord, it was not thus.

But now the gears mesh and the tires burn
and the ice chatters in the shaker and the priest
in the pulpit and Thy Name, O Lord,
is kept before the public, while the fruits
ripen and religion booms and the level rises
and every modern convenience runneth over,
that it may never be with us as it hath been
with Athens and Karnak and Nagasaki,[8]
nor Thy sun for one instant refrain from shining
on the rainbow Buick by the breezeway
or the Chris Craft with the uplift life raft;
that we may continue to be the just folks we are,
plain people with ordinary superliners and
disposable diaperliners, people of the stop'n'shop
'n'pray as you go, of hotel, motel, boatel,

---

4. According to the Book of Job, he was afflicted with the loss of prosperity, children, and health as a test of his faith. His name means, in Hebrew, "he cries"; see especially Job 2.7-13.
5. "Father Damien" (Joseph Damien de Veuster, 1840-1889), a Roman Catholic missionary from Belgium, was known for his work among lepers in Hawaii; he ultimately contracted leprosy himself and died there.
6. St. Francis of Assisi, thirteenth-century founder of the Franciscan order, was noted for his love of all living things, and one of the most famous stories about him tells of his preaching to the birds.
7. Dante's journey through Hell, Purgatory, and Paradise (in *The Divine Comedy*) takes a week, beginning on Good Friday, 1300. It rains in the third chasm of Hell.
8. A large Japanese port city, virtually destroyed by a U.S. atomic bomb in 1945. *Athens:* the cultural center of ancient Greek civilization. *Karnak:* a village on the Nile, built on the site of ancient Thebes.

the humble pilgrims of no deposit no return
and please adjust thy clothing, who will give to Thee,
if Thee will keep us going, our annual
45 Miss Universe, for Thy Name's Sake, Amen.

1960

MARIANNE MOORE

## Love in America?

Whatever it is, it's a passion—
a benign dementia that should be
engulfing America, fed in a way
   the opposite of the way
5 in which the Minotaur[9] was fed.
It's a Midas[1] of tenderness;
   from the heart;
nothing else. From one with ability
to bear being misunderstood—
10 take the blame, with "nobility
that is action,"[2] identifying itself with
   pioneer unperfunctoriness

without brazenness[3] or
bigness of overgrown
15 undergrown shallowness.

Whatever it is, let it be without
   affectation.
Yes, yes, yes, *yes*.

1967

---

9. The Minotaur demanded a virgin to devour once a year [Moore's note; notes 1–3 are also Moore's].
1. Midas, who had the golden touch, was inconvenienced when eating or picking things up.
2. Unamuno said that what we need as a cure for unruly youth is "nobility that is action."
3. *without brazenness or bigness* . . . Winston Churchill: "Modesty becomes a man."

## ROBERT HOLLANDER

### *You Too? Me Too—Why Not? Soda Pop*

```
        I am
        look
        ing at
        the Co
        caCola
        bottle
        which is
        green wi
        th ridges
        just–like
      c     c     c
      o     o     o
      l     l     l
      u     u     u
      m     m     m
      n     n     n
      s     s     s
   and on itself it says
        COCA-COLA
        reg.u.s.pat.off.
```

    exactly like an art pop
    statue of that kind of
    bottle but not so green
    that the juice inside
    gives other than the co-
    lor it has when I pour
    it out in a clear glass
    glass on this table top
    (It's making me thirsty
    all this winking and
    beading of Hippocrene
    please let me pause drink-
    ing the fluid in)
    ah! it is enticing how each
    color is the same
    brown in green bottle
    brown in uplifted glass
    making each utensil on
    the table laid a brown
    fork in a brown shade
    making me long to watch
    them harvesting the crop
   which makes the deep-aged
  rich brown wine of America
that is to say which makes
soda               pop

1968

WILLIAM SHAKESPEARE

## [Not marble, nor the gilded monuments]

Not marble, nor the gilded monuments
Of princes, shall outlive this powerful rhyme;
But you shall shine more bright in these conténts
Than unswept stone, besmeared with sluttish time.
5 When wasteful war shall statues overturn,
And broils[4] root out the work of masonry,
Nor[5] Mars his sword nor war's quick fire shall burn
The living record of your memory.
'Gainst death and all-oblivious enmity
10 Shall you pace forth; your praise shall still find room
Even in the eyes of all posterity
That wear this world out to the ending doom.[6]
So, till the judgment that yourself arise,
You live in this, and dwell in lovers' eyes.

1609

## POETIC "KINDS"

By now you have experienced all sorts of poems, on a variety of subjects and with all kinds of tones—short poems, long poems, poems that rhyme and poems that don't. And there are, of course, many other sorts of poems that we haven't looked at. Some poems, for example, have thousands of lines and differ substantially from the poems that can be included in an anthology like this.

Poems may be classified in a variety of ways—by subject or theme; by their length, appearance, and formal features; by the way they are organized; by the level of language they use; by the poet's intention and the kinds of effects the poem tries to generate.

Classification may be, of course, simply an intellectual exercise. Recognizing that a poem is, for example, an elegy, a parody, or a satire may provide a satisfaction like that of identifying a scarlet tanager, a weeping willow, a French phrase, or a 1967 Ford Thunderbird. Just *knowing* what others don't know may give us a sense of importance, accomplishment, and power. But we can also experience a poem more fully if we understand early on what kind of poem it is, and if we know that the poet has consciously played by certain rules. The **conventions** a poet employs indicate certain standard ways of saying things to achieve certain expected effects, and thus the tradition involved in a particular poetic kind yields certain standard responses—or variations on them, depending on a particular poem's relation to that tradition. For example, the humor and fun of the following poem depend entirely on readers' recognizing the *kind* of poem they are reading.

---

4. Riots.   5. Neither. *Mars his:* Mars's.   6. Judgment Day.

# CHRISTOPHER MARLOWE

## The Passionate Shepherd to His Love

Come live with me and be my love,
And we will all the pleasures prove[1]
That valleys, groves, hills, and fields,
Woods, or steepy mountain yields.

5 And we will sit upon the rocks,
Seeing the shepherds feed their flocks,
By shallow rivers to whose falls
Melodious birds sing madrigals.

And I will make thee beds of roses
10 And a thousand fragrant posies,
A cap of flowers, and a kirtle[2]
Embroidered all with leaves of myrtle;

A gown made of the finest wool
Which from our pretty lambs we pull;
15 Fair linéd slippers for the cold,
With buckles of the purest gold;

A belt of straw and ivy buds,
With coral clasps and amber studs:
And if these pleasures may thee move,
20 Come live with me, and be my love.

The shepherd swains[3] shall dance and sing
For thy delight each May morning:
If these delights thy mind may move,
Then live with me and be my love.

1600

    A beginning reader of poetry might easily protest that such a plea is unrealistic and fanciful, and thus feel unsure of the poem's tone. What could such a reader think of a speaker who constructs his argument in such a dreamlike way? But the traditions behind the poem and the conventions of the poetic kind make its intention and effects clear. "The Passionate Shepherd to His Love" is a **pastoral poem**, a poetic kind that concerns itself with the simple life of country folk and describes that life in stylized, idealized terms. The people in a pastoral poem are usually (as here) shepherds, although they may be fishermen or other rustics who lead an outdoor life and tend to basic human needs in a simplified society; the world of the poem is one of simplicity, beauty, music, and love. Life always seems timeless in pastoral; people are eternally young, and the season is always spring, usually May. Nature seems endlessly green and the future entirely golden. Difficulty, frus-

---

1. Experience.  2. Gown.  3. Youths.

tration, disappointment, and obligation do not exist in this world, which is blissfully free of problems. Shepherds sing instead of tending sheep, and they make love and play music instead of having to watch out for wolves in the night. If only the shepherd boy and shepherd girl can agree with each other to make love joyously and passionately, they will live happily ever after. Their language, though informal and fairly simple, always seems a bit more sophisticated than that of real shepherds with real problems and real sheep.

Unrealistic? Of course. No real shepherd spends even a single day like that, and certainly the world of simple country folk includes ferocities of nature, human deceit and mischief, disease, bad weather, old age, moments that are not all green and gold. Probably no poet ever thought that shepherds really live that way, but it is an attractive fantasy, and poets who write pastoral simply choose this one formulaic way to isolate a series of idealized moments. Fantasies can be personal and private, of course, but a certain pleasure comes from shared public fantasies, such as the central moment when two people first contemplate the joys of ecstatic love uncomplicated by the realities of duty or limit. To present a certain tone, attitude, and wholeness, poets self-consciously construct this vision of a world that is self-existent, self-contained, and self-referential.

Other poetic kinds included in this book are:

| | | |
|---|---|---|
| epic | From *Paradise Lost* | p. 931 |
| lyric | "The Lamb" | p. 1134 |
| ballad | "Sir Patrick Spens" | p. 1008 |
| aubade | "The Sun Rising" | p. 1242 |
| meditation | "Love Calls Us to the Things of This World" | p. 1280 |
| dramatic monologue | "My Last Duchess" | p. 1076 |
| soliloquy | "Soliloquy of the Spanish Cloister" | p. 866 |
| confessional | "Skunk Hour" | p. 1257 |
| protest | "Hard Rock Returns..." | p. 840 |

You will find brief definitions of these terms in the glossary. Each kind has its own characteristics and conventions—established by tradition and habit—and each deserves detailed study and discussion. Meanwhile, in the following section we will examine numerous examples of yet another poetic kind.

## HAIKU

The **haiku**, an import into the English poetic tradition, has a long history in its original tradition, Japanese. Originally, the haiku (then called *hokku*) was a short section of a longer poem (called a *renga* or *haikai*) composed by several poets who wrote segments in response to one another in a long, cumulative poetic exercise or game. But early on, at least as early as the seventeenth century, the distinctive subject matter and mode of the haiku, together with the creative discipline required by its formal demands, made it an attractive form in itself, and several major poets built their reputations largely on the basis of their skill in the form.

Traditionally, the Japanese haiku was an unrhymed poem consisting of seventeen sounds (or, rather, characters representing seventeen sounds) and distributed over three lines in a five-seven-five pattern—that is, five distinctive sounds in the first line, seven in the second, and five in the third. "Sounds" in the Japanese language are not exactly the same as "syllables" in English, but there is a rough parallel—close enough so that when English writers began to compose haiku about a century ago, they ordinarily translated the sound requirement into syllables. Here, for example, is a haiku (in translation) that conforms in its Japanese original to the standard formal definition:

## CHIYOJO

### [Whether astringent][1]

Whether astringent
I do not know. This is my first
Persimmon picking.

Haiku aim for conciseness and compression. They leave a lot unsaid, suggesting connections and causes but seldom making them explicit. Typically, haiku describe a natural object—a flower, say, or an animal, or a place—and imply a relationship between that perception and some human feeling or state of mind. Haiku thus depend heavily on emotive language, and they try not to be definitive. Instead of conclusions, summaries, closures, and neat answers, haiku seek openings; they alert the mind to possibility.

Three other traditional characteristics of haiku affect readers' expectations. First, haiku have a "seasonal" requirement, so that each poem associates itself with one season of the year and thus "dates" itself in relation to a predictable, revolving pattern of change. This seasonal association may be quite subtle and indirect—through, for example, some flower, event, or condition normally connected with a particular season. Second, haiku more generally involve descriptions of nature: a poem often begins with the observation of a specific natural phenomenon—a plant, an animal, or an aspect of landscape—that becomes connected, implicitly or explicitly, with a human feeling or emotion. This use of nature develops out of the Buddhist sense of nature as orderly and benign but also contingent and transient. Since human beings are a part of that unified order, other parts of nature serve as "natural" reflections of human states. Haiku adapted into other languages and cultures cannot, of course, rely on the same spiritual assumptions or worldview, but most haiku strive to retain a sense of the human and natural as being mutually reflective and interdependent. Third, haiku often connect the "natural" and the human through a combination of observation and imagination. They blur the Western distinction between seeing something literally and having some "vision" of its end or meaning, though they seldom explicitly connect that claim to a larger, visionary perspective.

Some of the traditional Japanese "masters" of haiku from the seventeenth to

---

1. Chiyojo (1703–1775) is probably the most famous Japanese woman haiku poet. Tradition has it that she wrote this poem at the time of (and about) her engagement. Translation by Daniel C. Buchanan.

the early twentieth century—Bashō, Issa, and Buson, for example—are represented (in English translations) in the examples that follow. But haiku has become an international form, and during the last half century or so, poets around the world have made conscious, concentrated attempts to create a haiku tradition in at least fifty languages. The habits and traditions of different languages and literatures have influenced and modified the way haiku are written, something that might offend some traditional masters of haiku, just as it would amuse others to see their work so readily but loosely adapted. Later poets and even translators of classic verses have not always observed the seventeen-syllable and three-line requirements, for example. As in any other poetic kind, the conventions prove both demanding and adaptable to the particular needs of different situations, different languages, and different individual poets. (If you would like to try writing haiku, you might consult one of the guides written for this purpose, such as William S. Higginson's *Haiku Handbook: How to Write, Share, and Teach Haiku* [1992].)

## BASHŌ

### [*A village without bells*—][2]

A village without bells—
how do they live?
spring dusk.

### [*This road*]

This road—
no one goes down it,
autumn evening.

## BUSON

### [*Coolness*—][3]

Coolness—
the sound of the bell
as it leaves the bell.

---

2. Matsuo Bashō (1644–1694) is usually considered the first great master poet of haiku. Translations by Robert Hass.   3. Yosa Buson (1716–1783). Translations by Robert Hass.

[*Listening to the moon*]

Listening to the moon,
gazing at the croaking of frogs
in a field of ripe rice.


**SEIFŪ**
[*The faces of dolls*][4]

The faces of dolls.
In unavoidable ways
I must have grown old.

Perhaps the single most famous haiku poem is by Bashō. Here are four different translations into English of that poem. (The source of these poems, Hiroaki Sato's *One Hundred Frogs: From Matsu [i.e. Matsuo] Basho to Allen Ginsberg*, contains an even greater variety of examples.)


**LAFCADIO HEARN**
[*Old pond—*]

Old pond—frogs jumped in—sound of water.
                            1898


**CLARA A. WALSH**
[*An old-time pond*]

An old-time pond, from off whose shadowed depth
Is heard the splash where some lithe frog leaps in.
                            1910

---

4. Seifū (1650–1721) was a nun. Translation by Daniel C. Buchanan.

EARL MINER

[*The still old pond*]

    The still old pond
    and as a frog leaps in it
      the sound of a splash.
              1979

ALLEN GINSBERG

[*The old pond*]

    The old pond—a frog jumps in, kerplunk!
              1979

**The following haiku were all written in English:**

BABETTE DEUTSCH

[*The falling flower*][5]

    The falling flower
    I saw drift back to the branch
    Was a butterfly.
              1957

ETHERIDGE KNIGHT

[*Eastern guard tower*]

    Eastern guard tower
    glints in sunset; convicts rest
    like lizards on rocks.
              1960

---

5. An adaptation of a poem by Arakida Moritake (1473–1549).

ALLEN GINSBERG

## [Looking over my shoulder]

Looking over my shoulder
my behind was covered
with cherry blossoms.
                    1955

RICHARD WRIGHT

## [In the falling snow]

In the falling snow
A laughing boy holds out his palms
Until they are white.
                    1960

JAMES A. EMANUEL

## Ray Charles

His get-aboard smile,
picnic knees, back-up bounce: JAZZ,
all there, ounce by ounce.
                    1999

## IMITATING AND ANSWERING

A poem will often respond directly—sometimes point by point or even line by line or word by word—to another poem. The tactic may be teasing or comic, but often, too, a real challenge exists behind such a facetious answer, perhaps a serious criticism of the first poem's point or the tradition it represents, or an attempt to provide a different perspective. While it may follow its model slavishly, the poem may also alter key words or details so that readers will easily notice the differences in tone or attitude.

The result usually seems self-conscious, as if the poet were trying to do something a little different in light of the shared tradition. However "sincere" the poem may be, its sense of play is equally important. The first three poems below, for example, playfully pick on Marlowe's "The Passionate Shepherd to His Love" (earlier in this chapter). In effect, all of them provide "answers" to that poem, as if his "love" were telling the shepherd what is wrong with his argument. Of course, the poets are answering Marlowe, too. These poets know full well what Marlowe was doing in the pastoral fantasy of his original poem, and they clearly enjoy telling him how people in various circumstances might feel about his fantasy. There is in the end a lot of playfulness and not much hostility in their "realistic" deflation of his magic. The poems by Koch and Skirrow, for example, poke gentle fun at other famous works, offering a summary or another version of what might have happened in each (see, respectively, Williams's "This Is Just to Say" in chapter 16, and Keats's "Ode on a Grecian Urn" in chapter 22).

Strictly speaking, only one of the poems that follows (the one by Koch) is a **parody**—that is, it pretends to write in the style of the original poem but exaggerates that style and changes the content for comic effect. The others make fun of an original in less direct ways, but they share the objective of answering an original, even though they use very different styles to alter the poetic intention of that original.

### SIR WALTER RALEGH

## The Nymph's Reply to the Shepherd

If all the world and love were young,
And truth in every shepherd's tongue,
These pretty pleasures might me move
To live with thee and be thy love.

5  Time drives the flocks from field to fold,
When rivers rage, and rocks grow cold,
And Philomel[1] becometh dumb;
The rest complain of cares to come.

The flowers do fade, and wanton fields
10  To wayward winter reckoning yields:
A honey tongue, a heart of gall,
Is fancy's spring, but sorrow's fall.

Thy gowns, thy shoes, thy beds of roses,
Thy cap, thy kirtle, and thy posies
15  Soon break, soon wither, soon forgotten;
In folly ripe, in reason rotten.

Thy belt of straw and ivy buds,
Thy coral clasps and amber studs,
All these in me no means can move
20  To come to thee and be thy love.

But could youth last, and love still breed,
Had joys no date,[2] nor age no need,
Then these delights my mind might move
To live with thee and be thy love.

1600

1. The nightingale.   2. End.

## WILLIAM CARLOS WILLIAMS

### Raleigh Was Right

We cannot go to the country
for the country will bring us no peace
What can the small violets tell us
that grow on furry stems in
the long grass among lance shaped leaves?

Though you praise us
and call to mind the poets
who sung of our loveliness
it was long ago!
long ago! when country people
would plow and sow with
flowering minds and pockets at ease—
if ever this were true.

Not now. Love itself a flower
with roots in a parched ground.
Empty pockets make empty heads.
Cure it if you can but
do not believe that we can live
today in the country
for the country will bring us no peace.

1941


## ALLEN GINSBERG

### A Further Proposal

Come live with me and be my love,
And we will some old pleasures prove.
Men like me have paid in verse
This costly courtesy, or curse;

But I would bargain with my art
(As to the mind, now to the heart),
My symbols, images, and signs
Please me more outside these lines.

For your share and recompense,
You will be taught another sense:
The wisdom of the subtle worm
Will turn most perfect in your form.

Not that your soul need tutored be
By intellectual decree,

15  But graces that the mind can share
    Will make you, as more wise, more fair,

    Till all the world's devoted thought
    Find all in you it ever sought,
    And even I, of skeptic mind,
20  A Resurrection of a kind.

    This compliment, in my own way,
    For what I would receive, I pay;
    Thus all the wise have writ thereof,
    And all the fair have been their love.

1947

## E. E. CUMMINGS

### [(ponder,darling,these busted statues)]

(ponder,darling,these busted statues
of yon motheaten forum be aware
notice what hath remained
—the stone cringes
5    clinging to the stone,how obsolete

lips utter their extant smile....
remark

a few deleted of texture
or meaning monuments and dolls

10   resist Them Greediest Paws of careful
time all of which is extremely
unimportant)whereas Life

matters if or

when the your- and my-
15   idle vertical worthless
self unite in a peculiarly
momentary

partnership(to instigate
constructive
20              Horizontal
business....even so,let us make haste
—consider well this ruined aqueduct

lady,
which used to lead something into somewhere)

1926

**KENNETH KOCH**

## Variations on a Theme by William Carlos Williams

### 1

I chopped down the house that you had been saving to live in next
   summer.
I am sorry, but it was morning, and I had nothing to do
and its wooden beams were so inviting.

### 2

We laughed at the hollyhocks together
5 and then I sprayed them with lye.
Forgive me. I simply do not know what I am doing.

### 3

I gave away the money that you had been saving to live on for the next
   ten years.
The man who asked for it was shabby
and the firm March wind on the porch was so juicy and cold.

### 4

10 Last evening we went dancing and I broke your leg.
Forgive me. I was clumsy, and
I wanted you here in the wards, where I am the doctor!

1962

**DESMOND SKIRROW**

## Ode on a Grecian Urn Summarized

Gods chase
Round vase.
What say?
What play?
5 Don't know.
Nice, though.

1960

## ANTHONY HECHT

### *The Dover Bitch*

A Criticism of Life

*for Andrews Wanning*

So there stood Matthew Arnold and this girl
With the cliffs of England crumbling away behind them,
And he said to her, "Try to be true to me,
And I'll do the same for you, for things are bad
5 All over, etc., etc."
Well now, I knew this girl. It's true she had read
Sophocles in a fairly good translation
And caught that bitter allusion to the sea,[3]
But all the time he was talking she had in mind
10 The notion of what his whiskers would feel like
On the back of her neck. She told me later on
That after a while she got to looking out
At the lights across the channel, and really felt sad,
Thinking of all the wine and enormous beds
15 And blandishments in French and the perfumes.
And then she got really angry. To have been brought
All the way down from London, and then be addressed
As a sort of mournful cosmic last resort
Is really tough on a girl, and she was pretty.
20 Anyway, she watched him pace the room
And finger his watch-chain and seem to sweat a bit,
And then she said one or two unprintable things.
But you mustn't judge her by that. What I mean to say is,
She's really all right. I still see her once in a while
25 And she always treats me right. We have a drink
And I give her a good time, and perhaps it's a year
Before I see her again, but there she is,
Running to fat, but dependable as they come.
And sometimes I bring her a bottle of *Nuit d'Amour*.

1968

## WENDY COPE

### *[Not only marble, but the plastic toys]*

Not only marble, but the plastic toys
From cornflake packets will outlive this rhyme:
I can't immortalize you, love—our joys

---

3. In Sophocles' *Antigone*, lines 583–91. See "Dover Beach," lines 9–18.

    Will lie unnoticed in the vault of time.
5   When Mrs Thatcher has been cast in bronze
    And her administration is a page
    In some O-level text-book, when the dons[4]
    Have analysed the story of our age,
    When travel firms sell tours of outer space
10  And aeroplanes take off without a sound
    And Tulse Hill has become a trendy place
    And Upper Norwood's on the underground[5]
    Your beauty and my name will be forgotten—
    My love is true, but all my verse is rotten.

                                            1986

## CULTURAL BELIEF AND TRADITION

The poems in this group draw on a tradition that is larger than just "literary." Mythologies involve whole systems of belief, usually cultural in scope, and the familiar literary formulations of these mythologies are just the surface articulations of a larger view of why the world works the way it does.

Every culture develops stories to explain itself. These stories, about who we are and why we are the way we are, constitute what are often called **myths**. Calling something a myth does not mean claiming that it is false. In fact, it means nearly the opposite, for cultures that subscribe or have ever subscribed to particular myths about culture or history become infused with, and even defined by, those views. Myth, in the sense in which it is used here, involves explanations of life that are more or less universally relied on within a particular culture; it is a frame of reference that people within the culture understand and share. This sharing of a frame of reference does not mean that all people within a culture are carbon copies of each other or that popular stereotypes represent reality accurately, nor does it mean that every individual in the culture *knows* the perceived history and can articulate its events, ideas, and values. But it does mean that a shared history and a shared set of symbols lie behind any particular culture and that the culture is to some extent aware of its distinctiveness from other cultures.

A **culture** may be of many sizes and shapes. Often we think of a nation as a culture (and so speak of American culture, American history, the myth of America, the American dream, the American frame of reference), and we may make smaller and larger divisions—as long as the group has some common history and a somewhat cohesive purpose. We speak of southern culture, for example, or of urban culture, or of the drug culture, or of the various popular-music cultures, or of a culture associated with a particular political belief, economic class, or social group. Most of us belong, willingly or not, to a number of such cultures at one time, and to some extent our identities and destinies are linked to the distinctive features of those cultures and the ways each culture perceives its identity, values, and history. Some of these cultures we choose to join; some are thrust upon us by birth and

---

4. Academics. *Mrs Thatcher:* Margaret Thatcher (b. 1925), British Conservative politician and prime minister, 1979–90. *O-level text-book:* a book that prepared British secondary-school students for standardized examinations ("ordinary-level").   5. London subway.

circumstances. It is these larger and more persistent forms of culture—not those chosen by an individual—that we illustrate in this section.

Poets aware of their heritage often like to probe its history and beliefs and plumb its depths, just as they like to articulate and play variations on the poetic tradition they feel a part of. For poetry written in the English language over the last four hundred years or so, both the Judeo-Christian frame of reference and the classical frame of reference (drawing on the civilizations of ancient Greece and Rome) have been important. Western culture, a broad culture that includes many nations and many religious and social groups, is largely defined within these two frames of reference—or it has been until quite recently. As religious belief in the West has changed over the past two or three centuries, and as classical civilization has been less emphasized and less studied, poets have felt less and less comfortable in assuming that their audiences share this cultural knowledge, but many have continued to use it in order to articulate human traits that have cultural continuity and importance. More recently, poets have drawn on other cultural myths—Native American, African, and Asian, for example—to expand our sense of common heritage and give new meaning to the "American" and "Western" experience. The poems that follow draw on different myths in a variety of ways and tones.

## JOHN HOLLANDER

### *Adam's Task*

> And Adam gave names to all cattle, and to the fowl of the air, and to every beast of the field...
> —Gen. 2:20

Thou, paw-paw-paw; thou, glurd; thou, spotted
Glurd; thou, whitestap, lurching through
The high-grown brush; thou, pliant-footed,
Implex; thou, awagabu.

5   Every burrower, each flier
    Came for the name he had to give:
Gay, first work, ever to be prior,
    Not yet sunk to primitive.

Thou, verdle; thou, McFleery's pomma;
10  Thou; thou; thou—three types of grawl;
Thou, flisket; thou, kabasch; thou, comma-
Eared mashawk; thou, all; thou, all.

Were, in a fire of becoming,
    Laboring to be burned away,
15  Then work, half-measuring, half-humming,
    Would be as serious as play.

Thou, pambler; thou, rivarn; thou, greater
    Wherret, and thou, lesser one;
Thou, sproal; thou, zant; thou, lily-eater.
20  Naming's over. Day is done.

1971

SUSAN DONNELLY

## Eve Names the Animals

To me, *lion* was sun on a wing
over the garden. *Dove,*
a burrowing, blind creature.

I swear that man
5   never knew animals. Words
he lined up according to size,

while elephants slipped flat-eyed
through water

and trout
10   hurtled from the underbrush, tusked
and ready for battle.

The name he gave me stuck
me to him. He did it to comfort me,
for not being first.

15   Mornings, while he slept,
I got away. Pickerel
hopped on the branches above me.
Only spider accompanied me,
nosing everywhere,
20   running up to lick my hand.

Poor finch. I suppose I was
woe to him—
the way he'd come looking for me,
not wanting either of us
25   to be ever alone

But to myself I was
palomino
      raven
           fox...

30   I strung words
by their stems and wore them
as garlands on my long walks.

The next day
I'd find them withered.

35   I liked change.

1985

MIRIAM WADDINGTON

## Ulysses Embroidered

You've come
at last from
all your journeying
to the old blind woman
5  in the tower,
Ulysses.[1]

After all adventurings
through seas and
mountains through
10 giant battles,
storms and death,
from pinnacles
to valleys;

Past sirens
15 naked on rocks
between Charybdis
and Scylla, from
dragons' teeth,
from sleep in
20 stables choking
on red flowers
walking through weeds
and through shipwreck.

And now you are
25 climbing the stairs,
taking shape,
a figure in shining
thread rising from
a golden shield:
30 a medallion
emblazoned in
tapestry you grew
from the blind hands
of Penelope.

35 Her tapestry
saw everything,
her stitches
embroidered the

---

1. After the Trojan War, Ulysses (or Odysseus), king of Ithaca and one of the Greek heroes of the war, journeyed for ten years to return to his island home and to his wife, Penelope. To ward off suitors, Penelope had craftily been weaving and unraveling a tapestry that had to be finished before she would remarry. See Homer's *Odyssey* for accounts of these events and others mentioned in the poem.

painful colors
40 of her breath the
long sighing touch
of her hands.

She made many
journeys.
                    1992

## ALFRED, LORD TENNYSON

### The Kraken

Below the thunders of the upper deep,
Far, far beneath in the abysmal sea,
His ancient, dreamless, uninvaded sleep
The Kraken[2] sleepeth: faintest sunlights flee
5 About his shadowy sides; above him swell
Huge sponges of millennial growth and height;
And far away into the sickly light,
From many a wondrous grot and secret cell
Unnumbered and enormous polypi[3]
10 Winnow with giant arms the slumbering green.
There hath he lain for ages, and will lie
Battening upon huge sea worms in his sleep,
Until the latter fire[4] shall heat the deep;
Then once by man and angels to be seen,
15 In roaring he shall rise and on the surface die.
                            1830

## PHILLIS WHEATLEY

### On Being Brought from Africa to America

'Twas mercy brought me from my Pagan land,
Taught my benighted soul to understand
That there's a God, that there's a Saviour too:
Once I redemption neither sought nor knew.
5 Some view our sable race with scornful eye,
"Their colour is a diabolic die."
Remember, Christians, Negroes, black as Cain,[5]
May be refin'd, and join th' angelic train.
                            1773

---

2. A gigantic mythical sea beast.    3. Octopuses.
4. According to the biblical Book of Revelation, fire that will consume the world.
5. One of Adam's sons, he killed his brother Abel. See Genesis 4.

JUNE JORDAN

## Something Like a Sonnet for Phillis Miracle Wheatley

Girl from the realm of birds florid and fleet
flying full feather in far or near weather
Who fell to a dollar lust coffled like meat
Captured by avarice and hate spit together
5 Trembling asthmatic alone on the slave block
built by a savagery travelling by carriage
viewed like a species of flaw in the livestock
A child without safety of mother or marriage

Chosen by whimsy but born to surprise
10 They taught you to read but you learned how to write
Begging the universe into your eyes:
They dressed you in light but you dreamed with the night.
From Africa singing of justice and grace,
Your early verse sweetens the fame of our Race.

1989

MAYA ANGELOU

## Africa

Thus she had lain
sugar cane sweet
deserts her hair
golden her feet
5 mountains her breasts
two Niles her tears
Thus she has lain
Black through the years.

Over the white seas
10 rime white and cold
brigands ungentled
icicle bold
took her young daughters
sold her strong sons
15 churched her with Jesus
bled her with guns.
Thus she has lain.

Now she is rising
remember her pain

20　remember the losses
　　her screams loud and vain
　　remember her riches
　　her history slain
　　now she is striding
25　although she had lain.

1975

**DEREK WALCOTT**

## A Far Cry from Africa

A wind is ruffling the tawny pelt
Of Africa. Kikuyu,[6] quick as flies,
Batten upon the bloodstreams of the veldt.[7]
Corpses are scattered through a paradise.
5　Only the worm, colonel of carrion, cries:
"Waste no compassion on these separate dead!"
Statistics justify and scholars seize
The salients of colonial policy.
What is that to the white child hacked in bed?
10　To savages, expendable as Jews?

Threshed out by beaters,[8] the long rushes break
In a white dust of ibises whose cries
Have wheeled since civilization's dawn
From the parched river or beast-teeming plain.
15　The violence of beast on beast is read
As natural law, but upright man
Seeks his divinity by inflicting pain.
Delirious as these worried beasts, his wars
Dance to the tightened carcass of a drum,
20　While he calls courage still that native dread
Of the white peace contracted by the dead.

Again brutish necessity wipes its hands
Upon the napkin of a dirty cause, again
A waste of our compassion, as with Spain,[9]
25　The gorilla wrestles with the superman.
I who am poisoned with the blood of both,

---

6. An East African tribe whose members, as Mau Mau fighters, conducted an eight-year insurrection against British colonial settlers in Kenya.　7. Open plains, neither cultivated nor thickly forested (Afrikaans).
8. In big-game hunting, natives are hired to beat the brush, driving birds—such as ibises—and animals into the open.
9. The Spanish Civil War (1936-39), in which the Republican loyalists were supported politically by liberals in the West and militarily by Soviet Communists, and the Nationalist rebels by Nazi Germany and Fascist Italy.

    Where shall I turn, divided to the vein?
    I who have cursed
    The drunken officer of British rule, how choose
30  Between this Africa and the English tongue I love?
    Betray them both, or give back what they give?
    How can I face such slaughter and be cool?
    How can I turn from Africa and live?

                                                    1962


ALBERTO ALVARO RÍOS

## Advice to a First Cousin

    The way the world works is like this:
    for the bite of scorpions, she says,
    my grandmother to my first cousin,
    because I might die and someone must know,
 5  go to the animal jar
    the one with the soup of green herbs
    mixed with the scorpions I have been putting in
    still alive. Take one out
    put it on the bite. It has had time to think
10  there with the others—put the lid back tight—
    and knows that a biting is not the way to win
    a finger or a young girl's foot.
    It will take back into itself the hurting
    the redness and the itching and its marks.

15  But the world works like this, too:
    look out for the next scorpion you see,
    she says, and makes a big face to scare me
    thereby instructing my cousin, look out!
    for one of the scorpion's many
20  illegitimate and unhappy sons.
    It will be smarter, more of the devil.
    It will have lived longer than these dead ones.
    It will know from them something more
    about the world, in the way mothers know
25  when something happens to a child, or how
    I knew from your sadness you had been bitten.
    It will learn something stronger than biting.
    Look out most for that scorpion, she says,
    making a big face to scare me again and it works
30  I go—crying—she lets me go—they laugh,
    the way you must look out for men
    who have not yet bruised you.

                                                    1985

**LOUISE ERDRICH**

## *Jacklight*

*The same Chippewa word is used both for flirting and hunting game, while another Chippewa word connotes both using force in intercourse and also killing a bear with one's bare hands.*
—DUNNING 1959

We have come to the edge of the woods,
out of brown grass where we slept, unseen,
out of knotted twigs, out of leaves creaked shut,
out of hiding.

5 At first the light wavered, glancing over us.
Then it clenched to a fist of light that pointed,
searched out, divided us.
Each took the beams like direct blows the heart answers.
Each of us moved forward alone.

10 We have come to the edge of the woods,
drawn out of ourselves by this night sun,
this battery of polarized acids,
that outshines the moon.

We smell them behind it
15 but they are faceless, invisible,
We smell the raw steel of their gun barrels,
mink oil on leather, their tongues of sour barley.
We smell their mother buried chin-deep in wet dirt.

We smell their fathers with scoured knuckles,
20 teeth cracked from hot marrow.
We smell their sisters of crushed dogwood, bruised apples,
of fractured cups and concussions of burnt hooks.

We smell their breath steaming lightly behind the jacklight.
We smell the itch underneath the caked guts on their clothes.
25 We smell their minds like silver hammers
cocked back, held in readiness
for the first of us to step into the open.

We have come to the edge of the woods,
out of brown grass where we slept, unseen,
30 out of leaves creaked shut, out of our hiding.
We have come here too long.

It is their turn now,
their turn to follow us. Listen,
they put down their equipment.
35 It is useless in the tall brush.

And now they take the first steps, not knowing
how deep the woods are and lightless.
How deep the woods are.

1984

## SUGGESTIONS FOR WRITING

1. Write an essay in which you examine the way William Blake's "The Lamb" draws its imagery from the Bible. Whom does the speaker refer to in saying "he calls himself a Lamb"? What, exactly, does "Lamb" imply in this context? Is "The Lamb" a Christian poem? Why or why not?
2. What does Howard Nemerov's "Boom!" allude to in its language and its form? What picture of American politics and culture does the poem paint? Write an essay in which you analyze the satire of "Boom!"
3. Consider Christopher Marlowe's "The Passionate Shepherd to His Love" and the "answers" that poem has inspired: Sir Walter Ralegh's "The Nymph's Reply to the Shepherd," William Carlos Williams's "Raleigh Was Right," and Allen Ginsberg's "A Further Proposal." What issues are illuminated by this poetic "debate"? What might account for the vigorous responses to a simple poem written in the well-established tradition of the pastoral? Write an essay examining the phenomenon of Marlowe's original poem and the poems it inspired.
4. What is gained, and what is lost, when an artistic tradition like Japanese haiku is imported, through translation, imitation, and inspiration, into another culture? Using the poems in this chapter and your own research, write an essay in which you analyze the way that haiku has established itself as a part of English-language literary culture.
5. How closely does E. E. Cummings's "(ponder,darling,these busted statues" echo Andrew Marvell's "To His Coy Mistress"? What images are derived from Marvell? In what specific ways does Cummings's poem undercut Marvell's argument, or its own? Write an essay in which you compare and contrast the two poems. What seem to be Marvell's real intentions, and what are Cummings's?
6. Write an essay in which you compare William Shakespeare's sonnet "Not marble, nor the gilded monuments" and Wendy Cope's "Not only marble, but the plastic toys," based on Shakespeare's original. Do the two poems share thematic concerns? Would Cope's poem be amusing to readers unfamiliar with Shakespeare's?
7. Write an essay in which you discuss the adaptation of Greek myth in Miriam Waddington's "Ulysses Embroidered." What details of Waddington's poem seem consistent with Homer's account in the *Odyssey*? What details seem to challenge Homer's account? What might be Waddington's purpose in adapting the myth in this way?
8. How does naming, and the use of language in general, help shape and define our perception of ourselves and the world around us? With reference to "Adam's Task" by John Hollander and "Eve Names the Animals" by Susan Donnelly, as well as the story "She Unnames Them" by Ursula K. Le Guin (chapter 10), write an essay discussing the way writers have seen naming as emblematic of our power to see and understand our experience.

9. Each of the "Africa" poems in this chapter displays a distinctive mix of anger and sorrow at the way Africa has been ravaged by history, and also pride in the way that Africans have adopted and mastered the Western culture that has been forced upon them. Write an essay in which you compare and contrast the attitudes that inform Phillis Wheatley's "On Being Brought from Africa to America," June Jordan's "Something Like a Sonnet for Phillis Miracle Wheatley," Maya Angelou's "Africa," and Derek Walcott's "A Far Cry from Africa."
10. Using research and your own analysis, write an essay in which you examine the cultural traditions and historical background behind any poem or group of poems in this book.

## 24 CULTURAL AND HISTORICAL CONTEXTS: THE HARLEM RENAISSANCE

Poetry may be read in private moments or experienced in a great variety of communal settings—in classrooms or theaters, for example, or at poetry slams or public readings. But it is almost always *written* in solitude by a single author. Collaboration is rare in poetry, even rarer than in other arts, though artistic creation in general (with a few exceptions like film) is usually a lonely process. Still, there is a sense in which many poems represent collaborative acts. We have seen, in chapter 23, how themes and poetic traditions and conventions are passed down over centuries so that they reappear in even the most original and experimental of poets and poems, and how the beliefs and ideologies of groups and cultures are identified, recorded, renewed, and reinterpreted by new poets in new poems. And we have seen, in chapter 21, how public events and shared cultural moments are transformed into poetic accounts and reflections. But sometimes traditions, group identities, shared experiences, desires, and communal needs come together in a particular moment and location to produce poetry (and other arts and artifacts) that has a distinctive stamp of time, place, and vision. One such phenomenon was the "Harlem Renaissance," a period of ten or fifteen years early in the twentieth century when an extraordinary (and extraordinarily talented) group of people came together in uptown Manhattan to celebrate (and embody) the awakening of a new American black consciousness. It was an unprecedented moment in American poetry and in American culture more generally, and it produced some of the twentieth century's most dramatic, compelling, and original poems, as well as significant works of art in a variety of other categories.

> *One ever feels his twoness—an American, a Negro; two souls, two thoughts, two unreconciled strivings; two warring ideals in one dark body, whose dogged strength alone keeps it from being torn asunder.*
> —W. E. B. DU BOIS

The Harlem Renaissance was not exactly a movement in the usual sense of structure and leadership; no one originated it or called it to order, and in fact it was not consciously planned or organized by any person or group. There was no founder, no architect, no leader, and it is hard to say why or how—or even exactly when—it began or ended. It happened, as needs and desires of African American intellectuals and artists became manifest and began to coalesce in a particular time and place, and it ended—or rather sputtered and scattered its energy—when conditions and circumstances in the world at large dictated that other priorities, especially economic ones, began to trump the forces that had brought it together. But it was not, of course, independent of history or without cause. It was a product of many circumstances, most of them involving the long-term aftereffects of slavery and the increasingly articulated desire of African Americans to produce a dis-

The Cotton Club, circa 1930

tinctive black American culture within the larger national culture that they had been introduced into forcibly. They drew consciously on features and habits of African culture but imported and naturalized them into a distinctively American, decidedly urban setting. The art they produced—only two generations after slavery—recognized the complications, unhappiness, resistance, awkwardness, and coercive constraints of being black in America, where they were patronized, distrusted, feared, and alternately treated as alien or invisible. But the Harlem Renaissance taught black artists that they were also somehow—though it was not very clear how—central to a melting-pot America that repeatedly tried to define itself without them. The Harlem Renaissance represented powerful assertions: that America had to include the voices of black Americans in order to find its own full definition, and, equally, that artistic creativity—including literary creativity—had to be fully realized and recognized if black Americans were to find their full human identity in their American homeland. To live in Harlem and to be black and creative was not an altogether happy experience, and the poetry that exploded out of that time and place was a poetry of anger, resentment, conflict and torn loyalties. But it was also a poetry of energy, sensitivity, humanity, and high ideals.

What was the Harlem Renaissance? To call it a movement is to make it seem more coherent, goal-centered, and idealistic than it appeared to be at the time, but out of leaderless and haphazard beginnings it focused needs and desires in a forceful and effective way. It was first of all a migration or, rather, part of a migration: around the end of World War I (the "War to End All Wars"), American blacks relocated in large numbers from the south to the north and from rural agricultural areas to cities. New York was only one of many destinations; Chicago, Philadelphia, Detroit, Washington, Cleveland, Buffalo, and other urban centers all received huge

# Harlem, New York
## in the 1920s and '30s

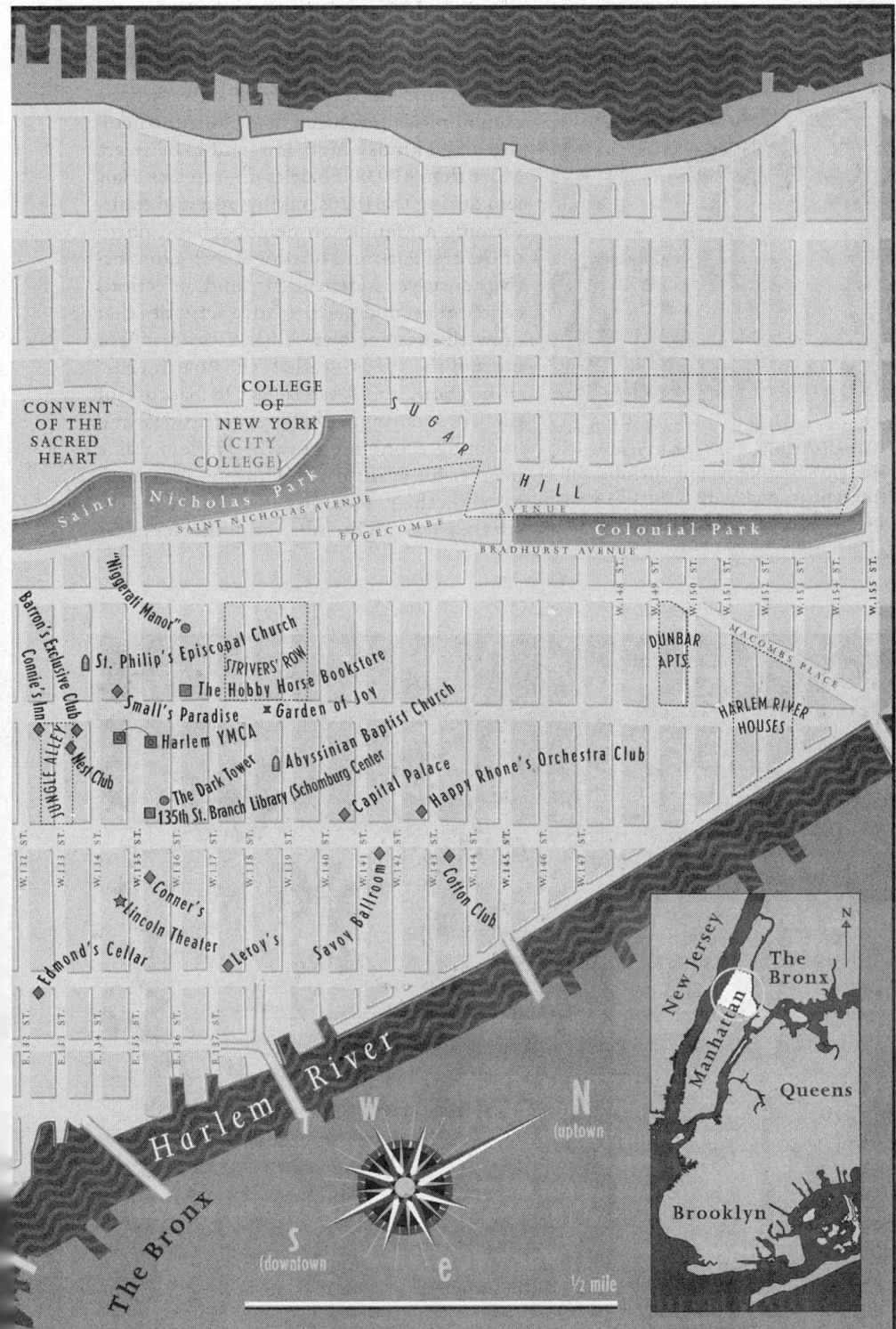

A dancer entertains a crowd at Small's Paradise Club, 1929. As at many of Harlem's best-known nightclubs, the entertainers and staff at Small's were primarily African American, and the clientele was mainly white.

numbers of black migrants. But New York was the largest and most vibrant seat of culture in America, beginning to rival European capitals as a site where active artistic communities produced and consumed culture of all kinds—high, low, and in between. More than 100,000 blacks migrated to Harlem during the 1920s, taking over and transforming a Manhattan neighborhood north of Central Park and turning it into a distinctive, creative, independent, and infectious center of art and performance activities that drew the rest of New York City to it. For most of the 1920s—called "the Roaring 20s" throughout the Western world because of the era's daring, rebellious attitudes and booming economic growth—Harlem was a magnet for avant-garde whites in New York to take their pleasures. They flocked to speakeasies, nightclubs, and theaters (see

Prominent African Americans (including W. E. B. Du Bois, third from the right in the second row) parade down New York's Fifth Avenue on July 28, 1917, to protest a race riot in East St. Louis, Illinois. Thirty-nine African Americans were killed and hundreds were seriously injured in the melee, one of the deadliest outbreaks of racial violence in America.

map, p. 1164), and they were fascinated by the kinds of of music, dance, and performance art they could find there—productions quite different from those on Broadway or in other parts of the city, though increasingly the white venues tried to capture, in their own productions, something of the life and energy that patrons sought in Harlem. White readers, and many white artists, showed enormous—sometimes mawkish or even ghoulish—curiosity about black life in America. Before the Harlem Renaissance had ended, a large number of Broadway productions—Marc Connelly's *Green Pastures*, Eugene O'Neill's *Emperor Jones* and *All God's Chillun Got Wings*, for example—and many novels tried to represent the black experience for white audiences. Black artists and writers (and their readers) were not always happy with the way white writers portrayed black experience and black concerns, but the widespread curiosity—some of it piqued by the flourishing of the Harlem group and some by "intruders" from the white establishment—provided a wider audience for black concerns than had existed in earlier generations.

> *I swear to the Lord*
> *I still can't see*
> *Why Democracy means*
> *Everybody but me.*
> —LANGSTON HUGHES

The height of the Harlem Renaissance was the 1920s, though it is hard to pin down just when the period began and ended. Some historians, pointing to the political ferment caused by U.S. entry into the war in 1917, date the beginnings in the mid to late teens, and some regard it as lasting until the outbreak of World War II in the late 1930s. But the decade of the 1920s saw most of the productivity and creative energy that we associate with the flourishing of Harlem. And it was in the early '20s when most of the leading writers in the group actually moved to New York. Many historians regard the stock-market crash of 1929 and the depression that followed as signs of the end. Certainly the mood of the whole nation changed rapidly then, and by the early 1930s most of the leading figures had moved away from New York, forming smaller communities elsewhere or becoming individually isolated. The Harlem neighborhood itself began a slow economic decline.

The cover of Volume I, Number 1 of *Fire!!*, a journal "Devoted to Younger Negro Artists," established by the self-designated "niggerati," the younger generation of African American intellectuals and writers—including Wallace Thurman, Langston Hughes, Zora Neale Hurston, and others—who wanted to (in Hughes's words) "burn up a lot of the old, dead, conventional Negro-white ideas of the past."

Between the wars, though, Harlem's productivity and impact were dramatic. Before 1917, there had been few publishing outlets hospitable to young black writers; only Paul Lawrence Dunbar among African American poets was widely read or known, and he had died in 1906. But rising political and social concerns during and immediately after World War I produced several new periodicals: *The Messenger*, founded in 1917 by A. Philip Randolph and Chandler Owen, claimed to be "The only Radical Negro Magazine in America," and in 1923 the Urban League started its own magazine, *Opportunity*. Both of these new journals saw themselves as activist alternatives to the NAACP's

Claude McKay, photographed circa 1930 by Carl Van Vechten

Portrait of Alain Locke, by Betsy G. Reyneau

official journal, *Crisis*, edited by W. E. B. Du Bois. Other magazines came and went. *Fire!!* managed only a single issue, but brought verbal and visual art spectacularly together. Meanwhile—and perhaps just as important in a different way—mainstream magazines (*Vanity Fair*, for example) and publishers (Knopf, Macmillan, Harper, and Harcourt Brace) began to feature younger black writers who soon developed a growing readership.

Some historians date the Harlem Renaissance from the composition of Claude McKay's fiery sonnet "If We Must Die," written in the summer of 1919. McKay later denied that the poem referred specifically to blacks and whites, but the many antiblack riots that broke out in several American cities that summer—sometimes called "the Red Summer"—certainly inspired and contextualized the poem. Another milestone was the publication in 1922 of James Weldon Johnson's *Book of American Negro Poetry*, which, in the words of the editors of the *Norton Anthology of African American Literature*, "emphasized the youthful promise of the new writers and established some of the terms of the emerging movement." But it was Alain Locke's landmark anthology, *The New Negro*, that, in 1925, effectively announced the significance of the Harlem Renaissance. Locke, a sociology professor at Howard University and an Oxford graduate as the first African American Rhodes

Langston Hughes, circa 1925, in a pastel portrait by Winold Reiss. The original hangs in the National Portrait Gallery in Washington, D.C.

Scholar, gathered all kinds of material—poems, fiction, essays, visual art—by authors old and young, black and white—into a working definition of what the "new Negro" was all about.

The major figures of the Harlem Renaissance were, however, highly individual, and (although they shared many ideals and aspirations) never confined themselves to a creed or hardened into a "school." Langston Hughes, with a wonderful lyric voice and an eye for telling small details, pursued the relationship of poetry to black music and experimented with a variety of forms and rhythms; look, for example, at the award-winning "Weary Blues." Countee Cullen, on the other hand, was deeply committed to conventional poetic forms and felt most at home poetically when he was working in traditional fixed formal structures. Claude McKay, born in Jamaica, lived briefly in New York but mostly in Greenwich Village rather than Harlem, and spent much of his career abroad (Russia, France, North Africa). He always followed his own star in poetry too; his poetry was sometimes violent and incendiary, but equally strong was his sense of nostalgia and natural spiritualism. "The Tropics in New York" shows his sensuous and romantic side, and in spite of setting a militant tone in a founding poem of the Harlem Renaissance, "If I Must Die," he wrote only two poems that were directly about Harlem experiences and themes. Likewise, novelists like Zora Neale Hurston, Jean Toomer, Jesse Fauset, and Nella Larsen pursued individual styles and themes in their fiction. What held the group together conceptually was a dedication to producing first-rate writing, on the one hand, and, on the other, a commitment to raising the aspirations of American blacks of all backgrounds and abilities.

Countee Cullen, circa 1935

*What is Africa to me?*
—COUNTEE CULLEN

Vendor selling books and pamphlets from a cart on 125th Street in Harlem, June 1943

The question of who was to benefit from the ambitious art of the Harlem Renaissance was hotly debated. Was it ordinary people, who could stretch the horizons of their reading and their own ambitions? African Americans generally? Or was it primarily intellectuals and artists who might raise expectations for black thought and art? W. E. B. Du Bois, who was a lightning rod for many members of the militant and radical new generation, had famously championed the "talented tenth," a select group whose natural gifts authoritatively raised them above others, and

The Dark Tower, a forum for African American intellectuals, met frequently in the home of A'Lelia Walker, a prominent Harlem heiress and socialite. Countee Cullen's poem "From the Dark Tower" is painted on the wall.

opinions split over whether the beneficiaries of the Harlem Renaissance were to be ordinary readers and viewers or the creative geniuses themselves, in the service of a higher aesthetic quite distinct from social progress. It's fair to say that the writers themselves remained divided, alternately championing the triumph of art and hoping for a larger cultural impact that would benefit readers (especially black readers) more generally.

The role of whites in the Harlem Renaissance is a matter of some dispute. The most controversial (though undeniably influential) figure was Carl Van Vechten, whose parties legendarily brought young black writers into the company of famous and powerful white celebrities, many of whom could be helpful to their careers. Van Vechten was a gifted photographer whose portraits of many rising figures chronicle the Harlem years brilliantly (see the photo of Arna Bontemps on p. 1172), and he undeniably fostered many useful connections that resulted in publication and fame. But some felt his motives were self-serving and meretricious, and his well-meaning novel about everyday Harlem life, *Nigger Heaven*, was widely disparaged, though critics equally suspected "realistic" accounts of everyday life by black writers. (See, for example, the Du Bois review of a Claude McKay novel on p. 1193). There is no doubt that figures like Van Vechten fostered considerable interaction between prominent whites and rising figures in the black artistic community, but not everyone regarded the results

Carl Van Vechten, 1926

as helpful to the black cause overall. Some historians view white participation in the Harlem Renaissance more generally as exploitative, others as sincere but bumbling; and still others view black-white collaboration then as an early demonstration of racial unity in behalf of art and communal relations.

A second set of issues involves questions about elitism and whether the renaissance had truly salutary effects on the larger black community. Du Bois insisted on the obligation of "the talented tenth" to use their artistic and intellectual gifts to improve the lot of others. Critics of Du Bois find his position divisive and patronizing toward the majority of the black community; defenders see the idea as a strategy for community improvement by emphasizing the responsibility of potential leaders. At the heart of this controversy is disagreement about how leadership works to promote both improved social conditions and audience engagement. (Similar arguments rage today over the stardom of African American athletes and entertainers.) Was the Harlem Renaissance a phenomenon that benefited only a talented few, or did it enhance the lives of ordinary readers, residents of Harlem, and African Americans more generally?

Two related controversies concern the influence of the church on black culture and the relationship of the ambitious new "high art" of poetry, novels, and painting to popular-culture phenomena such as jazz, blues, and dance. Many of the younger writers resisted religion and resented its powerful influence on the black experience, even when they thought highly of the specifically black contributions to religious music. There is little doubt that religion was a powerful force in the black community, but observers continue to debate, as the artists themselves then did, whether it fostered and furthered artistic expression or served as a restraining and discouraging force. Often readers can see in poetry about even the most secular subjects traces of religious ideas and traditions; you will have to decide for yourself whether the effects are positive or not. The relationship of radical art to popular culture was even more vexed. Some central figures in the Harlem Renaissance regarded their own aims as "above" the "attractions" and "spectacles" that drew large numbers of whites to Harlem, and they regarded the performance arts as, at best, distractions from or dilutions of the main thrust of radical artistic expression. And while nearly everyone agrees that the quality of various theatrical arts in the many venues of Harlem was very high, the question of whether, beyond jazz and blues, the influence of popular arts on poetry was good or bad remains open.

Known as the "Empress of the Blues," Bessie Smith was one of the most popular entertainers in America during the 1920s. A protégé of the legendary Ma Rainey, Smith spent much of the mid-1920s touring the United States as the star attraction on the vaudeville circuit.

• • •

No easy summary of the Harlem Renaissance will do. Its ambitions—often radical, sometimes revolutionary—made enormous waves in both the black urban community and the world of art. The poems of figures like McKay, Hughes, and Cullen, read in the context of their times, provide an invaluable gloss on particular events and issues; the history, in turn, adds resonance to the concerns expressed in the poems. However one measures the Harlem Renaissance in terms of its impact on later writers, black and white, the poems themselves continue to speak to readers across divides of time and culture. You will find that some of the poems can hardly be understood without knowledge of the specific circumstances and conditions that produced them; you will also find that many of the poems reach insistently for connections both to the past and to the enduring concerns of poets and readers in far-flung times and places.

Arna Bontemps, photographed by Carl Van Vechten, 1939

## ARNA BONTEMPS

### A Black Man Talks of Reaping

I have sown beside all waters in my day.
I planted deep, within my heart the fear
That wind or fowl would take the grain away.
I planted safe against this stark, lean year.

5 I scattered seed enough to plant the land
In rows from Canada to Mexico
But for my reaping only what the hand
Can hold at once is all that I can show.

Yet what I sowed and what the orchard yields
10 My brother's sons are gathering stalk and root,
Small wonder then my children glean in fields
They have not sown, and feed on bitter fruit.

1926

## COUNTEE CULLEN

 ### Yet Do I Marvel

I doubt not God is good, well-meaning, kind,
And did He stoop to quibble could tell why
The little buried mole continues blind,
Why flesh that mirrors Him must some day die,
5 Make plain the reason tortured Tantalus[1]

---

1. In Greek myth he was condemned, for ambiguous reasons, to stand up to his neck in water he couldn't drink and to be within sight of fruit he couldn't reach to eat.

Is baited by the fickle fruit, declare
If merely brute caprice dooms Sisyphus[2]
To struggle up a never-ending stair.
Inscrutable His ways are, and immune
10 To catechism by a mind too strewn
With petty cares to slightly understand
What awful brain compels His awful hand.
Yet do I marvel at this curious thing:
To make a poet black, and bid him sing!

1925

## Saturday's Child[3]

Some are teethed on a silver spoon,
    With the stars strung for a rattle;
I cut my teeth as the black raccoon—
    For implements of battle.

5 Some are swaddled in silk and down,
    And heralded by a star;[4]
They swathed my limbs in a sackcloth gown
    On a night that was black as tar.

For some, godfather and goddame
10     The opulent fairies be;
Dame Poverty gave me my name,
    And Pain godfathered me.

For I was born on Saturday—
    "Bad time for planting a seed,"
15 Was all my father had to say,
    And, "One mouth more to feed."

Death cut the strings that gave me life,
    And handed me to Sorrow,
The only kind of middle wife
20     My folks could beg or borrow.

1925

---

2. The king of Corinth who, in Greek myth, was condemned eternally to roll a huge stone uphill.
3. According to a popular nursery rhyme, "Saturday's child works hard for his living."
4. According to Matthew 2.7-10, Jesus' birth was accompanied by the appearance of a new star.

## From the Dark Tower

(*To Charles S. Johnson*)[5]

We shall not always plant while others reap
The golden increment of bursting fruit,
Not always countenance, abject and mute,
That lesser men should hold their brothers cheap;
5   Not everlastingly while others sleep
Shall we beguile their limbs with mellow flute,
Not always bend to some more subtle brute;
We were not made eternally to weep.

The night whose sable breast relieves the stark,
10  White stars is no less lovely being dark,
And there are buds that cannot bloom at all
In light, but crumple, piteous, and fall;
So in the dark we hide the heart that bleeds,
And wait, and tend our agonizing seeds.

1927

## ANGELINA GRIMKE

### The Black Finger

I have just seen a beautiful thing
  Slim and still,
Against a gold, gold sky,
  A straight cypress,
5   Sensitive
  Exquisite,
A black finger
Pointing upwards.
Why, beautiful, still finger are you black?
10 And why are you pointing upwards?

1925

Angelina Grimke, circa 1905

### Tenebris[6]

There is a tree, by day,
That, at night,
Has a shadow,
A hand huge and black,

---

5. Founder and editor of *Opportunity* magazine.   6. In darkness (Latin).

5 With fingers long and black.
    All through the dark,
Against the white man's house,
    In the little wind,
The black hand plucks and plucks
10     At the bricks.
The bricks are the color of blood and very small.
    Is it a black hand,
    Or is it a shadow?

1927

# LANGSTON HUGHES

## The Weary Blues

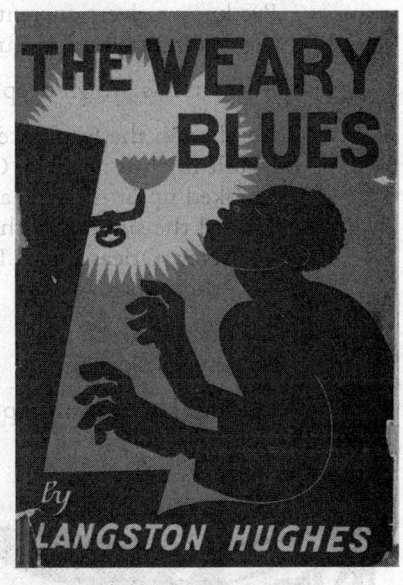

Droning a drowsy syncopated tune,
Rocking back and forth to a mellow croon,
   I heard a Negro play.
Down on Lenox Avenue[7] the other night
5 By the pale dull pallor of an old gas light
   He did a lazy sway. . . .
   He did a lazy sway. . . .
To the tune o' those Weary Blues.
With his ebony hands on each ivory key
10 He made that poor piano moan with melody.
   O Blues!
Swaying to and fro on his rickety stool
He played that sad raggy tune like a musical
    fool.
   Sweet Blues!
15 Coming from a black man's soul.
   O Blues!
In a deep song voice with a melancholy tone
I heard that Negro sing, that old piano moan—
   "Ain't got nobody in all this world,
20   Ain't got nobody but ma self.
   I's gwine to quit ma frownin'
   And put ma troubles on the shelf."
Thump, thump, thump, went his foot on the floor.
He played a few chords then he sang some more—
25   "I got the Weary Blues
   And I can't be satisfied.
   Got the Weary Blues
   And can't be satisfied—
   I ain't happy no mo'
30   And I wish that I had died."

---

7. Major Harlem thoroughfare, now Malcolm X Boulevard.

And far into the night he crooned that tune.
The stars went out and so did the moon.
The singer stopped playing and went to bed
While the Weary Blues echoed through his head.
35 He slept like a rock or a man that's dead.

1923                                                                  1925

## The Negro Speaks of Rivers

I've known rivers:
I've known rivers ancient as the world and older than the flow of human blood in human veins.

My soul has grown deep like the rivers.

I bathed in the Euphrates when dawns were young.
5 I built my hut near the Congo and it lulled me to sleep.
I looked upon the Nile and raised the pyramids above it.
I heard the singing of the Mississippi when Abe Lincoln went down to New Orleans, and I've seen its muddy bosom turn all golden in the sunset.

I've known rivers:
Ancient, dusky rivers.

10 My soul has grown deep like the rivers.

                                                                      1926

A pen-and-ink illustration by the artist Aaron Douglas made specifically to accompany Hughes's "The Negro Speaks of Rivers"

## I, Too

I, too, sing America.

I am the darker brother.
They send me to eat in the kitchen
When company comes,
5 But I laugh,
And eat well,
And grow strong.

Tomorrow,
I'll sit at the table.
10 When company comes
Nobody'll dare
Say to me,
"Eat in the kitchen,"
Then.

15 Besides,
They'll see how beautiful I am
And be ashamed—

I, too, am America.

                    1932


## HELENE JOHNSON

## Sonnet to a Negro in Harlem

You are disdainful and magnificent—
Your perfect body and your pompous gait,
Your dark eyes flashing solemnly with hate,
Small wonder that you are incompetent
5 To imitate those whom you so despise—
Your shoulders towering high above the throng,
Your head thrown back in rich, barbaric song,
Palm trees and mangoes stretched before your eyes.
Let others toil and sweat for labor's sake
10 And wring from grasping hands their meed[8] of gold.
Why urge ahead your supercilious feet?
Scorn will efface each footprint that you make.
I love your laughter arrogant and bold.
You are too splendid for this city street.

                    1927

8. Reward.

CLAUDE McKAY

## Harlem Shadows

I hear the halting footsteps of a lass
   In Negro Harlem when the night lets fall
Its veil. I see the shapes of girls who pass
   To bend and barter at desire's call.
5 Ah, little dark girls who in slippered feet
   Go prowling through the night from street to street!

Through the long night until the silver break
   Of day the little gray feet know no rest;
Through the lone night until the last snow-flake
10   Has dropped from heaven upon the earth's white breast,
The dusky, half-clad girls of tired feet
   Are trudging, thinly shod, from street to street.

Ah, stern harsh world, that in the wretched way
   Of poverty, dishonor and disgrace,
15 Has pushed the timid little feet of clay,
   The sacred brown feet of my fallen race!
Ah, heart of me, the weary, weary feet
   In Harlem wandering from street to street.

1918

## If We Must Die

If we must die, let it not be like hogs
Hunted and penned in an inglorious spot,
While round us bark the mad and hungry dogs,
Making their mock at our accursed lot.
5 If we must die, O let us nobly die,
So that our precious blood may not be shed
In vain; then even the monsters we defy
Shall be constrained to honor us though dead!
O kinsmen! we must meet the common foe!
10 Though far outnumbered let us show us brave,
And for their thousand blows deal one deathblow!
What though before us lies the open grave?
Like men we'll face the murderous, cowardly pack,
Pressed to the wall, dying, but fighting back!

1919

## The Tropics in New York

Bananas ripe and green, and ginger-root,
    Cocoa in pods and alligator pears,
And tangerines and mangoes and grape fruit,
    Fit for the highest prize at parish fairs,

5  Set in the window, bringing memories
    Of fruit-trees laden by low-singing rills,
And dewy dawns, and mystical blue skies
    In benediction over nun-like hills.

My eyes grew dim, and I could no more gaze;
10  A wave of longing through my body swept,
And, hungry for the old, familiar ways,
    I turned aside and bowed my head and wept.

                        1920

## The Harlem Dancer

Applauding youths laughed with young prostitutes
And watched her perfect, half-clothed body sway;
Her voice was like the sound of blended flutes
Blown by black players upon a picnic day.
5  She sang and danced on gracefully and calm,
The light gauze hanging loose about her form;
To me she seemed a proudly-swaying palm
Grown lovelier for passing through a storm.
Upon her swarthy neck black shiny curls
10  Luxuriant fell; and tossing coins in praise,
The wine-flushed, bold-eyed boys, and even the girls,
Devoured her shape with eager, passionate gaze;
But looking at her falsely-smiling face,
I knew her self was not in that strange place.

                        1922

## The White House

Your door is shut against my tightened face,
And I am sharp as steel with discontent;
But I possess the courage and the grace
To bear my anger proudly and unbent.
5  The pavement slabs burn loose beneath my feet,

And passion rends my vitals as I pass,
A chafing savage, down the decent street,
Where boldly shines your shuttered door of glass.
Oh, I must search for wisdom every hour,
10 Deep in my wrathful bosom sore and raw,
And find in it the superhuman power
To hold me to the letter of your law!
Oh, I must keep my heart inviolate
Against the poison of your deadly hate.

1937

## JAMES WELDON JOHNSON

## From the Preface to *The Book of American Negro Poetry*

This power of the Negro to suck up the national spirit from the soil and create something artistic and original, which, at the same time, possesses the note of universal appeal, is due to a remarkable racial gift of adaptability; it is more than adaptability, it is a transfusive[1] quality. And the Negro has exercised this transfusive quality not only here in America, where the race lives in large numbers, but in European countries, where the number has been almost infinitesimal.

James Weldon Johnson, circa 1920

Is it not curious to know that the greatest poet of Russia is Alexander Pushkin, a man of African descent; that the greatest romancer of France is Alexandre Dumas,[2] a man of African descent; and that one of the greatest musicians of England is Coleridge-Taylor,[3] a man of African descent?

The fact is fairly well known that the father of Dumas was a Negro of the French West Indies, and that the father of Coleridge-Taylor was a native-born African; but the facts concerning Pushkin's African ancestry are not so familiar.

When Peter the Great[4] was Czar of Russia, some potentate presented him with a full-blooded Negro of gigantic size. Peter, the most eccentric ruler of modern times,

---

1. Having the ability to transfer.
2. French novelist and dramatist (1802–1870). Pushkin (1799–1837), Russian man of letters.
3. Samuel Coleridge-Taylor (1875–1912), English composer.
4. Peter I (1672–1725), ruled from 1682 to 1725.

dressed this Negro up in soldier clothes, christened him Hannibal,[5] and made him a special body-guard.

But Hannibal had more than size, he had brain and ability. He not only looked picturesque and imposing in soldier clothes, he showed that he had in him the making of a real soldier. Peter recognized this, and eventually made him a general. He afterwards ennobled him, and Hannibal, later, married one of the ladies of the Russian court. This same Hannibal was great-grandfather of Pushkin, the national poet of Russia, the man who bears the same relation to Russian literature that Shakespeare bears to English literature.

I know the question naturally arises: If out of the few Negroes who have lived in France there came a Dumas; and out of the few Negroes who have lived in England there came a Coleridge-Taylor; and if from the man who was at the time, probably, the only Negro in Russia there sprang that country's national poet, why have not the millions of Negroes in the United States with all the emotional and artistic endowment claimed for them produced a Dumas, or a Coleridge-Taylor, or a Pushkin?

The question seems difficult, but there is an answer. The Negro in the United States is consuming all of his intellectual energy in this grueling race-struggle. And the same statement may be made in a general way about the white South. Why does not the white South produce literature and art? The white South, too, is consuming all of its intellectual energy in this lamentable conflict. Nearly all of the mental efforts of the white South run through one narrow channel. The life of every Southern white man and all of his activities are impassably limited by the ever present Negro problem. And that is why, as Mr. H. L. Mencken[6] puts it, in all that vast region, with its thirty or forty million people and its territory as large as a half dozen Frances or Germanys, there is not a single poet, not a serious historian, not a creditable composer, not a critic good or bad, not a dramatist dead or alive.[7]

\* \* \*

This preface has gone far beyond what I had in mind when I started. It was my intention to gather together the best verses I could find by Negro poets and present them with a bare word of introduction. It was not my plan to make this collection inclusive nor to make the book in any sense a book of criticism. I planned to present only verses by contemporary writers; but, perhaps, because this is the first collection of its kind, I realized the absence of a starting-point and was led to provide one and to fill in with historical data what I felt to be a gap.

It may be surprising to many to see how little of the poetry being written by Negro poets today is being written in Negro dialect. The newer Negro poets show a tendency to discard dialect; much of the subject-matter which went into the making of traditional dialect poetry, 'possums, watermelons, etc., they have discarded altogether, at least, as poetic material. This tendency will, no doubt, be regretted by the majority of white readers; and, indeed, it would be a distinct loss if the American Negro poets threw away this quaint and musical folk speech

---

5. After the North African general (247–c. 183 B.C.E.) who made war on Rome.
6. Henry Louis Mencken (1880–1956), American editor, critic, and essayist.
7. This statement was quoted in 1921. The reader may consider for himself the changes wrought in the decade [Johnson's note, 1931 edition].

as a medium of expression. And yet, after all, these poets are working through a problem not realized by the reader, and, perhaps, by many of these poets themselves not realized consciously. They are trying to break away from, not Negro dialect itself, but the limitations on Negro dialect imposed by the fixing effects of long convention.

The Negro in the United States has achieved or been placed in a certain artistic niche. When he is thought of artistically, it is as a happy-go-lucky, singing, shuffling, banjo-picking being or as a more or less pathetic figure. The picture of him is in a log cabin amid fields of cotton or along the levees. Negro dialect is naturally and by long association the exact instrument for voicing this phase of Negro life; and by that very exactness it is an instrument with but two full stops, humor and pathos. So even when he confines himself to purely racial themes, the Aframerican poet realizes that there are phases of Negro life in the United States which cannot be treated in the dialect either adequately or artistically. Take, for example, the phases rising out of life in Harlem, that most wonderful Negro city in the world. I do not deny that a Negro in a log cabin is more picturesque than a Negro in a Harlem flat, but the Negro in the Harlem flat is here, and he is but part of a group growing everywhere in the country, a group whose ideals are becoming increasingly more vital than those of the traditionally artistic group, even if its members are less picturesque.

What the colored poet in the United States needs to do is something like what Synge[8] did for the Irish; he needs to find a form that will express the racial spirit by symbols from within rather than by symbols from without, such as the mere mutilation of English spelling and pronunciation. He needs a form that is freer and larger than dialect, but which will still hold the racial flavor; a form expressing the imagery, the idioms, the peculiar turns of thought, and the distinctive humor and pathos, too, of the Negro, but which will also be capable of voicing the deepest and highest emotions and aspirations, and allow of the widest range of subjects and the widest scope of treatment.

Negro dialect is at present a medium that is not capable of giving expression to the varied conditions of Negro life in America, and much less is it capable of giving the fullest interpretation of Negro character and psychology. This is no indictment against the dialect as dialect, but against the mold of convention in which Negro dialect in the United States has been set. In time these conventions may become lost, and the colored poet in the United States may sit down to write in dialect without feeling that his first line will put the general reader in a frame of mind which demands that the poem be humorous or pathetic. In the meantime, there is no reason why these poets should not continue to do the beautiful things that can be done, and done best, in the dialect.

In stating the need for Aframerican poets in the United States to work out a new and distinctive form of expression I do not wish to be understood to hold any theory that they should limit themselves to Negro poetry, to racial themes; the sooner they are able to write *American* poetry spontaneously, the better. Nevertheless, I believe that the richest contribution the Negro poet can make to the American literature of the future will be the fusion into it of his own individual artistic gifts.

1921

---

8. John Middleton Synge (1871–1909), Irish dramatist whose works celebrate Irish traditions.

## ALAIN LOCKE

### From *The New Negro*

The tide of Negro migration, northward and city-ward, is not to be fully explained as a blind flood started by the demands of war industry coupled with the shutting off of foreign migration, or by the pressure of poor crops coupled with increased social terrorism in certain sections of the South and Southwest. Neither labor demand, the bollweevil[9] nor the Ku Klux Klan is a basic factor, however contributory any or all of them may have been. The wash and rush of this human tide on the beach line of the northern city centers is to be explained primarily in terms of a new vision of opportunity, of social and economic freedom, of a spirit to seize, even in the face of an extortionate and heavy toll, a chance for the improvement of conditions. With each successive wave of it, the movement of the Negro becomes more and more a mass movement toward the larger and the more democratic chance—in the Negro's case a deliberate flight not only from countryside to city, but from medieval America to modern.

Take Harlem as an instance of this. Here in Manhattan is not merely the largest Negro community in the world, but the first concentration in history of so many diverse elements of Negro life. It has attracted the African, the West Indian, the Negro American; has brought together the Negro of the North and the Negro of the South; the man from the city and the man from the town and village; the peasant, the student, the business man, the professional man, artist, poet, musician, adventurer and worker, preacher and criminal, exploiter and social outcast. Each group has come with its own separate motives and for its own special ends, but their greatest experience has been the finding of one another. Proscription and prejudice have thrown these dissimilar elements into a common area of contact and interaction. Within this area, race sympathy and unity have determined a further fusing of sentiment and experience. So what began in terms of segregation becomes more and more, as its elements mix and react, the laboratory of a great race-welding. Hitherto, it must be admitted that American Negroes have been a race more in name than in fact, or to be exact, more in sentiment than in experience. The chief bond between them has been that of a common condition rather than a common consciousness; a problem in common rather than a life in common. In Harlem, Negro life is seizing upon its first chances for group expression and self-determination. It is—or promises at least to be—a race capital. That is why our comparison is taken with those nascent centers of folk-expression and self-determination which are playing a creative part in the world today. Without pretense to their political significance, Harlem has the same role to play for the New Negro as Dublin has had for the New Ireland or Prague for the New Czechoslovakia.

Harlem, I grant you, isn't typical—but it is significant, it is prophetic. No sane observer, however sympathetic to the new trend, would contend that the great masses are articulate as yet, but they stir, they move, they are more than physically restless. The challenge of the new intellectuals among them is clear enough—the "race radicals" and realists who have broken with the old epoch of philanthropic

---

9. A snout beetle notorious for destroying cotton crops.

guidance, sentimental appeal and protest. But are we after all only reading into the stirrings of a sleeping giant the dreams of an agitator? The answer is in the migrating peasant. It is the "man farthest down" who is most active in getting up. One of the most characteristic symptoms of this is the professional man, himself migrating to recapture his constituency after a vain effort to maintain in some Southern corner what for years back seemed an established living and clientele. The clergyman following his errant flock, the physician or lawyer trailing his clients, supply the true clues. In a real sense it is the rank and file who are leading, and the leaders who are following. A transformed and transforming psychology permeates the masses.

When the racial leaders of twenty years ago spoke of developing race-pride and stimulating race-consciousness, and of the desirability of race solidarity, they could not in any accurate degree have anticipated the abrupt feeling that has surged up and now pervades the awakened centers. Some of the recognized Negro leaders and a powerful section of white opinion identified with "race work" of the older order have indeed attempted to discount this feeling as a "passing phase," an attack of "race nerves" so to speak, an "aftermath of the war," and the like. It has not abated, however, if we are to gauge by the present tone and temper of the Negro press, or by the shift in popular support from the officially recognized and orthodox spokesmen to those of the independent, popular, and often radical type who are unmistakable symptoms of a new order. It is a social disservice to blunt the fact that the Negro of the Northern centers has reached a stage where tutelage, even of the most interested and well-intentioned sort, must give place to new relationships, where positive self-direction must be reckoned with in ever increasing measure. The American mind must reckon with a fundamentally changed Negro.

The Negro too, for his part, has idols of the tribe to smash. If on the one hand the white man has erred in making the Negro appear to be that which would excuse or extenuate his treatment of him, the Negro, in turn, has too often unnecessarily excused himself because of the way he has been treated. The intelligent Negro of today is resolved not to make discrimination an extenuation for his shortcomings in performance, individual or collective; he is trying to hold himself at par, neither inflated by sentimental allowances nor depreciated by current social discounts. For this he must know himself and be known for precisely what he is, and for that reason he welcomes the new scientific rather than the old sentimental interest. Sentimental interest in the Negro has ebbed. We used to lament this as the falling off of our friends; now we rejoice and pray to be delivered both from self-pity and condescension. The mind of each racial group has had a bitter weaning, apathy or hatred on one side matching disillusionment or resentment on the other; but they face each other today with the possibility at least of entirely new mutual attitudes.

It does not follow that if the Negro were better known, he would be better liked or better treated. But mutual understanding is basic for any subsequent cooperation and adjustment. The effort toward this will at least have the effect of remedying in large part what has been the most unsatisfactory feature of our present stage of race relationships in America, namely the fact that the more intelligent and representative elements of the two race groups have at so many points got quite out of vital touch with one another.

The fiction is that the life of the races is separate, and increasingly so. The fact is that they have touched too closely at the unfavorable and too lightly at the favorable levels.

While inter-racial councils have sprung up in the South, drawing on forward elements of both races, in the Northern cities manual laborers may brush elbows in their everyday work, but the community and business leaders have experienced no such interplay or far too little of it. These segments must achieve contact or the race situation in America becomes desperate. Fortunately this is happening. There is a growing realization that in social effort the cooperative basis must supplant long-distance philanthropy, and that the only safeguard for mass relations in the future must be provided in the carefully maintained contacts of the enlightened minorities of both race groups. In the intellectual realm a renewed and keen curiosity is replacing the recent apathy; the Negro is being carefully studied, not just talked about and discussed. In art and letters, instead of being wholly caricatured, he is being seriously portrayed and painted.

To all of this the New Negro is keenly responsive as an augury of a new democracy in American culture. He is contributing his share to the new social understanding. But the desire to be understood would never in itself have been sufficient to have opened so completely the protectively closed portals of the thinking Negro's mind. There is still too much possibility of being snubbed or patronized for that. It was rather the necessity for fuller, truer self-expression, the realization of the unwisdom of allowing social discrimination to segregate him mentally, and a counter-attitude to cramp and fetter his own living—and so the "spite-wall" that the intellectuals built over the "color-line" has happily been taken down. Much of this reopening of intellectual contacts has centered in New York and has been richly fruitful not merely in the enlarging of personal experience, but in the definite enrichment of American art and letters and in the clarifying of our common vision of the social tasks ahead.

The particular significance in the re-establishment of contact between the more advanced and representative classes is that it promises to offset some of the unfavorable reactions of the past, or at least to re-surface race contacts somewhat for the future. Subtly the conditions that are molding a New Negro are molding a new American attitude.

However, this new phase of things is delicate; it will call for less charity but more justice; less help, but infinitely closer understanding. This is indeed a critical stage of race relationships because of the likelihood, if the new temper is not understood, of engendering sharp group antagonism and a second crop of more calculated prejudice. In some quarters, it has already done so. Having weaned the Negro, public opinion cannot continue to paternalize. The Negro today is inevitably moving forward under the control largely of his own objectives. What are these objectives? Those of his outer life are happily already well and finally formulated, for they are none other than the ideals of American institutions and democracy. Those of his inner life are yet in process of formation, for the new psychology at present is more of a consensus of feeling than of opinion, of attitude rather than of program. Still some points seem to have crystallized.

Up to the present one may adequately describe the Negro's "inner objectives" as an attempt to repair a damaged group psychology and reshape a warped social perspective. Their realization has required a new mentality for the American Negro. And as it matures we begin to see its effects; at first, negative, iconoclastic, and then positive and constructive. In this new group psychology we note the lapse of sentimental appeal, then the development of a more positive self-respect and self-reliance; the repudiation of social dependence, and then the gradual recovery from hyper-sensitiveness and "touchy" nerves, the repudiation of the double standard of judgment with its special philanthropic allowances and then the sturdier desire for objective and scientific appraisal; and finally the rise from social disillusionment to race pride, from the sense of social debt to the responsibilities of social contribution, and offsetting the necessary working and commonsense acceptance of restricted conditions, the belief in ultimate esteem and recognition. Therefore the Negro today wishes to be known for what he is, even in his faults and shortcomings, and scorns a craven and precarious survival at the price of seeming to be what he is not. He resents being spoken of as a social ward or minor, even by his own, and to being regarded a chronic patient for the sociological clinic, the sick man of American Democracy. For the same reasons, he himself is through with those social nostrums and panaceas, the so-called "solutions" of his "problem," with which he and the country have been so liberally dosed in the past. Religion, freedom, education, money—in turn, he has ardently hoped for and peculiarly trusted these things; he still believes in them, but not in blind trust that they alone will solve his life-problem.

Each generation, however, will have its creed, and that of the present is the belief in the efficacy of collective effort, in race cooperation. This deep feeling of race is at present the mainspring of Negro life. It seems to be the outcome of the reaction to proscription and prejudice; an attempt, fairly successful on the whole, to convert a defensive into an offensive position, a handicap into an incentive. It is radical in tone, but not in purpose and only the most stupid forms of opposition, misunderstanding or persecution could make it otherwise. Of course, the thinking Negro has shifted a little toward the left with the world-trend, and there is an increasing group who affiliate with radical and liberal movements. But fundamentally for the present the Negro is radical on race matters, conservative on others, in other words, a "forced radical," a social protestant rather than a genuine radical. Yet under further pressure and injustice iconoclastic thought and motives will inevitably increase. Harlem's quixotic radicalisms call for their ounce of democracy today lest tomorrow they be beyond cure.

The Negro mind reaches out as yet to nothing but American wants, American ideas. But this forced attempt to build his Americanism on race values is a unique social experiment, and its ultimate success is impossible except through the fullest sharing of American culture and institutions. There should be no delusion about this. American nerves in sections unstrung with race hysteria are often fed the opiate that the trend of Negro advance is wholly separatist, and that the effect of its operation will be to encyst the Negro as a benign foreign body in the body politic. This cannot be—even if it were desirable. The racialism of the Negro is no limitation or reservation with respect to American life; it is only a constructive effort to build the obstructions in the stream of his progress into an efficient dam of social energy and power. Democracy itself is obstructed and stagnated to the extent that any of its channels are closed. Indeed they cannot be selectively closed. So the choice is not between one way for the Negro and another way for the rest, but between American institutions frustrated on the one hand and American ideals progressively fulfilled and realized on the other.

There is, of course, a warrantably comfortable feeling in being on the right side of the country's professed ideals. We realize that we cannot be undone without America's undoing. It is within the gamut of this attitude that the thinking Negro faces America, but with variations of mood that are if anything more significant than the attitude itself. Sometimes we have it taken with the defiant ironic challenge of McKay:[1]

> Mine is the future grinding down to-day
> Like a great landslip moving to the sea,
> Bearing its freight of débris far away
> Where the green hungry waters restlessly
> Heave mammoth pyramids, and break and roar
> Their eerie challenge to the crumbling shore.

Sometimes, perhaps more frequently as yet, it is taken in the fervent and almost filial appeal and counsel of Weldon Johnson's:

> O Southland, dear Southland!
> Then why do you still cling
> To an idle age and a musty page,
> To a dead and useless thing?[2]

But between defiance and appeal, midway almost between cynicism and hope, the prevailing mind stands in the mood of the same author's *To America*,[3] an attitude of sober query and stoical challenge:

> How would you have us, as we are?
>   Or sinking 'neath the load we bear,
> Our eyes fixed forward on a star,
>   Or gazing empty at despair?
>
> Rising or falling? Men or things?
>   With dragging pace or footsteps fleet?
> Strong, willing sinews in your wings,
>   Or tightening chains about your feet?

More and more, however, an intelligent realization of the great discrepancy between the American social creed and the American social practice forces upon the Negro the taking of the moral advantage that is his. Only the steadying and sobering effect of a truly characteristic gentleness of spirit prevents the rapid rise of a definite cynicism and counter-hate and a defiant superiority feeling. Human as this reaction would be, the majority still deprecate its advent, and would gladly see it forestalled by the speedy amelioration of its causes. We wish our race pride to be a healthier, more positive achievement than a feeling based upon a realization of the shortcomings of others. But all paths toward the attainment of a sound social attitude have been difficult; only a relatively few enlightened minds have been able as the phrase puts it "to rise above" prejudice. The ordinary man has had until recently only a hard choice between the alternatives of supine and humiliating submission and stimulating but hurtful counter-prejudice. Fortunately from some inner, desperate resourcefulness has recently sprung up the simple expedient of fighting prejudice by mental passive resistance, in other words by trying to ignore it. For the few, this manna may perhaps be effective, but the masses cannot thrive upon it.

---

1. Claude McKay.   2. From "O Southland!" (1907).   3. Published in 1917.

Fortunately there are constructive channels opening out into which the balked social feelings of the American Negro can flow freely.

Without them there would be much more pressure and danger than there is. These compensating interests are racial but in a new and enlarged way. One is the consciousness of acting as the advance-guard of the African peoples in their contact with Twentieth Century civilization; the other, the sense of a mission of rehabilitating the race in world esteem from that loss of prestige for which the fate and conditions of slavery have so largely been responsible. Harlem, as we shall see, is the center of both these movements; she is the home of the Negro's "Zionism."[4] The pulse of the Negro world has begun to beat in Harlem. A Negro newspaper carrying news material in English, French and Spanish, gathered from all quarters of America, the West Indies and Africa has maintained itself in Harlem for over five years. Two important magazines,[5] both edited from New York, maintain their news and circulation consistently on a cosmopolitan scale. Under American auspices and backing, three pan-African congresses have been held abroad for the discussion of common interests, colonial questions and the future cooperative development of Africa. In terms of the race question as a world problem, the Negro mind has leapt, so to speak, upon the parapets of prejudice and extended its cramped horizons. In so doing it has linked up with the growing group consciousness of the dark-peoples and is gradually learning their common interests. As one of our writers has recently put it: "It is imperative that we understand the white world in its relations to the non-white world." As with the Jew, persecution is making the Negro international.

As a world phenomenon this wider race consciousness is a different thing from the much asserted rising tide of color. Its inevitable causes are not of our making. The consequences are not necessarily damaging to the best interests of civilization. Whether it actually brings into being new Armadas of conflict or argosies[6] of cultural exchange and enlightenment can only be decided by the attitude of the dominant races in an era of critical change. With the American Negro, his new internationalism is primarily an effort to recapture contact with the scattered peoples of African derivation. Garveyism[7] may be a transient, if spectacular, phenomenon, but the possible role of the American Negro in the future development of Africa is one of the most constructive and universally helpful missions that any modern people can lay claim to.

1925

## RUDOLPH FISHER

### *The Caucasian Storms Harlem*

I

It might not have been such a jolt had my five years' absence from Harlem been spent otherwise. But the study of medicine includes no courses in cabareting; and, anyway, the Negro cabarets in Washington, where I studied, are all uncom-

---

4. An international movement aimed at securing a homeland for the Jewish people.
5. Probably *Opportunity* and the *Crisis*.    6. Merchant ships. *Armadas*: fleets of warships.
7. The Back to Africa movement of Marcus Garvey (1887–1940).

promisingly black. Accordingly I was entirely unprepared for what I found when I returned to Harlem recently.

I remembered one place especially where my own crowd used to hold forth; and, hoping to find some old-timers there still, I sought it out one midnight. The old, familiar plunkety-plunk welcomed me from below as I entered. I descended the same old narrow stairs, came into the same smoke-misty basement, and found myself a chair at one of the ancient white-porcelain, mirror-smooth tables. I drew a deep breath and looked about, seeking familiar faces. "What a lot of 'fays!"[8] I thought, as I noticed the number of white guests. Presently I grew puzzled and began to stare, then I gaped—and gasped. I found myself wondering if this was the right place—if, indeed, this was Harlem at all. I suddenly became aware that, except for the waiters and members of the orchestra, I was the only Negro in the place.

After a while I left it and wandered about in a daze from night-club to night-club. I tried the Nest, Small's, Connie's Inn, the Capitol, Happy's, the Cotton Club. There was no mistake; my discovery was real and was repeatedly confirmed. No wonder my old crowd was not to be found in any of them. The best of Harlem's black cabarets have changed their names and turned white.

Such a discovery renders a moment's recollection irresistible. As irresistible as were the cabarets themselves to me seven or eight years ago. Just out of college in a town where cabarets were something only read about. A year of graduate work ahead. A Summer of rest at hand. Cabarets. Cabarets night after night, and one after another. There was no cover-charge then, and a fifteen-cent bottle of Whistle lasted an hour. It was just after the war[9]—the heroes were home—cabarets were the thing.

How the Lybia prospered in those happy days! It was the gathering place of the swellest Harlem set: if you didn't go to the Lybia, why, my dear, you just didn't belong. The people you saw at church in the morning you met at the Lybia at night. What romance in those war-tinged days and nights! Officers from Camp Upton,[1] with pretty maids from Brooklyn! Gay lieutenants, handsome captains—all whirling the lively onestep. Poor non-coms[2] completely ignored; what sensible girl wanted a corporal or even a sergeant? That white, old-fashioned house, standing alone in 138th street, near the corner of Seventh avenue—doomed to be torn down a few months thence—how it shook with the dancing and laughter of the dark merry crowds!

But the first place really popular with my friends was a Chinese restaurant in 136th street, which had been known as Hayne's Café and then became the Oriental. It occupied an entire house of three stories, and had carpeted floors and a quiet, superior air. There was excellent food and incredibly good tea and two unusual entertainers: a Cuban girl, who could so vary popular airs that they sounded like real music, and a slender little "brown" with a voice of silver and a way of singing a song that made you forget your food. One could dance in the Oriental if one liked, but one danced to a piano only, and wound one's way between linen-clad tables over velvety, noiseless floors.

Here we gathered: Fritz Pollard, All-American halfback,[3] selling Negro stock

---

8. Short for "ofays," a derogatory term for whites.    9. I.e., World War I. *Whistle:* a beverage.
1. A military facility near Manhattan.    2. Noncommissioned officers.
3. In 1916 at Brown University. He was the first black professional football player (Akron Indians, 1919).

to prosperous Negro physicians; Henry Creamer and Turner Layton, who had written "After You've Gone" and a dozen more songs, and were going to write "Strut, Miss Lizzie;" Paul Robeson,[4] All-American end, on the point of tackling law, quite unaware that the stage would intervene; Preacher Harry Bragg, Harvard Jimmie MacLendon and a half a dozen others. Here at a little table, just inside the door, Bert Williams[5] had supper every night, and afterward sometimes joined us upstairs and sang songs with us and lampooned the Actors' Equity Association, which had barred him because of his color. Never did white guests come to the Oriental except as guests of Negroes. But the manager soon was stricken with a psychosis of some sort, became a black Jew, grew himself a bushy, square-cut beard, donned a skull-cap and abandoned the Oriental. And so we were robbed of our favorite resort, and thereafter became mere rounders.

II

Such places, those real Negro cabarets that we met in the course of our rounds! There was Edmonds' in Fifth avenue at 130th street. It was a sure-enough honky-tonk, occupying the cellar of a saloon. It was the social center of what was then, and still is, Negro Harlem's kitchen. Here a tall brown-skin girl, unmistakably the one guaranteed in the song to make a preacher lay his Bible down, used to sing and dance her own peculiar numbers, vesting them with her own originality. She was known simply as Ethel,[6] and was a genuine drawing-card. She knew her importance, too. Other girls wore themselves ragged trying to rise above the inattentive din of conversation, and soon, literally, yelled themselves hoarse; eventually they lost whatever music there was in their voices and acquired that familiar throaty roughness which is so frequent among blues singers, and which, though admired as characteristically African, is as a matter of fact nothing but a form of chronic laryngitis. Other girls did these things, but not Ethel. She took it easy. She would stride with great leisure and self-assurance to the center of the floor, stand there with a half-contemptuous nonchalance, and wait. All would become silent at once. Then she'd begin her song, genuine blues, which, for all their humorous lines, emanated tragedy and heartbreak:

> Woke up this mawnin'
> The day was dawnin'
> And I was sad and blue, so blue, Lord—
> Didn' have nobody
> To tell my troubles to—

It was Ethel who first made popular the song, "Tryin' to Teach My Good Man Right from Wrong," in the slow, meditative measures in which she complained:

> I'm gettin' sick and tired of my railroad man
> I'm gettin' sick and tired of my railroad man—
> Can't get him when I want him—
> I get him when I can.

It wasn't long before this song-bird escaped her dingy cage. Her name is a vaude-ville attraction now, and she uses it all—Ethel Waters. Is there anyone who hasn't heard her sing "Shake That Thing!"?

---

4. A star football player at Rutgers before entering the Columbia University Law School in 1919 (1898–1976).   5. Popular black comedian and actor (c. 1874–1922).   6. Ethel Waters (1896–1977).

A second place was Connor's in 135th street near Lenox avenue. It was livelier, less languidly sensuous, and easier to breathe in than Edmonds'. Like the latter, it was in a basement, reached by the typical narrow, headlong stairway. One of the girls there specialized in the Jelly-Roll song, and mad habitués[7] used to fling petitions of greenbacks at her feet—pretty nimble feet they were, too—when she sang that she loved 'em but she had to turn 'em down. Over in a corner a group of 'fays would huddle and grin and think they were having a wild time. Slumming. But they were still very few in those days.

And there was the Oriental, which borrowed the name that the former Hayne's Café had abandoned. This was beyond Lenox avenue on the south side of 135th street. An upstairs place, it was nevertheless as dingy as any of the cellars, and the music fairly fought its way through the babble and smoke to one's ears, suffering in transit weird and incredible distortion. The prize pet here was a slim, little lad, unbelievably black beneath his high-brown powder, wearing a Mexican bandit costume with a bright-colored head-dress and sash. I see him now, poor kid, in all his glory, shimmying for enraptured women, who marveled at the perfect control of his voluntary abdominal tremors. He used to let the women reach out and put their hands on his sash to palpate[8] those tremors—for a quarter.

Finally, there was the Garden of Joy, an open-air cabaret between 138th and 139th streets in Seventh avenue, occupying a plateau high above the sidewalk—a large, well-laid, smooth wooden floor with tables and chairs and a tinny orchestra, all covered by a propped-up roof, that resembled an enormous lampshade, directing bright light downward and outward. Not far away the Abysinnian Church used to hold its Summer camp-meetings in a great round circus-tent. Night after night there would arise the mingled strains of blues and spirituals, those peculiarly Negro forms of song, the one secular and the other religious, but both born of wretchedness in travail, both with their soarings of exultation and sinkings of despair. I used to wonder if God, hearing them both, found any real distinction.

There were the Lybia, then, and Hayne's, Connor's, the Oriental, Edmonds' and the Garden of Joy, each distinctive, standing for a type, some living up to their names, others living down to them, but all predominantly black. Regularly I made the rounds among these places and saw only incidental white people. I have seen them occasionally in numbers, but such parties were out on a lark. They weren't in their natural habitat and they often weren't any too comfortable.

But what of Barron's, you say? Certainly they were at home there. Yes, I know about Barron's. I have been turned away from Barron's because I was too dark to be welcome. I have been a member of a group that was told, "No more room," when we could see plenty of room. Negroes were never actually wanted in Barron's save to work. Dark skins were always discouraged or barred. In short, the fact about Barron's was this: it simply wasn't a Negro cabaret; it was a cabaret run by Negroes for whites. It wasn't even on the lists of those who lived in Harlem—they'd no more think of going there than of going to the Winter Garden Roof.[9] But these other places were Negro through and through. Negroes supported them, not merely in now-and-then parties, but steadily, night after night.

---

7. Regular patrons.   8. Examine by touch.   9. A prominent Manhattan night club.

## IV

Some think it's just a fad. White people have always more or less sought Negro entertainment as diversion. The old shows of the early nineteen hundreds, Williams and Walker[1] and Cole and Johnson, are brought to mind as examples. The howling success—literally that—of J. Leubrie Hill[2] around 1913 is another; on the road his "Darktown Follies" played in numerous white theatres. In Harlem it played at the black Lafayette and, behold, the Lafayette temporarily became white. And so now, it is held, we are observing merely one aspect of a meteoric phenomenon, which simply presents itself differently in different circumstances: Roland Hayes and Paul Robeson, Jean Toomer and Walter White, Charles Gilpin[3] and Florence Mills—"Green Thursday," "Porgy," "In Abraham's Bosom"[4]—Negro spirituals—the startling new African groups proposed for the Metropolitan Museum of Art. Negro stock is going up, and everybody's buying.

## V

It may be a season's whim, then, this sudden, contagious interest in everything Negro. If so, when I go into a familiar cabaret, or the place where a familiar cabaret used to be, and find it transformed and relatively colorless, I may be observing just one form that the season's whim has taken.

But suppose it is a fad—to say that explains nothing. How came the fad? What occasions the focusing of attention on this particular thing—rounds up and gathers these seasonal whims, and centers them about the Negro? Cabarets are peculiar, mind you. They're not like theatres and concert halls. You don't just go to a cabaret and sit back and wait to be entertained. You get out on the floor and join the pow-wow and help entertain yourself. Granted that white people have long enjoyed the Negro entertainment as a diversion, is it not something different, something more, when they bodily throw themselves into Negro entertainment in cabarets? "Now Negroes go to their own cabarets to see how white people act."

And what do we see? Why, we see them actually playing Negro games. I watch them in that epidemic Negroism, the Charleston. I look on and envy them. They camel and fish-tail and turkey, they geche and black-bottom and scronch, they skate and buzzard and mess-around[5]—and they do them all better than I! This interest in the Negro is an active and participating interest. It is almost as if a traveler from the North stood watching an African tribe-dance, then suddenly found himself swept wildly into it, caught in its tidal rhythm.

Willingly would I be an outsider in this if I could know that I read it aright—that out of this change in the old familiar ways some finer thing may come. Is this interest akin to that of the Virginians on the veranda of a plantation's big-house—sitting genuinely spellbound as they hear the lugubrious strains floating up from the Negro quarters? Is it akin to that of the African explorer, Stanley,[6] leaving a village far behind, but halting in spite of himself to catch the boom of

---

1. Bert Williams and George Nash Walker formed an immensely popular vaudeville team in 1895.
2. Songwriter (1869–1916).
3. Actor (1878–1930). Hayes (1887–1976), singer. Toomer (1894–1967), author of *Cane*. White (1893–1955), writer and civil rights leader.
4. A 1926 play by white writer Paul Green. *Porgy* (1925) is a novel by Du Bose Heyward.
5. Various popular dances.   6. Sir Henry Morgan Stanley (1841–1904), English explorer.

its distant drum? Is it significant of basic human responses, the effect of which, once admitted, will extend far beyond cabarets? Maybe these Nordics at last have tuned in on our wave-length. Maybe they are at last learning to speak our language.

1927

## W. E. B. DU BOIS

## Two Novels

Nella Larsen[7] *Quicksand* (Knopf)
Claude McKay *Home to Harlem* (Harper and Brothers)

I have just read the last two novels of Negro America. The one I liked; the other I distinctly did not. I think that Mrs. Imes, writing under the pen name of Nella Larsen, has done a fine, thoughtful and courageous piece of work in her novel. It is, on the whole, the best piece of fiction that Negro America has produced since the heyday of Chesnutt, and stands easily with Jesse Fauset's *There is Confusion*,[8] in its subtle comprehension of the curious cross currents that swirl about the black American.

Claude McKay's *Home to Harlem*, on the other hand, for the most part nauseates me, and after the dirtier parts of its filth I feel distinctly like taking a bath. This does not mean that the book is wholly bad. McKay is too great a poet to make any complete failure in writing. There are bits of *Home to Harlem* beautiful and fascinating: the continued changes upon the theme of the beauty of colored skins; the portrayal of the fascination of their new yearnings for each other which Negroes are developing. The chief character, Jake, has something appealing, and the glimpses of the Haitian, Ray, have all the materials of a great piece of fiction.

But it looks as though, despite this, McKay has set out to cater for that prurient demand on the part of white folk for a portrayal in Negroes of that utter licentiousness which conventional civilization holds white folk back from enjoying—if enjoyment it can be called. That which a certain decadent section of the white American world, centered particularly in New York, longs for with fierce and unrestrained passions, it wants to see written out in black and white, and saddled on black Harlem. This demand, as voiced by a number of

The cover of the first edition of McKay's *Home to Harlem*

---

7. Nella Larsen (1891–1964), novelist. 8. A novel published in 1924.

New York publishers, McKay has certainly satisfied, and added much for good measure. He has used every art and emphasis to paint drunkenness, fighting, lascivious sexual promiscuity and utter absence of restraint in as bold and as bright colors as he can.

If this had been done in the course of a well-conceived plot or with any artistic unity, it might have been understood if not excused. But *Home to Harlem* is padded. Whole chapters here and there are inserted with no connection to the main plot, except that they are on the same dirty subject. As a picture of Harlem life or of Negro life anywhere, it is, of course, nonsense. Untrue, not so much as on account of its facts, but on account of its emphasis and glaring colors. I am sorry that the author of *Harlem Shadows* stooped to this. I sincerely hope that he will some day rise above it and give us in fiction the strong, well-knit as well as beautiful theme, that it seems to me he might do.

Nella Larsen on the other hand has seized an interesting character and fitted her into a close yet delicately woven plot. There is no "happy ending" and yet the theme is not defeatist like the work of Peterkin and Green.[9] Helga Crane sinks at last still master of her whimsical, unsatisfied soul. In the end she will be beaten down even to death but she never will utterly surrender to hypocrisy and convention. Helga is typical of the new, honest, young fighting Negro woman—the one on whom "race" sits negligibly and Life is always first and its wandering path is but darkened, not obliterated by the shadow of the Veil. White folk will not like this book. It is not near nasty enough for New York columnists. It is too sincere for the South and middle West. Therefore, buy it and make Mrs. Imes write many more novels.

1928

# ZORA NEALE HURSTON

## How It Feels to Be Colored Me

I am colored but I offer nothing in the way of extenuating circumstances except the fact that I am the only Negro in the United States whose grandfather on the mother's side was *not* an Indian chief.

I remember the very day that I became colored. Up to my thirteenth year I lived in the little Negro town of Eatonville, Florida. It is exclusively a colored town. The only white people I knew passed through the town going to or coming from Orlando. The native whites rode dusty horses, the Northern tourists chugged down the sandy village road in automobiles. The town knew the Southerners and never stopped cane chewing when they passed. But the Northerners were something else again. They were peered at cautiously from behind curtains by the timid. The more venturesome would come out on the porch to watch them go past and got just as much pleasure out of the tourists as the tourists got out of the village.

The front porch might seem a daring place for the rest of the town, but it

---

9. Paul Green (1894–1981), white dramatist who often dealt with interracial subjects. Julia Peterkin (1880–1961), white novelist of southern African American life.

Zora Neale Hurston

was a gallery seat for me. My favorite place was atop the gate-post. Proscenium box[1] for a born first-nighter. Not only did I enjoy the show, but I didn't mind the actors knowing that I liked it. I usually spoke to them in passing. I'd wave at them and when they returned my salute, I would say something like this: "Howdy-do-well-I-thank-you-where-you-goin'?" Usually automobile or the horse paused at this, and after a queer exchange of compliments, I would probably "go a piece of the way" with them, as we say in farthest Florida. If one of my family happened to come to the front in time to see me, of course negotiations would be rudely broken off. But even so, it is clear that I was the first "welcome-to-our-state" Floridian, and I hope the Miami Chamber of Commerce will please take notice.

During this period, white people differed from colored to me only in that they rode through town and never lived there. They liked to hear me "speak pieces" and sing and wanted to see me dance the parse-me-la, and gave me generously of their small silver for doing these things, which seemed strange to me for I wanted to do them so much that I needed bribing to stop. Only they didn't know it. The colored people gave no dimes. They deplored any joyful tendencies in me, but I was their Zora nevertheless. I belonged to them, to the nearby hotels, to the county—everybody's Zora.

But changes came in the family when I was thirteen, and I was sent to school in Jacksonville. I left Eatonville, the town of the oleanders, as Zora. When I disembarked from the river-boat at Jacksonville, she was no more. It seemed that I had suffered a sea change. I was not Zora of Orange County any more, I was now a little colored girl. I found it out in certain ways. In my heart as well as in the mirror, I became a fast[2] brown—warranted not to rub nor run.

But I am not tragically colored. There is no great sorrow dammed up in my soul, nor lurking behind my eyes. I do not mind at all. I do not belong to the sobbing school of Negrohood who hold that nature somehow has given them a lowdown dirty deal and whose feelings are all hurt about it. Even in the helter-skelter skirmish that is my life, I have seen that the world is to the strong regardless of a little pigmentation more or less. No, I do not weep at the world—I am too busy sharpening my oyster knife.[3]

Someone is always at my elbow reminding me that I am the grand-daughter of slaves. It fails to register depression with me. Slavery is sixty years in the past. The operation was successful and the patient is doing well, thank you. The ter-

---

1. The box seats in a theater on either side of and nearest to the stage.  2. Colorfast.
3. An allusion to Shakespeare's *The Merry Wives of Windsor* 2.2.4–5: "Why, then the world's mine oyster, / Which I with sword will open."

rible struggle that made me an American out of a potential slave said "On the line!" The Reconstruction said "Get set!"; and the generation before said "Go!" I am off to a flying start and I must not halt in the stretch to look behind and weep. Slavery is the price I paid for civilization, and the choice was not with me. It is a bully adventure and worth all that I have paid through my ancestors for it. No one on earth ever had a greater chance for glory. The world to be won and nothing to be lost. It is thrilling to think—to know that for any act of mine, I shall get twice as much praise or twice as much blame. It is quite exciting to hold the center of the national stage, with the spectators not knowing whether to laugh or to weep.

The position of my white neighbor is much more difficult. No brown specter pulls up a chair beside me when I sit down to eat. No dark ghost thrusts its leg against mine in bed. The game of keeping what one has is never so exciting as the game of getting.

I do not always feel colored. Even now I often achieve the unconscious Zora of Eatonville before the Hegira.[4] I feel most colored when I am thrown against a sharp white background.

For instance at Barnard. "Beside the waters of the Hudson" I feel my race. Among the thousand white persons, I am a dark rock surged upon, and overswept, but through it all, I remain myself. When covered by the waters, I am; and the ebb but reveals me again.

Sometimes it is the other way around. A white person is set down in our midst, but the contrast is just as sharp for me. For instance, when I sit in the drafty basement that is The New World Cabaret with a white person, my color comes. We enter chatting about any little nothing that we have in common and are seated by the jazz waiters. In the abrupt way that jazz orchestras have, this one plunges into a number. It loses no time in circumlocutions, but gets right down to business. It constricts the thorax and splits the heart with its tempo and narcotic harmonies. This orchestra grows rambunctious, rears on its hind legs and attacks the tonal veil with primitive fury, rending it, clawing it until it breaks through to the jungle beyond. I follow those heathen—follow them exultingly. I dance wildly inside myself; I yell within, I whoop; I shake my assegai[5] above my head, I hurl it true to the mark *yeeeeooww!* I am in the jungle and living in the jungle way. My face is painted red and yellow and my body is painted blue. My pulse is throbbing like a war drum. I want to slaughter something—give pain, give death to what, I do not know. But the piece ends. The men of the orchestra wipe their lips and rest their fingers. I creep back slowly to the veneer we call civilization with the last tone and find the white friend sitting motionless in his seat, smoking calmly.

"Good music they have here," he remarks, drumming the table with his fingertips.

Music. The great blobs of purple and red emotion have not touched him. He has only heard what I felt. He is far away and I see him but dimly across the ocean and the continent that have fallen between us. He is so pale with his whiteness then and I am *so* colored.

---

4. In Islam, Muhammad's emigration from Mecca to Medina in 622 C.E.; here, the journey to Jacksonville.
5. Spear.

At certain times I have no race, I am *me*. When I set my hat at a certain angle and saunter down Seventh Avenue, Harlem City, feeling as snooty as the lions in front of the Forty-Second Street Library,[6] for instance. So far as my feelings are concerned, Peggy Hopkins Joyce on the Boule Mich[7] with her gorgeous raiment, stately carriage, knees knocking together in a most aristocratic manner, has nothing on me. The cosmic Zora emerges. I belong to no race nor time. I am the eternal feminine with its string of beads.

I have no separate feeling about being an American citizen and colored. I am merely a fragment of the Great Soul that surges within the boundaries. My country, right or wrong.

Sometimes, I feel discriminated against, but it does not make me angry. It merely astonishes me. How *can* any deny themselves the pleasure of my company? It's beyond me.

But in the main, I feel like a brown bag of miscellany propped against a wall. Against a wall in company with other bags, white, red and yellow. Pour out the contents, and there is discovered a jumble of small things priceless and worthless. A first-water diamond,[8] an empty spool, bits of broken glass, lengths of string, a key to a door long since crumbled away, a rusty knife-blade, old shoes saved for a road that never was and never will be, a nail bent under the weight of things too heavy for any nail, a dried flower or two still a little fragrant. In your hand is the brown bag. On the ground before you is the jumble it held—so much like the jumble in the bags, could they be emptied, that all might be dumped in a single heap and the bags refilled without altering the content of any greatly. A bit of colored glass more or less would not matter. Perhaps that is how the Great Stuffer of Bags filled them in the first place—who knows?

1928

## LANGSTON HUGHES

### From *The Big Sea*

#### Harlem Literati

The summer of 1926, I lived in a rooming house on 137th Street, where Wallace Thurman and Harcourt Tynes[9] also lived. Thurman was then managing editor of the *Messenger*, a Negro magazine that had a curious career. It began by being very radical, racial, and socialistic, just after the war. I believe it received a grant from the Garland Fund[1] in its early days. Then it later became a kind of Negro society magazine and a plugger for Negro business, with photographs of prominent colored ladies and their nice homes in it. A. Phillip Randolph, now President of the Brotherhood of Sleeping Car Porters, Chandler Owen, and George

---

6. The headquarters of the New York Public Library.
7. The elegant Boulevard St. Michel in Paris. Peggy Hopkins Joyce was an American showgirl, actress, and celebrity (1893?–1957), famed as "the original gold digger" for her scandalous lifestyle.
8. A diamond of the highest quality.
9. A friend of Thurman's. *House on 137th Street:* the rooming house appears in Thurman's *Infants of the Spring* as "Niggerati Manor."  1. The American Fund for Public Service, established in 1920 by Charles Garland.

S. Schuyler were connected with it. Schuyler's editorials, à la Mencken,[2] were the most interesting things in the magazine, verbal brickbats that said sometimes one thing, sometimes another, but always vigorously. I asked Thurman what kind of magazine the *Messenger* was, and he said it reflected the policy of whoever paid off best at the time.

Anyway, the *Messenger* bought my first short stories. They paid me ten dollars a story. Wallace Thurman wrote me that they were very bad stories, but better than any others they could find, so he published them.

Thurman had recently come from California to New York. He was a strangely brilliant black boy, who had read everything, and whose critical mind could find something wrong with everything he read. I have no critical mind, so I usually either like a book or don't. But I am not capable of liking a book and then finding a million things wrong with it, too—as Thurman was capable of doing.

Thurman had read so many books because he could read eleven lines at a time. He would get from the library a great pile of volumes that would have taken me a year to read. But he would go through them in less than a week, and be able to discuss each one at great length with anybody. That was why, I suppose, he was later given a job as a reader at Macaulay's—the only Negro reader, so far as I know, to be employed by any of the larger publishing firms.

Later Thurman became a ghost writer for *True Story,* and other publications, writing under all sorts of fantastic names, like Ethel Belle Mandrake or Patrick Casey. He did Irish and Jewish and Catholic "true confessions." He collaborated with William Jordan Rapp[3] on plays and novels. Later he ghosted books. In fact, this quite dark young Negro is said to have written *Men, Women, and Checks.*

Wallace Thurman wanted to be a great writer, but none of his own work ever made him happy. *The Blacker the Berry,*[4] his first book, was an important novel on a subject little dwelt upon in Negro fiction—the plight of the very dark Negro woman, who encounters in some communities a double wall of color prejudice within and without the race. His play, *Harlem,* considerably distorted for box office purposes, was, nevertheless, a compelling study—and the only one in the theater—of the impact of Harlem on a Negro family fresh from the South. And his *Infants of the Spring,* a superb and bitter study of the bohemian fringe of Harlem's literary and artistic life, is a compelling book.

But none of these things pleased Wallace Thurman. He wanted to be a *very* great writer, like Gorki or Thomas Mann,[5] and he felt that he was merely a journalistic writer. His critical mind, comparing his pages to the thousands of other pages he had read, by Proust, Melville, Tolstoy, Galsworthy, Dostoyevski, Henry James, Sainte-Beuve, Taine, Anatole France,[6] found his own pages vastly

2. Henry Louis Mencken (1880–1956), prominent Baltimore essayist, critic, and editor who was a friend of Schuyler's. Randolph (1889–1976) and Owen (1889–1967), editors at the *Messenger,* who hired Schuyler as a writer in 1923. Schuyler (1895–1977), conservative black writer.
3. White playwright (1895–1942), editor of *True Story* magazine. The only work certain to be a collaboration of Thurman and Rapp is the play *Harlem* (1929).   4. Published in 1929.
5. German novelist (1875–1955). Maxim Gorki was the pen name of Russian writer Aleksey Maksimovich Pyeshkov (1868–1936).
6. Pen name of French novelist and essayist Jacques Antole Francois Thibault (1844–1924). Marcel Proust (1871–1922), French novelist. Herman Melville (1819–1891), U.S. writer. Leo Tolstoy (1828–1910), Russian novelist and social critic. John Galsworthy (1867–1933), English novelist. Fyodor Dostoyevski (1821–1881), Russian novelist. James (1843–1916), U.S. novelist and critic. Charles Augustin Sainte-Beuve (1804–1869), French critic and poet. Hippolyte Adolphe Taine (1828–1893), French critic and historian.

wanting. So he contented himself by writing a great deal for money, laughing bitterly at his fabulously concocted "true stories," creating two bad motion pictures[7] of the "Adults Only" type for Hollywood, drinking more and more gin, and then threatening to jump out of windows at people's parties and kill himself.

During the summer of 1926, Wallace Thurman, Zora Neale Hurston, Aaron Douglas, John P. Davis, Bruce Nugent, Gwendolyn Bennett,[8] and I decided to publish "a Negro quarterly of the arts" to be called *Fire*—the idea being that it would burn up a lot of the old, dead conventional Negro-white ideas of the past, *épater le bourgeois*[9] into a realization of the existence of the younger Negro writers and artists, and provide us with an outlet for publication not available in the limited pages of the small Negro magazines then existing, the *Crisis*, *Opportunity*, and the *Messenger*—the first two being house organs of inter-racial organizations, and the latter being God knows what.

Sweltering summer evenings we met to plan *Fire*. Each of the seven of us agreed to give fifty dollars to finance the first issue. Thurman was to edit it, John P. Davis to handle the business end, and Bruce Nugent to take charge of distribution. The rest of us were to serve as an editorial board to collect material, contribute our own work, and act in any useful way that we could. For artists and writers, we got along fine and there were no quarrels. But October came before we were ready to go to press. I had to return to Lincoln,[1] John Davis to Law School at Harvard, Zora Hurston to her studies at Barnard, from whence she went about Harlem with an anthropologist's ruler, measuring heads for Franz Boas.[2]

Only three of the seven had contributed their fifty dollars, but the others faithfully promised to send theirs out of tuition checks, wages, or begging. Thurman went on with the work of preparing the magazine. He got a printer. He planned the layout. It had to be on good paper, he said, worthy of the drawings of Aaron Douglas. It had to have beautiful type, worthy of the first Negro art quarterly. It had to be what we seven young Negroes dreamed our magazine would be—so in the end it cost almost a thousand dollars, and nobody could pay the bills.

I don't know how Thurman persuaded the printer to let us have all the copies to distribute, but he did. I think Alain Locke, among others, signed notes guaranteeing payments. But since Thurman was the only one of the seven of us with a regular job, for the next three or four years his checks were constantly being attached and his income seized to pay for *Fire*. And whenever I sold a poem, mine went there, too—to *Fire*.

None of the older Negro intellectuals would have anything to do with *Fire*. Dr. DuBois[3] in the *Crisis* roasted it. The Negro press called it all sorts of bad names, largely because of a green and purple story by Bruce Nugent, in the Oscar Wilde[4] tradition, which we had included. Rean Graves, the critic for the *Baltimore Afro-American*, began his review by saying: "I have just tossed the first issue of

---

7. *Tomorrow's Children* (1934) and *High School Girl* (1935).
8. Poet (1902–1981). Hurston (1891–1960), novelist and folklore collector. Douglas (1898–1979), artist. Davis (1905–1973), lawyer and prominent leftist. Nugent (1906–1987), illustrator and writer.
9. Shock the middle class (French). 1. I.e., Lincoln University in Pennsylvania.
2. German-born American anthropologist (1858–1942).
3. W. E. B. Du Bois (1868–1963), African American writer, editor of *Crisis*, and co-founder of the NAACP.
4. Irish playwright (1854–1900), a proponent of the Art for Art's Sake movement. *Green and purple story*: the first installment of a novel called *Smoke, Lilies and Jade*.

*Fire* into the fire." Commenting upon various of our contributors, he said: "Aaron Douglas who, in spite of himself and the meaningless grotesqueness of his creations, has gained a reputation as an artist, is permitted to spoil three perfectly good pages and a cover with his pen and ink hudge pudge. Countee Cullen has written a beautiful poem in his 'From a Dark Tower,' but tries his best to obscure the thought in superfluous sentences. Langston Hughes displays his usual ability to say nothing in many words."

So *Fire* had plenty of cold water thrown on it by the colored critics. The white critics (except for an excellent editorial in the *Bookman* for November, 1926) scarcely noticed it at all. We had no way of getting it distributed to bookstands or news stands. Bruce Nugent took it around New York on foot and some of the Greenwich Village bookshops put it on display, and sold it for us. But then Bruce, who had no job, would collect the money and, on account of salary, eat it up before he got back to Harlem.

Finally, irony of ironies, several hundred copies of *Fire* were stored in the basement of an apartment where an actual fire occurred and the bulk of the whole issue was burned up. Even after that Thurman had to go on paying the printer.

Now *Fire* is a collector's item, and very difficult to get, being mostly ashes.

That taught me a lesson about little magazines. But since white folks had them, we Negroes thought we could have one, too. But we didn't have the money.

Wallace Thurman laughed a long bitter laugh. He was a strange kind of fellow, who liked to drink gin, but *didn't* like to drink gin; who liked being a Negro, but felt it a great handicap; who adored bohemianism, but thought it wrong to be a bohemian. He liked to waste a lot of time, but he always felt guilty wasting time. He loathed crowds, yet he hated to be alone. He almost always felt bad, yet he didn't write poetry.

Once I told him if I could feel as bad as he did *all* the time, I would surely produce wonderful books. But he said you had to know how to *write*, as well as how to feel bad. I said I didn't have to know how to feel bad, because, every so often, the blues just naturally overtook me, like a blind beggar with an old guitar:

> You don't know,
> You don't know my mind—
> When you see me laughin',
> I'm laughin' to keep from cryin'.[5]

About the future of Negro literature Thurman was very pessimistic. He thought the Negro vogue had made us all too conscious of ourselves, had flattered and spoiled us, and had provided too many easy opportunities for some of us to drink gin and more gin, on which he thought we would always be drunk. With his bitter sense of humor, he called the Harlem literati, the "niggerati."

Of this "niggerati," Zora Neale Hurston was certainly the most amusing. Only to reach a wider audience, need she ever write books—because she is a perfect book of entertainment in herself. In her youth she was always getting scholarships and things from wealthy white people, some of whom simply paid her just to sit around and represent the Negro race for them, she did it in such a racy fashion. She was full of side-splitting anecdotes, humorous tales, and tragicomic

---

5. Hughes later titled a collection of his short stories *Laughing to Keep from Crying* (1952).

stories, remembered out of her life in the South as a daughter of a travelling minister of God. She could make you laugh one minute and cry the next. To many of her white friends, no doubt, she was a perfect "darkie," in the nice meaning they give the term—that is a naïve, childlike, sweet, humorous, and highly colored Negro.

But Miss Hurston was clever, too—a student who didn't let college give her a broad *a* and who had great scorn for all pretensions, academic or otherwise. That is why she was such a fine folk-lore collector,[6] able to go among the people and never act as if she had been to school at all. Almost nobody else could stop the average Harlemite on Lenox Avenue and measure his head with a strange-looking, anthropological device and not get bawled out for the attempt, except Zora, who used to stop anyone whose head looked interesting, and measure it.

When Miss Hurston graduated from Barnard she took an apartment in West 66th Street near the park, in that row of Negro houses there. She moved in with no furniture at all and no money, but in a few days friends had given her everything, from decorative silver birds, perched atop the linen cabinet, down to a footstool. And on Saturday night, to christen the place, she had a *hand*-chicken dinner, since she had forgotten to say she needed forks.

She seemed to know almost everybody in New York. She had been a secretary to Fannie Hurst,[7] and had met dozens of celebrities whose friendship she retained. Yet she was always having terrific ups-and-downs about money. She tells this story on herself, about needing a nickel to go downtown one day and wondering where on earth she would get it. As she approached the subway, she was stopped by a blind beggar holding out his cup.

"Please help the blind! Help the blind! A nickel for the blind!"

"I need money worse than you today," said Miss Hurston, taking five cents out of his cup. "Lend me this! Next time, I'll give it back." And she went on downtown.

Harlem was like a great magnet for the Negro intellectual, pulling him from everywhere. Or perhaps the magnet was New York—but once in New York, he had to live in Harlem, for rooms were hardly to be found elsewhere unless one could pass for white or Mexican or Eurasian and perhaps live in the Village—which always seemed to me a very arty locale, in spite of the many real artists and writers who lived there. Only a few of the New Negroes lived in the Village, Harlem being their real stamping ground.

The wittiest of these New Negroes of Harlem, whose tongue was flavored with the sharpest and saltiest humor, was Rudolph Fisher, whose stories appeared in the *Atlantic Monthly*. His novel, *Walls of Jericho*,[8] captures but slightly the raciness of his own conversation. He was a young medical doctor and X-ray specialist, who always frightened me a little, because he could think of the most incisively clever things to say—and I could never think of anything to answer. He and Alain Locke together were great for intellectual wise-cracking. The two would fling big and witty words about with such swift and punning innuendo that an ordinary mortal just sat and looked wary for fear of being caught in a net of witticisms beyond his cultural ken. I used to wish I could talk like Rudolph Fisher. Besides being a good writer, he was an excellent singer, and had sung with Paul Robeson

---

6. Hurston published two such collections: *Mules and Men* (1935) and *Tell My Horse* (1938).
7. American fiction writer (1899–1968).   8. Published in 1928.

during their college days. But I guess Fisher was too brilliant and too talented to stay long on this earth. During the same week, in December, 1934, he and Wallace Thurman both died.

Thurman died of tuberculosis in the charity ward at Bellevue Hospital, having just flown back to New York from Hollywood.

1940

## SUGGESTIONS FOR WRITING

1. Many poets of the Harlem Renaissance made extensive use of the sonnet form; this chapter contains such examples as Countee Cullen's "From the Dark Tower," Helene Johnson's "Sonnet to a Negro in Harlem," and Claude McKay's "If We Must Die." Write an essay in which you compare and contrast some of the sonnets written during the Harlem Renaissance. How do different approaches to the sonnet form signal different thematic concerns?
2. In 1921, James Weldon Johnson wrote of "the need for Aframerican poets in the United States to work out a new and distinctive form of expression." Judging from the selections in this chapter, do you think that poets such as Langston Hughes and Claude McKay met the need articulated by Johnson? Write an essay in which you examine both traditionalism and innovation in the poetry of the Harlem Renaissance. How distinct are the works of black and white poets during this period?
3. In *The New Negro*, Alain Locke declared, "In Harlem, Negro life is seizing upon its first chances for group expression and self-determination." Do poems such as Arna Bontemps's "A Black Man Talks of Reaping," Angelina Grimke's "The Black Finger," and Langston Hughes's "I, Too" achieve a common social consciousness—Locke's "group expression"? What political effect do you think these poets hoped to achieve through their work? Write an essay in which you analyze the political ideas in the poetry of the Harlem Renaissance.
4. Some poems of the Harlem Renaissance—Langston Hughes's "The Weary Blues" and Claude McKay's "The Harlem Dancer," for example—are explicitly about music; others, such as Countee Cullen's "Saturday's Child," with its ballad form, and Angelina Grimke's improvisational "Tenebris," take a distinctly musical approach. Write an essay about the interplay of words and music in the poetry of this period.
5. In his review of Claude McKay's *Home to Harlem*, W. E. B. Du Bois laments that McKay "stooped" to betraying the black cause by portraying "drunkenness, fighting, lascivious sexual promiscuity and utter absence of restraint" in his novel's black characters. Do writers have a particular duty to portray positive role models? Do writers from ethnic groups engaged in social struggle have a particular duty to participate in that struggle? Citing evidence from the selections in this chapter, write an essay in which you weigh the demands of artistic duty against the demands of artistic freedom.
6. What does it mean for a group of artists to be considered a "school"—that is, a group whose work appears to share common themes, styles, and goals? Write an essay in which you discuss whether or not the writers of the Harlem Renaissance spoke with a unified voice. Does a grouping like "the Harlem Renaissance" help our understanding of this period and the art it produced, or does it obscure the individual achievements of the artists themselves?

# 25. CRITICAL CONTEXTS: A POETRY CASEBOOK

As the previous context chapters have suggested, poems draw on all kinds of earlier texts, experiences, and events. But they also produce new contexts of discussion and interpretation, ongoing conversations about the poems themselves. Different readers of poems see different things in them, so naturally a variety of interpretations and evaluations develop around any poem that is read repeatedly by various readers. Many of those interpretations are published in specialized journals and books (the selections that follow are all reprinted from published sources), and a kind of dialogue develops among readers, producing a body of commentary about the poem. Professional interpreters of texts are called **literary critics,** and the textual analysis they provide is called **criticism**—not because their work is necessarily negative or corrective, but because they ask hard, analytical, "critical" questions and interpret texts through a wide variety of literary, historical, biographical, psychological, aesthetic, moral, political, or social perspectives.

Your own interpretive work may seem to you more private and far removed from such "professional" writing about poems. But once you engage in class discussion with your teacher or even talk informally with a fellow student about a poem, you are in effect practicing your own literary criticism—offering comments, analyzing, judging, putting the poem into some kind of perspective that makes it more knowable and understandable to yourself or to other readers. You are, in effect, joining the ongoing conversation about the poem. The accumulated criticism on any particular poem is, in fact, basically just public conversation and discussion—give and take, competing interpretations, accumulation of relevant facts and information—on the topic of how that poem should be experienced, interpreted, and evaluated. And when you *write* about the poem, you may often engage specifically the opinions of others—your teacher, fellow students, or published "criticism." You may not have the experience or specific expertise of professional critics, but you can modify or answer the work of others and use it in your own work.

There are many different ways to engage literary criticism and put it to work for you. The most common is to draw on published work for specific information about the poem: glossings of particular terms; explanations of references or situations you don't recognize; accounts of how, when, and under what circumstances the poem was written. Another common use of such material is as a springboard for your own interpretation, either building upon what someone else has said or, if you disagree, using it as a point of departure to launch a different view. In either case, your own paper may readily develop out of your reading or out of a class lecture or class discussion, which you may draw on just as you would written accounts. When you use the work of others, you must give full credit, carefully detailing the source of all direct quotations and all borrowed ideas. You must always tell your reader exactly how to find the material you have quoted or summarized. Usually, you do this through careful notes and a list of citations (that is, a bibliography) at the end of your paper. Your instructor will guide you to handbooks—for example, the *MLA Handbook* or *The Chicago Manual of Style*—that demonstrate how to cite each item in the appropriate way.

It can seem intimidating to become involved in critical dialogue, especially with those who are "authorities" or "experts" whose work has been published and widely read. But your own reading experience gives you a legitimate perspective, too, and often you can sharpen your skills by articulating your views against those with extensive interpretive experience. Besides, as you will quickly discover when you read several critical pieces on a particular poem, even the experts disagree. In fact, one measure of a poem's greatness is its ability to stimulate disagreement and a broad range of interpretation.

Procedurally, it is usually best to do your own extensive analysis of a poem *before* consulting what other critics have said. That way, you can confront other views from a firm (if tentative) position. You always want to take in new information and to challenge both your first impressions and your considered analyses—but don't be too quick to adopt somebody else's ideas. The best way to test the views of others is to compare them critically to your own conclusions, which you might then want to supplement, refine, extend, or even scrap altogether. In other words, proceed just as you have been proceeding—asking the questions you have learned to ask, sorting out the evidence you have noticed, and moving toward an integrated interpretation of the poem.

Before you read the criticism on Sylvia Plath's "Daddy" reprinted in this chapter, carefully read the poem itself several times. Ask all the analytical questions you have found useful in other cases: Who is speaking? To whom? When? Under what conditions? What is the full dramatic situation behind the poem? What kind of language does the poem use? To what effect? How does the poem use metaphor? allusion? historical reference? What strategies of rhythm and sound does the poem use? To what effect? What is the poem's tone? In what ways is this poem like other poems or other texts on similar topics? When was the poem written? What do you know about the person who wrote the poem? In what ways is this poem like others you have read by this poet or by this poet's contemporaries? How do the poem's themes and attitudes reflect the culture and times in which it was written?

**SYLVIA PLATH**

## *Daddy*[1]

    You do not do, you do not do
    Any more, black shoe
    In which I have lived like a foot
    For thirty years, poor and white,
5  Barely daring to breathe or Achoo.

---

1. First published in *Ariel*, a volume of poems that appeared two years after Plath's suicide.

Daddy, I have had to kill you.
You died before I had time—
Marble-heavy, a bag full of God,
Ghastly statue with one gray toe[2]
10 Big as a Frisco seal

And a head in the freakish Atlantic
Where it pours bean green over blue
In the waters off beautiful Nauset.[3]
I used to pray to recover you.
15 Ach, du.[4]

In the German tongue, in the Polish town[5]
Scraped flat by the roller
Of wars, wars, wars.
But the name of the town is common.
20 My Polack friend

Says there are a dozen or two.
So I never could tell where you
Put your foot, your root,
I never could talk to you.
25 The tongue stuck in my jaw.

It stuck in a barb wire snare.
Ich,[6] ich, ich, ich,
I could hardly speak.
I thought every German was you.
30 And the language obscene

An engine, an engine
Chuffing me off like a Jew.
A Jew to Dachau, Auschwitz, Belsen.[7]
I began to talk like a Jew.
35 I think I may well be a Jew.

The snows of the Tyrol, the clear beer of Vienna[8]
Are not very pure or true.
With my gypsy-ancestress and my weird luck
And my Taroc[9] pack and my Taroc pack
40 I may be a bit of a Jew.

I have always been scared of *you*,
With your Luftwaffe,[1] your gobbledygoo.
And your neat moustache

---

2. Otto Plath, Sylvia's father, lost a toe to gangrene that resulted from diabetes.   3. An inlet on Cape Cod.
4. Oh, you (German). Plath often portrays herself as Jewish and her oppressors as German.
5. Otto Plath, an ethnic German, was born in Grabow, Poland.   6. German for "I."
7. Sites of World War II Nazi death camps.
8. The snow in the Tyrol (an Alpine region in Austria and northern Italy) is, legendarily, as pure as the beer is clear in Vienna.   9. Tarot, playing cards used mainly for fortune-telling.
1. The German air force.

And your Aryan[2] eye, bright blue.
45 Panzer[3]-man, panzer-man, O You—

Not God but a swastika
So black no sky could squeak through.
Every woman adores a Fascist,
The boot in the face, the brute
50 Brute heart of a brute like you.

You stand at the blackboard, daddy,
In the picture I have of you,
A cleft in your chin instead of your foot
But no less a devil for that, no not
55 Any less the black man who

Bit my pretty red heart in two.
I was ten when they buried you.
At twenty I tried to die
And get back, back, back to you.
60 I thought even the bones would do.

But they pulled me out of the sack,
And they stuck me together with glue.[4]
And then I knew what to do.
I made a model of you,
65 A man in black with a Meinkampf[5] look

And a love of the rack and the screw.
And I said I do, I do.
So daddy, I'm finally through.
The black telephone's off at the root,
70 The voices just can't worm through.

If I've killed one man, I've killed two—
The vampire who said he was you
And drank my blood for a year,
Seven years, if you want to know.
75 Daddy, you can lie back now.

There's a stake in your fat black heart
And the villagers never liked you.
They are dancing and stamping on you.
They always *knew* it was you.
80 Daddy, daddy, you bastard, I'm through.

1966

---

2. People of Germanic lineage, often blond-haired and blue-eyed.
3. Literally "panther," the Nazi tank corps' term for an armored vehicle.
4. An allusion to Plath's recovery from her first suicide attempt.
5. The title of Adolf Hitler's autobiography and manifesto (1925–27); German for "my struggle."

Once you have a "reading" of your own and have made notes about your conclusions, look at the selections that follow. You can read them in a variety of ways:

- skim them all quickly, and look for things that surprise you or that provide you with specific challenges; or
- read each critical piece carefully, one by one, and keep close track of all the things with which you agree and (even more important) of those things with which you disagree; or
- look specifically for facts or apparently crucial information new to you, examine and question the information carefully, and see how it affects the interpretation you have previously decided on; or
- look for points of disagreement in the different interpretations, make a list of the most important issues raised, and look for the crucial parts of the poem where the basis for these disagreements occurs.

You will also find your own ways to respond to and use the various critical views you come upon here. Working the views of others into your own arguments and your own writing is complicated; while supporting your own conclusions, you must be fair to what others say. But learning to use the facts, opinions, and interpretations of others will clarify your own thoughts, hone or add to your analytical skills, and deepen your views. And participating in the larger conversation about a specific poem—or about poetry in general—will help you read, respond, and write more effectively.

Sylvia Plath

Sylvia Plath's father, Otto Plath

## GEORGE STEINER

### From *Dying Is an Art**

[N]o group of poems since Dylan Thomas' *Deaths and Entrances* has had as vivid and disturbing an impact on English critics and readers as has *Ariel*. Sylvia Plath's last poems have already passed into legend as both representative of our present tone of emotional life and unique in their implacable, harsh brilliance. Those among the young who read new poetry will know "Daddy," "Lady Lazarus," and "Death & Co." almost by heart, and reference to Sylvia Plath is constant where poetry and the conditions of its present existence are discussed.

The spell does not lie wholly in the poems themselves. The suicide of Sylvia Plath at the age of thirty-one in 1963, and the personality of this young woman who had come from Massachusetts to study and live in England (where she married Ted Hughes, himself a gifted poet), are vital parts of it. To those who knew her and to the greatly enlarged circle who were electrified by her last poems and sudden death, she had come to signify the specific honesties and risks of the poet's condition. Her personal style, and the price in private harrowing she so obviously paid to achieve the intensity and candor of her principal poems, have taken on their own dramatic authority.

All this makes it difficult to judge the poems. I mean that the vehemence and intimacy of the verse is such as to constitute a very powerful rhetoric of sincerity. The poems play on our nerves with their own proud nakedness, making claims so immediate and sharply urged that the reader flinches, embarrassed by the routine discretions and evasions of his own sensibility. Yet if these poems are to take life among us, if they are to be more than exhibits in the history of modern psychological stress, they must be read with all the intelligence and scruple we can muster. They are too honest, they have cost too much, to be yielded to myth.

... It requires no biographical impertinence to realize that Sylvia Plath's life was harried by bouts of physical pain, that she sometimes looked on the accumulated exactions of her own nerve and body as "a trash To annihilate each decade." She was haunted by the piecemeal, strung-together mechanics of the flesh, by what could be so easily broken and then mended with such searing ingenuity. The hospital ward was her exemplary ground:

> My patent leather overnight case like a black pillbox,
> My husband and child smiling out of the family photo;
> Their smiles catch onto my skin, little smiling hooks.

This brokenness, so sharply feminine and contemporary, is, I think, her principal realization. It is by the graphic expression she gave to it that she will be judged and remembered. Sylvia Plath carries forward, in an intensely womanly and aggravated note, from Robert Lowell's *Life Studies*, a book that obviously had a great impact on her. This new frankness of women about the specific hurts and tangles of their nervous-physiological makeup is as vital to the poetry of

---

*From George Steiner, *Language and Silence: Essays on Language, Literature, and the Inhuman* (1967; New York: Atheneum, 1974), pp. 295–302.

Sylvia Plath as it is to the tracts of Simone de Beauvoir or to the novels of Edna O'Brien and Brigid Brophy. Women speak out as never before:

> The womb
> Rattles its pod, the moon
> Discharges itself from the tree with nowhere to go.
> ("Childless Woman")

> They have swabbed me clear of my loving associations.
> Scared and bare on the green plastic-pillowed trolley....
> ("Tulips")

It is difficult to think of a precedent to the fearful close of "Medusa" (the whole poem is extraordinary):

> I shall take no bite of your body,
> Bottle in which I live,
> Ghastly Vatican.
> I am sick to death of hot salt.
> Green as eunuchs, your wishes
> Hiss at my sin.
> Off, off, eely tentacle!
> There is nothing between us.

The ambiguity and dual flash of insight in this final line are of a richness and obviousness that only a very great poem can carry off.

The progress registered between the early and the mature poems is one of concretion. The general Gothic means with which Sylvia Plath was so fluently equipped become singular to herself and therefore fiercely honest. What had been style passes into need. It is the need of a superbly intelligent, highly literate young woman to cry out about her especial being, about the tyrannies of blood and gland, of nervous spasm and sweating skin, the rankness of sex and childbirth in which a woman is still compelled to be wholly of her organic condition. Where Emily Dickinson could—indeed was obliged to—shut the door on the riot and humiliations of the flesh, thus achieving her particular dry lightness, Sylvia Plath "fully assumed her own condition." This alone would assure her of a place in modern literature. But she took one step further, assuming a burden that was not naturally or necessarily hers.

Born in Boston in 1932 of German and Austrian parents, Sylvia Plath had no personal, immediate contact with the world of the concentration camps. I may be mistaken, but so far as I know there was nothing Jewish in her background. But her last, greatest poems culminate in an act of identification, of total communion with those tortured and massacred. The poet sees herself on

> An engine, an engine
> Chuffing me off like a Jew.
> A Jew to Dachau, Auschwitz, Belsen.
> I began to talk like a Jew.
> I think I may well be a Jew.

> The snows of the Tyrol, the clear beer of Vienna
> Are not very pure or true.
> With my gypsy ancestress and my weird luck

> And my Taroc pack and my Taroc pack
> I may be a bit of a Jew.

Distance is no help; nor the fact that one is "guilty of nothing." The dead men cry out of the yew hedges. The poet becomes the loud cry of their choked silence:

> Herr God, Herr Lucifer
> Beware
> Beware.
> Out of the ash
> I rise with my red hair
> And I eat men like air.

Here the almost surrealistic wildness of the gesture is kept in place by the insistent obviousness of the language and beat; a kind of Hieronymus Bosch[1] nursery rhyme.

Sylvia Plath is only one of a number of young contemporary poets, novelists, and playwrights, themselves in no way implicated in the actual holocaust, who have done most to counter the general inclination to forget the death camps. Perhaps it is only those who had no part in the events who *can* focus on them rationally and imaginatively; to those who experienced the thing, it has lost the hard edges of possibility, it has stepped outside the real.

Committing the whole of her poetic and formal authority to the metaphor, to the mask of language, Sylvia Plath *became* a woman being transported to Auschwitz on the death trains. The notorious shards of massacre seemed to enter into her own being:

> A cake of soap,
> A wedding ring,
> A gold filling.

In "Daddy" she wrote one of the very few poems I know of in any language to come near the last horror. It achieves the classic act of generalization, translating a private, obviously intolerable hurt into a code of plain statement, of instantaneously public images which concern us all. It is the "Guernica"[2] of modern poetry. And it is both histrionic and, in some ways, "arty," as is Picasso's outcry.

Are these final poems entirely legitimate? In what sense does anyone, himself uninvolved and long after the event, commit a subtle larceny when he invokes the echoes and trappings of Auschwitz and appropriates an enormity of ready emotion to his own private design? Was there latent in Sylvia Plath's sensibility, as in that of many of us who remember only by fiat of imagination, a fearful envy, a dim resentment at not having been there, of having missed the rendezvous with hell? In "Lady Lazarus" and "Daddy" the realization seems to me so complete, the sheer rawness and control so great, that only irresistible need could have brought it off. These poems take tremendous risks, extending Sylvia Plath's essentially austere manner to the very limit. They are a bitter triumph, proof of the capacity of poetry to give to reality the greater permanence of the imagined. She could not return from them.

---

1. Dutch artist (c. 1450–c. 1516) whose nightmarish paintings are filled with obscure symbolism.
2. Picasso's famous painting (1937) depicting the brutalities of war.

IRVING HOWE

## From *The Plath Celebration: A Partial Dissent**

Sylvia Plath's most famous poem, adored by many sons and daughters, is "Daddy." It is a poem with an affecting theme, the feelings of the speaker as she regathers the pain of her father's premature death and her persuasion that he has betrayed her by dying:

> I was ten when they buried you.
> At twenty I tried to die
> And get back, back, back to you.

In the poem Sylvia Plath identifies the father (we recall his German birth) with the Nazis ("Panzer-man, panzer-man, O You") and flares out with assaults for which nothing in the poem (nor, so far as we know, in Sylvia Plath's own life) offers any warrant: "A cleft in your chin instead of your foot / But no less a devil for that...." Nor does anything in the poem offer warrant, other than the free-flowing hysteria of the speaker, for the assault of such lines as, "There's a stake in your fat black heart / And the villagers never liked you." Or for the snappy violence of

> Every woman adores a Fascist,
> The boot in the face, the brute
> Brute heart of a brute like you.

What we have here is a revenge fantasy, feeding upon filial love-hatred, and thereby mostly of clinical interest. But seemingly aware that the merely clinical can't provide the materials for a satisfying poem, Sylvia Plath tries to enlarge upon the personal plight, give meaning to the personal outcry, by fancying the girl as victim of a Nazi father:

> An engine, an engine
> Chuffing me off like a Jew.
> A Jew to Dachau, Auschwitz, Belsen.
> I began to talk like a Jew.
> I think I may well be a Jew.

The more sophisticated admirers of this poem may say that I fail to see it as a dramatic presentation, a monologue spoken by a disturbed girl not necessarily to be identified with Sylvia Plath, despite the similarities of detail between the events of the poem and the events of her life. I cannot accept this view. The personal-confessional element, strident and undisciplined, is simply too obtrusive to suppose the poem no more than a dramatic picture of a certain style of disturbance. If, however, we did accept such a reading of "Daddy," we would fatally narrow its claims to emotional or moral significance, for we would be confining it to a mere vivid imagining of pathological state. That, surely, is not how its admirers really take the poem.

---

* From Irving Howe, *The Critical Point of Literature and Culture* (1973; New York: Horizon Press, 1977), pp. 231–33.

It is clearly not how the critic George Steiner takes the poem when he calls it "the 'Guernica' of modern poetry." But then, in an astonishing turn, he asks: "In what sense does anyone, himself uninvolved and long after the event, commit a subtle larceny when he invokes the echoes and trappings of Auschwitz and appropriates an enormity of ready emotion to his own private design?" The question is devastating to his early comparison with "Guernica." Picasso's painting objectifies the horrors of Guernica, through the distancing of art; no one can suppose that he shares or participates in them. Plath's poem aggrandizes on the "enormity of ready emotion" invoked by references to the concentration camps, in behalf of an ill-controlled if occasionally brilliant outburst. There is something monstrous, utterly disproportionate, when tangled emotions about one's father are deliberately compared with the historical fate of the European Jews; something sad, if the comparison is made spontaneously. "Daddy" persuades once again, through the force of negative example, of how accurate T. S. Eliot was in saying, "The more perfect the artist, the more completely separate in him will be the man who suffers and the mind which creates."

## A. ALVAREZ

### From *Sylvia Plath**

The reasons for Sylvia Plath's images are always there, though sometimes you have to work hard to find them. She is, in short, always in intelligent control of her feelings. Her work bears out her theories:

> I think my poems come immediately out of the sensuous and emotional experiences I have, but I must say I cannot sympathise with these cries from the heart that are informed by nothing except a needle or a knife or whatever it is. I believe that one should be able to control and manipulate experiences, even the most terrifying—like madness, being tortured, this kind of experience—and one should be able to manipulate these experiences with an informed and intelligent mind. I think that personal experience shouldn't be a kind of shut box and mirror-looking narcissistic experience. I believe it should be generally relevant, to such things as Hiroshima and Dachau, and so on.

It seems to me that it was only by her determination both to face her most inward and terrifying experiences and to use her intelligence in doing so—so as not to be overwhelmed by them—that she managed to write these extraordinary last poems, which are at once deeply autobiographical and yet detached, generally relevant.

"Lady Lazarus" is a stage further on from "Fever 103°"; its subject is the total purification of achieved death. It is also far more intimately concerned with the drift of Sylvia Plath's life. The deaths of Lady Lazarus correspond to her own crises: the first just after her father died, the second when she had her nervous breakdown, the third perhaps a presentiment of the death that was shortly to come. Maybe this closeness of the subject helped make the poem so direct. The

---

* From A. Alvarez, *Beyond All This Fiddle* (London: Penguin, 1968), pp. 56–57.

details don't clog each other: they are swept forward by the current of immediate feeling, marshalled by it and ordered. But what is remarkable about the poem is the objectivity with which she handles such personal material. She is not just talking about her own private suffering. Instead, it is the very closeness of her pain which gives it a general meaning; through it she assumes the suffering of all the modern victims. Above all, she becomes an imaginary Jew. I think this is a vitally important element in her work. For two reasons. First, because anyone whose subject is suffering has a ready-made modern example of hell on earth in the concentration camps. And what matters in them is not so much the physical torture—since sadism is general and perennial—but the way modern, as it were industrial, techniques can be used to destroy utterly the human identity. Individual suffering can be heroic provided it leaves the person who suffers a sense of his own individuality—provided, that is, there is an illusion of choice remaining to him. But when suffering is mass-produced, men and women become as equal and identity-less as objects on an assembly line, and nothing remains—certainly no values, no humanity. This anonymity of pain, which makes all dignity impossible, was Sylvia Plath's subject. Second, she seemed convinced, in these last poems, that the root of her suffering was the death of her father, whom she loved, who abandoned her, and who dragged her after him into death. And in her fantasies her father was pure German, pure Aryan, pure anti-semite.

It all comes together in the most powerful of her last poems, "Daddy"..., about which she wrote the following bleak note:

> The poem is spoken by a girl with an Electra complex. Her father died while she thought he was God. Her case is complicated by the fact that her father was also a Nazi and her mother very possibly part Jewish. In the daughter the two strains marry and paralyse each other—she has to act out the awful little allegory once over before she is free of it.[1]

... What comes through most powerfully, I think, is the terrible *unforgivingness* of her verse, the continual sense not so much of violence—although there is a good deal of that—as of violent resentment that this should have been done to *her*. What she does in the poem is, with a weird detachment, to turn the violence against herself so as to show that she can equal her oppressors with her self-inflicted oppression. And this is the strategy of the concentration camps. When suffering is there whatever you do, by inflicting it upon yourself you achieve your identity, you set yourself free.

Yet the tone of the poem, like its psychological mechanisms, is not single or simple, and she uses a great deal of skill to keep it complex. Basically, her trick is to tell this horror story in a verse form as insistently jaunty and ritualistic as a nursery rhyme. And this helps her to maintain towards all the protagonists—her father, her husband and herself—a note of hard and sardonic anger, as though she were almost amused that her own suffering should be so extreme, so grotesque. The technical psychoanalytic term for this kind of insistent gaiety to protect you from what, if faced nakedly, would be insufferable, is "manic defence." But what, in a neurotic, is a means of avoiding reality can become, for an artist, a source of creative strength, a way of handling the unhandleable, and

---

1. From the introductory notes to "New Poems," a reading prepared for the BBC Third Programme but never broadcast [Alvarez's note].

presenting the situation in all its fullness. When she first read me the poem a few days after she wrote it, she called it a piece of "light verse." It obviously isn't, yet equally obviously it also isn't the racking personal confession that a mere description or précis of it might make it sound.

Yet neither is it unchangingly vindictive or angry. The whole poem works on one single, returning note and rhyme, echoing from start to finish:

> You do not do, you do not do . . .
> . . . I used to pray to recover you.
> Ach, du . . .

There is a kind of cooing tenderness in this which complicates the other, more savage note of resentment. It brings in an element of pity, less for herself and her own suffering than for the person who made her suffer. Despite everything, "Daddy" is a love poem.

## JUDITH KROLL

### From *Rituals of Exorcism: "Daddy"*\*

Poems explicitly about the protagonist's father, read in order of composition, show that the attitude toward him evolves from nostalgic mournfulness, regret, and guilt, to resentment and a bitter resolve to break his hold on her. . . .

The recital of the myth in "Daddy" ends in a ritual intended to cancel the earlier "sacred marriage" which has suffocated her:

> You do not do, you do not do
> Any more, black shoe
> In which I have lived like a foot
> For thirty years, poor and white,
> Barely daring to breathe or Achoo.[1]

In this image of passive and victimized domesticity, the speaker implicitly compares her past self to the "old woman who lived in a shoe" who "didn't know what to do"; now, however, she makes it clear that she does know what to do.

As a preamble to the exorcism, she recounts the development of her father's image, beginning with his earlier status as a "bag full of God, / Ghastly statue" (that is, a godlike colossus—mentioning the ghastliness, the ghostly, deathlike, pallid nature of the statue, anticipates the inversions to come) and then introduces the revised images: "panzer-man," "swastika," "Fascist," "brute," "devil," "bastard." Daddy must be cast in this new light, transformed from god to devil, if he is to be successfully expelled, but there must also be some real basis for it. To be effectively exposed, he must first appear as godly. But the speaker soon

---

\* From Judith Kroll, *Chapters in a Mythology: The Poetry of Sylvia Plath* (New York: Harper & Row, 1976), pp. 122–26. Unless otherwise specified, all notes are Kroll's.
1. When Plath introduced "Daddy" as being about "a girl with an Electra complex" (with, in effect, the female version of an Oedipus complex), she gave a clue to what may be a play on words in the poem. "Oedipus" means "swell-foot," and therefore the speaker's identification of herself as a "foot" may be a private way of saying "I am Oedipus" and incorporating into the poem an allusion to the Electra complex.

shows that she now attributes his godliness in part to his authoritarianism and personal inaccessibility—qualities which became intensified through his death, and which later became transferred to "a model of you"—her husband. Both men are really variations on a familiar type, even a stereotype: the "god" who, like Marco the "woman-hater" in *The Bell Jar*, is "chock-full of power" ... over women precisely because of his deadness, or ultimate inaccessibility, to them. Loving a man literally or metaphorically dead ("The face that lived in this mirror is the face of a dead man" ["The Courage of Shutting-Up"]) becomes a kind of persecution or punishment; and so, by the end of the incantation, Daddy deserves to be cast out. The "black telephone ... off at the root," conveys the finality of the intended exorcism.

The "venomousness," ambiguous from the beginning, is not the whole story. "Daddy" is not primarily a poem of "father-hatred" or abuse as Robert Lowell, Elizabeth Hardwick, and others have contended. The need for exorcising her father's ghost lies, after all, in the extremity of her attachment to him. Alvarez very justly remarks that

> The whole poem works on one single, returning note and rhyme, echoing from start to finish:
>
> > You do not do, you do not do ...
> > ... I used to pray to recover you.
> > Ach, du ...
>
> There is a kind of cooing tenderness in this which complicates the other, more savage note of resentment. It brings in an element of pity, less for herself and her own suffering than for the person who made her suffer. Despite everything, "Daddy" is a love poem.[2]

The love is not merely conveyed by the rhythm and sound of the poem, it is a necessary part of the poem's meaning, a part of the logic of its act.

The exorcism serves another purpose because through it she attempts to reject the pattern of being abandoned and made to suffer by a god, a man who is "chock-full of power": she creates "a model of you"—an image of her father—and marries this proxy. Then she kills both father and husband at once, magically using each as the other's representative.[3] Each death entails that of the other: the stake in her father's heart also kills the "vampire who said he was you"; and the killing of her marriage (for which she now claims to take responsibility, as she does for having allowed her marriage to perpetuate, by proxy, her relationship to her father) finally permits Daddy to "lie back." Formerly an acquiescent victim, she now vengefully cancels that role. The marriage to and killing of her father by proxy are acts of what Frazer[4] calls "sympathetic magic," in which "things act on each other at a distance through a secret sympathy".... Such magic, which assumes that human beings can either directly influence the course of nature or can induce gods to influence nature in the desired way, nearly always constitutes the logic of the rituals Frazer discusses. The ritual marriage of a Whitsun bride and bridegroom, for example, aims at assuring abundant crops by sympatheti-

---

2. Alvarez, "Sylvia Plath," p. 66.
3. The biographical basis for this identification is evident in *Letters Home*....
4. Sir James George Frazer (1854–1941), Scottish anthropologist whose book *The Golden Bough* analyzes early religious and magical practices [Editor's note].

cally encouraging a marriage between the powers of fertility. Likewise, diseases may be either inflicted or drawn off by sympathetic magic on the principle that "as the image suffers, so does the man"....

Plath was familiar with and used such ideas; for example, she transcribed, from *The Golden Bough,* Frazer's remark about the fertility or barrenness of a man's wife affecting his garden; and she echoes Frazer again in a line, excised from her poem "The Other," in which opening doors and windows is connected with the facilitation of childbirth. (Also, being "lame in the memory" and self, associated with the lameness and death of her father, is at once a homeopathic wound and a sympathetic attachment to him.) The notion that "as the image suffers, so does the man"—affecting the real subject through a proxy—nicely describes marriage to a model of Daddy, and explains why "If I've killed one man, I've killed two." The earlier attempt of the speaker in "Daddy" to recover her father also involved sympathetic magic; she had tried to rejoin him by dying and becoming like him:

> At twenty I tried to die
> And get back, back, back to you.

She finally exorcises her father as if he were a scapegoat invested with the evils of her spoiled history. Frazer's discussion of rituals in which the dying god is also a scapegoat is germane here. He conjectures that two originally separate rituals merged to form this combination, and the father in "Daddy" may well be described as such a divine scapegoat figure.[5]

Sometimes it is a place from which a devil must be cast out, but usually it is a person who is possessed. In Plath's mythology the speaker is not possessed by her father in this sense, but by the false self who is in his thrall. That is why the true self is released (as in "Purdah" and "Lady Lazarus") when the oppressor is made hateful, and thereby overthrown. Rituals of exorcism in Plath's poetry therefore inherently involve the idea of rebirth. When exorcism, or attempted exorcism, of father or proxy occurs, it is preliminary to a rebirth which will entail expulsion of the false self and spoiled history. And even when a ritual of rebirth does not involve an explicit exorcism, one is usually implied.

The logic of sympathetic magic, which appears widely in Plath's late poetry, might well be called one of the physical laws of her poems.... Such a logic seems poetically appropriate for a mythology: that the Moon-muse (or one of her agents, such as "The Rival") governs and affects her by a "secret sympathy" seems natural to a mythic drama.

The motifs "released"—or triggered—in her late poems contain the potential for a sympathetic association of those details which express the same motif. Because the details are not incidental, called forth as they are by her mythology, the sympathy is in a sense guaranteed. The images of blood, violent death, and red poppies, all of which release the death and rebirth motif, have the potential

---

5. Frazer says:"If we ask why a dying god should be chosen to take upon himself and carry away the sins and sorrows of the people, it may be suggested that in the practice of using the divinity as a scapegoat we have a combination of two customs.... [T]he result would be the employment of the dying god as a scapegoat. He was killed, not originally to take away sin, but to save the divine life from the degeneracy of old age; but, since he had to be killed at any rate, people may have thought that they might as well seize the opportunity to lay upon him the burden of their sufferings and sins, in order that he might bear it away with him to the unknown world beyond the grave" [pp. 667–68]....

for sympathetically affecting one another through their family resemblance. "Tulips" contains an example of the secret sympathy which operates through such resemblance (that is, through expressing the same motif):

> The tulips are too red in the first place, they hurt me.
> . . .
> Their redness talks to my wound, it corresponds.[6]

The word "corresponds" refers both to the communication between tulips and wound and to their underlying likeness. The tulips stand in the same relation to the incipient health or normalcy of the speaker that the poppies in later poems do to her suppressed true self, to (or with) which the poppies correspond. In a sense, this correspondence, and the contrast between it and the speaker's death-in-life existence, *is* the underlying motif in these poems.

It has already been suggested that the Moon-muse has a "sympathetic"—even though not entirely welcome—relation with the speaker[7] (as mother, totem, familiar, emblem) which can be activated without her consent, just as in "Tulips" she cannot prevent her wound from corresponding with the red flowers. Similarly, the coldness and sterility of the Moon-muse may infect the speaker, causing and not merely representing her state of being. The Moon therefore functions as both "emblem" and "real agent."

**MARY LYNN BROE**

## From *Protean Poetic**

Among the other poems that display the performing self, "Daddy" and "Lady Lazarus" are two of the most often quoted, but most frequently misunderstood, poems in the Plath canon. The speaker in "Daddy" performs a mock poetic exorcism of an event that has already happened—the death of her father, who she feels withdrew his love from her by dying prematurely: "Daddy, I have had to kill you. / You died before I had time—."

The speaker attempts to exorcise not just the memory of her father but her own *Mein Kampf* model of him as well as her inherited behavioral traits that lead her graveward under the Freudian banner of death instinct or Thanatos's libido. But her ritual reenactment simply does not take. The event comically backfires

---

6. By the time "Tulips" was written, she had clearly developed much of the technique, imagery, and themes (such as the logic of sympathetic magic) of the late poems.
7. The belief Frazer mentions, that "a barren wife infects her husband's garden with her own sterility," is the sort of contagion that occurs in *Three Women*, in which the Secretary has been infected by the Moon's sterility and by that of the men with whom she works. Men, who cannot bear children, have the disease of "flatness," for they create only negations of and abstractions about life rather than life itself. This disease can (through the mediumship of the Moon) be caught from men, and it is therefore also an inversion or parody of conception. Referring to her miscarriage, the Secretary says: "I watched the men walk about me in the office. They were so flat! / There was something about them like cardboard, and now I had caught it. . . ."

* From Mary Lynn Broe, *Protean Poetic: The Poetry of Sylvia Plath* (Columbia and London: University of Missouri Press, 1980), pp. 172–75.

as pure self-parody: the metaphorical murder of the father dwindles into Hollywood spectacle, while the poet is lost in the clutter of the collective unconscious.

Early in the poem, the ritual gets off on the wrong foot both literally and figuratively. A sudden rhythmic break midway through the first stanza interrupts the insistent and mesmeric chant of the poet's own freedom:

> You do not do, you do not do
> Any more, black shoe
> In which I have lived like a foot
> For thirty years, poor and white,
> Barely daring to breathe or Achoo.

The break suggests, on the one hand, that the nursery-rhyme world of contained terror is here abandoned; on the other, that the poet-exorcist's mesmeric control is superficial, founded in a shaky faith and an unsure heart—the worst possible state for the strong, disciplined exorcist.

At first she kills her father succinctly with her own words, demythologizing him to a ludicrous piece of statuary that is hardly a Poseidon or the Colossus of Rhodes:[1]

> Marble-heavy, a bag full of God,
> Ghastly statue with one grey toe
> Big as a Frisco seal
>
> And a head in the freakish Atlantic
> Where it pours bean green over blue
> In the waters off beautiful Nauset.
> I used to pray to recover you.
> Ach, du.

Then as she tries to patch together the narrative of him, his tribal myth (the "common" town, the "German tongue," the war-scraped culture), she begins to lose her own powers of description to a senseless Germanic prattle ("The tongue stuck in my jaw. / It stuck in a barb wire snare. / Ich, ich, ich, ich"). The individual man is absorbed by his inhuman archetype, the "panzer man," "an engine / Chuffing me off like a Jew." Losing the exorcist's power that binds the spirit and then casts out the demon, she is the classic helpless victim of the swastika man. As she calls up her own picture of him as a devil, he refuses to adopt this stereotype. Instead he jumbles his trademark:

> A cleft in your chin instead of your foot
> But no less a devil for that, no not
> Any less the black man who
>
> Bit my pretty red heart in two.

The overt Nazi-Jew allegory throughout the poem suggests that, by a simple inversion of power, father and daughter grow more alike. But when she tries to imitate his action of dying, making all the appropriate grand gestures, she once again fails: "but they pulled me out of the sack, / And they stuck me together

---

1. One of the seven wonders of the ancient world, a gigantic statue of the Greek sun god, Helios; *Poseidon*: the chief sea god in the Greek pantheon [Editor's note].

with glue." She retreats to a safe world of icons and replicas, but even the doll image she constructs turns out to be "the vampire who said he was you." At last, she abandons her father to the collective unconscious where it is *he* who is finally recognized ("they always *knew* it was you"). *She* is lost, impersonally absorbed by his irate persecutors, bereft of both her power and her conjuror's discipline, and possessed by the incensed villagers. The exorcist's ritual, one of purifying, cleansing, commanding silence and then ordering the evil spirit's departure, has dwindled to a comic picture from the heart of darkness. Mad villagers stamp on the devil-vampire creation.

In the course of performing the imaginative "killing," the speaker moves through a variety of emotions, from viciousness ("a stake in your fat black heart"), to vengefulness ("You bastard, I'm through"), finally to silence ("the black telephone's off at the root"). It would seem that the real victim is the poet-performer who, despite her straining toward identification with the public events of holocaust and destruction of World War II, becomes more murderously persecuting than the "panzer-man" who smothered her, and who abandoned her with a paradoxical love, guilt, and fear. Unlike him, she kills three times: the original subject, the model to whom she said "I do, I do," and herself, the imitating victim. But each of these killings is comically inverted. Each backfires. Instead of successfully binding the spirits, commanding them to remain silent and cease doing harm, and then ordering them to an appointed place, the speaker herself is stricken dumb.

The failure of the exorcism and the emotional ambivalence are echoed in the curious rhythm. The incantatory safety of the nursery-rhyme thump (seemingly one of controlled, familiar terrors) also suggests some sinister brooding by its repetition. The poem opens with a suspiciously emphatic protest, a kind of psychological whistling-in-the-dark. As it proceeds, "Daddy"'s continuous life-rhythms—the assonance, consonance, and especially the sustained *oo* sounds—triumph over either the personal or the cultural-historical imagery. The sheer sense of organic life in the interwoven sounds carries the verse forward in boisterous spirit and communicates an underlying feeling of comedy that is also echoed in the repeated failure of the speaker to perform her exorcism.

Ultimately, "Daddy" is like an emotional, psychological, and historical autopsy, a final report. There is no real progress. The poet is in the same place in the beginning as in the end. She begins the poem as a hesitant but familiar fairy-tale daughter who parodies her attempt to reconstruct the myth of her father. Suffocating in her shoe house, she is unable to do much with that "bag full of God." She ends as a murderous member of a mythical community enacting the ritual or vampire killing, but only for a surrogate vampire, not the real thing ("the vampire who said he was you"). Although it seems that the speaker has moved from identification with the persecuted to identity as persecutor, Jew to vampire-killer, powerless to powerful, she has simply enacted a performance that allows her to live with what is unchangeable. She has used her art to stave off suffocation, and performs her self-contempt with a degree of bravado.[2]

---

2. What remains the most thorough and enlightening account of the poem is A. R. Jones, "On 'Daddy,'" *The Art of Sylvia Plath,* [ed. Newman], pp. 230–36 [Broe's note].

MARGARET HOMANS

## From *A Feminine Tradition**

To place an exclusive valuation on the literal, expecially to identify the self as literal, is simply to ratify women's age-old and disadvantageous position as the other and the object. Contemporary poetry by women that takes up this self-defeating strategy risks encounters with death that are destructive both poetically and actually. The current belief in a literal "I" present in poetry is responsible for the popular superstition that Sylvia Plath's death was the purposeful completion of her poetry's project, the assumption being that if the speaker is precisely the same as the biographical Plath, the poetry's self-destructive violence is directed toward Plath herself, not toward an imagined speaker. This reading of Plath is unfair to the woman and, by calling it merely unmediated self-expression, obscures her poetry's real power. In poem after poem depicting or wishing for physical violence, the imagery of violence is part of a symmetrical figurative system, and death is figured as a way of achieving rebirth or some other transcendence.[1] Plath's project may not thus be very different from that of Dickinson, who speaks quite often from beyond the grave, reimagining and repossessing death as her own in order to dispel the terrors of literal death. However, within that figurative system the poet embraces a self-destructive program that must soon have been poetically terminal, even if it did not bring about the actual death.

Several of Plath's late poems come to terms with a father figure (who may include the poetic fathers she acknowledges in *The Colossus*), whose crime, no different from that identified by nineteenth-century women, is of attempting to transform the feminine self into objects. "Lady Lazarus" borrows the most appalling of Nazi imagery to accuse a generalized figure of male power of the ultimate reification. Not only is the dead victim of "Herr Doktor" and "Herr Enemy" an object in being dead, but she is also reduced to the actual physical objects from which the Nazis profited by destroying human bodies: "a Nazi lampshade,"

> A cake of soap,
> A wedding ring,
> A gold filling.

The poem combines the tradition of woman as medium of exchange with that of woman as object to produce a desperately concise picture of literalization.

> I am your opus,
> I am your valuable,
> The pure gold baby
>
> That melts to a shriek.

---

* From Margaret Homans, *Women Writers and Poetic Identity: Dorothy Wordsworth, Emily Brontë, and Emily Dickinson* (Princeton: Princeton University Press, 1982), pp. 218–21.

1. I am indebted here, for their persuasively positive readings of Plath, to Judith Kroll, *Chapters in a Mythology: The Poetry of Sylvia Plath* (New York: Harper & Row, 1976), and to Stacy Pies, "Coming Clear of the Shadow: The Poetry of Sylvia Plath," unpublished essay (Yale University, 1979) [Homans's note].

Though the poet is here objecting to literalization, not embracing it, the poetic myth of suicide through which the oppression may be lifted amounts to the same thing: the speaker must submit to this literalization in order to transcend it.

> Out of the ash
> I rise with my red hair
> And I eat men like air.

Their death costs her death, and powerful though the poem is, this is an extraordinarily high price for retribution. And as always, it is the process of objectification that makes up the poem, not the final, scarcely articulable transcendence.

"Daddy" uses Nazi imagery to make the same accusation about objectification brought against men as oppressors in "Lady Lazarus" and makes the corollary accusation against the father (and the husband modelled after him) that objectification has silenced her:

> I never could talk to you.
> The tongue stuck in my jaw.
>
> It stuck in a barb wire snare.
> Ich, ich, ich, ich,
> I could hardly speak.

In this context defiance and retribution take the form of her speaking, but again this counterattack is counterproductive. Punning on the expression "being through" to mean both establishing a telephone connection and being finished, she at once makes and conclusively severs communication:

> So daddy, I'm finally through.
> The black telephone's off at the root,
> The voices just can't worm through.

The poem concludes, "Daddy, daddy, you bastard, I'm through." Suppressing the power of the one who silenced her, she simultaneously returns herself to the silence that the poem came into being to protest.


**PAMELA J. ANNAS**

## From *A Disturbance in Mirrors*\*

... [T]he particular sexual metaphor in "Daddy" is sado-masochism, which stands for the authority structure of a partriarchal and war-making society.... "Daddy" is an analysis of the structure of the society in which the individual is enmeshed. Intertwined with the image of sadist and masochist in "Daddy" is a parallel image of vampire and victim. In "Daddy," father, husband, and a larger patriarchal and competitive authority structure, which the speaker of the poem sees as having been responsible for the various imperialisms of the twentieth

---

\* From Pamela J. Annas, *A Disturbance in Mirrors: The Poetry of Sylvia Plath*, Contributions in Women's Studies no. 89 (New York, Westport, and London: Greenwood Press, 1988), pp. 139–43. All notes are Annas's.

century, all melt together and become demonic, finally a gigantic vampire figure. In the modulation from one image to another to form an accumulated image that is characteristic of many of Plath's late poems, the male figure at the center of "Daddy" takes four major forms: the statue, the Gestapo officer, the professor, and the vampire. The poem begins, however, with an image of a black shoe, an image which, like the black shoe in "The Munich Mannequins" and like the black suit in "The Applicant," can be seen to stand for corporate man. The second stanza of the poem refers back to the title poem of *The Colossus*, where the speaker's father, representative of a gigantic male other, so dominated her world that her horizon was bounded by his scattered pieces. In "Daddy," she describes him as:

> Marble-heavy, a bag full of God,
> Ghastly statue with one grey toe
> Big as a Frisco seal
>
> And a head in the freakish Atlantic
> Where it pours bean green over blue
> In the waters off beautiful Nauset.

Between "The Colossus" and "Daddy" there has been a movement from a mythic and natural landscape to one with social and political boundaries. Here the image of her father, grown larger than the earlier Colossus of Rhodes, stretches across and subsumes the whole of the United States, from the Pacific to the Atlantic ocean.

The next seven stanzas of "Daddy" construct the image of the Gestapo officer, using her family background—her parents were both of German origin—to mediate between her personal sense of suffocation and the social history of the Nazi invasions. The black shoe of the first stanza in which she says she has been wedged like a foot "barely daring to breathe" becomes in stanza ten, at the end of the Nazi section, a larger social image of suffocation: "Not God but a swastika / So black no sky could squeak through." The Gestapo figure recurs briefly three stanzas later as the speaker of the poem transfers the image from father to husband and incidentally suggests that the victim has some control in a brutalized association—at least to the extent she chooses to be there.[1]

---

1. See Wilhelm Reich's *The Mass Psychology of Fascism* (New York: Simon and Schuster, 1969), particularly his chapter on "The Authoritarian Personality," for an analysis of how an oppressed class can contribute to its own oppression. Judith Lewis Herman, in *Father-Daughter Incest* (Cambridge, Mass.: Harvard University Press, 1981), discusses the history of the suppression of incest beginning with Freud and continuing into contemporary psychological literature, the attribution of reports of incest to hysterical female oedipal fantasizing or, when the fact of incest is impossible to deny, assigning blame to the victim: what Herman calls the Seductive Daughter and/or the Collusive Mother (Chapter 1, "A Common Occurence"). Writing in the early 1960s and familiar with some of these attitudes, ... Plath [not surprisingly] assigns some culpability to the victim. Herman goes on to say, "Even when the girl does give up her erotic attachment to her father, she is encouraged to persist in the fantasy that some other man, like her father, will some day take possession of her, raising her above the common lot of womankind" (p. 57).

I am not of course suggesting that Plath literally had an incestuous relationship with her father—there is no evidence one way or the other—but she does make recurrent use of father/daughter incest as a symbol for male/female relations in a patriarchal society. . . .

> I made a model of you,
> A man in black with a Meinkampf look
>
> And a love of the rack and the screw.
> And I said I do, I do.

The Gestapo figure becomes "Herr Professor" in stanza eleven, an actual image of Plath's father, and also an image of what has for centuries been seen as the prototypical and even ideal relationship between a man and a woman.[2] The professor, who is a man, talks and is active; the woman, who is a student, listens and is passive. A patriarchal social structure is at its purest and, superficially, at its most benign in the stereotyped relationship of male teacher and female student and is a stock romantic fantasy even in women's literature—Emma and Mr. Knightley, Lucy Snowe and the professor in *Villette*.[3] But Plath places this image between the images of Nazi/Jew and vampire/victim so that it becomes the center of a series. Indeed, the image of daddy as teacher turns almost immediately into a devil/demon/vampire:

> A cleft in your chin instead of your foot
> But no less a devil for that, no not
> Any less the black man who
>
> Bit my pretty red heart in two.

The last two stanzas of "Daddy" are like the conclusion of "Lady Lazarus" in their assertion that the speaker of the poem is breaking out of the cycle and that, in order to do so, she must turn on and kill Herr God, Herr Lucifer in the one poem, and Daddy in his final metamorphosis as vampire in the other poem. Plath explained this in Freudian terms in an introductory note to the poem for a BBC Third Programme reading:

> The poem is spoken by a girl with an Electra complex. The father died while she thought he was God. Her case is complicated by the fact that her father was also a Nazi and her mother very possibly part Jewish. In the daughter the two strains marry and paralyze each other—she has to act out the awful little allegory once over before she is free of it.[4]

This reenacting of the allegory becomes at the end of "Daddy" a frenzied communal ritual of exorcism.

> Daddy, you can lie back now.
>
> There's a stake in your fat black heart
> And the villagers never liked you.
> They are dancing and stamping on you.
> They always *knew* it was you.
> Daddy, daddy, you bastard, I'm through.

This cycle of victim/vampire is, left alone, a closed and repetitious cycle, like the repeated suicides of "Lady Lazarus." According to the legends and the Holly-

---

2. This photograph of Otto Plath is reproduced on page 17 of *Letters Home*.
3. [Mary] Ellmann, *Thinking About Women* [New York: Harcourt Brace Jovanovich, 1968], pp. 119-23.
4. Quoted in [M. L.] Rosenthal, *The New Poets* [New York: Oxford University Press, 1967], p. 82.

wood film versions of these legends we all grew up on, once consumed by a vampire, one dies and is reborn a vampire and preys upon others, who in their turn die and become vampires. The vampire imagery in Sylvia Plath's poetry intersects on one level with her World War II imagery and its exploitation and victimization and on another level intersects with her images of a bureaucratic, fragmented, and dead—in the sense of numbed and unaware—society. The connections are sometimes confused, but certainly World War II is often imaged in her poetry as a kind of grisly, vampiric feast....

The whole of "Daddy" is an exorcism to banish the demon, put a stake through the vampire's heart, and thus break the cycle of vampire→victim. It is crucial to the poem that the exorcism is accomplished through communal action by the "villagers." The rhythm of the poem is powerfully and deliberately primitive: a child's chant, a formal curse. The hard sounds, short lines, and repeated rhymes of "do," "you," "Jew," and "through" give a hard pounding quality to the poem that is close to the sound of a heart beat. "Daddy," as well as "Lady Lazarus" and, to a lesser extent, "Fever 103°," is structured as a magical formula or incantation. In the *Colossus* poems, Plath also used poetry as a ritual incantation, but in those early poems it was most often directed toward transformation of self. By 1961, she is less often attempting to transform self into some other, but rather attempting to rid herself and her world of demons. That is, rebirth cannot occur until after the demons have been exorcised. In all three of these poems, the possibilities of the individual are very much tied to those of her society.

Purity, which is what exorcism aims at, is for Plath an ambiguous concept. On the one hand it means integrity of self, wholeness rather than fragmentation, as unspoiled state of being, rest, perfection, aesthetic beauty, and loss of self through transformation into some reborn other. On the other hand, it also means absence, isolation, blindness, a kind of autism which shuts out the world, stasis and death, and a loss of self through dispersal into some other. In "Lady Lazarus" and "Fever 103°" the emphasis is on exorcising the poet's previous selves, though within a social context that makes that unlikely. "Daddy," however, is a purification of the world; in "Daddy" it is the various avatars of the other—the male figure who represents the patriarchal society she lives in—that are being exorcised. In all three cases, the exorcism is violent and, perhaps, provisional. Does she believe, in any of these cases, that a rebirth under such conditions is really possible, that an exorcism is truly taking place, that once the allegory is reenacted, she will be rid of it? The more the speaker of the poems defines her situation as desperate, the more violent and vengeful becomes the agent of purification and transformation. All three of these poems are retaliatory fantasies: in "Lady Lazarus" she swallows men, in "Fever 103°" she leaves them behind, in "Daddy" she kills them....

# STEVEN GOULD AXELROD

## From *Jealous Gods**

[Although "Daddy"] has traditionally been read as "personal" (Aird 78)[1] or "confessional" (M. L. Rosenthal 82),[2] Margaret Homans has more recently suggested that it concerns a woman's dislocated relations to speech (*Women Writers* 220-21).[3] Plath herself introduced it on the BBC as the opposite of confession, as a constructed fiction: "Here is a poem spoken by a girl with an Electra complex. Her father died while she thought he was God. Her case is complicated by the fact that her father was also a Nazi and her mother very possibly part Jewish. In the daughter the two strains marry and paralyze each other—she has to act out the awful little allegory once over before she is free of it" (*CP* 293).[4] We might interpret this preface as an accurate retelling of the poem; or we might regard it as a case of an author's estrangement from her text, on the order of Coleridge's preface to "Kubla Khan" in which he claims to be unable to finish the poem, having forgotten what it was about. However we interpret Plath's preface, we must agree that "Daddy" is dramatic and allegorical, since its details depart freely from the facts of her biography. In this poem she again figures her unresolved conflicts with paternal authority as a textual issue. Significantly, her father was a published writer, and his successor, her husband, was also a writer. Her preface asserts that the poem concerns a young woman's paralyzing self-division, which she can defeat only through allegorical representation. Recalling that paralysis was one of Plath's main tropes for literary incapacity, we begin to see that the poem evokes the female poet's anxiety of authorship and specifically Plath's strategy of delivering herself from that anxiety by making it the topic of her discourse. Viewed from this perspective, "Daddy" enacts the woman poet's struggle with "daddy-poetry." It represents her effort to eject the "buried male muse" from her invention process and the "jealous gods" from her audience (*J* 223;[5] *CP* 179).

Plath wrote "Daddy" several months after Hughes left her, on the day she learned that he had agreed to a divorce (October 12, 1962). George Brown and Tirril Harris have shown that early loss makes one especially vulnerable to subsequent loss (Bowlby 250-59),[6] and Plath seems to have defended against depression by almost literally throwing herself into her poetry. She followed "Daddy" with a host of poems that she considered her greatest achievement to date: "Medusa," "The Jailer," "Lady Lazarus," "Ariel," the bee sequence, and others. The letters she wrote to her mother and brother on the day of "Daddy," and then again four days later, brim with a sense of artistic self-discovery: "Writing like mad. . . . Terrific stuff, as if domesticity had choked me" (*LH* 466).[7] Composing

---

* From Steven Gould Axelrod, *Sylvia Plath: The Wound and the Cure of Words* (Baltimore: Johns Hopkins University Press, 1990), pp. 51-70, 237. Unless otherwise indicated, all notes are Axelrod's.
1. Eileen Aird, *Sylvia Plath: Her Life and Work* (New York: Harper & Row, 1973).
2. M. L. Rosenthal, *The New Poets: American and British Poetry since World War II* (London: Oxford University Press, 1967).
3. Margaret Homans, *Women Writers and Poetic Identity: Dorothy Wordsworth, Emily Brontë, and Emily Dickinson* (Princeton: Princeton University Press, 1980).   4. *CP* = *The Collected Poems*.   5. *J* = *The Journals*.
6. John Bowlby, *Attachment and Loss*, III: *Loss: Sadness and Depression* (London: Hogarth, 1980).
7. *LH* = *Letters Home*.

at the "still blue, almost eternal hour before the baby's cry, before the glassy music of the milkman, settling his bottles" (quoted in Alvarez, *Savage God* 21),[8] she experienced an "enormous" surge in creative energy (*LH* 467). Yet she also expressed feelings of misery: "The half year ahead seems like a lifetime, and the half behind an endless hell" (*LH* 468). She was again contemplating things German: a trip to the Austrian Alps, a renewed effort to learn the language. If "German" was Randall Jarrell's "favorite country," it was not hers, yet it returned to her discourse like clock work at times of psychic distress. Clearly Plath was attempting to find and to evoke in her art what she could not find or communicate in her life. She wished to compensate for her fragmenting social existence by investing herself in her texts: "Hope, when free, to write myself out of this hole" (*LH* 466). Desperately eager to sacrifice her "flesh," which was "wasted," to her "mind and spirit," which were "fine" (*LH* 470), she wrote "Daddy" to demonstrate the existence of her voice, which had been silent or subservient for so long. She wrote it to prove her "genius" (*LH* 468).

Plath projected her struggle for textual identity onto the figure of a partly Jewish young woman who learns to express her anger at the patriarch and at his language of male mastery, which is as foreign to her as German, as "obscene" as murder (st. 6), and as meaningless as "gobbledygoo" (st. 9). The patriarch's death "off beautiful Nauset" (st. 3) recalls Plath's journal entry in which she associated the "green seaweeded water" at "Nauset Light" with "the deadness of a being . . . who no longer creates" (*J* 164). Daddy's deadness—suggesting Plath's unwillingness to let her father, her education, her library, or her husband inhibit her any longer—inspires the poem's speaker to her moment of illumination. At a basic level, "Daddy" concerns its own violent, transgressive birth as a text, its origin in a culture that regards it as illegitimate—a judgment the speaker hurls back on the patriarch himself when she labels *him* a bastard (st. 16). Plath's unaccommodating worldview, which was validated by much in her childhood and adult experience, led her to understand literary tradition not as an expanding universe of beneficial influence (as depicted in Eliot's "Tradition and the Individual Talent") but as a closed universe in which every addition required a corresponding subtraction—a Spencerian agon in which only the fittest survived. If Plath's speaker was to be born as a poet, a patriarch must die.

As in "The Colossus," the father here appears as a force or an object rather than as a person. Initially he takes the form of an immense "black shoe," capable of stamping on his victim (st. 1). Immediately thereafter he becomes a marble "statue" (st. 2), cousin to the monolith of the earlier poem. He then transforms into Nazi Germany (st. 6-7, 9-10), the archetypal totalitarian state. When the protagonist mentions Daddy's "boot in the face" (st. 10), she may be alluding to Orwell's comment in *1984*, "If you want a picture of the future, imagine a boot stomping on a human face—forever" (3.3). Eventually the father declines in stature from God (st. 2) to a devil (st. 11) to a dying vampire (st. 15). Perhaps he shrinks under the force of his victim's denunciation, which de-creates him as a power as it creates him as figure. But whatever his size, he never assumes human dimensions, aspirations, and relations—except when posing as a teacher in a photograph (st. 11). Like the colossus, he remains figurative and symbolic, not individual.

---

8. A. Alvarez, *The Savage God: A Study of Suicide* (1971; New York, Bantam, 1973).

Nevertheless, the male figure of "Daddy" does differ significantly from that of "The Colossus." In the earlier poem, which emphasizes his lips, mouth, throat, tongue, and voice, the colossus allegorically represents the power of speech, however fragmented and resistant to the protagonist's ministrations. In the later poem Daddy remains silent, apart from the gobbledygoo attributed to him once (st. 9). He uses his mouth primarily for biting and for drinking blood. The poem emphasizes his feet and, implicitly, his phallus. He is a "black shoe" (st. 1), a statue with "one gray toe" (st. 2), a "boot" (st. 10). The speaker, estranged from him by fear, could never tell where he put his "foot," his "root" (st. 5). Furthermore, she is herself silenced by his shoe: "I never could talk to you" (st. 5). Daddy is no "male muse" (*J* 223), not even one in ruins, but frankly a male censor. His boot in the face of "every woman" is presumably lodged in her mouth (st. 10). He stands for all the elements in the literary situation and in the female ephebe's internalization of it, that prevent her from producing any words at all, even copied or subservient ones. Appropriately, Daddy can be killed only by being stamped on: he lives and dies by force, not language. If "The Colossus" tells a tale of the patriarch's speech, his grunts and brays, "Daddy" tells a tale of the daughter's effort to speak.

Thus we are led to another important difference between the two poems. The "I" of "The Colossus" acquires her identity only through serving her "father," whereas the "I" of "Daddy" actuates her gift only through opposition to him. The latter poem precisely inscribes the plot of Plath's dream novel of 1958: "a girl's search for her dead father—for an outside authority which must be developed, instead, from the inside" (*J* 258). As the child of a Nazi, the girl could "hardly speak" (st. 6), but as a Jew she begins "to talk" and to acquire an identity (st. 7). In Plath's allegory, the outsider Jew corresponds to "the rebel, the artist, the odd" (*JP* 55),[9] and particularly to the woman artist. Otto Rank's *Beyond Psychology*,[1] which had a lasting influence on her, explicitly compares women to Jews, since "woman . . . has suffered from the very beginning a fate similar to that of the Jew, namely, suppression, slavery, confinement, and subsequent persecution" (287–88). Rank, whose discourse I would consider tainted by anti-Semitism, argues that Jews speak a language of pessimistic "self-hatred" that differs essentially from the language of the majority cultures in which they find themselves (191, 281–84). He analogously, though more sympathetically, argues that woman speaks in a language different from man's, and that as a result of man's denial of woman's world, "woman's 'native tongue' has hitherto been unknown or at least unheard" (248). Although Rank's essentializing of woman's "nature" lapses into the sexist clichés of his time ("intuitive," "irrational" [249]), his idea of linguistic difference based on gender and his analogy between Jewish and female speech seem to have embedded themselves in the substructure of "Daddy" (and in many of Plath's other texts as well). For Plath, as later for Adrienne Rich, the Holocaust and the patriarchy's silencing of women were linked outcomes of the masculinist interpretation of the world. Political insurrection and female self-assertion also interlaced symbolically. In "Daddy," Plath's speaker finds her voice and motive by identifying herself as antithetical to her Fascist father. Rather than getting the colossus "glued" and properly jointed, she wishes to stick herself

---

9. *JP* = *Johnny Panic and the Bible of Dreams*.
1. Otto Rank, *Beyond Psychology* (Baltimore: Johns Hopkins University Press, 1990).

"together with glue" (st. 13), an act that seems to require her father's dismemberment. Previously devoted to the patriarch—both in "The Colossus" and in memories evoked in "Daddy" of trying to "get back" to him (st. 12)—she now seeks only to escape from him and to see him destroyed.

Plath has unleashed the anger, normal in mourning as well as in revolt, that she suppressed in the earlier poem. But she has done so at a cost. Let us consider her childlike speaking voice. The language of "Daddy," beginning with its title, is often regressive. The "I" articulates herself by moving backward in time, using the language of nursery rhymes and fairy tales (the little old woman who lived in a shoe, the black man of the forest). Such language accords with a child's conception of the world, not an adult's. Plath's assault on the language of "daddy-poetry" has turned inward, on the language of her own poem, which teeters precariously on the edge of a preverbal abyss—represented by the eerie, keening "oo" sound with which a majority of the verses end. And then let us consider the play on "through" at the poem's conclusion. Although that last line allows for multiple readings, one interpretation is that the "I" has unconsciously carried out her father's wish: her discourse, by transforming itself into cathartic oversimplifications, has undone itself.

Yet the poem does contain its verbal violence by means more productive than silence. In a letter to her brother, Plath referred to "Daddy" as "gruesome" (*LH* 472), while on almost the same day she described it to A. Alvarez as a piece of "light verse" (Alvarez, *Beyond* 56).[2] She later read it on the BBC in a highly ironic tone of voice. The poem's unique spell derives from its rhetorical complexity: its variegated and perhaps bizarre fusion of the horrendous and the comic. As Uroff has remarked, it both shares and remains detached from the fixation of its protagonist (159).[3] The protagonist herself seems detached from her own fixation. She is "split in the most complex fashion," as Plath wrote of Ivan Karamazov[4] in her Smith College honors thesis. Plath's speaker uses potentially self-mocking melodramatic terms to describe both her opponent ("so black no sky could squeak through" [st. 10]) and herself ("poor and white" [st. 1]). While this aboriginal speaker quite literally expresses black-and-white thinking, her civilized double possesses a sensibility sophisticated enough to subject such thinking to irony. Thus the poem expresses feelings that it simultaneously parodies—it may be parodying the very idea of feeling. The tension between erudition and simplicity in the speaker's voice appears in her pairings that juxtapose adult with childlike diction: "breathe or Achoo," "your Luftewaffe, your gobbledygoo" (st. 1, 9). She can expound such adult topics as Taroc packs, Viennese beer, and Tyrolean snowfall; can specify death camps by name; and can employ an adult vocabulary of "recover," "ancestress," "Aryan," "*Meinkampf,*" "obscene," and "bastard." Yet she also has recourse to a more primitive lexicon that includes "chuffing," "your fat black heart," and "my pretty red heart." She proves herself capable of careful intellectual discriminations ("so I never could tell" [st. 5]), conventionalized description ("beautiful Nauset" [st. 3]), and moral analogy ("if I've killed one man, I've killed two" [st. 15]), while also exhibiting regressive fantasies (vam-

---

2. A. Alvarez, *Beyond All This Fiddle* (London: Allen Lane–Penguin, 1968).
3. Margaret Dickie Uroff, *Sylvia Plath and Ted Hughes* (Urbana: University of Illinois Press, 1979).
4. A character in Fyodor Dostoyevsky's novel *The Brothers Karamazov* who suffers debilitating guilt for having wished for his father's death [Editor's note].

pires), repetitions ("wars, wars, wars" [st. 4]), and inarticulateness ("panzer-man, panzer-man, O You—" [st. 9]). She oscillates between calm reflection ("You stand at the blackboard, daddy, / In the picture I have of you" [st. 11]) and mad incoherence ("Ich, ich, ich, ich" [st. 6]). Her sophisticated language puts her wild language in an ironic perspective, removing the discourse from the control of the archaic self who understands experience only in extreme terms.

The ironies in "Daddy" proliferate in unexpected ways, however. When the speaker proclaims categorically that "every woman adores a Fascist" (st. 10), she is subjecting her victimization to irony by suggesting that sufferers choose, or at least accommodate themselves to, their suffering. But she is also subjecting her authority to irony, since her claim about "every woman" is transparently false. It simply parodies patriarchal commonplaces, such as those advanced by Helene Deutsch concerning "feminine masochism" (192–99, 245–85).[5] The adult, sophisticated self seems to be speaking here: Who else would have the confidence to make a sociological generalization? Yet the content of the assertion, if taken straightforwardly, returns us to the regressive self who is dominated by extravagant emotions she cannot begin to understand. Plath's mother wished that Plath would write about "decent, courageous people" (*LH* 477), and she herself heard an inner voice demanding that she be a perfect "paragon" in her language and feeling (*J* 176). But in the speaker of "Daddy," she inscribed the opposite of such a paragon: a divided self whose veneer of civilization is breached and infected by unhealthy instincts.

Plath's irony cuts both ways. At the same time that the speaker's sophisticated voice undercuts her childish voice, reducing its melodrama to comedy, the childish or maddened voice undercuts the pretensions of the sophisticated voice, revealing the extremity of suffering masked by its ironies. While demonstrating the inadequacy of thinking and feeling in opposites, the poem implies that such a mode can locate truths denied more complex cognitive and affective systems. The very moderation of the normal adult intelligence, its tolerance of ambiguity, its defenses against the primal energies of the id, results in falsification. Reflecting Schiller's idea that the creative artist experiences a "momentary and passing madness" (quoted by Freud in a passage of *The Interpretation of Dreams* [193][6] that Plath underscored), "Daddy" gives voice to that madness. Yet the poem's sophisticated awareness, its comic vision, probably wins out in the end, since the poem concludes by curtailing the power of its extreme discourse.... Furthermore, Plath distanced herself from the poem's aboriginal voice by introducing her text as "a poem spoken by a girl with an Electra complex"—that is, as a study of the *girl's* pathology rather than her father's—and as an allegory that will "free" her from that pathology. She also distanced herself by reading the poem in a tone that emphasized its irony. And finally, she distanced herself by laying the poem's wild voice permanently to rest after October. The aboriginal vision was indeed purged. "Daddy" represents not Dickinson's madness that is divinest sense, but rather an entry into a style of discourse and a mastery of it. The poem realizes the trope of suffering by means of an inherent irony that both questions and validates the trope in the same gestures, and that finally allows the speaker

---

5. Helen Deutsch, *The Psychology of Women*, I: *Girlhood* (1944; repr. New York: Bantam, 1973).
6. Sigmund Freud, *The Interpretation of Dreams*, ed. James Strachey, Standard Edition, IV (1900; New York: Norton, 1976).

to conclude the discourse and to remove herself from the trope with a sense of completion rather than wrenching, since the irony was present from the very beginning.

Plath's poetic revolt in "Daddy" liberated her pent-up creativity, but the momentary success sustained her little more than self-sacrifice had done. "Daddy" became another stage in her development, an unrepeatable experiment, a vocal opening that closed itself at once. The poem is not only an elegy for the power of "daddy-poetry" but for the powers of speech Plath discovered in composing it.

When we consider "Daddy" generically, a further range of implications presents itself. Although we could profitably consider the poem as the dramatic monologue Plath called it in her BBC broadcast, let us regard it instead as the kind of poem most readers have taken it to be: a domestic poem. I have chosen this term, rather than M. L. Rosenthal's better-known "confessional poem" or the more neutral "autobiographical poem," because "confessional poem" implies a confession rather than a making (though Steven Hoffman[7] and Lawrence Kramer[8] have recently indicated the mode's conventions) and because "autobiographical poem" is too general for our purpose. I shall define the domestic poem as one that represents and comments on a protagonist's relationship to one or more family members, usually a parent, child, or spouse. To focus our discussion even further, I shall emphasize poetry that specifically concerns a father.

... In the 1950s the "domestic poem" proper appeared on the scene, with its own conventions and expectations, and with its own complex cultural and literary reasons for being. Perhaps the precursive poems made the genre's eventual flowering inevitable, while its precise timing depended on a reaction against modernism's aesthetic of impersonality. Theodore Roethke wrote several early poems that initiated the genre: "My Papa's Waltz" (1948), "The Lost Son" (1948), and "Where Knock Is Open Wide" (1951). Lowell's "Life Studies" sequence (1959) was, and is, the genre's most prominent landmark. Other poems in the genre include John Berryman's *The Dream Songs* (1969); Frank Bidart's "Golden State" (1973) and "Confessional" (1983); Robert Duncan's "My Mother Would Be a Falconress" (1968); Allen Ginsberg's *Kaddish* (1960); Randall Jarrell's "The Lost World" (1965); Maxine Kumin's "The Thirties Revisited" (1975), "My Father's Neckties" (1978), and "Marianne, My Mother, and Me" (1989); Stanley Kunitz's "Father and Son" (1958) and "The Testing Tree" (1971); Lowell's "To Mother" (1977), "Robert T. S. Lowell" (1977), and "Unwanted" (1977); James Merrill's "Scenes of Childhood" (1962); Adrienne Rich's "After Dark" (1966); Anne Sexton's "Division of the Parts" (1960) and "The Death of the Fathers" (1972); W. D. Snodgrass' "Heart's Needle" (1959); Diane Wakoski's "The Father of My Country" (1968); and of course Sylvia Plath's "Daddy" (1962). In all these poems, the parent-child relationship serves as a locus for psychological investigation. In many of them it also serves as a means of representing the acquisition of poetic identity and of exploring the bounds of textuality itself. Because later writers

---

7. Steven Hoffman, "Impersonal Personalism: The Making of a Confessional Poetic," *English Literary History* 45 (Winter 1978): 687–709.
8. Lawrence Kramer, "Freud and the Skunks: Genre and Language in *Life Studies*," in *Robert Lowell: Essays on the Poetry*, ed. Steven Gould Axelrod and Helen Deese (New York: Cambridge University Press, 1986).

were conscious of the Roethke-Lowell domestic poem as at least a genre in embryo, they chose to use its features, or perhaps the power of the genre was such that the features chose them. The "domestic poem" became a system of signs in which each individual text's adherence to the system and deviations within the system produced its particular literary meaning.

In 1959 Plath did not consciously attempt to write in the domestic poem genre, perhaps because she was not yet ready to assume her majority. Her journal entries of that period bristle with an impatience at herself that may derive from this reluctance. She may have feared asserting her "I am I am I am," which seemed to carry with it a countervailing impulse of self-retribution. But by fall 1962, when she had already lost so much, she was ready to chance tackling poetic tradition, and specifically her chief male instructors, Roethke and Lowell. In "Daddy" she achieved her victory in two ways. First, as we have seen, she symbolically assaults a father figure who is identified with male control of language. All her anxiety of influence comes to the fore in the poem: her sense of belatedness, her awareness of constraint, her fears of inadequacy, her furious need to overcome her dependency, her guilt at her own aggressivity. Since the precursors "do not do / Any more" (st. 1), she wishes to escape their paralyzing influence and to empty the "bag full of God" that has kept her tongue stuck in her jaw for so long (st. 2, 5). The father whose power she attacks is not simply Roethke or Lowell, or even Hughes or Otto Plath, but a literary character who includes reference to all of them as categories of masculine authority. Although the Daddy of poetry has already "died" (st. 2)—the fate of all published texts in Plath's postromantic perspective—the speaker must symbolically "kill" him from her own discourse. The poem ironically depicts poetry as both an aggression and a suicide. The female ephebe herself becomes a "brute" in the act of voicing (st. 10), just as have her teachers before her. But the aggression of her speech yields to the self-annihilation of language. By the end of the poem she too, like her male precursors, is "through." The speaker's textual life will be misread on innumerable occasions in innumerable ways, whereas her own misreading and miswriting of the precursors is finished. In its conclusion, the poem acknowledges its alienation from itself, confessing the transitoriness of its unbounded power.

In addition to killing the father in its fictional plot, the poem seeks to discredit the forefathers through its status as poetic act. Taking a genre established by Roethke and Lowell, "Daddy" fundamentally alters it through antithesis and parody. Like all strong poems, it transforms its genre and therefore the way we perceive the precursive examples, making them seem not fulfillments but anticipations. Thus the later work projects its anxiety retrospectively back through its predecessors. Haunted by fears of inadequacy and redundancy, it seeks to make the earlier poems seem incompetent by comparison—a kind of juvenilia in the career of the genre, to represent the final possible stroke, or at the very least to inaugurate some new and important genre, of which the whole domestic genre was but a foreshadowing.

This point comes clearer if we compare "Daddy" with two analogues, Roethke's "The Lost Son" (1948) and Lowell's "Commander Lowell" (1959). In the Freudian drama of "The Lost Son," the protagonist subjectively relives his childhood fears and fantasies. Like the speaker of the companion piece, "My Papa's Waltz," he is still enmeshed in the family romance, remembering the father ambivalently as powerful, protective, and threatening. After locating himself at his father's grave, where he feels both grief and estrangement (in a scene that adumbrates "Electra on Azalea Path"), he descends into his unconscious, seeking, as Roethke later explained, "some clue to existence" (*Poet* 38).[9] He encounters his death wish, his memory of his father as "Father Fear," his sexual anxieties, and finally the "dark swirl" of a blackout, after which a childhood memory of his "Papa" shouting "order" in German returns him to consciousness. Although the figure of "Papa" blends earthly and heavenly father (*Poet* 39), he also symbolizes the superego, restoring order to a psyche and a poem that had fallen into chaos. At the poem's conclusion, as the "lost son" waits for his "understandable spirit" to revive, he appears to be purged, though not cured, of the conflicts that incapacitated him.

The speaker of "Commander Lowell," in contrast, is objective, precise, and witty. His discourse reflects a detached perspective on the past rather than a psychic reimmersion in it. He portrays his father as one who threatened him only through weakness. This father "was nothing to shout / about to the summer colony at 'Matt' "; took "four shots with his putter to sink his putt"; sang "Anchors Aweigh" in the bathtub; was fired from his job; and squandered his inheritance. Whereas Roethke's poem represents a cathartic experience, Lowell's converts chaotic feelings into intellectual irony. Whereas Roethke's poem can be read as an allegory of man's relationship to God or as a model of the Freudian psyche, Lowell's remains a realistic narrative, though it does suggest the cultural and financial decline of a social class.

Plath's poem combines features of both of these precursors: Roethke's evocation of a German-speaking authoritarian with Lowell's sarcastic deflation of a man without qualities; Roethke's subjective anguish with Lowell's social comedy. Like Roethke's Papa, Plath's title character is an intimidating patriarch; like Lowell's Father, he is a buffoon ("big as a Frisco seal"). Finally, Plath's poem, like those of her predecessors, has little to do with psychological cure: the speaker's defenses remain in place. But in a deeper sense, "Daddy" swerves sharply from its precursors, curtailing their power. It turns the psychological depth of Roethke's poem and the ironically detached surface of Lowell's poem into a fury of denunciation, an extravagance of emotion, an exaggeration of acts and effects, perhaps revealing the subtexts of both precursors. If in a sense the texts by Roethke and Lowell constitute what Ned Lukacher[1] might term the primal scene of "Daddy," the latter poem's raw intensity succeeds in reversing the relationship, making itself resemble *their* primal scene. It unmasks Roethke's implicitly oppressive father figure as a monster and Lowell's sophisticated comedy as slapstick. It transforms the domestic genre alternately into a horror show, encapsulating every political, cultural, and familial atrocity of the age, and a theater of cruelty, evoking nervous laughter. "Daddy" takes the genre as far as it can go—and then further.

---

9. *On the Poet and His Craft: Selected Prose of Theodore Roethke*, ed. Ralph J. Mills, Jr. (Seattle and London: University of Washington Press, 1965).

1. Ned Lukacher, *Primal Scenes: Literature, Philosophy, Psychoanalysis* (Ithaca and London: Cornell University Press, 1986).

## SUGGESTIONS FOR WRITING

1. In his essay "Dying Is an Art," George Steiner argues that Plath's poems "are too honest, they have cost too much, to be yielded to myth." Do you think that "Daddy" is an "honest" poem? Write an essay exploring what "honesty" means in modern poetry and whether or not "Daddy" is an "honest" poem. Draw on the critical essays found in this chapter, and be sure to cite them as appropriate.
2. Several of the critics in this chapter make competing claims about the meaning and significance of the form of "Daddy," particularly its nursery-rhyme-like qualities. Using those claims as a springboard, write an essay in which you make your own argument about the relationship between form and content in "Daddy."
3. In "The Plath Celebration: A Partial Dissent," Irving Howe argues, "There is something monstrous, utterly disproportionate, when tangled emotions about one's father are deliberately compared with the historical fate of the European Jews." Is Plath's personal, artistic use of a great historical tragedy truly "monstrous," as Howe says, or is it simply a case of what George Steiner calls "subtle larceny"? Write an essay in which you discuss whether or not it is appropriate for an artist to use the sufferings of others as material for personal artistic expression.
4. Broe, Kroll, Homans, Annas, and Axelrod all claim that "Daddy" portrays the speaker's attempt to successfully "exorcise" one demon or another, though they disagree rather dramatically both about what that demon is and about whether and how that exorcism (not the poem) succeeds. Using their arguments as a starting point, write an essay in which you offer your own interpretation of the process of exorcism enacted in the poem.
5. In "Sylvia Plath," A. Alvarez quotes Plath's own interpretation of "Daddy" as a poem "spoken by a girl with an Electra complex." Research the term "Electra Complex," which originated with Sigmund Freud. Is it useful to interpret "Daddy" through the lens of the "Electra complex"? Citing critics included in this chapter, write an essay in which you discuss Plath's Freudian explanation of "Daddy" and, more generally, the reliability of artists' interpretations of their own works.
6. Write an essay comparing Plath's "Daddy" to at least two of the "domestic poems" mentioned by Axelrod in "Jealous Gods." To what extent do you agree and disagree with Axelrod's interpretation of the similarities and differences between "Daddy" and these other poems by Plath's contemporaries?
7. Is "Daddy" a "feminist" poem? Does examination of the poem from a feminist viewpoint, like that of Margaret Homans, help to illuminate the poem, or does it obscure understanding? Citing the essays by Homans and other critics in this chapter, write an essay in which you discuss a feminist reading of "Daddy" and then argue for or against its validity.

# Reading More Poetry

**WILLIAM BLAKE**

## The Tyger

Tyger! Tyger! burning bright
In the forests of the night,
What immortal hand or eye
Could frame thy fearful symmetry?

5 In what distant deeps or skies
Burnt the fire of thine eyes?
On what wings dare he aspire?
What the hand dare seize the fire?

And what shoulder, & what art,
10 Could twist the sinews of thy heart?
And when thy heart began to beat,
What dread hand? & what dread feet?

What the hammer? what the chain?
In what furnace was thy brain?
15 What the anvil? what dread grasp
Dare its deadly terrors clasp?

When the stars threw down their spears
And water'd heaven with their tears,
Did he smile his work to see?
20 Did he who made the Lamb make thee?

Tyger! Tyger! burning bright
In the forests of the night,
What immortal hand or eye
Dare frame thy fearful symmetry?

1790

## Holy Thursday[1]

'Twas on a Holy Thursday, their innocent faces clean,
The children walking two & two, in red & blue & green;
Grey headed beadles walkd before with wands as white as snow,
Till into the high dome of Paul's they like Thames' waters flow.

5 O what a multitude they seemd, these flowers of London town!
Seated in companies they sit with radiance all their own.
The hum of multitudes was there, but multitudes of lambs,
Thousands of little boys & girls raising their innocent hands.

Now like a mighty wind they raise to heaven the voice of song,
10 Or like harmonious thunderings the seats of heaven among.
Beneath them sit the agèd men, wise guardians of the poor;
Then cherish pity, lest you drive an angel from your door.[2]

1789

## Holy Thursday

Is this a holy thing to see,
In a rich and fruitful land,
Babes reduced to misery,
Fed with cold and usurous hand?

5 Is that trembling cry a song?
Can it be a song of joy?
And so many children poor?
It is a land of poverty!

And their sun does never shine,
10 And their fields are bleak & bare,
And their ways are fill'd with thorns;
It is eternal winter there.

For where-e'er the sun does shine,
And where-e'er the rain does fall,
15 Babe can never hunger there,
Nor poverty the mind appall.

1794

---

1. In the English Church, the Thursday celebrating Christ's ascension, thirty-nine days after Easter. It was customary on this day to march the poor, frequently orphaned children from the charity schools of London to a service at St. Paul's Cathedral.
    This poem is from Blake's *Songs of Innocence*. The one that follows—with the same title—is from his *Songs of Experience*.
2. See Hebrews 13.2: "Be not forgetful to entertain strangers: for thereby some have entertained angels unawares."

## GWENDOLYN BROOKS

### To the Diaspora

*you did not know you were Afrika*

When you set out for Afrika
you did not know you were going.
Because
you did not know you were Afrika.
5 You did not know the Black continent
that had to be reached
was you.

I could not have told you then that some sun
would come,
10 somewhere over the road,
would come evoking the diamonds
of you, the Black continent—
somewhere over the road.
You would not have believed my mouth.

15 When I told you, meeting you somewhere close
to the heat and youth of the road,
liking my loyalty, liking belief,
you smiled and you thanked me but very little believed me.

Here is some sun. Some.
20 Now off into the places rough to reach.
Though dry, though drowsy, all unwillingly a-wobble,
into the dissonant and dangerous crescendo.
Your work, that was done, to be done to be done to be done.

1981

## ROBERT BROWNING

### Porphyria's Lover[3]

The rain set early in tonight,
   The sullen wind was soon awake,
It tore the elm-tops down for spite,
   And did its worst to vex the lake:
5 I listened with heart fit to break.
When glided in Porphyria; straight
   She shut the cold out and the storm,

---

3. A monologue originally published under the title *Madhouse Cells*.

And kneeled and made the cheerless grate
   Blaze up, and all the cottage warm;
10 Which done, she rose, and from her form
Withdrew the dripping cloak and shawl,
   And laid her soiled gloves by, untied
Her hat and let the damp hair fall,
   And, last, she sat down by my side
15 And called me. When no voice replied,
   She put my arm about her waist,
And made her smooth white shoulder bare,
   And all her yellow hair displaced,
And, stooping, made my cheek lie there,
20 And spread, o'er all, her yellow hair,
   Murmuring how she loved me—she
Too weak, for all her heart's endeavor,
   To set its struggling passion free
From pride, and vainer ties dissever,
25 And give herself to me forever.
But passion sometimes would prevail,
   Nor could tonight's gay feast restrain
A sudden thought of one so pale
   For love of her, and all in vain:
30 So, she was come through wind and rain.
Be sure I looked up at her eyes
   Happy and proud; at last I knew
Porphyria worshiped me: surprise
   Made my heart swell, and still it grew
35 While I debated what to do.
That moment she was mine, mine, fair,
   Perfectly pure and good: I found
A thing to do, and all her hair
   In one long yellow string I wound
40 Three times her little throat around,
And strangled her. No pain felt she;
   I am quite sure she felt no pain.
As a shut bud that holds a bee,
   I warily oped her lids: again
45 Laughed the blue eyes without a stain.
And I untightened next the tress
   About her neck; her cheek once more
Blushed bright beneath my burning kiss:
   I propped her head up as before,
50 Only, this time my shoulder bore
Her head, which droops upon it still:
   The smiling rosy little head,
So glad it has its utmost will,
   That all it scorned at once is fled,
55 And I, its love, am gained instead!
Porphyria's love: she guessed not how

Her darling one wish would be heard.
And thus we sit together now,
    And all night long we have not stirred
60  And yet God has not said a word!

                                    1836, 1842

## SAMUEL TAYLOR COLERIDGE

### *Kubla Khan*

Or, a Vision in a Dream[4]

In Xanadu did Kubla Khan
A stately pleasure-dome decree:
Where Alph, the sacred river, ran
Through caverns measureless to man
5   Down to a sunless sea.
So twice five miles of fertile ground
With walls and towers were girdled round:
And here were gardens bright with sinuous rills
Where blossomed many an incense-bearing tree;
10  And here were forests ancient as the hills,
Enfolding sunny spots of greenery.

But oh! that deep romantic chasm which slanted
Down the green hill athwart a cedarn cover![5]
A savage place! as holy and enchanted
15  As e'er beneath a waning moon was haunted
By woman wailing for her demon-lover![6]
And from this chasm, with ceaseless turmoil seething,
As if this earth in fast thick pants were breathing,
A mighty fountain momently[7] was forced,
20  Amid whose swift half-intermitted burst
Huge fragments vaulted like rebounding hail,
Or chaffy grain beneath the thresher's flail:
And 'mid these dancing rocks at once and ever
It flung up momently the sacred river.
25  Five miles meandering with a mazy motion
Through wood and dale the sacred river ran,
Then reached the caverns measureless to man,
And sank in tumult to a lifeless ocean:
And 'mid this tumult Kubla heard from far

---

4. Coleridge said he wrote this fragment immediately after waking from an opium dream and that after he was interrupted by a caller he was unable to finish the poem.
5. From side to side beneath a cover of cedar trees.
6. In a famous and often-imitated German ballad, the lady Lenore is carried off on horseback by the specter of her lover and married to him at his grave.   7. Suddenly.

30  Ancestral voices prophesying war!

    The shadow of the dome of pleasure
    Floated midway on the waves;
    Where was heard the mingled measure
    From the fountain and the caves.
35  It was a miracle of rare device,
    A sunny pleasure-dome with caves of ice!

    A damsel with a dulcimer
    In a vision once I saw:
    It was an Abyssinian maid,
40  And on her dulcimer she played,
    Singing of Mount Abora.
    Could I revive within me
    Her symphony and song,
    To such a deep delight 'twould win me,
45  That with music loud and long,
    I would build that dome in air,
    That sunny dome! those caves of ice!
    And all who heard should see them there,
    And all should cry, Beware! Beware!
50  His flashing eyes, his floating hair!
    Weave a circle round him thrice,
    And close your eyes with holy dread,
    For he on honey-dew hath fed,
    And drunk the milk of Paradise.

1798

## EMILY DICKINSON

### [Because I could not stop for Death—]

Because I could not stop for Death—
He kindly stopped for me—
The Carriage held but just Ourselves—
And Immortality.

5  We slowly drove—He knew no haste
And I had put away
My labor and my leisure too,
For His Civility—

We passed the School, where Children strove
10  At Recess—in the Ring—
We passed the Fields of Gazing Grain—
We passed the Setting Sun—

Or rather—He passed Us—
The Dews drew quivering and chill—

15  For only Gossamer,[8] my Gown—
    My Tippet—only Tulle[9]—

    We paused before a House that seemed
    A Swelling of the Ground—
    The Roof was scarcely visible—
20  The Cornice—in the Ground—

    Since then—'tis Centuries—and yet
    Feels shorter than the Day
    I first surmised the Horses' Heads
    Were toward Eternity—

ca. 1863

## [I stepped from Plank to Plank]

   I stepped from Plank to Plank
   A slow and cautious way
   The Stars about my Head I felt
   About my Feet the Sea.

5  I knew not but the next
   Would be my final inch—
   This gave me that precarious Gait
   Some call Experience.

ca. 1864

## [We do not play on Graves—]

   We do not play on Graves—
   Because there isn't Room—
   Besides—it isn't even—it slants
   And People come—

5  And put a Flower on it—
   And hang their faces so—
   We're fearing that their Hearts will drop—
   And crush our pretty play—

   And so we move as far
10 As Enemies—away—
   Just looking round to see how far
   It is—Occasionally—

ca. 1862

---

8. A soft, sheer fabric.   9. A fine net fabric. *Tippet:* scarf.

## [The Brain—is wider than the Sky—]

The Brain—is wider than the Sky—
For—put them side by side—
The one the other will contain
With ease—and You—beside—
5  The Brain is deeper than the sea—
For—hold them—Blue to Blue—
The one the other will absorb—
As Sponges—Buckets—do—

The Brain is just the weight of God—
10 For—Heft them—Pound for Pound—
And they will differ—if they do—
As Syllable from Sound—

ca. 1862

## [She dealt her pretty words like Blades—]

She dealt her pretty words like Blades—
How glittering they shone—
And every One unbared a Nerve
Or wantoned with a Bone—
5  She never deemed—she hurt—
That—is not Steel's Affair—
A vulgar grimace in the Flesh—
How ill the Creatures bear—

To Ache is human—not polite—
10 The Film upon the eye
Mortality's old Custom—
Just locking up—to Die.

1862

# JOHN DONNE

## [Death, be not proud]

Death be not proud, though some have callèd thee
Mighty and dreadful, for thou art not so;
For those whom thou think'st thou dost overthrow

Die not, poor Death, nor yet canst thou kill me.
5 From rest and sleep, which but thy pictures[1] be,
Much pleasure; then from thee much more must flow,
And soonest[2] our best men with thee do go,
Rest of their bones, and soul's delivery.[3]
Thou art slave to Fate, Chance, kings, and desperate men,
10 And dost with Poison, War, and Sickness dwell;
And poppy or charms can make us sleep as well,
And better than thy stroke; why swell'st[4] thou then?
One short sleep past, we wake eternally
And death shall be no more; Death, thou shalt die.

1633

## The Sun Rising

Busy old fool, unruly sun,
    Why dost thou thus,
Through windows, and through curtains, call on us?
Must to thy motions lovers' seasons run?
5     Saucy pedantic wretch, go chide
    Late schoolboys, and sour prentices,[5]
Go tell court-huntsmen that the king will ride,
Call country ants[6] to harvest offices;
Love, all alike, no season knows, nor clime,
10 Nor hours, days, months, which are the rags of time.
    Thy beams, so reverend and strong
    why shouldst thou think?
I could eclipse and cloud them with a wink,
But that I would not lose her sight so long:
15     If her eyes have not blinded thine,
    Look, and tomorrow late, tell me
Whether both the Indias[7] of spice and mine
Be where thou left'st them, or lie here with me.
Ask for those kings whom thou saw'st yesterday,
20 And thou shalt hear, all here in one bed lay.

    She is all states, and all princes I,
    Nothing else is.
Princes do but play us; compared to this,
All honor's mimic,[8] all wealth alchemy.
25     Thou, sun, art half as happy as we,
    In that the world's contracted thus;
Thine age asks[9] ease, and since thy duties be

---

1. Likenesses.   2. Most willingly.   3. Deliverance.   4. Puff with pride.   5. Apprentices.
6. Farmworkers.   7. The East and West Indies, commercial sources of spices and gold.   8. Hypocritical.
9. Requires.

To warm the world, that's done in warming us.
Shine here to us, and thou art every where;
30 This bed thy center[1] is, these walls thy sphere.
                    1633


## Song

Go, and catch a falling star,
  Get with child a mandrake root,[2]
Tell me, where all past years are,
  Or who cleft the devil's foot,
5 Teach me to hear mermaids singing
Or to keep off envy's stinging,
    And find
    What wind
Serves to advance an honest mind.

10 If thou beest born to strange sights,[3]
  Things invisible to see,
Ride ten thousand days and nights,
  Till age snow white hairs on thee;
Thou, when thou return'st, wilt tell me
15 All strange wonders that befell thee,
    And swear
    No where
Lives a woman true, and fair.

If thou find'st one, let me know:
20   Such a pilgrimage were sweet.
Yet do not, I would not go,
  Though at next door we might meet:
Though she were true when you met her,
And last till you write your letter,
25     Yet she
    Will be
False, ere I come, to two, or three.
                    1633

---

1. Of orbit.  2. The forked mandrake root looks vaguely like a pair of human legs.
3. That is, if you have supernatural powers.

## A Valediction: Forbidding Mourning

As virtuous men pass mildly away,
   And whisper to their souls to go,
Whilst some of their sad friends do say,
   "The breath goes now," and some say, "No,"

5 So let us melt, and make no noise,
   No tear-floods, nor sigh-tempests move;
'Twere profanation of our joys
   To tell the laity our love.

Moving of the earth[4] brings harms and fears,
10   Men reckon what it did and meant;
But trepidation of the spheres,[5]
   Though greater far, is innocent.

Dull sublunary[6] lovers' love
   (Whose soul is sense) cannot admit
15 Absence, because it doth remove
   Those things which elemented[7] it.

But we, by a love so much refined
   That our selves know not what it is,
Inter-assured of the mind,
20   Care less, eyes, lips, and hands to miss.

Our two souls therefore, which are one,
   Though I must go, endure not yet
A breach, but an expansion,
   Like gold to airy thinness beat.

25 If they be two, they are two so
   As stiff twin compasses are two:
Thy soul, the fixed foot, makes no show
   To move, but doth, if the other do;

And though it in the center sit,
30   Yet when the other far doth roam,
It leans, and hearkens after it,
   And grows erect, as that comes home.

Such wilt thou be to me, who must,
   Like the other foot, obliquely run;

---

4. Earthquakes.
5. The Renaissance hypothesis that the celestial spheres trembled and thus caused unexpected variations in their orbits. Such movements are "innocent" because earthlings do not observe or fret about them.
6. Below the moon—that is, changeable. According to the traditional cosmology that Donne invokes here, the moon was considered the dividing line between the immutable celestial world and the earthly mortal one.    7. Comprised.

35  Thy firmness makes my circle[8] just,
       And makes me end where I begun.

1611?

## PAUL LAURENCE DUNBAR

### Sympathy

   I know what the caged bird feels, alas!
       When the sun is bright on the upland slopes;
   When the wind stirs soft through the springing grass,
       And the river flows like a stream of glass;
5      When the first bird sings and the first bud opens,
       And the faint perfume from its chalice steals—
   I know what the caged bird feels!

   I know why the caged bird beats his wing
       Till its blood is red on the cruel bars;
10 For he must fly back to his perch and cling
       When he fain[9] would be on the bough a-swing;
       And a pain still throbs in the old, old scars
       And they pulse again with a keener sting—
   I know why he beats his wing!

15 I know why the caged bird sings, ah me,
       When his wing is bruised and his bosom sore,—
   When he beats his bars and he would be free;
   It is not a carol of joy or glee,
       But a prayer that he sends from his heart's deep core,
20 But a plea, that upward to Heaven he flings—
   I know why the caged bird sings!

                                                     1893

### We Wear the Mask

   We wear the mask that grins and lies,
   It hides our cheeks and shades our eyes,—
   This debt we pay to human guile;
       With torn and bleeding hearts we smile,
5  And mouth with myriad subtleties.

   Why should the world be over-wise,
   In counting all our tears and sighs?

---

8. A traditional symbol of perfection.   9. Gladly.

Nay, let them only see us, while
      We wear the mask.

10 We smile, but, O great Christ, our cries
   To thee from tortured souls arise.
   We sing, but oh the clay is vile
   Beneath our feet, and long the mile;
   But let the world dream otherwise,
15    We wear the mask!
                                    1895


## T. S. ELIOT

## *Journey of the Magi*[1]

"A cold coming we had of it,
Just the worst time of the year
For a journey, and such a long journey:
The ways deep and the weather sharp,
5 The very dead of winter."[2]
And the camels galled, sore-footed, refractory,
Lying down in the melting snow.
There were times we regretted
The summer palaces on slopes, the terraces,
10 And the silken girls bringing sherbet.
Then the camel men cursing and grumbling
And running away, and wanting their liquor and women,
And the night-fires going out, and the lack of shelters,
And the cities hostile and the towns unfriendly
15 And the villages dirty and charging high prices:
A hard time we had of it.
At the end we preferred to travel all night,
Sleeping in snatches,
With the voices singing in our ears, saying
20 That this was all folly.

   Then at dawn we came down to a temperate valley,
Wet, below the snow line, smelling of vegetation;
With a running stream and a water-mill beating the darkness,
And three trees on the low sky,[3]
25 And an old white horse galloped away in the meadow.

---

1. The wise men who followed the star of Bethlehem. See Matthew 2.1–12.
2. An adaptation of a passage from a 1622 sermon by Lancelot Andrews.
3. Suggesting the three crosses of the Crucifixion (Luke 23.32–33). The Magi see several objects that suggest later events in Christ's life: pieces of silver (see Matthew 26.14–16), the dicing (see Matthew 27.35), the white horse (see Revelation 6.2 and 19.11–16), and the empty wine skins (see Matthew 9.17, possibly relevant also to lines 41–42).

Then we came to a tavern with vine-leaves over the lintel,
Six hands at an open door dicing for pieces of silver,
And feet kicking the empty wine-skins.
But there was no information, and so we continued
30 And arrived at evening, not a moment too soon
Finding the place; it was (you may say) satisfactory.

    All this was a long time ago, I remember,
And I would do it again, but set down
This set down
35 This: were we led all that way for
Birth or Death? There was a Birth, certainly,
We had evidence and no doubt. I had seen birth and death,
But had thought they were different; this Birth was
Hard and bitter agony for us, like Death, our death.
40 We returned to our places, these Kingdoms,[4]
But no longer at ease here, in the old dispensation,
With an alien people clutching their gods.
I should be glad of another death.

                                         1927

## ROBERT FROST

### The Road Not Taken

Two roads diverged in a yellow wood,
And sorry I could not travel both
And be one traveler, long I stood
And looked down one as far as I could
5 To where it bent in the undergrowth;

Then took the other, as just as fair,
And having perhaps the better claim,
Because it was grassy and wanted wear;
Though as for that the passing there
10 Had worn them really about the same,

And both that morning equally lay
In leaves no step had trodden black.
Oh, I kept the first for another day!
Yet knowing how way leads on to way,
15 I doubted if I should ever come back.

I shall be telling this with a sigh
Somewhere ages and ages hence:
Two roads diverged in a wood, and I—

---

4. The Bible identifies the wise men only as "from the east," and subsequent tradition has made them kings. In Persia, magi were members of an ancient priestly caste.

I took the one less traveled by,
20 And that has made all the difference.

1916

## Stopping by Woods on a Snowy Evening

Whose woods these are I think I know.
His house is in the village, though;
He will not see me stopping here
To watch his woods fill up with snow.

5 My little horse must think it queer
To stop without a farmhouse near
Between the woods and frozen lake
The darkest evening of the year.

He gives his harness bells a shake
10 To ask if there is some mistake.
The only other sound's the sweep
Of easy wind and downy flake.

The woods are lovely, dark, and deep,
But I have promises to keep,
15 And miles to go before I sleep,
And miles to go before I sleep.

1923

### ALLEN GINSBERG

## Velocity of Money

*For Lee Berton*

I'm delighted by the velocity of money as it whistles through
   windows of Lower East Side
Delighted skyscrapers rise grungy apartments fall on 84th Street's
   pavement
Delighted this year inflation drives me out on the street
with double digit interest rates in Capitalist worlds
5 I always was a communist, now we'll win
as usury makes walls thinner, books thicker & dumber
Usury makes my poetry more valuable
Manuscripts worth their weight in useless gold—
The velocity's what counts as the National Debt gets trillions higher
10 Everybody running after the rising dollar

Crowds of joggers down Broadway past City Hall on the way to the Fed
Nobody reads Dostoyevsky books anymore so they'll have to give passing ear
to my fragmented ravings in between President's speeches
Nothing's happening but the collapse of the Economy
15 so I can go back to sleep till the landlord wins his eviction suit in court

February 18, 1986, 10:00 A.M.

**THOMAS GRAY**

## Elegy Written in a Country Churchyard

The curfew tolls the knell of parting day,
    The lowing herd wind slowly o'er the lea,
The plowman homeward plods his weary way,
    And leaves the world to darkness and to me.

5 Now fades the glimmering landscape on the sight,
    And all the air a solemn stillness holds,
Save where the beetle wheels his droning flight,
    And drowsy tinklings lull the distant folds;

Save that from yonder ivy-mantled tower
10    The moping owl does to the moon complain
Of such, as wandering near her secret bower,
    Molest her ancient solitary reign.

Beneath those rugged elms, that yew tree's shade,
    Where heaves the turf in many a moldering heap,
15 Each in his narrow cell forever laid,
    The rude[5] forefathers of the hamlet sleep.

The breezy call of incense-breathing Morn,
    The swallow twittering from the straw-built shed,
The cock's shrill clarion, or the echoing horn.[6]
20    No more shall rouse them from their lowly bed.

For them no more the blazing hearth shall burn,
    Or busy housewife ply her evening care;
No children run to lisp their sire's return,
    Or climb his knees the envied kiss to share.

25 Oft did the harvest to their sickle yield,
    Their furrow oft the stubborn glebe[7] has broke;
How jocund did they drive their team afield!
    How bowed the woods beneath their sturdy stroke!

5. Unlearned.   6. The hunter's horn.   7. Soil.

>           Let not Ambition mock their useful toil,
> 30    Their homely joys, and destiny obscure;
>        Nor Grandeur hear with a disdainful smile
>           The short and simple annals of the poor.
>
>        The boast of heraldry,[8] the pomp of power,
>           And all that beauty, all that wealth e'er gave,
> 35    Awaits alike the inevitable hour.
>           The paths of glory lead but to the grave.
>
>        Nor you, ye proud, impute to these the fault,
>           If Memory o'er their tomb no trophies[9] raise,
>        Where through the long-drawn aisle and fretted[1] vault
> 40       The pealing anthem swells the note of praise
>
>        Can storied urn or animated[2] bust
>           Back to its mansion call the fleeting breath?
>        Can Honor's voice provoke the silent dust,
>           Or Flattery soothe the dull cold ear of Death?
>
> 45    Perhaps in this neglected spot is laid
>           Some heart once pregnant with celestial fire;
>        Hands that the rod of empire might have swayed,
>           Or waked to ecstasy the living lyre.
>
>        But Knowledge to their eyes her ample page
> 50       Rich with the spoils of time did ne'er unroll;
>        Chill Penury repressed their noble rage,
>           And froze the genial current of the soul.
>
>        Full many a gem of purest ray serene,
>           The dark unfathomed caves of ocean bear:
> 55    Full many a flower is born to blush unseen,
>           And waste its sweetness on the desert air.
>
>        Some village Hampden,[3] that with dauntless breast
>           The little tyrant of his fields withstood;
>        Some mute inglorious Milton[4] here may rest,
> 60       Some Cromwell[5] guiltless of his country's blood.
>
>        The applause of listening senates to command,
>           The threats of pain and ruin to despise,
>        To scatter plenty o'er a smiling land,
>           And read their history in a nation's eyes,

---

8. Noble birth.
9. An ornamental or symbolic group of figures depicting the achievements of the deceased.
1. Decorated with intersecting lines in relief.
2. Lifelike. *Storied urn:* a funeral urn with an epitaph or pictured story inscribed on it.
3. John Hampden (1594–1643), who, both as a private citizen and as a member of Parliament, zealously defended the rights of the people against the autocratic policies of Charles I.
4. John Milton (1608–1674), great English poet.
5. Oliver Cromwell (1599–1658), lord protector of England during the Interregnum, noted for military genius but also cruelty and intolerance.

65 Their lot forbade: nor circumscribed alone
   Their growing virtues, but their crimes confined;
Forbade to wade through slaughter to a throne,
   And shut the gates of mercy on mankind,

The struggling pangs of conscious truth to hide,
70 To quench the blushes of ingenuous shame,
Or heap the shrine of Luxury and Pride
   With incense kindled at the Muse's flame.

Far from the madding crowd's ignoble strife,
   Their sober wishes never learned to stray;
75 Along the cool sequestered vale of life
   They kept the noiseless tenor of their way.

Yet even these bones from insult to protect
   Some frail memorial still erected nigh,
With uncouth rhymes and shapeless sculpture decked,[6]
80    Implores the passing tribute of a sigh.

Their name, their years, spelt by the unlettered Muse,
   The place of fame and elegy supply:
And many a holy text around she strews,
   That teach the rustic moralist to die.

85 For who to dumb Forgetfulness a prey,
   This pleasing anxious being e'er resigned,
Left the warm precincts of the cheerful day,
   Nor cast one longing lingering look behind?

On some fond breast the parting soul relies,
90    Some pious drops the closing eye requires;
Even from the tomb the voice of Nature cries,
   Even in our ashes live their wonted fires.

For thee, who mindful of the unhonored dead
   Dost in these lines their artless tale relate;
95 If chance, by lonely contemplation led,
   Some kindred spirit shall inquire thy fate,

Haply some hoary-headed swain may say,
   "Oft have we seen him at the peep of dawn
Brushing with hasty steps the dews away
100    To meet the sun upon the upland lawn.

"There at the foot of yonder nodding beech
   That wreathes its old fantastic roots so high,
His listless length at noontide would he stretch,
   And pore upon the brook that babbles by.

105 "Hard by yon wood, now smiling as in scorn,
   Muttering his wayward fancies he would rove,

---

6. Cf. the "storied urn or animated bust" (line 41) dedicated inside the church to the "proud" (line 37).

Now drooping, woeful wan, like one forlorn,
   Or crazed with care, or crossed in hopeless love.

"One morn I missed him on the customed hill,
110   Along the heath and near his favorite tree;
Another came; nor yet beside the rill,
   Nor up the lawn, nor at the wood was he;

"The next with dirges due in sad array
   Slow through the churchway path we saw him borne.
115  Approach and read (for thou canst read) the lay,
   Graved on the stone beneath yon aged thorn."

*The Epitaph*

*Here rests his head upon the lap of Earth*
   *A youth to Fortune and to Fame unknown.*
*Fair Science[7] frowned not on his humble birth,*
120  *And Melancholy marked him for her own.*

*Large was his bounty, and his soul sincere,*
   *Heaven did a recompense as largely send:*
*He gave to Misery all he had, a tear,*
   *He gained from Heaven ('twas all he wished) a friend.*

125  *No farther seek his merits to disclose,*
   *Or draw his frailties from their dread abode*
*(There they alike in trembling hope repose),*
   *The bosom of his Father and his God.*

                                          1751

## ROBERT HAYDEN

### *The Whipping*

The old woman across the way
   is whipping the boy again
and shouting to the neighborhood
   her goodness and his wrongs.

5  Wildly he crashes through elephant ears,
   pleads in dusty zinnias,
while she in spite of crippling fat
   pursues and corners him.

She strikes and strikes the shrilly circling
10  boy till the stick breaks
in her hand. His tears are rainy weather
   to woundlike memories:

---

7. Learning.

My head gripped in bony vise
  of knees, the writhing struggle
15 to wrench free, the blows, the fear
  worse than blows that hateful

Words could bring, the face that I
  no longer knew or loved....
Well, it is over now, it is over,
20  and the boy sobs in his room,

And the woman leans muttering against
  a tree, exhausted, purged—
avenged in part for lifelong hidings
  she has had to bear.
                              1962, 1966


**SEAMUS HEANEY**

## Digging

Between my finger and my thumb
The squat pen rests; snug as a gun.

Under my window, a clean rasping sound
When the spade sinks into gravelly ground:
5 My father, digging. I look down

Till his straining rump among the flowerbeds
Bends low, comes up twenty years away
Stooping in rhythm through potato drills[8]
Where he was digging.

10 The coarse boot nestled on the lug, the shaft
Against the inside knee was levered firmly.
He rooted out tall tops, buried the bright edge deep
To scatter new potatoes that we picked
Loving their cool hardness in our hands.

15 By God, the old man could handle a spade.
Just like his old man.

My grandfather cut more turf[9] in a day
Than any other man on Toner's bog.
Once I carried him milk in a bottle
20 Corked sloppily with paper. He straightened up
To drink it, then fell to right away.
Nicking and slicing neatly, heaving sods
Over his shoulder, going down and down
For the good turf. Digging.

8. Small furrows in which seeds are sown.
9. Peat cut into slabs and dried to be used as fuel in stoves and furnaces.

25 The cold smell of potato mould, the squelch and slap
   Of soggy peat, the curt cuts of an edge
   Through living roots awaken in my head.
   But I've no spade to follow men like them.

   Between my finger and my thumb
30 The squat pen rests.
   I'll dig with it.

                                          1966


## Punishment[1]

I can feel the tug
of the halter at the nape
of her neck, the wind
on her naked front.

5 It blows her nipples
to amber beads,
it shakes the frail rigging
of her ribs.

I can see her drowned
10 body in the bog,
the weighing stone,
the floating rods and boughs.

Under which at first
she was a barked sapling
15 that is dug up
oak-bone, brain-firkin:

her shaved head
like a stubble of black corn,
her blindfold a soiled bandage,
20 her noose a ring

to store
the memories of love.
Little adulteress,
before they punished you

25 you were flaxen-haired,
undernourished, and your
tar-black face was beautiful.
My poor scapegoat,

---

1. According to the Roman historian Tacitus (ca. 56–ca. 120 C.E.), Germanic peoples punished adulterous women by shaving their heads, then either banishing or killing them. In 1951, in Windeby, Germany, the naked body of a young girl from the first century C.E. was pulled from the bog where she had been murdered. In contemporary Ireland, "betraying sisters" (line 38) have sometimes been punished by the IRA for associating with British soldiers.

I almost love you
but would have cast, I know,
the stones of silence.
I am the artful voyeur

of your brain's exposed
and darkened combs,
your muscles' webbing
and all your numbered bones:

I who have stood dumb
when your betraying sisters,
cauled[2] in tar,
wept by the railings,

who would connive
in civilized outrage
yet understand the exact
and tribal, intimate revenge.

1975


### GERARD MANLEY HOPKINS

## God's Grandeur

The world is charged with the grandeur of God.
  It will flame out, like shining from shook foil;[3]
  It gathers to a greatness, like the ooze of oil
Crushed. Why do men then now not reck his rod?[4]
Generations have trod, have trod, have trod;
  And all is seared with trade; bleared, smeared with toil;
  And wears man's smudge and shares man's smell: the soil
Is bare now, nor can foot feel, being shod.

And for all this, nature is never spent;
  There lives the dearest freshness deep down things;
And though the last lights off the black West went
  Oh, morning, at the brown brink eastward, springs—
Because the Holy Ghost over the bent
  World broods with warm breast and with ah! bright wings.

1918

---

2. Wrapped or enclosed as if in a caul (the inner fetal membrane of higher vertebrates that sometimes covers the head at birth).
3. "I mean foil in its sense of leaf or tinsel. . . . Shaken goldfoil gives off broad glares like sheet lightning and also, and this is true of nothing else, owing to its zig-zag dints and creasings and network of small many cornered facets, a sort of fork lightning too" (*Letters of Gerard Manley Hopkins to Robert Bridges,* ed. C. C. Abbott [1955], p. 169).   4. Heed his authority.

## The Windhover[5]

### To Christ our Lord

I caught this morning morning's minion,[6] king-
   dom of daylight's dauphin,[7] dapple-dawn-drawn Falcon, in his riding
   Of the rolling level underneath him steady air, and striding
High there, how he rung upon the rein of a wimpling[8] wing
5 In his ecstasy! then off, off forth on swing,
   As a skate's heel sweeps smooth on a bow-bend: the hurl and gliding
   Rebuffed the big wind. My heart in hiding
Stirred for a bird,—the achieve of, the mastery of the thing!

Brute beauty and valor and act, oh, air, pride, plume, here
10 Buckle![9] AND the fire that breaks from thee then, a billion
Times told lovelier, more dangerous, O my chevalier![1]

No wonder of it: shéer plód makes plow down sillion[2]
Shine, and blue-bleak embers, ah my dear,
   Fall, gall themselves, and gash gold-vermilion.

1877

## GALWAY KINNELL

### Blackberry Eating

I love to go out in late September
among the fat, overripe, icy, black blackberries
to eat blackberries for breakfast,
the stalks very prickly, a penalty
5 they earn for knowing the black art
of blackberry-making; and as I stand among them
lifting the stalks to my mouth, the ripest berries
fall almost unbidden to my tongue,
as words sometimes do, certain peculiar words
10 like *strengths* or *squinched,*
many-lettered, one-syllabled lumps,
which I squeeze, squinch open, and splurge well
in the silent, startled, icy, black language
of blackberry-eating in late September.

1980

---

5. A small hawk, the kestrel, which habitually hovers in the air, headed into the wind.   6. Favorite, beloved.
7. Heir to regal splendor.   8. Rippling.
9. Several meanings may apply: to join closely, to prepare for battle, to grapple with, to collapse.
1. Horseman, knight.
2. The narrow strip of land between furrows in an open field divided for separate cultivation.

## ROBERT LOWELL

### Skunk Hour

*for Elizabeth Bishop*

Nautilus Island's hermit
heiress still lives through winter in her Spartan cottage;
her sheep still graze above the sea.
Her son's a bishop. Her farmer
5 is first selectman[3] in our village,
she's in her dotage.

Thirsting for
the hierarchic privacy
of Queen Victoria's century,
10 she buys up all
the eyesores facing her shore,
and lets them fall.

The season's ill—
we've lost our summer millionaire,
15 who seemed to leap from an L. L. Bean[4]
catalogue. His nine-knot yawl
was auctioned off to lobstermen.
A red fox stain covers Blue Hill.

And now our fairy
20 decorator brightens his shop for fall,
his fishnet's filled with orange cork,
orange, his cobbler's bench and awl,
there is no money in his work,
he'd rather marry.

25 One dark night,
my Tudor Ford climbed the hill's skull,
I watched for love-cars. Lights turned down,
they lay together, hull to hull,
where the graveyard shelves on the town. . . .
30 My mind's not right.

A car radio bleats,
"Love, O careless Love. . . ."[5] I hear
my ill-spirit sob in each blood cell,
as if my hand were at its throat. . . .
35 I myself am hell;
nobody's here—

---

3. An elected New England town official.  4. Famous old Maine sporting goods firm.
5. A popular folk song recorded many times, as by Frankie Laine (1959).

only skunks, that search
in the moonlight for a bite to eat.
They march on their soles up Main Street:
40 white stripes, moonstruck eyes' red fire
under the chalk-dry and spar spire
of the Trinitarian Church.

I stand on top
of our back steps and breathe the rich air—
45 a mother skunk with her column of kittens swills the garbage pail.
She jabs her wedge head in a cup
of sour cream, drops her ostrich tail,
and will not scare.

1959

ANDREW MARVELL

## The Garden

How vainly men themselves amaze[6]
To win the palm, the oak, or bays,[7]
And their incessant labors see
Crowned from some single herb, or tree,
5 Whose short and narrow-vergèd[8] shade
Does prudently their toils upbraid;
While all flowers and all trees do close[9]
To weave the garlands of repose!

Fair Quiet, have I found thee here,
10 And Innocence, thy sister dear?
Mistaken long, I sought you then
In busy companies of men.
Your sacred plants,[1] if here below,
Only among the plants will grow;
15 Society is all but rude[2]
To[3] this delicious solitude.

No white nor red was ever seen
So am'rous as this lovely green.
Fond lovers, cruel as their flame,
20 Cut in these trees their mistress' name:
Little, alas, they know, or heed
How far these beauties hers exceed!
Fair trees, wheresoe'er your barks I wound,
No name shall but your own be found.

---

6. Become frenzied.   7. Awards for athletic, civic, and literary achievements.   8. Narrowly cropped.
9. Unite.   1. Cuttings.   2. Barbarous.   3. Compared to.

25   When we have run our passion's heat,
     Love hither makes his best retreat.
     The gods, that mortal beauty chase,
     Still in a tree did end their race:
     Apollo hunted Daphne so,
30   Only that she might laurel grow;
     And Pan did after Syrinx speed,
     Not as a nymph, but for a reed.[4]

     What wondrous life is this I lead!
     Ripe apples drop about my head;
35   The luscious clusters of the vine
     Upon my mouth do crush their wine;
     The nectarine and curious[5] peach
     Into my hands themselves do reach;
     Stumbling on melons, as I npass,
40   Insnared with flowers, I fall on grass.

     Meanwhile the mind, from pleasure less,
     Withdraws into its happiness;[6]
     The mind, that ocean where each kind
     Does straight its own resemblance find;[7]
45   Yet it creates, transcending these,
     Far other worlds and other seas,
     Annihilating[8] all that's made
     To a green thought in a green shade.

     Here at the fountain's sliding foot,
50   Or at some fruit tree's mossy root,
     Casting the body's vest[9] aside,
     My soul into the boughs does glide:
     There, like a bird, it sits and sings,
     Then whets[1] and combs its silver wings,
55   And, till prepared for longer flight,
     Waves in its plumes the various[2] light.

     Such was that happy garden-state,
     While man there walked without a mate:
     After a place so pure, and sweet,
60   What other help could yet be meet![3]
     But 'twas beyond a mortal's share
     To wander solitary there:
     Two paradises 'twere in one
     To live in paradise alone.

---

4. In Ovid's *Metamorphoses*, Daphne, pursued by Apollo, is turned into a laurel, and Syrinx, pursued by Pan, into a reed that Pan makes into a flute.   5. Exquisite.
6. That is, the mind withdraws from lesser-sense pleasure into contemplation.
7. All land creatures supposedly had corresponding sea creatures.   8. Reducing to nothing by comparison.
9. Vestment, clothing; the flesh is being considered as simply clothing for the soul.   1. Preens.
2. Many-colored.   3. Appropriate.

65    How well the skillful gardener drew
       Of flowers and herbs this dial[4] new,
       Where, from above, the milder sun
       Does through a fragrant zodiac run;
       And as it works, th' industrious bee
70 Computes its time as well as we!
       How could such sweet and wholesome hours
       Be reckoned but with herbs and flowers?

                                              1681

## SYLVIA PLATH

### *Barren Woman*

    Empty, I echo to the least footfall,
    Museum without statues, grand with pillars, porticoes, rotundas.
    In my courtyard a fountain leaps and sinks back into itself,
    Nun-hearted and blind to the world. Marble lilies
5  Exhale their pallor like scent.

    I imagine myself with a great public,
    Mother of a white Nike and several bald-eyed Apollos.[5]
    Instead, the dead injure me with attentions, and nothing can happen.
    The moon lays a hand on my forehead,
10 Blank-faced and mum as a nurse.

February 21, 1963

### *Black Rook in Rainy Weather*

    On the stiff twig up there
    Hunches a wet black rook
    Arranging and rearranging its feathers in the rain.
    I do not expect a miracle
5  Or an accident

    To set the sight on fire
    In my eye, nor seek
    Any more in the desultory weather some design,
    But let spotted leaves fall as they fall,
10 Without ceremony, or portent

    Although, I admit, I desire,
    Occasionally, some backtalk

---

4. A garden planted in the shape of a sundial, complete with zodiac.
5. That is, gods of poetic inspiration. *Nike:* goddess of victory.

From the mute sky, I can't honestly complain:
A certain minor light may still
15 Leap incandescent

Out of kitchen table or chair
As if a celestial burning took
Possession of the most obtuse objects now and then—
Thus hallowing an interval
20 Otherwise inconsequent

By bestowing largesse, honor,
One might say love. At any rate, I now walk
Wary (for it could happen
Even in this dull, ruinous landscape); skeptical,
25 Yet politic; ignorant

Of whatever angel may choose to flare
Suddenly at my elbow. I only know that a rook
Ordering its black feathers can so shine
As to seize my senses, haul
30 My eyelids up, and grant

A brief respite from fear
Of total neutrality. With luck,
Trekking stubborn through this season
Of fatigue, I shall
35 Patch together a content

Of sorts. Miracles occur,
If you care to call those spasmodic
Tricks of radiance miracles. The wait's begun again,
The long wait for the angel,
40 For that rare, random descent.[6]

                                        1960


## Lady Lazarus

I have done it again.
One year in every ten
I manage it—

A sort of walking miracle, my skin
5 Bright as a Nazi lampshade,
My right foot

---

6. According to Acts 2, the Holy Ghost at Pentecost descended like a tongue of fire upon Jesus' disciples.

A paperweight,
My face a featureless, fine
Jew linen.[7]

10 Peel off the napkin
O my enemy.
Do I terrify?—

The nose, the eye pits, the full set of teeth?
The sour breath
15 Will vanish in a day.

Soon, soon the flesh
The grave cave ate will be
At home on me

And I a smiling woman.
20 I am only thirty.
And like the cat I have nine times to die.

This is Number Three.
What a trash
To annihilate each decade.

25 What a million filaments.
The peanut-crunching crowd
Shoves in to see

Them unwrap me hand and foot—
The big strip tease.
30 Gentlemen, ladies

These are my hands
My knees.
I may be skin and bone,

Nevertheless, I am the same, identical woman.
35 The first time it happened I was ten.
It was an accident.

The second time I meant
To last it out and not come back at all.
I rocked shut

40 As a seashell.
They had to call and call
And pick the worms off me like sticky pearls.

Dying
Is an art, like everything else.
45 I do it exceptionally well.

---

7. During World War II, in some Nazi camps, prisoners were gassed to death and their body parts then turned into objects such as lampshades and paperweights.

I do it so it feels like hell.
I do it so it feels real.
I guess you could say I've a call.

It's easy enough to do it in a cell.
50 It's easy enough to do it and stay put.
It's the theatrical

Comeback in broad day
To the same place, the same face, the same brute
Amused shout:

55 "A miracle!"
That knocks me out.
There is a charge

For the eyeing of my scars, there is a charge
For the hearing of my heart—
60 It really goes.

And there is a charge, a very large charge
For a word or a touch
Or a bit of blood

Or a piece of my hair or my clothes.
65 So, so Herr Doktor.
So, Herr Enemy.

I am your opus,
I am your valuable,
The pure gold baby

70 That melts to a shriek.
I turn and burn.
Do not think I underestimate your great concern.

Ash, ash—
You poke and stir.
75 Flesh, bone, there is nothing there—

A cake of soap,
A wedding ring,
A gold filling.

Herr God, Herr Lucifer
80 Beware
Beware.

Out of the ash
I rise with my red hair
And I eat men like air.

1965

EZRA POUND

## In a Station of the Metro[8]

The apparition of these faces in the crowd;
Petals on a wet, black bough.

                                    1913

## A Virginal

No, no! Go from me. I have left her lately.
I will not spoil my sheath with lesser brightness,
For my surrounding air hath a new lightness;
Slight are her arms, yet they have bound me straitly
5  And left me cloaked as with a gauze of aether;
As with sweet leaves; as with a subtle clearness.
Oh, I have picked up magic in her nearness
To sheathe me half in half the things that sheathe her.
No, no! Go from me, I have still the flavor,
10 Soft as spring wind that's come from birchen bowers.
Green come the shoots, aye April in the branches,
As winter's wound with her sleight hand she staunches,
Hath of the trees a likeness of the savor:
As white their bark, so white this lady's hours.

                                    1912

FRANCIS QUARLES

## On Change of Weathers

And were it for thy profit, to obtain
All sunshine? No vicissitude of rain?
Think'st thou that thy laborious plough requires
Not winter frosts as well as summer fires?
5  There must be both: sometimes these hearts of ours
Must have the sweet, the seasonable showers
Of tears; sometimes the frost of chill despair
Makes our desired sunshine seem more fair;
Weathers that most oppose the flesh and blood
10 Are such as help to make our harvest good.
We may not choose, great God: it is they task;
We know not what to have, nor how to ask.

                                    1632

---

8. The Paris subway.

**JOHN CROWE RANSOM**

## Bells for John Whiteside's Daughter

There was such speed in her little body,
And such lightness in her footfall,
It is no wonder her brown study[9]
Astonishes us all.

5  Her wars were bruited in our high window.
We looked among orchard trees and beyond
Where she took arms against her shadow,
Or harried unto the pond

The lazy geese, like a snow cloud
10 Dripping their snow on the green grass,
Tricking and stopping, sleepy and proud,
Who cried in goose, Alas,

For the tireless heart within the little
Lady with rod that made them rise
15 From their noon apple-dreams and scuttle
Goose-fashion under the skies!

But now go the bells, and we are ready,
In one house we are sternly stopped
To say we are vexed at her brown study,
20 Lying so primly propped.

                                        1924


**THEODORE ROETHKE**

## I Knew a Woman

I knew a woman, lovely in her bones,
When small birds sighed, she would sigh back at them;
Ah, when she moved, she moved more ways than one:
The shapes a bright container can contain!
5  Of her choice virtues only gods should speak;
Or English poets who grew up on Greek
(I'd have them sing in chorus, cheek to cheek).

How well her wishes went! She stroked my chin,
She taught me Turn, and Counter-turn, and Stand;[1]
10 She taught me Touch, that undulant white skin;
I nibbled meekly from her proffered hand;

---

9. Stillness, as if in meditation or deep thought.   1. Literary terms for the parts of a Pindaric ode.

She was the sickle; I, poor I, the rake,
Coming behind her for her pretty sake
(But what prodigious mowing we did make).

15 Love likes a gander, and adores a goose:
Her full lips pursed, the errant note to seize;
She played it quick, she played it light and loose;
My eyes, they dazzled at her flowing knees;
Her several parts could keep a pure repose,
20 Or one hip quiver with a mobile nose
(She moved in circles, and those circles moved).

Let seed be grass, and grass turn into hay:
I'm martyr to a motion not my own;
What's freedom for? To know eternity.
25 I swear she cast a shadow white as stone.
But who would count eternity in days?
These old bones live to learn her wanton ways:
(I measure time by how a body sways).

1958

## *The Waking*

I wake to sleep, and take my waking slow.
I feel my fate in what I cannot fear.
I learn by going where I have to go.

We think by feeling. What is there to know?
5 I hear my being dance from ear to ear.
I wake to sleep, and take my waking slow.

Of those so close beside me, which are you?
God bless the Ground! I shall walk softly there,
And learn by going where I have to go.

10 Light takes the Tree; but who can tell us how?
The lowly worm climbs up a winding stair;
I wake to sleep, and take my waking slow.

Great Nature has another thing to do
To you and me; so take the lively air,
15 And, lovely, learn by going where to go.

This shaking keeps me steady. I should know.
What falls away is always. And is near.
I wake to sleep, and take my waking slow.
I learn by going where I have to go.

1953

# WALLACE STEVENS

## The Idea of Order at Key West

She sang beyond the genius of the sea.
The water never formed to mind or voice,
Like a body wholly body, fluttering
Its empty sleeves; and yet its mimic motion
5 Made constant cry, caused constantly a cry,
That was not ours although we understood,
Inhuman, of the veritable ocean.

The sea was not a mask. No more was she.
The song and water were not medleyed sound
10 Even if what she sang was what she heard,
Since what she sang was uttered word by word.
It may be that in all her phrases stirred
The grinding water and the gasping wind;
But it was she and not the sea we heard.

15 For she was the maker of the song she sang.
The ever-hooded, tragic-gestured sea
Was merely a place by which she walked to sing.
Whose spirit is this? we said, because we knew
It was the spirit that we sought and knew
20 That we should ask this often as she sang.

If it was only the dark voice of the sea
That rose, or even colored by many waves;
If it was only the outer voice of sky
And cloud, of the sunken coral water-walled,
25 However clear, it would have been deep air,
The heaving speech of air, a summer sound
Repeated in a summer without end
And sound alone. But it was more than that,
More even than her voice, and ours, among
30 The meaningless plungings of water and the wind,
Theatrical distances, bronze shadows heaped
On high horizons, mountainous atmospheres
Of sky and sea.
            It was her voice that made
The sky acutest at its vanishing.
35 She measured to the hour its solitude.
She was the single artificer of the world
In which she sang. And when she sang, the sea,
Whatever self it had, became the self
That was her song, for she was the maker. Then we,
40 As we beheld her striding there alone,
Knew that there never was a world for her
Except the one she sang and, singing, made.

Ramon Fernandez,[2] tell me, if you know,
Why, when the singing ended and we turned
45 Toward the town, tell why the glassy lights,
The lights in the fishing boats at anchor there,
As the night descended, tilting in the air,
Mastered the night and portioned out the sea,
Fixing emblazoned zones and fiery poles,
50 Arranging, deepening, enchanting night.

Oh! Blessed rage for order, pale Ramon,
The maker's rage to order words of the sea,
Words of the fragrant portals, dimly-starred,
And of ourselves and of our origins,
55 In ghostlier demarcations, keener sounds.

1935

## The Emperor of Ice-Cream

Call the roller of big cigars,
The muscular one, and bid him whip
In kitchen cups concupiscent curds.[3]
Let the wenches dawdle in such dress
5 As they are used to wear, and let the boys
Bring flowers in last month's newspapers.
Let be be finale of seem.[4]
The only emperor is the emperor of ice-cream.

Take from the dresser of deal,
10 Lacking the three glass knobs, that sheet
On which she embroidered fantails[5] once
And spread it so as to cover her face.
If her horny feet protrude, they come
To show how cold she is, and dumb.
15 Let the lamp affix its beam.
The only emperor is the emperor of ice-cream.

1923

---

2. French classicist and critic (1894–1944), who emphasized the ordering role of a writer's consciousness upon the materials he or she used. Stevens denied that he had Fernandez in mind, saying that he combined a Spanish first name and surname at random: "I knew of Ramon Fernandez, the critic, and had read some of his criticisms, but I did not have him in mind" (*Letters of Wallace Stevens*, ed. Holly Stevens [1966], p. 798). Later, Stevens wrote to another correspondent that he did not have the critic "consciously" in mind (*Letters*, p. 823).
3. "The words 'concupiscent curds' have no genealogy; they are merely expressive: at least, I hope they are expressive. They express the concupiscence of life, but, by contrast with the things in relation in the poem, they express or accentuate life's destitution, and it is this that gives them something more than a cheap lustre" (*Letters*, p. 500).
4. "[T]he true sense of *Let be be the finale of seem* is let being become the conclusion of denouement of appearing to be: in short, ice cream is an absolute good. The poem is obviously not about ice cream, but about being as distinguished from seeming to be" (*Letters*, p. 341).  5. Fantall pigeons.

## Anecdote of the Jar

I placed a jar in Tennessee,
And round it was, upon a hill.
It made the slovenly wilderness
Surround that hill.

5 The wilderness rose up to it,
And sprawled around, no longer wild.
The jar was round upon the ground
And tall and of a port in air.

It took dominion everywhere.
10 The jar was gray and bare.
It did not give of bird or bush,
Like nothing else in Tennessee.

1923

## Sunday Morning

I

Complacencies of the peignoir, and late
Coffee and oranges in a sunny chair,
And the green freedom of a cockatoo
Upon a rug mingle to dissipate
5 The holy hush of ancient sacrifice.
She dreams a little, and she feels the dark
Encroachment of that old catastrophe,[6]
As a calm darkens among water-lights.
The pungent oranges and bright, green wings
10 Seem things in some procession of the dead,
Winding across wide water, without sound,
The day is like wide water, without sound,
Stilled for the passing of her dreaming feet
Over the seas, to silent Palestine,
15 Dominion of the blood and sepulchre.

II

Why should she give her bounty to the dead?
What is divinity if it can come
Only in silent shadows and in dreams?
Shall she not find in comforts of the sun,
20 In pungent fruit and bright, green wings, or else

---

6. The Crucifixion.

In any balm or beauty of the earth,
Things to be cherished like the thought of heaven?
Divinity must live within herself
Passions of rain, or moods in falling snow;
25 Grievings in loneliness, or unsubdued
Elations when the forest blooms; gusty
Emotions on wet roads on autumn nights;
All pleasures and all pains, remembering
The bough of summer and the winter branch.
30 These are the measures destined for her soul.

### III

Jove in the clouds has his inhuman birth.
No mother suckled him, no sweet land gave
Large-mannered motions to his mythy mind
He moved among us, as a muttering king,
35 Magnificent, would move among his hinds,[7]
Until our blood, commingling, virginal,
With heaven, brought such requital to desire
The very hinds discerned it, in a star.[8]
Shall our blood fail? Or shall it come to be
40 The blood of paradise? And shall the earth
Seem all of paradise that we shall know?
The sky will be much friendlier then than now,
A part of labor and a part of pain,
And next in glory to enduring love,
45 Not this dividing and indifferent blue.

### IV

She says, "I am content when wakened birds,
Before they fly, test the reality
Of misty fields, by their sweet questionings;
But when the birds are gone, and their warm fields
50 Return no more, where, then, is paradise?"
There is not any haunt of prophecy,
Nor any old chimera of the grave,
Neither the golden underground, nor isle
Melodious, where spirits gat[9] them home,
55 Nor visionary south, nor cloudy palm
Remote on heaven's hill, that has endured
As April's green endures, or will endure
Like her remembrance of awakened birds,
Or her desire for June and evening, tipped
60 By the consummation of the swallow's wings.

---

7. Lowliest rural subjects.    8. The star of Bethlehem.    9. Got.

### V

She says, "But in contentment I still feel
The need of some imperishable bliss."
Death is the mother of beauty; hence from her,
Alone, shall come fulfillment to our dreams
65 And our desires. Although she strews the leaves
Of sure obliteration on our paths,
The path sick sorrow took, the many paths
Where triumph rang its brassy phrase, or love
Whispered a little out of tenderness,
70 She makes the willow shiver in the sun
For maidens who were wont to sit and gaze
Upon the grass, relinquished to their feet.
She causes boys to pile new plums and pears
On disregarded plate.[1] The maidens taste
75 And stray impassioned in the littering leaves.

### VI

Is there no change of death in paradise?
Does ripe fruit never fall? Or do the boughs
Hang always heavy in that perfect sky,
Unchanging, yet so like our perishing earth,
80 With rivers like our own that seek for seas
They never find, the same receding shores
That never touch with inarticulate pang?
Why set the pear upon those river-banks
Or spice the shores with odors of the plum?
85 Alas, that they should wear our colors there,
The silken weavings of our afternoons,
And pick the strings of our insipid lutes!
Death is the mother of beauty, mystical,
Within whose burning bosom we devise
90 Our earthly mothers awaiting, sleeplessly.

### VII

Supple and turbulent, a ring of men
Shall chant in orgy[2] on a summer morn
Their boisterous devotion to the sun,
Not as a god, but as a god might be,
95 Naked among them, like a savage source.
Their chant shall be a chant of paradise,
Out of their blood, returning to the sky;
And in their chant shall enter, voice by voice,
The windy lake wherein their lord delights,

---

1. "Plate is used in the sense of so-called family plate. Disregarded refers to the disuse into which things fall that have been possessed for a long time. I mean, therefore, that death releases and renews. What the old have come to disregard, the young inherit and make use of" (*Letters*, pp. 183–84).
2. Ceremonial revelry.

100 The trees, like serafin,³ and echoing hills,
That choir among themselves long afterward.
They shall know well the heavenly fellowship
Of men that perish and of summer morn.
And whence they came and whither they shall go
105 The dew upon their feet shall manifest.

### VIII

She hears, upon that water without sound,
A voice that cries, "The tomb in Palestine
Is not the porch of spirits lingering.
It is the grave of Jesus, where he lay."
110 We live in an old chaos of the sun,
Or old dependency of day and night,
Or island solitude, unsponsored, free,
Of that wide water, inescapable.
Deer walk upon our mountains, and the quail
115 Whistle about us their spontaneous cries;
Sweet berries ripen in the wilderness;
And, in the isolation of the sky,
At evening, casual flocks of pigeons make
Ambiguous undulations as they sink,
120 Downward to darkness, on extended wings.

1915

## ALFRED, LORD TENNYSON

### *Now Sleeps the Crimson Petal*⁴

Now sleeps the crimson petal, now the white;
Nor waves the cypress in the palace walk;
Nor winks the gold fin in the porphyry font;⁵
The firefly wakens; waken thou with me.

5   Now droops the milk-white peacock like a ghost,
And like a ghost she glimmers on to me.

Now lies the Earth all Danaë⁶ to the stars,
And all thy heart lies open unto me.

Now slides the silent meteor on, and leaves
10  A shining furrow, as thy thoughts in me.

---

3. Seraphim, the highest of the nine orders of angels.
4. A song from *The Princess*, a long narrative poem about what the mid-nineteenth century called the "new woman."   5. Stone fishbowl. *Porphyry:* a red stone containing fine white crystals.
6. A princess in Greek mythology, seduced by Zeus after he became a shower of gold to enter the tower in which she was confined.

Now folds the lily all her sweetness up,
And slips into the bosom of the lake;
So fold thyself, my dearest, thou, and slip
Into my bosom and be lost in me.
                                        1847


## Tears, Idle Tears[7]

Tears, idle tears, I know not what they mean,
Tears from the depth of some divine despair
Rise in the heart, and gather to the eyes,
In looking on the happy autumn-fields,
5 And thinking of the days that are no more.

Fresh as the first beam glittering on a sail,
That brings our friends up from the underworld,
Sad as the last which reddens over one
That sinks with all we love below the verge;
10 So sad, so fresh, the days that are no more.

Ah, sad and strange as in dark summer dawns
The earliest pipe of half-awakened birds
To dying ears, when unto dying eyes
The casement slowly grows a glimmering square;
15 So sad, so strange, the days that are no more.

Dear as remembered kisses after death,
And sweet as those by hopeless fancy feigned
On lips that are for others; deep as love,
Deep as first love, and wild with all regret;
20 O Death in Life, the days that are no more!
                                        1847


## Tithonus[8]

The woods decay, the woods decay and fall,
The vapors weep their burthen[9] to the ground,
Man comes and tills the field and lies beneath,
And after many a summer dies the swan.
5 Me only cruel immortality
Consumes; I wither slowly in thine arms,
Here at the quiet limit of the world,

---

7. A song from *The Princess*.
8. Prince of Troy, loved by Aurora, goddess of the dawn, to whom he speaks the poem. Aurora obtained for him the gift of eternal life but forgot to ask for eternal youth.   9. Burden.

        A white-haired shadow roaming like a dream
        The ever-silent spaces of the East,
10      Far-folded mists, and gleaming halls of morn.
           Alas! for this gray shadow, once a man—
        So glorious in his beauty and thy choice,
        Who madest him thy chosen, that he seemed
        To his great heart none other than a God!
15      I asked thee, "Give me immortality."
        Then didst thou grant mine asking with a smile,
        Like wealthy men who care not how they give.
        But thy strong Hours indignant worked their wills,
        And beat me down and marred and wasted me,
20      And though they could not end me, left me maimed
        To dwell in presence of immortal youth,
        Immortal age beside immortal youth,
        And all I was in ashes. Can thy love,
        Thy beauty, make amends, though even now,
25      Close over us, the silver star, thy guide,
        Shines in those tremulous eyes that fill with tears
        To hear me? Let me go; take back thy gift.
        Why should a man desire in any way
        To vary from the kindly race of men,
30      Or pass beyond the goal of ordinance
        Where all should pause, as is most meet[1] for all?
           A soft air fans the cloud apart; there comes
        A glimpse of that dark world where I was born.
        Once more the old mysterious glimmer steals
35      From thy pure brows, and from thy shoulders pure
        And bosom beating with a heart renewed.
        Thy cheek begins to redden through the gloom,
        Thy sweet eyes brighten slowly close to mine,
        Ere yet they blind the stars, and the wild team
40      Which love thee, yearning for thy yoke, arise,
        And shake the darkness from their loosened manes,
        And beat the twilight into flakes of fire.
           Lo! ever thus thou growest beautiful
        In silence, then before thine answer given
45      Departest, and thy tears are on my cheek.
           Why wilt thou ever scare me with thy tears,
        And make me tremble lest a saying learnt,
        In days far-off, on that dark earth, be true?
        "The Gods themselves cannot recall their gifts."
50         Ay me! ay me! with what another heart
        In days far-off, and with what other eyes
        I used to watch—if I be he that watched—
        The lucid outline forming round thee; saw
        The dim curls kindle into sunny rings;

1. Proper.

55  Changed with thy mystic change, and felt my blood
    Glow with the glow that slowly crimsoned all
    Thy presence and thy portals, while I lay,
    Mouth, forehead, eyelids, growing dewy-warm
    With kisses balmier than half-opening buds
60  Of April, and could hear the lips that kissed
    Whispering I knew not what of wild and sweet,
    Like that strange song I heard Apollo sing,
    While Ilion like a mist rose into towers.[2]
        Yet hold me not forever in thine East;
65  How can my nature longer mix with thine?
    Coldly thy rosy shadows bathe me, cold
    Are all thy lights, and cold my wrinkled feet
    Upon thy glimmering thresholds, when the steam
    Floats up from those dim fields about the homes
70  Of happy men that have the power to die,
    And grassy barrows of the happier dead.
    Release me, and restore me to the ground.
    Thou seest all things, thou wilt see my grave;
    Thou wilt renew thy beauty morn by morn,
75  I earth in earth forget these empty courts,
    And thee returning on thy silver wheels.

                                                1860

## Ulysses[3]

   It little profits that an idle king,
   By this still hearth, among these barren crags,
   Matched with an agéd wife,[4] I mete and dole
   Unequal laws unto a savage race,
5  That hoard, and sleep, and feed, and know not me.

        I cannot rest from travel; I will drink
   Life to the lees.[5] All times I have enjoyed
   Greatly, have suffered greatly, both with those
   That loved me, and alone; on shore, and when
10 Through scudding drifts the rainy Hyades[6]
   Vexed the dim sea. I am become a name;
   For always roaming with a hungry heart
   Much have I seen and known—cities of men

---

2. According to Ovid's *Heroides*, music by the god of poetic inspiration accompanied the creation of walls and towers around Troy (Ilion).
3. After the end of the Trojan War, Ulysses (or Odysseus), king of Ithaca and one of the Greek heroes of the war, returned to his island home (line 34). Homer's account of the situation is in the *Odyssey* 11, but Dante's account of Ulysses in the *Inferno* 26 is the more immediate background of the poem.
4. Penelope.    5. All the way down to the bottom of the cup.
6. A group of stars that were supposed to predict the rain when they rose at the same time as the sun.

            And manners, climates, councils, governments,
15      Myself not least, but honored of them all—
            And drunk delight of battle with my peers,
            Far on the ringing plains of windy Troy.
            I am a part of all that I have met;
            Yet all experience is an arch wherethrough
20      Gleams that untraveled world, whose margin fades
            For ever and for ever when I move.
            How dull it is to pause, to make an end,
            To rust unburnished, not to shine in use!
            As though to breathe were life. Life piled on life
25      Were all too little, and of one to me
            Little remains; but every hour is saved
            From that eternal silence, something more,
            A bringer of new things; and vile it were
            For some three suns to store and hoard myself,
30      And this gray spirit yearning in desire
            To follow knowledge like a sinking star,
            Beyond the utmost bound of human thought.

             This is my son, mine own Telemachus,
            To whom I leave the scepter and the isle—
35      Well-loved of me, discerning to fulfill
            This labor by slow prudence to make mild
            A rugged people, and through soft degrees
            Subdue them to the useful and the good.
            Most blameless is he, centered in the sphere
40      Of common duties, decent not to fail
            In offices of tenderness, and pay
            Meet adoration to my household gods,
            When I am gone. He works his work, I mine.

             There lies the port; the vessel puffs her sail:
45      There gloom the dark, broad seas. My mariners,
            Souls that have toiled, and wrought, and thought with me—
            That ever with a frolic welcome took
            The thunder and the sunshine, and opposed
            Free hearts, free foreheads—you and I are old;
50      Old age hath yet his honor and his toil.
            Death closes all; but something ere the end,
            Some work of noble note, may yet be done,
            Not unbecoming men that strove with Gods.
            The lights begin to twinkle from the rocks;
55      The long day wanes; the slow moon climbs; the deep
            Moans round with many voices. Come, my friends.
            'Tis not too late to seek a newer world.
            Push off, and sitting well in order smite
            The sounding furrows; for my purpose holds
60      To sail beyond the sunset, and the baths
            Of all the western stars, until I die.

It may be that the gulfs will wash us down;[7]
It may be we shall touch the Happy Isles,[8]
And see the great Achilles, whom we knew.
65 Though much is taken, much abides; and though
We are not now that strength which in old days
Moved earth and heaven, that which we are, we are:
One equal temper of heroic hearts,
Made weak by time and fate, but strong in will
70 To strive, to seek, to find, and not to yield.

1833

## DYLAN THOMAS

### Fern Hill

Now as I was young and easy under the apple boughs
About the lilting house and happy as the grass was green,
   The night above the dingle starry,
     Time let me hail and climb
5   Golden in the heydays of his eyes,
And honored among wagons I was prince of the apple towns
And once below a time I lordly had the trees and leaves
   Trail with daisies and barley
     Down the rivers of the windfall light.

10 And as I was green and carefree, famous among the barns
About the happy yard and singing as the farm was home,
   In the sun that is young once only,
     Time let me play and be
Golden in the mercy of his means,
15 And green and golden I was huntsman and herdsman, the calves
Sang to my horn, the foxes on the hills barked clear and cold,
   And the sabbath rang slowly
     In the pebbles of the holy streams.

All the sun long it was running, it was lovely, the hay
20 Fields high as the house, the tunes from the chimneys, it was air
   And playing, lovely and watery
     And fire green as grass.
     And nightly under the simple stars
As I rode to sleep the owls were bearing the farm away,
25 All the moon long I heard, blessed among stables, the nightjars[9]

---

7. Beyond the Gulf of Gibraltar was supposed to be a chasm that led to Hades.
8. Elysium, the Islands of the Blessed, where heroes like Achilles (line 64) go after death.
9. Birds also known as goatsuckers.

Flying with the ricks,[1] and the horses
  Flashing into the dark.

And then to awake, and the farm, like a wanderer white
With the dew, come back, the cock on his shoulder: it was all
30 Shining, it was Adam and maiden,
  The sky gathered again
  And the sun grew round that very day.
So it must have been after the birth of the simple light
In the first, spinning place, the spellbound horses walking warm
35 Out of the whinnying green stable
  On to the fields of praise.

And honored among foxes and pheasants by the gay house
Under the new made clouds and happy as the heart was long,
  In the sun born over and over,
40 I ran my heedless ways,
  My wishes raced through the house-high hay
And nothing I cared, at my sky-blue trades, that time allows
In all his tuneful turning so few and such morning songs
  Before the children green and golden
45 Follow him out of grace,

Nothing I cared, in the lamb white days, that time would take me
Up to the swallow-thronged loft by the shadow of my hand,
  In the moon that is always rising,
    Nor that riding to sleep
50 I should hear him fly with the high fields
And wake to the farm forever fled from the childless land.
Oh as I was young and easy in the mercy of his means,
  Time held me green and dying
  Though I sang in my chains like the sea.

1946

## WALT WHITMAN

### *Facing West from California's Shores*

Facing west, from California's shores,
Inquiring, tireless, seeking what is yet unfound,
I, a child, very old, over waves, towards the house of maternity,[2] the
  land of migrations, look afar,
Look off the shores of my Western sea, the circle almost circled:
5 For starting westward from Hindustan, from the vales of Kashmere,
From Asia, from the north, from the God, the sage, and the hero,
From the south, from the flowery peninsulas and the spice islands,

---

1. Haystacks.   2. Asia, as the supposed birthplace of the human race.

Long having wandered since, round the earth having wandered,
Now I face home again, very pleased and joyous;
10 (But where is what I started for, so long ago?
And why is it yet unfound?)

                                                                    1860

## I Hear America Singing

I hear America singing, the varied carols I hear,
Those of mechanics, each one singing his as it should be blithe and
    strong,
The carpenter singing his as he measures his plank or beam,
The mason singing his as he makes ready for work, or leaves off work,
5 The boatman singing what belongs to him in his boat, the deckhand
    singing on the steamboat deck,
The shoemaker singing as he sits on his bench, the hatter singing as he
    stands,
The wood-cutter's song, the ploughboy's on his way in the morning,
    or at noon intermission or at sundown,
The delicious singing of the mother, or of the young wife at work, or
    of the girl sewing or washing,
Each singing what belongs to him or her and to none else,
10 The day what belongs to the day—at night the party of young fellows,
    robust, friendly,
Singing with open mouths their strong melodious songs.

                                                                    1860

## A Noiseless Patient Spider

A noiseless patient spider,
I marked where on a little promontory it stood isolated,
Marked how to explore the vacant vast surrounding,
It launched forth filament, filament, filament, out of itself,
5 Ever unreeling them, ever tirelessly speeding them.

And you O my soul where you stand,
Surrounded, detached, in measureless oceans of space,
Ceaselessly musing, venturing, throwing, seeking the spheres to
    connect them,
Till the bridge you will need be formed, till the ductile anchor hold,
10 Till the gossamer thread you fling catch somewhere, O my soul.

                                                                    1881

### RICHARD WILBUR

## Love Calls Us to the Things of This World

    The eyes open to a cry of pulleys,
And spirited from sleep, the astounded soul
Hangs for a moment bodiless and simple
As false dawn.
5           Outside the open window
The morning air is all awash with angels.

    Some are in bed-sheets, some are in blouses,
Some are in smocks: but truly there they are.
Now they are rising together in calm swells
10 Of halcyon[3] feeling, filling whatever they wear
With the deep joy of their impersonal breathing;

    Now they are flying in place,[4] conveying
The terrible speed of their omnipresence, moving
And staying like white water; and now of a sudden
15 They swoon down into so rapt a quiet
That nobody seems to be there.
                    The soul shrinks

    From all that it is about to remember,
From the punctual rape of every blessed day,
20 And cries,
          "Oh, let there be nothing on earth but laundry,
Nothing but rosy hands in the rising steam
And clear dances done in the sight of heaven."

    Yet, as the sun acknowledges
25 With a warm look the world's hunks and colors,
The soul descends once more in bitter love
To accept the waking body, saying now
In a changed voice as the man yawns and rises,

    "Bring them down from their ruddy gallows;
30 Let there be clean linen for the backs of thieves;
Let lovers go fresh and sweet to be undone,
And the heaviest nuns walk in a pure floating
Of dark habits,
          keeping their difficult balance."

                              1956

---

3. Serene.    4. Like planes in a formation.

**C. K. WILLIAMS**

## Alzheimer's: The Wife

*for Renée Mauger*

She answers the bothersome telephone, takes the message, forgets the
    message, forgets who called.
One of their daughters, her husband guesses: the one with the dogs,
    the babies, the boy Jed?
Yes, perhaps, but how tell which, how tell anything when all the
    name tags have been lost or switched,
when all the lonely flowers of sense and memory bloom and die now
    in adjacent bites of time?
5 Sometimes her own face will suddenly appear with terrifying
    inappropriateness before her in a mirror.
She knows that if she's patient, its gaze will break, demurely,
    decorously, like a well-taught child's,
It will turn from her as though it were embarrassed by the secrets of
    this awful hide-and-seek.
If she forgets, though, and glances back again, it will still be in there,
    furtively watching, crying.

1987

**WILLIAM WORDSWORTH**

## Lines Written a Few Miles above Tintern Abbey, On Revisiting the Banks of the Wye during a Tour, July 13, 1798[5]

  Five years have passed; five summers, with the length
Of five long winters! and again I hear
These waters, rolling from their mountain-springs
With a soft inland murmur. Once again
5 Do I behold these steep and lofty cliffs,
That on a wild secluded scene impress
Thoughts of more deep seclusion; and connect
The landscape with the quiet of the sky.
The day is come when I again repose
10 Here, under this dark sycamore, and view
These plots of cottage-ground, these orchard tufts,
Which at this season, with their unripe fruits,

---

5. Wordsworth had first visited the Wye valley and the ruins of the medieval abbey there in 1793, while on a solitary walking tour. He was twenty-three then, twenty-eight when he wrote this poem.

Are clad in one green hue, and lose themselves
'Mid groves and copses.[6] Once again I see
15 These hedge-rows, hardly hedge-rows, little lines
Of sportive wood run wild: these pastoral farms,
Green to the very door; and wreaths of smoke
Sent up, in silence, from among the trees!
With some uncertain notice, as might seem
20 Of vagrant dwellers in the houseless woods,
Or of some hermit's cave, where by his fire
The hermit sits alone.
                    These beauteous forms,
Through a long absence, have not been to me
As is a landscape to a blind man's eye;
25 But oft, in lonely rooms, and 'mid the din
Of towns and cities, I have owed to them,
In hours of weariness, sensations sweet,
Felt in the blood, and felt along the heart;
And passing even into my purer mind,
30 With tranquil restoration—feelings too
Of unremembered pleasure: such, perhaps,
As have no slight or trivial influence
On that best portion of a good man's life,
His little, nameless, unremembered acts
35 Of kindness and of love. Nor less, I trust,
To them I may have owed another gift,
Of aspect more sublime; that blessèd mood,
In which the burthen[7] of the mystery,
In which the heavy and the weary weight
40 Of all this unintelligible world,
Is lightened—that serene and blessèd mood,
In which the affections gently lead us on—
Until, the breath of this corporeal frame
And even the motion of our human blood
45 Almost suspended, we are laid asleep
In body, and become a living soul;
While with an eye made quiet by the power
Of harmony, and the deep power of joy,
We see into the life of things.
                        If this
50 Be but a vain belief, yet, oh! how oft—
In darkness and amid the many shapes
Of joyless daylight; when the fretful stir
Unprofitable, and the fever of the world,
Have hung upon the beatings of my heart—
55 How oft, in spirit, have I turned to thee,
O sylvan Wye! thou wanderer through the woods,
How often has my spirit turned to thee!

6. Thickets.   7. Burden.

And now, with gleams of half-extinguished thought,
With many recognitions dim and faint,
60 And somewhat of a sad perplexity,
The picture of the mind revives again;
While here I stand, not only with the sense
Of present pleasure, but with pleasing thoughts
That in this moment there is life and food
65 For future years. And so I dare to hope,
Though changed, no doubt, from what I was when first
I came among these hills; when like a roe
I bounded o'er the mountains, by the sides
Of the deep rivers, and the lonely streams,
70 Wherever nature led: more like a man
Flying from something that he dreads than one
Who sought the thing he loved. For nature then
(The coarser[8] pleasures of my boyish days,
And their glad animal movements all gone by)
75 To me was all in all—I cannot paint
What then I was. The sounding cataract
Haunted me like a passion; the tall rock,
The mountain, and the deep and gloomy wood,
Their colors and their forms, were then to me
80 An appetite; a feeling and a love,
That had no need of a remoter charm,
By thought supplied, nor any interest
Unborrowed from the eye. That time is past,
And all its aching joys are now no more,
85 And all its dizzy raptures. Not for this
Faint I,[9] nor mourn nor murmur; other gifts
Have followed; for such loss, I would believe,
Abundant recompense. For I have learned
To look on nature, not as in the hour
90 Of thoughtless youth; but hearing oftentimes
The still, sad music of humanity,
Nor[1] harsh nor grating, though of ample power
To chasten and subdue. And I have felt
A presence that disturbs me with the joy
95 Of elevated thoughts, a sense sublime
Of something far more deeply interfused,
Whose dwelling is the light of setting suns,
And the round ocean and the living air,
And the blue sky, and in the mind of man:
100 A motion and a spirit, that impels
All thinking things, all objects of all thought,
And rolls through all things. Therefore am I still
A lover of the meadows and the woods
And mountains; and of all that we behold
105 From this green earth; of all the mighty world

8. Physical.    9. Am I discouraged.    1. Neither.

        Of eye, and ear—both what they half create,
        And what perceive; well pleased to recognize
        In nature and the language of the sense
        The anchor of my purest thoughts, the nurse,
110     The guide, the guardian of my heart, and soul
        Of all my moral being.
                            Nor perchance,
        If I were not thus taught, should I the more
        Suffer my genial spirits² to decay:
        For thou art with me here upon the banks
115     Of this fair river; thou my dearest Friend,³
        My dear, dear Friend; and in thy voice I catch
        The language of my former heart, and read
        My former pleasures in the shooting lights
        Of thy wild eyes. Oh! yet a little while
120     May I behold in thee what I was once,
        My dear, dear Sister! and this prayer I make,
        Knowing that Nature never did betray
        The heart that loved her; 'tis her privilege,
        Through all the years of this our life, to lead
125     From joy to joy: for she can so inform
        The mind that is within us, so impress
        With quietness and beauty, and so feed
        With lofty thoughts, that neither evil tongues,
        Rash judgments, nor the sneers of selfish men,
130     Nor greetings where no kindness is, nor all
        The dreary intercourse of daily life,
        Shall e'er prevail against us, or disturb
        Our cheerful faith that all which we behold
        Is full of blessings. Therefore let the moon
135     Shine on thee in thy solitary walk;
        And let the misty mountain-winds be free
        To blow against thee: and, in after years,
        When these wild ecstasies shall be matured
        Into a sober pleasure; when thy mind
140     Shall be a mansion for all lovely forms,
        Thy memory be as a dwelling-place
        For all sweet sounds and harmonies; oh! then,
        If solitude, or fear, or pain, or grief,
        Should be thy portion, with what healing thoughts
145     Of tender joy wilt thou remember me,
        And these my exhortations! No, perchance—
        If I should be where I no more can hear
        Thy voice, nor catch from thy wild eyes these gleams
        Of past existence—wilt thou then forget
150     That on the banks of this delightful stream
        We stood together; and that I, so long

2. Natural disposition; that is, the spirits are part of his individual genius.    3. His sister Dorothy.

A worshiper of Nature, hither came
Unwearied in that service; rather say
With warmer love—oh! with far deeper zeal
155 Of holier love. Nor wilt thou then forget,
That after many wanderings, many years
Of absence, these steep woods and lofty cliffs,
And this green pastoral landscape, were to me
More dear, both for themselves and for thy sake!

1798

## W. B. YEATS

### The Lake Isle of Innisfree[4]

I will arise and go now, and go to Innisfree,
And a small cabin build there, of clay and wattles made,
Nine bean-rows will I have there, a hive for the honey-bee,
And live alone in the bee-loud glade.

5 And I shall have some peace there, for peace comes dropping slow,
Dropping from the veils of the morning to where the cricket sings;
There midnight's all a glimmer, and noon a purple glow,
And evening full of the linnet's wings.

I will arise and go now, for always night and day
10 I hear lake water lapping with low sounds by the shore;
While I stand on the roadway, or on the pavements grey,
I hear it in the deep heart's core.

1890

### All Things Can Tempt Me

All things can tempt me from this craft of verse:
One time it was a woman's face, or worse—
The seeming needs of my fool-driven land;
Now nothing but comes readier to the hand
5 Than this accustomed toil. When I was young,
I had not given a penny for a song
Did not the poet sing it with such airs
That one believed he had a sword upstairs;
Yet would be now, could I but have my wish,
10 Colder and dumber and deafer than a fish.

1910

---

4. Island in Lough Gill, County Sligo, Ireland.

## Easter 1916[5]

I have met them at close of day
Coming with vivid faces
From counter or desk among gray
Eighteenth-century houses.
5 I have passed with a nod of the head
Or polite meaningless words,
Or have lingered awhile and said
Polite meaningless words,
And thought before I had done
10 Of a mocking tale or a gibe
To please a companion
Around the fire at the club,
Being certain that they and I
But lived where motley is worn:
15 All changed, changed utterly:
A terrible beauty is born.

That woman's[6] days were spent
In ignorant good-will,
Her nights in argument
20 Until her voice grew shrill.
What voice more sweet than hers
When, young and beautiful,
She rode to harriers?
This man[7] had kept a school
25 And rode our wingèd horse;[8]
This other[9] his helper and friend
Was coming into his force;
He might have won fame in the end,
So sensitive his nature seemed,
30 So daring and sweet his thought.
This other man[1] I had dreamed
A drunken, vainglorious lout.

---

5. On Easter Monday, 1916, nationalist leaders proclaimed an Irish Republic. After a week of street fighting, the British government put down the Easter Rebellion and executed a number of prominent nationalists, including the four mentioned in lines 75–76, all of whom Yeats knew personally.
6. Countess Constance Georgina Markiewicz, a beautiful and well-born young woman from County Sligo who became a vigorous and bitter nationalist. At first she was condemned to death, but her sentence was later commuted to life imprisonment, and she was granted amnesty in 1917.
7. Patrick Pearse, who led the assault on the Dublin Post Office, from which the proclamation of a republic was issued. A schoolmaster by profession, he had vigorously supported the restoration of the Gaelic language in Ireland and was an active political writer and poet.
8. Pegasus, a traditional symbol of poetic inspiration.
9. Thomas MacDonagh, also a writer and teacher.
1. Major John MacBride, who had married Yeats's beloved Maud Gonne in 1903 but separated from her two years later.

He had done most bitter wrong
To some who are near my heart,
35 Yet I number him in the song;
He, too, has resigned his part
In the casual comedy;
He, too, has been changed in his turn,
Transformed utterly:
40 A terrible beauty is born.

Hearts with one purpose alone
Through summer and winter seem
Enchanted to a stone
To trouble the living stream.
45 The horse that comes from the road,
The rider, the birds that range
From cloud to tumbling cloud,
Minute by minute they change;
A shadow of cloud on the stream
50 Changes minute by minute;
A horse-hoof slides on the brim,
And a horse plashes within it;
The long-legged moor-hens dive,
And hens to moor-cocks call;
55 Minute by minute they live:
The stone's in the midst of all.

Too long a sacrifice
Can make a stone of the heart.
O when may it suffice?
60 That is Heaven's part, our part
To murmur name upon name,
As a mother names her child
When sleep at last has come
On limbs that had run wild.
65 What is it but nightfall?
No, no, not night but death;
Was it needless death after all?
For England may keep faith[2]
For all that is done and said.
70 We know their dream; enough
To know they dreamed and are dead;
And what if excess of love
Bewildered them till they died?
I write it out in a verse—
75 MacDonagh and MacBride
And Connolly[3] and Pearse
Now and in time to be,

---

2. Before the uprising the English had promised eventual home rule to Ireland.
3. James Connolly, the leader of the Easter uprising.

Wherever green is worn,
Are changed, changed utterly;
80 A terrible beauty is born.

1916

## *The Second Coming*[4]

Turning and turning in the widening gyre[5]
The falcon cannot hear the falconer;
Things fall apart; the center cannot hold;
Mere anarchy is loosed upon the world,
5 The blood-dimmed tide is loosed, and everywhere
The ceremony of innocence is drowned;
The best lack all conviction, while the worst
Are full of passionate intensity.
Surely some revelation is at hand;
10 Surely the Second Coming is at hand.
The Second Coming! Hardly are those words out
When a vast image out of *Spiritus Mundi*[6]
Troubles my sight: somewhere in sands of the desert
A shape with lion body and the head of a man,
15 A gaze blank and pitiless as the sun,
Is moving its slow thighs, while all about it
Reel shadows of the indignant desert birds.[7]
The darkness drops again; but now I know
That twenty centuries of stony sleep
20 Were vexed to nightmare by a rocking cradle,
And what rough beast, its hour come round at last,
Slouches towards Bethlehem to be born?

January 1919

---

4. The Second Coming of Christ, according to Matthew 24.29–44, will be after a time of "tribulation." Disillusioned by Ireland's continued civil strife, Yeats saw his time as the end of another historical cycle. In *A Vision* (1937), Yeats describes his view of history as dependent on cycles of about two thousand years: the birth of Christ had ended the cycle of Greco-Roman civilization, and now the Christian cycle seemed near an end, to be followed by an antithetical cycle, ominous in its portents.
5. Literally, the widening spiral of a falcon's flight. "Gyre" is Yeats's term for a cycle of history, which he diagrammed as a series of interpenetrating cones.
6. Or *Anima Mundi*, the spirit or soul of the world. Yeats considered this universal consciousness or memory a fund from which poets drew their images and symbols.
7. Yeats later wrote of the "brazen winged beast... described in my poem *The Second Coming*" as "associated with laughing, ecstatic destruction."

## Leda and the Swan[8]

A sudden blow: the great wings beating still
Above the staggering girl, her thighs caressed
By the dark webs, her nape caught in his bill,
He holds her helpless breast upon his breast.

5 How can those terrified vague fingers push
The feathered glory from her loosening thighs?
And how can body, laid in that white rush,
But feel the strange heart beating where it lies?

A shudder in the loins engenders there
10 The broken wall, the burning roof and tower
And Agamemnon dead.
                      Being so caught up,
So mastered by the brute blood of the air,
Did she put on his knowledge with his power
Before the indifferent beak could let her drop?

1923

## Sailing to Byzantium[9]

### I

That[1] is no country for old men. The young
In one another's arms, birds in the trees
—Those dying generations—at their song,
The salmon-falls, the mackerel-crowded seas,
5 Fish, flesh, or fowl, commend all summer long
Whatever is begotten, born, and dies.
Caught in that sensual music all neglect
Monuments of unaging intellect.

### II

An aged man is but a paltry thing,
10 A tattered coat upon a stick, unless

---

8. According to Greek myth, Zeus took the form of a swan to rape Leda, who became the mother of Helen of Troy; of Castor; and also of Clytemnestra, Agamemnon's wife and murderer. Helen's abduction from her husband, Menelaus, brother of Agamemnon, began the Trojan War (line 10). Yeats described the visit of Zeus to Leda as an annunciation like that to Mary (see Luke 1.26–38); "I imagine the annunciation that founded Greece as made to Leda" (*A Vision*).

9. The ancient name of Istanbul, the capital and holy city of Eastern Christendom from the late fourth century until 1453. It was famous for its stylized and formal mosaics; its symbolic, nonnaturalistic art; and its highly developed intellectual life. Yeats repeatedly uses it to symbolize a world of artifice and timelessness, free from the decay and death of the natural and sensual world.

1. Ireland, as an instance of the natural, temporal world.

Soul clap its hands and sing, and louder sing
  For every tatter in its mortal dress,
  Nor is there singing school but studying
  Monuments of its own magnificence;
15 And therefore I have sailed the seas and come
  To the holy city of Byzantium.

### III

  O sages standing in God's holy fire
  As in the gold mosaic of a wall,
  Come from the holy fire, perne in a gyre,[2]
20 And be the singing-masters of my soul.
  Consume my heart away; sick with desire
  And fastened to a dying animal
  It knows not what it is; and gather me
  Into the artifice of eternity.

### IV

25 Once out of nature I shall never take
  My bodily form from any natural thing,
  But such a form as Grecian goldsmiths make
  Of hammered gold and gold enameling
  To keep a drowsy Emperor awake;[3]
30 Or set upon a golden bough[4] to sing
  To lords and ladies of Byzantium
  Of what is past, or passing, or to come.

                                        1927

## Among School Children

### I

  I walk through the long schoolroom questioning;
  A kind old nun in a white hood replies;
  The children learn to cipher and to sing,
  To study reading-books and history,
5 To cut and sew, be neat in everything
  In the best modern way—the children's eyes
  In momentary wonder stare upon
  A sixty-year-old smiling public man.[5]

---

2. That is, whirl in a coiling motion, so that his soul may merge with its motion as the timeless world invades the cycles of history and nature. "Perne" is Yeats's coinage (from the noun *pirn*): to spin around in the kind of spiral pattern that thread makes as it comes off a bobbin or spool.
3. "I have read somewhere that in the Emperor's palace at Byzantium was a tree made of gold and silver, and artificial birds that sang" [Yeats's note].
4. In Book 6 of the *Aeneid*, the sibyl tells Aeneas that he must pluck a golden bough from a nearby tree in order to descend to Hades. Each time Aeneas plucks the one such branch there, an identical one takes its place.    5. At sixty (in 1925), Yeats had been a senator of the Irish Free State.

## II

I dream of a Ledaean body,[6] bent
Above a sinking fire, a tale that she
Told of a harsh reproof, or trivial event
That changed some childish day to tragedy—
Told, and it seemed that our two natures blent
Into a sphere from youthful sympathy,
Or else, to alter Plato's parable,
Into the yolk and white of the one shell.[7]

## III

And thinking of that fit of grief or rage
I look upon one child or t'other there
And wonder if she stood so at that age—
For even daughters of the swan can share
Something of every paddler's heritage—
And had that color upon cheek or hair,
And thereupon my heart is driven wild:
She stands before me as a living child.

## IV

Her present image floats into the mind—
Did Quattrocento finger[8] fashion it
Hollow of cheek as though it drank the wind
And took a mess of shadows for its meat?
And I though never of Ledaean kind
Had pretty plumage once—enough of that,
Better to smile on all that smile, and show
There is a comfortable kind of old scarecrow.

## V

What youthful mother, a shape upon her lap
Honey of generation[9] had betrayed,
And that must sleep, shriek, struggle to escape
As recollection or the drug decide,
Would think her son, did she but see that shape
With sixty or more winters on its head,

---

6. Like that of Helen of Troy, daughter of Leda. The memory dream is of Maud Gonne (see also lines 29-30), with whom Yeats had long been hopelessly in love.
7. In Plato's *Symposium*, the origin of human love is explained by parable: Human beings were once spheres, but Zeus feared their power and cut them in half; now each half longs to be reunited with its missing half. Helen and Pollux were hatched from one of two eggs born to Leda after her union with Zeus in the form of a swan; the other contained Castor and Clytemnestra. According to Yeats in *A Vision*, "from one of [Leda's] eggs came Love and from the other War."
8. The hand of a fifteenth-century artist. Yeats especially admired Botticelli, and in *A Vision* praises his "deliberate strangeness everywhere [that] gives one an emotion of mystery which is new to painting."
9. Porphyry, a third-century Greek scholar and Neoplatonic philosopher, says "honey of generation" means the "pleasure arising from copulation" that draws souls "downward" to generation.

A compensation for the pang of his birth,
40 Or the uncertainty of his setting forth?

### VI

Plato thought nature but a spume that plays
Upon a ghostly paradigm of things;[1]
Solider Aristotle played the taws
Upon the bottom of a king of kings;[2]
45 World-famous golden-thighed Pythagoras[3]
Fingered upon a fiddle-stick or strings
What a star sang and careless Muses heard:
Old clothes upon old sticks to scare a bird.

### VII

Both nuns and mothers worship images,
50 But those the candles light are not as those
That animate a mother's reveries
But keep a marble or a bronze repose.
And yet they too break hearts—O Presences
That passion, piety or affection knows,
55 And that all heavenly glory symbolize—
O self-born mockers of man's enterprise;

### VIII

Labor is blossoming or dancing where
The body is not bruised to pleasure soul,
Nor beauty born out of its own despair,
60 Nor blear-eyed wisdom out of midnight oil.
O chestnut-tree, great-rooted blossomer,
Are you the leaf, the blossom or the bole?
O body swayed to music, O brightening glance,
How can we know the dancer from the dance?

1927

## Byzantium

The unpurged images of day recede;
The Emperor's drunken soldiery are abed;
Night resonance recedes, night-walkers' song
After great cathedral gong;

---

1. Plato considered the real world an imperfect and illusory copy of the ideal world.
2. Aristotle, the teacher of Alexander the Great, disciplined him with a strap ("taws," line 43). His philosophy, insisting on the interdependence of form and matter, took the real world far more seriously than did Plato's.
3. Greek mathematician and philosopher (580?–500? B.C.E.); one legend describes his godlike golden thighs.

5   A starlit or a moonlit dome[4] disdains
All that man is,
All mere complexities,
The fury and the mire of human veins.

Before me floats an image, man or shade,
10  Shade more than man, more image than a shade;
For Hades' bobbin bound in mummy-cloth
May unwind the winding path;
A mouth that has no moisture and no breath
Breathless mouths may summon;
15  I hail the superhuman;
I call it death-in-life and life-in-death.

Miracle, bird or golden handiwork,
More miracle than bird or handiwork,
Planted on the star-lit golden bough
20  Can like the cocks of Hades crow,[5]
Or, by the moon embittered, scorn aloud
In glory of changeless metal
Common bird or petal
And all complexities of mire or blood.

25  At midnight on the Emperor's pavement flit
Flames that no faggot[6] feeds, nor steel has lit,
Nor storm disturbs, flames begotten of flame,
Where blood-begotten spirits come
And all complexities of fury leave,
30  Dying into a dance,
An agony of trance,
An agony of flame that cannot singe a sleeve.

Astraddle on the dolphin's mire and blood,[7]
Spirit after spirit! The smithies break the flood,
35  The golden smithies of the Emperor!
Marbles of the dancing floor
Break bitter furies of complexity,
Those images that yet
Fresh images beget,
40  That dolphin-torn, that gong-tormented sea.

1932

---

4. According to Yeats's philosophy, the full moon ("moonlit") represents the mind "completely absorbed in being."
5. As the bird of dawn, the cock has from antiquity symbolized rebirth and resurrection.
6. Bundle of sticks used as fuel.
7. In ancient art, dolphins symbolize the soul moving from one state to another, and sometimes they provide a vehicle for the dead.

# Biographical Sketches
# Poets

Sketches are included for all poets represented by two or more poems.

### W. H. AUDEN
(1907–1973)

Wystan Hugh Auden was born in York, England, to a medical officer and a nurse. Intending at first to become a scientist, Auden studied at Oxford, where he became the center of the "Oxford Group" of poets and leftist intellectuals. His travels during the 1930s led him to Germany, Iceland, China, Spain (where he was an ambulance driver in the civil war), and the United States (where he taught at various universities and, in 1946, became a naturalized citizen). A prolific writer of poems, plays, essays, and criticism, Auden won the Pulitzer Prize in 1948 for his collection of poems *The Age of Anxiety*, set in a New York City bar. Late in life he returned to Christ Church College, Oxford, where he was writer in residence. He is regarded as a masterly poet of political and intellectual conscience as well as one of the twentieth century's greatest lyric craftsmen.

### BASHŌ (1644–1694)

Born Matsuo Munefusa, the second son of a low-ranking provincial samurai, the haiku poet who came to be known as Bashō at first put aside his literary interests and entered into service with the local ruling military house. In 1666, following the feudal lord's death, Bashō left for Edo (now Tokyo), the military capital of the shogun's new government, to pursue a career as a professional poet. He supported himself as a teacher and editor of other people's poetry but ultimately developed a following and a sizable group of students. A seasoned traveler, Bashō maintained an austere existence on the road as well as at home, casting himself in travel narratives such as *Oku no hosomichi* (*The Narrow Road to the Interior*, 1694) as a pilgrim devoted to nature and Zen.

### EARLE BIRNEY
(1904–1995)

Born in Calgary, Alberta, Earle Birney was educated in Canada and eventually earned a Ph.D. from the University of Toronto before teaching at the University of Utah. After serving as a major in the Canadian army during World War II, Birney returned to the University of British Columbia, where he had received his B.A. twenty years earlier, and developed the first course there in creative writing. Birney's many books include novels and criticism, but he is best known as a poet. His first collection, *David and Other Poems*, won the Governor General's Medal for Poetry in 1942; many volumes and many awards later, his final collection, *Last Makings*, appeared in 1991.

### ELIZABETH BISHOP
(1911–1979)

Born in Worcester, Massachusetts, Elizabeth Bishop endured the death of her father before she was a year old and the institutionalization of her mother when she was five. Bishop was raised by her maternal grandmother in Nova Scotia, then by her paternal grandparents back in Worcester. At Vassar College she met the poet Marianne Moore, who encouraged her to give up plans for medical school and pursue a career in poetry. Bishop traveled through Canada, Europe, and South America, finally settling in Rio de Janeiro, where she lived for nearly twenty years. Her four volumes of poetry are *North and South* (1946); *A Cold Spring* (1955), which won the Pulitzer Prize; *Questions of Travel* (1965); and *Geography III* (1976), which won the National Book Critics' Circle Award. *Complete Poems 1929–1979* and *Collected Prose* gather most of her published work.

## WILLIAM BLAKE
(1757–1828)

The son of a London haberdasher and his wife, William Blake studied drawing at ten and at fourteen was apprenticed to an engraver for seven years. After a first book of poems, *Poetical Sketches* (1783), he began experimenting with what he called "illuminated printing"—the words and pictures of each page were engraved in relief on copper, which was used to print sheets that were then partly colored by hand—a laborious and time-consuming process that resulted in books of singular beauty, no two of which were exactly alike. His great *Songs of Innocence* (1789) and *Songs of Experience* (1794) were produced in this manner, as were his increasingly mythic and prophetic books, including *The Marriage of Heaven and Hell* (1793), *The Four Zoas* (1803), *Milton* (1804), and *Jerusalem* (1809). Blake devoted his later life to pictorial art, illustrating *The Canterbury Tales,* the Book of Job, and *The Divine Comedy,* on which he was hard at work when he died.

## ELIZABETH BARRETT BROWNING
(1806–1861)

Elizabeth Barrett was born into a wealthy family in Durham, England, and raised in Herefordshire. She received no formal schooling, but was very well educated at home in the classics and in English literature, and published her first volume of poetry at the age of thirteen. Despite her status as a prominent woman of letters, deteriorating health forced Barrett to live in semi-seclusion. Her collection *Poems* (1844) inspired the poet Robert Browning to write to her in May 1845, and thus began a courtship that resulted in their eloping to Italy in 1846. Following the publication of *Sonnets from the Portuguese* (1850), Barrett Browning received serious consideration to succeed Wordsworth as Poet Laureate (although the laureateship went instead to Tennyson); one critic hailed her as "the greatest female poet that England has produced." Her most admired work is *Aurora Leigh* (1857), a nine-book verse novel.

## GWENDOLYN BROOKS
(1917–2000)

Gwendolyn Brooks was born in Topeka, Kansas, and raised in Chicago, where she began writing poetry at the age of seven, and where she graduated from Wilson Junior College in 1936. Shortly after beginning her formal study of modern poetry at Chicago's Southside Community Art Center, Brooks produced her first book of poems, *A Street in Bronzeville* (1945). With her second volume, *Annie Allen* (1949), she became the first African American to win the Pulitzer Prize. Though her early work focused on what Langston Hughes called the "ordinary aspects of black life," during the mid-1960s she devoted her poetry to raising African American consciousness and to social activism. In 1968, she was named the Poet Laureate of Illinois; from 1985 to 1986, she served as poetry consultant to the Library of Congress. Her *Selected Poems* appeared in 1999.

## ROBERT BROWNING
(1812–1889)

Born in London, Robert Browning attended London University but was largely self-educated, learning Latin, Greek, French, and Italian by the time he was fourteen. He was an accomplished but little-known poet and playwright when he began courting the already famous poet Elizabeth Barrett. After they eloped to Italy in 1846, the Brownings enjoyed a period of happiness during which they produced most of their best-known work. Following Elizabeth's death in 1861, Robert returned to England with their son and for the rest of his life enjoyed great literary and social success. His major collections are *Men and Women* (1855), dedicated to his wife, and *Dramatis Personae* (1864), which contains some of his finest dramatic monologues. Lionized as one of England's greatest poets by the time of his death, Browning is buried in the Poets' Corner at Westminster Abbey.

## ROBERT BURNS
(1759–1796)

Robert Burns was born and raised in Ayrshire, Scotland. The son of impoverished tenant farmers, he attended school sporadically but was largely self-taught. He collected subscriptions to publish his first collection, *Poems, Chiefly in the Scottish Dialect* (1786), which made his reputation in both Edinburgh and London. These poems were new in their rebellious individualism and in their pre-Romantic sensitivity to nature, yet they seemed to speak in an authentic "auld Scots" voice. A perennial failure as a farmer, Burns became a tax inspector and settled in the country town of Dumfries. Despite financial difficulties and failing health, he continued to write poems and songs (including "Auld Lang Syne") and devoted his last years to collecting Scottish folk songs for a cultural-preservation project. His work, frequently bawdy, politically zealous, and critical of organized religion, remains deeply loved throughout the world.

## BUSON (1716–1784)
Born into a wealthy family in Kemu, Settsu province, Japan, Taniguchi Buson renounced a life of privilege to pursue a career in the arts. In 1751, after several years of traveling and studying under haiku masters in northeastern Japan, he settled in Kyoto and established himself as a professional painter. Known in later life as Yosa Buson, or simply Buson, he was responsible for a revival of the work of his prominent predecessor, Bashō. His own poems, regarded in Japan as second only to those of Bashō, display a subtle complexity and painterly attention to visual detail.

## HELEN CHASIN (b. ca. 1940)
Helen Chasin was born in New York and attended Radcliffe College. Her first book of poems, *Coming Close* (1968), was chosen for the Yale Series of Younger Poets. In this collection and her next, *Casting Stones* (1975), Chasin employed a compressed voice dense with meaning: many of her poems are a mere ten or fifteen lines long, yet every word and one-syllable line resonates. A student of Robert Lowell's, she has taught poetry at the University of Iowa. Most recently, Chasin edited *Likeness and Unlikeness: Selected Paintings* (1997), a volume of visual art by the modern Chinese painter and poet Qi Baishi.

## SAMUEL TAYLOR COLERIDGE (1772–1834)

Born in the small town of Ottery St. Mary in rural Devonshire, England, Samuel Taylor Coleridge is among the greatest and most original of the nineteenth-century Romantic poets. He wrote three of the most haunting and powerful poems in English—*The Rime of the Ancient Mariner* (1798), *Christabel* (1816), and "Kubla Khan" (1816)—as well as immensely influential literary criticism and a treatise on biology. In 1795, in the midst of a failed experiment to establish a "Pantisocracy" (his form of ideal community), he met William Wordsworth, and in 1798 they jointly published their enormously influential *Lyrical Ballads*. Coleridge's physical ailments, addiction to opium, and profound sense of despair made his life difficult and tumultuous and certainly affected his work. Still, he remains a central figure in English literature.

## BILLY COLLINS (b. 1941)

Born in New York, Billy Collins received a B.A. from the College of the Holy Cross in Massachusetts and a Ph.D. from the University of California at Riverside before becoming a professor of English at Lehman College, City University of New York. His publications, several of which have broken sales records for poetry, include *Pokerface* (1977), *Video Poems* (1980), *The Apple That Astonished Paris* (1988), *Questions about Angels* (1991), *The Art of Drowning* (1995), *Picnic, Lightning* (1998), *Sailing around the Room: New and Selected Poems* (2000), *Taking off Emily Dickinson's Clothes* (2000), and *Nine Horses: Poems* (2002). He reads regularly on National Public Radio, performs live, and has recorded a spoken-word CD, *The Best Cigarette* (1997). He was named Poet Laureate of the United States in 2001.

## HENRY CONSTABLE (1562–1613)
Henry Constable, the son of Sir Robert Constable, was educated at Cambridge University. A Roman Catholic during a period of fierce religious conflict in England, Constable spent most of his life in exile in Paris, where he served as agent for the Pope in pressing the Scottish king James VI's claims to the English throne (though he may have secretly worked in the service of the English government). As

was the fashion for courtiers, Constable composed sonnets; in fact, his collection *Diana* (1592) was one of the first sonnet sequences, in which the poems create a fictional love narrative. His small body of poetry also includes his "Spiritual Sonnets" and a pastoral, "Venus and Adonis," said to have influenced Shakespeare. In 1604, Constable returned to England only to be imprisoned in the Tower of London on suspicion of treason; upon his release two years later he returned to the Continent and died, in 1613, in Liège.

## WENDY COPE (b. 1945)

Born in Kent, England, Wendy Cope studied modern history at Oxford University, where she went on to receive a postgraduate degree in education. While working as a primary-school teacher in the 1970s, she began writing poetry. Her trademark optimistic and witty verses have been collected in the volumes *Making Cocoa for Kingsley Amis* (1986); *Serious Concerns* (1992); a children's book, *Twiddling Your Thumbs: Hand Rhymes* (1988); and *If I Don't Know,* which was short-listed for the Whitbread Poetry Award in 2002. Discussing her work, Cope has stated, "I dislike the term 'light verse' because it is used as a way of dismissing poets who allow humor into their work. I believe that a humorous poem can also be 'serious,' deeply felt and saying something that matters."

## COUNTEE CULLEN
(1903–1946)

During his own lifetime, Countee Cullen was the most celebrated and honored poet of the Harlem Renaissance, and he claimed New York City as his birthplace. In fact, he may have been born in Louisville, Kentucky, and the circumstances of his childhood adoption by the Reverend Frederick Cullen remain obscure. It is certain, though, that the poet received a good education at New York's DeWitt Clinton High School and then New York University. After receiving his M.A. at Harvard, Cullen returned to New York in 1926 and soon established himself as the leading figure in the active Harlem literary world, winning numerous awards for his poetry and editing the influential monthly column "The Dark Tower" for *Opportunity: Journal of Negro Life.* A playwright, novelist, translator, and anthologist, Cullen is best remembered as a poet; his work has been collected in the volume *My Soul's High Song: The Collected Writings of Countee Cullen, Voice of the Harlem Renaissance* (1991).

## E. E. CUMMINGS
(1894–1962)

Born in Cambridge, Massachusetts, the son of a Congregationalist minister, Edward Estlin Cummings attended Harvard University, where he wrote poetry in the Pre-Raphaelite and Metaphysical traditions. He joined the ambulance corps in France the day after the United States entered World War I but was imprisoned by the French due to his outspokenness against the war; he transmuted the experience into his first literary success, the novel *The Enormous Room* (1922). After the war, Cummings established himself as a poet and artist in New York City's Greenwich Village, made frequent trips to France and New Hampshire, and showed little interest in wealth or his growing celebrity. His variety of modernism was distinguished by its playfulness, its formal experimentation, its lyrical directness, and above all its celebration of the individual. His poetry is collected in *Complete Poems 1904–62* (1991).

## JAMES DICKEY
(1923–1997)

James Dickey did not become seriously interested in poetry until he joined the Air Force in 1942. When he returned from World War II, he earned a B.A. and an M.A. at Vanderbilt University, publishing his first poem in *Sewanee Review* in his senior year. Following the publication of his first volume of poems, *Into the Stone* (1960), Dickey, while primarily a poet, worked in advertising, wrote novels, and taught at various universities. His 1965 collection, *Buckdancer's Choice,* received the National Book Award, and from 1967 to 1969 Dickey was consultant in poetry to the Library of Congress. He is widely known for his best-selling novel, *Deliverance* (1970), which he later adapted for Hollywood. Other publications include *The Whole Motion: Collected Poems 1949–1992* (1992) and another novel, *To the White Sea* (1993).

## EMILY DICKINSON
(1830–1886)

From childhood on, Emily Dickinson led a sequestered and obscure life. Yet her verse has traveled far beyond the cultured yet relatively circumscribed environment in which she lived: her room, her father's house, her family, a few close friends, and the small town of Amherst, Massachusetts. Indeed, along with Walt Whitman, her far more public contemporary, she all but invented American poetry. Born in Amherst, the daughter of a respected lawyer whom she revered ("His heart was pure and terrible," she once wrote), Dickinson studied for less than a year at the Mount Holyoke Female Seminary, returning permanently to her family home. She became more and more reclusive, dressing only in white, seeing no visitors, yet working ceaselessly at her poems—nearly eighteen hundred in all, only a few of which were published during her lifetime. After her death, her sister Lavinia discovered the rest in a trunk, neatly bound into packets with blue ribbons—among the most important bodies of work in all of American literature.

## JOHN DONNE
(1572–1631)

The first and greatest of the English writers who came to be known as the Metaphysical poets, John Donne wrote in a revolutionary style that combined highly intellectual conceits with complex, compressed phrasing. Born into an old Roman Catholic family at a time when Catholics were subject to constant harassment, Donne quietly abandoned his religion and had a promising legal career until a politically disastrous marriage ruined his worldly hopes. He struggled for years to support a large family; impoverished and despairing, he even wrote a treatise (*Biathanatos*) on the lawfulness of suicide. King James (who had ambitions for him as a preacher) eventually pressured Donne to take Anglican orders in 1615, and Donne became one of the great sermonizers of his day, rising to the position of dean of St. Paul's Cathedral in 1621. Donne's private devotions ("Meditations") were published in 1624, and he continued to write poetry until a few years before his death.

## RITA DOVE (b. 1952)

A native of Akron, Ohio, Rita Dove attended Miami University in Ohio, studied for a year in West Germany as a Fulbright scholar, and received an MFA in creative writing from the University of Iowa. She is now a professor of English at the University of Virginia as well as associate editor of *Callaloo*, a journal of African American arts and letters. In 1987, Dove became the second African American poet (after Gwendolyn Brooks, in 1950) to win the Pulitzer Prize (for *Thomas and Beulah*). In 1993, she was appointed Poet Laureate of the United States. Her books include *The Yellow House on the Corner* (1980), *Museum* (1983), *Grace Notes* (1989), *Mother Love* (1995), *On the Bus with Rosa Parks* (1999), and, most recently, *American Smooth* (2004). A tireless advocate for poetry, Dove edited *The Best American Poetry 2000* and, from 2000 to 2002, authored the weekly column "Poet's Choice" in the *Washington Post Book World*.

## PAUL LAURENCE DUNBAR (1872–1906)

The son of former slaves, Paul Laurence Dunbar was born in Dayton, Ohio. He attended a white high school, where he showed an early talent for writing and was elected class president. Unable to afford further education, he then worked as an elevator operator, writing poems and newspaper articles in his spare time. Dunbar took out a loan to subsidize the printing of his first book, *Oak and Ivy* (1893), but with the publication of *Majors and Minors* (1895) and *Lyrics of Lowly Life* (1896), his growing reputation enabled him to support himself by writing and lecturing. Though acclaimed during his lifetime for his lyrical use of rural black dialect in volumes such as *Candle-Lightin' Time* (1902), Dunbar was later criticized for adopting "white" literary conventions and accused of pandering to racist images of slaves and ex-slaves. He wrote novels and short stories in addition to poetry, and dealt frankly with racial injustice in works such as *The Sport of the Gods* (1903) and *The Fourth of July and Race Outrages* (1903).

## STEPHEN DUNN
(b. 1939)

Born in New York, Stephen Dunn received a B.A. in history from Hofstra University, served in the armed forces, played professional basketball in Pennsylvania for a year, and afterward worked in advertising. In 1966, Dunn went to Spain "to try to change my life and see if I could write poetry"; in 1970, he earned an M.A. in creative writing from Syracuse University. Known for his clear, quietly powerful poems, Dunn has taught poetry at several universities, including Columbia, and has published many collections. Some of these are *Five Impersonations* (1971), *Full of Lust and Good Usage* (1976), *Work and Love* (1981), *Local Time* (1986), *Between Angels* (1989), *New and Selected Poems: 1974–1994* (1994), *Loosestrife* (1996), and *Different Hours* (2000), which won the Pulitzer Prize.

## T. S. ELIOT (1888–1965)

Thomas Stearns Eliot—from his formally experimental and oblique writings to his brilliant arguments in defense of "orthodoxy" and "tradition"—dominated the world of English poetry between the world wars. Born in St. Louis, Missouri, into a family that hailed from New England, Eliot studied literature and philosophy at Harvard and later in France and Germany. He went to England in 1914, read Greek philosophy at Oxford, and published his first major poem, "The Love Song of J. Alfred Prufrock," the next year. In 1922, with the help of Ezra Pound, Eliot published *The Waste Land*, which profoundly influenced a generation of poets and became a cornerstone of literary modernism. In his later work, particularly the *Four Quartets* (completed in 1945), Eliot explored religious questions in a quieter, more controlled idiom. By the middle of the twentieth century, Eliot was regarded as a towering figure in modern literature, renowned as a poet, critic, essayist, editor, and dramatist. He was awarded the Nobel Prize for Literature in 1948.

## JAMES A. EMANUEL
(b. 1921)

Raised in Nebraska, James A. Emanuel earned a B.A. from Howard University, an M.A. from Northwestern, and a Ph.D. from Columbia; he then became an assistant professor of English at the City College of New York. As the 1960s passed, Emanuel became increasingly committed to reading and writing practices grounded in consciousness of his own racial identity, and he began to write poetry as well as literary criticism. His collections include *The Treehouse and Other Poems* (1968), *Panther Man* (1970), *Black Man Abroad: The Toulouse Poems* (1978), *A Chisel in the Dark: Poems Selected and New* (1980), *The Broken Bowl: New and Uncollected Poems* (1983), *Deadly James and Other Poems* (1987), *Whole Grain: Collected Poems 1958–1989* (1991), and *Jazz: From the Haiku King* (1999). Emanuel has lived in Paris for many years.

## DAVID FERRY (b. 1924)

Born in Orange, New Jersey, David Ferry received a B.A. from Amherst College and an M.A. and a Ph.D. from Harvard. A professor of English at Wellesley College, he has published several widely acclaimed translations: *Gilgamesh* (1992), *The Odes of Horace* (1997), *The Eclogues of Virgil* (1999), and *The Epistles of Horace* (2001). His own poetry, informed by his multilingual scholarship, has been collected in such volumes as *On the Way to the Island* (1960), *A Letter and Some Photographs: A Group of Poems* (1981), *Strangers: A Book of Poems* (1983), *Dwelling Places: Poems and Translations* (1993), and *Of No Country I Know: New and Selected Poems and Translations* (1999), which won the Lenore Marshall Prize and the New Yorker Prize for Poetry in 2000.

## ROBERT FROST
(1874–1963)

Though his poetry identifies Frost with rural New England, he was born and lived to the age of eleven in San Francisco. Moving to New England after his father's death, Frost studied classics in high school, entered and dropped out of both Dartmouth and Harvard, and spent difficult years as an unrecognized poet before his first book, *A Boy's Will* (1913), was accepted and published in England. Frost's character was full of contradiction—he held "that we get forward as much by hating as by loving"—yet by the end of his long life he was one of the most honored poets of his time, and the most widely read. In 1961, two years before his death, he was invited to read a poem at John F. Kennedy's presidential inauguration ceremony. Frost's poems—masterfully crafted, sometimes deceptively simple—are collected in *The Poetry of Robert Frost* (1969).

### ALLEN GINSBERG
(1926–1997)

After a childhood in Paterson, New Jersey, overshadowed by his mother's mental illness, Allen Ginsberg enrolled at Columbia University, intent upon following his father's advice and becoming a labor lawyer. At the center of a circle that included Lucien Carr, Jack Kerouac, William S. Burroughs, and Neal Cassady, Ginsberg became interested in experimental poetry and alternative lifestyles. He graduated in 1948 and then joined the literary scene in San Francisco. In 1956, he published *Howl and Other Poems*, with an introduction by his mentor William Carlos Williams. The title poem, which condemned bourgeois culture and celebrated the emerging counterculture, became a manifesto for the Beat movement and catapulted Ginsberg to fame. Deeply involved in radical politics and Eastern spiritualism, Ginsberg went on to write such prose works as *Declaration of Independence for Dr. Timothy Leary* (1971) in addition to many volumes of poetry. His *Collected Poems, 1947–1980* appeared in 1984 and *Selected Poems 1947–1995* in 1996.

### ANGELINA GRIMKE
(1880–1958)

Born in Boston, Angelina Grimke was the descendent of black slaves, white slaveholders, free blacks, and prominent white abolitionists, including her namesake, Angelina Weld Grimke. As a child, Angelina was abandoned by her white mother, whose middle-class family disapproved of her marriage to Archibald Grimke, a biracial lawyer and author who eventually became vice president of the NAACP. Grimke graduated from the Boston Normal School of Gymnastics in 1902 and then moved with her father to Washington, D.C., where she worked as a teacher and began to write poetry, essays, short stories, and plays. By the 1920s, she was publishing her work in the leading journals and anthologies of the Harlem Renaissance—*The Crisis, Opportunity,* Alain Locke's *The New Negro* (1925), Countee Cullen's *Caroling Dusk* (1927), and Robert Kerlin's *Negro Poets and Their Poems* (1928). Much of her finest writing can be found in *Selected Works of Angelina Weld Grimke* (1991).

### THOM GUNN
(1929–2004)

With the irony that characterizes much of his poetry, Thom Gunn once claimed, "I am a completely anonymous person—my life contains no events, and I lack any visible personality." Nevertheless, Gunn impressed himself on American poetry, producing more than thirty volumes and winning the Lenore Marshall Prize for *The Man with Night Sweats* (1992). Although he was born and educated in England, earning by 1958 both a B.A. and an M.A. from Trinity College, Cambridge, he lived and worked in California for many years. His poetry combines an appreciation of formal tradition with frank treatments of such subjects as homosexuality and hallucinogens. Much of his best work can be found in his *Selected Poems 1950–1975* (1979) and *Collected Poems* (1994). His last collection is *Boss Cupid* (2000). In 2003, Gunn received the David Cohen British Literature Award for lifetime achievement.

### THOMAS HARDY
(1840–1928)

In a preface dated 1901, Thomas Hardy called his poems "unadjusted impressions," which nevertheless might, by "humbly recording diverse readings of phenomena as they are forced upon us by chance and change," lead to a philosophy. Indeed, though he was essentially retrospective in his outlook and traditional in his technique, Hardy anticipated the concerns of modern poetry by treating the craft as an awkward, often skeptical means of penetrating the facade of language. Born at Upper Bockhampton in Dorset, England, the son of a master mason and his wife, Hardy began to write fiction while pursuing an architectural career. His eight novels, now considered classics, brought him moderate commercial and critical success, but when *Jude the Obscure* (1896) was attacked as indecent, Hardy, disgusted, turned exclusively to poetry, producing a body of work that is as distinguished as his fiction. His major novels include *Far from the Madding Crowd* (1887) and *Tess of the D'Urbervilles* (1891); his poems have been selected and collected in various editions.

## ROBERT HAYDEN (1913–1980)

Robert Hayden was born Asa Bundy Sheffey, in Detroit, Michigan, and raised by foster parents. He studied at Detroit City College (later Wayne State University), but left in 1936 to work for the Federal Writers' Project, where he researched black history and folk culture. He received an M.A. from the University of Michigan, taught at Fisk University from 1949 until 1969, and then taught at Michigan until his retirement. Although he published ten volumes of poetry, he did not receive acclaim until late in life. His collections include *Heart-Shape in the Dust* (1940), *The Lion and the Archer*, *Figures of Time* (1955), *A Ballad of Remembrance* (1962), *Selected Poems* (1966), *Words in the Mourning Time* (1970), *Night-Blooming Cereus* (1972), *Angle of Ascent* (1975), *American Journal* (1978 and 1982), and *Collected Poems* (1985).

## SEAMUS HEANEY (b. 1939)

Seamus Heaney, whose poems explore themes of rural life, memory, and history, was born on a farm in Mossbawn, County Derry (Castledawson, Londonderry), Northern Ireland. Educated at Queen's University in Belfast, he has taught at the University of California at Berkeley, Carysfort College in Dublin, and Oxford University; he currently teaches at Harvard. Once called by Robert Lowell "the most important Irish poet since Yeats," Heaney received the 1995 Nobel Prize for Literature. His poetry collections include *Eleven Poems* (1965), *Death of a Naturalist* (1966), *Wintering Out* (1972), *The Haw Lantern* (1987), *Seeing Things* (1991), *The Spirit Level* (1996), and *Electric Light* (2001). Heaney's translation of *Beowulf* (2000) from Anglo-Saxon into modern English gave new life to the oldest of English poems; it not only won Britain's prestigious Whitbread Award but also become a bestseller.

## GEORGE HERBERT (1593–1633)

After the early death of his Welsh father, George Herbert was raised by his mother, a literary patron of John Donne. Herbert graduated with honors from Cambridge and was subsequently elected public orator at the university. He twice represented Montgomery, Wales, as a member of Parliament in the 1620s, but in 1626 he set aside his secular ambitions in favor of service to the Anglican Church. He married, took holy orders in 1630, and spent the rest of his brief life as a country parson in Bemerton, near Salisbury, where he was beloved as "Holy Mr. Herbert." Dying of consumption in 1633, he handed over to a friend the manuscript of *The Temple,* asking him to publish it only if he thought these quietly meditative poems might do good to "any dejected poor soul." The book proved a popular success and placed Herbert, along with Donne, at the forefront of the Metaphysical poets.

## ROBERT HERRICK (1591–1674)

The son of a London goldsmith and his wife, Robert Herrick would have liked nothing better than a life of leisured study, spent discussing literature and drinking sack with his hero, Ben Jonson. Instead, he answered the call of religion, taking holy orders and reluctantly accepting a remote parish in Devonshire. Herrick eventually made himself at home there, inventing dozens of imaginary mistresses with exotic names and practicing, half-seriously, his own peculiar form of paganism. When the Puritans came to power, Herrick was driven from his post to London, where in 1648 he published a volume of over fourteen hundred poems with two titles: *Hesperides* for the secular poems and *Noble Numbers* for those with sacred subjects. The poems did not fit the harsh atmosphere of Puritanism, but after the restoration of the Stuart monarchy in 1660, Herrick was eventually returned to his Devonshire parish, where he lived out his last years quietly.

## GERARD MANLEY HOPKINS (1844–1889)

Born the eldest of eight children of a marine-insurance adjuster and his wife, Gerard Manley Hopkins attended Oxford, where his ambition was to become a painter—until, at the age of 22, he converted to Roman Catholicism and burned all his early poetry as too worldly. Not until after his seminary training and ordination as a Jesuit priest, in 1877, did he resume writing poetry, though he made few attempts to publish his verse, which many of his contemporaries found nearly incomprehensible. Near the end of his life, Hopkins was appointed professor of Greek at University College, Dublin, where—out of place, deeply depressed, and all but unknown—he died of typhoid. His poetry, collected and published by his friends, has been championed by modern poets, who admire its controlled tension, strong rhythm, and sheer exuberance.

## ANDREW HUDGINS (b. 1951)

Texas-born Andrew Hudgins, son of a career Air Force officer and his wife, lived all over the American South as a boy. He earned an M.A. from the University of Alabama in 1976, then taught English and composition for several years before turning to poetry. After receiving his MFA from the University of Iowa in 1983, Hudgins produced *Saints and Strangers* (1985); astonishingly, this first collection was short-listed for the 1986 Pulitzer Prize. Many reviewers called Hudgins's work "Southern Gothic" for its eerie, graphic imagery, though he came to dislike this label. His second book, *After the Lost War* (1988), is a narrative poem based on the life of Sidney Lanier, an all-but-forgotten Civil War poet and Confederate soldier. Hudgins's subsequent works include *The Never-Ending: New Poems* (1991), *The Glass Hammer: A Southern Childhood* (1994), *Babylon in a Jar* (1998), and *Ecstatic in the Poison: New Poems* (2003).

## LANGSTON HUGHES (1902–1967)

Born in Joplin, Missouri, Langston Hughes was raised mainly by his maternal grandmother, though he lived intermittently with each of his parents. He studied at Columbia University, but left to travel and work at a variety of jobs. Having already published poems in periodicals, anthologies, and his own first collection, *The Weary Blues* (1926), he graduated from Lincoln University; published a successful novel, *Not without Laughter* (1930); and became a major writer in the intellectual and literary movement called the Harlem Renaissance. During the 1930s, he became involved in radical politics and traveled the world as a correspondent and columnist; during the 1950s, though, the FBI classified him as a security risk and limited his ability to travel. In addition to poems and novels, he wrote essays, plays, screenplays, and an autobiography; he also edited anthologies of literature and folklore. His *Collected Poems* appeared in 1994.

## BEN JONSON (1572?–1637)

Poet, playwright, actor, scholar, critic, and translator, Ben Jonson was the posthumous son of a clergyman and the stepson of a master bricklayer of Westminster. Jonson had an eventful early life, going to war against the Spanish, working as an actor, killing an associate in a duel, and converting to Roman Catholicism. Meanwhile, Jonson wrote a number of plays that have remained popular to this day, including *Every Man in His Humour* (in which Shakespeare acted a leading role; 1598), *Volpone* (1606), and *The Alchemist* (1610). He was named Poet Laureate in 1616 and spent the latter part of his life at the center of a large circle of friends and admirers known as the "Tribe of Ben." Often considered the first English author to deem writing his primary career, he published *The Works of Benjamin Jonson* in 1616.

## JOHN KEATS (1795–1821)

John Keats was the son of a London livery stable owner and his wife; reviewers would later disparage him as a working-class "Cockney poet." At fifteen he was apprenticed to a surgeon, and at twenty-one he became a licensed pharmacist—in the same year that his first two published poems, including the sonnet "On First Looking into Chapman's

Homer," appeared in *The Examiner,* a journal edited by the critic and poet Leigh Hunt. Hunt introduced Keats to such literary figures as the poet Percy Bysshe Shelley and helped him publish his *Poems by John Keats* (1817). When his second book, the long poem *Endymion* (1818), was fiercely attacked by critics, Keats, suffering from a steadily worsening case of tuberculosis, knew that he would not live to realize his poetic promise. In July 1820, he published *Lamia, Isabella, The Eve of St. Agnes, and Other Poems,* which contained the poignant "To Autumn" and three great odes: "Ode on a Grecian Urn," "Ode on Melancholy," and "Ode to a Nightingale"; early the next year, he died in Rome. In the years after Keats's death, his letters became almost as famous as his poetry.

### GALWAY KINNELL
(b. 1927)

Born in Providence, Rhode Island, Galway Kinnell earned a B.A. from Princeton and an M.A. from the University of Rochester. He served in the navy and has been a journalist, a civil-rights field-worker, and a teacher at numerous colleges and universities. His early poetry, collected in *What a Kingdom It Was* (1960) and *First Poems 1946–1954* (1970), is highly formal; his subsequent work employs a more colloquial style. "Poetry," he has said, "is the attempt to find a language that can speak the unspeakable." He received both a Pulitzer Prize and the American Book Award for *Selected Poems* (1982), and in 2000 he culled *A New Selected Poems* from eight collections spanning twenty-four years. He lives in New York and Vermont.

### ETHERIDGE KNIGHT
(1931–1991)

A native of Corinth, Mississippi, Etheridge Knight spent much of his adolescence carousing in pool halls, bars, and juke joints, developing a skillful oratorical style in an environment that prized verbal agility. During this time he also became addicted to narcotics. He served in the U.S. Army from 1947 to 1951; in 1960 he was sentenced to eight years in prison for robbery. At the Indiana State Prison in Michigan City, he began to write poetry and in 1968 published his first collection, *Poems from Prison.* After his release, Knight joined the Black Arts movement taught at a number of universities, and published works including *Black Voices from Prison* (1970), *Belly Song and Other Poems* (1973), and *Born of a Woman* (1980).

### ANDREW MARVELL
(1621–1678)

The son of a clergyman and his wife, Andrew Marvell was born in Yorkshire, England, and educated at Trinity College, Cambridge. There is no evidence that he fought in the English Civil War, which broke out in 1642, but his poem "An Horatian Ode upon Cromwell's Return from Ireland" appeared in 1650, shortly after the beheading of King Charles I in 1649, and may represent straightforward praise of England's new Puritan leader. Some regard it as strong satire, however—Marvell was known in his day for his satirical prose and verse. Today he is better known for lyric poems, such as the carpe diem manifesto "To His Coy Mistress," which he probably wrote while serving as tutor to a Yorkshire noble's daughter. In 1657, on the recommendation of John Milton, Marvell accepted a position in Cromwell's government that he held until his election to Parliament in 1659. After helping restore the monarchy in 1660, he continued to write and to serve as a member of Parliament until the end of his life.

### CLAUDE McKAY
(1889–1948)

Festus Claudis McKay was born and raised in Sunny Ville, Clarendon Parish, Jamaica, the youngest of eleven children. He worked as a wheelwright and cabinetmaker, then briefly as a police constable, before writing and publishing two books of poetry in Jamaican dialect. In 1912, he emigrated to the United States, where he attended Booker T. Washington's Tuskegee Institute in Alabama, studied agricultural science at Kansas State College, and then moved to New York City. McKay supported himself through various jobs while becoming a prominent literary and political figure. The oldest Harlem Renaissance writer, McKay was also the first to publish, with the poetry collection *Harlem Shadows* (1922); his other works include the novels *Home to Harlem* (1928) and *Banana Bottom* (1933) and his autobiography, *A Long Way from Home* (1937).

## JAMES MERRILL
(1926–1995)

Born to wealth in New York City (his father co-founded the Merrill Lynch brokerage house), James Merrill was a precocious poet whose first collection, *Jim's Book*, was printed privately when he was only sixteen. After college at Amherst, which was interrupted by a year of military service, Merrill began teaching at Bard College and soon started publishing poetry, plays, and fiction. *First Poems* (1951) was followed by many other verse collections, including two National Book Award-winners, *Nights and Days* (1966) and *Mirabell* (1979); the Pulitzer Prize-winning *Divine Comedies* (1976); *From the First Nine: Poems 1946–1976* (1982); and *The Inner Room* (1988). His masterpiece, *The Changing Light at Sandover* (1982), grew out of spiritualist sessions with a Ouija board that Merrill conducted with his partner, David Jackson. Merrill served as Chancellor of the Academy of American Poets from 1979 until his death.

## EDNA ST. VINCENT MILLAY (1892–1950)

Born in Rockland, Maine, Edna St. Vincent Millay published her first poem at twenty, her first poetry collection at twenty-five. After graduating from Vassar College, she moved to New York City's Greenwich Village, where, as she gained a reputation as a brilliant poet, she also became notorious for her bohemian life and her association with prominent artists, writers, and radicals. In 1923, she won the Pulitzer Prize for her collection *The Ballad of the Harp-Weaver*; in 1925, growing weary of fame, she and her husband moved to Austerlitz, New York, where she lived for the rest of her life. Although her work fell out of favor with mid-twentieth century modernists, who rejected her formalism as old-fashioned, her poetry—witty, acerbic, and superbly crafted—has found many new admirers today.

## JOHN MILTON
(1608–1674)

Born in London, the elder son of a self-made businessman and his wife, John Milton exhibited unusual literary and scholarly gifts at an early age; even before entering Cambridge University, he was adept at Latin and Greek and was well on his way to mastering Hebrew and a number of European languages. After graduation, he spent six more years of intense study and composed, among other works, his great pastoral elegy, "Lycidas" (1637). After a year of travel in Europe, Milton return to England and found his country embroiled in religious strife and civil war. Milton took up the Puritan cause and, in 1641, began writing pamphlets defending everything from free speech to Cromwell's execution of Charles I; Milton also served as Cromwell's Latin secretary until, in 1651, he lost his sight. After the monarchy was restored in 1660, Milton was briefly imprisoned and his property was confiscated. Blind, impoverished, and isolated, he devoted himself to the great spiritual epics of his later years: *Paradise Lost* (1667), *Paradise Regained* (1671), and *Samson Agonistes* (1671).

## MARIANNE MOORE
(1887–1972)

Born in Kirkwood, Missouri, Marianne Moore was raised in Carlisle, Pennsylvania. After receiving a degree in biology from Bryn Mawr College, she studied business at Carlisle Commercial College, taught stenography at the U.S. Industrial Indian School in Carlisle, and traveled to Europe. She and her mother moved to New Jersey and New York's Greenwich Village before settling, in 1918, in Brooklyn, New York. From 1921 to 1925, Moore was a librarian at the New York Public Library. She had written and published poetry while still in college, but did not publish her first collection until 1921. A prolific critic, she also edited the influential modernist magazine *Dial* from 1926 to 1929. Her *Collected Poems* (1951) won the Bollingen Prize, the Pulitzer Prize, and a National Book Award and made her a public figure. Her *Complete Poems* appeared in 1967.

## PAT MORA (b. 1942)

Born to Mexican American parents in El Paso, Texas, Pat Mora earned a B.A. and an M.A. from the University of Texas at El Paso. She has been a consultant on U.S.-Mexico youth exchanges; a museum director and administrator at her alma mater; and a teacher of English at all levels. Her poetry—collected in *Chants* (1985), *Borders* (1986), *Com-*

munion (1991), *Agua Santa* (1995), and *Aunt Carmen's Book of Practical Saints* (1997)—reflects and addresses her Chicana and southwestern background. Mora's other publications include *Nepantla: Essays from the Land in the Middle* (1993); a family memoir, *House of Houses* (1997); and many works for children.

## HOWARD NEMEROV
(1920–1991)

Born and raised in New York City, Howard Nemerov graduated from Harvard University, served in the U.S. Army Air Corps during World War II, and returned to New York to complete his first book, *The Image and the Law* (1948). He taught at a number of colleges and universities and published books of poetry, plays, short stories, novels, and essays. His *Collected Poems* won the Pulitzer Prize and the National Book Award in 1978. He served as Consultant in Poetry to the Library of Congress from 1963 to 1964, and Poet Laureate of the United States from 1988 to 1990. *Trying Conclusions: New and Selected Poems 1961–1991* was published in 1991.

## SHARON OLDS (b. 1942)

Born in San Francisco, Sharon Olds earned a B.A. from Stanford University and a Ph.D. from Columbia University. She was founding chair of the Writing Program at Goldwater Hospital (a public facility for the severely physically disabled), and she currently chairs New York University's Creative Writing Program. She has received a National Endowment for the Arts Grant and a Guggenheim Fellowship and was named New York State Poet in 1998. Her books include *Satan Says* (1980); the National Book Critics Circle Award-winning *The Dead and the Living* (1983); *The Gold Cell* (1987); *The Father* (1992); *The Wellspring* (1997); *Blood, Tin, Straw* (1999); and *The Unswept Room*, a National Book Award nominee in 2002.

## WILFRED OWEN
(1893–1918)

Born in Oswestry, Shropshire, England, Wilfred Owen left school in 1911, having failed to win a scholarship to London University. He served as assistant to a vicar in Oxfordshire until 1913, when he left to teach English at a Berlitz school in Bordeaux. In 1915, Owen returned to England to enlist in the army and was sent to the front lines in France. Suffering from shell shock two years later, he was evacuated to Craiglockhart War Hospital, where he met the poets Siegfried Sassoon and Robert Graves. Five of Owen's poems were published in 1918, the year he returned to combat; he was killed one week before the signing of the armistice. His poems, which portray the horror of trench warfare and satirize the unthinking patriotism of those who cheered the war from their armchairs, are collected in the two-volume *Complete Poems and Fragments* (1983).

## DOROTHY PARKER
(1893–1967)

Born in West End, New Jersey, Dorothy Rothschild worked for both *Vogue* and *Vanity Fair* magazines before becoming a freelance writer. In 1917, she married Edwin Pond Parker II, whom she divorced in 1928. Her first book of verse, *Enough Rope* (1926), was a best-seller and was followed by *Sunset Gun* (1928), *Death and Taxes* (1931), and *Collected Poems: Not So Deep as a Well* (1936). In 1927, Parker became a book reviewer for *The New Yorker*, to which she contributed for most of her career. In 1933, Parker and her second husband, Alan Campbell, moved to Hollywood, where they collaborated as film writers. In addition, Parker wrote criticism, two plays, short stories, and news reports from the Spanish Civil War. She is probably best remembered, though, as the reigning wit at the "Round Table" at Manhattan's Algonquin Hotel, where, in the 1920s and '30s, she traded barbs with other prominent writers and humorists.

## LINDA PASTAN (b. 1932)

Linda Pastan was born in New York City and raised in nearby Westchester County. After graduating from Radcliffe College, she received an M.A. in literature from Brandeis University. Although her first published poems appeared in *Mademoiselle* in 1955, Pastan spent many years concentrating on her husband and children—indeed, much of her poetry deals with her own family life. Her many collections include *A Perfect Circle of Sun* (1971), *The Five Stages of Grief* (1978), American Book Award nominee *PM / AM: New and Selected Poems* (1982), *A Fraction of Darkness* (1985), *The Imperfect Paradise* (1988), *An Early Afterlife* (1995), *Carnival Evening: New and Selected Poems 1968–1998* (1998), and *The Last Uncle: Poems* (2002). She lives in Potomac, Maryland, and was named Poet Laureate of Maryland in 1991.

### MARGE PIERCY (b. 1936)

Born and raised in Detroit, Marge Piercy received a B.A. from the University of Michigan and an M.A. from Northwestern University. She taught for some time before the success of her novels allowed her to move to Cape Cod. While her well-known early poetry is vigorously feminist and political, her later work draws more upon her love of nature and her Jewish heritage. Her many books include the poetry collections *Living in the Open* (1976), *The Moon Is Always Female* (1980), *Stone, Paper, Knife* (1983), *Available Light* (1988), *Mars and Her Children* (1992), *What Are Big Girls Made Of?* (1997), and *The Art of Blessing the Day: Poems with a Jewish Theme* (2000); her most recent novel, *Three Women* (1999); and a memoir, *Sleeping with Cats* (2002).

### SYLVIA PLATH (1932–1963)

Sylvia Plath was born in Boston; her father, a Polish immigrant, died when she was eight. After graduating from Smith College, Plath attended Cambridge University on a Fulbright scholarship, and there she met and married the poet Ted Hughes, with whom she had two children. As she documented in her novel *The Bell Jar* (1963), in 1953—between her junior and senior years of college—Plath became seriously depressed, attempted suicide, and was hospitalized. In 1963, the break-up of her marriage led to another suicide attempt, this time successful. Plath has attained cult status as much for her poems as for her "martyrdom" to art and life. In addition to her first volume of poetry, *The Colossus* (1960), Plath's work has been collected in *Ariel* (1966), *Crossing the Water* (1971), and *Winter Trees* (1972). Her selected letters were published in 1975; her expurgated journals, in 1983; and her unabridged journals, in 2000.

### EZRA POUND (1885–1972)

Born in Hailey, Idaho, Ezra Pound studied at the University of Pennsylvania and Hamilton College before traveling to Europe in 1908. He remained there, living in Ireland, England, France, and Italy, for much of his life. Pound's tremendous ambition—to succeed in his own work and to influence the development of poetry and Western culture in general—led him to found the Imagist school of poetry, to advise and assist many great writers (Eliot, Joyce, Williams, Frost, and Hemingway, to name a few), and to write a number of highly influential critical works. His increasingly fiery and erratic behavior led to a charge of treason (he served as a propagandist for Mussolini during World War II), a diagnosis of insanity, and twelve years at St. Elizabeth's, an institution for the criminally insane. His verse is collected in *Personae: The Collected Poems* (1949) and *The Cantos* (1976).

### ADRIENNE RICH (b. 1929)

Adrienne Rich was born in Baltimore. Since the selection of her first volume by W. H. Auden for the Yale Series of Younger Poets (1951), her work has continually evolved, from the tightly controlled early poems to the politically and personally charged verse for which she is known today. Rich's books of poetry include *Collected Early Poems 1950–1970* (1993), *The Dream of a Common Language* (1978), *Your Native Land, Your Life* (1986), *Time's Power* (1988), *An Atlas of the Difficult World* (1991), *Dark Fields of the Republic* (1995), *Midnight Salvage* (1999), *Fox* (2001), and *The School among the Ruins* (2004). Her prose works include *Of Woman Born: Motherhood as Experience and Institution* (1976), *On Lies, Secrets, and Silence* (1979), and *Blood, Bread, and Poetry* (1986), all influential feminist texts; *What Is Found There: Notebooks on Poetry and Politics* (1993); and *Arts of the Possible: Essays and Conversations* (2001). Her many awards include a MacArthur Fellowship and a Lanning Foundation Lifetime Achievement Award.

## THEODORE ROETHKE
(1908–1963)

Born in Saginaw, Michigan, Theodore Roethke grew up around his father's twenty-five-acre greenhouse complex—plants and their associations with nurture and growth were an important subject in his later poetry. He worked for a time at Lafayette College, where he was professor of English and tennis coach, and later at the University of Washington, which appointed him poet-in-residence one year before he died. Roethke suffered from periodic mental breakdowns, yet the best of his poetry, with its reverence for and fear of the physical world, seems destined to last. His books include *Open House* (1942), *Praise to the End!* (1951), *The Far Field* (1964), which received a posthumous National Book Award, and *Collected Poems* (1966).

## LIZ ROSENBERG
(b. 1956)

A native of Long Island, New York, Liz Rosenberg received a B.A. from Bennington College, an M.A. from Johns Hopkins University, and a Ph.D. from the State University of New York at Binghamton, where she teaches English and currently directs the creative writing program. She has published several books of poetry, including *The Angel Poems* (1984), *The Fire Music* (1985), *Children of Paradise* (1994), and *These Happy Days* (2000); a novel, *Heart and Soul* (1996); and numerous children's books, such as *Eli's Night-Light*, illustrated by Joanna Yardley (2001), and *We Wanted You*, illustrated by Peter Catalanotto (2002). In addition, she is a book columnist for *The Boston Globe*.

## CHRISTINA ROSSETTI
(1830–1894)

The daughter of Italian political refugees, Christina Rossetti was born in London and educated at home. Though associated with the Pre-Raphaelite group of artists and writers through her brother, Dante Gabriel Rossetti, Christina withdrew into the more personal world of her quiet but intense devotion to poetry and Anglican spirituality. Published under the pseudonym "Ellen Alleyn," her first poems appeared when she was only eighteen; her first adult collection, *Goblin Market and Other Poems* (1862), was a popular and critical success. Never marrying, Rossetti instead devoted herself to her writing and to a variety of moral and educational causes. Her collected *Poetical Works* (1904) was published a decade after her death.

## WILLIAM SHAKESPEARE
(1554–1616)

Considering the great fame of his work, surprisingly little is known of William Shakespeare's life. Between 1585 and 1592, he left his birthplace of Stratford-upon-Avon for London to begin a career as playwright and actor. No dates of his professional career are recorded, however, nor can the order in which he composed his plays and poetry be determined with any certainty. By 1594, he had established himself as a poet with two long works—*Venus and Adonis* and *The Rape of Lucrece*—and his more than 150 sonnets are supreme expressions of the form. His reputation, though, rests on the works he wrote for the theater. Shakespeare produced perhaps thirty-five plays in twenty-five years, proving himself a master of every dramatic genre: tragedy (in works such as *Macbeth, Hamlet, King Lear,* and *Othello*); historical drama (for example, *Richard III* and *Henry IV*); comedy (*Twelfth Night, As You Like It*, and many more); and romance (in plays such as *The Tempest* and *Cymbaline*). Without question, Shakespeare is the most quoted, discussed, and beloved writer in English literature.

## WALLACE STEVENS
(1879–1955)

Born and raised in Reading, Pennsylvania, Wallace Stevens attended Harvard University and New York Law School. In New York City, he worked for a number of law firms, published poems in magazines, and befriended such literary figures as William Carlos Williams and Marianne Moore. In 1916, Stevens moved to Connecticut and began working for the Hartford Accident and Indemnity Company, where he became a vice-president in 1934 and where he worked for the rest of his life, writing poetry at night and during vacations. He published his first collection, *Harmonium*, in 1923, and followed it with a series of volumes from 1935 until 1950, establishing himself as one of the twentieth century's most important poets. His lectures were collected in *The Necessary Angel: Essays on Reality and Imagination* (1951); his *Collected Poems* appeared in 1954.

## ALFRED, LORD TENNYSON (1809–1892)

Perhaps the most important and certainly the most popular of the Victorian poets, Alfred, Lord Tennyson demonstrated his talents at an early age; he published his first volume in 1827. Encouraged to devote his life to poetry by a group of undergraduates at Cambridge University known as the "Apostles," Tennyson was particularly close to Arthur Hallam, whose sudden death in 1833 inspired the long elegy *In Memoriam* (1850). With that poem he achieved lasting fame and recognition; he was appointed Poet Laureate the year of its publication, succeeding Wordsworth. Despite the great popularity of his "journalistic" poems—"The Charge of the Light Brigade" (1854) is perhaps the best known—Tennyson's great theme was the past, both personal (*In the Valley of Cauteretz*, 1864) and national (*Idylls of the King*, 1869). Tennyson was made a baron in 1884; when he died, eight years later, he was buried in Poets' Corner in Westminster Abbey.

## DYLAN THOMAS (1914–1953)

Born in Swansea, Wales, into what he called "the smug darkness of a provincial town," Dylan Thomas published his first book, *Eighteen Poems* (1934), at twenty, in the same year that he moved to London. Thereafter he had a successful, though turbulent, career publishing poetry, short stories, and plays, including the highly successful *Under Milk Wood* (1954). In his last years he supported himself with lecture tours and poetry readings in the United States, but his excessive drinking caught up with him and he died in New York City of chronic alcoholism. His *Collected Poems, 1934–1952* (1952) was the last book he published during his short lifetime; his comic novel, *Adventures in the Skin Trade*, was never completed.

## DEREK WALCOTT (b. 1930)

Born of mixed heritage on the West Indian island of St. Lucia, Derek Walcott grew up speaking French and patois but was educated in English. In 1953, he earned his B.A. in English, French, and Latin from the University College of the West Indies in Jamaica. In 1950, with his twin brother, Roderick, he founded the St. Lucia Arts Guild, a dramatic society; nine years later, he founded the Little Carib Theatre Workshop in Trinidad, which he ran until 1976, writing many plays for production there. Walcott has published many volumes of poetry, including *In a Green Night* (1962), *The Castaway* (1965), *Another Life* (1973), *Sea Grapes* (1976), *The Fortunate Traveller* (1981), *Omeros* (1990), *The Bounty* (1997), *Tiepolo's Hound* (2000), and *The Prodigal* (2004). His work draws on diverse influences, from West Indian folk tales to Homer to Yeats. The first Caribbean poet to win the Nobel Prize (in 1992), Walcott now lives and teaches in the United States.

## WALT WHITMAN (1819–1892)

Walt Whitman was born on a farm in West Hills, Long Island, to a British father and a Dutch mother. After working as a journalist throughout New York for many years, he taught for a while and founded his own newspaper, *The Long Islander*, in 1838; he then left journalism to work on *Leaves of Grass*, originally intended as a poetic treatise on American democratic idealism. Published privately in multiple editions from 1855 to 1874, the book at first failed to reach a mass audience. In 1881, Boston's Osgood and Company published another edition of *Leaves of Grass*, which sold well until the district attorney called it "obscene literature" and stipulated that Whitman remove certain poems and phrases. He refused, and it was many years before his works were again published, this time in Philadelphia. By the time Whitman died, his work was revered, as it still is today, for its greatness of spirit and its exuberant American voice.

## RICHARD WILBUR
(b. 1921)

Born in New York City and raised in New Jersey, Richard Wilbur received his B.A. from Amherst College and his M.A. from Harvard. He started to write while serving as an army cryptographer during World War II, and his collections *The Beautiful Changes* (1947) and *Ceremony* (1950) established his reputation as a serious poet. In addition to subsequent volumes such as the Pulitzer Prize-winning *Things of This World* (1956), *Walking to Sleep* (1969), *The Mind Reader* (1976), the Pulitzer Prize-winning *New and Collected Poems* (1988), and *Mayflies: New Poems and Translations* (2000), he has published children's books, critical essays, and numerous translations of classic French works by Racine and Molière. He has taught at various colleges and universities, including Harvard, Wellesley, Wesleyan, and Smith. In 1987, he was named Poet Laureate of the United States.

## WILLIAM WORDSWORTH (1770–1850)

Regarded by many as the greatest of the Romantic poets, William Wordsworth was born in Cockermouth in the English Lake District, a beautiful, mountainous region that figured as a deep inspiration for his poetry. He studied at Cambridge and then spent a year in France, hoping to witness the French Revolution firsthand; as the Revolution's "glorious renovation" dissolved into anarchy and then tyranny, Wordsworth was forced to return to England. Remarkably, he managed to establish "a saving intercourse with my true self" and to write some of his finest poetry, including the early version of his masterpiece, *The Prelude*, which first appeared in 1805 and then again, much altered, in 1850. In 1798, Wordsworth and his friend Samuel Taylor Coleridge published *Lyrical Ballads,* which contained many of their greatest poems and can be considered the founding document of English Romanticism. Wordsworth was revered by the reading public and in 1843 was named Poet Laureate.

## WILLIAM BUTLER YEATS
(1865–1939)

William Butler Yeats was born in Dublin and, though he spent most of his youth in London, became the pre-eminent Irish poet of the twentieth century. Immersed in Irish history, folklore, and politics, as well as spiritualism and the occult, he attended art school for a time, but left to devote himself to poetry that was, early in his career, self-consciously dreamy and ethereal. Yeats's poems became tighter and more passionate with his reading of philosophers such as Nietzsche, his involvement (mainly through theater) with the Irish nationalist cause, and his desperate love for the actress and nationalist Maud Gonne. He was briefly a senator in the newly independent Irish government before withdrawing from active public life to Thoor Ballylee, a crumbling Norman tower that Yeats and his wife fashioned into a home. There he developed an elaborate mythology (published as *A Vision* in 1925) and wrote poems that explored fundamental questions of history and identity. He was awarded the Nobel Prize for Literature in 1923. His works, in many genres, have been selected and collected in various editions.

# DRAMA

# Drama: Reading, Responding, Writing

As we noted in our introduction, many cultures have had oral literatures: histories, romances, poems to be recited or sung. Our own era has its share of oral art forms, of course, but "literary" fiction and poetry are now most often read privately, silently, from the printed page. Most contemporary fiction writers and poets write with an understanding that this is how their work will be experienced and enjoyed.

In contrast, **drama** is written primarily to be performed—by actors, on a stage, for an audience. Playwrights work with an understanding that the words on the page are just the first step—a map of sorts—toward the ultimate goal: a collaborative, publicly performed work of art. They create plays fully aware of the possibilities that go beyond printed words and extend to physical actions, stage devices, and other theatrical techniques for creating special effects and modifying our responses. Although the script of a play may be the most essential piece in the puzzle that makes up the final work of art, the play text is not the final, complete work.

> *On the stage it is always now; the personages are standing on that razor-edge, between the past and the future, which is the essential character of conscious being; the words are rising to their lips in immediate spontaneity.*
> —THORNTON WILDER

To attend a play—that is, to be part of an audience—represents a very different kind of experience from the usually solitary act of reading. On the stage, real human beings, standing for imaginary characters, deliver lines and perform actions for you to see and hear. In turn, the actors adapt in subtle ways to the reactions of the people who attend the performance, and whose responses are no longer wholly private but have become, in part, communal.

When you attend the performance of a play, then, you become a collaborator in the creation of a unique work of art: not the play *text*, but instead a specific *interpretation* of that text. The play has been mediated by all the people involved in a particular production—the director, producers, actors, and designers of lighting, set, sound, costume, makeup—who help to interpret the author's text. These mediators have made decisions about how to convey the meaning and spirit of the play, and they perform for viewers part of the act of imagination that readers of a story or a poem must perform for themselves. Consciously or not, every director interprets every scene by the way he or she stages the action; casting, set design, the "blocking" or physical interaction of the actors, and the timing, phrasing, and tone of every speech affect how the play comes across. Every syllable uttered by every actor in some sense reshapes the play; the delivery of lines and even the slightest gestures correspond, for an actor, to the choices of words and sentence rhythms for a writer. With so many fine details affecting the outcome, it's inevitable that no two performances of a play can ever be identical.

Similarly, no two interpretations of a play can be exactly the same. We speak of "Olivier's Hamlet" (meaning the performance of the title role by Sir Laurence Olivier), of "Dame Maggie Smith's" or "Glenda Jackson's Hedda Gabler," or of "Baz Luhrmann's *Romeo and Juliet*" (meaning the film directed by Luhrmann), because in each case the actor or director creates a distinctive interpretation of the play. In the written text Hamlet may seem indecisive, melancholy, conniving, mad, vindictive, ambitious, or some combination of these qualities; individual performances emphasize one attribute or another, inevitably by downplaying other characteristics and interpretations. No play can be all things in any one performance or run (all the performances of a particular production).

The power of the best plays to be interpreted in so many ways, and the complementary limitation of the performed play (its necessary exclusion of many possible interpretations) once led the nineteenth-century writer Charles Lamb to come home from the theater vowing never to see another play of Shakespeare's on the stage. He found that no matter how good the performance, the enacted play restricted his imagination and robbed the play of some of the richness he found in reading it—and imagining it—for himself. Without having to renounce the theater as Lamb did or deprive ourselves of the thrilling experience of a brilliantly directed and performed interpretation of a play, we agree with Lamb that reading a play, rather than being a poor substitute for attending a performance, gives us an opportunity to be creative and collaborative in ways that are different from the ways we read a story or a poem.

In some respects, of course, reading drama is similar to reading fiction. In both cases we anticipate what will happen next; we imagine the characters, settings, and actions; we respond to the symbolic suggestiveness of images; and we notice thematic patterns that are likely to matter in the end. The chief difference between narrative fiction and drama on the page is the absence, in drama, of a mediator or narrator, someone standing between the reader and the events to help us relate to the characters, actions, and meanings. Description in drama is usually limited to a few **stage directions**—the italicized descriptions of the set, characters, and actions—while **exposition**—the explanation of the past and current situation—emerges only here and there in the dialogue.

For this reason, reading drama may place a greater demand on the imagination than reading fiction does: the reader must be his or her own narrator and interpreter. Such an exercise for the imagination can prove rewarding, however, for it has much in common with the imaginative work that a director, actors, and other artists involved in a staged production bring to their performance of a play. Recreating a play as we read it, we are essentially imagining the play as if it were being performed by live actors in real time. We "cast" the characters, we design the set with its furniture and props, and we choreograph or "block" the physical action, according to the cues in the text.

Those cues, of course, can be few and far between. Stage directions, which were rare in plays before the later nineteenth century, seldom spell out many details of the lighting, costume design, or other effects that live audiences see. In *The Real Inspector Hound,* Tom Stoppard simply calls for a "realistic" drawing room in a country estate, with French windows and a telephone, a setting that had become a standard in many twentieth-century plays. Susan Glaspell assumes directors or readers will easily re-create another standard realistic set

> *The dream is the theater where the dreamer is at once scene, actor, prompter, stage manager, author, audience, and critic.*
> —C. G. JUNG

for her play, *Trifles:* the kitchen of a farmhouse in the early twentieth century, one that is partially heated by a coal stove and not yet wired for a party-line telephone. Obviously, both of these one-act plays allow directors, actors, and readers considerable discretion in fleshing out the skeleton of the script. Making the most of this freedom is one of the unique pleasures of reading drama.

In reading drama even more than in reading fiction, we construct our ideas of character and personality from what a character says. In some plays, especially those with a modernist or experimental bent, certain lines of dialogue can be mystifying; other characters and the audience or readers can be left wondering what a speech meant. On the one hand, such puzzling lines can become clearer in performance, in which actors physically express the intentions and interactions of the characters. On the other hand, plays that call for several characters to speak at once or to talk at cross purposes can be much easier to understand from the printed script than in performance. In interpreting dialogue, you will naturally draw on your own experiences of comparable situations or similar personalities, as well as your familiarity with other plays or stories.

As you read scene by scene, you should not only make mental or written notes about your expectations, but you should raise some of the questions an actor might ask in preparing a role, or a director might ask before choosing a cast: How should this line be spoken? What kind of person is this character and what are his or her motives in each scene? What does the play imply or state about what made the character this way—family, environment, experience? Which characters are present or absent (onstage or off) in which scenes, and how do the characters onstage or off influence each other? What are characters aware of and what is the audience aware of? When and how does the audience know something that the characters don't? With these sorts of questions in mind, you may want to read both of the following short plays now. In the discussion that follows the play texts, we will trace stages of a first reading, but we necessarily reveal something of the ending. You will want to enjoy on your own the experience of a first reading when you don't yet know what will happen.

## SUSAN GLASPELL

### Trifles

**CHARACTERS**

SHERIFF  
COUNTY ATTORNEY  
HALE  
MRS. PETERS, *Sheriff's wife*  
MRS. HALE

SCENE: *The kitchen in the now abandoned farmhouse of* JOHN WRIGHT, *a gloomy kitchen, and left without having been put in order—unwashed pans under the sink, a loaf of bread outside the bread-box, a dish-towel on the table—other signs of incompleted work. At the rear the outer door opens and the* SHERIFF *comes in followed by the* COUNTY ATTORNEY *and* HALE. *The* SHERIFF *and* HALE *are men in middle life, the* COUNTY ATTORNEY *is a young man; all are much bundled up and go at once to the stove. They are followed by the two women—the* SHERIFF'S *wife first; she is a slight wiry woman, a thin nervous face.* MRS. HALE *is larger and would ordinarily be called more comfortable looking, but she is disturbed now and looks fearfully about as she enters. The women have come in slowly, and stand close together near the door.*

COUNTY ATTORNEY: [*Rubbing his hands.*] This feels good. Come up to the fire, ladies.
MRS. PETERS: [*After taking a step forward.*] I'm not—cold.
SHERIFF: [*Unbuttoning his overcoat and stepping away from the stove as if to mark the beginning of official business.*] Now, Mr. Hale, before we move things about, you explain to Mr. Henderson just what you saw when you came here yesterday morning.
COUNTY ATTORNEY: By the way, has anything been moved? Are things just as you left them yesterday?
SHERIFF: [*Looking about.*] It's just the same. When it dropped below zero last night I thought I'd better send Frank out this morning to make a fire for us—no use getting pneumonia with a big case on, but I told him not to touch anything except the stove—and you know Frank.
COUNTY ATTORNEY: Somebody should have been left here yesterday.
SHERIFF: Oh—yesterday. When I had to send Frank to Morris Center for that man who went crazy—I want you to know I had my hands full yesterday. I knew you could get back from Omaha by today and as long as I went over everything here myself—
COUNTY ATTORNEY: Well, Mr. Hale, tell just what happened when you came here yesterday morning.
HALE: Harry and I had started to town with a load of potatoes. We came along the road from my place and as I got here I said, "I'm going to see if I can't get John Wright to go in with me on a party telephone." I spoke to Wright about it once before and he put me off, saying folks talked too much anyway, and all he asked was peace and quiet—I guess you know about how much he talked himself; but I thought maybe if I went to the house and talked about it before his wife, though I said to Harry that I didn't know as what his wife wanted made much difference to John—
COUNTY ATTORNEY: Let's talk about that later, Mr. Hale. I do want to talk about that, but tell now just what happened when you got to the house.
HALE: I didn't hear or see anything; I knocked at the door, and still it was all quiet inside. I knew they must be up, it was past eight o'clock. So I knocked again, and I thought I heard somebody say, "Come in." I wasn't sure, I'm not sure yet, but I opened the door—this door [*Indicating the door by which the two women are still standing.*] and there in that rocker—[*Pointing to it.*] sat Mrs. Wright.

[*They all look at the rocker.*]

COUNTY ATTORNEY: What—was she doing?
HALE: She was rockin' back and forth. She had her apron in her hand and was kind of—pleating it.
COUNTY ATTORNEY: And how did she—look?
HALE: Well, she looked queer.
COUNTY ATTORNEY: How do you mean—queer?

HALE: Well, as if she didn't know what she was going to do next. And kind of done up.
COUNTY ATTORNEY: How did she seem to feel about your coming?
HALE: Why, I don't think she minded—one way or other. She didn't pay much attention. I said, "How do, Mrs. Wright, it's cold, ain't it?" And she said, "Is it?"—and went on kind of pleating at her apron. Well, I was surprised; she didn't ask me to come up to the stove, or to set down, but just sat there, not even looking at me, so I said, "I want to see John." And then she—laughed. I guess you would call it a laugh. I thought of Harry and the team outside, so I said a little sharp: "Can't I see John?" "No," she says, kind o' dull like. "Ain't he home?" says I. "Yes," says she, "he's home." "Then why can't I see him?" I asked her, out of patience. "'Cause he's dead," says she. "*Dead?*" says I. She just nodded her head, not getting a bit excited, but rockin' back and forth. "Why—where is he?" says I, not knowing what to say. She just pointed upstairs—like that. [*Himself pointing to the room above.*] I got up, with the idea of going up there. I walked from there to here—then I says, "Why, what did he die of?" "He died of a rope round his neck," says she, and just went on pleatin' at her apron. Well, I went out and called Harry. I thought I might—need help. We went upstairs and there he was lyin'—
COUNTY ATTORNEY: I think I'd rather have you go into that upstairs, where you can point it all out. Just go on now with the rest of the story.
HALE: Well, my first thought was to get that rope off. It looked . . . [*Stops, his face twitches.*] . . . but Harry, he went up to him, and he said, "No, he's dead all right, and we'd better not touch anything." So we went back down stairs. She was still sitting that same way. "Has anybody been notified?" I asked. "No," says she unconcerned. "Who did this, Mrs. Wright?" said Harry. He said it business-like—and she stopped pleatin' of her apron. "I don't know," she says. "You don't *know?*" says Harry. "No," says she. "Weren't you sleepin' in the bed with him?" says Harry. "Yes," says she, "but I was on the inside." "Somebody slipped a rope round his neck and strangled him and you didn't wake up?" says Harry. "I didn't wake up," she said after him. We must 'a looked as if we didn't see how that could be, for after a minute she said, "I sleep sound." Harry was going to ask her more questions but I said maybe we ought to let her tell her story first to the coroner, or the sheriff, so Harry went fast as he could to Rivers' place, where there's a telephone.
COUNTY ATTORNEY: And what did Mrs. Wright do when she knew that you had gone for the coroner?
HALE: She moved from that chair to this one over here [*Pointing to a small chair in the corner.*] and just sat there with her hands held together and looking down. I got a feeling that I ought to make some conversation, so I said I had come in to see if John wanted to put in a telephone, and at that she started to laugh, and then she stopped and looked at me—scared. [*The* COUNTY ATTORNEY, *who has had his notebook out, makes a note.*] I dunno, maybe it wasn't scared. I wouldn't like to say it was. Soon Harry got back, and then Dr. Lloyd came, and you, Mr. Peters, and so I guess that's all I know that you don't.
COUNTY ATTORNEY: [*Looking around.*] I guess we'll go upstairs first—and then out to the barn and around there. [*To the* SHERIFF.] You're convinced that there was nothing important here—nothing that would point to any motive?
SHERIFF: Nothing here but kitchen things.

[The COUNTY ATTORNEY, *after again looking around the kitchen, opens the door of a cupboard closet. He gets up on a chair and looks on a shelf. Pulls his hand away, sticky.*]

COUNTY ATTORNEY: Here's a nice mess.

[*The women draw nearer.*]

MRS. PETERS: [*To the other woman.*] Oh, her fruit; it did freeze. [*To the* LAWYER.] She worried about that when it turned so cold. She said the fire'd go out and her jars would break.

SHERIFF: Well, can you beat the women! Held for murder and worryin' about her preserves.

COUNTY ATTORNEY: I guess before we're through she may have something more serious than preserves to worry about.

HALE: Well, women are used to worrying over trifles.

[*The two women move a little closer together.*]

COUNTY ATTORNEY: [*With the gallantry of a young politician.*] And yet, for all their worries, what would we do without the ladies? [*The women do not unbend. He goes to the sink, takes a dipperful of water from the pail and pouring it into a basin, washes his hands. Starts to wipe them on the roller towel, turns it for a cleaner place.*] Dirty towels! [*Kicks his foot against the pans under the sink.*] Not much of a housekeeper, would you say, ladies?

MRS. HALE: [*Stiffly.*] There's a great deal of work to be done on a farm.

COUNTY ATTORNEY: To be sure. And yet [*With a little bow to her.*] I know there are some Dickson county farmhouses which do not have such roller towels. [*He gives it a pull to expose its length again.*]

MRS. HALE: Those towels get dirty awful quick. Men's hands aren't always as clean as they might be.

COUNTY ATTORNEY: Ah, loyal to your sex, I see. But you and Mrs. Wright were neighbors. I suppose you were friends, too.

MRS. HALE: [*Shaking her head.*] I've not seen much of her of late years. I've not been in this house—it's more than a year.

COUNTY ATTORNEY: And why was that? You didn't like her?

MRS. HALE: I liked her all well enough. Farmers' wives have their hands full, Mr. Henderson. And then—

COUNTY ATTORNEY: Yes—?

MRS. HALE: [*Looking about.*] It never seemed a very cheerful place.

COUNTY ATTORNEY: No—it's not cheerful. I shouldn't say she had the homemaking instinct.

MRS. HALE: Well, I don't know as Wright had, either.

COUNTY ATTORNEY: You mean that they didn't get on very well?

MRS. HALE: No, I don't mean anything. But I don't think a place'd be any cheerfuller for John Wright's being in it.

COUNTY ATTORNEY: I'd like to talk more of that a little later. I want to get the lay of things upstairs now. [*He goes to the left, where three steps lead to a stair door.*]

SHERIFF: I suppose anything Mrs. Peters does'll be all right. She was to take in some clothes for her, you know, and a few little things. We left in such a hurry yesterday.

COUNTY ATTORNEY: Yes, but I would like to see what you take, Mrs. Peters, and keep an eye out for anything that might be of use to us.

MRS. PETERS: Yes, Mr. Henderson. [*The women listen to the men's steps on the stairs, then look about the kitchen.*]

MRS. HALE: I'd hate to have men coming into my kitchen, snooping around and criticizing. [*She arranges the pans under sink which the* LAWYER *had shoved out of place.*]

MRS. PETERS: Of course it's no more than their duty.

MRS. HALE: Duty's all right, but I guess that deputy sheriff that came out to make the fire might have got a little of this on. [*Gives the roller towel a pull.*] Wish I'd thought of that sooner. Seems mean to talk about her for not having things slicked up when she had to come away in such a hurry.

MRS. PETERS: [*Who has gone to a small table in the left rear corner of the room, and lifted one end of a towel that covers a pan.*] She had bread set. [*Stands still.*]

MRS. HALE: [*Eyes fixed on a loaf of bread beside the bread box, which is on a low shelf at the other side of the room. Moves slowly toward it.*] She was going to put this in there. [*Picks up loaf, then abruptly drops it. In a manner of returning to familiar things.*] It's a shame about her fruit. I wonder if it's all gone. [*Gets up on the chair and looks.*] I think there's some here that's all right, Mrs. Peters. Yes—here; [*Holding it toward the window.*] this is cherries, too. [*Looking again.*] I declare I believe that's the only one. [*Gets down, bottle in her hand. Goes to the sink and wipes it off on the outside.*] She'll feel awful bad after all her hard work in the hot weather. I remember the afternoon I put up my cherries last summer. [*She puts the bottle on the big kitchen table, center of the room. With a sigh, is about to sit down in the rocking-chair. Before she is seated realizes what chair it is; with a slow look at it, steps back. The chair, which she has touched, rocks back and forth.*]

MRS. PETERS: Well, I must get those things from the front room closet. [*She goes to the door at the right, but after looking into the other room, steps back.*] You coming with me, Mrs. Hale? You could help me carry them. [*They go in the other room; reappear,* MRS. PETERS *carrying a dress and skirt,* MRS. HALE *following with a pair of shoes.*] My, it's cold in there. [*She puts the clothes on the big table, and hurries to the stove.*]

MRS. HALE: [*Examining the skirt.*] Wright was close. I think maybe that's why she kept so much to herself. She didn't even belong to the Ladies Aid. I suppose she felt she couldn't do her part, and then you don't enjoy things when you feel shabby. She used to wear pretty clothes and be lively, when she was Minnie Foster, one of the town girls singing in the choir. But that—oh, that was thirty years ago. This all you was to take in?

MRS. PETERS: She said she wanted an apron. Funny thing to want, for there isn't much to get you dirty in jail, goodness knows. But I suppose just to make her feel more natural. She said they was in the top drawer in this cupboard. Yes, here. And then her little shawl that always hung behind the door. [*Opens stair door and looks.*] Yes, here it is. [*Quickly shuts door leading upstairs.*]

MRS. HALE: [*Abruptly moving toward her.*] Mrs. Peters?

MRS. PETERS: Yes, Mrs. Hale?

MRS. HALE: Do you think she did it?

MRS. PETERS: [*In a frightened voice.*] Oh, I don't know.

MRS. HALE: Well, I don't think she did. Asking for an apron and her little shawl. Worrying about her fruit.

MRS. PETERS: [*Starts to speak, glances up, where footsteps are heard in the room above. In a low voice.*] Mr. Peters says it looks bad for her. Mr. Henderson is awful sarcastic in a speech and he'll make fun of her sayin' she didn't wake up.

MRS. HALE: Well, I guess John Wright didn't wake when they was slipping that rope under his neck.

MRS. PETERS: No, it's strange. It must have been done awful crafty and still. They say it was such a—funny way to kill a man, rigging it all up like that.

MRS. HALE: That's just what Mr. Hale said. There was a gun in the house. He says that's what he can't understand.

MRS. PETERS: Mr. Henderson said coming out that what was needed for the case was a motive; something to show anger, or—sudden feeling.

MRS. HALE: [*Who is standing by the table.*] Well, I don't see any signs of anger around here. [*She puts her hand on the dish towel which lies on the table, stands looking down at table, one half of which is clean, the other half messy.*] It's wiped to here. [*Makes a move as if to finish work, then turns and looks at loaf of bread outside the bread box. Drops towel. In that voice of coming back to familiar things.*] Wonder how they are finding things upstairs. I hope she had it a little more red-up[1] up there. You know, it seems kind of *sneaking*. Locking her up in town and then coming out here and trying to get her own house to turn against her!

MRS. PETERS: But Mrs. Hale, the law is the law.

MRS. HALE: I s'pose 'tis. [*Unbuttoning her coat.*] Better loosen up your things, Mrs. Peters. You won't feel them when you go out.

[MRS. PETERS *takes off her fur tippet, goes to hang it on hook at back of room, stands looking at the under part of the small corner table.*]

MRS. PETERS: She was piecing a quilt. [*She brings the large sewing basket and they look at the bright pieces.*]

MRS. HALE: It's log cabin pattern. Pretty, isn't it? I wonder if she was goin' to quilt it or just knot it?

[*Footsteps have been heard coming down the stairs. The* SHERIFF *enters followed by* HALE *and the* COUNTY ATTORNEY.]

SHERIFF: They wonder if she was going to quilt it or just knot it!

[*The men laugh, the women look abashed.*]

COUNTY ATTORNEY: [*Rubbing his hands over the stove.*] Frank's fire didn't do much up there, did it? Well, let's go out to the barn and get that cleared up.

[*The men go outside.*]

MRS. HALE: [*Resentfully.*] I don't know as there's anything so strange, our takin' up our time with little things while we're waiting for them to get the evidence. [*She sits down at the big table smoothing out a block with decision.*] I don't see as it's anything to laugh about.

MRS. PETERS: [*Apologetically.*] Of course they've got awful important things on their minds. [*Pulls up a chair and joins* MRS. HALE *at the table.*]

MRS. HALE: [*Examining another block.*] Mrs. Peters, look at this one. Here, this is the one she was working on, and look at the sewing! All the rest of it has

1. Tidied up.

been so nice and even. And look at this! It's all over the place! Why, it looks as if she didn't know what she was about! [*After she has said this they look at each other, then start to glance back at the door. After an instant* MRS. HALE *has pulled at a knot and ripped the sewing.*]

MRS. PETERS: Oh, what are you doing, Mrs. Hale?

MRS. HALE: [*Mildly.*] Just pulling out a stitch or two that's not sewed very good. [*Threading the needle.*] Bad sewing always made me fidgety.

MRS. PETERS: [*Nervously.*] I don't think we ought to touch things.

MRS. HALE: I'll just finish up this end. [*Suddenly stopping and leaning forward.*] Mrs. Peters?

MRS. PETERS: Yes, Mrs. Hale?

MRS. HALE: What do you suppose she was so nervous about?

MRS. PETERS: Oh—I don't know. I don't know as she was nervous. I sometimes sew awful queer when I'm just tired. [MRS. HALE *starts to say something, looks at* MRS. PETERS, *then goes on sewing.*] Well I must get these things wrapped up. They may be through sooner than we think. [*Putting apron and other things together.*] I wonder where I can find a piece of paper, and string.

MRS. HALE: In that cupboard, maybe.

MRS. PETERS: [*Looking in cupboard.*] Why, here's a bird-cage. [*Holds it up.*] Did she have a bird, Mrs. Hale?

MRS. HALE: Why, I don't know whether she did or not—I've not been here for so long. There was a man around last year selling canaries cheap, but I don't know as she took one; maybe she did. She used to sing real pretty herself.

MRS. PETERS: [*Glancing around.*] Seems funny to think of a bird here. But she must have had one, or why would she have a cage? I wonder what happened to it.

MRS. HALE: I s'pose maybe the cat got it.

MRS. PETERS: No, she didn't have a cat. She's got that feeling some people have about cats—being afraid of them. My cat got in her room and she was real upset and asked me to take it out.

MRS. HALE: My sister Bessie was like that. Queer, ain't it?

MRS. PETERS: [*Examining the cage.*] Why, look at this door. It's broke. One hinge is pulled apart.

MRS. HALE: [*Looking too.*] Looks as if someone must have been rough with it.

MRS. PETERS: Why, yes. [*She brings the cage forward and puts it on the table.*]

MRS. HALE: I wish if they're going to find any evidence they'd be about it. I don't like this place.

MRS. PETERS: But I'm awful glad you came with me, Mrs. Hale. It would be lonesome for me sitting here alone.

MRS. HALE: It would, wouldn't it? [*Dropping her sewing.*] But I tell you what I do wish, Mrs. Peters. I wish I had come over sometimes when *she* was here. I—[*Looking around the room.*]—wish I had.

MRS. PETERS: But of course you were awful busy, Mrs. Hale—your house and your children.

MRS. HALE: I could've come. I stayed away because it weren't cheerful—and that's why I ought to have come. I—I've never liked this place. Maybe because it's down in a hollow and you don't see the road. I dunno what it is, but it's a lonesome place and always was. I wish I had come over to see Minnie Foster sometimes. I can see now—[*Shakes her head.*]

MRS. PETERS: Well, you mustn't reproach yourself, Mrs. Hale. Somehow we just don't see how it is with other folks until—something comes up.

MRS. HALE: Not having children makes less work—but it makes a quiet house, and Wright out to work all day, and no company when he did come in. Did you know John Wright, Mrs. Peters?

MRS. PETERS: Not to know him; I've seen him in town. They say he was a good man.

MRS. HALE: Yes—good; he didn't drink, and kept his word as well as most, I guess, and paid his debts. But he was a hard man, Mrs. Peters. Just to pass the time of day with him—[*Shivers.*] Like a raw wind that gets to the bone. [*Pauses, her eye falling on the cage.*] I should think she would 'a wanted a bird. But what do you suppose went with it?

MRS. PETERS: I don't know, unless it got sick and died. [*She reaches over and swings the broken door, swings it again, both women watch it.*]

MRS. HALE: You weren't raised round here, were you? [MRS. PETERS *shakes her head.*] You didn't know—her?

MRS. PETERS: Not till they brought her yesterday.

MRS. HALE: She—come to think of it, she was kind of like a bird herself—real sweet and pretty, but kind of timid and—fluttery. How—she—did—change. [*Silence; then as if struck by a happy thought and relieved to get back to everyday things.*] Tell you what, Mrs. Peters, why don't you take the quilt in with you? It might take up her mind.

MRS. PETERS: Why, I think that's a real nice idea, Mrs. Hale. There couldn't possibly be any objection to it, could there? Now, just what would I take? I wonder if her patches are in here—and her things. [*They look in the sewing basket.*]

MRS. HALE: Here's some red. I expect this has got sewing things in it. [*Brings out a fancy box.*] What a pretty box. Looks like something somebody would give you. Maybe her scissors are in here. [*Opens box. Suddenly puts her hand to her nose.*] Why—[MRS. PETERS *bends nearer, then turns her face away.*] There's something wrapped up in this piece of silk.

MRS. PETERS: Why, this isn't her scissors.

MRS. HALE: [*Lifting the silk.*] Oh, Mrs. Peters—it's—

[MRS. PETERS *bends closer.*]

MRS. PETERS: It's the bird.

MRS. HALE: [*Jumping up.*] But, Mrs. Peters—look at it! Its neck! Look at its neck! It's all—other side *to*.

MRS. PETERS: Somebody—wrung—its—neck.

[*Their eyes meet. A look of growing comprehension, of horror. Steps are heard outside.* MRS. HALE *slips box under quilt pieces, and sinks into her chair. Enter* SHERIFF *and* COUNTY ATTORNEY. MRS. PETERS *rises.*]

COUNTY ATTORNEY: [*As one turning from serious things to little pleasantries.*] Well ladies, have you decided whether she was going to quilt it or knot it?

MRS. PETERS: We think she was going to—knot it.

COUNTY ATTORNEY: Well, that's interesting, I'm sure. [*Seeing the bird-cage.*] Has the bird flown?

MRS. HALE: [*Putting more quilt pieces over the box.*] We think the—cat got it.
COUNTY ATTORNEY: [*Preoccupied.*] Is there a cat?

[MRS. HALE *glances in a quick covert way at* MRS. PETERS.]

MRS. PETERS: Well, not *now*. They're superstitious, you know. They leave.
COUNTY ATTORNEY: [*To* SHERIFF PETERS, *continuing an interrupted conversation.*] No sign at all of anyone having come from the outside. Their own rope. Now let's go up again and go over it piece by piece. [*They start upstairs.*] It would have to have been someone who knew just the—

[MRS. PETERS *sits down. The two women sit there not looking at one another, but as if peering into something and at the same time holding back. When they talk now it is in the manner of feeling their way over strange ground, as if afraid of what they are saying, but as if they cannot help saying it.*]

MRS. HALE: She liked the bird. She was going to bury it in that pretty box.
MRS. PETERS: [*In a whisper.*] When I was a girl—my kitten—there was a boy took a hatchet, and before my eyes—and before I could get there—[*Covers her face an instant.*] If they hadn't held me back I would have—[*Catches herself, looks upstairs where steps are heard, falters weakly.*]—hurt him.
MRS. HALE: [*With a slow look around her.*] I wonder how it would seem never to have had any children around. [*Pause.*] No, Wright wouldn't like the bird—a thing that sang. She used to sing. He killed that, too.
MRS. PETERS: [*Moving uneasily.*] We don't know who killed the bird.
MRS. HALE: I knew John Wright.
MRS. PETERS: It was an awful thing was done in this house that night, Mrs. Hale. Killing a man while he slept, slipping a rope around his neck that choked the life out of him.
MRS. HALE: His neck. Choked the life out of him. [*Her hand goes out and rests on the bird-cage.*]
MRS. PETERS: [*With rising voice.*] We don't know who killed him. We don't *know*.
MRS. HALE: [*Her own feeling not interrupted.*] If there's been years and years of nothing, then a bird to sing to you, it would be awful—still, after the bird was still.
MRS. PETERS: [*Something within her speaking.*] I know what stillness is. When we homesteaded in Dakota, and my first baby died—after he was two years old, and me with no other then—
MRS. HALE: [*Moving.*] How soon do you suppose they'll be through, looking for the evidence?
MRS. PETERS: I know what stillness is. [*Pulling herself back.*] The law has got to punish crime, Mrs. Hale.
MRS. HALE: [*Not as if answering that.*] I wish you'd seen Minnie Foster when she wore a white dress with blue ribbons and stood up there in the choir and sang. [*A look around the room.*] Oh, I *wish* I'd come over here once in a while! That was a crime! That was a crime! Who's going to punish that?
MRS. PETERS: [*Looking upstairs.*] We mustn't—take on.
MRS. HALE: I might have known she needed help! I know how things can be—for women. I tell you, it's queer, Mrs. Peters. We live close together and we live far apart. We all go through the same things—it's all just a different kind of the same thing. [*Brushes her eyes, noticing the bottle of fruit, reaches out for it.*] If I was you, I wouldn't tell her her fruit was gone. Tell her it *ain't*.

Tell her it's all right. Take this in to prove it to her. She—she may never know whether it was broke or not.

MRS. PETERS: [*Takes the bottle, looks about for something to wrap it in; takes petticoat from the clothes brought from the other room, very nervously begins winding this around the bottle. In a false voice.*] My, it's a good thing the men couldn't hear us. Wouldn't they just laugh! Getting all stirred up over a little thing like a—dead canary. As if that could have anything to do with—with—wouldn't they *laugh!*

[*The men are heard coming down stairs.*]

MRS. HALE: [*Under her breath.*] Maybe they would—maybe they wouldn't.

COUNTY ATTORNEY: No, Peters, it's all perfectly clear except a reason for doing it. But you know juries when it comes to women. If there was some definite thing. Something to show—something to make a story about—a thing that would connect up with this strange way of doing it—

[*The women's eyes meet for an instant. Enter* HALE *from outer door.*]

HALE: Well, I've got the team around. Pretty cold out there.

COUNTY ATTORNEY: I'm going to stay here a while by myself. [*To the* SHERIFF.] You can send Frank out for me, can't you? I want to go over everything. I'm not satisfied that we can't do better.

SHERIFF: Do you want to see what Mrs. Peters is going to take in?

[*The* LAWYER *goes to the table, picks up the apron, laughs.*]

COUNTY ATTORNEY: Oh, I guess they're not very dangerous things the ladies have picked out. [*Moves a few things about, disturbing the quilt pieces which cover the box. Steps back.*] No, Mrs. Peters doesn't need supervising. For that matter, a sheriff's wife is married to the law. Ever think of it that way, Mrs. Peters?

MRS. PETERS: Not—just that way.

SHERIFF: [*Chuckling.*] Married to the law. [*Moves toward the other room.*] I just want you to come in here a minute, George. We ought to take a look at these windows.

COUNTY ATTORNEY: [*Scoffingly.*] Oh, windows!

SHERIFF: We'll be right out, Mr. Hale.

[HALE *goes outside. The* SHERIFF *follows the* COUNTY ATTORNEY *into the other room. Then* MRS. HALE *rises, hands tight together, looking intensely at* MRS. PETERS, *whose eyes make a slow turn, finally meeting* MRS. HALE's. *A moment* MRS. HALE *holds her, then her own eyes point the way to where the box is concealed. Suddenly* MRS. PETERS *throws back quilt pieces and tries to put the box in the bag she is wearing. It is too big. She opens box, starts to take bird out, cannot touch it, goes to pieces, stands there helpless. Sound of a knob turning in the other room.* MRS. HALE *snatches the box and puts it in the pocket of her big coat. Enter* COUNTY ATTORNEY *and* SHERIFF.]

COUNTY ATTORNEY: [*Facetiously.*] Well, Henry, at least we found out that she was not going to quilt it. She was going to—what is it you call it, ladies?

MRS. HALE: [*Her hand against her pocket.*] We call it—knot it, Mr. Henderson.

CURTAIN

1916

## QUESTIONS

1. If we were watching a production of *Trifles* and had no cast list, how would we gradually piece together the fact that Mrs. Peters is the Sheriff's wife? What are the earliest lines of dialogue that allow an audience to infer this fact?
2. What lines in the play characterize Mrs. Hale's reaction to the men's behavior and attitudes? What lines characterize Mrs. Peters's reaction to the men early in the play, and what lines show her feelings changing later in the play? What might account for both their initial differences and then their evolving solidarity with Mrs. Wright?
3. What are the "trifles" that the men ignore and the two women notice? Why do the men dismiss them, and why do the women see these things as significant clues? What is the thematic importance of these "trifles"?
4. How would you stage the key moment of the play, Mrs. Hale's discovery inside the sewing basket? What facial expression would she have, what body language? Where would you place Mrs. Peters, and what would she be doing? How would you use lighting to heighten the effectiveness of the scene?
5. To what degree are each of the characters in the play "round," or well developed? To what degree are they stereotypes?
6. If a twenty-first-century playwright were to write an updated version of *Trifles*, what details of plot, character, and setting would be different from those in Glaspell's play? What would be the same? What are some possible "trifles" that might serve the same dramatic functions as those in Glaspell's play?

A title is always a key to an interpretation. Does the title "*Trifles*" lead you to expect a light comedy, something "trifling"? The list of characters that follows Glaspell's title, however, includes a sheriff and a county attorney along with some common Anglo American names, suggesting a serious situation involving the law (compare these ordinary names with Stoppard's inventions of an inspector named Hound, or a housekeeper named Drudge, which is another word for a servant). A few lines into Glaspell's play, the county attorney asks Mr. Hale if "things are just as you left them," and then asks him to "tell just what happened." Probably most readers expect at this point that the house is the scene of a crime. What does a reader expect Hale to say in the next lines as he describes his visit the day before? Are your expectations confirmed or altered when you find out more?

> What is drama but life with the dull bits cut out?
> —ALFRED HITCHCOCK

As the talkative Hale describes his visit to the home of people who seldom talk and don't answer the door, you probably feel curious. You don't yet know more than Hale did at the time, so you probably expect nothing too alarming. Why do the stage directions instruct all the actors to look at the rocking chair, if Mrs. Wright is obviously not there? It is a cue to imagine her and the rather strange behavior that Hale describes. When Hale reports that Mrs. Wright said her husband "died of a rope round his neck," curiosity changes to suspicion. Could she actually have slept so soundly that she didn't know someone had put a rope around his neck and pulled him upright, killing him? Though we anticipate the discovery of the murderer—or perhaps Mrs. Wright's confession—our attention is really more focused on the behavior of the people on stage. Why does Hale remark that "women are used to worrying over trifles"? Why do the men scoff at the women's discussion of Mrs. Wright's intentions for finishing the quilt, whether to quilt-stitch or knot it? Depending on how alert we are, we may have noticed that the county attorney dismisses information about Mr. Wright's treatment of

Mrs. Wright, and that the sheriff remarks that there is "nothing here but kitchen things." With the help of the title, we begin to see the flaw in the habitual way male characters devalue what women care about: they will miss the clues to a motive for the murder.

The situation now raises a number of questions. How offensive are these sexist remarks? Do you prefer the "gallantry" of the county attorney, who consistently flatters the women? Maybe the women's concerns are too trivial and practical. Obviously, losing all but one of the bottles of preserves, or leaving a quilt unfinished, is less important than the death of a husband. The women's sympathies and concerns evolve during the scene, whereas the men learn little from the visit to the house except that the rope belonged to the Wrights. Can you find the moments that Mrs. Peters shifts her allegiance from her husband and the law to Mrs. Hale? To what extent do the men's assumptions justify the women's suppression of their evidence (which the men might not have thought "real" evidence anyway)? Where do your own sympathies lie? Should Mrs. Wright get away with it? Does the play strongly suggest an answer to these questions? Does the answer make you like or dislike the play? How important is your acceptance or rejection of the social theme to your emotional response to the play?

There is nothing particularly difficult or unfamiliar about *Trifles* as a "story." (Glaspell did, indeed, turn the play into a story—"A Jury of Her Peers"—included earlier in this text; see "Reading More Fiction.") Like some detective stories, it asks not "who done it?" but why the murder was committed. Its **mode** of representation is a familiar type—domestic realism—in which the places, people, and even events are more or less ordinary (unfortunately, domestic violence is too common to be extraordinary). Its staging is also conventional in the modern theater: it shows three walls of a room, with the front of the stage—the **proscenium arch**—where the imaginary fourth wall would be. It also has—though somewhat in miniature—the traditional five-part structure: the **exposition**—the situation at the beginning of a play (here, Mr. Hale's description of what happened); the **rising action**—the complicating of the plot (the men leaving the women alone with the evidence that reveals the motive); the **climax**—the turning point (here, perhaps, the discovery of the dead bird); the **falling action**—the unwinding of the plot toward the conclusion (the women covering up the "trifling" evidence); and the **conclusion.** This does not suggest that the play is *too* conventional, but only that its type, subject matter, manner of presentation, and form are familiar—which might also be said, for example, of *Oedipus* or *Hamlet*.

Working with the conventions of her time, Glaspell made ingenious decisions about how to dramatize her story. To dramatize the story of what happened, Glaspell could have designed several scene changes over a longer period of time, showing the deteriorating marriage, the crisis over the bird, the murder itself, the sleepless night for Mrs. Wright, and the arrival of Mr. Hale the day before the scene we witness. Instead, the story unfolds in a single scene after the fact: in one room, on the second morning after the murder, between the entrance and exit of Mrs. Hale and Mrs. Peters. Mrs. Wright never appears. Instead, her old neighbors, Mr. and Mrs. Hale, describe her both as she is now and as she was when young. (When directors choose the plays they will put on, they have to think about the availability of actors and, if it is a professional production, the cost of paying them; plays with smaller casts are easier as well as cheaper to stage.) What is the effect of such a deliberate omission? Rather than watching Mrs. Wright to judge her guilt, the audience or readers focus on the process of detection and the motivation of the two visiting women. The other crucial omission from the play is the victim himself. The men go offstage to look at the corpse that everyone knows (or imagines) is lying upstairs. (Again, no actor is needed.) This separation of the women from the men brings out the theme of the different outlooks and values of the sexes. The growing allegiance of the two women with the absent housewife elicits the audience's sympathy as the secrets of Mrs. Wright's motivation are discovered. This evidence remains invisible to the men when they return to the kitchen, Mrs. Wright's environment. The audience now knows that space quite intimately.

## TOM STOPPARD

### The Real Inspector Hound

CHARACTERS

| MOON | SIMON | MAGNUS |
|---|---|---|
| BIRDBOOT | FELICITY | INSPECTOR HOUND |
| MRS. DRUDGE | CYNTHIA | |

*The first thing is that the audience appear to be confronted by their own reflection in a huge mirror. Impossible. However, back there in the gloom—not at the footlights—a bank of plush seats and pale smudges of faces. (The total effect having been established, it can be progressively faded out as the play goes on, until the front row remains to remind us of the rest and then, finally, merely two seats in that row—one of which is now occupied by* MOON. *Between* MOON *and the auditorium is an acting area which represents, in as realistic an idiom as possible, the drawing-room of Muldoon Manor. French windows at one side. A telephone fairly well upstage (i.e. towards* MOON). *The body of a man lies sprawled face down on the floor in front of a large settee. This settee must be of a size and design to allow it to be wheeled over the body, hiding it completely. Silence. The room. The body.* MOON.

MOON *stares blankly ahead. He turns his head to one side then the other, then up, then down—waiting. He picks up his programme and reads the front cover. He turns over the page and reads.*

*He turns over the page and reads.*

*He turns over the page and reads.*

*He turns over the page and reads.*

*He looks at the back cover and reads.*

*He puts it down and crosses his legs and looks about. He stares front. Behind him and to one side, barely visible, a man enters and sits down:* BIRDBOOT.

*Pause.* MOON *picks up his programme, glances at the front cover and puts it down impatiently. Pause . . . Behind him there is the crackle of a chocolate-box, absurdly loud.* MOON *looks round. He and* BIRDBOOT *see each other. They are clearly known to each other. They acknowledge each other with constrained waves.* MOON *looks straight ahead.* BIRDBOOT *comes down to join him.*

Note: *Almost always,* MOON *and* BIRDBOOT *converse in tones suitable for an auditorium, sometimes a whisper. However good the acoustics might be, they will have to have* microphones where they are sitting. The effect must be not of sound picked up, amplified and flung out at the audience, but of sound picked up, carried and gently dispersed around the auditorium.

Anyway, BIRDBOOT, with a box of Black Magic,[1] makes his way down to join MOON and plumps himself down next to him, plumpish middle-aged BIRDBOOT and younger taller, less-relaxed MOON.

BIRDBOOT: [sitting down; conspiratorially] Me and the lads have had a meeting in the bar and decided it's first-class family entertainment but if it goes on beyond half-past ten it's self-indulgent—pass it on . . . [and laughs jovially] I'm on my own tonight, don't mind if I join you?

MOON: Hello, Birdboot.

BIRDBOOT: Where's Higgs?

MOON: I'm standing in.

MOON AND BIRDBOOT: Where's Higgs?

MOON: Every time.

BIRDBOOT: What?

MOON: It is as if we only existed one at a time, combining to achieve continuity. I keep space warm for Higgs. My presence defines his absence, his absence confirms my presence, his presence precludes mine . . . When Higgs and I walk down this aisle together to claim our common seat, the oceans will fall into the sky and the trees will hang with fishes.

BIRDBOOT: [he has not been paying attention, looking around vaguely, now catches up] Where's Higgs?

MOON: The very sight of me with a complimentary ticket is enough. The streets are impassable tonight, the country is rising and the cry goes up from hill to hill—Where—is—Higgs? [Small pause.] Perhaps he's dead at last, or trapped in a lift[2] somewhere, or succumbed to amnesia, wandering the land with his turn-ups stuffed with ticket-stubs.

[BIRDBOOT regards him doubtfully for a moment.]

BIRDBOOT: Yes. . . . Yes, well I didn't bring Myrtle tonight—not exactly her cup of tea, I thought, tonight.

MOON: Over her head, you mean?

BIRDBOOT: Well, no—I mean it's a sort of a *thriller*, isn't it?

MOON: Is it?

BIRDBOOT: That's what I heard. Who killed thing?—no one will leave the house.

MOON: I suppose so. Underneath.

BIRDBOOT: *Underneath*?!? It's a whodunnit, man!—Look at it!

[They look at it. The room. The body. Silence.]

Has it started yet?

MOON: Yes.

[Pause. They look at it.]

BIRDBOOT: Are you sure?

---

1. Popular brand of chocolates sold in London theaters.   2. Elevator. *Turn-ups*: trouser cuffs.

MOON: It's a pause.
BIRDBOOT: You can't start with a *pause*! If you want my opinion there's total panic back there. [*Laughs and subsides.*] Where's Higgs tonight, then?
MOON: It will follow me to the grave and become my epitaph—Here lies Moon the second string: where's Higgs? . . . Sometimes I dream of revolution, a bloody *coup d'etat* by the second rank—troupes of actors slaughtered by their understudies, magicians sawn in half by indefatigably smiling glamour girls, cricket teams wiped out by marauding bands of twelfth men[3]—I dream of champions chopped down by rabbit-punching sparring partners while eternal bridesmaids turn and rape the bridegrooms over the sausage rolls and parliamentary private secretaries plant bombs in the Minister's Humber[4]—comedians die on provincial stages, robbed of their feeds by mutely triumphant stooges—
—and—march
—an army of assistants and deputies, the seconds-in-command, the runners-up, the right-hand men—storming the palace gates wherein the second son has already mounted the throne having committed regicide with a croquet-mallet—stand-ins of the world stand up!—

[*Beat.*][5] Sometimes I dream of Higgs.

[*Pause.* BIRDBOOT *regards him doubtfully. He is at a loss, and grasps reality in the form of his box of chocolates.*]

BIRDBOOT: [*Chewing into mike.*] Have a chocolate!
MOON: What kind?
BIRDBOOT: [*Chewing into mike.*] Black Magic.
MOON: No thanks.

[*Chewing stops dead.*]
[*Of such tiny victories and defeats. . . .* ]

BIRDBOOT: I'll give you a tip, then. Watch the girl.
MOON: You think she did it?
BIRDBOOT: No, no—the *girl*, watch her.
MOON: What girl?
BIRDBOOT: You won't know her, I'll give you a nudge.
MOON: *You* know her, do you?
BIRDBOOT: [*suspiciously, bridling*] What's *that* supposed to mean?
MOON: I beg your pardon?
BIRDBOOT: I'm trying to tip you a wink—give you a nudge as good as a tip—for God's sake, Moon, what's the matter with you?—you could do yourself some good, spotting her first time out—she's new, from the provinces, going straight to the top. I don't want to put words into your mouth but a word from us and we could make her.
MOON: I suppose you've made dozens of them, like that.
BIRDBOOT: [*instantly outraged.*] I'll have you know I'm a family man devoted to my homely but good-natured wife, and if you're suggesting—

---

3. Substitutes. A cricket team ("side") fields eleven players at a time.
4. A car once manufactured in Britain. *Feeds:* cues provided to comedians by straight men, "stooges."
5. In drama, a "beat" is a pause.

MOON: No, no—
BIRDBOOT: —A man of my scrupulous morality—
MOON: I'm sorry—
BIRDBOOT: —falsely besmirched.
MOON: Is that her?

[*For* MRS. DRUDGE *has entered.*]

BIRDBOOT: —don't be absurd, wouldn't be seen dead with the old—ah.

[MRS. DRUDGE *is the char,*[6] *middle-aged, turbanned. She heads straight for the radio, dusting on the trot.*]

MOON: [*reading his programme*] Mrs. Drudge the Help.
RADIO: [*without preamble, having been switched on by* MRS. DRUDGE] We interrupt our programme for a special police message.

[MRS. DRUDGE *stops to listen.*]

The search still goes on for the escaped madman who is on the run in Essex.
MRS. DRUDGE: [*fear and dismay*] Essex!
RADIO: County police led by Inspector Hound have received a report that the man has been seen in the desolate marshes around Muldoon Manor.

[*Fearful gasp from* MRS. DRUDGE.]

The man is wearing a darkish suit with a lightish shirt. He is of medium height and build and youngish. Anyone seeing a man answering to this description and acting suspiciously, is advised to phone the nearest police station.

[*A man answering this description has appeared behind* MRS. DRUDGE. *He is acting suspiciously. He creeps in. He creeps out.* MRS. DRUDGE *does not see him. He does not see the body.*]

That is the end of the police message.

[MRS. DRUDGE *turns off the radio and resumes her cleaning. She does not see the body. Quite fortuitously, her view of the body is always blocked, and when it isn't she has her back to it. However, she is dusting and polishing her way towards it.*]

BIRDBOOT: So that's what they say about me, is it?
MOON: What?
BIRDBOOT: Oh, I know what goes on behind my back—sniggers—slanders—hole-in-corner innuendo—What have you heard?
MOON: Nothing.
BIRDBOOT: [*urbanely*] Tittle tattle. Tittle, my dear fellow, tattle. I take no notice of it—the sly envy of scandal mongers—I can afford to ignore them, I'm a respectable married man—
MOON: Incidentally—
BIRDBOOT: Water off a duck's back, I assure you.
MOON: Who was that lady I saw you with last night?

---

6. British term for cleaning lady or maid who does not live in the house.

BIRDBOOT: [*unexpectedly stung into fury*] How dare you! [*More quietly*] How dare you. Don't you come here with your slimy insinuations! My wife Myrtle understands perfectly well that a man of my critical standing is obliged occasionally to mingle with the world of the footlights, simply by way of keeping *au fait*[7] with the latest—

MOON: I'm sorry—

BIRDBOOT: That a critic of my scrupulous integrity should be vilified and pilloried in the stocks of common gossip—

MOON: Ssssh—

BIRDBOOT: I have nothing to hide!—why, if this should reach the ears of my beloved Myrtle—

MOON: Can I have a chocolate?

BIRDBOOT: What? Oh— [*Mollified.*] Oh yes—my dear fellow—yes, let's have a chocolate— No point in—yes, good show. [*Pops chocolate into his mouth and chews.*] Which one do you fancy?—Cherry? Strawberry? Coffee cream? Turkish delight?

MOON: I'll have montelimar.

[*Chewing stops.*]

BIRDBOOT: Ah. Sorry. [*Just missed that one.*]

MOON: Gooseberry fondue?

BIRDBOOT: No.

MOON: Pistacchio fudge? Nectarine cluster? Hickory nut praline? Chateau Neuf du Pape '55 cracknell?[8]

BIRDBOOT: I'm afraid not . . . Caramel?

MOON: Yes, all right.

BIRDBOOT: Thanks very much. [*He gives* MOON *a chocolate. Pause.*] Incidentally, old chap, I'd be grateful if you didn't mention—I mean, you know how these misunderstandings get about. . . .

MOON: What?

BIRDBOOT: The fact is, Myrtle simply doesn't *like* the theatre. . . .

[*He tails off hopelessly.* MRS. DRUDGE, *whose discovery of the body has been imminent, now—by way of tidying the room—slides the couch over the corpse, hiding it completely. She resumes dusting and humming.*]

MOON: By the way, congratulations, Birdboot.

BIRDBOOT: What?

MOON: At the Theatre Royal. Your entire review reproduced in neon!

BIRDBOOT: [*pleased.*] Oh . . . that old thing.

MOON: You've seen it, of course.

BIRDBOOT: [*vaguely.*] Well, I was passing. . . .

MOON: I definitely intend to take a second look when it has settled down.

BIRDBOOT: As a matter of fact I have a few colour transparencies—I don't know whether you'd care to . . . ?

MOON: Please, please—love to, love to. . . .

---

7. In touch; knowledgeable (French).
8. A hard, sweet biscuit. *Chateau Neuf du Pape '55:* a fine wine in an excellent vintage year. The flavors that Moon requests, after "montelimar," are all fanciful—not found in any Black Magic box.

[BIRDBOOT *hands over a few colour slides and a battery-powered viewer which* MOON *holds up to his eyes as he speaks.*]

Yes... yes... lovely... awfully sound. It has scale, it has colour, it is, in the best sense of the word, electric. Large as it is, it is a small masterpiece—I would go so far as to say—kinetic without being pop, and having said that, I think it must be said that here we have a review that adds a new dimension to the critical scene. I urge you to make haste to the Theatre Royal, for this is the stuff of life itself. [*Handing back the slides, morosely*]: All I ever got was "Unforgettable" on the posters for... What was it?

BIRDBOOT: Oh—yes—I know.... Was that you? I thought it was Higgs.

[*The phone rings.* MRS. DRUDGE *seems to have been waiting for it to do so and for the last few seconds has been dusting it with an intense concentration. She snatches it up.*]

MRS. DRUDGE: [*into phone*] Hello, the drawing-room of Lady Muldoon's country residence one morning in early spring?... He*llo*!—the draw—— Who? Who did you wish to speak to? I'm afraid there is no one of that name here, this is all very mysterious and I'm sure it's leading up to something. I hope nothing is amiss for we, that is Lady Muldoon and her houseguests, are here cut off from the world, including Magnus, the wheelchair-ridden half-brother of her ladyship's husband Lord Albert Muldoon who ten years ago went out for a walk on the cliffs and was never seen again—and all alone, for they had no children.

MOON: Derivative, of course.

BIRDBOOT: But quite sound.

MRS. DRUDGE: Should a stranger enter our midst, which I very much doubt, I will tell him you called. Good-bye.

[*She puts down the phone and catches sight of the previously seen suspicious character who has now entered again, more suspiciously than ever, through the french windows. He senses her stare, freezes, and straightens up.*]

SIMON: Ah!—hello there! I'm Simon Gascoyne, I hope you don't mind, the door was open so I wandered in. I'm a friend of Lady Muldoon, the lady of the house, having made her acquaintance through a mutual friend, Felicity Cunningham, shortly after moving into this neighbourhood just the other day.

MRS. DRUDGE: I'm Mrs. Drudge. I don't live in but I pop in on my bicycle when the weather allows to help in the running of charming though somewhat isolated Muldoon Manor. Judging by the time [*she glances at the clock*] you did well to get here before high water cut us off for all practical purposes from the outside world.

SIMON: I took the short cut over the cliffs and followed one of the old smugglers' paths through the treacherous swamps that surround this strangely inaccessible house.

MRS. DRUDGE: Yes, many visitors have remarked on the topographical quirk in the local strata whereby there are no roads leading from the Manor, though there *are* ways of getting *to* it, weather allowing.

SIMON: Yes, well I must say it's a lovely day so far.

MRS. DRUDGE: Ah, but now that the cuckoo-beard is in bud there'll be fog before the sun hits Foster's Ridge.

SIMON: I say, it's wonderful how you country people really know weather.
MRS. DRUDGE: [*suspiciously*] Know whether what?
SIMON: [*glancing out of the window.*] Yes, it does seem to be coming on a bit foggy.
MRS. DRUDGE: The fog is very treacherous around here—it rolls off the sea without warning, shrouding the cliffs in a deadly mantle of blind man's buff.
SIMON: Yes, I've heard it said.
MRS. DRUDGE: I've known whole week-ends when Muldoon Manor, as this lovely old Queen Anne House is called, might as well have been floating on the pack ice for all the good it would have done phoning the police. It was on such a week-end as this that Lord Muldoon who had lately brought his beautiful bride back to the home of his ancestors, walked out of this house ten years ago, and his body was never found.
SIMON: Yes, indeed, poor Cynthia.
MRS. DRUDGE: His name was Albert.
SIMON: Yes indeed, poor Albert. But tell me, is Lady Muldoon about?
MRS. DRUDGE: I believe she is playing tennis on the lawn with Felicity Cunningham.
SIMON: [*startled*] Felicity Cunningham?
MRS. DRUDGE: A mutual friend, I believe you said. A happy chance. I will tell them you are here.
SIMON: Well, I can't really stay as a matter of fact—please don't disturb them—I really should be off.
MRS. DRUDGE: They would be very disappointed. It is some time since we have had a four for pontoon bridge at the Manor, and I don't play cards myself.
SIMON: There is another guest, then?
MRS. DRUDGE: Major Magnus, the crippled half-brother of Lord Muldoon who turned up out of the blue from Canada just the other day, completes the house-party.

[MRS. DRUDGE *leaves on this,* SIMON *is undecided.*]

MOON: [*ruminating quietly*] I think I must be waiting for Higgs to die.
BIRDBOOT: What?
MOON: Half afraid that I will vanish when he does.

[*The phone rings.* SIMON *picks it up.*]

SIMON: Hello?
MOON: I wonder if it's the same for Puckeridge?
BIRDBOOT AND SIMON: [*together*] Who?
MOON: Third string.
BIRDBOOT: Your stand-in?
MOON: Does he wait for Higgs and I to write each other's obituary—does he dream—?
SIMON: To whom did you wish to speak?
BIRDBOOT: What's he like?
MOON: Bitter.
SIMON: There is no one of that name here.
BIRDBOOT: No—as a critic, what's Puckeridge like as a critic?
MOON: [*laughs poisonously*] Nobody knows—

SIMON: You must have got the wrong number!
MOON: —there's always been me and Higgs.

> [SIMON *replaces the phone and paces nervously. Pause.* BIRDBOOT *consults his programme.*]

BIRDBOOT: Simon Gascoyne. It's not him, of course.
MOON: What?
BIRDBOOT: I said it's not him.
MOON: Who is it, then?
BIRDBOOT: My guess is Magnus.
MOON: In disguise, you mean?
BIRDBOOT: What?
MOON: You think he's Magnus in disguise?
BIRDBOOT: I don't think you're concentrating, Moon.
MOON: I thought you said—
BIRDBOOT: You keep chattering on about Higgs and Puckeridge—what's the matter with you?
MOON: [*thoughtfully*] I wonder if they talk about me . . . ?

> [*A strange impulse makes* SIMON *turn on the radio.*]

RADIO: Here is another police message. Essex county police are still searching in vain for the madman who is at large in the deadly marshes of the coastal region. Inspector Hound who is masterminding the operation, is not available for comment but it is widely believed that he has a secret plan. . . . Meanwhile police and volunteers are combing the swamps with loud-hailers, shouting, "Don't be a madman, give yourself up." That is the end of the police message.
> [SIMON *turns off the radio. He is clearly nervous.* MOON *and* BIRDBOOT *are on separate tracks.*]

BIRDBOOT: [*knowingly*] Oh yes. . . .
MOON: Yes, I should think my name is seldom off Puckeridge's lips . . . sad, really. I mean, it's no life at all, a stand-in's stand-in.
BIRDBOOT: Yes . . . yes . . .
MOON: Higgs never gives me a second thought. I can tell by the way he nods.
BIRDBOOT: Revenge, of course.
MOON: What?
BIRDBOOT: Jealousy.
MOON: Nonsense—there's nothing *personal* in it—
BIRDBOOT: The paranoid grudge—
MOON: [*sharply first, then starting to career . . .*] It is merely that it is not enough to wax at another's wane, to be held in reserve, to be on hand, on call, to step in or not at all, the substitute—the near offer—the temporary-acting—for I am Moon, continuous Moon, in my own shoes, Moon in June, April, September and no member of the human race keeps warm my bit of space—yes, I can tell by the way he nods.
BIRDBOOT: Quite mad, of course.
MOON: What?
BIRDBOOT: The answer lies out there in the swamps.
MOON: Oh.
BIRDBOOT: The skeleton in the cupboard is coming home to roost.

MOON: Oh yes. [*He clears his throat... for both he and* BIRDBOOT *have a "public" voice, a critic voice which they turn on for sustained pronouncements of opinion.*] Already in the opening stages we note the classic impact of the catalytic figure—the outsider—plunging through to the centre of an ordered world and setting up the disruptions—the shock waves—which unless I am much mistaken, will strip these comfortable people—these crustaceans in the rock pool of society—strip them of their shells and leave them exposed as the trembling raw meat which, at heart, is all of us. But there is more to it than that——

BIRDBOOT: I agree—keep your eye on Magnus.

[*A tennis ball bounces through the french windows, closely followed by* FELICITY, *who is in her 20's. She wears a pretty tennis outfit, and carries a racket.*]

FELICITY: [*calling behind her*] Out!

[*It takes her a moment to notice* SIMON *who is standing shiftily to one side.* MOON *is stirred by a memory.*]

MOON: I say, Birdboot....
BIRDBOOT: That's the one.
FELICITY: [*catching sight of* SIMON] You!

[FELICITY's *manner at the moment is one of great surprise but some pleasure.*]

SIMON: [*nervously*] Er, yes—hello again.
FELICITY: What are you doing here?
SIMON: Well, I....
MOON: She's——
BIRDBOOT: Sssh....
SIMON: No doubt you're surprised to see me.
FELICITY: Honestly, darling, you really are extraordinary.
SIMON: Yes, well, here I am.
FELICITY: You must have been desperate to see me—I mean, I'm *flattered*, but couldn't it wait till I got back?
SIMON: [*bravely*] There is something you don't know.
FELICITY: What is it?
SIMON: Look, about the things I said—it may be that I got carried away a little— we both did——
FELICITY: [*stiffly*] What are you trying to say?
SIMON: I love another!
FELICITY: I see.
SIMON: I didn't make any promises—I merely——
FELICITY: You don't have to say any more——
SIMON: Oh, I didn't want to hurt you——
FELICITY: Of all the nerve!
SIMON: Well, I——
FELICITY: You philandering coward——
SIMON: Let me explain——
FELICITY: This is hardly the time and place—you think you can barge in anywhere, whatever I happen to be doing——
SIMON: But I want you to know that my admiration for you is sincere—I don't want you to think that I didn't mean those things I said——
FELICITY: I'll kill you for this, Simon Gascoyne!

[*She leaves in tears, passing* MRS. DRUDGE *who has entered in time to overhear her last remark.*]

MOON: It was her.
BIRDBOOT: I told you—straight to the top—
MOON: No, no—
BIRDBOOT: Sssh....
SIMON: [*to* MRS. DRUDGE] Yes, what is it?
MRS. DRUDGE: I have come to set up the card table, sir.
SIMON: I don't think I can stay.
MRS. DRUDGE: Oh, Lady Muldoon *will* be disappointed.
SIMON: Does she know I'm here?
MRS. DRUDGE: Oh yes, sir, I just told her and it put her in quite a tizzy.
SIMON: Really?... Well, I suppose now that I've cleared the air.... Quite a tizzy, you say ... really ... really ...

[*He and* MRS. DRUDGE *start setting up for card game.* MRS. DRUDGE *leaves when this is done.*]

MOON: Felicity!—she's the one.
BIRDBOOT: Nonsense—red herring.
MOON: I mean, it was *her*!
BIRDBOOT: [*exasperated*] *What* was?
MOON: That lady I saw you with last night!
BIRDBOOT: [*inhales with fury*] Are you suggesting that a man of my scrupulous integrity would trade his pen for a mess of potage?![9] Simply because in the course of my profession I happen to have struck up an acquaintance—to have, that is, a warm regard, if you like, for a fellow toiler in the vineyard of greasepaint—I find it simply intolerable to be pillified and villoried—
MOON: I never implied—
BIRDBOOT: —to find myself the object of uninformed malice, the petty slanders of little men—
MOON: I'm sorry—
BIRDBOOT: —to suggest that my good opinion in a journal of unimpeachable integrity is at the disposal of the first coquette who gives me what I want—
MOON: Sssssh—
BIRDBOOT: A ladies' man!... Why, Myrtle and I have been together now for—Christ!—who's *that*?

[*Enter* LADY CYNTHIA MULDOON *through french windows. A beautiful woman in her thirties. She wears a cocktail dress, is formally coiffured, and carries a tennis racket.*]
[*Her effect on* BIRDBOOT *is also impressive. He half rises and sinks back agape.*]

CYNTHIA: [*entering*] Simon!

[*A dramatic freeze between her and* SIMON.]

---

9. In the Bible, Jacob persuades his elder brother Esau to give up his right of inheritance in exchange for a "mess of potage" or dish of stew—that is, for a very cheap price. *Toiler in the vineyard of greasepaint:* theater professional. *Pillified and villoried:* vilified and pilloried.

MOON: Lady Muldoon.
BIRDBOOT: No, I mean—who *is* she?
SIMON: [*coming forward*] Cynthia!
CYNTHIA: Don't say anything for a moment—just hold me.

[*He seizes her and glues his lips to hers, as they say. While their lips are glued——*]

BIRDBOOT: She's *beautiful*—a vision of eternal grace, a poem . . .
MOON: I think she's got her mouth open.

[CYNTHIA *breaks away dramatically.*]

CYNTHIA: We can't go on meeting like this!
SIMON: We have nothing to be ashamed of!
CYNTHIA: But darling, this is madness!
SIMON: Yes!—I am mad with love for you!
CYNTHIA: Please—remember where we are!
SIMON: Cynthia, I love you!
CYNTHIA: Don't—I love Albert!
SIMON: He's dead! [*Shaking her.*] Do you understand me—Albert's dead!
CYNTHIA: No—I'll never give up hope! Let me go! We are not free!
SIMON: I don't care, we were meant for each other—had we but met in time.
CYNTHIA: You're a cad, Simon! You will use me and cast me aside as you have cast aside so many others.
SIMON: No, Cynthia!—you can make me a better person!
CYNTHIA: You're ruthless—so strong, so cruel——

[*Ruthlessly he kisses her.*]

MOON: The son she never had, now projected in this handsome stranger and transformed into lover—youth, vigour, the animal, the athlete as aesthete—breaking down the barriers at the deepest level of desire.
BIRDBOOT: By jove, I think you're right. Her mouth *is* open.

[CYNTHIA *breaks away.* MRS. DRUDGE *has entered.*]

CYNTHIA: Stop—can't you see you're making a fool of yourself!
SIMON: I'll kill anyone who comes between us!
CYNTHIA: Yes, what is it, Mrs. Drudge?
MRS. DRUDGE: Should I close the windows, my lady? The fog is beginning to roll off the sea like a deadly——
CYNTHIA: Yes, you'd better. It looks as if we're in for one of those days. Are the cards ready?
MRS. DRUDGE: Yes, my lady.
CYNTHIA: Would you tell Miss Cunningham we are waiting.
MRS. DRUDGE: Yes, my lady.
CYNTHIA: And fetch the Major down.
MRS. DRUDGE: I think I hear him coming downstairs now [*as she leaves*].

[*She does: the sound of a wheelchair approaching down several flights of stairs with landings in between. It arrives bearing* MAGNUS *at about 15 m.p.h., knocking* SIMON *over violently.*]

CYNTHIA: Simon!
MAGNUS: [*roaring*] Never had a chance! Ran under the wheels!

CYNTHIA: Darling, are you all right?
MAGNUS: I have witnesses!
CYNTHIA: Oh, Simon—say something!
SIMON: [*sitting up suddenly*] I'm most frightfully sorry.
MAGNUS: [*shouting yet*] How long have you been a pedestrian?
SIMON: Ever since I could walk.
CYNTHIA: Can you walk now . . . ?

[SIMON *rises and walks.*]

Thank God! Magnus, this is Simon Gascoyne.
MAGNUS: What's he doing here?
CYNTHIA: He just turned up.
MAGNUS: Really? How do you like it here?
SIMON: [*to* CYNTHIA] I could stay for ever.

[FELICITY *enters.*]

FELICITY: So—you're still here.
CYNTHIA: Of course he's still here. We're going to play cards. There's no need to introduce you two, is there, for I recall now that you, Simon, met me through Felicity, our mutual friend.
FELICITY: Yes, Simon is an old friend, though not as old as you, Cynthia dear.
SIMON: Yes, I haven't seen Felicity since——
FELICITY: Last night.
CYNTHIA: Indeed? Well, you deal, Felicity. Simon, you help me with the sofa. Will you partner Felicity, Magnus, against Simon and me?
MAGNUS: [*aside*] Will Simon and you always be partnered against me, Cynthia?
CYNTHIA: What do you mean, Magnus?
MAGNUS: You are a damned attractive woman, Cynthia.
CYNTHIA: Please! Please! Remember Albert!
MAGNUS: Albert's dead, Cynthia—and you are still young. I'm sure he would have wished that you and I——
CYNTHIA: No, Magnus, this is not to be!
MAGNUS: It's Gascoyne, isn't it? I'll kill him if he comes between us!
CYNTHIA: [*calling*] Simon!

[*The sofa is shoved towards the card table, once more revealing the corpse, though not to the players.*]

BIRDBOOT: Simon's for the chop[1] all right.
CYNTHIA: Right! Who starts?
MAGNUS: I do. No bid.
CYNTHIA: Did I hear you say you saw Felicity last night, Simon?
SIMON: Did I?—Ah yes, yes, quite—your turn, Felicity.
FELICITY: I've had my turn, haven't I, Simon?—now, it seems, it's Cynthia's turn.
CYNTHIA: That's my trick, Felicity dear.
FELICITY: Hell hath no fury like a woman scorned,[2] Simon.
SIMON: Yes, I've heard it said.

---

1. In danger; slated for execution.
2. A saying adapted from a line in William Congreve's play *The Mourning Bride* (1697), warning that rejected or jealous women are roused to overwhelming, violent revenge.

FELICITY: So I hope you have not been cheating, Simon.
SIMON: [*standing up and throwing down his cards*] No, Felicity, it's just that I hold the cards!
CYNTHIA: Well done, Simon!

[MAGNUS *pays* SIMON, *while* CYNTHIA *deals*]

FELICITY: Strange how Simon appeared in the neighborhood from nowhere. We know so little about him.
SIMON: It doesn't always pay to show your hand!
CYNTHIA: Right! Simon, it's your opening on the minor bid.

[SIMON *plays*.]

CYNTHIA: Hm, let's see.... [*Plays.*]
FELICITY: I hear there's a dangerous madman on the loose.
CYNTHIA: Simon?
SIMON: Yes—yes—sorry. [*Plays.*]
CYNTHIA: I meld.
FELICITY: Yes—personally, I think he's been hiding out in the deserted cottage [*plays*] on the cliffs.
SIMON: Flush!
CYNTHIA: No! Simon—your luck's in tonight!
FELICITY: We shall see—the night is not over yet, Simon Gascoyne! [*She exits.*]

[MAGNUS *pays* SIMON *again.*]

SIMON: [*to* MAGNUS] So you're the crippled half-brother of Lord Muldoon who turned up out of the blue from Canada just the other day, are you? It's taken you a long time to get here. What did you do—walk? Oh, I say, I'm most frightfully sorry!
MAGNUS: Care for a spin round the rose garden, Cynthia?
CYNTHIA: No, Magnus, I must talk to Simon.
SIMON: My round, I think, Major.
MAGNUS: You think so?
SIMON: Yes, Major—I do.
MAGNUS: There's an old Canadian proverb handed down from the Bladfoot Indians, which says: He who laughs last laughs longest.[3]
SIMON: Yes, I've heard it said.

[SIMON *turns away to* CYNTHIA]

MAGNUS: Well, I think I'll go and oil my gun. [*He exits.*]
CYNTHIA: I think Magnus suspects something. And Felicity... Simon, was there anything between you and Felicity?
SIMON: No, no—it's over between her and me, Cynthia—it was a mere passing fleeting thing we had—but now that I have found you—
CYNTHIA: If I find that you have been untrue to me—if I find that you have falsely seduced me from my dear husband Albert—I will kill you, Simon Gascoyne!

---

3. The usual proverb, possibly of Italian origin, is "He who laughs last laughs best." The Bladfoot Indians, like Magnus's association with Canada, are fictitious.

[MRS. DRUDGE *has entered silently to witness this. On this tableau, pregnant with significance, the act ends, the body still undiscovered. Perfunctory applause.*]
[MOON *and* BIRDBOOT *seem to be completely preoccupied, becoming audible, as it were.*]

MOON: Camps it around the Old Vic in his opera cloak and passes me the tat.[4]
BIRDBOOT: Do you believe in love at first sight?
MOON: It's not that I think I'm a better critic—
BIRDBOOT: I feel my whole life changing—
MOON: I am but it's not that.
BIRDBOOT: Oh, the world will laugh at me, I know....
MOON: It is not that they are much in the way of shoes to step into....
BIRDBOOT: ... call me an infatuated old fool....
MOON: ... They are not.
BIRDBOOT: ... condemn me....
MOON: He is standing in my light, that is all.
BIRDBOOT: ... betrayer of my class....
MOON: ... an almost continuous eclipse, interrupted by the phenomenon of moonlight.
BIRDBOOT: I don't care, I'm a goner.
MOON: And I dream....
BIRDBOOT: The Blue Angel[5] all over again.
MOON: ... of the day his temperature climbs through the top of his head....
BIRDBOOT: Ah, the sweet madness of love....
MOON: ... of the spasm on the stairs....
BIRDBOOT: Myrtle, farewell...
MOON: ... dreaming of the stair he'll never reach—
BIRDBOOT: ... for I only live but once....
MOON: Sometimes I dream that I've killed him.
BIRDBOOT: What?
MOON: What?

[*They pull themselves together.*]

BIRDBOOT: Yes... yes.... A beautiful performance, a collector's piece. I shall say so.
MOON: A very promising debut. I'll put in a good word.
BIRDBOOT: It would be as hypocritical of me to withhold praise on grounds of personal feelings, as to withhold censure.
MOON: You're right. Courageous.
BIRDBOOT: Oh, I know what people will say— There goes Birdboot buttering up his latest—
MOON: Ignore them—
BIRDBOOT: But I rise above that— The fact is I genuinely believe her performance to be one of the summits in the range of contemporary theatre.
MOON: Trim-buttocked, that's the word for her.

---

4. That is, puts on a grand act when he goes to the Old Vic (a prestigious London theater) and treats Moon as an underling.
5. A 1931 film directed by Josef von Sternberg and starring Marlene Dietrich and Emil Jennings; it tells the story of a middle-aged professor falling for a nightclub performer.

BIRDBOOT: —the radiance, the inner sadness—
MOON: Does she actually come across with it?
BIRDBOOT: The part as written is a mere cypher but she manages to make Cynthia a real person—
MOON: Cynthia?
BIRDBOOT: And should she, as a result, care to meet me over a drink, simply by way of er—thanking me, as it were—
MOON: Well, you fickle old bastard!
BIRDBOOT: [*aggressively*] Are you suggesting . . . ?

[BIRDBOOT *shudders to a halt and clears his throat.*]

BIRDBOOT: Well now—shaping up quite nicely, wouldn't you say?
MOON: Oh yes, yes. A nice trichotomy of forces. One must reserve judgement of course, until the confrontation, but I think it's pretty clear where we're heading.
BIRDBOOT: I agree. It's Magnus a mile off.

[*Small pause.*]

MOON: What's Magnus a mile off?
BIRDBOOT: If we knew that we wouldn't be here.
MOON: [*clears throat*] Let me at once say that it has *élan*[6] while at the same time avoiding *éclat*. Having said that, and I think it must be said, I am bound to ask—does this play know where it is going?
BIRDBOOT: Well, it seems open and shut to me, Moon—Magnus is not what he pretends to be and he's got his next victim marked down—
MOON: Does it, I repeat, declare its affiliations? There are moments, and I would not begrudge it this, when the play, if we can call it that, and I think on balance we can, aligns itself uncompromisingly on the side of life. *Je suis*, it seems to be saying, *ergo sum*.[7] But is that enough? I think we are entitled to ask. For what in fact is this play concerned with? It is my belief that here we are concerned with what I have referred to elsewhere as the nature of identity. I think we are entitled to ask—and here one is irresistibly reminded of Voltaire's cry, "*Violà!*"—I think we are entitled to ask—*Where is God?*
BIRDBOOT: [*stunned*] Who?
MOON: Go-od.
BIRDBOOT: [*peeping furtively into his programme*] God?
MOON: I think we are entitled to ask.

[*The phone rings.*]
[*The set re-illumines to reveal* CYNTHIA, FELICITY *and* MAGNUS *about to take coffee, which is being taken round by* MRS. DRUDGE. SIMON *is missing. The body lies in position.*]

---

6. Flair; grace (French). *Éclat:* a public sensation; a splashy production (French).
7. Moon misquotes and misapplies the French philosopher Descartes's principle *Cogito, ergo sum*, Latin for "I think, therefore I am." "*Je suis*" means "I am" in French; that is, Moon says, "I am . . . therefore I am." *Voilà:* French expression meaning "Look!" or "You see!" There is no common reference to the French philosopher Voltaire (1694–1778) ever saying this.

MRS. DRUDGE: [*into phone*] The same, half an hour later?... No, I'm sorry—there's no one of that name here. [*She replaces phone and goes round with coffee. To* CYNTHIA]: Black or white, my lady?
CYNTHIA: White please.

[MRS. DRUDGE *pours.*]

MRS. DRUDGE: [*to* FELICITY] Black or white, miss?
FELICITY: White please.

[MRS. DRUDGE *pours.*]

MRS. DRUDGE: [*to* MAGNUS] Black or white, Major?
MAGNUS: White please.

[*Ditto.*]

MRS. DRUDGE: [*to* CYNTHIA] Sugar, my lady?
CYNTHIA: Yes please.

[*Puts sugar in.*]

MRS. DRUDGE: [*to* FELICITY] Sugar, miss?
FELICITY: Yes please.

[*Ditto.*]

MRS. DRUDGE: [*to* MAGNUS] Sugar, Major?
MAGNUS: Yes please.

[*Ditto.*]

MRS. DRUDGE: [*to* CYNTHIA] Biscuit, my lady?
CYNTHIA: No thank you.
BIRDBOOT: [*writing elaborately in his notebook*] The second act, however, fails to fulfil the promise....
FELICITY: If you ask me, there's something funny going on.

[MRS. DRUDGE'S *approach to* FELICITY *makes* FELICITY *jump to her feet in impatience. She goes to the radio while* MAGNUS *declines his biscuit, and* MRS. DRUDGE *leaves.*]

RADIO: We interrupt our programme for a special police message. The search for the dangerous madman who is on the loose in Essex has now narrowed to the immediate vicinity of Muldoon Manor. Police are hampered by the deadly swamps and the fog, but believe that the madman spent last night in a deserted cottage on the cliffs. The public is advised to stick together and make sure none of their number is missing. That is the end of the police message.

[FELICITY *turns off the radio nervously. Pause.*]

CYNTHIA: Where's Simon?
FELICITY: Who?
CYNTHIA: Simon. Have you seen him?
FELICITY: No.
CYNTHIA: Have you, Magnus?
MAGNUS: No.

CYNTHIA: Oh.
FELICITY: Yes, there's something foreboding in the air, it is as if one of *us*—
CYNTHIA: Oh, Felicity, the house is locked up tight—no one can get in—and the police are practically on the doorstep.
FELICITY: I don't know—it's just a feeling.
CYNTHIA: It's only the fog.
MAGNUS: Hound will never get through on a day like this.
CYNTHIA: [*shouting at him*] Fog!
FELICITY: He means the Inspector.
CYNTHIA: Is he bringing a dog?
FELICITY: Not that I know of.
MAGNUS: —never get through the swamps. Yes, I'm afraid the madman can show his hand in safety now.

[*A mournful baying hooting is heard in the distance, scary.*]

CYNTHIA: What's that?!
FELICITY: [*tensely*] It sounded like the cry of a gigantic hound!
MAGNUS: Poor devil!
CYNTHIA: Sssh!

[*They listen. The sound is repeated, nearer.*]

FELICITY: There it is again!
CYNTHIA: It's coming this way—it's right outside the house!

[MRS. DRUDGE *enters.*]

MRS. DRUDGE: Inspector Hound!
CYNTHIA: A *police* dog?

[*Enter* INSPECTOR HOUND. *On his feet are his swamp boots. These are two inflatable—and inflated—pontoons with flat bottoms about two feet across. He carries a foghorn.*]

HOUND: Lady Muldoon?
CYNTHIA: Yes.
HOUND: I came as soon as I could. Where shall I put my foghorn and my swamp boots?
CYNTHIA: Mrs. Drudge will take them out. Be prepared, as the Force's motto has it, eh, Inspector? How very resourceful!
HOUND: [*divesting himself of boots and foghorn*] It takes more than a bit of weather to keep a policeman from his duty.

[MRS. DRUDGE *leaves with chattels. A pause.*]

CYNTHIA: Oh—er, Inspector Hound—Felicity Cunningham, Major Magnus Muldoon.
HOUND: Good evening.

[*He and* CYNTHIA *continue to look expectantly at each other.*]

CYNTHIA AND HOUND: [*together*] Well?—Sorry—
CYNTHIA: No, do go on.
HOUND: Thank you. Well, tell me about it in your own words—take your time, begin at the beginning and don't leave anything out.

CYNTHIA: I beg your pardon?
HOUND: Fear nothing. You are in safe hands now. I hope you haven't touched anything.
CYNTHIA: I'm afraid I don't understand.
HOUND: I'm Inspector Hound.
CYNTHIA: Yes.
HOUND: Well, what's it all about?
CYNTHIA: I really have no idea.
HOUND: How did it begin?
CYNTHIA: What?
HOUND: The ... thing.
CYNTHIA: What thing?
HOUND: [*rapidly losing confidence but exasperated*] The trouble!
CYNTHIA: There hasn't *been* any trouble!
HOUND: Didn't you phone the police?
CYNTHIA: No.
FELICITY: I didn't.
MAGNUS: What for?
HOUND: I see. [*Pause.*] This puts me in a very difficult position. [*A steady pause.*] Well, I'll be getting along, then. [*He moves towards the door.*]
CYNTHIA: I'm terribly sorry.
HOUND: [*stiffly*] That's perfectly all right.
CYNTHIA: Thank you so much for coming.
HOUND: Not at all. You never know, there might have been a serious matter.
CYNTHIA: Drink?
HOUND: More serious than that, even.
CYNTHIA: [*correcting*] Drink before you go?
HOUND: No thank you. [*Leaves.*]
CYNTHIA: [*through the door*] I do hope you find him.
HOUND: [*reappearing at once*] Find who, Madam?—out with it!
CYNTHIA: I thought you were looking for the lunatic.
HOUND: And what do you know about that?
CYNTHIA: It was on the radio.
HOUND: Was it, indeed? Well, that's what I'm here about, really. I didn't want to mention it because I didn't know how much you knew. No point in causing unnecessary panic, even with a murderer in our midst.
FELICITY: Murderer, did you say?
HOUND: Ah—so that was not on the radio?
CYNTHIA: Whom has he murdered, Inspector?
HOUND: Perhaps no one—yet. Let us hope we are in time.
MAGNUS: You believe he is in our midst, Inspector?
HOUND: I do. If anyone of you have recently encountered a youngish good-looking fellow in a smart suit, white shirt, hatless, well-spoken—someone possibly claiming to have just moved into the neighbourhood, someone who on the surface seems as sane as you or I, then now is the time to speak!
FELICITY: I—
HOUND: Don't interrupt!
FELICITY: Inspector—
HOUND: Very well.
CYNTHIA: No. Felicity!

HOUND: Please, Lady Cynthia, we are all in this together. I must ask you to put yourself completely in my hands.
CYNTHIA: Don't, Inspector. I love Albert.
HOUND: I don't think you quite grasp my meaning.
MAGNUS: Is one of us in danger, Inspector?
HOUND: Didn't it strike you as odd that on his escape the madman made a beeline for Muldoon Manor? It is my guess that he bears a deep-seated grudge against someone in this very house! Lady Muldoon—where is your husband?
CYNTHIA: My husband?—you don't mean——?
HOUND: I don't know—but I have a reason to believe that one of you is the real McCoy![8]
FELICITY: The real what?
HOUND: William Herbert McCoy who as a young man, meeting the madman in the street and being solicited for sixpence for a cup of tea, replied, "Why don't you do a decent day's work, you shifty old bag of horse manure," in Canada all those many years ago and went on to make his fortune. [*He starts to pace intensely.*] The madman was a mere boy at the time but he never forgot that moment, and thenceforth carried in his heart the promise of revenge! [*At which point he finds himself standing on top of the corpse. He looks down carefully.*]
HOUND: Is there anything you have forgotten to tell me?

[*They all see the corpse for the first time.*]

FELICITY: So the madman has struck!
CYNTHIA: Oh—it's horrible—horrible——
HOUND: Yes, just as I feared. Now you see the sort of man you are protecting.
CYNTHIA: I can't believe it!
FELICITY: I'll have to tell him, Cynthia—Inspector, a stranger of that description has indeed appeared in our midst—Simon Gascoyne. Oh, he had charm, I'll give you that, and he took me in completely. I'm afraid I made a fool of myself over him, and so did Cynthia.
HOUND: Where is he now?
MAGNUS: He must be around the house—he couldn't get away in these conditions.
HOUND: You're right. Fear naught, Lady Muldoon—I shall apprehend the man who killed your husband.
CYNTHIA: My husband? I don't understand.
HOUND: Everything points to Gascoyne.
CYNTHIA: But who's that? [*The corpse.*]
HOUND: Your husband.
CYNTHIA: No, it's not.
HOUND: Yes, it is.
CYNTHIA: I tell you it's not.
HOUND: *I'm* in charge of this case!
CYNTHIA: But that's not my husband.
HOUND: Are you sure?
CYNTHIA: For goodness sake!

---

8. This expression, meaning the genuine original, the real article among fakes, has many possible origins, none of which has anything to do with the fanciful explanation in Inspector Hound's next speech.

HOUND: Then who is it?
CYNTHIA: I don't know.
HOUND: Anybody?
FELICITY: I've never seen him before.
MAGNUS: Quite unlike anybody I've ever met.
HOUND: This case is becoming an utter shambles.
CYNTHIA: But what are we going to do?
HOUND: [*snatching the phone*] I'll phone the police!
CYNTHIA: But you are the police!
HOUND: Thank God I'm here—the lines have been cut!
CYNTHIA: You mean——?
HOUND: Yes!—we're on our own, cut off from the world and in grave danger!
FELICITY: You mean——?
HOUND: Yes!—I think the killer will strike again!
MAGNUS: You mean——?
HOUND: Yes! One of us ordinary mortals thrown together by fate and cut off by the elements, is the murderer! He must be found—search the house!

[*All depart speedily in different directions leaving a momentarily empty stage.* SIMON *strolls on.*]

SIMON: [*entering, calling*] Anyone about?—funny . . .

[*He notices the corpse and is surprised. He approaches it and turns it over. He stands up and looks about in alarm.*]

BIRDBOOT: This is where Simon gets the chop.

[*There is a shot.* SIMON *falls dead.*]
[INSPECTOR HOUND *runs on and crouches down by* SIMON's *body.* CYNTHIA *appears at the french windows. She stops there and stares.*]

CYNTHIA: What happened, Inspector?!

[HOUND *turns to face her.*]

HOUND: He's dead . . . Simon Gascoyne, I presume. Rough justice even for a killer—unless—unless—We assumed that the body could not have been lying there before Simon Gascoyne entered the house . . . but . . . [*he slides the sofa over the body*] there's your answer. And now—who killed Simon Gascoyne? And why?

[*"Curtain", freeze, applause, exeunt.*]

MOON: Why not?
BIRDBOOT: Exactly. Good riddance.
MOON: Yes, getting away with murder must be quite easy provided that one's motive is sufficiently inscrutable.
BIRDBOOT: Fickle young pup! He was deceiving her right, left and centre.
MOON: [*thoughtfully*] Of course. I'd still have Puckeridge behind *me*—
BIRDBOOT: She needs someone steadier, more mature—
MOON: —And if I could, so could he—
BIRDBOOT: Yes, I know of this rather nice hotel, very discreet, run by a man of the world—

MOON: Uneasy lies the head that wears the crown.[9]
BIRDBOOT: Breakfast served in one's room and no questions asked.
MOON: Does Puckeridge dream of me?
BIRDBOOT: [*pause*] Hello—what's happened?
MOON: What? Oh yes—what do you make of it, so far?
BIRDBOOT: [*clears throat*] It is at this point that the play for me comes alive. The groundwork has been well and truly laid, and the author has taken the trouble to learn from the masters of the genre. He has created a real situation, and few will doubt his ability to resolve it with a startling denouement. Certainly that is what it so far lacks, but it has a beginning, a middle and I have no doubt it will prove to have an end. For this let us give thanks, and double thanks for a good clean show without a trace of smut. But perhaps even all this would be for nothing were it not for a performance which I consider to be one of the summits in the range of contemporary theatre. In what is possibly the finest Cynthia since the war—
MOON: If we examine this more closely, and I think close examination is the least tribute that this play deserves, I think we will find that within the austere framework of what is seen to be on one level a country-house week-end, and what a useful symbol that is, the author has given us—yes, I will go so far—he has given us the human condition—
BIRDBOOT: More talent in her little finger—
MOON: An uncanny ear that might have belonged to a Van Gogh[1]—
BIRDBOOT: —a public scandal that the Birthday Honours[2] to date have neglected—
MOON: Faced as we are with such ubiquitous obliquity, it is hard, it is hard indeed, and therefore I will not attempt, to refrain from invoking the names of Kafka, Sartre, Shakespeare, St. Paul, Beckett, Birkett, Pinero, Pirandello, Dante and Dorothy L. Sayers.[3]
BIRDBOOT: A rattling good evening out. I was held.

[*The phone starts to ring on the empty stage.* MOON *tries to ignore it.*]

MOON: Harder still—— Harder still if possible—— Harder still if it is possible to be—— Neither do I find it easy—Dante and Dorothy L. Sayers. Harder still——
BIRDBOOT: Others taking part included—*Moon!*

[*For* MOON *has lost patience and is bearing down on the ringing phone. He is frankly irritated.*]

MOON: [*picking up phone, barks*] Hel-lo! [*Pause, turns to* BIRDBOOT, *quietly.*] It's for you. [*Pause.*]

---

9. Shakespeare, *2 Henry IV* 3.1.31. The king is lamenting his insomnia, in contrast with a poor sailor boy's ability to sleep soundly during a storm at sea.
1. Dutch artist (1853–1890); Van Gogh cut off his ear, possibly because of suffering from Meniere's disease, which causes ringing in the inner ear and loss of balance.
2. A list of honorees for public service in various fields; the list is issued yearly in Britain to mark Queen Elizabeth's birthday.
3. A range of writers' names, biblical, classic, and modern, ending with one of the most famous detective novelists. "Birkett" apparently is an invention to chime with "Beckett."

[BIRDBOOT *gets up. He approaches cautiously.* MOON *gives him the phone and moves back to his seat.* BIRDBOOT *watches him go. He looks round and smiles weakly, expiating himself.*]

BIRDBOOT: [*into phone*] Hello . . . [*Expolosion.*] Oh, for God's sake, Myrtle!—I've told you never to phone me at work! [*He is naturally embarrassed, looking about with surreptitious fury.*] What? Last night? Good God, woman, this is hardly the time to—I assure you, Myrtle, there is absolutely nothing going on between me and—I took her to dinner simply by way of keeping *au fait* with the world of the paint and the motley[4]— Yes, I promise— Yes, I do— Yes, I *said* yes— I *do*—and you are mine too, Myrtle—darling—I can't—[*whispers*] I'm not alone—[*up*]. No, she's not!—[*he looks around furtively, licks his lips and mumbles*]. All *right*! I love your little pink ears and you are my own fluffy bunny-boo— Now for God's sake— Good-bye, Myrtle—[*puts down phone*].

[BIRDBOOT *mops his brow with his handkerchief. As he turns, a tennis ball bounces in through the french windows, followed by* FELICITY, *as before, in tennis outfit. The lighting is as it was. Everything is at it was. It is, let us say, the same moment of time.*]

FELICITY: [*calling*] Out! [*She catches sight of* BIRDBOOT *and is amazed.*] You!
BIRDBOOT: Er, yes—hello again.
FELICITY: What are you doing here?!
BIRDBOOT: Well, I . . .
FELICITY: Honestly, darling, you really are extraordinary—
BIRDBOOT: Yes, well, here I am. [*He looks round sheepishly.*]
FELICITY: You must have been desperate to see me—I mean, I'm flattered, but couldn't it wait till I got back?
BIRDBOOT: No, no, you've got it all wrong—
FELICITY: What is it?
BIRDBOOT: And about last night—perhaps I gave you the wrong impression—got carried away a bit, perhaps—
FELICITY: [*stiffly*] What are you trying to say?
BIRDBOOT: I want to call it off.
FELICITY: I see.
BIRDBOOT: I didn't promise anything—and the fact is, I have my reputation—people do talk—
FELICITY: You don't have to say any more—
BIRDBOOT: And my wife, too—I don't know how she got to hear of it, but—
FELICITY: Of all the nerve! To march in here and—
BIRDBOOT: I'm sorry you had to find out like this—the fact is I didn't mean it this way—
FELICITY: You philandering coward!
BIRDBOOT: I'm sorry—but I want you to know that I meant those things I said—oh yes—shows brilliant promise—I shall say so—
FELICITY: I'll kill you for this, Simon Gascoyne!

[*She leaves in tears, passing* MRS. DRUDGE *who has entered in time to overhear her last remark.*]

---

4. The world of the theater. ("Motley" refers to a jester's patchwork costume.)

BIRDBOOT: [wide-eyed] Good God....
MRS. DRUDGE: I have come to set up the card table, sir.
BIRDBOOT: [wildly] I can't stay for a game of *cards*!
MRS. DRUDGE: Oh, Lady Muldoon *will* be disappointed.
BIRDBOOT: You mean ... you mean, she wants to meet me ... ?
MRS. DRUDGE: Oh yes, sir, I just told her and it put her in quite a tizzy.
BIRDBOOT: Really? Yes, well, a man of my influence is not to be sneezed at—I think I have some small name for the making of reputations—mmm, yes, quite a tizzy, you say?

[MRS. DRUDGE *is busied with the card table.* BIRDBOOT *stands marooned and bemused for a moment.*]

MOON: [*from his seat*] Birdboot!—[*a tense whisper*]. Birdboot!

[BIRDBOOT *looks round vaguely.*]

What the hell are you doing?
BIRDBOOT: Nothing.
MOON: Stop making an ass of yourself. Come back.
BIRDBOOT: Oh, I know what you're thinking—but the fact is I genuinely consider her performance to be one of the summits—

[CYNTHIA *enters as before.* MRS. DRUDGE *has gone.*]

CYNTHIA: Darling!
BIRDBOOT: Ah, good evening—may I say that I genuinely consider——
CYNTHIA: Don't say anything for a moment—just hold me.

[*She falls into his arms.*]

BIRDBOOT: All right! [*They kiss.*] My God!—she *does* have her mouth open! Dear lady, from the first moment I saw you, I felt my whole life changing—
CYNTHIA: [*breaking free*] We can't go on meeting like this!
BIRDBOOT: I am not ashamed to proclaim nightly my love for you!—but fortunately that will not be necessary—— I know of a very good hotel, discreet—run by a man of the world—
CYNTHIA: But darling, this is madness!
BIRDBOOT: Yes! I am mad with love.
CYNTHIA: Please!—remember where we are!
BIRDBOOT: I don't care! Let them think what they like, I love you!
CYNTHIA: Don't—I love Albert!
BIRDBOOT: He's dead. [*Shaking her.*] Do you understand me—Albert's dead!
CYNTHIA: No—I'll never give up hope! Let me go! We are not free!
BIRDBOOT: You mean Myrtle? She means nothing to me—nothing!—she's all cocoa and blue nylon fur slippers—not a spark of creative genius in her whole slumping knee-length-knickered body—
CYNTHIA: You're a cad, Simon! You will use me and cast me aside as you have cast aside so many others!
BIRDBOOT: No, Cynthia—now that I have found you—
CYNTHIA: You're ruthless—so strong—so cruel—

[BIRDBOOT *seizes her in an embrace, during which* MRS. DRUDGE *enters, and* MOON's *fevered voice is heard.*]

MOON: Have you taken leave of your tiny mind?

[CYNTHIA *breaks free.*]

CYNTHIA: Stop—can't you see you're making a fool of yourself!
MOON: She's right.
BIRDBOOT: [*to* MOON] You keep out of this.
CYNTHIA: Yes, what is it, Mrs. Drudge?
MRS. DRUDGE: Should I close the windows, my lady? The fog—
CYNTHIA: Yes, you'd better.
MOON: Look, they've got your number—
BIRDBOOT: I'll leave in my own time, thank you very much.
MOON: It's the finish of you, I suppose you know that—
BIRDBOOT: I don't need your twopenny Grubb Street prognostications[5]—I have found something bigger and finer—
MOON: [*bemused, to himself*] If only it were Higgs....
CYNTHIA: ... And fetch the Major down.
MRS. DRUDGE: I think I hear him coming down stairs now.

[*She leaves. The sound of a wheelchair's approach as before.* BIRDBOOT *prudently keeps out of the chair's former path but it enters from the next wing down and knocks him flying. A babble of anguish and protestation.*]

CYNTHIA: Simon—say something!
BIRDBOOT: That reckless bastard [*as he sits up.*]
CYNTHIA: Thank God!—
MAGNUS: What's *he* doing here?
CYNTHIA: He just turned up.
MAGNUS: Really? How do you like it here?
BIRDBOOT: I couldn't take it night after night.

[FELICITY *enters.*]

FELICITY: So—you're still here.
CYNTHIA: Of course he's still here. We're going to play cards. There is no need to introduce you two, is there, for I recall now that you, Simon, met me through Felicity, our mutual friend.
FELICITY: Yes, Simon is an old friend—
BIRDBOOT: Ah—yes—well, I like to give young up and comers the benefit of my—er—Of course, she lacks technique as yet—
FELICITY: Last night.
BIRDBOOT: I'm not talking about last night!
CYNTHIA: Indeed? Well, you deal, Felicity. Simon, you help me with the sofa.
BIRDBOOT: [*to* MOON] Did you see that? Tried to kill me. I told you it was Magnus—not that it *is* Magnus.
MOON: Who did it, you mean?

---

5. Cheap predictions from hack journalists. Grubb Street, in London, was once home to low-market writers and publishers.

BIRDBOOT: What?
MOON: You think it's not Magnus who did it?
BIRDBOOT: Get a grip on yourself, Moon—the facts are staring you in the face. He's after Cynthia for one thing.
MAGNUS: It's Gascoyne, isn't it?
BIRDBOOT: Over my dead body!
MAGNUS: If he comes between us...
MOON: [*angrily*] For God's sake sit down!
CYNTHIA: Simon!
BIRDBOOT: She needs me, Moon. I've got to make up a four.

[CYNTHIA *and* BIRDBOOT *move the sofa as before, and they all sit at the table.*]

CYNTHIA: Right! Who starts?
MAGNUS: I do. I'll dummy for a no-bid ruff and double my holding on South's queen.[6] [*While he moves cards.*]
CYNTHIA: Did I hear you say you saw Felicity last night, Simon?
BIRDBOOT: Er—er—
FELICITY: Pay twenty-ones or trump my contract. [*Discards.*] Cynthia's turn.
CYNTHIA: I'll trump your contract with five dummy no-trumps there [*discards*], and I'll move West's rook for the re-bid with a banker ruff on his second trick there. [*Discards.*] Simon?
BIRDBOOT: Would you mind doing that again?
CYNTHIA: And I'll ruff your dummy with five no-bid trumps there, [*discards*] and I support your re-bid with a banker for the solo ruff in the dummy trick there. [*discards*].
BIRDBOOT: [*standing up and throwing down his cards*] And I call your bluff!
CYNTHIA: Well done, Simon!

[MAGNUS *pays* BIRDBOOT *while* CYNTHIA *deals.*]

FELICITY: Strange how Simon appeared in the neighbourhood from nowhere, we know so little about him.
CYNTHIA: Right, Simon, it's your opening on the minor bid. Hmm. Let's see. I think I'll overbid the spade convention with two no-trumps and King's gambit offered there—[*discards*] and West's dummy split double to Queen's Bishop four there!
MAGNUS: [*as he plays cards*] Faites vos jeux.[7] Rien ne va plus. Rouge et noir. Zero.
CYNTHIA: Simon?
BIRDBOOT: [*triumphant, leaping to his feet*] And I call your bluff!
CYNTHIA: [*imperturbably*] I meld.
FELICITY: I huff.
MAGNUS: I ruff.
BIRDBOOT: I bluff.
CYNTHIA: Twist.
FELICITY: Bust.

---

6. Like much of the dialogue that follows, a fanciful mishmash of card-game terminology.
7. Place your bets. *Rien ne va plus:* The betting is closed. (Literally: "No more.") *Rouge et noir:* Red and black. These are all French phrases that would be used at a roulette table (though not a card table) by a croupier—a casino employee in charge of table games like blackjack and roulette.

MAGNUS: Check.
BIRDBOOT: Snap.
CYNTHIA: How's that?
FELICITY: Not out.
MAGNUS: Double top.
BIRDBOOT: Bingo!
CYNTHIA: No! Simon—your luck's in tonight.
FELICITY: We shall see—the night is not over yet, Simon Gascoyne! [*She quickly exits.*]
BIRDBOOT: [*looking after* FELICITY] Red herring[8]—smell it a mile off. [*To* MAGNUS.] Oh, yes, she's as clean as a whistle, I've seen it a thousand times. And I've seen you before too, haven't I? Strange—there's something about you—
MAGNUS: Care for a spin round the rose garden, Cynthia?
CYNTHIA: No, Magnus, I must talk to Simon.
BIRDBOOT: There's nothing for you there, you know.
MAGNUS: You think so?
BIRDBOOT: Oh, yes, she knows which side her bread is buttered. I am a man not without a certain influence among those who would reap the limelight—she's not going to throw me over for a heavily disguised cripple.
MAGNUS: There's an old Canadian proverb——
BIRDBOOT: Don't give me that—I tumbled to you[9] right from the start—oh, yes, you chaps are not as clever as you think. . . . Sooner or later you make your mistake. . . . Incidentally, where was it I saw you? . . . I've definitely——
MAGNUS: [*leaving*] Well, I think I'll go and oil my gun. [*Exit.*]
BIRDBOOT: [*after* MAGNUS] Double bluff!—[*to* CYNTHIA] I've seen it a thousand times.
CYNTHIA: I think Magnus suspects something. And Felicity? Simon, was there anything between you and Felicity?
BIRDBOOT: No, no—that's all over now. I merely flattered her a little over a drink, told her she'd go far, that sort of thing. Dear me, the fuss that's been made over a simple flirtation—
CYNTHIA: [*as* MRS. DRUDGE *enters behind*] If I find you have falsely seduced me from my dear husband Albert, I will kill you, Simon Gascoyne!

[*The* "CURTAIN" *as before.* MRS. DRUDGE *and* CYNTHIA *leave.* BIRDBOOT *starts to follow them.*]

MOON: *Birdboot!*

[BIRDBOOT *stops.*]

MOON: For God's sake pull yourself together.
BIRDBOOT: I can't help it.
MOON: What do you think you're doing? You're turning it into a complete farce!
BIRDBOOT: I know, I know—but I can't live without her. [*He is making erratic neurotic journeys about the stage.*] I shall resign my position, of course. I don't care I'm a goner, I tell you—— [*He has arrived at the body. He looks at it in surprise, hesitates, bends and turns it over.*]

8. False lead; distraction.    9. I was on to you; I suspected you.

MOON: Birdboot, think of your family, your friends—your high standing the world of letters—I say, what are you doing?

[BIRDBOOT *is staring at the body's face.*]

Birdboot... leave it alone. Come and sit down—what's the matter with you?
BIRDBOOT: [*dead-voiced*] It's Higgs.
MOON: What?
BIRDBOOT: It's Higgs.

[*Pause.*]

MOON: Don't be silly.
BIRDBOOT: I tell you it's Higgs!

[MOON *half rises. Bewildered.*]

I don't understand.... He's dead.
MOON: Dead?
BIRDBOOT: Who would want to...?
MOON: He must have been lying there all the time...
BIRDBOOT: ...kill Higgs?
MOON: But what's he doing here? I was standing in tonight....
BIRDBOOT: [*turning*] Moon?...
MOON: [*in wonder, quietly*] So it's me and Puckeridge now.
BIRDBOOT: *Moon*...?
MOON: [*faltering*] But I swear I....
BIRDBOOT: I've got it—
MOON: But I didn't—
BIRDBOOT: [*quietly*] My God... so that was it.... [*Up.*] Moon—now I see—
MOON: —I swear I didn't—
BIRDBOOT: Now—finally—I see it all—

[*There is a shot and* BIRDBOOT *falls dead.*]

MOON: Birdboot! [*He runs on, to* BIRDBOOT's *body.*]

[CYNTHIA *appears at the french windows. She stops and stares. All as before.*]

CYNTHIA: Oh my God—what happened, Inspector?
MOON: [*almost to himself*] He's dead.... [*He rises.*] That's a bit rough, isn't it?—A bit extreme!—He may have had his faults—I admit he was a fickle old... Who did this, and why?

[MOON *turns to face her. He stands up and makes swiftly for his seat. Before he gets there he is stopped by the sound of voices.*]
[SIMON *and* HOUND *are occupying the critics' seats.*]
[MOON *freezes.*]

SIMON: To say that it is without pace, point, focus, interest, drama, wit or originality is to say simply that it does not happen to be my cup of tea. One has only to compare this ragbag with the masters of the genre to see that here we have a trifle that is not my cup of tea at all.
HOUND: I'm sorry to be blunt but there is no getting away from it. It lacks pace. A complete ragbag.

SIMON: I will go further. Those of you who were fortunate enough to be at the Comedie Française on Wednesday last, will not need to be reminded that hysterics are no substitute for *éclat*.

HOUND: It lacks *élan*.

SIMON: Some of the cast seem to have given up acting altogether, apparently aghast, with every reason, at finding themselves involved in an evening that would, and indeed will, make the angels weep.

HOUND: I am not a prude but I fail to see any reason for the shower of filth and sexual allusion foisted on to an unsuspecting public in the guise of modernity at all costs....

[*Behind* MOON, FELICITY, MAGNUS *and* MRS. DRUDGE *have made their entrances, so that he turns to face their semicircle.*]

MAGNUS: [*pointing to* BIRDBOOT's *body*] Well, Inspector, is this your man?

MOON: [*warily*] ... Yes.... Yes....

CYNTHIA: It's Simon ...

MOON: Yes ... yes ... poor.... [*Up.*] Is this some kind of joke?

MAGNUS: If it is, Inspector, it's in very poor taste.

[MOON *pulls himself together and becomes galvanic, a little wild, in grief for* BIRDBOOT.]

MOON: All right! I'm going to find out who did this! I want everyone to go to the positions they occupied when the shot was fired—[*they move; hysterically*]: No one will leave the house! [*They move back.*]

MAGNUS: I think we all had the opportunity to fire the shot, Inspector—

MOON: [*furious*] I am not—

MAGNUS: —but which of us would want to?

MOON: Perhaps you, Major Magnus!

MAGNUS: Why should I want to kill him?

MOON: Because he was on to you—yes, he tumbled you right from the start—and you shot him just when he was about to reveal that you killed—[MOON *points, pauses and then crosses to Higgs's body and falters*]—killed—[*he turns Higgs over*]—this ... chap.

MAGNUS: But what motive would there be for killing him? [*Pause.*] Who *is* this chap? [*Pause.*] Inspector?

MOON: [*rising*] I don't know. Quite unlike anyone I've ever met. [*Long pause.*] Well ... now ...

MRS. DRUDGE: Inspector?

MOON: [*eagerly*] Yes? Yes, what is it, dear lady?

MRS. DRUDGE: Happening to enter this room earlier in the day to close the windows, I chanced to overhear a remark made by the deceased Simon Gascoyne to her ladyship, viz.—"I will kill anyone who comes between us."

MOON: Ah—yes—well, that's it, then. This ... chap ... [*pointing*] was obviously killed by [*pointing*] er ... by [*pause*] Simon.

CYNTHIA: But he didn't come between us!

MAGNUS: And who, then, killed Simon?

MRS. DRUDGE: Subsequent to that reported remark, I also happened to be in earshot of a remark made by Lady Muldoon to the deceased, to the effect, "I will kill you, Simon Gascoyne!" I hope you don't mind my mentioning it.

MOON: Not at all. I'm glad you did. It is from these chance remarks that we in the force build up our complete picture before moving in to make the arrest. It will not be long now, I fancy, and I must warn you, Lady Muldoon that anything you say—

CYNTHIA: Yes!—I hated Simon Gascoyne, for he had me in his power!—But I didn't kill him!

MRS. DRUDGE: Prior to that, Inspector, I also chanced to overhear a remark made by Miss Cunningham, no doubt in the heat of the moment, but it stuck in my mind as these things do, viz., "I will kill you for this, Simon Gascoyne!"

MOON: Ah! The final piece of the jigsaw! I think I am now in a position to reveal the mystery. This man [*the corpse*] was, of course, McCoy, the Canadian who, as we heard, meeting Gascoyne in the street and being solicited for sixpence for a toffee apple, smacked him across the ear, with the cry, "How's that for a grudge to harbour, you sniffling little workshy!"[1] all those many years ago. Gascoyne bided his time, but in due course tracked McCoy down to this house, having, on the way, met, in the neighbourhood, a simple ambitious girl from the provinces. He was charming, persuasive—told her, I have no doubt, that she would go straight to the top—and she, flattered by his sophistication, taken in by his promises to see her all right on the night, gave in to his simple desires. Perhaps she loved him. We shall never know. But in the very hour of her promised triumph, his eye fell on another—yes, I refer to Lady Cynthia Muldoon. From the moment he caught sight of her there was no other woman for him—he was in her spell, willing to sacrifice anything, even you, Felicity Cunningham. It was only today—unexpectedly finding him here—that you learned the truth. There was a bitter argument which ended with your promise to kill him—a promise that you carried out in this very room at your first opportunity! And I must warn you that anything you say—

FELICITY: But it doesn't make sense!

MOON: Not at first glance, *perhaps*.

MAGNUS: Could not Simon have been killed by the same person who killed McCoy?

FELICITY: But why should any of us want to kill a perfect stranger?

MAGNUS: Perhaps he was not a stranger to *one* of us.

MOON: [*faltering*] But Simon was the madman, wasn't he?

MAGNUS: We only have your word for that, Inspector. We only have your word for a lot of things. For instance—McCoy. Who is he? Is his name McCoy? Is there any truth in that fantastic and implausible tale of the insult inflicted in the Canadian streets? Or is there something else, something quite unknown to us, behind all this? Suppose for a moment that the madman, having killed this unknown stranger for private and inscrutable reasons of his own, was disturbed before he could dispose of the body, so having cut the telephone wires he decided to return to the scene of the crime, masquerading as—Police Inspector Hound!

MOON: But . . . I'm not mad . . . I'm almost sure I'm not mad . . .

MAGNUS: . . . only to discover that in the house was a man, Simon Gascoyne, who recognized the corpse as a man against whom you had held a deep-seated grudge——!

---

1. Shirker.

MOON: But I didn't kill—I'm almost sure I——
MAGNUS: I put it to you!—are you the real Inspector Hound?!
MOON: You know damn well I'm not! What's it all about?
MAGNUS: I thought as much.
MOON: I only dreamed . . . sometimes I dreamed——
CYNTHIA: So it was you!
MRS. DRUDGE: The madman!
FELICITY: The killer!
CYNTHIA: Oh, it's horrible, horrible.
MRS. DRUDGE: The stranger in our midst!
MAGNUS: Yes, we had a shrewd suspicion he would turn up here—and he walked into the trap!
MOON: What *trap*?
MAGNUS: I am not the real Magnus Muldoon!—It was a mere subterfuge!—and [*standing up and removing his mustaches.*] I now reveal myself as——
CYNTHIA: You mean——?
MAGNUS: Yes!—I am the real Inspector Hound!
MOON: [*pause*] Puckeridge!
MAGNUS: [*with pistol*] Stand where you are, or I shoot!
MOON: [*backing*] Puckeridge! You killed Higgs—and Birdboot tried to tell me—
MAGNUS: Stop in the name of the law!

[MOON *turns to run.* MAGNUS *fires.* MOON *drops to his knees.*]

I have waited a long time for this moment.
CYNTHIA: So you are the real Inspector Hound.
MAGNUS: Not only that!—I have been leading a double life—at *least*!
CYNTHIA: You mean——?
MAGNUS: Yes!—It's been ten long years, but don't you know me?
CYNTHIA: You mean——?
MAGNUS: Yes!—it is me, Albert!—who lost his memory and joined the force, rising by merit to the rank of Inspector, his past blotted out—until fate cast him back into the home he left behind, back to the beautiful woman he had brought here as his girlish bride—in short, my darling, my memory has returned and your long wait is over!
CYNTHIA: Oh, Albert!

[*They embrace.*]

MOON: [*with a trace of admiration*] Puckeridge . . . you cunning bastard.

[MOON *dies.*]

THE END

1968

## QUESTIONS

1. How does Stoppard differentiate Moon from Birdboot? What can the reader infer about their respective characters—education and class background, attitude toward drama, etc.—from their speeches in the play?

2. If you were the set designer for a production of *The Real Inspector Hound*, how would you create the illusion that the audience is actually backstage, looking out over the stage and the "audience" that includes the critics Moon and Birdboot? How would you deploy the actors onstage so that their faces could be seen clearly by the real audience?
3. When does the imaginary barrier between the critics and the actors onstage first become blurred? When does it disappear entirely?
4. What is the dramatic function of Mrs. Drudge in the play? Is she a "static" character or "dynamic"—that is, does her character change over the course of the play?
5. For the comedy of *The Real Inspector Hound* to "work," what conventions of fiction and drama (standard settings, plots, characters) must be familiar to the audience? What must an audience know about the theater world of critics, reviews, etc.?

In spite of striking differences in style and tone as well as structure and substance, both *Trifles* and *The Real Inspector Hound* deal directly with expectations, differing awareness, and mistaken interpretation as themes. Glaspell's play has the manner of domestic realism that was current when the play was first performed in 1916, whereas Stoppard's play is an absurdist or postmodern farce, in keeping with its appearance in 1967. Yet each play uses a single set that represents a house in the country in which a murder has taken place.

*The Real Inspector Hound*, like *Trifles*, refers to actions and characters that never appear onstage and exposes gaps between what various characters and the audience know. First, the title of the play makes a reader or spectator wonder if a *false* inspector will be detected, or if the play will make fun of the detective genre that has been popular ever since Arthur Conan Doyle's Sherlock Holmes series. The stage directions, more serious in tone than the title, immediately call attention to theatricality itself: "The first thing is that the audience appear to be confronted by their own reflection." That is, Stoppard reverses the usual proscenium arrangement, and gives the drawing room set only two side walls. Seated in a theater watching Stoppard's play, we would feel as though we were backstage, or where backstage would be, looking across the stage itself toward the audience. This layout shows us Moon and Birdboot, the main characters, who are professional theater critics, each possibly guilty of a misdeed. As in Glaspell's play, the emphasis is on the characters who interpret the scene of a crime, and on shared guilt or responsibility.

> *We do on the stage the things that are supposed to happen off. Which is a kind of integrity, if you look on every exit being an entrance somewhere else.*
> —TOM STOPPARD

In Stoppard's play in contrast with Glaspell's, though, the audience can see the corpse most of the time, whereas characters are comically oblivious to it. (A director could decide that a man, who would need patience more than acting skill, would lie on the stage throughout the play; or, subverting the idea of realism, could use an obviously artificial dummy.) Part of the joke of the play is that Moon's and Birdboot's first repeated question, "Where's Higgs?" is just the right question for the play they have come to review, a *"thriller,"* a "whodunnit." Stoppard intentionally twists the very conventions that Glaspell skillfully employs. Instead of a clear rising action, climax, and resolution, the play begins with a pause—and "you can't start with a *pause!*" Before the action at Muldoon Manor begins, Moon, the substitute reviewer, reveals that he is obsessed with his rivals: Higgs, the "first string" reviewer, and Puckeridge, the backup or stand-in for Moon. Birdboot, who works for another newspaper, meanwhile reveals that he is a hypocrite who loves both cheap chocolates and pretty actresses whom he seduces by promising to make their careers. He lives in fear of his wife Myrtle's jealousy. As Stoppard portrays them, the reviewers are biased and distracted, ready to flourish phrases to show off or to curry favor. Stoppard is no more flattering to playwrights, who write the sort of predictable stuff we see on the stage in front of Moon and Birdboot. According to formula, this play-within-a-play establishes multiple motives for murder in act one; act two brings in the detective, reveals the corpse (in plain sight), and yields another murder; and act three combines climactic revelations of identity with fresh murders that end the conflict.

Throughout the play, Stoppard makes fun of the illusions and clichés of theater, such as stilted exposition—lines early in plays that include more information than anyone would realistically say. In her very first speech, Mrs. Drudge answers the phone with stage directions: "Hello, the drawing-room of Lady Muldoon's country residence one morning in early spring. . . . I hope nothing is amiss for we . . . are here cut off from the world, including Magnus, the wheelchair-ridden halfbrother of her ladyship's husband. . . ." The ludicrous stage business of repeated phone calls and radio announcements is supposed to rouse dread about the mad murderer on the loose. Moon and Birdboot, like typical critics, jump to their own conclusions according to their particular preoccupations. They constantly misunderstand each other, as when Moon, spouting phrases from the pompous review he plans to write, asks where God is; Birdboot promptly looks for God in the cast list. The critics gradually detect each other's guilt in the midst of guessing the outcome of the staged play's love triangles, jealousies, and revenge plots. The game of mistaken identity and double meanings continues, as the critics become part of the play and the actors become critics. Many plots are initiated by the arrival of a stranger—or as Moon in his overwrought review puts it, "the catalystic figure, the outsider"—but here this stock figure keeps multiplying: first Simon Gascoyne, then Inspector Hound, and then Birdboot (who is mistaken for Simon), followed by Moon (who is mistaken for the Inspector). Finding out "who done it" turns out to be the end for both critics in a very literal way. The shock, comically, is that for this jaded audience the play becomes all too real; this time the stage bullets are not blanks.

For us as readers or spectators, of course, Moon and Birdboot are just as fictitious as Felicity Cunningham or Magnus; everyone is "leading a double life—at least." It may be difficult to keep track of who is who and what is happening in this bloody, fast-paced farce, but Stoppard intended the effect to be entertaining, a "recreation" not about "anything grander than itself." Even if you don't know much about the London theater and professional reviewers, you can enjoy the comic repetitions, misunderstandings, and word play, such as the absurd cardgame terminology when Birdboot joins the game: "I'll ruff your dummy with five no-bid trumps"; "I huff" / "I ruff" / "I bluff," etc. Reading closely, you will find other places where characters begin to speak in rhyme. A performance would be more likely to make you laugh aloud, but a careful reading of the play allows you to examine the method in Stoppard's madness.

When you read and interpreted *Trifles*, you probably formulated the play's theme, a statement about the way preconceptions shape perceptions or about the importance of everyday details in revealing motives. Can you derive anything similar from *The Real Inspector Hound*? The play makes fun of the critic Moon, who tries to read profound themes about "the nature of identity" into the plays he sees. But the critic Birdboot, who is only interested in effective family entertainment, is no better. In a silly way, Moon is on to something about Stoppard. The form of *The Real Inspector Hound* does point to twentieth-century philosophical preoccupations with perception, reality, and the self, as well as to a tradition of experimental theater. (Moon happens to mention some of the philosophers and writers who would have influenced Stoppard, including Sartre and Beckett.) Perhaps Stoppard's play is an attempt to jolt the audience into an awareness of theater as an art form, much as Glaspell raises questions about gender differences.

• • •

How do you write about a play? If you are not a reviewer assigned to evaluate the acting, the staging, or the script, why should you analyze the elements of the play or present an interpretation of what it means? As with fiction and poetry, writing an essay about drama can sharpen your responses and focus your reading, while it can demonstrate effects in the work that other readers may have missed. When you write about drama, in a very real sense you perform the role that directors and actors take on in a stage performance: you offer your "reading" of the text, interpreting it in order to guide other readers' responses. But as when you write about a story or a poem, you also shape and refine your own response by attempting to express it clearly. Normally, you consider the whole play before you actually write about it, but jotting down your initial impressions as you read can be a constructive first step in writing an essay. Recording your thoughts before you've finished a play may help you clarify your expectations, much as Moon and Birdboot guess out loud who the murderer is and rehearse the reviews they will write. Try stopping your reading at some reasonable point—the end of a scene or an act, or when you are puzzled, or where the action seems to pause briefly—and writing out your current expectations for the play. Very likely you will choose what the playwright expected the audience to expect at this point. Why would the clues have been designed this way? When you find out that your expectations are met—or not met—ask what difference it makes for a playwright to have prepared a surprise for the audience, or to have led them to confirm their own predictions.

With such notes, however informal, you can now return to the text to locate the specific lines that have contributed to your expectations or your discoveries. Are these lines at the beginning, the middle, or the end of the play? Who gives most of the hints or misleading information? If there is one character who is especially unseeing, especially devious, or especially insightful, you might decide to write an essay describing the function of that character in the play. A good way to undertake such a study of a character in drama (as in fiction) is to imagine the work without that character. Mrs. Hale in *Trifles* is certainly the cleverest "detective"; why do we need Mrs. Peters as well? Similarly, Moon is cleverer than Birdboot, but *The Real Inspector Hound* would be incomplete without Moon's more conservative and complacent counterpart. Why? One answer is that plays need dialogue, and we would find it artificial if Mrs. Hale or Moon talked mainly to themselves. But a more interesting answer is that in each play the audience learns by witnessing different temperaments responding to a situation. Mrs. Peters speaks for our misgivings about protecting a murderer, and Birdboot stands in for our ordinary appetites, whether for chocolates or romance. As these remarks suggest, you can also develop essays that compare characters with similar roles in two plays. To do so, however, you need to take into account the different styles and forms of their respective plays. A brief essay comparing two characters is usually best limited to a single play.

In addition to character studies, essays on drama can focus on the kinds of observations we made above: expectations and structure of plot, from its rising action to its turning point and resolution; the presence and absence of characters or actions onstage; the different degrees of awareness of characters and audience at various points in the action; titles, stage directions, and other stylistic details including metaphors or other imagery; and, of course, themes such as the importance of feminine "trifles" or the illusoriness of reality, onstage or off. As you write, you will probably discover that you can imagine directing or acting in a performance of the play, and you'll realize that interpreting a play is a crucial step in bringing it to life.

## SUGGESTIONS FOR WRITING

1. How do your sympathies for Mrs. Peters change over the course of *Trifles*? What might Mrs. Peters be said to represent in the clash of attitudes at the heart of the play? Write an essay in which you examine both Mrs. Peters's evolving character as it is revealed in *Trifles* and her dramatic function in relation to the other characters and to the plot.
2. How would you characterize Susan Glaspell's feminism as revealed in *Trifles*—does it seem radical or moderate? How does it compare to feminist political and social ideas of our own time? (Consult three or more educational or library Web sites for biographical background on Glaspell; there are several sites offering teaching materials on *Trifles* as well. If time allows, you might also pursue sources that provide an overview of women's movements in the United States in the twentieth century.) Write an essay in which you explore the political leanings apparent in *Trifles*, both in the context of Glaspell's play (published in 1920) and in the broader historical context of the struggle for women's rights over the past century.
3. Write an essay in which you propose a production of *Trifles*, complete with details of how you would handle the casting, costumes, set design, lighting, and direction of the actors. What would be your overall controlling vision for the production? Would you attempt to reproduce faithfully the look and feel of the play as it might have been in 1916, or would you introduce innovations? How would you justify your choices in terms of dramatic effectiveness?
4. Write an essay in which you compare and contrast the way Glaspell presents the same material in the short story "A Jury of Her Peers" (included in "Reading More Fiction") as in the play *Trifles*. In what ways is the play more or less effective than the short story? What might make Glaspell's material better suited to one medium than the other?
5. Can a farce like *The Real Inspector Hound* be considered a "serious" play? What is *Inspector Hound* really about—drama? illusion? identity? Write an essay in which you argue that Stoppard's play should be taken seriously, that his aim is more than mere entertainment. What would you say is the play's main theme?
6. In *The Real Inspector Hound*, what does it mean that the critics seem to have formulated their reviews of the play-within-a-play in advance, or that they become more and more involved in the action onstage? Write an essay in which you examine the different critical approaches of Moon and Birdboot and Stoppard's depiction of the relationship between drama and drama criticism.
7. How would you stage *The Real Inspector Hound*? Write an essay in which you present a proposal for all aspects of a production—casting, direction, costumes, set design, lighting, sound, etc. What special challenges and opportunities does *Inspector Hound* present? What would be your overarching vision for a production of the play?

# Understanding the Text

## 26 ELEMENTS OF DRAMA

Most of us read more fiction than drama and are likely to encounter drama by watching videotaped or filmed versions of it. Nonetheless, the skills you have developed in reading stories and poems come in handy when reading plays. Just as with fiction and poetry, you will understand and appreciate drama more fully by becoming familiar with the various elements of the genre.

### Character

**Character** is possibly the most familiar and accessible of the elements; both fiction and drama feature one or more imaginary persons who take part in the action. The word "character" refers not only to a person represented in an imagined plot, whether narrated or acted out, but also to the unique qualities that make up a personality. From one point of view, "character" as a part in a plot and "character" as a kind of personality are both predictions: this sort of person is likely to see things from a certain angle and behave in certain ways. Notice that the idea of character includes both the individual differences among people and the classification of similar people into types. To have character is positive, but to have too much of it can be objectionable. A person has "a lot of character" if he or she has integrity and stands up to pressure; but to *be* "a character" is to provoke laughter, annoyance, or reproach. Whereas much realistic fiction emphasizes unique individuals rather than general character types, drama usually compresses and simplifies personalities—a play has only about two hours in which to show situations, appearances, and behaviors, without description or background other than exposition spoken by the actors. The advantage of portraying character in broader strokes is that it heightens the contrasts between character types, adding to the drama: differences provoke stronger reactions. Whether a play favors exceptional or typical characters, authors, actors, and readers collaborate in creating these roles, drawing on their experience of varieties of personality in life and in literature.

Plays are especially concerned with characters because of the concrete manner in which they portray people on the stage. With a few exceptions (such as experiments in multimedia performance), the only words in the performance of a play are spoken by actors, and usually these actors are *in character*—that is, speaking as though they really were the people they play in the drama. (Sometimes plays have a narrator who observes and comments on the action from the sidelines, and in some plays a character may address the audience directly, but even when apparently stepping outside of the imaginary frame the actors are still part of the play.) In fiction, the narrator's description and commentary can guide a reader's judgment about characters. Reading a play, you will have no such guide; apart from some clues about characters in the stage directions, you will need to imagine the appearance, manners, and movement of someone speaking the lines assigned to any one character. You can do this even as you read through a play for the first time, discovering the characters' attitudes and motivations as the scenes unfold. This ability to predict character and then to revise expectations as situations change is based not only on our experiences of people in real life, but also on our familiarity with types of characters or roles that occur in many dramatic forms.

Consider the patterns of characters in many stories that are narrated or acted out, whether in novels, children's books, comic books, cartoons, television series, Hollywood feature films, animated films by Disney or Pixar, and even some kinds of video games. In many of these forms, there is a leading role, a main character: the **protagonist.** The titles of plays such as *Hamlet, Antigone,* or, a little less obviously, *Death of a Salesman* imply that the play will be about a central character, the chief object of the playwright's and the reader's or audience's concern. Understanding the character of the protagonist—sometimes in contrast with an **antagonist,** the counterpart or opponent of the main character—becomes the consuming interest of such a play. Especially in more traditional or popular genres, the protagonist may be called a **hero** or **heroine,** and the antagonist may be called the **villain.** We have been trained since infancy to identify with the good guys and to oppose the bully, the stepmother, the madman out to destroy the planet, or other agents of hostility and evil. This lifelong training helps us quickly immerse ourselves in the conflict between characters in a play, even if the style and form are far removed from more typical examples of their genres.

Most characterization in professional theater avoids depicting pure good and pure evil in a fight to the death. Not only are most roles qualified with flaws or redeeming qualities, but most plays portray more than two imagined people, so the conflicts are necessarily more complex than a simple good-guy-vs.-bad-guy comic-book plot. As in other genres that represent people in action, in drama too there are minor characters or supporting roles. At least since ancient Rome, romantic comedies have been structured around a leading man, a leading woman, and a comparable pair whose problems may be less serious, whose characters may be less complex, or who in other ways support rather than lead the action. Sometimes a supporting role can be said to be a **foil,** a character designed to bring out qualities in another character by contrast. Curiously, actors who are usually cast in the minor parts are sometimes called *character actors*. We might exclaim "what a character!" about a supporting role. But usually the less important parts could be said to have less character, or to require less characterization; they reveal a few traits in brief, sharp contrast rather than complex development. The main point to remember is that all the characters in a drama are interdependent and help to characterize each other. In dialogue and in behavior, each brings out what is characteristic in the others.

Like movies and other "shows," plays must respect certain limitations: the time an audience can be expected to sit and watch; the attention and sympathy an audience is likely to give to various characters; the amount of exposition that can be shown rather than spoken aloud. Because of these constraints, playwrights, screenwriters, casting directors, and actors must rely on shortcuts to convey character. Everyone involved, including the audience, consciously or unconsciously relies on **stereotypes** of various social roles to flesh out the dramatic action that is concentrated into two hours, more or less. Even a play that seeks to undermine stereotypes must still invoke them. In the United States today, casting—or typecasting—usually relies on an actor's social identity, from gender and race to occupation, region, age, and values. It might be difficult to cast someone to play the part of a middle-aged Korean American truck driver from Georgia, and even more difficult if the part specifies that this truck driver is a woman who spends her days off learning to tap dance. Such a unique role might be very desirable to an actress who has found that there are few parts for Asian American women or older women. The fact that the role defies stereotypes makes it more interesting to perform and more interesting to watch. If an actor is cast too far "against type," however, it begins to be funny, which can be an intentional effect in a play that is making fun of stereotypes. Or the role can be so exceptional and unfamiliar that audiences will fail to recognize any connection to people they might meet, and their response will fall flat. At times, however, plays or other dramatic forms can rely too much on stereotypes, positive or negative, and the familiarity leaves everyone disappointed (or offended).

> Art always aims at the **individual**. . . . Nothing could be more unique than the character of Hamlet. Though he may resemble other men in some respects, it is clearly not on that account that he interests us most.
> —HENRI BERGSON

All dramatic roles, then, must have some connection to types of personality, and good roles modify such types just enough to make the character deeper and more interesting. Playwrights often overturn or modify expectations of character in order to surprise an audience. Some theatrical roles have become famous because of their larger-than-life complexity within certain types, and because they have been performed to great acclaim. In *A Streetcar Named Desire*, Blanche DuBois does to some extent fit the type of the southern aristocrat who has lost wealth, status, and her "mansion" in the Civil War and is too frail for the rapid changes of the new postwar, industrial society. In fact, she likes to imagine herself in this tragic role in spite of the generations and World Wars that have made her pre-Civil-War dream obsolete. It is the way that she simultaneously conforms to this stereotype, artificially impersonates it, and contradicts it that makes this role so rich and compelling. It is one of the great women's roles of the twentieth century, and in 1951 it earned Vivien Leigh an Oscar for Best Actress. A similarly complex leading role, likewise from a play that became a hit film, is Henry Higgins in *Pygmalion*. Rex Harrison immortalized the part in both the stage and film versions of the musical *My Fair Lady*, which closely follows Shaw's play. Higgins is an irascible middle-aged bachelor "rather like a very impetuous baby," a brilliant linguist who is ignorant about people, an idealistic reformer who hates any threats to his own privileges; he treats everyone alike—as a true gentleman should—but treats everyone badly, and his manners and vocabulary are crude. Should an actor in this role try to match Harrison's performance—including even his rough style of talking through his songs? Should he reveal that he is actually a soft romantic under his gruff exterior? Or would it be more authentic and interesting to give the impression that he enjoys other people's suffering and has no heart for his protégée, Eliza?

Every production of a play is an interpretation. Not just "adaptations"—Greek or Elizabethan plays set in modern times and performed in modern dress, for example—but even productions that seek the "essence" of a play are interpretations of what is vital or essential in it. John Malkovich, in the 1983–84 production of *Death of a Salesman*, did not project Biff Loman as an outgoing, successful, hail-fellow-well-met jock, though that is what Arthur Miller intended and how he wanted the part played. Malkovich saw Biff as only pretending to be a jock. Big-time athletes, he insisted, don't glad-hand people; they wait for people to come to them. The actor did not change the author's words, but by intonation, body language, and "stage business" (wordless gestures and actions) he suggested his own view of the character's nature. In other words, he broke with the expectations associated with the character's type. As you read and develop your own interpretation or imaginary performance of a play, try adding unexpected qualities to one or more of the characters, to reveal different possible meanings in the drama.

## Plot and Structure

An important part of any storyteller's task, whether in narrative or dramatic forms, is the invention, selection, and arrangement of the action. Even carefully structured action cannot properly be called a full-scale **plot** without some unifying sense of purpose that joins character, story line, and theme. That is, what happens should seem to happen for meaningful reasons. This does not mean, of course, that characters or audience need be satisfied in their hopes or expectations, or that effective plays need to wrap up all loose ends of cause and effect. It does mean that a reader or theatergoer should feel that the playwright has completed *this* play—that nothing essential is missing—though the play's outcome or overall effect may be difficult to sum up.

Conflict is the engine that drives plot, and the presentation of conflict shapes the dramatic structure of a play. A conflict whose outcome is never in doubt may have other kinds of interest, but it is not truly dramatic. In a dramatic conflict each of the opposing forces must at some point seem likely to triumph or worthy of such triumph—whether it is one character versus another, one group of characters versus another group, the values of an individual versus those of a group or society or nature, or one idea or ideology versus another one. In *Hamlet*, for example, our interest in the struggle between Hamlet and Claudius depends on their being evenly matched, though few viewers would ever wish the new king to defeat the young hero. Claudius has possession of the throne and the queen, but Hamlet's role as the heir to the late king and his popularity with the people offset his opponent's strength. As we have seen in the previous chapter, the typical structure of a dramatic plot involves five stages in the progression of the conflict: exposition, rising action, climax, falling action, and conclusion. Even a short play such as *Trifles* contains all five stages.

> *The plot is the first principle and, as it were, the soul of tragedy; character comes second.*
> —ARISTOTLE

In addition to plot, there are other devices that can give a play coherent structure and effect. Thematic concerns are a primary means of holding together varieties of characters and expansive plots. In *The Piano Lesson*, for example, the desire to define family, ancestry, and identity brings together the various conflicts—between races, classes, generations, genders, individuals, and ways of life—just as class conflict and the artificiality of rank and status underlie much of the plot (and most of the humor) of *Pygmalion*.

The intricate developments of conflict between characters—and hence the plot—

may be supported not only by events and themes but also by such elements as symbols or controlling metaphors. In *The Piano Lesson,* the constant presence of the piano onstage reminds us of the family's past and its relationship to slavery, and the ways that people have treated human beings as material property. In *Wit,* the religious sonnets of John Donne serve a unifying purpose similar to that of the piano in *The Piano Lesson*—they echo the protagonist's own use of "wit" to cope with her fears in the face of death.

Another structural device that often supports and propels plot is **dramatic irony,** the fulfillment of a plan, action, or expectation in a surprising way, often the opposite of what the characters intend. One example occurs in *Trifles,* when the women notice all the everyday things in the house while the official investigators—the men—keep looking for large and unusual things. Of course, the women's "trifles" reveal the truth about the murder while the men's search for evidence has missed it.

In addition to the above kinds of elements that provide structural unity in a play, most plays also have formal divisions such as acts and scenes that emphasize the five phases of the plot. In the Greek theater, scenes were separated by choral odes (see *Oedipus the King*). In many French plays, a new scene begins with any significant entrance or exit of a character. Many "classic" plays, like *Hamlet,* have five acts, but modern plays tend to have two or three acts. It has become customary to have at least one intermission in the performance of a play that is longer than one act, in part for the practical reasons of the audience's need for restrooms or refreshments. Breaks may be signaled by turning down stage lighting and turning up the house lights, lowering the curtain (if there is one), or other means. Playwrights since the early twentieth century have sometimes deliberately challenged audience expectations concerning the beginning, middle, and end—the rising action, climax, and resolution. (Every now and then, audiences find themselves wondering whether the play is over or whether there is still more to come. When the actors all come out and take their bows, it is a safe bet the play is over!) Experimental playwrights of the later twentieth century sometimes crossed the boundaries of the stage and introduced actors into the audience or induced audiences to participate in the action. Most of the plays in this collection follow the traditions of theater that maintain a realistic illusion and a separation (sometimes called "the fourth wall") between actors and audience. The recent plays *Wit* and *How I Learned to Drive,* however, show a contemporary flexibility in their treatment of time, with brief scenes out of chronological order, and of structure, with the protagonist developing an understanding of her life story as she now and then addresses the audience directly.

One-act plays like *The Real Inspector Hound* can have a tight, intense impact, without time for subplots or character development. In its length, *Wit* resembles a two-act play, but it has no intermission because Margaret Edson, the playwright, and the director who helped develop the play before its New York production realized that audiences might not want to return from an intermission to face the protagonist's painful death (which will come as no surprise, since it is announced in the first few lines of the play) or to continue the intense intellectual exercise of thinking about Donne's poetry. With its simple set, small cast of characters, thematic concentration, and sparing details, *Wit* has one intense emotional arc. With only two significant supporting roles, the play is dominated by one character who seems to direct some of the scenes; it spans months of this protagonist's life and includes memories from her childhood and youth. Thus it develops character to an unusual extent for a rather short play. On rare occasions, very long plays (such as Tony Kushner's *Angels in America*) are performed over more than one evening, with the obvious problems of finding an audience willing and able to pay and find the time for more than one performance; those who read such play "cycles" at their own pace at home have a certain advantage. In short, the form of a play and the breaks between scenes or acts result from the nature of the play. Breaks can create suspense—a curtain comes down after an unexplained gun shot—or they can provide relief from tension or an emotional crisis.

## Stages, Sets, and Setting

Most of us have been to a theater at one time or another, if only for a school play, and we know what a conventional modern stage (the proscenium stage) looks like: a room with the wall missing between us and it. So when we read a modern play—that is, one written during the past two or three hundred years—and imagine it taking place before us, we think of its happening on such a stage. There are other types of modern stages—the **thrust stage,** where the audience sits around three sides of the major acting area, and the **arena stage,** where the audience sits all the way around the acting area and players make their entrances and their exits through the auditorium—but most plays are set on a proscenium stage. Most of the plays in this textbook can be readily imagined to be taking place on such a stage.

The two Shakespeare plays and the two Greek plays here were staged quite differently, and although they may be played today on a proscenium stage, we might be confused as we read if we are unaware of the original layout of the staging. In the Greek theater, the audience sat on a raised semicircle of seats (**amphitheater**) halfway around a circular area (**orchestra**) used primarily for dancing by the chorus. At the back of the orchestra was the **skene,** or stage house, representing the palace or temple before which the action took place. Shakespeare's stage, in contrast, basically involved a rectangular area built inside one end of a large enclosure like a circular walled-in yard; the audience stood on the ground or sat in stacked balconies around three sides of the principal acting area (rather like a thrust stage). There were additional acting areas on either side of this stage, as well as a recessed area at the back of the stage (which could represent Gertrude's chamber in *Hamlet,* for example) and an upper acting area (which could serve as Juliet's balcony). There was a trap door in the stage floor used for occasional effects; the ghost of Hamlet's father probably came and went this way. Until three centuries ago—and certainly in Shakespeare's time—plays for large paying audiences were performed outdoors in daylight, due to the difficulty and expense of lighting. If you are curious about Shakespeare's stage, you can visit a reconstruction of his Globe Theatre (according to what scholars have been able to determine) in Southwark, London, England, whether you are able to go there in person or online at <www.shakespeares-globe.org>. Every summer, plays by Shakespeare are performed there for large international audiences willing to sit on hard benches around the arena or to stand with the "groundlings" (of whom a lucky few can lean on the stage near the feet of the actors). The walls in the background of the stage are beautifully carved and painted, but there is no painted scenery, minimal furniture, few costume changes, no lighting, and no curtain around the stage (a cloth hanging usually covers the recessed area at the back of the stage). Three or four musicians may play period instruments on the balcony.

As the design of the Globe suggests, the conventions of dramatic writing and stage production have changed considerably since the advent of theater. Certainly this is true of the way playwrights convey a sense of location. Usually the audience is asked to imagine that the featured section of the auditorium is actually a particular place or **setting** somewhere else. The audience of course knows it is a stage, more or less bare or disguised, but they accept it as a public square, a wooded park, an open road, or a room in a castle or a hut. *Oedipus the King* takes place entirely before the palace at Thebes. Following the general convention of Greek drama, the play never changes place. When the action demands the presence of Teiresias, for example, the scene does not shift to him, but instead escorts bring him to the front of the palace. Similarly, important events that take place elsewhere are described by witnesses who arrive on the scene.

In Shakespeare's theater the conventions of place are quite different: the acting arena does not represent a specific place, but assumes a temporary identity according to the characters who inhabit it, the costumes, and their speeches. At the opening of *Hamlet* we know we are at a sentry station because a man dressed as a soldier challenges two others. By line 15, we know that we are in Denmark because the actors profess to be "liegemen to the Dane." At the end of the scene the actors leave the stage and in a sense take the sentry station with them. Shortly a group of people dressed in court costumes and a man and a woman wearing crowns appear. As a theater audience, we must surmise from costumes and dialogue that the acting area has now become a royal court; when we read the play, the stage directions give us a cue that the place has changed.

In a modern play like *Pygmalion*, there are likely to be several changes of scene. The staging of Shaw's original play was relatively simple, however. Each of the five acts had only one scene: the portico of St. Paul's Church in the first act, Higgins's laboratory in acts 2 and 4, and his mother's drawing room in acts 3 and 5. (The revised version of the play that we print here, complete with the prose conclusion— Shaw also wrote a preface—is more complicated; it includes a scene at the Embassy party with characters not listed in the original cast list, and a glimpse of the inside of Eliza's bedroom. In other words, this version is designed more to be read than performed.)

The scene changes in modern plays involve lowering a curtain or darkening the stage while different sets and props are arranged. **Sets** (the design, decoration, and scenery) and **props** (articles or objects used on stage) vary greatly in modern productions of plays written in any period. Sometimes space is merely suggested—a circle of sand at one end of the stage, a blank wall behind—to emphasize abstraction and universal themes, or to exercise the audience's imagination. More typically, a set uses realistic aids to the imagination. The set of *Trifles*, for example, must include at least a sink, a cupboard, a stove, a small table, a large kitchen table, and a rocking chair, as well as certain props: a bird cage, quilting pieces, and an ornamental box.

In addition to representing place and the changing of place, dramatic conventions represent time and the changing of times, and these conventions, too, have altered across the centuries. Three or four centuries ago, European dramatists and critics admired the conventions of classical Greek drama which, they believed, dictated that the action of a play should represent a very short time—sometimes as short as the actual performance time (two or three hours), and certainly no longer than a single day. This **unity of time**, one of the so-called **classical unities**, impels a dramatist to select the moment when a stable situation should change and to fill in the necessary prior details by exposition. (These same critics maintained that a play should be unified in place and action as well; the kind of leaping from Denmark to England, or from court to forest, that happens in Shakespeare's plays was off limits according to such standards.) Thus, as we noted in *Trifles*, all the action before the investigators' visit to the farmhouse is summarized by characters during their brief visit, and the kitchen is the only part of the house that is seen by the audience.

Sometimes plays will use a more elaborate device to reveal characters' memories, as when Vivian Bearing in *Wit* imagines (and she and the other actors perform) her own classroom in years past, or as when Willy Loman's dreams or memories are acted out in *Death of a Salesman*. Gaps in time are often indicated between scenes, with the help of scenery, sound effects, stage directions, or notes in the program. Actors must assist in conveying the idea of time if their character appears at different ages, as in *How I Learned to Drive*. Various conventions of classical or Elizabethan drama have also worked effectively to communicate to the audience the idea of the passage of time, from the choral odes in *Oedipus the King* to the breaks between scenes in Shakespeare plays. There is a short time, for example, between Hamlet's departure to see his mother at the end of act 3, scene 2, and the entrance of the king with Rosencrantz and Guildenstern at the beginning of the next scene; in other parts of the play the elapsed time might be as long as that between scenes 4 and 5 of act 4, during which the news of Polonius's death reaches Paris and Laertes returns to Denmark and there rallies his friends. Action from the beginning to the end of a play thus can reach across a wide range of locations and represent many years rather than remaining in one place for the twenty-four hours demanded by critics who believed in the classical unities.

## *Tone, Style, Imagery, and Allusion*

In plays as in other literary genres, the **tone**—the style or manner of expression—is difficult to specify or explain. Perhaps tone is more important in drama than in other genres because it is, in performance, a spoken form, and vocal tone always affects the meaning of spoken words to some extent, in any culture or language. The actor—and any reader who wishes to imagine a play as spoken aloud—must infer from the written language just how to read a line, what tone of voice to use. The choice of tone must be a negotiation between the words of the playwright and the interpretation and skill of the actor. At times the stage directions will specify the tone of a line of dialogue, though even that must be only a hint, since there are many ways of speaking "intensely" or "angrily." Try it yourself; find a line in one of the plays printed here that has a stage direction telling the actor how to deliver it, and with one or two other people take turns saying it that way. (*Trifles, The Real Inspector Hound,* and *Pygmalion* have many such instructions on tone.) If nothing else, such an experiment may help all of us appreciate the talent of good actors who can put on a certain tone of voice and make it seem natural and convincing. But it will also show you the many options for interpreting tone.

**Dramatic irony,** in which a character's knowledge or expectation is contradicted by what the audience knows or by the outcome of events, is relatively easy to detect; **verbal irony,** in which speech and action don't match, or the audience recognizes meanings the speaker doesn't realize, can be fairly subtle and easy to miss. There is a combination of both kinds of irony in the scene in *Pygmalion* after Eliza Doolittle's triumph at the Embassy party. The stage business may look trivial: Higgins wonders where his slippers are and notices neither Eliza's silent protest nor her subsequent delivery of the wanted items at his feet. He is looking back over the evening as a kind of sporting event that bored him. "[*Yawning again.*] Oh Lord! . . . What a silly tomfoolery!" Then, "[ . . . *He stops unlacing (his shoe) and looks at (his slippers) as if they had appeared there of their own accord.*] Oh! theyre here, are they?" After Pickering responds with his own comments on the social events that tested Eliza, Higgins replies: "[*Fervently.*] Thank God it's over! [*Eliza flinches violently; but they take no notice of her. . . .* ]" Actions, dialogue, the tone in which it is spoken, and silent reactions all underline the irony in this scene: the gap between what the mentors consider important and what their human experiment has gone through. Tone may modulate the meaning of a few words, dominate an entire act, or pervade virtually an entire play, as in *Pygmalion*. Those who miss the cruelty of Higgins's and Pickering's cheerful indifference may be misled by another tone that does surface in the play, the romantic or sentimental. Certainly, the subtitle and aspects of the plot do refer to romance, and romantically inclined readers, directors, and viewers have given the play an ending the author did not intend, Eliza's marriage to Higgins.

Never hesitate to apply the skills you have developed in interpreting poetry to drama; after all, most early plays were written in some form of verse. Aspects of poetry emerge in modern plays; for example, **monologues** or extended speeches by one character, while they rarely rhyme or have regular meter, may allow greater eloquence than is usual in everyday speech, expressing character and theme in well-chosen images or metaphors. Moon in *The Real Inspector Hound*, for instance, often embarks on strange fantasy monologues, as in his description of his dream of the violent uprising of "the stand-ins of the world," or more briefly, his comment on his name and role: "It is merely that it is not enough to wax at another's wane, to be held in reserve . . . to step in or not at all, the substitute . . . for I am Moon, continuous Moon, in my own shoes, Moon in June, April, September and no member of the human race keeps warm my bit of space. . . ." Without line breaks, you may not notice that moon and June, September and member, race and space rhyme, and you may miss at first the point that Moon, like the moon itself, is in shadow (or wanes) when the first-string critic is in place. Stoppard is not using poetic devices seriously, but in parodic fun. Tennessee Williams and other playwrights may use these resources more straightforwardly, as in the names of characters and places (*Blanche DuBois*, or "White of the Woods"; *Belle Reve*, or "Beautiful Dream").

Not only can names, monologues, or recurrent memories stand in for webs of meaning in a play, but so can simple actions or objects. Effective plays often use props almost metaphorically. For instance, Vivian Bearing in *Wit*—named with reference to life (as in sur*viv*al or *viv*acious) and to the suffering she bears—is attached by an intravenous tube to an "IV pole." This becomes almost a lifeline, not unlike the umbilical cord, as well as a visual reminder of her weakness. Boy Willie and Lymon, in *The Piano Lesson,* bring a load of watermelons rather than squash or other produce, because watermelons have become part of a nasty caricature of rural African Americans, who supposedly lived a happy life consuming the cheap, sweet fruit. The carved family heirloom is a piano for several good reasons: it can be seen on stage as something difficult to move and impossible to divide without destruction; characters can play it and the child of the next generation can be taught to play it; and it can symbolize both the great art of African American music and the way African Americans might take on European forms of culture and art and make them their own. Compare the metaphor of piano lessons to the metaphor of driving lessons in Paula Vogel's play. The idea of a car, and images of cars, dominate *How I Learned to Drive* much as the piano stands at the center of August Wilson's play. As you read, pay close attention to metaphors or images, whether in language, concepts, or concrete forms.

Allusions too can enrich the text as well as the performance in similar ways. Usually the reference is intentional and clear, as in a title such as *Pygmalion*, so that you can look it up in a reference work if you are not sure what it means. In *Wit*, the doctor who signs Professor Bearing's "DNR" order (Do Not Resuscitate) is named Kelekian. Although there are many doctors of Armenian descent in the United States, this appears to be a reference to the famous Dr. Kevorkian who has defied the law against assisted suicide; in the play, Kelekian has presided over Bearing's treatment, which adds to her suffering, but he allows her to choose to die rather than continue to submit to the interests of research. Awareness of all the stylistic choices in the work, whether the playwright made these choices consciously or not, can help you reach a clearer interpretation of the whole play.

## Theme

**Theme**—usually defined as a statement or assertion about the subject of a work—is by its very nature the most comprehensive of the elements, embracing the impact of the entire work. Theme indeed is not part of the work, but abstracted from it by the reader or audience. Since we, as interpreters, infer the theme and put it in our own words, we understandably often disagree about nuances of emphasis or phrasing or even entire conceptions. Our assessments of theme usually entail judgments of the characters and plot. If *Pygmalion*'s theme is the artificiality of class (or if you take at face value the assertion that the play is a romance), then it may seem that Eliza in the end should marry Higgins, who has lifted her from the gutter. In addition, if you rely on the title's allusion to the myth of Pygmalion, who falls in love with the statue of a woman he has created, and who marries her when Aphrodite answers his prayer to bring the statue to life, then Eliza should love and marry Higgins. Yet Ovid's Pygmalion myth can also be interpreted as a criticism of egotistical fantasies that distort or exploit the object of one's love. Moreover, the characterization in Shaw's play suggests that Higgins and Eliza are incompatible (though somewhat alike at first). Eliza is enraged at Higgins's attitude toward her and grateful to the loving Freddy; she has always wanted an everyday middle-class existence running a flower shop, and manages to get it in the end. Shaw evidently intended Eliza to marry Freddy. The theme then is much more about the egotism of a Pygmalion who denies the autonomy of the creature he thinks he has created, though indeed he has irrevocably changed her. Higgins would be an unbearable husband, after all. The outcome that Shaw intended is in any case more consistent with the play's ironic and unsentimental tone—even if audiences may prefer a Cinderella story.

To arrive at your own statement of a theme it is necessary to consider all the elements of a play together: character, structure, setting (including time and place), tone, and other aspects of the style or the potential staging that create the entire effect. Above all, try to understand a play on its own terms. You may dislike symbolic or unrealistic drama until you get more used to it; if a play is not supposed to represent what real people would do in everyday life in that place and time, then it should not be criticized for failing to do so. Or you may find realistic plays about ordinary adults in middle America in the mid-twentieth century to be devoid of excitement or appeal. Yet if you read carefully, you may discover vigorous, moving portrayals of people trapped in situations all too familiar to them, if alien to you. Tastes may vary as widely as tones of speech, but equipped with familiarity with the elements of drama and the ways they have changed over time you can become a good judge of theatrical literature, and notice more and more of the fine effects it can achieve. Nothing replaces the exhilaration of the one-time immediacy of a live theater performance, but reading and rereading plays can yield a rich and rewarding appreciation of the dramatic art.

## BERNARD SHAW

# *Pygmalion*

### A Romance in Five Acts

**CHARACTERS**

| | | |
|---|---|---|
| CLARA EYNSFORD HILL | ELIZA DOOLITTLE | MRS. PEARCE |
| MRS. EYNSFORD HILL | COLONEL PICKERING | ALFRED DOOLITTLE |
| A BYSTANDER | HENRY HIGGINS | MRS. HIGGINS |
| FREDDY EYNSFORD HILL | A SARCASTIC BYSTANDER | PARLORMAID |

*Period: The present.*
ACT I: *The Portico of St. Paul's, Covent Garden. 11:15 P.M.*
ACT II: PROFESSOR HIGGINS's *phonetic laboratory, Wimpole Street. Next day. 11 A.M.*
ACT III: *The drawing room in* MRS. HIGGINS's *flat on Chelsea Embankment. Several months later. At-home day.*
ACT IV: *The same as Act II. Several months later. Midnight.*
ACT V: *The same as Act III. The following morning.*
NOTE: *In the dialogue an e upside down indicates the indefinite vowel, sometimes called obscure or neutral, for which, though it is one of the commonest sounds in English speech, our wretched alphabet has no letter.*

## ACT I

*London at 11:15 P.M. Torrents of heavy summer rain. Cab whistles blowing frantically in all directions.* PEDESTRIANS *running for shelter into the portico of St. Paul's church (not Wren's cathedral but Inigo Jones's church in Covent Garden vegetable market), among them a* LADY *and her* DAUGHTER *in evening dress. All are peering out gloomily at the rain, except one* MAN *with his back turned to the rest, wholly preoccupied with a notebook in which he is writing.*

*The church clock strikes the first quarter.*

THE DAUGHTER: [*In the space between the central pillars, close to the one on her left.*] I'm getting chilled to the bone. What can Freddy be doing all this time? He's been gone twenty minutes.

THE MOTHER: [*On her* DAUGHTER*'s right.*] Not so long. But he ought to have got us a cab by this.

A BYSTANDER: [*On the* LADY*'s right.*] He wont[1] get no cab not until half-past eleven, missus, when they come back after dropping their theatre fares.

THE MOTHER: But we must have a cab. We cant stand here until half-past eleven. It's too bad.

THE BYSTANDER: Well, it aint my fault, missus.

THE DAUGHTER: If Freddy had a bit of gumption, he would have got one at the theatre door.

THE MOTHER: What could he have done, poor boy?

THE DAUGHTER: Other people got cabs. Why couldnt he?

[FREDDY *rushes in out of the rain from the Southampton Street side, and comes between them closing a dripping umbrella. He is a young man of twenty, in evening dress, very wet round the ankles.*]

THE DAUGHTER: Well, havnt you got a cab?

FREDDY: Theres not one to be had for love or money.

THE MOTHER: Oh, Freddy, there must be one. You cant have tried.

THE DAUGHTER: It's too tiresome. Do you expect us to go and get one ourselves?

FREDDY: I tell you theyre all engaged. The rain was so sudden: nobody was prepared; and everybody had to take a cab. Ive been to Charing Cross one way and nearly to Ludgate Circus the other; and they were all engaged.

THE MOTHER: Did you try Trafalgar Square?

FREDDY: There wasnt one at Trafalgar Square.

THE DAUGHTER: Did you try?

FREDDY: I tried as far as Charing Cross Station. Did you expect me to walk to Hammersmith?[2]

THE DAUGHTER: You havnt tried at all.

THE MOTHER: You really are very helpless, Freddy. Go again; and dont come back until you have found a cab.

FREDDY: I shall simply get soaked for nothing.

THE DAUGHTER: And what about us? Are we to stay here all night in this draught, with next to nothing on? You selfish pig—

FREDDY: Oh, very well: I'll go, I'll go. [*He opens his umbrella and dashes off Strandwards, but comes into collision with a* FLOWER GIRL *who is hurrying in for shelter, knocking her basket out of her hands. A blinding flash of lightning, followed instantly by a rattling peal of thunder, orchestrates the incident.*]

THE FLOWER GIRL: Nah then, Freddy: look wh' y' gowin, deah.

FREDDY: Sorry. [*He rushes off.*]

THE FLOWER GIRL: [*Picking up her scattered flowers and replacing them in the basket.*] Theres menners f' yer! Tə-oo banches o voylets trod into the mad. [*She sits

---

1. Shaw insisted on eliminating apostrophes from most contractions—*wont, cant, didnt,* etc.
2. Freddie has walked more than half a mile in either direction to reach Charing Cross Station and Ludgate Circus. Trafalgar Square is several hundred yards beyond Charing Cross Station, and Hammersmith is several miles beyond that.

down on the plinth of the column, sorting her flowers, on the LADY's right. She is not at all a romantic figure. She is perhaps eighteen, perhaps twenty, hardly older. She wears a little sailor hat of black straw that has long been exposed to the dust and soot of London and has seldom if ever been brushed. Her hair needs washing rather badly: its mousy color can hardly be natural. She wears a shoddy black coat that reaches nearly to her knees and is shaped to her waist. She has a brown skirt with a coarse apron. Her boots are much the worse for wear. She is no doubt as clean as she can afford to be; but compared to the ladies she is very dirty. Her features are no worse than theirs; but their condition leaves something to be desired; and she needs the services of a dentist.]

THE MOTHER: How do you know that my son's name is Freddy, pray?

THE FLOWER GIRL: Ow, eez yə-ooa san, is e? Wal, fewd dan y' də-ooty bawmz a mather should, eed now bettern to spawl a pore gel's flahrzn than ran awy athaht pyin. Will ye-oo py me f'them? [*Here, with apologies, this desperate attempt to represent her dialect without a phonetic alphabet must be abandoned as unintelligible outside London.*]

THE DAUGHTER: Do nothing of the sort, mother. The idea!

THE MOTHER: Please allow me, Clara. Have you any pennies?

THE DAUGHTER: No. Ive nothing smaller than sixpence.

THE FLOWER GIRL: [*Hopefully.*] I can give you change for a tanner,[3] kind lady.

THE MOTHER: [*To* CLARA.] Give it to me. [CLARA *parts reluctantly.*] Now. [*To the* GIRL.] This is for your flowers.

THE FLOWER GIRL: Thank you kindly, lady.

THE DAUGHTER: Make her give you the change. These things are only a penny a bunch.

THE MOTHER: Do hold your tongue, Clara. [*To the* GIRL.] You can keep the change.

THE FLOWER GIRL: Oh, thank you, lady.

THE MOTHER: Now tell me how you know that young gentleman's name.

THE FLOWER GIRL: I didnt.

THE MOTHER: I heard you call him by it. Dont try to deceive me.

THE FLOWER GIRL: [*Protesting.*] Who's trying to deceive you? I called him Freddy or Charlie same as you might yourself if you was talking to a stranger and wished to be pleasant.

THE DAUGHTER: Sixpence thrown away! Really, mamma, you might have spared Freddy that. [*She retreats in disgust behind the pillar.*]

[*An elderly* GENTLEMAN *of the amiable military type rushes into the shelter, and closes a dripping umbrella. He is in the same plight as* FREDDY, *very wet about the ankles. He is in evening dress, with a light overcoat. He takes the place left vacant by the* DAUGHTER.]

THE GENTLEMAN: Phew!

THE MOTHER: [*To the* GENTLEMAN.] Oh sir, is there any sign of its stopping?

THE GENTLEMAN: I'm afraid not. It started worse than ever about two minutes ago. [*He goes to the plinth beside the* FLOWER GIRL; *puts up his foot on it; and stoops to turn down his trouser ends.*]

THE MOTHER: Oh dear! [*She retires sadly and joins her* DAUGHTER.]

THE FLOWER GIRL: [*Taking advantage of the military* GENTLEMAN's *proximity to estab-*

---

3. Slang for sixpence (six pennies), loosely equivalent to two and a half dollars in the United States today.

lish friendly relations with him.] If it's worse, it's a sign it's nearly over. So cheer up, Captain; and buy a flower off a poor girl.

THE GENTLEMAN: I'm sorry. I havnt any change.

THE FLOWER GIRL: I can give you change, Captain.

THE GENTLEMAN: For a sovereign?[4] Ive nothing less.

THE FLOWER GIRL: Garn![5] Oh do buy a flower off me, Captain. I can change half-a-crown.[6] Take this for tuppence.[7]

THE GENTLEMAN: Now dont be troublesome: theres a good girl. [*Trying his pockets.*] I really havnt any change—Stop: heres three hapence,[8] if thats any use to you. [*He retreats to the other pillar.*]

THE FLOWER GIRL: [*Disappointed, but thinking three halfpence better than nothing.*] Thank you, sir.

THE BYSTANDER: [*To the* GIRL.] You be careful: give him a flower for it. Theres a bloke here behind taking down every blessed word youre saying. [*All turn to the* MAN *who is taking notes.*]

THE FLOWER GIRL: [*Springing up terrified.*] I aint done nothing wrong by speaking to the gentleman. Ive a right to sell flowers if I keep off the kerb. [*Hysterically.*] I'm a respectable girl: so help me, I never spoke to him except to ask him to buy a flower off me.

> [*General hubbub, mostly sympathetic to the* FLOWER GIRL, *but deprecating her excessive sensibility. Cries of* Dont start hollerin. Who's hurting you? Nobody's going to touch you. Whats the good of fussing? Steady on. Easy easy, etc., *come from the elderly staid spectators, who pat her comfortingly. Less patient ones bid her shut her head, or ask her roughly what is wrong with her. A remoter group, not knowing what the matter is, crowd in and increase the noise with question and answer:* Whats the row? What-she do? Where is he? A tec[9] taking her down. What! him? Yes: him over there: Took money off the gentleman, *etc.*]

THE FLOWER GIRL: [*Breaking through them to the* GENTLEMAN, *crying wildly.*] Oh, sir, dont let him charge me. You dunno what it means to me. Theyll take away my character and drive me on the streets for speaking to gentlemen. They—

THE NOTE TAKER: [*Coming forward on her right, the rest crowding after him.*] There! there! there! there! who's hurting you, you silly girl? What do you take me for?

THE BYSTANDER: It's aw rawt: e's a genleman: look at his b-oots [*Explaining to the* NOTE TAKER.] She thought you was a copper's nark, sir.

THE NOTE TAKER: [*With quick interest.*] Whats a copper's nark?

THE BYSTANDER: [*Inapt at definition.*] It's a—well, it's a copper's nark, as you might say. What else would you call it? A sort of informer.

THE FLOWER GIRL: [*Still hysterical.*] I take my Bible oath I never said a word—

THE NOTE TAKER: [*Overbearing but good-humored.*] Oh, shut up, shut up. Do I look like a policeman?

THE FLOWER GIRL: [*Far from reassured.*] Then what did you take down my words for? How do I know whether you took me down right? You just shew me what youve wrote about me. [*The* NOTE TAKER *opens his book and holds it steadily*

---

4. Gold coin worth a pound (twenty shillings), equivalent to over 100 dollars in the United States today.
5. Go on!   6. Two and a half shillings, loosely equivalent to 14 dollars in the United States today.
7. Coin worth two pennies.   8. Half-penny coin.   9. Detective.

*under her nose, though the pressure of the mob trying to read it over his shoulders would upset a weaker man.*] Whats that? That aint proper writing. I cant read that.

THE NOTE TAKER: I can. [*Reads, reproducing her pronunciation exactly.*] "Cheer ap, Keptin; n' baw ya flahr orf a pore gel."

THE FLOWER GIRL: [*Much distressed.*] It's because I called him Captain. I meant no harm. [*To the* GENTLEMAN.] Oh, sir, dont let him lay a charge agen me for a word like that. You—

THE GENTLEMAN: Charge! I make no charge. [*To the* NOTE TAKER.] Really, sir, if you are a detective, you need not begin protecting me against molestation by young women until I ask you. Anybody could see that the girl meant no harm.

THE BYSTANDERS GENERALLY: [*Demonstrating against police espionage.*] Course they could. What business is it of yours? You mind your own affairs. He wants promotion, he does. Taking down people's words! Girl never said a word to him. What harm if she did? Nice thing a girl cant shelter from the rain without being insulted, etc., etc., etc. [*She is conducted by the more sympathetic demonstrators back to her plinth, where she resumes her seat and struggles with her emotion.*]

THE BYSTANDER: He aint a tec. He's a blooming busybody: thats what he is. I tell you, look at his bə-oots.

THE NOTE TAKER: [*Turning on him genially.*] And how are all your people down at Selsey?

THE BYSTANDER: [*Suspiciously.*] Who told you my people come from Selsey?

THE NOTE TAKER: Never you mind. They did. [*To the* GIRL.] How do you come to be up so far east? You were born in Lisson Grove.

THE FLOWER GIRL: [*Appalled.*] Oh, what harm is there in my leaving Lisson Grove? It wasnt fit for a pig to live in; and I had to pay four-and-six a week. [*In tears.*] Oh, boo—hoo—oo—

THE NOTE TAKER: Live where you like; but stop that noise.

THE GENTLEMAN: [*To the* GIRL.] Come, come! he cant touch you: you have a right to live where you please.

A SARCASTIC BYSTANDER: [*Thrusting himself between the* NOTE TAKER *and the* GENTLEMAN.] Park Lane, for instance. I'd like to go into the Housing Question with you, I would.

THE FLOWER GIRL: [*Subsiding into a brooding melancholy over her basket, and talking very low-spiritedly to herself.*] I'm a good girl, I am.

THE SARCASTIC BYSTANDER: [*Not attending to her.*] Do you know where *I* come from?

THE NOTE TAKER: [*Promptly.*] Hoxton. [*Titterings. Popular interest in the* NOTE TAKER'*s performance increases.*]

THE SARCASTIC ONE: [*Amazed.*] Well, who said I didnt? Bly me! you know everything, you do.

THE FLOWER GIRL: [*Still nursing her sense of injury.*] Aint no call to meddle with me, he aint.

THE BYSTANDER: [*To her.*] Of course he aint. Dont you stand it from him. [*To the* NOTE TAKER.] See here: what call have you to know about people what never offered to meddle with you?

THE FLOWER GIRL: Let him say what he likes. I dont want to have no truck with him.

THE BYSTANDER: You take us for dirt under your feet, dont you? Catch you taking liberties with a gentleman!

THE SARCASTIC BYSTANDER: Yes: tell him where he come from if you want to go fortune-telling.
THE NOTE TAKER: Cheltenham, Harrow, Cambridge, and India.
THE GENTLEMAN: Quite right. [*Great laughter. Reaction in the* NOTE TAKER'*s favor. Exclamations of* He knows all about it. Told him proper. Hear him tell the toff[1] where he come from? *etc.*] May I ask, sir, do you do this for your living at a music hall?
THE NOTE TAKER: I've thought of that. Perhaps I shall some day.

[*The rain has stopped; and the persons on the outside of the crowd begin to drop off.*]

THE FLOWER GIRL: [*Resenting the reaction.*] He's no gentleman, he aint, to interfere with a poor girl.
THE DAUGHTER: [*Out of patience, pushing her way rudely to the front and displacing the* GENTLEMAN, *who politely retires to the other side of the pillar.*] What on earth is Freddy doing? I shall get pneumownia if I stay in this draught any longer.
THE NOTE TAKER: [*To himself, hastily making a note of her pronunciation of "*monia.*"*] Earlscourt.
THE DAUGHTER: [*Violently.*] Will you please keep your impertinent remarks to yourself.
THE NOTE TAKER: Did I say that out loud? I didnt mean to. I beg your pardon. Your mother's Epsom, unmistakeably.
THE MOTHER: [*Advancing between her* DAUGHTER *and the* NOTE TAKER.] How very curious! I was brought up in Largelady Park, near Epsom.
THE NOTE TAKER: [*Uproariously amused.*] Ha! ha! What a devil of a name! Excuse me. [*To the* DAUGHTER.] You want a cab, do you?
THE DAUGHTER: Dont dare speak to me.
THE MOTHER: Oh please, please, Clara. [*Her* DAUGHTER *repudiates her with an angry shrug and retires haughtily.*] We should be so grateful to you, sir, if you found us a cab. [*The* NOTE TAKER *produces a whistle.*] Oh, thank you. [*She joins her* DAUGHTER.]

[*The* NOTE TAKER *blows a piercing blast.*]

THE SARCASTIC BYSTANDER: There! I knowed he was a plainclothes copper.
THE BYSTANDER: That aint a police whistle: thats a sporting whistle.
THE FLOWER GIRL: [*Still preoccupied with her wounded feelings.*] He's no right to take away my character. My character is the same to me as any lady's.
THE NOTE TAKER: I dont know whether youve noticed it; but the rain stopped about two minutes ago.
THE BYSTANDER: So it has. Why didnt you say so before? and us losing our time listening to your silliness! [*He walks off towards the Strand.*]
THE SARCASTIC BYSTANDER: I can tell where you come from. You come from Anwell. Go back there.
THE NOTE TAKER: [*Helpfully.*] Hanwell.[2]
THE SARCASTIC BYSTANDER: [*Affecting great distinction of speech.*] Thenk you, teacher.

---

1. Slang for "gentleman," slightly derogatory.
2. Parish in Middlesex County, eight miles west of London.

Haw haw! So long [*He touches his hat with mock respect and strolls off.*]

THE FLOWER GIRL: Frightening people like that! How would he like it himself?

THE MOTHER: It's quite fine now, Clara. We can walk to a motor bus. Come. [*She gathers her skirts above her ankles and hurries off towards the Strand.*]

THE DAUGHTER: But the cab—[*Her* MOTHER *is out of hearing.*] Oh, how tiresome! [*She follows angrily.*]

> [*All the rest have gone except the* NOTE TAKER, *the* GENTLEMAN, *and the* FLOWER GIRL, *who sits arranging her basket, and still pitying herself in murmurs.*]

THE FLOWER GIRL: Poor girl! Hard enough for her to live without being worrited and chivied.[3]

THE GENTLEMAN: [*Returning to his former place on the* NOTE TAKER's *left.*] How do you do it, if I may ask?

THE NOTE TAKER: Simply phonetics. The science of speech. Thats my profession: also my hobby. Happy is the man who can make a living by his hobby! You can spot an Irishman or a Yorkshireman by his brogue. *I* can place any man within six miles. I can place him within two miles in London. Sometimes within two streets.

THE FLOWER GIRL: Ought to be ashamed of himself, unmanly coward!

THE GENTLEMAN: But is there a living in that?

THE NOTE TAKER: Oh yes. Quite a fat one. This is an age of upstarts. Men begin in Kentish Town with £80 a year, and end in Park Lane with a hundred thousand. They want to drop Kentish Town; but they give themselves away every time they open their mouths. Now I can teach them—

THE FLOWER GIRL: Let him mind his own business and leave a poor girl—

THE NOTE TAKER: [*Explosively.*] Woman: cease this detestable boohooing instantly; or else seek the shelter of some other place of worship.

THE FLOWER GIRL: [*With feeble defiance.*] Ive a right to be here if I like, same as you.

THE NOTE TAKER: A woman who utters such depressing and disgusting sounds has no right to be anywhere—no right to live. Remember that you are a human being with a soul and the divine gift of articulate speech: that your native language is the language of Shakespear and Milton and The Bible; and dont sit there crooning like a bilious pigeon.

THE FLOWER GIRL: [*Quite overwhelmed, looking up at him in mingled wonder and deprecation without daring to raise her head.*] Ah-ah-ah-ow-ow-ow-oo!

THE NOTE TAKER: [*Whipping out his book.*] Heavens! what a sound! [*He writes; then holds out the book and reads, reproducing her vowels exactly.*] Ah-ah-ah-ow-ow-ow-oo!

THE FLOWER GIRL: [*Tickled by the performance, and laughing in spite of herself.*] Garn!

THE NOTE TAKER: You see this creature with her kerbstone English: the English that will keep her in the gutter to the end of her days. Well, sir, in three months I could pass that girl off as a duchess at an ambassador's garden party. I could even get her a place as lady's maid or shop assistant, which requires better English.

THE FLOWER GIRL: Whats that you say?

THE NOTE TAKER: Yes, you squashed cabbage leaf, you disgrace to the noble

---

3. Worried and hounded.

architecture of these columns, you incarnate insult to the English language: I could pass you off as the Queen of Sheba. [*To the* GENTLEMAN.] Can you believe that?

THE GENTLEMAN: Of course I can. I am myself a student of Indian dialects; and—

THE NOTE TAKER: [*Eagerly.*] Are you? Do you know Colonel Pickering, the author of Spoken Sanscrit?

THE GENTLEMAN: I am Colonel Pickering. Who are you?

THE NOTE TAKER: Henry Higgins, author of Higgins's Universal Alphabet.

PICKERING: [*With enthusiasm.*] I came from India to meet you.

HIGGINS: I was going to India to meet you.

PICKERING: Where do you live?

HIGGINS: 27A Wimpole Street. Come and see me tomorrow.

PICKERING: I'm at the Carlton. Come with me now and lets have a jaw over some supper.

HIGGINS: Right you are.

THE FLOWER GIRL: [*To* PICKERING, *as he passes her.*] Buy a flower, kind gentleman. I'm short for my lodging.

PICKERING: I really havnt any change. I'm sorry. [*He goes away.*]

HIGGINS: [*Shocked at the* GIRL'*s mendacity.*] Liar. You said you could change half-a-crown.

THE FLOWER GIRL: [*Rising in desperation.*] You ought to be stuffed with nails, you ought. [*Flinging the basket at his feet.*] Take the whole blooming basket for sixpence.

[*The church clock strikes the second quarter.*]

HIGGINS: [*Hearing in it the voice of God, rebuking him for his Pharisaic want of charity to the poor* GIRL.] A reminder. [*He raises his hat solemnly; then throws a handful of money into the basket and follows* PICKERING.]

THE FLOWER GIRL: [*Picking up a half-crown.*] Ah-ow-ooh! [*Picking up a couple of florins.*[4]] Aaah-ow-ooh! [*Picking up several coins.*] Aaaaaah-ow-ooh! [*Picking up a half-sovereign.*[5]] Aaaaaaaaaaaah-ow-ooh!!!

FREDDY: [*Springing out of a taxicab.*] Got one at last. Hallo! [*To the* GIRL.] Where are the two ladies that were here?

THE FLOWER GIRL: They walked to the bus when the rain stopped.

FREDDY: And left me with a cab on my hands! Damnation!

THE FLOWER GIRL: [*With grandeur.*] Never mind, young man. I'm going home in a taxi. [*She sails off to the cab. The driver puts his hand behind him and holds the door firmly shut against her. Quite understanding his mistrust, she shews him her handful of money.*] A taxi fare aint no object to me, Charlie. [*He grins and opens the door.*] Here. What about the basket?

THE TAXIMAN: Give it here. Tuppence extra.

LIZA: No: I dont want nobody to see it. [*She crushes it into the cab and gets in, continuing the conversation through the window.*] Goodbye, Freddy.

FREDDY: [*Dazedly raising his hat.*] Goodbye.

TAXIMAN: Where to?

LIZA: Bucknam Pellis [Buckingham Palace].

---

4. Two shillings, loosely equivalent to 11 dollars in the United States today.
5. Ten shillings (half a pound), loosely equivalent to 55 dollars in the United States today.

TAXIMAN: What d'ye mean—Bucknam Pellis?
LIZA: Dont you know where it is? In the Green Park, where the King lives. Goodbye, Freddy. Dont let me keep you standing there. Goodbye.
FREDDY: Goodbye. [*He goes.*].
TAXIMAN: Here? Whats this about Bucknam Pellis? What business have you at Bucknam Pellis?
LIZA: Of course I havnt none. But I wasnt going to let him know that. You drive me home.
TAXIMAN: And wheres home?
LIZA: Angel Court, Drury Lane, next Meiklejohn's oil shop.
TAXIMAN: That sounds more like it, Judy. [*He drives off.*]

---

*Let us follow the taxi to the entrance to Angel Court, a narrow little archway between two shops, one of them Meiklejohn's oil shop. When it stops there, Eliza gets out, dragging her basket with her.*

LIZA: How much?
TAXIMAN: [*Indicating the taximeter.*] Cant you read? A shilling.
LIZA: A shilling for two minutes!!
TAXIMAN: Two minutes or ten: it's all the same.
LIZA: Well, I dont call it right.
TAXIMAN: Ever been in a taxi before?
LIZA: [*With dignity.*] Hundreds and thousands of times, young man.
TAXIMAN: [*Laughing at her.*] Good for you, Judy. Keep the shilling, darling, with best love from all at home. Good luck! [*He drives off.*]
LIZA: [*Humiliated.*] Impidence!

[*She picks up the basket and trudges up the alley with it to her lodging: a small room with very old wall paper hanging loose in the damp places. A broken pane in the window is mended with paper. A portrait of a popular actor and a fashion plate of ladies' dresses, all wildly beyond poor* ELIZA'*s means, both torn from newspapers, are pinned up on the wall. A birdcage hangs in the window; but its tenant died long ago: it remains as a memorial only.*

*These are the only visible luxuries: the rest is the irreducible minimum of poverty's needs: a wretched bed heaped with all sorts of coverings that have any warmth in them, a draped packing case with a basin and jug on it and a little looking glass over it, a chair and table, the refuse of some suburban kitchen, and an American alarum clock on the shelf above the unused fireplace: the whole lighted with a gas lamp with a penny in the slot meter. Rent: four shillings a week.*]

Here ELIZA, *chronically weary, but too excited to go to bed, sits, counting her new riches and dreaming and planning what to do with them, until the gas goes out, when she enjoys for the first time the sensation of being able to put in another penny without grudging it. This prodigal mood does not extinguish her gnawing sense of the need for economy sufficiently to prevent her from calculating that she can dream and plan in bed more cheaply and warmly than sitting up without a fire. So she takes off her shawl and skirt and adds them to the miscellaneous bedclothes. Then she kicks off her shoes and gets into bed without any further change.*

## ACT II

*Next day at 11 A.M. HIGGINS's laboratory in Wimpole Street. It is a room on the first floor, looking on the street, and was meant for the drawing room. The double doors are in the middle of the back wall; and persons entering find in the corner to their right two tall file cabinets at right angles to one another against the walls. In this corner stands a flat writing-table, on which are a phonograph, a laryngoscope, a row of tiny organ pipes with a bellows, a set of lamp chimneys for singing flames with burners attached to a gas plug in the wall by an indiarubber tube, several tuning-forks of different sizes, a life-size image of half a human head, shewing in section the vocal organs, and a box containing a supply of wax cylinders for the phonograph.*

*Further down the room, on the same side, is a fireplace, with a comfortable leather-covered easy-chair at the side of the hearth nearest the door, and a coal-scuttle. There is a clock on the mantel-piece. Between the fireplace and the phonograph table is a stand for newspapers.*

*On the other side of the central door, to the left of the visitor, is a cabinet of shallow drawers. On it is a telephone and the telephone directory. The corner beyond, and most of the side wall, is occupied by a grand piano, with the keyboard at the end furthest from the door, and a bench for the player extending the full length of the keyboard. On the piano is a dessert dish heaped with fruit and sweets, mostly chocolates.*

*The middle of the room is clear. Besides the easy-chair, the piano bench, and two chairs at the phonograph table, there is one stray chair. It stands near the fireplace. On the walls, engravings: mostly Piranesis[6] and mezzotint portraits. No paintings.*

*PICKERING is seated at the table, putting down some cards and a tuning-fork which he has been using. HIGGINS is standing up near him, closing two or three file drawers which are hanging out. He appears in the morning light as a robust, vital, appetizing sort of man of forty or thereabouts, dressed in a professional-looking black frock-coat with a white linen collar and black silk tie. He is of the energetic, scientific type, heartily, even violently interested in everything that can be studied as a scientific subject, and careless about himself and other people, including their feelings. He is, in fact, but for his years and size, rather like a very impetuous baby "taking notice" eagerly and loudly, and requiring almost as much watching to keep him out of unintended mischief. His manner varies from genial bullying when he is in a good humor to stormy petulance when anything goes wrong; but he is so entirely frank and void of malice that he remains likeable even in his least reasonable moments.*

HIGGINS: [*As he shuts the last drawer.*] Well, I think thats the whole show.
PICKERING: It's really amazing. I havnt taken half of it in, you know.
HIGGINS: Would you like to go over any of it again?
PICKERING: [*Rising and coming to the fireplace, where he plants himself with his back to the fire.*] No, thank you: not now. I'm quite done up for this morning.
HIGGINS: [*Following him, and standing beside him on his left.*] Tired of listening to sounds?
PICKERING: Yes. It's a fearful strain. I rather fancied myself because I can pro-

---

6. Giovanni Battista Piranesi (1720–1778), a neoclassical master of etching whose prints of Roman architecture helped stimulate eighteenth-century enthusiasm for the classical style.

nounce twenty-four distinct vowel sounds; but your hundred and thirty beat me. I cant hear a bit of difference between most of them.

HIGGINS: [*Chuckling, and going over to the piano to eat sweets.*] Oh, that comes with practice. You hear no difference at first; but you keep on listening, and presently you find theyre all as different as A from B. [MRS. PEARCE *looks in: she is* HIGGINS's *housekeeper.*] Whats the matter?

MRS. PEARCE: [*Hesitating, evidently perplexed.*] A young woman asks to see you, sir.

HIGGINS: A young woman! What does she want?

MRS. PEARCE: Well, sir, she says youll be glad to see her when you know what she's come about. She's quite a common girl, sir. Very common indeed. I should have sent her away, only I thought perhaps you wanted her to talk into your machines. I hope Ive not done wrong; but really you see such queer people sometimes—youll excuse me, I'm sure, sir—

HIGGINS: Oh, thats all right, Mrs. Pearce. Has she an interesting accent?

MRS. PEARCE: Oh, something dreadful, sir, really. I dont know how you can take an interest in it.

HIGGINS: [*To* PICKERING.] Lets have her up. Shew her up, Mrs. Pearce [*He rushes across to his working table and picks out a cylinder to use on the phonograph.*]

MRS. PEARCE: [*Only half resigned to it.*] Very well, sir. It's for you to say. [*She goes downstairs.*]

HIGGINS: This is rather a bit of luck. I'll shew you how I make records. We'll set her talking; and I'll take it down first in Bell's Visible Speech; then in broad Romic;[7] and then we'll get her on the phonograph so that you can turn her on as often as you like with the written transcript before you.

MRS. PEARCE: [*Returning.*] This is the young woman, sir.

[*The* FLOWER GIRL *enters in state. She has a hat with three ostrich feathers, orange, sky-blue, and red. She has a nearly clean apron, and the shoddy coat has been tidied a little. The pathos of this deplorable figure, with its innocent vanity and consequential air, touches* PICKERING, *who has already straightened himself in the presence of* MRS. PEARCE. *But as to* HIGGINS, *the only distinction he makes between men and women is that when he is neither bullying nor exclaiming to the heavens against some feather-weight cross, he coaxes women as a child coaxes its nurse when it wants to get anything out of her.*]

HIGGINS: [*Brusquely, recognizing her with unconcealed disappointment, and at once, babylike, making an intolerable grievance of it.*] Why, this is the girl I jotted down last night. She's no use: Ive got all the records I want of the Lisson Grove lingo; and I'm not going to waste another cylinder on it. [*To the* GIRL.] Be off with you: I dont want you.

THE FLOWER GIRL: Dont you be so saucy. You aint heard what I come for yet. [*To* MRS. PEARCE, *who is waiting at the door for further instructions.*] Did you tell him I come in a taxi?

MRS. PEARCE: Nonsense, girl! what do you think a gentleman like Mr. Higgins cares what you came in?

THE FLOWER GIRL: Oh, we are proud! He aint above giving lessons, not him: I heard him say so. Well, I aint come here to ask for any compliment; and if my money's not good enough I can go elsewhere.

---

7. A system of phonetic transcription devised by Dr. Henry Sweet.

HIGGINS: Good enough for what?
THE FLOWER GIRL: Good enough for y-oo. Now you know, dont you? I'm come to have lessons, I am. And to pay for em te-oo: make no mistake.
HIGGINS: [Stupent.][8] Well!!! [Recovering his breath with a gasp.] What do you expect me to say to you?
THE FLOWER GIRL: Well, if you was a gentleman, you might ask me to sit down, I think. Dont I tell you I'm bringing you business?
HIGGINS: Pickering: shall we ask this baggage to sit down, or shall we throw her out of the window?
THE FLOWER GIRL: [Running away in terror to the piano, where she turns at bay.] Ah-ah-oh-ow-ow-ow-oo! [Wounded and whimpering.] I wont be called a baggage when Ive offered to pay like any lady.

[Motionless, the TWO MEN stare at her from the other side of the room, amazed.]

PICKERING: [Gently.] But what is it you want?
THE FLOWER GIRL: I want to be a lady in a flower shop stead of sellin at the corner of Tottenham Court Road. But they wont take me unless I can talk more genteel. He said he could teach me. Well, here I am ready to pay him—not asking any favor—and he treats me zif I was dirt.
MRS. PEARCE: How can you be such a foolish ignorant girl as to think you could afford to pay Mr. Higgins?
THE FLOWER GIRL: Why shouldnt I? I know what lessons cost as well as you do; and I'm ready to pay.
HIGGINS: How much?
THE FLOWER GIRL: [Coming back to him, triumphant.] Now youre talking! I thought youd come off it when you saw a chance of getting back a bit of what you chucked at me last night. [Confidentially.] Youd had a drop in,[9] hadnt you?
HIGGINS: [Peremptorily.] Sit down.
THE FLOWER GIRL: Oh, if youre going to make a compliment of it—
HIGGINS: [Thundering at her.] Sit down.
MRS. PEARCE: [Severely.] Sit down, girl. Do as youre told.
THE FLOWER GIRL: Ah-ah-ah-ow-ow-oo! [She stands, half rebellious, half bewildered.]
PICKERING: [Very courteous.] Wont you sit down? [He places the stray chair near the hearthrug between himself and HIGGINS.]
LIZA: [Coyly.] Dont mind if I do. [She sits down. PICKERING returns to the hearthrug.]
HIGGINS: Whats your name?
THE FLOWER GIRL: Liza Doolittle.
HIGGINS: [Declaiming gravely.]

    Eliza, Elizabeth, Betsy and Bess,
    They went to the woods to get a bird's nes':

PICKERING: They found a nest with four eggs in it:
HIGGINS: They took one apiece, and left three in it.

[They laugh heartily at their own fun.]

LIZA: Oh, dont be silly.

---

8. In a state of stupor or amazement.   9. That is, You'd had something to drink.

MRS. PEARCE: [*Placing herself behind* ELIZA's *chair.*] You mustnt speak to the gentleman like that.

LIZA: Well, why wont he speak sensible to me?

HIGGINS: Come back to business. How much do you propose to pay me for the lessons?

LIZA: Oh, I know whats right. A lady friend of mine gets French lessons for eighteenpence an hour from a real French gentleman. Well, you wouldnt have the face to ask me the same for teaching me my own language as you would for French; so I wont give more than a shilling. Take it or leave it.

HIGGINS: [*Walking up and down the room, rattling his keys and his cash in his pockets.*] You know, Pickering, if you consider a shilling, not as a simple shilling, but as a percentage of this girl's income, it works out as fully equivalent to sixty or seventy guineas from a millionaire.

PICKERING: How so?

HIGGINS: Figure it out. A millionaire has about £150 a day. She earns about half-a-crown.

LIZA: [*Haughtily.*] Who told you I only—

HIGGINS: [*Continuing.*] She offers me two-fifths of her day's income for a lesson. Two-fifths of a millionaire's income for a day would be somewhere about £60. It's handsome. By George, it's enormous! it's the biggest offer I ever had.

LIZA: [*Rising, terrified.*] Sixty pounds! What are you talking about? I never offered you sixty pounds. Where would I get—

HIGGINS: Hold your tongue.

LIZA: [*Weeping.*] But I aint got sixty pounds. Oh—

MRS. PEARCE: Dont cry, you silly girl. Sit down. Nobody is going to touch your money.

HIGGINS: Somebody is going to touch you, with a broomstick, if you dont stop snivelling. Sit down.

LIZA: [*Obeying slowly.*] Ah-ah-ah-ow-oo-o! One would think you was my father.

HIGGINS: If I decide to teach you, I'll be worse than two fathers to you. Here! [*He offers her his silk handkerchief.*]

LIZA: Whats this for?

HIGGINS: To wipe your eyes. To wipe any part of your face that feels moist. Remember: thats your handkerchief; and thats your sleeve. Dont mistake the one for the other if you wish to become a lady in a shop.

[LIZA, *utterly bewildered, stares helplessly at him.*]

MRS. PEARCE: It's no use talking to her like that, Mr. Higgins: she doesnt understand you. Besides, youre quite wrong: she doesnt do it that way at all. [*She takes the handkerchief.*]

LIZA: [*Snatching it.*] Here! You give me that handkerchief. He gev it to me, not to you.

PICKERING: [*Laughing.*] He did. I think it must be regarded as her property, Mrs. Pearce.

MRS. PEARCE: [*Resigning herself.*] Serve you right, Mr. Higgins.

PICKERING: Higgins: I'm interested. What about the ambassador's garden party? I'll say youre the greatest teacher alive if you make that good. I'll bet you all the expenses of the experiment you cant do it. And I'll pay for the lessons.

LIZA: Oh, you are real good. Thank you, Captain.

HIGGINS: [*Tempted, looking at her.*] It's almost irresistible. She's so deliciously low—so horribly dirty—

LIZA: [*Protesting extremely.*] Ah-ah-ah-ah-ow-ow-oo-oo!!! I aint dirty: I washed my face and hands afore I come, I did.

PICKERING: Youre certainly not going to turn her head with flattery, Higgins.

MRS. PEARCE: [*Uneasy.*] Oh, dont say that, sir: theres more ways than one of turning a girl's head; and nobody can do it better than Mr. Higgins, though he may not always mean it. I do hope, sir, you wont encourage him to do anything foolish.

HIGGINS: [*Becoming excited as the idea grows on him.*] What is life but a series of inspired follies? The difficulty is to find them to do. Never lose a chance: it doesnt come every day. I shall make a duchess of this draggletailed guttersnipe.

LIZA: [*Strongly deprecating this view of her.*] Ah-ah-ah-ow-ow-oo!

HIGGINS: [*Carried away.*] Yes: in six months—in three if she has a good ear and a quick tongue—I'll take her anywhere and pass her off as anything. We'll start today: now! this moment! Take her away and clean her, Mrs. Pearce. Monkey Brand,[1] if it wont come off any other way. Is there a good fire in the kitchen?

MRS. PEARCE: [*Protesting.*] Yes; but—

HIGGINS: [*Storming on.*] Take all her clothes off and burn them. Ring up Whiteley or somebody for new ones. Wrap her up in brown paper til they come.

LIZA: Youre no gentleman, youre not, to talk of such things. I'm a good girl, I am; and I know what the like of you are, I do.

HIGGINS: We want none of your Lisson Grove prudery here, young woman. Youve got to learn to behave like a duchess. Take her away, Mrs. Pearce. If she gives you any trouble, wallop her.

LIZA: [*Springing up and running between* PICKERING *and* MRS. PEARCE *for protection.*] No! I'll call the police, I will.

MRS. PEARCE: But Ive no place to put her.

HIGGINS: Put her in the dustbin.

LIZA: Ah-ah-ah-ow-ow-oo!

PICKERING: Oh come, Higgins! be reasonable.

MRS. PEARCE: [*Resolutely.*] You must be reasonable, Mr. Higgins: really you must. You cant walk over everybody like this.

[HIGGINS, *thus scolded, subsides. The hurricane is succeeded by a zephyr of amiable surprise.*]

HIGGINS: [*With professional exquisiteness of modulation.*] I walk over everybody! My dear Mrs. Pearce, my dear Pickering, I never had the slightest intention of walking over anyone. All I propose is that we should be kind to this poor girl. We must help her to prepare and fit herself for her new station in life. If I did not express myself clearly it was because I did not wish to hurt her delicacy, or yours.

[LIZA, *reassured, steals back to her chair.*]

MRS. PEARCE: [*To* PICKERING.] Well, did you ever hear anything like that, sir?

PICKERING: [*Laughing heartily.*] Never, Mrs. Pearce: never.

---

1. A brand of harsh soap.

HIGGINS: [*Patiently.*] Whats the matter?
MRS. PEARCE: Well, the matter is, sir, that you cant take a girl up like that as if you were picking up a pebble on the beach.
HIGGINS: Why not?
MRS. PEARCE: Why not! But you dont know anything about her. What about her parents? She may be married.
LIZA: Garn!
HIGGINS: There! As the girl very properly says, Garn! Married indeed! Dont you know that a woman of that class looks a worn out drudge of fifty a year after she's married?
LIZA: Whood marry me?
HIGGINS: [*Suddenly resorting to the most thrillingly beautiful low tones in his best elocutionary style.*] By George, Eliza, the streets will be strewn with the bodies of men shooting themselves for your sake before Ive done with you.
MRS. PEARCE: Nonsense, sir. You mustnt talk like that to her.
LIZA: [*Rising and squaring herself determinedly.*] I'm going away. He's off his chump,[2] he is. I dont want no balmies teaching me.
HIGGINS: [*Wounded in his tenderest point by her insensibility to his elocution.*] Oh, indeed! I'm mad, am I? Very well, Mrs. Pearce: you neednt order the new clothes for her. Throw her out.
LIZA: [*Whimpering.*] Nah-ow. You got no right to touch me.
MRS. PEARCE: You see now what comes of being saucy. [*Indicating the door.*] This way, please.
LIZA: [*Almost in tears.*] I didnt want no clothes. I wouldnt have taken them. [*She throws away the handkerchief.*] I can buy my own clothes.
HIGGINS: [*Deftly retrieving the handkerchief and intercepting her on her reluctant way to the door.*] Youre an ungrateful wicked girl. This is my return for offering to take you out of the gutter and dress you beautifully and make a lady of you.
MRS. PEARCE: Stop, Mr. Higgins. I wont allow it. It's you that are wicked. Go home to your parents, girl; and tell them to take better care of you.
LIZA: I aint got no parents. They told me I was big enough to earn my own living and turned me out.
MRS. PEARCE: Wheres your mother?
LIZA: I aint got no mother. Her that turned me out was my sixth stepmother. But I done without them. And I'm a good girl, I am.
HIGGINS: Very well, then, what on earth is all this fuss about? The girl doesnt belong to anybody—is no use of anybody but me. [*He goes to* MRS. PEARCE *and begins coaxing.*] You can adopt her, Mrs. Pearce: I'm sure a daughter would be a great amusement to you. Now dont make any more fuss. Take her downstairs; and—
MRS. PEARCE: But whats to become of her? Is she to be paid anything? Do be sensible, sir.
HIGGINS: Oh, pay her whatever is necessary: put it down in the housekeeping book. [*Impatiently.*] What on earth will she want with money? She'll have her food and her clothes. She'll only drink if you give her money.
LIZA: [*Turning on him.*] Oh you are a brute. It's a lie: nobody ever saw the sign of

---

2. That is, He's crazy. *Balmies:* crazy people.

liquor on me. [*To* PICKERING.] Oh, sir: youre a gentleman: dont let him speak to me like that.

PICKERING: [*In good-humored remonstrance.*] Does it occur to you, Higgins, that the girl has some feelings?

HIGGINS: [*Looking critically at her.*] Oh no, I dont think so. Not any feelings that we need bother about. [*Cheerily.*] Have you, Eliza?

LIZA: I got my feelings same as anyone else.

HIGGINS: [*To* PICKERING, *reflectively.*] You see the difficulty?

PICKERING: Eh? What difficulty?

HIGGINS: To get her to talk grammar. The mere pronunciation is easy enough.

LIZA: I dont want to talk grammar. I want to talk like a lady in a flower-shop.

MRS. PEARCE: Will you please keep to the point, Mr. Higgins. I want to know on what terms the girl is to be here. Is she to have any wages? And what is to become of her when youve finished your teaching? You must look ahead a little.

HIGGINS: [*Impatiently.*] Whats to become of her if I leave her in the gutter? Tell me that, Mrs. Pearce.

MRS. PEARCE: Thats her own business, not yours, Mr. Higgins.

HIGGINS: Well, when Ive done with her, we can throw her back into the gutter; and then it will be her own business again; so thats all right.

LIZA: Oh, youve no feeling heart in you: you dont care for nothing but yourself. [*She rises and takes the floor resolutely.*] Here! Ive had enough of this. I'm going. [*Making for the door.*] You ought to be ashamed of yourself, you ought.

HIGGINS: [*Snatching a chocolate cream from the piano, his eyes suddenly beginning to twinkle with mischief.*] Have some chocolates, Eliza.

LIZA: [*Halting, tempted.*] How do I know what might be in them? Ive heard of girls being drugged by the like of you.

[HIGGINS *whips out his penknife; cuts a chocolate in two; puts one half into his mouth and bolts it; and offers her the other half.*]

HIGGINS: Pledge of good faith, Eliza. I eat one half: you eat the other. [LIZA *opens her mouth to retort: he pops the half chocolate into it.*] You shall have boxes of them, barrels of them, every day. You shall live on them. Eh?

LIZA: [*Who has disposed of the chocolate after being nearly choked by it.*] I wouldnt have ate it, only I'm too ladylike to take it out of my mouth.

HIGGINS: Listen, Eliza. I think you said you came in a taxi.

LIZA: Well, what if I did? Ive as good a right to take a taxi as anyone else.

HIGGINS: You have, Eliza; and in future you shall have as many taxis as you want. You shall go up and down and round the town in a taxi every day. Think of that, Eliza.

MRS. PEARCE: Mr. Higgins: youre tempting the girl. It's not right. She should think of the future.

HIGGINS: At her age! Nonsense! Time enough to think of the future when you havnt any future to think of. No, Eliza: do as this lady does: think of other people's futures; but never think of your own. Think of chocolates, and taxis, and gold, and diamonds.

LIZA: No: I dont want no gold and no diamonds. I'm a good girl, I am. [*She sits down again, with an attempt at dignity.*]

HIGGINS: You shall remain so, Eliza, under the care of Mrs. Pearce. And you shall marry an officer in the Guards, with a beautiful moustache: the son of a marquis, who will disinherit him for marrying you, but will relent when he sees your beauty and goodness—

PICKERING: Excuse me, Higgins; but I really must interfere. Mrs. Pearce is quite right. If this girl is to put herself in your hands for six months for an experiment in teaching, she must understand thoroughly what she's doing.

HIGGINS: How can she? She's incapable of understanding anything. Besides, do any of us understand what we are doing? If we did, would we ever do it?

PICKERING: Very clever, Higgins; but not to the present point. [*To* ELIZA.] Miss Doolittle—

LIZA: [*Overwhelmed.*] Ah-ah-ow-oo!

HIGGINS: There! Thats all youll get out of Eliza. Ah-ah-ow-oo! No use explaining. As a military man you ought to know that. Give her her orders: thats enough for her. Eliza: you are to live here for the next six months, learning how to speak beautifully, like a lady in a florist's shop. If youre good and do whatever youre told, you shall sleep in a proper bedroom, and have lots to eat, and money to buy chocolates and take rides in taxis. If youre naughty and idle you will sleep in the back kitchen among the black beetles, and be walloped by Mrs. Pearce with a broomstick. At the end of six months you shall go to Buckingham Palace in a carriage, beautifully dressed. If the King finds out youre not a lady, you will be taken by the police to the Tower of London, where your head will be cut off as a warning to other presumptuous flower girls. If you are not found out, you shall have a present of seven-and-sixpence to start life with as a lady in a shop. If you refuse this offer you will be a most ungrateful wicked girl; and the angels will weep for you. [*To* PICKERING.] Now are you satisfied, Pickering? [*To* MRS. PEARCE.] Can I put it more plainly and fairly, Mrs. Pearce?

MRS. PEARCE: [*Patiently.*] I think youd better let me speak to the girl properly in private. I dont know that I can take charge of her or consent to the arrangement at all. Of course I know you dont mean her any harm; but when you get what you call interested in people's accents, you never think or care what may happen to them or you. Come with me, Eliza.

HIGGINS: Thats all right. Thank you, Mrs. Pearce. Bundle her off to the bathroom.

LIZA: [*Rising reluctantly and suspiciously.*] Youre a great bully, you are. I wont stay here if I dont like. I wont let nobody wallop me. I never asked to go to Bucknam Palace, I didnt. I was never in trouble with the police, not me. I'm a good girl—

MRS. PEARCE: Dont answer back, girl. You dont understand the gentleman. Come with me. [*She leads the way to the door, and holds it open for* ELIZA.]

LIZA: [*As she goes out.*] Well, what I say is right. I wont go near the King, not if I'm going to have my head cut off. If I'd known what I was letting myself in for, I wouldnt have come here. I always been a good girl; and I never offered to say a word to him; and I dont owe him nothing; and I dont care; and I wont be put upon; and I have my feelings the same as anyone else—

[MRS. PEARCE *shuts the door; and* ELIZA'*s plaints are no longer audible.*]

ELIZA *is taken upstairs to the third floor greatly to her surprise; for she expected to be taken down to the scullery. There* MRS. PEARCE *opens a door and takes her into a spare bedroom.*

MRS. PEARCE: I will have to put you here. This will be your bedroom.
LIZA: O-h, I couldnt sleep here, missus. It's too good for the likes of me. I should be afraid to touch anything. I aint a duchess yet, you know.
MRS. PEARCE: You have got to make yourself as clean as the room: then you wont be afraid of it. And you must call me Mrs. Pearce, not missus. [*She throws open the door of the dressingroom, now modernized as a bathroom.*]
LIZA: Gawd! whats this? Is this where you wash clothes? Funny sort of copper I call it.
MRS. PEARCE: It is not a copper. This is where we wash ourselves, Eliza, and where I am going to wash you.
LIZA: You expect me to get into that and wet myself all over! Not me. I should catch my death. I knew a woman did it every Saturday night; and she died of it.
MRS. PEARCE: Mr. Higgins has the gentlemen's bathroom downstairs; and he has a bath every morning, in cold water.
LIZA: Ugh! He's made of iron, that man.
MRS. PEARCE: If you are to sit with him and the Colonel and be taught you will have to do the same. They wont like the smell of you if you dont. But you can have the water as hot as you like. There are two taps: hot and cold.
LIZA: [*Weeping.*] I couldnt. I dursnt. It's not natural: it would kill me. Ive never had a bath in my life: not what youd call a proper one.
MRS. PEARCE: Well, dont you want to be clean and sweet and decent, like a lady? You know you can't be a nice girl inside if youre a dirty slut outside.
LIZA: Boohoo!!!!
MRS. PEARCE: Now stop crying and go back into your room and take off all your clothes. Then wrap yourself in this [*Taking down a gown from its peg and handing it to her.*] and come back to me. I will get the bath ready.
LIZA: [*All tears.*] I cant. I wont. I'm not used to it. Ive never took off all my clothes before. It's not right: it's not decent.
MRS. PEARCE: Nonsense, child. Dont you take off all your clothes every night when you go to bed?
LIZA: [*Amazed.*] No. Why should I? I should catch my death. Of course I take off my skirt.
MRS. PEARCE: Do you mean that you sleep in the underclothes you wear in the daytime?
LIZA: What else have I to sleep in?
MRS. PEARCE: You will never do that again as long as you live here. I will get you a proper nightdress.
LIZA: Do you mean change into cold things and lie awake shivering half the night? You want to kill me, you do.
MRS. PEARCE: I want to change you from a frowzy slut to a clean respectable girl fit to sit with the gentlemen in the study. Are you going to trust me and do what I tell you or be thrown out and sent back to your flower basket?
LIZA: But you dont know what the cold is to me. You dont know how I dread it.

MRS. PEARCE: Your bed wont be cold here: I will put a hot water bottle in it. [*Pushing her into the bedroom.*] Off with you and undress.

LIZA: Oh, if only I'd a known what a dreadful thing it is to be clean I'd never have come. I didnt know when I was well off. I—[MRS. PEARCE *pushes her through the door, but leaves it partly open lest her prisoner should take to flight.*]

> [MRS. PEARCE *puts on a pair of white rubber sleeves, and fills the bath, mixing hot and cold, and testing the result with the bath thermometer. She perfumes it with a handful of bath salts and adds a palmful of mustard. She then takes a formidable looking long handled scrubbing brush and soaps it profusely with a ball of scented soap.*
> 
> ELIZA *comes back with nothing on but the bath gown huddled tightly round her, a piteous spectacle of abject terror.*]

MRS. PEARCE: Now come along. Take that thing off.

LIZA: Oh I couldnt, Mrs. Pearce: I reely couldnt. I never done such a thing.

MRS. PEARCE: Nonsense. Here: step in and tell me whether it's hot enough for you.

LIZA: Ah-oo! Ah-oo! It's too hot.

MRS. PEARCE: [*Deftly snatching the gown away and throwing* ELIZA *down on her back.*] It wont hurt you. [*She sets to work with the scrubbing brush.*]

> [ELIZA's *screams are heartrending.*]

---

Meanwhile the COLONEL has been having it out with HIGGINS about ELIZA. PICKERING *has come from the hearth to the chair and seated himself astride of it with his arms on the back to cross-examine him.*

PICKERING: Excuse the straight question, Higgins. Are you a man of good character where women are concerned?

HIGGINS: [*Moodily.*] Have you ever met a man of good character where women are concerned?

PICKERING: Yes: very frequently.

HIGGINS: [*Dogmatically, lifting himself on his hands to the level of the piano, and sitting on it with a bounce.*] Well, I havnt. I find that the moment I let a woman make friends with me, she becomes jealous, exacting, suspicious, and a damned nuisance. I find that the moment I let myself make friends with a woman, I become selfish and tyrannical. Women upset everything. When you let them into your life, you find that the woman is driving at one thing and youre driving at another.

PICKERING: At what, for example?

HIGGINS: [*Coming off the piano restlessly.*] Oh, Lord knows! I suppose the woman wants to live her own life; and the man wants to live his; and each tries to drag the other on to the wrong tack. One wants to go north and the other south; and the result is that both have to go east, though they both hate the east wind. [*He sits down on the bench at the keyboard.*] So here I am, a confirmed old bachelor, and likely to remain so.

PICKERING: [*Rising and standing over him gravely.*] Come, Higgins! You know what I mean. If I'm to be in this business I shall feel responsible for that girl. I hope it's understood that no advantage is to be taken of her position.

HIGGINS: What! That thing! Sacred, I assure you. [*Rising to explain.*] You see, she'll be a pupil; and teaching would be impossible unless pupils were sacred. Ive taught scores of American millionairesses how to speak English: the best looking women in the world. I'm seasoned. They might as well be blocks of wood. *I* might as well be a block of wood. It's—

[MRS. PEARCE *opens the door. She has* ELIZA's *hat in her hand.* PICKERING *retires to the easy-chair at the hearth and sits down.*]

HIGGINS: [*Eagerly.*] Well, Mrs. Pearce: is it all right?

MRS. PEARCE: [*At the door.*] I just wish to trouble you with a word, if I may, Mr. Higgins.

HIGGINS: Yes, certainly. Come in. [*She comes forward.*] Dont burn that, Mrs. Pearce. I'll keep it as a curiosity. [*He takes the hat.*]

MRS. PEARCE: Handle it carefully, sir, please. I had to promise her not to burn it; but I had better put it in the oven for a while.

HIGGINS: [*Putting it down hastily on the piano.*] Oh! thank you. Well, what have you to say to me?

PICKERING: Am I in the way?

MRS. PEARCE: Not at all, sir. Mr. Higgins: will you please be very particular what you say before the girl?

HIGGINS: [*Sternly.*] Of course. I'm always particular about what I say. Why do you say this to me?

MRS. PEARCE: [*Unmoved.*] No, sir: youre not at all particular when youve mislaid anything or when you get a little impatient. Now it doesnt matter before me: I'm used to it. But you really must not swear before the girl.

HIGGINS: [*Indignantly.*] I swear! [*Most emphatically.*] I never swear. I detest the habit. What the devil do you mean?

MRS. PEARCE: [*Stolidly.*] Thats what I mean, sir. You swear a great deal too much. I dont mind your damning and blasting, and what the devil and where the devil and who the devil—

HIGGINS: Mrs. Pearce: this language from your lips! Really!

MRS. PEARCE: [*Not to be put off.*]—but there is a certain word I must ask you not to use.[3] The girl used it herself when she began to enjoy the bath. It begins with the same letter as bath. She knows no better: she learnt it at her mother's knee. But she must not hear it from your lips.

HIGGINS: [*Loftily.*] I cannot charge myself with having ever uttered it, Mrs. Pearce. [*She looks at him steadfastly. He adds, hiding an uneasy conscience with a judicial air.*] Except perhaps in a moment of extreme and justifiable excitement.

MRS. PEARCE: Only this morning, sir, you applied it to your boots, to the butter, and to the brown bread.

HIGGINS: Oh, that! Mere alliteration, Mrs. Pearce, natural to a poet.

MRS. PEARCE: Well, sir, whatever you choose to call it, I beg you not to let the girl hear you repeat it.

HIGGINS: Oh, very well, very well. Is that all?

---

3. The word is "bloody," which, when used as an expletive, derives from "by His (God's) body" and was considered very vulgar.

MRS. PEARCE: No, sir. We shall have to be very particular with this girl as to personal cleanliness.

HIGGINS: Certainly. Quite right. Most important.

MRS. PEARCE: I mean not to be slovenly about her dress or untidy in leaving things about.

HIGGINS: [*Going to her solemnly.*] Just so. I intended to call your attention to that. [*He passes on to* PICKERING, *who is enjoying the conversation immensely.*] It is these little things that matter, Pickering. Take care of the pence and the pounds will take care of themselves is as true of personal habits as of money. [*He comes to anchor on the hearthrug, with the air of a man in an unassailable position.*]

MRS. PEARCE: Yes, sir. Then might I ask you not to come down to breakfast in your dressing-gown, or at any rate not to use it as a napkin to the extent you do, sir. And if you would be so good as not to eat everything off the same plate, and to remember not to put the porridge saucepan out of your hand on the clean tablecloth, it would be a better example to the girl. You know you nearly choked yourself with a fishbone in the jam only last week.

HIGGINS: [*Routed from the hearthrug and drifting back to the piano.*] I may do these things sometimes in absence of mind; but surely I dont do them habitually. [*Angrily.*] By the way: my dressing-gown smells most damnably of benzine.

MRS. PEARCE: No doubt it does, Mr. Higgins. But if you will wipe your fingers—

HIGGINS: [*Yelling.*] Oh very well, very well: I'll wipe them in my hair in future.

MRS. PEARCE: I hope youre not offended, Mr. Higgins.

HIGGINS: [*Shocked at finding himself thought capable of an unamiable sentiment.*] Not at all, not at all. Youre quite right, Mrs. Pearce: I shall be particularly careful before the girl. Is that all?

MRS. PEARCE: No, sir. Might she use some of those Japanese dresses you brought from abroad? I really cant put her back into her old things.

HIGGINS: Certainly. Anything you like. Is that all?

MRS. PEARCE: Thank you, sir. Thats all. [*She goes out.*]

HIGGINS: You know, Pickering, that woman has the most extraordinary ideas about me. Here I am, a shy, diffident sort of man. Ive never been able to feel really grown-up and tremendous, like other chaps. And yet she's firmly persuaded that I'm an arbitrary overbearing bossing kind of person. I cant account for it.

[MRS. PEARCE *returns.*]

MRS. PEARCE: If you please, sir, the trouble's beginning already. Theres a dustman[4] downstairs, Alfred Doolittle, wants to see you. He says you have his daughter here.

PICKERING: [*Rising.*] Phew! I say!

HIGGINS: [*Promptly.*] Send the blackguard up.

MRS. PEARCE: Oh, very well, sir. [*She goes out.*]

PICKERING: He may not be a blackguard, Higgins.

HIGGINS: Nonsense. Of course he's a blackguard.

PICKERING: Whether he is or not, I'm afraid we shall have some trouble with him.

HIGGINS: [*Confidently.*] Oh no: I think not. If theres any trouble he shall have it

---

4. Trash hauler.

with me, not I with him. And we are sure to get something interesting out of him.
PICKERING: About the girl?
HIGGINS: No. I mean his dialect.
PICKERING: Oh!
MRS. PEARCE: [*At the door.*] Doolittle, sir. [*She admits* DOOLITTLE *and retires.*]

[ALFRED DOOLITTLE *is an elderly but vigorous dustman, clad in the costume of his profession, including a hat with a back brim covering his neck and shoulders. He has well marked and rather interesting features, and seems equally free from fear and conscience. He has a remarkably expressive voice, the result of a habit of giving vent to his feelings without reserve. His present pose is that of wounded honor and stern resolution.*]

DOOLITTLE: [*At the door, uncertain which of the two gentlemen is his man.*] Professor Iggins?
HIGGINS: Here. Good morning. Sit down.
DOOLITTLE: Morning, Governor. [*He sits down magisterially.*] I come about a very serious matter, Governor.
HIGGINS: [*To* PICKERING.] Brought up in Hounslow. Mother Welsh, I should think. [DOOLITTLE *opens his mouth, amazed.* HIGGINS *continues.*] What do you want, Doolittle?
DOOLITTLE: [*Menacingly.*] I want my daughter: thats what I want. See?
HIGGINS: Of course you do. Youre her father, arnt you? You dont suppose anyone else wants her, do you? I'm glad to see you have some spark of family feeling left. She's upstairs. Take her away at once.
DOOLITTLE: [*Rising, fearfully taken aback.*] What!
HIGGINS: Take her away. Do you suppose I'm going to keep your daughter for you?
DOOLITTLE: [*Remonstrating.*] Now, now, look here, Governor. Is this reasonable? Is it fairity to take advantage of a man like this? The girl belongs to me. You got her. Where do I come in? [*He sits down again.*]
HIGGINS: Your daughter had the audacity to come to my house and ask me to teach her how to speak properly so that she could get a place in a flower-shop. This gentleman and my housekeeper have been here all the time. [*Bullying him.*] How dare you come here and attempt to blackmail me? You sent her here on purpose.
DOOLITTLE: [*Protesting.*] No, Governor.
HIGGINS: You must have. How else could you possibly know that she is here?
DOOLITTLE: Dont take a man up like that, Governor.
HIGGINS: The police shall take you up. This is a plant—a plot to extort money by threats. I shall telephone for the police. [*He goes resolutely to the telephone and opens the directory.*]
DOOLITTLE: Have I asked you for a brass farthing? I leave it to the gentleman here: have I said a word about money?
HIGGINS: [*Throwing the book aside and marching down on* DOOLITTLE *with a poser.*] What else did you come for?
DOOLITTLE: [*Sweetly.*] Well, what would a man come for? Be human, Governor.
HIGGINS: [*Disarmed.*] Alfred: did you put her up to it?
DOOLITTLE: So help me, Governor, I never did. I take my Bible oath I aint seen the girl these two months past.

HIGGINS: Then how did you know she was here?

DOOLITTLE: [*"Most musical, most melancholy."*] I'll tell you, Governor, if youll only let me get a word in. I'm willing to tell you. I'm wanting to tell you. I'm waiting to tell you.

HIGGINS: Pickering: this chap has a certain natural gift of rhetoric. Observe the rhythm of his native woodnotes wild.[5] "I'm willing to tell you: I'm wanting to tell you: I'm waiting to tell you." Sentimental rhetoric! thats the Welsh strain in him. It also accounts for his mendacity and dishonesty.

PICKERING: Oh, please, Higgins: I'm west country[6] myself. [*To* DOOLITTLE.] How did you know the girl was here if you didnt send her?

DOOLITTLE: It was like this, Governor. The girl took a boy in the taxi to give him a jaunt. Son of her landlady, he is. He hung about on the chance of her giving him another ride home. Well, she sent him back for her luggage when she heard you was willing for her to stop here. I met the boy at the corner of Long Acre and Endell Street.

HIGGINS: Public house.[7] Yes?

DOOLITTLE: The poor man's club, Governor: why shouldnt I?

PICKERING: Do let him tell his story, Higgins.

DOOLITTLE: He told me what was up. And I ask you, what was my feelings and my duty as a father? I says to the boy, "You bring me the luggage," I says—

PICKERING: Why didnt you go for it yourself?

DOOLITTLE: Landlady wouldnt have trusted me with it, Governor. She's that kind of woman: you know. I had to give the boy a penny afore he trusted me with it, the little swine. I brought it to her just to oblige you like, and make myself agreeable. Thats all.

HIGGINS: How much luggage?

DOOLITTLE: Musical instrument, Governor. A few pictures, a trifle of jewelry, and a bird-cage. She said she didnt want no clothes. What was I to think from that, Governor? I ask you as a parent what was I to think?

HIGGINS: So you came to rescue her from worse than death, eh?

DOOLITTLE: [*Appreciatively: relieved at being so well understood.*] Just so, Governor. Thats right.

PICKERING: But why did you bring her luggage if you intended to take her away?

DOOLITTLE: Have I said a word about taking her away? Have I now?

HIGGINS: [*Determinedly.*] Youre going to take her away, double quick. [*He crosses to the hearth and rings the bell.*]

DOOLITTLE: [*Rising.*] No, Governor. Dont say that. I'm not the man to stand in my girl's light. Heres a career opening for her, as you might say; and—

[MRS. PEARCE *opens the door and awaits orders.*]

HIGGINS: Mrs. Pearce: this is Eliza's father. He has come to take her away. Give her to him. [*He goes back to the piano, with an air of washing his hands of the whole affair.*]

---

5. Higgins quotes the poem "L'Allegro" by John Milton (1608-1674): "... sweetest Shakespeare, fancy's darling child, / Warbled for me his native woodnotes wild."
6. Wales is in western Britain; "West Country" usually refers to southwestern England—Cornwall, Devon, Dorset, and Somerset.   7. That is, pub or alehouse.

DOOLITTLE: No. This is a misunderstanding. Listen here—
MRS. PEARCE: He cant take her away, Mr. Higgins: how can he? You told me to burn her clothes.
DOOLITTLE: Thats right. I cant carry the girl through the streets like a blooming monkey, can I? I put it to you.
HIGGINS: You have put it to me that you want your daughter. Take your daughter. If she has no clothes go out and buy her some.
DOOLITTLE: [*Desperate.*] Wheres the clothes she come in? Did I burn them or did your missus here?
MRS. PEARCE: I am the housekeeper, if you please. I have sent for some clothes for your girl. When they come you can take her away. You can wait in the kitchen. This way, please.

[DOOLITTLE, *much troubled, accompanies her to the door; then hesitates; finally turns confidentially to* HIGGINS.]

DOOLITTLE: Listen here, Governor. You and me is men of the world aint we?
HIGGINS: Oh! Men of the world, are we? Youd better go, Mrs. Pearce.
MRS. PEARCE: I think so, indeed, sir. [*She goes, with dignity.*]
PICKERING: The floor is yours, Mr. Doolittle.
DOOLITTLE: [*To* PICKERING] I thank you, Governor. [*To* HIGGINS, *who takes refuge on the piano bench, a little overwhelmed by the proximity of his visitor; for* DOOLITTLE *has a professional flavour of dust about him.*] Well, the truth is, Ive taken a sort of fancy to you, Governor; and if you want the girl, I'm not so set on having her back home again but what I might be open to an arrangement. Regarded in the light of a young woman, she's a fine handsome girl. As a daughter she's not worth her keep; and so I tell you straight. All I ask is my rights as a father; and youre the last man alive to expect me to let her go for nothing; for I can see youre one of the straight sort, Governor. Well, whats a five-pound note to you? and whats Eliza to me? [*He turns to his chair and sits down judicially.*]
PICKERING: I think you ought to know, Doolittle, that Mr. Higgins's intentions are entirely honorable.
DOOLITTLE: Course they are, Governor. If I thought they wasn't, I'd ask fifty.
HIGGINS: [*Revolted.*] Do you mean to say that you would sell your daughter for £50?
DOOLITTLE: Not in a general way I wouldnt; but to oblige a gentleman like you I'd do a good deal, I do assure you.
PICKERING: Have you no morals, man?
DOOLITTLE: [*Unabashed.*] Cant afford them, Governor. Neither could you if you was as poor as me. Not that I mean any harm, you know. But if Liza is going to have a bit out of this, why not me too?
HIGGINS: [*Troubled.*] I dont know what to do, Pickering. There can be no question that as a matter of morals it's a positive crime to give this chap a farthing. And yet I feel a sort of rough justice in his claim.
DOOLITTLE: Thats it, Governor. Thats all I say. A father's heart, as it were.
PICKERING: Well, I know the feeling; but really it seems hardly right—
DOOLITTLE: Dont say that, Governor. Dont look at it that way. What am I, Governors both? I ask you, what am I? I'm one of the undeserving poor: thats what I am. Think of what that means to a man. It means that he's up agen middle class morality all the time. If theres anything going, and I put in for

a bit of it, it's always the same story: "Youre undeserving; so you cant have it." But my needs is as great as the most deserving widow's that ever got money out of six different charities in one week for the death of the same husband. I dont need less than a deserving man: I need more. I dont eat less hearty than him; and I drink a lot more. I want a bit of amusement, cause I'm a thinking man. I want cheerfulness and a song and a band when I feel low. Well, they charge me just the same for everything as they charge the deserving. What is middle class morality? Just an excuse for never giving me anything. Therefore, I ask you, as two gentlemen, not to play that game on me. I'm playing straight with you. I aint pretending to be deserving. I'm undeserving; and I mean to go on being undeserving. I like it; and thats the truth. Will you take advantage of a man's nature to do him out of the price of his own daughter what he's brought up and fed and clothed by the sweat of his brow until she's growed big enough to be interesting to you two gentlemen? Is five pounds unreasonable? I put it to you; and I leave it to you.

HIGGINS: [*Rising, and going over to* PICKERING.] Pickering: if we were to take this man in hand for three months, he could choose between a seat in the Cabinet and a popular pulpit in Wales.

PICKERING: What do you say to that, Doolittle?

DOOLITTLE: Not me, Governor, thank you kindly. Ive heard all the preachers and all the prime ministers—for I'm a thinking man and game for politics or religion or social reform same as all the other amusements—and I tell you it's a dog's life any way you look at it. Undeserving poverty is my line. Taking one station in society with another, it's—it's—well, it's the only one that has any ginger in it, to my taste.

HIGGINS: I suppose we must give him a fiver.

PICKERING: He'll make a bad use of it, I'm afraid.

DOOLITTLE: Not me, Governor, so help me I wont. Dont you be afraid that I'll save it and spare it and live idle on it. There wont be a penny of it left by Monday: I'll have to go to work same as if I'd never had it. It wont pauperize me, you bet. Just one good spree for myself and the missus, giving pleasure to ourselves and employment to others, and satisfaction to you to think it's not been throwed away. You couldnt spend it better.

HIGGINS: [*Taking out his pocket book and coming between* DOOLITTLE *and the piano.*] This is irresistible. Lets give him ten. [*He offers two notes to the* DUSTMAN.]

DOOLITTLE: No, Governor. She wouldnt have the heart to spend ten; and perhaps I shouldnt neither. Ten pounds is a lot of money: it makes a man feel prudent like; and then goodbye to happiness. You give me what I ask you, Governor: not a penny more, and not a penny less.

PICKERING: Why dont you marry that missus of yours? I rather draw the line at encouraging that sort of immorality.

DOOLITTLE: Tell her so, Governor: tell her so. *I'm* willing. It's me that suffers by it. Ive no hold on her. I got to be agreeable to her. I got to give her presents. I got to buy her clothes something sinful. I'm a slave to that woman, Governor, just because I'm not her lawful husband. And she knows it too. Catch her marrying me! Take my advice, Governor: marry Eliza while she's young and dont know no better. If you dont youll be sorry for it after. If you do, she'll be sorry for it after; but better her than you, because youre a man, and she's only a woman and dont know how to be happy anyhow.

HIGGINS: Pickering: if we listen to this man another minute, we shall have no convictions left. [*To* DOOLITTLE.] Five pounds I think you said.
DOOLITTLE: Thank you kindly, Governor.
HIGGINS: Youre sure you wont take ten?
DOOLITTLE: Not now. Another time, Governor.
HIGGINS: [*Handing him a five-pound note.*] Here you are.
DOOLITTLE: Thank you, Governor. Good morning. [*He hurries to the door, anxious to get away with his booty. When he opens it he is confronted with a dainty and exquisitely clean young* JAPANESE LADY *in a simple blue cotton kimono printed cunningly with small white jasmine blossoms.* MRS. PEARCE *is with her. He gets out of her way deferentially and apologizes.*] Beg pardon, miss.
THE JAPANESE LADY: Garn! Dont you know your own daughter?
DOOLITTLE:  ⎱ *exclaiming*   ⎰ Bly me! it's Eliza!
HIGGINS:    ⎰ *simultaneously* ⎱ Whats that? This!
PICKERING:                         By Jove!
LIZA: Don't I look silly?
HIGGINS: Silly?
MRS. PEARCE: [*At the door.*] Now, Mr. Higgins, please dont say anything to make the girl conceited about herself.
HIGGINS: [*Conscientiously.*] Oh! Quite right, Mrs. Pearce. [*To* ELIZA.] Yes: damned silly.
MRS. PEARCE: Please, sir.
HIGGINS: [*Correcting himself.*] I mean extremely silly.
LIZA: I should look all right with my hat on. [*She takes up her hat; puts it on; and walks across the room to the fireplace with a fashionable air.*]
HIGGINS: A new fashion, by George! And it ought to look horrible!
DOOLITTLE: [*With fatherly pride.*] Well, I never thought she'd clean up as good looking as that, Governor. She's a credit to me, aint she?
LIZA: I tell you, it's easy to clean up here. Hot and cold water on tap, just as much as you like, there is. Woolly towels, there is; and a towel horse[8] so hot, it burns your fingers. Soft brushes to scrub yourself, and a wooden bowl of soap smelling like primroses. Now I know why ladies is so clean. Washing's a treat for them. Wish they could see what it is for the like of me!
HIGGINS: I'm glad the bathroom met with your approval.
LIZA: It didnt: not all of it; and I dont care who hears me say it. Mrs. Pearce knows.
HIGGINS: What was wrong, Mrs. Pearce?
MRS. PEARCE: [*Blandly.*] Oh, nothing, sir. It doesnt matter.
LIZA: I had a good mind to break it. I didnt know which way to look. But I hung a towel over it, I did.
HIGGINS: Over what?
MRS. PEARCE: Over the looking-glass, sir.
HIGGINS: Doolittle: you have brought your daughter up too strictly.
DOOLITTLE: Me! I never brought her up at all, except to give her a lick of a strap now and again. Dont put it on me, Governor. She aint accustomed to it, you see: thats all. But she'll soon pick up your free-and-easy ways.
LIZA: I'm a good girl, I am; and I wont pick up no free-and-easy ways.

---

8. Towel rack of pipes through which hot water runs, heating the towels.

HIGGINS: Eliza: if you say again that youre a good girl, your father shall take you home.
LIZA: Not him. You dont know my father. All he come here for was to touch you for some money to get drunk on.
DOOLITTLE: Well, what else would I want money for? To put into the plate in church, I suppose. [*She puts out her tongue at him. He is so incensed by this that* PICKERING *presently finds it necessary to step between them.*] Dont you give me none of your lip; and dont let me hear you giving this gentleman any of it neither, or youll hear from me about it. See?
HIGGINS: Have you any further advice to give her before you go, Doolittle? Your blessing, for instance.
DOOLITTLE: No, Governor: I aint such a mug as to put up my children to all I know myself. Hard enough to hold them in without that. If you want Eliza's mind improved, Governor, you do it yourself with a strap. So long, gentlemen. [*He turns to go.*]
HIGGINS: [*Impressively.*] Stop. Youll come regularly to see your daughter. It's your duty, you know. My brother is a clergyman; and he could help you in your talks with her.
DOOLITTLE: [*Evasively.*] Certainly, I'll come, Governor. Not just this week, because I have a job at a distance. But later on you may depend on me. Afternoon, gentlemen. Afternoon, maam. [*He touches his hat to* MRS. PEARCE, *who disdains the salutation and goes out. He winks at* HIGGINS, *thinking him probably a fellow sufferer from* MRS. PEARCE's *difficult disposition, and follows her.*]
LIZA: Dont you believe the old liar. He'd as soon you set a bulldog on him as a clergyman. You wont see him again in a hurry.
HIGGINS: I dont want to, Eliza. Do you?
LIZA: Not me. I dont want never to see him again, I dont. He's a disgrace to me, he is, collecting dust, instead of working at his trade.
PICKERING: What is his trade, Eliza?
LIZA: Talking money out of other people's pockets into his own. His proper trade's a navvy;[9] and he works at it sometimes too—for exercise—and earns good money at it. Aint you going to call me Miss Doolittle any more?
PICKERING: I beg your pardon, Miss Doolittle. It was a slip of the tongue.
LIZA: Oh, I dont mind; only it sounded so genteel. I should just like to take a taxi to the corner of Tottenham Court Road and get out there and tell it to wait for me, just to put the girls in their place a bit. I wouldnt speak to them, you know.
PICKERING: Better wait til we get you something really fashionable.
HIGGINS: Besides, you shouldnt cut your old friends now that you have risen in the world. Thats what we call snobbery.
LIZA: You dont call the like of them my friends now, I should hope. Theyve took it out of me often enough with their ridicule when they had the chance; and now I mean to get a bit of my own back. But if I'm to have fashionable clothes, I'll wait. I should like to have some. Mrs. Pearce says youre going to give me some to wear in bed at night different to what I wear in the daytime; but it do seem a waste of money when you could get something to shew. Besides, I never could fancy changing into cold things on a winter night.

---

9. Unskilled laborer.

MRS. PEARCE: [*Coming back.*] Now, Eliza. The new things have come for you to try on.
LIZA: Ah-ow-oo-ooh! [*She rushes out.*]
MRS. PEARCE: [*Following her.*] Oh, don't rush about like that, girl. [*She shuts the door behind her.*]
HIGGINS: Pickering: we have taken on a stiff job.
PICKERING: [*With conviction.*] Higgins: we have.

---

*There seems to be some curiosity as to what* HIGGINS'*s lessons to* ELIZA *were like. Well, here is a sample: the first one.*

*Picture* ELIZA, *in her new clothes, and feeling her inside put out of step by a lunch, dinner, and breakfast of a kind to which it is unaccustomed, seated with* HIGGINS *and the* COLONEL *in the study, feeling like a hospital out-patient at a first encounter with the doctors.*

HIGGINS, *constitutionally unable to sit still, discomposes her still more by striding restlessly about. But for the reassuring presence and quietude of her friend the* COLONEL *she would run for her life, even back to Drury Lane.*

HIGGINS: Say your alphabet.
LIZA: I know my alphabet. Do you think I know nothing? I dont need to be taught like a child.
HIGGINS: [*Thundering.*] Say your alphabet.
PICKERING: Say it, Miss Doolittle. You will understand presently. Do what he tells you; and let him teach you in his own way.
LIZA: Oh well, if you put it like that—Ahyee, bəyee, cəyee, dəyee—
HIGGINS: [*With the roar of a wounded lion.*] Stop. Listen to this, Pickering. This is what we pay for as elementary education. This unfortunate animal has been locked up for nine years in school at our expense to teach her to speak and read the language of Shakespear and Milton. And the result is Ahyee, Bə-yee, Cə-yee, Də-yee. [*To* ELIZA.] Say A, B, C, D.
LIZA: [*Almost in tears.*] But I'm sayin it. Ahyee, Bəyee, Cə-yee—
HIGGINS: Stop. Say a cup of tea.
LIZA: A cappətə-ee.
HIGGINS: Put your tongue forward until it squeezes against the top of your lower teeth. Now say cup.
LIZA: C-c-c—I cant. C-Cup.
PICKERING: Good. Splendid, Miss Doolittle.
HIGGINS: By Jupiter, she's done it at the first shot. Pickering: We shall make a duchess of her. [*To* ELIZA.] Now do you think you could possibly say tea? Not tə-yee, mind: if you ever say bə-yee cə-yee də-yee again you shall be dragged round the room three times by the hair of your head. [*Fortissimo.*] T, T, T, T.
LIZA: [*Weeping.*] I cant hear no difference cep that it sounds more genteel-like when you say it.
HIGGINS: Well, if you can hear that difference, what the devil are you crying for? Pickering: give her a chocolate.
PICKERING: No, no. Never mind crying a little, Miss Doolittle: you are doing very well; and the lessons wont hurt. I promise you I wont let him drag you round the room by your hair.

HIGGINS: Be off with you to Mrs. Pearce and tell her about it. Think about it. Try to do it by yourself: and keep your tongue well forward in your mouth instead of trying to roll it up and swallow it. Another lesson at half-past four this afternoon. Away with you.

[ELIZA, *still sobbing, rushes from the room.*]

And that is the sort of ordeal poor ELIZA has to go through for months before we meet her again on her first appearance in London society of the professional class.

## ACT III

*It is* MRS. HIGGINS's *at-home[1] day. Nobody has yet arrived. Her drawing room, in a flat on Chelsea Embankment, has three windows looking on the river; and the ceiling is not so lofty as it would be in an older house of the same pretension. The windows are open, giving access to a balcony with flowers in pots. If you stand with your face to the windows, you have the fireplace on your left and the door in the right-hand wall close to the corner nearest the windows.*

MRS. HIGGINS *was brought up on Morris and Burne Jones;[2] and her room, which is very unlike her son's room in Wimpole Street, is not crowded with furniture and little tables and nicknacks. In the middle of the room there is a big ottoman; and this, with the carpet, the Morris wall-papers, and the Morris chintz window curtains and brocade covers of the ottoman and its cushions, supply all the ornament, and are much too handsome to be hidden by odds and ends of useless things. A few good oil-paintings from the exhibitions in the Grosvenor Gallery thirty years ago (the Burne Jones, not the Whistler[3] side of them) are on the walls. The only landscape is a Cecil Lawson on the scale of a Rubens.[4] There is a portrait of* MRS. HIGGINS *as she was when she defied fashion in her youth in one of the beautiful Rossettian[5] costumes which, when caricatured by people who did not understand, led to the absurdities of popular estheticism in the eighteen-seventies.*

*In the corner diagonally opposite the door* MRS. HIGGINS, *now over sixty and long past taking the trouble to dress out of the fashion, sits writing at an elegantly simple writing-table with a bell button within reach of her hand. There is a Chippendale chair further back in the room between her and the window nearest her side. At the other side of the room, further forward, is an Elizabethan chair roughly carved in the taste of Inigo Jones.[6] On the same side a piano in a decorated case. The corner between the fireplace and the window is occupied by a divan cushioned in Morris chintz.*

*It is between four and five in the afternoon.*

*The door is opened violently; and* HIGGINS *enters with his hat on.*

---

1. Day on which someone is prepared to receive visitors.
2. William Morris (1834–1896), poet, painter, designer, and leading figure in the nineteenth-century decorative arts; Edward Burne-Jones (1833–1898), late Pre-Raphaelite painter and associate of Morris's spartan aesthetic movement.
3. James A. McNeill Whistler (1834–1903), American painter whose early work was associated with the realism of Courbet et al., and thus antithetical to the Pre-Raphaelite influences associated with Burne-Jones.
4. Cecil Lawson (1851–1882), English landscape painter. Peter Paul Rubens (1577–1640), a Flemish painter of the Baroque style, known for dynamic, large-scale works.
5. After Dante Gabriel Rossetti (1828–1882), a Pre-Raphaelite painter whose subject matter was exotically beautiful women from medieval literature and romantic legend.
6. Inigo Jones (1573–1652), architect to James I and Charles I, responsible for England's move toward Italian Renaissance architectural principles in the early seventeenth century. (It was Jones who designed St. Paul's Church, the front of which provides the setting for *Pygmalion*'s opening scene.)

MRS. HIGGINS: [*Dismayed.*] Henry! [*Scolding him.*] What are you doing here today? It is my at-home day: you promised not to come. [*As he bends to kiss her, she takes his hat off, and presents it to him.*]
HIGGINS: Oh bother! [*He throws the hat down on the table.*]
MRS. HIGGINS: Go home at once.
HIGGINS: [*Kissing her.*] I know, mother. I came on purpose.
MRS. HIGGINS: But you mustnt. I'm serious, Henry. You offend all my friends: they stop coming whenever they meet you.
HIGGINS: Nonsense! I know I have no small talk; but people dont mind. [*He sits on the settee.*]
MRS. HIGGINS: Oh! dont they? Small talk indeed! What about your large talk? Really, dear, you mustnt stay.
HIGGINS: I must. Ive a job for you. A phonetic job.
MRS. HIGGINS: No use, dear. I'm sorry; but I cant get round your vowels; and though I like to get pretty postcards in your patent shorthand, I always have to read the copies in ordinary writing you so thoughtfully send me.
HIGGINS: Well, this isnt a phonetic job.
MRS. HIGGINS: You said it was.
HIGGINS: Not your part of it. Ive picked up a girl.
MRS. HIGGINS: Does that mean that some girl has picked you up?
HIGGINS: Not at all. I dont mean a love affair.
MRS. HIGGINS: What a pity!
HIGGINS: Why?
MRS. HIGGINS: Well, you never fall in love with anyone under forty-five. When will you discover that there are some rather nice-looking young women about?
HIGGINS: Oh, I cant be bothered with young women. My idea of a lovable woman is somebody as like you as possible. I shall never get into the way of seriously liking young women: some habits lie too deep to be changed. [*Rising abruptly and walking about, jingling his money and his keys in his trouser pockets.*] Besides, theyre all idiots.
MRS. HIGGINS: Do you know what you would do if you really loved me, Henry?
HIGGINS: Oh bother! What? Marry, I suppose.
MRS. HIGGINS: No. Stop fidgeting and take your hands out of your pockets. [*With a gesture of despair, he obeys and sits down again.*] Thats a good boy. Now tell me about the girl.
HIGGINS: She's coming to see you.
MRS. HIGGINS: I dont remember asking her.
HIGGINS: You didnt. *I* asked her. If youd known her you wouldnt have asked her.
MRS. HIGGINS: Indeed! Why?
HIGGINS: Well, it's like this. She's a common flower girl. I picked her off the kerbstone.
MRS. HIGGINS: And invited her to my at-home!
HIGGINS: [*Rising and coming to her to coax her.*] Oh, thatll be all right. Ive taught her to speak properly; and she has strict orders as to her behavior. She's to keep to two subjects: the weather and everybody's health—Fine day and How do you do, you know—and not to let herself go on things in general. That will be safe.
MRS. HIGGINS: Safe! To talk about our health! about our insides! perhaps about our outsides! How could you be so silly, Henry?

HIGGINS: [*Impatiently.*] Well, she must talk about something. [*He controls himself and sits down again.*] Oh, she'll be all right: dont you fuss. Pickering is in it with me. Ive a sort of bet on that I'll pass her off as a duchess in six months. I started on her some months ago; and she's getting on like a house on fire. I shall win my bet. She has a quick ear; and she's been easier to teach than my middle-class pupils because she's had to learn a complete new language. She talks English almost as you talk French.

MRS. HIGGINS: Thats satisfactory, at all events.

HIGGINS: Well, it is and it isnt.

MRS. HIGGINS: What does that mean?

HIGGINS: You see, Ive got her pronunciation all right; but you have to consider not only how a girl pronounces, but what she pronounces; and that's where—

[*They are interrupted by the* PARLORMAID, *announcing guests.*]

THE PARLORMAID: Mrs. and Miss Eynsford Hill. [*She withdraws.*]

HIGGINS: Oh Lord! [*He rises; snatches his hat from the table; and makes for the door; but before he reaches it his mother introduces him.*]

[MRS. *and* MISS EYNSFORD HILL *are the mother and daughter who sheltered from the rain in Covent Garden. The mother is well bred, quiet, and has the habitual anxiety of straitened means. The daughter has acquired a gay air of being very much at home in society: the bravado of genteel poverty.*]

MRS. EYNSFORD HILL: [*To* MRS. HIGGINS.] How do you do? [*They shake hands.*]

MISS EYNSFORD HILL: How d'you do? [*She shakes.*]

MRS. HIGGINS: [*Introducing.*] My son Henry.

MRS. EYNSFORD HILL: Your celebrated son! I have so longed to meet you, Professor Higgins.

HIGGINS: [*Glumly, making no movement in her direction.*] Delighted. [*He backs against the piano and bows brusquely.*]

MISS EYNSFORD HILL: [*Going to him with confident familiarity.*] How do you do?

HIGGINS: [*Staring at her.*] Ive seen you before somewhere. I havnt the ghost of a notion where; but Ive heard your voice. [*Drearily.*] It doesnt matter. Youd better sit down.

MRS. HIGGINS: I'm sorry to say that my celebrated son has no manners. You mustnt mind him.

MISS EYNSFORD HILL: [*Gaily.*] I dont. [*She sits in the Elizabethan chair.*]

MRS. EYNSFORD HILL: [*A little bewildered.*] Not at all. [*She sits on the ottoman between her* DAUGHTER *and* MRS. HIGGINS, *who has turned her chair away from the writing-table.*]

HIGGINS: Oh, have I been rude? I didnt mean to be.

[*He goes to the central window, through which, with his back to the company, he contemplates the river and the flowers in Battersea Park on the opposite bank as if they were a frozen desert.*
  *The* PARLORMAID *returns, ushering in* PICKERING.]

THE PARLORMAID: Colonel Pickering. [*She withdraws.*]

PICKERING: How do you do, Mrs. Higgins?

MRS. HIGGINS: So glad youve come. Do you know Mrs. Eynsford Hill—Miss Eynsford Hill? [*Exchange of bows. The* COLONEL *brings the Chippendale chair a little forward between* MRS. HILL *and* MRS. HIGGINS, *and sits down.*]

PICKERING: Has Henry told you what weve come for?

HIGGINS: [*Over his shoulder.*] We were interrupted: damn it!

MRS. HIGGINS: Oh Henry, Henry, really!

MRS. EYNSFORD HILL: [*Half rising.*] Are we in the way?

MRS. HIGGINS: [*Rising and making her sit down again.*] No, no. You couldnt have come more fortunately: we want you to meet a friend of ours.

HIGGINS: [*Turning hopefully.*] Yes, by George! We want two or three people. Youll do as well as anybody else.

[*The* PARLORMAID *returns, ushering* FREDDY.]

THE PARLORMAID: Mr. Eynsford Hill.

HIGGINS: [*Almost audibly, past endurance.*] God of Heaven! another of them.

FREDDY: [*Shaking hands with* MRS. HIGGINS.] Ahdedo?

MRS. HIGGINS: Very good of you to come. [*Introducing.*] Colonel Pickering.

FREDDY: [*Bowing.*] Ahdedo?

MRS. HIGGINS: I dont think you know my son, Professor Higgins.

FREDDY: [*Going to* HIGGINS.] Ahdedo?

HIGGINS: [*Looking at him much as if he were a pickpocket.*] I'll take my oath Ive met you before somewhere. Where was it?

FREDDY: I dont think so.

HIGGINS: [*Resignedly.*] It dont matter, anyhow. Sit down.

[*He shakes* FREDDY's *hand, and almost slings him on to the ottoman with his face to the windows; then comes round to the other side of it.*]

HIGGINS: Well, here we are, anyhow! [*He sits down on the ottoman next to* FREDDY.] And now what the devil are we going to talk about until Eliza comes?

MRS. HIGGINS: Henry: you are the life and soul of the Royal Society's soirées; but really youre rather trying on more commonplace occasions.

HIGGINS: Am I? Very sorry. [*Beaming suddenly.*] I suppose I am, you know. [*Uproariously.*] Ha, ha!

MISS EYNSFORD HILL: [*Who considers* HIGGINS *quite eligible matrimonially.*] I sympathize. *I* havnt any small talk. If people would only be frank and say what they really think!

HIGGINS: [*Relapsing into gloom.*] Lord forbid!

MRS. EYNSFORD HILL: [*Taking up her daughter's cue.*] But why?

HIGGINS: What they think they ought to think is bad enough, Lord knows; but what they really think would break up the whole show. Do you suppose it would be really agreeable if I were to come out now with what *I* really think?

MISS EYNSFORD HILL: [*Gaily.*] Is it so very cynical?

HIGGINS: Cynical! Who the dickens said it was cynical? I mean it wouldnt be decent.

MRS. EYNSFORD HILL: [*Seriously.*] Oh! I'm sure you dont mean that, Mr. Higgins.

HIGGINS: You see, we're all savages, more or less. We're supposed to be civilized and cultured—to know all about poetry and philosophy and art and science, and so on; but how many of us know even the meanings of these names? [*To* MISS HILL.] What do you know of poetry? [*To* MRS. HILL.] What do you know of science? [*Indicating* FREDDY.] What does he know of art or science or anything else? What the devil do you imagine I know of philosophy?

MRS. HIGGINS: [*Warningly.*] Or of manners, Henry?

THE PARLORMAID: [*Opening the door.*] Miss Doolittle. [*She withdraws.*]

HIGGINS: [*Rising hastily and running to* MRS. HIGGINS.] Here she is, mother. [*He stands on tiptoe and makes signs over his mother's head to* ELIZA *to indicate to her which lady is her hostess.*]

> [ELIZA, *who is exquisitely dressed, produces an impression of such remarkable distinction and beauty as she enters that they all rise, quite fluttered. Guided by* HIGGINS's *signals, she comes to* MRS. HIGGINS *with studied grace.*]

LIZA: [*Speaking with pedantic correctness of pronunciation and great beauty of tone.*] How do you do, Mrs. Higgins? [*She gasps slightly in making sure of the H in Higgins, but is quite successful.*] Mr. Higgins told me I might come.

MRS. HIGGINS: [*Cordially.*] Quite right: I'm very glad indeed to see you.

PICKERING: How do you do, Miss Doolittle?

LIZA: [*Shaking hands with him.*] Colonel Pickering, is it not?

MRS. EYNSFORD HILL: I feel sure we have met before, Miss Doolittle. I remember your eyes.

LIZA: How do you do? [*She sits down on the ottoman gracefully in the place just left vacant by* HIGGINS.]

MRS. EYNSFORD HILL: [*Introducing.*] My daughter Clara.

LIZA: How do you do?

CLARA: [*Impulsively.*] How do you do? [*She sits down on the ottoman beside* ELIZA, *devouring her with her eyes.*]

FREDDY: [*Coming to their side of the ottoman.*] Ive certainly had the pleasure.

MRS. EYNSFORD HILL: [*Introducing.*] My son Freddy.

LIZA: How do you do?

> [FREDDY *bows and sits down in the Elizabethan chair, infatuated.*]

HIGGINS: [*Suddenly.*] By George, yes: it all comes back to me! [*They stare at him.*] Covent Garden! [*Lamentably.*] What a damned thing!

MRS. HIGGINS: Henry, please! [*He is about to sit on the edge of the table.*] Dont sit on my writing-table: youll break it.

HIGGINS: [*Sulkily.*] Sorry.

> [*He goes to the divan, stumbling into the fender*[7] *and over the fire-irons on his way; extricating himself with muttered imprecations; and finishing his disastrous journey by throwing himself so impatiently on the divan that he almost breaks it.* MRS. HIGGINS *looks at him, but controls herself and says nothing.*
> *A long and painful pause ensues.*]

MRS. HIGGINS: [*At last, conversationally.*] Will it rain, do you think?

LIZA: The shallow depression in the west of these islands is likely to move slowly in an easterly direction. There are no indications of any great change in the barometrical situation.

FREDDY: Ha! ha! how awfully funny!

LIZA: What is wrong with that, young man? I bet I got it right.

FREDDY: Killing!

---

7. Fire screen.

MRS. EYNSFORD HILL: I'm sure I hope it wont turn cold. Theres so much influenza about. It runs right through our whole family regularly every spring.
LIZA: [*Darkly.*] My aunt died of influenza: so they said.
MRS. EYNSFORD HILL: [*Clicks her tongue sympathetically.*]!!!
LIZA: [*In the same tragic tone.*] But it's my belief they done the old woman in.
MRS. HIGGINS: [*Puzzled.*] Done her in?
LIZA: Y-e-e-e-es, Lord love you! Why should she die of influenza? She come through diptheria right enough the year before. I saw her with my own eyes. Fairly blue with it, she was. They all thought she was dead; but my father he kept ladling gin down her throat til she came to so sudden that she bit the bowl off the spoon.
MRS. EYNSFORD HILL: [*Startled.*] Dear me!
LIZA: [*Piling up the indictment.*] What call would a woman with that strength in her have to die of influenza? What become of her new straw hat that should have come to me? Somebody pinched it; and what I say is, them as pinched it done her in.
MRS. EYNSFORD HILL: What does doing her in mean?
HIGGINS: [*Hastily.*] Oh, thats the new small talk. To do a person in means to kill them.
MRS. EYNSFORD HILL: [*To* ELIZA, *horrified.*] You surely dont believe that your aunt was killed?
LIZA: Do I not! Them she lived with would have killed her for a hat-pin, let alone a hat.
MRS. EYNSFORD HILL: But it cant have been right for your father to pour spirits down her throat like that. It might have killed her.
LIZA: Not her. Gin was mother's milk to her. Besides, he'd poured so much down his own throat that he knew the good of it.
MRS. EYNSFORD HILL: Do you mean that he drank?
LIZA: Drank! My word! Something chronic.
MRS. EYNSFORD HILL: How dreadful for you!
LIZA: Not a bit. It never did him no harm what I could see. But then he did not keep it up regular. [*Cheerfully.*] On the burst, as you might say, from time to time. And always more agreeable when he had a drop in. When he was out of work, my mother used to give him fourpence and tell him to go out and not come back until he'd drunk himself cheerful and loving-like. Theres lots of women has to make their husbands drunk to make them fit to live with. [*Now quite at her ease.*] You see, it's like this. If a man has a bit of a conscience, it always takes him when he's sober; and then it makes him low-spirited. A drop of booze just takes that off and makes him happy. [*To* FREDDY, *who is in convulsions of suppressed laughter.*] Here! what are you sniggering at?
FREDDY: The new small talk. You do it so awfully well.
LIZA: If I was doing it proper, what was you laughing at? [*To* HIGGINS.] Have I said anything I oughtnt?
MRS. HIGGINS: [*Interposing.*] Not at all, Miss Doolittle.
LIZA: Well, thats a mercy, anyhow. [*Expansively.*] What I always say is—
HIGGINS: [*Rising and looking at his watch.*] Ahem!
LIZA: [*Looking round at him; taking the hint; and rising.*] Well: I must go. [*They all rise.* FREDDY *goes to the door.*] So pleased to have met you. Goodbye. [*She shakes hands with* MRS. HIGGINS.]
MRS. HIGGINS: Goodbye.

LIZA: Goodbye, Colonel Pickering.
PICKERING: Goodbye, Miss Doolittle. [*They shake hands.*]
LIZA: [*Nodding to the others.*] Goodbye, all.
FREDDY: [*Opening the door for her.*] Are you walking across the Park, Miss Doolittle? If so—
LIZA: [*With perfectly elegant diction.*] Walk! Not bloody likely. [*Sensation.*] I am going in a taxi. [*She goes out.*]

> [PICKERING *gasps and sits down.* FREDDY *goes out on the balcony to catch another glimpse of* ELIZA.]

MRS. EYNSFORD HILL: [*Suffering from shock.*] Well, I really cant get used to the new ways.
CLARA: [*Throwing herself discontentedly into the Elizabethan chair.*] Oh, it's all right, mamma, quite right. People will think we never go anywhere or see anybody if you are so old-fashioned.
MRS. EYNSFORD HILL: I daresay I am very old-fashioned; but I do hope you wont begin using that expression, Clara. I have got accustomed to hear you talking about men as rotters, and calling everything filthy and beastly; though I do think it horrible and unladylike. But this last is really too much. Dont you think so, Colonel Pickering?
PICKERING: Dont ask me. Ive been away in India for several years; and manners have changed so much that I sometimes dont know whether I'm at a respectable dinner-table or in a ship's forecastle.
CLARA: It's all a matter of habit. Theres no right or wrong in it. Nobody means anything by it. And it's so quaint, and gives such a smart emphasis to things that are not in themselves very witty. I find the new small talk delightful and quite innocent.
MRS. EYNSFORD HILL: [*Rising.*] Well, after that, I think it's time for us to go.

> [PICKERING *and* HIGGINS *rise.*]

CLARA: [*Rising.*] Oh yes: we have three at-homes to go to still. Goodbye, Mrs. Higgins. Goodbye, Colonel Pickering. Goodbye, Professor Higgins.
HIGGINS: [*Coming grimly at her from the divan, and accompanying her to the door.*] Goodbye. Be sure you try on that small talk at the three at-homes. Dont be nervous about it. Pitch it in strong.
CLARA: [*All smiles.*] I will. Goodbye. Such nonsense, all this early Victorian prudery!
HIGGINS: [*Tempting her.*] Such damned nonsense!
CLARA: Such bloody nonsense!
MRS. EYNSFORD HILL: [*Convulsively.*] Clara!
CLARA: Ha! ha! [*She goes out radiant, conscious of being thoroughly up to date, and is heard descending the stairs in a stream of silvery laughter.*]
FREDDY: [*To the heavens at large.*] Well, I ask you—[*He gives it up, and comes to* MRS. HIGGINS.] Goodbye.
MRS. HIGGINS: [*Shaking hands.*] Goodbye. Would you like to meet Miss Doolittle again?
FREDDY: [*Eagerly.*] Yes, I should, most awfully.
MRS. HIGGINS: Well, you know my days.
FREDDY: Yes. Thanks awfully. Goodbye. [*He goes out.*]
MRS. EYNSFORD HILL: Goodbye, Mr. Higgins.

HIGGINS: Goodbye. Goodbye.
MRS. EYNSFORD HILL: [*To* PICKERING.] It's no use. I shall never be able to bring myself to use that word.
PICKERING: Dont. It's not compulsory, you know. Youll get on quite well without it.
MRS. EYNSFORD HILL: Only, Clara is so down on me if I am not positively reeking with the latest slang. Goodbye.
PICKERING: Goodbye. [*They shake hands.*]
MRS. EYNSFORD HILL: [*To* MRS. HIGGINS.] You mustnt mind Clara. [PICKERING, *catching from her lowered tone that this is not meant for him to hear, discreetly joins* HIGGINS *at the window.*] We're so poor! and she gets so few parties, poor child! She doesnt quite know. [MRS. HIGGINS, *seeing that her eyes are moist, takes her hand sympathetically and goes with her to the door.*] But the boy is nice. Dont you think so?
MRS. HIGGINS: Oh, quite nice. I shall always be delighted to see him.
MRS. EYNSFORD HILL: Thank you, dear. Goodbye. [*She goes out.*]
HIGGINS: [*Eagerly.*] Well? Is Eliza presentable? [*He swoops on his mother and drags her to the ottoman, where she sits down in* ELIZA'*s place with her son on her left.*]

[PICKERING *returns to his chair on her right.*]

MRS. HIGGINS: You silly boy, of course she's not presentable. She's a triumph of your art and of her dressmaker's; but if you suppose for a moment that she doesnt give herself away in every sentence she utters, you must be perfectly cracked about her.
PICKERING: But dont you think something might be done? I mean something to eliminate the sanguinary element[8] from her conversation.
MRS. HIGGINS: Not as long as she is in Henry's hands.
HIGGINS: [*Aggrieved.*] Do you mean that my language is improper?
MRS. HIGGINS: No, dearest: it would be quite proper—say on a canal barge; but it would not be proper for her at a garden party.
HIGGINS: [*Deeply injured.*] Well I must say—
PICKERING: [*Interrupting him.*] Come, Higgins: you must learn to know yourself. I havnt heard such language as yours since we used to review the volunteers[9] in Hyde Park twenty years ago.
HIGGINS: [*Sulkily.*] Oh, well, if you say so, I suppose I dont always talk like a bishop.
MRS. HIGGINS: [*Quieting* HENRY *with a touch.*] Colonel Pickering: will you tell me what is the exact state of things in Wimpole Street?
PICKERING: [*Cheerfully: as if this completely changed the subject.*] Well, I have come to live there with Henry. We work together at my Indian Dialects; and we think it more convenient—
MRS. HIGGINS: Quite so. I know all about that: it's an excellent arrangement. But where does this girl live?
HIGGINS: With us, of course. Where should she live?
MRS. HIGGINS: But on what terms? Is she a servant? If not, what is she?
PICKERING: [*Slowly.*] I think I know what you mean, Mrs. Higgins.
HIGGINS: Well, dash me if *I* do! Ive had to work at the girl every day for months

---

8. That is, the word "bloody."    9. Inspect the troops.

to get her to her present pitch. Besides, she's useful. She knows where my things are, and remembers my appointments and so forth.

MRS. HIGGINS: How does your housekeeper get on with her?

HIGGINS: Mrs. Pearce? Oh, she's jolly glad to get so much taken off her hands; for before Eliza came, she used to have to find things and remind me of my appointments. But she's got some silly bee in her bonnet about Eliza. She keeps saying "You dont think, sir": doesnt she, Pick?

PICKERING: Yes: thats the formula. "You dont think, sir." Thats the end of every conversation about Eliza.

HIGGINS: As if I ever stop thinking about the girl and her confounded vowels and consonants. I'm worn out, thinking about her, and watching her lips and her teeth and her tongue, not to mention her soul, which is the quaintest of the lot.

MRS. HIGGINS: You certainly are a pretty pair of babies, playing with your live doll.

HIGGINS: Playing! The hardest job I ever tackled: make no mistake about that, mother. But you have no idea how frightfully interesting it is to take a human being and change her into a quite different human being by creating a new speech for her. It's filling up the deepest gulf that separates class from class and soul from soul.

PICKERING: [*Drawing his chair closer to* MRS. HIGGINS *and bending over to her eagerly.*] Yes: it's enormously interesting. I assure you, Mrs. Higgins, we take Eliza very seriously. Every week—every day almost—there is some new change. [*Closer again.*] We keep records of every stage—dozens of gramophone disks and photographs—

HIGGINS: [*Assailing her at the other ear.*] Yes, by George: it's the most absorbing experiment I ever tackled. She regularly fills our lives up: doesnt she, Pick?

PICKERING: We're always talking Eliza.

HIGGINS: Teaching Eliza.

PICKERING: Dressing Eliza.

MRS. HIGGINS: What!

HIGGINS: Inventing new Elizas.

HIGGINS: [*Speaking together.*] You now, she has the most extraordinary quickness of ear:
PICKERING: I assure you, my dear Mrs. Higgins, that girl
HIGGINS: just like a parrot. Ive tried her with every
PICKERING: is a genius. She can play the piano quite beautifully.
HIGGINS: possible sort of sound that a human being can make:
PICKERING: We have taken her to classical concerts and to music
HIGGINS: Continental dialects, African dialects, Hottentot
PICKERING: halls; and it's all the same to her: she plays everything
HIGGINS: [*Speaking together.*] clicks, things it took me years to get hold of; and
PICKERING: she hears right off when she comes home, whether it's
HIGGINS: she picks them up like a shot, right away, as if she had
PICKERING: Beethoven and Brahms or Lehar and Lionel Monckton;[1]

---

1. German composers Ludwig van Beethoven (1770–1827) and Johannes Brahms (1833–1897); Hungarian operetta composer Franz Lehar (1870–1948) and English operetta composer Lionel Monckton (1861–1924).

HIGGINS: } { been at it all her life.
PICKERING: } { though six months ago, she'd never as much as touched a piano—
MRS. HIGGINS: [*Putting her fingers in her ears, as they are by this time shouting one another down with an intolerable noise.*] Sh-sh-sh—sh! [*They stop.*]
PICKERING: I beg your pardon. [*He draws his chair back apologetically.*]
HIGGINS: Sorry. When Pickering starts shouting nobody can get a word in edgeways.
MRS. HIGGINS: Be quiet, Henry. Colonel Pickering: dont you realize that when Eliza walked into Wimpole Street, something walked in with her?
PICKERING: Her father did. But Henry soon got rid of him.
MRS. HIGGINS: It would have been more to the point if her mother had. But as her mother didnt something else did.
PICKERING: But what?
MRS. HIGGINS: [*Unconsciously dating herself by the word.*] A problem.
PICKERING: Oh, I see. The problem of how to pass her off as a lady.
HIGGINS: I'll solve that problem. Ive half solved it already.
MRS. HIGGINS: No, you two infinitely stupid male creatures: the problem of what is to be done with her afterwards.
HIGGINS: I dont see anything in that. She can go her own way, with all the advantages I have given her.
MRS. HIGGINS: The advantages of that poor woman who was here just now! The manners and habits that disqualify a fine lady from earning her own living without giving her a fine lady's income! Is that what you mean?
PICKERING: [*Indulgently, being rather bored.*] Oh, that will be all right, Mrs. Higgins. [*He rises to go.*]
HIGGINS: [*Rising also.*] We'll find her some light employment.
PICKERING: She's happy enough. Dont you worry about her. Goodbye. [*He shakes hands as if he were consoling a frightened child, and makes for the door.*]
HIGGINS: Anyhow, theres no good bothering now. The thing's done. Goodbye, mother. [*He kisses her, and follows* PICKERING.]
PICKERING: [*Turning for a final consolation.*] There are plenty of openings. We'll do whats right. Goodbye.
HIGGINS: [*To* PICKERING *as they go out together.*] Lets take her to the Shakespear exhibition at Earls Court.
PICKERING: Yes: lets. Her remarks will be delicious.
HIGGINS: She'll mimic all the people for us when we get home.
PICKERING: Ripping. [*Both are heard laughing as they go downstairs.*]
MRS. HIGGINS: [*Rises with an impatient bounce, and returns to her work at the writing-table. She sweeps a litter of disarranged papers out of her way; snatches a sheet of paper from her stationery case; and tries resolutely to write. At the third line she gives it up; flings down her pen; grips the table angrily and exclaims.*] Oh, men! men!! men!!!

---

Clearly ELIZA *will not pass as a duchess yet; and* HIGGINS'*s bet remains unwon. But the six months are not yet exhausted; and just in time* ELIZA *does actually pass as a princess. For a glimpse of how she did it imagine an Embassy in London one summer evening after dark. The hall door has an awning and a carpet across the sidewalk to the kerb, because a grand reception is in progress. A small crowd is lined up to see the guests arrive.*

*A Rolls-Royce car drives up.* PICKERING *in evening dress, with medals and orders, alights, and hands out* ELIZA, *in opera cloak, evening dress, diamonds, fan, flowers and all accessories.* HIGGINS *follows. The car drives off; and the three go up the steps and into the house, the door opening for them as they approach.*

*Inside the house they find themselves in a spacious hall from which the grand staircase rises. On the left are the arrangements for the gentlemen's cloaks. The male guests are depositing their hats and wraps there.*

*On the right is a door leading to the ladies' cloakroom. Ladies are going in cloaked and coming out in splendor.* PICKERING *whispers to* ELIZA *and points out the ladies' room. She goes into it.* HIGGINS *and* PICKERING *take off their overcoats and take tickets for them from the attendant.*

*One of the guests, occupied in the same way, has his back turned. Having taken his ticket, he turns round and reveals himself as an important looking* YOUNG MAN *with an astonishingly hairy face. He has an enormous moustache, flowing out into luxuriant whiskers. Waves of hair cluster on his brow. His hair is cropped closely at the back, and glows with oil. Otherwise he is very smart.*[2] *He wears several worthless orders. He is evidently a foreigner, guessable as a whiskered Pandour from Hungary; but in spite of the ferocity of his moustache he is amiable and genially voluble.*

*Recognizing* HIGGINS, *he flings his arms wide apart and approaches him enthusiastically.*

WHISKERS: Maestro, maestro. [*He embraces* HIGGINS *and kisses him on both cheeks.*] You remember me?

HIGGINS: No I dont. Who the devil are you?

WHISKERS: I am your pupil: your first pupil, your best and greatest pupil. I am little Nepommuck, the marvellous boy. I have made your name famous throughout Europe. You teach me phonetic. You cannot forget ME.

HIGGINS: Why dont you shave?

NEPOMMUCK: I have not your imposing appearance, your chin, your brow. Nobody notice me when I shave. Now I am famous: they call me Hairy Faced Dick.

HIGGINS: And what are you doing here among all these swells?

NEPOMMUCK: I am interpreter. I speak 32 languages. I am indispensable at these international parties. You are great cockney specialist: you place a man anywhere in London the moment he open his mouth. I place any man in Europe.

[*A* FOOTMAN *hurries down the grand staircase and comes to* NEPOMMUCK.]

FOOTMAN: You are wanted upstairs. Her Excellency cannot understand the Greek gentleman.

NEPOMMUCK: Thank you, yes, immediately.

[*The* FOOTMAN *goes and is lost in the crowd.*]

NEPOMMUCK: [*To* HIGGINS.] This Greek diplomatist pretends he cannot speak nor understand English. He cannot deceive me. He is the son of a Clerkenwell watchmaker. He speaks English so villainously that he dare not utter a word of it without betraying his origin. I help him to pretend; but I make him pay through the nose. I make them all pay. Ha Ha! [*He hurries upstairs.*]

2. Dapper; well groomed.

PICKERING: Is this fellow really an expert? Can he find out Eliza and blackmail her?
HIGGINS: We shall see. If he finds her out I lose my bet.

[ELIZA *comes from the cloakroom and joins them.*]

PICKERING: Well, Eliza, now for it. Are you ready?
LIZA: Are you nervous, Colonel?
PICKERING: Frightfully. I feel exactly as I felt before my first battle. It's the first time that frightens.
LIZA: It is not the first time for me, Colonel. I have done this fifty times—hundreds of times—in my little piggery in Angel Court in my day-dreams. I am in a dream now. Promise me not to let Professor Higgins wake me; for if he does I shall forget everything and talk as I used to in Drury Lane.
PICKERING: Not a word, Higgins. [*To* ELIZA.] Now, ready?
LIZA: Ready.
PICKERING: Go.

[*They mount the stairs,* HIGGINS *last.* PICKERING *whispers to the* FOOTMAN *on the first landing.*]

FIRST LANDING FOOTMAN: Miss Doolittle, Colonel Pickering, Professor Higgins.
SECOND LANDING FOOTMAN: Miss Doolittle, Colonel Pickering, Professor Higgins.

[*At the top of the staircase the* AMBASSADOR *and his* WIFE, *with* NEPOMMUCK *at her elbow, are receiving.*]

HOSTESS: [*Taking* ELIZA'*s hand.*] How d'ye do?
HOST: [*Same play.*] How d'ye do? How d'ye do, Pickering?
LIZA: [*With a beautiful gravity that awes her* HOSTESS.] How do you do? [*She passes on to the drawingroom.*]
HOSTESS: Is that your adopted daughter, Colonel Pickering? She will make a sensation.
PICKERING: Most kind of you to invite her for me. [*He passes on.*]
HOSTESS: [*To* NEPOMMUCK.] Find out all about her.
NEPOMMUCK: [*Bowing.*] Excellency—[*He goes into the crowd.*]
HOST: How d'ye do, Higgins? You have a rival here tonight. He introduced himself as your pupil. Is he any good?
HIGGINS: He can learn a language in a fortnight—knows dozens of them. A sure mark of a fool. As a phonetician, no good whatever.
HOSTESS: How d'ye do, Professor?
HIGGINS: How do you do? Fearful bore for you this sort of thing. Forgive my part in it. [*He passes on.*]

[*In the drawingroom and its suite of salons the reception is in full swing.* ELIZA *passes through. She is so intent on her ordeal that she walks like a somnambulist in a desert instead of a débutante in a fashionable crowd. They stop talking to look at her, admiring her dress, her jewels, and her strangely attractive self. Some of the younger ones at the back stand on their chairs to see.*]

[*The* HOST *and* HOSTESS *come in from the staircase and mingle with their guests.* HIGGINS, *gloomy and contemptuous of the whole business, comes into the group where they are chatting.*]

HOSTESS: Ah, here is Professor Higgins: he will tell us. Tell us all about the wonderful young lady, Professor.

HIGGINS: [*Almost morosely.*] What wonderful young lady?

HOSTESS: You know very well. They tell me there has been nothing like her in London since people stood on their chairs to look at Mrs. Langtry.[3]

[NEPOMMUCK *joins the group, full of news.*]

HOSTESS: Ah, here you are at last, Nepommuck. Have you found out all about the Doolittle lady?

NEPOMMUCK: I have found out all about her. She is a fraud.

HOSTESS: A fraud! Oh no.

NEPOMMUCK: YES, yes. She cannot deceive me. Her name cannot be Doolittle.

HIGGINS: Why?

NEPOMMUCK: Because Doolittle is an English name. And she is not English.

HOSTESS: Oh, nonsense! She speaks English perfectly.

NEPOMMUCK: Too perfectly. Can you shew me any English woman who speaks English as it should be spoken? Only foreigners who have been taught to speak it speak it well.

HOSTESS: Certainly she terrified me by the way she said How d'ye do. I had a schoolmistress who talked like that; and I was mortally afraid of her. But if she is not English what is she?

NEPOMMUCK: Hungarian.

ALL THE REST: Hungarian!

NEPOMMUCK: Hungarian. And of royal blood. I am Hungarian. My blood is royal.

HIGGINS: Did you speak to her in Hungarian?

NEPOMMUCK: I did. She was very clever. She said "Please speak to me in English: I do not understand French." French! She pretends not to know the difference between Hungarian and French. Impossible: she knows both.

HIGGINS: And the blood royal? How did you find that out?

NEPOMMUCK: Instinct, maestro, instinct. Only the Magyar races[4] can produce that air of the divine right, those resolute eyes. She is a princess.

HOST: What do you say, Professor?

HIGGINS: I say an ordinary London girl out of the gutter and taught to speak by an expert. I place her in Drury Lane.

NEPOMMUCK: Ha ha ha! Oh, maestro, maestro, you are mad on the subject of cockney dialects. The London gutter is the whole world for you.

HIGGINS: [*To the* HOSTESS.] What does your Excellency say?

HOSTESS: Oh, of course I agree with Nepommuck. She must be a princess at least.

HOST: Not necessarily legitimate, of course. Morganatic[5] perhaps. But that is undoubtedly her class.

---

3. English actress Lillie Langtry (1852–1929), a renowned beauty.  4. Hungarians.
5. Relating to the marriage of a noble to a commoner.

HIGGINS: I stick to my opinion.
HOSTESS: Oh, you are incorrigible.

[*The group breaks up, leaving* HIGGINS *isolated.* PICKERING *joins him.*]

PICKERING: Where is Eliza? We must keep an eye on her.

[ELIZA *joins them.*]

LIZA: I dont think I can bear much more. The people all stare so at me. An old lady has just told me that I speak exactly like Queen Victoria. I am sorry if I have lost your bet. I have done my best; but nothing can make me the same as these people.
PICKERING: You have not lost it, my dear. You have won it ten times over.
HIGGINS: Let us get out of this. I have had enough of chattering to these fools.
PICKERING: Eliza is tired; and I am hungry. Let us clear out and have supper somewhere.

## ACT IV

*The Wimpole Street laboratory. Midnight. Nobody in the room. The clock on the mantelpiece strikes twelve. The fire is not alight: it is a summer night.*

*Presently* HIGGINS *and* PICKERING *are heard on the stairs.*

HIGGINS: [*Calling down to* PICKERING.] I say, Pick: lock up, will you? I shant be going out again.
PICKERING: Right. Can Mrs. Pearce go to bed? We dont want anything more, do we?
HIGGINS: Lord, no!

[ELIZA *opens the door and is seen on the lighted landing in all the finery in which she has just won* HIGGINS's *bet for him. She comes to the hearth, and switches on the electric lights there. She is tired: her pallor contrasts strongly with her dark eyes and hair; and her expression is almost tragic. She takes off her cloak; puts her fan and gloves on the piano; and sits down on the bench, brooding and silent.* HIGGINS, *in evening dress, with overcoat and hat, comes in, carrying a smoking jacket which he has picked up downstairs. He takes off the hat and overcoat; throws them carelessly on the newspaper stand; disposes of his coat in the same way; puts on the smoking jacket; and throws himself wearily into the easy-chair at the hearth.* PICKERING, *similarly attired, comes in. He also takes off his hat and overcoat, and is about to throw them on* HIGGINS's *when he hesitates.*]

PICKERING: I say: Mrs. Pearce will row[6] if we leave these things lying about in the drawing room.
HIGGINS: Oh, chuck them over the bannisters into the hall. She'll find them there in the morning and put them away all right. She'll think we were drunk.
PICKERING: We are, slightly. Are there any letters?
HIGGINS: I didnt look. [PICKERING *takes the overcoats and hats and goes downstairs.*

---

6. That is, will start a quarrel. ("Row" rhymes with "cow.")

HIGGINS *begins half singing half yawning an air from La Fanciulla del Golden West.*[7] *Suddenly he stops and exclaims.*] I wonder where the devil my slippers are!

[ELIZA *looks at him darkly; then rises suddenly and leaves the room.*
HIGGINS *yawns again, and resumes his song.*
PICKERING *returns, with the contents of the letter-box in his hand.*]

PICKERING: Only circulars,[8] and this coroneted billet-doux for you. [*He throws the circulars into the fender, and posts himself on the hearthrug, with his back to the grate.*]

HIGGINS: [*Glancing at the billet-doux.*] Money-lender. [*He throws the letter after the circulars.*]

[ELIZA *returns with a pair of large down-at-heel slippers. She places them on the carpet before* HIGGINS, *and sits as before without a word.*]

HIGGINS: [*Yawning again.*] Oh Lord! What an evening! What a crew! What a silly tomfoolery! [*He raises his shoe to unlace it, and catches sight of the slippers. He stops unlacing and looks at them as if they had appeared there of their own accord.*] Oh! theyre there, are they?

PICKERING: [*Stretching himself.*] Well, I feel a bit tired. It's been a long day. The garden party, a dinner party, and the reception! Rather too much of a good thing. But youve won your bet, Higgins. Eliza did the trick, and something to spare, eh?

HIGGINS: [*Fervently.*] Thank God it's over!

[ELIZA *flinches violently; but they take no notice of her; and she recovers herself and sits stonily as before.*]

PICKERING: Were you nervous at the garden party? *I* was. Eliza didnt seem a bit nervous.

HIGGINS: Oh, she wasnt nervous. I knew she'd be all right. No: it's the strain of putting the job through all these months that has told on me. It was interesting enough at first, while we were at the phonetics; but after that I got deadly sick of it. If I hadnt backed myself to do it I should have chucked the whole thing up two months ago. It was a silly notion: the whole thing has been a bore.

PICKERING: Oh come! the garden party was frightfully exciting. My heart began beating like anything.

HIGGINS: Yes, for the first three minutes. But when I saw we were going to win hands down, I felt like a bear in a cage, hanging about doing nothing. The dinner was worse: sitting gorging there for over an hour, with nobody but a damned fool of a fashionable woman to talk to! I tell you, Pickering, never again for me. No more artificial duchesses. The whole thing has been simple purgatory.

PICKERING: Youve never been broken in properly to the social routine. [*Strolling over to the piano.*] I rather enjoy dipping into it occasionally myself: it makes me feel young again. Anyhow, it was a great success: an immense success. I

---

7. *The Golden Girl of the West* (1910), a three-act opera by Puccini. (Shaw misstates the title of the Italian original, *La Fanciulla del West.*)
8. Advertising brochures. *Coroneted billet-doux:* love letter on fine stationery (coronets indicate nobility).

was quite frightened once or twice because Eliza was doing it so well. You see, lots of the real people cant do it at all: theyre such fools that they think style comes by nature to people in their position; and so they never learn. Theres always something professional about doing a thing superlatively well.

HIGGINS: Yes: thats what drives me mad: the silly people dont know their own silly business. [*Rising.*] However, it's over and done with; and now I can go to bed at last without dreading tomorrow.

[ELIZA's *beauty becomes murderous.*]

PICKERING: I think I shall turn in too. Still, it's been a great occasion: a triumph for you. Goodnight. [*He goes*].

HIGGINS: [*Following him.*] Goodnight. [*Over his shoulder, at the door.*] Put out the lights, Eliza; and tell Mrs. Pearce not to make coffee for me in the morning: I'll take tea. [*He goes out.*]

[ELIZA *tries to control herself and feel indifferent as she rises and walks across to the hearth to switch off the lights. By the time she gets there she is on the point of screaming. She sits down in* HIGGINS's *chair and holds on hard to the arms. Finally she gives way and flings herself furiously on the floor, raging.*]

HIGGINS: [*In despairing wrath outside.*] What the devil have I done with my slippers? [*He appears at the door.*]

LIZA: [*Snatching up the slippers, and hurling them at him one after the other with all her force.*] There are your slippers. And there. Take your slippers; and may you never have a day's luck with them!

HIGGINS: [*Astounded.*] What on earth—! [*He comes to her.*] Whats the matter? Get up. [*He pulls her up.*] Anything wrong?

LIZA: [*Breathless.*] Nothing wrong—with you. Ive won your bet for you, havent I? Thats enough for you. *I* dont matter, I suppose.

HIGGINS: You won my bet! You! Presumptuous insect! *I* won it. What did you throw those slippers at me for?

LIZA: Because I wanted to smash your face. I'd like to kill you, you selfish brute. Why didnt you leave me where you picked me out of—in the gutter? You thank God it's all over, and that now you can throw me back again there, do you? [*She crisps*[9] *her fingers frantically.*]

HIGGINS: [*Looking at her in cool wonder.*] The creature is nervous, after all.

LIZA: [*Gives a suffocated scream of fury, and instinctively darts her nails at his face.*]!!

HIGGINS: [*Catching her wrists.*] Ah! would you? Claws in, you cat. How dare you shew your temper to me? Sit down and be quiet. [*He throws her roughly into the easy-chair.*]

LIZA: [*Crushed by superior strength and weight.*] Whats to become of me? Whats to become of me?

HIGGINS: How the devil do I know whats to become of you? What does it matter what becomes of you?

LIZA: You dont care. I know you dont care. You wouldnt care if I was dead. I'm nothing to you—not so much as them slippers.

HIGGINS: [*Thundering.*] Those slippers.

---

9. Curls or clenches.

LIZA: [*With bitter submission.*] Those slippers. I didnt think it made any difference now.

[*A pause.* ELIZA *hopeless and crushed.* HIGGINS *a little uneasy.*]

HIGGINS: [*In his loftiest manner.*] Why have you begun going on like this? May I ask whether you complain of your treatment here?

LIZA: No.

HIGGINS: Has anybody behaved badly to you? Colonel Pickering? Mrs. Pearce? Any of the servants?

LIZA: No.

HIGGINS: I presume you dont pretend that *I* have treated you badly?

LIZA: No.

HIGGINS: I am glad to hear it. [*He moderates his tone.*] Perhaps youre tired after the strain of the day. Will you have a glass of champagne? [*He moves towards the door.*]

LIZA: No. [*Recollecting her manners.*] Thank you.

HIGGINS: [*Good-humored again.*] This has been coming on you for some days. I suppose it was natural for you to be anxious about the garden party. But thats all over now. [*He pats her kindly on the shoulder. She writhes.*] Theres nothing more to worry about.

LIZA: No. Nothing more for you to worry about. [*She suddenly rises and gets away from him by going to the piano bench, where she sits and hides her face.*] Oh God! I wish I was dead.

HIGGINS: [*Staring after her in sincere surprise.*] Why? In heaven's name, why? [*Reasonably, going to her.*] Listen to me, Eliza. All this irritation is purely subjective.

LIZA: I dont understand. I'm too ignorant.

HIGGINS: It's only imagination. Low spirits and nothing else. Nobody's hurting you. Nothing's wrong. You go to bed like a good girl and sleep it off. Have a little cry and say your prayers: that will make you comfortable.

LIZA: I heard your prayers. "Thank God it's all over!"

HIGGINS: [*Impatiently.*] Well, dont you thank God it's all over? Now you are free and can do what you like.

LIZA: [*Pulling herself together in desperation.*] What am I fit for? What have you left me fit for? Where am I to go? What am I to do? Whats to become of me?

HIGGINS: [*Enlightened, but not at all impressed.*] Oh, thats whats worrying you, is it? [*He thrusts his hands into his pockets, and walks about in his usual manner, rattling the contents of his pockets, as if condescending to a trivial subject out of pure kindness.*] I shouldnt bother about it if I were you. I should imagine you wont have much difficulty in settling yourself somewhere or other, though I hadnt quite realized that you were going away. [*She looks quickly at him: he does not look at her, but examines the dessert stand on the piano and decides that he will eat an apple.*] You might marry, you know. [*He bites a large piece out of the apple and munches it noisily.*] You see, Eliza, all men are not confirmed old bachelors like me and the Colonel. Most men are the marrying sort (poor devils!); and youre not bad-looking: it's quite a pleasure to look at you sometimes—not now, of course, because youre crying and looking as ugly as the very devil; but when youre all right and quite yourself, youre what I should call attractive. That is, to the people in the marrying line, you understand. You go to bed and have a good nice rest; and then get up and look at yourself in the glass; and you wont feel so cheap.

[ELIZA *again looks at him, speechless, and does not stir.*
*The look is quite lost on him: he eats his apple with a dreamy expression of happiness, as it is quite a good one.*]

HIGGINS: [*A genial afterthought occurring to him.*] I daresay my mother could find some chap or other who would do very well.
LIZA: We were above that at the corner of Tottenham Court Road.
HIGGINS: [*Waking up.*] What do you mean?
LIZA: I sold flowers. I didnt sell myself. Now youve made a lady of me I'm not fit to sell anything else. I wish youd left me where you found me.
HIGGINS: [*Slinging the core of the apple decisively into the grate.*] Tosh, Eliza. Dont you insult human relations by dragging all this cant about buying and selling into it. You neednt marry the fellow if you dont like him.
LIZA: What else am I to do?
HIGGINS: Oh, lots of things. What about your old idea of a florist's shop? Pickering could set you up in one: he has lots of money. [*Chuckling.*] He'll have to pay for all those togs you have been wearing today; and that, with the hire of the jewellery, will make a big hole in two hundred pounds. Why, six months ago you would have thought it the millennium to have a flower shop of your own. Come! youll be all right. I must clear off to bed: I'm devilish sleepy. By the way, I came down for something: I forget what it was.
LIZA: Your slippers.
HIGGINS: Oh yes, of course. You shied[1] them at me. [*He picks them up, and is going out when she rises and speaks to him.*]
LIZA: Before you go, sir—
HIGGINS: [*Dropping the slippers in his surprise at her calling him Sir.*] Eh?
LIZA: Do my clothes belong to me or to Colonel Pickering?
HIGGINS: [*Coming back into the room as if her question were the very climax of unreason.*] What the devil use would they be to Pickering?
LIZA: He might want them for the next girl you pick up to experiment on.
HIGGINS: [*Shocked and hurt.*] Is that the way you feel towards us?
LIZA: I dont want to hear anything more about that. All I want to know is whether anything belongs to me. My own clothes were burnt.
HIGGINS: But what does it matter? Why need you start bothering about that in the middle of the night?
LIZA: I want to know what I may take away with me. I dont want to be accused of stealing.
HIGGINS: [*Now deeply wounded.*] Stealing! You shouldnt have said that, Eliza. That shews a want of feeling.
LIZA: I'm sorry. I'm only a common ignorant girl; and in my station I have to be careful. There cant be any feelings between the like of you and the like of me. Please will you tell me what belongs to me and what doesnt?
HIGGINS: [*Very sulky.*] You may take the whole damned houseful if you like. Except the jewels. Theyre hired. Will that satisfy you? [*He turns on his heel and is about to go in extreme dudgeon.*]

1. Threw.

LIZA: [*Drinking in his emotion like nectar, and nagging him to provoke a further supply.*] Stop, please. [*She takes off her jewels.*] Will you take these to your room and keep them safe? I dont want to run the risk of their being missing.
HIGGINS: [*Furious.*] Hand them over. [*She puts them into his hands.*] If these belonged to me instead of to the jeweller, I'd ram them down your ungrateful throat. [*He perfunctorily thrusts them into his pockets, unconsciously decorating himself with the protruding ends of the chains.*]
LIZA: [*Taking a ring off.*] This ring isnt the jeweller's: it's the one you bought me in Brighton. I dont want it now. [HIGGINS *dashes the ring violently into the fireplace, and turns on her so threateningly that she crouches over the piano with her hands over her face, and exclaims.*] Dont you hit me.
HIGGINS: Hit you! You infamous creature, how dare you accuse me of such a thing? It is you who have hit me. You have wounded me to the heart.
LIZA: [*Thrilling with hidden joy.*] I'm glad. Ive got a little of my own back, anyhow.
HIGGINS: [*With dignity, in his finest professional style.*] You have caused me to lose my temper: a thing that has hardly ever happened to me before. I prefer to say nothing more tonight. I am going to bed.
LIZA: [*Pertly.*] Youd better leave a note for Mrs. Pearce about the coffee; for she wont be told by me.
HIGGINS: [*Formally.*] Damn Mrs. Pearce; and damn the coffee; and damn you; and [*Wildly.*] damn my own folly in having lavished my hard-earned knowledge and the treasure of my regard and intimacy on a heartless guttersnipe. [*He goes out with impressive decorum, and spoils it by slamming the door savagely.*]

> [ELIZA *goes down on her knees on the hearthrug to look for the ring. When she finds it she considers for a moment what to do with it. Finally she flings it down on the dessert stand and goes upstairs in a tearing rage.*]

---

*The furniture of* ELIZA'*s room has been increased by a big wardrobe and a sumptuous dressing-table. She comes in and switches on the electric light. She goes to the wardrobe; opens it; and pulls out a walking dress, a hat, and a pair of shoes, which she throws on the bed. She takes off her evening dress and shoes; then takes a padded hanger from the wardrobe; adjusts it carefully in the evening dress; and hangs it in the wardrobe, which she shuts with a slam. She puts on her walking shoes, her walking dress, and hat. She takes her wrist watch from the dressing-table and fastens it on. She pulls on her gloves; takes her vanity bag; and looks into it to see that her purse is there before hanging it on her wrist. She makes for the door. Every movement expresses her furious resolution.*

*She takes a last look at herself in the glass.*

*She suddenly puts out her tongue at herself; then leaves the room, switching off the electric light at the door.*

*Meanwhile, in the street outside,* FREDDY EYNSFORD HILL, *lovelorn, is gazing up at the second floor, in which one of the windows is still lighted.*

*The light goes out.*

FREDDY: Goodnight, darling, darling, darling.

> [ELIZA *comes out, giving the door a considerable bang behind her.*]

LIZA: Whatever are you doing here?
FREDDY: Nothing. I spend most of my nights here. It's the only place where I'm happy. Dont laugh at me, Miss Doolittle.

LIZA: Dont you call me Miss Doolittle, do you hear? Liza's good enough for me. [*She breaks down and grabs him by the shoulders.*] Freddy: you dont think I'm a heartless guttersnipe, do you?

FREDDY: Oh no, no, darling: how can you imagine such a thing? You are the loveliest, dearest—

> [*He loses all self-control and smothers her with kisses. She, hungry for comfort, responds. They stand there in one another's arms.*
> *An elderly police* CONSTABLE *arrives.*]

CONSTABLE: [*Scandalized.*] Now then! Now then!! Now then!!!

> [*They release one another hastily.*]

FREDDY: Sorry, constable. Weve only just become engaged.

> [*They run away.*]

> The CONSTABLE *shakes his head, reflecting on his own courtship and on the vanity of human hopes. He moves off in the opposite direction with slow professional steps.*
> *The flight of the lovers takes them to Cavendish Square. There they halt to consider their next move.*

LIZA: [*Out of breath.*] He didnt half give me a fright, that copper. But you answered him proper.

FREDDY: I hope I havent taken you out of your way. Where were you going?

LIZA: To the river.

FREDDY: What for?

LIZA: To make a hole in it.

FREDDY: [*Horrified.*] Eliza, darling. What do you mean? What's the matter?

LIZA: Never mind. It doesnt matter now. There's nobody in the world now but you and me, is there?

FREDDY: Not a soul.

> [*They indulge in another embrace, and are again surprised by a much younger* CONSTABLE.]

SECOND CONSTABLE: Now then, you two! Whats this? Where do you think you are? Move along here, double quick.

FREDDY: As you say, sir, double quick.

> [*They run away again, and are in Hanover Square before they stop for another conference.*]

FREDDY: I had no idea the police were so devilishly prudish.

LIZA: It's their business to hunt girls off the streets.

FREDDY: We must go somewhere. We cant wander about the streets all night.

LIZA: Cant we? I think it'd be lovely to wander about for ever.

FREDDY: Oh, darling.

> [*They embrace again, oblivious of the arrival of a crawling taxi. It stops.*]

TAXIMAN: Can I drive you and the lady anywhere, sir?

> [*They start asunder.*]

LIZA: Oh, Freddy, a taxi. The very thing.
FREDDY: But, damn it, Ive no money.
LIZA: I have plenty. The Colonel thinks you should never go out without ten pounds in your pocket. Listen. We'll drive about all night; and in the morning I'll call on old Mrs. Higgins and ask her what I ought to do. I'll tell you all about it in the cab. And the police wont touch us there.
FREDDY: Righto! Ripping. [*To the* TAXIMAN.] Wimbledon Common. [*They drive off.*]

## ACT V

MRS. HIGGINS's *drawing room. She is at her writing-table as before. The* PARLORMAID *comes in.*

THE PARLORMAID: [*At the door.*] Mr. Henry, maam, is downstairs with Colonel Pickering.
MRS. HIGGINS: Well, shew them up.
THE PARLORMAID: Theyre using the telephone, maam. Telephoning to the police, I think.
MRS. HIGGINS: What!
THE PARLORMAID: [*Coming further in and lowering her voice.*] Mr. Henry is in a state, maam. I thought I'd better tell you.
MRS. HIGGINS: If you had told me that Mr. Henry was not in a state it would have been more surprising. Tell them to come up when theyve finished with the police. I suppose he's lost something.
THE PARLORMAID: Yes, maam [*Going.*]
MRS. HIGGINS: Go upstairs and tell Miss Doolittle that Mr. Henry and the Colonel are here. Ask her not to come down til I send for her.
THE PARLORMAID: Yes, maam.

[HIGGINS *bursts in. He is, as the* PARLORMAID *has said, in a state.*]

HIGGINS: Look here, mother: heres a confounded thing!
MRS. HIGGINS: Yes, dear. Good morning. [*He checks his impatience and kisses her, whilst the* PARLORMAID *goes out.*] What is it?
HIGGINS: Eliza's bolted.
MRS. HIGGINS: [*Calmly continuing her writing.*] You must have frightened her.
HIGGINS: Frightened her! nonsense! She was left last night, as usual, to turn out the lights and all that; and instead of going to bed she changed her clothes and went right off: her bed wasnt slept in. She came in a cab for her things before seven this morning; and that fool Mrs. Pearce let her have them without telling me a word about it. What am I to do?
MRS. HIGGINS: Do without, I'm afraid, Henry. The girl has a perfect right to leave if she chooses.
HIGGINS: [*Wandering distractedly across the room.*] But I cant find anything. I dont know what appointments Ive got. I'm—

[PICKERING *comes in.* MRS. HIGGINS *puts down her pen and turns away from the writing-table.*]

PICKERING: [*Shaking hands.*] Good morning, Mrs. Higgins. Has Henry told you? [*He sits down on the ottoman.*]

HIGGINS: What does that ass of an inspector say? Have you offered a reward?
MRS. HIGGINS: [*Rising in indignant amazement.*] You dont mean to say you have set the police after Eliza.
HIGGINS: Of course. What are the police for? What else could we do? [*He sits in the Elizabethan chair.*]
PICKERING: The inspector made a lot of difficulties. I really think he suspected us of some improper purpose.
MRS. HIGGINS: Well, of course he did. What right have you to go to the police and give the girl's name as if she were a thief, or a lost umbrella, or something? Really! [*She sits down again, deeply vexed.*]
HIGGINS: But we want to find her.
PICKERING: We cant let her go like this, you know, Mrs. Higgins. What were we to do?
MRS. HIGGINS: You have no more sense, either of you, than two children. Why—

[*The* PARLORMAID *comes in and breaks off the conversation.*]

THE PARLORMAID: Mr. Henry: a gentleman wants to see you very particular. He's been sent on from Wimpole Street.
HIGGINS: Oh, bother! I cant see anyone now. Who is it?
THE PARLORMAID: A Mr. Doolittle, sir.
PICKERING: Doolittle! Do you mean the dustman?
THE PARLORMAID: Dustman! Oh no, sir: a gentleman.
HIGGINS: [*Springing up excitedly.*] By George, Pick, it's some relative of hers that she's gone to. Somebody we know nothing about. [*To the* PARLORMAID.] Send him up, quick.
THE PARLORMAID: Yes, sir. [*She goes.*]
HIGGINS: [*Eagerly, going to his mother.*] Genteel relatives! now we shall hear something. [*He sits down in the Chippendale chair.*]
MRS. HIGGINS: Do you know any of her people?
PICKERING: Only her father: the fellow we told you about.
THE PARLORMAID: [*Announcing.*] Mr. Doolittle. [*She withdraws.*]

[DOOLITTLE *enters. He is resplendently dressed as for a fashionable wedding, and might, in fact, be the bridegroom. A flower in his buttonhole, a dazzling silk hat, and patent leather shoes complete the effect. He is too concerned with the business he has come on to notice* MRS. HIGGINS. *He walks straight to* HIGGINS, *and accosts him with vehement reproach.*]

DOOLITTLE: [*Indicating his own person.*] See here! Do you see this? You done this.
HIGGINS: Done what, man?
DOOLITTLE: This, I tell you. Look at it. Look at this hat. Look at this coat.
PICKERING: Has Eliza been buying you clothes?
DOOLITTLE: Eliza! not she. Why would she buy me clothes?
MRS. HIGGINS: Good morning, Mr. Doolittle. Wont you sit down?
DOOLITTLE: [*Taken aback as he becomes conscious that he has forgotten his hostess.*] Asking your pardon, maam. [*He approaches her and shakes her proffered hand.*] Thank you. [*He sits down on the ottoman, on* PICKERING'*s right.*] I am that full of what has happened to me that I cant think of anything else.
HIGGINS: What the dickens has happened to you?
DOOLITTLE: I shouldnt mind if it had only happened to me: anything might happen to anybody and nobody to blame but Providence, as you might say.

But this is something that you done to me: yes, you, Enry Iggins.

HIGGINS: Have you found Eliza?

DOOLITTLE: Have you lost her?

HIGGINS: Yes.

DOOLITTLE: You have all the luck, you have. I aint found her; but she'll find me quick enough now after what you done to me.

MRS. HIGGINS: But what has my son done to you, Mr. Doolittle?

DOOLITTLE: Done to me! Ruined me. Destroyed my happiness. Tied me up and delivered me into the hands of middle class morality.

HIGGINS: [*Rising intolerantly and standing over* DOOLITTLE.] Youre raving. Youre drunk. Youre mad. I gave you five pounds. After that I had two conversations with you, at half-a-crown an hour. Ive never seen you since.

DOOLITTLE: Oh! Drunk am I? Mad am I? Tell me this. Did you or did you not write a letter to an old blighter in America that was giving five millions to found Moral Reform Societies all over the world, and that wanted you to invent a universal language for him?

HIGGINS: What! Ezra D. Wannafeller![2] He's dead. [*He sits down again carelessly.*]

DOOLITTLE: Yes: he's dead; and I'm done for. Now did you or did you not write a letter to him to say that the most original moralist at present in England, to the best of your knowledge, was Alfred Doolittle, a common dustman?

HIGGINS: Oh, after your first visit I remember making some silly joke of the kind.

DOOLITTLE: Ah! you may well call it a silly joke. It put the lid on me right enough. Just give him the chance he wanted to shew that Americans is not like us: that they reckonize and respect merit in every class of life, however humble. Them words is in his blooming will, in which, Henry Higgins, thanks to your silly joking, he leaves me a share in his Predigested Cheese Trust worth three thousand a year[3] on condition that I lecture for his Wannafeller Moral Reform World League as often as they ask me up to six times a year.

HIGGINS: The devil he does! Whew! [*Brightening suddenly.*] What a lark!

PICKERING: A safe thing for you, Doolittle. They wont ask you twice.

DOOLITTLE: It aint the lecturing I mind. I'll lecture them blue in the face, I will, and not turn a hair. It's making a gentleman of me that I object to. Who asked him to make a gentleman of me? I was happy. I was free. I touched pretty nigh everybody for money when I wanted it, same as I touched you, Enry Iggins. Now I am worried; tied neck and heels; and everybody touches me for money. It's a fine thing for you, says my solicitor. Is it? says I. You mean it's a good thing for you, I says. When I was a poor man and had a solicitor once when they found a pram in the dust cart, he got me off, and got shut of me and got me shut of him as quick as he could. Same with the doctors: used to shove me out of the hospital before I could hardly stand on my legs, and nothing to pay. Now they finds out that I'm not a healthy man and cant live unless they looks after me twice a day. In the house I'm not let do a hand's turn for myself: somebody else must do it and touch me for it. A year ago I hadnt a relative in the world except two or three that wouldnt speak to me. Now Ive fifty, and not a decent week's wages among the lot of them. I

---

2. Shaw's sly stereotype of American millionaires such as John Wannamaker (1838–1922) and John D. Rockefeller (1839–1937).
3. A substantial annuity; roughly $340,000 per year in American currency today.

have to live for others and not for myself: thats middle class morality. You talk of losing Eliza. Dont you be anxious: I bet she's on my doorstep by this: she that could support herself easy by selling flowers if I wasnt respectable. And the next one to touch me will be you, Enry Iggins. I'll have to learn to speak middle class language from you, instead of speaking proper English. Thats where youll come in; and I daresay thats what you done it for.

MRS. HIGGINS: But, my dear Mr. Doolittle, you need not suffer all this if you are really in earnest. Nobody can force you to accept this bequest. You can repudiate it. Isnt that so, Colonel Pickering?

PICKERING: I believe so.

DOOLITTLE: [*Softening his manner in deference to her sex.*] Thats the tragedy of it, maam. It's easy to say chuck it; but I havnt the nerve. Which of us has? We're all intimidated. Intimidated, maam: thats what we are. What is there for me if I chuck it but the workhouse in my old age? I have to dye my hair already to keep my job as a dustman. If I was one of the deserving poor, and had put by a bit, I could chuck it; but then why should I, acause the deserving poor might as well be millionaires for all the happiness they ever has. They dont know what happiness is. But I, as one of the undeserving poor, have nothing between me and the pauper's uniform but this here blasted three thousand a year that shoves me into the middle class. (Excuse the expression, maam; youd use it yourself if you had my provocation.) Theyve got you every way you turn: it's a choice between the Skilly of the workhouse and the Char Bydis[4] of the middle class; and I havnt the nerve for the workhouse. Intimidated: thats what I am. Broke. Bought up. Happier men than me will call for my dust, and touch me for their tip; and I'll look on helpless, and envy them. And thats what your son has brought me to. [*He is overcome by emotion.*]

MRS. HIGGINS: Well, I'm very glad youre not going to do anything foolish, Mr. Doolittle. For this solves the problem of Eliza's future. You can provide for her now.

DOOLITTLE: [*With melancholy resignation.*] Yes, maam: I'm expected to provide for everyone now, out of three thousand a year.

HIGGINS: [*Jumping up.*] Nonsense! he cant provide for her. He shant provide for her. She doesnt belong to him. I paid him five pounds for her. Doolittle: either youre an honest man or a rogue.

DOOLITTLE: [*Tolerantly.*] A little of both, Henry, like the rest of us: a little of both.

HIGGINS: Well, you took that money for the girl; and you have no right to take her as well.

MRS. HIGGINS: Henry: dont be absurd. If you want to know where Eliza is, she is upstairs.

HIGGINS: [*Amazed.*] Upstairs!!! Then I shall jolly soon fetch her downstairs. [*He makes resolutely for the door.*]

MRS. HIGGINS: [*Rising and following him.*] Be quiet, Henry. Sit down.

HIGGINS: I—

MRS. HIGGINS: Sit down, dear; and listen to me.

---

4. Mistake for the Greek mythological monsters Scylla, associated with a deadly rock jutting out of the Strait of Messina, and Charybdis, linked with a nearby whirlpool off the Sicilian coast. Used allusively, it refers to the danger of avoiding one peril only to encounter its opposite. (In Homer's *Odyssey*, Odysseus's ship narrowly makes it past Charybdis but six of his men are lost to the six-headed monster, Scylla.)

HIGGINS: Oh very well, very well, very well. [*He throws himself ungraciously on the ottoman, with his face towards the windows.*] But I think you might have told us this half an hour ago.

MRS. HIGGINS: Eliza came to me this morning. She told me of the brutal way you two treated her.

HIGGINS: [*Bounding up again.*] What!

PICKERING: [*Rising also.*] My dear Mrs. Higgins, she's been telling you stories. We didnt treat her brutally. We hardly said a word to her; and we parted on particularly good terms. [*Turning on* HIGGINS.] Higgins: did you bully her after I went to bed?

HIGGINS: Just the other way about. She threw my slippers in my face. She behaved in the most outrageous way. I never gave her the slightest provocation. The slippers came bang into my face the moment I entered the room—before I had uttered a word. And used perfectly awful language.

PICKERING: [*Astonished.*] But why? What did we do to her?

MRS. HIGGINS: I think I know pretty well what you did. The girl is naturally rather affectionate, I think. Isnt she, Mr. Doolittle?

DOOLITTLE: Very tender-hearted, maam. Takes after me.

MRS. HIGGINS: Just so. She had become attached to you both. She worked very hard for you, Henry. I dont think you quite realize what anything in the nature of brain work means to a girl of her class. Well, it seems that when the great day of trial came, and she did this wonderful thing for you without making a single mistake, you two sat there and never said a word to her, but talked together of how glad you were that it was all over and how you had been bored with the whole thing. And then you were surprised because she threw your slippers at you! *I* should have thrown the fire-irons at you.

HIGGINS: We said nothing except that we were tired and wanted to go to bed. Did we, Pick?

PICKERING: [*Shrugging his shoulders.*] That was all.

MRS. HIGGINS: [*Ironically.*] Quite sure?

PICKERING: Absolutely. Really, that was all.

MRS. HIGGINS: You didnt thank her, or pet her, or admire her, or tell her how splendid she'd been.

HIGGINS: [*Impatiently.*] But she knew all about that. We didnt make speeches to her, if thats what you mean.

PICKERING: [*Conscience stricken.*] Perhaps we were a little inconsiderate. Is she very angry?

MRS. HIGGINS: [*Returning to her place at the writing-table.*] Well, I'm afraid she wont go back to Wimpole Street, especially now that Mr. Doolittle is able to keep up the position you have thrust on her; but she says she is quite willing to meet you on friendly terms and to let bygones be bygones.

HIGGINS: [*Furious.*] Is she, by George? Ho!

MRS. HIGGINS: If you promise to behave yourself, Henry, I'll ask her to come down. If not, go home; for you have taken up quite enough of my time.

HIGGINS: Oh, all right. Very well. Pick: you behave yourself. Let us put on our best Sunday manners for this creature that we picked out of the mud. [*He flings himself sulkily into the Elizabethan chair.*]

DOOLITTLE: [*Remonstrating.*] Now, now, Enry Iggins! Have some consideration for my feelings as a middle class man.

MRS. HIGGINS: Remember your promise, Henry. [*She presses the bell-button on the writing-table.*] Mr. Doolittle: will you be so good as to step out on the balcony for a moment. I dont want Eliza to have the shock of your news until she has made it up with these two gentlemen. Would you mind?

DOOLITTLE: As you wish, lady. Anything to help Henry to keep her off my hands. [*He disappears through the window.*]

[*The* PARLORMAID *answers the bell.* PICKERING *sits down in* DOOLITTLE'*s place.*]

MRS. HIGGINS: Ask Miss Doolittle to come down, please.
THE PARLORMAID: Yes, maam. [*She goes out.*]
MRS. HIGGINS: Now, Henry: be good.
HIGGINS: I am behaving myself perfectly.
PICKERING: He is doing his best, Mrs. Higgins.

[*A pause.* HIGGINS *throws back his head; stretches out his legs; and begins to whistle.*]

MRS. HIGGINS: Henry, dearest, you dont look at all nice in that attitude.
HIGGINS: [*Pulling himself together.*] I was not trying to look nice, mother.
MRS. HIGGINS: It doesnt matter, dear. I only wanted to make you speak.
HIGGINS: Why?
MRS. HIGGINS: Because you cant speak and whistle at the same time.

[HIGGINS *groans. Another very trying pause.*]

HIGGINS: [*Springing up, out of patience.*] Where the devil is that girl? Are we to wait here all day?

[ELIZA *enters, sunny, self-possessed, and giving a staggeringly convincing exhibition of ease of manner. She carries a little work-basket, and is very much at home.* PICKERING *is too much taken aback to rise.*]

LIZA: How do you do, Professor Higgins? Are you quite well?
HIGGINS: [*Choking.*] Am I—[*He can say no more.*]
LIZA: But of course you are: you are never ill. So glad to see you again, Colonel Pickering. [*He rises hastily; and they shake hands.*] Quite chilly this morning, isnt it? [*She sits down on his left. He sits beside her.*]
HIGGINS: Dont you dare try this game on me. I taught it to you; and it doesnt take me in. Get up and come home; and dont be a fool.

[ELIZA *takes a piece of needlework from her basket, and begins to stitch at it, without taking the least notice of this outburst.*]

MRS. HIGGINS: Very nicely put, indeed, Henry. No woman could resist such an invitation.
HIGGINS: You let her alone, mother. Let her speak for herself. You will jolly soon see whether she has an idea that I havnt put into her head or a word that I havnt put into her mouth. I tell you I have created this thing out of the squashed cabbage leaves of Covent Garden; and now she pretends to play the fine lady with me.
MRS. HIGGINS: [*Placidly.*] Yes, dear; but youll sit down, wont you?

[HIGGINS *sits down again, savagely.*]

LIZA: [*To* PICKERING, *taking no apparent notice of* HIGGINS, *and working away deftly.*] Will you drop me altogether now that the experiment is over, Colonel Pickering?

PICKERING: Oh dont. You mustnt think of it as an experiment. It shocks me, somehow.

LIZA: Oh, I'm only a squashed cabbage leaf—

PICKERING: [*Impulsively.*] No.

LIZA: [*Continuing quietly.*]—but I owe so much to you that I should be very unhappy if you forgot me.

PICKERING: It's very kind of you to say so, Miss Doolittle.

LIZA: It's not because you paid for my dresses. I know you are generous to everybody with money. But it was from you that I learnt really nice manners; and that is what makes one a lady, isnt it? You see it was so very difficult for me with the example of Professor Higgins always before me. I was brought up to be just like him, unable to control myself, and using bad language on the slightest provocation. And I should never have known that ladies and gentlemen didnt behave like that if you hadnt been there.

HIGGINS: Well!!

PICKERING: Oh, thats only his way, you know. He doesnt mean it.

LIZA: Oh, *I* didnt mean it either, when I was a flower girl. It was only my way. But you see I did it; and thats what makes the difference after all.

PICKERING: No doubt. Still, he taught you to speak; and I couldnt have done that, you know.

LIZA: [*Trivially.*] Of course: that is his profession.

HIGGINS: Damnation!

LIZA: [*Continuing.*] It was just like learning to dance in the fashionable way: there was nothing more than that in it. But do you know what began my real education?

PICKERING: What?

LIZA: [*Stopping her work for a moment.*] Your calling me Miss Doolittle that day when I first came to Wimpole Street. That was the beginning of self-respect for me. [*She resumes her stitching.*] And there were a hundred little things you never noticed, because they came naturally to you. Things about standing up and taking off your hat and opening doors—

PICKERING: Oh, that was nothing.

LIZA: Yes: things that shewed you thought and felt about me as if I were something better than a scullery-maid; though of course I know you would have been just the same to a scullery-maid if she had been let into the drawing room. You never took off your boots in the dining room when I was there.

PICKERING: You mustnt mind that. Higgins takes off his boots all over the place.

LIZA: I know. I am not blaming him. It is his way, isnt it? But it made such a difference to me that you didnt do it. You see, really and truly, apart from the things anyone can pick up (the dressing and the proper way of speaking, and so on), the difference between a lady and a flower girl is not how she behaves, but how she's treated. I shall always be a flower girl to Professor Higgins, because he always treats me as a flower girl, and always will; but I know I can be a lady to you, because you always treat me as a lady, and always will.

MRS. HIGGINS: Please dont grind your teeth, Henry.

PICKERING: Well, this is really very nice of you, Miss Doolittle.

LIZA: I should like you to call me Eliza, now, if you would.

PICKERING: Thank you. Eliza, of course.

LIZA: And I should like Professor Higgins to call me Miss Doolittle.

HIGGINS: I'll see you damned first.

MRS. HIGGINS: Henry! Henry!

PICKERING: [*Laughing.*] Why dont you slang back at him? Dont stand it. It would do him a lot of good.

LIZA: I cant. I could have done it once; but now I cant go back to it. You told me, you know, that when a child is brought to a foreign country, it picks up the language in a few weeks, and forgets its own. Well, I am a child in your country. I have forgotten my own language, and can speak nothing but yours. Thats the real break-off with the corner of Tottenham Court Road. Leaving Wimpole Street finishes it.

PICKERING: [*Much alarmed.*] Oh! but youre coming back to Wimpole Street, arnt you? Youll forgive Higgins?

HIGGINS: [*Rising.*] Forgive! Will she, by George! Let her go. Let her find out how she can get on without us. She will relapse into the gutter in three weeks without me at her elbow.

> [DOOLITTLE *appears at the centre window. With a look of dignified reproach at* HIGGINS, *he comes slowly and silently to his daughter, who, with her back to the window, is unconscious of his approach.*]

PICKERING: He's incorrigible, Eliza. You wont relapse, will you?

LIZA: No: not now. Never again. I have learnt my lesson. I dont believe I could utter one of the old sounds if I tried. [DOOLITTLE *touches her on her left shoulder. She drops her work, losing her self-possession utterly at the spectacle of her father's splendor.*] A-a-a-a-a-ah-ow-ooh!

HIGGINS: [*With a crow of triumph.*] Aha! Just so. A-a-a-a-ahowooh! A-a-a-a-ah-ow-ooh! A-a-a-a-ahowooh! Victory! Victory! [*He throws himself on the divan, folding his arms, and spraddling arrogantly.*]

DOOLITTLE: Can you blame the girl? Dont look at me like that, Eliza. It aint my fault. Ive come into some money.

LIZA: You must have touched a millionaire this time, dad.

DOOLITTLE: I have. But I'm dressed something special today. I'm going to St. George's, Hanover Square. Your stepmother is going to marry me.

LIZA: [*Angrily.*] Youre going to let yourself down to marry that low common woman!

PICKERING: [*Quietly.*] He ought to, Eliza. [*To* DOOLITTLE.] Why has she changed her mind?

DOOLITTLE: [*Sadly.*] Intimidated, Governor. Intimidated. Middle class morality claims its victim. Wont you put on your hat, Liza, and come and see me turned off?

LIZA: If the Colonel says I must, I—I'll [*Almost sobbing.*] I'll demean myself. And get insulted for my pains, like enough.

DOOLITTLE: Dont be afraid: she never comes to words with anyone now, poor woman! respectability has broke all the spirit out of her.

PICKERING: [*Squeezing* ELIZA's *elbow gently.*] Be kind to them, Eliza. Make the best of it.

LIZA: [*Forcing a little smile for him through her vexation.*] Oh well, just to shew theres no ill feeling. I'll be back in a moment. [*She goes out.*]

DOOLITTLE: [*Sitting down beside* PICKERING.] I feel uncommon nervous about the ceremony, Colonel. I wish youd come and see me through it.

PICKERING: But youve been through it before, man. You were married to Eliza's mother.
DOOLITTLE: Who told you that, Colonel?
PICKERING: Well, nobody told me. But I concluded—naturally—
DOOLITTLE: No: that aint the natural way, Colonel: it's only the middle class way. My way was always the undeserving way. But dont say nothing to Eliza. She dont know: I always had a delicacy about telling her.
PICKERING: Quite right. We'll leave it so, if you dont mind.
DOOLITTLE: And youll come to the church, Colonel, and put me through straight?
PICKERING: With pleasure. As far as a bachelor can.
MRS. HIGGINS: May I come, Mr. Doolittle? I should be very sorry to miss your wedding.
DOOLITTLE: I should indeed be honored by your condescension, maam; and my poor old woman would take it as a tremenjous compliment. She's been very low, thinking of the happy days that are no more.
MRS. HIGGINS: [*Rising.*] I'll order the carriage and get ready. [*The men rise, except* HIGGINS.] I shant be more than fifteen minutes. [*As she goes to the door* ELIZA *comes in, hatted and buttoning her gloves.*] I'm going to the church to see your father married, Eliza. You had better come in the brougham[5] with me. Colonel Pickering can go on with the bridegroom.

[MRS. HIGGINS *goes out.* ELIZA *comes to the middle of the room between the centre window and the ottoman.* PICKERING *joins her.*]

DOOLITTLE: Bridegroom! What a word! It makes a man realize his position, somehow. [*He takes up his hat and goes towards the door.*]
PICKERING: Before I go, Eliza, do forgive Higgins and come back to us.
LIZA: I dont think dad would allow me. Would you, dad?
DOOLITTLE: [*Sad but magnanimous.*] They played you off very cunning, Eliza, them two sportsmen. It if had been only one of them, you could have nailed him. But you see, there was two; and one of them chaperoned the other, as you might say. [*To* PICKERING.] It was artful of you, Colonel; but I bear no malice: I should have done the same myself. I been the victim of one woman after another all my life; and I dont grudge you two getting the better of Eliza. I shant interfere. It's time for us to go, Colonel. So long, Henry. See you in St. George's, Eliza. [*He goes out.*]
PICKERING: [*Coaxing.*] Do stay with us, Eliza. [*He follows* DOOLITTLE.]

[ELIZA *goes out on the balcony to avoid being alone with* HIGGINS. *He rises and joins her there. She immediately comes back into the room and makes for the door; but he goes along the balcony quickly and gets his back to the door before she reaches it.*]

HIGGINS: Well, Eliza, youve had a bit of your own back, as you call it. Have you had enough? and are you going to be reasonable? Or do you want any more?
LIZA: You want me back only to pick up your slippers and put up with your tempers and fetch and carry for you.

---

5. A closed carriage.

HIGGINS: I havnt said I wanted you back at all.
LIZA: Oh, indeed. Then what are we talking about?
HIGGINS: About you, not about me. If you come back I shall treat you just as I have always treated you. I cant change my nature; and I dont intend to change my manners. My manners are exactly the same as Colonel Pickering's.
LIZA: Thats not true. He treats a flower girl as if she was a duchess.
HIGGINS: And I treat a duchess as if she was a flower girl.
LIZA: I see. [*She turns away composedly, and sits on the ottoman, facing the window.*] The same to everybody.
HIGGINS: Just so.
LIZA: Like father.
HIGGINS: [*Grinning, a little taken down.*] Without accepting the comparison at all points, Eliza, it's quite true that your father is not a snob, and that he will be quite at home in any station of life to which his eccentric destiny may call him. [*Seriously.*] The great secret, Eliza, is not having bad manners or good manners or any other particular sort of manners, but having the same manner for all human souls: in short, behaving as if you were in Heaven, where there are no third-class carriages, and one soul is as good as another.
LIZA: Amen. You are a born preacher.
HIGGINS: [*Irritated.*] The question is not whether I treat you rudely, but whether you ever heard me treat anyone else better.
LIZA: [*With sudden sincerity.*] I dont care how you treat me. I dont mind your swearing at me. I shouldnt mind a black eye: Ive had one before this. But [*Standing up and facing him.*] I wont be passed over.
HIGGINS: Then get out of my way; for I wont stop for you. You talk about me as if I were a motor bus.
LIZA: So you are a motor bus: all bounce and go, and no consideration for anyone. But I can do without you: dont think I cant.
HIGGINS: I know you can. I told you you could.
LIZA: [*Wounded, getting away from him to the other side of the ottoman with her face to the hearth.*] I know you did, you brute. You wanted to get rid of me.
HIGGINS: Liar.
LIZA: Thank you. [*She sits down with dignity.*]
HIGGINS: You never asked yourself, I suppose, whether *I* could do without *you.*
LIZA: [*Earnestly.*] Dont you try to get round me.[6] Youll have to do without me.
HIGGINS: [*Arrogant.*] I can do without anybody. I have my own soul: my own spark of divine fire. But [*With sudden humility.*] I shall miss you, Eliza. [*He sits down near her on the ottoman.*] I have learnt something from your idiotic notions: I confess that humbly and gratefully. And I have grown accustomed to your voice and appearance. I like them, rather.
LIZA: Well, you have both of them on your gramophone and in your book of photographs. When you feel lonely without me, you can turn the machine on. It's got no feelings to hurt.
HIGGINS: I cant turn your soul on. Leave me those feelings; and you can take away the voice and the face. They are not you.
LIZA: Oh, you are a devil. You can twist the heart in a girl as easy as some could

---

6. That is, Don't try to deceive me.

twist her arms to hurt her. Mrs. Pearce warned me. Time and again she has wanted to leave you; and you always got round her at the last minute. And you dont care a bit for her. And you dont care a bit for me.

HIGGINS: I care for life, for humanity; and you are a part of it that has come my way and been built into my house. What more can you or anyone ask?

LIZA: I wont care for anybody that doesnt care for me.

HIGGINS: Commercial principles, Eliza. Like [*Reproducing her Covent Garden pronunciation with professional exactness.*] s'yollin voylets [selling violets], isnt it?

LIZA: Dont sneer at me. It's mean to sneer at me.

HIGGINS: I have never sneered in my life. Sneering doesnt become either the human face or the human soul. I am expressing my righteous contempt for Commercialism. I dont and wont trade in affection. You call me a brute because you couldnt buy a claim on me by fetching my slippers and finding my spectacles. You were a fool: I think a woman fetching a man's slippers is a disgusting sight: did I ever fetch your slippers? I think a good deal more of you for throwing them in my face. No use slaving for me and then saying you want to be cared for: who cares for a slave? If you come back, come back for the sake of good fellowship; for youll get nothing else. Youve had a thousand times as much out of me as I have out of you; and if you dare to set up your little dog's tricks of fetching and carrying slippers against my creation of a Duchess Eliza, I'll slam the door in your silly face.

LIZA: What did you do it for if you didnt care for me?

HIGGINS: [*Heartily.*] Why, because it was my job.

LIZA: You never thought of the trouble it would make for me.

HIGGINS: Would the world ever have been made if its maker had been afraid of making trouble? Making life means making trouble. Theres only one way of escaping trouble; and thats killing things. Cowards, you notice, are always shrieking to have troublesome people killed.

LIZA: I'm no preacher: I dont notice things like that. I notice that you dont notice me.

HIGGINS: [*Jumping up and walking about intolerantly.*] Eliza: youre an idiot. I waste the treasures of my Miltonic mind by spreading them before you. Once for all, understand that I go my way and do my work without caring twopence what happens to either of us. I am not intimidated, like your father and your stepmother. So you can come back or go to the devil: which you please.

LIZA: What am I to come back for?

HIGGINS: [*Bouncing up on his knees on the ottoman and leaning over it to her.*] For the fun of it. Thats why I took you on.

LIZA: [*With averted face.*] And you may throw me out tomorrow if I dont do everything you want me to?

HIGGINS: Yes; and you may walk out tomorrow if I dont do everything you want me to.

LIZA: And live with my stepmother?

HIGGINS: Yes, or sell flowers.

LIZA: Oh! if I only could go back to my flower basket! I should be independent of both you and father and all the world! Why did you take my independence from me? Why did I give it up? I'm a slave now, for all my fine clothes.

HIGGINS: Not a bit. I'll adopt you as my daughter and settle money on you if you like. Or would you rather marry Pickering?

LIZA: [*Looking fiercely round at him.*] I wouldnt marry you if you asked me; and youre nearer my age than what he is.

HIGGINS: [*Gently.*] Than he is: not "than what he is."

LIZA: [*Losing her temper and rising.*] I'll talk as I like. Youre not my teacher now.

HIGGINS: [*Reflectively.*] I dont suppose Pickering would, though. He's as confirmed an old bachelor as I am.

LIZA: Thats not what I want; and dont you think it. Ive always had chaps enough wanting me that way. Freddy Hill writes to me twice and three times a day, sheets and sheets.

HIGGINS: [*Disagreeably surprised.*] Damn his impudence! [*He recoils and finds himself sitting on his heels.*]

LIZA: He has a right to if he likes, poor lad. And he does love me.

HIGGINS: [*Getting off the ottoman.*] You have no right to encourage him.

LIZA: Every girl has a right to be loved.

HIGGINS: What! By fools like that?

LIZA: Freddy's not a fool. And if he's weak and poor and wants me, may be he'd make me happier than my betters that bully me and dont want me.

HIGGINS: Can he make anything of you? Thats the point.

LIZA: Perhaps I could make something of him. But I never thought of us making anything of one another; and you never think of anything else. I only want to be natural.

HIGGINS: In short, you want me to be as infatuated about you as Freddy? Is that it?

LIZA: No I dont. Thats not the sort of feeling I want from you. And dont you be too sure of yourself or of me. I could have been a bad girl if I'd liked. Ive seen more of some things than you, for all your learning. Girls like me can drag gentlemen down to make love to them easy enough. And they wish each other dead the next minute.

HIGGINS: Of course they do. Then what in thunder are we quarrelling about?

LIZA: [*Much troubled.*] I want a little kindness. I know I'm a common ignorant girl, and you a book-learned gentleman; but I'm not dirt under your feet. What I done [*Correcting herself.*] what I did was not for the dresses and the taxis: I did it because we were pleasant together and I come—came—to care for you; not to want you to make love to me, and not forgetting the difference between us, but more friendly like.

HIGGINS: Well, of course. Thats just how I feel. And how Pickering feels. Eliza: youre a fool.

LIZA: Thats not a proper answer to give me. [*She sinks on the chair at the writing-table in tears.*]

HIGGINS: It's all youll get until you stop being a common idiot. If youre going to be a lady, youll have to give up feeling neglected if the men you know dont spend half their time snivelling over you and the other half giving you black eyes. If you cant stand the coldness of my sort of life, and the strain of it, go back to the gutter. Work til youre more a brute than a human being; and then cuddle and squabble and drink til you fall asleep. Oh, it's a fine life, the life of the gutter. It's real: it's warm: it's violent: you can feel it through the thickest skin: you can taste it and smell it without any training or any work. Not like Science and Literature and Classical Music and Philosophy and Art. You find me cold, unfeeling, selfish, dont you? Very well: be off with you to the sort of people you like. Marry some sentimental hog or other with lots of money, and a thick pair of lips to kiss you with and a thick pair of boots to kick you with. If you cant appreciate what youve got, youd better get what you can appreciate.

LIZA: [*Desperate.*] Oh, you are a cruel tyrant. I cant talk to you: you turn everything against me: I'm always in the wrong. But you know very well all the time that youre nothing but a bully. You know I cant go back to the gutter, as you call it, and that I have no real friends in the world but you and the Colonel. You know well I couldnt bear to live with a low common man after you two; and it's wicked and cruel of you to insult me by pretending I could. You think I must go back to Wimpole Street because I have nowhere else to go but father's. But dont you be too sure that you have me under your feet to be trampled on and talked down. I'll marry Freddy, I will, as soon as I'm able to support him.

HIGGINS: [*Thunderstruck.*] Freddy!!! that young fool! That poor devil who couldnt get a job as an errand boy even if he had the guts to try for it! Woman: do you not understand that I have made you a consort for a king?

LIZA: Freddy loves me: that makes him king enough for me. I dont want him to work: he wasnt brought up to it as I was. I'll go and be a teacher.

HIGGINS: Whatll you teach, in heaven's name?

LIZA: What you taught me. I'll teach phonetics.

HIGGINS: Ha! ha! ha!

LIZA: I'll offer myself as an assistant to that hairy-faced Hungarian.

HIGGINS: [*Rising in a fury.*] What! That impostor! that humbug! that toadying ignoramus! Teach him my methods! my discoveries! You take one step in his direction and I'll wring your neck. [*He lays hands on her.*] Do you hear?

LIZA: [*Defiantly non-resistant.*] Wring away. What do I care? I knew youd strike me some day. [*He lets her go, stamping with rage at having forgotten himself, and recoils so hastily that he stumbles back into his seat on the ottoman.*] Aha! Now I know how to deal with you. What a fool I was not to think of it before! You cant take away the knowledge you gave me. You said I had a finer ear than you. And I can be civil and kind to people, which is more than you can. Aha! [*Purposely dropping her aitches to annoy him.*] Thats done you, Enry Iggins, it az. Now I dont care that [*Snapping her fingers.*] for your bullying and your big talk. I'll advertize it in the papers that your duchess is only a flower girl that you taught, and that she'll teach anybody to be a duchess just the same in six months for a thousand guineas. Oh, when I think of myself crawling under your feet and being trampled on and called names, when all the time I had only to lift up my finger to be as good as you. I could just kick myself.

HIGGINS: [*Wondering at her.*] You damned impudent slut, you! But it's better than snivelling; better than fetching slippers and finding spectacles, isnt it? [*Rising.*] By George, Eliza, I said I'd make a woman of you; and I have. I like you like this.

LIZA: Yes: you turn round and make up to me now that I'm not afraid of you, and can do without you.

HIGGINS: Of course I do, you little fool. Five minutes ago you were like a millstone round my neck. Now youre a tower of strength: a consort battleship. You and I and Pickering will be three old bachelors together instead of only two men and a silly girl.

[MRS. HIGGINS, *returns, dressed for the wedding.* ELIZA *instantly becomes cool and elegant.*]

MRS. HIGGINS: The carriage is waiting, Eliza. Are you ready?

LIZA: Quite. Is the Professor coming?

MRS. HIGGINS: Certainly not. He cant behave himself in church. He makes remarks out loud all the time on the clergyman's pronunciation.

LIZA: Then I shall not see you again, Professor. Goodbye. [*She goes to the door.*]

MRS. HIGGINS: [*Coming to* HIGGINS.] Goodbye, dear.

HIGGINS: Goodbye, mother. [*He is about to kiss her, when he recollects something.*] Oh, by the way, Eliza, order a ham and a Stilton cheese, will you? And buy me a pair of reindeer gloves, number eights, and a tie to match that new suit of mine. You can choose the color. [*His cheerful, careless, vigorous voice shews that he is incorrigible.*]

LIZA: [*Disdainfully.*] Number eights are too small for you if you want them lined with lamb's wool. You have three new ties that you have forgotten in the drawer of your washstand. Colonel Pickering prefers double Gloucester to Stilton; and you dont notice the difference. I telephoned Mrs. Pearce this morning not to forget the ham. What you are to do without me I cannot imagine. [*She sweeps out.*]

MRS. HIGGINS: I'm afraid youve spoilt that girl, Henry. I should be uneasy about you and her if she were less fond of Colonel Pickering.

HIGGINS: Pickering! Nonsense: she's going to marry Freddy. Ha ha! Freddy! Freddy!! Ha ha ha ha ha!!!!! [*He roars with laughter as the play ends*].

CURTAIN

The rest of the story need not be shewn in action, and indeed, would hardly need telling if our imaginations were not so enfeebled by their lazy dependence on the ready-mades and reach-me-downs of the ragshop in which Romance keeps its stock of "happy endings" to misfit all stories. Now, the history of Eliza Doolittle, though called a romance because the transfiguration it records seems exceedingly improbable, is common enough. Such transfigurations have been achieved by hundreds of resolutely ambitious young women since Nell Gwynne[7] set them the example by playing queens and fascinating kings in the theatre in which she began by selling oranges. Nevertheless, people in all directions have assumed, for no other reason than that she became the heroine of a romance, that she must have married the hero of it. This is unbearable, not only because her little drama, if acted on such a thoughtless assumption, must be spoiled, but because the true sequel is patent to anyone with a sense of human nature in general, and of feminine instinct in particular.

Eliza, in telling Higgins she would not marry him if he asked her, was not coquetting: she was announcing a well-considered decision. When a bachelor interests, and dominates, and teaches, and becomes important to a spinster, as Higgins with Eliza, she always, if she has character enough to be capable of it, considers very seriously indeed whether she will play for becoming that bachelor's wife, especially if he is so little interested in marriage that a determined and devoted woman might capture him if she set herself resolutely to do it. Her

---

7. Eleanor Gwyn (1650–1687), celebrated English actress who became a mistress of King Charles II (1669).

decision will depend a good deal on whether she is really free to choose; and that, again, will depend on her age and income. If she is at the end of her youth, and has no security for her livelihood, she will marry him because she must marry anybody who will provide for her. But at Eliza's age a good-looking girl does not feel that pressure: she feels free to pick and choose. She is therefore guided by her instinct in the matter. Eliza's instinct tells her not to marry Higgins. It does not tell her to give him up. It is not in the slightest doubt as to his remaining one of the strongest personal interests in her life. It would be very sorely strained if there was another woman likely to supplant her with him. But as she feels sure of him on that last point, she has no doubt at all as to her course, and would not have any, even if the difference of twenty years in age, which seems so great to youth, did not exist between them.

As our own instincts are not appealed to by her conclusion, let us see whether we cannot discover some reason in it. When Higgins excused his indifference to young women on the ground that they had an irresistible rival in his mother, he gave the clue to his inveterate old-bachelordom. The case is uncommon only to the extent that remarkable mothers are uncommon. If an imaginative boy has a sufficiently rich mother who has intelligence, personal grace, dignity of character without harshness, and a cultivated sense of the best art of her time to enable her to make her house beautiful, she sets a standard for him against which very few women can struggle, besides effecting for him a disengagement of his affections, his sense of beauty, and his idealism from his specifically sexual impulses. This makes him a standing puzzle to the huge number of uncultivated people who have been brought up in tasteless homes by commonplace or disagreeable parents, and to whom, consequently, literature, painting, sculpture, music, and affectionate personal relations come as modes of sex if they come at all. The word passion means nothing else to them; and that Higgins could have a passion for phonetics and idealize his mother instead of Eliza, would seem to them absurd and unnatural. Nevertheless, when we look round and see that hardly anyone is too ugly or disagreeable to find a wife or a husband if he or she wants one, whilst many old maids and bachelors are above the average in quality and culture, we cannot help suspecting that the disentanglement of sex from the associations with which it is so commonly confused, a disentanglement which persons of genius achieve by sheer intellectual analysis, is sometimes produced or aided by parental fascination.

Now, though Eliza was incapable of thus explaining to herself Higgins's formidable powers of resistance to the charm that prostrated Freddy at the first glance, she was instinctively aware that she could never obtain a complete grip of him, or come between him and his mother (the first necessity of the married woman). To put it shortly, she knew that for some mysterious reason he had not the makings of a married man in him, according to her conception of a husband as one to whom she would be his nearest and fondest and warmest interest. Even had there been no mother-rival, she would still have refused to accept an interest in herself that was secondary to philosophic interests. Had Mrs. Higgins died, there would still have been Milton and the Universal Alphabet. Landor's[8] remark that to those who have the greatest power of loving, love is a secondary affair, would not have recommended Landor to Eliza. Put that along with her resentment of Higgins's domineering superiority, and her mistrust of his coaxing clev-

---

8. Walter Savage Landor (1775–1864), English poet.

erness in getting round her and evading her wrath when he had gone too far with his impetuous bullying, and you will see that Eliza's instinct had good grounds for warning her not to marry her Pygmalion.

And now, whom did Eliza marry? For if Higgins was a predestinate old bachelor, she was most certainly not a predestinate old maid. Well, that can be told very shortly to those who have not guessed it from the indications she has herself given them.

Almost immediately after Eliza is stung into proclaiming her considered determination not to marry Higgins, she mentions the fact that young Mr. Frederick Eynsford Hill is pouring out his love for her daily through the post. Now Freddy is young, practically twenty years younger than Higgins: he is a gentleman (or, as Eliza would qualify him, a toff), and speaks like one. He is nicely dressed, is treated by the Colonel as an equal, loves her unaffectedly, and is not her master, nor ever likely to dominate her in spite of his advantage of social standing. Eliza has no use for the foolish romantic tradition that all women love to be mastered, if not actually bullied and beaten. "When you go to women," says Nietzsche[9] "take your whip with you." Sensible despots have never confined that precaution to women: they have taken their whips with them when they have dealt with men, and been slavishly idealized by the men over whom they have flourished the whip much more than by women. No doubt there are slavish women as well as slavish men; and women, like men, admire those that are stronger than themselves. But to admire a strong person and to live under that strong person's thumb are two different things. The weak may not be admired and heroworshipped; but they are by no means disliked or shunned; and they never seem to have the least difficulty in marrying people who are too good for them. They may fail in emergencies; but life is not one long emergency: it is mostly a string of situations for which no exceptional strength is needed, and with which even rather weak people can cope if they have a stronger partner to help them out. Accordingly, it is a truth everywhere in evidence that strong people, masculine or feminine, not only do not marry stronger people, but do not shew any preference for them in selecting their friends. When a lion meets another with a louder roar "the first lion thinks the last a bore."[1] The man or woman who feels strong enough for two, seeks for every other quality in a partner than strength.

The converse is also true. Weak people want to marry strong people who do not frighten them too much; and this often leads them to make the mistake we describe metaphorically as "biting off more than they can chew." They want too much for too little; and when the bargain is unreasonable beyond all bearing, the union becomes impossible: it ends in the weaker party being either discarded or borne as a cross, which is worse. People who are not only weak, but silly or obtuse as well, are often in these difficulties.

This being the state of human affairs, what is Eliza fairly sure to do when she is placed between Freddy and Higgins? Will she look forward to a lifetime of fetching Higgins's slippers or to a lifetime of Freddy fetching hers? There can be no doubt about the answer. Unless Freddy is biologically repulsive to her, and Higgins biologically attractive to a degree that overwhelms all her other instincts, she will, if she marries either of them, marry Freddy.

And that is just what Eliza did.

---

9. German philosopher Friedrich Nietzsche (1844–1900).  1. Allusion unidentified.

Complications ensued; but they were economic, not romantic. Freddy had no money and no occupation. His mother's jointure, a last relic of the opulence of Largelady Park, had enabled her to struggle along in Earlscourt with an air of gentility, but not to procure any serious secondary education for her children, much less give the boy a profession. A clerkship at thirty shillings a week was beneath Freddy's dignity, and extremely distasteful to him besides. His prospects consisted of a hope that if he kept up appearances somebody would do something for him. The something appeared vaguely to his imagination as a private secretaryship or a sinecure of some sort. To his mother it perhaps appeared as a marriage to some lady of means who could not resist her boy's niceness. Fancy her feelings when he married a flower girl who had become disclassed under extraordinary circumstances which were now notorious!

It is true that Eliza's situation did not seem wholly ineligible. Her father, though formerly a dustman, and now fantastically disclassed, had become extremely popular in the smartest society by a social talent which triumphed over every prejudice and every disadvantage. Rejected by the middle class, which he loathed, he had shot up at once into the highest circles by his wit, his dustmanship (which he carried like a banner), and his Nietzschean transcendence of good and evil. At intimate ducal dinners he sat on the right hand of the Duchess; and in country houses he smoked in the pantry and was made much of by the butler when he was not feeding in the dining room and being consulted by cabinet ministers. But he found it almost as hard to do all this on four thousand a year as Mrs. Eynsford Hill to live in Earlscourt on an income so pitiably smaller that I have not the heart to disclose its exact figure. He absolutely refused to add the last straw to his burden by contributing to Eliza's support.

Thus Freddy and Eliza, now Mr. and Mrs. Eynsford Hill, would have spent a penniless honeymoon but for a wedding present of £500[2] from the Colonel to Eliza. It lasted a long time because Freddy did not know how to spend money, never having had any to spend, and Eliza, socially trained by a pair of old bachelors, wore her clothes as long as they held together and looked pretty, without the least regard to their being many months out of fashion. Still, £500 will not last two young people for ever; and they both knew, and Eliza felt as well, that they must shift for themselves in the end. She could quarter herself on Wimpole Street because it had come to be her home; but she was quite aware that she ought not to quarter Freddy there, and that it would not be good for his character if she did.

Not that the Wimpole Street bachelors objected. When she consulted them, Higgins declined to be bothered about her housing problem when that solution was so simple. Eliza's desire to have Freddy in the house with her seemed of no more importance than if she had wanted an extra piece of bedroom furniture. Pleas as to Freddy's character, and the moral obligation on him to earn his own living, were lost on Higgins. He denied that Freddy had any character, and declared that if he tried to do any useful work some competent person would have the trouble of undoing it: a procedure involving a net loss to the community, and great unhappiness to Freddy himself, who was obviously intended by Nature for such light work as amusing Eliza, which, Higgins declared, was a much more useful and honorable occupation than working in the city.[3] When

---

2. Roughly equivalent to $55,000 in today's American currency.
3. That is, working in London's finance industry.

Eliza referred again to her project of teaching phonetics, Higgins abated not a jot of his violent opposition to it. He said she was not within ten years of being qualified to meddle with his pet subject; and as it was evident that the Colonel agreed with him, she felt she could not go against them in this grave matter, and that she had no right, without Higgins's consent, to exploit the knowledge he had given her; for his knowledge seemed to her as much his private property as his watch: Eliza was no communist. Besides, she was superstitiously devoted to them both, more entirely and frankly after her marriage than before it.

It was the Colonel who finally solved the problem, which had cost him much perplexed cogitation. He one day asked Eliza, rather shyly, whether she had quite given up her notion of keeping a flower shop. She replied that she had thought of it, but had put it out of her head, because the Colonel had said, that day at Mrs. Higgins's, that it would never do. The Colonel confessed that when he said that, he had not quite recovered from the dazzling impression of the day before. They broke the matter to Higgins that evening. The sole comment vouchsafed by him very nearly led to a serious quarrel with Eliza. It was to the effect that she would have in Freddy an ideal errand boy.

Freddy himself was next sounded on the subject. He said he had been thinking of a shop himself; though it had presented itself to his pennilessness as a small place in which Eliza should sell tobacco at one counter whilst he sold newspapers at the opposite one. But he agreed that it would be extraordinarily jolly to go early every morning with Eliza to Covent Garden and buy flowers on the scene of their first meeting: a sentiment which earned him many kisses from his wife. He added that he had always been afraid to propose anything of the sort, because Clara would make an awful row about a step that must damage her matrimonial chances, and his mother could not be expected to like it after clinging for so many years to that step of the social ladder on which retail trade is impossible.

This difficulty was removed by an event highly unexpected by Freddy's mother. Clara, in the course of her incursions into those artistic circles which were the highest within her reach, discovered that her conversational qualifications were expected to include a grounding in the novels of Mr. H. G. Wells.[4] She borrowed them in various directions so energetically that she swallowed them all within two months. The result was a conversion of a kind quite common today. A modern Acts of the Apostles[5] would fill fifty whole Bibles if anyone were capable of writing it.

Poor Clara, who appeared to Higgins and his mother as a disagreeable and ridiculous person, and to her own mother as in some inexplicable way a social failure, had never seen herself in either light; for, though to some extent ridiculed and mimicked in West Kensington like everybody else there, she was accepted as a rational and normal—or shall we say inevitable?—sort of human being. At worst they called her The Pusher;[6] but to them no more than to herself had it ever occurred that she was pushing the air, and pushing it in a wrong direction. Still, she was not happy. She was growing desperate. Her one asset, the fact that her mother was what the Epsom greengrocer called a carriage lady, had no exchange value, apparently. It had prevented her from getting educated, because the only education she could have afforded was education with the Earlscourt greengro-

---

4. English novelist, scientific visionary, and social prophet (1866–1946).
5. Fifth book of the New Testament.   6. That is, The Social Climber.

cer's daughter. It had led her to seek the society of her mother's class; and that class simply would not have her, because she was much poorer than the greengrocer, and, far from being able to afford a maid, could not afford even a housemaid, and had to scrape along at home with an illiberally treated general servant. Under such circumstances nothing could give her an air of being a genuine product of Largelady Park. And yet its tradition made her regard a marriage with anyone within her reach as an unbearable humiliation. Commercial people and professional people in a small way were odious to her. She ran after painters and novelists; but she did not charm them; and her bold attempts to pick up and practise artistic and literary talk irritated them. She was, in short, an utter failure, an ignorant, incompetent, pretentious, unwelcome, penniless, useless little snob; and though she did not admit these disqualifications (for nobody ever faces unpleasant truths of this kind until the possibility of a way out dawns on them) she felt their effects too keenly to be satisfied with her position.

Clara had a startling eyeopener when, on being suddenly wakened to enthusiasm by a girl of her own age who dazzled her and produced in her a gushing desire to take her for a model, and gain her friendship, she discovered that this exquisite apparition had graduated from the gutter in a few months time. It shook her so violently, that when Mr. H. G. Wells lifted her on the point of his puissant pen, and placed her at the angle of view from which the life she was leading and the society to which she clung appeared in its true relation to real human needs and worthy social structure, he effected a conversion and a conviction of sin comparable to the most sensational feats of General Booth or Gypsy Smith.[7] Clara's snobbery went bang. Life suddenly began to move with her. Without knowing how or why, she began to make friends and enemies. Some of the acquaintances to whom she had been a tedious or indifferent or ridiculous affliction, dropped her: others became cordial. To her amazement she found that some "quite nice" people were saturated with Wells, and that this accessibility to ideas was the secret of their niceness. People she had thought deeply religious, and had tried to conciliate on that tack with disastrous results, suddenly took an interest in her, and revealed a hostility to conventional religion which she had never conceived possible except among the most desperate characters. They made her read Galsworthy;[8] and Galsworthy exposed the vanity of Largelady Park and finished her. It exasperated her to think that the dungeon in which she had languished for so many unhappy years had been unlocked all the time, and that the impulses she had so carefully struggled with and stifled for the sake of keeping well with society, were precisely those by which alone she could have come into any sort of sincere human contact. In the radiance of these discoveries, and the tumult of their reaction, she made a fool of herself as freely and conspicuously as when she so rashly adopted Eliza's expletive in Mrs. Higgins's drawing room; for the new-born Wellsian had to find her bearings almost as ridiculously as a baby; but nobody hates a baby for its ineptitudes, or thinks the worse of it for trying to eat the matches; and Clara lost no friends by her follies. They laughed at her to her face this time; and she had to defend herself and fight it out as best she could.

---

7. Gypsy Rodney Smith (1860-1947), English evangelist with the National Free Church Council and an associate of General William Booth (1829-1912), founder and leader of the Salvation Army.
8. English playwright and novelist John Galsworthy (1867-1933).

When Freddy paid a visit to Earlscourt (which he never did when he could possibly help it) to make the desolating announcement that he and his Eliza were thinking of blackening the Largelady scutcheon[9] by opening a shop, he found the little household already convulsed by a prior announcement from Clara that she also was going to work in an old furniture shop in Dover Street, which had been started by a fellow Wellsian. This appointment Clara owed, after all, to her old social accomplishment of Push. She had made up her mind that, cost what it might, she would see Mr. Wells in the flesh; and she had achieved her end at a garden party. She had better luck than so rash an enterprise deserved. Mr. Wells came up to her expectations. Age had not withered him, nor could custom stale his infinite variety in half an hour.[1] His pleasant neatness and compactness, his small hands and feet, his teeming ready brain, his unaffected accessibility, and a certain fine apprehensiveness which stamped him as susceptible from his topmost hair to his tipmost toe, proved irresistible. Clara talked of nothing else for weeks and weeks afterwards. And as she happened to talk to the lady of the furniture shop, and that lady also desired above all things to know Mr. Wells and sell pretty things to him, she offered Clara a job on the chance of achieving that end through her.

And so it came about that Eliza's luck held, and the expected opposition to the flower shop melted away. The shop is in the arcade of a railway station not very far from the Victoria and Albert Museum; and if you live in that neighborhood you may go there any day and buy a buttonhole from Eliza.

Now here is a last opportunity for romance. Would you not like to be assured that the shop was an immense success, thanks to Eliza's charms and her early business experience in Covent Garden? Alas! the truth is the truth: the shop did not pay for a long time, simply because Eliza and her Freddy did not know how to keep it. True, Eliza had not to begin at the very beginning: she knew the names and prices of the cheaper flowers; and her elation was unbounded when she found that Freddy, like all youths educated at cheap, pretentious, and thoroughly inefficient schools, knew a little Latin. It was very little, but enough to make him appear to her a Porson or Bentley,[2] and to put him at his ease with botanical nomenclature. Unfortunately he knew nothing else; and Eliza, though she could count money up to eighteen shillings or so, and had acquired a certain familiarity with the language of Milton from her struggles to qualify herself for winning Higgins's bet, could not write out a bill without utterly disgracing the establishment. Freddy's power of stating in Latin that Balbus built a wall and that Gaul was divided into three parts[3] did not carry with it the slightest knowledge of accounts or business: Colonel Pickering had to explain to him what a cheque book and a bank account meant. And the pair were by no means easily teachable. Freddy backed up Eliza in her obstinate refusal to believe that they could save money by engaging a bookkeeper with some knowledge of the business. How, they argued, could you possibly save money by going to extra expense when you

---

9. Heraldic shield; here meaning "reputation."
1. Shakespeare's *Antony and Cleopatra* 2.2.240–41: "Age cannot wither her, nor custom stale / Her infinite variety."
2. Classical scholars Richard Porson (1759–1808) and Richard Bentley (1662–1742).
3. Freddie's ability to say such things in Latin reflects his fragmented and partial "schoolboy's" understanding of Roman history.

already could not make both ends meet? But the Colonel, after making the ends meet over and over again, at last gently insisted; and Eliza, humbled to the dust by having to beg from him so often, and stung by the uproarious derision of Higgins, to whom the notion of Freddy succeeding at anything was a joke that never palled, grasped the fact that business, like phonetics, has to be learned.

On the piteous spectacle of the pair spending their evenings in shorthand schools and polytechnic classes, learning bookkeeping and typewriting with incipient junior clerks, male and female, from the elementary schools, let me not dwell. There were even classes at the London School of Economics, and a humble personal appeal to the director of that institution to recommend a course bearing on the flower business. He, being a humorist, explained to them the method of the celebrated Dickensian essay on Chinese Metaphysics by the gentleman who read an article on China and an article on Metaphysics and combined the information. He suggested that they should combine the London School with Kew Gardens. Eliza, to whom the procedure of the Dickensian gentleman seemed perfectly correct (as in fact it was) and not in the least funny (which was only her ignorance), took the advice with entire gravity. But the effort that cost her the deepest humiliation was a request to Higgins, whose pet artistic fancy, next to Milton's verse, was caligraphy, and who himself wrote a most beautiful Italian hand, that he would teach her to write. He declared that she was congenitally incapable of forming a single letter worthy of the least of Milton's words; but she persisted; and again he suddenly threw himself into the task of teaching her with a combination of stormy intensity, concentrated patience, and occasional bursts of interesting disquisition on the beauty and nobility, the august mission and destiny, of human handwriting. Eliza ended by acquiring an extremely uncommercial script which was a positive extension of her personal beauty, and spending three times as much on stationery as anyone else because certain qualities and shapes of paper became indispensable to her. She could not even address an envelope in the usual way because it made the margins all wrong.

Their commercial schooldays were a period of disgrace and despair for the young couple. They seemed to be learning nothing about flower shops. At last they gave it up as hopeless, and shook the dust of the shorthand schools, and the polytechnics, and the London School of Economics from their feet for ever. Besides, the business was in some mysterious way beginning to take care of itself. They had somehow forgotten their objections to employing other people. They came to the conclusion that their own way was the best, and that they had really a remarkable talent for business. The Colonel, who had been compelled for some years to keep a sufficient sum on current account at his bankers to make up their deficits, found that the provision was unnecessary: the young people were prospering. It is true that there was not quite fair play between them and their competitors in trade. Their week-ends in the country cost them nothing, and saved them the price of their Sunday dinners; for the motor car was the Colonel's; and he and Higgins paid the hotel bills. Mr. F. Hill, florist and greengrocer (they soon discovered that there was money in asparagus; and asparagus led to other vegetables), had an air which stamped the business as classy; and in private life he was still Frederick Eynsford Hill, Esquire. Not that there was any swank about him: nobody but Eliza knew that he had been christened Frederick Challoner. Eliza herself swanked like anything.

That is all. That is how it has turned out. It is astonishing how much Eliza still manages to meddle in the housekeeping at Wimpole Street in spite of the shop and her own family. And it is notable that though she never nags her husband, and frankly loves the Colonel as if she were his favorite daughter, she has never got out of the habit of nagging Higgins that was established on the fatal night when she won his bet for him. She snaps his head off on the faintest provocation, or on none. He no longer dares to tease her by assuming an abysmal inferiority of Freddy's mind to his own. He storms and bullies and derides; but she stands up to him so ruthlessly that the Colonel has to ask her from time to time to be kinder to Higgins; and it is the only request of his that brings a mulish expression into her face. Nothing but some emergency or calamity great enough to break down all likes and dislikes, and throw them both back on their common humanity—and may they be spared any such trial!—will ever alter this. She knows that Higgins does not need her, just as her father did not need her. The very scrupulousness with which he told her that day that he had become used to having her there, and dependent on her for all sorts of little services, and that he should miss her if she went away (it would never have occurred to Freddy or the Colonel to say anything of the sort) deepens her inner certainty that she is "no more to him than them slippers"; yet she has a sense, too, that his indifference is deeper than the infatuation of commoner souls. She is immensely interested in him. She has even secret mischievous moments in which she wishes she could get him alone, on a desert island, away from all ties and with nobody else in the world to consider, and just drag him off his pedestal and see him making love like any common man. We all have private imaginations of that sort. But when it comes to business, to the life that she really leads as distinguished from the life of dreams and fancies, she likes Freddy and she likes the Colonel; and she does not like Higgins and Mr. Doolittle. Galatea[4] never does quite like Pygmalion: his relation to her is too godlike to be altogether agreeable.

1914, revised 1941

## QUESTIONS

1. How does *Pygmalion*'s first scene, set in front of St. Paul's Church, serve to introduce the play's principal themes? How do the setting and the first actions and speeches reflect on the values of the characters and the differences between men and women, upper and lower classes? Consider that Covent Garden was known as the heart of London's theater district, but after 11:15, it turned into a sexual as well as produce market (both prostitutes and small-scale grocers worked through the night hours before the market opened at dawn). Why does Shaw have the play open after a play, in front of a landmark church that is serving as a shelter in which to wait for a taxi? Why does he introduce his heroine as "The Flower Girl"?
2. What is your first impression of Eliza? Can you understand the first lines she speaks, which Shaw has rendered phonetically? How does your impression of Eliza change after Shaw's announcement, in a stage direction, that he will abandon his "desperate attempt to represent her dialect"? Do you think that Shaw's brief experiment gives the reader special insights into Eliza's character that an audience in a theater might miss?

---

4. Remarkably, this is Shaw's first mention of the name of the statue that, in Greek myth, comes to life when the goddess Aphrodite answers the prayers of Pygmalion, king of Cyprus, who longs for such a beautiful wife.

3. When Higgins first appears as "The Note Taker" early in the play, what are the thematic implications of his uncanny ability to place accents? How does Shaw use language and accent to identify the place of birth, upbringing, and later relocations, as well as rank of everyone Higgins meets? Which class comes off best?
4. How convincing are Higgins's assertions of disdain for the class system? Does his behavior (toward Eliza, toward Doolittle, toward the Eynsford Hills) measure up to his declarations about the "soul and the divine gift of articulate speech"? In what ways does Higgins embody the class system that he professes to despise?
5. Act 1 ends with a glimpse of Eliza's squalid "lodging"; this is followed immediately by the action of act 2, set in Higgins's fine town house. What is the dramatic effect of this juxtaposition? If you were producing the play, how would you handle the change of setting?
6. What do the stage directions at the beginning of act 2, describing Higgins's home and his lab, reveal about his character? The text goes on to describe Higgins himself as a "robust, vital, appetizing sort of man of forty or thereabouts," an "energetic, scientific type," yet "careless about himself and other people" and "rather like a very impetuous baby." If you were the casting director for a production of *Pygmalion*, whom would you select for the role of Higgins—would you play to the stereotypes that Shaw is invoking here or would you "cast against type"? How could either approach to casting affect the audience's perception of the play's main themes?
7. In what way are Higgins's and Alfred Doolittle's attitudes and behavior similar? Why will Doolittle take five pounds for his daughter but not ten? What use does he promise to put the money to? Why will the woman he lives with not marry him? How does this relate to the reversal of conventional expectations?
8. What do you think Higgins really means when, in act 3, he exclaims to Clara Eynsford Hill that "we're all savages, more or less"? Is this consistent with Higgins's professed disdain for England's highly evolved social order? Why or why not?
9. What is the "new small talk" (act 3)? In what way is that "small talk" like the fairy tale of the emperor's new clothes? Though this scene seems comically exaggerated, what elements of "truth" or "reality" are in it? What does it suggest about society and its "rules"? What is the "sanguinary element" in the "new small talk"?
10. How is act 4 the climax or turning point? How does it initiate and present the falling action? What is the tone of this act? How does it differ from that of much of the rest of the play? To what extent is your opinion of Higgins changed?
11. Given the play's subtitle ("A Romance in Five Acts") and the many romantic conventions employed in the play, were you surprised by the play's ending? What had Shaw led the audience to expect? Why do you think Shaw chose to subvert those expectations?

## SUGGESTIONS FOR WRITING

1. Shaw's postscript tells us that Eliza marries Freddy, not Higgins. Write an argumentative essay that takes one of the two following positions and both uses concrete evidence from the text and takes into account your "opponent's" possible counter-arguments: (a) If we are to trust the tale and not the teller, as D. H. Lawrence advises us to do, then Shaw's postscript is either deliberately and perversely provocative, or simply wrong; the play itself contains ample hints that Eliza really does marry Higgins, as shown in both the movie *Pygmalion* and the later musical, *My Fair Lady*; (b) Bernard Shaw knows best: the whole tone of the play is ironic and undermines conventional expectation. Since Eliza's marrying Higgins is the expected comic resolution, it would not be an ending that is consistent with this anti-conventional play.
2. Is Higgins a sexist? Write an essay in which you analyze the attitudes toward gender relations in *Pygmalion*. If Higgins were to marry Eliza, how would it reinforce or change what the play seems to be saying about gender?

3. From the beginning of the play to the very end there are reversals of conventions and thus of conventional expectations. List as many of these as you can find. Taken together, do they form a consistent view of society and morality, or are some of them as questionable (sexist, inhumane, snobbish in their own way, and so forth) as the conventions they subvert? Write an essay in which you examine the complex moral order in *Pygmalion*.
4. Look up the classical myth of Pygmalion and Galatea, and consider its underlying themes and its "moral." Is Shaw's play fundamentally consistent with the ancient story, or is Shaw using the myth as an ironic vehicle for his many social concerns (regarding class, gender, speech, and so forth)? Write an essay in which you discuss the relationship between Shaw's *Pygmalion* and the play's classical source.
5. Is the dramatic art of live theater inherently different from (or inherently similar to) the dramatic art of movies? Watch one of the several movie versions of *Pygmalion* and the musical *My Fair Lady*, and then write an essay in which you compare and contrast Shaw's play with the movie adaptations. How faithful are the movie versions to Shaw's story and his thematic intentions? Is fidelity to the original important, or are the alterations justified?

## AUGUST WILSON

## *The Piano Lesson*

> Gin my cotton
> Sell my seed
> Buy my baby
> Everything she need
> —Skip James

### CHARACTERS

| | |
|---|---|
| DOAKER | MARETHA |
| BOY WILLIE | AVERY |
| LYMON | WINING BOY |
| BERNIECE | GRACE |

THE SETTING: *The action of the play takes place in the kitchen and parlor of the house where* DOAKER CHARLES *lives with his niece,* BERNIECE, *and her eleven-year-old daughter,* MARETHA. *The house is sparsely furnished, and although there is evidence of a woman's touch, there is a lack of warmth and vigor.* BERNIECE *and* MARETHA *occupy the upstairs rooms.* DOAKER's *room is prominent and opens onto the kitchen. Dominating the parlor is an old upright piano. On the legs of the piano, carved in the manner of African sculpture, are mask-like figures resembling totems. The carvings are rendered with a grace and power of invention that lifts them out of the realm of craftsmanship and into the realm of art. At left is a staircase leading to the upstairs.*

## ACT I

### Scene 1

[*The lights come up on the Charles household. It is five o'clock in the morning. The dawn is beginning to announce itself, but there is something in the air that belongs* to the night. A stillness that is a portent, a gathering, a coming together of something akin to a storm. There is a loud knock at the door.]

BOY WILLIE: [Off stage, calling.] Hey, Doaker . . . Doaker! [He knocks again and calls.] Hey, Doaker! Hey, Berniece! Berniece!

[DOAKER enters from his room. He is a tall, thin man of forty-seven, with severe features, who has for all intents and purposes retired from the world though he works full-time as a railroad cook.]

DOAKER: Who is it?
BOY WILLIE: Open the door, nigger! It's me . . . Boy Willie!
DOAKER: Who?
BOY WILLIE: Boy Willie! Open the door!

[DOAKER opens the door and BOY WILLIE and LYMON enter. BOY WILLIE is thirty years old. He has an infectious grin and a boyishness that is apt for his name. He is brash and impulsive, talkative and somewhat crude in speech and manner. LYMON is twenty-nine. BOY WILLIE's partner, he talks little, and then with a straightforwardness that is often disarming.]

DOAKER: What you doing up here?
BOY WILLIE: I told you, Lymon. Lymon talking about you might be sleep. This is Lymon. You remember Lymon Jackson from down home? This my Uncle Doaker.
DOAKER: What you doing up here? I couldn't figure out who that was. I thought you was still down in Mississippi.
BOY WILLIE: Me and Lymon selling watermelons. We got a truck out there. Got a whole truckload of watermelons. We brought them up here to sell. Where's Berniece? [Calls.] Hey, Berniece!
DOAKER: Berniece up there sleep.
BOY WILLIE: Well, let her get up. [Calls.] Hey, Berniece!
DOAKER: She got to go to work in the morning.
BOY WILLIE: Well she can get up and say hi. It's been three years since I seen her. [Calls.] Hey, Berniece! It's me . . . Boy Willie.
DOAKER: Berniece don't like all that hollering now. She got to work in the morning.
BOY WILLIE: She can go on back to bed. Me and Lymon been riding two days in that truck . . . the least she can do is get up and say hi.
DOAKER: [Looking out the window.] Where you all get that truck from?
BOY WILLIE: It's Lymon's. I told him let's get a load of watermelons and bring them up here.
LYMON: Boy Willie say he going back, but I'm gonna stay. See what it's like up here.
BOY WILLIE: You gonna carry me down there first.
LYMON: I told you I ain't going back down there and take a chance on that truck breaking down again. You can take the train. Hey, tell him Doaker, he can take the train back. After we sell them watermelons he have enough money he can buy him a whole railroad car.
DOAKER: You got all them watermelons stacked up there no wonder the truck broke down. I'm surprised you made it this far with a load like that. Where you break down at?

BOY WILLIE: We broke down three times! It took us two and a half days to get here. It's a good thing we picked them watermelons fresh.
LYMON: We broke down twice in West Virginia. The first time was just as soon as we got out of Sunflower. About forty miles out she broke down. We got it going and got all the way to West Virginia before she broke down again.
BOY WILLIE: We had to walk about five miles for some water.
LYMON: It got a hole in the radiator but it runs pretty good. You have to pump the brakes sometime before they catch. Boy Willie have his door open and be ready to jump when that happens.
BOY WILLIE: Lymon think that's funny. I told the nigger I give him ten dollars to get the brakes fixed. But he thinks that funny.
LYMON: They don't need fixing. All you got to do is pump them till they catch.

[BERNIECE *enters on the stairs. Thirty-five years old, with an eleven-year-old daughter, she is still in mourning for her husband after three years.*]

BERNIECE: What you doing all that hollering for?
BOY WILLIE: Hey, Berniece. Doaker said you was sleep. I said at least you could get up and say hi.
BERNIECE: It's five o'clock in the morning and you come in here with all this noise. You can't come like normal folks. You got to bring all that noise with you.
BOY WILLIE: Hell, I ain't done nothing but come in and say hi. I ain't got in the house good.
BERNIECE: That's what I'm talking about. You start all that hollering and carry on as soon as you hit the door.
BOY WILLIE: Aw hell, woman, I was glad to see Doaker. You ain't had to come down if you didn't want to. I come eighteen hundred miles to see my sister I figure she might want to get up and say hi. Other than that you can go back upstairs. What you got, Doaker? Where your bottle? Me and Lymon want a drink. [*To* BERNIECE.] This is Lymon. You remember Lymon Jackson from down home.
LYMON: How you doing, Berniece. You look just like I thought you looked.
BERNIECE: Why you all got to come in hollering and carrying on? Waking the neighbors with all that noise.
BOY WILLIE: They can come over and join the party. We fixing to have a party. Doaker, where your bottle? Me and Lymon celebrating. The Ghosts of the Yellow Dog got Sutter.
BERNIECE: Say what?
BOY WILLIE: Ask Lymon, they found him the next morning. Say he drowned in his well.
DOAKER: When this happen, Boy Willie?
BOY WILLIE: About three weeks ago. Me and Lymon was over in Stoner County when we heard about it. We laughed. We thought it was funny. A great big old three-hundred-and-forty-pound man gonna fall down his well.
LYMON: It remind me of Humpty Dumpty.
BOY WILLIE: Everybody say the Ghosts of the Yellow Dog pushed him.
BERNIECE: I don't want to hear that nonsense. Somebody down there pushing them people in their wells.
DOAKER: What was you and Lymon doing over in Stoner County?

BOY WILLIE: We was down there working. Lymon got some people down there.
LYMON: My cousin got some land down there. We was helping him.
BOY WILLIE: Got near about a hundred acres. He got it set up real nice. Me and Lymon was down there chopping down trees. We was using Lymon's truck to haul the wood. Me and Lymon used to haul wood all around them parts. [*To* BERNIECE.] Me and Lymon got a truckload of watermelons out there.

[BERNIECE *crosses to the window to the parlor.*]

Doaker, where your bottle? I know you got a bottle stuck up in your room. Come on, me and Lymon want a drink.

[DOAKER *exits into his room.*]

BERNIECE: Where you all get that truck from?
BOY WILLIE: I told you it's Lymon's.
BERNIECE: Where you get the truck from, Lymon?
LYMON: I bought it.
BERNIECE: Where he get that truck from, Boy Willie?
BOY WILLIE: He told you he bought it. Bought it for a hundred and twenty dollars. I can't say where he got that hundred and twenty dollars from . . . but he bought that old piece of truck from Henry Porter. [*To* LYMON.] Where you get that hundred and twenty dollars from, nigger?
LYMON: I got it like you get yours. I know how to take care of money.

[DOAKER *brings a bottle and sets it on the table.*]

BOY WILLIE: Aw hell, Doaker got some of that good whiskey. Don't give Lymon none of that. He ain't used to good whiskey. He liable to get sick.
LYMON: I done had good whiskey before.
BOY WILLIE: Lymon bought that truck so he have him a place to sleep. He down there wasn't doing no work or nothing. Sheriff looking for him. He bought that truck to keep away from the sheriff. Got Stovall looking for him too. He down there sleeping in that truck ducking and dodging both of them. I told him come on let's go up and see my sister.
BERNIECE: What the sheriff looking for you for, Lymon?
BOY WILLIE: The man don't want you to know all his business. He's my company. He ain't asking you no questions.
LYMON: It wasn't nothing. It was just a misunderstanding.
BERNIECE: He in my house. You say the sheriff looking for him, I wanna know what he looking for him for. Otherwise you all can go back out there and be where nobody don't have to ask you nothing.
LYMON: It was just a misunderstanding. Sometimes me and the sheriff we don't think alike. So we just got crossed on each other.
BERNIECE: Might be looking for him about that truck. He might have stole that truck.
BOY WILLIE: We ain't stole no truck, woman. I told you Lymon bought it.
DOAKER: Boy Willie and Lymon got more sense than to ride all the way up here in a stolen truck with a load of watermelons. Now they might have stole them watermelons, but I don't believe they stole that truck.
BOY WILLIE: You don't even know the man good and you calling him a thief. And we ain't stole them watermelons either. Them old man Pitterford's water-

melons. He give me and Lymon all we could load for ten dollars.

DOAKER: No wonder you got them stacked up out there. You must have five hundred watermelons stacked up out there.

BERNIECE: Boy Willie, when you and Lymon planning on going back?

BOY WILLIE: Lymon say he staying. As soon as we sell them watermelons I'm going on back.

BERNIECE: [*Starts to exit up the stairs.*] That's what you need to do. And you need to do it quick. Come in here disrupting the house. I don't want all that loud carrying on around here. I'm surprised you ain't woke Maretha up.

BOY WILLIE: I was fixing to get her now. [*Calls.*] Hey, Maretha!

DOAKER: Berniece don't like all that hollering now.

BERNIECE: Don't you wake that child up!

BOY WILLIE: You going up there... wake her up and tell her her uncle's here. I ain't seen her in three years. Wake her up and send her down here. She can go back to bed.

BERNIECE: I ain't waking that child up... and don't you be making all that noise. You and Lymon need to sell them watermelons and go on back.

[BERNIECE *exits up the stairs.*]

BOY WILLIE: I see Berniece still try to be stuck up.

DOAKER: Berniece alright. She don't want you making all that noise. Maretha up there sleep. Let her sleep until she get up. She can see you then.

BOY WILLIE: I ain't thinking about Berniece. You hear from Wining Boy? You know Cleotha died?

DOAKER: Yeah, I heard that. He come by here about a year ago. Had a whole sack of money. He stayed here about two weeks. Ain't offered nothing. Berniece asked him for three dollars to buy some food and he got mad and left.

LYMON: Who's Wining Boy?

BOY WILLIE: That's my uncle. That's Doaker's brother. You heard me talk about Wining Boy. He play piano. He done made some records and everything. He still doing that, Doaker?

DOAKER: He made one or two records a long time ago. That's the only ones I ever known him to make. If you let him tell it he a big recording star.

BOY WILLIE: He stopped down home about two years ago. That's what I hear. I don't know. Me and Lymon was up on Parchman Farm doing them three years.

DOAKER: He don't never stay in one place. Now, he been here about eight months ago. Back in the winter. Now, you subject not to see him for another two years. It's liable to be that long before he stop by.

BOY WILLIE: If he had a whole sack of money you liable never to see him. You ain't gonna see him until he get broke. Just as soon as that sack of money is gone you look up and he be on your doorstep.

LYMON: [*Noticing the piano.*] Is that the piano?

BOY WILLIE: Yeah... look here, Lymon. See how it's carved up real nice and polished and everything? You never find you another piano like that.

LYMON: Yeah, that look real nice.

BOY WILLIE: I told you. See how it's polished? My mama used to polish it every day. See all them pictures carved on it? That's what I was talking about. You can get a nice price for that piano.

LYMON: That's all Boy Willie talked about the whole trip up here. I got tired of hearing him talk about the piano.
BOY WILLIE: All you want to talk about is women. You ought to hear this nigger, Doaker. Talking about all the women he gonna get when he get up here. He ain't had none down there but he gonna get a hundred when he get up here.
DOAKER: How your people doing down there, Lymon?
LYMON: They alright. They still there. I come up here to see what it's like up here. Boy Willie trying to get me to go back and farm with him.
BOY WILLIE: Sutter's brother selling the land. He say he gonna sell it to me. That's why I come up here. I got one part of it. Sell them watermelons and get me another part. Get Berniece to sell that piano and I'll have the third part.
DOAKER: Berniece ain't gonna sell that piano.
BOY WILLIE: I'm gonna talk to her. When she see I got a chance to get Sutter's land she'll come around.
DOAKER: You can put that thought out your mind. Berniece ain't gonna sell that piano.
BOY WILLIE: I'm gonna talk to her. She been playing on it?
DOAKER: You know she won't touch that piano. I ain't never known her to touch it since Mama Ola died. That's over seven years now. She say it got blood on it. She got Maretha playing on it though. Say Maretha can go on and do everything she can't do. Got her in an extra school down at the Irene Kaufman Settlement House. She want Maretha to grow up and be a schoolteacher. Say she good enough she can teach on the piano.
BOY WILLIE: Maretha don't need to be playing on no piano. She can play on the guitar.
DOAKER: How much land Sutter got left?
BOY WILLIE: Got a hundred acres. Good land. He done sold it piece by piece, he kept the good part for himself. Now he got to give that up. His brother come down from Chicago for the funeral . . . he up there in Chicago got some kind of business with soda fountain equipment. He anxious to sell the land, Doaker. He don't want to be bothered with it. He called me to him and said cause of how long our families done known each other and how we been good friends and all, say he wanted to sell the land to me. Say he'd rather see me with it than Jim Stovall. Told me he'd let me have it for two thousand dollars cash money. He don't know I found out the most Stovall would give him for it was fifteen hundred dollars. He trying to get that extra five hundred out of me telling me he doing me a favor. I thanked him just as nice. Told him what a good man Sutter was and how he had my sympathy and all. Told him to give me two weeks. He said he'd wait on me. That's why I come up here. Sell them watermelons. Get Berniece to sell that piano. Put them two parts with the part I done saved. Walk in there. Tip my hat. Lay my money down on the table. Get my deed and walk on out. This time I get to keep all the cotton. Hire me some men to work it for me. Gin my cotton. Get my seed. And I'll see you again next year. Might even plant some tobacco or some oats.
DOAKER: You gonna have a hard time trying to get Berniece to sell that piano. You know Avery Brown from down there don't you? He up here now. He followed Berniece up here trying to get her to marry him after Crawley got killed. He been up here about two years. He call himself a preacher now.
BOY WILLIE: I know Avery. I know him from when he used to work on the Willshaw place. Lymon know him too.

DOAKER: He after Berniece to marry him. She keep telling him no but he won't give up. He keep pressing her on it.
BOY WILLIE: Avery think all white men is bigshots. He don't know there some white men ain't got as much as he got.
DOAKER: He supposed to come past here this morning. Berniece going down to the bank with him to see if he can get a loan to start his church. That's why I know Berniece ain't gonna sell that piano. He tried to get her to sell it to help him start his church. Sent the man around and everything.
BOY WILLIE: What man?
DOAKER: Some white fellow was going around to all the colored people's houses looking to buy up musical instruments. He'd buy anything. Drums. Guitars. Harmonicas. Pianos. Avery sent him past here. He looked at the piano and got excited. Offered her a nice price. She turned him down and got on Avery for sending him past. The man kept on her about two weeks. He seen where she wasn't gonna sell it, he gave her his number and told her if she ever wanted to sell it to call him first. Say he'd go one better than what anybody else would give her for it.
BOY WILLIE: How much he offer her for it?
DOAKER: Now you know me. She didn't say and I didn't ask. I just know it was a nice price.
LYMON: All you got to do is find out who he is and tell him somebody else wanna buy it from you. Tell him you can't make up your mind who to sell it to, and if he like Doaker say, he'll give you anything you want for it.
BOY WILLIE: That's what I'm gonna do. I'm gonna find out who he is from Avery.
DOAKER: It ain't gonna do you no good. Berniece ain't gonna sell that piano.
BOY WILLIE: She ain't got to sell it. I'm gonna sell it. I own just as much of it as she does.
BERNIECE: [*Offstage, hollers.*] Doaker! Go on get away. Doaker!
DOAKER: [*Calling.*] Berniece?

[DOAKER *and* BOY WILLIE *rush to the stairs,* BOY WILLIE *runs up the stairs, passing* BERNIECE *as she enters, running.*]

DOAKER: Berniece, what's the matter? You alright? What's the matter?

[BERNIECE *tries to catch her breath. She is unable to speak.*]

DOAKER: That's alright. Take your time. You alright. What's the matter? [*He calls.*] Hey, Boy Willie?
BOY WILLIE: [*Offstage.*] Ain't nobody up here.
BERNIECE: Sutter... Sutter's standing at the top of the steps.
DOAKER: [*Calls.*] Boy Willie!

[LYMON *crosses to the stairs and looks up.* BOY WILLIE *enters from the stairs.*]

BOY WILLIE: Hey Doaker, what's wrong with her? Berniece, what's wrong? Who was you talking to?
DOAKER: She say she seen Sutter's ghost standing at the top of the stairs.
BOY WILLIE: Seen what? Sutter? She ain't seen no Sutter.
BERNIECE: He was standing right up there.
BOY WILLIE: [*Entering on the stairs.*] That's all in Berniece's head. Ain't nobody up there. Go on up there, Doaker.
DOAKER: I'll take your word for it. Berniece talking about what she seen. She say

Sutter's ghost standing at the top of the steps. She ain't just make all that up.

BOY WILLIE: She up there dreaming. She ain't seen no ghost.

LYMON: You want a glass of water, Berniece? Get her a glass of water, Boy Willie.

BOY WILLIE: She don't need no water. She ain't seen nothing. Go on up there and look. Ain't nobody up there but Maretha.

DOAKER: Let Berniece tell it.

BOY WILLIE: I ain't stopping her from telling it.

DOAKER: What happened, Berniece?

BERNIECE: I come out my room to come back down here and Sutter was standing there in the hall.

BOY WILLIE: What he look like?

BERNIECE: He look like Sutter. He look like he always look.

BOY WILLIE: Sutter couldn't find his way from Big Sandy to Little Sandy. How he gonna find his way all the way up here to Pittsburgh? Sutter ain't never even heard of Pittsburgh.

DOAKER: Go on, Berniece.

BERNIECE: Just standing there with the blue suit on.

BOY WILLIE: The man ain't never left Marlin County when he was living . . . and he's gonna come all the way up here now that he's dead?

DOAKER: Let her finish. I want to hear what she got to say.

BOY WILLIE: I'll tell you this. If Berniece had seen him like she think she seen him she'd still be running.

DOAKER: Go on, Berniece. Don't pay Boy Willie no mind.

BERNIECE: He was standing there . . . had his hand on top of his head. Look like he might have thought if he took his hand down his head might have fallen off.

LYMON: Did he have on a hat?

BERNIECE: Just had on that blue suit . . . I told him to go away and he just stood there looking at me . . . calling Boy Willie's name.

BOY WILLIE: What he calling my name for?

BERNIECE: I believe you pushed him in the well.

BOY WILLIE: Now what kind of sense that make? You telling me I'm gonna go out there and hide in the weeds with all them dogs and things he got around there . . . I'm gonna hide and wait till I catch him looking down his well just right . . . then I'm gonna run over and push him in. A great big old three-hundred-and-forty-pound man.

BERNIECE: Well, what he calling your name for?

BOY WILLIE: He bending over looking down his well, woman . . . how he know who pushed him? It could have been anybody. Where was you when Sutter fell in his well? Where was Doaker? Me and Lymon was over in Stoner County. Tell her, Lymon. The Ghosts of the Yellow Dog got Sutter. That's what happened to him.

BERNIECE: You can talk all that Ghosts of the Yellow Dog stuff if you want. I know better.

LYMON: The Ghosts of the Yellow Dog pushed him. That's what the people say. They found him in his well and all the people say it must be the Ghosts of the Yellow Dog. Just like all them other men.

BOY WILLIE: Come talking about he looking for me. What he come all the way up here for? If he looking for me all he got to do is wait. He could have saved himself a trip if he looking for me. That ain't nothing but in Berniece's head. Ain't no telling what she liable to come up with next.

BERNIECE: Boy Willie, I want you and Lymon to go ahead and leave my house. Just go on somewhere. You don't do nothing but bring trouble with you everywhere you go. If it wasn't for you Crawley would still be alive.

BOY WILLIE: Crawley what? I ain't had nothing to do with Crawley getting killed. Crawley three time seven.[1] He had his own mind.

BERNIECE: Just go on and leave. Let Sutter go somewhere else looking for you.

BOY WILLIE: I'm leaving. Soon as we sell them watermelons. Other than that I ain't going nowhere. Hell, I just got here. Talking about Sutter looking for me. Sutter was looking for that piano. That's what he was looking for. He had to die to find out where that piano was at... If I was you I'd get rid of it. That's the way to get rid of Sutter's ghost. Get rid of that piano.

BERNIECE: I want you and Lymon to go on and take all this confusion out of my house!

BOY WILLIE: Hey, tell her, Doaker. What kind of sense that make? I told you, Lymon, as soon as Berniece see me she was gonna start something. Didn't I tell you that? Now she done made up that story about Sutter just so she could tell me to leave her house. Well, hell, I ain't going nowhere till I sell them watermelons.

BERNIECE: Well why don't you go out there and sell them! Sell them and go on back!

BOY WILLIE: We waiting till the people get up.

LYMON: Boy Willie say if you get out there too early and wake the people up they get mad at you and won't buy nothing from you.

DOAKER: You won't be waiting long. You done let the sun catch up with you. This the time everybody be getting up around here.

BERNIECE: Come on, Doaker, walk up here with me. Let me get Maretha up and get her started. I got to get ready myself. Boy Willie, just go on out there and sell them watermelons and you and Lymon leave my house.

[BERNIECE *and* DOAKER *exit up the stairs.*]

BOY WILLIE: [*Calling after them.*] If you see Sutter up there... tell him I'm down here waiting on him.

LYMON: What if she see him again?

BOY WILLIE: That's all in her head. There ain't no ghost up there. [*Calls.*] Hey, Doaker... I told you ain't nothing up there.

LYMON: I'm glad he didn't say he was looking for me.

BOY WILLIE: I wish I would see Sutter's ghost. Give me a chance to put a whupping on him.

LYMON: You ought to stay up here with me. You be down there working his land ... he might come looking for you all the time.

BOY WILLIE: I ain't thinking about Sutter. And I ain't thinking about staying up here. You stay up here. I'm going back and get Sutter's land. You think you ain't got to work up here. You think this the land of milk and honey. But I ain't scared of work. I'm going back and farm every acre of that land.

---

1. That is, Crawley was 21 years old—an adult.

[DOAKER *enters from the stairs.*]

I told you there ain't nothing up there, Doaker. Berniece dreaming all that.

DOAKER: I believe Berniece seen something. Berniece levelheaded. She ain't just made all that up. She say Sutter had on a suit. I don't believe she ever seen Sutter in a suit. I believe that's what he was buried in, and that's what Berniece saw.

BOY WILLIE: Well, let her keep on seeing him then. As long as he don't mess with me.

[DOAKER *starts to cook his breakfast.*]

I heard about you, Doaker. They say you got all the women looking out for you down home. They be looking to see you coming. Say you got a different one every two weeks. Say they be fighting one another for you to stay with them. [*To* LYMON.] Look at him, Lymon. He know it's true.

DOAKER: I ain't thinking about no women. They never get me tied up with them. After Coreen I ain't got no use for them. I stay up on Jack Slattery's place when I be down there. All them women want is somebody with a steady payday.

BOY WILLIE: That ain't what I hear. I hear every two weeks the women all put on their dresses and line up at the railroad station.

DOAKER: I don't get down there but once a month. I used to go down there every two weeks but they keep switching me around. They keep switching all the fellows around.

BOY WILLIE: Doaker can't turn that railroad loose. He was working the railroad when I was walking around crying for sugartit. My mama used to brag on him.

DOAKER: I'm cooking now, but I used to line track. I pieced together the Yellow Dog stitch by stitch. Rail by rail. Line track all up around there. I lined track all up around Sunflower and Clarksdale. Wining Boy worked with me. He helped put in some of that track. He'd work it for six months and quit. Go back to playing piano and gambling.

BOY WILLIE: How long you been with the railroad now?

DOAKER: Twenty-seven years. Now, I'll tell you something about the railroad. What I done learned after twenty-seven years. See, you got North. You got West. You look over here you got South. Over there you got East. Now, you can start from anywhere. Don't care where you at. You got to go one of them four ways. And whichever way you decide to go they got a railroad that will take you there. Now, that's something simple. You think anybody would be able to understand that. But you'd be surprised how many people trying to go North get on a train going West. They think the train's supposed to go where they going rather than where it's going.

Now, why people going? Their sister's sick. They leaving before they kill somebody . . . and they sitting across from somebody who's leaving to keep from getting killed. They leaving cause they can't get satisfied. They going to meet someone. I wish I had a dollar for every time that someone wasn't at the station to meet them. I done seen that a lot. In between the time they sent the telegram and the time the person get there . . . they done forgot all about them.

They got so many trains out there they have a hard time keeping them from running into each other. Got trains going every whichaway. Got people on all of them. Somebody going where somebody just left. If everybody stay in one place I believe this would be a better world. Now what I done learned after twenty-seven years of railroading is this . . . if the train stays on the track . . . it's going to get where it's going. It might not be where you going. If it ain't, then all you got to do is sit and wait cause the train's coming back to get you. The train don't never stop. It'll come back every time. Now I'll tell you another thing . . .

BOY WILLIE: What you cooking over there, Doaker? Me and Lymon's hungry.

DOAKER: Go on down there to Wylie and Kirkpatrick to Eddie's restaurant. Coffee cost a nickel and you can get two eggs, sausage, and grits for fifteen cents. He even give you a biscuit with it.

BOY WILLIE: That look good what you got. Give me a little piece of that grilled bread.

DOAKER: Here . . . go on take the whole piece.

BOY WILLIE: Here you go, Lymon . . . you want a piece?

[*He gives* LYMON *a piece of toast.* MARETHA *enters from the stairs.*]

BOY WILLIE: Hey, sugar. Come here and give me a hug. Come on give Uncle Boy Willie a hug. Don't be shy. Look at her, Doaker. She done got bigger. Ain't she got big?

DOAKER: Yeah, she getting up there.

BOY WILLIE: How you doing, sugar?

MARETHA: Fine.

BOY WILLIE: You was just a little old thing last time I seen you. You remember me, don't you? This your Uncle Boy Willie from down South. That there's Lymon. He my friend. We come up here to sell watermelons. You like watermelons?

[MARETHA *nods.*]

We got a whole truckload out front. You can have as many as you want. What you been doing?

MARETHA: Nothing.

BOY WILLIE: Don't be shy now. Look at you getting all big. How old is you?

MARETHA: Eleven. I'm gonna be twelve soon.

BOY WILLIE: You like it up here? You like the North?

MARETHA: It's alright.

BOY WILLIE: That there's Lymon. Did you say hi to Lymon?

MARETHA: Hi.

LYMON: How you doing? You look just like your mama. I remember you when you was wearing diapers.

BOY WILLIE: You gonna come down South and see me? Uncle Boy Willie gonna get him a farm. Gonna get a great big old farm. Come down there and I'll teach you how to ride a mule. Teach you how to kill a chicken, too.

MARETHA: I seen my mama do that.

BOY WILLIE: Ain't nothing to it. You just grab him by his neck and twist it. Get you a real good grip and then you just wring his neck and throw him in the pot. Cook him up. Then you got some good eating. What you like to eat? What kind of food you like?

MARETHA: I like everything... except I don't like no black-eyed peas.

BOY WILLIE: Uncle Doaker tell me your mama got you playing that piano. Come on play something for me.

[BOY WILLIE *crosses over to the piano followed by* MARETHA.]

Show me what you can do. Come on now. Here... Uncle Boy Willie give you a dime... show me what you can do. Don't be bashful now. That dime say you can't be bashful.

[MARETHA *plays. It is something any beginner first learns.*]

Here, let me show you something.

[BOY WILLIE *sits and plays a simple boogie-woogie.*]

See that? See what I'm doing? That's what you call the boogie-woogie. See now... you can get up and dance to that. That's how good it sound. It sound like you wanna dance. You can dance to that. It'll hold you up. Whatever kind of dance you wanna do you can dance to that right there. See that? See how it go? Ain't nothing to it. Go on you do it.

MARETHA: I got to read it on the paper.

BOY WILLIE: You don't need no paper. Go on. Do just like that there.

BERNIECE: Maretha! You get up here and get ready to go so you be on time. Ain't no need you trying to take advantage of company.

MARETHA: I got to go.

BOY WILLIE: Uncle Boy Willie gonna get you a guitar. Let Uncle Doaker teach you how to play that. You don't need to read no paper to play the guitar. Your mama told you about that piano? You know how them pictures got on there?

MARETHA: She say it just always been like that since she got it.

BOY WILLIE: You hear that, Doaker? And you sitting up here in the house with Berniece.

DOAKER: I ain't got nothing to do with that. I don't get in the way of Berniece's raising her.

BOY WILLIE: You tell your mama to tell you about that piano. You ask her how them pictures got on there. If she don't tell you I'll tell you.

BERNIECE: Maretha!

MARETHA: I got to get ready to go.

BOY WILLIE: She getting big, Doaker. You remember her, Lymon?

LYMON: She used to be real little.

[*There is a knock on the door.* DOAKER *goes to answer it.* AVERY *enters. Thirty-eight years old, honest and ambitious, he has taken to the city like a fish to water, finding in it opportunities for growth and advancement that did not exist for him in the rural South. He is dressed in a suit and tie with a gold cross around his neck. He carries a small Bible.*]

DOAKER: Hey, Avery, come on in. Berniece upstairs.

BOY WILLIE: Look at him... look at him... he don't know what to say. He wasn't expecting to see me.

AVERY: Hey, Boy Willie. What you doing up here?

BOY WILLIE: Look at him, Lymon.
AVERY: Is that Lymon? Lymon Jackson?
BOY WILLIE: Yeah, you know Lymon.
DOAKER: Berniece be ready in a minute, Avery.
BOY WILLIE: Doaker say you a preacher now. What . . . we supposed to call you Reverend? You used to be plain old Avery. When you get to be a preacher, nigger?
LYMON: Avery say he gonna be a preacher so he don't have to work.
BOY WILLIE: I remember when you was down there on the Willshaw place planting cotton. You wasn't thinking about no Reverend then.
AVERY: That must be your truck out there. I saw that truck with them watermelons, I was trying to figure out what it was doing in front of the house.
BOY WILLIE: Yeah, me and Lymon selling watermelons. That's Lymon's truck.
DOAKER: Berniece say you all going down to the bank.
AVERY: Yeah, they give me a half day off work. I got an appointment to talk to the bank about getting a loan to start my church.
BOY WILLIE: Lymon say preachers don't have to work. Where you working at, nigger?
DOAKER: Avery got him one of them good jobs. He working at one of them skyscrapers downtown.
AVERY: I'm working down there at the Gulf Building running an elevator. Got a pension and everything. They even give you a turkey on Thanksgiving.
LYMON: How you know the rope ain't gonna break? Ain't you scared the rope's gonna break?
AVERY: That's steel. They got steel cables hold it up. It take a whole lot of breaking to break that steel. Naw, I ain't worried about nothing like that. It ain't nothing but a little old elevator. Now, I wouldn't get in none of them airplanes. You couldn't pay me to do nothing like that.
LYMON: That be fun. I'd rather do that than ride in one of them elevators.
BOY WILLIE: How many of them watermelons you wanna buy?
AVERY: I thought you was gonna give me one seeing as how you got a whole truck full.
BOY WILLIE: You can get one, get two. I'll give you two for a dollar.
AVERY: I can't eat but one. How much are they?
BOY WILLIE: Aw, nigger, you know I'll give you a watermelon. Go on, take as many as you want. Just leave some for me and Lymon to sell.
AVERY: I don't want but one.
BOY WILLIE: How you get to be a preacher, Avery? I might want to be a preacher one day. Have everybody call me Reverend Boy Willie.
AVERY: It come to me in a dream. God called me and told me he wanted me to be a shepherd for his flock. That's what I'm gonna call my church . . . The Good Shepherd Church of God in Christ.
DOAKER: Tell him what you told me. Tell him about the three hobos.
AVERY: Boy Willie don't want to hear all that.
LYMON: I do. Lots a people say your dreams can come true.
AVERY: Naw. You don't want to hear all that.
DOAKER: Go on. I told him you was a preacher. He didn't want to believe me. Tell him about the three hobos.
AVERY: Well, it come to me in a dream. See . . . I was sitting out in this railroad

yard watching the trains go by. The train stopped and these three hobos got off. They told me they had come from Nazareth and was on their way to Jerusalem. They had three candles. They gave me one and told me to light it ... but to be careful that it didn't go out. Next thing I knew I was standing in front of this house. Something told me to go knock on the door. This old woman opened the door and said they had been waiting on me. Then she led me into this room. It was a big room and it was full of all kinds of different people. They looked like anybody else except they all had sheep heads and was making noise like sheep make. I heard somebody call my name. I looked around and there was these same three hobos. They told me to take off my clothes and they give me a blue robe with gold thread. They washed my feet and combed my hair. Then they showed me these three doors and told me to pick one.

I went through one of them doors and that flame leapt off that candle and it seemed like my whole head caught fire. I looked around and there was four or five other men standing there with these same blue robes on. Then we heard a voice tell us to look out across this valley. We looked out and saw the valley was full of wolves. The voice told us that these sheep people that I had seen in the other room had to go over to the other side of this valley and somebody had to take them. Then I heard another voice say, "Who shall I send?" Next thing I knew I said, "Here I am. Send me." That's when I met Jesus. He say, "If you go, I'll go with you." Something told me to say, "Come on. Let's go." That's when I woke up. My head still felt like it was on fire ... but I had a peace about myself that was hard to explain. I knew right then that I had been filled with the Holy Ghost and called to be a servant of the Lord. It took me a while before I could accept that. But then a lot of little ways God showed me that it was true. So I became a preacher.

LYMON: I see why you gonna call it the Good Shepherd Church. You dreaming about them sheep people. I can see that easy.

BOY WILLIE: Doaker say you sent some white man past the house to look at that piano. Say he was going around to all the colored people's houses looking to buy up musical instruments.

AVERY: Yeah, but Berniece didn't want to sell that piano. After she told me about it ... I could see why she didn't want to sell it.

BOY WILLIE: What's this man's name?

AVERY: Oh, that's a while back now. I done forgot his name. He give Berniece a card with his name and telephone number on it, but I believe she threw it away.

[BERNIECE and MARETHA enter from the stairs.]

BERNIECE: Maretha, run back upstairs and get my pocketbook. And wipe that hair grease off your forehead. Go ahead, hurry up.

[MARETHA exits up the stairs.]

How you doing, Avery? You done got all dressed up. You look nice. Boy Willie, I thought you and Lymon was going to sell them watermelons.

BOY WILLIE: Lymon done got sleepy. We liable to get some sleep first.

LYMON: I ain't sleepy.

DOAKER: As many watermelons as you got stacked up on that truck out there, you ought to have been gone.
BOY WILLIE: We gonna go in a minute. We going.
BERNIECE: Doaker. I'm gonna stop down there on Logan Street. You want anything?
DOAKER: You can pick up some ham hocks if you going down there. See if you can get the smoked ones. If they ain't got that get the fresh ones. Don't get the ones that got all that fat under the skin. Look for the long ones. They nice and lean. [*He gives her a dollar.*] Don't get the short ones lessen they smoked. If you got to get the fresh ones make sure that they the long ones. If they ain't got them smoked then go ahead and get the short ones. [*Pause.*] You may as well get some turnip greens while you down there. I got some buttermilk . . . if you pick up some cornmeal I'll make me some cornbread and cook up them turnip greens.

[MARETHA *enters from the stairs.*]

MARETHA: We gonna take the streetcar?
BERNIECE: Me and Avery gonna drop you off at the settlement house. You mind them people down there. Don't be going down there showing your color. Boy Willie, I done told you what to do. I'll see you later, Doaker.
AVERY: I'll be seeing you again, Boy Willie.
BOY WILLIE: Hey, Berniece . . . what's the name of that man Avery sent past say he want to buy the piano?
BERNIECE: I knew it. I knew it when I first seen you. I knew you was up to something.
BOY WILLIE: Sutter's brother say he selling the land to me. He waiting on me now. Told me he'd give me two weeks. I got one part. Sell them watermelons get me another part. Then we can sell that piano and I'll have the third part.
BERNIECE: I ain't selling that piano, Boy Willie. If that's why you come up here you can just forget about it. [*To* DOAKER.] Doaker, I'll see you later. Boy Willie ain't nothing but a whole lot of mouth. I ain't paying him no mind. If he come up here thinking he gonna sell that piano then he done come up here for nothing.

[BERNIECE, AVERY, *and* MARETHA *exit the front door.*]

BOY WILLIE: Hey, Lymon! You ready to go sell these watermelons.

[BOY WILLIE *and* LYMON *start to exit. At the door* BOY WILLIE *turns to* DOAKER.]

Hey, Doaker . . . if Berniece don't want to sell that piano . . . I'm gonna cut it in half and go on and sell my half.

[BOY WILLIE *and* LYMON *exit.*]

[*The lights go down on the scene.*]

Scene 2

[*The lights come up on the kitchen. It is three days later.* WINING BOY *sits at the kitchen table. There is a half-empty pint bottle on the table.* DOAKER *busies himself washing pots.* WINING BOY *is fifty-six years old.* DOAKER's *older brother, he tries to present the image of a successful musician and gambler, but his music, his clothes, and even his manner of presentation are old. He is a man who looking back over his life continues to live it with an odd mixture of zest and sorrow.*]

WINING BOY: So the Ghosts of the Yellow Dog got Sutter. That just go to show you I believe I always lived right. They say every dog gonna have his day and time it go around it sure come back to you. I done seen that a thousand times. I know the truth of that. But I'll tell you outright ... if I see Sutter's ghost I'll be on the first thing I find that got wheels on it.

[DOAKER *enters from his room.*]

DOAKER: Wining Boy!

WINING BOY: And I'll tell you another thing ... Berniece ain't gonna sell that piano.

DOAKER: That's what she told him. He say he gonna cut it in half and go on and sell his half. They been around here three days trying to sell them watermelons. They trying to get out to where the white folks live but the truck keep breaking down. They go a block or two and it break down again. They trying to get out to Squirrel Hill and can't get around the corner. He say soon as he can get that truck empty to where he can set the piano up in there he gonna take it out of here and go sell it.

WINING BOY: What about them boys Sutter got? How come they ain't farming that land?

DOAKER: One of them going to school. He left down there and come North to school. The other one ain't got as much sense as that frying pan over yonder. That is the dumbest white man I ever seen. He'd stand in the river and watch it rise till it drown him.

WINING BOY: Other than seeing Sutter's ghost how's Berniece doing?

DOAKER: She doing alright. She still got Crawley on her mind. He been dead three years but she still holding on to him. She need to go out here and let one of these fellows grab a whole handful of whatever she got. She act like it done got precious.

WINING BOY: They always told me any fish will bite if you got good bait.

DOAKER: She stuck up on it. She think it's better than she is. I believe she messing around with Avery. They got something going. He a preacher now. If you let him tell it the Holy Ghost sat on his head and heaven opened up with thunder and lightning and God was calling his name. Told him to go out and preach and tend to his flock. That's what he gonna call his church. The Good Shepherd Church.

WINING BOY: They had that joker down in Spear walking around talking about he Jesus Christ. He gonna live the life of Christ. Went through the Last Supper and everything. Rented him a mule on Palm Sunday and rode through the town. Did everything ... talking about he Christ. He did everything until they got up to that crucifixion part. Got up to that part and told everybody to go home and quit pretending. He got up to the crucifixion part and changed his mind. Had a whole bunch of folks come down there to see him get nailed to the cross. I don't know who's the worse fool. Him or them. Had all them folks come down there ... even carried the cross up this little hill. People standing around waiting to see him get nailed to the cross and he stop everything and preach a little sermon and told everybody to go home. Had enough nerve to tell them to come to church on Easter Sunday to celebrate his resurrection.

DOAKER: I'm surprised Avery ain't thought about that. He trying every little thing to get him a congregation together. They meeting over at his house till he get him a church.

WINING BOY: Ain't nothing wrong with being a preacher. You got the preacher on one hand and the gambler on the other. Sometimes there ain't too much difference in them.

DOAKER: How long you been in Kansas City?

WINING BOY: Since I left here. I got tied up with some old gal down there. [*Pause.*] You know Cleotha died.

DOAKER: Yeah, I heard that last time I was down there. I was sorry to hear that.

WINING BOY: One of her friends wrote and told me. I got the letter right here. [*He takes the letter out of his pocket.*] I was down in Kansas City and she wrote and told me Cleotha had died. Name of Willa Bryant. She say she know cousin Rupert. [*He opens the letter and reads.*] Dear Wining Boy: I am writing this letter to let you know Miss Cleotha Holman passed on Saturday the first of May she departed this world in the loving arms of her sister Miss Alberta Samuels. I know you would want to know this and am writing as a friend of Cleotha. There have been many hardships since last you seen her but she survived them all and to the end was a good woman whom I hope have God's grace and is in His Paradise. Your cousin Rupert Bates is my friend also and he give me your address and I pray this reaches you about Cleotha. Miss Willa Bryant. A friend. [*He folds the letter and returns it to his pocket.*] They was nailing her coffin shut by the time I heard about it. I never knew she was sick. I believe it was that yellow jaundice. That's what killed her mama.

DOAKER: Cleotha wasn't but forty-some.

WINING BOY: She was forty-six. I got ten years on her. I met her when she was sixteen. You remember I used to run around there. Couldn't nothing keep me still. Much as I loved Cleotha I loved to ramble. Couldn't nothing keep me still. We got married and we used to fight about it all the time. Then one day she asked me to leave. Told me she loved me before I left. Told me, Wining Boy, you got a home as long as I got mine. And I believe in my heart I always felt that and that kept me safe.

DOAKER: Cleotha always did have a nice way about her.

WINING BOY: Man that woman was something. I used to thank the Lord. Many a night I sat up and looked out over my life. Said, well, I had Cleotha. When it didn't look like there was nothing else for me, I said, thank God, at least I had that. If ever I go anywhere in this life I done known a good woman. And that used to hold me till the next morning. [*Pause.*] What you got? Give me a little nip. I know you got something stuck up in your room.

DOAKER: I ain't seen you walk in here and put nothing on the table. You done sat there and drank up your whiskey. Now you talking about what you got.

WINING BOY: I got plenty money. Give me a little nip.

[DOAKER *carries a glass into his room and returns with it half-filled. He sets it on the table in front of* WINING BOY.]

WINING BOY: You hear from Coreen?

DOAKER: She up in New York. I let her go from my mind.

WINING BOY: She was something back then. She wasn't too pretty but she had a way of looking at you made you know there was a whole lot of woman there. You got married and snatched her out from under us and we all got mad at you.

DOAKER: She up in New York City. That's what I hear.

[*The door opens and* BOY WILLIE *and* LYMON *enter.*]

BOY WILLIE: Aw hell . . . look here! We was just talking about you. Doaker say you left out of here with a whole sack of money. I told him we wasn't going see you till you got broke.

WINING BOY: What you mean broke? I got a whole pocketful of money.

DOAKER: Did you all get that truck fixed?

BOY WILLIE: We got it running and got halfway out there on Centre and it broke down again. Lymon went out there and messed it up some more. Fellow told us we got to wait till tomorrow to get it fixed. Say he have it running like new. Lymon going back down there and sleep in the truck so the people don't take the watermelons.

LYMON: Lymon nothing. You go down there and sleep in it.

BOY WILLIE: You was sleeping in it down home, nigger! I don't know nothing about sleeping in no truck.

LYMON: I ain't sleeping in no truck.

BOY WILLIE: They can take all the watermelons. I don't care. Wining Boy, where you coming from? Where you been?

WINING BOY: I been down in Kansas City.

BOY WILLIE: You remember Lymon? Lymon Jackson.

WINING BOY: Yeah, I used to know his daddy.

BOY WILLIE: Doaker say you don't never leave no address with nobody. Say he got to depend on your whim. See when it strike you to pay a visit.

WINING BOY: I got four or five addresses.

BOY WILLIE: Doaker say Berniece asked you for three dollars and you got mad and left.

WINING BOY: Berniece try and rule over you too much for me. That's why I left. It wasn't about no three dollars.

BOY WILLIE: Where you getting all these sacks of money from? I need to be with you. Doaker say you had a whole sack of money . . . turn some of it loose.

WINING BOY: I was just fixing to ask you for five dollars.

BOY WILLIE: I ain't got no money. I'm trying to get some. Doaker tell you about Sutter? The Ghosts of the Yellow Dog got him about three weeks ago. Berniece done seen his ghost and everything. He right upstairs. [*Calls.*] Hey Sutter! Wining Boy's here. Come on, get a drink!

WINING BOY: How many that make the Ghosts of the Yellow Dog done got?

BOY WILLIE: Must be about nine or ten, eleven or twelve. I don't know.

DOAKER: You got Ed Saunders. Howard Peterson. Charlie Webb.

WINING BOY: Robert Smith. That fellow that shot Becky's boy . . . say he was stealing peaches . . .

DOAKER: You talking about Bob Mallory.

BOY WILLIE: Berniece say she don't believe all that about the Ghosts of the Yellow Dog.

WINING BOY: She ain't got to believe. You go ask them white folks in Sunflower County if they believe. You go ask Sutter if he believe. I don't care if Berniece believe or not. I done been to where the Southern cross the Yellow Dog and called out their names. They talk back to you, too.

LYMON: What they sound like? The wind or something?

BOY WILLIE: You done been there for real, Wining Boy?

WINING BOY: Nineteen thirty. July of nineteen thirty I stood right there on that spot. It didn't look like nothing was going right in my life. I said everything can't go wrong all the time... let me go down there and call on the Ghosts of the Yellow Dog, see if they can help me. I went down there and right there where them two railroads cross each other... I stood right there on that spot and called out their names. They talk back to you, too.

LYMON: People say you can ask them questions. They talk to you like that?

WINING BOY: A lot of things you got to find out on your own. I can't say how they talked to nobody else. But to me it just filled me up in a strange sort of way to be standing there on that spot. I didn't want to leave. It felt like the longer I stood there the bigger I got. I seen the train coming and it seem like I was bigger than the train. I started not to move. But something told me to go ahead and get on out the way. The train passed and I started to go back up there and stand some more. But something told me not to do it. I walked away from there feeling like a king. Went on and had a stroke of luck that run on for three years. So I don't care if Berniece believe or not. Berniece ain't got to believe. I know cause I been there. Now Doaker'll tell you about the Ghosts of the Yellow Dog.

DOAKER: I don't try and talk that stuff with Berniece. Avery got her all tied up in that church. She just think it's a whole lot of nonsense.

BOY WILLIE: Berniece don't believe in nothing. She just think she believe. She believe in anything if it's convenient for her to believe. But when that convenience run out then she ain't got nothing to stand on.

WINING BOY: Let's not get on Berniece now. Doaker tell me you talking about selling that piano.

BOY WILLIE: Yeah... hey, Doaker, I got the name of that man Avery was talking about. The man what's fixing the truck gave me his name. Everybody know him. Say he buy up anything you can make music with. I got his name and his telephone number. Hey, Wining Boy, Sutter's brother say he selling the land to me. I got one part. Sell them watermelons get me the second part. Then... soon as I get them watermelons out that truck I'm gonna take and sell that piano and get the third part.

DOAKER: That land ain't worth nothing no more. The smart white man's up here in these cities. He cut the land loose and step back and watch you and the dumb white man argue over it.

WINING BOY: How you know Sutter's brother ain't sold it already? You talking about selling the piano and the man's liable to sold the land two or three times.

BOY WILLIE: He say he waiting on me. He say he give me two weeks. That's two weeks from Friday. Say if I ain't back by then he might gonna sell it to somebody else. He say he wanna see me with it.

WINING BOY: You know as well as I know the man gonna sell the land to the first one walk up and hand him the money.

BOY WILLIE: That's just who I'm gonna be. Look, you ain't gotta know he waiting on me. I know. Okay, I know what the man told me. Stovall already done tried to buy the land from him and he told him no. The man say he waiting on me... he waiting on me. Hey, Doaker... give me a drink. I see Wining Boy got his glass.

[DOAKER *exits into his room.*]

Wining Boy, what you doing in Kansas City? What they got down there?
LYMON: I hear they got some nice-looking women in Kansas City. I sure like to go down there and find out.
WINING BOY: Man, the women down there is something else.

[DOAKER *enters with a bottle of whiskey. He sets it on the table with some glasses.*]

DOAKER: You wanna sit up here and drink up my whiskey, leave a dollar on the table when you get up.
BOY WILLIE: You ain't doing nothing but showing your hospitality. I know we ain't got to pay for your hospitality.
WINING BOY: Doaker say they had you and Lymon down on the Parchman Farm. Had you on my old stomping grounds.
BOY WILLIE: Me and Lymon was down there hauling wood for Jim Miller and keeping us a little bit to sell. Some white fellows tried to run us off of it. That's when Crawley got killed. They put me and Lymon in the penitentiary.
LYMON: They ambushed us right there where that road dip down and around that bend in the creek. Crawley tried to fight them. Me and Boy Willie got away but the sheriff got us. Say we was stealing wood. They shot me in my stomach.
BOY WILLIE: They looking for Lymon down there now. They rounded him up and put him in jail for not working.
LYMON: Fined me a hundred dollars. Mr. Stovall come and paid my hundred dollars and the judge say I got to work for him to pay him back his hundred dollars. I told them I'd rather take my thirty days but they wouldn't let me do that.
BOY WILLIE: As soon as Stovall turned his back, Lymon was gone. He down there living in that truck dodging the sheriff and Stovall. He got both of them looking for him. So I brought him up here.
LYMON: I told Boy Willie I'm gonna stay up here. I ain't going back with him.
BOY WILLIE: Ain't nobody twisting your arm to make you go back. You can do what you want to do.
WINING BOY: I'll go back with you. I'm on my way down there. You gonna take the train? I'm gonna take the train.
LYMON: They treat you better up here.
BOY WILLIE: I ain't worried about nobody mistreating me. They treat you like you let them treat you. They mistreat me I mistreat them right back. Ain't no difference in me and the white man.
WINING BOY: Ain't no difference as far as how somebody supposed to treat you. I agree with that. But I'll tell you the difference between the colored man and the white man. Alright. Now you take and eat some berries. They taste real good to you. So you say I'm gonna go out and get me a whole pot of these berries and cook them up to make a pie or whatever. But you ain't looked to see them berries is sitting in the white fellow's yard. Ain't got no fence around them. You figure anybody want something they'd fence it in. Alright. Now the

white man come along and say that's my land. Therefore everything that grow on it belong to me. He tell the sheriff, "I want you to put this nigger in jail as a warning to all the other niggers. Otherwise first thing you know these niggers have everything that belong to us."

BOY WILLIE: I'd come back at night and haul off his whole patch while he was sleep.

WINING BOY: Alright. Now Mr. So and So, he sell the land to you. And he come to you and say, "John, you own the land. It's all yours now. But them is my berries. And come time to pick them I'm gonna send my boys over. You got the land . . . but them berries, I'm gonna keep them. They mine." And he go and fix it with the law that them is his berries. Now that's the difference between the colored man and the white man. The colored man can't fix nothing with the law.

BOY WILLIE: I don't go by what the law say. The law's liable to say anything. I go by if it's right or not. It don't matter to me what the law say. I take and look at it for myself.

LYMON: That's why you gonna end up back down there on the Parchman Farm.

BOY WILLIE: I ain't thinking about no Parchman Farm. You liable to go back before me.

LYMON: They work you too hard down there. All that weeding and hoeing and chopping down trees. I didn't like all that.

WINING BOY: You ain't got to like your job on Parchman. Hey, tell him, Doaker, the only one got to like his job is the waterboy.

DOAKER: If he don't like his job he need to set that bucket down.

BOY WILLIE: That's what they told Lymon. They had Lymon on water and everybody got mad at him cause he was lazy.

LYMON: That water was heavy.

BOY WILLIE: They had Lymon down there singing:

[*Sings.*]

O Lord Berta Berta O Lord gal oh-ah
O Lord Berta Berta O Lord gal well

[LYMON *and* WINING BOY *join in.*]

Go 'head marry don't you wait on me oh-ah
Go 'head marry don't you wait on me well
Might not want you when I go free oh-ah
Might not want you when I go free well

BOY WILLIE: Come on, Doaker. Doaker know this one.

[As DOAKER *joins in the men stamp and clap to keep time. They sing in harmony with great fervor and style.*]

O Lord Berta Berta O Lord gal oh-ah
O Lord Berta Berta O Lord gal well

Raise them up higher, let them drop on down oh-ah
Raise them up higher, let them drop on down well
Don't know the difference when the sun go down oh-ah
Don't know the difference when the sun go down well

> Berta in Meridan and she living at ease oh-ah
> Berta in Meridan and she living at ease well
> I'm on old Parchman, got to work or leave oh-ah
> I'm on old Parchman, got to work or leave well
>
> O Alberta, Berta, O Lord gal oh-ah
> O Alberta, Berta, O Lord gal well
>
> When you marry, don't marry no farming man oh-ah
> When you marry, don't marry no farming man well
> Everyday Monday, hoe handle in your hand oh-ah
> Everyday Monday, hoe handle in your hand well
>
> When you marry, marry a railroad man, oh-ah
> When you marry, marry a railroad man, well
> Everyday Sunday, dollar in your hand oh-ah
> Everyday Sunday, dollar in your hand well
>
> O Alberta, Berta, O Lord gal oh-ah
> O Alberta, Berta, O Lord gal well

BOY WILLIE: Doaker like that part. He like that railroad part.
LYMON: Doaker sound like Tangleye.[2] He can't sing a lick.
BOY WILLIE: Hey, Doaker, they still talk about you down on Parchman. They ask me, "You Doaker Boy's nephew?" I say, "Yeah, me and him is family." They treated me alright soon as I told them that. Say, "Yeah, he my uncle."
DOAKER: I don't never want to see none of them niggers no more.
BOY WILLIE: I don't want to see them either. Hey, Wining Boy, come on play some piano. You a piano player, play some piano. Lymon wanna hear you.
WINING BOY: I give that piano up. That was the best thing that ever happened to me, getting rid of that piano. That piano got so big and I'm carrying it around on my back. I don't wish that on nobody. See, you think it's all fun being a recording star. Got to carrying that piano around and man did I get slow. Got just like molasses. The world just slipping by me and I'm walking around with that piano. Alright. Now, there ain't but so many places you can go. Only so many road wide enough for you and that piano. And that piano get heavier and heavier. Go to a place and they find out you play piano, the first thing they want to do is give you a drink, find you a piano, and sit you right down. And that's where you gonna be for the next eight hours. They ain't gonna let you get up! Now, the first three or four years of that is fun. You can't get enough whiskey and you can't get enough women and you don't never get tired of playing that piano. But that only last so long. You look up one day and you hate the whiskey, and you hate the women, and you hate the piano. But that's all you got. You can't do nothing else. All you know how to do is play that piano. Now, who am I? Am I me? Or am I the piano player? Sometime it seem like the only thing to do is shoot the piano player cause he the cause of all the trouble I'm having.
DOAKER: What you gonna do when your troubles get like mine?

---

2. Or Tangle Eye, one of the prisoners field-recorded at Parchman Farm by Alan Lomax in the 1930s and 1940s.

LYMON: If I knew how to play it, I'd play it. That's a nice piano.
BOY WILLIE: Whoever playing better play quick. Sutter's brother say he waiting on me. I sell them watermelons. Get Berniece to sell that piano. Put them two parts with the part I done saved...
WINING BOY: Berniece ain't gonna sell that piano. I don't see why you don't know that.
BOY WILLIE: What she gonna do with it? She ain't doing nothing but letting it sit up there and rot. That piano ain't doing nobody no good.
LYMON: That's a nice piano. If I had it I'd sell it. Unless I knew how to play like Wining Boy. You can get a nice price for that piano.
DOAKER: Now I'm gonna tell you something, Lymon don't know this... but I'm gonna tell you why me and Wining Boy say Berniece ain't gonna sell that piano.
BOY WILLIE: She ain't got to sell it! I'm gonna sell it! Berniece ain't got no more rights to that piano than I do.
DOAKER: I'm talking to the man... let me talk to the man. See, now... to understand why we say that... to understand about that piano... you got to go back to slavery time. See, our family was owned by a fellow named Robert Sutter. That was Sutter's grandfather. Alright. The piano was owned by a fellow named Joel Nolander. He was one of the Nolander brothers from down in Georgia. It was coming up on Sutter's wedding anniversary and he was looking to buy his wife... Miss Ophelia was her name... he was looking to buy her an anniversary present. Only thing with him... he ain't had no money. But he had some niggers. So he asked Mr. Nolander to see if maybe he could trade off some of his niggers for that piano. Told him he would give him one and a half niggers for it. That's the way he told him. Say he could have one full grown and one half grown. Mr. Nolander agreed only he say he had to pick them. He didn't want Sutter to give him just any old nigger. He say he wanted to have the pick of the litter. So Sutter lined up his niggers and Mr. Nolander looked them over and out of the whole bunch he picked my grandmother... her name was Berniece... same like Berniece... and he picked my daddy when he wasn't nothing but a little boy nine years old. They made the trade off and Miss Ophelia was so happy with that piano that it got to be just about all she would do was play on that piano.
WINING BOY: Just get up in the morning, get all dressed up and sit down and play on that piano.
DOAKER: Alright. Time go along. Time go along. Miss Ophelia got to missing my grandmother... the way she would cook and clean the house and talk to her and what not. And she missed having my daddy around the house to fetch things for her. So she asked to see if maybe she could trade back that piano and get her niggers back. Mr. Nolander said no. Said a deal was a deal. Him and Sutter had a big falling out about it and Miss Ophelia took sick to the bed. Wouldn't get out of the bed in the morning. She just lay there. The doctor said she was wasting away.
WINING BOY: That's when Sutter called our granddaddy up to the house.
DOAKER: Now, our granddaddy's name was Boy Willie. That's who Boy Willie's named after... only they called him Willie Boy. Now, he was a worker of wood. He could make you anything you wanted out of wood. He'd make you a desk. A table. A lamp. Anything you wanted. Them white fellows around there used

to come up to Mr. Sutter and get him to make all kinds of things for them. Then they'd pay Mr. Sutter a nice price. See, everything my granddaddy made Mr. Sutter owned cause he owned him. That's why when Mr. Nolander offered to buy him to keep the family together Mr. Sutter wouldn't sell him. Told Mr. Nolander he didn't have enough money to buy him. Now . . . am I telling it right, Wining Boy?

WINING BOY: You telling it.

DOAKER: Sutter called him up to the house and told him to carve my grandmother and my daddy's picture on the piano for Miss Ophelia. And he took and carved this . . .

[DOAKER *crosses over to the piano.*]

See that right there? That's my grandmother, Berniece. She looked just like that. And he put a picture of my daddy when he wasn't nothing but a little boy the way he remembered him. He made them up out of his memory. Only thing . . . he didn't stop there. He carved all this. He got a picture of his mama . . . Mama Esther . . . and his daddy, Boy Charles.

WINING BOY: That was the first Boy Charles.

DOAKER: Then he put on the side here all kinds of things. See that? That's when him and Mama Berniece got married. They called it jumping the broom. That's how you got married in them days. Then he got here when my daddy was born . . . and here he got Mama Esther's funeral . . . and down here he got Mr. Nolander taking Mama Berniece and my daddy away down to his place in Georgia. He got all kinds of things what happened with our family. When Mr. Sutter seen the piano with all them carvings on it he got mad. He didn't ask for all that. But see . . . there wasn't nothing he could do about it. When Miss Ophelia seen it . . . she got excited. Now she had her piano and her niggers too. She took back to playing it and played on it right up till the day she died. Alright . . . now see, our brother Boy Charles . . . that's Berniece and Boy Willie's daddy . . . he was the oldest of us three boys. He's dead now. But he would have been fifty-seven if he had lived. He died in 1911 when he was thirty-one years old. Boy Charles used to talk about that piano all the time. He never could get it off his mind. Two or three months go by and he be talking about it again. He be talking about taking it out of Sutter's house. Say it was the story of our whole family and as long as Sutter had it . . . he had us. Say we was still in slavery. Me and Wining Boy tried to talk him out of it but it wouldn't do any good. Soon as he quiet down about it he'd start up again. We seen where he wasn't gonna get it off his mind . . . so, on the Fourth of July, 1911 . . . when Sutter was at the picnic what the county give every year . . . me and Wining Boy went on down there with him and took that piano out of Sutter's house. We put it on a wagon and me and Wining Boy carried it over into the next county with Mama Ola's people. Boy Charles decided to stay around there and wait until Sutter got home to make it look like business as usual.

Now, I don't know what happened when Sutter came home and found that piano gone. But somebody went up to Boy Charles's house and set it on fire. But he wasn't in there. He must have seen them coming cause he went down and caught the 3:57 Yellow Dog. He didn't know they was gonna come down and stop the train. Stopped the train and found Boy Charles in the boxcar with four of them hobos. Must have got mad when they couldn't find the piano cause they set the boxcar afire and killed everybody. Now, nobody know who done that. Some people say it was Sutter cause it was his piano. Some people say it was Sheriff Carter. Some people say it was Robert Smith and Ed Saunders. But don't nobody know for sure. It was about two months after that that Ed Saunders fell down his well. Just upped and fell down his well for no reason. People say it was the ghost of them men who burned up in the boxcar that pushed him in his well. They started calling them the Ghosts of the Yellow Dog. Now, that's how all that got started and that why we say Berniece ain't gonna sell that piano. Cause her daddy died over it.

BOY WILLIE: All that's in the past. If my daddy had seen where he could have traded that piano in for some land of his own, it wouldn't be sitting up here now. He spent his whole life farming on somebody else's land. I ain't gonna do that. See, he couldn't do no better. When he come along he ain't had nothing he could build on. His daddy ain't had nothing to give him. The only thing my daddy had to give me was that piano. And he died over giving me that. I ain't gonna let it sit up there and rot without trying to do something with it. If Berniece can't see that, then I'm gonna go ahead and sell my half. And you and Wining Boy know I'm right.

DOAKER: Ain't nobody said nothing about who's right and who's wrong. I was just telling the man about the piano. I was telling him why we say Berniece ain't gonna sell it.

LYMON: Yeah, I can see why you say that now. I told Boy Willie he ought to stay up here with me.

BOY WILLIE: You stay! I'm going back! That's what I'm gonna do with my life! Why I got to come up here and learn to do something I don't know how to do when I already know how to farm? You stay up here and make your own way if that's what you want to do. I'm going back and live my life the way I want to live it.

[WINING BOY *gets up and crosses to the piano.*]

WINING BOY: Let's see what we got here. I ain't played on this thing for a while.
DOAKER: You can stop telling that. You was playing on it the last time you was through here. We couldn't get you off of it. Go on and play something.

[WINING BOY *sits down at the piano and plays and sings. The song is one which has put many dimes and quarters in his pocket, long ago, in dimly remembered towns and way stations. He plays badly, without hesitation, and sings in a forceful voice.*]

WINING BOY: [*Singing.*]

>   I am a rambling gambling man
>   I gambled in many towns
>   I rambled this wide world over
>   I rambled this world around
>   I had my ups and downs in life
>   And bitter times I saw
>   But I never knew what misery was
>   Till I lit on old Arkansas.

I started out one morning
To meet that early train
He said, "You better work for me
I have some land to drain.
I'll give you fifty cents a day,
Your washing, board and all
And you shall be a different man
In the state of Arkansas."

I worked six months for the rascal
Joe Herrin was his name
He fed me old corn dodgers
They was hard as any rock
My tooth is all got loosened
And my knees begin to knock
That was the kind of hash I got
In the state of Arkansas.

Traveling man
I've traveled all around this world
Traveling man
I've traveled from land to land
Traveling man
I've traveled all around this world
Well it ain't no use
Writing no news
I'm a traveling man.

[*The door opens and* BERNIECE *enters with* MARETHA.]

BERNIECE: Is that . . . Lord, I know that ain't Wining Boy sitting there.
WINING BOY: Hey, Berniece.
BERNIECE: You all had this planned. You and Boy Willie had this planned.
WINING BOY: I didn't know he was gonna be here. I'm on my way down home. I stopped by to see you and Doaker first.
DOAKER: I told the nigger he left out of here with that sack of money, we thought we might never see him again. Boy Willie say he wasn't gonna see him till he got broke. I looked up and seen him sitting on the doorstep asking for two dollars. Look at him laughing. He know it's the truth.
BERNIECE: Boy Willie, I didn't see that truck out there. I thought you was out selling watermelons.
BOY WILLIE: We done sold them all. Sold the truck too.
BERNIECE: I don't want to go through none of your stuff. I done told you to go back where you belong.
BOY WILLIE: I was just teasing you, woman. You can't take no teasing?
BERNIECE: Wining Boy, when you get here?
WINING BOY: A little while ago. I took the train from Kansas City.
BERNIECE: Let me go upstairs and change and then I'll cook you something to eat.
BOY WILLIE: You ain't cooked me nothing when I come.
BERNIECE: Boy Willie, go on and leave me alone. Come on, Maretha, get up here and change your clothes before you get them dirty.

[BERNIECE *exits up the stairs, followed by* MARETHA.]

WINING BOY: Maretha sure getting big, ain't she, Doaker. And just as pretty as she want to be. I didn't know Crawley had it in him.

[BOY WILLIE *crosses to the piano.*]

BOY WILLIE: Hey, Lymon . . . get up on the other side of this piano and let me see something.

WINING BOY: Boy Willie, what is you doing?

BOY WILLIE: I'm seeing how heavy this piano is. Get up over there, Lymon.

WINING BOY: Go on and leave that piano alone. You ain't taking that piano out of here and selling it.

BOY WILLIE: Just as soon as I get them watermelons out that truck.

WINING BOY: Well, I got something to say about that.

BOY WILLIE: This my daddy's piano.

WINING BOY: He ain't took it by himself. Me and Doaker helped him.

BOY WILLIE: He died by himself. Where was you and Doaker at then? Don't come telling me nothing about this piano. This is me and Berniece's piano. Am I right, Doaker?

DOAKER: Yeah, you right.

BOY WILLIE: Let's see if we can lift it up, Lymon. Get a good grip on it and pick it up on your end. Ready? Lift!

[*As they start to move the piano, the sound of* SUTTER'S GHOST *is heard.* DOAKER *is the only one to hear it. With difficulty they move the piano a little bit so it is out of place.*]

BOY WILLIE: What you think?

LYMON: It's heavy . . . but you can move it. Only it ain't gonna be easy.

BOY WILLIE: It wasn't that heavy to me. Okay, let's put it back.

[*The sound of* SUTTER'S GHOST *is heard again. They all hear it as* BERNIECE *enters on the stairs.*]

BERNIECE: Boy Willie . . . you gonna play around with me one too many times. And then God's gonna bless you and West is gonna dress you. Now set that piano back over there. I done told you a hundred times I ain't selling that piano.

BOY WILLIE: I'm trying to get me some land, woman. I need that piano to get me some money so I can buy Sutter's land.

BERNIECE: Money can't buy what that piano cost. You can't sell your soul for money. It won't go with the buyer. It'll shrivel and shrink to know that you ain't taken on to it. But it won't go with the buyer.

BOY WILLIE: I ain't talking about all that, woman. I ain't talking about selling my soul. I'm talking about trading that piece of wood for some land. Get something under your feet. Land the only thing God ain't making no more of. You can always get you another piano. I'm talking about some land. What you get something out the ground from. That's what I'm talking about. You can't do nothing with that piano but sit up there and look at it.

BERNIECE: That's just what I'm gonna do. Wining Boy, you want me to fry you some pork chops?

BOY WILLIE: Now, I'm gonna tell you the way I see it. The only thing that make that piano worth something is them carvings Papa Willie Boy put on there. That's what make it worth something. That was my great-grandaddy. Papa Boy Charles brought that piano into the house. Now, I'm supposed to build on what they left me. You can't do nothing with that piano sitting up here in the house. That's just like if I let them watermelons sit out there and rot. I'd be a fool. Alright now, if you say to me, Boy Willie, I'm using that piano. I give out lessons on it and that help me make my rent or whatever. Then that be something else. I'd have to go on and say, well, Berniece using that piano. She building on it. Let her go on and use it. I got to find another way to get Sutter's land. But Doaker say you ain't touched that piano the whole time it's been up here. So why you wanna stand in my way? See, you just looking at the sentimental value. See, that's good. That's alright. I take my hat off whenever somebody say my daddy's name. But I ain't gonna be no fool about no sentimental value. You can sit up here and look at the piano for the next hundred years and it's just gonna be a piano. You can't make more than that. Now I want to get Sutter's land with that piano. I get Sutter's land and I can go down and cash in the crop and get my seed. As long as I got the land and the seed then I'm alright. I can always get me a little something else. Cause that land give back to you. I can make me another crop and cash that in. I still got the land and the seed. But that piano don't put out nothing else. You ain't got nothing working for you. Now, the kind of man my daddy was he would have understood that. I'm sorry you can't see it that way. But that's why I'm gonna take that piano out of here and sell it.

BERNIECE: You ain't taking that piano out of my house. [*She crosses to the piano.*] Look at this piano. Look at it. Mama Ola polished this piano with her tears for seventeen years. For seventeen years she rubbed on it till her hands bled. Then she rubbed the blood in . . . mixed it up with the rest of the blood on it. Every day that God breathed life into her body she rubbed and cleaned and polished and prayed over it. "Play something for me, Berniece. Play something for me, Berniece." Every day. "I cleaned it up for you, play something for me, Berniece." You always talking about your daddy but you ain't never stopped to look at what his foolishness cost your mama. Seventeen years' worth of cold nights and an empty bed. For what? For a piano? For a piece of wood? To get even with somebody? I look at you and you're all the same. You, Papa Boy Charles, Wining Boy, Doaker, Crawley . . . you're all alike. All this thieving and killing and thieving and killing. And what it ever lead to? More killing and more thieving. I ain't never seen it come to nothing. People getting burned up. People getting shot. People falling down their wells. It don't never stop.

DOAKER: Come on now, Berniece, ain't no need in getting upset.

BOY WILLIE: I done a little bit of stealing here and there, but I ain't never killed nobody. I can't be speaking for nobody else. You all got to speak for yourself, but I ain't never killed nobody.

BERNIECE: You killed Crawley just as sure as if you pulled the trigger.

BOY WILLIE: See, that's ignorant. That's downright foolish for you to say something like that. You ain't doing nothing but showing your ignorance. If the nigger was here I'd whup his ass for getting me and Lymon shot at.

BERNIECE: Crawley ain't knew about the wood.

BOY WILLIE: We told the man about the wood. Ask Lymon. He knew all about the wood. He seen we was sneaking it. Why else we gonna be out there at night? Don't come telling me Crawley ain't knew about the wood. Them fellows come up on us and Crawley tried to bully them. Me and Lymon seen the sheriff with them and give in. Wasn't no sense in getting killed over fifty dollars' worth of wood.

BERNIECE: Crawley ain't knew you stole that wood.

BOY WILLIE: We ain't stole no wood. Me and Lymon was hauling wood for Jim Miller and keeping us a little bit on the side. We dumped our little bit down there by the creek till we had enough to make a load. Some fellows seen us and we figured we better get it before they did. We come up there and got Crawley to help us load it. Figured we'd cut him in. Crawley trying to keep the wolf from his door . . . we was trying to help him.

LYMON: Me and Boy Willie told him about the wood. We told him some fellows might be trying to beat us to it. He say let me go back and get my thirty-eight. That's what caused all the trouble.

BOY WILLIE: If Crawley ain't had the gun he'd be alive today.

LYMON: We had it about half loaded when they come up on us. We seen the sheriff with them and we tried to get away. We ducked around near the bend in the creek . . . but they was down there too. Boy Willie say let's give in. But Crawley pulled out his gun and started shooting. That's when they started shooting back.

BERNIECE: All I know is Crawley would be alive if you hadn't come up there and got him.

BOY WILLIE: I ain't had nothing to do with Crawley getting killed. That was his own fault.

BERNIECE: Crawley's dead and in the ground and you still walking around here eating. That's all I know. He went off to load some wood with you and ain't never come back.

BOY WILLIE: I told you, woman . . . I ain't had nothing to do with . . .

BERNIECE: He ain't here, is he? He ain't here!

[BERNIECE *hits* BOY WILLIE.]

I said he ain't here. Is he?

[BERNIECE *continues to hit* BOY WILLIE, *who doesn't move to defend himself, other than back up and turning his head so that most of the blows fall on his chest and arms.*]

DOAKER: [*Grabbing* BERNIECE.] Come on, Berniece . . . let it go, it ain't his fault.

BERNIECE: He ain't here, is he? Is he?

BOY WILLIE: I told you I ain't responsible for Crawley.

BERNIECE: He ain't here.

BOY WILLIE: Come on now, Berniece . . . don't do this now. Doaker get her. I ain't had nothing to do with Crawley . . .

BERNIECE: You come up there and got him!

BOY WILLIE: I done told you now. Doaker, get her. I ain't playing.

DOAKER: Come on. Berniece.

[MARETHA *is heard screaming upstairs. It is a scream of stark terror.*]

MARETHA: Mama! . . . Mama!

[*The lights go down to black. End of Act One.*]

## ACT II

### Scene 1

[*The lights come up on the kitchen. It is the following morning.* DOAKER *is ironing the pants to his uniform. He has a pot cooking on the stove at the same time. He is singing a song. The song provides him with the rhythm for his work and he moves about the kitchen with the ease born of many years as a railroad cook*]

DOAKER:

Gonna leave Jackson Mississippi
And go to Memphis
And double back to Jackson
Come on down to Hattiesburg
Change cars on the Y.D.
Coming through the territory to
Meridian
And Meridian to Greenville
And Greenville to Memphis
I'm on my way and I know where

Change cars on the Katy
Leaving Jackson
And going through Clarksdale
Hello Winona!
Courtland!
Bateville!
Como!
Senitobia!
Lewisberg!
Sunflower!
Glendora!
Sharkey!
And double back to Jackson
Hello Greenwood
I'm on my way Memphis
Clarksdale
Moorhead
Indianola
Can a highball pass through?
Highball on through sir
Grand Carson!
Thirty First Street Depot
Fourth Street Depot
Memphis!

[WINING BOY *enters carrying a suit of clothes.*]

DOAKER: I thought you took that suit to the pawnshop?
WINING BOY: I went down there and the man tell me the suit is too old. Look at this suit. This is one hundred percent silk! How a silk suit gonna get too old?

I know what it was he just didn't want to give me five dollars for it. Best he wanna give me is three dollars. I figure a silk suit is worth five dollars all over the world. I wasn't gonna part with it for no three dollars so I brought it back.

DOAKER: They got another pawnshop up on Wylie.

WINING BOY: I carried it up there. He say he don't take no clothes. Only thing he take is guns and radios. Maybe a guitar or two. Where's Berniece?

DOAKER: Berniece still at work. Boy Willie went down there to meet Lymon this morning. I guess they got that truck fixed, they had been out there all day and ain't come back yet. Maretha scared to sleep up there now. Berniece don't know, but I seen Sutter before she did.

WINING BOY: Say what?

DOAKER: About three weeks ago. I had just come back from down there. Sutter couldn't have been dead more than three days. He was sitting over there at the piano. I come out to go to work . . . and he was sitting right there. Had his hand on top of his head just like Berniece said. I believe he broke his neck when he fell in the well. I kept quiet about it. I didn't see no reason to upset Berniece.

WINING BOY: Did he say anything? Did he say he was looking for Boy Willie?

DOAKER: He was just sitting there. He ain't said nothing. I went on out the door and left him sitting there. I figure as long as he was on the other side of the room everything be alright. I don't know what I would have done if he had started walking toward me.

WINING BOY: Berniece say he was calling Boy Willie's name.

DOAKER: I ain't heard him say nothing. He was just sitting there when I seen him. But I don't believe Boy Willie pushed him in the well. Sutter here cause of that piano. I heard him playing on it one time. I thought it was Berniece but then she don't play that kind of music. I come out here and ain't seen nobody, but them piano keys was moving a mile a minute. Berniece need to go on and get rid of it. It ain't done nothing but cause trouble.

WINING BOY: I agree with Berniece. Boy Charles ain't took it to give it back. He took it cause he figure he had more right to it than Sutter did. If Sutter can't understand that . . . then that's just the way that go. Sutter dead and in the ground . . . don't care where his ghost is. He can hover around and play on the piano all he want. I want to see him carry it out the house. That's what I want to see. What time Berniece get home? I don't see how I let her get away from me this morning.

DOAKER: You up there sleep. Berniece leave out of here early in the morning. She out there in Squirrel Hill cleaning house for some bigshot down there at the steel mill. They don't like you to come late. You come late they won't give you your carfare. What kind of business you got with Berniece?

WINING BOY: My business. I ain't asked you what kind of business you got.

DOAKER: Berniece ain't got no money. If that's why you was trying to catch her. She having a hard enough time trying to get by as it is. If she go ahead and marry Avery . . . he working every day . . . she go ahead and marry him they could do alright for themselves. But as it stands she ain't got no money.

WINING BOY: Well, let me have five dollars.

DOAKER: I just give you a dollar before you left out of here. You ain't gonna take my five dollars out there and gamble and drink it up.

WINING BOY: Aw, nigger, give me five dollars. I'll give it back to you.
DOAKER: You wasn't looking to give me five dollars when you had that sack of money. You wasn't looking to throw nothing my way. Now you wanna come in here and borrow five dollars. If you going back with Boy Willie you need to be trying to figure out how you gonna get train fare.
WINING BOY: That's why I need the five dollars. If I had five dollars I could get me some money.

[DOAKER *goes into his pocket.*]

Make it seven.
DOAKER: You take this five dollars . . . and you bring my money back here too.

[BOY WILLIE *and* LYMON *enter. They are happy and excited. They have money in all of their pockets and are anxious to count it.*]

DOAKER: How'd you do out there?
BOY WILLIE: They was lining up for them.
LYMON: Me and Boy Willie couldn't sell them fast enough. Time we got one sold we'd sell another.
BOY WILLIE: I seen what was happening and told Lymon to up the price on them.
LYMON: Boy Willie say charge them a quarter more. They didn't care. A couple of people give me a dollar and told me to keep the change.
BOY WILLIE: One fellow bought five. I say now what he gonna do with five watermelons? He can't eat them all. I sold him the five and asked him did he want to buy five more.
LYMON: I ain't never seen nobody snatch a dollar fast as Boy Willie.
BOY WILLIE: One lady asked me say, "Is they sweet?" I told her say, "Lady, where we grow these watermelons we put sugar in the ground." You know, she believed me. Talking about she had never heard of that before. Lymon was laughing his head off. I told her, "Oh, yeah, we put the sugar right in the ground with the seed." She say, "Well, give me another one." Them white folks is something else . . . ain't they, Lymon?
LYMON: Soon as you holler watermelons they come right out their door. Then they go and get their neighbors. Look like they having a contest to see who can buy the most.
WINING BOY: I got something for Lymon.

[WINING BOY *goes to get his suit.* BOY WILLIE *and* LYMON *continue to count their money.*]

BOY WILLIE: I know you got more than that. You ain't sold all them watermelons for that little bit of money.
LYMON: I'm still looking. That ain't all you got either. Where's all them quarters?
BOY WILLIE: You let me worry about the quarters. Just put the money on the table.
WINING BOY: [*Entering with his suit.*] Look here, Lymon . . . see this? Look at his eyes getting big. He ain't never seen a suit like this. This is one hundred percent silk. Go ahead . . . put it on. See if it fit you.

[LYMON *tries the suit coat on.*]

Look at that. Feel it. That's one hundred percent genuine silk. I got that in Chicago. You can't get clothes like that nowhere but New York and Chicago. You can't get clothes like that in Pittsburgh. These folks in Pittsburgh ain't never seen clothes like that.

LYMON: This is nice, feel real nice and smooth.

WINING BOY: That's a fifty-five-dollar suit. That's the kind of suit the bigshots wear. You need a pistol and a pocketful of money to wear that suit. I'll let you have it for three dollars. The women will fall out their windows they see you in a suit like that. Give me three dollars and go on and wear it down the street and get you a woman.

BOY WILLIE: That looks nice, Lymon. Put the pants on. Let me see it with the pants.

[LYMON *begins to try on the pants.*]

WINING BOY: Look at that... see how it fits you? Give me three dollars and go on and take it. Look at that, Doaker... don't he look nice?

DOAKER: Yeah... that's a nice suit.

WINING BOY: Got a shirt to go with it. Cost you an extra dollar. Four dollars you got the whole deal.

LYMON: How this look, Boy Willie?

BOY WILLIE: That look nice... if you like that kind of thing. I don't like them dress-up kind of clothes. If you like it, look real nice.

WINING BOY: That's the kind of suit you need for up here in the North.

LYMON: Four dollars for everything? The suit and the shirt?

WINING BOY: That's cheap. I should be charging you twenty dollars. I give you a break cause you a homeboy. That's the only way I let you have it for four dollars.

LYMON: [*Going into his pocket.*] Okay... here go the four dollars.

WINING BOY: You got some shoes? What size you wear?

LYMON: Size nine.

WINING BOY: That's what size I got! Size nine. I let you have them for three dollars.

LYMON: Where they at? Let me see them.

WINING BOY: They real nice shoes, too. Got a nice tip to them. Got pointy toe just like you want.

[WINING BOY *goes to get his shoes.*]

LYMON: Come on, Boy Willie, let's go out tonight. I wanna see what it looks like up here. Maybe we go to a picture show. Hey, Doaker, they got picture shows up here?

DOAKER: The Rhumba Theater. Right down there on Fullerton Street. Can't miss it. Got the speakers outside on the sidewalk. You can hear it a block away. Boy Willie know where it's at.

[DOAKER *exits into his room.*]

LYMON: Let's go to the picture show, Boy Willie. Let's go find some women.

BOY WILLIE: Hey, Lymon, how many of them watermelons would you say we got left? We got just under a half a load... right?

LYMON: About that much. Maybe a little more.
BOY WILLIE: You think that piano will fit up in there?
LYMON: If we stack them watermelons you can sit it up in the front there.
BOY WILLIE: I'm gonna call that man tomorrow.
WINING BOY: [*Returns with his shoes.*] Here you go . . . size nine. Put them on. Cost you three dollars. That's a Florsheim shoe. That's the kind Staggerlee[3] wore.
LYMON: [*Trying on the shoes.*] You sure these size nine?
WINING BOY: You can look at my feet and see we wear the same size. Man, you put on that suit and them shoes and you got something there. You ready for whatever's out there. But is they ready for you? With them shoes on you be the King of the Walk. Have everybody stop to look at your shoes. Wishing they had a pair. I'll give you a break. Go on and take them for two dollars.

[LYMON *pays* WINING BOY *two dollars.*]

LYMON: Come on, Boy Willie . . . let's go find some women. I'm gonna go upstairs and get ready. I'll be ready to go in a minute. Ain't you gonna get dressed?
BOY WILLIE: I'm gonna wear what I got on. I ain't dressing up for these city niggers.

[LYMON *exits up the stairs.*]

That's all Lymon think about is women.
WINING BOY: His daddy was the same way. I used to run around with him. I know his mama too. Two strokes back and I would have been his daddy! His daddy's dead now . . . but I got the nigger out of jail one time. They was fixing to name him Daniel and walk him through the Lion's Den.[4] He got in a tussle with one of them white fellows and the sheriff lit on him like white on rice. That's how the whole thing come about between me and Lymon's mama. She knew me and his daddy used to run together and he got in jail and she went down there and took the sheriff a hundred dollars. Don't get me to lying about where she got it from. I don't know. The sheriff *looked at that hundred dollars and turned his nose up.* Told her, say, "That ain't gonna do him no good. You got to put another hundred on top of that." She come up *there and got me where I was playing at this saloon* . . . said she had all but fifty dollars and asked me if I could help. Now the way I figured it . . . without that fifty dollars the sheriff was gonna turn him over to Parchman. The sheriff turn him over to Parchman it be three years before anybody see him again. Now I'm gonna say it right . . . I will give anybody fifty dollars to keep them out of jail for three years. I give her the fifty dollars and she told me to come over to the house. I ain't asked her. I figure if she was nice enough to invite me I ought to go. I ain't had to say a word. She invited me over just as nice. Say, "Why don't you come over to the house?" She ain't had to say nothing else. Them words rolled off her tongue just as nice. I went on down there and sat about three hours. Started to leave and changed my mind. She grabbed hold to me

---

3. In African American folklore, a flashy figure (also called Stagger Lee, Stagolee, Stagalee, Stackolee, Stack O'Lee, Stack-o-lee, and so on) who murdered the man who stole his Stetson hat. The story is frequently retold (and reinterpreted) in song.
4. See Daniel 6.23: "My God has sent his angel and closed the lions' mouths so that they have not hurt me."

and say, "Baby, it's all night long." That was one of the shortest nights I have ever spent on this earth! I could have used another eight hours. Lymon's daddy didn't even say nothing to me when he got out. He just looked at me funny. He had a good notion something had happened between me an' her. L. D. Jackson. That was one bad-luck nigger. Got killed at some dance. Fellow walked in and shot him thinking he was somebody else.

[DOAKER *enters from his room.*]

Hey, Doaker, you remember L. D. Jackson?
DOAKER: That's Lymon's daddy. That was one bad-luck nigger.
BOY WILLIE: Look like you ready to railroad some.
DOAKER: Yeah, I got to make that run.

[LYMON *enters from the stairs. He is dressed in his new suit and shoes, to which he has added a cheap straw hat.*]

LYMON: How I look?
WINING BOY: You look like a million dollars. Don't he look good, Doaker? Come on, let's play some cards. You wanna play some cards?
BOY WILLIE: We ain't gonna play no cards with you. Me and Lymon gonna find some women. Hey, Lymon, don't play no cards with Wining Boy. He'll take all your money.
WINING BOY: [*To* LYMON.] You got a magic suit there. You can get you a woman easy with that suit . . . but you got to know the magic words. You know the magic words to get you a woman?
LYMON: I just talk to them to see if I like them and they like me.
WINING BOY: You just walk right up to them and say, "If you got the harbor I got the ship." If that don't work ask them if you can put them in your pocket. The first thing they gonna say is, "It's too small." That's when you look them dead in the eye and say, "Baby, ain't nothing small about me." If that don't work then you move on to another one. Am I telling him right, Doaker?
DOAKER: That man don't need you to tell him nothing about no women. These women these days ain't gonna fall for that kind of stuff. You got to buy them a present. That's what they looking for these days.
BOY WILLIE: Come on, I'm ready. You ready, Lymon? Come on, let's go find some women.
WINING BOY: Here, let me walk out with you. I wanna see the women fall out their window when they see Lymon.

[*They all exit and the lights go down on the scene.*]

Scene 2

[*The lights come up on the kitchen. It is late evening of the same day.* BERNIECE *has set a tub for her bath in the kitchen. She is heating up water on the stove. There is a knock at the door.*]

BERNIECE: Who is it?
AVERY: It's me, Avery.

[BERNIECE *opens the door and lets him in.*]

BERNIECE: Avery, come on in. I was just fixing to take my bath.
AVERY: Where Boy Willie? I see that truck out there almost empty. They done sold almost all them watermelons.
BERNIECE: They was gone when I come home. I don't know where they went off to. Boy Willie around here about to drive me crazy.
AVERY: They sell them watermelons . . . he'll be gone soon.
BERNIECE: What Mr. Cohen say about letting you have the place?
AVERY: He say he'll let me have it for thirty dollars a month. I talked him out of thirty-five and he say he'll let me have it for thirty.
BERNIECE: That's a nice spot next to Benny Diamond's store.
AVERY: Berniece . . . I be at home and I get to thinking you up here an' I'm down there. I get to thinking how that look to have a preacher that ain't married. It makes for a better congregation if the preacher was settled down and married.
BERNIECE: Avery . . . not now. I was fixing to take my bath.
AVERY: You know how I feel about you, Berniece. Now . . . I done got the place from Mr. Cohen. I get the money from the bank and I can fix it up real nice. They give me a ten cents a hour raise down there on the job . . . now Berniece, I ain't got much in the way of comforts. I got a hole in my pockets near about as far as money is concerned. I ain't never found no way through life to a woman I care about like I care about you. I need that. I need somebody on my bond side. I need a woman that fits in my hand.
BERNIECE: Avery, I ain't ready to get married now.
AVERY: You too young a woman to close up, Berniece.
BERNIECE: I ain't said nothing about closing up. I got a lot of woman left in me.
AVERY: Where's it at? When's the last time you looked at it?
BERNIECE: [*Stunned by his remark.*] That's a nasty thing to say. And you call yourself a preacher.
AVERY: Anytime I get anywhere near you . . . you push me away.
BERNIECE: I got enough on my hands with Maretha. I got enough people to love and take care of.
AVERY: Who you got to love you? Can't nobody get close enough to you. Doaker can't half say nothing to you. You jump all over Boy Willie. Who you got to love you, Berniece?
BERNIECE: You trying to tell me a woman can't be nothing without a man. But you alright, huh? You can just walk out of here without me—without a woman—and still be a man. That's alright. Ain't nobody gonna ask you, "Avery, who you got to love you?" That's alright for you. But everybody gonna be worried about Berniece. "How Berniece gonna take care of herself? How she gonna raise that child without a man? Wonder what she do with herself. How she gonna live like that?" Everybody got all kinds of questions for Berniece. Everybody telling me I can't be a woman unless I got a man. Well, you tell me, Avery—you know—how much woman am I?
AVERY: It wasn't me, Berniece. You can't blame me for nobody else. I'll own up to my own shortcomings. But you can't blame me for Crawley or nobody else.
BERNIECE: I ain't blaming nobody for nothing. I'm just stating the facts.
AVERY: How long you gonna carry Crawley with you, Berniece? It's been over three years. At some point you got to let go and go on. Life's got all kinds of twists and turns. That don't mean you stop living. That don't mean you cut

yourself off from life. You can't go through life carrying Crawley's ghost with you. Crawley's been dead three years. Three years, Berniece.

BERNIECE: I know how long Crawley's been dead. You ain't got to tell me that. I just ain't ready to get married right now.

AVERY: What is you ready for, Berniece? You just gonna drift along from day to day. Life is more than making it from one day to another. You gonna look up one day and it's all gonna be past you. Life's gonna be gone out of your hands—there won't be enough to make nothing with. I'm standing here now, Berniece—but I don't know how much longer I'm gonna be standing here waiting on you.

BERNIECE: Avery, I told you . . . when you get your church we'll sit down and talk about this. I got too many other things to deal with right now. Boy Willie and the piano . . . and Sutter's ghost. I thought I might have been seeing things, but Maretha done seen Sutter's ghost, too.

AVERY: When this happen, Berniece?

BERNIECE: Right after I came home yesterday. Me and Boy Willie was arguing about the piano and Sutter's ghost was standing at the top of the stairs. Maretha scared to sleep up there now. Maybe if you bless the house he'll go away.

AVERY: I don't know, Berniece. I don't know if I should fool around with something like that.

BERNIECE: I can't have Maretha scared to go to sleep up there. Seem like if you bless the house he would go away.

AVERY: You might have to be a special kind of preacher to do something like that.

BERNIECE: I keep telling myself when Boy Willie leave he'll go on and leave with him. I believe Boy Willie pushed him in the well.

AVERY: That's been going on down there a long time. The Ghosts of the Yellow Dog been pushing people in their wells long before Boy Willie got grown.

BERNIECE: Somebody down there pushing them people in their wells. They ain't just upped and fell. Ain't no wind pushed nobody in their well.

AVERY: Oh, I don't know. God works in mysterious ways.

BERNIECE: He ain't pushed nobody in their wells.

AVERY: He caused it to happen. God is the Great Causer. He can do anything. He parted the Red Sea.[5] He say I will smite my enemies. Reverend Thompson used to preach on the Ghosts of the Yellow Dog as the hand of God.

BERNIECE: I don't care who preached what. Somebody down there pushing them people in their wells. Somebody like Boy Willie. I can see him doing something like that. You ain't gonna tell me that Sutter just upped and fell in his well. I believe Boy Willie pushed him so he could get his land.

AVERY: What Doaker say about Boy Willie selling the piano?

BERNIECE: Doaker don't want no part of that piano. He ain't never wanted no part of it. He blames himself for not staying behind with Papa Boy Charles. He washed his hands of that piano a long time ago. He didn't want me to bring it up here—but I wasn't gonna leave it down there.

AVERY: Well, it seems to me somebody ought to be able to talk to Boy Willie.

---

5. See Exodus 14.21: "Then Moses stretched out his hand over the sea, and the Lord swept the sea with a strong east wind throughout the night and so turned it into dry land."

BERNIECE: You can't talk to Boy Willie. He been that way all his life. Mama Ola had her hands full trying to talk to him. He don't listen to nobody. He just like my daddy. He get his mind fixed on something and can't nobody turn him from it.

AVERY: You ought to start a choir at the church. Maybe if he seen you was doing something with it—if you told him you was gonna put it in my church—maybe he'd see it different. You ought to put it down in the church and start a choir. The Bible say "Make a joyful noise unto the Lord." Maybe if Boy Willie see you was doing something with it he'd see it different.

BERNIECE: I done told you I don't play on that piano. Ain't no need in you to keep talking this choir stuff. When my mama died I shut the top on that piano and I ain't never opened it since. I was only playing it for her. When my daddy died seem like all her life went into that piano. She used to have me playing on it . . . had Miss Eula come in and teach me . . . say when I played it she could hear my daddy talking to her. I used to think them pictures came alive and walked through the house. Sometime late at night I could hear my mama talking to them. I said that wasn't gonna happen to me. I don't play that piano cause I don't want to wake them spirits. They never be walking around in this house.

AVERY: You got to put all that behind you, Berniece.

BERNIECE: I got Maretha playing on it. She don't know nothing about it. Let her go on and be a schoolteacher or something. She don't have to carry all of that with her. She got a chance I didn't have. I ain't gonna burden her with that piano.

AVERY: You got to put all of that behind you. Berniece. That's the same thing like Crawley. Everybody got stones in their passway. You got to step over them or walk around them. You picking them up and carrying them with you. All you got to do is set them down by the side of the road. You ain't got to carry them with you. You can walk over there right now and play that piano. You can walk over there right now and God will walk over there with you. Right now you can set that sack of stones down by the side of the road and walk away from it. You don't have to carry it with you. You can do it right now.

[AVERY *crosses over to the piano and raises the lid.*]

Come on, Berniece . . . set it down and walk away from it. Come on, play "Old Ship of Zion." Walk over here and claim it as an instrument of the Lord. You can walk over here right now and make it into a celebration.

[BERNIECE *moves toward the piano.*]

BERNIECE: Avery . . . I done told you I don't want to play that piano. Now or no other time.

AVERY: The Bible say, "The Lord is my refuge . . . and my strength!" With the strength of God you can put the past behind you, Berniece. With the strength of God you can do anything! God got a bright tomorrow. God don't ask what you done . . . God ask what you gonna do. The strength of God can move mountains! God's got a bright tomorrow for you . . . all you got to do is walk over here and claim it.

BERNIECE: Avery, just go on and let me finish my bath. I'll see you tomorrow.

AVERY: Okay, Berniece. I'm gonna go home. I'm gonna go home and read up on my Bible. And tomorrow... if the good Lord give me strength tomorrow... I'm gonna come by and bless the house... and show you the power of the Lord.

[AVERY *crosses to the door.*]

It's gonna be alright, Berniece. God say he will soothe the troubled waters. I'll come by tomorrow and bless the house.

[*The lights go down to black.*]

## Scene 3

[*Several hours later. The house is dark.* BERNIECE *has retired for the night.* BOY WILLIE *enters the darkened house with* GRACE.]

BOY WILLIE: Come on in. This is my sister's house. My sister live here. Come on, I ain't gonna bite you.
GRACE: Put some light on. I can't see.
BOY WILLIE: You don't need to see nothing, baby. This here is all you need to see. All you need to do is see me. If you can't see me you can feel me in the dark. How's that, sugar? [*He attempts to kiss her.*]
GRACE: Go on now... wait!
BOY WILLIE: Just give me one little old kiss.
GRACE: [*Pushing him away.*] Come on, now. Where I'm gonna sleep at?
BOY WILLIE: We got to sleep out here on the couch. Come on, my sister don't mind. Lymon come back he just got to sleep on the floor. He run off with Dolly somewhere he better stay there. Come on, sugar.
GRACE: Wait now... you ain't told me nothing about no couch. I thought you had a bed. Both of us can't sleep on that little old couch.
BOY WILLIE: It don't make no difference. We can sleep on the floor. Let Lymon sleep on the couch.
GRACE: You ain't told me nothing about no couch.
BOY WILLIE: What difference it make? You just wanna be with me.
GRACE: I don't want to be with you on no couch. Ain't you got no bed?
BOY WILLIE: You don't need no bed, woman. My granddaddy used to take women on the backs of horses. What you need a bed for? You just want to be with me.
GRACE: You sure is country. I didn't know you was this country.
BOY WILLIE: There's a lot of things you don't know about me. Come on, let me show you what this country boy can do.
GRACE: Let's go to my place. I got a room with a bed if Leroy don't come back there.
BOY WILLIE: Who's Leroy? You ain't said nothing about no Leroy.
GRACE: He used to be my man. He ain't coming back. He gone off with some other gal.
BOY WILLIE: You let him have your key?
GRACE: He ain't coming back.
BOY WILLIE: Did you let him have your key?
GRACE: He got a key but he ain't coming back. He took off with some other gal.

BOY WILLIE: I don't wanna go nowhere he might come. Let's stay here. Come on, sugar. [*He pulls her over to the couch.*] Let me heist your hood and check your oil. See if your battery needs charged. [*He pulls her to him. They kiss and tug at each other's clothing. In their anxiety they knock over a lamp.*]
BERNIECE: Who's that . . . Wining Boy?
BOY WILLIE: It's me . . . Boy Willie. Go on back to sleep. Everything's alright. [*To* GRACE.] That's my sister. Everything's alright, Berniece. Go on back to sleep.
BERNIECE: What you doing down there? What you done knocked over?
BOY WILLIE: It wasn't nothing. Everything's alright. Go on back to sleep. [*To* GRACE.] That's my sister. We alright. She gone back to sleep.

[*They begin to kiss.* BERNIECE *enters from the stairs dressed in a nightgown. She cuts on the light.*]

BERNIECE: Boy Willie, what you doing down here?
BOY WILLIE: It was just that there lamp. It ain't broke. It's okay. Everything's alright. Go on back to bed.
BERNIECE: Boy Willie, I don't allow that in my house. You gonna have to take your company someplace else.
BOY WILLIE: It's alright. We ain't doing nothing. We just sitting here talking. This here is Grace. That's my sister Berniece.
BERNIECE: You know I don't allow that kind of stuff in my house.
BOY WILLIE: Allow what? We just sitting here talking.
BERNIECE: Well, your company gonna have to leave. Come back and talk in the morning.
BOY WILLIE: Go on back upstairs now.
BERNIECE: I got an eleven-year-old girl upstairs. I can't allow that around here.
BOY WILLIE: Ain't nobody said nothing about that. I told you we just talking.
GRACE: Come on . . . let's go to my place. Ain't nobody got to tell me to leave but once.
BOY WILLIE: You ain't got to be like that, Berniece.
BERNIECE: I'm sorry, Miss. But he know I don't allow that in here.
GRACE: You ain't got to tell me but once. I don't stay nowhere I ain't wanted.
BOY WILLIE: I don't know why you want to embarrass me in front of my company.
GRACE: Come on, take me home.
BERNIECE: Go on, Boy Willie. Just go on with your company.

[BOY WILLIE *and* GRACE *exit.* BERNIECE *puts the light on in the kitchen and puts on the teakettle. Presently there is a knock at the door.* BERNIECE *goes to answer it.* BERNIECE *opens the door.* LYMON *enters.*]

LYMON: How you doing, Berniece? I thought you'd be asleep. Boy Willie been back here?
BERNIECE: He just left out of here a minute ago.
LYMON: I went out to see a picture show and never got there. We always end up doing something else. I was with this woman she just wanted to drink up all my money. So I left her there and came back looking for Boy Willie.
BERNIECE: You just missed him. He just left out of here.
LYMON: They got some nice-looking women in this city. I'm gonna like it up here real good. I like seeing them with their dresses on. Got them high heels. I like

that. Make them look like they real precious. Boy Willie met a real nice one today. I wish I had met her before he did.
BERNIECE: He come by here with some woman a little while ago. I told him to go on and take all that out of my house.
LYMON: What she look like, the woman he was with? Was she a brown-skinned woman about this high? Nice and healthy? Got nice hips on her?
BERNIECE: She had on a red dress.
LYMON: That's her! That's Grace. She real nice. Laugh a lot. Lot of fun to be with. She don't be trying to put on. Some of these woman act like they the Queen of Sheba. I don't like them kind. Grace ain't like that. She real nice with herself.
BERNIECE: I don't know what she was like. He come in here all drunk knocking over the lamp, and making all kind of noise. I told them to take that somewhere else. I can't really say what she was like.
LYMON: She real nice. I seen her before he did. I was trying not to act like I seen her. I wanted to look at her a while before I said something. She seen me when I come into the saloon. I tried to act like I didn't see her. Time I looked around Boy Willie was talking to her. She was talking to him kept looking at me. That's when her friend Dolly came. I asked her if she wanted to go to the picture show. She told me to buy her a drink while she thought about it. Next thing I knew she done had three drinks talking about she too tired to go. I bought her another drink, then I left. Boy Willie was gone and I thought he might have come back here. Doaker gone, huh? He say he had to make a trip.
BERNIECE: Yeah, he gone on his trip. This is when I can usually get me some peace and quiet, Maretha asleep.
LYMON: She look just like you. Got them big eyes. I remember her when she was in diapers.
BERNIECE: Time just keep on. It go on with or without you. She going on twelve.
LYMON: She sure is pretty. I like kids.
BERNIECE: Boy Willie say you staying . . . what you gonna do up here in this big city? You thought about that?
LYMON: They never get me back down there. The sheriff looking for me. All because they gonna try and make me work for somebody when I don't want to. They gonna try and make me work for Stovall when he don't pay nothing. It ain't like that up here. Up here you more or less do what you want to. I figure I find me a job and try to get set up and then see what the year brings. I tried to do that two or three times down there . . . but it never would work out. I was always in the wrong place.
BERNIECE: This ain't a bad city once you get to know your way around.
LYMON: Up here is different. I'm gonna get me a job unloading boxcars or something. One fellow told me say he know a place. I'm gonna go over there with him next week. Me and Boy Willie finish selling them watermelons I'll have enough money to hold me for a while. But I'm gonna go over there and see what kind of jobs they have.
BERNIECE: You shouldn't have too much trouble finding a job. It's all in how you present yourself. See now, Boy Willie couldn't get no job up here. Somebody hire him they got a pack of trouble on their hands. Soon as they find that out they fire him. He don't want to do nothing unless he do it his way.
LYMON: I know. I told him let's go to the picture show first and see if there was

any women down there. They might get tired of sitting at home and walk down to the picture show. He say he wanna look around first. We never did get down there. We tried a couple of places and then we went to this saloon where he met Grace. I tried to meet her before he did but he beat me to her. We left Wining Boy sitting down there running his mouth. He told me if I wear this suit I'd find me a woman. He was almost right.

BERNIECE: You don't need to be out there in them saloons. Ain't no telling what you liable to run into out there. This one liable to cut you as quick as that one shoot you. You don't need to be out there. You start out that fast life you can't keep it up. It makes you old quick. I don't know what them women out there be thinking about.

LYMON: Mostly they be lonely and looking for somebody to spend the night with them. Sometimes it matters who it is and sometimes it don't. I used to be the same way. Now it got to matter. That's why I'm here now. Dolly liable not to even recognize me if she sees me again. I don't like women like that. I like my women to be with me in a nice and easy way. That way we can both enjoy ourselves. The way I see it we the only two people like us in the world. We got to see how we fit together. A woman that don't want to take the time to do that I don't bother with. Used to. Used to bother with all of them. Then I woke up one time with this woman and I didn't know who she was. She was the prettiest woman I had ever seen in my life. I spent the whole night with her and didn't even know it. I had never taken the time to look at her. I guess she kinda knew I ain't never really looked at her. She must have known that cause she ain't wanted to see me no more. If she had wanted to see me I believe we might have got married. How come you ain't married? It seem like to me you would be married. I remember Avery from down home. I used to call him plain old Avery. Now he Reverend Avery. That's kinda funny about him becoming a preacher. I like when he told about how that come to him in a dream about them sheep people and them hobos. Nothing ever come to me in a dream like that. I just dream about women. Can't never seem to find the right one.

BERNIECE: She out there somewhere. You just got to get yourself ready to meet her. That's what I'm trying to do. Avery's alright. I ain't really got nobody in mind.

LYMON: I get me a job and a little place and get set up to where I can make a woman comfortable I might get married. Avery's nice. You ought to go ahead and get married. You be a preacher's wife you won't have to work. I hate living by myself. I didn't want to be no strain on my mama so I left home when I was about sixteen. Everything I tried seem like it just didn't work out. Now I'm trying this.

BERNIECE: You keep trying it'll work out for you.

LYMON: You ever go down there to the picture show?

BERNIECE: I don't go in for all that.

LYMON: Ain't nothing wrong with it. It ain't like gambling and sinning. I went to one down in Jackson once. It was fun.

BERNIECE: I just stay home most of the time. Take care of Maretha.

LYMON: It's getting kind of late. I don't know where Boy Willie went off to. He's liable not to come back. I'm gonna take off these shoes. My feet hurt. Was you in bed? I don't mean to be keeping you up.

BERNIECE: You ain't keeping me up. I couldn't sleep after that Boy Willie woke me up.
LYMON: You got on that nightgown. I likes women when they wear them fancy nightclothes and all. It makes their skin look real pretty.
BERNIECE: I got this at the five-and-ten-cents store. It ain't so fancy.
LYMON: I don't too often get to see a woman dressed like that. [*There is a long pause.* LYMON *takes off his suit coat.*] Well, I'm gonna sleep here on the couch. I'm supposed to sleep on the floor but I don't reckon Boy Willie's coming back tonight. Wining Boy sold me this suit. Told me it was a magic suit. I'm gonna put it on again tomorrow. Maybe it bring me a woman like he say. [*He goes into his coat pocket and takes out a small bottle of perfume.*] I almost forgot I had this. Some man sold me this for a dollar. Say it come from Paris. This is the same kind of perfume the Queen of France wear. That's what he told me. I don't know if it's true or not. I smelled it. It smelled good to me. Here ... smell it see if you like it. I was gonna give it to Dolly. But I didn't like her too much.
BERNIECE: [*Takes the bottle.*] It smells nice.
LYMON: I was gonna give it to Dolly if she had went to the picture with me. Go on, you take it.
BERNIECE: I can't take it. Here ... go on you keep it. You'll find somebody to give it to.
LYMON: I wanna give it to you. Make you smell nice. [*He takes the bottle and puts perfume behind* BERNIECE'*s ear.*] They tell me you supposed to put it right here behind your ear. Say if you put it there you smell nice all day.

[BERNIECE *stiffens at his touch.* LYMON *bends down to smell her.*]

There ... you smell real good now. [*He kisses her neck.*] You smell real good for Lymon.

[*He kisses her again.* BERNIECE *returns the kiss, then breaks the embrace and crosses to the stairs. She turns and they look silently at each other.* LYMON *hands her the bottle of perfume.* BERNIECE *exits up the stairs.* LYMON *picks up his suit coat and strokes it lovingly with the full knowledge that it is indeed a magic suit. The lights go down on the scene.*]

## Scene 4

[*It is late the next morning. The lights come up on the parlor.* LYMON *is asleep on the sofa.* BOY WILLIE *enters the front door.*]

BOY WILLIE: Hey, Lymon! Lymon, come on get up.
LYMON: Leave me alone.
BOY WILLIE: Come on, get up, nigger! Wake up, Lymon.
LYMON: What you want?
BOY WILLIE: Come on, let's go. I done called the man about the piano.
LYMON: What piano?
BOY WILLIE: [*Dumps* LYMON *on the floor.*] Come on, get up!
LYMON: Why you leave, I looked around and you was gone.
BOY WILLIE: I come back here with Grace, then I went looking for you. I figured you'd be with Dolly.

LYMON: She just want to drink and spend up your money. I come on back here looking for you to see if you wanted to go to the picture show.
BOY WILLIE: I been up at Grace's house. Some nigger named Leroy come by but I had a chair up against the door. He got mad when he couldn't get in. He went off somewhere and I got out of there before he could come back. Berniece got mad when we came here.
LYMON: She say you was knocking over the lamp busting up the place.
BOY WILLIE: That was Grace doing all that.
LYMON: Wining Boy seen Sutter's ghost last night.
BOY WILLIE: Wining Boy's liable to see anything. I'm surprised he found the right house. Come on, I done called the man about the piano.
LYMON: What he say?
BOY WILLIE: He say to bring it on out. I told him I was calling for my sister, Miss Berniece Charles. I told him some man wanted to buy it for eleven hundred dollars and asked him if he would go any better. He said yeah, he would give me eleven hundred and fifty dollars for it if it was the same piano. I described it to him again and he told me to bring it out.
LYMON: Why didn't you tell him to come and pick it up?
BOY WILLIE: I didn't want to have no problem with Berniece. This way we just take it on out there and it be out the way. He want to charge twenty-five dollars to pick it up.
LYMON: You should have told him the man was gonna give you twelve hundred for it.
BOY WILLIE: I figure I was taking a chance with that eleven hundred. If I had told him twelve hundred he might have run off. Now I wish I had told him twelve-fifty. It's hard to figure out white folks sometimes.
LYMON: You might have been able to tell him anything. White folks got a lot of money.
BOY WILLIE: Come on, let's get it loaded before Berniece come back. Get that end over there. All you got to do is pick it up on that side. Don't worry about this side. You wanna stretch you' back for a minute?
LYMON: I'm ready.
BOY WILLIE: Get a real good grip on it now.

[*The sound of* SUTTER'S GHOST *is heard. They do not hear it.*]

LYMON: I got this end. You get that end.
BOY WILLIE: Wait till I say ready now. Alright. You got it good? You got a grip on it?
LYMON: Yeah, I got it. You lift up on that end.
BOY WILLIE: Ready? Lift!

[*The piano will not budge.*]

LYMON: Man, this piano is heavy! It's gonna take more than me and you to move this piano.
BOY WILLIE: We can do it. Come on—we did it before.
LYMON: Nigger—you crazy! That piano weighs five hundred pounds!
BOY WILLIE: I got three hundred pounds of it! I know you can carry two hundred pounds! You be lifting them cotton sacks! Come on lift this piano!

[*They try to move the piano again without success.*]

LYMON: It's stuck. Something holding it.
BOY WILLIE: How the piano gonna be stuck? We just moved it. Slide you' end out.
LYMON: Naw—we gonna need two or three more people. How this big old piano get in the house?
BOY WILLIE: I don't know how it got in the house. I know how it's going out though! You get on this end. I'll carry three hundred and fifty pounds of it. All you got to do is slide your end out. Ready?

[*They switch sides and try again without success.* DOAKER *enters from his room as they try to push and shove it.*]

LYMON: Hey, Doaker . . . how this piano get in the house?
DOAKER: Boy Willie, what you doing?
BOY WILLIE: I'm carrying this piano out the house. What it look like I'm doing? Come on, Lymon, let's try again.
DOAKER: Go on let the piano sit there till Berniece come home.
BOY WILLIE: You ain't got nothing to do with this, Doaker. This my business.
DOAKER: This is my house, nigger! I ain't gonna let you or nobody else carry nothing out of it. You ain't gonna carry nothing out of here without my permission!
BOY WILLIE: This is my piano. I don't need your permission to carry my belongings out of your house. This is mine. This ain't got nothing to do with you.
DOAKER: I say leave it over there till Berniece come home. She got part of it too. Leave it set there till you see what she say.
BOY WILLIE: I don't care what Berniece say. Come on, Lymon. I got this side.
DOAKER: Go on and cut it half in two if you want to. Just leave Berniece's half sitting over there. I can't tell you what to do with your piano. But I can't let you take her half out of here.
BOY WILLIE: Go on, Doaker. You ain't got nothing to do with this. I don't want you starting nothing now. Just go on and leave me alone. Come on, Lymon. I got this end.

[DOAKER *goes into his room.* BOY WILLIE *and* LYMON *prepare to move the piano.*]

LYMON: How we gonna get it in the truck?
BOY WILLIE: Don't worry about how we gonna get it on the truck. You got to get it out the house first.
LYMON: It's gonna take more than me and you to move this piano.
BOY WILLIE: Just lift up on that end, nigger!

[DOAKER *comes to the doorway of his room and stands.*]

DOAKER: [*Quietly with authority.*] Leave that piano set over there till Berniece come back. I don't care what you do with it then. But you gonna leave it sit over there right now.
BOY WILLIE: Alright. . . . I'm gonna tell you this, Doaker. I'm going out of here . . . I'm gonna get me some rope . . . find me a plank and some wheels . . . and I'm coming back. Then I'm gonna carry that piano out of here . . . sell it and give Berniece half the money. See . . . now that's what I'm gonna do. And you

... or nobody else is gonna stop me. Come on, Lymon... let's go get some rope and stuff. I'll be back, Doaker.

[BOY WILLIE *and* LYMON *exit. The lights go down on the scene.*]

## Scene 5

[*The lights come up.* BOY WILLIE *sits on the sofa, screwing casters on a wooden plank.* MARETHA *is sitting on the piano stool.* DOAKER *sits at the table playing solitaire.*]

BOY WILLIE: [*To* MARETHA.] Then after that them white folks down around there started falling down their wells. You ever seen a well? A well got a wall around it. It's hard to fall down a well. You got to be leaning way over. Couldn't nobody figure out too much what was making these fellows fall down their well... so everybody says the Ghosts of the Yellow Dog must have pushed them. That's what everybody called them four men what got burned up in the boxcar.

MARETHA: Why they call them that?

BOY WILLIE: Cause the Yazoo Delta railroad got yellow boxcars. Sometime the way the whistle blow sound like an old dog howling so the people call it the Yellow Dog.

MARETHA: Anybody ever see the Ghosts?

BOY WILLIE: I told you they like the wind. Can you see the wind?

MARETHA: No.

BOY WILLIE: They like the wind you can't see them. But sometimes you be in trouble they might be around to help you. They say if you go where the Southern cross the Yellow Dog... you go to where them two railroads cross each other... and call out their names... they say they talk back to you. I don't know, I ain't never done that. But Uncle Wining Boy he say he been down there and talked to them. You have to ask him about that part.

[BERNIECE *has entered from the front door.*]

BERNIECE: Maretha, you go on and get ready for me to do your hair.

[MARETHA *crosses to the steps.*]

Boy Willie, I done told you to leave my house. [*To* MARETHA.] Go on, Maretha.

[MARETHA *is hesitant about going up the stairs.*]

BOY WILLIE: Don't be scared. Here, I'll go up there with you. If we see Sutter's ghost I'll put a whupping on him. Come on, Uncle Boy Willie going with you.

[BOY WILLIE *and* MARETHA *exit up the stairs.*]

BERNIECE: Doaker—what is going on here?

DOAKER: I come home and him and Lymon was moving the piano. I told them to leave it over there till you got home. He went out and got that board and them wheels. He say he gonna take that piano out of here and ain't nobody gonna stop him.

BERNIECE: I ain't playing with Boy Willie. I got Crawley's gun upstairs. He don't know but I'm through with it. Where Lymon go?
DOAKER: Boy Willie sent him for some rope just before you come in.
BERNIECE: I ain't studying Boy Willie or Lymon—or the rope. Boy Willie ain't taking that piano out this house. That's all there is to it.

[BOY WILLIE *and* MARETHA *enter on the stairs.* MARETHA *carries a hot comb and a can of hair grease.* BOY WILLIE *crosses over and continues to screw the wheels on the board.*]

MARETHA: Mama, all the hair grease is gone. There ain't but this little bit left.
BERNIECE: [*Gives her a dollar.*] Here . . . run across the street and get another can. You come straight back, too. Don't you be playing around out there. And watch the cars. Be careful when you cross the street.

[MARETHA *exits out the front door.*]

Boy Willie, I done told you to leave my house.
BOY WILLIE: I ain't in you' house. I'm in Doaker's house. If he ask me to leave then I'll go on and leave. But consider me done left your part.
BERNIECE: Doaker, tell him to leave. Tell him to go on.
DOAKER: Boy Willie ain't done nothing for me to put him out of the house. I told you if you can't get along just go on and don't have nothing to do with each other.
BOY WILLIE: I ain't thinking about Berniece. [*He gets up and draws a line across the floor with his foot.*] There! Now I'm out of your part of the house. Consider me done left your part. Soon as Lymon come back with that rope, I'm gonna take that piano out of here and sell it.
BERNIECE: You ain't gonna touch that piano.
BOY WILLIE: Carry it out of here just as big and bold. Do like my daddy would have done come time to get Sutter's land.
BERNIECE: I got something to make you leave it over there.
BOY WILLIE: It's got to come better than this thirty-two-twenty.[6]
DOAKER: Why don't you stop all that! Boy Willie, go on and leave her alone. You know how Berniece get. Why you wanna sit there and pick with her?
BOY WILLIE: I ain't picking with her. I told her the truth. She the one talking about what she got. I just told her what she better have.
BERNIECE: That's alright, Doaker. Leave him alone.
BOY WILLIE: She trying to scare me. Hell, I ain't scared of dying. I look around and see people dying every day. You got to die to make room for somebody else. I had a dog that died. Wasn't nothing but a puppy. I picked it up and put it in a bag and carried it up there to Reverend C. L. Thompson's church. I carried it up there and prayed and asked Jesus to make it live like he did the man in the Bible.[7] I prayed real hard. Knelt down and everything. Say ask in Jesus' name. Well, I must have called Jesus' name two hundred times. I called his name till my mouth got sore. I got up and looked in the bag and the dog still dead. It ain't moved a muscle! I say, "Well, ain't nothing precious." And then I went out and killed me a cat. That's when I discovered the power of

---

6. That is, this thirty-two-twenty-caliber gun I'm (figuratively) holding.
7. Lazarus, who was raised from the dead by Jesus; see John 11.1–44.

death. See, a nigger that ain't afraid to die is the worse kind of nigger for the white man. He can't hold that power over you. That's what I learned when I killed that cat. I got the power of death too. I can command him. I can call him up. The white man don't like to see that. He don't like for you to stand up and look him square in the eye and say, "I got it too." Then he got to deal with you square up.

BERNIECE: That's why I don't talk to him, Doaker. You try and talk to him and that's the only kind of stuff that comes out his mouth.

DOAKER: You say Avery went home to get his Bible?

BOY WILLIE: What Avery gonna do? Avery can't do nothing with me. I wish Avery would say something to me about this piano.

DOAKER: Berniece ain't said about that. Avery went home to get his Bible. He coming by to bless the house see if he can get rid of Sutter's ghost.

BOY WILLIE: Ain't nothing but a house full of ghosts down there at the church. What Avery look like chasing away somebody's ghost?

[MARETHA *enters the front door.*]

BERNIECE: Light that stove and set that comb over there to get hot. Get something to put around your shoulders.

BOY WILLIE: The Bible say an eye for an eye, a tooth for a tooth, and a life for a life. Tit for tat. But you and Avery don't want to believe that. You gonna pass up that part and pretend it ain't in there. Everything else you gonna agree with. But if you gonna agree with part of it you got to agree with all of it. You can't do nothing halfway. You gonna go at the Bible halfway. You gonna act like that part ain't in there. But you pull out the Bible and open it and see what it say. Ask Avery. He a preacher. He'll tell you it's in there. He the Good Shepherd. Unless he gonna shepherd you to heaven with half the Bible.

BERNIECE Maretha, bring me that comb. Make sure it's hot.

[MARETHA *brings the comb.* BERNIECE *begins to do her hair.*]

BOY WILLIE: I will say this for Avery. He done figured out a path to go through life. I don't agree with it. But he done fixed it so he can go right through it real smooth. Hell, he liable to end up with a million dollars that he done got from selling bread and wine.

MARETHA: OWWWWWW!

BERNIECE: Be still, Maretha. If you was a boy I wouldn't be going through this.

BOY WILLIE: Don't you tell that girl that. Why you wanna tell her that?

BERNIECE: You ain't got nothing to do with this child.

BOY WILLIE: Telling her you wished she was a boy. How's that gonna make her feel?

BERNIECE: Boy Willie, go on and leave me alone.

DOAKER: Why don't you leave her alone? What you got to pick with her for? Why don't you go on out and see what's out there in the streets? Have something to tell the fellows down home.

BOY WILLIE: I'm waiting on Lymon to get back with that truck. Why don't you go on out and see what's out there in the streets? You ain't got to work tomorrow. Talking about me . . . why don't you go out there? It's Friday night.

DOAKER: I got to stay around here and keep you all from killing one another.

BOY WILLIE: You ain't got to worry about me. I'm gonna be here just as long as it takes Lymon to get back here with that truck. You ought to be talking to Berniece. Sitting up there telling Maretha she wished she was a boy. What kind of thing is that to tell a child? If you want to tell her something tell her about that piano. You ain't even told her about that piano. Like that's something to be ashamed of. Like she supposed to go off and hide somewhere about that piano. You ought to mark down on the calendar the day that Papa Boy Charles brought that piano into the house. You ought to mark that day down and draw a circle around it . . . and every year when it come up throw a party. Have a celebration. If you did that she wouldn't have no problem in life. She could walk around here with her head held high. I'm talking about a big party!

Invite everybody! Mark that day down with a special meaning. That way she know where she at in the world. You got her going out here thinking she wrong in the world. Like there ain't no part of it belong to her.

BERNIECE: Let me take care of my child. When you get one of your own then you can teach it what you want to teach it.

[DOAKER exits into his room.]

BOY WILLIE: What I want to bring a child into this world for? Why I wanna bring somebody else into all this for? I'll tell you this . . . If I was Rockefeller[8] I'd have forty or fifty. I'd make one every day. Cause they gonna start out in life with all the advantages. I ain't got no advantages to offer nobody. Many is the time I looked at my daddy and seen him staring off at his hands. I got a little older I know what he was thinking. He sitting there saying, "I got these big old hands but what I'm gonna do with them? Best I can do is make a fifty-acre crop for Mr. Stovall. Got these big old hands capable of doing anything. I can take and build something with these hands. But where's the tools? All I got is these hands. Unless I go out here and kill me somebody and take what they got . . . it's a long row to hoe for me to get something of my own. So what I'm gonna do with these big old hands? What would you do?"

See now . . . if he had his own land he wouldn't have felt that way. If he had something under his feet that belonged to him he could stand up taller. That's what I'm talking about. Hell, the land is there for everybody. All you got to do is figure out how to get you a piece. Ain't no mystery to life. You just got to go out and meet it square on. If you got a piece of land you'll find everything else fall right into place. You can stand right up next to the white man and talk about the price of cotton . . . the weather, and anything else you want to talk about. If you teach that girl that she living at the bottom of life, she's gonna grow up and hate you.

BERNIECE: I'm gonna teach her the truth. That's just where she living. Only she ain't got to stay there. [*To* MARETHA.] Turn you' head over to the other side.

BOY WILLIE: This might be your bottom but it ain't mine. I'm living at the top of life. I ain't gonna just take my life and throw it away at the bottom. I'm in

---

8. John D. Rockefeller (1839–1937), American oil magnate and philanthropist; the Rockefeller family is known for its wealth.

the world like everybody else. The way I see it everybody else got to come up a little taste to be where I am.

BERNIECE: You right at the bottom with the rest of us.

BOY WILLIE: I'll tell you this . . . and ain't a living soul can put a come back on it. If you believe that's where you at then you gonna act that way. If you act that way then that's where you gonna be. It's as simple as that. Ain't no mystery to life. I don't know how you come to believe that stuff. Crawley didn't think like that. He wasn't living at the bottom of life. Papa Boy Charles and Mama Ola wasn't living at the bottom of life. You ain't never heard them say nothing like that. They would have taken a strap to you if they heard you say something like that.

[DOAKER *enters from his room.*]

Hey, Doaker . . . Berniece say the colored folks is living at the bottom of life. I tried to tell her if she think that . . . that's where she gonna be. You think you living at the bottom of life? Is that how you see yourself?

DOAKER: I'm just living the best way I know how. I ain't thinking about no top or no bottom.

BOY WILLIE: That's what I tried to tell Berniece. I don't know where she got that from. That sound like something Avery would say. Avery think cause the white man give him a turkey for Thanksgiving that makes him better than everybody else. That's gonna raise him out of the bottom of life. I don't need nobody to give me a turkey. I can get my own turkey. All you have to do is get out my way. I'll get me two or three turkeys.

BERNIECE: You can't even get a chicken let alone two or three turkeys. Talking about get out your way. Ain't nobody in your way. [*To* MARETHA.] Straighten your head, Maretha! Don't be bending down like that. Hold your head up! [*To* BOY WILLIE.] All you got going for you is talk. You' whole life that's all you ever had going for you.

BOY WILLIE: See now . . . I'll tell you something about me. I done strung along and strung along. Going this way and that. Whatever way would lead me to a moment of peace. That's all I want. To be as easy with everything. But I wasn't born to that. I was born to a time of fire.

The world ain't wanted no part of me. I could see that since I was about seven. The world say it's better off without me. See, Berniece accept that. She trying to come up to where she can prove something to the world. Hell, the world a better place cause of me. I don't see it like Berniece. I got a heart that beats here and it beats just as loud as the next fellow's. Don't care if he black or white. Sometime it beats louder. When it beats louder, then everybody can hear it. Some people get scared of that. Like Berniece. Some people get scared to hear a nigger's heart beating. They think you ought to lay low with that heart. Make it beat quiet and go along with everything the way it is. But my mama ain't birthed me for nothing. So what I got to do? I got to mark my passing on the road. Just like you write on a tree, "Boy Willie was here."

That's all I'm trying to do with that piano. Trying to put my mark on the road. Like my daddy done. My heart say for me to sell that piano and get me some land so I can make a life for myself to live in my own way. Other than that I ain't thinking about nothing Berniece got to say.

[*There is a knock at the door.* BOY WILLIE *crosses to it and yanks it open thinking it is* LYMON. AVERY *enters. He carries a Bible.*]

BOY WILLIE: Where you been, nigger? Aw... I thought you was Lymon. Hey, Berniece, look who's here.

BERNIECE: Come on in, Avery. Don't you pay Boy Willie no mind.

BOY WILLIE: Hey... Hey, Avery... tell me this... can you get to heaven with half the Bible?

BERNIECE: Boy Willie... I done told you to leave me alone.

BOY WILLIE: I just ask the man a question. He can answer. He don't need you to speak for him. Avery... if you only believe on half the Bible and don't want to accept the other half... you think God let you in heaven? Or do you got to have the whole Bible? Tell Berniece... if you only believe in part of it... when you see God he gonna ask you why you ain't believed in the other part ... then he gonna send you straight to Hell.

AVERY: You got to be born again. Jesus say unless a man be born again he cannot come unto the Father and who so ever heareth my words and believeth them not shall be cast into a fiery pit.

BOY WILLIE: That's what I was trying to tell Berniece. You got to believe in it all. You can't go at nothing halfway. She think she going to heaven with half the Bible. [*To* BERNIECE.] You hear that... Jesus say you got to believe in it all.

BERNIECE: You keep messing with me.

BOY WILLIE: I ain't thinking about you.

DOAKER: Come on in, Avery, and have a seat. Don't pay neither one of them no mind. They been arguing all day.

BERNIECE: Come on in, Avery.

AVERY: How's everybody in here?

BERNIECE: Here, set this comb back over there on that stove. [*To* AVERY.] Don't pay Boy Willie no mind. He been around here bothering me since I come home from work.

BOY WILLIE: Boy Willie ain't bothering you. Boy Willie ain't bothering nobody. I'm just waiting on Lymon to get back. I ain't thinking about you. You heard the man say I was right and you still don't want to believe it. You just wanna go and make up anythin'. Well there's Avery... there's the preacher... go on and ask him.

AVERY: Berniece believe in the Bible. She been baptized.

BOY WILLIE: What about that part that say an eye for an eye a tooth for a tooth and a life for a life? Ain't that in there?

DOAKER: What they say down there at the bank, Avery?

AVERY: Oh, they talked to me real nice. I told Berniece... they say maybe they let me borrow the money. They done talked to my boss down at work and everything.

DOAKER: That's what I told Berniece. You working every day you ought to be able to borrow some money.

AVERY: I'm getting more people in my congregation every day. Berniece says she gonna be the Deaconess. I get me my church I can get married and settled down. That's what I told Berniece.

DOAKER: That be nice. You all ought to go ahead and get married. Berniece don't need to be by herself. I tell her that all the time.

BERNIECE: I ain't said nothing about getting married. I said I was thinking about it.
DOAKER: Avery get him his church you all can make it nice. [*To* AVERY.] Berniece said you was coming by to bless the house.
AVERY: Yeah, I done read up on my Bible. She asked me to come by and see if I can get rid of Sutter's ghost.
BOY WILLIE: Ain't no ghost in this house. That's all in Berniece's head. Go on up there and see if you see him. I'll give you a hundred dollars if you see him. That's all in her imagination.
DOAKER: Well, let her find that out then. If Avery blessing the house is gonna make her feel better . . . what you got to do with it?
AVERY: Berniece say Maretha seen him too. I don't know, but I found a part in the Bible to bless the house. If he is here then that ought to make him go.
BOY WILLIE: You worse than Berniece believing all that stuff. Talking about . . . if he here. Go on up there and find out. I been up there I ain't seen him. If you reading from that Bible gonna make him leave out of Berniece imagination, well, you might be right. But if you talking about . . .
DOAKER: Boy Willie, why don't you just be quiet? Getting all up in the man's business. This ain't got nothing to do with you. Let him go ahead and do what he gonna do.
BOY WILLIE: I ain't stopping him. Avery ain't got no power to do nothing.
AVERY: Oh, I ain't got no power. God got the power! God got power over everything in His creation. God can do anything. God say, "As I commandeth so it shall be." God said, "Let there be light," and there was light.[9] He made the world in six days and rested on the seventh. God's got a wonderful power. He got power over life and death. Jesus raised Lazareth from the dead. They was getting ready to bury him and Jesus told him say, "Rise up and walk." He got up and walked and the people made great rejoicing at the power of God. I ain't worried about him chasing away a little old ghost!

[*There is a knock at the door.* BOY WILLIE *goes to answer it.* LYMON *enters carrying a coil of rope.*]

BOY WILLIE: Where you been? I been waiting on you and you run off somewhere.
LYMON: I ran into Grace. I stopped and bought her drink. She say she gonna go to the picture show with me.
BOY WILLIE: I ain't thinking about no Grace nothing.
LYMON: Hi, Berniece.
BOY WILLIE: Give me that rope and get up on this side of the piano.
DOAKER: Boy Willie, don't start nothing now. Leave the piano alone.
BOY WILLIE: Get that board there, Lymon. Stay out of this, Doaker.

[BERNIECE *exits up the stairs.*]

DOAKER: You just can't take the piano. How you gonna take the piano? Berniece ain't said nothing about selling that piano.
BOY WILLIE: She ain't got to say nothing. Come on, Lymon. We got to lift one end at a time up on the board. You got to watch so that the board don't slide up under there.

---

9. See Genesis 1.3. *Lazareth:* Lazarus.

LYMON: What we gonna do with the rope?
BOY WILLIE: Let me worry about the rope. You just get up on this side over here with me.

[BERNIECE *enters from the stairs. She has her hand in her pocket where she has Crawley's gun.*]

AVERY: Boy Willie . . . Berniece . . . why don't you all sit down and talk this out now?
BERNIECE: Ain't nothing to talk out.
BOY WILLIE: I'm through talking to Berniece. You can talk to Berniece till you get blue in the face, and it don't make no difference. Get up on that side, Lymon. Throw that rope around there and tie it to the leg.
LYMON: Wait a minute . . . wait a minute, Boy Willie. Berniece got to say. Hey, Berniece . . . did you tell Boy Willie he could take this piano?
BERNIECE: Boy Willie ain't taking nothing out of my house but himself. Now you let him go ahead and try.
BOY WILLIE: Come on, Lymon, get up on this side with me.

[LYMON *stands undecided.*]

Come on, nigger! What you standing there for?
LYMON: Maybe Berniece is right, Boy Willie. Maybe you shouldn't sell it.
AVERY: You all ought to sit down and talk it out. See if you can come to an agreement.
DOAKER: That's what I been trying to tell them. Seem like one of them ought to respect the other one's wishes.
BERNIECE: I wish Boy Willie would go on and leave my house. That's what I wish. Now, he can respect that. Cause he's leaving here one way or another.
BOY WILLIE: What you mean one way or another? What's that supposed to mean? I ain't scared of no gun.
DOAKER: Come on, Berniece, leave him alone with that.
BOY WILLIE: I don't care what Berniece say. I'm selling my half. I can't help it if her half got to go along with it. It ain't like I'm trying to cheat her out of her half. Come on, Lymon.
LYMON: Berniece . . . I got to do this . . . Boy Willie say he gonna give you half of the money . . . say he want to get Sutter's land.
BERNIECE: Go on, Lymon. Just go on . . . I done told Boy Willie what to do.
BOY WILLIE: Here, Lymon . . . put that rope up over there.
LYMON: Boy Willie, you sure you want to do this? The way I figure it . . . I might be wrong . . . but I figure she gonna shoot you first.
BOY WILLIE: She just gonna have to shoot me.
BERNIECE: Maretha, get on out the way. Get her out the way, Doaker.
DOAKER: Go on, do what your mama told you.
BERNIECE: Put her in your room.

[MARETHA *exits to Doaker's room.* BOY WILLIE *and* LYMON *try to lift the piano. The door opens and* WINING BOY *enters. He has been drinking.*]

WINING BOY: Man, these niggers around here! I stopped down there at Seefus. . . . These folks standing around talking about Patchneck Red's coming. They jumping back and getting off the sidewalk talking about Patchneck Red this and Patchneck Red that. Come to find out . . . you know who they was talking about? Old John D. from up around Tyler! Used to run around with Otis Smith. He got everybody scared of him. Calling him Patchneck Red. They don't know I whupped the nigger's head in one time.

BOY WILLIE: Just make sure that board don't slide, Lymon.

LYMON: I got this side. You watch that side.

WINING BOY: Hey, Boy Willie, what you got? I know you got a pint stuck up in your coat.

BOY WILLIE: Wining Boy, get out the way!

WINING BOY: Hey, Doaker. What you got? Gimme a drink. I want a drink.

DOAKER: It look like you had enough of whatever it was. Come talking about "What you got?" You ought to be trying to find somewhere to lay down.

WINING BOY: I ain't worried about no place to lay down. I can always find me a place to lay down in Berniece's house. Ain't that right, Berniece?

BERNIECE: Wining Boy, sit down somewhere. You been out there drinking all day. Come in here smelling like an old polecat. Sit on down there, you don't need nothing to drink.

DOAKER: You know Berniece don't like all that drinking.

WINING BOY: I ain't disrespecting Berniece. Berniece, am I disrespecting you? I'm just trying to be nice. I been with strangers all day and they treated me like family. I come in here to family and you treat me like a stranger. I don't need your whiskey. I can buy my own. I wanted your company, not your whiskey.

DOAKER: Nigger, why don't you go upstairs and lay down? You don't need nothing to drink.

WINING BOY: I ain't thinking about no laying down. Me and Boy Willie fixing to party. Ain't that right, Boy Willie? Tell him. I'm fixing to play me some piano. Watch this.

[WINING BOY *sits down at the piano.*]

BOY WILLIE: Come on, Wining Boy! Me and Lymon fixing to move the piano.

WINING BOY: Wait a minute . . . wait a minute. This a song I wrote for Cleotha. I wrote this song in memory of Cleotha. [*He begins to play and sing.*]

> Hey little woman what's the matter with you now
> Had a storm last night and blowed the line all down
> 
> Tell me how long
> Is I got to wait
> Can I get it now
> Or must I hesitate
> 
> It takes a hesitating stocking in her hesitating shoe
> It takes a hesitating woman wanna sing the blues
> 
> Tell me how long
> Is I got to wait
> Can I kiss you now
> Or must I hesitate.

BOY WILLIE: Come on, Wining Boy, get up! Get up, Wining Boy! Me and Lymon's fixing to move the piano.

WINING BOY: Naw . . . Naw . . . you ain't gonna move this piano!

BOY WILLIE: Get out the way, Wining Boy.

[WINING BOY, *his back to the piano, spreads his arms out over the piano.*]

WINING BOY: You ain't taking this piano out the house. You got to take me with it!

BOY WILLIE: Get on out the way, Wining Boy! Doaker get him!

[*There is a knock on the door.*]

BERNIECE: I got him, Doaker. Come on, Wining Boy. I done told Boy Willie he ain't taking the piano.

[BERNIECE *tries to take* WINING BOY *away from the piano.*]

WINING BOY: He got to take me with it!

[DOAKER *goes to answer the door.* GRACE *enters.*]

GRACE: Is Lymon here?
DOAKER: Lymon.
WINING BOY: He ain't taking that piano.
BERNIECE: I ain't gonna let him take it.
GRACE: I thought you was coming back. I ain't gonna sit in that truck all day.
LYMON: I told you I was coming back.
GRACE: [*Sees* BOY WILLIE.] Oh, hi, Boy Willie. Lymon told me you was gone back down South.
LYMON: I said he was going back. I didn't say he had left already.
GRACE: That's what you told me.
BERNIECE: Lymon, you got to take your company someplace else.
LYMON: Berniece, this is Grace. That there is Berniece. That's Boy Willie's sister.
GRACE: Nice to meet you. [*To* LYMON.] I ain't gonna sit out in that truck all day. You told me you was gonna take me to the movie.
LYMON: I told you I had something to do first. You supposed to wait on me.
BERNIECE: Lymon, just go on and leave. Take Grace or whoever with you. Just go on get out my house.
BOY WILLIE: You gonna help me move this piano first, nigger!
LYMON: [*To* GRACE.] I got to help Boy Willie move the piano first.

[*Everybody but* GRACE *suddenly senses* SUTTER's *presence.*]

GRACE: I ain't waiting on you. Told me you was coming right back. Now you got to move a piano. You just like all the other men. [GRACE *now senses something.*] Something ain't right here. I knew I shouldn't have come back up in this house. [GRACE *exits.*]
LYMON: Hey, Grace! I'll be right back, Boy Willie.
BOY WILLIE: Where you going, nigger?
LYMON: I'll be back. I got to take Grace home.
BOY WILLIE: Come on, let's move the piano first!
LYMON: I got to take Grace home. I told you I'll be back.

[LYMON *exits.* BOY WILLIE *exits and calls after him.*]

BOY WILLIE: Come on, Lymon! Hey . . . Lymon! Lymon . . . come on!

[*Again, the presence of* SUTTER *is felt.*]

WINING BOY: Hey, Doaker, did you feel that? Hey, Berniece . . . did you get cold? Hey, Doaker . . .
DOAKER: What you calling me for?
WINING BOY: I believe that's Sutter.
DOAKER: Well, let him stay up there. As long as he don't mess with me.
BERNIECE: Avery, go on and bless the house.
DOAKER: You need to bless that piano. That's what you need to bless. It ain't done nothing but cause trouble. If you gonna bless anything go on and bless that.
WINING BOY: Hey, Doaker, if he gonna bless something let him bless everything. The kitchen . . . the upstairs. Go on and bless it all.
BOY WILLIE: Ain't no ghost in this house. He need to bless Berniece's head. That's what he need to bless.
AVERY: Seem like that piano's causing all the trouble. I can bless that. Berniece, put me some water in that bottle.

[AVERY *takes a small bottle from his pocket and hands it to* BERNIECE, *who goes into the kitchen to get water.* AVERY *takes a candle from his pocket and lights it. He gives it to* BERNIECE *as she gives him the water.*]

Hold this candle. Whatever you do make sure it don't go out.

O Holy Father we gather here this evening in the Holy Name to cast out the spirit of one James Sutter. May this vial of water be empowered with thy spirit. May each drop of it be a weapon and a shield against the presence of all evil and may it be a cleansing and blessing of this humble abode.

Just as Our Father taught us how to pray so He say, "I will prepare a table for you in the midst of mine enemies," and in His hands we place ourselves to come unto his presence. Where there is Good so shall it cause Evil to scatter to the Four Winds. [*He throws water at the piano at each commandment.*] Get thee behind me, Satan! Get thee behind the face of Righteousness as we Glorify His Holy Name! Get thee behind the Hammer of Truth that breaketh down the Wall of Falsehood! Father. Father. Praise. Praise. We ask in Jesus' name and call forth the power of the Holy Spirit as it is written. . . . [*He opens the Bible and reads from it.*] I will sprinkle clean water upon thee and ye shall be clean.

BOY WILLIE: All this old preaching stuff. Hell, just tell him to leave.

[AVERY *continues reading throughout* BOY WILLIE*'s outburst.*]

AVERY: I will sprinkle clean water upon you and you shall be clean: from all your uncleanliness, and from all your idols, will I cleanse you. A new heart also will I give you, and a new spirit will I put within you: and I will take out of your flesh the heart of stone, and I will give you a heart of flesh. And I will put my spirit within you, and cause you to walk in my statutes, and ye shall keep my judgments, and do them.

[BOY WILLIE *grabs a pot of water from the stove and begins to fling it around the room.*]

BOY WILLIE: Hey Sutter! Sutter! Get your ass out this house! Sutter! Come on and get some of this water! You done drowned in the well, come on and get some more of this water!

[BOY WILLIE *is working himself into a frenzy as he runs around the room throwing water and calling* SUTTER's *name.* AVERY *continues reading.*]

BOY WILLIE: Come on, Sutter! [*He starts up the stairs.*] Come on, get some water! Come on, Sutter!

[*The sound of* SUTTER's GHOST *is heard. As* BOY WILLIE *approaches the steps he is suddenly thrown back by the unseen force, which is choking him. As he struggles he frees himself, then dashes up the stairs.*]

BOY WILLIE: Come on, Sutter!

AVERY: [*Continuing.*] A new heart also will I give you and a new spirit will I put within you: and I will take out of your flesh the heart of stone, and I will give you a heart of flesh. And I will put my spirit within you, and cause you to walk in my statutes, and ye shall keep my judgments, and do them.

[*There are loud sounds heard from upstairs as* BOY WILLIE *begins to wrestle with* SUTTER's GHOST. *It is a life-and-death struggle fraught with perils and faultless terror.* BOY WILLIE *is thrown down the stairs.* AVERY *is stunned into silence.* BOY WILLIE *picks himself up and dashes back upstairs.*]

AVERY: Berniece, I can't do it.

[*There are more sounds heard from upstairs.* DOAKER *and* WINING BOY *stare at one another in stunned disbelief. It is in this moment, from somewhere old, that* BERNIECE *realizes what she must do. She crosses to the piano. She begins to play. The song is found piece by piece. It is an old urge to song that is both a commandment and a plea. With each repetition it gains in strength. It is intended as an exorcism and a dressing for battle. A rustle of wind blowing across two continents.*]

BERNIECE: [*Singing.*]

    I want you to help me
    I want you to help me
    I want you to help me
    I want you to help me
    I want you to help me
    I want you to help me
    Mama Berniece
    I want you to help me
    Mama Esther
    I want you to help me
    Papa Boy Charles
    I want you to help me
    Mama Ola
    I want you to help me

    I want you to help me
    I want you to help me
    I want you to help me
    I want you to help me
    I want you to help me
    I want you to help me

> I want you to help me
> I want you to help me

[*The sound of a train approaching is heard. The noise upstairs subsides.*]

BOY WILLIE: Come on, Sutter! Come back, Sutter!

[BERNIECE *begins to chant:*]

BERNIECE:

> Thank you.
> Thank you.
> Thank you.

[*A calm comes over the house.* MARETHA *enters from* DOAKER's *room.* BOY WILLIE *enters on the stairs. He pauses a moment to watch* BERNIECE *at the piano.*]

BERNIECE:

> Thank you.
> Thank you.
> Thank you.

BOY WILLIE: Wining Boy, you ready to go back down home? Hey, Doaker, what time the train leave?

DOAKER: You still got time to make it.

[MARETHA *crosses and embraces* BOY WILLIE.]

BOY WILLIE: Hey Berniece . . . if you and Maretha don't keep playing on that piano . . . ain't no telling . . . me and Sutter both liable to be back. [*He exits.*]

BERNIECE: Thank you.

[*The lights go down to black.*]

1987

## QUESTIONS

1. If you were producing the play, where would you place the piano onstage? How would the characters move and stand in relation to the piano? How would you direct them to approach the piano when they try to lift it or play it or gesture toward it? What kind of piano would you use, and how would you represent the carvings?
2. What, specifically, do the carvings on the piano represent? What different past does the piano represent for each of the characters? How important is the past ownership of the piano? What is the significance of the way the family acquired it? In what ways do different characters' attitudes toward the piano reveal their sense of the past?
3. Why is Boy Willie portrayed in the first scene as so loud and intrusive? What does this behavior achieve for the play dramatically? What aspects of Boy Willie's character does the opening scene illustrate? What aspects of his character are revealed later? What does "land" represent to him?
4. How would you describe Doaker's role in the play? Is he a minor character? How does he contribute to the play thematically? How does he affect the way events

unfold, or the dramatic climax? Given the importance of family in this play and his role as the family's acting patriarch, could we call him a kind of hero?

5. What functions does Maretha have in the play? In what ways is her age important? If you were directing the play, how would you have Maretha behave? How would she be costumed?
6. In what ways is geography important to the play? What does "Mississippi" represent to the different characters? What does "Pittsburgh" represent to the different characters? What does Doaker's continued employment with the railroad symbolize?
7. What does the truckload of watermelons represent to Boy Willie? to Lymon? In what sense does the offstage presence of the watermelons keep time for the play and mark the progression of the plot? Describe the rising action and climax of the play in relation to the truck's load.
8. Clearly the past—and the effort to keep it alive—dominates Berniece's thinking, whereas Boy Willie believes he can transcend the past if he can reverse the historic sense of racial ownership. Describe the complications of this tension as they develop throughout the play. Where do other characters fit into the opposition? What is Doaker's relationship to the past?
9. What plot functions does Grace perform? In what ways does her presence complicate the play's gender themes?
10. What does Avery represent to Berniece? What attracts her to him, and what, on the other hand, makes her hesitate in accepting his offer of marriage? If you were producing the play, how would you present the critical scene of Avery preaching? of the exorcism?
11. What does "Lesson" in the title mean? What lesson does the piano teach each of the characters?

## SUGGESTIONS FOR WRITING

1. What is the role of music in *The Piano Lesson*? How does the music function to reveal character and to provide a counterpoint to the action of the plot? What is the thematic importance of the music? Write an essay in which you explore the many uses of music in Wilson's play.
2. What is the legacy of slavery in the lives of the African American characters in *The Piano Lesson*? How fully does each character acknowledge slavery's influence on the late-twentieth-century lives depicted in the play? How does each character try to break free of this influence? Write an essay in which you explore slavery's lingering power to shape the attitudes and behavior of the characters in *The Piano Lesson*.
3. How does *The Piano Lesson* present gender roles and sexual politics? What expectations do the men and women in the play have of each other? Write an essay in which you discuss the play's themes of gender differences.
4. Were you surprised by the play's ending? A longstanding "rule" for playwrights is that if a gun appears onstage, it must be fired by the end of the play. *The Piano Lesson*, though, seems to build steadily toward a violent climax that is averted at the last moment. Write an essay in which you examine the way August Wilson both uses and subverts the audience's conventional expectations that drama is resolved by violence.
5. Write a series of "newsy" letters from Boy Willie, Berniece, Maretha, and Lymon, in which each character, in turn, describes the conflict over the piano. How would they describe their own feelings and actions? How would they account for the values and motivations of the other characters? What resolution of the conflict would each character hope for?

# MARGARET EDSON

## *Wit*

**CHARACTERS**
VIVIAN BEARING, PH.D., 50, *Professor of Seventeenth-Century Poetry at the University*
HARVEY KELEKIAN, M.D., 50, *Chief of Medical Oncology, University Hospital*
JASON POSNER, M.D., 28, *Clinical Fellow, Medical Oncology Branch*
SUSIE MONAHAN, R.N., B.S.N., 28, *Primary Nurse, Cancer Inpatient Unit*
E. M. ASHFORD, D.PHIL., 80, *Professor Emerita of English Literature*
MR. BEARING, *Vivian's father*
LAB TECHNICIANS
CLINICAL FELLOWS
STUDENTS
CODE TEAM

*The play may be performed with a cast of nine: the four* TECHNICIANS, FELLOWS, STUDENTS, *and* CODE TEAM MEMBERS *should double;* DR. KELEKIAN *and* MR. BEARING *should double.*

---

VIVIAN BEARING *walks on the empty stage pushing her IV pole. She is fifty, tall and very thin, barefoot, and completely bald. She wears two hospital gowns—one tied in the front and one tied in the back—a baseball cap, and a hospital ID bracelet. The house lights are at half strength.* VIVIAN *looks out at the audience, sizing them up.*

VIVIAN: [*In false familiarity, waving and nodding to the audience.*]
Hi. How are you feeling today? Great. That's just great.
[*In her own professorial tone.*] This is not my standard greeting, I assure you.
I tend toward something a little more formal, a little less inquisitive, such as, say, "Hello."
But it is the standard greeting here.
There is some debate as to the correct response to this salutation. Should one reply "I feel good," using "feel" as a copulative to link the subject, "I," to its subjective complement, "good"; or "I feel well," modifying with an adverb the subject's state of being?
I don't know. I am a professor of seventeenth-century poetry, specializing in the Holy Sonnets of John Donne.[1]
So I just say, "Fine."
Of course it is not very often that I do feel fine.
I have been asked "How are you feeling today?" while I was throwing up into a plastic washbasin. I have been asked as I was emerging from a four-hour operation with a tube in every orifice, "How are you feeling today?"

---

1. John Donne (1572–1631), poet and high-ranking minister of the Church of England known for his wit as well as his contributions to Christian theology. Several examples of his poetry appear in this volume. One of the Holy Sonnets, "Batter my heart, three-personed God," appears on page 950.

I am waiting for the moment when someone asks me this question and I am dead.

I'm a little sorry I'll miss that.

It is unfortunate that this remarkable line of inquiry has come to me so late in my career. I could have exploited its feigned solicitude to great advantage: as I was distributing the final examination to the graduate course in seventeenth-century textual criticism—[2] "Hi. How are you feeling today?"

Of course I would not be wearing this costume at the time, so the question's *ironic significance* would not be fully apparent.

As I trust it is now.

*Irony* is a literary device that will necessarily be deployed to great effect.

I ardently wish this were not so. I would prefer that a play about me be cast in the mythic-heroic-pastoral mode; but the facts, most notably stage-four metastatic ovarian cancer,[3] conspire against that. *The Faerie Queene* this is not.

And I was dismayed to discover that the play would contain elements of ... *humor*.

I have been, at best, an *unwitting* accomplice. (*She pauses.*) It is not my intention to give away the plot; but I think I die at the end.

They've given me less than two hours.

If I were poetically inclined, I might employ a threadbare metaphor—the sands of time slipping through the hour-glass, the two-hour glass.

> Now our sands are almost run;
> More a little, and then dumb.[4]

Shakespeare. I trust the name is familiar.

At the moment, however, I am disinclined to poetry.

I've got less than two hours. Then: curtain. [*She disconnects herself from the IV pole and shoves it to a crossing technician. The house lights go out. Scene change.*]

I'll never forget the time I found out I had cancer. [DR. HARVEY KELEKIAN *enters at a big desk piled high with papers.*]

KELEKIAN: You have cancer.

VIVIAN: [*To audience.*] See? Unforgettable. It was something of a shock. I had to sit down. [*She plops down.*]

KELEKIAN: Please sit down. Miss Bearing, you have advanced metastatic ovarian cancer.

VIVIAN: Go on.

KELEKIAN: You are a professor, Miss Bearing.

VIVIAN: Like yourself, Dr. Kelekian.

KELEKIAN: Well, yes. Now then. You present with a growth that, unfortunately, went undetected in stages one, two, and three. Now it is an insidious adeno-

---

2. Professor Bearing's course would study the variations among manuscripts and printed versions of literary works produced in the 1600s in Britain, according to different methods or principles for establishing the version closest to the original, to the author's final intentions, or to a correct and readable text for readers today.
3. Advanced cancer of the ovaries that has spread to other parts of the body; *The Faerie Queene*: allegorical narrative poem in twelve books, written in a deliberately archaic style, by Edmund Spenser (1552–1599).
4. A couplet from Shakespeare's unfinished romance *Pericles* (5.2.1–2); like *The Faerie Queene*, it recalls the premodern world in a magical rather than realistic way.

carcinoma, which has spread from the primary adnexal mass—[5]
VIVIAN: "Insidious"?
KELEKIAN: "Insidious" means undetectable at an—
VIVIAN: "Insidious" *means* treacherous.
KELEKIAN: Shall I continue?
VIVIAN: By all means.
KELEKIAN: Good. In invasive epithelial carcinoma, the most effective treatment modality is a chemotherapeutic agent. We are developing an experimental combination of drugs designed for primary-site ovarian, with a target specificity of stage three—and—beyond administration.

Am I going too fast?

Good.

You will be hospitalized as an inpatient for treatment each cycle. You will be on complete intake-and-output measurement for three days after each treatment to monitor kidney function. After the initial eight cycles, you will have another battery of tests.

The antineoplastic will inevitably affect some healthy cells, including those lining the gastro-intestinal tract from the lips to the anus, and the hair follicles. We will of course be relying on your resolve to withstand some of the more pernicious side effects.

VIVIAN: Insidious. Hmm. Curious word choice.
Cancer.          Cancel.

"By cancer nature's changing course untrimmed."[6] No—that's not it.

[*To* KELEKIAN.] No.

Must read something about cancer.

Must get some books, articles. Assemble a bibliography.

Is anyone doing research on cancer?
Concentrate.

Antineoplastic. Anti: against. Neo: new. Plastic. To mold. Shaping. Antineoplastic. Against new shaping.

Hair follicles. My resolve.

"Pernicious." That doesn't seem—

KELEKIAN: Miss Bearing?
VIVIAN: I beg your pardon?
KELEKIAN: Do you have any questions so far?
VIVIAN: Please, go on.
KELEKIAN: Perhaps some of these terms are new. I realize—

---

5. Adenocarcinoma is a cancer that begins in cells in the lining of internal organs. An adnexal mass, common in women, is a growth, benign or cancerous, associated with the ovaries. Students may easily find definitions of these and subsequent medical terms; the patient herself looks them up.
6. A play on line 8 of Shakespeare's sonnet XVIII, "Shall I compare thee to a summer's day": "By chance, or nature's changing course untrimmed." (See p. 948.)

VIVIAN: No, no. Ah. You're being very thorough.
KELEKIAN: I make a point of it. And I always emphasize it with my students—
VIVIAN: So do I. "Thoroughness"—I always tell my students, but they are constitutionally averse to painstaking work.
KELEKIAN: Yours, too.
VIVIAN: Oh, it's worse every year.
KELEKIAN: And this is not dermatology, it's medical oncology, for Chrissake.
VIVIAN: My students read through a text once—once!—and think it's time for a break.
KELEKIAN: Mine are blind.
VIVIAN: Well, mine are deaf.
KELEKIAN: [*Resigned, but warmly.*] You just have to hope....
VIVIAN: [*Not so sure.*] I suppose. [*Pause.*]
KELEKIAN: Where were we, Dr. Bearing?
VIVIAN: I believe I was being thoroughly diagnosed.
KELEKIAN: Right. Now. The tumor is spreading very quickly, and this treatment is very aggressive. So far, so good?
VIVIAN: Yes.
KELEKIAN: Better not teach next semester.
VIVIAN: [*Indignant.*] Out of the question.
KELEKIAN: The first week of each cycle you'll be hospitalized for chemotherapy; the next week you may feel a little tired; the next two weeks'll be fine, relatively. This cycle will repeat eight times, as I said before.
VIVIAN: Eight months like that?
KELEKIAN: This treatment is the strongest thing we have to offer you. And, as research, it will make a significant contribution to our knowledge.
VIVIAN: Knowledge, yes.
KELEKIAN: [*Giving her a piece of paper.*] Here is the informed-consent form. Should you agree, you sign there, at the bottom. Is there a family member you want me to explain this to?
VIVIAN: [*Signing.*] That won't be necessary.
KELEKIAN: [*Taking back the paper.*] Good. The important thing is for you to take the full dose of chemotherapy. There may be times when you'll wish for a lesser dose, due to the side effects. But we've got to go full-force. The experimental phase has got to have the maximum dose to be of any use. Dr. Bearing—
VIVIAN: Yes?
KELEKIAN: You must be very tough. Do you think you can be very tough?
VIVIAN: You needn't worry.
KELEKIAN: Good. Excellent. [KELEKIAN *and the desk exit as* VIVIAN *stands and walks forward.*]
VIVIAN: [*Hesitantly.*] I should have asked more questions, because I know there's going to be a test.

I have cancer, insidious cancer, with pernicious side effects—No, the *treatment* has pernicious side effects.

I have stage-four metastatic ovarian cancer. There is no stage five. Oh, and I have to be very tough. It appears to be a matter, as the saying goes, of life and death.

I know all about life and death. I am, after all, a scholar of Donne's Holy

Sonnets, which explore mortality in greater depth than any other body of work in the English language.

And I know for a fact that I am tough. A demanding professor. Uncompromising. Never one to turn from a challenge. That is why I chose, while a student of the great E. M. Ashford, to study Donne. [PROFESSOR E. M. ASHFORD, *fifty-two, enters, seated at the same desk as* KELEKIAN *was. The scene is twenty-eight years ago.* VIVIAN *suddenly turns twenty-two, eager and intimidated.*]

Professor Ashford?

E.M.: Do it again.

VIVIAN: [*To audience.*] It was something of a shock. I had to sit down. [*She plops down.*]

E.M.: Please sit down. Your essay on Holy Sonnet Six, Miss Bearing, is a melodrama, with a veneer of scholarship unworthy of you—to say nothing of Donne. Do it again.

VIVIAN: I, ah . . .

E.M.: You must begin with a text, Miss Bearing, not with a feeling.

> Death be not proud, though some have called thee
> Mighty and dreadfull, for, thou art not soe[7]

You have entirely missed the point of the poem, because, I must tell you, you have used an edition of the text that is inauthentically punctuated. In the Gardner edition—

VIVIAN: That edition was checked out of the library—

E.M.: Miss Bearing!

VIVIAN: Sorry.

E.M.: You take this too lightly, Miss Bearing. This is Metaphysical Poetry, not The Modern Novel. The standards of scholarship and critical reading which one would apply to any other text are simply insufficient. The effort must be total for the results to be meaningful. Do you think the punctuation of the last line of this sonnet is merely an insignificant detail?

The sonnet begins with a valiant struggle with death, calling on all the forces of intellect and drama to vanquish the enemy. But it is ultimately about overcoming the seemingly insuperable barriers separating life, death, and eternal life.

In the edition you chose, this profoundly simple meaning is sacrificed to hysterical punctuation:

> And Death—*capital D*—shall be no more—*semicolon!*
> Death—*capital D*—*comma*—thou shalt die—*ex-clamation point!*

If you go in for this sort of thing, I suggest you take up Shakespeare.

Gardner's edition of the Holy Sonnets returns to the Westmoreland manuscript source of 1610—not for sentimental reasons, I assure you, but because Helen Gardner is a *scholar*. It reads:

> And death shall be no more, *comma*, Death thou shalt die.

[*As she recites this line, she makes a little gesture at the comma.*]

---

7. From John Donne's Holy Sonnet 6. (See p. 1241.)

Nothing but a breath—a comma—separates life from life everlasting. It is very simple really. With the original punctuation restored, death is no longer something to act out on a stage, with exclamation points. It's a comma, a pause.

This way, the *uncompromising* way, one learns something from this poem, wouldn't you say? Life, death. Soul, God. Past, present. Not insuperable barriers, not semicolons, just a comma.

VIVIAN: Life, death . . . I see. [*Standing.*] It's a metaphysical conceit.[8] It's wit! I'll go back to the library and rewrite the paper—

E. M.: [*Standing, emphatically.*] It is *not wit*, Miss Bearing. It is truth. [*Walking around the desk to her.*] The paper's not the point.

VIVIAN: It isn't?

E. M.: [*Tenderly.*] Vivian. You're a bright young woman. Use your intelligence. Don't go back to the library. Go out. Enjoy yourself with your friends. Hmm? [VIVIAN *walks away.* E. M. *Slides off.*]

VIVIAN: [*As she gradually returns to the hospital.*] I, ah, went outside. The sun was very bright. I, ah, walked around, past the . . . There were students on the lawn, talking about nothing, laughing. The insuperable barrier between one thing and another is . . . just a comma? Simple human truth, uncompromising scholarly standards? They're *connected*? I just couldn't. . . .

I went back to the library.

Anyway.

All right. Significant contribution to knowledge.

Eight cycles of chemotherapy. Give me the full dose, the full dose every time. [*Scene change. In a burst of activity, the hospital scene is created.*]

The attention was flattering. For the first five minutes. Now I know how poems feel. [SUSIE MONAHAN, *Vivian's primary nurse, gives* VIVIAN *her chart, then puts her in a wheelchair and takes her to her first appointment: chest X-ray. This and all other diagnostic tests are suggested by light and sound.*]

TECHNICIAN 1: Name.

VIVIAN: My name? Vivian Bearing.

TECHNICIAN 1: Huh?

VIVIAN: Bearing. B-E-A-R-I-N-G. Vivian. V-I-V-I-A-N.

TECHNICIAN 1: Doctor.

VIVIAN: Yes, I have a Ph.D.

TECHNICIAN 1: *Your* doctor.

VIVIAN: Oh. Dr. Harvey Kelekian. [TECHNICIAN 1 *positions her so that she is leaning forward and embracing the metal plate, then steps offstage.*] I am a doctor of philosophy—

TECHNICIAN 1: [*From offstage.*] Take a deep breath, and hold it. [*Pause, with light and sound.*] Okay.

VIVIAN: —a scholar of seventeenth-century poetry.

TECHNICIAN 1: Turn sideways, arms behind your head, and hold it. [*Pause.*] Okay.

VIVIAN: I have made an immeasurable contribution to the discipline of English

---

8. The work of John Donne and other "metaphysical" poets uses extended figures of speech, "conceits," that seem paradoxical or puzzling because they link very different entities, often common things and spiritual concepts. The seventeenth-century concept of "wit" is more a matter of brilliant intellect and verbal irony than clever jokes.

literature. [TECHNICIAN 1 *returns and puts her in the wheelchair.*] I am, in short, a force. [TECHNICIAN 1 *rolls her to upper GI series, where* TECHNICIAN 2 *picks up.*]

TECHNICIAN 2: Name.

VIVIAN: Lucy, Countess of Bedford.⁹

TECHNICIAN 2: [*Checking a printout.*] I don't see it here.

VIVIAN: My name is Vivian Bearing. B-E-A-R-I-N-G. Dr. Kelekian is my doctor.

TECHNICIAN 2: Okay. Lie down. [TECHNICIAN 2 *positions her on a stretcher and leaves. Light and sound suggest the filming.*]

VIVIAN: After an outstanding undergraduate career, I studied with Professor E. M. Ashford for three years, during which time I learned by instruction and example what it means to be a scholar of distinction.

As her research fellow, my principal task was the alphabetizing of index cards for Ashford's monumental critical edition of Donne's *Devotions upon Emergent Occasions*. [*During the procedure, another* TECHNICIAN *takes the wheelchair away.*]

I am thanked in the preface: "Miss Vivian Bearing for her able assistance."

My dissertation, "Ejaculations in Seventeenth-Century Manuscript and Printed Editions of the Holy Sonnets: A Comparison,"¹ was revised for publication in the *Journal of English Texts*, a very prestigious venue for a first appearance.

TECHNICIAN 2: Where's your wheelchair?

VIVIAN: I do not know. I was busy just now.

TECHNICIAN 2: Well, how are you going to get out of here?

VIVIAN: Well, I do not know. Perhaps you would like me to stay.

TECHNICIAN 2: I guess I got to go find you a chair.

VIVIAN: [*Sarcastically.*] Don't inconvenience yourself on my behalf. [TECHNICIAN 2 *leaves to get a wheelchair.*]

My second article, a classic explication of Donne's sonnet "Death be not proud," was published in *Critical Discourse*.

The success of the essay prompted the University Press to solicit a volume on the twelve Holy Sonnets in the 1633 edition, which I produced in the remarkably short span of three years. My book, entitled *Made Cunningly*, remains an immense success, in paper as well as cloth.

In it, I devote one chapter to a thorough examination of each sonnet, discussing every word in extensive detail. [TECHNICIAN 2 *returns with a wheelchair.*]

TECHNICIAN 2: Here.

VIVIAN: I summarize previous critical interpretations of the text and offer my own analysis. It is exhaustive. [TECHNICIAN 2 *deposits her at CT scan.*] Bearing. B-E-A-R-I-N-G. Kelekian. [TECHNICIAN 3 *has* VIVIAN *lie down on a metal stretcher. Light and sound suggest the procedure.*]

TECHNICIAN 3: Here. Hold still.

---

9. Ben Jonson (1572–1637), poet and playwright who was a contemporary of Shakespeare, wrote an epigrammatic poem published along with John Donne's *Satires* that praises the talented patroness Lucy, Countess of Bedford. The poem suggests that the Countess was among the few people who can appreciate satire.
1. *Ejaculations* (from Latin, meaning "to throw out") here refers to exclamations (such as "O God!"). This dissertation and journal are invented. The details of scholarship throughout the play, including scholars' names and journal titles, are sometimes fictitious and sometimes genuine, but are always plausible.

VIVIAN: For how long?

TECHNICIAN 3: Just a little while. [TECHNICIAN 3 *leaves. Silence.*]

VIVIAN: The scholarly study of poetic texts requires a capacity for scrupulously detailed examination, particularly the poetry of John Donne.

The salient characteristic of the poems is wit: "Itchy outbreaks of far-fetched wit," as Donne himself said.

To the common reader—that is to say, the undergraduate with a B-plus or better average—wit provides an invaluable exercise for sharpening the mental faculties, for stimulating the flash of comprehension that can only follow hours of exacting and seemingly pointless scrutiny. [TECHNICIAN 3 *puts* VIVIAN *back in the wheelchair and wheels her toward the unit. Partway,* TECHNICIAN 3 *gives the chair a shove and* SUSIE *takes over.* SUSIE *rolls* VIVIAN *to the exam room.*]

To the scholar, to the mind comprehensively trained in the subtleties of seventeenth-century vocabulary, versification, and theological, historical, geographical, political, and mythological allusions, Donne's wit is . . . a way to see how good you really are.

After twenty years, I can say with confidence, no one is quite as good as I. [*By now,* SUSIE *has helped* VIVIAN *sit on the exam table.* DR. JASON POSNER, *clinical fellow, stands in the doorway.*]

JASON: Ah, Susie?

SUSIE: Oh, hi.

JASON: Ready when you are.

SUSIE: Okay. Go ahead. Ms. Bearing, this is Jason Posner. He's going to do your history, ask you a bunch of questions. He's Dr. Kelekian's fellow. [SUSIE *is busy in the room, setting up for the exam.*]

JASON: Hi, Professor Bearing. I'm Dr. Posner, clinical fellow in the medical oncology branch, working with Dr. Kelekian.

Professor Bearing, I, ah, I was an undergraduate at the U. I took your course in seventeenth-century poetry.

VIVIAN: You did?

JASON: Yes. I thought it was excellent.

VIVIAN: Thank you. Were you an English major?

JASON: No. Biochemistry. But you can't get into medical school unless you're well-rounded. And I made a bet with myself that I could get an A in the three hardest courses on campus.

SUSIE: Howdja do, Jace?

JASON: Success.

VIVIAN: [*Doubtful.*] Really?

JASON: A minus. It was a very tough course. [*To* SUSIE.] I'll call you.

SUSIE: Okay. [*She leaves.*]

JASON: I'll just pull this over. [*He gets a little stool on wheels.*] Get the proxemics[2] right here. There. [*Nervously.*] Good. Now. I'm going to be taking your history. It's a medical interview, and then I give you an exam.

VIVIAN: I believe Dr. Kelekian has already done that.

JASON: Well, I know, but Dr. Kelekian wants me to do it, too. Now. I'll be taking a few notes as we go along.

VIVIAN: Very well.

---

2. The study of spatial sense.

JASON: Okay. Let's get started. How are you feeling today?
VIVIAN: Fine, thank you.
JASON: Good. How is your general health?
VIVIAN: Fine.
JASON: Excellent. Okay. We know you are an academic.
VIVIAN: Yes, we've established that.
JASON: So we don't need to talk about your interesting work.
VIVIAN: No. [*The following questions and answers go extremely quickly.*]
JASON: How old are you?
VIVIAN: Fifty.
JASON: Are you married?
VIVIAN: No.
JASON: Are your parents living?
VIVIAN: No.
JASON: How and when did they die?
VIVIAN: My father, suddenly, when I was twenty, of a heart attack. My mother, slowly, when I was forty-one and forty-two, of cancer. Breast cancer.
JASON: Cancer?
VIVIAN: Breast cancer.
JASON: I see. Any siblings?
VIVIAN: No.
JASON: Do you have any questions so far?
VIVIAN: Not so far.
JASON: Well, that about does it for your life history.
VIVIAN: Yes, that's all there is to my life history.
JASON: Now I'm going to ask you about your past medical history. Have you ever been hospitalized?
VIVIAN: I had my tonsils out when I was eight.
JASON: Have you ever been pregnant?
VIVIAN: No.
JASON: Ever had heart murmurs? High blood pressure?
VIVIAN: No.
JASON: Stomach, liver, kidney problems?
VIVIAN: No.
JASON: Venereal diseases? Uterine infections?
VIVIAN: No.
JASON: Thyroid, diabetes, cancer?
VIVIAN: No—cancer, yes.
JASON: When?
VIVIAN: Now.
JASON: Well, not including now.
VIVIAN: In that case, no.
JASON: Okay. Clinical depression? Nervous breakdowns? Suicide attempts?
VIVIAN: No.
JASON: Do you smoke?
VIVIAN: No.
JASON: Ethanol?
VIVIAN: I'm sorry?
JASON: Alcohol.

VIVIAN: Oh. Ethanol. Yes, I drink wine.
JASON: How much? How often?
VIVIAN: A glass with dinner occasionally. And perhaps a Scotch every now and then.
JASON: Do you use substances?
VIVIAN: Such as.
JASON: Marijuana, cocaine, crack cocaine, PCP, ecstasy, poppers—
VIVIAN: No.
JASON: Do you drink caffeinated beverages?
VIVIAN: Oh, yes!
JASON: Which ones?
VIVIAN: Coffee. A few cups a day.
JASON: How many?
VIVIAN: Two . . . to six. But I really don't think that's immoderate—
JASON: How often do you undergo routine medical checkups?
VIVIAN: Well, not as often as I should, probably, but I've felt fine, I really have.
JASON: So the answer is?
VIVIAN: Every three to . . . five years.
JASON: What do you do for exercise?
VIVIAN: Pace.
JASON: Are you having sexual relations?
VIVIAN: Not at the moment.
JASON: Are you pre- or post-menopausal?
VIVIAN: Pre.
JASON: When was the first day of your last period?
VIVIAN: Ah, ten days—two weeks ago.
JASON: Okay. When did you first notice your present complaint?
VIVIAN: This time, now?
JASON: Yes.
VIVIAN: Oh, about four months ago. I felt a pain in my stomach, in my abdomen, like a cramp, but not the same.
JASON: How did it feel?
VIVIAN: Like a cramp.
JASON: But not the same?
VIVIAN: No, duller, and stronger. I can't describe it.
JASON: What came next?
VIVIAN: Well, I just, I don't know, I started noticing my body, little things. I would be teaching, and feel a sharp pain.
JASON: What kind of pain?
VIVIAN: Sharp, and sudden. Then it would go away. Or I would be tired. Exhausted. I was working on a major project, the article on John Donne for *The Oxford Encyclopedia of English Literature*. It was a great honor. But I had a very strict deadline.
JASON: So you would say you were under stress?
VIVIAN: It wasn't so much more stress than usual, I just couldn't withstand it this time. I don't know.
JASON: So?
VIVIAN: So I went to Dr. Chin, my gynecologist, after I had turned in the article, and explained all this. She examined me, and sent me to Jefferson the internist,

and he sent me to Kelekian because he thought I might have a tumor.
JASON: And that's it?
VIVIAN: Till now.
JASON: Hmmm. Well, that's very interesting. [*Nervous pause.*]

Well, I guess I'll start the examination. It'll only take a few minutes. Why don't you, um, sort of lie back, and—oh—relax. [*He helps her lie back on the table, raises the stirrups out of the table, raises her legs and puts them in the stirrups, and puts a paper sheet over her.*]

Be very relaxed. This won't hurt. Let me get this sheet. Okay. Just stay calm. Okay. Put your feet in these stirrups. Okay. Just. There. Okay? Now. Oh, I have to go get Susie. Got to have a girl here. Some crazy clinical rule. Um. I'll be right back. Don't move. [JASON *leaves. Long pause. He is seen walking quickly back and forth in the hall, and calling* SUSIE's *name as he goes by.*]

VIVIAN: [*To herself.*] I wish I had given him an A. [*Silence.*]

Two times one is two. Two times two is four.
Two times three is six.
Um.
Oh.

Death be not proud, though some have called thee
Mighty and dreadful, for, thou art not soe,
For, those, whom thou think'st, thou dost overthrow,
Die not, poore death, nor yet canst thou kill mee; . . .

JASON: [*In the hallway.*] Has anybody seen Susie?
VIVIAN: [*Losing her place for a second.*] Ah.

Thou'art slave to Fate, chance, kings, and desperate men,
And dost with poyson, warre, and sicknesse dwell,
And poppie, or charmes can make us sleepe as well,
And better than thy stroake: why swell'st thou then?

JASON: [*In the hallway.*] She was here just a minute ago.
VIVIAN:

One short sleepe past, wee wake eternally,
And death shall be no more—*comma*—Death thou shalt die.

[JASON *and* SUSIE *return.*]

JASON: Okay. Here's everything. Okay.
SUSIE: What is this? Why did you leave her—
JASON: [*To* SUSIE.] I had to find you. Now, come on. [*To* VIVIAN.] We're ready, Professor Bearing. [*To himself, as he puts on exam gloves.*] Get these on. Okay. Just lift this up. Ooh. Okay. [*As much to himself as to her.*] Just relax. [*He begins the pelvic exam, with one hand on her abdomen and the other inside her, looking blankly at the ceiling as he feels around.*] Okay. [*Silence.*] Susie, isn't that interesting, that I had Professor Bearing.
SUSIE: Yeah. I wish I had taken some literature. I don't know anything about poetry.
JASON: [*Trying to be casual.*] Professor Bearing was very highly regarded on campus. It looked very good on my transcript that I had taken her course. [*Silence.*] They even asked me about it in my interview for med school—[*He feels the mass*

*and does a double take.*] Jesus! [*Tense silence. He is amazed and fascinated.*]
SUSIE: What?
VIVIAN: What?
JASON: Um. [*He tries for composure.*] Yeah. I survived Bearing's course. No problem. Heh. [*Silence.*] Yeah, John Donne, those metaphysical poets, that metaphysical wit. Hardest poetry in the English department. Like to see them try biochemistry. [*Silence.*] Okay. We're about done. Okay. That's it. Okay, Professor Bearing. Let's take your feet out, there. [*He takes off his gloves and throws them away.*] Okay. I gotta go. I gotta go. [JASON *quickly leaves.* VIVIAN *slowly gets up from this scene and walks stiffly away.* SUSIE *cleans up the exam room and exits. Scene change.*]
VIVIAN: [*Walking D to audience.*] That ... was ... hard. That ... was ...

One thing can be said for an eight-month course of cancer treatment: it is highly educational. I am learning to suffer.

Yes, it is mildly uncomfortable to have an electrocardiogram, but the ... agony ... of a proctosigmoidoscopy[3] sweeps it from memory. Yes, it was embarrassing to have to wear a nightgown all day long—two nightgowns!—but that seemed like a positive privilege compared to watching myself go bald. Yes, having a former student give me a pelvic exam was thoroughly degrading—and I use the term deliberately—but I could not have imagined the depths of humiliation that—

Oh, God— [VIVIAN *runs across the stage to her hospital room, dives onto the bed, and throws up into a large plastic washbasin.*]

Oh, God.

Oh. Oh. [*She lies slumped on the bed, fastened to the IV, which now includes a small bottle with a bright orange label.*]

Oh, God.

It can't be.

[*Silence.*]

Oh, God.

Please.

Steady. Steady.

[*Silence.*]

Oh—

Oh, no! [*She throws up again, moans, and retches in agony.*]

Oh, God.

What's left?

I haven't eaten in two days.

What's left to puke?

[*Silence.*]

You may remark that my vocabulary has taken a turn for the Anglo-Saxon. God, I'm going to barf my brains out.

[*She begins to relax.*] If I actually did barf my brains out, it would be a great loss to my discipline. Of course, not a few of my colleagues would be relieved. To say nothing of my students.

It's not that I'm controversial. Just uncompromising. Ooh— [*She lunges for the basin. Nothing.*] Oh. [*Silence.*] False alarm. If the word went round that Vivian Bearing had barfed her brains out ...

---

3. Diagnostic examination of the lower intestinal tract.

Well, first my colleagues, most of whom are my former students, would scramble madly for my position. Then their consciences would flare up, so to honor *my* memory they would put together a collection of *their* essays about John Donne. The volume would begin with a warm introduction, capturing my most endearing qualities. It would be short. But sweet.

Published *and* perished.[4]

Now, watch this. I have to ring the bell [*She presses the button on the bed.*] to get someone to come and measure this emesis, and record the amount on a chart of my intake and output. This counts as output. [SUSIE *enters.*]

SUSIE: [*Brightly.*] How you doing, Ms. Bearing? You having some nausea?
VIVIAN: [*Weakly.*] Uhh, yes.
SUSIE: Why don't I take that? Here.
VIVIAN: It's about 300 cc's.
SUSIE: That all?
VIVIAN: It was very hard work. [SUSIE *takes the basin to the bathroom and rinses it.*]
SUSIE: Yup. Three hundred. Good guess. [*She marks the graph.*] Okay.
  Anything else I can get for you? Some Jell-O or anything?
VIVIAN: Thank you, no.
SUSIE: You okay all by yourself here?
VIVIAN: Yes.
SUSIE: You're not having a lot of visitors, are you?
VIVIAN: [*Correcting.*] None, to be precise.
SUSIE: Yeah, I didn't think so. Is there somebody you want me to call for you?
VIVIAN: That won't be necessary.
SUSIE: Well, I'll just pop my head in every once in a while to see how you're coming along. Kelekian and the fellows should be in soon. [*She touches* VIVIAN'*s arm.*] If there's anything you need, you just ring.
VIVIAN: [*Uncomfortable with kindness.*] Thank you.
SUSIE: Okay. Just call. [SUSIE *disconnects the IV bottle with the orange label and takes it with her as she leaves.* VIVIAN *lies still. Silence. Scene change.*]
VIVIAN: In this dramatic structure you will see the most interesting aspects of my tenure as an inpatient receiving experimental chemotherapy for advanced metastatic ovarian cancer.
  But as I am a *scholar* before ... an impresario,[5] I feel obliged to document what it is like here most of the time, between the dramatic climaxes. Between the spectacles.
  In truth, it is like this: [*She ceremoniously lies back and stares at the ceiling.*] You cannot imagine how time ... can be ... so still.
  It hangs. It weighs. And yet there is so little of it.
  It goes so slowly, and yet it is so scarce. [*Pause.*]
  If I were writing this scene, it would last a full fifteen minutes. I would lie here, and you would sit there. [*She looks at the audience, daring them.*]

---

[4]. In colleges and universities the common saying is "publish or perish," because a professor's promotion and tenure or job security depend on publishing scholarly research. Vivian Bearing has just imagined a predictable memorial for a scholar of her eminence, a *festschrift* or collection of essays in honor of a senior scholar in a field. *Emesis:* vomiting.    [5]. Theatrical manager or producer; showman.

Not to worry. Brevity is the soul of wit.[6]

But if you think eight months of cancer treatment is tedious for the *audience*, consider how it feels to play my part.

All right. All right. It is Friday morning: Grand Rounds. [*Loudly, giving a cue.*] Action. [KELEKIAN *enters, followed by* JASON *and four other* FELLOWS.]

KELEKIAN: Dr. Bearing.

VIVIAN: Dr. Kelekian.

KELEKIAN: Jason. [JASON *moves to the front of the group.*]

JASON: Professor Bearing. How are you feeling today?

VIVIAN: Fine.

JASON: That's great. That's just great. [*He takes a sheet and carefully covers her legs and groin, then pulls up her gown to reveal her entire abdomen. He is barely audible, but his gestures are clear.*]

VIVIAN: "Grand Rounds."

The term is theirs. Not "Grand" in the traditional sense of sweeping or magnificent. Not "Rounds" as in a musical canon, or a *round* of applause (though either would be refreshing at this point). Here, "Rounds" seems to signify darting *around* the main issue ... which I suppose would be the struggle for life ... *my* life ... with heated discussions of *side* effects, *other* complaints, *additional* treatments.

Grand Rounds is not Grand Opera. But compared to lying here, it is positively *dramatic*.

Full of subservience, hierarchy, gratuitous displays, sublimated rivalries—I feel right at home. It is just like a graduate seminar.

With one important difference: in Grand Rounds, *they* read *me* like a book. Once I did the teaching; now I am taught. This is much easier. I just hold still and look cancerous. It requires less acting every time.

Excellent command of details

JASON: Very late detection. Staged as a four upon admission. Hexamethophosphacil with Vinplatin to potentiate.[7] Hex at 300 mg. per meter squared, Vin at 100. Today is cycle two, day three. Both cycles at the *full dose.* [*The* FELLOWS *are impressed.*]

The primary site is—here, [*He puts his finger on the spot on her abdomen.*] behind the left ovary. Metastases are suspected in the peritoneal cavity—here. And—here. [*He touches those spots.*]

Full lymphatic involvement. [*He moves his hands over her entire body.*]

At the time of first-look surgery, a significant part of the tumor was de-bulked, mostly in this area—here. [*He points to each organ, poking her abdomen.*] Left, right ovaries. Fallopian tubes. Uterus. All out.

Evidence of primary-site shrinkage. Shrinking in metastatic tumors has not been documented. Primary mass frankly palpable in pelvic exam, frankly, all through here—here. [*Some* FELLOWS *reach and press where he is pointing.*]

---

6. From Shakespeare's *Hamlet* 2.2, spoken by the verbose Polonius.
7. Hexamethophosphacil and Vinplatin ("Hex" and "Vin"), powerful chemicals used as anti-cancer medicines in chemotherapy.

KELEKIAN: Excellent command of details.
VIVIAN: [*To herself.*] I taught him, you know—
KELEKIAN: Okay. Problem areas with Hex and Vin. [*He addresses all the* FELLOWS, *but* JASON *answers first and they resent him.*]
FELLOW 1: Myelosu—
JASON: [*Interrupting.*] Well, first of course is myelosuppression, a lowering of blood-cell counts. It goes without saying. With this combination of agents, nephrotoxicity will be next.
KELEKIAN: Go on.
JASON: The kidneys are designed to filter out impurities in the bloodstream. In trying to filter the chemotherapeutic agent out of the bloodstream, the kidneys shut down.
KELEKIAN: Intervention.
JASON: Hydration.
KELEKIAN: Monitoring.
JASON: Full recording of fluid intake and output, as you see here on these graphs, to monitor hydration and kidney function. Totals monitored daily by the clinical fellow, as per the protocol.
KELEKIAN: Anybody else. Side effects.
FELLOW 1: Nausea and vomiting.
KELEKIAN: Jason.
JASON: Routine.
FELLOW 2: Pain while urinating.
JASON: Routine. [*The* FELLOWS *are trying to catch* JASON.]
FELLOW 3: Psychological depression.
JASON: No way. [*The* FELLOWS *are silent.*]
KELEKIAN: [*Standing by* VIVIAN *at the head of the bed.*] Anything else. Other complaints with Hexamethophosphacil and Vinplatin. Come on. [*Silence.* KELEKIAN *and* VIVIAN *wait together for the correct answer.*]
FELLOW 4: Mouth sores.
JASON: Not yet.
FELLOW 2: [*Timidly.*] Skin rash?
JASON: Nope.
KELEKIAN: [*Sharing this with* VIVIAN.] Why do we waste our time, Dr. Bearing?
VIVIAN: [*Delighted.*] I do not know, Dr. Kelekian.
KELEKIAN: [*To the* FELLOWS.] Use your eyes. [*All* FELLOWS *look closely at* VIVIAN.] Jesus God. Hair loss.
FELLOWS: [*All protesting.* VIVIAN *and* KELEKIAN *are amused.*]
—Come on.
—You can see it.
—It doesn't count.
—No fair.
KELEKIAN: Jason.
JASON: [*Begrudgingly.*] Hair loss after first cycle of treatment.
KELEKIAN: That's better. [*To* VIVIAN.] Dr. Bearing. Full dose. Excellent. Keep pushing the fluids. [*The* FELLOWS *leave.* KELEKIAN *stops* JASON.] Jason.
JASON: Huh?
KELEKIAN: Clinical.
JASON: Oh, right. [*To* VIVIAN.] Thank you, Professor Bearing. You've been very cooperative. [*They leave her with her stomach uncovered.*]

VIVIAN: Wasn't that . . . Grand? [*She gets up without the IV pole.*] At times, this obsessively detailed examination, this *scrutiny* seems to me to be a nefarious business. On the other hand, what is the alternative? Ignorance? Ignorance may be . . . bliss; but it is not a very noble goal.

So I play my part. [*Pause.*]

I receive chemotherapy, throw up, am subjected to countless indignities, feel better, go home. Eight cycles. Eight neat little strophes.[8] Oh, there have been the usual variations, subplots, red herrings: hepatotoxicity (liver poison), neuropathy (nerve death).

[*Righteously.*] They are medical terms. I look them up.

It has always been my custom to treat words with respect.

I can recall the time—the very hour of the very day—when I knew words would be my life's work.

[*Scene change. A pile of six little white books appears, with* MR. BEARING, *Vivian's father, seated behind an open newspaper.*] It was my fifth birthday. [VIVIAN, *now a child, flops down to the books.*] I liked that one best.

MR. BEARING: [*Disinterested but tolerant, never distracted from his newspaper.*] Read another.

VIVIAN: I think I'll read . . . [*She takes a book from the stack and reads its spine intently.*] *The Tale of the Flopsy Bunnies*. [*Reading the front cover.*] *The Tale of the Flopsy Bunnies*. It has little bunnies on the front. [*Opening to the title page.*] *The Tale of the Flopsy Bunnies* by Beatrix Potter.[9] [*She turns the page and begins to read.*]

It is said that the effect of eating too much lettuce is sopor—sop—or—

what is that word?

MR. BEARING: Sound it out.

VIVIAN: Sop—or—fic. Sop—or—i—fic. Soporific. What does that mean?

MR. BEARING: Soporific. Causing sleep.

VIVIAN: Causing sleep.

MR. BEARING: Makes you sleepy.

VIVIAN: "Soporific" means "makes you sleepy"?

MR. BEARING: Correct.

VIVIAN: "Soporific" means "makes you sleepy." Soporific.

MR. BEARING: Now use it in a sentence. What has a soporific effect on you?

VIVIAN: A soporific effect on me.

MR. BEARING: What makes you sleepy?

VIVIAN: Aahh—nothing.

MR. BEARING: Correct.

VIVIAN: What about you?

MR. BEARING: What has a soporific effect on me? Let me think: boring conversation, I suppose, after dinner.

VIVIAN: Me too, boring conversation.

MR. BEARING: Carry on.

VIVIAN:

It is said that the effect of eating too much lettuce is soporific.

---

8. Sections of a poem.
9. Beatrix Potter (1866–1943) wrote and illustrated many children's tales, including *The Tale of Peter Rabbit* (1902) and *The Tale of the Flopsy Bunnies* (1909).

The little bunnies in the picture are asleep! They're sleeping! Like you said, because of *soporific!* [*She stands up, and* MR. BEARING *exits.*]

The illustration bore out the meaning of the word, just as he had explained it. At the time, it seemed like magic.

So imagine the effect that the words of John Donne first had on me: ratiocination, concatenation, coruscation, tergiversation.[1]

Medical terms are less evocative. Still, I want to know what the doctors mean when they . . . anatomize me. And I will grant that in this particular field of endeavor they possess a more potent arsenal of terminology than I. My only defense is the acquisition of vocabulary.

[*Scene change.* SUSIE *enters and puts her arm around* VIVIAN's *shoulders to hold her up.* VIVIAN *is shaking, feverish, and weak. All at once.*] Fever-and-neutropenia.[2]

SUSIE: When did it start?

VIVIAN: [*Having difficulty speaking.*] I—I was at home—reading—and I—felt so bad. I called. Fever and neutropenia. They said to come in.

SUSIE: You did the right thing to come. Did somebody drive you?

VIVIAN: Cab. I took a taxi.

SUSIE: [*She grabs a wheelchair and helps* VIVIAN *sit. As* SUSIE *speaks, she takes* VIVIAN's *temperature, pulse, and respiration rate.*] Here, why don't you sit? Just sit there a minute. I'll get Jason. He's on call tonight. We'll get him to give you some meds. I'm glad I was here on nights. I'll make sure you get to bed soon, okay? It'll just be a minute. I'll get you some juice, some nice juice with lots of ice. [SUSIE *leaves quickly.* VIVIAN *sits there, agitated, confused, and very sick.* SUSIE *returns with the juice.*]

VIVIAN: Lights. I left all the lights on at my house.

SUSIE: Don't you worry. It'll be all right. [JASON *enters, roused from his sleep and not fully awake. He wears surgical scrubs and puts on a lab coat as he enters.*]

JASON: [*Without looking at* VIVIAN.] How are you feeling, Professor Bearing?

VIVIAN: My teeth—are chattering.

JASON: Vitals.

SUSIE: [*Giving* VIVIAN *juice and a straw, without looking at* JASON.] Temp 39.4. Pulse 120. Respiration 36. Chills and sweating.

JASON: Fever and neutropenia. It's a "shake and bake." Blood cultures and urine, stat. Admit her. Prepare for reverse isolation. Start with acetaminophen. Vitals every four hours. [*He starts to leave.*]

SUSIE: [*Following him.*] Jason—I think you need to talk to Kelekian about lowering the dose for the next cycle. It's too much for her like this.

JASON: Lower the dose? No way. Full dose. She's tough. She can take it. Wake me up when the counts come from the lab. [*He pads off.* SUSIE *wheels* VIVIAN *to her room, and* VIVIAN *collapses on the bed.* SUSIE *connects* VIVIAN's *IV, then wets a washcloth and rubs her face and neck.* VIVIAN *remains delirious.* SUSIE *checks the IV and leaves with the wheelchair.*]

[*After a while,* KELEKIAN *appears in the doorway holding a surgical mask near his face.* JASON *is with him, now dressed and clean-shaven.*]

---

1. That is, thought, connection, flash of wit or insight, and ambiguity or equivocation.
2. Fever and chills.

KELEKIAN: Good morning, Dr. Bearing. Fifth cycle. Full dose. Definite progress. Everything okay.
VIVIAN: [*Weakly.*] Yes.
KELEKIAN: You're doing swell. Isolation is no problem. Couple of days. Think of it as a vacation.
VIVIAN: Oh. [JASON *starts to enter, holding a mask near his face, just like* KELEKIAN.]
KELEKIAN: Jason.
JASON: Oh, Jesus. Okay, okay. [*He returns to the doorway, where he puts on a paper gown, mask, and gloves.* KELEKIAN *leaves.*]
VIVIAN: [*To audience.*] In isolation, I am isolated. For once I can use a term literally. The chemotherapeutic agents eradicating my cancer have also eradicated my immune system. In my present condition, every living thing is a health hazard to me . . . [JASON *comes in to check the intake-and-output.*]
JASON: [*Complaining to himself.*] I really have not got time for this . . .
VIVIAN: . . . particularly health-care professionals.
JASON: [*Going right to the graph on the wall.*] Just to look at the I&O sheets for one minute, and it takes me half an hour to do precautions. Four, seven, eleven. Two-fifty twice. Okay. [*Remembering.*] Oh, Jeez. Clinical. Professor Bearing. How are you feeling today?
VIVIAN: [*Very sick.*] Fine. Just shaking sometimes from the chills.
JASON: IV will kick in anytime now. No problem. Listen, gotta go. Keep pushing the fluids. [*As he exits, he takes off the gown, mask, and gloves.*]
VIVIAN: [*Getting up from bed with her IV pole and resuming her explanation.*] I am not in isolation because I have cancer, because I have a tumor the size of a grapefruit. No. I am in isolation because I am being treated for cancer. My treatment imperils my health.

Herein lies the paradox. John Donne would revel in it. I would revel in it, if he wrote a poem about it. My students would flounder in it, because paradox is too difficult to understand. Think of it as a puzzle, I would tell them, an intellectual game. [*She is trapped.*]

Or, I *would have* told them. Were it a game. Which it is not.

[*Escaping.*] If they were here, if I were lecturing: How I would *perplex* them! I could work my students into a frenzy. Every ambiguity, every shifting awareness. I could draw so much from the poems.

I could be so powerful.

[*Scene change. Vivian stands still, as if conjuring a scene. Now at the height of her powers, she grandly disconnects herself from the IV.* TECHNICIANS *remove the bed and hand her a pointer.*] The poetry of the early seventeenth century, what has been called the metaphysical school, considers an intractable mental puzzle by exercising the outstanding human faculty of the era, namely wit.

The greatest wit—the greatest English poet, some would say—was John Donne. In the Holy Sonnets, Donne applied his capacious, agile wit to the larger aspects of the human experience: life, death, and God.

In his poems, metaphysical quandaries are addressed, but never resolved. Ingenuity, virtuosity, and a vigorous intellect that jousts with the most exalted concepts: these are the tools of wit. [*The lights dim. A screen lowers, and the sonnet "If poysonous mineralls," from the Gardner edition, appears on it.* VIVIAN *recites.*]

> If poysonous mineralls, and if that tree,
> Whose fruit threw death on else immortall us,
> If lecherous goats, if serpents envious
> Cannot be damn'd; Alas; why should I bee?
> Why should intent or reason, borne in mee,
> Make sinnes, else equall, in mee, more heinous?
> And mercy being easie, and glorious
> To God, in his sterne wrath, why threatens hee?
> But who am I, that dare dispute with thee?
> O God, Oh! of thine onely worthy blood,
> And my teares, make a heavenly Lethean flood,
> And drowne in it my sinnes blacke memorie.
> That thou remember them, some claime as debt,
> I thinke it mercy, if thou wilt forget.

[VIVIAN *whacks the word on the screen with a pointer at every asterisk (\*). She moves around as she lectures.*]

Aggressive intellect. [*Line 1.*] Pious melodrama. [*Line 10.*] And a final, fearful point. [*Line 14.*] Donne's Holy Sonnet Five, 1609. From the Ashford edition, based on Gardner.

The speaker of the sonnet has a brilliant mind, and he plays the part convincingly; but in the end he finds God's *forgiveness* hard to believe, so he crawls under a rock to *hide*.

If [\*] arsenic [\**mineralls*] and serpents [\*] are not damned, then why is he? In asking the question, the speaker turns eternal damnation into an intellectual game. Why would God choose to do what is *hard*, to condemn, rather than what is *easy*, and also *glorious*—to show mercy?

(Several scholars have disputed Ashford's third comma [\*] in line six, but none convincingly.)

But. [\*] Exception. Limitation. Contrast. The argument shifts from cleverness to melodrama, an unconvincing eruption of piety: "O" [\*] "God" [\*] "Oh." [\*]

A typical prayer would plead "Remember me, O Lord." (This point is nicely explicated in an article by Richard Strier—a former student of mine who once sat where you do now, although I dare say *he* was *awake*—in the May 1989 issue of *Modern Philology*.) True believers ask to be *remembered* by God. The speaker of this sonnet asks God to *forget*. [\*] [VIVIAN *moves in front of the screen, and the projection of the poem is cast directly upon her.*] Where is the hyperactive intellect of the first section? Where is the histrionic outpouring of the second? When the speaker considers his own *sins*, and the inevitability of God's *judgment*, he can conceive of but one resolution: to *disappear*. [VIVIAN *moves away from the screen.*] Doctrine assures us that no sinner is denied *forgiveness*, not even one whose sins are overweening *intellect* [\* *Top half.*] or overwrought *dramatics*. [\**Bottom half.*] The speaker does not need to *hide* from God's *judgment*, only to *accept* God's *forgiveness*. It is very simple. Suspiciously simple.

We want to correct the speaker, to remind him of the assurance of salvation. But it is too late. The poetic encounter is over. We are left to our own consciences. Have we outwitted Donne? Or have we been outwitted? [SUSIE *comes on.*]

SUSIE: Ms. Bearing?
VIVIAN: [*Continuing.*] Will the po—
SUSIE: Ms. Bearing?
VIVIAN: [*Crossly.*] What is it?
SUSIE: You have to go down for a test. Jason just called. They want another ultrasound. They're concerned about a bowel obstruction— Is it okay if I come in?
VIVIAN: No. Not now.
SUSIE: I'm sorry, but they want it now.
VIVIAN: Not right now. It's not *supposed* to be now.
SUSIE: Yes, they want to do it now. I've got the chair.
VIVIAN: It should not be now. I am in the middle of—this. I have *this* planned for now, not ultrasound. No more tests. We've covered that.
SUSIE: I know, I know, but they need for it to be now. It won't take long, and it isn't a bad procedure. Why don't you just come along.
VIVIAN: *I do not want to go now!*
SUSIE: Ms. Bearing. [*Silence.* VIVIAN *raises the screen, walks away from the scene, hooks herself to the IV, and gets in the wheelchair.* SUSIE *wheels* VIVIAN, *and a* TECHNICIAN *takes her.*]
TECHNICIAN: Name.
VIVIAN: B-E-A-R-I-N-G. Kelekian.
TECHNICIAN: It'll just be a minute.
VIVIAN: Time for your break.
TECHNICIAN: Yup. [*The* TECHNICIAN *leaves.*]
VIVIAN: [*Mordantly.*] Take a break! [*Scene change.* VIVIAN *sits weakly in the wheelchair.*]

> This is my playes last scene, here heavens appoint
> My pilgrimages last mile; and my race
> Idly, yet quickly runne, hath this last pace,
> My spans last inch, my minutes last point,
> And gluttonous death will instantly unjoynt
> My body, and soule

John Donne. 1609.[3] I have always particularly liked that poem. In the abstract. Now I find the image of "my minute's last point" a little too, shall we say, *pointed*.

I don't mean to complain, but I am becoming very sick. Very, very sick. Ultimately sick, as it were.

In everything I have done, I have been steadfast, resolute—some would say in the extreme. Now, as you can see, I am distinguishing myself in illness.

I have survived eight treatments of Hexamethophosphacil and Vinplatin at the *full* dose, ladies and gentlemen. I have broken the record. I have become something of a celebrity. Kelekian and Jason are simply delighted. I think they foresee celebrity status for themselves upon the appearance of the journal article they will no doubt write about me.

But I flatter myself. The article will not be about me, it will be about my ovaries. It will be about my peritoneal cavity, which, despite their best intentions, is now crawling with cancer.

---

3. Vivian Bearing has quoted, with some variants, the first lines of a sonnet by Donne.

What we have come to think of as *me* is, in fact, just the specimen jar, just the dust jacket, just the white piece of paper that bears the little black marks.

My next line is supposed to be something like this:

"It is such a *relief* to get back to my room after those infernal tests."

This is hardly true. It would be a *relief* to be a cheerleader on her way to Daytona Beach for Spring Break.

To get back to my room after those infernal tests is just the next thing that happens.

[*Scene change. She returns to her bed, which now has a commode next to it. She is very sick.*] Oh, God. It is such a relief to get back to my goddamn room after those goddamn tests. [JASON *enters.*]

JASON: Professor Bearing. Just want to check the I&O. Four-fifty, six, five. Okay. How are you feeling today? [*He makes notations on his clipboard throughout the scene.*]

VIVIAN: Fine.

JASON: That's great. Just great.

VIVIAN: How are my fluids?

JASON: Pretty good. No kidney involvement yet. That's pretty amazing, with Hex and Vin.

VIVIAN: How will you know when the kidneys are involved?

JASON: Lots of in, not much out.

VIVIAN: That simple.

JASON: Oh, no way. Compromised kidney function is a highly complex reaction. I'm simplifying for you.

VIVIAN: Thank you.

JASON: We're supposed to.

VIVIAN: Bedside manner.

JASON: Yeah, there's a whole course on it in med school. It's required. Colossal waste of time for researchers. [*He turns to go.*]

VIVIAN: I can imagine. [*Trying to ask something important.*] Jason?

JASON: Huh?

VIVIAN: [*Not sure of herself.*] Ah, what . . . [*Quickly.*] What were you just saying?

JASON: When?

VIVIAN: Never mind.

JASON: Professor Bearing?

VIVIAN: Yes.

JASON: Are you experiencing confusion? Short-term memory loss?

VIVIAN: No.

JASON: Sure?

VIVIAN: Yes. [*Pause.*] I was just wondering: why cancer?

JASON: Why cancer?

VIVIAN: Why not open-heart surgery?

JASON: Oh yeah, why not *plumbing*. Why not run a *lube rack,* for all the surgeons know about *Homo sapiens sapiens*. No way. Cancer's the only thing I ever wanted.

VIVIAN: [*Intrigued.*] Huh.

JASON: No, really. Cancer is . . . [*Searching.*]

VIVIAN: [*Helping.*] Awesome.

JASON: [*Pause.*] Yeah. Yeah, that's right. It is. It is awesome. How does it do it?

The intercellular regulatory mechanisms—especially for proliferation and differentiation—the malignant neoplasia just don't get it. You grow normal cells in tissue culture in the lab, and they replicate just enough to make a nice, confluent monolayer. They divide twenty times, or fifty times, but eventually they conk out. You grow cancer cells, and they never stop. No contact inhibition whatsoever. They just pile up, just keep replicating forever. [*Pause.*] That's got a funny name. Know what it is?

VIVIAN: No. What?

JASON: Immortality in culture.

VIVIAN: Sounds like a symposium.

JASON: It's an error in judgment, in a molecular way. But *why*? Even on the protistic level[4] the normal cell-cell interactions are so subtle they'll take your breath away. Golden-brown algae, for instance, the lowest multicellular life form on earth—they're *idiots*—and it's incredible. It's perfect. So what's up with the cancer cells? Smartest guys in the world, with the best labs, funding—they don't know what to make of it.

VIVIAN: What about you?

JASON: Me? Oh, I've got a couple of ideas, things I'm kicking around. Wait till I get a lab of my own. If I can survive this . . . *fellowship*.

VIVIAN: The part with the human beings.

JASON: Everybody's got to go through it. All the great researchers. They want us to be able to converse intelligently with the clinicians. As though *researchers* were the impediments. The clinicians are such troglodytes. So smarmy. Like we have to hold hands to discuss creatinine clearance.[5] Just cut the crap, I say.

VIVIAN: Are you going to be sorry when— Do you ever miss people?

JASON: Everybody asks that. Especially girls.

VIVIAN: What do you tell them?

JASON: I tell them yes.

VIVIAN: Are they persuaded?

JASON: Some.

VIVIAN: Some. I see. [*With great difficulty.*] And what do you say when a patient is . . . apprehensive . . . frightened.

JASON: Of who?

VIVIAN: I just . . . Never mind.

JASON: Professor Bearing, who is the President of the United States?

VIVIAN: I'm fine, really. It's all right.

JASON: You sure? I could order a test—

VIVIAN: No! No, I'm fine. Just a little tired.

JASON: Okay. Look. Gotta go. Keep pushing the fluids. Try for 2,000 a day, okay?

VIVIAN: Okay. To use your word. Okay. [JASON *leaves. Getting out of bed, without her IV.*]

So. The young doctor, like the senior scholar, prefers research to humanity. At the same time the senior scholar, in her pathetic state as a simpering victim, wishes the young doctor would take more interest in personal contact.

---

4. That is, on the level of one-celled microbes.   5. Urination.

Now I suppose we shall see, through a series of flashbacks, how the senior scholar ruthlessly denied her simpering students the touch of human kindness she now seeks.

[*Scene change.* STUDENTS *appear, sitting at chairs with writing desks attached to the right arm. She suddenly commands attention.*]

How then would you characterize [*Pointing to a* STUDENT.]—you.
STUDENT 1: Huh?
VIVIAN: How would you characterize the animating force of this sonnet?
STUDENT 1: Huh?
VIVIAN: In this sonnet; what is the principal poetic device? I'll give you a hint. It has nothing to do with football. What propels this sonnet?
STUDENT 1: Um.
VIVIAN: [*Speaking to the audience.*] Did I say [*Tenderly.*] "You are nineteen years old. You are so young. You don't know a sonnet from a steak sandwich." [*Pause.*] By no means.

[*Sharply, to* STUDENT 1.] You can come to this class prepared, or you can excuse yourself from this class, this department, and this university. Do not think for a moment that I will tolerate anything in between.

[*To the audience, defensively.*] I was teaching him a lesson. [*She walks away from* STUDENT 1, *then turns and addresses the class.*]

So we have another instance of John Donne's agile wit at work: not so much *resolving* the issues of life and God as *reveling* in their complexity.
STUDENT 2: But why?
VIVIAN: Why what?
STUDENT 2: Why does Donne make everything so *complicated*? [*The other* STUDENTS *laugh in agreement.*] No, really, *why*?
VIVIAN: [*To the audience.*] You know, someone asked me that every year. And it was always one of the smart ones. What could I say? [*To* STUDENT 2.] What do you think?
STUDENT 2: I think it's like he's hiding. I think he's really confused, I don't know, maybe he's scared, so he hides behind all this complicated stuff, hides behind this *wit*.
VIVIAN: *Hides* behind *wit*?
STUDENT 2: I mean, if it's really something he's sure of, he can say it more simple—simply. He doesn't have to be such a brain, or such a performer. It doesn't have to be such a big deal. [*The other* STUDENTS *encourage him.*]
VIVIAN: Perhaps he is suspicious of simplicity.
STUDENT 2: Perhaps, but that's pretty stupid.
VIVIAN: [*To the audience.*] That observation, despite its infelicitous phrasing, contained the seed of a perspicacious remark. Such an unlikely occurrence left me with two choices. I could draw it out, or I could allow the brain to rest after that heroic effort. If I pursued, there was the chance of great insight, or the risk of undergraduate banality. I could never predict. [*To* STUDENT 2.] Go on.
STUDENT 2: Well, if he's trying to figure out God, and the meaning of life, and big stuff like that, why does he keep running away, you know?
VIVIAN: [*To the audience, moving closer to* STUDENT 2.] So far so good, but they can think for themselves only so long before they begin to self-destruct.

STUDENT 2: Um, it's like, the more you hide, the less—no, wait—the more you are getting closer—although you don't know it—and the simple thing is there—you see what I mean?
VIVIAN: [*To the audience, looking at* STUDENT 2, *as suspense collapses.*] Lost it.

[*She walks away and speaks to the audience.*] I distinctly remember an exchange between two students after my lecture on pronunciation and scansion. I overheard them talking on their way out of class. They were young and bright, gathering their books and laughing at the expense of seventeenth-century poetry, at my expense.

[*To the class.*] To scan the line properly, we must take advantage of the contemporary flexibility in "i-o-n" endings, as in "expansion." The quatrain stands:

> Our two souls therefore, which are one,
>    Though I must go, endure not yet
> A breach, but an ex-*pan*-see-on,
>    Like gold to airy thinness beat.[6]

Bear this in mind in your reading. That's all for today.

[*The* STUDENTS *get up in a chaotic burst.* STUDENT 3 *and* STUDENT 4 *pass by* VIVIAN *on their way out.*]

STUDENT 3: I hope I can get used to this pronuncia-see-on.
STUDENT 4: I know. I hope I can survive this course and make it to gradua-see-on. [*They laugh.* VIVIAN *glowers at them. They fall silent, embarrassed.*]
VIVIAN: [*To the audience.*] That was a witty little exchange, I must admit. It showed the mental acuity I would praise in a poetic text. But I admired only the studied application of wit, not its spontaneous eruption. [STUDENT 1 *interrupts.*]
STUDENT 1: Professor Bearing? Can I talk to you for a minute?
VIVIAN: You may.
STUDENT 1: I need to ask for an extension on my paper. I'm really sorry, and I know your policy, but see—
VIVIAN: Don't tell me. Your grandmother died.
STUDENT 1: You knew.
VIVIAN: It was a guess.
STUDENT 1: I have to go home.
VIVIAN: Do what you will, but the paper is due when it is due. [*As* STUDENT 1 *leaves and the classroom disappears,* VIVIAN *watches. Pause.*]

I don't know. I feel so much—what is the word? I look back, I see these scenes, and I . . . [*Long silence.* VIVIAN *walks absently around the stage, trying to think of something. Finally, giving up, she trudges back to bed. Scene change.*]

It was late at night, the graveyard shift. Susie was on. I could hear her in the hall.

I wanted her to come and see me. So I had to create a little emergency. Nothing dramatic. [VIVIAN *pinches the IV tubing. The pump alarm beeps.*]

It worked. [SUSIE *enters, concerned.*]

---

6. From Donne's poem "A Valediction: Forbidding Mourning," lines 21–24. (See page 1244.)

SUSIE: Ms. Bearing? Is that you beeping at four in the morning? [*She checks the tubing and presses buttons on the pump. The alarm stops.*] Did that wake you up? I'm sorry. It just gets occluded sometimes.
VIVIAN: I was awake.
SUSIE: You were? What's the trouble, sweetheart?
VIVIAN: [*To the audience, roused.*] Do not think for a minute that anyone calls me "Sweetheart." But then . . . I allowed it. [*To* SUSIE.] Oh, I don't know.
SUSIE: You can't sleep?
VIVIAN: No. I just keep thinking.
SUSIE: If you do that too much, you can get kind of confused.
VIVIAN: I know. I can't figure things out. I'm in a . . . *quandary,* having these . . . doubts.
SUSIE: What you're doing is very hard.
VIVIAN: Hard things are what I like best.
SUSIE: It's not the same. It's like it's out of control, isn't it?
VIVIAN: [*Crying, in spite of herself.*] I'm scared.
SUSIE: [*Stroking her.*] Oh, honey, of course you are.
VIVIAN: I want . . .
SUSIE: I know. It's hard.
VIVIAN: I don't feel sure of myself anymore.
SUSIE: And you used to feel sure.
VIVIAN: [*Crying.*] Oh, yes, I used to feel sure.
SUSIE: Vivian. It's all right. I know. It hurts. I know. It's all right. Do you want a tissue? It's all right. [*Silence.*] Vivian, would you like a Popsicle?
VIVIAN: [*Like a child.*] Yes, please.
SUSIE: I'll get it for you. I'll be right back.
VIVIAN: Thank you. [SUSIE *leaves. Pulling herself together.*] The epithelial cells in my GI tract have been killed by the chemo.[7] The cold Popsicle feels good, it's something I can digest, and it helps keep me hydrated. For your information.
    [SUSIE *returns with an orange two-stick Popsicle.* VIVIAN *unwraps it and breaks it in half.*] Here.
SUSIE: Sure?
VIVIAN: Yes.
SUSIE: Thanks. [SUSIE *sits on the commode by the bed. Silence.*] When I was a kid, we used to get these from a truck. The man would come around and ring his bell and we'd all run over. Then we'd sit on the curb and eat our Popsicles.
    Pretty profound, huh?
VIVIAN: It sounds nice. [*Silence.*]
SUSIE: Vivian, there's something we need to talk about, you need to think about. [*Silence.*]
VIVIAN: My cancer is not being cured, is it.
SUSIE: Huh-uh.
VIVIAN: They never expected it to be, did they.
SUSIE: Well, they thought the drugs would make the tumor get smaller, and it has gotten a lot smaller. But the problem is that it started in new places too. They've learned a lot for their research. It was the best thing they had

---

7. That is, the cells of the inner surface of my gastrointestinal tract have been killed by the chemotherapy.

to give you, the strongest drugs. There just isn't a good treatment for what you have yet, for advanced ovarian. I'm sorry. They should have explained this—

VIVIAN: I knew.

SUSIE: You did.

VIVIAN: I read between the lines.

SUSIE: What you have to think about is your "code status." What you want them to do if your heart stops.

VIVIAN: Well.

SUSIE: You can be "full code," which means that if your heart stops, they'll call a Code Blue and the code team will come and resuscitate you and take you to Intensive Care until you stabilize again. Or you can be "Do Not Resuscitate," so if your heart stops we'll . . . well, we'll just let it. You'll be "DNR." You can think about it, but I wanted to present both choices before Kelekian and Jason talk to you.

VIVIAN: You don't agree about this?

SUSIE: Well, they like to save lives. So anything's okay, as long as life continues. It doesn't matter if you're hooked up to a million machines. Kelekian is a great researcher and everything. And the fellows, like Jason, they're really smart. It's really an honor for them to work with him. But they always . . . want to know more things.

VIVIAN: I always want to know more things. I'm a scholar. Or I was when I had shoes, when I had eyebrows.

SUSIE: Well, okay then. You'll be full code. That's fine. [*Silence.*]

VIVIAN: No, don't complicate the matter.

SUSIE: It's okay. It's up to you—

VIVIAN: Let it stop.

SUSIE: Really?

VIVIAN: Yes.

SUSIE: So if your heart stops beating—

VIVIAN: Just let it stop.

SUSIE: Sure?

VIVIAN: Yes.

SUSIE: Okay. I'll get Kelekian to give the order, and then—

VIVIAN: Susie?

SUSIE: Uh-huh?

VIVIAN: You're still going to take care of me, aren't you?

SUSIE: 'Course, sweetheart. Don't you worry. [*As* SUSIE *leaves,* VIVIAN *sits upright, full of energy and rage.*]

VIVIAN: That certainly was a *maudlin* display. Popsicles? "Sweetheart"? I can't believe my life has become so . . . corny.

But it can't be helped. I don't see any other way. We are discussing life and death, and not in the abstract, either; we are discussing *my* life and *my* death, and my brain is dulling and poor Susie's was never very sharp to begin with, and I can't conceive of any other . . . *tone.*

[*Quickly.*] Now is not the time for verbal swordplay, for unlikely flights of imagination and wildly shifting perspectives, for metaphysical conceit, for wit.

And nothing would be worse than a detailed scholarly analysis. Erudition. Interpretation. Complication.

[*Slowly.*] Now is a time for simplicity. Now is a time for, dare I say it, kindness.

[*Searchingly.*] I thought being extremely smart would take care of it. But I see that I have been found out. Ooohhh.

I'm scared. Oh, God. I want . . . I want . . . No. I want to hide. I just want to curl up in a little ball. [*She dives under the covers. Scene change.* VIVIAN *wakes in horrible pain. She is tense, agitated, fearful. Slowly she calms down and addresses the audience. Trying extremely hard.*]

I want to tell you how it feels. I want to explain it, to use *my* words. It's as if . . . I can't . . . There aren't . . . I'm like a student and this is the final exam and I don't know what to put down because I don't understand the question and I'm *running out of time.* [*Pause.*]

The time for extreme measures has come. I am in terrible pain. Susie says that I need to begin aggressive pain management if I am going to stand it.

"It": such a little word. In this case, I think "it" signifies "being alive."

I apologize in advance for what this palliative treatment modality[8] does to the dramatic coherence of my play's last scene. It can't be helped. They have to do something. I'm in terrible pain.

Say it, Vivian. It hurts like hell. It really does. [SUSIE *enters.* VIVIAN *is writhing in pain.*]

Oh, God. Oh, God.

SUSIE: Sshh. It's okay. Sshh. I paged Kelekian up here, and we'll get you some meds.

VIVIAN: Oh, God, it is so painful. So painful. So much pain. So much pain.

SUSIE: I know, I know, it's okay. Sshh. Just try and clear your mind. It's all right. We'll get you a Patient-Controlled Analgesic. It's a little pump, and you push a little button, and you decide how much medication you want. [*Importantly.*] It's very simple, and it's up to you. [KELEKIAN *storms in;* JASON *follows with chart.*]

KELEKIAN: Dr. Bearing. Susie.

SUSIE: Time for Patient-Controlled Analgesic. The pain is killing her.

KELEKIAN: Dr. Bearing, are you in pain? [KELEKIAN *holds out his hand for chart;* JASON *hands it to him. They read.*]

VIVIAN: [*Sitting up, unnoticed by the staff.*] Am I in pain? I don't believe this. Yes, I'm in goddamn pain. [*Furious.*] I have a fever of 101 spiking to 104. And I have bone metastases in my pelvis and both femurs.[9] [*Screaming.*] There is cancer eating away at my goddamn bones, and I did not know there could be such pain on this earth.

[*She flops back on the bed and cries audibly to them.*] Oh, God.

KELEKIAN: [*Looking at* VIVIAN *intently.*] I want a morphine drip.

SUSIE: What about Patient-Controlled? She could be more alert—

KELEKIAN: [*Teaching.*] Ordinarily, yes. But in her case, no.

SUSIE: But—

KELEKIAN: [*To* SUSIE.] She's earned a rest. [*To* JASON.] Morphine, ten push now, then start at ten an hour. [*To* VIVIAN.] Dr. Bearing, try to relax. We're going to help you through this, don't worry. Dr. Bearing? Excellent. [*He squeezes* VIVIAN's *shoulder. They all leave.*]

---

8. That is, method of treatment for pain.
9. That is, cancerous tumors in my pelvis bone and both thighbones.

VIVIAN: [*Weakly, painfully, leaning on her IV pole, she moves to address the audience.*] Hi. How are you feeling today? [*Silence.*]

These are my last coherent lines. I'll have to leave the action to the professionals.

It came so quickly, after taking so long. Not even time for a proper conclusion. [VIVIAN *concentrates with all her might, and she attempts a grand summation, as if trying to conjure her own ending.*]

> And Death—*capital D*—shall be no more—*semicolon.*
> Death—*capital D*—thou shalt die—*ex-cla-mation point!*

[*She looks down at herself, looks out at the audience, and sees that the line doesn't work. She shakes her head and exhales with resignation.*]

I'm sorry.

[*Scene change. She gets back into bed as* SUSIE *injects morphine into the IV tubing.* VIVIAN *lies down and, in a final melodramatic gesture, shuts the lids of her own eyes and folds her arms over her chest.*] I trust this will have a soporific effect.

SUSIE: Well, I don't know about that, but it sure makes you sleepy. [*This strikes* VIVIAN *as delightfully funny. She starts to giggle, then laughs out loud.* SUSIE *doesn't get it.*] What's so funny? [VIVIAN *keeps laughing.*] What?

VIVIAN: Oh! It's that—"Soporific" means "makes you sleepy."

SUSIE: It does?

VIVIAN: Yes. [*Another fit of laughter.*]

SUSIE: [*Giggling.*] Well, that was pretty dumb—

VIVIAN: No! No, no! It was *funny!*

SUSIE: [*Starting to catch on.*] Yeah, I guess so. [*Laughing.*] In a dumb sort of way. [*This sets them both off laughing again.*] I never would have gotten it. I'm glad you explained it.

VIVIAN: [*Simply.*] I'm a teacher. [*They laugh a little together. Slowly the morphine kicks in, and* VIVIAN's *laugh become long sighs. Finally she falls asleep.* SUSIE *checks everything out, then leaves. Long silence. Scene change.* JASON *and* SUSIE *chat as they enter to insert a catheter.*]

JASON: Oh, yeah. She was a great scholar. Wrote tons of books, articles, was the head of everything. [*He checks the I&O sheet.*] Two hundred. Seventy-five. Five-twenty. Let's up the hydration. She won't be drinking anymore. See if we can keep her kidneys from fading. Yeah, I had a lot of respect for her, which is more than I can say for the *entire* biochemistry department.

SUSIE: What do you want? Dextrose?

JASON: Give her saline.

SUSIE: Okay.

JASON: She gave a hell of a lecture. No notes, not a word out of place. It was pretty impressive. A lot of students hated her, though.

SUSIE: Why?

JASON: Well, she wasn't exactly a cupcake.

SUSIE: [*Laughing, fondly.*] Well, she hasn't exactly been a cupcake here, either. [*Leaning over* VIVIAN *and talking loudly and slowly in her ear.*] Now, Ms. Bearing, Jason and I are here, and we're going to insert a catheter to collect your urine. It's not going to hurt, don't you worry. [*During the conversation she inserts the catheter.*]

JASON: Like she can hear you.

SUSIE: It's just nice to do.

JASON: Eight cycles of Hex and Vin at the full dose. Kelekian didn't think it was possible. I wish they could all get through it at full throttle. Then we could really have some data.

SUSIE: She's not what I imagined. I thought somebody who studied poetry would be sort of dreamy, you know?

JASON: Oh, not the way she did it. It felt more like boot camp than English class. This guy John Donne was incredibly intense. Like your whole brain had to be in knots before you could get it.

SUSIE: He made it hard on purpose?

JASON: Well, it has to do with the subject. The Holy Sonnets we worked on most, they were mostly about Salvation Anxiety. That's a term I made up in one of my papers, but I think it fits pretty well. Salvation Anxiety. You're this brilliant guy, I mean, brilliant—this guy makes Shakespeare sound like a Hallmark card. And you know you're a sinner. And there's this promise of salvation, the whole religious thing. But you just can't deal with it.

SUSIE: How come?

JASON: It just doesn't stand up to scrutiny. But you can't face life without it either. So you write these screwed-up sonnets. Everything is brilliantly convoluted. Really tricky stuff. Bouncing off the walls. Like a game, to make the puzzle so complicated. [*The catheter is inserted.* SUSIE *puts things away.*]

SUSIE: But what happens in the end?

JASON: End of what?

SUSIE: To John Donne. Does he ever get it?

JASON: Get what?

SUSIE: His Salvation Anxiety. Does he ever understand?

JASON: Oh, no way. The puzzle takes over. You're not even trying to solve it anymore. Fascinating, really. Great training for lab research. Looking at things in increasing levels of complexity.

SUSIE: Until what?

JASON: What do you mean?

SUSIE: Where does it end? Don't you get to solve the puzzle?

JASON: Nah. When it comes right down to it, research is just trying to quantify the complications of the puzzle.

SUSIE: But you *help* people! You save lives and stuff.

JASON: Oh, yeah, I save some guy's life, and then the poor slob gets hit by a bus!

SUSIE: [*Confused.*] Yeah, I guess so. I just don't think of it that way. Guess you can tell I never took a class in poetry.

JASON: Listen, if there's one thing we learned in Seventeenth-Century Poetry, it's that you can forget about that sentimental stuff. *Enzyme Kinetics* was more poetic than Bearing's class. Besides, you can't think about that *meaning-of-life* garbage all the time or you'd go nuts.

SUSIE: Do you believe in it?

JASON: In what?

SUSIE: Umm. I don't know, the meaning-of-life garbage. [*She laughs a little.*]

JASON: What do they *teach* you in nursing school? [*Checking Vivian's pulse.*] She's out of it. Shouldn't be too long. You done here?

SUSIE: Yeah, I'll just . . . tidy up.

JASON: See ya. [*He leaves.*]

SUSIE: Bye, Jace. [*She thinks for a minute, then carefully rubs baby oil on* VIVIAN*'s hands. She checks the catheter, then leaves. Scene change.* PROFESSOR E. M. ASHFORD, *now eighty, enters.*]

E. M.: Vivian? Vivian? It's Evelyn. Vivian?

VIVIAN: [*Waking, slurred.*] Oh, God. [*Surprised.*] Professor Ashford. Oh, God.

E. M.: I'm in town visiting my great-grandson, who is celebrating his fifth birthday. I went to see you at your office, and they directed me here. [*She lays her jacket, scarf, and parcel on the bed.*] I have been walking all over town. I had forgotten how early it gets chilly here.

VIVIAN: [*Weakly.*] I feel so bad.

E. M.: I know you do. I can see. [VIVIAN *cries.*] Oh, dear, there, there. There, there. [VIVIAN *cries more, letting the tears flow.*] Vivian, Vivian.

[E. M. *looks toward the hall, then furtively slips off her shoes and swings up on the bed. She puts her arm around* VIVIAN.] There, there. There, there, Vivian. [*Silence.*] It's a windy day. [*Silence.*]

Don't worry, dear. [*Silence.*]

Let's see. Shall I recite to you? Would you like that? I'll recite something by Donne.

VIVIAN: [*Moaning.*] Nooooooo.

E.M.: Very well. [*Silence.*] Hmmm. [*Silence.*] Little Jeffrey is very sweet. Gets into everything.

[*Silence.* E. M. *takes a children's book out of the paper bag and begins reading.* VIVIAN *nestles in, drifting in and out of sleep.*] Let's see. *The Runaway Bunny.* By Margaret Wise Brown. Pictures by Clement Hurd. Copyright 1942. First Harper Trophy Edition, 1972.[1]

Now then.

> Once there was a little bunny who wanted to run away.
> So he said to his mother, "I am running away."
> "If you run away," said his mother, "I will run after you. For you are my little bunny."
> "If you run after me," said the little bunny, "I will become a fish in a trout stream and I will swim away from you."
> "If you become a fish in a trout stream," said his mother, "I will become a fisherman and I will fish for you."

[*Thinking out loud.*] Look at that. A little allegory of the soul.

No matter where it hides, God will find it. See, Vivian?

VIVIAN: [*Moaning.*] Uhhhhhh.

E. M.:

> "If you become a fisherman," said the little bunny, "I will be a bird and fly away from you."
> "If you become a bird and fly away from me," said his mother, "I will be a tree that you come home to."

---

1. Margaret Wise Brown (1910–1952) wrote numerous children's books. *The Runaway Bunny,* which is still in print, is represented in accurate detail in the play.

[*To herself.*] Very clever.

"Shucks," said the little bunny, "I might just as well stay where I am and be your little bunny."
And so he did.

"Have a carrot," said the mother bunny.

[*To herself.*] Wonderful. [VIVIAN *is now fast asleep.* E. M. *slowly gets down and gathers her things. She leans over and kisses her.*]

It's time to go. And flights of angels sing thee to thy rest.[2]

[*She leaves.* JASON *strides in and goes directly to the I&O sheet without looking at* VIVIAN.]

JASON: Professor Bearing. How are you feeling today? Three P.M. IV hydration totals. Two thousand in. Thirty out. Uh-oh. That's it. Kidneys gone.

[*He looks at* VIVIAN.] Professor Bearing? Highly unresponsive. Wait a second— [*Puts his head down to her mouth and chest to listen for heartbeat and breathing.*] Wait a sec—Jesus Christ! [*Yelling.*] CALL A CODE! [JASON *throws down the chart, dives over the bed, and lies on top of her body as he reaches for the phone and punches in the numbers. To himself.*]

Code: 4-5-7-5. [*To operator.*] Code Blue, room 707. Code Blue, room 707. Dr. Posner—P-O-S-N-E-R. Hurry up!

[*He throws down the phone and lowers the head of the bed.*] Come on, come on, COME ON.

[*He begins CPR, kneeling over* VIVIAN, *alternately pounding frantically and giving mouth-to-mouth resuscitation. Over the loud-speaker in the hall, a droning voice repeats* "Code Blue, room 707. Code Blue, room 707."] One! Two! Three! Four! Five! [*He breathes in her mouth.* SUSIE, *hearing the announcement, runs into the room.*]

SUSIE: WHAT ARE YOU DOING?
JASON: A GODDAMN CODE. GET OVER HERE!
SUSIE: She's DNR! [*She grabs him.*]
JASON: [*He pushes* SUSIE *away.*] She's Research!
SUSIE: She's NO CODE! [*She grabs* JASON *and hurls him off the bed.*]
JASON: Ooowww! Goddamnit, Susie!
SUSIE: She's no code!
JASON: Aaargh!
SUSIE: Kelekian put the order in—you saw it! You were right there, Jason! Oh, God, the code! [*She runs to the phone.* JASON *struggles to stand. Into the phone.*] 4-5-7-5.

[*The* CODE TEAM *swoops in. Everything changes. Frenzy takes over. The* CODE TEAM *knocks* SUSIE *out of the way with their equipment.* SUSIE, *into the phone.*] Cancel code, room 707. Sue Monahan, primary nurse. Cancel code. Dr. Posner is here.

JASON: [*In agony.*] Oh, God.
CODE TEAM: —Get out of the way!
—Unit staff out!
—Get the board!

---

2. Professor Ashford quotes Horatio's line at the end of Shakespeare's *Hamlet*, addressed to the dead hero: "Good night, sweet prince, / And flights of angels sing thee to thy rest!" (5.2.329–30).

—Over here! [*They throw* VIVIAN's *body up at the waist and stick a board underneath for CPR. In a whirlwind of sterile packaging and barked commands, one* TEAM MEMBER *attaches a respirator, one begins CPR,*[3] *and one prepares the defibrillator.* SUSIE *and* JASON *try to stop them but are pushed away. The loudspeaker in the hall announces* "Cancel code, room 707. Cancel code, room 707."]
  —Bicarb amp!
  —I got it! [*To* SUSIE.] Get out!
  —One, two, three, four, five!
  —Get ready to shock! [*To* JASON.] Move it!
SUSIE: [*Running to each person, yelling.*] STOP! Patient is DNR!
JASON: [*At the same time, to the* CODE TEAM.] No, no! Stop doing this. STOP!
CODE TEAM: —Keep it going!
  —What do you get?
  —Bicarb amp!
  —No pulse!
SUSIE: She's NO CODE! Order was given— [*She dives for the chart and holds it up as she cries out.*] Look! Look at this! DO NOT RESUSCITATE. KELEKIAN.
CODE TEAM: [*As they administer electric shock,* VIVIAN's *body arches and bounces back down.*]
  —Almost ready!
  —Hit her!
  —CLEAR!
  —Pulse? Pulse?
JASON: [*Howling*]. I MADE A MISTAKE! [*Pause. The* CODE TEAM *looks at him. He collapses on the floor.*]
SUSIE: No code! Patient is no code.
CODE TEAM HEAD: Who the hell are you?
SUSIE: Sue Monahan, primary nurse.
CODE TEAM HEAD: Let me see the goddamn chart. CHART!
CODE TEAM: [*Slowing down.*]
  —What's going on?
  —Should we stop?
  —What's it say?
SUSIE: [*Pushing them away from the bed.*] Patient is no code. Get away from her!

[*Susie lifts the blanket.*
*Vivian steps out of the bed.*

*She walks away from the scene, toward*
*a little light.*

*She is now attentive and eager, moving*
*slowly toward the light.*

*She takes off her cap and lets it drop.*]

CODE TEAM HEAD: [*Reading.*] Do Not Resuscitate. Kelekian. Shit.

[*The* CODE TEAM *stops working.*]

JASON: [*Whispering.*] Oh, God.

CODE TEAM HEAD: Order was put in yesterday.

---

3. Cardiopulmonary resuscitation to restart the heart. *Defibrillator:* electrical device for restarting the heart's rhythm.

*She slips off her bracelet.*

*She loosens the ties and the top gown slides to the floor. She lets the second gown fall.*

*The instant she is naked, and beautiful, reaching for the light—*

*Lights out.*]

CODE TEAM:
—It's a doctor fuck-up.
—What is he, a resident?
—Got us up here on a DNR.
—Called a code on a no-code.

JASON: Oh, God. [*The bedside scene fades.*]

## QUESTIONS

1. What are some possible connotations of the name "Vivian Bearing"? How does this name help to orient the audience in a play so concerned with the derivations and meanings of words?
2. How does the play's title serve to introduce the play's secondary subject matter, the poetry of John Donne? What are some other implications of the word "wit" and how well do they apply to the play? To what degree does Vivian use wit to shield herself from her predicament? To what degree does wit become a means for her to attain insight and even some degree of comfort?
3. One meaning of "wit," of course, is humor. What is the nature of the play's humor? How well does the play's humor coexist with the play's grim subject matter?
4. If you were staging a production of *Wit*, what dramatic techniques would you use to present the play's many abrupt flashbacks, when the dying Vivian portrays herself as, variously, a child, a student, and a teacher? When Vivian is teaching specific passages of poetry, what techniques would you use to preserve the humor and rapid pace of the play and to help the audience visualize the words themselves?
5. What distinction, exactly, is Professor Ashford making in her insistence that it is a comma, not a semicolon, that separates the clauses in Donne's line "And death shall be no more, Death thou shalt die"? What are the thematic implications of this distinction? At what point in her life does Vivian fully grasp Professor Ashford's meaning?
6. In the very different ways they care for a dying patient, what do Dr. Kelekian, Jason, and Susie represent? By the end of the play, which of these characters seems to have the deepest insight into Vivian's life and her suffering? If you were directing a production of *Wit*, what kind of vocal tone and body language would you want each of these characters to project?
7. What are some of the ironies Vivian finds in medical terminology like "Grand Rounds" or "immortality in culture"? How does her scholarly dissection of this terminology serve the play's thematic purposes?
8. Why do you think that Vivian, once she has received her terminal diagnosis, opts for a painful and aggressive experimental treatment rather than the kind of palliative comfort care she would receive as a hospice patient? Is this a heroic choice on her part? a tragic choice? Could the play's dramatic effects have been fulfilled in a hospice setting?
9. When two students joke about Vivian's "pronuncia-see-on," she comments that she "admired only the studied application of wit, not its spontaneous eruption." Later she tells the audience, "Do not think for a minute that anyone calls me 'Sweetheart.'" What do these remarks reveal about her character? How do they affect the audience's sympathy for her?

10. What do you think of the play's ending—is it what you expected? Is it a suitable conclusion, consistent with the rest of the play? Is it disappointing? If you were producing the play, how would you stage the final scene?

## SUGGESTIONS FOR WRITING

1. Research the literary meanings of "wit" and "metaphysical conceit" as they relate to the poetry of the seventeenth century and especially to the poems of John Donne. How do these concepts inform *Wit*? Write an essay in which you discuss how Edson has applied Donne's poetic techniques to a late-twentieth-century drama.
2. Is Vivian "witty" in either the modern or the seventeenth-century senses of the word? Is she arrogant? Is she honest with herself and others? Why has she never married? How does her authority as a leading professor of literature relate to her role as a cancer patient? How do her career and personality affect her relationships with the medical personnel? Write an essay in which you interpret Vivian Bearing's character and how it influences the effect of the play. Would a different protagonist produce a different plot or different themes?
3. *Wit* examines how John Donne's Holy Sonnets represent an artistic attempt to understand mortality. How well does the play itself fulfill that same function? Write an essay in which you explore the various ways that *Wit* approaches the subject of death and dying. Does the play come to any specific "conclusion" about death, or about how to face one's death?
4. How is the American medical establishment portrayed in *Wit*? What different approaches and attitudes are represented by various characters in the play? To what degree is Vivian the beneficiary of her medical treatment? To what degree is she its victim? Write an essay in which you discuss *Wit*'s depiction of modern medicine.

# 27 THE WHOLE TEXT

Now that you have read more plays and have encountered the various elements of drama, you are ready to put a few works in a broader perspective. This chapter invites you to view three plays in their entirety, both in comparison to other plays and in the context of theater history. This larger scope can be approached with some of the specific skills you already have. The ultimate purpose of contemplating several plays along with trends in theater and playwriting is to enhance your ability to appreciate any individual play, whether read or performed.

The first selection in this chapter, *A Streetcar Named Desire* by Tennessee Williams, is an American drama written in the middle of the twentieth century. The second, *The Cherry Orchard* by Anton Chekhov, is a Russian play written at the beginning of the twentieth century. Both are frequently performed and studied. The third play, *How I Learned to Drive* by Paula Vogel, had its New York debut in 1997, and in 1998 won the Pulitzer Prize along with four other awards for best play of the year. Whereas Vogel is still shaping her career and reputation, Williams and Chekhov have long been established as among the leading playwrights of the twentieth century. Very few people have seen more than one production of *How I Learned to Drive*, and little has been written about it apart from newspaper reviews. In contrast, reputations have been made for directors, actors, and even literary critics by their association with *A Streetcar Named Desire* (as play and movie) or with the plays of Chekhov. Only a handful of actors—some famous, some not—have performed in Vogel's play, and no movie has been made of it. Your role in responding to and writing about a play may depend on whether it has a long-standing tradition of performances and criticism or is a fresh addition to the repertoire of drama studies and theatrical production.

> A critic is a man who knows the way but can't drive the car.
> —KENNETH TYNAN

As you read each play, consider its title, the cast of characters and stage directions, and the representation of time and place (in terms of both the historical period and geographical setting as well as the timing and location of the scenes shown on stage). Imagine the appearance, costumes, vocal styles, movements of each of the characters, and "run" each scene before your mental vision: who is on stage, who is claiming the attention or yielding to whom, who walks, who sits, who busies himself or herself with a book, game, or chore? Would there be any sound or lighting effects needed? Any props to be picked up, brought on stage or carried off? Once you have a good idea of what happens step by step in a performance of a play, you are in a better position to raise questions about what it all means. Especially if you know you will write about this play, you should make notes on a first reading. Mark passages directly on the page as you read, or use post-it flags that can be removed. Then write down your observations and questions. Which differences between the characters seem most important? What causes the decisive conflict that must be resolved or at least softened by the play's end? For the sake of analysis, pinpoint which portion of the play corresponds with each of the five stages of plot: exposition, rising action, climax, falling action, and conclusion. Are there surprises, delays, or disappointments in how the conflict is set up, how it is brought out in the open, how it is resolved? What does each character know at the end that he or she did not know earlier? Has the power shifted from one character to another at the end? Once you understand the characters and the plot or structure, look again more closely at specific scenes and lines. Why is any scene or exchange of dialogue necessary to the understanding of the whole play? (To understand the effect of any aspect or element of a literary work, it always helps to imagine what would be lost if it were missing.) Do you notice intriguing or puzzling language in any of the dialogue? Are there interesting patterns of imagery, or is there a symbol or concept that unites the whole play? How would you state the theme of the play?

If you follow the sequence of questions that we suggest above, you can accumulate specific observations about the parts of a play, and from these you can shape an overview—a sense of the play's spirit, coherence, or fundamental aim. Of course, a literary work, being more than the sum of its parts, may trace more than one thematic pattern.

Inevitably, your critical assessment of the whole play will entail one matter that is often the beginning and the end of discussion: do you like it? We have had little to say about this factor in your response because it does indeed tend to stop discussion. You either like the play or you don't. But very interesting and productive questions can follow when you ask what it is in the play or in this kind of play that pleases or alienates you. You might be encouraged to articulate what you think a better play would be like, or how this play might be improved. Or you might learn to classify different plays, recognizing that the one you don't like belongs with a class of plays that you tend not to like, though others might value plays of this kind. Your judgment will always be your own, but others will respect it if it is based on fair standards of comparison and on accurate observation of each work.

Tastes and preferences in drama as in other genres can be placed in historical perspective. Each reader, student, or critic is part of a time, place, and culture—a context that will influence any interpretation of a play. If theater reviewers from Moscow in 1904 or New York in 1947 were somehow to attend the opening night of *How I Learned to Drive* in New York in 1997, they might feel almost as alienated and dumbfounded as if they had suddenly been dropped into an ancient Athenian arena to watch a play by Sophocles. Though the conflicts of incest, frustrated desire, blocked ambition, and social censure remain remarkably constant over thousands of years, social and dramatic conventions change radically. You may find it easier to appreciate a recent play with a contemporary style and current themes. Or like many subscribers to repertory theaters, you may prefer classics of forty or a hundred years ago—or even four centuries ago, if it's Shakespeare you want. Or you may enjoy plays of many different contexts, reaching beyond your first reactions to engage with each work as much as possible on its own terms.

> *All theories of what a good play is, or how a good play should be written, are futile. A good play is a play which when acted upon the boards makes an audience interested and pleased. A play that fails in this is a bad play.*
> —MAURICE BARING

Samuel Johnson, the most respected arbiter of taste in England in the late eighteenth century, said that "nothing can please many and please long but just representations of general nature." Johnson was trying to explain why Shakespeare had continued to charm readers and playgoers for a century and a half, and his comments form both a commonsense argument about actual responses to texts (based on consensus and durability) and a proposition about the relation between literature and reality. Good literature, says Johnson, accurately reflects patterns that exist across culture and time; to last, literature must have something appropriate and valid ("just") to say about what is true regardless of time or place ("general nature").

Not everyone in Johnson's time agreed that such a universal standard could be found, and in the early twenty-first century's enlarged and varied world, fewer still believe that there are any universals that are shared by all human beings. Yet even if we no longer expect plots and characters that assure us that we are all essentially alike, and even if we try not to measure a play from Iran or Sri Lanka by the same yardstick as one from London or New York, we still seek some shared ground in order to understand any play. We must find a way to translate it, to some extent, into our language and our sense of what is human.

Our response to a play depends a great deal on how it is interpreted in performance, which in turn is influenced by the artistic standards of the playwright's time as well as our own. An examination of the three plays in this chapter brings out some significant historical trends in the theater. Anton Chekhov's last play, *The Cherry Orchard*, was produced just weeks before the playwright's death from tuberculosis. Already celebrated as a short-story writer (see "The Lady with the Dog," in chapter 4), Chekhov had a reputation as a comic playwright when he began to produce the serious dramas for which he is known today. Audiences were slow to appreciate these plays, as they had to get used to a style of drama and acting that were closer to the circumstances and manners of everyday life. As he wrote *The Cherry Orchard*, Chekhov asserted that it would "definitely be funny, very funny," but many directors and actors have interpreted it as a tragedy. Such interpretations ignore the fact that it is chock-full of running jokes, such as the old butler's mumbling and deafness, Pishtchik's falling asleep midsentence or begging for money, Gaev's pretending to play billiards all the time, and Lyubov's constant squandering of cash. The overly serious interpretations grow out of the twentieth-century fashion for seeing Chekhov as a bleak and uncompromising spiritual philosopher.

Chekhov's innovations were well accepted by the middle of the twentieth century, and indeed there is a connection between Russian acting techniques associated with Chekhov and the work of Tennessee Williams. Konstantin Stanislavsky (1863–1938), the Russian actor and producer, dismissed the old, melodramatic, "stagy" style of acting that preceded Chekhov. He recommended instead that an actor prepare a role by reconstructing a history for the character and drawing on memories of similar experiences to arouse the feelings and physical responses needed to perform the part. Stanislavsky's "Method" became the standard training for actors in the U.S. by the middle of the twentieth century. Method acting was popularized, in fact, by Marlon Brando, who played Stanley in Elia Kazan's stage and movie versions of *A Streetcar Named Desire*. (Tributes to Brando when he died in 2004 gave him credit for changing the way actors act.) Actors who perform in more recent plays such as Vogel's will usually have learned some "Method" techniques, though schools of acting in other countries approach this art quite differently. When you read a play from an earlier century, though, you should bear in mind that the style of acting then would probably strike us as artificial, if we could see it now. And there may come another revolution in acting styles during the twenty-first century.

Styles of production and staging, like styles of acting, follow historical trends. *A Streetcar Named Desire* and Arthur Miller's *Death of a Salesman* were first staged within two years of each other. Both plays express the harshness of the competitive postwar world. In their original Broadway productions, the sets of *Streetcar* and *Salesman* showed the inside and outside of cramped, low-income homes; both plays used invasive shadows and sounds to convey the characters' confinement. And with their intermixing of symbolic staging, poetic monologues, realistic, everyday action, and explicit psychological and sexual motivation, Tennessee Williams and Arthur Miller together influenced theater across the globe. A more recent play, *How I Learned to Drive* has some elements in common with these mid-twentieth-century classics, but the recent style is likely to be more playful than tragic, with more personal connection between characters and audience. Vogel's play, in the manner known as "postmodern," borrows devices from many periods of drama that call attention to the illusion of theater. The program and the printed text of the play tell us that three of the actors should function like an ancient **chorus**—unnamed members of the community who may address comments to the audience. In a similar effect, the main character, Li'l Bit, sometimes delivers a **soliloquy**—a monologue spoken as though to herself and overheard by the audience but not the other characters—or she addresses the audience directly, speaking the stage directions aloud: "1969. A typical family dinner."

*A good theatre critic is one who perceives what is happening in the theatre of his time. A great drama critic also perceives what is not happening.*
—KENNETH TYNAN

Different dramatic styles have developed to express different themes or different conceptions of character and experience. Realistic theater allows us to pretend that we are observing real people who would behave this way even if we were not watching; often such plays will imply that sincere self-expression, listening, and forgiveness can resolve conflict. Experimental staging may do little to hide its fictionality and may have the effect of "breaking down the fourth wall," so that we become aware of ourselves in the seats watching a performance on a set that represents only three sides of a room or other location. Such plays tend to distance the audience from characters, and may suggest the impossibility of honest communication and reconciliation between people. Yet in comparing the structure and staging of plays from different stylistic periods, we should remember to consider each play as a whole, on its own terms. For instance, *How I Learned to Drive* is clearly not a realistic drama presenting a family conflict exactly as it might have happened, yet the play does deal with recognizable experiences. In a convincing if stylized way, it recreates the feelings of those experiences through the therapeutic process of telling an audience about them. The structure and staging of Vogel's play are broken up in a contemporary fashion, as if bad memories are reconstructed in bits and pieces by someone reluctant to confess and forgive. This fragmentary, self-conscious, humorous style at the same time helps the audience to develop sympathy rather than disgust for the niece and her uncle. Thus it would be a mistake to generalize that plays that refer to their own theatricality are cynical or emotionally shallow compared to classic drama, just as it would be false to view long-established dramatic tradition as inherently predictable or sentimental. A well-designed play should create an effect (in reading or performance) that coordinates well with all its elements and that can be expressed in a coherent theme. Comparing plays in different styles that deal with similar themes can help you to understand how each play produces its unique effects.

The three plays in this chapter invite comparison with each other. Notice that *The Cherry Orchard* and *A Streetcar Named Desire* focus on a similar problem, the loss of a family estate that represents an older, more hierarchical way of life, which depended on slavery (or serfdom) a couple of generations earlier. In *The Cherry Orchard*, this problem drives the plot; in *A Streetcar Named Desire*, on the other hand, it provides the background and a source of conflict. Williams stages a violent confrontation—a rape—between new and old social elements, whereas Chekhov postpones indefinitely the proposal of marriage between Lopahin and Varya. Sexuality drives Stanley and ruins Blanche in Williams's play, and it permeates the entire seductive consumer culture of 1960s America in Vogel's play (in which advertisements feature women draped over cars), whereas Chekhov's characters seem almost unaware of the power of sexual attraction. On another front, Chekhov's characters seem aware of history, the social order, and coming political change in a way unimaginable in either American play. But in all three plays, characters struggle to escape their narrow circumstances and their guilty or grieving memories.

Through a careful reading of details, connecting parts to the whole, discovering themes, and noticing the tone, whether tragic or comic, as well as considering other works, we can approach a sound interpretation of a literary work. In the process, it helps to place each work historically and to approach the spirit in which it was first created. If we ask a Disney cartoon to be a classical ballet, or imagine a Shakespeare play performed in the manner of *Star Trek*—or vice versa—the works lose their integrity, and we will be disappointed all around. Some sense of historical context is indispensable to an evaluation that goes beyond current fashions or personal likes and dislikes.

What we bring to a text, from our own lives and experience, will likely influence our judgment at every point. But the fact that our judgments are both highly subjective and influenced by our ideologies and cultural identities does not mean that our responses are predetermined and beyond discussion or change. The better we can articulate our values and adduce evidence from the text, the more we will be able to learn, to grow, and to teach. You may never convince someone else that a particular play is as good or bad as you think it is. And you may never be convinced by someone else's arguments. But the grounds of judgment are ultimately more important than the judgment of any single play, and argument helps clarify your grounds of judgment. Knowing the reasons behind your interpretation of the whole play will certainly make it more interesting and meaningful to you, and probably help you to enjoy it more.

Your challenge now is to read these three plays, imagining how you would see and hear them on a stage. Reading, you can pay extra attention to the words, which might fly past you in a theatrical performance. Pay attention as well to your changing responses and, as you respond, begin the open-ended process of understanding the whole play. Don't be alarmed if at times you come to a moment of speechless admiration. It is all right to hold your breath with excitement, to laugh aloud, or to let tears come to your eyes—no one is watching you read, and the house lights in the theater are turned down! Remember that plays are supposed to be physical experiences. Applause was invented to let audiences discharge all that pent-up feeling. Writing about a play is just a more sustained and shared way than these physical reactions to express the kind of response that drama can provoke in performance or even in reading.

## TENNESSEE WILLIAMS

## A Streetcar Named Desire

> And so it was I entered the broken world
> To trace the visionary company of love, its voice
> An instant in the wind (I know not whither hurled)
> But not for long to hold each desperate choice.
> —"The Broken Tower" by HART CRANE[1]

### CHARACTERS

| | | |
|---|---|---|
| BLANCHE | EUNICE | A DOCTOR |
| STELLA | STEVE | A NURSE (MATRON) |
| STANLEY | PABLO | A YOUNG COLLECTOR |
| MITCH | A NEGRO WOMAN | A MEXICAN WOMAN |

### Scene 1

*The exterior of a two-story corner building on a street in New Orleans which is named Elysian Fields and runs between the L & N tracks and the river.[2] The section is poor but, unlike corresponding sections in other American cities, it has a raffish charm. The houses are mostly white frame, weathered grey, with rickety outside stairs and galleries and quaintly ornamented gables. This building contains two flats, upstairs and down. Faded white stairs ascend to the entrances of both.*

*It is first dark of an evening early in May. The sky that shows around the dim white building is a peculiarly tender blue, almost a turquoise, which invests the scene with a kind of lyricism and gracefully attenuates the atmosphere of decay. You can almost feel the warm breath of the brown river beyond the river warehouses with their faint redolences of bananas and coffee. A corresponding air is evoked by the music of Negro entertainers at a barroom around the corner. In this part of New Orleans you are practically always just around the corner, or a few doors down the street, from a tinny piano being played with the infatuated fluency of brown fingers. This "Blue Piano" expresses the spirit of the life which goes on here.*

*Two women, one white and one colored, are taking the air on the steps of the building. The white woman is* EUNICE, *who occupies the upstairs flat; the* NEGRO WOMAN, *a neighbor, for New Orleans is a cosmopolitan city where there is a relatively warm and easy intermingling of races in the old part of town.*

---

1. American poet (1899-1932).
2. Elysian Fields is in fact a New Orleans street at the northern tip of the French Quarter, between the Louisville & Nashville railroad tracks and the Mississippi River. In Greek mythology, the Elysian Fields are the abode of the blessed in the afterlife; in Paris, the Champs-Élysées ("Elysian Fields") is a grand boulevard.

*Above the music of the "Blue Piano" the voices of people on the street can be heard overlapping.*

[*Two men come around the corner,* STANLEY KOWALSKI *and* MITCH. *They are about twenty-eight, or thirty years old, roughly dressed in blue denim work clothes.* STANLEY *carries his bowling jacket and a red-stained package from a butcher's. They stop at the foot of the steps.*]

STANLEY: [*Bellowing.*] Hey there! Stella, baby!

[STELLA *comes out on the first floor landing, a gentle young woman, about twenty-five, and of a background obviously quite different from her husband's.*]

STELLA: [*Mildly.*] Don't holler at me like that. Hi, Mitch.
STANLEY: Catch!
STELLA: What?
STANLEY: Meat!

[*He heaves the package at her. She cries out in protest but manages to catch it: then she laughs breathlessly. Her husband and his companion have already started back around the corner.*]

STELLA: [*Calling after him.*] Stanley! Where are you going?
STANLEY: Bowling!
STELLA: Can I come watch?
STANLEY: Come on. [*He goes out.*]
STELLA: Be over soon. [*To the* WHITE WOMAN.] Hello, Eunice. How are you?
EUNICE: I'm all right. Tell Steve to get him a poor boy's sandwich[3] 'cause nothing's left here.

[*They all laugh; the* NEGRO WOMAN *does not stop.* STELLA *goes out.*]

NEGRO WOMAN: What was that package he th'ew at 'er? [*She rises from steps, laughing louder.*]
EUNICE: You hush, now!
NEGRO WOMAN: Catch *what!*

[*She continues to laugh.* BLANCHE *comes around the corner, carrying a valise. She looks at a slip of paper, then at the building, then again at the slip and again at the building. Her expression is one of shocked disbelief. Her appearance is incongruous to this setting. She is daintily dressed in a white suit with a fluffy bodice, necklace and earrings of pearl, white gloves and hat, looking as if she were arriving at a summer tea or cocktail party in the garden district.[4] She is about five years older than* STELLA. *Her delicate beauty must avoid a strong light. There is something about her uncertain manner, as well as her white clothes, that suggests a moth.*]

EUNICE: [*Finally.*] What's the matter, honey? Are you lost?
BLANCHE: [*With faintly hysterical humor.*] They told me to take a street-car named

---

3. Usually called just "poor boy" or "po' boy"; similar to a hero or submarine sandwich.
4. Wealthy, fashionable section of New Orleans.

Desire, and then transfer to one called Cemeteries[5] and ride six blocks and get off at—Elysian Fields!
EUNICE: That's where you are now.
BLANCHE: At Elysian Fields?
EUNICE: This here is Elysian Fields.
BLANCHE: They mustn't have—understood—what number I wanted...
EUNICE: What number you lookin' for?

[BLANCHE *wearily refers to the slip of paper.*]

BLANCHE: Six thirty-two.
EUNICE: You don't have to look no further.
BLANCHE: [*Uncomprehendingly.*] I'm looking for my sister, Stella DuBois, I mean—Mrs. Stanley Kowalski.
EUNICE: That's the party.—You just did miss her, though.
BLANCHE: This—can this be—her home?
EUNICE: She's got the downstairs here and I got the up.
BLANCHE: Oh. She's—out?
EUNICE: You noticed that bowling alley around the corner?
BLANCHE: I'm—not sure I did.
EUNICE: Well, that's where she's at, watchin' her husband bowl. [*There is a pause.*] You want to leave your suitcase here an' go find her?
BLANCHE: No.
NEGRO WOMAN: I'll go tell her you come.
BLANCHE: Thanks.
NEGRO WOMAN: You welcome. [*She goes out.*]
EUNICE: She wasn't expecting you?
BLANCHE: No. No, not tonight.
EUNICE: Well, why don't you just go in and make yourself at home till they get back.
BLANCHE: How could I—do that?
EUNICE: We own this place so I can let you in.

[*She gets up and opens the downstairs door. A light goes on behind the blind, turning it light blue.* BLANCHE *slowly follows her into the downstairs flat. The surrounding areas dim out as the interior is lighted. Two rooms can be seen, not too clearly defined. The one first entered is primarily a kitchen but contains a folding bed to be used by* BLANCHE. *The room beyond this is a bedroom. Off this room is a narrow door to a bathroom.*]

EUNICE: [*Defensively, noticing* BLANCHE'*s look.*] It's sort of messed up right now but when it's clean it's real sweet.
BLANCHE: Is it?
EUNICE: Uh-huh, I think so. So you're Stella's sister?
BLANCHE: Yes. [*Wanting to get rid of her.*] Thanks for letting me in.
EUNICE: *Por nada*, as the Mexicans say, *por nada!*[6] Stella spoke of you.
BLANCHE: Yes?
EUNICE: I think she said you taught school.

---

5. Desire is a street in New Orleans, Cemeteries the end of a streetcar line that stopped at a cemetery.
6. It's nothing.

BLANCHE: Yes.
EUNICE: And you're from Mississippi, huh?
BLANCHE: Yes.
EUNICE: She showed me a picture of your home-place, the plantation.
BLANCHE: Belle Reve?[7]
EUNICE: A great big place with white columns.
BLANCHE: Yes . . .
EUNICE: A place like that must be awful hard to keep up.
BLANCHE: If you will excuse me, I'm just about to drop.
EUNICE: Sure, honey. Why don't you set down?
BLANCHE: What I meant was I'd like to be left alone.
EUNICE: [*Offended.*] Aw. I'll make myself scarce, in that case.
BLANCHE: I didn't mean to be rude, but—
EUNICE: I'll drop by the bowling alley an' hustle her up. [*She goes out the door.*]

> [BLANCHE *sits in a chair very stiffly with her shoulders slightly hunched and her legs pressed close together and her hands tightly clutching her purse as if she were quite cold. After a while the blind look goes out of her eyes and she begins to look slowly around. A cat screeches. She catches her breath with a startled gesture. Suddenly she notices something in a half opened closet. She springs up and crosses to it, and removes a whiskey bottle. She pours a half tumbler of whiskey and tosses it down. She carefully replaces the bottle and washes out the tumbler at the sink. Then she resumes her seat in front of the table.*]

BLANCHE: [*Faintly to herself.*] I've got to keep hold of myself!

> [STELLA *comes quickly around the corner of the building and runs to the door of the downstairs flat.*]

STELLA: [*Calling out joyfully.*] Blanche!

> [*For a moment they stare at each other. Then* BLANCHE *springs up and runs to her with a wild cry.*]

BLANCHE: Stella, oh, Stella, Stella! Stella for Star! [*She begins to speak with feverish vivacity as if she feared for either of them to stop and think. They catch each other in a spasmodic embrace.*] Now, then, let me look at you. But don't you look at me, Stella, no, no, no, not till later, not till I've bathed and rested! And turn that over-light off! Turn that off! I won't be looked at in this merciless glare! [STELLA *laughs and complies.*] Come back here now! Oh, my baby! Stella! Stella for Star! [*She embraces her again.*] I thought you would never come back to this horrible place! What am I saying? I didn't mean to say that. I meant to be nice about it and say—Oh, what a convenient location and such—Ha-a-ha! Precious lamb! You haven't said a *word* to me.
STELLA: You haven't given me a chance to, honey! [*She laughs, but her glance at* BLANCHE *is a little anxious.*]
BLANCHE: Well, now you talk. Open your pretty mouth and talk while I look around for some liquor! I know you must have some liquor on the place! Where could it be, I wonder? Oh, I spy, I spy! [*She rushes to the closet and removes*

---

7. Beautiful Dream.

the bottle; she is shaking all over and panting for breath as she tries to laugh. The bottle nearly slips from her grasp.]

STELLA: [*Noticing.*] Blanche, you sit down and let me pour the drinks. I don't know what we've got to mix with. Maybe a Coke in the icebox. Look'n see, honey, while I'm—

BLANCHE: No Coke, honey, not with my nerves tonight! Where—where—where is—?

STELLA: Stanley? Bowling! He loves it. They're having a—found some soda!—tournament...

BLANCHE: Just water, baby, to chase it! Now don't get worried, your sister hasn't turned into a drunkard, she's just all shaken up and hot and tired and dirty! You sit down, now, and explain this place to me! What are you doing in a place like this?

STELLA: Now, Blanche—

BLANCHE: Oh, I'm not going to be hypocritical, I'm going to be honestly critical about it! Never, never, never in my worst dreams could I picture—Only Poe! Only Mr. Edgar Allan Poe!—could do it justice! Out there I suppose is the ghoul-haunted woodland of Weir![8] [*She laughs.*]

STELLA: No, honey, those are the L & N tracks.

BLANCHE: No, now seriously, putting joking aside. Why didn't you tell me, why didn't you write me, honey, why didn't you let me know?

STELLA: [*Carefully, pouring herself a drink.*] Tell you what, Blanche?

BLANCHE: Why, that you had to live in these conditions!

STELLA: Aren't you being a little intense about it? It's not that bad at all! New Orleans isn't like other cities.

BLANCHE: This has got nothing to do with New Orleans. You might as well say—forgive me, blessed baby! [*She suddenly stops short.*] The subject is closed!

STELLA: [*A little drily.*] Thanks.

[*During the pause,* BLANCHE *stares at her. She smiles at* BLANCHE.]

BLANCHE: [*Looking down at her glass, which shakes in her hand.*] You're all I've got in the world, and you're not glad to see me!

STELLA: [*Sincerely.*] Why, Blanche, you know that's not true.

BLANCHE: No?—I'd forgotten how quiet you were.

STELLA: You never did give me a chance to say much, Blanche. So I just got in the habit of being quiet around you.

BLANCHE: [*Vaguely.*] A good habit to get into ... [*Then, abruptly.*] You haven't asked me how I happened to get away from the school before the spring term ended.

STELLA: Well, I thought you'd volunteer that information—if you wanted to tell me.

BLANCHE: You thought I'd been fired?

STELLA: No, I—thought you might have—resigned ...

BLANCHE: I was so exhausted by all I'd been through my—nerves broke. [*Nervously tamping cigarette.*] I was on the verge of—lunacy, almost! So Mr. Graves—Mr. Graves is the high school superintendent—he suggested I take a leave of

---

8. From the refrain of Poe's gothic ballad "Ulalume" (1847).

absence. I couldn't put all of those details into the wire[9] . . . [*She drinks quickly.*] Oh, this buzzes right through me and feels so *good!*

STELLA: Won't you have another?

BLANCHE: No, one's my limit.

STELLA: Sure?

BLANCHE: You haven't said a word about my appearance.

STELLA: You look just fine.

BLANCHE: God love you for a liar! Daylight never exposed so total a ruin! But you—you've put on some weight, yes, you're just as plump as a little partridge! And it's so becoming to you!

STELLA: Now, Blanche—

BLANCHE: Yes, it is, it is or I wouldn't say it! You just have to watch around the hips a little. Stand up.

STELLA: Not now.

BLANCHE: You hear me? I said stand up! [STELLA *complies reluctantly.*] You messy child, you, you've spilt something on that pretty white lace collar! About your hair—you ought to have it cut in a feather bob with your dainty features. Stella, you have a maid, don't you?

STELLA: No. With only two rooms it's—

BLANCHE: What? *Two* rooms, did you say?

STELLA: This one and— [*She is embarrassed.*]

BLANCHE: The other one? [*She laughs sharply. There is an embarrassed silence.*] I am going to take just one little tiny nip more, sort of to put the stopper on, so to speak. . . . Then put the bottle away so I won't be tempted. [*She rises.*] I want you to look at *my* figure! [*She turns around.*] You know I haven't put on one ounce in ten years, Stella? I weigh what I weighed the summer you left Belle Reve. The summer Dad died and you left us . . .

STELLA: [*A little wearily.*] It's just incredible, Blanche, how well you're looking.

BLANCHE: [*They both laugh uncomfortably.*] But, Stella, there's only two rooms, I don't see where you're going to put me!

STELLA: We're going to put you in here.

BLANCHE: What kind of bed's this—one of those collapsible things? [*She sits on it.*]

STELLA: Does it feel all right?

BLANCHE: [*Dubiously.*] Wonderful, honey. I don't like a bed that gives much. But there's no door between the two rooms, and Stanley—will it be decent?

STELLA: Stanley is Polish, you know.

BLANCHE: Oh, yes. They're something like Irish, aren't they?

STELLA: Well—

BLANCHE: Only not so—highbrow? [*They both laugh again in the same way.*] I brought some nice clothes to meet all your lovely friends in.

STELLA: I'm afraid you won't think they are lovely.

BLANCHE: What are they like?

STELLA: They're Stanley's friends.

BLANCHE: Polacks?

STELLA: They're a mixed lot, Blanche.

BLANCHE: Heterogeneous—types?

---

9. Telegram.

STELLA: Oh, yes. Yes, types is right!
BLANCHE: Well—anyhow—I brought nice clothes and I'll wear them. I guess you're hoping I'll say I'll put up at a hotel, but I'm not going to put up at a hotel. I want to be *near* you, got to be *with* somebody, I *can't* be *alone!* Because—as you must have noticed—I'm—*not* very *well* . . . [*Her voice drops and her look is frightened.*]
STELLA: You seem a little bit nervous or overwrought or something.
BLANCHE: Will Stanley like me, or will I be just a visiting in-law, Stella? I couldn't stand that.
STELLA: You'll get along fine together, if you'll just try not to—well—compare him with men that we went out with at home.
BLANCHE: Is he so—different?
STELLA: Yes. A different species.
BLANCHE: In what way; what's he like?
STELLA: Oh, you can't describe someone you're in love with! Here's a picture of him! [*She hands a photograph to* BLANCHE.]
BLANCHE: An officer?
STELLA: A Master Sergeant in the Engineers' Corps. Those are decorations!
BLANCHE: He had those on when you met him?
STELLA: I assure you I wasn't just blinded by all the brass.
BLANCHE: That's not what I—
STELLA: But of course there were things to adjust myself to later on.
BLANCHE: Such as his civilian background! [STELLA *laughs uncertainly.*] How did he take it when you said I was coming?
STELLA: Oh, Stanley doesn't know yet.
BLANCHE: [*Frightened.*] You—haven't told him?
STELLA: He's on the road a good deal.
BLANCHE: Oh. Travels?
STELLA: Yes.
BLANCHE: Good. I mean—isn't it?
STELLA: [*Half to herself.*] I can hardly stand it when he is away for a night . . .
BLANCHE: Why, Stella!
STELLA: When he's away for a week I nearly go wild!
BLANCHE: Gracious!
STELLA: And when he comes back I cry on his lap like a baby . . . [*She smiles to herself.*]
BLANCHE: I guess that is what is meant by being in love . . . [STELLA *looks up with a radiant smile.*] Stella—
STELLA: What?
BLANCHE: [*In an uneasy rush.*] I haven't asked you the things you probably thought I was going to ask. And so I'll expect you to be understanding about what *I* have to tell *you.*
STELLA: What, Blanche? [*Her face turns anxious.*]
BLANCHE: Well, Stella—you're going to reproach me, I know that you're bound to reproach me—but before you do—take into consideration—you left! I stayed and struggled! You came to New Orleans and looked out for yourself! *I* stayed at Belle Reve and tried to hold it together! I'm not meaning this in any reproachful way, but *all* the burden descended on *my* shoulders.
STELLA: The best I could do was make my own living, Blanche.

[BLANCHE *begins to shake again with intensity.*]

BLANCHE: I know, I know. But you are the one that abandoned Belle Reve, not I! I stayed and fought for it, bled for it, almost died for it!
STELLA: Stop this hysterical outburst and tell me what's happened? What do you mean fought and bled? What kind of—
BLANCHE: I knew you would, Stella. I knew you would take this attitude about it!
STELLA: About—what?—please!
BLANCHE: [*Slowly.*] The loss—the loss . . .
STELLA: Belle Reve? Lost, is it? No!
BLANCHE: Yes, Stella.

[*They stare at each other across the yellow-checked linoleum of the table.* BLANCHE *slowly nods her head and* STELLA *looks slowly down at her hands folded on the table. The music of the "Blue Piano" grows louder.* BLANCHE *touches her handkerchief to her forehead.*]

STELLA: But how did it go? What happened?
BLANCHE: [*Springing up.*] You're a fine one to ask me how it went!
STELLA: Blanche!
BLANCHE: You're a fine one to sit there *accusing me* of it!
STELLA: *Blanche!*
BLANCHE: I, I, *I* took the blows in my face and my body! All of those deaths! The long parade to the graveyard! Father, Mother! Margaret, that dreadful way! So big with it, it couldn't be put in a coffin! But had to be burned like rubbish! You just came home in time for the funerals, Stella. And funerals are pretty compared to deaths. Funerals are quiet, but deaths—not always. Sometimes their breathing is hoarse, and sometimes it rattles, and sometimes they even cry out to you, "Don't let me go!" Even the old, sometimes, say, "Don't let me go." As if you were able to stop them! But funerals are quiet, with pretty flowers. And, oh, what gorgeous boxes they pack them away in! Unless you were there at the bed when they cried out, "Hold me!" you'd never suspect there was the struggle for breath and bleeding. You didn't dream, but I saw! *Saw! Saw!* And now you sit there telling me with your eyes that I let the place go! How in hell do you think all that sickness and dying was paid for? Death is expensive, Miss Stella! And old Cousin Jessie's right after Margaret's, hers! Why, the Grim Reaper[1] had put up his tent on our doorstep! . . . Stella. Belle Reve was his headquarters! Honey—that's how it slipped through my fingers! Which of them left us a fortune? Which of them left a cent of insurance even? Only poor Jessie—one hundred to pay for her coffin. That was all, Stella! And I with my pitiful salary at the school. Yes, accuse me! Sit there and stare at me, thinking I let the place go! *I* let the place go? Where were *you!* In bed with your—Polack!
STELLA: [*Springing.*] Blanche! You be still! That's enough! [*She starts out.*]
BLANCHE: Where are you going?
STELLA: I'm going into the bathroom to wash my face.
BLANCHE: Oh, Stella, Stella, you're crying!

1. Death.

STELLA: Does that surprise you?
BLANCHE: Forgive me—I didn't mean to—

[*The sound of men's voices is heard.* STELLA *goes into the bathroom, closing the door behind her. When the men appear, and* BLANCHE *realizes it must be* STANLEY *returning, she moves uncertainly from the bathroom door to the dressing table, looking apprehensively toward the front door.* STANLEY *enters, followed by* STEVE *and* MITCH. STANLEY *pauses near his door,* STEVE *by the foot of the spiral stair, and* MITCH *is slightly above and to the right of them, about to go out. As the men enter, we hear some of the following dialogue.*]

STANLEY: Is that how he got it?
STEVE: Sure that's how he got it. He hit the old weather-bird for 300 bucks on a six-number-ticket.
MITCH: Don't tell him those things; he'll believe it. [MITCH *starts out.*]
STANLEY: [*Restraining* MITCH.] Hey, Mitch—come back here.

[BLANCHE, *at the sound of voices, retires in the bedroom. She picks up* STANLEY'S *photo from dressing table, looks at it, puts it down. When* STANLEY *enters the apartment, she darts and hides behind the screen at the head of bed.*]

STEVE: [*To* STANLEY *and* MITCH.] Hey, are we playin' poker tomorrow?
STANLEY: Sure—at Mitch's.
MITCH: [*Hearing this, returns quickly to the stair rail.*] No—not at my place. My mother's still sick!
STANLEY: Okay, at my place . . . [MITCH *starts out again.*] But you bring the beer!

[MITCH *pretends not to hear—calls out "Good night, all," and goes out, singing.* EUNICE'S *voice is heard, above.*]

EUNICE: Break it up down there! I made the spaghetti dish and ate it myself.
STEVE: [*Going upstairs.*] I told you and phoned you we was playing. [*To the men.*] Jax[2] beer!
EUNICE: You never phoned me once.
STEVE: I told you at breakfast—and phoned you at lunch . . .
EUNICE: Well, never mind about that. You just get yourself home here once in a while.
STEVE: You want it in the papers?

[*More laughter and shouts of parting come from the men.* STANLEY *throws the screen door of the kitchen open and comes in. He is of medium height, about five feet eight or nine, and strongly, compactly built. Animal joy in his being is implicit in all his movements and attitudes. Since earliest manhood the center of his life has been pleasure with women, the giving and taking of it, not with weak indulgence, dependently, but with the power and pride of a richly feathered male bird among hens. Branching out from this complete and satisfying center are all the auxiliary channels of his life, such as his heartiness with men, his appreciation of rough humor, his love of good drink and food and games, his car, his radio, everything that is his, that bears his emblem of the gaudy seed-bearer. He sizes women up at a glance, with*

---

2. A local brand.

*sexual classifications, crude images flashing into his mind and determining the way he smiles at them.*]

BLANCHE: [*Drawing involuntarily back from his stare.*] You must be Stanley. I'm Blanche.
STANLEY: Stella's sister?
BLANCHE: Yes.
STANLEY: H'lo. Where's the little woman?
BLANCHE: In the bathroom.
STANLEY: Oh. Didn't know you were coming in town.
BLANCHE: I—uh—
STANLEY: Where you from, Blanche?
BLANCHE: Why, I—live in Laurel.

[*He has crossed to the closet and removed the whiskey bottle.*]

STANLEY: In Laurel, huh? Oh, yeah. Yeah, in Laurel, that's right. Not in my territory. Liquor goes fast in hot weather. [*He holds the bottle to the light to observe its depletion.*] Have a shot?
BLANCHE: No, I—rarely touch it.
STANLEY: Some people rarely touch it, but it touches them often.
BLANCHE: [*Faintly.*] Ha-ha.
STANLEY: My clothes're stickin' to me. Do you mind if I make myself comfortable?

[*He starts to remove his shirt.*]

BLANCHE: Please, please do.
STANLEY: Be comfortable is my motto.
BLANCHE: It's mine, too. It's hard to stay looking fresh. I haven't washed or even powdered my face and—here you are!
STANLEY: You know you can catch cold sitting around in damp things, especially when you been exercising hard like bowling is. You're a teacher, aren't you?
BLANCHE: Yes.
STANLEY: What do you teach, Blanche?
BLANCHE: English.
STANLEY: I never was a very good English student. How long you here for, Blanche?
BLANCHE: I—don't know yet.
STANLEY: You going to shack up here?
BLANCHE: I thought I would if it's not inconvenient for you all.
STANLEY: Good.
BLANCHE: Traveling wears me out.
STANLEY: Well, take it easy.

[*A cat screeches near the window.* BLANCHE *springs up.*]

BLANCHE: What's that?
STANLEY: Cats... Hey, Stella!
STELLA: [*Faintly, from the bathroom.*] Yes, Stanley.
STANLEY: Haven't fallen in, have you? [*He grins at* BLANCHE. *She tries unsuccessfully*

to smile back. *There is a silence.*] I'm afraid I'll strike you as being the unrefined type. Stella's spoke of you a good deal. You were married once, weren't you?

[*The music of the polka rises up, faint in the distance.*]

BLANCHE: Yes. When I was quite young.
STANLEY: What happened?
BLANCHE: The boy—the boy died. [*She sinks back down.*] I'm afraid I'm—going to be sick! [*Her head falls on her arms.*]

## Scene 2

It is six o'clock the following evening. BLANCHE *is bathing.* STELLA *is completing her toilette.* BLANCHE's *dress, a flowered print, is laid out on* STELLA's *bed.*

STANLEY *enters the kitchen from outside, leaving the door open on the perpetual "Blue Piano" around the corner.*

STANLEY: What's all this monkey doings?
STELLA: Oh, Stan! [*She jumps up and kisses him, which he accepts with lordly composure.*] I'm taking Blanche to Galatoire's[3] for supper and then to a show, because it's your poker night.
STANLEY: How about my supper, huh? I'm not going to no Galatoire's for supper!
STELLA: I put you a cold plate on ice.
STANLEY: Well, isn't that just dandy!
STELLA: I'm going to try to keep Blanche out till the party breaks up because I don't know how she would take it. So we'll go to one of the little places in the Quarter afterward and you'd better give me some money.
STANLEY: Where is she?
STELLA: She's soaking in a hot tub to quiet her nerves. She's terribly upset.
STANLEY: Over what?
STELLA: She's been through such an ordeal.
STANLEY: Yeah?
STELLA: Stan, we've—lost Belle Reve!
STANLEY: The place in the country?
STELLA: Yes.
STANLEY: How?
STELLA: [*Vaguely.*] Oh, it had to be—sacrificed or something. [*There is a pause while* STANLEY *considers.* STELLA *is changing into her dress.*] When she comes in be sure to say something nice about her appearance. And, oh! Don't mention the baby. I haven't said anything yet, I'm waiting until she gets in a quieter condition.
STANLEY: [*Ominously.*] So?
STELLA: And try to understand her and be nice to her, Stan.
BLANCHE: [*Singing in the bathroom.*] "From the land of the sky blue water, They brought a captive maid!"[4]

---

3. A famous old restaurant on Bourbon Street, the principal street in the French Quarter.
4. From the song "From the Land of Sky-Blue Water" (1908), by Nelle Richmond Eberhart (1871–1944) and Charles Wakefield Cadman (1881–1946), popularized by the Andrews Sisters in the late 1930s.

STELLA: She wasn't expecting to find us in such a small place. You see I'd tried to gloss things over a little in my letters.

STANLEY: So?

STELLA: And admire her dress and tell her she's looking wonderful. That's important with Blanche. Her little weakness!

STANLEY: Yeah. I get the idea. Now let's skip back a little to where you said the country place was disposed of.

STELLA: Oh!—yes...

STANLEY: How about that? Let's have a few more details on that subjeck.

STELLA: It's best not to talk much about it until she's calmed down.

STANLEY: So that's the deal, huh? Sister Blanche cannot be annoyed with business details right now!

STELLA: You saw how she was last night.

STANLEY: Uh-hum, I saw how she was. Now let's have a gander at the bill of sale.

STELLA: I haven't seen any.

STANLEY: She didn't show you no papers, no deed of sale or nothing like that, huh?

STELLA: It seems like it wasn't sold.

STANLEY: Well, what in hell was it then, give away? To charity?

STELLA: Shhh! She'll hear you.

STANLEY: I don't care if she hears me. Let's see the papers!

STELLA: There weren't any papers, she didn't show any papers, I don't care about papers.

STANLEY: Have you ever heard of the Napoleonic code?[5]

STELLA: No, Stanley, I haven't heard of the Napoleonic code and if I have, I don't see what it—

STANLEY: Let me enlighten you on a point or two, baby.

STELLA: Yes?

STANLEY: In the state of Louisiana we have the Napoleonic code according to which what belongs to the wife belongs to the husband and vice versa. For instance if I had a piece of property, or you had a piece of property—

STELLA: My head is swimming!

STANLEY: All right. I'll wait till she gets through soaking in a hot tub and then I'll inquire if *she* is acquainted with the Napoleonic code. It looks to me like you have been swindled, baby, and when you're swindled under the Napoleonic code I'm swindled *too*. And I don't like to be *swindled*.

STELLA: There's plenty of time to ask her questions later but if you do now she'll go to pieces again. I don't undertand what happened to Belle Reve but you don't know how ridiculous you are being when you suggest that my sister or I or anyone of our family could have perpetrated a swindle on anyone else.

STANLEY: Then where's the money if the place was sold?

STELLA: Not sold—*lost, lost!* [*He stalks into bedroom, and she follows him.*] Stanley!

[*He pulls open the wardrobe trunk standing in middle of room and jerks out an armful of dresses.*]

---

5. This codification of French law (1802), made by Napoleon as emperor, is the basis for Louisiana's civil law.

STANLEY: Open your eyes to this stuff! You think she got them out of a teacher's pay?
STELLA: Hush!
STANLEY: Look at these feathers and furs that she come here to preen herself in! What's this here? A solid-gold dress, I believe! And this one! What is these here? Fox-pieces! [*He blows on them.*] Genuine fox fur-pieces, a half a mile long! Where are your fox-pieces, Stella? Bushy snowwhite ones, no less! Where are your white fox-pieces?
STELLA: Those are inexpensive summer furs that Blanche has had a long time.
STANLEY: I got an acquaintance who deals in this sort of merchandise. I'll have him in here to appraise it. I'm willing to bet you there's thousands of dollars invested in this stuff here!
STELLA: Don't be such an idiot, Stanley!

[*He hurls the furs to the day bed. Then he jerks open small drawer in the trunk and pulls up a fistful of costume jewelry.*]

STANLEY: And what have we here? The treasure chest of a pirate!
STELLA: Oh, Stanley!
STANLEY: Pearls! Ropes of them! What is this sister of yours, a deep-sea diver? Bracelets of solid gold, too! Where are your pearls and gold bracelets?
STELLA: Shhh! Be still, Stanley!
STANLEY: And diamonds! A crown for an empress!
STELLA: A rhinestone tiara she wore to a costume ball.
STANLEY: What's rhinestone?
STELLA: Next door to glass.
STANLEY: Are you kidding? I have an acquaintance that works in a jewelry store. I'll have him in here to make an appraisal of this. Here's your plantation, or what was left of it, here!
STELLA: You have no idea how stupid and horrid you're being! Now close that trunk before she comes out of the bathroom!

[*He kicks the trunk partly closed and sits on the kitchen table.*]

STANLEY: The Kowalskis and the DuBoises have different notions.
STELLA: [*Angrily.*] Indeed they have, thank heavens!—*I'm* going outside. [*She snatches up her white hat and gloves and crosses to the outside door.*] You come out with me while Blanche is getting dressed.
STANLEY: Since when do you give me orders?
STELLA: Are you going to stay here and insult her?
STANLEY: You're damn tootin' I'm going to stay here.

[STELLA *goes out to the porch.* BLANCHE *comes out of the bathroom in a red satin robe.*]

BLANCHE: [*Airily.*] Hello, Stanley! Here I am, all freshly bathed and scented, and feeling like a brand new human being!

[*He lights a cigarette.*]

STANLEY: That's good.
BLANCHE: [*Drawing the curtains at the windows.*] Excuse me while I slip on my pretty new dress!
STANLEY: Go right ahead, Blanche.

[*She closes the drapes between the rooms.*]

BLANCHE: I understand there's to be a little card party to which we ladies are cordially *not* invited!
STANLEY: [*Ominously.*] Yeah?

[BLANCHE *throws off her robe and slips into a flowered print dress.*]

BLANCHE: Where's Stella?
STANLEY: Out on the porch.
BLANCHE: I'm going to ask a favor of you in a moment.
STANLEY: What could that be, I wonder?
BLANCHE: Some buttons in back! You may enter! [*He crosses through drapes with a smoldering look.*] How do I look?
STANLEY: You look all right.
BLANCHE: Many thanks! Now the buttons!
STANLEY: I can't do nothing with them.
BLANCHE: You men with your big clumsy fingers. May I have a drag on your cig?
STANLEY: Have one for yourself.
BLANCHE: Why, thanks! . . . It looks like my trunk has exploded.
STANLEY: Me an' Stella were helping you unpack.
BLANCHE: Well, you certainly did a fast and thorough job of it!
STANLEY: It looks like you raided some stylish shops in Paris.
BLANCHE: Ha-ha! Yes—clothes are my passion!
STANLEY: What does it cost for a string of fur-pieces like that?
BLANCHE: Why, those were a tribute from an admirer of mine!
STANLEY: He must have had a lot of—admiration!
BLANCHE: Oh, in my youth I excited some admiration. But look at me now! [*She smiles at him radiantly.*] Would you think it possible that I was once considered to be—attractive?
STANLEY: Your looks are okay.
BLANCHE: I was fishing for a compliment, Stanley.
STANLEY: I don't go in for that stuff.
BLANCHE: What—stuff?
STANLEY: Compliments to women about their looks. I never met a woman that didn't know if she was good-looking or not without being told, and some of them give themselves credit for more than they've got. I once went out with a doll who said to me, "I am the glamorous type, I am the glamorous type!" I said, "So what?"
BLANCHE: And what did she say then?
STANLEY: She didn't say nothing. That shut her up like a clam.
BLANCHE: Did it end the romance?
STANLEY: It ended the conversation—that was all. Some men are took in by this Hollywood glamor stuff and some men are not.
BLANCHE: I'm sure you belong in the second category.
STANLEY: That's right.
BLANCHE: I cannot imagine any witch of a woman casting a spell over you.
STANLEY: That's—right.
BLANCHE: You're simple, straightforward and honest, a little bit on the primitive side I should think. To interest you a woman would have to— [*She pauses with an indefinite gesture.*]

STANLEY: [*Slowly.*] Lay . . . her cards on the table.
BLANCHE: [*Smiling.*] Well, I never cared for wishy-washy people. That was why, when you walked in here last night, I said to myself—"My sister has married a man!"—Of course that was all that I could tell about you.
STANLEY: [*Booming.*] Now let's cut the re-bop![6]
BLANCHE: [*Pressing hands to her ears.*] Ouuuuu!
STELLA: [*Calling from the steps.*] Stanley! You come out here and let Blanche finish dressing!
BLANCHE: I'm through dressing, honey.
STELLA: Well, you come out, then.
STANLEY: Your sister and I are having a little talk.
BLANCHE: [*Lightly.*] Honey, do me a favor. Run to the drugstore and get me a lemon Coke with plenty of chipped ice in it!—Will you do that for me, sweetie?
STELLA: [*Uncertainly.*] Yes. [*She goes around the corner of the building.*]
BLANCHE: The poor little thing was out there listening to us, and I have an idea she doesn't understand you as well as I do. . . . All right; now, Mr. Kowalski, let us proceed without any more double-talk. I'm ready to answer all questions. I've nothing to hide. What is it?
STANLEY: There is such a thing in this state of Louisiana as the Napoleonic code, according to which whatever belongs to my wife is also mine—and vice versa.
BLANCHE: My, but you have an impressive judicial air!

> [*She sprays herself with her atomizer; then playfully sprays him with it. He seizes the atomizer and slams it down on the dresser. She throws back her head and laughs.*]

STANLEY: If I didn't know that you was my wife's sister I'd get ideas about you!
BLANCHE: Such as what!
STANLEY: Don't play so dumb. You know what!
BLANCHE: [*She puts the atomizer on the table.*] All right. Cards on the table. That suits me. [*She turns to* STANLEY.] I know I fib a good deal. After all, a woman's charm is fifty per cent illusion, but when a thing is important I tell the truth, and this is the truth: I haven't cheated my sister or you or anyone else as long as I have lived.
STANLEY: Where's the papers? In the trunk?
BLANCHE: Everything that I own is in that trunk. [STANLEY *crosses to the trunk, shoves it roughly open and begins to open compartments.*] What in the name of heaven are you thinking of! What's in the back of that little boy's mind of yours? That I am absconding with something, attempting some kind of treachery on my sister?—Let me do that! It will be faster and simpler . . . [*She crosses to the trunk and takes out a box.*] I keep my papers mostly in this tin box. [*She opens it.*]
STANLEY: What's them underneath? [*He indicates another sheaf of paper.*]
BLANCHE: These are love-letters, yellowing with antiquity, all from one boy. [*He snatches them up. She speaks fiercely.*] Give those back to me!
STANLEY: I'll have a look at them first!
BLANCHE: The touch of your hands insults them!
STANLEY: Don't pull that stuff!

---

6. Nonsense (from "bop," a form of jazz).

[*He rips off the ribbon and starts to examine them.* BLANCHE *snatches them from him, and they cascade to the floor.*]

BLANCHE: Now that you've touched them I'll burn them!

STANLEY: [*Staring, baffled.*] What in hell are they?

BLANCHE: [*On the floor gathering them up.*] Poems a dead boy wrote. I hurt him the way that you would like to hurt me, but you can't! I'm not young and vulnerable any more. But my young husband was and I—never mind about that! Just give them back to me!

STANLEY: What do you mean by saying you'll have to burn them?

BLANCHE: I'm sorry, I must have lost my head for a moment. Everyone has something he won't let others touch because of their—intimate nature . . . [*She now seems faint with exhaustion and she sits down with the strong box and puts on a pair of glasses and goes methodically through a large stack of papers.*] Ambler & Ambler. Hmmmmm. . . . Crabtree. . . . More Ambler & Ambler.

STANLEY: What is Ambler & Ambler?

BLANCHE: A firm that made loans on the place.

STANLEY: Then it *was* lost on a mortgage?

BLANCHE: [*Touching her forehead.*] That must've been what happened.

STANLEY: I don't want no ifs, ands or buts! What's all the rest of them papers?

[*She hands him the entire box. He carries it to the table and starts to examine the papers.*]

BLANCHE: [*Picking up a large envelope containing more papers.*] There are thousands of papers, stretching back over hundreds of years, affecting Belle Reve as, piece by piece, our improvident grandfathers and father and uncles and brothers exchanged the land for their epic fornications—to put it plainly! [*She removes her glasses with an exhausted laugh.*] The four-letter word deprived us of our plantation, till finally all that was left—and Stella can verify that!—was the house itself and about twenty acres of ground, including a graveyard, to which now all but Stella and I have retreated. [*She pours the contents of the envelope on the table.*] Here all of them are, all papers! I hereby endow you with them! Take them, peruse them—commit them to memory, even! I think it's wonderfully fitting that Belle Reve should finally be this bunch of old papers in your big, capable hands! . . . I wonder if Stella's come back with my lemon Coke . . . [*She leans back and closes her eyes.*]

STANLEY: I have a lawyer acquaintance who will study these out.

BLANCHE: Present them to him with a box of aspirin tablets.

STANLEY: [*Becoming somewhat sheepish.*] You see, under the Napoleonic code—a man has to take an interest in his wife's affairs—especially now that she's going to have a baby.

[BLANCHE *opens her eyes. The "Blue Piano" sounds louder.*]

BLANCHE: Stella? Stella going to have a baby? [*Dreamily.*] I didn't know she was going to have a baby! [*She gets up and crosses to the outside door.* STELLA *appears around the corner with a carton from the drugstore.* STANLEY *goes into the bedroom with the envelope and the box. The inner rooms fade to darkness and the outside wall of the house is visible.* BLANCHE *meets* STELLA *at the foot of the steps to the sidewalk.*] Stella, Stella for star! How lovely to have a baby! It's all right. Everything's all right.

STELLA: I'm sorry he did that to you.
BLANCHE: Oh, I guess he's just not the type that goes for jasmine perfume, but maybe he's what we need to mix with our blood now that we've lost Belle Reve. We thrashed it out. I feel a bit shaky, but I think I handled it nicely, I laughed and treated it all as a joke. [STEVE and PABLO *appear, carrying a case of beer.*] I called him a little boy and laughed and flirted. Yes, I was flirting with your husband! [*As the men approach.*] The guests are gathering for the poker party. [*The two men pass between them, and enter the house.*] Which way do we go now, Stella—this way?
STELLA: No, this way. [*She leads* BLANCHE *away.*]
BLANCHE: [*Laughing.*] The blind are leading the blind!⁷

[*A tamale* VENDOR *is heard calling.*]

VENDOR'S VOICE: Red-hot!

## Scene 3. The Poker Night

*There is a picture of Van Gogh's of a billiard-parlor at night.⁸ The kitchen now suggests that sort of lurid nocturnal brilliance, the raw colors of childhood's spectrum. Over the yellow linoleum of the kitchen table hangs an electric bulb with a vivid green glass shade. The poker players—*STANLEY, STEVE, MITCH *and* PABLO*—wear colored shirts, solid blues, a purple, a red-and-white check, a light green, and they are men at the peak of their physical manhood, as coarse and direct and powerful as the primary colors. There are vivid slices of watermelon on the table, whiskey bottles and glasses. The bedroom is relatively dim with only the light that spills between the portieres and through the wide window on the street.*

*For a moment, there is absorbed silence as a hand is dealt.*

STEVE: Anything wild this deal?
PABLO: One-eyed jacks are wild.
STEVE: Give me two cards.
PABLO: You, Mitch?
MITCH: I'm out.
PABLO: One.
MITCH: Anyone want a shot?
STANLEY: Yeah. Me.
PABLO: Why don't somebody go to the Chinaman's and bring back a load of chop suey?
STANLEY: When I'm losing you want to eat! Ante up! Openers? Openers! Get y'r ass off the table, Mitch. Nothing belongs on a poker table but cards, chips and whiskey. [*He lurches up and tosses some watermelon rinds to the floor.*]
MITCH: Kind of on your high horse, ain't you?
STANLEY: How many?
STEVE: Give me three.
STANLEY: One.
MITCH: I'm out again. I oughta go home pretty soon.

---

7. See Matthew 15.14—"If a blind person leads a blind person, both will fall into a pit." *Red-hot!:* Hot dog!
8. *The Night Café,* by Vincent van Gogh (1853–1890), Dutch Postimpressionist painter. *The Poker Night* was Williams's first title for *A Streetcar Named Desire.*

STANLEY: Shut up.
MITCH: I gotta sick mother. She don't go to sleep until I come in at night.
STANLEY: Then why don't you stay home with her?
MITCH: She says to go out, so I go, but I don't enjoy it. All the while I keep wondering how she is.
STANLEY: Aw, for the sake of Jesus, go home, then!
PABLO: What've you got?
STEVE: Spade flush.
MITCH: You all are married. But I'll be alone when she goes.—I'm going to the bathroom.
STANLEY: Hurry back and we'll fix you a sugar-tit.
MITCH: Aw, go rut. [*He crosses through the bedroom into the bathroom.*]
STEVE: [*Dealing a hand.*] Seven card stud. [*Telling his joke as he deals.*] This ole farmer is out in back of his house sittin' down th'owing corn to the chickens when all at once he hears a loud cackle and this young hen comes lickety split around the side of the house with the rooster right behind her and gaining on her fast.
STANLEY: [*Impatient with the story.*] Deal!
STEVE: But when the rooster catches sight of the farmer th'owing the corn he puts on the brakes and lets the hen get away and starts pecking corn. And the old farmer says, "Lord God, I hopes I never gits *that* hongry!"

[STEVE *and* PABLO *laugh. The sisters appear around the corner of the building.*]

STELLA: The game is still going on.
BLANCHE: How do I look?
STELLA: Lovely, Blanche.
BLANCHE: I feel so hot and frazzled. Wait till I powder before you open the door. Do I look done in?
STELLA: Why no. You are as fresh as a daisy.
BLANCHE: One that's been picked a few days.

[STELLA *opens the door and they enter.*]

STELLA: Well, well, well. I see you boys are still at it?
STANLEY: Where you been?
STELLA: Blanche and I took in a show. Blanche, this is Mr. Gonzales and Mr. Hubbell.
BLANCHE: Please don't get up.
STANLEY: Nobody's going to get up, so don't be worried.
STELLA: How much longer is this game going to continue?
STANLEY: Till we get ready to quit.
BLANCHE: Poker is so fascinating. Could I kibitz?[9]
STANLEY: You could not. Why don't you women go up and sit with Eunice?
STELLA: Because it is nearly two-thirty. [BLANCHE *crosses into the bedroom and partially closes the portieres.*] Couldn't you call it quits after one more hand?

[*A chair scrapes.* STANLEY *gives a loud whack of his hand on her thigh.*]

---

9. Watch a card player from behind and offer advice.

STELLA: [*Sharply.*] That's not fun, Stanley. [*The men laugh.* STELLA *goes into the bedroom.*] It makes me so mad when he does that in front of people.
BLANCHE: I think I will bathe.
STELLA: Again?
BLANCHE: My nerves are in knots. Is the bathroom occupied?
STELLA: I don't know.

[BLANCHE *knocks.* MITCH *opens the door and comes out, still wiping his hands on a towel.*]

BLANCHE: Oh!—good evening.
MITCH: Hello. [*He stares at her.*]
STELLA: Blanche, this is Harold Mitchell. My sister, Blanche DuBois.
MITCH: [*With awkward courtesy.*] How do you do, Miss DuBois.
STELLA: How is your mother now, Mitch?
MITCH: About the same, thanks. She appreciated your sending over that custard.—Excuse me, please.

[*He crosses slowly back into the kitchen, glancing back at* BLANCHE *and coughing a little shyly. He realizes he still has the towel in his hands and with an embarrassed laugh hands it to* STELLA. BLANCHE *looks after him with a certain interest.*]

BLANCHE: That one seems—superior to the others.
STELLA: Yes, he is.
BLANCHE: I thought he had a sort of sensitive look.
STELLA: His mother is sick.
BLANCHE: Is he married?
STELLA: No.
BLANCHE: Is he a wolf?
STELLA: Why, Blanche! [BLANCHE *laughs.*] I don't think he would be.
BLANCHE: What does—what does he do? [*She is unbuttoning her blouse.*]
STELLA: He's on the precision bench in the spare parts department. At the plant Stanley travels for.
BLANCHE: Is that something much?
STELLA: No. Stanley's the only one of his crowd that's likely to get anywhere.
BLANCHE: What makes you think Stanley will?
STELLA: Look at him.
BLANCHE: I've looked at him.
STELLA: Then you should know.
BLANCHE: I'm sorry, but I haven't noticed the stamp of genius even on Stanley's forehead.

[*She takes off the blouse and stands in her pink silk brassiere and white skirt in the light through the portieres. The game has continued in undertones.*]

STELLA: It isn't on his forehead and it isn't genius.
BLANCHE: Oh. Well, what is it, and where? I would like to know.
STELLA: It's a drive that he has. You're standing in the light, Blanche!
BLANCHE: Oh, am I!

[*She moves out of the yellow streak of light.* STELLA *has removed her dress and put on a light blue satin kimona.*]

STELLA: [*With girlish laughter.*] You ought to see their wives.
BLANCHE: [*Laughingly.*] I can imagine. Big, beefy things, I suppose.
STELLA: You know that one upstairs? [*More laughter.*] One time [*Laughing.*] the plaster— [*Laughing.*] cracked—
STANLEY: You hens cut out that conversation in there!
STELLA: You can't hear us.
STANLEY: Well, you can hear me and I said to hush up!
STELLA: This is my house and I'll talk as much as I want to!
BLANCHE: Stella, don't start a row.
STELLA: He's half drunk!—I'll be out in a minute.

> [*She goes into the bathroom.* BLANCHE *rises and crosses leisurely to a small white radio and turns it on.*]

STANLEY: Awright, Mitch, you in?
MITCH: What? Oh!—No, I'm out!

> [BLANCHE *moves back into the streak of light. She raises her arms and stretches, as she moves indolently back to the chair. Rhumba music comes over the radio.* MITCH *rises at the table.*]

STANLEY: Who turned that on in there?
BLANCHE: I did. Do you mind?
STANLEY: Turn it off!
STEVE: Aw, let the girls have their music.
PABLO: Sure, that's good, leave it on!
STEVE: Sounds like Xavier Cugat![1] [STANLEY *jumps up and, crossing to the radio, turns it off. He stops short at the sight of* BLANCHE *in the chair. She returns his look without flinching. Then he sits again at the poker table. Two of the men have started arguing hotly.*] I didn't hear you name it.
PABLO: Didn't I name it, Mitch?
MITCH: I wasn't listenin'.
PABLO: What were you doing, then?
STANLEY: He was looking through them drapes. [*He jumps up and jerks roughly at curtains to close them.*] Now deal the hand over again and let's play cards or quit. Some people get ants when they win.

> [MITCH *rises as* STANLEY *returns to his seat.*]

STANLEY: [*Yelling.*] Sit down!
MITCH: I'm going to the "head." Deal me out.
PABLO: Sure he's got ants now. Seven five-dollar bills in his pants pocket folded up tight as spitballs.
STEVE: Tomorrow you'll see him at the cashier's window getting them changed into quarters.
STANLEY: And when he goes home he'll deposit them one by one in a piggy bank his mother give him for Christmas. [*Dealing.*] This game is Spit in the Ocean.

> [MITCH *laughs uncomfortably and continues through the portieres. He stops just inside.*]

---

1. Spanish-born Cuban bandleader (1900–1990), well known for composing and playing rhumbas.

BLANCHE: [*Softly.*] Hello! The Little Boys' Room is busy right now.
MITCH: We've—been drinking beer.
BLANCHE: I hate beer.
MITCH: It's—a hot weather drink.
BLANCHE: Oh, I don't think so; it always makes me warmer. Have you got any cigs?

[*She has slipped on the dark red satin wrapper.*]

MITCH: Sure.
BLANCHE: What kind are they?
MITCH: Luckies.
BLANCHE: Oh, good. What a pretty case. Silver?
MITCH: Yes. Yes; read the inscription.
BLANCHE: Oh, is there an inscription? I can't make it out. [*He strikes a match and moves closer.*] Oh! [*Reading with feigned difficulty.*] "And if God choose,/I shall but love thee better—after—death!" Why, that's from my favorite sonnet by Mrs. Browning![2]
MITCH: You know it?
BLANCHE: Certainly I do!
MITCH: There's a story connected with that inscription.
BLANCHE: It sounds like a romance.
MITCH: A pretty sad one.
BLANCHE: Oh?
MITCH: The girl's dead now.
BLANCHE: [*In a tone of deep sympathy.*] Oh!
MITCH: She knew she was dying when she give me this. A very strange girl, very sweet—very!
BLANCHE: She must have been fond of you. Sick people have such deep, sincere attachments.
MITCH: That's right, they certainly do.
BLANCHE: Sorrow makes for sincerity, I think.
MITCH: It sure brings it out in people.
BLANCHE: The little there is belongs to people who have experienced some sorrow.
MITCH: I believe you are right about that.
BLANCHE: I'm positive that I am. Show me a person who hasn't known any sorrow and I'll show you a shuperficial—Listen to me! My tongue is a little—thick! You boys are responsible for it. The show let out at eleven and we couldn't come home on account of the poker game so we had to go somewhere and drink. I'm not accustomed to having more than one drink. Two is the limit—and *three*! [*She laughs.*] Tonight I had three.
STANLEY: Mitch!
MITCH: Deal me out. I'm talking to Miss—
BLANCHE: DuBois.
MITCH: Miss DuBois?
BLANCHE: It's a French name. It means woods and Blanche means white, so the

---

2. Elizabeth Barrett Browning (1806–1861), British poet, famous for her sequence of love poems, *Sonnets from the Portuguese.*

two together mean white woods. Like an orchard in spring! You can remember it by that.

MITCH: You're French?

BLANCHE: We are French by extraction. Our first American ancestors were French Huguenots.[3]

MITCH: You are Stella's sister, are you not?

BLANCHE: Yes, Stella is my precious little sister. I call her little in spite of the fact she's somewhat older than I. Just slightly. Less than a year. Will you do something for me?

MITCH: Sure. What?

BLANCHE: I bought this adorable little colored paper lantern at a Chinese shop on Bourbon. Put it over the light bulb! Will you, please?

MITCH: Be glad to.

BLANCHE: I can't stand a naked light bulb, any more than I can a rude remark or a vulgar action.

MITCH: [*Adjusting the lantern.*] I guess we strike you as being a pretty rough bunch.

BLANCHE: I'm very adaptable—to circumstances.

MITCH: Well, that's a good thing to be. You are visiting Stanley and Stella?

BLANCHE: Stella hasn't been so well lately, and I came down to help her for a while. She's very run down.

MITCH: You're not—?

BLANCHE: Married? No, no. I'm an old maid schoolteacher!

MITCH: You may teach school but you're certainly not an old maid.

BLANCHE: Thank you, sir! I appreciate your gallantry!

MITCH: So you are in the teaching profession?

BLANCHE: Yes. Ah, yes . . .

MITCH: Grade school or high school or—

STANLEY: [*Bellowing.*] Mitch!

MITCH: Coming!

BLANCHE: Gracious, what lung-power! . . . I teach high school. In Laurel.

MITCH: What do you teach? What subject?

BLANCHE: Guess!

MITCH: I bet you teach art or music? [BLANCHE *laughs delicately.*] Of course I could be wrong. You might teach arithmetic.

BLANCHE: Never arithmetic, sir; never arithmetic! [*With a laugh.*] I don't even know my multiplication tables! No, I have the misfortune of being an English instructor. I attempt to instill a bunch of bobby-soxers and drugstore Romeos with reverence for Hawthorne and Whitman and Poe!

MITCH: I guess that some of them are more interested in other things.

BLANCHE: How very right you are! Their literary heritage is not what most of them treasure above all else! But they're sweet things! And in the spring, it's touching to notice them making their first discovery of love! As if nobody had ever known it before! [*The bathroom door opens and* STELLA *comes out.* BLANCHE *continues talking to* MITCH.] Oh! Have you finished? Wait—I'll turn on the radio.

---

3. Protestants who fled persecution in Catholic France after the Edict of Nantes (1685); many settled in the American South.

[*She turns the knobs on the radio and it begins to play "Wien, Wien, nur du allein."*[4]
BLANCHE *waltzes to the music with romantic gestures.* MITCH *is delighted and moves in awkward imitation like a dancing bear.* STANLEY *stalks fiercely through the portieres into the bedroom. He crosses to the small white radio and snatches it off the table. With a shouted oath, he tosses the instrument out the window.*]

STELLA: Drunk—drunk—animal thing, you! [*She rushes through to the poker table.*] All of you—please go home! If any of you have one spark of decency in you—
BLANCHE: [*Wildly.*] Stella, watch out, he's—

[STANLEY *charges after* STELLA.]

MEN: [*Feebly.*] Take it easy, Stanley. Easy, fellow.—Let's all—
STELLA: You lay your hands on me and I'll—

[*She backs out of sight. He advances and disappears. There is the sound of a blow,* STELLA *cries out.* BLANCHE *screams and runs into the kitchen. The men rush forward and there is grappling and cursing. Something is overturned with a crash.*]

BLANCHE: [*Shrilly.*] My sister is going to have a baby!
MITCH: This is terrible.
BLANCHE: Lunacy, absolute lunacy!
MITCH: Get him in here, men.

[STANLEY *is forced, pinioned by the two men, into the bedroom. He nearly throws them off. Then all at once he subsides and is limp in their grasp. They speak quietly and lovingly to him and he leans his face on one of their shoulders.*]

STELLA: [*In a high, unnatural voice, out of sight.*] I want to go away, I want to go away!
MITCH: Poker shouldn't be played in a house with women.

[BLANCHE *rushes into the bedroom.*]

BLANCHE: I want my sister's clothes! We'll go to that woman's upstairs!
MITCH: Where is the clothes?
BLANCHE: [*Opening the closet.*] I've got them! [*She rushes through to* STELLA.] Stella, Stella, precious! Dear, dear little sister, don't be afraid!

[*With her arm around* STELLA, BLANCHE *guides her to the outside door and upstairs.*]

STANLEY: [*Dully.*] What's the matter; what's happened?
MITCH: You just blew your top, Stan.
PABLO: He's okay, now.

---

4. "Vienna, Vienna, you are my only," a waltz from an operetta by Franz Lehár (1870–1948).

STEVE: Sure, my boy's okay!
MITCH: Put him on the bed and get a wet towel.
PABLO: I think coffee would do him a world of good, now.
STANLEY: [*Thickly.*] I want water.
MITCH: Put him under the shower!

[*The men talk quietly as they lead him to the bathroom.*]

STANLEY: Let the rut go of me, you sons of bitches!

[*Sounds of blows are heard. The water goes on full tilt.*]

STEVE: Let's get quick out of here!

[*They rush to the poker table and sweep up their winnings on their way out.*]

MITCH: [*Sadly but firmly.*] Poker should not be played in a house with women.

[*The door closes on them and the place is still. The Negro entertainers in the bar around the corner play "Paper Doll"[5] slow and blue. After a moment* STANLEY *comes out of the bathroom dripping water and still in his clinging wet polka dot drawers.*]

STANLEY: Stella! [*There is a pause.*] My baby doll's left me! [*He breaks into sobs. Then he goes to the phone and dials, still shuddering with sobs.*] Eunice? I want my baby! [*He waits a moment; then he hangs up and dials again.*] Eunice! I'll keep on ringin' until I talk with my baby! [*An indistinguishable shrill voice is heard. He hurls phone to floor. Dissonant brass and piano sounds as the rooms dim out to darkness and the outer walls appear in the night light. The "Blue Piano" plays for a brief interval. Finally,* STANLEY *stumbles half-dressed out to the porch and down the wooden steps to the pavement before the building. There he throws back his head like a baying hound and bellows his wife's name:* "STELLA! STELLA, *sweetheart!* STELLA!"] Stell-*lahhhhh*!
EUNICE: [*Calling down from the door of her upper apartment.*] Quit that howling out there an' go back to bed!
STANLEY: I want my baby down here. Stella, Stella!
EUNICE: She ain't comin' down so you quit! Or you'll git th' law on you!
STANLEY: Stella!
EUNICE: You can't beat on a woman an' then call 'er back! She won't come! And her goin' t' have a baby! . . . You stinker! You whelp of a Polack, you! I hope they do haul you in and turn the fire hose on you, same as the last time!
STANLEY: [*Humbly.*] Eunice, I want my girl to come down with me!
EUNICE: Hah! [*She slams her door.*]
STANLEY: [*With heaven-splitting violence.*] STELL-LAHHHHH!

[*The low-tone clarinet moans. The door upstairs opens again.* STELLA *slips down the rickety stairs in her robe. Her eyes are glistening with tears and her hair loose about her throat and shoulders. They stare at each other. Then they come together with low, animal moans. He falls to his knees on the steps and presses his face to her belly, curving a little with maternity. Her eyes go blind with tenderness as she catches his head and raises him level with her. He snatches the screen door open and lifts*

---

5. Song by Johnny S. Black (1915), popularized by the Mills Brothers in the early 1940s.

her off her feet and bears her into the dark flat. BLANCHE *comes out the upper landing in her robe and slips fearfully down the steps.*]

BLANCHE: Where is my little sister? Stella? Stella?

[*She stops before the dark entrance of her sister's flat. Then catches her breath as if struck. She rushes down to the walk before the house. She looks right and left as if for a sanctuary. The music fades away.* MITCH *appears from around the corner.*]

MITCH: Miss DuBois?
BLANCHE: Oh!
MITCH: All quiet on the Potomac now?[6]
BLANCHE: She ran downstairs and went back in there with him.
MITCH: Sure she did.
BLANCHE: I'm terrified!
MITCH: Ho-ho! There's nothing to be scared of. They're crazy about each other.
BLANCHE: I'm not used to such—
MITCH: Naw, it's a shame this had to happen when you just got here. But don't take it serious.
BLANCHE: Violence! Is so—
MITCH: Set down on the steps and have a cigarette with me.
BLANCHE: I'm not properly dressed.
MITCH: That don't make no difference in the Quarter.
BLANCHE: Such a pretty silver case.
MITCH: I showed you the inscription, didn't I?
BLANCHE: Yes. [*During the pause, she looks up at the sky.*] There's so much—so much confusion in the world . . . [*He coughs diffidently.*] Thank you for being so kind! I need kindness now.

## Scene 4

*It is early the following morning. There is a confusion of street cries like a choral chant.*
STELLA *is lying down in the bedroom. Her face is serene in the early morning sunlight. One hand rests on her belly, rounding slightly with new maternity. From the other dangles a book of colored comics. Her eyes and lips have that almost narcotized tranquility that is in the faces of Eastern idols.*

*The table is sloppy with remains of breakfast and the debris of the preceding night, and* STANLEY's *gaudy pyjamas lie across the threshold of the bathroom. The outside door is slightly ajar on a sky of summer brilliance.*

BLANCHE *appears at this door. She has spent a sleepless night and her appearance entirely contrasts with* STELLA's. *She presses her knuckles nervously to her lips as she looks through the door, before entering.*

BLANCHE: Stella?
STELLA: [*Stirring lazily.*] Hmmh?

[BLANCHE *utters a moaning cry and runs into the bedroom, throwing herself down beside* STELLA *in a rush of hysterical tenderness.*]

---

6. "All Quiet on the Potomac" was a Civil War catchphrase, attributed to Union general George McClellan, who pushed the Confederate army back over the Potomac River in 1862.

BLANCHE: Baby, my baby sister!
STELLA: [*Drawing away from her.*] Blanche, what is the matter with you?

> [BLANCHE *straightens up slowly and stands beside the bed looking down at her sister with knuckles pressed to her lips.*]

BLANCHE: He's left?
STELLA: Stan? Yes.
BLANCHE: Will he be back?
STELLA: He's gone to get the car greased. Why?
BLANCHE: Why! I've been half crazy, Stella! When I found out you'd been insane enough to come back in here after what happened—I started to rush in after you!
STELLA: I'm glad you didn't.
BLANCHE: What were you thinking of? [STELLA *makes an indefinite gesture.*] Answer me! What? What?
STELLA: Please, Blanche! Sit down and stop yelling.
BLANCHE: All right, Stella. I will repeat the question quietly now. How could you come back in this place last night? Why, you must have slept with him!

> [STELLA *gets up in a calm and leisurely way.*]

STELLA: Blanche, I'd forgotten how excitable you are. You're making much too much fuss about this.
BLANCHE: Am I?
STELLA: Yes, you are, Blanche. I know how it must have seemed to you and I'm awful sorry it had to happen, but it wasn't anything as serious as you seem to take it. In the first place, when men are drinking and playing poker anything can happen. It's always a powder-keg. He didn't know what he was doing.... He was as good as a lamb when I came back and he's really very, very ashamed of himself.
BLANCHE: And that—that makes it all right?
STELLA: No, it isn't all right for anybody to make such a terrible row, but—people do sometimes. Stanley's always smashed things. Why, on our wedding night— soon as we came in here—he snatched off one of my slippers and rushed about the place smashing light bulbs with it.
BLANCHE: He did—*what*?
STELLA: He smashed all the lightbulbs with the heel of my slipper! [*She laughs.*]
BLANCHE: And you—you *let* him? Didn't *run*, didn't *scream*?
STELLA: I was—sort of—thrilled by it. [*She waits for a moment.*] Eunice and you had breakfast?
BLANCHE: Do you suppose I wanted any breakfast?
STELLA: There's some coffee left on the stove.
BLANCHE: You're so—matter-of-fact about it, Stella.
STELLA: What other can I be? He's taken the radio to get it fixed. It didn't land on the pavement so only one tube was smashed.
BLANCHE: And you are standing there smiling!
STELLA: What do you want me to do?
BLANCHE: Pull yourself together and face the facts.
STELLA: What are they, in your opinion?
BLANCHE: In my opinion? You're married to a madman!

STELLA: No!
BLANCHE: Yes, you are, your fix is worse than mine is! Only you're not being sensible about it. I'm going to *do* something. Get hold of myself and make myself a new life!
STELLA: Yes?
BLANCHE: But you've given in. And that isn't right, you're not old! You can get out.
STELLA: [*Slowly and emphatically.*] I'm not in anything I want to get out of.
BLANCHE: [*Incredulously.*] What—Stella?
STELLA: I said I am not in anything that I have a desire to get out of. Look at the mess in this room! And those empty bottles! They went through two cases last night! He promised this morning that he was going to quit having these poker parties, but you know how long such a promise is going to keep. Oh, well, it's his pleasure, like mine is movies and bridge. People have got to tolerate each other's habits, I guess.
BLANCHE: I don't understand you. [STELLA *turns toward her.*] I don't understand your indifference. Is this a Chinese philosophy you've—cultivated?
STELLA: Is what—what?
BLANCHE: This—shuffling about and mumbling—"One tube smashed—beer bottles—mess in the kitchen!"—as if nothing out of the ordinary has happened! [STELLA *laughs uncertainly and picking up the broom, twirls it in her hands.*] Are you deliberately shaking that thing in my face?
STELLA: No.
BLANCHE: Stop it. Let go of that broom. I won't have you cleaning up for him!
STELLA: Then who's going to do it? Are you?
BLANCHE: I? I!
STELLA: No, I didn't think so.
BLANCHE: Oh, let me think, if only my mind would function! We've got to get hold of some money, that's the way out!
STELLA: I guess that money is always nice to get hold of.
BLANCHE: Listen to me. I have an idea of some kind. [*Shakily she twists a cigarette into her holder.*] Do you remember Shep Huntleigh? [STELLA *shakes her head.*] Of course you remember Shep Huntleigh. I went out with him at college and wore his pin for a while. Well—
STELLA: Well?
BLANCHE: I ran into him last winter. You know I went to Miami during the Christmas holidays?
STELLA: No.
BLANCHE: Well, I did. I took the trip as an investment, thinking I'd meet someone with a million dollars.
STELLA: Did you?
BLANCHE: Yes. I ran into Shep Huntleigh—I ran into him on Biscayne Boulevard, on Christmas Eve, about dusk ... getting into his car—Cadillac convertible; must have been a block long!
STELLA: I should think it would have been—inconvenient in traffic!
BLANCHE: You've heard of oil wells?
STELLA: Yes—remotely.
BLANCHE: He has them, all over Texas. Texas is literally spouting gold in his pockets.

STELLA: My, my.
BLANCHE: Y'know how indifferent I am to money. I think of money in terms of what it does for you. But he could do it, he could certainly do it!
STELLA: Do what, Blanche?
BLANCHE: Why—set us up in a—shop!
STELLA: What kind of shop?
BLANCHE: Oh, a—shop of some kind! He could do it with half what his wife throws away at the races.
STELLA: He's married?
BLANCHE: Honey, would I be here if the man weren't married? [STELLA *laughs a little.* BLANCHE *suddenly springs up and crosses to phone. She speaks shrilly.*] How do I get Western Union?[7]—Operator! Western Union!
STELLA: That's a dial phone, honey.
BLANCHE: I can't dial, I'm too—
STELLA: Just dial O.
BLANCHE: O?
STELLA: Yes, "O" for Operator!

[BLANCHE *considers a moment; then she puts the phone down.*]

BLANCHE: Give me a pencil. Where is a slip of paper? I've got to write it down first—the message, I mean... [*She goes to the dressing table, and grabs up a sheet of Kleenex and an eyebrow pencil for writing equipment.*] Let me see now... [*She bites the pencil.*] "Darling Shep. Sister and I in desperate situation."
STELLA: I beg your pardon!
BLANCHE: "Sister and I in desperate situation. Will explain details later. Would you be interested in—?" [*She bites the pencil again.*] "Would you be—interested—in..." [*She smashes the pencil on the table and springs up.*] You never get anywhere with direct appeals!
STELLA: [*With a laugh.*] Don't be so ridiculous, darling!
BLANCHE: But I'll think of something, I've *got* to think of—something! Don't laugh at me, Stella! Please, please don't—I—I want you to look at the contents of my purse! Here's what's in it! [*She snatches her purse open.*] Sixty-five measly cents in coin of the realm!
STELLA: [*Crossing to bureau.*] Stanley doesn't give me a regular allowance, he likes to pay bills himself, but—this morning he gave me ten dollars to smooth things over. You take five of it, Blanche, and I'll keep the rest.
BLANCHE: Oh, no. No, Stella.
STELLA: [*Insisting.*] I know how it helps your morale just having a little pocket-money on you.
BLANCHE: No, thank you—I'll take to the streets!
STELLA: Talk sense! How did you happen to get so low on funds?
BLANCHE: Money just goes—it goes places. [*She rubs her forehead.*] Sometime today I've got to get hold of a Bromo![8]
STELLA: I'll fix you one now.
BLANCHE: Not yet—I've got to keep thinking!
STELLA: I wish you'd just let things go, at least for a—while.

---

7. The largest American telegraph company throughout most of the twentieth century.
8. Short for "Bromo Seltzer," a headache remedy.

BLANCHE: Stella, I can't live with him! You can, he's your husband. But how could I stay here with him, after last night, with just those curtains between us?

STELLA: Blanche, you saw him at his worst last night.

BLANCHE: On the contrary, I saw him at his best! What such a man has to offer is animal force and he gave a wonderful exhibition of that! But the only way to live with such a man is to—go to bed with him! And that's your job—not mine!

STELLA: After you've rested a little, you'll see it's going to work out. You don't have to worry about anything while you're here. I mean—expenses...

BLANCHE: I have to plan for us both, to get us both—out!

STELLA: You take it for granted that I am in something that I want to get out of.

BLANCHE: I take it for granted that you still have sufficient memory of Belle Reve to find this place and these poker players impossible to live with.

STELLA: Well, you're taking entirely too much for granted.

BLANCHE: I can't believe you're in earnest.

STELLA: No?

BLANCHE: I understand how it happened—a little. You saw him in uniform, an officer, not here but—

STELLA: I'm not sure it would have made any difference where I saw him.

BLANCHE: Now don't say it was one of those mysterious electric things between people! If you do I'll laugh in your face.

STELLA: I am not going to say anything more at all about it!

BLANCHE: All right, then, don't!

STELLA: But there are things that happen between a man and a woman in the dark—that sort of make everything else seem—unimportant. [*Pause.*]

BLANCHE: What you are talking about is brutal desire—just—Desire!—the name of that rattle-trap streetcar that bangs through the Quarter, up one old narrow street and down another...

STELLA: Haven't you ever ridden on that streetcar?

BLANCHE: It brought me here.—Where I'm not wanted and where I'm ashamed to be...

STELLA: Then don't you think your superior attitude is a bit out of place?

BLANCHE: I am not being or feeling at all superior, Stella. Believe me I'm not! It's just this. This is how I look at it. A man like that is someone to go out with—once—twice—three times when the devil is in you. But live with? Have a child by?

STELLA: I have told you I love him.

BLANCHE: Then I *tremble* for you! I just—*tremble* for you....

STELLA: I can't help your trembling if you insist on trembling!

[*There is a pause.*]

BLANCHE: May I—speak—*plainly?*

STELLA: Yes, do. Go ahead. As plainly as you want to.

[*Outside, a train approaches. They are silent till the noise subsides. They are both in the bedroom. Under cover of the train's noise* STANLEY *enters from outside. He stands unseen by the women, holding some packages in his arms, and overhears their following conversation. He wears an undershirt and grease-stained seersucker pants.*]

BLANCHE: Well—if you'll forgive me—he's *common*!

STELLA: Why, yes, I suppose he is.

BLANCHE: Suppose! You can't have forgotten that much of our bringing up, Stella, that you just *suppose* that any part of a gentleman's in his nature! *Not one particle, no!* Oh, if he was just—*ordinary!* Just *plain*—but good and wholesome, but—*no.* There's something downright—*bestial*—about him! You're hating me saying this, aren't you?

STELLA: [*Coldly.*] Go on and say it all, Blanche.

BLANCHE: He acts like an animal, has an animal's habits! Eats like one, moves like one, talks like one! There's even something—sub-human—something not quite to the stage of humanity yet! Yes, something—ape-like about him, like one of those pictures I've seen in—anthropological studies! Thousands and thousands of years have passed him right by, and there he is—Stanley Kowalski—survivor of the Stone Age! Bearing the raw meat home from the kill in the jungle! And you—*you* here—*waiting* for him! Maybe he'll strike you or maybe grunt and kiss you! That is, if kisses have been discovered yet! Night falls and the other apes gather! There in the front of the cave, all grunting like him, and swilling and gnawing and hulking! His poker night! you call it—this party of apes! Somebody growls—some creature snatches at something—the fight is on! *God!* Maybe we are a long way from being made in God's image, but Stella—my sister—there has been *some* progress since then! Such things as art—as poetry and music—such kinds of new light have come into the world since then! In some kinds of people some tenderer feelings have had some little beginning! That we have got to make *grow!* And *cling* to, and hold as our flag! In this dark march toward whatever it is we're approaching.... *Don't—don't hang back with the brutes!*

[*Another train passes outside.* STANLEY *hesitates, licking his lips. Then suddenly he turns stealthily about and withdraws through front door. The women are still unaware of his presence. When the train has passed he calls through the closed front door.*]

STANLEY: Hey! Hey, Stella!

STELLA: [*Who has listened gravely to* BLANCHE.] Stanley!

BLANCHE: Stell, I—

[*But* STELLA *has gone to the front door.* STANLEY *enters casually with his packages.*]

STANLEY: Hiyuh, Stella. Blanche back?

STELLA: Yes, she's back.

STANLEY: Hiyuh, Blanche. [*He grins at her.*]

STELLA: You must've got under the car.

STANLEY: Them darn mechanics at Fritz's don't know their ass fr'm—*Hey!*

[STELLA *has embraced him with both arms, fiercely, and full in the view of* BLANCHE. *He laughs and clasps her head to him. Over her head he grins through the curtains at* BLANCHE. *As the lights fade away, with a lingering brightness on their embrace, the music of the "Blue Piano" and trumpet and drums is heard.*]

## Scene 5

BLANCHE *is seated in the bedroom fanning herself with a palm leaf as she reads over a just-completed letter. Suddenly she bursts into a peal of laughter.* STELLA *is dressing in the bedroom.*

STELLA: What are you laughing at, honey?
BLANCHE: Myself, myself, for being such a liar! I'm writing a letter to Shep. [*She picks up the letter.*] "Darling Shep. I am spending the summer on the wing, making flying visits here and there. And who knows, perhaps I shall take a sudden notion to *swoop* down on *Dallas!* How would you feel about that? Ha-ha! [*She laughs nervously and brightly, touching her throat as if actually talking to Shep.*] Forewarned is forearmed, as they say!"—How does that sound?
STELLA: Uh-huh...
BLANCHE: [*Going on nervously.*] "Most of my sister's friends go north in the summer but some have homes on the Gulf and there has been a continued round of entertainments, teas, cocktails, and luncheons—"

[*A disturbance is heard upstairs at the Hubbells' apartment.*]

STELLA: Eunice seems to be having some trouble with Steve. [EUNICE's *voice shouts in terrible wrath.*]
EUNICE: I heard about you and that blonde!
STEVE: That's a damn lie!
EUNICE: You ain't pulling the wool over my eyes! I wouldn't mind if you'd stay down at the Four Deuces, but you always going up.
STEVE: Who ever seen me up?
EUNICE: I seen you chasing her 'round the balcony—I'm gonna call the vice squad!
STEVE: Don't you throw that at me!
EUNICE: [*Shrieking.*] You hit me! I'm gonna call the police!

[*A clatter of aluminum striking a wall is heard, followed by a man's angry roar, shouts and overturned furniture. There is a crash; then a relative hush.*]

BLANCHE: [*Brightly.*] Did he *kill* her?

[EUNICE *appears on the steps in daemonic disorder.*]

STELLA: No! She's coming downstairs.
EUNICE: Call the police, I'm going to call the police! [*She rushes around the corner.*]

[*They laugh lightly.* STANLEY *comes around the corner in his green and scarlet silk bowling shirt. He trots up the steps and bangs into the kitchen.* BLANCHE *registers his entrance with nervous gestures.*]

STANLEY: What's a matter with Eun-uss?
STELLA: She and Steve had a row. Has she got the police?
STANLEY: Naw. She's gettin' a drink.
STELLA: That's much more practical!

[STEVE *comes down nursing a bruise on his forehead and looks in the door.*]

STEVE: She here?
STANLEY: Naw, naw. At the Four Deuces.

STEVE: That rutting hunk! [*He looks around the corner a bit timidly, then turns with affected boldness and runs after her.*]
BLANCHE: I must jot that down in my notebook. Ha-ha! I'm compiling a notebook of quaint little words and phrases I've picked up here.
STANLEY: You won't pick up nothing here you ain't heard before.
BLANCHE: Can I count on that?
STANLEY: You can count on it up to five hundred.
BLANCHE: That's a mighty high number. [*He jerks open the bureau drawer, slams it shut and throws shoes in a corner. At each noise* BLANCHE *winces slightly. Finally she speaks.*] What sign were you born under?
STANLEY: [*While he is dressing.*] Sign?
BLANCHE: Astrological sign. I bet you were born under Aries. Aries people are forceful and dynamic. They dote on noise! They love to bang things around! You must have had lots of banging around in the army and now that you're out, you make up for it by treating inanimate objects with such a fury!

[STELLA *has been going in and out of closet during this scene. Now she pops her head out of the closet.*]

STELLA: Stanley was born just five minutes after Christmas.
BLANCHE: Capricorn—the Goat!
STANLEY: What sign were *you* born under?
BLANCHE: Oh, my birthday's next month, the fifteenth of September; that's under Virgo.
STANLEY: What's Virgo?
BLANCHE: Virgo is the Virgin.
STANLEY: [*Contemptuously.*] Hah! [*He advances a little as he knots his tie.*] Say, do you happen to know somebody named Shaw?

[*Her face expresses a faint shock. She reaches for the cologne bottle and dampens her handkerchief as she answers carefully.*]

BLANCHE: Why, everybody knows somebody named Shaw!
STANLEY: Well, this somebody named Shaw is under the impression he met you in Laurel, but I figure he must have got you mixed up with some other party because this other party is someone he met at a hotel called the Flamingo.

[BLANCHE *laughs breathlessly as she touches the cologne-dampened handkerchief to her temples.*]

BLANCHE: I'm afraid he does have me mixed up with this "other party." The Hotel Flamingo is not the sort of establishment I would dare to be seen in!
STANLEY: You know of it?
BLANCHE: Yes, I've seen it and smelled it.
STANLEY: You must've got pretty close if you could smell it.
BLANCHE: The odor of cheap perfume is penetrating.
STANLEY: That stuff you use is expensive?
BLANCHE: Twenty-five dollars an ounce! I'm nearly out. That's just a hint if you want to remember my birthday! [*She speaks lightly but her voice has a note of fear.*]
STANLEY: Shaw must've got you mixed up. He goes in and out of Laurel all the time so he can check on it and clear up any mistake.

[*He turns away and crosses to the portieres.* BLANCHE *closes her eyes as if faint. Her hand trembles as she lifts the handkerchief again to her forehead.* STEVE *and* EUNICE *come around corner.* STEVE's *arm is around* EUNICE's *shoulder and she is sobbing luxuriously and he is cooing love-words. There is a murmur of thunder as they go slowly upstairs in a tight embrace.*]

STANLEY: [*To* STELLA.] I'll wait for you at the Four Deuces!
STELLA: Hey! Don't I rate one kiss?
STANLEY: Not in front of your sister.

[*He goes out.* BLANCHE *rises from her chair. She seems faint; looks about her with an expression of almost panic.*]

BLANCHE: Stella! What have you heard about me?
STELLA: Huh?
BLANCHE: What have people been telling you about me?
STELLA: Telling?
BLANCHE: You haven't heard any—unkind—gossip about me?
STELLA: Why, no, Blanche, of course not!
BLANCHE: Honey, there was—a good deal of talk in Laurel.
STELLA: About *you,* Blanche?
BLANCHE: I wasn't so good the last two years or so, after Belle Reve had started to slip through my fingers.
STELLA: All of us do things we—
BLANCHE: I never was hard or self-sufficient enough. When people are soft—soft people have got to shimmer and glow—they've got to put on soft colors, the colors of butterfly wings, and put a—paper lantern over the light.... It isn't enough to be soft *and attractive.* And I—I'm fading now! I don't know how much longer I can turn the trick. [*The afternoon has faded to dusk.* STELLA *goes into the bedroom and turns on the light under the paper lantern. She holds a bottled soft drink in her hand.*] Have you been listening to me?
STELLA: I don't listen to you when you are being morbid! [*She advances with the bottled Coke.*]
BLANCHE: [*With abrupt change to gaiety.*] Is that Coke for me?
STELLA: Not for anyone else!
BLANCHE: Why, you precious thing, you! Is it just Coke?
STELLA: [*Turning.*] You mean you want a shot in it!
BLANCHE: Well, honey, a shot never does a Coke any harm! Let me! You mustn't wait on me!
STELLA: I like to wait on you, Blanche. It makes it seem more like home. [*She goes into the kitchen, finds a glass and pours a shot of whiskey into it.*]
BLANCHE: I have to admit I love to be waited on ... [*She rushes into the bedroom.* STELLA *goes to her with the glass.* BLANCHE *suddenly clutches* STELLA's *free hand with a moaning sound and presses the hand to her lips.* STELLA *is embarrassed by her show of emotion.* BLANCHE *speaks in a choked voice.*] You're—you're—so *good* to me! And I—
STELLA: Blanche.
BLANCHE: I know, I won't! You hate me to talk sentimental! But honey, *believe* I feel things more than I *tell* you! I *won't* stay long! I won't, I *promise* I—
STELLA: Blanche!

BLANCHE: [*Hysterically.*] I won't, I promise, *I'll* go! Go *soon!* I will *really!* I *won't* hang around until he—throws me out...

STELLA: Now will you stop talking foolish?

BLANCHE: Yes, honey. Watch how you pour—that fizzy stuff foams over!

> [BLANCHE *laughs shrilly and grabs the glass, but her hand shakes so it almost slips from her grasp.* STELLA *pours the Coke into the glass. It foams over and spills.* BLANCHE *gives a piercing cry.*]

STELLA: [*Shocked by the cry.*] Heavens!

BLANCHE: Right on my pretty white skirt!

STELLA: Oh... Use my hanky. Blot gently.

BLANCHE: [*Slowly recovering.*] I know—gently—gently...

STELLA: Did it stain?

BLANCHE: Not a bit. Ha-ha! Isn't that lucky? [*She sits down shakily, taking a grateful drink. She holds the glass in both hands and continues to laugh a little.*]

STELLA: Why did you scream like that?

BLANCHE: I don't know why I screamed! [*Continuing nervously.*] Mitch—Mitch is coming at seven. I guess I am just feeling nervous about our relations. [*She begins to talk rapidly and breathlessly.*] He hasn't gotten a thing but a good-night kiss, that's all I have given him, Stella. I want his respect. And men don't want anything they get too easy. But on the other hand men lose interest quickly. Especially when the girl is over—thirty. They think a girl over thirty ought to—the vulgar term is—"put out."... And I—I'm not "putting out." Of course he—he doesn't know—I mean I haven't informed him—of my real age!

STELLA: Why are you sensitive about your age?

BLANCHE: Because of hard knocks my vanity's been given. What I mean is—he thinks I'm sort of—prim and proper, you know! [*She laughs out sharply.*] I want to *deceive* him enough to make him—want me...

STELLA: Blanche, do you want *him*?

BLANCHE: I want to *rest*! I want to breathe quietly again! Yes—I *want* Mitch... very badly! Just think! If it happens! I can leave here and not be anyone's problem...

> [STANLEY *comes around the corner with a drink under his belt.*]

STANLEY: [*Bawling.*] Hey, Steve! Hey, Eunice! Hey, Stella!

> [*There are joyous calls from above. Trumpet and drums are heard from around the corner.*]

STELLA: [*Kissing* BLANCHE *impulsively.*] It *will* happen!

BLANCHE: [*Doubtfully.*] It will?

STELLA: It *will*! [*She goes across into the kitchen, looking back at* BLANCHE.] It will, honey, it will.... But don't take another drink! [*Her voice catches as she goes out the door to meet her husband.*]

> [BLANCHE *sinks faintly back in her chair with her drink.* EUNICE *shrieks with laughter and runs down the steps.* STEVE *bounds after her with goat-like screeches and chases her around corner.* STANLEY *and* STELLA *twine arms as they follow, laughing. Dusk settles deeper. The music from the Four Deuces is slow and blue.*]

BLANCHE: Ah, me, ah, me, ah, me... [*Her eyes fall shut and the palm leaf fan drops from her fingers. She slaps her hand on the chair arm a couple of times. There is a little* glimmer of lightning about the building. A YOUNG MAN comes along the street and rings the bell.] Come in. [The YOUNG MAN appears through the portieres. She regards him with interest.] Well, well! What can I do for *you*?

YOUNG MAN: I'm collecting for *The Evening Star*.

BLANCHE: I didn't know that stars took up collections.

YOUNG MAN: It's the paper.

BLANCHE: I know, I was joking—feebly! Will you—have a drink?

YOUNG MAN: No, ma'am. No, thank you. I can't drink on the job.

BLANCHE: Oh, well, now, let's see.... No, I don't have a dime! I'm not the lady of the house. I'm her sister from Mississippi. I'm one of those poor relations you've heard about.

YOUNG MAN: That's all right. I'll drop by later. [*He starts to go out. She approaches a little.*]

BLANCHE: Hey! [*He turns back shyly. She puts a cigarette in a long holder.*] Could you give me a light? [*She crosses toward him. They meet at the door between the two rooms.*]

YOUNG MAN: Sure. [*He takes out a lighter.*] This doesn't always work.

BLANCHE: It's temperamental? [*It flares.*] Ah!—thank you. [*He starts away again.*] Hey! [*He turns again, still more uncertainly. She goes close to him.*] Uh—what time is it?

YOUNG MAN: Fifteen of seven, ma'am.

BLANCHE: So late? Don't you just love these long rainy afternoons in New Orleans when an hour isn't just an hour—but a little piece of eternity dropped into your hands—and who knows what to do with it? [*She touches his shoulders.*] You—uh—didn't get wet in the rain?

YOUNG MAN: No, ma'am. I stepped inside.

BLANCHE: In a drugstore? And had a soda?

YOUNG MAN: Uh-huh.

BLANCHE: Chocolate?

YOUNG MAN: No, ma'am. Cherry.

BLANCHE: [*Laughing.*] Cherry!

YOUNG MAN: A cherry soda.

BLANCHE: You make my mouth water. [*She touches his cheek lightly, and smiles. Then she goes to the trunk.*]

YOUNG MAN: Well, I'd better be going—

BLANCHE: [*Stopping him.*] Young man! [*He turns. She takes a large, gossamer scarf from the trunk and drapes it about her shoulders. In the ensuing pause, the "Blue Piano" is heard. It continues through the rest of this scene and the opening of the next. The* YOUNG MAN *clears his throat and looks yearningly at the door.*] Young man! Young, young, young man! Has anyone ever told you that you look like a young Prince out of the Arabian Nights? [*The* YOUNG MAN *laughs uncomfortably and stands like a bashful kid.* BLANCHE *speaks softly to him.*] Well, you do, honey lamb! Come here. I want to kiss you, just once, softly and sweetly on your mouth! [*Without waiting for him to accept, she crosses quickly to him and presses her lips to his.*] Now run along, now, quickly! It would be nice to keep you, but I've got to be good—and keep my hands off children.

[*He stares at her a moment. She opens the door for him and blows a kiss at him as he goes down the steps with a dazed look. She stands there a little dreamily after he has disappeared. Then* MITCH *appears around the corner with a bunch of roses.*]

BLANCHE: [*Gaily.*] Look who's coming! My Rosenkavalier! Bow to me first... now present them! *Ahhhh—Merciiii!*[9] [*She looks at him over them, coquettishly pressing them to her lips. He beams at her self-consciously.*]

## Scene 6

*It is about two a.m. on the same evening. The outer wall of the building is visible.* BLANCHE *and* MITCH *come in. The utter exhaustion which only a neurasthenic personality can know is evident in* BLANCHE*'s voice and manner.* MITCH *is stolid but depressed. They have probably been out to the amusement park on Lake Pontchartrain,*[1] *for* MITCH *is bearing, upside down, a plaster statuette of Mae West, the sort of prize won at shooting galleries and carnival games of chance.*

BLANCHE: [*Stopping lifelessly at the steps.*] Well—[MITCH *laughs uneasily.*] Well...
MITCH: I guess it must be pretty late—and you're tired.
BLANCHE: Even the hot tamale man has deserted the street, and he hangs on till the end. [MITCH *laughs uneasily again.*] How will you get home?
MITCH: I'll walk over to Bourbon and catch an owl-car.[2]
BLANCHE: [*Laughing grimly.*] Is that street-car named Desire still grinding along the tracks at this hour?
MITCH: [*Heavily.*] I'm afraid you haven't gotten much fun out of this evening, Blanche.
BLANCHE: I spoiled it for *you*.
MITCH: No, you didn't, but I felt all the time that I wasn't giving you much—entertainment.
BLANCHE: I simply couldn't rise to the occasion. That was all. I don't think I've ever tried so hard to be gay and made such a dismal mess of it. I get ten points for trying!—I *did* try.
MITCH: Why did you try if you didn't feel like it, Blanche?
BLANCHE: I was just obeying the law of nature.
MITCH: Which law is that?
BLANCHE: The one that says the lady must entertain the gentleman—or no dice! See if you can locate my door key in this purse. When I'm so tired my fingers are all thumbs!
MITCH: [*Rooting in her purse.*] This it?
BLANCHE: No, honey, that's the key to my trunk which I must soon be packing.
MITCH: You mean you are leaving here soon?
BLANCHE: I've outstayed my welcome.
MITCH: This it?

[*The music fades away.*]

BLANCHE: Eureka! Honey, you open the door while I take a last look at the sky. [*She leans on the porch rail. He opens the door and stands awkwardly behind her.*] I'm looking for the Pleiades,[3] the Seven Sisters, but these girls are not out tonight.

---

9. *Merci:* thank you (French). *Rosenkavalier: Knight of the Rose,* title of a romantic opera (1911) by Richard Strauss (1864–1949).
1. Large coastal inlet in southern Louisiana; New Orleans is located on its south shore. *Mae West:* American star of stage and film (1892–1980). 2. All-night streetcar.
3. The seven daughters of Atlas who were changed into stars.

Oh, yes they are, there they are! God bless them! All in a bunch going home from their little bridge party.... Y' get the door open? Good boy! I guess you— want to go now...

[*He shuffles and coughs a little.*]

MITCH: Can I—uh—kiss you—good night?
BLANCHE: Why do you always ask me if you may?
MITCH: I don't know whether you want me to or not.
BLANCHE: Why should you be so doubtful?
MITCH: That night when we parked by the lake and I kissed you, you—
BLANCHE: Honey, it wasn't the kiss I objected to. I liked the kiss very much. It was the other little—familiarity—that I—felt obliged to—discourage.·... I didn't resent it! Not a bit in the world! In fact, I was somewhat flattered that you—desired me! But, honey, you know as well as I do that a single girl, a girl alone in the world, has got to keep a firm hold on her emotions or she'll be lost!
MITCH: [*Solemnly.*] Lost?
BLANCHE: I guess you are used to girls that like to be lost. The kind that get lost immediately, on the first date!
MITCH: I like you to be exactly the way that you are, because in all my—experience—I have never known anyone like you. [BLANCHE *looks at him gravely; then she bursts into laughter and then claps a hand to her mouth.*] Are you laughing at me?
BLANCHE: No, honey. The lord and lady of the house have not yet returned, so come in. We'll have a nightcap. Let's leave the lights off. Shall we?
MITCH: You just—do what you want to.

[BLANCHE *precedes him into the kitchen. The outer wall of the building disappears and the interiors of the two rooms can be dimly seen.*]

BLANCHE: [*Remaining in the first room.*] The other room's more comfortable—go on in. This crashing around in the dark is my search for some liquor.
MITCH: You want a drink?
BLANCHE: I want *you* to have a drink! You have been so anxious and solemn all evening, and so have I; we have both been anxious and solemn and now for these few last remaining moments of our lives together—I want to create—*joie de vivre!*[4] I'm lighting a candle.
MITCH: That's good.
BLANCHE: We are going to be very Bohemian. We are going to pretend that we are sitting in a little artists' cafe on the Left Bank in Paris! [*She lights a candle stub and puts it in a bottle.*] *Je suis la Dame aux Camellias! Vous êtes—Armand!*[5] Understand French?
MITCH: [*Heavily.*] Naw. Naw, I—

---

4. Joy of life (French).
5. I am the Lady of the Camellias! You are—Armand! (Both are characters in the popular romantic play *La Dame aux Camélias* [1852] by the French author Alexandre Dumas [1824–1895]; she is a courtesan who gives up her true love, Armand.) *Left Bank:* section of Paris on the westward ("left") bank of the river Seine, long associated with students and artists.

BLANCHE: *Voulez-vous couchez avec moi ce soir? Vous ne comprenez pas? Ah, quelle dommage!*[6]—I mean it's a damned good thing.... I've found some liquor! Just enough for two shots without any dividends, honey...

MITCH: [*Heavily.*] That's—good.

[*She enters the bedroom with the drinks and the candle.*]

BLANCHE: Sit down! Why don't you take off your coat and loosen your collar?

MITCH: I better leave it on.

BLANCHE: No. I want you to be comfortable.

MITCH: I am ashamed of the way I perspire. My shirt is sticking to me.

BLANCHE: Perspiration is healthy. If people didn't perspire they would die in five minutes. [*She takes his coat from him.*] This is a nice coat. What kind of material is it?

MITCH: They call that stuff alpaca.

BLANCHE: Oh. Alpaca.

MITCH: It's very light-weight alpaca.

BLANCHE: Oh. Light-weight alpaca.

MITCH: I don't like to wear a wash-coat[7] even in summer because I sweat through it.

BLANCHE: Oh.

MITCH: And it don't look neat on me. A man with a heavy build has got to be careful of what he puts on him so he don't look too clumsy.

BLANCHE: You are not too heavy.

MITCH: You don't think I am?

BLANCHE: You are not the delicate type. You have a massive bone-structure and a very imposing physique.

MITCH: Thank you. Last Christmas I was given a membership to the New Orleans Athletic Club.

BLANCHE: Oh, good.

MITCH: It was the finest present I ever was given. I work out there with the weights and I swim and I keep myself fit. When I started there, I was getting soft in the belly but now my belly is hard. It is so hard now that a man can punch me in the belly and it don't hurt me. Punch me! Go on! See? [*She pokes lightly at him.*]

BLANCHE: Gracious. [*Her hand touches her chest.*]

MITCH: Guess how much I weigh, Blanche?

BLANCHE: Oh, I'd say in the vicinity of—one hundred and eighty?

MITCH: Guess again.

BLANCHE: Not that much?

MITCH: No. More.

BLANCHE: Well, you're a tall man and you can carry a good deal of weight without looking awkward.

MITCH: I weigh two hundred and seven pounds and I'm six feet one and one half inches tall in my bare feet—without shoes on. And that is what I weigh stripped.

BLANCHE: Oh, my goodness, me! It's awe-inspiring.

---

6. Would you like to sleep with me this evening? You don't understand? Ah, what a pity!
7. Light washable jacket.

MITCH: [*Embarrassed.*] My weight is not a very interesting subject to talk about. [*He hesitates for a moment.*] What's yours?
BLANCHE: My weight?
MITCH: Yes.
BLANCHE: Guess!
MITCH: Let me lift you.
BLANCHE: Samson![8] Go on, lift me. [*He comes behind her and puts his hands on her waist and raises her lightly off the ground.*] Well?
MITCH: You are light as a feather.
BLANCHE: Ha-ha! [*He lowers her but keeps his hands on her waist.* BLANCHE *speaks with an affectation of demureness.*] You may release me now.
MITCH: Huh?
BLANCHE: [*Gaily.*] I said unhand me, sir. [*He fumblingly embraces her. Her voice sounds gently reproving.*] Now, Mitch. Just because Stanley and Stella aren't at home is no reason why you shouldn't behave like a gentleman.
MITCH: Just give me a slap whenever I step out of bounds.
BLANCHE: That won't be necessary. You're a natural gentleman, one of the very few that are left in the world. I don't want you to think that I am severe and old maid school-teacherish or anything like that. It's just—well—
MITCH: Huh?
BLANCHE: I guess it is just that I have—old-fashioned ideals! [*She rolls her eyes, knowing he cannot see her face.* MITCH *goes to the front door. There is a considerable silence between them.* BLANCHE *sighs and* MITCH *coughs self-consciously.*]
MITCH: [*Finally.*] Where's Stanley and Stella tonight?
BLANCHE: They have gone out. With Mr. and Mrs. Hubbell upstairs.
MITCH: Where did they go?
BLANCHE: I think they were planning to go to a midnight prevue at Loew's State.
MITCH: We should all go out together some night.
BLANCHE: No. That wouldn't be a good plan.
MITCH: Why not?
BLANCHE: You are an old friend of Stanley's?
MITCH: We was together in the Two-forty-first.[9]
BLANCHE: I guess he talks to you frankly?
MITCH: Sure.
BLANCHE: Has he talked to you about me?
MITCH: Oh—not very much.
BLANCHE: The way you say that, I suspect that he has.
MITCH: No, he hasn't said much.
BLANCHE: But what he *has* said. What would you say his attitude toward me was?
MITCH: Why do you want to ask that?
BLANCHE: Well—
MITCH: Don't you get along with him?
BLANCHE: What do you think?
MITCH: I don't think he understands you.
BLANCHE: That is putting it mildly. If it weren't for Stella about to have a baby, I wouldn't be able to endure things here.
MITCH: He isn't—nice to you?

---

8. Legendary strong man, in the Old Testament.   9. Battalion of engineers, in World War II.

BLANCHE: He is insufferably rude. Goes out of his way to offend me.
MITCH: In what way, Blanche?
BLANCHE: Why, in every conceivable way.
MITCH: I'm surprised to hear that.
BLANCHE: Are you?
MITCH: Well, I—don't see how anybody could be rude to you.
BLANCHE: It's really a pretty frightful situation. You see, there's no privacy here. There's just these portieres between the two rooms at night. He stalks through the rooms in his underwear at night. And I have to ask him to close the bathroom door. That sort of commonness isn't necessary. You probably wonder why I don't move out. Well, I'll tell you frankly. A teacher's salary is barely sufficient for her living expenses. I didn't save a penny last year and so I had to come here for the summer. That's why I have to put up with my sister's husband. And he has to put up with me, apparently so much against his wishes.... Surely he must have told you how much he hates he!
MITCH: I don't think he hates you.
BLANCHE: He hates me. Or why would he insult me? The first time I laid eyes on him I thought to myself, that man is my executioner! That man will destroy me, unless—
MITCH: Blanche—
BLANCHE: Yes, honey?
MITCH: Can I ask you a question?
BLANCHE: Yes. What?
MITCH: How old are you?

[*She makes a nervous gesture.*]

BLANCHE: Why do you want to know?
MITCH: I talked to my mother about you and she said, "How old is Blanche?" And I wasn't able to tell her. [*There is another pause.*]
BLANCHE: You talked to your mother about me?
MITCH: Yes.
BLANCHE: Why?
MITCH: I told my mother how nice you were, and I liked you.
BLANCHE: Were you sincere about that?
MITCH: You know I was.
BLANCHE: Why did your mother want to know my age?
MITCH: Mother is sick.
BLANCHE: I'm sorry to hear it. Badly?
MITCH: She won't live long. Maybe just a few months.
BLANCHE: Oh.
MITCH: She worries because I'm not settled.
BLANCHE: Oh.
MITCH: She wants me to be settled down before she— [*His voice is hoarse and he clears his throat twice, shuffling nervously around with his hands in and out of his pockets.*]
BLANCHE: You love her very much, don't you?
MITCH: Yes.
BLANCHE: I think you have a great capacity for devotion. You will be lonely when she passes on, won't you? [MITCH *clears his throat and nods.*] I understand what that is.

MITCH: To be lonely?
BLANCHE: I loved someone, too, and the person I loved I lost.
MITCH: Dead? [*She crosses to the window and sits on the sill, looking out. She pours herself another drink.*] A man?
BLANCHE: He was a boy, just a boy, when I was a very young girl. When I was sixteen, I made the discovery—love. All at once and much, much too completely. It was like you suddenly turned a blinding light on something that had always been half in shadow, that's how it struck the world for me. But I was unlucky. Deluded. There was something different about the boy, a nervousness, a softness and tenderness which wasn't like a man's, although he wasn't the least bit effeminate looking—still—that thing was there.... He came to me for help. I didn't know that. I didn't find out anything till after our marriage when we'd run away and come back and all I knew was I'd failed him in some mysterious way and wasn't able to give the help he needed but couldn't speak of! He was in the quicksands and clutching at me—but I wasn't holding him out, I was slipping in with him! I didn't know that. I didn't know anything except I loved him unendurably but without being able to help him or help myself. Then I found out. In the worst of all possible ways. By coming suddenly into a room that I thought was empty—which wasn't empty, but had two people in it... the boy I had married and an older man who had been his friend for years... [*A locomotive is heard approaching outside. She claps her hands to her ears and crouches over. The headlight of the locomotive glares into the room as it thunders past. As the noise recedes she straightens slowly and continues speaking.*] Afterward we pretended that nothing had been discovered. Yes, the three of us drove out to Moon Lake Casino, very drunk and laughing all the way. [*Polka music sounds, in a minor key faint with distance.*] We danced the "Varsouviana!"[1] Suddenly in the middle of the dance the boy I had married broke away from me and ran out of the casino. A few moments later—a shot! [*The polka stops abruptly.* BLANCHE *rises stiffly. Then, the polka resumes in a major key.*] I ran out—all did!—all ran and gathered about the terrible thing at the edge of the lake! I couldn't get near for the crowding. Then somebody caught my arm. "Don't go any closer! Come back! You don't want to see!" See? See what! Then I heard voices say—Allan! Allan! The Grey boy! He'd stuck the revolver into his mouth, and fired—so that the back of his head had been—blown away! [*She sways and covers her face.*] It was because—on the dance floor—unable to stop myself—I'd suddenly said—"I saw! I know! You disgust me...." And then the searchlight which had been turned on the world was turned off again and never for one moment since has there been any light that's stronger than this—kitchen—candle...

[MITCH *gets up awkwardly and moves toward her a little. The polka music increases.* MITCH *stands beside her.*]

MITCH: [*Drawing her slowly into his arms.*] You need somebody. And I need somebody, too. Could it be—you and me, Blanche?

[*She stares at him vacantly for a moment. Then with a soft cry huddles in his embrace. She makes a sobbing effort to speak but the words won't come. He kisses*

---

1. Fast Polish dance, similar to the polka.

*her forehead and her eyes and finally her lips. The polka tune fades out. Her breath is drawn and released in long, grateful sobs.*]

BLANCHE: Sometimes—there's God—so quickly!

## Scene 7

*It is late afternoon in mid-September.*
*The portieres are open and a table is set for a birthday supper, with cake and flowers.*
STELLA *is completing the decorations as* STANLEY *comes in.*

STANLEY: What's all this stuff for?
STELLA: Honey, it's Blanche's birthday.
STANLEY: She here?
STELLA: In the bathroom.
STANLEY: [*Mimicking.*] "Washing out some things"?
STELLA: I reckon so.
STANLEY: How long she been in there?
STELLA: All afternoon.
STANLEY: [*Mimicking.*] "Soaking in a hot tub"?
STELLA: Yes.
STANLEY: Temperature 100 on the nose, and she soaks herself in a hot tub.
STELLA: She says it cools her off for the evening.
STANLEY: And you run out an' get her cokes, I suppose? And serve 'em to Her Majesty in the tub? [STELLA *shrugs.*] Set down here a minute.
STELLA: Stanley, I've got things to do.
STANLEY: Set down! I've got th' dope on your big sister, Stella.
STELLA: Stanley, stop picking on Blanche.
STANLEY: That girl calls *me* common!
STELLA: Lately you been doing all you can think of to rub her the wrong way, Stanley, and Blanche is sensitive and you've got to realize that Blanche and I grew up under very different circumstances than you did.
STANLEY: So I been told. And told and told and told! You know she's been feeding us a pack of lies here?
STELLA: No, I don't and—
STANLEY: Well, she has, however. But now the cat's out of the bag! I found out some things!
STELLA: What—things?
STANLEY: Things I already suspected. But now I got proof from the most reliable sources—which I have checked on!

[BLANCHE *is singing in the bathroom a saccharine[2] popular ballad which is used contrapuntally with* STANLEY'S *speech.*]

STELLA: [*To* STANLEY.] Lower your voice!
STANLEY: Some canary bird, huh!
STELLA: Now please tell me quietly what you think you've found out about my sister.

---

2. Cloyingly sweet; overly sentimental. *Contrapuntally:* musical term meaning "in an alternating or contrasting manner."

STANLEY: Lie Number One: All this squeamishness she puts on! You should just know the line she's been feeding to Mitch. He thought she had never been more than kissed by a fellow! But Sister Blanche is no lily! Ha-ha! Some lily she is!

STELLA: What have you heard and who from?

STANLEY: Our supply-man down at the plant has been going through Laurel for years and he knows all about her and everybody else in the town of Laurel knows all about her. She is as famous in Laurel as if she was the President of the United States, only she is not respected by any party! This supply-man stops at a hotel called the Flamingo.

BLANCHE: [*Singing blithely.*] "Say, it's only a paper moon, Sailing over a cardboard sea /—But it wouldn't be make-believe If you believed in me!"[3]

STELLA: What about the—Flamingo?

STANLEY: She stayed there, too.

STELLA: My sister lived at Belle Reve.

STANLEY: This is after the home-place had slipped through her lily-white fingers! She moved to the Flamingo! A second-class hotel which has the advantage of not interfering in the private social life of the personalities there! The Flamingo is used to all kinds of goings-on. But even the management of the Flamingo was impressed by Dame Blanche! In fact they was so impressed by Dame Blanche that they requested her to turn in her room key—for permanently! This happened a couple of weeks before she showed here.

BLANCHE: [*Singing.*] "It's a Barnum and Bailey[4] world, Just as phony as it can be—/ But it wouldn't be make-believe If you believed in me!"

STELLA: What—contemptible—lies!

STANLEY: Sure, I can see how you would be upset by this. She pulled the wool over your eyes as much as Mitch's!

STELLA: It's pure invention! There's not a word of truth in it and if I were a man and this creature had dared to invent such things in my presence—

BLANCHE: [*Singing.*] "Without your love, / it's a honky-tonk parade! / Without your love, / It's a melody played In a penny arcade..."

STANLEY: Honey, I told you I thoroughly checked on these stories! Now wait till I finish. The trouble with Dame Blanche was that she couldn't put on her act any more in Laurel! They got wised up after two or three dates with her and then they quit, and she goes on to another, the same old line, same old act, same old hooey! But the town was too small for this to go on forever! And as time went by she became a town character. Regarded as not just different but downright loco—nuts. [STELLA *draws back.*] And for the last year or two she has been washed up like poison. That's why she's here this summer, visiting royalty, putting on all this act—because she's practically told by the mayor to get out of town! Yes, did you know there was an army camp near Laurel and your sister's was one of the places called "Out-of-Bounds"?

BLANCHE: "It's only a paper moon, Just as phony as it can be— / But it wouldn't be make-believe If you believed in me!"

---

3. From "It's Only a Paper Moon" (1933), a popular song by Harold Arlen (1905–1986).
4. P. T. Barnum (1810–1891) and James Bailey (1847–1906), circus promoters of "The Greatest Show on Earth."

STANLEY: Well, so much for her being such a refined and particular type of girl. Which brings us to Lie Number Two.
STELLA: I don't want to hear any more!
STANLEY: She's not going back to teach school! In fact I am willing to bet you that she never had no idea of returning to Laurel! She didn't resign temporarily from the high school because of her nerves! No, siree, Bob! She didn't. They kicked her out of that high school before the spring term ended—and I hate to tell you the reason that step was taken! A seventeen-year-old boy—she'd gotten mixed up with!
BLANCHE: "It's a Barnum and Bailey world, Just as phony as it can be—"

[*In the bathroom the water goes on loud; little breathless cries and peals of laughter are heard as if a child were frolicking in the tub.*]

STELLA: This is making me—sick!
STANLEY: The boy's dad learned about it and got in touch with the high school superintendent. Boy, oh, boy, I'd like to have been in that office when Dame Blanche was called on the carpet! I'd like to have seen her trying to squirm out of that one! But they had her on the hook good and proper that time and she knew that the jig was all up! They told her she better move on to some fresh territory. Yep, it was practickly a town ordinance passed against her!

[*The bathroom door is opened and* BLANCHE *thrusts her head out, holding a towel about her hair.*]

BLANCHE: Stella!
STELLA: [*Faintly.*] Yes, Blanche?
BLANCHE: Give me another bath-towel to dry my hair with. I've just washed it.
STELLA: Yes, Blanche. [*She crosses in a dazed way from the kitchen to the bathroom door with a towel.*]
BLANCHE: What's the matter, honey?
STELLA: Matter? Why?
BLANCHE: You have such a strange expression on your face!
STELLA: Oh—[*She tries to laugh.*] I guess I'm a little tired!
BLANCHE: Why don't you bathe, too, soon as I get out?
STANLEY: [*Calling from the kitchen.*] How soon is that going to be?
BLANCHE: Not so terribly long! Possess your soul in patience!⁵
STANLEY: It's not my soul, it's my kidneys I'm worried about! [BLANCHE *slams the door.* STANLEY *laughs harshly.* STELLA *comes slowly back into the kitchen.*] Well, what do you think of it?
STELLA: I don't believe all of those stories and I think your supply-man was mean and rotten to tell them. It's possible that some of the things he said are partly true. There are things about my sister I don't approve of—things that caused sorrow at home. She was always—flighty!
STANLEY: Flighty!
STELLA: But when she was young, very young, she married a boy who wrote poetry.... He was extremely good-looking. I think Blanche didn't just love

---

5. "In your patience you will possess your souls" (Luke 21.19).

him but worshipped the ground he walked on! Adored him and thought him almost too fine to be human! But then she found out—

STANLEY: What?

STELLA: This beautiful and talented young man was a degenerate. Didn't your supply-man give you that information?

STANLEY: All we discussed was recent history. That must have been a pretty long time ago.

STELLA: Yes, it was—a pretty long time ago . . .

[STANLEY *comes up and takes her by the shoulders rather gently. She gently withdraws from him. Automatically she starts sticking little pink candles in the birthday cake.*]

STANLEY: How many candles you putting in that cake?

STELLA: I'll stop at twenty-five.

STANLEY: Is company expected?

STELLA: We asked Mitch to come over for cake and ice-cream.

[STANLEY *looks a little uncomfortable. He lights a cigarette from the one he has just finished.*]

STANLEY: I wouldn't be expecting Mitch over tonight.

[STELLA *pauses in her occupation with candles and looks slowly around at* STANLEY.]

STELLA: *Why?*

STANLEY: Mitch is a buddy of mine. We were in the same outfit together—Two-forty-first Engineers. We work in the same plant and now on the same bowling team. You think I could face him if—

STELLA: Stanley Kowalski, did you—did you repeat what that—?

STANLEY: You're goddam right I told him! I'd have that on my conscience the rest of my life if I knew all that stuff and let my best friend get caught!

STELLA: Is Mitch through with her?

STANLEY: Wouldn't you be if—?

STELLA: I said, *Is Mitch through with her?*

[BLANCHE's *voice is lifted again, serenely as a bell. She sings "But it wouldn't be make-believe If you believed in me."*]

STANLEY: No, I don't think he's necessarily through with her—just wised up!

STELLA: Stanley, she thought Mitch was—going to—going to marry her. I was hoping so, too.

STANLEY: Well, he's not going to marry her. Maybe he *was,* but he's not going to jump in a tank with a school of sharks—now! [*He rises.*] Blanche! Oh, Blanche! Can I please get in my bathroom? [*There is a pause.*]

BLANCHE: Yes, indeed, sir! Can you wait one second while I dry?

STANLEY: Having waited one hour I guess one second ought to pass in a hurry.

STELLA: And she hasn't got her job? Well, what will she do!

STANLEY: She's not stayin' here after Tuesday. You know that, don't you? Just to make sure I bought her ticket myself. A bus ticket.

STELLA: In the first place, Blanche wouldn't go on a bus.

STANLEY: She'll go on a bus and like it.

STELLA: No, she won't, no, she won't, Stanley!
STANLEY: *She'll go!* Period. P.S. She'll go *Tuesday!*
STELLA: [*Slowly.*] What'll—she—do? What on earth will she—*do!*
STANLEY: Her future is mapped out for her.
STELLA: What do you mean?

[BLANCHE *sings.*]

STANLEY: Hey, canary bird! Toots! Get OUT of the BATHROOM!

[*The bathroom door flies open and* BLANCHE *emerges with a gay peal of laughter, but as* STANLEY *crosses past her, a frightened look appears in her face, almost a look of panic. He doesn't look at her but slams the bathroom door shut as he goes in.*]

BLANCHE: [*Snatching up a hairbrush.*] Oh, I feel so good after my long, hot bath, I feel so good and cool and—rested!
STELLA: [*Sadly and doubtfully from the kitchen.*] Do you, Blanche?
BLANCHE: [*Snatching up a hairbrush.*] Yes, I do, so refreshed! [*She tinkles her highball glass.*] A hot bath and a long, cold drink always give me a brand new outlook on life! [*She looks through the portieres at* STELLA, *standing between them, and slowly stops brushing.*] Something has happened!—What is it?
STELLA: [*Turning away quickly.*] Why, nothing has happened, Blanche.
BLANCHE: You're lying! Something has! [*She stares fearfully at* STELLA, *who pretends to be busy at the table. The distant piano goes into a hectic breakdown.*]

Scene 8

Three quarters of an hour later.
The view through the big windows is fading gradually into a still-golden dusk. A torch of sunlight blazes on the side of a big water-tank or oil-drum across the empty lot toward the business district which is now pierced by pinpoints of lighted windows or windows reflecting the sunset.
The three people are completing a dismal birthday supper. STANLEY looks sullen. STELLA is embarrassed and sad.
BLANCHE has a tight, artificial smile on her drawn face. There is a fourth place at the table which is left vacant.

BLANCHE: [*Suddenly.*] Stanley, tell us a joke, tell us a funny story to make us all laugh. I don't know what's the matter, we're all so solemn. Is it because I've been stood up by my beau? [STELLA *laughs feebly.*] It's the first time in my entire experience with men, and I've had a good deal of all sorts, that I've actually been stood up by anybody! Ha-ha! I don't know how to take it.... Tell us a funny little story, Stanley! Something to help us out.
STANLEY: I didn't think you liked my stories, Blanche.
BLANCHE: I like them when they're amusing but not indecent.
STANLEY: I don't know any refined enough for your taste.
BLANCHE: Then let me tell one.
STELLA: Yes, you tell one, Blanche. You used to know lots of good stories.

[*The music fades.*]

BLANCHE: Let me see, now. . . . I must run through my repertoire! Oh, yes—I love parrot stories! Do you all like parrot stories? Well, this one's about the old maid and the parrot. This old maid, she had a parrot that cursed a blue streak and knew more vulgar expressions than Mr. Kowalski!
STANLEY: Huh.
BLANCHE: And the only way to hush the parrot up was to put the cover back on its cage so it would think it was night and go back to sleep. Well, one morning the old maid had just uncovered the parrot for the day—when who should she see coming up the front walk but the preacher! Well, she rushed back to the parrot and slipped the cover back on the cage and then she let in the preacher. And the parrot was perfectly still, just as quiet as a mouse, but just as she was asking the preacher how much sugar he wanted in his coffee—the parrot broke the silence with a loud— [*She whistles.*] —and said—"God *damn,* but that was a short day!" [*She throws back her head and laughs.* STELLA *also makes an ineffectual effort to seem amused.* STANLEY *pays no attention to the story but reaches way over the table to spear his fork into the remaining chop which he eats with his fingers.*] Apparently Mr. Kowalski was not amused.
STELLA: Mr. Kowalski is too busy making a pig of himself to think of anything else!
STANLEY: That's right, baby.
STELLA: Your face and your fingers are disgustingly greasy. Go and wash up and then help me clear the table.

[*He hurls a plate to the floor.*]

STANLEY: That's how I'll clear the table! [*He seizes her arm.*] Don't ever talk that way to me! "Pig—Polack—disgusting—vulgar—greasy!"—them kind of words have been on your tongue and your sister's too much around here! What do you two think you are? A pair of queens? Remember what Huey Long[6] said—"Every Man is a King!" And I am the king around here, so don't forget it! [*He hurls a cup and saucer to the floor.*] My place is cleared! You want me to clear your places?

[STELLA *begins to cry weakly.* STANLEY *stalks out on the porch and lights a cigarette. The Negro entertainers around the corner are heard.*]

BLANCHE: What happened while I was bathing? What did he tell you, Stella?
STELLA: Nothing, nothing, nothing!
BLANCHE: I think he told you something about Mitch and me! You know why Mitch didn't come but you won't tell me! [STELLA *shakes her head helplessly.*] I'm going to call him!
STELLA: I wouldn't call him, Blanche.
BLANCHE: I am, I'm going to call him on the phone.
STELLA: [*Miserably.*] I wish you wouldn't.
BLANCHE: I intend to be given some explanation from someone!

[*She rushes to the phone in the bedroom.* STELLA *goes out on the porch and stares reproachfully at her husband. He grunts and turns away from her.*]

---

6. Demagogic Louisiana political leader, governor, and senator (1893–1935).

STELLA: I hope you're pleased with your doings. I never had so much trouble swallowing food in my life, looking at that girl's face and the empty chair! [*She cries quietly.*]
BLANCHE: [*At the phone.*] Hello. Mr. Mitchell, please. . . . Oh. . . . I would like to leave a number if I may. Magnolia 9047. And say it's important to call. . . . Yes, very important. . . . Thank you. [*She remains by the phone with a lost, frightened look.*]

   [STANLEY *turns slowly back toward his wife and takes her clumsily in his arms.*]

STANLEY: Stell, it's gonna be all right after she goes and after you've had the baby. It's gonna be all right again between you and me the way that it was. You remember the way that it was? Them nights we had together? God, honey, it's gonna be sweet when we can make noise in the night the way that we used to and get the colored lights going with nobody's sister behind the curtains to hear us! [*Their upstairs neighbors are heard in bellowing laughter at something.* STANLEY *chuckles.*] Steve an' Eunice. . . .
STELLA: Come on back in. [*She returns to the kitchen and starts lighting the candles on the white cake.*] Blanche?
BLANCHE: Yes. [*She returns from the bedroom to the table in the kitchen.*] Oh, those pretty, pretty little candles! Oh, don't burn them, Stella.
STELLA: I certainly will.

   [STANLEY *comes back in.*]

BLANCHE: You ought to save them for baby's birthdays. Oh, I hope candles are going to glow in his life and I hope that his eyes are going to be like candles, like two blue candles lighted in a white cake!
STANLEY: [*Sitting down.*] What poetry!
BLANCHE: [*She pauses reflectively for a moment.*] I shouldn't have called him.
STELLA: There's lots of things could have happened.
BLANCHE: There's no excuse for it, Stella. I don't have to put up with insults. I won't be taken for granted.
STANLEY: Goddamn, it's hot in here with the steam from the bathroom.
BLANCHE: I've said I was sorry three times. [*The piano fades out.*] I take hot baths for my nerves. Hydrotherapy, they call it. You healthy Polack, without a nerve in your body, of course you don't know what anxiety feels like!
STANLEY: I am not a Polack. People from Poland are Poles, not Polacks. But what I am is a one-hundred-per-cent American, born and raised in the greatest country on earth and proud as hell of it, so don't ever call me a Polack.

   [*The phone rings.* BLANCHE *rises expectantly.*]

BLANCHE: Oh, that's for me, I'm sure.
STANLEY: *I'm* not sure. Keep your seat. [*He crosses leisurely to phone.*] H'lo. Aw, yeh, hello, Mac.

   [*He leans against wall, staring insultingly in at* BLANCHE. *She sinks back in her chair with a frightened look.* STELLA *leans over and touches her shoulder.*]

BLANCHE: Oh, keep your hands off me, Stella. What is the matter with you? Why do you look at me with that pitying look?
STANLEY: [*Bawling.*] QUIET IN THERE!—We've got a noisy woman on the place.—

Go on, Mac. At Riley's? No, I don't wanta bowl at Riley's. I had a little trouble with Riley last week. I'm the team captain, ain't I? All right, then, we're not gonna bowl at Riley's, we're gonna bowl at the West Side or the Gala! All right, Mac. See you! [*He hangs up and returns to the table.* BLANCHE *fiercely controls herself, drinking quickly from her tumbler of water. He doesn't look at her but reaches in a pocket. Then he speaks slowly and with false amiability.*] Sister Blanche, I've got a little birthday remembrance for you.

BLANCHE: Oh, have you, Stanley? I wasn't expecting any, I—I don't know why Stella wants to observe my birthday! I'd much rather forget it—when you— reach twenty-seven! Well—age is a subject that you'd prefer to—ignore!

STANLEY: Twenty-seven?

BLANCHE: [*Quickly.*] What is it? Is it for *me*?

[*He is holding a little envelope toward her.*]

STANLEY: Yes, I hope you like it!

BLANCHE: Why, why—Why, it's a—

STANLEY: Ticket! Back to Laurel! On the Greyhound![7] Tuesday! [*The "Varsouviana" music steals in softly and continues playing.* STELLA *rises abruptly and turns her back.* BLANCHE *tries to smile. Then she tries to laugh. Then she gives both up and springs from the table and runs into the next room. She clutches her throat and then runs into the bathroom. Coughing, gagging sounds are heard.*] Well!

STELLA: You didn't need to do that.

STANLEY: Don't forget all that I took off her.

STELLA: You needn't have been so cruel to someone alone as she is.

STANLEY: Delicate piece she is.

STELLA: She is. She was. You didn't know Blanche as a girl. Nobody, nobody, was tender and trusting as she was. But people like you abused her, and forced her to change. [*He crosses into the bedroom, ripping off his shirt, and changes into a brilliant silk bowling shirt. She follows him.*] Do you think you're going bowling now?

STANLEY: Sure.

STELLA: You're not going bowling. [*She catches hold of his shirt.*] Why did you do this to her?

STANLEY: I done nothing to no one. Let go of my shirt. You've torn it.

STELLA: I want to know why. Tell me why.

STANLEY: When we first met, me and you, you thought I was common. How right you was, baby. I was common as dirt. You showed me the snapshot of the place with the columns. I pulled you down off them columns and how you loved it, having them colored lights going! And wasn't we happy together, wasn't it all okay till she showed here? [STELLA *makes a slight movement. Her look goes suddenly inward as if some interior voice had called her name. She begins a slow, shuffling progress from the bedroom to the kitchen, leaning and resting on the back of the chair and then on the edge of a table with a blind look and listening expression.* STANLEY, *finishing with his shirt, is unaware of her reaction.*] And wasn't we happy together? Wasn't it all okay? Till she showed here. Hoity-Toity,

---

7. Long-distance bus company.

describing me as an ape. [*He suddenly notices the change in* STELLA.] Hey, what is it, Stell? [*He crosses to her.*]
STELLA: [*Quietly.*] Take me to the hospital.

> [*He is with her now, supporting her with his arm, murmuring indistinguishably as they go outside.*]

## Scene 9

*A while later that evening.* BLANCHE *is seated in a tense hunched position in a bedroom chair that she has recovered with diagonal green and white stripes. She has on her scarlet satin robe. On the table beside chair is a bottle of liquor and a glass. The rapid, feverish polka tune, the "Varsouviana," is heard. The music is in her mind; she is drinking to escape it and the sense of disaster closing in on her, and she seems to whisper the words of the song. An electric fan is turning back and forth across her.*

MITCH *comes around the corner in work clothes: blue denim shirt and pants. He is unshaven. He climbs the steps to the door and rings.* BLANCHE *is startled.*

BLANCHE: Who is it, please?
MITCH: [*Hoarsely.*] Me. Mitch.

> [*The polka tune stops.*]

BLANCHE: Mitch!—Just a minute. [*She rushes about frantically, hiding the bottle in a closet, crouching at the mirror and dabbing her face with cologne and powder. She is so excited that her breath is audible as she dashes about. At last she rushes to the door in the kitchen and lets him in.*] Mitch!—Y'know, I really shouldn't let you in after the treatment I have received from you this evening! So utterly uncavalier! But hello, beautiful! [*She offers him her lips. He ignores it and pushes past her into the flat. She looks fearfully after him as he stalks into the bedroom.*] My, my, what a cold shoulder! And such uncouth apparel! Why, you haven't even shaved! The unforgivable insult to a lady! But I forgive you. I forgive you because it's such a relief to see you. You've stopped that polka tune that I had caught in my head. Have you ever had anything caught in your head? No, of course you haven't, you dumb angel-puss, you'd never get anything awful caught in your head!

> [*He stares at her while she follows him while she talks. It is obvious that he has had a few drinks on the way over.*]

MITCH: Do we have to have that fan on?
BLANCHE: No!
MITCH: I don't like fans.
BLANCHE: Then let's turn it off, honey. I'm not partial to them! [*She presses the switch and the fan nods slowly off. She clears her throat uneasily as* MITCH *plumps himself down on the bed in the bedroom and lights a cigarette.*] I don't know what there is to drink. I—haven't investigated.
MITCH: I don't want Stan's liquor.
BLANCHE: It isn't Stan's. Everything here isn't Stan's. Some things on the premises are actually mine! How is your mother? Isn't your mother well?
MITCH: Why?
BLANCHE: Something's the matter tonight, but never mind. I won't cross-examine

the witness. I'll just— [*She touches her forehead vaguely. The polka tune starts up again.*]—pretend I don't notice anything different about you! That—music again . . .

MITCH: What music?

BLANCHE: The "Varsouviana"! The polka tune they were playing when Allan— Wait! [*A distant revolver shot is heard.* BLANCHE *seems relieved.*] There now, the shot! It always stops after that. [*The polka music dies out again.*] Yes, now it's stopped.

MITCH: Are you boxed out of your mind?

BLANCHE: I'll go and see what I can find in the way of—[*She crosses into the closet, pretending to search for the bottle.*] Oh, by the way, excuse me for not being dressed. But I'd practically given you up! Had you forgotten your invitation to supper?

MITCH: I wasn't going to see you any more.

BLANCHE: Wait a minute. I can't hear what you're saying and you talk so little that when you do say something, I don't want to miss a single syllable of it. . . . What am I looking around here for? Oh, yes—liquor! We've had so much excitement around here this evening that I *am* boxed out of my mind! [*She pretends suddenly to find the bottle. He draws his foot up on the bed and stares at her contemptuously.*] Here's something. Southern Comfort! What is that, I wonder?

MITCH: If you don't know, it must belong to Stan.

BLANCHE: Take your foot off the bed. It has a light cover on it. Of course you boys don't notice things like that. I've done so much with this place since I've been here.

MITCH: I bet you have.

BLANCHE: You saw it before I came. Well, look at it now! This room is almost— dainty! I want to keep it that way. I wonder if this stuff ought to be mixed with something? Ummm, it's sweet! It's terribly, terribly sweet! Why, it's a *liqueur*, I believe! Yes, that's what it *is*, a liqueur! [MITCH *grunts.*] I'm afraid you won't like it, but try it, and maybe you will.

MITCH: I told you already I don't want none of his liquor and I mean it. You ought to lay off his liquor. He says you been lapping it up all summer like a wild cat!

BLANCHE: What a fantastic statement! Fantastic of him to say it, fantastic of you to repeat it! I won't descend to the level of such cheap accusations to answer them, even!

MITCH: Huh.

BLANCHE: What's in your mind? I see something in your eyes!

MITCH: [*Getting up.*] It's dark in here.

BLANCHE: I like it dark. The dark is comforting to me.

MITCH: I don't think I ever seen you in the light. [BLANCHE *laughs breathlessly.*] That's a fact!

BLANCHE: Is it?

MITCH: I've never seen you in the afternoon.

BLANCHE: Whose fault is that?

MITCH: You never want to go out in the afternoon.

BLANCHE: Why, Mitch, you're at the plant in the afternoon!

MITCH: Not Sunday afternoon. I've asked you to go out with me sometimes on Sundays but you always make an excuse. You never want to go out till after

six and then it's always some place that's not lighted much.
BLANCHE: There is some obscure meaning in this but I fail to catch it.
MITCH: What it means is I've never had a real good look at you, Blanche. Let's turn the light on here.
BLANCHE: [*Fearfully.*] Light? Which light? What for?
MITCH: This one with the paper thing on it.

[*He tears the paper lantern off the light bulb. She utters a frightened gasp.*]

BLANCHE: What did you do that for?
MITCH: So I can take a look at you good and plain!
BLANCHE: Of course you don't really mean to be insulting!
MITCH: No, just realistic.
BLANCHE: I don't want realism. I want magic! [MITCH *laughs.*] Yes, yes, magic! I try to give that to people. I misrepresent things to them. I don't tell truth, I tell what *ought* to be truth. And if that is sinful, then let me be damned for it!—Don't turn the light on!

[MITCH *crosses to the switch. He turns the light on and stares at her. She cries out and covers her face. He turns the lights off again.*]

MITCH: [*Slowly and bitterly.*] I don't mind you being older than what I thought. But all the rest of it—Christ! That pitch about your ideals being so old-fashioned and all the malarkey that you've dished out all summer. Oh, I knew you weren't sixteen any more. But I was a fool enough to believe you was straight.
BLANCHE: Who told you I wasn't—"straight"? My loving brother-in-law. And you believed him.
MITCH: I called him a liar at first. And then I checked on the story. First I asked our supply-man who travels through Laurel. And then I talked directly over long-distance to this merchant.
BLANCHE: Who is this merchant?
MITCH: Kiefaber.
BLANCHE: The merchant Kiefaber of Laurel! I know the man. He whistled at me. I put him in his place. So now for revenge he makes up stories about me.
MITCH: Three people, Kiefaber, Stanley and Shaw, swore to them!
BLANCHE: Rub-a-dub-dub, three men in a tub! And such a filthy tub!
MITCH: Didn't you stay at a hotel called The Flamingo?
BLANCHE: Flamingo? No! Tarantula was the name of it! I stayed at a hotel called The Tarantula Arms!
MITCH: [*Stupidly.*] Tarantula?
BLANCHE: Yes, a big spider! That's where I brought my victims. [*She pours herself another drink.*] Yes, I had many intimacies with strangers. After the death of Allan—intimacies with strangers was all I seemed able to fill my empty heart with. . . . I think it was panic, just panic, that drove me from one to another, hunting for some protection—here and there, in the most—unlikely places—even, at last, in a seventeen-year-old boy but—somebody wrote the superintendent about it—"This woman is morally unfit for her position!" [*She throws back her head with convulsive, sobbing laughter. Then she repeats the statement, gasps, and drinks.*] True? Yes, I suppose—unfit somehow—anyway. . . . So I came here. There was nowhere else I could go. I was played out. You know what played

out is? My youth was suddenly gone up the water-spout, and—I met you. You said you needed somebody. Well, I needed somebody, too. I thanked God for you, because you seemed to be gentle—a cleft in the rock of the world that I could hide in! But I guess I was asking, hoping—too much! Kiefaber, Stanley and Shaw have tied an old tin can to the tail of the kite.

[*There is a pause.* MITCH *stares at her dumbly.*]

MITCH: You lied to me, Blanche.
BLANCHE: Don't say I lied to you.
MITCH: Lies, lies, inside and out, all lies.
BLANCHE: Never inside, I didn't lie in my heart...

[*A vendor comes around the corner. She is a blind* MEXICAN WOMAN *in a dark shawl, carrying bunches of those gaudy tin flowers that lower-class Mexicans display at funerals and other festive occasions. She is calling barely audibly. Her figure is only faintly visible outside the building.*]

MEXICAN WOMAN: *Flores. Flores, Flores para los muertos.*[8] *Flores. Flores.*
BLANCHE: What? Oh! Somebody outside... [*She goes to the door, opens it and stares at the* MEXICAN WOMAN.]
MEXICAN WOMAN: [*She is at the door and offers* BLANCHE *some of her flowers.*] *Flores? Flores para los muertos?*
BLANCHE: [*Frightened.*] No, no! Not now! Not now! [*She darts back into the apartment, slamming the door.*]
MEXICAN WOMAN: [*She turns away and starts to move down the street.*] *Flores para los muertos.*

[*The polka tune fades in.*]

BLANCHE: [*As if to herself.*] Crumble and fade and—regrets—recriminations... "If you'd done this, it wouldn't've cost me that!"
MEXICAN WOMAN: *Corones*[9] *para los muertos. Corones*...
BLANCHE: Legacies! Huh.... And other things such as bloodstained pillow-slips— "Her linen needs changing"—"Yes, Mother. But couldn't we get a colored girl to do it?" No, we couldn't of course. Everything gone but the—
MEXICAN WOMAN: *Flores.*
BLANCHE: Death—I used to sit here and she used to sit over there and death was as close as you are.... We didn't dare even admit we had ever heard of it!
MEXICAN WOMAN: *Flores para los muertos, flores—flores*...
BLANCHE: The opposite is desire. So do you wonder? How could you possibly wonder! Not far from Belle Reve, before we had lost Belle Reve, was a camp where they trained young soldiers. On Sunday nights they would go in town to get drunk—
MEXICAN WOMAN: [*Softly.*] *Corones*...
BLANCHE: —and on the way back they would stagger onto my lawn and call— "Blanche! Blanche!"—the deaf old lady remaining suspected nothing. But sometimes I slipped outside to answer their calls.... Later the paddy-wagon[1] would gather them up like daisies... the long way home... [*The* MEXICAN WOMAN *turns slowly and drifts back off with her soft mournful cries.* BLANCHE *goes*

---

8. Flowers for the dead.   9. Wreaths.   1. Police van.

to the dresser and leans forward on it. After a moment, MITCH rises and follows her purposefully. The polka music fades away. He places his hands on her waist and tries to turn her about.] What do you want?

MITCH: [Fumbling to embrace her.] What I been missing all summer.

BLANCHE: Then marry me, Mitch!

MITCH: I don't think I want to marry you anymore.

BLANCHE: No?

MITCH: [Dropping his hands from her waist.] You're not clean enough to bring in the house with my mother.

BLANCHE: Go away, then. [He stares at her.] Get out of here quick before I start screaming fire! [Her throat is tightening with hysteria.] Get out of here quick before I start screaming fire. [He still remains staring. She suddenly rushes to the big window with its pale blue square of the soft summer light and cries wildly.] Fire! Fire! Fire!

[With a startled gasp, MITCH turns and goes out the outer door, clatters awkwardly down the steps and around the corner of the building. BLANCHE staggers back from the window and falls to her knees. The distant piano is slow and blue.]

## Scene 10

It is a few hours later that night.

BLANCHE has been drinking fairly steadily since MITCH left. She has dragged her wardrobe trunk into the center of the bedroom. It hangs open with flowery dresses thrown across it. As the drinking and packing went on, a mood of hysterical exhilaration came into her and she has decked herself out in a somewhat soiled and crumpled white satin evening gown and a pair of scuffed silver slippers with brilliants set in their heels.

Now she is placing the rhinestone tiara on her head before the mirror of the dressing-table and murmuring excitedly as if to a group of spectral admirers.

BLANCHE: How about taking a swim, a moonlight swim at the old rock-quarry? If anyone's sober enough to drive a car! Ha-ha! Best way in the world to stop your head buzzing! Only you've got to be careful to dive where the deep pool is—if you hit a rock you don't come up till tomorrow . . . [Tremblingly she lifts the hand mirror for a closer inspection. She catches her breath and slams the mirror face down with such violence that the glass cracks. She moans a little and attempts to rise. STANLEY appears around the corner of the building. He still has on the vivid green silk bowling shirt. As he rounds the corner the honky-tonk music is heard. It continues softly throughout the scene. He enters the kitchen, slamming the door. As he peers in at BLANCHE, he gives a low whistle. He has had a few drinks on the way and has brought some quart beer bottles home with him.] How is my sister?

STANLEY: She is doing okay.

BLANCHE: And how is the baby?

STANLEY: [Grinning amiably.] The baby won't come before morning so they told me to go home and get a little shut-eye.

BLANCHE: Does that mean we are to be alone in here?

STANLEY: Yep. Just me and you, Blanche. Unless you got somebody hid under the bed. What've you got on those fine feathers for?

BLANCHE: Oh, that's right. You left before my wire came.

STANLEY: You got a wire?

BLANCHE: I received a telegram from an old admirer of mine.
STANLEY: Anything good?
BLANCHE: I think so. An invitation.
STANLEY: What to? A fireman's ball?
BLANCHE: [*Throwing back her head.*] A cruise of the Caribbean on a yacht!
STANLEY: Well, well. What do you know?
BLANCHE: I have never been so surprised in my life.
STANLEY: I guess not.
BLANCHE: It came like a bolt from the blue!
STANLEY: Who did you say it was from?
BLANCHE: An old beau of mine.
STANLEY: The one that give you the white fox-pieces?
BLANCHE: Mr. Shep Huntleigh. I wore his ATO[2] pin my last year at college. I hadn't seen him again until last Christmas. I ran in to him on Biscayne Boulevard. Then—just now—this wire—inviting me on a cruise of the Caribbean! The problem is clothes. I tore into my trunk to see what I have that's suitable for the tropics!
STANLEY: And come up with that—gorgeous—diamond—tiara?
BLANCHE: This old relic? Ha-ha! It's only rhinestones.
STANLEY: Gosh. I thought it was Tiffany diamonds. [*He unbuttons his shirt.*]
BLANCHE: Well, anyhow, I shall be entertained in style.
STANLEY: Uh-huh. It goes to show, you never know what is coming.
BLANCHE: Just when I thought my luck had begun to fail me—
STANLEY: Into the picture pops this Miami millionaire.
BLANCHE: This man is not from Miami. This man is from Dallas.
STANLEY: This man is from Dallas?
BLANCHE: Yes, this man is from Dallas where gold spouts out of the ground!
STANLEY: Well, just so he's from somewhere! [*He starts removing his shirt.*]
BLANCHE: Close the curtains before you undress any further.
STANLEY: [*Amiably.*] This is all I'm going to undress right now. [*He rips the sack off a quart beer bottle.*] Seen a bottle-opener? [*She moves slowly toward the dresser, where she stands with her hands knotted together.*] I used to have a cousin who could open a beer bottle with his teeth. [*Pounding the bottle cap on the corner of table.*] That was his only accomplishment, all he could do—he was just a human bottle-opener. And then one time, at a wedding party, he broke his front teeth off! After that he was so ashamed of himself he used t' sneak out of the house when company came . . . [*The bottle cap pops off and a geyser of foam shoots up.* STANLEY *laughs happily, holding up the bottle over his head.*] Ha-ha! Rain from heaven! [*He extends the bottle toward her.*] Shall we bury the hatchet and make it a loving-cup? Huh?
BLANCHE: No, thank you.
STANLEY: Well, it's a red-letter night for us both. You having an oil millionaire and me having a baby. [*He goes to the bureau in the bedroom and crouches to remove something from the bottom drawer.*]
BLANCHE: [*Drawing back.*] What are you doing in here?
STANLEY: Here's something I always break out on special occasions like this. The silk pyjamas I wore on my wedding night!

2. Probably Alpha Tau Omega, a college fraternity.

BLANCHE: Oh.
STANLEY: When the telephone rings and they say, "You've got a son!" I'll tear this off and wave it like a flag! [*He shakes out a brilliant pyjama coat.*] I guess we are both entitled to put on the dog. [*He goes back to the kitchen with the coat over his arm.*]
BLANCHE: When I think of how divine it is going to be to have such a thing as privacy once more—I could weep with joy!
STANLEY: This millionaire from Dallas is not going to interfere with your privacy any?
BLANCHE: It won't be the sort of thing you have in mind. This man is a gentleman and he respects me. [*Improvising feverishly.*] What he wants is my companionship. Having great wealth sometimes makes people lonely! A cultivated woman, a woman of intelligence and breeding, can enrich a man's life—immeasurably! I have those things to offer, and this doesn't take them away. Physical beauty is passing. A transitory possession. But beauty of the mind and richness of the spirit and tenderness of the heart—and I have all of those things—aren't taken away, but grow! Increase with the years! How strange that I should be called a destitute woman! When I have all of these treasures locked in my heart. [*A choked sob comes from her.*] I think of myself as a very, very rich woman! But I have been foolish—casting my pearls before swine!³
STANLEY: Swine, huh?
BLANCHE: Yes, swine! Swine! And I'm thinking not only of you but of your friend, Mr. Mitchell. He came to see me tonight. He dared to come here in his work clothes! And to repeat slander to me, vicious stories that he had gotten from you! I gave him his walking papers...
STANLEY: You did, huh?
BLANCHE: But then he came back. He returned with a box of roses to beg my forgiveness! He implored my forgiveness. But some things are not forgivable. Deliberate cruelty is not forgivable. It is the one unforgivable thing in my opinion and it is the one thing of which I have never, ever been guilty. And so I told him, I said to him, "Thank you," but it was foolish of me to think that we could ever adapt ourselves to each other. Our ways of life are too different. Our attitudes and our backgrounds are incompatible. We have to be realistic about such things. So farewell, my friend! And let there be no hard feelings...
STANLEY: Was this before or after the telegram came from the Texas oil millionaire?
BLANCHE: What telegram? No! No, after! As a matter of fact, the wire came just as—
STANLEY: As a matter of fact there wasn't no wire at all!
BLANCHE: Oh, oh!
STANLEY: There isn't no millionaire! And Mitch didn't come back with roses 'cause I know where he is—
BLANCHE: Oh!
STANLEY: There isn't a goddam thing but imagination!
BLANCHE: Oh!

---

3. See Matthew 7.6: "Do not give what is holy to dogs, or throw your pearls before swine, lest they trample them underfoot, and turn and tear you to pieces."

STANLEY: And lies and conceit and tricks!
BLANCHE: Oh!
STANLEY: And look at yourself! Take a look at yourself in that worn-out Mardi Gras[4] outfit, rented for fifty cents from some ragpicker! And with the crazy crown on! What queen do you think you are?
BLANCHE: Oh—God...
STANLEY: I've been on to you from the start! Not once did you pull any wool over this boy's eyes! You come in here and sprinkle the place with powder and spray perfume and cover the light-bulb with a paper lantern, and lo and behold the place has turned into Egypt and you are the Queen of the Nile![5] Sitting on your throne and swilling down my liquor! I say—Ha!—Ha! Do you hear me? *Ha—ha—ha!* [*He walks into the bedroom.*]
BLANCHE: Don't come in here! [*Lurid reflections appear on the walls around* BLANCHE. *The shadows are of a grotesque and menacing form. She catches her breath, crosses to the phone and jiggles the hook.* STANLEY *goes into the bathroom and closes the door.*] Operator, operator! Give me long-distance, please.... I want to get in touch with Mr. Shep Huntleigh of Dallas. He's so well known he doesn't require any address. Just ask anybody who—Wait!!—No, I couldn't find it right now.... Please understand, I—No! No, wait!... One moment! Someone is—Nothing! Hold on, please! [*She sets the phone down and crosses warily into the kitchen. The night is filled with inhuman voices like cries in a jungle. The shadows and lurid reflections move sinuously as flames along the wall spaces. Through the back wall of the rooms, which have become transparent, can be seen the sidewalk. A prostitute has rolled[6] a drunkard. He pursues her along the walk, overtakes her and there is a struggle. A policeman's whistle breaks it up. The figures disappear. Some moments later the* NEGRO WOMAN *appears around the corner with a sequined bag which the prostitute had dropped on the walk. She is rooting excitedly through it.* BLANCHE *presses her knuckles to her lips and returns slowly to the phone. She speaks in a hoarse whisper.*] Operator! Operator! Never mind long-distance. Get Western Union. There isn't time to be—Western—Western Union! [*She waits anxiously.*] Western Union? Yes! I—want to—Take down this message! "In desperate, desperate circumstances! Help me! Caught in a trap. Caught in—" Oh!

> [*The bathroom door is thrown open and* STANLEY *comes out in the brilliant silk pyjamas. He grins at her as he knots the tassled sash about his waist. She gasps and backs away from the phone. He stares at her for a count of ten. Then a clicking becomes audible from the telephone, steady and rasping.*]

STANLEY: You left th' phone off th' hook.

> [*He crosses to it deliberately and sets it back on the hook. After he has replaced it, he stares at her again, his mouth slowly curving into a grin, as he weaves between* BLANCHE *and the outer door. The barely audible "Blue Piano" begins to drum up louder. The sound of it turns into the roar of an approaching locomotive.* BLANCHE *crouches, pressing her fists to her ears until it has gone by.*]

---

4. "Fat Tuesday" (French), the carnival before Lent, the Christian period of self-denial, which begins on Ash Wednesday.   5. Cleopatra, Queen of Egypt.   6. Robbed.

BLANCHE: [*Finally straightening.*] Let me—let me get by you!
STANLEY: Get by me? Sure. Go ahead. [*He moves back a pace in the doorway.*]
BLANCHE: You—you stand over there! [*She indicates a further position.*]
STANLEY: You got plenty of room to walk by me now.
BLANCHE: Not with you there! But I've got to get out somehow!
STANLEY: You think I'll interfere with you? Ha-ha! [*The "Blue Piano" goes softly. She turns confusedly and makes a faint gesture. The inhuman jungle voices rise up. He takes a step toward her, biting his tongue, which protrudes between his lips. Softly.*] Come to think of it—maybe you wouldn't be bad to—interfere with . . .

[BLANCHE *moves backward through the door into the bedroom.*]

BLANCHE: Stay back! Don't you come toward me another step or I'll—
STANLEY: What?
BLANCHE: Some awful thing will happen! It will!
STANLEY: What are you putting on now?

[*They are now both inside the bedroom.*]

BLANCHE: I warn you, don't, I'm in danger!

[*He takes another step. She smashes a bottle on the table and faces him, clutching the broken top.*]

STANLEY: What did you do that for?
BLANCHE: So I could twist the broken end in your face!
STANLEY: I bet you would do that!
BLANCHE: I would! I will if you—
STANLEY: Oh! So you want some roughhouse! All right, let's have some roughhouse! [*He springs toward her, overturning the table. She cries out and strikes at him with the bottle top but he catches her wrist.*] Tiger—tiger! Drop the bottle-top! Drop it! We've had this date with each other from the beginning!

[*She moans. The bottle-top falls. She sinks to her knees: He picks up her inert figure and carries her to the bed. The hot trumpet and drums from the Four Deuces sound loudly.*]

## Scene 11

It is some weeks later. STELLA *is packing* BLANCHE'*s things. Sounds of water can be heard running in the bathroom.*

*The portieres are partly open on the poker players—*STANLEY, STEVE, MITCH *and* PABLO—*who sit around the table in the kitchen. The atmosphere of the kitchen is now the same raw, lurid one of the disastrous poker night.*

*The building is framed by the sky of turquoise.* STELLA *has been crying as she arranges the flowery dresses in the open trunk.*

EUNICE *comes down the steps from her flat above and enters the kitchen. There is an outburst from the poker table.*

STANLEY: Drew to an inside straight and made it, by God.
PABLO: *Maldita sea tu suerto!*
STANLEY: Put it in English, greaseball.

PABLO: I am cursing your rutting luck.
STANLEY: [*Prodigiously elated.*] You know what luck is? Luck is believing you're lucky. Take at Salerno.[7] I believed I was lucky. I figured that 4 out of 5 would not come through but I would... and I did. I put that down as a rule. To hold front position in this rat-race you've got to believe you are lucky.
MITCH: You... you... you... Brag... brag... bull... bull.

[STELLA *goes into the bedroom and starts folding a dress.*]

STANLEY: What's the matter with him?
EUNICE: [*Walking past the table.*] I always did say that men are callous things with no feelings but this does beat anything. Making pigs of yourselves. [*She comes through the portieres into the bedroom.*]
STANLEY: What's the matter with her?
STELLA: How is my baby?
EUNICE: Sleeping like a little angel. Brought you some grapes. [*She puts them on a stool and lowers her voice.*] Blanche?
STELLA: Bathing.
EUNICE: How is she?
STELLA: She wouldn't eat anything but asked for a drink.
EUNICE: What did you tell her?
STELLA: I—just told her that—we'd made arrangements for her to rest in the country. She's got it mixed in her mind with Shep Huntleigh.

[BLANCHE *opens the bathroom door slightly.*]

BLANCHE: Stella.
STELLA: Yes.
BLANCHE: That cool yellow silk—the bouclé.[8] See if it's crushed. If it's not too crushed I'll wear it and on the lapel that silver and turquoise pin in the shape of a seahorse. You will find them in the heart-shaped box I keep my accessories in. And Stella... Try and locate a bunch of artificial violets in that box, too, to pin with the seahorse on the lapel of the jacket.

[*She closes the door.* STELLA *turns to* EUNICE.]

STELLA: I don't know if I did the right thing.
EUNICE: What else could you do?
STELLA: I couldn't believe her story and go on living with Stanley.
EUNICE: Don't ever believe it. Life has got to go on. No matter what happens, you've got to keep on going.

[*The bathroom door opens a little.*]

BLANCHE: [*Looking out.*] Is the coast clear?
STELLA: Yes, Blanche. [*To* EUNICE.] Tell her how well she's looking.
BLANCHE: Please close the curtains before I come out.
STELLA: They're closed.
STANLEY: —How many for you?

---

7. Important beachhead in the Allied invasion of Italy in World War II.
8. Textile woven with uneven yarn to produce a rough, uneven surface.

PABLO: Two.
STEVE: Three.

> [BLANCHE *appears in the amber light of the door. She has a tragic radiance in her red satin robe following the sculptural lines of her body. The "Varsouviana" rises audibly as* BLANCHE *enters the bedroom.*]

BLANCHE: [*With faintly hysterical vivacity.*] I have just washed my hair.
STELLA: Did you?
BLANCHE: I'm not sure I got the soap out.
EUNICE: Such fine hair!
BLANCHE: [*Accepting the compliment.*] It's a problem. Didn't I get a call?
STELLA: Who from, Blanche?
BLANCHE: Shep Huntleigh . . .
STELLA: Why, not yet, honey!
BLANCHE: How strange! I—

> [*At the sound of* BLANCHE'*s voice* MITCH'*s arm supporting his cards has sagged and his gaze is dissolved into space.* STANLEY *slaps him on the shoulder.*]

STANLEY: Hey, Mitch, come to!

> [*The sound of this new voice shocks* BLANCHE. *She makes a shocked gesture, forming his name with her lips.* STELLA *nods and looks quickly away.* BLANCHE *stands quite still for some moments—the silver-backed mirror in her hand and a look of sorrowful perplexity as though all human experience shows on her face.* BLANCHE *finally speaks but with sudden hysteria.*]

BLANCHE: What's going on here? [*She turns from* STELLA *to* EUNICE *and back to* STELLA. *Her rising voice penetrates the concentration of the game.* MITCH *ducks his head lower but* STANLEY *shoves back his chair as if about to rise.* STEVE *places a restraining hand on his arm. Continuing.*] What's happened here? I want an explanation of what's happened here.
STELLA: [*Agonizingly.*] Hush! Hush!
EUNICE: Hush! Hush! Honey.
STELLA: Please, Blanche.
BLANCHE: Why are you looking at me like that? Is something wrong with me?
EUNICE: You look wonderful, Blanche. Don't she look wonderful?
STELLA: Yes.
EUNICE: I understand you are going on a trip.
STELLA: Yes, Blanche *is*. She's going on a vacation.
EUNICE: I'm green with envy.
BLANCHE: Help me, help me get dressed!
STELLA: [*Handing her dress.*] Is this what you—
BLANCHE: Yes, it will do! I'm anxious to get out of here—this place is a trap!
EUNICE: What a pretty blue jacket.
STELLA: It's lilac colored.
BLANCHE: You're both mistaken. It's Della Robbia blue.[9] The blue of the robe in the old Madonna pictures. Are these grapes washed? [*She fingers the bunch of grapes which* EUNICE *had brought in.*]
EUNICE: Huh?

---

9. A shade of light blue seen in terra cottas made by the Della Robbia family during the Italian Renaissance.

BLANCHE: Washed, I said. Are they washed?
EUNICE: They're from the French Market.
BLANCHE: That doesn't mean they've been washed. [*The cathedral bells chime.*] Those cathedral bells—they're the only clean thing in the Quarter. Well, I'm going now. I'm ready to go.
EUNICE: [*Whispering.*] She's going to walk out before they get here.
STELLA: Wait, Blanche.
BLANCHE: I don't want to pass in front of those men.
EUNICE: Then wait'll the game breaks up.
STELLA: Sit down and . . .

[BLANCHE *turns weakly, hesitantly about. She lets them push her into a chair.*]

BLANCHE: I can smell the sea air. The rest of my time I'm going to spend on the sea. And when I die, I'm going to die on the sea. You know what I shall die of? [*She plucks a grape.*] I shall die of eating an unwashed grape one day out on the ocean. I will die—with my hand in the hand of some nice-looking ship's doctor, a very young one with a small blond mustache and a big silver watch. "Poor lady," they'll say, "the quinine did her no good. That unwashed grape has transported her soul to heaven." [*The cathedral chimes are heard.*] And I'll be buried at sea sewn up in a clean white sack and dropped overboard—at noon—in the blaze of summer—and into an ocean as blue as [*Chimes again.*] my first lover's eyes!

[A DOCTOR *and a* MATRON *have appeared around the corner of the building and climbed the steps to the porch. The gravity of their profession is exaggerated—the unmistakable aura of the state institution with its cynical detachment. The* DOCTOR *rings the doorbell. The murmur of the game is interrupted.*]

EUNICE: [*Whispering to* STELLA.] That must be them.

[STELLA *presses her fists to her lips.*]

BLANCHE: [*Rising slowly.*] What is it?
EUNICE: [*Affectedly casual.*] Excuse me while I see who's at the door.
STELLA: Yes.

[EUNICE *goes into the kitchen.*]

BLANCHE: [*Tensely.*] I wonder if it's for me.

[*A whispered colloquy takes place at the door.*]

EUNICE: [*Returning, brightly.*] Someone is calling for Blanche.
BLANCHE: It *is* for me, then! [*She looks fearfully from one to the other and then to the portieres. The "Varsouviana" faintly plays.*] Is it the gentleman I was expecting from Dallas?
EUNICE: I think it is, Blanche.
BLANCHE: I'm not quite ready.
STELLA: Ask him to wait outside.
BLANCHE: I . . .

[EUNICE *goes back to the portieres. Drums sound very softly.*]

STELLA: Everything packed?
BLANCHE: My silver toilet articles are still out.

STELLA: Ah!
EUNICE: [*Returning.*] They're waiting in front of the house.
BLANCHE: They! Who's "they"?
EUNICE: There's a lady with him.
BLANCHE: I cannot imagine who this "lady" could be! How is she dressed?
EUNICE: Just—just a sort of a—plain-tailored outfit.
BLANCHE: Possibly she's—[*Her voice dies out nervously.*]
STELLA: Shall we go, Blanche?
BLANCHE: Must we go through that room?
STELLA: I will go with you.
BLANCHE: How do I look?
STELLA: Lovely.
EUNICE: [*Echoing.*] Lovely.

[BLANCHE *moves fearfully to the portieres.* EUNICE *draws them open for her.* BLANCHE *goes into the kitchen.*]

BLANCHE: [*To the men.*] Please don't get up. I'm only passing through.

[*She crosses quickly to outside door.* STELLA *and* EUNICE *follow. The poker players stand awkwardly at the table—all except* MITCH, *who remains seated, looking down at the table.* BLANCHE *steps out on a small porch at the side of the door. She stops short and catches her breath.*]

DOCTOR: How do you do?
BLANCHE: You are not the gentleman I was expecting. [*She suddenly gasps and starts back up the steps. She stops by* STELLA, *who stands just outside the door, and speaks in a frightening whisper.*] That man isn't Shep Huntleigh.

[*The "Varsouviana" is playing distantly.* STELLA *stares back at* BLANCHE. EUNICE *is holding* STELLA'*s arm. There is a moment of silence—no sound but that of* STANLEY *steadily shuffling the cards.* BLANCHE *catches her breath again and slips back into the flat. She enters the flat with a peculiar smile, her eyes wide and brilliant. As soon as her sister goes past her,* STELLA *closes her eyes and clenches her hands.* EUNICE *throws her arms comfortingly about her. Then she starts up to her flat.* BLANCHE *stops just inside the door.* MITCH *keeps staring down at his hands on the table, but the other men look at her curiously. At last she starts around the table toward the bedroom. As she does,* STANLEY *suddenly pushes back his chair and rises as if to block her way. The* MATRON *follows her into the flat.*]

STANLEY: Did you forget something?
BLANCHE: [*Shrilly.*] Yes! Yes, I forgot something!

[*She rushes past him into the bedroom. Lurid reflections appear on the walls in odd, sinuous shapes. The "Varsouviana" is filtered into a weird distortion, accompanied by the cries and noises of the jungle.* BLANCHE *seizes the back of a chair as if to defend herself.*]

STANLEY: [*Sotto voce.*] Doc, you better go in.
DOCTOR: [*Sotto voce, motioning to the* MATRON.] Nurse, bring her out.

[*The* MATRON *advances on one side,* STANLEY *on the other. Divested of all the softer properties of womanhood, the* MATRON *is a peculiarly sinister figure in her severe dress. Her voice is bold and toneless as a firebell.*]

MATRON: Hello, Blanche.

[*The greeting is echoed and re-echoed by other mysterious voices behind the walls, as if reverberated through a canyon of rock.*]

STANLEY: She says that she forgot something.

[*The echo sounds in threatening whispers.*]

MATRON: That's all right.
STANLEY: What did you forget, Blanche?
BLANCHE: I—I—
MATRON: It don't matter. We can pick it up later.
STANLEY: Sure. We can send it along with the trunk.
BLANCHE: [*Retreating in panic.*] I don't know you—I don't know you. I want to be—left alone—please!
MATRON: Now, Blanche!
ECHOES: [*Rising and falling.*] Now, Blanche—now, Blanche—now, Blanche!
STANLEY: You left nothing here but spilt talcum and old empty perfume bottles—unless it's the paper lantern you want to take with you. You want the lantern?

[*He crosses to dressing table and seizes the paper lantern, tearing it off the light bulb, and extends it toward her. She cries out as if the lantern was herself. The* MATRON *steps boldly toward her. She screams and tries to break past the* MATRON. *All the men spring to their feet.* STELLA *runs out to the porch, with* EUNICE *following to comfort her, simultaneously with the confused voices of the men in the kitchen.* STELLA *rushes into* EUNICE's *embrace on the porch.*]

STELLA: Oh, my God, Eunice help me! Don't let them do that to her, don't let them hurt her! Oh, God, oh, please God, don't hurt her! What are they doing to her? What are they doing? [*She tries to break from* EUNICE's *arms.*]
EUNICE: No, honey, no, no, honey. Stay here. Don't go back in there. Stay with me and don't look.
STELLA: What have I done to my sister? Oh, God, what have I done to my sister?
EUNICE: You done the right thing, the only thing you could do. She couldn't stay here; there wasn't no other place for her to go.

[*While* STELLA *and* EUNICE *are speaking on the porch the voices of the men in the kitchen overlap them.* MITCH *has started toward the bedroom.* STANLEY *crosses to block him.* STANLEY *pushes him aside.* MITCH *lunges and strikes at* STANLEY. STANLEY *pushes* MITCH *back.* MITCH *collapses at the table, sobbing. During the preceding scenes, the* MATRON *catches hold of* BLANCHE's *arm and prevents her flight.* BLANCHE *turns wildly and scratches at the* MATRON. *The heavy woman pinions her arms.* BLANCHE *cries out hoarsely and slips to her knees.*]

MATRON: These fingernails have to be trimmed. [*The* DOCTOR *comes into the room and she looks at him.*] Jacket, Doctor?
DOCTOR: Not unless necessary. [*He takes off his hat and now he becomes personalized. The unhuman quality goes. His voice is gentle and reassuring as he crosses to* BLANCHE *and crouches in front of her. As he speaks her name, her terror subsides a little. The lurid reflections fade from the walls, the inhuman cries and noises die out and her own hoarse crying is calmed.*] Miss DuBois. [*She turns her face to him and stares at him*

*with desperate pleading. He smiles; then he speaks to the* MATRON.] It won't be necessary.

BLANCHE: [*Faintly.*] Ask her to let go of me.
DOCTOR: [*To the* MATRON.] Let go.

[*The* MATRON *releases her.* BLANCHE *extends her hands toward the* DOCTOR. *He draws her up gently and supports her with his arm and leads her through the portieres.*]

BLANCHE: [*Holding tight to his arm.*] Whoever you are—I have always depended on the kindness of strangers.

[*The poker players stand back as* BLANCHE *and the* DOCTOR *cross the kitchen to the front door. She allows him to lead her as if she were blind. As they go out on the porch,* STELLA *cries out her sister's name from where she is crouched a few steps up on the stairs.*]

STELLA: Blanche! Blanche, Blanche!

[BLANCHE *walks on without turning, followed by the* DOCTOR *and the* MATRON. *They go around the corner of the building.* EUNICE *descends to* STELLA *and places the child in her arms. It is wrapped in a pale blue blanket.* STELLA *accepts the child, sobbingly.* EUNICE *continues downstairs and enters the kitchen where the men, except for* STANLEY, *are returning silently to their places about the table.* STANLEY *has gone out on the porch and stands at the foot of the steps looking at* STELLA.]

STANLEY: [*A bit uncertainly.*] Stella? [*She sobs with inhuman abandon. There is something luxurious in her complete surrender to crying now that her sister is gone. Voluptuously, soothingly.*] Now, honey. Now, love. Now, now, love. [*He kneels beside her and his fingers find the opening of her blouse.*] Now, now, love. Now, love. . . .

[*The luxurious sobbing, the sensual murmur fade away under the swelling music of the "Blue Piano" and the muted trumpet.*]

STEVE: This game is seven-card stud.

CURTAIN

1947

## QUESTIONS

1. Does *A Streetcar Named Desire* begin with "exposition" in the traditional sense? How does Williams provide the audience with necessary background information? What is the "rising action"—the event that upsets the status quo and sets the plot in motion? What is the play's climax? How does the play present the "falling action" and the conclusion? Does such traditional dramatic terminology really apply to this play? Why or why not? Why do you think Williams divided the play into eleven scenes rather than three or five acts?
2. *A Streetcar Named Desire* centers on the conflict between Blanche DuBois and Stanley Kowalski. Why and how are their personalities and values in conflict? Can either of them be called a "hero" or a "villain" in the traditional senses of those words? Why or why not? Of these two characters, whom do you most sympathize with and/or admire at different moments of the play? At which point are you most aware of the faults of one or the other?

3. What role does Stella play in this conflict? What, for example, is the significance of the scene in which Blanche tries to convince Stella to leave Stanley? What is the full significance of Stella's line, in scene 11, that she couldn't believe Blanche's story "and go on living with Stanley"?
4. What is the significance of Stanley's allusion in scene 8 to Huey Long's remark that "Every Man is a King"? How might this remark resonate with the references to class sprinkled throughout the play, including the initial description of Stella as "of a background obviously quite different from her husband's" and Stanley's reference to how he "pulled [Stella] down off them columns"?
5. What emotional associations and values does Belle Reve have for Blanche? for Stella? What different memories does each woman associate with Belle Reve? What does the place symbolize for Blanche, Stella, and Stanley? How important are the particulars of Belle Reve's history? How does the name of the plantation (literally, "beautiful dream") comment on what happens in the play?
6. Much of the action of the play centers on the process whereby Stanley discovers and reveals what he sees as the truth about Blanche and about Blanche's past, and he more than once refers to her as a liar. Yet Blanche offers us a very different reading of her lies, particularly in her encounter with Mitch in scene 9. In what sense is and is not Blanche a liar? Why is Stanley so bent on discovering and revealing the truth?
7. A key moment in Blanche's past and one that we get both from her point of view and from Stella's is the night when her young husband shot himself. What is the significance of that moment? Why does it figure so largely, not only in Blanche's mind but also in the play? What does this long-dead character represent in the play?
8. What is the significance of the play's title? How did Williams change the play by naming it *A Streetcar Named Desire* rather than *The Poker Night*? What different kinds or notions of "desire" are at issue in the play? (Consider such references as when Blanche rebukes Stella for "talking about . . . brutal desire—just—Desire!" [scene 4] or when Blanche tells Mitch that desire is "[t]he opposite" of death" [scene 9]).
9. To what extent does Williams draw upon stereotypes of New Orleans, or the South? In what ways are Blanche and Stanley stereotypes, and in what ways do they confound the expectations created by these stereotypes? How does Williams make each of these characters emerge as a unique individual?
10. How are Williams's stage directions unlike those of other plays you have read? What are some examples of stage directions in *A Streetcar Named Desire* that go beyond what is necessary for staging a performance and indicate that Williams intended the play to be read as literature?

## SUGGESTIONS FOR WRITING

1. Is *A Streetcar Named Desire* a "realistic" play—that is, are the characters, setting, and situation plausible, recognizable? Do the characters speak in a natural idiom, or do they seem to be "speechifying" for the sake of the play? Write an essay in which you argue that the mode of the play is or is not one of realism, and be sure to support your position with specifics from the text.
2. Although *A Streetcar Named Desire* is set in New Orleans, the DuBois family plantation, Belle Reve, has critical significance in the play. What is evoked—about history, about social class—by the offstage presence of a Southern plantation? How does the story of Belle Reve affect each character and propel the plot? Write an essay in which you discuss the dramatic and thematic significance of Belle Reve in the play.

3. *A Streetcar Named Desire* is filled with paper and references to paper: the paper lantern, the deed to Belle Reve, the song "Paper Moon," among others. What is the effect of such accumulating details? How do they acquire thematic significance? Write an essay in which you examine the recurrence of paper imagery in the play. Why is it important?
4. Gender roles and sexuality are central to the drama of *A Streetcar Named Desire*. To what extent are Stanley Kowalski and Blanche DuBois caricatures of masculinity and femininity? Write an essay in which you discuss the play's depiction of gender roles. Do you think that Williams is trying to make a conclusive statement about gender, or is the play more open-ended and exploratory in this regard?
5. At one point Blanche tells Mitch, "The first time I laid eyes on [Stanley] I thought to myself, that man is my executioner! That man will destroy me." And indeed, at the play's climactic moment Stanley declares, "We've had this date with each other from the beginning!" Are the play's characters pawns of fate, acting out destinies over which they have little control, or are they fully conscious of and responsible for their actions? Write an essay in which you examine the role of free will in *A Streetcar Named Desire*.

# ANTON CHEKHOV

## *The Cherry Orchard*[1]

### CHARACTERS IN THE PLAY

MADAME RANEVSKY (LYUBOV ANDREYEVNA), *the owner of the Cherry Orchard*
ANYA, *her daughter, aged 17*
VARYA, *her adopted daughter, aged 24*
SEMYONOV-PISHTCHIK, *a landowner*
CHARLOTTA IVANOVNA, *a governess*
EPIHODOV (SEMYON PANTALEYEVITCH), *a clerk*
DUNYASHA, *a maid*
FIRS, *an old valet, aged 87*
GAEV (LEONID ANDREYEVITCH), *brother of Madame Ranevsky*
LOPAHIN (YERMOLAY ALEXEYEVITCH), *a merchant*
TROFIMOV (PYOTR SERGEYEVITCH), *a student*
YASHA, *a young valet*
A WAYFARER
THE STATION MASTER
A POST-OFFICE CLERK
VISITORS, SERVANTS

The action takes place on the estate of MADAME RANEVSKY.

## ACT I

A room, which has always been called the nursery. One of the doors leads into ANYA's room. Dawn, sun rises during the scene. May, the cherry trees in flower, but it is cold in the garden with the frost of early morning. Windows closed.

Enter DUNYASHA *with a candle and* LOPAHIN *with a book in his hand.*

---

1. Translated by Constance Garnett.

LOPAHIN: The train's in, thank God. What time is it?

DUNYASHA: Nearly two o'clock. [*Puts out the candle.*] It's daylight already.

LOPAHIN: The train's late! Two hours, at least. [*Yawns and stretches.*] I'm a pretty one; what a fool I've been. Came here on purpose to meet them at the station and dropped asleep.... Dozed off as I sat in the chair. It's annoying.... You might have waked me.

DUNYASHA: I thought you had gone. [*Listens.*] There, I do believe they're coming!

LOPAHIN: [*Listens.*] No, what with the luggage and one thing and another. [*A pause.*] Lyubov Andreyevna has been abroad five years; I don't know what she is like now.... She's a splendid woman. A good-natured, kind-hearted woman. I remember when I was a lad of fifteen, my poor father—he used to keep a little shop here in the village in those days—gave me a punch in the face with his fist and made my nose bleed. We were in the yard here, I forget what we'd come about—he had had a drop. Lyubov Andreyevna—I can see her now—she was a slim young girl then—took me to wash my face, and then brought me into this very room, into the nursery. "Don't cry, little peasant," says she, "it will be well in time for your wedding day." ... [*A pause.*] Little peasant.... My father was a peasant, it's true, but here am I in a white waistcoat and brown shoes, like a pig in a bun shop. Yes, I'm a rich man, but for all my money, come to think, a peasant I was, and a peasant I am. [*Turns over the pages of the book.*] I've been reading this book and I can't make head or tail of it. I fell asleep over it. [*A pause.*]

DUNYASHA: The dogs have been awake all night, they feel that the mistress is coming.

LOPAHIN: Why, what's the matter with you, Dunyasha?

DUNYASHA: My hands are all of a tremble. I feel as though I should faint.

LOPAHIN: You're a spoilt soft creature, Dunyasha. And dressed like a lady too, and your hair done up. That's not the thing. One must know one's place.

[*Enter* EPIHODOV *with a nosegay;*[2] *he wears a pea-jacket and highly polished creaking topboots; he drops the nosegay as he comes in.*]

EPIHODOV: [*Picking up the nosegay.*] Here! the gardener's sent this, says you're to put it in the dining-room. [*Gives* DUNYASHA *the nosegay.*]

LOPAHIN: And bring me some kvass.[3]

DUNYASHA: I will. [*Goes out.*]

EPIHODOV: It's chilly this morning, three degrees of frost,[4] though the cherries are all in flower. I can't say much for our climate. [*Sighs.*] I can't. Our climate is not often propitious to the occasion. Yermolay Alexeyevitch, permit me to call your attention to the fact that I purchased myself a pair of boots the day before yesterday, and they creak, I venture to assure you, so that there's no tolerating them. What ought I to grease them with?

LOPAHIN: Oh, shut up! Don't bother me.

EPIHODOV: Every day some misfortune befalls me. I don't complain, I'm used to it, and I wear a smiling face.

[DUNYASHA *comes in, hands* LOPAHIN *the kvass.*]

---

2. Bouquet.   3. Weak homemade beer.   4. That is, 29°F (−2°C).

EPIHODOV: I am going. [*Stumbles against a chair, which falls over.*] There! [*As though triumphant.*] There you see now, excuse the expression, an accident like that among others.... It's positively remarkable. [*Goes out.*]

DUNYASHA: Do you know, Yermolay Alexeyevitch, I must confess, Epihodov has made me a proposal.

LOPAHIN: Ah!

DUNYASHA: I'm sure I don't know.... He's a harmless fellow, but sometimes when he begins talking, there's no making anything of it. It's all very fine and expressive, only there's no understanding it. I've a sort of liking for him too. He loves me to distraction. He's an unfortunate man; every day there's something. They tease him about it—two and twenty misfortunes they call him.

LOPAHIN: [*Listening.*] There! I do believe they're coming.

DUNYASHA: They are coming! What's the matter with me?... I'm cold all over.

LOPAHIN: They really are coming. Let's go and meet them. Will she know me? It's five years since I saw her.

DUNYASHA: [*In a flutter.*] I shall drop this very minute.... Ah, I shall drop.

[*There is a sound of two carriages driving up to the house.* LOPAHIN *and* DUNYASHA *go out quickly. The stage is left empty. A noise is heard in the adjoining rooms.* FIRS, *who has driven to meet* MADAME RANEVSKY, *crosses the stage hurriedly leaning on a stick. He is wearing old-fashioned livery and a high hat. He says something to himself, but not a word can be distinguished. The noise behind the scenes goes on increasing. A voice: "Come, let's go in here." Enter* LYUBOV ANDREYEVNA, ANYA, *and* CHARLOTTA IVANOVNA *with a pet dog on a chain, all in traveling dresses.* VARYA *in an out-door coat with a kerchief over her head,* GAEV, SEMYONOV-PISHTCHIK, LOPAHIN, DUNYASHA *with bag and parasol, servants with other articles. All walk across the room.*]

ANYA: Let's come in here. Do you remember what room this is, mamma?

LYUBOV: [*Joyfully, through her tears.*] The nursery!

VARYA: How cold it is, my hands are numb. [*To* LYUBOV ANDREYEVNA.] Your rooms, the white room and the lavender one, are just the same as ever, mamma.

LYUBOV: My nursery, dear delightful room.... I used to sleep here when I was little.... [*Cries.*] And here I am, like a little child.... [*Kisses her brother and* VARYA, *and then her brother again.*] Varya's just the same as ever, like a nun. And I knew Dunyasha. [*Kisses* DUNYASHA.]

GAEV: The train was two hours late. What do you think of that? Is that the way to do things?

CHARLOTTA: [*To* PISHTCHIK.] My dog eats nuts, too.

PISHTCHIK: [*Wonderingly.*] Fancy that!

[*They all go out except* ANYA *and* DUNYASHA.]

DUNYASHA: We've been expecting you so long. [*Takes* ANYA's *hat and coat.*]

ANYA: I haven't slept for four nights on the journey. I feel dreadfully cold.

DUNYASHA: You set out in Lent, there was snow and frost, and now? My darling! [*Laughs and kisses her.*] I have missed you, my precious, my joy. I must tell you ... I can't put it off a minute....

ANYA: [*Wearily.*] What now?

DUNYASHA: Epihodov, the clerk, made me a proposal just after Easter.

ANYA: It's always the same thing with you.... [*Straightening her hair.*] I've lost all my hairpins.... [*She is staggering from exhaustion.*]
DUNYASHA: I don't know what to think, really. He does love me, he does love me so!
ANYA: [*Looking towards her door, tenderly.*] My own room, my windows just as though I had never gone away. I'm home! To-morrow morning I shall get up and run into the garden.... Oh, if I could get to sleep! I haven't slept all the journey, I was so anxious and worried.
DUNYASHA: Pyotr Sergeyevitch came the day before yesterday.
ANYA: [*Joyfully.*] Petya!
DUNYASHA: He's asleep in the bath house, he has settled in there. I'm afraid of being in their way, says he. [*Glancing at her watch.*] I was to have waked him, but Varvara Mihalovna told me not to. Don't you wake him, says she.

[*Enter* VARYA *with a bunch of keys at her waist.*]

VARYA: Dunyasha, coffee and make haste.... Mamma's asking for coffee.
DUNYASHA: This very minute. [*Goes out.*]
VARYA: Well, thank God, you've come. You're home again. [*Petting her.*] My little darling has come back! My precious beauty has come back again!
ANYA: I have had a time of it!
VARYA: I can fancy.
ANYA: We set off in Holy Week—it was so cold then, and all the way Charlotta would talk and show off her tricks. What did you want to burden me with Charlotta for?
VARYA: You couldn't have traveled all alone, darling. At seventeen!
ANYA: We got to Paris at last, it was cold there—snow. I speak French shockingly. Mamma lives on the fifth floor, I went up to her and there were a lot of French people, ladies, an old priest with a book. The place smelt of tobacco and so comfortless. I felt sorry, oh! so sorry for mamma all at once, I put my arms round her neck, and hugged her and wouldn't let her go. Mamma was as kind as she could be, and she cried....
VARYA: [*Through her tears.*] Don't speak of it, don't speak of it!
ANYA: She had sold her villa at Mentone, she had nothing left, nothing. I hadn't a farthing left either, we only just had enough to get here. And mamma doesn't understand! When we had dinner at the stations, she always ordered the most expensive things and gave the waiters a whole rouble. Charlotta's just the same. Yasha too must have the same as we do; it's simply awful. You know Yasha is mamma's valet now, we brought him here with us.
VARYA: Yes, I've seen the young rascal.
ANYA: Well, tell me—have you paid the arrears on the mortgage?
VARYA: How could we get the money?
ANYA: Oh, dear! Oh, dear!
VARYA: In August the place will be sold.
ANYA: My goodness!
LOPAHIN: [*Peeps in at the door and moos like a cow.*] Moo! [*Disappears.*]
VARYA: [*Weeping.*] There, that's what I could do to him. [*Shakes her fist.*]
ANYA: [*Embracing* VARYA, *softly.*] Varya, has he made you an offer? [VARYA *shakes her head.*] Why, but he loves you. Why is it you don't come to an understanding? What are you waiting for?

VARYA: I believe that there never will be anything between us. He has a lot to do, he has no time for me . . . and takes no notice of me. Bless the man, it makes me miserable to see him. . . . Everyone's talking of our being married, everyone's congratulating me, and all the while there's really nothing in it; it's all like a dream. [*In another tone.*] You have a new brooch like a bee.
ANYA: [*Mournfully.*] Mamma bought it. [*Goes into her own room and in a lighthearted childish tone.*] And you know, in Paris I went up in a balloon!
VARYA: My darling's home again! My pretty is home again!

[DUNYASHA *returns with the coffee-pot and is making the coffee.*]

VARYA: [*Standing at the door.*] All day long, darling, as I go about looking after the house, I keep dreaming all the time. If only we could marry you to a rich man, then I should feel more at rest. Then I would go off by myself on a pilgrimage to Kiev, to Moscow . . . and so I would spend my life going from one holy place to another. . . . I would go on and on. . . . What bliss!
ANYA: The birds are singing in the garden. What time is it?
VARYA: It must be nearly three. It's time you were asleep, darling. [*Going into* ANYA's *room.*] What bliss!

[YASHA *enters with a rug and a traveling bag.*]

YASHA: [*Crosses the stage, mincingly.*] May one come in here, pray?
DUNYASHA: I shouldn't have known you, Yasha. How you have changed abroad.
YASHA: H'm! . . . And who are you?
DUNYASHA: When you went away, I was that high. [*Shows distance from floor.*] Dunyasha, Fyodor's daughter. . . . You don't remember me!
YASHA: H'm! . . . You're a peach! [*Looks round and embraces her: she shrieks and drops a saucer.* YASHA *goes out hastily.*]
VARYA: [*In the doorway, in a tone of vexation.*] What now?
DUNYASHA: [*Through her tears.*] I have broken a saucer.
VARYA: Well, that brings good luck.
ANYA: [*Coming out of her room.*] We ought to prepare mamma: Petya is here.
VARYA: I told them not to wake him.
ANYA: [*Dreamily.*] It's six years since father died. Then only a month later little brother Grisha was drowned in the river, such a pretty boy he was, only seven. It was more than mamma could bear, so she went away, went away without looking back. [*Shuddering.*] . . . How well I understand her, if only she knew! [*A pause.*] And Petya Trofimov was Grisha's tutor, he may remind her.

[*Enter* FIRS: *he is wearing a pea-jacket and a white waistcoat.*]

FIRS: [*Goes up to the coffee-pot, anxiously.*] The mistress will be served here. [*Puts on white gloves.*] Is the coffee ready? [*Sternly to* DUNYASHA.] Girl! Where's the cream?
DUNYASHA: Ah, mercy on us! [*Goes out quickly.*]
FIRS: [*Fussing round the coffee-pot.*] Ech! you good-for-nothing! [*Muttering to himself.*] Come back from Paris. And the old master used to go to Paris too . . . horses all the way. [*Laughs.*]
VARYA: What is it, Firs?
FIRS: What is your pleasure? [*Gleefully.*] My lady has come home! I have lived to see her again! Now I can die. [*Weeps with joy.*]

[*Enter* LYUBOV ANDREYEVNA, GAEV *and* SEMYONOV-PISHTCHIK; *the latter is in a short-waisted full coat of fine cloth, and full trousers.* GAEV, *as he comes in, makes a gesture with his arms and his whole body, as though he were playing billiards.*]

LYUBOV: How does it go? Let me remember. Cannon off the red!
GAEV: That's it—in off the white! Why, once, sister, we used to sleep together in this very room, and now I'm fifty-one, strange as it seems.
LOPAHIN: Yes, time flies.
GAEV: What do you say?
LOPAHIN: Time, I say, flies.
GAEV: What a smell of patchouli!
ANYA: I'm going to bed. Good-night, mamma. [*Kisses her mother.*]
LYUBOV: My precious darling. [*Kisses her hands.*] Are you glad to be home? I can't believe it.
ANYA: Good-night, uncle.
GAEV: [*Kissing her face and hands.*] God bless you! How like you are to your mother! [*To his sister.*] At her age you were just the same, Lyuba.

[ANYA *shakes hands with* LOPAHIN *and* PISHTCHIK, *then goes out, shutting the door after her.*]

LYUBOV: She's quite worn out.
PISHTCHIK: Aye, it's a long journey, to be sure.
VARYA: [*To* LOPAHIN *and* PISHTCHIK.] Well, gentlemen? It's three o'clock and time to say good-bye.
LYUBOV: [*Laughs.*] You're just the same as ever, Varya. [*Draws her to her and kisses her.*] I'll just drink my coffee and then we will all go and rest. [FIRS *puts a cushion under her feet.*] Thanks, friend. I am so fond of coffee, I drink it day and night. Thanks, dear old man. [*Kisses* FIRS.]
VARYA: I'll just see whether all the things have been brought in. [*Goes out.*]
LYUBOV: Can it really be me sitting here? [*Laughs.*] I want to dance about and clap my hands. [*Covers her face with her hands.*] And I could drop asleep in a moment! God knows I love my country, I love it tenderly; I couldn't look out of the window in the train, I kept crying so. [*Through her tears.*] But I must drink my coffee, though. Thank you, Firs, thanks, dear old man. I'm so glad to find you still alive.
FIRS: The day before yesterday.
GAEV: He's rather deaf.
LOPAHIN: I have to set off for Harkov directly, at five o'clock.... It is annoying! I wanted to have a look at you, and a little talk.... You are just as splendid as ever.
PISHTCHIK: [*Breathing heavily.*] Handsomer, indeed.... Dressed in Parisian style ... completely bowled me over.
LOPAHIN: Your brother, Leonid Andreyevitch here, is always saying that I'm a low-born knave, that I'm a money-grubber, but I don't care one straw for that. Let him talk. Only I do want you to believe in me as you used to. I do want your wonderful tender eyes to look at me as they used to in the old days. Merciful God! My father was a serf of your father and of your grandfather, but you—you—did so much for me once, that I've forgotten all that; I love you as though you were my kin ... more than my kin.

LYUBOV: I can't sit still, I simply can't.... [*Jumps up and walks about in violent agitation.*] This happiness is too much for me.... You may laugh at me, I know I'm silly.... My own bookcase. [*Kisses the bookcase.*] My little table.

GAEV: Nurse died while you were away.

LYUBOV: [*Sits down and drinks coffee.*] Yes, the Kingdom of Heaven be hers! You wrote me of her death.

GAEV: And Anastasy is dead. Squinting Petruchka has left me and is in service now with the police captain in the town. [*Takes a box of caramels out of his pocket and sucks one.*]

PISHTCHIK: My daughter, Dashenka, wishes to be remembered to you.

LOPAHIN: I want to tell you something very pleasant and cheering. [*Glancing at his watch.*] I'm going directly... there's no time to say much... well, I can say it in a couple of words. I needn't tell you your cherry orchard is to be sold to pay your debts; the 22nd of August is the date fixed for the sale; but don't you worry, dearest lady, you may sleep in peace, there is a way of saving it.... This is what I propose. I beg your attention! Your estate is not twenty miles from the town, the railway runs close by it, and if the cherry orchard and the land along the river bank were cut up into building plots and then let on lease for summer villas, you would make an income of at least 25,000 roubles a year out of it.[5]

GAEV: That's all rot, if you'll excuse me.

LYUBOV: I don't quite understand you, Yermolay Alexeyevitch.

LOPAHIN: You will get a rent of at least 25 roubles a year for a three-acre plot from summer visitors, and if you say the word now, I'll bet you what you like there won't be one square foot of ground vacant by the autumn, all the plots will be taken up. I congratulate you; in fact, you are saved. It's a perfect situation with that deep river. Only, of course, it must be cleared—all the old buildings, for example, must be removed, this house too, which is really good for nothing and the old cherry orchard must be cut down.

LYUBOV: Cut down? My dear fellow, forgive me, but you don't know what you are talking about. If there is one thing interesting—remarkable indeed—in the whole province, it's just our cherry orchard.

LOPAHIN: The only thing remarkable about the orchard is that it's a very large one. There's a crop of cherries every alternate year, and then there's nothing to be done with them, no one buys them.

GAEV: This orchard is mentioned in the *Encyclopædia*.[6]

LOPAHIN: [*Glancing at his watch.*] If we don't decide on something and don't take some steps, on the 22nd of August the cherry orchard and the whole estate too will be sold by auction. Make up your minds! There is no other way of saving it, I'll take my oath on that. No, no!

FIRS: In old days, forty or fifty years ago, they used to dry the cherries, soak them, pickle them, make jam too, and they used—

GAEV: Be quiet, Firs.

FIRS: And they used to send the preserved cherries to Moscow and to Harkov by the wagon-load. That brought the money in! And the preserved cherries in

---

5. Over $400,000 per year in today's U.S. currency; a rental fee of 25 roubles is the equivalent of about $400.
6. Perhaps the *Great Russian Encyclopedic Dictionary*, an authoritative 86-volume reference work edited by Brockhaus and Efron.

those days were soft and juicy, sweet and fragrant.... They knew the way to do them then....

LYUBOV: And where is the recipe now?

FIRS: It's forgotten. Nobody remembers it.

PISHTCHIK: [*To* LYUBOV ANDREYEVNA.] What's it like in Paris? Did you eat frogs there?

LYUBOV: Oh, I ate crocodiles.

PISHTCHIK: Fancy that now!

LOPAHIN: There used to be only the gentlefolks and the peasants in the country, but now there are these summer visitors. All the towns, even the small ones, are surrounded nowadays by these summer villas. And one may say for sure, that in another twenty years there'll be many more of these people and that they'll be everywhere. At present the summer visitor only drinks tea in his verandah, but maybe he'll take to working his bit of land too, and then your cherry orchard would become happy, rich and prosperous....

GAEV: [*Indignant.*] What rot!

[*Enter* VARYA *and* YASHA.]

VARYA: There are two telegrams for you, mamma. [*Takes out keys and opens an old-fashioned bookcase with a loud crack.*] Here they are.

LYUBOV: From Paris. [*Tears the telegrams, without reading them.*] I have done with Paris.

GAEV: Do you know, Lyuba, how old that bookcase is? Last week I pulled out the bottom drawer and there I found the date branded on it. The bookcase was made just a hundred years ago. What do you say to that? We might have celebrated its jubilee. Though it's an inanimate object, still it is a *book* case.

PISHTCHIK: [*Amazed.*] A hundred years! Fancy that now.

GAEV: Yes.... It is a thing.... [*Feeling the bookcase.*] Dear, honored, bookcase! Hail to thee who for more than a hundred years hast served the pure ideals of good and justice; thy silent call to fruitful labor has never flagged in those hundred years, maintaining [*In tears.*] in the generations of man, courage and faith in a brighter future and fostering in us ideals of good and social consciousness. [*A pause.*]

LOPAHIN: Yes....

LYUBOV: You are just the same as ever, Leonid.

GAEV: [*A little embarrassed.*] Cannon off the right into the pocket!

LOPAHIN: [*Looking at his watch.*] Well, it's time I was off.

YASHA: [*Handing* LYUBOV ANDREYEVNA *medicine.*] Perhaps you will take your pills now.

PISHTCHIK: You shouldn't take medicines, my dear madam ... they do no harm and no good. Give them here ... honored lady. [*Takes the pill-box, pours the pills into the hollow of his hand, blows on them, puts them in his mouth and drinks off some kvass.*] There!

LYUBOV: [*In alarm.*] Why, you must be out of your mind!

PISHTCHIK: I have taken all the pills.

LOPAHIN: What a glutton! [*All laugh.*]

FIRS: His honor stayed with us in Easter week, ate a gallon and a half of cucumbers.... [*Mutters.*]

LYUBOV: What is he saying?

VARYA: He has taken to muttering like that for the last three years. We are used to it.

YASHA: His declining years!

[CHARLOTTA IVANOVNA, *a very thin, lanky figure in a white dress with a lorgnette in her belt, walks across the stage.*]

LOPAHIN: I beg your pardon, Charlotta Ivanovna, I have not had time to greet you. [*Tries to kiss her hand.*]

CHARLOTTA: [*Pulling away her hand.*] If I let you kiss my hand, you'll be wanting to kiss my elbow, and then my shoulder.

LOPAHIN: I've no luck to-day! [*All laugh.*] Charlotta Ivanovna, show us some tricks!

LYUBOV: Charlotta, do show us some tricks!

CHARLOTTA: I don't want to. I'm sleepy. [*Goes out.*]

LOPAHIN: In three weeks' time we shall meet again. [*Kisses* LYUBOV ANDREYEVNA's *hand.*] Good-bye till then—I must go. [*To* GAEV.] Good-bye. [*Kisses* PISHTCHIK.] Good-bye. [*Gives his hand to* VARYA, *then to* FIRS *and* YASHA.] I don't want to go. [*To* LYUBOV ANDREYEVNA.] If you think over my plan for the villas and make up your mind, then let me know; I will lend you 50,000 roubles.[7] Think of it seriously.

VARYA: [*Angrily.*] Well, do go, for goodness sake.

LOPAHIN: I'm going, I'm going. [*Goes out.*]

GAEV: Low-born knave! I beg pardon, though ... Varya is going to marry him, he's Varya's fiancé.

VARYA: Don't talk nonsense, uncle.

LYUBOV: Well, Varya, I shall be delighted. He's a good man.

PISHTCHIK: He is, one must acknowledge, a most worthy man. And my Dashenka ... says too that ... she says ... various things. [*Snores, but at once wakes up.*] But all the same, honored lady, could you oblige me ... with a loan of 240 roubles ... to pay the interest on my mortgage to-morrow?

VARYA: [*Dismayed.*] No, no.

LYUBOV: I really haven't any money.

PISHTCHIK: It will turn up. [*Laughs.*] I never lose hope. I thought everything was over, I was a ruined man, and lo and behold—the railway passed through my land and ... they paid me for it. And something else will turn up again, if not to-day, then to-morrow ... Dashenka'll win two hundred thousand ... she's got a lottery ticket.

LYUBOV: Well, we've finished our coffee, we can go to bed.

FIRS: [*Brushes* GAEV, *reprovingly.*] You have got on the wrong trousers again! What am I to do with you?

VARYA: [*Softly.*] Anya's asleep. [*Softly opens the window.*] Now the sun's risen, it's not a bit cold. Look, mamma, what exquisite trees! My goodness! And the air! The starlings are singing!

GAEV: [*Opens another window.*] The orchard is all white. You've not forgotten it, Lyuba? That long avenue that runs straight, straight as an arrow, how it shines on a moonlight night. You remember? You've not forgotten?

---

7. The equivalent of over $800,000 in today's U.S. currency. *A loan of 240 roubles:* a loan of nearly $4000 in today's U.S. currency.

LYUBOV: [*Looking out of the window into the garden.*] Oh, my childhood, my innocence! It was in this nursery I used to sleep, from here I looked out into the orchard, happiness waked with me every morning and in those days the orchard was just the same, nothing has changed. [*Laughs with delight.*] All, all white! Oh, my orchard! After the dark gloomy autumn, and the cold winter; you are young again, and full of happiness, the heavenly angels have never left you.... If I could cast off the burden that weighs on my heart, if I could forget the past!

GAEV: H'm! and the orchard will be sold to pay our debts; it seems strange....

LYUBOV: See, our mother walking ... all in white, down the avenue! [*Laughs with delight.*] It is she!

GAEV: Where?

VARYA: Oh, don't, mamma!

LYUBOV: There is no one. It was my fancy. On the right there, by the path to the arbor, there is a white tree bending like a woman....

[*Enter* TROFIMOV *wearing a shabby student's uniform and spectacles.*]

LYUBOV: What a ravishing orchard! White masses of blossom, blue sky....

TROFIMOV: Lyubov Andreyevna! [*She looks round at him.*] I will just pay my respects to you and then leave you at once. [*Kisses her hand warmly.*] I was told to wait until morning, but I hadn't the patience to wait any longer....

[LYUBOV ANDREYEVNA *looks at him in perplexity.*]

VARYA: [*Through her tears.*] This is Petya Trofimov.

TROFIMOV: Petya Trofimov, who was your Grisha's tutor.... Can I have changed so much?

[LYUBOV ANDREYEVNA *embraces him and weeps quietly.*]

GAEV: [*In confusion.*] There, there, Lyuba.

VARYA: [*Crying.*] I told you, Petya, to wait till to-morrow.

LYUBOV: My Grisha ... my boy ... Grisha ... my son!

VARYA: We can't help it, mamma, it is God's will.

TROFIMOV: [*Softly through his tears.*] There ... there.

LYUBOV: [*Weeping quietly.*] My boy was lost ... drowned. Why? Oh, why, dear Petya? [*More quietly.*] Anya is asleep in there, and I'm talking loudly ... making this noise.... But, Petya? Why have you grown so ugly? Why do you look so old?

TROFIMOV: A peasant-woman in the train called me a mangy-looking gentleman.

LYUBOV: You were quite a boy then, a pretty little student, and now your hair's thin—and spectacles. Are you really a student still? [*Goes towards the door.*]

TROFIMOV: I seem likely to be a perpetual student.

LYUBOV: [*Kisses her brother, then* VARYA.] Well, go to bed.... You are older too, Leonid.

PISHTCHIK: [*Follows her.*] I suppose it's time we were asleep.... Ugh! my gout. I'm staying the night! Lyubov Andreyevna, my dear soul, if you could ... tomorrow morning ... 240 roubles.

GAEV: That's always his story.

PISHTCHIK: 240 roubles ... to pay the interest on my mortgage.

LYUBOV: My dear man, I have no money.

PISHTCHIK: I'll pay it back, my dear . . . a trifling sum.
LYUBOV: Oh, well, Leonid will give it you. . . . You give him the money, Leonid.
GAEV: Me give it him! Let him wait till he gets it!
LYUBOV: It can't be helped, give it him. He needs it. He'll pay it back.

[LYUBOV ANDREYEVNA, TROFIMOV, PISHTCHIK and FIRS go out. GAEV, VARYA and YASHA remain.]

GAEV: Sister hasn't got out of the habit of flinging away her money. [To YASHA.] Get away, my good fellow, you smell of the hen-house.
YASHA: [With a grin.] And you, Leonid Andreyevitch, are just the same as ever.
GAEV: What's that? [To VARYA.] What did he say?
VARYA: [To YASHA.] Your mother has come from the village; she has been sitting in the servants' room since yesterday, waiting to see you.
YASHA: Oh, bother her!
VARYA: For shame!
YASHA: What's the hurry? She might just as well have come to-morrow. [Goes out.]
VARYA: Mamma's just the same as ever, she hasn't changed a bit. If she had her own way, she'd give away everything.
GAEV: Yes. [A pause.] If a great many remedies are suggested for some disease, it means that the disease is incurable. I keep thinking and racking my brains; I have many schemes, a great many, and that really means none. If we could only come in for a legacy from somebody, or marry our Anya to a very rich man, or we might go to Yaroslavl[8] and try our luck with our old aunt, the Countess. She's very, very rich, you know.
VARYA: [Weeps.] If God would help us.
GAEV: Don't blubber. Aunt's very rich, but she doesn't like us. First, sister married a lawyer instead of a nobleman. . . .

[ANYA appears in the doorway.]

GAEV: And then her conduct, one can't call it virtuous. She is good, and kind, and nice, and I love her, but, however one allows for extenuating circumstances, there's no denying that she's an immoral woman. One feels it in her slightest gesture.
VARYA: [In a whisper.] Anya's in the doorway.
GAEV: What do you say? [A pause.] It's queer, there seems to be something wrong with my right eye. I don't see as well as I did. And on Thursday when I was in the district Court . . .

[Enter ANYA.]

VARYA: Why aren't you asleep, Anya?
ANYA: I can't get to sleep.
GAEV: My pet. [Kisses ANYA's face and hands.] My child. [Weeps.] You are not my niece, you are my angel, you are everything to me. Believe me, believe. . . .
ANYA: I believe you, uncle. Everyone loves you and respects you . . . but, uncle dear, you must be silent . . . simply be silent. What were you saying just now about my mother, about your own sister? What made you say that?

---

8. Major industrial city located on the Volga River, 170 miles northeast of Moscow.

GAEV: Yes, yes.... [*Puts his hand over his face.*] Really, that was awful! My God, save me! And to-day I made a speech to the bookcase ... so stupid! And only when I had finished, I saw how stupid it was.

VARYA: It's true, uncle, you ought to keep quiet. Don't talk, that's all.

ANYA: If you could keep from talking, it would make things easier for you, too.

GAEV: I won't speak. [*Kisses* ANYA's *and* VARYA's *hands.*] I'll be silent. Only this is about business. On Thursday I was in the district Court; well, there was a large party of us there and we began talking of one thing and another, and this and that, and do you know, I believe that it will be possible to raise a loan on an I.O.U. to pay the arrears on the mortgage.

VARYA: If the Lord would help us!

GAEV: I'm going on Tuesday; I'll talk of it again. [*To* VARYA.] Don't blubber. [*To* ANYA.] Your mamma will talk to Lopahin; of course, he won't refuse her. And as soon as you're rested you shall go to Yaroslavl to the Countess, your great-aunt. So we shall all set to work in three directions at once, and the business is done. We shall pay off arrears, I'm convinced of it. [*Puts a caramel in his mouth.*] I swear on my honor, I swear by anything you like, the estate shan't be sold. [*Excitedly.*] By my own happiness, I swear it! Here's my hand on it, call me the basest, vilest of men, if I let it come to an auction! Upon my soul I swear it!

ANYA: [*Her equanimity has returned, she is quite happy.*] How good you are, uncle, and how clever! [*Embraces her uncle.*] I'm at peace now! Quite at peace! I'm happy!

[*Enter* FIRS.]

FIRS: [*Reproachfully.*] Leonid Andreyevitch, have you no fear of God? When are you going to bed?

GAEV: Directly, directly. You can go, Firs. I'll ... yes, I will undress myself. Come, children, bye-bye. We'll go into details to-morrow, but now go to bed. [*Kisses* ANYA *and* VARYA.] I'm a man of the eighties.[9] They run down that period, but still I can say I have had to suffer not a little for my convictions in my life, it's not for nothing that the peasant loves me. One must know the peasant! One must know how....

ANYA: At it again, uncle!

VARYA: Uncle dear, you'd better be quiet!

FIRS: [*Angrily.*] Leonid Andreyevitch!

GAEV: I'm coming. I'm coming. Go to bed. Potted the shot—there's a shot for you![1] A beauty! [*Goes out,* FIRS *hobbling after him.*]

ANYA: My mind's at rest now. I don't want to go to Yaroslavl, I don't like my great-aunt, but still my mind's at rest. Thanks to uncle. [*Sits down.*]

VARYA: We must go to bed. I'm going. Something unpleasant happened while you were away. In the old servants' quarters there are only the old servants, as you know—Efimyushka, Polya and Yevstigney—and Karp too. They began letting stray people in to spend the night—I said nothing. But all at once I heard they had been spreading a report that I gave them nothing but pease

---

9. That is, the 1880s, a period of reactionary conservatism in Russia under Tsar Alexander III.
1. Gaev is preoccupied with billiards; the terminology is fanciful because Chekhov admittedly knew nothing about the game.

pudding to eat. Out of stinginess, you know.... And it was all Yevstigney's doing.... Very well, I said to myself.... If that's how it is, I thought, wait a bit. I sent for Yevstigney.... [*Yawns.*] He comes.... "How's this, Yevstigney," I said, "you could be such a fool as to?..." [*Looking at* ANYA.] Anitchka! [*A pause.*] She's asleep. [*Puts her arm around* ANYA.] Come to bed... come along! [*Leads her.*] My darling has fallen asleep! Come.... [*They go.*]

[*Far away beyond the orchard a shepherd plays on a pipe.* TROFIMOV *crosses the stage and, seeing* VARYA *and* ANYA, *stands still.*]

VARYA: 'Sh! asleep, asleep. Come, my own.
ANYA: [*Softly, half asleep.*] I'm so tired. Still those bells. Uncle... dear... mamma and uncle....
VARYA: Come, my own, come along.

[*They go into* ANYA'S *room.*]

TROFIMOV: [*Tenderly.*] My sunshine! My spring.

CURTAIN

## ACT II

*The open country. An old shrine,[2] long abandoned and fallen out of the perpendicular; near it a well, large stones that have apparently once been tombstones, and an old garden seat. The road to* GAEV'S *house is seen. On one side rise dark poplars; and there the cherry orchard begins. In the distance a row of telegraph poles and far, far away on the horizon there is faintly outlined a great town, only visible in very fine clear weather. It is near sunset.* CHARLOTTA, YASHA *and* DUNYASHA *are sitting on the seat.* EPIHODOV *is standing near, playing something mournful on a guitar. All sit plunged in thought.* CHARLOTTA *wears an old forage cap; she has taken a gun from her shoulder and is tightening the buckle on the strap.*

CHARLOTTA: [*Musingly.*] I haven't a real passport[3] of my own, and I don't know how old I am, and I always feel that I'm a young thing. When I was a little girl, my father and mother used to travel about to fairs and give performances—very good ones. And I used to dance *salto-mortale*[4] and all sorts of things. And when papa and mamma died, a German lady took me and had me educated. And so I grew up and become a governess. But where I came from, and who I am, I don't know.... Who my parents were, very likely they weren't married.... I don't know. [*Takes a cucumber out of her pocket and eats.*] I know nothing at all. [*A pause.*] One wants to talk and has no one to talk to. ... I have nobody.
EPIHODOV: [*Plays on the guitar and sings.*] "What care I for the noisy world! What care I for friends or foes!"[5] How agreeable it is to play on the mandoline!
DUNYASHA: That's a guitar, not a mandoline. [*Looks in a hand-mirror and powders herself.*]

---

2. That is, a chapel.  3. A document required for travel within Russia.
4. *Salto mortal*, literally "deadly leap," is Spanish for "somersault."  5. Words of a popular ballad.

EPIHODOV: To a man mad with love, it's a mandoline. [*Sings.*] "Were her heart but aglow with love's mutual flame." [YASHA *joins in.*]

CHARLOTTA: How shockingly these people sing! Foo! Like jackals!

DUNYASHA: [*To* YASHA.] What happiness, though, to visit foreign lands.

YASHA: Ah, yes! I rather agree with you there. [*Yawns, then lights a cigar.*]

EPIHODOV: That's comprehensible. In foreign lands everything has long since reached full complexion.

YASHA: That's so, of course.

EPIHODOV: I'm a cultivated man, I read remarkable books of all sorts, but I can never make out the tendency I am myself precisely inclined for, whether to live or to shoot myself, speaking precisely, but nevertheless I always carry a revolver. Here it is.... [*Shows revolver.*]

CHARLOTTA: I've had enough, and now I'm going. [*Puts on the gun.*] Epihodov, you're a very clever fellow, and a very terrible one too, all the women must be wild about you. Br-r-r! [*Goes.*] These clever fellows are all so stupid; there's not a creature for me to speak to.... Always alone, alone, nobody belonging to me... and who I am, and why I'm on earth, I don't know. [*Walks away slowly.*]

EPIHODOV: Speaking precisely, not touching upon other subjects, I'm bound to admit about myself, that destiny behaves mercilessly to me, as a storm to a little boat. If, let us suppose, I am mistaken, then why did I wake up this morning, to quote an example, and look round, and there on my chest was a spider of fearful magnitude... like this. [*Shows with both hands.*] And then I take up a jug of kvass, to quench my thirst, and in it there is something in the highest degree unseemly of the nature of a cockroach. [*A pause.*] Have you read Buckle?[6] [*A pause.*] I am desirous of troubling you, Dunyasha, with a couple of words.

DUNYASHA: Well, speak.

EPIHODOV: I should be desirous to speak with you alone. [*Sighs.*]

DUNYASHA: [*Embarrassed.*] Well—only bring me my mantle first. It's by the cupboard. It's rather damp here.

EPIHODOV: Certainly. I will fetch it. Now I know what I must do with my revolver. [*Takes guitar and goes off playing on it.*]

YASHA: Two and twenty misfortunes! Between ourselves, he's a fool. [*Yawns.*]

DUNYASHA: God grant he doesn't shoot himself! [*A pause.*] I am so nervous, I'm always in a flutter. I was a little girl when I was taken into our lady's house, and now I have quite grown out of peasant ways, and my hands are white, as white as a lady's. I'm such a delicate, sensitive creature, I'm afraid of everything. I'm so frightened. And if you deceive me, Yasha, I don't know what will become of my nerves.

YASHA: [*Kisses her.*] You're a peach! Of course a girl must never forget herself; what I dislike more than anything is a girl being flighty in her behavior.

DUNYASHA: I'm passionately in love with you, Yasha; you are a man of culture—you can give your opinion about anything. [*A pause.*]

YASHA: [*Yawns.*] Yes, that's so. My opinion is this: if a girl loves anyone, that

---

6. Henry Thomas Buckle (1821–1861), a learned but eccentric historian known as a freethinker whose *History of Civilization in England* (1857) was the talk of Moscow a generation earlier. His work, initially respected for its empirical methods, quickly fell into disrepute in sophisticated intellectual circles.

means that she has no principles. [*A pause.*] It's pleasant smoking a cigar in the open air. [*Listens.*] Someone's coming this way . . . it's the gentlefolk. [DUNYASHA *embraces him impulsively.*] Go home, as though you had been to the river to bathe; go by that path, or else they'll meet you and suppose I have made an appointment with you here. That I can't endure.

DUNYASHA: [*Coughing softly.*] The cigar has made my head ache. . . . [*Goes off.*]

[YASHA *remains sitting near the shrine. Enter* LYUBOV ANDREYEVNA, GAEV *and* LOPAHIN.]

LOPAHIN: You must make up your mind once for all—there's no time to lose. It's quite a simple question, you know. Will you consent to letting the land for building or not? One word in answer: Yes or no? Only one word!

LYUBOV: Who is smoking such horrible cigars here? [*Sits down.*]

GAEV: Now the railway line has been brought near, it's made things very convenient. [*Sits down.*] Here we have been over and lunched in town. Cannon off the white! I should like to go home and have a game.

LYUBOV: You have plenty of time.

LOPAHIN: Only one word! [*Beseechingly.*] Give me an answer!

GAEV: [*Yawning.*] What do you say?

LYUBOV: [*Looks in her purse.*] I had quite a lot of money here yesterday, and there's scarcely any left to-day. My poor Varya feeds us all on milk soup for the sake of economy; the old folks in the kitchen get nothing but pease pudding, while I waste my money in a senseless way. [*Drops purse, scattering gold pieces.*] There, they have all fallen out! [*Annoyed.*]

YASHA: Allow me, I'll soon pick them up. [*Collects the coins.*]

LYUBOV: Pray do, Yasha. And what did I go off to the town to lunch for? Your restaurant's a wretched place with its music and the tablecloth smelling of soap. . . . Why drink so much, Leonid? And eat so much? And talk so much? To-day you talked a great deal again in the restaurant, and all so inappropriately. About the era of the seventies,[7] about the decadents. And to whom? Talking to waiters about decadents!

LOPAHIN: Yes.

GAEV: [*Waving his hand.*] I'm incorrigible; that's evident. [*Irritably to* YASHA.] Why is it you keep fidgeting about in front of us!

YASHA: [*Laughs.*] I can't help laughing when I hear your voice.

GAEV: [*To his sister.*] Either I or he. . . .

LYUBOV: Get along! Go away, Yasha.

YASHA: [*Gives* LYUBOV ANDREYEVNA *her purse.*] Directly. [*Hardly able to suppress his laughter.*] This minute. . . . [*Goes off.*]

LOPAHIN: Deriganov, the millionaire, means to buy your estate. They say he is coming to the sale himself.

LYUBOV: Where did you hear that?

LOPAHIN: That's what they say in town.

GAEV: Our aunt in Yaroslavl has promised to send help; but when, and how much she will send, we don't know.

---

7. The 1870s, a relatively liberal period in Russia that ended abruptly with the assassination of Alexander II in 1881. *The decadents*: probably a reference to the group of flamboyant French poets of the 1880s who called themselves *les décadents*.

LOPAHIN: How much will she send? A hundred thousand? Two hundred?

LYUBOV: Oh, well! . . . Ten or fifteen thousand, and we must be thankful to get that.

LOPAHIN: Forgive me, but such reckless people as you are—such queer, unbusiness-like people—I never met in my life. One tells you in plain Russian your estate is going to be sold, and you seem not to understand it.

LYUBOV: What are we to do? Tell us what to do.

LOPAHIN: I do tell you every day. Every day I say the same thing. You absolutely must let the cherry orchard and the land on building leases; and do it at once, as quick as may be—the auction's close upon us! Do understand! Once make up your mind to build villas, and you can raise as much money as you like, and then you are saved.

LYUBOV: Villas and summer visitors—forgive me saying so—it's so vulgar.

GAEV: There I perfectly agree with you.

LOPAHIN: I shall sob, or scream, or fall into a fit. I can't stand it! You drive me mad! [*To* GAEV.] You're an old woman!

GAEV: What do you say?

LOPAHIN: An old woman! [*Gets up to go.*]

LYUBOV: [*In dismay.*] No, don't go! Do stay, my dear friend! Perhaps we shall think of something.

LOPAHIN: What is there to think of?

LYUBOV: Don't go, I entreat you! With you here it's more cheerful, anyway. [*A pause.*] I keep expecting something, as though the house were going to fall about our ears.

GAEV: [*In profound dejection.*] Potted the white! It fails—a kiss.

LYUBOV: We have been great sinners. . . .

LOPAHIN: You have no sins to repent of.

GAEV: [*Puts a caramel in his mouth.*] They say I've eaten up my property in caramels. [*Laughs.*]

LYUBOV: Oh, my sins! I've always thrown my money away recklessly like a lunatic. I married a man who made nothing but debts. My husband died of champagne—he drank dreadfully. To my misery I loved another man, and immediately—it was my first punishment—the blow fell upon me, here, in the river . . . my boy was drowned and I went abroad—went away for ever, never to return, not to see that river again . . . I shut my eyes, and fled, distracted, and *he* after me . . . pitilessly, brutally. I bought a villa at Mentone, for *he* fell ill there, and for three years I had no rest day or night. His illness wore me out, my soul was dried up. And last year, when my villa was sold to pay my debts, I went to Paris and there he robbed me of everything and abandoned me for another woman; and I tried to poison myself. . . . So stupid, so shameful! . . . And suddenly I felt a yearning for Russia, for my country, for my little girl. . . . [*Dries her tears.*] Lord, Lord, be merciful! Forgive my sins! Do not chastise me more! [*Takes a telegram out of her pocket.*] I got this to-day from Paris. He implores forgiveness, entreats me to return. [*Tears up the telegram.*] I fancy there is music somewhere. [*Listens.*]

GAEV: That's our famous Jewish orchestra. You remember, four violins, a flute and a double bass.

LYUBOV: That still in existence? We ought to send for them one evening, and give a dance.

LOPAHIN: [*Listens.*] I can't hear.... [*Hums softly.*] "For money the Germans will turn a Russian into a Frenchman." [*Laughs.*] I did see such a piece at the theater yesterday! It was funny!

LYUBOV: And most likely there was nothing funny in it. You shouldn't look at plays, you should look at yourselves a little oftener. How gray your lives are! How much nonsense you talk.

LOPAHIN: That's true. One may say honestly, we live a fool's life. [*Pause.*] My father was a peasant, an idiot; he knew nothing and taught me nothing, only beat me when he was drunk, and always with his stick. In reality I am just such another blockhead and idiot. I've learnt nothing properly. I write a wretched hand. I write so that I feel ashamed before folks, like a pig.

LYUBOV: You ought to get married, my dear fellow.

LOPAHIN: Yes... that's true.

LYUBOV: You should marry our Varya, she's a good girl.

LOPAHIN: Yes.

LYUBOV: She's a good-natured girl, she's busy all day long, and what's more, she loves you. And you have liked her for ever so long.

LOPAHIN: Well? I'm not against it.... She's a good girl. [*Pause.*]

GAEV: I've been offered a place in the bank: 6,000 roubles a year.[8] Did you know?

LYUBOV: You would never do for that! You must stay as you are.

[*Enter* FIRS *with overcoat.*]

FIRS: Put it on, sir, it's damp.

GAEV: [*Putting it on.*] You bother me, old fellow.

FIRS: You can't go on like this. You went away in the morning without leaving word. [*Looks him over.*]

LYUBOV: You look older, Firs!

FIRS: What is your pleasure?

LOPAHIN: You look older, she said.

FIRS: I've had a long life. They were arranging my wedding before your papa was born.... [*Laughs.*] I was the head footman before the emancipation came.[9] I wouldn't consent to be set free then; I stayed on with the old master.... [*A pause.*] I remember what rejoicings they made and didn't know themselves what they were rejoicing over.

LOPAHIN: Those were fine old times. There was flogging anyway.

FIRS: [*Not hearing.*] To be sure! The peasants knew their place, and the masters knew theirs; but now they're all at sixes and sevens,[1] there's no making it out.

GAEV: Hold your tongue, Firs. I must go to town to-morrow. I have been promised an introduction to a general, who might let us have a loan.

LOPAHIN: You won't bring that off. And you won't pay your arrears, you may rest assured of that.

LYUBOV: That's all his nonsense. There is no such general.

[*Enter* TROFIMOV, ANYA *and* VARYA.]

---

8. Nearly $100,000 per year in today's U.S. currency.
9. In 1861 Tsar Alexander II issued the Edict of Emancipation, which freed the serfs (agricultural workers held in feudal bondage, who represented about one-third of Russia's population).
1. That is, they are confused, unsettled.

GAEV: Here come our girls.
ANYA: There's mamma on the seat.
LYUBOV: [*Tenderly.*] Come here, come along. My darlings! [*Embraces* ANYA *and* VARYA.] If you only knew how I love you both. Sit beside me, there, like that. [*All sit down.*]
LOPAHIN: Our perpetual student is always with the young ladies.
TROFIMOV: That's not your business.
LOPAHIN: He'll soon be fifty, and he's still a student.
TROFIMOV: Drop your idiotic jokes.
LOPAHIN: Why are you so cross, you queer fish?
TROFIMOV: Oh, don't persist!
LOPAHIN: [*Laughs.*] Allow me to ask you what's your idea of me?
TROFIMOV: I'll tell you my idea of you, Yermolay Alexeyevitch: you are a rich man, you'll soon be a millionaire. Well, just as in the economy of nature a wild beast is of use, who devours everything that comes in his way, so you too have your use.

[*All laugh.*]

VARYA: Better tell us something about the planets, Petya.
LYUBOV: No, let us go on with the conversation we had yesterday.
TROFIMOV: What was it about?
GAEV: About pride.
TROFIMOV: We had a long conversation yesterday, but we came to no conclusion. In pride, in your sense of it, there is something mystical. Perhaps you are right from your point of view; but if one looks at it simply, without subtlety, what sort of pride can there be, what sense is there in it, if man in his physiological formation is very imperfect, if in the immense majority of cases he is coarse, dull-witted, profoundly unhappy? One must give up glorification of self. One should work, and nothing else.
GAEV: One must die in any case.
TROFIMOV: Who knows? And what does it mean—dying? Perhaps man has a hundred senses, and only the five we know are lost at death, while the other ninety-five remain alive.
LYUBOV: How clever you are, Petya!
LOPAHIN: [*Ironically.*] Fearfully clever!
TROFIMOV: Humanity progresses, perfecting its powers. Everything that is beyond its ken now will one day become familiar and comprehensible; only we must work, we must with all our powers aid the seeker after truth. Here among us in Russia the workers are few in number as yet. The vast majority of the intellectual people I know, seek nothing, do nothing, are not fit as yet for work of any kind. They call themselves intellectual, but they treat their servants as inferiors, behave to the peasants as though they were animals, learn little, read nothing seriously, do practically nothing, only talk about science and know very little about art. They are all serious people, they all have severe faces, they all talk of weighty matters and air their theories, and yet the vast majority of us—ninety-nine per cent—live like savages, at the least thing fly to blows and abuse, eat piggishly, sleep in filth and stuffiness, bugs everywhere, stench and damp and moral impurity. And it's clear all our fine talk is only to divert our attention and other people's. Show me where to find

the *crèches* there's so much talk about, and the reading-rooms?² They only exist in novels: in real life there are none of them. There is nothing but filth and vulgarity and Asiatic apathy. I fear and dislike very serious faces. I'm afraid of serious conversations. We should do better to be silent.

LOPAHIN: You know, I get up at five o'clock in the morning, and I work from morning to night; and I've money, my own and other people's, always passing through my hands, and I see what people are made of all round me. One has only to begin to do anything to see how few honest, decent people there are. Sometimes when I lie awake at night, I think: "Oh! Lord, thou hast given us immense forests, boundless plains, the widest horizons, and living here we ourselves ought really to be giants."

LYUBOV: You ask for giants! They are no good except in story-books; in real life they frighten us.

[EPIHODOV *advances in the background, playing on the guitar.*]

LYUBOV: [*Dreamily.*] There goes Epihodov.
ANYA: [*Dreamily.*] There goes Epihodov.
GAEV: The sun has set, my friends.
TROFIMOV: Yes.
GAEV: [*Not loudly, but, as it were, declaiming.*] O nature, divine nature, thou art bright with eternal luster, beautiful and indifferent! Thou, whom we call mother, thou dost unite within thee life and death! Thou dost give life and dost destroy!
VARYA: [*In a tone of supplication.*] Uncle!
ANYA: Uncle, you are at it again!
TROFIMOV: You'd much better be cannoning off the red!
GAEV: I'll hold my tongue, I will.

[*All sit plunged in thought. Perfect stillness. The only thing audible is the muttering of* FIRS. *Suddenly there is a sound in the distance, as it were from the sky—the sound of a breaking harp-string, mournfully dying away.*]

LYUBOV: What is that?
LOPAHIN: I don't know. Somewhere far away a bucket fallen and broken in the pits. But somewhere very far away.
GAEV: It might be a bird of some sort—such as a heron.
TROFIMOV: Or an owl.
LYUBOV: [*Shudders.*] I don't know why, but it's horrid. [*A pause.*]
FIRS: It was the same before the calamity—the owl hooted and the samovar hissed all the time.
GAEV: Before what calamity?
FIRS: Before the emancipation. [*A pause.*]
LYUBOV: Come, my friends, let us be going; evening is falling. [*To* ANYA.] There are tears in your eyes. What is it, darling? [*Embraces her.*]
ANYA: Nothing, mamma; it's nothing.
TROFIMOV: There is somebody coming.

---

2. Nursery schools and centers offering free reading material—that is, the social services and civilizing influences that have been imagined but never created.

[*The* WAYFARER *appears in a shabby white forage cap and an overcoat; he is slightly drunk.*]

WAYFARER: Allow me to inquire, can I get to the station this way?
GAEV: Yes. Go along that road.
WAYFARER: I thank you most feelingly. [*Coughing.*] The weather is superb. [*Declaims.*] My brother, my suffering brother!³ ... Come out to the Volga! Whose groan do you hear? ... [*To* VARYA.] Mademoiselle, vouchsafe a hungry Russian thirty kopecks.⁴

[VARYA *utters a shriek of alarm.*]

LOPAHIN: [*Angrily.*] There's a right and a wrong way of doing everything!
LYUBOV: [*Hurriedly.*] Here, take this. [*Looks in her purse.*] I've no silver. No matter—here's gold for you.
WAYFARER: I thank you most feelingly! [*Goes off.*]

[*Laughter.*]

VARYA: [*Frightened.*] I'm going home—I'm going.... Oh, mamma, the servants have nothing to eat, and you gave him gold!
LYUBOV: There's no doing anything with me. I'm so silly! When we get home, I'll give you all I possess. Yermolay Alexeyevitch, you will lend me some more! ...
LOPAHIN: I will.
LYUBOV: Come, friends, it's time to be going. And Varya, we have made a match of it for you. I congratulate you.
VARYA: [*Through her tears.*] Mamma, that's not a joking matter.
LOPAHIN: "Ophelia, get thee to a nunnery!"⁵
GAEV: My hands are trembling; it's a long while since I had a game of billiards.
LOPAHIN: "Ophelia! Nymph, in thy orisons be all my sins remember'd."
LYUBOV: Come, it will soon be supper-time.
VARYA: How he frightened me! My heart's simply throbbing.
LOPAHIN: Let me remind you, ladies and gentlemen: on the 22nd of August the cherry orchard will be sold. Think about that! Think about it!

[*All go off, except* TROFIMOV *and* ANYA.]

ANYA: [*Laughing.*] I'm grateful to the wayfarer! He frightened Varya and we are left alone.
TROFIMOV: Varya's afraid we shall fall in love with each other, and for days together she won't leave us. With her narrow brain she can't grasp that we are above love. To eliminate the petty and transitory which hinder us from being free and happy—that is the aim and meaning of our life. Forward! We go forward irresistibly towards the bright star that shines yonder in the distance. Forward! Do not lag behind, friends.
ANYA: [*Claps her hands.*] How well you speak! [*A pause.*] It is divine here today.
TROFIMOV: Yes, it's glorious weather.

---

3. A line from a poem by Semen Nadson (1862–1887), persecuted in Russia because of his Jewish origins.
4. *Come out to the Volga!*: from a poem by Nikolai Nekrasov (1821–1878), a poet known as a champion of the lower classes. (The Volga is Europe's longest river and Russia's principal waterway.) Thirty kopecks is the equivalent of about $5 in today's U.S. currency.    5. For this quotation and the one below, see *Hamlet* 3.1.

ANYA: Somehow, Petya, you've made me so that I don't love the cherry orchard as I used to. I used to love it so dearly. I used to think that there was no spot on earth like our garden.

TROFIMOV: All Russia is our garden. The earth is great and beautiful—there are many beautiful places in it. [*A pause.*] Think only, Anya, your grandfather, and great-grandfather, and all your ancestors were slave-owners—the owners of living souls—and from every cherry in the orchard, from every leaf, from every trunk there are human creatures looking at you. Cannot you hear their voices? Oh, it is awful! Your orchard is a fearful thing, and when in the evening or at night one walks about the orchard, the old bark on the trees glimmers dimly in the dusk, and the old cherry trees seem to be dreaming of centuries gone by and tortured by fearful visions.[6] Yes! We are at least two hundred years behind, we have really gained nothing yet, we have no definite attitude to the past, we do nothing but theorize or complain of depression or drink vodka. It is clear that to begin to live in the present we must first expiate our past, we must break with it; and we can expiate it only by suffering, by extraordinary unceasing labor. Understand that, Anya.

ANYA: The house we live in has long ceased to be our own, and I shall leave it, I give you my word.

TROFIMOV: If you have the house keys, fling them into the well and go away. Be free as the wind.

ANYA: [*In ecstasy.*] How beautifully you said that!

TROFIMOV: Believe me, Anya, believe me! I am not thirty yet, I am young, I am still a student, but I have gone through so much already! As soon as winter comes I am hungry, sick, careworn, poor as a beggar, and what ups and downs of fortune have I not known! And my soul was always, every minute, day and night, full of inexplicable forebodings. I have a foreboding of happiness, Anya. I see glimpses of it already.

ANYA: [*Pensively.*] The moon is rising.

[EPIHODOV *is heard playing still the same mournful song on the guitar. The moon rises. Somewhere near the poplars* VARYA *is looking for* ANYA *and calling* "Anya! where are you?"]

TROFIMOV: Yes, the moon is rising. [*A pause.*] Here is happiness—here it comes! It is coming nearer and nearer; already I can hear its footsteps. And if we never see it—if we may never know it—what does it matter? Others will see it after us.

VARYA'S VOICE: Anya! Where are you?

TROFIMOV: That Varya again! [*Angrily.*] It's revolting!

ANYA: Well, let's go down to the river. It's lovely there.

TROFIMOV: Yes, let's go. [*They go.*]

VARYA'S VOICE: Anya! Anya!

CURTAIN

---

6. *Oh, it is awful!...fearful visions.* Chekhov wrote this passage to replace one that official censors found objectionable: "To own human beings has affected every one of you—those who lived before and those who live now. Your mother, your uncle, and you don't notice that you are living off the labors of others—in fact, the very people you won't even let in the front door." This passage was restored following the 1917 revolution.

## ACT III

*A drawing-room divided by an arch from a larger drawing-room.*[7] *A chandelier burning. The Jewish orchestra, the same that was mentioned in Act II, is heard playing in the ante-room. It is evening. In the larger drawing-room they are dancing the grand chain. The voice of* SEMYONOV-PISHTCHIK: *"Promenade à une paire!"*[8] *Then enter the drawing-room in couples first* PISHTCHIK *and* CHARLOTTA IVANOVA, *then* TROFIMOV *and* LYUBOV ANDREYEVNA, *thirdly* ANYA *with the* POST-OFFICE CLERK, *fourthly* VARYA *with the* STATION MASTER, *and other guests.* VARYA *is quietly weeping and wiping away her tears as she dances. In the last couple is* DUNYASHA. *They move across the drawing-room.* PISHTCHIK *shouts:* "Grand rond, balancez!" *and* "Les Cavaliers à genou et remerciez vos dames."

FIRS *in a swallow-tail coat brings in seltzer water on a tray.* PISHTCHIK *and* TROFIMOV *enter the drawing-room.*

PISHTCHIK: I am a full-blooded man; I have already had two strokes. Dancing's hard work for me, but as they say, if you're in the pack, you must bark with the rest. I'm as strong, I may say, as a horse. My parent, who would have his joke—may the Kingdom of Heaven be his!—used to say about our origin that the ancient stock of the Semyonov-Pishtchiks was derived from the very horse that Caligula made a member of the senate.[9] [*Sits down.*] But I've no money, that's where the mischief is. A hungry dog believes in nothing but meat. [*Snores, but at once wakes up.*] That's like me... I can think of nothing but money.

TROFIMOV: There really is something horsy about your appearance.

PISHTCHIK: Well... a horse is a fine beast... a horse can be sold.

[*There is the sound of billiards being played in an adjoining room.* VARYA *appears in the arch leading to the larger drawing-room.*]

TROFIMOV: [*Teasing.*] Madame Lopahin! Madame Lopahin!

VARYA: [*Angrily.*] Mangy-looking gentleman!

TROFIMOV: Yes, I am a mangy-looking gentleman, and I'm proud of it!

VARYA: [*Pondering bitterly.*] Here we have hired musicians and nothing to pay them! [*Goes out.*]

TROFIMOV: [*To* PISHTCHIK.] If the energy you have wasted during your lifetime in trying to find the money to pay your interest had gone to something else, you might in the end have turned the world upside down.

PISHTCHIK: Nietzsche, the philosopher, a very great and celebrated man[1]... of enormous intellect... says in his works, that one can make forged bank-notes.

TROFIMOV: Why, have you read Nietzsche?

---

7. That is, ballroom.
8. In this French phrase and those quoted below, Semyonov-Pishtchik is calling out the moves in the "grand chain" dance: promenade (walk) to a couple; grand circle, step to the side (that is, *balancez* as in ballet); and gentlemen (knights), kneel and thank your ladies. (French was widely spoken as a second language among the upper classes in pre-Soviet Russia.)
9. Caligula (12–41 C.E.), Roman emperor known for tyrannical cruelty, is said to have gone insane and to have appointed his horse as a consul.
1. Friedrich Wilhelm Nietzsche (1844–1900), German philosopher who rejected what he termed the "slave morality" of Western bourgeois civilization.

PISHTCHIK: What next... Dashenka told me.... And now I am in such a position, I might just as well forge banknotes. The day after to-morrow I must pay 310 roubles[2]—130 I have procured. [*Feels in his pockets, in alarm.*] The money's gone! I have lost my money! [*Through his tears.*] Where's the money? [*Gleefully.*] Why, here it is behind the lining.... It has made me hot all over.

[*Enter* LYUBOV ANDREYEVNA *and* CHARLOTTA IVANOVNA.]

LYUBOV: [*Hums the Lezginka.*] Why is Leonid so long? What can he be doing in town? [*To* DUNYASHA.] Offer the musicians some tea.
TROFIMOV: The sale hasn't taken place, most likely.
LYUBOV: It's the wrong time to have the orchestra, and the wrong time to give a dance. Well, never mind. [*Sits down and hums softly.*]
CHARLOTTA: [*Gives* PISHTCHIK *a pack of cards.*] Here's a pack of cards. Think of any card you like.
PISHTCHIK: I've thought of one.
CHARLOTTA: Shuffle the pack now. That's right. Give it here, my dear Mr. Pishtchik. *Ein, zwei, drei*[3]—now look, it's in your breast pocket.
PISHTCHIK: [*Taking a card out of his breast pocket.*] The eight of spades! Perfectly right! [*Wonderingly.*] Fancy that now!
CHARLOTTA: [*Holding pack of cards in her hands, to* TROFIMOV.] Tell me quickly which is the top card.
TROFIMOV: Well, the queen of spades.
CHARLOTTA: It is! [*To* PISHTCHIK.] Well, which card is uppermost?
PISHTCHIK: The ace of hearts.
CHARLOTTA: It is! [*Claps her hands, pack of cards disappears.*] Ah! what lovely weather it is to-day!

[*A mysterious feminine voice which seems coming out of the floor answers her.* "Oh, yes, it's magnificent weather, madam."]

CHARLOTTA: You are my perfect ideal.
VOICE: And I greatly admire you too, madam.
STATION MASTER: [*Applauding.*] The lady ventriloquist—bravo!
PISHTCHIK: [*Wonderingly.*] Fancy that now! Most enchanting Charlotta Ivanovna. I'm simply in love with you.
CHARLOTTA: In love? [*Shrugging shoulders.*] What do you know of love, *guter Mensch, aber schlechter Musikant.*[4]
TROFIMOV: [*Pats* PISHTCHIK *on the shoulder.*] You dear old horse....
CHARLOTTA: Attention, please! Another trick! [*Takes a traveling rug from a chair.*] Here's a very good rug; I want to sell it. [*Shaking it out.*] Doesn't anyone want to buy it?
PISHTCHIK: [*Wonderingly.*] Fancy that!
CHARLOTTA: *Ein, zwei, drei!* [*Quickly picks up rug she has dropped; behind the rug stands* ANYA; *she makes a curtsey, runs to her mother, embraces her and runs back into the larger drawing-room amidst general enthusiasm.*]
LYUBOV: [*Applauds.*] Bravo! Bravo!

---

2. The equivalent of over $5000 in today's U.S. currency.
3. One, two, three (German). Charlotta speaks the language she associates with her childhood of performing at carnivals.   4. A good man, but a poor musician (German).

CHARLOTTA: Now again! *Ein, zwei, drei!* [*Lifts up the rug; behind the rug stands* VARYA, *bowing.*]
PISHTCHIK: [*Wonderingly.*] Fancy that now!
CHARLOTTA: That's the end. [*Throws the rug at* PISHTCHIK, *makes a curtsey, runs into the larger drawing-room.*]
PISHTCHIK: [*Hurries after her.*] Mischievous creature! Fancy! [*Goes out.*]
LYUBOV: And still Leonid doesn't come. I can't understand what he's doing in the town so long! Why, everything must be over by now. The estate is sold, or the sale has not taken place. Why keep us so long in suspense?
VARYA: [*Trying to console her.*] Uncle's bought it. I feel sure of that.
TROFIMOV: [*Ironically.*] Oh, yes!
VARYA: Great-aunt sent him an authorization to buy it in her name, and transfer the debt. She's doing it for Anya's sake, and I'm sure God will be merciful. Uncle will buy it.
LYUBOV: My aunt in Yaroslavl sent fifteen thousand to buy the estate in her name, she doesn't trust us—but that's not enough even to pay the arrears. [*Hides her face in her hands.*] My fate is being sealed to-day, my fate....
TROFIMOV: [*Teasing* VARYA.] Madame Lopahin.
VARYA: [*Angrily.*] Perpetual student! Twice already you've been sent down[5] from the University.
LYUBOV: Why are you angry, Varya? He's teasing you about Lopahin. Well, what of that? Marry Lopahin if you like, he's a good man, and interesting; if you don't want to, don't! Nobody compels you, darling.
VARYA: I must tell you plainly, mamma, I look at the matter seriously; he's a good man, I like him.
LYUBOV: Well, marry him. I can't see what you're waiting for.
VARYA: Mamma. I can't make him an offer myself. For the last two years, everyone's been talking to me about him. Everyone talks; but he says nothing or else makes a joke. I see what it means. He's growing rich, he's absorbed in business, he has no thoughts for me. If I had money, were it ever so little, if I had only a hundred roubles, I'd throw everything up and go far away. I would go into a nunnery.
TROFIMOV: What bliss!
VARYA: [*To* TROFIMOV.] A student ought to have sense! [*In a soft tone with tears.*] How ugly you've grown, Petya! How old you look! [*To* LYUBOV ANDREYEVNA, *no longer crying.*] But I can't do without work, mamma; I must have something to do every minute.

[*Enter* YASHA.]

YASHA: [*Hardly restraining his laughter.*] Epihodov has broken a billiard cue! [*Goes out.*]
VARYA: What is Epihodov doing here? Who gave him leave to play billiards? I can't make these people out. [*Goes out.*]
LYUBOV: Don't tease her, Petya. You see she has grief enough without that.
TROFIMOV: She is so very officious, meddling in what's not her business. All the summer she's given Anya and me no peace. She's afraid of a love affair between

---

5. Expelled.

us. What's it to do with her? Besides, I have given no grounds for it. Such triviality is not in my line. We are above love!

LYUBOV: And I suppose I am beneath love. [*Very uneasily.*] Why is it Leonid's not here? If only I could know whether the estate is sold or not! It seems such an incredible calamity that I really don't know what to think. I am distracted... I shall scream in a minute... I shall do something stupid. Save me, Petya, tell me something, talk to me!

TROFIMOV: What does it matter whether the estate is sold to-day or not? That's all done with long ago. There's no turning back, the path is overgrown. Don't worry yourself, dear Lyubov Andreyevna. You mustn't deceive yourself; for once in your life you must face the truth!

LYUBOV: What truth? You see where the truth lies, but I seem to have lost my sight, I see nothing. You settle every great problem so boldly, but tell me, my dear boy, isn't it because you're young—because you haven't yet understood one of your problems through suffering? You look forward boldly, and isn't it that you don't see and don't expect anything dreadful because life is still hidden from your young eyes? You're bolder, more honest, deeper than we are, but think, be just a little magnanimous, have pity on me. I was born here, you know, my father and mother lived here, my grandfather lived here, I love this house. I can't conceive of life without the cherry orchard, and if it really must be sold, then sell me with the orchard. [*Embraces* TROFIMOV, *kisses him on the forehead.*] My boy was drowned here. [*Weeps.*] Pity me, my dear kind fellow.

TROFIMOV: You know I feel for you with all my heart.

LYUBOV: But that should have been said differently, so differently. [*Takes out her handkerchief, telegram falls on the floor.*] My heart is so heavy to-day. It's so noisy here, my soul is quivering at every sound, I'm shuddering all over, but I can't go away; I'm afraid to be quiet and alone. Don't be hard on me, Petya... I love you as though you were one of ourselves. I would gladly let you marry Anya—I swear I would—only, my dear boy, you must take your degree, you do nothing—you're simply tossed by fate from place to place. That's so strange. It is, isn't it? And you must do something with your beard to make it grow somehow. [*Laughs.*] You look so funny!

TROFIMOV: [*Picks up the telegram.*] I've no wish to be a beauty.

LYUBOV: That's a telegram from Paris. I get one every day. One yesterday and one to-day. That savage creature is ill again, he's in trouble again. He begs forgiveness, beseeches me to go, and really I ought to go to Paris to see him. You look shocked, Petya. What am I to do, my dear boy, what am I to do? He is ill, he is alone and unhappy, and who'll look after him, who'll keep him from doing the wrong thing, who'll give him his medicine at the right time? And why hide it or be silent? I love him, that's clear. I love him! I love him! He's a millstone about my neck, I'm going to the bottom with him, but I love that stone and can't live without it. [*Presses* TROFIMOV's *hand.*] Don't think ill of me, Petya, don't tell me anything, don't tell me....

TROFIMOV: [*Through his tears*] For God's sake forgive my frankness: why, he robbed you!

LYUBOV: No! No! No! You mustn't speak like that. [*Covers her ears.*]

TROFIMOV: He is a wretch! You're the only person that doesn't know it! He's a worthless creature! A despicable wretch!

LYUBOV: [*Getting angry, but speaking with restraint.*] You're twenty-six or twenty-seven years old, but you're still a schoolboy.

TROFIMOV: Possibly.

LYUBOV: You should be a man at your age! You should understand what love means! And you ought to be in love yourself. You ought to fall in love! [*Angrily.*] Yes, yes, and it's not purity in you, you're simply a prude, a comic fool, a freak.

TROFIMOV: [*In horror.*] The things she's saying!

LYUBOV: I am above love! You're not above love, but simply as our Firs here says, "You are a good-for-nothing." At your age not to have a mistress!

TROFIMOV: [*In horror.*] This is awful! The things she is saying! [*Goes rapidly into the larger drawing-room clutching his head.*] This is awful! I can't stand it! I'm going. [*Goes off, but at once returns.*] All is over between us! [*Goes off into the ante-room.*]

LYUBOV: [*Shouts after him.*] Petya! Wait a minute! You funny creature! I was joking! Petya! [*There is a sound of somebody running quickly downstairs and suddenly falling with a crash.* ANYA *and* VARYA *scream, but there is a sound of laughter at once.*]

LYUBOV: What has happened?

[ANYA *runs in.*]

ANYA: [*Laughing.*] Petya's fallen downstairs! [*Runs out.*]

LYUBOV: What a queer fellow that Petya is!

[*The* STATION MASTER *stands in the middle of the larger room and reads* The Magdalene, *by Alexey Tolstoy.*[6] *They listen to him, but before he has recited many lines strains of a waltz are heard from the ante-room and the reading is broken off. All dance.* TROFIMOV, ANYA, VARYA *and* LYUBOV ANDREYEVNA *come in from the ante-room.*]

LYUBOV: Come, Petya—come, pure heart! I beg your pardon. Let's have a dance! [*Dances with* PETYA.]

[ANYA *and* VARYA *dance.* FIRS *comes in, puts his stick down near the side door.* YASHA *also comes into the drawing-room and looks on at the dancing.*]

YASHA: What is it, old man?

FIRS: I don't feel well. In old days we used to have generals, barons and admirals dancing at our balls, and now we send for the post-office clerk and the station master and even they're not overanxious to come. I am getting feeble. The old master, the grandfather, used to give sealing-wax for all complaints. I have been taking sealing-wax for twenty years or more. Perhaps that's what's kept me alive.

YASHA: You bore me, old man! [*Yawns.*] It's time you were done with.

FIRS: Ach, you're a good-for-nothing! [*Mutters.*]

[TROFIMOV *and* LYUBOV ANDREYEVNA *dance in larger room and then on to the stage.*]

LYUBOV: *Merci.* I'll sit down a little. [*Sits down.*] I'm tired.

---

6. A poem sometimes translated as "The Sinful Woman," by Alexsey Tolstoy (1817–1875), a distant cousin of novelist Leo Tolstoy.

[*Enter* ANYA.]

ANYA: [*Excitedly.*] There's a man in the kitchen has been saying that the cherry orchard's been sold to-day.
LYUBOV: Sold to whom?
ANYA: He didn't say to whom. He's gone away.

[*She dances with* TROFIMOV, *and they go off into the larger room.*]

YASHA: There was an old man gossiping there, a stranger.
FIRS: Leonid Andreyevitch isn't here yet, he hasn't come back. He has his light overcoat on, *demi-saison*, he'll catch cold for sure. Ach! Foolish young things!
LYUBOV: I feel as though I should die. Go, Yasha, find out to whom it has been sold.
YASHA: But he went away long ago, the old chap. [*Laughs.*]
LYUBOV: [*With slight vexation.*] What are you laughing at? What are you pleased at?
YASHA: Epihodov is so funny. He's a silly fellow, two and twenty misfortunes.
LYUBOV: Firs, if the estate is sold, where will you go?
FIRS: Where you bid me, there I'll go.
LYUBOV: Why do you look like that? Are you ill? You ought to be in bed.
FIRS: Yes. [*Ironically.*] Me go to bed and who's to wait here? Who's to see to things without me? I'm the only one in all the house.
YASHA: [*To* LYUBOV ANDREYEVNA.] Lyubov Andreyevna, permit me to make a request of you; if you go back to Paris again, be so kind as to take me with you. It's positively impossible for me to stay here. [*Looking about him; in an undertone.*] There's no need to say it, you see for yourself—an uncivilized country, the people have no morals, and then the dullness! The food in the kitchen's abominable, and then Firs runs after one muttering all sorts of unsuitable words. Take me with you, please do!

[*Enter* PISHTCHIK.]

PISHTCHIK: Allow me to ask you for a waltz, my dear lady. [LYUBOV ANDREYEVNA *goes with him.*] Enchanting lady, I really must borrow of you just 180 roubles, [*Dances.*] only 180 roubles. [*They pass into the larger room.*]

[*In the larger drawing-room, a figure in a gray top hat and in check trousers is gesticulating and jumping about. Shouts of* "Bravo, Charlotta Ivanovna."]

DUNYASHA: [*She has stopped to powder herself.*] My young lady tells me to dance. There are plenty of gentlemen, and too few ladies, but dancing makes me giddy and makes my heart beat. Firs, the post-office clerk said something to me just now that quite took my breath away.

[*Music becomes more subdued.*]

FIRS: What did he say to you?
DUNYASHA: He said I was like a flower.
YASHA: [*Yawns.*] What ignorance! [*Goes out.*]
DUNYASHA: Like a flower. I am a girl of such delicate feelings, I am awfully fond of soft speeches.
FIRS: Your head's being turned.

[*Enter* EPIHODOV.]

EPIHODOV: You have no desire to see me, Dunyasha. I might be an insect. [*Sighs.*] Ah! life!
DUNYASHA: What is it you want?
EPIHODOV: Undoubtedly you may be right. [*Sighs.*] But, of course, if one looks at it from that point of view, if I may so express myself, you have, excuse my plain speaking, reduced me to a complete state of mind. I know my destiny. Every day some misfortune befalls me and I have long ago grown accustomed to it, so that I look upon my fate with a smile. You gave me your word, and though I——
DUNYASHA: Let us have a talk later, I entreat you, but now leave me in peace, for I am lost in reverie. [*Plays with her fan.*]
EPIHODOV: I have a misfortune every day, and if I may venture to express myself, I merely smile at it, I even laugh.

[VARYA *enters from the larger drawing-room.*]

VARYA: You still have not gone, Epihodov. What a disrespectful creature you are, really! [*To* DUNYASHA.] Go along, Dunyasha! [*To* EPIHODOV.] First you play billiards and break the cue, then you go wandering about the drawing-room like a visitor!
EPIHODOV: You really cannot, if I may so express myself, call me to account like this.
VARYA: I'm not calling you to account, I'm speaking to you. You do nothing but wander from place to place and don't do your work. We keep you as a counting-house clerk, but what use you are I can't say.
EPIHODOV: [*Offended.*] Whether I work or whether I walk, whether I eat or whether I play billiards, is a matter to be judged by persons of understanding and my elders.
VARYA: You dare to tell me that! [*Firing up.*] You dare! You mean to say I've no understanding. Begone from here! This minute!
EPIHODOV: [*Intimidated.*] I beg you to express yourself with delicacy.
VARYA: [*Beside herself with anger.*] This moment! get out! away! [*He goes towards the door, she following him.*] Two and twenty misfortunes! Take yourself off! Don't let me set eyes on you! [EPIHODOV *has gone out, behind the door his voice,* "I shall lodge a complaint against you."] What! You're coming back? [*Snatches up the stick* FIRS *has put down near the door.*] Come! Come! Come! I'll show you! What! you're coming? Then take that! [*She swings the stick, at the very moment that* LOPAHIN *comes in.*]
LOPAHIN: Very much obliged to you!
VARYA: [*Angrily and ironically.*] I beg your pardon!
LOPAHIN: Not at all! I humbly thank you for your kind reception!
VARYA: No need of thanks for it. [*Moves away, then looks round and asks softly.*] I haven't hurt you?
LOPAHIN: Oh, no! Not at all! There's an immense bump coming up, though!
VOICES FROM LARGER ROOM: Lopahin has come! Yermolay Alexeyevitch!
PISHTCHIK: What do I see and hear? [*Kisses* LOPAHIN.] There's a whiff of cognac about you, my dear soul, and we're making merry here too!

[*Enter* LYUBOV ANDREYEVNA.]

LYUBOV: Is it you, Yermolay Alexeyevitch? Why have you been so long? Where's Leonid?

LOPAHIN: Leonid Andreyevitch arrived with me. He is coming.
LYUBOV: [*In agitation.*] Well! Well! Was there a sale? Speak!
LOPAHIN: [*Embarrassed, afraid of betraying his joy.*] The sale was over at four o'clock. We missed our train—had to wait till half-past nine. [*Sighing heavily.*] Ugh! I feel a little giddy.

[*Enter* GAEV. *In his right hand he has purchases, with his left hand he is wiping away his tears.*]

LYUBOV: Well, Leonid? What news? [*Impatiently, with tears.*] Make haste, for God's sake!
GAEV: [*Makes her no answer, simply waves his hand. To* FIRS, *weeping.*] Here, take them; there's anchovies, Kertch herrings. I have eaten nothing all day. What I have been through! [*Door into the billiard room is open. There is heard a knocking of balls and the voice of* YASHA *saying "Eighty-seven."* GAEV's *expression changes, he leaves off weeping.*] I am fearfully tired. Firs, come and help me change my things. [*Goes to his own room across the larger drawing-room.*]
PISHTCHIK: How about the sale? Tell us, do!
LYUBOV: Is the cherry orchard sold?
LOPAHIN: It is sold.
LYUBOV: Who has bought it?
LOPAHIN: I have bought it. [*A pause.* LYUBOV *is crushed; she would fall down if she were not standing near a chair and table.*]

[VARYA *takes keys from her waistband, flings them on the floor in middle of drawing-room and goes out.*]

LOPAHIN: I have bought it! Wait a bit, ladies and gentlemen, pray. My head's a bit muddled, I can't speak. [*Laughs.*] We came to the auction. Deriganov was there already. Leonid Andreyevitch only had 15,000 and Deriganov bid 30,000, besides the arrears, straight off. I saw how the land lay. I bid against him. I bid 40,000, he bid 45,000, I said 55, and so he went on, adding 5 thousands and I adding 10. Well... So it ended. I bid 90, and it was knocked down to me.[7] Now the cherry orchard's mine! Mine! [*Chuckles.*] My God, the cherry orchard's mine! Tell me that I'm drunk, that I'm out of my mind, that it's all a dream. [*Stamps with his feet.*] Don't laugh at me! If my father and my grandfather could rise from their graves and see all that has happened! How their Yermolay, ignorant, beaten Yermolay, who used to run about barefoot in winter, how that very Yermolay has bought the finest estate in the world! I have bought the estate where my father and grandfather were slaves, where they weren't even admitted into the kitchen. I am asleep, I am dreaming! It is all fancy, it is the work of your imagination plunged in the darkness of ignorance. [*Picks up keys, smiling fondly.*] She threw away the keys; she means to show she's not the housewife now. [*Jingles the keys.*] Well, no matter. [*The orchestra is heard tuning up.*] Hey, musicians! Play! I want to hear you. Come, all of you, and look how Yermolay Lopahin will take the ax to the cherry orchard, how the

---

7. Lopahin's winning bid for the estate was 90,000 roubles, the equivalent of nearly $1.5 million in today's U.S. currency—about twice what Lopahin had offered to lend Lyubov and her family to save the estate (act 1).

trees will fall to the ground! We will build houses on it and our grandsons and great-grandsons will see a new life springing up there. Music! Play up!

[*Music begins to play.* LYUBOV ANDREYEVNA *has sunk into a chair and is weeping bitterly.*]

LOPAHIN: [*Reproachfully.*] Why, why didn't you listen to me? My poor friend! Dear lady, there's no turning back now. [*With tears.*] Oh, if all this could be over, oh, if our miserable disjointed life could somehow soon be changed!

PISHTCHIK: [*Takes him by the arm, in an undertone.*] She's weeping, let us go and leave her alone. Come. [*Takes him by the arm and leads him into the larger drawing-room.*]

LOPAHIN: What's that? Musicians, play up! All must be as I wish it. [*With irony.*] Here comes the new master, the owner of the cherry orchard! [*Accidentally tips over a little table, almost upsetting the candelabra.*] I can pay for everything! [*Goes out with* PISHTCHIK. *No one remains on the stage or in the larger drawing-room except* LYUBOV, *who sits huddled up, weeping bitterly. The music plays softly.* ANYA *and* TROFIMOV *come in quickly.* ANYA *goes up to her mother and falls on her knees before her.* TROFIMOV *stands at the entrance to the larger drawing-room.*]

ANYA: Mamma! Mamma, you're crying, dear, kind, good mamma! My precious! I love you! I bless you! The cherry orchard is sold, it is gone, that's true, that's true! But don't weep, mamma! Life is still before you, you have still your good, pure heart! Let us go, let us go, darling, away from here! We will make a new garden, more splendid than this one; you will see it, you will understand. And joy, quiet, deep joy, will sink into your soul like the sun at evening! And you will smile, mamma! Come, darling, let us go!

CURTAIN

## ACT IV

SCENE: *Same as in First Act. There are neither curtains on the windows nor pictures on the walls: only a little furniture remains piled up in a corner as if for sale. There is a sense of desolation; near the outer door and in the background of the scene are packed trunks, traveling bags, etc. On the left the door is open, and from here the voices of* VARYA *and* ANYA *are audible.* LOPAHIN *is standing waiting.* YASHA *is holding a tray with glasses full of champagne. In front of the stage* EPIHODOV *is tying up a box. In the background behind the scene a hum of talk from the peasants who have come to say good-bye. The voice of* GAEV: "*Thanks, brothers, thanks!*"

YASHA: The peasants have come to say good-bye. In my opinion, Yermolay Alexeyevitch, the peasants are good-natured, but they don't know much about things.

[*The hum of talk dies away. Enter across front of stage* LYUBOV ANDREYEVNA *and* GAEV. *She is not weeping, but is pale; her face is quivering—she cannot speak.*]

GAEV: You gave them your purse, Lyuba. That won't do—that won't do!
LYUBOV: I couldn't help it! I couldn't help it!

[*Both go out.*]

LOPAHIN: [*In the doorway, calls after them.*] You will take a glass at parting? Please do. I didn't think to bring any from the town, and at the station I could only get one bottle. Please take a glass. [*A pause.*] What? You don't care for any? [*Comes away from the door.*] If I'd known, I wouldn't have bought it. Well, and I'm not going to drink it. [YASHA *carefully sets the tray down on a chair.*] You have a glass, Yasha, anyway.

YASHA: Good luck to the travelers, and luck to those that stay behind! [*Drinks.*] This champagne isn't the real thing, I can assure you.

LOPAHIN: It cost eight roubles the bottle. [*A pause.*] It's devilish cold here.

YASHA: They haven't heated the stove today—it's all the same since we're going. [*Laughs.*]

LOPAHIN: What are you laughing for?

YASHA: For pleasure.

LOPAHIN: Though it's October, it's as still and sunny as though it were summer. It's just right for building! [*Looks at his watch; says in doorway.*] Take note, ladies and gentlemen, the train goes in forty-seven minutes; so you ought to start for the station in twenty minutes. You must hurry up!

[TROFIMOV *comes in from out of doors wearing a great-coat.*]

TROFIMOV: I think it must be time to start, the horses are ready. The devil only knows what's become of my goloshes; they're lost. [*In the doorway.*] Anya! My goloshes aren't here. I can't find them.

LOPAHIN: And I'm getting off to Harkov. I am going in the same train with you. I'm spending all the winter at Harkov. I've been wasting all my time gossiping with you and fretting with no work to do. I can't get on without work. I don't know what to do with my hands, they flap about so queerly, as if they didn't belong to me.

TROFIMOV: Well, we're just going away, and you will take up your profitable labors again.

LOPAHIN: Do take a glass.

TROFIMOV: No, thanks.

LOPAHIN: Then you're going to Moscow now?

TROFIMOV: Yes. I shall see them as far as the town, and to-morrow I shall go on to Moscow.

LOPAHIN: Yes, I daresay, the professors aren't giving any lectures, they're waiting for your arrival.

TROFIMOV: That's not your business.

LOPAHIN: How many years have you been at the University?

TROFIMOV: Do think of something newer than that—that's stale and flat. [*Hunts for goloshes.*] You know we shall most likely never see each other again, so let me give you one piece of advice at parting: don't wave your arms about—get out of the habit. And another thing, building villas, reckoning up that the summer visitors will in time become independent farmers—reckoning like that, that's not the thing to do either. After all, I am fond of you: you have fine delicate fingers like an artist, you've a fine delicate soul.

LOPAHIN: [*Embraces him.*] Good-bye, my dear fellow. Thanks for everything. Let me give you money for the journey, if you need it.

TROFIMOV: What for? I don't need it.

LOPAHIN: Why, you haven't got a half-penny.

TROFIMOV: Yes, I have, thank you. I got some money for a translation. Here it is in my pocket, [*Anxiously.*] but where can my goloshes be!
VARYA: [*From the next room.*] Take the nasty things! [*Flings a pair of goloshes on to the stage.*]
TROFIMOV: Why are you so cross, Varya? h'm! . . . but those aren't my goloshes.
LOPAHIN: I sowed three thousand acres with poppies in the spring, and now I have cleared forty thousand profit.[8] And when my poppies were in flower, wasn't it a picture! So here, as a I say, I made forty thousand, and I'm offering you a loan because I can afford to. Why turn up your nose? I am a peasant—I speak bluntly.
TROFIMOV: Your father was a peasant, mine was a chemist[9]—and that proves absolutely nothing whatever. [LOPAHIN *takes out his pocket-book.*] Stop that—stop that. If you were to offer me two hundred thousand I wouldn't take it. I am an independent man, and everything that all of you, rich and poor alike, prize so highly and hold so dear, hasn't the slightest power over me—it's like so much fluff fluttering in the air. I can get on without you. I can pass by you. I am strong and proud. Humanity is advancing towards the highest truth, the highest happiness, which is possible on earth, and I am in the front ranks.
LOPAHIN: Will you get there?
TROFIMOV: I shall get there. [*A pause.*] I shall get there, or I shall show others the way to get there.

[*In the distance is heard the stroke of an ax on a tree.*]

LOPAHIN: Good-bye, my dear fellow; it's time to be off. We turn up our noses at one another, but life is passing all the while. When I am working hard without resting, then my mind is more at ease, and it seems to me as though I too know what I exist for; but how many people there are in Russia, my dear boy, who exist, one doesn't know what for. Well, it doesn't matter. That's not what keeps things spinning. They tell me Leonid Andreyevitch has taken a situation. He is going to be a clerk at the bank—6,000 roubles a year.[1] Only, of course, he won't stick to it—he's too lazy.
ANYA: [*In the doorway.*] Mamma begs you not to let them chop down the orchard until she's gone.
TROFIMOV: Yes, really, you might have the tact. [*Walks out across the front of the stage.*]
LOPAHIN: I'll see to it! I'll see to it! Stupid fellows! [*Goes out after him.*]
ANYA: Has Firs been taken to the hospital?
YASHA: I told them this morning. No doubt they have taken him.
ANYA: [*To* EPIHODOV, *who passes across the drawing-room.*] Semyon Pantaleyevitch, inquire, please, if Firs has been taken to the hospital.
YASHA: [*In a tone of offence.*] I told Yegor this morning—why ask a dozen times?
EPIHODOV: Firs is advanced in years. It's my conclusive opinion no treatment would do him good; it's time he was gathered to his fathers. And I can only envy him. [*Puts a trunk down on a cardboard hat-box and crushes it.*] There, now, of course—I knew it would be so.
YASHA: [*Jeeringly.*] Two and twenty misfortunes!

---

8. That is, a profit equivalent to about $650,000 in today's U.S. currency.   9. Pharmacist.
1. A salary equivalent to nearly $100,000 in today's U.S. currency.

VARYA: [*Through the door.*] Has Firs been taken to the hospital?
ANYA: Yes.
VARYA: Why wasn't the note for the doctor taken too?
ANYA: Oh, then, we must send it after them. [*Goes out.*]
VARYA: [*From the adjoining room.*] Where's Yasha? Tell him his mother's come to say good-bye to him.
YASHA: [*Waves his hand.*] They put me out of all patience! [DUNYASHA *has all this time been busy about the luggage. Now, when* YASHA *is left alone, she goes up to him.*]
DUNYASHA: You might just give me one look, Yasha. You're going away. You're leaving me. [*Weeps and throws herself on his neck.*]
YASHA: What are you crying for? [*Drinks the champagne.*] In six days I shall be in Paris again. To-morrow we shall get into the express train and roll away in a flash. I can scarcely believe it! *Vive la France!* It doesn't suit me here—it's not the life for me; there's no doing anything. I have seen enough of the ignorance here. I have had enough of it. [*Drinks champagne.*] What are you crying for? Behave yourself properly, and then you won't cry.
DUNYASHA: [*Powders her face, looking in a pocket-mirror.*] Do send me a letter from Paris. You know how I loved you, Yasha—how I loved you! I am a tender creature, Yasha.
YASHA: Here they are coming!

[*Busies himself about the trunks, humming softly. Enter* LYUBOV ANDREYEVNA, GAEV, ANYA *and* CHARLOTTA IVANOVNA.]

GAEV: We ought to be off. There's not much time now. [*Looking at* YASHA.] What a smell of herrings!
LYUBOV: In ten minutes we must get into the carriage. [*Casts a look about the room.*] Farewell, dear house, dear old home of our fathers! Winter will pass and spring will come, and then you will be no more; they will tear you down! How much those walls have seen! [*Kisses her daughter passionately.*] My treasure, how bright you look! Your eyes are sparkling like diamonds! Are you glad? Very glad?
ANYA: Very glad! A new life is beginning, mamma.
GAEV: Yes, really, everything is all right now. Before the cherry orchard was sold, we were all worried and wretched, but afterwards, when once the question was settled conclusively, irrevocably, we all felt calm and even cheerful. I am a bank clerk now—I am a financier—cannon off the red. And you, Lyuba, after all, you are looking better; there's no question of that.
LYUBOV: Yes. My nerves are better, that's true. [*Her hat and coat are handed to her.*] I'm sleeping well. Carry out my things, Yasha. It's time. [*To* ANYA.] My darling, we shall soon see each other again. I am going to Paris. I can live there on the money your Yaroslavl auntie sent us to buy the estate with—hurrah for auntie—but that money won't last long.
ANYA: You'll come back soon, mamma, won't you? I'll be working up for my examination in the high school, and when I have passed that, I shall set to work and be a help to you. We will read all sorts of things together, mamma, won't we? [*Kisses her mother's hands.*] We will read in the autumn evenings. We'll read lots of books, and a new wonderful world will open out before us. [*Dreamily.*] Mamma, come soon.
LYUBOV: I shall come, my precious treasure. [*Embraces her.*]

[*Enter* LOPAHIN. CHARLOTTA *softly hums a song.*]

GAEV: Charlotta's happy; she's singing!
CHARLOTTA: [*Picks up a bundle like a swaddled baby.*] Bye, bye, my baby. [*A baby is heard crying: "Ooah! ooah!"*] Hush, hush, my pretty boy! [*Ooah! ooah!*] Poor little thing! [*Throws the bundle back.*] You must please find me a situation. I can't go on like this.
LOPAHIN: We'll find you one, Charlotta Ivanovna. Don't you worry yourself.
GAEV: Everyone's leaving us. Varya's going away. We have become of no use all at once.
CHARLOTTA: There's nowhere for me to be in the town. I must go away. [*Hums.*] What care I . . .

[*Enter* PISHTCHIK.]

LOPAHIN: The freak of nature!
PISHTCHIK: [*Gasping.*] Oh! . . . let me get my breath. . . . I'm worn out . . . my most honored . . . Give me some water.
GAEV: Want some money, I suppose? Your humble servant! I'll go out of the way of temptation. [*Goes out.*]
PISHTCHIK: It's a long while since I have been to see you . . . dearest lady. [*To* LOPAHIN.] You are here . . . glad to see you . . . a man of immense intellect . . . take . . . here. [*Gives* LOPAHIN.] 400 roubles.[2] That leaves me owing 840.
LOPAHIN: [*Shrugging his shoulders in amazement.*] It's like a dream. Where did you get it?
PISHTCHIK: Wait a bit . . . I'm hot . . . a most extraordinary occurrence! Some Englishmen came along and found in my land some sort of white clay. [*To* LYUBOV ANDREYEVNA.] And 400 for you . . . most lovely . . . wonderful. [*Gives money.*] The rest later. [*Sips water.*] A young man in the train was telling me just now that a great philosopher advises jumping off a house-top. "Jump!" says he; "the whole gist of the problem lies in that." [*Wonderingly.*] Fancy that, now! Water, please!
LOPAHIN: What Englishmen?
PISHTCHIK: I have made over to them the rights to dig the clay for twenty-four years . . . and now, excuse me . . . I can't stay . . . I must be trotting on. I'm going to Znoikovo . . . to Kardamanovo. . . . I'm in debt all round. [*Sips.*] . . . To your very good health! . . . I'll come in on Thursday.
LYUBOV: We are just off to the town, and to-morrow I start for abroad.
PISHTCHIK: What! [*In agitation.*] Why to the town? Oh, I see the furniture . . . the boxes. No matter . . . [*Through his tears.*] . . . no matter . . . men of enormous intellect . . . these Englishmen. . . . Never mind . . . be happy. God will succor you . . . no matter . . . everything in this world must have an end. [*Kisses* LYUBOV ANDREYEVNA'*s hand.*] If the rumor reaches you that my end has come, think of this . . . old horse, and say: "There once was such a man in the world . . . Semyonov-Pishtchik . . . the Kingdom of Heaven be his!" . . . most extraordinary weather . . . yes. [*Goes out in violent agitation, but at once returns and says in the doorway.*] Dashenka wishes to be remembered to you. [*Goes out.*]
LYUBOV: Now we can start. I leave with two cares in my heart. The first is leaving Firs ill. [*Looking at her watch.*] We have still five minutes.
ANYA: Mamma, Firs has been taken to the hospital. Yasha sent him off this morning.

---

2. About $6500 in today's U.S. currency.

LYUBOV: My other anxiety is Varya. She is used to getting up early and working; and now, without work, she's like a fish out of water. She is thin and pale, and she's crying, poor dear! [*A pause.*] You are well aware, Yermolay Alexeyevitch, I dreamed of marrying her to you, and everything seemed to show that you would get married. [*Whispers to* ANYA *and motions to* CHARLOTTA *and both go out.*] She loves you—she suits you. And I don't know—I don't know why it is you seem, as it were, to avoid each other. I can't understand it!

LOPAHIN: I don't understand it myself, I confess. It's queer somehow, altogether. If there's still time, I'm ready now at once. Let's settle it straight off, and go ahead; but without you, I feel I shan't make her an offer.

LYUBOV: That's excellent. Why, a single moment's all that's necessary. I'll call her at once.

LOPAHIN: And there's champagne all ready too. [*Looking into the glasses.*] Empty! Someone's emptied them already. [YASHA *coughs.*] I call that greedy.

LYUBOV: [*Eagerly.*] Capital! We will go out. Yasha, *allez!*[3] I'll call her in. [*At the door.*] Varya, leave all that; come here. Come along! [*Goes out with* YASHA.]

LOPAHIN: [*Looking at his watch.*] Yes.

[*A pause. Behind the door, smothered laughter and whispering, and, at last, enter* VARYA.]

VARYA: [*Looking a long while over the things.*] It is strange, I can't find it anywhere.

LOPAHIN: What are you looking for?

VARYA: I packed it myself, and I can't remember. [*A pause.*]

LOPAHIN: Where are you going now, Varvara Mihailova?

VARYA: I? To the Ragulins. I have arranged to go to them to look after the house—as a housekeeper.

LOPAHIN: That's in Yashnovo? It'll be seventy miles away. [*A pause.*] So this is the end of life in this house!

VARYA: [*Looking among the things.*] Where is it? Perhaps I put it in the trunk. Yes, life in this house is over—there will be no more of it.

LOPAHIN: And I'm just off to Harkov—by this next train. I've a lot of business there. I'm leaving Epihodov here, and I've taken him on.

VARYA: Really!

LOPAHIN: This time last year we had snow already, if you remember; but now it's so fine and sunny. Though it's cold, to be sure—three degrees of frost.

VARYA: I haven't looked. [*A pause.*] And besides, our thermometer's broken. [*A pause.*]

[*Voice at the door from the yard:* "Yermolay Alexeyevitch!"]

LOPAHIN: [*As though he had long been expecting this summons.*] This minute!

[LOPAHIN *goes out quickly.* VARYA *sitting on the floor and laying her head on a bag full of clothes, sobs quietly. The door opens.* LYUBOV ANDREYEVNA *comes in cautiously.*]

LYUBOV: Well? [*A pause.*] We must be going.

VARYA: [*Has wiped her eyes and is no longer crying.*] Yes, mamma, it's time to start.

---

3. Go! (French).

I shall have time to get to the Ragulins to-day, if only you're not late for the train.
LYUBOV: [*In the doorway.*] Anya, put your things on.

[*Enter* ANYA, *then* GAEV *and* CHARLOTTA IVANOVNA. GAEV *has on a warm coat with a hood. Servants and cabmen come in.* EPIHODOV *bustles about the luggage.*]

LYUBOV: Now we can start on our travels.
ANYA: [*Joyfully.*] On our travels!
GAEV: My friends—my dear, my precious friends! Leaving this house for ever, can I be silent? Can I refrain from giving utterance at leave-taking to those emotions which now flood all my being?
ANYA: [*Supplicatingly.*] Uncle!
VARYA: Uncle, you mustn't!
GAEV: [*Dejectedly.*] Cannon and into the pocket . . . I'll be quiet. . . .

[*Enter* TROFIMOV *and afterwards* LOPAHIN.]

TROFIMOV: Well, ladies and gentlemen, we must start.
LOPAHIN: Epihodov, my coat!
LYUBOV: I'll stay just one minute. It seems as though I have never seen before what the walls, what the ceilings in this house were like, and now I look at them with greediness, with such tender love.
GAEV: I remember when I was six years old sitting in that window on Trinity Day watching my father going to church.
LYUBOV: Have all the things been taken?
LOPAHIN: I think all. [*Putting on overcoat, to* EPIHODOV.] You, Epihodov, mind you see everything is right.
EPIHODOV: [*In a husky voice.*] Don't you trouble, Yermolay Alexeyevitch.
LOPAHIN: Why, what's wrong with your voice?
EPIHODOV: I've just had a drink of water, and I choked over something.
YASHA: [*Contemptuously.*] The ignorance!
LYUBOV: We are going—and not a soul will be left here.
LOPAHIN: Not till the spring.
VARYA: [*Pulls a parasol out of a bundle, as though about to hit someone with it.* LOPAHIN *makes a gesture as though alarmed.*] What is it? I didn't mean anything.
TROFIMOV: Ladies and gentlemen, let us get into the carriage. It's time. The train will be in directly.
VARYA: Petya, here they are, your goloshes, by that box. [*With tears.*] And what dirty old things they are!
TROFIMOV: [*Putting on his goloshes.*] Let us go, friends!
GAEV: [*Greatly agitated, afraid of weeping.*] The train—the station! Double baulk, ah!
LYUBOV: Let us go!
LOPAHIN: Are we all here? [*Locks the side-door on left.*] The things are all here. We must lock up. Let us go!
ANYA: Good-bye, home! Good-bye to the old life!
TROFIMOV: Welcome to the new life!

[TROFIMOV *goes out with* ANYA. VARYA *looks round the room and goes out slowly.* YASHA *and* CHARLOTTA IVANOVNA, *with her dog, go out.*]

LOPAHIN: Till the spring, then! Come, friends, till we meet! [*Goes out.*]

[LYUBOV ANDREYEVNA and GAEV remain alone. As though they had been waiting for this, they throw themselves on each other's necks, and break into subdued smothered sobbing, afraid of being overheard.]

GAEV: [In despair.] Sister, my sister!
LYUBOV: Oh, my orchard!—my sweet, beautiful orchard! My life, my youth, my happiness, good-bye! good-bye!
VOICE OF ANYA: [Calling gaily.] Mamma!
VOICE OF TROFIMOV: [Gaily, excitedly.] Aa—oo!
LYUBOV: One last look at the walls, at the windows. My dear mother loved to walk about this room.
GAEV: Sister, sister!
VOICE OF ANYA: Mamma!
VOICE OF TROFIMOV: Aa—oo!
LYUBOV: We are coming. [They go out.]

[The stage is empty. There is the sound of the doors being locked up, then of the carriages driving away. There is silence. In the stillness there is the dull stroke of an ax in a tree, clanging with a mournful lonely sound. Footsteps are heard. FIRS appears in the doorway on the right. He is dressed as always—in a pea-jacket and white waistcoat, with slippers on his feet. He is ill.]

FIRS: [Goes up to the doors, and tries the handles.] Locked! They have gone... [Sits down on sofa.] They have forgotten me.... Never mind... I'll sit here a bit.... I'll be bound Leonid Andreyevitch hasn't put his fur coat on and has gone off in his thin overcoat. [Sighs anxiously.] I didn't see after him.... These young people... [Mutters something that can't be distinguished.] Life has slipped by as though I hadn't lived. [Lies down.] I'll lie down a bit.... There's no strength in you, nothing left you—all gone! Ech! I'm good for nothing. [Lies motionless.]

[A sound is heard that seems to come from the sky, like a breaking harp-string, dying away mournfully. All is still again, and there is heard nothing but the strokes of the ax far away in the orchard.]

CURTAIN

1903–04

## QUESTIONS

1. What is the significance of the setting of the first scene in *The Cherry Orchard*, a room "that has always been called the nursery"? What are some of the connotations of "nursery," and what ironies are evoked by the term in the context of a house without children? What does the nursery represent to Lyubov?
2. Early in the play, Anya says of her mother, "How well I understand her, if only she knew!" How well *does* Anya understand her mother? How well does her mother, Lyubov, understand herself?
3. What is absurd about Firs's line "Now I can die," which he utters when Madame Ranevsky (Lyubov) returns home to her estate? If you were staging a production of the play, how would you direct the actor playing Firs? How would you direct the actor to mutter "Ech! you good-for-nothing!" in this early scene, and how should he say "Ech! I'm good for nothing" as the play's final line?

4. When Lopahin offers to get the family a loan so that they can build the summer cottages, he says, "Think of it seriously." But neither Lyubov nor anyone in her family can give serious consideration to such an offer. Why not? What are some of the nuances of class conflict reflected in Lopahin's offer and in Lyubov's refusal to "think of it seriously"?
5. When Lopahin innocently comments to Lyubov that he has recently seen a funny play, she snaps, "And most likely there was nothing funny in it. You shouldn't look at plays, you should look at yourselves a little oftener. How gray your lives are! How much nonsense you talk." In what ways is *The Cherry Orchard* funny? What are some of the ironies in Lyubov's insisting that "you should look at yourselves" instead of looking at plays?
6. In what respects is Gaev more realistic than his sister about the family's situation and what must be done about it? In what respects is Gaev as self-deluded as any other character in the play? Does he really think he can save the estate by becoming a bank manager? What does Gaev mean when he says, "I'm a man of the eighties"?
6. Right up until the end of the play it seems likely that Lopahin will propose marriage to Varya. Why is Varya ambivalent about this likelihood? What would such a marriage mean to her? Why do you think that Lopahin hesitates to make the proposal, especially since the marriage would be so advantageous to him socially? At what point in the play does the marriage become impossible? Why?
7. Lopahin offers Trofimov money, saying, "I'm offering you a loan because I can afford to. Why turn up your nose? I'm a peasant—I speak bluntly." Trofimov replies, "Your father was a peasant, and mine was a chemist—and that proves absolutely nothing whatever." What is Trofimov's point here? Why does he turn down the money? Does the play as a whole bear out the idea that parentage means "absolutely nothing"?
8. What does Trofimov mean when he insists that "Humanity is advancing"? Why does he then say, "I am in the front ranks"? In what ways is Trofimov a visionary, and in what ways is he a fool? Does Chekhov intend the audience to view Trofimov sympathetically, or to laugh at him, or both in some combination?
9. Just after Epihodov calmly remarks that he thinks he might shoot himself, Charlotta remarks, "Always alone, alone, nobody belonging to me . . . and who I am, and why I'm on earth, I don't know." Are these the stereotyped "stock" characters one would expect to find in a farce, or do real human beings say such things? What is the importance of minor characters such as these in *The Cherry Orchard*?
10. What do you make of all the play's compulsive behavior, such as Lyubov's extravagant generosity even though she is deeply in debt, or Gaev's preoccupation with billiards, or Pishtchik's obsessive grasping for loans? Is this simply the play's comedy, or does it have thematic significance?

## SUGGESTIONS FOR WRITING

1. At times, Chekhov's method of providing exposition—background information—may seem stiff and artificial, with characters saying things that the other characters know already. For example, to explain why Madame Ranevsky has been in Paris, Chekhov has Anya say, "It's six years since father died. Then only a month later little brother Grisha was drowned in the river, such a pretty boy he was, only seven years. It was more than mamma could bear, so she went away without looking back." There are numerous such expository set-pieces throughout the play. Do the play's key moments occur onstage, or are they contained in these set-pieces? Is such summary of the past believable? Is there a thematic significance in "looking back" or restating the past in this way? Write an essay in which you discuss Chekhov's

2. Throughout *The Cherry Orchard* Madame Ranevsky (Lyubov) keeps doing what she tells herself she should not do. For example, she gives money to a beggar although she has no money of her own to give; she hosts a dance on the eve of the estate's sale although she tells herself this is inappropriate. Write an essay in which you examine Lyubov's often self-contradictory behavior. What "should" Madame Ranevsky (Lyubov) do, given her circumstances? What options does she really have?
3. When Trofimov makes his grand declaration about how he will further the advancement of humanity, Chekhov answers him with the stage direction "[*In the distance is heard the stroke of an axe on a tree.*]" Focusing on this and other stage directions, write an essay in which you discuss various aspects of Chekhov's stagecraft besides the dialogue.
4. What are the politics of *The Cherry Orchard*, a play written during a period of great social upheaval in Russia, barely a decade before the revolution that brought the Communists to power? Is the play "conservative"? Is it "revolutionary"? Idealistic? Cynical? Citing specific passages from the play, write an essay in which you argue either for or against the interpretation that *The Cherry Orchard* is an indictment of an old social order that has grown corrupt and will soon be swept away.
5. What does the cherry orchard itself symbolize to the various characters in the play? What does it come to symbolize to the audience? Write an essay examining *The Cherry Orchard*'s central symbol. Is there, finally, any one "correct" interpretation? How does the ambiguity of this symbol serve Chekhov's overall artistic purposes in the play?

## PAULA VOGEL

### How I Learned to Drive

*This play is dedicated to Peter Franklin.*

#### CHARACTERS

LI'L BIT  *A woman who ages forty-something to eleven years old. (See Notes on the New York Production.)*

PECK  *Attractive man in his forties. Despite a few problems, he should be played by an actor one might cast in the role of Atticus in* To Kill a Mockingbird.

THE GREEK CHORUS  *If possible, these three members should be able to sing three-part harmony.*

  MALE GREEK CHORUS  *Plays Grandfather, Waiter, High School Boys. Thirties-forties. (See Notes on the New York Production.)*

  FEMALE GREEK CHORUS  *Plays Mother, Aunt Mary, High School Girls. Thirty-fifty. (See Notes on the New York Production.)*

  TEENAGE GREEK CHORUS  *Plays Grandmother, High School Girls and the voice of eleven-year-old Li'l Bit. Note on the casting of this actor: I would strongly recommend casting a young woman who is "of legal age," that is, twenty-one to twenty-five years old who can look as close to eleven as possible. The contrast with the other cast members will help. If the actor is too young, the audience may feel uncomfortable. (See Notes on the New York Production.)*

### PRODUCTION NOTES

I urge directors to use the Greek Chorus in staging as environment and, well, part of the family—with the exception of the Teenage Greek Chorus member who, after the last time she appears onstage, should perhaps disappear.

AS FOR MUSIC: *Please have fun. I wrote sections of the play listening to music like Roy Orbison's "Dream Baby" and The Mamas and the Papa's "Dedicated to the One I Love." The vaudeville sections go well to the Tijuana Brass or any music that sounds like a Laugh-In soundtrack. Other sixties music is rife with pedophilish (?) reference: the "You're Sixteen" genre hits; The Beach Boys' "Little Surfer Girl"; Gary Puckett and the Union Gap's "This Girl Is a Woman Now"; "Come Back When You Grow Up," etc.*

And whenever possible, please feel free to punctuate the action with traffic signs: "No Passing," "Slow Children," "Dangerous Curves," "One Way," and the visual signs for children, deer crossings, hills, school buses, etc. (See Notes on the New York Production.)

This script uses the notion of slides and projections, which were not used in the New York production of the play.

ON TITLES: *Throughout the script there are bold-faced titles. In production these should be spoken in a neutral voice (the type of voice that driver education films employ). In the New York production these titles were assigned to various members of the Greek Chorus and were done live.*

### NOTES ON THE NEW YORK PRODUCTION

The role of Li'l Bit was originally written as a character who is forty-something. When we cast Mary-Louise Parker in the role of Li'l Bit, we cast the Greek Chorus members with younger actors as the Female Greek and the Male Greek, and cast the Teenage Greek with an older (that is, mid-twenties) actor as well. There is a great deal of flexibility in age. Directors should change the age in the last monologue for Li'l Bit ("And before you know it, I'll be thirty-five....") to reflect the age of the actor who is playing Li'l Bit.

*As the house lights dim, a Voice announces:*

### Safety First—You and Driver Education.

*Then the sound of a key turning the ignition of a car.* LI'L BIT *steps into a spotlight on the stage; "well-endowed," she is a softer-looking woman in the present time than she was at seventeen.*

LI'L BIT: Sometimes to tell a secret, you first have to teach a lesson. We're going to start our lesson tonight on an early, warm summer evening.

In a parking lot overlooking the Beltsville Agricultural Farms in suburban Maryland.

Less than a mile away, the crumbling concrete of U.S. One[1] wends its way past one-room revival churches, the porno drive-in, and boarded up motels with For Sale signs tumbling down.

Like I said, it's a warm summer evening.

Here on the land the Department of Agriculture owns, the smell of sleeping farm animal is thick on the air. The smells of clover and hay mix in with the

---

1. Major highway passing through Washington, D.C., Baltimore, and northeastern Maryland.

smells of the leather dashboard. You can still imagine how Maryland used to be, before the malls took over. This countryside was once dotted with farmhouses—from their porches you could have witnessed the Civil War raging in the front fields.

Oh yes. There's a moon over Maryland tonight, that spills into the car where I sit beside a man old enough to be—did I mention how still the night is? Damp soil and tranquil air. It's the kind of night that makes a middle-aged man with a mortgage feel like a country boy again.

It's 1969. And I am very old, very cynical of the world, and I know it all. In short, I am seventeen years old, parking off a dark lane with a married man on an early summer night.

[*Lights up on two chairs facing front—or a Buick Riviera, if you will. Waiting patiently, with a smile on his face,* PECK *sits sniffing the night air.* LI'L BIT *climbs in beside him, seventeen years old and tense. Throughout the following, the two sit facing directly front. They do not touch. Their bodies remain passive. Only their facial expressions emote.*]

PECK: Ummm. I love the smell of your hair.
LI'L BIT: Uh-huh.
PECK: Oh, Lord. Ummmm. [*Beat.*][2] A man could die happy like this.
LI'L BIT: Well, *don't*.
PECK: What shampoo is this?
LI'L BIT: Herbal Essence.
PECK: Herbal Essence. I'm gonna buy me some. Herbal Essence. And when I'm all alone in the house, I'm going to get into the bathtub, and uncap the bottle and—
LI'L BIT: —Be good.
PECK: What?
LI'L BIT: Stop being . . . bad.
PECK: What did you think I was going to say? What do you think I'm going to do with the shampoo?
LI'L BIT: I don't want to know. I don't want to hear it.
PECK: I'm going to wash my hair. That's all.
LI'L BIT: Oh.
PECK: What did you think I was going to do?
LI'L BIT: Nothing. . . . I don't know. Something . . . nasty.
PECK: With shampoo? Lord, gal—your mind!
LI'L BIT: And whose fault is it?
PECK: Not mine. I've got the mind of a boy scout.
LI'L BIT: Right. A horny boy scout.
PECK: Boy scouts are always horny. What do you think the first Merit Badge is for?
LI'L BIT: There. You're going to be nasty again.
PECK: Oh, no. I'm good. Very good.
LI'L BIT: It's getting late.
PECK: Don't change the subject. I was talking about how good I am. [*Beat.*] Are you ever gonna let me show you how good I am?

---

2. In stage directions, a "beat" is a pause.

LI'L BIT: Don't go over the line now.
PECK: I won't. I'm not gonna do anything you don't want me to do.
LI'L BIT: That's right.
PECK: And I've been good all week.
LI'L BIT: You have?
PECK: Yes. All week. Not a single drink.
LI'L BIT: Good boy.
PECK: Do I get a reward? For not drinking?
LI'L BIT: A small one. It's getting late.
PECK: Just let me undo you. I'll do you back up.
LI'L BIT: All right. But be quick about it. [PECK *pantomimes undoing Li'l Bit's brassiere with one hand.*] You know, that's amazing. The way you can undo the hooks through my blouse with one hand.
PECK: Years of practice.
LI'L BIT: You would make an incredible brain surgeon with that dexterity.
PECK: I'll bet Clyde—what's the name of the boy taking you to the prom?
LI'L BIT: Claude Souders.
PECK: Claude Souders. I'll bet it takes him two hands, lights on, and you helping him on to get to first base.
LI'L BIT: Maybe.

[*Beat.*]

PECK: Can I . . . kiss them? Please?
LI'L BIT: I don't know.
PECK: Don't make a grown man beg.
LI'L BIT: Just one kiss.
PECK: I'm going to lift your blouse.
LI'L BIT: It's a little cold.

[PECK *laughs gently.*]

PECK: That's not why you're shivering. [*They sit, perfectly still, for a long moment of silence.* PECK *makes gentle, concentric circles with his thumbs in the air in front of him*] How does that feel?

[LI'L BIT *closes her eyes, carefully keeps her voice calm.*]

LI'L BIT: It's . . . okay.

[*Scared music, organ music or a boy's choir swells beneath the following.*]

PECK: I tell you, you can keep all the cathedrals of Europe. Just give me a second with these—these celestial orbs—

[PECK *bows his head as if praying. But he is kissing her nipple.* LI'L BIT, *eyes still closed, rears back her head on the leather Buick car seat.*]

LI'L BIT: Uncle Peck—we've got to go. I've got graduation rehearsal at school tomorrow morning. And you should get on home to Aunt Mary—
PECK: —All right, Li'l Bit.
LI'L BIT: —*Don't* call me that no more. [*Calmer.*] Any more. I'm a big girl now, Uncle Peck. As you know.

[LI'L BIT *pantomimes refastening her bra behind her back.*]

PECK: That you are. Going on eighteen. Kittens will turn into cats. [*Sighs.*] I live all week long for these few minutes with you—you know that?

LI'L BIT: I'll drive.

[*A Voice cuts in with:*]

## Idling in the Neutral Gear.

[*Sound of car revving cuts off the sacred music;* LI'L BIT, *now an adult, rises out of the car and comes to us.*]

LI'L BIT: In most families, relatives get names like "Junior," or "Brother," or "Bubba." In my family, if we call someone "Big Papa," it's not because he's tall. In my family, folks tend to get nicknamed for their genitalia. Uncle Peck, for example. My mama's adage was "the titless wonder," and my cousin Bobby got branded for life as "B.B."

[*In unison with* GREEK CHORUS:]

| LI'L BIT: | GREEK CHORUS: |
|---|---|
| For blue balls. | For blue balls. |

FEMALE GREEK CHORUS: [*As Mother.*] And of course, we were so excited to have a baby girl that when the nurse brought you in and said, "It's a girl! It's a baby girl!" I just had to see for myself. So we whipped your diapers down and parted your chubby little legs—and right between your legs there was—

[PECK *has come over during the above and chimes along:*]

| PECK: | GREEK CHORUS: |
|---|---|
| Just a little bit. | Just a little bit. |

FEMALE GREEK CHORUS: [*As Mother.*] And when you were born, you were so tiny that you fit in Uncle Peck's outstretched hand.

[PECK *stretches his hand out.*]

PECK: Now that's a fact. I held you, one day old, right in this hand.

[*A traffic signal is projected of a bicycle in a circle with a diagonal red slash.*]

LI'L BIT: Even with my family background, I was sixteen or so before I realized that pedophilia did not mean people who loved to bicycle....

[*A Voice intrudes:*]

## Driving in First Gear.

LI'L BIT: 1969. A typical family dinner.

FEMALE GREEK CHORUS: [*As Mother.*] Look, Grandma. Li'l Bit's getting to be as big in the bust as you are.

LI'L BIT: Mother! Could we please change the subject?

TEENAGE GREEK CHORUS: [*As Grandmother.*] Well, I hope you are buying her some decent bras. I never had a decent bra, growing up in the Depression, and now my shoulders are just crippled—crippled from the weight hanging on my shoulders—the dents from my bra straps are big enough to put your finger in.—Here, let me show you—

[As GRANDMOTHER *starts to open her blouse:*]

LI'L BIT: Grandma! Please don't undress at the dinner table.
PECK: I thought the entertainment came *after* the dinner.
LI'L BIT: [*To the audience.*] This is how it always starts. My grandfather, Big Papa, will chime in next with—
MALE GREEK CHORUS: [*As Grandfather.*] Yup. If Li'l Bit gets any bigger, we're gonna haveta buy her a wheelbarrow to carry in front of her—
LI'L BIT: —Damn it—
PECK: —How about those Redskins on Sunday, Big Papa?
LI'L BIT: [*To the audience.*] The only sport Big Papa followed was chasing Grandma around the house—
MALE GREEK CHORUS: [*As Grandfather.*]—Or we could write to Kate Smith. Ask her for somma her used brassieres she don't want anymore—she could maybe give to Li'l Bit here—
LI'L BIT: —I can't stand it. I can't.
PECK: Now, honey, that's just their way—
FEMALE GREEK CHORUS: [*As Mother.*] I tell you, Grandma, Li'l Bit's at that age. She's so sensitive, you can't say boo—
LI'L BIT: I'd like some privacy, that's all. Okay? Some goddamn privacy—
PECK: —Well, at least she didn't use the savior's name—
LI'L BIT: [*To the audience.*] And Big Papa wouldn't let a dead dog lie. No sirree.
MALE GREEK CHORUS: [*As Grandfather.*] Well, she'd better stop being so sensitive. 'Cause five minutes before Li'l Bit turns the corner, her tits turn first—
LI'L BIT: [*Starting to rise from the table.*]—That's it. That's it.
PECK: Li'l Bit, you can't let him get to you. Then he wins.
LI'L BIT: I hate him. *Hate* him.
PECK: That's fine. But hate him and eat a good dinner at the same time.

[LI'L BIT *calms down and sits with perfect dignity.*]

LI'L BIT: The gumbo is really good, Grandma.
MALE GREEK CHORUS: [*As Grandfather.*] A'course, Li'l Bit's got a big surprise coming for her when she goes to that fancy college this fall—
PECK: Big Papa—let it go.
MALE GREEK CHORUS: [*As Grandfather.*] What does she need a college degree for? She's got all the credentials she'll need on her chest—
LI'L BIT: —Maybe I want to learn things. Read. Rise above my cracker[3] background—
PECK: —Whoa, now, Li'l Bit—
MALE GREEK CHORUS: [*As Grandfather.*] What kind of things do you want to read?
LI'L BIT: There's a whole semester course, for example, on Shakespeare—

[GREEK CHORUS, *as Grandfather, laughs until he weeps.*]

MALE GREEK CHORUS: [*As Grandfather.*] Shakespeare. That's a good one. Shakespeare is really going to help you in life.
PECK: I think it's wonderful. And on scholarship!

---

3. Derogatory term for a poor white person, usually associated with the rural South.

MALE GREEK CHORUS: [*As Grandfather.*] How is Shakespeare going to help her lie on her back in the dark?

[LI'L BIT *is on her feet.*]

LI'L BIT: You're getting old, Big Papa. You are going to die—very very soon. Maybe even *tonight*. And when you get to heaven, God's going to be a beautiful black woman in a long white robe. She's gonna look at your chart and say: Uh-oh. Fornication. Dog-ugly mean with blood relatives. Oh. Uh-oh. Voted for George Wallace.[4] Well, one last chance: If you can name the play, all will be forgiven. And then she'll quote: "The quality of mercy is not strained." Your answer? Oh, too bad—*Merchant of Venice*: Act IV, Scene iii. And then she'll send your ass to fry in hell with all the other crackers. Excuse me, please.

[*To the audience.*] And as I left the house, I would always hear Big Papa say:

MALE GREEK CHORUS: [*As Grandfather.*] Lucy, your daughter's got a mouth on her. Well, no sense in wasting good gumbo. Pass me her plate, Mama.

LI'L BIT: And Aunt Mary would come up to Uncle Peck:

FEMALE GREEK CHORUS: [*As Aunt Mary.*] Peck, go after her, will you? You're the only one she'll listen to when she gets like this.

PECK: She just needs to cool off.

FEMALE GREEK CHORUS: [*As Aunt Mary.*] Please, honey—Grandma's been on her feet cooking all day.

PECK: All right.

LI'L BIT: And as he left the room, Aunt Mary would say:

FEMALE GREEK CHORUS: [*As Aunt Mary.*] Peck's so good with them when they get to be this age.

[LI'L BIT *has stormed to another part of the stage, her back turned, weeping with a teenage fury. Peck, cautiously, as if stalking a deer, comes to her. She turns away even more. He waits a bit.*]

PECK: I don't suppose you're talking to family. [*No response.*] Does it help that I'm in-law?

LI'L BIT: Don't you dare make fun of this.

PECK: I'm not. There's nothing funny about this. [*Beat.*] Although I'll bet when Big Papa is about to meet his maker, he'll remember *The Merchant of Venice*.

LI'L BIT: I've got to get away from here.

PECK: You're going away. Soon. Here, take this.

[PECK *hands her his folded handkerchief.* LI'L BIT *uses it, noisily. Hands it back. Without her seeing, he reverently puts it back.*]

LI'L BIT: I hate this family.

PECK: Your grandfather's ignorant. And you're right—he's going to die soon. But he's family. Family is . . . family.

LI'L BIT: Grown-ups are always saying that. Family.

PECK: Well, when you get a little older, you'll see what we're saying.

---

4. George Wallace (1919–1998), opponent of school desegregation as governor of Alabama in 1963–67, ran for U.S. president in 1968 on a third-party, anti-civil rights platform. Campaigning again in 1972, he was shot and paralyzed from the waist down. (He later served two more nonconsecutive terms as Alabama governor, renounced racism, and won support from African Americans.)

LI'L BIT: Uh-huh. So family is another acquired taste, like French kissing?
PECK: Come again?
LI'L BIT: You know, at first it really grosses you out, but in time you grow to like it?
PECK: Girl, you are . . . a handful.
LI'L BIT: Uncle Peck—you have the keys to your car?
PECK: Where do you want to go?
LI'L BIT: Just up the road.
PECK: I'll come with you.
LI'L BIT: No—please? I just need to . . . to drive for a little bit. Alone.

[PECK *tosses her the keys.*]

PECK: When can I see you alone again?
LI'L BIT: Tonight.

[LI'L BIT *crosses to center stage while the lights dim around her. A Voice directs:*]

### Shifting Forward from First to Second Gear.

LI'L BIT: There were a lot of rumors about why I got kicked out of that fancy school in 1970. Some say I got caught with a man in my room. Some say as a kid on scholarship I fooled around with a rich man's daughter.
[LI'L BIT *smiles innocently at the audience.*] I'm not talking.
But the real truth was I had a constant companion in my dorm room— who was less than discrete. Canadian V.O. A fifth a day.
1970. A Nixon recession. I slept on the floors of friends who were out of work themselves. Took factory work when I could find it. A string of deadend day jobs that didn't last very long.
What I did, most nights, was cruise the Beltway and the back roads of Maryland, where there was still country, past the battlefields and farm houses. Racing in a 1965 Mustang—and as long as I had gasoline for my car and whiskey for me, the nights would pass. Fully tanked, I would speed past the churches and the trees on the bend, thinking just one notch of the steering wheel would be all it would take, and yet some . . . reflex took over. My hands on the wheel in the nine and three o'clock position—I never so much as got a ticket. He taught me well.

[*A Voice announces:*]

### You and the Reverse Gear.

LI'L BIT: Back up. 1968. On the Eastern Shore. A celebration dinner.

[LI'L BIT *joins* PECK *at a table in a restaurant.*]

PECK: Feeling better, missy?
LI'L BIT: The bathroom's really amazing here, Uncle Peck! They have these little soaps—instead of borax or something—and they're in the shape of shells.
PECK: I'll have to take a trip to the gentleman's room just to see.
LI'L BIT: How did you know about this place?
PECK: This inn is famous on the Eastern Shore—it's been open since the seventeenth century. And I know how you like history . . .

[LI'L BIT *is shy and pleased.*]

LI'L BIT: It's great.

PECK: And you've just done your first, legal, long-distance drive. You must be hungry.

LI'L BIT: I'm starved.

PECK: I would suggest a dozen oysters to start, and the crab imperial... [LI'L BIT *is genuinely agog.*] You might be interested to know the town history. When the British sailed up this very river in the dead of night—see outside where I'm pointing?—they were going to bombard the heck out of this town. But the town fathers were ready for them. They crept up all the trees with lanterns so that the British would think they saw the town lights and they aimed their cannons too high. And that's why the inn is still here for business today.

LI'L BIT: That's a great story.

PECK: [*Casually.*] Would you like to start with a cocktail?

LI'L BIT: You're not... you're not going to start drinking, are you, Uncle Peck?

PECK: Not me. I told you, as long as you're with me, I'll never drink. I asked you if *you'd* like a cocktail before dinner. It's nice to have a little something with the oysters.

LI'L BIT: But... I'm not... legal. We could get arrested. Uncle Peck, they'll never believe I'm twenty-one!

PECK: So? Today we celebrate your driver's license—on the first try. This establishment reminds me a lot of places back home.

LI'L BIT: What does that mean?

PECK: In South Carolina, like here on the Eastern Shore, they're... [*Searches for the right euphemism.*]... "European." Not so puritanical. And very understanding if gentlemen wish to escort very attractive young ladies who might want a before-dinner cocktail. If you want one, I'll order one.

LI'L BIT: Well—sure. Just... one.

[*The* FEMALE GREEK CHORUS *appears in a spot.*]

FEMALE GREEK CHORUS: [*As Mother.*] A Mother's Guide to Social Drinking:

A lady never gets sloppy—she may, however, get tipsy and a little gay.

Never drink on an empty stomach. Avail yourself of the bread basket and generous portions of butter. *Slather* the butter on your bread.

Sip your drink, slowly, let the beverage linger in your mouth—interspersed with interesting, fascinating conversation. Sip, never... slurp or gulp. Your glass should always be three-quarters full when his glass is empty.

Stay away from *ladies'* drinks: drinks like pink ladies, sloe gin fizzes, daiquiris, gold cadillacs, Long Island iced teas, margaritas, piña coladas, mai tais, planters punch, white Russians, black Russians, red Russians, melon balls, blue balls, hummingbirds, hemorrhages and hurricanes. In short, avoid anything with sugar, or anything with an umbrella. Get your vitamin C from *fruit*. Don't order anything with Voodoo or Vixen in the title or sexual positions in the name like Dead Man Screw or the Missionary. [*She sort of titters.*]

Believe me, they are lethal.... I think you were conceived after one of those.

Drink, instead, like a man: straight up or on the rocks, with plenty of water in between.

Oh, yes. And never mix your drinks. Stay with one all night long, like the man you came in with: bourbon, gin, or tequila till dawn, damn the torpedoes, full speed ahead!

[*As the* FEMALE GREEK CHORUS *retreats, the* MALE GREEK CHORUS *approaches the table as a Waiter.*]

MALE GREEK CHORUS: [*As Waiter.*] I hope you all are having a pleasant evening. Is there something I can bring you, sir, before you order?

[LI'L BIT *waits in anxious fear. Carefully,* UNCLE PECK *says with command:*]

PECK: I'll have a plain iced tea. The lady would like a drink, I believe.

[*The* MALE GREEK CHORUS *does a double take; there is a moment when.* UNCLE PECK *and he are in silent communication.*]

MALE GREEK CHORUS: [*As Waiter.*] Very good. What would the . . . lady like?
LI'L BIT: [*A flushed.*] Is there . . . is there any sugar in a martini?
PECK: None that I know of.
LI'L BIT: That's what I'd like then—a dry martini. And could we maybe have some bread?
PECK: A drink fit for a woman of the world.—Please bring the lady a dry martini, be generous with the olives, straight up.

[*The* MALE GREEK CHORUS *anticipates a large tip.*]

MALE GREEK CHORUS: [*As Waiter.*] Right away. Very good, sir.

[*The* MALE GREEK CHORUS *returns with an empty martini glass which he puts in front of* LI'L BIT.]

PECK: Your glass is empty. Another martini, madam?
LI'L BIT: Yes, thank you. [PECK *signals the* MALE GREEK CHORUS, *who nods.*] So why did you leave South Carolina, Uncle Peck?
PECK: I was stationed in D.C. after the war, and decided to stay. Go North, Young Man, someone might have said.
LI'L BIT: What did you do in the service anyway?
PECK: [*Suddenly taciturn.*] I . . . I did just this and that. Nothing heroic or spectacular.
LI'L BIT: But did you see fighting? Or go to Europe?
PECK: I served in the Pacific Theater. It's really nothing interesting to talk about.
LI'L BIT: It is to me. [*The Waiter has brought another empty glass.*] Oh, goody. I love the color of the swizzle sticks. What were we talking about?
PECK: Swizzle sticks.
LI'L BIT: Do you ever think of going back?
PECK: To the Marines?
LI'L BIT: No—to South Carolina.
PECK: Well, we do go back. To visit.
LI'L BIT: No, I mean to live.
PECK: Not very likely. I think it's better if my mother doesn't have a daily reminder of her disappointment.
LI'L BIT: Are these floorboards slanted?

PECK: Yes, the floor is very slanted. I think this is the original floor.
LI'L BIT: Oh, good.

[*The* FEMALE GREEK CHORUS *as Mother enters swaying a little, a little past tipsy.*]

FEMALE GREEK CHORUS: [*As Mother.*] Don't leave your drink unattended when you visit the ladies' room. There is such a thing as white slavery; the modus operandi is to spike an unsuspecting young girl's drink with a "mickey" when she's left the room to powder her nose.

But if you feel you have had more than your sufficiency in liquor, do go to the ladies' room—often. Pop your head out of doors for a refreshing breath of the night air. If you must, wet your face and head with tap water. Don't be afraid to dunk your head if necessary. A wet woman is still less conspicuous than a drunk woman.

[*The Female Greek Chorus stumbles a little; conspiratorially.*] When in the course of human events it becomes necessary,[5] go to a corner stall and insert the index and middle finger down the throat almost to the epiglottis. Divulge your stomach contents by such persuasion, and then wait a few moments before rejoining your beau waiting for you at your table.

Oh, no. Don't be shy or embarrassed. In the very best of establishments, there's always one or two debutantes crouched in the corner stalls, their beaded purses tossed willy-nilly, sounding like cats in heat, heaving up the contents of their stomachs.

[*The* FEMALE GREEK CHORUS *begins to wander off.*] I wonder what it is they do in the men's rooms . . .

LI'L BIT: So why is your mother disappointed in you, Uncle Peck?
PECK: Every mother in Horry County has Great Expectations.
LI'L BIT: —Could I have another mar-ti-ni, please?
PECK: I think this is your last one.

[PECK *signals the Waiter. The Waiter looks at Li'l Bit and shakes his head no.* PECK *raises his eyebrow, raises his finger to indicate one more, and then rubs his fingers together. It looks like a secret code. The Waiter sighs, shakes his head sadly, and brings over another empty martini glass. He glares at* PECK.]

LI'L BIT: The name of the county where you grew up is "Horry?" [LI'L BIT, *plastered, begins to laugh. Then she stops.*] I think your mother should be proud of you.

[PECK *signals for the check.*]

PECK: Well, missy, she wanted me to do—to *be* everything my father was not. She wanted me to amount to something.
LI'L BIT: But you have! You've amounted a lot. . . .
PECK: I'm just a very ordinary man.

[*The Waiter has brought the check and waits.* PECK *draws out a large bill and hands it to the Waiter.* LI'L BIT *is in the soppy stage.*]

LI'L BIT: I'll bet your mother loves you, Uncle Peck.

[PECK *freezes a bit. To* MALE GREEK CHORUS *as Waiter:*]

---

5. The beginning of the Declaration of Independence, by Thomas Jefferson (1743–1826).

PECK: Thank you. The service was exceptional. Please keep the change.
MALE GREEK CHORUS: [*As Waiter, in a tone that could freeze.*] Thank you, sir. Will you be needing any help?
PECK: I think we can manage, thank you.

> [*Just then, the* FEMALE GREEK CHORUS *as Mother lurches on stage; the* MALE GREEK CHORUS *as Waiter escorts her off as she delivers:*]

FEMALE GREEK CHORUS: [*As Mother.*] Thanks to judicious planning and several trips to the ladies' loo, your mother once out-drank an entire regiment of British officers on a good-will visit to Washington! Every last man of them! Milquetoasts! How'd they ever kick Hitler's cahones,[6] huh? No match for an American lady—I could drink every man in here under the table.
> [*She delivers one last crucial hint before she is gently "bounced."*] As a last resort, when going out for an evening on the town, be sure to wear a skin-tight girdle—so tight that only a surgical knife or acetylene torch can get it off you—so that if you do pass out in the arms of your escort, he'll end up with rubber burns on his fingers before he can steal your virtue—

> [*A Voice punctures the interlude with:*]

**Vehicle Failure.**
**Even with careful maintenance and preventive operation of your automobile, it is all too common for us to experience an unexpected breakdown. If you are driving at any speed when a break-down occurs, you must slow down and guide the automobile to the side of the road.**

> [PECK *is slowly propping up* LI'L BIT *as they work their way to his car in the parking lot of the inn.*]

PECK: How are you doing, missy?
LI'L BIT: It's so far to the car, Uncle Peck. Like the lanterns in the trees the British fired on . . .

> [LI'L BIT *stumbles.* PECK *swoops her up in his arms.*]

PECK: Okay. I think we're going to take a more direct route.
> [LI'L BIT *closes her eyes.*] Dizzy? [*She nods her head.*] Don't look at the ground. Almost there—do you feel sick to your stomach? [LI'L BIT *nods. They reach the "car."* PECK *gently deposits her on the front seat.*] Just settle here a little while until things stop spinning. [LI'L BIT *opens her eyes.*]
LI'L BIT: What are we doing?
PECK: We're just going to sit here until your tummy settles down.
LI'L BIT: It's such nice upholst'ry—
PECK: Think you can go for a ride, now?
LI'L BIT: Where are you taking me?
PECK: Home.
LI'L BIT: You're not taking me—upstairs? There's no room at the inn? [LI'L BIT *giggles.*]
PECK: Do you want to go upstairs? [LI'L BIT *doesn't answer.*] Or home?

---

6. *Cojones*: Spanish-language obscenity, literally testicles, implying "guts" or "manhood." *Loo*: British slang for bathroom. *Milquetoasts*: old-fashioned insult for effeminate or weak men.

LI'L BIT: —This isn't right, Uncle Peck.
PECK: What isn't right?
LI'L BIT: What we're doing. It's wrong. It's very wrong.
PECK: What are we doing? [LI'L BIT *does not answer.*] We're just going out to dinner.
LI'L BIT: You know. It's not nice to Aunt Mary.
PECK: You let me be the judge of what's nice and not nice to my wife.

[*Beat.*]

LI'L BIT: Now you're mad.
PECK: I'm not mad. It's just that I thought you . . . understood me, Li'l Bit. I think you're the only one who does.
LI'L BIT: Someone will get hurt.
PECK: Have I forced you to do anything?

[*There is a long pause as* LI'L BIT *tries to get sober enough to think this through.*]

LI'L BIT: . . . I guess not.
PECK: We are just enjoying each other's company. I've told you, nothing is going to happen between us until you want it to. Do you know that?
LI'L BIT: Yes.
PECK: Nothing is going to happen until you want it to. [*A second more, with* PECK *staring ahead at the river while seated at the wheel of his car. Then, softly:*] Do you want something to happen?

[PECK *reaches over and strokes her face, very gently.* LI'L BIT *softens, reaches for him, and buries her head in his neck. Then she kisses him. Then she moves away, dizzy again.*]

LI'L BIT: . . . I don't know.

[PECK *smiles; this has been good news for him—it hasn't been a "no."*]

PECK: Then I'll wait. I'm a very patient man. I've been waiting for a long time. I don't mind waiting.
LI'L BIT: Someone is going to get hurt.
PECK: No one is going to get hurt. [LI'L BIT *closes her eyes*] Are you feeling sick?
LI'L BIT: Sleepy.

[*Carefully,* PECK *props* LI'L BIT *up on the seat.*]

PECK: Stay here a second.
LI'L BIT: Where're you going?
PECK: I'm getting something from the back seat.
LI'L BIT: [*Scared; too loud*] What? What are you going to do?

[PECK *reappears in the front seat with a lap rug.*]

PECK: Shhhh. [PECK *covers* LI'L BIT. *She calms down*] There. Think you can sleep?

[LI'L BIT *nods. She slides over to rest on his shoulder. With a look of happiness,* PECK *turns the ignition key. Beat.* PECK *leaves* LI'L BIT *sleeping in the car and strolls down to the audience. Wagner's* Flying Dutchman[7] *comes up faintly. A voice interjects:*]

---

7. *The Flying Dutchman* (1841), mythic opera by the German composer Richard Wagner (1813–1883).

### Idling in the Neutral Gear.

TEENAGE GREEK CHORUS: Uncle Peck Teaches Cousin Bobby How to Fish.

PECK: I get back once or twice a year—supposedly to visit Mama and the family, but the real truth is to fish. I miss this the most of all. There's a smell in the Low Country—where the swamp and fresh inlet join the saltwater—a scent of sand and cypress, that I haven't found anywhere yet.

I don't say this very often up North because it will just play into the stereotype everyone has, but I will tell you: I didn't wear shoes in the summertime until I was sixteen. It's unnatural down here to pen up your feet in leather. Go ahead—take 'em off. Let yourself breathe—it really will make you feel better.

We're going to aim for some pompano today—and I have to tell you, they're a very shy, mercurial fish. Takes patience, and psychology. You have to believe it doesn't matter if you catch one or not.

Sky's pretty spectacular—there's some beer in the cooler next to the crab salad I packed, so help yourself if you get hungry. Are you hungry? Thirsty? Holler if you are.

Okay. You don't want to lean over the bridge like that—pompano feed in shallow water, and you don't want to get too close—they're frisky and shy little things—wait, check your line. Yep, something's been munching while we were talking.

Okay, look: We take the sand flea and you take the hook like this—right through his little sand flea rump. Sand fleas should always keep their backs to the wall. Okay. Cast it in, like I showed you. That's great! I can taste that pompano now, sautéed with some pecans and butter, a little bourbon—now—let it lie on the bottom—now, reel, jerk, reel, jerk—

Look—look at your line. There's something calling, all right. Okay, tip the rod up—not too sharp—hook it—all right, now easy, reel and then rest—let it play. And reel—play it out, that's right—really good! I can't believe it! It's a pompano.—Good work! Way to go! You are an official fisherman now. Pompano are hard to catch. We are going to have a delicious little—

What? Well, I don't know how much pain a fish feels—you can't think of that. Oh, no, don't cry, come on now, it's just a fish—the other guys are going to see you.—No, no, you're just real sensitive, and I think that's wonderful at your age—look, do you want me to cut it free? You do?

Okay, hand me those pliers—look—I'm cutting the hook—okay? And we're just going to drop it in—no I'm not mad. It's just for fun, okay? There—it's going to swim back to its lady friend and tell her what a terrible day it had and she's going to stroke him with her fins until he feels better, and then they'll do something alone together that will make them both feel good and sleepy....

[PECK *bends down, very earnest*] I don't want you to feel ashamed about crying. I'm not going to tell anyone, okay? I can keep secrets. You know, men cry all the time. They just don't tell anybody, and they don't let anybody catch them. There's nothing you could do that would make me feel ashamed of you. Do you know that? Okay. [PECK *straightens up, smiles.*]

Do you want to pack up and call it a day? I tell you what—I think I can still remember—there's a really neat tree house where I used to stay for days.

I think it's still here—it was the last time I looked. But it's a secret place—you can't tell anybody we've gone there—least of all your mom or your sisters.—This is something special just between you and me. Sound good? We'll climb up there and have a beer and some crab salad—okay, B. B.? Bobby? Robert . . .

[LI'L BIT *sits at a kitchen table with the two* FEMALE GREEK CHORUS *members.*]

LI'L BIT: [*To the audience.*] Three women, three generations, sit at the kitchen table. On Men, Sex, and Women: Part I:

FEMALE GREEK CHORUS: [*As Mother.*] Men only want one thing.

LI'L BIT: [*Wide-eyed.*] But what? What is it they want?

FEMALE GREEK CHORUS: [*As Mother.*] And once they have it, they lose all interest. So Don't Give It to Them.

TEENAGE GREEK CHORUS: [*As Grandmother.*] I never had the luxury of the rhythm method. Your grandfather is just a big bull. A big bull. Every morning, every evening.

FEMALE GREEK CHORUS: [*As Mother, whispers to Li'l Bit.*] And he used to come home for lunch every day.

LI'L BIT: My god, Grandma!

TEENAGE GREEK CHORUS: [*As Grandmother.*] Your grandfather only cares that I do two things: have the table set and the bed turned down.

FEMALE GREEK CHORUS: [*As Mother.*] And in all that time, Mother, you never have experienced—?

LI'L BIT: [*To the audience.*]—Now my grandmother believed in all the sacraments of the church, to the day she died. She believed in Santa Claus and the Easter Bunny until she was fifteen. But she didn't believe in—

TEENAGE GREEK CHORUS: [*As Grandmother.*]—Orgasm! That's just something you and Mary have made up! I don't believe you.

FEMALE GREEK CHORUS: [*As Mother.*] Mother, it happens to women all the time—

TEENAGE GREEK CHORUS: [*As Grandmother.*]—Oh, now you're going to tell me about the G force![8]

LI'L BIT: No, Grandma, I think that's astronauts—

FEMALE GREEK CHORUS: [*As Mother.*] Well, Mama, after all, you were a child bride when Big Papa came and got you—you were a married woman and you still believed in Santa Claus.

TEENAGE GREEK CHORUS: [*As Grandmother.*] It was legal, what Daddy and I did! I was fourteen and in those days, fourteen was a grown-up woman—

[*Big Papa shuffles in the kitchen for a cookie.*]

MALE GREEK CHORUS: [*As Grandfather.*]—Oh, now we're off on Grandma and the Rape of the Sa-bean Women![9]

TEENAGE GREEK CHORUS: [*As Grandmother.*] Well, you were the one in such a big hurry—

MALE GREEK CHORUS: [*As Grandfather to Li'l Bit.*]—I picked your grandmother out

---

8. Grandmother here mistakes *G force*—an astronaut's term referring to G, the symbol for the constant of gravity in the universe as well as for acceleration of free fall due to Earth's gravity—for *G spot*, a bean-shaped mass of highly sensitive nerve tissue inside the vagina.

9. The legend of the mass rape of the Sabine women of central Italy by soldiers of ancient Rome, a scene of violent conquest often depicted in paintings.

of that herd of sisters just like a lion chooses the gazelle—the plump, slow, flaky gazelle dawdling at the edge of the herd—your sisters were too smart and too fast and too scrawny—

LI'L BIT: [*To the audience.*]—The family story is that when Big Papa came for Grandma, my Aunt Lily was waiting for him with a broom—and she beat him over the head all the way down the stairs as he was carrying out Grandma's hope chest—

MALE GREEK CHORUS: [*As Grandfather.*]—And they were *mean*. 'Specially Lily.

FEMALE GREEK CHORUS: [*As Mother.*] Well, you were robbing the baby of the family!

TEENAGE GREEK CHORUS: [*As Grandmother.*] I still keep a broom handy in the kitchen! And I know how to use it! So get your hand out of the cookie jar and don't you spoil your appetite for dinner—out of the kitchen!

[MALE GREEK CHORUS *as Grandfather leaves chuckling with a cookie.*]

FEMALE GREEK CHORUS: [*As Mother.*] Just one thing a married woman needs to know how to use—the rolling pin or the broom. I prefer a heavy, cast-iron fry pan—they're great on a man's head, no matter how thick the skull is.

TEENAGE GREEK CHORUS: [*As Grandmother.*] Yes, sir, your father is ruled by only two bosses! Mr. Gut and Mr. Peter! And sometimes, first thing in the morning, Mr. Sphincter Muscle!

FEMALE GREEK CHORUS: [*As Mother.*] It's true. Men are like children. Just like little boys.

TEENAGE GREEK CHORUS: [*As Grandmother.*] Men are bulls! Big bulls!

[*The* GREEK CHORUS *is getting aroused.*]

FEMALE GREEK CHORUS: [*As Mother*] They'd still be crouched on their haunches over a fire in a cave if we hadn't cleaned them up!

TEENAGE GREEK CHORUS: [*As Grandmother, flushed.*] Coming in smelling of sweat—

FEMALE GREEK CHORUS: [*As Mother.*]—Looking at those naughty pictures like boys in a dime store with a dollar in their pockets!

TEENAGE GREEK CHORUS: [*As Grandmother; raucous.*] No matter to them what they smell like! They've got to have it, right then, on the spot, right there! Nasty!—

FEMALE GREEK CHORUS: [*As Mother.*]—Vulgar!

TEENAGE GREEK CHORUS: [*As Grandmother.*] Primitive!—

FEMALE GREEK CHORUS: [*As Mother.*]—Hot!—

LI'L BIT: And just about then, Big Papa would shuffle in with—

MALE GREEK CHORUS: [*As Grandfather.*]—What are you all cackling about in here?

TEENAGE GREEK CHORUS: [*As Grandmother.*] Stay out of the kitchen! This is just for girls!

[*As Grandfather leaves:*]

MALE GREEK CHORUS: [*As Grandfather.*] Lucy, you'd better not be filling Mama's head with sex! Every time you and Mary come over and start in about sex, when I ask a simple question like, "What time is dinner going to be ready?," Mama snaps my head off!

TEENAGE GREEK CHORUS: [*As Grandmother.*] Dinner will be ready when I'm good and ready! Stay out of this kitchen!

[LI'L BIT *steps out. A Voice directs:*]

## When Making a Left Turn, You Must Downshift While Going Forward.

LI'L BIT: 1979. A long bus trip to Upstate New York. I settled in to read, when a young man sat beside me.

MALE GREEK CHORUS: [*As Young Man; voice cracking.*] "What are you reading?"

LI'L BIT: He asked. His voice broke into that miserable equivalent of vocal acne, not quite falsetto and not tenor, either. I glanced a side view. He was appealing in an odd way, huge ears at a defiant angle springing forward at ninety degrees. He must have been shaving, because his face, with a peach sheen, was speckled with nicks and styptic. "I have a class tomorrow," I told him.

MALE GREEK CHORUS: [*As Young Man.*] "You're taking a class?"

LI'L BIT: "I'm teaching a class." He concentrated on lowering his voice.

MALE GREEK CHORUS: [*As Young Man.*] "I'm a senior. Walt Whitman High."

LI'L BIT: The light was fading outside, so perhaps he was—with a very high voice.

I felt his "interest" quicken. Five steps ahead of the hopes in his head, I slowed down, waited, pretended surprise, acted at listening, all the while knowing we would get off the bus, he would just then seem to think to ask me to dinner, he would chivalrously insist on walking me home, he would continue to converse in the street until I would casually invite him up to my room—and—I was only into the second moment of conversation and I could see the whole evening before me.

And dramaturgically speaking, after the faltering and slightly comical "first act," there was the very briefest of intermissions, and an extremely capable and forceful and *sustained* second act. And after the second act climax and a gentle denouement—before the post-play discussion—I lay on my back in the dark and I thought about you, Uncle Peck. Oh. Oh—this is the allure. Being older. Being the first. Being the translator, the teacher, the epicure, the already jaded. This is how the giver gets taken.

[LI'L BIT *changes her tone.*] On Men, Sex, and Women: Part II:

[LI'L BIT *steps back into the scene as a fifteen-year-old, gawky and quiet, as the gazelle at the edge of the herd.*]

TEENAGE GREEK CHORUS: [*As Grandmother; to Li'l Bit.*] You're being mighty quiet, missy. Cat Got Your Tongue?

LI'L BIT: I'm just listening. Just thinking.

TEENAGE GREEK CHORUS: [*As Grandmother.*] Oh, yes, Little Miss Radar Ears? Soaking it all in? Little Miss Sponge? Penny for your thoughts?

[LI'L BIT *hesitates to ask but she really wants to know.*]

LI'L BIT: Does it—when you do it—you know, theoretically when I do it and I haven't done it before—I mean—does it hurt?

FEMALE GREEK CHORUS: [*As Mother.*] Does what hurt, honey?

LI'L BIT: When a . . . when a girl does it for the first time—with a man—does it hurt?

TEENAGE GREEK CHORUS: [*As Grandmother; horrified.*] *That's* what you're thinking about?

FEMALE GREEK CHORUS: [*As Mother; calm.*] Well, just a little bit. Like a pinch. And there's a little blood.

TEENAGE GREEK CHORUS: [*As Grandmother.*] Don't tell her that! She's too young to be thinking those things!
FEMALE GREEK CHORUS: [*As Mother.*] Well, if she doesn't find out from me, where is she going to find out? In the street?
TEENAGE GREEK CHORUS: [*As Grandmother.*] Tell her it hurts! It's agony! You think you're going to die! Especially if you do it before marriage!
FEMALE GREEK CHORUS: [*As Mother.*] Mama! I'm going to tell her the truth! Unlike you, you left me and Mary completely in the dark with fairy tales and told us to go to the priest! What does an eighty-year-old priest know about lovemaking with girls!
LI'L BIT: [*Getting upset.*] It's not fair!
FEMALE GREEK CHORUS: [*As Mother.*] Now, see, she's getting upset—you're scaring her.
TEENAGE GREEK CHORUS: [*As Grandmother.*] Good! Let her be good and scared! It hurts! You bleed like a stuck pig! And you lay there and say, "Why, O Lord, have you forsaken me?!"
LI'L BIT: It's not fair! Why does everything have to hurt for girls? Why is there always blood?
FEMALE GREEK CHORUS: [*As Mother.*] It's not a lot of blood—and it feels wonderful after the pain subsides . . .
TEENAGE GREEK CHORUS: [*As Grandmother.*] You're encouraging her to just go out and find out with the first drugstore joe who buys her a milk shake!
FEMALE GREEK CHORUS: [*As Mother.*] Don't be scared. It won't hurt you—if the man you go to bed with really loves you. It's important that he loves you.
TEENAGE GREEK CHORUS: [*As Grandmother.*]—Why don't you just go out and rent a motel room for her, Lucy?
FEMALE GREEK CHORUS: [*As Mother.*] I believe in telling my daughter the truth! We have a very close relationship! I want her to be able to ask me anything—I'm not scaring her with stories about Eve's sin and snakes crawling on their bellies for eternity and women bearing children in mortal pain—
TEENAGE GREEK CHORUS: [*As Grandmother.*]—If she stops and thinks before she takes her knickers off, maybe someone in this family will finish high school!

[LI'L BIT *knows what is about to happen and starts to retreat from the scene at this point.*]

FEMALE GREEK CHORUS: [*As Mother.*] Mother! If you and Daddy had helped me—I wouldn't have had to marry that—that no-good-son-of-a—
TEENAGE GREEK CHORUS: [*As Grandmother.*]—He was good enough for you on a full moon! I hold you responsible!
FEMALE GREEK CHORUS: [*As Mother.*]—You could have helped me! You could have told me something about the facts of life!
TEENAGE GREEK CHORUS: [*As Grandmother.*]—I told you what my mother told me! A girl with her skirt up can outrun a man with his pants down!

[*The* MALE GREEK CHORUS *enters the fray;* LI'L BIT *edges further downstage.*]

FEMALE GREEK CHORUS: [*As Mother.*] And when I turned to you for a little help, all I got afterwards was—
MALE GREEK CHORUS: [*As Grandfather.*] You Made Your Bed; Now Lie On It!

[*The* GREEK CHORUS *freezes, mouths open, argumentatively.*]

LI'L BIT: [*To the audience.*] Oh, please! I still can't bear to listen to it, after all these years—

[*The* MALE GREEK CHORUS *"unfreezes," but out of his open mouth, as if to his surprise, comes a base refrain from a Motown song.*]

MALE GREEK CHORUS: "Do-Bee-Do-Wah!"

[*The* FEMALE GREEK CHORUS *member is also surprised; but she, too, unfreezes.*]

FEMALE GREEK CHORUS: "Shoo-doo-be-doo-be-doo; shoo-doo-be-doo-be-doo."

[*The* MALE *and* FEMALE GREEK CHORUS *members continue with their harmony, until the* TEENAGE *member of the* CHORUS *starts in with Motown lyrics such as "Dedicated to the One I Love," or "In the Still of the Night," or "Hold Me"—any Sam Cooke[1] will do. The three modulate down into three-part harmony, softly, until they are submerged by the actual recording playing over the radio in the car in which* UNCLE PECK *sits in the driver's seat, waiting.* LI'L BIT *sits in the passenger's seat.*]

LI'L BIT: Ahh. That's better.

[UNCLE PECK *reaches over and turns the volume down; to* LI'L BIT:]

PECK: How can you hear yourself think?

[LI'L BIT *does not answer. A Voice insinuates itself in the pause:*]

**Before You Drive.**
**Always check under your car for obstructions—broken bottles, fallen tree branches, and the bodies of small children. Each year hundreds of children are crushed beneath the wheels of unwary drivers in their own driveways. Children depend on *you* to watch them.**

[*Pause. The Voice continues:*]

**You and the Reverse Gear.**

[*In the following section, it would be nice to have slides of erotic photographs of women and cars: women posed over the hood; women draped along the sideboards; women with water hoses spraying the car; and the actress playing* LI'L BIT *with a Bel Air or any 1950s car one can find for the finale.*]

LI'L BIT: 1967. In a parking lot of the Beltsville Agricultural Farms. The Initiation into a Boy's First Love.

PECK: [*With a soft look on his face.*] Of course, my favorite car will always be the 56 Bel Air Sports Coupe. Chevy sold more '55s, but the '56!—a V-8 with Corvette option, 225 horsepower; went from zero to sixty miles per hour in 8.9 seconds.

LI'L BIT: [*To the audience.*] Long after a mother's tits, but before a woman's breasts:

---

1. Successful gospel singer (1931–1964) who crossed over to secular music with such hits as "You Send Me" (1957) and "Only Sixteen" (1959); he was never a Motown recording artist. Stevie Wonder (b. 1950), a Motown artist influenced by Cooke, recorded a song called "Hold Me." "Dedicated to the One I Love" was a 1961 hit for the Shirelles and a 1967 hit for the Mamas and the Papas. "In the Still of the Night" was a 1956 hit for the Five Satins and a 1960 hit for Dion and the Belmonts.

PECK: Super-Turbo-Fire! What a Power Pack—mechanical lifters, twin four-barrel carbs, lightweight valves, dual exhausts—
LI'L BIT: [*To the audience.*] After the milk but before the beer:
PECK: A specific intake manifold, higher-lift camshaft, and the tightest squeeze Chevy had ever made—
LI'L BIT: [*To the audience.*] Long after he's squeezed down the birth canal but before he's pushed his way back in: The boy falls in love with the thing that bears his weight with speed.
PECK: I want you to know your automobile inside and out.—Are you there? Li'l Bit?

[*Slides end here.*]

LI'L BIT: —What?
PECK: You're drifting. I need you to concentrate.
LI'L BIT: Sorry.
PECK: Okay. Get into the driver's seat. [LI'L BIT *does.*] Okay. Now. Show me what you're going to do before you start the car.

[LI'L BIT *sits, with her hands in her lap. She starts to giggle.*]

LI'L BIT: I don't know, Uncle Peck.
PECK: Now, come on. What's the first thing you're going to adjust?
LI'L BIT: My bra strap?—
PECK: —Li'l Bit. What's the most important thing to have control of on the inside of the car?
LI'L BIT: That's easy. The radio. I tune the radio from Mama's old fart tunes to—

[LI'L BIT *turns the radio up so we can hear a 1960s tune. With surprising firmness,* PECK *commands:*]

PECK: —Radio off. Right now. [LI'L BIT *turns the radio off.*] When you are driving your car, with your license, you can fiddle with the stations all you want. But when you are driving with a learner's permit in my car, I want all your attention to be on the road.
LI'L BIT: Yes, sir.
PECK: Okay. Now the seat—forward and up. [LI'L BIT *pushes it forward.*] Do you want a cushion?
LI'L BIT: No—I'm good.
PECK: You should be able to reach all the switches and controls. Your feet should be able to push the accelerator, brake and clutch all the way down. Can you do that?
LI'L BIT: Yes.
PECK: Okay, the side mirrors. You want to be able to see just a bit of the right side of the car in the right mirror—can you?
LI'L BIT: Turn it out more.
PECK: Okay. How's that?
LI'L BIT: A little more.... Okay, that's good.
PECK: Now the left—again, you want to be able to see behind you—but the left lane—adjust it until you feel comfortable. [LI'L BIT *does so.*] Next. I want you to check the rearview mirror. Angle it so you have a clear vision of the back.

[LI'L BIT *does so.*] Okay. Lock your door. Make sure all the doors are locked.
LI'L BIT: [*Making a joke of it.*] But then I'm locked in with you.
PECK: Don't fool.
LI'L BIT: All right. We're locked in.
PECK: We'll deal with the air vents and defroster later. I'm teaching you on a manual—once you learn manual, you can drive anything. I want you to be able to drive any car, any machine. Manual gives you *control*. In ice, if your brakes fail, if you need more power—okay? It's a little harder at first, but then it becomes like breathing. Now. Put your hands on the wheel. I never want to see you driving with one hand. Always two hands. [LI'L BIT *hesitates.*] What? What is it now?
LI'L BIT: If I put my hands on the wheel—how do I defend myself?
PECK: [*Softly.*] Now listen. Listen up close. We're not going to fool around with this. This is serious business. I will never touch you when you are driving a car. Understand?
LI'L BIT: Okay.
PECK: Hands on the nine o'clock and three o'clock position gives you maximum control and turn.

[PECK *goes silent for a while.* LI'L BIT *waits for more instruction.*]

Okay. Just relax and listen to me, Li'l Bit, okay? I want you to lift your hands for a second and look at them. [LI'L BIT *feels a bit silly, but does it.*]

Those are your two hands. When you are driving, your life is in your own two hands. Understand? [LI'L BIT *nods.*],

I don't have any sons. You're the nearest to a son I'll ever have—and I want to give you something. Something that really matters to me.

There's something about driving—when you're in control of the car, just you and the machine and the road—that nobody can take from you. A power. I feel more myself in my car than anywhere else. And that's what I want to give to you.

There's a lot of assholes out there. Crazy men, arrogant idiots, drunks, angry kids, geezers who are blind—and you have to be ready for them. I want to teach you to drive like a man.
LI'L BIT: What does that mean?
PECK: Men are taught to drive with confidence—with aggression. The road belongs to them. They drive defensively—always looking out for the other guy. Women tend to be polite—to hesitate. And that can be fatal.

You're going to learn to think what the other guy is going to do before he does it. If there's an accident, and ten cars pile up, and people get killed, you're the one who's gonna steer through it, put your foot on the gas if you have to, and be the only one to walk away. I don't know how long you or I are going to live, but we're for damned sure not going to die in a car.

So if you're going to drive with me, I want you to take this very seriously.
LI'L BIT: I will, Uncle Peck. I want you to teach me to drive.
PECK: Good. You're going to pass your test on the first try. Perfect score. Before the next four weeks are over, you're going to know this baby inside and out. Treat her with respect.
LI'L BIT: Why is it a "she?"
PECK: Good question. It doesn't have to be a "she"—but when you close your eyes and think of someone who responds to your touch—someone who per-

forms just for you and gives you what you ask for—I guess I always see a "she." You can call her what you like.

LI'L BIT: [*To the audience.*] I closed my eyes—and decided not to change the gender.

[*A Voice:*]

**Defensive driving involves defending yourself from hazardous and sudden changes in your automotive environment. By thinking ahead, the defensive driver can adjust to weather, road conditions and road kill. Good defensive driving involves mental and physical preparation. Are you prepared?**

[*Another Voice chimes in:*]

**You and the Reverse Gear.**

LI'L BIT: 1966. The Anthropology of the Female Body in Ninth Grade—Or A Walk Down Mammary Lane.

[*Throughout the following, there is occasional rhythmic beeping, like a transmitter signalling.* LI'L BIT *is aware of it, but can't figure out where it is coming from. No one else seems to hear it.*]

MALE GREEK CHORUS: In the hallway of Francis Scott Key Middle School.

[*A bell rings; the* GREEK CHORUS *is changing classes and meets in the hall, conspiratorially.*]

TEENAGE GREEK CHORUS: She's coming!

[LI'L BIT *enters the scene; the* MALE GREEK CHORUS *member has a sudden, violent sneezing and lethal allergy attack.*]

FEMALE GREEK CHORUS: Jerome? Jerome? Are you all right?
MALE GREEK CHORUS: I—don't—know. I can't breathe—get Li'l Bit—
TEENAGE GREEK CHORUS: —He needs oxygen!—
FEMALE GREEK CHORUS: —Can you help us here?
LI'L BIT: What's wrong? Do you want me to get the school nurse—

[*The* MALE GREEK CHORUS *member wheezes, grabs his throat and sniffs at Li'l Bit's chest, which is beeping away.*]

MALE GREEK CHORUS: No—it's okay—I only get this way when I'm around an allergy trigger—
LI'L BIT: Golly. What are you allergic to?
MALE GREEK CHORUS: [*With a sudden grab of her breast.*] Foam rubber.

[*The* GREEK CHORUS *members break up with hilarity; Jerome leaps away from Li'l Bit's kicking rage with agility; as he retreats:*]

LI'L BIT: Jerome! Creep! Cretin! Cro-Magnon!
TEENAGE GREEK CHORUS: Rage is not attractive in a girl.
FEMALE GREEK CHORUS: Really. Get a Sense of Humor.

[*A voice echoes:*]

### Good defensive driving involves mental and physical preparation. Were you prepared?

FEMALE GREEK CHORUS: Gym Class: In the showers.

[*The sudden sound of water; the* FEMALE GREEK CHORUS *members and* LI'L BIT, *while fully clothed, drape towels across their fronts, miming nudity. They stand, hesitate, at an imaginary shower's edge.*]

LI'L BIT: Water looks hot.
FEMALE GREEK CHORUS: Yesss....

[FEMALE GREEK CHORUS *members are not going to make the first move. One dips a tentative toe under the water, clutching the towel around her.*]

LI'L BIT: Well, I guess we'd better shower and get out of here.
FEMALE GREEK CHORUS: Yep. You go ahead. I'm still cooling off.
LI'L BIT: Okay.—Sally? Are you gonna shower?
TEENAGE GREEK CHORUS: After you—

[LI'L BIT *takes a deep breath for courage, drops the towel and plunges in: The two* FEMALE GREEK CHORUS *members look at Li'l Bit in the all together, laugh, gasp and high-five each other.*]

TEENAGE GREEK CHORUS: Oh my god! Can you believe—
FEMALE GREEK CHORUS: Told you! It's not foam rubber! I win! Jerome owes me fifty cents!

[*A Voice editorializes:*]

### Were you prepared?

[LI'L BIT *tries to cover up; she is exposed, as suddenly 1960s Motown fills the room and we segue into:*]

FEMALE GREEK CHORUS: The Sock Hop.

[LI'L BIT *stands up against the wall with her female classmates. Teenage Greek Chorus is mesmerized by the music and just sways alone, lip-synching the lyrics.*]

LI'L BIT: I don't know. Maybe it's just me—but—do you ever feel like you're just a walking Mary Jane joke?
FEMALE GREEK CHORUS: I don't know what you mean.
LI'L BIT: You haven't heard the Mary Jane jokes? [FEMALE GREEK CHORUS *member shakes her head no.*] Okay. "Little Mary Jane is walking through the woods, when all of a sudden this man who was hiding behind a tree *jumps* out, *rips* open Mary Jane's blouse, and *plunges* his hands on her breasts. And Little Mary Jane just laughed and laughed because she knew her money was in her shoes."

[LI'L BIT *laughs; the* FEMALE GREEK CHORUS *does not.*]

FEMALE GREEK CHORUS: You're weird.

[*In another space, in a strange light,* UNCLE PECK *stands and stares at Li'l Bit's body. He is setting up a tripod, but he just stands, appreciative, watching her.*]

LI'L BIT: Well, don't you ever feel... self-conscious? Like you're being looked at all the time?

FEMALE GREEK CHORUS: That's not a problem for me.—Oh—look—Greg's coming over to ask you to dance.

> [TEENAGE GREEK CHORUS *becomes attentive, flustered.* MALE GREEK CHORUS *member, as Greg, bends slightly as a very short young man, whose head is at Li'l Bit's chest level. Ardent, sincere and socially inept, Greg will become a successful gynecologist.*]

TEENAGE GREEK CHORUS: [*Softly.*] Hi, Greg.

> [*Greg does not hear. He is intent on only one thing.*]

MALE GREEK CHORUS: [*As Greg, to Li'l Bit.*] Good Evening. Would you care to dance?

LI'L BIT: [*Gently.*] Thank you very much, Greg—but I'm going to sit this one out.

MALE GREEK CHORUS: [*As Greg.*] Oh. Okay. I'll try my luck later.

> [*He disappears.*]

TEENAGE GREEK CHORUS: Oohhh.

> [LI'L BIT *relaxes. Then she tenses, aware of Peck's gaze.*]

FEMALE GREEK CHORUS: Take pity on him. Someone should.

LI'L BIT: But he's so short.

TEENAGE GREEK CHORUS: He can't help it.

LI'L BIT: But his head comes up to [LI'L BIT *gestures.*] here. And I think he asks me on the fast dances so he can watch me—you know—jiggle.

FEMALE GREEK CHORUS: I wish I had your problems.

> [*The tune changes; Greg is across the room in a flash.*]

MALE GREEK CHORUS: [*As Greg.*] Evening again. May I ask you for the honor of a spin on the floor?

LI'L BIT: I'm... very complimented, Greg. But I... I just don't do fast dances.

MALE GREEK CHORUS: [*As Greg.*] Oh. No problem. That's okay.

> [*He disappears.* TEENAGE GREEK CHORUS *watches him go.*]

TEENAGE GREEK CHORUS: That is just so—*sad*.

> [LI'L BIT *becomes aware of* PECK *waiting.*]

FEMALE GREEK CHORUS: You know, you should take it as a compliment that the guys want to watch you jiggle. They're guys. That's what they're supposed to do.

LI'L BIT: I guess you're right. But sometimes I feel like these alien life forces, these two mounds of flesh have grafted themselves onto my chest, and they're using me until they can "propagate" and take over the world and they'll just keep growing, with a mind of their own until I collapse under their weight and they suck all the nourishment out of my body and I finally just waste away

while they get bigger and bigger and—[*Li'l Bit's classmates are just staring at her in disbelief.*]
FEMALE GREEK CHORUS: —You are the strangest girl I have ever met.

> [LI'L BIT*'s trying to joke but feels on the verge of tears.*]

LI'L BIT: Or maybe someone's implanted radio transmitters in my chest at a frequency I can't hear, that girls can't detect, but they're sending out these signals to men who get mesmerized, like sirens, calling them to dash themselves on these "rocks"—[2]

> [*Just then, the music segues into a slow dance, perhaps a Beach Boys tune like "Little Surfer," but over the music there's a rhythmic, hypnotic beeping transmitted, which both Greg and* PECK *hear.* LI'L BIT *hears it too, and in horror she stares at her chest. She, too, is almost hypnotized. In a trance, Greg responds to the signals and is called to her side—actually, her front. Like a zombie, he stands in front of her, his eyes planted on her two orbs.*]

MALE GREEK CHORUS: [*As Greg.*] This one's a slow dance. I hope your dance card isn't . . . filled?

> [LI'L BIT *is aware of* PECK; *but the signals are calling her to him. The signals are no longer transmitters, but an electromagnetic force, pulling* LI'L BIT *to his side, where he again waits for her to join him. She must get away from the dance floor.*]

LI'L BIT: Greg—you really are a nice boy. But I don't like to dance.
MALE GREEK CHORUS: [*As Greg.*]: That's okay. We don't have to move or anything. I could just hold you and we could just *sway* a little—
LI'L BIT: —No! I'm sorry—but I think I have to leave; I hear someone calling me—

> [LI'L BIT *starts across the dance floor, leaving Greg behind. The beeping stops. The lights change, although the music does not. As* LI'L BIT *talks to the audience, she continues to change and prepare for the coming session. She should be wearing a tight tank top or a sheer blouse and very tight pants. To the audience:*]

In every man's home some small room, some zone in his house, is set aside. It might be the attic, or the study, or a den. And there's an invisible sign as if from the old treehouse: Girls Keep Out.

Here, away from female eyes, lace doilies and crochet, he keeps his manly toys: the Vargas pinups, the tackle. A scent of tobacco and WD-40.[3] [*She inhales deeply.*] A dash of his Bay Rum. Ahhh. . . . [LI'L BIT *savors it for just a moment more.*]

Here he keeps his secrets: a violin or saxophone, drum set or darkroom, and the stacks of *Playboy*. [*In a whisper.*] Here, in my aunt's home, it was the basement. Uncle Peck's turf.

[*A Voice commands:*]

---

2. The Sirens, according to Greek mythology, were nymphs with women's heads and birds' bodies whose singing seduced sailors to shipwreck upon the rocks near Messina.
3. A brand of aerosol lubricant for mechanical parts. *Vargas*: Alberto Vargas (1896–1982), Peruvian-born illustrator for *Esquire, Playboy,* and other magazines, famous for his slick, good-humored, erotic images of semiclad or nude young women, which were often "pinned up" on walls by U.S. soldiers overseas.

### You and the Reverse Gear.

LI'L BIT: 1965. The Photo Shoot.

> [LI'L BIT *steps into the scene as a nervous but curious thirteen-year-old. Music, from the previous scene, continues to play, changing into something like Roy Orbison later—something seductive with a beat.* PECK *fiddles, all business, with his camera. As in the driving lesson, he is all competency and concentration.* LI'L BIT *stands awkwardly. He looks through the Leica camera on the tripod, adjusts the back lighting, etc.*]

PECK: Are you cold? The lights should heat up some in a few minutes—
LI'L BIT: —Aunt Mary is?
PECK: At the National Theatre matinee. With your mother. We have time.
LI'L BIT: But—what if—
PECK: —And so what if they return? I told them you and I were going to be working with my camera. They won't come down. [LI'L BIT *is quiet, apprehensive.*]—Look, are you sure you want to do this?
LI'L BIT: I said I'd do it. But—
PECK: —I know. You've drawn the line.
LI'L BIT: [*Reassured.*] That's right. No frontal nudity.
PECK: Good heavens, girl, where did you pick that up?
LI'L BIT: [*Defensive.*] I read.

> [PECK *tries not to laugh.*]

PECK: And I read *Playboy* for the interviews. Okay. Let's try some different music.

> [PECK *goes to an expensive reel-to-reel and forwards. Something like "Sweet Dreams"*[4] *begins to play.*]

LI'L BIT: I didn't know you listened to this.
PECK: I'm not dead, you know. I try to keep up. Do you like this song? [LI'L BIT *nods with pleasure.*] Good. Now listen—at professional photo shoots, they always play music for the models. Okay? I want you to just enjoy the music. Listen to it with your body, and just—respond.
LI'L BIT: Respond to the music with my . . . body?
PECK: Right. Almost like dancing. Here—let's get you on the stool, first. [PECK *comes over and helps her up.*]
LI'L BIT: But nothing showing—

> [PECK *firmly, with his large capable hands, brushes back her hair, angles her face.*
> LI'L BIT *turns to him like a plant to the sun.*]

PECK: Nothing showing. Just a peek.

> [*He holds her by the shoulder, looking at her critically. Then he unbuttons her blouse to the midpoint, and runs his hands over the flesh of her exposed sternum, arranging the fabric, just touching her. Deliberately, calmly. Asexually.* LI'L BIT *quiets, sits perfectly still, and closes her eyes.*]
>
> Okay?

---

4. Here and elsewhere, actually the early 1960s hit "Dream Baby (How Long Must I Dream)," by Roy Orbison (1936–1988).

LI'L BIT: Yes.

[PECK *goes back to his camera.*]

PECK: I'm going to keep talking to you. Listen without responding to what I'm saying; you want to *listen* to the music. Sway, move just your torso or your head—I've got to check the light meter.

LI'L BIT: But—you'll be watching.

PECK: No—I'm not here—just my voice. Pretend you're in your room all alone on a Friday night with your mirror—and the music feels good—just move for me, Li'l Bit—

[LI'L BIT *closes her eyes. At first self-conscious; then she gets more into the music and begins to sway. We hear the camera start to whir. Throughout the shoot, there can be a slide montage of actual shots of the actor playing Li'l Bit—interspersed with other models à la* Playboy, *Calvin Klein and Victoriana/Lewis Carroll's Alice Liddell.*][5]

That's it. That looks great. Okay. Just keep doing that. Lift your head up a bit more, good, good, just keep moving, that a girl—you're a very beautiful young woman. Do you know that? [LI'L BIT *looks up, blushes.* PECK *shoots the camera. The audience should see this shot on the screen.*]

LI'L BIT: No. I don't know that.

PECK: Listen to the music. [LI'L BIT *closes her eyes again.*] Well you are. For a thirteen-year-old, you have a body a twenty-year-old woman would die for.

LI'L BIT: The boys in school don't think so.

PECK: The boys in school are little Neanderthals in short pants. You're ten years ahead of them in maturity; it's gonna take a while for them to catch up.

[PECK *clicks another shot; we see a faint smile on Li'l Bit on the screen.*]

Girls turn into women long before boys turn into men.

LI'L BIT: Why is that?

PECK: I don't know, Li'l Bit. But it's a blessing for men.

[LI'L BIT *turns silent.*] Keep moving. Try arching your back on the stool, hands behind you, and throw your head back. [*The slide shows a* Playboy *model in this pose.*] Oohh, great. That one was great. Turn your head away, same position. [*Whir.*] Beautiful.

[LI'L BIT *looks at him a bit defiantly.*]

LI'L BIT: I think Aunt Mary is beautiful.

[PECK *stands still.*]

PECK: My wife is a very beautiful woman. Her beauty doesn't cancel yours out. [*More casually; he returns to the camera.*] All the women in your family are beautiful. In fact, I think all women are. You're not listening to the music. [PECK *shoots some more film in silence.*] All right, turn your head to the left. Good. Now take the back of your right hand and put in on your right cheek—your elbow

---

5. The slides would mix adult pornography with the images of seductive adolescents in Calvin Klein ads and examples of the Victorian fashion of photographing children in sensual poses. Lewis Carroll is the pseudonym of the English mathematician Charles Dodgson (1832–1898), author of *Alice in Wonderland* (1865). The original Alice, Alice Liddell, was ten years old—twenty years younger than Dodgson—when he first told the story; his photographs of her, some nude, suggest pedophilic eroticism.

angled up—now slowly, slowly, stroke your cheek, draw back your hair with the back of your hand. [*Another classic* Playboy *or Vargas.*] Good. One hand above and behind your head; stretch your body; smile. [*Another pose.*]

Li'l Bit. I want you to think of something that makes you laugh—

LI'L BIT: I can't think of anything.

PECK: Okay. Think of Big Papa chasing Grandma around the living room. [*li'l bit lifts her head and laughs. Click. We should see this shot.*] Good. Both hands behind your head. Great! Hold that. [*From behind his camera.*] You're doing great work. If we keep this up, in five years we'll have a really professional portfolio.

[LI'L BIT *stops.*]

LI'L BIT: What do you mean in five years?

PECK: You can't submit work to *Playboy* until you're eighteen.—

[PECK *continues to shoot; he knows he's made a mistake.*]

LI'L BIT: —Wait a minute. You're joking, aren't you, Uncle Peck?

PECK: Heck, no. You can't get into *Playboy* unless you're the very best. And you are the very best.

LI'L BIT: I would never do that!

[PECK *stops shooting. He turns off the music.*]

PECK: Why? There's nothing wrong with *Playboy*—it's a very classy maga—

LI'L BIT: [*More upset.*] But I thought you said I should go to college!

PECK: Wait—Li'l Bit—it's nothing like that. Very respectable women model for *Playboy*—actresses with major careers—women in college—there's an Ivy League issue every—

LI'L BIT: —I'm never doing anything like that! You'd show other people these— other *men*—these—what I'm doing.—Why would you do that?! Any *boy* around here could just pick up, just go into The Stop & Go and *buy*—Why would you ever want to—to share—

PECK: —Whoa, whoa. Just stop a second and listen to me. Li'l Bit. Listen. There's nothing wrong in what we're doing. I'm very proud of you. I think you have a wonderful body and an even more wonderful mind. And of course I want other people to *appreciate* it. It's not anything shameful.

LI'L BIT: [*Hurt.*] But this is something—that I'm only doing for you. This is something—that you said was just between us.

PECK: It is. And if that's how you feel, five years from now, it will remain that way. Okay? I know you're not going to do anything you don't feel like doing. [*He walks back to the camera.*] Do you want to stop now? I've got just a few more shots on this roll—

LI'L BIT: I don't want anyone seeing this.

PECK: I swear to you. No one will. I'll treasure this—that you're doing this only for me.

[LI'L BIT, *still shaken, sits on the stool. She closes her eyes.*] Li'l Bit? Open your eyes and look at me. [LI'L BIT *shakes her head no.*] Come on. Just open your eyes, honey.

LI'L BIT: If I look at you—if I look at the camera: You're gonna know what I'm thinking. You'll see right through me—

PECK: —No, I won't. I want you to look at me. All right, then. I just want you to listen. Li'l Bit. [*She waits.*] I love you. [LI'L BIT *opens her eyes; she is startled.* PECK *captures the shot. On the screen we see right though her.* PECK *says softly.*] Do you know that? [LI'L BIT *nods her head yes.*] I have loved you every day since the day you were born.

LI'L BIT: Yes.

[LI'L BIT *and* PECK *just look at each other. Beat. Beneath the shot of herself on the screen,* LI'L BIT, *still looking at her uncle, begins to unbutton her blouse. A neutral Voice cuts off the above scene with:*]

## Implied Consent.

**As an individual operating a motor vehicle in the state of Maryland, you must abide by "Implied Consent." If you do not consent to take the blood alcohol content test, there may be severe penalties: a suspension of license, a fine, community service and a possible *jail* sentence.**

[*The Voice shifts tone:*]

## Idling in the Neutral Gear.

MALE GREEK CHORUS: [*Announcing.*] Aunt Mary on behalf of her husband.

[FEMALE GREEK CHORUS *checks her appearance, and with dignity comes to the front of the stage and sits down to talk to the audience.*]

FEMALE GREEK CHORUS: [*As Aunt Mary.*] My husband was such a good man—is. Is such a good man. Every night, he does the dishes. The second he comes home, he's taking out the garbage, or doing yard work, lifting the heavy things I can't. Everyone in the neighborhood borrows Peck—it's true—women with husbands of their own, men who just don't have Peck's abilities—there's always a knock on our door for a jump start on cold mornings, when anyone needs a ride, or help shoveling the sidewalk—I look out, and there Peck is, without a coat, pitching in.

I know I'm lucky. The man works from dawn to dusk. And the overtime he does every year—my poor sister. She sits every Christmas when I come to dinner with a new stole, or diamonds, or with the tickets to Bermuda.

I know he has troubles. And we don't talk about them. I wonder, sometimes, what happened to him during the war. The men who fought World War II didn't have "rap sessions" to talk about their feelings. Men in his generation were expected to be quiet about it and get on with their lives. And sometimes I can feel him just fighting the trouble—whatever has burrowed deeper than the scar tissue—and we don't talk about it. I know he's having a bad spell because he comes looking for me in the house, and just hangs around me until it passes. And I keep my banter light—I discuss a new recipe, or sales, or gossip—because I think domesticity can be a balm for men when they're lost. We sit in the house and listen to the peace of the clock ticking in his well-ordered living room, until it passes.

[*Sharply.*] I'm not a fool. I know what's going on. I wish you could feel how hard Peck fights against it—he's swimming against the tide, and what he needs is to see me on the shore, believing in him, knowing he won't go under, he won't give up—

And I want to say this about my niece. She's a sly one, that one is. She knows exactly what she's doing; she's twisted Peck around her little finger and thinks it's all a big secret. Yet another one who's borrowing my husband until it doesn't suit her anymore.

Well, I'm counting the days until she goes away to school. And she manipulates someone else. And then he'll come back again, and sit in the kitchen while I bake, or beside me on the sofa when I sew in the evenings. I'm a very patient woman. But I'd like my husband back.

I am counting the days.

[*A Voice repeats:*]

### You and the Reverse Gear.

MALE GREEK CHORUS: Li'l Bit's Thirteenth Christmas. Uncle Peck Does the Dishes. Christmas 1964.

[PECK *stands in a dress shirt and tie, nice pants, with an apron. He is washing dishes. He's in a mood we haven't seen. Quiet, brooding.* LI'L BIT *watches him a moment before seeking him out.*]

LI'L BIT: Uncle Peck? [*He does not answer. He continues to work on the pots.*] I didn't know where you'd gone to. [*He nods. She takes this as a sign to come in.*] Don't you want to sit with us for a while?

PECK: No. I'd rather do the dishes.

[*Pause.* LI'L BIT *watches him.*]

LI'L BIT: You're the only man I know who does dishes. [*Peck says nothing.*] I think it's really nice.

PECK: My wife has been on her feet all day. So's your grandmother and your mother.

LI'L BIT: I know. [*Beat.*] Do you want some help?

PECK: No. [*He softens a bit towards her.*] You can help by just talking to me.

LI'L BIT: Big Papa never does the dishes. I think it's nice.

PECK: I think men should be nice to women. Women are always working for us. There's nothing particularly manly in wolfing down food and then sitting around in a stupor while the women clean up.

LI'L BIT: That looks like a really neat camera that Aunt Mary got you.

PECK: It is. It's a very nice one.

[*Pause, as* PECK *works on the dishes and some demon that* LI'L BIT *intuits.*]

LI'L BIT: Did Big Papa hurt your feelings?

PECK: [*Tired.*] What? Oh, no—it doesn't hurt me. Family is family. I'd rather have him picking on me than—I don't pay him any mind, Li'l Bit.

LI'L BIT: Are you angry with us?

PECK: No, Li'l Bit. I'm not angry.

[*Another pause.*]

LI'L BIT: We missed you at Thanksgiving. . . . I did. I missed you.

PECK: Well, there were . . . "things" going on. I didn't want to spoil anyone's Thanksgiving.

LI'L BIT: Uncle Peck? [*Very carefully.*] Please don't drink anymore tonight.
PECK: I'm not . . . overdoing it.
LI'L BIT: I know. [*Beat.*] Why do you drink so much?

[PECK *stops and thinks, carefully.*]

PECK: Well, Li'l Bit—let me explain it this way. There are some people who have a . . . a "fire" in the belly. I think they go to work on Wall Street or they run for office. And then there are people who have a "fire" in their heads—and they become writers or scientists or historians. [*He smiles a little at her.*] You. You've got a "fire" in the head. And then there are people like me.
LI'L BIT: Where do you have . . . a fire?
PECK: I have a fire in my heart. And sometimes the drinking helps.
LI'L BIT: There's got to be other things that can help.
PECK: I suppose there are.
LI'L BIT: Does it help—to talk to me?
PECK: Yes. It does. [*Quiet.*] I don't get to see you very much.
LI'L BIT: I know. [*Li'l Bit thinks.*] You could talk to me more.
PECK: Oh?
LI'L BIT: I could make a deal with you, Uncle Peck.
PECK: I'm listening.
LI'L BIT: We could meet and talk—once a week. You could just store up whatever's bothering you during the week—and then we could talk.
PECK: Would you like that?
LI'L BIT: As long as you don't drink. I'd meet you somewhere for lunch or for a walk—on the weekends—as long as you stop drinking. And we could talk about whatever you want.
PECK: You would do that for me?
LI'L BIT: I don't think I'd want Mom to know. Or Aunt Mary. I wouldn't want them to think—
PECK: —No. It would just be us talking.
LI'L BIT: I'll tell Mom I'm going to a girlfriend's. To study. Mom doesn't get home until six, so you can call me after school and tell me where to meet you.
PECK: You get home at four?
LI'L BIT: We can meet once a week. But only in public. You've got to let me—draw the line. And once it's drawn, you mustn't cross it.
PECK: Understood.
LI'L BIT: Would that help?

[PECK *is very moved.*]

PECK: Yes. Very much.
LI'L BIT: I'm going to join the others in the living room now. [LI'L BIT *turns to go.*]
PECK: Merry Christmas, Li'l Bit.

[LI'L BIT *bestows a very warm smile on him.*]

LI'L BIT: Merry Christmas, Uncle Peck.

[*A Voice dictates.*]

**Shifting Forward from Second to Third Gear.**

[*The* MALE *and* FEMALE GREEK CHORUS *members come forward.*]

MALE GREEK CHORUS: 1969. Days and Gifts: A Countdown:
FEMALE GREEK CHORUS: A note. "September 3, 1969. Li'l Bit: You've only been away two days and it feels like months. Hope your dorm room is cozy. I'm sending you this tape cassette—it's a new model—so you'll have some music in your room. Also that music you're reading about for class—*Carmina Burana*.[6] Hope you enjoy. Only ninety days to go!—Peck."
MALE GREEK CHORUS: September 22. A bouquet of roses. A note: "Miss you like crazy. Sixty-nine days . . ."
TEENAGE GREEK CHORUS: September 25. A box of chocolates. A card: "Don't worry about the weight gain. You still look great. Got a post office box—write to me there. Sixty-six days.—Love, your candy man."[7]
MALE GREEK CHORUS: October 16. A note: "Am trying to get through the Jane Austen you're reading—*Emma*—here's a book in return: *Liaisons Dangereuses*.[8] Hope you're saving time for me." Scrawled in the margin the number: "47."
FEMALE GREEK CHORUS: November 16. "Sixteen days to go!—Hope you like the perfume.—Having a hard time reaching you on the dorm phone. You must be in the library a lot. Won't you think about me getting you your own phone so we can talk?"
TEENAGE GREEK CHORUS: November 18. "Li'l Bit—got a package returned to the P.O. Box. Have you changed dorms? Call me at work, or write to the P.O. Am still on the wagon. Waiting to see you. Only two weeks more!"
MALE GREEK CHORUS: November 23. A letter. "Li'l Bit. So disappointed you couldn't come home for the turkey. Sending you some money for a nice dinner out—nine days and counting!"
GREEK CHORUS: [*In unison*] November 25th. A letter:
LI'L BIT: "Dear Uncle Peck: I am sending this to you at work. Don't come up next weekend for my birthday. I will not be here—"

[*A Voice directs:*]

**Shifting Forward from Third to Fourth Gear.**

MALE GREEK CHORUS: December 10, 1969. A hotel room. Philadelphia. There is no moon tonight.

[PECK *sits on the side of the bed while* LI'L BIT *paces. He can't believe she's in his room, but there's a desperate edge to his happiness.* LI'L BIT *is furious, edgy. There is a bottle of champagne in an ice bucket in a very nice hotel room.*]

PECK: Why don't you sit?
LI'L BIT: I don't want to.—What's the champagne for?

---

6. Popular, untraditional opera, set to thirteenth-century Latin and German lyrics, by the German composer Carl Orff (1895–1982).    7. Reference to another song by Roy Orbison, "Candy Man" (1961).
8. *Les Liaisons dangereuses* (1782; translated as *Dangerous Connections* in 1784 but generally known as *Dangerous Liaisons*), famous work by the French general and novelist Pierre Choderlos de Laclos (1741–1803); it concerns a conspiracy between two cynical former lovers to seduce an innocent young wife. In the classic novel *Emma* (1816), by the English writer Jane Austen (1775–1817), the heroine is morally educated by her older brother-in-law, whom she marries in the end.

PECK: I thought we might toast your birthday—
LI'L BIT: —I am so pissed off at you, Uncle Peck.
PECK: Why?
LI'L BIT: I mean, are you crazy?
PECK: What did I do?
LI'L BIT: You scared the holy crap out of me—sending me that stuff in the mail—
PECK: —They were gifts! I just wanted to give you some little perks your first semester—
LI'L BIT: —Well, what the hell were those numbers all about! Forty-four days to go—only two more weeks.—And then just numbers—69—68—67—like some serial killer!
PECK: Li'l Bit! Whoa! This is me you're talking to—I was just trying to pick up your spirits, trying to celebrate your birthday.
LI'L BIT: My *eighteenth* birthday. I'm not a child, Uncle Peck. You were counting down to my eighteenth birthday.
PECK: So?
LI'L BIT: So? So statutory rape is not in effect when a young woman turns eighteen. And you and I both know it.

[PECK *is walking on ice.*]

PECK: I think you misunderstand.
LI'L BIT: I think I understand all too well. I know what you want to do five steps ahead of you doing it. Defensive Driving 101.
PECK: Then why did you suggest we meet here instead of the restaurant?
LI'L BIT: I don't want to have this conversation in public.
PECK: Fine. Fine. We have a lot to talk about.
LI'L BIT: Yeah. We do. [LI'L BIT *doesn't want to do what she has to do*] Could I . . . have some of that champagne?
PECK: Of course, madam! [PECK *makes a big show of it.*] Let me do the honors. I wasn't sure which you might prefer—Taittingers or Veuve Clicquot—so I thought we'd start out with an old standard—Perrier Jouet.⁹ [*The bottle is popped.*]
   Quick—Li'l Bit—your glass! [UNCLE PECK *fills Li'l Bit's glass. He puts the bottle back in the ice and goes for a can of ginger ale.*] Let me get some of this ginger ale—my bubbly—and toast you.

[*He turns and sees that* LI'L BIT *has not waited for him.*]

LI'L BIT: Oh—sorry, Uncle Peck. Let me have another. [PECK *fills her glass and reaches for his ginger ale; she stops him.*] Uncle Peck—maybe you should join me in the champagne.
PECK: You want me to—drink?
LI'L BIT: It's not polite to let a lady drink alone.
PECK: Well, missy, if you insist. . . . [PECK *hesitates.*]—Just one. It's been a while. [PECKS *fills another flute for himself.*] There. I'd like to propose a toast to you and your birthday! [PECK *sips it tentatively.*] I'm not used to this anymore.
LI'L BIT: You don't have anywhere to go tonight, do you?

---

9. Like Taittingers and Veuve Clicquot, a good brand of champagne.

[PECK *hopes this is a good sign.*]

PECK: I'm all yours.—God, it's good to see you! I've gotten so used to . . . to . . . talking to you in my head. I'm used to seeing you every week—there's so much—I don't quite know where to begin. How's school, Li'l Bit?

LI'L BIT: I—it's hard, Uncle Peck. Harder than I thought it would be. I'm in the middle of exams and papers and—I don't know.

PECK: You'll pull through. You always do.

LI'L BIT: Maybe. I . . . might be flunking out.

PECK: You always think the worse, Li'l Bit, but when the going gets tough—[LI'L BIT *shrugs and pours herself another glass.*]—Hey, honey, go easy on that stuff, okay?

LI'L BIT: Is it very expensive?

PECK: Only the best for you. But the cost doesn't matter—champagne should be "sipped." [LI'L BIT *is quiet.*] Look—if you're in trouble in school—you can always come back home for a while.

LI'L BIT: *No*— [LI'L BIT *tries not to be so harsh.*] —Thanks, Uncle Peck, but I'll figure some way out of this.

PECK: You're supposed to get in scrapes, your first year away from home.

LI'L BIT: Right. How's Aunt Mary?

PECK: She's fine. [*Pause.*] Well—how about the new car?

LI'L BIT: It's real nice. What is it, again?

PECK: It's a Cadillac El Dorado.

LI'L BIT: Oh. Well, I'm real happy for you, Uncle Peck.

PECK: I got it for you.

LI'L BIT: What?

PECK: I always wanted to get a Cadillac—but I thought, Peck, wait until Li'l Bit's old enough—and thought maybe you'd like to drive it, too.

LI'L BIT: [*Confused.*] Why would I want to drive your car?

PECK: Just because it's the best—I want you to have the best.

[*They are running out of "gas"; small talk.*]

LI'L BIT:
Listen, Uncle Peck, I don't know how to begin this, but—

PECK:
I have been thinking of how to say this in my head, over and over—

PECK: Sorry.

LI'L BIT: You first.

PECK: Well, your going away—has just made me realize how much I miss you. Talking to you and being alone with you. I've really come to depend on you, Li'l Bit. And it's been so hard to get in touch with you lately—the distance and—and you're never in when I call—I guess you've been living in the library—

LI'L BIT: —No—the problem is, I haven't been in the library—

PECK: —Well, it doesn't matter—I hope you've been missing me as much.

LI'L BIT: Uncle Peck—I've been thinking a lot about this—and I came here tonight to tell you that—I'm not doing very well. I'm getting very confused—I can't concentrate on my work—and now that I'm away—I've been going over and over it in my mind—and I don't want us to "see" each other anymore. Other than with the rest of the family.

PECK: [*Quiet.*] Are you seeing other men?
LI'L BIT: [*Getting agitated.*] I—no, that's not the reason—I—well, yes, I am seeing other—listen, it's not really anybody's business!
PECK: Are you in love with anyone else?
LI'L BIT: That's not what this is about.
PECK: Li'l Bit—you're scared. Your mother and your grandparents have filled your head with all kinds of nonsense about men—I hear them working on you all the time—and you're scared. It won't hurt you—if the man you go to bed with really loves you. [LI'L BIT *is scared. She starts to tremble.*] And I have loved you since the day I held you in my hand. And I think everyone's just gotten you frightened to death about something that is just like breathing—
LI'L BIT: Oh, my god—[*She takes a breath.*] I can't see you anymore, Uncle Peck.

[PECK *downs the rest of his champagne.*]

PECK: Li'l Bit. Listen. Listen. Open your eyes and look at me. Come on. Just open your eyes, honey. [LI'L BIT, *eyes squeezed shut, refuses.*] All right then. I just want you to listen. Li'l Bit—I'm going to ask you just this once. Of your own free will. Just lie down on the bed with me—our clothes on—just lie down with me, a man and a woman . . . and let's . . . hold one another. Nothing else. Before you say anything else. I want the chance to . . . hold you. Because sometimes the body knows things that the mind isn't listening to . . . and after I've held you, then I want you to tell me what you feel.
LI'L BIT: You'll just . . . hold me?
PECK: Yes. And then you can tell me what you're feeling. [LI'L BIT—*half wanting to run, half wanting to get it over with, half wanting to be held by him:*]
LI'L BIT: Yes. All right. Just hold. Nothing else.

[PECK *lies down on the bed and holds his arms out to her.* LI'L BIT *lies beside him, putting her head on his chest. He looks as if he's trying to soak her into his pores by osmosis. He strokes her hair, and she lies very still. The* MALE GREEK CHORUS *member and the* FEMALE GREEK CHORUS *member as Aunt Mary come into the room.*]

MALE GREEK CHORUS: Recipe for a Southern Boy:
FEMALE GREEK CHORUS: [*As Aunt Mary.*] A drawl of molasses in the way he speaks.
MALE GREEK CHORUS: A gumbo of red and brown mixed in the cream of his skin.

[*While* PECK *lies, his eyes closed,* LI'L BIT *rises in the bed and responds to her aunt.*]

LI'L BIT: Warm brown eyes—
FEMALE GREEK CHORUS: [*As Aunt Mary.*] Bedroom eyes—
MALE GREEK CHORUS: A dash of Southern Baptist Fire and Brimstone—
LI'L BIT: A curl of Elvis on his forehead—
FEMALE GREEK CHORUS: [*As Aunt Mary.*] A splash of Bay Rum—
MALE GREEK CHORUS: A closely shaven beard that he razors just for you—
FEMALE GREEK CHORUS: [*As Aunt Mary.*] Large hands—rough hands—
LI'L BIT: Warm hands—
MALE GREEK CHORUS: The steel of the military in his walk—
LI'L BIT: The slouch of the fishing skiff in his walk—
MALE GREEK CHORUS: Neatly pressed khakis—
FEMALE GREEK CHORUS: [*As Aunt Mary.*] And under the wide leather of the belt—

LI'L BIT: Sweat of cypress and sand—
MALE GREEK CHORUS: Neatly pressed khakis—
LI'L BIT: His heart beating Dixie—
FEMALE GREEK CHORUS: [As Aunt Mary.] The whisper of the zipper—you could reach out with your hand and—
LI'L BIT: His mouth—
FEMALE GREEK CHORUS: [As Aunt Mary.] You could just reach out and—
LI'L BIT: Hold him in your hand—
FEMALE GREEK CHORUS: [As Aunt Mary.] And his mouth—

[LI'L BIT *rises above her uncle and looks at his mouth; she starts to lower herself to kiss him—and wrenches herself free. She gets up from the bed.*]

LI'L BIT: —I've got to get back.
PECK: Wait—Li'l Bit. Did you . . . feel nothing?
LI'L BIT: [*Lying.*] No. Nothing.
PECK: Do you—do you think of me?

[*The* GREEK CHORUS *whispers:*]

FEMALE GREEK CHORUS: Khakis—
MALE GREEK CHORUS: Bay Rum—
FEMALE GREEK CHORUS: The whisper of the—
LI'L BIT: —No.

[PECK, *in a rush, trembling, gets something out of his pocket.*]

PECK: I'm forty-five. That's not old for a man. And I haven't been able to do anything else but think of you. I can't concentrate on my work—Li'l Bit. You've got to—I want you to think about what I am about to ask you.
LI'L BIT: I'm listening.

[PECK *opens a small ring box.*]

PECK: I want you to be my wife.
LI'L BIT: This isn't happening.
PECK: I'll tell Mary I want a divorce. We're not blood-related. It would be legal—
LI'L BIT: —What have you been thinking! You are married to my aunt, Uncle Peck. She's my family. You have—you have gone way over the line. Family is family.

[*Quickly,* LI'L BIT *flies through the room, gets her coat.*] I'm leaving. Now. I am not seeing you. Again.

[PECK *lies down on the bed for a moment, trying to absorb the terrible news. For a moment, he almost curls into a fetal position.*]

I'm not coming home for Christmas. You should go home to Aunt Mary. Go home now, Uncle Peck.

[PECK *gets control, and sits, rigid.*]

Uncle Peck?—I'm sorry but I have to go.
[*Pause.*]
Are you all right?

[*With a discipline that comes from being told that boys don't cry,* PECK *stands upright.*]

PECK: I'm fine. I just think—I need a real drink.

[*The* MALE GREEK CHORUS *has become a bartender. At a small counter, he is lining up shots for* PECK. *As* LI'L BIT *narrates, we see* PECK *sitting, carefully and calmly downing shot glasses.*]

LI'L BIT: [*To the audience.*] I never saw him again. I stayed away from Christmas and Thanksgiving for years after.

It took my uncle seven years to drink himself to death. First he lost his job, then his wife, and finally his driver's license. He retreated to his house, and had his bottles delivered.

[PECK *stands, and puts his hands in front of him—almost like Superman flying.*]

One night he tried to go downstairs to the basement—and he flew down the steep basement stairs. My aunt came by weekly to put food on the porch, and she noticed the mail and the papers stacked up, uncollected.

They found him at the bottom of the stairs. Just steps away from his dark room.

Now that I'm old enough, there are some questions I would have liked to have asked him. Who did it to you, Uncle Peck? How old were you? Were you eleven?

[PECK *moves to the driver's seat of the car and waits.*]

Sometimes I think of my uncle as a kind of Flying Dutchman. In the opera, the Dutchman is doomed to wander the sea; but every seven years he can come ashore, and if he finds a maiden who will love him of her own free will—he will be released.

And I see Uncle Peck in my mind, in his Chevy '56, a spirit driving up and down the back roads of Carolina—looking for a young girl who, of her own free will, will love him. Release him.

[*A Voice states:*]

**You and the Reverse Gear.**

LI'L BIT: The summer of 1962. On Men, Sex, and Women: Part III:

[LI'L BIT *steps, as an eleven year old, into:*]

FEMALE GREEK CHORUS: [*As Mother.*] It is out of the question. End of Discussion.

LI'L BIT: But why?

FEMALE GREEK CHORUS: [*As Mother.*] Li'l Bit—we are not discussing this. I said no.

LI'L BIT: But I could spend an extra week at the beach! You're not telling me why!

FEMALE GREEK CHORUS: [*As Mother.*] Your uncle pays entirely too much attention to you.

LI'L BIT: He listens to me when I talk. And—and he talks to me. He teaches me about things. Mama—he knows an awful lot.

FEMALE GREEK CHORUS: [*As Mother.*] He's a small town hick who's learned how to mix drinks from Hugh Hefner.[1]

LI'L BIT: Who's Hugh Hefner?

[*Beat.*]

---

1. Founding publisher of *Playboy* magazine, known for promoting a flamboyant, extravagant lifestyle.

FEMALE GREEK CHORUS: [*As Mother.*] I am not letting an eleven-year-old girl spend seven hours alone in the car with a man.... I don't like the way your uncle looks at you.

LI'L BIT: For god's sake, mother! Just because you've gone through a bad time with my father—you think every man is evil!

FEMALE GREEK CHORUS: [*As Mother.*] Oh no, Li'l Bit—not all men.... We ... we just haven't been very lucky with the men in our family.

LI'L BIT: Just because you lost your husband—I still deserve a chance at having a father! Someone! A man who will look out for me! Don't I get a chance?

FEMALE GREEK CHORUS: [*As Mother.*] I will feel terrible if something happens.

LI'L BIT: Mother! It's in your head! Nothing will happen! I can take care of myself. And I can certainly handle Uncle Peck.

FEMALE GREEK CHORUS: [*As Mother.*] All right. But I'm warning you—if anything happens, I hold you responsible.

[LI'L BIT *moves out of this scene and toward the car.*]

LI'L BIT: 1962. On the Back Roads of Carolina: The First Driving Lesson.

[*The* TEENAGE GREEK CHORUS *member stands apart on stage. She will speak all of Li'l Bit's lines.* LI'L BIT *sits beside* PECK *in the front seat. She looks at him closely, remembering.*]

PECK: Li'l Bit? Are you getting tired?

TEENAGE GREEK CHORUS: A little.

PECK: It's a long drive. But we're making really good time. We can take the back road from here and see ... a little scenery. Say—I've got an idea—[PECK *checks his rearview mirror*]

TEENAGE GREEK CHORUS: Are we stopping, Uncle Peck?

PECK: There's no traffic here. Do you want to drive?

TEENAGE GREEK CHORUS: I can't drive.

PECK: It's easy. I'll show you how. I started driving when I was your age. Don't you want to?—

TEENAGE GREEK CHORUS: —But it's against the law at my age!

PECK: And that's why you can't tell anyone I'm letting you do this—

TEENAGE GREEK CHORUS: —But—I can't reach the pedals.

PECK: You can sit in my lap and steer. I'll push the pedals for you. Did your father ever let you drive his car?

TEENAGE GREEK CHORUS: No way.

PECK: Want to try?

TEENAGE GREEK CHORUS: Okay. [LI'L BIT *moves into Peck's lap. She leans against him, closing her eyes.*]

PECK: You're just a little thing, aren't you? Okay—now think of the wheel as a big clock—I want you to put your right hand on the clock where three o'clock would be; and your left hand on the nine—

[LI'L BIT *puts one hand to Peck's face, to stroke him. Then, she takes the wheel.*]

TEENAGE GREEK CHORUS: Am I doing it right?

PECK: That's right. Now, whatever you do, don't let go of the wheel. You tell me whether to go faster or slower—

TEENAGE GREEK CHORUS: Not so fast, Uncle Peck!

PECK: Li'l Bit—I need you to watch the road—

[PECK *puts his hands on Li'l Bit's breasts. She relaxes against him, silent, accepting his touch.*]

TEENAGE GREEK CHORUS: Uncle Peck—what are you doing?
PECK: Keep driving. [*He slips his hands under her blouse.*]
TEENAGE GREEK CHORUS: Uncle Peck—please don't do this—
PECK: —Just a moment longer . . . [PECK *tenses against* LI'L BIT.]
TEENAGE GREEK CHORUS: [*Trying not to cry.*] This isn't happening.

[PECK *tenses more, sharply. He buries his face in Li'l Bit's neck, and moans softly. The.* TEENAGE GREEK CHORUS *exits, and* LI'L BIT *steps out of the car.* PECK, *too, disappears. A Voice reflects.*]

### Driving in Today's World.

LI'L BIT: That day was the last day I lived in my body. I retreated above the neck, and I've lived inside the "fire" in my head ever since.

And now that seems like a long, long time ago. When we were both very young.

And before you know it, I'll be thirty-five. That's getting up there for a woman. And I find myself believing in things that a younger self vowed never to believe in. Things like family and forgiveness.

I know I'm lucky. Although I still have never known what it feels like to jog or dance. Any thing that . . . "jiggles." I do like to watch people on the dance floor, or out on the running paths, just jiggling away. And I say—good for them. [LI'L BIT *moves to the car with pleasure.*]

The nearest sensation I feel—of flight in the body—I guess I feel when I'm driving. On a day like today. It's five A.M. The radio says it's going to be clear and crisp. I've got five hundred miles of highway ahead of me—and some back roads too. I filled the tank last night, and had the oil checked. Checked the tires, too. You've got to treat her . . . with respect.

First thing I do is: Check under the car. To see if any two-year-olds or household cats have crawled beneath, and strategically placed their skulls behind my back tires. [LI'L BIT *crouches.*]

Nope. Then I get in the car. [LI'L BIT *does so.*]

I lock the doors. And turn the key. Then I adjust the most important control on the dashboard—the radio—[LI'L BIT *turns the radio on: We hear all of the Greek Chorus overlapping, and static:*]

FEMALE GREEK CHORUS: [*Overlapping.*]—"You were so tiny you fit in his hand—"
MALE GREEK CHORUS: [*Overlapping.*]—"How is Shakespeare gonna help her lie on her back in the—"
TEENAGE GREEK CHORUS: [*Overlapping.*]—"Am I doing it right?"

[LI'L BIT *fine-tunes the radio station. A song like "Dedicated to the One I Love" or Orbison's "Sweet Dreams" comes on, and cuts off the Greek Chorus.*]

LI'L BIT: Ahh . . . [*Beat.*] I adjust my seat. Fasten my seat belt. Then I check the right side mirror—check the left side. [*She does.*] Finally, I adjust the rearview mirror. [*As* LI'L BIT *adjusts the rearview mirror, a faint light strikes the spirit of* UNCLE PECK, *who is sitting in the back seat of the car. She sees him in the mirror. She smiles at him, and he nods at her. They are happy to be going for a long drive together.* LI'L BIT *slips the car into first gear; to the audience:*] And then—I floor it. [*Sound of a car taking off. Blackout.*]

END OF PLAY

1997

## QUESTIONS

1. *How I Learned to Drive* opens with the line "Sometimes to tell a secret, you first have to teach a lesson." What is the secret in the play, or are there several? What lesson or lessons are taught at the beginning and later? Do lessons usually involve secrets, or instructions in how to keep them? How successful is the play's use of "driver's education" language (printed in boldface type) to punctuate the scenes?
2. The play's stage directions and production notes communicate the playwright's desire that directors have great latitude in staging *How I Learned to Drive*. If you were producing the play, how would you deploy the three-member "Greek Chorus" on stage? How would they be costumed, and what lighting would you use for different scenes? How would you clearly differentiate the various roles of each chorus member?
3. How do the members of L'il Bit's family acquire their nicknames? What does this indicate about the family's history and values? What is the significance of each of the nicknames mentioned in the play?
4. What challenges would be faced by a director and a cast staging a production of *How I Learned to Drive*? What special opportunities does the play present? How would a production share with an audience the information that appears only in stage directions, such as "Greg will become a successful gynecologist" or "The signals are no longer transmitters, but an electromagnetic force"?
5. What are some actual commercial products named in the play? How important is it that the audience recognize these product names? What does the use of these names imply about the relationship between commercial culture and the "artistic culture" of theater? How is this relationship reflected in the theme and plot of the play? Should future productions of the play "update" the product names, or should they be retained as artifacts of the play's own time? Should the songs always be appropriate for L'il Bit's teenage years, or should they be updated along with the products to suggest the experience of contemporary teenagers?
6. Consider the play's device of time-shifting, especially the reverse chronology that takes us back to L'il Bit's very first driving lesson in 1962. Why do you think Vogel chose this method of "backward storytelling" for this play? How does this method mirror the workings of memory? What are some kinds of stories for which reverse chronology would or would not be effective?
7. Is L'il Bit a victim? Is Uncle Peck a villain? How sincere is he when he tells L'il Bit that he loves her? How significant is it that, at each stage of his "lessons," he insists that L'il Bit always has the choice to stop or proceed? Does this exonerate him to any degree? How responsible is L'il Bit for the choices she makes throughout the play?
8. In one scene L'il Bit says that "the most important thing to have control of on the inside of the car" is the radio. What is the role of music in *How I Learned to Drive*—that is, how is music used to establish the play's setting, tone, and theme?

## SUGGESTIONS FOR WRITING

1. In printed form, a play like August Wilson's *The Piano Lesson* is a bare script; the stage directions are minimal. Some playwrights, though, seem to consider readers as part of a play's audience; Tennessee Williams, for instance, paid attention to the "literary" style of the stage directions in *A Streetcar Named Desire,* and George Bernard Shaw's *Pygmalion* contains a great deal of material solely for readers, especially the lengthy prose afterword. Does *How I Learned to Drive* seem to have been written more for "stage or page"? Write an essay in which you explore the different ways of considering plays, as theatrical scripts or as literary artifacts, and the advantages of either way.

2. Is it too simplistic to say that *How I Learned to Drive* is a play about sexual abuse? To what extent does L'il Bit feel abused by Uncle Peck? Are there degrees of "abuse"? How are we to understand the scene in the bus in 1979, when L'il Bit picks up the high-school senior, calling herself "the translator, the teacher, the epicure"—has she become an abuser herself? Write an essay in which you examine the moral subtleties of *How I Learned to Drive.* Does the play offer any clear "lessons" about right and wrong in sexual politics?

3. Think about the three depictions of marriage in the play: L'il Bit's grandparents, her parents, and her Aunt Mary and Uncle Peck. What do they have in common? How do they relate to the play's themes of sexual desire, abuse, and initiation? Write an essay in which you discuss the different kinds of sexual relationships depicted in the play and how these are used to create the context for L'il Bit's relationship with Uncle Peck. In the moral world of Vogel's play, what would an "ideal" marriage be like?

4. *How I Learned to Drive* is, in many ways, a highly artificial play: it skips around chronologically, mainly going backward; it makes extensive use of "stagy" effects like the Greek Choruses, slide shows, and recorded music; actors play multiple roles and sometimes address the audience directly. Given all these contrivances, does *How I Learned to Drive* convey convincing characters involved in a traditional plot of rising action, climax, and falling action? Write an essay in which you explore the play's methods of presenting its underlying story and discuss whether these methods increase or decrease audience sympathy for the characters and their situation.

# Exploring Contexts

## 28   THE AUTHOR'S WORK AS CONTEXT: WILLIAM SHAKESPEARE

When we read, we inevitably compare. We compare the writer's style to the styles of other writers; we compare characters within a story or play to one another and to people we know; we compare our life experiences to the many imaginary experiences that unfold before us as we read. Our interpretations of literature are fueled by such comparisons.

Reading several works by a single author is one of the most rewarding and enlightening types of comparison we can employ as active readers of literature. Such comparisons serve a variety of purposes: they help us develop a sense of the overall shape of the writer's work (that is, the writer's **oeuvre**, or **canon**); they reveal the kinds of characters, plots, and dramatic situations the author likes to create; they offer a glimpse into the author's particular way of looking at the world. At the same time, such comparisons can enrich our understanding of any one work by drawing our attention to features we might not have thought much about otherwise.

This chapter offers you the opportunity to compare two plays by one of history's most vital and versatile playwrights: William Shakespeare. Shakespeare is a particularly enticing subject for this kind of comparative study in part because we know so little about him. While we can facilitate and enhance our reading of many writers by studying the letters, essays, diaries, and other documents in which the writers comment directly on their lives and works, Shakespeare left behind no such record. The only records that exist are official ones—marriage licenses, property deeds, and wills.

William Shakespeare

Those records tell a brief story. Shakespeare's origins were humble: his grandfather, Richard, rented the land he farmed, near Stratford-upon-Avon, a market town in the English midlands. Richard's son, John, married the daughter of one of Richard's former landlords and moved to town. There he became a tradesman prosperous and respected enough to buy quite a bit of property and to hold several civic offices, includ-

Shakespeare's birthplace

ing that of mayor. The family's star was on the rise by the time William was born (sometime in April 1564). Though most likely neither of Shakespeare's parents could read or write (certainly they had no formal schooling), his father's involvement in city government brought with it the privilege of enrolling William in the local free grammar school. Here Shakespeare learned how to read and write, not only in English but also in Latin and perhaps Greek. His schoolmasters also probably required him to read such standard classical works as Ovid's *Metamorphoses* and the plays of Plautus and Terence (which greatly influenced the plays he would later write). In 1582, Shakespeare married Anne Hathaway, the daughter of a local farmer; in the next three years, the couple had three children, including a set of twins.

> *Life's but a walking shadow,*
> *a poor player*
> *That struts and frets his*
> *hour upon the stage,*
> *And then is heard no*
> *more....*
> —SHAKESPEARE

From the time of the twins' birth in 1585 until 1592, Shakespeare's life becomes—for us—a blank: all we know is that by the latter date he was a successful actor and playwright spending most of his time in London. (We know this, in part, because Shakespeare was prominent enough to be called an "upstart crow" in a book published by a rival playwright in 1592; apparently, this London-born, university-educated author felt a bit threatened by the undereducated provincial.) Though, in 1594, the "upstart crow" achieved a measure of renown as a poet by publishing two lengthy narrative poems (*Venus and Adonis* and *The Rape of Lucrece*), his career from this time until his death centered mainly on his work with the Lord Chamberlain's (later King's) Men—one of the two most prominent acting companies of his day. Shakespeare's work with the company was multifaceted: an actor with the troupe and its chief dramatist, he was also a shareholder who helped manage the troupe's affairs (including the building of the Globe Theater, on the South Bank of the Thames River, in 1599).

Being a shareholder ensured that he prospered along with the company (especially after they secured the patronage of the king in 1603). As a result, Shakespeare enjoyed a level of economic prosperity and a kind of status that wouldn't have been possible to a mere actor, playwright, or poet. The Crown granted Shakespeare's father (and thus the playwright) the title of "gentleman" in the late 1590s. And at his death in 1616, Shakespeare left his family substantial property in both London and Stratford (where the family had continued to live).

The Globe Theater

Such facts remind us that Shakespeare was, after all, a real and in some ways rather ordinary person—who ultimately convinced audiences and rivals alike that he was more than an "upstart crow," but who did not, as a recent biographer reminds us, "in his own day inspire the mysterious veneration that afterwards came to surround him." These mundane facts tell us almost nothing, however, about the man's or the artist's inner life—his personal opinions, his motives, his loves, his dislikes, his politics, his "philosophy." These we can only infer, guess at, or imagine by reading and comparing his plays and poems. Luckily, Shakespeare left us a lot of these, including 154 sonnets (some of which are included in the poetry section of this book) and at least thirty-eight plays. (Scholars believe Shakespeare co-wrote at least one more play, and others may yet be discovered and authenticated.)

Given that the plays include thirteen comedies, ten tragedies, ten English histories, and five romances, variety is a distinctive feature of Shakespeare's work as a playwright. It is fitting, then, that the two plays included in this chapter—*A Midsummer Night's Dream* and *Hamlet*—seem, at first glance, so different. *A Midsummer Night's Dream*, written in about 1595, is generally considered one of the last of Shakespeare's "apprentice" plays—the work of a young writer just beginning to find his own voice and dramatic style, but still quite dependent on classical models. Though written only a few years later (ca. 1599-1601), *Hamlet* is nonetheless regarded as one of the greatest works of a seasoned writer. Differences proliferate: *Dream*, a comedy, culminates in marriage (several marriages, in fact); *Hamlet*, a tragedy, concludes with the death and destruction of an entire royal family. *Dream* is among Shakespeare's shortest plays; *Hamlet*, among his longest. *Hamlet* focuses squarely—almost relentlessly—on its title character, whom we leave the play feeling that we know inside and out. *Dream*, in contrast, flits among many characters. Though we may fall in love with some of them, we probably will not feel that we truly know them. (Indeed, part of the play's humor comes from our having as hard a time as the characters themselves do remembering who is who and who loves whom.)

But while the plays have important and revealing differences, they have equally significant similarities, and by attending to these similarities we may come to understand and appreciate Shakespeare's particular way of looking at the world. To begin with, we may approach such similarities (within these or any plays) by concentrating on their basic elements, looking for patterns in character, setting, structure, tone, and theme (remembering, of course, that these elements ultimately combine to shape our experience of any one play).

In thinking about character, for example, notice that both the protagonists and the antagonists of *A Midsummer Night's Dream* and *Hamlet* are persons of high birth and position. These characters' choices and behavior deeply affect the communities that they lead. In fact, both plays repeatedly remind us of the general effects and communal significance of such characters' actions, as when, for example, we are told in *A Midsummer Night's Dream* of the "progeny of evils" that come of the "debate" and "dissension" between Titania and Oberon (2.1.115–16). Like all Shakespeare's plays, this comedy and tragedy both take for granted the idea that "on [a leader's] choice depends / The safety and health of th[e] whole state" (*Hamlet* 1.3.20–21), and both trace the effects of the particular, often bad, choices made by kings, princes, and dukes.

Shakespeare and his contemporaries often compared the relationship between a king and his subjects to that between a father and his children or between a husband and his wife. For example, an early Shakespeare comedy, *The Taming of the Shrew*, concludes with a speech in which the tamed shrew declares, "Thy husband is thy lord, thy life, thy keeper, / Thy head, thy sovereign." Building on this idea, she argues both that a woman's duty to her husband is the same "as the subject owes the prince" and that a woman who refuses to obey her husband is exactly like "a foul contending rebel / And graceless traitor." We can see similar analogies at work in *A Midsummer Night's Dream* and *Hamlet*: one begins with a duke and a father provoking a group of young Athenians to rebel against them; the other shows us a son who is also a prince struggling to choose the right response to the murder of a father who was also a king.

We pay attention to the effects of these high-born characters on their environments in part because Shakespeare's plays also include characters who occupy positions much lower on the social scale than the main characters do. In addition to Titania, Oberon, Theseus, and Hippolyta (rulers of the divine and human realms), *A Midsummer Night's Dream* introduces us to the Athenian craftsmen (or "mechanicals") led by the fittingly named Bottom. And while *Hamlet* focuses predominantly on members of the Danish royal court, one of the most memorable scenes in the play features a lowly gravedigger and the skeletal remains of a court jester named Yorick. As a result, the two plays demonstrate Shakespeare's tendency to people his plays with a socially diverse cast of characters and to thereby create a socially inclusive dramatic world.

As inclusive as Shakespeare's dramatic world is, it is far from *democratic* (as the speech from *The Taming of the Shrew* suggests). As you read more plays by Shakespeare, you will probably become more attuned to the different ways in which they depict "high" and "low" characters. *A Midsummer Night's Dream* is typical, for example, in the way it associates socially low characters with **low** or **physical comedy** (as opposed to **high** or **verbal comedy**). Bottom, after all, wears an ass's head for much of the play. Yet Bottom is also typical of Shakespeare's socially humble characters because he possesses a kind of wisdom lacking in his social betters. Certainly, he has more imagination and a much greater appreciation of art's power than Duke Theseus, who refuses to believe in "fables," thinks lovers and poets are no better than madmen (5.1.3-6), and rather heartlessly ridicules the mechanicals' creative efforts.

Despite the tendency to distinguish high from low, then, Shakespearean drama draws our attention to fundamental human experiences that cut across social lines. *A Midsummer Night's Dream* reminds us that a fairy queen is no more immune to love's magic or foolishness than the lowliest of mortals; *Hamlet*, that a king's life lasts no longer than a court jester's. The joys of love, the pain of death—these experiences link us and remind us of our common humanity.

Shakespeare suggests such links, in part, by structuring each play so that the main plot is complemented by parallel, yet often contrasting, secondary plots. *A Midsummer Night's Dream* offers at least four plots, each featuring a pair of lovers whose happiness is, or has been, threatened by their own failures to understand each other or by others' opposition to their relationship. *Hamlet* revolves around three intersecting, but distinct, plots featuring Hamlet, Laertes, and Fortinbras—three very different young men who must each figure out how to respond to, and perhaps avenge, his father's murder. In these, as in other Shakespeare plays, the secondary plots can be divided into **underplots**, which are romantic or parodic versions of the main plot, and **overplots**, which foreground its political dimensions. In *A Midsummer Night's Dream,* Bottom becomes the protagonist of the underplot, Theseus and Hippolyta (and, perhaps, Titania and Oberon) of the overplot(s). In *Hamlet,* the underplot focuses on Laertes; the overplot, on Fortinbras. However, all the secondary plots encourage us (and sometimes, as in *Hamlet,* the characters themselves) to compare the way different people handle similar situations and thus to evaluate various choices, various responses. The parallel plots serve simultaneously as a structural device, a potent means of characterization, and a way of drawing our attention to general issues and themes.

Bottom, from *A Midsummer Night's Dream*

Reading *Hamlet* and *A Midsummer Night's Dream* side by side may also help us appreciate the tonal complexity of Shakespeare's plays—their incorporation of both comic and tragic elements. While *A Midsummer Night's Dream* plunges us into a nighttime world dominated by the intertwining forces of magic, love, and humor, it also continually reminds us of the dangerous aspects of the night, of the struggles that human beings endure in their pursuit of love and happiness, of the brevity and fragility of human joy and human

*Shakespeare's plays are not in the rigorous critical sense either tragedies or comedies, but compositions of a distinct kind; exhibiting the real state of sublunary nature, which partakes of good and evil, joy and sorrow.*
—SAMUEL JOHNSON

Sir Laurence Olivier as Hamlet

life, of what Hamlet calls the "thousand natural shocks / That flesh is heir to" (3.1.62–63). The specter of death hovers in the background of *A Midsummer Night's Dream* as surely as it occupies the foreground of *Hamlet*. And while *Hamlet*, like most tragedies, focuses primarily on mortality, violence, and time's destructive force, it also shows us the comic side of the human condition. In fact, one of the things that makes Hamlet such a sympathetic character is his sense of humor; he proves so adept at wordplay that we wish he could stick to that instead of resorting to swordplay.

Turning from tone to theme, we find that both *Hamlet* and *A Midsummer Night's Dream* say something about the order of things and the rhythm of life. Although *Hamlet* ends with a body-strewn stage, the play encourages us to see those deaths as the necessary prelude to a restoration of order and health to a kingdom diseased and disordered as a result of a sovereign's choices. For Claudius's crimes ultimately infect and poison everything and everyone, even innocent bystanders like Ophelia. Both to us and to Hamlet, Claudius's reign represents the triumph of humanity's worst impulses. By embracing his role as heaven's "scourge and minister" even at the risk of his own life (3.4.179–81), however, Hamlet reaffirms our faith in humanity's noblest qualities as he strives to set right all that is "rotten in Denmark" (1.4.90). In *A Midsummer Night's Dream*, we again see the actions of a sovereign turn the world upside down: the young rebel against the old, women chase men, old friends turn on each other, an ass consorts with a queen. Clearly, the kinds of dissension and disorder at work in *A Midsummer Night's Dream* make us laugh, while those in *Hamlet* make us cringe or cry. Yet the rhythm of both plays turns out to be surprisingly similar, tracing the movement from disorder to order, from dissension to harmony. In the process, both plays ask us to think about the nature and causes of social, political, and moral disorder, of dissension within states and families.

> [W]hen you are really reading **Hamlet**, the action and the characters are not something which you conceive apart from the words; you apprehend them . . . in the words, and the words are expressions of them.
> 
> —A. C. BRADLEY

As you read *Hamlet* and *A Midsummer Night's Dream*, you will discover many more parallels of theme, character, setting, and structure whose significance you will want to ponder and investigate. But you may also want to think about another, perhaps more elusive element: language. Shakespeare is justly celebrated for his use of language, and we pay homage to it, unwittingly or not, every time we use any one of the many idiomatic expressions that originated in the plays. (If, for example, you conclude that Shakespeare is "Greek to me," you have proven otherwise by quoting directly from his play *Julius Caesar*.) In Shakespearean drama, language is never an end in itself but instead establishes character and tone, structures the play, shapes our emotional response to it, and enunciates theme. *Hamlet*, for example, characterizes both Polonius and Hamlet in part through their penchant for wordplay. But as Polonius suggests, Hamlet's wordplay is "pregnant" with significance in a way that his own is not (2.2.201). While Polonius's use of language arguably demonstrates both his facile nature and his fondness for sham and trickery, Hamlet's displays his preoccupation with probing beneath the surface of language and much else.

In both *Hamlet* and *A Midsummer Night's Dream* the musical and visual qualities of Shakespeare's language are integral to its meaning. Though written mainly in verse, Shakespeare's plays include prose passages; and though most of the poetry is **blank verse** (unrhymed iambic pentameter), Shakespeare also uses rhyme and rhythmic variation to great effect. As you read the plays, then, you will want to pay attention to the texture and rhythm of the language—to the effect of *sound* on *sense*. You will also want to attend to the way Shakespeare uses language to appeal to your eye, as well as your ear. For visual imagery, like sound, consistently serves both structural and thematic ends, linking various moments and ideas, actions and themes. In *A Midsummer Night's Dream*, for example, characters frequently refer to their eyes. Such references begin in the very first scene: when Hermia wishes that her father "look'd but with my eyes," Theseus responds that "your eyes must with his judgment look" (lines 56–57). These lines prepare us for a drama in which eyes will play a major part, in which love and vision tend to go hand in hand, in which both love and vision often conflict with "judgment." Oberon's love potion, after all, works through the eyes, while Puck initially misapplies the potion largely because his eyes have deceived him. The characters' talk of eyes thus connects directly to the plot; through both, the play asks us to think about the tremendous power of vision and the dangers of relying on it.

Reading many plays by a single playwright will help you better recognize stylistic as well as structural and thematic patterns within each play: each additional Shakespeare play you read will bring you closer to an understanding and appreciation of his unique way of looking at the world and of the way his views and his technique changed over time. You will gain a sense of Shakespeare's development as a dramatist even as, ideally, you develop your own skills as a reader of drama.

# WILLIAM SHAKESPEARE

## *A Midsummer Night's Dream*[1]

### CHARACTERS

THESEUS, *Duke of Athens*
EGEUS, *father to Hermia*
LYSANDER,  ⎫
DEMETRIUS, ⎭ *in love with Hermia*
PHILOSTRATE, *Master of the Revels to Theseus*
QUINCE, *a carpenter*
SNUG, *a joiner*
BOTTOM, *a weaver*
FLUTE, *a bellows-maker*
SNOUT, *a tinker*
STARVELING, *a tailor*
Other FAIRIES *attending their king and queen*
ATTENDANTS *on Theseus and Hippolyta*

HIPPOLYTA, *Queen of the Amazons, betrothed to Theseus*
HERMIA, *daughter to Egeus, in love with Lysander*
HELENA, *in love with Demetrius*
OBERON, *King of the Fairies*
TITANIA, *Queen of the Fairies*
PUCK, *or Robin Goodfellow*
PEASEBLOSSOM, ⎫
COBWEB, ⎬ *fairies*
MOTH, ⎪
MUSTARDSEED ⎭

SCENE: *Athens, and a wood near it.*

## ACT I

### Scene 1[2]

*Enter* THESEUS, HIPPOLYTA, PHILOSTRATE, *with others.*

THESEUS: Now, fair Hippolyta, our nuptial hour
Draws on apace. Four happy days bring in
Another moon; but, O, methinks, how slow
This old moon wanes! She lingers[3] my desires,
5   Like to a step-dame or a dowager[4]
Long withering out a young man's revenue.
HIPPOLYTA: Four days will quickly steep themselves in night,
Four nights will quickly dream away the time;
And then the moon, like to a silver bow
10  New-bent in heaven, shall behold the night
Of our solemnities.
THESEUS:                Go, Philostrate,
Stir up the Athenian youth to merriments,
Awake the pert and nimble spirit of mirth,
Turn melancholy forth to funerals;

---

1. Edited and annotated by David Bevington (except footnotes set in brackets).
2. Location: Athens. The palace of Theseus.   3. Lengthens, protracts.
4. Widow with a jointure or dower. *Step-dame:* stepmother.

The pale companion is not for our pomp.⁵ [*Exit* PHILOSTRATE.]
Hippolyta, I woo'd thee with my sword,⁶
And won thy love doing thee injuries;
But I will wed thee in another key,
With pomp, with triumph,⁷ and with reveling.

[*Enter* EGEUS *and his daughter* HERMIA, *and* LYSANDER, *and* DEMETRIUS.]

EGEUS: Happy be Theseus, our renowned Duke!
THESEUS: Thanks, good Egeus. What's the news with thee?
EGEUS: Full of vexation come I, with complaint
    Against my child, my daughter Hermia.
    Stand forth, Demetrius. My noble lord,
    This man hath my consent to marry her.
    Stand forth, Lysander. And, my gracious Duke,
    This man hath bewitch'd the bosom of my child.
    Thou, thou, Lysander, thou hast given her rhymes
    And interchang'd love-tokens with my child.
    Thou hast by moonlight at her window sung
    With feigning⁸ voice verses of feigning love,
    And stol'n the impression of her fantasy⁹
    With bracelets of thy hair, rings, gauds, conceits,¹
    Knacks,² trifles, nosegays, sweetmeats—messengers
    Of strong prevailment in unhardened youth.
    With cunning hast thou filch'd my daughter's heart,
    Turn'd her obedience, which is due to me,
    To stubborn harshness. And, my gracious Duke,
    Be it so she will not here before your Grace
    Consent to marry with Demetrius,
    I beg the ancient privilege of Athens:
    As she is mine, I may dispose of her,
    Which shall be either to this gentleman
    Or to her death, according to our law
    Immediately³ provided in that case.
THESEUS: What say you, Hermia? Be advis'd, fair maid.
    To you your father should be as a god—
    One that compos'd your beauties, yea, and one
    To whom you are but as a form in wax
    By him imprinted and within his power
    To leave the figure or disfigure⁴ it.
    Demetrius is a worthy gentleman.
HERMIA: So is Lysander.
THESEUS:             In himself he is;

---

5. Ceremonial magnificence. *Companion:* fellow.
6. That is, in a military engagement against the Amazons, when Hippolyta was taken captive.
7. Public festivity.    8. (1) Counterfeiting; (2) faining, desirous.
9. Made her fall in love with you (imprinting your image on her imagination) by stealthy and dishonest means.    1. Fanciful trifles. *Gauds:* playthings.    2. Knickknacks.    3. Expressly.
4. Obliterate. *Leave:* that is, leave unaltered.

        But in this kind, wanting your father's voice,[5]
55    The other must be held the worthier.
    HERMIA: I would my father look'd but with my eyes.
    THESEUS: Rather your eyes must with his judgment look.
    HERMIA: I do entreat your Grace to pardon me.
        I know not by what power I am made bold,
60    Nor how it may concern[6] my modesty,
        In such a presence here to plead my thoughts;
        But I beseech your Grace that I may know
        The worst that may befall me in this case,
        If I refuse to wed Demetrius.
65   THESEUS: Either to die the death, or to abjure
        Forever the society of men.
        Therefore, fair Hermia, question your desires,
        Know of your youth, examine well your blood,[7]
        Whether, if you yield not to your father's choice,
70    You can endure the livery[8] of a nun,
        For aye to be in shady cloister mew'd,[9]
        To live a barren sister all your life,
        Chanting faint hymns to the cold fruitless moon.
        Thrice blessed they that master so their blood
75    To undergo such maiden pilgrimage;
        But earthlier happy[1] is the rose distill'd,
        Than that which withering on the virgin thorn
        Grows, lives, and dies in single blessedness.
    HERMIA: So will I grow, so live, so die, my lord,
80    Ere I will yield my virgin patent[2] up
        Unto his lordship, whose unwished yoke
        My soul consents not to give sovereignty.
    THESEUS: Take time to pause; and, by the next new moon—
        The sealing-day betwixt my love and me,
85    For everlasting bond of fellowship—
        Upon that day either prepare to die
        For disobedience to your father's will,
        Or[3] else to wed Demetrius, as he would,
        Or on Diana's altar to protest[4]
90    For aye austerity and single life.
    DEMETRIUS: Relent, sweet Hermia, and, Lysander, yield
        Thy crazed[5] title to my certain right.
    LYSANDER: You have her father's love, Demetrius;
        Let me have Hermia's. Do you marry him.
95   EGEUS: Scornful Lysander! True, he hath my love,
        And what is mine my love shall render him.
        And she is mine, and all my right of her
        I do estate unto[6] Demetrius.

---

5. Approval. *Kind:* respect. *Wanting:* lacking.   6. Befit.   7. Passions.   8. Habit.
9. Shut in (said of a hawk, poultry, and so on). *Aye:* ever.   1. Happier as respects this world.
2. Privilege.   3. Either.   4. Vow.   5. Cracked, unsound.   6. Settle or bestow upon.

LYSANDER: I am, my lord, as well deriv'd[7] as he,
  As well possess'd;[8] my love is more than his;
  My fortunes every way as fairly[9] rank'd,
  If not with vantage,[1] as Demetrius';
  And, which is more than all these boasts can be,
  I am belov'd of beauteous Hermia.
  Why should not I then prosecute my right?
  Demetrius, I'll avouch it to his head,[2]
  Made love to Nedar's daughter, Helena,
  And won her soul; and she, sweet lady, dotes,
  Devoutly dotes, dotes in idolatry,
  Upon this spotted[3] and inconstant man.
THESEUS: I must confess that I have heard so much,
  And with Demetrius thought to have spoke thereof;
  But, being over-full of self-affairs,
  My mind did lose it. But, Demetrius, come,
  And come, Egeus, you shall go with me;
  I have some private schooling for you both.
  For you, fair Hermia, look you arm[4] yourself
  To fit your fancies[5] to your father's will;
  Or else the law of Athens yields you up—
  Which by no means we may extenuate[6]—
  To death, or to a vow of single life.
  Come, my Hippolyta. What cheer, my love?
  Demetrius and Egeus, go[7] along.
  I must employ you in some business
  Against[8] our nuptial, and confer with you
  Of something nearly that[9] concerns yourselves.
EGEUS: With duty and desire we follow you.

  [*Exeunt (all but* LYSANDER *and* HERMIA*).*]

LYSANDER: How now, my love, why is your cheek so pale?
  How chance the roses there do fade so fast?
HERMIA: Belike[1] for want of rain, which I could well
  Beteem[2] them from the tempest of my eyes.
LYSANDER: Ay me! For aught that I could ever read,
  Could ever hear by tale or history,
  The course of true love never did run smooth;
  But either it was different in blood[3]—
HERMIA: O cross,[4] too high to be enthrall'd to low!
LYSANDER: Or else misgraffed[5] in respect of years—
HERMIA: O spite, too old to be engag'd to young!
LYSANDER: Or else it stood upon the choice of friends[6]—
HERMIA: O hell, to choose love by another's eyes!
LYSANDER: Or, if there were a sympathy in choice,

---

7. Descended; that is, as well born.   8. Endowed with wealth.   9. Handsomely.   1. Superiority.
2. That is, face.   3. That is, morally stained.   4. Take care you prepare.   5. Likings, thoughts of love.
6. Mitigate.   7. That is, come.   8. In preparation for.   9. That closely.   1. Very likely.
2. Grant, afford.   3. Hereditary station.   4. Vexation.   5. Ill grafted, badly matched.   6. Relatives.

    War, death, or sickness did lay siege to it,
    Making it momentany[7] as a sound,
    Swift as a shadow, short as any dream,
145  Brief as the lightning in the collied[8] night,
    That, in a spleen, unfolds[9] both heaven and earth,
    And ere a man hath power to say "Behold!"
    The jaws of darkness do devour it up.
    So quick bright things come to confusion.[1]
150 HERMIA: If then true lovers have been ever cross'd,[2]
    It stands as an edict in destiny.
    Then let us teach our trial patience,[3]
    Because it is a customary cross,
    As due to love as thoughts and dreams and sighs,
155  Wishes and tears, poor fancy's[4] followers.
  LYSANDER: A good persuasion. Therefore, hear me, Hermia.
    I have a widow aunt, a dowager
    Of great revenue, and she hath no child.
    From Athens is her house remote seven leagues;
160  And she respects[5] me as her only son.
    There, gentle Hermia, may I marry thee,
    And to that place the sharp Athenian law
    Cannot pursue us. If thou lovest me, then,
    Steal forth thy father's house tomorrow night;
165  And in the wood, a league without the town,
    Where I did meet thee once with Helena
    To do observance to a morn of May,[6]
    There will I stay for thee.
  HERMIA:      My good Lysander!
    I swear to thee, by Cupid's strongest bow,
170  By his best arrow[7] with the golden head,
    By the simplicity of Venus' doves,[8]
    By that which knitteth souls and prospers loves,
    And by that fire which burn'd the Carthage queen,
    When the false Troyan[9] under sail was seen,
175  By all the vows that ever men have broke,
    In number more than ever women spoke,
    In that same place thou hast appointed me
    Tomorrow truly will I meet with thee.
  LYSANDER: Keep promise, love. Look, here comes Helena.

---

7. Lasting but a moment.   8. Blackened (as with coal dust), darkened.
9. Discloses. *In a spleen:* in a swift impulse, in a violent flash.
1. Ruin. *Quick:* quickly; or, perhaps, living, alive.   2. Always thwarted.
3. That is, teach ourselves patience in this trial.   4. Amorous passion's.   5. Regards.
6. Perform the ceremonies of May Day.
7. [Cupid's best gold-pointed arrows were supposed to induce love; his blunt leaden arrows, aversion.]
8. That is, those that drew Venus's chariot. *Simplicity:* innocence.
9. [Dido, queen of Carthage, immolated herself on a funeral pyre after having been deserted by the Trojan hero Aeneas.]

[*Enter* HELENA.]

HERMIA: God speed fair[1] Helena, whither away?
HELENA: Call you me fair? That fair again unsay.
    Demetrius loves your fair. O happy fair![2]
    Your eyes are lodestars, and your tongue's sweet air[3]
    More tuneable[4] than lark to shepherd's ear
    When wheat is green, when hawthorn buds appear.
    Sickness is catching. O, were favor[5] so,
    Yours would I catch, fair Hermia, ere I go;
    My ear should catch your voice, my eye your eye,
    My tongue should catch your tongue's sweet melody.
    Were the world mine, Demetrius being bated,[6]
    The rest I'd give to be to you translated.[7]
    O, teach me how you look, and with what art
    You sway the motion[8] of Demetrius' heart.
HERMIA: I frown upon him, yet he loves me still.
HELENA: O that your frowns would teach my smiles such skill!
HERMIA: I give him curses, yet he gives me love.
HELENA: O that my prayers could such affection move![9]
HERMIA: The more I hate, the more he follows me.
HELENA: The more I love, the more he hateth me.
HERMIA: His folly, Helena, is no fault of mine.
HELENA: None, but your beauty. Would that fault were mine!
HERMIA: Take comfort. He no more shall see my face.
    Lysander and myself will fly this place.
    Before the time I did Lysander see,
    Seem'd Athens as a paradise to me.
    O, then, what graces in my love do dwell,
    That he hath turn'd a heaven unto a hell!
LYSANDER: Helen, to you our minds we will unfold.
    Tomorrow night, when Phoebe[1] doth behold
    Her silver visage in the wat'ry glass,[2]
    Decking with liquid pearl the bladed grass,
    A time that lovers' flights doth still[3] conceal,
    Through Athens' gates have we devis'd to steal.
HERMIA: And in the wood, where often you and I
    Upon faint[4] primrose beds were wont to lie,
    Emptying our bosoms of their counsel[5] sweet,
    There my Lysander and myself shall meet;
    And thence from Athens turn away our eyes,
    To seek new friends and stranger companies.
    Farewell, sweet playfellow. Pray thou for us,

---

1. Fair-complexioned (a fair complexion was generally regarded by the Elizabethans as more beautiful than a dark complexion).    2. Lucky fair one! *Fair:* beauty (even though Hermia is dark-complexioned).    3. Music. *Lodestars:* guiding stars.    4. Tuneful, melodious.    5. Appearance, looks.    6. Excepted.    7. Transformed.    8. Impulse.    9. Arouse. *Affection:* passion.    1. Diana, the moon.    2. Mirror.    3. Always.    4. Pale.    5. Secret thought.

And good luck grant thee thy Demetrius!
Keep word, Lysander. We must starve our sight
From lovers' food till morrow deep midnight.
LYSANDER: I will, my Hermia. [*Exit* HERMIA.]
    Helena, adieu.
225 As you on him, Demetrius dote on you! [*Exit.*]
HELENA: How happy some o'er other some can be!⁶
Through Athens I am thought as fair as she.
But what of that? Demetrius thinks not so;
He will not know what all but he do know.
230 And as he errs, doting on Hermia's eyes,
So I, admiring of⁷ his qualities.
Things base and vile, holding no quantity,⁸
Love can transpose to form and dignity.
Love looks not with the eyes, but with the mind,
235 And therefore is wing'd Cupid painted blind.
Nor hath Love's mind of any judgment taste;⁹
Wings, and no eyes, figure¹ unheedy haste.
And therefore is Love said to be a child,
Because in choice he is so oft beguil'd.
240 As waggish boys in game² themselves forswear,
So the boy Love is perjur'd everywhere.
For ere Demetrius look'd on Hermia's eyne,³
He hail'd down oaths that he was only mine;
And when this hail some heat from Hermia felt,
245 So he dissolv'd, and show'rs of oaths did melt.
I will go tell him of fair Hermia's flight.
Then to the wood will he tomorrow night
Pursue her; and for this intelligence⁴
If I have thanks, it is a dear expense.⁵
250 But herein mean I to enrich my pain,
To have his sight thither and back again. [*Exit.*]

## Scene 2⁶

*Enter* QUINCE *the Carpenter, and* SNUG *the Joiner, and* BOTTOM *the Weaver, and* FLUTE *the Bellows-mender, and* SNOUT *the Tinker, and* STARVELING *the Tailor.*

QUINCE: Is all our company here?
BOTTOM: You were best to call them generally,⁷ man by man, according to the scrip.⁸
QUINCE: Here is the scroll of every man's name which is thought fit, through
5    all Athens, to play in our interlude before the Duke and the Duchess on his wedding-day at night.

---

6. Can be in comparison to some others.   7. Wondering at.   8. That is, unsubstantial, unshapely.
9. That is, nor has Love, which dwells in the fancy or imagination, any taste or least bit of judgment or reason.   1. Are a symbol of.   2. Sport, jest.   3. Eyes (old form of plural).   4. Information.
5. That is, a trouble worth taking. *Dear:* costly.   6. Location: Athens. Quince's house (?).
7. [Bottom's blunder for *individually.*]   8. Script, written list.

BOTTOM: First, good Peter Quince, say what the play treats on, then read the names of the actors, and so grow to[9] a point.
QUINCE: Marry,[1] our play is "The most lamentable comedy and most cruel death of Pyramus and Thisby."
BOTTOM: A very good piece of work, I assure you, and a merry. Now, good Peter Quince, call forth your actors by the scroll. Masters, spread yourselves.
QUINCE: Answer as I call you. Nick Bottom, the weaver.
BOTTOM: Ready. Name what part I am for, and proceed.
QUINCE: You, Nick Bottom, are set down for Pyramus.
BOTTOM: What is Pyramus? A lover, or a tyrant?
QUINCE: A lover, that kills himself most gallant for love.
BOTTOM: That will ask some tears in the true performing of it. If I do it, let the audience look to their eyes. I will move storms; I will condole[2] in some measure. To the rest—yet my chief humor[3] is for a tyrant. I could play Ercles rarely, or a part to tear a cat in, to make all split.[4]

> "The raging rocks
> And shivering shocks
> Shall break the locks
>     Of prison gates;
> And Phibbus' car[5]
> Shall shine from far
> And make and mar
>     The foolish Fates."

This was lofty! Now name the rest of the players. This is Ercles' vein, a tyrant's vein. A lover is more condoling.
QUINCE: Francis Flute, the bellows-mender.
FLUTE: Here, Peter Quince.
QUINCE: Flute, you must take Thisby on you.
FLUTE: What is Thisby? A wand'ring knight?
QUINCE: It is the lady that Pyramus must love.
FLUTE: Nay, faith, let not me play a woman. I have a beard coming.
QUINCE: That's all one.[6] You shall play it in a mask, and you may speak as small[7] as you will.
BOTTOM: An[8] I may hide my face, let me play Thisby too. I'll speak in a monstrous little voice, "Thisne, Thisne!" "Ah, Pyramus, my lover dear! Thy Thisby dear, and lady dear!"
QUINCE: No, no; you must play Pyramus; and, Flute, you Thisby.
BOTTOM: Well, proceed.
QUINCE: Robin Starveling, the tailor.
STARVELING: Here, Peter Quince.
QUINCE: Robin Starveling, you must play Thisby's mother. Tom Snout, the tinker.

---

9. Come to.   1. [A mild oath, originally the name of the Virgin Mary.]   2. Lament, arouse pity.
3. Inclination, whim.
4. That is, cause a stir, bring the house down. *Ercles:* Hercules (the tradition of ranting came from Seneca's *Hercules Furens*). *Tear a cat:* that is, rant.   5. Phoebus's, the sun-god's, chariot.   6. It makes no difference.
7. High-pitched.   8. If.

SNOUT: Here, Peter Quince.

QUINCE: You, Pyramus' father; myself, Thisby's father; Snug, the joiner, you, the lion's part; and I hope here is a play fitted.

SNUG: Have you the lion's part written? Pray you, if it be, give it me, for I am slow of study.

QUINCE: You may do it extempore, for it is nothing but roaring.

BOTTOM: Let me play the lion too. I will roar that I will do any man's heart good to hear me. I will roar that I will make the Duke say, "Let him roar again, let him roar again."

QUINCE: An you should do it too terribly, you would fright the Duchess and the ladies, that they would shriek; and that were enough to hang us all.

ALL: That would hang us, every mother's son.

BOTTOM: I grant you, friends, if you should fright the ladies out of their wits, they would have no more discretion but to hang us; but I will aggravate[9] my voice so that I will roar[1] you as gently as any sucking dove; I will roar you an 'twere any nightingale.

QUINCE: You can play no part but Pyramus; for Pyramus is a sweet-fac'd man, a proper[2] man as one shall see in a summer's day, a most lovely gentlemanlike man. Therefore you must needs play Pyramus.

BOTTOM: Well, I will undertake it. What beard were I best to play it in?

QUINCE: Why, what you will.

BOTTOM: I will discharge it in either your[3] straw-color beard, your orange-tawny beard, your purple-in-grain beard, or your French-crown-color[4] beard, your perfect yellow.

QUINCE: Some of your French crowns[5] have no hair at all, and then you will play barefac'd. But, masters, here are your parts. [*He distributes parts.*] And I am to entreat you, request you, and desire you, to con[6] them by tomorrow night; and meet me in the palace wood, a mile without the town, by moonlight. There will we rehearse; for if we meet in the city, we shall be dogg'd with company, and our devices[7] known. In the meantime I will draw a bill[8] of properties, such as our play wants. I pray you, fail me not.

BOTTOM: We will meet, and there we may rehearse most obscenely[9] and courageously. Take pains, be perfect;[1] adieu.

QUINCE: At the Duke's oak we meet.

BOTTOM: Enough. Hold, or cut bow-strings.[2] [*Exeunt.*]

---

9. [Bottom's blunder for *diminish*.]   1. That is, roar for you.   2. Handsome.
3. That is, you know the kind I mean. *Discharge:* perform.
4. That is, color of a French crown, a gold coin. *Purple-in-grain:* dyed a very deep red (from *grain,* the name applied to the dried insect used to make the dye).   5. Heads bald from syphilis, the "French disease."
6. Learn by heart.   7. Plans.   8. List.
9. [An unintentionally funny blunder, whatever Bottom meant to say.]
1. That is, letter-perfect in memorizing your parts.
2. [An archer's expression not definitely explained, but probably meaning here "keep your promises, or give up the play."]

## ACT II

*Scene 1*[3]

*Enter a* FAIRY *at one door, and Robin Goodfellow (*PUCK*) at another.*

PUCK: How now, spirit! Whither wander you?
FAIRY: Over hill, over dale,
    Thorough[4] bush, thorough brier,
    Over park, over pale,[5]
    Thorough flood, thorough fire,                         5
    I do wander every where,
    Swifter than the moon's sphere;
    And I serve the Fairy Queen,
    To dew her orbs[6] upon the green.
    The cowslips tall her pensioners[7] be.                  10
    In their gold coats spots you see;
    Those be rubies, fairy favors,[8]
    In those freckles live their savors.[9]
I must go seek some dewdrops here
And hang a pearl in every cowslip's ear.                    15
Farewell, thou lob[1] of spirits; I'll be gone.
Our Queen and all her elves come here anon.[2]
PUCK: The King doth keep his revels here tonight.
Take heed the Queen come not within his sight.
For Oberon is passing fell and wrath,[3]                      20
Because that she as her attendant hath
A lovely boy, stolen from an Indian king;
She never had so sweet a changeling.[4]
And jealous Oberon would have the child
Knight of his train, to trace[5] the forests wild.               25
But she perforce[6] withholds the loved boy,
Crowns him with flowers and makes him all her joy.
And now they never meet in grove or green,
By fountain[7] clear, or spangled starlight sheen,
But they do square,[8] that all their elves for fear          30
Creep into acorn-cups and hide them there.
FAIRY: Either I mistake your shape and making quite,
Or else you are that shrewd and knavish sprite[9]
Call'd Robin Goodfellow. Are not you he
That frights the maidens of the villagery,                    35
Skim milk, and sometimes labor in the quern,[1]
And bootless[2] make the breathless huswife churn,
And sometime make the drink to bear no barm,[3]

---

3. Location: a wood near Athens.    4. Through.    5. Enclosure.    6. Circles; that is, fairy rings.
7. Retainers, members of the royal bodyguard.    8. Love tokens.    9. Sweet smells.
1. Country bumpkin.    2. At once.    3. Wrathful. *Fell:* exceedingly angry.
4. Child exchanged for another by the fairies.    5. Range through.    6. Forcibly.    7. Spring.
8. Quarrel.    9. Spirit. *Shrewd:* mischievous.    1. Handmill.    2. In vain.    3. Yeast, head on the ale.

                Mislead night-wanderers, laughing at their harm?
40              Those that Hobgoblin call you and sweet Puck,
                You do their work, and they shall have good luck.
                Are you not he?
        PUCK:           Thou speakest aright;
                I am that merry wanderer of the night.
                I jest to Oberon and make him smile
45              When I a fat and bean-fed horse beguile,
                Neighing in likeness of a filly foal;
                And sometime lurk I in a gossip's[4] bowl,
                In very likeness of a roasted crab,[5]
                And when she drinks, against her lips I bob
50              And on her withered dewlap[6] pour the ale.
                The wisest aunt, telling the saddest[7] tale,
                Sometime for three-foot stool mistaketh me;
                Then slip I from her bum, down topples she,
                And "tailor"[8] cries, and falls into a cough;
55              And then the whole quire[9] hold their hips and laugh,
                And waxen in their mirth and neeze[1] and swear
                A merrier hour was never wasted there.
                But, room, fairy! Here comes Oberon.
        FAIRY: And here my mistress. Would that he were gone!

        [Enter OBERON, *the King of Fairies, at one door, with his train; and* TITANIA, *the Queen, at another, with hers.*]

60      OBERON: Ill met by moonlight, proud Titania.
        TITANIA: What, jealous Oberon? Fairies, skip hence.
                I have forsworn his bed and company.
        OBERON: Tarry, rash wanton.[2] Am not I thy lord?
        TITANIA: Then I must be thy lady; but I know
65              When thou hast stolen away from fairy land,
                And in the shape of Corin[3] sat all day,
                Playing on pipes of corn[4] and versing love
                To amorous Phillida. Why art thou here,
                Come from the farthest steep[5] of India,
70              But that, forsooth, the bouncing Amazon,
                Your buskin'd[6] mistress and your warrior love,
                To Theseus must be wedded, and you come
                To give their bed joy and prosperity.
        OBERON: How canst thou thus for shame, Titania,
75              Glance at my credit with Hippolyta,[7]
                Knowing I know thy love to Theseus?

---

4. Old woman's.   5. Crab apple.   6. Loose skin on neck.   7. Most serious. *Aunt:* old woman.
8. [Possibly because she ends up sitting cross-legged on the floor, looking like a tailor.]   9. Company.
1. Sneeze. *Waxen:* increase.   2. Headstrong creature.
3. Corin and Phillida are conventional names of pastoral lovers.   4. [Here, oat stalks.]
5. Mountain range.   6. Wearing half boots called buskins.
7. Make insinuations about my favored relationship with Hippolyta.

Didst not thou lead him through the glimmering night
From Perigenia,[8] whom he ravished?
And make him with fair Aegles[9] break his faith,
With Ariadne and Antiopa?[1]                                                80
TITANIA: These are the forgeries of jealousy;
And never, since the middle summer's spring,[2]
Met we on hill, in dale, forest, or mead,
By paved fountain or by rushy[3] brook,
Or in the beached margent[4] of the sea,                                    85
To dance our ringlets[5] to the whistling wind,
But with thy brawls thou hast disturb'd our sport.
Therefore the winds, piping to us in vain,
As in revenge, have suck'd up from the sea
Contagious[6] fogs; which falling in the land                                90
Hath every pelting[7] river made so proud
That they have overborne their continents.[8]
The ox hath therefore stretch'd his yoke in vain,
The ploughman lost his sweat, and the green corn[9]
Hath rotted ere his youth attain'd a beard;                                  95
The fold[1] stands empty in the drowned field,
And crows are fatted with the murrion[2] flock;
The nine men's morris[3] is fill'd up with mud,
And the quaint mazes in the wanton[4] green
For lack of tread are undistinguishable.                                    100
The human mortals want their winter[5] here;
No night is now with hymn or carol bless'd.
Therefore[6] the moon, the governess of floods,
Pale in her anger, washes all the air,
That rheumatic[7] diseases do abound.                                       105
And thorough this distemperature[8] we see
The seasons alter: hoary-headed frosts
Fall in the fresh lap of the crimson rose,
And on old Hiems'[9] thin and icy crown
An odorous chaplet of sweet summer buds                                     110

8. That is, Perigouna, one of Theseus's conquests. (This and the following women are named in Thomas North's translation of Plutarch's *Life of Theseus*.)
9. That is, Aegle, for whom Theseus deserted Ariadne, according to some accounts.
1. Queen of the Amazons and wife of Theseus; elsewhere identified with Hippolyta, but here thought of as a separate woman. *Ariadne*: the daughter of Minos, king of Crete, who helped Theseus to escape the labyrinth after killing the Minotaur; later she was abandoned by Theseus.   2. Beginning of midsummer.
3. Bordered with rushes. *Paved*: with pebbled bottom.   4. Edge, border. *In*: on.
5. Dances in a ring. (See *orbs* in 2.1.9.)   6. Noxious.   7. Paltry; or striking, moving forcefully.
8. Banks that contain them.   9. Grain of any kind.   1. Pen for sheep or cattle.
2. Having died of the murrain, plague.
3. That is, portion of the village green marked out in a square for a game played with nine pebbles or pegs.
4. Luxuriant. *Mazes*: that is, intricate paths marked out on the village green to be followed rapidly on foot as a kind of contest.
5. That is, regular winter season; or proper observances of winter, such as the *hymn* or *carol* in the next line. *Want*: lack.   6. That is, as a result of our quarrel.   7. Colds, flu, and other respiratory infections.
8. Disturbance in nature.   9. The winter god's.

         Is, as in mockery, set. The spring, the summer,
         The childing[1] autumn, angry winter, change
         Their wonted liveries, and the mazed[2] world,
         By their increase,[3] now knows not which is which.
115      And this same progeny of evils comes
         From our debate,[4] from our dissension;
         We are their parents and original.[5]
    OBERON: Do you amend it then; it lies in you.
         Why should Titania cross her Oberon?
120      I do but beg a little changeling boy,
         To be my henchman.[6]
    TITANIA:                    Set your heart at rest.
         The fairy land buys not the child of me.
         His mother was a vot'ress of my order,
         And, in the spiced Indian air, by night,
125      Full often hath she gossip'd by my side,
         And sat with me on Neptune's yellow sands,
         Marking th' embarked traders on the flood,[7]
         When we have laugh'd to see the sails conceive
         And grow big-bellied with the wanton[8] wind;
130      Which she, with pretty and with swimming gait,
         Following—her womb then rich with my young squire—
         Would imitate, and sail upon the land
         To fetch me trifles, and return again,
         As from a voyage, rich with merchandise.
135      But she, being mortal, of that boy did die;
         And for her sake do I rear up her boy,
         And for her sake I will not part with him.
    OBERON: How long within this wood intend you stay?
    TITANIA: Perchance till after Theseus' wedding-day.
140      If you will patiently dance in our round[9]
         And see our moonlight revels, go with us;
         If not, shun me, and I will spare[1] your haunts.
    OBERON: Give me that boy, and I will go with thee.
    TITANIA: Not for thy fairy kingdom. Fairies, away!
145      We shall chide downright, if I longer stay.    [*Exeunt* TITANIA *with her train.*]
    OBERON: Well, go thy way. Thou shalt not from[2] this grove
         Till I torment thee for this injury.
         My gentle Puck, come hither. Thou rememb'rest
         Since[3] once I sat upon a promontory,
150      And heard a mermaid on a dolphin's back
         Uttering such dulcet and harmonious breath[4]
         That the rude sea grew civil at her song
         And certain stars shot madly from their spheres,
         To hear the sea-maid's music.

---

1. Fruitful, pregnant.   2. Bewildered. *Liveries:* usual apparel.   3. Their yield, what they produce.
4. Quarrel.   5. Origin.   6. Attendant, page.   7. Flood tide. *Traders:* trading vessels.   8. Sportive.
9. Circular dance.   1. Shun.   2. Go from.   3. When.   4. Voice, song.

PUCK:                         I remember.
OBERON: That very time I saw, but thou couldst not,
   Flying between the cold moon and the earth,
   Cupid all[5] arm'd. A certain aim he took
   At a fair vestal[6] throned by the west,
   And loos'd his love-shaft smartly from his bow,
   As[7] it should pierce a hundred thousand hearts;
   But I might[8] see young Cupid's fiery shaft
   Quench'd in the chaste beams of the wat'ry moon,
   And the imperial vot'ress passed on,
   In maiden meditation, fancy-free.[9]
   Yet mark'd I where the bolt of Cupid fell:
   It fell upon a little western flower,
   Before milk-white, now purple with love's wound,
   And maidens call it love-in-idleness.[1]
   Fetch me that flow'r; the herb I showed thee once.
   The juice of it on sleeping eyelids laid
   Will make or man or[2] woman madly dote
   Upon the next live creature that it sees.
   Fetch me this herb, and be thou here again
   Ere the leviathan[3] can swim a league.
PUCK: I'll put a girdle round about the earth
   In forty[4] minutes.                          [*Exit.*]
OBERON:              Having once this juice,
   I'll watch Titania when she is asleep,
   And drop the liquor of it in her eyes.
   The next thing then she waking looks upon,
   Be it on lion, bear, or wolf, or bull,
   On meddling monkey, or on busy ape,
   She shall pursue it with the soul of love.
   And ere I take this charm from off her sight,
   As I can take it with another herb,
   I'll make her render up her page to me.
   But who comes here? I am invisible,
   And I will overhear their conference.

     [*Enter* DEMETRIUS, HELENA *following him.*]

DEMETRIUS: I love thee not, therefore pursue me not.
   Where is Lysander and fair Hermia?
   The one I'll slay, the other slayeth me.
   Thou told'st me they were stol'n unto this wood;
   And here am I, and wode[5] within this wood,
   Because I cannot meet my Hermia.
   Hence, get thee gone, and follow me no more.

---

5. Fully.   6. Vestal virgin (contains a complimentary allusion to Queen Elizabeth as a votaress of Diana and probably refers to an actual entertainment in her honor at Elvetham in 1591).   7. As if.   8. Could.   9. Free of love's spell.   1. Pansy, heartsease.   2. Either . . . or.   3. Sea monster, whale.   4. [The time parameters are used indefinitely here.]   5. Mad (pronounced *wood* and often spelled so).

195 HELENA: You draw me, you hard-hearted adamant;[6]
   But yet you draw not iron, for my heart
   Is true as steel. Leave[7] you your power to draw,
   And I shall have no power to follow you.
DEMETRIUS: Do I entice you? Do I speak you fair?[8]
200 Or, rather, do I not in plainest truth
   Tell you I do not nor I cannot love you?
HELENA: And even for that do I love you the more.
   I am your spaniel; and, Demetrius,
   The more you beat me, I will fawn on you.
205 Use me but as your spaniel, spurn me, strike me,
   Neglect me, lose me; only give me leave,
   Unworthy as I am, to follow you.
   What worser place can I beg in your love—
   And yet a place of high respect with me—
210 Than to be used as you use your dog?
DEMETRIUS: Tempt not too much the hatred of my spirit,
   For I am sick when I do look on thee.
HELENA: And I am sick when I look not on you.
DEMETRIUS: You do impeach[9] your modesty too much
215 To leave the city and commit yourself
   Into the hands of one that loves you not,
   To trust the opportunity of night
   And the ill counsel of a desert[1] place
   With the rich worth of your virginity.
220 HELENA: Your virtue is my privilege. For that[2]
   It is not night when I do see your face,
   Therefore I think I am not in the night;
   Nor doth this wood lack worlds of company,
   For you in my respect[3] are all the world.
225 Then how can it be said I am alone,
   When all the world is here to look on me?
DEMETRIUS: I'll run from thee and hide me in the brakes,[4]
   And leave thee to the mercy of wild beasts.
HELENA: The wildest hath not such a heart as you.
230 Run when you will, the story shall be chang'd:
   Apollo flies and Daphne holds the chase,[5]
   The dove pursues the griffin, the mild hind[6]
   Makes speed to catch the tiger—bootless[7] speed,
   When cowardice pursues and valor flies.
235 DEMETRIUS: I will not stay thy questions.[8] Let me go!

6. Lodestone, magnet (with pun on *hard-hearted*, since adamant was also thought to be the hardest of all stones and was confused with the diamond). 7. Give up. 8. Courteously. 9. Call into question.
1. Deserted. 2. Because. *Virtue:* goodness or power to attract. *Privilege:* safeguard, warrant.
3. As far as I am concerned. 4. Thickets.
5. [In the ancient myth, Daphne fled from Apollo and was saved from rape by being transformed into a laurel tree; here it is the female who *holds the chase,* or pursues, instead of the male.]
6. Female deer. *Griffin:* a fabulous monster with the head of an eagle and the body of a lion. 7. Fruitless.
8. Talk or argument. *Stay:* wait for.

> Or if thou follow me, do not believe
> But I shall do thee mischief in the wood.

HELENA: Ay, in the temple, in the town, the field,
> You do me mischief. Fie, Demetrius!
> Your wrongs do set a scandal on my sex.
> We cannot fight for love, as men may do;
> We should be woo'd and were not made to woo.     [*Exit* DEMETRIUS.]
> I'll follow thee and make a heaven of hell,
> To die upon[9] the hand I love so well.     [*Exit.*]

OBERON: Fare thee well, nymph. Ere he do leave this grove,
> Thou shalt fly him and he shall seek thy love.

    [*Enter* PUCK.]

> Hast thou the flower there? Welcome, wanderer.

PUCK: Ay, there it is.     [*Offers the flower.*]

OBERON:     I pray thee, give it me.
> I know a bank where the wild thyme blows,[1]
> Where oxlips[2] and the nodding violet grows,
> Quite over-canopied with luscious woodbine,[3]
> With sweet musk-roses and with eglantine.[4]
> There sleeps Titania sometime of the night,
> Lull'd in these flowers with dances and delight;
> And there the snake throws[5] her enamel'd skin,
> Weed[6] wide enough to wrap a fairy in.
> And with the juice of this I'll streak[7] her eyes,
> And make her full of hateful fantasies.
> Take thou some of it, and seek through this grove.     [*Gives some love-juice.*]
> A sweet Athenian lady is in love
> With a disdainful youth. Anoint his eyes,
> But do it when the next thing he espies
> May be the lady. Thou shalt know the man
> By the Athenian garments he hath on.
> Effect it with some care, that he may prove
> More fond on[8] her than she upon her love;
> And look thou meet me ere the first cock crow.

PUCK: Fear not, my lord, your servant shall do so.     [*Exeunt.*]

## Scene 2[9]

*Enter* TITANIA, *Queen of Fairies, with her train.*

TITANIA: Come, now a roundel[1] and a fairy song;
> Then, for the third part of a minute, hence—
> Some to kill cankers[2] in the musk-rose buds,

---

9. By.    1. Blooms.    2. Flowers resembling cowslip and primrose.    3. Honeysuckle.
4. Sweetbriar, a kind of rose. *Musk-rose:* a kind of large, sweet-scented rose.    5. Sloughs off, sheds.
6. Garment.    7. Anoint, touch gently.    8. Doting on.    9. Location: the wood.    1. Dance in a ring.
2. Cankerworms.

        Some war with rere-mice[3] for their leathern wings,
5       To make my small elves coats, and some keep back
        The clamorous owl, that nightly hoots and wonders
        At our quaint[4] spirits. Sing me now asleep.
        Then to your offices and let me rest.

                    [FAIRIES *sing*.]

[FIRST FAIRY:]
            You spotted snakes with double[5] tongue,
10              Thorny hedgehogs, be not seen;
            Newts[6] and blindworms, do no wrong,
                Come not near our fairy queen.
        [*Chorus.*] Philomel,[7] with melody
            Sing in our sweet lullaby;
15      Lulla, lulla, lullaby, lulla, lulla, lullaby.
                Never harm,
                Nor spell nor charm,
            Come our lovely lady nigh.
            So, good night, with lullaby.

[FIRST FAIRY:]
20          Weaving spiders, come not here;
                Hence, you long-legg'd spinners, hence!
            Beetles black, approach not near;
                Worm nor snail, do no offense.
        [*Chorus.*] Philomel, with melody, etc.

                                        [TITANIA *sleeps*.]

[SECOND FAIRY:]
25          Hence, away! Now all is well.
                One aloof stand sentinel.

                                        [*Exeunt* FAIRIES.]

        [*Enter* OBERON *and squeezes the flower on* TITANIA'*s eyelids*.]

OBERON: What thou seest when thou dost wake,
            Do it for thy true-love take;
            Love and languish for his sake.
30      Be it ounce,[8] or cat, or bear,
            Pard,[9] or boar with bristled hair,
            In thy eye that shall appear
            When thou wak'st, it is thy dear.
            Wake when some vile thing is near.            [*Exit.*]

---

3. Bats.   4. Dainty.   5. Forked.
6. Water lizards (considered poisonous, as were *blindworms*—small snakes with tiny eyes—and spiders).
7. The nightingale (Philomela, daughter of King Pandion, was transformed into a nightingale, according to Ovid's *Metamorphoses* 6, after she had been raped by her sister Procne's husband, Tereus).   8. Lynx.
9. Leopard.

[*Enter* LYSANDER *and* HERMIA.]

LYSANDER: Fair love, you faint with wand'ring in the wood;
  And to speak troth,[1] I have forgot our way.
  We'll rest us, Hermia, if you think it good,
  And tarry for the comfort of the day.
HERMIA: Be 't so, Lysander. Find you out a bed,
  For I upon this bank will rest my head.
LYSANDER: One turf shall serve as pillow for us both,
  One heart, one bed, two bosoms, and one troth.[2]
HERMIA: Nay, good Lysander; for my sake, my dear,
  Lie further off yet, do not lie so near.
LYSANDER: O, take the sense, sweet, of my innocence![3]
  Love takes the meaning in love's conference.[4]
  I mean, that my heart unto yours is knit
  So that but one heart we can make of it;
  Two bosoms interchained with an oath—
  So then two bosoms and a single troth.
  Then by your side no bed-room me deny,
  For lying so, Hermia, I do not lie.[5]
HERMIA: Lysander riddles very prettily.
  Now much beshrew[6] my manners and my pride
  If Hermia meant to say Lysander lied.
  But, gentle friend, for love and courtesy
  Lie further off, in human[7] modesty;
  Such separation as may well be said
  Becomes a virtuous bachelor and a maid,
  So far be distant; and, good night, sweet friend.
  Thy love ne'er alter till thy sweet life end!
LYSANDER: Amen, amen, to that fair prayer, say I,
  And then end life when I end loyalty!
  Here is my bed. Sleep give thee all his rest!
HERMIA: With half that wish the wisher's eyes be press'd![8]

[*They sleep, separated by a short distance. Enter* PUCK.]

PUCK: Through the forest have I gone,
    But Athenian found I none
    On whose eyes I might approve[9]
    This flower's force in stirring love.
    Night and silence.—Who is here?
    Weeds of Athens he doth wear.
    This is he, my master said,
    Despised the Athenian maid;
    And here the maiden, sleeping sound,
    On the dank and dirty ground.

---

1. Truth.  2. Faith, trothplight.  3. That is, interpret my intention as innocent.
4. That is, when lovers confer, love teaches each lover to interpret the other's meaning lovingly.
5. Tell a falsehood (with a pun on *lie*, recline).  6. Curse (but mildly meant).  7. Courteous.
8. That is, may we share your wish, so that your eyes too are *press'd*, closed, in sleep.  9. Test.

Pretty soul! She durst not lie
Near this lack-love, this kill-courtesy.
Churl, upon thy eyes I throw
All the power this charm doth owe.[1]   *[Applies the love-juice.]*
80  When thou wak'st, let love forbid
Sleep his seat on thy eyelid.
So awake when I am gone,
For I must now to Oberon.                *[Exit.]*

*[Enter* DEMETRIUS *and* HELENA, *running.]*

HELENA: Stay, though thou kill me, sweet Demetrius.
85  DEMETRIUS: I charge thee, hence, and do not haunt me thus.
HELENA: O, wilt thou darkling[2] leave me? Do not so.
DEMETRIUS: Stay, on thy peril![3] I alone will go.    *[Exit.]*
HELENA: O, I am out of breath in this fond[4] chase!
The more my prayer, the lesser is my grace.[5]
90  Happy is Hermia, wheresoe'er she lies,[6]
For she hath blessed and attractive eyes.
How came her eyes so bright? Not with salt tears;
If so, my eyes are oft'ner wash'd than hers.
No, no, I am as ugly as a bear;
95  For beasts that meet me run away for fear.
Therefore no marvel though Demetrius
Do, as a monster, fly my presence thus.
What wicked and dissembling glass of mine
Made me compare with Hermia's sphery eyne?[7]
100  But who is here? Lysander, on the ground?
Dead, or asleep? I see no blood, no wound.
Lysander, if you live, good sir, awake.
LYSANDER: *[Awaking.]* And run through fire I will for thy sweet sake.
Transparent[8] Helena! Nature shows art,
105  That through thy bosom makes me see thy heart.
Where is Demetrius? O, how fit a word
Is that vile name to perish on my sword!
HELENA: Do not say so, Lysander, say not so.
What though he love your Hermia? Lord, what though?
110  Yet Hermia still loves you. Then be content.
LYSANDER: Content with Hermia? No! I do repent
The tedious minutes I with her have spent.
Not Hermia but Helena I love.
Who will not change a raven for a dove?
115  The will of man is by his reason sway'd,
And reason says you are the worthier maid.
Things growing are not ripe until their season;
So I, being young, till now ripe not to reason.[9]

---

1. Own.   2. In the dark.   3. That is, on pain of danger to you if you don't obey me and stay.
4. Doting.   5. The favor I obtain.   6. Dwells.   7. Eyes as bright as stars in their spheres.
8. (1) Radiant; (2) able to be seen through.   9. Mature enough to be reasonable.

    And touching now the point of human skill,[1]
    Reason becomes the marshal to my will 120
    And leads me to your eyes, where I o'erlook[2]
    Love's stories written in love's richest book.
HELENA: Wherefore was I to this keen mockery born?
    When at your hands did I deserve this scorn?
    Is 't not enough, is 't not enough, young man, 125
    That I did never, no, nor never can,
    Deserve a sweet look from Demetrius' eye,
    But you must flout my insufficiency?
    Good troth, you do me wrong, good sooth,[3] you do,
    In such disdainful manner me to woo. 130
    But fare you well. Perforce I must confess
    I thought you lord of more true gentleness.[4]
    O, that a lady, of[5] one man refus'd,
    Should of another therefore be abus'd![6] *[Exit.]*
LYSANDER: She sees not Hermia. Hermia, sleep thou there, 135
    And never mayst thou come Lysander near!
    For as a surfeit of the sweetest things
    The deepest loathing to the stomach brings,
    Or as the heresies that men do leave
    Are hated most of those they did deceive, 140
    So thou, my surfeit and my heresy,
    Of all be hated, but the most of me!
    And, all my powers, address your love and might
    To honor Helen and to be her knight! *[Exit.]*
HERMIA: *[Awaking.]* Help me, Lysander, help me! Do thy best 145
    To pluck this crawling serpent from my breast!
    Ay me, for pity! What a dream was here!
    Lysander, look how I do quake with fear.
    Methought a serpent eat[7] my heart away,
    And you sat smiling at his cruel prey.[8] 150
    Lysander! What, remov'd? Lysander! Lord!
    What, out of hearing? Gone? No sound, no word?
    Alack, where are you? Speak, an if you hear.
    Speak, of all loves![9] I swoon almost with fear.
    No? Then I well perceive you are not nigh. 155
    Either death, or you, I'll find immediately.

    *[Exit. Manet* TITANIA *lying asleep.]*

---

1. Judgment. *Touching:* reaching. *Point:* summit.   2. Read.   3. That is, indeed, truly.
4. Courtesy. *Lord of:* that is, possessor of.   5. By.   6. Ill treated.   7. Ate (pronounced *et*).
8. Act of preying.   9. For all love's sake.

## ACT III

*Scene 1*[1]

*Enter the Clowns* (QUINCE, SNUG, BOTTOM, FLUTE, SNOUT, *and* STARVELING.)

BOTTOM: Are we all met?

QUINCE: Pat, pat; and here's a marvailes convenient place for our rehearsal. This green plot shall be our stage, this hawthorn brake our tiring-house,[2] and we will do it in action as we will do it before the Duke.

BOTTOM: Peter Quince?

QUINCE: What sayest thou, bully[3] Bottom?

BOTTOM: There are things in this comedy of Pyramus and Thisby that will never please. First, Pyramus must draw a sword to kill himself, which the ladies cannot abide. How answer you that?

SNOUT: By 'r lakin, a parlous[4] fear.

STARVELING: I believe we must leave the killing out, when all is done.[5]

BOTTOM: Not a whit. I have a device to make all well. Write me[6] a prologue; and let the prologue seem to say, we will do no harm with our swords and that Pyramus is not kill'd indeed; and, for the more better assurance, tell them that I Pyramus am not Pyramus, but Bottom the weaver. This will put them out of fear.

QUINCE: Well, we will have such a prologue, and it shall be written in eight and six.[7]

BOTTOM: No, make it two more; let it be written in eight and eight.

SNOUT: Will not the ladies be afeard of the lion?

STARVELING: I fear it, I promise you.

BOTTOM: Masters, you ought to consider with yourselves, to bring in—God shield us!—a lion among ladies,[8] is a most dreadful thing. For there is not a more fearful[9] wild-fowl than your lion living; and we ought to look to 't.

SNOUT: Therefore another prologue must tell he is not a lion.

BOTTOM: Nay, you must name his name, and half his face must be seen through the lion's neck, and he himself must speak through, saying thus, or to the same defect:[1] "Ladies"—or "Fair ladies—I would wish you"—or "I would request you"—or "I would entreat you—not to fear, not to tremble; my life for yours.[2] If you think I come hither as a lion, it were pity of my life.[3] No, I am no such thing; I am a man as other men are." And there indeed let him name his name, and tell them plainly he is Snug the joiner.

QUINCE: Well, it shall be so. But there is two hard things: that is, to bring the moonlight into a chamber; for, you know, Pyramus and Thisby meet by moonlight.

SNOUT: Doth the moon shine that night we play our play?

---

1. Location: scene continues.  2. Attiring area, hence backstage. *Brake:* thicket.
3. That is, worthy, jolly, fine fellow.
4. Perilous. *By 'r lakin:* by our ladykin; that is, the Virgin Mary.  5. That is, when all is said and done.
6. That is, write at my suggestion.  7. Alternate lines of eight and six syllables, a common ballad measure.
8. [A contemporary pamphlet tells how at the christening in 1594 of Prince Henry, eldest son of King James VI of Scotland, later James I of England, a "blackmoor" instead of a lion drew the triumphal chariot since the lion's presence might have "brought some fear to the nearest."]  9. Fear-inspiring.
1. [Bottom's blunder for *effect*.]  2. That is, I pledge my life to make your lives safe.
3. My life would be endangered.

BOTTOM: A calendar, a calendar! Look in the almanac. Find out moonshine, find out moonshine. [*They consult an almanac.*]
QUINCE: Yes, it doth shine that night.
BOTTOM: Why then may you leave a casement of the great chamber window, where we play, open, and the moon may shine in at the casement.
QUINCE: Ay; or else one must come in with a bush of thorns and a lantern, and say he comes to disfigure,[4] or to present,[5] the person of Moonshine. Then there is another thing: we must have a wall in the great chamber; for Pyramus and Thisby, says the story, did talk through the chink of a wall.
SNOUT: You can never bring in a wall. What say you, Bottom?
BOTTOM: Some man or other must present Wall. And let him have some plaster, or some loam, or some roughcast[6] about him, to signify wall; and let him hold his fingers thus, and through that cranny shall Pyramus and Thisby whisper.
QUINCE: If that may be, then all is well. Come, sit down, every mother's son, and rehearse your parts. Pyramus, you begin. When you have spoken your speech, enter into that brake, and so every one according to his cue.

[*Enter Robin (PUCK).*]

PUCK: What hempen home-spuns have we swagg'ring here,
So near the cradle of the Fairy Queen?
What, a play toward?[7] I'll be an auditor;
An actor too perhaps, if I see cause.
QUINCE: Speak, Pyramus. Thisby, stand forth.
BOTTOM: "Thisby, the flowers of odious savors sweet,"—
QUINCE: Odors, odors.
BOTTOM: —"Odors savors sweet;
So hath thy breath, my dearest Thisby dear.
But hark, a voice! Stay thou but here awhile,
And by and by I will to thee appear." [*Exit.*]
PUCK: A stranger Pyramus than e'er played here.[8] [*Exit.*]
FLUTE: Must I speak now?
QUINCE: Ay, marry, must you; for you must understand he goes but to see a noise that he heard, and is to come again.
FLUTE: "Most radiant Pyramus, most lily-white of hue,
Of color like the red rose on triumphant brier,
Most brisky juvenal and eke most lovely Jew,[9]
As true as truest horse that yet would never tire.
I'll meet thee, Pyramus, at Ninny's tomb."
QUINCE: "Ninus'[1] tomb," man. Why, you must not speak that yet. That you answer to Pyramus. You speak all your part at once, cues and all. Pyramus, enter. Your cue is past; it is, "never tire."
FLUTE: O—"As true as truest horse, that yet would never tire."

4. [Quince's blunder for *prefigure*.] *Bush of thorns*: bundle of thornbush faggots (part of the accoutrements of the man in the moon, according to the popular notions of the time, along with his lantern and his dog).
5. Represent.   6. A mixture of lime and gravel used to plaster the outside of buildings.
7. About to take place.   8. That is, in this theater (?).
9. [Probably an absurd repetition of the first syllable of *juvenal*.] *Briskly juvenal*: brisk youth. *Eke*: also.
1. Mythical founder of Nineveh (whose wife, Semiramis, was supposed to have built the walls of Babylon, where the story of Pyramis and Thisbe takes place).

[*Enter* PUCK, *and* BOTTOM *as Pyramus with the ass head.*][2]

BOTTOM: "If I were fair,[3] Thisby, I were only thine."
QUINCE: O monstrous! O strange! We are haunted. Pray, masters! Fly, masters! Help!     [*Exeunt* QUINCE, SNUG, FLUTE, SNOUT, *and* STARVELING.]
PUCK: I'll follow you, I'll lead you about a round,[4]
    Through bog, through bush, through brake, through brier.
    Sometime a horse I'll be, sometime a hound,
    A hog, a headless bear, sometime a fire;[5]
    And neigh, and bark, and grunt, and roar, and burn,
    Like horse, hound, hog, bear, fire, at every turn.     [*Exit.*]
BOTTOM: Why do they run away? This is a knavery of them to make me afeard.

[*Enter* SNOUT.]

SNOUT: O Bottom, thou art chang'd! what do I see on thee?
BOTTOM: What do you see? You see an ass-head of your own, do you?     [*Exit* SNOUT.]

[*Enter* QUINCE.]

QUINCE: Bless thee, Bottom, bless thee! Thou art translated.[6]     [*Exit.*]
BOTTOM: I see their knavery. This is to make an ass of me, to fright me, if they could. But I will not stir from this place, do what they can. I will walk up and down here, and will sing, that they shall hear I am not afraid.

[*Sings.*]

    The woosel cock[7] so black of hue,
        With orange-tawny bill,
    The throstle[8] with his note so true,
        The wren with little quill[9]—

TITANIA: [*Awaking.*] What angel wakes me from my flow'ry bed?

[BOTTOM *sings.*]

    The finch, the sparrow, and the lark,
        The plain-song[1] cuckoo grey,
    Whose note full many a man doth mark,
        And dares not answer nay[2]—

For, indeed, who would set his wit to so foolish a bird? Who would give a bird the lie,[3] though he cry "cuckoo" never so?[4]
TITANIA: I pray thee, gentle mortal, sing again.
    Mine ear is much enamored of thy note;
    So is mine eye enthralled to thy shape;
    And thy fair virtue's force[5] perforce doth move me
    On the first view to say, to swear, I love thee.

---

2. [This stage direction, taken from the Folio, presumably refers to a standard stage property.]
3. Handsome.     4. Roundabout.     5. Will-o'-the-wisp.     6. Transformed.
7. Male ousel or ouzel, blackbird.     8. Song thrush.
9. [Literally, a reed pipe; hence, the bird's piping song.]     1. Singing a melody without variations.
2. That is, cannot deny that he is a cuckold.     3. Call the bird a liar.     4. Ever so much.
5. The power of your beauty.

BOTTOM: Methinks, mistress, you should have little reason for that. And yet, to say the truth, reason and love keep little company together nowadays. The more the pity that some honest neighbors will not make them friends. Nay, I can gleek[6] upon occasion.
TITANIA: Thou art as wise as thou art beautiful.
BOTTOM: Not so, neither. But if I had wit enough to get out of this wood, I have enough to serve mine own turn.[7]
TITANIA: Out of this wood do not desire to go.
Thou shalt remain here, whether thou wilt or no.
I am a spirit of no common rate.[8]
The summer still doth tend upon my state;[9]
And I do love thee. Therefore, go with me.
I'll give thee fairies to attend on thee,
And they shall fetch thee jewels from the deep,
And sing while thou on pressed flowers dost sleep.
And I will purge thy mortal grossness so
That thou shalt like an airy spirit go.
Peaseblossom, Cobweb, Moth,[1] and Mustardseed!

[*Enter four* FAIRIES (PEASEBLOSSOM, COBWEB, MOTH, *and* MUSTARDSEED).]

PEASEBLOSSOM: Ready.
COBWEB: And I.
MOTH: And I.
MUSTARDSEED: And I.
ALL: Where shall we go?
TITANIA: Be kind and courteous to this gentleman.
Hop in his walks and gambol in his eyes;
Feed him with apricocks and dewberries,
With purple grapes, green figs, and mulberries;
The honey-bags steal from the humble-bees,
And for night-tapers crop their waxen thighs
And light them at the fiery glow-worm's eyes,
To have my love to bed and to arise;
And pluck the wings from painted butterflies
To fan the moonbeams from his sleeping eyes.
Nod to him, elves, and do him courtesies.
PEASEBLOSSOM: Hail, mortal!
COBWEB: Hail!
MOTH: Hail!
MUSTARDSEED: Hail!
BOTTOM: I cry your worships mercy, heartily. I beseech your worship's name.
COBWEB: Cobweb.
BOTTOM: I shall desire you of more acquaintance, good Master Cobweb. If I cut my finger, I shall make bold with you.[2] Your name, honest gentleman?
PEASEBLOSSOM: Peaseblossom.

---

6. Scoff, jest. 7. Answer my purpose. 8. Rank, value.
9. Waits upon me as a part of my royal retinue. *Still:* ever, always.
1. That is, mote, speck. (The two words *moth* and *mote* were pronounced alike.)
2. [Cobwebs were used to stanch bleeding.]

BOTTOM: I pray you, commend me to Mistress Squash,³ your mother, and to Master Peascod,⁴ your father. Good Master Peaseblossom, I shall desire you of more acquaintance too. Your name, I beseech you, sir?
MUSTARDSEED: Mustardseed.
BOTTOM: Good Master Mustardseed, I know your patience well.⁵ That same cowardly, giant-like ox-beef hath devour'd many a gentleman of your house. I promise you your kindred hath made my eyes water ere now. I desire you of more acquaintance, good Master Mustardseed.
TITANIA: Come wait upon him; lead him to my bower.
    The moon methinks looks with a wat'ry eye;
    And when she weeps,⁶ weeps every little flower,
    Lamenting some enforced⁷ chastity.
    Tie up my lover's tongue, bring him silently.                    [*Exeunt.*]

## Scene 2⁸

*Enter* OBERON, *King of Fairies.*

OBERON: I wonder if Titania be awak'd;
    Then, what it was that next came in her eye,
    Which she must dote on in extremity.

        [*Enter Robin Goodfellow* (PUCK).]

    Here comes my messenger. How now, mad spirit?
5   What night-rule now about this haunted⁹ grove?
PUCK: My mistress with a monster is in love.
    Near to her close¹ and consecrated bower,
    While she was in her dull² and sleeping hour,
    A crew of patches, rude mechanicals,³
10  That work for bread upon Athenian stalls,
    Were met together to rehearse a play
    Intended for great Theseus' nuptial day.
    The shallowest thick-skin of that barren sort,⁴
    Who Pyramus presented,⁵ in their sport
15  Forsook his scene⁶ and ent'red in a brake.
    When I did him at this advantage take,
    An ass's nole⁷ I fixed on his head.
    Anon his Thisby must be answered,
    And forth my mimic⁸ comes. When they him spy,
20  As wild geese that the creeping fowler eye,
    Or russet-pated choughs, many in sort,⁹
    Rising and cawing at the gun's report,
    Sever¹ themselves and madly sweep the sky,

---

3. Unripe pea pod.   4. Ripe pea pod.   5. What you have endured.   6. That is, she causes dew.
7. Forced, violated, or, possibly, constrained (since Titania at this moment is hardly concerned about chastity).   8. Location: the wood.   9. Much frequented. *Night-rule:* diversion for the night.
1. Secret, private.   2. Drowsy.   3. Ignorant artisans. *Patches:* clowns, fools.   4. Stupid company or crew.
5. Acted.   6. Playing area.   7. Noddle, head.   8. Burlesque actor.
9. In a flock. *Russet-pated choughs:* gray-headed jackdaws.   1. That is, scatter.

So, at his sight, away his fellows fly;
And, at our stamp, here o'er and o'er one falls; 25
He murder cries and help from Athens calls.
Their sense thus weak, lost with their fears thus strong,
Made senseless things begin to do them wrong,
For briers and thorns at their apparel snatch;
Some, sleeves—some, hats; from yielders all things catch. 30
I led them on in this distracted fear
And left sweet Pyramus translated there,
When in that moment, so it came to pass,
Titania wak'd and straightway lov'd an ass.
OBERON: This falls out better than I could devise. 35
But hast thou yet latch'd[2] the Athenian's eyes
With the love-juice, as I did bid thee do?
PUCK: I took him sleeping—that is finish'd too—
And the Athenian woman by his side,
That, when he wak'd, of force[3] she must be ey'd. 40

[Enter DEMETRIUS and HERMIA.]

OBERON: Stand close. This is the same Athenian.
PUCK: This is the woman, but not this the man. [They stand aside.]
DEMETRIUS: O, why rebuke you him that loves you so?
Lay breath so bitter on your bitter foe.
HERMIA: Now I but chide; but I should use thee worse, 45
For thou, I fear, hast given me cause to curse.
If thou hast slain Lysander in his sleep,
Being o'er shoes in blood, plunge in the deep,
And kill me too.
The sun was not so true unto the day 50
As he to me. Would he have stolen away
From sleeping Hermia? I'll believe as soon
This whole[4] earth may be bor'd and that the moon
May through the center creep and so displease
Her brother's noontide with th' Antipodes.[5] 55
It cannot be but thou hast murd'red him;
So should a murderer look, so dead,[6] so grim.
DEMETRIUS: So should the murdered look, and so should I,
Pierc'd through the heart with your stern cruelty.
Yet you, the murderer, look as bright, as clear, 60
As yonder Venus in her glimmering sphere.
HERMIA: What's this to my Lysander? Where is he?
Ah, good Demetrius, wilt thou give him me?
DEMETRIUS: I had rather give his carcass to my hounds.
HERMIA: Out, dog! Out, cur! Thou driv'st me past the bounds 65
Of maiden's patience. Hast thou slain him, then?

2. Moistened, anointed.   3. Perforce.   4. Solid.
5. The people on the opposite side of the Earth. *Her brother's:* that is, the sun's.
6. Deadly, or deathly pale.

Henceforth be never numb'red among men!
O, once tell true, tell true, even for my sake!
Durst thou have look'd upon him being awake,
And hast thou kill'd him sleeping? O brave touch!⁷ 70
Could not a worm,⁸ an adder, do so much?
An adder did it; for with doubler tongue
Than thine, thou serpent, never adder stung.
DEMETRIUS: You spend your passion on a mispris'd mood.⁹
I am not guilty of Lysander's blood, 75
Nor is he dead, for aught that I can tell.
HERMIA: I pray thee, tell me then that he is well.
DEMETRIUS: An if I could, what should I get therefore?
HERMIA: A privilege never to see me more.
And from thy hated presence part I so. 80
See me no more, whether he be dead or no. [*Exit.*]
DEMETRIUS: There is no following her in this fierce vein.
Here therefore for a while I will remain.
So sorrow's heaviness doth heavier¹ grow
For debt that bankrupt² sleep doth sorrow owe; 85
Which now in some slight measure it will pay,
If for his tender here I make some stay.³ [*He lies down and sleeps.*]
OBERON: What hast thou done? Thou hast mistaken quite
And laid the love-juice on some true-love's sight.
Of thy misprision⁴ must perforce ensue 90
Some true love turn'd and not a false turn'd true.
PUCK: Then fate o'er-rules, that, one man holding troth,⁵
A million fail, confounding⁶ oath on oath.
OBERON: About the wood go swifter than the wind,
And Helena of Athens look thou find. 95
All fancy-sick she is and pale of cheer⁷
With sighs of love, that cost the fresh blood⁸ dear.
By some illusion see thou bring her here.
I'll charm his eyes against she do appear.⁹
PUCK: I go, I go; look how I go, 100
Swifter than arrow from the Tartar's bow.¹ [*Exit.*]
OBERON: Flower of this purple dye,
Hit with Cupid's archery.
Sink in apple of his eye. [*Applies love-juice to* DEMETRIUS's *eyes.*]
When his love he doth espy, 105
Let her shine as gloriously
As the Venus of the sky.

7. Noble exploit (said ironically).   8. Serpent.
9. Anger based on misconception. *Passion:* violent feelings.   1. (1) Harder to bear; (2) more drowsy.
2. [Demetrius is saying that his sleepiness adds to the weariness caused by sorrow.]
3. That is, to a small extent I will be able to "pay back" and hence find some relief from sorrow, if I pause here a while (*make some stay*) while sleep "tenders" or offers itself by way of paying the debt owed to sorrow.
4. Mistake.   5. Faith.   6. That is, invalidating one oath with another.   7. Face. *Fancy-sick:* lovesick.
8. [An allusion to the physiological theory that each sigh costs the heart a drop of blood.]
9. In anticipation of her coming.   1. [Tartars were famed for their skill with the bow.]

When thou wak'st, if she be by,
Beg of her for remedy.

[*Enter* PUCK.]

PUCK: Captain of our fairy band, 110
Helena is here at hand,
And the youth, mistook by me,
Pleading for a lover's fee.[2]
Shall we their fond pageant[3] see?
Lord, what fools these mortals be! 115
OBERON: Stand aside. The noise they make
Will cause Demetrius to awake.
PUCK: Then will two at once woo one;
That must needs be sport alone[4];
And those things do best please me 120
That befall prepost'rously.[5]  [*They stand aside.*]

[*Enter* LYSANDER *and* HELENA.]

LYSANDER: Why should you think that I should woo in scorn?
Scorn and derision never come in tears.
Look when[6] I vow, I weep; and vows so born,
In their nativity all truth appears.[7] 125
How can these things in me seem scorn to you,
Bearing the badge[8] of faith, to prove them true?
HELENA: You do advance[9] your cunning more and more.
When truth kills truth,[1] O devilish-holy fray!
These vows are Hermia's. Will you give her o'er? 130
Weigh oath with oath, and you will nothing weigh.
Your vows to her and me, put in two scales,
Will even weigh, and both as light as tales.[2]
LYSANDER: I had no judgment when to her I swore.
HELENA: Nor none, in my mind, now you give her o'er. 135
LYSANDER: Demetrius loves her, and he loves not you.
DEMETRIUS: [*Awaking.*] O Helen, goddess, nymph, perfect, divine!
To what, my love, shall I compare thine eyne?
Crystal is muddy. O, how ripe in show[3]
Thy lips, those kissing cherries, tempting grow! 140
That pure congealed white, high Taurus'[4] snow,
Fann'd with the eastern wind, turns to a crow[5]
When thou hold'st up thy hand. O, let me kiss
This princess of pure white, this seal[6] of bliss!
HELENA: O spite! O hell! I see you all are bent 145
To set against me for your merriment.

---

2. Privilege, reward.   3. Foolish exhibition.   4. Unequaled.   5. Out of the natural order.
6. Whenever.   7. That is, vows made by one who is weeping give evidence thereby of their sincerity.
8. Identifying device such as that worn on servants' livery.   9. Carry forward, display.
1. That is, one of Lysander's vows must invalidate the other.   2. Lies.   3. Appearance.
4. A lofty mountain range in Asia Minor.   5. That is, seems black by contrast.   6. Pledge.

>            If you were civil and knew courtesy,
>            You would not do me thus much injury.
>            Can you not hate me, as I know you do,
> 150        But you must join in souls to mock me too?
>            If you were men, as men you are in show,
>            You would not use a gentle lady so—
>            To vow, and swear, and superpraise my parts,[7]
>            When I am sure you hate me with your hearts.
> 155        You both are rivals, and love Hermia;
>            And now both rivals, to mock Helena.
>            A trim[8] exploit, a manly enterprise,
>            To conjure tears up in a poor maid's eyes
>            With your derision! None of noble sort
> 160        Would so offend a virgin and extort[9]
>            A poor soul's patience, all to make you sport.
> LYSANDER: You are unkind, Demetrius. Be not so;
>            For you love Hermia; this you know I know.
>            And here, with all good will, with all my heart,
> 165        In Hermia's love I yield you up my part;
>            And yours of Helena to me bequeath,
>            Whom I do love and will do till my death.
> HELENA: Never did mockers waste more idle breath.
> DEMETRIUS: Lysander, keep thy Hermia; I will none.[1]
> 170        If e'er I lov'd her, all that love is gone.
>            My heart to her but as guest-wise sojourn'd,
>            And now to Helen is it home return'd,
>            There to remain.
> LYSANDER:              Helen, it is not so.
> DEMETRIUS: Disparage not the faith thou dost not know,
> 175        Lest, to thy peril, thou aby[2] it dear.
>            Look, where thy love comes; yonder is thy dear.
>
>            [*Enter* HERMIA.]
>
> HERMIA: Dark night, that from the eye his[3] function takes,
>            The ear more quick of apprehension makes;
>            Wherein it doth impair the seeing sense,
> 180        It pays the hearing double recompense.
>            Thou art not by mine eye, Lysander, found;
>            Mine ear, I thank it, brought me to thy sound.
>            But why unkindly didst thou leave me so?
> LYSANDER: Why should he stay, whom love doth press to go?
> 185 HERMIA: What love could press Lysander from my side?
> LYSANDER: Lysander's love, that would not let him bide,
>            Fair Helena, who more engilds the night
>            Than all yon fiery oes[4] and eyes of light.
>            Why seek'st thou me? Could not this make thee know,

---

7. Qualities. *Superpraise*: overpraise.   8. Pretty, fine (said ironically).   9. Twist, torture.
1. That is, wish none of her.   2. Pay for.   3. Its.   4. That is, circles, orbs, stars.

    The hate I bear thee made me leave thee so?    190
HERMIA: You speak not as you think. It cannot be.
HELENA: Lo, she is one of this confederacy!
    Now I perceive they have conjoin'd all three
    To fashion this false sport, in spite of me.[5]
    Injurious Hermia, most ungrateful maid!    195
    Have you conspir'd, have you with these contriv'd[6]
    To bait[7] me with this foul derision?
    Is all the counsel[8] that we two have shar'd,
    The sisters' vows, the hours that we have spent,
    When we have chid the hasty-footed time    200
    For parting us—O, is all forgot?
    All school-days friendship, childhood innocence?
    We, Hermia, like two artificial[9] gods,
    Have with our needles created both one flower,
    Both on one sampler, sitting on one cushion,    205
    Both warbling of one song, both in one key,
    As if our hands, our sides, voices, and minds
    Had been incorporate. So we grew together,
    Like to a double cherry, seeming parted,
    But yet an union in partition;    210
    Two lovely[1] berries molded on one stem;
    So, with two seeming bodies, but one heart;
    Two of the first, like coats in heraldry,
    Due but to one and crowned with one crest.[2]
    And will you rent[3] our ancient love asunder,    215
    To join with men in scorning your poor friend?
    It is not friendly, 'tis not maidenly.
    Our sex, as well as I, may chide you for it,
    Though I alone do feel the injury.
HERMIA: I am amazed at your passionate words.    220
    I scorn you not. It seems that you scorn me.
HELENA: Have you not set Lysander, as in scorn,
    To follow me and praise my eyes and face?
    And made your other love, Demetrius,
    Who even but now did spurn me with his foot,    225
    To call me goddess, nymph, divine and rare,
    Precious, celestial? Wherefore speaks he this
    To her he hates? And wherefore doth Lysander
    Deny your love, so rich within his soul,
    And tender[4] me, forsooth, affection,    230
    But by your setting on, by your consent?
    What though I be not so in grace[5] as you,
    So hung upon with love, so fortunate,

---

5. To vex me.    6. Plotted.    7. Torment, as one sets on dogs to bait a bear.    8. Confidential talk.
9. Skilled in art or creation.    1. Loving.
2. That is, we have two separate bodies, just as a coat of arms in heraldry can be represented twice on a shield but surmounted by a single crest.    3. Rend.    4. Offer.    5. Favor.

But miserable most, to love unlov'd?
235 This you should pity rather than despise.
HERMIA: I understand not what you mean by this.
HELENA: Ay, do! Persever, counterfeit sad[6] looks,
Make mouths upon[7] me when I turn my back,
Wink each at other, hold the sweet jest up.
240 This sport, well carried,[8] shall be chronicled.
If you have any pity, grace, or manners,
You would not make me such an argument.[9]
But fare ye well. 'Tis partly my own fault,
Which death, or absence, soon shall remedy.
245 LYSANDER: Stay, gentle Helena; hear my excuse,
My love, my life, my soul, fair Helena!
HELENA: O excellent!
HERMIA:         Sweet, do not scorn her so.
DEMETRIUS: If she cannot entreat,[1] I can compel.
LYSANDER: Thou canst compel no more than she entreat.
250 Thy threats have no more strength than her weak prayers.
Helen, I love thee, by my life, I do!
I swear by that which I will lose for thee,
To prove him false that says I love thee not.
DEMETRIUS: I say I love thee more than he can do.
255 LYSANDER: If thou say so, withdraw, and prove it too.
DEMETRIUS: Quick, come!
HERMIA:         Lysander, whereto tends all this?
LYSANDER: Away, you Ethiope![2]    [*He tries to break away from* HERMIA.]
DEMETRIUS:         No, no; he'll
Seem to break loose; take on as you would follow,
But yet come not. You are a tame man, go!
260 LYSANDER: Hang off,[3] thou cat, thou burr! Vile thing, let loose,
Or I will shake thee from me like a serpent!
HERMIA: Why are you grown so rude? What change is this,
Sweet love?
LYSANDER:    Thy love? Out, tawny Tartar, out!
Out, loathed med'cine![4] O hated potion, hence!
HERMIA: Do you not jest?
265 HELENA:         Yes, sooth,[5] and so do you.
LYSANDER: Demetrius, I will keep my word with thee.
DEMETRIUS: I would I had your bond, for I perceive
A weak bond[6] holds you. I'll not trust your word.
LYSANDER: What, should I hurt her, strike her, kill her dead?
270 Although I hate her, I'll not harm her so.
HERMIA: What, can you do me greater harm than hate?

---

6. Grave, serious.   7. That is, makes mows, faces, grimaces at.   8. Managed.
9. Subject for a jest.   1. That is, succeed by entreaty.
2. [Referring to Hermia's relatively dark hair and complexion; see also *tawny Tartar* six lines later.]
3. Let go.   4. That is, poison.   5. Truly.
6. That is, Hermia's arm (with a pun on *bond*, oath, in the previous line).

Hate me? Wherefore? O me, what news,[7] my love?
Am not I Hermia? Are not you Lysander?
I am as fair now as I was erewhile.[8]
Since night you lov'd me; yet since night you left me. 275
Why, then you left me—O, the gods forbid!—
In earnest, shall I say?
LYSANDER: Ay, by my life!
And never did desire to see thee more.
Therefore be out of hope, of question, of doubt;
Be certain, nothing truer. 'Tis no jest 280
That I do hate thee and love Helena.
HERMIA: O me! You juggler! You cankerblossom![9]
You thief of love! What, have you come by night
And stol'n my love's heart from him?
HELENA: Fine, i' faith!
Have you no modesty, no maiden shame, 285
No touch of bashfulness? What, will you tear
Impatient answers from my gentle tongue?
Fie, fie! You counterfeit, you puppet,[1] you!
HERMIA: Puppet? Why so? Ay, that way goes the game.
Now I perceive that she hath made compare 290
Between our statures; she hath urg'd her height,
And with her personage, her tall personage,
Her height, forsooth, she hath prevail'd with him.
And are you grown so high in his esteem,
Because I am so dwarfish and so low? 295
How low am I, thou painted maypole? Speak!
How low am I? I am not yet so low
But that my nails can reach unto thine eyes.

[*She flails at* HELENA, *but is restrained.*]

HELENA: I pray you, though you mock me, gentlemen,
Let her not hurt me. I was never curst;[2] 300
I have no gift at all in shrewishness;
I am a right[3] maid for my cowardice.
Let her not strike me. You perhaps may think,
Because she is something[4] lower than myself,
That I can match her.
HERMIA: Lower! Hark, again! 305
HELENA: Good Hermia, do not be so bitter with me.
I evermore did love you, Hermia,
Did ever keep your counsels, never wrong'd you;
Save that, in love unto Demetrius,
I told him of your stealth[5] unto this wood. 310
He followed you; for love I followed him.
But he hath chid me hence and threat'ned me

---

7. What is the matter.    8. Just now.    9. Worm that destroys the flower bud (?).
1. (1) Counterfeit; (2) dwarfish woman (in reference to Hermia's smaller stature).    2. Shrewish.    3. True.
4. Somewhat.    5. Stealing away.

To strike me, spurn me, nay, to kill me too.
And now, so[6] you will let me quiet go,
315 To Athens will I bear my folly back
And follow you no further. Let me go.
You see how simple and how fond[7] I am.
HERMIA: Why, get you gone. Who is 't that hinders you?
HELENA: A foolish heart, that I leave here behind.
HERMIA: What, with Lysander?
320 HELENA:                With Demetrius.
LYSANDER: Be not afraid; she shall not harm thee, Helena.
DEMETRIUS: No, sir, she shall not, though you take her part.
HELENA: O, when she is angry, she is keen and shrewd![8]
She was a vixen when she went to school;
325 And though she be but little, she is fierce.
HERMIA: "Little" again! Nothing but "low" and "little"!
Why will you suffer her to flout me thus?
Let me come to her.
LYSANDER:           Get you gone, you dwarf!
You minimus, of hind'ring knot-grass[9] made!
You bead, you acorn!
330 DEMETRIUS:          You are too officious
In her behalf that scorns your services.
Let her alone. Speak not of Helena;
Take not her part. For, if thou dost intend[1]
Never so little show of love to her,
Thou shalt aby[2] it.
335 LYSANDER:          Now she holds me not;
Now follow, if thou dar'st, to try whose right,
Of thine or mine, is most in Helena.             [*Exit.*]
DEMETRIUS: Follow? Nay, I'll go with thee, cheek by jowl.[3]
                                           [*Exit, following* LYSANDER.]
HERMIA: You, mistress, all this coil is 'long of[4] you.
Nay, go not back.[5]
340 HELENA:            I will not trust you, I,
Nor longer stay in your curst company.
Your hands than mine are quicker for a fray;
My legs are longer, though, to run away.           [*Exit.*]
HERMIA: I am amaz'd, and know not what to say.           [*Exit.*]
345 OBERON: This is thy negligence. Still thou mistak'st,
Or else committ'st thy knaveries willfully.
PUCK: Believe me, king of shadows, I mistook.
Did not you tell me I should know the man
By the Athenian garments he had on?
350 And so far blameless proves my enterprise

---

6. If only.     7. Foolish.     8. Shrewish.
9. A weed, an infusion of which was thought to stunt the growth. *Minimus:* diminutive creature.
1. Give sign of.     2. Pay for.     3. That is, side by side.     4. On account of. *Coil:* turmoil, dissension.
5. That is, don't retreat (Hermia is again proposing a fight).

      That I have 'nointed an Athenian's eyes;
      And so far am I glad it so did sort[6]
      As this their jangling I esteem a sport.
OBERON: Thou see'st these lovers seek a place to fight.
      Hie therefore, Robin, overcast the night;     355
      The starry welkin[7] cover thou anon
      With drooping fog as black as Acheron,[8]
      And lead these testy rivals so astray
      As[9] one come not within another's way.
      Like to Lysander sometime frame thy tongue,     360
      Then stir Demetrius up with bitter wrong;[1]
      And sometime rail thou like Demetrius.
      And from each other look thou lead them thus,
      Till o'er their brows death-counterfeiting sleep
      With leaden legs and batty[2] wings doth creep.     365
      Then crush this herb[3] into Lysander's eye,     *[Gives herb.]*
      Whose liquor hath this virtuous[4] property,
      To take from thence all error with his[5] might
      And make his eyeballs roll with wonted[6] sight.
      When they next wake, all this derision[7]     370
      Shall seem a dream and fruitless vision,
      And back to Athens shall the lovers wend
      With league whose date[8] till death shall never end.
      Whiles I in this affair do thee employ,
      I'll to my queen and beg her Indian boy;     375
      And then I will her charmed eye release
      From monster's view, and all things shall be peace.
PUCK: My fairy lord, this must be done with haste,
      For night's swift dragons[9] cut the clouds full fast,
      And yonder shines Aurora's harbinger,[1]     380
      At whose approach, ghosts, wand'ring here and there,
      Troop home to churchyards. Damned spirits all,
      That in crossways and floods have burial,[2]
      Already to their wormy beds are gone.
      For fear lest day should look their shames upon,     385
      They willfully themselves exile from light
      And must for aye[3] consort with black-brow'd night.
OBERON: But we are spirits of another sort.
      I with the Morning's love[4] have oft made sport,

---

6. Turn out.    7. Sky.    8. River of Hades (here representing Hades itself).    9. That.
1. Insults.    2. Batlike.    3. That is, the antidote (mentioned in 2.1.184) to love-in-idleness.
4. Efficacious.    5. Its.    6. Accustomed.    7. Laughable business.    8. Term of existence.
9. [Supposed by Shakespeare to be yoked to the car of the goddess of night.]
1. The morning star, precursor of dawn.
2. [Those who had committed suicide were buried at crossways, with a stake driven through them; those drowned, that is, buried in floods or great waters, would be condemned to wander disconsolate for want of burial rites.]    3. Forever.
4. Cephalus, a beautiful youth beloved by Aurora; or perhaps the goddess of the dawn herself.

390 And, like a forester,[5] the groves may tread
Even till the eastern gate, all fiery-red,
Opening on Neptune with fair blessed beams,
Turns into yellow gold his salt green streams.
But, notwithstanding, haste; make no delay.
395 We may effect this business yet ere day. [*Exit.*]
PUCK: Up and down, up and down,
I will lead them up and down.
I am fear'd in field and town.
Goblin, lead them up and down.
400 Here comes one.

[*Enter* LYSANDER.]

LYSANDER: Where art thou, proud Demetrius? Speak thou now.
PUCK: [*Mimicking* DEMETRIUS.] Here, villain, drawn[6] and ready. Where art thou?
LYSANDER: I will be with thee straight.[7]
PUCK: Follow me, then,
To plainer[8] ground.

[LYSANDER *wanders about,*[9] *following the voice. Enter* DEMETRIUS.]

DEMETRIUS: Lysander! Speak again!
405 Thou runaway, thou coward, art thou fled?
Speak! In some bush? Where dost thou hide thy head?
PUCK: [*Mimicking* LYSANDER.] Thou coward, art thou bragging to the stars,
Telling the bushes that thou look'st for wars,
And wilt not come? Come, recreant;[1] come, thou child,
410 I'll whip thee with a rod. He is defil'd
That draws a sword on thee.
DEMETRIUS: Yea, art thou there?
PUCK: Follow my voice. We'll try[2] no manhood here. [*Exeunt.*]

[LYSANDER *returns.*]

LYSANDER: He goes before me and still dares me on.
When I come where he calls, then he is gone.
415 The villain is much lighter-heel'd than I.
I followed fast, but faster he did fly,
That fallen am I in dark uneven way,
And here will rest me. [*Lies down.*] Come, thou gentle day!
For if but once thou show me thy grey light,
420 I'll find Demetrius and revenge this spite. [*Sleeps.*]

[*Enter Robin* (PUCK) *and* DEMETRIUS.]

PUCK: Ho, ho, ho! Coward, why com'st thou not?
DEMETRIUS: Abide me, if thou dar'st; for well I wot[3]
Thou runn'st before me, shifting every place,

---

5. Keeper of a royal forest.   6. With drawn sword.   7. Immediately.   8. Smoother.
9. [It is not clearly necessary that Lysander exit at this point; neither exit nor reentrance is indicated in the early texts.]   1. Cowardly wretch.   2. Test.   3. Know.

And dar'st not stand nor look me in the face.
Where art thou now?
PUCK:                    Come hither. I am here.                                         425
DEMETRIUS: Nay, then, thou mock'st me. Thou shalt buy this dear,[4]
If ever I thy face by daylight see.
Now, go thy way. Faintness constraineth me
To measure out my length on this cold bed.
By day's approach look to be visited.          [*Lies down and sleeps.*]   430

   [*Enter* HELENA.]

HELENA: O weary night, O long and tedious night,
Abate[5] thy hours! Shine, comforts, from the east,
That I may back to Athens by daylight,
From these that my poor company detest;
And sleep, that sometimes shuts up sorrow's eye,                            435
Steal me awhile from mine own company.     [*Lies down and sleeps.*]
PUCK: Yet but three? Come one more;
   Two of both kinds makes up four.
   Here she comes, curst and sad.
   Cupid is a knavish lad,                                                            440
   Thus to make poor females mad.

   [*Enter* HERMIA.]

HERMIA: Never so weary, never so in woe,
Bedabbled with the dew and torn with briers,
I can no further crawl, no further go;
My legs can keep no pace with my desires.                                   445
Here will I rest me till the break of day.
Heavens shield Lysander, if they mean a fray!    [*Lies down and sleeps.*]
PUCK: On the ground
   Sleep sound.
   I'll apply                                                                             450
   To your eye,
Gentle lover, remedy.          [*Squeezing the juice on* LYSANDER's *eyes.*]
   When thou wak'st,
   Thou tak'st
   True delight                                                                        455
   In the sight
Of thy former lady's eye;
And the country proverb known,
That every man should take his own,
In your waking shall be shown:                                                 460
   Jack shall have Jill;
   Nought shall go ill;
The man shall have his mare again, and all
   shall be well.                            [*Exit. Manent the four lovers.*]

---

4. Pay dearly for this.   5. Lessen, shorten.

## ACT IV

### Scene 1[6]

*Enter* TITANIA, *Queen of Fairies, and* BOTTOM *the Clown, and* FAIRIES: *and* OBERON, *the King, behind them.*

TITANIA: Come, sit thee down upon this flow'ry bed,
While I thy amiable cheeks do coy,[7]
And stick musk-roses in thy sleek smooth head,
And kiss thy fair large ears, my gentle joy.

[*They recline.*]

5 BOTTOM: Where's Peaseblossom?
PEASEBLOSSOM: Ready.
BOTTOM: Scratch my head, Peaseblossom. Where's Mounsieur Cobweb?
COBWEB: Ready.
BOTTOM: Mounsieur Cobweb, good mounsieur, get you your weapons in your
10 hand, and kill me a red-hipp'd humble-bee on the top of a thistle; and, good mounsieur, bring me the honey-bag. Do not fret yourself too much in the action, mounsieur; and, good mounsieur, have a care the honey-bag break not; I would be loath to have you overflown with a honey-bag, signior. Where's Mounsieur Mustardseed? [*Exit* COBWEB.]
15 MUSTARDSEED: Ready.
BOTTOM: Give me your neaf,[8] Mounsieur Mustardseed. Pray you, leave your curtsy,[9] good mounsieur.
MUSTARDSEED: What's your will?
BOTTOM: Nothing, good mounsieur, but to help Cavalery Cobweb[1] to scratch. I
20 must to the barber's, mounsieur; for methinks I am marvailes hairy about the face; and I am such a tender ass, if my hair do but tickle me, I must scratch.
TITANIA: What, wilt thou hear some music, my sweet love?
BOTTOM: I have a reasonable good ear in music. Let's have the tongs and the bones.[2]

[*Music: tongs, rural music.*][3]

25 TITANIA: Or say, sweet love, what thou desirest to eat.
BOTTOM: Truly, a peck of provender. I could munch your good dry oats. Methinks I have a great desire to a bottle of hay. Good hay, sweet hay, hath no fellow.[4]
TITANIA: I have a venturous fairy that shall seek
30 The squirrel's hoard, and fetch thee new nuts.
BOTTOM: I had rather have a handful or two of dried peas. But, I pray you, let

---

6. Location: scene continues. The four lovers are still asleep on stage.    7. Caress. *Amiable:* lovely.
8. Fist.    9. That is, put on your hat.
1. [Seemingly an error since Cobweb has been sent to bring honey while Peaseblossom has been asked to scratch. *Cavalery:* form of address for a gentleman.]
2. Instruments for rustic music. (The tongs were played like a triangle, whereas the bones were held between the fingers and used as clappers.)    3. [This stage direction is added from the Folio.]
4. Equal. *Bottle:* bundle.

none of your people stir me. I have an exposition[5] of sleep come upon me.
TITANIA: Sleep thou, and I will wind thee in my arms.
    Fairies, be gone, and be all ways[6] away.         *[Exeunt* FAIRIES.*]*
    So doth the woodbine the sweet honeysuckle
    Gently entwist; the female ivy so
    Enrings the barky fingers of the elm.
    Oh, how I love thee! How I dote on thee!         *[They sleep.]*

    *[Enter Robin Goodfellow (*PUCK*).]*

OBERON: *[Advancing.]* Welcome, good Robin. See'st thou this sweet sight?
    Her dotage now I do begin to pity.
    For, meeting her of late behind the wood,
    Seeking sweet favors[7] for this hateful fool,
    I did upbraid her and fall out with her.
    For she his hairy temples then had rounded
    With coronet of fresh and fragrant flowers;
    And that same dew, which sometime[8] on the buds
    Was wont to swell like round and orient pearls,[9]
    Stood now within the pretty flouriets'[1] eyes
    Like tears that did their own disgrace bewail.
    When I had at my pleasure taunted her,
    And she in mild terms begg'd my patience,
    I then did ask of her her changeling child;
    Which straight she gave me, and her fairy sent
    To bear him to my bower in fairy land.
    And, now I have the boy, I will undo
    This hateful imperfection of her eyes.
    And, gentle Puck, take this transformed scalp
    From off the head of this Athenian swain,
    That he, awaking when the other[2] do,
    May all to Athens back again repair,
    And think no more of this night's accidents
    But as the fierce vexation of a dream.
    But first I will release the Fairy Queen.     *[Squeezes juice in her eyes.]*
        Be as thou wast wont to be;
        See as thou wast wont to see.
        Dian's bud[3] o'er Cupid's flower
        Hath such force and blessed power.
    Now, my Titania, wake you, my sweet queen.
TITANIA: *[Waking.]* My Oberon! What visions have I seen!
    Methought I was enamor'd of an ass.
OBERON: There lies your love.

---

5. [Bottom's word for *disposition.*]    6. In all directions.    7. That is, gifts of flowers.
8. Formerly.    9. That is, the most beautiful of all pearls, those coming from the Orient.
1. Flowerets'.    2. Others.
3. [Perhaps the flower of the *agnus castus,* or chaste-tree, supposed to preserve chastity; or perhaps referring simply to the herb by which Oberon can undo the effects of "Cupid's flower," the love-in-idleness of 2.1.166 f.]

TITANIA: How came these things to pass?
O, how mine eyes do loathe his visage now!
OBERON: Silence awhile. Robin, take off this head.
Titania, music call, and strike more dead
Than common sleep of all these five[4] the sense.
TITANIA: Music, ho! Music, such as charmeth sleep!

*[Music.]*

PUCK: *[Removing the ass's head.]* Now, when thou wak'st, with thine own fool's eyes peep.
OBERON: Sound, music! Come, my queen, take hands with me,
And rock the ground whereon these sleepers be.

*[Dance.]*

Now thou and I are new in amity,
And will tomorrow midnight solemnly[5]
Dance in Duke Theseus' house triumphantly
And bless it to all fair prosperity.
There shall the pairs of faithful lovers be
Wedded, with Theseus, all in jollity.
PUCK: Fairy King, attend, and mark:
I do hear the morning lark.
OBERON: Then, my queen, in silence sad,[6]
Trip we after night's shade.
We the globe can compass soon,
Swifter than the wand'ring moon.
TITANIA: Come, my lord, and in our flight
Tell me how it came this night
That I sleeping here was found
With these mortals on the ground. *[Exeunt.]*

*[Wind horn within. Enter* THESEUS *and all his train;* HIPPOLYTA, EGEUS.*]*

THESEUS: Go, one of you, find out the forester,
For now our observation[7] is perform'd;
And since we have the vaward[8] of the day,
My love shall hear the music of my hounds.
Uncouple in the western valley; let them go.
Dispatch, I say, and find the forester. *[Exit an Attendant.]*
We will, fair queen, up to the mountain's top
And mark the musical confusion
Of hounds and echo in conjunction.
HIPPOLYTA: I was with Hercules and Cadmus[9] once,
When in a wood of Crete they bay'd[1] the bear
With hounds of Sparta.[2] Never did I hear

---

4. That is, the four lovers and Bottom.   5. Ceremoniously.   6. Sober.
7. That is, observance to a morn of May (1.1.167).   8. Vanguard, that is, earliest part.
9. Mythical founder of Thebes. (This story about him is unknown.)   1. Brought to bay.
2. [A breed famous in antiquity for its hunting skill.]

Such gallant chiding; for, besides the groves,
The skies, the fountains, every region near
Seem'd all one mutual cry. I never heard
So musical a discord, such sweet thunder.
THESEUS: My hounds are bred out of the Spartan kind,
So flew'd, so sanded;[3] and their heads are hung
With ears that sweep away the morning dew;
Crook-knee'd, and dewlapp'd[4] like Thessalian bulls;
Slow in pursuit, but match'd in mouth like bells,
Each under each. A cry more tuneable[5]
Was never holla'd to, nor cheer'd with horn,
In Crete, in Sparta, nor in Thessaly.
Judge when you hear. [*Sees the sleepers.*] But, soft! What nymphs are these?
EGEUS: My lord, this' my daughter here asleep;
And this, Lysander; this Demetrius is;
This Helena, old Nedar's Helena.
I wonder of their being here together.
THESEUS: No doubt they rose up early to observe
The rite of May, and, hearing our intent,
Came here in grace of our solemnity.[6]
But speak, Egeus. Is not this the day
That Hermia should give answer of her choice?
EGEUS: It is, my lord.
THESEUS: Go, bid the huntsmen wake them with their horns.

[*Exit an Attendant.*]

[*Shout within. Wind horns. They all start up.*]

Good morrow, friends. Saint Valentine[7] is past.
Begin these wood-birds but to couple now?
LYSANDER: Pardon, my lord. [*They kneel.*]
THESEUS:         I pray you all, stand up.
I know you two are rival enemies;
How comes this gentle concord in the world,
That hatred is so far from jealousy
To sleep by hate and fear no enmity?
LYSANDER: My lord, I shall reply amazedly,
Half sleep, half waking; but as yet, I swear,
I cannot truly say how I came here.
But, as I think—for truly would I speak,
And now I do bethink me, so it is—
I came with Hermia hither. Our intent
Was to be gone from Athens, where[8] we might,

---

3. Of sandy color. *So flew'd:* similarly having large hanging chaps or fleshy covering of the jaw.
4. Having pendulous folds of skin under the neck.
5. Well tuned, melodious. *Match'd . . . each:* that is, harmoniously matched in their various cries like a set of bells, from treble down to bass. *Cry:* pack of hounds.    6. That is, observance of these same rites of May.
7. [Birds were supposed to choose their mates on St. Valentine's Day.]    8. Wherever, or to where.

Without[9] the peril of the Athenian law—
EGEUS: Enough, enough, my lord; you have enough.
I beg the law, the law, upon his head.
They would have stol'n away; they would, Demetrius,
Thereby to have defeated you and me,
You of your wife and me of my consent,
Of my consent that she should be your wife.
DEMETRIUS: My lord, fair Helen told me of their stealth,
Of this their purpose hither to this wood,
And I in fury hither followed them,
Fair Helena in fancy following me.
But, my good lord, I wot not by what power—
But by some power it is—my love to Hermia,
Melted as the snow, seems to me now
As the remembrance of an idle gaud[1]
Which in my childhood I did dote upon;
And all the faith, the virtue of my heart,
The object and the pleasure of mine eye,
Is only Helena. To her, my lord,
Was I betroth'd ere I saw Hermia,
But like a sickness did I loathe this food;
But, as in health, come to my natural taste,
Now I do wish it, love it, long for it,
And will for evermore be true to it.
THESEUS: Fair lovers, you are fortunately met.
Of this discourse we more will hear anon.
Egeus, I will overbear your will;
For in the temple, by and by, with us
These couples shall eternally be knit.
And, for the morning now is something[2] worn,
Our purpos'd hunting shall be set aside.
Away with us to Athens. Three and three,
We'll hold a feast in great solemnity.
Come, Hippolyta.        [*Exeunt* THESEUS, HIPPOLYTA, EGEUS, *and train.*]
DEMETRIUS: These things seem small and undistinguishable,
Like far-off mountains turned into clouds.
HERMIA: Methinks I see these things with parted[3] eye,
When every thing seems double.
HELENA:                           So methinks;
And I have found Demetrius like a jewel,
Mine own, and not mine own.[4]
DEMETRIUS:                    Are you sure
That we are awake? It seems to me
That yet we sleep, we dream. Do not you think
The Duke was here, and bid us follow him?

---

9. Outside of, beyond.    1. Worthless trinket.    2. Somewhat. *For*: since.    3. Improperly focused.
4. That is, like a jewel that one finds by chance and, therefore, possesses but cannot certainly consider one's own property.

HERMIA: Yea, and my father.
HELENA: And Hippolyta.
LYSANDER: And he did bid us follow to the temple.
DEMETRIUS: Why, then, we are awake. Let's follow him,
And by the way let us recount our dreams. [*Exeunt.*]
BOTTOM: [*Awaking.*] When my cue comes, call me, and I will answer. My next is, "Most fair Pyramus." Heigh-ho! Peter Quince! Flute, the bellows-mender! Snout, the tinker! Starveling! God's my life, stol'n hence, and left me asleep! I have had a most rare vision. I have had a dream, past the wit of man to say what dream it was. Man is but an ass, if he go about[5] to expound this dream. Methought I was—there is no man can tell what. Methought I was—and methought I had—but man is but a patch'd fool, if he will offer[6] to say what methought I had. The eye of man hath not heard, the ear of man hath not seen, man's hand is not able to taste, his tongue to conceive, nor his heart to report, what my dream was. I will get Peter Quince to write a ballad of this dream. It shall be called "Bottom's Dream," because it hath no bottom; and I will sing it in the latter end of a play, before the Duke. Peradventure, to make it the more gracious, I shall sing it at her[7] death. [*Exit.*]

Scene 2[8]

*Enter* QUINCE, FLUTE, SNOUT, *and* STARVELING.

QUINCE: Have you sent to Bottom's house? Is he come home yet?
STARVELING: He cannot be heard of. Out of doubt he is transported.[9]
FLUTE: If he come not, then the play is marr'd. It goes not forward, doth it?
QUINCE: It is not possible. You have not a man in all Athens able to discharge[1] Pyramus but he.
FLUTE: No, he hath simply the best wit of any handicraft man in Athens.
QUINCE: Yea, and the best person too; and he is a very paramour for a sweet voice.
FLUTE: You must say "paragon." A paramour is, God bless us, a thing of naught.

[*Enter* SNUG *the Joiner.*]

SNUG: Masters, the Duke is coming from the temple, and there is two or three lords and ladies more married. If our sport had gone forward, we had all been made men.
FLUTE: O sweet bully Bottom! Thus hath he lost sixpence a day[2] during his life; he could not have scap'd sixpence a day. An the Duke had not given him sixpence a day for playing Pyramus, I'll be hang'd. He would have deserv'd it. Sixpence a day in Pyramus, or nothing.

[*Enter* BOTTOM.]

BOTTOM: Where are these lads? Where are these hearts?[3]
QUINCE: Bottom! O most courageous day! O most happy hour!

---

5. Attempt.   6. Venture. *Patch'd:* wearing motley, that is, a dress of various colors.   7. Thisby's (?).
8. Location: Athens. Quince's house (?).   9. Carried off by fairies or, possibly, transformed.
1. Perform.   2. That is, as a royal pension.   3. Good fellows.

BOTTOM: Masters, I am to discourse wonders.[4] But ask me not what; for if I tell you, I am no true Athenian. I will tell you everything, right as it fell out.
QUINCE: Let us hear, sweet Bottom.
BOTTOM: Not a word of[5] me. All that I will tell you is, that the Duke hath din'd. Get your apparel together, good strings to your beards, new ribands[6] to your pumps; meet presently[7] at the palace; every man look o'er his part; for the short and the long is, our play is preferr'd.[8] In any case, let Thisby have clean linen; and let not him that plays the lion pare his nails, for they shall hang out for the lion's claws. And, most dear actors, eat no onions nor garlic, for we are to utter sweet breath; and I do not doubt but to hear them say, it is a sweet comedy. No more words. Away! Go away! [*Exeunt.*]

## ACT V

### Scene 1[9]

*Enter* THESEUS, HIPPOLYTA, *and* PHILOSTRATE, *Lords, and Attendants.*

HIPPOLYTA: 'Tis strange, my Theseus, that[1] these lovers speak of.
THESEUS: More strange than true. I never may[2] believe
    These antic fables, nor these fairy toys.[3]
    Lovers and madmen have such seething brains,
5     Such shaping fantasies,[4] that apprehend
    More than cool reason ever comprehends.
    The lunatic, the lover, and the poet
    Are of imagination all compact.[5]
    One sees more devils than vast hell can hold;
10     That is the madman. The lover, all as frantic,
    Sees Helen's beauty in a brow of Egypt.[6]
    The poet's eye, in a fine frenzy rolling,
    Doth glance from heaven to earth, from earth to heaven;
    And as imagination bodies forth
15     The forms of things unknown, the poet's pen
    Turns them to shapes and gives to airy nothing
    A local habitation and a name.
    Such tricks hath strong imagination
    That, if it would but apprehend some joy,
20     It comprehends some bringer[7] of that joy;
    Or in the night, imagining some fear,[8]
    How easy is a bush suppos'd a bear!
HIPPOLYTA: But all the story of the night told over,

---

4. Have wonders to relate.    5. Out of.    6. Ribbons. *Strings:* that is, to attach the beards.
7. Immediately.    8. Selected for consideration.    9. Location: Athens. The palace of Theseus.
1. That which.    2. Can.
3. Trifling stories about fairies. *Antic:* strange, grotesque (with additional punning sense of *antique,* ancient).
4. Imaginations.    5. Formed, composed.
6. That is, face of a gypsy. *Helen's:* that is, of Helen of Troy, pattern of beauty.    7. That is, source.
8. Object of fear.

And all their minds transfigur'd so together,
More witnesseth than fancy's images[9] 25
And grows to something of great constancy;[1]
But, howsoever, strange and admirable.[2]

[*Enter lovers:* LYSANDER, DEMETRIUS, HERMIA, *and* HELENA.]

THESEUS: Here come the lovers, full of joy and mirth.
    Joy, gentle friends! Joy and fresh days of love
    Accompany your hearts!
LYSANDER:               More than to us 30
    Wait in your royal walks, your board, your bed!
THESEUS: Come now, what masques, what dances shall we have,
    To wear away this long age of three hours
    Between our after-supper and bed-time?
    Where is our usual manager of mirth? 35
    What revels are in hand? Is there no play,
    To ease the anguish of a torturing hour?
    Call Philostrate.
PHILOSTRATE:       Here, mighty Theseus.
THESEUS: Say, what abridgement[3] have you for this evening?
    What masque? What music? How shall we beguile 40
    The lazy time, if not with some delight?
PHILOSTRATE: There is a brief[4] how many sports are ripe.
    Make choice of which your Highness will see first.     [*Giving a paper.*]
THESEUS: [*Reads.*] "The battle with the Centaurs,[5] to be sung
    By an Athenian eunuch to the harp." 45
    We'll none of that. That have I told my love,
    In glory of my kinsman[6] Hercules.
    [*Reads.*] "The riot of the tipsy Bacchanals,
    Tearing the Thracian singer in their rage."[7]
    That is an old device; and it was play'd 50
    When I from Thebes came last a conqueror.
    [*Reads.*] "The thrice three Muses mourning for the death
    Of Learning, late deceas'd in beggary."[8]
    That is some satire, keen and critical,
    Not sorting with[9] a nuptial ceremony. 55
    [*Reads.*] "A tedious brief scene of young Pyramus
    And his love Thisby; very tragical mirth."
    Merry and tragical? Tedious and brief?

---

9. Testifies to something more substantial than mere imaginings.    1. Certainty.
2. Source of wonder. *Howsoever:* in any case.    3. Pastime (to abridge or shorten the evening).
4. Short written statement, list.
5. [Probably refers to the battle of the Centaurs and the Lapithae, when the Centaurs attempted to carry off Hippodamia, bride of Theseus's friend Pirothous.]
6. [Plutarch's *Life of Theseus* states that Hercules and Theseus were near kinsmen. Theseus is referring to a version of the battle of the Centaurs in which Hercules was said to be present.]
7. [This was the story of the death of Orpheus, as told in *Metamorphoses* 11.]
8. [Possibly an allusion to Spenser's *Teares of the Muses* (1591), though "satires" deploring the neglect of learning and the creative arts were commonplace.]    9. Befitting.

That is, hot ice and wondrous strange[1] snow.
60 How shall we find the concord of this discord?
PHILOSTRATE: A play there is, my lord, some ten words long,
Which is as brief as I have known a play;
But by ten words, my lord, it is too long,
Which makes it tedious. For in all the play
65 There is not one word apt, one player fitted.
And tragical, my noble lord, it is,
For Pyramus therein doth kill himself.
Which, when I saw rehears'd, I must confess,
Made mine eyes water; but more merry tears
70 The passion of loud laughter never shed.
THESEUS: What are they that do play it?
PHILOSTRATE: Hard-handed men that work in Athens here,
Which never labor'd in their minds till now,
And now have toil'd their unbreathed[2] memories
75 With this same play, against[3] your nuptial.
THESEUS: And we will hear it.
PHILOSTRATE:           No, my noble lord,
It is not for you. I have heard it over,
And it is nothing, nothing in the world;
Unless you can find sport in their intents,
80 Extremely stretch'd and conn'd[4] with cruel pain,
To do you service.
THESEUS:           I will hear that play;
For never anything can be amiss
When simpleness and duty tender it.
Go, bring them in; and take your places, ladies.

[PHILOSTRATE *goes to summon the players.*]

85 HIPPOLYTA: I love not to see wretchedness o'ercharg'd[5]
And duty in his service[6] perishing.
THESEUS: Why, gentle sweet, you shall see no such thing.
HIPPOLYTA: He says they can do nothing in this kind.[7]
THESEUS: The kinder we, to give them thanks for nothing.
90 Our sport shall be to take what they mistake;
And what poor duty cannot do, noble respect
Takes it in might, not merit.[8]
Where I have come, great clerks[9] have purposed
To greet me with premeditated welcomes;
95 Where I have seen them shiver and look pale,
Make periods in the midst of sentences,
Throttle their practic'd accent[1] in their fears,

---

1. [Seemingly an error for some adjective that would contrast with *snow*, just as *hot* contrasts with *ice*.]
2. Unexercised. *Toil'd:* taxed.   3. In preparation for.   4. Memorized. *Stretch'd:* strained.
5. Incompetence overburdened.   6. Its attempt to serve.   7. Kind of thing.
8. Values it for the effort made rather than for the excellence achieved.   9. Learned men.
1. That is, rehearsed speech, or usual way of speaking.

And in conclusion dumbly have broke off,
Not paying me a welcome. Trust me, sweet,
Out of this silence yet I pick'd a welcome;
And in the modesty of fearful duty
I read as much as from the rattling tongue
Of saucy and audacious eloquence.
Love, therefore, and tongue-tied simplicity
In least speak most, to my capacity.[2]

[PHILOSTRATE *returns*.]

PHILOSTRATE: So please your Grace, the Prologue is address'd.[3]
THESEUS: Let him approach.

[*Flourish of trumpets. Enter the Prologue* (QUINCE).]

PROLOGUE: If we offend, it is with our good will.
That you should think, we come not to offend,
But with good will. To show our simple skill,
That is the true beginning of our end.
Consider, then, we come but in despite.
We do not come, as minding[4] to content you,
Our true intent is. All for your delight
We are not here. That you should here repent you,
The actors are at hand; and, by their show,
You shall know all that you are like to know.
THESEUS: This fellow doth not stand upon points.[5]
LYSANDER: He hath rid his prologue like a rough[6] colt; he knows not the stop.[7]
A good moral, my lord: it is not enough to speak, but to speak true.
HIPPOLYTA: Indeed he hath play'd on his prologue like a child on a recorder; a sound, but not in government.[8]
THESEUS: His speech was like a tangled chain, nothing[9] impair'd, but all disorder'd. Who is next?

[*Enter* PYRAMUS *and* THISBY, *and* WALL, *and* MOONSHINE, *and* LION.]

PROLOGUE: Gentles, perchance you wonder at this show;
But wonder on, till truth make all things plain.
This man is Pyramus, if you would know;
This beauteous lady Thisby is certain.
This man, with lime and rough-cast, doth present
Wall, that vile Wall which did these lovers sunder;
And through Wall's chink, poor souls, they are content
To whisper. At the which let no man wonder.
This man, with lantern, dog, and bush of thorn,

---

2. In my judgment and understanding. *Least:* that is, saying least.
3. Ready. *Prologue:* speaker of the prologue.    4. Intending.
5. (1) Heed niceties or small points; (2) pay attention to punctuation in his reading. (The humor of Quince's speech is in the blunders of its punctuation.)    6. Unbroken.
7. (1) The stopping of a colt by reining it in; (2) punctuation mark.
8. Control. *Recorder:* a wind instrument like a flute or flageolet.    9. Not at all.

Presenteth Moonshine; for, if you will know,
135  By moonshine did these lovers think no scorn[1]
To meet at Ninus' tomb, there, there to woo.
This grisly beast, which Lion hight[2] by name,
The trusty Thisby, coming first by night,
Did scare away, or rather did affright;
140  And, as she fled, her mantle she did fall,[3]
Which Lion vile with bloody mouth did stain.
Anon comes Pyramus, sweet youth and tall,[4]
And finds his trusty Thisby's mantle slain;
Whereat, with blade, with bloody blameful blade,
145  He bravely broach'd[5] his boiling bloody breast.
And Thisby, tarrying in mulberry shade,
His dagger drew, and died. For all the rest,
Let Lion, Moonshine, Wall, and lovers twain
At large[6] discourse, while here they do remain.

[*Exeunt* LION, THISBY, *and* MOONSHINE.]

150  THESEUS: I wonder if the lion be to speak.
DEMETRIUS: No wonder, my lord. One lion may, when many asses do.
WALL: In this same interlude it doth befall
That I, one Snout by name, present a wall;
And such a wall, as I would have you think,
155  That had in it a crannied hole or chink,
Through which the lovers, Pyramus and Thisby,
Did whisper often very secretly.
This loam, this rough-cast, and this stone doth show
That I am that same wall; the truth is so.
160  And this the cranny is, right and sinister,[7]
Through which the fearful lovers are to whisper.
THESEUS: Would you desire lime and hair to speak better?
DEMETRIUS: It is the wittiest partition[8] that ever I heard discourse, my lord.

[PYRAMUS *comes forward.*]

THESEUS: Pyramus draws near the wall. Silence!
165  PYRAMUS: O grim-look'd[9] night! O night with hue so black!
O night, which ever art when day is not!
O night, O night! Alack, alack, alack,
I fear my Thisby's promise is forgot.
And thou, O wall, O sweet, O lovely wall,
170  That stand'st between her father's ground and mine,
Thou wall, O wall, O sweet and lovely wall,
Show me thy chink, to blink through with mine eyne!

[WALL *holds up his fingers.*]

---

1. Think it no disgraceful matter.   2. Is called.   3. Let fall.   4. Courageous.   5. Stabbed.
6. In full, at length.
7. That is, the right side of it and the left; or running from right to left, horizontally.
8. (1) Wall; (2) section of a learned treatise or oration.   9. Grim-looking.

Thanks, courteous Wall. Jove shield thee well for this!
But what see I? No Thisby do I see.
O wicked wall, through whom I see no bliss!
Curs'd be thy stones for thus deceiving me!
THESEUS: The wall, methinks, being sensible,[1] should curse again.
PYRAMUS: No, in truth, sir, he should not. "Deceiving me" is Thisby's cue: she is
to enter now, and I am to spy her through the wall. You shall see, it will fall
pat as I told you. Yonder she comes.

   [*Enter* THISBY.]

THISBY: O wall, full often hast thou heard my moans,
For parting my fair Pyramus and me.
My cherry lips have often kiss'd thy stones,
Thy stones with lime and hair knit up in thee.
PYRAMUS: I see a voice. Now will I to the chink,
To spy an[2] I can hear my Thisby's face.
Thisby!
THISBY: My love! Thou art my love, I think.
PYRAMUS: Think what thou wilt, I am thy lover's grace;[3]
And, like Limander, am I trusty still.
THISBY: And I like Helen,[4] till the Fates me kill.
PYRAMUS: Not Shafalus to Procrus[5] was so true.
THISBY: As Shafalus to Procrus, I to you.
PYRAMUS: O, kiss me through the hole of this vile wall!
THISBY: I kiss the wall's hole, not your lips at all.
PYRAMUS: Wilt thou at Ninny's tomb meet me straightway?
THISBY: 'Tide life, 'tide[6] death, I come without delay.
                              [*Exeunt* PYRAMUS *and* THISBY.]
WALL: Thus have I, Wall, my part discharged so;
And, being done, thus Wall away doth go.                [*Exit.*]
THESEUS: Now is the mural down between the two neighbors.
DEMETRIUS: No remedy, my lord, when walls are so willful to hear without
warning.[7]
HIPPOLYTA: This is the silliest stuff that ever I heard.
THESEUS: The best in this kind are but shadows;[8] and the worst are no worse, if
imagination amend them.
HIPPOLYTA: It must be your imagination then, and not theirs.
THESEUS: If we imagine no worse of them than they of themselves, they may pass
for excellent men. Here come two noble beasts in, a man and a lion.

   [*Enter* LION *and* MOONSHINE.]

LION: You, ladies, you, whose gentle hearts do fear
The smallest monstrous mouse that creeps on floor,

---

1. Capable of feeling.   2. If.   3. That is, gracious lover.
4. [Blunders for "Leander" (*Limander*) and "Hero."]
5. [Blunders for "Cephalus" (*Shafalus*) and "Procris," also famous lovers.]   6. Betide, come.
7. That is, without warning the parents. *To hear:* as to hear.
8. Likenesses, representations. *In this kind:* of this sort.

May now perchance both quake and tremble here,
When lion rough in widest rage doth roar.
Then know that I, as Snug the joiner, am
A lion fell,[9] nor else no lion's dam;
215 For, if I should as lion come in strife
Into this place, 'twere pity on my life.
THESEUS: A very gentle beast, and of a good conscience.
DEMETRIUS: The very best at a beast, my lord, that e'er I saw.
LYSANDER: This lion is a very fox for his valor.[1]
220 THESEUS: True; and a goose for his discretion.[2]
DEMETRIUS: Not so, my lord; for his valor cannot carry his discretion; and the fox carries the goose.
THESEUS: His discretion, I am sure, cannot carry his valor; for the goose carries not the fox. It is well. Leave it to his discretion, and let us listen to the moon.
225 MOON: This lanthorn[3] doth the horned moon present—
DEMETRIUS: He should have worn the horns on his head.[4]
THESEUS: He is no crescent, and his horns are invisible within the circumference.
MOON: This lanthorn doth the horned moon present;
Myself the man i' th' moon do seem to be.
230 THESEUS: This is the greatest error of all the rest. The man should be put into the lanthorn. How is it else the man i' th' moon?
DEMETRIUS: He dares not come there for the[5] candle; for, you see, it is already in snuff.[6]
HIPPOLYTA: I am aweary of this moon. Would he would change!
235 THESEUS: It appears, by his small light of discretion, that he is in the wane; but yet, in courtesy, in all reason, we must stay the time.
LYSANDER: Proceed, Moon.
MOON: All that I have to say is to tell you that the lanthorn is the moon, I, the man in the moon, this thorn-bush my thorn-bush, and this dog my dog.
240 DEMETRIUS: Why, all these should be in the lanthorn; for all these are in the moon. But silence! Here comes Thisby.

[*Enter* THISBY.]

THISBY: This is old Ninny's tomb. Where is my love?
LION: [*Roaring.*] Oh—          [THISBY *runs off, dropping her mantle.*]
DEMETRIUS: Well roar'd, Lion.
245 THESEUS: Well run, Thisby.
HIPPOLYTA: Well shone, Moon. Truly, the moon shines with a good grace.

[*The* LION *shakes* THISBY'*s mantle, and exits.*]

THESEUS: Well mous'd,[7] Lion.
DEMETRIUS: And then came Pyramus.

---

9. Fierce lion (with a play on the idea of *lion skin*).   1. That is, his valor consists of craftiness and discretion.
2. That is, as discreet as a goose, meaning more foolish than discreet.
3. [This original spelling, *lanthorn*, may suggest a play on the *horn* of which lanterns were made, and also on a cuckold's horns; but the spelling *lanthorn* is not used consistently for comic effect in this play or elsewhere. At 5.1.133, for example, the word is *lantern* in the original.]   4. [As a sign of cuckoldry.]
5. Because of the.   6. (1) Offended; (2) in need of snuffing.   7. Shaken.

[*Enter* PYRAMUS.]

LYSANDER: And so the lion vanish'd.
PYRAMUS: Sweet Moon, I thank thee for thy sunny beams;
  I thank thee, Moon, for shining now so bright;
  For, by thy gracious, golden, glittering gleams,
  I trust to take of truest Thisby sight.
    But stay, O spite!
    But mark, poor knight,
  What dreadful dole[8] is here!
    Eyes, do you see?
    How can it be?
  O dainty duck! O dear!
    Thy mantle good,
    What, stain'd with blood!
  Approach, ye Furies fell![9]
    O Fates, come, come,
    Cut thread and thrum;[1]
  Quail, crush, conclude, and quell![2]

THESEUS: This passion, and the death of a dear friend, would go near to make a man look sad.[3]
HIPPOLYTA: Beshrew my heart, but I pity the man.
PYRAMUS: O wherefore, Nature, didst thou lions frame?
  Since lion vile hath here deflow'r'd my dear,
  Which is—no, no—which was the fairest dame
  That liv'd, that lov'd, that lik'd, that look'd with cheer.[4]
    Come, tears, confound,
    Out, sword, and wound
  The pap of Pyramus;
    Ay, that left pap,
    Where heart doth hop.     [*Stabs himself.*]
  Thus die I, thus, thus, thus.
    Now am I dead,
    Now am I fled;
  My soul is in the sky.
    Tongue, lose thy light;
    Moon, take thy flight.     [*Exit* MOONSHINE.]
  Now die, die, die, die, die.     [*Dies.*]

DEMETRIUS: No die, but an ace,[5] for him; for he is but one.[6]

---

8. Grievous event.    9. Fierce.    1. The warp in weaving and the loose end of the warp.
2. Kill, destroy. *Quail:* overpower.
3. That is, if one had other reason to grieve, one might be sad, but not from this absurd portrayal of passion.    4. Countenance.
5. The side of the die featuring the single pip, or spot. (The pun is on *die* as a singular of *dice*; Bottom's performance is not worth a whole *die* but rather one single face of it, one small portion.)
6. (1) An individual person; (2) unique.

LYSANDER: Less than an ace, man; for he is dead, he is nothing.
THESEUS: With the help of a surgeon he might yet recover, and yet prove an ass.[7]
HIPPOLYTA: How chance Moonshine is gone before Thisby comes back and finds her lover?
290 THESEUS: She will find him by starlight. Here she comes; and her passion ends the play.

[*Enter* THISBY.]

HIPPOLYTA: Methinks she should not use a long one for such a Pyramus. I hope she will be brief.
DEMETRIUS: A mote will turn the balance, which Pyramus, which[8] Thisby, is the
295 better: he for a man, God warr'nt us; she for a woman, God bless us.
LYSANDER: She hath spied him already with those sweet eyes.
DEMETRIUS: And thus she means, videlicet:[9]
THISBY: Asleep, my love?
    What, dead, my dove?
300   O Pyramus, arise!
    Speak, speak. Quite dumb?
    Dead, dead? A tomb
Must cover thy sweet eyes.
    These lily lips,
305     This cherry nose,
These yellow cowslip cheeks,
    Are gone, are gone!
    Lovers, make moan.
His eyes were green as leeks.
310   O Sisters Three,[1]
    Come, come to me,
With hands as pale as milk;
    Lay them in gore,
    Since you have shore[2]
315 With shears his thread of silk.
    Tongue, not a word.
    Come, trusty sword,
Come, blade, my breast imbrue![3]     [*Stabs herself.*]
    And farewell, friends.
320   Thus Thisby ends.
Adieu, adieu, adieu.     [*Dies.*]
THESEUS: Moonshine and Lion are left to bury the dead.
DEMETRIUS: Ay, and Wall too.
BOTTOM: [*Starting up.*] No, I assure you; the wall is down that parted their fathers.
325 Will it please you to see the epilogue, or to hear a Bergomask dance[4] between two of our company?
THESEUS: No epilogue, I pray you; for your play needs no excuse. Never excuse; for when the players are all dead, there need none to be blam'd. Marry, if

---

7. [With a pun on *ace*.]    8. Whether...or.    9. To wit. *Means:* moans, laments.    1. The Fates.
2. Shorn.    3. Stain with blood.
4. A rustic dance named from Bergamo, a province in the state of Venice.

he that writ it had play'd Pyramus and hang'd himself in Thisby's garter, it
would have been a fine tragedy; and so it is, truly, and very notably discharg'd.     330
But, come, your Bergomask. Let your epilogue alone.
   [*A dance.*]
The iron tongue of midnight hath told[5] twelve.
Lovers, to bed; 'tis almost fairy time.
I fear we shall outsleep the coming morn
As much as we this night have overwatch'd.[6]                                          335
This palpable-gross[7] play hath well beguil'd
The heavy[8] gait of night. Sweet friends, to bed.
A fortnight hold we this solemnity,
In nightly revels and new jollity.                                        [*Exeunt.*]

   [*Enter* PUCK, *carrying a broom.*]

PUCK: Now the hungry lion roars,                                                       340
   And the wolf behowls the moon;
Whilst the heavy ploughman snores,
   All with weary task fordone.[9]
Now the wasted brands[1] do glow,
   Whilst the screech-owl, screeching loud,                                            345
Puts the wretch that lies in woe
   In remembrance of a shroud.
Now it is the time of night
   That the graves, all gaping wide,
Every one lets forth his sprite,[2]                                                    350
   In the churchway paths to glide.
And we fairies, that do run
   By the triple Hecate's[3] team
From the presence of the sun,
   Following darkness like a dream,                                                    355
Now are frolic.[4] Not a mouse
Shall disturb this hallowed house.
I am sent with broom before,
To sweep the dust behind[5] the door.

   [*Enter* OBERON *and* TITANIA, *King and Queen of Fairies, with all their train.*]

OBERON: Through the house give glimmering light,                                       360
   By the dead and drowsy fire;
Every elf and fairy sprite
   Hop as light as bird from brier;
And this ditty, after me,
   Sing, and dance it trippingly.                                                      365

---

5. Counted, struck ("tolled").   6. Stayed up too late.   7. Palpably gross, obviously crude.
8. Drowsy, dull.   9. Exhausted.   1. Burned-out logs.   2. Every grave lets forth its ghost.
3. [Hecate ruled as Luna or Cynthia in Heaven, as Diana on Earth, and as Proserpina in Hell.]   4. Merry.
5. From behind. (Robin Goodfellow was a household spirit who helped good housemaids and punished lazy ones.)

TITANIA: First, rehearse your song by rote,
　　　　 To each word a warbling note.
　　　　 Hand in hand, with fairy grace,
　　　　 Will we sing, and bless this place.

　　　　 [Song and dance.]

370　OBERON: Now, until the break of day,
　　　　 Through this house each fairy stray.
　　　　 To the best bride-bed will we,
　　　　 Which by us shall blessed be;
　　　　 And the issue there create[6]
375　　　 Ever shall be fortunate.
　　　　 So shall all the couples three
　　　　 Ever true in loving be;
　　　　 And the blots of Nature's hand
　　　　 Shall not in their issue stand;
380　　　 Never mole, hare lip, nor scar,
　　　　 Nor mark prodigious,[7] such as are
　　　　 Despised in nativity,
　　　　 Shall upon their children be.
　　　　 With this field-dew consecrate,[8]
385　　　 Every fairy take his gait,[9]
　　　　 And each several[1] chamber bless,
　　　　 Through this palace, with sweet peace;
　　　　 And the owner of it blest
　　　　 Ever shall in safety rest.
390　　　 Trip away; make no stay;
　　　　 Meet me all by break of day.　　　　 [Exeunt OBERON, TITANIA, and train.]

　　PUCK: If we shadows have offended,
　　　　 Think but this, and all is mended,
　　　　 That you have but slumb'red here[2]
395　　　 While these visions did appear.
　　　　 And this weak and idle theme,
　　　　 No more yielding but[3] a dream,
　　　　 Gentles, do not reprehend.
　　　　 If you pardon, we will mend.
400　　　 And, as I am an honest Puck,
　　　　 If we have unearned luck
　　　　 Now to scape the serpent's tongue,[4]
　　　　 We will make amends ere long;
　　　　 Else the Puck a liar call.
405　　　 So, good night unto you all.
　　　　 Give me your hands,[5] if we be friends,
　　　　 And Robin shall restore amends.
　　　　　　　　　　　　　　　　　　　　　　　[Exit.]

　　　　　　　　　　　　　　　　　　　　　　ca. 1594–95

6. Created.　7. Monstrous, unnatural.　8. Consecrated.　9. Go his way.　1. Separate.
2. That is, that it is a "midsummer night's dream."　3. Yielding no more than.　4. That is, hissing.
5. Applaud.

# Hamlet

**CHARACTERS**

CLAUDIUS, *King of Denmark*
HAMLET, *son of the former and nephew to the present King*
POLONIUS, *Lord Chamberlain*
HORATIO, *friend of Hamlet*
LAERTES, *son of Polonius*
VOLTEMAND
CORNELIUS
ROSENCRANTZ } *courtiers*
GUILDENSTERN
OSRIC
A GENTLEMAN
A PRIEST
MARCELLUS } *officers*
BERNARDO
FRANCISCO, *a soldier*
REYNALDO, *servant to Polonius*
PLAYERS
TWO CLOWNS, *gravediggers*
FORTINBRAS, *Prince of Norway*
A NORWEGIAN CAPTAIN
ENGLISH AMBASSADORS
GERTRUDE, *Queen of Denmark, and mother of Hamlet*
OPHELIA, *daughter of Polonius*
GHOST OF HAMLET'S FATHER
LORDS, LADIES, OFFICERS, SOLDIERS, SAILORS, MESSENGERS, AND ATTENDANTS

SCENE: *The action takes place in or near the royal castle of Denmark at Elsinore.*

## ACT I

### Scene 1

*A guard station atop the castle. Enter* BERNARDO *and* FRANCISCO, *two sentinels.*

BERNARDO: Who's there?
FRANCISCO: Nay, answer me. Stand and unfold yourself.
BERNARDO: Long live the king!
FRANCISCO: Bernardo?
BERNARDO: He.   5
FRANCISCO: You come most carefully upon your hour.
BERNARDO: 'Tis now struck twelve. Get thee to bed, Francisco.
FRANCISCO: For this relief much thanks. 'Tis bitter cold,
  And I am sick at heart.
BERNARDO: Have you had quiet guard?
FRANCISCO:                          Not a mouse stirring.   10
BERNARDO: Well, good night.
  If you do meet Horatio and Marcellus,
  The rivals[1] of my watch, bid them make haste.

  [*Enter* HORATIO *and* MARCELLUS.]

FRANCISCO: I think I hear them. Stand, ho! Who is there?
HORATIO: Friends to this ground.
MARCELLUS:                    And liegemen to the Dane.[2]   15

---

1. Companions.
2. The "Dane" is the king of Denmark, who is also called "Denmark," as in line 48 of this scene. In line 61 the same figure is used for the king of Norway.

FRANCISCO: Give you good night.
MARCELLUS:                     O, farewell, honest soldier!
   Who hath relieved you?
FRANCISCO:            Bernardo hath my place.
   Give you good night.                              [*Exit* FRANCISCO.]
MARCELLUS:       Holla, Bernardo!
BERNARDO:                    Say—
   What, is Horatio there?
HORATIO:          A piece of him.
20 BERNARDO: Welcome, Horatio. Welcome, good Marcellus.
HORATIO: What, has this thing appeared again tonight?
BERNARDO: I have seen nothing.
MARCELLUS: Horatio says 'tis but our fantasy,
   And will not let belief take hold of him
25 Touching this dreaded sight twice seen of us.
   Therefore I have entreated him along
   With us to watch the minutes of this night,
   That if again this apparition come,
   He may approve[3] our eyes and speak to it.
HORATIO: Tush, tush, 'twill not appear.
30 BERNARDO:                     Sit down awhile,
   And let us once again assail your ears,
   That are so fortified against our story,
   What we have two nights seen.
HORATIO:                    Well, sit we down.
   And let us hear Bernardo speak of this.
35 BERNARDO: Last night of all,
   When yond same star that's westward from the pole[4]
   Had made his course t' illume that part of heaven
   Where now it burns, Marcellus and myself,
   The bell then beating one—

   [*Enter* GHOST.]

40 MARCELLUS: Peace, break thee off. Look where it comes again.
BERNARDO: In the same figure like the king that's dead.
MARCELLUS: Thou art a scholar; speak to it, Horatio.
BERNARDO: Looks 'a[5] not like the king? Mark it, Horatio.
HORATIO: Most like. It harrows me with fear and wonder.
BERNARDO: It would be spoke to.
45 MARCELLUS:                    Speak to it, Horatio.
HORATIO: What art thou that usurp'st this time of night
   Together with that fair and warlike form
   In which the majesty of buried Denmark
   Did sometimes march? By heaven I charge thee, speak.
MARCELLUS: It is offended.
50 BERNARDO:             See, it stalks away.
HORATIO: Stay. Speak, speak. I charge thee, speak.     [*Exit* GHOST.]

3. Confirm the testimony of.   4. Polestar.   5. He.

MARCELLUS: 'Tis gone and will not answer.
BERNARDO: How now, Horatio! You tremble and look pale.
   Is not this something more than fantasy?
   What think you on't?
HORATIO: Before my God, I might not this believe
   Without the sensible[6] and true avouch
   Of mine own eyes.
MARCELLUS:           It is not like the king?
HORATIO: As thou art to thyself.
   Such was the very armor he had on
   When he the ambitious Norway combated.
   So frowned he once when, in an angry parle,[7]
   He smote the sledded Polacks on the ice.
   'Tis strange.
MARCELLUS: Thus twice before, and jump[8] at this dead hour,
   With martial stalk hath he gone by our watch.
HORATIO: In what particular thought to work I know not,
   But in the gross and scope of mine opinion,
   This bodes some strange eruption to our state.
MARCELLUS: Good now, sit down, and tell me he that knows,
   Why this same strict and most observant watch
   So nightly toils the subject[9] of the land,
   And why such daily cast of brazen cannon
   And foreign mart for implements of war;
   Why such impress of shipwrights, whose sore task
   Does not divide the Sunday from the week.
   What might be toward that this sweaty haste
   Doth make the night joint-laborer with the day?
   Who is't that can inform me?
HORATIO:               That can I.
   At last, the whisper goes so. Our last king,
   Whose image even but now appeared to us,
   Was as you know by Fortinbras of Norway,
   Thereto pricked on by a most emulate pride,
   Dared to the combat; in which our valiant Hamlet
   (For so this side of our known world esteemed him)
   Did slay this Fortinbras; who by a sealed compact
   Well ratified by law and heraldry,
   Did forfeit, with his life, all those his lands
   Which he stood seized of,[1] to the conqueror;
   Against the which a moiety competent[2]
   Was gagéd[3] by our king; which had returned
   To the inheritance of Fortinbras,
   Had he been vanquisher; as, by the same covenant
   And carriage of the article designed,
   His fell to Hamlet. Now, sir, young Fortinbras,

---

6. Perceptible.   7. Parley.   8. Precisely.   9. People.   1. Possessed.   2. Portion of similar value.
3. Pledged.

        Of unimprovéd mettle hot and full,
        Hath in the skirts of Norway here and there
        Sharked up a list of lawless resolutes
        For food and diet to some enterprise
100   That hath a stomach in't; which is no other,
        As it doth well appear unto our state,
        But to recover of us by strong hand
        And terms compulsatory, those foresaid lands
        So by his father lost; and this, I take it,
105   Is the main motive of our preparations,
        The source of this our watch, and the chief head
        Of this post-haste and romage[4] in the land.
   BERNARDO: I think it be no other but e'en so.
        Well may it sort[5] that this portentous figure
110   Comes arméd through our watch so like the king
        That was and is the question of these wars.
   HORATIO: A mote[6] it is to trouble the mind's eye.
        In the most high and palmy state of Rome,
        A little ere the mightiest Julius fell,
115   The graves stood tenantless, and the sheeted dead
        Did squeak and gibber in the Roman streets;
        As stars with trains of fire, and dews of blood,
        Disasters in the sun; and the moist star,
        Upon whose influence Neptune's empire stands,[7]
120   Was sick almost to doomsday with eclipse.
        And even the like precurse[8] of feared events,
        As harbingers preceding still the fates
        And prologue to the omen coming on,
        Have heaven and earth together demonstrated
125   Unto our climatures[9] and countrymen.

        *[Enter GHOST.]*

        But soft, behold, lo where it comes again!
        I'll cross it[1] though it blast me.—Stay, illusion.

        *[It spreads (its) arms.]*

        If thou hast any sound or use of voice,
        Speak to me.
130   If there be any good thing to be done,
        That may to thee do ease, and grace to me,
        Speak to me.
        If thou art privy to thy country's fate,
        Which happily foreknowing may avoid,

---

4. Stir.   5. Chance.   6. Speck of dust.
7. Neptune was the Roman sea god; the "moist star" is the moon.   8. Precursor.   9. Regions.
1. Horatio means either that he will move across the ghost's path in order to stop him or that he will make the sign of the cross to gain power over him. The stage direction that follows is somewhat ambiguous. "It" seems to refer to the ghost, but the movement would be appropriate to Horatio.

O, speak!
Or if thou hast uphoarded in thy life
Extorted treasure in the womb of earth,
For which, they say, you spirits oft walk in death,

[*The cock crows.*]

Speak of it. Stay, and speak. Stop it, Marcellus.
MARCELLUS: Shall I strike at it with my partisan?[2]
HORATIO: Do, if it will not stand.
BERNARDO:                          'Tis here.
HORATIO:                                     'Tis here.
MARCELLUS: 'Tis gone.                         [*Exit* GHOST.]
We do it wrong, being so majestical,
To offer it the show of violence;
For it is as the air, invulnerable,
And our vain blows malicious mockery.
BERNARDO: It was about to speak when the cock crew.
HORATIO: And then it started like a guilty thing
Upon a fearful summons. I have heard
The cock, that is the trumpet to the morn,
Doth with his lofty and shrill-sounding throat
Awake the god of day, and at his warning,
Whether in sea or fire, in earth or air,
Th' extravagant and erring[3] spirit hies
To his confine; and of the truth herein
This present object made probation.[4]
MARCELLUS: It faded on the crowing of the cock.
Some say that ever 'gainst that season comes
Wherein our Savior's birth is celebrated,
This bird of dawning singeth all night long,
And then, they say, no spirit dare stir abroad,
The nights are wholesome, then no planets strike,
No fairy takes,[5] nor witch hath power to charm,
So hallowed and so gracious is that time.
HORATIO: So have I heard and do in part believe it.
But look, the morn in russet mantle clad
Walks o'er the dew of yon high eastward hill.
Break we our watch up, and by my advice
Let us impart what we have seen tonight
Unto young Hamlet, for upon my life
This spirit, dumb to us, will speak to him.
Do you consent we shall acquaint him with it,
As needful in our loves, fitting our duty?
MARCELLUS: Let's do't, I pray, and I this morning know
Where we shall find him most conveniently.    [*Exeunt.*]

2. Halberd.   3. Wandering out of bounds.   4. Proof.   5. Enchants.

## Scene 2

*A chamber of state. Enter* KING CLAUDIUS, QUEEN GERTRUDE, HAMLET, POLONIUS, LAERTES, VOLTEMAND, CORNELIUS *and other members of the court.*

KING: Though yet of Hamlet our dear brother's death
The memory be green, and that it us befitted
To bear our hearts in grief, and our whole kingdom
To be contracted in one brow of woe,
5 Yet so far hath discretion fought with nature
That we with wisest sorrow think on him,
Together with remembrance of ourselves.
Therefore our sometime sister, now our queen,
Th' imperial jointress[6] to this warlike state,
10 Have we, as 'twere with a defeated joy,
With an auspicious and a dropping eye,
With mirth in funeral, and with dirge in marriage,
In equal scale weighing delight and dole,
Taken to wife; nor have we herein barred
15 Your better wisdoms, which have freely gone
With this affair along. For all, our thanks.
Now follows that you know young Fortinbras,
Holding a weak supposal of our worth,
Or thinking by our late dear brother's death
20 Our state to be disjoint and out of frame,
Colleaguéd with this dream of his advantage,
He hath not failed to pester us with message
Importing the surrender of those lands
Lost by his father, with all bonds of law,
25 To our most valiant brother. So much for him.
Now for ourself, and for this time of meeting,
Thus much the business is: we have here writ
To Norway, uncle of young Fortinbras—
Who, impotent and bedrid, scarcely hears
30 Of this his nephew's purpose—to suppress
His further gait[7] herein, in that the levies,
The lists, and full proportions are all made
Out of his subject; and we here dispatch
You, good Cornelius, and you, Voltemand,
35 For bearers of this greeting to old Norway,
Giving to you no further personal power
To business with the king, more than the scope
Of these dilated[8] articles allow.
Farewell, and let your haste commend your duty.
CORNELIUS:⎫
40 VOLTEMAND:⎭ In that, and all things will we show our duty.

---

6. A "jointress" is a widow who holds a *jointure* or life interest in the estate of her deceased husband.
7. Progress.   8. Fully expressed.

KING: We doubt it nothing, heartily farewell.
             [*Exeunt* VOLTEMAND *and* CORNELIUS.]
    And now, Laertes, what's the news with you?
    You told us of some suit. What is't, Laertes?
    You cannot speak of reason to the Dane
    And lose your voice. What wouldst thou beg, Laertes,      45
    That shall not be my offer, not thy asking?
    The head is not more native to the heart,
    The hand more instrumental[9] to the mouth,
    Than is the throne of Denmark to thy father.
    What wouldst thou have, Laertes?
LAERTES:                    My dread lord,                    50
    Your leave and favor to return to France,
    From whence, though willingly, I came to Denmark
    To show my duty in your coronation,
    Yet now I must confess, that duty done,
    My thoughts and wishes bend again toward France,          55
    And bow them to your gracious leave and pardon.
KING: Have you your father's leave? What says Polonius?
POLONIUS: He hath, my lord, wrung from me my slow leave
    By laborsome petition, and at last
    Upon his will I sealed my hard consent.                   60
    I do beseech you give him leave to go.
KING: Take thy fair hour, Laertes. Time be thine,
    And thy best graces spend it at thy will.
    But now, my cousin[1] Hamlet, and my son—
HAMLET: [*Aside.*] A little more than kin, and less than kind. 65
KING: How is it that the clouds still hang on you?
HAMLET: Not so, my lord. I am too much in the sun.
QUEEN: Good Hamlet, cast thy nighted color off,
    And let thine eye look like a friend on Denmark.
    Do not for ever with thy vailéd lids[2]                    70
    Seek for thy noble father in the dust.
    Thou know'st 'tis common—all that lives must die,
    Passing through nature to eternity.
HAMLET: Ay, madam, it is common.
QUEEN:                      If it be,
    Why seems it so particular with thee?                     75
HAMLET: Seems, madam? Nay, it is. I know not "seems."
    'Tis not alone my inky cloak, good mother,
    Nor customary suits of solemn black,
    Nor windy suspiration of forced breath,
    No, nor the fruitful river in the eye,                    80
    Nor the dejected havior[3] of the visage,
    Together with all forms, moods, shapes of grief,
    That can denote me truly. These indeed seem,

9. Serviceable.  1. "Cousin" is used here as a general term of kinship.  2. Lowered eyes.
3. Appearance.

>        For they are actions that a man might play,
> 85     But I have that within which passes show—
>        These but the trappings and the suits of woe.
>    KING: 'Tis sweet and commendable in your nature, Hamlet,
>        To give these mourning duties to your father,
>        But you must know your father lost a father,
> 90     That father lost, lost his, and the survivor bound
>        In filial obligation for some term
>        To do obsequious[4] sorrow. But to persever
>        In obstinate condolement is a course
>        Of impious stubbornness. 'Tis unmanly grief.
> 95     It shows a will most incorrect to[5] heaven,
>        A heart unfortified, a mind impatient,
>        An understanding simple and unschooled.
>        For what we know must be, and is as common
>        As any the most vulgar thing to sense,
> 100    Why should we in our peevish opposition
>        Take it to heart? Fie, 'tis a fault to heaven,
>        A fault against the dead, a fault to nature,
>        To reason most absurd, whose common theme
>        Is death of fathers, and who still hath cried,
> 105    From the first corse[6] till he that died today,
>        "This must be so." We pray you throw to earth
>        This unprevailing woe, and think of us
>        As of a father, for let the world take note
>        You are the most immediate[7] to our throne,
> 110    And with no less nobility of love
>        Than that which dearest father bears his son
>        Do I impart toward you. For your intent
>        In going back to school in Wittenberg,
>        It is most retrograde[8] to our desire,
> 115    And we beseech you, bend you to remain
>        Here in the cheer and comfort of our eye,
>        Our chiefest courtier, cousin, and our son.
>    QUEEN: Let not thy mother lose her prayers, Hamlet.
>        I pray thee stay with us, go not to Wittenberg.
> 120 HAMLET: I shall in all my best obey you, madam.
>    KING: Why, 'tis a loving and a fair reply.
>        Be as ourself in Denmark. Madam, come.
>        This gentle and unforced accord of Hamlet
>        Sits smiling to my heart, in grace whereof,
> 125    No jocund health that Denmark drinks today
>        But the great cannon to the clouds shall tell,
>        And the king's rouse the heaven shall bruit[9] again,
>        Respeaking earthly thunder. Come away. [*Flourish. Exeunt all but* HAMLET.]
>    HAMLET: O, that this too too solid flesh would melt,

---

4. Suited for funeral obsequies.   5. Uncorrected toward.   6. Corpse.   7. Next in line.   8. Contrary.
9. Echo. *Rouse:* carousal.

Thaw, and resolve itself into a dew,
Or that the Everlasting had not fixed
His canon[1] 'gainst self-slaughter. O God, God,
How weary, stale, flat, and unprofitable
Seem to me all the uses of this world!
Fie on't, ah, fie, 'tis an unweeded garden
That grows to seed. Things rank and gross in nature
Possess it merely.[2] That it should come to this,
But two months dead, nay, not so much, not two.
So excellent a king, that was to this
Hyperion to a satyr,[3] so loving to my mother,
That he might not beteem[4] the winds of heaven
Visit her face too roughly. Heaven and earth,
Must I remember? Why, she would hang on him
As if increase of appetite had grown
By what it fed on, and yet, within a month—
Let me not think on't. Frailty, thy name is woman—
A little month, or ere those shoes were old
With which she followed my poor father's body
Like Niobe,[5] all tears, why she, even she—
O God, a beast that wants discourse of reason
Would have mourned longer—married with my uncle,
My father's brother, but no more like my father
Than I to Hercules.[6] Within a month,
Ere yet the salt of most unrighteous tears
Had left the flushing in her gallèd eyes,
She married. O, most wicked speed, to post
With such dexterity to incestuous sheets!
It is not, nor it cannot come to good.
But break my heart, for I must hold my tongue.

[*Enter* HORATIO, MARCELLUS, *and* BERNARDO.]

HORATIO: Hail to your lordship!
HAMLET:            I am glad to see you well.
   Horatio—or I do forget myself.
HORATIO: The same, my lord, and your poor servant ever.
HAMLET: Sir, my good friend, I'll change[7] that name with you.
   And what make you from Wittenberg, Horatio?
   Marcellus?
MARCELLUS: My good lord!
HAMLET: I am very glad to see you. [*To* BERNARDO.] Good even, sir.—

1. Law.  2. Entirely.
3. Hyperion, a Greek god, stands here for beauty in contrast to the monstrous satyr, a lecherous creature, half man and half goat.  4. Permit.
5. In Greek mythology, Niobe was turned to stone after a tremendous fit of weeping over the death of her fourteen children, a misfortune brought about by her boasting over her fertility.
6. The demigod Hercules was noted for his strength and the series of spectacular labors that it allowed him to accomplish.  7. Exchange.

But what, in faith, make you from Wittenberg?
HORATIO: A truant disposition, good my lord.
170 HAMLET: I would not hear your enemy say so,
Nor shall you do my ear that violence
To make it truster of your own report
Against yourself. I know you are no truant.
But what is your affair in Elsinore?
175 We'll teach you to drink deep ere you depart.
HORATIO: My lord, I came to see your father's funeral.
HAMLET: I prithee do not mock me, fellow-student,
I think it was to see my mother's wedding.
HORATIO: Indeed, my lord, it followed hard upon.
180 HAMLET: Thrift, thrift, Horatio. The funeral-baked meats
Did coldly furnish forth the marriage tables.
Would I had met my dearest[8] foe in heaven
Or ever I had seen that day, Horatio!
My father—methinks I see my father.
HORATIO: Where, my lord?
185 HAMLET:           In my mind's eye, Horatio.
HORATIO: I saw him once, 'a was a goodly king.
HAMLET: 'A was a man, take him for all in all,
I shall not look upon his like again.
HORATIO: My lord, I think I saw him yesternight.
190 HAMLET: Saw who?
HORATIO: My lord, the king your father.
HAMLET:           The king my father?
HORATIO: Season your admiration[9] for a while
With an attent ear till I may deliver[1]
Upon the witness of these gentlemen
This marvel to you.
195 HAMLET:           For God's love, let me hear!
HORATIO: Two nights together had these gentlemen,
Marcellus and Bernardo, on their watch
In the dead waste and middle of the night
Been thus encountered. A figure like your father,
200 Arméd at point exactly, cap-a-pe,[2]
Appears before them, and with solemn march
Goes slow and stately by them. Thrice he walked
By their oppressed and fear-surpriséd eyes
Within his truncheon's[3] length, whilst they, distilled
205 Almost to jelly with the act of fear,
Stand dumb and speak not to him. This to me
In dreadful secrecy impart they did,
And I with them the third night kept the watch,
Where, as they had delivered, both in time,
210 Form of the thing, each word made true and good,

---

8. Bitterest.    9. Moderate your wonder.    1. Relate. *Attent:* attentive.
2. From head to toe. *Exactly:* completely.    3. Baton of office.

The apparition comes. I knew your father.
　　These hands are not more like.
HAMLET:　　　　　　　　　　But where was this?
MARCELLUS: My lord, upon the platform where we watch.
HAMLET: Did you not speak to it?
HORATIO:　　　　　　　　　　My lord, I did,
　　But answer made it none. Yet once methought　　　　　　　　　　215
　　It lifted up it head and did address
　　Itself to motion, like as it would speak;
　　But even then the morning cock crew loud,
　　And at the sound it shrunk in haste away
　　And vanished from our sight.
HAMLET:　　　　　　　　　　'Tis very strange.　　　　　　　　　　220
HORATIO: As I do live, my honored lord, 'tis true,
　　And we did think it writ down in our duty
　　To let you know of it.
HAMLET:　　　　　　Indeed, sirs, but
　　This troubles me. Hold you the watch tonight?
ALL: We do, my lord.
HAMLET:　　　　　　　　　　Armed, say you?
ALL:　　　　　　　　　　Armed, my lord.　　　　　　　　　　225
HAMLET: From top to toe?
ALL:　　　　　　　　　　My lord, from head to foot.
HAMLET: Then saw you not his face.
HORATIO: O yes, my lord, he wore his beaver[4] up.
HAMLET: What, looked he frowningly?
HORATIO: A countenance more in sorrow than in anger.　　　　　　　　　　230
HAMLET: Pale or red?
HORATIO: Nay, very pale.
HAMLET:　　　　　　　　　　And fixed his eyes upon you?
HORATIO: Most constantly.
HAMLET:　　　　　　　　　　I would I had been there.
HORATIO: It would have much amazed you.
HAMLET:　　　　　　　　　　Very like.
　　Stayed it long?　　　　　　　　　　235
HORATIO: While one with moderate haste might tell a hundred.
BOTH: Longer, longer.
HORATIO:　　　　　　　　　　Not when I saw't.
HAMLET: His beard was grizzled, no?
HORATIO: It was as I have seen it in his life,
　　A sable silvered.
HAMLET:　　　　　　　　　　I will watch tonight.　　　　　　　　　　240
　　Perchance 'twill walk again.
HORATIO:　　　　　　　　　　I warr'nt it will.
HAMLET: If it assume my noble father's person,
　　I'll speak to it though hell itself should gape[5]
　　And bid me hold my peace. I pray you all,

---

4. Movable face protector.　　5. Open (its mouth) wide.

245    If you have hitherto concealed this sight,
       Let it be tenable[6] in your silence still,
       And whatsomever else shall hap tonight,
       Give it an understanding but no tongue.
       I will requite your loves. So fare you well.
250    Upon the platform 'twixt eleven and twelve
       I'll visit you.
  ALL:              Our duty to your honor.
  HAMLET: Your loves, as mine to you. Farewell.    [*Exeunt all but* HAMLET.]
       My father's spirit in arms? All is not well.
       I doubt[7] some foul play. Would the night were come!
255    Till then sit still, my soul. Foul deeds will rise,
       Though all the earth o'erwhelm them, to men's eyes.    [*Exit.*]

## Scene 3

*The dwelling of* POLONIUS. *Enter* LAERTES *and* OPHELIA.

  LAERTES: My necessaries are embarked. Farewell.
       And, sister, as the winds give benefit
       And convoy is assistant,[8] do not sleep,
       But let me hear from you.
  OPHELIA:                Do you doubt that?
5  LAERTES: For Hamlet, and the trifling of his favor,
       Hold it a fashion and a toy in blood,
       A violet in the youth of primy[9] nature,
       Forward, not permanent, sweet, not lasting,
       The perfume and suppliance of a minute,
       No more.
  OPHELIA:    No more but so?
10 LAERTES:              Think it no more.
       For nature crescent[1] does not grow alone
       In thews and bulk, but as this temple[2] waxes
       The inward service of the mind and soul
       Grows wide withal. Perhaps he loves you now,
15     And now no soil nor cautel[3] doth besmirch
       The virtue of his will, but you must fear,
       His greatness weighted,[4] his will is not his own,
       For he himself is subject to his birth.
       He may not, as unvalued persons do,
20     Carve for himself, for on his choice depends
       The safety and health of this whole state,
       And therefore must his choice be circumscribed
       Unto the voice[5] and yielding of that body
       Whereof he is the head. Then if he says he loves you,
25     It fits your wisdom so far to believe it

---

6. Held.   7. Suspect.   8. Means of transport is available.   9. Of the spring.   1. Growing.
2. Body.   3. Deceit.   4. Rank considered.   5. Assent.

As he in his particular act and place
May give his saying deed, which is no further
Than the main voice of Denmark goes withal.
Then weigh what loss your honor may sustain
If with too credent ear you list[6] his songs, 30
Or lose your heart, or your chaste treasure open
To his unmastered importunity.
Fear it, Ophelia, fear it, my dear sister,
And keep you in the rear of your affection,
Out of the shot and danger of desire. 35
The chariest[7] maid is prodigal enough
If she unmask her beauty to the moon.
Virtue itself scapes not calumnious strokes.
The canker[8] galls the infants of the spring
Too oft before their buttons[9] be disclosed, 40
And in the morn and liquid dew of youth
Contagious blastments[1] are most imminent.
Be wary then; best safety lies in fear.
Youth to itself rebels, though none else near.
OPHELIA: I shall the effect of this good lesson keep 45
As watchman to my heart. But, good my brother,
Do not as some ungracious pastors do,
Show me the steep and thorny way to heaven,
Whiles like a puffed and reckless libertine
Himself the primrose path of dalliance treads 50
And recks not his own rede.[2]
LAERTES:                    O, fear me not.

[*Enter* POLONIUS.]

I stay too long. But here my father comes.
A double blessing is a double grace;
Occasion smiles upon a second leave.
POLONIUS: Yet here, Laertes? Aboard, aboard, for shame! 55
The wind sits in the shoulder of your sail,
And you are stayed for. There—my blessing with thee,
And these few precepts in thy memory
Look thou character.[3] Give thy thoughts no tongue,
Nor any unproportioned thought his act. 60
Be thou familiar, but by no means vulgar.
Those friends thou hast, and their adoption tried,
Grapple them unto thy soul with hoops of steel;
But do not dull[4] thy palm with entertainment
Of each new-hatched, unfledged comrade. Beware 65
Of entrance to a quarrel, but being in,
Bear't that th' opposéd[5] may beware of thee.

---

6. Too credulous an ear you listen to.   7. Most circumspect.   8. Rose caterpillar.   9. Buds.
1. Blights.   2. Heeds not his own advice.   3. Write.   4. Make callous.
5. Conduct it so that the opponent.

```
          Give every man thy ear, but few thy voice;⁶
          Take each man's censure, but reserve thy judgment.
70        Costly thy habit as thy purse can buy,
          But not expressed in fancy; rich not gaudy,
          For the apparel oft proclaims the man,
          And they in France of the best rank and station
          Are of a most select and generous chief⁷ in that.
75        Neither a borrower nor a lender be,
          For loan oft loses both itself and friend,
          And borrowing dulls th' edge of husbandry.
          This above all, to thine own self be true,
          And it must follow as the night the day
80        Thou canst not then be false to any man.
          Farewell. My blessing season this in thee!
     LAERTES: Most humbly do I take my leave, my lord.
     POLONIUS: The time invests you. Go, your servants tend.⁸
     LAERTES: Farewell, Ophelia, and remember well
          What I have said to you.
85   OPHELIA:                        'Tis in my memory locked,
          And you yourself shall keep the key of it.
     LAERTES: Farewell.                                    [Exit.]
     POLONIUS: What is't, Ophelia, he hath said to you?
     OPHELIA: So please you, something touching the Lord Hamlet.
90   POLONIUS: Marry, well bethought.
          'Tis told me he hath very oft of late
          Given private time to you, and you yourself
          Have of your audience been most free and bounteous.
          If it be so—as so 'tis put on me,
95        And that in way of caution—I must tell you,
          You do not understand yourself so clearly
          As it behooves my daughter and your honor.
          What is between you? Give me up the truth.
     OPHELIA: He hath, my lord, of late made many tenders
100       Of his affection to me.
     POLONIUS: Affection? Pooh! You speak like a green girl,
          Unsifted in such perilous circumstance.
          Do you believe his tenders, as you call them?
     OPHELIA: I do not know, my lord, what I should think.
105  POLONIUS: Marry, I will teach you. Think yourself a baby
          That you have ta'en these tenders for true pay
          Which are not sterling. Tender yourself more dearly,
          Or (not to crack the wind of the poor phrase,
          Running it thus) you'll tender me a fool.
110  OPHELIA: My lord, he hath importuned me with love
          In honorable fashion.
     POLONIUS: Ay, fashion you may call it. Go to, go to.
     OPHELIA: And hath given countenance⁹ to his speech, my lord,
```

6. Approval.   7. Eminence.   8. Await.   9. Confirmation.

    With almost all the holy vows of heaven.
POLONIUS: Ay, springes[1] to catch woodcocks. I do know,
    When the blood burns, how prodigal the soul
    Lends the tongue vows. These blazes, daughter,
    Giving more light than heat, extinct in both
    Even in their promise, as it is a-making,
    You must not take for fire. From this time
    Be something scanter of your maiden presence.
    Set your entreatments[2] at a higher rate
    Than a command to parle. For Lord Hamlet,
    Believe so much in him that he is young,
    And with a larger tether may he walk
    Than may be given you. In few, Ophelia,
    Do not believe his vows, for they are brokers,[3]
    Not of that dye which their investments[4] show,
    But mere implorators[5] of unholy suits,
    Breathing like sanctified and pious bawds,
    The better to beguile. This is for all:
    I would not, in plain terms, from this time forth
    Have you so slander any moment leisure
    As to give words or talk with the Lord Hamlet.
    Look to't, I charge you. Come your ways.
OPHELIA: I shall obey, my lord.                                                 [*Exeunt.*]

## Scene 4

*The guard station. Enter* HAMLET, HORATIO *and* MARCELLUS.

HAMLET: The air bites shrewdly;[6] it is very cold.
HORATIO: It is a nipping and an eager[7] air.
HAMLET: What hour now?
HORATIO:                     I think it lacks of twelve.
MARCELLUS: No, it is struck.
HORATIO:                     Indeed? I heard it not.
    It then draws near the season
    Wherein the spirit held his wont to walk.

    [*A flourish of trumpets, and two pieces go off.*]

    What does this mean, my lord?
HAMLET: The king doth wake tonight and takes his rouse,
    Keeps wassail, and the swagg'ring up-spring[8] reels,
    And as he drains his draughts of Rhenish down,
    The kettledrum and trumpet thus bray out
    The triumph of his pledge.
HORATIO:                     Is it a custom?
HAMLET: Ay, marry, is't,

---

1. Snares.   2. Negotiations before a surrender.   3. Panderers.   4. Garments.   5. Solicitors.
6. Sharply.   7. Keen.   8. A German dance.

But to my mind, though I am native here
And to the manner born, it is a custom
More honored in the breach than the observance.
This heavy-headed revel east and west
Makes us traduced and taxed of other nations.
They clepe[9] us drunkards, and with swinish phrase
Soil our addition,[1] and indeed it takes
From our achievements, though performed at height,
The pith and marrow of our attribute.[2]
So oft it chances in particular men,
That for some vicious mole of nature in them,
As in their birth, wherein they are not guilty
(Since nature cannot choose his origin),
By their o'ergrowth of some complexion,
Oft breaking down the pales[3] and forts of reason,
Or by some habit that too much o'er-leavens
The form of plausive[4] manners—that these men,
Carrying, I say, the stamp of one defect,
Being nature's livery or fortune's star,
His virtues else, be they as pure as grace,
As infinite as man may undergo,
Shall in the general censure take corruption
From that particular fault. The dram of evil
Doth all the noble substance often doubt[5]
To his own scandal.

[*Enter* GHOST.]

HORATIO:            Look, my lord, it comes.
HAMLET: Angels and ministers of grace defend us!
Be thou a spirit of health or goblin damned,
Bring with thee airs from heaven or blasts from hell,
Be thy intents wicked or charitable,
Thou com'st in such a questionable[6] shape
That I will speak to thee. I'll call thee Hamlet,
King, father, royal Dane. O, answer me!
Let me not burst in ignorance, but tell
Why thy canonized[7] bones, hearsèd in death,
Have burst their cerements;[8] why the sepulchre
Wherein we saw thee quietly inurned
Hath oped his ponderous and marble jaws
To cast thee up again. What may this mean
That thou, dead corse, again in complete steel[9]
Revisits thus the glimpses of the moon,
Making night hideous, and we fools of nature
So horridly to shake our disposition
With thoughts beyond the reaches of our souls?
Say, why is this? wherefore? What should we do?

9. Call.   1. Reputation.   2. Honor.   3. Barriers.   4. Pleasing.   5. Put out.
6. Prompting question.   7. Buried in accordance with church canons.   8. Graveclothes.   9. Armor.

[GHOST *beckons*.]

HORATIO: It beckons you to go away with it,
   As if it some impartment[1] did desire
   To you alone.
MARCELLUS:      Look with what courteous action 60
   It waves you to a more removéd[2] ground.
   But do not go with it.
HORATIO:           No, by no means.
HAMLET: It will not speak; then I will follow it.
HORATIO: Do not, my lord.
HAMLET:          Why, what should be the fear?
   I do not set my life at a pin's fee,[3] 65
   And for my soul, what can it do to that,
   Being a thing immortal as itself?
   It waves me forth again. I'll follow it
HORATIO: What if it tempt you toward the flood, my lord,
   Or to the dreadful summit of the cliff 70
   That beetles[4] o'er his base into the sea,
   And there assume some other horrible form,
   Which might deprive your sovereignty of reason[5]
   And draw you into madness? Think of it.
   The very place puts toys of desperation,[6] 75
   Without more motive, into every brain
   That looks so many fathoms to the sea
   And hears it roar beneath.
HAMLET:          It wafts me still.
   Go on. I'll follow thee.
MARCELLUS: You shall not go, my lord.
HAMLET:          Hold off your hands. 80
HORATIO: Be ruled. You shall not go.
HAMLET:         My fate cries out
   And makes each petty artere in this body
   As hardy as the Nemean lion's nerve.[7]
   Still am I called. Unhand me, gentlemen.
   By heaven, I'll make a ghost of him that lets[8] me. 85
   I say, away! Go on. I'll follow thee. [*Exeunt* GHOST *and* HAMLET.]
HORATIO: He waxes desperate with imagination.
MARCELLUS: Let's follow. 'Tis not fit thus to obey him.
HORATIO: Have after. To what issue will this come?
MARCELLUS: Something is rotten in the state of Denmark. 90
HORATIO: Heaven will direct it.
MARCELLUS:      Nay, let's follow him. [*Exeunt.*]

---

1. Communication.   2. Beckons you to a more distant.   3. Price.   4. Juts out.
5. Rational power. *Deprive:* take away.   6. Desperate fancies.
7. The Nemean lion was a mythological monster slain by Hercules as one of his twelve labors.
8. Hinders.

## Scene 5

*Near the guard station. Enter* GHOST *and* HAMLET.

HAMLET: Whither wilt thou lead me? Speak. I'll go no further.
GHOST: Mark me.
HAMLET:        I will.
GHOST:                My hour is almost come,
  When I to sulph'rous and tormenting flames
  Must render up myself.
HAMLET:               Alas, poor ghost!
5 GHOST: Pity me not, but lend thy serious hearing
  To what I shall unfold.
HAMLET:               Speak. I am bound to hear.
GHOST: So art thou to revenge, when thou shalt hear.
HAMLET: What?
GHOST: I am thy father's spirit,
10   Doomed for a certain term to walk the night,
  And for the day confined to fast in fires,
  Till the foul crimes done in my days of nature[9]
  Are burnt and purged away. But that I am forbid
  To tell the secrets of my prison house,
15   I could a tale unfold whose lightest word
  Would harrow up thy soul, freeze thy young blood,
  Make thy two eyes like stars start from their spheres,
  Thy knotted and combinéd[1] locks to part,
  And each particular hair to stand an end,
20   Like quills upon the fretful porpentine.[2]
  But this eternal blazon[3] must not be
  To ears of flesh and blood. List, list, O, list!
  If thou didst every thy dear father love—
HAMLET: O God!
25 GHOST: Revenge his foul and most unnatural murder.
HAMLET: Murder!
GHOST: Murder most foul, as in the best it is,
  But this most foul, strange, and unnatural.
HAMLET: Haste me to know't, that I, with wings as swift
30   As meditation or the thoughts of love,
  May sweep to my revenge.
GHOST:               I find thee apt.
  And duller shouldst thou be than the fat weed
  That rots itself in ease on Lethe[4] wharf,—
  Wouldst thou not stir in this. Now, Hamlet, hear.
35   'Tis given out that, sleeping in my orchard,

---

9. That is, while I was alive.   1. Tangled.   2. Porcupine.   3. Description of eternity.
4. The waters of the Lethe, one of the rivers of the classical underworld, when drunk, induced forgetfulness. The "fat weed" is the asphodel that grew there; some texts have "roots" for "rots."

                A serpent stung me. So the whole ear of Denmark
                Is by a forgéd process[5] of my death
                Rankly abused. But know, thou noble youth,
                The serpent that did sting thy father's life
                Now wears his crown.
HAMLET:                    O my prophetic soul! 40
                My uncle!
GHOST: Ay, that incestuous, that adulterate beast,
                With witchcraft of his wits, with traitorous gifts—
                O wicked wit and gifts that have the power
                So to seduce!—won to his shameful lust 45
                The will of my most seeming virtuous queen.
                O Hamlet, what a falling off was there,
                From me, whose love was of that dignity
                That it went hand in hand even with the vow
                I made to her in marriage, and to decline[6] 50
                Upon a wretch whose natural gifts were poor
                To those of mine!
                But virtue, as it never will be moved,
                Though lewdness court it in a shape of heaven,
                So lust, though to a radiant angel linked, 55
                Will sate itself in a celestial bed
                And prey on garbage.
                But soft, methinks I scent the morning air.
                Brief let me be. Sleeping within my orchard,
                My custom always of the afternoon, 60
                Upon my secure hour thy uncle stole,
                With juice of cursed hebona[7] in a vial,
                And in the porches of my ears did pour
                The leperous distilment, whose effect
                Holds such an enmity with blood of man 65
                That swift as quicksilver it courses through
                The natural gates and alleys of the body,
                And with a sudden vigor it doth posset[8]
                And curd, like eager[9] droppings into milk,
                The thin and wholesome blood. So did it mine, 70
                And a most instant tetter barked about[1]
                Most lazar-like[2] with vile and loathsome crust
                All my smooth body.
                Thus was I sleeping by a brother's hand
                Of life, of crown, of queen at once dispatched, 75
                Cut off even in the blossoms of my sin,
                Unhouseled, disappointed, unaneled,[3]

---

5. False report.   6. Sink.   7. A poison.   8. Coagulate.   9. Acid. *Curd:* curdle.
1. Covered like bark. *Tetter:* a skin disease.   2. Leperlike.
3. The ghost means that he died without the customary rites of the church, that is, without receiving the Sacrament, without confession, and without Extreme Unction.

No reck'ning made, but sent to my account
With all my imperfections on my head.
80 O, horrible! O, horrible! most horrible!
If thou hast nature in thee, bear it not.
Let not the royal bed of Denmark be
A couch of luxury[4] and damnèd incest.
But howsomever thou pursues this act,
85 Taint not thy mind, nor let thy soul contrive
Against thy mother aught. Leave her to heaven,
And to those thorns that in her bosom lodge
To prick and sting her. Fare thee well at once.
The glowworm shows the matin[5] to be near,
90 And gins to pale his uneffectual fire.
Adieu, adieu, adieu. Remember me. [*Exit.*]
HAMLET: O all you host of heaven! O earth! What else?
And shall I couple hell? O, fie! Hold, hold, my heart,
And you, my sinews, grow not instant old,
95 But bear me stiffly up. Remember thee?
Ay, thou poor ghost, whiles memory holds a seat
In this distracted globe.[6] Remember thee?
Yea, from the table[7] of my memory
I'll wipe away all trivial fond[8] records,
100 All saws of books, all forms, all pressures past
That youth and observation copied there,
And thy commandment all alone shall live
Within the book and volume of my brain,
Unmixed with baser matter. Yes, by heaven!
105 O most pernicious woman!
O villain, villain, smiling, damnèd villain!
My tables—meet it is I set it down
That one may smile, and smile, and be a villain.
At least I am sure it may be so in Denmark.
110 So, uncle, there you are. Now to my word:[9]
It is "Adieu, adieu. Remember me."
I have sworn't.

[*Enter* HORATIO *and* MARCELLUS.]

HORATIO: My lord, my lord!
MARCELLUS:                Lord Hamlet!
HORATIO:                             Heavens secure him!
HAMLET: So be it!
115 MARCELLUS: Illo, ho, ho, my lord!
HAMLET: Hillo, ho, ho, boy![1] Come, bird, come.
MARCELLUS: How is't, my noble lord?
HORATIO:                           What news, my lord?

---

4. Lust.   5. Morning.   6. Skull.   7. Writing tablet.   8. Foolish.   9. For my motto.
1. A falconer's cry.

HAMLET: O, wonderful!
HORATIO: Good my lord, tell it.
HAMLET: No, you will reveal it.
HORATIO: Not I, my lord, by heaven.
MARCELLUS: Nor I, my lord.
HAMLET: How say you then, would heart of man once think it?
But you'll be secret?
BOTH: Ay, by heaven, my lord.
HAMLET: There's never a villain dwelling in all Denmark
But he's an arrant knave.
HORATIO: There needs no ghost, my lord, come from the grave
To tell us this.
HAMLET: Why, right, you are in the right,
And so without more circumstance at all
I hold it fit that we shake hands and part,
You, as your business and desire shall point you,
For every man hath business and desire
Such as it is, and for my own poor part,
Look you, I'll go pray.
HORATIO: These are but wild and whirling words, my lord.
HAMLET: I am sorry they offend you, heartily;
Yes, faith, heartily.
HORATIO: There's no offence, my lord.
HAMLET: Yes, by Saint Patrick, but there is, Horatio,
And much offence too. Touching this vision here,
It is an honest ghost, that let me tell you.
For your desire to know what is between us,
O'ermaster't as you may. And now, good friends,
As you are friends, scholars, and soldiers,
Give me one poor request.
HORATIO: What is't, my lord? We will.
HAMLET: Never make known what you have seen tonight.
BOTH: My lord, we will not.
HAMLET: Nay, but swear't.
HORATIO: In faith,
My lord, not I.
MARCELLUS: Nor I, my lord, in faith.
HAMLET: Upon my sword.
MARCELLUS: We have sworn, my lord, already.
HAMLET: Indeed, upon my sword, indeed.

[GHOST *cries under the stage.*]

GHOST: Swear.
HAMLET: Ha, ha, boy, say'st thou so? Art thou there, truepenny?[2]
Come on. You hear this fellow in the cellarage.[3]

2. Old fellow. 3. Below.

        Consent to swear.
HORATIO:               Propose the oath, my lord.
HAMLET: Never to speak of this that you have seen,
    Swear by my sword.
GHOST: [*Beneath.*] Swear.
155 HAMLET: Hic et ubique?[4] Then we'll shift our ground.
    Come hither, gentlemen,
    And lay your hands again upon my sword.
    Swear by my sword
    Never to speak of this that you have heard.
160 GHOST: [*Beneath.*] Swear by his sword.
HAMLET: Well said, old mole! Canst work i' th' earth so fast?
    A worthy pioneer![5] Once more remove, good friends.
HORATIO: O day and night, but this is wondrous strange!
HAMLET: And therefore as a stranger give it welcome.
165 There are more things in heaven and earth, Horatio,
    Than are dreamt of in your philosophy.
    But come.
    Here as before, never, so help you mercy,
    How strange or odd some'er I bear myself
170 (As I perchance hereafter shall think meet
    To put an antic[6] disposition on),
    That you, at such times, seeing me, never shall,
    With arms encumbered[7] thus, or this head-shake,
    Or by pronouncing of some doubtful phrase,
175 As "Well, we know," or "We could, and if we would"
    Or "If we list to speak," or "There be, and if they might"
    Or such ambiguous giving out, to note
    That you know aught of me—this do swear,
    So grace and mercy at your most need help you.
180 GHOST: [*Beneath.*] Swear.         [*They swear.*]
HAMLET: Rest, rest, perturbéd spirit! So, gentlemen,
    With all my love I do commend me to you,
    And what so poor a man as Hamlet is
    May do t'express his love and friending[8] to you,
185 God willing, shall not lack. Let us go in together,
    And still your fingers on your lips, I pray.
    The time is out of joint. O curséd spite
    That ever I was born to set it right!
    Nay, come, let's go together.         [*Exeunt.*]

---

4. Here and everywhere?    5. Soldier who digs trenches.    6. Mad.    7. Folded.    8. Friendship.

## ACT II

*Scene 1*

*The dwelling of* POLONIUS. *Enter* POLONIUS *and* REYNALDO.

POLONIUS: Give him this money and these notes, Reynaldo.
REYNALDO: I will, my lord.
POLONIUS: You shall do marvellous wisely, good Reynaldo,
    Before you visit him, to make inquire[9]
    Of his behavior.
REYNALDO:        My lord, I did intend it.     5
POLONIUS: Marry, well said, very well said. Look you, sir.
    Enquire me first what Danskers[1] are in Paris,
    And how, and who, what means, and where they keep,[2]
    What company, at what expense; and finding
    By this encompassment[3] and drift of question     10
    That they do know my son, come you more nearer
    Than your particular demands[4] will touch it.
    Take you as 'twere some distant knowledge of him,
    As thus, "I know his father and his friends,
    And in part him." Do you mark this, Reynaldo?     15
REYNALDO: Ay, very well, my lord.
POLONIUS: "And in part him, but," you may say, "not well,
    But if't be he I mean, he's very wild,
    Addicted so and so." And there put on him
    What forgeries you please; marry, none so rank[5]     20
    As may dishonor him. Take heed of that.
    But, sir, such wanton, wild, and usual slips
    As are companions noted and most known
    To youth and liberty.
REYNALDO:        As gaming, my lord.
POLONIUS: Ay, or drinking, fencing, swearing,     25
    Quarrelling, drabbing[6]—you may go so far.
REYNALDO: My lord, that would dishonor him.
POLONIUS: Faith, no, as you may season it in the charge.[7]
    You must not put another scandal on him,
    That he is open to incontinency.[8]     30
    That's not my meaning. But breathe his faults so quaintly[9]
    That they may seem the taints of liberty,[1]
    The flash and outbreak of a fiery mind,
    A savageness in unreclaiméd[2] blood,
    Of general assault.[3]
REYNALDO:        But, my good lord—     35
POLONIUS: Wherefore should you do this?

---

9. Inquiry.   1. Danes.   2. Live.   3. Indirect means.   4. Direct questions.   5. Foul. *Forgeries:* lies.
6. Whoring.   7. Soften the accusation.   8. Sexual excess.   9. With delicacy.   1. Faults of freedom.
2. Untamed.   3. Touching everyone.

REYNALDO: Ay, my lord,
 I would know that.
POLONIUS: Marry, sir, here's my drift,
 And I believe it is a fetch of warrant.[4]
 You laying these slight sullies on my son,
 As 'twere a thing a little soiled wi' th' working,
 Mark you,
 Your party in converse,[5] him you would sound,
 Having ever seen in the prenominate[6] crimes
 The youth you breathe[7] of guilty, be assured
 He closes with you in this consequence,
 "Good sir," or so, or "friend," or "gentleman,"
 According to the phrase or the addition
 Of man and country.
REYNALDO: Very good, my lord.
POLONIUS: And then, sir, does 'a this—'a does—What was I about to say?
 By the mass, I was about to say something.
 Where did I leave?
REYNALDO: At "closes in the consequence."
POLONIUS: At "closes in the consequence"—ay, marry,
 He closes thus: "I know the gentleman.
 I saw him yesterday, or th' other day,
 Or then, or then, with such, or such, and as you say,
 There was 'a gaming, there o'ertook in's rouse,
 There falling out at tennis," or perchance
 "I saw him enter such a house of sale,"
 Videlicet,[8] a brothel, or so forth.
 See you, now—
 Your bait of falsehood takes this carp of truth,
 And thus do we of wisdom and of reach,[9]
 With windlasses and with assays of bias,[1]
 By indirections find directions out;
 So by my former lecture and advice
 Shall you my son. You have me, have you not?
REYNALDO: My lord, I have.
POLONIUS: God b'wi' ye; fare ye well.
REYNALDO: Good my lord.
POLONIUS: Observe his inclination in yourself.
REYNALDO: I shall, my lord.
POLONIUS: And let him ply[2] his music.
REYNALDO: Well, my lord.
POLONIUS: Farewell. [*Exit* REYNALDO.]

[*Enter* OPHELIA.]

 How now, Ophelia, what's the matter?
OPHELIA: O my lord, my lord, I have been so affrighted!
POLONIUS: With what, i' th' name of God?

---

4. Permissible trick.  5. Conversation.  6. Already named.  7. Speak.  8. Namely.  9. Ability.
1. Indirect tests.  2. Practice.

OPHELIA: My lord, as I was sewing in my closet,[3]
  Lord Hamlet with his doublet all unbraced,[4]
  No hat upon his head, his stockings fouled,
  Ungartered and down-gyvéd[5] to his ankle,
  Pale as his shirt, his knees knocking each other,
  And with a look so piteous in purport
  As if he had been loosèd out of hell
  To speak of horrors—he comes before me.
POLONIUS: Mad for thy love?
OPHELIA:               My lord, I do not know,
  But truly I do fear it.
POLONIUS:           What said he?
OPHELIA: He took me by the wrist, and held me hard,
  Then goes he to the length of all his arm,
  And with his other hand thus o'er his brow,
  He falls to such perusal of my face
  As 'a would draw it. Long stayed he so.
  At last, a little shaking of mine arm,
  And thrice his head thus waving up and down,
  He raised a sigh so piteous and profound
  As it did seem to shatter all his bulk,[6]
  And end his being. That done, he lets me go,
  And with his head over his shoulder turned
  He seemed to find his way without his eyes,
  For out adoors he went without their helps,
  And to the last bended[7] their light on me.
POLONIUS: Come, go with me. I will go seek the king.
  This is the very ecstasy of love,
  Whose violent property fordoes[8] itself,
  And leads the will to desperate undertakings
  As oft as any passion under heaven
  That does afflict our natures. I am sorry.
  What, have you given him any hard words of late?
OPHELIA: No, my good lord, but as you did command
  I did repel[9] his letters, and denied
  His access to me.
POLONIUS:       That hath made him mad.
  I am sorry that with better heed and judgment
  I had not quoted[1] him. I feared he did but trifle,
  And meant to wrack[2] thee; but beshrew my jealousy.
  By heaven, it is as proper to our age
  To cast beyond ourselves in our opinions
  As it is common for the younger sort
  To lack discretion. Come, go we to the king.
  This must be known, which being kept close, might move
  More grief to hide than hate to utter love.
  Come.
                                    [*Exeunt.*]

---

3. Chamber.   4. Unlaced. *Doublet:* jacket.   5. Fallen down like fetters.   6. Body.   7. Directed.
8. Destroys. *Property:* character.   9. Refuse.   1. Observed.   2. Harm.

*Scene 2*

*A public room. Enter* KING, QUEEN, ROSENCRANTZ *and* GUILDENSTERN.

KING: Welcome, dear Rosencrantz and Guildenstern.
    Moreover that[3] we much did long to see you,
    The need we have to use you did provoke
    Our hasty sending. Something have you heard
5   Of Hamlet's transformation—so call it,
    Sith[4] nor th' exterior nor the inward man
    Resembles that it was. What it should be,
    More than his father's death, that thus hath put him
    So much from th' understanding of himself,
10  I cannot deem of. I entreat you both
    That, being of so young days[5] brought up with him,
    And sith so neighbored[6] to his youth and havior,
    That you vouchsafe your rest here in our court
    Some little time, so by your companies
15  To draw him on to pleasures, and to gather
    So much as from occasion you may glean,
    Whether aught to us unknown afflicts him thus,
    That opened lies within our remedy.
QUEEN: Good gentlemen, he hath much talked of you,
20  And sure I am two men there are not living
    To whom he more adheres. If it will please you
    To show us so much gentry[7] and good will
    As to expend your time with us awhile
    For the supply and profit of our hope,
25  Your visitation shall receive such thanks
    As fits a king's remembrance.
ROSENCRANTZ:           Both your majesties
    Might, by the sovereign power you have of us,
    Put your dread pleasures more into command
    Than to entreaty.
GUILDENSTERN:    But we both obey,
30  And here give up ourselves in the full bent[8]
    To lay our service freely at your feet,
    To be commanded.
KING: Thanks, Rosencrantz and gentle Guildenstern.
QUEEN: Thanks, Guildenstern and gentle Rosencrantz.
35  And I beseech you instantly to visit
    My too much changed son. Go, some of you,
    And bring these gentlemen where Hamlet is.
GUILDENSTERN: Heavens make our presence and our practices
    Pleasant and helpful to him!
QUEEN:                Ay, amen!
                [*Exeunt* ROSENCRANTZ *and* GUILDENSTERN.]

---

3. In addition to the fact that.   4. Since.   5. From childhood.   6. Closely allied.   7. Courtesy.
8. Completely.

[*Enter* POLONIUS.]

POLONIUS: Th' ambassadors from Norway, my good lord, 
    Are joyfully returned.
KING: Thou still[9] hast been the father of good news.
POLONIUS: Have I, my lord? I assure you, my good liege,
    I hold my duty as I hold my soul,
    Both to my God and to my gracious king;
    And I do think—or else this brain of mine
    Hunts not the trail of policy[1] so sure
    As it hath used to do—that I have found
    The very cause of Hamlet's lunacy.
KING: O, speak of that, that do I long to hear.
POLONIUS: Give first admittance to th' ambassadors.
    My news shall be the fruit[2] to that great feast.
KING: Thyself do grace to them, and bring them in.   [*Exit* POLONIUS.]
    He tells me, my dear Gertrude, he hath found
    The head and source of all your son's distemper.
QUEEN: I doubt it is no other but the main,
    His father's death and our o'erhasty marriage.
KING: Well, we shall sift[3] him.

[*Enter Ambassadors* (VOLTEMAND *and* CORNELIUS) *with* POLONIUS.]

            Welcome, my good friends,
    Say, Voltemand, what from our brother Norway?
VOLTEMAND: Most fair return of greetings and desires.
    Upon our first,[4] he sent out to suppress
    His nephew's levies, which to him appeared
    To be a preparation 'gainst the Polack,
    But better looked into, he truly found
    It was against your highness, whereat grieved,
    That so his sickness, age, and impotence
    Was falsely borne in hand, sends out arrests[5]
    On Fortinbras, which he in brief obeys,
    Receives rebuke from Norway, and in fine,
    Makes vow before his uncle never more
    To give th' assay[6] of arms against your majesty.
    Whereon old Norway, overcome with joy,
    Gives him three thousand crowns in annual fee,
    And his commission to employ those soldiers,
    So levied as before, against the Polack,
    With an entreaty, herein further shown,   [*Gives* CLAUDIUS *a paper.*]
    That it might please you to give quiet pass[7]
    Through your dominions for this enterprise,
    On such regards of safety and allowance
    As therein are set down.

---

9. Ever.    1. Statecraft.    2. Dessert.    3. Examine.    4. That is, first appearance.
5. Orders to stop. *Falsely borne in hand:* deceived.    6. Trial.    7. Safe conduct.

| | | |
|---|---|---|
| 80 | KING: | It likes[8] us well, |

    KING: It likes[8] us well,
      And at our more considered time[9] we'll read,
      Answer, and think upon this business.
      Meantime we thank you for your well-took[1] labor.
      Go to your rest; at night we'll feast together.
      Most welcome home!     [*Exeunt* AMBASSADORS.]
85 POLONIUS:     This business is well ended.
      My liege and madam, to expostulate[2]
      What majesty should be, what duty is,
      Why day is day, night night, and time is time,
      Were nothing but to waste night, day, and time.
90    Therefore, since brevity is the soul of wit,
      And tediousness the limbs and outward flourishes,[3]
      I will be brief. Your noble son is mad.
      Mad call I it, for to define true madness,
      What is't but to be nothing else but mad?
      But let that go.
95 QUEEN:     More matter with less art.
    POLONIUS: Madam, I swear I use no art at all.
      That he is mad, 'tis true: 'tis true 'tis pity,
      And pity 'tis 'tis true. A foolish figure,
      But farewell it, for I will use no art.
100   Mad let us grant him, then, and now remains
      That we find out the cause of this effect,
      Or rather say the cause of this defect,
      For this effect defective comes by cause.
      Thus it remains, and the remainder thus.
105   Perpend.[4]
      I have a daughter—have while she is mine—
      Who in her duty and obedience, mark,
      Hath given me this. Now gather, and surmise.
      "To the celestial, and my soul's idol, the most beautified Ophelia."—That's
110   an ill phrase, a vile phrase, "beautified" is a vile phrase. But you shall hear.
      Thus:
      "In her excellent white bosom, these, etc."
    QUEEN: Came this from Hamlet to her?
    POLONIUS: Good madam, stay awhile. I will be faithful.
115       "Doubt thou the stars are fire,
        Doubt that the sun doth move;
      Doubt truth to be a liar;
        But never doubt I love.

      O dear Ophelia, I am ill at these numbers.[5] I have not art to reckon my
120 groans, but that I love thee best, O most best, believe it. Adieu.
      Thine evermore, most dear lady, whilst this machine[6] is to him,
      Hamlet."

---

8. Pleases.   9. Time for more consideration.   1. Successful.   2. Discuss.   3. Adornments.
4. Consider.   5. Verses.   6. Body.

    This in obedience hath my daughter shown me,
    And more above, hath his solicitings,
    As they fell out by time, by means, and place,           125
    All given to mine ear.
KING:                       But how hath she
    Received his love?
POLONIUS:           What do you think of me?
KING: As of a man faithful and honorable.
POLONIUS: I would fain prove so. But what might you think,
    When I had seen this hot love on the wing.            130
    (As I perceived it, I must tell you that,
    Before my daughter told me), what might you,
    Or my dear majesty your queen here, think,
    If I had played the desk or table-book,
    Or given my heart a winking, mute and dumb,        135
    Or looked upon this love with idle sight,[7]
    What might you think? No, I went round[8] to work,
    And my young mistress thus I did bespeak:
    "Lord Hamlet is a prince out of thy star.[9]
    This must not be." And then I prescripts[1] gave her,      140
    That she should lock herself from his resort,
    Admit no messengers, receive no tokens.
    Which done, she took[2] the fruits of my advice;
    And he repelled, a short tale to make,
    Fell into a sadness, then into a fast,                 145
    Thence to a watch, thence into a weakness,
    Thence to a lightness, and by this declension,
    Into the madness wherein now he raves,
    And all we mourn for.
KING:                  Do you think 'tis this?
QUEEN: It may be, very like.                               150
POLONIUS: Hath there been such a time—I would fain know that—
    That I have positively said " 'Tis so,"
    When it proved otherwise?
KING:                      Not that I know.
POLONIUS: [*Pointing to his head and shoulder.*] Take this from this, if this be
    otherwise.
    If circumstances lead me, I will find                 155
    Where truth is hid, though it were hid indeed
    Within the centre.[3]
KING:                  How may we try it further?
POLONIUS: You know sometimes he walks four hours together
    Here in the lobby.
QUEEN:              So he does, indeed.

---

7. Polonius means that he would have been at fault if, having seen Hamlet's attention to Ophelia, he had winked at it or not paid attention, an "idle sight," and if he had remained silent and kept the information to himself, as if it were written in a "desk" or "table-book."   8. Directly.   9. Beyond your sphere.
1. Orders.   2. Followed.   3. Of the earth.

160 POLONIUS: At such a time I'll loose[4] my daughter to him.
　　　Be you and I behind an arras[5] then.
　　　Mark the encounter. If he love her not,
　　　And be not from his reason fall'n thereon,
　　　Let me be no assistant for a state,
　　　But keep a farm and carters.
165 KING: 　　　　　　　　We will try it.

[*Enter* HAMLET *reading a book.*]

QUEEN: But look where sadly the poor wretch comes reading.
POLONIUS: Away, I do beseech you both away,
　　　I'll board[6] him presently. 　　　[*Exeunt* KING *and* QUEEN.]
　　　　　　　　O, give me leave.
　　　How does my good Lord Hamlet?
170 HAMLET: Well, God-a-mercy.
POLONIUS: Do you know me, my lord?
HAMLET: Excellent well, you are a fishmonger.
POLONIUS: Not I, my lord.
HAMLET: Then I would you were so honest a man.
175 POLONIUS: Honest, my lord?
HAMLET: Ay, sir, to be honest as this world goes, is to be one man picked out of
　　　ten thousand.
POLONIUS: That's very true, my lord.
HAMLET: For if the sun breed maggots in a dead dog, being a god kissing
180 　　carrion[7]—Have you a daughter?
POLONIUS: I have, my lord.
HAMLET: Let her not walk i' th' sun. Conception is a blessing, but as your daughter may conceive—friend, look to't.
POLONIUS: How say you by that? [*Aside.*] Still harping on my daughter. Yet he
185 　　knew me not at first. 'A said I was a fishmonger. 'A is far gone. And truly in
　　　my youth I suffered much extremity for love. Very near this. I'll speak to him
　　　again.—What do you read, my lord?
HAMLET: Words, words, words.
POLONIUS: What is the matter, my lord?
190 HAMLET: Between who?
POLONIUS: I mean the matter that you read, my lord.
HAMLET: Slanders, sir; for the satirical rogue says here that old men have grey
　　　beards, that their faces are wrinkled, their eyes purging thick amber and plum-
　　　tree gum, and that they have a plentiful lack of wit, together with most weak
195 　　hams[8]—all which, sir, though I most powerfully and potently believe, yet I
　　　hold it not honesty to have it thus set down, for yourself, sir, shall grow old
　　　as I am, if like a crab you could go backward.
POLONIUS: [*Aside.*] Though this be madness, yet there is method in't.—Will you
　　　walk out of the air, my lord?
200 HAMLET: Into my grave?

---

4. Let loose.　5. Tapestry.　6. Accost.
7. A reference to the belief of the period that maggots were produced spontaneously by the action of sunshine on carrion.　8. Limbs.

POLONIUS: [*Aside.*] Indeed, that's out of the air. How pregnant sometime his replies are! a happiness that often madness hits on, which reason and sanity could not so prosperously be delivered of. I will leave him, and suddenly contrive the means of meeting between him and my daughter.—My honorable lord. I will most humbly take my leave of you.

HAMLET: You cannot take from me anything that I will more willingly part withal—except my life, except my life, except my life.

[*Enter* GUILDENSTERN *and* ROSENCRANTZ.]

POLONIUS: Fare you well, my lord.
HAMLET: These tedious old fools!
POLONIUS: You go to seek the Lord Hamlet. There he is.
ROSENCRANTZ: [*To* POLONIUS.] God save you, sir! [*Exit* POLONIUS.]
GUILDENSTERN: My honored lord!
ROSENCRANTZ: My most dear lord!
HAMLET: My excellent good friends! How dost thou, Guildenstern? Ah, Rosencrantz! Good lads, how do you both?
ROSENCRANTZ: As the indifferent[9] children of the earth.
GUILDENSTERN: Happy in that we are not over-happy;
On Fortune's cap we are not the very button.[1]
HAMLET: Nor the soles of her shoe?
ROSENCRANTZ: Neither, my lord.
HAMLET: Then you live about her waist, or in the middle of her favors?
GUILDENSTERN: Faith, her privates we.
HAMLET: In the secret parts of Fortune? O, most true, she is a strumpet.[2] What news?
ROSENCRANTZ: None, my lord, but that the world's grown honest.
HAMLET: Then is doomsday near. But your news is not true. Let me question more in particular. What have you, my good friends, deserved at the hands of Fortune, that she sends you to prison hither?
GUILDENSTERN: Prison, my lord?
HAMLET: Denmark's a prison.
ROSENCRANTZ: Then is the world one.
HAMLET: A goodly one, in which there are many confines, wards[3] and dungeons. Denmark being one o' th' worst.
ROSENCRANTZ: We think not so, my lord.
HAMLET: Why then 'tis none to you; for there is nothing either good or bad, but thinking makes it so. To me it is a prison.
ROSENCRANTZ: Why then your ambition makes it one. 'Tis too narrow for your mind.
HAMLET: O God, I could be bounded in a nutshell and count myself a king of infinite space, were it not that I have bad dreams.
GUILDENSTERN: Which dreams indeed are ambition; for the very substance of the ambitious is merely the shadow of a dream.

9. Ordinary.   1. That is, on top.
2. Prostitute. Hamlet is indulging in characteristic ribaldry. Guildenstern means that they are "privates" = ordinary citizens, but Hamlet takes him to mean "privates" = sexual organs and "middle of her favors" = waist = sexual organs.   3. Cells.

HAMLET: A dream itself is but a shadow.
ROSENCRANTZ: Truly, and I hold ambition of so airy and light a quality that it is but a shadow's shadow.
HAMLET: Then are our beggars bodies, and our monarchs and outstretched heroes the beggars' shadows. Shall we to th' court? for, by my fay,[4] I cannot reason.
BOTH: We'll wait upon you.
HAMLET: No such matter. I will not sort[5] you with the rest of my servants; for to speak to you like an honest man, I am most dreadfully attended. But in the beaten way of friendship, what make you at Elsinore?
ROSENCRANTZ: To visit you, my lord; no other occasion.
HAMLET: Beggar that I am, I am even poor in thanks, but I thank you; and sure, dear friends, my thanks are too dear a halfpenny.[6] Were you not sent for? Is it your own inclining? Is it a free visitation? Come, come, deal justly with me. Come, come, nay speak.
GUILDENSTERN: What should we say, my lord?
HAMLET: Anything but to th' purpose. You were sent for, and there is a kind of confession in your looks, which your modesties have not craft enough to color. I know the good king and queen have sent for you.
ROSENCRANTZ: To what end, my lord?
HAMLET: That you must teach me. But let me conjure you by the rights of our fellowship, by the consonancy of our youth, by the obligation of our ever-preserved love, and by what more dear a better proposer can charge you withal, be even and direct[7] with me whether you were sent for or no.
ROSENCRANTZ: [*Aside to* GUILDENSTERN.] What say you?
HAMLET: [*Aside.*] Nay, then, I have an eye of you.—If you love me, hold not off.
GUILDENSTERN: My lord, we were sent for.
HAMLET: I will tell you why; so shall my anticipation prevent your discovery,[8] and your secrecy to the king and queen moult no feather. I have of late—but wherefore I know not—lost all my mirth, forgone all custom of exercises; and indeed it goes so heavily with my disposition, that this goodly frame the earth seems to me a sterile promontory, this most excellent canopy the air, look you, this brave o'er-hanging firmament, this majestical roof fretted[9] with golden fire, why it appeareth nothing to me but a foul and pestilent congregation of vapors. What a piece of work is a man, how noble in reason, how infinite in faculties, in form and moving, how express[1] and admirable in action, how like an angel in apprehension, how like a god: the beauty of the world, the paragon of animals. And yet to me, what is this quintessence of dust? Man delights not me, nor woman neither, though by your smiling you seem to say so.
ROSENCRANTZ: My lord, there was no such stuff in my thoughts.
HAMLET: Why did ye laugh, then, when I said "Man delights not me"?
ROSENCRANTZ: To think, my lord, if you delight not in man, what lenten entertainment the players shall receive from you. We coted[2] them on the way, and hither are they coming to offer you service.

---

4. Faith.   5. Include.   6. Not worth a halfpenny.   7. Straightforward.   8. Disclosure.
9. Ornamented with fretwork.   1. Well built.   2. Passed. *Lenten:* scanty.

HAMLET: He that plays the king shall be welcome—his majesty shall have tribute of me; the adventurous knight shall use his foil and target; the lover shall not sigh gratis; the humorous[3] man shall end his part in peace; the clown shall make those laugh whose lungs are tickle o' th' sere;[4] and the lady shall say her mind freely, or the blank verse shall halt for't. What players are they?

ROSENCRANTZ: Even those you were wont to take such delight in, the tragedians of the city.

HAMLET: How chances it they travel? Their residence, both in reputation and profit, was better both ways.

ROSENCRANTZ: I think their inhibition comes by the means of the late innovation.

HAMLET: Do they hold the same estimation they did when I was in the city? Are they so followed?

ROSENCRANTZ: No, indeed, are they not.

HAMLET: How comes it? Do they grow rusty?

ROSENCRANTZ: Nay, their endeavor keeps in the wonted pace; but there is, sir, an eyrie of children, little eyases,[5] that cry out on the top of question,[6] and are most tyrannically clapped for't. These are now the fashion, and so berattle the common stages (so they call them) that many wearing rapiers are afraid of goose quills[7] and dare scarce come thither.[8]

HAMLET: What, are they children? Who maintains 'em? How are they escoted?[9] Will they pursue the quality no longer than they can sing? Will they not say afterwards, if they should grow themselves to common players (as it is most like, if their means are no better), their writers do them wrong to make them exclaim against their own succession?[1]

ROSENCRANTZ: Faith, there has been much todo on both sides; and the nation holds it no sin to tarre[2] them to controversy. There was for a while no money bid for argument,[3] unless the poet and the player went to cuffs[4] in the question.

HAMLET: Is't possible?

GUILDENSTERN: O, there has been much throwing about of brains.

HAMLET: Do the boys carry it away?

ROSENCRANTZ: Ay, that they do, my lord. Hercules and his load too.[5]

HAMLET: It is not very strange, for my uncle is King of Denmark, and those that would make mouths[6] at him while my father lived give twenty, forty, fifty, a hundred ducats apiece for his picture in little.[7] 'Sblood, there is something in this more than natural, if philosophy could find it out.

[*A flourish.*]

---

3. Eccentric. *Foil and target:* sword and shield.   4. Easily set off.   5. Little hawks.
6. With a loud, high delivery.   7. Pens of satirical writers.
8. The passage refers to the emergence at the time of the play of theatrical companies made up of children from London choir schools. Their performances became fashionable and hurt the business of the established companies. Hamlet says that if they continue to act, "pursue the quality," when they are grown, they will find that they have been damaging their own future careers.   9. Supported.   1. Future careers.
2. Urge.   3. Paid for a play plot.   4. Blows.
5. During one of his labors Hercules assumed for a time the burden of the Titan Atlas, who supported the heavens on his shoulders. Also a reference to the effect on business at Shakespeare's theater, the Globe.
6. Sneer.   7. Miniature.

GUILDENSTERN: There are the players.
HAMLET: Gentlemen, you are welcome to Elsinore. Your hands. Come then, th' appurtenance of welcome is fashion and ceremony. Let me comply with you in this garb, lest my extent[8] to the players, which I tell you must show fairly outwards should more appear like entertainment[9] than yours. You are welcome. But my uncle-father and aunt-mother are deceived.
GUILDENSTERN: In what, my dear lord?
HAMLET: I am but mad north-north-west; when the wind is southerly I know a hawk from a handsaw.[1]

[*Enter* POLONIUS.]

POLONIUS: Well be with you, gentlemen.
HAMLET: Hark you, Guildenstern—and you too—at each ear a hearer. That great baby you see there is not yet out of his swaddling clouts.[2]
ROSENCRANTZ: Happily he is the second time come to them, for they say an old man is twice a child.
HAMLET: I will prophesy he comes to tell me of the players. Mark it.—You say right, sir, a Monday morning, 'twas then indeed.
POLONIUS: My lord, I have news to tell you.
HAMLET: My lord, I have news to tell you. When Roscius was an actor in Rome—[3]
POLONIUS: The actors are come hither, my lord.
HAMLET: Buzz, buzz.
POLONIUS: Upon my honor—
HAMLET: Then came each actor on his ass—
POLONIUS: The best actors in the world, either for tragedy, comedy, history, pastoral, pastoral-comical, historical-pastoral, tragical-historical, tragical-comical-historical-pastoral, scene individable, or poem unlimited. Seneca cannot be too heavy nor Plautus too light. For the law of writ and the liberty, these are the only men.[4]
HAMLET: O Jephtha, judge of Israel, what a treasure hadst thou![5]
POLONIUS: What a treasure had he, my lord?
HAMLET: Why—

"One fair daughter, and no more,
The which he loved passing well."

POLONIUS: [*Aside.*] Still on my daughter.
HAMLET: Am I not i' th' right, old Jephtha?
POLONIUS: If you call me Jephtha, my lord, I have a daughter that I love passing well.
HAMLET: Nay, that follows not.

---

8. Fashion. *Comply with:* welcome.   9. Cordiality.
1. A "hawk" is a plasterer's tool; Hamlet may also be using "handsaw" = hernshaw = heron.
2. Wrappings for an infant.   3. Roscius was the most famous actor of classical Rome.
4. Seneca and Plautus were Roman writers of tragedy and comedy, respectively. The "law of writ" refers to plays written according to such rules as the three unities; the "liberty" to those written otherwise.
5. To insure victory, Jephtha promised to sacrifice the first creature to meet him on his return. Unfortunately, his only daughter outstripped his dog and was the victim of his vow. The biblical story is told in Judges 11.

POLONIUS: What follows then, my lord?
HAMLET: Why—

> "As by lot, God wot"

and then, you know,

> "It came to pass, as most like it was."

The first row of the pious chanson[6] will show you more, for look where my abridgement[7] comes.

[*Enter the* PLAYERS.]

You are welcome, masters; welcome, all.—I am glad to see thee well.—Welcome, good friends.—O, old friend! Why thy face is valanced[8] since I saw thee last. Com'st thou to beard me in Denmark?—What, my young lady and mistress? By'r lady, your ladyship is nearer to heaven than when I saw you last by the altitude of a chopine.[9] Pray God your voice, like a piece of uncurrent gold, be not cracked within the ring.—Masters, you are all welcome. We'll e'en to't like French falconers, fly at anything we see. We'll have a speech straight. Come give us a taste of your quality,[1] come a passionate speech.

FIRST PLAYER: What speech, my good lord?

HAMLET: I heard thee speak me a speech once, but it was never acted, or if it was, not above once, for the play, I remember, pleased not the million; 'twas caviary to the general.[2] But it was—as I received it, and others whose judgments in such matters cried in the top of[3] mine—an excellent play, well digested[4] in the scenes, set down with as much modesty as cunning. I remember one said there were no sallets[5] in the lines to make the matter savory, nor no matter in the phrase that might indict the author of affectation, but called it an honest method, as wholesome as sweet, and by very much more handsome than fine. One speech in't I chiefly loved. 'Twas Æneas' tale to Dido, and thereabout of it especially where he speaks of Priam's slaughter.[6] If it live in your memory, begin at this line—let me see, let me see:

> "The rugged Pyrrhus, like th' Hyrcanian beast"[7]—

'tis not so; it begins with Pyrrhus—

> "The rugged Pyrrhus, he whose sable arms,
> Black as his purpose, did the night resemble
> When he lay couchéd in th' ominous horse,[8]
> Hath now this dread and black complexion smeared
> With heraldry more dismal; head to foot

---

6. Song. *Row:* stanza.   7. That which cuts short by interrupting.   8. Fringed (with a beard).
9. A reference to the contemporary theatrical practice of using boys to play women's parts. The company's "lady" has grown in height by the size of a woman's thick-soled shoe, "chopine," since Hamlet saw him last. The next sentence refers to the possibility, suggested by his growth, that the young actor's voice may soon begin to change.   1. Trade.   2. Masses. *Caviary:* caviar.   3. Were weightier than.   4. Arranged.
5. Spicy passages.
6. Aeneas, fleeing with his band from fallen Troy (Ilium), arrives in Carthage, where he tells Dido, the queen of Carthage, of the fall of Troy. Here he is describing the death of Priam, the aged king of Troy, at the hands of Pyrrhus, the son of the slain Achilles.   7. Tiger.   8. That is, the Trojan horse.

>           Now is he total gules, horridly tricked[9]
>           With blood of fathers, mothers, daughters, sons,
>           Baked and impasted with the parching[1] streets,
> 400       That lend a tyrannous and a damnèd light
>           To their lord's murder. Roasted in wrath and fire,
>           And thus o'er-sizèd with coagulate[2] gore,
>           With eyes like carbuncles, the hellish Pyrrhus
>           Old grandsire Priam seeks."
>
> 405       So proceed you.
>
> POLONIUS: Fore God, my lord, well spoken, with good accent and good discretion.
>
> FIRST PLAYER:                        "Anon he finds him[3]
>           Striking too short at Greeks. His antique[4] sword,
> 410       Rebellious[5] to his arm, lies where it falls,
>           Repugnant to command. Unequal matched,
>           Pyrrhus at Priam drives, in rage strikes wide.
>           But with the whiff and wind of his fell sword
>           Th' unnervèd father falls. Then senseless[6] Ilium,
> 415       Seeming to feel this blow, with flaming top
>           Stoops[7] to his base, and with a hideous crash
>           Takes prisoner Pyrrhus' ear. For, lo! his sword,
>           Which was declining[8] on the milky head
>           Of reverend Priam, seemed i' th' air to stick.
> 420       So as a painted tyrant Pyrrhus stood,
>           And like a neutral to his will and matter,[9]
>           Did nothing.
>           But as we often see, against some storm,
>           A silence in the heavens, the rack[1] stand still,
> 425       The bold winds speechless, and the orb below
>           As hush as death, anon the dreadful thunder
>           Doth rend the region; so, after Pyrrhus' pause,
>           A rousèd vengeance sets him new awork,[2]
>           And never did the Cyclops' hammers fall
> 430       On Mars's armor, forged for proof eterne,[3]
>           With less remorse than Pyrrhus' bleeding sword
>           Now falls on Priam.
>           Out, out, thou strumpet, Fortune! All you gods,
>           In general synod take away her power,
> 435       Break all the spokes and fellies[4] from her wheel,
>           And bowl the round nave[5] down the hill of heaven
>           As low as to the fiends."
>
> POLONIUS: This is too long.

---

9. Adorned. *Total gules:* completely red.   1. Burning. *Impasted:* crusted.   2. Clotted. *O'er-sizèd:* glued over.
3. That is, Pyrrhus finds Priam.   4. Which he used when young.   5. Refractory.   6. Without feeling.
7. Falls.   8. About to fall.   9. Between his will and the fulfillment of it.   1. Clouds.   2. To work.
3. Mars, as befits a Roman war god, had armor made for him by the blacksmith god Vulcan and his assistants, the Cyclopes. It was suitably impenetrable, of "proof eterne."   4. Parts of the rim.
5. Hub. *Bowl:* roll.

HAMLET: It shall to the barber's with your beard.—Prithee say on. He's for a jig,[6] or a tale of bawdry, or he sleeps. Say on; come to Hecuba.[7]
FIRST PLAYER: "But who, ah woe! had seen the mobléd[8] queen—"
HAMLET: "The mobléd queen"?
POLONIUS: That's good. "Mobléd queen" is good.
FIRST PLAYER: "Run barefoot up and down, threat'ning the flames
With bisson rheum, a clout[9] upon that head
Where late the diadem stood, and for a robe,
About her lank and all o'er-teeméd loins,
A blanket, in the alarm of fear caught up—
Who this had seen, with tongue in venom steeped,
'Gainst Fortune's state[1] would treason have pronounced.
But if the gods themselves did see her then,
When she saw Pyrrhus make malicious sport
In mincing[2] with his sword her husband's limbs,
The instant burst of clamor that she made,
Unless things mortal move them not at all,
Would have made milch[3] the burning eyes of heaven,
And passion in the gods."
POLONIUS: Look whe'r[4] he has not turned his color, and has tears in's eyes. Prithee no more.
HAMLET: 'Tis well. I'll have thee speak out the rest of this soon.—Good my lord, will you see the players well bestowed?[5] Do you hear, let them be well used, for they are the abstract[6] and brief chronicles of the time; after your death you were better have a bad epitaph than their ill report while you live.
POLONIUS: My lord, I will use them according to their desert.
HAMLET: God's bodkin, man, much better. Use every man after his desert, and who shall 'scape whipping? Use them after your own honor and dignity. The less they deserve, the more merit is in your bounty. Take them in.
POLONIUS: Come, sirs.
HAMLET: Follow him, friends. We'll hear a play tomorrow.
          [*Aside to* FIRST PLAYER.]
Dost thou hear me, old friend, can you play "The Murder of Gonzago"?
FIRST PLAYER: Ay, my lord.
HAMLET: We'll ha't tomorrow night. You could for a need study a speech of some dozen or sixteen lines which I would set down and insert in't, could you not?
FIRST PLAYER: Ay, my lord.
HAMLET: Very well. Follow that lord, and look you mock him not.
          [*Exeunt* POLONIUS *and* PLAYERS.]
My good friends, I'll leave you till night. You are welcome to Elsinore.
ROSENCRANTZ: Good my lord.     [*Exeunt* ROSENCRANTZ *and* GUILDENSTERN.]
HAMLET: Ay, so God b'wi'ye. Now I am alone.
O, what a rogue and peasant slave am I!

---

6. A comic act.
7. Hecuba was the wife of Priam and queen of Troy. Her "loins" are described below as "o'erteeméd" because of her unusual fertility. The number of her children varies in different accounts, but twenty is a safe minimum.   8. Muffled (in a hood).   9. Cloth. *Bisson rheum:* blinding tears.   1. Government.
2. Cutting up.   3. Tearful (literally, milk-giving).   4. Whether.   5. Provided for.   6. Summary.

|     |                                                                                 |
| --- | ------------------------------------------------------------------------------- |
| 480 | Is it not monstrous that this player here,                                      |
|     | But in a fiction, in a dream of passion,                                        |
|     | Could force his soul so to his own conceit[7]                                   |
|     | That from her working all his visage wanned;[8]                                 |
|     | Tears in his eyes, distraction in his aspect[9]                                 |
| 485 | A broken voice, and his whole function suiting                                  |
|     | With forms to his conceit? And all for nothing,                                 |
|     | For Hecuba!                                                                     |
|     | What's Hecuba to him or he to Hecuba,                                           |
|     | That he should weep for her? What would he do                                   |
| 490 | Had he the motive and the cue for passion                                       |
|     | That I have? He would drown the stage with tears,                               |
|     | And cleave the general ear with horrid speech,                                  |
|     | Make mad the guilty, and appal the free,                                        |
|     | Confound the ignorant, and amaze indeed                                         |
| 495 | The very faculties of eyes and ears.                                            |
|     | Yet I,                                                                          |
|     | A dull and muddy-mettled rascal, peak[1]                                        |
|     | Like John-a-dreams, unpregnant[2] of my cause,                                  |
|     | And can say nothing; no, not for a king                                         |
| 500 | Upon whose property and most dear life                                          |
|     | A damned defeat was made. Am I a coward?                                        |
|     | Who calls me villain, breaks my pate across,                                    |
|     | Plucks off my beard and blows it in my face,                                    |
|     | Tweaks me by the nose, gives me the lie i' th' throat                           |
| 505 | As deep as to the lungs? Who does me this?                                      |
|     | Ha, 'swounds, I should take it; for it cannot be                                |
|     | But I am pigeon-livered and lack gall[3]                                        |
|     | To make oppression bitter, or ere this                                          |
|     | I should 'a fatted all the region kites[4]                                      |
| 510 | With this slave's offal. Bloody, bawdy villain!                                 |
|     | Remorseless, treacherous, lecherous, kindless[5] villain!                       |
|     | O, vengeance!                                                                   |
|     | Why, what an ass am I! This is most brave,                                      |
|     | That I, the son of a dear father murdered,                                      |
| 515 | Prompted to my revenge by heaven and hell,                                      |
|     | Must like a whore unpack[6] my heart with words,                                |
|     | And fall a-cursing like a very drab,                                            |
|     | A scullion![7] Fie upon't! foh!                                                 |
|     | About, my brains. Hum—I have heard                                              |
| 520 | That guilty creatures sitting at a play,                                        |
|     | Have by the very cunning of the scene                                           |
|     | Been struck so to the soul that presently                                       |

---

7. Imagination.   8. Grew pale.   9. Face.   1. Mope. *Muddy-mettled:* dull-spirited.
2. Not quickened by. *John-a-dreams:* a man dreaming.   3. Bitterness.   4. Birds of prey of the area.
5. Unnatural.   6. Relieve.
7. In some versions of the play, the word "stallion," a slang term for a prostitute, appears in place of "scullion."

They have proclaimed[8] their malefactions;
For murder, though it have no tongue, will speak
With most miraculous organ. I'll have these players                525
Play something like the murder of my father
Before mine uncle. I'll observe his looks.
I'll tent him to the quick. If 'a do blench,[9]
I know my course. The spirit that I have seen
May be a devil, and the devil hath power                           530
T' assume a pleasing shape, yea, and perhaps
Out of my weakness and my melancholy,
As he is very potent with such spirits,
Abuses me to damn me. I'll have grounds
More relative[1] than this. The play's the thing                   535
Wherein I'll catch the conscience of the king.          [*Exit.*]

ACT III

Scene 1

*A room in the castle. Enter* KING, QUEEN, POLONIUS, OPHELIA, ROSENCRANTZ *and* GUILDENSTERN.

KING: And can you by no drift of conference[2]
    Get from him why he puts on this confusion,
    Grating so harshly all his days of quiet
    With turbulent[3] and dangerous lunacy?
ROSENCRANTZ: He does confess he feels himself distracted,          5
    But from what cause 'a will by no means speak.
GUILDENSTERN: Nor do we find him forward to be sounded,[4]
    But with a crafty madness keeps aloof
    When we would bring him on to some confession
    Of his true state.
QUEEN:          Did he receive you well?                   10
ROSENCRANTZ: Most like a gentleman.
GUILDENSTERN: But with much forcing of his disposition.[5]
ROSENCRANTZ: Niggard of question, but of our demands[6]
    Most free in his reply.
QUEEN:          Did you assay[7] him
    To any pastime?                                              15
ROSENCRANTZ: Madam, it so fell out that certain players
    We o'er-raught[8] on the way. Of these we told him,
    And there did seem in him a kind of joy
    To hear of it. They are here about the court,
    And as I think, they have already order                      20
    This night to play before him.
POLONIUS:          'Tis most true,

---

8. Admitted.   9. Turn pale. *Tent:* try.   1. Conclusive.   2. Line of conversation.   3. Disturbing.
4. Questioned. *Forward:* eager.   5. Conversation.   6. To our questions.   7. Tempt.   8. Passed.

        And he beseeched me to entreat your majesties
        To hear and see the matter.[9]
    KING: With all my heart, and it doth much content me
25        To hear him so inclined.
        Good gentlemen, give him a further edge,
        And drive his purpose[1] into these delights.
    ROSENCRANTZ: We shall, my lord.    [*Exeunt* ROSENCRANTZ *and* GUILDENSTERN.]
    KING:                  Sweet Gertrude, leave us too,
        For we have closely sent for Hamlet hither,
30        That he, as 'twere by accident, may here
        Affront[2] Ophelia.
        Her father and myself (lawful espials[3])
        Will so bestow ourselves that, seeing unseen,
        We may of their encounter frankly judge,
35        And gather by him, as he is behaved,
        If't be th' affliction of his love or no
        That thus he suffers for.
    QUEEN:              I shall obey you.—
        And for your part, Ophelia, I do wish
        That your good beauties be the happy cause
40        Of Hamlet's wildness. So shall I hope your virtues
        Will bring him to his wonted[4] way again,
        To both your honors.
    OPHELIA:            Madam, I wish it may.    [*Exit* QUEEN.]
    POLONIUS: Ophelia, walk you here.—Gracious,[5] so please you,
        We will bestow ourselves.—[*To* OPHELIA.] Read on this book,
45        That show of such an exercise may color[6]
        Your loneliness.—We are oft to blame in this,
        'Tis too much proved, that with devotion's visage
        And pious action we do sugar o'er
        The devil himself.
    KING: [*Aside.*]        O, 'tis too true.
50        How smart a lash that speech doth give my conscience!
        The harlot's cheek, beautied with plast'ring[7] art,
        Is not more ugly to the thing that helps it
        Than is my deed to my most painted word.
        O heavy burden!
55    POLONIUS: I hear him coming. Let's withdraw, my lord.
                                  [*Exeunt* KING *and* POLONIUS.]

    [*Enter* HAMLET.]

    HAMLET: To be, or not to be, that is the question:
        Whether 'tis nobler in the mind to suffer
        The slings and arrows of outrageous fortune,
        Or to take arms against a sea of troubles,
60        And by opposing end them. To die, to sleep—

---

9. Performance.   1. Sharpen his intention.   2. Confront.   3. Justified spies.   4. Usual.   5. Majesty.
6. Explain. *Exercise:* act of devotion.   7. Thickly painted.

No more; and by a sleep to say we end
The heartache, and the thousand natural shocks
That flesh is heir to. 'Tis a consummation
Devoutly to be wished—to die, to sleep—
To sleep, perchance to dream, ay there's the rub; 65
For in that sleep of death what dreams may come
When we have shuffled off this mortal coil[8]
Must give us pause—there's the respect[9]
That makes calamity of so long life.
For who would bear the whips and scorns of time, 70
Th' oppressor's wrong, the proud man's contumely,[1]
The pangs of despised love, the law's delay,
The insolence of office, and the spurns[2]
That patient merit of th' unworthy takes,
When he himself might his quietus[3] make 75
With a bare bodkin? Who would fardels[4] bear,
To grunt and sweat under a weary life,
But that the dread of something after death,
The undiscovered country, from whose bourn[5]
No traveller returns, puzzles the will, 80
And makes us rather bear those ills we have
Than fly to others that we know not of?
Thus conscience does make cowards of us all;
And thus the native[6] hue of resolution
Is sicklied o'er with the pale cast of thought, 85
And enterprises of great pitch and moment[7]
With this regard their currents turn awry
And lose the name of action.—Soft you now,
The fair Ophelia.—Nymph, in thy orisons[8]
Be all my sins remembered.
OPHELIA: Good my lord, 90
How does your honor for this many a day?
HAMLET: I humbly thank you, well, well, well.
OPHELIA: My lord, I have remembrances of yours
That I have longéd long to re-deliver.
I pray you now receive them.
HAMLET: No, not I, 95
I never gave you aught.
OPHELIA: My honored lord, you know right well you did,
And with them words of so sweet breath composed
As made the things more rich. Their perfume lost,
Take these again, for to the noble mind 100
Rich gifts wax[9] poor when givers prove unkind.
There, my lord.
HAMLET: Ha, ha! are you honest?[1]

8. Turmoil.   9. Consideration.   1. Insulting behavior.   2. Rejections.   3. Settlement.
4. Burdens. *Bodkin:* dagger.   5. Boundary.   6. Natural.   7. Importance. *Pitch:* height.   8. Prayers.
9. Become.   1. Chaste.

OPHELIA: My lord?

HAMLET: Are you fair?

OPHELIA: What means your lordship?

HAMLET: That if you be honest and fair, your honesty should admit no discourse to your beauty.

OPHELIA: Could beauty, my lord, have better commerce[2] than with honesty?

HAMLET: Ay, truly, for the power of beauty will sooner transform honesty from what it is to a bawd than the force of honesty can translate beauty into his likeness. This was sometimes a paradox, but now the time gives it proof. I did love you once.

OPHELIA: Indeed, my lord, you made me believe so.

HAMLET: You should not have believed me, for virtue cannot so inoculate[3] our old stock but we shall relish of it. I loved you not.

OPHELIA: I was the more deceived.

HAMLET: Get thee to a nunnery.[4] Why wouldst thou be a breeder of sinners? I am myself indifferent[5] honest, but yet I could accuse me of such things that it were better my mother had not borne me: I am very proud, revengeful, ambitious, with more offences at my beck[6] than I have thoughts to put them in, imagination to give them shape, or time to act them in. What should such fellows as I do crawling between earth and heaven? We are arrant[7] knaves all; believe none of us. Go thy ways to a nunnery. Where's your father?

OPHELIA: At home, my lord.

HAMLET: Let the doors be shut upon him, that he may play the fool nowhere but in's own house. Farewell.

OPHELIA: O, help him, you sweet heavens!

HAMLET: If thou dost marry, I'll give thee this plague for thy dowry: be thou as chaste as ice, as pure as snow, thou shalt not escape calumny. Get thee to a nunnery, farewell. Or if thou wilt needs marry, marry a fool, for wise men know well enough what monsters[8] you make of them. To a nunnery, go, and quickly too. Farewell.

OPHELIA: Heavenly powers, restore him!

HAMLET: I have heard of your paintings, too, well enough. God hath given you one face, and you make yourselves another. You jig, you amble, and you lisp;[9] you nickname God's creatures, and make your wantonness your ignorance.[1] Go to, I'll no more on't, it hath made me mad. I say we will have no more marriage. Those that are married already, all but one, shall live. The rest shall keep as they are. To a nunnery, go. [*Exit.*]

OPHELIA: O, what a noble mind is here o'erthrown!
 The courtier's, soldier's, scholar's, eye, tongue, sword,
 Th' expectancy and rose[2] of the fair state,
 The glass of fashion and the mould[3] of form,
 Th' observed of all observers, quite quite down!

---

2. Intercourse.   3. Change by grafting.
4. With typical ribaldry Hamlet uses "nunnery" in two senses, the second as a slang term for brothel.
5. Moderately.   6. Command.   7. Thorough.   8. Horned because cuckolded.
9. Walk and talk affectedly.
1. Hamlet means that women call things by pet names and then blame the affectation on ignorance.
2. Ornament. *Expectancy:* hope.   3. Model. *Glass:* mirror.

And I of ladies most deject and wretched,
That sucked the honey of his music⁴ vows,
Now see that noble and most sovereign reason
Like sweet bells jangled, out of time and harsh;
That unmatched form and feature of blown⁵ youth       150
Blasted with ecstasy. O, woe is me
T' have seen what I have seen, see what I see!

[*Enter* KING *and* POLONIUS.]

KING: Love! His affections do not that way tend,
Nor what he spake, though it lacked form a little,
Was not like madness. There's something in his soul    155
O'er which his melancholy sits on brood,⁶
And I do doubt the hatch and the disclose⁷
Will be some danger; which to prevent,
I have in quick determination
Thus set it down: he shall with speed to England       160
For the demand of our neglected tribute.
Haply the seas and countries different,
With variable objects, shall expel
This something-settled matter in his heart
Whereon his brains still beating puts him thus         165
From fashion of himself. What think you on't?

POLONIUS: It shall do well. But yet do I believe
The origin and commencement of his grief
Sprung from neglected love.—How now, Ophelia?
You need not tell us what Lord Hamlet said,            170
We heard it all.—My lord, do as you please,
But if you hold it fit, after the play
Let his queen-mother all alone entreat him
To show his grief. Let her be round⁸ with him,
And I'll be placed, so please you, in the ear⁹         175
Of all their conference. If she find him not,¹
To England send him; or confine him where
Your wisdom best shall think.

KING:                               It shall be so.
Madness in great ones must not unwatched go.   [*Exeunt.*]

## Scene 2

*A public room in the castle. Enter* HAMLET *and three of the* PLAYERS.

HAMLET: Speak the speech, I pray you, as I pronounced it to you, trippingly on the tongue; but if you mouth it as many of our players do, I had as lief the town-crier spoke my lines. Nor do not saw the air too much with your hand thus, but use all gently, for in the very torrent, tempest, and as I may say,

---

4. Musical.   5. Full-blown.   6. That is, like a hen.   7. Result. *Doubt:* fear.   8. Direct.   9. Hearing.
1. Does not discover his problem.

whirlwind of your passion, you must acquire and beget a temperance that may give it smoothness. O, it offends me to the soul to hear a robustious periwig-pated[2] fellow tear a passion to tatters, to very rags, to split the ears of the groundlings, who for the most part are capable of[3] nothing but inexplicable dumb shows and noise. I would have such a fellow whipped for o'erdoing Termagant. It out-herods Herod.[4] Pray you avoid it.

FIRST PLAYER: I warrant your honor.

HAMLET: Be not too tame neither, but let your own discretion be your tutor. Suit the action to the word, the word to the action, with this special observance, that you o'erstep not the modesty of nature; for anything so o'erdone is from[5] the purpose of playing, whose end both at the first, and now, was and is, to hold as 'twere the mirror up to nature, to show virtue her own feature, scorn her own image, and the very age and body of the time his form and pressure.[6] Now this overdone, or come tardy off, though it makes the unskilful[7] laugh, cannot but make the judicious grieve, the censure[8] of the which one must in your allowance o'erweigh a whole theatre of others. O, there be players that I have seen play—and heard others praise, and that highly—not to speak it profanely, that neither having th' accent of Christians, nor the gait of Christian, pagan, nor man, have so strutted and bellowed that I have thought some of nature's journeymen[9] had made men, and not made them well, they imitated humanity so abominably.

FIRST PLAYER: I hope we have reformed that indifferently[1] with us, sir.

HAMLET: O, reform it altogether. And let those that play your clowns speak no more than is set down for them, for there be of them that will themselves laugh, to set on some quantity of barren[2] spectators to laugh too, though in the meantime some necessary question of the play be then to be considered. That's villainous, and shows a most pitiful ambition in the fool that uses it. Go, make you ready.               [*Exeunt* PLAYERS.]

[*Enter* POLONIUS, GUILDENSTERN, *and* ROSENCRANTZ.]

How now, my lord? Will the king hear this piece of work?

POLONIUS: And the queen too, and that presently.

HAMLET: Bid the players make haste.               [*Exit* POLONIUS.]
Will you two help to hasten them?

ROSENCRANTZ: Ay, my lord.               [*Exeunt they two.*]

HAMLET: What, ho, Horatio!

[*Enter* HORATIO.]

HORATIO: Here, sweet lord, at your service.

HAMLET: Horatio, thou art e'en as just a man
As e'er my conversation coped[3] withal.

HORATIO: O my dear lord!

HAMLET:               Nay, do not think I flatter,

---

2. Bewigged. *Robustious:* noisy.
3. That is, capable of understanding. *Groundlings:* the spectators who paid least.
4. Termagant, a "Saracen" deity, and the biblical Herod were stock characters in popular drama noted for the excesses of sound and fury used by their interpreters.     5. Contrary to.     6. Shape.     7. Ignorant.
8. Judgment.     9. Inferior craftsmen.     1. Somewhat.     2. Dull-witted.     3. Encountered.

For what advancement may I hope from thee,
That no revenue hast but thy good spirits
To feed and clothe thee? Why should the poor be flattered?
No, let the candied tongue lick absurd pomp,
And crook the pregnant⁴ hinges of the knee
Where thrift⁵ may follow fawning. Dost thou hear?
Since my dear soul was mistress of her choice
And could of men distinguish her election,
S'hath sealed thee for herself, for thou hast been
As one in suff'ring all that suffers nothing,
A man that Fortune's buffets and rewards
Hast ta'en with equal thanks; and blest are those
Whose blood and judgment are so well commingled
That they are not a pipe⁶ for Fortune's finger
To sound what stop⁷ she please. Give me that man
That is not passion's slave, and I will wear him
In my heart's core, ay, in my heart of heart,
As I do thee. Something too much of this.
There is a play tonight before the king.
One scene of it comes near the circumstance
Which I have told thee of my father's death.
I prithee, when thou seest that act afoot,
Even with the very comment⁸ of thy soul
Observe my uncle. If his occulted⁹ guilt
Do not itself unkennel¹ in one speech,
It is a damnéd ghost that we have seen,
And my imaginations are as foul
As Vulcan's stithy. Give him heedful note,²
For I mine eyes will rivet to his face,
And after we will both our judgments join
In censure of his seeming.³

HORATIO: Well, my lord.
If 'a steal aught the whilst this play in playing,
And 'scape detecting, I will pay⁴ the theft.

[*Enter Trumpets and Kettledrums,* KING, QUEEN, POLONIUS, OPHELIA, ROSEN-
CRANTZ, GUILDENSTERN, *and other* LORDS *attendant.*]

HAMLET: They are coming to the play. I must be idle.
    Get you a place.
KING: How fares our cousin Hamlet?
HAMLET: Excellent, i' faith, of the chameleon's dish.⁵ I eat the air, promise-
    crammed. You cannot feed capons so.
KING: I have nothing with this answer, Hamlet. These words are not mine.

---

4. Quick to bend.   5. Profit.   6. Musical instrument.   7. Note. *Sound:* play.   8. Keenest observation.
9. Hidden.   1. Break loose.   2. Careful attention. *Stithy:* smithy.   3. Manner.   4. Repay.
5. A reference to a popular belief that the chameleon subsisted on a diet of air. Hamlet has deliberately misunderstood the king's question.

HAMLET: No, nor mine now. [*To* POLONIUS.] My lord, you played once i' th' university, you say?
POLONIUS: That did I, my lord, and was accounted a good actor.
HAMLET: What did you enact?
85 POLONIUS: I did enact Julius Cæsar. I was killed i' th' Capitol; Brutus killed me.[6]
HAMLET: It was a brute part of him to kill so capital a calf there. Be the players ready?
ROSENCRANTZ: Ay, my lord, they stay upon your patience.[7]
QUEEN: Come hither, my dear Hamlet, sit by me.
90 HAMLET: No, good mother, here's metal more attractive.
POLONIUS: [*To the* KING.] O, ho! do you mark that?
HAMLET: Lady, shall I lie in your lap?

[*Lying down at* OPHELIA's *feet.*]

OPHELIA: No, my lord.
HAMLET: I mean, my head upon your lap?
95 OPHELIA: Ay, my lord.
HAMLET: Do you think I meant country matters?[8]
OPHELIA: I think nothing, my lord.
HAMLET: That's a fair thought to lie between maids' legs.
OPHELIA: What is, my lord?
100 HAMLET: Nothing.
OPHELIA: You are merry, my lord.
HAMLET: Who, I?
OPHELIA: Ay, my lord.
HAMLET: O God, your only jig-maker![9] What should a man do but be merry? For
105 look you how cheerfully my mother looks, and my father died within's two hours.
OPHELIA: Nay, 'tis twice two months, my lord.
HAMLET: So long? Nay then, let the devil wear black, for I'll have a suit of sables. O heavens! die two months ago, and not forgotten yet? Then there's hope a
110 great man's memory may outlive his life half a year, but by'r lady 'a must build churches then, or else shall 'a suffer not thinking on, with the hobby-horse, whose epitaph is "For O, for O, the hobby-horse is forgot!"[1]

> *The trumpets sound. Dumb Show follows. Enter a* KING *and a* QUEEN *very lovingly; the* QUEEN *embracing him and he her. She kneels, and makes show of protestation unto him. He takes her up, and declines[2] his head upon her neck. He lies him down upon a bank of flowers; she, seeing him asleep, leaves him. Anon come in another man, takes off his crown, kisses it, pours poison in the sleeper's ears, and leaves him. The* QUEEN *returns, finds the* KING *dead, makes passionate action. The* POISONER *with some three or four come in again, seem to condole with her. The dead body is carried away. The* POISONER *woos the* QUEEN *with gifts; she seems harsh awhile, but in the end accepts love.* [*Exeunt.*]

---

6. The assassination of Julius Caesar by Brutus and others is the subject of another play by Shakespeare.
7. Leisure. *Stay:* wait.
8. Presumably, rustic misbehavior, but here and elsewhere in this exchange Hamlet treats Ophelia to some ribald double meanings.    9. Writer of comic scenes.
1. In traditional games and dances one of the characters was a man represented as riding a horse. The horse was made of something like cardboard and was worn about the "rider's" waist.    2. Lays.

OPHELIA: What means this, my lord?
HAMLET: Marry, this is miching mallecho;³ it means mischief.
OPHELIA: Belike this show imports the argument⁴ of the play.

[*Enter* PROLOGUE.]

HAMLET: We shall know by this fellow. The players cannot keep counsel; they'll tell all.
OPHELIA: Will 'a tell us what this show meant?
HAMLET: Ay, or any show that you will show him. Be not you ashamed to show, he'll not shame to tell you what it means.
OPHELIA: You are naught, you are naught. I'll mark⁵ the play.
PROLOGUE: *For us, and for our tragedy,*
    *Here stooping to your clemency,*
    *We beg your hearing patiently.*                                      [*Exit.*]

HAMLET: Is this a prologue, or the posy⁶ of a ring?
OPHELIA: 'Tis brief, my lord.
HAMLET: As woman's love.

[*Enter the* PLAYER KING *and* QUEEN.]

PLAYER KING: *Full thirty times hath Phœbus' cart gone round*
    *Neptune's salt wash and Tellus' orbèd ground,*
    *And thirty dozen moons with borrowed sheen⁷*
    *About the world have times twelve thirties been,*
    *Since love our hearts and Hymen did our hands*
    *Unite comutual in most sacred bands.⁸*
PLAYER QUEEN: *So many journeys may the sun and moon*
    *Make us again count o'er ere love be done!*
    *But woe is me, you are so sick of late,*
    *So far from cheer and from your former state,*
    *That I distrust⁹ you. Yet though I distrust,*
    *Discomfort you, my lord, it nothing must.*
    *For women's fear and love hold quantity,¹*
    *In neither aught, or in extremity.²*
    *Now what my love is proof hath made you know,*
    *And as my love is sized,³ my fear is so.*
    *Where love is great, the littlest doubts are fear;*
    *Where little fears grow great, great love grows there.*
PLAYER KING: *Faith, I must leave thee, love, and shortly too;*
    *My operant powers their functions leave⁴ to do.*
    *And thou shalt live in this fair world behind,*
    *Honored, beloved, and haply one as kind*
    *For husband shalt thou—*

---

3. Sneaking crime.   4. Plot. *Imports*: explains.   5. Attend to. *Naught*: obscene.
6. Motto engraved inside.   7. Light.
8. The speech contains several references to Greek mythology. Phoebus was the sun god, and his chariot or "cart" is the sun. The "salt wash" of Neptune is the ocean; Tellus was an earth goddess, and her "orbèd ground" is the Earth, or globe. Hymen was the god of marriage. *Comutual*: mutually.   9. Fear for.
1. Agree in weight.   2. Without regard to too much or too little.   3. In size.
4. Cease. *Operant powers*: active forces.

150 PLAYER QUEEN:       O, confound the rest!
    Such love must needs be treason in my breast.
    In second husband let me be accurst!
    None wed the second but who killed the first.[5]
    HAMLET: That's wormwood.
155 PLAYER QUEEN: The instances[6] that second marriage move
    Are base respects[7] of thrift, but none of love.
    A second time I kill my husband dead,
    When second husband kisses me in bed.
    PLAYER KING: I do believe you think what now you speak,
160 But what we do determine oft we break.
    Purpose is but the slave to memory,
    Of violent birth, but poor validity;
    Which now, like fruit unripe, sticks on the tree,
    But fall unshaken when they mellow be.
165 Most necessary 'tis that we forget
    To pay ourselves what to ourselves is debt.
    What to ourselves in passion we propose,
    The passion ending, doth the purpose lose.
    The violence of either grief or joy
170 Their own enactures[8] with themselves destroy.
    Where joy most revels, grief doth most lament;
    Grief joys, joy grieves, on slender accident.
    This world is not for aye,[9] nor 'tis not strange
    That even our loves should with our fortunes change;
175 For 'tis a question left us yet to prove,
    Whether love lead fortune, or else fortune love.
    The great man down, you mark his favorite flies;
    The poor advanced makes friends of enemies;
    And hitherto doth love on fortune tend,
180 For who not needs shall never lack a friend,
    And who in want a hollow[1] friend doth try,
    Directly seasons him[2] his enemy.
    But orderly to end where I begun,
    Our wills and fates do so contrary run
185 That our devices[3] still are overthrown;
    Our thoughts are ours, their ends none of our own.
    So think thou wilt no second husband wed,
    But die thy thoughts when thy first lord is dead.
    PLAYER QUEEN: Nor earth to me give food, nor heaven light,
190 Sport and repose lock from me day and night,
    To desperation turn my trust and hope,
    An anchor's cheer[4] in prison be my scope,
    Each opposite that blanks[5] the face of joy
    Meet what I would have well, and it destroy,

---

5. Though there is some ambiguity, she seems to mean that the only kind of woman who would remarry is one who has killed or would kill her first husband.   6. Causes.   7. Concerns.   8. Actions.   9. Eternal.   1. False.   2. Ripens him into.   3. Plans.   4. Anchorite's food.   5. Blanches.

>     *Both here and hence*[6] *pursue me lasting strife,*
>     *If once a widow, ever I be wife!*
> HAMLET: If she should break it now!
> PLAYER KING: 'Tis deeply sworn. Sweet, leave me here awhile.
>     *My spirits grow dull, and fain I would beguile*
>     *The tedious day with sleep.*                                    [*Sleeps.*]
> PLAYER QUEEN:               *Sleep rock thy brain,*
>     *And never come mischance between us twain!*                [*Exit.*]
> HAMLET: Madam, how like you this play?
> QUEEN: The lady doth protest too much, methinks.
> HAMLET: O, but she'll keep her word.
> KING: Have you heard the argument? Is there no offence in't?
> HAMLET: No, no, they do but jest, poison in jest; no offence i' th' world.
> KING: What do you call the play?
> HAMLET: "The Mouse-trap." Marry, how? Tropically.[7] This play is the image of a murder done in Vienna. Gonzago is the duke's name; his wife, Baptista. You shall see anon. 'Tis a knavish piece of work, but what of that? Your majesty, and we that have free souls, it touches us not. Let the galled jade wince, our withers are unwrung.[8]
> 
>     [*Enter* LUCIANUS.]
> 
>     This is one Lucianus, nephew to the king.
> OPHELIA: You are as good as a chorus, my lord.
> HAMLET: I could interpret between you and your love, if I could see the puppets dallying.
> OPHELIA: You are keen, my lord, you are keen.
> HAMLET: It would cost you a groaning to take off mine edge.
> OPHELIA: Still better, and worse.
> HAMLET: So you mistake your husbands.—Begin, murderer. Leave thy damnable faces and begin. Come, the croaking raven doth bellow for revenge.
> LUCIANUS: *Thoughts black, hands apt, drugs fit, and time agreeing,*
>     *Confederate season,*[9] *else no creature seeing,*
>     *Thou mixture rank, of midnight weeds collected,*
>     *With Hecate's ban thrice blasted, thrice infected,*[1]
>     *Thy natural magic*[2] *and dire property*
>     *On wholesome life usurp immediately.*        [*Pours the poison in his ears.*]
> HAMLET: 'A poisons him i' th' garden for his estate. His name's Gonzago. The story is extant, and written in very choice Italian. You shall see anon how the murderer gets the love of Gonzago's wife.
> OPHELIA: The king rises.
> HAMLET: What, frighted with false fire?
> QUEEN: How fares my lord?
> POLONIUS: Give o'er the play.
> KING: Give me some light. Away!

---

6. In the next world.    7. Figuratively.
8. A "galled jade" is a horse, particularly one of poor quality, with a sore back. The "withers" are the ridge between a horse's shoulders; "unwrung withers" are not chafed by the harness.
9. A helpful time for the crime.    1. Hecate was a classical goddess of witchcraft.    2. Native power.

POLONIUS: Lights, lights, lights!       [*Exeunt all but* HAMLET *and* HORATIO.]
HAMLET:
> Why, let the strucken deer go weep,
>    The hart ungallèd[3] play.
> For some must watch while some must sleep;
>    Thus runs the world away.

Would not this, sir, and a forest of feathers[4]—if the rest of my fortunes turn Turk with me—with two Provincial roses on my razed shoes, get me a fellowship in a cry of players?[5]
HORATIO: Half a share.
HAMLET: A whole one, I.
> For thou dost know, O Damon dear,[6]
>    This realm dismantled was
> Of Jove himself, and now reigns here
>    A very, very—peacock.

HORATIO: You might have rhymed.
HAMLET: O good Horatio, I'll take the ghost's word for a thousand pound. Didst perceive?
HORATIO: Very well, my lord.
HAMLET: Upon the talk of the poisoning.
HORATIO: I did very well note[7] him.
HAMLET: Ah, ha! Come, some music. Come, the recorders.[8]
> For if the king like not the comedy.
> Why then, belike he likes it not, perdy.[9]

Come, some music.

[*Enter* ROSENCRANTZ *and* GUILDENSTERN.]

GUILDENSTERN: Good my lord, vouchsafe me a word with you.
HAMLET: Sir, a whole history.
GUILDENSTERN: The king, sir—
HAMLET: Ay, sir, what of him?
GUILDENSTERN: Is in his retirement marvellous distempered.[1]
HAMLET: With drink, sir?
GUILDENSTERN: No, my lord, with choler.[2]
HAMLET: Your wisdom should show itself more richer to signify this to the doctor, for for me to put him to his purgation[3] would perhaps plunge him into more choler.

---

3. Uninjured.     4. Plumes.
5. Hamlet asks Horatio if "this" recitation, accompanied with a player's costume, including plumes and rosettes on shoes that have been slashed for decorative effect, might not entitle him to become a shareholder in a theatrical company in the event that Fortune goes against him, "turn Turk." *Cry:* company.
6. Damon was a common name for a young man or a shepherd in lyric, especially pastoral poetry. Jove was the chief god of the Romans. Readers may supply for themselves the rhyme referred to by Horatio.
7. Observe.     8. Wooden, end-blown flutes.     9. *Par Dieu* (by God).
1. Vexed. *Retirement:* place to which he has retired.     2. Bile.     3. Treatment with a laxative.

GUILDENSTERN: Good my lord, put your discourse into some frame,[4] and start not so wildly from my affair.

HAMLET: I am tame, sir. Pronounce.

GUILDENSTERN: The queen your mother, in most great affliction of spirit, hath sent me to you.

HAMLET: You are welcome.

GUILDENSTERN: Nay, good my lord, this courtesy is not of the right breed. If it shall please you to make me a wholesome[5] answer, I will do your mother's commandment. If not, your pardon and my return[6] shall be the end of my business.

HAMLET: Sir, I cannot.

ROSENCRANTZ: What, my lord?

HAMLET: Make you a wholesome answer; my wit's diseased. But, sir, such answer as I can make, you shall command, or rather, as you say, my mother. Therefore no more, but to the matter. My mother, you say—

ROSENCRANTZ: Then thus she says: your behavior hath struck her into amazement and admiration.[7]

HAMLET: O wonderful son, that can so stonish a mother! But is there no sequel at the heels of his mother's admiration? Impart.[8]

ROSENCRANTZ: She desires to speak with you in her closet[9] ere you go to bed.

HAMLET: We shall obey, were she ten times our mother. Have you any further trade[1] with us?

ROSENCRANTZ: My lord, you once did love me.

HAMLET: And do still, by these pickers and stealers.[2]

ROSENCRANTZ: Good my lord, what is your cause of distemper? You do surely bar the door upon your own liberty, if you deny your griefs to your friend.

HAMLET: Sir, I lack advancement.

ROSENCRANTZ: How can that be, when you have the voice of the king himself for your succession in Denmark?

HAMLET: Ay, sir, but "while the grass grows"—the proverb[3] is something musty.

[Enter the PLAYERS with recorders.]

O, the recorders! Let me see one. To withdraw with you[4]—why do you go about to recover the wind of me, as if you would drive me into a toil?[5]

GUILDENSTERN: O my lord, if my duty be too bold, my love is too unmannerly.

HAMLET: I do not well understand that. Will you play upon this pipe?[6]

GUILDENSTERN: My lord, I cannot.

HAMLET: I pray you.

GUILDENSTERN: Believe me, I cannot.

HAMLET: I do beseech you.

GUILDENSTERN: I know no touch of it,[7] my lord.

HAMLET: It is as easy as lying. Govern these ventages[8] with your fingers and

---

4. Order. *Discourse:* speech.   5. Reasonable.   6. That is, to the queen.   7. Wonder.   8. Tell me.
9. Bedroom.   1. Business.   2. Hands.   3. The proverb ends "the horse starves."   4. Let me step aside.
5. The figure is from hunting. Hamlet asks why Guildenstern is attempting to get windward of him, as if he would drive him into a net.   6. Recorder.   7. Have no ability.   8. Holes. *Govern:* cover and uncover.

thumb, give it breath with your mouth, and it will discourse most eloquent music. Look you, these are the stops.[9]

GUILDENSTERN: But these cannot I command to any utt'rance of harmony. I have not the skill.

HAMLET: Why, look you now, how unworthy a thing you make of me! You would play upon me, you would seem to know my stops, you would pluck out the heart of my mystery, you would sound[1] me from my lowest note to the top of my compass;[2] and there is much music, excellent voice, in this little organ, yet cannot you make it speak. 'Sblood, do you think I am easier to be played on than a pipe? Call me what instrument you will, though you can fret[3] me, you cannot play upon me.

[*Enter* POLONIUS.]

God bless you, sir!

POLONIUS: My lord, the queen would speak with you, and presently.[4]

HAMLET: Do you see yonder cloud that's almost in shape of a camel?

POLONIUS: By th' mass, and 'tis like a camel indeed.

HAMLET: Methinks it is like a weasel.

POLONIUS: It is backed like a weasel.

HAMLET: Or like a whale.

POLONIUS: Very like a whale.

HAMLET: Then I will come to my mother by and by. [*Aside.*] They fool me to the top of my bent.[5]—I will come by and by.

POLONIUS: I will say so. [*Exit.*]

HAMLET: "By and by" is easily said. Leave me, friends. [*Exeunt all but* HAMLET.]
'Tis now the very witching time of night,
When churchyards yawn, and hell itself breathes out
Contagion to this world. Now could I drink hot blood,
And do such bitter business as the day
Would quake to look on. Soft, now to my mother.
O heart, lose not thy nature; let not ever
The soul of Nero[6] enter this firm bosom.
Let me be cruel, not unnatural;
I will speak daggers to her, but use none.
My tongue and soul in this be hypocrites—
How in my words somever she be shent,[7]
To give them seals[8] never, my soul, consent! [*Exit.*]

## Scene 3

*A room in the castle. Enter* KING, ROSENCRANTZ *and* GUILDENSTERN.

KING: I like him not,[9] nor stands it safe with us
To let his madness range.[1] Therefore prepare you.

---

9. Wind-holes.   1. Play.   2. Range.
3. "Fret" is used in a double sense, to annoy and to play a guitar or similar instrument using the "frets" or small bars on the neck.   4. At once.   5. Treat me as an utter fool.
6. The Roman emperor Nero, known for his excesses, was believed to have been responsible for the death of his mother.   7. Shamed.   8. Fulfillment in action.   9. Distrust him.   1. Roam freely.

                    I your commission will forthwith dispatch,
                    And he to England shall along with you.
                    The terms of our estate² may not endure
                    Hazard so near's as doth hourly grow
                    Out of his brows.
GUILDENSTERN:           We will ourselves provide,³
                    Most holy and religious fear it is
                    To keep those many many bodies safe
                    That live and feed upon your majesty.
ROSENCRANTZ: The single and peculiar⁴ life is bound
                    With all the strength and armor of the mind
                    To keep itself from noyance,⁵ but much more
                    That spirit upon whose weal⁶ depends and rests
                    The lives of many. The cess⁷ of majesty
                    Dies not alone, but like a gulf⁸ doth draw
                    What's near it with it. It is a massy⁹ wheel
                    Fixed on the summit of the highest mount,
                    To whose huge spokes ten thousand lesser things
                    Are mortised and adjoined,¹ which when it falls,
                    Each small annexment, petty consequence,
                    Attends² the boist'rous ruin. Never alone
                    Did the king sigh, but with a general groan.
KING:   Arm you, I pray you, to this speedy voyage,
                    For we will fetters put about this fear,
                    Which now goes too free-footed.
ROSENCRANTZ:                    We will haste us.
                                [Exeunt ROSENCRANTZ and GUILDENSTERN.]

                    [Enter POLONIUS.]

POLONIUS: My lord, he's going to his mother's closet.
                    Behind the arras I'll convey³ myself
                    To hear the process. I'll warrant she'll tax him home,⁴
                    And as you said, and wisely was it said,
                    'Tis meet that some more audience than a mother,
                    Since nature makes them partial, should o'erhear
                    The speech, of vantage.⁵ Fare you well, my liege.
                    I'll call upon you ere you go to bed,
                    And tell you what I know.
KING:                   Thanks, dear my lord.               [Exit POLONIUS.]
                    O, my offence is rank, it smells to heaven;
                    It hath the primal eldest curse⁶ upon't,
                    A brother's murder. Pray can I not,
                    Though inclination be as sharp as will.
                    My stronger guilt defeats my strong intent,

---

2. Condition of the state.   3. Equip (for the journey).   4. Individual.   5. Harm.   6. Welfare.
7. Cessation.   8. Whirlpool.   9. Massive.   1. Attached.   2. Joins in.   3. Station.
4. Sharply. *Process:* proceedings.   5. From a position of vantage.   6. That is, of Cain.

And like a man to double business[7] bound,
I stand in pause where I shall first begin,
And both neglect. What if this cursèd hand
Were thicker than itself with brother's blood,
Is there not rain enough in the sweet heavens
To wash it white as snow? Whereto serves mercy
But to confront the visage of offence?
And what's in prayer but this twofold force,
To be forestallèd[8] ere we come to fall,
Or pardoned being down?[9] Then I'll look up.
My fault is past, But, O, what form of prayer
Can serve my turn? "Forgive me my foul murder"?
That cannot be, since I am still possessed
Of those effects[1] for which I did the murder—
My crown, mine own ambition, and my queen.
May one be pardoned and retain th' offence?[2]
In the corrupted currents of this world
Offence's gilded[3] hand may shove by justice,
And oft 'tis seen the wicked prize itself
Buys out the law. But 'tis not so above.
There is no shuffling; there the action[4] lies
In his true nature, and we ourselves compelled,
Even to the teeth and forehead of[5] our faults,
To give in evidence. What then? What rests?[6]
Try what repentance can. What can it not?
Yet what can it when one cannot repent?
O wretched state! O bosom black as death!
O limèd[7] soul, that struggling to be free
Art more engaged! Help, angels! Make assay.
Bow, stubborn knees, and heart with strings of steel,
Be soft as sinews of the new-born babe.
All may be well.                                    [*He kneels.*]

[*Enter* HAMLET.]

HAMLET: Now might I do it pat,[8] now 'a is a-praying,
And now I'll do't—and so 'a goes to heaven,
And so am I revenged. That would be scanned.[9]
A villain kills my father, and for that,
I, his sole son, do this same villain send
To heaven.
Why, this is hire and salary, not revenge.
'A took my father grossly, full of bread,[1]
With all his crimes broad blown, as flush[2] as May;
And how his audit stands who knows save heaven?

---

7. Two mutually opposed interests.   8. Prevented (from sin).   9. Having sinned.   1. Gains.
2. That is, benefits of the offense.   3. Bearing gold as a bribe.   4. Case at law.   5. Face-to-face with.
6. Remains.   7. Caught as with birdlime.   8. Easily.   9. Deserves consideration.
1. In a state of sin and without fasting.   2. Vigorous. *Broad blown:* full-blown.

> But in our circumstance and course of thought
> 'Tis heavy with him; and am I then revenged
> To take him in the purging of his soul,
> When he is fit and seasoned[3] for his passage?
> No.
> Up, sword, and know thou a more horrid hent.[4]
> When he is drunk, asleep, or in his rage,
> Or in th' incestuous pleasure of his bed,
> At game a-swearing, or about some act
> That has no relish[5] of salvation in't—
> Then trip him, that his heels may kick at heaven,
> And that his soul may be as damned and black
> As hell, whereto it goes. My mother stays.
> This physic[6] but prolongs thy sickly days.   [*Exit.*]
> KING: [*Rising.*] My words fly up, my thoughts remain below.
> Words without thoughts never to heaven go.   [*Exit.*]

### Scene 4

*The Queen's chamber. Enter* QUEEN *and* POLONIUS.

POLONIUS: 'A will come straight. Look you lay home to[7] him.
  Tell him his pranks have been too broad[8] to bear with,
  And that your grace hath screen'd[9] and stood between
  Much heat and him. I'll silence me even here.
  Pray you be round with him.
HAMLET: [*Within.*] Mother, mother, mother!
QUEEN: I'll warrant you. Fear[1] me not.
  Withdraw, I hear him coming.

   [POLONIUS *goes behind the arras. Enter* HAMLET.]

HAMLET: Now, mother, what's the matter?
QUEEN: Hamlet, thou hast thy father much offended.
HAMLET: Mother, you have my father much offended.
QUEEN: Come, come, you answer with an idle tongue.
HAMLET: Go, go, you question with a wicked tongue.
QUEEN: Why, how now, Hamlet?
HAMLET:              What's the matter now?
QUEEN: Have you forgot me?
HAMLET:              No, by the rood,[2] not so.
  You are the queen, your husband's brother's wife,
  And would it were not so, you are my mother.
QUEEN: Nay, then I'll set those to you that can speak.
HAMLET: Come, come, and sit you down. You shall not budge.
  You go not till I set you up a glass[3]
  Where you may see the inmost part of you.

---

3. Ready.   4. Opportunity.   5. Flavor.   6. Medicine.   7. Be sharp with.   8. Outrageous.
9. Acted as a fire screen.   1. Doubt.   2. Cross.   3. Mirror.

QUEEN: What wilt thou do? Thou wilt not murder me?
    Help, ho!
POLONIUS: [*Behind.*] What, ho! help!
HAMLET: [*Draws.*] How now, a rat?
    Dead for a ducat, dead!

[*Kills* POLONIUS *with a pass through the arras.*]

POLONIUS: [*Behind.*] O, I am slain!
QUEEN: O me, what hast thou done?
HAMLET:                      Nay, I know not.
    Is it the king?
QUEEN: O, what a rash and bloody deed is this!
HAMLET: A bloody deed!—almost as bad, good mother,
    As kill a king and marry with his brother.
QUEEN: As kill a king?
HAMLET:          Ay, lady, it was my word.          [*Parting the arras.*]
    Thou wretched, rash, intruding fool, farewell!
    I took thee for thy better. Take thy fortune.
    Thou find'st to be too busy[4] is some danger.—
    Leave wringing of your hands. Peace, sit you down
    And let me wring your heart, for so I shall
    If it be made of penetrable stuff,
    If damnéd custom have not brazed it[5] so
    That it be proof and bulwark against sense.[6]
QUEEN: What have I done that thou dar'st wag thy tongue
    In noise so rude against me?
HAMLET:                  Such an act
    That blurs the grace and blush of modesty,
    Calls virtue hypocrite, takes off the rose
    From the fair forehead of an innocent love.
    And sets a blister[7] there, makes marriage-vows
    As false as dicers' oaths. O, such a deed
    As from the body of contraction[8] plucks
    The very soul, and sweet religion makes
    A rhapsody of words. Heaven's face does glow
    O'er this solidity and compound mass[9]
    With heated visage, as against the doom[1]—
    Is thought-sick at the act.
QUEEN:                Ay me, what act
    That roars so loud and thunders in the index?[2]
HAMLET: Look here upon this picture[3] and on this,
    The counterfeit presentment of two brothers.
    See what a grace was seated on this brow:
    Hyperion's curls, the front[4] of Jove himself,
    An eye like Mars, to threaten and command,

---

4. Officious.   5. Plated it with brass.   6. Feeling. *Proof:* armor.   7. Brand.   8. The marriage contract.
9. Meaningless mass (Earth).   1. Judgment Day.   2. Table of contents.   3. Portrait.   4. Forehead.

A station like the herald Mercury⁵
New lighted⁶ on a heaven-kissing hill—
A combination and a form indeed
Where every god did seem to set his seal,⁷
To give the world assurance of a man.   65
This was your husband. Look you now what follows.
Here is your husband, like a mildewed ear
Blasting his wholesome brother. Have you eyes?
Could you on this fair mountain leave to feed,
And batten⁸ on this moor? Ha! have you eyes?   70
You cannot call it love, for at your age
The heyday in the blood is tame, it's humble,
And waits upon the judgment, and what judgment
Would step from this to this? Sense sure you have
Else could you not have motion, but sure that sense   75
Is apoplexed⁹ for madness would not err,
Nor sense to ecstasy was ne'er so thralled
But it reserved some quantity¹ of choice
To serve in such a difference. What devil was't
That thus hath cozened you at hoodman-blind?²   80
Eyes without feeling, feeling without sight,
Ears without hands or eyes, smelling sans³ all,
Or but a sickly part of one true sense
Could not so mope.⁴ O shame! where is thy blush?
Rebellious hell,   85
If thou canst mutine⁵ in a matron's bones,
To flaming youth let virtue be as wax
And melt in her own fire. Proclaim no shame
When the compulsive ardor gives the charge,⁶
Since frost itself as actively doth burn,   90
And reason panders⁷ will.

QUEEN:             O Hamlet, speak no more!
Thou turn'st my eyes into my very soul;
And there I see such black and grainéd⁸ spots
As will not leave their tinct.⁹

HAMLET:                    Nay, but to live
In the rank sweat of an enseaméd¹ bed,   95
Stewed in curruption, honeying and making love
Over the nasty sty—

QUEEN:             O, speak to me no more!
These words like daggers enter in my ears;
No more, sweet Hamlet.

HAMLET:                 A murderer and a villain,
A slave that is not twentieth part the tithe²   100

---

5. In Roman mythology, Mercury served as the messenger of the gods. *Station:* bearing.   6. Newly alighted.
7. Mark of approval.   8. Feed greedily.   9. Paralyzed.   1. Power.
2. Blindman's buff. *Cozened:* cheated.   3. Without.   4. Be stupid.   5. Commit mutiny.   6. Attacks.
7. Pimps for.   8. Ingrained.   9. Lose their color.   1. Greasy.   2. One-tenth.

           Of your precedent lord, a vice of kings,[3]
           A cutpurse[4] of the empire and the rule,
           That from a shelf the precious diadem stole
           And put it in his pocket—
105 QUEEN: No more.

           [*Enter* GHOST.]

     HAMLET: A king of shreds and patches—
           Save me and hover o'er me with your wings,
           You heavenly guards! What would your gracious figure?
     QUEEN: Alas, he's mad.
110 HAMLET: Do you not come your tardy[5] son to chide,
           That lapsed in time and passion lets go by
           Th' important acting of your dread command?
           O, say!
     GHOST: Do not forget. This visitation
115        Is but to whet thy almost blunted purpose.
           But look, amazement on thy mother sits.
           O, step between her and her fighting soul!
           Conceit[6] in weakest bodies strongest works.
           Speak to her, Hamlet.
     HAMLET: How is it with you, lady?
120 QUEEN:                    Alas, how is't with you,
           That you do bend[7] your eye on vacancy,
           And with th' incorporal air do hold discourse?
           Forth at your eyes your spirits wildly peep,
           And as the sleeping soldiers in th' alarm,
125        Your bedded hairs like life in excrements[8]
           Start up and stand an end. O gentle son,
           Upon the heat and flame of thy distemper
           Sprinkle cool patience. Whereon do you look?
     HAMLET: On him, on him! Look you how pale he glares.
130        His form and cause conjoined,[9] preaching to stones,
           Would make them capable.[1]—Do not look upon me,
           Lest with this piteous action you convert
           My stern effects.[2] Then what I have to do
           Will want true color—tears perchance for blood.
135 QUEEN: To whom do you speak this?
     HAMLET: Do you see nothing there?
     QUEEN: Nothing at all, yet all that is I see.
     HAMLET: Nor did you nothing hear?
     QUEEN: No, nothing but ourselves.
140 HAMLET: Why, look you there. Look how it steals away.
           My father, in his habit[3] as he lived!
           Look where he goes even now out at the portal.   [*Exit* GHOST.]

---

3. The "Vice," a common figure in the popular drama, was a clown or buffoon. *Precedent lord:* first husband.
4. Pickpocket.   5. Slow to act.   6. Imagination.   7. Turn.   8. Nails and hair.   9. Working together.
1. Of responding.   2. Deeds.   3. Costume.

QUEEN: This is the very coinage[4] of your brain.
    Ths bodiless creation ecstasy[5]
    Is very cunning[6] in.
HAMLET:         Ecstasy?
    My pulse as yours doth temperately keep time,
    And makes as healthful music. It is not madness
    That I have uttered. Bring me to the test,
    And I the matter will re-word, which madness
    Would gambol[7] from. Mother, for love of grace,
    Lay not that flattering unction[8] to your soul,
    That not your trespass but my madness speaks.
    It will but skin and film the ulcerous place
    Whiles rank corruption, mining[9] all within,
    Infects unseen. Confess yourself to heaven,
    Repent what's past, avoid what is to come.
    And do not spread the compost on the weeds,
    To make them ranker. Forgive me this my virtue,
    For in the fatness of these pursy[1] times
    Virtue itself of vice must pardon beg,
    Yea, curb[2] and woo for leave to do him good.
QUEEN: O Hamlet, thou hast cleft my heart in twain.
HAMLET: O, throw away the worser part of it,
    And live the purer with the other half.
    Good night—but go not to my uncle's bed.
    Assume a virtue, if you have it not.
    That monster custom[3] who all sense doth eat
    Of habits devil, is angel yet in this,
    That to the use of actions fair and good
    He likewise gives a frock or livery
    That aptly[4] is put on. Refrain tonight,
    And that shall lend a kind of easiness
    To the next abstinence; the next more easy;
    For use almost can change the stamp of nature,
    And either curb the devil, or throw him out
    With wondrous potency. Once more, good night,
    And when you are desirous to be blest,
    I'll blessing beg of you. For this same lord
    I do repent; but heaven hath pleased it so,
    To punish me with this, and this with me,
    That I must be their scourge and minister.
    I will bestow[5] him and will answer well
    The death I gave him. So, again, good night.
    I must be cruel only to be kind.
    Thus bad begins and worse remains behind.
    One word more, good lady.
QUEEN:         What shall I do?

---

4. Invention.   5. Madness.   6. Skilled.   7. Shy away.   8. Ointment.   9. Undermining.
1. Bloated.   2. Bow.   3. Habit.   4. Easily.   5. Dispose of.

HAMLET: Not this, by no means, that I bid you do:
　　Let the bloat⁶ king tempt you again to bed,
　　Pinch wanton⁷ on your cheek, call you his mouse,
190　And let him, for a pair of reechy⁸ kisses,
　　Or paddling in your neck with his damned fingers,
　　Make you to ravel⁹ all this matter out,
　　That I essentially am not in madness,
　　But mad in craft. 'Twere good you let him know,
195　For who that's but a queen, fair, sober, wise,
　　Would from a paddock, from a bat, a gib,¹
　　Such dear concernings hide? Who would so do?
　　No, in despite of sense and secrecy,
　　Unpeg the basket on the house's top,
200　Let the birds fly, and like the famous ape,
　　To try conclusions, in the basket creep
　　And break your own neck down.²
QUEEN: Be thou assured, if words be made of breath
　　And breath of life, I have no life to breathe
205　What thou hast said to me.
HAMLET: I must to England; you know that?
QUEEN:　　　　　　　　　　　　　　　Alack,
　　I had forgot. 'Tis so concluded on.
HAMLET: There's letters sealed, and my two school-fellows,
　　Whom I will trust as I will adders fanged,
210　They bear the mandate; they must sweep³ my way
　　And marshal me to knavery. Let it work,
　　For 'tis the sport to have the enginer
　　Hoist with his own petard;⁴ and't shall go hard
　　But I will delve⁵ one yard below their mines
215　And blow them at the moon. O, 'tis most sweet
　　When in one line two crafts directly meet.
　　This man shall set me packing.
　　I'll lug the guts into the neighbor room.
　　Mother, good night. Indeed, this counsellor
220　Is now most still, most secret, and most grave,
　　Who was in life a foolish prating knave.
　　Come sir, to draw toward an end with you.
　　Good night, mother. [Exit the QUEEN. Then exit HAMLET tugging POLONIUS.]

---

6. Bloated.　　7. Lewdly.　　8. Foul.　　9. Reveal.　　1. Tomcat. *Paddock:* toad.
2. Apparently a reference to a now-lost fable in which an ape, finding a basket containing a cage of birds on a housetop, opens the cage. The birds fly away. The ape, thinking that if he were in the basket he too could fly, enters, jumps out, and breaks his neck.　　3. Prepare. *Mandate:* command.
4. The "enginer," or engineer, is a military man who is here described as being blown up by a bomb of his own construction, "hoist with his own petard." The military figure continues in the succeeding lines where Hamlet describes himself as digging a countermine or tunnel beneath the one Claudius is digging to defeat Hamlet. In line 216 the two tunnels unexpectedly meet.　　5. Dig.

## ACT IV

### Scene 1

*A room in the castle. Enter* KING, QUEEN, ROSENCRANTZ *and* GUILDENSTERN.

KING: There's matter in these sighs, these profound heaves,
   You must translate;[6] 'tis fit we understand them.
   Where is your son?
QUEEN: Bestow this place on us a little while.
   [*Exeunt* ROSENCRANTZ *and* GUILDENSTERN.]
   Ah, mine own lord, what have I seen tonight!    5
KING: What, Gertrude? How does Hamlet?
QUEEN: Mad as the sea and wind when both contend
   Which is the mightier. In his lawless fit,
   Behind the arras hearing something stir,
   Whips out his rapier, cries "A rat, a rat!"    10
   And in this brainish apprehension[7] kills
   The unseen good old man.
KING:                    O heavy deed!
   It had been so with us had we been there.
   His liberty is full of threats to all—
   To you yourself, to us, to every one.    15
   Alas, how shall this bloody deed be answered?
   It will be laid to us, whose providence[8]
   Should have kept short, restrained, and out of haunt,[9]
   This mad young man. But so much was our love,
   We would not understand what was most fit;    20
   But, like the owner of a foul disease,
   To keep it from divulging, let it feed
   Even on the pith of life. Where is he gone?
QUEEN: To draw apart the body he hath killed,
   O'er whom his very madness, like some ore    25
   Among a mineral of metals base,
   Shows itself pure: 'a weeps for what is done.
KING: O Gertrude, come away!
   The sun no sooner shall the mountains touch
   But we will ship him hence, and this vile deed    30
   We must with all our majesty and skill
   Both countenance and excuse. Ho, Guildenstern!

   [*Enter* ROSENCRANTZ *and* GUILDENSTERN.]

   Friends both, go join you with some further aid.
   Hamlet in madness hath Polonius slain,
   And from his mother's closet hath he dragged him.    35
   Go seek him out; speak fair, and bring the body

---

6. Explain.  7. Insane notion.  8. Prudence.  9. Away from court.

Into the chapel. I pray you haste in this.

[*Exeunt* ROSENCRANTZ *and* GUILDENSTERN.]

Come, Gertrude, we'll call up our wisest friends
And let them know both what we mean to do
40 And what's untimely done;
Whose whisper o'er the world's diameter,
As level as the cannon to his blank,[1]
Transports his poisoned shot—may miss our name,
And hit the woundless air. O, come away!
45 My soul is full of discord and dismay.             [*Exeunt.*]

### Scene 2

*A passageway. Enter* HAMLET.

HAMLET: Safely stowed.
ROSENCRANTZ *and* GUILDENSTERN: [*Within.*] Hamlet! Lord Hamlet!
HAMLET: But soft, what noise? Who calls on Hamlet?
    O, here they come.

[*Enter* ROSENCRANTZ, GUILDENSTERN, *and* OTHERS.]

5 ROSENCRANTZ: What have you done, my lord, with the dead body?
HAMLET: Compounded it with dust, whereto 'tis kin.
ROSENCRANTZ: Tell us where 'tis, that we may take it thence
    And bear it to the chapel.
HAMLET: Do not believe it.
10 ROSENCRANTZ: Believe what?
HAMLET: That I can keep your counsel and not mine own. Besides, to be demanded of a sponge—what replication[2] should be made by the son of a king?
ROSENCRANTZ: Take you me for a sponge, my lord?
15 HAMLET: Ay, sir, that soaks up the king's countenance,[3] his rewards, his authorities. But such officers do the king best service in the end. He keeps them like an apple in the corner of his jaw, first mouthed to be last swallowed. When he needs what you have gleaned, it is but squeezing you and, sponge, you you shall be dry again.
20 ROSENCRANTZ: I understand you not, my lord.
HAMLET: I am glad of it. A knavish speech sleeps in a foolish ear.
ROSENCRANTZ: My lord, you must tell us where the body is, and go with us to the king.
HAMLET: The body is with the king, but the king is not with the body.
25     The king is a thing—
GUILDENSTERN: A thing, my lord!
HAMLET: Of nothing. Bring me to him. Hide fox, and all after.[4]             [*Exeunt.*]

---

1. Mark. *Level:* direct.   2. Answer. *Demanded of:* questioned by.   3. Favor.
4. Apparently a reference to a children's game like hide-and-seek.

## Scene 3

*A room in the castle. Enter* KING.

KING: I have sent to seek him, and to find the body.
How dangerous is it that this man goes loose!
Yet must not we put the strong law on him.
He's loved of the distracted[5] multitude,
Who like not in their judgment but their eyes, 5
And where 'tis so, th' offender's scourge[6] is weighed,
But never the offence. To bear all smooth and even,
This sudden sending him away must seem
Deliberate pause.[7] Diseases desperate grown
By desperate appliance are relieved, 10
Or not at all.

[*Enter* ROSENCRANTZ, GUILDENSTERN, *and all the rest.*]

How now! what hath befall'n?
ROSENCRANTZ: Where the dead body is bestowed, my lord,
We cannot get from him.
KING:                         But where is he?
ROSENCRANTZ: Without, my lord; guarded, to know[8] your pleasure.
KING: Bring him before us.
ROSENCRANTZ:                 Ho! bring in the lord. 15

[*They enter with* HAMLET.]

KING: Now, Hamlet, where's Polonius?
HAMLET: At supper.
KING: At supper? Where?
HAMLET: Not where he eats, but where 'a is eaten. A certain convocation of politic[9] worms are e'en at him. Your worm is your only emperor for diet. We 20 fat all creatures else to fat us, and we fat ourselves for maggots. Your fat king and your lean beggar is but variable service—two dishes, but to one table. That's the end.
KING: Alas, alas!
HAMLET: A man may fish with the worm that hath eat of a king, and eat of the 25 fish that hath fed of that worm.
KING: What dost thou mean by this?
HAMLET: Nothing but to show you how a king may go a progress through the guts of a beggar.
KING: Where is Polonius? 30
HAMLET: In heaven. Send thither to see. If your messenger find him not there, seek him i' th' other place yourself. But if, indeed, you find him not within this month, you shall nose[1] him as you go up the stairs into the lobby.
KING: [*To* ATTENDANTS.] Go seek him there.
HAMLET: 'A will stay till you come.         [*Exeunt* ATTENDANTS.] 35

---

5. Confused.    6. Punishment.    7. That is, not an impulse.    8. Await.
9. Statesmanlike. *Convocation:* gathering.    1. Smell.

KING: Hamlet, this deed, for thine especial safety—
   Which we do tender, as we dearly[2] grieve
   For that which thou hast done—must send thee hence
   With fiery quickness. Therefore prepare thyself.
40 The bark is ready, and the wind at help,
   Th' associates tend, and everything is bent
   For England.
HAMLET:          For England?
KING:                      Ay, Hamlet.
HAMLET:                            Good.
KING: So it is, if thou knew'st our purposes.
HAMLET: I see a cherub that sees them. But come, for England!
45 Farewell, dear mother.
KING: Thy loving father, Hamlet.
HAMLET: My mother. Father and mother is man and wife, man and wife is one
   flesh. So, my mother. Come, for England.          [Exit.]
KING: Follow him at foot;[3] tempt him with speed aboard.
50 Delay it not; I'll have him hence tonight.
   Away! for everything is sealed and done
   That else leans on th' affair. Pray you make haste.   [Exeunt all but the KING.]
   And, England, if my love thou hold'st at aught—
   As my great power thereof may give thee sense,[4]
55 Since yet thy cicatrice[5] looks raw and red
   After the Danish sword, and thy free awe
   Pays homage to us—thou mayst not coldly set[6]
   Our sovereign process,[7] which imports at full
   By letters congruing[8] to that effect
60 The present death of Hamlet. Do it, England,
   For like the hectic[9] in my blood he rages,
   And thou must cure me. Till I know 'tis done,
   Howe'er my haps, my joys were ne'er begun.          [Exit.]

## Scene 4

*Near Elsinore. Enter* FORTINBRAS *with his army.*

FORTINBRAS: Go, captain, from me greet the Danish king.
   Tell him that by his license Fortinbras
   Craves the conveyance[1] of a promised march
   Over his kingdom. You know the rendezvous.
5 If that his majesty would aught with us,
   We shall express our duty in his eye,[2]
   And let him know so.
CAPTAIN:             I will do't, my lord.
FORTINBRAS: Go softly on.          [*Exeunt all but the* CAPTAIN.]

   [*Enter* HAMLET, ROSENCRANTZ, GUILDENSTERN, *and* OTHERS.]

---

2. Deeply. *Tender:* consider.   3. Closely.   4. Of its value.   5. Wound scar.   6. Set aside.
7. Mandate.   8. Agreeing.   9. Chronic fever.   1. Escort.   2. Presence.

HAMLET: Good sir, whose powers are these?
CAPTAIN: They are of Norway, sir.
HAMLET: How purposed, sir, I pray you?
CAPTAIN: Against some part of Poland.
HAMLET: Who commands them, sir?
CAPTAIN: The nephew to old Norway, Fortinbras.
HAMLET: Goes it against the main[3] of Poland, sir,
    Or for some frontier?
CAPTAIN: Truly to speak, and with no addition,[4]
    We go to gain a little patch of ground
    That hath in it no profit but the name.
    To pay five ducats,[5] five, I would not farm it;
    Nor will it yield to Norway or the Pole
    A ranker rate should it be sold in fee.[6]
HAMLET: Why, then the Polack never will defend it.
CAPTAIN: Yes, it is already garrisoned.
HAMLET: Two thousand souls and twenty thousand ducats
    Will not debate the question of this straw.
    This is th' imposthume[7] of much wealth and peace,
    That inward breaks, and shows no cause without
    Why the man dies. I humbly thank you, sir.
CAPTAIN: God b'wi'ye, sir.     [*Exit.*]
ROSENCRANTZ:     Will't please you go, my lord?
HAMLET: I'll be with you straight. Go a little before.     [*Exeunt all but* HAMLET.]
    How all occasions do inform against me,
    And spur my dull revenge! What is a man,
    If his chief good and market[8] of his time
    Be but to sleep and feed? A beast, no more.
    Sure he that made us with such large discourse,[9]
    Looking before and after, gave us not
    That capability and godlike reason
    To fust[1] in us unused. Now, whether it be
    Bestial oblivion, or some craven scruple
    Of thinking too precisely on th' event[2]—
    A thought which, quartered, hath but one part wisdom
    And ever three parts coward—I do not know
    Why yet I live to say "This thing's to do,"
    Sith[3] I have cause, and will, and strength, and means,
    To do't. Examples gross as earth exhort me.
    Witness this army of such mass and charge,[4]
    Led by a delicate and tender prince,
    Whose spirit, with divine ambition puffed,
    Makes mouths at[5] the invisible event,
    Exposing what is mortal and unsure
    To all that fortune, death, and danger dare,

---

3. Central part.   4. Exaggeration.   5. That is, in rent.   6. Outright. *Ranker:* higher.   7. Abscess.
8. Occupation.   9. Ample reasoning power.   1. Grow musty.   2. Outcome.   3. Since.   4. Expense.
5. Scorns.

         Even for an eggshell. Rightly to be great
         Is not to stir without great argument,
55       But greatly to find quarrel in a straw
         When honor's at the stake. How stand I then,
         That have a father killed, a mother stained,
         Excitements of my reason and my blood,
         And let all sleep, while to my shame I see
60       The imminent death of twenty thousand men
         That for a fantasy and trick of fame
         Go to their graves like beds, fight for a plot
         Whereon the numbers cannot try the cause,
         Which is not tomb enough and continent
65       To hide the slain?[6] O, from this time forth,
         My thoughts be bloody, or be nothing worth!          [*Exit.*]

    Scene 5

    *A room in the castle. Enter* QUEEN, HORATIO *and a* GENTLEMAN.

    QUEEN: I will not speak with her.
    GENTLEMAN: She is importunate, indeed distract.
         Her mood will needs to be pitied.
    QUEEN:                           What would she have?
    GENTLEMAN: She speaks much of her father, says she hears
5        There's tricks i' th' world, and hems, and beats her heart,
         Spurns enviously at straws,[7] speaks things in doubt
         That carry but half sense. Her speech is nothing,
         Yet the unshapèd use of it doth move
         The hearers to collection;[8] they yawn at it,
10       And botch the words up fit to their own thoughts,
         Which, as her winks and nods and gestures yield them,
         Indeed would make one think there might be thought,
         Though nothing sure, yet much unhappily.
    HORATIO: 'Twere good she were spoken with, for she may strew
15       Dangerous conjectures in ill-breeding minds.
    QUEEN: Let her come in.                              [*Exit* GENTLEMAN.]
         [*Aside.*] To my sick soul, as sin's true nature is,
         Each toy seems prologue to some great amiss.[9]
         So full of artless jealousy is guilt,
20       It spills itself in fearing to be spilt.

             [*Enter* OPHELIA *distracted.*]

    OPHELIA: Where is the beauteous majesty of Denmark?
    QUEEN: How now, Ophelia!

---

6. The plot of ground involved is so small that it cannot contain the number of men involved in fighting or furnish burial space for the number of those who will die.   7. Takes offense at trifles.
8. An attempt to order.   9. Catastrophe. *Toy:* trifle.

OPHELIA:

> [*Sings.*]
>
> How should I your true love know
>   From another one?
> By his cockle hat and staff,¹
>   And his sandal shoon.²

QUEEN: Alas, sweet lady, what imports this song?
OPHELIA: Say you? Nay, pray you mark.

> [*Sings.*]
>
> He is dead and gone, lady,
>   He is dead and gone;
> At his head a grass-green turf,
>   At his heels a stone.

  O, ho!
QUEEN: Nay, but Ophelia—
OPHELIA:             Pray you mark.

> [*Sings.*]
>
> White his shroud as the mountain snow—

[*Enter* KING.]

QUEEN: Alas, look here, my lord.
OPHELIA:

> [*Sings.*]
>
> Larded all with sweet flowers;
> Which bewept to the grave did not go
>   With true-love showers.

KING: How do you, pretty lady?
OPHELIA: Well, God dild³ you! They say the owl was a baker's daughter. Lord, we know what we are, but know not what we may be. God be at your table!
KING: Conceit⁴ upon her father.
OPHELIA: Pray let's have no words of this, but when they ask you what it means, say you this:

> [*Sings.*]
>
> Tomorrow is Saint Valentine's day,
>   All in the morning betime,
> And I a maid at your window,
>   To be your Valentine.
>
> Then up he rose, and donn'd his clo'es,
>   And dupped⁵ the chamber-door,

---

1. A cockle hat, one decorated with a shell, indicated that the wearer had made a pilgrimage to the shrine of St. James at Compostela in Spain. The staff also marked the carrier as a pilgrim.    2. Shoes.    3. Yield.    4. Thought.    5. Opened.

> Let in the maid, that out a maid
> Never departed more.

KING: Pretty Ophelia!
OPHELIA: Indeed, without an oath, I'll make an end on't.

[*Sings.*]

> 55 By Gis[6] and by Saint Charity,
> Alack, and fie for shame!
> Young men will do't, if they come to't;
> By Cock,[7] they are to blame.
> Quoth she "before you tumbled me,
> 60 You promised me to wed."

He answers:

> "So would I'a done, by yonder sun,
> An thou hadst not come to my bed."

KING: How long hath she been thus?
65 OPHELIA: I hope all will be well. We must be patient, but I cannot choose but weep to think they would lay him i' th' cold ground. My brother shall know of it, and so I thank you for your good counsel. Come, my coach! Good night, ladies, good night. Sweet ladies, good night, good night.　　　　[*Exit.*]
KING: Follow her close; give her good watch, I pray you.

[*Exeunt* HORATIO *and* GENTLEMAN.]

> 70 O, this is the poison of deep grief; it springs
> All from her father's death, and now behold!
> O Gertrude, Gertrude!
> When sorrows come, they come not single spies,
> But in battalions: first, her father slain;
> 75 Next, your son gone, and he most violent author
> Of his own just remove; the people muddied,[8]
> Thick and unwholesome in their thoughts and whispers
> For good Polonius' death; and we have done but greenly[9]
> In hugger-mugger[1] to inter him; poor Ophelia
> 80 Divided from herself and her fair judgment,
> Without the which we are pictures, or mere beasts;
> Last, and as much containing as all these,
> Her brother is in secret come from France,
> Feeds on his wonder, keeps himself in clouds,
> 85 And wants not buzzers to infect his ear
> With pestilent speeches of his father's death,
> Wherein necessity, of matter beggared,[2]
> Will nothing stick our person to arraign[3]
> In ear and ear.[4] O my dear Gertrude, this,
> 90 Like to a murd'ring piece,[5] in many places
> Gives me superfluous death.　　　　[*A noise within.*]

---

6. Jesus.　　7. God.　　8. Disturbed.　　9. Without judgment.　　1. Haste.　　2. Short on facts.
3. Accuse. *Stick:* hesitate.　　4. From both sides.　　5. A weapon designed to scatter its shot.

QUEEN: Alack, what noise is this?
KING: Attend!
   Where are my Switzers?[6] Let them guard the door.
   What is the matter?
MESSENGER:         Save yourself, my lord.
   The ocean, overpeering of his list,[7]
   Eats not the flats with more impiteous[8] haste
   Than young Laertes, in a riotous head,[9]
   O'erbears your officers. The rabble call him lord,
   And as the world were now but to begin,
   Antiquity forgot, custom not known,
   The ratifiers and props of every word,
   They cry "Choose we, Laertes shall be king."
   Caps, hands, and tongues, applaud it to the clouds,
   "Laertes shall be king, Laertes king."
QUEEN: How cheerfully on the false trail they cry![1]

   [*A noise within.*]

   O, this is counter,[2] you false Danish dogs!
KING: The doors are broke.

   [*Enter* LAERTES, *with* OTHERS.]

LAERTES: Where is this king?—Sirs, stand you all without.
ALL: No, let's come in.
LAERTES:         I pray you give me leave.
ALL: We will, we will.
LAERTES: I thank you. Keep[3] the door.      [*Exeunt his followers.*]
               O thou vile king,
   Give me my father!
QUEEN:         Calmly, good Laertes.
LAERTES: That drop of blood that's calm proclaims me bastard,
   Cries cuckold to my father, brands the harlot
   Even here between the chaste unsmirchéd brow
   Of my true mother.
KING:         What is the cause, Laertes,
   That thy rebellion looks so giant-like?
   Let him go, Gertrude. Do not fear[4] our person.
   There's such divinity doth hedge a king
   That treason can but peep to[5] what it would,
   Acts little of his will. Tell me, Laertes,
   Why thou art thus incensed. Let him go, Gertrude.
   Speak, man.
LAERTES:         Where is my father?
KING:         Dead.
QUEEN: But not by him.
KING:         Let him demand[6] his fill.

---

6. Swiss guards.   7. Towering above its limits.   8. Pitiless.   9. With an armed band.
1. As if following the scent.   2. Backward.   3. Guard.   4. Fear for.
5. Look at over or through a barrier.   6. Question.

LAERTES: How came he dead? I'll not be juggled with.
    To hell allegiance, vows to the blackest devil,
    Conscience and grace to the profoundest pit!
    I dare damnation. To this point I stand,
130   That both the worlds I give to negligence,[7]
    Let come what comes, only I'll be revenged
    Most throughly for my father.
KING: Who shall stay you?
LAERTES:               My will, not all the world's.
    And for my means, I'll husband[8] them so well
    They shall go far with little.
135 KING:               Good Laertes,
    If you desire to know the certainty
    Of your dear father, is't writ in your revenge
    That, swoopstake,[9] you will draw both friend and foe,
    Winner and loser?
LAERTES:           None but his enemies.
140 KING: Will you know them, then?
LAERTES: To his good friends thus wide I'll ope my arms,
    And like the kind life-rend'ring pelican,[1]
    Repast them with my blood.
KING:                 Why, now you speak
    Like a good child and a true gentleman.
145 That I am guiltless of your father's death,
    And am most sensibly in grief for it,
    It shall as level[2] to your judgment 'pear
    As day does to your eye.

    [*A noise within:* "Let her come in."]

LAERTES: How now? What noise is that?

    [*Enter* OPHELIA.]

150 O, heat dry up my brains! tears seven times salt
    Burn out the sense and virtue[3] of mine eye!
    By heaven, thy madness shall be paid with weight
    Till our scale turn the beam. O rose of May,
    Dear maid, kind sister, sweet Ophelia!
155 O heavens! is't possible a young maid's wits
    Should be as mortal as an old man's life?
    Nature is fine[4] in love, and where 'tis fine
    It sends some precious instances of itself
    After the thing it loves.[5]

---

7. Disregard. *Both the worlds:* that is, this and the next.   8. Manage.   9. Sweeping the board.
1. The pelican was believed to feed her young with her own blood.   2. Plain.   3. Function. *Sense:* feeling.
4. Refined.
5. Laertes means that Ophelia, because of her love for her father, gave up her sanity as a token of grief at his death.

OPHELIA:

> [*Sings.*]
>
> They bore him barefac'd on the bier; 160
>   Hey non nonny, nonny, hey nonny;
> And in his grave rain'd many a tear—

Fare you well, my dove!
LAERTES: Hadst thou thy wits, and didst persuade revenge,
  It could not move thus. 165
OPHELIA: You must sing "A-down, a-down, and you call him a-down-a." O, how the wheel becomes it! It is the false steward, that stole his master's daughter.[6]
LAERTES: This nothing's more than matter.
OPHELIA: There's a rosemary, that's for remembrance. Pray you, love, remember. And there is pansies, that's for thoughts. 170
LAERTES: A document[7] in madness, thoughts and remembrance fitted.
OPHELIA: There's fennel for you, and columbines. There's rue for you, and here's some for me. We may call it herb of grace a Sundays. O, you must wear your rue with a difference. There's a daisy. I would give you some violets, but they withered all when my father died. They say 'a made a good end. 175

> [*Sings.*]
>
> For bonny sweet Robin is all my joy.

LAERTES: Thought and affliction, passion, hell itself,
  She turns to favor[8] and to prettiness.
OPHELIA:

> [*Sings.*]
>
> And will 'a not come again?
> And will 'a not come again? 180
>   No, no, he is dead,
>   Go to thy death-bed,
> He never will come again.
>
> His beard was as white as snow,
> All flaxen was his poll;[9] 185
>   He is gone, he is gone,
>   And we cast away moan:
> God-a-mercy on his soul!

And of all Christian souls, I pray God. God b'wi'you. [*Exit.*]
LAERTES: Do you see this, O God? 190
KING: Laertes, I must commune with your grief,
  Or you deny me right. Go but apart,
  Make choice of whom your wisest friends you will,
  And they shall hear and judge 'twixt you and me.
  If by direct or by collateral[1] hand 195

---

6. The "wheel" refers to the "burden" or refrain of a song, in this case "A-down, a-down, and you call him a-down-a." The ballad to which she refers was about a false steward. Others have suggested that the "wheel" is the Wheel of Fortune, a spinning wheel to whose rhythm such a song might have been sung or a kind of dance movement performed by Ophelia as she sings.   7. Lesson.   8. Beauty.   9. Head.   1. Indirect.

They find us touched,[2] we will our kingdom give,
Our crown, our life, and all that we call ours,
To you in satisfaction; but if not,
Be you content to lend your patience to us,
And we shall jointly labor with your soul
To give it due content.

LAERTES:               Let this be so.
His means of death, his obscure funeral—
No trophy, sword, nor hatchment,[3] o'er his bones,
No noble rite nor formal ostentation[4]—
Cry to be heard, as 'twere from heaven to earth,
That I must call't in question.

KING:                   So you shall;
And where th' offence is, let the great axe fall.
I pray you go with me.                   [*Exeunt.*]

### Scene 6

*Another room in the castle. Enter* HORATIO *and a* GENTLEMAN.

HORATIO: What are they that would speak with me?
GENTLEMAN: Sea-faring men, sir. They say they have letters for you.
HORATIO: Let them come in.                [*Exit* GENTLEMAN.]
    I do not know from what part of the world
    I should be greeted, if not from Lord Hamlet.

[*Enter* SAILORS.]

SAILOR: God bless you, sir.
HORATIO: Let him bless thee too.
SAILOR: 'A shall, sir, an't please him. There's a letter for you, sir—it came from th' ambassador that was bound for England—if your name be Horatio, as I am let to know[5] it is.
HORATIO: [*Reads.*] "Horatio, when thou shalt have overlooked[6] this, give these fellows some means[7] to the king. They have letters for him. Ere we were two days old at sea, a pirate of very warlike appointment[8] gave us chase. Finding ourselves too slow of sail, we put on a compelled valor, and in the grapple I boarded them. On the instant they got clear of our ship, so I alone became their prisoner. They have dealt with me like thieves of mercy, but they knew what they did; I am to do a good turn for them. Let the king have the letters I have sent, and repair thou to me with as much speed as thou wouldest fly death. I have words to speak in thine ear will make thee dumb; yet are they much too light for the bore of the matter.[9] These good fellows will bring thee where I am. Rosencrantz and Guildenstern hold their course for England. Of them I have much to tell thee. Farewell.
                                He that thou knowest thine, Hamlet."

---

2. By guilt.   3. Coat of arms.   4. Pomp.   5. Informed.   6. Read through.   7. Access.
8. Equipment.
9. A figure from gunnery, referring to shot that is too small for the size of the weapons to be fired.

Come, I will give you way¹ for these your letters,
And do't the speedier that you may direct me                                25
To him from whom you brought them.                     [*Exeunt.*]

### Scene 7

*Another room in the castle. Enter* KING *and* LAERTES.

KING: Now must your conscience my acquittance seal,²
    And you must put me in your heart for friend,
    Sith you have heard, and with a knowing ear,
    That he which hath your noble father slain
    Pursued my life.
LAERTES:            It well appears. But tell me                            5
    Why you proceeded not against these feats,
    So criminal and so capital in nature,
    As by your safety, greatness, wisdom, all things else,
    You mainly were stirred up.
KING:                         O, for two special reasons,
    Which may to you, perhaps, seem much unsinewed,³                        10
    But yet to me th' are strong. The queen his mother
    Lives almost by his looks, and for myself—
    My virtue or my plague, be it either which—
    She is so conjunctive⁴ to my life and soul
    That, as the star moves not but in his sphere,⁵                         15
    I could not but by her. The other motive,
    Why to a public count⁶ I might not go,
    Is the great love the general gender⁷ bear him,
    Who, dipping all his faults in their affection,
    Work like the spring that turneth wood to stone,⁸                       20
    Convert his gyves⁹ to graces; so that my arrows,
    Too slightly timbered¹ for so loud a wind,
    Would have reverted to my bow again,
    But not where I had aimed them.
LAERTES: And so have I a noble father lost,                                 25
    A sister driven into desp'rate terms,
    Whose worth, if praises may go back again,
    Stood challenger on mount of all the age
    For her perfections. But my revenge will come.
KING: Break not your sleeps for that. You must not think                    30
    That we are made of stuff so flat and dull
    That we can let our beard be shook with danger,
    And think it pastime. You shortly shall hear more.
    I loved you father, and we love our self,

---

1. Means of delivery.   2. Grant me innocent.   3. Weak.   4. Closely joined.
5. A reference to the Ptolemaic cosmology, in which planets and stars were believed to revolve in crystalline spheres concentrically about the Earth.   6. Reckoning.   7. Common people.
8. Certain English springs contain so much lime that a lime covering will be deposited on a log placed in one of them for a length of time.   9. Fetters.   1. Shafted.

And that, I hope, will teach you to imagine—

[*Enter a* MESSENGER *with letters.*]

How now? What news?

MESSENGER: Letters, my lord, from Hamlet.
These to your majesty; this to the queen.

KING: From Hamlet! Who brought them?

MESSENGER: Sailors, my lord, they say. I saw them not.
They were given me by Claudio; he received them
Of him that brought them.

KING: Laertes, you shall hear them.—
Leave us. [*Exit* MESSENGER.]
[*Reads.*] "High and mighty, you shall know I am set naked on your kingdom. Tomorrow shall I beg leave to see your kingly eyes; when I shall, first asking your pardon thereunto, recount the occasion of my sudden and more strange return.
                Hamlet."
What should this mean? Are all the rest come back?
Or is it some abuse,[2] and no such thing?

LAERTES: Know you the hand?

KING: 'Tis Hamlet's character.[3] "Naked"!
And in a postscript here, he says "alone."
Can you devise[4] me?

LAERTES: I am lost in it, my lord. But let him come.
It warms the very sickness in my heart
That I shall live and tell him to his teeth
"Thus didest thou."

KING: If it be so, Laertes—
As how should it be so, how otherwise?—
Will you be ruled by me?

LAERTES: Ay, my lord,
So you will not o'errule me to a peace.

KING: To thine own peace. If he be now returned,
As checking at[5] his voyage, and that he means
No more to undertake it, I will work him
To an exploit now ripe in my device,
Under the which he shall not choose but fall;
And for his death no wind of blame shall breathe
But even his mother shall uncharge[6] the practice
And call it accident.

LAERTES: My lord, I will be ruled;
The rather if you could devise it so
That I might be the organ.[7]

KING: It falls right.
You have been talked of since your travel much,
And that in Hamlet's hearing, for a quality

---

2. Trick.  3. Handwriting.  4. Explain it to.  5. Turning aside from.  6. Not accuse.
7. Instrument.

    Wherein they say you shine. Your sum of parts
    Did not together pluck such envy from him
    As did that one, and that, in my regard,
    Of the unworthiest siege.[8]
LAERTES:                   What part is that, my lord?
KING: A very riband in the cap of youth,
    Yet needful too, for youth no less becomes
    The light and careless livery that it wears
    Than settled age his sables and his weeds,[9]
    Importing health and graveness. Two months since
    Here was a gentleman of Normandy.
    I have seen myself, and served against, the French,
    And they can[1] well on horseback, but this gallant
    Had witchcraft in't. He grew unto his seat,
    And to such wondrous doing brought his horse,
    As had he been incorpsed and demi-natured
    With the brave beast. So far he topped my thought
    That I, in forgery[2] of shapes and tricks,
    Come short of what he did.[3]
LAERTES:                   A Norman was't?
KING: A Norman.
LAERTES: Upon my life, Lamord.
KING:                        The very same.
LAERTES: I know him well. He is the brooch indeed
    And gem of all the nation.
KING: He made confession[4] of you,
    And gave you such a masterly report
    For art and exercise in your defence,[5]
    And for your rapier most especial,
    That he cried out 'twould be a sight indeed
    If one could match you. The scrimers[6] of their nation
    He swore had neither motion, guard, nor eye,
    If you opposed them. Sir, this report of his
    Did Hamlet so envenom with his envy
    That he could nothing do but wish and beg
    Your sudden coming o'er, to play with you.
    Now out of this—
LAERTES:             What out of this, my lord?
KING: Laertes, was your father dear to you?
    Or are you like the painting of a sorrow,
    A face without a heart?
LAERTES:                   Why ask you this?
KING: Not that I think you did not love your father,

---

8. Rank.   9. Dignified clothing.   1. Perform.   2. Imagination.
3. The gentleman referred to was so skilled in horsemanship that he seemed to share one body with the horse, "incorpsed." The king further extends the compliment by saying that he appeared like the mythical centaur, a creature who was man from the waist up and horse from the waist down, therefore "demi-natured."   4. Gave a report.   5. Skill in fencing.   6. Fencers.

|     | But that I know love is begun by time, |
| --- | --- |
| 110 | But that I know love is begun by time, |
|     | And that I see in passages of proof,[7] |
|     | Time qualifies the spark and fire of it. |
|     | There lives within the very flame of love |
|     | A kind of wick or snuff that will abate it, |
| 115 | And nothing is at a like goodness still, |
|     | For goodness, growing to a plurisy,[8] |
|     | Dies in his own too much.[9] That we would do, |
|     | We should do when we would; for this "would" changes, |
|     | And hath abatements and delays as many |
| 120 | As there are tongues, are hands, are accidents, |
|     | And then this "should" is like a spendthrift's sigh |
|     | That hurts by easing. But to the quick of th' ulcer— |
|     | Hamlet comes back; what would you undertake |
|     | To show yourself in deed your father's son |
|     | More than in words? |
| 125 | LAERTES:        To cut his throat i' th' church. |
|     | KING: No place indeed should murder sanctuarize;[1] |
|     | Revenge should have no bounds. But, good Laertes, |
|     | Will you do this? Keep close within your chamber. |
|     | Hamlet returned shall know you are come home. |
| 130 | We'll put on those shall praise your excellence, |
|     | And set a double varnish[2] on the fame |
|     | The Frenchman gave you, bring you in fine[3] together, |
|     | And wager on your heads. He, being remiss,[4] |
|     | Most generous, and free from all contriving, |
| 135 | Will not peruse[5] the foils, so that with ease, |
|     | Or with a little shuffling, you may choose |
|     | A sword unbated,[6] and in a pass of practice |
|     | Requite him for your father. |
|     | LAERTES:        I will do't, |
|     | And for that purpose I'll anoint my sword. |
| 140 | I bought an unction of a mountebank |
|     | So mortal that but dip a knife in it, |
|     | Where it draws blood no cataplasm[7] so rare, |
|     | Collected from all simples[8] that have virtue |
|     | Under the moon, can save the thing from death |
| 145 | That is but scratched withal. I'll touch my point |
|     | With this contagion, that if I gall[9] him slightly, |
|     | It may be death. |
|     | KING:        Let's further think of this, |
|     | Weigh what convenience both of time and means |
|     | May fit us to our shape. If this should fail, |
| 150 | And that our drift look[1] through our bad performance, |
|     | 'Twere better not assayed. Therefore this project |

7. Tests of experience.  8. Fullness.  9. Excess.  1. Provide sanctuary for murder.  2. Gloss.
3. In short.  4. Careless.  5. Examine.  6. Not blunted.  7. Poultice.  8. Herbs.  9. Scratch.
1. Intent become obvious.

Should have a back or second that might hold
If this did blast in proof.² Soft, let me see.
We'll make a solemn wager on your cunnings—
I ha't. 155
When in your motion you are hot and dry—
As make your bouts more violent to that end—
And that he calls for drink, I'll have prepared him
A chalice for the nonce, whereon but sipping,
If he by chance escape your venomed stuck,³ 160
Our purpose may hold there.—But stay, what noise?

[*Enter* QUEEN.]

QUEEN: One woe doth tread upon another's heel,
    So fast they follow. Your sister's drowned, Laertes.
LAERTES: Drowned? O, where?
QUEEN: There is a willow grows aslant the brook 165
    That shows his hoar leaves in the glassy stream.
    Therewith fantastic garlands did she make
    Of crowflowers, nettles, daisies, and long purples
    That liberal shepherds give a grosser⁴ name,
    But our cold⁵ maids do dead men's fingers call them. 170
    There on the pendent boughs her coronet weeds
    Clamb'ring to hang, an envious⁶ sliver broke,
    When down her weedy trophies and herself
    Fell in the weeping brook. Her clothes spread wide,
    And mermaid-like awhile they bore her up, 175
    Which time she chanted snatches of old tunes,
    As one incapable⁷ of her own distress,
    Or like a creature native and indued⁸
    Unto that element. But long it could not be
    Till that her garments, heavy with their drink, 180
    Pulled the poor wretch from her melodious lay
    To muddy death.
LAERTES:            Alas, then she is drowned?
QUEEN: Drowned, drowned.
LAERTES: Too much of water hast thou, poor Ophelia,
    And therefore I forbid my tears; but yet 185
    It is our trick; nature her custom holds,
    Let shame say what it will. When these are gone,
    The woman will be out. Adieu, my lord.
    I have a speech o' fire that fain would blaze
    But that this folly drowns it. [*Exit.*]
KING:                Let's follow, Gertrude. 190
    How much I had to do to calm his rage!
    Now fear I this will give it start again;
    Therefore let's follow. [*Exeunt.*]

2. Fail when tried.   3. Thrust.   4. Coarser. *Liberal:* vulgar.   5. Chaste.   6. Malicious.   7. Unaware.
8. Habituated.

## ACT V

### Scene 1

*A churchyard. Enter two* CLOWNS.[9]

CLOWN: Is she to be buried in Christian burial when she wilfully seeks her own salvation?

OTHER: I tell thee she is. Therefore make her grave straight. The crowner hath sat on her,[1] and finds it Christian burial.

CLOWN: How can that be, unless she drowned herself in her own defence?

OTHER: Why, 'tis found so.

CLOWN: It must be "se offendendo";[2] it cannot be else. For here lies the point: if I drown myself wittingly, it argues an act, and an act hath three branches—it is to act, to do, to perform; argal,[3] she drowned herself wittingly.

OTHER: Nay, but hear you, Goodman Delver.

CLOWN: Give me leave. Here lies the water; good. Here stands the man; good. If the man go to this water and drown himself, it is, will he, nill he, he goes—mark you that. But if the water come to him and drown him, he drowns not himself. Argal, he that is not guilty of his own death shortens not his own life.

OTHER: But is this law?

CLOWN: Ay, marry, is't; crowner's quest[4] law.

OTHER: Will you ha' the truth on't? If this had not been a gentlewoman, she should have been buried out o' Christian burial.

CLOWN: Why, there thou say'st. And the more pity that great folk should have count'nance[5] in this world to drown or hang themselves more than their even-Christen.[6] Come, my spade. There is no ancient gentlemen but gard'ners, ditchers, and grave-makers. They hold up Adam's profession.

OTHER: Was he a gentleman?

CLOWN: 'A was the first that ever bore arms.

OTHER: Why, he had none.

CLOWN: What, art a heathen? How dost thou understand the Scripture? The Scripture says Adam digged. Could he dig without arms? I'll put another question to thee. If thou answerest me not to the purpose, confess thyself—

OTHER: Go to.

CLOWN: What is he that builds stronger than either the mason, the shipwright, or the carpenter?

OTHER: The gallows-maker, for that frame outlives a thousand tenants.

CLOWN: I like thy wit well, in good faith. The gallows does well. But how does it well? It does well to those that do ill. Now thou dost ill to say the gallows is built stronger than the church. Argal, the gallows may do well to thee. To't again,[7] come.

OTHER: Who builds stronger than a mason, a shipwright, or a carpenter?

CLOWN: Ay tell me that, and unyoke.[8]

---

9. Rustics. 1. Held an inquest. *Crowner:* coroner. 2. An error for *se defendendo*, in self-defense. 3. Therefore. 4. Inquest. 5. Approval. 6. Fellow Christians. 7. Guess again. 8. Finish the matter.

OTHER: Marry, now I can tell.
CLOWN: To't.
OTHER: Mass, I cannot tell.
CLOWN: Cudgel thy brains no more about it, for your dull ass will not mend his pace with beating. And when you are asked this question next, say "a grave maker." The houses he makes lasts till doomsday. Go, get thee in, and fetch me a stoup[9] of liquor.                [*Exit* OTHER CLOWN.]

[*Enter* HAMLET *and* HORATIO *as* CLOWN *digs and sings.*]

> In youth, when I did love, did love,
>     Methought it was very sweet,
> To contract the time for-a my behove,[1]
>     O, methought there-a was nothing-a meet.[2]

HAMLET: Has this fellow no feeling of his business, that 'a sings in grave-making?
HORATIO: Custom hath made it in him a property of easiness.
HAMLET: 'Tis e'en so. The hand of little employment hath the daintier sense.
CLOWN:

[*Sings.*]

> But age, with his stealing steps,
>     Hath clawed me in his clutch,
> And hath shipped me into the land,
>     As if I had never been such.

[*Throws up a skull.*]

HAMLET: That skull had a tongue in it, and could sing once. How the knave jowls[3] it to the ground, as if 'twere Cain's jawbone, that did the first murder! This might be the pate of a politician, which this ass now o'erreaches;[4] one that would circumvent God, might it not?
HORATIO: It might, my lord.
HAMLET: Or of a courtier, which could say, "Good morrow, sweet lord! How does thou, sweet lord?" This might be my Lord Such-a-one, that praised my Lord Such-a-one's horse, when 'a meant to beg it, might it not?
HORATIO: Ay, my lord.
HAMLET: Why, e'en so, and now my Lady Worm's, chapless,[5] and knock'd about the mazzard[6] with a sexton's spade. Here's fine revolution,[7] an we had the trick to see't. Did these bones cost no more the breeding but to play at loggets with them?[8] Mine ache to think on't.
CLOWN:

[*Sings.*]

> A pick-axe and a spade, a spade,
>     For and a shrouding sheet:

---

9. Mug.   1. Advantage. *Contract:* shorten.
2. The gravedigger's song is a free version of "The aged lover renounceth love" by Thomas, Lord Vaux, published in *Tottel's Miscellany*, 1557.   3. Hurls.   4. Gets the better of.   5. Lacking a lower jaw.
6. Head.   7. Skill.   8. "Loggets" were small pieces of wood thrown as part of a game.

        O, a pit of clay for to be made
          For such a guest is meet.

        [*Throws up another skull.*]

75 HAMLET: There's another. Why may not that be the skull of a lawyer? Where be his quiddities now, his quillets, his cases, his tenures, and his tricks? Why does he suffer this mad knave now to knock him about the sconce[9] with a dirty shovel, and will not tell him of his action of battery? Hum! This fellow might be in's time a great buyer of land, with his statutes, his recognizances, his
80 fines, his double vouchers, his recoveries. Is this the fine[1] his fines, and the recovery of his recoveries, to have his fine pate full of fine dirt? Will his vouchers vouch him no more of his purchases, and double ones too, than the length and breadth of a pair of indentures?[2] The very conveyances of his lands will scarcely lie in this box, and must th' inheritor himself have no more, ha?[3]
85 HORATIO: Not a jot more, my lord.
HAMLET: Is not parchment made of sheepskins?
HORATIO: Ay, my lord, and of calves' skins too.
HAMLET: They are sheep and calves which seek out assurance in that. I will speak to this fellow. Whose grave's this, sirrah?
90 CLOWN: Mine, sir.

        [*Sings.*]

        O, a pit of clay for to be made
          For such a guest is meet.

HAMLET: I think it be thine indeed, for thou liest in't.
CLOWN: You lie out on't, sir, and therefore 'tis not yours. For my part, I do not
95 lie in't, yet it is mine.
HAMLET: Thou dost lie in't, to be in't and say it is thine. 'Tis for the dead, not for the quick;[4] therefore thou liest.
CLOWN: 'Tis a quick lie, sir; 'twill away again from me to you.
HAMLET: What man dost thou dig it for?
100 CLOWN: For no man, sir.
HAMLET: What woman, then?
CLOWN: For none neither.
HAMLET: Who is to be buried in't?
CLOWN: One that was a woman, sir; but, rest her soul, she's dead.
105 HAMLET: How absolute the knave is! We must speak by the card,[5] or equivocation will undo us. By the Lord, Horatio, this three years I have took note of it, the age is grown so picked[6] that the toe of the peasant comes so near the heel of the courtier, he galls his kibe.[7] How long hast thou been a grave-maker?
CLOWN: Of all the days i' th' year, I came to't that day that our last King Hamlet
110 overcame Fortinbras.
HAMLET: How long is that since?

---

9. Head.   1. End.   2. Contracts.
3. In this speech Hamlet reels off a list of legal terms relating to property transactions.   4. Living.
5. Exactly. *Absolute*: precise.   6. Refined.   7. Rubs a blister on his heel.

CLOWN: Cannot you tell that? Every fool can tell that. It was that very day that young Hamlet was born—he that is mad, and sent into England.
HAMLET: Ay, marry, why was he sent into England?
CLOWN: Why, because 'a was mad. 'A shall recover his wits there; or, if 'a do not, 'tis no great matter there.
HAMLET: Why?
CLOWN: 'Twill not be seen in him there. There the men are as mad as he.
HAMLET: How came he mad?
CLOWN: Very strangely, they say.
HAMLET: How strangely?
CLOWN: Faith, e'en with losing his wits.
HAMLET: Upon what ground?
CLOWN: Why, here in Denmark. I have been sexton here, man and boy, thirty years.
HAMLET: How long will a man lie i' th' earth ere he rot?
CLOWN: Faith, if 'a be not rotten before 'a die—as we have many pocky[8] corses now-a-days that will scarce hold the laying in—'a will last you some eight year or nine year. A tanner will last you nine year.
HAMLET: Why he more than another?
CLOWN: Why, sir, his hide is so tanned with his trade that 'a will keep out water a great while; and your water is a sore decayer of your whoreson dead body. Here's a skull now hath lien[9] you i' th' earth three and twenty years.
HAMLET: Whose was it?
CLOWN: A whoreson mad fellow's it was. Whose do you think it was?
HAMLET: Nay, I know not.
CLOWN: A pestilence on him for a mad rogue! 'A poured a flagon of Rhenish on my head once. This same skull, sir, was, sir, Yorick's skull, the king's jester.
HAMLET: [*Takes the skull.*] This?
CLOWN: E'en that.
HAMLET: Alas, poor Yorick! I knew him, Horatio—a fellow of infinite jest, of most excellent fancy. He hath bore me on his back a thousand times, and now how abhorred in my imagination it is! My gorge[1] rises at it. Here hung those lips that I have kissed I know not how oft. Where be your gibes now, your gambols, your songs, your flashes of merriment that were wont to set the table on a roar? Not one now to mock your own grinning? Quite chap-fall'n?[2] Now get you to my lady's chamber, and tell her, let her paint an inch thick, to this favor[3] she must come. Make her laugh at that. Prithee, Horatio, tell me one thing.
HORATIO: What's that, my lord?
HAMLET: Dost thou think Alexander looked o' this fashion i' th' earth?
HORATIO: E'en so.
HAMLET: And smelt so? Pah! [*Throws down the skull.*]
HORATIO: E'en so, my lord.
HAMLET: To what base uses we may return, Horatio! Why may not imagination trace the noble dust of Alexander till 'a find it stopping a bung-hole?

---

8. Corrupted by syphilis.   9. Lain. *Whoreson:* bastard (not literally).   1. Throat.   2. Lacking a lower jaw.
3. Appearance.

HORATIO: 'Twere to consider too curiously[4] to consider so.
HAMLET: No, faith, not a jot, but to follow him thither with modesty[5] enough, and likelihood to lead it. Alexander died, Alexander was buried, Alexander returneth to dust; the dust is earth; of earth we make loam; and why of that loam whereto he was converted might they not stop a beerbarrel?

> Imperious Cæsar, dead and turned to clay,
> Might stop a hole to keep the wind away.
> O, that that earth which kept the world in awe
> Should patch a wall t'expel the winter's flaw![6]

But soft, but soft awhile! Here comes the king,
The queen, the courtiers.

[*Enter* KING, QUEEN, LAERTES, *and the Corse with a* PRIEST *and* LORDS *attendant.*]

> Who is this they follow?
> And with such maiméd[7] rites? This doth betoken
> The corse they follow did with desperate hand
> Fordo its own life. 'Twas of some estate.[8]
> Couch[9] we awhile and mark. [*Retires with* HORATIO.]

LAERTES: What ceremony else?[1]
HAMLET: That is Laertes, a very noble youth. Mark.
LAERTES: What ceremony else?
PRIEST: Here obsequies have been as far enlarged[2]
As we have warranty. Her death was doubtful,
And but that great command o'ersways the order,[3]
She should in ground unsanctified been lodged
Till the last trumpet. For charitable prayers,
Shards, flints, and pebbles, should be thrown on her.
Yet here she is allowed her virgin crants,[4]
Her maiden strewments,[5] and the bringing home
Of bell and burial.
LAERTES: Must there no more be done?
PRIEST:                 No more be done.
We should profane the service of the dead
To sing a requiem and such rest to her
As to peace-parted souls.
LAERTES:         Lay her i' th' earth,
And from her fair and unpolluted flesh
May violets spring! I tell thee, churlish priest,
A minist'ring angel shall my sister be
When thou liest howling.[6]
HAMLET:         What, the fair Ophelia!
QUEEN: Sweets to the sweet. Farewell! [*Scatters flowers.*]
I hoped thou shouldst have been my Hamlet's wife.

---

4. Precisely.   5. Moderation.   6. Gusty wind.   7. Cut short.   8. Rank. *Fordo:* destroy.
9. Conceal ourselves.   1. More.   2. Extended.   3. Usual rules.   4. Wreaths.
5. Flowers strewn on the grave.   6. In Hell.

I thought thy bride-bed to have decked, sweet maid,
And not t' have strewed thy grave.

LAERTES: O, treble woe
Fall ten times treble on that curséd head
Whose wicked deed thy most ingenious sense[7]
Deprived thee of! Hold off the earth awhile,
Till I have caught her once more in mine arms. [*Leaps into the grave.*]
Now pile your dust upon the quick and dead,
Till of this flat a mountain you have made
T' o'er-top old Pelion or the skyish head
Of blue Olympus.[8]

HAMLET: [*Coming forward.*] What is he whose grief
Bears such an emphasis, whose phrase of sorrow
Conjures[9] the wand'ring stars, and makes them stand
Like wonder-wounded hearers? This is I,
Hamlet the Dane.

[HAMLET *leaps into the grave and they grapple.*]

LAERTES: The devil take thy soul!
HAMLET: Thou pray'st not well.
I prithee take thy fingers from my throat,
For though I am not splenitive[1] and rash,
Yet have I in me something dangerous,
Which let thy wisdom fear. Hold off thy hand.

KING: Pluck them asunder.
QUEEN: Hamlet! Hamlet!
ALL: Gentlemen!
HORATIO: Good my lord, be quiet.

[*The* ATTENDANTS *part them, and they come out of the grave.*]

HAMLET: Why, I will fight with him upon this theme
Until my eyelids will no longer wag.[2]
QUEEN: O my son, what theme?
HAMLET: I loved Ophelia. Forty thousand brothers
Could not with all their quantity of love
Make up my sum. What wilt thou do for her?
KING: O, he is mad, Laertes.
QUEEN: For love of God, forbear[3] him.
HAMLET: 'Swounds, show me what th'owt do.
Woo't[4] weep, woo't fight, woo't fast, woo't tear thyself,
Woo't drink up eisel,[5] eat a crocodile?
I'll do't. Dost come here to whine?

---

7. Lively mind.
8. The rivalry between Laertes and Hamlet in this scene extends even to their rhetoric. Pelion and Olympus, mentioned here by Laertes, and Ossa, mentioned below by Hamlet, are Greek mountains noted in mythology for their height. Olympus was the reputed home of the gods, and the other two were piled one on top of the other by the Giants in an attempt to reach the top of Olympus and overthrow the gods.
9. Casts a spell on.  1. Hot-tempered.  2. Move.  3. Bear with.  4. Will you.  5. Vinegar.

>                 To outface[6] me with leaping in her grave?
> 230             Be buried quick with her, and so will I.
>                 And if thou prate of mountains, let them throw
>                 Millions of acres on us, till our ground,
>                 Singeing his pate against the burning zone,[7]
>                 Make Ossa like a wart! Nay, an thou'lt mouth,
>                 I'll rant as well as thou.
> 235  QUEEN:                     This is mere madness
>                 And thus awhile the fit will work on him.
>                 Anon, as patient as the female dove
>                 When that her golden couplets[8] are disclosed,
>                 His silence will sit drooping.
>      HAMLET:                    Hear you, sir.
> 240            What is the reason that you use me thus?
>                 I loved you ever. But it is no matter.
>                 Let Hercules himself do what he may,
>                 The cat will mew, and dog will have his day.    [Exit.]
>      KING: I pray thee, good Horatio, wait upon[9] him.
>      [Exit HORATIO.]
> 245  [To LAERTES.] Strengthen your patience in our last night's speech.
>                 We'll put the matter to the present push.[1]—
>                 Good Gertrude, set some watch over your son.—
>                 This grave shall have a living monument.
>                 An hour of quiet shortly shall we see;
> 250            Till then in patience our proceeding be.           [Exeunt.]

### Scene 2

*A hall or public room. Enter* HAMLET *and* HORATIO.

> HAMLET: So much for this, sir; now shall you see the other.
>     You do remember all the circumstance?
> HORATIO: Remember it, my lord!
> HAMLET: Sir, in my heart there was a kind of fighting
> 5      That would not let me sleep. Methought I lay
>         Worse than the mutines in the bilboes.[2] Rashly,
>         And praised be rashness for it—let us know,
>         Our indiscretion sometime serves us well,
>         When our deep plots do pall; and that should learn[3] us
> 10     There's a divinity that shapes our ends,
>         Rough-hew them how we will—
> HORATIO:                    That is most certain.
> HAMLET: Up from my cabin,
>     My sea-gown scarfed[4] about me, in the dark
>     Groped I to find out them, had my desire,

---

6. Get the best of.   7. Sky in the torrid zone.   8. Pair of eggs.   9. Attend.   1. Immediate trial.
2. Stocks. *Mutines:* mutineers.   3. Teach.   4. Wrapped.

Fingered their packet, and in fine[5] withdrew
To mine own room again, making so bold,
My fears forgetting manners, to unseal
Their grand commission; where I found, Horatio—
Ah, royal knavery!—an exact[6] command,
Larded[7] with many several sorts of reasons,
Importing Denmark's health, and England's too,
With, ho! such bugs and goblins in my life,[8]
That on the supervise,[9] no leisure bated,
No, not to stay the grinding of the axe,
My head should be struck off.

HORATIO:                 Is't possible?

HAMLET: Here's the commission; read it at more leisure.
But wilt thou hear now how I did proceed?

HORATIO: I beseech you.

HAMLET: Being thus benetted[1] round with villainies,
Ere I could make a prologue to my brains,
They had begun the play. I sat me down,
Devised a new commission, wrote it fair.[2]
I once did hold it, as our statists[3] do,
A baseness to write fair, and labored much
How to forget that learning; but sir, now
It did me yeoman's service. Wilt thou know
Th' effect[4] of what I wrote?

HORATIO:                 Ay, good my lord.

HAMLET: An earnest conjuration from the king,
As England was his faithful tributary,[5]
As love between them like the palm might flourish,
As peace should still her wheaten garland wear
And stand a comma 'tween their amities[6]
And many such like as's of great charge,[7]
That on the view and knowing of these contents,
Without debatement[8] further more or less,
He should those bearers put to sudden death,
Not shriving-time allowed.[9]

HORATIO:                 How was this sealed?

HAMLET: Why, even in that was heaven ordinant,[1]
I had my father's signet in my purse,
Which was the model of that Danish seal,
Folded the writ up in the form of th' other,
Subscribed it, gave't th' impression,[2] placed it safely,
The changeling[3] never known. Now, the next day
Was our sea-fight, and what to this was sequent[4]
Thou knowest already.

---

5. Quickly. *Fingered:* stole.    6. Precisely stated.    7. Garnished.    8. Such dangers if I remained alive.
9. As soon as the commission was read.    1. Caught in a net.    2. Legibly. *Devised:* made.    3. Politicians.
4. Contents.    5. Vassal.    6. Link friendships.    7. Import.    8. Consideration.
9. Without time for confession.    1. Operative.    2. Of the seal.    3. Alteration.    4. Followed.

HORATIO: So Guildenstern and Rosencrantz go to't.
HAMLET: Why, man, they did make love to this employment.
    They are not near my conscience; their defeat[5]
    Does by their own insinuation grow.
60  'Tis dangerous when the baser nature comes
    Between the pass and fell[6] incensèd points
    Of mighty opposites.
HORATIO:               Why, what a king is this!
HAMLET: Does it not, think thee, stand me now upon—
    He that hath killed my king and whored my mother,
65  Popped in between th' election and my hopes,
    Thrown out his angle[7] for my proper life,
    And with such coz'nage[8]—is't not perfect conscience
    To quit[9] him with this arm? And is't not to be damned
    To let this canker of our nature come
70  In further evil?
HORATIO: It must be shortly known to him from England
    What is the issue[1] of the business there.
HAMLET: It will be short;[2] the interim is mine.
    And a man's life's no more than to say "one."
75  But I am very sorry, good Horatio,
    That to Laertes I forgot myself;
    For by the image of my cause I see
    The portraiture of his. I'll court his favors.
    But sure the bravery[3] of his grief did put me
    Into a tow'ring passion.
80 HORATIO:             Peace; who comes here?

    [*Enter* OSRIC.]

OSRIC: Your lordship is right welcome back to Denmark.
HAMLET: I humbly thank you, sir. [*Aside to* HORATIO.] Dost know this water-fly?
HORATIO: [*Aside to* HAMLET.] No, my good lord.
HAMLET: [*Aside to* HORATIO.] Thy state is the more gracious, for 'tis a vice to know
85  him. He hath much land, and fertile. Let a beast be lord of beasts, and his
    crib shall stand at the king's mess. 'Tis a chough,[4] but as I say, spacious in
    the possession of dirt.
OSRIC: Sweet lord, if your lordship were at leisure, I should impart a thing to
    you from his majesty.
90 HAMLET: I will receive it, sir, with all diligence of spirit. Put your bonnet to his
    right use. 'Tis for the head.
OSRIC: I thank your lordship, it is very hot.
HAMLET: No, believe me, 'tis very cold; the wind is northerly.
OSRIC: It is indifferent[5] cold, my lord, indeed.
95 HAMLET: But yet methinks it is very sultry and hot for my complexion.[6]
OSRIC: Exceedingly, my lord; it is very sultry, as 'twere—I cannot tell how. My

---

5. Death. *Are not near:* do not touch.   6. Cruel. *Pass:* thrust.   7. Fishhook.   8. Trickery.   9. Repay.
1. Outcome.   2. Soon.   3. Exaggerated display.   4. Jackdaw.   5. Moderately.   6. Temperament.

lord, his majesty bade me signify to you that 'a has laid a great wager on your head. Sir, this is the matter—
HAMLET: I beseech you, remember. [*Moves him to put on his hat.*]
OSRIC: Nay, good my lord; for my ease, in good faith. Sir, here is newly come to court Laertes; believe me, an absolute[7] gentleman, full of most excellent differences,[8] of very soft society and great showing.[9] Indeed, to speak feelingly of him, he is the card or calendar of gentry, for you shall find in him the continent[1] of what part a gentleman would see.
HAMLET: Sir, his definement[2] suffers no perdition in you, though I know to divide him inventorially would dozy[3] th' arithmetic of memory, and yet but yaw[4] neither in respect of his quick sail. But in the verity of extolment, I take him to be a soul of great article,[5] and his infusion[6] of such dearth and rareness as, to make true diction of him, his semblage[7] is his mirror, and who else would trace him, his umbrage,[8] nothing more.
OSRIC: Your lordship speaks most infallibly of him.
HAMLET: The concernancy,[9] sir? Why do we wrap the gentleman in our more rawer breath?[1]
OSRIC: Sir?
HORATIO: Is't not possible to understand in another tongue? You will to't, sir, really.
HAMLET: What imports the nomination[2] of this gentleman?
OSRIC: Of Laertes?
HORATIO: [*Aside.*] His purse is empty already. All's golden words are spent.
HAMLET: Of him, sir.
OSRIC: I know you are not ignorant—
HAMLET: I would you did, sir; yet, in faith, if you did, it would not much approve me. Well, sir.
OSRIC: You are not ignorant of what excellence Laertes is—
HAMLET: I dare not confess that, lest I should compare[3] with him in excellence; but to know a man well were to know himself.
OSRIC: I mean, sir, for his weapon; but in the imputation[4] laid on him by them, in his meed he's unfellowed.[5]
HAMLET: What's his weapon?
OSRIC: Rapier and dagger.
HAMLET: That's two of his weapons—but well.
OSRIC: The king, sir, hath wagered with him six Barbary horses, against the which he has impawned,[6] as I take it, six French rapiers and poniards, with their assigns,[7] as girdle, hangers, and so. Three of the carriages, in faith, are very dear to fancy,[8] very responsive to the hilts, most delicate carriages, and of very liberal conceit.[9]
HAMLET: What call you the carriages?
HORATIO: [*Aside to* HAMLET.] I knew you must be edified by the margent[1] ere you had done.

7. Perfect.   8. Qualities.   9. Good manners.   1. Sum total. *Calendar:* measure.   2. Description.
3. Daze. *Divide him inventorially:* examine bit by bit.   4. Steer wildly.   5. Scope.   6. Nature.
7. Rival. *Diction:* telling.   8. Shadow. *Trace:* keep pace with.   9. Meaning.   1. Cruder words.
2. Naming.   3. That is, compare myself.   4. Reputation.   5. Unequaled in his excellence.   6. Staked.
7. Appurtenances.   8. Finely designed.   9. Elegant design. *Delicate:* well adjusted.   1. Marginal gloss.

OSRIC: The carriages, sir, are the hangers.

HAMLET: The phrase would be more germane to the matter if we could carry a cannon by our sides. I would it might be hangers till then. But on! Six Barbary horses against six French swords, their assigns, and three liberal conceited carriages; that's the French bet against the Danish. Why is this all impawned, as you call it?

OSRIC: The king, sir, hath laid, sir, that in a dozen passes between yourself and him he shall not exceed you three hits; he hath laid on twelve for nine, and it would come to immediate trial if your lordship would vouchsafe the answer.

HAMLET: How if I answer no?

OSRIC: I mean, my lord, the opposition of your person in trial.

HAMLET: Sir, I will walk here in the hall. If it please his majesty, it is the breathing time[2] of day with me. Let the foils be brought, the gentleman willing, and the king hold his purpose; I will win for him an I can. If not, I will gain nothing but my shame and the odd hits.

OSRIC: Shall I deliver you so?

HAMLET: To this effect, sir, after what flourish your nature will.

OSRIC: I commend my duty to your lordship.

HAMLET: Yours, yours. [*Exit* OSRIC.] He does well to commend it himself; there are no tongues else for's turn.

HORATIO: This lapwing runs away with the shell on his head.[3]

HAMLET: 'A did comply, sir, with his dug[4] before 'a sucked it. Thus has he, and many more of the same bevy that I know the drossy age dotes on, only got the tune of the time; and out of an habit of encounter, a king of yesty[5] collection which carries them through and through the most fanned and winnowed opinions; and do but blow them to their trial, the bubbles are out.

[*Enter a* LORD.]

LORD: My lord, his majesty commended him to you by young Osric, who brings back to him that you attend[6] him in the hall. He sends to know if your pleasure hold to play with Laertes, or that you will take longer time.

HAMLET: I am constant to my purposes; they follow the king's pleasure. If his fitness speaks, mine is ready; now or whensoever, provided I be so able as now.

LORD: The king and queen and all are coming down.

HAMLET: In happy time.

LORD: The queen desires you to use some gentle entertainment[7] to Laertes before you fall to play.

HAMLET: She well instructs me.                                    [*Exit* LORD.]

HORATIO: You will lose this wager, my lord.

HAMLET: I do not think so. Since he went into France I have been in continual practice. I shall win at the odds. But thou wouldst not think how ill[8] all's here about my heart. But it's no matter.

HORATIO: Nay, good my lord—

HAMLET: It is but foolery, but it is such a kind of gaingiving[9] as would perhaps trouble a woman.

---

2. Time for exercise.
3. The lapwing was thought to be so precocious that it could run immediately after being hatched, even, as here, with bits of the shell still on its head.    4. Mother's breast. *Comply:* deal formally.    5. Yeasty.
6. Await.    7. Cordiality.    8. Uneasy.    9. Misgiving.

HORATIO: If your mind dislike anything, obey it. I will forestall their repair[1] hither, and say you are not fit.

HAMLET: Not a whit, we defy augury. There is special providence in the fall of a sparrow. If it be now, 'tis not to come; if it be not to come, it will be now; if it be not now, yet it will come. The readiness is all. Since no man of aught he leaves knows, what is't to leave betimes? Let be.

[*A table prepared. Enter* TRUMPETS, DRUMS, *and* OFFICERS *with cushions;* KING, QUEEN, OSRIC *and* ATTENDANTS *with foils, daggers, and* LAERTES.]

KING: Come, Hamlet, come and take this hand from me.

[*The* KING *puts* LAERTES' *hand into* HAMLET'*s*.]

HAMLET: Give me your pardon, sir. I have done you wrong,
But pardon 't as you are a gentleman.
This presence[2] knows, and you must needs have heard,
How I am punished with a sore distraction.
What I have done
That might your nature, honor, and exception,[3]
Roughly awake, I here proclaim was madness.
Was 't Hamlet wronged Laertes? Never Hamlet.
If Hamlet from himself be ta'en away,
And when he's not himself does wrong Laertes,
Then Hamlet does it not, Hamlet denies it.
Who does it then? His madness. If't be so,
Hamlet is of the faction that is wronged;
His madness is poor Hamlet's enemy.
Sir, in this audience,
Let my disclaiming from[4] a purposed evil
Free[5] me so far in your most generous thoughts
That I have shot my arrow o'er the house
And hurt my brother.

LAERTES:            I am satisfied in nature,
Whose motive in this case should stir me most
To my revenge. But in my terms of honor
I stand aloof, and will no reconcilement
Till by some elder masters of known honor
I have a voice[6] and precedent of peace
To keep my name ungored.[7] But till that time
I do receive your offered love like love,
And will not wrong it.

HAMLET:           I embrace it freely,
And will this brother's wager frankly[8] play.
Give us the foils. Come on.

LAERTES:           Come, one for me.

HAMLET: I'll be your foil, Laertes. In mine ignorance
Your skill shall, like a star i' th' darkest night,
Stick fiery off[9] indeed.

---

1. Coming.    2. Company.    3. Resentment.    4. Denying of.    5. Absolve.    6. Authority.
7. Unshamed.    8. Without rancor.    9. Shine brightly.

LAERTES: You mock me, sir.
HAMLET: No, by this hand.
KING: Give them the foils, young Osric. Cousin Hamlet,
  You know the wager?
HAMLET: Very well, my lord;
225 Your Grace has laid the odds o' th' weaker side.
KING: I do not fear it, I have seen you both;
  But since he is bettered[1] we have therefore odds.
LAERTES: This is too heavy; let me see another.
HAMLET: This likes me well. These foils have all a[2] length?

[*They prepare to play.*]

230 OSRIC: Ay, my good lord.
KING: Set me the stoups of wine upon that table.
  If Hamlet give the first or second hit,
  Or quit in answer of[3] the third exchange,
  Let all the battlements their ordnance fire.
235 The king shall drink to Hamlet's better breath,
  And in the cup an union[4] shall he throw,
  Richer than that which four successive kings
  In Denmark's crown have worn. Give me the cups,
  And let the kettle[5] to the trumpet speak,
240 The trumpet to the cannoneer without,
  The cannons to the heavens, the heaven to earth,
  "Now the king drinks to Hamlet." Come, begin—

[*Trumpets the while.*]

  And you, the judges, bear a wary eye.
HAMLET: Come on, sir.
LAERTES: Come, my lord.

[*They play.*]

HAMLET: One.
LAERTES: No.
HAMLET: Judgment?
245 OSRIC: A hit, a very palpable hit.

[*Drums, trumpets, and shot. Flourish; a piece goes off.*]

LAERTES: Well, again.
KING: Stay, give me drink. Hamlet, this pearl is thine.
  Here's to thy health. Give him the cup.
HAMLET: I'll play this bout first; set it by awhile.
250 Come.

[*They play.*]

  Another hit; what say you?
LAERTES: A touch, a touch, I do confess't.

---

1. Reported better.  2. The same. *Likes:* suits.  3. Repay.  4. Pearl.  5. Kettledrum.

KING: Our son shall win.
QUEEN:                He's fat,[6] and scant of breath.
　Here, Hamlet, take my napkin, rub thy brows.
　The queen carouses to thy fortune, Hamlet.
HAMLET: Good madam!
KING: Gertrude, do not drink.
QUEEN: I will, my lord; I pray you pardon me.
KING: [*Aside.*] It is the poisoned cup; it is too late.
HAMLET: I dare not drink yet, madam; by and by.
QUEEN: Come, let me wipe thy face.
LAERTES: My lord, I'll hit him now.
KING:                I do not think't.
LAERTES: [*Aside.*] And yet it is almost against my conscience.
HAMLET: Come, for the third, Laertes. You do but dally.
　I pray you pass[7] with your best violence;
　I am afeard you make a wanton of me.[8]
LAERTES: Say you so? Come on.

　　[*They play.*]

OSRIC: Nothing, neither way.
LAERTES: Have at you now!

　　[LAERTES *wounds* HAMLET: *then, in scuffling, they change rapiers, and* HAMLET
　　*wounds* LAERTES.]

KING: Part them. They are incensed.
HAMLET: Nay, come again.

　　[*The* QUEEN *falls.*]

OSRIC: Look to the queen there, ho!
HORATIO: They bleed on both sides. How is it, my lord?
OSRIC: How is't, Laertes?
LAERTES: Why, as a woodcock to mine own springe,[9] Osric.
　I am justly killed with mine own treachery.
HAMLET: How does the queen?
KING:                She swoons to see them bleed.
QUEEN: No, no, the drink, the drink! O my dear Hamlet!
　The drink, the drink! I am poisoned.                [*Dies.*]
HAMLET: O, villainy! Ho! let the door be locked.
　Treachery! seek it out.
LAERTES: It is here, Hamlet. Hamlet, thou art slain;
　No med'cine in the world can do thee good.
　In thee there is not half an hour's life.
　The treacherous instrument is in thy hand,
　Unbated[1] and envenomed. The foul practice
　Hath turned itself on me. Lo, here I lie,
　Never to rise again. Thy mother's poisoned.
　I can no more. The king, the king's to blame.

6. Out of shape.　7. Attack.　8. Trifle with me.　9. Snare.　1. Unblunted.

290 HAMLET: The point envenomed too?
   Then, venom, to thy work. [*Hurts the* KING.]
   ALL: Treason! treason!
   KING: O, yet defend me, friends. I am but hurt.[2]
   HAMLET: Here, thou incestuous, murd'rous, damnéd Dane,
295   Drink off this potion. Is thy union here?
   Follow my mother.

   [*The* KING *dies.*]

   LAERTES:         He is justly served.
   It is a poison tempered[3] by himself.
   Exchange forgiveness with me, noble Hamlet.
   Mine and my father's death come not upon thee,
300   Nor thine on me! [*Dies.*]
   HAMLET: Heaven make thee free of[4] it! I follow thee.
   I am dead, Horatio. Wretched queen, adieu!
   You that look pale and tremble at this chance,[5]
   That are but mutes or audience to this act,
305   Had I but time, as this fell sergeant Death
   Is strict in his arrest,[6] O, I could tell you—
   But let it be. Horatio, I am dead:
   Thou livest; report me and my cause aright
   To the unsatisfied.[7]
   HORATIO:         Never believe it.
310   I am more an antique Roman than a Dane.
   Here's yet some liquor left.
   HAMLET:         As th'art a man,
   Give me the cup. Let go. By heaven, I'll ha't.
   O God, Horatio, what a wounded name,
   Things standing thus unknown, shall live behind me!
315   If thou didst ever hold me in thy heart,
   Absent thee from felicity awhile,
   And in this harsh world draw thy breath in pain,
   To tell my story.

   [*A march afar off.*]

         What warlike noise is this?
   OSRIC: Young Fortinbras, with conquest come from Poland,
320   To th' ambassadors of England gives
   This warlike volley.[8]
   HAMLET:         O, I die, Horatio!
   The potent poison quite o'er-crows[9] my spirit.
   I cannot live to hear the news from England,
   But I do prophesy th' election lights

---

2. Wounded.   3. Mixed.   4. Forgive.   5. Circumstance.   6. Summons to court.   7. Uninformed.
8. The staging presents some difficulties here. Unless Osric is clairvoyant, he must have left the stage at some point and returned. One possibility is that he might have left to carry out Hamlet's order to lock the door (line 280) and returned when the sound of the distant march is heard.   9. Overcomes.

On Fortinbras. He has my dying voice.[1]
So tell him, with th' occurrents,[2] more and less,
Which have solicited[3]—the rest is silence. [*Dies.*]

HORATIO: Now cracks a noble heart. Good night, sweet prince,
And flights of angels sing thee to thy rest!

[*March within.*]

Why does the drum come hither?

[*Enter* FORTINBRAS, *with the* AMBASSADORS *and with drum, colors, and* ATTENDANTS.]

FORTINBRAS: Where is this sight?
HORATIO: What is it you would see?
If aught of woe or wonder, cease your search.
FORTINBRAS: This quarry cries on havoc.[4] O proud death,
What feast is toward[5] in thine eternal cell
That thou so many princes at a shot
So bloodily hast struck?
AMBASSADORS: The sight is dismal;
And our affairs from England come too late.
The ears are senseless[6] that should give us hearing
To tell him his commandment is fulfilled,
That Rosencrantz and Guildenstern are dead.
Where should we have our thanks?
HORATIO: Not from his mouth,
Had it th' ability of life to thank you.
He never gave commandment for their death.
But since, so jump[7] upon this bloody question,
You from the Polack wars, and you from England,
Are here arrived, give orders that these bodies
High on a stage be placed to the view,
And let me speak to th' yet unknowing world
How these things came about. So shall you hear
Of carnal, bloody, and unnatural acts;
Of accidental judgments, casual[8] slaughters;
Of deaths put on by cunning and forced cause;
And, in this upshot,[9] purposes mistook
Fall'n on th' inventors' heads. All this can I
Truly deliver.
FORTINBRAS: Let us haste to hear it,
And call the noblest to the audience.[1]
For me, with sorrow I embrace my fortune.
I have some rights of memory[2] in this kingdom,
Which now to claim my vantage[3] doth invite me.

1. Support.   2. Circumstances.   3. Brought about this scene.
4. The game killed in the hunt proclaims a slaughter.
5. In preparation.   6. Without sense of hearing.   7. Exactly.   8. Brought about by apparent accident.
9. Result.   1. Hearing.   2. Succession.   3. Position.

360 HORATIO: Of that I shall have also cause to speak,
    And from his mouth whose voice will draw on more.
    But let this same be presently performed,
    Even while men's minds are wild, lest more mischance
    On plots and errors happen.
  FORTINBRAS:              Let four captains
365   Bear Hamlet like a soldier to the stage,
    For he was likely, had he been put on,[4]
    To have proved most royal; and for his passage
    The soldier's music and the rite of war
    Speak loudly for him.
370   Take up the bodies. Such a sight as this
    Becomes the field, but here shows much amiss.
    Go, bid the soldiers shoot.     [*Exeunt marching. A peal of ordnance shot off.*]

ca. 1600

---

## SUGGESTIONS FOR WRITING

1. In *A Midsummer Night's Dream*'s best-known speech, Theseus asserts that "The lunatic, the lover, and the poet / Are of imagination all compact" (5.1.7–8). Citing evidence from the play, write an essay analyzing Shakespeare's characterization of love—not only in the play's action, but also in the words of the love-obsessed characters. Is Shakespearean love merely a kind of madness, or does it contain hints of a guiding wisdom beyond the awareness of lovers themselves?
2. Early in *A Midsummer Night's Dream* Helena remarks, "Love looks not with the eyes, but with the mind" (1.1.234). The play is filled with references to eyes and vision; indeed, the plot hinges on the differences between what characters see and what they think they see. Using specific examples, write an essay exploring the significance of eyes, sight, and seeing in this play. What does the play suggest about the power and the limitations of human vision?
3. In ancient Greek tragedy, misfortune is often the result of *hubris*—the excessive pride that leads a hero to overstep the bounds of his destiny and thus to offend the gods. More recent writing about tragedy develops the concept of *hamartia*—the notion that the protagonist's fate is brought about by a tragic flaw or failing of character. What propels *Hamlet*—the prince's proud wish to avenge his father's death and assert his rights? a tragic flaw in Hamlet's otherwise noble character? or something else altogether? Write an essay examining the circumstances and motivations that lead to Hamlet's death and the fall of Denmark.
4. Some critics have focused on the psychological underpinnings of *Hamlet*; others have seen the play as political commentary. In 1600 (the approximate date of *Hamlet*'s first performance), Queen Elizabeth I was sixty-seven and had no direct heirs, a situation that promised no end to the wars and rebellions over succession to the throne that had plagued England for the preceding two centuries. Drawing on the play and, if need be, your own research into the politics of Shakespeare's era, write an essay showing how England's historical circumstances may be reflected in *Hamlet*.
5. In both *A Midsummer Night's Dream* and *Hamlet*, characters perform a play. What are the functions and effects of this device? What might the plays within plays suggest

---

4. Elected king.

about the value of drama—including the value of plays like Shakespeare's own? What different attitudes toward drama are displayed by various characters in *A Midsummer Night's Dream* and *Hamlet*? Write an essay exploring the function and significance of these plays within plays. What attitudes toward drama does Shakespeare encourage us to adopt?

6. For centuries Shakespeare's plays have been celebrated for their originality and variety. Samuel Johnson, the great eighteenth-century literary critic, once wrote of Shakespeare that "Each change of many-colour'd life he drew." T. S. Eliot claimed that, of all writers, "Shakespeare gives the greatest width of human passion." Still, for all their variety, most of Shakespeare's plays follow fairly rigid formulas for either comedy or tragedy. Write an essay in which you discuss either (a) how *A Midsummer Night's Dream* and at least one other Shakespeare play (for example, *The Merchant of Venice, As You Like It, or Twelfth Night*) typify Shakespearean comedy, or (b) how *Hamlet* and at least one other Shakespeare play (for example, *Romeo and Juliet, Julius Caesar*, or *Macbeth*) embody Shakespearean tragedy.

# 29 LITERARY CONTEXT: TRAGEDY AND COMEDY

Classifying literary texts serves a variety of purposes for literary critics, who may need to "place" a work in history, suggest its relationship to other texts, or assess its literary quality or cultural value. But classification is not just an activity for "professionals." Classification can also be important to students and ordinary readers, for a knowledge of categories and what they stand for can aid in the enjoyment and interpretation of individual texts.

Authors sometimes label their texts specifically to help readers know what to expect, thereby entering into a kind of contract with readers. When fiction writers call their books "romances," for example, they tell readers to expect stories that are romantic, idealistic, improbable, full of fantasy, and characterized by love and emotional fulfillment. Playwrights have historically labeled their texts to inform both audiences and readers about what they may experience during a performance or reading of a work. **Pastoral plays** promise to be about shepherds living in an idealized world reminiscent of some primitive golden age. **Farces** promise broad humor and wild antics, perhaps slapstick, pratfalls, or other physical humor or perhaps easy puns and verbal high jinks, but certainly something entertaining, not too taxing, and not too serious. **Satires** promise critical commentary on a person or situation or event, often political or involving a specific cultural or social situation. Not all satires, farces, and pastoral plays do exactly what their labels promise, but those labels *do* lead readers to expect a certain kind of text—one that will treat predictable subject matter and behave in predictable fashion. Often these labels imply a certain kind of structure, language, and value system.

Not all plays (or texts of any other kind) are labeled by their authors, but many unlabeled texts draw on previous practice and traditional classifications and are therefore placed by critics or by viewers and readers within traditional categories. We might, for example, describe a film as a whodunit or a spaghetti Western, or we might call a TV program a sitcom or a soap, and reasonably expect that others will know, at least roughly speaking, what kind of film or show we are describing.

> *Comedy aims at representing man as worse, Tragedy as better than in actual life.*
> —ARISTOTLE

**Tragedy** and **comedy** are two of the oldest dramatic forms, and many contemporary playwrights and critics continue to apply these terms. Many people believe that tragedy and comedy still provide convenient ways to organize and present experience because they reflect basic ways of viewing human history. You can sometimes get into a pretty lively argument about whether a particular play should be called a tragedy; all kinds of critics, students, theatergoers, and readers argued with Arthur Miller and with each other about whether *Death of a Salesman* was truly tragic, for example. But while individuals often disagree about how to label particular texts, and about exactly what each label implies, most people admit the necessity of labels and believe that general agreement about definition is possible, despite quibbling over details.

The broad parameters of comedy and tragedy have been around since the time of Aristotle, the fourth century B.C.E.; in his *Poetics* Aristotle defined tragedy in terms of contemporary examples. Aristotle's definition depends on three things—the order of values implicit in the play, the nature of character in the play, and the nature of the conclusion.

In a tragedy like *Oedipus the King*, values are universal and beyond the control of humankind. Right and wrong stem not from any agreement between individuals, but from the will of the gods or from some other extrahuman force. When the oracle tells Oedipus that he is fated to kill his father and marry his mother, Oedipus is revolted. In human terms he must try to avoid this fate—but in terms of the value system that rules the play, his attempt to circumvent the will of the gods must destroy him. In a comedy like *The Importance of Being Earnest*, on the other hand, values are social and determined by the general opinion of society. In moral terms Jack and Gwendolen, being healthy and single, might marry and establish a family. They face, however, a social problem, in that Gwendolen's children cannot achieve their "proper" place in society unless her husband is a man of good family, some social position, and adequate means. Comedy tends to endorse the values of society, sometimes at the expense of individual needs or values. Lady Bracknell may be amusing, but she also understands how her society works, what is acceptable and what is not.

> *Tragic art, passionate art, ... the confounder of understanding, moves us ... almost to the intensity of trance. The persons upon the stage ... greaten until they are humanity itself.*
> —W. B. YEATS

Tragedy and comedy also differ in their treatment of character. Tragedy tends to focus on a single individual, a person of high rank who confronts the universe and his or her fate as an individual. The tragic figure is ultimately doomed because, although good and noble, this person has a flaw of character or a limitation of knowledge—some mark of humanity—that offsets all his or her goodness. Oedipus wishes to know and to control his own destiny, but he learns too much and is destroyed. Had Oedipus been the son of a shepherd rather than of a king, perhaps the gods would not have taken such an unfortunate interest in his fate.

By contrast, being concerned largely with society, comedies often define their characters in terms of social roles. In *The Importance of Being Earnest* both Jack and Algernon are, for plot purposes, unmarried young men but not eminently eligible husbands-to-be, Jack because of his uncertain parentage and Algernon because of his lack of money. They have individual traits—Algernon eats too much and is somewhat pretentious; Jack tries to be more straightforward—but what distinguishes them is not so important as what they have in common according to societal standards. Many comic characters become stereotypes. Lady Bracknell, for example, is a middle-aged, meddling matron, ideally placed by age and position to exert tremendous social influence. Other stereotypes in the play include Miss Prism, the desperate spinster, and Dr. Chasuble, the slightly dim clergyman.

Finally, tragedy and comedy can be defined by their endings. In most tragedies, the hero is enlightened, coming to understand the meaning of his or her deeds and to accept an appropriate punishment. At the end of *Oedipus the King* the blind hero sees and understands. Accepting his ostracism, he leaves Thebes a chastened but wiser man. Many tragic heroes die, as Hamlet does, but understanding, not death itself, ends the tragedy. Hamlet understands what has happened and in his last moments tries to restore order to the kingdom, asking for himself only that people may know the truth about what he has done. In comedy, on the other hand, the resolution occurs when one or more characters take a proper social role. Most frequently, this means the marriage of an eligible young woman and an equally eligible young man. The society of *Earnest* believes that young men like Jack and Algernon and young women like Gwendolen and Cecily should marry and get about the business of having children and raising them to continue the society. Even the marriage of Miss Prism and Dr. Chasuble serves social purposes. The society of the play prefers married clergymen to celibates and has no really useful function for a middle-aged spinster.

*Oedipus the King* and *The Importance of Being Earnest* clearly display the assumptions and features of tragedy and comedy, respectively. Many good plays provide less clear examples of these genres, and many other categories have been used over the centuries to describe the shape and conventions of groups of dramatic texts. Still, *tragedy* and *comedy* are two of the most important genres to explore in any study of the various classifications of drama.

# SOPHOCLES

## *Oedipus the King*[1]

CHARACTERS

OEDIPUS, *King of Thebes*
JOCASTA, *His Wife*
CREON, *His Brother-in-Law*
TEIRESIAS, *an Old Blind Prophet*
A PRIEST
FIRST MESSENGER
SECOND MESSENGER
A HERDSMAN
A CHORUS *of Old Men of Thebes*

SCENE: *In front of the palace of* OEDIPUS *at Thebes. To the right of the stage near the altar stands the* PRIEST *with a crowd of children.* OEDIPUS *emerges from the central door.*

OEDIPUS: Children, young sons and daughters of old Cadmus,[2]
why do you sit here with your suppliant crowns?
The town is heavy with a mingled burden
of sounds and smells, of groans and hymns and incense;
5  I did not think it fit that I should hear
of this from messengers but came myself,—
I Oedipus whom all men call the Great.

[*He turns to the* PRIEST.]

You're old and they are young; come, speak for them.
What do you fear or want, that you sit here
10  suppliant? Indeed I'm willing to give all

---

1. Translated by David Grene.  2. The founder of Thebes.

  that you may need; I would be very hard
  should I not pity suppliants like these.
PRIEST: O ruler of my country, Oedipus,
  you see our company around the altar;
  you see our ages; some of us, like these,         15
  who cannot yet fly far, and some of us
  heavy with age; these children are the chosen
  among the young, and I the priest of Zeus.
  Within the market place sit others crowned
  with suppliant garlands, at the double shrine      20
  of Pallas[3] and the temple where Ismenus
  gives oracles by fire. King, you yourself
  have seen our city reeling like a wreck
  already; it can scarcely lift its prow
  out of the depths, out of the bloody surf.        25
  A blight is on the fruitful plants of the earth,
  a blight is on the cattle in the fields,
  a blight is on our women that no children
  are born to them; a God that carries fire,
  a deadly pestilence, is on our town,          30
  strikes us and spares not, and the house of Cadmus
  is emptied of its people while black Death
  grows rich in groaning and in lamentation.
  We have not come as suppliants to this altar
  because we thought of you as of a God,        35
  but rather judging you the first of men
  in all the chances of this life and when
  we mortals have to do with more than man.
  You came and by your coming saved our city,
  freed us from tribute which we paid of old       40
  to the Sphinx, cruel singer. This you did
  in virtue of no knowledge we could give you,
  in virtue of no teaching; it was God
  that aided you, men say, and you are held
  with God's assistance to have saved our lives.      45
  Now Oedipus, Greatest in all men's eyes,
  here falling at your feet we all entreat you,
  find us some strength for rescue.
  Perhaps you'll hear a wise word from some God,
  perhaps you will learn something from a man      50
  (for I have seen that for the skilled of practice
  the outcome of their counsels live the most).
  Noblest of men, go, and raise up our city,
  go,—and give heed. For now this land of ours
  calls you its savior since you saved it once.       55
  So, let us never speak about your reign
  as of a time when first our feet were set

---

3. Athena, the goddess of wisdom.

secure on high, but later fell to ruin.
Raise up our city, save it and raise it up.
60 Once you have brought us luck with happy omen;
be no less now in fortune.
If you will rule this land, as now you rule it,
better to rule it full of men than empty.
For neither tower nor ship is anything
65 when empty, and none live in it together.
OEDIPUS: I pity you, children. You have come full of longing,
but I have known the story before you told it
only too well. I know you are all sick,
yet there is not one of you, sick though you are,
70 that is as sick as I myself.
Your several sorrows each have single scope
and touch but one of you. My spirit groans
for city and myself and you at once.
You have not roused me like a man from sleep;
75 know that I have given many tears to this,
gone many ways wandering in thought,
but as I thought I found only one remedy
and that I took. I sent Menoeceus' son
Creon, Jocasta's brother, to Apollo,
80 to his Pythian temple,
that he might learn there by what act or word
I could save this city. As I count the days,
it vexes me what ails him; he is gone
far longer than he needed for the journey.
85 But when he comes, then, may I prove a villain,
if I shall not do all the God commands.
PRIEST: Thanks for your gracious words. Your servants here
signal that Creon is this moment coming.
OEDIPUS: His face is bright. O holy Lord Apollo,
90 grant that his news too may be bright for us
and bring us safety.
PRIEST: It is happy news,
I think, for else his head would not be crowned
with sprigs of fruitful laurel.
OEDIPUS:                         We will know soon,
95 he's within hail. Lord Creon, my good brother,
what is the word you bring us from the God?

[CREON *enters*.]

CREON: A good word,—for things hard to bear themselves
if in the final issue all is well
I count complete good fortune.
OEDIPUS:                         What do you mean?
100 What you have said so far
leaves me uncertain whether to trust or fear.
CREON: If you will hear my news before these others

I am ready to speak, or else to go within.
OEDIPUS: Speak it to all;
the grief I bear, I bear it more for these
than for my own heart.
CREON: I will tell you, then,
what I heard from the God.
King Phoebus[4] in plain words commanded us
to drive out a pollution from our land,
pollution grown ingrained within the land;
drive it out, said the God, not cherish it,
till it's past cure.
OEDIPUS: What is the rite
of purification? How shall it be done?
CREON: By banishing a man, or expiation
of blood by blood, since it is murder guilt
which holds our city in this destroying storm.
OEDIPUS: Who is this man whose fate the God pronounces?
CREON: My Lord, before you piloted the state
we had a king called Laius.
OEDIPUS: I know of him by hearsay. I have not seen him.
CREON: The God commanded clearly: let some one
punish with force this dead man's murderers.
OEDIPUS: Where are they in the world? Where would a trace
of this old crime be found? It would be hard
to guess where.
CREON: The clue is in this land;
that which is sought is found;
the unheeded thing escapes:
so said the God.
OEDIPUS: Was it at home,
or in the country that death came upon him,
or in another country travelling?
CREON: He went, he said himself, upon an embassy,
but never returned when he set out from home.
OEDIPUS: Was there no messenger, no fellow traveller
who knew what happened? Such a one might tell
something of use.
CREON: They were all killed save one. He fled in terror
and he could tell us nothing in clear terms
of what he knew, nothing, but one thing only.
OEDIPUS: What was it?
If we could even find a slim beginning
in which to hope, we might discover much.
CREON: This man said that the robbers they encountered
were many and the hands that did the murder
were many; it was no man's single power.
OEDIPUS: How could a robber dare a deed like this

---

4. Apollo, the god of truth.

were he not helped with money from the city,
money and treachery?
CREON:                     That indeed was thought.
But Laius was dead and in our trouble
there was none to help.
150 OEDIPUS: What trouble was so great to hinder you
inquiring out the murder of your king?
CREON: The riddling Sphinx induced us to neglect
mysterious crimes and rather seek solution
of troubles at our feet.
155 OEDIPUS: I will bring this to light again. King Phoebus[5]
fittingly took this care about the dead,
and you too fittingly.
And justly you will see in me an ally,
a champion of my country and the God.
160 For when I drive pollution from the land
I will not serve a distant friend's advantage,
but act in my own interest. Whoever
he was that killed the king may readily
wish to dispatch me with his murderous hand;
165 so helping the dead king I help myself.

Come, children, take your supplicant boughs and go;
up from the altars now. Call the assembly
and let it meet upon the understanding
that I'll do everything. God will decide
170 whether we prosper or remain in sorrow.
PRIEST: Rise, children—it was this we came to seek,
which of himself the king now offers us.
May Phoebus who gave us the oracle
come to our rescue and stay the plague.

[*Exeunt*[6] *all but the* CHORUS.]

175 CHORUS: [*Strophe.*] What is the sweet spoken word of God from the shrine of Pythorich in gold
that has come to glorious Thebes?
I am stretched on the rack of doubt, and terror and trembling hold
my heart, O Delian Healer, and I worship full of fears
for what doom you will bring to pass, new or renewed in the revolving years.
180 Speak to me, immortal voice,
child of golden Hope.

[*Antistrophe.*]

---

5. Apollo, god of light.
6. Exit the stage (Latin for "they go out"). *Strophe* (line 175): in Greek stagecraft, a choral song and the corresponding dance of the chorus to one side. *Antistrophe* (stage direction following line 181): after the strophe, the chorus's answering song and returning dance.

First I call on you, Athene,[7] deathless daughter of Zeus,
and Artemis, Earth Upholder,
who sits in the midst of the market place in the throne which men call Fame,
and Phoebus, the Far Shooter, three averters of Fate, 185
come to us now, if ever before, when ruin rushed upon the state,
you drove destruction's flame away
out of our land.

[*Strophe.*]

Our sorrows defy number;
all the ship's timbers are rotten; 190
taking of thought is no spear for the driving away of the plague.
There are no growing children in this famous land;
there are no women bearing the pangs of childbirth.
You may see them one with another, like birds swift on the wing,
quicker than fire unmastered, 195
speeding away to the coast of the Western God.

[*Antistrophe.*]

In the unnumbered deaths
of its people the city dies;
those children that are born lie dead on the naked earth
unpitied, spreading contagion of death; and grey haired mothers and wives 200
everywhere stand at the altar's edge, suppliant, moaning;
the hymn to the healing God rings out but with it the wailing voices are
    blended.
From these our sufferings grant us, O golden Daughter of Zeus,
glad-faced deliverance.

[*Strophe.*]

There is no clash of brazen shields but our fight is with the War God, 205
a War God ringed with the cries of men, a savage God who burns us;
grant that he turn in racing course backwards out of our country's bounds
to the great palace of Amphitrite[8] or where the waves of the Thracian sea
deny the stranger safe anchorage.
Whatsoever escapes the night 210
at last the light of day revisits;
so smite the War God, Father Zeus,
beneath your thunderbolt,
for you are the Lord of the lightning, the lightning that carries fire.

[*Antistrophe.*]

And your unconquered arrow shafts, winged by the golden corded bow, 215
Lycean King, I beg to be at our side for help;
and the gleaming torches of Artemis with which she scours the Lycean hills,

---

7. Goddess of both war and peace as well as wisdom. Artemis (line 183): goddess of the earth and the hunt, twin sister of Apollo.
8. Queen of the sea and wife of Poseidon, sometimes said to dwell in the Atlantic Ocean.

and I call on the God with the turban of gold, who gave his name to this
   country of ours,
the Bacchic God with the wind flushed face,
220 Evian One, who travel
with the Maenad[9] company,
combat the God that burns us
with your torch of pine;
for the God that is our enemy is a God unhonoured among the Gods.

[OEDIPUS *returns*.]

225 OEDIPUS: For what you ask me—if you will hear my words,
and hearing welcome them and fight the plague,
you will find strength and lightening of your load.
Hark to me; what I say to you, I say
as one that is a stranger to the story
230 as stranger to the deed. For I would not
be far upon the track if I alone
were tracing it without a clue. But now,
since after all was finished, I became
a citizen among you, citizens—
235 now I proclaim to all the men of Thebes:
who so among you knows the murderer
by whose hand Laius, son of Labdacus,
died—I command him to tell everything
to me,—yes, though he fears himself to take the blame
240 on his own head; for bitter punishment
he shall have none, but leave this land unharmed.
Or if he knows the murderer, another,
a foreigner, still let him speak the truth.
For I will pay him and be grateful, too.
245 But if you shall keep silence, if perhaps
some one of you, to shield a guilty friend,
or for his own sake shall reject my words—
hear what I shall do then:
I forbid that man, whoever he be, my land,
250 my land where I hold sovereignty and throne;
and I forbid any to welcome him
or cry him greeting or make him a sharer
in sacrifice or offering to the gods,
or give him water for his hands to wash.
255 I command all to drive him from their homes,
since he is our pollution, as the oracle
of Pytho's god proclaimed him now to me.
So I stand forth a champion of the god
and of the man who died.
260 Upon the murderer I invoke this curse—

---

9. Female worshipers of Bacchus (see line 219): Dionysus (Bacchus to the Romans), god of fertility and wine. *Evian one* (line 220): Dionysus (also known as Evius).

whether he is one man and all unknown,
or one of many—may he wear out his life
in misery to miserable doom!
If with my knowledge he lives at my hearth
I pray that I myself may feel my curse. 265
On you I lay my charge to fulfill all this
for me, for the god, and for this land of ours
destroyed and blighted, by the god forsaken.

Even were this no matter of God's ordinance
it would not fit you so to leave it lie, 270
unpurified, since a good man is dead
and one that was a king. Search it out.
Since I am now the holder of his office,
and have his bed and wife that once was his,
and had his line not been unfortunate 275
we would have common children—(fortune leaped
upon his head)—because of all these things,
I fight in his defence as for my father,
and I shall try all means to take the murderer
of Laius the son of Labdacus 280
the son of Polydorus and before him
of Cadmus and before him of Agenor.
Those who do not obey me, may the Gods
grant no crops springing from the ground they plough
nor children to their women! May a fate 285
like this, or one still worse than this consume them!
For you whom these words please, the other Thebans,
may Justice as your ally and all the Gods
live with you, blessing you now and for ever!

CHORUS: As you have held me to my oath, I speak: 290
 I neither killed the king nor can declare
 the killer; but since Phoebus set the quest
 it is his part to tell who the man is.
OEDIPUS: Right; but to put compulsion on the Gods
 against their will—no man can do that. 295
CHORUS: May I then say what I think second best?
OEDIPUS: If there's a third best, too, spare not to tell it.
CHORUS: I know that what the Lord Teiresias
 sees, is most often what the Lord Apollo
 sees. If you should inquire of this from him 300
 you might find out most clearly.
OEDIPUS: Even in this my actions have not been sluggard.
 On Creon's word I have sent two messengers
 and why the prophet is not here already
 I have been wondering.
CHORUS:                His skill apart 305
 there is besides only an old faint story.
OEDIPUS: What is it?

I look at every story.
CHORUS: It was said
that he was killed by certain wayfarers.
310 OEDIPUS: I heard that, too, but no one saw the killer.
CHORUS: Yet if he has a share of fear at all,
his courage will not stand firm, hearing your curse.
OEDIPUS: The man who in the doing did not shrink
will fear no word.
CHORUS: Here comes his prosecutor:
315 led by your men the godly prophet comes
in whom alone of mankind truth is native.

[*Enter* TEIRESIAS, *led by a* LITTLE BOY.]

OEDIPUS: Teiresias, you are versed in everything,
things teachable and things not to be spoken,
things of the heaven and earth-creeping things.
320 You have no eyes but in your mind you know
with what a plague our city is afflicted.
My lord, in you alone we find a champion,
in you alone one that can rescue us.
Perhaps you have not heard the messengers,
325 but Phoebus sent in answer to our sending
an oracle declaring that our freedom
from this disease would only come when we
should learn the names of those who killed King Laius,
and kill them or expel from our country.
330 Do not begrudge us oracles from birds,
or any other way of prophecy
within your skill; save yourself and the city,
save me; redeem the debt of our pollution
that lies on us because of this dead man.
335 We are in your hands; pains are most nobly taken
to help another when you have means and power.
TEIRESIAS: Alas, how terrible is wisdom when
it brings no profit to the man that's wise!
This I knew well, but had forgotten it,
else I would not have come here.
340 OEDIPUS: What is this?
How sad you are now you have come!
TEIRESIAS: Let me
go home. It will be easiest for us both
to bear our several destinies to the end
if you will follow my advice.
OEDIPUS: You'd rob us
345 of this your gift of prophecy? You talk
as one who had no care for law nor love
for Thebes who reared you.
TEIRESIAS: Yes, but I see that even your own words
miss the mark; therefore I must fear for mine.

OEDIPUS: For God's sake if you know of anything, 350
  do not turn from us; all of us kneel to you,
  all of us here, your suppliants.
TEIRESIAS: All of you here know nothing. I will not
  bring to the light of day my troubles, mine—
  rather than call them yours.
OEDIPUS:           What do you mean? 355
  You know of something but refuse to speak.
  Would you betray us and destroy the city?
TEIRESIAS: I will not bring this pain upon us both,
  neither on you nor on myself. Why is it
  you question me and waste your labour? I 360
  will tell you nothing.
OEDIPUS: You would provoke a stone! Tell us, you villain,
  tell us, and do not stand there quietly
  unmoved and balking at the issue.
TEIRESIAS: You blame my temper but you do not see 365
  your own that lives within you; it is me
  you chide.
OEDIPUS: Who would not feel his temper rise
  at words like these with which you shame our city?
TEIRESIAS: Of themselves things will come, although I hide them 370
  and breathe no word of them.
OEDIPUS:           Since they will come
  tell them to me.
TEIRESIAS:           I will say nothing further.
  Against this answer let your temper rage
  as wildly as you will.
OEDIPUS:           Indeed I am
  so angry I shall not hold back a jot 375
  of what I think. For I would have you know
  I think you were complotter of the deed
  and doer of the deed save in so far
  as for the actual killing. Had you had eyes
  I would have said alone you murdered him. 380
TEIRESIAS: Yes? Then I warn you faithfully to keep
  the letter of your proclamation and
  from this day forth to speak no word of greeting
  to these nor me; you are the land's pollution.
OEDIPUS: How shamelessly you started up this taunt! 385
  How do you think you will escape?
TEIRESIAS:           I have.
  I have escaped; the truth is what I cherish
  and that's my strength.
OEDIPUS:           And who has taught you truth?
  Not your profession surely!
TEIRESIAS:           You have taught me,
  for you have made me speak against my will. 390
OEDIPUS: Speak what? Tell me again that I may learn it better.

TEIRESIAS: Did you not understand before or would you
    provoke me into speaking?
OEDIPUS:                    I did not grasp it,
    not so to call it known. Say it again.
395 TEIRESIAS: I say you are the murderer of the king
    whose murderer you seek.
OEDIPUS:            Not twice you shall
    say calumnies like this and stay unpunished.
TEIRESIAS: Shall I say more to tempt your anger more?
OEDIPUS: As much as you desire; it will be said
    in vain.
400 TEIRESIAS:        I say that with those you love best
    you live in foulest shame unconsciously
    and do not see where you are in calamity.
OEDIPUS: Do you imagine you can always talk
    like this, and live to laugh at it hereafter?
405 TEIRESIAS: Yes, if the truth has anything of strength.
OEDIPUS: It has, but not for you; it has no strength
    for you because you are blind in mind and ears
    as well as in your eyes.
TEIRESIAS:            You are a poor wretch
    to taunt me with the very insults which
410 every one soon will heap upon yourself.
OEDIPUS: Your life is one long night so that you cannot
    hurt me or any other who sees the light.
TEIRESIAS: It is not fate that I should be your ruin,
    Apollo is enough; it is his care
    to work this out.
415 OEDIPUS:            Was this your own design
    or Creon's?
TEIRESIAS:            Creon is no hurt to you,
    but you are to yourself.
OEDIPUS: Wealth, sovereignty and skill outmatching skill
    for the contrivance of an envied life!
420 Great store of jealousy fill your treasury chests,
    if my friend Creon, friend from the first and loyal,
    thus secretly attacks me, secretly
    desires to drive me out and secretly
    suborns this juggling, trick devising quack,
425 this wily beggar who has only eyes
    for his own gains, but blindness in his skill.
    For, tell me, where have you seen clear, Teiresias,
    with your prophetic eyes? When the dark singer,
    the sphinx, was in your country, did you speak
430 word of deliverance to its citizens?
    And yet the riddle's answer was not the province
    of a chance comer. It was a prophet's task
    and plainly you had no such gift of prophecy
    from birds nor otherwise from any God

    to glean a word of knowledge. But I came,
      Oedipus, who knew nothing, and I stopped her.
    I solved the riddle by my wit alone.
    Mine was no knowledge got from birds.[1] And now
    you would expel me,
    because you think that you will find a place
    by Creon's throne. I think you will be sorry,
    both you and your accomplice, for your plot
    to drive me out. And did I not regard you
    as an old man, some suffering would have taught you
    that what was in your heart was treason.
CHORUS: We look at this man's words and yours, my king,
    and we find both have spoken them in anger.
    We need no angry words but only thought
    how we may best hit the God's meaning for us.
TEIRESIAS: If you are king, at least I have the right
    no less to speak in my defence against you.
    Of that much I am master. I am no slave
    of yours, but Loxias',[2] and so I shall not
    enroll myself with Creon for my patron.
    Since you have taunted me with being blind,
    here is my word for you.
    You have your eyes but see not where you are
    in sin, nor where you live, nor whom you live with.
    Do you know who your parents are? Unknowing
    you are an enemy to kith and kin
    in death, beneath the earth, and in this life.
    A deadly footed, double striking curse,
    from father and mother both, shall drive you forth
    out of this land, with darkness on your eyes,
    that now have such straight vision. Shall there be
    a place will not be harbour to your cries,
    a corner of Cithaeron[3] will not ring
    in echo to your cries, soon, soon,—
    when you shall learn the secret of your marriage,
    which steered you to a haven in this house,—
    haven no haven, after lucky voyage?
    And of the multitude of other evils
    establishing a grim equality
    between you and your children, you know nothing.
    So, muddy with contempt my words and Creon's!
    Misery shall grind no man as it will you.
OEDIPUS: Is it endurable that I should hear
    such words from him? Go and a curse go with you
    Quick, home with you! Out of my house at once!
TEIRESIAS: I would not have come either had you not called me.

---

1. Prophetic knowledge derived from observing the flight of birds, or sometimes from inspecting bird entrails.   2. Yet another name for Apollo.   3. The mountain where Oedipus was abandoned as a child.

OEDIPUS: I did not know then you would talk like a fool—
or it would have been long before I called you.
TEIRESIAS: I am a fool then, as it seems to you—
but to the parents who have bred you, wise.
485 OEDIPUS: What parents? Stop! Who are they of all the world?
TEIRESIAS: This day will show your birth and will destroy you.
OEDIPUS: How needlessly your riddles darken everything.
TEIRESIAS: But it's in riddle answering you are strongest.
OEDIPUS: Yes. Taunt me where you will find me great.
490 TEIRESIAS: It is this very luck that has destroyed you.
OEDIPUS: I do not care, if it has saved this city.
TEIRESIAS: Well, I will go. Come, boy, lead me away.
OEDIPUS: Yes, lead him off. So long as you are here,
you'll be a stumbling block and a vexation;
once gone, you will not trouble me again.
495 TEIRESIAS: I have said
what I came here to say not fearing your
countenance: there is no way you can hurt me.
I tell you, king, this man, this murderer
(whom you have long declared you are in search of,
500 indicting him in threatening proclamation
as murderer of Laius)—he is here.
In name he is a stranger among citizens
but soon he will be shown to be a citizen
true native Theban, and he'll have no joy
505 of the discovery: blindness for sight
and beggary for riches his exchange,
he shall go journeying to a foreign country
tapping his way before him with a stick.
He shall be proved father and brother both
510 to his own children in his house; to her
that gave him birth, a son and husband both;
a fellow sower in his father's bed
with that same father that he murdered.
Go within, reckon that out, and if you find me
515 mistaken, say I have no skill in prophecy.

[*Exeunt separately* TEIRESIAS *and* OEDIPUS.]

CHORUS: [*Strophe.*] Who is the man proclaimed
by Delphi's prophetic rock
as the bloody handed murderer,
the doer of deeds that none dare name?
520 Now is the time for him to run
with a stronger foot
than Pegasus[4]
for the child of Zeus leaps in arms upon him
with fire and the lightning bolt,

4. Winged horse.

and terribly close on his heels
are the Fates[5] that never miss.

[*Antistrophe.*]

Lately from snowy Parnassus[6]
clearly the voice flashed forth,
bidding each Theban track him down,
the unknown murderer.
In the savage forests he lurks and in
the caverns like
the mountain bull.
He is sad and lonely, and lonely his feet
that carry him far from the navel of earth;
but its prophecies, ever living,
flutter around his head.

[*Strophe.*]

The augur has spread confusion,
terrible confusion;
I do not approve what was said
nor can I deny it.
I do not know what to say;
I am in a flutter of foreboding;
I never heard in the present
nor past of a quarrel between
the sons of Labdacus and Polybus,[7]
that I might bring as proof
in attacking the popular fame
of Oedipus, seeking
to take vengeance for undiscovered
death in the line of Labdacus.

[*Antistrophe.*]

Truly Zeus and Apollo are wise
and in human things all knowing;
but amongst men there is no
distinct judgment, between the prophet
and me—which of us is right.
One man may pass another in wisdom
but I would never agree
with those that find fault with the king
till I should see the word
proved right beyond doubt. For once
in visible form the Sphinx
came on him and all of us
saw his wisdom and in that test

---

5. Goddesses who decide the course of human life.   6. Mountain sacred to Apollo.
7. King who adopted Oedipus.

565     he saved the city. So he will not be condemned by my mind.

        [*Enter* CREON.]

CREON: Citizens, I have come because I heard
    deadly words spread about me, that the king
    accuses me. I cannot take that from him.
    If he believes that in these present troubles
570 he has been wronged by me in word or deed
    I do not want to live on with the burden
    of such a scandal on me. The report
    injures me doubly and most vitally—
    for I'll be called a traitor to my city
575 and traitor also to my friends and you.
CHORUS: Perhaps it was a sudden gust of anger
    that forced that insult from him, and no judgment.
CREON: But did he say that it was in compliance
    with schemes of mine that the seer told him lies?
580 CHORUS: Yes, he said that, but why, I do not know.
CREON: Were his eyes straight in his head? Was his mind right
    when he accused me in this fashion?
CHORUS: I do not know; I have no eyes to see
    what princes do. Here comes the king himself.

        [*Enter* OEDIPUS.]

585 OEDIPUS: You, sir, how is it you come here? Have you so much
    brazen-faced daring that you venture in
    my house although you are proved manifestly
    the murderer of that man, and though you tried,
    openly, highway robbery of my crown?
590 For God's sake, tell me what you saw in me,
    what cowardice or what stupidity,
    that made you lay a plot like this against me?
    Did you imagine I should not observe
    the crafty scheme that stole upon me or
595 seeing it, take no means to counter it?
    Was it not stupid of you to make the attempt,
    to try to hunt down royal power without
    the people at your back or friends? For only
    with the people at your back or money can
600 the hunt end in the capture of a crown.
CREON: Do you know what you're doing? Will you listen
    to words to answer yours, and then pass judgment?
OEDIPUS: You're quick to speak, but I am slow to grasp you,
    for I have found you dangerous,—and my foe.
605 CREON: First of all hear what I shall say to that.
OEDIPUS: At least don't tell me that you are not guilty.
CREON: If you think obstinacy without wisdom
    a valuable possession, you are wrong.
OEDIPUS: And you are wrong if you believe that one,

    a criminal, will not be punished only  
    because he is my kinsman.  
CREON:                      This is but just—  
    but tell me, then, of what offense I'm guilty?  
OEDIPUS: Did you or did you not urge me to send  
    to this prophetic mumbler?  
CREON:                      I did indeed,  
    and I shall stand by what I told you.  
OEDIPUS: How long ago is it since Laius . . .  
CREON: What about Laius? I don't understand.  
OEDIPUS: Vanished—died—was murdered?  
CREON:                      It is long,  
    a long, long time to reckon.  
OEDIPUS:                    Was this prophet  
    in the profession then?  
CREON:                      He was, and honoured  
    as highly as he is today.  
OEDIPUS: At that time did he say a word about me?  
CREON: Never, at least when I was near him.  
OEDIPUS: You never made a search for the dead man?  
CREON: We searched, indeed, but never learned of anything.  
OEDIPUS: Why did our wise old friend not say this then?  
CREON: I don't know; and when I know nothing, I  
    usually hold my tongue.  
OEDIPUS:                    You know this much,  
    and can declare this much if you are loyal.  
CREON: What is it? If I know, I'll not deny it.  
OEDIPUS: That he would not have said that I killed Laius  
    had he not met you first.  
CREON:                      You know yourself  
    whether he said this, but I demand that I  
    should hear as much from you as you from me.  
OEDIPUS: Then hear,—I'll not be proved a murderer.  
CREON: Well, then. You're married to my sister.  
OEDIPUS:                    Yes,  
    that I am not disposed to deny.  
CREON:                      You rule  
    this country giving her an equal share  
    in the government?  
OEDIPUS:                    Yes, everything she wants  
    she has from me.  
CREON:                      And I, as thirdsman to you,  
    am rated as the equal of you two?  
OEDIPUS: Yes, and it's there you've proved yourself false friend.  
CREON: Not if you will reflect on it as I do.  
    Consider, first, if you think any one  
    would choose to rule and fear rather than rule  
    and sleep untroubled by a fear if power  
    were equal in both cases. I, at least,

I was not born with such a frantic yearning
to be a king—but to do what kings do.
650 And so it is with every one who has learned
wisdom and self-control. As it stands now,
the prizes are all mine—and without fear.
But if I were the king myself, I must
do much that went against the grain.
655 How should despotic rule seem sweeter to me
than painless power and an assured authority?
I am not so besotted yet that I
want other honours than those that come with profit.
Now every man's my pleasure; every man greets me;
660 now those who are your suitors fawn on me,—
success for them depends upon my favour.
Why should I let all this go to win that?
My mind would not be traitor if it's wise;
I am no treason lover, of my nature,
665 nor would I ever dare to join a plot.
Prove what I say. Go to the oracle
at Pytho and inquire about the answers,
if they are as I told you. For the rest,
if you discover I laid any plot
670 together with the seer, kill me, I say,
not only by your vote but by my own.
But do not charge me on obscure opinion
without some proof to back it. It's not just
lightly to count your knaves as honest men,
675 nor honest men as knaves. To throw away
an honest friend is, as it were, to throw
your life away, which a man loves the best.
In time you will know all with certainty;
time is the only test of honest men,
680 one day is space enough to know a rogue.
CHORUS: His words are wise, king, if one fears to fall.
Those who are quick of temper are not safe.
OEDIPUS: When he that plots against me secretly
moves quickly, I must quickly counterplot.
685 If I wait taking no decisive measure
his business will be done, and mine be spoiled.
CREON: What do you want to do then? Banish me?
OEDIPUS: No, certainly; kill you, not banish you.[8]
CREON: I do not think that you've your wits about you.
OEDIPUS: For my own interests, yes.
690 CREON:                 But for mine, too,
you should think equally.

---

8. *Translator's note:* Two lines omitted here owing to the confusion in the dialogue consequent on the loss of a third line. The lines as they stand in Jebb's edition (1902) are: OED.: That you may show what manner of thing is envy. / CREON: You speak as one that will not yield or trust. / [OED. *lost line.*]

OEDIPUS: You are a rogue.
CREON: Suppose you do not understand?
OEDIPUS: But yet
  I must be ruler.
CREON: Not if you rule badly.
OEDIPUS: O, city, city!
CREON: I too have some share
  in the city; it is not yours alone.
CHORUS: Stop, my lords! Here—and in the nick of time
  I see Jocasta coming from the house;
  with her help lay the quarrel that now stirs you.

[*Enter* JOCASTA.]

JOCASTA: For shame! Why have you raised this foolish squabbling
  brawl? Are you not ashamed to air your private
  griefs when the country's sick? Go in, you, Oedipus,
  and you, too, Creon, into the house. Don't magnify
  your nothing troubles.
CREON: Sister, Oedipus,
  your husband, thinks he has the right to do
  terrible wrongs—he has but to choose between
  two terrors: banishing or killing me.
OEDIPUS: He's right, Jocasta; for I find him plotting
  with knavish tricks against my person.
CREON: That God may never bless me! May I die
  accursed, if I have been guilty of
  one tittle of the charge you bring against me!
JOCASTA: I beg you, Oedipus, trust him in this,
  spare him for the sake of this his oath to God,
  for my sake, and the sake of those who stand here.
CHORUS: Be gracious, be merciful,
  we beg of you.
OEDIPUS: In what would you have me yield?
CHORUS: He has been no silly child in the past.
  He is strong in his oath now.
  Spare him.
OEDIPUS: Do you know what you ask?
CHORUS: Yes.
OEDIPUS: Tell me then.
CHORUS: He has been your friend before all men's eyes; do not cast him
  away dishonoured on an obscure conjecture.
OEDIPUS: I would have you know that this request of yours
  really requests my death or banishment.
CHORUS: May the Sun God,[9] king of Gods, forbid! May I die without God's
  blessing, without friends' help, if I had any such thought. But my
  spirit is broken by my unhappiness for my wasting country; and
  this would but add troubles amongst ourselves to the other troubles.

---

9. Helios, closely associated with Apollo, the god of light.

OEDIPUS: Well, let him go then—if I must die ten times for it,
  or be sent out dishonoured into exile.
  It is your lips that prayed for him I pitied,
735  not his; wherever he is, I shall hate him.
CREON: I see you sulk in yielding and you're dangerous
  when you are out of temper; natures like yours
  are justly heaviest for themselves to bear.
OEDIPUS: Leave me alone! Take yourself off, I tell you.
740 CREON: I'll go, you have not known me, but they have,
  and they have known my innocence.

  [*Exit.*]

CHORUS: Won't you take him inside, lady?
JOCASTA: Yes, when I've found out what was the matter.
CHORUS: There was some misconceived suspicion of a story, and on the other
745  side the sting of injustice.
JOCASTA: So, on both sides?
CHORUS: Yes.
JOCASTA: What was the story?
CHORUS: I think it best, in the interests of the country, to leave it where it
  ended.
750 OEDIPUS: You see where you have ended, straight of judgment
  although you are, by softening my anger.
CHORUS: Sir, I have said before and I say again—be sure that I would have been
  proved a madman, bankrupt in sane council, if I should put you away, you
  who steered the country I love safely when she was crazed with troubles. God
755  grant that now, too, you may prove a fortunate guide for us.
JOCASTA: Tell me, my lord, I beg of you, what was it
  that roused your anger so?
OEDIPUS:             Yes, I will tell you.
  I honour you more than I honour them.
  It was Creon and the plots he laid against me.
760 JOCASTA: Tell me—if you can clearly tell the quarrel—
OEDIPUS:                Creon says
  that I'm the murderer of Laius.
JOCASTA: Of his own knowledge or on information?
OEDIPUS: He sent this rascal prophet to me, since
  he keeps his own mouth clean of any guilt.
765 JOCASTA: Do not concern yourself about this matter;
  listen to me and learn that human beings
  have no part in the craft of prophecy.
  Of that I'll show you a short proof.
  There was an oracle once that came to Laius,—
770 I will not say that it was Phoebus' own,
  but it was from his servants—and it told him
  that it was fate that he should die a victim
  at the hands of his own son, a son to be born
  of Laius and me. But, see now, he,
775 the king, was killed by foreign highway robbers

at a place where three roads meet—so goes the story;
and for the son—before three days were out
after his birth King Laius pierced his ankles
and by the hands of others cast him forth
upon a pathless hillside. So Apollo
failed to fulfill his oracle to the son,
that he should kill his father, and to Laius
also proved false in that the thing he feared,
death at his son's hands, never came to pass.
So clear in this case were the oracles,
so clear and false. Give them no heed, I say;
what God discovers need of, easily
he shows to us himself.

OEDIPUS:                 O dear Jocasta,
as I hear this from you, there comes upon me
a wandering of the soul—I could run mad.

JOCASTA: What trouble is it, that you turn again
and speak like this?

OEDIPUS:                 I thought I heard you say
that Laius was killed at a crossroads.

JOCASTA: Yes, that was how the story went and still
that word goes round.

OEDIPUS:               Where is this place, Jocasta,
where he was murdered?

JOCASTA:               Phocis is the country
and the road splits there, one of two roads from Delphi,
another comes from Daulia.

OEDIPUS:               How long ago is this?

JOCASTA: The news came to the city just before
you became king and all men's eyes looked to you.
What is it, Oedipus, that's in your mind?

OEDIPUS: What have you designed, O Zeus, to do with me?

JOCASTA: What is the thought that troubles your heart?

OEDIPUS: Don't ask me yet—tell me of Laius—
How did he look? How old or young was he?

JOCASTA: He was a tall man and his hair was grizzled
already—nearly white—and in his form
not unlike you.

OEDIPUS:               O God, I think I have
called curses on myself in ignorance.

JOCASTA: What do you mean? I am terrified
when I look at you.

OEDIPUS:               I have a deadly fear
that the old seer had eyes. You'll show me more
if you can tell me one more thing.

JOCASTA:               I will.
I'm frightened,—but if I can understand,
I'll tell you all you ask.

OEDIPUS:               How was his company?

Had he few with him when he went this journey,
or many servants, as would suit a prince?
JOCASTA: In all there were but five, and among them
a herald; and one carriage for the king.
820 OEDIPUS: It's plain—it's plain—who was it told you this?
JOCASTA: The only servant that escaped safe home.
OEDIPUS: Is he at home now?
JOCASTA:                        No, when he came home again
and saw you king and Laius was dead,
he came to me and touched my hand and begged
825 that I should send him to the fields to be
my shepherd and so he might see the city
as far off as he might. So I
sent him away. He was an honest man,
as slaves go, and was worthy of far more
830 than what he asked of me.
OEDIPUS: O, how I wish that he could come back quickly!
JOCASTA: He can. Why is your heart so set on this?
OEDIPUS: O dear Jocasta, I am full of fears
that I have spoken far too much; and therefore
I wish to see this shepherd.
835 JOCASTA:                        He will come;
but, Oedipus, I think I'm worthy too
to know what it is that disquiets you.
OEDIPUS: It shall not be kept from you, since my mind
has gone so far with its forebodings. Whom
840 should I confide in rather than you, who is there
of more importance to me who have passed
through such a fortune?
Polybus was my father, king of Corinth,
and Merope, the Dorian, my mother.
845 I was held greatest of the citizens
in Corinth till a curious chance befell me
as I shall tell you—curious, indeed,
but hardly worth the store I set upon it.
There was a dinner and at it a man,
850 a drunken man, accused me in his drink
of being bastard. I was furious
but held my temper under for that day.
Next day I went and taxed my parents with it;
they took the insult very ill from him,
855 the drunken fellow who had uttered it.
So I was comforted for their part, but
still this thing rankled always, for the story
crept about widely. And I went at last
to Pytho, though my parents did not know.
860 But Phoebus sent me home again unhonoured
in what I came to learn, but he foretold
other and desperate horrors to befall me,
that I was fated to lie with my mother,

and show to daylight an accursed breed
which men would not endure, and I was doomed 865
to be murderer of the father that begot me.
When I heard this I fled, and in the days
that followed I would measure from the stars
the whereabouts of Corinth—yes, I fled
to somewhere where I should not see fulfilled 870
the infamies told in that dreadful oracle.
And as I journeyed I came to the place
where, as you say, this king met with his death.
Jocasta, I will tell you the whole truth.
When I was near the branching of the crossroads, 875
going on foot, I was encountered by
a herald and a carriage with a man in it,
just as you tell me. He that led the way
and the old man himself wanted to thrust me
out of the road by force. I became angry 880
and struck the coachman who was pushing me.
When the old man saw this he watched his moment,
and as I passed he struck me from his carriage,
full on the head with his two pointed goad.
But he was paid in full and presently 885
my stick had struck him backwards from the car
and he rolled out of it. And then I killed them
all. If it happened there was any tie
of kinship twixt this man and Laius,
who is then now more miserable than I, 890
what man on earth so hated by the Gods,
since neither citizen nor foreigner
may welcome me at home or even greet me,
but drive me out of doors? And it is I,
I and no other have so cursed myself. 895
And I pollute the bed of him I killed
by the hands that killed him. Was I not born evil?
Am I not utterly unclean? I had to fly
and in my banishment not even see
my kindred nor set foot in my own country, 900
or otherwise my fate was to be yoked
in marriage with my mother and kill my father,
Polybus who begot me and had reared me.
Would not one rightly judge and say that on me
these things were sent by some malignant God? 905
O no, no, no—O holy majesty
of God on high, may I not see that day!
May I be gone out of men's sight before
I see the deadly taint of this disaster
come upon me. 910
CHORUS: Sir, we too fear these things. But until you see this man face to face
and hear his story, hope.
OEDIPUS: Yes, I have just this much of hope—to wait until the herdsman comes.

JOCASTA: And when he comes, what do you want with him?
915 OEDIPUS: I'll tell you; if I find that his story is the same as yours, I at least will be clear of this guilt.
JOCASTA: Why what so particularly did you learn from my story?
OEDIPUS: You said that he spoke of highway *robbers* who killed Laius. Now if he uses the same number, it was not I who killed him. One man cannot be the
920 same as many. But if he speaks of a man travelling alone, then clearly the burden of the guilt inclines towards me.
JOCASTA: Be sure, at least, that this was how he told the story. He cannot unsay it now, for every one in the city heard it—not I alone. But, Oedipus, even if he diverges from what he said then, he shall never prove that the murder of
925 Laius squares rightly with the prophecy—for Loxias declared that the king should be killed by his own son. And that poor creature did not kill him surely,—for he died himself first. So as far as prophecy goes, henceforward I shall not look to the right hand or the left.
OEDIPUS: Right. But yet, send some one for the peasant to bring him here; do
930 not neglect it.
JOCASTA: I will send quickly. Now let me go indoors. I will do nothing except what pleases you.

[*Exeunt.*]

CHORUS: [*Strophe.*] May destiny ever find me
pious in word and deed
935 prescribed by the laws that live on high:
laws begotten in the clear air of heaven,
whose only father is Olympus;
no mortal nature brought them to birth,
no forgetfulness shall lull them to sleep;
940 for God is great in them and grows not old.

[*Antistrophe.*]

Insolence breeds the tyrant, insolence
if it is glutted with a surfeit, unseasonable, unprofitable,
climbs to the roof-top and plunges
sheer down to the ruin that must be,
945 and there its feet are no service.
But I pray that the God may never
abolish the eager ambition that profits the state.
For I shall never cease to hold the God as our protector.

[*Strophe.*]

If a man walks with haughtiness
950 of hand or word and gives no heed
to Justice and the shrines of Gods
despises—may an evil doom
smite him for his ill-starred pride of heart!—
if he reaps gains without justice
955 and will not hold from impiety
and his fingers itch for untouchable things.

When such things are done, what man shall contrive
to shield his soul from the shafts of the God?
When such deeds are held in honour,
why should I honour the Gods in the dance? 960

[*Antistrophe.*]

No longer to the holy place,
to the navel of earth I'll go
to worship, nor to Abae
nor to Olympia,
unless the oracles are proved to fit, 965
for all men's hands to point at.
O Zeus, if you are rightly called
the sovereign lord, all-mastering,
let this not escape you nor your ever-living power!
The oracles concerning Laius 970
are old and dim and men regard them not.
Apollo is nowhere clear in honour; God's service perishes.

[*Enter* JOCASTA, *carrying garlands.*]

JOCASTA: Princes of the land, I have had the thought to go
to the Gods' temples, bringing in my hand
garlands and gifts of incense, as you see. 975
For Oedipus excites himself too much
at every sort of trouble, not conjecturing,
like a man of sense, what will be from what was,
but he is always at the speaker's mercy,
when he speaks terrors. I can do no good 980
by my advice, and so I came as suppliant
to you, Lycaean Apollo, who are nearest.
These are the symbols of my prayer and this
my prayer: grant us escape free of the curse.
Now when we look to him we are all afraid; 985
he's pilot of our ship and he is frightened.

[*Enter* MESSENGER.]

MESSENGER: Might I learn from you, sirs, where is the house of Oedipus? Or best
of all, if you know, where is the king himself?
CHORUS: This is his house and he is within doors. This lady is his wife and mother
of his children. 990
MESSENGER: God bless you, lady, and God bless your household! God bless Oedipus' noble wife!
JOCASTA: God bless you, sir, for your kind greeting! What do you want of us that
you have come here? What have you to tell us?
MESSENGER: Good news, lady. Good for your house and for your husband. 995
JOCASTA: What is your news? Who sent you to us?
MESSENGER: I come from Corinth and the news I bring will give you pleasure.
Perhaps a little pain too.
JOCASTA: What is this news of double meaning?

MESSENGER: The people of the Isthmus will choose Oedipus to be their king. That is the rumour there.

JOCASTA: But isn't their king still old Polybus?

MESSENGER: No. He is in his grave. Death has got him.

JOCASTA: Is that the truth? Is Oedipus' father dead?

MESSENGER: May I die myself if it be otherwise!

JOCASTA: [*To a* SERVANT.] Be quick and run to the King with the news! O oracles of the Gods, where are you now? It was from this man Oedipus fled, lest he should be his murderer! And now he is dead, in the course of nature, and not killed by Oedipus.

[*Enter* OEDIPUS.]

OEDIPUS: Dearest Jocasta, why have you sent for me?

JOCASTA: Listen to this man and when you hear reflect what is the outcome of the holy oracles of the Gods.

OEDIPUS: Who is he? What is his message for me?

JOCASTA: He is from Corinth and he tells us that your father Polybus is dead and gone.

OEDIPUS: What's this you say, sir? Tell me yourself.

MESSENGER: Since this is the first matter you want clearly told: Polybus has gone down to death. You may be sure of it.

OEDIPUS: By treachery or sickness?

MESSENGER: A small thing will put old bodies asleep.

OEDIPUS: So he died of sickness, it seems,—poor old man!

MESSENGER: Yes, and of age—the long years he had measured.

OEDIPUS: Ha! Ha! O dear Jocasta, why should one look to the Pythian hearth?[1] Why should one look to the birds screaming overhead? They prophesied that I should kill my father! But he's dead, and hidden deep in earth, and I stand here who never laid a hand on spear against him,— unless perhaps he died of longing for me, and thus I am his murderer. But they, the oracles, as they stand—he's taken them away with him, they're dead as he himself is, and worthless.

JOCASTA: That I told you before now.

OEDIPUS: You did, but I was misled by my fear.

JOCASTA: Then lay no more of them to heart, not one.

OEDIPUS: But surely I must fear my mother's bed?

JOCASTA: Why should man fear since chance is all in all for him, and he can clearly foreknow nothing? Best to live lightly, as one can, unthinkingly. As to your mother's marriage bed,—don't fear it. Before this, in dreams too, as well as oracles, many a man has lain with his own mother. But he to whom such things are nothing bears

1. Delphi.

his life most easily.
OEDIPUS: All that you say would be said perfectly
  if she were dead; but since she lives I must
  still fear, although you talk so well, Jocasta.
JOCASTA: Still in your father's death there's light of comfort?
OEDIPUS: Great light of comfort; but I fear the living.
MESSENGER: Who is the woman that makes you afraid?
OEDIPUS: Merope, old man, Polybus' wife.
MESSENGER: What about her frightens the queen and you?
OEDIPUS: A terrible oracle, stranger, from the Gods.
MESSENGER: Can it be told? Or does the sacred law
  forbid another to have knowledge of it?
OEDIPUS: O no! Once on a time Loxias said
  that I should lie with my own mother and
  take on my hands the blood of my own father.
  And so for these long years I've lived away
  from Corinth; it has been to my great happiness;
  but yet it's sweet to see the face of parents.
MESSENGER: This was the fear which drove you out of Corinth?
OEDIPUS: Old man, I did not wish to kill my father.
MESSENGER: Why should I not free you from this fear, sir,
  since I have come to you in all goodwill?
OEDIPUS: You would not find me thankless if you did.
MESSENGER: Why, it was just for this I brought the news,—
  to earn your thanks when you had come safe home.
OEDIPUS: No, I will never come near my parents.
MESSENGER:                    Son,
  it's very plain you don't know what you're doing.
OEDIPUS: What do you mean, old man? For God's sake, tell me.
MESSENGER: If your homecoming is checked by fears like these.
OEDIPUS: Yes, I'm afraid that Phoebus may prove right.
MESSENGER: The murder and the incest?
OEDIPUS:                    Yes, old man;
  that is my constant terror.
MESSENGER:              Do you know
  that all your fears are empty?
OEDIPUS:                How is that,
  if they are father and mother and I their son?
MESSENGER: Because Polybus was no kin to you in blood.
OEDIPUS: What, was not Polybus my father?
MESSENGER: No more than I but just so much.
OEDIPUS:                How can
  my father be my father as much as one
  that's nothing to me?
MESSENGER:          Neither he nor I
  begat you.
OEDIPUS:          Why then did he call me son?
MESSENGER: A gift he took you from these hands of mine.
OEDIPUS: Did he love so much what he took from another's hand?

MESSENGER: His childlessness before persuaded him.
OEDIPUS: Was I a child you bought or found when I
  was given to him?
MESSENGER:          On Cithaeron's slopes
  in the twisting thickets you were found.
OEDIPUS:           And why
  were you a traveller in those parts?
1090 MESSENGER:         I was
  in charge of mountain flocks.
OEDIPUS:          You were a shepherd?
  A hireling vagrant?
MESSENGER:          Yes, but at least at that time
  the man that saved your life, son.
OEDIPUS: What ailed me when you took me in your arms?
1095 MESSENGER: In that your ankles should be witnesses.
OEDIPUS: Why do you speak of that old pain?
MESSENGER:          I loosed you;
  the tendons of your feet were pierced and fettered,—
OEDIPUS: My swaddling clothes brought me a rare disgrace.
MESSENGER: So that from this you're called your present name.[2]
1100 OEDIPUS: Was this my father's doing or my mother's?
  For God's sake, tell me.
MESSENGER:          I don't know, but he
  who gave you to me has more knowledge than I.
OEDIPUS: You yourself did not find me then? You took me
  from someone else?
MESSENGER:          Yes, from another shepherd.
1105 OEDIPUS: Who was he? Do you know him well enough
  to tell?
MESSENGER:          He was called Laius' man.
OEDIPUS: You mean the king who reigned here in the old days?
MESSENGER: Yes, he was that man's shepherd.
OEDIPUS:           Is he alive
  still, so that I could see him?
MESSENGER:          You who live here
  would know that best.
1110 OEDIPUS:         Do any of you here
  know of this shepherd whom he speaks about
  in town or in the fields? Tell me. It's time
  that this was found out once for all.
CHORUS: I think he is none other than the peasant
1115 whom you have sought to see already; but
  Jocasta here can tell us best of that.
OEDIPUS: Jocasta, do you know about this man
  whom we have sent for? Is he the man he mentions?
JOCASTA: Why ask of whom he spoke? Don't give it heed;
1120 nor try to keep in mind what has been said.
  It will be wasted labour.

---

2. *Oedipus* means, literally, "swollen foot."

OEDIPUS:                    With such clues
    I could not fail to bring my birth to light.
JOCASTA: I beg you—do not hunt this out—I beg you,
    if you have any care for your own life.
    What I am suffering is enough.
OEDIPUS:                    Keep up
    your heart, Jocasta. Though I'm proved a slave,
    thrice slave, and though my mother is thrice slave,
    you'll not be shown to be of lowly lineage.
JOCASTA: O be persuaded by me, I entreat you;
    do not do this.
OEDIPUS: I will not be persuaded to let be
    the chance of finding out the whole thing clearly.
JOCASTA: It is because I wish you well that I
    give you this counsel—and it's the best counsel.
OEDIPUS: Then the best counsel vexes me, and has
    for some while since.
JOCASTA:                    O Oedipus, God help you!
    God keep you from the knowledge of who you are!
OEDIPUS: Here, someone, go and fetch the shepherd for me;
    and let her find her joy in her rich family!
JOCASTA: O Oedipus, unhappy Oedipus!
    that is all I can call you, and the last thing
    that I shall ever call you.

    [*Exit.*]

CHORUS: Why has the queen gone, Oedipus, in wild
    grief rushing from us? I am afraid that trouble
    will break out of this silence.
OEDIPUS: Break out what will! I at least shall be
    willing to see my ancestry, though humble.
    Perhaps she is ashamed of my low birth,
    for she has all a woman's high-flown pride.
    But I account myself a child of Fortune,
    beneficent Fortune, and I shall not be
    dishonoured. She's the mother from whom I spring;
    the months, my brothers, marked me, now as small,
    and now again as mighty. Such is my breeding,
    and I shall never prove so false to it,
    as not to find the secret of my birth.
CHORUS: [*Strophe.*] If I am a prophet and wise of heart
    you shall not fail, Cithaeron,
    by the limitless sky, you shall not!—
    to know at tomorrow's full moon
    that Oedipus honours you,
    as native to him and mother and nurse at once;
    and that you are honoured in dancing by us, as finding favour in sight of
        our king.
    Apollo, to whom we cry, find these things pleasing!

[*Antistrophe.*]

1165 Who was it bore you, child? One of
the long-lived nymphs who lay with Pan[3]—
the father who treads the hills?
Or was she a bride of Loxias, your mother? The grassy slopes
are all of them dear to him. Or perhaps Cyllene's[4] king
1170 or the Bacchants' God[5] that lives on the tops
of the hills received you a gift from some
one of the Helicon Nymphs,[6] with whom he mostly plays?

[*Enter an* OLD MAN, *led by* OEDIPUS' *servants.*]

OEDIPUS: If someone like myself who never met him
may make a guess,—I think this is the herdsman,
1175 whom we were seeking. His old age is consonant
with the other. And besides, the men who bring him
I recognize as my own servants. You
perhaps may better me in knowledge since
you've seen the man before.
CHORUS: You can be sure
1180 I recognize him. For if Laius
had ever an honest shepherd, this was he.
OEDIPUS: You, sir, from Corinth, I must ask you first,
is this the man you spoke of?
MESSENGER: This is he
before your eyes.
OEDIPUS: Old man, look here at me
1185 and tell me what I ask you. Were you ever
a servant of King Laius?
HERDSMAN: I was,—
no slave he bought but reared in his own house.
OEDIPUS: What did you do as work? How did you live?
HERDSMAN: Most of my life was spent among the flocks.
1190 OEDIPUS: In what part of the country did you live?
HERDSMAN: Cithaeron and the places near to it.
OEDIPUS: And somewhere there perhaps you knew this man?
HERDSMAN: What was his occupation? Who?
OEDIPUS: This man here
have you had any dealings with him?
HERDSMAN: No—
1195 not such that I can quickly call to mind.
MESSENGER: That is no wonder, master. But I'll make him remember what he
does not know. For I know, that he well knows the country of Cithaeron, how
he with two flocks, I with one kept company for three years—each year half a

---

3. God of nature; half man, half goat.
4. Mountain reputed to be the birthplace of Hermes, the messenger god.  5. Dionysus.
6. The Muses; nine sister goddesses who presided over poetry, music, and the arts.

year—from spring till autumn time and then when winter came I drove my flocks to our fold home again and he to Laius' steadings. Well—am I right or not in what I said we did?
HERDSMAN: You're right—although it's a long time ago.
MESSENGER: Do you remember giving me a child to bring up as my foster child?
HERDSMAN:         What's this?
Why do you ask this question?
MESSENGER:         Look old man,
here he is—here's the man who was that child!
HERDSMAN: Death take you! Won't you hold your tongue?
OEDIPUS:         No, no,
do not find fault with him, old man. Your words
are more at fault than his.
HERDSMAN:         O best of masters,
how do I give offense?
OEDIPUS:         When you refuse
to speak about the child of whom he asks you.
HERDSMAN: He speaks out of his ignorance, without meaning.
OEDIPUS: If you'll not talk to gratify me, you
will talk with pain to urge you.
HERDSMAN:         O please, sir,
don't hurt an old man, sir.
OEDIPUS: [*To the* SERVANTS.] Here, one of you,
twist his hands behind him.
HERDSMAN:         Why, God help me, why?
What do you want to know?
OEDIPUS:         You gave a child
to him,—the child he asked you of?
HERDSMAN:         I did.
I wish I'd died the day I did.
OEDIPUS:         You will
unless you tell me truly.
HERDSMAN:         And I'll die
far worse if I should tell you.
OEDIPUS:         This fellow
is bent on more delays, as it would seem.
HERDSMAN: O no, no! I have told you that I gave it.
OEDIPUS: Where did you get this child from? Was it your own or did you get it from another?
HERDSMAN:         Not
my own at all; I had it from someone.
OEDIPUS: One of these citizens? or from what house?
HERDSMAN: O master, please—I beg you, master, please don't ask me more.
OEDIPUS:         You're a dead man if I
ask you again.
HERDSMAN:         It was one of the children
of Laius.
OEDIPUS:         A slave? Or born in wedlock?

HERDSMAN: O God, I am on the brink of frightful speech.
OEDIPUS: And I of frightful hearing. But I must hear.
HERDSMAN: The child was called his child; but she within,
1235 your wife would tell you best how all this was.
OEDIPUS: *She* gave it to you?
HERDSMAN: Yes, she did, my lord.
OEDIPUS: To do what with it?
HERDSMAN: Make away with it.
OEDIPUS: She was so hard—its mother?
HERDSMAN: Aye, through fear
of evil oracles.
OEDIPUS: Which?
HERDSMAN: They said that he
should kill his parents.
1240 OEDIPUS: How was it that you
gave it away to this old man?
HERDSMAN: O master,
I pitied it, and thought that I could send it
off to another country and this man
was from another country. But he saved it
1245 for the most terrible troubles. If you are
the man he says you are, you're bred to misery.
OEDIPUS: O, O, O, they will all come,
all come out clearly! Light of the sun, let me
look upon you no more after today!
1250 I who first saw the light bred of a match
accursed, and accursed in my living
with them I lived with, cursed in my killing.

[*Exeunt all but the* CHORUS.]

CHORUS: [*Strophe.*] O generations of men, how I
count you as equal with those who live
1255 not at all!
What man, what man on earth wins more
of happiness than a seeming
and after that turning away?
Oedipus, you are my pattern of this,
1260 Oedipus, you and your fate!
Luckless Oedipus, whom of all men
I envy not at all.

[*Antistrophe.*]

In as much as he shot his bolt
beyond the others and won the prize
1265 of happiness complete—
O Zeus—and killed and reduced to nought
the hooked taloned maid of the riddling speech,[7]

---

7. The sphinx, who killed herself when Oedipus was the first to give a correct answer to her riddle: "What walks on four feet in the morning, on two at noon, and on three in the evening?"

standing a tower against death for my land:
hence he was called my king and hence
was honoured the highest of all
honours; and hence he ruled
in the great city of Thebes.

[*Strophe.*]

But now whose tale is more miserable?
Who is there lives with a savager fate?
Whose troubles so reverse his life as his?

O Oedipus, the famous prince
for whom a great haven
the same both as father and son
sufficed for generation,
how, O how, have the furrows ploughed
by your father endured to bear you, poor wretch,
and hold their peace so long?

[*Antistrophe.*]

Time who sees all has found you out
against your will; judges your marriage accursed,
begetter and begot at one in it.

O child of Laius,
would I had never seen you.
I weep for you and cry
a dirge of lamentation.

To speak directly, I drew my breath
from you at the first and so now I lull
my mouth to sleep with your name.

[*Enter a* SECOND MESSENGER.]

SECOND MESSENGER: O Princes always honoured by our country,
what deeds you'll hear of and what horrors see,
what grief you'll feel, if you as true born Thebans
care for the house of Labdacus' sons.[8]
Phasis nor Ister cannot purge this house,
I think, with all their streams, such things
it hides, such evils shortly will bring forth
into the light, whether they will or not;
and troubles hurt the most
when they prove self-inflicted.
CHORUS: What we had known before did not fall short
of bitter groaning's worth; what's more to tell?
SECOND MESSENGER: Shortest to hear and tell—our glorious queen

---

8. Labdacus, king of Thebes, was father of Laïus and grandfather of Oedipus. *Phasis . . . Ister* (line 1297): rivers near Thebes.

                Jocasta's dead.
    CHORUS:                    Unhappy woman! How?
    SECOND MESSENGER: By her own hand. The worst of what was done
        you cannot know. You did not see the sight.
        Yet in so far as I remember it
1310    you'll hear the end of our unlucky queen.
        When she came raging into the house she went
        straight to her marriage bed, tearing her hair
        with both her hands, and crying upon Laius
        long dead—Do you remember, Laius,
1315    that night long past which bred a child for us
        to send you to your death and leave
        a mother making children with her son?
        And then she groaned and cursed the bed in which
        she brought forth husband by her husband, children
1320    by her own child, an infamous double bond.
        How after that she died I do not know,—
        for Oedipus distracted us from seeing.
        He burst upon us shouting and we looked
        to him as he paced frantically around,
1325    begging us always: Give me a sword, I say,
        to find this wife no wife, this mother's womb,
        this field of double sowing whence I sprang
        and where I sowed my children! As he raved
        some god showed him the way—none of us there.
1330    Bellowing terribly and led by some
        invisible guide he rushed on the two doors,—
        wrenching the hollow bolts out of their sockets,
        he charged inside. There, there, we saw his wife
        hanging, the twisted rope around her neck.
1335    When he saw her, he cried out fearfully
        and cut the dangling noose. Then, as she lay,
        poor woman, on the ground, what happened after,
        was terrible to see. He tore the brooches—
        the gold chased[9] brooches fastening her robe—
1340    away from her and lifting them up high
        dashed them on his own eyeballs, shrieking out
        such things as: they will never see the crime
        I have committed or had done upon me!
        Dark eyes, now in the days to come look on
1345    forbidden faces, do not recognize
        those whom you long for—with such imprecations
        he struck his eyes again and yet again
        with the brooches. And the bleeding eyeballs gushed
        and stained his beard—no sluggish oozing drops
1350    but a black rain and bloody hail poured down.

---

9. Decorated with ornamental grooves.

So it has broken—and not on one head
but troubles mixed for husband and for wife.
The fortune of the days gone by was true
good fortune—but today groans and destruction
and death and shame—of all ills can be named 1355
not one is missing.
CHORUS: Is he now in any ease from pain?
SECOND MESSENGER:            He shouts
for someone to unbar the doors and show him
to all the men of Thebes, his father's killer,
his mother's—no I cannot say the word, 1360
it is unholy—for he'll cast himself,
out of the land, he says, and not remain
to bring a curse upon his house, the curse
he called upon it in his proclamation. But
he wants for strength, aye, and some one to guide him; 1365
his sickness is too great to bear. You, too,
will be shown that. The bolts are opening.
Soon you will see a sight to waken pity
even in the horror of it.

   [Enter the blinded OEDIPUS.]

CHORUS: This is a terrible sight for men to see! 1370
I never found a worse!
Poor wretch, what madness came upon you!
What evil spirit leaped upon your life
to your ill-luck—a leap beyond man's strength!
Indeed I pity you, but I cannot 1375
look at you, though there's much I want to ask
and much to learn and much to see.
I shudder at the sight of you.
OEDIPUS: O, O,
where am I going? Where is my voice 1380
borne on the wind to and fro?
Spirit, how far have you sprung?
CHORUS: To a terrible place whereof men's ears
may not hear, nor their eyes behold it.
OEDIPUS: Darkness! 1385
Horror of darkness enfolding, resistless, unspeakable visitant sped by an ill
   wind in haste!
madness and stabbing pain and memory
of evil deeds I have done!
CHORUS: In such misfortunes it's no wonder
if double weighs the burden of your grief. 1390
OEDIPUS: My friend,
you are the only one steadfast, the only one that attends on me;
you still stay nursing the blind man.
Your care is not unnoticed. I can know
your voice, although this darkness is my world. 1395

CHORUS: Doer of dreadful deeds, how did you dare
    so far to do despite to your own eyes?
    what spirit urged you to it?
OEDIPUS: It was Apollo, friends, Apollo,
1400    that brought this bitter bitterness, my sorrows to completion.
    But the hand that struck me
    was none but my own.
    Why should I see
    whose vision showed me nothing sweet to see?
1405 CHORUS: These things are as you say.
OEDIPUS: What can I see to love?
    What greeting can touch my ears with joy?
    Take me away, and haste—to a place out of the way!
    Take me away, my friends, the greatly miserable,
1410    the most accursed, whom God too hates
    above all men on earth!
CHORUS: Unhappy in your mind and your misfortune,
    would I had never known you!
OEDIPUS: Curse on the man who took
1415    the cruel bonds from off my legs, as I lay in the field.
    He stole me from death and saved me,
    no kindly service.
    Had I died then
    I would not be so burdensome to friends.
1420 CHORUS: I, too, could have wished it had been so.
OEDIPUS: Then I would not have come
    to kill my father and marry my mother infamously.
    Now I am godless and child of impurity,
    begetter in the same seed that created my wretched self.
1425    If there is any ill worse than ill,
    that is the lot of Oedipus.
CHORUS: I cannot say your remedy was good;
    you would be better dead than blind and living.
OEDIPUS: What I have done here was best done—don't tell me
1430    otherwise, do not give me further counsel.
    I do not know with what eyes I could look
    upon my father when I die and go
    under the earth, nor yet my wretched mother—
    those two to whom I have done things deserving
1435    worse punishment than hanging. Would the sight
    of children, bred as mine are, gladden me?
    No, not these eyes, never. And my city,
    its towers and sacred places of the Gods,
    of these I robbed my miserable self
1440    when I commanded all to drive *him* out,
    the criminal since proved by God impure
    and of the race of Laius.
    To this guilt I bore witness against myself—
    with what eyes shall I look upon my people?

No. If there were a means to choke the fountain
of hearing I would not have stayed my hand
from locking up my miserable carcase,
seeing and hearing nothing; it is sweet
to keep our thoughts out of the range of hurt.

Cithaeron, why did you receive me? why
having received me did you not kill me straight?
And so I had not shown to men my birth.

O Polybus and Corinth and the house,
the old house that I used to call my father's—
what fairness you were nurse to, and what foulness
festered beneath! Now I am found to be
a sinner and a son of sinners. Crossroads,
and hidden glade, oak and the narrow way
at the crossroads, that drank my father's blood
offered you by my hands, do you remember
still what I did as you looked on, and what
I did when I came here? O marriage, marriage!
you bred me and again when you had bred
bred children of your child and showed to men
brides, wives and mothers and the foulest deeds
that can be in this world of ours.

Come—it's unfit to say what is unfit
to do.—I beg of you in God's name hide me
somewhere outside your country, yes, or kill me,
or throw me into the sea, to be forever
out of your sight. Approach and deign to touch me
for all my wretchedness, and do not fear.
No man but I can bear my evil doom.

CHORUS: Here Creon comes in fit time to perform
or give advice in what you ask of us.
Creon is left sole ruler in your stead.

OEDIPUS: Creon! Creon! What shall I say to him?
How can I justly hope that he will trust me?
In what is past I have been proved towards him
an utter liar.

[*Enter* CREON.]

CREON:                    Oedipus, I've come
not so that I might laugh at you nor taunt you
with evil of the past. But if you still
are without shame before the face of men
reverence at least the flame that gives all life,
our Lord the Sun, and do not show unveiled
to him pollution such that neither land
nor holy rain nor light of day can welcome.

[*To a* SERVANT.]

Be quick and take him in. It is most decent
that only kin should see and hear the troubles
of kin.

1490 OEDIPUS: I beg you, since you've torn me from
my dreadful expectations and have come
in a most noble spirit to a man
that has used you vilely—do a thing for me.
I shall speak for your own good, not for my own.

1495 CREON: What do you need that you would ask of me?

OEDIPUS: Drive me from here with all the speed you can
to where I may not hear a human voice.

CREON: Be sure, I would have done this had not I
wished first of all to learn from the God the course
of action I should follow.

1500 OEDIPUS: But his word
has been quite clear to let the parricide,
the sinner, die.

CREON: Yes, that indeed was said.
But in the present need we had best discover
what we should do.

OEDIPUS: And will you ask about
a man so wretched?

1505 CREON: Now even you will trust
the God.

OEDIPUS: So. I command you—and will beseech you—
to her that lies inside that house give burial
as you would have it; she is yours and rightly
you will perform the rites for her. For me—
1510 never let this my father's city have me
living a dweller in it. Leave me live
in the mountains where Cithaeron is, that's called
*my* mountain, which my mother and my father
while they were living would have made my tomb.
1515 So I may die by their decree who sought
indeed to kill me. Yet I know this much:
no sickness and no other thing will kill me.
I would not have been saved from death if not
for some strange evil fate. Well, let my fate
go where it will.
1520 Creon, you need not care
about my sons; they're men and so wherever
they are, they will not lack a livelihood.
But my two girls—so sad and pitiful—
whose table never stood apart from mine,
1525 and everything I touched they always shared—
O Creon, have a thought for them! And most
I wish that you might suffer me to touch them
and sorrow with them.

[*Enter* ANTIGONE *and* ISMENE, OEDIPUS' *two daughters.*]

O my lord! O true noble Creon! Can I
really be touching them, as when I saw?
What shall I say?
Yes, I can hear them sobbing—my two darlings!
and Creon has had pity and has sent me
what I loved most?
Am I right?

CREON: You're right: it was I gave you this
because I knew from old days how you loved them
as I see now.

OEDIPUS: God bless you for it, Creon,
and may God guard you better on your road
than he did me!
            O children,
where are you? Come here, come to my hands,
a brother's hands which turned your father's eyes,
those bright eyes you knew once, to what you see,
a father seeing nothing, knowing nothing,
begetting you from his own source of life.
I weep for you—I cannot see your faces—
I weep when I think of the bitterness
there will be in your lives, how you must live
before the world. At what assemblages
of citizens will you make one? to what
gay company will you go and not come home
in tears instead of sharing in the holiday?
And when you're ripe for marriage, who will he be,
the man who'll risk to take such infamy
as shall cling to my children, to bring hurt
on them and those that marry with them? What
curse is not there? "Your father killed his father
and sowed the seed where he had sprung himself
and begot you out of the womb that held him."
These insults you will hear. Then who will marry you?
No one, my children; clearly you are doomed
to waste away in barrenness unmarried.
Son of Menoeceus,[1] since you are all the father
left these two girls, and we, their parents, both
are dead to them—do not allow them wander
like beggars, poor and husbandless.
They are of your own blood.
And do not make them equal with myself
in wretchedness; for you can see them now
so young, so utterly alone, save for you only.
Touch my hand, noble Creon, and say yes.
If you were older, children, and were wiser,
there's much advice I'd give you. But as it is,
let this be what you pray: give me a life

---

1. Father of Creon and Jocasta.

1575     wherever there is opportunity
        to live, and better life than was my father's.
    CREON: Your tears have had enough of scope; now go within the house.
    OEDIPUS: I must obey, though bitter of heart.
    CREON: In season, all is good.
    OEDIPUS: Do you know on what conditions I obey?
1580   CREON:                 You tell me them,
    and I shall know them when I hear.
    OEDIPUS:              That you shall send me out
    to live away from Thebes.
    CREON:                That gift you must ask of the Gods.
    OEDIPUS: But I'm now hated by the Gods.
    CREON:                So quickly you'll obtain your prayer.
    OEDIPUS: You consent then?
    CREON:                What I do not mean, I do not use to say.
    OEDIPUS: Now lead me away from here.
1585   CREON:                Let go the children, then, and come.
    OEDIPUS: Do not take them from me.
    CREON:                Do not seek to be master in everything,
    for the things you mastered did not follow you throughout your life.

    [*As* CREON *and* OEDIPUS *go out.*]

    CHORUS: You that live in my ancestral Thebes, behold this Oedipus,—
    him who knew the famous riddles and was a man most masterful;
1590   not a citizen who did not look with envy on his lot—
    see him now and see the breakers of misfortune swallow him!
    Look upon that last day always. Count no mortal happy till
    he has passed the final limit of his life secure from pain.

ca. 429 B.C.E.

OSCAR WILDE

## *The Importance of Being Earnest*

### CHARACTERS

ALGERNON MONCRIEFF    LADY AUGUSTA BRACKNELL    CECILY CARDEW
LANE    GWENDOLEN FAIRFAX    CANON CHASUBLE
ERNEST WORTHING    MISS PRISM    MERRIMAN

### ACT I

SCENE: *Morning room in* ALGERNON'S *flat in Half-Moon Street.*[1]
*The room is luxuriously and artistically furnished. The sound of a piano is heard in the adjoining room.*

[LANE *is arranging afternoon tea on the table, and after the music has ceased,* ALGERNON *enters.*]

ALGERNON: Did you hear what I was playing, Lane?

LANE: I didn't think it polite to listen, sir.

ALGERNON: I'm sorry for that, for your sake. I don't play accurately—anyone can play accurately—but I play with wonderful expression. As far as the piano is concerned, sentiment is my forte. I keep science for Life.

LANE: Yes, sir.

ALGERNON: And, speaking of the science of Life, have you got the cucumber sandwiches cut for Lady Bracknell?

LANE: Yes, sir. [*Hands them on a salver.*]

ALGERNON: [*Inspects them, takes two, and sits down on the sofa.*] Oh! . . . by the way, Lane, I see from your book that on Thursday night, when Lord Shoreham and Mr. Worthing were dining with me, eight bottles of champagne are entered as having been consumed.

LANE: Yes, sir; eight bottles and a pint.

ALGERNON: Why is it that at a bachelor's establishment the servants invariably drink the champagne? I ask merely for information.

LANE: I attribute it to the superior quality of the wine, sir. I have often observed that in married households the champagne is rarely of a first-rate brand.

ALGERNON: Good heavens! Is marriage so demoralizing as that?

LANE: I believe it *is* a very pleasant state, sir. I have had very little experience of it myself up to the present. I have only been married once. That was in consequence of a misunderstanding between myself and a young person.

ALGERNON: [*Languidly.*] I don't know that I am much interested in your family life, Lane.

LANE: No, sir; it is not a very interesting subject. I never think of it myself.

ALGERNON: Very natural, I am sure. That will do, Lane, thank you.

LANE: Thank you, sir. [LANE *goes out.*]

ALGERNON: Lane's views on marriage seem somewhat lax. Really, if the lower

---

1. Like many of the addresses in the play, Half-Moon Street is in Mayfair, a very fashionable section of London. It runs north from Piccadilly near Hyde Park.

orders don't set us a good example, what on earth is the use of them? They seem, as a class, to have absolutely no sense of moral responsibility.

[*Enter* LANE.]

LANE: Mr. Ernest Worthing.

[*Enter* JACK. LANE *goes out.*]

ALGERNON: How are you, my dear Ernest? What brings you up to town?
JACK: Oh, pleasure, pleasure! What else should bring one anywhere? Eating as usual, I see, Algy!
ALGERNON: [*Stiffly.*] I believe it is customary in good society to take some slight refreshment at five o'clock. Where have you been since last Thursday?
JACK: [*Sitting down on the sofa.*] In the country.
ALGERNON: What on earth do you do there?
JACK: [*Pulling off his gloves.*] When one is in town one amuses oneself. When one is in the country one amuses other people. It is excessively boring.
ALGERNON: And who are the people you amuse?
JACK: [*Airily.*] Oh, neighbors, neighbors.
ALGERNON: Got nice neighbors in your part of Shropshire?
JACK: Perfectly horrid! Never speak to one of them.
ALGERNON: How immensely you must amuse them! [*Goes over and takes sandwich.*] By the way, Shropshire is your county, is it not?
JACK: Eh? Shropshire? Yes, of course.[2] Hallo! Why all these cups? Why cucumber sandwiches? Why such reckless extravagance in one so young? Who is coming to tea?
ALGERNON: Oh! merely Aunt Augusta and Gwendolen.
JACK: How perfectly delightful!
ALGERNON: Yes, that is all very well; but I am afraid Aunt Augusta won't quite approve of your being here.
JACK: May I ask why?
ALGERNON: My dear fellow, the way you flirt with Gwendolen is perfectly disgraceful. It is almost as bad as the way Gwendolen flirts with you.
JACK: I am in love with Gwendolen. I have come up to town expressly to propose to her.
ALGERNON: I thought you had come up for pleasure? . . . I call that business.
JACK: How utterly unromantic you are!
ALGERNON: I really don't see anything romantic in proposing. It is very romantic to be in love. But there is nothing romantic about a definite proposal. Why, one may be accepted. One usually is, I believe. Then the excitement is all over. The very essence of romance is uncertainty. If ever I get married, I'll certainly try to forget the fact.
JACK: I have no doubt about that, dear Algy. The divorce court was specially invented for people whose memories are so curiously constituted.
ALGERNON: Oh! there is no use speculating on that subject. Divorces are made in heaven— [JACK *puts out his hand to take a sandwich.* ALGERNON *at once interferes.*]

---

2. Shropshire is a county on the Welsh border, to the west of London; Jack's country place is actually in Hertfordshire, to the north of London.

Please don't touch the cucumber sandwiches. They are ordered specially for Aunt Augusta. [*Takes one and eats it.*]

JACK: Well, you have been eating them all the time.

ALGERNON: That is quite a different matter. She is my aunt. [*Takes plate from below.*] Have some bread and butter. The bread and butter is for Gwendolen. Gwendolen is devoted to bread and butter.

JACK: [*Advancing to table and helping himself.*] And very good bread and butter it is too.

ALGERNON: Well, my dear fellow, you need not eat as if you were going to eat it all. You behave as if you were married to her already. You are not married to her already, and I don't think you ever will be.

JACK: Why on earth do you say that?

ALGERNON: Well, in the first place, girls never marry the men they flirt with. Girls don't think it right.

JACK: Oh, that is nonsense!

ALGERNON: It isn't. It is a great truth. It accounts for the extraordinary number of bachelors that one sees all over the place. In the second place, I don't give my consent.

JACK: Your consent!

ALGERNON: My dear fellow, Gwendolen is my first cousin. And before I allow you to marry her, you will have to clear up the whole question of Cecily. [*Rings bell.*]

JACK: Cecily! What on earth do you mean? What do you mean, Algy, by Cecily? I don't know anyone of the name of Cecily.

[*Enter* LANE.]

ALGERNON: Bring me that cigarette case Mr. Worthing left in the smoking-room the last time he dined here.

LANE: Yes, sir. [LANE *goes out.*]

JACK: Do you mean to say you have had my cigarette case all this time? I wish to goodness you had let me know. I have been writing frantic letters to Scotland Yard about it. I was very nearly offering a large reward.

ALGERNON: Well, I wish you would offer one. I happen to be more than usually hard up.

JACK: There is no good offering a large reward now that the thing is found.

[*Enter* LANE *with the cigarette case on a salver.* ALGERNON *takes it at once.* LANE *goes out.*]

ALGERNON: I think that is rather mean of you, Ernest, I must say. [*Opens case and examines it.*] However, it makes no matter, for, now that I look at the inscription inside, I find that the thing isn't yours after all.

JACK: Of course it's mine. [*Moving to him.*] You have seen me with it a hundred times, and you have no right whatsoever to read what is written inside. It is a very ungentlemanly thing to read a private cigarette case.

ALGERNON: Oh! it is absurd to have a hard-and-fast rule about what one should read and what one shouldn't. More than half of modern culture depends on what one shouldn't read.

JACK: I am quite aware of the fact, and I don't propose to discuss modern culture.

It isn't the sort of thing one should talk of in private. I simply want my cigarette case back.

ALGERNON: Yes; but this isn't your cigarette case. This cigarette case is a present from someone of the name of Cecily, and you said you didn't know anyone of that name.

JACK: Well, if you want to know, Cecily happens to be my aunt.

ALGERNON: Your aunt!

JACK: Yes. Charming old lady she is, too. Lives at Tunbridge Wells.[3] Just give it back to me, Algy.

ALGERNON: [*Retreating to back of sofa.*] But why does she call herself Cecily if she is your aunt and lives at Tunbridge Wells? [*Reading.*] "From little Cecily with her fondest love."

JACK: [*Moving to sofa and kneeling upon it.*] My dear fellow, what on earth is there in that? Some aunts are tall, some aunts are not tall. That is a matter that surely an aunt may be allowed to decide for herself. You seem to think that every aunt should be exactly like your aunt! That is absurd! For heaven's sake give me back my cigarette case. [*Follows* ALGY *round the room.*]

ALGERNON: Yes. But why does your aunt call you her uncle? "From little Cecily, with her fondest love to her dear Uncle Jack." There is no objection, I admit, to an aunt being a small aunt, but why an aunt, no matter what her size may be, should call her own nephew her uncle, I can't quite make out. Besides, your name isn't Jack at all; it is Ernest.

JACK: It isn't Ernest; it's Jack.

ALGERNON: You have always told me it was Ernest. I have introduced you to everyone as Ernest. You answer to the name of Ernest. You look as if your name was Ernest. You are the most earnest looking person I ever saw in my life. It is perfectly absurd your saying that your name isn't Ernest. It's on your cards. Here is one of them. [*Taking it from case.*] "Mr. Ernest Worthing, B. 4, The Albany."[4] I'll keep this as a proof that your name is Ernest if ever you attempt to deny it to me, or to Gwendolen, or to anyone else. [*Puts the card in his pocket.*]

JACK: Well, my name is Ernest in town and Jack in the country, and the cigarette case was given to me in the country.

ALGERNON: Yes, but that does not account for the fact that your small Aunt Cecily, who lives at Tunbridge Wells, calls you her dear uncle. Come, old boy, you had much better have the thing out at once.

JACK: My dear Algy, you talk exactly as if you were a dentist. It is very vulgar to talk like a dentist when one isn't a dentist. It produces a false impression.

ALGERNON: Well, that is exactly what dentists always do. Now, go on! Tell me the whole thing. I may mention that I have always suspected you of being a confirmed and secret Bunburyist; and I am quite sure of it now.

JACK: Bunburyist? What on earth do you mean by a Bunburyist?

ALGERNON: I'll reveal to you the meaning of that incomparable expression as soon as you are kind enough to inform me why you are Ernest in town and Jack in the country.

JACK: Well, produce my cigarette case first.

---

3. A resort town in Kent, southeast of London.
4. An apartment building for single gentlemen on Piccadilly, east of Algernon's flat.

ALGERNON: Here it is. [*Hands cigarette case.*] Now produce your explanation, and pray make it improbable. [*Sits on sofa.*]

JACK: My dear fellow, there is nothing improbable about my explanation at all. In fact it's perfectly ordinary. Old Mr. Thomas Cardew, who adopted me when I was a little boy, made me in his will guardian to his granddaughter, Miss Cecily Cardew. Cecily, who addresses me as her uncle from motives of respect that you could not possibly appreciate, lives at my place in the country under the charge of her admirable governess, Miss Prism.

ALGERNON: Where is that place in the country, by the way?

JACK: That is nothing to you, dear boy. You are not going to be invited. . . . I may tell you candidly that the place is not in Shropshire.

ALGERNON: I suspected that, my dear fellow! I have Bunburyed all over Shropshire on two separate occasions. Now, go on. Why are you Ernest in town and Jack in the country?

JACK: My dear Algy, I don't know whether you will be able to understand my real motives. You are hardly serious enough. When one is placed in the position of guardian, one has to adopt a very high moral tone on all subjects. It's one's duty to do so. And as a high moral tone can hardly be said to conduce very much to either one's health or one's happiness, in order to get up to town I have always pretended to have a younger brother of the name of Ernest, who lives in the Albany, and gets into the most dreadful scrapes. That, my dear Algy, is the whole truth pure and simple.

ALGERNON: The truth is rarely pure and never simple. Modern life would be very tedious if it were either, and modern literature a complete impossibility!

JACK: That wouldn't be at all a bad thing.

ALGERNON: Literary criticism is not your forte, my dear fellow. Don't try it. You should leave that to people who haven't been at a university. They do it so well in the daily papers. What you really are is a Bunburyist. I was quite right in saying you were a Bunburyist. You are one of the most advanced Bunburyists I know.

JACK: What on earth do you mean?

ALGERNON: You have invented a very useful young brother called Ernest, in order that you may be able to come up to town as often as you like. I have invented an invaluable permanent invalid called Bunbury, in order that I may be able to go down into the country whenever I choose. Bunbury is perfectly invaluable. If it wasn't for Bunbury's extraordinary bad health, for instance, I wouldn't be able to dine with you at Willis's[5] tonight, for I have been really engaged to Aunt Augusta for more than a week.

JACK: I haven't asked you to dine with me anywhere tonight.

ALGERNON: I know. You are absurdly careless about sending out invitations. It is very foolish of you. Nothing annoys people so much as not receiving invitations.

JACK: You had much better dine with your Aunt Augusta.

ALGERNON: I haven't the smallest intention of doing anything of the kind. To begin with, I dined there on Monday, and once a week is quite enough to dine with one's own relations. In the second place, whenever I do dine there I am always treated as a member of the family, and sent down with either

---

5. A well-known restaurant on King Street, off St. James's Street, near Piccadilly.

no woman at all, or two. In the third place, I know perfectly well whom she will place me next to, tonight. She will place me next Mary Farquhar, who always flirts with her own husband across the dinner table. That is not very pleasant. Indeed, it is not even decent . . . and that sort of thing is enormously on the increase. The amount of women in London who flirt with their own husbands is perfectly scandalous. It looks so bad. It is simply washing one's clean linen in public. Besides, now that I know you to be a confirmed Bunburyist, I naturally want to talk to you about Bunburying. I want to tell you the rules.

JACK: I'm not a Bunburyist at all. If Gwendolen accepts me, I am going to kill my brother, indeed I think I'll kill him in any case. Cecily is a little too much interested in him. It is rather a bore. So I am going to get rid of Ernest. And I strongly advise you to do the same with Mr. . . . with your invalid friend who has the absurd name.

ALGERNON: Nothing will induce me to part with Bunbury, and if you ever get married, which seems to me extremely problematic, you will be very glad to know Bunbury. A man who marries without knowing Bunbury has a very tedious time of it.

JACK: That is nonsense. If I marry a charming girl like Gwendolen, and she is the only girl I ever saw in my life that I would marry, I certainly won't want to know Bunbury.

ALGERNON: Then your wife will. You don't seem to realize, that in married life three is company and two is none.

JACK: [*Sententiously.*] That, my dear young friend, is the theory that the corrupt French drama has been propounding for the last fifty years.[6]

ALGERNON: Yes; and that the happy English home has proved in half the time.

JACK: For heaven's sake, don't try to be cynical. It's perfectly easy to be cynical.

ALGERNON: My dear fellow, it isn't easy to be anything nowadays. There's such a lot of beastly competition about. [*The sound of an electric bell is heard.*] Ah! that must be Aunt Augusta. Only relatives, or creditors, ever ring in that Wagnerian manner.[7] Now, if I get her out of the way for ten minutes, so that you can have an opportunity for proposing to Gwendolen, may I dine with you tonight at Willis's?

JACK: I suppose so, if you want to.

ALGERNON: Yes, but you must be serious about it. I hate people who are not serious about meals. It is so shallow of them.

[*Enter* LANE.]

LANE: Lady Bracknell and Miss Fairfax.

[ALGERNON *goes forward to meet them. Enter* LADY BRACKNELL *and* GWENDOLEN.]

---

6. Starting in the mid-nineteenth century, the French produced plays dealing with such subjects as adultery, prostitution, and illegitimacy. The heavily censored English theater either avoided such subjects or dealt with them more cautiously.

7. Many early listeners to the music of Richard Wagner found it extremely loud and, consequently, unpleasantly demanding.

LADY BRACKNELL: Good afternoon, dear Algernon, I hope you are behaving very well.
ALGERNON: I'm feeling very well, Aunt Augusta.
LADY BRACKNELL: That's not quite the same thing. In fact the two things rarely go together. [*Sees* JACK *and bows to him with icy coldness.*]
ALGERNON: [*To* GWENDOLEN.] Dear me, you are smart![8]
GWENDOLEN: I am always smart! Aren't I, Mr. Worthing?
JACK: You're quite perfect, Miss Fairfax.
GWENDOLEN: Oh! I hope I am not that. It would leave no room for developments, and I intend to develop in many directions. [GWENDOLEN *and* JACK *sit down together in the corner.*]
LADY BRACKNELL: I'm sorry if we are a little late, Algernon, but I was obliged to call on dear Lady Harbury. I hadn't been there since her poor husband's death. I never saw a woman so altered; she looks quite twenty years younger. And now I'll have a cup of tea, and one of those nice cucumber sandwiches you promised me.
ALGERNON: Certainly, Aunt Augusta. [*Goes over to teatable.*]
LADY BRACKNELL: Won't you come and sit here, Gwendolen?
GWENDOLEN: Thanks, mamma, I'm quite comfortable where I am.
ALGERNON: [*Picking up empty plate in horror.*] Good heavens! Lane! Why are there no cucumber sandwiches? I ordered them specially.
LANE: [*Gravely.*] There were no cucumbers in the market this morning, sir. I went down twice.
ALGERNON: No cucumbers!
LANE: No, sir. Not even for ready money.
ALGERNON: That will do, Lane, thank you.
LANE: Thank you, sir.
ALGERNON: I am greatly distressed, Aunt Augusta, about there being no cucumbers, not even for ready money.
LADY BRACKNELL: It really makes no matter, Algernon. I had some crumpets with Lady Harbury, who seems to me to be living entirely for pleasure now.
ALGERNON: I hear her hair has turned quite gold from grief.
LADY BRACKNELL: It certainly has changed its color. From what cause I, of course, cannot say. [ALGERNON *crosses and hands tea.*] Thank you. I've quite a treat for you tonight, Algernon. I am going to send you down with Mary Farquhar. She is such a nice woman, and so attentive to her husband. It's delightful to watch them.
ALGERNON: I am afraid, Aunt Augusta, I shall have to give up the pleasure of dining with you tonight after all.
LADY BRACKNELL: [*Frowning.*] I hope not, Algernon. It would put my table completely out. Your uncle would have to dine upstairs. Fortunately he is accustomed to that.
ALGERNON: It is a great bore, and, I need hardly say, a terrible disappointment to me, but the fact is I have just had a telegram to say that my poor friend Bunbury is very ill again. [*Exchanges glances with* JACK.] They seem to think I should be with him.

8. Neat and stylish in appearance.

LADY BRACKNELL: It is very strange. This Mr. Bunbury seems to suffer from curiously bad health.

ALGERNON: Yes; poor Bunbury is a dreadful invalid.

LADY BRACKNELL: Well, I must say, Algernon, that I think it is high time that Mr. Bunbury made up his mind whether he was going to live or to die. This shilly-shallying with the question is absurd. Nor do I in any way approve of the modern sympathy with invalids. I consider it morbid. Illness of any kind is hardly a thing to be encouraged in others. Health is the primary duty of life. I am always telling that to your poor uncle, but he never seems to take much notice . . . as far as any improvement in his ailments goes. I should be obliged if you would ask Mr. Bunbury, from me, to be kind enough not to have a relapse on Saturday, for I rely on you to arrange my music for me. It is my last reception, and one wants something that will encourage conversation, particularly at the end of the season when everyone has practically said whatever they had to say, which, in most cases, was probably not much.

ALGERNON: I'll speak to Bunbury, Aunt Augusta, if he is still conscious, and I think I can promise you he'll be all right by Saturday. Of course the music is a great difficulty. You see, if one plays good music, people don't listen, and if one plays bad music, people don't talk. But I'll run over the program I've drawn out, if you will kindly come into the next room for a moment.

LADY BRACKNELL: Thank you, Algernon. It is very thoughtful of you. [*Rising, and following* ALGERNON.] I'm sure the program will be delightful, after a few expurgations. French songs I cannot possibly allow. People always seem to think that they are improper, and either look shocked, which is vulgar, or laugh, which is worse. But German sounds a thoroughly respectable language, and indeed, I believe is so. Gwendolen, you will accompany me.

GWENDOLEN: Certainly, mamma.

[LADY BRACKNELL *and* ALGERNON *go into the music room,* GWENDOLEN *remains behind.*]

JACK: Charming day it has been, Miss Fairfax.

GWENDOLEN: Pray don't talk to me about the weather, Mr. Worthing. Whenever people talk to me about the weather, I always feel quite certain that they mean something else. And that makes me so nervous.

JACK: I do mean something else.

GWENDOLWN: I thought so. In fact, I am never wrong.

JACK: And I would like to be allowed to take advantage of Lady Bracknell's temporary absence . . .

GWENDOLEN: I would certainly advise you to do so. Mamma has a way of coming back suddenly into a room that I have often had to speak to her about.

JACK: [*Nervously.*] Miss Fairfax, ever since I met you I have admired you more than any girl . . . I have ever met since . . . I met you.

GWENDOLEN: Yes, I am quite aware of the fact. And I often wish that in public, at any rate, you had been more demonstrative. For me you have always had an irresistible fascination. Even before I met you I was far from indifferent to you. [JACK *looks at her in amazement.*] We live, as I hope you know, Mr. Worthing, in an age of ideals. The fact is constantly mentioned in the more expensive monthly magazines, and has reached the provincial pulpits, I am told: and my ideal has always been to love someone of the name of Ernest. There is something in that name that inspires absolute confidence. The moment Algernon first mentioned to me that he had a friend called Ernest, I knew I was destined to love you.

JACK: You really love me, Gwendolen?

GWENDOLEN: Passionately!

JACK: Darling! You don't know how happy you've made me.

GWENDOLEN: My own Ernest!

JACK: But you don't really mean to say that you couldn't love me if my name wasn't Ernest?

GWENDOLEN: But your name is Ernest.

JACK: Yes, I know it is. But supposing it was something else? Do you mean to say you couldn't love me then?

GWENDOLEN: [*Glibly.*] Ah! that is clearly a metaphysical speculation, and like most metaphysical speculations has very little reference at all to the actual facts of real life, as we know them.

JACK: Personally, darling, to speak quite candidly, I don't much care about the name of Ernest... I don't think the name suits me at all.

GWENDOLEN: It suits you perfectly. It is a divine name. It has a music of its own. It produces vibrations.

JACK: Well, really, Gwendolen, I must say that I think there are lots of other much nicer names. I think Jack, for instance, a charming name.

GWENDOLEN: Jack?... No, there is very little music in the name Jack, if any at all, indeed. It does not thrill. It produces absolutely no vibrations.... I have known several Jacks, and they all, without exception, were more than usually plain. Besides, Jack is a notorious domesticity for John! And I pity any woman who is married to a man called John. She would probably never be allowed to know the entrancing pleasure of a single moment's solitude. The only really safe name is Ernest.

JACK: Gwendolen, I must get christened at once—I mean we must get married at once. There is no time to be lost.

GWENDOLEN: Married, Mr. Worthing?

JACK: [*Astounded.*] Well... surely. You know that I love you, and you led me to believe, Miss Fairfax, that you were not absolutely indifferent to me.

GWENDOLEN: I adore you. But you haven't proposed to me yet. Nothing has been said at all about marriage. The subject has not even been touched on.

JACK: Well... may I propose to you now?

GWENDOLEN: I think it would be an admirable opportunity. And to spare you any possible disappointment, Mr. Worthing, I think it only fair to tell you quite frankly beforehand that I am fully determined to accept you.

JACK: Gwendolen!

GWENDOLEN: Yes, Mr. Worthing, what have you got to say to me?

JACK: You know what I have got to say to you.

GWENDOLEN: Yes, but you don't say it.

JACK: Gwendolen, will you marry me? [*Goes on his knees.*]

GWENDOLEN: Of course I will, darling. How long you have been about it! I am afraid you have had very little experience in how to propose.

JACK: My own one, I have never loved anyone in the world but you.
GWENDOLEN: Yes, but men often propose for practice. I know my brother Gerald does. All my girlfriends tell me so. What wonderfully blue eyes you have, Ernest! They are quite, quite blue. I hope you will always look at me just like that, especially when there are other people present.

[*Enter* LADY BRACKNELL.]

LADY BRACKNELL: Mr. Worthing! Rise, sir, from this semi-recumbent posture. It is most indecorous.
GWENDOLEN: Mamma! [*He tries to rise; she restrains him.*] I must beg you to retire. This is no place for you. Besides, Mr. Worthing has not quite finished yet.
LADY BRACKNELL: Finished what, may I ask?
GWENDOLEN: I am engaged to Mr. Worthing, mamma.

[*They rise together.*]

LADY BRACKNELL: Pardon me, you are not engaged to anyone. When you do become engaged to someone, I, or you father, should his health permit him, will inform you of the fact. An engagement should come on a young girl as a surprise, pleasant or unpleasant, as the case may be. It is hardly a matter that she could be allowed to arrange for herself.... And now I have a few questions to put to you, Mr. Worthing. While I am making these inquiries, you, Gwendolen, will wait for me below in the carriage.
GWENDOLEN: [*Reproachfully.*] Mamma!
LADY BRACKNELL: In the carriage, Gwendolen! [GWENDOLEN *goes to the door. She and* JACK *blow kisses to each other behind* LADY BRACKNELL*'s back.* LADY BRACKNELL *looks vaguely about as if she could not understand what the noise was. Finally turns round.*] Gwendolen, the carriage!
GWENDOLEN: Yes, mamma. [*Goes out, looking back at* JACK.]
LADY BRACKNELL: [*Sitting down.*] You can take a seat, Mr. Worthing.

[*Looks in her pocket for notebook and pencil.*]

JACK: Thank you, Lady Bracknell, I prefer standing.
LADY BRACKNELL: [*Pencil and notebook in hand.*] I feel bound to tell you that you are not down on my list of eligible young men, although I have the same list as the dear Duchess of Bolton has. We work together, in fact. However, I am quite ready to enter your name, should your answers be what a really affectionate mother requires. Do you smoke?
JACK: Well, yes, I must admit I smoke.
LADY BRACKNELL: I am glad to hear it. A man should always have an occupation of some kind. There are far too many idle men in London as it is. How old are you?
JACK: Twenty-nine.
LADY BRACKNELL: A very good age to be married at. I have always been of opinion that a man who desires to get married should know either everything or nothing. Which do you know?
JACK: [*After some hesitation.*] I know nothing, Lady Bracknell.
LADY BRACKNELL: I am pleased to hear it. I do not approve of anything that tampers with natural ignorance. Ignorance is like a delicate exotic fruit; touch it and the bloom is gone. The whole theory of modern education is radically

unsound. Fortunately in England, at any rate, education produces no effect whatsoever. If it did, it would prove a serious danger to the upper classes, and probably lead to acts of violence in Grosvenor Square.[9] What is your income?

JACK: Between seven and eight thousand a year.[1]

LADY BRACKNELL: [*Makes a note in her book.*] In land, or in investments?

JACK: In investments, chiefly.

LADY BRACKNELL: That is satisfactory. What between the duties expected of one during one's lifetime, and the duties exacted from one after one's death, land has ceased to be either a profit or a pleasure. It gives one position, and prevents one from keeping it up. That's all that can be said about land.

JACK: I have a country house with some land, of course, attached to it, about fifteen hundred acres, I believe; but I don't depend on that for my real income. In fact, as far as I can make out, the poachers are the only people who make anything out of it.

LADY BRACKNELL: A country house! How many bedrooms? Well, that point can be cleared up afterwards. You have a town house, I hope? A girl with a simple, unspoiled nature, like Gwendolen, could hardly be expected to reside in the country.

JACK: Well, I own a house in Belgrave Square,[2] but it is let by the year to Lady Bloxham. Of course, I can get it back whenever I like, at six months' notice.

LADY BRACKNELL: Lady Bloxham? I don't know her.

JACK: Oh, she goes about very little. She is a lady considerably advanced in years.

LADY BRACKNELL: Ah, nowadays that is no guarantee of respectability of character. What number in Belgrave Square?

JACK: 149.

LADY BRACKNELL: [*Shaking her head.*] The unfashionable side. I thought there was something. However, that could easily be altered.

JACK: Do you mean the fashion, or the side?

LADY BRACKNELL: [*Sternly.*] Both, if necessary, I presume. What are your politics?

JACK: Well, I am afraid I really have none. I am a Liberal Unionist.

LADY BRACKNELL: Oh, they count as Tories.[3] They dine with us. Or come in the evening, at any rate. Now to minor matters. Are your parents living?

JACK: I have lost both my parents.

LADY BRACKNELL: Both? To lose one parent may be regarded as a misfortune—to lose *both* seems like carelessness. Who was your father? He was evidently a man of some wealth. Was he born in what the Radical papers call the purple of commerce, or did he rise from the ranks of aristocracy?

JACK: I am afraid I really don't know. The fact is, Lady Bracknell, I said I had lost my parents. It would be nearer the truth to say that my parents seem to have lost me. . . . I don't actually know who I am by birth. I was . . . well, I was found.

LADY BRACKNELL: Found!

JACK: The late Mr. Thomas Cardew, an old gentleman of a very charitable and kindly disposition, found me, and gave me the name of Worthing, because he

---

9. A fashionable location in Mayfair.  1. Nearly $700,000 annually in today's U.S. currency.
2. Near the southeast corner of Hyde Park in Belgravia, another fashionable section of London.
3. Members of the Conservative party. Opposed to home rule for Ireland, they joined forces with the Liberal Unionists, who had split from the Liberal party over the issue.

happened to have a first-class ticket for Worthing in his pocket at the time. Worthing is a place in Sussex. It is a seaside resort.

LADY BRACKNELL: Where did the charitable gentleman who had a first-class ticket for this seaside resort find you?

JACK: [*Gravely.*] In a handbag.

LADY BRACKNELL: A handbag?

JACK: [*Very seriously.*] Yes, Lady Bracknell. I was in a handbag—a somewhat large, black leather handbag, with handles to it—an ordinary handbag, in fact.

LADY BRACKNELL: In what locality did this Mr. James, or Thomas, Cardew come across this ordinary handbag?

JACK: In the cloak room at Victoria Station.[4] It was given to him in mistake for his own.

LADY BRACKNELL: The cloak room at Victoria Station?

JACK: Yes. The Brighton line.

LADY BRACKNELL: The line is immaterial. Mr. Worthing, I confess I feel somewhat bewildered by what you have just told me. To be born, or at any rate, bred in a handbag, whether it had handles or not, seems to me to display a contempt for the ordinary decencies of family life that reminds one of the worst excesses of the French Revolution. And I presume you know what that unfortunate movement led to? As for the particular locality in which the handbag was found, a cloak room at a railway station might serve to conceal a social indiscretion—has probably, indeed, been used for that purpose before now—but it could hardly be regarded as an assured basis for a recognized position in good society.

JACK: May I ask you then what you would advise me to do? I need hardly say I would do anything in the world to ensure Gwendolen's happiness.

LADY BRACKNELL: I would strongly advise you, Mr. Worthing, to try and acquire some relations as soon as possible, and to make a definite effort to produce at any rate one parent, of either sex, before the season is quite over.

JACK: Well, I don't see how I could possibly manage to do that. I can produce the handbag at any moment, it is in my dressing room at home. I really think that should satisfy you, Lady Bracknell.

LADY BRACKNELL: Me, sir! What has it to do with me? You can hardly imagine that I and Lord Bracknell would dream of allowing our only daughter—a girl brought up with the utmost care—to marry into a cloak room, and form an alliance with a parcel? Good morning, Mr. Worthing!

[LADY BRACKNELL *sweeps out in majestic indignation.*]

JACK: Good morning! [ALGERNON, *from the other room, strikes up the Wedding March.* JACK *looks perfectly furious, and goes to the door.*] For goodness' sake don't play that ghastly tune, Algy! How idiotic you are!

[*The music stops, and* ALGERNON *enters cheerily.*]

ALGERNON: Didn't it go off all right, old boy? You don't mean to say Gwendolen refused you? I know it is a way she has. She is always refusing people. I think it is most ill-natured of her.

---

4. Major railroad station in London.

JACK: Oh, Gwendolen is as right as a trivet.[5] As far as she is concerned, we are engaged. Her mother is perfectly unbearable. Never met such a Gorgon[6] . . . I don't really know what a Gorgon is like, but I am quite sure that Lady Bracknell is one. In any case, she is a monster, without being a myth, which is rather unfair . . . I beg your pardon, Algy, I suppose I shouldn't talk about your own aunt in that way before you.

ALGERNON: My dear boy, I love hearing my relations abused. It is the only thing that makes me put up with them at all. Relations are simply a tedious pack of people who haven't got the remotest knowledge of how to live, nor the smallest instinct about when to die.

JACK: Oh, that is nonsense!

ALGERNON: It isn't!

JACK: Well, I won't argue about the matter. You always want to argue about things.

ALGERNON: That is exactly what things were originally made for.

JACK: Upon my word, if I thought that, I'd shoot myself . . . [*A pause.*] You don't think there is any chance of Gwendolen becoming like her mother in about a hundred and fifty years, do you, Algy?

ALGERNON: All women become like their mothers. That is their tragedy. No man does. That's his.

JACK: Is that clever?

ALGERNON: It is perfectly phrased! and quite as true as any observation in civilized life should be.

JACK: I am sick to death of cleverness. Everybody is clever nowadays. You can't go anywhere without meeting clever people. The thing has become an absolute public nuisance. I wish to goodness we had a few fools left.

ALGERNON: We have.

JACK: I should extremely like to meet them. What do they talk about?

ALGERNON: The fools? Oh! about the clever people, of course.

JACK: What fools!

ALGERNON: By the way, did you tell Gwendolen the truth about your being Ernest in town, and Jack in the country?

JACK: [*In a very patronizing manner.*] My dear fellow, the truth isn't quite the sort of thing one tells to a nice sweet refined girl. What extraordinary ideas you have about the way to behave to a woman!

ALGERNON: The only way to behave to a woman is to make love to her, if she is pretty, and to someone else if she is plain.

JACK: Oh, that is nonsense.

ALGERNON: What about your brother? What about the profligate Ernest?

JACK: Oh, before the end of the week I shall have got rid of him. I'll say he died in Paris of apoplexy. Lots of people die of apoplexy, quite suddenly, don't they?

ALGERNON: Yes, but it's hereditary, my dear fellow. It's a sort of thing that runs in families. You had much better say a severe chill.

JACK: You are sure a severe chill isn't hereditary, or anything of that kind?

---

5. A proverbial expression, referring to the solidity of a tripod on its three legs.
6. A mythological creature with a horrible face, the Gorgon had snakes in place of hair. According to myth, those who looked on a Gorgon were turned to stone.

ALGERNON: Of course it isn't!

JACK: Very well, then. My poor brother Ernest is carried off suddenly in Paris, by a severe chill. That gets rid of him.

ALGERNON: But I thought you said that . . . Miss Cardew was a little too much interested in your poor brother Ernest? Won't she feel his loss a good deal?

JACK: Oh, that is all right. Cecily is not a silly romantic girl, I am glad to say. She has got a capital appetite, goes on long walks, and pays no attention at all to her lessons.

ALGERNON: I would rather like to see Cecily.

JACK: I will take very good care you never do. She is excessively pretty, and she is only just eighteen.

ALGERNON: Have you told Gwendolen yet that you have an excessively pretty ward who is only just eighteen?

JACK: Oh! one doesn't blurt these things out to people. Cecily and Gwendolen are perfectly certain to be extremely great friends. I'll bet you anything you like that half an hour after they have met, they will be calling each other sister.

ALGERNON: Women only do that when they have called each other a lot of other things first. Now, my dear boy, if we want to get a good table at Willis's, we really must go and dress. Do you know it is nearly seven?

JACK: [*Irritably.*] Oh! it always is nearly seven.

ALGERNON: Well, I'm hungry.

JACK: I never knew you when you weren't. . . .

ALGERNON: What shall we do after dinner? Go to the theater?

JACK: Oh no! I loathe listening.

ALGERNON: Well, let us go to the club?

JACK: Oh, no! I hate talking.

ALGERNON: Well, we might trot around to the Empire[7] at ten?

JACK: Oh no! I can't bear looking at things. It is so silly.

ALGERNON: Well, what shall we do?

JACK: Nothing!

ALGERNON: It is awfully hard work doing nothing. However, I don't mind hard work where there is no definite object of any kind.

[*Enter* LANE.]

LANE: Miss Fairfax.

[*Enter* GWENDOLEN. LANE *goes out.*]

ALGERNON: Gwendolen, upon my word!

GWENDOLEN: Algy, kindly turn your back. I have something very particular to say to Mr. Worthing.

ALGERNON: Really, Gwendolen, I don't think I can allow this at all.

GWENDOLEN: Algy, you always adopt a strictly immoral attitude towards life. You are not quite old enough to do that.

[ALGERNON *retires to the fireplace.*]

JACK: My own darling!

GWENDOLEN: Ernest, we may never be married. From the expression on mamma's

---

7. The Empire Theatre of Varieties, a music hall on Leicester Square.

face I fear we never shall. Few parents nowadays pay any regard to what their children say to them. The old-fashioned respect for the young is fast dying out. Whatever influence I ever had over mamma, I lost at the age of three. But although she may prevent us from becoming man and wife, and I may marry someone else, and marry often, nothing that she can possibly do can alter my eternal devotion to you.

JACK: Dear Gwendolen!

GWENDOLEN: The story of your romantic origin, as related to me by mamma, with unpleasing comments, has naturally stirred the deeper fibers of my nature. Your Christian name has an irresistible fascination. The simplicity of your character makes you exquisitely incomprehensible to me. Your town address at the Albany I have. What is your address in the country?

JACK: The Manor House, Woolton, Hertfordshire.

[ALGERNON, *who has been carefully listening, smiles to himself, and writes the address on his shirt-cuff. Then picks up the Railway Guide.*]

GWENDOLEN: There is a good postal service, I suppose? It may be necessary to do something desperate. That of course will require serious consideration. I will communicate with you daily.

JACK: My own one!

GWENDOLEN: How long do you remain in town?

JACK: Till Monday.

GWENDOLEN: Good! Algy, you may turn round now.

ALGERNON: Thanks, I've turned round already.

GWENDOLEN: You may also ring the bell.

JACK: You will let me see you to your carriage, my own darling?

GWENDOLEN: Certainly.

JACK: [*To* LANE, *who now enters.*] I will see Miss Fairfax out.

LANE: Yes, sir.

[JACK *and* GWENDOLEN *go off.* LANE *presents several letters on a salver to* ALGERNON. *It is to be surmised that they are bills, as* ALGERNON, *after looking at the envelopes, tears them up.*]

ALGERNON: A glass of sherry, Lane.

LANE: Yes, sir.

ALGERNON: Tomorrow, Lane, I'm going Bunburying.

LANE: Yes, sir.

ALGERNON: I shall probably not be back till Monday. You can put up my dress clothes, my smoking jacket, and all the Bunbury suits...

LANE: Yes, sir. [*Handing sherry.*]

ALGERNON: I hope tomorrow will be a fine day, Lane.

LANE: It never is, sir.

ALGERNON: Lane, you're a perfect pessimist.

LANE: I do my best to give satisfaction, sir.

[*Enter* JACK. LANE *goes off.*]

JACK: There's a sensible, intellectual girl! the only girl I ever cared for in my life.

[ALGERNON *is laughing immoderately.*] What on earth are you so amused at?

ALGERNON: Oh, I'm a little anxious about poor Bunbury, that is all.

JACK: If you don't take care, your friend Bunbury will get you into a serious scrape some day.
ALGERNON: I love scrapes. They are the only things that are never serious.
JACK: Oh, that's nonsense, Algy. You never talk anything but nonsense.
ALGERNON: Nobody ever does.

[JACK *looks indignantly at him, and leaves the room.* ALGERNON *lights a cigarette, reads his shirt-cuff, and smiles.*]

ACT-DROP

## ACT II

SCENE: *Garden at the Manor House. A flight of gray stone steps leads up to the house. The garden, an old-fashioned one, full of roses. Time of year, July. Basket chairs, and a table covered with books, are set under a large yew tree.*

[MISS PRISM *discovered seated at the table.* CECILY *is at the back watering flowers.*]

MISS PRISM: [*Calling.*] Cecily, Cecily! Surely such a utilitarian occupation as the watering of flowers is rather Moulton's duty than yours? Especially at a moment when intellectual pleasures await you. Your German grammar is on the table. Pray open it at page fifteen. We will repeat yesterday's lesson.
CECILY: [*Coming over very slowly.*] But I don't like German. It isn't at all a becoming language. I know perfectly well that I look quite plain after my German lesson.
MISS PRISM: Child, you know how anxious your guardian is that you should improve yourself in every way. He laid particular stress on your German, as he was leaving for town yesterday. Indeed, he always lays stress on your German when he is leaving for town.
CECILY: Dear Uncle Jack is so very serious! Sometime he is so serious that I think he cannot be quite well.
MISS PRISM: [*Drawing herself up.*] Your guardian enjoys the best of health, and his gravity of demeanor is especially to be commended in one so comparatively young as he is. I know no one who has a higher sense of duty and responsibility.
CECILY: I suppose that is why he often looks a little bored when we three are together.
MISS PRISM: Cecily! I am surprised at you. Mr. Worthing has many troubles in his life. Idle merriment and triviality would be out of place in his conversation. You must remember his constant anxiety about that unfortunate young man his brother.
CECILY: I wish Uncle Jack would allow that unfortunate young man, his brother, to come down here sometimes. We might have a good influence over him, Miss Prism. I am sure you certainly would. You know German, and geology, and things of that kind influence a man very much. [CECILY *begins to write in her diary.*]
MISS PRISM: [*Shaking her head.*] I do not think that even I could produce any effect on a character that according to his own brother's admission is irretrievably weak and vacillating. Indeed I am not sure that I would desire to reclaim him. I am not in favor of this modern mania for turning bad people into good people at a moment's notice. As a man sows so let him reap. You must put

away your diary, Cecily. I really don't see why you should keep a diary at all.

CECILY: I keep a diary in order to enter the wonderful secrets of my life. If I didn't write them down I should probably forget all about them.

MISS PRISM: Memory, my dear Cecily, is the diary that we all carry about with us.

CECILY: Yes, but it usually chronicles the things that have never happened, and couldn't possibly have happened. I believe that memory is responsible for nearly all the three-volume novels that Mudie sends us.[8]

MISS PRISM: Do not speak slightingly of the three-volume novel, Cecily. I wrote one myself in earlier days.

CECILY: Did you really, Miss Prism? How wonderfully clever you are! I hope it did not end happily? I don't like novels that end happily. They depress me so much.

MISS PRISM: The good ended happily, and the bad unhappily. That is what fiction means.

CECILY: I suppose so. But it seems very unfair. And was your novel ever published?

MISS PRISM: Alas! no. The manuscript unfortunately was abandoned. I use the word in the sense of lost or mislaid. To your work, child—these speculations are profitless.

CECILY: [*Smiling.*] But I see dear Dr. Chasuble coming up through the garden.

MISS PRISM: [*Rising and advancing.*] Dr. Chasuble! This is indeed a pleasure.

[*Enter* CANON CHASUBLE.]

CHASUBLE: And how are we this morning? Miss Prism, you are, I trust, well?

CECILY: Miss Prism has just been complaining of a slight headache. I think it would do her so much good to have a short stroll with you in the park, Dr. Chasuble.

MISS PRISM: Cecily, I have not mentioned anything about a headache.

CECILY: No, dear Miss Prism, I know that, but I felt instinctively that you had a headache. Indeed I was thinking about that, and not about my German lesson, when the Rector came in.

CHASUBLE: I hope, Cecily, you are not inattentive.

CECILY: Oh, I am afraid I am.

CHASUBLE: That is strange. Were I fortunate enough to be Miss Prism's pupil, I would hang upon her lips. [MISS PRISM *glares.*] I spoke metaphorically.—My metaphor was drawn from bees. Ahem! Mr. Worthing, I suppose, has not returned from town yet?

MISS PRISM: We do not expect him till Monday afternoon.

CHASUBLE: Ah yes, he usually likes to spend his Sunday in London. He is not one of those whose sole aim is enjoyment, as, by all accounts, that unfortunate young man his brother seems to be. But I must not disturb Egeria[9] and her pupil any longer.

MISS PRISM: Egeria? My name is Laetitia, Doctor.

---

8. From the 1840s to the 1890s most novels were published in three volumes. Because of the price, most readers could not afford to buy copies and so obtained them by subscription from lending libraries, of which Mudie's in London was by far the largest.

9. In classical mythology, a nymph famous as the wise counselor of Numa Pompilius, the second of the legendary kings of Rome.

CHASUBLE: [*Bowing.*] A classical allusion merely, drawn from the Pagan authors. I shall see you both no doubt at Evensong?[1]

MISS PRISM: I think, dear Doctor, I will have a stroll with you. I find I have a headache after all, and a walk might do it good.

CHASUBLE: With pleasure, Miss Prism, with pleasure. We might go as far as the schools and back.

MISS PRISM: That would be delightful. Cecily, you will read your Political Economy[2] in my absence. The chapter on the Fall of the Rupee you may omit. It is somewhat too sensational. Even these metallic problems have their melodramatic side. [*Goes down the garden with* CANON CHASUBLE.]

CECILY: [*Picks up books and throws them back on table.*] Horrid Political Economy! Horrid Geography! Horrid, horrid German!

[*Enter* MERRIMAN *with a card on a salver.*]

MERRIMAN: Mr. Ernest Worthing has just driven over from the station. He has brought his luggage with him.

CECILY: [*Takes the card and reads it.*] "Mr. Ernest Worthing, B. 4, The Albany, W." Uncle Jack's brother! Did you tell him Mr. Worthing was in town?

MERRIMAN: Yes, Miss. He seemed very much disappointed. I mentioned that you and Miss Prism were in the garden. He said he was anxious to speak to you privately for a moment.

CECILY: Ask Mr. Ernest Worthing to come here. I suppose you had better talk to the housekeeper about a room for him.

MERRIMAN: Yes, Miss. [MERRIMAN *goes off.*]

CECILY: I have never met any really wicked person before. I feel rather frightened. I am so afraid he will look just like everyone else. [*Enter* ALGERNON, *very gay and debonair.*] He does!

ALGERNON: [*Raising his hat.*] You are my little cousin Cecily, I'm sure.

CECILY: You are under some strange mistake. I am not little. In fact, I believe I am more than usually tall for my age. [ALGERNON *is rather taken aback.*] But I am your cousin Cecily. You, I see from your card, are Uncle Jack's brother, my cousin Ernest, my wicked cousin Ernest.

ALGERNON: Oh! I am not really wicked at all, cousin Cecily. You mustn't think that I am wicked.

CECILY: If you are not, then you have certainly been deceiving us all in a very inexcusable manner. I hope you have not been leading a double life, pretending to be wicked and being really good all the time. That would be hypocrisy.

ALGERNON: [*Looks at her in amazement.*] Oh! Of course I have been rather reckless.

CECILY: I am glad to hear it.

ALGERNON: In fact, now you mention the subject, I have been very bad in my own small way.

CECILY: I don't think you should be so proud of that, though I am sure it must have been very pleasant.

ALGERNON: It is much pleasanter being here with you.

CECILY: I can't understand how you are here at all. Uncle Jack won't be back till Monday afternoon.

ALGERNON: That is a great disappointment. I am obliged to go up by the first

---

1. Evening church services.  2. That is, book about economics.

train on Monday morning. I have a business appointment that I am anxious . . . to miss.

CECILY: Couldn't you miss it anywhere but in London?

ALGERNON: No: the appointment is in London.

CECILY: Well, I know, of course, how important it is not to keep a business engagement, if one wants to retain any sense of the beauty of life, but still I think you had better wait till Uncle Jack arrives. I know he wants to speak to you about your emigrating.

ALGERNON: About my what?

CECILY: Your emigrating. He has gone up to buy your outfit.

ALGERNON: I certainly wouldn't let Jack buy my outfit. He has no taste in neckties at all.

CECILY: I don't think you will require neckties. Uncle Jack is sending you to Australia.

ALGERNON: Australia? I'd sooner die.

CECILY: Well, he said at dinner on Wednesday night, that you would have to choose between this world, the next world, and Australia.

ALGERNON: Oh, well! The accounts I have received of Australia and the next world are not particularly encouraging. This world is good enough for me, cousin Cecily.

CECILY: Yes, but are you good enough for it?

ALGERNON: I'm afraid I'm not that. That is why I want you to reform me. You might make that your mission, if you don't mind, cousin Cecily.

CECILY: I'm afraid I've no time, this afternoon.

ALGERNON: Well, would you mind my reforming myself this afternoon?

CECILY: It is rather Quixotic of you. But I think you should try.

ALGERNON: I will. I feel better already.

CECILY: You are looking a little worse.

ALGERNON: That is because I am hungry.

CECILY: How thoughtless of me. I should have remembered that when one is going to lead an entirely new life, one requires regular and wholesome meals. Won't you come in?

ALGERNON: Thank you. Might I have a buttonhole[3] first? I never have any appetite unless I have a buttonhole first.

CECILY: A Maréchal Niel? [*Picks up scissors.*]

ALGERNON: No, I'd sooner have a pink rose.

CECILY: Why? [*Cuts a flower.*]

ALGERNON: Because you are like a pink rose, cousin Cecily.

CECILY: I don't think it can be right for you to talk to me like that. Miss Prism never says such things to me.

ALGERNON: Then Miss Prism is a shortsighted old lady. [CECILY *puts the rose in his buttonhole.*] You are the prettiest girl I ever saw.

CECILY: Miss Prism says that all good looks are a snare.

ALGERNON: They are a snare that every sensible man would like to be caught in.

CECILY: Oh! I don't think I would care to catch a sensible man. I shouldn't know what to talk to him about.

---

3. A flower to be worn on the lapel of a man's coat, in this case the Maréchal Niel, a popular yellow rose of the period.

[*They pass into the house.* MISS PRISM *and* DR. CHASUBLE *return.*]

MISS PRISM: You are too much alone, dear Dr. Chasuble. You should get married. A misanthrope I can understand—a womanthrope, never!

CHASUBLE: [*With a scholar's shudder.*] Believe me, I do not deserve so neologistic a phrase. The precept as well as the practice of the Primitive Church was distinctly against matrimony.

MISS PRISM: [*Sententiously.*] That is obviously the reason why the Primitive Church has not lasted up to the present day. And you do not seem to realize, dear Doctor, that by persistently remaining single, a man converts himself into a permanent public temptation. Men should be more careful; this very celibacy leads weaker vessels astray.

CHASUBLE: But is a man not equally attractive when married?

MISS PRISM: No married man is ever attractive except to his wife.

CHASUBLE: And often, I've been told, not even to her.

MISS PRISM: That depends on the intellectual sympathies of the woman. Maturity can always be depended on. Ripeness can be trusted. Young women are green. [DR. CHASUBLE *starts.*] I spoke horticulturally. My metaphor was drawn from fruits. But where is Cecily?

CHASUBLE: Perhaps she followed us to the schools.

[*Enter* JACK *slowly from the back of the garden. He is dressed in the deepest mourning, with crape hat-band and black gloves.*]

MISS PRISM: Mr. Worthing!

CHASUBLE: Mr. Worthing?

MISS PRISM: This is indeed a surprise. We did not look for you till Monday afternoon.

JACK: [*Shakes* MISS PRISM'*s hand in a tragic manner.*] I have returned sooner than I expected. Dr. Chasuble, I hope you are well?

CHASUBLE: Dear Mr. Worthing, I trust this garb of woe does not betoken some terrible calamity?

JACK: My brother.

MISS PRISM: More shameful debts and extravagance?

CHASUBLE: Still leading his life of pleasure?

JACK: [*Shaking his head.*] Dead!

CHASUBLE: Your brother Ernest dead?

JACK: Quite dead.

MISS PRISM: What a lesson for him! I trust he will profit by it.

CHASUBLE: Mr. Worthing, I offer you my sincere condolence. You have at least the consolation of knowing that you were always the most generous and forgiving of brothers.

JACK: Poor Ernest! He had many faults, but it is a sad, sad blow.

CHASUBLE: Very sad indeed. Were you with him at the end?

JACK: No. He died abroad; in Paris, in fact. I had a telegram last night from the manager of the Grand Hotel.

CHASUBLE: Was the cause of death mentioned?

JACK: A severe chill, it seems.

MISS PRISM: As a man sows, so shall he reap.

CHASUBLE: [*Raising his hand.*] Charity, dear Miss Prism, charity! None of us are perfect. I myself am peculiarly susceptible to drafts. Will the interment take place here?

JACK: No. He seemed to have expressed a desire to be buried in Paris.

CHASUBLE: In Paris! [*Shakes his head.*] I fear that hardly points to any very serious state of mind at the last. You would no doubt wish me to make some slight allusion to this tragic domestic affliction next Sunday. [JACK *presses his hand convulsively.*] My sermon on the meaning of the manna in the wilderness can be adapted to almost any occasion, joyful, or, as in the present case, distressing. [*All sigh.*] I have preached it at harvest celebrations, christenings, confirmations, on days of humiliation and festal days. The last time I delivered it was in the Cathedral, as a charity sermon on behalf of the Society for the Prevention of Discontent among the Upper Orders. The Bishop, who was present, was much struck by some of the analogies I drew.

JACK: Ah! That reminds me, you mentioned christenings, I think, Dr. Chasuble? I suppose you know how to christen all right? [DR. CHASUBLE *looks astounded.*] I mean, of course, you are continually christening, aren't you?

MISS PRISM: It is, I regret to say, one of the Rector's most constant duties in this parish. I have often spoken to the poorer classes on the subject. But they don't seem to know what thrift is.

CHASUBLE: But is there any particular infant in whom you are interested, Mr. Worthing? Your brother was, I believe, unmarried, was he not?

JACK: Oh yes.

MISS PRISM: [*Bitterly.*] People who live entirely for pleasure usually are.

JACK: But it is not for any child, dear Doctor. I am very fond of children. No! the fact is, I would like to be christened myself, this afternoon, if you have nothing better to do.

CHASUBLE: But surely, Mr. Worthing, you have been christened already?

JACK: I don't remember anything about it.

CHASUBLE: But have you any grave doubts on the subject?

JACK: I certainly intend to have. Of course I don't know if the thing would bother you in any way, or if you think I am a little too old now.

CHASUBLE: Not at all. The sprinkling, and, indeed, the immersion of adults is a perfectly canonical practice.

JACK: Immersion!

CHASUBLE: You need have no apprehensions. Sprinkling is all that is necessary, or indeed I think advisable. Our weather is so changeable. At what hour would you wish the ceremony performed?

JACK: Oh, I might trot round about five if that would suit you.

CHASUBLE: Perfectly, perfectly! In fact I have two similar ceremonies to perform at that time. A case of twins that occurred recently in one of the outlying cottages on your own estate. Poor Jenkins the carter, a most hard-working man.

JACK: Oh! I don't see much fun in being christened along with other babies. It would be childish. Would half-past five do?

CHASUBLE: Admirably! Admirably! [*Takes out watch.*] And now, dear Mr. Worthing, I will not intrude any longer into a house of sorrow. I would merely beg you not to be too much bowed down by grief. What seem to us bitter trials are often blessings in disguise.

MISS PRISM: This seems to me a blessing of an extremely obvious kind.

[*Enter* CECILY *from the house.*]

CECILY: Uncle Jack! Oh, I am pleased to see you back. But what horrid clothes you have got on! Do go and change them.

MISS PRISM: Cecily!

CHASUBLE: My child! my child!

[CECILY *goes towards* JACK; *he kisses her brow in a melancholy manner.*]

CECILY: What is the matter, Uncle Jack? Do look happy! You look as if you had toothache, and I have got such a surprise for you. Who do you think is in the dining room? Your brother!

JACK: Who?

CECILY: Your brother Ernest. He arrived about half an hour ago.

JACK: What nonsense! I haven't got a brother!

CECILY: Oh, don't say that. However badly he may have behaved to you in the past he is still your brother. You couldn't be so heartless as to disown him. I'll tell him to come out. And you will shake hands with him, won't you, Uncle Jack? [*Runs back into the house.*]

CHASUBLE: These are very joyful tidings.

MISS PRISM: After we had all been resigned to his loss, his sudden return seems to me peculiarly distressing.

JACK: My brother is in the dining room? I don't know what it all means. I think it is perfectly absurd. [*Enter* ALGERNON *and* CECILY *hand in hand. They come slowly up to* JACK.] Good heavens! [*Motions* ALGERNON *away.*]

ALGERNON: Brother John, I have come down from town to tell you that I am very sorry for all the trouble I have given you, and that I intend to lead a better life in the future. [JACK *glares at him and does not take his hand.*]

CECILY: Uncle Jack, you are not going to refuse your own brother's hand?

JACK: Nothing will induce me to take his hand. I think his coming down here disgraceful. He knows perfectly well why.

CECILY: Uncle Jack, do be nice. There is some good in everyone. Ernest has just been telling me about his poor invalid friend Mr. Bunbury whom he goes to visit so often. And surely there must be much good in one who is kind to an invalid, and leaves the pleasures of London to sit by a bed of pain.

JACK: Oh! he has been talking about Bunbury, has he?

CECILY: Yes, he has told me all about poor Mr. Bunbury, and his terrible state of health.

JACK: Bunbury! Well, I won't have him talk to you about Bunbury or about anything else. It is enough to drive one perfectly frantic.

ALGERNON: Of course I admit that the faults were all on my side. But I must say that I think that Brother John's coldness to me is peculiarly painful. I expected a more enthusiastic welcome, especially considering it is the first time I have come here.

CECILY: Uncle Jack, if you don't shake hands with Ernest, I will never forgive you.

JACK: Never forgive me?

CECILY: Never, never, never!

JACK: Well, this is the last time I shall ever do it. [*Shakes hands with* ALGERNON *and glares.*]

CHASUBLE: It's pleasant, is it not, to see so perfect a reconciliation? I think we might leave the two brothers together.

MISS PRISM: Cecily, you will come with us.
CECILY: Certainly, Miss Prism. My little task of reconciliation is over.
CHASUBLE: You have done a beautiful action today, dear child.
MISS PRISM: We must not be premature in our judgments.
CECILY: I feel very happy.

[*They all go off.*]

JACK: You young scoundrel, Algy, you must get out of this place as soon as possible. I don't allow any Bunburying here.

[*Enter* MERRIMAN.]

MERRIMAN: I have put Mr. Ernest's things in the room next to yours, sir. I suppose that is all right?
JACK: What?
MERRIMAN: Mr. Ernest's luggage, sir. I have unpacked it and put it in the room next to your own.
JACK: His luggage?
MERRIMAN: Yes, sir. Three portmanteaus, a dressing case, two hat-boxes, and a large luncheon basket.
ALGERNON: I am afraid I can't stay more than a week this time.
JACK: Merriman, order the dogcart[4] at once. Mr. Ernest has been suddenly called back to town.
MERRIMAN: Yes, sir. [*Goes back into the house.*]
ALGERNON: What a fearful liar you are, Jack. I have not been called back to town at all.
JACK: Yes, you have.
ALGERNON: I haven't heard anyone call me.
JACK: Your duty as a gentleman calls you back.
ALGERNON: My duty as a gentleman has never interfered with my pleasures in the smallest degree.
JACK: I can quite understand that.
ALGERNON: Well, Cecily is a darling.
JACK: You are not to talk of Miss Cardew like that. I don't like it.
ALGERNON: Well, I don't like your clothes. You look perfectly ridiculous in them. Why on earth don't you go up and change? It is perfectly childish to be in deep mourning for a man who is actually staying for a whole week with you in your house as a guest. I call it grotesque.
JACK: You are certainly not staying with me for a whole week as a guest or anything else. You have got to leave . . . by the four-five train.
ALGERNON: I certainly won't leave you so long as you are in mourning. It would be most unfriendly. If I were in mourning you would stay with me, I suppose. I should think it very unkind if you didn't.
JACK: Well, will you go if I change my clothes?
ALGERNON: Yes, if you are not too long. I never saw anybody take so long to dress, and with such little result.
JACK: Well, at any rate, that is better than being always overdressed as you are.
ALGERNON: If I am occasionally a little overdressed, I make up for it by being always immensely overeducated.

---

4. A light, two-wheeled carriage, usually drawn by one horse.

JACK: Your vanity is ridiculous, your conduct an outrage, and your presence in my garden utterly absurd. However, you have got to catch the four-five, and I hope you will have a pleasant journey back to town. This Bunburying, as you call it, has not been a great success for you. [*Goes into the house.*]
ALGERNON: I think it has been a great success. I'm in love with Cecily, and that is everything. [*Enter* CECILY *at the back of the garden. She picks up the can and begins to water the flowers.*] But I must see her before I go, and make arrangements for another Bunbury. Ah, there she is.
CECILY: Oh, I merely came back to water the roses. I thought you were with Uncle Jack.
ALGERNON: He's gone to order the dogcart for me.
CECILY: Oh, is he going to take you for a nice drive?
ALGERNON: He's going to send me away.
CECILY: Then have we got to part?
ALGERNON: I am afraid so. It's very painful parting.
CECILY: It is always painful to part from people whom one has known for a very brief space of time. The absence of old friends one can endure with equanimity. But even a momentary separation from anyone to whom one has just been introduced is almost unbearable.
ALGERNON: Thank you.

[*Enter* MERRIMAN.]

MERRIMAN: The dogcart is at the door, sir. [ALGERNON *looks appealingly at* CECILY.]
CECILY: It can wait, Merriman . . . for . . . five minutes.
MERRIMAN: Yes, Miss. [*Exit* MERRIMAN.]
ALGERNON: I hope, Cecily, I shall not offend you if I state quite frankly and openly that you seem to me to be in every way the visible personification of absolute perfection.
CECILY: I think your frankness does you great credit, Ernest. If you will allow me I will copy your remarks into my diary. [*Goes over to table and begins writing in diary.*]
ALGERNON: Do you really keep a diary? I'd give anything to look at it. May I?
CECILY: Oh no. [*Puts her hand over it.*] You see, it is simply a very young girl's record of her own thoughts and impressions, and consequently meant for publication. When it appears in volume form I hope you will order a copy. But pray, Ernest, don't stop. I delight in taking down from dictation. I have reached "absolute perfection." You can go on. I am quite ready for more.
ALGERNON: [*Somewhat taken aback.*] Ahem! Ahem!
CECILY: Oh, don't cough, Ernest. When one is dictating one should speak fluently and not cough. Besides, I don't know how to spell a cough. [*Writes as* ALGERNON *speaks.*]
ALGERNON: [*Speaking very rapidly.*] Cecily, ever since I first looked upon your wonderful and incomparable beauty, I have dared to love you wildly, passionately, devotedly, hopelessly.
CECILY: I don't think that you should tell me that you love me wildly, passionately, devotedly, hopelessly. Hopelessly doesn't seem to make much sense, does it?
ALGERNON: Cecily!

[*Enter* MERRIMAN.]

MERRIMAN: The dogcart is waiting, sir.
ALGERNON: Tell it to come round next week, at the same hour.
MERRIMAN: [*Looks at* CECILY, *who makes no sign.*] Yes, sir. [MERRIMAN *retires.*]
CECILY: Uncle Jack would be very much annoyed if he knew you were staying on till next week, at the same hour.
ALGERNON: Oh, I don't care about Jack. I don't care for anybody in the whole world but you. I love you, Cecily. You will marry me, won't you?
CECILY: You silly boy! Of course. Why, we have been engaged for the last three months.
ALGERNON: For the last three months?
CECILY: Yes, it will be exactly three months on Thursday.
ALGERNON: But how did we become engaged?
CECILY: Well, ever since dear Uncle Jack first confessed to us that he had a younger brother who was very wicked and bad, you of course have formed the chief topic of conversation between myself and Miss Prism. And of course a man who is much talked about is always very attractive. One feels there must be something in him after all. I daresay it was foolish of me, but I fell in love with you, Ernest.
ALGERNON: Darling! And when was the engagement actually settled?
CECILY: On the 14th of February last. Worn out by your entire ignorance of my existence, I determined to end the matter one way or the other, and after a long struggle with myself I accepted you under this dear old tree here. The next day I bought this little ring in your name, and this is the little bangle with the true lovers' knot I promised you always to wear.
ALGERNON: Did I give you this? It's very pretty, isn't it?
CECILY: Yes, you've wonderfully good taste, Ernest. It's the excuse I've always given for your leading such a bad life. And this is the box in which I keep all your dear letters. [*Kneels at table, opens box, and produces letters tied up with blue ribbon.*]
ALGERNON: My letters! But my own sweet Cecily, I have never written you any letters.
CECILY: You need hardly remind me of that, Ernest. I remember only too well that I was forced to write your letters for you. I always wrote three times a week, and sometimes oftener.
ALGERNON: Oh, do let me read them, Cecily?
CECILY: Oh, I couldn't possibly. They would make you far too conceited. [*Replaces box.*] The three you wrote me after I had broken off the engagement are so beautiful, and so badly spelled, that even now I can hardly read them without crying a little.
ALGERNON: But was our engagement ever broken off?
CECILY: Of course it was. On the 22nd of last March. You can see the entry if you like. [*Shows diary.*] "Today I broke off my engagement with Ernest. I feel it is better to do so. The weather still continues charming."
ALGERNON: But why on earth did you break it off? What had I done? I had done nothing at all. Cecily, I am very much hurt indeed to hear you broke it off. Particularly when the weather was so charming.
CECILY: It would hardly have been a really serious engagement if it hadn't been broken off at least once. But I forgave you before the week was out.
ALGERNON: [*Crossing to her, and kneeling.*] What a perfect angel you are, Cecily.
CECILY: You dear romantic boy. [*He kisses her, she puts her fingers through his hair.*] I hope your hair curls naturally, does it?

ALGERNON: Yes, darling, with a little help from others.
CECILY: I am so glad.
ALGERNON: You'll never break off our engagement again, Cecily?
CECILY: I don't think I could break it off now that I have actually met you. Besides, of course, there is the question of your name.
ALGERNON: Yes, of course. [*Nervously.*]
CECILY: You must not laugh at me, darling, but it had always been a girlish dream of mine to love someone whose name was Ernest. [ALGERNON *rises,* CECILY *also.*] There is something in that name that seems to inspire absolute confidence. I pity any poor married woman whose husband is not called Ernest.
ALGERNON: But, my dear child, do you mean to say you could not love me if I had some other name?
CECILY: But what name?
ALGERNON: Oh, any name you like—Algernon—for instance...
CECILY: But I don't like the name of Algernon.
ALGERNON: Well, my own dear, sweet, loving little darling, I really can't see why you should object to the name of Algernon. It is not at all a bad name. In fact, it is rather an aristocratic name. Half of the chaps who get into the Bankruptcy Court are called Algernon. But seriously, Cecily... [*Moving to her.*] ... if my name was Algy, couldn't you love me?
CECILY: [*Rising.*] I might respect you, Ernest, I might admire your character, but I fear that I should not be able to give you my undivided attention.
ALGERNON: Ahem! Cecily! [*Picking up hat.*] Your Rector here is, I suppose, thoroughly experienced in the practice of all the rites and ceremonials of the Church?
CECILY: Oh, yes. Dr. Chasuble is a most learned man. He has never written a single book, so you can imagine how much he knows.
ALGERNON: I must see him at once on a most important christening—I mean on most important business.
CECILY: Oh!
ALGERNON: I shan't be away more than half an hour.
CECILY: Considering that we have been engaged since February the 14th, and that I only met you today for the first time, I think it is rather hard that you should leave me for so long a period as half an hour. Couldn't you make it twenty minutes?
ALGERNON: I'll be back in no time. [*Kisses her and rushes down the garden.*]
CECILY: What an impetuous boy he is! I like his hair so much. I must enter his proposal in my diary.

[*Enter* MERRIMAN.]

MERRIMAN: A Miss Fairfax has just called to see Mr. Worthing. On very important business, Miss Fairfax states.
CECILY: Isn't Mr. Worthing in his library?
MERRIMAN: Mr. Worthing went over in the direction of the rectory some time ago.
CECILY: Pray ask the lady to come out here; Mr. Worthing is sure to be back soon. And you can bring tea.
MERRIMAN: Yes, Miss. [*Goes out.*]
CECILY: Miss Fairfax! I suppose one of the many good elderly women who are

associated with Uncle Jack in some of his philanthropic work in London. I don't quite like women who are interested in philanthropic work. I think it is so forward of them.

[*Enter* MERRIMAN.]

MERRIMAN: Miss Fairfax.

[*Enter* GWENDOLEN. *Exit* MERRIMAN.]

CECILY: [*Advancing to meet her.*] Pray let me introduce myself to you. My name is Cecily Cardew.

GWENDOLEN: Cecily Cardew? [*Moving to her and shaking hands.*] What a very sweet name! Something tells me that we are going to be great friends. I like you already more than I can say. My first impressions of people are never wrong.

CECILY: How nice of you to like me so much after we have known each other such a comparatively short time. Pray sit down.

GWENDOLEN: [*Still standing up.*] I may call you Cecily, may I not?

CECILY: With pleasure!

GWENDOLEN: And you will always call me Gwendolen, won't you?

CECILY: If you wish.

GWENDOLEN: Then that is all quite settled, is it not?

CECILY: I hope so. [*A pause. They both sit down together.*]

GWENDOLEN: Perhaps this might be a favorable opportunity for my mentioning who I am. My father is Lord Bracknell. You have never heard of papa, I suppose?

CECILY: I don't think so.

GWENDOLEN: Outside the family circle, papa, I am glad to say, is entirely unknown. I think that is quite as it should be. The home seems to me to be the proper sphere for the man. And certainly once a man begins to neglect his domestic duties he becomes painfully effeminate, does he not? And I don't like that. It makes men so very attractive. Cecily, mamma, whose views on education are remarkably strict, has brought me up to be extremely short-sighted; it is part of her system; so do you mind my looking at you through my glasses?

CECILY: Oh! not at all, Gwendolen. I am very fond of being looked at.

GWENDOLEN: [*After examining* CECILY *carefully through a lorgnette.*] You are here on a short visit, I suppose.

CECILY: Oh no! I live here.

GWENDOLEN: [*Severely.*] Really? Your mother, no doubt, or some female relative of advanced years, resides here also?

CECILY: Oh no! I have no mother, nor, in fact, any relations.

GWENDOLEN: Indeed?

CECILY: My dear guardian, with the assistance of Miss Prism, has the arduous task of looking after me.

GWENDOLEN: Your guardian?

CECILY: Yes, I am Mr. Worthing's ward.

GWENDOLEN: Oh! It is strange he never mentioned to me that he had a ward. How secretive of him! He grows more interesting hourly. I am not sure, however, that the news inspires me with feelings of unmixed delight. [*Rising and going to her.*] I am very fond of you, Cecily; I have liked you ever since I met you! But I am bound to state that now that I know that you are Mr. Worthing's ward, I cannot help expressing a wish you were—well just a little older than you seem to be—and not quite so very alluring in appearance. In fact, if I may speak candidly—

CECILY: Pray do! I think that whenever one has anything unpleasant to say, one should always be quite candid.

GWENDOLEN: Well, to speak with perfect candor, Cecily, I wish that you were fully forty-two, and more than usually plain for your age. Ernest has a strong upright nature. He is the very soul of truth and honor. Disloyalty would be as impossible to him as deception. But even men of the noblest possible moral character are extremely susceptible to the influence of the physical charms of others. Modern, no less than ancient history, supplies us with many most painful examples of what I refer to. If it were not so, indeed, history would be quite unreadable.

CECILY: I beg your pardon, Gwendolen, did you say Ernest?

GWENDOLEN: Yes.

CECILY: Oh, but it is not Mr. Ernest Worthing who is my guardian. It is his brother—his elder brother.

GWENDOLEN: [*Sitting down again.*] Ernest never mentioned to me that he had a brother.

CECILY: I am sorry to say they have not been on good terms for a long time.

GWENDOLEN: Ah! that accounts for it. And now that I think of it I have never heard any man mention his brother. The subject seems distasteful to most men. Cecily, you have lifted a load from my mind. I was growing almost anxious. It would have been terrible if any cloud had come across a friendship like ours, would it not? Of course you are quite, quite sure that it is not Mr. Ernest Worthing who is your guardian?

CECILY: Quite sure. [*A pause.*] In fact, I am going to be his.

GWENDOLEN: [*Inquiringly.*] I beg your pardon?

CECILY: [*Rather shy and confidingly.*] Dearest Gwendolen, there is no reason why I should make a secret of it to you. Our little county newspaper is sure to chronicle the fact next week. Mr. Ernest Worthing and I are engaged to be married.

GWENDOLEN: [*Quite politely, rising.*] My darling Cecily, I think there must be some slight error. Mr. Ernest Worthing is engaged to me. The announcement will appear in the *Morning Post* on Saturday at the latest.

CECILY: [*Very politely, rising.*] I am afraid you must be under some misconception. Ernest proposed to me exactly ten minutes ago. [*Shows diary.*]

GWENDOLEN: [*Examines diary through her lorgnette carefully.*] It is certainly very curious, for he asked me to be his wife yesterday afternoon at 5:30. If you would care to verify the incident, pray do so. [*Produces diary of her own.*] I never travel without my diary. One should always have something sensational to read in the train. I am so sorry, dear Cecily, if it is any disappointment to you, but I am afraid *I* have the prior claim.

CECILY: It would distress me more than I can tell you, dear Gwendolen, if it caused you any mental or physical anguish, but I feel bound to point out that since Ernest proposed to you he clearly has changed his mind.

GWENDOLEN: [*Meditatively.*] If the poor fellow has been entrapped into any foolish promise I shall consider it my duty to rescue him at once, and with a firm hand.

CECILY: [*Thoughtfully and sadly.*] Whatever unfortunate entanglement my dear boy may have got into, I will never reproach him with it after we are married.

GWENDOLEN: Do you allude to me, Miss Cardew, as an entanglement? You are presumptuous. On an occasion of this kind it becomes more than a moral duty to speak one's mind. It becomes a pleasure.

CECILY: Do you suggest, Miss Fairfax, that I entrapped Ernest into an engagement? How dare you? This is no time for wearing the shallow mask of manners. When I see a spade I call it a spade.

GWENDOLEN: [*Satirically.*] I am glad to say that I have never seen a spade. It is obvious that our social spheres have been widely different.

[*Enter* MERRIMAN, *followed by the footman. He carries a salver, tablecloth, and plate stand.* CECILY *is about to retort. The presence of the servants exercises a restraining influence, under which both girls chafe.*]

MERRIMAN: Shall I lay tea here as usual, Miss?

CECILY: [*Sternly, in a calm voice.*] Yes, as usual.

[MERRIMAN *begins to clear table and lay cloth. A long pause.* CECILY *and* GWENDOLEN *glare at each other.*]

GWENDOLEN: Are there many interesting walks in the vicinity, Miss Cardew?

CECILY: Oh! yes! a great many. From the top of one of the hills quite close one can see five counties.

GWENDOLEN: Five counties! I don't think I should like that. I hate crowds.

CECILY: [*Sweetly.*] I suppose that is why you live in town?

[GWENDOLEN *bites her lip, and beats her foot nervously with her parasol.*]

GWENDOLEN: [*Looking round.*] Quite a well-kept garden this is, Miss Cardew.

CECILY: So glad you like it, Miss Fairfax.

GWENDOLEN: I had no idea there were any flowers in the country.

CECILY: Oh, flowers are as common here, Miss Fairfax, as people are in London.

GWENDOLEN: Personally I cannot understand how anybody manages to exist in the country, if anybody who is anybody does. The country always bores me to death.

CECILY: Ah! This is what the newspapers call agricultural depression, is it not? I believe the aristocracy are suffering very much from it just at present. It is almost an epidemic amongst them, I have been told. May I offer you some tea, Miss Fairfax?

GWENDOLEN: [*With elaborate politeness.*] Thank you. [*Aside.*] Detestable girl! But I require tea!

CECILY: [*Sweetly.*] Sugar?

GWENDOLEN: [*Superciliously.*] No, thank you. Sugar is not fashionable anymore.

[CECILY *looks angrily at her, takes up the tongs and puts four lumps of sugar into the cup.*]

CECILY: [*Severely.*] Cake or bread and butter?

GWENDOLEN: [*In a bored manner.*] Bread and butter, please. Cake is rarely seen at the best houses nowadays.

CECILY: [*Cuts a very large slice of cake, and puts it on the tray.*] Hand that to Miss Fairfax.

[MERRIMAN *does so, and goes out with footman.* GWENDOLEN *drinks the tea and makes a grimace. Puts down cup at once, reaches out her hand to the bread and butter, looks at it, and finds it is cake. Rises in indignation.*]

GWENDOLEN: You have filled my tea with lumps of sugar, and though I asked most distinctly for bread and butter, you have given me cake. I am known for the gentleness of my disposition, and the extraordinary sweetness of my nature, but I warn you, Miss Cardew, you may go too far.

CECILY: [*Rising.*] To save my poor, innocent, trusting boy from the machinations of any other girl there are no lengths to which I would not go.

GWENDOLEN: From the moment I saw you I distrusted you. I felt that you were false and deceitful. I am never deceived in such matters. My first impressions of people are invariably right.

CECILY: It seems to me, Miss Fairfax, that I am trespassing on your valuable time. No doubt you have many other calls of a similar character to make in the neighborhood.

[*Enter* JACK.]

GWENDOLEN: [*Catching sight of him.*] Ernest! My own Ernest!

JACK: Gwendolen! Darling! [*Offers to kiss her.*]

GWENDOLEN: [*Drawing back.*] A moment! May I ask if you are engaged to be married to this young lady? [*Points to* CECILY.]

JACK: [*Laughing.*] To dear little Cecily! Of course not! What could have put such an idea into your pretty little head?

GWENDOLEN: Thank you. You may! [*Offers her cheek.*]

CECILY: [*Very sweetly.*] I knew there must be some misunderstanding, Miss Fairfax. The gentleman whose arm is at present round your waist is my dear guardian, Mr. John Worthing.

GWENDOLEN: I beg your pardon?

CECILY: This is Uncle Jack.

GWENDOLEN: [*Receding.*] Jack! Oh!

[*Enter* ALGERNON.]

CECILY: Here is Ernest.

ALGERNON: [*Goes straight over to* CECILY *without noticing anyone else.*] My own love! [*Offers to kiss her.*]

CECILY: [*Drawing back.*] A moment, Ernest! May I ask you—are you engaged to be married to this young lady?

ALGERNON: [*Looking round.*] To what young lady? Good heavens! Gwendolen!

CECILY: Yes! to good heavens, Gwendolen, I mean to Gwendolen.

ALGERNON: [*Laughing.*] Of course not! What could have put such an idea into your pretty little head?

CECILY: Thank you. [*Presenting her cheek to be kissed.*] You may. [ALGERNON *kisses her.*]

GWENDOLEN: I felt there was some slight error, Miss Cardew. The gentleman who is now embracing you is my cousin, Mr. Algernon Moncrieff.

CECILY: [*Breaking away from* ALGERNON.] Algernon Moncrieff! Oh! [*The two girls*

*move towards each other and put their arms round each other's waists as if for protection.*] Are you called Algernon?
ALGERNON: I cannot deny it.
CECILY: Oh!
GWENDOLEN: Is your name really John?
JACK: [*Standing rather proudly.*] I could deny it if I liked, I could deny anything if I liked. But my name certainly is John. It has been John for years.
CECILY: [*To* GWENDOLEN.] A gross deception has been practiced on both of us.
GWENDOLEN: My poor wounded Cecily!
CECILY: My sweet wronged Gwendolen!
GWENDOLEN: [*Slowly and seriously.*] You will call me sister, will you not?

[*They embrace.* JACK *and* ALGERNON *groan and walk up and down.*]

CECILY: [*Rather brightly.*] There is just one question I would like to be allowed to ask my guardian.
GWENDOLEN: An admirable idea! Mr. Worthing, there is just one question I would like to be permitted to put to you. Where is your brother Ernest? We are both engaged to be married to your brother Ernest, so it is a matter of some importance to us to know where your brother Ernest is at present.
JACK: [*Slowly and hesitatingly.*] Gwendolen—Cecily—it is very painful for me to be forced to speak the truth. It is the first time in my life that I have ever been reduced to such a painful position, and I am really quite inexperienced in doing anything of the kind. However I will tell you quite frankly that I have no brother Ernest. I have no brother at all. I never had a brother in my life, and certainly have not the smallest intention of ever having one in the future.
CECILY: [*Surprised.*] No brother at all?
JACK: [*Cheerily.*] None!
GWENDOLEN: [*Severely.*] Had you never a brother of any kind?
JACK: [*Pleasantly.*] Never. Not even of any kind.
GWENDOLEN: I am afraid it is quite clear, Cecily, that neither of us is engaged to be married to anyone.
CECILY: It is not a very pleasant position for a young girl suddenly to find herself in. Is it?
GWENDOLEN: Let us go into the house. They will hardly venture to come after us there.
CECILY: No, men are so cowardly, aren't they?

[*They retire into the house with scornful looks.*]

JACK: This ghastly state of things is what you call Bunburying, I suppose?
ALGERNON: Yes, and a perfectly wonderful Bunbury it is. The most wonderful Bunbury I have ever had in my life.
JACK: Well, you've no right whatsoever to Bunbury here.
ALGERNON: That is absurd. One has a right to Bunbury anywhere one chooses. Every serious Bunburyist knows that.
JACK: Serious Bunburyist! Good heavens!
ALGERNON: Well, one must be serious about something, if one wants to have any amusement in life. I happen to be serious about Bunburying. What on earth you are serious about I haven't got the remotest idea. About everything, I should fancy. You have such an absolutely trivial nature.

JACK: Well, the only small satisfaction I have in the whole of this wretched business is that your friend Bunbury is quite exploded. You won't be able to run down to the country quite so often as you used to do, dear Algy. And a very good thing too.

ALGERNON: Your brother is a little off-color, isn't he, dear Jack? You won't be able to disappear to London quite so frequently as your wicked custom was. And not a bad thing either.

JACK: As for your conduct towards Miss Cardew, I must say that your taking in a sweet, simple, innocent girl like that is quite inexcusable. To say nothing of the fact that she is my ward.

ALGERNON: I can see no possible defense at all for your deceiving a brilliant, clever, thoroughly experienced young lady like Miss Fairfax. To say nothing of the fact that she is my cousin.

JACK: I wanted to be engaged to Gwendolen, that is all. I love her.

ALGERNON: Well, I simply wanted to be engaged to Cecily. I adore her.

JACK: There is certainly no chance of your marrying Miss Cardew.

ALGERNON: I don't think there is much likelihood, Jack, of you and Miss Fairfax being united.

JACK: Well, that is no business of yours.

ALGERNON: If it was my business, I wouldn't talk about it. [*Begins to eat muffins.*] It is very vulgar to talk about one's business. Only people like stockbrokers do that, and then merely at dinner parties.

JACK: How can you sit there, calmly eating muffins when we are in this horrible trouble, I can't make out. You seem to me to be perfectly heartless.

ALGERNON: Well, I can't eat muffins in an agitated manner. The butter would probably get on my cuffs. One should always eat muffins quite calmly. It is the only way to eat them.

JACK: I say it's perfectly heartless your eating muffins at all, under the circumstances.

ALGERNON: When I am in trouble, eating is the only thing that consoles me. Indeed, when I am in really great trouble, as anyone who knows me intimately will tell you, I refuse everything except food and drink. At the present moment I am eating muffins because I am unhappy. Besides, I am particularly fond of muffins. [*Rising.*]

JACK: [*Rising.*] Well, that is no reason why you should eat them all in that greedy way. [*Takes muffins from* ALGERNON.]

ALGERNON: [*Offering tea cake.*] I wish you would have tea cake instead. I don't like tea cake.

JACK: Good heavens! I suppose a man may eat his own muffins in his own garden.

ALGERNON: But you have just said it was perfectly heartless to eat muffins.

JACK: I said it was perfectly heartless of you, under the circumstances. That is a very different thing.

ALGERNON: That may be. But the muffins are the same. [*He seizes the muffin dish from* JACK.]

JACK: Algy, I wish to goodness you would go.

ALGERNON: You can't possibly ask me to go without having some dinner. It's absurd. I never go without my dinner. No one ever does, except vegetarians and people like that. Besides I have just made arrangements with Dr. Chasuble to be christened at a quarter to six under the name of Ernest.

JACK: My dear fellow, the sooner you give up that nonsense the better. I made arrangements this morning with Dr. Chasuble to be christened myself at 5:30, and I naturally will take the name of Ernest. Gwendolen would wish it. We can't both be christened Ernest. It's absurd. Besides, I have a perfect right to be christened if I like. There is no evidence at all that I ever have been christened by anybody. I should think it extremely probable I never was, and so does Dr. Chasuble. It is entirely different in your case. You have been christened already.

ALGERNON: Yes, but I have not been christened for years.

JACK: Yes, but you have been christened. That is the important thing.

ALGERNON: Quite so. So I know my constitution can stand it. If you are not quite sure about your ever having been christened, I must say I think it rather dangerous your venturing on it now. It might make you very unwell. You can hardly have forgotten that someone very closely connected with you was very nearly carried off this week in Paris by a severe chill.

JACK: Yes, but you said yourself that a severe chill was not hereditary.

ALGERNON: It usen't to be, I know—but I daresay it is now. Science is always making wonderful improvements in things.

JACK: [*Picking up the muffin dish.*] Oh, that is nonsense; you are always talking nonsense.

ALGERNON: Jack, you are at the muffins again! I wish you wouldn't. There are only two left. [*Takes them.*] I told you I was particularly fond of muffins.

JACK: But I hate tea cake.

ALGERNON: Why on earth then do you allow tea cake to be served up for your guests? What ideas you have of hospitality!

JACK: Algernon! I have already told you to go. I don't want you here. Why don't you go!

ALGERNON: I haven't quite finished my tea yet! and there is still one muffin left.

[JACK *groans, and sinks into a chair.* ALGERNON *still continues eating.*]

ACT-DROP

# ACT III

SCENE: *Morning room at the Manor House.*

[GWENDOLEN *and* CECILY *are at the window, looking out into the garden.*]

GWENDOLEN: The fact that they did not follow us at once into the house, as anyone else would have done, seems to me to show that they have some sense of shame left.

CECILY: They have been eating muffins. That looks like repentance.

GWENDOLEN: [*After a pause.*] They don't seem to notice us at all. Couldn't you cough?

CECILY: But I haven't got a cough.

GWENDOLEN: They're looking at us. What effrontery!

CECILY: They're approaching. That's very forward of them.

GWENDOLEN: Let us preserve a dignified silence.

CECILY: Certainly. It's the only thing to do now.

[*Enter* JACK *followed by* ALGERNON. *They whistle some dreadful popular air from a British Opera.*]

GWENDOLEN: This dignified silence seems to produce an unpleasant effect.
CECILY: A most distasteful one.
GWENDOLEN: But we will not be the first to speak.
CECILY: Certainly not.
GWENDOLEN: Mr. Worthing, I have something very particular to ask you. Much depends on your reply.
CECILY: Gwendolen, your common sense is invaluable. Mr. Moncrieff, kindly answer me the following question. Why did you pretend to be my guardian's brother?
ALGERNON: In order that I might have an opportunity of meeting you.
CECILY: [*To* GWENDOLEN.] That certainly seems a satisfactory explanation, does it not?
GWENDOLEN: Yes, dear, if you can believe him.
CECILY: I don't. But that does not affect the wonderful beauty of his answer.
GWENDOLEN: True. In matters of grave importance, style, not sincerity, is the vital thing. Mr. Worthing, what explanation can you offer to me for pretending to have a brother? Was it in order that you might have an opportunity of coming up to town to see me as often as possible?
JACK: Can you doubt it, Miss Fairfax?
GWENDOLEN: I have the gravest doubts upon the subject. But I intend to crush them. This is not the moment for German skepticism.[5] [*Moving to* CECILY.] Their explanations appear to be quite satisfactory, especially Mr. Worthing's. That seems to me to have the stamp of truth upon it.
CECILY: I am more than content with what Mr. Moncrieff said. His voice alone inspires one with absolute credulity.
GWENDOLEN: Then you think we should forgive them?
CECILY: Yes. I mean no.
GWENDOLEN: True! I had forgotten. There are principles at stake that one cannot surrender. Which of us should tell them? The task is not a pleasant one.
CECILY: Could we not both speak at the same time?
GWENDOLEN: An excellent idea! I nearly always speak at the same time as other people. Will you take the time from me?
CECILY: Certainly. [GWENDOLEN *beats time with uplifted finger.*]
GWENDOLEN AND CECILY: [*Speaking together.*] Your Christian names are still an insuperable barrier. That is all!
JACK AND ALGERNON: [*Speaking together.*] Our Christian names! Is that all? But we are going to be christened this afternoon.
GWENDOLEN: [*To* JACK.] For my sake you are prepared to do this terrible thing?
JACK: I am.
CECILY: [*To* ALGERNON.] To please me you are ready to face this fearful ordeal?
ALGERNON: I am!
GWENDOLEN: How absurd to talk of the equality of the sexes! Where questions

---

5. A reference to such philosophical movements as the Materialism of Ludwig Feuerbach (1804–1872) and such theological movements as the "Higher Criticism," which promoted studying the Bible in the same way as other books.

of self-sacrifice are concerned, men are infinitely beyond us.
JACK: We are. [*Clasps hands with* ALGERNON.]
CECILY: They have moments of physical courage of which we women know absolutely nothing.
GWENDOLEN: [*To* JACK.] Darling!
ALGERNON: [*To* CECILY.] Darling. [*They fall into each other's arms.*]

[*Enter* MERRIMAN. *When he enters he coughs loudly, seeing the situation.*]

MERRIMAN: Ahem! Ahem! Lady Bracknell!
JACK: Good heavens!

[*Enter* LADY BRACKNELL. *The couples separate in alarm. Exit* MERRIMAN.]

LADY BRACKNELL: Gwendolen! What does this mean?
GWENDOLEN: Merely that I am engaged to be married to Mr. Worthing, mamma.
LADY BRACKNELL: Come here. Sit down. Sit down immediately. Hesitation of any kind is a sign of mental decay in the young, of physical weakness in the old. [*Turns to* JACK.] Apprised, sir, of my daughter's sudden flight by her trusty maid, whose confidence I purchased by means of a small coin, I followed her at once by a luggage train. Her unhappy father is, I am glad to say, under the impression that she is attending a more than usually lengthy lecture by the University Extension Scheme on the Influence of a Permanent Income on Thought. I do not propose to undeceive him. Indeed I have never undeceived him on any question. I would consider it wrong. But of course, you will clearly understand that all communication between yourself and my daughter must cease immediately from this moment. On this point, as indeed on all points, I am firm.
JACK: I am engaged to be married to Gwendolen, Lady Bracknell!
LADY BRACKNELL: You are nothing of the kind, sir. And now, as regards Algernon! . . . Algernon!
ALGERNON: Yes, Aunt Augusta.
LADY BRACKNELL: May I ask if it is in this house that your invalid friend Mr. Bunbury resides?
ALGERNON: [*Stammering.*] Oh! No! Bunbury doesn't live here. Bunbury is somewhere else at present. In fact, Bunbury is dead.
LADY BRACKNELL: Dead! When did Mr. Bunbury die? His death must have been extremely sudden.
ALGERNON: [*Airily.*] Oh! I killed Bunbury this afternoon. I mean poor Bunbury died this afternoon.
LADY BRACKNELL: What did he die of?
ALGERNON: Bunbury? Oh, he was quite exploded.
LADY BRACKNELL: Exploded! Was he the victim of a revolutionary outrage? I was not aware that Mr. Bunbury was interested in social legislation. If so, he is well punished for his morbidity.
ALGERNON: My dear Aunt Augusta, I mean he was found out! The doctors found out that Bunbury could not live, that is what I mean—so Bunbury died.
LADY BRACKNELL: He seems to have had great confidence in the opinion of his physicians. I am glad, however, that he made up his mind at the last to some definite course of action, and acted under proper medical advice. And now that we have finally got rid of this Mr. Bunbury, may I ask, Mr. Worthing,

who is that young person whose hand my nephew Algernon is now holding in what seems to me a peculiarly unnecessary manner?

JACK: That lady is Miss Cecily Cardew, my ward.

[LADY BRACKNELL *bows coldly to* CECILY.]

ALGERNON: I am engaged to be married to Cecily, Aunt Augusta.

LADY BRACKNELL: I beg your pardon?

CECILY: Mr. Moncrieff and I are engaged to be married, Lady Bracknell.

LADY BRACKNELL: [*With a shiver, crossing to the sofa and sitting down.*] I do not know whether there is anything peculiarly exciting in the air of this particular part of Hertfordshire, but the number of engagements that go on seems to me considerably above the proper average that statistics have laid down for our guidance. I think some preliminary inquiry on my part would not be out of place. Mr. Worthing, is Miss Cardew at all connected with any of the larger railway stations in London? I merely desire information. Until yesterday I had no idea that there were any families or persons whose origin was a terminus.

[JACK *looks perfectly furious, but restrains himself.*]

JACK: [*In a clear, cold voice.*] Miss Cardew is the granddaughter of the late Mr. Thomas Cardew of 149, Belgrave Square, S.W.; Gervase Park, Dorking, Surrey; and the Sporran, Fifeshire, N.B.[6]

LADY BRACKNELL: That sounds not unsatisfactory. Three addresses always inspire confidence, even in tradesmen. But what proof have I of their authenticity?

JACK: I have carefully preserved the Court Guides[7] of the period. They are open to your inspection, Lady Bracknell.

LADY BRACKNELL: [*Grimly.*] I have known strange errors in that publication.

JACK: Miss Cardew's family solicitors are Messrs. Markby, Markby, and Markby.

LADY BRACKNELL: Markby, Markby, and Markby? A firm of the very highest position in their profession. Indeed I am told that one of the Mr. Markbys is occasionally to be seen at dinner parties. So far I am satisfied.

JACK: [*Very irritably.*] How extremely kind of you, Lady Bracknell! I have also in my possession, you will be pleased to hear, certificates of Miss Cardew's birth, baptism, whooping cough, registration, vaccination, confirmation, and the measles; both the German and the English variety.

LADY BRACKNELL: Ah! A life crowded with incident, I see; though perhaps somewhat too exciting for a young girl. I am not myself in favor of premature experiences. [*Rises, looks at her watch.*] Gwendolen! the time approaches for our departure. We have not a moment to lose. As a matter of form, Mr. Worthing, I had better ask you if Miss Cardew has any little fortune?

JACK: Oh! about a hundred and thirty thousand pounds in the Funds.[8] That is all. Good-bye, Lady Bracknell. So pleased to have seen you.

LADY BRACKNELL: [*Sitting down again.*] A moment, Mr. Worthing. A hundred and thirty thousand pounds! And in the Funds! Miss Cardew seems to me a most

---

6. In addition to his London residence in Belgrave Square (referred to in Act I), Mr. Cardew has homes in the south of England (Dorking, Surrey) and in Scotland (Fifeshire; N.B.: North Britain).
7. Records of civil and legal proceedings.
8. Nearly $12,000,000 in today's U.S. currency, invested in stock of the British National Debt.

attractive young lady, now that I look at her. Few girls of the present day have any really solid qualities, any of the qualities that last, and improve with time. We live, I regret to say, in an age of surfaces. [*To* CECILY.] Come over here, dear. [CECILY *goes across.*] Pretty child! your dress is sadly simple, and your hair seems almost as Nature might have left it. But we can soon alter all that. A thoroughly experienced French maid produces a really marvelous result in a very brief space of time. I remember recommending one to young Lady Lancing, and after three months her own husband did not know her.

JACK: [*Aside.*] And after six months nobody knew her.

LADY BRACKNELL: [*Glares at* JACK *for a few moments. Then bends, with a practiced smile, to* CECILY.] Kindly turn round, sweet child. [CECILY *turns completely round.*] No, the side view is what I want. [CECILY *presents her profile.*] Yes, quite as I expected. There are distinct social possibilities in your profile. The two weak points in our age are its want of principle and its want of profile. The chin a little higher, dear. Style largely depends on the way the chin is worn. They are worn very high, just at present. Algernon!

ALGERNON: Yes, Aunt Augusta!

LADY BRACKNELL: There are distinct social possibilities in Miss Cardew's profile.

ALGERNON: Cecily is the sweetest, dearest, prettiest girl in the whole world. And I don't care twopence about social possibilities.

LADY BRACKNELL: Never speak disrespectfully of Society, Algernon. Only people who can't get into it do that. [*To* CECILY.] Dear child, of course you know that Algernon has nothing but his debts to depend upon. But I do not approve of mercenary marriages. When I married Lord Bracknell I had no fortune of any kind. But I never dreamed for a moment of allowing that to stand in my way. Well, I suppose I must give my consent.

ALGERNON: Thank you, Aunt Augusta.

LADY BRACKNELL: Cecily, you may kiss me!

CECILY: [*Kisses her.*] Thank you, Lady Bracknell.

LADY BRACKNELL: You may also address me as Aunt Augusta for the future.

CECILY: Thank you, Aunt Augusta.

LADY BRACKNELL: The marriage, I think, had better take place quite soon.

ALGERNON: Thank you, Aunt Augusta.

CECILY: Thank you, Aunt Augusta.

LADY BRACKNELL: To speak frankly, I am not in favor of long engagements. They give people the opportunity of finding out each other's character before marriage, which I think is never advisable.

JACK: I beg your pardon for interrupting you, Lady Bracknell, but this engagement is quite out of the question. I am Miss Cardew's guardian, and she cannot marry without my consent until she comes of age. That consent I absolutely decline to give.

LADY BRACKNELL: Upon what grounds may I ask? Algernon is an extremely, I may almost say an ostentatiously, eligible young man. He has nothing, but he looks everything. What more can one desire?

JACK: It pains me very much to have to speak frankly to you, Lady Bracknell, about your nephew, but the fact is that I do not approve at all of his moral character. I suspect him of being untruthful.

[ALGERNON *and* CECILY *look at him in indignant amazement.*]

LADY BRACKNELL: Untruthful! My nephew Algernon? Impossible! He is an Oxonian.[9]

JACK: I fear there can be no possible doubt about the matter. This afternoon, during my temporary absence in London on an important question of romance, he obtained admission to my house by means of the false pretense of being my brother. Under an assumed name he drank, I've just been informed by the butler, an entire pint bottle of my Perrier-Jouet, Brut, '89;[1] a wine I was specially reserving for myself. Continuing his disgraceful deception, he succeeded in the course of the afternoon in alienating the affections of my only ward. He subsequently stayed to tea, and devoured every single muffin. And what makes his conduct all the more heartless is, that he was perfectly well aware from the first that I have no brother, that I never had a brother, and that I don't intend to have a brother, not even of any kind. I distinctly told him so myself yesterday afternoon.

LADY BRACKNELL: Ahem! Mr. Worthing, after careful consideration I have decided entirely to overlook my nephew's conduct to you.

JACK: That is very generous of you, Lady Bracknell. My own decision, however, is unalterable. I decline to give my consent.

LADY BRACKNELL: [*To* CECILY.] Come here, sweet child. [CECILY *goes over.*] How old are you, dear?

CECILY: Well, I am really only eighteen, but I always admit to twenty when I go to evening parties.

LADY BRACKNELL: You are perfectly right in making some slight alteration. Indeed, no woman should ever be quite accurate about her age. It looks so calculating.... [*In a meditative manner.*] Eighteen, but admitting to twenty at evening parties. Well, it will not be very long before you are of age and free from the restraints of tutelage. So I don't think your guardian's consent is, after all, a matter of any importance.

JACK: Pray excuse me, Lady Bracknell, for interrupting you again, but it is only fair to tell you that according to the terms of her grandfather's will Miss Cardew does not come legally of age till she is thirty-five.

LADY BRACKNELL: That does not seem to me to be a grave objection. Thirty-five is a very attractive age. London society is full of women of the very highest birth who have, of their own free choice, remained thirty-five for years. Lady Dumbleton is an instance in point. To my own knowledge she has been thirty-five ever since she arrived at the age of forty, which was many years ago now. I see no reason why our dear Cecily should not be even still more attractive at the age you mention than she is at present. There will be a large accumulation of property.

CECILY: Algy, could you wait for me till I was thirty-five?

ALGERNON: Of course I could, Cecily. You know I could.

CECILY: Yes, I felt it instinctively, but I couldn't wait all that time. I hate waiting even five minutes for anybody. It always makes me rather cross. I am not punctual myself, I know, but I do like punctuality in others, and waiting, even to be married, is quite out of the question.

ALGERNON: Then what is to be done, Cecily?

CECILY: I don't know, Mr. Moncrieff.

---

9. A graduate of Oxford University. 1. A very fine champagne.

LADY BRACKNELL: My dear Mr. Worthing, as Miss Cardew states positively that she cannot wait till she is thirty-five—a remark which I am bound to say seems to me to show a somewhat impatient nature—I would beg of you to reconsider your decision.

JACK: But my dear Lady Bracknell, the matter is entirely in your own hands. The moment you consent to my marriage with Gwendolen, I will most gladly allow your nephew to form an alliance with my ward.

LADY BRACKNELL: [*Rising and drawing herself up.*] You must be quite aware that what you propose is out of the question.

JACK: Then a passionate celibacy is all that any of us can look forward to.

LADY BRACKNELL: This is not the destiny I propose for Gwendolen. Algernon, of course, can choose for himself. [*Pulls out her watch.*] Come, dear; [GWENDOLEN *rises.*] we have already missed five, if not six, trains. To miss any more might expose us to comment on the platform.

[*Enter* CANON CHASUBLE.]

CHASUBLE: Everything is quite ready for the christenings.

LADY BRACKNELL: The christenings, sir! Is not that somewhat premature!

CHASUBLE: [*Looking rather puzzled, and pointing to* JACK *and* ALGERNON.] Both these gentlemen have expressed a desire for immediate baptism.

LADY BRACKNELL: At their age? The idea is grotesque and irreligious! Algernon, I forbid you to be baptized. I will not hear of such excesses. Lord Bracknell would be highly displeased if he learned that that was the way in which you wasted your time and money.

CHASUBLE: Am I to understand then that there are to be no christenings at all this afternoon?

JACK: I don't think that, as things are now, it would be of much practical value to either of us, Dr. Chasuble.

CHASUBLE: I am grieved to hear such sentiments from you, Mr. Worthing. They savor of the heretical views of the Anabaptists,[2] views that I have completely refuted in four of my unpublished sermons. However, as your present mood seems to be one peculiarly secular, I will return to the church at once. Indeed, I have just been informed by the pew-opener[3] that for the last hour and a half Miss Prism has been waiting for me in the vestry.

LADY BRACKNELL: [*Starting.*] Miss Prism! Did I hear you mention a Miss Prism?

CHASUBLE: Yes, Lady Bracknell. I am on my way to join her.

LADY BRACKNELL: Pray allow me to detain you for a moment. This matter may prove to be one of vital importance to Lord Bracknell and myself. Is this Miss Prism a female of repellent aspect, remotely connected with education?

CHASUBLE: [*Somewhat indignantly.*] She is the most cultivated of ladies, and the very picture of respectability.

LADY BRACKNELL: It is obviously the same person. May I ask what position she holds in your household?

---

2. A sixteenth-century religious group, somewhat like contemporary Mennonites. Dr. Chasuble, however, is probably using the term loosely to apply to a group more like contemporary Baptists.

3. An usher. Since most pews were enclosed, his duties would have included opening the gate that allowed worshipers to enter. In addition, since most pews were rented for the use of specific persons, he would have been responsible for seeing that worshipers were seated in the correct pews.

CHASUBLE: [*Severely.*] I am a celibate, madam.
JACK: [*Interposing.*] Miss Prism, Lady Bracknell, has been for the last three years Miss Cardew's esteemed governess and valued companion.
LADY BRACKNELL: In spite of what I hear of her, I must see her at once. Let her be sent for.
CHASUBLE: [*Looking off.*] She approaches; she is nigh.

[*Enter* MISS PRISM *hurriedly.*]

MISS PRISM: I was told you expected me in the vestry, dear Canon. I have been waiting for you there for an hour and three quarters. [*Catches sight of* LADY BRACKNELL, *who has fixed her with a stony glare.* MISS PRISM *grows pale and quails. She looks anxiously round as if desirous to escape.*]
LADY BRACKNELL: [*In a severe, judicial voice.*] Prism! [MISS PRISM *bows her head in shame.*] Come here, Prism! [MISS PRISM *approaches in a humble manner.*] Prism! Where is that baby? [*General consternation.* THE CANON *starts back in horror.* ALGERNON *and* JACK *pretend to be anxious to shield* CECILY *and* GWENDOLEN *from hearing the details of a terrible public scandal.*] Twenty-eight years ago, Prism, you left Lord Bracknell's house, Number 104, Upper Grosvenor Street, in charge of a perambulator that contained a baby, of the male sex. You never returned. A few weeks later, through the elaborate investigations of the Metropolitan police, the perambulator was discovered at midnight, standing by itself in a remote corner of Bayswater.[4] It contained the manuscript of a three-volume novel of more than usually revolting sentimentality. [MISS PRISM *starts in involuntary indignation.*] But the baby was not there! [*Everyone looks at* MISS PRISM.] Prism! Where is that baby? [*A pause.*]
MISS PRISM: Lady Bracknell, I admit with shame that I do not know. I only wish I did. The plain facts of the case are these. On the morning of the day you mention, a day that is forever branded on my memory, I prepared as usual to take the baby out in its perambulator. I had also with me a somewhat old, but capacious handbag, in which I had intended to place the manuscript of a work of fiction that I had written during my few unoccupied hours. In a moment of mental abstraction, for which I never can forgive myself, I deposited the manuscript in the bassinette, and placed the baby in the handbag.
JACK: [*Who has been listening attentively.*] But where did you deposit the handbag?
MISS PRISM: Do not ask me, Mr. Worthing.
JACK: Miss Prism, this is a matter of no small importance to me. I insist on knowing where you deposited the handbag that contained that infant.
MISS PRISM: I left it in the cloak room of one of the larger railway stations in London.
JACK: What railway station?
MISS PRISM: [*Quite crushed.*] Victoria. The Brighton line. [*Sinks into a chair.*]
JACK: I must retire to my room for a moment. Gwendolen, wait here for me.
GWENDOLEN: If you are not too long, I will wait here for you all my life.

[*Exit* JACK *in great excitement.*]

CHASUBLE: What do you think this means, Lady Bracknell?
LADY BRACKNELL: I dare not even suspect, Dr. Chasuble. I need hardly tell you

---

4. A fashionable residential section north of Hyde Park and Kensington Gardens.

that in families of high position strange coincidences are not supposed to occur. They are hardly considered the thing.

[*Noises heard overhead as if someone was throwing trunks about. Everyone looks up.*]

CECILY: Uncle Jack seems strangely agitated.
CHASUBLE: Your guardian has a very emotional nature.
LADY BRACKNELL: This noise is extremely unpleasant. It sounds as if he was having an argument. I dislike arguments of any kind. They are always vulgar, and often convincing.
CHASUBLE: [*Looking up.*] It has stopped now. [*The noise is redoubled.*]
LADY BRACKNELL: I wish he would arrive at some conclusion.
GWENDOLEN: This suspense is terrible. I hope it will last.

[*Enter* JACK *with a handbag of black leather in his hand.*]

JACK: [*Rushing over to* MISS PRISM.] Is this the handbag, Miss Prism? Examine it carefully before you speak. The happiness of more than one life depends on your answer.
MISS PRISM: [*Calmly.*] It seems to be mine. Yes, here is the injury it received through the upsetting of a Gower Street omnibus in younger and happier days. Here is the stain on the lining caused by the explosion of a temperance beverage,[5] an incident that occurred at Leamington. And here, on the lock, are my initials. I had forgotten that in an extravagant mood I had had them placed there. The bag is undoubtedly mine. I am delighted to have it so unexpectedly restored to me. It has been a great inconvenience being without it all these years.
JACK: [*In a pathetic voice.*] Miss Prism, more is restored to you than this handbag. I was the baby you placed in it.
MISS PRISM: [*Amazed.*] You!
JACK: [*Embracing her.*] Yes . . . mother!
MISS PRISM: [*Recoiling in indignant astonishment.*] Mr. Worthing! I am unmarried!
JACK: Unmarried! I do not deny that is a serious blow. But after all, who has the right to cast a stone against one who has suffered? Cannot repentance wipe out an act of folly? Why should there be one law for men, and another for women? Mother, I forgive you. [*Tries to embrace her again.*]
MISS PRISM: [*Still more indignant.*] Mr. Worthing, there is some error. [*Pointing to* LADY BRACKNELL.] There is the lady who can tell you who you really are.
JACK: [*After a pause.*] Lady Bracknell, I hate to seem inquisitive, but would you kindly inform me who I am?
LADY BRACKNELL: I am afraid that the news I have to give you will not altogether please you. You are the son of my poor sister, Mrs. Moncrieff, and consequently Algernon's elder brother.
JACK: Algy's elder brother! Then I have a brother after all. I knew I had a brother! I always said I had a brother! Cecily—how could you have ever doubted that I had a brother? [*Seizes hold of* ALGERNON.] Dr. Chasuble, my unfortunate brother. Miss Prism, my unfortunate brother. Gwendolen, my unfortunate

---

5. Carbonated soda drinks were marketed, in the 1890s, as "temperance beverages" (healthy alternatives to alcohol).

brother. Algy, you young scoundrel, you will have to treat me with more respect in the future. You have never behaved to me like a brother in all your life.

ALGERNON: Well, not till today, old boy, I admit. I did my best, however, though I was out of practice. [*Shakes hands.*]

GWENDOLEN: [*To* JACK.] My own! But what own are you? What is your Christian name, now that you have become someone else?

JACK: Good heavens! . . . I had quite forgotten that point. Your decision on the subject of my name is irrevocable, I suppose?

GWENDOLEN: I never change, except in my affections.

CECILY: What a noble nature you have, Gwendolen!

JACK: Then the question had better be cleared up at once. Aunt Augusta, a moment. At the time when Miss Prism left me in the handbag, had I been christened already?

LADY BRACKNELL: Every luxury that money could buy, including christening, had been lavished on you by your fond and doting parents.

JACK: Then I was christened! That is settled. Now, what name was I given? Let me know the worst.

LADY BRACKNELL: Being the eldest son you were naturally christened after your father.

JACK: [*Irritably.*] Yes, but what was my father's Christian name?

LADY BRACKNELL: [*Meditatively.*] I cannot at the present moment recall what the General's Christian name was. But I have no doubt he had one. He was eccentric, I admit. But only in later years. And that was the result of the Indian climate, and marriage, and indigestion, and other things of that kind.

JACK: Algy! Can't you recollect what our father's Christian name was?

ALGERNON: My dear boy, we were never even on speaking terms. He died before I was a year old.

JACK: His name would appear in the Army Lists of the period, I suppose, Aunt Augusta?

LADY BRACKNELL: The General was essentially a man of peace, except in his domestic life. But I have no doubt his name would appear in any military directory.

JACK: The Army Lists of the last forty years are here. These delightful records should have been my constant study. [*Rushes to bookcase and tears the books out.*] M. Generals . . . Mallam, Maxbohm, Magley, what ghastly names they have—Markby, Migsby, Mobbs, Moncrieff! Lieutenant 1840, Captain, Lieutenant Colonel, Colonel, General 1869, Christian names, Ernest John. [*Puts book very quietly down and speaks quite calmly.*] I always told you, Gwendolen, my name was Ernest, didn't I? Well it is Ernest after all. I mean it naturally is Ernest.

LADY BRACKNELL: Yes, I remember now that the General was called Ernest. I knew I had some particular reason for disliking the name.

GWENDOLEN: Ernest! My own Ernest! I felt from the first that you could have no other name!

JACK: Gwendolen, it is a terrible thing for a man to find out suddenly that all his life he has been speaking nothing but the truth. Can you forgive me?

GWENDOLEN: I can. For I feel that you are sure to change.

JACK: My own one!

CHASUBLE: [*To* MISS PRISM.] Laetitia! [*Embraces her.*]

MISS PRISM: [*Enthusiastically.*] Frederick! At last!
ALGERNON: Cecily! [*Embraces her.*] At last!
JACK: Gwendolen! [*Embraces her.*] At last!
LADY BRACKNELL: My nephew, you seem to be displaying signs of triviality.
JACK: On the contrary, Aunt Augusta, I've now realized for the first time in my life the vital Importance of Being Earnest.

CURTAIN

1899

## SUGGESTIONS FOR WRITING

1. *Oedipus the King* poses intriguing questions about the mysteries of sight and blindness, light and darkness. Why, for example, is it significant that Apollo, the sun god, is also a god of prophecy? Why is Teiresias, a prophet inspired by Apollo, blind? How does his blindness compare to that of Oedipus? What distinction does Sophocles draw between sight and insight? Citing specific actions, images, and passages, write an essay in which you examine what *seeing* means in *Oedipus the King*. With what kinds of enlightenment and darkness is the play concerned?
2. What is "tragic," and what is "heroic," about a tragic hero? To the modern sensibility, Oedipus's poor judgment and stubborn unwillingness to face facts are what bring down on him, and on his family and the people of Thebes, the fate shown in the play. But to the ancients, Oedipus was the model of nobility in his innate sense of justice, selfless concern for the well-being of his people, and ultimate embrace of his destiny. What, then, is the nature of Oedipus's responsibility for his fate and the fate of Thebes? Write an essay in which you discuss the role of the "tragic hero" in *Oedipus the King*. What is the play's intended "lesson"?
3. In his *Poetics*, Aristotle praised *Oedipus the King* as a model tragedy—nearly perfect in the simplicity of its plot, the nobility of its characterization, and the decorousness of its poetry. Write an essay in which you compare and contrast the dramatic elements of *Oedipus the King* with those of at least one other play by Sophocles, such as *Antigone* (chapter 31). How does Sophocles define and vary his dramatic formula?
4. In its traditional form as practiced, for example, by Shakespeare, a comedy nearly always depicts lovers who must overcome obstacles (such as misunderstandings, unjust laws, or family interference) in order to unite in marriage and in this way ensure the continuation of their society. By such a definition, is *The Importance of Being Earnest* a traditional "comedy"? Or might it instead be labeled an "anti-comedy," a play that subverts traditional social mores? Using research if necessary, write an essay in which you trace the ways in which *The Importance of Being Earnest* does and does not adhere to the classic comic formula.
5. Oscar Wilde was famous in his time as a champion of aestheticism—that is, the belief that art exists solely for its own sake and that artists should be free from any religious, political, or social interference. "All art," he declared, "is quite useless." Nevertheless, in its own witty way, *The Importance of Being Earnest* seems to address many of the same matters that concern moralists—the proper ordering of society, the use and abuse of language, the relations between men and women. Is Wilde's play truly "useless"? Write an essay in which you argue that the play either is or is not a mere entertainment. Does *The Importance of Being Earnest* have a "moral"?
6. Two of English literature's most renowned wits, George Bernard Shaw and Oscar Wilde, wrote comedies for the London stage at about the same time, and both used

stock characters and settings that would be familiar to playgoers of the day: the ardent social reformer, the overeducated idler, the domineering mother, the comfortably furnished "drawing room." Both writers were, in very different ways, sharp-eyed satirists, and we can hear more than a hint of rivalry in Wilde's remark about Shaw, "He hasn't an enemy in the world, and none of his friends like him." Write an essay in which you compare and contrast *Pygmalion* (ch. 26) and *The Importance of Being Earnest*; consider both plays' use of comic conventions as well as the targets of their satire.

# 30 CULTURAL AND HISTORICAL CONTEXT

Three different levels of time operate in most literary texts, dramatic or otherwise. First, a text represents some particular time—the temporal setting—in which the action takes place. We can call this **plot time**. Second, the text reflects the time when the author was writing, and, inevitably, the conditions and assumptions of that time inform the text's conception and style; this feature of textual time we may call **authorial time**. Third, readers read in a particular **reader time**, when conditions and assumptions may differ from those that obtain in either the text's or the author's present. (If we encounter a play on the stage, we might instead call this *performance time*.)

In some cases, plot, authorial, and reader time all differ. Wole Soyinka's *Death and the King's Horseman*, for example, is set in the early 1940s in the British colony of Nigeria. Yet it was written in the early 1970s, more than ten years after his country gained its independence. Thus, when we—as readers in the 2000s—read the play, three distinct historical and cultural contexts are operating at once. The play's plot unfolds in a time and a place quite remote from us. And the text also reflects values, writing conditions, habits of language, and dramatic conventions of yet another context—three decades after the events in the play occurred, but still almost twenty-five years earlier than, and thousands of miles away from, the time and place in which we read the text. Values in these three worlds will not be identical. How we interpret the actions and thoughts of the characters in part depends not only on our own assumptions about what they should or might do, but also on what we know about the conditions that shaped people's lives in two quite different historical and cultural milieus. Keeping these three contexts in mind as we read—and consciously making comparisons when we perceive conflicting values—is a vital part of our response and interpretation.

This can be equally true of plays that represent the times in which they were written. When, for example, Lorraine Hansberry's *A Raisin in the Sun* debuted in 1959, its audience watched scenes that might well have been unfolding at virtually the same moment just down the street. The stage directions, in fact, indicate that the action in the play occurs "in Chicago's Southside, sometime between World War II and the present." In this case, almost no difference exists between plot time and authorial time. Indeed, the play asked its original audiences to believe that there was no distinction between these times and their own, that they were confronting life exactly as it was happening and being invited to consider issues of immediate consequence. And the play also drew, at least to some extent, upon that audience's knowledge of current events, concerns, and issues—knowledge that we, living in a quite different reader time, may have to work to master.

Of course, this does not mean that *A Raisin in the Sun*, *Death and the King's Horseman*, or any great play can't speak to us unless we "study up" on the worlds about and in which they were written. "Inevitably, ... every [literary] work belongs to a given moment," as Wole Soyinka reminds us—but, he adds, "it transcends this" moment, too. Both of these plays remain relevant because they show us people that are as hopeful, complex, funny, and flawed as we are. Indeed, one of Hansberry's major objectives in writing *A Raisin in the Sun* was, as she explained in a letter, to "help ... people to understand how we ['Negroes'] are just as complicated as they are—and just as mixed up." And we see these characters confronting questions that we face, too—about family, cultural and personal identity, gender, race and ethnicity, ambition, human dignity and honor, historical change, and generational conflict. Much of what happens in both plays could and does still happen in our world, and in much the same way.

But not everything. Take, for example, the abortion that Ruth Younger contemplates near the end of *A Raisin in the Sun*'s first act. In 1959, abortion was illegal in the United States. Women who sought abortions had either to leave the country, usually traveling to Mexico or Puerto Rico (a relatively expensive option), or to seek out shady, back-alley practitioners like the one Ruth consults. Such abortionists typically had little medical expertise and often operated in highly unsanitary conditions. Disease and mortality rates were high, and some of the horror that the Younger family expresses at the thought of abortion can be attributed to reasonable fears about its physical consequences. But their horror also results from the moral and social stigma surrounding abortion. However individuals might themselves feel about the ethics of abortion, the law prohibited it in 1959, and public opinion—as well as the Christian doctrine so important to Mama and other African Americans of her generation—weighed heavily against the practice. To appreciate Ruth's situation, understand other characters' responses, and imagine the original audience's reactions, it helps to know about the prevailing legal climate, as well as the various social attitudes and concerns of the day, especially within a respectable, proud, and aspiring African American family like the Youngers.

Some plays offer us a good deal of information about setting that is relevant to the interpretation of specific episodes. But sometimes we have to supply facts that the text doesn't give us. People may share some characteristics across ages and cultures, but behavior and motivation are often conditioned by historically and culturally specific circumstances. Often we have to adjust our expectations because the world of the play or that of its author differs greatly from our own. Identifying the play's setting—in time and place—and considering carefully the historical and cultural context in which the play was written can be crucial to understanding what happens and why. With that in mind, the rest of this chapter seeks to introduce you to the contexts that inspired and shaped both *A Raisin in the Sun* and *Death and the King's Horseman*—two very different plays, yet ones connected, in part, through the complex web of history and culture that both plays explore.

* * *

The debut of *A Raisin in the Sun* was a significant historical and cultural event. The first play by an African American woman ever produced on Broadway, *A Raisin in the Sun* earned its creator, Lorraine Hansberry (1930–1965), the New York Drama Critics Circle Award as the year's best play just two months after it opened. Hansberry thus became—at twenty-nine—the youngest American playwright, the first

## CULTURAL AND HISTORICAL CONTEXT

Lorraine Hansberry, 1959

black writer, and only the fifth woman ever to receive this prestigious award. Yet when Hansberry's friend and fellow writer James Baldwin labeled her play a "historical achievement" of the greatest importance, he had something else in mind—the unprecedented way that *A Raisin in the Sun* brought African Americans into the theater and onto the stage. "I had never in my life seen so many black people in the theater," Baldwin recalled. "And the reason was that never before, in the entire history of the American theater, had so much of the truth of black people's lives been seen on the stage. Black people [had] ignored the theater because the theater had always ignored them." To Baldwin and others, *A Raisin in the Sun* was a "historical achievement" precisely because of its realism and contemporaneity, its truthful depiction of the lives of many ordinary African Americans in the late 1950s. In a sense, the play made history by accurately reflecting a historical and cultural reality previously ignored by dramatists.

One factor that undoubtedly made the Younger family seem so realistic was the fact that their situation closely resembled that of the 6.5 million African Americans who moved from the rural South to the urban North between 1910 and 1970 as part of the Great Migration. Though these migrants settled in every northern city, the majority eventually made their homes in New York City and Chicago. By 1960, Chicago's black population had grown to 813,000—twenty-five percent of the city's inhabitants.

Like Lena Younger and her husband, those migrant millions flew north on the wings of hope—hope for better jobs at higher wages and for greater safety and freedom than they enjoyed in the Jim Crow–era South. (By 1914, every southern state had passed "Jim Crow" laws mandating segregated railroad cars, waiting rooms, bathrooms, restaurants, theaters, recreation areas, and even hospitals.) Not coincidentally, migration increased when northern industries were expanding and when conditions in the South were particularly oppressive or violent. In the 1920s, when the Younger family would have arrived in Chicago, a government-sponsored report on race relations in that city pointed out that over 85 percent of the 2,881 lynchings that occurred in the United States between 1885 and 1918 occurred in southern states and "that numbers of migrants from towns where lynchings had occurred registered for jobs in Chicago very shortly after lynchings." The same report also concluded that southern blacks were drawn to the city as much for so-called "sentimental" reasons as for "economic" ones. When recent immigrants interviewed for the report were asked, "What do you like about the North?" their responses were remarkably similar:

1. Freedom in voting and conditions of colored people here.
2. Freedom and chance to make a living; privileges.
3. Freedom and opportunity to acquire something.

Segregated drinking fountain, Oklahoma City, 1939

10. Freedom of speech and action. Can live without fear. No Jim Crow.

Songs and poems of the 1920s, as well as the African American press, fueled such hopes and imbued them with religious significance. The Great Migration was cast as the "Flight out of Egypt"; migrants were encouraged to see themselves as "Bound for the Promised Land," "Going into Canaan."

In reality, the vast majority of blacks who came north found themselves not in Canaan, but in the all-black, inner-city enclaves—the "Smoketowns," "Bronzevilles," and "Black Belts"—that had begun to develop in all of the North's major cities before the First World War. In Chicago, that "distinct Negro world" was the South Side, a strip of land extending south along State Street from the Loop (the city's central business district) and bounded by Lake Michigan (to the east), Chicago's famous stockyards (to the west), and white neighborhoods (to the south). By the 1940s, the South Side had become what it remains to this day—"the largest contiguous settlement of African-Americans" (in the words of journalist Nicholas Lemann).

On the one hand, this "Black Metropolis" might well have looked very like the African American Promised Land, a city within a city in which "a black person could be somebody." By the 1940s, the South Side boasted bustling shopping districts; a spacious public park and lake-side beach; nationally known institutions such as the Regal Theater, the Savoy Ballroom, and the Hotel Grand; as well as countless movie houses and nightclubs featuring blues masters like Muddy Waters (1915–1983), himself a migrant from the Mississippi Delta. It was also, as Lemann notes,

> home to the heavyweight boxing champion of the world (and the most famous black man in America), Joe Louis; the only black member of Congress, William

Regal Theater, Chicago, 1953

Dawson; the most prominent black newspaper, the *Defender*; the largest black congregation, J. H. Jackson's Olivet Baptist Church; the greatest black singer, Mahalia Jackson; and a host of lesser-known prosperous people....

Undoubtedly, the presence of so many African American luminaries, as well as the sheer existence of such a large black community, fueled the pride and aspirations of ordinary people like the Youngers.

On the other hand, however, those "prosperous people" were few and far between. And what lay between them were the thousands who, like the Youngers, occupied the lower rungs of the social ladder. For even if northern cities offered African Americans much greater economic opportunities than they enjoyed in the South, they were still paid much lower wages than their white counterparts, barred entirely from many good jobs, fired first in bad economic times, and hired last in good ones. In 1950 (nine years before *A Raisin in the Sun*'s debut), the African American unemployment rate in Chicago was about three times that of white workers. Of those Chicagoans who were employed, 70 percent of black men (vs. 36 percent of white men) and 75 percent of black women (vs. 33 percent of white women) held unskilled jobs. At the same time, 22 percent of black men and almost 36 percent of black women worked, like the Youngers, in the lowest, "service" sector—as cooks, maids, janitors, and chauffeurs; only 14 percent of white men and 11 percent of white women did so.

If the Youngers' jobs make them representative, so, too, does the fact that they live in a small, "tired," roach-infested apartment. In the 1940s, population density on the South Side averaged about 90,000 people per square mile (as compared with 20,000 in white neighborhoods). Landlords often charged South Side residents much higher rents than were charged elsewhere, while doing little to maintain the apartments hastily carved out of existing buildings. In their 1960 study *Housing a Metropolis*, sociologists Beverly Duncan and Philip M. Hauser estimated that Chicago's non-white renters were more than twice as likely as whites to live in substandard housing. For homebuyers in the South Side, the situation was even worse. Duncan and Hauser estimated that, in the late 1940s, those buyers paid 28

Crowded conditions in a Chicago tenement, 1941

to 51 percent more than they would in white neighborhoods. And they often got less for their money: in 1960, non-white homeowners were, according to the same source, six times as likely as their white counterparts to live in substandard homes.

Though Chicago's Black Belt could and did expand southward and westward throughout the Great Migration, this expansion meant movement into formerly white residential areas—an extraordinarily difficult, slow, and often violent process. This was so, as sociologists St. Clair Drake and Horace R. Cayton explained in their classic *Black Metropolis* (1945), "primarily because of white people's attitudes toward having Negroes as neighbors. Because some white Chicagoans do not wish colored neighbors, formal and informal social controls are used to isolate the latter within congested all-Negro neighborhoods." The major "formal" means of maintaining residential segregation were restrictive covenants preventing property from being sold or rented to blacks. By 1930, about 75 percent of the city's residential property was bound by such agreements, while all agents who belonged to the real estate trade association were bound by a code of ethics that forbade moving blacks into white areas. The Supreme Court declared such covenants legally unenforceable, though not themselves illegal, in 1948. But both before and after that time—in Chicago and every other northern U.S. city—violence was the chief "informal" means adopted by whites when restrictive covenants and codes failed. According to Drake and Cayton, almost five hundred attacks on black residents were reported in Chicago between 1945 and 1950, most involving arson. In 1956 and 1957 alone, 164 such racial "incidents" occurred.

It is here that Hansberry's personal experience intersects with the historical and cultural context about and in which she wrote, though her family was much more comfortably middle class than was the fictional family she created. In 1938, when Lorraine was eight, her father, Carl—a prosperous real-estate broker and founder of one of Chicago's first black-owned banks—decided to test the legality of restrictive covenants by purchasing a house in an all-white neighborhood. When the local neighborhood association secured an injunction prohibiting him from occupying the property, Carl Hansberry, backed by the National Association for the Advancement of Colored People, took the case all the way to the Supreme Court. Though he won the case (on a technicality) in 1940, his victory was a limited and costly one. As Lorraine Hansberry later recalled,

> That fight . . . required that our family occupy the disputed property in a hellishly hostile "white neighborhood" in which, literally, howling mobs surrounded our house. One of their missiles almost took [my] life. . . . My memories . . . include being spat at, cursed, and pummeled in the daily trek to and from school. And I also remember my desperate and courageous mother, patrolling our house all night with a loaded German luger, doggedly guarding her four children, while my father fought . . . in the Washington court.
> 
> . . . The cost, in emotional turmoil, time, and money . . . led to my father's early death as a permanently embittered exile in a foreign country when he saw that after such sacrificial efforts the Negroes of Chicago were as ghetto-locked as ever. . . .

(The disillusioned Carl Hansberry was arranging to move his family to Mexico when he died in 1945.) Among other things, Hansberry's account of her experience might give readers of *A Raisin in the Sun* a deeper appreciation of the play's complex denouement and of the fact that its plot is propelled by a much-loved, hard-working father's death.

Hansberry's experiences remind us that the African American civil rights struggle was multi-faceted and began well before the 1960s. Yet there is no doubt that it was entering an entirely new phase in 1959. Just five years earlier, in 1954, the famous *Brown v. Board of Education* Supreme Court decision declared "separate but equal" education policies unconstitutional, initiating the long, often violent fight to integrate America's schools. One year later, in 1955, the Montgomery Bus Boycott began, eventually forcing full integration of public transportation and launching Martin Luther King, Jr. (1929–1968) on his career as one of the nation's most famous and influential civil rights leaders. The modern civil rights movement had begun—one in which "gradualism" gave way to direct action, and court battles to marches, sit-ins, and other forms of civil disobedience.

Though the modern civil rights movement involved people of every age, it was in some ways, as Howard Zinn would argue in 1964, the first major social movement in U.S. history "led by youngsters"—youngsters intent on "living, hour by hour, the very ideals which this country has often thought about, but not yet managed to practice" and thereby "creating new definitions of success, of happiness, of democracy." A political scientist and activist, Zinn was speaking specifically of the college students who, in 1960, began conducting sit-ins throughout the South and eventually formed the Student Non-Violent Coordinating Committee (SNCC). It's worth remembering too that Martin Luther King, Jr. was himself only twenty-six when he was chosen to lead the Montgomery boycott. In a

The Reverend Ralph Abernathy (center left) and the Reverend Martin Luther King, Jr. (center right), leaders of the Southern Christian Leadership Conference (SCLC), are arrested in Birmingham, Alabama, during a peaceful demonstration for civil rights, Good Friday, 1963. Held in solitary confinement for a week, King wrote the famous "Letter from Birmingham Jail" in response to an advertisement in the *Birmingham News*, written by a group of white ministers, in which King was denounced as a troublemaker.

sense, then, the modern civil rights movement was born out of the kinds of generational attitudes explored in *A Raisin in the Sun*. Hansberry, for example, saw her father as "typical of a generation of Negroes who believed that the 'American way' could successfully be made to work to democratize the United States." But, she said, it was "Negroes my own age and younger" who were beginning to question the "American way" and to advocate a more aggressively confrontational stance, "say[ing] that we must now lie down in the streets, tie up traffic, do whatever we can—take to the hills with guns if necessary—and fight back."

Determined to act on their frustration in ways that their parents wouldn't or couldn't, thousands of young people—many the city-born children of the Great Migration—turned to activism in the 1950s and 1960s. Yet, through Walter's drinking as well as the crime at the heart of her play, Hansberry also subtly reminds us that there were other ways in which that frustration could and did find expression. For as the following excerpt from Richard Wright's semi-autobiographical *Twelve Million Black Voices* suggests, the very same impulses and emotions that inspired SNCC members to head south led many of their peers in a very different direction.

In *A Raisin in the Sun*, differences between and within generations take a variety of shapes, but one such distinction whose meaning and significance may be especially dependent on a knowledge of historical and cultural context involves the character of Joseph Asagai. A Nigerian attending college in Chicago, Joseph plans to return home in order to help liberate his country from British colonial rule. Through him, Hansberry thus highlights connections and parallels between the situation of blacks in the U.S. and in Africa, drawing on her audience's knowledge of contemporary events in Africa even as she points up just how little real knowledge of Africa most Americans possess.

A poster printed and distributed by the Student Non-Violent Coordinating Committee in the late 1960s

Historically speaking, Hansberry's (and Beneatha's) keen interest in both traditional African culture and contemporary African liberation is no accident. As Earl Thorpe noted in 1959 (in an article excerpted below), various African American intellectuals and activists had worked to spread knowledge about Africa, to forge connections with African leaders, and to improve the situation of colonized Africans since at least the 1920s. But African American interest in Africa was becoming much more widespread and taking on a variety of unprecedented forms in the 1950s. First, between the late 1950s and early 1970s more African Americans than ever before would, like Beneatha, seek to learn about, and embrace, their African cultural heritage. Quite a few made pilgrimages to Africa. Thousands more did so symbolically, sporting dashikis, adopting African names, or giving up hair-straighteners in order to grow Afros. Second, some black activists and intellectuals would, in the early 1960s, begin to argue that the plight of African Americans closely resembled that of colonized peoples elsewhere, even describing African Americans as victims of systematic "domestic" or "internal" colonialism. This controversial argument was popularized through Stokely Carmichael and Charles V. Hamilton's influential *Black Power* (1967, excerpted below). Yet even moderates drew inspiration from events in Africa. In his "Letter from Birmingham City Jail" (1963), for example, Martin Luther King, Jr. defended civil disobedience and lamented the extremely slow pace of change in the United States by reminding his readers that, while "we still creep at horse and buggy pace toward the gaining of a cup of coffee at a lunch counter," "[t]he nations of Asia and Africa are moving with jet-like speed toward the goal of political independence."

In the 1950s and 1960s, Africa was indeed going through a process of change so rapid and dramatic that it might well have made America seem like a stagnant backwater. Between 1880 and 1912 all of Africa except Liberia and Ethiopia had come under the control of European powers. And for decades the situation changed only in two nations—white-controlled South Africa (which became virtually self-governing in 1910) and Egypt (which achieved a measure of sovereignty in 1922). But in the 1950s, "the winds of change" suddenly began to blow hard across Africa, beginning in the north where first Libya achieved independence (1951), and then Morocco, Sudan, and Tunisia (1956). One year later the process moved southward into sub-Saharan Africa when Britain's Gold Coast colony became independent Ghana. Thereafter, almost every year saw the birth of at least one new African nation. (See the timeline below.) No wonder, then, that Africa was often in the news and on American minds in the 1950s and 1960s.

For a variety of reasons, change in Africa and the United States was propelled by the shared experience of World War II (1939–45). James Baldwin was only one of many Americans to see that war as marking "a turning point in the Negro's relation to" his country because, as Baldwin wrote in *The Fire Next Time* (1963),

> a certain hope died, a certain respect for white Americans faded. One began to pity them, or to hate them. You must put yourself in the skin of a man who is wearing the uniform of his country, is a candidate for death in its defense, and who is called a "nigger" by his comrades-in-arms and his officers; who is almost always given the hardest, ugliest, most menial work to do; . . . who does not dance at the U.S.O. the night white soldiers dance there . . . ; and who watches German prisoners of war being treated by Americans with more human dignity than he has ever received at their hands. And who, at the same time, as a human being, is far freer in a strange land than he has ever been at home. . . . You must consider what happens to this citizen, after all he has endured, when he returns—home: search, in his shoes, for a job, for a place to live; ride, in his skin, on segregated buses; see, with his eyes, the signs saying "White" and "Colored" . . . ; look into the eyes of his wife; look into the eyes of his son; listen, with his ears, to political speeches, North and South; imagine yourself being told to "wait."

Something similar happened to the tens of thousands of African servicemen who fought for the Allies during the war. For, as the authors of *The Making of Modern Africa* suggest, these veterans, too, "came back with new ideas and attitudes" and with stories about Europeans who "worked as [mere] stewards, cooks, cleaners or even lived by begging." Proving that "Europeans were ordinary flesh and blood,"

An American soldier of the 12th Armored Division guarding captured German soldiers, Germany, 1945

such stories did much to undermine "the respect and fear which [colonial] administrators had excited before 1939." As Baldwin's *The Fire Next Time* emphasizes, too, the revelation of Nazi atrocities—atrocities perpetrated in the very heart of Christian Europe—further undermined the notions of Western civility and superiority so often used to justify segregation in the U.S. and colonialism worldwide:

> ... [T]he terms "civilized" and "Christian" begin to have a very strange ring, particularly in the ears of those who have been judged to be neither civilized nor Christian, when a Christian nation surrenders to a foul and violent orgy, as Germany did during the Third Reich.... From my own point of view, the fact of the Third Reich alone makes obsolete forever any question of Christian superiority, except in technological terms.

For these reasons, it is no accident that Hansberry sets her play in the aftermath of World War II or that Wole Soyinka chose to set *Death and the King's Horseman* during the war, even though the events that inspired it in fact occurred after the war's end.

If it was in part the shared experience of World War II that fueled—and indirectly linked—the American civil rights movement and the African independence movement, the latter drew the West's attention for yet another reason. African independence was, in many cases, the result of hard-fought popular campaigns spearheaded by extraordinarily charismatic men very like Joseph Asagai and Soyinka's Olunde—men educated partially in the West and quite familiar with its culture and ways, yet eager to liberate their people and to embrace and revitalize ancient African folkways. The first presidents of the Republics of Ghana and Nigeria, for example, were Kwame Nkrumah (1909-1972) and Benjamin Nnamdi ("Zik") Azikiwe (1904-1996), men who returned to their countries only after taking multiple degrees at U.S. and British universities. The first and most famous such leader to emerge on the world stage was Jomo Kenyatta (1893?-1978), whose career led him from an obscure village to the presidency of independent Kenya by way of the London School of Economics; a masterful book on the culture of his own people, the Kikuyu (*Facing Mount Kenya* [1938]); and a seven-year "detainment" for sedition against the British colonial state. At least in African American eyes, such leaders might very well seem like modern versions of the great warriors of African history and myth.

But, as *A Raisin in the Sun* reminds us, the differences between African Americans and Africans are just as deep-seated and significant as their historical and cultural ties. And "domestic colonialism"—if indeed it does exist—is not identical to the "classic" variety experienced by Africans. For all its interest in Africa, moreover, *A Raisin in the Sun* is a distinctly American play in terms of both content and style. Hansberry herself was well aware of the way it complemented and contrasted with American classics such as Arthur Miller's *Death of a Salesman*. As she pointed out, "Walter Younger is an American more than he is anything else," and there is "a simple line of descent between" her Walter and Miller's Willy Loman—"the last great hero in American drama to also *accept* the values of his [American] culture."

One way to appreciate the "Americanness" of Hansberry's play—and its distinctly American vision of Africa and Africans—is to compare it with Soyinka's *Death and the King's Horseman*—a play that invites us to explore African culture

Newly elected Prime Minister Jomo Kenyatta (right), independent Kenya's first head of state, greets supporters in Nairobi, 1963

from the inside and to think about the nature and complex effects of "classic" colonialism.

Like the fictional Joseph Asagai, Wole Soyinka and many of his characters are Africans. But they are also Nigerians and, more specifically, Yorubans—a dual (or even triple) identity that Americans like Lena Younger sometimes have difficulty understanding. Here, it is useful to remember that Nigeria, like most modern African nation-states, was itself the product of colonialism—in Soyinka's words, "an artificial creation" whose boundaries were determined by Europeans with little "consideration either [of] the wishes or the will *or* the interests of" African natives. Among other things, such states "lumped together"—to quote Soyinka again—a number of ethnically, linguistically, and culturally distinct groups. The West African state of Nigeria, for example, didn't exist until the British created it in 1914, in the process bringing together about 250 distinct peoples. The largest of these are the Hausa and Fulani, who dominate northern Nigeria; the Igbo (also known as the Ibo), who live primarily in the southeast; and the Yoruba of the southwest. Today Nigerians certainly see themselves as members of a single nation knit together, as Soyinka puts it, by the "unrolling of historical events, the sharing of certain experiences, political fortunes, economic arrangements, cultural relations, [and] cultural interaction." But cultural differences remain profoundly meaningful. Soyinka speaks of himself as "primarily a Yoruba writer"; his compatriot, novelist Chinua Achebe, sees himself as an Igbo writer.

Wole Soyinka of Nigeria, winner of the 1986 Nobel Prize for Literature

Yoruban cultural beliefs and traditions inform the style, as well as the content, of all of Soyinka's works, including *Death and the King's Horseman*. And one of the excerpts below—*Yoruba: Nine Centuries of African Art and Thought* by Henry John Drewal, John Pemberton III, and Rowland Abiodun—is included here in order to give you some sense of the unique history and culture of Yorubaland. Yet *Death and the King's Horseman* also draws our attention to the ways in which traditional African cultures have been challenged and changed by three linked forces—Islam, Christianity, and European colonialism.

Islam had become an important force in northern Nigeria as early as the eleventh century. By the early nineteenth century, northern Nigeria had, in fact, become part of a giant Muslim empire known as the Sokoto Caliphate. Today, almost half of the Nigerian population follows some version of Islam, and the vast majority of them live in the north.

West Africa's contact with European Christians began with the arrival of Portuguese traders in the fifteenth century. By about 1650, West Africa's main export was slaves, and British ships did much of the trafficking. For centuries, however, Europeans seldom ventured beyond the coastline. In the nineteenth century, all of that began to change. Fired with a mixture of economic, humanitarian, and political ambitions, Britons pushed into the interior in order to end the slave trade (declared illegal by Britain in 1807), foster other kinds of commerce, and convert the population to Christianity. Through treaties with local leaders and the use of force, Britain gradually gained control of much of West Africa. Britain's claims to the area were officially recognized at the 1885 Berlin Conference (where Western nations met to settle their ongoing disputes about what portions of Africa each would control).

From around 1900 until independence in 1960, the British governed Nigeria through the system known as "indirect rule." Under this system, a relatively small number of British officials—headed by a governor and several district commissioners—ruled the country via local, native leaders. In theory, the latter were men—like the king of Soyinka's play—already recognized as leaders by their communities. In this and other ways indirect rule ostensibly ensured minimal interference with traditional African culture and society. But in practice, British rule couldn't help but have profound, direct effects. For one thing, the British often found it necessary to supplant defiant native leaders with more compliant ones and to create "warrant chiefs" in communities (like those of the Igbo) that didn't traditionally have them. For another, British governors actively worked to stamp out any traditional practice that they saw as either interfering with trade (and thus with British economic interests) or violating Western notions of civilized human behavior. (This policy propels the tragic plot of *Death and the King's Horseman*.) Finally, the British government achieved the latter aim in part by actively encouraging the efforts of both Muslims in northern Nigeria and Christian missionaries in the south to convert and educate the populace. As a result, education and religion went hand in hand in Nigeria, as in much of colonial Africa, and together undermined traditional social structures as well as the beliefs and

British colonial administrators meeting tribal representatives in Lagos, Nigeria, ca. 1900

customs that sustained them. (Today, about 40 percent of Nigerians are Christians, the vast majority living in the south.)

Yet, as *Death and the King's Horseman* demonstrates, African culture has always had a remarkable resilience and capacity to adapt, which Soyinka attributes to its "attitude of philosophic accommodation." Today, both Islam and Christianity often take unique forms in Africa precisely because their doctrines and practices have had to accommodate traditional ones. In northern Nigeria, for example, some Muslim emirs lead prayers for the welfare of the state at the graves of royal ancestors, thus synthesizing Islam with the ancestor-worship at the heart of so many African belief systems. In the process, of course, these indigenous belief systems have themselves evolved: one of Soyinka's examples of this process and of the "accommodative nature" of African culture is the fact that Yorubans have come to regard Sango as the god of electricity, as well as lightning, effectively "extend[ing]" the god's ancient "territory... to embrace" a distinctly modern phenomenon. Likewise, Soyinka's own favorite deity, Ogun, has become "not merely the god of war but the god of revolution," a patron saint of sorts to revolutionaries and freedom fighters in Africa and the Americas.

Whatever the aims of educators and missionaries, then, neither a Western-style education nor conversion to Christianity or Islam necessarily led Africans like Soyinka (or his protagonist, Olunde) to completely reject ancient ways and values. Soyinka himself, born in Abeokuta in 1934, grew up in the 1940s—roughly the same time period in which his play is set. And he was, as literary scholar Simon Gikandi notes, raised in "one of the most [Christian] and Westernized families in colonial Nigeria." Soyinka's father was a schoolteacher, his maternal grandfather an Anglican minister, his uncle the principal of the local Anglican grammar school. Yet many in the community, including members of Soyinka's extended family, still embraced traditional Yoruban beliefs and practices. In a 1981 interview, Soyinka describes the world of his childhood as one in which African and European cultural traditions co-existed and combined as often as they conflicted:

> My family brought together what is generally, simplistically, referred to as the new and the old, the modern and the traditional.... [M]y father was a teacher and my mother, who also came from a teaching family, was a petty trader. I grew up among music, performances. I grew up to

*Annunciation of the Angel to Mary*, carved wood panel by Yoruba sculptor Lamidi Olonade Fakeye. Fakeye converted to Islam as a young man, but his woodwork incorporates Christian and traditional Yoruban imagery.

the sounds of poetry as women hawked their wares.... [F]ruit-sellers or market-women [didn't] just sit but actually s[a]ng their wares to attract customers.... I also had the advantage, this is where the question of being born into two societies, two forms, two levels, two patterns of creativity comes in, I had the advantage of actually being raised in a Christian family in the midst of "pagan" manifestations. So it was quite usual for me to be returning from church and suddenly find an *Egungun* masquerade, that's an ancestral masquerade cult, parading with very lively music, drums, etcetera, along the street, to the discomfiture of the Christian worshippers. Discomfiture, because they felt that their Sunday was being desecrated. I don't know what was so desecrating about it. I thought it was a glorious spectacle, and I suppose for following them around once or twice I received the requisite number of lashes or slaps. But I just thought they were all different forms of worship. I don't remember any time when I felt that *that* particular set of worship or belief was sinful. I am afraid that from a very early age I had a rather pagan outlook on the world, let's put it that way, and I think it has stood me in good stead. In any case, to be frank, their music was more enthralling to my ears than the hymns of the Christian church.... So I had this advantage of seeing how material belonging to one culture didn't really come to blows with material from another culture.

Moreover, Soyinka's schooling—like Olunde's—reinforced and deepened his knowledge and appreciation of various cultural traditions. Educated in some of Nigeria's most exclusive Western-style schools and at a British university, where the curricula focused on European history, literature, and culture, Soyinka nonetheless also devoted himself to the study of traditional African history and culture (especially drama), as well as East Asian literature.

Having thus "read widely in the world's literature," Soyinka is understandably impatient both with those contemporary African artists and intellectuals who declare that "the literature of Europe has no relevance whatever" to themselves and with those Western readers who find the world portrayed in his plays too "exotic" to enter fully. As he explains,

I grew up, as many of us did, on the fare of European literature. Even in school we didn't have too much problem understanding the worlds of William Shakespeare, Bernard Shaw, Galsworthy, Moliere, and Ibsen, and, frankly, I'm irritated when people from outside my world say they find it difficult to enter.... It's laziness, it's intellectual laziness ... especially today when communication is a matter of course.... I find no difficulty at all in entering into Chinese literature, Japanese literature, Russian literature, and this has always been so. I think the barrier is self-induced. "This is a world of the exotic, we cannot enter it." ... By now it has to be a two-way traffic. There can be no concessions at all; the effort simply has to be made.

*Death and the King's Horseman* directly challenges us to make that effort, to accept Africans on their own terms in a way that the play's Western characters will not or cannot—or, in Soyinka's words, to approach African people and culture "with some humility," fully "enter[ing] their philosophy, their world view" and "opening" ourselves "up to a new existence, a new scale of values." The play invites us to appreciate the distinctiveness of traditional African culture and the ways in which that culture has been undervalued and undermined by the West. Yet the play issues that invitation in part by itself demonstrating the very same openness toward non-African cultural traditions. Drawing as much on Greek and Shakespearean tragedy as on African ritual and drama, *Death and the King's Horseman* encourages us also to recognize the similarities—or what Soyinka calls the "complementarities"—among widely different literary and cultural traditions. In the process, Soyinka's play, like Hansberry's, offers you the perfect opportunity to think further about both how historical and cultural contexts shape literary texts and how those texts transcend their contexts, showing us everything that connects human beings across the boundaries of time and place, history and culture.

## The American Civil Rights and the African Liberation Struggles 1940–1970

1943  *U.S.:* In Beaumont, Texas, martial law is declared after a race riot injures 50 and kills two (June); a much larger race riot, in Detroit, kills 34 people (including 25 blacks), injures almost 700, and ends only after President Roosevelt calls in 6,000 National Guardsmen (June); race riot in Harlem injures 300 and kills six African Americans (August).

1946  *U.S.:* Race riot leads Chicago authorities to abandon their effort to move black families into the Airport Homes housing project.

*Africa:* In Kenya, a group of Kikuyus begins what will become known as the Mau Mau rebellion, urging Kenyans to take up arms to regain their rights and lands.

1947  *U.S.:* Race riot occurs in Chicago when local authorities attempt to move blacks into the Fernwood Park housing project.

*Africa:* Kwame Nkrumah returns to the Gold Coast from Britain and becomes General Secretary of the colony's most influential political party.

1948  *U.S.:* President Truman issues an executive order integrating the armed forces; Supreme Court rules restrictive covenants legally unenforceable.

*Africa:* The Afrikaner Nationalist Party wins general elections in South Africa after promising to strengthen the system of *apartheid* or racial segregation (which will last until 1991–92); in the Gold Coast, disturbances throughout the colony lead to the arrest and temporary detention of Kwame Nkrumah and several other nationalist political leaders.

1949  *U.S.:* Race riot occurs in Chicago's Park Manor when a black family attempts to move in; another riot breaks out in Englewood Park when a black man is seen visiting the home of a white union organizer.

*Africa:* In the Gold Coast, Kwame Nkrumah leads a series of strikes and boycotts to protest British rule and is imprisoned for sedition (until 1952).

1950  *Africa:* British authorities in Kenya outlaw the Mau Mau movement.

1951  *U.S.:* The National Guard is called in to quell a riot after a black family moves into an apartment complex in Cicero, a town bordering Chicago.

*Africa:* Libya gains independence from Britain and France.

1952  *Africa:* In response to the Mau Mau rebellion, British authorities in Kenya declare a state of emergency (which will last until 1956) and imprison or exile several African nationalist leaders, including Jomo Kenyatta (who will be detained until 1959); Eritrea gains independence, in federation with Ethiopia, from Britain.

1953 *U.S.:* Two neighborhood associations in Chicago lead a nine-month "campaign of terror" after local authorities try to move a black family into the Trumbull Park Homes housing project.

*Africa:* British authorities in Kenya outlaw all nationalist political parties and begin a policy of general, forced detention, escalating the Mau Mau rebellion into a full-scale war.

1954 *U.S.:* In *Brown v. Board of Education*, the Supreme Court declares school segregation unconstitutional.

1955 *U.S.:* Year-long bus boycott begins in Montgomery, Alabama.

1956 *U.S.:* Supreme Court declares segregation on buses unconstitutional.

*Africa:* Morocco gains independence from Spain and France; Sudan, from Britain; and Tunisia, from France.

1957 *U.S.:* When Arkansas's governor blocks nine black students from attending a Little Rock high school, President Eisenhower sends in federal troops to force compliance with court-ordered desegregation.

*Africa:* The Gold Coast becomes the independent state (later Republic) of Ghana under the leadership of Nkrumah.

1958 *Africa:* French Guinea becomes the independent state of Guinea.

1960 *U.S.:* Refused service at the lunch counter of a Woolworth's in Greensboro, North Carolina, four black college students stage the first sit-in (February); Student Non-Violent Coordinating Committee (SNCC) is founded in Raleigh, North Carolina (April).

*Africa:* Republic of Congo (formerly the Belgian Congo), Nigeria, Somalia (formerly Italian Somaliland), Togo (formerly French Togoland), and all of France's remaining sub-Saharan colonies gain independence.

1961 *U.S.:* Between May and August, approximately 1,000 volunteer "Freedom Riders" take buses to the South in support of integration.

*Africa:* Sierra Leone and Tanganyika gain independence from Britain. (In 1964, Tanganyika will join with newly independent Zanzibar to form Tanzania.)

1962 *U.S.:* African American James Meredith is denied admission to the University of Mississippi, resulting in contempt charges against the state's governor and race riots that kill two.

*Africa:* Algeria gains independence from France; Burundi and Rwanda, from Belgium; and Uganda, from Britain.

1963 *U.S.:* Martin Luther King, Jr. is arrested in Birmingham, Alabama, for leading civil rights demonstrations (April); Governor George Wallace attempts to block integration of the University of Alabama but is forced by President Kennedy to allow black enrollment (June); civil rights leader Medgar Evers is assassinated in Mississippi (June); 200,000 people participate in the March on Washington at which Martin Luther King, Jr. delivers his "I Have a Dream" speech (August); church bombing in Birmingham, Alabama, kills four black girls attending Sunday School and sparks riots in which two more African Americans are killed (September).

*Africa:* Kenya gains independence from Britain under the leadership of Kenyatta (president until his death in 1979); Nigeria is declared a republic under the leadership of Nnamdi Azikiwe.

1964 *U.S.:* Twenty-Fourth Amendment to the Constitution is ratified, abolishing the poll tax traditionally used to prevent blacks from voting (January); "Freedom Summer" begins with a massive effort to register black voters throughout the South; Congress overcomes 75-day filibuster to pass Civil Rights Act, which outlaws employment discrimination and segregation in public facilities (July); in Mississippi, three people working to register black voters are murdered, their bodies discovered only after President Johnson sends military personnel to aid in the search (June–August); Martin Luther King, Jr. wins the Nobel Peace Prize.

*Africa:* Former British colonies Northern Rhodesia and Nyasaland become the independent states of Zambia and Malawi.

1965 *U.S.:* Malcolm X is assassinated in Harlem (February); Martin Luther King, Jr. leads march from Selma to Montgomery, Alabama, to demand protection of voting rights, and, on "Bloody Sunday," fifty marchers are hospitalized after police use tear gas, whips, and clubs against them (March); Voting Rights Act makes it easier for southern blacks to register to vote by outlawing requirements such as literacy tests (August); race riots occur in several cities, the worst—in Los Angeles's Watts neighborhood—kills 34 and injures 1,000 (August).

*Africa:* Gambia gains independence from Britain.

1966 *U.S.:* In Chicago, Martin Luther King, Jr. leads a series of marches to protest housing segregation (July–March); Edward Brooke, of Massachusetts, becomes the first African American elected to the U.S. Senate in 85 years.

*Africa:* British Bechuanaland and Basutoland become the independent states of Botswana and Lesotho.

1967 *U.S.:* In the first nine months of the year, 164 race riots occur across the country, the worst in Detroit (43 people killed) and Newark, New Jersey (26 killed, over 1,000 injured); Supreme Court declares unconstitutional the bans against interracial marriage still enforced in 16 states (June); Thurgood Marshall becomes the first African American Supreme Court justice; Carl Stokes of Cleveland becomes the first African American elected as mayor of a major U.S. city.

1968 *U.S.:* Martin Luther King, Jr. is assassinated in Memphis, Tennessee, sparking riots in Chicago, Baltimore, Washington, and other cities across the country (April); Civil Rights Act of 1968 guarantees fair treatment in housing (April).

*Africa:* Equatorial Guinea gains independence from Spain; Mauritius and Swaziland, from Britain.

From left to right, Ruby Dee as Ruth, Sidney Poitier as Walter Lee Younger, and Diana Sands as Beneatha in the original 1959 Broadway production of *A Raisin in the Sun*

## LORRAINE HANSBERRY

[WEB] *A Raisin in the Sun*

> What happens to a dream deferred?
>
> Does it dry up
> Like a raisin in the sun?
> Or fester like a sore—
> And then run?
> Does it stink like rotten meat?
> Or crust and sugar over—
> Like a syrupy sweet?

Maybe it just sags
Like a heavy load.

Or does it explode?
—LANGSTON HUGHES[1]

CAST OF CHARACTERS

RUTH YOUNGER
TRAVIS YOUNGER
WALTER LEE YOUNGER (BROTHER)
BENEATHA YOUNGER
LENA YOUNGER (MAMA)
JOSEPH ASAGAI
GEORGE MURCHISON
KARL LINDNER
BOBO
MOVING MEN

*The action of the play is set in Chicago's Southside, sometime between World War II and the present.*

## ACT I

### Scene One

*The Younger living room would be a comfortable and well-ordered room if it were not for a number of indestructible contradictions to this state of being. Its furnishings are typical and undistinguished and their primary feature now is that they have clearly had to accommodate the living of too many people for too many years—and they are tired. Still, we can see that at some time, a time probably no longer remembered by the family (except perhaps for* MAMA*), the furnishings of this room were actually selected with care and love and even hope—and brought to this apartment and arranged with taste and pride.*

*That was a long time ago. Now the once loved pattern of the couch upholstery has to fight to show itself from under acres of crocheted doilies and couch covers which have themselves finally come to be more important than the upholstery. And here a table or a chair has been moved to disguise the worn places in the carpet; but the carpet has fought back by showing its weariness, with depressing uniformity, elsewhere on its surface.*

*Weariness has, in fact, won in this room. Everything has been polished, washed, sat on, used, scrubbed too often. All pretenses but living itself have long since vanished from the very atmosphere of this room.*

*Moreover, a section of this room, for it is not really a room unto itself, though the landlord's lease would make it seem so, slopes backward to provide a small kitchen area, where the family prepares the meals that are eaten in the living room proper, which must also serve as dining room. The single window that has been provided for these "two" rooms is located in this kitchen area. The sole natural light the family may enjoy in the course of a day is only that which fights its way through this little window.*

*At left, a door leads to a bedroom which is shared by* MAMA *and her daughter,* BENEATHA. *At right, opposite, is a second room (which in the beginning of the life of this apartment was probably a breakfast room) which serves as a bedroom for* WALTER *and his wife,* RUTH.

*Time: Sometime between World War II and the present.*

*Place: Chicago's Southside.*

*At Rise: It is morning dark in the living room.* TRAVIS *is asleep on the make-down bed*

---

1. Hughes's poem, published in 1951, is entitled "Harlem (A Dream Deferred)."

*at center. An alarm clock sounds from within the bedroom at right, and presently* RUTH *enters from that room and closes the door behind her. She crosses sleepily toward the window. As she passes her sleeping son she reaches down and shakes him a little. At the window she raises the shade and a dusky Southside morning light comes in feebly. She fills a pot with water and puts it on to boil. She calls to the boy, between yawns, in a slightly muffled voice.*

RUTH *is about thirty. We can see that she was a pretty girl, even exceptionally so, but now it is apparent that life has been little that she expected, and disappointment has already begun to hang in her face. In a few years, before thirty-five even, she will be known among her people as a "settled woman."*

*She crosses to her son and gives him a good, final, rousing shake.*

RUTH: Come on now, boy, it's seven thirty! [*Her son sits up at last, in a stupor of sleepiness.*] I say hurry up, Travis! You ain't the only person in the world got to use a bathroom! [*The child, a sturdy, handsome little boy of ten or eleven, drags himself out of the bed and almost blindly takes his towels and "today's clothes" from drawers and a closet and goes out to the bathroom, which is in an outside hall and which is shared by another family or families on the same floor.* RUTH *crosses to the bedroom door at right and opens it and calls in to her husband.*] Walter Lee! . . . It's after seven thirty! Lemme see you do some waking up in there now! [*She waits.*] You better get up from there, man! It's after seven thirty I tell you. [*She waits again.*] All right, you just go ahead and lay there and next thing you know Travis be finished and Mr. Johnson'll be in there and you'll be fussing and cussing round here like a mad man! And be late too! [*She waits, at the end of patience.*] Walter Lee—it's time for you to get up!

[*She waits another second and then starts to go into the bedroom, but is apparently satisfied that her husband has begun to get up. She stops, pulls the door to, and returns to the kitchen area. She wipes her face with a moist cloth and runs her fingers through her sleep-disheveled hair in a vain effort and ties an apron around her housecoat. The bedroom door at right opens and her husband stands in the doorway in his pajamas, which are rumpled and mismated. He is a lean, intense young man in his middle thirties, inclined to quick nervous movements and erratic speech habits—and always in his voice there is a quality of indictment.*]

WALTER: Is he out yet?
RUTH: What you mean *out*? He ain't hardly got in there good yet.
WALTER: [*Wandering in, still more oriented to sleep than to a new day.*] Well, what was you doing all that yelling for if I can't even get in there yet? [*Stopping and thinking.*] Check coming today?
RUTH: They *said* Saturday and this is just Friday and I hopes to God you ain't going to get up here first thing this morning and start talking to me 'bout no money—'cause I 'bout don't want to hear it.
WALTER: Something the matter with you this morning?
RUTH: No—I'm just sleepy as the devil. What kind of eggs you want?
WALTER: Not scrambled. [RUTH *starts to scramble eggs.*] Paper come? [RUTH *points impatiently to the rolled up* Tribune *on the table, and he gets it and spreads it out and vaguely reads the front page.*] Set off another bomb yesterday.
RUTH: [*Maximum indifference.*] Did they?
WALTER: [*Looking up.*] What's the matter with you?

RUTH: Ain't nothing the matter with me. And don't keep asking me that this morning.
WALTER: Ain't nobody bothering you. [*Reading the news of the day absently again.*] Say Colonel McCormick[2] is sick.
RUTH: [*Affecting tea-party interest.*] Is he now? Poor thing.
WALTER: [*Sighing and looking at his watch.*] Oh, me. [*He waits.*] Now what is that boy doing in that bathroom all this time? He just going to have to start getting up earlier. I can't be late to work on account of him fooling around in there.
RUTH: [*Turning on him.*] Oh, no he ain't going to be getting up no earlier no such thing! It ain't his fault that he can't get to bed no earlier nights 'cause he got a bunch of crazy good-for-nothing clowns sitting up running their mouths in what is supposed to be his bedroom after ten o'clock at night...
WALTER: That's what you mad about, ain't it? The things I want to talk about with my friends just couldn't be important in your mind, could they?

[*He rises and finds a cigarette in her handbag on the table and crosses to the little window and looks out, smoking and deeply enjoying this first one.*]

RUTH: [*Almost matter of factly, a complaint too automatic to deserve emphasis.*] Why you always got to smoke before you eat in the morning?
WALTER: [*At the window.*] Just look at 'em down there... Running and racing to work... [*He turns and faces his wife and watches her a moment at the stove, and then, suddenly.*] You look young this morning, baby.
RUTH: [*Indifferently.*] Yeah?
WALTER: Just for a second—stirring them eggs. It's gone now—just for a second it was—you looked real young again. [*Then, drily.*] It's gone now—you look like yourself again.
RUTH: Man, if you don't shut up and leave me alone.
WALTER: [*Looking out to the street again.*] First thing a man ought to learn in life is not to make love to no colored woman first thing in the morning. You all some evil people at eight o'clock in the morning.

[TRAVIS *appears in the hall doorway, almost fully dressed and quite wide awake now, his towels and pajamas across his shoulders. He opens the door and signals for his father to make the bathroom in a hurry.*]

TRAVIS: [*Watching the bathroom.*] Daddy, come on!

[WALTER *gets his bathroom utensils and flies out to the bathroom.*]

RUTH: Sit down and have your breakfast, Travis.
TRAVIS: Mama, this is Friday. [*Gleefully.*] Check coming tomorrow, huh?
RUTH: You get your mind off money and eat your breakfast.
TRAVIS: [*Eating.*] This is the morning we supposed to bring the fifty cents to school.
RUTH: Well, I ain't got no fifty cents this morning.
TRAVIS: Teacher say we have to.
RUTH: I don't care what teacher say. I ain't got it. Eat your breakfast, Travis.
TRAVIS: I *am* eating.
RUTH: Hush up now and just eat!

---

2. Robert Rutherford McCormick (1880–1955), owner-publisher of the *Chicago Tribune*.

[*The boy gives her an exasperated look for her lack of understanding, and eats grudgingly.*]

TRAVIS: You think Grandmama would have it?

RUTH: No! And I want you to stop asking your grandmother for money, you hear me?

TRAVIS: [*Outraged.*] Gaaaleee! I don't ask her, she just gimme it sometimes!

RUTH: Travis Willard Younger—I got too much on me this morning to be—

TRAVIS: Maybe Daddy—

RUTH: *Travis!*

[*The boy hushes abruptly. They are both quiet and tense for several seconds.*]

TRAVIS: [*Presently.*] Could I maybe go carry some groceries in front of the supermarket for a little while after school then?

RUTH: Just hush, I said. [TRAVIS *jabs his spoon into his cereal bowl viciously, and rests his head in anger upon his fists.*] If you through eating, you can get over there and make up your bed.

[*The boy obeys stiffly and crosses the room, almost mechanically, to the bed and more or less carefully folds the covering. He carries the bedding into his mother's room and returns with his books and cap.*]

TRAVIS: [*Sulking and standing apart from her unnaturally.*] I'm gone.

RUTH: [*Looking up from the stove to inspect him automatically.*] Come here. [*He crosses to her and she studies his head.*] If you don't take this comb and fix this here head, you better! [TRAVIS *puts down his books with a great sigh of oppression, and crosses to the mirror. His mother mutters under her breath about his "slubbornness."*] 'Bout to march out of here with that head looking just like chickens slept in it! I just don't know where you get your slubborn ways . . . And get your jacket, too. Looks chilly out this morning.

TRAVIS: [*With conspicuously brushed hair and jacket.*] I'm gone.

RUTH: Get carfare and milk money—[*Waving one finger.*]—and not a single penny for no caps, you hear me?

TRAVIS: [*With sullen politeness.*] Yes'm.

[*He turns in outrage to leave. His mother watches after him as in his frustration he approaches the door almost comically. When she speaks to him, her voice has become a very gentle tease.*]

RUTH: [*Mocking; as she thinks he would say it.*] Oh, Mama makes me so mad sometimes, I don't know what to do! [*She waits and continues to his back as he stands stock-still in front of the door.*] I wouldn't kiss that woman good-bye for nothing in this world this morning! [*The boy finally turns around and rolls his eyes at her, knowing the mood has changed and he is vindicated; he does not, however, move toward her yet.*] Not for nothing in this world! [*She finally laughs aloud at him and holds out her arms to him and we see that it is a way between them, very old and practiced. He crosses to her and allows her to embrace him warmly but keeps his face fixed with masculine rigidity. She holds him back from her presently and looks at him and runs her fingers over the features of his face. With utter gentleness—*] Now—whose little old angry man are you?

TRAVIS: [*The masculinity and gruffness start to fade at last.*] Aw gaalee—Mama . . .

RUTH: [*Mimicking.*] Aw—gaaaaalleeeee, Mama! [*She pushes him, with rough playfulness and finality, toward the door.*] Get on out of here or you going to be late.
TRAVIS: [*In the face of love, new aggressiveness.*] Mama, could I *please* go carry groceries?
RUTH: Honey, it's starting to get so cold evenings.
WALTER: [*Coming in from the bathroom and drawing a make-believe gun from a make-believe holster and shooting at his son.*] What is it he wants to do?
RUTH: Go carry groceries after school at the supermarket.
WALTER: Well, let him go . . .
TRAVIS: [*Quickly, to the ally.*] I *have* to—she won't gimme the fifty cents . . .
WALTER: [*To his wife only.*] Why not?
RUTH: [*Simply, and with flavor.*] 'Cause we don't have it.
WALTER: [*To* RUTH *only.*] What you tell the boy things like that for? [*Reaching down into his pants with a rather important gesture.*] Here, son—

[*He hands the boy the coin, but his eyes are directed to his wife's.* TRAVIS *takes the money happily.*]

TRAVIS: Thanks, Daddy.

[*He starts out.* RUTH *watches both of them with murder in her eyes.* WALTER *stands and stares back at her with defiance, and suddenly reaches into his pocket again on an afterthought.*]

WALTER: [*Without even looking at his son, still staring hard at his wife.*] In fact, here's another fifty cents . . . Buy yourself some fruit today—or take a taxicab to school or something!
TRAVIS: Whoopee—

[*He leaps up and clasps his father around the middle with his legs, and they face each other in mutual appreciation; slowly* WALTER LEE *peeks around the boy to catch the violent rays from his wife's eyes and draws his head back as if shot.*]

WALTER: You better get down now—and get to school, man.
TRAVIS: [*At the door.*] O.K. Good-bye.

[*He exits.*]

WALTER: [*After him, pointing with pride.*] That's *my* boy. [*She looks at him in disgust and turns back to her work.*] You know what I was thinking 'bout in the bathroom this morning?
RUTH: No.
WALTER: How come you always try to be so pleasant!
RUTH: What is there to be pleasant 'bout!
WALTER: You want to know what I was thinking 'bout in the bathroom or not!
RUTH: I know what you thinking 'bout.
WALTER: [*Ignoring her.*] 'Bout what me and Willy Harris was talking about last night.
RUTH: [*Immediately—a refrain.*] Willy Harris is a good-for-nothing loud mouth.
WALTER: Anybody who talks to me has got to be a good-for-nothing loud mouth, ain't he! And what you know about who is just a good-for-nothing loud mouth? Charlie Atkins was just a "good-for-nothing loud mouth" too, wasn't he! When he wanted me to go in the dry-cleaning business with him. And

now—he's grossing a hundred thousand a year. A hundred thousand dollars a year! You still call *him* a loud mouth!

RUTH: [*Bitterly.*] Oh, Walter Lee...

[*She folds her head on her arms over the table.*]

WALTER: [*Rising and coming to her and standing over her.*] You tired, ain't you? Tired of everything. Me, the boy, the way we live—this beat-up hole—everything. Ain't you? [*She doesn't look up, doesn't answer.*] So tired—moaning and groaning all the time, but you wouldn't do nothing to help, would you? You couldn't be on my side that long for nothing, could you?

RUTH: Walter, please leave me alone.

WALTER: A man needs for a woman to back him up...

RUTH: Walter—

WALTER: Mama would listen to you. You know she listen to you more than she do me and Bennie. She think more of you. All you have to do is just sit down with her when you drinking your coffee one morning and talking 'bout things like you do and— [*He sits down beside her and demonstrates graphically what he thinks her methods and tone should be.*] —you just sip your coffee, see, and say easy like that you been thinking 'bout that deal Walter Lee is so interested in, 'bout the store and all, and sip some more coffee, like what you saying ain't really that important to you—And the next thing you know, she be listening good and asking you questions and when I come home—I can tell her the details. This ain't no fly-by-night proposition, baby. I mean we figured it out, me and Willy and Bobo.

RUTH: [*With a frown.*] Bobo?

WALTER: Yeah. You see, this little liquor store we got in mind cost seventy-five thousand and we figured the initial investment on the place be 'bout thirty thousand, see. That be ten thousand each. Course, there's a couple of hundred you got to pay so's you don't spend your life just waiting for them clowns to let your license get approved—

RUTH: You mean graft?

WALTER: [*Frowning impatiently.*] Don't call it that. See there, that just goes to show you what women understand about the world. Baby, don't *nothing* happen for you in this world 'less you pay *somebody* off!

RUTH: Walter, leave me alone! [*She raises her head and stares at him vigorously—then says, more quietly.*] Eat your eggs, they gonna be cold.

WALTER: [*Straightening up from her and looking off.*] That's it. There you are. Man say to his woman: I got me a dream. His woman say: Eat your eggs. [*Sadly, but gaining in power.*] Man say: I got to take hold of this here world, baby! And a woman will say: Eat your eggs and go to work. [*Passionately now.*] Man say: I got to change my life, I'm choking to death, baby! And his woman say— [*In utter anguish as he brings his fists down on his thighs.*] —Your eggs is getting cold!

RUTH: [*Softly.*] Walter, that ain't none of our money.

WALTER: [*Not listening at all or even looking at her.*] This morning, I was lookin' in the mirror and thinking about it... I'm thirty-five years old; I been married eleven years and I got a boy who sleeps in the living room— [*Very, very quietly.*] —and all I got to give him is stories about how rich white people live...

RUTH: Eat your eggs, Walter.

WALTER: *Damn my eggs... damn all the eggs that ever was!*

RUTH: Then go to work.
WALTER: [*Looking up at her.*] See—I'm trying to talk to you 'bout myself— [*Shaking his head with the repetition.*] —and all you can say is eat them eggs and go to work.
RUTH: [*Wearily.*] Honey, you never say nothing new. I listen to you every day, every night and every morning, and you never say nothing new. [*Shrugging.*] So you would rather *be* Mr. Arnold than be his chauffeur. So—I would *rather* be living in Buckingham Palace.[3]
WALTER: That is just what is wrong with the colored woman in this world... Don't understand about building their men up and making 'em feel like they somebody. Like they can do something.
RUTH: [*Drily, but to hurt.*] There *are* colored men who do things.
WALTER: No thanks to the colored woman.
RUTH: Well, being a colored woman, I guess I can't help myself none.

[*She rises and gets the ironing board and sets it up and attacks a huge pile of rough-dried clothes, sprinkling them in preparation for the ironing and then rolling them into tight fat balls.*]

WALTER: [*Mumbling.*] We one group of men tied to a race of women with small minds.

[*His sister* BENEATHA *enters. She is about twenty, as slim and intense as her brother. She is not as pretty as her sister-in-law, but her lean, almost intellectual face has a handsomeness of its own. She wears a bright-red flannel nightie, and her thick hair stands wildly about her head. Her speech is a mixture of many things; it is different from the rest of the family's insofar as education has permeated her sense of English—and perhaps the Midwest rather than the South has finally—at last—won out in her inflection; but not altogether, because over all of it is a soft slurring and transformed use of vowels which is the decided influence of the Southside. She passes through the room without looking at either* RUTH *or* WALTER *and goes to the outside door and looks, a little blindly, out to the bathroom. She sees that it has been lost to the Johnsons. She closes the door with a sleepy vengeance and crosses to the table and sits down a little defeated.*]

BENEATHA: I am going to start timing those people.
WALTER: You should get up earlier.
BENEATHA: [*Her face in her hands. She is still fighting the urge to go back to bed.*] Really—would you suggest dawn? Where's the paper?
WALTER: [*Pushing the paper across the table to her as he studies her almost clinically, as though he has never seen her before.*] You a horrible-looking chick at this hour.
BENEATHA: [*Drily.*] Good morning, everybody.
WALTER: [*Senselessly.*] How is school coming?
BENEATHA: [*In the same spirit.*] Lovely. Lovely. And you know, biology is the greatest. [*Looking up at him.*] I dissected something that looked just like you yesterday.
WALTER: I just wondered if you've made up your mind and everything.
BENEATHA: [*Gaining in sharpness and impatience.*] And what did I answer yesterday morning—and the day before that?

---

3. Where the queen of Great Britain resides in London.

RUTH: [*From the ironing board, like someone disinterested and old.*] Don't be so nasty, Bennie.
BENEATHA: [*Still to her brother.*] And the day before that and the day before that!
WALTER: [*Defensively.*] I'm interested in you. Something wrong with that? Ain't many girls who decide—
WALTER AND BENEATHA: [*In unison.*] —"to be a doctor."

[*Silence.*]

WALTER: Have we figured out yet just exactly how much medical school is going to cost?
RUTH: Walter Lee, why don't you leave that girl alone and get out of here to work?
BENEATHA: [*Exits to the bathroom and bangs on the door.*] Come on out of there, please!

[*She comes back into the room.*]

WALTER: [*Looking at his sister intently.*] You know the check is coming tomorrow.
BENEATHA: [*Turning on him with a sharpness all her own.*] That money belongs to Mama, Walter, and it's for her to decide how she wants to use it. I don't care if she wants to buy a house or a rocket ship or just nail it up somewhere and look at it. It's hers. Not ours—*hers*.
WALTER: [*Bitterly.*] Now ain't that fine! You just got your mother's interest at heart, ain't you, girl? You such a nice girl—but if Mama got that money she can always take a few thousand and help you through school too—can't she?
BENEATHA: I have never asked anyone around here to do anything for me.
WALTER: No! And the line between asking and just accepting when the time comes is big and wide—ain't it!
BENEATHA: [*With fury.*] What do you want from me, Brother—that I quit school or just drop dead, which!
WALTER: I don't want nothing but for you to stop acting holy 'round here. Me and Ruth done made some sacrifices for you—why can't you do something for the family?
RUTH: Walter, don't be dragging me in it.
WALTER: You are in it—Don't you get up and go work in somebody's kitchen for the last three years to help put clothes on her back?
RUTH: Oh, Walter—that's not fair . . .
WALTER: It ain't that nobody expects you to get on your knees and say thank you, Brother; thank you, Ruth; thank you, Mama—and thank you, Travis, for wearing the same pair of shoes for two semesters—
BENEATHA: [*Dropping to her knees.*] Well—I *do*—all right?—thank everybody . . . and forgive me for ever wanting to be anything at all . . . forgive me, forgive me!
RUTH: Please stop it! Your mama'll hear you.
WALTER: Who the hell told you you had to be a doctor? If you so crazy 'bout messing 'round with sick people—then go be a nurse like other women—or just get married and be quiet . . .
BENEATHA: Well—you finally got it said . . . it took you three years but you finally got it said. Walter, give up; leave me alone—it's Mama's money.
WALTER: *He was my father, too!*
BENEATHA: So what? He was mine, too—and Travis' grandfather—but the insur-

ance money belongs to Mama. Picking on me is not going to make her give it to you to invest in any liquor stores— [*Underbreath, dropping into a chair.*] —and I for one say, God bless Mama for that!

WALTER: [*To* RUTH.] See—did you hear? Did you hear!

RUTH: Honey, please go to work.

WALTER: Nobody in this house is ever going to understand me.

BENEATHA: Because you're a nut.

WALTER: Who's a nut?

BENEATHA: You—you are a nut. Thee is mad, boy.

WALTER: [*Looking at his wife and his sister from the door, very sadly.*] The world's most backward race of people, and that's a fact.

BENEATHA: [*Turning slowly in her chair.*] And then there are all those prophets who would lead us out of the wilderness— [WALTER *slams out of the house.*] —into the swamps!

RUTH: Bennie, why you always gotta be pickin' on your brother? Can't you be a little sweeter sometimes? [*Door opens.* WALTER *walks in.*]

WALTER: [*To* RUTH.] I need some money for carfare.

RUTH: [*Looks at him, then warms; teasing, but tenderly.*] Fifty cents? [*She goes to her bag and gets money.*] Here, take a taxi.

[WALTER *exits.* MAMA *enters. She is a woman in her early sixties, full-bodied and strong. She is one of those women of a certain grace and beauty who wear it so unobtrusively that it takes a while to notice. Her dark-brown face is surrounded by the total whiteness of her hair, and, being a woman who has adjusted to many things in life and overcome many more, her face is full of strength. She has, we can see, wit and faith of a kind that keep her eyes lit and full of interest and expectancy. She is, in a word, a beautiful woman. Her bearing is perhaps most like the noble bearing of the women of the Hereros of Southwest Africa—rather as if she imagines that as she walks she still bears a basket or a vessel upon her head. Her speech, on the other hand, is as careless as her carriage is precise—she is inclined to slur everything—but her voice is perhaps not so much quiet as simply soft.*]

MAMA: Who that 'round here slamming doors at this hour?

[*She crosses through the room, goes to the window, opens it, and brings in a feeble little plant growing doggedly in a small pot on the window sill. She feels the dirt and puts it back out.*]

RUTH: That was Walter Lee. He and Bennie was at it again.

MAMA: My children and they tempers. Lord, if this little old plant don't get more sun than it's been getting it ain't never going to see spring again. [*She turns from the window.*] What's the matter with you this morning, Ruth? You looks right peaked. You aiming to iron all them things? Leave some for me. I'll get to 'em this afternoon. Bennie honey, it's too drafty for you to be sitting 'round half dressed. Where's your robe?

BENEATHA: In the cleaners.

MAMA: Well, go get mine and put it on.

BENEATHA: I'm not cold, Mama, honest.

MAMA: I know—but you so thin . . .

BENEATHA: [*Irritably.*] Mama, I'm not cold.

MAMA: [*Seeing the make-down bed as* TRAVIS *has left it.*] Lord have mercy, look at that poor bed. Bless his heart—he tries, don't he?

[*She moves to the bed* TRAVIS *has sloppily made up.*]

RUTH: No—he don't half try at all 'cause he knows you going to come along behind him and fix everything. That's just how come he don't know how to do nothing right now—you done spoiled that boy so.

MAMA: Well—he's a little boy. Ain't supposed to know 'bout housekeeping. My baby, that's what he is. What you fix for his breakfast this morning?

RUTH: [*Angrily.*] I feed my son, Lena!

MAMA: I ain't meddling— [*Underbreath; busy-bodyish.*] I just noticed all last week he had cold cereal, and when it starts getting this chilly in the fall a child ought to have some hot grits or something when he goes out in the cold—

RUTH: [*Furious.*] I gave him hot oats—is that all right!

MAMA: I ain't meddling. [*Pause.*] Put a lot of nice butter on it? [RUTH *shoots her an angry look and does not reply.*] He likes lots of butter.

RUTH: [*Exasperated.*] Lena—

MAMA: [*To* BENEATHA. MAMA *is inclined to wander conversationally sometimes.*] What was you and your brother fussing 'bout this morning?

BENEATHA: It's not important, Mama.

[*She gets up and goes to look out at the bathroom, which is apparently free, and she picks up her towels and rushes out.*]

MAMA: What was they fighting about?

RUTH: Now you know as well as I do.

MAMA: [*Shaking her head.*] Brother still worrying hisself sick about that money?

RUTH: You know he is.

MAMA: You had breakfast?

RUTH: Some coffee.

MAMA: Girl, you better start eating and looking after yourself better. You almost thin as Travis.

RUTH: Lena—

MAMA: Un-hunh?

RUTH: What are you going to do with it?

MAMA: Now don't you start, child. It's too early in the morning to be talking about money. It ain't Christian.

RUTH: It's just that he got his heart set on that store—

MAMA: You mean that liquor store that Willy Harris want him to invest in?

RUTH: Yes—

MAMA: We ain't no business people, Ruth. We just plain working folks.

RUTH: Ain't nobody business people till they go into business. Walter Lee say colored people ain't never going to start getting ahead till they start gambling on some different kinds of things in the world—investments and things.

MAMA: What done got into you, girl? Walter Lee done finally sold you on investing.

RUTH: No. Mama, something is happening between Walter and me. I don't know what it is—but he needs something—something I can't give him anymore. He needs this chance, Lena.

MAMA: [*Frowning deeply.*] But liquor, honey—

RUTH: Well—like Walter say—I spec people going to always be drinking themselves some liquor.
MAMA: Well—whether they drinks it or not ain't none of my business. But whether I go into business selling it to 'em *is,* and I don't want that on my ledger this late in life. [*Stopping suddenly and studying her daughter-in-law.*] Ruth Younger, what's the matter with you today? You look like you could fall over right there.
RUTH: I'm tired.
MAMA: Then you better stay home from work today.
RUTH: I can't stay home. She'd be calling up the agency and screaming at them, "My girl didn't come in today—send me somebody! My girl didn't come in!" Oh, she just have a fit...
MAMA: Well, let her have it. I'll just call her up and say you got the flu—
RUTH: [*Laughing.*] Why the flu?
MAMA: 'Cause it sounds respectable to 'em. Something white people get, too. They know 'bout the flu. Otherwise they think you been cut up or something when you tell 'em you sick.
RUTH: I got to go in. We need the money.
MAMA: Somebody would of thought my children done all but starved to death the way they talk about money here late. Child, we got a great big old check coming tomorrow.
RUTH: [*Sincerely, but also self-righteously.*] Now that's your money. It ain't got nothing to do with me. We all feel like that—Walter and Bennie and me—even Travis.
MAMA: [*Thoughtfully, and suddenly very far away.*] Ten thousand dollars—
RUTH: Sure is wonderful.
MAMA: Ten thousand dollars.
RUTH: You know what you should do, Miss Lena? You should take yourself a trip somewhere. To Europe or South America or someplace—
MAMA: [*Throwing up her hands at the thought.*] Oh, child!
RUTH: I'm serious. Just pack up and leave! Go on away and enjoy yourself some. Forget about the family and have yourself a ball for once in your life—
MAMA: [*Drily.*] You sound like I'm just about ready to die. Who'd go with me? What I look like wandering 'round Europe by myself?
RUTH: Shoot—these here rich white women do it all the time. They don't think nothing of packing up they suitcases and piling on one of them big steamships and—swoosh!—they gone, child.
MAMA: Something always told me I wasn't no rich white woman.
RUTH: Well—what are you going to do with it then?
MAMA: I ain't rightly decided. [*Thinking. She speaks now with emphasis.*] Some of it got to be put away for Beneatha and her schoolin'—and ain't nothing going to touch that part of it. Nothing. [*She waits several seconds, trying to make up her mind about something, and looks at* RUTH *a little tentatively before going on.*] Been thinking that we maybe could meet the notes on a little old two-story somewhere, with a yard where Travis could play in the summertime, if we use part of the insurance for a down payment and everybody kind of pitch in. I could maybe take on a little day work again, few days a week—
RUTH: [*Studying her mother-in-law furtively and concentrating on her ironing, anxious to encourage without seeming to.*] Well, Lord knows, we've put enough rent into this here rat trap to pay for four houses by now...

MAMA: [*Looking up at the words "rat trap" and then looking around and leaning back and sighing—in a suddenly reflective mood—*] "Rat trap"—yes, that's all it is. [*Smiling.*] I remember just as well the day me and Big Walter moved in here. Hadn't been married but two weeks and wasn't planning on living here no more than a year. [*She shakes her head at the dissolved dream.*] We was going to set away, little by little, don't you know, and buy a little place out in Morgan Park. We had even picked out the house. [*Chuckling a little.*] Looks right dumpy today. But Lord, child, you should know all the dreams I had 'bout buying that house and fixing it up and making me a little garden in the back— [*She waits and stops smiling.*] And didn't none of it happen.

[*Dropping her hands in a futile gesture.*]

RUTH: [*Keeps her head down, ironing.*] Yes, life can be a barrel of disappointments, sometimes.

MAMA: Honey, Big Walter would come in here some nights back then and slump down on that couch there and just look at the rug, and look at me and look at the rug and then back at me—and I'd know he was down then . . . really down. [*After a second very long and thoughtful pause; she is seeing back to times that only she can see.*] And then, Lord, when I lost that baby—little Claude—I almost thought I was going to lose Big Walter too. Oh, that man grieved hisself! He was one man to love his children.

RUTH: Ain't nothin' can tear at you like losin' your baby.

MAMA: I guess that's how come that man finally worked hisself to death like he done. Like he was fighting his own war with this here world that took his baby from him.

RUTH: He sure was a fine man, all right. I always liked Mr. Younger.

MAMA: Crazy 'bout his children! God knows there was plenty wrong with Walter Younger—hard-headed, mean, kind of wild with women—plenty wrong with him. But he sure loved his children. Always wanted them to have something—be something. That's where Brother gets all these notions, I reckon. Big Walter used to say, he'd get right wet in the eyes sometimes, lean his head back with the water standing in his eyes and say, "Seem like God didn't see fit to give the black man nothing but dreams—but He did give us children to make them dreams seem worthwhile." [*She smiles.*] He could talk like that, don't you know.

RUTH: Yes, he sure could. He was a good man, Mr. Younger.

MAMA: Yes, a fine man—just couldn't never catch up with his dreams, that's all.

[BENEATHA *comes in, brushing her hair and looking up to the ceiling, where the sound of a vacuum cleaner has started up.*]

BENEATHA: What could be so dirty on that woman's rugs that she has to vacuum them every single day?

RUTH: I wish certain young women 'round here who I could name would take inspiration about certain rugs in a certain apartment I could also mention.

BENEATHA: [*Shrugging.*] How much cleaning can a house need, for Christ's sakes.

MAMA: [*Not liking the Lord's name used thus.*] Bennie!

RUTH: Just listen to her—just listen!

BENEATHA: Oh, God!

MAMA: If you use the Lord's name just one more time—

BENEATHA: [*A bit of a whine.*] Oh, Mama—
RUTH: Fresh—just fresh as salt, this girl!
BENEATHA: [*Drily.*] Well—if the salt loses its savor—[4]
MAMA: Now that will do. I just ain't going to have you 'round here reciting the scriptures in vain—you hear me?
BENEATHA: How did I manage to get on everybody's wrong side by just walking into a room?
RUTH: If you weren't so fresh—
BENEATHA: Ruth, I'm twenty years old.
MAMA: What time you be home from school today?
BENEATHA: Kind of late. [*With enthusiasm.*] Madeline is going to start my guitar lessons today.

[MAMA *and* RUTH *look up with the same expression.*]

MAMA: Your *what* kind of lessons?
BENEATHA: Guitar.
RUTH: Oh, Father!
MAMA: How come you done taken it in your mind to learn to play the guitar?
BENEATHA: I just want to, that's all.
MAMA: [*Smiling.*] Lord, child, don't you know what to do with yourself? How long it going to be before you get tired of this now—like you got tired of that little play-acting group you joined last year? [*Looking at* RUTH.] And what was it the year before that?
RUTH: The horseback-riding club for which she bought that fifty-five-dollar riding habit that's been hanging in the closet ever since!
MAMA: [*To* BENEATHA.] Why you got to flit so from one thing to another, baby?
BENEATHA: [*Sharply.*] I just want to learn to play the guitar. Is there anything wrong with that?
MAMA: Ain't nobody trying to stop you. I just wonders sometimes why you has to flit so from one thing to another all the time. You ain't never done nothing with all that camera equipment you brought home—
BENEATHA: I don't flit! I—I experiment with different forms of expression—
RUTH: Like riding a horse?
BENEATHA: —People have to express themselves one way or another.
MAMA: What is it you want to express?
BENEATHA: [*Angrily.*] Me! [MAMA *and* RUTH *look at each other and burst into raucous laughter.*] Don't worry—I don't expect you to understand.
MAMA: [*To change the subject.*] Who you going out with tomorrow night?
BENEATHA: [*With displeasure.*] George Murchison again.
MAMA: [*Pleased.*] Oh—you getting a little sweet on him?
RUTH: You ask me, this child ain't sweet on nobody but herself— [*Underbreath.*] Express herself!

[*They laugh.*]

BENEATHA: Oh—I like George all right, Mama. I mean I like him enough to go out with him and stuff, but—

---

4. See Matthew 5.13: "You are the salt of the earth. But if the salt loses its taste, with what can it be seasoned? It is no longer good for anything but to be thrown out and trampled underfoot."

RUTH: [*For devilment.*] What does *and stuff* mean?
BENEATHA: Mind your own business.
MAMA: Stop picking at her now, Ruth. [*A thoughtful pause, and then a suspicious sudden look at her daughter as she turns in her chair for emphasis.*] What does it mean?
BENEATHA: [*Wearily.*] Oh, I just mean I couldn't ever really be serious about George. He's—he's so shallow.
RUTH: Shallow—what do you mean he's shallow? He's *rich!*
MAMA: Hush, Ruth.
BENEATHA: I know he's rich. He knows he's rich, too.
RUTH: Well—what other qualities a man got to have to satisfy you, little girl?
BENEATHA: You wouldn't even begin to understand. Anybody who married Walter could not possibly understand.
MAMA: [*Outraged.*] What kind of way is that to talk about your brother?
BENEATHA: Brother is a flip—let's face it.
MAMA: [*To* RUTH, *helplessly.*] What's a flip?
RUTH: [*Glad to add kindling.*] She's saying he's crazy.
BENEATHA: Not crazy. Brother isn't really crazy yet—he—he's an elaborate neurotic.
MAMA: Hush your mouth!
BENEATHA: As for George. Well. George looks good—he's got a beautiful car and he takes me to nice places and, as my sister-in-law says, he is probably the richest boy I will ever get to know and I even like him sometimes—but if the Youngers are sitting around waiting to see if their little Bennie is going to tie up the family with the Murchisons, they are wasting their time.
RUTH: You mean you wouldn't marry George Murchison if he asked you someday? That pretty, rich thing? Honey, I knew you was odd—
BENEATHA: No I would not marry him if all I felt for him was what I feel now. Besides, George's family wouldn't really like it.
MAMA: Why not?
BENEATHA: Oh, Mama—The Murchisons are honest-to-God-real-*live*-rich colored people, and the only people in the world who are more snobbish than rich white people are rich colored people. I thought everybody knew that. I've met Mrs. Murchison. She's a scene!
MAMA: You must not dislike people 'cause they well off, honey.
BENEATHA: Why not? It makes just as much sense as disliking people 'cause they are poor, and lots of people do that.
RUTH: [*A wisdom-of-the-ages manner. To* MAMA.] Well, she'll get over some of this—
BENEATHA: Get over it? What are you talking about, Ruth? Listen, I'm going to be a doctor. I'm not worried about who I'm going to marry yet—if I ever get married.
MAMA AND RUTH: *If!*
MAMA: Now, Bennie—
BENEATHA: Oh, I probably will . . . but first I'm going to be a doctor, and George, for one, still thinks that's pretty funny. I couldn't be bothered with that. I am going to be a doctor and everybody around here better understand that!
MAMA: [*Kindly.*] 'Course you going to be a doctor, honey, God willing.
BENEATHA: [*Drily.*] God hasn't got a thing to do with it.
MAMA: Beneatha—that just wasn't necessary.

BENEATHA: Well—neither is God. I get sick of hearing about God.
MAMA: Beneatha!
BENEATHA: I mean it! I'm just tired of hearing about God all the time. What has He got to do with anything? Does He pay tuition?
MAMA: You 'bout to get your fresh little jaw slapped!
RUTH: That's just what she needs, all right!
BENEATHA: Why? Why can't I say what I want to around here, like everybody else?
MAMA: It don't sound nice for a young girl to say things like that—you wasn't brought up that way. Me and your father went to trouble to get you and Brother to church every Sunday.
BENEATHA: Mama, you don't understand. It's all a matter of ideas, and God is just one idea I don't accept. It's not important. I am not going out and be immoral or commit crimes because I don't believe in God. I don't even think about it. It's just that I get tired of Him getting credit for all the things the human race achieves through its own stubborn effort. There simply is no blasted God—there is only man and it is he who makes miracles!

[MAMA *absorbs this speech, studies her daughter and rises slowly and crosses to* BENEATHA *and slaps her powerfully across the face. After, there is only silence and the daughter drops her eyes from her mother's face, and* MAMA *is very tall before her.*]

MAMA: Now—you say after me, in my mother's house there is still God. [*There is a long pause and* BENEATHA *stares at the floor wordlessly.* MAMA *repeats the phrase with precision and cool emotion.*] In my mother's house there is still God.
BENEATHA: In my mother's house there is still God.

[*A long pause.*]

MAMA: [*Walking away from* BENEATHA, *too disturbed for triumphant posture. Stopping and turning back to her daughter.*] There are some ideas we ain't going to have in this house. Not long as I am at the head of this family.
BENEATHA: Yes, ma'am.

[MAMA *walks out of the room.*]

RUTH: [*Almost gently, with profound understanding.*] You think you a woman, Bennie—but you still a little girl. What you did was childish—so you got treated like a child.
BENEATHA: I see. [*Quietly.*] I also see that everybody thinks it's all right for Mama to be a tyrant. But all the tyranny in the world will never put a God in the heavens!

[*She picks up her books and goes out.*]

RUTH: [*Goes to* MAMA'S *door.*] She said she was sorry.
MAMA: [*Coming out, going to her plant.*] They frightens me, Ruth. My children.
RUTH: You got good children, Lena. They just a little off sometimes—but they're good.
MAMA: No—there's something come down between me and them that don't let us understand each other and I don't know what it is. One done almost lost his mind thinking 'bout money all the time and the other done commence

to talk about things I can't seem to understand in no form or fashion. What is it that's changing, Ruth?

RUTH: [*Soothingly, older than her years.*] Now...you taking it all too seriously. You just got strong-willed children and it takes a strong woman like you to keep 'em in hand.

MAMA: [*Looking at her plant and sprinkling a little water on it.*] They spirited all right, my children. Got to admit they got spirit—Bennie and Walter. Like this little old plant that ain't never had enough sunshine or nothing—and look at it...

[*She has her back to* RUTH, *who has had to stop ironing and lean against something and put the back of her hand to her forehead.*]

RUTH: [*Trying to keep* MAMA *from noticing.*] You...sure...loves that little old thing, don't you?...

MAMA: Well, I always wanted me a garden like I used to see sometimes at the back of the houses down home. This plant is close as I ever got to having one. [*She looks out of the window as she replaces the plant.*] Lord, ain't nothing as dreary as the view from this window on a dreary day, is there? Why ain't you singing this morning, Ruth? Sing that "No Ways Tired." That song always lifts me up so— [*She turns at last to see that* RUTH *has slipped quietly into a chair, in a state of semiconsciousness.*] Ruth! Ruth honey—what's the matter with you...Ruth!

[CURTAIN.]

## Scene Two

*It is the following morning; a Saturday morning, and house cleaning is in progress at the Youngers. Furniture has been shoved hither and yon and* MAMA *is giving the kitchen-area walls a washing down.* BENEATHA, *in dungarees, with a handkerchief tied around her face, is spraying insecticide into the cracks in the walls. As they work, the radio is on and a Southside disk-jockey program is inappropriately filling the house with a rather exotic saxophone blues.* TRAVIS, *the sole idle one, is leaning on his arms, looking out of the window.*

TRAVIS: Grandmama, that stuff Bennie is using smells awful. Can I go downstairs, please?

MAMA: Did you get all them chores done already? I ain't seen you doing much.

TRAVIS: Yes'm—finished early. Where did Mama go this morning?

MAMA: [*Looking at* BENEATHA.] She had to go on a little errand.

TRAVIS: Where?

MAMA: To tend to her business.

TRAVIS: Can I go outside then?

MAMA: Oh, I guess so. You better stay right in front of the house, though...and keep a good lookout for the postman.

TRAVIS: Yes'm. [*He starts out and decides to give his aunt* BENEATHA *a good swat on the legs as he passes her.*] Leave them poor little old cockroaches alone, they ain't bothering you none.

[*He runs as she swings the spray gun at him both viciously and playfully.* WALTER *enters from the bedroom and goes to the phone.*]

MAMA: Look out there, girl, before you be spilling some of that stuff on that child!

TRAVIS: [*Teasing.*] That's right—look out now!

[*He exits.*]

BENEATHA: [*Drily.*] I can't imagine that it would hurt him—it has never hurt the roaches.
MAMA: Well, little boys' hides ain't as tough as Southside roaches.
WALTER: [*Into phone.*] Hello—Let me talk to Willy Harris.
MAMA: You better get over there behind the bureau. I seen one marching out of there like Napoleon yesterday.
WALTER: Hello, Willy? It ain't come yet. It'll be here in a few minutes. Did the lawyer give you the papers?
BENEATHA: There's really only one way to get rid of them, Mama—
MAMA: How?
BENEATHA: Set fire to this building.
WALTER: Good. Good. I'll be right over.
BENEATHA: Where did Ruth go, Walter?
WALTER: I don't know.

[*He exits abruptly.*]

BENEATHA: Mama, where did Ruth go?
MAMA: [*Looking at her with meaning.*] To the doctor, I think.
BENEATHA: The doctor? What's the matter? [*They exchange glances.*] You don't think—
MAMA: [*With her sense of drama.*] Now I ain't saying what I think. But I ain't never been wrong 'bout a woman neither.

[*The phone rings.*]

BENEATHA: [*At the phone.*] Hay-lo... [*Pause, and a moment of recognition.*] Well—when did you get back!... And how was it?... Of course I've missed you—in my way... This morning? No... house cleaning and all that and Mama hates it if I let people come over when the house is like this... You *have?* Well, that's different... What is it—Oh, what the hell, come on over... Right, see you then.

[*She hangs up.*]

MAMA: [*Who has listened vigorously, as is her habit.*] Who is that you inviting over here with this house looking like this? You ain't got the pride you was born with!
BENEATHA: Asagai doesn't care how houses look, Mama—he's an intellectual.
MAMA: *Who?*
BENEATHA: Asagai—Joseph Asagai. He's an African boy I met on campus. He's been studying in Canada all summer.
MAMA: What's his name?
BENEATHA: Asagai, Joseph. Ah-sah-guy... He's from Nigeria.
MAMA: Oh, that's the little country that was founded by slaves way back...
BENEATHA: No, Mama—that's Liberia.
MAMA: I don't think I never met no African before.
BENEATHA: Well, do me a favor and don't ask him a whole lot of ignorant questions about Africans. I mean, do they wear clothes and all that—
MAMA: Well, now, I guess if you think we so ignorant 'round here maybe you shouldn't bring your friends here—

BENEATHA: It's just that people ask such crazy things. All anyone seems to know about when it comes to Africa is Tarzan—
MAMA: [*Indignantly.*] Why should I know anything about Africa?
BENEATHA: Why do you give money at church for the missionary work?
MAMA: Well, that's to help save people.
BENEATHA: You mean save them from *heathenism*—
MAMA: [*Innocently.*] Yes.
BENEATHA: I'm afraid they need more salvation from the British and the French.

[RUTH *comes in forlornly and pulls off her coat with dejection. They both turn to look at her.*]

RUTH: [*Dispiritedly.*] Well, I guess from all the happy faces—everybody knows.
BENEATHA: You pregnant?
MAMA: Lord have mercy, I sure hope it's a little old girl. Travis ought to have a sister.

[BENEATHA *and* RUTH *give her a hopeless look for this grandmotherly enthusiasm.*]

BENEATHA: How far along are you?
RUTH: Two months.
BENEATHA: Did you mean to? I mean did you plan it or was it an accident?
MAMA: What do you know about planning or not planning?
BENEATHA: Oh, Mama.
RUTH: [*Wearily.*] She's twenty years old, Lena.
BENEATHA: Did you plan it, Ruth?
RUTH: Mind your own business.
BENEATHA: It is my business—where is he going to live, on the roof? [*There is silence following the remark as the three women react to the sense of it.*] Gee—I didn't mean that, Ruth, honest. Gee, I don't feel like that at all. I—I think it is wonderful.
RUTH: [*Dully.*] Wonderful.
BENEATHA: Yes—really.
MAMA: [*Looking at* RUTH, *worried.*] Doctor say everything going to be all right?
RUTH: [*Far away.*] Yes—she says everything is going to be fine . . .
MAMA: [*Immediately suspicious.*] "She"—What doctor you went to?

[RUTH *folds over, near hysteria.*]

MAMA: [*Worriedly hovering over* RUTH.] Ruth honey—what's the matter with you—you sick?

[RUTH *has her fists clenched on her thighs and is fighting hard to suppress a scream that seems to be rising in her.*]

BENEATHA: What's the matter with her, Mama?
MAMA: [*Working her fingers in* RUTH'*s shoulder to relax her.*] She be all right. Women gets right depressed sometimes when they get her way. [*Speaking softly, expertly, rapidly.*] Now you just relax. That's right . . . just lean back, don't think 'bout nothing at all . . . nothing at all—
RUTH: I'm all right . . .

[*The glassy-eyed look melts and then she collapses into a fit of heavy sobbing. The bell rings.*]

BENEATHA: Oh, my God—that must be Asagai.
MAMA: [*To* RUTH.] Come on now, honey. You need to lie down and rest awhile . . . then have some nice hot food.

[*They exit,* RUTH'*s weight on her mother-in-law.* BENEATHA, *herself profoundly disturbed, opens the door to admit a rather dramatic-looking young man with a large package.*]

ASAGAI: Hello, Alaiyo—
BENEATHA: [*Holding the door open and regarding him with pleasure.*] Hello . . . [*Long pause.*] Well—come in. And please excuse everything. My mother was very upset about my letting anyone come here with the place like this.
ASAGAI: [*Coming into the room.*] You look disturbed too . . . Is something wrong?
BENEATHA: [*Still at the door, absently.*] Yes . . . we've all got acute ghettoitus. [*She smiles and comes toward him, finding a cigarette and sitting.*] So—sit down! How was Canada?
ASAGAI: [*A sophisticate.*] Canadian.
BENEATHA: [*Looking at him.*] I'm very glad you are back.
ASAGAI: [*Looking back at her in turn.*] Are you really?
BENEATHA: Yes—very.
ASAGAI: Why—you were quite glad when I went away. What happened?
BENEATHA: You went away.
ASAGAI: Ahhhhhhhh.
BENEATHA: Before—you wanted to be so serious before there was time.
ASAGAI: How much time must there be before one knows what one feels?
BENEATHA: [*Stalling this particular conversation. Her hands pressed together, in a deliberately childish gesture.*] What did you bring me?
ASAGAI: [*Handing her the package.*] Open it and see.
BENEATHA: [*Eagerly opening the package and drawing out some records and the colorful robes of a Nigerian woman.*] Oh, Asagai! . . . You got them for me! . . . How beautiful . . . and the records too! [*She lifts out the robes and runs to the mirror with them and holds the drapery up in front of herself.*]
ASAGAI: [*Coming to her at the mirror.*] I shall have to teach you how to drape it properly. [*He flings the material about her for the moment and stands back to look at her.*] Ah—Oh-pay-gay-day, oh-gbah-mu-shay. [*A Yoruba exclamation for admiration.*] You wear it well . . . very well . . . mutilated hair and all.
BENEATHA: [*Turning suddenly.*] My hair—what's wrong with my hair?
ASAGAI: [*Shrugging.*] Were you born with it like that?
BENEATHA: [*Reaching up to touch it.*] No . . . of course not.

[*She looks back to the mirror, disturbed.*]

ASAGAI: [*Smiling.*] How then?
BENEATHA: You know perfectly well how . . . as crinkly as yours . . . that's how.
ASAGAI: And it is ugly to you that way?
BENEATHA: [*Quickly.*] Oh, no—not ugly . . . [*More slowly, apologetically.*] But it's so hard to manage when it's, well—raw.
ASAGAI: And so to accommodate that—you mutilate it every week?

BENEATHA: It's not mutilation!

ASAGAI: [*Laughing aloud at her seriousness.*] Oh... please! I am only teasing you because you are so very serious about these things. [*He stands back from her and folds his arms across his chest as he watches her pulling at her hair and frowning in the mirror.*] Do you remember the first time you met me at school?... [*He laughs.*] You came up to me and you said—and I thought you were the most serious little thing I had ever seen—you said: [*He imitates her.*] "Mr. Asagai—I want very much to talk with you. About Africa. You see, Mr. Asagai, I am looking for my *identity*!"

[*He laughs.*]

BENEATHA: [*Turning to him, not laughing.*] Yes—

[*Her face is quizzical, profoundly disturbed.*]

ASAGAI: [*Still teasing and reaching out and taking her face in his hands and turning her profile to him.*] Well... it is true that this is not so much a profile of a Hollywood queen as perhaps a queen of the Nile— [*A mock dismissal of the importance of the question.*] But what does it matter? Assimilationism is so popular in your country.

BENEATHA: [*Wheeling, passionately, sharply.*] I am not an assimilationist!

ASAGAI: [*The protest hangs in the room for a moment and* ASAGAI *studies her, his laughter fading.*] Such a serious one. [*There is a pause.*] So—you like the robes? You must take excellent care of them—they are from my sister's personal wardrobe.

BENEATHA: [*With incredulity.*] You—you sent all the way home—for me?

ASAGAI: [*With charm.*] For you—I would do much more... Well, that is what I came for. I must go.

BENEATHA: Will you call me Monday?

ASAGAI: Yes... We have a great deal to talk about. I mean about identity and time and all that.

BENEATHA: Time?

ASAGAI: Yes. About how much time one needs to know what one feels.

BENEATHA: You never understood that there is more than one kind of feeling which can exist between a man and a woman—or, at least, there should be.

ASAGAI: [*Shaking his head negatively but gently.*] No. Between a man and a woman there need be only one kind of feeling. I have that for you... Now even... right this moment...

BENEATHA: I know—and by itself—it won't do. I can find that anywhere.

ASAGAI: For a woman it should be enough.

BENEATHA: I know—because that's what it says in all the novels that men write. But it isn't. Go ahead and laugh—but I'm not interested in being someone's little episode in America or— [*With feminine vengeance.*] —one of them! [ASAGAI *has burst into laughter again.*] That's funny as hell, huh!

ASAGAI: It's just that every American girl I have known has said that to me. White—black—in this you are all the same. And the same speech, too!

BENEATHA: [*Angrily.*] Yuk, yuk, yuk!

ASAGAI: It's how you can be sure that the world's most liberated women are not liberated at all. You all talk about it too much!

[MAMA *enters and is immediately all social charm because of the presence of a guest.*]

BENEATHA: Oh—Mama—this is Mr. Asagai.

MAMA: How do you do?

ASAGAI: [*Total politeness to an elder.*] How do you do, Mrs. Younger. Please forgive me for coming at such an outrageous hour on a Saturday.

MAMA: Well, you are quite welcome. I just hope you understand that our house don't always look like this. [*Chatterish.*] You must come again. I would love to hear all about— [*Not sure of the name.*] —your country. I think it's so sad the way our American Negroes don't know nothing about Africa 'cept Tarzan and all that. And all that money they pour into these churches when they ought to be helping you people over there drive out them French and Englishmen done taken away your land.

   [*The mother flashes a slightly superior look at her daughter upon completion of the recitation.*]

ASAGAI: [*Taken aback by this sudden and acutely unrelated expression of sympathy.*] Yes . . . yes . . .

MAMA: [*Smiling at him suddenly and relaxing and looking him over.*] How many miles is it from here to where you come from?

ASAGAI: Many thousands.

MAMA: [*Looking at him as she would* WALTER.] I bet you don't half look after yourself, being away from your mama either. I spec you better come 'round here from time to time and get yourself some decent home-cooked meals . . .

ASAGAI: [*Moved.*] Thank you. Thank you very much. [*They are all quiet, then—*] Well . . . I must go. I will call you Monday, Alaiyo.

MAMA: What's that he call you?

ASAGAI: Oh—"Alaiyo." I hope you don't mind. It is what you would call a nickname, I think. It is a Yoruba word. I am a Yoruba.

MAMA: [*Looking at* BENEATHA.] I—I thought he was from—

ASAGAI: [*Understanding.*] Nigeria is my country. Yoruba is my tribal origin—

BENEATHA: You didn't tell us what Alaiyo means . . . for all I know, you might be calling me Little Idiot or something . . .

ASAGAI: Well . . . let me see . . . I do not know how just to explain it . . . The sense of a thing can be so different when it changes languages.

BENEATHA: You're evading.

ASAGAI: No—really it is difficult . . . [*Thinking.*] It means . . . it means One for Whom Bread—Food—Is Not Enough. [*He looks at her.*] Is that all right?

BENEATHA: [*Understanding, softly.*] Thank you.

MAMA: [*Looking from one to the other and not understanding any of it.*] Well . . . that's nice . . . You must come see us again—Mr.—

ASAGAI: Ah-sah-guy . . .

MAMA: Yes . . . Do come again.

ASAGAI: Good-bye.

   [*He exits.*]

MAMA: [*After him.*] Lord, that's a pretty thing just went out here! [*Insinuatingly, to her daughter.*] Yes, I guess I see why we done commence to get so interested in Africa 'round here. Missionaries my aunt Jenny!

   [*She exits.*]

BENEATHA: Oh, Mama! . . .

> [*She picks up the Nigerian dress and holds it up to her in front of the mirror again. She sets the headdress on haphazardly and then notices her hair again and clutches at it and then replaces the headdress and frowns at herself. Then she starts to wriggle in front of the mirror as she thinks a Nigerian woman might.* TRAVIS *enters and regards her.*]

TRAVIS: You cracking up?
BENEATHA: Shut up.

> [*She pulls the headdress off and looks at herself in the mirror and clutches at her hair again and squinches her eyes as if trying to imagine something. Then, suddenly, she gets her raincoat and kerchief and hurriedly prepares for going out.*]

MAMA: [*Coming back into the room.*] She's resting now. Travis, baby, run next door and ask Miss Johnson to please let me have a little kitchen cleanser. This here can is empty as Jacob's kettle.
TRAVIS: I just came in.
MAMA: Do as you told. [*He exits and she looks at her daughter.*] Where you going?
BENEATHA: [*Halting at the door.*] To become a queen of the Nile!

> [*She exits in a breathless blaze of glory.* RUTH *appears in the bedroom doorway.*]

MAMA: Who told you to get up?
RUTH: Ain't nothing wrong with me to be lying in no bed for. Where did Bennie go?
MAMA: [*Drumming her fingers.*] Far as I could make out—to Egypt. [RUTH *just looks at her.*] What time is it getting to?
RUTH: Ten twenty. And the mailman going to ring that bell this morning just like he done every morning for the last umpteen years.

> [TRAVIS *comes in with the cleanser can.*]

TRAVIS: She say to tell you that she don't have much.
MAMA: [*Angrily.*] Lord, some people I could name sure is tight-fisted! [*Directing her grandson.*] Mark two cans of cleanser down on the list there. If she that hard up for kitchen cleanser, I sure don't want to forget to get her none!
RUTH: Lena—maybe the woman is just short on cleanser—
MAMA: [*Not listening.*] —Much baking powder as she done borrowed from me all these years, she could of done gone into the baking business!

> [*The bell sounds suddenly and sharply and all three are stunned—serious and silent—mid-speech. In spite of all the other conversations and distractions of the morning, this is what they have been waiting for, even* TRAVIS, *who looks helplessly from his mother to his grandmother.* RUTH *is the first to come to life again.*]

RUTH: [*To* TRAVIS.] Get down them steps, boy!

> [TRAVIS *snaps to life and flies out to get the mail.*]

MAMA: [*Her eyes wide, her hand to her breast.*] You mean it done really come?
RUTH: [*Excited.*] Oh, Miss Lena!
MAMA: [*Collecting herself.*] Well . . . I don't know what we all so excited about 'round here for. We known it was coming for months.
RUTH: That's a whole lot different from having it come and being able to hold

it in your hands . . . a piece of paper worth ten thousand dollars . . . [TRAVIS *bursts back into the room. He holds the envelope high above his head, like a little dancer, his face is radiant and he is breathless. He moves to his grandmother with sudden slow ceremony and puts the envelope into her hands. She accepts it, and then merely holds it and looks at it.*] Come on! Open it . . . Lord have mercy, I wish Walter Lee was here!

TRAVIS: Open it, Grandmama!

MAMA: [*Staring at it.*] Now you all be quiet. It's just a check.

RUTH: Open it . . .

MAMA: [*Still staring at it.*] Now don't act silly . . . We ain't never been no people to act silly 'bout no money—

RUTH: [*Swiftly.*] We ain't never had none before—*open it!*

> [MAMA *finally makes a good strong tear and pulls out the thin blue slice of paper and inspects it closely. The boy and his mother study it raptly over* MAMA's *shoulders.*]

MAMA: *Travis!* [*She is counting off with doubt.*] Is that the right number of zeros.

TRAVIS: Yes'm . . . ten thousand dollars. Gaalee, Grandmama, you rich.

MAMA: [*She holds the check away from her, still looking at it. Slowly her face sobers into a mask of unhappiness.*] Ten thousand dollars. [*She hands it to* RUTH.] Put it away somewhere, Ruth. [*She does not look at* RUTH; *her eyes seem to be seeing something somewhere very far off.*] Ten thousand dollars they give you. Ten thousand dollars.

TRAVIS: [*To his mother, sincerely.*] What's the matter with Grandmama—don't she want to be rich?

RUTH: [*Distractedly.*] You go on out and play now, baby. [TRAVIS *exits.* MAMA *starts wiping dishes absently, humming intently to herself.* RUTH *turns to her, with kind exasperation.*] You've gone and got yourself upset.

MAMA: [*Not looking at her.*] I spec if it wasn't for you all . . . I would just put that money away or give it to the church or something.

RUTH: Now what kind of talk is that. Mr. Younger would just be plain mad if he could hear you talking foolish like that.

MAMA: [*Stopping and staring off.*] Yes . . . he sure would. [*Sighing.*] We got enough to do with that money, all right. [*She halts then, and turns and looks at her daughter-in-law hard;* RUTH *avoids her eyes and* MAMA *wipes her hands with finality and starts to speak firmly to* RUTH.] Where did you go today, girl?

RUTH: To the doctor.

MAMA: [*Impatiently.*] Now, Ruth . . . you know better than that. Old Doctor Jones is strange enough in his way but there ain't nothing 'bout him make somebody slip and call him "she"—like you done this morning.

RUTH: Well, that's what happened—my tongue slipped.

MAMA: You went to see that woman, didn't you?

RUTH: [*Defensively, giving herself away.*] What woman you talking about?

MAMA: [*Angrily.*] That woman who—

> [WALTER *enters in great excitement.*]

WALTER: Did it come?

MAMA: [*Quietly.*] Can't you give people a Christian greeting before you start asking about money?

WALTER: [*To* RUTH.] Did it come? [RUTH *unfolds the check and lays it quietly before* him, watching him intently with thoughts of her own. WALTER *sits down and grasps it close and counts off the zeros.*] Ten thousand dollars— [*He turns suddenly, frantically to his mother and draws some papers out of his breast pocket.*] Mama—look. Old Willy Harris put everything on paper—

MAMA: Son—I think you ought to talk to your wife... I'll go on out and leave you alone if you want—

WALTER: I can talk to her later—Mama, look—

MAMA: Son—

WALTER: WILL SOMEBODY PLEASE LISTEN TO ME TODAY!

MAMA: [*Quietly.*] I don't 'low no yellin' in this house, Walter Lee, and you know it— [WALTER *stares at them in frustration and starts to speak several times.*] And there ain't going to be no investing in no liquor stores. I don't aim to have to speak on that again.

[*A long pause.*]

WALTER: Oh—so you don't aim to have to speak on that again? So you have decided... [*Crumpling his papers.*] Well, *you* tell that to my boy tonight when you put him to sleep on the living-room couch... [*Turning to* MAMA *and speaking directly to her.*] Yeah—and tell it to my wife, Mama, tomorrow when she has to go out of here to look after somebody else's kids. And tell it to *me*, Mama, every time we need a new pair of curtains and I have to watch *you* go out and work in somebody's kitchen. Yeah, you tell me then!

[WALTER *starts out.*]

RUTH: Where you going?

WALTER: I'm going out!

RUTH: Where?

WALTER: Just out of this house somewhere—

RUTH: [*Getting her coat.*] I'll come too.

WALTER: I don't want you to come!

RUTH: I got something to talk to you about, Walter.

WALTER: That's too bad.

MAMA: [*Still quietly.*] Walter Lee— [*She waits and he finally turns and looks at her.*] Sit down.

WALTER: I'm a grown man, Mama.

MAMA: Ain't nobody said you wasn't grown. But you still in my house and my presence. And as long as you are—you'll talk to your wife civil. Now sit down.

RUTH: [*Suddenly.*] Oh, let him go on out and drink himself to death! He makes me sick to my stomach! [*She flings her coat against him.*]

WALTER: [*Violently.*] And you turn mine too, baby! [RUTH *goes into their bedroom and slams the door behind her.*] That was my greatest mistake—

MAMA: [*Still quietly.*] Walter, what is the matter with you?

WALTER: Matter with me? Ain't nothing the matter with *me*!

MAMA: Yes there is. Something eating you up like a crazy man. Something more than me not giving you this money. The past few years I been watching it happen to you. You get all nervous acting and kind of wild in the eyes— [WALTER *jumps up impatiently at her words.*] I said sit there now, I'm talking to you!

WALTER: Mama—I don't need no nagging at me today.

MAMA: Seem like you getting to a place where you always tied up in some kind of knot about something. But if anybody ask you 'bout it you just yell at 'em and bust out the house and go out and drink somewheres. Walter Lee, people can't live with that. Ruth's a good, patient girl in her way—but you getting to be too much. Boy, don't make the mistake of driving that girl away from you.

WALTER: Why—what she do for me?

MAMA: She loves you.

WALTER: Mama—I'm going out. I want to go off somewhere and be by myself for a while.

MAMA: I'm sorry 'bout your liquor store, son. It just wasn't the thing for us to do. That's what I want to tell you about—

WALTER: I got to go out, Mama—

[*He rises.*]

MAMA: It's dangerous, son.

WALTER: What's dangerous?

MAMA: When a man goes outside his home to look for peace.

WALTER: [*Beseechingly.*] Then why can't there never be no peace in this house then?

MAMA: You done found it in some other house?

WALTER: No—there ain't no woman! Why do women always think there's a woman somewhere when a man gets restless. [*Coming to her.*] Mama—Mama—I want so many things...

MAMA: Yes, son—

WALTER: I want so many things that they are driving me kind of crazy... Mama—look at me.

MAMA: I'm looking at you. You a good-looking boy. You got a job, a nice wife, a fine boy and—

WALTER: A job. [*Looks at her.*] Mama, a job? I open and close car doors all day long. I drive a man around in his limousine and I say, "Yes, sir; no, sir; very good, sir; shall I take the Drive, sir?" Mama, that ain't no kind of job... that ain't nothing at all. [*Very quietly.*] Mama, I don't know if I can make you understand.

MAMA: Understand what, baby?

WALTER: [*Quietly.*] Sometimes it's like I can see the future stretched out in front of me—just plain as day. The future, Mama. Hanging over there at the edge of my days. Just waiting for me—a big, looming blank space—full of *nothing*. Just waiting for *me*. [*Pause.*] Mama—sometimes when I'm downtown and I pass them cool, quiet-looking restaurants where them white boys are sitting back and talking 'bout things... sitting there turning deals worth millions of dollars... sometimes I see guys don't look much older than me—

MAMA: Son—how come you talk so much 'bout money?

WALTER: [*With immense passion.*] Because it is life, Mama!

MAMA: [*Quietly.*] Oh— [*Very quietly.*] So now it's life. Money is life. Once upon a time freedom used to be life—now it's money. I guess the world really do change...

WALTER: No—it was always money, Mama. We just didn't know about it.

MAMA: No... something has changed. [*She looks at him.*] You something new, boy. In my time we was worried about not being lynched and getting to the North if we could and how to stay alive and still have a pinch of dignity too... Now here come you and Beneatha—talking 'bout things we ain't never even thought about hardly, me and your daddy. You ain't satisfied or proud of nothing we done. I mean that you had a home; that we kept you out of trouble till you was grown; that you don't have to ride to work on the back of nobody's streetcar—You my children—but how different we done become.

WALTER: You just don't understand, Mama, you just don't understand.

MAMA: Son—do you know your wife is expecting another baby? [WALTER *stands, stunned, and absorbs what his mother has said.*] That's what she wanted to talk to you about. [WALTER *sinks down into a chair.*] This ain't for me to be telling—but you ought to know. [*She waits.*] I think Ruth is thinking 'bout getting rid of that child.⁵

WALTER: [*Slowly understanding.*] No—no—Ruth wouldn't do that.

MAMA: When the world gets ugly enough—a woman will do anything for her family. *The part that's already living.*

WALTER: You don't know Ruth, Mama, if you think she would do that.

[RUTH *opens the bedroom door and stands there a little limp.*]

RUTH: [*Beaten.*] Yes I would too, Walter. [*Pause.*] I gave her a five-dollar down payment.

[*There is total silence as the man stares at his wife and the mother stares at her son.*]

MAMA: [*Presently.*] Well— [*Tightly.*] Well—son, I'm waiting to hear you say something... I'm waiting to hear how you be your father's son. Be the man he was ... [*Pause.*] Your wife say she going to destroy your child. And I'm waiting to hear you talk like him and say we a people who give children life, not who destroys them— [*She rises.*] I'm waiting to see you stand up and look like your daddy and say we done give up one baby to poverty and that we ain't going to give up nary another one... I'm waiting.

WALTER: Ruth—

MAMA: If you a son of mine, tell her! [WALTER *turns, looks at her and can say nothing. She continues, bitterly.*] You ... you are a disgrace to your father's memory. Somebody get me my hat.

[CURTAIN.]

## ACT II

### Scene One

*Time: Later the same day.*

*At rise:* RUTH *is ironing again. She has the radio going. Presently* BENEATHA's *bedroom door opens and* RUTH's *mouth falls and she puts down the iron in fascination.*

RUTH: What have we got on tonight!

BENEATHA: [*Emerging grandly from the doorway so that we can see her thoroughly robed in the costume* ASAGAI *brought.*] You are looking at what a well-dressed Nigerian woman wears— [*She parades for* RUTH, *her hair completely hidden by the headdress;*

---

5. Abortions were illegal and dangerous in the United States at that time.

she is coquettishly fanning herself with an ornate oriental fan, mistakenly more like Butterfly[6] than any Nigerian that ever was.] Isn't it beautiful? [She promenades to the radio and, with an arrogant flourish, turns off the good loud blues that is playing.] Enough of this assimilationist junk! [RUTH follows her with her eyes as she goes to the phonograph and puts on a record and turns and waits ceremoniously for the music to come up. Then, with a shout—] OCOMOGOSIAY!

[RUTH jumps. The music comes up, a lovely Nigerian melody. BENEATHA listens, enraptured, her eyes far away—"back to the past." She begins to dance. RUTH is dumbfounded.]

RUTH: What kind of dance is that?
BENEATHA: A folk dance.
RUTH: [Pearl Bailey.][7] What kind of folks do that, honey?
BENEATHA: It's from Nigeria. It's a dance of welcome.
RUTH: Who you welcoming?
BENEATHA: The men back to the village.
RUTH: Where they been?
BENEATHA: How should I know—out hunting or something. Anyway, they are coming back now...
RUTH: Well, that's good.
BENEATHA: [With the record.]

*Alundi, alundi*
*Alundi alunya*
*Jop pu a jeepua*
*Ang gu sooooooooo*

*Ai yai yae...*
*Ayehaye—alundi...*

[WALTER comes in during this performance; he has obviously been drinking. He leans against the door heavily and watches his sister, at first with distaste. Then his eyes look off—"back to the past"—as he lifts both his fists to the roof, screaming.]

WALTER: YEAH...AND ETHIOPIA STRETCH FORTH HER HANDS AGAIN!...
RUTH: [Drily, looking at him.] Yes—and Africa sure is claiming her own tonight. [She gives them both up and starts ironing again.]
WALTER: [All in a drunken, dramatic shout.] Shut up!...I'm digging them drums ...them drums move me!... [He makes his weaving way to his wife's face and leans in close to her.] In my heart of hearts— [He thumps his chest.] —I am much warrior!
RUTH: [Without even looking up.] In your heart of hearts you are much drunkard.
WALTER: [Coming away from her and starting to wander around the room, shouting.] Me and Jomo... [Intently, in his sister's face. She has stopped dancing to watch him in this unknown mood.] That's my man, Kenyatta.[8] [Shouting and thumping his chest.] FLAMING SPEAR! HOT DAMN! [He is suddenly in possession of an imag-

---

6. Butterfly McQueen (1911-1995), African American actor who appeared in *Gone with the Wind*.
7. That is, in the manner of the popular African American singer and entertainer (1918-1990).
8. Jomo Kenyatta (1893-1978), African political leader and first president of Kenya (1964-1978).

*inary spear and actively spearing enemies all over the room.*] OCOMOGOSIAY... THE LION IS WAKING... OWIMOWEH! [*He pulls his shirt open and leaps up on a table and gestures with his spear. The bell rings.* RUTH *goes to answer.*]

BENEATHA: [*To encourage* WALTER, *thoroughly caught up with this side of him.*] OCOMOGOSIAY, FLAMING SPEAR!

WALTER: [*On the table, very far gone, his eyes pure glass sheets. He sees what we cannot, that he is a leader of his people, a great chief, a descendant of Chaka,*[9] *and that the hour to march has come.*] Listen, my black brothers—

BENEATHA: OCOMOGOSIAY!

WALTER: —Do you hear the waters rushing against the shores of the coastlands—

BENEATHA: OCOMOGOSIAY!

WALTER: —Do you hear the screeching of the cocks in yonder hills beyond where the chiefs meet in council for the coming of the mighty war—

BENEATHA: OCOMOGOSIAY!

WALTER: —Do you hear the beating of the wings of the birds flying low over the mountains and the low places of our land—

[RUTH *opens the door.* GEORGE MURCHISON *enters.*]

BENEATHA: OCOMOGOSIAY!

WALTER: —Do you hear the singing of the women, singing the war songs of our fathers to the babies in the great houses... singing the sweet war songs? OH, DO YOU HEAR, MY BLACK BROTHERS!

BENEATHA: [*Completely gone.*] We hear you, Flaming Spear—

WALTER: Telling us to prepare for the greatness of the time— [*To* GEORGE.] Black Brother!

[*He extends his hand for the fraternal clasp.*]

GEORGE: Black Brother, hell!

RUTH: [*Having had enough, and embarrassed for the family.*] Beneatha, you got company—what's the matter with you? Walter Lee Younger, get down off that table and stop acting like a fool...

[WALTER *comes down off the table suddenly and makes a quick exit to the bathroom.*]

RUTH: He's had a little to drink... I don't know what her excuse is.

GEORGE: [*To* BENEATHA.] Look honey, we're going *to* the theatre—we're not going to be *in* it... so go change, huh?

RUTH: You expect this boy to go out with you looking like that?

BENEATHA: [*Looking at* GEORGE.] That's up to George. If he's ashamed of his heritage—

GEORGE: Oh, don't be so proud of yourself, Bennie—just because you look eccentric.

BENEATHA: How can something that's natural be eccentric?

GEORGE: That's what being eccentric means—being natural. Get dressed.

BENEATHA: I don't like that, George.

---

9. Zulu chief (1786-1828), also known as "Shaka" and called "The Black Napoleon" for his strategic and organizational genius.

RUTH: Why must you and your brother make an argument out of everything people say?
BENEATHA: Because I hate assimilationist Negroes!
RUTH: Will somebody please tell me what assimila-who-ever means!
GEORGE: Oh, it's just a college girl's way of calling people Uncle Toms—but that isn't what it means at all.
RUTH: Well, what does it mean?
BENEATHA: [*Cutting* GEORGE *off and staring at him as she replies to* RUTH.] It means someone who is willing to give up his own culture and submerge himself completely in the dominant, and in this case, *oppressive* culture!
GEORGE: Oh, dear, dear, dear! Here we go! A lecture on the African past! On our Great West African Heritage! In one second we will hear all about the great Ashanti empires; the great Songhay civilizations; and the great sculpture of Bénin—and then some poetry in the Bantu—and the whole monologue will end with the word *heritage*! [*Nastily.*] Let's face it, baby, your heritage is nothing but a bunch of raggedy-assed spirituals and some grass huts!
BENEATHA: *Grass huts!* [RUTH *crosses to her and forcibly pushes her toward the bedroom.*] See there ... you are standing there in your splendid ignorance talking about people who were the first to smelt iron on the face of the earth! [RUTH *is pushing her through the door.*] The Ashanti were performing surgical operations when the English— [RUTH *pulls the door to, with* BENEATHA *on the other side, and smiles graciously at* GEORGE. BENEATHA *opens the door and shouts the end of the sentence defiantly at* GEORGE.] —were still tattooing themselves with blue dragons ... [*She goes back inside.*]
RUTH: Have a seat, George. [*They both sit.* RUTH *folds her hands rather primly on her lap, determined to demonstrate the civilization of the family.*] Warm, ain't it? I mean for September. [*Pause.*] Just like they always say about Chicago weather: If it's too hot or cold for you, just wait a minute and it'll change. [*She smiles happily at this cliché of clichés.*] Everybody say it's got to do with them bombs and things they keep setting off.[1] [*Pause.*] Would you like a nice cold beer?
GEORGE: No, thank you. I don't care for beer. [*He looks at his watch.*] I hope she hurries up.
RUTH: What time is the show?
GEORGE: It's an eight-thirty curtain. That's just Chicago, though. In New York standard curtain time is eight forty.

[*He is rather proud of this knowledge.*]

RUTH: [*Properly appreciating it.*] You get to New York a lot?
GEORGE: [*Offhand.*] Few times a year.
RUTH: Oh—that's nice. I've never been to New York.

[WALTER *enters. We feel he has relieved himself, but the edge of unreality is still with him.*]

WALTER: New York ain't got nothing Chicago ain't. Just a bunch of hustling people all squeezed up together—being "Eastern."

[*He turns his face into a screw of displeasure.*]

---

1. In the 1950s, people commonly blamed weather fluctuations on atomic testing.

GEORGE: Oh—you've been?
WALTER: *Plenty* of times.
RUTH: [*Shocked at the lie.*] Walter Lee Younger!
WALTER: [*Staring her down.*] Plenty! [*Pause.*] What we got to drink in this house? Why don't you offer this man some refreshment. [*To* GEORGE.] They don't know how to entertain people in this house, man.
GEORGE: Thank you—I don't really care for anything.
WALTER: [*Feeling his head; sobriety coming.*] Where's Mama?
RUTH: She ain't come back yet.
WALTER: [*Looking* MURCHISON *over from head to toe, scrutinizing his carefully casual tweed sports jacket over cashmere V-neck sweater over soft eyelet shirt and tie, and soft slacks, finished off with white buckskin shoes.*] Why all you college boys wear them fairyish-looking white shoes?
RUTH: Walter Lee!

[GEORGE MURCHISON *ignores the remark.*]

WALTER: [*To* RUTH.] Well, they look crazy as hell—white shoes, cold as it is.
RUTH: [*Crushed.*] You have to excuse him—
WALTER: No he don't! Excuse me for what? What you always excusing me for! I'll excuse myself when I needs to be excused! [*A pause.*] They look as funny as them black knee socks Beneatha wears out of here all the time.
RUTH: It's the college *style*, Walter.
WALTER: Style, hell, She looks like she got burnt legs or something!
RUTH: Oh, Walter—
WALTER: [*An irritable mimic.*] Oh, Walter! Oh, Walter! [*To* MURCHISON.] How's your old man making out? I understand you all going to buy that big hotel on the Drive?[2] [*He finds a beer in the refrigerator, wanders over to* MURCHISON, *sipping and wiping his lips with the back of his hand, and straddling a chair backwards to talk to the other man.*] Shrewd move. Your old man is all right, man. [*Tapping his head and half winking for emphasis.*] I mean he knows how to operate. I mean he thinks *big*, you know what I mean, I mean for a *home*, you know? But I think he's kind of running out of ideas now. I'd like to talk to him. Listen, man, I got some plans that could turn this city upside down. I mean I think like he does. *Big*. Invest big, gamble big, hell, lose *big* if you have to, you know what I mean. It's hard to find a man on this whole Southside who understands my kind of thinking—you dig? [*He scrutinizes* MURCHISON *again, drinks his beer, squints his eyes and leans in close, confidential, man to man.*] Me and you ought to sit down and talk sometimes, man. Man, I got me some ideas . . .
GEORGE: [*With boredom.*] Yeah—sometimes we'll have to do that, Walter.
WALTER: [*Understanding the indifference, and offended.*] Yeah—well, when you get the time, man. I know you a busy little boy.
RUTH: Walter, please—
WALTER: [*Bitterly, hurt.*] I know ain't nothing in this world as busy as you colored college boys with your fraternity pins and white shoes . . .
RUTH: [*Covering her face with humiliation.*] Oh, Walter Lee—
WALTER: I see you all the time—with the books tucked under your arms—going to your [*British A—a mimic.*] "clahsses." And for what! What the hell you learn-

---

2. Lake Shore Drive, a scenic thoroughfare along Lake Michigan.

ing over there? Filling up your heads— [*Counting off on his fingers.*] —with the sociology and the psychology—but they teaching you how to be a man? How to take over and run the world? They teaching you how to run a rubber plantation or a steel mill? Naw—just to talk proper and read books and wear white shoes . . .
GEORGE: [*Looking at him with distaste, a little above it all.*] You're all wacked up with bitterness, man.
WALTER: [*Intently, almost quietly, between the teeth, glaring at the boy.*] And you—ain't you bitter, man? Ain't you just about had it yet? Don't you see no stars gleaming that you can't reach out and grab? You happy?—You contented son-of-a-bitch—you happy? You got it made? Bitter? Man, I'm a volcano. Bitter? Here I am a giant—surrounded by ants! Ants who can't even understand what it is the giant is talking about.
RUTH: [*Passionately and suddenly.*] Oh, Walter—ain't you with nobody!
WALTER: [*Violently.*] No! 'Cause ain't nobody with me! Not even my own mother!
RUTH: Walter, that's a terrible thing to say!

[BENEATHA *enters, dressed for the evening in a cocktail dress and earrings.*]

GEORGE: Well—hey, you look great.
BENEATHA: Let's go, George. See you all later.
RUTH: Have a nice time.
GEORGE: Thanks. Good night. [*To* WALTER, *sarcastically.*] Good night, *Prometheus.*[3]

[BENEATHA *and* GEORGE *exit.*]

WALTER: [*To* RUTH.] Who is Prometheus?
RUTH: I don't know. Don't worry about it.
WALTER: [*In fury, pointing after* GEORGE.] See there—they get to a point where they can't insult you man to man—they got to go talk about something ain't nobody never heard of!
RUTH: How do you know it was an insult? [*To humor him.*] Maybe Prometheus is a nice fellow.
WALTER: Prometheus! I bet there ain't even no such thing! I bet that simple-minded clown—
RUTH: Walter—

[*She stops what she is doing and looks at him.*]

WALTER: [*Yelling.*] Don't start!
RUTH: Start what?
WALTER: Your nagging! Where was I? Who was I with? How much money did I spend?
RUTH: [*Plaintively.*] Walter Lee—why don't we just try to talk about it . . .
WALTER: [*Not listening.*] I been out talking with people who understand me. People who care about the things I got on my mind.
RUTH: [*Wearily.*] I guess that means people like Willy Harris.
WALTER: Yes, people like Willy Harris.

---

3. In Greek mythology, Prometheus represented the bold creative spirit; he stole fire from Olympus (the locale of the gods) and gave it to humankind.

RUTH: [*With a sudden flash of impatience.*] Why don't you all just hurry up and go into the banking business and stop talking about it!
WALTER: Why? You want to know why? 'Cause we all tied up in a race of people that don't know how to do nothing but moan, pray and have babies!

[*The line is too bitter even for him and he looks at her and sits down.*]

RUTH: Oh, Walter... [*Softly.*] Honey, why can't you stop fighting me?
WALTER: [*Without thinking.*] Who's fighting you? Who even cares about you?

[*This line begins the retardation of his mood.*]

RUTH: Well— [*She waits a long time, and then with resignation starts to put away her things.*] I guess I might as well go on to bed... [*More or less to herself.*] I don't know where we lost it... but we have... [*Then, to him.*] I—I'm sorry about this new baby, Walter. I guess maybe I better go on and do what I started... I guess I just didn't realize how bad things was with us... I guess I just didn't really realize— [*She starts out to the bedroom and stops.*] You want some hot milk?
WALTER: Hot milk?
RUTH: Yes—hot milk.
WALTER: Why hot milk?
RUTH: 'Cause after all that liquor you come home with you ought to have something hot in your stomach.
WALTER: I don't want no milk.
RUTH: You want some coffee then?
WALTER: No, I don't want no coffee. I don't want nothing hot to drink. [*Almost plaintively.*] Why you always trying to give me something to eat?
RUTH: [*Standing and looking at him helplessly.*] What else can I give you, Walter Lee Younger?

[*She stands and looks at him and presently turns to go out again. He lifts his head and watches her going away from him in a new mood which began to emerge when he asked her "Who cares about you?"*]

WALTER: It's been rough, ain't it, baby? [*She hears and stops but does not turn around and he continues to her back.*] I guess between two people there ain't never as much understood as folks generally thinks there is. I mean like between me and you— [*She turns to face him.*] How we gets to the place where we scared to talk softness to each other. [*He waits, thinking hard himself.*] Why you think it got to be like that? [*He is thoughtful, almost as a child would be.*] Ruth, what is it gets into people ought to be close?
RUTH: I don't know, honey. I think about it a lot.
WALTER: On account of you and me, you mean? The way things are with us. The way something done come down between us.
RUTH: There ain't so much between us, Walter... Not when you come to me and try to talk to me. Try to be with me... a little even.
WALTER: [*Total honesty.*] Sometimes... sometimes... I don't even know how to try.
RUTH: Walter—
WALTER: Yes?
RUTH: [*Coming to him, gently and with misgiving, but coming to him.*] Honey... life don't have to be like this. I mean sometimes people can do things so that

things are better . . . You remember how we used to talk when Travis was born . . . about the way we were going to live . . . the kind of house . . . [*She is stroking his head.*] Well, it's all starting to slip away from us . . .

[MAMA *enters, and* WALTER *jumps up and shouts at her.*]

WALTER: Mama, where have you been?
MAMA: My—them steps is longer than they used to be. Whew! [*She sits down and ignores him.*] How you feeling this evening, Ruth?

[RUTH *shrugs, disturbed some at having been prematurely interrupted and watching her husband knowingly.*]

WALTER: Mama, where have you been all day?
MAMA: [*Still ignoring him and leaning on the table and changing to more comfortable shoes.*] Where's Travis?
RUTH: I let him go out earlier and he ain't come back yet. Boy, is he going to get it!
WALTER: Mama!
MAMA: [*As if she has heard him for the first time.*] Yes, son?
WALTER: Where did you go this afternoon?
MAMA: I went downtown to tend to some business that I had to tend to.
WALTER: What kind of business?
MAMA: You know better than to question me like a child, Brother.
WALTER: [*Rising and bending over the table.*] Where were you, Mama? [*Bringing his fists down and shouting.*] Mama, you didn't go do something with that insurance money, something crazy?

[*The front door opens slowly, interrupting him, and* TRAVIS *peeks his head in, less than hopefully.*]

TRAVIS: [*To his mother.*] Mama, I—
RUTH: "Mama I" nothing! You're going to get it, boy! Get on in that bedroom and get yourself ready!
TRAVIS: But I—
MAMA: Why don't you all never let the child explain hisself.
RUTH: Keep out of it now, Lena.

[MAMA *clamps her lips together, and* RUTH *advances toward her son menacingly.*]

RUTH: A thousand times I have told you not to go off like that—
MAMA: [*Holding out her arms to her grandson.*] Well—at least let me tell him something. I want him to be the first one to hear . . . Come here, Travis. [*The boy obeys, gladly.*] Travis— [*She takes him by the shoulder and looks into his face.*] —you know that money we got in the mail this morning?
TRAVIS: Yes'm—
MAMA: Well—what you think your grandmama gone and done with that money?
TRAVIS: I don't know, Grandmama.
MAMA: [*Putting her finger on his nose for emphasis.*] She went out and she bought you a house! [*The explosion comes from* WALTER *at the end of the revelation and he jumps up and turns away from all of them in a fury.* MAMA *continues, to* TRAVIS.] You glad about the house? It's going to be yours when you get to be a man.
TRAVIS: Yeah—I always wanted to live in a house.

MAMA: All right, gimme some sugar then— [TRAVIS *puts his arms around her neck as she watches her son over the boy's shoulder. Then, to* TRAVIS, *after the embrace.*] Now when you say your prayers tonight, you thank God and your grandfather—'cause it was him who give you the house—in his way.
RUTH: [*Taking the boy from* MAMA *and pushing him toward the bedroom.*] Now you get out of here and get ready for your beating.
TRAVIS: Aw, Mama—
RUTH: Get on in there— [*Closing the door behind him and turning radiantly to her mother-in-law.*] So you went and did it!
MAMA: [*Quietly, looking at her son with pain.*] Yes, I did.
RUTH: [*Raising both arms classically.*] Praise God! [*Looks at* WALTER *a moment, who says nothing. She crosses rapidly to her husband.*] Please, honey—let me be glad... you be glad too. [*She has laid her hands on his shoulders, but he shakes himself free of her roughly, without turning to face her.*] Oh, Walter... a home... *a home*. [*She comes back to* MAMA.] Well—where is it? How big is it? How much it going to cost?
MAMA: Well—
RUTH: When we moving?
MAMA: [*Smiling at her.*] First of the month.
RUTH: [*Throwing back her head with jubilance.*] Praise God!
MAMA: [*Tentatively, still looking at her son's back turned against her and* RUTH.] It's—it's a nice house too... [*She cannot help speaking directly to him. An imploring quality in her voice, her manner, makes her almost like a girl now.*] Three bedrooms—nice big one for you and Ruth... Me and Beneatha still have to share our room, but Travis have one of his own—and [*With difficulty.*] I figure if the—new baby—is a boy, we could get one of them double-decker outfits... And there's a yard with a little patch of dirt where I could maybe get to grow me a few flowers... And a nice big basement...
RUTH: Walter honey, be glad—
MAMA: [*Still to his back, fingering things on the table.*] 'Course I don't want to make it sound fancier than it is... It's just a plain little old house—but it's made good and solid—and it will be *ours*. Walter Lee—it makes a difference in a man when he can walk on floors that belong to *him*...
RUTH: Where is it?
MAMA: [*Frightened at this telling.*] Well—well—it's out there in Clybourne Park—[4]

[RUTH's *radiance fades abruptly, and* WALTER *finally turns slowly to face his mother with incredulity and hostility.*]

RUTH: Where?
MAMA: [*Matter-of-factly.*] Four o six Clybourne Street, Clybourne Park.
RUTH: Clybourne Park? Mama, there ain't no colored people living in Clybourne Park.
MAMA: [*Almost idiotically.*] Well, I guess there's going to be some now.
WALTER: [*Bitterly.*] So that's the peace and comfort you went out and bought for us today!
MAMA: [*Raising her eyes to meet his finally.*] Son—I just tried to find the nicest place for the least amount of money for my family.

---

4. On Chicago's Near North Side.

RUTH: [*Trying to recover from the shock.*] Well—well—'course I ain't one never been 'fraid of no crackers[5] mind you—but—well, wasn't there no other houses nowhere?

MAMA: Them houses they put up for colored in them areas way out all seem to cost twice as much as other houses. I did the best I could.

RUTH: [*Struck senseless with the news, in its various degrees of goodness and trouble, she sits a moment, her fists propping her chin in thought, and then she starts to rise, bringing her fists down with vigor, the radiance spreading from cheek to cheek again.*] Well—well!—All I can say is—if this is my time in life—*my time*—to say good-bye— [*And she builds with momentum as she starts to circle the room with an exuberant, almost tearfully happy release.*] —to these Goddamned cracking walls!— [*She pounds the walls.*] —and these marching roaches!— [*She wipes at an imaginary army of marching roaches.*] —and this cramped little closet which ain't now or never was no kitchen!... then I say it loud and good, *Hallelujah!* and good-bye misery... I don't never want to see your ugly face again! [*She laughs joyously, having practically destroyed the apartment, and flings her arms up and lets them come down happily, slowly, reflectively, over her abdomen, aware for the first time perhaps that the life therein pulses with happiness and not despair.*] Lena?

MAMA: [*Moved, watching her happiness.*] Yes, honey?

RUTH: [*Looking off.*] Is there—is there a whole lot of sunlight?

MAMA: [*Understanding.*] Yes, child, there's a whole lot of sunlight.

[*Long pause.*]

RUTH: [*Collecting herself and going to the door of the room* TRAVIS *is in.*] Well—I guess I better see 'bout Travis. [*To* MAMA.] Lord, I sure don't feel like whipping nobody today!

[*She exits.*]

MAMA: [*The mother and son are left alone now and the mother waits a long time, considering deeply, before she speaks.*] Son—you—you understand what I done, don't you? [WALTER *is silent and sullen.*] I—I just seen my family falling apart today ... just falling to pieces in front of my eyes ... We couldn't of gone on like we was today. We was going backwards 'stead of forwards—talking 'bout killing babies and wishing each other was dead ... When it gets like that in life—you just got to do something different, push on out and do something bigger ... [*She waits.*] I wish you say something, son ... I wish you'd say how deep inside you you think I done the right thing—

WALTER: [*Crossing slowly to his bedroom door and finally turning there and speaking measuredly.*] What you need me to say you done right for? *You* the head of this family. You run our lives like you want to. It was your money and you did what you wanted with it. So what you need for me to say it was all right for? [*Bitterly, to hurt her as deeply as he knows is possible.*] So you butchered up a dream of mine—you—who always talking 'bout your children's dreams ...

MAMA: Walter Lee—

[*He just closes the door behind him.* MAMA *sits alone, thinking heavily.*]

[CURTAIN.]

---

5. Derogatory term for poor whites.

### Scene Two

*Time: Friday night. A few weeks later.*

*At rise: Packing crates mark the intention of the family to move.* BENEATHA *and* GEORGE *come in, presumably from an evening out again.*

GEORGE: O.K. . . . O.K., whatever you say . . . [*They both sit on the couch. He tries to kiss her. She moves away.*] Look, we've had a nice evening; let's not spoil it, huh? . . .

[*He again turns her head and tries to nuzzle in and she turns away from him, not with distaste but with momentary lack of interest; in a mood to pursue what they were talking about.*]

BENEATHA: I'm *trying* to talk to you.

GEORGE: We always talk.

BENEATHA: Yes—and I love to talk.

GEORGE: [*Exasperated; rising.*] I know it and I don't mind it sometimes . . . I want you to cut it out, see—The moody stuff, I mean. I don't like it. You're a nice-looking girl . . . all over. That's all you need, honey, forget the atmosphere. Guys aren't going to go for the atmosphere—they're going to go for what they see. Be glad for that. Drop the Garbo[6] routine. It doesn't go with you. As for myself, I want a nice— [*Groping.*] —simple [*Thoughtfully.*] —sophisticated girl . . . not a poet—O.K.?

[*She rebuffs him again and he starts to leave.*]

BENEATHA: Why are you angry?

GEORGE: Because this is stupid! I don't go out with you to discuss the nature of "quiet desperation"[7] or to hear all about your thoughts—because the world will go on thinking what it thinks regardless—

BENEATHA: Then why read books? Why go to school?

GEORGE: [*With artificial patience, counting on his fingers.*] It's simple. You read books—to learn facts—to get grades—to pass the course—to get a degree. That's all—it has nothing to do with thoughts.

[*A long pause.*]

BENEATHA: I see. [*A longer pause as she looks at him.*] Good night, George.

[GEORGE *looks at her a little oddly, and starts to exit. He meets* MAMA *coming in.*]

GEORGE: Oh—hello, Mrs. Younger.

MAMA: Hello, George, how you feeling?

GEORGE: Fine—fine, how are you?

MAMA: Oh, a little tired. You know them steps can get you after a day's work. You all have a nice time tonight?

GEORGE: Yes—a fine time. Well, good night.

---

6. Greta Garbo (1905–1990), Swedish-born American film star whose sultry, remote, and European femininity was widely imitated.
7. In *Walden* (1854), Henry Thoreau asserted that "the mass of men lead lives of quiet desperation."

MAMA: Good night. [*He exits.* MAMA *closes the door behind her.*] Hello, honey. What you sitting like that for?
BENEATHA: I'm just sitting.
MAMA: Didn't you have a nice time?
BENEATHA: No.
MAMA: No? What's the matter?
BENEATHA: Mama, George is a fool—honest. [*She rises.*]
MAMA: [*Hustling around unloading the packages she has entered with. She stops.*] Is he, baby?
BENEATHA: Yes.

[BENEATHA *makes up* TRAVIS' *bed as she talks.*]

MAMA: You sure?
BENEATHA: Yes.
MAMA: Well—I guess you better not waste your time with no fools.

[BENEATHA *looks up at her mother, watching her put groceries in the refrigerator. Finally she gathers up her things and starts into the bedroom. At the door she stops and looks back at her mother.*]

BENEATHA: Mama—
MAMA: Yes, baby—
BENEATHA: Thank you.
MAMA: For what?
BENEATHA: For understanding me this time.

[*She exits quickly and the mother stands, smiling a little, looking at the place where* BENEATHA *just stood.* RUTH *enters.*]

RUTH: Now don't you fool with any of this stuff, Lena—
MAMA: Oh, I just thought I'd sort a few things out.

[*The phone rings.* RUTH *answers.*]

RUTH: [*At the phone.*] Hello—Just a minute. [*Goes to door.*] Walter, it's Mrs. Arnold. [*Waits. Goes back to the phone. Tense.*] Hello. Yes, this is his wife speaking . . . He's lying down now. Yes . . . well, he'll be in tomorrow. He's been very sick. Yes—I know we should have called, but we were so sure he'd be able to come in today. Yes—yes, I'm very sorry. Yes . . . Thank you very much. [*She hangs up.* WALTER *is standing in the doorway of the bedroom behind her.*] That was Mrs. Arnold.
WALTER: [*Indifferently.*] Was it?
RUTH: She said if you don't come in tomorrow that they are getting a new man . . .
WALTER: Ain't that sad—ain't that crying sad.
RUTH: She said Mr. Arnold has had to take a cab for three days . . . Walter, you ain't been to work for three days! [*This is a revelation to her.*] Where you been, Walter Lee Younger? [WALTER *looks at her and starts to laugh.*] You're going to lose your job.
WALTER: That's right . . .
RUTH: Oh, Walter, and with your mother working like a dog every day—
WALTER: That's sad too—Everything is sad.
MAMA: What you been doing for these three days, son?

WALTER: Mama—you don't know all the things a man what got leisure can find to do in this city... What's this—Friday night? Well—Wednesday I borrowed Willy Harris' car and I went for a drive... just me and myself and I drove and drove... Way out... way past South Chicago, and I parked the car and I sat and looked at the steel mills all day long. I just sat in the car and looked at them big black chimneys for hours. Then I drove back and I went to the Green Hat. [*Pause.*] And Thursday—Thursday I borrowed the car again and I got in it and I pointed it the other way and I drove the other way—for hours—way, way up to Wisconsin, and I looked at the farms. I just drove and looked at the farms. Then I drove back and I went to the Green Hat. [*Pause.*] And today—today I didn't get the car. Today I just walked. All over the Southside. And I looked at the Negroes and they looked at me and finally I just sat down on the curb at Thirty-ninth and South Parkway and I just sat there and watched the Negroes go by. And then I went to the Green Hat. You all sad? You all depressed? And you know where I am going right now—

[RUTH *goes out quietly.*]

MAMA: Oh, Big Walter, is this the harvest of our days?
WALTER: You know what I like about the Green Hat? [*He turns the radio on and a steamy, deep blues pours into the room.*] I like this little cat they got there who blows a sax... He blows. He talks to me. He ain't but 'bout five feet tall and he's got a conked head[8] and his eyes is always closed and he's all music—
MAMA: [*Rising and getting some papers out of her handbag.*] Walter—
WALTER: And there's this other guy who plays the piano... and they got a sound. I mean they can work on some music... They got the best little combo in the world in the Green Hat... You can just sit there and drink and listen to them three men play and you realize that don't nothing matter worth a damn, but just being there—
MAMA: I've helped do it to you, haven't I, son? Walter, I been wrong.
WALTER: Naw—you ain't never been wrong about nothing, Mama.
MAMA: Listen to me, now. I say I been wrong, son. That I been doing to you what the rest of the world been doing to you. [*She stops and he looks up slowly at her and she meets his eyes pleadingly.*] Walter—what you ain't never understood is that I ain't got nothing, don't own nothing, ain't never really wanted nothing that wasn't for you. There ain't nothing as precious to me... There ain't nothing worth holding on to, money, dreams, nothing else—if it means—if it means it's going to destroy my boy. [*She puts her papers in front of him and he watches her without speaking or moving.*] I paid the man thirty-five hundred dollars down on the house. That leaves sixty-five hundred dollars. Monday morning I want you to take this money and take three thousand dollars and put it in a savings account for Beneatha's medical schooling. The rest you put in a checking account—with your name on it. And from now on any penny that come out of it or that go in it is for you to look after. For you to decide. [*She drops her hands a little helplessly.*] It ain't much, but it's all I got in the world and I'm putting it in your hands. I'm telling you to be the head of this family from now on like you supposed to be.

---

8. Straightened hair.

WALTER: [*Stares at the money.*] You trust me like that, Mama?
MAMA: I ain't never stop trusting you. Like I ain't never stop loving you.

> [*She goes out, and* WALTER *sits looking at the money on the table as the music continues in its idiom, pulsing in the room. Finally, in a decisive gesture, he gets up, and, in mingled joy and desperation, picks up the money. At the same moment,* TRAVIS *enters for bed.*]

TRAVIS: What's the matter, Daddy? You drunk?
WALTER: [*Sweetly, more sweetly than we have ever known him.*] No, Daddy ain't drunk. Daddy ain't going to never be drunk again....
TRAVIS: Well, good night, Daddy.

> [*The father has come from behind the couch and leans over, embracing his son.*]

WALTER: Son, I feel like talking to you tonight.
TRAVIS: About what?
WALTER: Oh, about a lot of things. About you and what kind of man you going to be when you grow up... Son—son, what do you want to be when you grow up?
TRAVIS: A bus driver.
WALTER: [*Laughing a little.*] A what? Man, that ain't nothing to want to be!
TRAVIS: Why not?
WALTER: 'Cause, man—it ain't big enough—you know what I mean.
TRAVIS: I don't know then. I can't make up my mind. Sometimes Mama asks me that too. And sometimes when I tell you I just want to be like you—she says she don't want me to be like that and sometimes she says she does...
WALTER: [*Gathering him up in his arms.*] You know what, Travis? In seven years you going to be seventeen years old. And things is going to be very different with us in seven years, Travis... One day when you are seventeen I'll come home—home from my office downtown somewhere—
TRAVIS: You don't work in no office, Daddy.
WALTER: No—but after tonight. After what your daddy gonna do tonight, there's going to be offices—a whole lot of offices...
TRAVIS: What you gonna do tonight, Daddy?
WALTER: You wouldn't understand yet, son, but your daddy's gonna make a transaction... a business transaction that's going to change our lives... That's how come one day when you 'bout seventeen years old I'll come home and I'll be pretty tired, you know what I mean, after a day of conferences and secretaries getting things wrong the way they do... 'cause an executive's life is hell, man— [*The more he talks the farther away he gets.*] And I'll pull the car up on the driveway... just a plain black Chrysler, I think, with white walls—no—black tires. More elegant. Rich people don't have to be flashy... though I'll have to get something a little sportier for Ruth—maybe a Cadillac convertible to do her shopping in... And I'll come up the steps to the house and the gardener will be clipping away at the hedges and he'll say, "Good evening, Mr. Younger." And I'll say, "Hello, Jefferson, how are you this evening?" And I'll go inside and Ruth will come downstairs and meet me at the door and we'll kiss each other and she'll take my arm and we'll go up to your room to see you sitting on the floor with the catalogues of all the great schools in America around you... All the great schools in the world. And—and I'll say, all right

son—it's your seventeenth birthday, what is it you've decided? . . . Just tell me where you want to go to school and you'll *go*. Just tell me, what it is you want to be—and you'll *be* it . . . Whatever you want to be—Yessir! [*He holds his arms open for* TRAVIS.] You just name it, son . . . [TRAVIS *leaps into them.*] and I hand you the world!

[WALTER's *voice has risen in pitch and hysterical promise and on the last line he lifts* TRAVIS *high.*]

[BLACKOUT.]

## Scene Three

*Time: Saturday, moving day, one week later.*
*Before the curtain rises,* RUTH's *voice, a strident, dramatic church alto, cuts through the silence.*
*It is, in the darkness, a triumphant surge, a penetrating statement of expectation:* "Oh, Lord, I don't feel no ways tired! Children, oh, glory hallelujah!"
*As the curtain rises we see that* RUTH *is alone in the living room, finishing up the family's packing. It is moving day. She is nailing crates and tying cartons.* BENEATHA *enters, carrying a guitar case, and watches her exuberant sister-in-law.*

RUTH: Hey!
BENEATHA: [*Putting away the case.*] Hi.
RUTH: [*Pointing at a package.*] Honey—look in that package there and see what I found on sale this morning at the South Center. [RUTH *gets up and moves to the package and draws out some curtains.*] Lookahere—hand-turned hems!
BENEATHA: How do you know the window size out there?
RUTH: [*Who hadn't thought of that.*] Oh—Well, they bound to fit something in the whole house. Anyhow, they was too good a bargain to pass up. [RUTH *slaps her head, suddenly remembering something.*] Oh, Bennie—I meant to put a special note on that carton over there. That's your mama's good china and she wants 'em to be very careful with it.
BENEATHA: I'll do it.

[BENEATHA *finds a piece of paper and starts to draw large letters on it.*]

RUTH: You know what I'm going to do soon as I get in that new house?
BENEATHA: What?
RUTH: Honey—I'm going to run me a tub of water up to here . . . [*With her fingers practically up to her nostrils.*] And I'm going to get in it—and I am going to sit . . . and sit . . . and sit in that hot water and the first person who knocks to tell *me* to hurry up and come out—
BENEATHA: Gets shot at sunrise.
RUTH: [*Laughing happily.*] You said it, sister! [*Noticing how large* BENEATHA *is absent-mindedly making the note.*] Honey, they ain't going to read that from no airplane.
BENEATHA: [*Laughing herself.*] I guess I always think things have more emphasis if they are big, somehow.
RUTH: [*Looking up at her and smiling.*] You and your brother seem to have that as

a philosophy of life. Lord, that man—done changed so 'round here. You know—you know what we did last night? Me and Walter Lee?

BENEATHA: What?

RUTH: [*Smiling to herself.*] We went to the movies. [*Looking at* BENEATHA *to see if she understands.*] We went to the movies. You know the last time me and Walter went to the movies together?

BENEATHA: No.

RUTH: Me neither. That's how long it been. [*Smiling again.*] But we went last night. The picture wasn't much good, but that didn't seem to matter. We went—and we held hands.

BENEATHA: Oh, Lord!

RUTH: We held hands—and you know what?

BENEATHA: What?

RUTH: When we come out of the show it was late and dark and all the stores and things was closed up ... and it was kind of chilly and there wasn't many people on the streets ... and we was still holding hands, me and Walter.

BENEATHA: You're killing me.

[WALTER *enters with a large package. His happiness is deep in him; he cannot keep still with his new-found exuberance. He is singing and wiggling and snapping his fingers. He puts his package in a corner and puts a phonograph record, which he has brought in with him, on the record player. As the music comes up he dances over to* RUTH *and tries to get her to dance with him. She gives in at last to his raunchiness and in a fit of giggling allows herself to be drawn into his mood and together they deliberately burlesque an old social dance of their youth.*]

BENEATHA: [*Regarding them a long time as they dance, then drawing in her breath for a deeply exaggerated comment which she does not particularly mean.*] Talk about—olddddddddddd-fashiondddddddd—Negroes!

WALTER: [*Stopping momentarily.*] What kind of Negroes?

[*He says this in fun. He is not angry with her today, nor with anyone. He starts to dance with his wife again.*]

BENEATHA: Old-fashioned.

WALTER: [*As he dances with* RUTH.] You know, when these *New Negroes* have their convention— [*Pointing at his sister.*] —that is going to be the chairman of the Committee on Unending Agitation. [*He goes on dancing, then stops.*] Race, race, race! ... Girl, I do believe you are the first person in the history of the entire human race to successfully brainwash yourself. [BENEATHA *breaks up and he goes on dancing. He stops again, enjoying his tease.*] Damn, even the N double A C P[9] takes a holiday sometimes! [BENEATHA *and* RUTH *laugh. He dances with* RUTH *some more and starts to laugh and stops and pantomimes someone over an operating table.*] I can just see that chick someday looking down at some poor cat on an operating table before she starts to slice him, saying ... [*Pulling his sleeves back maliciously.*] "By the way, what are your views on civil rights down there? ..."

---

9. National Association for the Advancement of Colored People, civil rights organization founded in 1909.

[*He laughs at her again and starts to dance happily. The bell sounds.*]

BENEATHA: Sticks and stones may break my bones but... words will never hurt me!

[BENEATHA *goes to the door and opens it as* WALTER *and* RUTH *go on with the clowning.* BENEATHA *is somewhat surprised to see a quiet-looking middle-aged white man in a business suit holding his hat and a briefcase in his hand and consulting a small piece of paper.*]

MAN: Uh—how do you do, miss. I am looking for a Mrs.— [*He looks at the slip of paper.*] Mrs. Lena Younger?

BENEATHA: [*Smoothing her hair with slight embarrassment.*] Oh—yes, that's my mother. Excuse me [*She closes the door and turns to quiet the other two.*] Ruth! Brother! Somebody's here. [*Then she opens the door. The* MAN *casts a curious quick glance at all of them.*] Uh—come in please.

MAN: [*Coming in.*] Thank you.

BENEATHA: My mother isn't here just now. Is it business?

MAN: Yes... well, of a sort.

WALTER: [*Freely, the Man of the House.*] Have a seat. I'm Mrs. Younger's son. I look after most of her business matters.

[RUTH *and* BENEATHA *exchange amused glances.*]

MAN: [*Regarding* WALTER, *and sitting.*] Well—My name is Karl Lindner...

WALTER: [*Stretching out his hand.*] Walter Younger. This is my wife— [RUTH *nods politely.*] —and my sister.

LINDNER: How do you do.

WALTER: [*Amiably, as he sits himself easily on a chair, leaning with interest forward on his knees and looking expectantly into the newcomer's face.*] What can we do for you, Mr. Lindner!

LINDNER: [*Some minor shuffling of the hat and briefcase on his knees.*] Well—I am a representative of the Clybourne Park Improvement Association—

WALTER: [*Pointing.*] Why don't you sit your things on the floor?

LINDNER: Oh—yes. Thank you. [*He slides the briefcase and hat under the chair.*] And as I was saying—I am from the Clybourne Park Improvement Association and we have had it brought to our attention at the last meeting that you people—or at least your mother—has bought a piece of residential property at— [*He digs for the slip of paper again.*] —four o six Clybourne Street...

WALTER: That's right. Care for something to drink? Ruth, get Mr. Lindner a beer.

LINDNER: [*Upset for some reason.*] Oh—no, really. I mean thank you very much, but no thank you.

RUTH: [*Innocently.*] Some coffee?

LINDNER: Thank you, nothing at all.

[BENEATHA *is watching the man carefully.*]

LINDNER: Well, I don't know how much you folks know about our organization. [*He is a gentle man; thoughtful and somewhat labored in his manner.*] It is one of these community organizations set up to look after—oh, you know, things like block upkeep and special projects and we also have what we call our New Neighbors Orientation Committee...

BENEATHA: [*Drily.*] Yes—and what do they do?

LINDNER: [*Turning a little to her and then returning the main force to* WALTER.] Well— it's what you might call a sort of welcoming committee, I guess. I mean they, we, I'm the chairman of the committee—go around and see the new people who move into the neighborhood and sort of give them the lowdown on the way we do things out in Clybourne Park.

BENEATHA: [*With appreciation of the two meanings, which escape* RUTH *and* WALTER.] Un-huh.

LINDNER: And we also have the category of what the association calls— [*He looks elsewhere.*] —uh—special community problems . . .

BENEATHA: Yes—and what are some of those?

WALTER: Girl, let the man talk.

LINDNER: [*With understated relief.*] Thank you. I would sort of like to explain this thing in my own way. I mean I want to explain to you in a certain way.

WALTER: Go ahead.

LINDNER: Yes. Well. I'm going to try to get right to the point. I'm sure we'll all appreciate that in the long run.

BENEATHA: Yes.

WALTER: Be still now!

LINDNER: Well—

RUTH: [*Still innocently.*] Would you like another chair—you don't look comfortable.

LINDNER: [*More frustrated than annoyed.*] No, thank you very much. Please. Well— to get right to the point I— [*A great breath, and he is off at last.*] I am sure you people must be aware of some of the incidents which have happened in various parts of the city when colored people have moved into certain areas— [BENEATHA *exhales heavily and starts tossing a piece of fruit up and down in the air.*] Well— because we have what I think is going to be a unique type of organization in American community life—not only do we deplore that kind of thing—but we are trying to do something about it. [BENEATHA *stops tossing and turns with a new and quizzical interest to the man.*] We feel— [*Gaining confidence in his mission because of the interest in the faces of the people he is talking to.*] —we feel that most of the trouble in this world, when you come right down to it— [*He hits his knee for emphasis.*] —most of the trouble exists because people just don't sit down and talk to each other.

RUTH: [*Nodding as she might in church, pleased with the remark.*] You can say that again, mister.

LINDNER: [*More encouraged by such affirmation.*] That we don't try hard enough in this world to understand the other fellow's problem. The other guy's point of view.

RUTH: Now that's right.

[BENEATHA *and* WALTER *merely watch and listen with genuine interest.*]

LINDNER: Yes—that's the way we feel out in Clybourne Park. And that's why I was elected to come here this afternoon and talk to you people. Friendly like, you know, the way people should talk to each other and see if we couldn't find some way to work this thing out. As I say, the whole business is a matter of *caring* about the other fellow. Anybody can see that you are a nice family of folks, hard working and honest I'm sure. [BENEATHA *frowns slightly, quizzi-*

*cally, her head tilted regarding him.*] Today everybody knows what it means to be on the outside of something. And of course, there is always somebody who is out to take the advantage of people who don't always understand.

WALTER: What do you mean?

LINDNER: Well—you see our community is made up of people who've worked hard as the dickens for years to build up that little community. They're not rich and fancy people; just hard-working, honest people who don't really have much but those little homes and a dream of the kind of community they want to raise their children in. Now, I don't say we are perfect and there is a lot wrong in some of the things they want. But you've got to admit that a man, right or wrong, has the right to want to have the neighborhood he lives in a certain kind of way. And at the moment the overwhelming majority of our people out there feel that people get along better, take more of a common interest in the life of the community, when they share a common background. I want you to believe me when I tell you that race prejudice simply doesn't enter into it. It is a matter of the people of Clybourne Park believing, rightly or wrongly, as I say, that for the happiness of all concerned that our Negro families are happier when they live in their *own* communities.

BENEATHA: [*With a grand and bitter gesture.*] This, friends, is the Welcoming Committee!

WALTER: [*Dumfounded, looking at* LINDNER.] Is this what you came marching all the way over here to tell us?

LINDNER: Well, now we've been having a fine conversation. I hope you'll hear me all the way through.

WALTER: [*Tightly.*] Go ahead, man.

LINDNER: You see—in the face of all things I have said, we are prepared to make your family a very generous offer . . .

BENEATHA: Thirty pieces and not a coin less![1]

WALTER: Yeah?

LINDNER: [*Putting on his glasses and drawing a form out of the briefcase.*] Our association is prepared, through the collective effort of our people, to buy the house from you at a financial gain to your family.

RUTH: Lord have mercy, ain't this the living gall!

WALTER: All right, you through?

LINDNER: Well, I want to give you the exact terms of the financial arrangement—

WALTER: We don't want to hear no exact terms of no arrangements. I want to know if you got any more to tell us 'bout getting together?

LINDNER: [*Taking off his glasses.*] Well—I don't suppose that you feel . . .

WALTER: Never mind how I feel—you got any more to say 'bout how people ought to sit down and talk to each other? . . . Get out of my house, man.

[*He turns his back and walks to the door.*]

LINDNER: [*Looking around at the hostile faces and reaching and assembling his hat and briefcase.*] Well—I don't understand why you people are reacting this way. What do you think you are going to gain by moving into a neighborhood where you just aren't wanted and where some elements—well—people can get awful worked up when they feel that their whole way of life and everything they've ever worked for is threatened.

---

1. See Matthew 26.15, in which Judas Iscariot is paid 30 pieces of silver to betray Jesus.

WALTER: Get out.
LINDNER: [*At the door, holding a small card.*] Well—I'm sorry it went like this.
WALTER: Get out.
LINDNER: [*Almost sadly regarding* WALTER.] You just can't force people to change their hearts, son.

> [*He turns and put his card on a table and exits.* WALTER *pushes the door to with stinging hatred, and stands looking at it.* RUTH *just sits and* BENEATHA *just stands. They say nothing.* MAMA *and* TRAVIS *enter.*]

MAMA: Well—this all the packing got done since I left out of here this morning. I testify before God that my children got all the energy of the dead. What time the moving men due?
BENEATHA: Four o'clock. You had a caller, Mama.

> [*She is smiling, teasingly.*]

MAMA: Sure enough—who?
BENEATHA: [*Her arms folded saucily.*] The Welcoming Committee.

> [WALTER *and* RUTH *giggle.*]

MAMA: [*Innocently.*] Who?
BENEATHA: The Welcoming Committee. They said they're sure going to be glad to see you when you get there.
WALTER: [*Devilishly.*] Yeah, they said they can't hardly wait to see your face.

> [*Laughter.*]

MAMA: [*Sensing their facetiousness.*] What's the matter with you all?
WALTER: Ain't nothing the matter with us. We just telling you 'bout the gentleman who came to see you this afternoon. From the Clybourne Park Improvement Association.
MAMA: What he want?
RUTH: [*In the same mood as* BENEATHA *and* WALTER.] To welcome you, honey.
WALTER: He said they can't hardly wait. He said the one thing they don't have, that they just *dying* to have out there is a fine family of colored people! [*To* RUTH *and* BENEATHA.] Ain't that right!
RUTH *and* BENEATHA: [*Mockingly.*] Yeah! He left his card in case—

> [*They indicate the card, and* MAMA *picks it up and throws it on the floor—understanding and looking off as she draws her chair up to the table on which she has put her plant and some sticks and some cord.*]

MAMA: Father, give us strength. [*Knowingly—and without fun.*] Did he threaten us?
BENEATHA: Oh—Mama—they don't do it like that anymore. He talked Brotherhood. He said everybody ought to learn how to sit down and hate each other with good Christian fellowship.

> [*She and* WALTER *shake hands to ridicule the remark.*]

MAMA: [*Sadly.*] Lord, protect us . . .
RUTH: You should hear the money those folks raised to buy the house from us. All we paid and then some.
BENEATHA: What they think we going to do—eat 'em?
RUTH: No, honey, marry 'em.

MAMA: [*Shaking her head.*] Lord, Lord, Lord...
RUTH: Well—that's the way the crackers crumble. Joke.
BENEATHA: [*Laughingly noticing what her mother is doing.*] Mama, what are you doing?
MAMA: Fixing my plant so it won't get hurt none on the way...
BEANEATHA: Mama, you going to take *that* to the new house?
MAMA: Un-huh—
BENEATHA: That raggedy-looking old thing?
MAMA: [*Stopping and looking at her.*] It expresses *me*.
RUTH: [*With delight, to* BENEATHA.] So there, Miss Thing!

[WALTER *comes to* MAMA *suddenly and bends down behind her and squeezes her in his arms with all his strength. She is overwhelmed by the suddenness of it and, though delighted, her manner is like that of* RUTH *with* TRAVIS.]

MAMA: Look out now, boy! You make me mess up my thing here!
WALTER: [*His face lit, he slips down on his knees beside her, his arms still about her.*] Mama... you know what it means to climb up in the chariot?
MAMA: [*Gruffly, very happy.*] Get on away from me now...
RUTH: [*Near the gift-wrapped package, trying to catch* WALTER's *eye.*] Psst—
WALTER: What the old song say, Mama...
RUTH: Walter—Now?

[*She is pointing at the package.*]

WALTER: [*Speaking the lines, sweetly, playfully, in his mother's face.*]

I got wings... you got wings...
All God's Children got wings[2]...

MAMA: Boy—get out of my face and do some work...
WALTER:
When I get to heaven gonna put on my wings,
Gonna fly all over God's heaven...

BENEATHA: [*Teasingly, from across the room.*] Everybody talking 'bout heaven ain't going there!
WALTER: [*To* RUTH, *who is carrying the box across to them.*] I don't know, you think we ought to give her that... Seems to me she ain't been very appreciative around here.
MAMA: [*Eying the box, which is obviously a gift.*] What is that?
WALTER: [*Taking it from* RUTH *and putting it on the table in front of* MAMA.] Well—what you all think? Should we give it to her?
RUTH: Oh—she was pretty good today.
MAMA: I'll good you—

[*She turns her eyes to the box again.*]

BENEATHA: Open it, Mama.

---

2. Lines from an African American spiritual. Walter's and Beneatha's next lines are also from the song.

[*She stands up, looks at it, turns and looks at all of them, and then presses her hands together and does not open the package.*]

WALTER: [*Sweetly.*] Open it, Mama. It's for you. [MAMA *looks in his eyes. It is the first present in her life without its being Christmas. Slowly she opens her package and lifts out, one by one, a brand-new sparkling set of gardening tools.* WALTER *continues, prodding.*] Ruth made up the note—read it...
MAMA: [*Picking up the card and adjusting her glasses.*] "To our own Mrs. Miniver[3]— Love from Brother, Ruth and Beneatha." Ain't that lovely...
TRAVIS: [*Tugging at his father's sleeve.*] Daddy, can I give her mine now?
WALTER: All right, son. [TRAVIS *flies to get his gift.*] Travis didn't want to go in with the rest of us, Mama. He got his own. [*Somewhat amused.*] We don't know what it is...
TRAVIS: [*Racing back in the room with a large hatbox and putting it in front of his grandmother.*] Here!
MAMA: Lord have mercy, baby. You done gone and bought your grandmother a hat?
TRAVIS: [*Very proud.*] Open it!

[*She does and lifts out an elaborate, but very elaborate, wide gardening hat, and all the adults break up at the sight of it.*]

RUTH: Travis, honey, what is that?
TRAVIS: [*Who thinks it is beautiful and appropriate.*] It's a gardening hat! Like the ladies always have on in the magazines when they work in their gardens.
BENEATHA: [*Giggling fiercely.*] Travis—we were trying to make Mama Mrs. Miniver—not Scarlett O'Hara![4]
MAMA: [*Indignantly.*] What's the matter with you all! This here is a beautiful hat! [*Absurdly.*] I always wanted me one just like it!

[*She pops it on her head to prove it to her grandson, and the hat is ludicrous and considerably oversized.*]

RUTH: Hot dog! Go, Mama!
WALTER: [*Doubled over with laughter.*] I'm sorry, Mama—but you look like you ready to go out and chop you some cotton sure enough!

[*They all laugh except* MAMA, *out of deference to* TRAVIS' *feelings.*]

MAMA: [*Gathering the boy up to her.*] Bless your heart—this is the prettiest hat I ever owned— [WALTER, RUTH *and* BENEATHA *chime in—noisily, festively and insincerely congratulating* TRAVIS *on his gift.*] What are we all standing around here for? We ain't finished packin' yet. Bennie, you ain't packed one book.

[*The bell rings.*]

BENEATHA: That couldn't be the movers... it's not hardly two good yet—

[BENEATHA *goes into her room.* MAMA *starts for door.*]

WALTER: [*Turning, stiffening.*] Wait—wait—I'll get it.

---

3. The courageous, charismatic title character of a 1942 film starring Greer Garson.
4. The glamorous, headstrong heroine in *Gone with the Wind*.

[*He stands and looks at the door.*]

MAMA: You expecting company, son?
WALTER: [*Just looking at the door.*] Yeah—yeah...

[MAMA *looks at* RUTH, *and they exchange innocent and unfrightened glances.*]

MAMA: [*Not understanding.*] Well, let them in, son.
BENEATHA: [*From her room.*] We need some more string.
MAMA: Travis—you run to the hardware and get me some string cord.

[MAMA *goes out and* WALTER *turns and looks at* RUTH. TRAVIS *goes to a dish for money.*]

RUTH: Why don't you answer the door, man?
WALTER: [*Suddenly bounding across the floor to her.*] 'Cause sometimes it hard to let the future begin! [*Stooping down in her face.*]

I got wings! You got wings!
All God's children got wings!

[*He crosses to the door and throws it open. Standing there is a very slight little man in a not too prosperous business suit and with haunted frightened eyes and a hat pulled down tightly, brim up, around his forehead.* TRAVIS *passes between the men and exits.* WALTER *leans deep in the man's face, still in his jubilance.*]

When I get to heaven gonna put on my wings,
Gonna fly all over God's heaven...

[*The little man just stares at him.*]

Heaven—

[*Suddenly he stops and looks past the little man into the empty hallway.*] Where's Willy, man?

BOBO: He ain't with me.
WALTER: [*Not disturbed.*] Oh—come on in. You know my wife.
BOBO: [*Dumbly, taking off his hat.*] Yes—h'you, Miss Ruth.
RUTH: [*Quietly, a mood apart from her husband already, seeing* BOBO.] Hello, Bobo.
WALTER: You right on time today... Right on time. That's the way! [*He slaps* BOBO *on his back.*] Sit down... lemme hear.

[RUTH *stands stiffly and quietly in back of them, as though somehow she senses death, her eyes fixed on her husband.*]

BOBO: [*His frightened eyes on the floor, his hat in his hands.*] Could I please get a drink of water, before I tell you about it, Walter Lee?

[WALTER *does not take his eyes off the man.* RUTH *goes blindly to the tap and gets a glass of water and brings it to* BOBO.]

WALTER: There ain't nothing wrong, is there?
BOBO: Lemme tell you—
WALTER: Man—didn't nothing go wrong?
BOBO: Lemme tell you—Walter Lee. [*Looking at* RUTH *and talking to her more than*

*to* WALTER.] You know how it was. I got to tell you how it was. I mean first I got to tell you how it was all the way ... I mean about the money I put in, Walter Lee ...

WALTER: [*With taut agitation now.*] What about the money you put in?

BOBO: Well—it wasn't much as we told you—me and Willy— [*He stops.*] I'm sorry, Walter. I got a bad feeling about it. I got a real bad feeling about it ...

WALTER: Man, what you telling me about all this for? ... Tell me what happened in Springfield ...

BOBO: Springfield.

RUTH: [*Like a dead woman.*] What was supposed to happen in Springfield?

BOBO: [*To her.*] This deal that me and Walter went into with Willy—Me and Willy was going to go down to Springfield and spread some money 'round so's we wouldn't have to wait so long for the liquor license ... That's what we were going to do. Everybody said that was the way you had to do, you understand, Miss Ruth?

WALTER: Man—what happened down there?

BOBO: [*A pitiful man, near tears.*] I'm trying to tell you, Walter.

WALTER: [*Screaming at him suddenly.*] THEN TELL ME, GODDAMMIT ... WHAT'S THE MATTER WITH YOU?

BOBO: Man ... I didn't go to no Springfield, yesterday.

WALTER: [*Halted, life hanging in the moment.*] Why not?

BOBO: [*The long way, the hard way to tell.*] 'Cause I didn't have no reasons to ...

WALTER: Man, what are you talking about!

BOBO: I'm talking about the fact that when I got to the train station yesterday morning—eight o'clock like we planned ... Man—*Willy didn't never show up.*

WALTER: Why ... where was he ... where is he?

BOBO: That's what I'm trying to tell you ... I don't know ... I waited six hours ... I called his house ... and I waited ... six hours ... I waited in that train station six hours ... [*Breaking into tears.*] That was all the extra money I had in the world ... [*Looking up at* WALTER *with the tears running down his face.*] Man, Willy is gone.

WALTER: Gone, what you mean Willy is gone? Gone where? You mean he went by himself. You mean he went off to Springfield by himself—to take care of getting the license— [*Turns and looks anxiously at* RUTH.] You mean maybe he didn't want too many people in on the business down there? [*Looks to* RUTH *again, as before.*] You know Willy got his own ways. [*Looks back to* BOBO.] Maybe you was late yesterday and he just went on down there without you. Maybe—maybe—he's been callin' you at home tryin' to tell you what happened or something. Maybe—maybe—he just got sick. He's somewhere—he's got to be somewhere. We just got to find him—me and you got to find him. [*Grabs* BOBO *senselessly by the collar and starts to shake him.*] We got to!

BOBO: [*In sudden angry, frightened agony.*] What's the matter with you, Walter! When a cat take off with your money he don't leave you no maps!

WALTER: [*Turning madly, as though he is looking for* WILLY *in the very room.*] Willy! ... Willy ... don't do it ... Please don't do it ... Man, not with that money ... Man, please, not with that money ... Oh, God ... Don't let it be true ... [*He is wandering around, crying out for* WILLY *and looking for him or perhaps for help from God.*] Man ... I trusted you ... Man, I put my life in your hands ... [*He starts to crumple down on the floor as* RUTH *just covers her face in horror.* MAMA *opens the door and comes into the room, with* BENEATHA *behind her.*] Man... [*He starts to pound the floor with his fists, sobbing wildly.*] *That money is made out of my father's flesh*...

BOBO: [*Standing over him helplessly.*] I'm sorry, Walter.... [*Only* WALTER's *sobs reply.* BOBO *puts on his hat.*] I had my life staked on this deal, too....

[*He exits.*]

MAMA: [*To* WALTER.] Son— [*She goes to him, bends down to him, talks to his bent head.*] Son... Is it gone? Son, I gave you sixty-five hundred dollars. Is it gone? All of it? Beneatha's money too?

WALTER: [*Lifting his head slowly.*] Mama... I never... went to the bank at all....

MAMA: [*Not wanting to believe him.*] You mean... your sister's school money... you used that too... Walter?

WALTER: Yessss!... All of it.... It's all gone.... [*There is total silence.* RUTH *stands with her face covered with her hands*; BENEATHA *leans forlornly against a wall, fingering a piece of red ribbon from the mother's gift.* MAMA *stops and looks at her son without recognition and then, quite without thinking about it, starts to beat him senselessly in the face.* BENEATHA *goes to them and stops it.*]

BENEATHA: Mama!

[MAMA *stops and looks at both of her children and rises slowly and wanders vaguely, aimlessly away from them.*]

MAMA: I seen... him... night after night... come in... and look at that rug... and then look at me... the red showing in his eyes... the veins moving in his head... I seen him grow thin and old before he was forty... working and working and working like somebody's old horse... killing himself... and you—you give it all away in a day....

BENEATHA: Mama—

MAMA: Oh, God... [*She looks up to Him.*] Look down here—and show me the strength.

BENEATHA: Mama—

MAMA: [*Folding over.*] Strength....

BENEATHA: [*Plaintively.*] Mama...

MAMA: Strength!

[CURTAIN.]

## ACT III

*An hour later.*

*At curtain, there is a sullen light of gloom in the living room, gray light not unlike that which began the first scene of Act I. At left we can see* WALTER *within his room, alone with himself. He is stretched out on the bed, his shirt out and open, his arms under his head. He does not smoke, he does not cry out, he merely lies there, looking up at the ceiling, much as if he were alone in the world.*

*In the living room* BENEATHA *sits at the table, still surrounded by the now almost ominous packing crates. She sits looking off. We feel that this is a mood struck perhaps an hour before, and it lingers now, full of the empty sound of profound disappointment. We see on a line from her brother's bedroom the sameness of their attitudes. Presently the bell rings and* BENEATHA *rises without ambition or interest in answering. It is* ASAGAI, *smiling broadly, striding into the room with energy and happy expectation and conversation.*

ASAGAI: I came over... I had some free time. I thought I might help with the packing. Ah, I like the look of packing crates! A household in preparation for a journey! It depresses some people... but for me... it is another feeling. Something full of the flow of life, do you understand? Movement, progress ... It makes me think of Africa.
BENEATHA: Africa!
ASAGAI: What kind of a mood is this? Have I told you how deeply you move me?
BENEATHA: He gave away the money, Asagai...
ASAGAI: Who gave away what money?
BENEATHA: The insurance money. My brother gave it away.
ASAGAI: Gave it away?
BENEATHA: He made an investment! With a man even Travis wouldn't have trusted.
ASAGAI: And it's gone?
BENEATHA: Gone!
ASAGAI: I'm very sorry... And you, now?
BENEATHA: Me?... Me?... Me, I'm nothing... Me. When I was very small... we used to take our sleds out in the wintertime and the only hills we had were the ice-covered stone steps of some houses down the street. And we used to fill them in with snow and make them smooth and slide down them all day ... and it was very dangerous you know... far too steep... and sure enough one day a kid named Rufus came down too fast and hit the sidewalk... and we saw his face just split open right there in front of us... And I remember standing there looking at his bloody open face thinking that was the end of Rufus. But the ambulance came and they took him to the hospital and they fixed the broken bones and they sewed it all up... and the next time I saw Rufus he just had a little line down the middle of his face... I never got over that...

[WALTER *sits up, listening on the bed. Throughout this scene it is important that we feel his reaction at all times, that he visibly respond to the words of his sister and* ASAGAI.]

ASAGAI: What?
BENEATHA: That that was what one person could do for another, fix him up— sew up the problem, make him all right again. That was the most marvelous thing in the world... I wanted to do that. I always thought it was the one concrete thing in the world that a human being could do. Fix up the sick, you know—and make them whole again. This was truly being God...
ASAGAI: You wanted to be God?
BENEATHA: No—I wanted to cure. It used to be so important to me. I wanted to cure. It used to matter. I used to care. I mean about people and how their bodies hurt...
ASAGAI: And you've stopped caring?
BENEATHA: Yes—I think so.
ASAGAI: Why?

[WALTER *rises, goes to the door of his room and is about to open it, then stops and stands listening, leaning on the door jamb.*]

BENEATHA: Because it doesn't seem deep enough, close enough to what ails mankind—I mean this thing of sewing up bodies or administering drugs. Don't you understand? It was a child's reaction to the world. I thought that doctors had the secret to all the hurts . . . That's the way a child sees things—or an idealist.

ASAGAI: Children see things very well sometimes—and idealists even better.

BENEATHA: I know that's what you think. Because you are still where I left off—you still care. This is what you see for the world, for Africa. You with the dreams of the future will patch up all Africa—you are going to cure the Great Sore of colonialism with Independence—

ASAGAI: Yes!

BENEATHA: Yes—and you think that one word is the penicillin of the human spirit: "Independence!" But then what?

ASAGAI: That will be the problem for another time. First we must get there.

BENEATHA: And where does it end?

ASAGAI: End? Who even spoke of an end? To life? To living?

BENEATHA: An end to misery!

ASAGAI: [*Smiling.*] You sound like a French intellectual.

BENEATHA: No! I sound like a human being who just had her future taken right out of her hands! While I was sleeping in my bed in there, things were happening in this world that directly concerned me—and nobody asked me, consulted me—they just went out and did things—and changed my life. Don't you see there isn't any real progress, Asagai, there is only one large circle that we march in, around and around, each of us with our own little picture—in front of us—our own little mirage that we think is the future.

ASAGAI: That is the mistake.

BENEATHA: What?

ASAGAI: What you just said—about the circle. It isn't a circle—it is simply a long line—as in geometry, you know, one that reaches into infinity. And because we cannot see the end—we also cannot see how it changes. And it is very odd but those who see the changes are called "idealists"—and those who cannot, or refuse to think, they are the "realists." It is very strange, and amusing too, I think.

BENEATHA: You—you are almost religious.

ASAGAI: Yes . . . I think I have the religion of doing what is necessary in the world—and of worshipping man—because he is so marvelous, you see.

BENEATHA: Man is foul! And the human race deserves its misery!

ASAGAI: You see: *you* have become the religious one in the old sense. Already, and after such a small defeat, you are worshipping despair.

BENEATHA: From now on, I worship the truth—and the truth is that people are puny, small and selfish . . .

ASAGAI: Truth? Why is it that you despairing ones always think that only you have the truth? I never thought to see *you* like that. You! Your brother made a stupid, childish mistake—and you are grateful to him. So that now you can give up the ailing human race on account of it. You talk about what good is struggle; what good is anything? Where are we all going? And why are we bothering?

BENEATHA: *And you cannot answer it!* All your talk and dreams about Africa and

Independence. Independence and then what? What about all the crooks and petty thieves and just plain idiots who will come into power to steal and plunder the same as before—only now they will be black and do it in the name of the new Independence—You cannot answer that.

ASAGAI: [*Shouting over her.*] I live the answer! [*Pause.*] In my village at home it is the exceptional man who can even read a newspaper... or who ever *sees* a book at all. I will go home and much of what I will have to say will seem strange to the people of my village... But I will teach and work and things will happen, slowly and swiftly. At times it will seem that nothing changes at all... and then again... the sudden dramatic events which make history leap into the future. And then quiet again. Retrogression even. Guns, murder, revolution. And I even will have moments when I wonder if the quiet was not better than all that death and hatred. But I will look about my village at the illiteracy and disease and ignorance and I will not wonder long. And perhaps... perhaps I will be a great man... I mean perhaps I will hold on to the substance of truth and find my way always with the right course... and perhaps for it I will be butchered in my bed some night by the servants of empire...

BENEATHA: *The martyr!*

ASAGAI: ... or perhaps I shall live to be a very old man, respected and esteemed in my new nation... And perhaps I shall hold office and this is what I'm trying to tell you, Alaiyo; perhaps the things I believe now for my country will be wrong and outmoded, and I will not understand and do terrible things to have things my way or merely to keep my power. Don't you see that there will be young men and women, not British soldiers then, but my own black countrymen... to step out of the shadows some evening and slit my then useless throat? Don't you see they have always been there... that they always will be. And that such a thing as my own death will be an advance? They who might kill me even... actually replenish me!

BENEATHA: Oh, Asagai, I know all that.

ASAGAI: Good! Then stop moaning and groaning and tell me what you plan to do.

BENEATHA: Do?

ASAGAI: I have a bit of a suggestion.

BENEATHA: What?

ASAGAI: [*Rather quietly for him.*] That when it is all over—that you come home with me—

BENEATHA: [*Slapping herself on the forehead with exasperation born of misunderstanding.*] Oh—Asagai—at this moment you decide to be romantic!

ASAGAI: [*Quickly understanding the misunderstanding.*] My dear, young creature of the New World—I do not mean across the city—I mean across the ocean; home—to Africa.

BENEATHA: [*Slowly understanding and turning to him with murmured amazement.*] To—to Nigeria?

ASAGAI: Yes!... [*Smiling and lifting his arms playfully.*] Three hundred years later the African Prince rose up out of the seas and swept the maiden back across the middle passage over which her ancestors had come—

BENEATHA: [*Unable to play.*] Nigeria?

ASAGAI: Nigeria. Home. [*Coming to her with genuine romantic flippancy.*] I will show you our mountains and our stars; and give you cool drinks from gourds and teach you the old songs and the ways of our people—and, in time, we will pretend that— [*Very softly.*] —you have only been away for a day—

[*She turns her back to him, thinking. He swings her around and takes her full in his arms in a long embrace which proceeds to passion.*]

BENEATHA: [*Pulling away.*] You're getting me all mixed up—
ASAGAI: Why?
BENEATHA: Too many things—too many things have happened today. I must sit down and think. I don't know what I feel about anything right this minute.

[*She promptly sits down and props her chin on her fist.*]

ASAGAI: [*Charmed.*] All right, I shall leave you. No—don't get up. [*Touching her, gently, sweetly.*] Just sit awhile and think... Never be afraid to sit awhile and think. [*He goes to door and looks at her.*] How often I have looked at you and said, "Ah—so this is what the New World hath finally wrought..."

[*He exits.* BENEATHA *sits on alone. Presently* WALTER *enters from his room and starts to rummage through things, feverishly looking for something. She looks up and turns in her seat.*]

BENEATHA: [*Hissingly.*] Yes—just look at what the New World hath wrought!... Just look! [*She gestures with bitter disgust.*] There he is! *Monsieur le petit bourgeois noir*—himself! There he is—Symbol of a Rising Class! Entrepreneur! Titan of the system! [WALTER *ignores her completely and continues frantically and destructively looking for something and hurling things to the floor and tearing things out of their place in his search.* BENEATHA *ignores the eccentricity of his actions and goes on with the monologue of insult.*] Did you dream of yachts on Lake Michigan, Brother? Did you see yourself on that Great Day sitting down at the Conference Table, surrounded by all the mighty bald-headed men in America? All halted, waiting, breathless, waiting for your pronouncements on industry? Waiting for you—Chairman of the Board? [WALTER *finds what he is looking for—a small piece of white paper—and pushes it in his pocket and puts on his coat and rushes out without ever having looked at her. She shouts after him.*] I look at you and I see the final triumph of stupidity in the world!

[*The door slams and she returns to just sitting again.* RUTH *comes quickly out of* MAMA's *room.*]

RUTH: Who was that?
BENEATHA: Your husband.
RUTH: Where did he go?
BENEATHA: Who knows—maybe he has an appointment at U.S. Steel.
RUTH: [*Anxiously, with frightened eyes.*] You didn't say nothing bad to him, did you?
BENEATHA: Bad? Say anything bad to him? No—I told him he was a sweet boy and full of dreams and everything is strictly peachy keen, as the ofay[5] kids say!

[MAMA *enters from her bedroom. She is lost, vague, trying to catch hold, to make some sense of her former command of the world, but it still eludes her. A sense of waste overwhelms her gait; a measure of apology rides on her shoulders. She goes to her plant, which has remained on the table, looks at it, picks it up and takes it to the window sill and sits it outside, and she stands and looks at it a long moment.*]

5. White.

*Then she closes the window, straightens her body with effort and turns around to her children.*]

MAMA: Well—ain't it a mess in here, though? [*A false cheerfulness, a beginning of something.*] I guess we all better stop moping around and get some work done. All this unpacking and everything we got to do. [RUTH *raises her head slowly in response to the sense of the line; and* BENEATHA *in similar manner turns very slowly to look at her mother.*] One of you all better call the moving people and tell 'em not to come.

RUTH: Tell 'em not to come?

MAMA: Of course, baby. Ain't no need in 'em coming all the way here and having to go back. They charges for that too. [*She sits down, fingers to her brow, thinking.*] Lord, ever since I was a little girl, I always remembers people saying, "Lena—Lena Eggleston, you aims too high all the time. You needs to slow down and see life a little more like it is. Just slow down some." That's what they always used to say down home—"Lord, that Lena Eggleston is a high-minded thing. She'll get her due one day!"

RUTH: No, Lena...

MAMA: Me and Big Walter just didn't never learn right.

RUTH: Lena, no! We gotta go. Bennie—tell her... [*She rises and crosses to* BENEATHA *with her arms outstretched.* BENEATHA *doesn't respond.*] Tell her we can still move ... the notes ain't but a hundred and twenty-five a month. We got four grown people in this house—we can work...

MAMA: [*To herself.*] Just aimed too high all the time—

RUTH: [*Turning and going to* MAMA *fast—the words pouring out with urgency and desperation.*] Lena—I'll work... I'll work twenty hours a day in all the kitchens in Chicago... I'll strap my baby on my back if I have to and scrub all the floors in America and wash all the sheets in America if I have to—but we got to move... We got to get out of here...

[MAMA *reaches out absently and pats* RUTH'*s hand.*]

MAMA: No—I sees things differently now. Been thinking 'bout some of the things we could do to fix this place up some. I seen a second-hand bureau over on Maxwell Street[6] just the other day that could fit right there. [*She points to where the new furniture might go.* RUTH *wanders away from her.*] Would need some new handles on it and then a little varnish and then it look like something brand-new. And—we can put up them new curtains in the kitchen... Why this place be looking fine. Cheer us all up so that we forget trouble ever came... [*To* RUTH.] And you could get some nice screens to put up in your room round the baby's bassinet... [*She looks at both of them, pleadingly.*] Sometimes you just got to know when to give up some things... and hold on to what you got.

[WALTER *enters from the outside, looking spent and leaning against the door, his coat hanging from him.*]

MAMA: Where you been, son?
WALTER: [*Breathing hard.*] Made a call.
MAMA: To who, son?

---

6. A street market southwest of the Loop.

WALTER: To The Man.
MAMA: What man, baby?
WALTER: The Man, Mama. Don't you know who The Man is?
RUTH: Walter Lee?
WALTER: *The Man.* Like the guys in the streets say—The Man. Captain Boss—Mistuh Charley... Old Captain Please Mr. Bossman...
BENEATHA: [*Suddenly.*] Lindner!
WALTER: That's right! That's good. I told him to come right over.
BENEATHA: [*Fiercely, understanding.*] For what? What do you want to see him for!
WALTER: [*Looking at his sister.*] We going to do business with him.
MAMA: What you talking 'bout, son?
WALTER: Talking 'bout life, Mama. You all always telling me to see life like it is. Well—I laid in there on my back today... and I figured it out. Life just like it is. Who gets and who don't get. [*He sits down with his coat on and laughs.*] Mama, you know it's all divided up. Life is. Sure enough. Between the takers and the "tooken." [*He laughs.*] I've figured it out finally. [*He looks around at them.*] Yeah. Some of us always getting "tooken." [*He laughs.*] People like Willy Harris, they don't never get "tooken." And you know why the rest of us do? 'Cause we all mixed up. Mixed up bad. We get to looking 'round for the right and the wrong, and we worry about it and cry about it and stay up nights trying to figure out 'bout the wrong and the right of things all the time... And all the time, man, them takers is out there operating, just taking and taking. Willy Harris? Shoot—Willy Harris don't even count. He don't even count in the big scheme of things. But I'll say one thing for old Willy Harris... he's taught me something. He's taught me to keep my eye on what counts in this world. Yeah—[*Shouting out a little.*] Thanks, Willy!
RUTH: What did you call that man for, Walter Lee?
WALTER: Called him to tell him to come on over to the show. Gonna put on a show for the man. Just what he wants to see. You see, Mama, the man came here today and he told us that them people out there where you want us to move—well they so upset they willing to pay us not to move out there. [*He laughs again.*] And—and oh, Mama—you would of been proud of the way me and Ruth and Bennie acted. We told him to get out... Lord have mercy! We told the man to get out. Oh, we was some proud folks this afternoon, yeah. [*He lights a cigarette.*] We were still full of that old-time stuff...
RUTH: [*Coming toward him slowly.*] You talking 'bout taking them people's money to keep us from moving in that house?
WALTER: I ain't just talking 'bout it, baby—I'm telling you that's what's going to happen.
BENEATHA: Oh, God! Where is the bottom! Where is the real honest-to-God bottom so he can't go any farther!
WALTER: See—that's the old stuff. You and that boy that was here today. You all want everybody to carry a flag and a spear and sing some marching songs, huh? You wanna spend your life looking into things and trying to find the right and the wrong part, huh? Yeah. You know what's going to happen to that boy someday—he'll find himself sitting in a dungeon, locked in forever—and the takers will have the key! Forget it, baby! There ain't no causes—there ain't nothing but taking in this world, and he who takes most is smartest—and it don't make a damn bit of difference *how.*
MAMA: You making something inside me cry, son. Some awful pain inside me.

WALTER: Don't cry, Mama. Understand. That white man is going to walk in that door able to write checks for more money than we ever had. It's important to him and I'm going to help him . . . I'm going to put on the show, Mama.
MAMA: Son—I come from five generations of people who was slaves and sharecroppers—but ain't nobody in my family never let nobody pay 'em no money that was a way of telling us we wasn't fit to walk the earth. We ain't never been that poor. [*Raising her eyes and looking at him.*] We ain't never been that dead inside.
BENEATHA: Well—we are dead now. All the talk about dreams and sunlight that goes on in this house. All dead.
WALTER: What's the matter with you all! I didn't make this world! It was give to me this way! Hell, yes, I want me some yachts someday! Yes, I want to hang some real pearls 'round my wife's neck. Ain't she supposed to wear no pearls? Somebody tell me—tell me, who decides which women is suppose to wear pearls in this world. I tell you I am a *man*—and I think my wife should wear some pearls in this world!

[*This last line hangs a good while and* WALTER *begins to move about the room. The word "Man" has penetrated his consciousness; he mumbles it to himself repeatedly between strange agitated pauses as he moves about.*]

MAMA: Baby, how you going to feel on the inside?
WALTER: Fine! . . . Going to feel fine . . . a man . . .
MAMA: You won't have nothing left then, Walter Lee.
WALTER: [*Coming to her.*] I'm going to feel fine, Mama. I'm going to look that son-of-a-bitch in the eyes and say— [*He falters.*] —and say, "All right, Mr. Lindner— [*He falters even more.*] —that's your neighborhood out there. You got the right to keep it like you want. You got the right to have it like you want. Just write the check and—the house is yours." And, and I am going to say— [*His voice almost breaks.*] And you—you people just put the money in my hand and you won't have to live next to this bunch of stinking niggers! . . . [*He straightens up and moves away from his mother, walking around the room.*] Maybe—maybe I'll just get down on my black knees . . . [*He does so;* RUTH *and* BENNIE *and* MAMA *watch him in frozen horror.*] Captain, Mistuh, Bossman. [*He starts crying.*] A-hee-hee-hee! [*Wringing his hands in profoundly anguished imitation.*] Yassss-suh! Great White Father, just gi' ussen de money, fo' God's sake, and we's ain't gwine come out deh and dirty up yo' white folks neighborhood . . .

[*He breaks down completely, then gets up and goes into the bedroom.*]

BENEATHA: That is not a man. That is nothing but a toothless rat.
MAMA: Yes—death done come in this here house. [*She is nodding, slowly, reflectively.*] Done come walking in my house. On the lips of my children. You what supposed to be my beginning again. You—what supposed to be my harvest. [*To* BENEATHA.] You—you mourning your brother?
BENEATHA: He's no brother of mine.
MAMA: What you say?
BENEATHA: I said that that individual in that room is no brother of mine.
MAMA: That's what I thought you said. You feeling like you better than he is today? [BENEATHA *does not answer.*] Yes? What you tell him a minute ago? That he wasn't a man? Yes? You give him up for me? You done wrote his epitaph too—like the rest of the world? Well, who give you the privilege?

BENEATHA: Be on my side for once! You saw what he just did, Mama! You saw him—down on his knees. Wasn't it you who taught me—to despise any man who would do that. Do what he's going to do.

MAMA: Yes—I taught you that. Me and your daddy. But I thought I taught you something else too . . . I thought I taught you to love him.

BENEATHA: Love him? There is nothing left to love.

MAMA: There is always something left to love. And if you ain't learned that, you ain't learned nothing. [*Looking at her.*] Have you cried for that boy today? I don't mean for yourself and for the family 'cause we lost the money. I mean for him; what he been through and what it done to him. Child, when do you think is the time to love somebody the most; when they done good and made things easy for everybody? Well then, you ain't through learning—because that ain't the time at all. It's when he's at his lowest and can't believe in hisself 'cause the world done whipped him so. When you starts measuring somebody, measure him right, child, measure him right. Make sure you done taken into account what hills and valleys he come through before he got to wherever he is.

[TRAVIS *bursts into the room at the end of the speech, leaving the door open.*]

TRAVIS: Grandmama—the moving men are downstairs! The truck just pulled up.

MAMA: [*Turning and looking at him.*] Are they, baby? They downstairs?

[*She sighs and sits.* LINDNER *appears in the doorway. He peers in and knocks lightly, to gain attention, and comes in. All turn to look at him.*]

LINDNER: [*Hat and briefcase in hand.*] Uh—hello . . . [RUTH *crosses mechanically to the bedroom door and opens it and lets it swing open freely and slowly as the lights come up on* WALTER *within, still in his coat, sitting at the far corner of the room. He looks up and out through the room to* LINDNER.]

RUTH: He's here.

[*A long minute passes and* WALTER *slowly gets up.*]

LINDNER: [*Coming to the table with efficiency, putting his briefcase on the table and starting to unfold papers and unscrew fountain pens.*] Well, I certainly was glad to hear from you people. [WALTER *has begun the trek out of the room, slowly and awkwardly, rather like a small boy, passing the back of his sleeve across his mouth from time to time.*] Life can really be so much simpler than people let it be most of the time. Well—with whom do I negotiate? You, Mrs. Younger, or your son here? [MAMA *sits with her hands folded on her lap and her eyes closed as* WALTER *advances.* TRAVIS *goes close to* LINDNER *and looks at the papers curiously.*] Just some official papers, sonny.

RUTH: Travis, you go downstairs.

MAMA: [*Opening her eyes and looking into* WALTER's.] No. Travis, you stay right here. And you make him understand what you doing, Walter Lee. You teach him good. Like Willy Harris taught you. You show where our five generations done come to. Go ahead, son—

WALTER: [*Looks down into his boy's eyes.* TRAVIS *grins at him merrily and* WALTER *draws him beside him with his arm lightly around his shoulders.*] Well, Mr. Lindner. [BENEATHA *turns away.*] We called you— [*There is a profound, simple groping quality in his speech.*] —because, well, me and my family [*He looks around and shifts from one foot to the other.*] Well—we are very plain people . . .

LINDNER: Yes—
WALTER: I mean—I have worked as a chauffeur most of my life—and my wife here, she does domestic work in people's kitchens. So does my mother. I mean—we are plain people . . .
LINDNER: Yes, Mr. Younger—
WALTER: [*Really like a small boy, looking down at his shoes and then up at the man.*] And—uh—well, my father, well, he was a laborer most of his life.
LINDNER: [*Absolutely confused.*] Uh, yes—
WALTER: [*Looking down at his toes once again.*] My father almost beat a man to death once because this man called him a bad name or something, you know what I mean?
LINDNER: No, I'm afraid I don't.
WALTER: [*Finally straightening up.*] Well, what I mean is that we come from people who had a lot of pride. I mean—we are very proud people. And that's my sister over there and she's going to be a doctor—and we are very proud—
LINDNER: Well—I am sure that is very nice, but—
WALTER: [*Starting to cry and facing the man eye to eye.*] What I am telling you is that we called you over here to tell you that we are very proud and that this is—this is my son, who makes the sixth generation of our family in this country, and that we have all thought about your offer and we have decided to move into our house because my father—my father—he earned it. [MAMA *has her eyes closed and is rocking back and forth as though she were in church, with her head nodding the amen yes.*] We don't want to make no trouble for nobody or fight no causes—but we will try to be good neighbors. That's all we got to say. [*He looks the man absolutely in the eyes.*] We don't want your money.

[*He turns and walks away from the man.*]

LINDNER: [*Looking around at all of them.*] I take it then that you have decided to occupy.
BENEATHA: That's what the man said.
LINDNER: [*To* MAMA *in her reverie.*] Then I would like to appeal to you, Mrs. Younger. You are older and wiser and understand things better I am sure . . .
MAMA: [*Rising.*] I am afraid you don't understand. My son said we was going to move and there ain't nothing left for me to say. [*Shaking her head with double meaning.*] You know how these young folks is nowadays, mister. Can't do a thing with 'em. Good-bye.
LINDNER: [*Folding up his materials.*] Well—if you are that final about it . . . There is nothing left for me to say. [*He finishes. He is almost ignored by the family, who are concentrating on* WALTER LEE. *At the door* LINDNER *halts and looks around.*] I sure hope you people know what you're doing.

[*He shakes his head and exits.*]

RUTH: [*Looking around and coming to life.*] Well, for God's sake—if the moving men are here—LET'S GET THE HELL OUT OF HERE!
MAMA: [*Into action.*] Ain't it the truth! Look at all this here mess. Ruth, put Travis' good jacket on him . . . Walter Lee, fix your tie and tuck your shirt in, you look just like somebody's hoodlum. Lord have mercy, where is my plant? [*She flies to get it amid the general bustling of the family, who are deliberately trying to ignore the nobility of the past moment.*] You all start on down . . . Travis child, don't go empty-handed . . . Ruth, where did I put that box with my skillets in it? I want

to be in charge of it myself... I'm going to make us the biggest dinner we ever ate tonight... Beneatha, what's the matter with them stockings? Pull them things up, girl...

[*The family starts to file out as two moving men appear and begin to carry out the heavier pieces of furniture, bumping into the family as they move about.*]

BENEATHA: Mama, Asagai—asked me to marry him today and go to Africa—
MAMA: [*In the middle of her getting-ready activity.*] He did? You ain't old enough to marry nobody— [*Seeing the moving men lifting one of her chairs precariously.*] Darling, that ain't no bale of cotton, please handle it so we can sit in it again. I had that chair twenty-five years...

[*The movers sigh with exasperation and go on with their work.*]

BENEATHA: [*Girlishly and unreasonably trying to pursue the conversation.*] To go to Africa, Mama—be a doctor in Africa...
MAMA: [*Distracted.*] Yes, baby—
WALTER: Africa! What he want you to go to Africa for?
BENEATHA: To practice there...
WALTER: Girl, if you don't get all them silly ideas out your head! You better marry yourself a man with some loot...
BENEATHA: [*Angrily, precisely as in the first scene of the play.*] What have you got to do with who I marry!
WALTER: Plenty. Now I think George Murchison—

[*He and* BENEATHA *go out yelling at each other vigorously;* BENEATHA *is heard saying that she would not marry* GEORGE MURCHISON *if he were Adam and she were Eve, etc. The anger is loud and real till their voices diminish.* RUTH *stands at the door and turns to* MAMA *and smiles knowingly.*]

MAMA: [*Fixing her hat at last.*] Yeah—they something all right, my children...
RUTH: Yeah—they're something. Let's go, Lena.
MAMA: [*Stalling, starting to look around at the house.*] Yes—I'm coming. Ruth—
RUTH: Yes?
MAMA: [*Quietly, woman to woman.*] He finally come into his manhood today, didn't he? Kind of like a rainbow after the rain...
RUTH: [*Biting her lip lest her own pride explode in front of* MAMA.] Yes, Lena.

[WALTER's *voice calls for them raucously.*]

MAMA: [*Waving* RUTH *out vaguely.*] All right, honey—go on down. I be down directly.

[RUTH *hesitates, then exits.* MAMA *stands, at last alone in the living room, her plant on the table before her as the lights start to come down. She looks around at all the walls and ceilings and suddenly, despite herself, while the children call below, a great heaving thing rises in her and she puts her fist to her mouth, takes a final desperate look, pulls her coat about her, pats her hat and goes out. The lights dim down. The door opens and she comes back in, grabs her plant, and goes out for the last time.*]

[CURTAIN.]

1959

Norman Matlock (left) as Elesin and Ben Halley, Jr. (middle) as the Praise-Singer in the 1979 Kennedy Center production of *Death and the King's Horseman*

## WOLE SOYINKA

 *Death and the King's Horseman*

### CHARACTERS

PRAISE-SINGER
ELESIN, *Horseman of the King*
IYALOJA, *"Mother"[1] of the market*
SIMON PILKINGS, *District Officer*
JANE PILKINGS, *his wife*
SERGEANT AMUSA
JOSEPH, *houseboy to the Pilkingses*
BRIDE
H.R.H. THE PRINCE
THE RESIDENT[2]
AIDE-DE-CAMP
OLUNDE, *eldest son of Elesin*
DRUMMERS, WOMEN, YOUNG GIRLS, DANCERS AT THE BALL

*The play should run without an interval. For rapid scene changes, one adjustable outline set is very appropriate.*

---

1. Leader of the market women.
2. Senior colonial administrator who outranks and oversees the district officer.

## Scene 1

*A passage through a market in its closing stages. The stalls are being emptied, mats folded. A few* WOMEN *pass through on their way home, loaded with baskets. On a cloth-stand, bolts of cloth are taken down, display pieces folded and piled on a tray.* ELESIN OBA *enters along a passage before the market, pursued by his* DRUMMERS *and* PRAISE-SINGERS. *He is a man of enormous vitality, speaks, dances and sings with that infectious enjoyment of life which accompanies all his actions.*

PRAISE-SINGER: Elesin o! Elesin Oba! Howu![3] What tryst is this the cockerel[4] goes to keep with such haste that he must leave his tail behind?

ELESIN: [*Slows down a bit, laughing.*] A tryst where the cockerel needs no adornment.

PRAISE-SINGER: O-oh, you hear that, my companions? That's the way the world goes. Because the man approaches a brand-new bride he forgets the long-faithful mother of his children.

ELESIN: When the horse sniffs the stable does he not strain at the bridle? The market is the long-suffering home of my spirit and the women are packing up to go. That Esu[5]-harassed day slipped into the stewpot while we feasted. We ate it up with the rest of the meat. I have neglected my women.

PRAISE-SINGER: We know all that. Still it's no reason for shedding your tail on this day of all days. I know the women will cover you in damask and *alari*[6] but when the wind blows cold from behind, that's when the fowl knows his true friends.

ELESIN: Olohun-iyo![7]

PRAISE-SINGER: Are you sure there will be one like me on the other side?

ELESIN: Olohun-iyo!

PRAISE-SINGER: Far be it for me to belittle the dwellers of that place but, a man is either born to his art or he isn't. And I don't know for certain that you'll meet my father, so who is going to sing these deeds in accents that will pierce the deafness of the ancient ones. I have prepared my going—just tell me: Olohun-iyo, I need you on this journey and I shall be behind you.

ELESIN: You're like a jealous wife. Stay close to me, but only on this side. My fame, my honour are legacies to the living; stay behind and let the world sip its honey from your lips.

PRAISE-SINGER: Your name will be like the sweet berry a child places under his tongue to sweeten the passage of food. The world will never spit it out.

ELESIN: Come then. This market is my roost. When I come among the women I am a chicken with a hundred mothers. I become a monarch whose palace is built with tenderness and beauty.

PRAISE-SINGER: They love to spoil you but beware. The hands of women also weaken the unwary.

ELESIN: This night I'll lay my head upon their lap and go to sleep. This night I'll touch feet with their feet in a dance that is no longer of this earth. But the smell of their flesh, their sweat, the smell of indigo[8] on their cloth, this is the

---

3. "Why have you come?"   4. Young domestic rooster.
5. Yoruba trickster god often associated with doubleness, ambivalence, and duplicity.
6. A rich, woven cloth, brightly coloured [Soyinka's glossary].   7. Praise-singer.
8. Blue dye obtained from plants; it is associated with royalty and power.

last air I wish to breathe as I go to meet my great forebears.
PRAISE-SINGER: In their time the world was never tilted from its groove, it shall not be in yours.
ELESIN: The gods have said, No.
PRAISE-SINGER: In their time the great wars came and went, the little wars came and went; the white slavers came and went, they took away the heart of our race, they bore away the mind and muscle of our race.[9] The city fell and was rebuilt; the city fell and our people trudged through mountain and forest to found a new home[1] but—Elesin Oba, do you hear me?
ELESIN: I hear your voice, Olohun-iyo.
PRAISE-SINGER: Our world was never wrenched from its true course.
ELESIN: The gods have said, No.
PRAISE-SINGER: There is only one home to the life of a river-mussel; there is only one home to the life of a tortoise; there is only one shell to the soul of man; there is only one world to the spirit of our race. If that world leaves its course and smashes on boulders of the great void, whose world will give us shelter?
ELESIN: It did not in the time of my forebears, it shall not in mine.
PRAISE-SINGER: The cockerel must not be seen without his feathers.
ELESIN: Nor will the Not-I bird[2] be much longer without his nest.
PRAISE-SINGER: [*Stopped in his lyric stride.*] The Not-I bird, Elesin?
ELESIN: I said, The Not-I bird.
PRAISE-SINGER: All respect to our elders but, is there really such a bird?
ELESIN: What! Could it be that he failed to knock on your door?
PRAISE-SINGER: [*Smiling.*] Elesin's riddles are not merely the nut in the kernel[3] that breaks human teeth; he also buries the kernel in hot embers and dares a man's fingers to draw it out.
ELESIN: I am sure he called on you, Olohun-iyo. Did you hide in the loft and push out the servant to tell him you were out?

[ELESIN *executes a brief, half-taunting dance. The* DRUMMER *moves in and draws a rhythm out of his steps.* ELESIN *dances towards the market-place as he chants the story of the Not-I bird, his voice changing dexterously to mimic his characters. He performs like a born raconteur, infecting his retinue with his humour and energy. More* WOMEN *arrive during his recital, including* IYALOJA.]

Death came calling.
Who does not know his rasp of reeds?
A twilight whisper in the leaves before
The great araba[4] falls? Did you hear it?
Not I! swears the farmer. He snaps
His fingers round his head, abandons
A hard-worn harvest and begins
A rapid dialogue with his legs.

---

9. Reference to the numerous wars among Yoruba kingdoms in the eighteenth and nineteenth centuries and to the transatlantic slave trade and its consequences.
1. As it sought to consolidate its authority in the sixteenth century, the Yoruba kingdom of Oyo had to build and rebuild its capital several times.
2. Bird whose chirping sounds like it is saying "Not I" in Yoruba.   3. Soft, edible part of a palm nut.
4. Silk cotton tree or kapok.

"Not I," shouts the fearless hunter, "but—
It's getting dark, and this night-lamp
Has leaked out all its oil. I think
It's best to go home and resume my hunt
Another day." But now he pauses, suddenly
Lets out a wail: "Oh foolish mouth, calling
Down a curse on your own head! Your lamp
Has leaked out all its oil, has it?"
Forwards or backwards now he dare not move.
To search for leaves and make *etutu*[5]
On that spot? Or race home to the safety
Of his hearth? Ten market-days have passed
My friends, and still he's rooted there
Rigid as the plinth of Orayan.[6]
The mouth of the courtesan barely
Opened wide enough to take a ha'penny *robo*[7]
When she wailed: "Not I." All dressed she was
To call upon my friend the Chief Tax Officer.
But now she sends her go-between instead:
"Tell him I'm ill: my period has come suddenly
But not—I hope—my time."

Why is the pupil crying?
His hapless head was made to taste
The knuckles of my friend the Mallam.[8]
"If you were then reciting the Koran
Would you have ears for idle noises
Darkening the trees, you child of ill omen?"
He shuts down school before its time
Runs home and rings himself with amulets.

And take my good kinsman, Ifawomi.
His hands were like a carver's, strong
And true. I saw them
Tremble like wet wings of a fowl
One day he cast his time-smoothed *opele*[9]
Across the divination board. And all because
The suppliant looked him in the eye and asked,
"Did you hear that whisper in the leaves?"
"Not I," was his reply; "perhaps I'm growing deaf—
Good-day." And Ifa spoke no more that day
The priest locked fast his doors,
Sealed up his leaking roof—but wait!

---

5. Placatory rites or medicine [Soyinka's glossary].
6. Tall plinth or landmark in Ile-Ife, considered to be the ancestral home of the Yoruba. Orayan was one of the children of Oduduwa, the founding father of the Yoruba people.
7. Delicacy made from crushed melon seeds, fried in tiny balls [Soyinka's glossary].   8. Muslim teacher.
9. String of beads used in Ifa divination [Soyinka's glossary].

This sudden care was not for Fawomi[1]
But for Osanyin,[2] courier-bird of Ifa's
Heart of wisdom. I did not know a kite
Was hovering in the sky
And Ifa now a twittering chicken in
The brood of Fawomi the Mother Hen.

Ah, but I must not forget my evening
Courier from the abundant palm, whose groan
Became Not I, as he constipated down
A wayside bush. He wonders if Elegbara[3]
Has tricked his buttocks to discharge
Against a sacred grove. Hear him
Mutter spells to ward off penalties
For an abomination he did not intend.
If any here.
Stumbles on a gourd of wine, fermenting
Near the road, and nearby hears a stream
Of spells issuing from a crouching form,
Brother to a *sigidi*,[4] bring home my wine,
Tell my tapper[5] I have ejected
Fear from home and farm. Assure him,
All is well.

PRAISE-SINGER: In your time we do not doubt the peace of farmstead and home, the peace of road and hearth, we do not doubt the peace of the forest.

ELESIN: There was fear in the forest too.
Not I was lately heard even in the lair
Of beasts. The hyena cackled loud: Not I,
The civet twitched his fiery tail and glared:
Not I. Not-I became the answering-name
Of the restless bird, that little one
Whom Death found nesting in the leaves
When whisper of his coming ran
Before him on the wind. Not-I
Has long abandoned home. This same dawn
I heard him twitter in the gods' abode.
Ah, companions of this living world
What a thing this is, that even those
We call immortal
Should fear to die.

IYALOJA: But you, husband of multitudes?

ELESIN: I, when that Not-I bird perched

---

1. Contraction of "Ifawomi," meaning "Ifa watches over me." Ifa is the Yoruba god of divination.
2. Patron deity of diviners and medicine men in Yoruba culture.
3. Another name for Esu, the trickster god.
4. Squat, carved figure, endowed with the powers of an incubus [Soyinka's glossary]. An incubus is an imaginary evil spirit that descends on sleeping people.
5. Person whose profession is to tap palm trees for their sap, which is fermented into a wine.

    Upon my roof, bade him seek his nest again,
    Safe, without care or fear. I unrolled
    My welcome mat for him to see. Not-I
    Flew happily away, you'll hear his voice
    No more in this lifetime—You all know
    What I am.

PRAISE-SINGER: That rock which turns its open lodes
    Into the path of lightning. A gay
    Thoroughbred whose stride disdains
    To falter though an adder reared
    Suddenly in his path.

ELESIN: My rein is loosened.
    I am master of my Fate. When the hour comes
    Watch me dance along the narrowing path
    Glazed by the soles of my great precursors.
    My soul is eager. I shall not turn aside.

WOMEN: You will not delay?

ELESIN: Where the storm pleases, and when, it directs
    The giants of the forest. When friendship summons
    Is when the true comrade goes.

WOMEN: Nothing will hold you back?

ELESIN: Nothing. What! Has no one told you yet?
    I go to keep my friend and master company.
    Who says the mouth does not believe in
    "No, I have chewed all that before?" I say I have.
    The world is not a constant honey-pot.
    Where I found little I made do with little.
    Where there was plenty I gorged myself.
    My master's hands and mine have always
    Dipped together and, home or sacred feast,
    The bowl was beaten bronze, the meats
    So succulent our teeth accused us of neglect.
    We shared the choicest of the season's
    Harvest of yams. How my friend would read
    Desire in my eyes before I knew the cause—
    However rare, however precious, it was mine.

WOMEN: The town, the very land was yours.

ELESIN: The world was mine. Our joint hands
    Raised houseposts of trust that withstood
    The siege of envy and the termites of time.
    But the twilight hour brings bats and rodents—
    Shall I yield them cause to foul the rafters?

PRAISE-SINGER: Elesin Oba! Are you not that man who
    Looked out of doors that stormy day
    The god of luck[6] limped by, drenched
    To the very lice that held

---

6. Possibly a reference to Esu Elegba, the trickster god, who, especially in New World versions, limps because one leg is shorter than the other.

His rags together? You took pity upon
His sores and wished him fortune.
Fortune was footloose this dawn, he replied,
Till you trapped him in a heartfelt wish
That now returns to you. Elesin Oba!
I say you are that man who
Chanced upon the calabash[7] of honour
You thought it was palm wine and
Drained its contents to the final drop.

ELESIN: Life has an end. A life that will outlive
Fame and friendship begs another name.
What elder takes his tongue to his plate,
Licks it clean of every crumb? He will encounter
Silence when he calls on children to fulfill
The smallest errand! Life is honour.
It ends when honour ends.

WOMEN: We know you for a man of honour.

ELESIN: Stop! Enough of that!

WOMEN: [*Puzzled, they whisper among themselves, turning mostly to* IYALOJA.] What is it? Did we say something to give offence? Have we slighted him in some way?

ELESIN: Enough of that sound I say. Let me hear no more in that vein. I've heard enough.

IYALOJA: We must have said something wrong. [*Comes forward a little.*] Elesin Oba, we ask forgiveness before you speak.

ELESIN: I am bitterly offended.

IYALOJA: Our unworthiness has betrayed us. All we can do is ask your forgiveness. Correct us like a kind father.

ELESIN: This day of all days . . .

IYALOJA: It does not bear thinking. If we offend you now we have mortified the gods. We offend heaven itself. Father of us all, tell us where we went astray. [*She kneels, the other women follow.*]

ELESIN: Are you not ashamed? Even a tear-veiled
Eye preserves its function of sight.
Because my mind was raised to horizons
Even the boldest man lowers his gaze
In thinking of, must my body here
Be taken for a vagrant's?

IYALOJA: Horseman of the King, I am more baffled than ever.

PRAISE-SINGER: The strictest father unbends his brow when the child is penitent, Elesin. When time is short, we do not spend it prolonging the riddle. Their shoulders are bowed with the weight of fear lest they have marred your day beyond repair. Speak now in plain words and let us pursue the ailment to the home of remedies.

ELESIN: Words are cheap. "We know you for
A man of honour." Well tell me, is this how
A man of honour should be seen?

---

7. Half of a gourd usually used to serve food or drink.

Are these not the same clothes in which
I came among you a full half-hour ago?

> [*He roars with laughter and the* WOMEN, *relieved, rise and rush into stalls to fetch rich cloths.*]

WOMEN: The gods are kind. A fault soon remedied is soon forgiven.
Elesin Oba, even as we match our words with deed, let your heart forgive us completely.

ELESIN: You who are breath and giver of my being
How shall I dare refuse you forgiveness
Even if the offence were real.

IYALOJA: [*Dancing round him. Sings.*]
He forgives us. He forgives us.
What a fearful thing it is when
The voyager sets forth
But a curse remains behind.

WOMEN: For a while we truly feared
Our hands had wrenched the world adrift
In emptiness.

IYALOJA: Richly, richly, robe him richly
The cloth of honour is *alari*
*Sanyan*[8] is the band of friendship
Boa-skin[9] makes slippers of esteem.

WOMEN: For a while we truly feared
Our hands had wrenched the world adrift
In emptiness.

PRAISE-SINGER: He who must, must voyage forth
The world will not roll backwards.
It is he who must, with one
Great gesture overtake the world.

WOMEN: For a while we truly feared
Our hands had wrenched the world
In emptiness.

PRAISE-SINGER: The gourd you bear is not for shirking.
The gourd is not for setting down
At the first crossroad or wayside grove.
Only one river may know its contents.

WOMEN: We shall all meet at the great market.[1]
We shall all meet at the great market
He who goes early takes the best bargains
But we shall meet, and resume our banter.

> [ELESIN *stands resplendent in rich clothes, cap, shawl, etc. His sash is of a bright red* alari *cloth. The* WOMEN *dance round him. Suddenly, his attention is caught by an object off-stage.*]

ELESIN: The world I know is good.
WOMEN: We know you'll leave it so.

---

8. A richly valued woven cloth [Soyinka's glossary].   9. Skin from a boa constrictor.   1. In the afterlife.

ELESIN: The world I know is the bounty
　　Of hives after bees have swarmed.
　　No goodness teems with such open hands
　　Even in the dreams of deities.
WOMEN: And we know you'll leave it so.
ELESIN: I was born to keep it so. A hive
　　Is never known to wander. An anthill
　　Does not desert its roots. We cannot see
　　The still great womb of the world—
　　No man beholds his mother's womb—
　　Yet who denies it's there? Coiled
　　To the navel of the world is that
　　Endless cord that links us all
　　To the great origin. If I lose my way
　　The trailing cord will bring me to the roots.
WOMEN: The world is in your hands.

　　　[*The earlier distraction, a beautiful* YOUNG GIRL, *comes along the passage through which* ELESIN *first made his entry.*]

ELESIN: I embrace it. And let me tell you, women—
　　I like this farewell that the world designed,
　　Unless my eyes deceive me, unless
　　We are already parted, the world and I,
　　And all that breeds desire is lodged
　　Among our tireless ancestors. Tell me, friends,
　　Am I still earthed in that beloved market
　　Of my youth? Or could it be my will
　　Has outleapt the conscious act and I have come
　　Among the great departed?
PRAISE-SINGER: Elesin-Oba, why do your eyes roll like a bush rat who sees his fate like his father's spirit, mirrored in the eye of a snake? And all these questions! You're standing on the same earth you've always stood upon. This voice you hear is mine, Oluhun-iyo, not that of an acolyte in heaven.
ELESIN: How can that be? In all my life
　　As Horseman of the King, the juiciest
　　Fruit on every tree was mine. I saw,
　　I touched, I wooed, rarely was the answer No.
　　The honour of my place, the veneration I
　　Received in the eye of man or woman
　　Prospered my suit and
　　Played havoc with my sleeping hours.
　　And they tell me my eyes were a hawk
　　In perpetual hunger. Split an iroko[2] tree
　　In two, hide a woman's beauty in its heartwood
　　And seal it up again—Elesin, journeying by,
　　Would make his camp beside that tree

---

2. An African teak, a large tree believed, in Yoruba folklore, to be inhabited by a roguish fairy or spirit. The "heartwood," or inside, of the iroko tree is multi-colored.

Of all the shades in the forest.
PRAISE-SINGER: Who would deny your reputation, snake-on-the-loose in dark passages of the market! Bed-bug who wages war on the mat and receives the thanks of the vanquished! When caught with his bride's own sister he protested—but I was only prostrating myself to her as becomes a grateful in-law. Hunter who carries his powder-horn[3] on the hips and fires crouching or standing! Warrior who never makes that excuse of the whining coward—but how can I go to battle without my trousers?—trouserless or shirtless it's all one to him. Oka[4]-rearing-from-a-camouflage-of-leaves, before he strikes the victim is already prone! Once they told him, Howu, a stallion does not feed on the grass beneath him: he replied, true, but surely he can roll on it!
WOMEN: Ba-a-a-ba O!
PRAISE-SINGER: Ah, but listen yet. You know there is the leaf-nibbling grub and there is the cola-chewing beetle; the leaf-nibbling grub lives on the leaf, the cola-chewing beetle lives in the colanut.[5] Don't we know what our man feeds on when we find him cocooned in a woman's wrapper?
ELESIN: Enough, enough, you all have cause
To know me well. But, if you say this earth
Is still the same as gave birth to those songs,
Tell me who was that goddess through whose lips
I saw the ivory pebbles of Oya's[6] riverbed.
Iyaloja, who is she? I saw her enter
Your stall; all your daughters I know well.
No, not even Ogun[7]-of-the-farm toiling.
Dawn till dusk on his tuber patch
Not even Ogun with the finest hoe he ever
Forged at the anvil could have shaped
That rise of buttocks, not though he had
The richest earth between his fingers.
Her wrapper was no disguise
For thighs whose ripples shamed the river's
Coils around the hills of Ilesi.[8] Her eyes
Were new-laid eggs glowing in the dark.
Her skin . . .
IYALOJA: Elesin Oba . . .
ELESIN: What! Where do you all say I am?
IYALOJA: Still among the living.
ELESIN: And that radiance which so suddenly
Lit up this market I could boast
I knew so well?
IYALOJA: Has one step already in her husband's home. She is betrothed.
ELESIN: [*Irritated.*] Why do you tell me that?

[IYALOJA *falls silent. The* WOMEN *shuffle uneasily.*]

3. Yoruba hunters carry their gunpowder in a horn. 4. Python.
5. Seed of the cola (kola) nut tree valued by long-distance drivers for its caffeine, but also used as a ritual symbol of welcome. 6. Oya is the goddess of the Niger River and patron of fishermen and sailors.
7. God of iron and war, of hunters, soldiers, and blacksmiths; also considered the patron of artists.
8. District and town in Oyo, western Nigeria.

IYALOJA: Not because we dare give you offence, Elesin. Today is your day and the whole world is yours. Still, even those who leave town to make a new dwelling elsewhere like to be remembered by what they leave behind.

ELESIN: Who does not seek to be remembered?
　Memory is Master of Death, the chink
　In his armour of conceit. I shall leave
　That which makes my going the sheerest
　Dream of an afternoon. Should voyagers
　Not travel light? Let the considerate traveller
　Shed, of his excessive load, all
　That may benefit the living.

WOMEN: [*Relieved.*] Ah Elesin Oba, we knew you for a man of honour.

ELESIN: Then honour me. I deserve a bed of honour to lie upon.

IYALOJA: The best is yours. We know you for a man of honour. You are not one who eats and leaves nothing on his plate for children. Did you not say it yourself? Not one who blights the happiness of others for a moment's pleasure.

ELESIN: Who speaks of pleasure? O women, listen!
　Pleasure palls. Our acts should have meaning.
　The sap of the plantain[9] never dries.
　You have seen the young shoot swelling
　Even as the parent stalk begins to wither.
　Women, let my going be likened to
　The twilight hour of the plantain.

WOMEN: What does he mean, Iyaloja? This language is the language of our elders, we do not fully grasp it.

IYALOJA: I dare not understand you yet, Elesin.

ELESIN: All you who stand before the spirit that dares
　The opening of the last door of passage,
　Dare to rid my going of regrets! My wish
　Transcends the blotting out of thought
　In one mere moment's tremor of the senses.
　Do me credit. And do me honour.
　I am girded for the route beyond
　Burdens of waste and longing.
　Then let me travel light. Let
　Seed that will not serve the stomach
　On the way remain behind. Let it take root
　In the earth of my choice, in this earth
　I leave behind.

IYALOJA: [*Turns to* WOMEN.] The voice I hear is already touched by the waiting fingers of our departed. I dare not refuse.

WOMAN: But Iyaloja...

IYALOJA: The matter is no longer in our hands.

WOMAN: But she is betrothed to your own son. Tell him.

IYALOJA: My son's wish is mine. I did the asking for him, the loss can be remedied. But who will remedy the blight of closed hands on the day when all should

---

9. A variety of banana, a popular staple of the tropical regions of Africa.

be openness and light? Tell him, you say! You wish that I burden him with knowledge that will sour his wish and lay regrets on the last moments of his mind. You pray to him who is your intercessor to the world—don't set this world adrift in your own time; would you rather it was my hand whose sacrilege wrenched it loose?

WOMAN: Not many men will brave the curse of a dispossessed husband.

IYALOJA: Only the curses of the departed are to be feared. The claims of one whose foot is on the threshold of their abode surpasses even the claims of blood. It is impiety even to place hindrances in their ways.

ELESIN: What do my mothers say? Shall I step
Burdened into the unknown?

IYALOJA: Not we, but the very earth says No. The sap in the plantain does not dry. Let grain that will not feed the voyager at his passage drop here and take root as he steps beyond this earth and us. Oh you who fill the home from hearth to threshold with the voices of children, you who now bestride the hidden gulf and pause to draw the right foot across and into the resting-home of the great forebears, it is good that your loins be drained into the earth we know, that your last strength be ploughed back into the womb that gave you being.

PRAISE-SINGER: Iyaloja, mother of multitudes in the teeming market of the world, how your wisdom transfigures you!

IYALOJA: [*Smiling broadly, completely reconciled.*] Elesin, even at the narrow end of the passage I know you will look back and sigh a last regret for the flesh that flashed past your spirit in flight. You always had a restless eye. Your choice has my blessing. [*To the* WOMEN.] Take the good news to our daughter and make her ready. [*Some* WOMEN *go off.*]

ELESIN: Your eyes were clouded at first.

IYALOJA: Not for long. It is those who stand at the gateway of the great change to whose cry we must pay heed. And then, think of this—it makes the mind tremble. The fruit of such a union is rare. It will be neither of this world nor of the next. Nor of the one behind us. As if the timelessness of the ancestor world and the unborn have joined spirits to wring an issue of the elusive being of passage . . . Elesin!

ELESIN: I am here. What is it?

IYALOJA: Did you hear all I said just now?

ELESIN: Yes.

IYALOJA: The living must eat and drink. When the moment comes, don't turn the food to rodents' droppings in their mouth. Don't let them taste the ashes of the world when they step out at dawn to breathe the morning dew.

ELESIN: This doubt is unworthy of you, Iyaloja.

IYALOJA: Eating the awusa[1] nut is not so difficult as drinking water afterwards.

ELESIN: The waters of the bitter stream are honey to a man
Whose tongue has savoured all.

IYALOJA: No one knows when the ants desert their home; they leave the mound intact. The swallow is never seen to peck holes in its nest when it is time to move with the season. There are always throngs of humanity behind the leave-

---

1. A climbing plant.

taker. The rain should not come through the roof for them, the wind must not blow through the walls at night.
ELESIN: I refuse to take offence.
IYALOJA: You wish to travel light. Well, the earth is yours. But be sure the seed you leave in it attracts no curse.
ELESIN: You really mistake my person, Iyaloja.
IYALOJA: I said nothing. Now we must go prepare your bridal chamber. Then these same hands will lay your shrouds.
ELESIN: [*Exasperated.*] Must you be so blunt? [*Recovers.*] Well, weave your shrouds, but let the fingers of my bride seal my eyelids with earth and wash my body.
IYALOJA: Prepare yourself, Elesin.

[*She gets up to leave. At that moment the* WOMEN *return, leading the* BRIDE. ELESIN's *face glows with pleasure. He flicks the sleeves of his agbada*[2] *with renewed confidence and steps forward to meet the group. As the girl kneels before* IYALOJA, *lights fade out on the scene.*]

## Scene 2

*The verandah of the District Officer's bungalow. A tango is playing from an old hand-cranked gramophone and, glimpsed through the wide windows and doors which open onto the forestage verandah are the shapes of* SIMON PILKINGS *and his wife,* JANE, *tangoing in and out of shadows in the living-room. They are wearing what is immediately apparent as some form of fancy-dress.*[3] *The dance goes on for some moments and then the figure of a "*NATIVE ADMINISTRATION*"* POLICEMAN[4] *emerges and climbs up the steps onto the verandah. He peeps through and observes the dancing couple, reacting with what is obviously a long-standing bewilderment. He stiffens suddenly, his expression changes to one of disbelief and horror. In his excitement he upsets a flowerpot and attracts the attention of the couple. They stop dancing.*

PILKINGS: Is there anyone out there?
JANE: I'll turn off the gramophone.
PILKINGS: [*Approaching the verandah.*] I'm sure I heard something fall over. [*The* CONSTABLE *retreats slowly, open-mouthed as* PILKINGS *approaches the verandah.*] Oh, it's you, Amusa. Why didn't you just knock instead of knocking things over?
AMUSA: [*Stammers badly and points a shaky finger at his dress.*] Mista Pirinkin... Mista Pirinkin...
PILKINGS: What is the matter with you?
JANE: [*Emerging.*] Who is it dear? Oh, Amusa...
PILKINGS: Yes, it's Amusa, and acting most strangely.
AMUSA: [*His attention now transferred to* MRS PILKINGS.] Mammadam... you too!
PILKINGS: What the hell is the matter with you, man!
JANE: Your costume, darling. Our fancy dress.
PILKINGS: Oh hell, I'd forgotten all about that. [*Lifts the face mask over his head showing his face. His wife follows suit.*]

---

2. Large, flowing robe usually worn by men and often embroidered at the neck and chest.
3. Costume, usually representing some historical or fictitious character.
4. Policeman belonging to a unit charged with the policing of Africans and considered inferior to the regular police.

JANE: I think you've shocked his big pagan heart, bless him.
PILKINGS: Nonsense, he's a Moslem. Come on, Amusa, you don't believe in all this nonsense, do you? I thought you were a good Moslem.
AMUSA: Mista Pirinkin, I beg you sir, what you think you do with that dress? It belong to dead cult, not for human being.
PILKINGS: Oh Amusa, what a let-down you are. I swear by you at the club you know—thank God for Amusa, he doesn't believe in any mumbo-jumbo. And now look at you!
AMUSA: Mista Pirinkin, I beg you, take it off. Is not good for man like you to touch that cloth.
PILKINGS: Well, I've got it on. And what's more, Jane and I have bet on it we're taking first prize at the ball. Now, if you can just pull yourself together and tell me what you wanted to see me about...
AMUSA: Sir, I cannot talk this matter to you in that dress. I no fit.
PILKINGS: What's that rubbish again?
JANE: He is dead earnest too, Simon. I think you'll have to handle this delicately.
PILKINGS: Delicately my...! Look here, Amusa, I think this little joke has gone far enough, hm? Let's have some sense. You seem to forget that you are a police officer in the service of His Majesty's Government. I order you to report your business at once or face disciplinary action.
AMUSA: Sir, it is a matter of death. How can man talk against death to person in uniform of death? Is like talking against government to person in uniform of police. Please sir, I go and come back.
PILKINGS: [*Roars.*] Now! [AMUSA *switches his gaze to the ceiling suddenly, remains mute.*]
JANE: Oh Amusa, what is there to be scared of in the costume? You saw it confiscated last month from those *egungun*[5] men who were creating trouble in town. You helped arrest the cult leaders yourself—if the *juju*[6] didn't harm you at the time how could it possibly harm you now? And merely by looking at it?
AMUSA: [*Without looking down.*] Madam, I arrest the ringleaders who make trouble but me I no touch *egungun*. That *egungun* itself, I no touch. And I no abuse 'am. I arrest ringleader but I treat *egungun* with respect.
PILKINGS: It's hopeless. We'll merely end up missing the best part of the ball. When they get this way there is nothing you can do. It's simply hammering against a brick wall. Write your report or whatever it is on that pad, Amusa, and take yourself out of here. Come on, Jane. We only upset his delicate sensibilities by remaining here.

[AMUSA *waits for them to leave, then writes in the notebook, somewhat laboriously. Drumming from the direction of the town wells up.* AMUSA *listens, makes a movement as if he wants to recall* PILKINGS *but changes his mind. Completes his note and goes. A few moments later* PILKINGS *emerges, picks up the pad and reads.*]

PILKINGS: Jane!
JANE: [*From the bedroom.*] Coming, darling. Nearly ready.
PILKINGS: Never mind being ready, just listen to this.

---

5. Ancestral masquerade [Soyinka's glossary]. The masked figures in the masquerade are considered to be the reincarnated spirits of ancestors; their dress is often a long grass robe and a wooden mask representing the face or head of an animal. 6. Magic, usually attributed to a fetish.

JANE: What is it?
PILKINGS: Amusa's report. Listen. "I have to report that it come to my information that one prominent chief, namely, the Elesin Oba, is to commit death tonight as a result of native custom. Because this is criminal offence I await further instruction at charge office. Sergeant Amusa."

[JANE *comes out onto the verandah while he is reading.*]

JANE: Did I hear you say commit death?
PILKINGS: Obviously he means murder.
JANE: You mean a ritual murder?
PILKINGS: Must be. You think you've stamped it all out but it's always lurking under the surface somewhere.
JANE: Oh. Does it mean we are not getting to the ball at all?
PILKINGS: No-o. I'll have the man arrested. Everyone remotely involved. In any case there may be nothing to it. Just rumours.
JANE: Really? I thought you found Amusa's rumours generally reliable.
PILKINGS: That's true enough. But who knows what may have been giving him the scare lately. Look at his conduct tonight.
JANE: [*Laughing.*] You have to admit he had his own peculiar logic. [*Deepens her voice.*] How can man talk against death to person in uniform of death? [*Laughs.*] Anyway, you can't go into the police station dressed like that.
PILKINGS: I'll send Joseph with instructions. Damn it, what a confounded nuisance!
JANE: But don't you think you should talk first to the man, Simon?
PILKINGS: Do you want to go to the ball or not?
JANE: Darling, why are you getting rattled? I was only trying to be intelligent. It seems hardly fair just to lock up a man—and a chief at that—simply on the er . . . what is the legal word again?—uncorroborated word of a sergeant.
PILKINGS: Well, that's easily decided. Joseph!
JOSEPH: [*From within.*] Yes, master.
PILKINGS: You're quite right of course, I am getting rattled. Probably the effect of those bloody drums. Do you hear how they go on and on?
JANE: I wondered when you'd notice. Do you suppose it has something to do with this affair?
PILKINGS: Who knows? They always find an excuse for making a noise . . . [*Thoughtfully.*] Even so . . .
JANE: Yes Simon?
PILKINGS: It's different, Jane. I don't think I've heard this particular—sound—before. Something unsettling about it.
JANE: I thought all bush drumming sounded the same.
PILKINGS: Don't tease me now, Jane. This may be serious.
JANE: I'm sorry. [*Gets up and throws her arms around his neck. Kisses him. The* HOUSEBOY *enters, retreats and knocks.*]
PILKINGS: [*Wearily.*] Oh, come in, Joseph! I don't know where you pick up all these elephantine notions of tact. Come over here.
JOSEPH: Sir?
PILKINGS: Joseph, are you a Christian or not?
JOSEPH: Yessir.
PILKINGS: Does seeing me in this outfit bother you?

JOSEPH: No sir, it has no power.

PILKINGS: Thank God for some sanity at last. Now Joseph, answer me on the honour of a Christian—what is supposed to be going on in town tonight?

JOSEPH: Tonight, sir? You mean the chief who is going to kill himself?

PILKINGS: What?

JANE: What do you mean, kill himself?

PILKINGS: You do mean he is going to kill somebody, don't you?

JOSEPH: No, master. He will not kill anybody and no one will kill him. He will simply die.

JANE: But why, Joseph?

JOSEPH: It is native law and custom. The King die last month. Tonight is his burial. But before they can bury him, the Elesin must die so as to accompany him to heaven.

PILKINGS: I seem to be fated to clash more often with that man than with any of the other chiefs.

JOSEPH: He is the King's Chief Horseman.

PILKINGS: [*In a resigned way.*] I know.

JANE: Simon, what's the matter?

PILKINGS: It would have to be him!

JANE: Who is he?

PILKINGS: Don't you remember? He's that chief with whom I had a scrap some three or four years ago. I helped his son get to a medical school in England, remember? He fought tooth and nail to prevent it.

JANE: Oh, now I remember. He was that very sensitive young man. What was his name again?

PILKINGS: Olunde. Haven't replied to his last letter, come to think of it. The old pagan wanted him to stay and carry on some family tradition or the other. Honestly I couldn't understand the fuss he made. I literally had to help the boy escape from close confinement and load him onto the next boat. A most intelligent boy, really bright.

JANE: I rather thought he was much too sensitive, you know. The kind of person you feel should be a poet munching rose petals in Bloomsbury.[7]

PILKINGS: Well, he's going to make a first-class doctor. His mind is set on that. And as long as he wants my help he is welcome to it.

JANE: [*After a pause.*] Simon.

PILKINGS: Yes?

JANE: This boy, he was the eldest son, wasn't he?

PILKINGS: I'm not sure. Who could tell with that old ram?

JANE: Do you know, Joseph?

JOSEPH: Oh yes, madam. He was the eldest son. That's why Elesin cursed master good and proper. The eldest son is not supposed to travel away from the land.

JANE: [*Giggling.*] Is that true, Simon? Did he really curse you good and proper?

PILKINGS: By all accounts I should be dead by now.

JOSEPH: Oh no, master is white man. And good Christian. Black man juju can't touch master.

JANE: If he was his eldest, it means that he would be the Elesin to the next king. It's a family thing, isn't it, Joseph?

---

7. Area of central London next to the British Museum; it is associated with art and high culture.

JOSEPH: Yes, madam. And if this Elesin had died before the King, his eldest son must take his place.
JANE: That would explain why the old chief was so mad you took the boy away.
PILKINGS: Well, it makes me all the more happy I did.
JANE: I wonder if he knew.
PILKINGS: Who? Oh, you mean Olunde?
JANE: Yes. Was that why he was so determined to get away? I wouldn't stay if I knew I was trapped in such a horrible custom.
PILKINGS: [*Thoughtfully.*] No, I don't think he knew. At least he gave no indication. But you couldn't really tell with him. He was rather close you know, quite unlike most of them. Didn't give much away, not even to me.
JANE: Aren't they all rather close, Simon?
PILKINGS: These natives here? Good gracious. They'll open their mouths and yap with you about their family secrets before you can stop them. Only the other day...
JANE: But Simon, do they really give anything away? I mean, anything that really counts. This affair for instance, we didn't know they still practised that custom, did we?
PILKINGS: Ye-e-es, I suppose you're right there. Sly, devious bastards.
JOSEPH: [*Stiffly.*] Can I go now, master? I have to clean the kitchen.
PILKINGS: What? Oh, you can go. Forgot you were still there.

[JOSEPH *goes.*]

JANE: Simon, you really must watch your language. Bastard isn't just a simple swear-word in these parts, you know.
PILKINGS: Look, just when did you become a social anthropologist, that's what I'd like to know.
JANE: I'm not claiming to know anything. I just happen to have overheard quarrels among the servants. That's how I know they consider it a smear.
PILKINGS: I thought the extended family system took care of all that. Elastic family, no bastards.
JANE: [*Shrugs.*] Have it your own way.

[*Awkward silence. The drumming increases in volume.* JANE *gets up suddenly, restless.*]

That drumming, Simon, do you think it might really be connected with this ritual? It's been going on all evening.
PILKINGS: Let's ask our native guide. Joseph! Just a minute, Joseph. [JOSEPH *re-enters.*] What's the drumming about?
JOSEPH: I don't know, master.
PILKINGS: What do you mean, you don't know? It's only two years since your conversion. Don't tell me all that holy water nonsense also wiped out your tribal memory.
JOSEPH: [*Visibly shocked.*] Master!
JANE: Now you've done it.
PILKINGS: What have I done now?
JANE: Never mind. Listen, Joseph, just tell me this. Is that drumming connected with dying or anything of that nature?

JOSEPH: Madam, this is what I am trying to say: I am not sure. It sounds like the death of a great chief and then, it sounds like the wedding of a great chief. It really mix me up.

PILKINGS: Oh, get back to the kitchen. A fat lot of help you are.

JOSEPH: Yes, master. [*Goes.*]

JANE: Simon . . .

PILKINGS: Alright, alright. I'm in no mood for preaching.

JANE: It isn't my preaching you have to worry about, it's the preaching of the missionaries who preceded you here. When they make converts they really convert them. Calling holy water nonsense to our Joseph is really like insulting the Virgin Mary before a Roman Catholic. He's going to hand in his notice tomorrow, you mark my word.

PILKINGS: Now you're being ridiculous.

JANE: Am I? What are you willing to bet that tomorrow we are going to be without a steward-boy?[8] Did you see his face?

PILKINGS: I am more concerned about whether or not we will be one native chief short by tomorrow. Christ! Just listen to those drums. [*He strides up and down, undecided.*]

JANE: [*Getting up.*] I'll change and make us some supper.

PILKINGS: What's that?

JANE: Simon, it's obvious we have to miss this ball.

PILKINGS: Nonsense. It's the first bit of real fun the European club has managed to organise for over a year, I'm damned if I'm going to miss it. And it is a rather special occasion. Doesn't happen every day.

JANE: You know this business has to be stopped, Simon. And you are the only man who can do it.

PILKINGS: I don't have to stop anything. If they want to throw themselves off the top of a cliff or poison themselves for the sake of some barbaric custom what is that to me? If it were ritual murder or something like that I'd be duty-bound to do something. I can't keep an eye on all the potential suicides in this province. And as for that man—believe me, it's good riddance.

JANE: [*Laughs.*] I know you better than that, Simon. You are going to have to do something to stop it—after you've finished blustering.

PILKINGS: [*Shouts after her.*] And suppose after all it's only a wedding. I'd look a proper fool if I interrupted a chief on his honeymoon, wouldn't I? [*Resumes his angry stride, slows down.*] Ah well, who can tell what those chiefs actually do on their honeymoon anyway? [*He takes up the pad and scribbles rapidly on it.*] Joseph! Joseph! Joseph! [*Some moments later* JOSEPH *puts in a sulky appearance.*] Did you hear me call you? Why the hell didn't you answer?

JOSEPH: I didn't hear, master.

PILKINGS: You didn't hear me! How come you are here, then?

JOSEPH: [*Stubbornly.*] I didn't hear, master.

PILKINGS: [*Controls himself with an effort.*] We'll talk about it in the morning. I want you to take this note directly to Sergeant Amusa. You'll find him at the charge office.[9] Get on your bicycle and race there with it. I expect you back in twenty minutes exactly. Twenty minutes, is that clear?

JOSEPH: Yes, master. [*Going.*]

---

8. Houseboy, servant.   9. Booking office of a police station.

PILKINGS: Oh er.... Joseph.
JOSEPH: Yes, master?
PILKINGS: [*Between gritted teeth.*] Er... forget what I said just now. The holy water is not nonsense. I was talking nonsense.
JOSEPH: Yes, master. [*Goes.*]
JANE: [*Pokes her head round the door.*] Have you found him?
PILKINGS: Found who?
JANE: Joseph. Weren't you shouting for him?
PILKINGS: Oh yes, he turned up finally.
JANE: You sounded desperate. What was it all about?
PILKINGS: Oh, nothing. I just wanted to apologise to him. Assure him that the holy water isn't really nonsense.
JANE: Oh? And how did he take it?
PILKINGS: Who the hell gives a damn! I had a sudden vision of our Very Reverend Macfarlane drafting another letter of complaint to the Resident about my unchristian language towards his parishioners.
JANE: Oh, I think he's given up on you by now.
PILKINGS: Don't be too sure. And anyway, I wanted to make sure Joseph didn't "lose" my note on the way. He looked sufficiently full of the holy crusade to do some such thing.
JANE: If you've finished exaggerating, come and have something to eat.
PILKINGS: No, put it all away. We can still get to the ball.
JANE: Simon...
PILKINGS: Get your costume back on. Nothing to worry about. I've instructed Amusa to arrest the man and lock him up.
JANE: But that station is hardly secure, Simon. He'll soon get his friends to help him escape.
PILKINGS: A-ah, that's where I have out-thought you. I'm not having him put in the station cell. Amusa will bring him right here and lock him up in my study. And he'll stay with him till we get back. No one will dare come here to incite him to anything.
JANE: How clever of you, darling. I'll get ready.
PILKINGS: Hey.
JANE: Yes, darling.
PILKINGS: I have a surprise for you. I was going to keep it until we actually got to the ball.
JANE: What is it?
PILKINGS: You know the Prince is on a tour of the colonies, don't you? Well, he docked in the capital only this morning but he is already at the Residency. He is going to grace the ball with his presence later tonight.
JANE: Simon! Not really.
PILKINGS: Yes, he is. He's been invited to give away the prizes and he has agreed. You must admit old Engleton is the best Club Secretary we ever had. Quick off the mark, that lad.
JANE: But how thrilling.
PILKINGS: The other provincials are going to be damned envious.
JANE: I wonder what he'll come as.
PILKINGS: Oh, I don't know. As a coat-of-arms perhaps. Anyway it won't be anything to touch this.

JANE: Well, that's lucky. If we are to be presented I won't have to start looking for a pair of gloves. It's all sewn on.
PILKINGS: [*Laughing.*] Quite right. Trust a woman to think of that. Come on, let's get going.
JANE: [*Rushing off.*] Won't be a second. [*Stops.*] Now I see why you've been so edgy all evening. I thought you weren't handling this affair with your usual brilliance—to begin with that is.
PILKINGS: [*His mood is much improved.*] Shut up, woman, and get your things on.
JANE: Alright, boss—coming.

[PILKINGS *suddenly begins to hum the tango to which they were dancing before. Starts to execute a few practice steps. Lights fade.*]

## Scene 3

*A swelling, agitated hum of women's voices rises immediately in the background. The lights come on and we see the frontage of a converted cloth stall in the market. The floor leading up to the entrance is covered in rich velvets and woven cloth. The* WOMEN *come on stage, borne backwards by the determined progress of Sergeant* AMUSA *and his two* CONSTABLES, *who already have their batons out and use them as a pressure against the* WOMEN. *At the edge of the cloth-covered floor, however, the* WOMEN *take a determined stand and block all further progress of the men. They begin to tease them mercilessly.*

AMUSA: I am tell you women for last time to commot my road.[1] I am here on official business.
WOMAN: Official business, you white man's eunuch? Official business is taking place where you want to go and it's a business you wouldn't understand.
WOMAN: [*Makes a quick tug at the* CONSTABLE's *baton.*] That doesn't fool anyone, you know. It's the one you carry under your government knickers[2] that counts. [*She bends low as if to peep under the baggy shorts. The embarrassed* CONSTABLE *quickly puts his knees together. The* WOMEN *roar.*]
WOMAN: You mean there is nothing there at all?
WOMAN: Oh, there was something. You know that handbell which the whiteman uses to summon his servants . . . ?
AMUSA: [*He manages to preserve some dignity throughout.*] I hope you women know that interfering with officer in execution of his duty is criminal offence.
WOMAN: Interfere? He says we're interfering with him. You foolish man, we're telling you there's nothing to interfere with.
AMUSA: I am order you now to clear the road.
WOMAN: What road? The one your father built?
WOMAN: You are a policeman, not so? Then you know what they call trespassing in court. Or— [*Pointing to the cloth-lined steps.*] —do you think that kind of road is built for every kind of feet?
WOMAN: Go back and tell the white man who sent you to come himself.
AMUSA: If I go I will come back with reinforcement. And we will all return carrying weapons.

---

1. "Get out of my way"; literally translated from pidgin English as "come out of my road."
2. Women's underpants. The reference here is to the khaki shorts worn by colonial policemen.

WOMAN: Oh, now I understand. Before they can put on those knickers the white man first cuts off their weapons.
WOMAN: What a cheek! You mean you come here to show power to women and you don't even have a weapon.
AMUSA: [*Shouting above the laughter.*] For the last time, I warn you women to clear the road.
WOMAN: To where?
AMUSA: To that hut. I know he dey dere.
WOMAN: Who?
AMUSA: The chief who call himself Elesin Oba.
WOMAN: You ignorant man. It is not he who calls himself Elesin Oba, it is his blood that says it. As it called out to his father before him and will to his son after him. And that is in spite of everything your white man can do.
WOMAN: Is it not the same ocean that washes this land and the white man's land? Tell your white man he can hide our son away as long as he likes. When the time comes for him, the same ocean will bring him back.
AMUSA: The government say dat kin' ting[3] must stop.
WOMAN: Who will stop it? You? Tonight our husband and father will prove himself greater than the laws of strangers.
AMUSA: I tell you nobody go prove anything tonight or anytime. Is ignorant and criminal to prove dat kin' prove.
IYALOJA: [*Entering, from the hut. She is accompanied by a group of* YOUNG GIRLS *who have been attending the* BRIDE.] What is it, Amusa? Why do you come here to disturb the happiness of others?
AMUSA: Madame Iyaloja, I glad you come. You know me, I no like trouble but duty is duty. I am here to arrest Elesin for criminal intent. Tell these women to stop obstructing me in the performance of my duty.
IYALOJA: And you? What gives you the right to obstruct our leader of men in the performance of his duty?
AMUSA: What kin' duty be dat one, Iyaloja?
IYALOJA: What kin' duty? What kin' duty does a man have to his new bride?
AMUSA: [*Bewildered, looks at the* WOMEN *and at the entrance to the hut.*] Iyaloja, is it wedding you call dis kin' ting?
IYALOJA: You have wives, haven't you? Whatever the white man has done to you he hasn't stopped you having wives. And if he has, at least he is married. If you don't know what a marriage is, go and ask him to tell you.
AMUSA: This no to wedding.
IYALOJA: And ask him at the same time what he would have done if anyone had come to disturb him on his wedding night.
AMUSA: Iyaloja, I say dis no to wedding.
IYALOJA: You want to look inside the bridal chamber? You want to see for yourself how a man cuts the virgin knot?
AMUSA: Madam . . .
WOMAN: Perhaps his wives are still waiting for him to learn.
AMUSA: Iyaloja, make you tell dese women make den no insult me again. If I hear dat kin' insult once more . . .
GIRL: [*Pushing her way through.*] You will do what?

---

3. "That kind of thing" in pidgin English.

GIRL: He's out of his mind. It's our mothers you're talking to, do you know that? Not to any illiterate villager you can bully and terrorise. How dare you intrude here anyway?
GIRL: What a cheek, what impertinence!
GIRL: You've treated them too gently. Now let them see what it is to tamper with the mothers of this market.
GIRL: Your betters dare not enter the market when the women say no!
GIRL: Haven't you learnt that yet, you jester in khaki and starch?
IYALOJA: Daughters . . .
GIRL: No no, Iyaloja, leave us to deal with him. He no longer knows his mother, we'll teach him.

[*With a sudden movement they snatch the batons of the two* CONSTABLES. *They begin to hem them in.*]

GIRL: What next? We have your batons? What next? What are you going to do?

[*With equally swift movements they knock off their hats.*]

GIRL: Move if you dare. We have your hats, what will you do about it? Didn't the white man teach you to take off your hats before women?
IYALOJA: It's a wedding night. It's a night of joy for us. Peace . . .
GIRL: Not for him. Who asked him here?
GIRL: Does he dare go to the Residency without an invitation?
GIRL: Not even where the servants eat the leftovers.
GIRL: [*In turn. In an "English" accent.*] Well well, it's Mister Amusa. Were you invited? [*Playacting to one another. The older* WOMEN *encourage them with their titters.*]
—Your invitation card please?
—Who are you? Have we been introduced?
—And who did you say you were?
—Sorry, I didn't quite catch your name.
—May I take your hat?
—If you insist. May I take yours? [*Exchanging the* POLICEMEN's *hats.*]
—How very kind of you.
—Not at all. Won't you sit down?
—After you.
—Oh no.
—I insist.
—You're most gracious.
—And how do you find the place?
—The natives are alright.
—Friendly?
—Tractable.
—Not a teeny-weeny bit restless?
—Well, a teeny-weeny bit restless.
—One might even say, difficult?
—Indeed one might be tempted to say, difficult.
—But you do manage to cope?
—Yes, indeed I do. I have a rather faithful ox called Amusa.
—He's loyal?
—Absolutely.

—Lay down his life for you what?
—Without a moment's thought.
—Had one like that once. Trust him with my life.
—Mostly of course they are liars.
—Never known a native to tell the truth.
—Does it get rather close around here?
—It's mild for this time of the year.
—But the rains may still come.
—They are late this year aren't they?
—They are keeping African time.
—Ha ha ha ha
—Ha ha ha ha
—The humidity is what gets me.
—It used to be whisky.
—Ha ha ha ha
—Ha ha ha ha
—What's your handicap, old chap?
—Is there racing by golly?
—Splendid golf course, you'll like it.
—I'm beginning to like it already.
—And a European club, exclusive.
—You've kept the flag flying.
—We do our best for the old country.
—It's a pleasure to serve.
—Another whisky, old chap?
—You are indeed too too kind.
—Not at all sir. Where is that boy? [*With a sudden bellow.*] Sergeant!
AMUSA: [*Snaps to attention.*] Yessir!

[*The* WOMEN *collapse with laughter.*]

GIRL: Take your men out of here.
AMUSA: [*Realising the trick, he rages from loss of face.*] I'm give you warning . . .
GIRL: Alright then. Off with his knickers! [*They surge slowly forward.*]
IYALOJA: Daughters, please.
AMUSA: [*Squaring himself for defence.*] The first woman wey touch me . . .
IYALOJA: My children, I beg of you . . .
GIRL: Then tell him to leave this market. This is the home of our mothers. We don't want the eater of white left-overs at the feast their hands have prepared.
IYALOJA: You heard them, Amusa. You had better go.
GIRL: Now!
AMUSA: [*Commencing his retreat.*] We dey go now, but make you no say we no warn you.
GIRL: Now!
GIRL: Before we read the riot act—you should know all about that.
AMUSA: Make we go. [*They depart, more precipitately.*]

[*The* WOMEN *strike their palms across in the gesture of wonder.*]

WOMEN: Do they teach you all that at school?
WOMAN: And to think I nearly kept Apinke away from the place.
WOMAN: Did you hear them? Did you see how they mimicked the white man?

WOMAN: The voices exactly. Hey, there are wonders in this world!
IYALOJA: Well, our elders have said it: Dada may be weak, but he has a younger sibling who is truly fearless.[4]
WOMAN: The next time the white man shows his face in this market I will set Wuraola[5] on his tail.

[A WOMAN *bursts into song and dance of euphoria—'Tani l'awa o l'ogbeja? Kayi! A l'ogbeja. Omo Kekere l'ogbeja.'*[6] *The rest of the* WOMEN *join in, some placing the* GIRLS *on their back like infants, others dancing round them. The dance becomes general, mounting in excitement.* ELESIN *appears, in wrapper only. In his hands a white velvet cloth folded loosely as if it held some delicate object. He cries out.*]

ELESIN: Oh, you mothers of beautiful brides! [*The dancing stops. They turn and see him, and the object in his hands.* IYALOJA *approaches and gently takes the cloth from him.*] Take it. It is no mere virgin stain, but the union of life and the seeds of passage. My vital flow, the last from this flesh is intermingled with the promise of future life. All is prepared. Listen! [*A steady drum-beat from the distance.*] Yes. It is nearly time. The King's dog has been killed. The King's favourite horse is about to follow his master. My brother chiefs know their task and perform it well. [*He listens again.*]

[*The* BRIDE *emerges, stands shyly by the door. He turns to her.*]

Our marriage is not yet wholly fulfilled. When earth and passage wed, the consummation is complete only when there are grains of earth on the eyelids of passage. Stay by me till then. My faithful drummers, do me your last service. This is where I have chosen to do my leave-taking, in this heart of life, this hive which contains the swarm of the world in its small compass. This is where I have known love and laughter away from the palace. Even the richest food cloys when eaten days on end; in the market, nothing ever cloys. Listen. [*They listen to the drums.*] They have begun to seek out the heart of the King's favourite horse. Soon it will ride in its bolt of raffia[7] with the dog at its feet. Together they will ride on the shoulders of the King's grooms through the pulse centres of the town. They know it is here I shall await them. I have told them. [*His eyes appear to cloud. He passes his hand over them as if to clear his sight. He gives a faint smile.*] It promises well; just then I felt my spirit's eagerness. The kite makes for wide spaces and the wind creeps up behind its tail; can the kite say less than—thank you, the quicker the better? But wait a while my spirit. Wait. Wait for the coming of the courier of the King. Do you know, friends, the horse is born to this one destiny, to bear the burden that is man upon its back. Except for this night, this night alone when the spotless stallion will ride in triumph on the back of man. In the time of my father I witnessed the strange sight. Perhaps tonight also I shall see it for the last time. If they arrive before the drums beat for me, I shall tell them to let the Alafin[8] know I follow swiftly. If they come after the drums have sounded, why then, all is

---

4. Dada, the mythical king of Oyo and patron god of newborns, reputedly abdicated in favor of his fierce younger brother, Shango, the god of thunder and lightning.   5. "Rich gold," a common name for a girl.   6. "Who says we haven't a defender? Silence! We have our defenders. Little children are our champions" [Soyinka's translation].   7. Fiber from raffia palms, used in making skirts for masqueraders.   8. King of the Yoruba.

well for I have gone ahead. Our spirits shall fall in step along the great passage. [*He listens to the drums. He seems again to be falling into a state of semi-hypnosis; his eyes scan the sky but it is in a kind of daze. His voice is a little breathless.*] The moon has fed, a glow from its full stomach fills the sky and air, but I cannot tell where is that gateway through which I must pass. My faithful friends, let our feet touch together this last time, lead me into the other market with sounds that cover my skin with down yet make my limbs strike earth like a thoroughbred. Dear mothers, let me dance into the passage even as I have lived beneath your roofs. [*He comes down progressively among them. They make way for him, the* DRUMMERS *playing. His dance is one of solemn, regal motions, each gesture of the body is made with a solemn finality. The* WOMEN *join him, their steps a somewhat more fluid version of his. Beneath the* PRAISE-SINGER's *exhortations the women dirge* "Alẹ lẹ lẹ, awo mi lọ."[9]].

PRAISE-SINGER: Elesin Alafin, can you hear my voice?
ELESIN: Faintly, my friend, faintly.
PRAISE-SINGER: Elesin Alafi, can you hear my call?
ELESIN: Faintly, my king, faintly.
PRAISE-SINGER: Is your memory sound, Elesin?
   Shall my voice be a blade of grass and
   Tickle the armpit of the past?
ELESIN: My memory needs no prodding but
   What do you wish to say to me?
PRAISE-SINGER: Only what has been spoken. Only what concerns
   The dying wish of the father of all.
ELESIN: It is buried like seed-yam in my mind.
   This is the season of quick rains, the harvest
   Is this moment due for gathering.
PRAISE-SINGER: If you cannot come, I said, swear
   You'll tell my favourite horse. I shall
   Ride on through the gates alone.
ELESIN: Elesin's message will be read
   Only when his loyal heart no longer beats.
PRAISE-SINGER: If you cannot come, Elesin, tell my dog.
   I cannot stay the keeper too long
   At the gate.
ELESIN: A dog does not outrun the hand
   That feeds it meat. A horse that throws its rider
   Slows down to a stop. Elesin Alafin
   Trusts no beasts with messages between
   A king and his companion.
PRAISE-SINGER: If you get lost my dog will track
   The hidden path to me.
ELESIN: The seven-way crossroads[1] confuses
   Only the stranger. The Horseman of the King
   Was born in the recesses of the house.

---

9. "Night has fallen, the seasoned initiate is leaving."
1. In Yoruba cosmology, Esu Elegba, the god of confusion and doubleness, is often to be found at the crossroads.

PRAISE-SINGER: I know the wickedness of men. If there is
    Weight on the loose end of your sash, such weight
    As no mere man can shift; if your sash is earthed
    By evil minds who mean to part us at the last...
ELESIN: My sash is of the deep purple *alari*;
    It is no tethering-rope. The elephant
    Trails no tethering-rope; that king
    Is not yet crowed who will peg[2] an elephant—
    Not even you, my friend and King.
PRAISE-SINGER: And yet this fear will not depart from me
    The darkness of this new abode is deep—
    Will your human eyes suffice?
ELESIN: In a night which falls before our eyes
    However deep, we do not miss our way.
PRAISE-SINGER: Shall I now not acknowledge I have stood
    Where wonders met their end? The elephant deserves
    Better than that we say, "I have caught
    A glimpse of something." If we see the tamer
    Of the forest let us say plainly, we have seen
    An elephant.
ELESIN: [*His voice is drowsy.*]
    I have freed myself of earth and now
    It's getting dark. Strange voices guide my feet.
PRAISE-SINGER: The river is never so high that the eyes
    Of a fish are covered. The night is not so dark
    That the albino fails to find his way. A child
    Returning homewards craves no leading by the hand.
    Gracefully does the mask regain his grove at the end of the day...
    Gracefully. Gracefully does the mask dance
    Homeward at the end of the day, gracefully...

    [ELESIN's *trance appears to be deepening, his steps heavier.*]

IYALOJA: It is the death of war that kills the valiant,
    Death of water is how the swimmer goes
    It is the death of markets that kills the trader
    And death of indecision takes the idle away
    The trade of the cutlass blunts its edge
    And the beautiful die the death of beauty.
    It takes an Elesin to die the death of death...
    Only Elesin... dies the unknowable death of death...
    Gracefully, gracefully does the horseman regain
    The stables at the end of day, gracefully...
PRAISE-SINGER: How shall I tell what my eyes have seen? The Horseman gallops on before the courier, how shall I tell what my eyes have seen? He says a dog may be confused by new scents of beings he never dreamt of, so he must precede the dog to heaven. He says a horse may stumble on strange boulders and be lamed, so he races on before the horse to heaven. It is best, he says, to

---

2. Confine, pin down.

trust no messenger who may falter at the outer gate; oh how shall I tell what my ears have heard? But do you hear me still, Elesin, do you hear your faithful one?

[ELESIN *in his motions appears to feel for a direction of sound, subtly, but he only sinks deeper into his trance-dance.*]

Elesin Alafin, I no longer sense your flesh. The drums are changing now but you have gone far ahead of the world. It is not yet noon in heaven; let those who claim it is begin their own journey home. So why must you rush like an impatient bride: why do you race to desert your Olohun-iyo?

[ELESIN *is now sunk fully deep in his trance, there is no longer sign of any awareness of his surroundings.*]

Does the deep voice of *gbedu*[3] cover you then, like the passage of royal elephants? Those drums that brook no rivals, have they blocked the passage to your ears that my voice passes into wind, a mere leaf floating in the night? Is your flesh lightened, Elesin, is that lump of earth I slid between your slippers to keep you longer slowly sifting from your feet? Are the drums on the other side now tuning skin to skin with ours in *osugbo*?[4] Are there sounds there I cannot hear, do footsteps surround you which pound the earth like *gbedu*, roll like thunder round the dome of the world? Is the darkness gathering in your head, Elesin? Is there now a streak of light at the end of the passage, a light I dare not look upon? Does it reveal whose voices we often heard, whose touches we often felt, whose wisdoms come suddenly into the mind when the wisest have shaken their heads and murmured: It cannot be done? Elesin Alafin, don't think I do not know why your lips are heavy, why your limbs are drowsy as palm oil in the cold of harmattan.[5] I would call you back but when the elephant heads for the jungle, the tail is too small a handhold for the hunter that would pull him back. The sun that heads for the sea no longer heeds the prayers of the farmer. When the river begins to taste the salt of the ocean, we no longer know what deity to call on, the river-god or Olokun.[6] No arrow flies back to the string, the child does not return through the same passage that gave it birth. Elesin Oba, can you hear me at all? Your eyelids are glazed like a courtesan's, is it that you see the dark groom and master of life? And will you see my father? Will you tell him that I stayed with you to the last? Will my voice ring in your ears awhile, will you remember Olohun-iyo even if the music on the other side surpasses his mortal craft? But will they know you over there? Have they eyes to gauge your worth, have they the heart to love you, will they know what thoroughbred prances towards them in caparisons[7] of honour? If they do not, Elesin, if any there cuts your yam with a small knife, or pours you wine in a small calabash, turn back and return to welcoming hands. If the world were not greater than the wishes of Olohun-iyo, I would not let you go . . .

---

3. A deep-timbred royal drum [Soyinka's glossary].
4. Secret 'executive' cult of the Yoruba; its meeting place [Soyinka's glossary].
5. In west Africa, a dry, parching seasonal breeze carrying dusty winds from the Sahara Desert.
6. God of the ocean, worshiped by fishermen and sailors.
7. Cloths spread over the saddle or harness of a horse, often gaily ornamented.

[*He appears to break down.* ELESIN *dances on, completely in a trance. The dirge wells up louder and stronger.* ELESIN's *dance does not lose its elasticity but his gestures become, if possible, even more weighty. Lights fade slowly on the scene.*]

## Scene 4

A Masque.[8] *The front side of the stage is part of a wide corridor around the great hall of the Residency extending beyond vision into the rear and wings. It is redolent of the tawdry decadence of a far-flung but key imperial frontier. The couples in a variety of fancy-dress are ranged around the walls, gazing in the same direction. The guest-of-honour is about to make an appearance. A portion of the local police brass band with its white conductor is just visible. At last, the entrance of Royalty. The band plays "Rule Britannia," badly, beginning long before he is visible. The couples bow and curtsey as he passes by them. Both he and his companions are dressed in seventeenth-century European costume. Following behind are the* RESIDENT *and his partner similarly attired. As they gain the end of the hall where the orchestra dais begins the music comes to an end. The* PRINCE *bows to the guests. The band strikes up a Viennese waltz and the* PRINCE *formally opens the floor. Several bars later the* RESIDENT *and his companion follow suit. Others follow in appropriate pecking order. The orchestra's waltz rendition is not of the highest musical standard.*

*Some time later the* PRINCE *dances again into view and is settled into a corner by the* RESIDENT *who then proceeds to select couples as they dance past for introduction, sometimes threading his way through the dancers to tap the lucky couple on the shoulder. Desperate efforts from many to ensure that they are recognised in spite of, perhaps, their costume. The ritual of introductions soon takes in* PILKINGS *and his wife. The* PRINCE *is quite fascinated by their costume and they demonstrate the adaptations they have made to it, pulling down the mask to demonstrate how the* egungun *normally appears, then showing the various press-button controls they have innovated for the face flaps, the sleeves, etc. They demonstrate the dance steps and the guttural sounds made by the* egungun, *harass other dancers in the hall,* MRS. PILKINGS *playing the "restrainer"[9] to* PILKINGS' *manic darts. Everyone is highly entertained, the Royal Party especially who lead the applause.*

*At this point a liveried footman comes in with a note on a salver and is intercepted almost absent-mindedly by the* RESIDENT *who takes the note and reads it. After polite coughs he succeeds in excusing the* PILKINGS *from the* PRINCE *and takes them aside. The* PRINCE *considerately offers the* RESIDENT's *wife his hand and dancing is resumed.*

*On their way out the* RESIDENT *gives an order to his* AIDE-DE-CAMP.[1] *They come into the side corridor where the* RESIDENT *hands the note to* PILKINGS.

RESIDENT: As you see, it says "emergency" on the outside. I took the liberty of opening it because His Highness was obviously enjoying the entertainment. I didn't want to interrupt unless really necessary.
PILKINGS: Yes, yes of course, sir.
RESIDENT: Is it really as bad as it says? What's it all about?
PILKINGS: Some strange custom they have, sir. It seems because the King is dead some important chief has to commit suicide.
RESIDENT: The King? Isn't it the same one who died nearly a month ago?

---

8. Formal, European-style costume party with elaborate dress and masks.
9. Person who controls the movements of the dancing mask when its movements seem excessive.
1. Military assistant to a civilian administrator.

PILKINGS: Yes, sir.
RESIDENT: Haven't they buried him yet?
PILKINGS: They take their time about these things, sir. The pre-burial ceremonies last nearly thirty days. It seems tonight is the final night.
RESIDENT: But what has it got to do with the market women? Why are they rioting? We've waived that troublesome tax,[2] haven't we?
PILKINGS: We don't quite know that they are exactly rioting yet, sir. Sergeant Amusa is sometimes prone to exaggerations.
RESIDENT: He sounds desperate enough. That comes out even in his rather quaint grammar. Where is the man, anyway? I asked my aide-de-camp to bring him here.
PILKINGS: They are probably looking in the wrong verandah. I'll fetch him myself.
RESIDENT: No no you stay here. Let your wife go and look for them. Do you mind, my dear . . . ?
JANE: Certainly not, your Excellency. [*Goes.*]
RESIDENT: You should have kept me informed, Pilkings. You realise how disastrous it would have been if things had erupted while His Highness was here.
PILKINGS: I wasn't aware of the whole business until tonight, sir.
RESIDENT: Nose to the ground, Pilkings, nose to the ground. If we all let these little things slip past us, where would the empire be, eh? Tell me that. Where would we all be?
PILKINGS: [*Low voice.*] Sleeping peacefully at home, I bet.
RESIDENT: What did you say, Pilkings?
PILKINGS: It won't happen again, sir.
RESIDENT: It mustn't, Pilkings. It mustn't. Where is that damned sergeant? I ought to get back to His Highness as quickly as possible and offer him some plausible explanation for my rather abrupt conduct. Can you think of one, Pilkings?
PILKINGS: You could tell him the truth, sir.
RESIDENT: I could? No no no, Pilkings, that would never do. What! Go and tell him there is a riot just two miles away from him? This is supposed to be a secure colony of His Majesty, Pilkings.
PILKINGS: Yes, sir.
RESIDENT: Ah, there they are. No, these are not our native police. Are these the ring-leaders of the riot?
PILKINGS: Sir, these are my police officers.
RESIDENT: Oh, I beg your pardon, officers. You do look a little . . . I say, isn't there something missing in their uniform? I think they used to have some rather colourful sashes. If I remember rightly I recommended them myself in my young days in the service. A bit of colour always appeals to the natives, yes, I remember putting that in my report. Well well well, where are we? Make your report man.
PILKINGS: [*Moves close to* AMUSA, *between his teeth.*] And let's have no more superstitious nonsense from you Amusa or I'll throw you in the guardroom for a month and feed you pork![3]
RESIDENT: What's that? What has pork to do with it?

---

2. Taxes levied on market women were often the cause of riots in colonial West Africa.
3. Muslims consider it a sacrilege to eat pork.

PILKINGS: Sir, I was just warning him to be brief. I'm sure you are most anxious to hear his report.
RESIDENT: Yes yes yes, of course. Come on man, speak up. Hey, didn't we give them some colourful fez hats with all those wavy things, yes, pink tassels...
PILKINGS: Sir, I think if he was permitted to make his report we might find that he lost his hat in the riot.
RESIDENT: Ah yes, indeed. I'd better tell His Highness that. Lost his hat in the riot, ha ha. He'll probably say, Well, as long as he didn't lose his head. [*Chuckles to himself.*] Don't forget to send me a report first thing in the morning, young Pilkings.
PILKINGS: No, sir.
RESIDENT: And whatever you do, don't let things get out of hand. Keep a cool head and—nose to the ground, Pilkings. [*Wanders off in the general direction of the hall.*]
PILKINGS: Yes, sir.
AIDE-DE-CAMP: Would you be needing me, sir?
PILKINGS: No thanks, Bob. I think His Excellency's need of you is greater than ours.
AIDE-DE-CAMP: We have a detachment of soldiers from the capital, sir. They accompanied His Highness up here.
PILKINGS: I doubt if it will come to that but, thanks, I'll bear it in mind. Oh, could you send an orderly[4] with my cloak.
AIDE-DE-CAMP: Very good, sir. [*Goes.*]
PILKINGS: Now, sergeant.
AMUSA: Sir... [*Makes an effort, stops dead. Eyes to the ceiling.*]
PILKINGS: Oh, not again.
AMUSA: I cannot against death to dead cult. This dress get power of dead.
PILKINGS: Alright, let's go. You are relieved of all further duty, Amusa. Report to me first thing in the morning.
JANE: Shall I come, Simon?
PILKINGS: No, there's no need for that. If I can get back later I will. Otherwise get Bob to bring you home.
JANE: Be careful, Simon... I mean, be clever.
PILKINGS: Sure I will. You two, come with me. [*As he turns to go, the clock in the Residency begins to chime.* PILKINGS *looks at his watch then turns, horror-stricken, to stare at his wife. The same thought clearly occurs to her. He swallows hard. An orderly brings his cloak.*] It's midnight. I had no idea it was that late.
JANE: But surely... they don't count the hours the way we do. The moon, or something...
PILKINGS: I am... not so sure.

[*He turns and breaks into a sudden run. The two* CONSTABLES *follow, also at a run.* AMUSA, *who has kept his eyes on the ceiling throughout waits until the last of the footsteps has faded out of hearing. He salutes suddenly, but without once looking in the direction of the woman.*]

AMUSA: Goodnight, madam.
JANE: Oh. [*She hesitates.*] Amusa... [*He goes off without seeming to have heard.*] Poor

---

4. Soldier assigned to perform duties for a superior, like carrying orders or messages.

Simon... [*A figure emerges from the shadows, a young black man dressed in a sober western suit. He peeps into the hall, trying to make out the figures of the dancers.*] Who is that?

OLUNDE: [*Emerging into the light.*] I didn't mean to startle you, madam. I am looking for the District Officer.

JANE: Wait a minute... don't I know you? Yes, you are Olunde, the young man who...

OLUNDE: Mrs. Pilkings! How fortunate. I came here to look for your husband.

JANE: Olunde! Let's look at you. What a fine young man you've become. Grand but solemn. Good God, when did you return? Simon never said a word. But you do look well, Olunde. Really!

OLUNDE: You are... well, you look quite well yourself, Mrs. Pilkings. From what little I can see of you.

JANE: Oh, this. It's caused quite a stir, I assure you, and not all of it very pleasant. You are not shocked, I hope?

OLUNDE: Why should I be? But don't you find it rather hot in there? Your skin must find it difficult to breathe.

JANE: Well, it is a little hot I must confess, but it's all in a good cause.

OLUNDE: What cause, Mrs. Pilkings?

JANE: All this. The ball. And His Highness being here in person and all that.

OLUNDE: [*Mildly.*] And that is the good cause for which you desecrate an ancestral mask?

JANE: Oh, so you are shocked after all. How disappointing.

OLUNDE: No, I am not shocked, Mrs. Pilkings. You forget that I have now spent four years among your people. I discovered that you have no respect for what you do not understand.

JANE: Oh. So you've returned with a chip on your shoulder. That's a pity, Olunde. I am sorry.

[*An uncomfortable silence follows.*]

I take it then that you did not find your stay in England altogether edifying.

OLUNDE: I don't say that. I found your people quite admirable in many ways, their conduct and courage in this war,[5] for instance.

JANE: Ah yes, the war. Here, of course, it is all rather remote. From time to time we have a black-out drill just to remind us that there is a war on. And the rare convoy passes through on its way somewhere or on manoeuvres. Mind you, there is the occasional bit of excitement like that ship that was blown up in the harbour.

OLUNDE: Here? Do you mean through enemy action?

JANE: Oh no, the war hasn't come that close. The captain did it himself. I don't quite understand it, really. Simon tried to explain. The ship had to be blown up because it had become dangerous to the other ships, even to the city itself. Hundreds of the coastal population would have died.

OLUNDE: Maybe it was loaded with ammunition and had caught fire. Or some of those lethal gases they've been experimenting on.

JANE: Something like that. The captain blew himself up with it. Deliberately. Simon said someone had to remain on board to light the fuse.

---

5. World War II.

OLUNDE: It must have been a very short fuse.
JANE: [*Shrugs.*] I don't know much about it. Only that there was no other way to save lives. No time to devise anything else. The captain took the decision and carried it out.
OLUNDE: Yes... I quite believe it. I met men like that in England.
JANE: Oh, just look at me! Fancy welcoming you back with such morbid news. Stale too. It was at least six months ago.
OLUNDE: I don't find it morbid at all. I find it rather inspiring. It is an affirmative commentary on life.
JANE: What is?
OLUNDE: That captain's self-sacrifice.
JANE: Nonsense. Life should never be thrown deliberately away.
OLUNDE: And the innocent people round the harbour?
JANE: Oh, how does one know? The whole thing was probably exaggerated anyway.
OLUNDE: That was a risk the captain couldn't take. But please, Mrs. Pilkings, do you think you could find your husband for me? I have to talk to him.
JANE: Simon? Oh. [*As she recollects for the first time the full significance of* OLUNDE'S *presence.*] Simon is... there is a little problem in town. He was sent for. But ... when did you arrive? Does Simon know you're here?
OLUNDE: [*Suddenly earnest.*] I need your help, Mrs. Pilkings. I've always found you somewhat more understanding than your husband. Please find him for me and when you do, you must help me talk to him.
JANE: I'm afraid I don't quite... follow you. Have you seen my husband already?
OLUNDE: I went to your house. Your houseboy told me you were here. [*He smiles.*] He even told me how I would recognise you and Mr. Pilkings.
JANE: Then you must know what my husband is trying to do for you.
OLUNDE: For me?
JANE: For you. For your people. And to think he didn't even know you were coming back! But how do you happen to be here? Only this evening we were talking about you. We thought you were still four thousand miles away.
OLUNDE: I was sent a cable.
JANE: A cable? Who did? Simon? The business of your father didn't begin till tonight.
OLUNDE: A relation sent it weeks ago, and it said nothing about my father. All it said was, Our King is dead. But I knew I had to return home at once so as to bury my father. I understood that.
JANE: Well, thank God you don't have to go through that agony. Simon is going to stop it.
OLUNDE: That's why I want to see him. He's wasting his time. And since he has been so helpful to me I don't want him to incur the enmity of our people. Especially over nothing.
JANE: [*Sits down open-mouthed.*] You... you Olunde!
OLUNDE: Mrs. Pilkings, I came home to bury my father. As soon as I heard the news I booked my passage home. In fact we were fortunate. We travelled in the same convoy as your Prince, so we had excellent protection.
JANE: But you don't think your father is also entitled to whatever protection is available to him?
OLUNDE: How can I make you understand? He *has* protection. No one can under-

take what he does tonight without the deepest protection the mind can conceive. What can you offer him in place of his peace of mind, in place of the honour and veneration of his own people? What would you think of your Prince if he refused to accept the risk of losing his life on this voyage? This ... showing-the-flag tour of colonial possessions.

JANE: I see. So it isn't just medicine you studied in England.

OLUNDE: Yet another error into which your people fall. You believe that everything which appears to make sense was learnt from you.

JANE: Not so fast, Olunde. You have learnt to argue I can tell that, but I never said you made sense. However clearly you try to put it, it is still a barbaric custom. It is even worse—it's feudal! The king dies and a chieftain must be buried with him. How feudalistic can you get!

OLUNDE: [*Waves his hand towards the background. The* PRINCE *is dancing past again—to a different step—and all the guests are bowing and curtseying as he passes.*] And this? Even in the midst of a devastating war, look at that. What name would you give to that?

JANE: Therapy, British style. The preservation of sanity in the midst of chaos.

OLUNDE: Others would call it decadence. However, it doesn't really interest me. You white races know how to survive; I've seen proof of that. By all logical and natural laws this war should end with all the white races wiping out one another, wiping out their so-called civilisation for all time and reverting to a state of primitivism the like of which has so far only existed in your imagination when you thought of us. I thought all that at the beginning. Then I slowly realised that your greatest art is the art of survival. But at least have the humility to let others survive in their own way.

JANE: Through ritual suicide?

OLUNDE: Is that worse than mass suicide? Mrs. Pilkings, what do you call what those young men are sent to do by their generals in this war? Of course you have also mastered the art of calling things by names which don't remotely describe them.

JANE: You talk! You people with your long-winded, roundabout way of making conversation.

OLUNDE: Mrs. Pilkings, whatever we do, we never suggest that a thing is the opposite of what it really is. In your newsreels[6] I heard defeats, thorough, murderous defeats described as strategic victories. No wait, it wasn't just on your newsreels. Don't forget I was attached to hospitals all the time. Hordes of your wounded passed through those wards. I spoke to them. I spent long evenings by their bedsides while they spoke terrible truths of the realities of that war. I know now how history is made.

JANE: But surely, in a war of this nature, for the morale of the nation you must expect...

OLUNDE: That a disaster beyond human reckoning be spoken of as a triumph? No. I mean, is there no mourning in the home of the bereaved that such blasphemy is permitted?

JANE: [*After a moment's pause.*] Perhaps I can understand you now. The time we picked for you was not really one for seeing us at our best.

---

6. Tapes of news and features shown in movie houses before the main features. This was common before the age of television, especially during World War II.

OLUNDE: Don't think it was just the war. Before that even started I had plenty of time to study your people. I saw nothing, finally, that gave you the right to pass judgment on other peoples and their ways. Nothing at all.
JANE: [*Hesitantly.*] Was it the . . . colour thing? I know there is some discrimination.
OLUNDE: Don't make it so simple, Mrs. Pilkings. You make it sound as if when I left, I took nothing at all with me.
JANE: Yes . . . and to tell the truth, only this evening, Simon and I agreed that we never really knew what you left with.
OLUNDE: Neither did I. But I found out over there. I am grateful to your country for that. And I will never give it up.
JANE: Olunde, please . . . promise me something. Whatever you do, don't throw away what you have started to do. You want to be a doctor. My husband and I believe you will make an excellent one, sympathetic and competent. Don't let anything make you throw away your training.
OLUNDE: [*Genuinely surprised.*] Of course not. What a strange idea. I intend to return and complete my training. Once the burial of my father is over.
JANE: Oh, please . . . !
OLUNDE: Listen! Come outside. You can't hear anything against that music.
JANE: What is it?
OLUNDE: The drums. Can you hear the changes? Listen.

[*The drums come over, still distant but more distinct. There is a change of rhythm, it rises to a crescendo and then, suddenly, it is cut off. After a silence, a new beat begins, slow and resonant.*]

There, it's all over.
JANE: You mean he's . . .
OLUNDE: Yes, Mrs. Pilkings, my father is dead. His willpower has always been enormous; I know he is dead.
JANE: [*Screams.*] How can you be so callous! So unfeeling! You announce your father's own death like a surgeon looking down on some strange . . . stranger's body! You're just a savage like all the rest.
AIDE-DE-CAMP: [*Rushing out.*] Mrs. Pilkings. Mrs. Pilkings. [*She breaks down, sobbing.*] Are you all right, Mrs. Pilkings?
OLUNDE: She'll be all right. [*Turns to go.*]
AIDE-DE-CAMP: Who are you? And who the hell asked your opinion?
OLUNDE: You're quite right, nobody. [*Going.*]
AIDE-DE-CAMP: What the hell! Did you hear me ask you who you were?
OLUNDE: I have business to attend to.
AIDE-DE-CAMP: I'll give you business in a moment, you impudent nigger. Answer my question!
OLUNDE: I have a funeral to arrange. Excuse me. [*Going.*]
AIDE-DE-CAMP: I said stop! Orderly!
JANE: No, no, don't do that. I'm alright. And for heaven's sake, don't act so foolishly. He's a family friend.
AIDE-DE-CAMP: Well, he'd better learn to answer civil questions when he's asked them. These natives put a suit on and they get high opinions of themselves.
OLUNDE: Can I go now?
JANE: No no, don't go. I must talk to you. I'm sorry about what I said.
OLUNDE: It's nothing, Mrs. Pilkings. And I'm really anxious to go. I couldn't see

my father before, it's forbidden for me, his heir and successor, to set eyes on him from the moment of the king's death. But now.... I would like to touch his body while it is still warm.

JANE: You will. I promise I shan't keep you long. Only, I couldn't possibly let you go like that. Bob, please excuse us.

AIDE-DE-CAMP: If you're sure...

JANE: Of course I'm sure. Something happened to upset me just then, but I'm alright now. Really.

[*The* AIDE-DE-CAMP *goes, somewhat reluctantly.*]

OLUNDE: I mustn't stay long.

JANE: Please, I promise not to keep you. It's just that... oh, you saw yourself what happens to one in this place. The Resident's man thought he was being helpful, that's the way we all react. But I can't go in among that crowd just now and if I stay by myself somebody will come looking for me. Please, just say something for a few moments and then you can go. Just so I can recover myself.

OLUNDE: What do you want me to say?

JANE: Your calm acceptance, for instance—can you explain that? It was so unnatural. I don't understand that at all. I feel a need to understand all I can.

OLUNDE: But you explained it yourself. My medical training perhaps. I have seen death too often. And the soldiers who returned from the front, they died on our hands all the time.

JANE: No. It has to be more than that. I feel it has to do with the many things we don't really grasp about your people. At least you can explain.

OLUNDE: All these things are part of it. And anyway, my father has been dead in my mind for nearly a month. Ever since I learnt of the King's death. I've lived with my bereavement so long now that I cannot think of him alive. On that journey on the boat, I kept my mind on my duties as the one who must perform the rites over his body. I went through it all again and again in my mind as he himself had taught me. I didn't want to do anything wrong, something which might jeopardise the welfare of my people.

JANE: But he had disowned you. When you left he swore publicly you were no longer his son.

OLUNDE: I told you, he was a man of tremendous will. Sometimes that's another way of saying stubborn. But among our people, you don't disown a child just like that. Even if I had died before him I would still be buried like his eldest son. But it's time for me to go.

JANE: Thank you. I feel calmer. Don't let me keep you from your duties.

OLUNDE: Goodnight, Mrs. Pilkings.

JANE: Welcome home. [*She holds out her hand. As he takes it footsteps are heard approaching the drive. A short while later a woman's sobbing is also heard.*]

PILKINGS: [*Off.*] Keep them here till I get back. [*He strides into view, reacts at the sight of* OLUNDE *but turns to his wife.*] Thank goodness you're still here.

JANE: Simon, what happened?

PILKINGS: Later, Jane, please. Is Bob still here?

JANE: Yes, I think so. I'm sure he must be.

PILKINGS: Try and get him out here as quickly as you can. Tell him it's urgent.

JANE: Of course. Oh Simon, you remember...

PILKINGS: Yes yes. I can see who it is. Get Bob out here. [*She runs off.*] At first I thought I was seeing a ghost.
OLUNDE: Mr. Pilkings, I appreciate what you tried to do. I want you to believe that. I can tell you it would have been a terrible calamity if you'd succeeded.
PILKINGS: [*Opens his mouth several times, shuts it.*] You . . . said what?
OLUNDE: A calamity for us, the entire people.
PILKINGS: [*Sighs.*] I see. Hm.
OLUNDE: And now I must go. I must see him before he turns cold.
PILKINGS: Oh ah . . . em . . . but this is a shock to see you. I mean, er, thinking all this while you were in England and thanking God for that.
OLUNDE: I came on the mail boat. We travelled in the Prince's convoy.
PILKINGS: Ah yes, a-ah, hm . . . er, well . . .
OLUNDE: Goodnight. I can see you are shocked by the whole business. But you must know by now there are things you cannot understand—or help.
PILKINGS: Yes. Just a minute. There are armed policemen that way and they have instructions to let no one pass. I suggest you wait a little. I'll, er . . . give you an escort.
OLUNDE: That's very kind of you. But do you think it could be quickly arranged?
PILKINGS: Of course. In fact, yes, what I'll do is send Bob over with some men to the er . . . place. You can go with them. Here he comes now. Excuse me a minute.
AIDE-DE-CAMP: Anything wrong, sir?
PILKINGS: [*Takes him to one side.*] Listen, Bob, that cellar in the disused annexe of the Residency, you know, where the slaves were stored before being taken down to the coast. . . .
AIDE-DE-CAMP: Oh yes, we use it as a storeroom for broken furniture.
PILKINGS: But it's still got the bars on it?
AIDE-DE-CAMP: Oh yes, they are quite intact.
PILKINGS: Get the keys please. I'll explain later. And I want a strong guard over the Residency tonight.
AIDE-DE-CAMP: We have that already. The detachment from the coast . . .
PILKINGS: No, I don't want them at the gates of the Residency. I want you to deploy them at the bottom of the hill, a long way from the main hall so they can deal with any situation long before the sound carries to the house.
AIDE-DE-CAMP: Yes, of course.
PILKINGS: I don't want His Highness alarmed.
AIDE-DE-CAMP: You think the riot will spread here?
PILKINGS: It's unlikely but I don't want to take a chance. I made them believe I was going to lock the man up in my house, which was what I had planned to do in the first place. They are probably assailing it by now. I took a roundabout route here so I don't think there is any danger at all. At least not before dawn. Nobody is to leave the premises of course—the native employees I mean. They'll soon smell something is up and they can't keep their mouths shut.
AIDE-DE-CAMP: I'll give instructions at once.
PILKINGS: I'll take the prisoner down myself. Two policemen will stay with him throughout the night. Inside the cell.
AIDE-DE-CAMP: Right, sir. [*Salutes and goes off at the double.*]
PILKINGS: Jane. Bob is coming back in a moment with a detachment. Until he gets back please stay with Olunde. [*He makes an extra warning gesture with his eyes.*]

OLUNDE: Please, Mr. Pilkings...

PILKINGS: I hate to be stuffy, old son, but we have a crisis on our hands. It has to do with your father's affair, if you must know. And it happens also at a time when we have His Highness here. I am responsible for security so you'll simply have to do as I say. I hope that's understood. [*Marches off quickly, in the direction from which he made his first appearance.*]

OLUNDE: What's going on? All this can't be just because he failed to stop my father killing himself.

JANE: I honestly don't know. Could it have sparked off a riot?

OLUNDE: No. If he'd succeeded that would be more likely to start the riot. Perhaps there were other factors involved. Was there a chieftancy dispute?

JANE: None that I know of.

ELESIN: [*An animal bellow from off*[7].] Leave me alone! Is it not enough that you have covered me in shame! White man, take your hand from my body!

[OLUNDE *stands frozen to the spot.* JANE, *understanding at last, tries to move him.*]

JANE: Let's go in. It's getting chilly out here.

PILKINGS: [*Off.*] Carry him.

ELESIN: Give me back the name you have taken away from me, you ghost from the land of the nameless!

PILKINGS: Carry him! I can't have a disturbance here. Quickly! stuff up his mouth.

JANE: Oh God! Let's go in. Please, Olunde. [OLUNDE *does not move.*]

ELESIN: Take your albino's hand from me, you...

[*Sounds of a struggle. His voice chokes as he is gagged.*]

OLUNDE: [*Quietly.*] That was my father's voice.

JANE: Oh you poor orphan, what have you come home to?

[*There is a sudden explosion of rage from off-stage and powerful steps come running up the drive.*]

PILKINGS: You bloody fools, after him!

[*Immediately* ELESIN, *in handcuffs, comes pounding in the direction of* JANE *and* OLUNDE, *followed some moments afterwards by* PILKINGS *and the* CONSTABLES. ELESIN, *confronted by the seeming statue of his son, stops dead.* OLUNDE *stares above his head into the distance. The* CONSTABLES *try to grab him.* JANE *screams at them.*]

JANE: Leave him alone! Simon, tell them to leave him alone.

PILKINGS: All right, stand aside, you. [*Shrugs.*] Maybe just as well. It might help to calm him down.

[*For several moments they hold the same position.* ELESIN *moves a step forward, almost as if he's still in doubt.*]

ELESIN: Olunde? [*He moves his head, inspecting him from side to side.*] Olunde! [*He collapses slowly at* OLUNDE's *feet.*] Oh son, don't let the sight of your father turn you blind!

---

7. A loud, hollow sound usually associated with animals, especially cows; in some cases, it was considered to be a feature of the language of *egungun* and other masked figures.

OLUNDE: [*He moves for the first time since he heard his voice, brings his head slowly down to look on him.*] I have no father, eater of leftovers.

[*He walks slowly down the way his father had run. Light fades out on* ELESIN, *sobbing into the ground.*]

## Scene 5

*A wide iron-barred gate stretches almost the whole width of the cell in which* ELESIN *is imprisoned. His wrists are encased in thick iron bracelets, chained together; he stands against the bars, looking out. Seated on the ground to one side on the outside is his recent* BRIDE, *her eyes bent perpetually to the ground. Figures of the two* GUARDS *can be seen deeper inside the cell, alert to every movement* ELESIN *makes.* PILKINGS *now in a police officer's uniform, enters noiselessly, observes him a while. Then he coughs ostentatiously and approaches. Leans against the bars near a corner, his back to* ELESIN. *He is obviously trying to fall in mood with him. Some moments' silence.*

PILKINGS: You seem fascinated by the moon.
ELESIN: [*After a pause.*] Yes, ghostly one. Your twin-brother up there engages my thoughts.
PILKINGS: It is a beautiful night.
ELESIN: Is that so?
PILKINGS: The light on the leaves, the peace of the night...
ELESIN: The night is not at peace, District Officer.
PILKINGS: No? I would have said it was. You know, quiet...
ELESIN: And does quiet mean peace for you?
PILKINGS: Well, nearly the same thing. Naturally there is a subtle difference...
ELESIN: The night is not at peace, ghostly one. The world is not at peace. You have shattered the peace of the world forever. There is no sleep in the world tonight.
PILKINGS: It is still a good bargain if the world should lose one night's sleep as the price of saving a man's life.
ELESIN: You did not save my life, District Officer. You destroyed it.
PILKINGS: Now come on...
ELESIN: And not merely my life but the lives of many. The end of the night's work is not over. Neither this year nor the next will see it. If I wished you well, I would pray that you do not stay long enough on our land to see the disaster you have brought upon us.
PILKINGS: Well, I did my duty as I saw it. I have no regrets.
ELESIN: No. The regrets of life always come later.

[*Some moments' pause.*]

You are waiting for dawn, white man. I hear you saying to yourself: Only so many hours until dawn and then the danger is over. All I must do is to keep him alive tonight. You don't quite understand it all but you know that tonight is when what ought to be must be brought about. I shall ease your mind even more, ghostly one. It is not an entire night but a moment of the night, and that moment is past. The moon was my messenger and guide. When it reached a certain gateway in the sky, it touched that moment for which my whole life has been spent in blessings. Even I do not know the gateway. I have stood here and scanned the sky for a glimpse of that door, but I cannot see it. Human eyes are useless for a search of this nature. But in the house of *osugbo*, those who keep watch through the spirit recognised the moment, they sent word to me through the voice of our sacred drums to prepare myself. I heard them and I shed all thoughts of earth began to follow the moon to the abode of the gods . . . servant of the white king, that was when you entered my chosen place of departure on feet of desecration.

PILKINGS: I'm sorry, but we all see our duty differently.

ELESIN: I no longer blame you. You stole from me my first-born, sent him to your country so you could turn him into something in your own image. Did you plan it all beforehand? There are moments when it seems part of a larger plan. He who must follow my footsteps is taken from me, sent across the ocean: Then, in my turn, I am stopped from fulfilling my destiny. Did you think it all out before, this plan to push our world from its course and sever the cord that links us to the great origin?

PILKINGS: You don't really believe that. Anyway, if that was my intention with your son, I appear to have failed.

ELESIN: You did not fail in the main thing, ghostly one. We know the roof covers the rafters, the cloth covers blemishes; who would have known that the white skin covered our future, preventing us from seeing the death our enemies had prepared for us? The world is set adrift and its inhabitants are lost. Around them, there is nothing but emptiness.

PILKINGS: Your son does not take so gloomy a view.

ELESIN: Are you dreaming now, white man? Were you not present at the reunion of shame? Did you not see when the world reversed itself and the father fell before his son, asking forgiveness?

PILKINGS: That was in the heat of the moment. I spoke to him and . . . if you want to know, he wishes he could cut out his tongue for uttering the words he did.

ELESIN: No. What he said must never be unsaid. The contempt of my own son rescued something of my shame at your hands. You have stopped me in my duty but I know now that I did give birth to a son. Once I mistrusted him for seeking the companionship of those my spirit knew as enemies of our race. Now I understand. One should seek to obtain the secrets of his enemies. He will avenge my shame, white one. His spirit will destroy you and yours.

PILKINGS: That kind of talk is hardly called for. If you don't want my consolation . . .

ELESIN: No, white man, I do not want your consolation.

PILKINGS: As you wish. Your son, anyway, sends his consolation. He asks your forgiveness. When I asked him not to despise you his reply was: I cannot judge him, and if I cannot judge him, I cannot despise him. He wants to come to you and say goodbye and to receive your blessing.

ELESIN: Goodbye? Is he returning to your land?

PILKINGS: Don't you think that's the most sensible thing for him to do? I advised him to leave at once, before dawn, and he agrees that is the right course of action.

ELESIN: Yes, it is best. And even if I did not think so, I have lost the father's place of honour. My voice is broken.

PILKINGS: Your son honours you. If he didn't he would not ask your blessing.

ELESIN: No. Even a thoroughbred is not without pity for the turf he strikes with his hoof. When is he coming?

PILKINGS: As soon as the town is a little quieter. I advised it.

ELESIN: Yes, white man, I am sure you advised it. You advise all our lives, although on the authority of what gods, I do not know.

PILKINGS: [*Opens his mouth to reply, then appears to change his mind. Turns to go. Hesitates and stops again.*] Before I leave you, may I ask just one thing of you?

ELESIN: I am listening.

PILKINGS: I wish to ask you to search the quiet of your heart and tell me—do you not find great contradictions in the wisdom of your own race?

ELESIN: Make yourself clear, white one.

PILKINGS: I have lived among you long enough to learn a saying or two. One came to my mind tonight when I stepped into the market and saw what was going on. You were surrounded by those who egged you on with song and praises. I thought, are these not the same people who say: "The elder grimly approaches heaven and you ask him to bear your greetings yonder; do you really think he makes the journey willingly?" After that, I did not hesitate.

[*A pause.* ELESIN *sighs. Before he can speak a sound of running feet is heard.*]

JANE: [*Off.*] Simon! Simon!

PILKINGS: What on earth . . . ! [*Runs off.*]

[ELESIN *turns to his new wife, gazes on her for some moments.*]

ELESIN: My young bride, did you hear the ghostly one? You sit and sob in your silent heart but say nothing to all this. First I blamed the white man, then I blamed my gods for deserting me. Now I feel I want to blame you for the mystery of the sapping of my will. But blame is a strange peace offering for a man to bring a world he has deeply wronged, and to its innocent dwellers. Oh little mother, I have taken countless women in my life but you were more than a desire of the flesh. I needed you as the abyss across which my body must be drawn, I filled it with earth and dropped my seed in it at the moment of preparedness for my crossing. You were the final gift of the living to their emissary to the land of the ancestors, and perhaps your warmth and youth brought new insights of this world to me and turned my feet leaden on this side of the abyss. For I confess to you, daughter, my weakness came not merely from the abomination of the white man who came violently into my fading presence, there was also a weight of longing on my earth-held limbs. I would have shaken it off, already my foot had begun to lift, but then the white ghost entered and all was defiled.

[*Approaching voices of* PILKINGS *and his wife.*]

JANE: Oh Simon, you will let her in, won't you?

PILKINGS: I really wish you'd stop interfering.

[*They come into view.* JANE *is in a dressing-gown.* PILKINGS *is holding a note to which he refers from time to time.*]

JANE: Good gracious, I didn't initiate this. I was sleeping quietly, or trying to anyway, when the servant brought it. It's not my fault if one can't sleep undisturbed even in the Residency.

PILKINGS: He'd have done the same thing if we were sleeping at home, so don't sidetrack the issue. He knows he can get round you or he wouldn't send you the petition in the first place.

JANE: Be fair, Simon. After all, he was thinking of your own interests. He is grateful, you know—you seem to forget that. He feels he owes you something.

PILKINGS: I just wish they'd leave this man alone tonight, that's all.

JANE: Trust him, Simon. He's pledged his word it will all go peacefully.

PILKINGS: Yes, and that's the other thing. I don't like being threatened.

JANE: Threatened? [*Takes the note.*] I didn't spot any threat.

PILKINGS: It's there. Veiled, but it's there. The only way to prevent serious rioting tomorrow—what a cheek!

JANE: I don't think he's threatening you, Simon.

PILKINGS: He's picked up the idiom, alright. Wouldn't surprise me if he's been mixing with commies or anarchists over there. The phrasing sounds too good to be true. Damn! If only the Prince hadn't picked this time for his visit.

JANE: Well, even so, Simon, what have you got to lose? You don't want a riot on your hands, not with the Prince here.

PILKINGS: [*Going up to* ELESIN.] Let's see what he has to say. Chief Elesin, there is yet another person who wants to see you. As she is not a next-of-kin I don't really feel obliged to let her in. But your son sent a note with her, so it's up to you.

ELESIN: I know who that must be. So she found out your hiding-place. Well, it was not difficult. My stench of shame is so strong, it requires no hunter's dog to follow it.

PILKINGS: If you don't want to see her, just say so and I'll send her packing.

ELESIN: Why should I not want to see her? Let her come. I have no more holes in my rag of shame. All is laid bare.

PILKINGS: I'll bring her in. [*Goes off.*]

JANE: [*Hesitates, then goes to* ELESIN.] Please, try and understand. Everything my husband did was for the best.

ELESIN: [*He gives her a long strange stare, as if he is trying to understand who she is.*] You are the wife of the District Officer?

JANE: Yes. My name is Jane.

ELESIN: That is my wife sitting down there. You notice how still and silent she sits? My business is with your husband.

[PILKINGS *returns with* IYALOJA.]

PILKINGS: Here she is. Now first I want your word of honour that you will try nothing foolish.

ELESIN: Honour? White one, did you say you wanted my word of honour?

PILKINGS: I know you to be an honourable man. Give me your word of honour you will receive nothing from her.

ELESIN: But I am sure you have searched her clothing as you would never dare touch your own mother. And there are these two lizards of yours who roll their eyes even when I scratch.

PILKINGS: And I shall be sitting on that tree trunk watching even how you blink. Just the same I want your word that you will not let her pass anything to you.

ELESIN: You have my honour already. It is locked up in that desk in which you will put away your report of this night's events. Even the honour of my people you have taken already; it is tied together with those papers of treachery which make you masters in this land.

PILKINGS: Alright. I am trying to make things easy but if you must bring in politics we'll have to do it the hard way. Madam, I want you to remain along this line and move no nearer to the cell door. Guards! [*They spring to attention.*] If she moves beyond this point, blow your whistle. Come on, Jane. [*They go off.*]

IYALOJA: How boldly the lizard struts before the pigeon when it was the eagle itself he promised us he would confront.

ELESIN: I don't ask you to take pity on me, Iyaloja. You have a message for me or you would not have come. Even if it is the curses of the world, I shall listen.

IYALOJA: You made so bold with the servant of the white king who took your side against death. I must tell your brother chiefs when I return how bravely you waged war against him. Especially with words.

ELESIN: I more than deserve your scorn.

IYALOJA: [*With sudden anger.*] I warned you, if you must leave a seed behind, be sure it is not tainted with the curses of the world. Who are you to open a new life when you dared not open the door to a new existence? I say who are you to make so bold? [*The* BRIDE *sobs and* IYALOJA *notices her. Her contempt noticeably increases as she turns back to* ELESIN.] Oh, you self-vaunted stem of the plantain, how hollow it all proves. The pith is gone in the parent stem, so how will it prove with the new shoot? How will it go with that earth that bears it? Who are you to bring this abomination on us!

ELESIN: My powers deserted me. My charms, my spells, even my voice lacked strength when I made to summon the powers that would lead me over the last measure of earth into the land of the fleshless. You saw it, Iyaloja. You saw me struggle to retrieve my will from the power of the stranger whose shadow fell across the doorway and left me floundering and blundering in a maze I had never before encountered. My senses were numbed when the touch of cold iron came upon my wrists. I could do nothing to save myself.

IYALOJA: You have betrayed us. We fed you sweetmeats[8] such as we hoped awaited you on the other side. But you said, No, I must eat the world's leftovers. We said you were the hunter who brought the quarry down; to you belonged the vital portions of the game. No, you said, I am the hunter's dog and I shall eat the entrails of the game and the faeces of the hunter. We said you were the hunter returning home in triumph, a slain buffalo pressing down on his neck; you said, Wait, I first must turn up this cricket hole with my toes. We said yours was the doorway at which we first spy the tapper when he comes down from the tree, yours was the blessing of the twilight wine,[9] the purl that brings night spirits out of doors to steal their portion before the light of day. We said yours was the body of wine whose burden shakes the tapper like a sudden gust on his perch. You said, No, I am content to lick the dregs from each calabash when the drinkers are done. We said the dew on earth's surface was for you to wash your feet along the slopes of honour. You said, No, I shall step in the vomit of cats and the droppings of mice; I shall fight them for the left-overs of the world.

---

8. Delicacies made with sugar or honey; pastries or candies.
9. Palm wine tapped before dawn is considered especially fresh and potent.

ELESIN: Enough, Iyaloja, enough.
IYALOJA: We called you leader and oh, how you led us on. What we have no intention of eating should not be held to the nose.
ELESIN: Enough, enough. My shame is heavy enough.
IYALOJA: Wait. I came with a burden.
ELESIN: You have more than discharged it.
IYALOJA: I wish I could pity you.
ELESIN: I need neither your pity nor the pity of the world. I need understanding. Even I need to understand. You were present at my defeat. You were part of the beginnings. You brought about the renewal of my tie to earth, you helped in the binding of the cord.
IYALOJA: I gave you warning. The river which fills up before our eyes does not sweep us away in its flood.
ELESIN: What were warnings beside the moist contact of living earth between my fingers? What were warnings beside the renewal of famished embers lodged eternally in the heart of man. But even that, even if it overwhelmed one with a thousandfold temptations to linger a little while, a man could overcome it. It is when the alien hand pollutes the source of will,[1] when a stranger force of violence shatters the mind's calm resolution, this is when a man is made to commit the awful treachery of relief, commit in his thought the unspeakable blasphemy of seeing the hand of the gods in this alien rupture of his world. I know it was this thought that killed me, sapped my powers and turned me into an infant in the hands of unnamable strangers. I made to utter my spells anew but my tongue merely rattled in my mouth. I fingered hidden charms and the contact was damp; there was no spark left to sever the life-strings that should stretch from every fingertip. My will was squelched in the spittle of an alien race, and all because I had committed this blasphemy of thought—that there might be the hand of the gods in a stranger's intervention.
IYALOJA: Explain it how you will, I hope it brings you peace of mind. The bush rat fled his rightful cause, reached the market and set up a lamentation. "Please save me!"—are these fitting words to hear from an ancestral mask? "There's a wild beast at my heels" is not becoming language from a hunter.
ELESIN: May the world forgive me.
IYALOJA: I came with a burden, I said. It approaches the gates which are so well guarded by those jackals whose spittle will from this day be on your food and drink. But first, tell me, you who were once Elesin Oba, tell me, you who know so well the cycle of the plantain: is it the parent shoot which withers to give sap to the younger, or does your wisdom see it running the other way?
ELESIN: I don't see your meaning, Iyaloja.
IYALOJA: Did I ask you for a meaning? I asked a question. Whose trunk withers to give sap to the other? The parent shoot or the younger?
ELESIN: The parent.
IYALOJA: Ah. So you do know that. There are sights in this world which say different, Elesin. There are some who choose to reverse the cycle of our being. Oh, you emptied bark that the world once saluted for a pith-laden being, shall I tell you what the gods have claimed of you?

---

1. In Yoruba cosmology, will is the life source that makes everything happen.

[*In her agitation she steps beyond the line indicated by* PILKINGS *and the air is rent by piercing whistles. The two* GUARDS *also leap forward and place safe-guarding hands on* ELESIN. IYALOJA *stops, astonished.* PILKINGS *comes racing in, followed by* JANE.]

PILKINGS: What is it? Did they try something?

GUARD: She stepped beyond the line.

ELESIN: [*In a broken voice.*] Let her alone. She meant no harm.

IYALOJA: Oh Elesin, see what you've become. Once you had no need to open your mouth in explanation because evil-smelling goats, itchy of hand and foot, had lost their senses. And it was a brave man indeed who dared lay hands on you because Iyaloja stepped from one side of the earth onto another. Now look at the spectacle of your life. I grieve for you.

PILKINGS: I think you'd better leave. I doubt you have done him much good by coming here. I shall make sure you are not allowed to see him again. In any case we are moving him to a different place before dawn, so don't bother to come back.

IYALOJA: We foresaw that. Hence the burden I trudged here to lay beside your gates.

PILKINGS: What was that you said?

IYALOJA: Didn't our son explain? Ask that one. He knows what it is. At least we hope the man we once knew as Elesin remembers the lesser oaths he need not break.

PILKINGS: Do you know what she is talking about?

ELESIN: Go to the gates, ghostly one. Whatever you find there, bring it to me.

IYALOJA: Not yet. It drags behind me on the slow, weary feet of women. Slow as it is, Elesin, it has long overtaken you. It rides ahead of your laggard will.

PILKINGS: What is she saying now? Christ! Must your people forever speak in riddles?

ELESIN: It will come, white man, it will come. Tell your men at the gates to let it through.

PILKINGS: [*Dubiously.*] I'll have to see what it is.

IYALOJA: You will. [*Passionately.*] But this is one oath he cannot shirk. White one, you have a king here, a visitor from your land. We know of his presence here. Tell me, were he to die would you leave his spirit roaming restlessly on the surface of earth? Would you bury him here among those you consider less than human? In your land have you no ceremonies of the dead?

PILKINGS: Yes. But we don't make our chiefs commit suicide to keep him company.

IYALOJA: Child, I have not come to help your understanding. [*Points to* ELESIN.] This is the man whose weakened understanding holds us in bondage to you. But ask him if you wish. He knows the meaning of a king's passage; he was not born yesterday. He knows the peril to the race when our dead father, who goes as intermediary, waits and waits and knows he is betrayed. He knows when the narrow gate was opened and he knows it will not stay for laggards who drag their feet in dung and vomit, whose lips are reeking of the leftovers of lesser men. He knows he has condemned our King to wander in the void of evil with beings who are enemies of life.

PILKINGS: Yes, er... but look here...
IYALOJA: What we ask is little enough. Let him release our King so he can ride on homewards alone. The messenger is on his way on the backs of women. Let him send word through the heart that is folded up within the bolt. It is the least of all his oaths, it is the easiest fulfilled.

[*The* AIDE-DE-CAMP *runs in.*]

PILKINGS: Bob?
AIDE-DE-CAMP: Sir, there's a group of women chanting up the hill.
PILKINGS: [*Rounding on* IYALOJA.] If you people want trouble...
JANE: Simon, I think that's what Olunde referred to in his letter.
PILKINGS: He knows damned well I can't have a crowd here! Damn it, I explained the delicacy of my position to him. I think it's about time I got him out of town. Bob, send a car and two or three soldiers to bring him in. I think the sooner he takes his leave of his father and gets out the better.
IYALOJA: Save your labour, white one. If it is the father of your prisoner you want, Olunde, he who until this night we knew as Elesin's son, he comes soon himself to take his leave. He has sent the women ahead, so let them in.

[PILKINGS *remains undecided.*]

AIDE-DE-CAMP: What do we do about the invasion? We can still stop them far from here.
PILKINGS: What do they look like?
AIDE-DE-CAMP: They're not many. And they seem quite peaceful.
PILKINGS: No men?
AIDE-DE-CAMP: Mm, two or three at the most.
JANE: Honestly, Simon, I'd trust Olunde. I don't think he'll deceive you about their intentions.
PILKINGS: He'd better not. Alright then, let them in, Bob. Warn them to control themselves. Then hurry Olunde here. Make sure he brings his baggage because I'm not returning him into town.
AIDE-DE-CAMP: Very good, sir. [*Goes.*]
PILKINGS: [*To* IYALOJA.] I hope you understand that if anything goes wrong it will be on your head. My men have orders to shoot at the first sign of trouble.
IYALOJA: To prevent one death you will actually make other deaths? Ah, great is the wisdom of the white race. But have no fear. Your Prince will sleep peacefully. So at long last will ours. We will disturb you no further, servant of the white King. Just let Elesin fulfil his oath and we will retire home and pay homage to our King.
JANE: I believe her, Simon, don't you?
PILKINGS: Maybe.
ELESIN: Have no fear, ghostly one. I have a message to send my King and then you have nothing more to fear.
IYALOJA: Olunde would have done it. The chiefs asked him to speak the words but he said no, not while you lived.
ELESIN: Even from the depths to which my spirit has sunk, I find some joy that this little has been left to me.

[*The* WOMEN *enter, intoning the dirge* "Alẹ lẹ lẹ" *and swaying from side to side. On their shoulders is borne a longish object roughly like a cylindrical bolt, covered in cloth. They set it down on the spot where* IYALOJA *had stood earlier, and form a semi-circle round it. The* PRAISE-SINGER *and* DRUMMER *stand on the inside of the semi-circle but the drum is not used at all. The* DRUMMER *intones under the* PRAISE-SINGER's *invocations.*]

PILKINGS: [*As they enter.*] What is *that*?
IYALOJA: The burden you have made, white one, but we bring it in peace.
PILKINGS: I said *what* is it?
ELESIN: White man, you must let me out. I have a duty to perform.
PILKINGS: I most certainly will not.
ELESIN: There lies the courier of my King. Let me out so I can perform what is demanded of me.
PILKINGS: You'll do what you need to do from inside there or not at all. I've gone as far as I intend to with this business.
ELESIN: The worshipper who lights a candle in your church to bear a message to his god bows his head and speaks in a whisper to the flame. Have I not seen it, ghostly one? His voice does not ring out to the world. Mine are no words for anyone's ears. They are not words even for the bearers of this load. They are words I must speak secretly, even as my father whispered them in my ears and I in the ears of my first-born. I cannot shout them to the wind and the open night sky.
JANE: Simon . . .
PILKINGS: Don't interfere. Please!
IYALOJA: They have slain the favourite horse of the King and slain his dog. They have borne them from pulse to pulse centre of the land receiving prayers for their King. But the rider has chosen to stay behind. Is it too much to ask that he speak his heart to heart of the waiting courier? [PILKINGS *turns his back on her.*] So be it, Elesin Oba, you see how even the mere leavings are denied you. [*She gestures to the* PRAISE-SINGER.]
PRAISE-SINGER: Elesin Oba! I call you by that name only this last time. Remember when I said, If you cannot come, tell my horse. [*Pause.*] What? I cannot hear you? I said, If you cannot come, whisper in the ears of my horse. Is your tongue severed from the roots, Elesin? I can hear no response. I said, If there are boulders you cannot climb, mount my horse's back, this spotless black stallion, he'll bring you over them. [*Pauses.*] Elesin Oba, once you had a tongue that darted like a drummer's stick. I said, If you get lost my dog will track a path to me. My memory fails me but I think you replied: My feet have found the path, Alafin.

[*The dirge rises and falls.*]

I said at the last, If evil hands hold you back, just tell my horse there is weight on the hem of your smock. I dare not wait too long.

[*The dirge rises and falls.*]

There lies the swiftest ever messenger of a king, so set me free with the errand of your heart. There lie the head and heart of the favourite of the gods, whisper in his ears. Oh my companion, if you had followed when you should, we would not say that the horse preceded its rider. If you had followed when it was time, we would not say the dog has raced beyond and left his master behind. If you had raised your will to cut the thread of life at the summons of the drums, we would not say your mere shadow fell across the gateway and took its owner's place at the banquet. But the hunter, laden with slain buffalo, stayed to root in the cricket's hole with his toes. What now is left? If there is a dearth of bats, the pigeon must serve us for the offering. Speak the words over your shadow which must now serve in your place.

ELESIN: I cannot approach. Take off the cloth. I shall speak my message from heart to heart of silence.

IYALOJA: [*Moves forward and removes the covering.*] Your courier, Elesin, cast your eyes on the favoured companion of the King.

> [*Rolled up in the mat, his head and feet showing at either end, is the body of* OLUNDE.]

There lies the honour of your household and of our race. Because he could not bear to let honour fly out of doors, he stopped it with his life. The son has proved the father, Elesin, and there is nothing left in your mouth to gnash but infant gums.

PRAISE-SINGER: Elesin, we placed the reins of the world in your hands yet you watched it plunge over the edge of the bitter precipice. You sat with folded arms while evil strangers tilted the world from its course and crashed it beyond the edge of emptiness—you muttered, There is little that one man can do, you left us floundering in a blind future. Your heir has taken the burden on himself. What the end will be, we are not gods to tell. But this young shoot has poured its sap into the parent stalk, and we know this is not the way of life. Our world is tumbling in the void of strangers, Elesin.

> [ELESIN *has stood rock-still, his knuckles taut on the bars, his eyes glued to the body of his son. The stillness seizes and paralyses everyone, including* PILKINGS, *who has turned to look. Suddenly* ELESIN *flings one arm round his neck, once, and with the loop of the chain, strangles himself in a swift, decisive pull. The* GUARDS *rush forward to stop him but they are only in time to let his body down.* PILKINGS *has leapt to the door at the same time and struggles with the lock. He rushes within, fumbles with the handcuffs and unlocks them, raises the body to a sitting position while he tries to give resuscitation. The* WOMEN *continue their dirge, unmoved by the sudden event.*]

IYALOJA: Why do you strain yourself? Why do you labour at tasks for which no one, not even the man lying there, would give you thanks? He is gone at last into the passage but oh, how late it all is. His son will feast on the meat and throw him bones. The passage is clogged with droppings from the King's stallion; he will arrive all stained in dung.

PILKINGS: [*In a tired voice.*] Was this what you wanted?

IYALOJA: No child, it is what you brought to be, you who play with strangers' lives, who even usurp the vestments of our dead, yet believe that the stain of death will not cling to you. The gods demanded only the old expired plantain but you cut down the sap-laden shoot to feed your pride. There is your board, filled to overflowing. Feast on it. [*She screams at him suddenly, seeing that* PILKINGS *is about to close* ELESIN'S *staring eyes.*] Let him alone! However sunk he was in debt he is no pauper's carrion abandoned on the road. Since when have strangers donned clothes of indigo before the bereaved cries out his loss?

[*She turns to the* BRIDE *who has remained motionless throughout.*]

Child.

[*The girl takes up a little earth, walks calmly into the cell and closes* ELESIN'S *eyes. She then pours some earth over each eyelid and comes out again.*]

IYALOJA: Now forget the dead, forget even the living. Turn your mind only to the unborn.

[*She goes off, accompanied by the* BRIDE. *The dirge rises in volume and the* WOMEN *continue their sway. Lights fade to a black-out.*]

THE END                                                                 1975

• • •

The materials that make up the rest of this chapter are included to deepen your understanding of the plays. First is a semi-autobiographical account of life in the mid-twentieth century, "Black Metropolis," written by one of the United States' most revered African American writers—Richard Wright (1908–1960), who moved from the Mississippi Delta to Chicago's South Side in the 1920s. Connections between Africa and African Americans are the main concern of the four excerpts that follow Wright's. Taken from articles and books published between 1959 and 1969, each of these excerpts offers a very different view of these connections. Finally, the chapter concludes with an excerpt that focuses on Yoruba history and culture.

RICHARD WRIGHT

# From *Twelve Million Black Voices: A Folk History of the Negro in the United States* (1941)

Perhaps never in history has a more utterly unprepared folk wanted to go to the city; we were barely born as a folk when we headed for the tall and sprawling centers of steel and stone. We, who were landless upon the land; we, who had barely managed to live in family groups; . . . we who had never belonged to any organizations except the church and burial societies; we, who had had our personalities blasted with two hundred years of slavery and had been turned loose to shift for ourselves—we were such a folk as this when we moved into a world that was destined to test all we were, that threw us into the scales of competition to weigh our mettle. And how were we to know that, the moment we landless millions of the land—we men who were struggling to be born—set our awkward feet upon the pavements of the city, life would begin to exact of us a heavy toll in death?

We did not know what would happen, what was in store for us. We went innocently, longing and hoping for a life that the Lords of the Land would not let us live. Our hearts were high as we moved northward to the cities. What emotions, fears, what a complex of sensations we felt when, looking out of a train window at the revolving fields, we first glimpsed the sliding waters of the gleaming Ohio! What memories that river evoked in us, memories black and gloomy, yet tinged with the bright border of a wild and desperate hope! The Ohio is more than a river. It is a symbol, a line that runs through our hearts, dividing hope from despair, just as once it bisected the nation, dividing freedom from slavery.

* * *

[Once in the North] we . . . live in the clinging soot just beyond the factory areas, behind the railroad tracks, near the river banks, under the viaducts, by the steel and iron mills, on the edges of the coal and lumber yards. We live in crowded, barn-like rooms, in old rotting buildings where once dwelt rich native whites of a century ago. . . . When we return home at night from our jobs, we are afraid to venture into other sections of the city, for we fear that the white boys will gang up and molest us. When we do go out into white neighborhoods, we always go in crowds, for that is the best mode of protection.

White people say that they are afraid of us, and it often makes us laugh. When they see one of us, they either smile with contempt or amusement. . . . When they see *six* of us, they become downright apprehensive and alarmed. And because they are afraid of us, we are afraid of them. Especially do we feel fear when we meet the gangs of white boys who have been taught—at home and at school—that we black folk are making their parents lose their homes and life's savings because we have moved into their neighborhoods.

They say our presence in their neighborhoods lowers the value of their property. We do not understand why this should be so. We are poor; but they were once poor, too. They make up their minds, because othes tell them to, that they must move at once if we rent an apartment near them. Having been warned against us by the Bosses of the Buildings, having heard tall tales about us, about how "bad" we are, they react emotionally as though we had the plague when we move into their neighborhoods. Is it any wonder, then, that their homes are suddenly and drastically reduced in value? They hastily abandon them, sacrificing them to the Bosses of the Buildings....

And the Bosses of the Buildings take these old houses and convert them into "kitchenettes," and then rent them to us at rates so high that they make fabulous fortunes before the houses are too old for habitation. What they do is this: they take, say, a seven-room apartment, . . . and cut it up into seven small apartments, of one room each; they install one small gas stove and one small sink in each room.

\* \* \*

Sometimes five or six of us live in a one-room kitchenette, a place where simple folk such as we should never be held captive. A war sets up in our emotions: one part of our feelings tells us that it is good to be in the city, that we have a chance at life here, that we need but turn a corner to become a stranger, that we no longer need bow and dodge at the sight of the Lords of the Land. Another part of our feelings tells us that, in terms of worry and strain, the cost of living in the kitchenettes is too high, that the city heaps too much responsibility upon us and gives too little security in return.

The kitchenette is the author of the glad tidings that new suckers are in town, ready to be cheated, plundered, and put in their places.

The kitchenette is our prison, our death sentence without a trial, the new form of mob violence that assaults not only the lone individual, but all of us, in its ceaseless attacks.

The kitchenette, with its filth and foul air, with its one toilet for thirty or more tenants, kills our black babies so fast that in many cities twice as many of them die as white babies.

The kitchenette is the seed bed for scarlet fever, dysentery, typhoid, tuberculosis, gonorrhea, syphilis, pneumonia, and malnutrition.

The kitchenette scatters death so widely among us that our death rate exceeds our birth rate, and if it were not for the trains and autos bringing us daily into the city from the plantations, we black folks who dwell in northern cities would die out entirely over the course of a few years.

The kitchenette, with its crowded rooms and incessant bedlam, provides an enticing place for crimes of all sort—crimes against women and children or any stranger who happens to stray into its dark hallways. The noise of our living, boxed in stone and steel, is so loud that even a pistol shot is smothered.

The kitchenette throws desperate and unhappy people into an unbearable closeness of association, thereby increasing latent friction, giving birth to never-ending quarrels of recrimination, accusation, and vindictiveness, producing warped personalities.

The kitchenette injects pressure and tension into our individual personalities, making many of us give up the struggle, walk off and leave wives, husbands, and even children behind to shift as best they can.

The kitchenette creates thousands of one-room homes where our black mothers sit, deserted, with their children about their knees.

The kitchenette blights the personalities of our growing children, disorganizes them, blinds them to hope, creates problems whose effects can be traced in the characters of its child victims for years afterward.

The kitchenette jams our farm girls, while still in their teens, into rooms with men who are restless and stimulated by the noise and lights of the city; and more of our girls have bastard babies than the girls in any other sections of the city.

The kitchenette fills our black boys with longing and restlessness, urging them to run off from home, to join together with other restless black boys in gangs, that brutal form of city courage.

The kitchenette piles up mountains of profits for the Bosses of the Buildings and makes them ever more determined to keep things as they are.

The kitchenette reaches out with fingers full of golden bribes to the officials of the city, persuading them to allow old firetraps to remain standing and occupied long after they should have been torn down.

The kitchenette is the funnel through which our pulverized lives flow to ruin and death on the city pavements, at a profit....

\* \* \*

Despite our new worldliness, ... we keep our churches alive. In fact, we have built more of them than ever here on the city pavements, for it is only when we are within the walls of our churches that we are wholly ourselves, that we keep alive a sense of our personalities in relation to the total world in which we live, that we maintain a quiet and constant communion with all that is deepest in us. Our going to church of a Sunday is like placing one's ear to another's chest to hear the unquenchable murmur of the human heart. In our collective outpourings of song and prayer, the fluid emotions of others make us feel the strength in ourselves.... Our churches are where we dip our tired bodies in cool springs of hope, where we retain our wholeness and humanity....

Our churches are centers of social and community life, for we have virtually no other mode of communion and we are usually forbidden to worship God in the temples of the Bosses of the Buildings....

In the Black Belts of the northern cities, our women are the most circumscribed and tragic objects to be found in our lives, and it is to the churches that our black women cling for emotional security and the release of their personalities. Because their orbit of life is narrow—from their kitchenette to the white folk's kitchen and back home again—they love the church more than do our men, who find a large measure of the expression of their lives in the mills and factories. Surrounding our black women are many almost insuperable barriers: they are black, they are women, they are workers; they are triply anchored and restricted in their movements within and without the Black Belts.

So they keep thousands of Little Bethels and Pilgrims and Calvarys and White Rocks and Good Hopes and Mount Olives going with their nickels and dimes. ... Sometimes, even in crowded northern cities, elderly black women, hungry for the South but afraid to return, will cultivate tiny vegetable gardens in the narrow squares of ground in front of their hovels.

\* \* \*

Many of our children scorn us; they say that we still wear the red bandanna about our heads, that we are still Uncle Toms. We lean upon our God and scold our children and try to drag them to church with us, but just as we once, years ago, left the plantation to roam the South, so now they leave us for the city pavements. But deep down in us we are glad that our children feel the world hard enough to yearn to wrestle with it. We, the mothers and fathers of the black children, try to hold them back from death, but if we persuade them to stay, or if they come back because we call them, we will pour out our pity upon them. Always our deepest love is toward those children of ours who turn their backs upon our way of life, for our instincts tell us that those brave ones who struggle against death are the ones who bring new life into the world, even though they die to do so, even though our hearts are broken when they die.

We watch strange moods fill our children, and our hearts swell with pain. The streets, with their noise and flaring lights, the taverns, the automobiles, and the poolrooms claim them, and no voice of ours can call them back. They spend their nights away from home; they forget our ways of life, our language, our God. Their swift speech and impatient eyes make us feel weak and foolish. We cannot keep them in school.... We fall upon our knees and pray for them, but in vain. The city has beaten us, evaded us; but they, with young bodies filled with warm blood, feel bitter and frustrated at the sight of the alluring hopes and prizes denied them. It is not their eagerness to fight that makes us afraid, but that they go to death on the city pavements faster than even disease and starvation can take them.... [T]he courts and the morgues become crowded with our lost children....

**EARL E. THORPE**

# From *Africa in the Thought of Negro Americans* (1959)

The continent of Africa is daily growing in economic, political, and cultural significance. Recently a Negro newspaper in St. Louis, Missouri contained the statement that the newly independent state of Ghana holds a significance for Negro Americans which is comparable to that which Israel holds for Jewish Americans. How much truth is there in such a statement? Or better still, what does Africa and its history mean to American Negroes? Opinions on this vary greatly, for in an opposite vein from that contained in the St. Louis newspaper, recently the most eminent of all Negro Sociologists[1] stated that most educated Negroes have little but contempt and disdain for Africa and its peoples.

\* \* \*

What is the truth between these two rather extreme views? While the following does not give a categorical answer to this question, ... a survey of the statements which Afro-Americans have made from time to time respecting this continent and its peoples may shed light on the question.

\* \* \*

---

1. E. Franklin Frazier (1894–1962), author of several influential sociological studies of African American life and first black president of the American Sociological Society.

In the early decades of the nineteenth century, the work of the American Colonization Society and the founding of Liberia projected Africa into the thought of Negroes in America as never before.... [M]any slaves became possessed by the dream and hope of being freed and sent to Africa....

But if the slave regarded expatriation to Africa as a welcome eventuality, the majority of free Negroes, many of whom were active abolitionists, did not share this attitude. Through mass meetings, orations, petitions, editorials, letters, and other means they remonstrated against the effort to remove them from the United States. Yet the free Negroes revealed ambivalence in their attitude toward Africa. When they were describing the kidnapping of their forebearers from the ancestral home and the horrors of the slave trade, they painted the continent and its people in beautiful glowing terms, but when efforts were made to force free Negroes to "return" to Africa, the overwhelming majority refused to go there and depicted Africa and its people in a quite different light.

\* \* \*

... [I]n the antebellum period, Afro-Americans evidenced a desire to help lift Africa to a greater respectability through extending Christianity to the continent. In his 1827 address on the occasion of New York's emancipation of slaves, the Reverend Nathaniel Paul hoped that his race might yet produce "one whose devotedness towards the cause of God, and whose zeal for the salvation of Africa, shall cause him to leave the land which gave him birth and cross the Atlantic, eager to plant the standard of the cross upon every hill of that vast continent, that has hitherto ignobly submitted to the haleful crescent, or crouched under the iron bondage of the vilest superstition."

Previous to W. E. B. Du Bois, George Washington Williams was the most distinguished of all Negro historians. Together with the colored abolitionists, and most Negro historians of the nineteenth century, Williams accepted many of the then-current stereotypes about his race. However, Williams and others tended to assign to Afro-Americans only the stereotypes which were favorable and to leave the remainder for Negroes who were still in Africa.... [O]f the African, he declared:

> The Negro type is the result of degradation. It is nothing more than the lowest strata of the African race.... His blood infected with the poison of his low habitation, his body shrivelled by disease, his intellect veiled in pagan superstitions, the noblest yearnings of his soul strangled at birth by the savage passions of a nature abandoned to sensuality,—the poor Negro of Africa deserves more our pity than our contempt.

\* \* \*

After the brief flurry of talk in the 1880s and '90s about emigration to Africa, and a mild protest against late nineteenth century imperialism, Afro-American interest in the so-called "Dark Continent" appears to have subsided until the 1920s, when, coincident with the Harlem or Negro Renaissance, interest in Africa burgeoned anew. W. E. B. Du Bois led in the sponsorship of meetings designed to bring Negroid peoples closer together. The first Pan-African Congress, held in Paris in 1919, ... was attended by fifty-seven delegates from the United States of America, the West Indies, and Africa. Racial concord and advancement were the primary objectives. In 1921 a second Pan-African Congress was held which drew 113 delegates to Europe, two years later a third was held, and the last Congress met in New York City in 1927.

\* \* \*

While most Afro-Americans have wished to be a part of the midstream of [American] national life and culture, not all have wanted this integration. A few, either because they felt that the race actually is inferior and could not compete with whites, or because they went to the opposite extreme and came to believe that Negroes were superior and would lose their distinctive qualities, have desired continued segregation in some form, either here or abroad. Marcus Garvey belonged to the latter group....

The movement of the 1920s with which the West Indian immigrant Marcus Garvey has been prominently identified, revolved around an organization called the Universal Improvement Association. Centered in the North, though by no means limited to it, this movement had its genesis in the World War I stimulus to the desire for equality. But while it originated out of the desire for a full share in democracy, the movement really fed on the lynchings . . . and racial strife which characterized the twenties, and on the growing maturity of the race. Sharing the pessimism and disillusionment, as well as the optimism of the period, Marcus Garvey became convinced that the position of his race within the United States was eternally without hope. Thus he advocated a "back to Africa" movement, and in step with the new appreciation which artists and scholars were beginning to show for African culture, Garvey created a veritable cult of blackness. Reacting against the contempt for dark complexions which many white and Negro Americans held, he proclaimed that black is actually the best and "superior" color. Since it coincided with the efforts of . . . scholars in the social sciences, as well as with . . . trends in art, music, and creative literature, the movement "put steel into the spine of many Negroes who had previously been ashamed of their color." Especially did Garveyism appeal to lower class Negroes, and even yet it represents the nearest semblance to a mass movement which has existed among Afro-Americans. Most Negro organizations and intellectuals opposed the movement, however.

\* \* \*

With the Depression of the thirties and the events leading to World War II, in many ways Afro-American thought gained a new international concern, and Africa, long the focal point of the international interests of Negro Americans, became more integrated in a larger world setting....

During the thirties Negro historians reflected this continuing interest in Africa. Appearing in this general period were [Carter G.] Woodson's *The African Background Outlined* and *African Heroes and Heroines*.... "History should be reconstructed," declared Charles Wesley, "so that Africa . . . shall have its proper place." This was a major theme with Negro historians of the period.... About one-third of Du Bois's *Black Folk Then and Now*, published in 1939, deals with the African background of the Afro-American, and in 1947 this same author's *The World and Africa* was published.... [T]he author stated that he was seeking to "remind readers of . . . how critical a part Africa has played in human history, past and present, and how impossible it is to forget this and rightly explain the present plight of mankind."

\* \* \*

[T]he prominence of the African theatre of battle during the early years of the war, participation of native African troops in the allied cause, and the possible demise of colonialism as a consequence of the war kept Africa prominent in the thought of Negro Americans. With the return of peace, Afro-American race consciousness and pride were bolstered not only by the phenomenal overthrow of imperialism and colonialism by yellow, brown and black people in Asia and Africa, but by the dramatic achievements in racial integration within their own country. And just as the personality and efforts of Mahatma Gandhi had inspired Afro-Americans in the twenties and thirties, he, Kwame Nkrumah, Jomo Kenyatta, Gamel Nasser,[2] and other nationalist leaders in Asia and Africa were great sources of inspiration to them in the late forties and fifties.

It seems almost paradoxical that rampant nationalism in Asia and Africa have evoked a greater internationalism in the thought of Afro-Americans.

... In the fifties, in *Black Power*, Richard Wright lifted his cudgel in defense of nationalist aspirations in Africa, while Era Bell Thompson struck a similar note in her *Land of My Fathers*.... [B]oth Wright and Thompson based their convictions on direct observation of conditions in Africa. Indeed, a dominant characteristic of the mid-twentieth century Negro vis-a-vis Africa is the greatly increased number who have visited that continent.... This travel is helping to dispel much of the ignorance about Africa and Africans which has been evident among Negro Americans. Thus many of the old stereotypes once commonly accepted are now rapidly being discarded.

\* \* \*

As a consequence of the degradation of slavery, Negroes have been unique among Americans in the rejection of the land of their fathers. Now a greater maturity and developing race pride are bringing an end to this rejection, and it would not be surprising, to the present writer at least, to see the masses of Afro-Americans soon embrace Africa with a force comparable to that which the Irish and Jewish Americans show for the lands of their fathers.

PHAON GOLDMAN

## From *The Significance of African Freedom for the Negro American* (1960)

With Africa in the headlines every day it behooves us as alert, adult Americans, to know more about Africa and her peoples and the new nations being born almost monthly on this the world's second largest continent. One of my professors used to say that all we know (as Negro Americans) about Africa was that it was shaped like a "po'k chop"—and it is, too, if you'll notice the map. It's a pork chop that's sizzling nowadays.

---

2. Gamel Nasser (1918–1970), first president of the republic of Egypt (1956–70). Kwame Nkrumah (1909–1972), first prime minister, then first president, of Ghana (1957–66). Jomo Kenyatta (1893–1978), first president of Kenya (1964–78).

Africa is significant not only because it's in the news, but also because we have an ancestral connection with the peoples of Africa—a connection we need to review and re-appraise. We have only heard since we were wee tots about Africa in terms of the exotic, the outlandish—land of cannibals, slithering snakes, and people who go around boiling missionaries in a pot. These are the one-sided views of Africa we have been taught; these would furnish material for books and movies that would sell. Seldom, if ever, did we hear the appraisals of Africa made by the most learned scholars of old, such as Ibn Batuda, greatest of the Moslem travelers of the Middle Ages—a man who had traveled throughout most of the then known world, said this of West Africa (in contrast to Spain, Syria, India, China, Turkey, etc.), "Nowhere is there a higher regard for justice or greater security. One can travel throughout the kingdom of the blacks without fear of thieves, robbers, vagabonds, or other evil persons." ...

\* \* \*

There is also another instance of our background and connection with Africa which we have come to see only in one light, and that is our outlook on the system of slavery—the instrument that brought us to these shores. When we think of slavery we too often visualize happy-go-lucky slaves captured easily and without a struggle. But the truth of the matter is that the Portuguese, Dutch, and British, fought many a pitched battle to capture most of the Africans that were taken into slavery. Those men, sold into the chains of the European slave-traders by other Africans, were most often warriors who had been captured in inter-village battles. Tens of thousands of these men died by their own hand on the long middle passage rather than submit to that day's form of man's inhumanity to man. So you can see that our ancestors represent not a bunch of cringing cowards but the most valiant of men in body and spirit.

\* \* \*

The valor and sense of justice of the ancient peoples of West Africa can most clearly be seen ... in the determined, forthright, and courageous stand for freedom now being taken by our young Negro youth of the South who in spite of threats, insults, and violence, stand by their right to be accorded the simple human decencies that all other people on earth get in America. The strength of our forefathers is with us still, and make no mistake about it, the students' inspiration came from the fight for freedom now being waged all over the African continent ....

These are sides of our past which have been deliberately buried, for if a man can convince you that you came from nothing, that you are nothing, and that you never will be anything, he doesn't need to worry about you trying to break down segregation barriers, for he has already convinced you that you are different from other human beings and you will be content with your lot.

There are other ways in which we have come to disrespect ourselves too—subtle ways, ways that affect our subconscious mind and blunt our demand for "Freedom Now," and the human dignity accorded all other peoples.

\* \* \*

[One] subconscious factor causing us to feel we're different from others and therefore perhaps should be treated differently, is the American standard of beauty.... [T]he faces we see on TV, in the movies and in the magazine ads, reflect the Anglo-Saxon characteristics of the thin nose, a white skin, and straight hair. Being a minority people of physically diametrically opposite characteristics, but set down in the middle of other values, we begin to subconsciously feel that we need to make ourselves over, physically, in order to become acceptable to the majority. So we're told that certain skin preparations will make us "lighter, brighter and more acceptable" and similar positive attributes are assigned to hair preparations that give us 'straight' hair instead of the curly variety we have.

* * *

So to sum up, with Africa in the news every day we must re-view our past concepts of Africa and our relations with the African people, we must view their current battle for "Freedom Now" through the pressures of boycotts, strikes, and mass protests as that stage of man's eternal quest for human dignity that brings the issues out into the open and forces a decision. We must keep ever in mind that the cry of "Freedom Now" is but the present day application of the ideas of men like Thomas Jefferson and Patrick Henry whose cry of "Give me liberty or give me death" brought freedom to this country and still inspires men to fight for freedom around the world.

Perhaps the greatest significance of African freedom for the Negro American is that it may light the way for those of us of African descent here in America to re-vitalize America's conscience by moving together now for our freedom and force America to solve her moral dilemma of the race question and resume her rightful place as a world leader by showing in deed as well as in preachment that she is truly the land of "liberty and justice for all."

NAACP POLITICAL ACTION COMMITTEE

## STOKELY CARMICHAEL AND CHARLES V. HAMILTON

### From *Black Power: The Politics of Liberation in America* (1967)

... [B]lack people in this country form a colony, and it is not in the interest of the colonial power to liberate them. Black people are legal citizens of the United States with, for the most part, the same *legal* rights as other citizens. Yet they stand as colonial subjects in relation to the white society. Thus institutional racism has another name: colonialism.

Obviously, the analogy is not perfect. One normally associates a colony with a land and people subjected to, and physically separated from, the "Mother Country." This is not always the case, however; in South Africa and Rhodesia, black and white inhabit the same land—with blacks subordinated to whites just as in the English, French, Italian, Portuguese, and Spanish colonies. It is the objective relationship which counts, not rhetoric (such as constitutions *articulating* equal rights) or geography.

The analogy is not perfect in another respect. Under classic colonialism, the colony is a source of cheaply produced raw materials (usually agricultural or mineral) which the "Mother Country" then processes into finished goods and sells at high profit—sometimes back to the colony itself. The black communities of the United States do not export anything except human labor. But is the differentiation more than a technicality? Essentially, the African colony is selling its labor; the product itself does not belong to the "subjects" because the land is not theirs. At the same time, let us look at the black people of the South: cultivating cotton at $3.00 for a ten-hour day and from that buying cotton dresses (and food and other goods) from white manufacturers.... Black people in the United States have a colonial relationship to the larger society, a relationship characterized by institutional racism. That colonial status operates in three areas—political, economic, social....

Colonial subjects have their political decisions made for them by the colonial masters, and those decisions are handed down directly or through a process of "indirect rule." Politically, decisions which affect black lives have always been made by white people—the "white power structure."

\* \* \*

The black community perceives the "white power structure" in very concrete terms. The man in the ghetto sees his white landlord come only to collect exorbitant rents and fail to make necessary repairs, while both know that the white-dominated city building inspection department will wink at violations or impose only slight fines. The man in the ghetto sees the white policeman on the corner brutally manhandle a black drunkard in a doorway, and at the same time accept a pay-off from one of the agents of the white-controlled rackets.... He looks at the absence of a meaningful curriculum in the ghetto schools—for example, the history books that woefully overlook the historical achievements of black people—and he knows that the school board is controlled by whites. He is not about to listen to intellectual discourses on the pluralistic and fragmented nature of political power. He is faced with a "white power structure" as monolithic as Europe's colonial offices have been to African and Asian colonies.

There is another aspect of colonial politics frequently found in colonial Africa and in the United States: the process of indirect rule.... In other words, the white power structure rules the black community through local blacks who are responsive to the white leaders, the downtown, white machine, not to the black populace. These black politicians do not exercise effective power. They cannot be relied upon to make forceful demands in behalf of their black constituents, and they become no more than puppets.

\* \* \*

This process of cooptation and a subsequent widening of the gap between the black elites and the masses is common under colonial rule. There has developed in this country an entire class of "captive leaders" in the black communities. These are black people with certain technical and administrative skills who could provide useful leadership roles in the black communities but do not because they have become beholden to the white power structure. These are black school teachers, county agents, junior executives in management positions with companies, etc....

Historically, colonies have existed for the sole purpose of enriching, in one form or another, the "colonizer"; the consequence is to maintain the economic dependency of the "colonized." All too frequently we hear of the missionary motive behind colonization: to "civilize," to "Christianize" the underdeveloped, backward peoples.... One is immediately reminded of the bitter maxim voiced by many black Africans today: the missionaries came for our goods, not for our good. Indeed, the missionaries turned the Africans' eyes toward heaven, and then robbed them blind in the process.

\* \* \*

Professor Kenneth Clark described the economic colonization of the *Dark Ghetto* [1965] as follows:

> The ghetto feeds upon itself; it does not produce goods or contribute to the prosperity of the city. It has few large businesses.... Even though the white community has tried to keep the Negro confined in ghetto pockets, the white businessman has not stayed out of the ghetto. A ghetto, too, offers opportunities for profit, and in a competitive society profit is to be made where it can.
>
> In Harlem there is only one large department store and that is owned by whites. Negroes own a savings and loan association; and one Negro-owned bank has recently been organized. The other banks are branches of white-owned downtown banks. Property—apartment houses, stores, businesses, bars, concessions, and theaters—are for the most part owned by persons who live outside the community and take their profits home...
>
> When tumult arose in ghetto streets in the summer of 1964, most of the stores broken into and looted belonged to white men. Many of these owners responded to the destruction with bewilderment and anger, for they felt that they had been serving a community that needed them. *They did not realize* that the residents were not grateful for this service but bitter, as natives often feel toward the functionaries of a colonial power who in the very act of service, keep the hated *structure of oppression intact.*

\* \* \*

This is not to say that every single white American consciously oppresses black people. He does not need to. Institutional racism has been maintained deliberately by the power structure and through indifference, inertia and lack of courage on the part of white masses as well as petty officials. Whenever black demands for change become loud and strong, indifference is replaced by active opposition based on fear and self-interest. The line between purposeful suppression and indifference blurs. One way or another, most whites participate in economic colonialism.

\* \* \*

The social and psychological effects on black people of all their degrading experiences are also very clear.... Born into this society today, black people begin to doubt themselves, their worth as human beings. Self-respect becomes almost impossible. Kenneth Clark describes the process in *Dark Ghetto*:

> Human beings who are forced to live under ghetto conditions and whose daily experience tells them that almost nowhere in society are they respected

and granted the ordinary dignity and courtesy accorded to others will, as a matter of course, begin to doubt their own worth. Since every human being depends upon his cumulative experiences with others for clues as to how he should view and value himself, children who are consistently rejected understandably begin to question and doubt whether they, their family, and their group really deserve no more respect from the larger society than they receive. These doubts become the seeds of a pernicious self- and group-hatred, the Negro's complex and debilitating prejudice against himself.

The preoccupation of many Negroes with hair straighteners, skin bleachers, and the like illustrates this tragic aspect of American racial prejudice—Negroes have come to believe in their own inferiority.

There was the same result in Africa. . . .

In a manner similar to that of the colonial powers in Africa, American society indicates avenues of escape from the ghetto for those individuals who adapt to the "mainstream." This adaptation means to disassociate oneself from the black race, its culture, community and heritage, and become immersed (dispersed is another term) in the white world. What actually happens, as Professor E. Franklin Frazier pointed out in his book, *Black Bourgeoisie* [1957], is that the black person ceases to identify himself with black people yet is obviously unable to assimilate with whites. He becomes a "marginal man," living on the fringes of both societies in a world largely of "make believe." This black person is urged to adopt American middle-class standards and values. As with the black African who had to become a "Frenchman" in order to be accepted, so to be an American, the black man must strive to become "white." To the extent that he does, he is considered "well adjusted"—one who has "risen above the race question." These people are frequently held up by the white Establishment as living examples of the progress being made by the society in solving the race problem. Suffice it to say that precisely because they are required to denounce—overtly or covertly—their black race, *they are reinforcing racism in this country.*

## ROBERT BLAUNER

### From *Internal Colonialism and Ghetto Revolt* (1969)

Colonialism traditionally refers to the establishment of domination over a geographically external political unit, most often inhabited by people of a different race and culture, where this domination is political and economic, and the colony exists subordinated to and dependent upon the mother country. Typically the colonizers exploit the land, the raw materials, the labor, and other resources of the colonized nation; in addition a formal recognition is given to the difference in power, autonomy, and political status, and various agencies are set up to maintain this subordination.

\* \* \*

Classic colonialism involved the control and exploitation of the majority of a nation by a minority of outsiders. Whereas in America the people who are oppressed were themselves originally outsiders and are a numerical minority.

* * *

[T]he classical colonialism of the imperialist era and American racism developed out of the same historical situation and reflected a common world economic and power stratification. The slave trade for the most part preceded the imperialist partition and economic exploitation of Africa, and in fact may have been a necessary prerequisite for colonial conquest—since it helped deplete and pacify Africa, undermining the resistance to direct occupation. Slavery contributed one of the basic raw materials for the textile industry which provided much of the capital for the West's industrial development and need for economic expansionism. The essential condition for both American slavery and European colonialism was the power domination and the technological superiority of the Western world in its relation to peoples of non-Western and non-white origins. This objective supremacy in technology and military power buttressed the West's sense of cultural superiority, laying the basis for racist ideologies that were elaborated to justify control and exploitation of non-white people. Thus because classical colonialism and America's internal version developed out of a similar balance of technological, cultural, and power relations, a common *process* of social oppression characterized the racial patterns in the two contexts—despite the variation in political and social structure.

* * *

The crucial difference between the colonized Americans and the ethnic immigrant minorities is that the latter have always been able to operate fairly competitively within that relatively open section of the social and economic order because these groups came voluntarily in search of a better life, because their movements in society were not administratively controlled, and because they transformed their culture at their own pace—giving up ethnic values and institutions when it was seen as a desirable exchange for improvements in social position.

In present-day America, a major device of Black colonization is the powerless ghetto....

Of course many ethnic groups in America have lived in ghettoes. What make the Black ghettoes an expression of colonized status are three special features. First, the ethnic ghettoes arose more from voluntary choice, both in the sense of the choice to immigrate to America and the decision to live among one's fellow ethnics. Second, the immigrant ghettoes tended to be one and two generation phenomenon; they were actually way-stations in the process of acculturation and assimilation.... The Black ghetto on the other hand has been a more permanent phenomenon, although some individuals do escape it. But most relevant is the third point. European ethnic groups like the Poles, Italians, and Jews generally only experienced a brief period, often less than a generation, during which their residential buildings, commercial stores, and other enterprises were owned by outsiders. The Chinese and Japanese faced handicaps of color prejudice that were almost as strong as the Blacks faced, but very soon gained control of their internal communities, because their traditional ethnic culture and social organization had not been destroyed by slavery and internal colonization. But Afro-Americans are distinct in the extent to which their segregated communities have remained controlled economically, politically, and administratively from the outside...

... [T]he most important expressions of protest in the Black community during the recent years reflect the colonized status of Afro-America. Riots, programs of separation, politics of community control, the Black revolutionary movements, and cultural nationalism each represent a different strategy of attack on domestic colonialism in America. Let us now examine some of these movements.

* * *

Despite the appeal of Frantz Fanon[1] to young Black revolutionaries, America is not Algeria. It is difficult to foresee how riots in our cities can play a role equivalent to rioting in the colonial situation as an integral phase in a movement for national liberation.

* * *

But despite the difference in objective conditions, the violence of the 1960s seems to serve the same psychic function, assertions of dignity and manhood for young Blacks in urban ghettoes, as it did for the colonized of North Africa described by Fanon. ...

Cultural conflict is generic to the colonial relation because colonization involves the domination of Western technological values over the more communal cultures of non-Western peoples. Colonialism played havoc with the national integrity of the peoples it brought under its sway. ...

The most total destruction of culture in the colonization process took place not in traditional colonialism but in America. ... [T]he integral cultures of the diverse African peoples who furnished the slave trade were destroyed because slaves from different tribes, kingdoms, and linguistic groups were purposely separated to maximize domination and control. Thus language, religion, and national loyalties were lost in North America much more completely than [elsewhere] ...

Yet a similar cultural process unfolds in both contexts of colonialism. To the extent that they are involved in the larger society and economy, the colonized are caught up in a conflict between two cultures. Fanon has described how the assimilation-oriented schools of Martinique taught him to reject his own culture and Blackness in favor of Westernized, French, and white values. Both the colonized elites under traditional colonialism and perhaps the majority of Afro-Americans today experience a parallel split in identity, cultural loyalty, and political orientation.

The colonizers use their culture to socialize the colonized elites (intellectuals, politicians, and middle class) into an identification with the colonial system. Because Western culture has the prestige, the power, and the key to open the limited opportunity that a minority of the colonized may achieve, the first reaction seems to be an acceptance of the dominant values.

Cultural revitalization movements play a key role in anti-colonial movements. They follow an inner necessity and logic of their own that comes from the consequences of colonialism on groups and personal identities; they are also essential to provide the solidarity which the political or military phase of the anti-colonial

---

1. Fanon (1925–1961), French West Indian psychiatrist, leader of the Algerian National Front, and author of the influential anticolonial works *Black Skin, White Masks* (1952) and *The Wretched of the Earth* (1961).

revolution requires.... That Afro-Americans are moving toward cultural nationalism in a period when ethnic loyalties tend to be weak (and perhaps on the decline) in this country is another confirmation of the unique colonized position of the Black group.

## HENRY JOHN DREWAL, JOHN PEMBERTON III, AND ROWLAND ABIODUN

### From *Yoruba: Nine Centuries of African Art and Thought* (1989)

The Yoruba-speaking peoples of Nigeria and the Popular Republic of Benin, together with their countless descendants in other parts of Africa and the Americas, have made remarkable contributions to world civilization.[1] Their urbanism is ancient and legendary, probably dating to A.D. 800–1000, according to the results of archeological excavations at two ancient city sites, Oyo and Ife.[2] These were only two of numerous complex city-states headed by sacred rulers (both women and men) and councils of elders and chiefs. Many have flourished up to our own time. The dynasty of kings at Ife, for example, regarded by the Yoruba as the place of origin of life itself and of human civilization, remains unbroken to the present day.

In the arts, the Yoruba are heirs to one of the oldest and finest artistic traditions in Africa, a tradition that remains vital and influential today. By A.D. 1100 the artists at Ife had already developed an exquisitely refined and highly naturalistic sculptural tradition in terracotta and stone that was soon followed by works in copper, brass and bronze....

Of the series of remarkable Yoruba kingdoms over the last nine centuries, one of the earliest was Oyo, sited near the Niger River, the "Nile" of West Africa. Straddling this important trading corridor Oyo and its feared cavalry flourished between 1600 and 1830 and came to dominate a vast territory....

The Ijebu Yoruba kingdoms (1400–1900)... were the first Yoruba to establish trading ties with Europeans in the late fifteenth century. Over the next four centuries, the Yoruba kingdoms prospered and then declined as the devastating effects of the slave trade and internecine warfare of the nineteenth century took their toll. The stage was set for the ascendancy of the British and the advent of colonial rule at the end of the nineteenth century.

One of the effects of eighteenth- and nineteenth-century disruptions was the dispersal of millions of Yoruba peoples over the globe, primarily to the Americas—Haiti, Cuba, Trinidad, and Brazil—where their late arrival and enormous

---

1. Throughout this [selection] we use the term Yoruba as shorthand for Yoruba-speaking peoples who historically identified themselves by their independent but interactive city-states, such as Ife, Ijebu, Owo, Ekiti, Oyo, and others. Despite significant cultural diversity, Yoruba-speaking peoples assert their common origins at Ile-Ife and share certain fundamental social, political, religious, philosophical, and artistic concepts that justify the now widely used and accepted designation of Yoruba.
2. See R. S. Smith, *Kingdoms of the Yoruba* (London: Methuen, 1969).

numbers ensured a strong Yoruba character in the artistic, religious, and social lives of Africans in the New World. That imprint persists today in many arts and in a variety of African-American faiths that have arisen not only in the Caribbean and South America, but also in urban centers across the United States.[3] Yoruba philosophical, religious, and artistic tenets, ideas, and icons have transformed and continue to transform religious beliefs and practices and the arts of persons far beyond Africa's shores.

There are several fundamental concepts that are distinctive to a Yoruba world view.

## The Yoruba Cosmos

The Yoruba conceive of the cosmos as consisting of two distinct yet inseparable realms—*aye* (the visible, tangible world of the living) and *orun* (the invisible, spiritual realm of the ancestors, gods, and spirits) (see the diagram on p. 2067)....

... [T]he Yoruba conceive of the past as accessible and essential as a model for the present. They believe that persons live, depart, and are reborn and that every individual comes from either the gods or one's ancestors on the mother's or the father's side. In addition, rituals are efficacious only when they are performed regularly according to tenets from the past and creatively re-presented to suit the present.

## Orun: The Otherworld

Olodumare (also known as Odumare, Olorun, Eleda, Eleemi) is conceived as the creator of existence, without sexual identity and generally distant, removed from the affairs of both divine and worldly beings. Olodumare is the source of *ase*, the life force possessed by everything that exists. *Orun* (the otherworld), the abode of the sacred, is populated by countless forces such as *orisa* (gods), *ara orun* (ancestors) and *oro, iwin, ajogun*, and *egbe* (various spirits), who are close to the living and frequently involved in human affairs.

The *orisa* are deified ancestors and/or personified natural forces. They are grouped broadly into two categories depending upon their personalities and modes of action—the "cool, temperate, symbolically white gods" (*orisa funfun*), and the "hot, temperamental gods" (*orisa gbigbona*). The former tend to be gentle, soothing, calm, and reflective and include: Obatala/Orisanla, the divine sculptor; Osoosi/Eyinle, hunter and water lord; Osanyin, lord of leaves and medicines; Oduduwa, first monarch at Ile-Ife; Yemoja, Osun, Yewa, and Oba, queens of their respective rivers; Olosa, ruler of the lagoon; and Olokun, goddess of the sea. Many of the "hot gods" are male, although some are female. They include: Ogun, god of Iron; Sango, former king of Oyo and lord of thunder; Obaluaye, lord of pestilence; and Oya, Sango's wife and queen of the whirlwind. The latter tend to be harsh, demanding, aggressive and quick-tempered.

This characterization of the *orisa* has nothing to do with issues of good and evil. All gods, like humans, possess both positive and negative values—strengths as well as foibles. Only their modes of action differ, which is the actualization of their distinctive *ase* (life force), as expressed by their natures or personalities (*iwa*). Furthermore, the gods are not ranked in any hierarchy. Their relative

---

3. The African-American religious communities include Lucumi, Candomble, Shango, Santeria, Vodun, Umbanda, and Macumba.

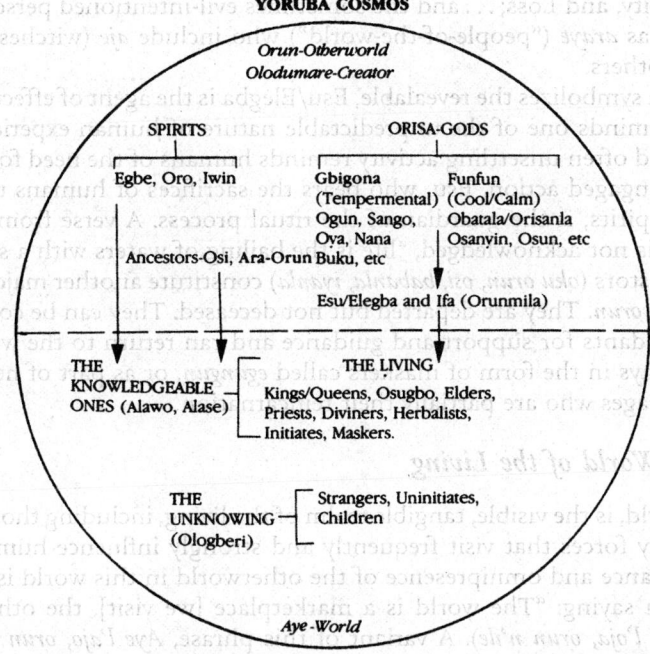

A diagram of some of the key elements of the Yoruba cosmos. It consists of two distinct yet interactive realms—*aye*, the tangible world of the living and *orun*, the invisible realm of spiritual forces such as the gods, ancestors, and spirits. All beings, whether living or spiritual, possess life force, *ase*. Those wise individuals such as priests, initiates, diviners, rulers and elders who learn to use it for the benefit of themselves and those around them are known as *alase* or *alawo*. Drawing by H. J. Drewal.

importance in any given part of the Yoruba world reflects their relative local popularity, reputation, and influence, and the order in which they are invoked in ceremonies has to do with their roles in the ritual and their relationships to each other.

The gods regularly enter the world through their mediums—worshippers who have been trained and prepared to receive the spirit of their divinities during possession trances in the course of religious ceremonies. When the gods are made manifest in this way, they speak through their devotees, praying and giving guidance.

While all the gods periodically journey to the world, two sacred powers, Ifa and Esu/Elegba, stand at the threshold between the realms of *orun* and *aye*, assisting in communication between the divine and human realms. Ifa, actually a Yoruba system of divination, is presided over by Orunmila, its deified mythic founder, who is also sometimes called Ifa. . . .

Ifa offers humans the possibility of knowing the forces at work in specific situations in their lives and of influencing the course of events through prayer and sacrifice. The diviner, or *babalawo* ("father of ancient wisdom"), uses the rituals and poetry of Ifa to identify cosmic forces: the gods, ancestors, and spirits, and the machinations of the enemies of humankind personified as Death, Disease, Infirmity, and Loss; . . . and the sometimes evil-intentioned persons known collectively as *araye* ("people-of-the-world") who include *aje* (witches), *oso* (wizards), and others.

While Ifa symbolizes the revealable, Esu/Elegba is the agent of effective action, who also reminds one of the unpredictable nature of human experience. Esu's constant and often unsettling activity reminds humans of the need for guidance in lives of engaged action. Esu, who bears the sacrifices of humans to the *orisa* and other spirits, is the guardian of the ritual process. A verse from Ifa warns that if Esu is not acknowledged, "life is the bailing of waters with a sieve."

The ancestors (*oku orun, osi, babanla, iyanla*) constitute another major category of beings in *orun*. They are departed but not deceased. They can be contacted by their descendants for support and guidance and can return to the world either for short stays in the form of maskers called *egungun*, or as part of new persons in their lineages who are partially their reincarnation.

## Aye: The World of the Living

*Aye*, the world, is the visible, tangible realm of the living, including those invisible otherworldly forces that visit frequently and strongly influence human affairs. The importance and omnipresence of the otherworld in this world is expressed in a Yoruba saying: "The world is a marketplace [we visit], the otherworld is home" (*Aye l'oja, orun n'ile*). A variant of this phrase, *Aye l'ajo, orun n'ile* ("The world [life] is a journey, the otherworld [afterlife] is home"), contrasts the movement and unpredictability of life with the haven of the afterworld that promises spiritual existence for eternity.[4] Individual goals and aspirations in the world include long life, peace, prosperity, progeny, and good reputation. Ideally, these can be achieved through the constant search for *ogbon* (wisdom), *imo* (knowledge), and *oye* (understanding).

Yoruba society is traditionally open, but with a long history of monarchical and hierarchical organization. Nevertheless, decision making is shared widely—consensual rather than autocratic or dictatorial—and an elaborate series of checks and balances ensures an essentially egalitarian system. Just as all the gods are equal in relation to Olodumare, so too all lineages are structurally equal in their relation to the sacred king. At the same time, the possibility of mobility is fundamental, depending on how one marshals the forces in the environment. The situation is remarkably fluid and dynamic. Within this context, there is some recognition of rank, yet distribution of responsibilities and authority are given more importance than hierarchy. Seniority is based on the age of the person, the antiquity of the title, and the person's tenure in office. Such an ideal for social interaction is rooted in the concept of *ase*, the life force possessed by all individuals and unique to each one. Thus *ase* must be acknowledged and used in all social matters and in dealings with divine forces as well.

## Ase: Life Force

*Ase* is given by Olodumare to everything—gods, ancestors, spirits, humans, animals, plants, rocks, rivers, and voiced words such as songs, prayers, praises, curses,

---

4. For the importance of the metaphor of the "journey" in Yoruba thought and in ritual practice, see M. T. Drewal, "Performer, Play, and Agency: Yoruba Ritual Process." Ph.D Thesis, New York University, 1989.

or even everyday conversation. Existence, according to Yoruba thought, is dependent upon it; it is the power to make things happen and change. In addition to its sacred characteristics, *ase* also has important social ramifications, reflected in its translation as "power, authority, command." A person who, through training, experience, and initiation, learns how to use the essential life force of things is called an *alaase*. Theoretically, every individual possesses a unique blend of performative power and knowledge—the potential for certain achievements. Yet because no one can know with certainty the potential of others, *eso* (caution), *ifarabale* (composure), *owo* (respect), and *suuru* (patience) are highly valued in Yoruba society and shape all social interactions and organization.

Social processes encourage the participation of all and the contribution of the *ase* of every person. For example, members of the council of elder men and women, known as Osugbo among the Ijebu Yoruba and Ogboni in the Oyo area, have hereditary titles that rotate among many lineages, and there are other positions that are open to all in the society, as well as honorary titles bestowed on those who have made special contributions to the community. Members stress the equality of such positions in emphasizing their distinctive rights and responsibilities. All are seen as crucial to the successful functioning of the society as evident in Osugbo rituals. The members share kola nut, the drummers play the praises of titles, individuals take turns hosting a series of celebrations, each person has the opportunity to state opinions during debates, and all decisions are consensual. Osugbo members stress the autonomy of their individual roles while at the same time asserting their equality in decision making. At various times some will dominate while others acquiesce, which is entirely in keeping with Yoruba notions of the distinctive *ase* of individuals and the fluid social reality of competing powers that continually shape society.

Rituals to invoke divine forces reflect this same concern for the autonomous *ase* of particular entities. Those invoked first are not more important or higher in rank, rather they are called first in order to perform specific tasks—such as the divine mediator Esu/Elegba who "opens the way" for communication between humans and gods. The recognition of the uniqueness and autonomy of the *ase* of persons and gods is what structures society and its relationship with the otherworld.

---

## SUGGESTIONS FOR WRITING

1. Langston Hughes's poem "Harlem (A Dream Deferred)" poses a question: "What happens to a dream deferred?" Why do you think Lorraine Hansberry chose this poem as the epigraph for *A Raisin in the Sun*? Which of the different "dreams" in the play does the play as a whole endorse? Write an essay in which you discuss the various "dreams" that are so central to the play. Does the play ultimately answer Hughes's question?

2. In *Twelve Million Black Voices: A Folk History of the Negro in the United States*, Richard Wright describes the hopes of black migrants to the North and the sometimes-squalid conditions that awaited them. With reference to Wright's essay and the other primary materials in this chapter, write an essay in which you explore how *A Raisin in the Sun* illustrates various currents in black intellectual thought of the mid-twentieth century.

3. *A Raisin in the Sun* is set in Chicago, but in many ways its heart is in Africa—the

Africa of the mythical past, the Africa of the slave trade, and the Africa of the play's own temporal setting. Write an essay in which you explore the many ways in which African history and culture inform Hansberry's play. How African are the play's African American characters? To what extent does the play illustrate the ideas found in Earl E. Thorpe's *Africa in the Thought of Negro Americans* and Phaon Goldman's *The Significance of African Freedom for the Negro American*?

4. Hansberry's play explores not only the evolving social and economic position of African Americans in the mid-twentieth century, but also their evolving gender roles. On the one hand, we are reminded of the patriarchal nature of traditional African cultures; on the other hand, the Younger household seems to fulfill the more modern stereotype of the African American family dominated by women. Write an essay in which you discuss the crucial role that gender plays in the action of the play. Does *A Raisin in the Sun* seem to endorse any particular family structure as "ideal" for African Americans?

5. In *A Raisin in the Sun*'s third act, Beneatha asserts that "there isn't any real progress ... there is only one large circle that we march in, around and around, each of us with our own little picture—in front of us—our own little mirage that we think is the future." Asagai counters that progress follows "a long line—as in geometry, you know, one that reaches into infinity." Write an essay in which you compare and contrast these two views of history as they are depicted in *A Raisin in the Sun*. Does the play seem to endorse one view over the other? Does the play seem to contain seeds of the ideas found in Stokely Carmichael and Charles V. Hamilton's *Black Power*, or the essay by Robert Blauner?

6. *Death and the King's Horseman* depicts a clash of cultures. Is the misunderstanding between the native Africans and their British colonial masters mutual? What seems to be at the core of this misunderstanding—is it mainly cultural, political, economic, or some combination of these factors? Write an essay in which you discuss the issues at the heart of the conflict in Wole Soyinka's play.

7. What must a Western audience know—or be shown—in order to appreciate the Yoruba culture of *Death and the King's Horseman*? Research traditional Yoruba dress, music, and dance, and write an essay in which you discuss how you would stage a production of the play for American or European audiences.

8. How well does Soyinka's play illustrate the ideas about colonialism found in *Black Power* by Stokely Carmichael and Charles V. Hamilton? What evidence of "cooptation" and "captive leaders" do you see in the play? Write an essay in which you discuss the depiction of colonialism in *Death and the King's Horseman*.

9. Soyinka's play offers a rare glimpse into the richly complex traditional culture of the Yoruba. Using the information found in *Yoruba: Nine Centuries of African Art and Thought* by Henry John Drewal, John Pemberton III, and Rowland Abiodun, as well as other materials you might find through research, write a detailed introduction to the play, outlining the Yoruban social and spiritual beliefs at the center of the play's drama.

10. Both Hansberry's *A Raisin in the Sun* and Soyinka's *Death and the King's Horseman* feature characters who are students straddling the very different worlds of traditional Africa and the modern West. Write an essay in which you compare and contrast Hansberry's Asagai and Soyinka's Olunde. How do the characters function dramatically in their respective plays? What different ideas about cultural understanding does each seem to represent? How might they illustrate what Soyinka calls "complementarities" between Western and African cultures?

# 31    CRITICAL CONTEXTS: A DRAMA CASEBOOK

Even more than other forms of literature, drama has a relatively stable canon—that is, a select group of plays that the theater community thinks of as especially worthy of frequent performance. New plays join this canon, of course, but theater companies worldwide tend to perform the same ones over and over, especially those by Shakespeare, Ibsen, and Sophocles. The reasons are many, involving the plays' themes and continued appeal across times and cultures as well as their formal literary and theatrical accomplishments. But their repeated performance means that a relatively small number of plays become a lot better known than all the others and that there is a tradition of "talk" about those plays. A lot of this talk is informal and local, resulting from the fact that people see plays communally—that is, they see performances together—and often compare responses afterward. But more permanent and more formal records of canonical responses also exist; critics almost always review individual productions of plays in newspapers and magazines, on radio and television, and on the Internet. For the most part, reviews concentrate primarily on the details of a performance. But because every production of a play involves a particular interpretation of the text, cumulative accounts of performances add up to a body of interpretive criticism—that is, analytical commentary about many aspects of the play as text and as performance.

Any oral or written text can provoke disagreement, partly because of the slippery nature of verbal and visual language and partly because different readers and listeners bring different interests, experiences, and perspectives to the text. Differences in response may result from differing temperaments and preferences and from differing circumstances and cultural assumptions—all readers and viewers are influenced by the times and places in which they live. But plays in particular, because of their many productions in varied locations by different acting companies and directors, carry with them an especially varied accumulation of critical responses. New productions of a play often draw consciously on previous productions, sometimes imitating particular features and sometimes reacting against well-known interpretations. The many famous productions of *Hamlet*, for example, consciously compare themselves to each other in their emphasis on political intrigue, mother/son and father/son relationships, the hesitations or "indecisiveness" of the hero, and so forth. As a reader of plays in a textbook like this one, you may or may not bring to your reading an awareness of what others have thought about a particular play, but that body of material is available if you choose to use it as a way of getting additional perspectives on the text.

Sophocles' *Antigone*, for instance, attracts attention from a wide variety of perspectives—from Greek scholars, who view it in relation to classical myth or the ancient Greek language; from philosophers, who may see in it examinations of classic ideas and ethical problems; from theater historians, who may think about it in relation to traditions of staging and visualization or the particulars of gestures and stage business; and from historians of rhetoric, who may consider the interactions between the chorus and the players. Some of these examinations draw on deep historical knowledge in order to study the play; others depend more on working out a particular critical theory or simply a coherent interpretation. You don't have to read this accumulated criticism to understand what happens in a text; indeed, some of this work may seem irrelevant to you. But reading what others have said about a text can help you—by offering historical information that you hadn't known or hadn't considered relevant, by pointing to problems or possibilities of interpretation you had not yet thought of, or by supporting a reading you had already arrived at. In a sense, reading published criticism is a lot like talking with your fellow students or being involved in a class discussion. In general, you shouldn't read "the critics" until after you have read the complete play at least once, just as you should read the text in full before you discuss it with others. That way, your initial responses to the play are your own; if you don't understand some things, you can always discuss them later or read a few pieces of good criticism.

A bust of Sophocles

> *A play should give you something to think about. When I see a play and understand it the first time, then I know it can't be much good.*
>
> —T. S. ELIOT

Reading critics can be especially helpful when you have to write a paper. Critics will often guide you to crucial points of debate or to a place in the text that is a crux for deciding on a particular interpretation. You will likely get the most help if you read several critics with different perspectives—not because more is better, but because you will see their differences and, more important, the *grounds* for their differences in the kinds of evidence they use. Their disagreements will likely be very useful to you as a new interpreter. But don't regard critics as "authorities" (an interpretation is not true simply because it is published or written by somebody famous); instead, look to critics and their work for indicators of what the issues are.

Often, when you're just starting to think about the paper you want to write, reading a few pieces of criticism can help you see some of the critical issues in the play. Critics frequently disagree on the interpretation of particular issues or passages or even on what the issues really are, but reading their work can make your own thoughts concrete, especially when you're just starting to sort things out. Reacting to someone else's view, especially one that it is strongly argued, can help you articulate what you think and can suggest a line of interpretation and argument for your own writing.

Sorting out the important issues can be complicated, and issues do shift from era to era and culture to culture. But often the arguments posed in one era interest subsequent critics in whatever age and from whatever perspective. *Antigone*'s performance history goes back more than twenty-four centuries, and over that time readers and viewers have recorded many thousands of responses. Following the text of the play below, we reprint only a small sample, all from the twentieth century. But earlier views are often referred to and sometimes still argued about. The famous comments of the German philosopher G. W. F. Hegel (1770–1831), for example, continue to set the agenda for an astonishing number of interpreters. Many answer him directly; others use him to sharpen, complicate, or detail their views or simply to position themselves in some larger debate about specific issues in the play or about literary criticism or philosophy more generally.

In the following selections you will find various interpretations of crucial scenes and issues in *Antigone*. Especially prominent are questions about how to read the opinions of the chorus, how to interpret the character of Antigone, and how to assess Creon's flaws. As you read the critics, pay attention to the way they argue—the kinds of textual evidence they use to back up their points and how they structure their arguments—as well as the main interpretive points they make.

A production of *Antigone*
(New York Shakespeare Festival, 1982)

If you draw on published criticism in your papers (or to back up a point in class or in a discussion with a fellow student), you will want to acknowledge the critic upfront and then work his or her words into your paper or conversation the way you have learned to do with lines or phrases from a text. Sometimes a particular critic can be especially helpful in focusing your thoughts because you so clearly disagree with what she or he says. In that case, you may well get a good paper out of a rebuttal in which you answer or attack that critic's argument point by point. Pitting one critic against another—sorting out the issues that different interpreters disagree on and showing what their differences consist of—can also be a good way to focus on your own contribution. But remember that the point of reading criticism is to *use* it for your own interpretive purposes, to make your responses more sensitive and resonant, to make you a more-informed reader of the play, and to make you a better reader in general.

## SOPHOCLES

## Antigone[1]

CHARACTERS

| | |
|---|---|
| ANTIGONE | HAEMON |
| ISMENE | TEIRESIAS |
| CHORUS OF THEBAN ELDERS | A MESSENGER |
| CREON | EURYDICE |
| A SENTRY | SECOND MESSENGER |

*The two sisters* ANTIGONE *and* ISMENE *meet in front of the palace gates in Thebes.*

ANTIGONE: Ismene, my dear sister,
whose father was my father, can you think of any
of all the evils that stem from Oedipus[2]
that Zeus does not bring to pass for us, while we yet live?
5   No pain, no ruin, no shame, and no dishonor
but I have seen it in our mischiefs,
yours and mine.
And now what is the proclamation that they tell of
made lately by the commander, publicly,
10  to all the people? Do you know it? Have you heard it?
Don't you notice when the evils due to enemies
are headed towards those we love?
ISMENE: Not a word, Antigone, of those we love,
either sweet or bitter, has come to me since the moment
15  when we lost our two brothers,
on one day, by their hands dealing mutual death.
Since the Argive army fled in this past night,
I know of nothing further, nothing
of better fortune or of more destruction.
20 ANTIGONE: *I* knew it well; that is why I sent for you
to come outside the palace gates
to listen to me, privately.
ISMENE: What is it? Certainly your words
come of dark thoughts.
25 ANTIGONE: Yes, indeed; for those two brothers of ours, in burial
has not Creon honored the one, dishonored the other?
Eteocles, they say he has used justly
with lawful rites and hid him in the earth
to have his honor among the dead men there.

---

1. Translated by David Grene.
2. In Greek legend, Oedipus became king of Thebes by inadvertently fulfilling his destiny that he would kill his father and marry his mother (as depicted in Sophocles' *Oedipus the King*); for these offenses against nature and the gods, Creon sent Oedipus, along with his daughters Antigone and Ismene, into exile at Colonus. Soon Oedipus's sons, Eteocles and Polyneices, battled to the death for the throne of Thebes.

But the unhappy corpse of Polyneices
he has proclaimed to all the citizens,
they say, no man may hide
in a grave nor mourn in funeral,
but leave unwept, unburied, a dainty treasure
for the birds that see him, for their feast's delight.
That is what, they say, the worthy Creon
has proclaimed for you and me—for me, I tell you—
and he comes here to clarify to the unknowing
his proclamation; he takes it seriously;
for whoever breaks the edict death is prescribed,
and death by stoning publicly.
There you have it; soon you will show yourself
as noble both in your nature and your birth,
or yourself as base, although of noble parents.
ISMENE: If things are as you say, poor sister, how
    can I better them? how loose or tie the knot?
ANTIGONE: Decide if you will share the work, the deed.
ISMENE: What kind of danger is there? How far have your thoughts gone?
ANTIGONE: Here is this hand. Will you help it to lift the dead man?
ISMENE: Would you bury him, when it is forbidden the city?
ANTIGONE: At least he is my brother—and yours, too,
    though you deny him. I will not prove false to him.
ISMENE: You are so headstrong. Creon has forbidden it.
ANTIGONE: It is not for him to keep me from my own.
ISMENE: O God!
    Consider, sister, how our father died,
hated and infamous; how he brought to light
his own offenses; how he himself struck out
the sight of his two eyes;
his own hand was their executioner.
Then, mother and wife, two names in one, did shame
violently on her life, with twisted cords.
Third, our two brothers, on a single day,
poor wretches, themselves worked out their mutual doom.
Each killed the other, hand against brother's hand.
Now there are only the two of us, left behind,
and see how miserable our end shall be
if in the teeth of law we shall transgress
against the sovereign's decree and power.
You ought to realize we are only women,
not meant in nature to fight against men,
and that we are ruled, by those who are stronger,
to obedience in this and even more painful matters.
I do indeed beg those beneath the earth
to give me their forgiveness,
since force constrains me,
that I shall yield in this to the authorities.
Extravagant action is not sensible.

ANTIGONE: I would not urge you now; nor if you wanted
 to act would I be glad to have you with me.
 Be as you choose to be; but for myself
 I myself will bury him. It will be good
 to die, so doing. I shall lie by his side,
 loving him as he loved me; I shall be
 a criminal—but a religious one.
 The time in which I must please those that are dead
 is longer than I must please those of this world.
 For there I shall lie forever. You, if you like,
 can cast dishonor on what the gods have honored.
ISMENE: I will not put dishonor on them, but
 to act in defiance of the citizenry,
 my nature does not give me means for that.
ANTIGONE: Let that be your excuse. But I will go
 to heap the earth on the grave of my loved brother.
ISMENE: How I fear for you, my poor sister!
ANTIGONE: Do not fear for me. Make straight your own path to destiny.
ISMENE: At least do not speak of this act to anyone else;
 bury him in secret; I will be silent, too.
ANTIGONE: Oh, oh, no! shout it out. I will hate you still worse
 for silence—should you not proclaim it,
 to everyone.
ISMENE: You have a warm heart for such chilly deeds.
ANTIGONE: I know I am pleasing those I should please most.
ISMENE: *If* you can do it. But you are in love
 with the impossible.
ANTIGONE: No. When I can no more, then I will stop.
ISMENE: It is better not to hunt the impossible
 at all.
ANTIGONE: If you will talk like this I will loathe you,
 and you will be adjudged an enemy—
 justly—by the dead's decision. Let me alone
 and my folly with me, to endure this terror.
 No suffering of mine will be enough
 to make me die ignobly.
ISMENE: Well, if you will, go on.
 Know this; that though you are wrong to go, your friends
 are right to love you.
CHORUS: Sun's beam, fairest of all
  that ever till now shone
  on seven-gated Thebes;
  O golden eye of day, you shone
  coming over Dirce's stream;[3]
  You drove in headlong rout
  the whiteshielded man from Argos,
  complete in arms;

---

3. River near Thebes.

his bits rang sharper
under your urging.

Polyneices brought him here
against our land, Polyneices,
roused by contentious quarrel;                                          130
like an eagle he flew into our country,
with many men-at-arms,
with many a helmet crowned with horsehair.

He stood above the halls, gaping with murderous lances,
encompassing the city's                                                 135
seven-gated mouth.
But before his jaws would be sated
with our blood, before the fire,
pine fed, should capture our crown of towers,
he went hence—                                                          140
such clamor of war stretched behind his back,
from his dragon foe, a thing he could not overcome.

For Zeus, who hates the most
the boasts of a great tongue,
saw them coming in a great tide,                                        145
insolent in the clang of golden armor.
The god struck him down with hurled fire,
as he strove to raise the victory cry,
now at the very winning post.

The earth rose to strike him as he fell swinging.                       150
In his frantic onslaught, possessed, he breathed upon us
with blasting winds of hate.
Sometimes the great god of war was on one side,
and sometimes he struck a staggering blow on the other;
the god was a very wheel horse[4] on the right trace.                   155

At seven gates stood seven captains,
ranged equals against equals, and there left
their brazen suits of armor
to Zeus, the god of trophies.
Only those two wretches born of one father and mother                   160
set their spears to win a victory on both sides;
they worked out their share in a common death.

Now Victory, whose name is great, has come
to Thebes of many chariots
with joy to answer her joy,                                             165
to bring forgetfulness of these wars;
let us go to all the shrines of the gods
and dance all night long.

---

4. The strongest and ablest horse in a team pulling a vehicle, harnessed nearest the front wheels "on the right trace."

>           Let Bacchus lead the dance,
> 170       shaking Thebes to trembling.
>
>           But here is the king of our land,
>           Creon,[5] son of Menoeceus;
>           in our new contingencies with the gods,
>           he is our new ruler.
> 175       He comes to set in motion some design—
>           what design is it? Because he has proposed
>           the convocation of the elders.
>           He sent a public summons for our discussion.
>
> CREON: Gentlemen: as for our city's fortune,
> 180   the gods have shaken her, when the great waves broke,
>       but the gods have brought her through again to safety.
>       For yourselves, I chose you out of all and summoned you
>       to come to me, partly because I knew you
>       as always loyal to the throne—at first,
> 185   when Laïus[6] was king, and then again
>       when Oedipus saved our city and then again
>       when he died and you remained with steadfast truth
>       to their descendants,
>       until they met their double fate upon one day,
> 190   striking and stricken, defiled each by a brother's murder.
>       Now here I am, holding all authority
>       and the throne, in virtue of kinship with the dead.
>       It is impossible to know any man—
>       I mean his soul, intelligence, and judgment—
> 195   until he shows his skill in rule and law.
>       I think that a man supreme ruler of a whole city,
>       if he does not reach for the best counsel for her,
>       but through some fear, keeps his tongue under lock and key,
>       him I judge the worst of any;
> 200   I have always judged so; and anyone thinking
>       another man more a friend than his own country,
>       I rate him nowhere. For my part, God is my witness,
>       who sees all, always, I would not be silent
>       if I saw ruin, not safety, on the way
> 205   towards my fellow citizens. I would not count
>       any enemy of my country as a friend—
>       because of what I know, that she it is
>       which gives us our security. If she sails upright
>       and we sail on her, friends will be ours for the making.
> 210   In the light of rules like these, I will make her greater still.
>
>       In consonance with this, I here proclaim
>       to the citizens about Oedipus' sons.
>       For Eteocles, who died this city's champion,

---

5. The brother of Jocasta, mother and wife of Oedipus; he became king of Thebes after the deaths of Oedipus's sons.  6. The father of Oedipus.

showing his valor's supremacy everywhere,
he shall be buried in his grave with every rite 215
of sanctity given to heroes under earth.
However, his brother, Polyneices, a returned exile,
who sought to burn with fire from top to bottom
his native city, and the gods of his own people;
who sought to taste the blood he shared with us, 220
and lead the rest of us to slavery—
I here proclaim to the city that this man
shall no one honor with a grave and none shall mourn.
You shall leave him without burial; you shall watch him
chewed up by birds and dogs and violated. 225
Such is my mind in the matter; never by me
shall the wicked man have precedence in honor
over the just. But he that is loyal to the state
in death, in life alike, shall have my honor.

CHORUS: Son of Menoeceus, so it is your pleasure 230
to deal with foe and friend of this our city.
To use any legal means lies in your power,
both about the dead and those of us who live.

CREON: I understand, then, you will do my bidding.

CHORUS: Please lay this burden on some younger man. 235

CREON: Oh, watchers of the corpse I have already.

CHORUS: What else, then, do your commands entail?

CREON: That you should not side with those who disagree.

CHORUS: There is none so foolish as to love his own death.

CREON: Yes, indeed those are the wages, but often greed 240
has with its hopes brought men to ruin.

[*The* SENTRY *whose speeches follow represents a remarkable experiment in Greek tragedy in the direction of naturalism of speech. He speaks with marked clumsiness, partly because he is excited and talks almost colloquially. But also the royal presence makes him think apparently that he should be rather grand in his show of respect. He uses odd bits of archaism or somewhat stale poetical passages, particularly in catch phrases. He sounds something like lower-level Shakespearean characters, e.g. Constable Elbow, with his uncertainty about benefactor and malefactor.*]

SENTRY: My lord, I will never claim my shortness of breath
is due to hurrying, nor were there wings in my feet.
I stopped at many a lay-by in my thinking;
I circled myself till I met myself coming back. 245
My soul accosted me with different speeches.
"Poor fool, yourself, why are you going somewhere
when once you get there you will pay the piper?"
"Well, aren't you the daring fellow! stopping again?
and suppose Creon hears the news from someone else— 250
don't you realize that you will smart for that?"
I turned the whole matter over. I suppose I may say
"I made haste slowly" and the short road became long.
However, at last I came to a resolve:

255 I must go to you; even if what I say
is nothing, really, still I shall say it.
I come here, a man with a firm clutch on the hope
that nothing can betide him save what is fated.
CREON: What is it then that makes you so afraid?
260 SENTRY: No, I want first of all to tell you my side of it.
I didn't do the thing; I never saw who did it.
It would not be fair for me to get into trouble.
CREON: You hedge, and barricade the thing itself.
Clearly you have some ugly news for me.
265 SENTRY: Well, you know how disasters make a man
hesitate to be their messenger.
CREON: For God's sake, tell me and get out of here!
SENTRY: Yes, I *will* tell you. Someone just now
buried the corpse and vanished. He scattered on the skin
270 some thirsty dust; he did the ritual,
duly, to purge the body of desecration.
CREON: What! Now who on earth could have done that?
SENTRY: I do not know. For there was there no mark
of axe's stroke nor casting up of earth
275 of any mattock; the ground was hard and dry,
unbroken; there were no signs of wagon wheels.
The doer of the deed had left no trace.
But when the first sentry of the day pointed it out,
there was for all of us a disagreeable
280 wonder. For the body had disappeared;
not in a grave, of course; but there lay upon him
a little dust as of a hand avoiding
the curse of violating the dead body's sanctity.
There were no signs of any beast nor dog
285 that came there; he had clearly not been torn.
There was a tide of bad words at one another,
guard taunting guard, and it might well have ended
in blows, for there was no one there to stop it.
Each one of us was the criminal but no one
290 manifestly so; all denied knowledge of it.
We were ready to take hot bars in our hands
or walk through fire,[7] and call on the gods with oaths
that we had neither done it nor were privy
to a plot with anyone, neither in planning
295 nor yet in execution.
At last when nothing came of all our searching,
there was one man who spoke, made every head
bow to the ground in fear. For we could not

---

7. Ancient legal customs in which an accused person was required to undergo a "trial by ordeal," such as walking through fire; if the resulting injuries were not serious, the person was thought to be innocent and therefore divinely protected.

    either contradict him nor yet could we see how
    if we did what he said we would come out all right.    300
    His word was that we must lay information
    about the matter to yourself; we could not cover it.
    This view prevailed and the lot of the draw chose me,
    unlucky me, to win that prize. So here
    I am. I did not want to come,    305
    and you don't want to have me. I know that.
    For no one likes the messenger of bad news.

CHORUS: My lord: I wonder, could this be God's doing?
    This is the thought that keeps on haunting me.

CREON: Stop, before your words fill even me with rage,    310
    that you should be exposed as a fool, and you so old.
    For what you say is surely insupportable
    when you say the gods took forethought for this corpse.
    Is it out of excess of honor for the man,
    for the favors that he did them, they should cover him?    315
    This man who came to burn their pillared temples,
    their dedicated offerings—and this land
    and laws he would have scattered to the winds?
    Or do you see the gods as honoring
    criminals? This is not so. But what I am doing    320
    now, and other things before this, some men disliked,
    within this very city, and muttered against me,
    secretly shaking their heads; they would not bow
    justly beneath the yoke to submit to me.
    I am very sure that these men hired others    325
    to do this thing. I tell you the worse currency
    that ever grew among mankind is money. This
    sacks cities, this drives people from their homes,
    this teaches and corrupts the minds of the loyal
    to acts of shame. This displays    330
    all kinds of evil for the use of men,
    instructs in the knowledge of every impious act.
    Those that have done this deed have been paid to do it,
    but in the end they will pay for what they have done.

    It is as sure as I still reverence Zeus—    335
    know this right well—and I speak under oath—
    if you and your fellows do not find this man
    who with his own hand did the burial
    and bring him here before me face to face,
    your death alone will not be enough for me.    340
    You will hang alive till you open up this outrage.
    That will teach you in the days to come from what
    you may draw profit—safely—from your plundering.
    It's not from anything and everything
    you can grow rich. You will find out    345
    that ill-gotten gains ruin more than they save.

SENTRY: Have I your leave to say something—or should
    I just turn and go?
CREON: Don't you know your talk is painful enough already?
350 SENTRY: Is the ache in your ears or in your mind?
CREON: Why do you dissect the whereabouts of my pain?
SENTRY: Because it is he who did the deed who hurts your
    mind. I only hurt your ears that listen.
CREON: I am sure you have been a chatterbox since you were born.
355 SENTRY: All the same, I did not do this thing.
CREON: You might have done this, too, if you sold your soul.
SENTRY: It's a bad thing if one judges and judges wrongly.
CREON: You may talk as wittily as you like of judgment.
    Only, if you don't bring to light those men
360 who have done this, you will yet come to say
    that your wretched gains have brought bad consequences.
SENTRY: [*Aside.*] It were best that he were found, but whether
    the criminal is taken or he isn't—
    for that chance will decide—one thing is certain,
365 you'll never see me coming here again.
    I never hoped to escape, never thought I could.
    But now I have come off safe, I thank God heartily.
CHORUS: Many are the wonders, none
        is more wonderful than what is man.
370     This it is that crosses the sea
        with the south winds storming and the waves swelling,
        breaking around him in roaring surf.
        He it is again who wears away
        the Earth, oldest of gods, immortal, unwearied,
375     as the ploughs wind across her from year to year
        when he works her with the breed that comes from horses.

        The tribe of the lighthearted birds he snares
        and takes prisoner the races of savage beasts
        and the brood of the fish of the sea,
380     with the close-spun web of nets.
        A cunning fellow is man. His contrivances
        make him master of beasts of the field
        and those that move in the mountains.
        So he brings the horse with the shaggy neck
385     to bend underneath the yoke;
        and also the untamed mountain bull;
        and speech and windswift thought
        and the tempers that go with city living
        he has taught himself, and how to avoid
390     the sharp frost, when lodging is cold
        under the open sky
        and pelting strokes of the rain.
        He has a way against everything,
        and he faces nothing that is to come

without contrivance.
Only against death
can he call on no means of escape;
but escape from hopeless diseases
he has found in the depths of his mind.
With some sort of cunning, inventive
beyond all expectation
he reaches sometimes evil,
and sometimes good.

If he honors the laws of earth,
and the justice of the gods he has confirmed by oath,
high is his city; no city
has he with whom dwells dishonor
prompted by recklessness.
He who is so, may he never
share my hearth!
may he never think my thoughts!

Is this a portent sent by God?
I cannot tell.
I know her. How can I say
that this is not Antigone?
Unhappy girl, child of unhappy Oedipus,
what is this?
Surely it is not you they bring here
as disobedient to the royal edict,
surely not you, taken in such folly.

SENTRY: She is the one who did the deed;
we took her burying him. But where is Creon?
CHORUS: He is just coming from the house, when you most need him.
CREON: What is this? What has happened that I come
so opportunely?
SENTRY: My lord, there is nothing
that a man should swear he would never do.
Second thoughts make liars of the first resolution.
I would have vowed it would be long enough
before I came again, lashed hence by your threats.
But since the joy that comes past hope, and against all hope,
is like no other pleasure in extent,
I have come here, though I break my oath in coming.
I bring this girl here who has been captured
giving the grace of burial to the dead man.
This time no lot chose me; this was my jackpot,
and no one else's. Now, my lord, take her
and as you please judge her and test her; I
am justly free and clear of all this trouble.
CREON: This girl—how did you take her and from where?
SENTRY: She was burying the man. Now you know all.
CREON: Do you know what you are saying? Do you mean it?

SENTRY: She is the one; I saw her burying
   the dead man you forbade the burial of.
445   Now, do I speak plainly and clearly enough?
CREON: How was she seen? How was she caught in the act?
SENTRY: This is how it was. When we came there,
   with those dreadful threats of yours upon us,
   we brushed off all the dust that lay upon
450   the dead man's body, heedfully
   leaving it moist and naked.
   We sat on the brow of the hill, to windward,
   that we might shun the smell of the corpse upon us.
   Each of us wakefully urged his fellow
455   with torrents of abuse, not to be careless
   in this work of ours. So it went on,
   until in the midst of the sky the sun's bright circle
   stood still; the heat was burning. Suddenly
   a squall lifted out of the earth a storm of dust,
460   a trouble in the sky. It filled the plain,
   ruining all the foliage of the wood
   that was around it. The great empty air
   was filled with it. We closed our eyes, enduring
   this plague sent by the gods. When at long last
465   we were quit of it, why, then we saw the girl.

   She was crying out with the shrill cry
   of an embittered bird
   that sees its nest robbed of its nestlings
   and the bed empty. So, too, when she saw
470   the body stripped of its cover, she burst out in groans,
   calling terrible curses on those that had done that deed;
   and with her hands immediately
   brought thirsty dust to the body; from a shapely brazen
   urn, held high over it, poured a triple stream
475   of funeral offerings; and crowned the corpse.
   When we saw that, we rushed upon her and
   caught our quarry then and there, not a bit disturbed.
   We charged her with what she had done, then and the first time.
   She did not deny a word of it—to my joy,
480   but to my pain as well. It is most pleasant
   to have escaped oneself out of such troubles
   but painful to bring into it those whom we love.
   However, it is but natural for me
   to count all this less than my own escape.
485 CREON: You there, that turn your eyes upon the ground,
   do you confess or deny what you have done?
ANTIGONE: Yes, I confess; I will not deny my deed.
CREON: [*To the* SENTRY.] You take yourself off where you like.
   You are free of a heavy charge.
490   Now, Antigone, tell me shortly and to the point,
   did you know the proclamation against your action?

ANTIGONE: I knew it; of course I did. For it was public.
CREON: And did you dare to disobey that law?
ANTIGONE: Yes, it was not Zeus that made the proclamation;
nor did Justice, which lives with those below, enact      495
such laws as that, for mankind. I did not believe
your proclamation had such power to enable
one who will someday die to override
God's ordinances, unwritten and secure.
*They* are not of today and yesterday;                    500
they live forever; none knows when first they were.
These are the laws whose penalties I would not
incur from the gods, through fear of any man's temper.

I know that I will die—of course I do—
even if you had not doomed me by proclamation.            505
If I shall die before my time, I count that
a profit. How can such as I, that live
among such troubles, not find a profit in death?
So for such as me, to face such a fate as this
is pain that does not count. But if I dared to leave      510
the dead man, my mother's son, dead and unburied,
that would have been real pain. The other is not.
Now, if you think me a fool to act like this,
perhaps it is a fool that judges so.

CHORUS: The savage spirit of a savage father              515
    shows itself in this girl. She does not know
    how to yield to trouble.
CREON: I would have you know the most fanatic spirits
    fall most of all. It is the toughest iron,
    baked in the fire to hardness, you may see            520
    most shattered, twisted, shivered to fragments.
    I know hot horses are restrained
    by a small curb. For he that is his neighbor's slave cannot
    be high in spirit. This girl had learned her insolence
    before this, when she broke the established laws.     525
    But here is still another insolence
    in that she boasts of it, laughs at what she did.
    I swear I am no man and she the man
    if she can win this and not pay for it.
    No; though she were my sister's child or closer       530
    in blood than all that my hearth god acknowledges
    as mine, neither she nor her sister should escape
    the utmost sentence—death. For indeed I accuse her,
    the sister, equally of plotting the burial.
    Summon her. I saw her inside, just now,               535
    crazy, distraught. When people plot
    mischief in the dark, it is the mind which first
    is convicted of deceit. But surely I hate indeed
    the one that is caught in evil and then makes
    that evil look like good.                             540

ANTIGONE: Do you want anything
    beyond my taking and my execution?
CREON: Oh, nothing! Once I have that I have everything.
ANTIGONE: Why do you wait, then? Nothing that you say
545    pleases me; God forbid it ever should.
    So my words, too, naturally offend you.
    Yet how could I win a greater share of glory
    than putting my own brother in his grave?
    All that are here would surely say that's true,
550    if fear did not lock their tongues up. A prince's power
    is blessed in many things, not least in this,
    that he can say and do whatever he likes.
CREON: You are alone among the people of Thebes
    to see things in that way.
555 ANTIGONE: No, these do, too,
    but keep their mouths shut for the fear of you.
CREON: Are you not ashamed to think so differently
    from them?
ANTIGONE: There is nothing shameful in honoring my brother.
560 CREON: Was not he that died on the other side your brother?
ANTIGONE: Yes, indeed, of my own blood from father and mother.
CREON: Why then do you show a grace that must be impious
    in *his* sight?
ANTIGONE: *That* other dead man
565    would never bear you witness in what you say.
CREON: Yes he would, if you put him only on equality
    with one that was a desecrator.
ANTIGONE: It was his brother, not his slave, that died.
CREON: He died destroying the country the other defended.
570 ANTIGONE: The god of death demands these rites for both.
CREON: But the good man does not seek an *equal* share only,
    with the bad.
ANTIGONE:           Who knows
    if in that other world this is true piety?
CREON: My enemy is still my enemy, even in death.
575 ANTIGONE: My nature is to join in love, not hate.
CREON: Go then to the world below, yourself, if you
    must love. Love *them*. When I am alive no woman shall rule.
CHORUS: Here before the gates comes Ismene
    shedding tears for the love of a brother.
580    A cloud over her brow casts shame
    on her flushed face, as the tears wet
    her fair cheeks.
CREON: You there, who lurked in my house, viper-like—
    secretly drawing its lifeblood; I never thought
585    that I was raising two sources of destruction,
    two rebels against my throne. Come tell me now,
    will you, too, say you bore a hand in the burial
    or will you swear that you know nothing of it?

ISMENE: I did it, yes—if she will say I did it
   I bear my share in it, bear the guilt, too.
ANTIGONE: Justice will not allow you what you refused
   and I will have none of your partnership.
ISMENE: But in your troubles I am not ashamed
   to sail with you the sea of suffering.
ANTIGONE: Where the act was death, the dead are witnesses.
   I do not love a friend who loves in words.
ISMENE: Sister, do not dishonor me, denying me
   a common death with you, a common honoring
   of the dead man.
ANTIGONE: Don't die with me, nor make your own
   what you have never touched. I that die am enough.
ISMENE: What life is there for me, once I have lost you?
ANTIGONE: Ask Creon; all your care was on his behalf.
ISMENE: Why do you hurt me, when you gain nothing by it?
ANTIGONE: I am hurt by my own mockery—if I mock you.
ISMENE: Even now—what can I do to help you still?
ANTIGONE: Save yourself; I do not grudge you your escape.
ISMENE: I cannot bear it! Not even to share your death!
ANTIGONE: Life was your choice, and death was mine.
ISMENE: You cannot say I accepted that choice in silence.
ANTIGONE: You were right in the eyes of one party, I in the other.
ISMENE: Well then, the fault is equally between us.
ANTIGONE: Take heart; you are alive, but my life died
   long ago, to serve the dead.
CREON: Here are two girls; I think that one of them
   has suddenly lost her wits—the other was always so.
ISMENE: Yes, for, my lord, the wits that they are born with
   do not stay firm for the unfortunate.
   They go astray.
CREON:         Certainly yours do,
   when you share troubles with the troublemaker.
ISMENE: What life can be mine alone without her?
CREON:                     Do not
   speak of *her*. *She* isn't, anymore.
ISMENE: Will you kill your son's wife to be?[8]
CREON: Yes, there are other fields for him to plough.
ISMENE: Not with the mutual love of him and her.
CREON: I hate a bad wife for a son of mine.
ANTIGONE: Dear Haemon, how your father dishonors you.
CREON: There is too much of you—and of your marriage!
CHORUS: Will you rob your son of this girl?
CREON: Death—it is death that will stop the marriage for me.
CHORUS: Your decision it seems is taken: she shall die.
CREON: Both you and I have decided it. No more delay.

---

8. Antigone, betrothed to Creon's son Haemon.

[*He turns to the* SERVANTS.]

Bring her inside, you. From this time forth,
these must be women, and not free to roam.
For even the stout of heart shrink when they see
the approach of death close to their lives.

CHORUS: Lucky are those whose lives
know no taste of sorrow.
But for those whose house has been shaken by God
there is never cessation of ruin;
it steals on generation after generation
within a breed. Even as the swell
is driven over the dark deep
by the fierce Thracian winds
I see the ancient evils of Labdacus' house[9]
are heaped on the evils of the dead.
No generation frees another, some god
strikes them down; there is no deliverance.
Here was the light of hope stretched
over the last roots of Oedipus' house,
and the bloody dust due to the gods below
has mowed it down—that and the folly of speech
and ruin's enchantment of the mind.

Your power, O Zeus, what sin of man can limit?
All-aging sleep does not overtake it,
nor the unwearied months of the gods; and you,
for whom time brings no age,
you hold the glowing brightness of Olympus.
For the future near and far,
and the past, this law holds good:
nothing very great
comes to the life of mortal man
without ruin to accompany it.
For Hope, widely wandering, comes to many of mankind
as a blessing,
but to many as the deceiver,
using light-minded lusts;
she comes to him that knows nothing
till he burns his foot in the glowing fire.
With wisdom has someone declared
a word of distinction:
that evil seems good to one whose mind
the god leads to ruin,
and but for the briefest moment of time
is his life outside of calamity.
Here is Haemon, youngest of your sons.

---

9. The Theban royal lineage that included Labdacus, his son, Laïus, and his grandson, Oedipus.

>     Does he come grieving
>     for the fate of his bride to be,
>     in agony at being cheated of his marriage?
> CREON: Soon we will know that better than the prophets.
>     My son, can it be that you have not heard
>     of my final decision on your betrothed?
>     Can you have come here in your fury against your father?
>     Or have I your love still, no matter what I do?
> HAEMON: Father, I am yours; with your excellent judgment
>     you lay the right before me, and I shall follow it.
>     No marriage will ever be so valued by me
>     as to override the goodness of your leadership.
> CREON: Yes, my son, this should always be
>     in your very heart, that everything else
>     shall be second to your father's decision.
>     It is for this that fathers pray to have
>     obedient sons begotten in their halls,
>     that they may requite with ill their father's enemy
>     and honor his friend no less than he would himself.
>     If a man have sons that are no use to him,
>     what can one say of him but that he has bred
>     so many sorrows to himself, laughter to his enemies?
>     Do not, my son, banish your good sense
>     through pleasure in a woman, since you know
>     that the embrace grows cold
>     when an evil woman shares your bed and home.
>     What greater wound can there be than a false friend?
>     No. Spit on her, throw her out like an enemy,
>     this girl, to marry someone in Death's house.
>     I caught her openly in disobedience
>     alone out of all this city and I shall not make
>     myself a liar in the city's sight. No, I will kill her.
>     So let her cry if she will on the Zeus of kinship;
>     for if I rear those of my race and breeding
>     to be rebels, surely I will do so with those outside it.
>     For he who is in his household a good man
>     will be found a just man, too, in the city.
>     But he that breaches the law or does it violence
>     or thinks to dictate to those who govern him
>     shall never have my good word.
>     The man the city sets up in authority
>     must be obeyed in small things and in just
>     but also in their opposites.
>     I am confident such a man of whom I speak
>     will be a good ruler, and willing to be well ruled.
>     He will stand on his country's side, faithful and just,
>     in the storm of battle. There is nothing worse
>     than disobedience to authority.
>     It destroys cities, it demolishes homes;

it breaks and routs one's allies. Of successful lives
the most of them are saved by discipline.
So we must stand on the side of what is orderly;
we cannot give victory to a woman.
730 If we must accept defeat, let it be from a man;
we must not let people say that a woman beat us.
CHORUS: We think, if we are not victims of Time the Thief,
that you speak intelligently of what you speak.
HAEMON: Father, the natural sense that the gods breed
735 in men is surely the best of their possessions.
I certainly could not declare you wrong—
may I never know how to do so!—Still there might
be something useful that some other than you might think.
It is natural for me to be watchful on your behalf
740 concerning what all men say or do or find to blame.
Your face is terrible to a simple citizen;
it frightens him from words you dislike to hear.
But what *I* can hear, in the dark, are things like these:
the city mourns for this girl; they think she is dying
745 most wrongly and most undeservedly
of all womenkind, for the most glorious acts.
Here is one who would not leave her brother unburied,
a brother who had fallen in bloody conflict,
to meet his end by greedy dogs or by
750 the bird that chanced that way. Surely what she merits
is golden honor, isn't it? That's the dark rumor
that spreads in secret. Nothing I own
I value more highly, father, than your success.
What greater distinction can a son have than the glory
755 of a successful father, and for a father
the distinction of successful children?
Do not bear this single habit of mind, to think
that what you say and nothing else is true
A man who thinks that he alone is right,
760 or what he says, or what he *is* himself,
unique, such men, when opened up, are seen
to be quite empty. For a man, though he be wise,
it is no shame to learn—learn many things,
and not maintain his views too rigidly.
765 You notice how by streams in wintertime
the trees that yield preserve their branches safely,
but those that fight the tempest perish utterly.
The man who keeps the sheet[1] of his sail tight
and never slackens capsizes his boat
770 and makes the rest of his trip keel uppermost.
Yield something of your anger, give way a little.
If a much younger man, like me, may have

---

1. Rope attached to the corner of a sail to hold it at the proper angle to the wind.

a judgment, I would say it were far better
to be one altogether wise by nature, but,
as things incline not to be so, then it is good        775
also to learn from those who advise well.
CHORUS: My lord, if he says anything to the point,
you should learn from him, and you, too, Haemon,
learn from your father. Both of you
have spoken well.                                       780
CREON: Should we that are my age learn wisdom
from young men such as he is?
HAEMON: Not learn injustice, certainly. If I am young,
do not look at my years but what I do.
CREON: Is what you do to have respect for rebels?
HAEMON: I                                               785
would not urge you to be scrupulous
towards the wicked.
CREON: Is *she* not tainted by the disease of wickedness?
HAEMON: The entire people of Thebes says no to that.
CREON: Should the city tell me how I am to rule them?   790
HAEMON: Do you see what a young man's words these are of yours?
CREON: Must I rule the land by someone else's judgment
rather than my own?
HAEMON: There is no city
possessed by one man only.
CREON: Is not the city thought to be the ruler's?       795
HAEMON: You would be a fine dictator of a desert.
CREON: It seems this boy is on the woman's side.
HAEMON: If you are a woman—my care is all for you.
CREON: You villain, to bandy words with your own father!
HAEMON: I see your acts as mistaken and unjust.         800
CREON: Am I mistaken, reverencing my own office?
HAEMON: There is no reverence in trampling on God's honor.
CREON: Your nature is vile, in yielding to a woman.
HAEMON: You will not find me yield to what is shameful.
CREON: At least, your argument is all for her.          805
HAEMON: Yes, and for you and me—and for the gods below.
CREON: You will never marry her while her life lasts.
HAEMON: Then she must die—and dying destroy another.
CREON: Has your daring gone so far, to threaten me?
HAEMON: What threat is it to speak against empty judgments?  810
CREON: Empty of sense yourself, you will regret
your schooling of me in sense.
HAEMON: If you were not
my father, I would say you are insane.
CREON: You woman's slave, do not try to wheedle me.
HAEMON: You want to talk but never to hear and listen.  815
CREON: Is that so? By the heavens above you will not—
be sure of that—get off scot-free, insulting,
abusing me.

[*He speaks to the* SERVANTS.]

              You people bring out this creature,
this hated creature, that she may die before
820   his very eyes, right now, next her would-be husband.
HAEMON: Not at my side! Never think that! She will not
   die by my side. But you will never again
   set eyes upon my face. Go then and rage
   with such of your friends as are willing to endure it.
825 CHORUS: The man is gone, my lord, quick in his anger.
   A young man's mind is fierce when he is hurt.
CREON: Let him go, and do and think things superhuman.
   But these two girls he shall not save from death.
CHORUS: Both of them? Do you mean to kill them both?
830 CREON: No, not the one that didn't do anything.
   You are quite right there.
CHORUS: And by what form of death do you mean to kill her?
CREON: I will bring her where the path is loneliest,
   and hide her alive in a rocky cavern there.
835   I'll give just enough of food as shall suffice
   for a bare expiation, that the city may avoid pollution.
   In that place she shall call on Hades, god of death,
   in her prayers. That god only she reveres.
   Perhaps she will win from him escape from death
840   or at least in that last moment will recognize
   her honoring of the dead is labor lost.
CHORUS: Love undefeated in the fight,
     Love that makes havoc of possessions,
     Love who lives at night in a young girl's soft cheeks,
845     Who travels over sea, or in huts in the countryside—
     there is no god able to escape you
     nor anyone of men, whose life is a day only,
     and whom you possess is mad.

     You wrench the minds of just men to injustice,
850     to their disgrace; this conflict among kinsmen
     it is you who stirred to turmoil.
     The winner is desire. She gleaming kindles
     from the eyes of the girl good to bed.
     Love shares the throne with the great powers that rule.
855     For the golden Aphrodite[2] holds her play there
     and then no one can overcome her.

     Here I too am borne out of the course of lawfulness
     when I see these things, and I cannot control
     the springs of my tears
860     when I see Antigone making her way

---

2. Goddess of love and beauty.

  to her bed—but the bed
  that is rest for everyone.
ANTIGONE: You see me, you people of my country,
  as I set out on my last road of all,
  looking for the last time on this light of this sun—    865
  never again. I am alive but Hades who gives sleep to everyone
  is leading me to the shores of Acheron,[3]
  though I have known nothing of marriage songs
  nor the chant that brings the bride to bed.
  My husband is to be the Lord of Death.    870
CHORUS: Yes, you go to the place where the dead are hidden,
  but you go with distinction and praise.
  You have not been stricken by wasting sickness;
  you have not earned the wages of the sword;
  it was your own choice and alone among mankind    875
  you will descend, alive,
  to that world of death.
ANTIGONE: But indeed I have heard of the saddest of deaths—
  of the Phrygian stranger,[4] daughter of Tantalus,
  whom the rocky growth subdued, like clinging ivy.    880
  The rains never leave her, the snow never fails,
  as she wastes away. That is how men tell the story.
  From streaming eyes her tears wet the crags;
  most like to her the god brings me to rest.
CHORUS: Yes, but she was a god, and god born,    885
  and you are mortal and mortal born.
  Surely it is great renown
  for a woman that dies, that in life and death
  her lot is a lot shared with demigods.
ANTIGONE: You mock me. In the name of our fathers' gods    890
  why do you not wait till I am gone to insult me?
  Must you do it face to face?
  My city! Rich citizens of my city!
  You springs of Dirce, you holy groves of Thebes,
  famed for its chariots! I would still have you as my witnesses,    895
  with what dry-eyed friends, under what laws
  I make my way to my prison sealed like a tomb.
  Pity me. Neither among the living nor the dead
  do I have a home in common—
  neither with the living nor the dead.    900
CHORUS: You went to the extreme of daring
  and against the high throne of Justice
  you fell, my daughter, grievously.
  But perhaps it was for some ordeal of your father
  that you are paying requital.    905

---

3. River in Hades.
4. Niobe, whose children were slain because of her boastfulness and who was herself turned into a stone on Mount Siphylus. Her tears became the mountain's streams.

ANTIGONE: You have touched the most painful of my cares—
  the pity for my father, ever reawakened,
  and the fate of all of our race, the famous Labdacids;
  the doomed self-destruction of my mother's bed
910 when she slept with her own son,
  my father.
  What parents I was born of, God help me!
  To them I am going to share their home,
  the curse on me, too, and unmarried.
915 Brother, it was a luckless marriage you made,
  and dying killed my life.
CHORUS: There *is* a certain reverence for piety.
  But for him in authority,
  he cannot see that authority defied;
920 it is your own self-willed temper
  that has destroyed you.
ANTIGONE: No tears for me, no friends, no marriage. Brokenhearted
  I am led along the road ready before me.
  I shall never again be suffered
925 to look on the holy eye of the day.
  But my fate claims no tears—
  no friend cries for me.
CREON: [*To the* SERVANTS.] Don't you know that weeping and wailing before death
  would never stop if one is allowed to weep and wail?
930 Lead her away at once. Enfold her
  in that rocky tomb of hers—as I told you to.
  There leave her alone, solitary,
  to die if she so wishes
  or live a buried life in such a home;
935 we are guiltless in respect of her, this girl.
  But living above, among the rest of us, this life
  she shall certainly lose.
ANTIGONE: Tomb, bridal chamber, prison forever
  dug in rock, it is to you I am going
940 to join my people, that great number that have died,
  whom in their death Persephone[5] received.
  I am the last of them and I go down
  in the worst death of all—for I have not lived
  the due term of my life. But when I come
945 to that other world my hope is strong
  that my coming will be welcome to my father,
  and dear to you, my mother, and dear to you,
  my brother deeply loved. For when you died,
  with my own hands I washed and dressed you all,
950 and poured the lustral offerings on your graves.

---

5. Abducted by Pluto (known to the Greeks as Hades), god of the underworld.

And now, Polyneices, it was for such care of your body
that I have earned these wages.
Yet those who think rightly will think I did right
in honoring you. Had I been a mother
of children, and my husband been dead and rotten, 955
I would not have taken this weary task upon me
against the will of the city. What law backs me
when I say this? I will tell you:
If my husband were dead, I might have another,
and child from another man, if I lost the first. 960
But when father and mother both were hidden in death
no brother's life would bloom for me again.
That is the law under which I gave you precedence,
my dearest brother, and that is why Creon thinks me
wrong, even a criminal, and now takes me 965
by the hand and leads me away,
unbedded, without bridal, without share
in marriage and in nurturing of children;
as lonely as you see me; without friends;
with fate against me I go to the vault of death 970
while still alive. What law of God have I broken?
Why should I still look to the gods in my misery?
Whom should I summon as ally? For indeed
because of piety I was called impious.
If this proceeding is good in the gods' eyes 975
I shall know my sin, once I have suffered.
But if Creon and his people are the wrongdoers
let their suffering be no worse than the injustice
they are meting out to me.
CHORUS: It is the same blasts, the tempests of the soul, 980
   possess her.
CREON:        Then for this her guards,
   who are so slow, will find themselves in trouble.
ANTIGONE: [*Cries out.*] Oh, that word has come
   very close to death.
CREON: I will not comfort you 985
   with hope that the sentence will not be accomplished.
ANTIGONE: O my father's city, in Theban land,
   O gods that sired my race,
   I am led away, I have no more stay.
   Look on me, princes of Thebes, 990
   the last remnant of the old royal line;
   see what I suffer and who makes me suffer
   because I gave reverence to what claims reverence.
CHORUS: Danae suffered, too, when, her beauty lost, she gave
      the light of heaven in exchange for brassbound walls, 995
      and in the tomb-like cell was she hidden and held;
      yet she was honored in her breeding, child,
      and she kept, as guardian, the seed of Zeus

that came to her in a golden shower.[6]
But there is some terrible power in destiny
and neither wealth nor war
nor tower nor black ships, beaten by the sea,
can give escape from it.

The hot-tempered son of Dryas,[7] the Edonian king,
in fury mocked Dionysus,
who then held him in restraint
in a rocky dungeon.
So the terrible force and flower of his madness
drained away. He came to know the god
whom in frenzy he had touched with his mocking tongue,
when he would have checked the inspired women
and the fire of Dionysus,
when he provoked the Muses[8] that love the lyre.
By the black rocks, dividing the sea in two,
are the shores of the Bosporus, Thracian Salmydessus.[9]
There the god of war who lives near the city
saw the terrible blinding wound
dealt by his savage wife
on Phineus' two sons.[1]
She blinded and tore with the points of her shuttle,
and her bloodied hands, those eyes
that else would have looked on her vengefully.
As they wasted away, they lamented
their unhappy fate that they were doomed
to be born of a mother cursed in her marriage.
She traced her descent from the seed
of the ancient Erechtheidae.
In far-distant caves she was raised
among her father's storms, that child of Boreas
quick as a horse, over the steep hills,
a daughter of the gods.
But, my child, the long-lived Fates[2]
bore hard upon her, too.

[*Enter* TEIRESIAS, *the blind prophet, led by a* BOY.]

TEIRESIAS: My lords of Thebes, we have come here together,
one pair of eyes serving us both. For the blind

---

6. Danae was locked away because it was prophesized that her son would kill her father. Zeus entered her cell as a shower of gold, impregnated her, and thus fathered Perseus, the child who fulfilled the prophecy.
7. Stricken with madness by Dionysus.   8. Nine sister goddesses of poetry, music, and the arts.
9. City in the land of Thrace, in ancient times erroneously believed to lie on the Bosporus, the strait separating Europe and Asia at the outlet of the Black Sea.
1. King Phineus's second wife blinded the children of his first wife, whom Phineus had imprisoned in a cave.
2. Supernatural forces, usually represented as three old women, who determine the quality and length of life.

such must be the way of going, by a guide's leading.
CREON: What is the news, my old Teiresias?
TEIRESIAS: I will tell you; and you, listen to the prophet.
CREON: Never in the past have I turned from your advice.
TEIRESIAS: And so you have steered well the ship of state. 1040
CREON: I have benefited and can testify to that.
TEIRESIAS: Then realize you are on the razor edge
of danger.
CREON: What can that be? I shudder to hear those words.
TEIRESIAS: When you learn the signs recognized by my art 1045
you will understand.
I sat at my ancient place of divination
for watching the birds, where every bird finds shelter;
and I heard an unwonted voice among them;
they were horribly distressed, and screamed unmeaningly. 1050
I knew they were tearing each other murderously;
the beating of their wings was a clear sign.
I was full of fear; at once on all the altars,
as they were fully kindled, I tasted the offerings,
but the god of fire refused to burn from the sacrifice, 1055
and from the thighbones a dark stream of moisture
oozed from the embers, smoked and sputtered.
The gall bladder burst and scattered to the air
and the streaming thighbones lay exposed
from the fat wrapped round them— 1060
so much I learned from this boy here,
the fading prophecies of a rite that failed.
This boy here is my guide, as I am others'.
This is the city's sickness—and your plans are the cause of it.
For our altars and our sacrificial hearths 1065
are filled with the carrion meat of birds and dogs,
torn from the flesh of Oedipus' poor son.
So the gods will not take our prayers or sacrifice
nor yet the flame from the thighbones, and no bird
cries shrill and clear, so glutted 1070
are they with fat of the blood of the killed man.
Reflect on these things, son. All men
can make mistakes; but, once mistaken,
a man is no longer stupid nor accursed
who, having fallen on ill, tries to cure that ill, 1075
not taking a fine undeviating stand.
It is obstinacy that convicts of folly.
Yield to the dead man; do not stab him—
now he is gone—what bravery is this,
to inflict another death upon the dead? 1080
I mean you well and speak well for your good.
It is never sweeter to learn from a good counselor
than when he counsels to your benefit.
CREON: Old man, you are all archers, and I am your mark.

1085 I must be tried by your prophecies as well.
By the breed of you I have been bought and sold
and made a merchandise, for ages now.
But I tell you: make your profit from silver-gold
from Sardis and the gold from India
1090 if you will. But this dead man you shall not hide
in a grave, not though the eagles of Zeus should bear
the carrion, snatching it to the throne of Zeus itself.
Even so, I shall not so tremble at the pollution
to let you bury him.
                No, I am certain
1095 no human has the power to pollute the gods.
They fall, you old Teiresias, those men,
—so very clever—in a bad fall whenever
they eloquently speak vile words for profit.
TEIRESIAS: I wonder if there's a man who dares consider—
1100 CREON: What do you mean? What sort of generalization
is this talk of yours?
TEIRESIAS: How much the best of possessions is the ability
to listen to wise advice?
CREON: As I should imagine that the worst
1105 injury must be native stupidity.
TEIRESIAS: Now that is exactly where your mind is sick.
CREON: I do not like to answer a seer with insults.
TEIRESIAS: But you do, when you say my prophecies are lies.
CREON: Well,
1110 the whole breed of prophets certainly loves money.
TEIRESIAS: And the breed that comes from princes loves to take
advantage—base advantage.
CREON:                 Do you realize
you are speaking in such terms of your own prince?
TEIRESIAS: I know. But it is through me you have saved the city.
1115 CREON: You are a wise prophet, but what you love is wrong.
TEIRESIAS: You will force me to declare what should be hidden
in my own heart.
CREON:              Out with it—
but only if your words are not for gain.
TEIRESIAS: They won't be for *your* gain—that I am sure of.
1120 CREON: But realize you will not make a merchandise
of my decisions.
TEIRESIAS:           And you must realize
that you will not outlive many cycles more
of this swift sun before you give in exchange
one of your own loins bred, a corpse for a corpse,
1125 for you have thrust one that belongs above
below the earth, and bitterly dishonored
a living soul by lodging her in the grave;
while one that belonged indeed to the underworld
gods you have kept on this earth without due share

of rites of burial, of due funeral offerings,
a corpse unhallowed. With all of this you, Creon,
have nothing to do, nor have the gods above.
These acts of yours are violence, on your part.
And in requital the avenging Spirits
of Death itself and the gods' Furies shall
after *your* deeds, lie in ambush for you, and
in their hands you shall be taken cruelly.
Now, look at this and tell me I was bribed
to say it! The delay will not be long
before the cries of mourning in your house,
of men and women. All the cities will stir in hatred
against you, because their sons in mangled shreds
received their burial rites from dogs, from wild beasts
or when some bird of the air brought a vile stink
to each city that contained the hearths of the dead.
These are the arrows that archer-like I launched—
you vexed me so to anger—at your heart.
You shall not escape their sting. You, boy,
lead me away to my house, so he may discharge
his anger on younger men; so may he come to know
to bear a quieter tongue in his head and a better
mind than that now he carries in him.

CHORUS: That was a terrible prophecy, my lord.
 The man has gone. Since these hairs of mine grew white
 from the black they once were, he has never spoken
 a word of a lie to our city.

CREON: I know, I know.
 My mind is all bewildered. To yield is terrible.
 But by opposition to destroy my very being
 with a self-destructive curse must also be reckoned
 in what is terrible.

CHORUS: You need good counsel, son of Menoeceus,
 and need to take it.

CREON: What must I do, then? Tell me; I shall agree.

CHORUS: The girl—go now and bring her up from her cave,
 and for the exposed dead man, give him his burial.

CREON: That is really your advice? You would have me yield.

CHORUS: And quickly as you may, my lord. Swift harms
 sent by the gods cut off the paths of the foolish.

CREON: Oh, it is hard; I must give up what my heart
 would have me do. But it is ill to fight
 against what must be.

CHORUS: Go now, and do this;
 do not give the task to others.

CREON: I will go,
 just as I am. Come, servants, all of you;
 take axes in your hands; away with you
 to the place you see, there.

> For my part, since my intention is so changed,
1180 as I bound her myself, myself will free her.
> I am afraid it may be best, in the end
> of life, to have kept the old accepted laws.

CHORUS: You of many names,[3] glory of the Cadmeian
bride, breed of loud thundering Zeus;
1185 you who watch over famous Italy;
you who rule where all are welcome in Eleusis;
in the sheltered plains of Deo—
O Bacchus that dwells in Thebes,
the mother city of Bacchanals,
1190 by the flowing stream of Ismenus,
in the ground sown by the fierce dragon's teeth.

You are he on whom the murky gleam of torches glares,
above the twin peaks of the crag
where come the Corycean nymphs
1195 to worship you, the Bacchanals;
and the stream of Castalia has seen you, too;
and you are he that the ivy-clad
slopes of Nisaean hills,
and the green shore ivy-clustered,
1200 sent to watch over the roads of Thebes,
where the immortal Evoe chant[4] rings out.

It is Thebes which you honor most of all cities,
you and your mother both,
she who died by the blast of Zeus' thunderbolt.
1205 And now when the city, with all its folk,
is gripped by a violent plague,
come with healing foot, over the slopes of Parnassus,[5]
over the moaning strait.
You lead the dance of the fire-breathing stars,
1210 you are master of the voices of the night.
True-born child of Zeus, appear,
my lord, with your Thyiad attendants,
who in frenzy all night long
dance in your house, Iacchus,
1215 dispenser of gifts.

MESSENGER: You who live by the house of Cadmus and Amphion,[6]
hear me. There is no condition of man's life
that stands secure. As such I would not
praise it or blame. It is chance that sets upright;
1220 it is chance that brings down the lucky and the unlucky,
each in his turn. For men, that belong to death,
there is no prophet of established things.

---

3. Refers to Dionysus.   4. Come forth, come forth!
5. Mountain in central Greece sacred to Apollo, Dionysus, and the Muses; Apollo's shrine, Delphi, lies at the foot of Parnassus.   6. A name for Thebes.

Once Creon was a man worthy of envy—
of my envy, at least. For he saved this city
of Thebes from her enemies, and attained
the throne of the land, with all a king's power.
He guided it right. His race bloomed
with good children. But when a man forfeits joy
I do not count his life as life, but only
a life trapped in a corpse.
Be rich within your house, yes greatly rich,
if so you will, and live in a prince's style.
If the gladness of these things is gone, I would not
give the shadow of smoke for the rest,
as against joy.

CHORUS: What is the sorrow of our princes
of which you are the messenger?

MESSENGER: Death; and the living are guilty of their deaths.

CHORUS: But who is the murderer? Who the murdered? Tell us.

MESSENGER: Haemon is dead; the hand that shed his blood
was his very own.

CHORUS: Truly his own hand? Or his father's?

MESSENGER: His own hand, in his anger
against his father for a murder.

CHORUS: Prophet, how truly you have made good your word!

MESSENGER: These things are so; you may debate the rest.
Here I see Creon's wife Eurydice
approaching. Unhappy woman!
Does she come from the house as hearing about her son
or has she come by chance?

EURYDICE: I heard your words, all you men of Thebes, as I
was going out to greet Pallas[7] with my prayers.
I was just drawing back the bolts of the gate
to open it when a cry struck through my ears
telling of my household's ruin. I fell backward
in terror into the arms of my servants; I fainted.
But tell me again, what is the story? I
will hear it as one who is no stranger to sorrow.

MESSENGER: Dear mistress, I will tell you, for I was there,
and I will leave out no word of the truth.
Why should I comfort you and then tomorrow
be proved a liar? The truth is always best.
I followed your husband, at his heels, to the end of the plain
where Polyneices' body still lay unpitied,
and torn by dogs. We prayed to Hecate, goddess
of the crossroads, and also to Pluto[8]
that they might restrain their anger and turn kind.
And him we washed with sacred lustral water

---

7. Athena, goddess of wisdom.
8. King of the underworld, known to the Greeks as Hades. *Hecate:* goddess of witchcraft.

and with fresh-cut boughs we burned what was left of him
1270 and raised a high mound of his native earth;
then we set out again for the hollowed rock,
death's stone bridal chamber for the girl.
Someone then heard a voice of bitter weeping
while we were still far off, coming from that unblest room.
1275 The man came to tell our master Creon of it.
As the king drew nearer, there swarmed about him
a cry of misery but no clear words.
He groaned and in an anguished mourning voice
cried "Oh, am I a true prophet? Is this the road
1280 that I must travel, saddest of all my wayfaring?
It is my son's voice that haunts my ear. Servants,
get closer, quickly. Stand around the tomb
and look. There is a gap there where the stones
have been wrenched away; enter there, by the very mouth,
1285 and see whether I recognize the voice of Haemon
or if the gods deceive me." On the command
of our despairing master we went to look.
In the furthest part of the tomb we saw her, hanging
by her neck. She had tied a noose of muslin on it.
1290 Haemon's hands were about her waist embracing her,
while he cried for the loss of his bride gone to the dead,
and for all his father had done, and his own sad love.
When Creon saw him he gave a bitter cry,
went in and called to him with a groan: "Poor son!
1295 what have you done? What can you have meant?
What happened to destroy you? Come out, I pray you!"
The boy glared at him with savage eyes, and then
spat in his face, without a word of answer.
He drew his double-hilted sword. As his father
1300 ran to escape him, Haemon failed to strike him,
and the poor wretch in anger at himself
leaned on his sword and drove it halfway in,
into his ribs. Then he folded the girl to him,
in his arms, while he was conscious still,
1305 and gasping poured a sharp stream of bloody drops
on her white cheeks. There they lie,
the dead upon the dead. So he has won
the pitiful fulfillment of his marriage
within death's house. In this human world he has shown
1310 how the wrong choice in plans is for a man
his greatest evil.

CHORUS: What do you make of this? My lady is gone,
without a word of good or bad.

MESSENGER: I, too,
am lost in wonder. I am inclined to hope
1315 that hearing of her son's death she could not
open her sorrow to the city, but chose rather

within her house to lay upon her maids
the mourning for the household grief. Her judgment
is good; she will not make any false step.
CHORUS: I do not know. To me this over-heavy silence
seems just as dangerous as much empty wailing.
MESSENGER: I will go in and learn if in her passionate
heart she keeps hidden some secret purpose.
You are right; there is sometimes danger in too much silence.
CHORUS: Here comes our king himself. He bears in his hands
a memorial all too clear;
it is a ruin of none other's making,
purely his own if one dare to say that.
CREON: The mistakes of a blinded man
are themselves rigid and laden with death.
You look at us the killer and the killed
of the one blood. Oh, the awful blindness
of those plans of mine. My son, you were so young,
so young to die. You were freed from the bonds of life
through no folly of your own—only through mine.
CHORUS: I think you have learned justice—but too late.
CREON: Yes, I have learned it to my bitterness. At this moment
God has sprung on my head with a vast weight
and struck me down. He shook me in my savage ways;
he has overturned my joy, has trampled it,
underfoot. The pains men suffer
are pains indeed.
SECOND MESSENGER: My lord, you have troubles and a store besides;
some are there in your hands, but there are others
you will surely see when you come to your house.
CREON: What trouble can there be beside these troubles?
SECOND MESSENGER: The queen is dead. She was indeed true mother
of the dead son. She died, poor lady,
by recent violence upon herself.
CREON: Haven of death, you can never have enough.
Why, why do you destroy me?
You messenger, who have brought me bitter news,
what is this tale you tell?
It is a dead man that you kill again—
what new message of yours is this, boy?
Is this new slaughter of a woman
a doom to lie on the pile of the dead?
CHORUS: You can see. It is no longer
hidden in a corner.

[*By some stage device, perhaps the so-called eccyclema, the inside of the palace is shown, with the body of the dead* QUEEN.]

CREON: Here is yet another horror
for my unhappy eyes to see.
What doom still waits for me?

       I have but now taken in my arms my son,
       and again I look upon another dead face.
1365    Poor mother and poor son!
    SECOND MESSENGER: She stood at the altar, and with keen whetted knife
       she suffered her darkening eyes to close.
       First she cried in agony recalling the noble fate of Megareus,[9]
       who died before all this,
1370   and then for the fate of this son; and in the end
       she cursed you for the evil you had done
       in killing her sons.
    CREON: I am distracted with fear. Why does not someone
       strike a two-edged sword right through me?
1375   I am dissolved in an agony of misery.
    SECOND MESSENGER: You were indeed accused
       by her that is dead
       of Haemon's and of Megareus' death.
    CREON: By what kind of violence did she find her end?
1380 SECOND MESSENGER: Her own hand struck her to the entrails
       when she heard of her son's lamentable death.
    CREON: These acts can never be made to fit another
       to free me from the guilt. It was I that killed her.
       Poor wretch that I am, I say it is true!
1385   Servants, lead me away, quickly, quickly.
       I am no more a live man than one dead.
    CHORUS: What you say is for the best—if there be a best
       in evil such as this. For the shortest way
       is best with troubles that lie at our feet.
1390 CREON: O, let it come, let it come,
       that best of fates that waits on my last day.
       Surely best fate of all. Let it come, let it come!
       That I may never see one more day's light!
    CHORUS: These things are for the future. We must deal
1395   with what impends. What in the future is to care for
       rests with those whose duty it is
       to care for them.
    CREON: At least, all that *I* want
       is in that prayer of mine.
1400 CHORUS: Pray for no more at all. For what is destined
       for us, men mortal, there is no escape.
    CREON: Lead me away, a vain silly man
       who killed you, son, and you, too, lady.
       I did not mean to, but I did.
1405   I do not know where to turn my eyes
       to look to, for support.
       Everything in my hands is crossed. A most unwelcome fate
       has leaped upon me.
    CHORUS: Wisdom is far the chief element in happiness

---

9. Another son of Creon who died defending Thebes.

and, secondly, no irreverence towards the gods.
But great words of haughty men exact
in retribution blows as great
and in old age teach wisdom.

THE END

ca. 441 B.C.

**RICHARD C. JEBB**

*From* The *Antigone* of Sophocles*

The issue defined in the opening scene,—the conflict of divine with human law,—remains the central interest throughout. The action, so simple in plan, is varied by masterly character-drawing, both in the two principal figures, and in those lesser persons who contribute gradations of light and shade to the picture. There is no halting in the march of the drama; at each successive step we become more and more keenly interested to see how this great conflict is to end; and when the tragic climax is reached, it is worthy of such a progress.

The simplicity of the plot is due to the clearness with which two principles are opposed to each other. *Creon represents the duty of obeying the State's laws; Antigone, the duty of listening to the private conscience.* The definiteness and the power with which the play puts the case on each side are conclusive proofs that the question had assumed a distinct shape before the poet's mind. It is the only instance in which a Greek play has for its central theme a practical problem of conduct, involving issues, moral and political, which might be discussed on similar grounds in any age and in any country of the world. Greek Tragedy, owing partly to the limitations which it placed on detail, was better suited than modern drama to raise such a question in a general form. The *Antigone*, indeed, raises the question in a form as nearly abstract as is compatible with the nature of drama. The case of Antigone is a thoroughly typical one for the private conscience, because the particular thing which she believes that she ought to do was, in itself, a thing which every Greek of that age recognised as a most sacred duty,—viz.,[1] to render burial rites to kinsfolk. This advantage was not devised by Sophocles; it came to him as part of the story which he was to dramatise; but it forms an additional reason for thinking that, when he dramatised that story in the precise manner which he has chosen, he had a consciously dialectical purpose. Such a purpose was wholly consistent, in this instance, with the artist's first aim,—to produce a work of art. It is because Creon and Antigone are so human that the controversy which they represent becomes so vivid.

But how did Sophocles intend us to view the result? What is the drift of the words at the end, which say that "wisdom is the supreme part of happiness"? If this wisdom, or prudence, means, generally, the observance of due limit, may not

---

*From Sir Richard C. Jebb, ed., *The* Antigone *of Sophocles*, abr. by E. S. Shuckburgh (orig. ed., 1902; repr. Cambridge and New York: Cambridge UP, 1984) xvii-xix.
1. Namely (abbreviation of the Latin *videlicet*) [Editor's note].

the suggested moral be that both the parties to the conflict were censurable? As Creon overstepped the due limit when, by his edict, he infringed the divine law, so Antigone also overstepped it when she defied the edict. The drama would thus be a conflict between two persons, each of whom defends an intrinsically sound principle, but defends it in a mistaken way; and both persons are therefore punished. This view, of which Boeckh[2] is the chief representative, has found several supporters. Among them is Hegel:—"In the view of the Eternal Justice, both were wrong, because they were one-sided, but at the same time both were right."[3]

Or does the poet rather intend us to feel that Antigone is wholly in the right,—*i.e.*, that nothing of which the human lawgiver could complain in her was of a moment's account beside the supreme duty which she was fulfilling;—and that Creon was wholly in the wrong,—*i.e.*, that the intrinsically sound maxims of government on which he relies lose all validity when opposed to the higher law which he was breaking? If that was the poet's meaning, then the "wisdom" taught by the issue of the drama means the sense which duly subordinates human to divine law,—teaching that, if the two come into conflict, human law must yield.

A careful study of the play itself will suffice (I think) to show that the second of these two views is the true one. Sophocles has allowed Creon to put his case ably, and (in a measure from which an inferior artist might have shrunk) he has been content to make Antigone merely a nobly heroic woman, not a being exempt from human passion and human weakness; but none the less does he mean us to feel that, in this controversy, the right is wholly with her, and the wrong wholly with her judge.

MAURICE BOWRA

## *From* Sophoclean Tragedy*

Modern critics who do not share Sophocles' conviction about the paramount duty of burying the dead and who attach more importance than he did to the claims of political authority have tended to underestimate the way in which he justifies Antigone against Creon. To their support they have called in the great name of Hegel, who was fascinated by the play and advanced remarkable views on it. His remarks have been taken out of their context, and he has been made responsible for the opinion that Sophocles dramatized a conflict not between right and wrong but between right and right, that Antigone and Creon are equally justified in their actions and that the tragedy arises out of this irreconcilable conflict. Hegel's own words lend some support to this view: "In the view of eternal justice both were wrong, because they were one-sided; but at the same time both were right." But if we look at Hegel's observations in their own place, we find that this summary hardly conveys his full meaning. He was thinking of something much vaster than the play, of the whole logic of history which is here symbolized in a concrete example. In this the conflict of opposites ends by pro-

---

2. August Boeckh (1785–1867), German classical scholar [Editor's note].
3. *Religionsphilosophie*, II. 114 [Jebb's note].
*From Maurice Bowra, *Sophoclean Tragedy* (Oxford: Clarendon, 1944) 65–67.

ducing a synthesis which is itself right. The conclusion is what matters, and that is different from saying that both sides in the conflict are themselves right. The tragic conclusion is, so to speak, a lesson of history, a fact which cannot be denied, real and therefore right, but the conflict which precedes it cannot be judged in isolation and neither side in it is right or wrong except in a relative sense. Hegel used the *Antigone* to illustrate his view of tragedy and his view of existence. He drew his own conclusions about the actions portrayed in it, as he was fully entitled to do. But his views are not those of Sophocles, and he should not be thought to maintain that Creon and Antigone were equally right in the eyes of their creator.

Sophocles leaves no doubt what conclusion should be drawn from the *Antigone*. He closes with a moral on the lips of the Chorus which tells the audience what to think:

> Wisdom has first place in happiness,
> And to fail not in reverence to the gods.
> The big words of the arrogant
> Lay big stripes on the boasters' backs.
> They pay the price
> And learn in old age to be wise.[1]

This can refer to no one but Creon, whose lack of wisdom has brought him to misery, who has shown irreverence to the gods in refusing burial to Polynices, been chastened for his proud words, and learned wisdom in his old age. To this lesson the preceding action in which Creon has lost son and wife and happiness has already made its effective contribution. We may be sure that the Chorus speak for the poet. It is as silent about Antigone as it is emphatic about Creon. There is no hint that she has in any way acted wrongly or that her death should be regarded as a righteous punishment. Of course the final words do not sum up everything important in the play, but we may reasonably assume that they pass judgement on its salient events as they appear in retrospect when the action is finished. There is no real problem about the ethical intention of the *Antigone*. It shows the fall of a proud man, and its lesson is that the gods punish pride and irreverence. But what matters much more than the actual conclusion is the means by which it is reached, the presentation of the different parties in the conflict, the view that we take of each, the feelings that are forced on us. The interest and power of the *Antigone* lie in the tangled issues which are unravelled in it.

A conclusion so clear as this is only worth reaching if it has been preceded by a drama in which the issues are violent and complex. The rights and wrongs of the case must not throughout be so obvious as they are at the end; the audience must feel that the issue is difficult, that there is much to be said on both sides, that the ways of the gods are hard to discern. Without this the play will fail in dramatic and human interest. And Sophocles has taken great care to show the issues in their full difficulty before he provides a solution for them. He makes the two protagonists appear in such a light that at intervals we doubt if all the right is really with Antigone and all the wrong with Creon. To Creon, who defies the divine ordinance of burial, he gives arguments and sentiments which sound

---

1. Bowra's translation.

convincing enough when they are put forward, and many must feel that he has some good reason to act as he does. On the other hand Antigone, who fearlessly vindicates the laws of the gods, is by no means a gentle womanly creature who suffers martyrdom for the right. She may be right, but there are moments when we qualify our approval of her, when she seems proud and forbidding in her determination to do her duty and to do it alone. For these variations in our feelings Sophocles is responsible. He makes us find some right in Creon, some wrong in Antigone, even if we are misled about both. He built his play on a contrast not between obvious wrong and obvious right but between the real arrogance of Creon and the apparent arrogance of Antigone. The first deceives by its fine persuasive sentiments; the second works through Antigone's refusal to offer concessions or to consider any point of view but her own. This contrast runs through much of the play, accounts for misunderstandings of what takes place in it, provides false clues and suggests wrong conclusions, and adds greatly to the intensity of the drama. When a play is written round a moral issue, that issue must be a real problem about which more than one view is tenable until all the relevant facts are known. So the *Antigone* dramatizes a conflict which was familiar to the Periclean age,[2] would excite divergent judgements and feelings, and make some support Antigone, some Creon, until the end makes all clear.

## BERNARD KNOX

### *Introduction to* The Three Theban Plays*

The opening scenes show us the conflicting claims and loyalties of the two adversaries, solidly based, in both cases, on opposed political and religious principles. This is of course the basic insight of Hegel's famous analysis of the play: he sees it as "a collision between the two highest moral powers." What is wrong with them, in his view, is that they are both "one-sided." But Hegel goes much further than that. He was writing in the first half of the nineteenth century, a period of fervent German nationalism in which the foundations of the unified German state were laid: his views on loyalty to the state were very much those of Creon. "Creon," he says, "is not a tyrant, he is really a moral power. He is not in the wrong."

However, as the action develops the favorable impression created by Creon's opening speech is quickly dissipated. His announcement of his decision to expose the corpse, the concluding section of his speech, is couched in violent, vindictive terms—"carrion for the birds and dogs to tear"[1]—which stand in shocking contrast to the ethical generalities that precede it. This hint of a cruel disposition underlying the statesmanlike façade is broadened by the threat of torture leveled at the sentry and the order to execute Antigone in the presence of Haemon, her

---

2. The height of Athenian culture and political power in the time of the Athenian statesman Pericles (ca. 495–429 B.C.E.).

* From Sophocles, *The Three Theban Plays: Antigone, Oedipus the King, Oedipus at Colonus*, trans. by Robert Fagles, intro. and notes by Bernard Knox (New York: Penguin, 1982) 41–47, 53.

1. Knox's references are to Robert Fagles's translation, printed in *The Three Theban Plays.*

betrothed. And as he meets resistance from a series of opponents—Antigone's contemptuous defiance, the rational, political advice of his son Haemon, the imperious summons to obedience of the gods' spokesman, Tiresias—he swiftly abandons the temperate rhetoric of his inaugural address for increasingly savage invective. Against the two sanctions invoked by Antigone, the demands of blood relationship, the rights and privileges of the gods below, he rages in terms ranging from near-blasphemous defiance to scornful mockery.

> Sister's child or closer in blood
> than all my family clustered at my altar
> worshiping Guardian Zeus—she'll never escape,
> ... the most barbaric death.

He will live to regret this wholesale denial of the family bond, for it is precisely through that family clustered at his altar that his punishment will be administered, in the suicides of his son and his wife, both of whom die cursing him.

And for Antigone's appeals to Hades, the great god of the underworld to whom the dead belong, Creon has nothing but contempt; for him "Hades" is simply a word meaning "death," a sentence he is prepared to pass on anyone who stands in his way. He threatens the sentry with torture as a prelude: "simple death won't be enough for you." When asked if he really intends to deprive Haemon of his bride he answers sarcastically: "Death will do it for me." He expects to see Antigone and Ismene turn coward "once they see Death coming for their lives." With a derisive comment he tells his son to abandon Antigone: "Spit her out, / ... Let her find a husband down among the dead [in Hades' house]." And he dismisses Antigone's reverence for Hades and the rights of the dead with mockery as he condemns her to be buried alive: "There let her pray to the one god she worships: / Death." But this Hades is not something to be so lightly referred to, used or mocked. In the great choral ode which celebrated Man's progress and powers this was the one insurmountable obstacle that confronted him:

> ready, Never without man!
> Never without resources
> never an impasse as he marches on the future—
> only Death, from Death alone he will find no rescue ...

And Creon, in the end, looking at the corpse of his son and hearing the news of his wife's suicide, speaks of Hades for the first time with the fearful respect that is his due, not as an instrument of policy or a subject for sardonic word-play, but as a divine power, a dreadful presence: "harbor of Death, so choked, so hard to cleanse!— / why me? why are you killing me?"

Creon is forced at last to recognize the strength of those social and religious imperatives that Antigone obeys, but long before this happens he has abandoned the principles which he had proclaimed as authority for his own actions. His claim to be representative of the whole community is forgotten as he refuses to accept Haemon's report that the citizens, though they dare not speak out, disapprove of his action; he denies the relevance of such a report even if true—"And is Thebes about to tell me how to rule?"—and finally repudiates his principles in specific terms by an assertion that the city belongs to him—"The city *is* the king's—that's the law!" This autocratic phrase puts the finishing touch to the picture Sophocles is drawing for his audience: Creon has now displayed all the characteristics of the "tyrant," a despotic ruler who seizes power and retains it by intimidation and force. Athens had lived under the rule of a "tyrant" before the democracy was established in 508 B.C., and the name and institution were still regarded with abhorrence. Creon goes on to abandon the gods whose temples crown the city's high places, the gods he once claimed as his own, and his language is even more violent. The blind prophet Tiresias tells him that the birds and dogs are fouling the altars of the city's gods with the carrion flesh of Polynices; he must bury the corpse. His furious reply begins with a characteristic accusation that the prophet has been bribed (the sentry had this same accusation flung at him), but what follows is a hideously blasphemous defiance of those gods Creon once claimed to serve:

> You'll never bury that body in the grave,
> not even if Zeus's eagles rip the corpse
> and wing their rotten pickings off to the throne of god!

At this high point in his stubborn rage (he will break by the end of the scene and try, too late, to avoid the divine wrath), he is sustained by nothing except his tyrannical insistence on his own will, come what may, and his outraged refusal to be defeated by a woman. "No woman," he says, "is going to lord it over me." "I'm not the man, not now: she is the man / if this victory goes to her and she goes free."

Antigone, on her side, is just as indifferent to Creon's principles of action as he is to hers. She mentions the city only in her last agonized laments before she is led off to her living death:

> O my city, all your fine rich sons!
> ... springs of the Dirce,
> holy grove of Thebes ...

But here she is appealing for sympathy to the city over the heads of the chorus, the city's symbolic representative on stage. In all her arguments with Creon and Ismene she speaks as one wholly unconscious of the rights and duties membership in the city confers and imposes, as if no unit larger than the family existed. It is a position just as extreme as Creon's insistence that the demands of the city take precedence over all others, for the living and the dead alike.

Like Creon, she acts in the name of gods, but they are different gods. There is more than a little truth in Creon's mocking comment that Hades is "the one god she worships." She is from the beginning "much possessed by death"; together with Ismene she is the last survivor of a doomed family, burdened with such sorrow that she finds life hardly worth living. "Who on earth," she says to Creon, "alive in the midst of so much grief as I, / could fail to find his death a rich reward?" She has performed the funeral rites for mother, father and her brother Eteocles:

> I washed you with my hands,
> I dressed you all, I poured the cups
> across your tombs.

She now sacrifices her life to perform a symbolic burial, a handful of dust sprinkled on the corpse, for Polynices, the brother left to rot on the battlefield. She looks forward to her reunion with her beloved dead in that dark kingdom where Persephone, the bride of Hades, welcomes the ghosts. It is in the name of Hades, one of the three great gods who rule the universe, that she defends the right of Polynices and of all human beings to proper burial. "Death [Hades] longs for the same rites for all," she tells Creon—for patriot and traitor alike; she rejects Ismene's plea to be allowed to share her fate with an appeal to the same stern authority: "Who did the work? / Let the dead and the god of death bear witness!" In Creon's gods, the city's patrons and defenders, she shows no interest at all. Zeus she mentions twice: once as the source of all the calamities that have fallen and are still to fall on the house of Oedipus, and once again at the beginning of her famous speech about the unwritten laws. But the context here suggests strongly that she is thinking about Zeus in his special relationship to the underworld, Zeus *Chthonios* (Underworld Zeus). "It wasn't Zeus," she says,

>who made this proclamation....
>Nor did that Justice, dwelling with the gods
>beneath the earth, ordain such laws for men.

From first to last her religious devotion and duty are to the divine powers of the world below, the masters of that world where lie her family dead, to which she herself, reluctant but fascinated, is irresistibly drawn.

But, like Creon, she ends by denying the great sanctions she invoked to justify her action. In his case the process was spread out over the course of several scenes, as he reacted to each fresh pressure that was brought to bear on him; Antigone turns her back on the claims of blood relationship and the nether gods in one sentence: three lines in Greek, no more. They are the emotional high point of the speech she makes just before she is led off to her death.

>Never, I tell you,
>if I had been the mother of children
>or if my husband died, exposed and rotting—
>I'd never have taken this ordeal upon myself,
>never defied our people's will.

These unexpected words are part of the long speech that concludes a scene of lyric lamentation and is in effect her farewell to the land of the living. They are certainly a total repudiation of her proud claim that she acted as the champion of the unwritten laws and the infernal gods, for, as she herself told Creon, those laws and those gods have no preferences, they long "for the same rites for all." And her assertion that she would not have done for her children what she has done for Polynices is a spectacular betrayal of that fanatical loyalty to blood relationship which she urged on Ismene and defended against Creon, for there is no closer relationship imaginable than that between the mother and the children of her own body. Creon turned his back on his guiding principles step by step, in reaction to opposition based on those principles; Antigone's rejection of her public values is just as complete, but it is the sudden product of a lonely, brooding introspection, a last-minute assessment of her motives, on which the imminence of death confers a merciless clarity. She did it because Polynices was her brother; she would not have done it for husband or child. She goes on to justify this disturbing statement by an argument which is more disturbing still: husband and children, she says, could be replaced by others but, since her parents are dead, she could never have another brother. It so happens that we can identify the source of this strange piece of reasoning; it is a story in the *Histories* of Sophocles' friend Herodotus (a work from which Sophocles borrowed material more than once). Darius the Great King had condemned to death for treason a Persian noble, Intaphrenes, and all the men of his family. The wife of Intaphrenes begged importunately for their lives; offered one, she chose her brother's. When Darius asked her why, she replied in words that are unmistakably the original of Antigone's lines. But what makes sense in the story makes less in the play. The wife of Intaphrenes saves her brother's life, but Polynices is already dead; Antigone's phrase "no brother could ever spring to light again" would be fully appropriate only if Antigone had managed to save Polynices' life rather than bury his corpse.

For this reason, and also because of some stylistic anomalies in this part of the speech, but most of all because they felt that the words are unworthy of the Antigone who spoke so nobly for the unwritten laws, many great scholars and also a great poet and dramatist, Goethe, have refused to believe that Sophocles wrote them. "I would give a great deal," Goethe told his friend Eckermann in 1827, "if some talented scholar could prove that these lines were interpolated, not genuine." Goethe did not know that the attempt had already been made, six years earlier; many others have tried since—Sir Richard Jebb, the greatest English editor of Sophocles, pronounced against them—and opinion today is still divided. Obviously a decision on this point is of vital significance for the interpretation of the play as a whole: with these lines removed, Antigone goes to her prison-tomb with no flicker of self-doubt, the flawless champion of the family bond and the unwritten laws, "whole as the marble, founded as the rock"—unlike Creon, she is not, in the end, reduced to recognizing that her motive is purely personal.

The gods do not praise Antigone, nor does anyone else in the play—except the young man who loves her so passionately that he cannot bear to live without her. Haemon tells his father what the Thebans are saying behind his back, the "murmurs in the dark": that Antigone deserves not death but "a glowing crown of gold!" Whether this is a true report (and the chorus does not praise Antigone even when they have been convinced that she was right) or just his own feelings attributed to others for the sake of his argument, it is a timely reminder of Antigone's heroic status. In the somber world of the play, against the background of so many sudden deaths and the dark mystery of the divine dispensation, her courage and steadfastness are a gleam of light; she is the embodiment of the only consolation tragedy can offer—that in certain heroic natures unmerited suffering and death can be met with a greatness of soul which, because it is purely human, brings honor to us all.

MARTHA C. NUSSBAUM

## *From* The Fragility of Goodness: Luck and Ethics in Greek Tragedy and Philosophy*

[A]lmost all interpreters of [*Antigone*] have agreed that the play shows Creon to be morally defective, though they might not agree about the particular nature of his defect. The situation of Antigone is more controversial. Hegel assimilated her defect to Creon's; some more recent writers uncritically hold her up as a blameless heroine. Without entering into an exhaustive study of her role in the tragedy, I should like to claim (with the support of an increasing number of recent critics) that there is at least some justification for the Hegelian assimilation—though the criticism needs to be focused more clearly and specifically than it is in Hegel's brief remarks. I want to suggest that Antigone, like Creon, has engaged in a ruthless simplification of the world of value which effectively eliminates conflicting obligations. Like Creon, she can be blamed for refusal of vision. But there are important differences, as well, between her project and Creon's. When these are seen, it will also emerge that this criticism of Antigone is not incompatible with the judgment that she is morally superior to Creon.

> O kindred, own-sisterly head of Ismene, do you know that there is not one of the evils left by Oedipus that Zeus does not fulfill for us while we live?... Do you grasp anything? Have you heard anything? Or has it escaped your notice that the evils that belong to enemies are advancing against our friends?[1]

A person is addressed with a periphrasis that is both intimate and impersonal. In the most emphatic terms available, it characterizes her as a close relative of the speaker. And yet its attitude towards the addressee is strangely remote. Antigone sees Ismene simply as the form of a close family relation. As such, she presses on her, with anxious insistence, the knowledge of the family: that "loved ones" (*philoi*) are being penalized as if they were enemies (*echthroi*). Loving relatives must "see" the shame and dishonour of "the evils that are yours and mine."

There has been a war. On one side was an army led by Eteocles, brother of Antigone and Ismene. On the other side was an invading army, made up partly of foreigners, but led by a Theban brother, Polynices. This heterogeneity is denied, in different ways, by both Creon and Antigone. Creon's strategy is to draw, in thought, a line between the invading and defending forces. What falls to one side of this line is a foe, bad, unjust; what falls to the other (if loyal to the city's cause) becomes, indiscriminately, friend or loved one. Antigone, on the other hand, denies the relevance of this distinction entirely. She draws, in imagination, a small circle around the members of her family: what is inside (with further restrictions which we shall mention) is family, therefore loved one and friend; what is outside is non-family, therefore, in any conflict with the family, enemy. If one listened only to Antigone, one would not know that a war had

---

*From Martha C. Nussbaum, *The Fragility of Goodness: Luck and Ethics in Greek Tragedy and Philosophy* (Cambridge and New York: Cambridge UP, 1986) 63–67.
1. All translations are Nussbaum's, based on the Oxford Classical Text of A. C. Pearson.

taken place or that anything called "city" was ever in danger. To her it is a simple injustice that Polynices should not be treated like a friend.

"Friend" (*philos*) and "enemy," then, are functions solely of family relationship. When Antigone says, "It is my nature to join in loving, not to join in hating," she is expressing not a general attachment to love, but a devotion to the *philia* of the family. It is the nature of these *philia* bonds to make claims on one's commitments and actions regardless of one's occurrent desires. This sort of love is not something one decides about; the relationships involved may have little to do with liking or fondness. We might say (to use terminology borrowed from Kant[2]) that Antigone, in speaking of love, means "practical," not "pathological" love (a love that has its source in fondness or inclination). "He is my own brother," she says to Ismene in explanation of her defiance of the city's decree, "and yours too, even if you don't want it. I certainly will never be found a traitor to him." Relationship is itself a source of obligation, regardless of the feelings involved. When Antigone speaks of Polynices as "my dearest brother," even when she proclaims, "I shall lie with him as a loved one with a loved one," there is no sense of closeness, no personal memory, no particularity animating her speech. Ismene, the one person who ought, historically, to be close to her, is treated from the beginning with remote coldness; she is even called enemy when she takes the wrong stand on matters of pious obligation. It is Ismene whom we see weeping "sister-loving tears," who acts out of commitment to a felt love. "What life is worth living for me, bereft of you?" she asks with an intensity of feeling that never animates her sister's piety. To Haemon, the man who passionately loves and desires her, Antigone never addresses a word throughout the entire play. It is Haemon, not Antigone, whom the Chorus views as inspired by *erōs*. Antigone is as far from *erōs* as Creon. For Antigone, the dead are "those whom it is most important to please." "You have a warm heart for the cold," observes her sister, failing to comprehend this impersonal and single-minded passion.

Duty to the family dead is the supreme law and the supreme passion. And Antigone structures her entire life and her vision of the world in accordance with this simple, self-contained system of duties. Even within this system, should a conflict ever arise, she is ready with a fixed priority ordering that will clearly dictate her choice. The strange speech in which she ranks duties to different family dead, placing duty to brother above duties to husband and children, is in this sense (if genuine) highly revealing: it makes us suspect that she is capable of a strangely ruthless simplification of duties, corresponding not so much to any known religious law as to the exigencies of her own practical imagination.

Other values fall into place, confirming these suspicions. Her single-minded identification with duties to the dead (and only some of these) effects a strange reorganization of piety, as well as of honor and justice. She is truly, in her own words, *hosia panourgēsasa*, one who will do anything for the sake of the pious; and her piety takes in only a part of conventional religion. She speaks of her allegiance to Zeus, but she refuses to recognize his role as guardian of the city and backer of Eteocles. The very expression of her devotion is suspect: "Zeus did not decree this, as far as I am concerned." She sets herself up as the arbiter of what Zeus can and cannot have decreed, just as Creon took it upon himself to say whom the gods could and could not have covered: no other character bears out her

---

2. Immanuel Kant (1724–1804), German philosopher who uses these terms in his *Critique of Pure Reason*.

view of Zeus as single-mindedly backing the rights of the dead. She speaks, too, of the goddess *Dikē,* Justice; but *Dikē* for her is, simply, "the Justice who lives together with the gods below." The Chorus recognizes another *Dikē.* Later they will say to her, "Having advanced to the utmost limit of boldness, you struck hard against the altar of *Dikē* on high, o child." Justice is up here in the city, as well as below the earth. It is not as simple as she says it is. Antigone, accordingly, is seen by them not as a conventionally pious person, but as one who improvised her piety, making her own decisions about what to honor. She is a "maker of her own law"; her defiance is "self-invented passion." Finally they tell her unequivocally that her pious respect is incomplete: "[This] reverent action is a part of piety." Antigone's rigid adherence to a single narrow set of duties has caused her to misinterpret the nature of piety itself, a virtue within which a more comprehensive understanding would see the possibility of conflict.

Creon's strategy of simplification led him to regard others as material for his aggressive exploitation. Antigone's dutiful subservience to the dead leads to an equally strange, though different (and certainly less hideous) result. Her relation to others in the world above is characterized by an odd coldness. "You are alive," she tells her sister, "but my life is long since dead, to the end of serving the dead." The safely dutiful human life requires, or is, life's annihilation. Creon's attitude towards others is like necrophilia: he aspires to possess the inert and unresisting. Antigone's subservience to duty is, finally, the ambition to be a *nekros,* a corpse beloved of corpses. (Her apparent similarity to martyrs in our own tradition, who expect a fully active life after death, should not conceal from us the strangeness of this goal.) In the world below, there are no risks of failure or wrongdoing.

Neither Creon nor Antigone, then, is a loving or passionate being in anything like the usual sense. Not one of the gods, not one human being escapes the power of *erōs,* says the Chorus; but these two oddly inhuman beings do, it appears, escape. Creon sees loved persons as functions of the civic good, replaceable producers of citizens. For Antigone, they are either dead, fellow servants of the dead, or objects of complete indifference. No living being is loved for his or her personal qualities, loved with the sort of love that Haemon feels and Ismene praises. By altering their beliefs about the nature and value of persons, they have, it seems, altered or restructured the human passions themselves. They achieve harmony in this way; but at a cost. The Chorus speaks of *erōs* as a force as important and obligating as the ancient *thesmoi* or laws of right, a force against which it is both foolish and, apparently, blameworthy to rebel.

Antigone learns too—like Creon, by being forced to recognize a problem that lies at the heart of her single-minded concern. Creon saw that the city itself is pious and loving; that he could not be its champion without valuing what it values, in all its complexity. Antigone comes to see that the service of the dead requires the city, that her own religious aims cannot be fulfilled without civic institutions. By being her own law, she has not only ignored a part of piety, she has also jeopardized the fulfillment of the very pious duties to which she is so attached. Cut off from friends, from the possibility of having children, she cannot keep herself alive in order to do further service to the dead; nor can she guarantee the pious treatment of her own corpse. In her last speeches she laments not so much the fact of imminent death as, repeatedly, her isolation from the continuity of offspring, from friends and mourners. She emphasizes the fact that she will never marry; she will remain childless. Acheron will be her husband, the tomb her bridal chamber. Unless she can successfully appeal to the citizens whose needs as citizens she had refused to consider, she will die without anyone to mourn her death or to replace her as guardian of her family religion. She turns therefore increasingly, in this final scene, to the citizens and the gods of the city, until her last words closely echo an earlier speech made by Creon and blend his concerns with hers:

> O city of my fathers in this land of Thebes. O gods, progenitors of our race. I am led away, and wait no longer. Look, leaders of Thebes, the last of your royal line. Look what I suffer, at whose hands, for having respect for piety.

We have, then, two narrowly limited practical worlds, two strategies of avoidance and simplification. In one, a single human value has become *the* final end; in the other, a single set of duties has eclipsed all others. But we can now acknowledge that we admire Antigone, nonetheless, in a way that we do not admire Creon. It seems important to look for the basis of this difference.

First, in the world of the play, it seems clear that Antigone's actual choice is preferable to Creon's. The dishonour to civic values involved in giving pious burial to an enemy's corpse is far less radical than the violation of religion involved in Creon's act. Antigone shows a deeper understanding of the community and its values than Creon does when she argues that the obligation to bury the dead is an unwritten law, which cannot be set aside by the decree of a particular ruler. The belief that not all values are utility-relative, that there are certain claims whose neglect will prove deeply destructive of communal attunement and individual character, is a part of Antigone's position left untouched by the play's implicit criticism of her single-mindedness.

Furthermore, Antigone's pursuit of virtue is her own. It involves nobody else and commits her to abusing no other person. Rulership must be rulership *of* something; Antigone's pious actions are executed alone, out of a solitary commitment. She may be strangely remote from the world; but she does no violence to it.

Finally, and perhaps most important, Antigone remains ready to risk and to sacrifice her ends in a way that is not possible for Creon, given the singleness of his conception of value. There is a complexity in Antigone's virtue that permits genuine sacrifice *within* the defense of piety. She dies recanting nothing; but still she is torn by a conflict. Her virtue is, then, prepared to admit a contingent conflict, at least in the extreme case where its adequate exercise requires the cancellation of the conditions of its exercise. From within her single-minded devotion to the dead, she recognizes the power of these contingent circumstances and yields to them, comparing herself to Niobe wasted away by nature's snow and rain. (Earlier she had been compared, in her grief, to a mother bird crying out over an empty nest; so she is, while heroically acting, linked with the openness and vulnerability of the female.) The Chorus here briefly tries to console her with the suggestion that her bad luck does not really matter, in view of her future fame; she calls their rationalization a mockery of her loss. This vulnerability in virtue, this ability to acknowledge the world of nature by mourning the constraints that it imposes on virtue, surely contributes to making her the more humanly rational and the richer of the two protagonists: both active and receptive, neither exploiter nor simply victim.

# REBECCA W. BUSHNELL

## *From* Prophesying Tragedy: Sign and Voice in Sophocles' Theban Plays*

It is primarily through the power of speech, against silence, that Creon's suffering is distinguished from Antigone's, as Creon becomes "nothing" in his disaster, whereas Antigone leaves the stage as herself. She has clearly lost in her battle for any kind of political autonomy, in her effort to counteract Creon's *kērygma*[1] (the Chorus, not Antigone, makes him change his mind). Further, neither the other characters in the play nor the gods confer heroic status on her. While the "punishment" of Creon may be seen as her vindication, Creon never mentions her again, nor does Tiresias defend her directly in his prophecy. Yet she leaves the stage, neither abject nor resigned to oblivion, but proclaiming her importance as the last of the Cadmeans. While Creon speaks his "sentence" of death, Antigone responds by invoking the gods and the city of Thebes, calling upon the Chorus to look on her and acknowledge her right to have buried Polynices. Antigone's last act on stage is thus an act of apostrophe or invocation, meant to establish the presence and power of her own voice. For her, it matters little that neither god nor city responds; for one last time, Antigone relies on her voice to define herself, as she claims her link to her city, her lineage, and the gods of her race. Antigone is denied personal and political autonomy in the city of Thebes— what she cannot have as a woman; yet at the same time Antigone maintains her freedom of speech in public, which was the essence of freedom in Athens, where the worst punishment of exile was considered the loss of *parrēsia* or "free speech." Antigone speaks, too, as the bride of death, both in this world and beyond; like Hector, she has the authority that those on the brink of death possess over the living, and yet she already stands apart from the rest of the citizens, who must find a way to rule in the days to come.

Creon's loss of his power to invoke and command marks the loss of his role in the family and the city. Creon, too, laments his disaster, but his speech lacks the ceremony and self-reflection of Antigone's. Crying forth the ritual sound of wailing, *aiai*, he calls himself wretched (*deilaios*). Creon's penultimate gesture, matching Antigone's, is to utter a prayer for death. It may be addressed to the gods, but it is heard only by the Chorus, who refuse to answer the prayer: "That will come," they say, "but now we must do what is before us." When Creon protests that he prayed for what he desires most, the Chorus answers that he must not pray now. Creon thus ends in the world he created for himself, where "fate" is inflexible, yet there are no gods to hear his prayers. The gods will not help Creon, and he can no longer help himself. His words become meaningless when he himself becomes "nothing," having lost his family and his city. Earlier, Haemon compared Creon to writing tablets which, when unfolded, are blank. In the end, Creon fulfills that image, becoming someone who is nothing, a voice which is *asēmos*, "without significance."

---

*From Rebecca W. Bushnell, *Prophesying Tragedy: Sign and Voice in Sophocles' Theban Plays* (Ithaca: Cornell UP, 1988) 64–66. All notes are the editor's.   1. Proclamation.

In the *Iliad*, Hector's defiance of prophecy[2] plays out a conflict of discourse in the struggle between man and god for the right to declare *anankē*.[3] In *Antigone*, Sophocles dramatizes that conflict in the context of the city, where the king strives to emulate the gods in making the signs of "fate," and king, prophet, and citizen compete for the right to speak for the city's needs and future. Antigone loses this battle when Creon condemns her to death, just as Hector must die, according to the sentence of "fate." But Creon is silenced by the gods—and by the playwright. Both Creon and Antigone threaten the order of the city and are destroyed, but Sophocles gives the victory to her, in the dramatic authority of her voice. Although the gods themselves never answer her pleas for recognition, her voice commands the audience's and Chorus' attention. Creon, however, trails off in inarticulate confusion, just as he has no recognizable "self" when stripped of his roles of *tyrannos*,[4] husband, and father. Antigone never loses her ability to speak for herself, and in this way, is given her freedom. Thus it is she, not Creon, who is Hector's heir, and she who most closely imitates his defiance of fatal authority. But Antigone is not only Hector's heir; she is also the forerunner[5] of her own father, Oedipus, who in *Oedipus the King* masters human speech in his pride and his shame.

## MARY WHITLOCK BLUNDELL

### *From* Helping Friends and Harming Enemies: A Study in Sophocles and Greek Ethics*

Creon and Antigone are alike in several ways, especially the inconsistency of their values and the way they are driven by passion below a surface of rational argument. Both are also one-sided in their commitments. The poet could have given the champion of the *polis*[1] a much stronger case. But he could also have let Antigone meet and conquer Creon on his own ground (for example by arguing that her two brothers were equally responsible for the war). The narrowness of both is revealed by their failure really to engage in argument. Creon's two main statements of principle actually occur in Antigone's absence. When they do confront each other, in the brief passage of stichomythia[2] with which we began, they argue at cross purposes, repeatedly missing each other's point.

This does not mean, however, that they are equally limited in the values to which they adhere. Antigone is sometimes accused of being as narrowly one-sided as Creon in her allegiance to the family and disregard for the interests and *nomoi*[3] of the *polis*: "If one listened only to Antigone, one would not know that a war had taken place or that anything called 'city' was ever in danger" (Nuss-

---

2. Perhaps a reference to Book 22 of the *Iliad*, in which Hector mistakenly disbelieves Achilles' boast that Zeus will allow Achilles to kill Hector in battle.  3. Necessity, fate.  4. Ruler.
5. In that the play *Antigone* was written and first performed more than ten years before *Oedipus the King*.
*From Mary Whitlock Blundell, *Helping Friends and Harming Enemies: A Study in Sophocles and Greek Ethics* (Cambridge and New York: Cambridge UP, 1989) 145–48. All notes are the editor's.
1. City-state.  2. Dialogue delivered in alternating lines; often used to show vigorous dispute.
3. Laws, standards (singular, *nomos*) (Greek).

baum, p. 2113, above). Nor can it be denied that she ignores competing concepts of *nomos* and justice which have their claims, no matter how shoddily Creon may represent them. Creon's misapplication of his principles does not undermine their claim to consideration, and the rightness of Antigone's cause does not of itself justify the passionate narrowness with which she pursues it. But although she does not acknowledge the authority of the *polis*, she never explicitly rejects it, as Creon does the family. Moreover she acts ultimately to the city's advantage. As Creon himself so ironically puts it, "the man who is worthwhile in family matters will also turn out to be just in the *polis*." It is Creon's own scorn not just for the family but for public opinion which finally brings the *polis* "doom instead of *soteria*."[4] He who began by saving Thebes from its enemies ends by stirring up other cities with enmity. He tells Antigone she is alone in her views, but she retorts that, on the contrary, all those present (namely the chorus of the city's elders) are on her side. Moreover she foresees great glory from her deed, which the context suggests is to derive from none other than her fellow citizens. Creon can make no such claims for himself. Indeed Haemon will hint that his father's behaviour may be destroying a glorious reputation. With the loss of his son's loyalty, Creon also loses the last shreds of his claim to represent the *polis*. But Antigone's words are vindicated when Haemon reports the admiration of the ordinary citizens, echoing her own evaluation of her deed. Even the chorus, while withholding direct approval of Antigone's actions, promise her praise and glory for the manner of her death.

Antigone does once suggest that she is violating the will of the *polis* as represented by its citizens. But she does so only in the extremity of her isolation, lamenting that she is "friendless" and even questioning her divine support. She has cut herself off from her sister and quarrelled with the chorus, and has not, of course, heard Haemon's report of public sympathy for her fate. Under the circumstances it is not unreasonable that she should now believe she is defying the will of the citizens. But she claims that she would do so under the most extreme provocation, implying respect for the *polis* if not its present king. She restricts her defiance to the drastic circumstances of the present crisis, acknowledging the potential conflict between her own priorities and the demands of civic life.

As Antigone goes to her death, she emphatically calls the city itself, its gods and its most prominent citizens, the chorus, to bear witness to her fate. Does this tell us that she has learned the limitations of her own narrow principles? Or is it a reproach to the apathetic chorus? Surely the latter. She shows no sign of regret or new-found insight into the civic value of obedience. But she addresses the chorus in ways suggesting their special responsibility not just as citizens, but as Theban aristocrats who might be expected to play a role in public life. She calls them "citizens of the fatherland," "wealthy men of the *polis*," "leading men of Thebes." When she refers to herself as "the last remaining daughter of the royal house," she is reasserting her status as a member of the ruling family, to which the chorus are supposedly loyal, and to which Creon is tied only by marriage. This royal status is linked with her reverence for the gods, especially her ancestral gods. Her obligations to the *polis* and her dead family are not mutually exclusive. She has not failed the citizens, for the burial was both in their best

---

4. Salvation; the root, *soter*, means "savior."

interest and called for by their "established laws." But they, intimidated by Creon, have abandoned her. She therefore accuses the chorus of mockery and *hubris*,[5] the same hostile laughter that she inflicted on her sister and (in his view) on Creon.

One-sided and "autonomous" though she may be, Antigone's obsession is less sterile and destructive than Creon's. He, as he so much likes to remind us, is the sole ruler of the *polis*. In order to achieve a just and stable social order, such a ruler must acknowledge and balance competing claims and values. If these are ultimately incommensurable, he must attempt a compromise, however uneasy. As Haemon eloquently insists, he must know how to bend with the storm. He must respect the ties of natural *philia*,[6] and at the same time promote political *philia* by adopting policies that meet the citizens' approval. Antigone abides heroically by the first variety of *philia* as she interprets it, and can make some claim to the second, but Creon is a failure at both.

---

5. A complex term in Greek ethical thought that implies an impious overreaching of human limits.
6. Love, affinity.

# Reading More Drama

CD **ARTHUR MILLER**

## Death of a Salesman

Certain Private Conversations in Two Acts and a Requiem

CHARACTERS

| | | |
|---|---|---|
| WILLY LOMAN | THE WOMAN | STANLEY |
| LINDA | CHARLEY | MISS FORSYTHE |
| BIFF | UNCLE BEN | LETTA |
| HAPPY | HOWARD WAGNER | |
| BERNARD | JENNY | |

The action takes place in WILLY LOMAN's house and yard and in various places he visits in the New York and Boston of today.

## ACT I

A melody is heard, playing upon a flute. It is small and fine, telling of grass and trees and the horizon. The curtain rises.

Before us is the Salesman's house. We are aware of towering, angular shapes behind it, surrounding it on all sides. Only the blue light of the sky falls upon the house and forestage; the surrounding area shows an angry flow of orange. As more light appears, we see a solid vault of apartment houses around the small, fragile-seeming home. An air of the dream clings to the place, a dream rising out of reality. The kitchen at center seems actual enough, for there is a kitchen table with three chairs, and a refrigerator. But no other fixtures are seen. At the back of the kitchen there is a draped entrance, which leads to the living-room. To the right of the kitchen, on a level raised two feet, is a bedroom furnished only with a brass bedstead and a straight chair. On a shelf over the bed a silver athletic trophy stands. A window opens onto the apartment house at the side.

Behind the kitchen, on a level raised six and a half feet, is the boys' bedroom, at present barely visible. Two beds are dimly seen, and at the back of the room a dormer window. (This bedroom is above the unseen living-room.) At the left a stairway curves up to it from the kitchen.

The entire setting is wholly or, in some places, partially transparent. The roof-line of the house is one-dimensional; under and over it we see the apartment buildings. Before the house lies an apron, curving beyond the forestage into the orchestra. This forward area serves as the back yard as well as the locale of all WILLY's imaginings and of his city scenes.

*Whenever the action is in the present the actors observe the imaginary wall-lines, entering the house only through its door at the left. But in the scenes of the past these boundaries are broken, and characters enter or leave a room by stepping "through" a wall onto the forestage.*

*From the right,* WILLY LOMAN, *the Salesman, enters, carrying two large sample cases. The flute plays on. He hears but is not aware of it. He is past sixty years of age, dressed quietly. Even as he crosses the stage to the doorway of the house, his exhaustion is apparent. He unlocks the door, comes into the kitchen, and thankfully lets his burden down, feeling the soreness of his palms. A word-sigh escapes his lips—it might be "Oh, boy, oh, boy." He closes the door, then carries his cases out into the living-room, through the draped kitchen doorway.*

LINDA, *his wife, has stirred in her bed at the right. She gets out and puts on a robe, listening. Most often jovial, she has developed an iron repression of her exceptions to* WILLY'S *behavior—she more than loves him, she admires him, as though his mercurial nature, his temper, his massive dreams and little cruelties, served her only as sharp reminders of the turbulent longings within him, longings which she shares but lacks the temperament to utter and follow to their end.*

LINDA: [*Hearing* WILLY *outside the bedroom, calls with some trepidation.*] Willy!
WILLY: It's all right. I came back.
LINDA: Why? What happened? [*Slight pause.*] Did something happen, Willy?
WILLY: No, nothing happened.
LINDA: You didn't smash the car, did you?
WILLY: [*With casual irritation.*] I said nothing happened. Didn't you hear me?
LINDA: Don't you feel well?
WILLY: I'm tired to the death. [*The flute has faded away. He sits on the bed beside her, a little numb.*] I couldn't make it. I just couldn't make it, Linda.
LINDA: [*Very carefully, delicately.*] Where were you all day? You look terrible.
WILLY: I got as far as a little above Yonkers. I stopped for a cup of coffee. Maybe it was the coffee.
LINDA: What?
WILLY: [*After a pause.*] I suddenly couldn't drive any more. The car kept going off onto the shoulder, y'know?
LINDA: [*Helpfully.*] Oh. Maybe it was the steering again. I don't think Angelo knows the Studebaker.
WILLY: No, it's me, it's me. Suddenly I realize I'm goin' sixty miles an hour and I don't remember the last five minutes. I'm—I can't seem to—keep my mind to it.
LINDA: Maybe it's your glasses. You never went for your new glasses.
WILLY: No, I see everything. I came back ten miles an hour. It took me nearly four hours from Yonkers.
LINDA: [*Resigned.*] Well, you'll just have to take a rest, Willy, you can't continue this way.
WILLY: I just got back from Florida.
LINDA: But you didn't rest your mind. Your mind is overactive, and the mind is what counts, dear.
WILLY: I'll start out in the morning. Maybe I'll feel better in the morning. [*She is taking off his shoes.*] These goddam arch supports are killing me.
LINDA: Take an aspirin. Should I get you an aspirin? It'll soothe you.

WILLY: [*With wonder.*] I was driving along, you understand? And I was fine. I was even observing the scenery. You can imagine, me looking at scenery, on the road every week of my life. But it's so beautiful up there, Linda, the trees are so thick, and the sun is warm. I opened the windshield and just let the warm air bathe over me. And then all of a sudden I'm goin' off the road! I'm tellin' ya, I absolutely forgot I was driving. If I'd've gone the other way over the white line I might've killed somebody. So I went on again—and five minutes later I'm dreamin' again, and I nearly—[*He presses two fingers against his eyes.*] I have such thoughts, I have such strange thoughts.

LINDA: Willy, dear. Talk to them again. There's no reason why you can't work in New York.

WILLY: They don't need me in New York. I'm the New England man. I'm vital in New England.

LINDA: But you're sixty years old. They can't expect you to keep traveling every week.

WILLY: I'll have to send a wire[1] to Portland. I'm supposed to see Brown and Morrison tomorrow morning at ten o'clock to show the line. Goddammit, I could sell them! [*He starts putting on his jacket.*]

LINDA: [*Taking the jacket from him.*] Why don't you go down to the place tomorrow and tell Howard you've simply got to work in New York? You're too accommodating, dear.

WILLY: If old man Wagner was alive I'da been in charge of New York now! That man was a prince, he was a masterful man. But that boy of his, that Howard, he don't appreciate. When I went north the first time, the Wagner Company didn't know where New England was!

LINDA: Why don't you tell those things to Howard, dear?

WILLY: [*Encouraged.*] I will, I definitely will. Is there any cheese?

LINDA: I'll make you a sandwich.

WILLY: No, go to sleep. I'll take some milk. I'll be up right away. The boys in?

LINDA: They're sleeping. Happy took Biff on a date tonight.

WILLY: [*Interested.*] That so?

LINDA: It was so nice to see them shaving together, one behind the other, in the bathroom. And going out together. You notice? The whole house smells of shaving lotion.

WILLY: Figure it out. Work a lifetime to pay off a house. You finally own it, and there's nobody to live in it.

LINDA: Well, dear, life is a casting off. It's always that way.

WILLY: No, no, some people—some people accomplish something. Did Biff say anything after I went this morning?

LINDA: You shouldn't have criticized him, Willy, especially after he just got off the train. You mustn't lose your temper with him.

WILLY: When the hell did I lose my temper? I simply asked him if he was making any money. Is that a criticism?

LINDA: But, dear, how could he make any money?

WILLY: [*Worried and angered.*] There's such an undercurrent in him. He became a moody man. Did he apologize when I left this morning?

1. Telegram.

LINDA: He was crestfallen, Willy. You know how he admires you. I think if he finds himself, then you'll both be happier and not fight any more.

WILLY: How can he find himself on a farm? Is that a life? A farmhand? In the beginning, when he was young, I thought, well, a young man, it's good for him to tramp around, take a lot of different jobs. But it's more than ten years now and he has yet to make thirty-five dollars a week!

LINDA: He's finding himself, Willy.

WILLY: Not finding yourself at the age of thirty-four is a disgrace!

LINDA: Shh!

WILLY: The trouble is he's lazy, goddammit!

LINDA: Willy, please!

WILLY: Biff is a lazy bum!

LINDA: They're sleeping. Get something to eat. Go on down.

WILLY: Why did he come home? I would like to know what brought him home.

LINDA: I don't know. I think he's still lost, Willy. I think he's very lost.

WILLY: Biff Loman is lost. In the greatest country in the world a young man with such—personal attractiveness, gets lost. And such a hard worker. There's one thing about Biff—he's not lazy.

LINDA: Never.

WILLY: [*With pity and resolve.*] I'll see him in the morning; I'll have a nice talk with him. I'll get him a job selling. He could be big in no time. My God! Remember how they used to follow him around in high school? When he smiled at one of them their faces lit up. When he walked down the street... [*He loses himself in reminiscences.*]

LINDA: [*Trying to bring him out of it.*] Willy, dear, I got a new kind of American-type cheese today. It's whipped.

WILLY: Why do you get American when I like Swiss?

LINDA: I just thought you'd like a change—

WILLY: I don't want a change! I want Swiss cheese. Why am I always being contradicted?

LINDA: [*With a covering laugh.*] I thought it would be a surprise.

WILLY: Why don't you open a window in here, for God's sake?

LINDA: [*With infinite patience.*] They're all open, dear.

WILLY: The way they boxed us in here. Bricks and windows, windows and bricks.

LINDA: We should've bought the land next door.

WILLY: The street is lined with cars. There's not a breath of fresh air in the neighborhood. The grass don't grow any more, you can't raise a carrot in the back yard. They should've had a law against apartment houses. Remember those two beautiful elm trees out there? When I and Biff hung the swing between them?

LINDA: Yeah, like being a million miles from the city.

WILLY: They should've arrested the builder for cutting those down. They massacred the neighborhood. [*Lost.*] More and more I think of those days, Linda. This time of year it was lilac and wisteria. And then the peonies would come out, and the daffodils. What fragrance in this room!

LINDA: Well, after all, people had to move somewhere.

WILLY: No, there's more people now.

LINDA: I don't think there's more people. I think—

WILLY: There's more people! That's what ruining this country! Population is getting out of control. The competition is maddening! Smell the stink from that apartment house! And another one on the other side... How can they whip cheese?

[*On* WILLY's *last line,* BIFF *and* HAPPY *raise themselves up in their beds, listening.*]

LINDA: Go down, try it. And be quiet.
WILLY: [*Turning to* LINDA, *guiltily.*] You're not worried about me, are you, sweetheart?
BIFF: What's the matter?
HAPPY: Listen!
LINDA: You've got too much on the ball to worry about.
WILLY: You're my foundation and my support, Linda.
LINDA: Just try to relax, dear. You make mountains out of mole-hills.
WILLY: I won't fight with him anymore. If he wants to go back to Texas, let him go.
LINDA: He'll find his way.
WILLY: Sure. Certain men just don't get started till later in life. Like Thomas Edison, I think. Or B. F. Goodrich. One of them was deaf. [*He starts for the bedroom doorway.*] I'll put my money on Biff.
LINDA: And Willy—if it's warm Sunday we'll drive in the country. And we'll open the windshield, and take lunch.
WILLY: No, the windshields don't open on the new cars.
LINDA: But you opened it today.
WILLY: Me? I didn't. [*He stops.*] Now isn't that peculiar! Isn't that a remarkable—
[*He breaks off in amazement and fright as the flute is heard distantly.*]
LINDA: What, darling?
WILLY: That is the most remarkable thing.
LINDA: What, dear?
WILLY: I was thinking of the Chevvy. [*Slight pause.*] Nineteen twenty-eight... when I had that red Chevvy—[*Breaks off.*] That funny? I coulda sworn I was driving that Chevvy today.
LINDA: Well, that's nothing. Something must've reminded you.
WILLY: Remarkable. Ts.[2] Remember those days? The way Biff used to simonize that car? The dealer refused to believe there was eighty thousand miles on it. [*He shakes his head.*] Heh! [*To* LINDA.] Close your eyes, I'll be right up. [*He walks out of the bedroom.*]
HAPPY: [*To* BIFF.] Jesus, maybe he smashed up the car again!
LINDA: [*Calling after* WILLY.] Be careful on the stairs, dear! The cheese is on the middle shelf! [*She turns, goes over to the bed, takes his jacket, and goes out of the bedroom.*]

[*Light has risen on the boys' room. Unseen,* WILLY *is heard talking to himself, "Eighty thousand miles," and a little laugh.* BIFF *gets out of bed, comes downstage a bit, and stands attentively.* BIFF *is two years older than his brother,* HAPPY, *well built, but in these days bears a worn air and seems less self-assured. He has succeeded less, and his dreams are stronger and less acceptable than* HAPPY's. HAPPY *is tall, powerfully*

---

2. Ford Model Ts, extraordinarily popular cars manufactured from 1908 to 1928. *Simonize:* polish with car wax.

*made. Sexuality is like a visible color on him, or a scent that many women have discovered. He, like his brother, is lost, but in a different way, for he has never allowed himself to turn his face toward defeat and is thus more confused and hard-skinned, although seemingly more content.*]

HAPPY: [*Getting out of bed.*] He's going to get his license taken away if he keeps that up. I'm getting nervous about him, y'know, Biff?
BIFF: His eyes are going.
HAPPY: No, I've driven with him. He sees all right. He just doesn't keep his mind on it. I drove into the city with him last week. He stops at a green light and then it turns red and he goes. [*He laughs.*]
BIFF: Maybe he's color-blind.
HAPPY: Pop? Why he's got the finest eye for color in the business. You know that.
BIFF: [*Sitting down on his bed.*] I'm going to sleep.
HAPPY: You're not still sour on Dad, are you Biff?
BIFF: He's all right, I guess.
WILLY: [*Underneath them, in the living-room.*] Yes, sir, eighty thousand miles—eighty-two thousand!
BIFF: You smoking?
HAPPY: [*Holding out a pack of cigarettes.*] Want one?
BIFF: [*Taking a cigarette.*] I can never sleep when I smell it.
WILLY: What a simonizing job, heh!
HAPPY: [*With deep sentiment.*] Funny, Biff, y'know? Us sleeping in here again? The old beds. [*He pats his bed affectionately.*] All the talk that went across those two beds, huh? Our whole lives.
BIFF: Yeah. Lotta dreams and plans.
HAPPY: [*With a deep and masculine laugh.*] About five hundred women would like to know what was said in this room.

[*They share a soft laugh.*]

BIFF: Remember that big Betsy something—what the hell was her name—over on Bushwick Avenue?
HAPPY: [*Combing his hair.*] With the collie dog!
BIFF: That's the one. I got you in there, remember?
HAPPY: Yeah, that was my first time—I think. Boy, there was a pig! [*They laugh, almost crudely.*] You taught me everything I know about women. Don't forget that.
BIFF: I bet you forgot how bashful you used to be. Especially with girls.
HAPPY: Oh, I still am, Biff.
BIFF: Oh, go on.
HAPPY: I just control it, that's all. I think I got less bashful and you got more so. What happened, Biff? Where's the old humor, the old confidence? [*He shakes* BIFF's *knee.* BIFF *gets up and moves restlessly about the room.*] What's the matter?
BIFF: Why does Dad mock me all the time?
HAPPY: He's not mocking you, he—
BIFF: Everything I say there's a twist of mockery on his face. I can't get near him.
HAPPY: He just wants you to make good, that's all. I wanted to talk to you about Dad for a long time, Biff. Something's—happening to him. He—talks to himself.

BIFF: I noticed that this morning. But he always mumbled.
HAPPY: But not so noticeable. It got so embarrassing I sent him to Florida. And you know something? Most of the time he's talking to you.
BIFF: What's he say about me?
HAPPY: I can't make it out.
BIFF: What's he say about me?
HAPPY: I think the fact that you're not settled, that you're still kind of up in the air...
BIFF: There's one or two things depressing him, Happy.
HAPPY: What do you mean?
BIFF: Never mind. Just don't lay it all to me.
HAPPY: But I think if you just got started—I mean—is there any future for you out there?
BIFF: I tell ya, Hap, I don't know what the future is. I don't know—what I'm supposed to want.
HAPPY: What do you mean?
BIFF: Well, I spent six or seven years after high school trying to work myself up. Shipping clerk, salesman, business of one kind or another. And it's a measly manner of existence. To get on that subway on the hot mornings in summer. To devote your whole life to keeping stock, or making phone calls, or selling or buying. To suffer fifty weeks of the year for the sake of a two-week vacation, when all you really desire is to be outdoors, with your shirt off. And always to have to get ahead of the next fella. And still—that's how you build a future.
HAPPY: Well, you really enjoy it on a farm? Are you content out there?
BIFF: [*With rising agitation.*] Hap, I've had twenty or thirty different kinds of jobs since I left home before the war, and it always turns out the same. I just realized it lately. In Nebraska when I herded cattle, and the Dakotas, and Arizona, and now in Texas. It's why I came home now, I guess, because I realized it. This farm I work on, it's spring there now, see? And they've got about fifteen new colts. There's nothing more inspiring or—beautiful than the sight of a mare and a new colt. And it's cool there now, see? Texas is cool now, and it's spring. And whenever spring comes to where I am, I suddenly get the feeling, my God, I'm not gettin' anywhere! What the hell am I doing, playing around with horses, twenty-eight dollars a week! I'm thirty-four years old. I oughta be makin' my future. That's when I come running home. And now, I get there, and I don't know what to do with myself. [*After a pause.*] I've always made a point of not wasting my life, and everytime I come back here I know that all I've done is to waste my life.
HAPPY: You're a poet, you know that, Biff? You're a—you're an idealist!
BIFF: No, I'm mixed up very bad. Maybe I oughta get married. Maybe I oughta get stuck into something. Maybe that's my trouble. I'm like a boy. I'm not married. I'm not in business, I just—I'm like a boy. Are you content, Hap? You're a success, aren't you? Are you content?
HAPPY: Hell, no!
BIFF: Why? You're making money, aren't you?
HAPPY: [*Moving about with energy, expressiveness.*] All I can do now is wait for the merchandise manager to die. And suppose I get to be merchandise manager? He's a good friend of mine, and he just built a terrific estate on Long Island. And he lived there about two months and sold it, and now he's building

another one. He can't enjoy it once it's finished. And I know that's just what I would do. I don't know what the hell I'm workin' for. Sometimes I sit in my apartment—all alone. And I think of the rent I'm paying. And it's crazy. But then, it's what I always wanted. My own apartment, a car, and plenty of women. And still, goddammit, I'm lonely.

BIFF: [*With enthusiasm.*] Listen, why don't you come out West with me?

HAPPY: You and I, heh?

BIFF: Sure, maybe we could buy a ranch. Raise cattle, use our muscles. Men built like we are should be working out in the open.

HAPPY: [*Avidly.*] The Loman Brothers, heh?

BIFF: [*With vast affection.*] Sure, we'd be known all over the counties!

HAPPY: [*Enthralled.*] That's what I dream about, Biff. Sometimes I want to just rip my clothes off in the middle of the store and outbox that goddam merchandise manager. I mean I can outbox, outrun, and outlift anybody in that store, and I have to take orders from those common, petty sons-of-bitches till I can't stand it any more.

BIFF: I'm tellin' you, kid, if you were with me I'd be happy out there.

HAPPY: [*Enthused.*] See, Biff, everybody around me is so false that I'm constantly lowering my ideals . . .

BIFF: Baby, together we'd stand up for one another, we'd have someone to trust.

HAPPY: If I were around you—

BIFF: Hap, the trouble is we weren't brought up to grub for money. I don't know how to do it.

HAPPY: Neither can I!

BIFF: Then let's go!

HAPPY: The only thing is—what can you make out there?

BIFF: But look at your friend. Builds an estate and then hasn't the peace of mind to live in it.

HAPPY: Yeah, but when he walks into the store the waves part in front of him. That's fifty-two thousand dollars a year coming through the revolving door, and I got more in my pinky finger than he's got in his head.

BIFF: Yeah, but you just said—

HAPPY: I gotta show some of those pompous, self-important executives over there that Hap Loman can make the grade. I want to walk into the store the way he walks in. Then I'll go with you, Biff. We'll be together yet, I swear. But take those two we had tonight. Now weren't they gorgeous creatures?

BIFF: Yeah, yeah, most gorgeous I've had in years.

HAPPY: I get that any time I want, Biff. Whenever I feel disgusted. The only trouble is, it gets like bowling or something. I just keep knockin' them over and it doesn't mean anything. You still run around a lot?

BIFF: Naa. I'd like to find a girl—steady, somebody with substance.

HAPPY: That's what I long for.

BIFF: Go on! You'd never come home.

HAPPY: I would! Somebody with character, with resistance! Like Mom, y'know? You're gonna call me a bastard when I tell you this. That girl Charlotte I was with tonight is engaged to be married in five weeks. [*He tries on his new hat.*]

BIFF: No kiddin'!

HAPPY: Sure, the guy's in line for the vice-presidency of the store. I don't know what gets into me, maybe I just have an overdeveloped sense of competition or something, but I went and ruined her, and furthermore I can't get rid of her. And he's the third executive I've done that to. Isn't that a crummy characteristic? And to top it all, I go to their weddings! [*Indignantly, but laughing.*] Like I'm not supposed to take bribes. Manufacturers offer me a hundred-dollar bill now and then to throw an order their way. You know how honest I am, but it's like this girl, see. I hate myself for it. Because I don't want the girl, and, still, I take it and—I love it!

BIFF: Let's go to sleep.

HAPPY: I guess we didn't settle anything, heh?

BIFF: I just got one idea that I'm going to try.

HAPPY: What's that?

BIFF: Remember Bill Oliver?

HAPPY: Sure, Oliver is very big now. You want to work for him again?

BIFF: No, but when I quit he said something to me. He put his arm on my shoulder, and he said, "Biff, if you ever need anything, come to me."

HAPPY: I remember that. That sounds good.

BIFF: I think I'll go to see him. If I could get ten thousand or even seven or eight thousand dollars I could buy a beautiful ranch.

HAPPY: I bet he'd back you. 'Cause he thought highly of you, Biff. I mean, they all do. You're well liked, Biff. That's why I say to come back here, and we both have the apartment. And I'm tellin' you, Biff, any babe you want...

BIFF: No, with a ranch I could do the work I like and still be something. I just wonder though. I wonder if Oliver still thinks I stole that carton of basketballs.

HAPPY: Oh, he probably forgot that long ago. It's almost ten years. You're too sensitive. Anyway, he didn't really fire you.

BIFF: Well, I think he was going to. I think that's why I quit. I was never sure whether he knew or not. I know he thought the world of me, though. I was the only one he'd let lock up the place.

WILLY: [*Below.*] You gonna wash the engine, Biff?

HAPPY: Shh! [BIFF *looks at* HAPPY, *who is gazing down, listening.* WILLY *is mumbling in the parlor.*] You hear that?

[*They listen.* WILLY *laughs warmly.*]

BIFF: [*Growing angry.*] Doesn't he know Mom can hear that?

WILLY: Don't get your sweater dirty, Biff!

[*A look of pain crosses* BIFF's *face.*]

HAPPY: Isn't that terrible? Don't leave again, will you? You'll find a job here. You gotta stick around. I don't know what to do about him, it's getting embarrassing.

WILLY: What a simonizing job!

BIFF: Mom's hearing that!

WILLY: No kiddin', Biff, you got a date? Wonderful!

HAPPY: Go on to sleep. But talk to him in the morning, will you?

BIFF: [*Reluctantly getting into bed.*] With her in the house. Brother!

HAPPY: [*Getting into bed.*] I wish you'd have a good talk with him.

[*The light on their room begins to fade.*]

BIFF: [*To himself in bed.*] That selfish, stupid...

HAPPY: Sh... Sleep, Biff.

[*Their light is out. Well before they have finished speaking,* WILLY's *form is dimly seen below in the darkened kitchen. He opens the refrigerator, searches in there, and takes out a bottle of milk. The apartment houses are fading out, and the entire house and surroundings become covered with leaves. Music insinuates itself as the leaves appear.*]

WILLY: Just wanna be careful with those girls, Biff, that's all. Don't make any promises. No promises of any kind. Because a girl, y'know, they always believe what you tell 'em, and you're very young, Biff, you're too young to be talking seriously to girls. [*Light rises on the kitchen.* WILLY, *talking, shuts the refrigerator door and comes downstage to the kitchen table. He pours milk into a glass. He is totally immersed in himself, smiling faintly.*] Too young entirely, Biff. You want to watch your schooling first. Then when you're all set, there'll be plenty of girls for a boy like you. [*He smiles broadly at a kitchen chair.*] That so? The girls pay for you? [*He laughs.*] Boy, you must really be makin' a hit. [WILLY *is gradually addressing—physically—a point offstage, speaking through the wall of the kitchen, and his voice has been rising in volume to that of a normal conversation.*] I been wondering why you polish the car so careful. Ha! Don't leave the hubcaps, boys. Get the chamois to the hubcaps. Happy, use newspaper on the windows, it's the easiest thing. Show him how to do it, Biff! You see, Happy? Pad it up, use it like a pad. That's it, that's it, good work. You're doin' all right, Hap. [*He pauses, then nods in approbation for a few seconds, then looks upward.*] Biff, first thing we gotta do when we get time is clip that big branch over the house. Afraid it's gonna fall in a storm and hit the roof. Tell you what. We get a rope and sling her around, and then we climb up there with a couple of saws and take her down. Soon as you finish the car, boys, I wanna see ya. I got a surprise for you, boys.

BIFF: [*Offstage.*] Whatta ya got, Dad?

WILLY: No, you finish first. Never leave a job till you're finished—remember that. [*Looking toward the "big trees."*] Biff, up in Albany I saw a beautiful hammock. I think I'll buy it next trip, and we'll hang it right between those two elms. Wouldn't that be something? Just swingin' there under those branches. Boy, that would be...

[YOUNG BIFF *and* YOUNG HAPPY *appear from the direction* WILLY *was addressing.* HAPPY *carries rags and a pail of water.* BIFF, *wearing a sweater with a block "S," carries a football.*]

BIFF: [*Pointing in the direction of the car offstage.*] How's that, Pop, professional?
WILLY: Terrific. Terrific job, boys. Good work, Biff.
HAPPY: Where's the surprise, Pop?
WILLY: In the back seat of the car.
HAPPY: Boy! [*He runs off.*]
BIFF: What is it, Dad? Tell me, what'd you buy?
WILLY: [*Laughing, cuffs him.*] Never mind, something I want you to have.
BIFF: [*Turns and starts off.*] What is it, Hap?
HAPPY: [*Offstage.*] It's a punching bag!
BIFF: Oh, Pop!
WILLY: It's got Gene Tunney's[3] signature on it!

[HAPPY *runs onstage with a punching bag.*]

3. Tunney (1897–1978) was world heavyweight boxing champion from 1926 to 1928 and retired undefeated.

BIFF: Gee, how'd you know we wanted a punching bag?
WILLY: Well, it's the finest thing for the timing.
HAPPY: [*Lies down on his back and pedals with his feet.*] I'm losing weight, you notice, Pop?
WILLY: [*To* HAPPY.] Jumping rope is good too.
BIFF: Did you see the new football I got?
WILLY: [*Examining the ball.*] Where'd you get a new ball?
BIFF: The coach told me to practice my passing.
WILLY: That so? And he gave you the ball, heh?
BIFF: Well, I borrowed it from the locker room. [*He laughs confidentially.*]
WILLY: [*Laughing with him at the theft.*] I want you to return that.
HAPPY: I told you he wouldn't like it!
BIFF: [*Angrily.*] Well, I'm bringing it back!
WILLY: [*Stopping the incipient argument, to* HAPPY.] Sure, he's gotta practice with a regulation ball, doesn't he? [*To* BIFF.] Coach'll probably congratulate you on your initiative!
BIFF: Oh, he keeps congratulating my initiative all the time, Pop.
WILLY: That's because he likes you. If somebody else took that ball there'd be an uproar. So what's the report, boys, what's the report?
BIFF: Where'd you go this time, Dad? Gee we were lonesome for you.
WILLY: [*Pleased, puts an arm around each boy and they come down to the apron.*] Lonesome, heh?
BIFF: Missed you every minute.
WILLY: Don't say? Tell you a secret, boys. Don't breathe it to a soul. Someday I'll have my own business, and I'll never have to leave home anymore.
HAPPY: Like Uncle Charley, heh?
WILLY: Bigger than Uncle Charley! Because Charley is not—liked. He's liked, but he's not—well liked.
BIFF: Where'd you go this time, Dad?
WILLY: Well, I got on the road, and I went north to Providence. Met the mayor.
BIFF: The mayor of Providence!
WILLY: He was sitting in the hotel lobby.
BIFF: What'd he say?
WILLY: He said, "Morning!" And I said, "You got a fine city here, Mayor." And then he had coffee with me. And then I went to Waterbury. Waterbury is a fine city. Big clock city, the famous Waterbury clock. Sold a nice bill there. And then Boston—Boston is the cradle of the Revolution. A fine city. And a couple of other towns in Mass., and on to Portland and Bangor and straight home!
BIFF: Gee, I'd love to go with you sometime, Dad.
WILLY: Soon as summer comes.
HAPPY: Promise?
WILLY: You and Hap and I, and I'll show you all the towns. America is full of beautiful towns and fine, upstanding people. And they know me, boys, they know me up and down New England. The finest people. And when I bring you fellas up, there'll be open sesame for all of us, 'cause one thing, boys: I have friends. I can park my car in any street in New England, and the cops protect it like their own. This summer, heh?
BIFF and HAPPY: [*Together.*] Yeah! You bet!
WILLY: We'll take our bathing suits.

HAPPY: We'll carry your bags, Pop!
WILLY: Oh, won't that be something! Me comin' into the Boston stores with you boys carryin' my bags. What a sensation! [BIFF *is prancing around, practicing passing the ball.*] You nervous, Biff, about the game?
BIFF: Not if you're gonna be there.
WILLY: What do they say about you in school, now that they made you captain?
HAPPY: There's a crowd of girls behind him everytime the classes change.
BIFF: [*Taking* WILLY's *hand.*] This Saturday, Pop, this Saturday—just for you, I'm going to break through for a touchdown.
HAPPY: You're supposed to pass.
BIFF: I'm takin' one play for Pop. You watch me, Pop, and when I take off my helmet, that means I'm breakin' out. Then you watch me crash through that line!
WILLY: [*Kisses* BIFF.] Oh, wait'll I tell this in Boston!

[BERNARD *enters in knickers. He is younger than* BIFF, *earnest and loyal, a worried boy.*]

BERNARD: Biff, where are you? You're supposed to study with me today.
WILLY: Hey, looka Bernard. What're you lookin' so anemic about, Bernard?
BERNARD: He's gotta study, Uncle Willy. He's got Regents[4] next week.
HAPPY: [*Tauntingly, spinning* BERNARD *around.*] Let's box, Bernard!
BERNARD: Biff! [*He gets away from* HAPPY.] Listen, Biff, I heard Mr. Birnbaum say that if you don't start studyin' math he's gonna flunk you, and you won't graduate. I heard him!
WILLY: You better study with him, Biff. Go ahead now.
BERNARD: I heard him!
BIFF: Oh, Pop, you didn't see my sneakers! [*He holds up a foot for* WILLY *to look at.*]
WILLY: Hey, that's a beautiful job of printing!
BERNARD: [*Wiping his glasses.*] Just because he printed University of Virginia on his sneakers doesn't mean they've got to graduate him, Uncle Willy!
WILLY: [*Angrily.*] What're you talking about? With scholarships to three universities they're gonna flunk him?
BERNARD: But I heard Mr. Birnbaum say—
WILLY: Don't be a pest, Bernard! [*To his boys.*] What an anemic!
BERNARD: Okay, I'm waiting for you in my house, Biff.

[BERNARD *goes off. The* LOMANS *laugh.*]

WILLY: Bernard is not well liked, is he?
BIFF: He's liked, but he's not well liked.
HAPPY: That's right, Pop.
WILLY: That's just what I mean. Bernard can get the best marks in school, y'understand, but when he gets out in the business world, y'understand, you are going to be five times ahead of him. That's why I thank Almighty God you're both built like Adonises. Because the man who makes an appearance in the business world, the man who creates personal interest, is the man who gets ahead. Be liked and you will never want. You take me, for instance. I never

---

4. Examinations administered to New York State high-school students.

have to wait in line to see a buyer. "Willy Loman is here!" That's all they have to know, and I go right through.

BIFF: Did you knock them dead, Pop?

WILLY: Knocked 'em cold in Providence, slaughtered 'em in Boston.

HAPPY: [*On his back, pedaling again.*] I'm losing weight, you notice, Pop?

[LINDA *enters, as of old, a ribbon in her hair, carrying a basket of washing.*]

LINDA: [*With youthful energy.*] Hello, dear!

WILLY: Sweetheart!

LINDA: How'd the Chevvy run?

WILLY: Chevrolet, Linda, is the greatest car ever built. [*To the boys.*] Since when do you let your mother carry wash up the stairs?

BIFF: Grab hold there, boy!

HAPPY: Where to, Mom?

LINDA: Hang them up on the line. And you better go down to your friends, Biff. The cellar is full of boys. They don't know what to do with themselves.

BIFF: Ah, when Pop comes home they can wait!

WILLY: [*Laughs appreciatively.*] You better go down and tell them what to do, Biff.

BIFF: I think I'll have them sweep out the furnace room.

WILLY: Good work, Biff.

BIFF: [*Goes through wall-line of kitchen to doorway at back and calls down.*] Fellas! Everybody sweep out the furnace room! I'll be right down!

VOICES: All right! Okay, Biff.

BIFF: George and Sam and Frank, come out back! We're hangin' up the wash! Come on, Hap, on the double!

[*He and* HAPPY *carry out the basket.*]

LINDA: The way they obey him!

WILLY: Well, that training, the training. I'm tellin' you, I was sellin' thousands and thousands, but I had to come home.

LINDA: Oh, the whole block'll be at that game. Did you sell anything?

WILLY: I did five hundred gross in Providence and seven hundred gross in Boston.

LINDA: No! Wait a minute, I've got a pencil. [*She pulls pencil and paper out of her apron pocket.*] That makes your commission . . . Two hundred—my God! Two hundred and twelve dollars!

WILLY: Well, I didn't figure it yet, but . . .

LINDA: How much did you do?

WILLY: Well, I—I did—about a hundred and eighty gross in Providence. Well, no—it came to—roughly two hundred gross on the whole trip.

LINDA: [*Without hesitation.*] Two hundred gross. That's . . . [*She figures.*]

WILLY: The trouble was that three of the stores were half closed for inventory in Boston. Otherwise I woulda broke records.

LINDA: Well, it makes seventy dollars and some pennies. That's very good.

WILLY: What do we owe?

LINDA: Well, on the first there's sixteen dollars on the refrigerator—

WILLY: Why sixteen?

LINDA: Well, the fan belt broke, so it was a dollar eighty.

WILLY: But it's brand new.

LINDA: Well, the man said that's the way it is. Till they work themselves in, y'know.

[*They move through the wall-line into the kitchen.*]

WILLY: I hope we didn't get stuck on that machine.
LINDA: They got the biggest ads of any of them!
WILLY: I know, it's a fine machine. What else?
LINDA: Well, there's nine-sixty for the washing machine. And for the vacuum cleaner there's three and a half due on the fifteenth. Then the roof, you got twenty-one dollars remaining.
WILLY: It don't leak, does it?
LINDA: No, they did a wonderful job. Then you owe Frank for the carburetor.
WILLY: I'm not going to pay that man! That goddam Chevrolet, they ought to prohibit the manufacture of that car!
LINDA: Well, you owe him three and a half. And odds and ends, comes to around a hundred and twenty dollars by the fifteenth.
WILLY: A hundred and twenty dollars! My God, if business don't pick up I don't know what I'm gonna do!
LINDA: Well, next week you'll do better.
WILLY: Oh, I'll knock 'em dead next week. I'll go to Hartford. I'm very well liked in Hartford. You know, the trouble is, Linda, people don't seem to take to me.

[*They move onto the forestage.*]

LINDA: Oh, don't be foolish.
WILLY: I know it when I walk in. They seem to laugh at me.
LINDA: Why? Why would they laugh at you? Don't talk that way, Willy.

[WILLY *moves to the edge of the stage.* LINDA *goes into the kitchen and starts to darn stockings.*]

WILLY: I don't know the reason for it, but they just pass me by. I'm not noticed.
LINDA: But you're doing wonderful, dear. You're making seventy to a hundred dollars a week.
WILLY: But I gotta be at it ten, twelve hours a day. Other men—I don't know—they do it easier. I don't know why—I can't stop myself—I talk too much. A man oughta come in with a few words. One thing about Charley. He's a man of few words, and they respect him.
LINDA: You don't talk too much, you're just lively.
WILLY: [*Smiling.*] Well, I figure, what the hell, life is short, a couple of jokes. [*To himself.*] I joke too much! [*The smile goes.*]
LINDA: Why? You're—
WILLY: I'm fat. I'm very—foolish to look at, Linda. I didn't tell you, but Christmas time I happened to be calling on F. H. Stewarts, and a salesman I know, as I was going in to see the buyer I heard him say something about—walrus. And I—I cracked him right across the face. I won't take that. I simply will not take that. But they do laugh at me. I know that.
LINDA: Darling...
WILLY: I gotta overcome it. I know I gotta overcome it. I'm not dressing to advantage, maybe.

LINDA: Willy, darling, you're the handsomest man in the world—
WILLY: Oh, no, Linda.
LINDA: To me you are. [*Slight pause.*] The handsomest. [*From the darkness is heard the laughter of a woman.* WILLY *doesn't turn to it, but it continues through* LINDA'*s lines.*] And the boys, Willy. Few men are idolized by their children the way you are.

[*Music is heard as behind a scrim, to the left of the house,* THE WOMAN, *dimly seen, is dressing.*]

WILLY: [*With great feeling.*] You're the best there is, Linda, you're a pal, you know that? On the road—on the road I want to grab you sometimes and just kiss the life outa you. [*The laughter is loud now, and he moves into a brightening area at the left, where* THE WOMAN *has come from behind the scrim and is standing, putting on her hat, looking into a "mirror" and laughing.*] 'Cause I get so lonely—especially when business is bad and there's nobody to talk to. I get the feeling that I'll never sell anything again, that I won't make a living for you, or a business, a business for the boys. [*He talks through* THE WOMAN'*s subsiding laughter.* THE WOMAN *primps at the "mirror."*] There's so much I want to make for—
THE WOMAN: Me? You didn't make me, Willy. I picked you.
WILLY: [*Pleased.*] You picked me?
THE WOMAN: [*Who is quite proper-looking,* WILLY'*s age.*] I did. I've been sitting at that desk watching all the salesmen go by, day in, day out. But you've got such a sense of humor, and we do have such a good time together, don't we?
WILLY: Sure, sure. [*He takes her in his arms.*] Why do you have to go now?
THE WOMAN: It's two o'clock...
WILLY: No, come on in! [*He pulls her.*]
THE WOMAN: ... my sisters'll be scandalized. When'll you be back?
WILLY: Oh, two weeks about. Will you come up again?
THE WOMAN: Sure thing. You do make me laugh. It's good for me. [*She squeezes his arm, kisses him.*] And I think you're a wonderful man.
WILLY: You picked me, heh?
THE WOMAN: Sure. Because you're so sweet. And such a kidder.
WILLY: Well, I'll see you next time I'm in Boston.
THE WOMAN: I'll put you right through to the buyers.
WILLY: [*Slapping her bottom.*] Right. Well, bottoms up!
THE WOMAN: [*Slaps him gently and laughs.*] You just kill me, Willy. [*He suddenly grabs her and kisses her roughly.*] You kill me. And thanks for the stockings. I love a lot of stockings. Well, good night.
WILLY: Good night. And keep your pores open!
THE WOMAN: Oh, Willy!

[THE WOMAN *bursts out laughing, and* LINDA'*s laughter blends in.* THE WOMAN *disappears into the dark. Now the area at the kitchen table brightens.* LINDA *is sitting where she was at the kitchen table, but now is mending a pair of her silk stockings.*]

LINDA: You are, Willy. The handsomest man. You've got no reason to feel that—
WILLY: [*Coming out of* THE WOMAN'*s dimming area and going over to* LINDA.] I'll make it all up to you, Linda. I'll—
LINDA: There's nothing to make up, dear. You're doing fine, better than—

WILLY: [*Noticing her mending.*] What's that?
LINDA: Just mending my stockings. They're so expensive—
WILLY: [*Angrily, taking them from her.*] I won't have you mending stockings in this house! Now throw them out!

[LINDA *puts the stockings in her pocket.*]

BERNARD: [*Entering on the run.*] Where is he? If he doesn't study!
WILLY: [*Moving to the forestage, with great agitation.*] You'll give him the answers!
BERNARD: I do, but I can't on a Regents! That's a state exam! They're liable to arrest me!
WILLY: Where is he? I'll whip him, I'll whip him!
LINDA: And he'd better give back that football, Willy, it's not nice.
WILLY: Biff! Where is he? Why is he taking everything?
LINDA: He's too rough with the girls, Willy. All the mothers are afraid of him!
WILLY: I'll whip him!
BERNARD: He's driving the car without a license!

[THE WOMAN'S *laugh is heard.*]

WILLY: Shut up!
LINDA: All the mothers—
WILLY: Shut up!
BERNARD: [*Backing quietly away and out.*] Mr. Birnbaum says he's stuck up.
WILLY: Get outa here!
BERNARD: If he doesn't buckle down he'll flunk math! [*He goes off.*]
LINDA: He's right, Willy, you've gotta—
WILLY: [*Exploding at her.*] There's nothing the matter with him! You want him to be a worm like Bernard? He's got spirit, personality... [*As he speaks,* LINDA, *almost in tears, exits into the living room.* WILLY *is alone in the kitchen, wilting and staring. The leaves are gone. It is night again, and the apartment houses look down from behind.*] Loaded with it. Loaded! What is he stealing? He's giving it back, isn't he? Why is he stealing? What did I tell him? I never in my life told him anything but decent things.

[HAPPY *in pajamas has come down the stairs;* WILLY *suddenly becomes aware of* HAPPY's *presence.*]

HAPPY: Let's go now, come on.
WILLY: [*Sitting down at the kitchen table.*] Huh! Why did she have to wax the floors herself? Everytime she waxes the floors she keels over. She knows that!
HAPPY: Shh! Take it easy. What brought you back tonight?
WILLY: I got an awful scare. Nearly hit a kid in Yonkers. God! Why didn't I go to Alaska with my brother Ben that time! Ben! That man was a genius, that man was success incarnate! What a mistake! He begged me to go.
HAPPY: Well, there's no use in—
WILLY: You guys! There was a man started with the clothes on his back and ended up with diamond mines!
HAPPY: Boy, someday I'd like to know how he did it.
WILLY: What's the mystery? The man knew what he wanted and went out and got it! Walked into a jungle, and comes out, the age of twenty-one, and he's rich! The world is an oyster, but you don't crack it open on a mattress!
HAPPY: Pop, I told you I'm gonna retire you for life.

WILLY: You'll retire me for life on seventy goddam dollars a week? And your women and your car and your apartment, and you'll retire me for life! Christ's sake, I couldn't get past Yonkers today! Where are you guys, where are you? The woods are burning! I can't drive a car!

[CHARLEY *has appeared in the doorway. He is a large man, slow of speech, laconic, immovable. In all he says, despite what he says, there is pity, and now, trepidation. He has a robe over pajamas, slippers on his feet. He enters the kitchen.*]

CHARLEY: Everything all right?
HAPPY: Yeah, Charley, everything's . . .
WILLY: What's the matter?
CHARLEY: I heard some noise. I thought something happened. Can't we do something about the walls? You sneeze in here, and in my house hats blow off.
HAPPY: Let's go to bed, Dad. Come on.

[CHARLEY *signals to* HAPPY *to go.*]

WILLY: You go ahead, I'm not tired at the moment.
HAPPY: [*To* WILLY.] Take it easy, huh? [*He exits.*]
WILLY: What're you doin' up?
CHARLEY: [*Sitting down at the kitchen table opposite* WILLY.] Couldn't sleep good. I had a heartburn.
WILLY: Well, you don't know how to eat.
CHARLEY: I eat with my mouth.
WILLY: No, you're ignorant. You gotta know about vitamins and things like that.
CHARLEY: Come on, let's shoot. Tire you out a little.
WILLY: [*Hesitantly.*] All right. You got cards?
CHARLEY: [*Taking a deck from his pocket.*] Yeah, I got them. Someplace. What is it with those vitamins?
WILLY: [*Dealing.*] They build up your bones. Chemistry.
CHARLEY: Yeah, but there's no bones in a heartburn.
WILLY: What are you talkin' about? Do you know the first thing about it?
CHARLEY: Don't get insulted.
WILLY: Don't talk about something you don't know anything about.

[*They are playing. Pause.*]

CHARLEY: What're you doin' home?
WILLY: A little trouble with the car.
CHARLEY: Oh. [*Pause.*] I'd like to take a trip to California.
WILLY: Don't say.
CHARLEY: You want a job?
WILLY: I got a job, I told you that. [*After a slight pause.*] What the hell are you offering me a job for?
CHARLEY: Don't get insulted.
WILLY: Don't insult me.
CHARLEY: I don't see no sense in it. You don't have to go on this way.
WILLY: I got a good job. [*Slight pause.*] What do you keep comin' in here for?
CHARLEY: You want me to go?
WILLY: [*After a pause, withering.*] I can't understand it. He's going back to Texas again. What the hell is that?
CHARLEY: Let him go.

WILLY: I got nothin' to give him, Charley, I'm clean, I'm clean.
CHARLEY: He won't starve. None a them starve. Forget about him.
WILLY: Then what have I got to remember?
CHARLEY: You take it too hard. To hell with it. When a deposit bottle is broken you don't get your nickel back.
WILLY: That's easy enough for you to say.
CHARLEY: That ain't easy for me to say.
WILLY: Did you see the ceiling I put up in the living-room?
CHARLEY: Yeah, that's a piece of work. To put up a ceiling is a mystery to me. How do you do it?
WILLY: What's the difference?
CHARLEY: Well, talk about it.
WILLY: You gonna put up a ceiling?
CHARLEY: How could I put up a ceiling?
WILLY: Then what the hell are you bothering me for?
CHARLEY: You're insulted again.
WILLY: A man who can't handle tools is not a man. You're disgusting.
CHARLEY: Don't call me disgusting, Willy.

[UNCLE BEN, *carrying a valise and an umbrella, enters the forestage from around the right corner of the house. He is a stolid man, in his sixties, with a mustache and an authoritative air. He is utterly certain of his destiny, and there is an aura of far places about him. He enters exactly as* WILLY *speaks.*]

WILLY: I'm getting awfully tired, Ben.

[BEN's *music is heard.* BEN *looks around at everything.*]

CHARLEY: Good, keep playing; you'll sleep better. Did you call me Ben?

[BEN *looks at his watch.*]

WILLY: That's funny. For a second there you reminded me of my brother Ben.
BEN: I only have a few minutes. [*He strolls, inspecting the place.* WILLY *and* CHARLEY *continue playing.*]
CHARLEY: You never heard from him again, heh? Since that time?
WILLY: Didn't Linda tell you? Couple of weeks ago we got a letter from his wife in Africa. He died.
CHARLEY: That so.
BEN: [*Chuckling.*] So this is Brooklyn, eh?
CHARLEY: Maybe you're in for some of his money.
WILLY: Naa, he had seven sons. There's just one opportunity I had with that man . . .
BEN: I must make a train, William. There are several properties I'm looking at in Alaska.
WILLY: Sure, sure! If I'd gone with him to Alaska that time, everything would've been totally different.
CHARLEY: Go on, you'da froze to death up there.
WILLY: What're you talking about?
BEN: Opportunity is tremendous in Alaska, William. Surprised you're not up there.
WILLY: Sure, tremendous.

CHARLEY: Heh?
WILLY: There was the only man I ever met who knew the answers.
CHARLEY: Who?
BEN: How are you all?
WILLY: [*Taking a pot, smiling.*] Fine, fine.
CHARLEY: Pretty sharp tonight.
BEN: Is Mother living with you?
WILLY: No, she died a long time ago.
CHARLEY: Who?
BEN: That's too bad. Fine specimen of a lady, Mother.
WILLY: [*To* CHARLEY.] Heh?
BEN: I'd hoped to see the old girl.
CHARLEY: Who died?
BEN: Heard anything from Father, have you?
WILLY: [*Unnerved.*] What do you mean, who died?
CHARLEY: [*Taking a pot.*] What're you talkin' about?
BEN: [*Looking at his watch.*] William, it's half-past eight!
WILLY: [*As though to dispel his confusion he angrily stops* CHARLEY*'s hand.*] That's my build!
CHARLEY: I put the ace—
WILLY: If you don't know how to play the game I'm not gonna throw my money away on you!
CHARLEY: [*Rising.*] It was my ace, for God's sake!
WILLY: I'm through, I'm through!
BEN: When did Mother die?
WILLY: Long ago. Since the beginning you never knew how to play cards.
CHARLEY: [*Picks up the cards and goes to the door.*] All right! Next time I'll bring a deck with five aces.
WILLY: I don't play that kind of game!
CHARLEY: [*Turning to him.*] You ought to be ashamed of yourself!
WILLY: Yeah?
CHARLEY: Yeah! [*He goes out.*]
WILLY: [*Slamming the door after him.*] Ignoramus!
BEN: [*As* WILLY *comes toward him through the wall-line of the kitchen.*] So you're William.
WILLY: [*Shaking* BEN*'s hand.*] Ben! I've been waiting for you so long! What's the answer? How did you do it?
BEN: Oh, there's a story in that.

[LINDA *enters the forestage, as of old, carrying the wash basket.*]

LINDA: Is this Ben?
BEN: [*Gallantly.*] How do you do, my dear.
LINDA: Where've you been all these years? Willy's always wondered why you—
WILLY: [*Pulling* BEN *away from her impatiently.*] Where is Dad? Didn't you follow him? How did you get started?
BEN: Well, I don't know how much you remember.
WILLY: Well, I was just a baby, of course, only three or four years old—
BEN: Three years and eleven months.
WILLY: What a memory, Ben!

BEN: I have many enterprises, William, and I have never kept books.
WILLY: I remember I was sitting under the wagon in—was it Nebraska?
BEN: It was South Dakota, and I gave you a bunch of wild flowers.
WILLY: I remember you walking away down some open road.
BEN: [*Laughing.*] I was going to find Father in Alaska.
WILLY: Where is he?
BEN: At that age I had a very faulty view of geography, William. I discovered after a few days that I was heading due south, so instead of Alaska, I ended up in Africa.
LINDA: Africa!
WILLY: The Gold Coast!
BEN: Principally diamond mines.
LINDA: Diamond mines!
BEN: Yes, my dear. But I've only a few minutes—
WILLY: No! Boys! Boys! [*Young* BIFF *and* HAPPY *appear.*] Listen to this. This is your Uncle Ben, a great man! Tell my boys, Ben!
BEN: Why, boys, when I was seventeen I walked into the jungle, and when I was twenty-one I walked out. [*He laughs.*] And by God I was rich.
WILLY: [*To the boys.*] You see what I been talking about? The greatest things can happen!
BEN: [*Glancing at his watch.*] I have an appointment in Ketchikan Tuesday week.
WILLY: No, Ben! Please tell about Dad. I want my boys to hear. I want them to know the kind of stock they spring from. All I remember is a man with a big beard, and I was in Mamma's lap, sitting around a fire, and some kind of high music.
BEN: His flute. He played the flute.
WILLY: Sure, the flute, that's right!

[*New music is heard, a high, rollicking tune.*]

BEN: Father was a very great and a very wild-hearted man. We would start in Boston, and he'd toss the whole family into the wagon, and then he'd drive the team right across the country; through Ohio, and Indiana, Michigan, Illinois, and all the Western states. And we'd stop in the towns and sell the flutes that he'd made on the way. Great inventor, Father. With one gadget he made more in a week than a man like you could make in a lifetime.
WILLY: That's just the way I'm bringing them up, Ben—rugged, well liked, all-around.
BEN: Yeah? [*To* BIFF.] Hit that, boy—hard as you can. [*He pounds his stomach.*]
BIFF: Oh, no, sir!
BEN: [*Taking boxing stance.*] Come on, get to me! [*He laughs.*]
WILLY: Go to it, Biff! Go ahead, show him!
BIFF: Okay! [*He cocks his fist and starts in.*]
LINDA: [*To* WILLY.] Why must he fight, dear?
BEN: [*Sparring with* BIFF.] Good boy! Good boy!
WILLY: How's that, Ben, heh?
HAPPY: Give him the left, Biff!
LINDA: Why are you fighting?
BEN: Good boy! [*Suddenly comes in, trips* BIFF, *and stands over him, the point of his umbrella poised over* BIFF's *eye.*]

LINDA: Look out, Biff!
BIFF: Gee!
BEN: [*Patting* BIFF's *knee.*] Never fight fair with a stranger, boy. You'll never get out of the jungle that way. [*Taking* LINDA's *hand and bowing.*] It was an honor and a pleasure to meet you, Linda.
LINDA: [*Withdrawing her hand coldly, frightened.*] Have a nice—trip.
BEN: [*To* WILLY.] And good luck with your—what do you do?
WILLY: Selling.
BEN: Yes. Well... [*He raises his hand in farewell to all.*]
WILLY: No, Ben, I don't want you to think... [*He takes* BEN's *arm to show him.*] It's Brooklyn, I know, but we hunt too.
BEN: Really, now.
WILLY: Oh, sure, there's snakes and rabbits and—that's why I moved out here. Why, Biff can fell any one of these trees in no time! Boys! Go right over to where they're building the apartment house and get some sand. We're gonna rebuild the entire front stoop right now! Watch this, Ben!
BIFF: Yes, sir! On the double, Hap!
HAPPY: [*As he and* BIFF *run off.*] I lost weight, Pop, you notice?

[CHARLEY *enters in knickers, even before the boys are gone.*]

CHARLEY: Listen, if they steal any more from that building the watchman'll put the cops on them!
LINDA: [*To* WILLY.] Don't let Biff...

[BEN *laughs lustily.*]

WILLY: You shoulda seen the lumber they brought home last week. At least a dozen six-by-tens worth all kinds a money.
CHARLEY: Listen, if that watchman—
WILLY: I gave them hell, understand. But I got a couple of fearless characters there.
CHARLEY: Willy, the jails are full of fearless characters.
BEN: [*Clapping* WILLY *on the back, with a laugh at* CHARLEY.] And the stock exchange, friend!
WILLY: [*Joining in* BEN's *laughter.*] Where are the rest of your pants?
CHARLEY: My wife bought them.
WILLY: Now all you need is a golf club and you can go upstairs and go to sleep. [*To* BEN.] Great athlete! Between him and his son Bernard they can't hammer a nail!
BERNARD: [*Rushing in.*] The watchman's chasing Biff!
WILLY: [*Angrily.*] Shut up! He's not stealing anything!
LINDA: [*Alarmed, hurrying off left.*] Where is he? Biff, dear! [*She exits.*]
WILLY: [*Moving toward the left, away from* BEN.] There's nothing wrong. What's the matter with you?
BEN: Nervy boy. Good!
WILLY: [*Laughing.*] Oh, nerves of iron, that Biff!
CHARLEY: Don't know what it is. My New England man comes back and he's bleedin', they murdered him up there.
WILLY: It's contacts, Charley, I got important contacts!
CHARLEY: [*Sarcastically.*] Glad to hear it, Willy. Come in later, we'll shoot a little

casino. I'll take some of your Portland money. [*He laughs at* WILLY *and exits.*]
WILLY: [*Turning to* BEN.] Business is bad, it's murderous. But not for me, of course.
BEN: I'll stop by on my way back to Africa.
WILLY: [*Longingly.*] Can't you stay a few days? You're just what I need, Ben, because I—I have a fine position here, but I—well, Dad left when I was such a baby and I never had a chance to talk to him and I still feel—kind of temporary about myself.
BEN: I'll be late for my train.

[*They are at opposite ends of the stage.*]

WILLY: Ben, my boys—can't we talk? They'd go into the jaws of hell for me, see, but I—
BEN: William, you're being first-rate with your boys. Outstanding, manly chaps!
WILLY: [*Hanging on to his words.*] Oh, Ben, that's good to hear! Because sometimes I'm afraid that I'm not teaching them the right kind of—Ben, how should I teach them?
BEN: [*Giving great weight to each word, and with a certain vicious audacity.*] William, when I walked into the jungle, I was seventeen. When I walked out I was twenty-one. And, by God, I was rich! [*He goes off into darkness around the right corner of the house.*]
WILLY: . . . was rich! That's just the spirit I want to imbue them with! To walk into a jungle! I was right! I was right! I was right!

[BEN *is gone, but* WILLY *is still speaking to him as* LINDA, *in nightgown and robe, enters the kitchen, glances around for* WILLY, *then goes to the door of the house, looks out and sees him. Comes down to his left. He looks at her.*]

LINDA: Willy, dear? Willy?
WILLY: I was right!
LINDA: Did you have some cheese? [*He can't answer.*] It's very late, darling. Come to bed, heh?
WILLY: [*Looking straight up.*] Gotta break your neck to see a star in this yard.
LINDA: You coming in?
WILLY: Whatever happened to that diamond watch fob? Remember? When Ben came from Africa that time? Didn't he give me a watch fob with a diamond in it?
LINDA: You pawned it, dear. Twelve, thirteen years ago. For Biff's radio correspondence course.
WILLY: Gee, that was a beautiful thing. I'll take a walk.
LINDA: But you're in your slippers.
WILLY: [*Starting to go around the house at the left.*] I was right! I was! [*Half to* LINDA, *as he goes, shaking his head.*] What a man! There was a man worth talking to. I was right!
LINDA: [*Calling after* WILLY.] But in your slippers, Willy!

[WILLY *is almost gone when* BIFF, *in his pajamas, comes down the stairs and enters the kitchen.*]

BIFF: What is he doing out there?
LINDA: Sh!
BIFF: God Almighty, Mom, how long has he been doing this?

LINDA: Don't, he'll hear you.
BIFF: What the hell is the matter with him?
LINDA: It'll pass by morning.
BIFF: Shouldn't we do anything?
LINDA: Oh, my dear, you should do a lot of things, but there's nothing to do, so go to sleep.

[HAPPY *comes down the stairs and sits on the steps.*]

HAPPY: I never heard him so loud, Mom.
LINDA: Well, come around more often; you'll hear him. [*She sits down at the table and mends the lining of* WILLY'S *jacket.*]
BIFF: Why didn't you ever write me about this, Mom?
LINDA: How would I write to you? For over three months you had no address.
BIFF: I was on the move. But you know I thought of you all the time. You know that, don't you, pal?
LINDA: I know, dear, I know. But he likes to have a letter. Just to know that there's still a possibility for better things.
BIFF: He's not like this all the time, is he?
LINDA: It's when you come home he's always the worst.
BIFF: When I come home?
LINDA: When you write you're coming, he's all smiles, and talks about the future, and—he's just wonderful. And then the closer you seem to come, the more shaky he gets, and then, by the time you get here, he's arguing, and he seems angry at you. I think it's just that maybe he can't bring himself to—to open up to you. Why are you so hateful to each other? Why is that?
BIFF: [*Evasively.*] I'm not hateful, Mom.
LINDA: But you no sooner come in the door than you're fighting!
BIFF: I don't know why. I mean to change. I'm tryin', Mom, you understand?
LINDA: Are you home to stay now?
BIFF: I don't know. I want to look around, see what's doin'.
LINDA: Biff, you can't look around all your life, can you?
BIFF: I just can't take hold, Mom. I can't take hold of some kind of a life.
LINDA: Biff, a man is not a bird, to come and go with the springtime.
BIFF: Your hair... [*He touches her hair.*] Your hair got so gray.
LINDA: Oh, it's been gray since you were in high school. I just stopped dyeing it, that's all.
BIFF: Dye it again, will ya? I don't want my pal looking old. [*He smiles.*]
LINDA: You're such a boy! You think you can go away for a year and... You've got to get it into your head now that one day you'll knock on this door and there'll be strange people here—
BIFF: What are you talking about? You're not even sixty, Mom.
LINDA: But what about your father?
BIFF: [*Lamely.*] Well, I meant him too.
HAPPY: He admires Pop.
LINDA: Biff, dear, if you don't have any feeling for him, then you can't have any feeling for me.
BIFF: Sure I can, Mom.
LINDA: No. You can't just come to see me, because I love him. [*With a threat, but only a threat, of tears.*] He's the dearest man in the world to me, and I won't

have anyone making him feel unwanted and low and blue. You've got to make up your mind now, darling, there's no leeway anymore. Either he's your father and you pay him that respect, or else you're not to come here. I know he's not easy to get along with—nobody knows that better than me—but . . .

WILLY: [*From the left, with a laugh.*] Hey, hey, Biffo!

BIFF: [*Starting to go out after* WILLY.] What the hell is the matter with him? [HAPPY *stops him.*]

LINDA: Don't—don't go near him!

BIFF: Stop making excuses for him! He always, always wiped the floor with you. Never had an ounce of respect for you.

HAPPY: He's always had respect for—

BIFF: What the hell do you know about it?

HAPPY: [*Surlily.*] Just don't call him crazy!

BIFF: He's got no character—Charley wouldn't do this. Not in his own house—spewing out that vomit from his mind.

HAPPY: Charley never had to cope with what he's got to.

BIFF: People are worse off than Willy Loman. Believe me, I've seen them!

LINDA: Then make Charley your father, Biff. You can't do that, can you? I don't say he's a great man. Willy Loman never made a lot of money. His name was never in the paper. He's not the finest character that ever lived. But he's a human being, and a terrible thing is happening to him. So attention must be paid. He's not to be allowed to fall into his grave like an old dog. Attention, attention must be finally paid to such a person. You called him crazy—

BIFF: I didn't mean—

LINDA: No, a lot of people think he's lost his—balance. But you don't have to be very smart to know what his trouble is. The man is exhausted.

HAPPY: Sure!

LINDA: A small man can be just as exhausted as a great man. He works for a company thirty-six years this March, opens up unheard-of territories to their trademark, and now in his old age they take his salary away.

HAPPY: [*Indignantly.*] I didn't know that, Mom.

LINDA: You never asked, my dear! Now that you get your spending money someplace else you don't trouble your mind with him.

HAPPY: But I gave you money last—

LINDA: Christmas time, fifty dollars! To fix the hot water it cost ninety-seven fifty! For five weeks he's been on straight commission, like a beginner, an unknown!

BIFF: Those ungrateful bastards!

LINDA: Are they any worse than his sons? When he brought them business, when he was young, they were glad to see him. But now his old friends, the old buyers that loved him so and always found some order to hand him in a pinch—they're all dead, retired. He used to be able to make six, seven calls a day in Boston. Now he takes his valises out of the car and puts them back and takes them out again and he's exhausted. Instead of walking he talks now. He drives seven hundred miles, and when he gets there no one knows him anymore, no one welcomes him. And what goes through a man's mind, driving seven hundred miles home without having earned a cent? Why shouldn't he talk to himself? Why? When he has to go to Charley and borrow fifty dollars a week and pretend to me that it's his pay? How long can that go on? How long? You see what I'm sitting here and waiting for? And you tell me he has no character? The man who never worked a day but for your benefit? When does he get the medal for that? Is this his reward—to turn around at the age of sixty-three and find his sons, who he loved better than his life, one a philandering bum—

HAPPY: Mom!

LINDA: That's all you are, my baby! [*To* BIFF.] And you! What happened to the love you had for him? You were such pals! How you used to talk to him on the phone every night! How lonely he was till he could come home to you!

BIFF: All right, Mom. I'll live here in my room, and I'll get a job. I'll keep away from him, that's all.

LINDA: No, Biff. You can't stay here and fight all the time.

BIFF: He threw me out of this house, remember that.

LINDA: Why did he do that? I never knew why.

BIFF: Because I know he's a fake and he doesn't like anybody around who knows!

LINDA: Why a fake? In what way? What do you mean?

BIFF: Just don't lay it all at my feet. It's between me and him—that's all I have to say. I'll chip in from now on. He'll settle for half my paycheck. He'll be all right. I'm going to bed. [*He starts for the stairs.*]

LINDA: He won't be all right.

BIFF: [*Turning on the stairs, furiously.*] I hate this city and I'll stay here. Now what do you want?

LINDA: He's dying, BIFF.

[HAPPY *turns quickly to her, shocked.*]

BIFF: [*After a pause.*] Why is he dying?

LINDA: He's been trying to kill himself.

BIFF: [*With great horror.*] How?

LINDA: I live from day to day.

BIFF: What're you talking about?

LINDA: Remember I wrote you that he smashed up the car again? In February?

BIFF: Well?

LINDA: The insurance inspector came. He said that they have evidence. That all these accidents in the last year—weren't—weren't—accidents.

HAPPY: How can they tell that? That's a lie.

LINDA: It seems there's a woman . . . [*She takes a breath as. . . .*]

{ BIFF: [*Sharply but contained.*] What woman?
{ LINDA: [*Simultaneously.*] . . . and this woman . . .

LINDA: What?

BIFF: Nothing. Go ahead.

LINDA: What did you say?

BIFF: Nothing. I just said what woman?

HAPPY: What about her?

LINDA: Well, it seems she was walking down the road and saw his car. She says that he wasn't driving fast at all, and that he didn't skid. She says he came to that little bridge, and then deliberately smashed into the railing, and it was only the shallowness of the water that saved him.

BIFF: Oh, no, he probably just fell asleep again.

LINDA: I don't think he fell asleep.

BIFF: Why not?

LINDA: Last month . . . [*With great difficulty.*] Oh, boys, it's so hard to say a thing like this! He's just a big stupid man to you, but I tell you there's more good in him than in many other people. [*She chokes, wipes her eyes.*] I was looking for a fuse. The lights blew out, and I went down the cellar. And behind the fuse box—it happened to fall out—was a length of rubber pipe—just short.

HAPPY: No kidding?

LINDA: There's a little attachment on the end of it. I knew right away. And sure enough, on the bottom of the water heater there's a new little nipple on the gas pipe.

HAPPY: [*Angrily.*] That—jerk.

BIFF: Did you have it taken off?

LINDA: I'm—I'm ashamed to. How can I mention it to him? Every day I go down and take away that little rubber pipe. But, when he comes home, I put it back where it was. How can I insult him that way? I don't know what to do. I live from day to day, boys. I tell you, I know every thought in his mind. It sounds so old-fashioned and silly, but I tell you he put his whole life into you and you've turned your backs on him. [*She is bent over in the chair, weeping, her face in her hands.*] Biff, I swear to God! Biff, his life is in your hands!

HAPPY: [*To* BIFF.] How do you like that damned fool!

BIFF: [*Kissing her.*] All right, pal, all right. It's all settled now. I've been remiss. I know that, Mom. But now I'll stay, and I swear to you, I'll apply myself. [*Kneeling in front of her, in a fever of self-reproach.*] It's just—you see, Mom, I don't fit in business. Not that I won't try. I'll try, and I'll make good.

HAPPY: Sure you will. The trouble with you in business was you never tried to please people.

BIFF: I know, I—

HAPPY: Like when you worked for Harrison's. Bob Harrison said you were tops, and then you go and do some damn fool thing like whistling whole songs in the elevator like a comedian.

BIFF: [*Against* HAPPY.] So what? I like to whistle sometimes.

HAPPY: You don't raise a guy to a responsible job who whistles in the elevator!

LINDA: Well, don't argue about it now.

HAPPY: Like when you'd go off and swim in the middle of the day instead of taking the line around.

BIFF: [*His resentment rising.*] Well, don't you run off? You take off sometimes, don't you? On a nice summer day?

HAPPY: Yeah, but I cover myself!

LINDA: Boys!

HAPPY: If I'm going to take a fade the boss can call any number where I'm supposed to be and they'll swear to him that I just left. I'll tell you something that I hate to say, Biff, but in the business world some of them think you're crazy.

BIFF: [*Angered.*] Screw the business world!

HAPPY: All right, screw it! Great, but cover yourself!

LINDA: Hap, Hap!

BIFF: I don't care what they think! They've laughed at Dad for years, and you know why? Because we don't belong in this nuthouse of a city! We should be mixing cement on some open plain, or—or carpenters. A carpenter is allowed to whistle!

[WILLY *walks in from the entrance of the house, at left.*]

WILLY: Even your grandfather was better than a carpenter. [*Pause. They watch him.*] You never grew up. Bernard does not whistle in the elevator, I assure you.
BIFF: [*As though to laugh* WILLY *out of it.*] Yeah, but you do, Pop.
WILLY: I never in my life whistled in an elevator! And who in the business world thinks I'm crazy?
BIFF: I didn't mean it like that, Pop. Now don't make a whole thing out of it, will ya?
WILLY: Go back to the West! Be a carpenter, a cowboy, enjoy yourself!
LINDA: Willy, he was just saying—
WILLY: I heard what he said!
HAPPY: [*Trying to quiet* WILLY.] Hey, Pop, come on now...
WILLY: [*Continuing over* HAPPY's *line.*] They laugh at me, heh? Go to Filene's, go to the Hub, go to Slattery's Boston. Call out the name Willy Loman and see what happens! Big shot!
BIFF: All right, Pop.
WILLY: Big!
BIFF: All right!
WILLY: Why do you always insult me?
BIFF: I didn't say a word. [*To* LINDA.] Did I say a word?
LINDA: He didn't say anything, Willy.
WILLY: [*Going to the doorway of the living-room.*] All right, good night, good night.
LINDA: Willy, dear, he just decided...
WILLY: [*To* BIFF.] If you get tired hanging around tomorrow, paint the ceiling I put up in the living-room.
BIFF: I'm leaving early tomorrow.
HAPPY: He's going to see Bill Oliver, Pop.
WILLY: [*Interestedly.*] Oliver? For what?
BIFF: [*With reserve, but trying, trying.*] He always said he'd stake me. I'd like to go into business, so maybe I can take him up on it.
LINDA: Isn't that wonderful?
WILLY: Don't interrupt. What's wonderful about it? There's fifty men in the City of New York who'd stake him. [*To* BIFF.] Sporting goods?
BIFF: I guess so. I know something about it and—
WILLY: He knows something about it! You know sporting goods better than Spalding,[5] for God's sake! How much is he giving you?
BIFF: I don't know, I didn't even see him yet, but—
WILLY: Then what're you talkin' about?
BIFF: [*Getting angry.*] Well, all I said was I'm gonna see him, that's all!
WILLY: [*Turning away.*] Ah, you're counting your chickens again.
BIFF: [*Starting left for the stairs.*] Oh, Jesus, I'm going to sleep!
WILLY: [*Calling after him.*] Don't curse in this house!
BIFF: [*Turning.*] Since when did you get so clean?
HAPPY: [*Trying to stop them.*] Wait a...
WILLY: Don't use that language to me! I won't have it!
HAPPY: [*Grabbing* BIFF, *shouts.*] Wait a minute! I got an idea. I got a feasible idea. Come here, Biff, let's talk this over now, let's talk some sense here. When I was down in Florida last time, I thought of a great idea to sell sporting goods.

---

5. Albert G. Spalding (1850–1915), American baseball player and sporting-goods manufacturer.

It just came back to me. You and I, Biff—we have a line, the Loman Line. We train a couple of weeks, and put on a couple of exhibitions, see?

WILLY: That's an idea!

HAPPY: Wait! We form two basketball teams, see? Two water-polo teams. We play each other. It's a million dollars' worth of publicity. Two brothers, see? The Loman Brothers. Displays in the Royal Palms—all the hotels. And banners over the ring and the basketball court: "Loman Brothers." Baby, we could sell sporting goods!

WILLY: That is a one-million-dollar idea!

LINDA: Marvelous!

BIFF: I'm in great shape as far as that's concerned.

HAPPY: And the beauty of it is, Biff, it wouldn't be like a business. We'd be out playin' ball again . . .

BIFF: [*Enthused.*] Yeah, that's . . .

WILLY: Million-dollar . . .

HAPPY: And you wouldn't get fed up with it, Biff. It'd be the family again. There'd be the old honor, and comradeship, and if you wanted to go off for a swim or somethin'—well, you'd do it! Without some smart cooky gettin' up ahead of you!

WILLY: Lick the world! You guys together could absolutely lick the civilized world.

BIFF: I'll see Oliver tomorrow. Hap, if we could work that out . . .

LINDA: Maybe things are beginning to—

WILLY: [*Wildly enthused, to* LINDA.] Stop interrupting! [*To* BIFF.] But don't wear sport jacket and slacks when you see Oliver.

BIFF: No, I'll—

WILLY: A business suit, and talk as little as possible, and don't crack any jokes.

BIFF: He did like me. Always liked me.

LINDA: He loved you!

WILLY: [*To* LINDA.] Will you stop! [*To* BIFF.] Walk in very serious. You are not applying for a boy's job. Money is to pass. Be quiet, fine, and serious. Everybody likes a kidder, but nobody lends him money.

HAPPY: I'll try to get some myself, Biff. I'm sure I can.

WILLY: I see great things for you kids, I think your troubles are over. But remember, start big and you'll end big. Ask for fifteen. How much you gonna ask for?

BIFF: Gee, I don't know—

WILLY: And don't say "Gee." "Gee" is a boy's word. A man walking in for fifteen thousand dollars does not say "Gee!"

BIFF: Ten, I think, would be top though.

WILLY: Don't be so modest. You always started too low. Walk in with a big laugh. Don't look worried. Start off with a couple of your good stories to lighten things up. It's not what you say, it's how you say it—because personality always wins the day.

LINDA: Oliver always thought the highest of him—

WILLY: Will you let me talk?

BIFF: Don't yell at her, Pop, will ya?

WILLY: [*Angrily.*] I was talking, wasn't I?

BIFF: I don't like you yelling at her all the time, and I'm tellin' you, that's all.

WILLY: What're you, takin' over this house?

LINDA: Willy—

WILLY: [*Turning on her.*] Don't take his side all the time, goddammit!
BIFF: [*Furiously.*] Stop yelling at her!
WILLY: [*Suddenly pulling on his cheek, beaten down, guilt ridden.*] Give my best to Bill Oliver—he may remember me. [*He exits through the living-room doorway.*]
LINDA: [*Her voice subdued.*] What'd you have to start that for? [BIFF *turns away.*] You see how sweet he was as soon as you talked hopefully? [*She goes over to* BIFF.] Come up and say good night to him. Don't let him go to bed that way.
HAPPY: Come on, Biff, let's buck him up.
LINDA: Please, dear. Just say good night. It takes so little to make him happy. Come. [*She goes through the living-room doorway, calling upstairs from within the living-room.*] Your pajamas are hanging in the bathroom, Willy!
HAPPY: [*Looking toward where* LINDA *went out.*] What a woman! They broke the mold when they made her. You know that, Biff?
BIFF: He's off salary. My God, working on commission!
HAPPY: Well, let's face it: he's no hot-shot selling man. Except that sometimes, you have to admit, he's a sweet personality.
BIFF: [*Deciding.*] Lend me ten bucks, will ya? I want to buy some new ties.
HAPPY: I'll take you to a place I know. Beautiful stuff. Wear one of my striped shirts tomorrow.
BIFF: She got gray. Mom got awful old. Gee, I'm gonna go in to Oliver tomorrow and knock him for a—
HAPPY: Come on up. Tell that to Dad. Let's give him a whirl. Come on.
BIFF: [*Steamed up.*] You know, with ten thousand bucks, boy!
HAPPY: [*As they go into the living-room.*] That's the talk, Biff, that's the first time I've heard the old confidence out of you! [*From within the living-room, fading off.*] You're gonna live with me, kid, and any babe you want just say the word...

[*The last lines are hardly heard. They are mounting the stairs to their parents' bedroom.*]

LINDA: [*Entering her bedroom and addressing* WILLY, *who is in the bathroom. She is straightening the bed for him.*] Can you do anything about the shower? It drips.
WILLY: [*From the bathroom.*] All of a sudden everything falls to pieces! Goddam plumbing, oughta be sued, those people. I hardly finished putting it in and the thing... [*His words rumble off.*]
LINDA: I'm just wondering if Oliver will remember him. You think he might?
WILLY: [*Coming out of the bathroom in his pajamas.*] Remember him? What's the matter with you, you crazy? If he'd've stayed with Oliver he'd be on top by now! Wait'll Oliver gets a look at him. You don't know the average caliber anymore. The average young man today—[*He is getting into bed.*]—is got a caliber of zero. Greatest thing in the world for him was to bum around. [BIFF *and* HAPPY *enter the bedroom. Slight pause.* WILLY *stops short, looking at* BIFF.] Glad to hear it, boy.
HAPPY: He wanted to say good night to you, sport.
WILLY: [*To* BIFF.] Yeah. Knock him dead, boy. What'd you want to tell me?
BIFF: Just take it easy, Pop. Good night. [*He turns to go.*]
WILLY: [*Unable to resist.*] And if anything falls off the desk while you're talking to him—like a package or something—don't you pick it up. They have office boys for that.
LINDA: I'll make a big breakfast—

WILLY: Will you let me finish? [*To* BIFF.] Tell him you were in the business in the West. Not farm work.
BIFF: All right, Dad.
LINDA: I think everything—
WILLY: [*Going right through her speech.*] And don't undersell yourself. No less than fifteen thousand dollars.
BIFF: [*Unable to bear him.*] Okay. Good night, Mom. [*He starts moving.*]
WILLY: Because you got a greatness in you, Biff, remember that. You got all kinds of greatness . . . [*He lies back, exhausted.* BIFF *walks out.*]
LINDA: [*Calling after* BIFF.] Sleep well, darling!
HAPPY: I'm gonna get married, Mom. I wanted to tell you.
LINDA: Go to sleep, dear.
HAPPY: [*Going.*] I just wanted to tell you.
WILLY: Keep up the good work. [HAPPY *exits.*] God . . . remember that Ebbets Field[6] game? The championship of the city?
LINDA: Just rest. Should I sing to you?
WILLY: Yeah. Sing to me. [LINDA *hums a soft lullaby.*] When that team came out—he was the tallest, remember?
LINDA: Oh, yes. And in gold.

[BIFF *enters the darkened kitchen, takes a cigarette, and leaves the house. He comes downstage into a golden pool of light. He smokes, staring at the night.*]

WILLY: Like a young god. Hercules—something like that. And the sun, the sun all around him. Remember how he waved to me? Right up from the field, with the representatives of three colleges standing by? And the buyers I brought, and the cheers when he came out—Loman, Loman, Loman! God Almighty, he'll be great yet. A star like that, magnificent, can never really fade away!

[*The light on* WILLY *is fading. The gas heater begins to glow through the kitchen wall, near the stairs, a blue flame beneath red coils.*]

LINDA: [*Timidly.*] Willy dear, what has he got against you?
WILLY: I'm so tired. Don't talk anymore.

[BIFF *slowly returns to the kitchen. He stops, stares toward the heater.*]

LINDA: Will you ask Howard to let you work in New York?
WILLY: First thing in the morning. Everything'll be all right.

[BIFF *reaches behind the heater and draws out a length of rubber tubing. He is horrified and turns his head toward* WILLY'S *room, still dimly lit, from which the strains of* LINDA'S *desperate but monotonous humming rise.*]

WILLY: [*Staring through the window into the moonlight.*] Gee, look at the moon moving between the buildings!

[BIFF *wraps the tubing around his hand and quickly goes up the stairs.*]

CURTAIN

---

6. Stadium where the Dodgers, Brooklyn's major-league baseball team, played from 1913 to 1957.

## ACT II

*Music is heard, gay and bright. The curtain rises as the music fades away.* WILLY, *in shirt sleeves, is sitting at the kitchen table, sipping coffee, his hat in his lap.* LINDA *is filling his cup when she can.*

WILLY: Wonderful coffee. Meal in itself.
LINDA: Can I make you some eggs?
WILLY: No. Take a breath.
LINDA: You look so rested, dear.
WILLY: I slept like a dead one. First time in months. Imagine, sleeping till ten on a Tuesday morning. Boys left nice and early, heh?
LINDA: They were out of here by eight o'clock.
WILLY: Good work!
LINDA: It was so thrilling to see them leaving together. I can't get over the shaving lotion in this house!
WILLY: [*Smiling.*] Mmm—
LINDA: Biff was very changed this morning. His whole attitude seemed to be hopeful. He couldn't wait to get downtown to see Oliver.
WILLY: He's heading for a change. There's no question, there simply are certain men that take longer to get—solidified. How did he dress?
LINDA: His blue suit. He's so handsome in that suit. He could be a—anything in that suit!

[WILLY *gets up from the table.* LINDA *holds his jacket for him.*]

WILLY: There's no question, no question at all. Gee, on the way home tonight I'd like to buy some seeds.
LINDA: [*Laughing.*] That'd be wonderful. But not enough sun gets back there. Nothing'll grow any more.
WILLY: You wait, kid, before it's all over we're gonna get a little place out in the country, and I'll raise some vegetables, a couple of chickens...
LINDA: You'll do it yet, dear.

[WILLY *walks out of his jacket.* LINDA *follows him.*]

WILLY: And they'll get married, and come for a weekend. I'd build a little guest house. 'Cause I got so many fine tools, all I'd need would be a little lumber and some peace of mind.
LINDA: [*Joyfully.*] I sewed the lining...
WILLY: I could build two guest houses, so they'd both come. Did he decide how much he's going to ask Oliver for?
LINDA: [*Getting him into the jacket.*] He didn't mention it, but I imagine ten or fifteen thousand. You going to talk to Howard today?
WILLY: Yeah. I'll put it to him straight and simple. He'll just have to take me off the road.
LINDA: And Willy, don't forget to ask for a little advance, because we've got the insurance premium. It's the grace period now.
WILLY: That's a hundred...?
LINDA: A hundred and eight, sixty-eight. Because we're a little short again.
WILLY: Why are we short?

LINDA: Well, you had the motor job on the car...
WILLY: That goddam Studebaker!
LINDA: And you got one more payment on the refrigerator...
WILLY: But it just broke again!
LINDA: Well, it's old, dear.
WILLY: I told you we should've bought a well-advertised machine. Charley bought a General Electric and it's twenty years old and it's still good, that son-of-a-bitch.
LINDA: But, Willy—
WILLY: Whoever heard of a Hastings refrigerator? Once in my life I would like to own something outright before it's broken! I'm always in a race with the junkyard! I just finished paying for the car and it's on its last legs. The refrigerator consumes belts like a goddam maniac. They time those things. They time them so when you finally paid for them, they're used up.
LINDA: [*Buttoning up his jacket as he unbuttons it.*] All told, about two hundred dollars would carry us, dear. But that includes the last payment on the mortgage. After this payment, Willy, the house belongs to us.
WILLY: It's twenty-five years!
LINDA: Biff was nine years old when we bought it.
WILLY: Well, that's a great thing. To weather a twenty-five year mortgage is—
LINDA: It's an accomplishment.
WILLY: All the cement, the lumber, the reconstruction I put in this house! There ain't a crack to be found in it anymore.
LINDA: Well, it served its purpose.
WILLY: What purpose? Some stranger'll come along, move in, and that's that. If only Biff would take this house, and raise a family... [*He starts to go.*] Goodbye, I'm late.
LINDA: [*Suddenly remembering.*] Oh, I forgot! You're supposed to meet them for dinner.
WILLY: Me?
LINDA: At Frank's Chop House on Forty-eighth near Sixth Avenue.
WILLY: Is that so! How about you?
LINDA: No, just the three of you. They're gonna blow you to a big meal!
WILLY: Don't say! Who thought of that?
LINDA: Biff came to me this morning, Willy, and he said, "Tell Dad, we want to blow him to a big meal." Be there six o'clock. You and your two boys are going to have dinner.
WILLY: Gee whiz! That's really somethin'. I'm gonna knock Howard for a loop, kid. I'll get an advance, and I'll come home with a New York job. Goddammit, now I'm gonna do it!
LINDA: Oh, that's the spirit, Willy!
WILLY: I will never get behind a wheel the rest of my life!
LINDA: It's changing, Willy, I can feel it changing!
WILLY: Beyond a question. G'bye, I'm late. [*He starts to go again.*]
LINDA: [*Calling after him as she runs to the kitchen table for a handkerchief.*] You got your glasses?
WILLY: [*Feels for them, then comes back in.*] Yeah, yeah, got my glasses.
LINDA: [*Giving him the handkerchief.*] And a handkerchief.
WILLY: Yeah, handkerchief.

LINDA: And your saccharine?[7]
WILLY: Yeah, my saccharine.
LINDA: Be careful on the subway stairs.

[*She kisses him, and a silk stocking is seen hanging from her hand.* WILLY *notices it.*]

WILLY: Will you stop mending stockings? At least while I'm in the house. It gets me nervous. I can't tell you. Please.

[LINDA *hides the stocking in her hand as she follows* WILLY *across the forestage in front of the house.*]

LINDA: Remember, Frank's Chop House.
WILLY: [*Passing the apron.*] Maybe beets would grow out there.
LINDA: [*Laughing.*] But you tried so many times.
WILLY: Yeah. Well, don't work hard today. [*He disappears around the right corner of the house.*]
LINDA: Be careful! [*As* WILLY *vanishes,* LINDA *waves to him. Suddenly the phone rings. She runs across the stage and into the kitchen and lifts it.*] Hello? Oh, Biff! I'm so glad you called, I just . . . Yes, sure, I just told him. Yes, he'll be there for dinner at six o'clock, I didn't forget. Listen, I was just dying to tell you. You know that little rubber pipe I told you about? That he connected to the gas heater? I finally decided to go down the cellar this morning and take it away and destroy it. But it's gone! Imagine? He took it away himself, it isn't there! [*She listens.*] When? Oh, then you took it. Oh—nothing, it's just that I'd hoped he'd taken it away himself. Oh, I'm not worried, darling, because this morning he left in such high spirits, it was like the old days! I'm not afraid anymore. Did Mr. Oliver see you? . . . Well, you wait there then. And make a nice impression on him, darling. Just don't perspire too much before you see him. And have a nice time with Dad. He may have big news too! . . . That's right, a New York job. And be sweet to him tonight, dear. Be loving to him. Because he's only a little boat looking for a harbor. [*She is trembling with sorrow and joy.*] Oh, that's wonderful, Biff, you'll save his life. Thanks, darling. Just put your arm around him when he comes into the restaurant. Give him a smile. That's the boy . . . Good-bye, dear . . . You got your comb? . . . That's fine. Good-bye, Biff dear.

[*In the middle of her speech,* HOWARD WAGNER, *thirty-six, wheels on a small typewriter table on which is a wire-recording machine and proceeds to plug it in. This is on the left forestage. Light slowly fades on* LINDA *as it rises on* HOWARD. HOWARD *is intent on threading the machine and only glances over his shoulder as* WILLY *appears.*]

WILLY: Pst! Pst!
HOWARD: Hello, Willy, come in.
WILLY: Like to have a little talk with you, Howard.
HOWARD: Sorry to keep you waiting. I'll be with you in a minute.
WILLY: What's that, Howard?
HOWARD: Didn't you ever see one of these? Wire recorder.
WILLY: Oh. Can we talk a minute?

---

7. Artificial sweetener once recommended as a healthy alternative to sugar.

HOWARD: Records things. Just got delivery yesterday. Been driving me crazy, the most terrific machine I ever saw in my life. I was up all night with it.
WILLY: What do you do with it?
HOWARD: I bought it for dictation, but you can do anything with it. Listen to this. I had it home last night. Listen to what I picked up. The first one is my daughter. Get this. [*He flicks the switch and "Roll out the Barrel" is heard being whistled.*] Listen to that kid whistle.
WILLY: That is lifelike, isn't it?
HOWARD: Seven years old. Get that tone.
WILLY: Ts, ts. Like to ask a little favor if you . . .

[*The whistling breaks off, and the voice of* HOWARD's *daughter is heard.*]

HIS DAUGHTER: "Now you, Daddy."
HOWARD: She's crazy for me! [*Again the same song is whistled.*] That's me! Ha! [*He winks.*]
WILLY: You're very good!

[*The whistling breaks off again. The machine runs silent for a moment.*]

HOWARD: Sh! Get this now, this is my son.
HIS SON: "The capital of Alabama is Montgomery; the capital of Arizona is Phoenix; the capital of Arkansas is Little Rock; the capital of California is Sacramento . . ." [*And on, and on.*]
HOWARD: [*Holding up five fingers.*] Five years old, Willy!
WILLY: He'll make an announcer some day!
HIS SON: [*Continuing.*] "The capital . . ."
HOWARD: Get that—alphabetical order! [*The machine breaks off suddenly.*] Wait a minute. The maid kicked the plug out.
WILLY: It certainly is a—
HOWARD: Sh, for God's sake!
HIS SON: "It's nine o'clock, Bulova watch time.[8] So I have to go to sleep."
WILLY: That really is—
HOWARD: Wait a minute! The next is my wife.

[*They wait.*]

HOWARD'S VOICE: "Go on, say something." [*Pause.*] "Well, you gonna talk?"
HIS WIFE: "I can't think of anything."
HOWARD'S VOICE: "Well, talk—it's turning."
HIS WIFE: [*Shyly, beaten.*] "Hello." [*Silence.*] "Oh, Howard, I can't talk into this . . ."
HOWARD: [*Snapping the machine off.*] That was my wife.
WILLY: That is a wonderful machine. Can we—
HOWARD: I tell you, Willy, I'm gonna take my camera, and my bandsaw, and all my hobbies, and out they go. This is the most fascinating relaxation I ever found.
WILLY: I think I'll get one myself.
HOWARD: Sure, they're only a hundred and a half. You can't do without it. Sup-

---

8. Phrase commonly heard on radio programs sponsored by the Bulova Watch Company.

posing you wanna hear Jack Benny,[9] see? But you can't be at home at that hour. So you tell the maid to turn the radio on when Jack Benny comes on, and this automatically goes on with the radio . . .

WILLY: And when you come home you . . .

HOWARD: You can come home twelve o'clock, one o'clock, any time you like, and you get yourself a Coke and sit yourself down, throw the switch, and there's Jack Benny's program in the middle of the night!

WILLY: I'm definitely going to get one. Because lots of time I'm on the road, and I think to myself, what I must be missing on the radio!

HOWARD: Don't you have a radio in the car?

WILLY: Well, yeah, but who ever thinks of turning it on?

HOWARD: Say, aren't you supposed to be in Boston?

WILLY: That's what I want to talk to you about, Howard. You got a minute? [*He draws a chair in from the wing.*]

HOWARD: What happened? What're you doing here?

WILLY: Well . . .

HOWARD: You didn't crack up again, did you?

WILLY: Oh, no. No . . .

HOWARD: Geez, you had me worried there for a minute. What's the trouble?

WILLY: Well, tell you the truth, Howard. I've come to the decision that I'd rather not travel anymore.

HOWARD: Not travel! Well, what'll you do?

WILLY: Remember, Christmas time, when you had the party here? You said you'd try to think of some spot for me here in town.

HOWARD: With us?

WILLY: Well, sure.

HOWARD: Oh, yeah, yeah. I remember. Well, I couldn't think of anything for you, Willy.

WILLY: I tell ya, Howard. The kids are all grown up, y'know. I don't need much anymore. If I could take home—well, sixty-five dollars a week, I could swing it.

HOWARD: Yeah, but Willy, see I—

WILLY: I tell ya why, Howard. Speaking frankly and between the two of us, y'know—I'm just a little tired.

HOWARD: Oh, I could understand that, Willy. But you're a road man, Willy, and we do a road business. We've only got a half-dozen salesmen on the floor here.

WILLY: God knows, Howard, I never asked a favor of any man. But I was with the firm when your father used to carry you in here in his arms.

HOWARD: I know that, Willy, but—

WILLY: Your father came to me the day you were born and asked me what I thought of the name of Howard, may he rest in peace.

HOWARD: I appreciate that, Willy, but there just is no spot here for you. If I had a spot I'd slam you right in, but I just don't have a single solitary spot.

[*He looks for his lighter.* WILLY *has picked it up and gives it to him. Pause.*]

---

9. A vaudeville, radio, television, and movie star (1894–1974); he hosted America's most popular radio show from 1932 to 1955.

WILLY: [*With increasing anger.*] Howard, all I need to set my table is fifty dollars a week.
HOWARD: But where am I going to put you, kid?
WILLY: Look, it isn't a question of whether I can sell merchandise, is it?
HOWARD: No, but it's a business, kid, and everybody's gotta pull his own weight.
WILLY: [*Desperately.*] Just let me tell you a story, Howard—
HOWARD: 'Cause you gotta admit, business is business.
WILLY: [*Angrily.*] Business is definitely business, but just listen for a minute. You don't understand this. When I was a boy—eighteen, nineteen—I was already on the road. And there was a question in my mind as to whether selling had a future for me. Because in those days I had a yearning to go to Alaska. See, there were three gold strikes in one month in Alaska, and I felt like going out. Just for the ride, you might say.
HOWARD: [*Barely interested.*] Don't say.
WILLY: Oh, yeah, my father lived many years in Alaska. He was an adventurous man. We've got quite a little streak of self-reliance in our family. I thought I'd go out with my older brother and try to locate him, and maybe settle in the North with the old man. And I was almost decided to go, when I met a salesman in the Parker House. His name was Dave Singleman. And he was eighty-four years old, and he'd drummed merchandise in thirty-one states. And old Dave, he'd go up to his room, y'understand, put on his green velvet slippers—I'll never forget—and pick up his phone and call the buyers, and without ever leaving his room, at the age of eighty-four, he made a living. And when I saw that, I realized that selling was the greatest career a man could want. 'Cause what could be more satisfying than to be able to go, at the age of eighty-four, into twenty or thirty different cities, and pick up his phone and be remembered and loved and helped by so many different people? Do you know? when he died—and by the way he died the death of a salesman, in his green velvet slippers in the smoker of the New York, New Haven and Hartford, going into Boston—when he died, hundreds of salesmen and buyers were at his funeral. Things were sad on a lotta trains for months after that. [*He stands up.* HOWARD *has not looked at him.*] In those days there was personality in it, Howard. There was respect, and comradeship, and gratitude in it. Today, it's all cut and dried, and there's no chance for bringing friendship to bear— or personality. You see what I mean? They don't know me anymore.
HOWARD: [*Moving away, toward the right.*] That's just the thing, Willy.
WILLY: If I had forty dollars a week—that's all I'd need. Forty dollars, Howard.
HOWARD: Kid, I can't take blood from a stone, I—
WILLY: [*Desperation is on him now.*] Howard, the year Al Smith[1] was nominated, your father came to me and—
HOWARD: [*Starting to go off.*] I've got to see some people, kid.
WILLY: [*Stopping him.*] I'm talking about your father! There were promises made across this desk! You mustn't tell me you've got people to see—I put thirty-four years into this firm, Howard, and now I can't pay my insurance! You can't eat the orange and throw the peel away—a man is not a piece of fruit! [*After a pause.*] Now pay attention. Your father—in 1928 I had a big year. I averaged a hundred and seventy dollars a week in commissions.

1. Alfred E. Smith (1873-1944), Democratic presidential nominee who lost to Herbert Hoover in 1928.

HOWARD: [*Impatiently.*] Now, Willy, you never averaged—
WILLY: [*Banging his hand on the desk.*] I averaged a hundred and seventy dollars a week in the year of 1928! And your father came to me—or rather, I was in the office here—it was right over this desk—and he put his hand on my shoulder—
HOWARD: [*Getting up.*] You'll have to excuse me, Willy, I gotta see some people. Pull yourself together. [*Going out.*] I'll be back in a little while.

[*On* HOWARD'*s exit, the light on his chair grows very bright and strange.*]

WILLY: Pull myself together! What the hell did I say to him? My God, I was yelling at him! How could I! [WILLY *breaks off, staring at the light, which occupies the chair, animating it. He approaches this chair, standing across the desk from it.*] Frank, Frank, don't you remember what you told me that time? How you put your hand on my shoulder, and Frank ... [*He leans on the desk and as he speaks the dead man's name he accidentally switches on the recorder, and instantly.*]
HOWARD'S SON: "... of New York is Albany. The capital of Ohio is Cincinnati, the capital of Rhode Island is ..." [*The recitation continues.*]
WILLY: [*Leaping away with fright, shouting.*] Ha! Howard! Howard! Howard!
HOWARD: [*Rushing in.*] What happened?
WILLY: [*Pointing at the machine, which continues nasally, childishly, with the capital cities.*] Shut it off! Shut it off!
HOWARD: [*Pulling the plug out.*] Look, Willy ...
WILLY: [*Pressing his hands to his eyes.*] I gotta get myself some coffee. I'll get some coffee ...

[WILLY *starts to walk out.* HOWARD *stops him.*]

HOWARD: [*Rolling up the cord.*] Willy, look ...
WILLY: I'll go to Boston.
HOWARD: Willy, you can't go to Boston for us.
WILLY: Why can't I go?
HOWARD: I don't want you to represent us. I've been meaning to tell you for a long time now.
WILLY: Howard, are you firing me?
HOWARD: I think you need a good long rest, Willy.
WILLY: Howard—
HOWARD: And when you feel better, come back, and we'll see if we can work something out.
WILLY: But I gotta earn money, Howard. I'm in no position to—
HOWARD: Where are your sons? Why don't your sons give you a hand?
WILLY: They're working on a very big deal.
HOWARD: This is no time for false pride, Willy. You go to your sons and you tell them that you're tired. You've got two great boys, haven't you?
WILLY: Oh, no question, no question, but in the meantime ...
HOWARD: Then that's that, heh?
WILLY: All right, I'll go to Boston tomorrow.
HOWARD: No, no.
WILLY: I can't throw myself on my sons. I'm not a cripple!
HOWARD: Look, kid, I'm busy, I'm busy this morning.
WILLY: [*Grasping* HOWARD'*s arm.*] Howard, you've got to let me go to Boston!
HOWARD: [*Hard, keeping himself under control.*] I've got a line of people to see this

morning. Sit down, take five minutes, and pull yourself together, and then go home, will ya? I need the office, Willy. [*He starts to go, turns, remembering the recorder, starts to push off the table holding the recorder.*] Oh, yeah. Whenever you can this week, stop by and drop off the samples. You'll feel better, Willy, and then come back and we'll talk. Pull yourself together, kid, there's people outside.

[HOWARD *exits, pushing the table off left.* WILLY *stares into space, exhausted. Now the music is heard—*BEN'S *music—first distantly, then closer, closer. As* WILLY *speaks,* BEN *enters from the right. He carries valise and umbrella.*]

WILLY: Oh, Ben, how did you do it? What is the answer? Did you wind up the Alaska deal already?

BEN: Doesn't take much time if you know what you're doing. Just a short business trip. Boarding ship in an hour. Wanted to say good-by.

WILLY: Ben, I've got to talk to you.

BEN: [*Glancing at his watch.*] Haven't the time, William.

WILLY: [*Crossing the apron to* BEN.] Ben, nothing's working out. I don't know what to do.

BEN: Now, look here, William. I've bought timberland in Alaska and I need a man to look after things for me.

WILLY: God, timberland! Me and my boys in those grand outdoors!

BEN: You've a new continent at your doorstep, William. Get out of these cities, they're full of talk and time payments and courts of law. Screw on your fists and you can fight for a fortune up there.

WILLY: Yes, yes! Linda, Linda!

[LINDA *enters as of old, with the wash.*]

LINDA: Oh, you're back?

BEN: I haven't much time.

WILLY: No, wait! Linda, he's got a proposition for me in Alaska.

LINDA: But you've got—[*To* BEN.] He's got a beautiful job here.

WILLY: But in Alaska, kid, I could—

LINDA: You're doing well enough, Willy!

BEN: [*To* LINDA.] Enough for what, my dear?

LINDA: [*Frightened of* BEN *and angry at him.*] Don't say those things to him! Enough to be happy right here, right now. [*To* WILLY, *while* BEN *laughs.*] Why must everybody conquer the world? You're well liked, and the boys love you, and someday—[*To* BEN.]—why, old man Wagner told him just the other day that if he keeps it up he'll be a member of the firm, didn't he, Willy?

WILLY: Sure, sure. I am building something with this firm, Ben, and if a man is building something he must be on the right track, mustn't he?

BEN: What are you building? Lay your hand on it. Where is it?

WILLY: [*Hesitantly.*] That's true, Linda, there's nothing.

LINDA: Why? [*To* BEN.] There's a man eighty-four years old—

WILLY: That's right, Ben, that's right. When I look at that man I say, what is there to worry about?

BEN: Bah!

WILLY: It's true, Ben. All he has to do is go into any city, pick up the phone, and he's making his living and you know why?

BEN: [*Picking up his valise.*] I've got to go.
WILLY: [*Holding* BEN *back.*] Look at this boy! [BIFF, *in his high school sweater, enters carrying suitcase.* HAPPY *carries* BIFF's *shoulder guards, gold helmet, and football pants.*] Without a penny to his name, three great universities are begging for him, and from there the sky's the limit, because it's not what you do, Ben. It's who you know and the smile on your face! It's contacts, Ben, contacts! The whole wealth of Alaska passes over the lunch table at the Commodore Hotel, and that's the wonder, the wonder of this country, that a man can end with diamonds here on the basis of being liked! [*He turns to* BIFF.] And that's why when you get out on that field today it's important. Because thousands of people will be rooting for you and loving you. [*To* BEN, *who has again begun to leave.*] And Ben! when he walks into a business office his name will sound out like a bell and all the doors will open to him! I've seen it, Ben, I've seen it a thousand times! You can't feel it with your hand like timber, but it's there!
BEN: Good-by, William.
WILLY: Ben, am I right? Don't you think I'm right? I value your advice.
BEN: There's a new continent at your doorstep, William. You could walk out rich. Rich! [*He is gone.*]
WILLY: We'll do it here, Ben! You hear me? We're gonna do it here!

[*Young* BERNARD *rushes in. The gay music of the Boys is heard.*]

BERNARD: Oh, gee, I was afraid you left already!
WILLY: Why? What time is it?
BERNARD: It's half-past one!
WILLY: Well, come on, everybody! Ebbets Field next stop! Where's the pennants? [*He rushes through the wall-line of the kitchen and out into the living room.*]
LINDA: [*To* BIFF.] Did you pack fresh underwear?
BIFF: [*Who has been limbering up.*] I want to go!
BERNARD: Biff, I'm carrying your helmet, ain't I?
HAPPY: No, I'm carrying the helmet.
BERNARD: Oh, Biff, you promised me.
HAPPY: I'm carrying the helmet.
BERNARD: How am I going to get in the locker room?
LINDA: Let him carry the shoulder guards. [*She puts her coat and hat on in the kitchen.*]
BERNARD: Can I, Biff? 'Cause I told everybody I'm going to be in the locker room.
HAPPY: In Ebbets Field it's the clubhouse.
BERNARD: I meant the clubhouse, Biff!
HAPPY: Biff!
BIFF: [*Grandly, after a slight pause.*] Let him carry the shoulder guards.
HAPPY: [*As he gives* BERNARD *the shoulder guards.*] Stay close to us now.

[WILLY *rushes in with the pennants.*]

WILLY: [*Handing them out.*] Everybody wave when Biff comes out on the field. [HAPPY *and* BERNARD *run off.*] You set now, boy?

[*The music has died away.*]

BIFF: Ready to go, Pop. Every muscle is ready.
WILLY: [*At the edge of the apron.*] You realize what this means?

BIFF: That's right, Pop.
WILLY: [*Feeling* BIFF's *muscles.*] You're comin' home this afternoon captain of the All-Scholastic Championship Team of the City of New York.
BIFF: I got it, Pop. And remember, pal, when I take off my helmet, that touchdown is for you.
WILLY: Let's go! [*He is starting out, with his arm around* BIFF, *when* CHARLEY *enters, as of old, in knickers.*] I got no room for you, Charley.
CHARLEY: Room? For what?
WILLY: In the car.
CHARLEY: You goin' for a ride? I wanted to shoot some casino.
WILLY: [*Furiously.*] Casino! [*Incredulously.*] Don't you realize what today is?
LINDA: Oh, he knows, Willy. He's just kidding you.
WILLY: That's nothing to kid about!
CHARLEY: No, Linda, what's goin' on?
LINDA: He's playing in Ebbets Field.
CHARLEY: Baseball in this weather?
WILLY: Don't talk to him. Come on, come on! [*He is pushing them out.*]
CHARLEY: Wait a minute, didn't you hear the news?
WILLY: What?
CHARLEY: Don't you listen to the radio? Ebbets Field just blew up.
WILLY: You go to hell! [CHARLEY *laughs. Pushing them out.*] Come on, come on! We're late.
CHARLEY: [*As they go.*] Knock a homer, Biff, knock a homer!
WILLY: [*The last to leave, turning to* CHARLEY.] I don't think that was funny, Charley. This is the greatest day of my life.
CHARLEY: Willy, when are you going to grow up?
WILLY: Yeah, heh? When this game is over, Charley, you'll be laughing out of the other side of your face. They'll be calling him another Red Grange.[2] Twenty-five thousand a year.
CHARLEY: [*Kidding.*] Is that so?
WILLY: Yeah, that's so.
CHARLEY: Well, then, I'm sorry, Willy. But tell me something.
WILLY: What?
CHARLEY: Who is Red Grange?
WILLY: Put up your hands. Goddam you, put up your hands! [CHARLEY, *chuckling, shakes his head and walks away, around the left corner of the stage.* WILLY *follows him. The music rises to a mocking frenzy.*] Who the hell do you think you are, better than everybody else? You don't know everything, you big, ignorant, stupid ... Put up your hands!

[*Light rises, on the right side of the forestage, on a small table in the reception room of* CHARLEY's *office. Traffic sounds are heard.* BERNARD, *now mature, sits whistling to himself. A pair of tennis rackets and an overnight bag are on the floor beside him.*]

WILLY: [*Offstage.*] What are you walking away for? Don't walk away! If you're going to say something say it to my face! I know you laugh at me behind my

---

2. Harold Edward Grange (1903–1991), All-American halfback at the University of Illinois from 1923 to 1925; he played professionally for the Chicago Bears.

back. You'll laugh out of the other side of your goddam face after this game. Touchdown! Touchdown! Eighty thousand people! Touchdown! Right between the goal posts.

[BERNARD *is a quiet, earnest, but self-assured young man.* WILLY's *voice is coming from right upstage now.* BERNARD *lowers his feet off the table and listens.* JENNY, *his father's secretary, enters.*]

JENNY: [*Distressed.*] Say, Bernard, will you go out in the hall?
BERNARD: What is that noise? Who is it?
JENNY: Mr. Loman. He just got off the elevator.
BERNARD: [*Getting up.*] Who's he arguing with?
JENNY: Nobody. There's nobody with him. I can't deal with him anymore, and your father gets all upset everytime he comes. I've got a lot of typing to do, and your father's waiting to sign it. Will you see him?
WILLY: [*Entering.*] Touchdown! Touch—[*He sees* JENNY.] Jenny, Jenny, good to see you. How're ya? Workin'? Or still honest?
JENNY: Fine. How've you been feeling?
WILLY: Not much anymore, Jenny. Ha, ha! [*He is surprised to see the rackets.*]
BERNARD: Hello, Uncle Willy.
WILLY: [*Almost shocked.*] Bernard! Well, look who's here! [*He comes quickly, guiltily to* BERNARD *and warmly shakes his hand.*]
BERNARD: How are you? Good to see you.
WILLY: What are you doing here?
BERNARD: Oh, just stopped by to see Pop. Get off my feet till my train leaves. I'm going to Washington in a few minutes.
WILLY: Is he in?
BERNARD: Yes, he's in his office with the accountant. Sit down.
WILLY: [*Sitting down.*] What're you going to do in Washington?
BERNARD: Oh, just a case I've got there, Willy.
WILLY: That so? [*Indicating the rackets.*] You going to play tennis there?
BERNARD: I'm staying with a friend who's got a court.
WILLY: Don't say. His own tennis court. Must be fine people, I bet.
BERNARD: They are, very nice. Dad tells me Biff's in town.
WILLY: [*With a big smile.*] Yeah, Biff's in. Working on a very big deal, Bernard.
BERNARD: What's Biff doing?
WILLY: Well, he's been doing very big things in the West. But he decided to establish himself here. Very big. We're having dinner. Did I hear your wife had a boy?
BERNARD: That's right. Our second.
WILLY: Two boys! What do you know!
BERNARD: What kind of a deal has Biff got?
WILLY: Well, Bill Oliver—very big sporting-goods man—he wants Biff very badly. Called him in from the West. Long distance, carte blanche, special deliveries. Your friends have their own private tennis court?
BERNARD: You still with the old firm, Willy?
WILLY: [*After a pause.*] I'm—I'm overjoyed to see how you made the grade, Bernard, overjoyed. It's an encouraging thing to see a young man really—really—Looks very good for Biff—very—[*He breaks off, then.*] Bernard—[*He is so full of emotion, he breaks off again.*]

BERNARD: What is it, Willy?
WILLY: [*Small and alone.*] What—what's the secret?
BERNARD: What secret?
WILLY: How—how did you? Why didn't he ever catch on?
BERNARD: I wouldn't know that, Willy.
WILLY: [*Confidentially, desperately.*] You were his friend, his boyhood friend. There's something I don't understand about it. His life ended after that Ebbets Field game. From the age of seventeen nothing good ever happened to him.
BERNARD: He never trained himself for anything.
WILLY: But he did, he did. After high school he took so many correspondence courses. Radio mechanics; television; God knows what, and never made the slightest mark.
BERNARD: [*Taking off his glasses.*] Willy, do you want to talk candidly?
WILLY: [*Rising, faces* BERNARD.] I regard you as a very brilliant man, Bernard. I value your advice.
BERNARD: Oh, the hell with the advice, Willy. I couldn't advise you. There's just one thing I've always wanted to ask you. When he was supposed to graduate, and the math teacher flunked him—
WILLY: Oh, that son-of-a-bitch ruined his life.
BERNARD: Yeah, but, Willy, all he had to do was go to summer school and make up that subject.
WILLY: That's right, that's right.
BERNARD: Did you tell him not to go to summer school?
WILLY: Me? I begged him to go. I ordered him to go!
BERNARD: Then why wouldn't he go?
WILLY: Why? Why! Bernard, that question has been trailing me like a ghost for the last fifteen years. He flunked the subject, and laid down and died like a hammer hit him!
BERNARD: Take it easy, kid.
WILLY: Let me talk to you—I got nobody to talk to. Bernard, Bernard, was it my fault? Y'see? It keeps going around in my mind, maybe I did something to him. I got nothing to give him.
BERNARD: Don't take it so hard.
WILLY: Why did he lay down? What is the story there? You were his friend!
BERNARD: Willy, I remember, it was June, and our grades came out. And he'd flunked math.
WILLY: That son-of-a-bitch!
BERNARD: No, it wasn't right then. Biff just got very angry, I remember, and he was ready to enroll in summer school.
WILLY: [*Surprised.*] He was?
BERNARD: He wasn't beaten by it at all. But then, Willy, he disappeared from the block for almost a month. And I got the idea that he'd gone up to New England to see you. Did he have a talk with you then? [WILLY *stares in silence.*] Willy?
WILLY: [*With a strong edge of resentment in his voice.*] Yeah, he came to Boston. What about it?
BERNARD: Well, just that when he came back—I'll never forget this, it always mystifies me. Because I'd thought so well of Biff, even though he'd always taken advantage of me. I loved him, Willy, y'know? And he came back after

that month and took his sneakers—remember those sneakers with "University of Virginia" printed on them? He was so proud of those, wore them every day. And he took them down in the cellar, and burned them up in the furnace. We had a fist fight. It lasted at least half an hour. Just the two of us, punching each other down the cellar, and crying right through it. I've often thought of how strange it was that I knew he'd given up his life. What happened in Boston, Willy? [WILLY *looks at him as at an intruder.*] I just bring it up because you asked me.

WILLY: [*Angrily.*] Nothing. What do you mean, "What happened?" What's that got to do with anything?

BERNARD: Well, don't get sore.

WILLY: What are you trying to do, blame it on me? If a boy lays down is that my fault?

BERNARD: Now, Willy, don't get—

WILLY: Well, don't—don't talk to me that way! What does that mean, "What happened?"

[CHARLEY *enters. He is in his vest, and he carries a bottle of bourbon.*]

CHARLEY: Hey, you're going to miss that train. [*He waves the bottle.*]

BERNARD: Yeah, I'm going. [*He takes the bottle.*] Thanks, Pop. [*He picks up his rackets and bag.*] Good-bye, Willy, and don't worry about it. You know, "If at first you don't succeed . . ."

WILLY: Yes, I believe in that.

BERNARD: But sometimes, Willy, it's better for a man just to walk away.

WILLY: Walk away?

BERNARD: That's right.

WILLY: But if you can't walk away?

BERNARD: [*After a slight pause.*] I guess that's when it's tough. [*Extending his hand.*] Good-bye, Willy.

WILLY: [*Shaking* BERNARD's *hand.*] Good-bye, boy.

CHARLEY: [*An arm on* BERNARD's *shoulder.*] How do you like this kid? Gonna argue a case in front of the Supreme Court.

BERNARD: [*Protesting.*] Pop!

WILLY: [*Genuinely shocked, pained, and happy.*] No! The Supreme Court!

BERNARD: I gotta run. 'Bye, Dad!

CHARLEY: Knock 'em dead, Bernard!

[BERNARD *goes off.*]

WILLY: [As CHARLEY *takes out his wallet.*] The Supreme Court! And he didn't even mention it!

CHARLEY: [*Counting out money on the desk.*] He don't have to—he's gonna do it.

WILLY: And you never told him what to do, did you? You never took any interest in him.

CHARLEY: My salvation is that I never took any interest in anything. There's some money—fifty dollars. I got an accountant inside.

WILLY: Charley, look . . . [*With difficulty.*] I got my insurance to pay. If you can manage it—I need a hundred and ten dollars. [CHARLEY *doesn't reply for a moment; merely stops moving.*] I'd draw it from my bank but Linda would know, and I . . .

CHARLEY: Sit down, Willy.

WILLY: [*Moving toward the chair.*] I'm keeping an account of everything, remember. I'll pay every penny back. [*He sits.*]
CHARLEY: Now listen to me, Willy.
WILLY: I want you to know I appreciate . . .
CHARLEY: [*Sitting down on the table.*] Willy, what're you doin'? What the hell is goin' on in your head?
WILLY: Why? I'm simply . . .
CHARLEY: I offered you a job. You can make fifty dollars a week. And I won't send you on the road.
WILLY: I've got a job.
CHARLEY: Without pay? What kind of job is a job without pay? [*He rises.*] Now, look kid, enough is enough. I'm no genius but I know when I'm being insulted.
WILLY: Insulted!
CHARLEY: Why don't you want to work for me?
WILLY: What's the matter with you? I've got a job.
CHARLEY: Then what're you walkin' in here every week for?
WILLY: [*Getting up.*] Well, if you don't want me to walk in here—
CHARLEY: I am offering you a job!
WILLY: I don't want your goddam job!
CHARLEY: When the hell are you going to grow up?
WILLY: [*Furiously.*] You big ignoramus, if you say that to me again I'll rap you one! I don't care how big you are! [*He's ready to fight. Pause.*]
CHARLEY: [*Kindly, going to him.*] How much do you need, Willy?
WILLY: Charley, I'm strapped, I'm strapped. I don't know what to do. I was just fired.
CHARLEY: Howard fired you?
WILLY: That snotnose. Imagine that? I named him. I named him Howard.
CHARLEY: Willy, when're you gonna realize that them things don't mean anything? You named him Howard, but you can't sell that. The only thing you got in this world is what you can sell. And the funny thing is that you're a salesman, and you don't know that.
WILLY: I've always tried to think otherwise, I guess. I always felt that if a man was impressive, and well liked, that nothing—
CHARLEY: Why must everybody like you? Who liked J. P. Morgan?[3] Was he impressive? In a Turkish bath he'd look like a butcher. But with his pockets on he was very well liked. Now listen, Willy, I know you don't like me, and nobody can say I'm in love with you, but I'll give you a job because—just for the hell of it, put it that way. Now what do you say?
WILLY: I—I just can't work for you, Charley.
CHARLEY: What're you, jealous of me?
WILLY: I can't work for you, that's all, don't ask me why.
CHARLEY: [*Angered, takes out more bills.*] You been jealous of me all your life, you damned fool! Here, pay your insurance. [*He puts the money in* WILLY's *hand.*]
WILLY: I'm keeping strict accounts.
CHARLEY: I've got some work to do. Take care of yourself. And pay your insurance.

3. American financier (1837–1890), widely criticized for his business dealings with the U.S. government.

WILLY: [*Moving to the right.*] Funny, y'know? After all the highways and the trains, and the appointments, and the years, you end up worth more dead than alive.
CHARLEY: Willy, nobody's worth nothin' dead. [*After a slight pause.*] Did you hear what I said? [WILLY *stands still, dreaming.*] Willy!
WILLY: Apologize to Bernard for me when you see him. I didn't mean to argue with him. He's a fine boy. They're all fine boys, and they'll end up big—all of them. Someday they'll all play tennis together. Wish me luck, Charley. He saw Bill Oliver today.
CHARLEY: Good luck.
WILLY: [*On the verge of tears.*] Charley, you're the only friend I got. Isn't that a remarkable thing? [*He goes out.*]
CHARLEY: Jesus!

[CHARLEY *stares after him a moment and follows. All light blacks out. Suddenly raucous music is heard, and a red glow rises behind the screen at right.* STANLEY, *a young waiter, appears, carrying a table, followed by* HAPPY, *who is carrying two chairs.*]

STANLEY: [*Putting the table down.*] That's all right, Mr. Loman, I can handle it myself. [*He turns and takes the chairs from* HAPPY *and places them at the table.*]
HAPPY: [*Glancing around.*] Oh, this is better.
STANLEY: Sure, in the front there you're in the middle of all kinds a noise. Whenever you got a party. Mr. Loman, you just tell me and I'll put you back here. Y'know, there's a lotta people they don't like it private, because when they go out they like to see a lotta action around them because they're sick and tired to stay in the house by theirself. But I know you, you ain't from Hackensack. You know what I mean?
HAPPY: [*Sitting down.*] So how's it coming, Stanley?
STANLEY: Ah, it's a dog life. I only wish during the war they'd a took me in the Army. I couda been dead by now.
HAPPY: My brother's back, Stanley.
STANLEY: Oh, he come back, heh? From the Far West.
HAPPY: Yeah, big cattle man, my brother, so treat him right. And my father's coming too.
STANLEY: Oh, your father too!
HAPPY: You got a couple of nice lobsters?
STANLEY: Hundred per cent, big.
HAPPY: I want them with the claws.
STANLEY: Don't worry, I don't give you no mice. [HAPPY *laughs.*] How about some wine? It'll put a head on the meal.
HAPPY: No. You remember, Stanley, that recipe I brought you from overseas? With the champagne in it?
STANLEY: Oh, yeah, sure. I still got it tacked up yet in the kitchen. But that'll have to cost a buck apiece anyways.
HAPPY: That's all right.
STANLEY: What'd you, hit a number or somethin'?
HAPPY: No, it's a little celebration. My brother is—I think he pulled off a big deal today. I think we're going into business together.
STANLEY: Great! That's the best for you. Because a family business, you know what I mean?—that's the best.

HAPPY: That's what I think.
STANLEY: 'Cause what's the difference? Somebody steals? It's in the family. Know what I mean? [*Sotto voce.*] Like this bartender here. The boss is goin' crazy what kinda leak he's got in the cash register. You put it in but it don't come out.
HAPPY: [*Raising his head.*] Sh!
STANLEY: What?
HAPPY: You notice I wasn't lookin' right or left, was I?
STANLEY: No.
HAPPY: And my eyes are closed.
STANLEY: So what's the—?
HAPPY: Strudel's comin'.
STANLEY: [*Catching on, looks around.*] Ah, no, there's no—[*He breaks off as a furred, lavishly dressed* GIRL *enters and sits at the next table. Both follow her with their eyes.*] Geez, how'd ya know?
HAPPY: I got radar or something. [*Staring directly at her profile.*] Oooooooo... Stanley.
STANLEY: I think, that's for you, Mr. Loman.
HAPPY: Look at that mouth. Oh, God. And the binoculars.
STANLEY: Geez, you got a life, Mr. Loman.
HAPPY: Wait on her.
STANLEY: [*Going to the* GIRL'S *table.*] Would you like a menu, ma'am?
GIRL: I'm expecting someone, but I'd like a—
HAPPY: Why don't you bring her—excuse me, miss, do you mind? I sell champagne, and I'd like you to try my brand. Bring her a champagne, Stanley.
GIRL: That's awfully nice of you.
HAPPY: Don't mention it. It's all company money. [*He laughs.*]
GIRL: That's a charming product to be selling, isn't it?
HAPPY: Oh, gets to be like everything else. Selling is selling, y'know.
GIRL: I suppose.
HAPPY: You don't happen to sell, do you?
GIRL: No, I don't sell.
HAPPY: Would you object to a compliment from a stranger? You ought to be on a magazine cover.
GIRL: [*Looking at him a little archly.*] I have been.

[STANLEY *comes in with a glass of champagne.*]

HAPPY: What'd I say before, Stanley? You see? She's a cover girl.
STANLEY: Oh, I could see, I could see.
HAPPY: [*To the* GIRL.] What magazine?
GIRL: Oh, a lot of them. [*She takes the drink.*] Thank you.
HAPPY: You know what they say in France, don't you? "Champagne is the drink of the complexion"—Hya, Biff!

[BIFF *has entered and sits with* HAPPY.]

BIFF: Hello, kid. Sorry I'm late.
HAPPY: I just got here. Uh, Miss—?
GIRL: Forsythe.
HAPPY: Miss Forsythe, this is my brother.

BIFF: Is Dad here?
HAPPY: His name is Biff. You might've heard of him. Great football player.
GIRL: Really? What team?
HAPPY: Are you familiar with football?
GIRL: No, I'm afraid I'm not.
HAPPY: Biff is quarterback with the New York Giants.
GIRL: Well, that's nice, isn't it? [*She drinks.*]
HAPPY: Good health.
GIRL: I'm happy to meet you.
HAPPY: That's my name, Hap. It's really Harold, but at West Point they called me Happy.
GIRL: [*Now really impressed.*] Oh, I see. How do you do? [*She turns her profile.*]
BIFF: Isn't Dad coming?
HAPPY: You want her?
BIFF: Oh, I could never make that.
HAPPY: I remember the time that idea would never come into your head. Where's the old confidence, Biff?
BIFF: I just saw Oliver—
HAPPY: Wait a minute. I've got to see that old confidence again. Do you want her? She's on call.
BIFF: Oh, no. [*He turns to look at the* GIRL.]
HAPPY: I'm telling you. Watch this. [*Turning to see the* GIRL.] Honey? [*She turns to him.*] Are you busy?
GIRL: Well, I am . . . but I could make a phone call.
HAPPY: Do that, will you, honey? And see if you can get a friend. We'll be here for a while. Biff is one of the greatest football players in the country.
GIRL: [*Standing up.*] Well, I'm certainly happy to meet you.
HAPPY: Come back soon.
GIRL: I'll try.
HAPPY: Don't try, honey, try hard. [*The* GIRL *exits.* STANLEY *follows, shaking his head in bewildered admiration.*] Isn't that a shame now? A beautiful girl like that? That's why I can't get married. There's not a good woman in a thousand. New York is loaded with them, kid!
BIFF: Hap, look—
HAPPY: I told you she was on call!
BIFF: [*Strangely unnerved.*] Cut it out, will ya? I want to say something to you.
HAPPY: Did you see Oliver?
BIFF: I saw him all right. Now look, I want to tell Dad a couple of things and I want you to help me.
HAPPY: What? Is he going to back you?
BIFF: Are you crazy? You're out of your goddam head, you know that?
HAPPY: Why? What happened?
BIFF: [*Breathlessly.*] I did a terrible thing today, Hap. It's been the strangest day I ever went through. I'm all numb, I swear.
HAPPY: You mean he wouldn't see you?
BIFF: Well, I waited six hours for him, see? All day. Kept sending my name in. Even tried to date his secretary so she'd get me to him, but no soap.
HAPPY: Because you're not showin' the old confidence, Biff. He remembered you, didn't he?

BIFF: [*Stopping* HAPPY *with a gesture.*] Finally, about five o'clock, he comes out. Didn't remember who I was or anything. I felt like such an idiot, Hap.
HAPPY: Did you tell him my Florida idea?
BIFF: He walked away. I saw him for one minute. I got so mad I could've torn the walls down! How the hell did I ever get the idea I was a salesman there? I even believed myself that I'd been a salesman for him! And then he gave me one look and—I realized what a ridiculous lie my whole life has been! We've been talking in a dream for fifteen years. I was a shipping clerk.
HAPPY: What'd you do?
BIFF: [*With great tension and wonder.*] Well, he left, see. And the secretary went out. I was all alone in the waiting-room. I don't know what came over me, Hap. The next thing I know I'm in his office—paneled walls, everything. I can't explain it. I—Hap, I took his fountain pen.
HAPPY: Geez, did he catch you?
BIFF: I ran out. I ran down all eleven flights. I ran and ran and ran.
HAPPY: That was an awful dumb—what'd you do that for?
BIFF: [*Agonized.*] I don't know, I just—wanted to take something, I don't know. You gotta help me, Hap, I'm gonna tell Pop.
HAPPY: You crazy? What for?
BIFF: Hap, he's got to understand that I'm not the man somebody lends that kind of money to. He thinks I've been spiting him all these years and it's eating him up.
HAPPY: That's just it. You tell him something nice.
BIFF: I can't.
HAPPY: Say you got a lunch date with Oliver tomorrow.
BIFF: So what do I do tomorrow?
HAPPY: You leave the house tomorrow and come back at night and say Oliver is thinking it over. And he thinks it over for a couple of weeks, and gradually it fades away and nobody's the worse.
BIFF: But it'll go on forever!
HAPPY: Dad is never so happy as when he's looking forward to something! [WILLY *enters.*] Hello, scout!
WILLY: Gee, I haven't been here in years!

[STANLEY *has followed* WILLY *in and sets a chair for him.* STANLEY *starts off but* HAPPY *stops him.*]

HAPPY: Stanley!

[STANLEY *stands by, waiting for an order.*]

BIFF: [*Going to* WILLY *with guilt, as to an invalid.*] Sit down, Pop. You want a drink?
WILLY: Sure, I don't mind.
BIFF: Let's get a load on.
WILLY: You look worried.
BIFF: N-no. [*To* STANLEY.] Scotch all around. Make it doubles.
STANLEY: Doubles, right. [*He goes.*]
WILLY: You had a couple already, didn't you?
BIFF: Just a couple, yeah.
WILLY: Well, what happened, boy? [*Nodding affirmatively, with a smile.*] Everything go all right?

BIFF: [*Takes a breath, then reaches out and grasps* WILLY's *hand.*] Pal . . . [*He is smiling bravely, and* WILLY *is smiling too.*] I had an experience today.
HAPPY: Terrific, Pop.
WILLY: That so? What happened?
BIFF: [*High, slightly alcoholic, above the earth.*] I'm going to tell you everything from first to last. It's been a strange day. [*Silence. He looks around, composes himself as best he can, but his breath keeps breaking the rhythm of his voice.*] I had to wait quite a while for him, and—
WILLY: Oliver?
BIFF: Yeah, Oliver. All day, as a matter of cold fact. And a lot of—instances—facts, Pop, facts about my life came back to me. Who was it, Pop? Who ever said I was a salesman with Oliver?
WILLY: Well, you were.
BIFF: No, Dad, I was shipping clerk.
WILLY: But you were practically—
BIFF: [*With determination.*] Dad, I don't know who said it first, but I was never a salesman for Bill Oliver.
WILLY: What're you talking about?
BIFF: Let's hold on to the facts tonight, Pop. We're not going to get anywhere bullin' around. I was a shipping clerk.
WILLY: [*Angrily.*] All right, now listen to me—
BIFF: Why don't you let me finish?
WILLY: I'm not interested in stories about the past or any crap of that kind because the woods are burning, boys, you understand? There's a big blaze going on all around. I was fired today.
BIFF: [*Shocked.*] How could you be?
WILLY: I was fired, and I'm looking for a little good news to tell your mother, because the woman has waited and the woman has suffered. The gist of it is that I haven't got a story left in my head, Biff. So don't give me a lecture about facts and aspects. I am not interested. Now what've you got to say to me? [STANLEY *enters with three drinks. They wait until he leaves.*] Did you see Oliver?
BIFF: Jesus, Dad!
WILLY: You mean you didn't go up there?
HAPPY: Sure he went up there.
BIFF: I did. I—saw him. How could they fire you?
WILLY: [*On the edge of his chair.*] What kind of a welcome did he give you?
BIFF: He won't even let you work on commission?
WILLY: I'm out. [*Driving.*] So tell me, he gave you a warm welcome?
HAPPY: Sure, Pop, sure!
BIFF: [*Driven.*] Well, it was kind of—
WILLY: I was wondering if he'd remember you. [*To* HAPPY.] Imagine, man doesn't see him for ten, twelve years and gives him that kind of a welcome!
HAPPY: Damn right!
BIFF: [*Trying to return to the offensive.*] Pop, look—
WILLY: You know why he remembered you, don't you? Because you impressed him in those days.
BIFF: Let's talk quietly and get this down to the facts, huh?
WILLY: [*As though* BIFF *had been interrupting.*] Well, what happened? It's great news,

Biff. Did he take you into his office or'd you talk in the waiting-room?
BIFF: Well, he came in, see and—
WILLY: [*With a big smile.*] What'd he say? Betcha he threw his arm around you.
BIFF: Well, he kinda—
WILLY: He's a fine man. [*To* HAPPY.] Very hard man to see, y'know.
HAPPY: [*Agreeing.*] Oh, I know.
WILLY: [*To* BIFF.] Is that where you had the drinks?
BIFF: Yeah, he gave me a couple of—no, no!
HAPPY: [*Cutting in.*] He told him my Florida idea.
WILLY: Don't interrupt. [*To* BIFF.] How'd he react to the Florida idea?
BIFF: Dad, will you give me a minute to explain?
WILLY: I've been waiting for you to explain since I sat down here! What happened? He took you into his office and what?
BIFF: Well—I talked. And—he listened, see.
WILLY: Famous for the way he listens, y'know. What was his answer?
BIFF: His answer was—[*He breaks off, suddenly angry.*] Dad, you're not letting me tell you what I want to tell you!
WILLY: [*Accusing, angered.*] You didn't see him, did you?
BIFF: I did see him!
WILLY: What'd you insult him or something? You insulted him, didn't you?
BIFF: Listen, will you let me out of it, will you just let me out of it!
HAPPY: What the hell!
WILLY: Tell me what happened!
BIFF: [*To* HAPPY.] I can't talk to him!

[*A single trumpet note jars the ear. The light of green leaves stains the house, which holds the air of night and a dream.* YOUNG BERNARD *enters and knocks on the door of the house.*]

YOUNG BERNARD: [*Frantically.*] Mrs. Loman, Mrs. Loman!
HAPPY: Tell him what happened!
BIFF: [*To* HAPPY.] Shut up and leave me alone!
WILLY: No, no. You had to go and flunk math!
BIFF: What math? What're you talking about?
YOUNG BERNARD: Mrs. Loman, Mrs. Loman!

[LINDA *appears in the house, as of old.*]

WILLY: [*Wildly.*] Math, math, math!
BIFF: Take it easy, Pop!
YOUNG BERNARD: Mrs. Loman!
WILLY: [*Furiously.*] If you hadn't flunked you'd've been set by now!
BIFF: Now, look, I'm gonna tell you what happened, and you're going to listen to me.
YOUNG BERNARD: Mrs. Loman!
BIFF: I waited six hours—
HAPPY: What the hell are you saying?
BIFF: I kept sending in my name but he wouldn't see me. So finally he . . . [*He continues unheard as light fades low on the restaurant.*]
YOUNG BERNARD: Biff flunked math!
LINDA: No!

YOUNG BERNARD: Birnbaum flunked him! They won't graduate him!
LINDA: But they have to. He's gotta go to the university. Where is he? Biff! Biff!
YOUNG BERNARD: No, he left. He went to Grand Central.
LINDA: Grand—You mean he went to Boston!
YOUNG BERNARD: Is Uncle Willy in Boston?
LINDA: Oh, maybe Willy can talk to the teacher. Oh, the poor, poor boy!

[*Light on house area snaps out.*]

BIFF: [*At the table, now audible, holding up a gold fountain pen.*] ... so I'm washed up with Oliver, you understand? Are you listening to me?
WILLY: [*At a loss.*] Yeah, sure. If you hadn't flunked—
BIFF: Flunked what? What're you talking about?
WILLY: Don't blame everything on me! I didn't flunk math—you did! What pen?
HAPPY: That was awful dumb, Biff, a pen like that is worth—
WILLY: [*Seeing the pen for the first time.*] You took Oliver's pen?
BIFF: [*Weakening.*] Dad, I just explained it to you.
WILLY: You stole Bill Oliver's fountain pen!
BIFF: I didn't exactly steal it! That's just what I've been explaining to you!
HAPPY: He had it in his hand and just then Oliver walked in, so he got nervous and stuck it in his pocket!
WILLY: My God, Biff!
BIFF: I never intended to do it, Dad!
OPERATOR'S VOICE: Standish Arms, good evening!
WILLY: [*Shouting.*] I'm not in my room!
BIFF: [*Frightened.*] Dad, what's the matter? [*He and* HAPPY *stand up.*]
OPERATOR: Ringing Mr. Loman for you!
BIFF: [*Horrified, gets down on one knee before* WILLY.] Dad, I'll make good, I'll make good. [WILLY *tries to get to his feet.* BIFF *holds him down.*] Sit down now.
WILLY: No, you're no good, you're no good for anything.
BIFF: I am, Dad, I'll find something else, you understand? Now don't worry about anything. [*He holds up* WILLY'S *face.*] Talk to me, Dad.
OPERATOR: Mr. Loman does not answer. Shall I page him?
WILLY: [*Attempting to stand, as though to rush and silence the* OPERATOR.] No, no, no!
HAPPY: He'll strike something, Pop.
WILLY: No, no ...
BIFF: [*Desperately, standing over* WILLY.] Pop, listen! Listen to me! I'm telling you something good. Oliver talked to his partner about the Florida idea. You listening? He—he talked to his partner, and he came to me ... I'm going to be all right, you hear? Dad, listen to me, he said it was just a question of the amount!
WILLY: Then you ... got it?
HAPPY: He's gonna be terrific, Pop!
WILLY: [*Trying to stand.*] Then you got it, haven't you? You got it! You got it!
BIFF: [*Agonized, holds* WILLY *down.*] No, no. Look, Pop. I'm supposed to have lunch with them tomorrow. I'm just telling you this so you'll know that I can still make an impression, Pop. And I'll make good somewhere, but I can't go tomorrow, see?
WILLY: Why not? You simply—
BIFF: But the pen, Pop!

WILLY: You give it to him and tell him it was an oversight!
HAPPY: Sure, have lunch tomorrow!
BIFF: I can't say that—
WILLY: You were doing a crossword puzzle and accidentally used his pen!
BIFF: Listen, kid, I took those balls years ago, now I walk in with his fountain pen? That clinches it, don't you see? I can't face him like that! I'll try elsewhere.
PAGE'S VOICE: Paging Mr. Loman!
WILLY: Don't you want to be anything?
BIFF: Pop, how can I go back?
WILLY: You don't want to be anything, is that what's behind it?
BIFF: [*Now angry at* WILLY *for not crediting his sympathy.*] Don't take it that way! You think it was easy walking into that office after what I'd done to him? A team of horses couldn't have dragged me back to Bill Oliver!
WILLY: Then why'd you go?
BIFF: Why did I go? Why did I go! Look at you! Look at what's become of you!

[*Off left*, THE WOMAN *laughs.*]

WILLY: Biff, you're going to go to that lunch tomorrow, or—
BIFF: I can't go. I've got an appointment!
HAPPY: Biff, for . . . !
WILLY: Are you spiting me?
BIFF: Don't take it that way! Goddammit!
WILLY: [*Strikes* BIFF *and falters away from the table.*] You rotten little louse! Are you spiting me?
THE WOMAN: Someone's at the door, Willy!
BIFF: I'm no good, can't you see what I am?
HAPPY: [*Separating them.*] Hey, you're in a restaurant! Now cut it out, both of you! [*The* GIRLS *enter.*] Hello, girls, sit down.

[THE WOMAN *laughs, off left.*]

MISS FORSYTHE: I guess we might as well. This is Letta.
THE WOMAN: Willy, are you going to wake up?
BIFF: [*Ignoring* WILLY.] How're ya, miss, sit down. What do you drink?
MISS FORSYTHE: Letta might not be able to stay long.
LETTA: I gotta get up early tomorrow. I got jury duty. I'm so excited! Were you fellows ever on a jury?
BIFF: No, but I been in front of them! [*The* GIRLS *laugh.*] This is my father.
LETTA: Isn't he cute? Sit down with us, Pop.
HAPPY: Sit him down, Biff!
BIFF: [*Going to him.*] Come on, slugger, drink us under the table. To hell with it! Come on, sit down, pal.

[*On* BIFF's *last insistence*, WILLY *is about to sit.*]

THE WOMAN: [*Now urgently.*] Willy, are you going to answer the door!

[THE WOMAN's *call pulls* WILLY *back. He starts right, befuddled.*]

BIFF: Hey, where are you going?
WILLY: Open the door.
BIFF: The door?

WILLY: The washroom . . . the door . . . where's the door?
BIFF: [*Leading* WILLY *to the left.*] Just go straight down.

[WILLY *moves left.*]

THE WOMAN: Willy, Willy, are you going to get up, get up, get up, get up?

[WILLY *exits left.*]

LETTA: I think it's sweet you bring your daddy along.
MISS FORSYTHE: Oh, he isn't really your father!
BIFF: [*At left, turning to her resentfully.*] Miss Forsythe, you've just seen a prince walk by. A fine, troubled prince. A hardworking, unappreciated prince. A pal, you understand? A good companion. Always for his boys.
LETTA: That's so sweet.
HAPPY: Well, girls, what's the program? We're wasting time. Come on, Biff. Gather round. Where would you like to go?
BIFF: Why don't you do something for him?
HAPPY: Me!
BIFF: Don't you give a damn for him, Hap?
HAPPY: What're you talking about? I'm the one who—
BIFF: I sense it, you don't give a good goddam about him. [*He takes the rolled-up hose from his pocket and puts it on the table in front of* HAPPY.] Look what I found in the cellar, for Christ's sake. How can you bear to let it go on?
HAPPY: Me? Who goes away? Who runs off and—
BIFF: Yeah, but he doesn't mean anything to you. You could help him—I can't! Don't you understand what I'm talking about? He's going to kill himself, don't you know that?
HAPPY: Don't I know it! Me!
BIFF: Hap, help him! Jesus . . . help him . . . Help me, help me, I can't bear to look at his face! [*Ready to weep, he hurries out, up right.*]
HAPPY: [*Starting after him.*] Where are you going?
MISS FORSYTHE: What's he so mad about?
HAPPY: Come on, girls, we'll catch up with him.
MISS FORSYTHE: [*As* HAPPY *pushes her out.*] Say, I don't like that temper of his!
HAPPY: He's just a little overstrung, he'll be all right!
WILLY: [*Off left, as* THE WOMAN *laughs.*] Don't answer! Don't answer!
LETTA: Don't you want to tell your father—
HAPPY: No, that's not my father. He's just a guy. Come on, we'll catch Biff, and, honey, we're going to paint this town! Stanley, where's the check! Hey, Stanley!

[*They exit.* STANLEY *looks toward left.*]

STANLEY: [*Calling to* HAPPY *indignantly.*] Mr. Loman! Mr. Loman!

[STANLEY *picks up a chair and follows them off. Knocking is heard off left.* THE WOMAN *enters, laughing.* WILLY *follows her. She is in a black slip; he is buttoning his shirt. Raw, sensuous music accompanies their speech.*]

WILLY: Will you stop laughing? Will you stop?
THE WOMAN: Aren't you going to answer the door? He'll wake the whole hotel.
WILLY: I'm not expecting anybody.

THE WOMAN: Whyn't you have another drink, honey, and stop being so damn self-centered?
WILLY: I'm so lonely.
THE WOMAN: You know you ruined me, Willy? From now on, whenever you come to the office, I'll see that you go right through to the buyers. No waiting at my desk anymore, Willy. You ruined me.
WILLY: That's nice of you to say that.
THE WOMAN: Gee, you are self-centered! Why so sad? You are the saddest, self-centeredest soul I ever did see-saw. [*She laughs. He kisses her.*] Come on inside, drummer boy. It's silly to be dressing in the middle of the night. [*As knocking is heard.*] Aren't you going to answer the door?
WILLY: They're knocking on the wrong door.
THE WOMAN: But I felt the knocking. And he heard us talking in here. Maybe the hotel's on fire!
WILLY: [*His terror rising.*] It's a mistake.
THE WOMAN: Then tell them to go away!
WILLY: There's nobody there.
THE WOMAN: It's getting on my nerves, Willy. There's somebody standing out there and it's getting on my nerves!
WILLY: [*Pushing her away from him.*] All right, stay in the bathroom here, and don't come out. I think there's a law in Massachusetts about it, so don't come out. It may be that new room clerk. He looked very mean. So don't come out. It's a mistake, there's no fire.

[*The knocking is heard again. He takes a few steps away from her, and she vanishes into the wing. The light follows him, and now he is facing* YOUNG BIFF, *who carries a suitcase.* BIFF *steps toward him. The music is gone.*]

BIFF: Why didn't you answer?
WILLY: Biff! What are you doing in Boston?
BIFF: Why didn't you answer? I've been knocking for five minutes, I called you on the phone—
WILLY: I just heard you. I was in the bathroom and had the door shut. Did anything happen home?
BIFF: Dad—I let you down.
WILLY: What do you mean?
BIFF: Dad . . .
WILLY: Biffo, what's this about? [*Putting his arm around* BIFF.] Come on, let's go downstairs and get you a malted.
BIFF: Dad, I flunked math.
WILLY: Not for the term?
BIFF: The term. I haven't got enough credits to graduate.
WILLY: You mean to say Bernard wouldn't give you the answers?
BIFF: He did, he tried, but I only got a sixty-one.
WILLY: And they wouldn't give you four points?
BIFF: Birnbaum refused absolutely. I begged him, Pop, but he won't give me those points. You gotta talk to him before they close the school. Because if he saw the kind of man you are, and you just talked to him in your way, I'm sure he'd come through for me. The class came right before practice, see, and I didn't go enough. Would you talk to him? He'd like you, Pop. You know the way you could talk.

WILLY: You're on. We'll drive right back.
BIFF: Oh, Dad, good work! I'm sure he'll change for you!
WILLY: Go downstairs and tell the clerk I'm checkin' out. Go right down.
BIFF: Yes, sir! See, the reason he hates me, Pop—one day he was late for class so I got up at the blackboard and imitated him. I crossed my eyes and talked with a lithp.
WILLY: [*Laughing.*] You did? The kids like it?
BIFF: They nearly died laughing!
WILLY: Yeah? What'd you do?
BIFF: The thquare root of thixthy twee is . . . [WILLY *bursts out laughing;* BIFF *joins him.*] And in the middle of it he walked in!

[WILLY *laughs and* THE WOMAN *joins in offstage.*]

WILLY: [*Without hesitation.*] Hurry downstairs and—
BIFF: Somebody in there?
WILLY: No, that was next door.

[THE WOMAN *laughs offstage.*]

BIFF: Somebody got in your bathroom!
WILLY: No, it's the next room, there's a party—
THE WOMAN: [*Enters laughing. She lisps this.*] Can I come in? There's something in the bathtub, Willy, and it's moving!

[WILLY *looks at* BIFF, *who is staring open-mouthed and horrified at* THE WOMAN.]

WILLY: Ah—you better go back to your room. They must be finished painting by now. They're painting her room so I let her take a shower here. Go back, go back . . . [*He pushes her.*]
THE WOMAN: [*Resisting.*] But I've got to get dressed, Willy, I can't—
WILLY: Get out of here! Go back, go back . . . [*Suddenly striving for the ordinary.*] This is Miss Francis, Biff, she's a buyer. They're painting her room. Go back, Miss Francis, go back . . .
THE WOMAN: But my clothes, I can't go out naked in the hall!
WILLY: [*Pushing her offstage.*] Get outa here! Go back, go back!

[BIFF *slowly sits down on his suitcase as the argument continues offstage.*]

THE WOMAN: Where's my stockings? You promised me stockings, Willy!
WILLY: I have no stockings here!
THE WOMAN: You had two boxes of size nine sheers for me, and I want them!
WILLY: Here, for God's sake, will you get outa here!
THE WOMAN: [*Enters holding a box of stockings.*] I just hope there's nobody in the hall. That's all I hope. [*To* BIFF.] Are you football or baseball?
BIFF: Football.
THE WOMAN: [*Angry, humiliated.*] That's me too. G'night. [*She snatches her clothes from* WILLY, *and walks out.*]
WILLY: [*After a pause.*] Well, better get going. I want to get to the school first thing in the morning. Get my suits out of the closet. I'll get my valise. [BIFF *doesn't move.*] What's the matter? BIFF *remains motionless, tears falling.*] She's a buyer. Buys for J. H. Simmons. She lives down the hall—they're painting. You don't imagine—[*He breaks off. After a pause.*] Now listen, pal, she's just a buyer. She sees merchandise in her room and they have to keep it looking just so . . .

[*Pause. Assuming command.*] All right, get my suits. [BIFF *doesn't move.*] Now stop crying and do as I say. I gave you an order. Biff, I gave you an order! Is that what you do when I give you an order? How dare you cry! [*Putting his arm around* BIFF.] Now look, Biff, when you grow up you'll understand about these things. You mustn't—you mustn't overemphasize a thing like this. I'll see Birnbaum first thing in the morning.

BIFF: Never mind.

WILLY: [*Getting down beside* BIFF.] Never mind! He's going to give you those points. I'll see to it.

BIFF: He wouldn't listen to you.

WILLY: He certainly will listen to me. You need those points for the U. of Virginia.

BIFF: I'm not going there.

WILLY: Heh? If I can't get him to change that mark you'll make it up in summer school. You've got all summer to—

BIFF: [*His weeping breaking from him.*] Dad . . .

WILLY: [*Infected by it.*] Oh, my boy . . .

BIFF: Dad . . .

WILLY: She's nothing to me, Biff. I was lonely, I was terribly lonely.

BIFF: You—you gave her Mama's stockings! [*His tears break through and he rises to go.*]

WILLY: [*Grabbing for* BIFF.] I gave you an order!

BIFF: Don't touch me, you—liar!

WILLY: Apologize for that!

BIFF: You fake! You phony little fake! You fake!

[*Overcome, he turns quickly and weeping fully goes out with his suitcase.* WILLY *is left on the floor on his knees.*]

WILLY: I gave you an order! Biff, come back here or I'll beat you! Come back here! I'll whip you! [STANLEY *comes quickly in from the right and stands in front of* WILLY. WILLY *shouts at* STANLEY.] I gave you an order . . .

STANLEY: Hey, let's pick it up, pick it up, Mr. Loman. [*He helps* WILLY *to his feet.*] Your boys left with the chippies. They said they'll see you home.

[*A* SECOND WAITER *watches some distance away.*]

WILLY: But we were supposed to have dinner together.

[*Music is heard,* WILLY's *theme.*]

STANLEY: Can you make it?

WILLY: I'll—sure, I can make it. [*Suddenly concerned about his clothes.*] Do I—I look all right?

STANLEY: Sure, you look all right. [*He flicks a speck off* WILLY's *lapel.*]

WILLY: Here—here's a dollar.

STANLEY: Oh, your son paid me. It's all right.

WILLY: [*Putting it in* STANLEY's *hand.*] No, take it. You're a good boy.

STANLEY: Oh, no, you don't have to . . .

WILLY: Here—here's some more, I don't need it anymore. [*After a slight pause.*] Tell me—is there a seed store in the neighborhood?

STANLEY: Seeds? You mean like to plant?

[*As* WILLY *turns,* STANLEY *slips the money back into his jacket pocket.*]

WILLY: Yes. Carrots, peas...
STANLEY: Well, there's hardware stores on Sixth Avenue, but it may be too late now.
WILLY: [*Anxiously.*] Oh, I'd better hurry. I've got to get some seeds. [*He starts off to the right.*] I've got to get some seeds, right away. Nothing's planted. I don't have a thing in the ground.

[WILLY *hurries out as the light goes down.* STANLEY *moves over to the right after him, watches him off. The other* WAITER *has been staring at* WILLY.]

STANLEY: [*To the* WAITER.] Well, whatta you looking at?

[*The* WAITER *picks up the chairs and moves off right.* STANLEY *takes the table and follows him. The light fades on this area. There is a long pause, the sound of the flute coming over. The light gradually rises on the kitchen, which is empty.* HAPPY *appears at the door of the house, followed by* BIFF. HAPPY *is carrying a large bunch of long-stemmed roses. He enters the kitchen, looks around for* LINDA. *Not seeing her, he turns to* BIFF, *who is just outside the house door, and makes a gesture with his hands, indicating "Not here, I guess." He looks into the living-room and freezes. Inside,* LINDA, *unseen, is seated,* WILLY's *coat on her lap. She rises ominously and quietly and moves toward* HAPPY, *who backs up into the kitchen, afraid.*]

HAPPY: Hey, what're you doing up? [LINDA *says nothing but moves toward him implacably.*] Where's Pop? [*He keeps backing to the right, and now* LINDA *is in full view in the doorway to the living-room.*] Is he sleeping?
LINDA: Where were you?
HAPPY: [*Trying to laugh it off.*] We met two girls, Mom, very fine types. Here, we brought you some flowers. [*Offering them to her.*] Put them in your room, Ma. [*She knocks them to the floor at* BIFF's *feet. He has now come inside and closed the door behind him. She stares at* BIFF, *silent.*] Now what'd you do that for? Mom, I want you to have some flowers—
LINDA: [*Cutting* HAPPY *off, violently to* BIFF.] Don't you care whether he lives or dies?
HAPPY: [*Going to the stairs.*] Come upstairs, Biff.
BIFF: [*With a flare of disgust, to* HAPPY.] Go away from me! [*To* LINDA.] What do you mean, lives or dies? Nobody's dying around here, pal.
LINDA: Get out of my sight! Get out of here!
BIFF: I wanna see the boss.
LINDA: You're not going near him!
BIFF: Where is he? [*He moves into the living-room and* LINDA *follows.*]
LINDA: [*Shouting after* BIFF.] You invite him for dinner. He looks forward to it all day—[BIFF *appears in his parents' bedroom, looks around and exits.*]—and then you desert him there. There's no stranger you'd do that to!
HAPPY: Why? He had a swell time with us. Listen, when I—[LINDA *comes back into the kitchen.*]—desert him I hope I don't outlive the day!
LINDA: Get out of here!
HAPPY: Now look, Mom...
LINDA: Did you have to go to women tonight? You and your lousy rotten whores!

[BIFF *re-enters the kitchen.*]

HAPPY: Mom, all we did was follow Biff around trying to cheer him up! [*To* BIFF.] Boy, what a night you gave me!

LINDA: Get out of here, both of you, and don't come back! I don't want you tormenting him anymore. Go on now, get your things together! [*To* BIFF.] You can sleep in his apartment. [*She starts to pick up the flowers and stops herself.*] Pick up this stuff, I'm not your maid anymore. Pick it up, you bum, you! [HAPPY *turns his back to her in refusal.* BIFF *slowly moves over and gets down on his knees, picking up the flowers.*] You're a pair of animals! Not one, not another living soul would have had the cruelty to walk out on that man in a restaurant!

BIFF: [*Not looking at her.*] Is that what he said?

LINDA: He didn't have to say anything. He was so humiliated he nearly limped when he came in.

HAPPY: But, Mom, he had a great time with us—

BIFF: [*Cutting him off violently.*] Shut up!

[*Without another word,* HAPPY *goes upstairs.*]

LINDA: You! You didn't even go in to see if he was all right!

BIFF: [*Still on the floor in front of* LINDA, *the flowers in his hand; with self-loathing.*] No. Didn't. Didn't do a damned thing. How do you like that, heh? Left him babbling in a toilet.

LINDA: You louse. You...

BIFF: Now you hit it on the nose! [*He gets up, throws the flowers in the wastebasket.*] The scum of the earth, and you're looking at him!

LINDA: Get out of here!

BIFF: I gotta talk to the boss, Mom. Where is he?

LINDA: You're not going near him. Get out of this house!

BIFF: [*With absolute assurance, determination.*] No. We're gonna have an abrupt conversation, him and me.

LINDA: You're not talking to him! [*Hammering is heard from outside the house, off right.* BIFF *turns toward the noise. Suddenly pleading.*] Will you please leave him alone?

BIFF: What's he doing out there?

LINDA: He's planting the garden!

BIFF: [*Quietly.*] Now? Oh, my God!

[BIFF *moves outside,* LINDA *following. The light dies down on them and comes up on the center of the apron as* WILLY *walks into it. He is carrying a flashlight, a hoe, and a handful of seed packets. He raps the top of the hoe sharply to fix it firmly, and then moves to the left, measuring off the distance with his foot. He holds the flashlight to look at the seed packets, reading off the instructions. He is in the blue of night.*]

WILLY: Carrots... quarter-inch apart. Rows... one-foot rows. [*He measures it off.*] One foot. [*He puts down a package and measures off.*] Beets. [*He puts down another package and measures again.*] Lettuce. [*He reads the package, puts it down.*] One foot—[*He breaks off as* BEN *appears at the right and moves slowly down to him.*] What a proposition, ts, ts. Terrific, terrific. 'Cause she's suffered, Ben, the woman has suffered. You understand me? A man can't go out the way he came in, Ben, a man has got to add up to something. You can't, you can't— [BEN *moves toward him as though to interrupt.*] You gotta consider, now. Don't answer so quick. Remember, it's a guaranteed twenty-thousand-dollar proposition. Now look, Ben, I want you to go through the ins and outs of this thing with me. I've got nobody to talk to, Ben, and the woman has suffered, you hear me?

BEN: [*Standing still, considering.*] What's the proposition?

WILLY: It's twenty thousand dollars on the barrelhead. Guaranteed, gilt-edged, you understand?

BEN: You don't want to make a fool of yourself. They might not honor the policy.

WILLY: How can they dare refuse? Didn't I work like a coolie to meet every premium on the nose? And now they don't pay off! Impossible!

BEN: It's called a cowardly thing, William.

WILLY: Why? Does it take more guts to stand here the rest of my life ringing up a zero?

BEN: [*Yielding.*] That's a point, William. [*He moves, thinking, turns.*] And twenty thousand—that *is* something one can feel with the hand, it is there.

WILLY: [*Now assured, with rising power.*] Oh, Ben, that's the whole beauty of it! I see it like a diamond, shining in the dark, hard and rough, that I can pick up and touch in my hand. Not like—like an appointment! This would not be another damned-fool appointment, Ben, and it changes all the aspects. Because he thinks I'm nothing, see, and so he spites me. But the funeral— [*Straightening up.*] Ben, that funeral will be massive! They'll come from Maine, Massachusetts, Vermont, New Hampshire! All the old-timers with the strange license plates—that boy will be thunder-struck, Ben, because he never realized—I am known! Rhode Island, New York, New Jersey—I am known, Ben, and he'll see it with his eyes once and for all. He'll see what I am, Ben! He's in for a shock, that boy!

BEN: [*Coming down to the edge of the garden.*] He'll call you a coward.

WILLY: [*Suddenly fearful.*] No, that would be terrible.

BEN: Yes. And a damned fool.

WILLY: No, no, he mustn't, I won't have that! [*He is broken and desperate.*]

BEN: He'll hate you, William.

[*The gay music of the Boys is heard.*]

WILLY: Oh, Ben, how do we get back to all the great times? Used to be so full of light, and comradeship, the sleigh-riding in winter, and the ruddiness on his cheeks. And always some kind of good news coming up, always something nice coming up ahead. And never even let me carry the valises in the house, and simonizing, simonizing that little red car! Why, why can't I give him something and not have him hate me?

BEN: Let me think about it. [*He glances at his watch.*] I still have a little time. Remarkable proposition, but you've got to be sure you're not making a fool of yourself.

[BEN *drifts off upstage and goes out of sight.* BIFF *comes down from the left.*]

WILLY: [*Suddenly conscious of* BIFF, *turns and looks up at him, then begins picking up the packages of seeds in confusion.*] Where the hell is that seed? [*Indignantly.*] You can't see nothing out here! They boxed in the whole goddam neighborhood!

BIFF: There are people all around here. Don't you realize that?

WILLY: I'm busy. Don't bother me.

BIFF: [*Taking the hoe from* WILLY.] I'm saying good-bye to you, Pop. [WILLY *looks at him, silent, unable to move.*] I'm not coming back anymore.
WILLY: You're not going to see Oliver tomorrow?
BIFF: I've got no appointment, Dad.
WILLY: He put his arm around you, and you've got no appointment?
BIFF: Pop, get this now, will you? Everytime I've left it's been a fight that sent me out of here. Today I realized something about myself and I tried to explain it to you and I—I think I'm just not smart enough to make any sense out of it for you. To hell with whose fault it is or anything like that. [*He takes* WILLY'S *arm.*] Let's just wrap it up, heh? Come on in, we'll tell Mom. [*He gently tries to pull* WILLY *to left.*]
WILLY: [*Frozen, immobile, with guilt in his voice.*] No, I don't want to see her.
BIFF: Come on! [*He pulls again, and* WILLY *tries to pull away.*]
WILLY: [*Highly nervous.*] No, no, I don't want to see her.
BIFF: [*Tries to look into* WILLY'S *face, as if to find the answer there.*] Why don't you want to see her?
WILLY: [*More harshly now.*] Don't bother me, will you?
BIFF: What do you mean, you don't want to see her? You don't want them calling you yellow, do you? This isn't your fault; it's me, I'm a bum. Now come inside! [WILLY *strains to get away.*] Did you hear what I said to you?

[WILLY *pulls away and quickly goes by himself into the house.* BIFF *follows.*]

LINDA: [*To* WILLY.] Did you plant, dear?
BIFF: [*At the door, to* LINDA.] All right, we had it out. I'm going and I'm not writing anymore.
LINDA: [*Going to* WILLY *in the kitchen.*] I think that's the best way, dear. 'Cause there's no use drawing it out, you'll just never get along.

[WILLY *doesn't respond.*]

BIFF: People ask where I am and what I'm doing, you don't know, and you don't care. That way it'll be off your mind and you can start brightening up again. All right? That clears it, doesn't it? [WILLY *is silent, and* BIFF *goes to him.*] You gonna wish me luck, scout? [*He extends his hand.*] What do you say?
LINDA: Shake his hand, Willy.
WILLY: [*Turning to her, seething with hurt.*] There's no necessity to mention the pen at all, y'know.
BIFF: [*Gently.*] I've got no appointment, Dad.
WILLY: [*Erupting fiercely.*] He put his arm around . . . ?
BIFF: Dad, you're never going to see what I am, so what's the use of arguing? If I strike oil I'll send you a check. Meantime forget I'm alive.
WILLY: [*To* LINDA.] Spite, see?
BIFF: Shake hands, Dad.
WILLY: Not my hand.
BIFF: I was hoping not to go this way.
WILLY: Well, this is the way you're going. Good-bye. [BIFF *looks at him a moment, then turns sharply and goes to the stairs.* WILLY *stops him with.*] May you rot in hell if you leave this house!
BIFF: [*Turning.*] Exactly what is it that you want from me?
WILLY: I want you to know, on the train, in the mountains, in the valleys, wherever you go, that you cut down your life for spite!

BIFF: No, no.
WILLY: Spite, spite, is the word of your undoing! And when you're down and out, remember what did it. When you're rotting somewhere beside the railroad tracks, remember, and don't you dare blame it on me!
BIFF: I'm not blaming it on you!
WILLY: I won't take the rap for this, you hear?

[HAPPY *comes down the stairs and stands on the bottom step, watching.*]

BIFF: That's just what I'm telling you!
WILLY: [*Sinking into a chair at the table, with full accusation.*] You're trying to put a knife in me—don't think I don't know what you're doing!
BIFF: All right, phony! Then let's lay it on the line. [*He whips the rubber tube out of his pocket and puts it on the table.*]
HAPPY: You crazy—
LINDA: Biff!

[*She moves to grab the hose, but* BIFF *holds it down with his hand.*]

BIFF: Leave it there! Don't move it!
WILLY: [*Not looking at it.*] What is that?
BIFF: You know goddam well what that is.
WILLY: [*Caged, wanting to escape.*] I never saw that.
BIFF: You saw it. The mice didn't bring it into the cellar! What is this supposed to do, make a hero out of you? This supposed to make me sorry for you?
WILLY: Never heard of it.
BIFF: There'll be no pity for you, you hear it? No pity!
WILLY: [*To* LINDA.] You hear the spite!
BIFF: No, you're going to hear the truth—what you are and what I am!
LINDA: Stop it!
WILLY: Spite!
HAPPY: [*Coming down toward* BIFF.] You cut it now!
BIFF: [*To* HAPPY.] The man don't know who we are! The man is gonna know! [*To* WILLY.] We never told the truth for ten minutes in this house!
HAPPY: We always told the truth!
BIFF: [*Turning on him.*] You big blow, are you the assistant buyer? You're one of the two assistants to the assistant, aren't you?
HAPPY: Well, I'm practically—
BIFF: You're practically full of it! We all are! And I'm through with it. [*To* WILLY.] Now hear this, Willy, this is me.
WILLY: I know you!
BIFF: You know why I had no address for three months? I stole a suit in Kansas City and I was in jail. [*To* LINDA, *who is sobbing.*] Stop crying. I'm through with it.

[LINDA *turns away from them, her hands covering her face.*]

WILLY: I suppose that's my fault!
BIFF: I stole myself out of every good job since high school!
WILLY: And whose fault is that?
BIFF: And I never got anywhere because you blew me so full of hot air I could never stand taking orders from anybody! That's whose fault it is!
WILLY: I hear that!

LINDA: Don't, Biff!

BIFF: It's goddam time you heard that! I had to be boss big shot in two weeks, and I'm through with it!

WILLY: Then hang yourself! For spite, hang yourself!

BIFF: No! Nobody's hanging himself, Willy! I ran down eleven flights with a pen in my hand today. And suddenly I stopped, you hear me? And in the middle of that office building, do you hear this? I stopped in the middle of that building and I saw—the sky. I saw the things that I love in this world. The work and the food and time to sit and smoke. And I looked at the pen and said to myself, what the hell am I grabbing this for? Why am I trying to become what I don't want to be? What am I doing in an office, making a contemptuous, begging fool of myself, when all I want is out there, waiting for me the minute I say I know who I am! Why can't I say that, Willy? [*He tries to make* WILLY *face him, but* WILLY *pulls away and moves to the left.*]

WILLY: [*With hatred, threateningly.*] The door of your life is wide open!

BIFF: Pop! I'm a dime a dozen, and so are you!

WILLY: [*Turning on him now in an uncontrolled outburst.*] I am not a dime a dozen! I am Willy Loman, and you are Biff Loman!

[BIFF *starts for* WILLY, *but is blocked by* HAPPY. *In his fury,* BIFF *seems on the verge of attacking his father.*]

BIFF: I am not a leader of men, Willy, and neither are you. You were never anything but a hard-working drummer who landed in the ash can like all the rest of them! I'm one dollar an hour, Willy! I tried seven states and couldn't raise it. A buck an hour! Do you gather my meaning? I'm not bringing home any prizes anymore, and you're going to stop waiting for me to bring them home!

WILLY: [*Directly to* BIFF.] You vengeful, spiteful mut!

[BIFF *breaks from* HAPPY. WILLY, *in fright, starts up the stairs.* BIFF *grabs him.*]

BIFF: [*At the peak of his fury.*] Pop, I'm nothing! I'm nothing, Pop. Can't you understand that? There's no spite in it anymore. I'm just what I am, that's all.

[BIFF's *fury has spent itself, and he breaks down, sobbing, holding on to* WILLY, *who dumbly fumbles for* BIFF's *face.*]

WILLY: [*Astonished.*] What're you doing? What're you doing? [*To* LINDA.] Why is he crying?

BIFF: [*Crying, broken.*] Will you let me go, for Christ's sake? Will you take that phony dream and burn it before something happens? [*Struggling to contain himself, he pulls away and moves to the stairs.*] I'll go in the morning. Put him—put him to bed. [*Exhausted,* BIFF *moves up the stairs to his room.*]

WILLY: [*After a long pause, astonished, elevated.*] Isn't that—isn't that remarkable? Biff—he likes me!

LINDA: He loves you, Willy!

HAPPY: [*Deeply moved.*] Always did, Pop.

WILLY: Oh, Biff! [*Staring wildly.*] He cried! Cried to me. [*He is choking with his love, and now cries out his promise.*] That boy—that boy is going to be magnificent!

[BEN *appears in the light just outside the kitchen.*]

BEN: Yes, outstanding, with twenty thousand behind him.
LINDA: [*Sensing the racing of his mind, fearfully, carefully.*] Now come to bed, Willy. It's all settled now.
WILLY: [*Finding it difficult not to rush out of the house.*] Yes, we'll sleep. Come on. Go to sleep, Hap.
BEN: And it does take a great kind of man to crack the jungle.

[*In accents of dread,* BEN'S *idyllic music starts up.*]

HAPPY: [*His arm around* LINDA.] I'm getting married, Pop, don't forget it. I'm changing everything. I'm gonna run that department before the year is up. You'll see, Mom. [*He kisses her.*]
BEN: The jungle is dark but full of diamonds, Willy.

[WILLY *turns, moves, listening to* BEN.]

LINDA: Be good. You're both good boys, just act that way, that's all.
HAPPY: 'Night, Pop. [*He goes upstairs.*]
LINDA: [*To* WILLY.] Come, dear.
BEN: [*With greater force.*] One must go in to fetch a diamond out.
WILLY: [*To* LINDA, *as he moves slowly along the edge of the kitchen, toward the door.*] I just want to get settled down, Linda. Let me sit alone for a little.
LINDA: [*Almost uttering her fear.*] I want you upstairs.
WILLY: [*Taking her in his arms.*] In a few minutes, Linda. I couldn't sleep right now. Go on, you look awful tired. [*He kisses her.*]
BEN: Not like an appointment at all. A diamond is rough and hard to the touch.
WILLY: Go on now. I'll be right up.
LINDA: I think this is the only way, Willy.
WILLY: Sure, it's the best thing.
BEN: Best thing!
WILLY: The only way. Everything is gonna be—go on, kid, get to bed. You look so tired.
LINDA: Come right up.
WILLY: Two minutes. [LINDA *goes into the living-room, then reappears in her bedroom.* WILLY *moves just outside the kitchen door.*] Loves me. [*Wonderingly.*] Always loved me. Isn't that a remarkable thing? Ben, he'll worship me for it!
BEN: [*With promise.*] It's dark there, but full of diamonds.
WILLY: Can you imagine that magnificence with twenty thousand dollars in his pocket?
LINDA: [*Calling from her room.*] Willy! Come up!
WILLY: [*Calling into the kitchen.*] Yes! Yes. Coming! It's very smart, you realize that, don't you, sweetheart? Even Ben sees it. I gotta go, baby. 'Bye! 'Bye! [*Going over to* BEN, *almost dancing.*] Imagine? When the mail comes he'll be ahead of Bernard again!
BEN: A perfect proposition all around.
WILLY: Did you see how he cried to me? Oh, if I could kiss him, Ben!
BEN: Time, William, time!
WILLY: Oh, Ben, I always knew one way or another we were gonna make it, Biff and I!
BEN: [*Looking at his watch.*] The boat. We'll be late. [*He moves slowly off into the darkness.*]

WILLY: [*Elegiacally, turning to the house.*] Now when you kick off, boy, I want a seventy-yard boot, and get right down the field under the ball, and when you hit, hit low and hit hard, because it's important, boy. [*He swings around and faces the audience.*] There's all kinds of important people in the stands, and the first thing you know... [*Suddenly realizing he is alone.*] Ben! Ben, where do I...? [*He makes a sudden movement of search.*] Ben, how do I...?

LINDA: [*Calling.*] Willy, you coming up?

WILLY: [*Uttering a gasp of fear, whirling about as if to quiet her.*] Sh! [*He turns around as if to find his way; sounds, faces, voices, seem to be swarming in upon him and he flicks at them, crying.*] Sh! Sh! [*Suddenly music, faint and high, stops him. It rises in intensity, almost to an unbearable scream. He goes up and down on his toes, and rushes off around the house.*] Shhh!

LINDA: Willy? [*There is no answer.* LINDA *waits.* BIFF *gets up off his bed. He is still in his clothes.* HAPPY *sits up.* BIFF *stands listening.*] [*With real fear.*] Willy, answer me! Willy! [*There is the sound of a car starting and moving away at full speed.*] No!

BIFF: [*Rushing down the stairs.*] Pop!

[*As the car speeds off, the music crashes down in a frenzy of sound, which becomes the soft pulsation of a single cello string.* BIFF *slowly returns to his bedroom. He and* HAPPY *gravely don their jackets.* LINDA *slowly walks out of her room. The music has developed into a dead march. The leaves of day are appearing over everything.* CHARLEY *and* BERNARD, *somberly dressed, appear and knock on the kitchen door.* BIFF *and* HAPPY *slowly descend the stairs to the kitchen as* CHARLEY *and* BERNARD *enter. All stop a moment when* LINDA, *in clothes of mourning, bearing a little bunch of roses, comes through the draped doorway into the kitchen. She goes to* CHARLEY *and takes his arm. Now all move toward the audience, through the wall-line of the kitchen. At the limit of the apron,* LINDA *lays down the flowers, kneels, and sits back on her heels. All stare down at the grave.*]

# REQUIEM

CHARLEY: It's getting dark, Linda.

[LINDA *doesn't react. She stares at the grave.*]

BIFF: How about it, Mom? Better get some rest, heh? They'll be closing the gate soon.

[LINDA *makes no move. Pause.*]

HAPPY: [*Deeply angered.*] He had no right to do that. There was no necessity for it. We would've helped him.

CHARLEY: [*Grunting.*] Hmmm.

BIFF: Come along, Mom.

LINDA: Why didn't anybody come?

CHARLEY: It was a very nice funeral.

LINDA: But where are all the people he knew? Maybe they blame him.

CHARLEY: Naa. It's a rough world, Linda. They wouldn't blame him.

LINDA: I can't understand it. At this time especially. First time in thirty-five years we were just about free and clear. He only needed a little salary. He was even finished with the dentist.

CHARLEY: No man only needs a little salary.

LINDA: I can't understand it.
BIFF: There were a lot of nice days. When he'd come home from a trip; or on Sundays, making the stoop; finishing the cellar; putting on the new porch; when he built the extra bathroom; and put up the garage. You know something, Charley, there's more of him in that front stoop than in all the sales he ever made.
CHARLEY: Yeah. He was a happy man with a batch of cement.
LINDA: He was so wonderful with his hands.
BIFF: He had the wrong dreams. All, all, wrong.
HAPPY: [*Almost ready to fight* BIFF.] Don't say that!
BIFF: He never knew who he was.
CHARLEY: [*Stopping* HAPPY's *movement and reply. To* BIFF.] Nobody dast blame this man. You don't understand: Willy was a salesman. And for a salesman, there is no rock bottom to the life. He don't put a bolt to a nut, he don't tell you the law or give you medicine. He's a man way out there in the blue, riding on a smile and a shoeshine. And when they start not smiling back—that's an earthquake. And then you get yourself a couple of spots on your hat, and you're finished. Nobody dast blame this man. A salesman is got to dream, boy. It comes with the territory.
BIFF: Charley, the man didn't know who he was.
HAPPY: [*Infuriated.*] Don't say that!
BIFF: Why don't you come with me, Happy?
HAPPY: I'm not licked that easily. I'm staying right in this city, and I'm gonna beat this racket! [*He looks at* BIFF, *his chin set.*] The Loman Brothers!
BIFF: I know who I am, kid.
HAPPY: All right, boy. I'm gonna show you and everybody else that Willy Loman did not die in vain. He had a good dream. It's the only dream you can have—to come out number-one-man. He fought it out here, and this is where I'm gonna win it for him.
BIFF: [*With a hopeless glance at* HAPPY, *bends toward his mother.*] Let's go, Mom.
LINDA: I'll be with you in a minute. Go on, Charley. [*He hesitates.*] I want to, just for a minute. I never had a chance to say good-bye. [CHARLEY *moves away, followed by* HAPPY. BIFF *remains a slight distance up and left of* LINDA. *She sits there, summoning herself. The flute begins, not far away, playing behind her speech.*] Forgive me, dear. I can't cry. I don't know what it is, but I can't cry. I don't understand it. Why did you ever do that? Help me, Willy, I can't cry. It seems to me that you're just on another trip. I keep expecting you. Willy, dear, I can't cry. Why did you do it? I search and search and I search, and I can't understand it, Willy. I made the last payment on the house today. Today, dear. And there'll be nobody home. [*A sob rises in her throat.*] We're free and clear. [*Sobbing more fully, released.*] We're free. [BIFF *comes slowly toward her.*] We're free... We're free...

[BIFF *lifts her to her feet and moves out up right with her in his arms.* LINDA *sobs quietly.* BERNARD *and* CHARLEY *come together and follow them, followed by* HAPPY. *Only the music of the flute is left on the darkening stage as over the house the hard towers of the apartment buildings rise into sharp focus.*]

CURTAIN

1949

HENRIK IBSEN

# A Doll House[1]

CHARACTERS

TORVALD HELMER, *a lawyer*
NORA, *his wife*
DR. RANK
MRS. LINDE
NILS KROGSTAD, *a bank clerk*
THE HELMERS' THREE SMALL CHILDREN
ANNE-MARIE, *their nurse*
HELENE, *a maid*
A DELIVERY BOY

*The action takes place in* HELMER'*s residence.*

## ACT I

*A comfortable room, tastefully but not expensively furnished. A door to the right in the back wall leads to the entryway; another to the left leads to* HELMER'*s study. Between these doors, a piano. Midway in the left-hand wall a door, and further back a window. Near the window a round table with an armchair and a small sofa. In the right-hand wall, toward the rear, a door, and nearer the foreground a porcelain stove with two armchairs and a rocking chair beside it. Between the stove and the side door, a small table. Engravings on the walls. An etagère with china figures and other small art objects; a small bookcase with richly bound books; the floor carpeted; a fire burning in the stove. It is a winter day.*

*A bell rings in the entryway; shortly after we hear the door being unlocked.* NORA *comes into the room, humming happily to herself; she is wearing street clothes and carries an armload of packages, which she puts down on the table to the right. She has left the hall door open; and through it a* DELIVERY BOY *is seen, holding a Christmas tree and a basket, which he gives to the* MAID *who let them in.*

NORA: Hide the tree well, Helene. The children mustn't get a glimpse of it till this evening, after it's trimmed. [*To the* DELIVERY BOY, *taking out her purse.*] How much?
DELIVERY BOY: Fifty, ma'am.
NORA: There's a crown. No, keep the change. [*The* BOY *thanks her and leaves.* NORA *shuts the door. She laughs softly to herself while taking off her street things. Drawing a bag of macaroons from her pocket, she eats a couple, then steals over and listens at her husband's study door.*] Yes, he's home. [*Hums again as she moves to the table right.*]
HELMER: [*From the study.*] Is that my little lark twittering out there?
NORA: [*Busy opening some packages.*] Yes, it is.
HELMER: Is that my squirrel rummaging around?
NORA: Yes!
HELMER: When did my squirrel get in?
NORA: Just now. [*Putting the macaroon bag in her pocket and wiping her mouth.*] Do come in, Torvald, and see what I've bought.
HELMER: Can't be disturbed. [*After a moment he opens the door and peers in, pen in*

---

1. Translated by Rolf Fjelde.

hand.] Bought, you say? All that there? Has the little spendthrift been out throwing money around again?

NORA: Oh, but Torvald, this year we really should let ourselves go a bit. It's the first Christmas we haven't had to economize.

HELMER: But you know we can't go squandering.

NORA: Oh yes, Torvald, we can squander a little now. Can't we? Just a tiny, wee bit. Now that you've got a big salary and are going to make piles and piles of money.

HELMER: Yes—starting New Year's. But then it's a full three months till the raise comes through.

NORA: Pooh! We can borrow that long.

HELMER: Nora! [*Goes over and playfully takes her by the ear.*] Are your scatterbrains off again? What if today I borrowed a thousand crowns, and you squandered them over Christmas week, and then on New Year's Eve a roof tile fell on my head, and I lay there—

NORA: [*Putting her hand on his mouth.*] Oh! Don't say such things!

HELMER: Yes, but what if it happened—then what?

NORA: If anything so awful happened, then it just wouldn't matter if I had debts or not.

HELMER: Well, but the people I'd borrowed from?

NORA: Them? Who cares about them! They're strangers.

HELMER: Nora, Nora, how like a woman! No, but seriously, Nora, you know what I think about that. No debts! Never borrow! Something of freedom's lost—and something of beauty, too—from a home that's founded on borrowing and debt. We've made a brave stand up to now, the two of us; and we'll go right on like that the little while we have to.

NORA: [*Going toward the stove.*] Yes, whatever you say, Torvald.

HELMER: [*Following her.*] Now, now, the little lark's wings mustn't droop. Come on, don't be a sulky squirrel. [*Taking out his wallet.*] Nora, guess what I have here.

NORA: [*Turning quickly.*] Money!

HELMER: There, see. [*Hands her some notes.*] Good grief, I know how costs go up in a house at Christmastime.

NORA: Ten—twenty—thirty—forty. Oh, thank you, Torvald; I can manage no end on this.

HELMER: You really will have to.

NORA: Oh yes, I promise I will. But come here so I can show you everything I bought. And so cheap! Look, new clothes for Ivar here—and a sword. Here a horse and a trumpet for Bob. And a doll and a doll's bed here for Emmy; they're nothing much, but she'll tear them to bits in no time anyway. And here I have dress material and handkerchiefs for the maids. Old Anne-Marie really deserves something more.

HELMER: And what's in that package there?

NORA: [*With a cry.*] Torvald, no! You can't see that till tonight!

HELMER: I see. But tell me now, you little prodigal, what have you thought of for yourself?

NORA: For myself? Oh, I don't want anything at all.

HELMER: Of course you do. Tell me just what—within reason—you'd most like to have.

NORA: I honestly don't know. Oh, listen, Torvald—
HELMER: Well?
NORA: [*Fumbling at his coat buttons, without looking at him.*] If you want to give me something, then maybe you could—you could—
HELMER: Come, on, out with it.
NORA: [*Hurriedly.*] You could give me money, Torvald. No more than you think you can spare; then one of these days I'll buy something with it.
HELMER: But Nora—
NORA: Oh, please, Torvald darling, do that! I beg you, please. Then I could hang the bills in pretty gilt paper on the Christmas tree. Wouldn't that be fun?
HELMER: What are those little birds called that always fly through their fortunes?
NORA: Oh yes, spendthrifts; I know all that. But let's do as I say, Torvald; then I'll have time to decide what I really need most. That's very sensible, isn't it?
HELMER: [*Smiling.*] Yes, very—that is, if you actually hung onto the money I give you, and you actually used it to buy yourself something. But it goes for the house and for all sorts of foolish things, and then I only have to lay out some more.
NORA: Oh, but Torvald—
HELMER: Don't deny it, my dear little Nora. [*Putting his arm around her waist.*] Spendthrifts are sweet, but they use up a frightful amount of money. It's incredible what it costs a man to feed such birds.
NORA: Oh, how can you say that! Really, I save everything I can.
HELMER: [*Laughing.*] Yes, that's the truth. Everything you can. But that's nothing at all.
NORA: [*Humming, with a smile of quiet satisfaction.*] Hm, if you only knew what expenses we larks and squirrels have, Torvald.
HELMER: You're an odd little one. Exactly the way your father was. You're never at a loss for scaring up money; but the moment you have it, it runs right out through your fingers; you never know what you've done with it. Well, one takes you as you are. It's deep in your blood. Yes, these things are hereditary, Nora.
NORA: Ah, I could wish I'd inherited many of Papa's qualities.
HELMER: And I couldn't wish you anything but just what you are, my sweet little lark. But wait; it seems to me you have a very—what should I call it?—a very suspicious look today—
NORA: I do?
HELMER: You certainly do. Look me straight in the eye.
NORA: [*Looking at him.*] Well?
HELMER: [*Shaking an admonitory finger.*] Surely my sweet tooth hasn't been running riot in town today, has she?
NORA: No. Why do you imagine that?
HELMER: My sweet tooth really didn't make a little detour through the confectioner's?
NORA: No, I assure you, Torvald—
HELMER: Hasn't nibbled some pastry?
NORA: No, not at all.
HELMER: Not even munched a macaroon or two?
NORA: No, Torvald, I assure you, really—
HELMER: There, there now. Of course I'm only joking.

NORA: [*Going to the table, right.*] You know I could never think of going against you.
HELMER: No, I understand that; and you *have* given me your word. [*Going over to her.*] Well, you keep your little Christmas secrets to yourself, Nora darling. I expect they'll come to light this evening, when the tree is lit.
NORA: Did you remember to ask Dr. Rank?
HELMER: No. But there's no need for that; it's assumed he'll be dining with us. All the same, I'll ask him when he stops by here this morning. I've ordered some fine wine. Nora, you can't imagine how I'm looking forward to this evening.
NORA: So am I. And what fun for the children, Torvald!
HELMER: Ah, it's so gratifying to know that one's gotten a safe, secure job, and with a comfortable salary. It's a great satisfaction, isn't it?
NORA: Oh, it's wonderful!
HELMER: Remember last Christmas? Three whole weeks before, you shut yourself in every evening till long after midnight, making flowers for the Christmas tree, and all the other decorations to surprise us. Ugh, that was the dullest time I've ever lived through.
NORA: It wasn't at all dull for me.
HELMER: [*Smiling.*] But the outcome *was* pretty sorry, Nora.
NORA: Oh, don't tease me with that again. How could I help it that the cat came in and tore everything to shreds.
HELMER: No, poor thing, you certainly couldn't. You wanted so much to please us all, and that's what counts. But it's just as well that the hard times are past.
NORA: Yes, it's really wonderful.
HELMER: Now I don't have to sit here alone, boring myself, and you don't have to tire your precious eyes and your fair little delicate hands—
NORA: [*Clapping her hands.*] No, is it really true, Torvald, I don't have to? Oh, how wonderfully lovely to hear! [*Taking his arm.*] Now I'll tell you just how I've thought we should plan things. Right after Christmas—[*The doorbell rings.*] Oh, the bell. [*Straightening the room up a bit.*] Somebody would have to come. What a bore!
HELMER: I'm not at home to visitors, don't forget.
MAID: [*From the hall doorway.*] Ma'am, a lady to see you—
NORA: All right, let her come in.
MAID: [*To* HELMER.] And the doctor's just come too.
HELMER: Did he go right to my study?
MAID: Yes, he did.

[HELMER *goes into his room. The* MAID *shows in* MRS. LINDE, *dressed in traveling clothes, and shuts the door after her.*]

MRS. LINDE: [*In a dispirited and somewhat hesitant voice.*] Hello, Nora.
NORA: [*Uncertain.*] Hello—
MRS. LINDE: You don't recognize me.
NORA: No, I don't know—but wait, I think—[*Exclaiming.*] What! Kristine! Is it really you?
MRS. LINDE: Yes, it's me.
NORA: Kristine! To think I didn't recognize you. But then, how could I? [*More quietly.*] How you've changed, Kristine!

MRS. LINDE: Yes, no doubt I have. In nine—ten long years.
NORA: Is it so long since we met! Yes, it's all of that. Oh, these last eight years have been a happy time, believe me. And so now you've come in to town, too. Made the long trip in the winter. That took courage.
MRS. LINDE: I just got here by ship this morning.
NORA: To enjoy yourself over Christmas, of course. Oh, how lovely! Yes, enjoy ourselves, we'll do that. But take your coat off. You're not still cold? [*Helping her.*] There now, let's get cozy here by the stove. No, the easy chair there! I'll take the rocker here. [*Seizing her hands.*] Yes, now you have your old look again; it was only in that first moment. You're a bit more pale, Kristine—and maybe a bit thinner.
MRS. LINDE: And much, much older, Nora.
NORA: Yes, perhaps a bit older; a tiny, tiny bit; not much at all. [*Stopping short; suddenly serious.*] Oh, but thoughtless me, to sit here, chattering away. Sweet, good Kristine, can you forgive me?
MRS. LINDE: What do you mean, Nora?
NORA: [*Softly.*] Poor Kristine, you've become a widow.
MRS. LINDE: Yes, three years ago.
NORA: Oh, I knew it, of course; I read it in the papers. Oh, Kristine, you must believe me; I often thought of writing you then, but I kept postponing it, and something always interfered.
MRS. LINDE: Nora dear, I understand completely.
NORA: No, it was awful of me, Kristine. You poor thing, how much you must have gone through. And he left you nothing?
MRS. LINDE: No.
NORA: And no children?
MRS. LINDE: No.
NORA: Nothing at all, then?
MRS. LINDE: Not even a sense of loss to feed on.
NORA: [*Looking incredulously at her.*] But Kristine, how could that be?
MRS. LINDE: [*Smiling wearily and smoothing her hair.*] Oh, sometimes it happens, Nora.
NORA: So completely alone. How terribly hard that must be for you. I have three lovely children. You can't see them now; they're out with the maid. But now you must tell me everything—
MRS. LINDE: No, no, no, tell me about yourself.
NORA: No, you begin. Today I don't want to be selfish. I want to think only of you today. But there *is* something I must tell you. Did you hear of the wonderful luck we had recently?
MRS. LINDE: No, what's that?
NORA: My husband's been made manager in the bank, just think!
MRS. LINDE: Your husband? How marvelous!
NORA: Isn't it? Being a lawyer is such an uncertain living, you know, especially if one won't touch any cases that aren't clean and decent. And of course Torvald would never do that, and I'm with him completely there. Oh, we're simply delighted, believe me! He'll join the bank right after New Year's and start getting a huge salary and lots of commissions. From now on we can live quite differently—just as we want. Oh, Kristine, I feel so light and happy! Won't it be lovely to have stacks of money and not a care in the world?

MRS. LINDE: Well, anyway, it would be lovely to have enough for necessities.
NORA: No, not just for necessities, but stacks and stacks of money!
MRS. LINDE: [*Smiling.*] Nora, Nora, aren't you sensible yet? Back in school you were such a free spender.
NORA: [*With a quiet laugh.*] Yes, that's what Torvald still says. [*Shaking her finger.*] But "Nora, Nora" isn't as silly as you all think. Really, we've been in no position for me to go squandering. We've had to work, both of us.
MRS. LINDE: You too?
NORA: Yes, at odd jobs—needlework, crocheting, embroidery, and such—[*Casually.*] and other things too. You remember that Torvald left the department when we were married? There was no chance of promotion in his office, and of course he needed to earn more money. But that first year he drove himself terribly. He took on all kinds of extra work that kept him going morning and night. It wore him down, and then he fell deathly ill. The doctors said it was essential for him to travel south.
MRS. LINDE: Yes, didn't you spend a whole year in Italy?
NORA: That's right. It wasn't easy to get away, you know. Ivar had just been born. But of course we had to go. Oh, that was a beautiful trip, and it saved Torvald's life. But it cost a frightful sum, Kristine.
MRS. LINDE: I can well imagine.
NORA: Four thousand, eight hundred crowns it cost. That's really a lot of money.
MRS. LINDE: But it's lucky you had it when you needed it.
NORA: Well, as it was, we got it from Papa.
MRS. LINDE: I see. It was just about the time your father died.
NORA: Yes, just about then. And, you know, I couldn't make that trip out to nurse him. I had to stay here, expecting Ivar any moment, and with my poor sick Torvald to care for. Dearest Papa, I never saw him again, Kristine. Oh, that was the worst time I've known in all my marriage.
MRS. LINDE: I know how you loved him. And then you went off to Italy?
NORA: Yes. We had the means now, and the doctors urged us. So we left a month after.
MRS. LINDE: And your husband came back completely cured?
NORA: Sound as a drum!
MRS. LINDE: But—the doctor?
NORA: Who?
MRS. LINDE: I thought the maid said he was a doctor, the man who came in with me.
NORA: Yes, that was Dr. Rank—but he's not making a sick call. He's our closest friend, and he stops by at least once a day. No, Torvald hasn't had a sick moment since, and the children are fit and strong, and I am, too. [*Jumping up and clapping her hands.*] Oh, dear God, Kristine, what a lovely thing to live and be happy! But how disgusting of me—I'm talking of nothing but my own affairs. [*Sits on a stool close by* KRISTINE, *arms resting across her knees.*] Oh, don't be angry with me! Tell me, is it really true that you weren't in love with your husband? Why did you marry him, then?
MRS. LINDE: My mother was still alive, but bedridden and helpless—and I had my two younger brothers to look after. In all conscience, I didn't think I could turn him down.
NORA: No, you were right there. But was he rich at the time?

MRS. LINDE: He was very well off, I'd say. But the business was shaky, Nora. When he died, it all fell apart, and nothing was left.

NORA: And then—?

MRS. LINDE: Yes, so I had to scrape up a living with a little shop and a little teaching and whatever else I could find. The last three years have been like one endless workday without a rest for me. Now it's over, Nora. My poor mother doesn't need me, for she's passed on. Nor the boys, either; they're working now and can take care of themselves.

NORA: How free you must feel—

MRS. LINDE: No—only unspeakably empty. Nothing to live for now. [*Standing up anxiously.*] That's why I couldn't take it any longer out in that desolate hole. Maybe here it'll be easier to find something to do and keep my mind occupied. If I could only be lucky enough to get a steady job, some office work—

NORA: Oh, but Kristine, that's so dreadfully tiring, and you already look so tired. It would be much better for you if you could go off to a bathing resort.

MRS. LINDE: [*Going toward the window.*] I have no father to give me travel money, Nora.

NORA: [*Rising.*] Oh, don't be angry with me.

MRS. LINDE: [*Going to her.*] Nora dear, don't you be angry with me. The worst of my kind of situation is all the bitterness that's stored away. No one to work for, and yet you're always having to snap up your opportunities. You have to live; and so you grow selfish. When you told me the happy change in your lot, do you know I was delighted less for your sakes than for mine?

NORA: How so? Oh, I see. You think maybe Torvald could do something for you.

MRS. LINDE: Yes, that's what I thought.

NORA: And he will, Kristine! Just leave it to me; I'll bring it up so delicately—find something attractive to humor him with. Oh, I'm so eager to help you.

MRS. LINDE: How very kind of you, Nora, to be so concerned over me—doubly kind, considering you really know so little of life's burdens yourself.

NORA: I—? I know so little—?

MRS. LINDE: [*Smiling.*] Well, my heavens—a little needlework and such—Nora, you're just a child.

NORA: [*Tossing her head and pacing the floor.*] You don't have to act so superior.

MRS. LINDE: Oh?

NORA: You're just like the others. You all think I'm incapable of anything serious—

MRS. LINDE: Come now—

NORA: That I've never had to face the raw world.

MRS. LINDE: Nora dear, you've just been telling me all your troubles.

NORA: Hm! Trivia! [*Quietly.*] I haven't told you the big thing.

MRS. LINDE: Big thing? What do you mean?

NORA: You look down on me so, Kristine, but you shouldn't. You're proud that you worked so long and hard for your mother.

MRS. LINDE: I don't look down on a soul. But it *is* true: I'm proud—and happy, too—to think it was given to me to make my mother's last days almost free of care.

NORA: And you're also proud thinking of what you've done for your brothers.

MRS. LINDE: I feel I've a right to be.

NORA: I agree. But listen to this, Kristine—I've also got something to be proud and happy for.

MRS. LINDE: I don't doubt it. But whatever do you mean?

NORA: Not so loud. What if Torvald heard! He mustn't, not for anything in the world. Nobody must know, Kristine. No one but you.

MRS. LINDE: But what is it, then?

NORA: Come here. [*Drawing her down beside her on the sofa.*] It's true—I've also got something to be proud and happy for. I'm the one who saved Torvald's life.

MRS. LINDE: Saved—? Saved how?

NORA: I told you about the trip to Italy. Torvald never would have lived if he hadn't gone south—

MRS. LINDE: Of course; your father gave you the means—

NORA: [*Smiling.*] That's what Torvald and all the rest think, but—

MRS. LINDE: But—?

NORA: Papa didn't give us a pin. I was the one who raised the money.

MRS. LINDE: You? That whole amount?

NORA: Four thousand, eight hundred crowns. What do you say to that?

MRS. LINDE: But Nora, how was it possible? Did you win the lottery?

NORA: [*Disdainfully.*] The lottery? Pooh! No art to that.

MRS. LINDE: But where did you get it from then?

NORA: [*Humming, with a mysterious smile.*] Hmm, tra-la-la-la.

MRS. LINDE: Because you couldn't have borrowed it.

NORA: No? Why not?

MRS. LINDE: A wife can't borrow without her husband's consent.

NORA: [*Tossing her head.*] Oh, but a wife with a little business sense, a wife who knows how to manage—

MRS. LINDE: Nora, I simply don't understand—

NORA: You don't have to. Whoever said I *borrowed* the money? I could have gotten it other ways. [*Throwing herself back on the sofa.*] I could have gotten it from some admirer or other. After all, a girl with my ravishing appeal—

MRS. LINDE: You lunatic.

NORA: I'll bet you're eaten up with curiosity, Kristine.

MRS. LINDE: Now listen here, Nora—you haven't done something indiscreet?

NORA: [*Sitting up again.*] Is it indiscreet to save your husband's life?

MRS. LINDE: I think it's indiscreet that without his knowledge you—

NORA: But that's the point: he mustn't know! My Lord, can't you understand? He mustn't ever know the close call he had. It was to *me* the doctors came to say his life was in danger—that nothing could save him but a stay in the south. Didn't I try strategy then! I began talking about how lovely it would be for me to travel abroad like other young wives; I begged and I cried; I told him please to remember my condition, to be kind and indulge me; and then I dropped a hint that he could easily take out a loan. But at that, Kristine, he nearly exploded. He said I was frivolous, and it was his duty as man of the house not to indulge me in whims and fancies—as I think he called them. Aha, I thought, now you'll just have to be saved—and that's when I saw my chance.

MRS. LINDE: And your father never told Torvald the money wasn't from him?

NORA: No, never. Papa died right about then. I'd considered bringing him into my secret and begging him never to tell. But he was too sick at the time—and then, sadly, it didn't matter.

MRS. LINDE: And you've never confided in your husband since?

NORA: For heaven's sake, no! Are you serious? He's so strict on that subject. Besides—Torvald, with all his masculine pride—how painfully humiliating for him if he ever found out he was in debt to me. That would just ruin our relationship. Our beautiful, happy home would never be the same.

MRS. LINDE: Won't you ever tell him?

NORA: [*Thoughtfully.*] Yes—maybe sometime years from now, when I'm no longer so attractive. Don't laugh! I only mean when Torvald loves me less than now, when he stops enjoying my dancing and dressing up and reciting for him. Then it might be wise to have something in reserve—[*Breaking off.*] How ridiculous! That'll never happen—Well, Kristine, what do you think of my big secret? I'm capable of something too, hm? You can imagine, of course, how this thing hangs over me. It really hasn't been easy meeting the payments on time. In the business world there's what they call quarterly interest and what they call amortization, and these are always so terribly hard to manage. I've had to skimp a little here and there, wherever I could, you know. I could hardly spare anything from my house allowance, because Torvald has to live well. I couldn't let the children go poorly dressed; whatever I got for them, I felt I had to use up completely—the darlings!

MRS. LINDE: Poor Nora, so it had to come out of your own budget, then?

NORA: Yes, of course. But I was the one most responsible, too. Every time Torvald gave me money for new clothes and such, I never used more than half; always bought the simplest, cheapest outfits. It was a godsend that everything looks so well on me that Torvald never noticed. But it did weigh me down at times, Kristine. It *is* such a joy to wear fine things. You understand.

MRS. LINDE: Oh, of course.

NORA: And then I found other ways of making money. Last winter I was lucky enough to get a lot of copying to do. I locked myself in and sat writing every evening till late in the night. Ah, I was tired so often, dead tired. But still it was wonderful fun, sitting and working like that, earning money. It was almost like being a man.

MRS. LINDE: But how much have you paid off this way so far?

NORA: That's hard to say, exactly. These accounts, you know, aren't easy to figure. I only know that I've paid out all I could scrape together. Time and again I haven't known where to turn. [*Smiling.*] Then I'd sit here dreaming of a rich old gentleman who had fallen in love with me—

MRS. LINDE: What! Who is he?

NORA: Oh, really! And that he'd died, and when his will was opened, there in big letters it said, "All my fortune shall be paid over in cash, immediately, to that enchanting Mrs. Nora Helmer."

MRS. LINDE: But Nora dear—who *was* this gentleman?

NORA: Good grief, can't you understand? The old man never existed; that was only something I'd dream up time and again whenever I was at my wits' end for money. But it makes no difference now; the old fossil can go where he pleases for all I care; I don't need him or his will—because now I'm free. [*Jumping up.*] Oh, how lovely to think of that, Kristine! Carefree! To know you're carefree, utterly carefree; to be able to romp and play with the children, and to keep up a beautiful, charming home—everything just the way Torvald likes it! And think, spring is coming, with big blue skies. Maybe we can travel a little then. Maybe I'll see the ocean again. Oh yes, it *is* so marvelous to live and be happy!

[*The front doorbell rings.*]

MRS. LINDE: [*Rising.*] There's the bell. It's probably best that I go.
NORA: No, stay. No one's expected. It must be for Torvald.
MAID: [*From the hall doorway.*] Excuse me, ma'am—there's a gentleman here to see Mr. Helmer, but I didn't know—since the doctor's with him—
NORA: Who is the gentleman?
KROGSTAD: [*From the doorway.*] It's me, Mrs. Helmer.

[MRS. LINDE *starts and turns away toward the window.*]

NORA: [*Stepping toward him, tense, her voice a whisper.*] You? What is it? Why do you want to speak to my husband?
KROGSTAD: Bank business—after a fashion. I have a small job in the investment bank, and I hear now your husband is going to be our chief—
NORA: In other words, it's—
KROGSTAD: Just dry business, Mrs. Helmer. Nothing but that.
NORA: Yes, then please be good enough to step into the study. [*She nods indifferently as she sees him out by the hall door, then returns and begins stirring up the stove.*]
MRS. LINDE: Nora—who was that man?
NORA: That was a Mr. Krogstad—a lawyer.
MRS. LINDE: Then it really was him.
NORA: Do you know that person?
MRS. LINDE: I did once—many years ago. For a time he was a law clerk in our town.
NORA: Yes, he's been that.
MRS. LINDE: How he's changed.
NORA: I understand he had a very unhappy marriage.
MRS. LINDE: He's a widower now.
NORA: With a number of children. There now, it's burning. [*She closes the stove door and moves the rocker a bit to one side.*]
MRS. LINDE: They say he has a hand in all kinds of business.
NORA: Oh? That may be true; I wouldn't know. But let's not think about business. It's so dull.

[DR. RANK *enters from* HELMER'S *study.*]

RANK: [*Still in the doorway.*] No, no, really—I don't want to intrude, I'd just as soon talk a little while with your wife. [*Shuts the door, then notices* MRS. LINDE.] Oh, beg pardon. I'm intruding here too.
NORA: No, not at all. [*Introducing him.*] Dr. Rank, Mrs. Linde.
RANK: Well now, that's a name much heard in this house. I believe I passed the lady on the stairs as I came.
MRS. LINDE: Yes, I take the stairs very slowly. They're rather hard on me.
RANK: Uh-hm, some touch of internal weakness?
MRS. LINDE: More overexertion, I'd say.
RANK: Nothing else? Then you're probably here in town to rest up in a round of parties?
MRS. LINDE: I'm here to look for work.

RANK: Is that the best cure for overexertion?
MRS. LINDE: One has to live, Doctor.
RANK: Yes, there's a common prejudice to that effect.
NORA: Oh, come on, Dr. Rank—you really do want to live yourself.
RANK: Yes, I really do. Wretched as I am, I'll gladly prolong my torment indefinitely. All my patients feel like that. And it's quite the same, too, with the morally sick. Right at this moment there's one of those moral invalids in there with Helmer—
MRS. LINDE: [*Softly.*] Ah!
NORA: Who do you mean?
RANK: Oh, it's a lawyer, Krogstad, a type you wouldn't know. His character is rotten to the root—but even he began chattering all-importantly about how he had to *live*.
NORA: Oh? What did he want to talk to Torvald about?
RANK: I really don't know. I only heard something about the bank.
NORA: I didn't know that Krog—that this man Krogstad had anything to do with the bank.
RANK: Yes, he's gotten some kind of berth down there. [*To* MRS. LINDE.] I don't know if you also have, in your neck of the woods, a type of person who scuttles about breathlessly, sniffing out hints of moral corruption, and then maneuvers his victim into some sort of key position where he can keep an eye on him. It's the healthy these days that are out in the cold.
MRS. LINDE: All the same, it's the sick who most need to be taken in.
RANK: [*With a shrug.*] Yes, there we have it. That's the concept that's turning society into a sanatorium.

[NORA, *lost in her thoughts, breaks out into quiet laughter and claps her hands.*]

RANK: Why do you laugh at that? Do you have any real idea of what society is?
NORA: What do I care about dreary old society? I was laughing at something quite different—something terribly funny. Tell me, Doctor—is everyone who works in the bank dependent now on Torvald?
RANK: Is that what you find so terribly funny?
NORA: [*Smiling and humming.*] Never mind, never mind [*Pacing the floor.*] Yes, that's really immensely amusing: that we—that Torvald has so much power now over all those people. [*Taking the bag out of her pocket.*] Dr. Rank, a little macaroon on that?
RANK: See here, macaroons! I thought they were contraband here.
NORA: Yes, but these are some that Kristine gave me.
MRS. LINDE: What? I—?
NORA: Now, now, don't be afraid. You couldn't possibly know that Torvald had forbidden them. You see, he's worried they'll ruin my teeth. But hmp! Just this once! Isn't that so, Dr. Rank? Help yourself! [*Puts a macaroon in his mouth.*] And you too, Kristine. And I'll also have one, only a little one—or two, at the most. [*Walking about again.*] Now I'm really tremendously happy. Now there's just one last thing in the world that I have an enormous desire to do.
RANK: Well! And what's that?
NORA: It's something I have such a consuming desire to say so Torvald could hear.
RANK: And why can't you say it?

NORA: I don't dare. It's quite shocking.
MRS. LINDE: Shocking?
RANK: Well, then it isn't advisable. But in front of us you certainly can. What do you have such a desire to say so Torvald could hear?
NORA: I have such a huge desire to say—to hell and be damned!
RANK: Are you crazy?
MRS. LINDE: My goodness, Nora!
RANK: Go on, say it. Here he is.
NORA: [*Hiding the macaroon bag.*] Shh, shh, shh!

[HELMER *comes in from his study, hat in hand, overcoat over his arm.*]

NORA: [*Going toward him.*] Well, Torvald dear, are you through with him?
HELMER: Yes, he just left.
NORA: Let me introduce you—this is Kristine, who's arrived here in town.
HELMER: Kristine—? I'm sorry, but I don't know—
NORA: Mrs. Linde, Torvald dear. Mrs. Kristine Linde.
HELMER: Of course. A childhood friend of my wife's, no doubt?
MRS. LINDE: Yes, we knew each other in those days.
NORA: And just think, she made the long trip down here in order to talk with you.
HELMER: What's this?
MRS. LINDE: Well, not exactly—
NORA: You see, Kristine is remarkably clever in office work, and so she's terribly eager to come under a capable man's supervision and add more to what she already knows—
HELMER: Very wise, Mrs. Linde.
NORA: And then when she heard that you'd become a bank manager—the story was wired out to the papers—then she came in as fast as she could and— Really, Torvald, for my sake you can do a little something for Kristine, can't you?
HELMER: Yes, it's not at all impossible. Mrs. Linde, I suppose you're a widow?
MRS. LINDE: Yes.
HELMER: Any experience in office work?
MRS. LINDE: Yes, a good deal.
HELMER: Well, it's quite likely that I can make an opening for you—
NORA: [*Clapping her hands.*] You see, you see!
HELMER: You've come at a lucky moment, Mrs. Linde.
MRS. LINDE: Oh, how can I thank you?
HELMER: Not necessary. [*Putting his overcoat on.*] But today you'll have to excuse me—
RANK: Wait, I'll go with you. [*He fetches his coat from the hall and warms it at the stove.*]
NORA: Don't stay out long, dear.
HELMER: An hour; no more.
NORA: Are you going too, Kristine?
MRS. LINDE: [*Putting on her winter garments.*] Yes, I have to see about a room now.
HELMER: Then perhaps we can all walk together.
NORA: [*Helping her.*] What a shame we're so cramped here, but it's quite impossible for us to—

MRS. LINDE: Oh, don't even think of it! Good-bye, Nora dear, and thanks for everything.

NORA: Good-bye for now. Of course you'll be back this evening. And you too, Dr. Rank. What? If you're well enough? Oh, you've got to be! Wrap up tight now.

[*In a ripple of small talk the company moves out into the hall; children's voices are heard outside on the steps.*]

NORA: There they are! There they are! [*She runs to open the door. The children come in with their nurse,* ANNE-MARIE.] Come in, come in! [*Bends down and kisses them.*] Oh, you darlings—! Look at them, Kristine. Aren't they lovely!

RANK: No loitering in the draft here.

HELMER: Come, Mrs. Linde—this place is unbearable now for anyone but mothers.

[DR. RANK, HELMER, *and* MRS. LINDE *go down the stairs.* ANNE-MARIE *goes into the living room with the children.* NORA *follows, after closing the hall door.*]

NORA: How fresh and strong you look. Oh, such red cheeks you have! Like apples and roses. [*The children interrupt her throughout the following.*] And it was so much fun? That's wonderful. Really? You pulled both Emmy and Bob on the sled? Imagine, all together! Yes, you're a clever boy, Ivar. Oh, let me hold her a bit, Anne-Marie. My sweet little doll baby! [*Takes the smallest from the nurse and dances with her.*] Yes, yes, Mama will dance with Bob as well. What? Did you throw snowballs? Oh, if I'd only been there! No, don't bother, Anne-Marie— I'll undress them myself. Oh yes, let me. It's such fun. Go in and rest; you look half frozen. There's hot coffee waiting for you on the stove. [*The nurse goes into the room to the left.* NORA *takes the children's winter things off, throwing them about, while the children talk to her all at once.*] Is that so? A big dog chased you? But it didn't bite? No, dogs never bite little, lovely doll babies. Don't peek in the packages, Ivar! What is it? Yes, wouldn't you like to know. No, no, it's an ugly something. Well? Shall we play? What shall we play? Hide-and-seek? Yes, let's play hide-and-seek. Bob must hide first. I must? Yes, let me hide first. [*Laughing and shouting, she and the children play in and out of the living room and the adjoining room to the right. At last* NORA *hides under the table. The children come storming in, search, but cannot find her, then hear her muffled laughter, dash over to the table, lift the cloth up and find her. Wild shouting. She creeps forward as if to scare them. More shouts. Meanwhile, a knock at the hall door; no one has noticed it. Now the door half opens, and* KROGSTAD *appears. He waits a moment; the game goes on.*]

KROGSTAD: Beg pardon, Mrs. Helmer—

NORA: [*With a strangled cry, turning and scrambling to her knees.*] Oh! What do you want?

KROGSTAD: Excuse me. The outer door was ajar; it must be someone forgot to shut it—

NORA: [*Rising.*] My husband isn't home, Mr. Krogstad.

KROGSTAD: I know that.

NORA: Yes—then what do you want here?

KROGSTAD: A word with you.

NORA: With—? [*To the children, quietly.*] Go in to Anne-Marie. What? No, the strange man won't hurt Mama. When he's gone, we'll play some more. [*She leads the children into the room to the left and shuts the door after them. Then, tense and nervous:*] You want to speak to me?

KROGSTAD: Yes, I want to.

NORA: Today? But it's not yet the first of the month—

KROGSTAD: No, it's Christmas Eve. It's going to be up to you how merry a Christmas you have.

NORA: What is it you want? Today I absolutely can't—

KROGSTAD: We won't talk about that till later. This is something else. You do have a moment to spare, I suppose?

NORA: Oh yes, of course—I do, except—

KROGSTAD: Good. I was sitting over at Olsen's Restaurant when I saw your husband go down the street—

NORA: Yes?

KROGSTAD: With a lady.

NORA: Yes. So?

KROGSTAD: If you'll pardon my asking: wasn't that lady a Mrs. Linde?

NORA: Yes.

KROGSTAD: Just now come into town?

NORA: Yes, today.

KROGSTAD: She's a good friend of yours?

NORA: Yes, she is. But I don't see—

KROGSTAD: I also knew her once.

NORA: I'm aware of that.

KROGSTAD: Oh? You know all about it. I thought so. Well, then let me ask you short and sweet: is Mrs. Linde getting a job in the bank?

NORA: What makes you think you can cross-examine me, Mr. Krogstad—you, one of my husband's employees? But since you ask, you might as well know—yes, Mrs. Linde's going to be taken on at the bank. And I'm the one who spoke for her, Mr. Krogstad. Now you know.

KROGSTAD: So I guessed right.

NORA: [*Pacing up and down.*] Oh, one does have a tiny bit of influence, I should hope. Just because I am a woman, don't think it means that—When one has a subordinate position, Mr. Krogstad, one really ought to be careful about pushing somebody who—hm—

KROGSTAD: Who has influence?

NORA: That's right.

KROGSTAD: [*In a different tone.*] Mrs. Helmer, would you be good enough to use your influence on my behalf?

NORA: What? What do you mean?

KROGSTAD: Would you please make sure that I keep my subordinate position in the bank?

NORA: What does that mean? Who's thinking of taking away your position?

KROGSTAD: Oh, don't play the innocent with me. I'm quite aware that your friend would hardly relish the chance of running into me again; and I'm also aware now whom I can thank for being turned out.

NORA: But I promise you—

KROGSTAD: Yes, yes, yes, to the point: there's still time, and I'm advising you to use your influence to prevent it.

NORA: But Mr. Krogstad, I have absolutely no influence.
KROGSTAD: You haven't? I thought you were just saying—
NORA: You shouldn't take me so literally. I! How can you believe that I have any such influence over my husband?
KROGSTAD: Oh, I've known your husband from our student days. I don't think the great bank manager's more steadfast than any other married man.
NORA: You speak insolently about my husband, and I'll show you the door.
KROGSTAD: The lady has spirit.
NORA: I'm not afraid of you any longer. After New Year's, I'll soon be done with the whole business.
KROGSTAD: [*Restraining himself.*] Now listen to me, Mrs. Helmer. If necessary, I'll fight for my little job in the bank as if it were life itself.
NORA: Yes, so it seems.
KROGSTAD: It's not just a matter of income; that's the least of it. It's something else—All right, out with it! Look, this is the thing. You know, just like all the others, of course, that once, a good many years ago, I did something rather rash.
NORA: I've heard rumors to that effect.
KROGSTAD: The case never got into court; but all the same, every door was closed in my face from then on. So I took up those various activities you know about. I had to grab hold somewhere; and I dare say I haven't been among the worst. But now I want to drop all that. My boys are growing up. For their sakes, I'll have to win back as much respect as possible here in town. That job in the bank was like the first rung in my ladder. And now your husband wants to kick me right back down in the mud again.
NORA: But for heaven's sake, Mr. Krogstad, it's simply not in my power to help you.
KROGSTAD: That's because you haven't the will to—but I have the means to make you.
NORA: You certainly won't tell my husband that I owe you money?
KROGSTAD: Hm—what if I told him that?
NORA: That would be shameful of you. [*Nearly in tears.*] This secret—my joy and my pride—that he should learn it in such a crude and disgusting way—learn it from you. You'd expose me to the most horrible unpleasantness—
KROGSTAD: Only unpleasantness?
NORA: [*Vehemently.*] But go on and try. It'll turn out the worse for you, because then my husband will really see what a crook you are, and then you'll *never* be able to hold your job.
KROGSTAD: I asked if it was just domestic unpleasantness you were afraid of?
NORA: If my husband finds out, then of course he'll pay what I owe at once, and then we'd be through with you for good.
KROGSTAD: [*A step closer.*] Listen, Mrs. Helmer—you've either got a very bad memory, or else no head at all for business. I'd better put you a little more in touch with the facts.
NORA: What do you mean?
KROGSTAD: When your husband was sick, you came to me for a loan of four thousand, eight hundred crowns.
NORA: Where else could I go?
KROGSTAD: I promised to get you that sum—

NORA: And you got it.
KROGSTAD: I promised to get you that sum, on certain conditions. You were so involved in your husband's illness, and so eager to finance your trip, that I guess you didn't think out all the details. It might just be a good idea to remind you. I promised you the money on the strength of a note I drew up.
NORA: Yes, and that I signed.
KROGSTAD: Right. But at the bottom I added some lines for your father to guarantee the loan. He was supposed to sign down there.
NORA: Supposed to? He did sign.
KROGSTAD: I left the date blank. In other words, your father would have dated his signature himself. Do you remember that?
NORA: Yes, I think—
KROGSTAD: Then I gave you the note for you to mail to your father. Isn't that so?
NORA: Yes.
KROGSTAD: And naturally you sent it at once—because only some five, six days later you brought me the note, properly signed. And with that, the money was yours.
NORA: Well, then; I've made my payments regularly, haven't I?
KROGSTAD: More or less. But—getting back to the point—those were hard times for you then, Mrs. Helmer.
NORA: Yes, they were.
KROGSTAD: Your father was very ill, I believe.
NORA: He was near the end.
KROGSTAD: He died soon after?
NORA: Yes.
KROGSTAD: Tell me, Mrs. Helmer, do you happen to recall the date of your father's death? The day of the month, I mean.
NORA: Papa died the twenty-ninth of September.
KROGSTAD: That's quite correct; I've already looked into that. And now we come to a curious thing—[*Taking out a paper.*] which I simply cannot comprehend.
NORA: Curious thing? I don't know—
KROGSTAD: This is the curious thing: that your father co-signed the note for your loan three days after his death.
NORA: How—? I don't understand.
KROGSTAD: Your father died the twenty-ninth of September. But look. Here your father dated his signature October second. Isn't that curious, Mrs. Helmer? [NORA *is silent.*] Can you explain it to me? [NORA *remains silent.*] It's also remarkable that the words "October second" and the year aren't written in your father's hand, but rather in one that I think I know. Well, it's easy to understand. Your father forgot perhaps to date his signature, and then someone or other added it, a bit sloppily, before anyone knew of his death. There's nothing wrong in that. It all comes down to the signature. And there's no question about *that*, Mrs. Helmer. It really *was* your father who signed his own name here, wasn't it?
NORA: [*After a short silence, throwing her head back and looking squarely at him.*] No, it wasn't. *I* signed papa's name.
KROGSTAD: Wait, now—are you fully aware that this is a dangerous confession?

NORA: Why? You'll soon get your money.
KROGSTAD: Let me ask you a question—why didn't you send the paper to your father?
NORA: That was impossible. Papa was so sick. If I'd asked him for his signature, I also would have had to tell him what the money was for. But I couldn't tell him, sick as he was, that my husband's life was in danger. That was just impossible.
KROGSTAD: Then it would have been better if you'd given up the trip abroad.
NORA: I couldn't possibly. The trip was to save my husband's life. I couldn't give that up.
KROGSTAD: But didn't you ever consider that this was a fraud against me?
NORA: I couldn't let myself be bothered by that. You weren't any concern of mine. I couldn't stand you, with all those cold complications you made, even though you knew how badly off my husband was.
KROGSTAD: Mrs. Helmer, obviously you haven't the vaguest idea of what you've involved yourself in. But I can tell you this: it was nothing more and nothing worse that I once did—and it wrecked my whole reputation.
NORA: You? Do you expect me to believe that you ever acted bravely to save your wife's life?
KROGSTAD: Laws don't inquire into motives.
NORA: Then they must be very poor laws.
KROGSTAD: Poor or not—if I introduce this paper in court, you'll be judged according to law.
NORA: This I refuse to believe. A daughter hasn't a right to protect her dying father from anxiety and care? A wife hasn't a right to save her husband's life? I don't know much about laws, but I'm sure that somewhere in the books these things are allowed. And you don't know anything about it—you who practice the law? You must be an awful lawyer, Mr. Krogstad.
KROGSTAD: Could be. But business—the kind of business we two are mixed up in—don't you think I know about that? All right. Do what you want now. But I'm telling you *this*: if I get shoved down a second time, you're going to keep me company. [*He bows and goes out through the hall.*]
NORA: [*Pensive for a moment, then tossing her head.*] Oh, really! Trying to frighten me! I'm not so silly as all that. [*Begins gathering up the children's clothes, but soon stops.*] But—? No, but that's impossible! I did it out of love.
THE CHILDREN: [*In the doorway, left.*] Mama, that strange man's gone out the door.
NORA: Yes, yes, I know it. But don't tell anyone about the strange man. Do you hear? Not even Papa!
THE CHILDREN: No, Mama. But now will you play again?
NORA: No, not now.
THE CHILDREN: Oh, but Mama, you promised.
NORA: Yes, but I can't now. Go inside; I have too much to do. Go in, go in, my sweet darlings. [*She herds them gently back in the room and shuts the door after them. Settling on the sofa, she takes up a piece of embroidery and makes some stitches, but soon stops abruptly.*] No! [*Throws the work aside, rises, goes to the hall door and calls out.*] Helene! Let me have the tree in here. [*Goes to the table, left, opens the table drawer, and stops again.*] No, but that's utterly impossible!
MAID: [*With the Christmas tree.*] Where should I put it, ma'am?
NORA: There. The middle of the floor.

MAID: Should I bring anything else?
NORA: No, thanks. I have what I need.

[*The* MAID, *who has set the tree down, goes out.*]

NORA: [*Absorbed in trimming the tree.*] Candles here—and flowers here. That terrible creature! Talk, talk, talk! There's nothing to it at all. The tree's going to be lovely. I'll do anything to please you, Torvald. I'll sing for you, dance for you—

[HELMER *comes in from the hall, with a sheaf of papers under his arm.*]

NORA: Oh! You're back so soon?
HELMER: Yes. Has anyone been here?
NORA: Here? No.
HELMER: That's odd. I saw Krogstad leaving the front door.
NORA: So? Oh yes, that's true. Krogstad was here a moment.
HELMER: Nora, I can see by your face that he's been here, begging you to put in a good word for him.
NORA: Yes.
HELMER: And it was supposed to seem like your own idea? You were to hide it from me that he'd been here. He asked you that, too, didn't he?
NORA: Yes, Torvald, but—
HELMER: Nora, Nora, and you could fall for that? Talk with that sort of person and promise him anything? And then in the bargain, tell me an untruth.
NORA: An untruth—?
HELMER: Didn't you say that no one had been here? [*Wagging his finger.*] My little songbird must never do that again. A songbird needs a clean beak to warble with. No false notes. [*Putting his arm about her waist.*] That's the way it should be, isn't it? Yes, I'm sure of it. [*Releasing her.*] And so, enough of that. [*Sitting by the stove.*] Ah, how snug and cozy it is here. [*Leafing among his papers.*]
NORA: [*Busy with the tree, after a short pause.*] Torvald!
HELMER: Yes.
NORA: I'm so much looking forward to the Stenborgs' costume party, day after tomorrow.
HELMER: And I can't wait to see what you'll surprise me with.
NORA: Oh, that stupid business!
HELMER: What?
NORA: I can't find anything that's right. Everything seems so ridiculous, so inane.
HELMER: So my little Nora's come to *that* recognition?
NORA: [*Going behind his chair, her arms resting on its back.*] Are you very busy, Torvald?
HELMER: Oh—
NORA: What papers are those?
HELMER: Bank matters.
NORA: Already?
HELMER: I've gotten full authority from the retiring management to make all necessary changes in personnel and procedure. I'll need Christmas week for that. I want to have everything in order by New Year's.
NORA: So that was the reason this poor Krogstad—
HELMER: Hm.
NORA: [*Still leaning on the chair and slowly stroking the nape of his neck.*] If you weren't so very busy, I would have asked you an enormous favor, Torvald.

HELMER: Let's hear. What is it?
NORA: You know, there isn't anyone who has your good taste—and I want so much to look well at the costume party. Torvald, couldn't you take over and decide what I should be and plan my costume?
HELMER: Ah, is my stubborn little creature calling for a lifeguard?
NORA: Yes, Torvald, I can't get anywhere without your help.
HELMER: All right—I'll think it over. We'll hit on something.
NORA: Oh, how sweet of you. [*Goes to the tree again. Pause.*] Aren't the red flowers pretty—? But tell me, was it really such a crime that this Krogstad committed?
HELMER: Forgery. Do you have any idea what that means?
NORA: Couldn't he have done it out of need?
HELMER: Yes, or thoughtlessness, like so many others. I'm not so heartless that I'd condemn a man categorically for just one mistake.
NORA: No, of course not, Torvald!
HELMER: Plenty of men have redeemed themselves by openly confessing their crimes and taking their punishment.
NORA: Punishment—?
HELMER: But now Krogstad didn't go that way. He got himself out by sharp practices, and that's the real cause of his moral breakdown.
NORA: Do you really think that would—?
HELMER: Just imagine how a man with that sort of guilt in him has to lie and cheat and deceive on all sides, has to wear a mask even with the nearest and dearest he has, even with his own wife and children. And with the children, Nora—that's where it's most horrible.
NORA: Why?
HELMER: Because that kind of atmosphere of lies infects the whole life of a home. Every breath the children take in is filled with the germs of something degenerate.
NORA: [*Coming closer behind him.*] Are you sure of that?
HELMER: Oh, I've seen it often enough as a lawyer. Almost everyone who goes bad early in life has a mother who's a chronic liar.
NORA: Why just—the mother?
HELMER: It's usually the mother's influence that's dominant, but the father's works in the same way, of course. Every lawyer is quite familiar with it. And still this Krogstad's been going home year in, year out, poisoning his own children with lies and pretense; that's why I call him morally lost. [*Reaching his hands out toward her.*] So my sweet little Nora must promise me never to plead his cause. Your hand on it. Come, come, what's this? Give me your hand. There, now. All settled. I can tell you it'd be impossible for me to work alongside of him. I literally feel physically revolted when I'm anywhere near such a person.
NORA: [*Withdraws her hand and goes to the other side of the Christmas tree.*] How hot it is here! And I've got so much to do.
HELMER: [*Getting up and gathering his papers.*] Yes, and I have to think about getting some of these read through before dinner. I'll think about your costume, too. And something to hang on the tree in gilt paper, I may even see about that. [*Putting his hand on her head.*] Oh you, my darling little songbird. [*He goes into his study and closes the door after him.*]

NORA: [*Softly, after a silence.*] Oh, really! it isn't so. It's impossible. It must be impossible.
ANNE-MARIE: [*In the doorway, left.*] The children are begging so hard to come in to Mama.
NORA: No, no, no, don't let them in to me! You stay with them, Anne-Marie.
ANNE-MARIE: Of course, ma'am. [*Closes the door.*]
NORA: [*Pale with terror*]. Hurt my children—! Poison my home? [*A moment's pause; then she tosses her head.*] That's not true. Never. Never in all the world.

## ACT II

*Same room. Beside the piano the Christmas tree now stands stripped of ornament, burned-down candle stubs on its ragged branches.* NORA's *street clothes lie on the sofa.* NORA, *alone in the room, moves restlessly about; at last she stops at the sofa and picks up her coat.*

NORA: [*Dropping the coat again.*] Someone's coming! [*Goes toward the door, listens.*] No—there's no one. Of course—nobody's coming today, Christmas Day—or tomorrow, either. But maybe—[*Opens the door and looks out.*] No, nothing in the mailbox. Quite empty. [*Coming forward.*] What nonsense! He won't do anything serious. Nothing terrible could happen. It's impossible. Why, I have three small children.

   [ANNE-MARIE, *with a large carton, comes in from the room to the left.*]

ANNE-MARIE: Well, at last I found the box with the masquerade clothes.
NORA: Thanks. Put it on the table.
ANNE-MARIE: [*Does so.*] But they're all pretty much of a mess.
NORA: Ahh! I'd love to rip them in a million pieces!
ANNE-MARIE: Oh, mercy, they can be fixed right up. Just a little patience.
NORA: Yes, I'll go get Mrs. Linde to help me.
ANNE-MARIE: Out again now? In this nasty weather? Miss Nora will catch cold—get sick.
NORA: Oh, worse things could happen—How are the children?
ANNE-MARIE: The poor mites are playing with their Christmas presents, but—
NORA: Do they ask for me much?
ANNE-MARIE: They're so used to having Mama around, you know.
NORA: Yes, but Anne-Marie, I *can't* be together with them as much as I was.
ANNE-MARIE: Well, small children get used to anything.
NORA: You think so? Do you think they'd forget their mother if she was gone for good?
ANNE-MARIE: Oh, mercy—gone for good!
NORA: Wait, tell me, Anne-Marie—I've wondered so often—how could you ever have the heart to give your child over to strangers?
ANNE-MARIE: But I had to, you know, to become little Nora's nurse.
NORA: Yes, but how could you *do* it?
ANNE-MARIE: When I could get such a good place? A girl who's poor and who's gotten in trouble is glad enough for that. Because that slippery fish, he didn't do a thing for me, you know.
NORA: But your daughter's surely forgotten you.

ANNE-MARIE: Oh, she certainly has not. She's written to me, both when she was confirmed and when she was married.

NORA: [*Clasping her about the neck.*] You old Anne-Marie, you were a good mother for me when I was little.

ANNE-MARIE: Poor little Nora, with no other mother but me.

NORA: And if the babies didn't have one, then I know that you'd—What silly talk! [*Opening the carton.*] Go in to them. Now I'll have to—Tomorrow you can see how lovely I'll look.

ANNE-MARIE: Oh, there won't be anyone at the party as lovely as Miss Nora. [*She goes off into the room, left.*]

NORA: [*Begins unpacking the box, but soon throws it aside.*] Oh, if I dared to go out. If only nobody would come. If only nothing would happen here while I'm out. What craziness—nobody's coming. Just don't think. This muff—needs a brushing. Beautiful gloves, beautiful gloves. Let it go. Let it go! One, two, three, four, five, six—[*With a cry.*] Oh, there they are! [*Poises to move toward the door, but remains irresolutely standing.* MRS. LINDE *enters from the hall, where she has removed her street clothes.*]

NORA: Oh, it's you, Kristine. There's no one else out there? How good that you've come.

MRS. LINDE: I hear you were up asking for me.

NORA: Yes, I just stopped by. There's something you really can help me with. Let's get settled on the sofa. Look, there's going to be a costume party tomorrow evening at the Stenborgs' right above us, and now Torvald wants me to go as a Neapolitan peasant girl and dance the tarantella[2] that I learned in Capri.

MRS. LINDE: Really, are you giving a whole performance?

NORA: Torvald says yes, I should. See, here's the dress. Torvald had it made for me down there; but now it's all so tattered that I just don't know—

MRS. LINDE: Oh, we'll fix that up in no time. It's nothing more than the trimmings—they're a bit loose here and there. Needle and thread? Good, now we have what we need.

NORA: Oh, how sweet of you!

MRS. LINDE: [*Sewing.*] So you'll be in disguise tomorrow, Nora. You know what? I'll stop by then for a moment and have a look at you all dressed up. But listen, I've absolutely forgotten to thank you for that pleasant evening yesterday.

NORA: [*Getting up and walking about.*] I don't think it was as pleasant as usual yesterday. You should have come to town a bit sooner, Kristine—Yes, Torvald really knows how to give a home elegance and charm.

MRS. LINDE: And you do, too, if you ask me. You're not your father's daughter for nothing. But tell me, is Dr. Rank always so down in the mouth as yesterday?

NORA: No, that was quite an exception. But he goes around critically ill all the time—tuberculosis of the spine, poor man. You know, his father was a disgusting thing who kept mistresses and so on—and that's why the son's been sickly from birth.

---

2. Lively folk dance of southern Italy, thought to cure the bite of the tarantula.

MRS. LINDE: [*Lets her sewing fall to her lap.*] But my dearest Nora, how do you know about such things?
NORA: [*Walking more jauntily.*] Hmp! When you've had three children, then you've had a few visits from—from women who know something of medicine, and they tell you this and that.
MRS. LINDE: [*Resumes sewing; a short pause.*] Does Dr. Rank come here every day?
NORA: Every blessed day. He's Torvald's best friend from childhood, and *my* good friend, too. Dr. Rank almost belongs to this house.
MRS. LINDE: But tell me—is he quite sincere? I mean, doesn't he rather enjoy flattering people?
NORA: Just the opposite. Why do you think that?
MRS. LINDE: When you introduced us yesterday, he was proclaiming that he'd often heard my name in this house; but later I noticed that your husband hadn't the slightest idea who I really was. So how could Dr. Rank—?
NORA: But it's all true, Kristine. You see, Torvald loves me beyond words, and, as he puts it, he'd like to keep me all to himself. For a long time he'd almost be jealous if I even mentioned any of my old friends back home. So of course I dropped that. But with Dr. Rank I talk a lot about such things, because he likes hearing about them.
MRS. LINDE: Now listen, Nora; in many ways you're still like a child. I'm a good deal older than you, with a little more experience. I'll tell you something: you ought to put an end to all this with Dr. Rank.
NORA: What should I put an end to?
MRS. LINDE: Both parts of it, I think. Yesterday you said something about a rich admirer who'd provide you with money—
NORA: Yes, one who doesn't exist—worse luck. So?
MRS. LINDE: Is Dr. Rank well off?
NORA: Yes, he is.
MRS. LINDE: With no dependents?
NORA: No, no one. But—
MRS. LINDE: And he's over here every day?
NORA: Yes, I told you that.
MRS. LINDE: How can a man of such refinement be so grasping?
NORA: I don't follow you at all.
MRS. LINDE: Now don't try to hide it, Nora. You think I can't guess who loaned you the forty-eight hundred crowns?
NORA: Are you out of your mind? How could you think such a thing! A friend of ours, who comes here every single day. What an intolerable situation that would have been!
MRS. LINDE: Then it really wasn't him.
NORA: No, absolutely not. It never even crossed my mind for a moment—And he had nothing to lend in those days; his inheritance came later.
MRS. LINDE: Well, I think that was a stroke of luck for you, Nora dear.
NORA: No, it never would have occurred to me to ask Dr. Rank—Still, I'm quite sure that if I had asked him—
MRS. LINDE: Which you won't, of course.
NORA: No, of course not. I can't see that I'd ever need to. But I'm quite positive that if I talked to Dr. Rank—
MRS. LINDE: Behind your husband's back?

NORA: I've got to clear up this other thing; *that's* also behind his back. I've *got* to clear it all up.
MRS. LINDE: Yes, I was saying that yesterday, but—
NORA: [*Pacing up and down.*] A man handles these problems so much better than a woman—
MRS. LINDE: One's husband does, yes.
NORA: Nonsense. [*Stopping.*] When you pay everything you owe, then you get your note back, right?
MRS. LINDE: Yes, naturally.
NORA: And can rip it into a million pieces and burn it up—that filthy scrap of paper!
MRS. LINDE: [*Looking hard at her, laying her sewing aside, and rising slowly.*] Nora, you're hiding something from me.
NORA: You can see it in my face?
MRS. LINDE: Something's happened to you since yesterday morning. Nora, what is it?
NORA: [*Hurrying toward her.*] Kristine! [*Listening.*] Shh! Torvald's home. Look, go in with the children a while. Torvald can't bear all this snipping and stitching. Let Anne-Marie help you.
MRS. LINDE: [*Gathering up some of the things.*] All right, but I'm not leaving here until we've talked this out. [*She disappears into the room, left, as* TORVALD *enters from the hall.*]
NORA: Oh, how I've been waiting for you, Torvald dear.
HELMER: Was that the dressmaker?
NORA: No, that was Kristine. She's helping me fix up my costume. You know, it's going to be quite attractive.
HELMER: Yes, wasn't that a bright idea I had?
NORA: Brilliant! But then wasn't I good as well to give in to you?
HELMER: Good—because you give in to your husband's judgment? All right, you little goose, I know you didn't mean it like that. But I won't disturb you. You'll want to have a fitting, I suppose.
NORA: And you'll be working?
HELMER: Yes. [*Indicating a bundle of papers.*] See. I've been down to the bank. [*Starts toward his study.*]
NORA: Torvald.
HELMER: [*Stops.*] Yes.
NORA: If your little squirrel begged you, with all her heart and soul, for something—?
HELMER: What's that?
NORA: Then would you do it?
HELMER: First, naturally, I'd have to know what it was.
NORA: Your squirrel would scamper about and do tricks, if you'd only be sweet and give in.
HELMER: Out with it.
NORA: Your lark would be singing high and low in every room—
HELMER: Come on, she does that anyway.
NORA: I'd be a wood nymph and dance for you in the moonlight.
HELMER: Nora—don't tell me it's that same business from this morning?
NORA: [*Coming closer.*] Yes, Torvald, I beg you, please!

HELMER: And you actually have the nerve to drag that up again?
NORA: Yes, yes, you've got to give in to me; you *have* to let Krogstad keep his job in the bank.
HELMER: My dear Nora, I've slated his job for Mrs. Linde.
NORA: That's awfully kind of you. But you could just fire another clerk instead of Krogstad.
HELMER: This is the most incredible stubbornness! Because you go and give an impulsive promise to speak up for him, I'm expected to—
NORA: That's not the reason, Torvald. It's for your own sake. That man does writing for the worst papers; you said it yourself. He could do you any amount of harm. I'm scared to death of him—
HELMER: Ah, I understand. It's the old memories haunting you.
NORA: What do you mean by that?
HELMER: Of course, you're thinking about your father.
NORA: Yes, all right. Just remember how those nasty gossips wrote in the papers about Papa and slandered him so cruelly. I think they'd have had him dismissed if the department hadn't sent you up to investigate, and if you hadn't been so kind and open-minded toward him.
HELMER: My dear Nora, there's a notable difference between your father and me. Your father's official career was hardly above reproach. But mine is; and I hope it'll stay that way as long as I hold my position.
NORA: Oh, who can ever tell what vicious minds can invent? We could be so snug and happy now in our quiet, carefree home—you and I and the children, Torvald! That's why I'm pleading with you so—
HELMER: And just by pleading for him you make it impossible for me to keep him on. It's already known at the bank that I'm firing Krogstad. What if it's rumored around now that the new bank manager was vetoed by his wife—
NORA: Yes, what then—?
HELMER: Oh yes—as long as our little bundle of stubbornness gets her way—! I should go and make myself ridiculous in front of the whole office—give people the idea I can be swayed by all kinds of outside pressure. Oh, you can bet I'd feel the effects of that soon enough! Besides—there's something that rules Krogstad right out at the bank as long as I'm the manager.
NORA: What's that?
HELMER: His moral failings I could maybe overlook if I had to—
NORA: Yes, Torvald, why not?
HELMER: And I hear he's quite efficient on the job. But he was a crony of mine back in my teens—one of those rash friendships that crop up again and again to embarrass you later in life. Well, I might as well say it straight out: we're on a first-name basis. And that tactless fool makes no effort at all to hide it in front of others. Quite the contrary—he thinks that entitles him to take a familiar air around me, and so every other second he comes booming out with his "Yes, Torvald!" and "Sure thing, Torvald!" I tell you, it's been excruciating for me. He's out to make my place in the bank unbearable.
NORA: Torvald, you can't be serious about all this.
HELMER: Oh no? Why not?
NORA: Because these are such petty considerations.
HELMER: What are you saying? Petty? You think I'm petty!
NORA: No, just the opposite, Torvald dear. That's exactly why—

HELMER: Never mind. You call my motives petty; then I might as well be just that. Petty! All right! We'll put a stop to this for good. [*Goes to the hall door and calls.*] Helene!

NORA: What do you want?

HELMER: [*Searching among his papers.*] A decision. [*The* MAID *comes in.*] Look here; take this letter; go out with it at once. Get hold of a messenger and have him deliver it. Quick now. It's already addressed. Wait, here's some money.

MAID: Yes, sir. [*She leaves with the letter.*]

HELMER: [*Straightening his papers.*] There, now, little Miss Willful.

NORA: [*Breathlessly.*] Torvald, what was that letter?

HELMER: Krogstad's notice.

NORA: Call it back, Torvald! There's still time. Oh, Torvald, call it back! Do it for my sake—for your sake, for the children's sake! Do you hear, Torvald; do it! You don't know how this can harm us.

HELMER: Too late.

NORA: Yes, too late.

HELMER: Nora dear, I can forgive you this panic, even though basically you're insulting me. Yes, you are! Or isn't it an insult to think that *I* should be afraid of a courtroom hack's revenge? But I forgive you anyway, because this shows so beautifully how much you love me. [*Takes her in his arms.*] This is the way it should be, my darling Nora. Whatever comes, you'll see: when it really counts, I have strength and courage enough as a man to take on the whole weight myself.

NORA: [*Terrified.*] What do you mean by that?

HELMER: The whole weight, I said.

NORA: [*Resolutely.*] No, never in all the world.

HELMER: Good. So we'll share it, Nora, as man and wife. That's as it should be. [*Fondling her.*] Are you happy now? There, there, there—not these frightened dove's eyes. It's nothing at all but empty fantasies—Now you should run through your tarantella and practice your tambourine. I'll go to the inner office and shut both doors, so I won't hear a thing; you can make all the noise you like. [*Turning in the doorway.*] And when Rank comes, just tell him where he can find me. [*He nods to her and goes with his papers into the study, closing the door.*]

NORA: [*Standing as though rooted, dazed with fright, in a whisper.*] He really could do it. He will do it. He'll do it in spite of everything. No, not that, never, never! Anything but that! Escape! A way out—[*The doorbell rings.*] Dr. Rank! Anything but that! *Anything*, whatever it is! [*Her hands pass over her face, smoothing it; she pulls herself together, goes over and opens the hall door.* DR. RANK *stands outside, hanging his fur coat up. During the following scene, it begins getting dark.*]

NORA: Hello, Dr. Rank. I recognized your ring. But you mustn't go in to Torvald yet; I believe he's working.

RANK: And you?

NORA: For you, I always have an hour to spare—you know that. [*He has entered, and she shuts the door after him.*]

RANK: Many thanks. I'll make use of these hours while I can.

NORA: What do you mean by that? While you can?

RANK: Does that disturb you?

NORA: Well, it's such an odd phrase. Is anything going to happen?

RANK: What's going to happen is what I've been expecting so long—but I honestly didn't think it would come so soon.

NORA: [*Gripping his arm.*] What is it you've found out? Dr. Rank, you have to tell me!

RANK: [*Sitting by the stove.*] It's all over with me. There's nothing to be done about it.

NORA: [*Breathing easier.*] Is it you—then—?

RANK: Who else? There's no point in lying to one's self. I'm the most miserable of all my patients, Mrs. Helmer. These past few days I've been auditing my internal accounts. Bankrupt! Within a month I'll probably be laid out and rotting in the churchyard.

NORA: Oh, what a horrible thing to say.

RANK: The thing itself is horrible. But the worst of it is all the other horror before it's over. There's only one final examination left; when I'm finished with that, I'll know about when my disintegration will begin. There's something I want to say. Helmer with his sensitivity has such a sharp distaste for anything ugly. I don't want him near my sickroom.

NORA: Oh, but Dr. Rank—

RANK: I won't have him in there. Under no condition. I'll lock my door to him—As soon as I'm completely sure of the worst, I'll send you my calling card marked with a black cross, and you'll know then the wreck has started to come apart.

NORA: No, today you're completely unreasonable. And I wanted you so much to be in a really good humor.

RANK: With death up my sleeve? And then to suffer this way for somebody else's sins. Is there any justice in that? And in every single family, in some way or another, this inevitable retribution of nature goes on—

NORA: [*Her hands pressed over her ears.*] Oh, stuff! Cheer up! Please—be gay!

RANK: Yes, I'd just as soon laugh at it all. My poor, innocent spine, serving time for my father's gay army days.

NORA: [*By the table, left.*] He was so infatuated with asparagus tips and *pâté de foie gras*, wasn't that it?

RANK: Yes—and with truffles.

NORA: Truffles, yes. And then with oysters, I suppose?

RANK: Yes, tons of oysters, naturally.

NORA: And then the port and champagne to go with it. It's so sad that all these delectable things have to strike at our bones.

RANK: Especially when they strike at the unhappy bones that never shared in the fun.

NORA: Ah, that's the saddest of all.

RANK: [*Looks searchingly at her.*] Hm.

NORA: [*After a moment.*] Why did you smile?

RANK: No, it was you who laughed.

NORA: No, it was you who smiled, Dr. Rank!

RANK: [*Getting up.*] You're even a bigger tease than I'd thought.

NORA: I'm full of wild ideas today.

RANK: That's obvious.

NORA: [*Putting both hands on his shoulders.*] Dear, dear Dr. Rank, you'll never die for Torvald and me.

RANK: Oh, that loss you'll easily get over. Those who go away are soon forgotten.
NORA: [*Looks fearfully at him.*] You believe that?
RANK: One makes new connections, and then—
NORA: Who makes new connections?
RANK: Both you and Torvald will when I'm gone. I'd say you're well under way already. What was that Mrs. Linde doing here last evening?
NORA: Oh, come—you can't be jealous of poor Kristine?
RANK: Oh yes, I am. She'll be my successor here in the house. When I'm down under, that woman will probably—
NORA: Shh! Not so loud. She's right in there.
RANK: Today as well. So you see.
NORA: Only to sew on my dress. Good gracious, how unreasonable you are. [*Sitting on the sofa.*] Be nice now, Dr. Rank. Tomorrow you'll see how beautifully I'll dance; and you can imagine then that I'm dancing only for you—yes, and of course for Torvald, too—that's understood. [*Takes various items out of the carton.*] Dr. Rank, sit over here and I'll show you something.
RANK: [*Sitting.*] What's that?
NORA: Look here. Look.
RANK: Silk stockings.
NORA: Flesh-colored. Aren't they lovely? Now it's so dark here, but tomorrow— No, no, no, just look at the feet. Oh well, you might as well look at the rest.
RANK: Hm—
NORA: Why do you look so critical? Don't you believe they'll fit?
RANK: I've never had any chance to form an opinion on that.
NORA: [*Glancing at him a moment.*] Shame on you. [*Hits him lightly on the ear with the stockings.*] That's for you. [*Puts them away again.*]
RANK: And what other splendors am I going to see now?
NORA: Not the least bit more, because you've been naughty. [*She hums a little and rummages among her things.*]
RANK: [*After a short silence.*] When I sit here together with you like this, completely easy and open, then I don't know—I simply can't imagine—whatever would have become of me if I'd never come into this house.
NORA: [*Smiling.*] Yes, I really think you feel completely at ease with us.
RANK: [*More quietly, staring straight ahead.*] And then to have to go away from it all—
NORA: Nonsense, you're not going away.
RANK: [*His voice unchanged.*]—and not even be able to leave some poor show of gratitude behind, scarcely a fleeting regret—no more than a vacant place that anyone can fill.
NORA: And if I asked you now for—? No—
RANK: For what?
NORA: For a great proof of your friendship—
RANK: Yes, yes?
NORA: No, I mean—for an exceptionally big favor—
RANK: Would you really, for once, make me so happy?
NORA: Oh, you haven't the vaguest idea what it is.
RANK: All right, then tell me.
NORA: No, but I can't, Dr. Rank—it's all out of reason. It's advice and help, too—and a favor—

RANK: So much the better. I can't fathom what you're hinting at. Just speak out. Don't you trust me?

NORA: Of course. More than anyone else. You're my best and truest friend, I'm sure. That's why I want to talk to you. All right, then, Dr. Rank: there's something you can help me prevent. You know how deeply, how inexpressibly dearly Torvald loves me; he'd never hesitate a second to give up his life for me.

RANK: [*Leaning close to her.*] Nora—do you think he's the only one—

NORA: [*With a slight start.*] Who—?

RANK: Who'd gladly give up his life for you.

NORA: [*Heavily.*] I see.

RANK: I swore to myself you should know this before I'm gone. I'll never find a better chance. Yes, Nora, now you know. And also you know now that you can trust me beyond anyone else.

NORA: [*Rising, natural and calm.*] Let me by.

RANK: [*Making room for her, but still sitting.*] Nora—

NORA: [*In the hall doorway.*] Helene, bring the lamp in. [*Goes over to the stove.*] Ah, dear Dr. Rank, that was really mean of you.

RANK: [*Getting up.*] That I've loved you just as deeply as somebody else? Was *that* mean?

NORA: No, but that you came out and told me. That was quite unnecessary—

RANK: What do you mean? Have you known—?

[*The* MAID *comes in with the lamp, sets it on the table, and goes out again.*]

RANK: Nora—Mrs. Helmer—I'm asking you: have you known about it?

NORA: Oh, how can I tell what I know or don't know? Really, I don't know what to say—Why did you have to be so clumsy, Dr. Rank! Everything was so good.

RANK: Well, in any case, you now have the knowledge that my body and soul are at your command. So won't you speak out?

NORA: [*Looking at him.*] After that?

RANK: Please, just let me know what it is.

NORA: You can't know anything now.

RANK: I have to. You mustn't punish me like this. Give me the chance to do whatever is humanly possible for you.

NORA: Now there's nothing you can do for me. Besides, actually, I don't need any help. You'll see—it's only my fantasies. That's what it is. Of course! [*Sits in the rocker, looks at him, and smiles.*] What a nice one you are, Dr. Rank. Aren't you a little bit ashamed, now that the lamp is here?

RANK: No, not exactly. But perhaps I'd better go—for good?

NORA: No, you certainly can't do that. You must come here just as you always have. You know Torvald can't do without you.

RANK: Yes, but *you*?

NORA: You know how much I enjoy it when you're here.

RANK: That's precisely what threw me off. You're a mystery to me. So many times I've felt you'd almost rather be with me than with Helmer.

NORA: Yes—you see, there are some people that one loves most and other people that one would almost prefer being with.

RANK: Yes, there's something to that.

NORA: When I was back home, of course I loved Papa most. But I always thought

it was so much fun when I could sneak down to the maids' quarters, because they never tried to improve me, and it was always so amusing, the way they talked to each other.
RANK: Aha, so it's *their* place that I've filled.
NORA: [*Jumping up and going to him.*] Oh, dear, sweet Dr. Rank, that's not what I meant at all. But you can understand that with Torvald it's just the same as with Papa—

[*The* MAID *enters from the hall.*]

MAID: Ma'am—please! [*She whispers to* NORA *and hands her a calling card.*]
NORA: Ah [*Glancing at the card.*]! [*Slips it into her pocket.*]
RANK: Anything wrong?
NORA: No, no, not at all. It's only some—it's my new dress—
RANK: Really? But—there's your dress.
NORA: Oh, that. But this is another one—I ordered it—Torvald mustn't know—
RANK: Ah, now we have the big secret.
NORA: That's right. Just go in with him—he's back in the inner study. Keep him there as long as—
RANK: Don't worry. He won't get away. [*Goes into the study.*]
NORA: [*To the* MAID.] And he's standing waiting in the kitchen?
MAID: Yes, he came up by the back stairs.
NORA: But didn't you tell him somebody was here?
MAID: Yes, but that didn't do any good.
NORA: He won't leave?
MAID: No, he won't go till he's talked with you, ma'am.
NORA: Let him come in, then—but quietly. Helene, don't breathe a word about this. It's a surprise for my husband.
MAID: Yes, yes, I understand—[*Goes out.*]
NORA: This horror—it's going to happen. No, no, no, it can't happen, it mustn't.

[*She goes and bolts* HELMER's *door. The* MAID *opens the hall door for* KROGSTAD *and shuts it behind him. He is dressed for travel in a fur coat, boots, and a fur cap.*]

NORA: [*Going toward him.*] Talk softly. My husband's home.
KROGSTAD: Well, good for him.
NORA: What do you want?
KROGSTAD: Some information.
NORA: Hurry up, then. What is it?
KROGSTAD: You know, of course, that I got my notice.
NORA: I couldn't prevent it, Mr. Krogstad. I fought for you to the bitter end, but nothing worked.
KROGSTAD: Does your husband's love for you run so thin? He knows everything I can expose you to, and all the same he dares to—
NORA: How can you imagine he knows anything about this?
KROGSTAD: Ah, no—I can't imagine it either, now. It's not at all like my fine Torvald Helmer to have so much guts—
NORA: Mr. Krogstad, I demand respect for my husband!
KROGSTAD: Why, of course—all due respect. But since the lady's keeping it so carefully hidden, may I presume to ask if you've also a bit better informed than yesterday about what you've actually done?

NORA: More than you ever could teach me.
KROGSTAD: Yes, I *am* such an awful lawyer.
NORA: What is it you want from me?
KROGSTAD: Just a glimpse of how you are, Mrs. Helmer. I've been thinking about you all day long. A cashier, a night-court scribbler, a—well, a type like me also has a little of what they call a heart, you know.
NORA: Then show it. Think of my children.
KROGSTAD: Did you or your husband ever think of mine? But never mind. I simply wanted to tell you that you don't need to take this thing too seriously. For the present, I'm not proceeding with any action.
NORA: Oh no, really! Well—I knew that.
KROGSTAD: Everything can be settled in a friendly spirit. It doesn't have to get around town at all; it can stay just among us three.
NORA: My husband must never know anything of this.
KROGSTAD: How can you manage that? Perhaps you can pay me the balance?
NORA: No, not right now.
KROGSTAD: Or you know some way of raising the money in a day or two?
NORA: No way that I'm willing to use.
KROGSTAD: Well, it wouldn't have done you any good, anyway. If you stood in front of me with a fistful of bills, you still couldn't buy your signature back.
NORA: Then tell me what you're going to do with it.
KROGSTAD: I'll just hold onto it—keep it on file. There's no outsider who'll even get wind of it. So if you've been thinking of taking some desperate step—
NORA: I have.
KROGSTAD: Been thinking of running away from home—
NORA: I have!
KROGSTAD: Or even of something worse—
NORA: How could you guess that?
KROGSTAD: You can drop those thoughts.
NORA: How could you guess I was thinking of *that*?
KROGSTAD: Most of us think about *that* at first. I thought about it too, but I discovered I hadn't the courage—
NORA: [*Lifelessly.*] I don't either.
KROGSTAD: [*Relieved.*] That's true, you haven't the courage? You too?
NORA: I don't have it—I don't have it.
KROGSTAD: It would be terribly stupid, anyway. After that first storm at home blows out, why, then—I have here in my pocket a letter for your husband—
NORA: Telling everything?
KROGSTAD: As charitably as possible.
NORA: [*Quickly.*] He mustn't ever get that letter. Tear it up. I'll find some way to get money.
KROGSTAD: Beg pardon, Mrs. Helmer, but I think I just told you—
NORA: Oh, I don't mean the money I owe you. Let me know how much you want from my husband, and I'll manage it.
KROGSTAD: I don't want any money from your husband.
NORA: What do you want, then?
KROGSTAD: I'll tell you what. I want to recoup, Mrs. Helmer; I want to get on in the world—and there's where your husband can help me. For a year and a half I've kept myself clean of anything disreputable—all that time struggling with

the worst conditions; but I was satisfied, working my way up step by step. Now I've been written right off, and I'm just not in the mood to come crawling back. I tell you, I want to move on. I want to get back in the bank—in a better position. Your husband can set up a job for me—

NORA: He'll never do that!

KROGSTAD: He'll do it. I know him. He won't dare breathe a word of protest. And once I'm in there together with him, you just wait and see! Inside of a year, I'll be the manager's right-hand man. It'll be Nils Krogstad, not Torvald Helmer, who runs the bank.

NORA: You'll never see the day!

KROGSTAD: Maybe you think you can—

NORA: I have the courage now—for *that*.

KROGSTAD: Oh, you don't scare me. A smart, spoiled lady like you—

NORA: You'll see; you'll see!

KROGSTAD: Under the ice, maybe? Down in the freezing, coal-black water? There, till you float up in the spring, ugly, unrecognizable, with your hair falling out—

NORA: You don't frighten me.

KROGSTAD: Nor do you frighten me. One doesn't do these things, Mrs. Helmer. Besides, what good would it be? I'd still have him safe in my pocket.

NORA: Afterwards? When I'm no longer—?

KROGSTAD: Are you forgetting that *I'll* be in control then over your final reputation? [NORA *stands speechless, staring at him.*] Good; now I've warned you. Don't do anything stupid. When Helmer's read my letter, I'll be waiting for his reply. And bear in mind that it's your husband himself who's forced me back to my old ways. I'll never forgive him for that. Good-bye, Mrs. Helmer. [*He goes out through the hall.*]

NORA: [*Goes to the hall door, opens it a crack, and listens.*] He's gone. Didn't leave the letter. Oh no, no, that's impossible too! [*Opening the door more and more.*] What's that? He's standing outside—not going downstairs. He's thinking it over? Maybe he'll—? [*A letter falls in the mailbox; then* KROGSTAD's *footsteps are heard, dying away down a flight of stairs.* NORA *gives a muffled cry and runs over toward the sofa table. A short pause.*] In the mailbox. [*Slips warily over to the hall door.*] It's lying there. Torvald, Torvald—now we're lost!

MRS. LINDE: [*Entering with the costume from the room, left.*] There now, I can't see anything else to mend. Perhaps you'd like to try—

NORA: [*In a hoarse whisper.*] Kristine, come here.

MRS. LINDE: [*Tossing the dress on the sofa.*] What's wrong? You look upset.

NORA: Come here. See that letter? *There!* Look—through the glass in the mailbox.

MRS. LINDE: Yes, yes, I see it.

NORA: That letter's from Krogstad—

MRS. LINDE: Nora—it's Krogstad who loaned you the money!

NORA: Yes, and now Torvald will find out everything.

MRS. LINDE: Believe me, Nora, it's best for both of you.

NORA: There's more you don't know. I forged a name.

MRS. LINDE: But for heaven's sake—?

NORA: I only want to tell you that, Kristine, so that you can be my witness.

MRS. LINDE: Witness? Why should I—?

NORA: If I should go out of my mind—it could easily happen—

MRS. LINDE: Nora!

NORA: Or anything else occurred—so I couldn't be present here—
MRS. LINDE: Nora, Nora, you aren't yourself at all!
NORA: And someone should try to take on the whole weight, all of the guilt, you follow me—
MRS. LINDE: Yes, of course, but why do you think—?
NORA: Then you're the witness that it isn't true, Kristine. I'm very much myself; my mind right now is perfectly clear; and I'm telling you: nobody else has known about this; I alone did everything. Remember that.
MRS. LINDE: I will. But I don't understand all this.
NORA: Oh, how could you ever understand it? It's the miracle now that's going to take place.
MRS. LINDE: The miracle?
NORA: Yes, the miracle. But it's so awful, Kristine. It mustn't take place, not for anything in the world.
MRS. LINDE: I'm going right over and talk with Krogstad.
NORA: Don't go near him; he'll do you some terrible harm!
MRS. LINDE: There was a time once when he'd gladly have done anything for me.
NORA: He?
MRS. LINDE: Where does he live?
NORA: Oh, how do I know? Yes. [*Searches in her pocket.*] Here's his card. But the letter, the letter—!
HELMER: [*From the study, knocking on the door.*] Nora!
NORA: [*With a cry of fear.*] Oh! What is it? What do you want?
HELMER: Now, now, don't be so frightened. We're not coming in. You locked the door—are you trying on the dress?
NORA: Yes, I'm trying it. I'll look just beautiful, Torvald.
MRS. LINDE: [*Who has read the card.*] He's living right around the corner.
NORA: Yes, but what's the use? We're lost. The letter's in the box.
MRS. LINDE: And your husband has the key?
NORA: Yes, always.
MRS. LINDE: Krogstad can ask for his letter back unread; he can find some excuse—
NORA: But it's just this time that Torvald usually—
MRS. LINDE: Stall him. Keep him in there. I'll be back as quick as I can. [*She hurries out through the hall entrance.*]
NORA: [*Goes to* HELMER's *door, opens it, and peers in.*] Torvald!
HELMER: [*From the inner study.*] Well—does one dare set foot in one's own living room at last? Come on, Rank, now we'll get a look—[*In the doorway.*] But what's this?
NORA: What, Torvald dear?
HELMER: Rank had me expecting some grand masquerade.
RANK: [*In the doorway.*] That was my impression, but I must have been wrong.
NORA: No one can admire me in my splendor—not till tomorrow.
HELMER: But Nora dear, you look so exhausted. Have you practiced too hard?
NORA: No, I haven't practiced at all yet.
HELMER: You know, it's necessary—
NORA: Oh, it's absolutely necessary, Torvald. But I can't get anywhere without your help. I've forgotten the whole thing completely.
HELMER: Ah, we'll soon take care of that.
NORA: Yes, take care of me, Torvald, please! Promise me that? Oh, I'm so nervous.

That big party—You must give up everything this evening for me. No business—don't even touch your pen. Yes? Dear Torvald, promise?

HELMER: It's a promise. Tonight I'm totally at your service—you little helpless thing. Hm—but first there's one thing I want to—[*Goes toward the hall door.*]

NORA: What are you looking for?

HELMER: Just to see if there's any mail.

NORA: No, no, don't do that, Torvald!

HELMER: Now what?

NORA: Torvald, please. There isn't any.

HELMER: Let me look, though. [*Starts out.* NORA, *at the piano, strikes the first notes of the tarantella.* HELMER, *at the door, stops.*] Aha!

NORA: I can't dance tomorrow if I don't practice with you.

HELMER: [*Going over to her.*] Nora dear, are you really so frightened?

NORA: Yes, so terribly frightened. Let me practice right now; there's still time before dinner. Oh, sit down and play for me, Torvald. Direct me. Teach me, the way you always have.

HELMER: Gladly, if it's what you want. [*Sits at the piano.*]

NORA: [*Snatches the tambourine up from the box, then a long, varicolored shawl, which she throws around herself, whereupon she springs forward and cries out:*] Play for me now! Now I'll dance!

[HELMER *plays and* NORA *dances.* RANK *stands behind* HELMER *at the piano and looks on.*]

HELMER: [*As he plays.*] Slower. Slow down.

NORA: Can't change it.

HELMER: Not so violent, Nora!

NORA: Has to be just like this.

HELMER: [*Stopping.*] No, no, that won't do at all.

NORA: [*Laughing and swinging her tambourine.*] Isn't that what I told you?

RANK: Let me play for her.

HELMER: [*Getting up.*] Yes, go on. I can teach her more easily then.

[RANK *sits at the piano and plays;* NORA *dances more and more wildly.* HELMER *has stationed himself by the stove and repeatedly gives her directions; she seems not to hear them; her hair loosens and falls over her shoulders; she does not notice, but goes on dancing.* MRS. LINDE *enters.*]

MRS. LINDE: [*Standing dumbfounded at the door.*] Ah—!

NORA: [*Still dancing.*] See what fun, Kristine!

HELMER: But Nora darling, you dance as if your life were at stake.

NORA: And it is.

HELMER: Rank, stop! This is pure madness. Stop it, I say!

[RANK *breaks off playing, and* NORA *halts abruptly.*]

HELMER: [*Going over to her.*] I never would have believed it. You've forgotten everything I taught you.

NORA: [*Throwing away the tambourine.*] You see for yourself.

HELMER: Well, there's certainly room for instruction here.

NORA: Yes, you see how important it is. You've got to teach me to the very last minute. Promise me that, Torvald?

HELMER: You can bet on it.

NORA: You mustn't, either today or tomorrow, think about anything else but me; you mustn't open any letters—or the mailbox—
HELMER: Ah, it's still the fear of that man—
NORA: Oh yes, yes, that too.
HELMER: Nora, it's written all over you—there's already a letter from him out there.
NORA: I don't know. I guess so. But you mustn't read such things now; there mustn't be anything ugly between us before it's all over.
RANK: [*Quietly to* HELMER.] You shouldn't deny her.
HELMER: [*Putting his arm around her.*] The child can have her way. But tomorrow night, after you've danced—
NORA: Then you'll be free.
MAID: [*In the doorway, right.*] Ma'am, dinner is served.
NORA: We'll be wanting champagne, Helene.
MAID: Very good, ma'am. [*Goes out.*]
HELMER: So—a regular banquet, hm?
NORA: Yes, a banquet—champagne till daybreak! [*Calling out.*] And some macaroons, Helene. Heaps of them—just this once.
HELMER: [*Taking her hands.*] Now, now, now—no hysterics. Be my own little lark again.
NORA: Oh, I will soon enough. But go on in—and you, Dr. Rank. Kristine, help me put up my hair.
RANK: [*Whispering, as they go.*] There's nothing wrong—really wrong, is there?
HELMER: Oh, of course not. It's nothing more than this childish anxiety I was telling you about. [*They go out, right.*]
NORA: Well?
MRS. LINDE: Left town.
NORA: I could see by your face.
MRS. LINDE: He'll be home tomorrow evening. I wrote him a note.
NORA: You shouldn't have. Don't try to stop anything now. After all, it's a wonderful joy, this waiting here for the miracle.
MRS. LINDE: What is it you're waiting for?
NORA: Oh, you can't understand that. Go in to them; I'll be along in a moment.

[MRS. LINDE *goes into the dining room.* NORA *stands a short while as if composing herself; then she looks at her watch.*]

NORA: Five. Seven hours to midnight. Twenty-four hours to the midnight after, and then the tarantella's done. Seven and twenty-four? Thirty-one hours to live.
HELMER: [*In the doorway, right.*] What's become of the little lark?
NORA: [*Going toward him with open arms.*] Here's your lark!

# ACT III

*Same scene. The table, with chairs around it, has been moved to the center of the room. A lamp on the table is lit. The hall door stands open. Dance music drifts down from the floor above.* MRS. LINDE *sits at the table, absently paging through a book, trying to read, but apparently unable to focus her thoughts. Once or twice she pauses, tensely listening for a sound at the outer entrance.*

MRS. LINDE: [*Glancing at her watch.*] Not yet—and there's hardly any time left. If only he's not—[*Listening again.*] Ah, there he is. [*She goes out in the hall and cautiously opens the outer door. Quiet footsteps are heard on the stairs. She whispers:*] Come in. Nobody's here.

KROGSTAD: [*In the doorway.*] I found a note from you at home. What's back of all this?

MRS. LINDE: I just *had* to talk to you.

KROGSTAD: Oh? And it just *had* to be here in this house?

MRS. LINDE: At my place it was impossible; my room hasn't a private entrance. Come in; we're all alone. The maid's asleep, and the Helmers are at the dance upstairs.

KROGSTAD: [*Entering the room.*] Well, well, the Helmers are dancing tonight? Really?

MRS. LINDE: Yes, why not?

KROGSTAD: How true—why not?

MRS. LINDE: All right, Krogstad, let's talk.

KROGSTAD: Do we two have anything more to talk about?

MRS. LINDE: We have a great deal to talk about.

KROGSTAD: I wouldn't have thought so.

MRS. LINDE: No, because you've never understood me, really.

KROGSTAD: Was there anything more to understand—except what's all too common in life? A calculating woman throws over a man the moment a better catch comes by.

MRS. LINDE: You think I'm so thoroughly calculating? You think I broke it off lightly?

KROGSTAD: Didn't you?

MRS. LINDE: Nils—is that what you really thought?

KROGSTAD: If you cared, then why did you write me the way you did?

MRS. LINDE: What else could I do? If I had to break off with you, then it was my job as well to root out everything you felt for me.

KROGSTAD: [*Wringing his hands.*] So that was it. And this—all this, simply for money!

MRS. LINDE: Don't forget I had a helpless mother and two small brothers. We couldn't wait for you, Nils; you had such a long road ahead of you then.

KROGSTAD: That may be; but you still hadn't the right to abandon me for somebody else's sake.

MRS. LINDE: Yes—I don't know. So many, many times I've asked myself if I did have that right.

KROGSTAD: [*More softly.*] When I lost you, it was as if all the solid ground dissolved from under my feet. Look at me; I'm a half-drowned man now, hanging onto a wreck.

MRS. LINDE: Help may be near.

KROGSTAD: It was near—but then you came and blocked it off.

MRS. LINDE: Without my knowing it, Nils. Today for the first time I learned that it's you I'm replacing at the bank.

KROGSTAD: All right—I believe you. But now that you know, will you step aside?

MRS. LINDE: No, because that wouldn't benefit you in the slightest.

KROGSTAD: Not "benefit" me, hm! I'd step aside anyway.

MRS. LINDE: I've learned to be realistic. Life and hard, bitter necessity have taught me that.

KROGSTAD: And life's taught me never to trust fine phrases.
MRS. LINDE: Then life's taught you a very sound thing. But you do have to trust in actions, don't you?
KROGSTAD: What does that mean?
MRS. LINDE: You said you were hanging on like a half-drowned man to a wreck.
KROGSTAD: I've good reason to say that.
MRS. LINDE: I'm also like a half-drowned woman on a wreck. No one to suffer with; no one to care for.
KROGSTAD: You made your choice
MRS. LINDE: There wasn't any choice then.
KROGSTAD: So—what of it?
MRS. LINDE: Nils, if only we two shipwrecked people could reach across to each other.
KROGSTAD: What are you saying?
MRS. LINDE: Two on one wreck are at least better off than each on his own.
KROGSTAD: Kristine!
MRS. LINDE: Why do you think I came into town?
KROGSTAD: Did you really have some thought of me?
MRS. LINDE: I have to work to go on living. All my born days, as long as I can remember, I've worked, and it's been my best and my only joy. But now I'm completely alone in the world; it frightens me to be so empty and lost. To work for yourself—there's no joy in that. Nils, give me something—someone to work for.
KROGSTAD: I don't believe all this. It's just some hysterical feminine urge to go out and make a noble sacrifice.
MRS. LINDE: Have you ever found me to be hysterical?
KROGSTAD: Can you honestly mean this? Tell me—do you know everything about my past?
MRS. LINDE: Yes.
KROGSTAD: And you know what they think I'm worth around here.
MRS. LINDE: From what you were saying before, it would seem that with me you could have been another person.
KROGSTAD: I'm positive of that.
MRS. LINDE: Couldn't it happen still?
KROGSTAD: Kristine—you're saying this in all seriousness? Yes, you are! I can see it in you. And do you really have the courage, then—?
MRS. LINDE: I need to have someone to care for; and your children need a mother. We both need each other. Nils, I have faith that you're good at heart—I'll risk everything together with you.
KROGSTAD: [*Gripping her hands.*] Kristine, thank you, thank you—Now I know I can win back a place in their eyes. Yes—but I forgot—
MRS. LINDE: [*Listening.*] Shh! The tarantella. Go now! Go on!
KROGSTAD: Why? What is it?
MRS. LINDE: Hear the dance up there? When that's over, they'll be coming down.
KROGSTAD: Oh, then I'll go. But—it's all pointless. Of course, you don't know the move I made against the Helmers.
MRS. LINDE: Yes, Nils, I know.
KROGSTAD: And all the same, you have the courage to—?
MRS. LINDE: I know how far despair can drive a man like you.
KROGSTAD: Oh, if I only could take it all back.

MRS. LINDE: You easily could—your letter's still lying in the mailbox.
KROGSTAD: Are you sure of that?
MRS. LINDE: Positive. But—
KROGSTAD: [*Looks at her searchingly.*] Is that the meaning of it, then? You'll save your friend at any price. Tell me straight out. Is that it?
MRS. LINDE: Nils—anyone who's sold herself for somebody else once isn't going to do it again.
KROGSTAD: I'll demand my letter back.
MRS. LINDE: No, no.
KROGSTAD: Yes, of course. I'll stay here till Helmer comes down; I'll tell him to give me my letter again—that it only involves my dismissal—that he shouldn't read it—
MRS. LINDE: No, Nils, don't call the letter back.
KROGSTAD: But wasn't that exactly why you wrote me to come here?
MRS. LINDE: Yes, in that first panic. But it's been a whole day and night since then, and in that time I've seen such incredible things in this house. Helmer's got to learn everything; this dreadful secret has to be aired; those two have to come to a full understanding; all these lies and evasions can't go on.
KROGSTAD: Well, then, if you want to chance it. But at least there's one thing I can do, and do right away—
MRS. LINDE: [*Listening.*] Go now, go, quick! The dance is over. We're not safe another second.
KROGSTAD: I'll wait for you downstairs.
MRS. LINDE: Yes, please do; take me home.
KROGSTAD: I can't believe it; I've never been so happy. [*He leaves by way of the outer door; the door between the room and the hall stays open.*]
MRS. LINDE: [*Straightening up a bit and getting together her street clothes.*] How different now! How different! Someone to work for, to live for—a home to build. Well, it is worth the try! Oh, if they'd only come! [*Listening.*] Ah, there they are. Bundle up. [*She picks up her hat and coat.* NORA's *and* HELMER's *voices can be heard outside; a key turns in the lock, and* HELMER *brings* NORA *into the hall almost by force. She is wearing the Italian costume with a large black shawl about her; he has on evening dress, with a black domino*[3] *open over it.*]
NORA: [*Struggling in the doorway.*] No, no, no, not inside! I'm going up again. I don't want to leave so soon.
HELMER: But Nora dear—
NORA: Oh, I beg you, please, Torvald. From the bottom of my heart, *please*—only an hour more!
HELMER: Not a single minute, Nora darling. You know our agreement. Come on, in we go; you'll catch cold out here. [*In spite of her resistance, he gently draws her into the room.*]
MRS. LINDE: Good evening.
NORA: Kristine!
HELMER: Why, Mrs. Linde—are you here so late?
MRS. LINDE: Yes, I'm sorry, but I did want to see Nora in costume.
NORA: Have you been sitting here, waiting for me?

---

3. Hood worn by members of some religious orders.

MRS. LINDE: Yes. I didn't come early enough; you were all upstairs; and then I thought I really couldn't leave without seeing you.
HELMER: [*Removing* NORA's *shawl.*] Yes, take a good look. She's worth looking at, I can tell you that, Mrs. Linde. Isn't she lovely?
MRS. LINDE: Yes, I should say—
HELMER: A dream of loveliness, isn't she? That's what everyone thought at the party, too. But she's horribly stubborn—this sweet little thing. What's to be done with her? Can you imagine, I almost had to use force to pry her away.
NORA: Oh, Torvald, you're going to regret you didn't indulge me, even for just a half hour more.
HELMER: There, you see. She danced her tarantella and got a tumultuous hand—which was well earned, although the performance may have been a bit too naturalistic—I mean it rather overstepped the proprieties of art. But never mind—what's important is, she made a success, an overwhelming success. You think I could let her stay on after that and spoil the effect? Oh no; I took my lovely little Capri girl—my capricious little Capri girl, I should say—took her under my arm; one quick tour of the ballroom, a curtsy to every side, and then—as they say in novels—the beautiful vision disappeared. An exit should always be effective, Mrs. Linde, but that's what I can't get Nora to grasp. Phew, it's hot in here. [*Flings the domino on a chair and opens the door to his room.*] Why's it dark in here? Oh yes, of course. Excuse me. [*He goes in and lights a couple of candles.*]
NORA: [*In a sharp, breathless whisper.*] So?
MRS. LINDE: [*Quietly.*] I talked with him.
NORA: And—?
MRS. LINDE: Nora—you must tell your husband everything.
NORA: [*Dully.*] I knew it.
MRS. LINDE: You've got nothing to fear from Krogstad, but you have to speak out.
NORA: I won't tell.
MRS. LINDE: Then the letter will.
NORA: Thanks, Kristine. I know now what's to be done. Shh!
HELMER: [*Reentering.*] Well, then, Mrs. Linde—have you admired her?
MRS. LINDE: Yes, and now I'll say good night.
HELMER: Oh, come, so soon? Is this yours, this knitting?
MRS. LINDE: Yes, thanks. I nearly forgot it.
HELMER: Do you knit, then?
MRS. LINDE: Oh yes.
HELMER: You know what? You should embroider instead.
MRS. LINDE: Really? Why?
HELMER: Yes, because it's a lot prettier. See here, one holds the embroidery so, in the left hand, and then one guides the needle with the right—so—in an easy, sweeping curve—right?
MRS. LINDE: Yes, I guess that's—
HELMER: But, on the other hand, knitting—it can never be anything but ugly. Look, see here, the arms tucked in, the knitting needles going up and down—there's something Chinese about it. Ah, that was really a glorious champagne they served.
MRS. LINDE: Yes, good night, Nora, and don't be stubborn anymore.

HELMER: Well put, Mrs. Linde!
MRS. LINDE: Good night, Mr. Helmer.
HELMER: [*Accompanying her to the door.*] Good night, good night. I hope you get home all right. I'd be very happy to—but you don't have far to go. Good night, good night. [*She leaves. He shuts the door after her and returns.*] There, now, at last we got her out the door. She's a deadly bore, that creature.
NORA: Aren't you pretty tired, Torvald?
HELMER: No, not a bit.
NORA: You're not sleepy?
HELMER: Not at all. On the contrary, I'm feeling quite exhilarated. But you? Yes, you really look tired and sleepy.
NORA: Yes, I'm very tired. Soon now I'll sleep.
HELMER: See! You see! I was right all along that we shouldn't stay longer.
NORA: Whatever you do is always right.
HELMER: [*Kissing her brow.*] Now my little lark talks sense. Say, did you notice what a time Rank was having tonight?
NORA: Oh, was he? I didn't get to speak with him.
HELMER: I scarcely did either, but it's a long time since I've seen him in such high spirits. [*Gazes at her a moment, then comes nearer her.*] Hm—it's marvelous, though, to be back home again—to be completely alone with you. Oh, you bewitchingly lovely young woman!
NORA: Torvald, don't look at me like that!
HELMER: Can't I look at my richest treasure? At all that beauty that's mine, mine alone—completely and utterly.
NORA: [*Moving around to the other side of the table.*] You mustn't talk to me that way tonight.
HELMER: [*Following her.*] The tarantella is still in your blood, I can see—and it makes you even more enticing. Listen. The guests are beginning to go. [*Dropping his voice.*] Nora—it'll soon be quiet through this whole house.
NORA: Yes, I hope so.
HELMER: You do, don't you, my love? Do you realize—when I'm out at a party like this with you—do you know why I talk to you so little, and keep such a distance away; just send you a stolen look now and then—you know why I do it? It's because I'm imagining then that you're my secret darling, my secret young bride-to-be, and that no one suspects there's anything between us.
NORA: Yes, yes; oh, yes, I know you're always thinking of me.
HELMER: And then when we leave and I place the shawl over those fine young rounded shoulders—over that wonderful curving neck—then I pretend that you're my young bride, that we're just coming from the wedding, that for the first time I'm bringing you into my house—that for the first time I'm alone with you—completely alone with you, your trembling young beauty! All this evening I've longed for nothing but you. When I saw you turn and sway in the tarantella—my blood was pounding till I couldn't stand it—that's why I brought you down here so early—
NORA: Go away, Torvald! Leave me alone. I don't want all this.
HELMER: What do you mean? Nora, you're teasing me. You will, won't you? Aren't I your husband—?

[*A knock at the outside door.*]

NORA: [*Startled.*] What's that?
HELMER: [*Going toward the hall.*] Who is it?
RANK: [*Outside.*] It's me. May I come in a moment?
HELMER: [*With quiet irritation.*] Oh, what does he want now? [*Aloud.*] Hold on. [*Goes and opens the door.*] Oh, how nice that you didn't just pass us by!
RANK: I thought I heard your voice, and then I wanted so badly to have a look in. [*Lightly glancing about.*] Ah, me, these old familiar haunts. You have it snug and cozy in here, you two.
HELMER: You seemed to be having it pretty cozy upstairs, too.
RANK: Absolutely. Why shouldn't I? Why not take in everything in life? As much as you can, anyway, and as long as you can. The wine was superb—
HELMER: The champagne especially.
RANK: You noticed that too? It's amazing how much I could guzzle down.
NORA: Torvald also drank a lot of champagne this evening.
RANK: Oh?
NORA: Yes, and that always makes him so entertaining.
RANK: Well, why shouldn't one have a pleasant evening after a well-spent day?
HELMER: Well spent? I'm afraid I can't claim that.
RANK: [*Slapping him on the back.*] But I can, you see!
NORA: Dr. Rank, you must have done some scientific research today.
RANK: Quite so.
HELMER: Come now—little Nora talking about scientific research!
NORA: And can I congratulate you on the results?
RANK: Indeed you may.
NORA: Then they were good?
RANK: The best possible for both doctor and patient—certainty.
NORA: [*Quickly and searchingly.*] Certainty?
RANK: Complete certainty. So don't I owe myself a gay evening afterwards?
NORA: Yes, you're right, Dr. Rank.
HELMER: I'm with you—just so long as you don't have to suffer for it in the morning.
RANK: Well, one never gets something for nothing in life.
NORA: Dr. Rank—are you very fond of masquerade parties?
RANK: Yes, if there's a good array of odd disguises—
NORA: Tell me, what should we two go as at the next masquerade?
HELMER: You little featherhead—already thinking of the next!
RANK: We two? I'll tell you what: you must go as Charmed Life—
HELMER: Yes, but find a costume for *that!*
RANK: Your wife can appear just as she looks every day.
HELMER: That was nicely put. But don't you know what you're going to be?
RANK: Yes, Helmer, I've made up my mind.
HELMER: Well?
RANK: At the next masquerade I'm going to be invisible.
HELMER: That's a funny idea.
RANK: They say there's a hat—black, huge—have you never heard of the hat that makes you invisible? You put it on, and then no one on earth can see you.
HELMER: [*Suppressing a smile.*] Ah, of course.
RANK: But I'm quite forgetting what I came for. Helmer, give me a cigar, one of the dark Havanas.

HELMER: With the greatest pleasure. [*Holds out his case.*]
RANK: Thanks. [*Takes one and cuts off the tip.*]
NORA: [*Striking a match*] Let me give you a light.
RANK: Thank you. [*She holds the match for him; he lights the cigar.*] And now good-bye.
HELMER: Good-bye, good-bye, old friend.
NORA: Sleep well, Doctor.
RANK: Thanks for that wish.
NORA: Wish me the same.
RANK: You? All right, if you like—Sleep well. And thanks for the light. [*He nods to them both and leaves.*]
HELMER: [*His voice subdued.*] He's been drinking heavily.
NORA: [*Absently.*] Could be. [HELMER *takes his keys from his pocket and goes out in the hall.*] Torvald—what are you after?
HELMER: Got to empty the mailbox; it's nearly full. There won't be room for the morning papers.
NORA: Are you working tonight?
HELMER: You know I'm not. Why—what's this? Someone's been at the lock.
NORA: At the lock—?
HELMER: Yes, I'm positive. What do you suppose—? I can't imagine one of the maids—? Here's a broken hairpin. Nora, it's yours—
NORA: [*Quickly.*] Then it must be the children—
HELMER: You'd better break them of that. Hm, hm—well, opened it after all. [*Takes the contents out and calls into the kitchen.*] Helene! Helene, would you put out the lamp in the hall. [*He returns to the room, shutting the hall door, then displays the handful of mail.*] Look how it's piled up. [*Sorting through them.*] Now what's this?
NORA: [*At the window.*] The letter! Oh, Torvald, no!
HELMER: Two calling cards—from Rank.
NORA: From Dr. Rank?
HELMER: [*Examining them.*] "Dr. Rank, Consulting Physician." They were on top. He must have dropped them in as he left.
NORA: Is there anything on them?
HELMER: There's a black cross over the name. See? That's a gruesome notion. He could almost be announcing his own death.
NORA: That's just what he's doing.
HELMER: What! You've heard something? Something he's told you?
NORA: Yes. That when those cards came, he'd be taking his leave of us. He'll shut himself in now and die.
HELMER: Ah, my poor friend! Of course I knew he wouldn't be here much longer. But so soon—And then to hide himself away like a wounded animal.
NORA: If it has to happen, then it's best it happens in silence—don't you think so, Torvald?
HELMER: [*Pacing up and down.*] He'd grown right into our lives. I simply can't imagine him gone. He with his suffering and loneliness—like a dark cloud setting off our sunlit happiness. Well, maybe it's best this way. For him, at least. [*Standing still.*] And maybe for us too, Nora. Now we're thrown back on each other, completely. [*Embracing her.*] Oh you, my darling wife, how can I hold you close enough? You know what, Nora—time and again I've wished

you were in some terrible danger, just so I could stake my life and soul and everything, for your sake.

NORA: [*Tearing herself away, her voice firm and decisive.*] Now you must read your mail, Torvald.

HELMER: No, no, not tonight. I want to stay with you, dearest.

NORA: With a dying friend on your mind?

HELMER: You're right. We've both had a shock. There's ugliness between us—these thoughts of death and corruption. We'll have to get free of them first. Until then—we'll stay apart.

NORA: [*Clinging about his neck.*] Torvald—good night! Good night!

HELMER: [*Kissing her on the cheek.*] Good night, little songbird. Sleep well, Nora. I'll be reading my mail now. [*He takes the letters into his room and shuts the door after him.*]

NORA: [*With bewildered glances, groping about, seizing* HELMER's *domino, throwing it around her, and speaking in short, hoarse, broken whispers.*] Never see him again. Never, never. [*Putting her shawl over her head.*] Never see the children either—them, too. Never, never. Oh, the freezing black water! The depths—down—Oh, I wish it were over—He has it now; he's reading it—now. Oh no, no, not yet. Torvald, good-bye, you and the children—[*She starts for the hall; as she does,* HELMER *throws open his door and stands with an open letter in his hand.*]

HELMER: Nora!

NORA: [*Screams.*] Oh—!

HELMER: What is this? You know what's in this letter?

NORA: Yes, I know. Let me go! Let me out!

HELMER: [*Holding her back.*] Where are you going?

NORA: [*Struggling to break loose.*] You can't save me, Torvald!

HELMER: [*Slumping back.*] True! Then it's true what he writes? How horrible! No, no, it's impossible—it can't be true.

NORA: It *is* true. I've loved you more than all this world.

HELMER: Ah, none of your slippery tricks.

NORA: [*Taking one step toward him.*] Torvald—!

HELMER: What *is* this you've blundered into!

NORA: Just let me loose. You're not going to suffer for my sake. You're not going to take on my guilt.

HELMER: No more playacting. [*Locks the hall door.*] You stay right here and give me a reckoning. You understand what you've done? Answer! You understand?

NORA: [*Looking squarely at him, her face hardening.*] Yes. I'm beginning to understand everything now.

HELMER: [*Striding about.*] Oh, what an awful awakening! In all these eight years—she who was my pride and joy—a hypocrite, a liar—worse, worse—a criminal! How infinitely disgusting it all is! The shame! [NORA *says nothing and goes on looking straight at him. He stops in front of her.*] I should have suspected something of the kind. I should have known. All your father's flimsy values—Be still! All your father's flimsy values have come out in you. No religion, no morals, no sense of duty—Oh, how I'm punished for letting him off! I did it for your sake, and you repay me like this.

NORA: Yes, like this.

HELMER: Now you've wrecked all my happiness—ruined my whole future. Oh, it's awful to think of. I'm in a cheap little grafter's hands; he can do anything he wants with me, ask for anything, play with me like a puppet—and I can't breathe a word. I'll be swept down miserably into the depths on account of a featherbrained woman.

NORA: When I'm gone from this world, you'll be free.

HELMER: Oh, quit posing. Your father had a mess of those speeches too. What good would that ever do me if you were gone from this world, as you say? Not the slightest. He can still make the whole thing known; and if he does, I could be falsely suspected as your accomplice. They might even think that I was behind it—that I put you up to it. And all that I can thank you for—you that I've coddled the whole of our marriage. Can you see now what you've done to me?

NORA: [*Icily calm.*] Yes.

HELMER: It's so incredible, I just can't grasp it. But we'll have to patch up whatever we can. Take off the shawl. I said, take it off! I've got to appease him somehow or other. The thing has to be hushed up at any cost. And as for you and me, it's got to seem like everything between us is just as it was—to the outside world, that is. You'll go right on living in this house, of course. But you can't be allowed to bring up the children; I don't dare trust you with them—Oh, to have to say this to someone I've loved so much, and that I still—! Well, that's done with. From now on happiness doesn't matter; all that matters is saving the bits and pieces, the appearance—[*The doorbell rings.* HELMER *starts.*] What's that? And so late. Maybe the worst—? You think he'd—? Hide, Nora! Say you're sick. [NORA *remains standing motionless.* HELMER *goes and opens the door.*]

MAID: [*Half dressed, in the hall.*] A letter for Mrs. Helmer.

HELMER: I'll take it. [*Snatches the letter and shuts the door.*] Yes, it's from him. You don't get it; I'm reading it myself.

NORA: Then read it.

HELMER: [*By the lamp.*] I hardly dare. We may be ruined, you and I. But—I've got to know. [*Rips open the letter, skims through a few lines, glances at an enclosure, then cries out joyfully.*] Nora! [NORA *looks inquiringly at him.*] Nora! Wait—better check it again—Yes, yes, it's true. I'm saved. Nora, I'm saved!

NORA: And I?

HELMER: You too, of course. We're both saved, both of us. Look. He's sent back your note. He says he's sorry and ashamed—that a happy development in his life—oh, who cares what he says! Nora, we're saved! No one can hurt you. Oh, Nora, Nora—but first, this ugliness all has to go. Let me see—[*Takes a look at the note.*] No, I don't want to see it; I want the whole thing to fade like a dream. [*Tears the note and both letters to pieces, throws them into the stove and watches them burn.*] There—now there's nothing left—He wrote that since Christmas Eve you—Oh, they must have been three terrible days for you, Nora.

NORA: I fought a hard fight.

HELMER: And suffered pain and saw no escape but—No, we're not going to dwell on anything unpleasant. We'll just be grateful and keep on repeating: it's over now, it's over! You hear me, Nora? You don't seem to realize—it's over. What's it mean—that frozen look? Oh, poor little Nora, I understand. You can't believe I've forgiven you. But I have, Nora; I swear I have. I know that what you did, you did out of love for me.

NORA: That's true.

HELMER: You loved me the way a wife ought to love her husband. It's simply the means that you couldn't judge. But you think I love you any the less for not knowing how to handle your affairs? No, no—just lean on me; I'll guide you and teach you. I wouldn't be a man if this feminine helplessness didn't make you twice as attractive to me. You mustn't mind those sharp words I said— that was all in the first confusion of thinking my world had collapsed. I've forgiven you, Nora; I swear I've forgiven you.

NORA: My thanks for your forgiveness. [*She goes out through the door, right.*]
HELMER: No, wait—[*Peers in.*] What are you doing in there?
NORA: [*Inside.*] Getting out of my costume.
HELMER: [*By the open door.*] Yes, do that. Try to calm yourself and collect your thoughts again, my frightened little songbird. You can rest easy now; I've got wide wings to shelter you with. [*Walking about close by the door.*] How snug and nice our home is, Nora. You're safe here; I'll keep you like a hunted dove I've rescued out of a hawk's claws. I'll bring peace to your poor, shuddering heart. Gradually it'll happen, Nora; you'll see. Tomorrow all this will look different to you; then everything will be as it was. I won't have to go on repeating I forgive you; you'll feel it for yourself. How can you imagine I'd ever conceivably want to disown you—or even blame you in any way? Ah, you don't know a man's heart, Nora. For a man there's something indescribably sweet and satisfying in knowing he's forgiven his wife—and forgiven her out of a full and open heart. It's as if she belongs to him in two ways now: in a sense he's given her fresh into the world again, and she's become his wife and his child as well. From now on that's what you'll be to me—you little, bewildered, helpless thing. Don't be afraid of anything, Nora; just open your heart to me, and I'll be conscience and will to you both—[NORA *enters in her regular clothes.*] What's this? Not in bed? You've changed your dress?
NORA: Yes, Torvald, I've changed my dress.
HELMER: But why now, so late?
NORA: Tonight I'm not sleeping.
HELMER: But Nora dear—
NORA: [*Looking at her watch.*] It's still not so very late. Sit down, Torvald; we have a lot to talk over. [*She sits at one side of the table.*]
HELMER: Nora—what is this? That hard expression—
NORA: Sit down. This'll take some time. I have a lot to say.
HELMER: [*Sitting at the table directly opposite her.*] You worry me, Nora. And I don't understand you.
NORA: No, that's exactly it. You don't understand me. And I've never understood you either—until tonight. No, don't interrupt. You can just listen to what I say. We're closing out accounts, Torvald.
HELMER: How do you mean that?
NORA: [*After a short pause.*] Doesn't anything strike you about our sitting here like this?
HELMER: What's that?
NORA: We've been married now eight years. Doesn't it occur to you that this is the first time we two, you and I, man and wife, have ever talked seriously together?
HELMER: What do you mean—seriously?
NORA: In eight whole years—longer even—right from our first acquaintance, we've never exchanged a serious word on any serious thing.

HELMER: You mean I should constantly go and involve you in problems you couldn't possibly help me with?
NORA: I'm not talking of problems. I'm saying that we've never sat down seriously together and tried to get to the bottom of anything.
HELMER: But dearest, what good would that ever do you?
NORA: That's the point right there: you've never understood me. I've been wronged greatly, Torvald—first by Papa, and then by you.
HELMER: What! By us—the two people who've loved you more than anyone else?
NORA: [*Shaking her head.*] You never loved me. You've thought it fun to be in love with me, that's all.
HELMER: Nora, what a thing to say!
NORA: Yes, it's true now, Torvald. When I lived at home with Papa, he told me all his opinions, so I had the same ones too; or if they were different I hid them, since he wouldn't have cared for that. He used to call me his doll-child, and he played with me the way I played with my dolls. Then I came into your house—
HELMER: How can you speak of our marriage like that?
NORA: [*Unperturbed.*] I mean, then I went from Papa's hands into yours. You arranged everything to your own taste, and so I got the same taste as you—or I pretended to; I can't remember. I guess a little of both, first one, then the other. Now when I look back, it seems as if I'd lived here like a beggar—just from hand to mouth. I've lived by doing tricks for you, Torvald. But that's the way you wanted it. It's a great sin what you and Papa did to me. You're to blame that nothing's become of me.
HELMER: Nora, how unfair and ungrateful you are! Haven't you been happy here?
NORA: No, never. I thought so—but I never have.
HELMER: Not—not happy!
NORA: No, only lighthearted. And you've always been so kind to me. But our home's been nothing but a playpen. I've been your doll-wife here, just as at home I was Papa's doll-child. And in turn the children have been my dolls. I thought it was fun when you played with me, just as they thought it fun when I played with them. That's been our marriage, Torvald.
HELMER: There's some truth in what you're saying—under all the raving exaggeration. But it'll all be different after this. Playtime's over; now for the schooling.
NORA: Whose schooling—mine or the children's?
HELMER: Both yours and the children's, dearest.
NORA: Oh, Torvald, you're not the man to teach me to be a good wife to you.
HELMER: And you can say that?
NORA: And I—how am I equipped to bring up children?
HELMER: Nora!
NORA: Didn't you say a moment ago that that was no job to trust me with?
HELMER: In a flare of temper! Why fasten on that?
NORA: Yes, but you were so very right. I'm not up to the job. There's another job I have to do first. I have to try to educate myself. You can't help me with that. I've got to do it alone. And that's why I'm leaving you now.
HELMER: [*Jumping up.*] What's that?
NORA: I have to stand completely alone, if I'm ever going to discover myself and the world out there. So I can't go on living with you.
HELMER: Nora, Nora!

NORA: I want to leave right away. Kristine should put me up for the night—
HELMER: You're insane! You've no right! I forbid you!
NORA: From here on, there's no use forbidding me anything. I'll take with me whatever is mine. I don't want a thing from you, either now or later.
HELMER: What kind of madness is this!
NORA: Tomorrow I'm going home—I mean, home where I came from. It'll be easier up there to find something to do.
HELMER: Oh, you blind, incompetent child!
NORA: I must learn to be competent, Torvald.
HELMER: Abandon your home, your husband, your children! And you're not even thinking what people will say.
NORA: I can't be concerned about that. I only know how essential this is.
HELMER: Oh, it's outrageous. So you'll run out like this on your most sacred vows.
NORA: What do you think are my most sacred vows?
HELMER: And I have to tell you that! Aren't they your duties to your husband and children?
NORA: I have other duties equally sacred.
HELMER: That isn't true. What duties are they?
NORA: Duties to myself.
HELMER: Before all else, you're a wife and a mother.
NORA: I don't believe in that anymore. I believe that, before all else, I'm a human being, no less than you—or anyway, I ought to try to become one. I know the majority thinks you're right, Torvald, and plenty of books agree with you, too. But I can't go on believing what the majority says, or what's written in books. I have to think over these things myself and try to understand them.
HELMER: Why can't you understand your place in your own home? On a point like that, isn't there one everlasting guide you can turn to? Where's your religion?
NORA: Oh, Torvald, I'm really not sure what religion is.
HELMER: What—?
NORA: I only know what the minister said when I was confirmed. He told me religion was this thing and that. When I get clear and away by myself, I'll go into that problem too. I'll see if what the minister said was right, or, in any case, if it's right for me.
HELMER: A young woman your age shouldn't talk like that. If religion can't move you, I can try to rouse your conscience. You do have some moral feeling? Or, tell me—has that gone too?
NORA: It's not easy to answer that, Torvald. I simply don't know. I'm all confused about these things. I just know I see them so differently from you. I find out, for one thing, that the law's not at all what I'd thought—but I can't get it through my head that the law is fair. A woman hasn't a right to protect her dying father or save her husband's life! I can't believe that.
HELMER: You talk like a child. You don't know anything of the world you live in.
NORA: No, I don't. But now I'll begin to learn for myself. I'll try to discover who's right, the world or I.
HELMER: Nora, you're sick; you've got a fever. I almost think you're out of your head.
NORA: I've never felt more clearheaded and sure in my life.

HELMER: And—clearheaded and sure—you're leaving your husband and children?
NORA: Yes.
HELMER: Then there's only one possible reason.
NORA: What?
HELMER: You no longer love me.
NORA: No. That's exactly it.
HELMER: Nora! You can't be serious!
NORA: Oh, this is so hard, Torvald—you've been so kind to me always. But I can't help it. I don't love you anymore.
HELMER: [*Struggling for composure.*] Are you also clearheaded and sure about that?
NORA: Yes, completely. That's why I can't go on staying here.
HELMER: Can you tell me what I did to lose your love?
NORA: Yes, I can tell you. It was this evening when the miraculous thing didn't come—then I knew you weren't the man I'd imagined.
HELMER: Be more explicit; I don't follow you.
NORA: I've waited now so patiently eight long years—for, my Lord, I know miracles don't come every day. Then this crisis broke over me, and such a certainty filled me: *now* the miraculous event would occur. While Krogstad's letter was lying out there, I never for an instant dreamed that you could give in to his terms. I was so utterly sure you'd say to him: go on, tell your tale to the whole wide world. And when he'd done that—
HELMER: Yes, what then? When I'd delivered my own wife into shame and disgrace—!
NORA: When he'd done that, I was so utterly sure that you'd step forward, take the blame on yourself and say: I am the guilty one.
HELMER: Nora—!
NORA: You're thinking I'd never accept such a sacrifice from you? No, of course not. But what good would my protests be against you? That was the miracle I was waiting for, in terror and hope. And to stave that off, I would have taken my life.
HELMER: I'd gladly work for you day and night, Nora—and take on pain and deprivation. But there's no one who gives up honor for love.
NORA: Millions of women have done just that.
HELMER: Oh, you think and talk like a silly child.
NORA: Perhaps. But you neither think nor talk like the man I could join myself to. When your big fright was over—and it wasn't from any threat against me, only for what might damage you—when all the danger was past, for you it was just as if nothing had happened. I was exactly the same, your little lark, your doll, that you'd have to handle with double care now that I'd turned out so brittle and frail. [*Gets up.*] Torvald—in that instant it dawned on me that for eight years I've been living here with a stranger, and that I'd even conceived three children—oh, I can't stand the thought of it! I could tear myself to bits.
HELMER: [*Heavily.*] I see. There's a gulf that's opened between us—that's clear. Oh, but Nora, can't we bridge it somehow?
NORA: The way I am now, I'm no wife for you.
HELMER: I have the strength to make myself over.
NORA: Maybe—if your doll gets taken away.
HELMER: But to part! To part from you! No, Nora, no—I can't imagine it.

NORA: [*Going out, right.*] All the more reason why it has to be. [*She reenters with her coat and a small overnight bag, which she puts on a chair by the table.*]
HELMER: Nora, Nora, not now! Wait till tomorrow.
NORA: I can't spend the night in a strange man's room.
HELMER: But couldn't we live here like brother and sister—
NORA: You know very well how long that would last. [*Throws her shawl about her.*] Good-bye, Torvald. I won't look in on the children. I know they're in better hands than mine. The way I am now, I'm no use to them.
HELMER: But someday, Nora—someday—?
NORA: How can I tell? I haven't the least idea what'll become of me.
HELMER: But you're my wife, now and wherever you go.
NORA: Listen, Torvald—I've heard that when a wife deserts her husband's house just as I'm doing, then the law frees him from all responsibility. In any case, I'm freeing you from being responsible. Don't feel yourself bound, any more than I will. There has to be absolute freedom for us both. Here, take your ring back. Give me mine.
HELMER: That too?
NORA: That too.
HELMER: There it is.
NORA: Good. Well, now it's all over. I'm putting the keys here. The maids know all about keeping up the house—better than I do. Tomorrow, after I've left town, Kristine will stop by to pack up everything that's mine from home. I'd like those things shipped up to me.
HELMER: Over! All over! Nora, won't you ever think about me?
NORA: I'm sure I'll think of you often, and about the children and the house here.
HELMER: May I write you?
NORA: No—never. You're not to do that.
HELMER: Oh, but let me send you—
NORA: Nothing. Nothing.
HELMER: Or help you if you need it.
NORA: No. I accept nothing from strangers.
HELMER: Nora—can I never be more than a stranger to you?
NORA: [*Picking up the overnight bag.*] Ah, Torvald—it would take the greatest miracle of all—
HELMER: Tell me the greatest miracle!
NORA: You and I both would have to transform ourselves to the point that—Oh, Torvald, I've stopped believing in miracles.
HELMER: But I'll believe. Tell me! Transform ourselves to the point that—?
NORA: That our living together could be a true marriage. [*She goes out down the hall.*]
HELMER: [*Sinks down on a chair by the door, face buried in his hands.*] Nora! Nora! [*Looking about and rising.*] Empty. She's gone. [*A sudden hope leaps in him.*] The greatest miracle—?

[*From below, the sound of a door slamming shut.*]

1879

# Biographical Sketches: Playwrights

**ANTON CHEKHOV**
(1860–1904)

The son of a grocer and the grandson of an emancipated serf, Anton Pavlovich Chekhov was born in the Russian town of Taganrog. In 1875, his father, facing bankruptcy and imprisonment, fled to Moscow; shortly after, the rest of the family lost their house to a former friend and lodger, a misfortune that Chekhov would revisit in *The Cherry Orchard*. In 1884, Chekhov received his M.D. from the University of Moscow; in the early 1890s, he purchased an estate near Moscow and became both an industrious landowner and a doctor to the local peasants. Throughout the 1880s, he supported his family and financed his medical studies by writing the sketches and stories that would eventually win him enduring international acclaim. Chekhov began writing for the stage in 1887. Early productions of his plays were poorly received: *The Wood Demon* (later rewritten as *Uncle Vanya*) was performed only a few times in 1889 before closing; the 1896 premiere of *The Seagull* turned into a riot when an audience expecting comedy found themselves watching an experimental tragedy. Konstantin Stanislavsky, director at the Moscow Art Theater, helped restore Chekhov's reputation with successful productions of *The Seagull* and *Uncle Vanya* in 1899, *The Three Sisters* in 1901, and *The Cherry Orchard* in 1904.

**MARGARET EDSON**
(b. 1961)

When Margaret Edson's *Wit* won the Pulitzer Prize for Drama in 1999, the theater world was astounded to learn that a play about the death and journey to grace of a cancer-stricken professor of seventeenth-century poetry had been written by an Atlanta kindergarten teacher. Edson, a native of Washington, D.C., graduated from Smith College in 1983 with a degree in Renaissance history. The inspiration for her play came from a brief stint as a clerk in the cancer and AIDS unit of a research hospital. Edson began writing *Wit* while working in a Washington bicycle shop; before completing the play she earned an M.A. in English from Georgetown University and began her work as a teacher. Even after *Wit* made her famous, Edson said she had no plans to leave the classroom to write more plays. "Every single day," she told an interviewer, "I'm working to the bone to bring more justice to the world. This work ... is where the action is."

**SUSAN GLASPELL**
(1876–1948)

Born and raised in Davenport, Iowa, Susan Glaspell graduated from Drake University and worked on the staff of the Des Moines *Daily News* until her stories began appearing in magazines such as *Harper's* and *Ladies' Home Journal*. In 1911, Glaspell moved to New York City, where, two years later, she married the theater director George Cram Cook. In 1915 they founded the Provincetown Playhouse (later the Playwright's Theater), an extraordinary Cape Cod gathering of actors, directors, and playwrights, including Eugene O'Neill, Edna St. Vincent Millay, and John Reed. The Provincetown Players produced several of Glaspell's early plays, including *Trifles* (1916); her later plays include *The Inheritors* (1921), *The Verge* (1921), *Bernice* (1924), and *Alison's House* (1930), for which she won the Pulitzer Prize. Glaspell spent the last part of her life writing fiction in Provincetown; among her many books are *Visioning* (1911), *Lifted Masks: Stories* (1912), *Fidelity* (1915), *The Road to the Temple* (1926), and *The Morning Is Near Us* (1940).

**LORRAINE HANSBERRY**
(1930–1965)

The first African American woman to have a play produced on Broadway, Lorraine Hansberry was born in Chicago to a prominent family and even at a young age showed an interest in writing. She attended the University of Wisconsin, the Art Institute of Chicago, and Roosevelt University, then moved to New York City in order to concentrate on writing for the stage. After extensive fund-raising, Hansberry's play *A Raisin in the Sun* (loosely based on events involving her own family) opened in 1959 at the Ethel Barrymore Theatre on Broadway, received critical acclaim, and won the New York Drama Critics' Circle Award for Best Play. Hansberry's second production, *The Sign in Sidney Brustein's Window,* had a short run on Broadway in 1964. Shortly after, Hansberry died of cancer. *To Be Young, Gifted, and Black,* adapted from her writing, was produced off-Broadway in 1969 and published the next year, when her drama *Les Blancs* was also produced.

## HENRIK IBSEN
(1828–1906)

Born in Skien, Norway, Henrik Ibsen was apprenticed to an apothecary until 1850, when he left for Oslo and published his first play, *Catilina,* a verse tragedy. By 1857 Ibsen was director of Oslo's Norwegian Theater, but his early plays, such as *Love's Comedy* (1862), were poorly received. Disgusted with what he saw as Norway's backwardness, Ibsen left in 1864 for Rome, where he wrote two more verse plays, *Brand* (1866) and *Peer Gynt* (1867), before turning to the realistic style and harsh criticism of traditional social mores for which he is best known. *The League of Youth* (1869), *Pillars of Society* (1877), *A Doll House* (1879), *Ghosts* (1881), *An Enemy of the People* (1882), *The Wild Duck* (1884), and *Hedda Gabler* (1890) won him a reputation throughout Europe as a controversial and outspoken advocate of moral and social reform. Near the end of his life, Ibsen explored the human condition in the explicitly symbolic terms of *The Master Builder* (1892) and *When We Dead Awaken* (1899). Ibsen's works had enormous influence over the drama of the twentieth century.

## ARTHUR MILLER
(1915–2005)

Arthur Miller was born in New York City to a prosperous family whose fortunes were ruined by the Depression, a circumstance that would shape his political outlook and imbue him with a deep sense of social responsibility. Miller studied history, economics, and journalism at the University of Michigan, began writing plays, and joined the Federal Theater Project, a proving ground for some of the best playwrights of the period. He had his first Broadway success, *All My Sons,* in 1947, followed two years later by his Pulitzer Prize–winning masterpiece, *Death of a Salesman,* a starkly poetic depiction of the American dream as a hollow sham. In 1953, against the backdrop of Senator Joseph McCarthy's anti-Communist "witch-hunts," Miller fashioned another modern parable, his Tony Award–winning *The Crucible,* based on the seventeenth-century Salem witch trials. Among his other works for the stage are the Pulitzer Prize–winner *A View from the Bridge* (1955), *After the Fall* (1964), *Incident at Vichy* (1965), *The Price* (1968), *The Ride Down Mt. Morgan* (1991), *Broken Glass* (1994), and *Resurrection Blues* (2004). In addition, Miller wrote a novel, *Focus* (1945); the screenplay for the film *The Misfits* (1961), which starred his second wife, Marilyn Monroe; *The Theater Essays* (1971), a collection of his writings about dramatic literature; and *Timebends* (1987), his autobiography.

## WILLIAM SHAKESPEARE
(1554–1616)

Considering the great and well-deserved fame of his work, surprisingly little is known of William Shakespeare's life. Between 1585 and 1592, he left his birthplace of Stratford-upon-Avon for London to begin a career as playwright and actor. No dates of his professional career are recorded, however, nor can the order in which he composed his plays and poetry be determined with certainty. By 1594, he had established himself as a poet with two long works—*Venus and Adonis* and *The Rape of Lucrece;* his more than 150 sonnets are supreme expressions of the form. His matchless reputation, though, rests on his works for the theater. Shakespeare produced perhaps thirty-five plays in twenty-five years, proving himself a master of every dramatic genre: tragedy (in works such as *Macbeth, Hamlet, King Lear,* and *Othello*); historical drama (for example, *Richard III* and *Henry IV*); comedy (*A Midsummer Night's Dream, Twelfth Night, As You Like It,* and many more); and romance or "tragi-comedy" (in plays such as *The Tempest* and *Cymbeline*). Without question, Shakespeare is the most quoted, discussed, and beloved writer in English literature.

## GEORGE BERNARD SHAW (1856–1950)

Born in Dublin to English parents, George Bernard Shaw left school at fourteen to work in a real estate agent's office; at nineteen he left for London to become a writer. An ardent socialist, he took up journalism, eventually becoming a music and drama critic best known for championing the operas of Richard Wagner and the plays of Henrik Ibsen. After five novels that were largely ignored, his first play, *Widowers' Houses*, an attack on slum housing, was produced in 1891. His second play, *Mrs. Warren's Profession* (1893), was banned for its frank depiction of prostitution, but *The Devil's Disciple* (1899), dealing with the American Revolution, brought him great success in New York. Shaw's realistic dramas, enlivened by his famous wit, address the platitudes and hypocrisies of turn-of-the-century society with unsparing satire; his favorite targets were the idealization of war and sentimental notions about love. Among his most popular works are *Arms and the Man* (1894), *Man and Superman* (1904), *Major Barbara* (1907), *Pygmalion* (1912), *Heartbreak House* (1919), and *Saint Joan* (1923), all of which are still frequently produced. In 1925 Shaw was awarded the Nobel Prize for Literature.

## SOPHOCLES (496?–406 B.C.E.)

Sophocles lived at a time when Athens and Greek civilization were at the peak of their power and influence. He not only served as a general under Pericles and played a prominent role in the city's affairs but also was arguably the greatest of the Greek tragic playwrights, winning the annual dramatic competition about twenty times, a feat unmatched by even his great contemporaries, Aeschylus and Euripides. An innovator, Sophocles fundamentally changed the nature of dramatic performance by adding a third actor, enlarging the chorus, and introducing the use of painted scenery. Aristotle held that Sophocles' *Oedipus the King* (c. 429 B.C.E.) was the perfect tragedy and used it as his model when he discussed the nature of tragedy in his *Poetics*. Today only seven of Sophocles' tragedies survive—the Oedipus trilogy (*Oedipus the King*, *Oedipus at Colonus*, and *Antigone*), *Philoctetes*, *Ajax*, *Trachiniae*, and *Electra*—though he is believed to have written as many as 123 plays.

## WOLE SOYINKA (b. 1934)

Akinwande Oluwole Soyinka was born in 1934 in Abeokuta, southwestern Nigeria, then a British colony. He studied at the universities of Ibadan, in Nigeria, and Leeds, in England, before joining London's Royal Court Theatre as an actor and director. In 1960 Soyinka returned to Nigeria to study African drama and to teach. *A Dance of the Forests* (1960) was commissioned in celebration of Nigeria's independence, but like many of Soyinka's subsequent works, the play angered Nigerian authorities. Soyinka's appeal for a ceasefire during Nigeria's civil war led to his arrest in 1967; for nearly two years he was a political prisoner. His many plays, ranging from satirical comedies to politically charged tragedies, chronicle Africa's difficult transition from traditional to modern life. Among the best known are *The Trial of Brother Jero* (1963), *Death and the King's Horseman* (1975), *A Play of Giants* (1984), and *King Baabu* (2001). Other works include such novels as *The Interpreters* (1965), *Season of Anomy* (1973), and *Isara* (1988); his prison memoir, *The Man Died* (1972), and an account of his childhood, *Aké* (1983); a collection of literary essays, *Myth, Literature and the African World* (1975); and numerous volumes of poetry. In 1986 Soyinka became the first black African awarded the Nobel Prize for Literature.

## TOM STOPPARD (b. 1937)

Tom Stoppard was born in Zlin, Czechoslovakia. In 1939 his family moved to Singapore to escape the Nazis. His mother then fled with Tom and his brother to Darjeeling, India, in advance of the Japanese invasion of Singapore; his father, who remained behind, was killed. In 1946 the family moved to England, where Tom's mother married Kenneth Stoppard, a major in the British army. Stoppard dropped out of high school before his junior year, worked as a journalist and freelance drama critic, and began to write plays for radio and television. His first television play, *A Walk on the Water* (1963), was later adapted for the stage as *Enter a Free Man* (1968). Stoppard's first major success was *Rosencrantz and Guildenstern Are Dead* (1966), which won a Tony Award for Best Play in 1968. Subsequent popular dramas include *The Real Inspector Hound* (1968), *Jumpers* (1972), and *Travesties* (1974). *Every Good Boy Deserves*

*Favour* (1977), *Dogg's Hamlet* (1979), and *Squaring the Circle* (1984) attack the oppressive regimes of Eastern Europe. Among Stoppard's more recent plays are *Arcadia* (1993) and *The Invention of Love* (1997). Stoppard has written a number of screenplays, including *Shakespeare in Love* (1998), which he coauthored with Marc Norman and which won the 1999 Academy Award for Best Screenplay.

## PAULA VOGEL (b. 1951)

Paula Vogel grew up in Washington, D.C., and earned a B.A. in drama from Catholic University. She was turned down for graduate study at the Yale School of Drama and found it difficult to get her early plays produced, but she kept working at her craft and took on controversial themes: *The Oldest Profession* (1981) depicts aging prostitutes; *And Baby Makes Seven* (1988) concerns lesbian motherhood; and the Obie Award–winning *The Baltimore Waltz* (1991) is based on the death of her brother Carl from AIDS. Her most famous play, the Pulitzer Prize–winning *How I Learned to Drive* (1997), portrays the sexual relationship between a young girl and her uncle. Vogel now teaches at Brown University. Recent work includes *The Mineola Twins* (1999) and *The Long Christmas Ride Home* (2004).

## OSCAR WILDE
(1854–1900)

Born and raised in Dublin, Oscar Wilde studied classical languages at Trinity College and took his degree from Oxford in 1878. While at Oxford, he was captivated by the aesthetic theories of John Ruskin and Walter Pater. Upon graduation, he moved to London to write, soon becoming both a much-quoted wit and the most visible exponent of the "art for art's sake" movement, for which he was lampooned by Gilbert and Sullivan in their operetta *Patience*. Wilde wrote criticism, poetry, and fiction, most notably his novel *The Picture of Dorian Gray* (1891). However, he achieved his greatest success as a comic dramatist, with clever, witty plays such as *Lady Windermere's Fan* (1892), *A Woman of No Importance* (1893), and his masterpiece, *The Importance of Being Earnest* (1895). At the height of his career, Wilde was accused of homosexuality by his lover's father, the marquess of Queensbury; he sued for libel, lost the case, and was imprisoned for two years, a ruinous experience that inspired his best-known poem, "The Ballad of Reading Gaol" (1898). Upon his release, he emigrated to France under an assumed name, dying there three years later. "In this world," he wrote, "there are only two tragedies. One is not getting what one wants, and the other is getting it."

## TENNESSEE WILLIAMS
(1911–1983)

Born in Columbus, Mississippi, Thomas Lanier Williams moved to St. Louis with his family at the age of seven. Williams's father was a violent alcoholic, his mother was ill, and his sister, Rose, suffered from a variety of mental illnesses; each of them became a model for the domineering men and sensitive women of his plays. He attended the University of Missouri and Washington University in St. Louis, but earned his B.A. from the University of Iowa. While there, Williams won prizes for his fiction and began to write plays. His extensive body of work, with its explosive dramatic tension and dazzling dialogue, confronts issues of adultery, homosexuality, incest, and mental illness. In 1944, *The Glass Menagerie* won the New York Drama Critics' Circle Award. In 1948, he earned his first Pulitzer Prize, with *A Streetcar Named Desire;* in 1955, he won a second Pulitzer Prize, for *Cat on a Hot Tin Roof.* His other dramas include *Camino Real* (1953), *Suddenly Last Summer* (1958), *The Night of the Iguana* (1961), *The Two-Character Play* (1969; later revised as *Out Cry*), and *Clothes for a Summer Hotel* (1980). Williams also published short fiction, poetry, and a film script.

## AUGUST WILSON
(b. 1945)

Frederick August Kittel was born in a lower-class black neighborhood of Pittsburgh, Pennsylvania. At fifteen, disgusted by treatment he considered racist, he left school and sought to educate himself at the local library. A black nationalist and participant in the Black Arts Movement during the 1960s and '70s, Wilson disavowed his white father and adopted his black mother's surname. In 1968 he cofounded the Black Horizons Theater Company, in St. Paul, Minnesota; he later founded the Playwrights Center in Minneapolis. The 1984 Broadway production of *Ma Rainey's Black Bottom* established his theatrical reputation, and since then he has been writing a series of ten plays dealing with the black experience in America, each one set during a different decade of the twentieth century. Among his plays are *Jitney* (1982); *Fences* (1985), winner of the 1987 Pulitzer Prize; *Joe Turner's Come and Gone* (1986); *The Piano Lesson* (1987), which won a Tony Award, the Drama Critics Circle Award, the American Theater Critics Outstanding Play Award, and the 1990 Pulitzer Prize; *Two Trains Running* (1992); *Seven Guitars* (1995); *King Hedley II* (2001); and *Gem of the Ocean* (2003).

### TENNESSEE WILLIAMS
(1911–1983)

(1945–2005)

# Writing about Literature

When it comes to the study of literature, reading and writing are closely interrelated—even mutually dependent—activities. On the one hand, the quality of whatever we write about a literary text depends entirely upon the quality of our work as readers. On the other hand, our reading isn't truly complete until we've tried to capture our sense of a text in writing. Indeed, we often read a literary work much more actively and attentively when we integrate informal writing into the reading process—pausing periodically to mark especially important or confusing passages, to jot down significant facts, to describe the impressions and responses the text provokes—or when we imagine our reading (and our informal writing) as preparation for writing about the work in a more sustained and formal way.

Writing about literature can take any number of forms, ranging from the very informal and personal to the very formal and public. In fact, your instructor may well ask you to try your hand at more than one form. However, the essay is by far the most common and complex form that writing about literature takes. As a result, the following chapters will focus on the essay.* A first, short chapter covers three basic ways of writing about literature. The second chapter, "The Elements of the Essay," seeks to answer a very basic set of questions: *When an instructor says, "Write an essay," what precisely does that mean? What is the purpose of an essay, and what form does it need to take in order to achieve that purpose?* The third chapter, "The Writing Process," addresses questions about how an essay is produced, while the fourth chapter explores the special steps and strategies involved in writing a research essay—a type of essay about literature that draws on secondary sources. "Quotation, Citation, and Documentation" explains the rules and strategies involved in quoting and citing both literary texts and secondary sources using the documentation system recommended by the Modern Language Association (MLA). And, finally, we present a sample research essay, annotated to point out some its most important features.

## 32 PARAPHRASE, SUMMARY, DESCRIPTION

Before turning to the essay, let's briefly consider three other basic ways of writing about literature: *paraphrase, summary,* and *description.* Each of these can be useful both as an exercise to prepare for writing an essay and as part of a completed essay. That is, an essay about a literary text must do more than paraphrase, summarize, or describe the text; yet a good essay about a literary text almost always incorporates some paraphrase, summary, and description of the literature and, in the case of a research essay, of secondary sources as well.

---

*In chapters 32–36, unless otherwise specified, page numbers in the examples refer to this volume, *The Norton Introduction to Literature,* 9th edition.

## 32.1 PARAPHRASE

To paraphrase a statement is to restate it in your own words. Since the goal of paraphrase is to represent a statement fully and faithfully, paraphrases tend to be at least as long as the original, and one usually wouldn't try to paraphrase an entire work of any length. The following examples offer paraphrases of sentences from a work of fiction (Jane Austen's *Pride and Prejudice*), a poem (W. B. Yeats's "All Things Can Tempt Me"), and an essay (George L. Dillon's "Styles of Reading").

| ORIGINAL SENTENCE | PARAPHRASE |
| --- | --- |
| It is a truth universally acknowledged that a single man in possession of a good fortune must be in want of a wife. | Everyone agrees that a propertied bachelor needs (or wants) to find a woman to marry. |
| All things can tempt me from this craft of verse:<br>One time it was a woman's face, or worse—<br>The seeming needs of my fool-driven land;<br>Now nothing but comes readier to the hand<br>Than this accustomed toil.... | Anything can distract me from writing poetry: One time I was distracted by a woman's face, but I was even more distracted by (or I found an even less worthy distraction in) the attempt to fulfill what I imagined to be the needs of a country governed by idiots. At this point in my life I find any task easier than the work I'm used to doing (writing poetry). |
| ...making order out of Emily's life is a complicated matter, since the narrator recalls the details through a nonlinear filter. | It's difficult to figure out the order in which events in Emily's life occurred because the narrator doesn't relate them chronologically. |

Paraphrase resembles translation. Indeed, the paraphrase of Yeats is essentially a "translation" of poetry into prose, and the paraphrases of Austen and of Dillon are "translations" of one kind of prose (formal nineteenth-century British prose, the equally formal but quite different prose of a twentieth-century literary critic) into another kind (colloquial twentieth-century American prose).

But what good is that? First, paraphrasing tests that you truly understand what you've read; it can be especially helpful when an author's diction and syntax seem difficult, complex, or "foreign" to you. Second, paraphrasing can direct your attention to nuances of tone or potentially significant details. For example, paraphrasing Austen's sentence might highlight its irony and call attention to the multiple meanings of phrases such as *a good fortune* and *in want of*. Similarly, paraphrasing Yeats might help you to think about all that he gains by making himself the object rather than the subject of his sentence. Third, paraphrase can help you begin generating the kind of interpretive questions that can drive an essay. For example, the Austen paraphrase might suggest the following questions: *What competing definitions of "a good fortune" are set out in* Pride and Prejudice? *Which definition, if any, does the novel as a whole seem to endorse?*

## 32.2 SUMMARY

A summary is a fairly succinct restatement or overview of the content of an entire text or source (or a significant portion thereof). Like paraphrases, summaries should always be stated in your own words.

A summary of a literary text is generally called a *plot summary* because it focuses on the action or plot. Here, for example, is a summary of Edgar Allan Poe's "The Raven":

> The speaker of Poe's "The Raven" is sitting in his room late at night reading in order to forget the death of his beloved Lenore. There's a tap at the door; after some hesitation he opens it and calls Lenore's name, but there is only an echo. When he goes back into his room he hears the rapping again, this time at his window, and when he opens it a raven enters. He asks the raven its name, and it answers very clearly, "Nevermore." As the speaker's thoughts run back to Lenore, he realizes the aptness of the raven's word: she shall sit there nevermore. But, he says, sooner or later he will forget her, and the grief will lessen. "Nevermore," the raven says again, too aptly. Now the speaker wants the bird to leave, but "Nevermore," the raven says once again. At the end, the speaker knows he'll never escape the raven or its dark message.

Though a summary should be significantly shorter than the original, it can be any length you need it to be. Above, the 108 lines of Poe's poem have been reduced to about 160 words. But one could summarize this or any other work in as little as one sentence. Here, for example, are three viable one-sentence summaries of *Hamlet*:

> A young man seeking to avenge his uncle's murder of his father kills his uncle, while also bringing about his own and many others' deaths.

> A young Danish prince avenges the murder of his father, the king, by his uncle, who had usurped the throne, but the prince himself is killed, as are others, and a well-led foreign army has no trouble successfully invading the decayed and troubled state.

> When, from the ghost of his murdered father, a young prince learns that his uncle, who has married the prince's mother, is the father's murderer, the prince plots revenge, feigning madness, acting erratically—even insulting the woman he loves—and, though gaining his revenge, causes the suicide of his beloved and the deaths of others and, finally, of himself.

As these *Hamlet* examples suggest, different readers—or even the same reader on different occasions—will almost certainly summarize the same text in dramatically different ways. Summarizing entails selection and emphasis. As a result, any summary reflects a particular point of view and may even imply a particular interpretation or argument. When writing a summary, you should try to be as objective as possible; nevertheless, your summary will reflect your own understanding and attitudes. For this reason, summarizing a literary text may help you to begin figuring out just what your particular understanding of a text is, especially if you then compare your summary to those of other readers.

## 32.3 DESCRIPTION

Whereas both summary and paraphrase focus on content, a description of a literary text focuses on its overall form or structure or some particular aspect thereof. Here, for example, is a description (rather than a summary) of the rhyme scheme of "The Raven":

Poe's "The Raven" is a poem of 108 lines divided into eighteen six-line stanzas. If you were to look just at the ends of the lines, you would notice only one or two unusual features: not only is there only one rhyme sound per stanza—lines 2, 4, 5, and 6 rhyming—but one rhyme sound is the same in all eighteen stanzas, so that seventy-two lines end with the sound "ore." In addition, the fourth and fifth lines of each stanza end with an identical word; in six of the stanzas that word is "door" and in four others "Lenore." There is even more repetition: the last line of six of the first seven stanzas ends with the words "nothing more," and the last eleven stanzas end with the word "Nevermore." The rhyming lines—other than the last, which is very short—in each stanza are fifteen syllables long, the rhymed line sixteen. The longer lines give the effect of shorter ones, however, and add still further to the frequency of repeated sounds, for the first half of each opening line rhymes with the second half of the line, and so do the halves of line 3. There is still more: the first half of line 4 rhymes with the halves of line 3 (in the first stanza the rhymes are "dreary" / "weary" and "napping" / "tapping" / "rapping"). So at least nine words in each six-line stanza are involved in the regular rhyme scheme, and many stanzas have added instances of rhyme or repetition. As if this were not enough, all the half-line rhymes are rich feminine rhymes, where both the accented and the following unaccented syllables rhyme—"dreary" / "wary."

You could similarly describe many other formal elements of the poem—images and symbols, for example. You can describe a play in comparable terms—acts, scenes, settings, time lapses, perhaps—and you might describe a novel in terms of chapters, books, summary narration, dramatized scenes. In addition to describing the narrative structure or focus and voice of a short story, you might describe the diction (word choice), the sentence structure, the amount and kind of description of characters or landscape, and so on.

# 33 THE ELEMENTS OF THE ESSAY

As you move from reading literary works to writing essays about them, remember that the essay—like the short story, poem, or play—is a distinctive subgenre with unique elements and conventions. Just as you come to a poem or play with a certain set of expectations, so will readers approach your essay. They will be looking for particular elements, anticipating that the work will unfold in a specific way. This chapter explains and explores those elements so that you can develop a clear sense of what makes a piece of writing an essay and why some essays are more effective than others.

An essay has particular elements and a particular form because it serves a specific purpose. Keeping this in mind, consider what an essay is and what it does. An essay is a relatively short written composition that articulates, supports, and develops an idea or claim. Like any work of expository prose, it aims to explain something complex. Explaining in this case entails both *analysis* (breaking the complex "thing" down into its constituent parts and showing how they work together to form a meaningful whole) and *argument* (working to convince someone that the analysis is valid). In an essay about literature, the literary work is the complex thing that you are helping a reader to better understand. The essay needs to show the reader a particular way to understand the work, to interpret or read it. That interpretation or reading starts with the essayist's own personal response. But an essay also needs to persuade the reader that this interpretation is reasonable and enlightening—that it is, though it is distinctive and new, it is more than merely idiosyncratic or subjective.

To achieve these ends, an essay must incorporate four elements: an appropriate *tone*, a clear *thesis*, a coherent *structure*, and ample, appropriate *evidence*.

## 33.1 TONE (AND AUDIENCE)

Although your reader or audience isn't an element *in* your essay, tone is. And tone and audience are closely interrelated. In everyday life, the tone we adopt has everything to do with whom we are talking to and what situation we're in. For example, we talk very differently to our parents than to our best friends. And in different situations we talk to the same person in different ways. What tone do you adopt with your best friends when you want to borrow money? when you need advice? when you're giving advice? when you're deciding whether to eat pizza or sushi? In each case you act on your knowledge of who your friends are, what information they already have, and what their response is likely to be. But you also try to adopt a tone that will encourage them to respond in a certain way.

In writing, as in everyday life, your audience, situation, and purpose should shape your tone. Conversely, your tone will shape your audience's response. You need to figure out both who your readers are and what response you want to elicit. Who is your audience? When you write an essay for class, the obvious answer is your instructor. But in an important sense, that is the wrong answer. Although your instructor could literally be the only person besides you who will ever read your essay, you write about literature to learn how to write for an audience of peers—people a lot like you who are sensible and educated and who will appreciate having a literary work explained so that they can understand it more fully. Picture your reader as someone about your own age with roughly the same educational background. Assume the person has some experience in reading literature, but that he or she has read this particular work only once and has not yet closely analyzed it. You should neither be insulting and explain the obvious nor assume that your reader has noticed, considered, and remembered every detail.

Should you, then, altogether ignore the obvious fact that an instructor—who probably has a master's degree or doctorate in literature—is your actual reader? Not altogether: you don't want to get so carried away with speaking to people of your own age and interests that you slip into slang, or feel the need to explain what a stanza is, or leave unexplained an allusion to your favorite movie. Even though you do want to learn from the advice and guidelines your instructor has given, try not to be preoccupied with the idea that you are writing for someone "in authority" or someone utterly different from yourself.

Above all, don't think of yourself as writing for a captive audience, for readers who have to read what you write or who already see the text as you do. (If that were the case, there wouldn't be much point in writing at all.) It is not always easy to know how interested your readers will be or how their views might differ from yours, so you must make the most of every word. Remember that the purpose of your essay is to persuade readers to see the text your way. That process begins with persuading them that you deserve their attention and respect. The tone of your paper should be serious and straightforward, respectful toward your readers and the literary work. But its approach and vocabulary, while formal enough for academic writing, should be lively enough to interest someone like you. Try to imagine, as your ideal reader, the person in class whom you most respect but who often seems to see things differently from you. Write to capture and hold that person's attention and respect. Encourage your reader to adopt a desirable stance *toward* your essay by adopting that same stance *in* your essay. Engage and convince your reader by demonstrating your engagement and conviction. Encourage your reader to keep an open mind by showing that you have done the same.

## 33.2 THESIS

A thesis is to an essay what a theme is to a short story, play, or poem: it's the governing idea, proposition, claim, or point. Good theses come in many shapes and sizes. A thesis cannot always be conveyed in one sentence, nor will it always appear in the same place in every essay. But you will risk both appearing confused and confusing the reader if you can't state the thesis in one to three sentences or if the thesis doesn't appear somewhere in your introduction, usually near its end.

Regardless of its length or location, a thesis must be debatable—a claim that all readers won't automatically accept. It's a proposition that *can* be proven with evidence from the text. Yet it's one that *has* to be proven, that isn't obviously true or factual, that must be supported with evidence in order to be fully understood or accepted by the reader. The following examples juxtapose a series of inarguable topics or fact statements—ones that are merely factual or descriptive—with thesis statements, each of which makes a debatable claim about the topic or fact:

| TOPIC OR FACT STATEMENTS | THESIS STATEMENTS |
| --- | --- |
| "The Story of an Hour" explores the topic of marriage. | In "The Story of an Hour," Chopin poses a troubling question: Does marriage inevitably encourage people to "impose [their] private will upon a fellow-creature" (537)? |
| "The Blind Man," "Cathedral," and "The Lame Shall Enter First" all feature characters with physical handicaps. | "The Blind Man," "Cathedral," and "The Lame Shall Enter First" feature protagonists who learn about their own emotional or spiritual shortcomings through an encounter with a physically handicapped person. In this way, all three stories invite us to question traditional definitions of "disability." |
| The experience of the speaker in "How I Discovered Poetry" is very ambiguous. | In "How I Discovered Poetry," what the speaker discovers is the ambiguous power of words—their capacity both to inspire and unite and to denigrate and divide. |
| "London" consists of three discrete stanzas that each end with a period; two-thirds of the lines are end-stopped. | In "London," William Blake uses a variety of formal techniques to suggest the unnatural rigidity and constraints of urban life. |
| *A Streetcar Named Desire* uses a lot of Darwinian language. | *A Streetcar Named Desire* asks whether or not it is truly the "fittest" who "survive" in contemporary America. |
| Creon and Antigone are both similar and different. | Creon and Antigone are alike in several ways, especially the inconsistency of their values and the way they are driven by passion below the surface of rational argument. Both are also one-sided in their commitments.... This does not mean, however, that they are equally limited in the values to which they adhere. —Mary Whitlock Blundell, "Helping Friends..." (ch. 31) |

All of the thesis statements above are arguable, but they share other traits as well. All are clear and emphatic. Each implicitly answers a compelling interpretive question—for instance, *What do Antigone and Creon stand for? Which character and worldview, if any, does the play as a whole ultimately champion?* Yet each statement entices us to read further by generating more questions in our minds—*How and why do Creon and Antigone demonstrate "inconsistency" and "one-sidedness"? If these two characters are not equally limited, which of them is more limited?* An effective thesis enables the reader to enter the essay with a clear sense of what its writer will try to prove, and it inspires the reader with the desire to see the writer do it. We want to understand how the writer arrived at this view, to test whether it's valid, and to see how the writer will answer the other questions the thesis has generated in our minds. A good thesis captures the reader's interest and shapes his or her expectations. It also makes promises that the rest of the essay should fulfill.

At the same time, an arguable claim is not one-sided or narrow-minded. A thesis needs to stake out a position, but a position can and should admit complexity. Literary texts tend to focus more on exploring problems, conflicts, and questions than on offering solutions, resolutions, and answers. Their goal is to complicate, not simplify, our way of looking at the world. The best essays about literature and the theses that drive them often share a similar quality.

### 33.2.1 Interpretive versus Evaluative Claims

All the theses in the previous examples involve *interpretive* claims—claims about how a literary text works, what it says, how one should understand it. And interpretive claims generally work best as theses.

Yet it's useful to remember that in reading and writing about literature we often make (and debate) a different type of claim—the *evaluative*. Evaluation entails judging or assessing. Evaluative claims about literature tend to be of two kinds. The first involves aesthetic judgment, the question being whether a text (or a part or element thereof) succeeds in artistic terms. (This kind of claim features prominently in book reviews, for example.) The second involves philosophical, ethical, or even socially or politically based judgment, the question being whether an idea or action is wise or good, valid or admirable. All interpretive and evaluative claims involve informed opinion (which is why they are debatable). But whereas interpretive claims aim to elucidate the opinions expressed *in* and *by* the text, the second kind of evaluative claim assesses the value or validity of those opinions, often by comparing them with the writer's own.

The following examples juxtapose a series of interpretive claims with evaluative claims of both types:

| INTERPRETIVE CLAIMS | EVALUATIVE CLAIMS |
|---|---|
| "A Conversation with My Father" explores the relative values of realistic and fantastic fiction. Rather than advocating one type of fiction, however, the story ends up affirming just how much we need stories of any and every kind. | "A Conversation with My Father" fails because it ends up being more a stilted Platonic dialogue about works of fiction than a true work of fiction in its own right. |
| | The father in "A Conversation with My Father" is absolutely right: realistic stories are more effective and satisfying than fantastic ones. |
| The speaker of John Donne's "Song" is an angry and disillusioned man obsessed with the infidelity of women. | In "Song," John Donne does a very effective job of characterizing the speaker, an angry and disillusioned man obsessed with the infidelity of women. |
| | John Donne's "Song" is a horribly misogynistic poem because it ends up endorsing the idea that women are incapable of fidelity. |
| "How I Learned to Drive" demonstrates that, in Paula Vogel's words, "it takes a whole village to molest a child." | "How I Learned to Drive" is at once too preachy and too self-consciously theatrical to be dramatically effective. |
| | By insisting that sexual abuse is a crime perpetrated by a "whole village" rather than by an individual, Paula Vogel lets individual abusers off the hook, encouraging us to see them as victims rather than as the villains they really are. |

In practice, the line between these different types of claims can become very thin. For instance, an essay claiming that Vogel's play conveys a socially dangerous or morally bad message about abuse may also claim that it is, as a result, an aesthetically flawed play. Further, an essay defending an interpretive claim about a text implies that it is at least aesthetically or philosophically worthy enough to merit interpretation. Conversely, defending and developing an evaluative claim about a text always requires a certain amount of interpretation. (You have to figure out what the text says in order to figure out whether the text says it well or says something worthwhile.)

To some extent, then, the distinctions are ones of emphasis. But they are important nonetheless. And unless instructed otherwise, you should generally make your thesis an interpretive claim, reserving evaluative claims for conclusions. (On conclusions, see 33.3.3.)

## 33.3 STRUCTURE

Like any literary text, an essay needs to have a beginning (or introduction), a middle (or body), and an ending (or conclusion). Each of these parts has a distinct function.

### 33.3.1 Beginning: The Introduction

Your essay's beginning, or introduction, should draw readers in and prepare them for what's to come by:

- articulating the thesis;
- providing whatever basic information—about the text, the author, and/or the topic—readers will need to follow the argument; and
- creating interest in the thesis by demonstrating that there is a problem or question that it resolves or answers.

This final task involves showing readers why your thesis isn't dull or obvious, establishing a specific *motive* for the essay and its readers. There are numerous possible motives, but writing expert Gordon Harvey has identified three especially common ones:

1. The truth isn't what one would expect or what it might appear to be on a first reading.
2. There's an interesting wrinkle in the text—a paradox, a contradiction, a tension.
3. A seemingly tangential or insignificant matter is actually important or interesting.

(On motives specific to research essays, see 35.1.1.)

### 33.3.2 Middle: The Body

The middle, or body, of your essay is its beating heart, the place where you do the essential work of supporting and developing the thesis by presenting and analyzing evidence. Each of the body paragraphs needs to articulate, support, and develop one specific claim—a debatable idea directly related to, but smaller and more specific than, the thesis. This claim should be stated fairly early in the paragraph in a *topic sentence*. And every sentence in the paragraph should help prove, or elaborate on, that claim. Indeed, each paragraph ideally should build from an initial, general statement of the claim to the more complex form of it that you develop by presenting and analyzing evidence. In this way, each paragraph functions like a miniature essay with its own thesis, body, and conclusion.

Your essay as a whole should develop logically just as each paragraph does. To ensure that that happens, you need to:

- order your paragraphs so that each builds on the last, with one idea following another in a logical sequence. The goal is to lay out a clear path for the reader. Like any path, it should go somewhere. Don't just prove your point; develop it.
- present each idea/paragraph so that the logic behind the sequential order is clear. Try to start each paragraph with a sentence that functions as a bridge, carrying the reader from one point to the next. Don't make the reader have to leap.

### 33.3.3 Ending: The Conclusion

In terms of their purpose (not their content), conclusions are introductions in reverse. Whereas introductions draw readers away from their world and into your essay, conclusions send them back. Introductions work to convince readers that they should read the essay. Conclusions work to show them why and how the experience was worthwhile. You should approach conclusions, then, by thinking about what sort of lasting impression you want to create. What precisely do you want readers to take with them as they journey back into the "real world"?

Effective conclusions often consider three things:

1. *Implications*—What picture of your author's work or worldview does your argument imply or suggest? Alternatively, what might your argument imply about some real-world issue or situation? Implications don't have to be earth-shattering. For example, it's unlikely that your reading of O'Connor's "Everything That Rises Must Converge" will rock your readers' world. Moreover, trying to convince readers that it can may well have the opposite effect. Yet your argument should in some small but significant way change the way readers see O'Connor's work; alternatively, it might give them new insight into how racism works, or how difficult it is for human beings to adjust to changes in the world around us, or how mistaken it can be to see ourselves as more enlightened than our elders, and so on.
2. *Evaluation*—What might your argument about the text reveal about the literary quality or effectiveness of the text as a whole or of some specific element? Alternatively, to what extent and how do you agree and/or disagree with the author's conclusions about a particular issue? How, for example, does your own view of how racism works compare to the viewpoint implied in "Everything That Rises Must Converge"? (For more on evaluative claims, see 33.2.1.)

3. *Areas of ambiguity or unresolved questions*—Are there any remaining puzzles or questions that your argument and/or the text itself doesn't resolve or answer? Alternatively, might your argument suggest a new question or puzzle worth investigating?

Above all, don't repeat what you've already said. If the essay has done its job to this point, and especially if the essay is relatively short, your readers may feel bored and insulted if they get a mere summary. You should clarify anything that needs clarifying, but go a little beyond that. The best essays are rounded wholes in which conclusions do, in a sense, circle back to the place where they started. However, the best essays remind readers of where they began only in order to give them a more palpable sense of how far they've come.

## 33.4 EVIDENCE

In terms of convincing readers that your claims are valid, both the amount and the quality of your evidence count. And the quality of your evidence will depend, in great part, on how you prepare and present it. Each of the ideas that makes up the body of your essay must be supported and developed with ample, appropriate evidence. Colloquially speaking, the term *evidence* simply refers to facts. But it's helpful to remember that a fact by itself isn't really evidence for anything, or rather that—as lawyers well know—any one fact can be evidence for many things. Like lawyers, essayists turn a fact into evidence by interpreting it; drawing an inference from it; giving the reader a vivid sense of why and how the fact supports a specific claim. You need, then, both to present specific facts and to actively interpret them. *Show* readers why and how each fact matters.

Quotations are an especially important form of evidence in essays about literature; indeed, an essay about literature that contains no quotations will likely be relatively weak. The reader of such an essay may doubt whether its argument emerges out of a thorough knowledge of the work. However, quotations are by no means the only facts on which you should draw. Indeed, a quotation will lead your reader to expect commentary on, and interpretation of, its language. As a general rule, you should quote directly from the text only when its wording is significant. Otherwise, simply paraphrase, describe, or summarize. The following example demonstrates the use of both summary and quotation. (On effective quotation, see 36.1; on paraphrase, summary, and description, see ch. 32.)

> At many points in the novel, religion is represented as having degenerated into a system of social control by farmers over workers. Only respectable young men can come courting at Upper Weatherbury farm, and no swearing is allowed (ch. 8). Similarly, the atmosphere in Boldwood's farm kitchen is "like a Puritan Sunday lasting all the week." Bathsheba tries to restrict her workers to drinking mild liquor, and church attendance is taken as the mark of respectability.
> —Fred Reid, "Art and Ideology in *Far from the Madding Crowd*,"
> *Thomas Hardy Annual 4* (London: Macmillan, 1986)

> NOTE: Pay special attention to the way this writer uses paraphrase, summary, and quotation. At the beginning of the paragraph, he simply paraphrases certain rules; at its end, he summarizes or describes one character's action. Here, he can use his own words because it's the rules and actions that illustrate his point, not the words that the novelist uses to describe them. However, Reid does quote the text when its (religious) language is the crucial, evidentiary element.

## 33.5 CONVENTIONS THAT CAN CAUSE PROBLEMS

A mastery of basic mechanics and writing conventions is essential to convincing your readers that you are a knowledgeable and careful writer whose ideas they should respect. This section explores three conventions that are especially crucial to essays about literature.

### 33.5.1 Tenses

Essays about literature tend to function almost wholly in the present tense, a practice that can take some getting used to. The rationale is that the action within any literary work never stops: a text simply, always *is*. Thus yesterday, today, and tomorrow, Ophelia *goes* mad; "The Lost World" *asks* what it means to grow up; Wordsworth *sees* nature as an avenue to God; and so on. When in doubt, stick to the present tense when writing about literature.

An important exception to this general rule is demonstrated in the following example. As you read the excerpt, pay attention to the way the writer shifts between tenses, using various past tenses to refer to completed actions that took place in the actual past, and using the present tense to refer to actions that occur within, or are performed by, the text.

> In 1959 Plath **did not** consciously **attempt** to write in the domestic poem genre, perhaps because she **was not** yet ready to assume her majority. Her journal entries of that period **bristle** with an impatience at herself that **may derive** from this reluctance.... But by fall 1962, when she **had** already **lost** so much, she **was** ready.... In "Daddy" she **achieved** her victory in two ways. First, ... she symbolically **assaults** a father figure who **is identified** with male control of language.
> —Steven Gould Axelrod, "Jealous Gods" (ch. 25)

### 33.5.2 Titles

Underline or italicize the titles of all books and works published independently, including:

- long poems (*Endymion; Paradise Lost*)
- plays (*A Midsummer Night's Dream; Death and the King's Horseman*)
- periodicals: newspapers, magazines, scholarly journals, and the like (*New York Times; College English*)

Use quotation marks for the titles of works that have been published as part of longer works, including:

- short stories ("A Rose for Emily"; "Happy Endings")
- essays and periodical articles ("A Rose for 'A Rose for Emily' "; "Art and Ideology in *Far from the Madding Crowd*")
- poems ("Daddy"; "Ode to a Nightingale")

Generally speaking, you should capitalize the first word of every title, as well as all the other words that aren't either articles (e.g., *the, a*); prepositions (e.g., *among, in, through*); or conjunctions (e.g., *and, but*). One exception to this rule is the poem in which the first line substitutes for a missing title (a category that includes everything by Emily Dickinson, as well as the sonnets of Shakespeare and Edna St. Vincent Millay). In such cases, only the first word is capitalized. Often, the entire phrase is placed in brackets—as in "[Let me not to the marriage of true minds]"—but you will just as often see such titles without brackets.

### 33.5.3 Names

When first referring to an author, use his or her full name; thereafter, use the last name. (For example, although you may feel a real kinship with Robert Frost, you will appear disrespectful if you refer to him as Robert.)

With characters' names, use the literary work as a guide. Because "Bartleby, the Scrivener" always refers to its characters as *Bartleby, Turkey,* and *Nippers,* so should you. But because "The Management of Grief" refers to Judith Templeton either by her full name or by her first name, it would be odd and confusing to call her *Templeton.*

# 34 THE WRITING PROCESS

It's fairly easy to describe the purpose and formal elements of an essay. Actually writing one is more difficult. So, too, is prescribing a precise formula for how to do so. In practice, the writing process will vary from writer to writer and from assignment to assignment. No one can give you a recipe. However, this chapter presents a menu of possible approaches and exercises, which you should test out and refine for yourself.

As you do so, keep in mind that writing needn't be a solitary enterprise. Most writers—working in every genre, at every level—get inspiration, guidance, help, and feedback from other people throughout the writing process, and so can you. Your instructor may well create opportunities for collaboration, having you and your colleagues work together to plan essays, critique drafts, and so on. Even if that isn't the case, you can always reach out to others on your own. Since every essay will ultimately have to engage readers, why not bring some actual readers and fellow writers into the writing process? Use class discussions to generate and test out essay topics and theses. Ask the instructor to clarify assignments or to talk with you about your plans. Have classmates, friends, or roommates read your drafts.

Of course, your essay ultimately needs to be your own work. You, the individual writer, must be the ultimate arbiter, critically scrutinizing the advice you receive, differentiating valid reader responses from idiosyncratic ones. But in writing about literature, as in reading it, we all can get a much better sense of what we think by considering others' views.

## 34.1 GETTING STARTED

### 34.1.1 Scrutinizing the Assignment

For student essayists, as for most professional ones, the writing process usually begins with an assignment. Though assignments vary greatly, all impose certain restrictions. These are designed not to hinder your creativity but to direct it into productive channels, ensuring that you hone certain skills, try out various approaches, and avoid common pitfalls. Your first task as a writer is thus to scrutinize the assignment. Make sure that you fully understand what you are being asked to do (and not do), and ask questions about anything unclear or puzzling.

Almost all assignments restrict the length of the essay by giving word or page limits. Keep those limits in mind as you generate and evaluate potential essay topics, making sure that you choose a topic you can handle in the space allowed. Many assignments impose further restrictions, often indicating the texts and/or topics to be explored. As a result, any given assignment will significantly shape the rest of the writing process—determining, for example, whether and how you should tackle a step such as "Choosing a Text" or "Identifying Topics."

Here are three representative essay assignments, each of which imposes a different set of restrictions:

1. Choose any story in this anthology and write an essay analyzing the way in which its protagonist changes.
2. Write an essay analyzing one of the following sonnets: "The New Colossus," "Range-Finding," or "London, 1802." Be sure to consider how the poem's form contributes to its meaning.
3. Write an essay exploring the significance of references to eyes and vision in *A Midsummer Night's Dream*. What, through them, does the play suggest about both the power and the limitations of human vision?

The first assignment dictates the topic and main question. It also provides the kernel of a thesis: *In [story title], [protagonist's name] goes from being a _____ to a _____ OR By the end of [story title], [protagonist's name] has learned that _____*. The assignment leaves you free to choose which story you will write about, although it limits you to those in which the protagonist clearly changes or learns a lesson of some kind. The second assignment limits your choice of texts to three. Though it also requires that your essay address the effects of the poet's choice to use the sonnet form, it doesn't require this to be the main topic of the essay. Rather, it leaves you free to pursue any topic that focuses on the poem's meaning. The third assignment is the most restrictive. It indicates both the text and the general topic to be explored, while requiring you to narrow the topic and formulate a specific thesis.

### 34.1.2 Choosing a Text

If the assignment allows you to choose which text to write about, try letting your initial impressions or "gut reactions" guide you. If you do so, your first impulse may be to choose a text that you like or "get" right away. Perhaps its language resembles your own; it depicts speakers, characters, or situations that you easily relate to; or it explores issues that you care deeply about. Following that first impulse can be a great idea. Writing an engaging essay requires being engaged with whatever we're writing about, and we all find it easier to engage with texts, authors, and/or characters that we like immediately.

You may discover, however, that you have little interesting or new to say about such a text. Perhaps you're too emotionally invested to analyze it closely, or maybe its meaning seems so obvious that there's no puzzle or problem to drive an argument. You might, then, find it more productive to choose a work that provokes the opposite reaction—one that initially puzzles or angers you, one whose characters or situations seem alien, one that investigates an issue you haven't previously thought much about or that articulates a theme you don't agree with. Sometimes such negative responses can have surprisingly positive results when it comes to writing. One student writer, for example, summed up her basic response to William Blake's *The Marriage of Heaven and Hell* with the words "He's crazy." Initially, the poem made no sense to her. And that's precisely why she decided to write about it: she needed to do so, to make sense of it for other readers, in order to make sense of it for herself. In the end, she wrote a powerful essay exploring how the poem defined, and why it celebrated, seeming insanity.

When writing about a text that you've discussed in class, you might make similar use of your "gut responses" to that conversation. Did you strongly agree or disagree with one of your classmate's interpretations of a particular text? If so, why not write about it?

### 34.1.3 Identifying Topics

When an assignment allows you to create your own topic, you will much more likely build a lively and engaging essay from a particular insight or question that captures your attention and makes you want to say something, solve a problem, or stake out a position. The best papers originate in an individual response to a text and focus on a genuine question about it. Even when an instructor assigns a topic, the effectiveness of your essay will largely depend on whether or not you have made the topic your own, turning it into a question to which you discover your own answer.

Often we refer to "finding" a topic, as if there are a bevy of topics "out there" just waiting to be plucked like ripe fruit off the topic-tree. In at least two ways, that's true. For one thing, as we read a literary work, certain topics often do jump out and say, "Hey, look at me! I'm a topic!" A title alone may have that effect: What rises and converges in "Everything That Rises Must Converge"? Why is Keats so keen on that darn nightingale; what does it symbolize for him? Why does Wilde think it's important *not* to be earnest?

For another thing, certain general topics can be adapted to fit almost any literary work. In fact, that's just another way of saying that there are certain common types (or subgenres) of literary essays, just as there are of short stories, plays, and poems. For example, one very common kind of literary essay explores the significance of a seemingly insignificant aspect or element of a work—a word or group of related words, an image or image-cluster, a minor character, an incident or action, and so on. Equally common are character-focused essays of three types. The first explores the outlook or worldview of a character and its consequences. The second considers the way a major character develops from the beginning of a literary work to its end. The third analyzes the nature and significance of a conflict between two characters (or two groups of characters) and the way this conflict is ultimately resolved. (Many of the arguments about *Antigone* excerpted in chapter 31 do this.) Especially when you're utterly befuddled about where to begin, it can be very useful to keep in mind these generic topics and essay types and to use them as starting points. But remember that they are just starting points. One always has to adapt and narrow a generic topic such as "imagery" or "character change" in order to produce an effective essay. In practice, then, no writer simply "finds" a topic; he or she *makes* one.

Similarly, though the topic that leaps out at you immediately might end up being the one you find most interesting, you can only discover that by giving yourself some options. It's always a good idea to initially come up with as many topics as you can. Test out various topics to see which one will work best. Making yourself identify multiple topics will lead you to think harder, look more closely, and reach deeper into yourself and the work.

Here are some additional techniques to identify potential topics. In each case, write your thoughts down. Don't worry at this point about what form your writing takes or how good it is.

- *Analyze your initial response.*

  If you've chosen a text that you feel strongly about, start with those responses. Try to describe your feelings and trace them to their source. Be as specific as possible. What moments, aspects, or elements of the text most affected you? Exactly how and why did they affect you? What was most puzzling? amusing? annoying? intriguing? Try to articulate the question behind your feelings. Often, strong responses result when a work either challenges or affirms an expectation, assumption, or conviction that you, the reader, bring to the work. Think about whether and how that's true here. Define the specific expectation, assumption, or conviction. How, where, and why does the text challenge it? fulfill and affirm it? Which of your responses and expectations are objectively valid, likely to be shared by other readers?

- *Think through the elements.*

  Start with a list of elements and work your way through them, thinking about what's unique or interesting or puzzling about the text in terms of each. When it comes to tone, what stands out? What about the speaker? the situation? other elements? Come up with a statement about each. Look for patterns among your statements. Also, think about the questions implied or overlooked by your statements.

- *Pose motive questions.*

  In articulating a motive in your essay's introduction, your concern is primarily with the readers, your goal being to give them a solid reason to keep on reading. But you can often work your way toward a topic (or topics) by considering motive. As suggested earlier (33.3.1), there are three common motives. Turn each one into a question in order to identify potential topics:

  1. What element(s) or aspect(s) of this work might a casual reader misinterpret?
  2. What interesting paradox(es), contradiction(s), or tension(s) do you see in this text?
  3. What seemingly minor, insignificant, easily ignored element(s) or aspect(s) of this text might in fact have major significance?

### 34.1.4 Formulating a Question and a Thesis

Almost any element, aspect, or point of interest in a text can become a topic for a short essay. Before you can begin writing an essay on that topic, however, you need to come up with a thesis or hypothesis—an arguable statement about the topic. Quite often, one comes up with topic and thesis simultaneously: you might well decide to write about a topic precisely because you've got a specific claim to make about it. At other times, that's not the case: the topic comes much more easily than the thesis. In those cases, it helps to formulate a specific question about the topic and to develop a specific answer. That answer will be your thesis.

Again, remember that your question and thesis should focus on something specific, yet they need to be generally valid, involving more than your personal feelings. Who, after all, can really argue with you about how you feel? The following example demonstrates the way you might freewrite your way from an initial, subjective response to an arguable thesis:

> *I really admire Bartleby.*
> *But why? What in the story encourages me to respond that way to him? Well, he sticks to his guns and insists on doing only what he "prefers" to do. He doesn't just follow orders. That makes him really different from all the other characters in the story (especially the narrator). And also from a lot of people I know, even me. He's a nonconformist.*
> *Do I think other readers should feel the same way? Maybe, but maybe not. After all, his refusal to conform does cause problems for everyone around him. And actually it doesn't do him a lot of good either. Plus, he would be really annoying in real life. And, even if you admire him, you can't really care about him because he doesn't seem to care about anybody else.*
> *Maybe that's the point. Through Bartleby, Melville explores both how rare and important, and how dangerous, nonconformity can be.*

Regardless of how you arrive at your thesis or how strongly you believe in it, it's still helpful at this early stage to think of it as a working hypothesis—a claim that's provisional, still open to rethinking and revision.

## 34.2 PLANNING

Once you've formulated a tentative thesis, you need to (1) identify the relevant evidence, and (2) figure out how to structure your argument, articulating and ordering your claims or sub-ideas. Generally speaking, it works best to tackle structure first—that is, to first figure out your claims and create an outline—because doing so will help you get a sense of what kind of evidence you need. However, you may sometimes get stuck and need to reverse this process, gathering evidence first in order to then formulate and order your claims.

### 34.2.1 Moving from Claims to Evidence

If you want to focus first on structure, start by looking closely at your thesis. As in many other aspects of writing, it helps to temporarily fill your readers' shoes, trying to see your thesis and the promises it makes from the readers' point of view. What will they need to be shown, and in what order?

If a good thesis shapes readers' expectations, it can also guide you, as a writer. A good thesis often implies what the essay's claims should be and how they should be ordered. For instance, a thesis that focuses on the development of a character implies both that the first body paragraphs will explain what the character is initially like and that later paragraphs will explore how and why that character changes over the course of the story, poem, or play. Similarly, the Bartleby thesis developed in the previous example—*Through Bartleby, Melville explores both how rare and important, and how dangerous, nonconformity can be.*—implies that the writer's essay will address four major issues and will thus have four major parts. The first part must show that Bartleby is a nonconformist. The second part should establish that this nonconformity is rare, a quality that isn't shared by the other characters in the story. Finally, the third and fourth parts should explore, respectively, the positive and negative aspects or consequences of Bartleby's nonconformist behavior. Some or all of these parts may need to include multiple paragraphs, each devoted to a more specific claim.

At this stage, it's very helpful to create an outline. Write down or type out your thesis, and then list each claim (to create a *sentence outline*) or each of the topics to be covered (to create a *topic outline*). Now you can return to the text, rereading it in order to gather evidence for each claim. In the process, you might discover facts that seem relevant to the thesis but that don't relate directly to any of the claims you've articulated. In that case, you may need to insert a new claim into the outline. Additionally, you may find (and should actively look for) facts that challenge your argument. Test and reassess your claims against those facts.

### 34.2.2 Moving From Evidence to Claims

If you are focusing first on evidence, start by rereading the literary work in a more strategic way, searching for everything relevant to your topic—words, phrases, structural devices, changes of tone, and so forth. As you read (slowly and single-mindedly, with your thesis in mind), keep your pen constantly poised to mark or note down useful facts. Be ready to say something about the facts as you come upon them; immediately write down any ideas that occur to you. Some of these will appear in your essay; some won't. Just like most of the footage shot in making a film, many of your notes will end up on the cutting-room floor. As in filmmaking, however, having too much raw material is preferable to not having enough.

No one can tell you exactly how to take notes. But here is one process that you might try. Be forewarned: this process involves using notecards or uniform sheets of paper. Having your notes on individual cards makes it easier to separate and sort them, a concrete, physical process that can aid the mental process of organizing thoughts and facts. If you are working on a computer, create notecards by putting page breaks between each note or by leaving enough space so that you can cut each page down to a uniform size.

1. Keep your thesis constantly in mind as you reread and take notes. Mark all the passages in the text that bear on your thesis. For each, create a notecard that contains both (a) a single sentence describing how the passage relates to your thesis, and (b) the specific information about the passage's location that you will need to create a parenthetical citation. (The information you need will depend on the kind of text you're working with; for specifics, see 36.2.1.) Also, make cards for other relevant, evidentiary facts—like aspects of a poem's rhyme scheme.

2. Keep reading and taking notes until you experience any of the following:
   - get too tired and lose your concentration. (Stop, take a break, come back later.)
   - stop finding relevant evidence or perceive a noticeable drying up of your ideas. (Again, it's time to pause. Later, when your mind is fresh, read the text one more time to ensure that you didn't miss anything.)
   - find yourself annotating every sentence or line, with the evidence all running together into a single blob. (If this happens, your thesis is probably too broad. Simplify and narrow it. Then continue notetaking.)

- become impatient with your notetaking and can't wait to get started writing. (Start drafting immediately. But be prepared to go back to systematic notetaking if your ideas stop coming or your energy fades.)
- find that the evidence is insufficient for your thesis, that it points in another direction, or that it contradicts your thesis. (Revise your thesis to accommodate the evidence, and begin rereading once more.)

3. When you think you have finished notetaking, read all your notecards over slowly, one by one, and jot down any further ideas as they occur to you, each one on a separate notecard.

Use your notecards to work toward an outline. Again, there are many ways to go about doing this. Here's one process:

1. Sort your cards into logical groups or clusters. Come up with a keyword for that group, and write that word at the top of each card in the group.
2. Set your notecards aside. On a fresh sheet of paper or in a separate document on your computer, write all the major points you want to make. Write them randomly, as they occur to you. Then read quickly through your notecards, and add to your list any important points you have left out.
3. Now it's time to order your points. Putting your points in order is something of a guess at this point, and you may well want to re-order later. For now, take your best guess. Taking your random list, put a "1" in front of the point you will probably begin with, a "2" before the probable second point, and so on.
4. Copy the list in numerical order, revising (if necessary) as you go.
5. Match up your notes (and examples) with the points on your outline. Prepare a title card for each point in the outline, writing on it the point and its probable place in the essay. Then line them up in order before you begin writing. If you're working on a computer, use the search function to find each instance of a keyword, phrase, or name. Then cut and paste in order to arrange your electronic "cards" under the headings you've identified.
6. At this point, you may discover cards that resist classification, cards that belong in two or more places, and/or cards that don't belong anywhere at all. If a card relates to more than one point, put it in the pile with the lowest number, but write on it the number or numbers of other possible locations. Try to find a place for the cards that don't seem to fit, and then put any that remain unsorted into a special file marked "?" or "use in revision."

Before you begin drafting, you may want to develop a more elaborate outline, incorporating examples and including topic sentences for each paragraph; or you may wish to work directly from your sketchy outline and cards.

## 34.3 DRAFTING

If you've taken enough time with the planning process, you may already be quite close to a first draft. If you've instead jumped straight into writing, you may have to move back and forth between composing and taking some of the steps described in the last section. Either way, remember that first drafts are often called *rough drafts* for a reason. Think of yourself as a painter "roughing out" a sketch in preparation for the more detailed painting to come. The most important thing is to start writing and keep at it.

Try to start with your thesis and work your way step by step through the entire body of the essay at one sitting. (However, you don't actually have to sit the whole time; if you get stuck, jump up and down, walk around the room, water your plants. Then get back to work.) You will almost certainly feel frustrated at times—as you search for the right word, struggle to decide how the next sentence should begin, or discover that you need to tackle ideas in a different order from what you originally had planned.

Stick to it. If you become truly stuck, try to explain your point to another person, or get out a piece of paper or open a new computer file and try working out your ideas or freewriting for a few minutes before returning to your draft. Or, if you get to a section you simply can't write at the moment, make a note about what needs to go in that spot. Then move on and come back to that point later.

Whatever it takes, stay with your draft until you've at least got a middle, or body, that you're relatively satisfied with. Then take a break. Later or even tomorrow come back and take another shot, attaching an introduction and conclusion to the body, filling in any gaps, doing your utmost to create a relatively satisfying whole. Now pat yourself on the back and take another break.

## 34.4 REVISING

Revision is one of the most important and difficult tasks for any writer. It's a crucial stage in the writing process, yet one that is all too easy to ignore or mismanage. The difference between a so-so essay and a good one, between a good essay and a great one, often depends entirely on effective revision. Give yourself time to revise and develop revision strategies that work for you; the investment in time and effort will pay rich dividends.

Ideally, the process of revision should involve three distinct tasks: assessing the elements, improving the argument, and editing and proofreading. Each of these may require a separate draft. Before considering those three tasks, however, you should be aware of the following three general tips.

First, effective revision requires you to temporarily play the role of reader, as well as writer, of your essay. Take a step back from your draft, doing your utmost to look at it from a more objective point of view. Revision demands re-vision—looking again, seeing anew. As a result, this is an especially good time to involve other people. Have a classmate or friend read and critique your draft.

Second, at this stage it helps to think less in absolute terms (right and wrong, good and bad) than in terms of strengths and weaknesses (elements and aspects of the draft that work well and those that can be improved through revision). If you can understand what's making your essay work as well as what's detracting from it, then you're better able to improve it. Don't get distracted from this important work by grammatical errors, spelling mistakes, or other minutiae; there will be time to correct them later.

Third, learn to take full advantage of all the capabilities of the computer, but also recognize its limitations. Cutting and pasting make experimenting with different organizational strategies a breeze; word-processing programs identify problems with grammar, spelling, and syntax; the search function can locate repetitive or problematic wording; and so on. You should familiarize yourself with, and use, all of the tools your computer provides and be thankful that you barely know the meaning of the word *white-out*. But you should also remember that the computer is just a tool with limits and that you must be its master. Like any tool, it can create new problems in the process of solving old ones. When it comes to grammar, syntax, and spelling, for instance, you should always pay attention to your program's queries and suggestions. But if you let it make all the decisions, you may end up with an essay full of malapropisms at once hilarious and tragic (one student essay consistently referred to human beings as *human beans*!) or of sentences that are all exactly the same size and shape—all perfectly correct, and all perfectly boring. Also, because the computer makes cutting and pasting so easy and only shows an essay one screen at a time, it's much easier to reorganize but much harder to recognize the effects of doing so. During revision, then, you should at times move away from the computer screen. Print out a hard copy periodically so that you can assess your essay as a whole, identifying problems that you can return to the computer to fix.

### 34.4.1 Assessing the Elements

The first step in revision is to make sure that all the elements or working parts of the essay are indeed working. To help with that process, run through the following checklist in order to identify the strengths and weaknesses of your draft. Try to answer each question honestly.

*Thesis*
- ☐ Is there *one* claim that effectively controls the essay?
- ☐ Is the claim debatable?
- ☐ Does the claim demonstrate real thought? Does it truly illuminate the text and the topic?

*Structure*

BEGINNING
- ☐ Does the introduction establish a clear motive for readers, effectively convincing them that there's something worth thinking, reading, and writing about here?
- ☐ Does it give readers all (and only) the basic information they need about the text, author, and/or topic?
- ☐ Does the introduction clearly state the central claim or thesis? Is it obvious which claim is the thesis?

MIDDLE
- ☐ Does each paragraph state one debatable claim? Is the main claim always obvious? Does everything in the paragraph relate to, and help to support and develop, that claim?
- ☐ Is each of those claims clearly related to (but different from) the thesis?
- ☐ Are the claims/paragraphs logically ordered?
- ☐ Is that logic clear? Is each claim clearly linked to those that come before and after? Are there any logical "leaps" that readers might have trouble taking?
- ☐ Does each claim/paragraph clearly build on the last one? Does the argu-

ment move forward, or does it seem more like a list or a tour through a museum of interesting observations?
☐ Do any key claims or steps in the argument seem to be missing?

> TIP: You may be better able to discover structural weaknesses if you:
> 1. re-outline your draft as it is. Copy your thesis statement and each of your topic sentences into a separate document. Then pose the above questions.
> OR
> 2. read through the essay with highlighters of various colors in hand. As you read, color-code parts that could be restatements of the same or closely related ideas. Then reorganize to match up the colors.

ENDING
☐ Does the conclusion give readers the sense that they've gotten somewhere and that the journey has been worthwhile?
☐ Does it indicate the implications of the argument, consider relevant evaluative questions, and/or discuss questions that remain unanswered?

*Evidence*
☐ Is there ample, appropriate evidence for each claim?
☐ Are the appropriateness and significance of each fact—its relevance to the claim—perfectly clear?
☐ Are there any weak examples or inferences that aren't reasonable? Are there moments when readers might ask, "But couldn't that fact instead mean this?"
☐ Is all the evidence considered? What about facts that might complicate or contradict the argument? Are there moments when readers might think, "But what about this other fact?"
☐ Is each piece of evidence clearly presented? Do readers have all the contextual information they need to understand a quotation?
☐ Is each piece of evidence gracefully presented? Are quotations varied by length and presentation? Are they ever too long? Are there any unnecessary block quotations, or block quotations that require additional analysis? (For more specific explanations and advice on effective quotation, see 36.1.)

Though you want to pay attention to all of the elements, first drafts often have similar weaknesses. There are three especially common ones:

- *Mismatch between thesis and argument or between introduction and body*
  Sometimes a first or second draft ends up being a tool for discovering what your thesis really is. As a result, you may find that the thesis of your draft (or your entire introduction) doesn't fit the argument you've ended up making. You thus need to start your revision by reworking the thesis and introduction. Then work your way back through the essay, making sure that each claim or topic sentence fits the new thesis.

- *The list, or "museum tour," structure*
  In a draft, writers sometimes present each claim as if it were just an item on a list (*First, second,* and so on) or as a stop on a tour of ideas (*And this is also important . . .*). But presenting your ideas in this way keeps you and your readers from making logical connections between ideas. It may also

prevent your argument from developing. Sometimes it can even be a symptom of the fact that you've ceased arguing entirely, falling into mere plot summary or description. Check to see if number-like words or phrases appear prominently at the beginning of your paragraphs or if your paragraphs could be put into a different order without fundamentally changing what you're saying. At times, solving this problem will require wholesale rethinking and reorganizing. But at other times, you will just need to add or rework topic sentences. Make sure that there's a clearly stated, debatable claim up-front and in charge of each paragraph and that each claim relates to, but differs from, the thesis.

- *Missing sub-ideas*
You may find that you've skipped a logical step in your argument—that the claim you make in, say, body paragraph 3 actually depends on, or makes sense only in light of, a more basic claim that you took for granted in your draft. In that case, you'll need to create and insert a new paragraph that articulates, supports, and develops this key claim.

### 34.4.2 Enriching the Argument

Step 1 of the revision process aims to ensure that your essay does the best possible job of making your argument. But revision is also an opportunity to go beyond that—to think about ways in which your overall argument might be made more thorough and complex. In drafting an essay our attention is often and rightly focused on emphatically staking out a particular position and proving its validity. This is the fundamental task of any essay, and you certainly don't want to do anything at this stage to compromise that. At the same time, you do want to make sure that you haven't purchased clarity at the cost of oversimplification by, for example, ignoring evidence that might undermine or complicate your claims, alternative interpretations of the evidence you do present, or alternative claims or points of view. Remember, you have a better chance of persuading readers to accept your point of view if you show them that it's based on a thorough, open-minded exploration of the text and topic. Don't invent unreasonable or irrelevant complications or counterarguments. Do try to assess your argument objectively and honestly, perhaps testing it against the text one more time. Think like a reader rather than a writer: Are there points where a reasonable reader might object to, or disagree with, the argument? Have you ignored or glossed over any questions or issues that a reasonable reader might expect an essay on this topic to address?

### 34.4.3 Editing and Proofreading

Once you've gotten the overall argument in good shape, it's time to focus on the small but important stuff—words and sentences. Your prose should not only convey your ideas to your readers but also demonstrate how much you care about your essay. Flawless prose can't disguise a vapid or illogical argument, but faulty, flabby prose can destroy a potentially persuasive and thoughtful one. Don't sabotage all your hard work by failing to correct misspelled words, grammatical problems, misquotations, incorrect citations, or typographical errors. Little oversights make all the difference when it comes to clarity and credibility.

Though you will want to check all of the following aspects of your essay, it will probably be easier to spot mistakes and weaknesses if you read through the essay several times, concentrating each time on one specific aspect.

Every writer has individual weaknesses and strengths, and every writer tends to be overly fond of certain phrases and sentence structures. With practice, you will learn to watch out for the kinds of mistakes to which you are most prone. Eventually, you can and should develop your own *personalized* editing checklist.

### Sentences
- ☐ Does each one read clearly and crisply?
- ☐ Are they varied in length, structure, and word order?
- ☐ Is my phrasing direct rather than roundabout?

> **TIPS:**
> 1. Try circling, or using your computer to search for, every preposition and *to be* verb. Since these can lead to confusion or roundabout phrasing, weed out as many as you can.
> 2. Try reading your paper aloud or having your roommate read it to you. Note places where you stumble, and listen for sentences that are hard to get through or understand.

### Words
- ☐ Have I used any words whose meaning I'm not sure of?
- ☐ Are the idioms used correctly? Is my terminology correct?
- ☐ Do my key words always mean *exactly* the same thing?
- ☐ Do I ever use a fancy word or phrase where a simpler one might do?
- ☐ Are there any unnecessary words or phrases?
- ☐ Do my metaphors and figures of speech make literal sense?
- ☐ Are my verbs active and precise?
- ☐ Are my pronoun references clear and correct?
- ☐ Do my subjects and verbs always agree?

### Mechanics
- ☐ Is every quotation correctly worded and punctuated?
- ☐ Is the source of each quotation clearly indicated through parenthetical citation?
- ☐ Have I checked the spelling of words I'm not sure of? (Remember that spell-checks won't indicate how to spell every word and that they sometimes create mistakes by substituting the wrong word for the misspelled one.)
- ☐ Are my pages numbered?
- ☐ Does the first page of my essay clearly indicate my name (and any other required identifying information), as well as my essay's title?

## 34.5 CRAFTING A TITLE

Complete your essay by giving it a title. As any researcher trying to locate and assess sources by browsing titles will tell you, titles are extremely important. They're the first thing readers encounter and a writer's first opportunity to create a good impression and to shape readers' expectations. Every good essay deserves a good title. And a good title is one that both *informs* and *interests*. Inform readers by telling them both the work(s) your essay will analyze and something about your topic. Interest them with an especially vivid and telling word or a short phrase from the literary work (" 'We all said, "she will kill herself" ' : The Narrator/Detective in William Faulkner's 'A Rose for Emily' "), with a bit of wordplay (" 'Tintern Abbey' and the Art of Artlessness"), or with a little of both ("A Rose for 'A Rose for Emily' ").

# 35  THE RESEARCH ESSAY

Writing a research essay may seem like a daunting task that requires specialized skills and considerable time and effort. Research does add a few more steps to the writing process, so that process will take more time. And those steps require you to draw upon, and develop, skills somewhat different from those involved in creating other kinds of essays. But a research essay is, after all, an essay. Its core elements are those of any essay, its basic purpose exactly the same—to articulate and develop a debatable claim about a literary text. As a result, this kind of essay draws upon many of the same skills and strategies you've already begun to develop. Similarly, though you will need to add a few new steps, the writing process still involves getting started, planning, drafting, and revising—exactly the same dance whose rhythms you've already begun to master.

Indeed, the only distinctive thing about a research essay is that it requires the use of secondary sources. Though that adds to your burden in some ways, it can lighten it in others. Think of secondary sources not as another ball you have to juggle but as another tool you get to add to your toolbelt: you're still being asked to build a cabinet, but now you get to use a hammer *and* a screwdriver. This chapter will help you make the best use of this powerful tool.

## 35.1 TYPES AND FUNCTIONS OF SECONDARY SOURCES

Whenever we write an essay about literature, we engage in a conversation with other readers about the meaning and significance of a particular work (or works). Effective argumentation always depends on imagining how other readers are likely to respond to, and interpret, the literary text. As the "Critical Contexts" chapters in this anthology demonstrate, however, almost all texts and authors are the subject of actual public conversations, often extending over many years and involving numerous scholarly readers. A research essay can be an opportunity to investigate this conversation and to contribute to it. In this case, your secondary sources will be works in which literary scholars analyze a specific text or an author's body of work.

As the "Author's Work as Context" and "Cultural and Historical Contexts" chapters show, each literary work is significantly shaped by, and speaks to, its author's unique experience and outlook, as well as the events and debates of the era in which the author lived. So a research assignment can be an opportunity to learn more about a particular author, about that author's canon, or about the place and time in which the author lived and worked. The goal of the essay will be to show how context informs text or vice versa. Secondary sources for this sort of research essay will be biographies of the author, essays or letters by the author, and/or historical works of some kind.

Generally speaking, three types of secondary sources are used in essays about literature: *literary criticism, biography,* and *history.* The goal of a particular essay and the kinds of questions it raises will determine which kind of sources you use.

In practice, however, many secondary sources cross these boundaries. Biographies of a particular author often offer literary critical interpretations of that author's work; works of literary criticism sometimes make use of historical or biographical information; and so on. And you, too, may want or need to draw on more than one kind of source in a single essay. Your instructor will probably give you guidance about what kinds of sources and research topics or questions are appropriate. So make sure that you have a clear sense of the assignment before you get started.

Unless your instructor indicates otherwise, *your* argument should be the focus of your essay, and secondary sources should be just that—secondary. They should merely serve as tools that you use to deepen and enrich your argument about the literary text. They shouldn't substitute for it. Your essay should never simply repeat or report on what other people have already said.

Thus even though secondary sources are important to the development of your research essay, they should not be the source of your ideas. Instead, as one popular guide to writing suggests,* they are sources of:

- *opinion* (or *debatable claims*)—other readers' views and interpretations of the text, author, or topic, which "you support, criticize, or develop";
- *information*—facts (which "you interpret") about the author's life; the text's composition, publication, or reception; the era during, or about which, the author wrote; or the literary movement of which the author was a part;
- *concept*—general terms or theoretical frameworks that you borrow and apply to your author or text.

Again, any one source will likely offer more than one of these things. For example, the excerpt from Stephen Gould Axelrod's "Jealous Gods" in chapter 25 provides Axelrod's *opinion* on (or interpretation of) Sylvia Plath's "Daddy"; *information* about the status of the domestic poem in the 1950s; and *concepts* drawn from Freud's theories of psychological development.

Nonetheless, the distinction between opinion (debatable claim) and information (factual statement) is crucial. As you read a source, you must discriminate between the two. And when drawing upon sources in your essay, remember that an opinion about a text, no matter how well informed, isn't the same as evidence. Only facts can serve that function. Suppose, for example, that you are writing an essay on "Daddy." You claim that the speaker adopts two voices, that of her child self and that of her adult self—an opinion also set forth in Axelrod's "Jealous Gods." You cannot prove this claim to be true by merely saying that Axelrod makes the same claim. Like any debatable claim, this one must be backed up with evidence from the primary text.

In this situation, however, you must indicate that a source has made the same claim that you do in order to:

- give the source credit for having this idea or stating this opinion before you did (see 35.4.1);

---

* Gordon Harvey, *Writing with Sources* (Indianapolis: Hackett, 1998) 1.

- encourage readers to see you as a knowledgeable and trustworthy writer, one who has taken the time to explore, digest, and fairly represent others' opinions;
- demonstrate that your opinion isn't merely idiosyncratic because another informed, even "expert," reader agrees with you.

Were you to disagree with the source's opinion, you would need to acknowledge that disagreement in order to demonstrate the originality of your own interpretation, while also (again) encouraging readers to see you as a knowledgeable, careful, trustworthy writer.

You will need to cite sources throughout your essay whenever you make (1) a claim that complements or contradicts the opinion-claim of a source, or (2) a claim that requires secondary-source information or concepts. In essays that draw upon literary critical sources, those sources may prove especially helpful when articulating motive (see 35.1.1).

> TIP: In addition to being secondary sources of the type you might use in a research essay, many of the pieces excerpted in the "Critical Contexts" chapters draw on other secondary sources. Look over these pieces to see what kinds of sources professional literary critics use and how they use them. For example, Lawrence R. Rodgers's essay on "A Rose for Emily" (ch. 12) makes use of *information* garnered from biographies of Faulkner (¶3), applies to the story *concepts* taken from another literary critic's argument about detective fiction (¶4), and refers to other critics' *opinions* about the story in order to suggest the distinctiveness and value of his own (¶11, 18).

### 35.1.1 Source-Related Motives

Not all research essays use sources to establish motive. However, this is one technique you can use to ensure that your own ideas are the focus of your essay and to demonstrate that (and how) your essay contributes to a literary critical conversation rather than just reporting on it or repeating what others have already said.

In addition to the general motives described above (33.3.1), writing expert Gordon Harvey has identified three common source-related motives:

1. Sources offer different opinions about a particular issue, thus suggesting that there is still a problem or a puzzle worth investigating.

   > [A]lmost all interpreters of [*Antigone*] have agreed that the play shows Creon to be morally defective, though they might not agree about the particular nature of his defect. [examples] . . . I want to suggest [instead] that. . . .
   > —Martha Nussbaum, *"The Fragility of Goodness . . . "* (ch. 31)

2. A source (or sources) makes a faulty claim that needs to be challenged or clarified.

   > Modern critics who do not share Sophocles' conviction about the paramount duty of burying the dead and who attach more importance than he did to the claims of political authority have tended to underestimate the way in which he justifies Antigone against Creon. [examples] —Maurice Bowra, *"Sophoclean Tragedy"* (ch. 31)

3. Sources neglect a significant aspect or element of the text, or they make a claim that needs to be further developed or applied in a new way.

> At first sight, there appears little need for further study of the lovers in *Far from the Madding Crowd*, and even less of their environment. To cite but a few critics, David Cecil has considered the courtship of Bathsheba, Virginia Hyman her moral development through her varied experience in love, George Wing her suitors, Douglas Brown her relation to the natural environment, Merryn Williams that of Gabriel Oak in contrast to Sergeant Troy's alienation from nature, and, most recently, Peter Casagrande Bathsheba's reformation through her communion with both Gabriel and the environment. To my knowledge, none has considered the modes or styles in which those and other characters express love and how far these may result from or determine their attitude to the land and its dependents, nor the tragic import in the Wessex novels of incompatibility in this sense between human beings, as distinct from that between the human psyche and the cosmos.
> —Lionel Adey, "Styles of Love in *Far from the Madding Crowd*," *Thomas Hardy Annual 5* (London: Macmillan, 1987)

## 35.2 RESEARCH AND THE WRITING PROCESS

Keeping in mind the overall goal of making secondary sources secondary, you have two options about when and how to integrate research into the writing process: (1) you may consult sources in the exploratory phase, using them to generate potential topics and theses for your essay, or (2) you may consult sources during (or even after) the planning or drafting phases, using them to refine and test a tentative thesis. Each approach has advantages and disadvantages.

### 35.2.1 Using Research to Generate Topic and Thesis

You may consult secondary sources very early in the writing process, using them to help generate your essay topic and thesis (or several potential ones from which you will need to choose). This approach has three advantages. First, you approach the research with a thoroughly open mind and formulate your own opinion about the text(s) only after having considered the range of opinions and information that the sources offer. Second, as you investigate others' opinions, you may find yourself disagreeing, thereby discovering that your mind isn't nearly as open as you'd thought—that you do, indeed, have an opinion of which you weren't fully aware. (Since you've discovered this by disagreeing with a published opinion, you're well on your way to having a motive as well as a thesis.) Third, because you begin by informing yourself about what others have already said, you may be in less danger of simply repeating or reporting.

The potential disadvantage is that you may become overwhelmed by the sheer number of sources or by the amount and diversity of information and opinion they offer. You may agree with everyone, being unable to discriminate among others' opinions or to formulate your own. Or you may find that the conversation seems so exhaustive that you despair of finding anything new to add. If you take this approach, you should maximize the advantages and minimize the disadvantages by keeping in mind a set of clearly defined motive-related questions.

If your sources are works of literary criticism, your goal is to answer two general questions: *What's the conversation about? How can I contribute to it?* To answer those questions, it helps to recall the various motives described in section 35.1.1. Turn them into questions that you can pose about each source:

- ☐ Do the critics tend to disagree about a particular issue? Might I take one side or another in this debate? Might I offer an alternative?
- ☐ Do any critics make a claim that I think deserves to be challenged or clarified?
- ☐ Do the critics ignore a particular element or aspect of the text that I think needs to be investigated? Do any of the critics make a claim that they don't really develop? Or do they make a claim about one text that I might apply to another?

If your sources are historical or biographical, you will instead need to ask questions such as:

- ☐ Is there information here that might help readers understand some aspect of the literary work in a new way?
- ☐ Does any of this information challenge or complicate my previous interpretation of the text, or an interpretation that I think other readers might adopt if they weren't aware of these facts?

### 35.2.2 Using Research to Refine and Test a Thesis

Because of the potential problems of consulting secondary sources in the exploratory phase of the writing process (35.2.1), your instructor may urge you to delay research until later—after you've formulated a tentative thesis, gathered evidence, or written a complete rough draft. This approach may be especially appealing when you begin an assignment with a firm sense of what you want to write. The chief advantage of this approach is that you can look at secondary sources more selectively and critically, seeking information and opinions that will deepen, confirm, or challenge your argument. And since you've already formulated your opinion, you may be in less danger of becoming overwhelmed by others'.

There are, however, several things to watch out for if you take this approach. First, you must be especially careful not to ignore, distort, or misrepresent any source's argument in the interest of maintaining your own. Second, you must strive to keep your mind open, remembering that the goal of your research is to *test* and *refine* your opinion, not just to *confirm* it. A compelling argument or new piece of information may well require you to modify or broaden your original argument. Third, you still need to pose the general questions outlined above (35.2.1).

## 35.3 THE RESEARCH PROCESS

Regardless of when you begin your research, the process will involve four tasks:

- creating and maintaining a working bibliography;
- identifying and locating potentially useful secondary sources;
- evaluating the credibility of sources;
- taking notes.

### 35.3.1 Creating a Working Bibliography

A working bibliography lists all the sources that you *might* use in your research essay. It is a "working" document in two ways. For one thing, it will change throughout the research process—expanding each time you add a potentially useful source and contracting when you omit sources that turn out to be less relevant than you anticipated. Also, once you have written your essay, your working bibliography will evolve one last time, becoming your list of works cited. For another thing, you can use your bibliography to organize and keep track of your research "work." To this end, some researchers divide the bibliography into three parts: (1) sources that they need to locate, (2) sources that they have located and think they will use, and (3) sources that they have located but think they probably won't use. (Keeping track of "rejects" ensures, first, that you won't have to start from scratch if you later change your mind; second, that you won't forget that you've already located and rejected a source if you come across another reference to it.)

Because you will need to update your bibliography regularly and because it will ultimately become the kernel of your list of works cited, you should consider using a computer. In that case, you'll need to print a copy or take your laptop along each time you head to the library. However, some researchers find it helpful to also or instead use notecards, creating a separate card for each source. You can then physically separate cards dedicated to sources to be located, sources already located, and "rejected" sources. Just in case your cards get mixed up, however, you should also always note the status of the source on the card (by writing at the top "find," "located," or "rejected").

Regardless of the format you use, your record for each source should include all the information you will need in order both to locate the source and to cite it in your essay. Helpful location information might include the library in which it's found (if you're using multiple libraries), the section of the library in which it's held (e.g., "Reference," "Stacks"), and its call number. As for citation or publication information, it's tempting to ignore this until the very end of the writing process, and some writers do. But if you give in to that temptation, you will, at best, create much more work for yourself down the road. At worst, you'll find yourself unable to use a great source in your essay because you can't relocate the necessary information about it. To avoid these fates, note down all facts you will need for a works cited entry (see 36.2.2). Finally, consider noting where you first discovered each source, just in case you later need to double-check citation information or to remind yourself why you considered a source potentially useful or authoritative. (Though you can use abbreviations, make sure they're ones you'll recognize later.)

Here are two sample entries from the working bibliography of a student researching Adrienne Rich's poetry. Each entry includes all the required citation information, as well as notes on where the student discovered the source and where it is located.

*Sample Working Bibliography Entries*

> Boyers, Robert. "On Adrienne Rich: Intelligence and Will." <u>Salmagundi</u> 22–23 (Spring–Summer 1973): 132–48. Source: *DLB* 5. Loc.: UNLV LASR AS30.S33
>
> Martin, Wendy. <u>American Triptych: Anne Bradstreet, Emily Dickinson, Adrienne Rich</u>. U of North Carolina P, 1984. Source: *LRC/CLC*. UNLV Stacks PS310.F45 M3 1984

Once you locate a source, double-check the accuracy and thoroughness of your citation information and update your working bibliography. (Notice, for example, that this student will need to check *American Triptych* to find out the city where it was published and then add this information to her bibliography.)

### 35.3.2 Identifying and Locating Sources

Regardless of your author, text, or topic, you will almost certainly find a wealth of sources to consult. Your first impulse may be to head straight for the library catalog. But the conversation about literature occurs in periodicals as well as books, and not all contributions to that conversation are equally credible or relevant. For all these reasons, consider starting with one of the reference works or bibliographies described in this section. Then you can head to the catalog armed with a clear sense of what you're looking for.

Once you find one good secondary source, you can use its bibliography to refine your own. Checking the footnotes and bibliographies of several (especially recent) sources will give you a good sense of what other sources are available and which ones experts consider the most significant.

#### REFERENCE WORKS

Your library will contain many reference works that can be helpful starting points, and some may be accessible via the library's Web page. Here are six especially useful ones.

***Literature Resource Center (LRC)***

One online source to which your library may subscribe is Gale's *Literature Resource Center*. Designed with undergraduate researchers in mind, it's an excellent place to start. Here you can access and search:

- all the material in two of the reference works described below (*Dictionary of Literary Biography* and *Contemporary Authors*) and in both Merriam-Webster's *Encyclopedia of Literature* and Gale's For Students series (*Novels for Students, Literature of Developing Nations for Students*, etc.);
- much (though not all) of the material contained in Gale's Literary Criticism series (another of the reference works described below);
- selected full-text critical essays (or articles) from more than 250 literary journals.

Depending upon your library's subscription arrangement, *LRC* may also give you access to the *MLA Bibliography* (from 1963) and/or to the Twayne's Authors series (both described below).

You can search the database in numerous ways, but you should probably start with an author search. Results will appear as a list of sources divided into four files: Biographies; Literary Criticism, Articles, and Work Overviews; Bibliographies (of works by and about the author); Additional Resources (such as author-focused Web sites). You can access each file or list by simply clicking on the appropriate tab. (There will be a good deal of overlap among the files.) You can then click any item on the list in order to open and read it. Once an item is open, you can also print or e-mail it by clicking on the appropriate icons and following the directions.

If your library doesn't subscribe to *LRC*, consider starting with the printed reference works listed below. Because each is a multivolume work, you will need to consult its cumulative index to find out which volumes contain entries on your author. None of these series can keep up to the minute with the literary critical conversation about a particular author or work, and all offer only selective bibliographies. Such selectivity is both the greatest strength and the greatest limitation of these reference works.

### *Dictionary of Literary Biography (DLB)*

One of the most important and authoritative reference works for students of literature, the *Dictionary of Literary Biography* covers primarily British and American authors, both living and dead. Each volume focuses on writers working in a particular genre and period. (Volume 152, 4th series, for example, covers *American Novelists since World War II*.) Written by a scholar in the field, each entry includes a photo or sketch of the author, a list of his or her publications, a bibliography of selected secondary sources, and an overview of the author's life and work. The overviews are often very thorough, incorporating brief quotations from letters, interviews, reviews, and so on. You will find multiple entries on any major author, each focusing on a particular portion of his or her canon. The volume titles will give you a good sense of which entry will be most relevant to you. Entries on W. B. Yeats, for example, appear in volume 10, *Modern British Dramatists, 1900–1945*; volume 19, *British Poets, 1880–1914*; volume 98, *Modern British Essayists, First Series*; and volume 156, *British Short-Fiction Writers, 1880–1914: The Romantic Tradition*.

### *Contemporary Authors: A Biobibliographical Guide to Current Authors and Their Works (CA)*

Gale's *Contemporary Authors* focuses on twentieth- and twenty-first-century writers from around the world and in a range of fields (including the social and natural sciences). In terms of content, its entries closely resemble those in the *DLB* (see above). But *CA* entries tend to be much shorter.

### *Literary Criticism (LC)*

Also published by Gale, the Literary Criticism series is, in effect, a series of series, each of which covers a particular historical period. (See below for individual series titles, as well as information about the periods covered by each one.) Each entry includes a very brief overview of the author's life and work. (There is often overlap between these overviews and those in *CA*.) But there are two key differences between the *LC* series and both the *DLB* and *CA*. First, the *LC* series includes entries devoted entirely to some individual works, as well as entries on an author's entire canon. (For example, Nineteenth-Century Literature Criticism contains both a general entry on Charlotte Brontë and one devoted exclusively to *Jane Eyre*.) Second, the bulk of each entry is devoted to excerpts (often lengthy) from some of the most important reviews and literary criticism on an author and/or work, and coverage extends from the author's day up to the time when the *LC* entry was written. Each entry concludes with a bibliography of additional secondary sources. The *LC* series will thus give a lot of guidance in identifying authoritative sources, as well as access to excerpts from sources that your library doesn't own.

Here are the titles of the five series, along with information about the period each one covers. To identify the appropriate series, you will need to know the year in which your author died.

- Contemporary Literary Criticism (living authors and those who died from 1960 on)

- Twentieth-Century Literary Criticism (authors who died 1900–1959)
- Nineteenth-Century Literature Criticism (authors who died 1800–1899)
- Literature Criticism from 1400 to 1800 (authors [except Shakespeare] who died 1400–1799)
- Shakespearean Criticism

*The Critical Heritage*

For some major authors, you can find information and excerpts like those offered by *LC* within the individual volumes of the Critical Heritage series. Unlike the reference works described above, this series is a collection of discrete publications such as *The Brontës: The Critical Heritage*. Each will be held not in the reference department, but in the section of the stacks devoted to scholarship on a specific author. You will thus need to search your library's catalog to find it. These volumes are not regularly updated, so each will give a good sense of your author's reception only up to the time it was published.

*Twayne's Authors*

The Twayne's Authors series incorporates three distinct series: Twayne's United States Authors, Twayne's English Authors, and Twayne's World Authors. Each volume in each series is a distinct book focusing on one author and typically offering both biographical information and interpretation of major works. All aim to be generally accessible and introductory. (As the publishers themselves put it, "The intent of each volume in these series is to present a critical-analytical study of the works of the writer; to include biographical and historical material that may be necessary for understanding, appreciation, and critical appraisal of the writer; and to present all material in clear, concise English.") Yet because each volume is the work of an individual specialist, it represents that scholar's particular point of view (or opinion), and volumes differ a good deal in terms of organization, approach, and level of difficulty.

Each volume will be held not in the reference department, but in the section of the stacks devoted to scholarship on a specific author. To find it, you will need to search the catalog.

### MLA INTERNATIONAL BIBLIOGRAPHY

For much more thorough, up-to-date lists of secondary sources—especially periodical articles—you should consult scholarly bibliographies. In terms of literary criticism, the most comprehensive and useful general bibliography is *The MLA International Bibliography of Books and Articles on the Modern Languages and Literatures*. Since 1969, the *MLA Bibliography* has aimed to provide a comprehensive list of all scholarship published anywhere in the world on literature and modern languages, including books, dissertations, book chapters, and articles in over two thousand periodicals. Though it doesn't quite live up to that aim, it comes closer than any other reference work. (The *Bibliography* in fact began in 1922 but initially included only American scholarship; international coverage began in 1956, but the range of publications remained limited until 1969.) Updated annually, the bibliography is available in print, CD-ROM, and online versions, so what the bibliography encompasses, how many years it covers, and how you use it will depend on the version you consult.

In the print version, each volume lists articles and books published in a specific year, so you should start with the most recent volume and then work your way backward through earlier volumes. Each volume is arranged by nationality or language, then by period, then by author and title.

The CD-ROM and online versions allow you to do topic or keyword searches to find all relevant publications, regardless of the year of publication. Ask a librarian for help with accessing and searching the database.

### ONLINE AND CARD CATALOGS

Your library's catalog will guide you to books about the author's work. However, the title of a potentially useful book may be too general to indicate whether it covers the text and topic in which you're interested. If your library's catalog is online, use keyword searches to limit the number and range of books that the computer finds. For example, if you're writing about William Faulkner's "A Rose for Emily," first limit the search to items that include both "Faulkner" and "A Rose for Emily." If you find few matches or none, broaden the search to include all books about William Faulkner.

The books that you find through a catalog search will lead you to a section of the library where other books on your subject are held (because each will have a similar Library of Congress call number). Even if you locate the books you were looking for right away, take a moment to browse. Books shelved nearby probably cover similar topics, and they may prove even more useful than the ones you originally sought. You can also do this kind of browsing online because most online catalogs offer the option of moving from the record of one book to the records of those that appear just before and after it in the catalog.

### THE INTERNET

With its innumerable links and pathways, the Internet seems the perfect resource for research of any kind. And in fact some excellent online resources are available to students of literature. *Bartleby.com* is a good, general information site. Here you can access and search several reference works, including the *Columbia Encyclopedia*, the *American Heritage Dictionary of the English Language*, and the eighteen-volume *Cambridge History of English and American Literature*, as well as full-text versions of numerous poems and works of fiction and nonfiction.

There are also many scholarly sites dedicated to specific authors, works, and literary periods. Most sites provide links to others. One site especially useful as a gateway to thousands of more specific sites is *The Voice of the Shuttle* <http://vos.ucsb.edu/>.

If you don't find an appropriate link on *The Voice of the Shuttle*, you will probably want to conduct a search using one of the commonly available search engines. Searches using keywords such as "Chekhov" or "poetry" will lead you to thousands of possible matches, however, so you should limit your search by creating search strings longer than one word. Read onscreen directions carefully to make sure that the search engine treats the search string as a unit and doesn't find every mention of each individual word.

Despite the obvious benefits of the Internet, you should be cautious in your use of online sources for two reasons. First, although many sites provide solid information and informed opinion, many more offer misinformation or unsubstantiated opinion. Unlike journal articles and books, which are rigorously reviewed by experts before they are accepted for publication, many Internet sources are posted without any sort of review process, and authorship is often difficult to pin down. As a result, you need to be especially careful to identify and evaluate the ultimate source of the information and opinions you find in cyberspace. (For more on evaluating sources, see 35.3.3.)

Second, because the Internet enables you to jump easily from one site to another and to copy whole pages of text merely by cutting and pasting, you may lose your place and be unable to provide readers with precise citations. More serious, you may lose track of where your own words end and those of your source begin, thereby putting yourself at risk of plagiarizing (see 35.4.1). In addition, the Internet is itself constantly mutating; what's there today may not be there tomorrow. All this makes it difficult to achieve the goal of all citation: to enable readers to retrace your steps and check your sources. When you find sites that seem potentially useful, bookmark them if you can. If not, make sure that you accurately write down (or, better, copy directly into a document) the URL of each, as well as the other information you will need for your list of works cited: the author's name, if available; the site or page title; the date the site was last revised or originally published; and the date you accessed it. If the material on the site has been taken from a printed source, note all of the particulars about this source as well.

As a general rule, Internet sources should supplement print sources, not substitute for them.

### 35.3.3 Evaluating Sources

Not all sources are equally reliable or credible. The credibility and persuasiveness of your essay will depend, in part, on the credibility of the sources you draw on. This is a good reason to start with reference works that will guide you to credible sources.

Nonetheless, it is very important to learn how to gauge for yourself the credibility of sources. As you do so, keep in mind that finding a source to be credible isn't the same as agreeing with everything it says. At this stage, concentrate on whether the opinions expressed in a source are worthy of serious consideration, not on whether you agree with them. Here are some especially important questions to consider:

1. *How credible is the publisher (in the case of books), the periodical (in the case of essays, articles, and reviews), or the sponsoring organization (in the case of Internet sources)?*

    Generally speaking, academics give most credence to books published by academic and university presses and to articles published in scholarly or professional journals because all such publications undergo a rigorous peer-review process. As a result, you can trust that these publications have been judged credible by more than one recognized expert. For periodicals aimed at a more general audience, you should prefer prominent, highly respected publications such as the *Los Angeles Times* or the *New Yorker* to, say, the *National Enquirer* or *People* magazine.

    Internet sources are not subjected to rigorous review processes, but many sites are created and sponsored by organizations. Be sure to identify the sponsoring organization and carefully consider its nature, status, and purpose. The last part of the domain name will indicate the kind of organization it is: the suffix *.com* indicates that the ultimate source is a *company* or commercial, for-profit enterprise; *.org*, a nonprofit or charitable *organization*; *.gov*, a *government* agency; and *.edu*, an *educational* institution.

Though you will often find more reliable information via *.gov* or *.edu* sites, this won't always be the case. Bartleby.com is, for example, only one of many extremely useful commercial sites, whereas many *.edu* sites feature the work of students who may have much less expertise than you do.

2. *How credible is the author? Is he or she a recognized expert in the relevant field or on the relevant subject?*

Again, publication by a reputable press or in a reputable periodical generally indicates that its author is considered an expert. But you can also investigate further by checking the thumbnail biographies that usually appear within the book or journal (typically near the beginning or end). Has this person been trained or held positions at respected institutions? What else has he or she published?

3. *How credible is the actual argument?*

Assess the source's argument by applying all that you've learned about what makes an argument effective. Does it draw on ample, appropriate, convincing evidence? Does it consider all the relevant evidence? Are its inferences reasonable? Are its claims sound? Does the whole seem fair, balanced, and thorough? Has the author considered possible counter-arguments or alternative points of view?

Finally, researchers in many fields would encourage you to consider the source's publication date and the currency of the information it contains. In the sciences, for example, preference is almost always given to the most recently published work on a given topic because new scholarly works tend to render older ones obsolete. In the humanities, too, new scholarly works build on old ones. You should consult recently published sources in order to get a sense of what today's scholars consider the most significant, debatable questions and what answers they offer. Though originality is as important in the humanities as in other scholarly fields, new work in the humanities doesn't necessarily render older work utterly obsolete. For example, a 1922 article on Shakespeare's *Hamlet* may still be as valid and influential as one published in 2002. As a result, you should consider the date of publication in evaluating a source, but don't let age alone determine its credibility or value.

### 35.3.4 Taking Notes

Once you've acquired the books and articles you determine to be most credible and potentially useful, it's a good idea to skim each one. (In the case of a book, concentrate on the introduction and on the chapter that seems most relevant.) Focus at this point on assessing the relevance of each source to your topic. Or, if you're working your way toward a topic, look for things that spark your interest. Either way, try to get a rough sense of the overall conversation—of the issues and topics that come up again and again across the various sources.

After identifying the sources most pertinent to your argument, begin reading more carefully and taking notes. Again, some researchers find it easier to organize (and reorganize) notes by using notecards, creating one card for each key point. (If you use this method, make sure that each card clearly indicates the source author and short title because cards have a tendency to get jumbled.) Today, however, most researchers take notes on the computer, creating a separate document or file for each source.

Regardless of their form, your notes should be as thorough and accurate as possible. Be thorough because memory is a treacherous thing; it's best not to rely too heavily on it. Be accurate to avoid a range of serious problems, including plagiarism (see 35.4.1).

Your notes for each source should include four things: summary, paraphrase, and quotation, as well as your own comments and thoughts. It's crucial to visually discriminate among these by, for instance, always recording your own comments and thoughts in a separate computer document or file or on a separate set of clearly labeled or differently colored notecards.

Whenever you write down, type out, or paste in more than two consecutive words from a source, you should:

- place these words in quotation marks so that you will later recognize them as quotations;
- make sure to quote with absolute accuracy every word and punctuation mark;
- record the page where the quotation is found (in the case of print sources).

Keep such quotations to a minimum, recording only the most vivid or telling.

In lieu of extensive quotations, try to summarize and paraphrase as much as possible. You can't decide how to use the source or whether you agree with its argument unless you've first understood it, and you can best understand and test your understanding through summary and paraphrase. Start with a two- or three-sentence summary of the author's overall argument. Then summarize each of the relevant major subsections of the argument. Paraphrase especially important points, making sure to note the page on which each appears.

You may want to try putting your notes in the form of an outline. Again, start with a brief general summary. Then paraphrase each of the major relevant subclaims, incorporating summaries and quotations where appropriate.

Especially if you're dealing with literary criticism, it can be useful to complete the note-taking process by writing a summary that covers all of your sources. Your goal is to show how all the arguments fit together to form one coherent conversation. Doing so will require that you both define the main questions at issue in the conversation and indicate what stance each source takes on each question—where and how their opinions coincide and differ. One might say, for example, that the main questions about *Antigone* that preoccupy all the various scholars represented in chapter 31 are (1) *What is the exact nature of the conflict between Creon and Antigone, or what two conflicting worldviews do they represent?* and (2) *How is that conflict resolved? Which, if any, character and worldview does the play as a whole endorse?* A synthetic summary of these sources would explain how each critic answers each question. This kind of summary can be especially helpful when you haven't yet identified a specific essay topic or crafted a thesis because it may help you to see gaps in the conversation, places where you can enter and contribute.

## 35.4 INTEGRATING SOURCE MATERIAL INTO THE ESSAY

In research essays, you can refer to sources in a number of ways. You can

*briefly allude to them*:

Many critics, including Maurice Bowra and Bernard Knox, see Creon as morally inferior to Antigone.

*summarize or paraphrase their contents*:

> According to Maurice Bowra, Creon's arrogance is his downfall. However prideful Antigone may occasionally seem, Bowra insists that Creon is genuinely, deeply, and consistently so (2108).

*quote them directly*:

> For Bowra, Creon is the prototypical "proud man" (2107); where Antigone's arrogance is only "apparent," Creon's is all too "real" (2108).

With secondary sources, be very careful about how often you quote and when and how you do so. Keep the number and length of quotations to a minimum. After all, this is *your* essay, and you should use your own words whenever possible, even to describe someone else's ideas. Save quotations for when you really need them: when the source's author has expressed an idea with such precision, clarity, or vividness that you simply can't say it any better; or when a key passage from your source is so rich or difficult that you need to analyze its ideas and language closely. As with primary texts, lengthy quotation will lead the reader to expect sustained analysis. And only rarely will you want to devote a large amount of your limited time and space to thoroughly analyzing the language of a source (as opposed to a primary text). (For more on responsible and effective quotation, see 36.1.)

One advantage of direct quotation is that it's an easy way to indicate that ideas derive from a source rather than from you. But whether you are quoting, summarizing, or paraphrasing a source, use other techniques as well to ensure that there's no doubt about where your ideas and words leave off and those of a source begin (see 35.4.1). A parenthetical citation within a sentence indicates that something in it comes from a specific source, but unless you indicate otherwise, it will also imply that the entire sentence is a paraphrase of the source. For clarity's sake, then, you should also mention the source or its author in your text, using signal phrases (*According to X; As X argues; X notes that*, etc.) to announce that you are about to introduce someone else's ideas. If your summary of a source goes on for more than a sentence or two, keep on using signal phrases to remind readers that you're still summarizing someone else's ideas rather than stating your own, as Lawrence Rodgers does in the example below.

> The ways of interpreting Emily's decision to murder Homer are numerous. . . . For simple clarification, they can be summarized along two lines. One group finds the murder growing out of Emily's demented attempt to forestall the inevitable passage of time—toward her abandonment by Homer, toward her own death, and toward the steady encroachment of the North and the New South on something loosely defined as the "tradition" of the Old South. Another view sees the murder in more psychological terms. It grows out of Emily's complex relationship to her father, who, by elevating her above all of the eligible men of Jefferson, insured that to yield what one commentator called the "normal emotions" associated with desire, his daughter had to "retreat into a marginal world, into fantasy" (O'Connor 184).
>
> These lines of interpretation complement more than critique each other. . . . Together, they de-emphasize the element of detection, viewing the murder and its solution not as the central action but as manifestations of the principal element, the decline of the Grierson lineage and all it represents. Recognizing the way in which the story makes use of the detective genre, however, adds another interpretive layer to the story by making the narrator . . . a central player in the pattern of action.
> —Lawrence R. Rodgers, " 'We All Said . . .' " (ch. 12)

NOTE: In the first paragraph, Rodgers summarizes other critics' arguments in his own words, briefly but clearly. To ensure that we know he's about to summarize, he actually announces this intention ("*For simple clarification, they can be summarized...*"). As he begins summarizing each view, he reminds us that it is a "view," that he's still not describing his own thoughts. Finally, he uses this unusually long summary to make a very clear and important point: *everyone except me has ignored this element!*

### 35.4.1 Using Sources Responsibly

Both the clarity and the credibility of any research essay depend upon the responsible use of sources. And using sources responsibly entails accurately representing them and clearly discriminating between your own words and ideas and those that come from sources. Since ideas, words, information, and concepts not directly and clearly attributed to a source will be taken as your own, any lack of clarity on this score amounts to *plagiarism*. Representing anyone else's ideas or data as your own, even if you state them in your own words, is plagiarism—whether you do so intentionally or unintentionally; whether ideas are taken from a published book or article, another student's paper, the Internet, or any other source. Plagiarism is the most serious of offenses within academe because it amounts to stealing ideas, the resource most precious to this community and its members. As a result, the punishments for plagiarism are severe—including failure, suspension, and expulsion.

To avoid both the offense and its consequences, you must always:

- put quotation marks around any quotation from a source (a quotation being any two or more consecutive words or any one especially distinctive word, label, or concept);

- credit a source whenever you take from it any of the following:
  —a quotation (as described above);
  —a nonfactual or debatable claim (an idea, opinion, interpretation, evaluation, or conclusion) stated in your own words;
  —a fact or piece of data that isn't common knowledge; or
  —a distinctive way of organizing factual information.

To clarify, a fact counts as common knowledge—and therefore doesn't need to be credited to a source—whenever you can find it in multiple, readily available sources, none of which seriously question its validity. For example, it is common knowledge that Sherman Alexie is Native American, that he was born in 1966, and that he published a collection of short stories entitled *Ten Little Indians*. No source can "own" or get credit for these facts. However, a source can still "own" a particular way of arranging or presenting such facts. If, for example, you begin your essay by stating—in your own words—a series of facts about Alexie's life in exactly the same order they appear in, say, the *Dictionary of Literary Biography*, then you would need to acknowledge that by citing the *Dictionary*. When in doubt, cite. (For guidance about *how* to do so, see 36.2.)

# 36 QUOTATION, CITATION, AND DOCUMENTATION

The bulk of any essay you write should consist of your own ideas expressed in your own words. Yet you can develop your ideas and persuade readers to accept them only if you present and analyze evidence. In essays about literature, quotations are an especially privileged kind of evidence. If your essay also makes use of secondary sources, you will need to quote (selectively) from some of these as well. In either case, your clarity and credibility will depend on how responsibly, effectively, and gracefully you move between others' words and your own. Clarity and credibility will also depend on letting your readers know—through precise citation and documentation—exactly where they can find each quotation and each fact or idea that you paraphrase. This chapter addresses the issue of *how* to quote, cite, and document texts and sources. (For a discussion of *when* to do so, see 33.4 and 35.4.)

## 36.1 EFFECTIVE QUOTATION

When it comes to quoting, there are certain rules that you must follow and certain strategies that, though not required, will help to make your argument more clear and effective.

### 36.1.1 Rules You Must Follow

1. Generally speaking, you should reproduce a quotation exactly as it appears in the original: include every word and preserve original spelling, capitalization, italics, and so on. However, there are a few exceptions:

   - When absolutely necessary, you may make minor changes to the quotation as long as (a) they do not distort the sense of the quotation, and (b) you clearly acknowledge them. For instance:

     —Additions and substitutions (e.g., of verb endings or pronouns) may be necessary in order to reconcile the quotation's grammar and syntax with your own or to ensure that the quotation makes sense out of its original context. Enclose these additions and changes in brackets.

     —Omit material from quotations to ensure you stay focused only on what's truly essential. Indicate omissions with ellipsis points unless the quotation is obviously a sentence fragment.

Notice how these rules are followed in the two examples below:

> Sethe, like Jacobs, experiences the wish to give up the fight for survival and die, but while Jacobs says she was "willing to bear on" "for the children's sakes" (127), the reason that Sethe gives for enduring is the physical presence of the baby in her womb: "[I]t didn't seem such a bad idea [to die], ... but the thought of herself stretched out dead while the little antelope lived on ... in her lifeless body grieved her so" that she persevered (31).
>
> When Denver tries to leave the haunted house to get food for her mother and Beloved, she finds herself imprisoned within her mother's time—a time that, clinging to places, is always happening again: "Out there ... were places in which things so bad had happened that when you went near them it would happen again...."
> —Jean Wyatt, "Giving Body to the Word: The Maternal Symbolic in Toni Morrison's *Beloved*," *PMLA* 108 (May 1993): 474–88

NOTE: In the first example, Wyatt uses brackets to indicate two changes, the capitalization of "it" and the addition of the words "to die." Ellipses indicate that she's omitted a word or words within the sentence that follows the colon. However, she doesn't need to begin or end the phrases *"willing to bear on"* and *"for the children's sake"* with ellipses because both are obviously sentence fragments. In the second example, notice that Wyatt does need to end the quotation with ellipsis points. Even though it reads like a complete sentence, this isn't the case; the sentence continues in the original text.

> —Occasionally, you may want to draw your readers' attention to a particular word or phrase within the quotation by using italics. Indicate this change by putting the words "emphasis added" (not underlined or in italics) into your parenthetical citation.

Like his constant references to "Tragedy," the wording of the father's question demonstrates that he is almost as hesitant as his daughter to confront death head-on: "When will you look *it* in the face?" he asks her (34; emphasis added).

- Although you should also accurately reproduce original punctuation, there is one exception to this rule: when incorporating a quotation into a sentence, you may *end* it with whatever punctuation mark your sentence requires. You do not need to indicate this particular change with brackets.

Whether portrayed as "queen," "saint," or "angel," the same "nameless girl" "looks out from all his canvases" (Rossetti, lines 5–7, 1).

NOTE: In the poem quoted ("In an Artist's Studio"), the words *queen* and *angel* are not followed by commas. Yet the syntax of this sentence requires that commas be added. Similarly, the word *canvases* is followed by a comma in the poem, but the sentence requires that this comma be changed to a period.

2. When incorporating short quotations into a sentence, put them in quotation marks and make sure that they fit into the sentence grammatically and syntactically. If necessary, you may make changes to the quotation (e.g., altering verb endings or pronouns) in order to reconcile its grammar and syntax with your own. But you should—again—always indicate changes with brackets.

It isn't until Mr. Kapasi sees the "topless women" carved on the temple that it "occur[s] to him ... that he had never seen his own wife fully naked" (333).

3. When quoting fewer than three lines of poetry, indicate any line break with a slash mark, any stanza break with a double slash mark.

   Before Milton's speaker can question his "Maker" for allowing him to go blind, "Patience" intervenes "to prevent / That murmur" (lines 8–9), urging him to see that "God doth not need / Either man's work or his own gifts . . ." (lines 9–10).

   "The cane appears // in our dreams," the speaker explains (Dove, lines 15–16).

4. Long quotations—four or more lines of prose, three of poetry—should be indented and presented without quotation marks to create a *block quotation*. In the case of poetry, reproduce original line and stanza breaks.

   Whereas the second stanza individualizes the dead martyrs, the third considers the characteristics they shared with each other and with all those who dedicate themselves utterly to any one cause:
   >  Hearts with one purpose alone
   >  Through summer and winter seem
   >  Enchanted to a stone
   >  To trouble the living stream. (lines 41–44)
   
   Whereas all other "living" people and things are caught up in the "stream" of change represented by the shift of seasons, those who fill their "Hearts with one purpose alone" become as hard, unchanging, and immoveable as stones.

5. Unless they are indented, quotations belong in double quotation marks; quotations within quotations get single quotation marks. However, if everything in your quotation appears in quotation marks in the original, you do not need to reproduce the single quotation marks.

   The words of Rufus Johnson come ringing back to the reader: " 'Listen here,' he hissed, 'I don't care if he's good or not. He ain't *right!*' " (468).

   As Rufus Johnson says of Sheppard, "I don't care if he's good or not. He ain't *right!*" (468).

6. Follow a word-group introducing a quotation with whatever punctuation is appropriate to your sentence. For instance:

   —If you introduce a quotation with a full independent clause (other than something like *She says*), separate the two with a colon.

   Ironically, Mr. Lindner's description of the neighborhood's white residents makes them sound exactly like the Youngers, the very family he's trying to exclude: "They're not rich and fancy people; just hard-working, honest people who don't really have much but . . . a dream of the kind of community they want to raise their children in" (1986).

   —If you introduce or interrupt a quotation with an expression such as *she says* or *he writes*, use a comma (or commas) or add a *that*. Likewise, use a comma if you end a quotation with an expression such as *he says*, unless the quotation ends with a question mark or exclamation point.

Alvarez claims, "The whole poem works on one single, returning note and rhyme . . ." (1214).

Alvarez suggests that "The whole poem works on one single, returning note and rhyme . . ." (1214).

"The whole poem," Alvarez argues, "works on one single, returning note and rhyme . . ." (1214).

"Here comes one," says Puck. "Where art thou, proud Demetrius?" asks Lysander (Shakespeare 3.2.400–401).

—If quoted words are blended into your sentence, use the same punctuation (or lack thereof) that you would if the words *were not* quoted.

Miriam Allott suggests that the odes, like "all Keats's major poetry," trace the same one "movement of thought and feeling," which "at first carries the poet . . . into an ideal world of beauty and permanence, and finally returns him to what is actual and inescapable."

Keats's poetry just as powerfully evokes the beauty of ordinary, natural things—of "the sun, the moon, / Trees," and "simple sheep"; of "daffodils" and "musk-rose blooms" (*Endymion*, lines 13–14, 15, 19); of nightingales, grasshoppers, and crickets; of "the stubble-plains" and "barred clouds" of a "soft-dying" autumn day ("To Autumn," lines 25–26).

When the narrator's eighty-six-year-old father asks her to tell him a "simple story" with "recognizable people" and a plot that explains "what happened to them next" (31), he gets "an unadorned and miserable tale" whose protagonist ends up "Hopeless and alone" (31).

7. **Commas and periods belong inside quotation marks, semicolons outside. Question marks and exclamation points go inside quotation marks if they are part of the quotation, outside if they aren't.** (Since parenthetical citations will often alter your punctuation, they have been omitted in the following examples. On the placement and punctuation of parenthetical citations, see 4.2.1.)

"You have a nice sense of humor," the narrator's father notes, but "you can't tell a plain story."

Wordsworth calls nature a "homely Nurse"; she has "something of a Mother's Mind."

What does Johnson mean when he says, "I don't care if he's good or not. He ain't *right!*"?

Bobby Lee speaks volumes about the grandmother when he says, "She was a talker, wasn't she?"

### 36.1.2 Useful Strategies

1. **Make the connection between quotations and inferences as seamless as possible.** Try to put them next to each other (in one sentence, if possible). Avoid drawing attention to your evidence as evidence. Don't waste time with phrases such as *This statement is proof that . . . ; This phrase is significant because . . . ; This idea is illustrated by . . . ; There is good evidence for this . . .* ; and

the like. Show why facts are meaningful or interesting rather than simply saying that they are.

| INEFFECTIVE QUOTING | EFFECTIVE QUOTING |
|---|---|
| Wordsworth calls nature a "homely Nurse" and says she has "something of a Mother's mind" (lines 81, 79). This diction supports the idea that he sees nature as a beneficent, maternal force. He is saying that nature is an educator and a healer. | Wordsworth describes nature as a beneficent, maternal force. A "homely Nurse" with "something of a Mother's Mind," nature both heals and educates (lines 81, 79). |
| Tennyson advocates decisive action, even as he highlights the forces that often prohibited his contemporaries from taking it. This is suggested by the lines "Made weak by time and fate, but strong in will, / To strive, to seek, to find, and not to yield" (lines 69-70). | Tennyson advocates forceful action, encouraging his contemporaries "To strive, to seek, to find, and not to yield" (line 70). Yet he recognizes that his generation is more tempted to "yield" than earlier ones because they have been "Made weak by time and fate" (line 69). |

2. Introduce or follow a quotation from a source (as well as a paraphrase or summary) with a *signal phrase* that includes the source author's name; you might also include the author's title and/or a bit of information about his or her status, if that information helps to establish credibility.

   In his study of the Frankenstein myth, Chris Baldick claims that "[m]ost myths, in literate societies at least, prolong their lives not by being retold at great length, but by being alluded to" (3)—a claim that definitely applies to the Hamlet myth.

   Oyin Ogunba, himself a scholar of Yoruban descent, suggests that many of Soyinka's plays attempt to capture the mood and rhythm of traditional Yoruban festivals (8).

   As historian R. K. Webb observes, "Britain is a country in miniature" (1).

   To avoid boring your readers, vary the content and placement of these phrases while always choosing the most accurate verb. (*Says*, for example, implies that words are spoken, not written.) You may find it useful to consult the following list of verbs that describe what sources do.

   *Verbs to Use in Signal Phrases*

   | | | | | |
   |---|---|---|---|---|
   | affirms | considers | explains | insists | shows |
   | argues | contends | explores | investigates | sees |
   | asks | demonstrates | finds | maintains | speculates |
   | asserts | describes | focuses on | notes | states |
   | believes | discusses | identifies | observes | stresses |
   | claims | draws atten- | illustrates | points out | suggests |
   | comments | tion to | implies | remarks | surmises |
   | concludes | emphasizes | indicates | reports | writes |

3. Lead your readers into fairly long quotations by giving them:
   - a clear sense of what to look for in the quotation;
   - any information they need to understand the quotation and to appreciate its significance. Quite often, contextual information—for instance, about who's speaking to whom and in what situation—is crucial to a

quotation's meaning; this is especially true when quoting dialogue. Also pay attention to pronouns: if the quotation contains a pronoun without an obvious referent, either indicate the specific referent in advance or add the appropriate noun into the quotation. (Again, place added words in brackets.)

| INEFFECTIVE QUOTING | EFFECTIVE QUOTING |
|---|---|
| *A Raisin in the Sun* seems to endorse traditional gender roles: "I'm telling you to be the head of this family... like you supposed to be" (1980); "the colored woman" should be "building their men up and making 'em feel like they somebody" (1949). | *A Raisin in the Sun* seems to endorse traditional gender roles. When Mama tells Walter "to be the head of this family from now on like you supposed to be" (1980), she affirms that Walter, rather than she or Ruth or Beneatha, is the rightful leader of the family. Implicitly she's also doing what Walter elsewhere says "the colored woman" should do—"building their men up and making 'em feel like they somebody" (1949). |
| Julian expresses disgust for the class distinctions so precious to his mother: "Rolling his eyes upward, he put his tie back on. 'Restored to my class,' he muttered" (490). | Julian professes disgust for the class distinctions so precious to his mother. At her request, he puts back on his tie, but he can't do so without "[r]olling his eyes" and making fun of the idea that he is thereby "[r]estored to [his] class" (490). |

NOTE: Here, the more effective examples offer crucial information about who is speaking (*"When Lena tells Walter"*) or what is happening (*"At her request, he puts back on his tie"*). They also include statements about the implications of the quoted words (*"she affirms that Walter... is the rightful leader of the family"*). At the same time, background facts are subordinated to the truly important, evidentiary ones.

4. **Follow each block quotation with a sentence or more of analysis.** It often helps to incorporate into that analysis certain key words and phrases from the quotation.

The second stanza of the poem refers back to the title poem of *The Colossus*, where the speaker's father, representative of the gigantic male other, so dominated her world that her horizon was bounded by his scattered pieces. In "Daddy," she describes him as

> Marble-heavy, a bag full of God,
> Ghastly statue with one grey toe
> Big as a Frisco seal
>
> And a head in the freakish Atlantic
> Where it pours bean green over blue
> In the waters off beautiful Nanset.

... Here the image of her father, grown larger than the earlier Colossus of Rhodes, stretches across and subsumes the whole of the United States, from the Pacific to the Atlantic ocean.     —Pamela J. Annas, "*A Disturbance of Mirrors*" (ch. 25)

5. **Be aware that even though long (especially block) quotations can be effective, they should be used sparingly.** Long quotations can create information overload or confusion for readers, making it hard for them to see what is most significant. When you quote only individual words or short

phrases, weaving them into your sentences, readers stay focused on what's significant, and it's easier to show them why it's significant, to get inferences and facts right next to each other.

6. Vary the length of quotations and the way you present them, using a variety of strategies. Choose the strategy that best suits your purpose at a specific moment in your essay, while fairly and fully representing the text. It can be very tempting to fall into a pattern—always, for example, choosing quotations that are at least a sentence long and introducing each with an independent clause and a colon. But overusing any one technique can easily render your essay monotonous. It might even prompt readers to focus more on the (inelegant) way you present evidence than on its appropriateness and significance.

## 36.2 CITATION AND DOCUMENTATION

In addition to indicating which facts, ideas, or words derive from someone else, always let your readers know where each can be found. You want to enable readers not only to "check up" on you, but also to follow in your footsteps and build on your work. After all, you hope that your analysis of a text will entice readers to reread certain passages from a different point of view.

At the same time, you don't want information about how to find others' work to interfere with readers' engagement with your work. Who, after all, could really make sense of an essay full of sentences such as these: (1) *"I know not 'seems,' " Hamlet claims in line 76 of Act 1, Scene 2,* and (2) *On the fourth page of her 1993* PMLA *article (which was that journal's 108th volume), Jean Wyatt insists that Morrison's "plot . . . cannot move forward because Sethe's space is crammed with the past."*

To ensure that doesn't happen, it is important to have a system for conveying this information in a concise, unobtrusive way. There are, in fact, many such systems currently in use. Different disciplines, publications, and even instructors prefer or require different systems. In literary studies (and the humanities generally), the preferred system is that developed by the Modern Language Association (MLA).

In this system, parenthetical citations embedded in an essay are keyed to an alphabetized list of works cited that appears at its end. Parenthetical citations allow the writer to briefly indicate where an idea, fact, or quotation appears, while the list of works cited gives readers all the information they need to find that source. Here is a typical sentence with parenthetical citation, as well as the works cited entry to which it refers.

*Sample Parenthetical Citation*

> In one critic's view, "Ode on a Grecian Urn" explores "what great art means" not to the ordinary person, but only "to those who create it" (Bowra 148).

> NOTE: Here, the parenthetical citation indicates that readers can find this quotation on page 148 of some work by an author named Bowra. To find out more, readers must turn to the list of works cited and scan it for an entry, like the following, that begins with the name "Bowra."

*Sample Works Cited Entry*

> Bowra, C. M. The Romantic Imagination. Oxford: Oxford UP, 1950.

This example gives a basic sense of how parenthetical citations and the list of works cited work together in the MLA system. Note that each parenthetical citation must "match up" with one (and only one) works cited entry.

The exact content of each parenthetical citation and works cited entry will depend upon a host of factors. The next two sections focus on these factors.

### 36.2.1 Parenthetical Citation

#### THE GENERIC PARENTHETICAL CITATION: AUTHOR(S) AND PAGE NUMBER(S)

The generic MLA parenthetical citation includes an author's name and a page number (or numbers). If the source has two or three authors, include all last names, as in (Gilbert and Gubar 57). If it has four or more, use the first author's name followed by *et al.* (Latin for "and others") in roman type, as in the second example below. In all cases, nothing but a space separates author's name(s) from page number(s).

> Most domestic poems of the 1950s foreground the parent-child relationship (Axelrod 1230).
>
> Given their rigid structure, it is perhaps "[n]ot surprisin[g]" that many sonnets explore the topic of "confinement" (Booth et al. 1022).

Notice the placement of the parenthetical citations in these examples. In each one the citation comes at the end of the sentence, yet it appears *inside* the period (because it is part of the sentence) and *outside* the quotation marks (because it isn't part of the quotation). Such placement of parenthetical citations should be your practice in all but two situations (both described in the next section).

#### VARIATIONS IN PLACEMENT

In terms of placement, the first exception is the block quotation. In this case, the parenthetical citation should immediately *follow* (not precede) the punctuation mark that ends the quotation.

> As historian Michael Crowder insists, Western-style education was the single "most radical influence on Nigeria introduced by the British" because it
>> came to be seen as a means not only of economic betterment but of social elevation. It opened doors to an entirely new world, the world of the white man. Since missionaries had a virtual monopoly on schools, they were able to use them as a means of further proselytization, and continued to warn their pupils of the evils of their former way of life. (195)

The second exception is the sentence that either incorporates material from multiple sources or texts (as in the first example below) or refers both to something from a source or text and to your own idea (as in the second example below). In either situation, you will need to put the appropriate parenthetical citation in mid-sentence right next to the material to which it refers, even at the risk of interrupting the flow of the sentence.

> Critics describe Caliban as a creature with an essentially "unalterable natur[e]" (Garner 458), "incapable of comprehending the good or of learning from the past" (Peterson 442), "impervious to genuine moral improvement" (Wright 451).

If Caliban is "incapable of . . . learning from the past" (Peterson 442), then how do we explain the changed attitude he seems to demonstrate at the end of the play?

## VARIATIONS IN CONTENT

The generic MLA citation may contain the author's name(s) and the relevant page number(s), but variations are the rule when it comes to content. The six most common variations occur when you do the following:

1. *Name the author in a signal phrase*
   Parenthetical citations should include only information that isn't crucial to the sense and credibility of your argument. Yet in nine cases out of ten, information about *whose* ideas, data, or words you are referring to is crucial in precisely this way. As a result, it is usually a good idea to indicate this in your text. When you do so, the parenthetical citation need only include the relevant page number(s).

   > Jefferson's "new generation" are, in Judith Fetterley's words, just "as much bound by the code of gentlemanly behavior as their fathers were" (619).

   > According to Steven Gould Axelrod, most domestic poems of the 1950s foreground the parent-child relationship (1230).

2. *Cite a poem or play*
   In the case of most poetry, refer to line (not page) numbers.

   > Ulysses encourages his men "To strive, to seek, to find, and not to yield" (line 70).

   In the case of classic plays, indicate act, scene, and line numbers, and separate them with periods.

   > "I know not 'seems,' " Hamlet claims (1.2.76).

3. *Cite multiple works by the same author or a work whose author is unknown*
   When citing multiple works by the same author or an anonymous work, you will need to indicate the title of the specific work to which you refer. Either indicate the title in your text, putting only the page number(s) in a parenthetical citation (as in the first example below), or create a parenthetical citation in which the first word or two of the title is followed by the page number(s) (as in the third example below). In the latter case, you should format the title words exactly as you would the full title, using quotation marks for essays, short stories, and short poems, and using italics or underlining for books.

   > As Judith Fetterley argues in "A Rose for 'A Rose for Emily,' " Jefferson's younger generation is just "as much bound by the code of gentlemanly behavior as their fathers were" (619).

   > Jefferson's "new generation" is, in Judith Fetterley's words, just "as much bound by the code of gentlemanly behavior as their fathers were" ("A Rose" 562).

   > Arguably, Jefferson's "new generation" is just "as much bound by the code of gentlemanly behavior as their fathers were" (Fetterley, "A Rose" 619).

4. *Cite a source quoted in another source*
   When quoting the words of one person as they appear in another author's work, mention the person's name in a signal phrase. Then create a parenthetical citation in which the abbreviation "qtd. in" is followed by the author's name and the relevant page number(s).

   Hegel describes Creon as "a moral power," "not a tyrant" (qtd. in Knox 2108).

5. *Cite multiple authors with the same last name*
   In this case, you should either use the author's full name in a signal phrase (as above) or add the author's first initial to the parenthetical citation (as below).

   *Beloved* depicts a "a specifically female quest powered by the desire to get one's milk to one's baby" (J. Wyatt 475).

6. *Cite multiple sources for the same idea or fact*
   In this case, put both citations within a single set of parentheses and separate them with a semicolon.

   Though many scholars attribute Caliban's bestiality to a seemingly innate inability to learn or change (Garner 458; Peterson 442; Wright 451), others highlight how inefficient or problematic Prospero's teaching methods are (Willis 443) and how invested Prospero might be in keeping Caliban ignorant (Taylor 384).

7. *Cite a work without numbered pages*
   Omit page numbers from parenthetical citations if you cite:
   - an electronic work that isn't paginated;
   - a print work whose pages aren't numbered;
   - a print work that is only one page long;
   - a print work, such as an encyclopedia, that is organized alphabetically.

   If at all possible, mention the author's name and/or the work's title in your text (so that you don't need any parenthetical citation). Otherwise, create a parenthetical citation that contains, as appropriate, the author's name and/or the first word(s) of the title.

8. *Italicize words that aren't italicized in the original*
   If you draw your readers' attention to a particular word or phrase within a quotation by using italics or underlining, your parenthetical citation must include the words "emphasis added."

   Like his constant references to "Tragedy," the wording of the father's question demonstrates that he is almost as hesitant as his daughter to confront death head-on: "When will you look *it* in the face?" he asks her (34; emphasis added).

### 36.2.2 The List of Works Cited

The alphabetized list of works cited should appear at the end of your completed essay. It must include all, and only, the texts and sources that you cite in your essay; it also must provide full publication information about each one.

If you're writing a research essay and have created and maintained a working bibliography (see 3.3.1), that bibliography will become the core of your works cited list. To turn the former into the latter, you will need to:

- delete sources that you did not ultimately cite in your essay;
- add an entry for each primary text you did cite;
- delete notes about where you found sources (call numbers, etc.).

## FORMATTING THE LIST OF WORKS CITED

The list of works cited should appear on a separate page (or pages) at the end of your essay. (If you conclude your essay on page 5, for example, you would start the list of works cited on page 6.) Center the heading "Works Cited" (without quotation marks) at the top of the first page, and double-space throughout.

The first line of each entry should begin at the left margin; the second and subsequent lines should be indented 5 spaces or ½ inch.

Alphabetize your list by the last names of the authors or editors. In the case of anonymous works, alphabetize by the first word of the title other than *A*, *An*, or *The*.

If your list includes multiple works by the same author, begin the first entry with the author's name and each subsequent entry with three hyphens followed by a period. Alphabetize these listings by the first word of the title, again ignoring the words *A*, *An*, or *The*.

## FORMATTING WORKS CITED ENTRIES

The exact content and style of each entry in your list of works cited will depend upon the type of source it is. Following are examples of some of the most frequently used types of entries in lists of works cited. For all other types, consult the sixth edition of the *MLA Handbook*.

*Book by a single author or editor*

Webb, R. K. Modern England: From the Eighteenth Century to the Present. New York: Columbia UP, 1969.

Wu, Duncan, ed. A Companion to Romanticism. Oxford: Blackwell, 1998.

*Book with an author and an editor*

Keats, John. Complete Poems. Ed. Jack Stillinger. Cambridge: Belknap-Harvard UP, 1982.

*Book by two or three authors or editors*

Gallagher, Catherine, and Thomas Laqueur, eds. The Making of the Modern Body: Sexuality and Society in the Nineteenth Century. Berkeley: U of California P, 1987.

*Book by more than three authors or editors*

Zipes, Jack, et al. The Norton Anthology of Children's Literature. New York: Norton, 2005.

*Introduction, preface, or foreword*

O'Prey, Paul. Introduction. Heart of Darkness. By Joseph Conrad. New York: Viking, 1983. 7-24.

*Essay, poem, or any other work in an edited collection or anthology*

>Shaw, Philip. "Britain at War: The Historical Context." <u>A Companion to Romanticism</u>. Ed. Duncan Wu. Oxford: Blackwell, 1998. 48-60.
>Yeats, W. B. "The Lake Isle of Innisfree." <u>The Norton Introduction to Literature</u>. 9th ed. Ed. Alison Booth, J. Paul Hunter, and Kelly J. Mays. New York: Norton, 2005. 1285.

*Multiple short works from one collection or anthology*

>Booth, Alison, J. Paul Hunter, and Kelly J. Mays, eds. <u>The Norton Introduction to Literature</u>. 9th ed. New York: Norton, 2005.
>Frost, Robert. "The Road Not Taken." Booth, Hunter, and Mays. 1247-48.
>Keats, John. "Ode to a Nightingale." Booth, Hunter, and Mays. 1098-99.

*Article in a reference work*

>"Magna Carta." <u>Encyclopaedia Britannica</u>. 14th ed. 630–35.

*Article in a scholarly journal*

>Wyatt, Jean. "Giving Body to the Word: The Maternal Symbolic in Toni Morrison's <u>Beloved</u>." PMLA 108 (May 1993): 474-88.

*Article in a newspaper or magazine*

>McNulty, Charles. "All the World's a Stage Door." <u>Village Voice</u> 13 Feb. 2001: 69.

*Review or editorial*

>Leys, Simon. "Balzac's Genius and Other Paradoxes." Rev. of <u>Balzac: A Life</u>, by Graham Robb. <u>New Republic</u> 20 Dec. 1994: 26-27.

> NOTE: The first name here is that of the reviewer, the second that of the author whose book is being reviewed.

*Internet site*

><u>U.S. Department of Education (ED) Home Page</u>. US Dept. of Education. 12 Aug. 2004 <http://www.ed.gov/index.jhtml>.
><u>Yeats Society Sligo Home Page</u>. Yeats Society Sligo. 12 Nov. 2004 <http://www.yeats-sligo.com/>.

*Article on a Web site*

>Padgett, John B. "William Faulkner." <u>The Mississippi Writers Page</u>. 29 Mar. 1999. 8 Feb. 2004 <http://www.olemiss.edu/depts/english/ms-writers/dir/faulkner_william/>.

> NOTE: The first date indicates when material was published or last updated. The second date indicates when you accessed the site.

# 37 SAMPLE RESEARCH PAPER

The student essay below was written in response to the following assignment:

Write an essay of 10–15 pages that analyzes at least two poems by any one author in your text and draws upon three or more secondary sources. At least one of these sources must be a work of literary criticism (a book or article in which a scholar interprets your author's work).

Richard Gibson's response to this assignment is an essay that explores the treatment of religion in four poems by Emily Dickinson; Gibson asks how conventional that treatment was in its original historical and social context. Notice that Gibson uses a variety of sources: literary critical studies of Dickinson's poetry; Dickinson biographies; historical studies of nineteenth-century American religious beliefs and practices; letters written by and to Dickinson; and a dictionary. At the same time, notice that Gibson's thesis is an original, debatable interpretive claim about Dickinson's poetry and that he supports and develops that claim by carefully analyzing four poems.

---

Gibson 1

Richard Gibson
Professor William Barksdale
English 301
4 March 2004

Keeping the Sabbath Separately:
Emily Dickinson's Rebellious Faith

When cataloguing Christian poets, it might be tempting to place Emily Dickinson between Dante and John Donne. She built many poems around biblical quotations, locations, and characters. She meditated often on the afterlife, prayer, and trust in God. Yet Dickinson was also intensely doubtful of the strand of Christianity that she inherited; in fact, she never became a Christian by the standards of her community in nineteenth-century Amherst, Massachusetts. Rather, like many of her contemporaries in Boston, Dickinson recognized the tension between traditional religious teaching and modern ideas. And these tensions, between hope and doubt, between tradition and modernity, animate her poetry. In "Some keep

*Gibson establishes a motive for his essay by first stating a claim about Dickinson's poetry that a casual reader might be tempted to adopt and then pointing out the problems with that claim in order to set up the more subtle and complex claim that is his thesis.*

the Sabbath going to church—," "The Brain—is wider than the Sky—," "Because I could not stop for Death—," and "The Bible is an antique Volume," the poet uses traditional religious terms and biblical allusions. But she does so in order both to criticize traditional doctrines and practices and to articulate her own unorthodox beliefs.

In some ways, Emily Dickinson seemed destined by birth and upbringing to be a creature of tradition. After all, her ancestry stretched back to the origin of the Massachusetts Bay Colony; her ancestor Nathaniel Dickinson "was among the four hundred or so settlers who accompanied John Winthrop in the migration that began in 1630" (Lundin 8). Winthrop and his followers were Puritans, a group of zealous Christians who believed in the literal truth and authority of the Bible; the innate corruption of humanity; the doctrine of salvation by faith, not works; and the idea that only certain people were "predestined" for heaven (Noll 21). A few decades after his immigration, Nathaniel Dickinson moved to western Massachusetts, where he and his descendants would become farmers and stalwarts in local churches (Lundin 9). Although Emily Dickinson's grandfather, Samuel Fowler Dickinson, and her father, Edward Dickinson, would give up farming to become lawyers, they, too, subscribed to the articles of their inherited religion (9). In short, for more than three hundred years prior to her birth, Emily Dickinson's family faithfully adhered to the Puritan tradition.

From early life to her year at college, Dickinson received an education that was "overwhelmingly religious" and traditional (Jones 295). The daily routine of the Dickinson household included prayer and readings from the Bible (296). She also received religious teaching regularly at the First Congregational Church and its "Sabbath [Sunday] school" (296). In her weekday schooling, Dickinson read textbooks such as <u>The New England Primer</u> and Amherst resident Noah Webster's spelling book that included "catechisms," or methodical teachings in religious doctrine and morality (296).

In the early nineteenth century, though, traditional churchgoers in western Massachusetts began to look warily to the east, especially to Boston, where nontraditional religious thinking had developed among both the "liberal Congregationalists" and the "free-thinking rationalists," or "deists" (Noll 138–42, 143–45). Because these theologies were

---

Gibson does a great job of establishing key terms—"traditional religious teaching," "modern ideas," and "unorthodox beliefs." Notice how he repeats these terms and variations on them throughout the essay in order to link his various subideas.

Gibson simply paraphrases because his focus is the information in the source, not its words. Nonetheless, Gibson uses parenthetical citations to indicate where in the source one can find this information.

Gibson omits the author's name in this parenthetical citation because he is referring to the source indicated in the preceding parenthetical citation.

Gibson refers readers to all the pages in the source that discuss the debate to which he refers—not just to those pages where the quoted phrases appear.

distinctly European and philosophical, they won few converts outside Boston (143, 145). The greater threat was Unitarianism, which had sprung up in Congregational churches. The Unitarians rejected many of the foundational beliefs of the Puritans and instead "promoted a benevolent God, a balanced universe, and a sublime human potential" (284). Former Unitarian minister and transcendentalist philosopher Ralph Waldo Emerson, an author whom Dickinson admired, gained national attention through his writings and speeches on self-reliance and the individual's "direct access" to the "divine spirit" that is behind all "religious systems" (Doriani 18; Norberg xiii–xv). Binding these Bostonian theologies together is an agreement that reason should be applied to religious beliefs. Each then concluded that some—or, in a few minds, most—of the traditional Christian doctrines (to which Amherst adhered) should be abandoned or revised.

Many Bostonian thinkers were influenced by recent developments in science and philosophy that contested the traditional Christian conception of the universe and of the Bible's literal truth. Earlier generations of scientists and philosophers had postulated that the universe obeys fixed laws, which led to ongoing debates about whether the miracles described in the Bible were plausible, even possible (Noll 108). The new astronomy discredited biblical passages describing irregular movements of the sun and the stars. The foremost contemporary dispute, though, concerned the age of the universe. The traditional Christian interpretation of the Bible stated that the universe had existed for about six thousand years (Lundin 32). Early-nineteenth-century geologists, though, had discovered fossils and rock formations that suggested that the Earth was significantly older. Some Christians dug in their heels, while others, like Amherst College professor Edward Hitchcock, attempted to "reconcile orthodoxy and the new geology"—an effort in which the young Dickinson "took comfort" (32). The intellectual scene of Massachusetts at the time of Dickinson's youth thus offered many competing answers to questions about divinity, the historicity of the Bible, and the cosmos. The reign of the old Puritan beliefs over the minds of New England was beginning to wane.

Dickinson herself began to confess doubts about her ability to join the First Congregational Church while still a teenager. In nineteenth-century Amherst, "to 'become a Christian' and

*Gibson uses double quotation marks to enclose words he's taken from a source, single quotation marks to enclose words quoted in that source.*

Gibson 4

join the church" required "only" that one "subscribe to the articles of faith and offer the briefest of assurance [sic] of belief in Christ" (Lundin 51). At age fifteen, though, Dickinson felt unable to do even this much, writing to her friend Abiah Root that she "had not yet made [her] peace with God." Unable to "feel that [she] could give up all for Christ, were [she] called to die," she asked her friend to pray for her, "that [she] may yet enter into the kingdom [of God], that there may be room left for [her] in the shining courts above" (8 Sept. 1846).

During her stay at Mount Holyoke Women's Seminary, from September 1847 to May 1848, Dickinson was frequently invited, even pressured, to become a Christian. Mary Lyon, headmistress of the college, "laid stress on the salvation of souls" and asked her "students to classify themselves according to their religious condition at the beginning of the year" (Jones 314). Asked to identify herself as a "No-Hoper," "Hoper," or "Christian," Dickinson chose the first of these options (Lundin 40–41). A few months into the school year, she informed Root that "there is a great deal of [religious] interest here and many are flocking to the ark of safety." Dickinson confessed, though, that she "[had] not yet given up to the claims of Christ," but was "not entirely thoughtless on so important & serious a subject" (17 Jan. 1848). In her final letter to Root from Mount Holyoke, Dickinson describes herself as "filled with self-recrimination about the opportunities [for salvation] [she had] missed," fearful that she might never "cast her burden on Christ" (16 May 1848). She thus left Mount Holyoke just as she came to it—a "No-Hoper."

Many critics, including recent biographer Roger Lundin, see the year at Mount Holyoke as a turning point in Emily Dickinson's life, the time when it became clear that she would never "become a Christian" according to Amherst's standards (47–48). Dickinson would never join the First Congregationalist Church and, by the age of thirty, stopped going to services altogether (99). She would likewise never join the Unitarians. Many of her spiritual ideas would resemble those of the transcendentalist Emerson, yet important distinctions remained (171). Throughout her life, she wrote to Christian friends, including ministers, on spiritual topics, despite their doctrinal differences (Lease 50–51). Dickinson thus eschewed New England's religious congregations and asserted her independence in spiritual matters. Yet she always remained

*The term* sic *indicates that a spelling or grammar problem within the quotation is present in the original. Gibson encloses the term in brackets to indicate that it is his addition.*

*In order to make quoted material fit grammatically and syntactically into his sentences, Gibson changes pronouns and adds explanatory words, enclosing all changed or added words in brackets.*

*The author's name is omitted from this parenthetical citation because it is included in the sentence.*

interested in the traditional perspective, and, as a poet, she relied on the traditional terminology in order to relate her new thinking.

Dickinson's well-known poem "Some keep the Sabbath going to church—," which she wrote around 1860, demonstrates this tendency. The opening line places the poem's events on the "Sabbath," the day of worship in Judeo-Christian traditions (Oxford). Thus, while the speaker does not follow her traditional peers "to Church," she nonetheless observes the traditional day (line 1). The speaker finds a "Bobolink," a native bird, to be the service's "Chorister" (line 3), the official term for the leader of a church choir (Oxford). A few lines later, the speaker calls this bird "Our little Sexton," the title of the manager of the church grounds. Normally, the sexton "[tolls] the Bell, for Church" (line 7), yet this sexton "sings" (line 8). The "Orchard" where she sits resembles an important part of church architecture, "a Dome." In this intimate setting, "God preaches, a noted Clergyman— / and the sermon is never long" (lines 9–10). The sermon satisfies two desires that most people have at church: first, to encounter God, and, second, not to be bored. In this natural scene "instead of getting to Heaven, at last— / [She's] going, all along" (lines 11–12).

The poem is so pleasant that it is easy to overlook the fact that its central message, that staying at home can be a spiritual experience, is subversive, for church attendance was important in traditional Congregationalist towns like Amherst (Rabinowitz 64–77). In fact, the word "some" might be an understatement, as, in 1860, most citizens in Amherst probably attended a church on Sunday. The speaker's situation instead resembles Emerson's 1842 description of the transcendentalists, those "lonely" and "sincere and religious" people who "repel influences" and "shun general society" (104–05). Furthermore, the speaker claims access to God without the aid of a religious community, a pastor, or a sacred text, all of which, as seen above, were essential to Puritan religious experience. In this poem, then, the speaker frames her spiritual experience in traditional terms and even keeps a few of the traditional practices, yet she simultaneously describes the benefits of departing from traditional practice.

While "Some keep the Sabbath going to church—" reveals Dickinson's changes in practice, "The Brain—is wider than the

Sky—," composed perhaps two years later, shows her shift in theology. The speaker asserts a confidence in the power of the human intellect that resembles that of Boston's nontraditional thinkers. In each stanza, she invites the reader to measure the brain by comparing it to some other enormous entity. First, she finds that the brain "is wider than the Sky" and urges the reader to "put them side by side" and see that "the one the other will contain / with ease" and the reader "beside" (lines 1–4). Second, she observes that the brain "is deeper than the sea" and, again, urges the reader to "hold them" and see that "the one the other will absorb / as Sponges—Buckets—do" (lines 5–8). The speaker has a complicated imaginative method: her materials thus far are all physical—brain, sky, sea—but the qualities that she compares are mixed—physical length and depth versus metaphysical length and depth.

> Gibson carefully leads the reader from one section of his essay to another with a transitional sentence that first summarizes the claim developed in the last section and then articulates the claim that he will develop in the next section.

In the third stanza, when the speaker observes that the brain "is just the weight of God" (line 9), she introduces theological material into her experiment. She asks the reader to "Heft," or weigh (Oxford), the two "Pound for Pound" and forecasts that "they will differ—if they do— / as Syllable from Sound" (lines 10–12). The poet switches from physical science to linguistics in this closing simile, the meaning of which divides scholars. William Sherwood argues that "each syllable is . . . finite" and "includes only a fraction of the total range of sound," yet "at the same time the syllable is the instrument by which sound is articulated" (127–28). Robert Weisbuch tries to take into account the context of the simile, arguing,

> Gibson's reference to "scholars" tells the reader that he's about to describe and consider other interpretations.

> We must take the qualifying "if they do" ironically. The difference of weight between "Syllable" and "Sound" is at once minute and absolute, the difference of a hair. It is the difference between the thing itself and its imperfect, itemized explanation. It is the difference, say, between paraphrase and poetry, poetry and thought. The brain is not quite and not at all the weightless weight of God. (84)

> Because this quotation is over four lines, it is indented to create a block quotation. Gibson doesn't need to enclose the whole quotation in quotation marks, but he does use quotation marks to set off words quoted within the quotation.

Weisbuch is right to note that the phrase "if they do" is ironic, as "Syllable" and "Sound" undeniably differ. Sherwood helpfully argues that these are differences in quantity and clarity. Thus, though the brain "As Syllable" is, ultimately, less than "the weight of God," it is more intelligible, perhaps more intelligent, than "the total range of sound."

> Rather than letting other scholarly interpreters have the last word, Gibson concludes the paragraph by stating his own interpretive claim.

The speaker of this poem is of a scientific bent; her

> Again, notice how Gibson touches back on key terms: "Amherst," "Boston," "traditional theology," etc.

measurements of length, depth, and weight recall the instruction in science that Dickinson received throughout her schooling (Jones 309; Lundin 30). Yet the speaker also believes that there are things beyond or outside the physical world of science and is just as eager to apply her scientific method to them. She perceives both that the human intellect is enormously expansive and that there is a God behind the cosmos. The divinity that she describes, though, is not the one her ancestors worshipped in Amherst: the speaker's God is more like a force than a person, more like the spirit of the universe than its sovereign. In "Some keep the Sabbath going to church—" Dickinson's orchard still seemed planted in Amherst. In "The Brain—is wider than the Sky," it becomes conspicuously a satellite of Boston.

This departure from traditional theology caused Dickinson to revise her vision of the afterlife, as suggested by her 1863 "Because I could not stop for Death—." The poem begins by personifying Death as a carriage-driver (lines 1–3). This personification of death echoes several biblical passages; Dickinson's Death "may," for example, "represent one of the Four Horsemen of the Apocalypse" (Bennett 208). The poet's "kindly" personification is, of course, both more benevolent than the destructive biblical figure and, with his carriage, more modern (line 2). The carriage ride takes the speaker past a school, "Fields of Gazing Grain," the "Setting Sun," and then "[pauses]" at a "House," before proceeding "toward Eternity" (lines 9, 11, 12, 17, 24). The "House" "[seems] / a Swelling of the Ground," and is, in fact, a grave (lines 10–11). Thus, the carriage drives the speaker through the stages of life—from youth to maturity, decline, death, and, ultimately, the afterlife.

Although Dickinson may draw her image of Death from the Christian tradition, her Death drives the speaker into a distinctly nontraditional afterlife. The speaker tells the reader early on that Death's carriage "[holds]" "Immortality" and then, in the closing stanza, that she has "surmised" that the carriage's direction is "toward Eternity" (lines 3, 4, 23, 24). In the Puritan theological tradition, death leads to Heaven or Hell, paradise or perdition. Yet Dickinson's carriage does not drive toward either destination; rather, the afterlife is just a continuous movement, a continuation of consciousness. "Some keep the Sabbath going to church—" prepared us, quite subtly, for this conception of the afterlife; there, too, Heaven is not a not place one "[gets] to," "at last," but a state to which one can be "going all along" (lines 11–12). In "Because I could not stop for Death—," the speaker sounds neither blissful nor pessimistic about this state. Her consciousness has adapted to her new existence: "centuries" pass now, "and yet / [it] feels shorter than the Day" when she "first surmised" the carriage's direction (lines 21–23). The word "surmised," though, signals that she is not entirely certain about what, if anything, is to come.

Uncertainty about the afterlife would remain with Dickinson throughout her life and, in 1882, would result in her asking the Reverend Washington Gladden, a somewhat unorthodox Congregationalist, "Is immortality true?" (Lease 50; Gladden). At this time, one of Dickinson's friends, a pastor, had recently died and another friend had become seriously ill (Gladden). Gladden's attempt to reassure her of the truth of immortality draws mostly from his argument that the authoritative figure "Jesus Christ taught" immortality. At the same time, he admits that "absolute demonstration there can be none of this truth."

> No page number is needed in the parenthetical citations for Gladden because the source is only one page long (see Works Cited).

In perhaps the same year, Dickinson wrote "The Bible is an antique Volume," which shows a mix of skepticism and optimism about the source of Gladden's arguments. The first three lines undermine the Bible's authority; it is an "antique Volume," authored by "faded Men / at the suggestion of Holy Spectres." The poet then provides a list of biblical "Subjects" that "reads like the playbill of a cheap traveling show" (Lundin 203): Eden is "the ancient Homestead"; Satan "the brigadier"; Judas "the Great Defaulter"; David "the Troubadour"; and sin "a distinguished Precipice / others must resist" (lines 4–10). The speaker then uses quotation marks to show her dissatisfaction with religious categories, saying, "Boys that 'believe' are very lonesome / other boys are 'lost' " (lines 11–12). Thus far, the speaker has given us every reason to abandon the Bible—she has discredited its authors, shown the silliness of its subjects, and revealed the tragic culture that surrounds it.

> Notice how Gibson leads the reader from one idea/paragraph to the next with a transition sentence that states the coming paragraph's main idea (This poem "shows a mix of skepticism and optimism about the" Bible) by referring back to the concerns of the last paragraph ("Gladden's arguments").

Yet the speaker believes that "had but the Tale [the Bible] a warbling Teller— / all the Boys would come" (lines 13–14). A "warbling Teller" is one whose voice is "thrilling," "ardent," or "friendly" (Bennett 430). For an example, she borrows the poet Orpheus from Greek mythology. His "Sermon," unlike the one the "believing" and "lost" boys now hear, "captivated— / it did not condemn" (lines 15–16). In addition to drawing distinct lines between the saved and the damned, like headmistress Mary Lyon, Puritans often used condemnation, in the now-infamous "fire and brimstone" style, to rouse the immoral to seek salvation (Lundin 11–12; Rabinowitz 5). Instead Dickinson here favors a passionate or intellectual response to a captivating speech over a moral response to a condemning one. She remains a believer in "the emotional force of the Scriptures and [their] expositors," even if she doubts the Bible's historical accuracy and rejects the claims of traditionalist preachers (Doriani 198). The implication of these closing lines, then, is that the Bible is—when read in the right spirit—still a valuable "Volume" for building a community. The Bible has reduced religious authority, but, when performed properly, retains inspirational power. The subtle magic of the poem is that Dickinson herself, in her parodies of biblical "Subjects," enlivens the Bible, "captivates" readers with the old "Tale" through her "warbling" poem.

> Gibson begins his conclusion by returning to the issue he raised in his introduction (Dickinson's status as a "Christian poet"). He then summarizes his argument by briefly reiterating his key points and using a few key words from Dickinson to do so, thus reminding us of how grounded his argument is in textual evidence. Finally, he moves from summarizing his argument to considering its implications for our overall view of Dickinson's poetry.

Though Emily Dickinson might not be a "Christian poet" in the traditional sense of the term, she does beautify and hand down a few beloved pieces of her inheritance, New England Puritanism. She "[keeps] the Sabbath," but at home. She imagines eternity, but without a Heaven or a Hell. She calls the Bible's authors "faded men," but frequently enlivens their "antique" passages in her poems. Over the years, her ideas about God, the universe, and the afterlife changed, but her yearnings to encounter the divine and to experience immortality remained. Emily Dickinson may have physically withdrawn from Amherst society, yet her mind did not withdraw from the intellectual struggles between traditional Amherst and modern Boston. Her spiritual questions and insights are distinctively personal and deeply honest; she is neither a purely skeptical nor a purely religious poet. Her intellect kept her, to her death in 1886, a "No-Hoper" by Mary Lyon's standards, yet, for modern readers, who understand her doubts and share her longings, she is a refreshingly hopeful poet.

## Works Cited

Bennett, Fordyce R. A Reference Guide to the Bible in Emily Dickinson's Poetry. Lanham: Scarecrow, 1997.

Dickinson, Emily. "Because I could not stop for Death." Dickinson, Complete Poems 350.

---. "The Bible is an antique Volume." Dickinson, Complete Poems 644.

---. "The Brain—is wider than the Sky—." Dickinson, Complete Poems 312.

---. The Complete Poems of Emily Dickinson. Ed. Thomas H. Johnson. Boston: Little, 1960.

---. Letters. Ed. Thomas H. Johnson. Vol. 1. Cambridge: Belknap, 1958.

---. "Some keep the Sabbath going to church." Dickinson, Complete Poems 153–54.

---. "To Abiah Root." 8 Sept. 1846. Dickinson, Letters 36.

---. "To Abiah Root." 17 Jan. 1848. Dickinson, Letters 60.

---. "To Abiah Root." 16 May 1848. Dickinson, Letters 67–68.

Doriani, Beth M. Emily Dickinson: Daughter of Prophecy. Amherst: U of Massachusetts P, 1996.

Gladden, Washington. "To Emily Dickinson." 27 May 1882. Letter 752a of Emily Dickinson: Selected Letters. Ed. Thomas H. Johnson. Cambridge: Belknap, 1971. 282.

Jones, Rowena Revis. "The Preparation of a Poet: Puritan Directions in Emily Dickinson's Education." Studies in the American Renaissance, 1982. Boston: Twayne, 1982.

Lease, Benjamin. " 'This World is not Conclusion': Dickinson, Amherst, and 'the local conditions of the soul.' " Emily Dickinson Journal 3.2 (1994): 38–55.

Lundin, Roger. Emily Dickinson and the Art of Belief. 2nd ed. Grand Rapids: Eerdmans, 2004.

Noll, Mark A. America's God: From Jonathan Edwards to Abraham Lincoln. New York: Oxford UP, 2002.

Norberg, Peter. Introduction. Essays and Poems by Ralph Waldo Emerson. New York: Barnes and Noble Classics, 2004. xiii–xxxii.

The Oxford English Dictionary. 2nd ed. 1989.

Rabinowitz, Richard. The Spiritual Self in Everyday Life: The Transformation of Personal Religious Experience in Nineteenth-Century New England. Boston: Northeastern UP, 1989.

Sherwood, William R. Circumference and Circumstance: Stages in the Mind and Art of Emily Dickinson. New York: Columbia UP, 1968.

Weisbuch, Robert. "The Necessary Veil: A Quest Fiction." Emily Dickinson. Ed. Harold Bloom. New York: Chelsea, 1985.

# Critical Approaches

Few human abilities are more remarkable than the ability to read and interpret literature. A computer program or a database can't perform the complex process of reading and interpreting—not to mention writing about—a literary text, although computers can easily exceed human powers of processing codes and information. Readers follow the sequence of printed words and as if by magic recreate a scene between characters in a novel or play, or they respond to the almost inexpressible emotional effect of a poem's figurative language. Experienced readers can pick up on a multitude of literary signals all at once. With rereading and some research, readers can draw on information such as the author's life or the time period when this work and others like it were first published. Varied and complex as the approaches to literary criticism may be, they are not difficult to learn. For the most part schools of criticism and theory have developed to address questions that any reader can begin to answer.

As we noted in the introduction, there are essentially three participants in what could be called the literary exchange or interaction: the *text,* the *source* (the *author* and other factors that produce the text), and the *receiver* (the *reader* and other aspects of *reception*). All the varieties of literary analysis concern themselves with these aspects of the literary exchange in varying degrees and with varying emphases. Although each of these elements has a role in any form of literary analysis, systematic studies of literature and its history have defined approaches or methods that focus on the different elements and circumstances of the literary interaction. The first three sections below—"Emphasis on the Text," "Emphasis on the Source," and "Emphasis on the Receiver"—describe briefly those schools or modes of literary analysis that have concentrated on one of the three elements while de-emphasizing the others. These different emphases, plainly speaking, are habits of asking different kinds of questions. Answers or interpretations will vary according to the questions we ask of a literary work. In practice the range of questions can be—to some extent *should* be—combined whenever we develop a literary interpretation. Such questions can always generate the thesis or argument of a critical essay.

Although some approaches to literary analysis treat the literary exchange (text, source, receiver) in isolation from the world surrounding that exchange (the world of economics, politics, religion, cultural tradition, and sexuality—in other words, the world in which we live), most contemporary modes of analysis acknowledge the importance of that world to the literary exchange. These days, even if a literary scholar wants to focus primarily on the text or its source or receiver, she or he will often incorporate some of the observations and methods developed by theorists and critics who have turned their attention toward the changing world surrounding the formal conventions of literature, the writing process and writer's career, and the reception or response to literature. We describe the work of such theorists and critics in the fourth section below, "Historical and Ideological Criticism."

Before expanding on the kinds of critical approaches within these four categories, let's consider one example in which questions concerning the text, source, and receiver, as well as a consideration of historical and ideological questions, would contribute to a richer interpretation of a text. To begin as usual with preliminary questions about the *text: What* is "First Fight. Then Fiddle." (see p. 1026)? Printed correctly on a separate piece of paper, the text would tell us at once that it is a poem because of its form: rhythm, repeating word sounds, lines that leave very wide margins on the page. Because you are reading this poem in this book, you know even more about its form (in this way, the publication *source* gives clues about the *text*). By putting it in a section with other poetry, we have told you it is a poem worth reading, rereading, and thinking about. (What other ways do you encounter poems, and what does the medium of presenting a poem tell you about it?)

You should pursue other questions focused on the text. What *kind* of poem is it? Here we have helped you, especially if you are not already familiar with the sonnet form, by grouping this poem with other sonnets. Classifying "First Fight. Then Fiddle." as a sonnet might then prompt you to interpret the ways that this poem is or is not like other sonnets. Well and good: you can check off its fourteen lines of (basically) iambic pentameter, and note its somewhat unusual rhyme scheme and meter, in relation to the rules of **Italian** and **English sonnets.** *Why* does this experiment with the sonnet form matter?

To answer questions about the purpose of form, you need to answer some basic questions about *source*, such as: *When* was this sonnet written and published? *Who* wrote it? What do you know about Gwendolyn Brooks, about 1949, about African American women and/or poets in the United States at that time? A short historical and biographical essay answering such questions might help put the sonnetness of "First Fight. Then Fiddle." in context. But assembling all the available information about the source and original context of the poem, even some sort of documented testimony from Brooks about her intentions or interpretation of it, would still leave room for other questions leading to new interpretations.

What about the *receiver* of "First Fight. Then Fiddle."? Even within the poem a kind of audience exists. This sonnet seems to be a set of instructions addressed to "you." (Although many sonnets are addressed by a speaker, "I," to an auditor, "you," such address rarely sounds like military commands, as it does here.) This internal audience is not of course to be confused with real people responding to the poem. How did readers respond to it when it was first published? Can you find any published reviews, or any criticism of this sonnet published in studies of Gwendolyn Brooks?

Questions about the receiver, like those about the author and other sources, readily connect with historical questions. Would a reader or someone listening to this poem read aloud respond differently in the years after World War II than in an age of global terrorism? Does it make a difference if the audience addressed by the speaker *inside* the poem is imagined as a group of African American men and women or as a group of European American male commanders? (The latter question could be regarded as involving questions about the text and the source as well as about the receiver.) Does a reader need to identify with any of the particular groups the poem fictitiously addresses, or would any reader, from any background, respond to it the same way? Even the formal qualities of the text could be examined through historical lenses: the sonnet form has been associated with prestigious European literature, and with themes of love and mortality, since the Renaissance. It is significant that a twentieth-century African American poet chose *this* traditional form to twist "threadwise" into an antiwar protest.

The above are only some of the worthwhile questions concerning this short, intricate poem. (We will develop a few more thoughts about it in illustrating different approaches to the text and to the source.) Similarly, the complexity of critical approaches far exceeds our four categories. While a great deal of worthwhile scholarship and criticism borrows from a range of theories and methods, below we give necessarily simplified descriptions of various critical approaches that have continuing influence. We cannot trace a history of the issues involved, or the complexity and controversies within these movements. Instead think of what follows as a road map to the terrain of literary analysis. Many available resources describe the entire landscape of literary analysis in more precise detail. If you are interested in learning more about these or any other analytical approaches, consult the works listed in the bibliography at the end of this chapter.

## EMPHASIS ON THE TEXT

This broad category encompasses approaches that minimize the elements associated with the author/source or the reader/reception to focus on the work. In a sense any writing about literature presupposes recognition of form, in that it deems the object of study to *be* a literary work, and to belong to a type or genre of literature, as Brooks's poem belongs with sonnets. Moreover, almost all literary criticism notes some details of style or structure, some *intrinsic* features such as the relation between dialogue or narrated summary, or the pattern of rhyme and meter. But *formalist* approaches go further by foregrounding the design of the text as inherent to the meaning of the whole work.

Some formalists, reasonably denying the division of content from form (since the form is part of the content or meaning), have more controversially excluded any discussion of *extrinsic* matters such as the author's biography or questions of psychology, sociology, or history. This has led to accusations that formalism, in avoiding relevance to actual authors and readers or to the world of economic power or social change, also avoids political issues or commitments. Some historical or ideological critics have therefore argued that formalism supports the powers that be, since it precludes protest. Conversely, some formalists charge that any extrinsic—that is, historical, political, ideological, as well as biographical or psychological—interpretations of literature reduce the text to a set of more or less cleverly encoded messages or propaganda. A formalist might maintain that the inventive wonders of art exceed any practical function it serves. In practice influential formalisms have generated modes of *close reading* that balance attention to form, significance, and social context, with some acknowledgment of the political implications of literature. In the early twenty-first century the formalist methods of close reading remain influential, especially in classrooms. Indeed, *The Norton Introduction to Literature* adheres to these methods in its presentation of elements and interpretation of form.

### New Criticism

One strain of formalism, loosely identified as the New Criticism, dominated literary studies from approximately the 1920s to the 1970s. New Critics rejected both of the approaches that prevailed then in the relatively new field of English studies: the dry analysis of the development of the English language, and the misty appreciation and evaluation of great works. Generally, New Criticism minimizes consideration of both the source and the receiver, favoring the intrinsic qualities of a unified literary work. Psychological or historical information about the author, the intentions or feelings of authors or readers, and any philosophical or socially relevant "messages" derived from the work all are out of bounds in a New Critical reading. The text in a fundamental way refers to itself: its medium is its message. Although interested in ambiguity and irony as well as figurative language, a New Critical reader establishes the organic unity of the unique work. Like an organism, the work develops in a synergetic relation of parts to whole.

A New Critic might, for example, publish an article titled "A Reading of 'First Fight. Then Fiddle.'" (The method works best with lyric or other short forms because it requires painstaking attention to details such as metaphors or alliteration.) Little if anything would be said of Gwendolyn Brooks or the poem's relation to modernist poetry. The critic's task is to give credit to the poem, not the poet or the period, and if it is a good poem, implicitly, it can't be merely "about" World War II or civil rights. New Criticism presumes that a good literary work symbolically embodies universal human themes and may be interpreted objectively on many levels. These levels may be related more by tension and contradiction than harmony, yet that relation demonstrates the coherence of the whole poem.

Thus the New Critic's essay might include some of the following observations. The title—which reappears as half of the first line—consists of a pair of two-word imperative sentences, and most statements in the poem paraphrase these two sentences, especially the first of them, "First fight." Thus an alliterative two-word command, "Win war" (line 12), follows a longer version of such a command: "But first to arms, to armor" (line 9). Echoes of this sort of exhortation appear throughout. We, as audience, begin to feel "bewitch[ed], bewilder[ed]" (line 4) by a buildup of undesirable urgings, whether at the beginning of a line ("Be deaf," line 11) or the end of a line ("Be remote," line 7; "Carry hate," line 9) or in the middle of a line ("Rise bloody," line 12). It's hardly what we would want to do. Yet the speaker makes a strong case for the practical view that a society needs to take care of defense before it can "devote" itself to "silks and honey" (lines 6–7), that is, the soft and sweet pleasures of art. But what kind of culture would place "hate / In front of... harmony" and try to ignore "music" and "beauty" (lines 9–11)? What kind of people are only "remote / A while from malice and from murdering" (lines 6–7)? A society of warlike heroes would rally to this speech. Yet on rereading, many of the words jar with the tone of heroic battle cry.

The New Critic examines not only the speaker's style and words but the order of ideas and lines in the poem. Ironically, the poem defies the speaker's command; it fiddles first, and then fights, as the **octave** (first eight lines) concern art, and the **sestet** (last six) concern war. The New Critic might be delighted by the irony that the two segments of the poem in fact unite, in that their topics—octave on how to fiddle, sestet on how to fight—mirror each other. The beginning of the poem plays with metaphors for music and art as means of inflicting "hurting love" (line 3) or emotional conquest, that is, ways to "fight." War and art are both, as far as we know, universal in all human societies. The poem, then, is an organic whole that restates ancient themes.

Later critics have pointed out that New Criticism, despite its avoidance of extrinsic questions, had a political context of its own. The affirmation of unity for the artwork and humanities in general should be regarded as a strategy adapted during the Cold War as a counterbalance to the politicization of art in fascist and communist regimes. New Criticism also provided a program for literary reading that is accessible to beginners regardless of their social background, in keeping with the opening of college-level English studies to more women, minorities, and members of the working class. By the 1970s these same groups had helped generate two sources of opposition to New Criticism's ostensible neutrality and transparency: critical studies that emphasized the politics of social differences (e.g., feminist criticism); and theoretical approaches, based on linguistics, philosophy, and political theory, that effectively distanced nonspecialists once more.

### Structuralism

Whereas New Criticism was largely a British and American phenomenon, structuralism and its successor, poststructuralism, derive primarily from French theorists. Strains of structuralism also emerged in the Soviet Union and in Prague, influenced by the demand for a science of criticism that would avoid direct political confrontation. Each of these movements was drawn to scientific objectivity—difficult to attain in literature, arts, and other "humanities"—and at the same time wary of political commitment. Politics, after all, had been the rallying cry for censorship of science, art, and inquiry throughout centuries and in recent memory.

Structuralist philosophy, however, was something rather new. Influenced by the French linguist Ferdinand de Saussure (1857–1913), structuralists sought an objective system for studying the principles of language. Saussure distinguished between individual uses of language, such as the sentences you or I just spoke or wrote (*parole*), and the sets of rules of English or any language (*langue*). Just as a structuralist linguist would study the interrelations of signs in the *langue* rather than the variations in specific utterances in *parole*, a structuralist critic of literature or culture would study shared systems of meaning, such as genres or myths that pass from one country or period to another, rather than a certain poem in isolation (the favored subject of New Criticism).

Another structuralist principle derived from Saussure is the emphasis on the arbitrary association between a word and what it is said to signify, the *signifier* and the *signified*. The word "horse," for example, has no divine, natural, or necessary connection to that four-legged, domesticated mammal, which is named by other combinations of sounds and letters in other languages. Any language is a network of relations among such arbitrary signifiers, just as each word in the dictionary must be defined using other words in that dictionary. Structuralists largely attribute the meanings of words to rules of differentiation from other words. Such differences may be phonetic (as among the words "cat" and "bat" and "hat") or they may belong to conceptual associations (as among the words "dinky," "puny," "tiny," "small," "miniature," "petite," "compact"). Structuralist thought has particularly called attention to the way that opposites or dualisms such as "night" and "day" or "feminine" and "masculine" define each other through their differences rather than in direct reference to objective reality. For example, the earth's motion around the sun produces changing exposure to sunlight daily and seasonally, but by linguistic convention we call it "night" between, let's say, 8 p.m. and 5 a.m., no matter how light it is. (We may differ in opinions about "evening" or "dawn." But our "day" at work may begin or end in the dark.) The point is that arbitrary labels divide what in fact is continuous.

Structuralism's linguistic insights have greatly influenced literary studies. Like New Criticism, structuralism shows little interest in the creative process or in authors, their intentions, or their circumstances. Similarly, structuralism discounts the idiosyncrasies of particular readings; it takes texts to represent interactions of words and ideas that stand apart from individual human identities or sociopolitical commitments. Structuralist approaches have applied less to lyric poetry than to myths, narratives, and cultural practices, such as sports or fashion. Although structuralism tends to affirm a universal humanity as the New Critics might do, its work in comparative mythology and anthropology challenged the absolute value that New Criticism tended to grant to time-honored canons of great literature.

The structuralist would regard a text not as a self-sufficient icon but as part of a network of conventions. A structuralist essay on "First Fight. Then Fiddle." might ask why the string is plied with the "feathery sorcery" (line 2) of the "bow" (line 7). These words suggest the art of a Native American trickster or primitive sorcerer, while at the same time the instrument is a disguised weapon: a stringed bow with feathered arrows (the term "muzzle" is a similar pun, suggesting an animal's snout and the discharging end of a gun). Or is the fiddle—a violin played in musical forms such as bluegrass—a metaphor for popular art or folk resistance to official culture? In many folk tales a hero is taught to play the fiddle by the devil or tricks the devil with a fiddle or similar instrument. Further, a structuralist reading might attach great significance to the sonnet form as a paradigm that has shaped poetic expression for centuries. The classic "turn" or reversal of thought in a sonnet may imitate the form of many narratives of departure and return, separation and reconciliation. Brooks's poem repeats in the numerous short reversing imperatives, as well as in the structure of octave versus sestet, the eternal oscillation between love and death, creation and destruction.

### Poststructuralism

By emphasizing the paradoxes of dualisms and the ways that language constructs our awareness, structuralism planted the seeds of its own destruction or, rather, deconstruction. Dualisms (e.g., masculine/feminine, mind/body, culture/nature) cannot be separate-but-equal; rather they take effect as differences of power in which one dominates the other. Yet as the German philosopher of history Georg Wilhelm Friedrich Hegel (1770–1831) insisted, the relations of the dominant and subordinate, of master and slave readily invert themselves. The master is dominated by his need for the slave's subordination; the possession of subordinates defines his mastery. As Brooks's poem implies, each society reflects its own identity through an opposing "they," in a dualism of civilized/barbaric. The instability of the speaker's position in this poem (is he or she among the conquerors or the conquered?) is a model of the instability of roles throughout the human world. There is no transcendent ground—except on another planet, perhaps—from which to measure the relative positions of the polar opposites on Earth. Roland Barthes (1915–1980) and others, influenced by the radical movements of the 1960s and the increasing complexity of culture in an era of mass consumerism and global media, extended structuralism into more profoundly relativist perspectives.

Poststructuralism is the broad term used to designate the philosophical position that attacks the objective, universalizing claims of most fields of knowledge since the eighteenth century. Poststructuralists, distrusting the optimism of a positivist philosophy that suggests the world is knowable and explainable, ultimately doubt the possibility of certainties of any kind, since language signifies only through a chain of other words rather than through any fundamental link to reality. This argument derives from structuralism, yet it also criticizes structuralist universalism and avoidance of political issues. *Ideology* is a key conceptual ingredient in the poststructuralist argument against structuralism. Ideology is a slippery term that can broadly be defined as a socially shared set of ideas that shape behavior; often it refers to the values that legitimate the ruling interests in a society, and in many accounts it is the hidden code that is officially denied. (We discuss kinds of "ideological" criticism later.) Poststructuralist theory has played a part in a number of critical schools introduced below, not all of them focused on the text. But in literary criticism, poststructuralism has marshaled most forces under the banner of deconstruction.

### Deconstruction

Deconstruction insists on the logical impossibility of knowledge that is not influenced or biased by the words used to express it. Deconstruction also claims that language is incapable of representing any sort of reality directly. As practiced by its most famous proponent, the French philosopher Jacques Derrida (1930–2004), deconstruction endeavors to trace the way texts imply the contradiction of their explicit meanings. The deconstructionist delights in the sense of dizziness as the grounds of conviction crumble away; *aporia*, or irresolvable doubt, is the desired, if fleeting, end of an encounter with a text. Deconstruction threatens *humanism*, or the worldview that is centered on human values and the self-sufficient individual, because it denies that there is an ultimate, solid reality on which to base truth or the identity of the self. All values and identities are constructed by the competing systems of meaning, or *discourses*. This is a remarkably influential set of ideas that you will meet again as we discuss other approaches.

The traditional concept of the author as creative origin of the text comes under fire in deconstructionist criticism, which emphasizes instead the creative power of language or the text, and the ingenious work of the critic in detecting gaps and contradictions in writing. Thus like New Criticism, deconstruction disregards the author and concentrates on textual close reading, but unlike New Criticism, it features the role of the reader as well. Moreover, the text need not be respected as a pure and coherent icon. Deconstructionists might "read" many kinds of writing and representation in other media in much the same way that they might read Milton's *Paradise Lost*, that is, irreverently. Indeed, when deconstruction erupted in university departments of literature, traditional critics and scholars feared the breakdown of the distinctions between literature and criticism and between literature and many other kinds of text. Many attacks on literary theory have particularly lambasted deconstructionists for apparently rejecting all the reasons to care about literature in the first place and for writing in a style so flamboyantly obscure that no one but specialists can understand. Yet in practice Derrida and others have carried harmony before them, to paraphrase Brooks; their readings can delight in the play of figurative language, thereby enhancing rather than debunking the value of literature.

A deconstructionist might read "First Fight. Then Fiddle." in a manner somewhat similar to the New Critic's, but with even more focus on puns and paradoxes and with resistance to organic unity. For instance, the two alliterative commands, "fight" and "fiddle," might be opposites, twins, or inseparable consequences of each other. The word "fiddle" is tricky. Does it suggest that art is trivial? Does it allude to a dictator who "fiddles while Rome burns," as the saying goes? Someone who "fiddles" is not performing a grand, honest, or even competent act: one fiddles with a hobby, with the books, with car keys in the dark. The artist in this poem defies the orthodoxy of the sonnet form, instead making a kind of harlequin patchwork out of different traditions, breaking the rhythm, intermixing endearments and assaults.

To the deconstructionist the recurring broken antitheses of war and art, art and war cancel each other out. The very metaphors undermine the speaker's summons to war. The command "Be deaf to music and to beauty blind," which takes the form of a *chiasmus*, or X-shaped sequence (adjective, noun; noun, adjective), is a kind of miniature version of this chiasmic poem. (We are supposed to follow a sequence, fight then fiddle, but instead reverse that by imagining ways to do violence with art or to create beauty through destruction.) The poem, a lyric written but imagined as spoken or sung, puts the senses and the arts under erasure; we are somehow not to hear music (by definition audible), not to see beauty (here a visual attribute). "Maybe not too late" comes rather too late: at the end of the poem it will be too late to start over, although "having first to civilize a space / Wherein to play your violin with grace" (lines 12–14) comes across as a kind of beginning. These comforting lines form the only heroic couplet in the poem, the only two lines that run smoothly from end to end. (All the other lines have **caesuras, enjambments,** or balanced pairs of concepts, as in "from malice and from murdering" [line 8].) But the violence behind "civilize," the switch to the high-art term "violin," and the use of the Christian term "grace" suggest that the pagan erotic art promised at the outset, the "sorcery" of "hurting love" that can "bewitch," will be suppressed.

Like other formalisms, deconstruction can appear apolitical or conservative because of its skepticism about the referential connection between literature and the world of economics, politics, and other social forms. Yet poststructuralist linguistics provides a theory of *difference* that clearly pertains to the rankings of status and power in society, as in earlier examples of masculine/feminine, master/slave. The *Other*, the negative of the norm, is always less than an equal counterpart. Deconstruction has been a tool for various poststructuralist thinkers—including the historian Michel Foucault (1926–1984), the feminist theorist and psychoanalyst Julia Kristeva (b. 1941), and the psychoanalytic theorist Jacques Lacan (1901–1981).

### Narrative Theory

Before concluding the discussion of text-centered approaches, we should mention the schools of narratology and narrative theory that have shaped study of the novel and other kinds of narrative. Criticism of fiction has been in a boom period since the 1950s, but the varieties of narrative theory per se have had more limited effect than the approaches we have discussed above. Since the 1960s different analysts of the forms and techniques of narrative, most notably the Chicago formalists and the structuralist narratologists, have developed terminology for the various interactions of author, implied author, narrator, and characters; of plot and the treatment of time in the selection and sequence of scenes; of voice, point of view, or focus and other aspects of fiction. As formalisms, narrative theories tend to exclude the author's biography, individual reader response, and the historical context of the work or its actual reception.

Narratology began by presenting itself as a structuralist science; its branches have grown from psychoanalytic theory or extended to reader-response criticism. In recent decades studies of narrative technique and form have responded to Marxist, feminist, and other ideological criticism that insists on the political contexts of literature. One important influence on this shift has been the revival of the work of Mikhail Bakhtin (1895–1975), which features the novel as a *dialogic* form that pulls together the many discourses and voices of a culture and its history. Part of the appeal of Bakhtin's work has been the fusion of textual close reading with comprehension of material factors such as economics and class, and a sense of the open-endedness and contradictoriness of writing (in the spirit of deconstruction more than of New Criticism). Like other Marxist-trained European formalists, Bakhtin sought to place the complex literary modes of communication in the light of politics and history.

## EMPHASIS ON THE SOURCE

As the above examples suggest, a great deal can be drawn from a text without any reference to its source or author. For millennia many anonymous works were shared in oral or manuscript form, and even after printing spread in Europe it was not necessary to know the author's name or anything about him or her. Yet criticism from its beginnings in ancient Greece has been interested in the designing intention "behind" the text. Even when no evidence remained about the author, a legendary personality has been invented to satisfy readers' curiosity. From the legend of blind Homer to the latest debates about biographical evidence and portraits of William Shakespeare, literary criticism has been accompanied by interest in the author's life.

### Biographical Criticism

This approach reached its height in an era when humanism prevailed in literary studies (roughly 1750s to 1960s). At this time there was widely shared confidence in the ideas that art and literature were the direct expressions of the artist's or writer's genius and that criticism of great works supported veneration of the great persons who created them. The lives of some famous writers became the models that aspiring writers emulated. Criticism at times was skewed by social judgments of personalities, as when Keats was put down as a "Cockney" poet, that is, London-bred and lower-class. Many writers have struggled to get their work taken seriously because of mistaken biographical criticism. Women or minorities have at times used pseudonyms or published anonymously to avoid having their work put down or having it read only through the expectations, negative or positive, of what a woman or person of color might write. Biographical criticism can be diminishing in this respect. Others have objected to reading literature as a reflection of the author's personality. Such critics have supported the idea that the highest literary art is pure form, untouched by gossip or personal emotion. In this spirit some early twentieth-century critics as well as modernist writers such as T. S. Eliot, James Joyce, and Virginia Woolf tried to dissociate the text from the personality or political commitments of the author. (The theories of these writers and their actual practices did not quite coincide.)

In the early twentieth century, psychoanalytic interpretations placed the text in light of the author's emotional conflicts, and other interpretations relied heavily on the author's stated intentions. (Although psychoanalytic criticism entails more than analysis of the author, we will introduce it as an approach that primarily concerns the human source[s] of literature; it usually has less to say about the form and receiver of the text.) Author-based readings can be reductive. All the accessible information about a writer's life cannot explain the writings. As a young man D. H. Lawrence might have hated his father and loved his mother, but all men who hate their fathers and love their mothers do not write fiction as powerful as Lawrence's. Indeed, Lawrence cautioned that we should "trust the tale, not the teller."

Any kind of criticism benefits, however, from being informed by the writer's life and career to some extent. Certain critical approaches, devoted to recognition of separate literary traditions, make sense only in light of supporting biographical evidence. Studies that concern traditions such as Irish literature, Asian American literature, or literature by Southern women require reliable information about the writers' birth and upbringing and even some judgment of the writers' intentions to write *as* members of such traditions. (We discuss feminist, African American, and other studies of distinct literatures in the "Historical and Ideological Criticism" section, although such studies recognize the biographical "source" as a starting point.)

A reading of "First Fight. Then Fiddle." becomes rather different when we know more about Gwendolyn Brooks. An African American, she was raised in Chicago in the 1920s. These facts begin to provide a context for her work. Some of the biographical information has more to do with her time and place than with her race and sex. Brooks began in the 1940s to associate with Harriet Monroe's magazine, *Poetry,* which had been influential in promoting modernist poetry. Brooks early received acclaim for books of poetry that depict the everyday lives of poor, urban African Americans; in 1950 she was the first African American to win a Pulitzer Prize. In 1967 she became an outspoken advocate for the Black Arts movement, which promoted a separate tradition rather than integration into the aesthetic mainstream. But even before this political commitment, her work never sought to "pass" or to distance itself from racial difference, nor did it become any less concerned with poetic tradition and form when she published it through small, independent black presses in her "political" phase.

It is reasonable, then, to read "First Fight. Then Fiddle.," published in 1949, in relation to the role of a racial outsider mastering and adapting the forms of a dominant tradition. Perhaps Brooks's speaker addresses an African American audience in the voice of a revolutionary, calling for violence to gain the right to express African American culture. Perhaps the lines "the music that they wrote / Bewitch, bewilder. Qualify to sing / Threadwise" (lines 3–5) suggest the way that the colonized may transform the empire's music rather than the other way around. Ten years before the poem was published, a famous African American singer, Marian Anderson, had more than "qualif[ied] to sing" opera and classical concert music, but had still encountered the color barrier in the United States. Honored throughout Europe as the greatest living contralto, Anderson was barred in 1939 from performing at Constitution Hall in Washington, D.C., because of her race. Instead she performed at the Lincoln Memorial on Easter Sunday to an audience of seventy-five thousand people. It was not easy to find a "space" in which to practice her art. Such a contextual reference, whether or not intended, relates biographically to Brooks's role as an African American woman wisely reweaving classical traditions "threadwise" rather than straining them into "hempen" (line 5) ropes. Beneath the manifest reference to the recent world war, this poem refers to the segregation of the arts in America. (Questions of source and historical context often interrelate.)

Besides readings that derive from biographical and historical information, there are still other ways to read aspects of the *source* rather than the *text* or the *receiver*. The source of the work extends beyond the life of the person who wrote it to include not only the writer's other works but also the circumstances of contemporary publishing; contemporary literary movements; the history of the composition and publication of this particular text, with all the variations; and other contributing factors. While entire schools of literary scholarship have been devoted to each of these matters, any analyst of a particular work should bear in mind what is known about the circumstances of writers at that time, the material conditions of the work's first publication, and the means of dissemination ever since. It makes a difference in our interpretation to know that a certain sonnet circulated in manuscript in a small courtly audience or that a particular novel was serialized in a weekly journal.

### Psychoanalytic Criticism

With the development of psychology and psychoanalysis toward the end of the nineteenth century, many critics were tempted to apply psychological theories to literary analysis. Symbolism, dreamlike imagery, emotional rather than rational logic, a pleasure in language all suggested that literature profoundly evoked a mental and emotional landscape, often one of disorder or abnormality. From mad poets to patients speaking in verse, imaginative literature might be regarded as a representation of shared irrational structures within all *psyches* (i.e., souls) or selves. While psychoanalytic approaches have developed along with structuralism and poststructuralist linguistics and philosophy, they rarely focus on textual form. Rather, they attribute latent or hidden meaning to unacknowledged desires in some person, usually the author or source behind the character in a narrative or drama. A psychoanalytic critic could focus on the response of readers and, in recent decades, usually accepts the influence of changing social history on the structures of sexual desire represented in the work. Nevertheless, psychoanalysis has typically aspired to a universal, unchanging theory of the mind and personality, and criticism that applies it has tended to emphasize the authorial source.

#### FREUDIAN CRITICISM

For most of the twentieth century, the dominant school of psychoanalytic critics was the Freudian, based on the work of Sigmund Freud (1856–1939). Many of its practitioners assert that the meaning of a literary work exists not on its surface but in the psyche (some would even claim, in the neuroses) of the author. Classic psychoanalytic criticism read works as though they were the recorded dreams of patients; interpreted the life histories of authors as keys to the works; or analyzed characters as though like real people they have a set of repressed childhood memories. (In fact, many novels and most plays leave out information about characters' development from infancy through adolescence, the period that psychoanalysis especially strives to reconstruct.)

A well-known Freudian reading of *Hamlet*, for example, insists that Hamlet suffers from an Oedipus complex, a Freudian term for a group of repressed desires and memories that corresponds with the Greek myth that is the basis of Sophocles' play *Oedipus the King*. In this view Hamlet envies his uncle because the son unconsciously wants to sleep with his mother, who was the first object of his desire as a baby. The ghost of Hamlet Sr. may then be a manifestation of Hamlet's unconscious desire or a figure for his guilt for wanting to kill his father, the person who has a right to the desired mother's body. Hamlet's madness is not just acting but the result of this frustrated desire; his cruel mistreatment of Ophelia is a deflection of his disgust at his mother's being "unfaithful" in her love for him. Some Freudian critics stress the author's psyche and so might read *Hamlet* as the expression of Shakespeare's own Oedipus complex. In another mode psychoanalytic critics, reading imaginative literature as symbolic fulfillment of unconscious wishes much as an analyst would interpret a dream, decipher objects, spaces, or actions that appear to relate to sexual anatomy or activity. Much as if tracing out the extended metaphors of an erotic poem by Donne or a blues or Motown lyric, the Freudian reads containers, empty spaces, or bodies of water as female; tools, weapons, towers or trees, trains or planes as male.

Psychoanalytic criticism, learning from Freud's ventures in literary criticism, has favored narrative fiction with uncanny, supernatural, or detective elements. Plots with excessive, inexplicable fatalities seem to express wishes unconsciously shared by all readers as well as the writer. The method has often been applied to writers of such stories whose biographies are well documented. The life and works of Edgar Allan Poe (1809-1849) therefore have attracted psychoanalytic readings. An orphan who quarreled with the surrogate father who raised him, Poe seems to have been tormented by an unresolved desire for a mother figure. A series of beloved mother figures died prematurely, including his mother and Mrs. Allan, the woman who raised him. He became attached to his aunt and fell in love with her daughter, Virginia Clemm, whom he married in 1836 when she was thirteen, and who died of tuberculosis in 1847. He famously asserted that the most apt subject of poetry is the death of a beautiful woman. In Poe's "The Raven" a macabre talking bird intrudes in the speaker's room and induces an obsession with the dead beloved, a woman named Lenore. In a Freudian reading Poe's "The Cask of Amontillado" appears to transpose a fantasy of return to the womb—an enclosed space holding liquids—into a fulfilled desire to kill a male rival.

### JUNGIAN AND MYTH CRITICISM

Just as a Freudian assumes that all human psyches have similar histories and structures, the Jungian critic assumes that we all share a universal or collective unconscious (as well as having a racial and individual unconscious). According to Carl Gustav Jung (1875-1961) and his followers, the unconscious harbors universal patterns and forms of human experiences, or archetypes. We can never know these archetypes directly, but they surface in art in an imperfect, shadowy way, taking the form of archetypal images—the snake with its tail in its mouth, rebirth, mother, the double, the descent into hell. In the classic quest narrative, the hero struggles to free himself (the gender of the pronoun is significant) from the Great Mother, to become a separate, self-sufficient being (combating a demonic antagonist), surviving trials to gain the reward of union with his ideal other, the feminine anima. In a related school of *archetypal criticism,* influenced by Northrop Frye (1912–1991), the prevailing myth follows a seasonal cycle of death and rebirth. Frye proposed a system for literary criticism that classified all literary forms in all ages according to a cycle of genres associated with the phases of human experience from birth to death and the natural cycle of seasons (e.g., Spring/Romance).

These approaches have been useful in the study of folklore and early literatures as well as in comparative studies of various national literatures. While most myth critics focus on the hero's quest, there have been forays into feminist archetypal criticism. These emphasize variations on the myths of Isis and Demeter, goddesses of fertility or seasonal renewal, who take different forms to restore either the sacrificed woman (Persephone's season in the underworld) or the sacrificed man (Isis's search for Osiris and her rescue of their son, Horus). Many twentieth-century poets were drawn to the heritage of archetypes and myths. Adrienne Rich's "Diving into the Wreck," for example, self-consciously rewrites a number of gendered archetypes, with a female protagonist on a quest into a submerged world. Most critics today, influenced by poststructuralism, have become wary of universal patterns. Like structuralists, Jungians and archetypal critics strive to compare and unite the ages and peoples of the world and to reveal fundamental truths. Rich, as a feminist poet, suggests that the "book of myths" is an eclectic anthology that needs to be revised. Claims of universality tend to obscure the detailed differences between cultures and often appeal to some idea of *biological determinism.* Such determinism diminishes the power of individuals to design alternative life patterns and even implies that no literature can really surprise us.

## LACANIAN CRITICISM

As it has absorbed the indeterminacies of poststructuralism under the influence of thinkers such as Jacques Lacan and Julia Kristeva, psychological criticism has become increasingly complex. Few critics today are direct Freudian analysts of authors or texts, and few maintain that universal archetypes explain the meaning of a tree or water in a text. Yet psychoanalytic theory continues to inform many varieties of criticism, and most new work in this field is affiliated with Lacanian psychoanalysis. Lacan's theory unites poststructuralist linguistics with Freudian theory. The Lacanian critic, like a deconstructionist, focuses on the text that defies conscious authorial control, foregrounding the powerful interpretation of the critic rather than the author or any other reader. Accepting the Oedipal paradigm and the unconscious as the realm of repressed desire, Lacanian theory aligns the development and structure of the individual human *subject* with the development and structure of language. To simplify a purposefully dense theory: The very young infant inhabits the Imaginary, in a preverbal, undifferentiated phase dominated by a sense of union with Mother. Recognition of identity begins with the Mirror Stage, ironically with a disruption of a sense of oneness. For when one first looks into a mirror, one begins to recognize a split or difference between one's body and the image in the mirror. This splitting prefigures a sense that the *object* of desire is Other and distinct from the subject. With difference or the splitting of subject and object comes language and entry into the Symbolic Order, since we use words to summon the absent object of desire (as a child would cry "Mama" to bring her back). But what language signifies most is the lack of that object. The imaginary, perfectly nurturing Mother would never need to be called.

As in the biblical Genesis, the Lacanian "genesis" of the subject tells of a loss of paradise through knowledge of the difference between subject and object or Man and Woman (eating of the Tree of the Knowledge of Good and Evil leads to the sense of shame that teaches Adam and Eve to hide their nakedness). In Lacanian theory the Father governs language or the Symbolic Order; the Word spells the end of a child's sense of oneness with the Mother. Further, the Father's power claims omnipotence, the possession of male prerogative symbolized by the Phallus, which is not the anatomical difference between men and women but the idea or construction of that difference. Thus it is language or culture rather than nature that generates the difference and inequality between the sexes. Some feminist theorists have adopted aspects of Lacanian psychoanalytic theory, particularly the concept of *the gaze*. This concept notes that the masculine subject is the one who looks, whereas the feminine object is to be looked at.

Another influential concept is *abjection*. Julia Kristeva's theory of abjection most simply reimagines the infant's blissful sense of union with the mother and the darker side of such possible union. To return to the mother's body would be death, as metaphorically we are buried in Mother Earth. Yet according to the theory, people both desire and dread such loss of boundaries. A sense of self or *subjectivity* and hence of independence and power depends on resisting abjection. The association of the maternal body with abjection or with the powerlessness symbolized by the female's Lack of the Phallus can help explain negative cultural images of women. Many narrative genres seem to split the images of women between an angelic and a witchlike type. Lacanian or Kristevan theory has been well adapted to film and to the fantasy and other popular forms favored by structuralism or archetypal criticism.

Psychoanalytic literary criticism today—as distinct from specialized discussion of Lacanian theory, for example—treads more lightly than in the past. In James Joyce's "Araby" a young Dublin boy, orphaned and raised by an aunt and uncle, likes to haunt a back room in the house; there the "former tenant, ... a priest, had died" (paragraph 2). (Disused rooms at the margins of houses resemble the unconscious, and a dead celibate "father" suggests a kind of failure of the Law, conscience, or in Freudian terms, superego.) The priest had left behind a "rusty bicycle-pump" in the "wild garden" with "a central apple tree" (these echoes of the garden of Eden suggesting the impotence of Catholic religious symbolism). The boy seems to gain consciousness of a separate self—or his subjectivity is constructed—through his gaze upon an idealized female object, Mangan's sister, whose "name was like a summons to all my foolish blood" (paragraph 4). Though he secretly watches and follows her, she is not so much a sexual fantasy as a beautiful art object (paragraph 9). He retreats to the back room to think of her in a kind of ecstasy that resembles masturbation. Yet it is not masturbation: it is preadolescent, dispersed through all orifices—the rain feels like "incessant needles ... playing in the sodden beds"; and it is sublimated, that is, repressed and redirected into artistic or religious forms rather than directly expressed by bodily pleasure: "All my senses seemed to desire to veil themselves" (paragraph 6).

It is not in the back room but on the street that the girl finally speaks to the hero, charging him to go on a quest to *Araby*. After several trials the hero carrying the talisman arrives in a darkened hall "girdled at half its height by a gallery," an underworld or maternal space that is also a deserted temple (paragraph 25). The story ends without his grasping the prize to carry back, the "chalice" or holy grail (symbolic of female sexuality) that he had once thought to bear "safely through a throng of foes" (paragraph 5).

Such a reading seems likely to raise objections that it is overreading: *you're seeing too much in it; the author didn't mean that.* This has been a popular reaction to psychoanalysis for over a hundred years, but it is only a heightened version of a response to many kinds of criticism. This sample reading pays close attention to the text, but does not really follow a formal approach because its goal is to explain the psychological motivations or sources of the story's details. We have mentioned nothing about the author, though we could have placed the above reading within a psychoanalytic reading of Joyce's biography.

## EMPHASIS ON THE RECEIVER

In some sense critical schools develop in reaction to the excesses of other critical schools. By the 1970s, in a time of political upheaval that placed a value on individual expression, a number of critics felt that the various routes toward objective criticism had proven dead ends. New Critics, structuralists, and psychoanalytic or myth critics had sought objective, scientific systems that disregarded changing times, political issues, or the reader's personal response. New Critics and other formalists tended to value a literary canon made up of works that were regarded as complete, unchanging objects to be comprehended as if spatially in a photograph according to timeless standards.

### Reader-Response Criticism

Among critics who challenged New Critical assumptions, the reader-response critics regarded the work not as what is printed on the page but as what is experienced temporally through each act of reading. In effect the reader performs the poem into existence the way a musician performs a score. Reader-response critics ask not what a work means but what a work does or, rather, what it makes a reader do. Literary texts especially leave gaps that experienced readers fill according to expectations or conventions. Individual readers differ, of course, and gaps in a text provide space for different readings or interpretations. Some of these lacunae are temporary—such as the withholding of the murderer's name until the end of a mystery novel—and are closed by the text sooner or later, though each reader will in the meantime fill them differently. But other lacunae are permanent and can never be filled with certainty; they result in a degree of uncertainty or indeterminacy in the text.

The reader-response critic observes the expectations aroused by a text, how they are satisfied or modified, and how the reader projects a comprehension of the work when all of it has been read, and when it is reread in whole or in part. Such criticism attends to the reading habits associated with different genres and to the shared assumptions of a cultural context that seem to furnish what is left unsaid in the text. Margaret Atwood's "Happy Endings" could almost be an essay on reader response in the guise of do-it-yourself instructions to a simpleminded reader: "John and Mary meet. What happens next? If you want a happy ending, try A" (paragraphs 1–3). This beginning seems to steer the reader to follow alphabetized instructions to assist in designing the narrative. It also satirizes romance plot conventions. Every romance fan knows that if a male and a female character meet, they will fall in love, and that some conflict will delay their marriage until it is resolved—unless the conflict proves insurmountable. As Atwood humorously shows, various love triangles or death will change the outcome. In spite of the scanty details given in the text, each reader will fill in the gaps and imagine "How and Why" (paragraph 23), the realistic details and rounded characterization that he or she has learned to imagine from reading other fiction.

Beyond theoretical formulations about reading, there are other approaches to literary study that concern the receiver rather than the text or source. A critic might examine specific documents of a work's reception, from contemporary reviews to critical essays written across the generations since the work was first published. Sometimes we have available diaries or autobiographical evidence about readers' encounters with particular works. Just as there are histories of publishing and of the book, there are histories of literacy and reading practices. Poetry, fiction, and drama often directly represent the theme of reading as well as writing. Many published works over the centuries have debated the benefits and perils of reading works such as sermons or novels. Different genres and particular works construct different classes or kinds of readers in the way they address them or supply what they are supposed to want. Some scholars have found quantitative measures for reading, from sales and library lending rates to questionnaires.

Finally, the role of the reader or receiver in literary exchange has been portrayed from a political perspective. Literature helps shape social identity, and social status shapes access to different kinds of literature. Feminist critics adapted reader-response criticism, for example, to note that girls often do not identify with many American literary classics as boys do, and thus girls do not simply accept the idea of women as angels, temptresses, or scolds who should be abandoned for the sake of all-male adventures. Studies of African American literature and other ethnic literatures have often featured discussion of literacy and of the obstacles for readers who cannot find their counterparts within the texts or who encounter negative stereotypes of their group. Thus, as we will discuss below, most forms of historical and ideological criticism include some consideration of the reader.

## HISTORICAL AND IDEOLOGICAL CRITICISM

Approaches to the text, the author, and the reader, outlined above, each may take some note of historical contexts, including changes in formal conventions, the writer's milieu, or audience expectations. In the nineteenth century, historical criticism took the obvious facts that a work is created in a specific historical and cultural context and that the author is a part of that context as reasons to treat literature as a reflection of society. Twentieth-century formalists rejected the *reflectivist* model of art in the old historical criticism, that is, the assumption that literature and other arts straightforwardly express the collective spirit of the society at that time. But as we have remarked, formalist rules for isolating the work of art from social and historical context met resistance in the last decades of the twentieth century. In a revival of historical approaches, critics have replaced the reflectivist model with a *constructivist* model, whereby literature and other cultural discourses help construct social relations and roles rather than merely reflecting them. In other words, art is not just the frosting on the cake but an integral part of the recipe's ingredients and instructions. A society's ideology, its inherent system of representations (ideas, myths, images), is inscribed in and by literature and other cultural forms, which in turn help shape identities and social practices.

Since the 1980s historical approaches have regained great influence in literary studies. Some critical schools have been insistently *materialist,* that is, seeking causes more in concrete conditions such as technology, production, and distribution of wealth, or the exploitation of markets and labor in and beyond Western countries. Such criticism usually owes an acknowledged debt to Marxism. Other historical approaches have been influenced to a degree by Marxist critics and cultural theorists, but work within the realm of ideology, textual production, and interpretation, using some of the methods and concerns of traditional literary history. Still others emerge from the civil rights movement and the struggles for recognition of women and racial, ethnic, and sexual constituencies.

Feminist studies, African American studies, gay and lesbian studies, and studies of the cultures of different immigrant and ethnic populations within the United States have each developed along similar theoretical lines. These schools, like Marxist criticism, adopt a constructivist position; literature is not simply a reflection of prejudices and norms, but helps define as well as reshape social identities, such as what it means to be an African American woman. Each of these schools has moved through stages of first claiming *equality* with the literature dominated by white Anglo American men, then affirming the *difference* of their own separate culture, and then theoretically *questioning the terms and standards* of such comparisons. At a certain point in the thought process, each group rejects *essentialism,* the notion of innate or biological bases for the differences between the sexes, races, or other groups. This rejection of essentialism is usually called the constructivist position, in a somewhat different but related sense to our definition above. Constructivism maintains that identity is socially formed rather than biologically determined. Differences of anatomical sex, skin color, first language, parental ethnicity, and eventual sexual practices have great impact on how one is classified, brought up, and treated socially, and on one's subjectivity or conception of identity. These differences are, however, more constructed by ideology and the resulting behaviors than by any natural programming.

### Marxist Criticism

The most insistent and vigorous historical approach through the twentieth century to the present has been Marxism, based on the work of Karl Marx (1818–1883). With roots in nineteenth-century historicism, Marxist criticism was initially reflectivist. Economics, the underlying cause of history, was thus the *base,* and culture, including literature and the other arts, was the *superstructure,* an outcome or reflection of the base. Viewed from the Marxist perspective, the literary works of a period were economically determined; they would *reflect* the state of the struggle between classes in any place and time. History enacted recurrent three-step cycles, a pattern that Hegel had defined as *dialectic* (Hegel was cited above on the interdependence of master and slave). Each socioeconomic phase, or *thesis,* is counteracted by its *antithesis,* and the resulting conflict yields a *synthesis,* which becomes the ensuing *thesis,* and so on. As with early Freudian criticism, early Marxist criticism was often overly concerned with labeling and exposing illusions or deceptions. A novel might be read as thinly disguised defense of the power of bourgeois industrial capital; its appeal on behalf of the suffering poor might be dismissed as an effort to fend off a class rebellion.

As a rationale for state control of the arts, Marxism was abused in the Soviet Union and in other totalitarian states. In the hands of sophisticated critics, however, Marxism has been richly rewarding. Various schools that unite formal close reading and political analysis developed in the early twentieth century under Soviet communism and under fascism in Europe, often in covert resistance. These schools in turn have influenced critical movements in North American universities through translations or through members who came to the United States; New Criticism, structuralist linguistics, deconstruction, and narrative theory have each borrowed from European Marxist critics.

Most recently, a new mode of Marxist theory has developed, largely guided by the thinking of Walter Benjamin (1892-1940) and Theodor Adorno (1903-1969) of the Frankfurt School in Germany, Louis Althusser (1918-1990) in France, and Raymond Williams (1921-1998) in Britain. This work has generally tended to modify the base/superstructure distinction and to interrelate public and private life, economics and culture. Newer Marxist interpretation assumes that the relation of a literary work to its historical context is *overdetermined*—the relation has multiple determining factors rather than a sole cause or aim. This thinking similarly acknowledges that neither the source nor the receiver of the literary interaction is a mere tool or victim of the ruling powers or state. Representation of all kinds, including literature, always has a political dimension, according to this approach; conversely, political and material conditions such as work, money, or institutions depend on representation.

Showing some influence of psychoanalytic and poststructuralist theories, recent Marxist literary studies examine the effects of ideology by focusing on the works' gaps and silences: ideology may be conveyed in what is repressed or contradicted. In many ways Marxist criticism has adapted to the conditions of consumer rather than industrial capitalism and to global rather than national economies. The revolution that was to come when the proletariat or working classes overthrew the capitalists has never taken place; in many countries industrial labor has been swallowed up by the service sector, and workers reject the political Left that would seem their most likely ally. Increasingly, Marxist criticism has acknowledged that the audience of literature may be active rather than passive, just as the text and source may be more than straightforward instructions for toeing the political line. Marxist criticism has been especially successful with the novel, since that genre more than drama or short fiction is capable of representing numerous people from different classes as they develop over a significant amount of time.

### Feminist Criticism

Like Marxist criticism and the schools discussed below, feminist criticism derives from a critique of a history of oppression, in this case the history of women's inequality. Feminist criticism has no single founder like Freud or Marx; it has been practiced to some extent since the 1790s, when praise of women's cultural achievements went hand in hand with arguments that women were rational beings deserving equal rights and education. Contemporary feminist criticism emerged from a "second wave" of feminist activism, in the 1960s and 1970s, associated with the civil rights and antiwar movements. One of the first disciplines in which women's activism took root was literary criticism, but feminist theory and women's studies quickly became recognized methods across the disciplines.

Feminist literary studies began by denouncing the misrepresentation of women in literature and affirming women's writings, before quickly adopting the insights of poststructuralist theory; yet the early strategies continue to have their use. At first, feminist criticism in the 1970s, like early Marxist criticism, regarded literature as a reflection of patriarchal society's sexist base; the demeaning images of women in literature were symptoms of a system that had to be overthrown. Feminist literary studies soon began, however, to claim the *equal* worth if distinctive themes of writings by women and men. Critics such as Elaine Showalter (b. 1941), Sandra M. Gilbert (b. 1936), and Susan Gubar (b. 1944) featured the canonical works by women, relying on close reading with some aid from historical and psychoanalytic methods. Yet by the 1980s it was widely recognized that a New Critical method would leave most of the male-dominated canon intact and most women writers still in obscurity, because many women had written in different genres and styles, on different themes, and for different audiences than had male writers.

To affirm the *difference* of female literary traditions, some feminist studies claimed women's innate or universal affinity for fluidity and cycle rather than solidity and linear progress. Others concentrated on the role of the mother in human psychological development. According to this argument, girls, not having to adopt a gender role different from that of their first object of desire, the mother, grow up with less rigid boundaries of self and a relational rather than judgmental ethic. The dangers of these intriguing generalizations soon became apparent. If the reasons for women's differences from men were biologically based or were due to universal archetypes, there was no solution to women's oppression, which many cultures worldwide had justified in terms of biological reproduction or archetypes of nature.

At this point in the debate, feminist literary studies intersected with poststructuralist linguistic theory in *questioning the terms and standards* of comparison. French feminist theory, articulated most prominently by Hélène Cixous (b. 1935) and Luce Irigaray (b. 1932), deconstructed the supposed archetypes of gender written into the founding discourses of Western culture. We have seen that deconstruction helps expose the power imbalance in every dualism. Thus man is to woman as culture is to nature or mind is to body, and in each case the second term is held to be inferior or Other. The language and hence the worldview and social formations of our culture, not nature or eternal archetypes, constructed woman as Other. This insight was helpful in avoiding essentialism or biological determinism.

Having reached a theoretical criticism of the terms on which women might claim equality or difference from men in the field of literature, feminist studies also confronted other issues in the 1980s. Deconstructionist readings of gender difference in texts by men as well as women could lose sight of the real world, in which women are paid less and are more likely to be victims of sexual violence. Some feminist critics with this in mind pursued links with Marxist or African American studies; gender roles, like those of class and race, were interdependent systems for registering the material consequences of people's differences. It no longer seemed so easy to say what the term "women" referred to, when the interests of different kinds of women had been opposed to each other. African American women asked if feminism was really their cause, when white women had so long enjoyed power over both men and women of their race. In a classic Marxist view, women allied with men of their class rather than with women of other classes. It became more difficult to make universal claims about women's literature, as the horizon of the college-educated North American feminists expanded to recognize the range of conditions of women and literature worldwide. Feminist literary studies have continued to consider famous and obscure women writers; the way women and gender are portrayed in writings by men as well as women; feminist issues concerning the text, source, or receiver in any national literature; theoretical and historical questions about the representation of differences such as gender, race, class, and nationality, and the way these differences shape each other.

### Gender Studies and Queer Theory

From the 1970s, feminists sought recognition for lesbian writers and lesbian culture, which they felt had been even less visible than male homosexual writers and gay culture. Concurrently, feminist studies abandoned the simple dualism of male/female, part of the very binary logic of patriarchy that seemed to cause the oppression of women. Thus feminists recognized a zone of inquiry, the study of gender, as distinct from historical studies of women, and increasingly they included masculinity as a subject of investigation. As gender studies turned to interpretation of the text in ideological context regardless of the sex or intention of the author, it incorporated the ideas of Michel Foucault's *History of Sexuality* (1976). Foucault helped show that there was nothing natural, universal, or timeless in the constructions of sexual difference or sexual practices. Foucault also introduced a history of the concept of homosexuality, which had once been regarded in terms of taboo acts and in the later nineteenth century became defined as a disease associated with a personality type. Literary scholars began to study the history of sexuality as a key to the shifts in modern culture that had also shaped literature.

In the 1980s, gender had come to be widely regarded as a discourse that imposed binary social norms on human beings' diversity. Theorists such as Donna Haraway (b. 1944) and Judith Butler (b. 1956) insisted further that sex and sexuality have no natural basis; even the anatomical differences are representations from the moment the newborn is put in a pink or blue blanket. Moreover, these theorists claimed that gender and sexuality are *performative* and malleable positions, enacted in many more than two varieties. From cross-dressing to surgical sex changes, the alternatives chosen by real people have collaborated with the critical theories and generated both writings and literary criticism about those writings. Perhaps biographical and feminist studies face new challenges when identity seems subject to radical change and it is less easy to determine the sex of an author.

Gay and lesbian literary studies have included practices that parallel feminist criticism. At times critics identify oppressive or positive representations of homosexuality in works by men or women, gay, lesbian, or straight. At other times critics seek to establish the equivalent stature of a work by a gay or lesbian writer or, because these identities tended to be hidden in the past, to reveal that a writer *was* gay or lesbian. Again stages of *equality* and *difference* have yielded to a *questioning of the terms of difference,* in this case what has been called queer theory (the stages have not superseded each other). The field of queer theory hopes to leave everyone guessing rather than to identify gay or lesbian writers, characters, or themes. One of its founding texts, *Between Men* (1985), by Eve Kosofsky Sedgwick (b. 1950), drew upon structuralist insight into desire as well as anthropological models of kinship to show that, in canonical works of English literature, male characters bond together through their rivalry for and exchange of a woman. Queer theory, because it rejects the idea of a fixed identity or innate or essential gender, likes to discover resistance to heterosexuality in unexpected places. Queer theorists value gay writers such as Oscar Wilde, but they also find queer implications regardless of the author's acknowledged identity. This approach emphasizes not the surface signals of the text but what the audience or receiver might detect. It encompasses elaborate close reading of varieties of work; characteristically, a leading queer theorist, D. A. Miller (b. 1948), has written in loving detail about Jane Austen and about Broadway musicals.

### African American and Ethnic Literary Studies

Critics sought to define an African American literary tradition as early as the turn of the twentieth century. A period of literary success in the 1920s, known as the Harlem Renaissance, produced some of the first classic essays on writings by African Americans. Criticism and histories of African American literature tended to ignore and dismiss women writers, while feminist literary histories, guided by the Virginia Woolf's classic *A Room of One's Own* (1929), neglected women writers of color. Only after feminist critics began to succeed in the academy and African American studies programs were established did the whiteness of feminist studies and masculinity of African American studies became glaring; both fields have for some time corrected this problem of vision. The study of African American literature followed the general pattern that we have noted, first striving to claim equality, on established aesthetic grounds, of works such as Ralph Ellison's magnificent *Invisible Man* (1952). Then in the 1960s the Black Arts or Black Aesthetic emerged. Once launched in the academy, however, African American studies has been devoted less to celebrating an essential racial difference than to tracing the historical construction of a racial Other and a subordinated literature. The field sought to recover genres in which African Americans have written, such as slave narratives, and traced common elements in fiction or poetry to the conditions of slavery and segregation. By the 1980s feminist and poststructuralist theory had an impact in the work of some African American critics such as Henry Louis Gates Jr. (b. 1950), Houston A. Baker Jr. (b. 1943), Hazel V. Carby (b. 1948), and Deborah E. McDowell (b. 1951), while others objected that the doubts raised by "theory" stood in the way of political commitment. African Americans' cultural contributions to America have gained much more recognition than before. New histories of American culture have been written with the view that racism is not an aberration but inherent to the guiding narratives of national progress. Many critics now regard race as a discourse with only slight basis in genetics but with weighty investments in ideology. This poststructuralist position coexists with scholarship that takes into account the race of the author or reader or that focuses on African American characters or themes.

In recent years a series of fields has arisen in recognition of the literatures of other American ethnic groups, large and small: Asian Americans, Native Americans, and Chicano/as. Increasingly, such studies avoid romanticizing an original, pure culture or assuming that these literatures by their very nature undermine the values and power of the dominant culture. Instead, critics emphasize the *hybridity* of all cultures in a global economy. The contact and intermixture of cultures across geographical borders and languages (translations, the "creole" speech made up of native and acquired languages, dialects) may be read as enriching themes for literature and art, albeit they are caused by economic exploitation. In method and in aim these fields have much in common with African American studies, though each cultural and historical context is very different. Each field deserves the separate study that we cannot offer here.

Not so very long ago, critics might have been charged with a fundamental misunderstanding of the nature of literature if they pursued matters considered the business of sociologists, matters—such as class, race, and gender—that seemed extrinsic to the text. The rise of the above fields has made it expected that a critic will address questions about class, race, and gender to place a text, its source, and its reception in historical and ideological context. One brief example might illustrate the way Marxist, feminist, queer, and African American criticism can contribute to a literary reading.

Tennessee Williams's *A Streetcar Named Desire* was first produced in 1947 and won the Pulitzer Prize in 1948. Part of its acclaim was likely due to its fashionable blend of naturalism and symbolism: the action takes place in a shabby tenement on an otherworldly street, Elysian Fields—in an "atmosphere of decay" laced with "lyricism," as Williams's stage directions put it. After the Depression and World War II, American audiences welcomed a turn away from world politics into the psychological core of human sexuality. This turn to ostensibly individual conflict was a kind of alibi for at least two sets of issues that Williams and the middle-class theatergoers in New York and elsewhere sought to avoid. First, the racial questions that relate to questions of gender and class: what is the play's attitude to race, and what is Williams's attitude? Biography seems relevant, though not the last word on what the play means. Williams's family had included slave-holding cotton growers, and he chose to spend much of his adult life in the South, which he saw as representing a beautiful but dying way of life. He was deeply attached to women in his family who might be models for the brilliant, fragile, cultivated Southern white woman, Blanche DuBois. Blanche ("white" in French), representative of a genteel, feminine past that has gambled, prostituted, dissipated itself, speaks some of the most eloquent lines in the play when she mourns the faded Delta plantation society. Neither the playwright nor his audience wished to deal with segregation in the South, a region that since the Civil War had festered as a kind of agricultural working class in relation to the dominant North—which had its racism, too.

The play scarcely notices race. The main characters are white. The cast includes a "Negro Woman" as servant, and a blind Mexican woman who offers artificial flowers to remember the dead, but these figures seem either stage business or symbolism. Instead, racial difference is transposed as ethnic and class difference, in the story of a working-class Pole intruding into a family clinging to French gentility. Stella warns Blanche that she lives among "heterogeneous types" and that Stanley is "a different species." The play thus transfigures of contemporary anxieties about miscegenation, as the virile (black) man dominates the ideal white woman and rapes the spirit of the plantation South. A former army man who works in a factory, Stanley represents as well the defeat of the old, agricultural economy by industrialization.

The second set of issues that neither the playwright nor his audience confronts directly is the disturbance of sexual and gender roles that would in later decades lead to movements for women's and gay rights. It was well known in New Orleans at least that Williams was gay. In the 1940s he lived with his lover, Pancho Rodriguez y Gonzales, in the French Quarter. Like many homosexual writers in different eras, Williams recasts homosexual desire in heterosexual costume. Blanche, performing femininity with a kind of camp excess, might be a fading queen pursuing and failing to capture younger men. Stanley, hypermasculine, might caricature the object of desire of both men and women as well as the anti-intellectual, brute force in postwar America. His conquest of women (he had "the power and pride of a richly feathered male bird among hens") appears to be biologically determined. By the same token it seems natural that Stanley and his buddies go out to work and their wives become homemakers in the way now seen as typical of the 1950s. In this world, artists, homosexuals, or unmarried working women like Blanche would be both vulnerable and threatening. Blanche after all has secret pleasures—drinking and sex—that Stanley indulges in openly. Blanche is the one who is taken into custody by the medical establishment, which in this period diagnosed homosexuality as a form of insanity.

### New Historicism

Three interrelated schools of historical and ideological criticism have been important innovations in the past two decades. These are part of the swing of the pendulum away from formal analysis of the text and toward historical analysis of context. New historicism has less obvious political commitments than Marxism, feminism, or queer theory, but it shares their interest in the power of discourse to shape ideology. Old historicism, in the 1850s–1950s, confidently told a story of civilization's progress from the point of view of a Western nation; a historicist critic would offer a close reading of the plays of Shakespeare and then locate them within the prevailing Elizabethan "worldview." "New Historicism," labeled in 1982 by Stephen Greenblatt (b. 1943), rejected the technique of plugging samples of a culture into a history of ideas. Influenced by poststructuralist anthropology, New Historicism tried to take a multilayered impression or "thick description" of a culture at one moment in time, including popular as well as elite forms of representation. As a method, New Historicism belongs with those that deny the unity of the text, defy the authority of the source, and license the receiver—much like deconstructionism. Accordingly, New Historicism doubts the accessibility of the past; all we have is discourse. One model for New Historicism was the historiography of Michel Foucault, who as we have said insisted on the power of discourses, that is, not only writing but all structuring myths or ideologies that underlie social relations. The New Historicist, like Foucault, is interested in the transition from the external powers of the state and church in the feudal order to modern forms of power. The rule of the modern state and middle-class ideology is enforced insidiously by systems of surveillance and by each individual's internalization of discipline (not unlike Freud's idea of the superego).

No longer so "new," the New Historicists have had a lasting influence on a more narrative and concrete style of criticism even among those who espouse poststructuralist and Marxist theories. A New Historicist article begins with an anecdote, often a description of a public spectacle, and teases out the many contributing causes that brought disparate social elements together in that way.

It usually applies techniques of close reading to forms that would not traditionally have received such attention. Although it often concentrates on events several hundred years ago, in some ways it defies historicity, flouting the idea that a complete objective impression of the entire context could ever be achieved.

## Cultural Studies

Popular culture often gets major attention in the work of New Historicists. Yet today most studies of popular culture would acknowledge their debt instead to cultural studies, as filtered through the now-defunct Center for Contemporary Cultural Studies, founded in 1964 by Stuart Hall (b. 1932) and others at the University of Birmingham in England. Method, style, and subject matter may be similar in New Historicism and cultural studies: both attend to historical context, theoretical method, political commitment, and textual analysis. But whereas the American movement shares Foucault's paranoid view of state domination through discourse, the British school, influenced by Raymond Williams and his concept of "structures of feeling," emphasizes the possibility that ordinary people, the receivers of cultural forms, may resist dominant ideology. The documents examined in a cultural-studies essay may be recent, such as artifacts of tourism at Shakespeare's birthplace rather than sixteenth-century maps. Cultural studies today influences history, sociology, communications and media, and literature departments; its studies may focus on television, film, romance novels, advertising, or on museums and the art market, sports and stadiums, New Age religious groups, or other forms and practices.

The questions raised by cultural studies would encourage a critic to place a poem like Marge Piercy's "Barbie Doll" in the context of the history of that toy, a doll whose slender, impossibly long legs, tiptoe feet (not unlike the bound feet of Chinese women of an earlier era), small nose, and torpedo breasts enforced a 1950s ideal for the female body. A critic influenced by cultural studies might align the poem with other works published around 1973 that express feminist protest concerning cosmetics, body image, consumption, and the objectification of women, while she or he would draw on research into the founding and marketing of Mattel toys. The poem reverses the Sleeping Beauty story: this heroine puts herself into the coffin rather than waking up. The poem omits any hero—Ken?—who would rescue her. "Barbie Doll" protests the pressure a girl feels to fit into a heterosexual plot of romance and marriage; no one will buy her if she is not the right toy or accessory.

Indeed, accessories such as "GE stoves and irons" (line 3) taught girls to plan their lives as domestic consumers, and Barbie's lifestyle is decidedly middle-class and suburban (everyone has a house, car, pool, and lots of handbags). The whiteness of the typical "girlchild" (line 1) goes without saying. Although Mattel produced Barbie's African American friend, Christie, in 1968, Piercy's title makes the reader imagine Barbie, not Christie. In 1997 Mattel issued Share a Smile Becky, a friend in a wheelchair, as though in answer to the humiliation of the girl in Piercy's poem, who feels so deformed, in spite of her "strong arms and back, / abundant sexual drive and manual dexterity" (lines 8–9), that she finally cripples herself. The icon, in short, responds to changing ideology. Perhaps responding to generations of objections like Piercy's, Barbies over the years have had feminist career goals, yet women's lives are still plotted according to physical image.

In this manner a popular product might be "read" alongside a literary work.

The approach would be influenced by Marxist, feminist, gender, and racial studies, but it would not be driven by a desire to destroy Barbie as sinister, misogynist propaganda. Piercy's kind of protest against indoctrination has gone out of style. Girls have found ways to respond to such messages and divert them into stories of empowerment. Such at least is the outlook of cultural studies, which usually affirms popular culture. A researcher could gather data on Barbie sales and could interview girls or videotape their play, to establish the actual effects of the dolls. Whereas traditional anthropology examined non-European or preindustrial cultures, cultural studies may direct its "field work," or ethnographic research, inward, at home. Nevertheless, many contributions to cultural studies rely on methods of textual close reading or Marxist and Freudian literary criticism developed in the mid-twentieth century.

### Postcolonial Criticism and Studies of World Literature

A Web site on the invention of the Barbie doll says that Barbies are sold in over 150 countries around the world and that "more than one billion Barbie dolls (and family members) have been sold since 1959, and placed head-to-toe, the dolls would circle the earth more than seven times" <http://www.ideafinder.com/history/inventions/story081.htm>. Such a global reach for an American toy begins to seem less like play and more like imperial domination. In the middle of the twentieth century, meanwhile, the remaining colonies of the European nations struggled toward independence. French-speaking Frantz Fanon (1925–1961) of Martinique was one of the most compelling voices for the point of view of the colonized or exploited countries, which like the feminine Other had been objectified and denied the right to look and talk back. Edward Said (1935–2003), in *Orientalism* (1978), brought a poststructuralist analysis to bear on the history of colonization, illustrating the ways that Western culture feminized and objectified the East. Postcolonial literary studies developed into a distinct field in the 1990s in light of globalization and the replacement of direct colonial power with international corporations. In general this field cannot share the optimism of some cultural studies, given the histories of slavery and economic exploitation of colonies and the violence committed in the name of civilization's progress. Studies by Gayatri Chakravorty Spivak (b. 1942) and Homi K. Bhabha (b. 1949) have further mingled Marxist, feminist, and poststructuralist theory to reread both canonical Western works and the writings of people from beyond centers of dominant culture. Colonial or postcolonial literatures may include works set or published in countries during colonial rule or after independence, or they may feature texts produced in the context of international cultural exchange, such as a novel in English by a woman of Chinese descent writing in Malaysia.

Like feminist studies and studies of African American or other literatures, the field is inspired by recovery of neglected works, redress of a systematic denial of rights and recognition, and increasing realization that the dualisms of opposing groups reveal interdependence. In this field the stage of difference came early, with the celebrations of African heritage known as *Négritude*, but the danger of that essentialist claim was soon apparent: the Dark Continent or wild island might be romanticized and idealized as a source of innate qualities of vitality long repressed in Enlightened Europe. Currently, most critics accept that the context for literature in all countries is hybrid, with immigration and educational intermixing. Close readings of texts are always linked to the author's biography and literary influences and placed within the context of contemporary international politics as well as colonial history. Many fiction writers, from Salman Rushdie to Jhumpa Lahiri, make the theme of cultural mixture or hybridity part of their work, whether in a pastiche of Charles Dickens or a story of an Indian family growing up in New Jersey and returning as tourists to the supposed "native" land. Poststructuralist theories of trauma, and theories of the interrelation of narrative and memory, provide explanatory frames for interpreting writings from Afghanistan to the former Zaire.

Studies of postcolonial culture retain a clear political mission that feminist and Marxist criticism have found difficult to sustain. Perhaps this is because the scale of the power relations is so vast, between nations rather than the sexes or classes within those nations. Imperialism can be called an absolute evil, and the destruction of local cultures a crime against humanity. Today some of the most exciting literature in English emerges from countries once under the British Empire, and all the techniques of criticism will be brought to bear on it. If history is any guide, in later decades some critical school will attempt to read the diverse literatures of the early twenty-first century in pure isolation from authorship and national origin, as self-enclosed form. The themes of hybridity, indeterminacy, trauma, and memory will be praised as universal. It is even possible that readers' continuing desire to revere authors as creative geniuses in control of their meanings will regain respectability among specialists. For the elements of the literary exchange—text, source, and receiver—are always there to provoke questions that generate criticism, which in turn produces articulations of the methods of that criticism. It is an ongoing discussion worth participating in.

## BIBLIOGRAPHY

For good introductions to the issues discussed here, see the following books, from which we have drawn in our discussion and definitions. Some of these provide bibliographies of the works of critics and schools mentioned above.

Alter, Robert. *The Pleasure of Reading in an Ideological Age.* New York: Norton, 1996. Rpt. of *The Pleasures of Reading: Thinking about Literature in an Ideological Age.* 1989.
Barnet, Sylvan, and William E. Cain. *A Short Guide to Writing about Literature.* 10th ed. New York: Longman, 2005.
Barry, Peter. *Beginning Theory: An Introduction to Literary and Cultural Theory.* 2nd ed. Manchester: Manchester UP, 2002.
Bressler, Charles E. *Literary Criticism: An Introduction to Theory and Practice.* 3rd ed. Upper Saddle River: Prentice, 2003.
Culler, Jonathan. *Literary Theory: A Very Short Introduction.* Oxford: Oxford UP, 1997.
Davis, Robert Con, and Ronald Schleifer. *Contemporary Literary Criticism: Literary and Cultural Studies.* 4th ed. New York: Addison, 1999.
During, Simon. *Cultural Studies: A Critical Introduction.* New York: Routledge, 2005.
———. *The Cultural Studies Reader.* New York: Routledge, 1999.
Eagleton, Mary, ed. *Feminist Literary Theory: A Reader.* 2nd ed. Malden: Blackwell, 1996.

Eagleton, Terry. *Literary Theory: An Introduction.* 2nd rev. ed. Minneapolis: U of Minnesota P, 1996.
Groden, Michael, and Martin Kreiswirth. *The Johns Hopkins Guide to Literary Theory and Criticism.* Baltimore: Johns Hopkins UP, 1994.
Hawthorn, Jeremy. *A Glossary of Contemporary Literary Theory.* 3rd ed. London: Arnold, 1998.
Leitch, Vincent B. *American Literary Criticism from the Thirties to the Eighties.* New York: Columbia UP, 1989.
———, et al. *The Norton Anthology of Theory and Criticism.* New York: Norton, 2001.
Lentricchia, Frank. *After the New Criticism.* Chicago: U of Chicago P, 1981.
Macksey, Richard, and Eugenio Donato, eds. *The Structuralist Controversy: The Languages of Criticism and the Sciences of Man.* 1972. Ann Arbor: Books on Demand, n.d.
Moi, Toril. *Sexual-Textual Politics.* New York: Routledge, 1985.
Murfin, Ross, and Supryia M. Ray. *The Bedford Glossary of Critical and Literary Terms.* Boston: Bedford, 1997.
Piaget, Jean. *Structuralism.* Trans. and ed. Chaninah Maschler. New York: Basic, 1970.
Selden, Raman, and Peter Widdowson. *A Reader's Guide to Contemporary Literary Theory.* 3rd ed. Lexington: U of Kentucky P, 1993.
Todorov, Tzvetan. *Mikhail Bakhtin: The Dialogic Principle.* Trans. Wlad Godzich. Minneapolis: U of Minnesota P, 1984.
Turco, Lewis. *The Book of Literary Terms.* Hanover: UP of New England, 1999.
Veeser, Harold, ed. *The New Historicism.* New York: Routledge, 1989.
———. *The New Historicism Reader.* New York: Routledge, 1994.
Warhol, Robyn R., and Diane Price Herndl. *Feminisms.* 2nd ed. New Brunswick: Rutgers UP, 1997.
Wolfreys, Julian. *Literary Theories: A Reader and Guide.* Edinburgh: Edinburgh UP, 1999.

# Glossary

Boldface words within definitions are themselves defined in the glossary.

**acting** the last of the four steps of **characterization** in a performed play.

**action** an imagined event or series of events; an event may be verbal as well as physical, so that saying something or telling a story within the story may be an event.

**allegory** as in **metaphor**, one thing (usually nonrational, abstract, religious) is implicitly spoken of in terms of something concrete, but in an allegory the comparison is extended to include an entire work or large portion of a work.

**alliteration** the repetition of initial consonant sounds through a sequence of words—for example, "While I nodded, nearly napping" in Edgar Allan Poe's "The Raven."

**allusion** a reference—whether explicit or implicit, to history, the Bible, myth, literature, painting, music, and so on—that suggests the meaning or generalized implication of details in the story, poem, or play.

**ambiguity** the use of a word or expression to mean more than one thing.

**amphitheater** the design of classical Greek theaters, consisting of a stage area surrounded by a semicircle of tiered seats.

**analogy** a comparison based on certain resemblances between things that are otherwise unlike.

**anapestic** a metrical form in which each foot consists of two unstressed syllables followed by a stressed one.

**antagonist** a neutral term for a **character** who opposes the leading male or female character. *See* hero/heroine and **protagonist**.

**antihero** a leading **character** who is not, like a **hero**, perfect or even outstanding, but is rather ordinary and representative of the more or less average person.

**archetype** a plot or **character** element that recurs in cultural or cross-cultural **myths**, such as "the quest" or "descent into the underworld" or "scapegoat."

**arena stage** a stage design in which the audience is seated all the way around the acting area; actors make their entrances and exits through the auditorium.

**assonance** the repetition of vowel sounds in a sequence of words with different endings—for example, "The d*ea*th of the poet was k*e*pt from his poems" in W. H. Auden's "In Memory of W. B. Yeats."

**aubade** a morning song in which the coming of dawn is either celebrated or denounced as a nuisance.

**auditor** someone other than the reader—a **character** within the fiction—to whom the story or "speech" is addressed.

**authorial time** distinct from **plot time** and **reader time**, authorial time denotes the influence that the time in which the author was writing had upon the **conception** and **style** of the text.

**ballad** a narrative poem that is, or originally was, meant to be sung. Characterized by repetition and often by a repeated refrain (recurrent phrase or series of phrases), ballads were originally a folk creation, transmitted orally from person to person and age to age.

**ballad stanza** a common **stanza** form, consisting of a quatrain that alternates four-beat and three-beat lines; lines 1 and 3 are unrhymed iambic tetrameter (four beats), and lines 2 and 4 are rhymed iambic trimeter (three beats).

**blank verse** the verse form most like everyday human speech; blank verse consists of unrhymed lines in **iambic pentameter**. Many of Shakespeare's plays are in blank verse.

**caesura** a short pause within a line of poetry; often but not always signaled by punctuation. Note the two caesuras in this line from Poe's "The Raven": "Once upon a midnight dreary, while I pondered, weak and weary."

**canon** when applied to an individual author, *canon* (like **oeuvre**) means the sum total of works written by that author. When used generally, it means the range of works that a consensus of scholars, teachers, and readers of a particular time and culture consider "great" or "major." This second sense of the word is a matter of debate since the literary canon in Europe and America has long been dominated by the works of white men. During the last several decades, the canon in the United States has expanded considerably to include more works by women and writers from various ethnic and racial backgrounds.

**casting** the third step in the creation of a **character** on the stage; deciding which actors are to play which parts.

**centered (central) consciousness** a limited third-person **point of view**, one tied to a single **character** throughout the story; this character often reveals his or her inner thoughts but is unable to read the thoughts of others.

**character** (1) a fictional personage who acts, appears, or is referred to in a work; (2) a combination of a person's qualities, especially moral qualities, so that such terms as "good" and "bad," "strong" and "weak," often apply. *See* **nature** and **personality**.

**characterization** the fictional or artistic presentation of a fictional personage. A term like "a good character" can, then, be ambiguous—it may mean that the personage is virtuous or that he or she is well presented regardless of his or her characteristics or moral qualities.

**chorus** in classical Greek plays, a group of actors who commented on and described the **action** of a play. Members of the chorus were often masked and relied on song, dance, and recitation to make their commentary.

**classical unities** as derived from Aristotle's *Poetics,* the principles of structure that require a play to have one action that occurs in one place and within one day.

**climax** also called the **turning point,** the third part of **plot structure,** the point at which the **action** stops rising and begins falling or reversing.

**colloquial diction** a level of language in a work that approximates the speech of ordinary people. The language used by characters in Toni Cade Bambara's "Gorilla, My Love" is a good example.

**comedy** a broad category of dramatic works that are intended primarily to entertain and amuse an audience. Comedies take many different forms, but they share three basic characteristics: (1) the values that are expressed and that typically present the conflict within the play are social and determined by the general opinion of society (as opposed to being universal and beyond the control of humankind, as in **tragedy**); (2) **characters** in comedies are often defined primarily in terms of their society and their role within it; (3) comedies often end with a restoration of social order in which one or more characters take a proper social role.

**conception** the first step in the creation of any work of art, but especially used to indicate the first step in the creation of a dramatic **character,** whether for written text or performed play; the original idea, when the playwright first begins to construct (or even dream about) a **plot,** the **characters,** the **structure,** or a **theme.**

**conclusion** the fifth part of **plot structure,** the point at which the situation that was destabilized at the beginning of the story becomes stable once more.

**concrete poetry** poetry shaped to look like an object. Robert Herrick's "Pillar of Fame," for example, is arranged to look like a pillar. Also called **shaped verse.**

**confessional poem** a relatively recent (or recently defined) **kind** in which the speaker describes a state of mind, which becomes a **metaphor** for the larger world.

**conflict** a struggle between opposing forces, such as between two people, between a person and something in nature or society, or even between two drives, impulses, or parts of the self.

**connotation** what is suggested by a word, apart from what it explicitly describes. *See* **denotation.**

**controlling metaphors** **metaphors** that dominate or organize an entire poem. In Linda Pastan's "Marks," for example, the controlling metaphor is of marks (grades) as a way of talking about the speaker's performance of roles within her family.

**conventions** standard or traditional ways of saying things in literary works, employed to achieve certain expected effects.

**cosmic irony** a type of irony that arises out of the difference between what a character aspires to and what so-called universal forces deal him or her; such irony implies that a god or fate controls and toys with human actions, feelings, lives, outcomes.

**criticism** *See* **literary criticism.**

**culture** a broad and relatively indistinct term that implies a commonality of history and some cohesiveness of purpose within a group. One can speak of southern culture, for example, or urban culture, or American culture, or rock culture; at any one time, each of us belongs to a number of these cultures.

**dactylic** the metrical pattern in which each foot consists of a stressed syllable followed by two unstressed ones.

**denotation** a direct and specific meaning. *See* **connotation.**

**descriptive structure** a textual organization determined by the requirements of describing someone or something.

**diction** an author's choice of words.

**discriminated occasion** the first specific event in a story, usually in the form of a specific scene.

**discursive structure** a textual organization based on the form of a treatise, argument, or essay.

**dramatic irony** a plot device in which a **character** holds a position or has an expectation that is reversed or fulfilled in a way that the character did not expect but that we, as readers or as audience members, have anticipated because our knowledge of events or individuals is more complete than the character's.

**dramatic monologue** a monologue set in a specific situation and spoken to an imaginary audience.

**dramatic structure** a textual organization based on a series of scenes, each of which is presented vividly and in detail.

**dramatis personae** the list of **characters** that appears either in the play's program or at the top of the first page of the written play.

**echo** a verbal reference that recalls a word, phrase, or sound in another text.

**elegy** in classical times, any poem on any subject written in "elegiac" **meter**; since the Renaissance, usually a formal lament on the death of a particular person.

**English sonnet** *see* **Shakespearean sonnet**.

**enjambment** running over from one line of poetry to the next without stop, as in the following lines by Wordsworth: "My heart leaps up when I behold / A rainbow in the sky."

**epic** a poem that celebrates, in a continuous narrative, the achievements of mighty **heroes** and **heroines**, usually in founding a nation or developing a **culture**, and uses elevated language and a grand, high style.

**epigram** originally any poem carved in stone (on tombstones, buildings, gates, and so forth), but in modern usage a very short, usually witty verse with a quick turn at the end.

**expectation** the anticipation of what is to happen next (*see* **curiosity** and **suspense**), what a **character** is like or how he or she will develop, what the **theme** or meaning of the story will prove to be, and so on.

**exposition** that part of the **structure** that sets the scene, introduces and identifies **characters**, and establishes the situation at the beginning of a story or play. Additional exposition is often scattered throughout the work.

**extended metaphor** a detailed and complex metaphor that stretches through a long section of a work.

**falling action** the fourth part of **plot structure**, in which the complications of the **rising action** are untangled.

**farce** a play characterized by broad humor, wild antics, and often slapstick, pratfalls, or other physical humor.

**figurative** usually applied to language that uses **figures of speech**. Figurative language heightens meaning by implicitly or explicitly representing something in terms of some other thing, the assumption being that the "other thing" will be more familiar to the reader.

**figures of speech** comparisons in which something is pictured or figured in other, more familiar terms.

**first-person narrator** a character, "I," who tells the story and necessarily has a **limited point of view**; may also be an **unreliable narrator**.

**flashback** a plot-structuring device whereby a scene from the fictional past is inserted into the fictional present or dramatized out of order.

**flat character** a fictional **character**, often but not always a minor character, who is relatively simple; who is presented as having few, though sometimes dominant, traits; and who thus does not change much in the course of a story. *See* **round character**.

**focus** the point from which people, events, and other details in a story are viewed. *See* **point of view**.

**foil** one **character** that serves as a contrast to another.

**formal diction** language that is lofty, dignified, and impersonal. *See* **colloquial diction** and **informal diction**.

**free verse** poetry characterized by varying line lengths, lack of traditional **meter**, and nonrhyming lines.

**genre** the largest category for classifying literature—fiction, poetry, drama. *See* **kind** and **subgenre**.

**haiku** an unrhymed poetic form, Japanese in origin, that contains seventeen syllables arranged in three lines of five, seven, and five syllables, respectively.

**hero/heroine** the leading male/female character, usually larger than life, sometimes almost godlike. *See* **antihero**, **protagonist**, and **villain**.

**heroic couplet** rhymed pairs of lines in iambic pentameter.

**hexameter** a line of poetry with six feet: "She comes, | she comes | again, | like ring | dove frayed | and fled" (Keats, *The Eve of St. Agnes*).

**high (verbal) comedy** humor that employs subtlety, wit, or the representation of refined life. *See* **low (physical) comedy**.

**hyperbole** overstatement characterized by exaggerated language.

**iamb** a metrical foot consisting of an unstressed syllable followed by a stressed one.

**iambic pentameter** a metrical form in which the basic foot is an **iamb** and most lines consist of five iambs; iambic pentameter is the most common poetic meter in English: "One com | mon note | on ei | ther lyre | did strike" (Dryden, "To the Memory of Mr. Oldham")

**imagery** broadly defined, any sensory detail or evocation in a work; more narrowly, the use of **figurative** language to evoke a feeling, to call to mind an idea, or to describe an object.

**imitative structure** a textual organization that mirrors as exactly as possible the structure of something that already exists as an object and can be seen.

**implied author** the guiding personality or value system behind a text; the implied author is not necessarily synonymous with the actual author.

**informal diction** language that is not as lofty or impersonal as **formal diction**; similar to everyday speech. *See* **colloquial diction**, which is one variety of informal diction.

**initiation story** a kind of short story in which a **character**—often but not always a child or young person—first learns a significant, usually life-changing truth about the universe, society, people, himself or herself.

**in medias res** "in the midst of things"; refers to opening a story in the middle of the action, necessitating filling in past details by **exposition** or **flashback**.

**irony** a situation or statement characterized by a significant difference between what is expected or understood and what actually happens or is meant. *See* **cosmic irony**, **dramatic irony**, and **situational irony**.

**Italian sonnet** *see* **Petrarchan sonnet**.

**limerick** a light or humorous verse form of mainly **anapestic** verses of which the first, second, and fifth lines are of three feet; the third and fourth lines are of two feet; and the rhyme scheme is *aabba*.

**limited point of view** or **limited focus** a perspective pinned to a single **character**, whether a first-person- or a third-person-centered consciousness, so that we cannot know for sure what is going on in the minds of other characters; thus, when the focal character leaves the room in a story we must go, too, and cannot know what is going on while our "eyes" or "camera" is gone. A variation on this, which generally has no name and is often lumped with the **omniscient point of view**, is the **point of view** that can wander like a camera from one character to another and close in or move back but cannot (or at least does not) get inside anyone's head and does not present from the inside any character's thoughts.

**literary criticism** the evaluative or interpretive work written by professional interpreters of texts. It is "criticism" not because it is negative or corrective, but rather because those who write criticism ask hard, analytical, crucial, or "critical" questions about the works they read.

**litotes** a figure of speech that emphasizes its subject by conscious **understatement**. An example from common speech is to say "Not bad" as a form of high praise.

**low (physical) comedy** humor that employs burlesque, horseplay, or the representation of unrefined life. *See* **high (verbal) comedy**.

**lyric** originally, a poem meant to be sung to the accompaniment of a lyre; now, any short poem in which the **speaker** expresses intense personal emotion rather than describing a narrative or dramatic situation.

**major (main) characters** those **characters** whom we see and learn about the most.

**meditation** a contemplation of some physical object as a way of reflecting upon some larger truth, often (but not necessarily) a spiritual one.

**memory devices** also called *mnemonic devices*; these devices—including rhyme, repetitive phrasing, and **meter**—when part of the structure of a longer work, make that work easier to memorize.

**metaphor** (1) one thing pictured as if it were something else, suggesting a likeness or **analogy** between them; (2) an implicit comparison or identification of one thing with another unlike itself without the use of a verbal signal. Sometimes used as a general term for **figure of speech**.

**meter** the more or less regular pattern of stressed and unstressed syllables in a line of poetry. This is determined by the kind of "foot" (**iambic** and **dactylic**, for example) and by the number of feet per line (five feet = pentameter, six feet = hexameter, for example).

**minor characters** those figures who fill out

the story but who do not figure prominently in it.

**mode** style, manner, way of proceeding, as in "tragic mode"; often used synonymously with **genre, kind,** and **subgenre.**

**monologue** a speech of more than a few sentences, usually in a play but also in other genres, spoken by one person and uninterrupted by the speech of anyone else. *See* **soliloquy.**

**motif** a recurrent device, formula, or situation that deliberately connects a poem with common patterns of existing thought.

**myth** like **allegory**, myth usually is symbolic and extensive, including an entire work or story. Though it no longer is necessarily specific to or pervasive in a single **culture**—individual authors may now be said to create myths—myth still seems communal or cultural, while the symbolic can often involve private or personal myths. Thus stories more or less universally shared within a culture to explain its history and traditions are frequently called myths.

**narrative structure** a textual organization based on sequences of connected events usually presented in a straightforward chronological framework.

**narrator** the **character** who "tells" the story.

**occasional poem** a poem written about or for a specific occasion, public or private.

**octameter** a line of poetry with eight feet: "Once u | pon a | midnight | dreary | while I | pondered, | weak and | weary" (Poe, "The Raven").

**octave** the first eight lines of the Italian, or Petrarchan, sonnet. See also **sestet.**

**ode** a lyric poem characterized by a serious topic and formal tone but no prescribed formal pattern. See Keats's odes and Shelley's "Ode to the West Wind."

**oeuvre** the sum total of works verifiably written by an author. See **canon.**

**omniscient point of view** also called **unlimited point of view;** a perspective that can be seen from one **character**'s view, then another's, then another's, or can be moved in or out of any character's mind at any time. Organization in which the reader has access to the perceptions and thoughts of all the characters in the story.

**onomatopoeia** a word capturing or approximating the sound of what it describes; *buzz* is a good example.

**orchestra** in classical Greek theater, a semicircular area used mostly for dancing by the **chorus.**

**overplot** a main plot in fiction or drama.

**overstatement** exaggerated language; also called **hyperbole.**

**oxymoron** a **figure of speech** that combines two apparently contradictory elements, as in *wise fool (sophomore).*

**parable** a short fiction that illustrates an explicit moral lesson.

**paradox** a statement that seems contradictory but may actually be true, such as "That I may rise and stand, o'erthrow me" in Donne's "Batter My Heart."

**parody** a work that imitates another work for comic effect by exaggerating the style and changing the content of the original.

**pastoral** a poem (also called an eclogue, a bucolic, or an idyll) that describes the simple life of country folk, usually shepherds who live a timeless, painless (and sheepless) life in a world full of beauty, music, and love.

**pastoral play** a play that features the sort of idyllic world described in the definition for **pastoral.**

**pentameter** a line of poetry with five feet: "Nuns fret | not at | their con | vent's nar | row room" (Wordsworth).

**persona** the voice or figure of the author who tells and structures the story and who may or may not share the values of the actual author.

**personification** (or *prosopopeia*) treating an abstraction as if it were a person by endowing it with humanlike qualities.

**Petrarchan sonnet** also called **Italian sonnet;** a **sonnet** form that divides the poem into one section of eight lines (**octave**) and a second section of six lines (**sestet**), usually following the *abbaabba cdecde* rhyme scheme or, more loosely, an *abbacddc* pattern.

**plot/plot structure** the arrangement of the **action.**

**plot summary** a description of the arrangement of the **action** in the order in which it actually appears in a story. The term is popularly used to mean the description of the history, or chronological order, of the action as it would have appeared in reality. It is important to indicate exactly in which sense you are using the term.

**plot time** the temporal setting in which the **action** takes place in a story or play.

**point of view** also called **focus;** the point from which people, events, and other details in a story are viewed. This term is sometimes used to include both **focus** and **voice.**

**precision** exactness, accuracy of language or description.

**presentation** the second step in the creation of a **character** for the written text and the performed play; the representation of the character by the playwright in the words and actions specified in the text.

**props** articles and objects used on the stage.

**proscenium arch** an arch over the front of a stage; the proscenium serves as a "frame" for the **action** on stage.

**protagonist** the main **character** in a work, who may be male or female, heroic or not heroic. See **antagonist, antihero,** and **hero/heroine.** *Protagonist* is the most neutral term.

**protest poem** a poetic attack, usually quite direct, on allegedly unjust institutions or social injustices.

**psychological realism** a modification of the concept of **realism,** or telling it like it is, which recognizes that what is real to the individual is that which he or she perceives. It is the ground for the use of the **centered consciousness,** or the first-person narrator, since both of these present reality only as something perceived by the focal **character.**

**reader time** the actual time it takes a reader to read a work.

**realism** the practice in literature of attempting to describe nature and life without idealization and with attention to detail.

**red herring** a false lead, something that misdirects expectations.

**referential** when used to describe a poem, play, or story, *referential* means making textual use of a specific historical moment or event or, more broadly, making use of external, "natural," or "actual" detail.

**reflective (meditative) structure** a textual organization based on the pondering of a **subject, theme,** or event, and letting the mind play with it, skipping from one sound to another or to related thoughts or objects as the mind receives them.

**represent** to verbally depict an image so that readers can "see" it.

**rhetorical trope** traditional **figure of speech,** used for specific persuasive effects.

**rhyme scheme** the pattern of end rhymes in a poem, often noted by small letters, e.g., *abab* or *abba,* etc.

**rhythm** the modulation of weak and strong (or stressed and unstressed) elements in the flow of speech. In most poetry written before the twentieth century, rhythm was often expressed in regular, metrical forms; in prose and in **free verse,** rhythm is present but in a much less predictable and regular manner.

**rising action** the second of the five parts of **plot structure,** in which events complicate the situation that existed at the beginning of a work, intensifying the **conflict** or introducing new conflict.

**rite of passage** a ritual or ceremony marking an individual's passing from one stage or state to a more advanced one, or an event in one's life that seems to have such significance; a formal initiation. Rites of passage are common in **initiation stories.**

**round characters** complex **characters,** often major characters, who can grow and change and "surprise convincingly"—that is, act in a way that you did not expect from what had gone before but now accept as possible, even probable, and "realistic."

**sarcasm** a form of **verbal irony** in which apparent praise is actually harshly or bitterly critical.

**satire** a literary work that holds up human failings to ridicule and censure.

**scanning/scansion** *Scansion* is the process of *scanning* a poem, analyzing the verse to show its **meter,** line by line.

**second-person narrator** a character, "you," who tells the story and necessarily has a **limited point of view;** may be seen as an extension of the reader, an external figure acting out a story, or an **auditor;** may also be an **unreliable narrator.**

**sestet** the last six lines of the Italian, or Petrarchan, **sonnet.** See also **octave.**

**sestina** an elaborate verse **structure** written in **blank verse** that consists of six **stanzas** of six lines each followed by a three-line stanza. The final words of each line in the first stanza appear in variable order in the next five stanzas, and are repeated in the middle and at the end of the three lines in the final stanza, as in Elizabeth Bishop's "Sestina."

**set** the design, decoration, and scenery of the stage during a play.

**setting** the time and place of the **action** in a story, poem, or play.

**Shakespearean sonnet** also called an English sonnet; a **sonnet** form that divides the poem into three units of four lines each and a final unit of two lines (4+4+4+2 structure). Its classic rhyme scheme is *abab cdcd efef gg,* but there are variations.

**shaped verse** another name for **concrete poetry;** poetry that is shaped to look like an object.

**simile** a direct, explicit comparison of one thing to another, usually using the words *like* or *as* to draw the connection. See **metaphor.**

**situation** the context of the literary work's **action,** what is happening when the story, poem, or play begins.

**situational irony** in a narrative, the incongruity between what the reader and/or character expects to happen and what actually does happen.

**skene** a low building in the back of the stage area in classical Greek theaters. It represented the palace or temple in front of which the **action** took place.

**soliloquy** a monologue in which the **character** in a play is alone and speaking only to him- or herself.

**sonnet** a fixed verse form consisting of fourteen lines usually in **iambic pentameter**. *See* **Italian sonnet** and **Shakespearean sonnet**.

**spatial setting** the place of a poem, story, or play.

**speaker** the person, not necessarily the author, who is the voice of a poem.

**Spenserian stanza** a stanza that consists of eight lines of **iambic pentameter** (five feet) followed by a ninth line of iambic hexameter (six feet). The rhyme scheme is *ababbcbcc*.

**spondee** a metrical foot consisting of a pair of stressed syllables ("Dead set").

**stage directions** The words in the printed text of a play that inform the director, crew, actors, and readers how to stage, perform, or imagine the play. Stage directions are not spoken aloud and may appear at the beginning of a play, before any scene, or attached to a line of dialogue. The place and time of the action, the design of the set itself, and at times the characters' actions or tone of voice are dictated through stage directions and interpreted by the group of people that put on a performance.

**stanza** a section of a poem demarcated by extra line spacing. Some distinguish between a stanza, a division marked by a single pattern of **meter** or rhyme, and a verse paragraph, a division governed by thought rather than sound pattern.

**stereotype** a **characterization** based on conscious or unconscious assumptions that some one aspect—such as gender, age, ethnic or national identity, religion, occupation, marital status, and so on—is predictably accompanied by certain **character** traits, actions, even values.

**stock character** a **character** that appears in a number of stories or plays, such as the cruel stepmother, the braggart, and so forth.

**structure** the organization or arrangement of the various elements in a work.

**style** a distinctive manner of expression; each author's style is expressed through his/her **diction, rhythm, imagery,** and so on.

**subgenre** a division within the category of a genre; *novel, novella,* and *short story* are subgenres of the genre *fiction*.

**subject** (1) the concrete and literal description of what a story is about; (2) the general or specific area of concern of a poem—also called **topic**; (3) also used in fiction commentary to denote a **character** whose inner thoughts and feelings are recounted.

**subplot** another name for an **underplot**; a subordinate **plot** in fiction or drama.

**suspense** the expectation of and doubt about what is going to happen next.

**syllabic verse** a form in which the poet establishes a precise number of syllables to a line and repeats it in subsequent **stanzas**.

**symbol** a person, place, thing, event, or pattern in a literary work that designates itself and at the same time figuratively represents or "stands for" something else. Often the thing or idea represented is more abstract, general, non- or superrational; the symbol, more concrete and particular.

**symbolic poem** a poem in which the use of symbols is so pervasive and internally consistent that the larger referential world is distanced, if not forgotten.

**syntax** the way words are put together to form phrases, clauses, and sentences.

**technopaegnia** the art of "shaped" poems in which the visual force is supposed to work spiritually or magically.

**temporal setting** the time of a story, poem, or play.

**terza rima** a verse form consisting of three-line **stanzas** in which the second line of each stanza rhymes with the first and third of the next.

**tetrameter** a line of poetry with four feet: "The Grass | divides | as with | a comb" (Dickinson).

**tetrameter couplet** rhymed pairs of lines that contain (in classical **iambic, trochaic,** and **anapestic** verse) four measures of two feet or (in modern English verse) four metrical feet.

**theme** (1) a generalized, abstract paraphrase of the inferred central or dominant idea or concern of a work; (2) the statement a poem makes about its subject.

**third-person narrator** a character, "he" or "she," who "tells" the story; may have either a **limited point of view** or an **omniscient point of view**; may also be an **unreliable narrator**.

**thrust stage** a stage design that allows the audience to sit around three sides of the major acting area.

**tone** the attitude a literary work takes toward its **subject** and **theme**.

**topic** (1) the concrete and literal description of what a story is about; (2) a poem's general or specific area of concern. Also called **subject**.

**tradition** an inherited, established, or customary practice.

**traditional symbols** symbols that, through years of usage, have acquired an agreed-upon significance, an accepted meaning. *See* **archetype**.

**tragedy** a drama in which a **character** (usually a good and noble person of high rank) is brought to a disastrous end in his or her confrontation with a superior force (fortune, the gods, social forces, universal values), but also comes to understand the meaning of his or her deeds and to accept an appropriate punishment. Often the **protagonist**'s downfall is a direct result of a fatal flaw in his or her character.

**trochaic** a metrical form in which the basic foot is a **trochee**.

**trochee** a metrical foot consisting of a stressed syllable followed by an unstressed one ("Homer").

**turning point** the third part of **plot structure**, the point at which the **action** stops rising and begins falling or reversing. Also called **climax**.

**underplot** a subordinate **plot** in fiction or drama. Also called a **subplot**.

**understatement** language that avoids obvious emphasis or embellishment; **litotes** is one form of it.

**unity of time** one of the three unities of drama as described by Aristotle in his *Poetics*. Unity of time refers to the limitation of a play's action to a short period—usually the time it takes to present the play or, at any rate, no longer than a day. *See* **classical unities**.

**unlimited point of view** also called **omniscient point of view**; a perspective that can be seen from one **character**'s view, then another's, then another's, or can be moved in or out of any character's mind at any time. Organization in which the reader has access to the perceptions and thoughts of all the characters in the story.

**unreliable narrator** a speaker or voice whose vision or version of the details of a story are consciously or unconsciously deceiving; such a **narrator**'s version is usually subtly undermined by details in the story or the reader's general knowledge of facts outside the story. If, for example, the narrator were to tell you that Columbus was Spanish and that he discovered America in the fourteenth century when his ship the *Golden Hind* landed on the coast of Florida near present-day Gainesville, you might not trust other things he tells you.

**verbal irony** a statement in which the literal meaning differs from the implicit meaning. *See* **dramatic irony** and **situational irony**.

**verse paragraph** *see* **stanza**.

**villain** the one who opposes the hero and heroine—that is, the "bad guy." *See* **antagonist** and **hero/heroine**.

**villanelle** a verse form consisting of nineteen lines divided into six **stanzas**—five tercets (three-line stanzas) and one quatrain (four-line stanza). The first and third lines of the first tercet rhyme, and this rhyme is repeated through each of the next four tercets and in the last two lines of the concluding quatrain. The villanelle is also known for its repetition of select lines. A good example of a twentieth-century villanelle is Dylan Thomas's "Do Not Go Gentle into That Good Night."

**voice** the acknowledged or unacknowledged source of a story's words; the **speaker**; the "person" telling the story.

**word order** the positioning of words in relation to one another.

# Permissions Acknowledgments

## Texts

### FICTION

MARGARET ATWOOD: "Happy Endings" from *Good Bones and Simple Murders* by Margaret Atwood. Copyright © 1983, 1992, 1994 by O. W. Toad Ltd. A Nan A. Talese Book. Used by permission of Doubleday, a division of Random House, Inc. Used by permission McClelland & Stewart Ltd., The Canadian Publishers.

JAMES BALDWIN: "Sonny's Blues." Originally published in *Partisan Review*. Collected in *Going to Meet the Man* by James Baldwin. Copyright © 1965 by James Baldwin. Copyright renewed. Published by Vintage Books. Reprinted by arrangement with the James Baldwin Estate.

TONI CADE BAMBARA: "Gorilla, My Love" from *Gorilla, My Love* by Toni Cade Bambara. Copyright © 1971 by Toni Cade Bambara. Reprinted by permission of Random House, Inc.

ANDREA BARRETT: "The Littoral Zone" from *Ship Fever and Other Stories* by Andrea Barrett. Copyright © 1996 by Andrea Barrett. Used by permission of W. W. Norton & Company.

ANN BEATTIE: "Janus" from *Where You'll Find Me* by Ann Beattie. Copyright © 1986 by Irony & Pity, Inc. Reprinted with the permission of Simon & Schuster.

JORGE LUIS BORGES: "The Garden of Forking Paths," translated by Donald A. Yates, from *Labyrinths*. Copyright © 1962, 1964 by New Directions Publishing Corp. Reprinted by permission of New Directions Publishing Corp. Reprinted by permission of New Directions.

LINDA BREWER: "20/20" from *Micro Fiction: An Anthology of Really Short Stories* edited by Jerome Stern. Reprinted with the permission of the author.

A. S. BYATT: "The Thing in the Forest" Reprinted by permission of SII/sterling Lord Literistic, Inc. Copyright © 2002 by Antonia Byatt.

PETER CAREY: "'Do You Love Me?'" from *Collected Stories*. Copyright © 1994 Peter Carey. Reproduced by permission of the author c/o Rogers, Coleridge & White Ltd., 20 Powis Mews, London W11 1JN.

ANGELA CARTER: "A Souvenir from Japan." Originally published in *Fireworks*. Copyright © 1995 by the Estate of Angela Carter. Reprinted by permission of the Estate of Angela Carter, c/o Rogers, Coleridge and White Ltd., 20 Powis Mews, London W11 1JN.

RAYMOND CARVER: "Cathedral" from *Cathedral* by Raymond Carver. Copyright © 1981, 1982, 1983 by Raymond Carver. Reprinted by permission of Alfred A. Knopf, Inc.

MICHAEL CHABON: "The Lost World," from *A Model World*. Copyright © 1991 by Michael Chabon. Reprinted by permission of HarperCollins Publishers, Inc.

JOHN CHEEVER: "The Country Husband" from *The Short Stories of John Cheever* by John Cheever. Copyright © 1978 by John Cheever. Reprinted by permission of Alfred A. Knopf, Inc., a division of Random House, Inc.

MALCOLM COWLEY: excerpts from *Exile's Return* by Malcolm Cowley. Copyright © 1934, 1935, 1941, and 1951 by Malcolm Cowley. Used by permission of Viking Penguin, a division of Penguin Putnam, Inc.

EDWIDGE DANTICAT: "The Wall of Fire Rising" from *Krik? Krak!* by Edwidge Danticat. Reprinted by permission of Soho Press.

GEORGE L. DILLON: "Styles of Reading" from *Poetics Today* 3.2 (Spring 1982): 77–88. Copyright © 1982, Porter Institute for Poetics and Semiotics. Reprinted by permission of Duke University Press.

RICHARD DOKEY: "Sánchez." Originally published in *Southwest Review*. Copyright © 1967 by Richard Dokey. Reprinted by permission of the author.

**LOUISE ERDRICH:** "Love Medicine" from *Love Medicine* by Louise Erdrich. Copyright © 1984, 1993 by Louise Erdrich. Reprinted by permission of Henry Holt & Company, LLC.

**WILLIAM FAULKNER:** "Barn Burning" and "A Rose for Emily" from *Collected Stories of William Faulkner* (New York: Random House, 1950). Reprinted by permission.

**JUDITH FETTERLEY:** "A Rose for 'A Rose for Emily'" from *Resisting Reader*, Second Edition. Reprinted by permission of Indiana University Press.

**F. SCOTT FITZGERALD:** excerpts from "Echoes of the Jazz Age" from *The Crack-Up*, edited by Edmund Wilson. Copyright © 1945 by New Directions Publishing Company. Copyright © 1945 by Elena Wilson. "Babylon Revisited" from *The Short Stories of F. Scott Fitzgerald*, edited by Matthew J. Bruccoli. Copyright © 1931 by The Curtis Publishing Company. Copyright renewed © 1959 by Frances Scott Fitzgerald Lanahan.

**NADINE GORDIMER:** "Good Climate, Friendly Inhabitants" from *Selected Stories* by Nadine Gordimer. Copyright © 1964 by Nadine Gordimer, renewed. Used by permission of Viking Penguin, a division of Penguin Putnam, Inc.

**ERNEST R. GROVES:** excerpts from *Social Problems of the Family* by Ernest R. Groves. Copyright © 1927 by Lippincott Company. Reprinted by permission of HarperCollins, Inc.

**ERNEST HEMINGWAY:** "Hills Like White Elephants" from *Men Without Women* by Ernest Hemingway. Copyright © 1927 by Charles Scribner's Sons. Copyright renewed 1955 by Ernest Hemingway. Reprinted by permission of Scribner, a division of Simon & Schuster, and the Hemingway Foreign Rights Trust.

**HA JIN:** "In Broad Daylight." Originally published in *The Kenyon Review*. Reprinted by permission of the author.

**JAMES JOYCE:** "Araby" from *Dubliners* by James Joyce, copyright 1916 by B.W. Heubsch. Definitive text copyright © 1967 by the Estate of James Joyce. Used by permission of Viking Penguin, a division of Penguin Group (USA), Inc.

**FRANZ KAFKA:** "A Hunger Artist" from *Franz Kafka: The Complete Stories* by Nahum N. Glatzer, Editor. Copyright © 1946, 1947, 1948, 1949, 1954, 1958, 1971 by Schocken Books, Inc. Reprinted by permission of Schocken Books, published by Pantheon Books, a division of Random House, Inc.

**YASUNARI KAWABATA:** "The Grasshopper and the Bell Cricket" from *Palm-of-the-Hand Stories* by Yasunari Kawabata. Translated by Lane Dunlop and J. Martin Holman. Translation copyright © 1988 by Lane Dunlop and J. Martin Holman. Reprinted by permission of North Point Press, a division of Farrar, Straus & Giroux, Inc.

**JAMAICA KINCAID:** "Girl" from *At the Bottom of the River* by Jamaica Kincaid. Copyright © 1983 by Jamaica Kincaid. Reprinted by permission of Farrar, Straus & Giroux, Inc.

**JHUMPA LAHIRI:** "Interpreter of Maladies" from *Interpreter of Maladies* by Jhumpa Lahiri. Copyright © 1999 by Jhumpa Lahiri. Reprinted by permission of Houghton Mifflin Company. All rights reserved.

**D. H. LAWRENCE:** "The Rocking-Horse Winner" from *The Complete Short Stories of D. H. Lawrence*. Copyright © 1933 by the Estate of D. H. Lawrence, renewed 1961 by Angelo Ravagli and C. M. Weekley, Executors of the Estate of Frieda Lawrence. Excerpts from "Art and Morality," "Love," "Morality and the Novel," "Nottingham and the Mining Countryside," "Why the Novel Matters," and "Women Are So Cocksure" from *Phoenix: The Posthumous Papers of D. H. Lawrence* and edited by Edward McDonald. Copyright © 1936 by Frieda Lawrence, renewed © 1964 by the Estate of the late Frieda Lawrence Ravagli. Excerpt from "Autobiographical Sketch" from *Phoenix II: Uncollected Papers of D. H. Lawrence* by D. H. Lawrence, edited by Roberts and Moore. Copyright © 1959, 1963, 1968 by the Estate of Frieda Lawrence Ravagli. Used by permission of Viking Penguin, a division of Penguin Books USA Inc., Laurence Pollinger Limited, and The Estate of Frieda Lawrence Ravagli. "Odour of Chrysanthemums" from *Selected Stories of D. H. Lawrence*. Used by permission of Laurence Pollinger Limited and the Estate of Frieda Lawrence Ravagli.

**URSULA K. LE GUIN:** "She Unnames Them" from *Buffalo Gals and Other Animal Presences* by Ursula K. Le Guin. Copyright © 1985 by Ursula K. Le Guin. First appeared in *The New Yorker*.

Reprinted by permission of the author and the author's agents, the Virginia Kidd Agency, Inc.

DORIS LESSING: "Our Friend Judith" from *A Man and Two Women* by Doris Lessing. Copyright © 1963 Doris Lessing. Also from *Stories* by Doris Lessing. Copyright © 1978 by Doris Lessing. Usage by kind permission of Jonathan Clowes Ltd., London, on behalf of Doris Lessing and Alfred A. Knopf, Inc.

KATHERINE MANSFIELD: "Bliss," from *The Short Stories of Katherine Mansfield* by Katherine Mansfield, copyright 1923 by Alfred A. Knopf, a division of Random House, Inc., and renewed 1951 by John Middleton Murry. Used by permission of Alfred A. Knopf, a division of Random House, Inc.

GABRIEL GARCÍA MÁRQUEZ: "A Very Old Man with Enormous Wings" from *Leaf Storm and Other Stories* by Gabriel García Márquez and translated by Gregory Rabassa. Copyright © 1971 by Gabriel García Márquez. Reprinted by permission of HarperCollins Publishers, Inc.

BOBBIE ANN MASON: "Shiloh" from *Shiloh and Other Stories* by Bobbie Ann Mason. Originally published in *The New Yorker*. Copyright © 1982 by Bobbie Ann Mason. Reprinted by permission of International Creative Management.

GENE M. MOORE: "Of Time and Its Mathematical Progression: Problems of Chronology in Faulkner's 'A Rose for Emily.' " From *Studies in Short Fiction*. Copyright © 1992 by Studies in Short Fiction, Inc.

LORRIE MOORE: "How." From *Self-Help* by Lorrie Moore. Copyright © 1985 by M. L. Moore. Used by permission of Alfred A. Knopf, a division of Random House, Inc.

TONI MORRISON: "Recitatif" reprinted by permission of International Creative Management, Inc. Copyright © by Toni Morrison.

BHARATI MUKHERJEE: "The Management of Grief" from *The Middleman and Other Stories* by Bharati Mukherjee. Copyright © 1988 by Bharati Mukherjee. Reprinted by permission of Grove/Atlantic, Inc., and Penguin Books Canada Ltd.

ALICE MUNRO: "Boys and Girls" from *Dance of the Happy Shades* by Alice Munro. Copyright © 1968 by Alice Munro. Published by McGraw-Hill Ryerson Ltd. Reprinted by arrangement with the Virginia Barber Literary Agency and McGraw-Hill Ryerson Ltd. All rights reserved. Reprinted by permission of William Morris Agency, Inc., on behalf of the author.

NEW YORK TIMES: "Crowds at Tickers See Fortunes Wane," "Stocks Collapse in 16,410,030-Share Day, but Rally at Close Cheers Brokers," and "Women Traders Going Back to Bridge Games." Copyright © 1929 by the New York Times Co. Reprinted by permission.

JOYCE CAROL OATES: "The Lady with the Pet Dog" from *Marriages and Infidelities* (Vanguard Press, 1972). Copyright © 1972 by Ontario Review Press, Inc. Reprinted by permission of John Hawkins & Associates, Inc.

FLANNERY O'CONNOR: "Everything That Rises Must Converge" and "The Lame Shall Enter First" from *The Complete Stories* by Flannery O'Connor. Copyright © 1971 by the Estate of Mary Flannery O'Connor and copyright renewed © 1993 by Regina O'Connor. "A Good Man Is Hard to Find" from *A Good Man Is Hard to Find and Other Stories* by Flannery O'Connor. Copyright © 1953 by Flannery O'Connor and renewed 1981 by Regina O'Connor. Reprinted by permission of Harcourt Brace & Company. Excerpts from pp. 437, 438, 443, 446, 456, 457, 490, 498, 524, and 537 from *The Habit of Being* by Flannery O'Connor, edited by Sally Fitzgerald. Copyright © 1979 by Regina O'Connor. Excerpts from "The Fiction Writer and His Country", "The Nature and Aim of Fiction", "Writing Short Stories", "On Her Own Work", and "Novelist and Believer" from *Mystery and Manners* by Flannery O'Connor. Copyright © 1969 by the Estate of Mary Flannery O'Connor. Reprinted by permission of Farrar, Straus & Giroux, Inc.

GRACE PALEY: "A Conversation with My Father" from *Enormous Changes at the Last Minute* by Grace Paley. Copyright © 1971, 1974 by Grace Paley.

KATHERINE ANNE PORTER: "Flowering Judas" from *Flowering Judas and Other Stories* by Katherine Anne Porter. Copyright © 1930 by Katherine Anne Porter, renewed 1958 by Katherine Anne Porter. Reprinted by permission of Harcourt, Inc.

**A12   PERMISSIONS ACKNOWLEDGMENTS: POETRY**

LAWRENCE RODGERS: " 'We all said, "she will kill herself" ': The Narrator/Detective in William Faulkner's 'A Rose for Emily.' " Originally published in *Clues* magazine. Reprinted by permission of the author.

SALMAN RUSHDIE: "The Prophet's Hair" from *East, West: Stories* by Salman Rushdie. Copyright © 1994 by Salman Rushdie. Reprinted by permission of Pantheon Books, a division of Random House, Inc.

CAROL SHIELDS: "Dressing Down" from *Dressing Up for the Carnival* by Carol Shields. Copyright © 2000 by Carol Shields. Used by permission of Viking Penguin, a division of Penguin Putnam, Inc. Reprinted with the permission of Random House Canada.

AMY TAN: "A Pair of Tickets" from *The Joy Luck Club* by Amy Tan. Copyright © 1989 by Amy Tan. Reprinted by permission of G. P. Putnam's Sons, a division of Penguin Putnam, Inc.

EUDORA WELTY: "Why I Live at the P.O." from *A Curtain of Green and Other Stories* by Eudora Welty. Copyright © 1941 and renewed 1969 by Eudora Welty, reprinted by permission of Harcourt Brace & Company.

WILLIAM CARLOS WILLIAMS: "The Use of Force" from *The Collected Stories of William Carlos Williams*. Copyright © 1938 by William Carlos Williams. Reprinted by permission of New Directions Publishing Corp.

## POETRY

DIANE ACKERMAN: "Sweep Me Through Your Many-Chambered Heart" from *Jaguar of Sweet Laughter: New and Selected Poems* by Diane Ackerman. Copyright © 1991 by Diane Ackerman. Reprinted by permission of Random House, Inc.

VIRGINIA HAMILTON ADAIR: "Peeling an Orange" from *Ants on the Melon* by Virginia Hamilton Adair. Copyright © 1996 by Virginia Hamilton Adair. Used by permission of Random House, Inc.

ELIZABETH ALEXANDER: "West Indian Primer" from *The Venus Hottentot* by Elizabeth Alexander. Copyright © 1990. Reprinted by permission of the author.

AGHA SHAHID ALI: "Postcard from Kashmir" from *The Half-Inch Himalayas* by Agha Shahid Ali. Copyright © 1987 by Wesleyan University Press. Reprinted by permission of the publisher.

A. ALVAREZ: "Sylvia Plath" from *Beyond All This Fiddle*. Copyright © 1968 by Al Alvarez. Reprinted by permission of the author and Gillon Aitken Associates Ltd.

MAYA ANGELOU: "Africa" from *Oh Pray My Wings Are Gonna Fit Me Well* by Maya Angelou. Copyright © 1975 by Maya Angelou. Reprinted by permission of Random House, Inc.

PAMELA J. ANNAS: excerpt from *A Disturbance in Mirrors: The Poetry of Sylvia Plath* by Pamela J. Annas. Copyright © 1988 by Pamela J. Annas. Reproduced with permission of Greenwood Publishing Group, Inc. (Westport CT).

MARGARET ATWOOD: "Death of a Young Son by Drowning" from *Selected Poems 1966–1984* by Margaret Atwood. Copyright © Margaret Atwood, 1990. Reprinted by permission of Oxford University Press. "Death of a Young Son by Drowning" from *The Journals of Susanna Moodie* by Margaret Atwood. Copyright © 1976 by Oxford University Press. Reprinted by permission of Houghton Mifflin Company. "Scarlet Ibis" from *Bluebeard's Egg* by Margaret Atwood. Copyright © 1983 by O.W. Toad, Ltd. Reprinted by permission of Houghton Mifflin Company. All rights reserved.

W. H. AUDEN: "In Memory of W. B. Yeats," and "Stop all the clocks" from *W. H. Auden: Collected Poems* by W. H. Auden, edited by Edward Mendelson. Copyright © 1940 and renewed 1968 by W. H. Auden. Reprinted by permission of Random House, Inc. "Musée des Beaux Arts" from *W. H. Auden: Collected Poems* by W. H. Auden, edited by Edward Mendelson. Copyright © 1940 and renewed 1968 by W. H. Auden. Reprinted by permission of Random House, Inc., and Faber & Faber Ltd.

STEVEN GOULD AXELROD: excerpt from *Sylvia Plath: The Wound and the Cure of Words* by Steven Gould Axelrod (pp. 51-70). Copyright © 1980 by the Johns Hopkins University Press. Reprinted by permission of John Hopkins University Press.

JIMMY SANTIAGO BACA: "Green Chile" from *Black Mesa Poems*. Copyright © 1989 by Jimmy Santiago Baca. Reprinted by permission of the New Directions Publishing Corp.

BASHŌ: "This road" and "A village without bells" from *The Essential Haiku*, edited and with verse translations by Robert Hass. Copyright © 1994 by Robert Hass. Reprinted with the permission of HarperCollins

JEANNE MARIE BEAUMONT: "Rorschach" from *Placebo Effects* by Jeanne Marie Beaumont. Copyright © 1997 by Jeanne Marie Beaumont. Used by permission of W. W. Norton & Company, Inc.

CHARLES BERNSTEIN: "Of Time and the Line" from *Rough Trade* by Charles Bernstein. Reprinted by permission of the author.

JOHN BETJEMAN: "In Westminster Abbey" from *Collected Poems* by John Betjeman. Reprinted by permission of John Murray (Publishers) Ltd.

EARLE BIRNEY: "Anglosaxon Street" from *Selected Poems* by Earle Birney. Used by permission of McClelland & Stewart, Inc., Toronto, The Canadian Publishers.

ELIZABETH BISHOP: "Casabianca," "Exchanging Hats," and "Sestina" from *The Collected Poems 1927–1979* by Elizabeth Bishop. Copyright © 1979, 1980 by Alice Helen Methfessel. Reprinted by permission of Farrar, Straus & Giroux, Inc.

LOUISE BOGAN: "Evening in the Sanitarium" from *Blue Estuaries*. Copyright © 1968 by Louise Bogan. Copyright renewed © 1996 by Ruth Limmer. Reprinted by permission of Farrar, Straus & Giroux, Inc.

ARNA BONTEMPS: "A Black Man Talks of Reaping," copyright © 1963 by Arna Bontemps. Reprinted by permission of Harold Ober Associates, Inc.

ROO BORSON: "After a Death" by Roo Borson, reprinted by permission of the author. From *Night Walk: Selected Poems*, Oxford University Press, Toronto, 1994.

MARY LYNN BROE: excerpt from *Protean Poetic: The Poetry of Sylvia Plath* by Mary Lynn Broe. Copyright © 1980 by the Curators of the University of Missouri Press. Reprinted by permission of the publisher.

GWENDOLYN BROOKS: "First Fight, Then Fiddle" and "We Real Cool" from *Blacks* by Gwendolyn Brooks. "To the Diaspora" from *Children Coming Home* by Gwendolyn Brooks. Copyright © 1991 by Gwendolyn Brooks. Reprinted by consent of Brooks Permissions

LEE ANN BROWN: "Foolproof Loofah" from *Polyverse* (Los Angeles: Green Integer Books, 1999), page 118. Copyright © 1999 by Lee Ann Brown. Reprinted with the permission of the publisher.

BUSON: "Coolness" and "Listening to the Moon" from *The Essential Haiku*, edited and with verse translations by Robert Hass. Copyright © 1994 by Robert Hass. Reprinted by permission of the Ecco Press.

FRED CHAPPELL: "Recovery of Sexual Desire after a Bad Cold," reprinted by permission of Louisiana State Unversity Press from *Spring Garden* by Fred Chappell. Copyright © 1995 by Fred Chappell.

KAREN CHASE: "Venison." Originally published in *The New Yorker*. Copyright © 1995 by Karen Chase. Reprinted by permission of Harold Matson Co., Inc.

HELEN CHASIN: "Joy Sonnet in a Random Universe" and "The Word *Plum*" from *Coming Close and Other Poems* by Helen Chasin. Copyright © 1968 by Helen Chasin. Reprinted by permission of Yale University Press.

KELLY CHERRY: "Alzheimer's" from *Death and Transfiguration*. Copyright © 1997. Reprinted by permission of Louisiana State University Press.

MARILYN CHIN: "Summer Love" from *The Phoenix Gone, The Terrace Empty* by Marilyn Chin (Milkweed Editions, 1994). Copyright © 1994 by Marilyn Chin. Reprinted by permission of Milkweed Editions.

CHIYOJO: "Whether astringent I do not know" from *One Hundred Famous Haiku*, selected and translated by Daniel Buchanan. Reprinted by permission of Japan Publications, Inc.

JUDITH ORTIZ COFER: "The Changeling" from *Prairie Schooner* 66.3, by Judith Ortiz Cofer. Copyright © 1992 by the University of Nebraska Press. Reprinted by permission of the publisher.

BILLY COLLINS: "Morning" from *Picnic, Lightning* by Billy Collins. Copyright © 1998. Reprinted by permission of the University of Pittsburgh Press. "Sonnet" copyright © 2001 by Billy Collins from *Sailing Alone Around the Room* by Billy Collins. Used by permission of Random House, Inc.

MARTHA COLLINS: "Lies" from *Some Things Words Can Do*. Copyright © 1998 by Martha Collins. Reprinted by permission of the author.

WENDY COPE: "Emily Dickinson" and "From Strugnell's Sonnets IV, 'Not only marble, but the plastic toys'" from *Making Cocoa for Kingsley Amis* by Wendy Cope. Reprinted by permission of Faber & Faber Ltd.

COUNTEE CULLEN: "Yet Do I Marvel" and "The Dark Tower" from *Color* by Countee Cullen. Copyright © 1925 by Harper & Brothers, copyright renewed 1953 by Ida M. Cullen. "Harlem Wine" and "Saturday's Child" from *Voices of Harlem*. Reprinted by permission of GRM Associates, agents for the Estate of Ida M. Cullen.

E. E. CUMMINGS: "l(a," and "(ponder, darling, these busted statues" from *Complete Poems: 1904–1962* by E. E. Cummings, edited by George J. Firmage. "l(a," copyright © 1958, 1986, 1991 by the Trustees for the E. E. Cummings Trust. "(ponder, darling, these busted statues," copyright © 1926, 1954, 1991 by the Trustees for the E. E. Cummings Trust. Copyright © 1985 by George James Firmage. "Buffalo Bill's" and "in Just-" from *Complete Poems: 1904–1962* by E. E. Cummings, edited by George J. Firmage. Copyright © 1923, 1951, 1991 by the Trustees for the E. E. Cummings Trust. Copyright © 1976 by George James Firmage. Reprinted by permission of Liveright Publishing Corporation.

WALTER DE LA MARE: "Slim Cunning Hands" from *The Complete Poems of Walter de la Mare*. Reprinted by permission of the Literary Trustees of Walter de la Mare and the Society of Authors as their representative.

GREG DELANTY: "The Blind Stitch," from *The Blind Stitch*. Reprinted with the permission of Carcanet Press Limited.

BABETTE DEUTSCH: "The Falling Flower..." from *Poetry Handbook: A Dictionary of Terms* by Babette Deutsch. Copyright © 1974, 1969, 1962, 1957 by Babette Deutsch. Reprinted by permission of HarperCollins Publishers, Inc.

JAMES DICKEY: "Cherrylog Road" and "The Leap" from *Poems, 1957–1967*. Copyright © 1964 and 1967 by Wesleyan University Press. Reprinted by permission of the publisher.

EMILY DICKINSON: #479 [She dealt her pretty words like Blades], #341 [After great pain, a formal feeling comes] #712 [Because I could not stop for death] from *The Poems of Emily Dickinson* edited by Thomas H. Johnson (Cambridge, Mass.: The Belknap Press of Harvard University Press). Copyright © 1951, 1955, 1979, 1983 by the President and Fellows of Harvard College. Copyright © 1929, 1935 by Martha Dickinson Bianchi; copyright © renewed 1957, 1963 by Mary L. Hampson. Reprinted by permission of the publishers and the Trustees of Amherst College. #467 [We do not play on Graves—], #632 [The Brain is Wider than the Sky], and #875 [I stepped from Plank to Plank] from *The Poems of Emily Dickinson* edited by Thomas H. Johnson (Cambridge, Mass.: The Belknap Press of Harvard University Press). Copyright © 1951, 1955, 1979, 1983 by the President and Fellows of Harvard College. Reprinted by permission of the publishers and the Trustees of Amherst College.

SUSAN DONNELLY: "Eve Names the Animals" from *Eve Names the Animals* by Susan Donnelly. Copyright © 1985 by Susan Donnelly. Reprinted by permission of Northeastern University Press.

RITA DOVE: "Fifth Grade Autobiography" from *Grace Notes* by Rita Dove. Copyright © 1989 by Rita Dove. Reprinted by permission of W. W. Norton & Company, Inc. "Daystar" from *Thomas and Beulah* by Rita Dove (Carnegie-Mellon University Press, 1986). Copyright © 1983 and 1986 by Rita Dove. Reprinted by permission of the author.

W. E. B. DU BOIS: "Two Novels: *Home to Harlem* and *Quicksand*" from *Crisis*, 1928. Reprinted with the permission of the Estate of W. E. B. Du Bois.

STEPHEN DUNN: "Dancing with God" from *Between Angels* by Stephen Dunn. Copyright ©

1989 by Stephen Dunn. "Poetry" from *Loosestrife* by Stephen Dunn. Copyright © 1996 by Stephen Dunn.

BOB DYLAN: "Mister Tambourine Man," lyrics and music by Bob Dylan. Copyright © 1964 by Warner Bros. Music. Copyright © renewed 1993 by Special Rider Music. All rights reserved. International copyright secured. Reprinted by permission

T. S. ELIOT: "Journey of the Magi" from *Collected Poems 1909–1962* by T. S. Eliot. Copyright © 1936 by Harcourt Brace & Company, copyright © 1964, 1963 by T. S. Eliot. Reprinted by permission of Harcourt Brace & Company and Faber & Faber Ltd.

JAMES A. EMANUEL: "Emmett Till" from *Whole Grain: Collected Poems, 1958–1989* by James A. Emanuel. Reprinted by permission of the author. "Ray Charles" from *Jazz from the Haiku King* by James A. Emanuel. Reprinted by permission of Broadside Press.

LOUISE ERDRICH: "Jacklight" from *Jacklight* by Louise Erdrich. Copyright © 1984 by Louise Erdrich. Reprinted by permission of Henry Holt & Company, LLC., and the Wylie Agency.

KENNETH FEARING: "Dirge" from *New and Selected Poems* by Kenneth Fearing. We have made diligent efforts to contact the copyright holder to obtain permission to reprint this selection. If you have information that would help us, please write to W. W. Norton & Company, Inc., 500 Fifth Avenue, New York, NY 10110.

DAVID FERRY: "At the Hospital" (p. 145), and "Evening News" (p. 115) from *Of No Country I Know: New and Selected Poems*, University of Chicago Press, 1999. Reprinted by permission of the author.

ROBERT FROST: "Design," "Stopping by Woods on a Snowy Evening," "The Road Not Taken" and "Fireflies in the Garden" from *The Poetry of Robert Frost*, edited by Edward Connery Lathem. Copyright © 1936, 1951, 1956 by Robert Frost, © 1964 by Lesley Frost Ballantine, © 1923, 1928, 1969 by Henry Holt & Co., Inc. Reprinted by permission of Henry Holt & Company, LLC.

TESS GALLAGHER: "Sudden Journey" from *Amplitude: New and Selected Poems* by Tess Gallagher. Copyright © 1984, 1987 by Tess Gallagher. Reprinted with the permission of Graywolf Press (Saint Paul, Minnesota).

SANDRA GILBERT: "Sonnet: *The Ladies' Home Journal*" from *Emily's Bread* by Sandra M. Gilbert. Copyright © 1984 by Sandra M. Gilbert. Reprinted by permission of W. W. Norton & Company, Inc.

ALLEN GINSBERG: "A Further Proposal" (all lines), copyright © 1984 by Allen Ginsberg; [Looking over my shoulder] (all lines), copyright © 1984 by Allen Ginsberg; from *Collected Poems 1947–1980* by Allen Ginsberg. "Velocity of Money" from *Cosmopolitan Greetings, Poems 1986–1992* by Allen Ginsberg. Copyright © 1994 by Allen Ginsberg. [The Old Pond] (all lines), copyright © 1984 by Allen Ginsberg. Reprinted by permission of HarperCollins Publishers, Inc.

PHAON GOLDMAN: "The Significance of African Freedom for the Negro Americans" from *The Negro History Bulletin*. Property of the Association for the study of African American Life and History, Inc.

ANGELINA GRIMKE: "Tenebris" and "The Black Finger" from *Selected Works of Angelina Grimke*, Angelina Grimke Papers, Moorland-Spingarn Research Center, Howard University.

EMILY GROSHOLZ: "Eden" from *Rebel Angels* (1996). Reprinted by permission of the author and Storyline Press.

THOM GUNN: "In Time of Plague," "A Blank," and "A Map of the City" from *Collected Poems* by Thom Gunn. Copyright © 1994 by Thom Gunn. Reprinted by permission of Farrar, Straus, & Giroux, Inc., and Faber and Faber Ltd.

MARILYN HACKER: "[Who would divorce her lover ...]" from *Love, Death, and the Changing of the Seasons* by Marilyn Hacker. Copyright © 1986 by Marilyn Hacker. Reprinted by permission of Frances Collin, Literary Agent.

MICHAEL S. HARPER: "Dear John, Dear Coltrane" from *Dear John, Dear Coltrane* by Michael S. Harper. Copyright © 1970 by Michael S. Harper. Reprinted by permission of the author.

GWEN HARWOOD: "In the Park" from *Selected Poems* by Gwen Harwood (ETT Imprint, Watsons Bay, 1997). Reprinted by permission of the publisher Penguin Australia.

ROBERT HAYDEN: "Frederick Douglass," "Those Winter Sundays," "The Whipping" and "Homage to the Empress of the Blues" from *Collected Poems of Robert Hayden* edited by Frederick Glaysher. Copyright © 1966 by Robert Hayden. Reprinted by permission of Liveright Publishing Corporation.

SEAMUS HEANEY: "Digging," "Mid-Term Break," and "Mother of the Groom" from *Poems 1965–1975* by Seamus Heaney. Copyright © 1980 by Seamus Heaney. Reprinted by permission of Farrar, Straus & Giroux, Inc., and Faber & Faber Ltd. "Punishment" from *North* by Seamus Heaney. Copyright © 1985 by Seamus Heaney. Reprinted by permission of Farrar, Straus & Giroux, Inc., and Faber & Faber Ltd.

ANTHONY HECHT: "The Dover Bitch" from *Collected Earlier Poems* by Anthony Hecht. Copyright © 1990 by Anthony E. Hecht. Reprinted by permission of Alfred A. Knopf, Inc.

JOHN HOLLANDER: "Adam's Task" from *Selected Poetry* by John Hollander. Copyright © 1993 by John Hollander. Reprinted by permission of Alfred A. Knopf, Inc., a division of Random House.

ROBERT HOLLANDER: "You Too? Me Too—Why Not? Soda Pop" from *The Massachusetts Review*. Copyright © 1968 by The Massachusetts Review, Inc. Reprinted by permission of the publisher.

MARGARET HOMANS: excerpt from "A Feminine Tradition" from *Women Writers and Poetic Identity* by Margaret Homans. Copyright © 1980 by Princeton University Press. Reprinted by permission of Princeton University Press.

IRVING HOWE: "The Plath Celebration: A Partial Dissent" from *The Critical Point of Literature and Culture* by Irving Howe (Horizon Press, 1973). Reprinted by permission of the Literary Estate of Irving Howe.

MARIE HOWE: "Practicing" from *What the Living Do* by Mary Howe. Copyright © 1997 by Marie Howe. Used by permission of W. W. Norton & Company, Inc.

ANDREW HUDGINS: "Most of my Nightmares Are Dull" from *The Never Ending* by Andrew Hudgins. Copyright © 1991 by Andrew Hudgins. "Begotten" from *The Glass Hammer* by Andrew Hudgins. Copyright © 1994 by Andrew Hudgins. Reprinted by permission of Houghton Mifflin Company. All rights reserved.

LANGSTON HUGHES: "Harlem (A Dream Deferred)" from *The Panther and the Lash* by Langston Hughes. Copyright © 1951 by Langston Hughes. Reprinted by permission of Alfred A. Knopf, Inc. "The Negro Speaks of Rivers" from *Selected Poems* by Langston Hughes. Copyright © 1926 by Alfred A. Knopf, Inc., and renewed 1954 by Langston Hughes. Reprinted by permission of the publisher. "Theme for English B," "The Weary Blues" and "I, Too" from *Collected Poems* by Langston Hughes. Copyright © 1994 by the Estate of Langston Hughes. Reprinted by permission of Alfred A. Knopf, Inc. "Harlem Literati" from *The Big Sea* by Langston Hughes. Copyright © 1940 by Langston Hughes. Copyright renewed 1968 by Arna Bontemps and George Houston Bass. Reprinted by permission of Hill and Wang, a division of Farrar, Straus, and Giroux, LLC.

ZORA NEALE HURSTON: "How It Feels to Be Colored Me" by Zora Neale Hurston. Copyright © 1928. Used by permission of the Zora Neale Hurston Trust.

RANDALL JARRELL: "The Death of the Ball Turret Gunner" from *The Complete Poems* by Randall Jarrell. Copyright © 1969 by Mrs. Randall Jarrell. Reprinted by permission of Farrar, Straus & Giroux, Inc.

ELIZABETH JENNINGS: "Delay" from *Collected Poems* by Elizabeth Jennings. Reprinted by permission of David Higham Associates, Ltd.

PAULETTE JILES: "Paper Matches" from *Celestial Navigation* by Paulette Jiles. Reprinted by permission of McClelland & Stewart, Ltd.

HELENE JOHNSON: "Sonnet to a Negro in Harlem," Copyright © 2000 by the University of Massachusetts Press, Afterword and Helene Johnson's poems Copyright © 2000 by Abigail McGarth.

JAMES WELDON JOHNSON: "Preface" from *The Book of American Negro Poetry* by James Weldon Johnson, copyright 1922 by Harcourt, Inc., and renewed 1950 by Grace Nail Johnson; reprinted by permission of the publisher.

JUNE JORDAN: "Something Like a Sonnet for Phillis Miracle Wheatley" from *Naming Our Destiny: New and Selected Poems* by June Jordan. Copyright © 1989 by June Jordan. Appears by permission of the publisher, Thunder's Mouth Press, a division of Avalon Publishing Group.

X. J. KENNEDY: "In a Prominent Bar in Secaucus One Day" from *Nude Descending a Staircase* by X. J. Kennedy. Copyright © 1961 by X. J. Kennedy, renewed. Reprinted by permission of Curtis Brown Ltd.

GALWAY KINNELL: "After Making Love We Hear Footsteps" and "Blackberry Eating" from *Three Books* by Galway Kinnell. Copyright © 1993 by Galway Kinnell. Originally published in *Mortal Acts, Mortal Words* (1980). Reprinted by permission of Houghton Mifflin Company. All rights reserved.

AUGUST KLEINZAHLER: "Aubade on East 12th Street" from *Red Sauce, Whiskey, and Snow* by August Kleinzahler. Copyright © 1995 by August Kleinzahler. Reprinted by permission of Farrar, Straus and Giroux, LLC.

ETHERIDGE KNIGHT: "Eastern guard tower" from *The Essential Etheridge Knight* by Etheridge Knight, copyright © 1986. Reprinted by permission of the University of Pittsburgh Press. "Hard Rock Returns to Prison from the Hospital for the Criminal Insane" from *Poems from Prison* by Etheridge Knight. Permission to reprint granted by Broadside Press.

KENNETH KOCH: "Variations on a Theme by William Carlos Williams" from *Thank You and Other Poems* by Kenneth Koch. Copyright © 1962 and 1994 by Kenneth Koch. Reprinted by permission of the Kenneth Koch Literary Estate.

YUSEF KOMUNYAKAA: "Tu Do Street" from *Dien Cai Dau* by Yusef Komunyakaa. Copyright © 1988 by Yusef Komunyakaa. Reprinted by permission of Wesleyan University Press.

JUDITH KROLL: "Rituals of Exorcism: 'Daddy' " from *Chapters in a Mythology: The Poetry of Sylvia Plath* by Judith Kroll (HarperCollins, 1976). Copyright © 1997 by Judith Kroll.

MAXINE KUMIN: "Woodchucks" from *Selected Poems 1960–1990* by Maxine Kumin. Copyright © 1972 by Maxine Kumin. Reprinted by permission of W. W. Norton & Company, Inc.

PHILIP LARKIN: "Church Going" from *The Less Deceived* by Philip Larkin. Reprinted by permission of The Marvell Press, England and Australia.

D. H. LAWRENCE: "I Am Like a Rose" from *The Complete Poems of D. H. Lawrence*. Copyright © 1964, 1971 by the Estate of D. H. Lawrence, renewed by the Executors of the Estate of Frieda Lawrence Ravagli. Used by permission of Laurence Pollinger Limited and the Estate of Frieda Lawrence Ravagli.

IRVING LAYTON: "Street Funeral" from *Collected Poems of Irving Layton* by Irving Layton. Used by permission of McClelland & Stewart, Inc., The Canadian Publishers.

LI-YOUNG LEE: "Persimmons" from *Rose* by Li-Young Lee. Copyright © 1986 by Li-Young Lee. Reprinted by permission of BOA Editions Ltd.

DENISE LEVERTOV: "Wedding Ring" from *Life in the Forest* by Denise Levertov. Copyright © 1978 by Denise Levertov. Reprinted by permission of New Directions Publishing Corp.

ALAIN LOCKE: "The New Negro" reprinted with the permission of Scribner, an imprint of Simon and Schuster Adult Publishing Group, from *The New Negro: Voices of the Harlem Renaissance* by Alain Locke. Copyright © 1925 by Albert & Charles Boni, Inc.

AUDRE LORDE: "Hanging Fire" from *The Black Unicorn* by Audre Lorde. Copyright © 1978 by Audre Lorde. Reprinted by permission of W. W. Norton & Company, Inc.

ROBERT LOWELL: "Skunk Hour" from *Life Studies* by Robert Lowell. Copyright © 2003 by Harriet Lowell and Sheridan Lowell. Reprinted by permission of Farrar, Straus & Giroux, Inc.

ARCHIBALD MACLEISH: "Ars Poetica" from *Collected Poems 1917–1982* by Archibald MacLeish. Copyright © 1985 by the Estate of Archibald MacLeish. Reprinted by permission of Houghton Mifflin Company. All rights reserved.

CLAUDE MCKAY: "The White House," "Harlem Dancer," "Harlem Shadows," "If we must die," "The Tropics in New York," and "Dawn in New York" courtesy of the Literary Representative of the Works of Claude McKay, Schomburg Center for Research in Black Culture, The New York Public Library, Astor, Lenox and Tilden Foundations.

ROGER MCGOUGH: "Here I Am" from *Melting into the Foreground*. Reprinted by permission of PFD on behalf of Roger McGough, © 1986, Roger McGough.

JAMES MERRILL: "Watching the Dance" and "body" from *Nights and Days* by James Merrill. Copyright © 1966, 1992 by James Merrill. *Selected Poems 1946–1985* by James Merrill, published by Alfred A. Knopf in 1992. Reprinted with permission of Alfred A. Knopf, Inc.

EDNA ST. VINCENT MILLAY: "I shall forget you presently," "I, being born a woman and distressed," and "What lips my lips have kissed" by Edna St. Vincent Millay. From *Collected Poems*, HarperCollins. Copyright © 1922, 1923, 1931, 1951, 1958 by Edna St. Vincent Millay and Norma Millay Ellis. "Sonnet XXVI [Women have loved before as I love now]" from *Fatal Interview* by Edna St. Vincent Millay. From *Collected Poems*, HarperCollins. Copyright © 1922, 1931, 1950, 1958 by Edna St. Vincent Millay and Norma Millay Ellis. All rights reserved. Reprinted by permission of Elizabeth Barnett, literary executor.

EARL MINER: "The still old pond" from *Japanese Linked Poetry* by Earl Miner. Copyright © 1979 by Earl Miner. Reprinted by permission of the author.

MARIANNE MOORE: "Love in America?" from *The Complete Poems of Marianne Moore* by Marianne Moore. Copyright © 1981 by Clive E. Driver, Literary Executor of the Estate of Marianne Moore. Used by permission of Viking Penguin, a division of Penguin Books USA, Inc. "Poetry" from *The Complete Poems of Marianne Moore*. Copyright © 1935 by Marianne Moore; copyright renewed © 1963 by Marianne Moore and T. S. Eliot. Reprinted with the permission of Simon & Schuster.

PAT MORA: "Gentle Communion" from *Communion* (Houston: Arte Publico Press–University of Houston, 1991) by Pat Mora. "La Migra" from *Agua Santa: Holy Water* by Pat Mora. Copyright © 1995 by Pat Mora. Reprinted by permission of Beacon Press, Boston. "Sonrisas" from *Borders* by Pat Mora (Houston: Arte Publico Press–University of Houston, 1986). Reprinted with permission from the publisher. "Elena" by Pat Mora is reprinted with permission from the publisher of Chants (Houston: Arte Publico Press–University of Houston, 1985).

PAUL MULDOON: "Milkweed and Monarch" from *Poems 1968–1988* by Paul Muldoon. Copyright © 2001 by Paul Muldoon. Reprinted by permission of Farrar, Straus and Giroux, LLC.

HOWARD NEMEROV: "Boom!," "The Goose Fish," "The Town Dump," "The Vacuum," and "A Way of Life" from *The Collected Poems of Howard Nemerov*. Copyright © 1977 by Howard Nemerov. Reprinted by permission of Margaret Nemerov.

SHARON OLDS: "Sex Without Love" and "The Victims" from *The Dead and the Living* by Sharon Olds. Copyright © 1983 by Sharon Olds. Reprinted by permission of Alfred A. Knopf, Inc. "Leningrad Cemetery, Winter of 1941" from *The New Yorker*, December 31, 1979. Copyright © 1979 by The New Yorker Magazine, Inc. Reprinted by permission of the publisher.

MARY OLIVER: "Singapore" from *House of Light* by Mary Oliver. Copyright © 1990 by Mary Oliver. Reprinted by permission of Beacon Press, Boston.

SIMON ORTIZ: "My Father's Song." Reprinted by the permission of the author

WILFRED OWEN: "Dulce et Decorum Est" and "Disabled" from *The Collected Poems of Wilfred Owen*, copyright © 1963 by Chatto & Windus, Ltd. Reprinted by permission of New Directions Publishing Corp.

DOROTHY PARKER: "A Certain Lady" and "One Perfect Rose" copyright © 1926, renewed 1954 by Dorothy Parker from *The Portable Dorothy Parker* by Dorothy Parker. Copyright © 1928, renewed 1956 by Dorothy Parker. Used by permission of Viking Penguin, a division of Penguin Putnam, Inc.

LINDA PASTAN: "love poem" and "To a Daughter Leaving Home" from *The Imperfect Paradise* by Linda Pastan. Copyright © 1988 by Linda Pastan. "Marks" from *PM / AM: New and Selected Poems* by Linda Pastan. Copyright © 1978 by Linda Pastan. Reprinted by permission of W. W. Norton & Company, Inc.

BOB PERELMAN: "The Masque of Rhyme" from *The Future of Memory*, published by Roof Books, NY, 1998. Reprinted with the permission of the author.

WILLIE PERDOMO: "123rd Street Rap" from *Where a Nickel Costs a Dime* by Willie Perdomo. Copyright © 1996 by Willie Perdomo. Used by permission of W. W. Norton & Company, Inc.

MARGE PIERCY: "Barbie Doll" and "What's That Smell in the Kitchen?" from *Circles on the Water* by Marge Piercy. Copyright © 1982 by Marge Piercy. Reprinted by permission of Alfred A. Knopf, Inc.

SYLVIA PLATH: "Point Shirley" from *The Colossus and Other Poems* by Sylvia Plath. Copyright © 1959 by Sylvia Plath. Reprinted by permission of Alfred A. Knopf, Inc. "Black Rook in Rainy Weather" (all lines) from *Crossing the Water* by Sylvia Plath. Copyright © 1960 by Ted Hughes. "Morning Song" (all lines) copyright © 1961 by Ted Hughes, copyright renewed; "Daddy" (all lines) copyright © 1963 by Ted Hughes; and "Lady Lazarus" (all lines) copyright © 1963 by Ted Hughes from *Ariel* by Sylvia Plath. Copyright © 1963 by Ted Hughes, copyright renewed. "Barren Women" from *The Collected Poems of Sylvia Plath* edited by Ted Hughes. Copyright © 1960, 1965, 1971, 1981 by the Estate of Sylvia Plath. Editorial material copyright © 1981 by Ted Hughes. Reprinted by permission of HarperCollins Publishers, Inc., and Faber & Faber Ltd.

EZRA POUND: "In a Station of the Metro," "The River-Merchant's Wife: A Letter," and "A Virginal" from *Personae* by Ezra Pound. Copyright © 1926 by Ezra Pound. Reprinted by permission of New Directions Publishing Corp.

JAROLD RAMSEY: "The Tally Stick." Reprinted by permission of the author.

DUDLEY RANDALL: "Ballad of Birmingham" from *Poem Counter Poem* by Dudley Randall (Michigan: Broadside Press, 1969). Reprinted by permission of the publisher.

JOHN CROWE RANSOM: "Bells for John Whiteside's Daughter" from *Selected Poems* by John Crowe Ransom. Copyright © 1924, 1927 by Alfred A. Knopf, Inc., and renewed 1952, 1955 by John Crowe Ransom. Used by permission of Alfred A. Knopf, a division of Random House, Inc.

ISHMAEL REED: "beware: do not read this poem" Copyright © 1972 by Ishmael Reed. Reprinted by permission of Ishmael Reed.

ADRIENNE RICH: "At a Bach Concert," "Aunt Jennifer's Tigers," "Dialogue," "Diving into the Wreck," "For the Record," "Living in Sin," "Planetarium," "Power," "Snapshots of a Daughter-in-Law," "Storm Warnings," and "Two Songs" from *The Fact of a Doorframe, Poems Selected and New 1950–1984* by Adrienne Rich. Copyright © 1984 by Adrienne Rich. Copyright © 1975, 1978 by W. W. Norton & Company, Inc. Copyright © 1981 by Adrienne Rich. Poem 3 of "Contradictions: Tracking Poems" [my mouth hovers across your breasts] from *Your Native Land, Your Life: Poems* by Adrienne Rich. Copyright © 1986 by Adrienne Rich. "Four: history" from "Inscriptions" from *Dark Fields of the Republic: Poems 1991–1995* by Adrienne Rich. Copyright © 1995 by Adrienne Rich. Excerpts from "A Communal Poetry" and "How Does a Poet Put Bread on the Table?" from *What Is Found There: Notebooks on Poetry and Politics* by Adrienne Rich. Copyright © 1993 by Adrienne Rich. Excerpt from "When We Dead Awaken: Writing as Re-Vision" from *On Lies, Secrets, and Silence: Selected Prose 1966–1978* by Adrienne Rich. Copyright © 1979 by W. W. Norton & Company, Inc. "Why I Refused the National Medal for the Arts" from *Arts of the Possible: Essays and Conversations* by Adrienne Rich. Copyright © 2001 by Adrienne Rich. "Modotti" from *Midnight Salvage: Poems 1995–1998* by Adrienne Rich. Copyright © 1999 by Adrienne Rich. All reprinted by permission of the author and W. W. Norton & Company, Inc.

E. E. RICH: from *Hudson's Bay Copy Booke of Letters Commissions Instructions Outwards 1688–1696*. Reprinted with the permission of Hudson's Bay Company Archives, Archives of Manitoba.

ALBERTO ALVARO RÍOS: "Advice to a First Cousin" First published in *Five Indiscretions: A Book of Poems* (Sheep Meadow Press). Copyright 1985 by Alberto Rios. Reprinted by permission of author.

THEODORE ROETHKE: "I Knew a Woman," copyright © 1953 by Theodore Roethke; "My Papa's Waltz," copyright © 1942 by Hearst Magazines, Inc.; and "The Waking," copyright © 1953 by Theodore Roethke; from *The Collected Poems of Theodore Roethke* by Theodore Roethke. Used by permission of Doubleday, a division of Random House, Inc.

LIZ ROSENBERG: "Married Love" from *The Fire Music* by Liz Rosenberg. Copyright © 1986. Reprinted by permission of the author. "The Silence of Women" from *Children of Paradise* by Liz Rosenberg. Copyright © 1994. Reprinted by permission of the University of Pittsburgh Press.

MARY JO SALTER: "Welcome to Hiroshima" from *Henry Purcell in Japan* by Mary Jo Salter. Copyright © 1984 by Mary Jo Salter. Reprinted by permission of Alfred A. Knopf, Inc.

SEIFU: "The faces of dolls" from *One Hundred Famous Haiku*, selected and translated by Daniel Buchanan. Reprinted by permission of Japan Publications, Inc.

OLIVE SENIOR: "Ancestral Poem" from *Talking of Trees*. Copyright © 1985 by Olive Senior. Reprinted by permission of author.

ANNE SEXTON: "The Fury of Overshoes" from *The Death Notebooks*. Copyright © 1974 by Anne Sexton. Reprinted by permission of Houghton Mifflin. All rights reserved.

DESMOND SKIRROW: "Ode on a Grecian Urn Summarized." We have made diligent efforts to contact the copyright holder to obtain permission to reprint this selection. If you have information that would help us, please write to W. W. Norton & Company, Inc., 500 Fifth Avenue, New York, NY 10110.

STEVIE SMITH: "The Jungle Husband" from *Collected Poems of Stevie Smith* by Stevie Smith. Copyright © 1972 by Stevie Smith. Reprinted by permission of the New Directions Publishing Corp.

W. D. SNODGRASS: "Leaving the Motel." Reprinted by permission of the author.

CATHY SONG: "Heaven" from *Frameless Windows, Squares of Light: Poems* by Cathy Song. Copyright © 1988 by Cathy Song. Reprinted by permission of W. W. Norton & Company, Inc.

GEORGE STEINER: "Dying Is an Art" from *Language and Silence* by George Steiner. Copyright © 1958, 1960, 1961, 1962, 1963, 1964, 1965, 1966, 1967 by George Steiner. Reprinted by permission of Georges Borchardt, Inc., for the author.

WALLACE STEVENS: "Anecdote of the Jar," "The Emperor of Ice Cream," and "Sunday Morning" from *Collected Poems* by Wallace Stevens. Copyright © 1923 and renewed 1951 by Wallace Stevens. "The Idea of Order at Key West" from *Collected Poems* by Wallace Stevens. Copyright © 1936 by Wallace Stevens and renewed 1964 by Holly Stevens. Reprinted by permission of Alfred A. Knopf, Inc.

DYLAN THOMAS: "Do Not Go Gentle into That Good Night," "Fern Hill," from *The Poems of Dylan Thomas* by Dylan Thomas. Copyright © 1945 by the Trustees for the Copyrights of Dylan Thomas. Reprinted by permission of David Higham Associates and New Directions Publishing Corp.

EARL E. THORPE: "Africa in the Thought of Negro Americans" from *The Negro History Bulletin*. Property of the Association for the Study of African American Life and History, Inc.

DANIEL TOBIN: "The Clock" from *Where the World Is Made*, © 1999 by Daniel Tobin. Reprinted by permission of the University of New England Press.

MONA VAN DUYN: "What the Motorcycle Said" from *If It Be Not I* by Mona Van Duyn. Copyright © 1973 by Mona Van Duyn. Reprinted by permission of Alfred A. Knopf, Inc., a division of Random House, Inc.

MIRIAM WADDINGTON: "Ulysses Embroidered" from *The Last Landscape* by Miriam Waddington. Copyright © 1992 by Miriam Waddington. Reprinted by permission Jonathon Waddington.

DAVID WAGONER: "My Father's Garden" from *Traveling Light: Collected and New Poems* by David Wagoner. Copyright © 1999 by David Wagoner. Used by permission of the poet.

DEREK WALCOTT: "A Far Cry from Africa" and "Midsummer" from *Collected Poems 1948–1984* by Derek Walcott. Copyright © 1986 by Derek Walcott. Reprinted by permission of Faber and Faber Ltd. and Farrar, Straus & Giroux, Inc. "A Far Cry from Africa" and "Midsummer" from *The Castaway* by Derek Walcott, published by Jonathan Cape. Used by permission of The Random House Group Limited.

RICHARD WILBUR: "The Beautiful Changes" from *The Beautiful Changes and Other Poems* by Richard Wilbur. Copyright © 1947 and renewed 1975 by Richard Wilbur. "Love Calls Us to the Things of This World" from *Things Of This World* by Richard Wilbur. Copyright © 1956 and renewed 1984 by Richard Wilbur. Reprinted by permission of Harcourt Brace & Company.

C. K. WILLIAMS: "Alzheimer's Wife" from *Selected Poems* by C. K. Williams. Copyright © 1994 by C. K. Williams. Reprinted by permission of Farrar, Straus, & Giroux, Inc.

MILLER WILLIAMS: "Thinking about Bill, Dead of AIDS" from *Living on the Surface: New and Selected Poems* by Miller Williams. Copyright © 1989 by Miller Williams. Reprinted by permission of Louisiana State University Press.

WILLIAM CARLOS WILLIAMS: "The Red Wheelbarrow" and "This Is Just to Say" from *Collected Poems 1909–1939, Volume I.* Copyright © 1938 by New Directions Publishing Corp. "Raleigh Was Right" and "The Dance" from *Collected Poems 1939–1962, Volume II.* Copyright © 1944, 1953 by William Carlos Williams. Reprinted by permission of New Directions Publishing Corp.

YVOR WINTERS: "At the San Francisco Airport" from *The Selected Poems of Yvor Winters* (1999). Reprinted with the permission of Ohio University Press/Swallow Press, Athens, Ohio.

RICHARD WRIGHT: "In the falling snow" from *The Richard Wright Reader.* Copyright © 1978 by Richard Wright. Reprinted by permission of John Hawkins & Associates, Inc.

W. B. YEATS: "Among School Children," "Leda and the Swan," and "Sailing to Byzantium" from *The Collected Works of W. B. Yeats, Volume 1: The Poems.* Revised and edited by Richard J. Finneran. Copyright © 1928 by Macmillan Publishing Company; copyright renewed © 1956 by Bertha Georgie Yeats. Reprinted with the permission of Simon & Schuster and A. P. Watt Ltd. on the behalf of Michael Yeats. "Byzantium" from *The Collected Works of W. B. Yeats, Volume 1: The Poems.* Revised and edited by Richard J. Finneran. Copyright © 1933 by Macmillan Publishing Company; copyright renewed © 1961 by Bertha Georgie Yeats. Reprinted with the permission of Simon & Schuster and A. P. Watt Ltd. on the behalf of Anne and Michael Yeats. "A Last Confession" from *The Collected Works of W. B. Yeats, Volume 1: The Poems.* Revised and edited by Richard J. Finneran. Copyright © 1933 by Macmillan Publishing Company, renewed 1961 by Bertha Georgie Yeats. Reprinted with the permission of Simon & Schuster. "The Second Coming" and "Easter, 1916" from *The Collected Poems of W. B. Yeats, Revised Second Edition,* edited by Richard J. Finneran. Copyright © 1924 by Macmillian Publishing Company, renewed 1952 by Bertha Georgie Yeats.

## DRAMA

ROBERT BLAUNER: "Internal Colonialism and Ghetto Revolt," copyright © 1969 The Society for the Study of Social Problems.

MARY WHITLOCK BLUNDELL: excerpt from *Helping Friends and Harming Enemies: A Study in Sophocles and Greek Ethics* by Mary Whitlock Blundell. Copyright © 1991 by Mary Whitlock Blundell. Reprinted with permission of Cambridge University Press.

MAURICE BOWRA: excerpt from *Sophoclean Tragedy* (1944). Reprinted by permission of Oxford University Press.

REBECCA W. BUSHNELL: excerpt from *Prophesying Tragedy: Sign and Voice in Sophocles' Theban Plays.* Copyright © 1990 by Cornell University. Used by permission of publisher, Cornell University Press.

STOKELY CARMICHAEL AND CHARLES HAMILTON: from *Black Power* by Stokely Carmichael and Charles Hamilton, copyright © 1967 by Stokely Carmichael and Charles Hamilton. Used by permission of Random House, Inc.

MARGARET EDSON: entire text of *Wit* by Margaret Edson. Copyright © 1993, 1999 by Margaret

Edson. Reprinted by permission of Faber & Faber, an affiliate of Farrar, Straus and Giroux, LLC.
LORRAINE HANSBERRY: *A Raisin in the Sun* from *A Raisin in the Sun* by Lorraine Hansberry. Copyright © 1958 by Robert Nemiroff, as an unpublished work. Copyright © 1959, 1966, 1984 by Robert Nemiroff. Reprinted by permission of Random House, Inc.
HENRIK IBSEN: *A Doll House* from *The Complete Major Prose Plays of Henrik Ibsen* by Henrik Ibsen, translated by Rolf Fjelde. Copyright © 1965, 1970, 1978 by Rolf Fjelde. Used by permission of Penguin Putnam, Inc.
BERNARD KNOX: from the Introduction to *Three Theban Plays*. Copyright © 1982 by Bernard Knox. From *Three Theban Plays* by Sophocles, translated by Robert Fagles, translation copyright © 1982 by Robert Fagles. Used by permission of Viking Penguin, a division of Penguin Books USA, Inc.
ARTHUR MILLER: *Death of a Salesman* from *Death of a Salesman* by Arthur Miller. Copyright © 1949, renewed 1977 by Arthur Miller. Used by permission of Viking Penguin, a division of Penguin Books USA, Inc.
MARTHA C. NUSSBAUM: excerpt from *The Fragility of Goodness: Luck and Ethics in Greek Tragedy and Philosophy*, Second Edition, by Martha C. Nussbaum. Copyright © 1986 by Cambridge University Press. Copyright © 2001 by Martha C. Nussbaum. Reprinted with permission of Cambridge University Press.
BERNARD SHAW: *Pygmalion* from *The Collected Plays of George Bernard Shaw* by Bernard Shaw. Copyright © 1913, 1914, 1916, 1930, 1941 by George Bernard Shaw. Copyright © 1957 by the Public Trustee as Executor of the Estate of Bernard Shaw. Reprinted by permission of the Society of Authors on behalf of George Bernard Shaw.
SOPHOCLES: *Oedipus the King* and *Antigone* from *Complete Greek Tragedies*, translated by D. Grene, edited by Grene and Lattimore. Copyright © 1942 by the University of Chicago. Reprinted by permission of The University of Chicago Press.
WOLE SOYINKA: *Death and the King's Horseman*. Copyright © 1975, 2003 by Wole Soyinka. Reprinted by permission of Melanie Jackson Agency, LLC. Used by permission of W.W. Norton & Company.
TOM STOPPARD: *The Real Inspector Hound*. Copyright © 1968 by Tom Stoppard. Used by permission of Grove/Atlantic, Inc.
PAULA VOGEL: *How I Learned to Drive* from *Mammary Plays* by Paula Vogel. Copyright © 1998 by Paula Vogel. Published by Theatre Communications Group.
TENNESSEE WILLIAMS: *A Streetcar Named Desire* by Tennessee Williams. Copyright © 1947 by Tennessee Williams. CAUTION: Professionals and amateurs are hereby warned that *A Streetcar Named Desire*, being fully protected under the copyright laws of the United States of America, the British Empire including the Dominion of Canada, and all other countries of the Copyright Union, is subject to royalty. All rights, including professional, amateur, motion picture, recitation, lecturing, public reading, radio and television broadcasting, and the rights of translation into foreign languages are strictly reserved. Particular emphasis is laid on the question of readings, permission for which must be secured from the author's agent, Luis Sanjurjo, c / o International Creative Management, 40 West 57th Street, New York, NY 10019. Inquiries concerning the amateur acting rights of *A Streetcar Named Desire* should be directed to the Dramatists' Play Service, Inc., 440 Park Avenue South, New York, NY 10016, without whose permission in writing no amateur performance may be given.
AUGUST WILSON: *The Piano Lesson* by August Wilson. Copyright © 1988, 1990 by August Wilson. Used by permission of Dutton Signet, a division of Penguin Putnam, Inc.

# Illustrations

### FICTION

D. H. Lawrence as a young schoolmaster. University of Nottingham Library, D. H. Lawrence Collection. Reprinted by permission of the University of Nottingham.

Flannery O'Connor. Photograph by Ralph Morrissey. Reprinted by the courtesy of the Morrissey Collection and the Photographic Archives, Vanderbilt University, Nashville, Tennessee.

Lawrence's hometown—Eastwood, ca. 1911. University of Nottingham Library, D. H. Lawrence Collection. Reprinted by permission of the University of Nottingham.

A collier undercutting coal at Brinsley Colliery. Courtesy of Nottinghamshire County Library Service.

D. H. Lawrence with his wife, Frieda Lawrence. University of Nottingham Library, D. H. Lawrence Collection. Reprinted by permission of the University of Nottingham.

Flannery O'Connor alongside self-portrait with peacock. Bettmann/Corbis.

The Fitzgeralds celebrate Christmas. Brown Brothers.

Teaching Old Dogs New Tricks. Cover of *Life* magazine, February 18, 1926. The Granger Collection, New York.

Stockmarket Collapse. Aerial view of Wall Street. Bettmann/Corbis.

Wall Street investor tries to sell a car. Bettmann/Corbis.

Illegal beer being poured away during Prohibition. Getty Images.

## POETRY

John Keats. Portrait by Joseph Severn. Reprinted by courtesy of the National Portrait Gallery, London.

George Keats. Sketch by Joseph Severn. Photographed by Chris Warde Jones. Reprinted with the kind permission of the Keats-Shelley Memorial House, Rome.

Tom Keats. Sketch by Joseph Severn. Reprinted with the kind permission of the Keats-Shelley Memorial House, Rome.

John Hamilton Reynolds. Miniature by Joseph Severn. Reprinted by permission of the Corporation of London, Keats House.

Adrienne Rich in the classroom, circa 1978. © Lynda Koolish. Reprinted by permission of the photographer.

Adrienne Rich in the 1990s. © Jason Langer, photographer. Reprinted by permission.

Cotton Club exterior. Underwood & Underwood/Corbis.

Harlem cabaret. Bettmann/Corbis.

Negro silent parade, 1917. Bettmann/Corbis.

First issue of *Fire!!* Yale Collection of American Literature, Beinecke Rare Book and Manuscript Library.

Claude McKay (older). Carl Van Vechten/Library of Congress.

Alain Locke. National Portrait Gallery, Smithsonian Institution/Art Resource, NY.

Langston Hughes, circa 1925, portrait by Winold Reiss. National Portrait Gallery, Smithsonian Institution/Art Resource, NY.

Countee Cullen, circa 1935. Bettmann/Corbis.

Vendor selling books and pamphlets from a cart on 125th street in Harlem, June 1943. Library of Congress.

Dark Tower Salon. Donna Mussenden VanDerZee.

Carl Van Vechten, 1926. E. O. Hoppé/Corbis.

Bessie Smith. Bettmann/Corbis.

Arna Bontemps. Carl Van Vechten/ Library of Congress.

Angelina Weld Grimke, circa 1905. Moorland-Spingarn Research Center, Howard University.

*Weary Blues* cover. Yale Collection of American Literature, Beinecke Rare Book and Manuscript Library. Reproduced by permission of Alfred A. Knopf Publishers, Inc.

A pen-and-ink illustration by Aaron Douglas made specifically to accompany Hughes's "The Negro Speaks of Rivers." Walter O. Evans Collection.

James Weldon Johnson, circa 1920. Corbis.

The cover of the first edition of McKay's *Home to Harlem*. Reprinted by permission of HarperCollins Publishers, Inc. Yale Collection of American Literature, Beinecke Rare Book and Manuscript Library.

Sylvia Plath. Mortimer Rare Book Room, Smith College, © Estate of Sylvia Plath.

Sylvia Plath's father, Otto Plath. Mortimer Rare Book Room, Smith College, © Estate of Sylvia Plath.

## DRAMA

William Shakespeare. Droeshout engraving. Chris Hellier/Corbis.

Shakespeare's birthplace. Michael Maslan Historic Photographs/Corbis.

The Globe Theatre. Bettmann/Corbis.

Bottom from *Midsummer Night's Dream*. Nineteenth-century print. Corbis.

Sir Laurence Olivier in *Hamlet*. Bettmann/Corbis.

*Sophocles*. Greek playwright of the fifth century B.C.E., head-and-shoulders sculpture. Bettmann/Corbis.

Production of *Antigone* (The New York Shakespeare Festival, 1982). Photo by Martha Swope. Reprinted by permission of the photographer.

Lorraine Hansberry. Bettman/Corbis.

Jim Crow segregation. Bettmann/Corbis.

Regal Theater, Chicago. Bettmann/Corbis.

Sleeping children in Chicago. Library of Congress.

Martin Luther King Jr. arrest. AP/Wide World Photos.

Zora Neale Hurston. Carl Van Vechten/ Library of Congress.

SNCC poster, "Black Power." AP/Wide World Photos.

Black GIs, Nazi prisoners. National Archives.

Kenyatta. Bettmann/Corbis.

Colonials in Nigeria. Hulton-Deutsch Collection/Corbis.

Soyinka portrait. Pelletier Micheline/Corbis.

Carved wood panel (Annunciation of the Angel to Mary) by Lamidi Olonade Fakeye. National Archives.

*A Raisin in the Sun.* Bettmann/Corbis.

*Death and the King's Horseman.* © The Washington Post. Photograph by Harry Naltchayan. Reprinted with permission.

## AUTHOR BIOGRAPHIES

### Fiction

Sherman Alexie. Christopher Felver/Corbis.

Margaret Atwood. Christopher Felver/Corbis.

James Baldwin. Sophie Bassouls/Corbis.

Toni Cade Bambara. © Joyce Middler, Courtesy of Vintage/Random House.

Andrea Barrett. Courtesy of Barry Goldstein.

Ann Beattie. Courtesy of Simon & Schuster.

Ambrose Bierce. Bettmann/Corbis.

Jorge Luis Borges. Bettmann/Corbis.

Linda Brewer. Courtesy of the author.

A. S. Byatt. Sophie Bassouls/Corbis.

Peter Carey. Reuters/Corbis.

Angela Carter. Mike Laye/Corbis.

Raymond Carver. Sophie Bassouls/Corbis.

Michael Chabon. Lisa O'Connor/Corbis.

John Cheever. Bettmann/Corbis.

Anton Chekhov. Archivo Iconografico, S.A./Corbis.

Kate Chopin. The Granger Collection, New York.

Joseph Conrad. Corbis.

Stephen Crane. Bettmann/Corbis.

Edwidge Danticat. AP/World Wide Photos.

Richard Dokey. Courtesy of University of Missouri Press.

Ralph Ellison. Bettmann/Corbis.

Louise Erdrich. AP/World Wide Photos.

William Faulkner. Bettmann/Corbis.

F. Scott Fitzgerald. Bettmann/Corbis.

Gabriel García Márquez. Colita/Corbis.

Charlotte Perkins Gilman. Corbis.

Susan Glaspell. AP/World Wide Photos.

Nadine Gordimer. Sophie Bassouls/Corbis.

Ha Jin. Reuters/Corbis.

Nathaniel Hawthorne. Corbis.

Ernest Hemingway. John Springer Collection/Corbis.

Henry James. Bettmann/Corbis.

James Joyce. Hulton-Deutsch Collection/Corbis.

Franz Kafka. Bettmann/Corbis.

Yasunari Kawabata. Bettmann/Corbis.

Jamaica Kincaid. Jeremy Bembara/Corbis.

Jhumpa Lahiri. Nancy Kaszerman/Zuma/Corbis.

D. H. Lawrence. University of Nottingham Library, D. H. Lawrence Collection. Reprinted by permission of the University of Nottingham.

Ursula K. Le Guin. Bettmann/Corbis.

Doris Lessing. Christopher Felver/Corbis.

Katherine Mansfield. Bettmann/Corbis.

Bobbie Ann Mason. Courtesy of Viking/Penguin.

Guy de Maupassant. Bettmann/Corbis.

Herman Melville. Bettmann/Corbis.

Lorrie Moore. Courtesy of Vintage/Anchor. Photo by Joyce Ravid.

Toni Morrison. Christopher Felver/Corbis.

Bharati Mukherjee. Courtesy of Hyperion.

Alice Munro. AP/Wide World Photos.

Joyce Carol Oates. Christopher Felver/Corbis.

Flannery O'Connor. Photo by Ralph Morrissey. Reprinted by the courtesy of the Morrissey Collection and the photographic archives, Vanderbilt University, Nashville, Tennessee.

Grace Paley. Christopher Felver/Corbis.

Edgar Allan Poe. Bettmann/Corbis.

Katherine Anne Porter. Bettmann/Corbis.

Salmon Rushdie. Christopher Felver/Corbis.

Carol Shields. Christopher J. Morris/Corbis.

Amy Tan. Christopher Felver/Corbis.

Eudora Welty. Bettmann/Corbis.

Edith Wharton. Bettmann/Corbis.

William Carlos Williams. Pach Brothers/Corbis.

## Poetry

W. H. Auden. Corbis.

Bashō. Asian Art & Archaeology, Inc./Corbis.

Earle Birney. Courtesy of Wailan Low.

Elizabeth Bishop. Bettmann/Corbis.

William Blake. Bettmann/Corbis.

Gwendolyn Brooks. AP/Wide World Photos.

Elizabeth Barrett Browning. Bettmann/Corbis.

Robert Browning. Bettmann/Corbis.

Robert Burns. Bettmann/Corbis.

Samuel Taylor Coleridge. Bettmann/Corbis.

Billy Collins. AP/Wide World Photos.

Wendy Cope. Photograph by Steve McGarrity-Alderice. Courtesy of Faber & Faber.

Countee Cullen. Bettmann/Corbis.

E. E. Cummings. Library of Congress.

James Dickey. Oscar White/Corbis.

Emily Dickinson. Bettmann/Corbis.

John Donne. Bettmann/Corbis.

Rita Dove. Fred Viebahn.

Paul Laurence Dunbar. Corbis.

Stephen Dunn. Matt Valentine.

T. S. Eliot. Hulton-Deutsch Collection/Corbis.

James A. Emanuel. Godelieve Simons.

David Ferry. Stephen Ferry.

Robert Frost. E. O. Hoppé/Corbis.

Allen Ginsberg. AP/Wide World Photos.

Angelina Grimke. Moorland-Spingarn Research Center, Howard University.

Thomas Gunn. Christopher Felver/Corbis.

Thomas Hardy. Bettmann/Corbis.

Seamus Heaney. Christopher Felver/Corbis.

George Herbert. Michael Nicholson/Corbis.

Robert Herrick. Hulton-Deutsch Collection/Corbis.

Gerard Manley Hopkins. The Granger Collection, New York.

Andrew Hudgins. Photograph by Jo McCulty. Courtesy of Overlook Press.

Ben Jonson. Corbis.

John Keats. Bettmann/Corbis.

Galway Kinnell. Christopher Felver/Corbis.

Etheridge Knight. Photograph by Judy Ray. American Poetry Review Collection, University of Pennsylvania.

Andrew Marvell. Mary Evans Picture Library.

Claude McKay. Corbis.

James Merrill. Oscar White/Corbis.

Edna St. Vincent Millay. Underwood & Underwood/Corbis.

John Milton. Stefano Bianchetti/Corbis.

Marianne Moore. Bettmann/Corbis.

## PERMISSIONS ACKNOWLEDGMENTS: AUDIO CDS  A27

Pat Mora. Cheron Bayna.

Howard Nemerov. Bettmann/Corbis.

Sharon Olds. Christopher Felver/Corbis.

Wilfred Owen. Hulton-Deutsch Collection/Corbis.

Dorothy Parker. AP/Wide World Photos.

Linda Pastan. Margaretta K. Mitchell.

Marge Piercy. Ira Wood.

Sylvia Plath. Courtesy of the Sylvia Plath Collection, Mortimer Rare Book Room, Smith College.

Ezra Pound. E. O. Hoppé/Corbis.

Adrienne Rich. Lilian Kemp.

Theodore Roethke. Bettmann/Corbis.

Liz Rosenberg. Courtesy of the author.

Christina Rossetti. Bettmann/Corbis.

William Shakespeare. Droeshout engraving. Chris Hellier/Corbis.

Wallace Stevens. Bettmann/Corbis.

Lord Alfred Tennyson. Bettmann/Corbis.

Dylan Thomas. Hulton-Deutsch Collection/Corbis.

Derek Walcott. Christopher Felver/Corbis.

Walt Whitman. Warder Collection.

Richard Wilbur. Oscar White/Corbis.

William Wordsworth. Hulton-Deutsch Collection/Corbis.

William Butler Yeats. Bettmann/Corbis.

### Drama

Anton Chekhov. Archivo Iconografico, S.A./Corbis.

Margaret Edson. Photograph by Dave Smiley. Courtesy of Fifi Oscard Agency.

Susan Glaspell. AP/Wide World Photos.

Lorraine Hansberry. Bettmann/Corbis.

Henrik Ibsen. Bettmann/Corbis.

Arthur Miller. Christopher Felver/Corbis.

William Shakespeare. Droeshout engraving. Chris Hellier/Corbis.

Bernard Shaw. Bettmann/Corbis.

Sophocles. Bettmann/Corbis.

Wole Soyinka. Micheline Pelletier/Corbis.

Tom Stoppard. Christopher Felver/Corbis.

Paula Vogel. © Carol Rosegg. Courtesy of William Morris Agency.

Oscar Wilde. Bettmann/Corbis.

Tennessee Williams. Bettmann.Corbis.

August Wilson. AP/Wide World Photos.

## *Audio CDs*

© 2001 W. W. Norton & Company, Inc.

Maya Angelou "Africa." Copyright © 1996 by Random House, Inc. Copyright © 1975 by Maya Angelou, from *Oh Pray My Wings Are Gonna Fit Me Well* by Maya Angelou. Used by permission of Random House Audio Publishing Group, a division of Random House, Inc.

W. H. Auden "Musée des Beaux Arts." Used by permission of Curtis Brown Ltd. Copyright © 1940 by W. H. Auden, renewed. All rights reserved.

Elizabeth Bishop "Casabianca." From *The Complete Poems 1927–1979* by Elizabeth Bishop. Copyright © 1979, 1983 by Alice Helen Methfessel.

William Blake "London." Read by Jon Stallworthy, Oxford University. Copyright © 1996 W. W. Norton & Company, Inc.

Gwendolyn Brooks "We Real Cool." From *Blacks* by Gwendolyn Brooks. Copyright © 1987, 1997. Used by permission of the Estate of Gwendolyn Brooks.

Emily Dickinson "A narrow fellow in the grass"
Emily Dickinson "After great pain a formal feeling comes"
Emily Dickinson "Because I could not stop for Death"
As read by Julie Harris, from *Poems and Letters of Emily Dickinson, Read by Julie Harris*. © 1960, 1987, 1991 HarperCollins Publishers, Inc. All rights reserved. Recorded by permission of HarperAudio, a division of HarperCollins Publishers, Inc.

Emily Dickinson "I Dwell in Possibility." Read by Garrison Keillor. From the audio recording "3 Doz. Poems." Copyright © 1995 Minnesota Public Radio. All rights reserved. Used by permission of Minnesota Public Radio.

Robert Frost "The Road Not Taken." From *Robert Frost Reads His Poetry*. Copyright © 1956 by HarperCollins Publishers, Inc. All rights reserved. Recorded by permission of HarperAudio, a division of HarperCollins Publishers, Inc.

Michael S. Harper "Dear John, Dear Coltrane." Copyright © 1970 by Michael S. Harper. Used by permission of Michael S. Harper.

Gerard Manley Hopkins "Spring and Fall." Read by M. H. Abrams, Cornell University. Copyright © 1996. W. W. Norton & Company, Inc.

Li-Young Lee "Persimmons." Copyright © 1986 by Li-Young Lee. From *Rose*, poems by Li-Young Lee. Used with the permission of BOA Editions Ltd.

Robert Lowell "Skunk Hour." Copyright © 2000 by HarperCollins Publishers, Inc. All rights reserved. Recorded by permission of HarperAudio, a division of HarperCollins Publishers, Inc.

Christopher Marlowe "The Passionate Shepherd to His Love." Read by Garrison Keillor. From the audio recording "3 Doz. Poems." Copyright © 1995 Minnesota Public Radio. All rights reserved. Used by permission of Minnesota Public Radio.

Willie Perdomo "123rd Street Rap." Copyright © 1996 by Willie Perdomo. Used by permission of Marie Brown Associates.

Adrienne Rich "Diving into the Wreck." From *The Fact of a Doorframe: Poems Selected and New, 1950–1984* by Adrienne Rich. Copyright © 1984 by Adrienne Rich. Copyright © 1975, 1978 by W. W. Norton & Company, Inc. Used by permission of the author and W. W. Norton & Company, Inc.

Anne Sexton "The Fury of Overshoes." From *Anne Sexton Reads*. © 1974, 1999 HarperCollins Publishers, Inc. Caedmon. All rights reserved. Recorded by permission of HarperAudio, a division of HarperCollins Publishers, Inc.

William Shakespeare "Let me not to the marriage of true minds." Read by Patrick Stewart. Read by Ossie Davis. Courtesy of AIRPLAY, Inc., producers of *The Complete Shakespeare Sonnets*.

William Shakespeare "That time of year thou mayst in me behold." Read by Natasha Richardson. Courtesy of AIRPLAY, Inc., producers of *The Complete Shakespeare Sonnets*.

William Shakespeare "Like as the waves." As read by Sir John Gielgud, from *William Shakespeare: The Sonnets*. Copyright © 1963, 1996 HarperCollins Publishers, Inc. All rights reserved. Recorded by permission of HarperAudio, a division of HarperCollins Publishers, Inc.

Wallace Stevens "The Idea of Order at Key West." Recorded courtesy of Harper & Row Publishers. Copyright © 1956, 1998 by Wallace Stevens. All rights reserved. Recorded by permission of HarperAudio, a division of HarperCollins Publishers, Inc.

Dylan Thomas "Do Not Go Gentle..." As read by Dylan Thomas, from *Dylan Thomas Reading His Poetry*. Copyright © 1956 by HarperCollins Publishers, Inc. All rights reserved. Recorded by permission of HarperAudio, a division of HarperCollins Publishers, Inc.

Derek Walcott "A Far Cry from Africa." From *Collected Poems 1948–1984* by Derek Walcott. Copyright © 1986 by Derek Walcott. Used by permission of Farrar, Straus and Giroux, LLC.

Richard Wilbur "Love Calls Us to the Things of This World." Recorded courtesy of Harper & Row Publishers. Copyright © 1972 by Richard Wilbur. All rights reserved. Recorded by permission of HarperAudio, a division of HarperCollins Publishers, Inc.

William Carlos Williams "This Is Just to Say." from *Collected Poems: 1909–1939*, Volume I. Copyright © 1938 by New Directions Publishing Corp. Reprinted by permission of New Directions Publishing Corp.

William Butler Yeats "The Lake Isle of Innisfree." Recorded courtesy of Harper & Row Publishers. Copyright © 1968 by HarperCollins Publishers, Inc. All rights reserved. Recorded by permission of HarperAudio, a division of HarperCollins Publishers, Inc.

Arthur Miller Excerpt from Act I of *Death of a Salesman*. From *Death of a Salesman: The Complete Play with Introduction by Arthur Miller*. Copyright © 1965, 1991, 1998 HarperCollins Publishers, Inc. Recorded by permission of HarperAudio, a division of HarperCollins Publishers, Inc.

George Bernard Shaw. Excerpt from *Pygmalion*, Act 2. Copyright © 1971, 1996 by HarperCollins Publishers, Inc. All rights reserved. Recorded by permission of HarperAudio, a division of HarperCollins Publishers, Inc.

William Shakespeare *Hamlet*, Act 3, Scene 4. As read by Paul Scofield, from *Hamlet: The Complete Play in Five Acts*. Copyright © 1963, 1995 by HarperCollins Publishers, Inc. All rights reserved. Recorded by permission of HarperAudio, a division of HarperCollins Publishers, Inc.

Jamaica Kincaid "Girl." Copyright © 1986 American Audio Prose Library, Inc. All rights reserved.

Raymond Carver "Cathedral." Read by Peter Reigert. Used by permission of International Creative Management, Inc. Copyright © 1981, 1982, 1983 by Raymond Carver.

James Joyce "Araby." Read by Colm Meaney. From *Dubliners*. Copyright © 2000 HarperCollins Publishers, Inc. Recorded by permission of HarperAudio, a division of HarperCollins Publishers, Inc.

Eudora Welty "Why I Live at the P.O." Courtesy of Harper & Row Publishers. Copyright © 1954 by Eudora Welty. All rights reserved. Recorded by permission of HarperAudio, a division of HarperCollins Publishers, Inc.

CD Mastered by Precision Powerhouse, Minneapolis, MN.

Every effort has been made to contact the copyright holders of each of these selections. Rights holders of any selection not credited should contact W. W. Norton & Company, Inc., Permissions Department, 500 Fifth Avenue, New York, NY 10110, in order for a correction to be made in the text or on the CD.

# Index of Authors

Ackerman, Diane
  *Sweep Me through Your Many-Chambered Heart*, 1034
Adair, Virginia Hamilton
  *Peeling an Orange*, 898
Adams, Franklin P.
  *Composed in the Composing Room*, 1043
Alexander, Elizabeth
  *West Indian Primer*, 908
Alexie, Sherman
  *Flight Patterns*, 49
Ali, Agha Shahid
  *Postcard from Kashmir*, 852
Alvarez, A.
  FROM *Sylvia Plath*, 1212
Angelou, Maya
  *Africa*, 1156
Annas, Pamela J.
  *A Disturbance in Mirrors*, 1221
Anonymous
  *Sir Patrick Spens*, 1008
  [*There was a young girl from St. Paul*], 979
  *The Twenty-third Psalm*, 949
  *Western Wind*, 1052
Arnold, Matthew
  *Dover Beach*, 893
Atwood, Margaret
  *Death of a Young Son by Drowning*, 864
  *Happy Endings*, 67
  *Scarlet Ibis*, 757
Auden, W. H.
  *In Memory of W. B. Yeats*, 1016
  *Musée des Beaux Arts*, 1055
  [*Stop all the clocks, cut off the telephone*], 825
Axelrod, Steven Gould
  *Jealous Gods*, 1225

Baca, Jimmy Santiago
  *Green Chile*, 854
Baldwin, James
  *Sonny's Blues*, 91
Bambara, Toni Cade
  *Gorilla My Love*, 505
Barrett, Andrea
  *Littoral Zone, The*, 221
Bashō
  [*This road—*], 1142
  [*A village without bells—*], 1142
Beattie, Ann
  *Janus*, 280
Beaumont, Jeanne Marie
  *Rorschach*, 936
Behn, Aphra
  *On Her Loving Two Equally*, 828
Bernstein, Charles
  *Of Time and the Line*, 915
Betjeman, John
  *In Westminster Abbey*, 907
Bierce, Ambrose
  *An Occurrence at Owl Creek Bridge*, 639
Birney, Earle
  *Anglosaxon Street*, 1047
  *Irapuato*, 912
Bishop, Elizabeth
  *Casabianca*, 1070
  *Exchanging Hats*, 1073
  *Sestina*, 1039
Blake, William
  *Holy Thursday* (1789), 1235
  *Holy Thursday* (1794), 1235
  *The Lamb*, 1134
  *London*, 841
  *The Sick Rose*, 962
  *The Tyger*, 1234
Blauner, Robert
  *Internal Colonialism and Ghetto Revolt*, 2062
Blundell, Mary Whitlock
  *Helping Friends and Harming Enemies: A Study in Sophocles and Greek Ethics*, 2118
Bogan, Louise
  *Evening in the Sanitarium*, 905
Bontemps, Arna
  *A Black Man Talks of Reaping*, 1172
Borges, Jorge Luis
  *The Garden of the Forking Paths*, 722
Borson, Roo
  *After a Death*, 967
Bourdillon, Francis William
  *The Night Has a Thousand Eyes*, 953
Bowra, Maurice
  *Sophoclean Tragedy*, 2106
Bradstreet, Anne
  *To My Dear and Loving Husband*, 826
Brewer, Linda
  *20/20*, 15
Broe, Mary Lynn
  *Protean Poetic*, 1217
Brontë, Emily
  *The Night-Wind*, 895
Brooks, Gwendolyn
  *First Fight. Then Fiddle.*, 1026
  *To the Diaspora*, 1236
  *We Real Cool*, 879
Brown, Lee Ann
  *Foolproof Loofah*, 987
Browning, Elizabeth Barrett
  *How Do I Love Thee?*, 811
  *To George Sand* [*A Desire*], 1079
  *To George Sand* [*A Recognition*], 1080
  [*When our two souls stand up erect and strong*], 1029
Browning, Robert
  *My Last Duchess*, 1076
  *Porphyria's Lover*, 1236
  *Soliloquy of the Spanish Cloister*, 866
  *A Woman's Last Word*, 1078
Burns, Robert
  *A Red, Red Rose*, 945
  *To a Louse*, 876

## INDEX OF AUTHORS

Bushnell, Rebecca W.
 *Prophesying Tragedy: Sign and Voice in Sophocles' Theban Plays*, 2117
Buson
 [*Coolness*—], 1142
 [*Listening to the moon*], 1143
Byatt, A. S.
 *The Thing in the Forest*, 35

Calverton, V. F.
 *The Bankruptcy of Marriage*, 587
Campion, Thomas
 *When to Her Lute Corinna Sings*, 989
Carey, Peter
 "*Do You Love Me?*" 142
Carmichael, Stokely, and Charles V. Hamilton
 *Black Power: The Politics of Liberation in America*, 2059
Carter, Angela
 *Souvenir of Japan, A*, 298
Carver, Raymond
 *Cathedral*, 20
Cavendish, Margaret, Duchess of Newcastle
 *Of the Theme of Love*, 953
Chabon, Michael
 *The Lost World*, 524
Chappell, Fred
 *Recovery of Sexual Desire after a Bad Cold*, 875
Chase, Karen
 *Venison*, 874
Chasin, Helen
 *Joy Sonnet in a Random Universe*, 1035
 *The Word Plum*, 969
Cheever, John
 *The Country Husband*, 74
Chekhov, Anton
 *The Cherry Orchard*, 1604
 *The Lady with the Dog*, 250
Cherry, Kelly
 *Alzheimer's*, 856
Chin, Marilyn
 *Summer Love*, 897
Chiyojo
 [*Whether astringent*], 1141
Chopin Kate
 *The Story of an Hour*, 536

Cleghorn, Sarah
 [*The golf links lie so near the mill*], 914
Cofer, Judith Ortiz
 *The Changeling*, 873
Coleridge, Samuel Taylor
 *Kubla Khan*, 1238
 *Metrical Feet*, 978
Collins, Billy
 *Morning*, 903
 *Sonnet*, 1035
Collins, Martha
 *Lies*, 925
Conrad, Joseph
 *The Secret Sharer*, 341
Constable, Henry
 [*My lady's presence makes the roses red*], 1024
 [*Wonder it is, and pity*], 1032
Cope, Wendy
 [*Not only marble, but the plastic toys*], 1150
 *Emily Dickinson*, 978
Cowley, Malcolm
 *Exile's Return: A Literary Odyssey of the 1920s*, 577
Crane, Stephen
 *The Open Boat*, 385
Cullen, Countee
 *From the Dark Tower*, 1174
 *Saturday's Child*, 1173
 *Yet Do I Marvel*, 1172
Cummings, E. E.
 [*Buffalo Bill 's*], 1044
 [*in Just-*], 928
 [*l(a*], 1042
 [*(ponder,darling,these busted statues*], 1148

Danticat, Edwidge
 *A Wall of Fire Rising*, 284
de la Mare, Walter
 *Slim Cunning Hands*, 919
de Maupassant, Guy
 *The Jewelry*, 634
Delanty, Greg
 *The Blind Stitch*, 954
Deutsch, Babette
 [*The falling flower*], 1144
Dickey, James
 *Cherrylog Road*, 883
 *The Leap*, 957
Dickinson, Emily
 [*After great pain, a formal feeling comes—*], 922

[*Because I could not stop for Death—*], 1239
[*The Brain—is wider than the Sky—*], 1241
[*I dwell in Possibility—*], 926
[*I stepped from Plank to Plank*], 1240
[*A narrow Fellow in the Grass*], 987
[*My Life had stood—a Loaded Gun—*], 1058
[*She dealt her pretty words like Blades—*], 1241
[*We do not play on Graves—*], 1240
[*Wild Night—Wild Nights!*], 954
[*The Wind begun to knead the Grass—*], 1010
Dillon, George L.
 *Styles of Reading*, 608
Dokey, Richard
 *Sánchez*, 227
Donne, John
 [*Batter my heart*], 950
 *The Canonization*, 951
 *The Computation*, 950
 [*Death, be not proud*], 1241
 *The Flea*, 886
 *The Good-Morrow*, 902
 *Song*, 1243
 *The Sun Rising*, 1242
 *A Valediction: Forbidding Mourning*, 1244
Donnelly, Susan
 *Eve Names the Animals*, 1153
Dove, Rita
 *Daystar*, 887
 *Fifth Grade Autobiography*, 821
Drewal, Henry John, John Pemberton III, and Rowland Abiodun
 *Yoruba: Nine Centuries of African Art and Thought*, 2065
Dryden, John
 *To the Memory of Mr. Oldham*, 980
Du Bois, W. E. B.
 *Two Novels*, 1193
Dunbar, Paul Laurence
 *Sympathy*, 1245
 *We Wear the Mask*, 1245

Dunn, Stephen
  *Dancing with God*, 963
  *Poetry*, 1013
Dylan, Bob
  *Mr. Tambourine Man*, 993

Edson, Margaret
  *Wit*, 1500
Eliot, T. S.
  *Journey of the Magi*, 1246
Elizabeth I
  *When I Was Fair and Young*, 1083
Ellison, Ralph
  *King of the Bingo Game*, 729
Emanuel, James A.
  *Emmett Till*, 1062
  *Ray Charles*, 1145
Erdrich, Louise
  *Jacklight*, 1159
  *Love Medicine*, 369

Faulkner, William
  *Barn Burning*, 710
  *A Rose for Emily*, 594
Fearing, Kenneth
  *Dirge*, 972
Ferry, David
  *At the Hospital*, 952
  *Evening News*, 1048
Fetterley, Judith
  *A Rose for "A Rose for Emily,"* 616
Finch, Anne, Countess of Winchelsea
  *There's No To-morrow*, 915
Fisher, Rudolph
  *The Caucasian Storms Harlem*, 1188
Fitzgerald, F. Scott
  *Babylon Revisited*, 560
  *Echoes of the Jazz Age*, 575
Frost, Robert
  *Design*, 1057
  *Fireflies in the Garden*, 963
  *Range-Finding*, 1027
  *The Road Not Taken*, 1247
  *Stopping by Woods on a Snowy Evening*, 1248

Gallagher, Tess
  *Sudden Journey*, 868
García Márquez, Gabriel
  *A Very Old Man with Enormous Wings*, 538

Gilbert, Sandra
  *Sonnet: The Ladies' Home Journal*, 1064
Gilman, Charlotte Perkins
  *The Yellow Wallpaper*, 667
Ginsberg, Allen
  *A Further Proposal*, 1147
  *[Looking over my shoulder]*, 1145
  *[The old pond]*, 1144
  *Velocity of Money*, 1248
Glaspell, Susan
  *A Jury of Her Peers*, 678
  *Trifles*, 1314
Goldman, Phaon
  *The Significance of African Freedom for the Negro American*, 2057
Gordimer, Nadine
  *Good Climate, Friendly Inhabitants*, 316
Gray, Thomas
  *Elegy Written in a Country Churchyard*, 1249
Griffin, Bartholomew
  *Care-charmer Sleep*, 1033
Grimke, Angelina
  *The Black Finger*, 1174
  *Tenebris*, 1174
Grosholz, Emily
  *Eden*, 846
Groves, Ernest R.
  *Social Problems of the Family*, 585
Gunn, Thom
  *A Blank*, 1086
  *In Time of Plague*, 838
  *A Map of the City*, 910

Ha Jin
  *In Broad Daylight*, 768
Hacker, Marilyn
  *[Who would divorce her lover]*, 1084
Hamilton, Charles V., and Stokely Carmichael
  *Black Power: The Politics of Liberation in America*, 2059
Hansberry, Lorraine
  *A Raisin in the Sun*, 1942
Hardy, Thomas
  *Channel Firing*, 1063
  *The Ruined Maid*, 861

Harper, Michael
  *Dear John, Dear Coltrane*, 992
Harwood, Gwen
  *In the Park*, 1031
Hawthorne, Nathaniel
  *Young Goodman Brown*, 264
Hayden, Robert
  *Frederick Douglass*, 1069
  *Homage to the Empress of the Blues*, 991
  *Those Winter Sundays*, 850
  *The Whipping*, 1252
Heaney, Seamus
  *Digging*, 1253
  *Mid-Term Break*, 820
  *Mother of the Groom*, 851
  *Punishment*, 1254
Hearn, Lafcadio
  *[Old pond—]*, 1143
Hecht, Anthony
  *The Dover Bitch*, 1150
Hemans, Felicia Dorothea
  *Casabianca*, 1069
Hemingway, Ernest
  *Hills Like White Elephants*, 132
Herbert, George
  *The Collar*, 1056
  *Easter Wings*, 1046
Herrick, Robert
  *Delight in Disorder*, 931
  *Upon Julia's Clothes*, 1053
Hollander, John
  *Adam's Task*, 1152
Hollander, Robert
  *You Too? Me Too—Why Not? Soda Pop*, 1137
Homans, Margaret
  *A Feminine Tradition*, 1220
Hopkins, Gerard Manley
  *God's Grandeur*, 1255
  *Pied Beauty*, 927
  *Spring and Fall*, 986
  *The Windhover*, 1256
Howe, Irving
  *The Plath Celebration: A Partial Dissent*, 1211
Howe, Marie
  *Practicing*, 1074
Hudgins, Andrew
  *Begotten*, 856
  *Mostly My Nightmares Are Dull*, 857

Hughes, Langston
  The Big Sea, 1197
  Harlem, 1068
  I, Too, 1177
  The Negro Speaks of Rivers, 1176
  The Weary Blues, 1175
Hughes, Ted
  To Paint a Water Lily, 938
Hurston, Zora Neale
  How It Feels to Be Colored Me, 1194

Ibsen, Henrik
  A Doll House, 2186

James, Henry
  The Jolly Corner, 645
Jarrell, Randall
  The Death of the Ball Turret Gunner, 953
Jebb, Richard C.
  The Antigone of Sophocles, 2105
Jennings, Elizabeth
  Delay, 1050
Jiles, Paulette
  Paper Matches, 1083
Johnson, Helene
  Sonnet to a Negro in Harlem, 1177
Johnson, James Weldon
  Preface to The Book of American Negro Poetry, 1180
Jonson, Ben
  [Come, my Celia, let us prove], 1133
  Epitaph on Elizabeth, L. H., 1059
  On My First Son, 818
  Still to Be Neat, 930
Jordan, June
  Something Like a Sonnet for Phillis Miracle Wheatley, 1156
Joyce, James
  Araby, 519

Kafka, Franz
  A Hunger Artist, 274
Kawabata, Yasunari
  The Grasshopper and the Bell Cricket, 544
Keats, John
  Endymion (Book 1), 1096
  Letter to Benjamin Bailey, Nov. 22, 1817, 1101
  Letter to George and Thomas Keats, Dec. 21, 1817, 1102
  Letter to John Hamilton Reynolds, Feb. 19, 1818, 1101
  Letter to John Taylor, Feb. 27, 1818, 1105
  Ode on a Grecian Urn, 1099
  Ode to a Nightingale, 1097
  On First Looking into Chapman's Homer, 1094
  On Seeing the Elgin Marbles, 1095
  On the Grasshopper and the Cricket, 1094
  On the Sonnet, 1025
  Preface to Endymion, 1106
  Sonnet to Sleep, 1095
  To Autumn, 1100
Kennedy, X. J.
  In a Prominent Bar in Secaucus One Day, 863
Kincaid, Jamaica
  Girl, 543
King, Henry
  Sic Vita, 949
Kinnell, Galway
  After Making Love We Hear Footsteps, 845
  Blackberry Eating, 1256
Kleinzahler, August
  Aubade on East 12th Street, 904
Knight, Etheridge
  [Eastern guard tower], 1144
  Hard Rock Returns to Prison from the Hospital for the Criminal Insane, 840
Knox, Bernard
  Introduction to Sophocles: Three Theban Plays, 2108
Koch, Kenneth
  Variations on a Theme by William Carlos Williams, 1149
Komunyakaa, Yusef
  Tu Do Street, 1080
Kroll, Judith
  Rituals of Exorcism: "Daddy," 1214
Kumin, Maxine
  Woodchucks, 843

Lahiri, Jhumpa
  Interpreter of Maladies, 325
Lampman, Archibald
  Winter Evening, 906
Larkin, Philip
  Church Going, 1002
Lawrence, D. H.
  The Blind Man, 423
  I Am Like a Rose, 961
  Odour of Chrysanthemums, 409
  Passages from Essays and Letters, 446
  The Rocking-Horse Winner, 436
Layton, Irving
  From Colony to Nation, 1068
Lazarus, Emma
  The New Colossus, 1027
Le Guin, Ursula K.
  She Unnames Them, 549
Lee, Li-Young
  Persimmons, 847
Lessing, Doris
  Our Friend Judith, 189
Levertov, Denise
  Wedding-Ring, 829
Locke, Alain
  The New Negro, 1183
Lorde, Audre
  Hanging Fire, 872
Lovelace, Richard
  Song: To Lucasta, Going to the Wars, 1075
Lowell, Amy
  The Lonely Wife, 1085
Lowell, Robert
  Skunk Hour, 1257

MacLeish, Archibald
  Ars Poetica, 1041
Mansfield, Katherine
  Bliss, 692
Marlowe, Christopher
  The Passionate Shepherd to His Love, 1139
Marvell, Andrew
  The Garden, 1258
  On a Drop of Dew, 940
  To His Coy Mistress, 896
Mary, Lady Chudleigh
  To the Ladies, 829
Mason, Bobbie Ann
  Shiloh, 747

## INDEX OF AUTHORS A35

McGough, Roger
   *Here I Am*, 1046
McKay, Claude
   *The Harlem Dancer*, 1179
   *Harlem Shadows*, 1178
   *If We Must Die*, 1178
   *The Tropics in New York*, 1179
   *The White House*, 1179
Melville, Herman
   *Bartleby, the Scrivener*, 164
Merrill, James
   *body*, 939
   *Watching the Dance*, 985
Millay, Edna St. Vincent
   [*I, being born a woman and distressed*], 879
   [*I shall forget you presently, my dear*], 1031
   [*What lips my lips have kissed*], 1030
   [*Women have loved before as I love now*], 878
Miller, Arthur
   *Death of a Salesman*, 2121
Milton, John
   *On the Late Massacre in Piedmont*, 889
   *Paradise Lost*, 931
   [*When I consider how my light is spent*], 1028
Miner, Earl
   [*The still old pond*], 1144
Montagu, Lady Mary Wortley
   *Written the First Year I Was Marry'd*, 1082
Moore, Gene M.
   *Of Time and Its Mathematical Progression: Problems of Chronology in Faulkner's "A Rose for Emily,"* 622
Moore, Lorrie
   *How*, 135
Moore, Marianne
   *Love in America?* 1136
   *Poetry*, 1037
Mora, Pat
   *Elena*, 854
   *Gentle Communion*, 920
   *La Migra*, 877
   *Sonrisas*, 1005
Morrison, Toni
   *Recitatif*, 202
Mukherjee Bharati
   *The Management of Grief*, 304

Muldoon, Paul
   *Milkweed and Monarch*, 849
Munro, Alice
   *Boys and Girls*, 509
Nemerov, Howard
   *Boom!* 1134
   *The Goose Fish*, 1000
   *The Vacuum*, 819
   *A Way of Life*, 900
New York Times
   *Crowds at Tickers See Fortunes Wane*, 584
   *Stocks Collapse*, 583
   *Women Traders Going Back to Bridge Games*, 585
Nussbaum, Martha C.
   *The Fragility of Goodness: Luck and Ethics in Greek Tragedy and Philosophy*, 2113
O'Connor, Flannery
   *Everything That Rises Must Converge*, 487
   *A Good Man Is Hard to Find*, 451
   *The Lame Shall Enter First*, 462
   *Passages from Essays and Letters*, 497
Oates, Joyce Carol
   *The Lady with the Pet Dog*, 735
Olds, Sharon
   *Last Night*, 827
   *Leningrad Cemetery, Winter of 1941*, 956
   *Sex without Love*, 924
   *The Victims*, 1006
Oliver, Mary
   *Singapore*, 911
Ortiz, Simon J.
   *My Father's Song*, 858
Owen, Wilfred
   *Disabled*, 1075
   *Dulce et Decorum Est*, 1071
Paley, Grace
   *A Conversation with My Father*, 31
Parker, Dorothy
   *A Certain Lady*, 869
   *One Perfect Rose*, 961
Pastan, Linda
   *love poem*, 813

*Marks*, 944
   *To a Daughter Leaving Home*, 888
Perdomo, Willie
   *123rd Street Rap*, 995
Perelman, Bob
   *The Masque of Rhyme*, 929
Philips, Katherine
   *L'amitié: To Mrs. M. Awbrey*, 880
Phillpotts, Eden
   *The Learned*, 1058
Piercy, Marge
   *Barbie Doll*, 835
   *What's That Smell in the Kitchen?*, 1082
Plath, Sylvia
   *Barren Woman*, 1260
   *Black Rook in Rainy Weather*, 1260
   *Daddy*, 1204
   *Lady Lazarus*, 1261
   *Morning Song*, 903
   *Point Shirley*, 891
Poe, Edgar Allan
   *The Cask of Amontillado*, 127
   *The Raven*, 982
Pope, Alexander
   *Sound and Sense*, 974
Porter, Katherine Anne
   *Flowering Judas*, 701
Pound, Ezra
   *In a Station of the Metro*, 1264
   *The River-Merchant's Wife: A Letter*, 815
   *A Virginal*, 1264
Quarles, Francis
   *On Change of Weathers*, 1264
Ralegh, Sir Walter
   *The Nymph's Reply to the Shepherd*, 1146
Ramsey, Jarold
   *The Tally Stick*, 812
Randall, Dudley
   *Ballad of Birmingham*, 1072
Ransom, John Crowe
   *Bells for John Whiteside's Daughter*, 1265
Reed, Ishmael
   *beware : do not read this poem*, 1040

# INDEX OF AUTHORS

Rich, Adrienne
  *Aunt Jennifer's Tigers*, 844
  *At a Bach Concert*, 1109
  *A Communal Poetry*, 1123
  *Diving into the Wreck*, 965
  *For the Record*, 1117
  *History*, 1118
  *How Does a Poet Put Bread on the Table?* 1122
  *Living in Sin*, 1111
  *Modotti*, 1119
  *[My mouth hovers across your breasts]*, 1118
  *Planetarium*, 1115
  *Snapshots of a Daughter-in-Law*, 1111
  *Storm Warnings*, 1110
  *Two Songs*, 947
  *When We Dead Awaken: Writing as Re-Vision*, 1120
  *Why I Refused the National Medal for the Arts*, 1124
Ríos, Alberto Alvaro
  *Advice to a First Cousin*, 1158
  *Mi Abuelo*, 858
Robinson, Edwin Arlington
  *Mr. Flood's Party*, 997
Rodgers, Lawrence R.
  *"We all said, 'She will kill herself' ": The Narrator/Detective in William Faulkner's "A Rose for Emily,"* 601
Roethke, Theodore
  *I Knew a Woman*, 1265
  *My Papa's Waltz*, 923
  *The Waking*, 1266
Rosenberg, Liz
  *Married Love*, 816
  *The Silence of Women*, 1986
Rossetti, Christina
  *In an Artist's Studio*, 1029
  *Cobwebs*, 1030
Rossetti, Dante Gabriel
  *A Sonnet Is a Moment's Monument*, 1025
Rushdie, Salman
  *The Prophet's Hair*, 776

Salter, Mary Jo
  *Welcome to Hiroshima*, 899
Seifu
  *[The faces of dolls]*, 1143
Senior, Olive
  *Ancestral Poem*, 852

Sexton, Anne
  *The Fury of Overshoes*, 822
Shakespeare, William
  *[Th'expense of spirit in a waste of shame]*, 1011
  *[Full many a glorious morning have I seen]*, 901
  *Hamlet*, 1743
  *[Let me not to the marriage of true minds]*, 827
  *[Like as the waves make towards the pebbled shore]*, 985
  *A Midsummer Night's Dream*, 1690
  *[My mistress' eyes are nothing like the sun]*, 1034
  *[Not marble, nor the gilded monuments]*, 1138
  *[Shall I compare thee to a summer's day?]*, 948
  *Spring*, 990
  *[That time of year thou mayst in me behold]*, 942
Shaw, Bernard
  *Pygmalion*, 1370
Shelley, Percy Bysshe
  *Ode to the West Wind*, 1014
Shields, Carol
  *Dressing Down*, 786
Sidney, Sir Philip
  *[Come sleep! Oh sleep]*, 1033
Skirrow, Desmond
  *Ode on a Grecian Urn Summarized*, 1149
Smith, Stevie
  *The Jungle Husband*, 1045
Snodgrass, W. D.
  *Leaving the Motel*, 836
Song, Cathy
  *Heaven*, 1011
Sophocles
  *Antigone*, 2074
  *Oedipus the King*, 1840
Soyinka, Wole
  *Death and the King's Horseman*, 2003
Steiner, George
  *Dying Is an Art*, 1208
Stevens, Wallace
  *Anecdote of the Jar*, 1269
  *The Emperor of Ice-Cream*, 1268
  *The Idea of Order at Key West*, 1267
  *Sunday Morning*, 1269

Stoppard, Tom
  *The Real Inspector Hound*, 1326
Suckling, Sir John
  *Song*, 979
Swift, Jonathan
  *A Description of the Morning*, 905

Tan, Amy
  *A Pair of Tickets*, 236
Tennyson, Alfred, Lord
  *The Kraken*, 1155
  *Now Sleeps the Crimson Petal*, 1272
  *Tears, Idle Tears*, 1273
  *Tithonus*, 1273
  *Ulysses*, 1275
Thomas, Dylan
  *Do Not Go Gentle into That Good Night*, 1037
  *Fern Hill*, 1277
Thorpe, Earl E.
  *Africa in the Thought of Negro Americans*, 2054
Tobin, Daniel
  *The Clock*, 850
Toplady, Augustus Montague
  *A Prayer, Living and Dying*, 990

Van Duyn, Mona
  *What the Motorcycle Said*, 970
Vogel, Paula
  *How I Learned to Drive*, 1642

Waddington, Miriam
  *Ulysses Embroidered*, 1154
Wagoner, David
  *My Father's Garden*, 944
Walcott, Derek
  *A Far Cry from Africa*, 1157
  *Midsummer*, 909
Waller, Edmund
  *Song*, 960
Walsh, Clara A.
  *[An old-time pond]*, 1143
Welty, Eudora
  *Why I Live at the P.O.*, 155
Wharton, Edith
  *Roman Fever*, 113
Wheatley, Phillis
  *On Being Brought from Africa to America*, 1155

Whitman, Walt
  *Facing West from California's Shores*, 1278
  *[I celebrate myself, and sing myself]*, 881
  *I Hear America Singing*, 1279
  *A Noiseless Patient Spider*, 1279
Wilbur, Richard
  *The Beautiful Changes*, 938
  *Love Calls Us to the Things of This World*, 1280
Wilde, Oscar
  *The Importance of Being Earnest*, 1879
  *Symphony in Yellow*, 937
William, William Carlos
  *The Dance*, 1009
  *Raleigh Was Right*, 1147
  *The Red Wheelbarrow*, 926
  *This Is Just to Say*, 927
  *The Use of Force*, 546

Williams, C. K.
  *Alzheimer's: The Wife*, 1284
Williams, Miller
  *Thinking about Bill, Dead of AIDS*, 1067
Williams, Tennessee
  *A Streetcar Named Desire*, 1539
Wilson, August
  *The Piano Lesson*, 1441
Winters, Yvor
  *At the San Francisco Airport*, 917
Wordsworth, William
  *Lines Written a Few Miles above Tintern Abbey*, 1281
  *London, 1802*, 1028
  *Nuns Fret Not*, 1023
  *She Dwelt among the Untrodden Ways*, 871

Wright, Richard
  *[In the falling snow]*, 1145
  *Twelve Million Black Voices: A Folk History of the Negro in the United States*, 2051
Wyatt, Sir Thomas
  *They Flee from Me*, 875
Yeats, W. B.
  *All Things Can Tempt Me*, 1285
  *Among School Children*, 1290
  *Byzantium*, 1292
  *Easter 1916*, 1286
  *The Lake Isle of Innisfree*, 1285
  *A Last Confession*, 830
  *Leda and the Swan*, 1289
  *Sailing to Byzantium*, 1289
  *The Second Coming*, 1288

# Index of Titles and First Lines

About suffering they were never wrong, 1055
"A cold coming we had of it, 1246
*Adam's Task* (Hollander), 1152
A day on, 995
Adding my pee to the sea, 929
A dull people, 1068
*Advice to a First Cousin* (Ríos), 1158
*Africa* (Angelou), 1156
*Africa in the Thought of Negro Americans* (Thorpe), 000
*After a Death* (Borson), 967
[*After great pain, a formal feeling comes—*] (Dickinson), 922
*After Making Love We Hear Footsteps* (Kinnell), 845
A green level of lily leaves, 938
All over America women are burning dinners, 1082
*All Things Can Tempt Me* (Yeats), 1285
All things can tempt me from this craft of verse, 1285
All we need is fourteen lines, well, thirteen now, 1035
*Alzheimer's* (Cherry), 856
*Alzheimer's: The Wife* (Williams), 1284
*Among School Children* (Yeats), 1290
A narrow Fellow in the Grass, 987
*Ancestral Poem* (Senior), 852
And were it for thy profit, to obtain, 1264
*Anecdote of the Jar* (Stevens), 1269
*Anglosaxon Street* (Birney), 1047
An old-time pond, 1143
An omnibus across the bridge, 937
*Antigone* (Sophocles), 2074
*Antigone of Sophocles, The*, 2105
Anyone can get it wrong, laying low, 925
A poem should be palpable and mute, 1041
Applauding youths laughed with young prostitutes, 1179
*Araby* (Joyce), 519
*Ars Poetica* (MacLeish), 1041
As a young girl, 873
As he knelt by the grave of his mother and father, 849
A single flow'r he sent me, since we met, 961
A sudden blow: the great wings beating still, 1289
As virtuous men pass mildly away, 1244
A sweet disorder in the dress, 931

*At a Bach Concert* (Rich), 1109
At first the surprise, 963
A thing of beauty is a joy for ever, 1096
At stated ic. times, 1043
*At the Hospital* (Ferry), 952
*At the San Francisco Airport* (Winters), 917
*Aubade on East 12th Street* (Kleinzahler), 904
*Aunt Jennifer's Tigers* (Rich), 844
Aunt Jennifer's tigers prance across a screen, 844
Avenge, O Lord, thy slaughtered saints, whose bones, 889
A village without bells—, 1042
A wind is ruffling the tawny pelt, 1157
A woman in the shape of a monster, 1115

*Babylon Revisited* (Fitzgerald), 560
*Ballad of Birmingham* (Randall), 1072
Bananas ripe and green, and ginger-root, 1179
*Bankruptcy of Marriage, The* (Calverton), 587
*Barbie Doll* (Piercy), 835
*Barn Burning* (Faulkner), 710
*Barren Woman* (Plath), 1260
*Bartleby, the Scrivener* (Melville), 164
[*Batter my heart, three-personed God*] (Donne), 950
*Beautiful Changes, The* (Wilbur), 938
[*Because I could not stop for Death—*] (Dickinson), 1239
Because there isn't Room—, 1240
Because there was a man somewhere in a candystripe silk shirt, 991
*Begotten* (Hudgins), 856
*Bells for John Whiteside's Daughter* (Ransom), 1265
Below the thunders of the upper deep, 1155
Bent double, like old beggars under sacks, 1071
Between my finger and thumb, 1253
Between you and a bowl of oranges I lie nude, 898
*beware : do not read this poem* (Reed), 1040
*Big Sea, The* (Hughes), 1197
*Black Finger, The* (Grimke), 1174
*Black Man Talks of Reaping, A* (Bontemps), 1172
*Black Power: The Politics of Liberation in America* (Carmichael), 2059

## INDEX OF TITLES AND FIRST LINES   A39

Black Rook in Rainy Weather (Plath), 1260
Blackberry Eating (Kinnell), 1256
Blank, A (Gunn), 1086
Blind Man, The (Lawrence), 423
Blind Stitch, The (Delanty), 954
Bliss (Mansfield), 692
body (Merrill), 939
Boom! (Nemerov), 1134
Bored with plastic armies, 850
Boys and Girls (Munro), 509
[Brain—is wider than the Sky—, The] (Dickinson), 1241
Br-r-r-am-m-m, rackery-am-m, OM, Am, 970
[Buffalo Bill 's] (Cummings), 1044
Busy old fool, unruly sun, 1242
But most by numbers judge a poet's song, 974
Byzantium (Yeats), 1292

Call the roller of big cigars, 1268
Canonization, The (Donne), 951
Care-charmer Sleep (Griffin), 1033
Care-charmer sleep, sweet ease in restless misery, 1033
Casabianca (Bishop), 1070
Casabianca (Hemans), 1069
Cask of Amontillado, The (Poe), 127
Cathedral (Carver), 20
Caucasian Storms Harlem, The (Fisher), 1188
Certain Lady, A (Parker), 869
Certain things here are quietly American—, 909
Changeling, The (Cofer), 873
Channel Firing (Hardy), 1063
Cherrylog Road (Dickey), 883
Cherry Orchard, The (Chekhov), 1604
Church Going (Larkin), 1002
Clock, The (Tobin), 850
Cobwebs (Rossetti), 1030
Collar, The (Herbert), 1056
Come live with me and be my love (Ginsberg), 1147
Come live with me and be my love (Marlowe), 1139
[Come, my Celia, let us prove] (Jonson), 1133
[Come sleep! Oh sleep] (Sidney), 1033
Come sleep! Oh Sleep, the certain knot of peace, 1033
Coming by evening through the wintry city, 1109
Communal Poetry, A (Rich), 1123
Complacencies of the peignoir, and late, 1269
Composed in the Composing Room (Adams), 1043
Computation, The (Donne), 950
Conversation with My Father, A (Paley), 31

[Coolness—] (Buson), 1142
Country Husband, The (Cheever), 74

Daddy (Plath), 1204
Dance, The (Williams), 1009
Dancing with God (Dunn), 963
Dawn drizzle ended dampness steams from, 1047
Daystar (Dove), 887
Dearest Evelyn, I often think of you, 1045
Dear John, Dear Coltrane (Harper), 992
Death and the King's Horseman (Soyinka), 2003
[Death, be not proud] (Donne), 1241
Death of a Salesman (Miller), 2121
Death of a Young Son by Drowning (Atwood), 864
Death of the Ball Turret Gunner, The (Jarrell), 953
Delay (Jennings), 1050
Delight in Disorder (Herrick), 931
Description of the Morning, A (Swift), 905
Design (Frost), 1057
Digging (Heaney), 1253
Dirge (Fearing), 972
Disabled (Owen), 1075
Disturbance in Mirrors, A (Annas), 1221
Diving into the Wreck (Rich), 965
Doll House, A (Ibsen), 2186
Do Not Go Gentle into That Good Night (Thomas), 1037
Dover Beach (Arnold), 893
Dover Bitch, The (Hecht), 1150
"Do You Love Me?" 142
Dressing Down (Shields), 786
Droning a drowsy syncopated tune, 1175
Dulce et Decorum Est (Owen), 1071
Dying Is an Art (Steiner), 1208

[Eastern guard tower] (Knight), 1144
Easter 1916 (Yeats), 1286
Easter Wings (Herbert), 1046
Echoes of the Jazz Age (Fitzgerald), 575
Eden (Grosholz), 846
Elegy Written in a Country Churchyard (Gray), 1249
Elena (Mora), 854
Emily Dickinson (Cope), 978
Emmett Till (Emanuel), 1062
Emperor of Ice-Cream, The (Stevens), 1268
Empty, I echo to the least footfall, 1260
Endymion (Book 1) (Keats), 1096
Epitaph on Elizabeth, L. H. (Jonson), 1059
Eve Names the Animals (Donnelly), 1153
Evening in the Sanitarium (Bogan), 905
Evening News (Ferry), 1048
Even the long-dead are willing to move, 920

*Everything That Rises Must Converge* (O'Conner), 487
*Exchanging Hats* (Bishop), 1073
*Exile's Return: A Literary Odyssey of the 1920s* (Cowley), 577

[*faces of dolls, The*] (Seifū), 1143
*Facing West from California's Shores* (Whitman), 1278
[*falling flower, The*] (Deutsch), 1144
*Far Cry from Africa, A* (Walcott), 1157
Farewell, thou child of my right hand, and joy, 818
Farewell, too little, and too lately known, 980
*Feminine Tradition, A* (Homans), 1220
*Fern Hill* (Thomas), 1277
*Fifth Grade Autobiography* (Dove), 821
*Fireflies in the Garden* (Frost), 963
*First Fight. Then Fiddle.* (Brooks), 1026
First fight. Then fiddle. Ply the slipping string, 1026
First having read the book of myths, 965
Five years have passed; five summers, with the length, 1281
*Flea, The* (Donne), 886
*Flight Patterns* (Alexie), 49
*Flowering Judas* (Porter), 701
*Foolproof Loofah* (Brown), 987
For God's sake hold your tongue and let me love!, 951
For I can snore like a bullhorn, 845
For reasons any, 912
For the first twenty years, since yesterday, 950
*For the Record* (Rich), 1117
*Fragility of Goodness: Luck and Ethics in Greek Tragedy and Philosophy, The* (Nussbaum), 2113
*Frederick Douglass* (Hayden), 1069
*From Colony to Nation* (Layton), 1068
From my mother's sleep I fell into the State, 953
*From the Dark Tower* (Cullen), 1174
From Water-Tower Hill to the brick prison, 891
[*Full many a glorious morning have I seen*] (Shakespeare), 901
*Further Proposal, A* (Ginsberg), 1147
*Fury of Overshoes, The* (Sexton), 822

*Garden of the Forking Paths, The* (Borges), 722
*Garden, The* (Marvell), 1258
Gassing the woodchucks didn't turn out right, 843
*Gentle Communion* (Mora), 920

George Burns likes to insist that he always, 915
*Girl* (Kincaid), 543
Girl from the realm of birds florid and fleet, 1156
Glory be to God for dappled things—, 927
Go, and catch a falling star, 1243
*God's Grandeur* (Hopkins), 1255
[*golf links lie so near the mill, The*] (Cleghorn), 914
Go, lovely rose! 960
*Good Climate, Friendly Inhabitants* (Gordimer), 316
*Good Man Is Hard to Find, A* (O'Connor), 451
*Good-Morrow, The* (Donne), 902
*Goose Fish, The* (Nemerov), 1000
*Gorilla My Love* (Bambara), 505
*Grasshopper and the Bell Cricket, The* (Kawabata), 544
*Green Chile* (Baca), 854
Gr-r-r-there go, my heart's abhorrence! 866

Had we but world enough, and time, 896
*Hamlet* (Shakespeare), 1743
*Hanging Fire* (Lorde), 872
*Happy Endings* (Atwood), 67
*Hard Rock Returns to Prison from the Hospital for the Criminal Insane* (Knight), 840
Hard Rock was "known not to take no shit, 840
*Harlem* (Hughes), 1068
*Harlem Dancer, The* (McKay), 1179
*Harlem Shadows* (McKay), 1178
Ha! whare ya gaun, ye crowlan ferlie!, 876
*Heaven* (Song), 1011
He disappeared in the dead of winter, 1016
*Helping Friends and Harming Enemies: A Study in Sophocles and Greek Ethics* (Blundell), 2118
Here at the Vespasian-Carlton, it's just one, 1134
Here come real stars to fill the upper skies, 963
Here from the start, from our first days, look, 812
*Here I Am* (McGough), 1046
He sat in a wheeled chair, waiting for dark, 1075
He stands at the door, a crazy old man, 856
He thinks when we die we'll go to China, 1011
He, who navigated with success, 864
Hey! Mr. Tambourine Man, play a song for me, 993
Higgledy-piggledy, 978
*Hills Like White Elephants* (Hemingway), 132
His get-aboard smile, 1145

*History* (Rich), 1118
*Holy Thursday* (1789) (Blake), 1235
*Homage to the Empress of the Blues* (Hayden), 991
*How* (Moore), 135
*How Does a Poet Put Bread on the Table?* (Rich), 1122
*How Do I Love Thee?* (Browning), 811
How do I love thee? Let me count the ways, 811
How do they do it, the ones who make love, 924
*How I Learned to Drive* (Vogel), 1642
*How It Feels to Be Colored Me* (Hurston), 1194
How strongly does my passion flow, 828
How vainly men themselves amaze, 1258
*Hunger Artist, A* (Kafka), 274

I am, 1137
I am fourteen, 872
*I Am Like a Rose* (Lawrence), 961
I am myself at last; now I achieve, 961
[*I, being born a woman and distressed*] (Millay), 879
I can feel the tug, 1254
I can't say why rightly, but suddenly it's clear once more, 954
I caught this morning morning's minion, 1256
[*I celebrate myself, and sing myself*] (Whitman), 881
I chopped down the house that you had been saving to live in, 1149
*Idea of Order at Key West, The* (Stevens), 1267
I doubt not God is good, well-meaning, kind, 1172
[*I dwell in Possibility—*] (Dickinson), 926
If all the world and love were young, 1146
If by dull rhymes our English must be chained, 1025
If ever two were one, then surely we, 826
I found a dimpled spider, fat and white, 1057
*If We Must Die* (McKay), 1178
If we must die, let it not be like hogs, 1178
I have done it again, 1261
I have eaten, 927
I have just seen a beautiful thing, 1174
I have met them at close of day, 1286
I have sown beside all waters in my day, 1172
*I Hear America Singing* (Whitman), 1279
I hear America singing, the varied carols I hear, 1279
I hear a whistling, 1062
I hear the halting footsteps of a lass, 1178
*I Knew a Woman* (Roethke), 1265

I knew a woman, lovely in her bones, 1265
I know what the caged bird feels, alas!, 1245
I live in a doorway, 1005
I love to go out in late September, 1256
I'm delighted by the velocity of money as it whistles through, 1248
*Importance of Being Earnest, The* (Wilde), 1879
*In an Artist's Studio* (Rossetti), 1029
*In a Prominent Bar in Secaucus One Day* (Kennedy), 863
*In a Station of the Metro* (Pound), 1264
*In Broad Daylight* (Ha Jin), 768
In Brueghel's great picture, The Kermess, 1009
In Xanadu did Kubla Khan, 1238
In lurid cartoon colors, the big baby, 846
*In Memory of W. B. Yeats* (Auden), 1016
In Singapore, in the airport, 911
In sixth grade Mrs. Walker, 847
In summer's mellow midnight, 895
*Internal Colonialism and Ghetto Revolt* (Blauner), 2062
*Interpreter of Maladies* (Lahiri), 325
*In the Park* (Harwood), 1031
*In Time of Plague* (Gunn), 838
*Introduction to* Sophocles: Three Theban Plays (Knox), 2108
[*in Just-*] (Cummings), 928
[*In the falling snow*] (Wright), 1145
*In Westminster Abbey* (Betjeman), 907
I placed a jar in Tennessee, 1269
I prefer red chile over my eggs, 854
*Irapuato* (Birney), 912
I sat all morning in the college sick bay, 820
[*I shall forget you presently, my dear*] (Millay), 1031
I stand upon a hill and see, 910
[*I stepped from Plank to Plank*] (Dickinson), 1240
Is this a Holy thing to see, 1235
I struck the board and cried, "No more, 1056
is what you first see, stepping off the train, 899
It is a land with neither night nor day, 1030
It little profits that an idle king, 1275
It makes no difference where one starts, 1013
It's been going on a long time, 900
*I, Too* (Hughes), 1177
I, too, dislike it: there are things that are important beyond all this fiddle, 1037
I, too, sing America, 1177
I wake to sleep, and take my waking slow, 1266
I walk through the long schoolroom questioning, 1290

## INDEX OF TITLES AND FIRST LINES

I wander through each chartered street, 841
I want to write a love poem for the girls I kissed in seventh grade, 1074
I want to write you, 813
I was four in this photograph fishing, 821
I will arise and go now, and go to Innisfree, 1285
I wonder, by my troth, what thou and I, 902
I've known rivers, 1176
I've never, as some children do, 856

*Jacklight* (Erdrich), 1159
*Janus* (Beattie), 280
*Jealous Gods* (Axelrod), 1225
*Jewelry, The* (Maupassant), 634
*Jolly Corner, The* (James), 645
*Journey of the Magi* (Eliot), 1246
*Joy Sonnet in a Random Universe* (Chasin), 1035
*Jungle Husband, The* (Smith), 1045
*Jury of Her Peers, A* (Glaspell), 678

Kashmir shrinks into my mailbox, 852
*King of the Bingo Game* (Ellison), 729
*Kraken, The* (Tennyson), 1155
*Kubla Khan* (Coleridge), 1238

*[l(a]* (Cummings), 1042
*Lady Lazarus* (Plath), 1261
*Lady with the Dog, The* (Chekhov), 250
*Lady with the Pet Dog, The* (Oates), 735
*Lake Isle of Innisfree, The* (Yeats), 1285
*Lamb, The* (Blake), 1134
*Lame Shall Enter First, The*, 462
*La Migra* (Mora), 877
*L'amitié: To Mrs. M. Awbrey* (Philips), 880
*Last Confession, A* (Yeats), 830
*Last Night* (Olds), 827
*Leap, The* (Dickey), 957
*Learned, The* (Phillpotts), 1058
*Leaving the Motel* (Snodgrass), 836
*Leda and the Swan* (Yeats), 1289
*Leningrad Cemetery, Winter of 1941* (Olds), 956
*[Let me not to the marriage of true minds]* (Shakespeare), 827
Let me take this other glove off, 907
Let's contend no more, Love, 1078
Let's play *La Migra*, 877
*Letter to Benjamin Bailey* (Keats), 1101
*Letter to George and Thomas Keats* (Keats), 1102
*Letter to John Hamilton Reynolds* (Keats), 1101
*Letter to John Taylor* (Keats), 1105
*Lies* (Collins), 925
*[Like as the waves make towards the pebbled shore]* (Shakespeare), 985

Like to the falling of a star, 949
*Lines Written a Few Miles above Tintern Abbey* (Wordsworth), 1281
*[Listening to the moon]* (Buson), 1143
*Little Lamb, who made thee?* 1134
*Littoral Zone, The* (Barrett), 221
*Living in Sin* (Rich), 1111
Lo! I fill prol pills, 987
*London* (Blake), 841
*London, 1802* (Wordsworth), 1028
*Lonely Wife, The* (Lowell), 1085
Look closely at the letters. Can you see, 939
*[Looking over my shoulder]* (Ginsberg), 1145
Lord, who createdst man in wealth and store, 1046
*Lost World, The* (Chabon), 524
*Love Calls Us to the Things of This World* (Wilbur), 1280
*Love in America?* (Moore), 1136
*Love Medicine* (Erdrich), 369
*love poem* (Pastan), 813
Love set you going like a fat gold watch, 903
Love's the boy stood on the burning deck, 1070

*Management of Grief, The* (Mukherjee), 304
*Map of the City, A* (Gunn), 910
Márgárét áre you grieving, 986
*Mark but this flea, and mark in this*, 886
*Marks* (Pastan), 944
*Married Love* (Rosenberg), 816
*Masque of Rhyme, The* (Perelman), 929
Maybe I'm seven in the open field—, 868
*Metrical Feet* (Coleridge), 978
*Mi Abuelo* (Ríos), 858
*Midsummer* (Walcott), 909
*Midsummer Night's Dream, A* (Shakespeare), 1690
*Mid-Term Break* (Heaney), 820
*Milkweed and Monarch* (Muldoon), 849
Milton! Thou should'st be living at this hour, 1028
*Modotti* (Rich), 1119
*Morning* (Collins), 903
*Morning Song* (Plath), 903
*Mostly My Nightmares Are Dull* (Hudgins), 857
Mostly my nightmares are dull. On autumn nights, 857
"Mother dear, may I go downtown, 1072
*Mother of the Groom* (Heaney), 851
*Mr. Flood's Party* (Robinson), 997
*Mr. Tambourine Man* (Dylan), 993
Much have I traveled in the realms of gold, 1094
*Musée des Beaux Arts* (Auden), 1055
My ancestors are nearer, 852

INDEX OF TITLES AND FIRST LINES  **A43**

My aunts washed dishes while the uncles, 1082
*My Father's Song* (Ortiz), 858
*My Father's Garden* (Wagoner), 944
My heart aches, and a drowsy numbness pains, 1097
My husband gives me an A, 944
*My Last Duchess* (Browning), 1076
[*My lady's presence makes the roses red*] (Constable), 1024
[*My Life had stood—a Loaded Gun—*] (Dickinson), 1058
[*My mistress' eyes are nothing like the sun*] (Shakespeare), 1034
[*My mouth hovers across your breasts*] (Rich), 1118
*My Papa's Waltz* (Roethke), 923
My Spanish isn't enough, 854
My spirit is too weak—mortality, 1095
My thoughts are crowded with death, 838
My wedding-ring lies in a basket, 829

[*narrow Fellow in the Grass, A*] (Dickinson), 987
Nautilus Island's hermit, 1257
*Negro Speaks of Rivers, The* (Hughes), 1176
*New Colossus, The* (Lazarus), 1027
*New Negro, The* (Locke), 1183
*Night Has a Thousand Eyes, The* (Bourdillon), 953
*Night-Wind, The* (Brontë), 895
*Noiseless Patient Spider, A* (Whitman), 1279
No no! Go from me. I have left her lately, 1264
Not like the brazen giant of Greek fame, 1027
[*Not marble, nor the gilded monuments*] (Shakespeare), 1138
[*Not only marble, but the plastic toys*] (Cope), 1150
Now hardly here and there a hackney-coach, 905
*Now Sleeps the Crimson Petal* (Tennyson), 1272
Now sleeps the crimson petal, now the white, 1272
Now as I was young and easy under the apple boughs, 1277
*Nuns Fret Not* (Wordsworth), 1023
Nuns fret not at their convent's narrow room, 1023
*Nymph's Reply to the Shepherd, The* (Ralegh), 1146

*Occurrence at Owl Creek Bridge, An* (Bierce), 639
*Ode on a Grecian Urn* (Keats), 1099

*Ode on a Grecian Urn Summarized* (Skirrow), 1149
*Ode to a Nightingale* (Keats), 1097
*Ode to the West Wind* (Shelley), 1014
*Odour of Chrysanthemums* (Lawrence), 409
*Oedipus the King* (Sophocles), 1840
Off Highway 106, 883
Of man's first disobedience, and the fruit, 931
*Of the Theme of Love* (Cavendish), 953
*Of Time and Its Mathematical Progression: Problems of Chronology in Faulkner's "A Rose for Emily"* (Moore), 622
*Of Time and the Line* (Bernstein), 915
Oh, I can smile for you, and tilt my head, 869
Old Eben Flood, climbing alone one night, 997
Old men, as time goes on, grow softer, sweeter, 1086
[*Old pond—*] (Hearn), 1143
[*old pond, The*] (Ginsberg), 1144
[*old-time pond, An*] (Walsh), 1143
O love, how thou art tired out with rhyme! 953
"O 'Melia, my dear, this does everything crown, 861
O, my luve's like a red, red rose, 945
*On a Drop of Dew* (Marvell), 940
*On Being Brought from Africa to America* (Wheatley), 1155
Once I am sure there's nothing going on, 1002
Once upon a midnight dreary, while I pondered, weak and weary, 982
*On Change of Weathers* (Quarles), 1264
One face looks out from all his canvases, 1029
1-2-3 was the number he played but today the number came 3-2-1, 972
*123rd Street Rap* (Perdomo), 995
*One Perfect Rose* (Parker), 961
One wading a Fall meadow finds on all sides, 938
*On First Looking into Chapman's Homer* (Keats), 1094
*On Her Loving Two Equally* (Behn), 828
On his way to the open hearth where white-hot steel, 944
*On My First Son* (Jonson), 818
*On Seeing the Elgin Marbles* (Keats), 1095
*On the Grasshopper and the Cricket* (Keats), 1094
*On the Late Massacre in Piedmont* (Milton), 889
On the long shore, lit by the moon, 1000
"On the road between Spanish Town, 908

## A44 INDEX OF TITLES AND FIRST LINES

On the Sonnet (Keats), 1025
On the stiff twig up there, 1260
Open Boat, The, 385
O rose, thou art sick, 962
O soft embalmer of the still midnight, 1095
Our Friend Judith, 189
Outside, the last kids holler, 836
O wild West Wind, thou breath of Autumn's being, 1014

Pair of Tickets, A (Tan), 236
Paper Matches (Jiles), 1083
Paradise Lost (Milton), 931
Passionate Shepherd to His Love, The (Marlowe), 1139
Paul sets the bags down, told how they had split, 874
Peeling an Orange (Adair), 898
Persimmons (Lee), 847
Piano Lesson, The (Wilson), 1441
Pied Beauty (Hopkins), 927
Planetarium (Rich), 1115
Plath Celebration: A Partial Dissent, The (Howe), 1211
Poetry (Dunn), 1013
Poetry (Moore), 1037
Point Shirley (Plath), 891
[(ponder,darling,these busted statues] (Cummings), 1148
Poor savage, doubting that a river flows, 985
Porphyria's Lover (Browning), 1236
Postcard from Kashmir (Ali), 852
Practicing (Howe), 1074
Prayer, Living and Dying, A (Toplady), 990
Preface to Endymion (Keats), 1106
Preface to The Book of American Negro Poetry (Johnson), 1180
Prophesying Tragedy: Sign and Voice in Sophocles' Theban Plays (Bushnell), 2117
Prophet's Hair, The (Rushdie), 776
Protean Poetic (Broe), 1217
Punishment (Heaney), 1254
Pygmalion (Shaw), 1370

Raisin in the Sun, A (Hansberry), 1942
Raleigh Was Right (Williams), 1147
Range-Finding (Frost), 1027
Raven, The (Poe), 982
Ray Charles (Emanuel), 1145
Real Inspector Hound, The (Stoppard), 1326
Recitatif (Morrison), 202
Recovery of Sexual Desire after a Bad Cold (Chappell), 875
Red, Red Rose, A (Burns), 945
Red Wheelbarrow, The (Williams), 926
Rituals of Exorcism: "Daddy" (Kroll), 1214

River-Merchant's Wife: A Letter, The (Pound), 815
Road Not Taken, The (Frost), 1247
Rocking-Horse Winner, The (Lawrence), 436
ROCK of ages, cleft for me, 990
Roman Fever (Wharton), 113
Rorschach (Beaumont), 936
Rose for "A Rose for Emily," A (Fetterley), 616
Rose for Emily, A (Faulkner), 594
Ruined Maid, The (Hardy), 861

Sailing to Byzantium (Yeats), 1289
Sánchez (Dokey), 227
Saturday's Child (Cullen), 1173
Scarlet Ibis (Atwood), 757
Searching for love, a woman, 1080
Season of mists and mellow fruitfulness, 1100
Second Coming, The (Yeats), 1288
Secret Sharer, The (Conrad), 341
See how the orient dew, 940
Seeing that there's no other way, 967
September rain falls on the house, 1039
Sestina (Bishop), 1039
Sex, as they harshly call it, 947
Sex fingers toes, 992
Sex without Love (Olds), 924
[Shall I compare thee to a summer's day?] (Shakespeare), 948
She answers the bothersome telephone, 1284
[She dealt her pretty words like Blades—] (Dickinson), 1241
She Dwelt among the Untrodden Ways (Wordsworth), 871
She had thought the studio would keep itself, 1111
She sang beyond the genius of the sea, 1267
She sits in the park. Her clothes are out of date, 1031
She Unnames Them (Le Guin), 549
She wanted a little room for thinking, 887
She was the sentence the cancer spoke at last, 952
Shiloh (Mason), 747
Should I simplify my life for you? 1118
Sick Rose, The (Blake), 962
Sic Vita (King), 949
Significance of African Freedom for the Negro American, The (Goldman), 2057
Silence of Women, The (Rosenberg), 1086
Singapore (Oliver), 911
Sir Patrick Spens, 1008
Skunk Hour (Lowell), 1257
Slim Cunning Hands (de la Mare), 919

# INDEX OF TITLES AND FIRST LINES  A45

Slim cunning hands at rest, and cozening eyes—, 919
*Snapshots of a Daughter-in-Law* (Rich), 1111
Snow patches along the creek bank, 936
*Social Problems of the Family* (Groves), 585
*Soliloquy of the Spanish Cloister* (Browning), 866
Some are teethed on a silver spoon, 1173
*Something Like a Sonnet for Phillis Miracle Wheatley* (Jordan), 1156
Sometimes I'm happy: la la la la la la, 1035
so much depends, 926
*Song* (Donne), 1243
*Song* (Suckling), 979
*Song* (Waller), 960
*Song: To Lucasta, Going to the Wars* (Lovelace), 1075
*Sonnet* (Collins), 1035
*Sonnet Is a Moment's Monument, A* (Rossetti), 1025
*Sonnet: The Ladies' Home Journal* (Gilbert), 1064
*Sonnet to a Negro in Harlem* (Johnson), 1177
*Sonnet to Sleep* (Keats), 1095
*Sonny's Blues* (Baldwin), 91
*Sonrisas* (Mora), 1005
*Sophoclean Tragedy* (Bowra), 2106
So there stood Matthew Arnold and this girl, 1150
Soul of my soul, my Joy, my crown, my friend! 880
*Sound and Sense* (Pope), 974
*Souvenir of Japan, A* (Carter), 298
*Spring* (Shakespeare), 990
*Spring and Fall* (Hopkins), 986
[*still old pond, The*] (Miner), 1144
*Still to Be Neat* (Jonson), 930
Still to be neat, still to be dressed, 930
[*Stop all the clocks, cut off the telephone*] (Auden), 825
*Stopping by Woods on a Snowy Evening* (Frost), 1248
*Storm Warnings* (Rich), 1110
*Story of an Hour, The* (Chopin), 536
*Streetcar Named Desire, A* (Williams), 1539
*Styles of Reading* (Dillon), 608
*Sudden Journey* (Gallagher), 868
*Summer Love* (Chin), 897
*Sunday Morning* (Stevens), 1269
Sundays too my father got up early, 850
*Sun Rising, The* (Donne), 1242
*Sweep Me through Your Many-Chambered Heart* (Ackerman), 1034
*Sylvia Plath* (Alvarez), 1212
*Sympathy* (Dunbar), 1245
*Symphony in Yellow* (Wilde), 937

*Tally Stick, The* (Ramsey), 812
*Tears, Idle Tears* (Tennyson), 1273
Tears, idle tears, I know not what they mean, 1273
Tell me not, sweet, I am unkind, 1075
*Tenebris* (Grimke), 1174
That is no country for old men. The young, 1289
That night your great guns, unawares, 1063
That's my last Duchess painted on the wall, 1076
[*That time of year thou mayst in me behold*] (Shakespeare), 942
That winter, the dead could not be buried, 956
The apparition of these faces in the crowd, 1264
The battle rent a cobweb diamond-string, 1027
The black smoke rising means that I am cooking, 897
The boy stood on the burning deck, 1069
The Brain—is wider than the sky—, 1241
The brilliant stills of food, the cozy, 1064
The faces of dolls, 1143
The clouds and the stars didn't wage this war, 1117
The curfew tolls the knell of parting day, 1249
The eyes open to a cry of pulleys, 1280
The falling flower, 1144
The free evening fades, outside the windows, 905
The glass has been falling all afternoon, 1110
The golf links lie so near the mill, 914
The grey beards wag, the bald heads nod, 1058
The house is so quiet now, 819
The king sits in Dumferling toune, 1008
The Lord is my shepherd; I shall not want, 949
The mist is thick. On the wide river, the water-plants float smoothly, 1085
The next day, I am almost afraid, 827
The old pond, 1144
The old woman across the way, 1252
The only thing I have of Jane MacNaughton, 957
The poetry of earth is never dead, 1094
The radiance of that star that leans on me, 1050
The rain set early in tonight, 1236
The sea is calm tonight, 893
The skylight silvers, 904
There is a tree, by day, 1174

There's No To-morrow (Finch), 915
[There was a young girl from St. Paul], 979
There was such speed in her little body, 1265
The still old pond, 1144
The tree are uncurling their first, 816
The unpurged images of day recede, 1292
The way the world works is like this, 1158
The Wind begun to knead the Grass—, 1010
The whiskey on your breath, 923
The woods decay, the woods decay and fall, 1273
The word *plum* is delicious, 969
The world is charged with the grandeur of God, 1255
Th'expense of spirit in a waste of shame, 1011
The year of griefs being through, they had to merge, 1086
They Flee from Me (Wyatt), 875
They flee from me, that sometime did me seek, 875
They sit in a row, 822
Thing in the Forest, The (Byatt), 35
Thinking about Bill, Dead of AIDS (Williams), 1067
This girlchild was born as usual, 835
This Is Just to Say (Williams), 927
This is the terminal: the light, 917
[This road—] (Bashō), 1142
Those Winter Sundays (Hayden), 850
Thou large-brained woman and large-hearted man, 1079
Thou still unravished bride of quietness, 1099
Thou, paw-paw-paw; thou, glurd; thou, spotted, 1152
Thus she had lain, 1156
Tithonus (Tennyson), 1273
To a Daughter Leaving Home (Pastan), 888
To a Louse (Burns), 876
To Autumn (Keats), 1100
To George Sand [A Desire] (Browning), 1079
To George Sand [A Recognition] (Browning), 1080
To His Coy Mistress (Marvell), 896
To me, *lion* was sun on a wing, 1153
To My Dear and Loving Husband (Bradstreet), 826
To-night the very horses springing by, 906
tonite, thriller was, 1040
To Paint a Water Lily (Hughes), 938
To the Disapora (Brooks), 1236
To the Ladies (Chudleigh), 829
To the Memory of Mr. Oldham (Dryden), 980
Toward morning I dreamed of the Ace of Spades reversed, 875

Trifles (Glaspell), 1314
Trŏchĕ trīps frŏm lōng tŏ shŏrt, 978
Tropics in New York, The (McKay), 1179
True genius, but true woman! Dost deny, 1080
Tu Do Street (Komunyakaa), 1080
Turning and turning in the widening gyre, 1288
'Twas mercy brought me from my Pagan land, 1155
'Twas on a Holy Thursday, their innocent faces clean, 1235
Twelve Million Black Voices: A Folk History of the Negro in the United States (Wright), 2051
Twenty-third Psalm, The, 949
20/20 (Brewer), 15
Two long had Lov'd, and now the Nymph desir'd, 915
Two Novels (du Bois), 1193
Two roads diverged in a yellow wood, 1247
Two Songs (Rich), 947
Tyger, The (Blake), 1234
Tyger Tyger! Burning bright, 1234

Ulysses (Tennyson), 1275
Ulysses Embroidered (Waddington), 1154
Unfunny uncles who insist, 1073
Upon Julia's Clothes (Herrick), 1053
Use of Force, The (Williams), 546

Vacuum, The (Nemerov), 819
Valediction: Forbidding Mourning, A (Donne), 1244
Variations on a Theme by William Carlos Williams (Koch), 1149
Velocity of Money (Ginsberg), 1248
Venison (Chase), 874
Very Old Man with Enormous Wings, A (Márquez), 538
Victims, The (Olds), 1006
[village without bells—, A] (Bashō), 1142
Virginal, A (Pound), 1264

Waking, The (Roethke), 1266
Wall of Fire Rising, A (Danticat), 284
Wanting to say things, 858
Watching the Dance (Merrill), 985
Way of Life, A (Nemerov), 900
"We all said, 'She will kill herself'": The Narrator/Detective in William Faulkner's "A Rose for Emily" (Rodgers), 601
Weary Blues, The (Hughes), 1175
We cannot go to the country, 1147
Wedding-Ring (Levertov), 829
We did not know the first thing about, 1067
[We do not play on Graves—] (Dickinson), 1240

## INDEX OF TITLES AND FIRST LINES  A47

We have been there, 1048
We have come to the edge of the woods, 1159
*Welcome to Hiroshima* (Salter), 899
*We Real Cool* (Brooks), 879
We shall not always plant while others reap, 1174
*Western Wind*, 1052
Western wind, when wilt thou blow, 1052
*West Indian Primer* (Alexander), 908
*We Wear the Mask* (Dunbar), 1245
We wear the mask that grins and lies, 1245
Whatever it is, it's a passion—, 1136
What happens to a dream deferred?, 1068
[*What lips my lips have kissed, and where and why*] (Millay), 1030
What lively lad most pleasured me, 830
What she remembers, 851
*What's That Smell in the Kitchen?* (Piercy), 1082
*What the Motorcycle Said* (Duyn), 970
Whenas in silks my Julia goes, 1053
When daisies pied and violets blue, 990
[*When I consider how my light is spent*] (Milton), 1028
When I taught you, 888
*When I Was Fair and Young* (Elizabeth I), 1083
When I was fair and young, and favor graced me, 1083
[*When our two souls stand up erect and strong*] (Browning), 1029
When it is finally ours, this freedom, this liberty, this beautiful, 1069
*When to Her Lute Corinna Sings* (Campion), 989
*When We Dead Awaken: Writing as Re-Vision* (Rich), 1120
When you set out for Afrika, 1236
[*Whether astringent*] (Chiyojo), 1141
Where my grandfather is in the ground, 858
While my hair was still cut straight across my forehead, 815
While thirst for power, and desire of fame, 1081

*Whipping, The* (Hayden), 1252
*White House, The* (McKay), 1179
Whose woods these are I think I know, 1248
[*Who would divorce her lover*] (Hacker), 1084
Why do we bother with the rest of the day, 903
*Why I Live at the P.O.* (Welty), 155
*Why I Refused the National Medal for the Arts* (Rich), 1124
Why so pale and wan, fond Lover? 979
Wife and servant are the same, 829
[*Wild Nights—Wild Nights!*] (Dickinson), 954
*Windhover, The* (Hopkins), 1256
[*Wind begun to knead the Grass—, The*] (Dickinson), 1010
*Winter Evening* (Lampman), 906
*Wit* (Edson), 1500
*Woman's Last Word, A* (Browning), 1078
[*Women have loved before as I love now*] (Millay), 878
[*Wonder it is, and pity*] (Constable), 1032
*Woodchucks* (Kumin), 843
*Word Plum, The* (Chasin), 969
Wouldst thou hear what man can say, 1059
*Written the First Year I Was Marry'd* (Montagu), 1082

*Yellow Wallpaper, The* (Gilman), 667
*Yet Do I Marvel* (Cullen), 1172
*Yoruba: Nine Centuries of African Art and Thought* (Abiodun), 2065
You are disdainful and magnificent—, 1177
You do not do, you do not do, 1204
*Young Goodman Brown* (Hawthorne), 264
You, once a belle in Shreveport, 1111
Your door is shut against my tightened face, 1179
Your footprints of light on sensitive paper, 1119
*You Too? Me Too—Why Not? Soda Pop* (Hollander), 1137
You've come, 1154

REGISTRATION NUMBER:

**BTLO-BDOM**

NORTON LITERATURE ONLINE

# wwnorton.com/literature

Visit this exciting gateway to the outstanding online literary resources available from Norton.

Detach your registration card. On the back you will find a registration code. This code offers free access to the site for twelve months. Once you register, you can change your password however you wish.

If the registration card has been removed from your textbook, visit wwnorton.com/literature for instructions regarding site access.

HOW TO REGISTER FOR
## Norton Literature Online

- Go to wwnorton.com/literature.

- Select "Access Norton Literature Online."

- Click "Register" and enter the registration code printed on this card.
  You will be asked to provide an e-mail address. We will send you an individual password that will give you access to the site for twelve months. You will be able to change both the e-mail address and the password later.

Please visit our help desk at wwnorton.com/techsupport/helpdesk if you have any difficulties or need assistance.